VICTOR HUGO

LIBRARY OF ESSENTIAL WRITERS

VICTOR
HUGO

◆

THREE NOVELS

◆

COMPLETE AND UNABRIDGED

The Hunchback of Notre-Dame ◆ Les Misérables ◆

The Man Who Laughs

BARNES & NOBLE

NEW YORK

Barnes & Noble, Inc.
122 Fifth Avenue
New York, NY 10011

ISBN-13: 978-0-7607-9323-7

Printed and bound in China

1 3 5 7 9 10 8 6 4 2

CONTENTS

Contents

INTRODUCTION

VICTOR-MARIE HUGO BECAME THE ACKNOWLEDGED FIGUREHEAD OF THE FRENCH ROMANTIC Movement in the 1830s, and survived the decline of that movement in the 1840s to remain the dominant figure of nineteenth-century French literature until his death in 1885. In 1851, following Louis-Napoleon's *coup d'état*, he was exiled from his homeland. He took up residence on the island of Jersey, although his visiting card indicated his address thereafter with the single word, *Ocean*. He remained as towering a figure in his absence as he had been while his home was the focal point of literary Paris. Unlike the similarly exiled Alexandre Dumas, who accepted an amnesty and returned to Paris in 1853, Hugo refused to return while the Second Empire endured, and was mortified when the way was eventually opened for his return by France's ignominious defeat in the Franco-Prussian war of 1870.

Hugo's father, Joseph-Léopold-Sigisbert Hugo, had been an officer in the Republican army following the revolution. He met Victor's Breton mother, Sophie, in 1793 while suppressing a rebellion in the fervently Royalist Vendée. They were married in 1796, and Victor, their third child, was born six years later. Although Joseph Hugo's progress in Napoleon's imperial army was relentless—he was promoted to the rank of general and granted the title of Comte—the necessity of being perpetually on the move greatly increased the strain on the mismatched union, ensuring a highly colorful childhood for Victor and his two older brothers, Abel and Eugène.

Victor's first experience of stability came when the marriage broke up in 1812—when he was ten years old—and Sophie settled in Paris, determined to provide her children with a good education. He began writing plays and stories almost immediately, and completed the first draft of his first long work of prose fiction at sixteen. In 1819 he and his brothers founded a Royalist literary journal, *Le Conservateur littéraire*, which published sixteen issues and to which he was the leading contributor of poetry and criticism. In 1822, already widely hailed as a budding genius, he published a volume of *Odes*, for which he was awarded a royal pension.

The pension gave Hugo sufficient security to marry the woman with whom he had fallen in love, Adèle Foucher. Although their first child died in infancy they had four more in the next seven years, and settled down to a long domestic contentment that contrasted sharply with the turbulent private lives of many nineteenth-century French writers. The French Romantic Movement had been led for some years by Charles Nodier, who hosted meetings of his *"cénacle"* at the Arsenal, where he had been appointed librarian; Hugo attended Nodier's *cénacle* regularly before hosting its principal successor at his house in the Rue Notre-Dame-des-Champs.

The influence of his fellow Romantics—who took considerable inspiration from the radical philosophical writings of Jean-Jacques Rousseau—combined with the renewed influence of his fervently Bonapartist father, with whom he was reconciled after his mother's death, to urge Hugo away from Royalism towards Republicanism. He took up his new cause with the zeal that often characterizes converts, and he became a relentless campaigner against all the social evils that he associated with conservatism in politics and religion.

Hugo's fervor for Republican ideals became the most important influence on the content and tone of his literary work, but he also became deeply interested in the aesthetics of Romantic art. The formal aspects distinguishing Romanticism from the Classicism against which it opposed itself were even more interesting to Hugo than the ideological aspects of its rebellion, and he was determined to produce work of a new and distinctive kind in all the literary forms in which he worked. Poetry was his primary medium, but he was almost as passionate about drama, and labored hard to provoke the revolution in the theatre that he finally accomplished with a sensational première performance of *Hernani* in 1830, at which the members of his *cénacle* turned out *en masse* to comprise an unusually cultured claque. He also set out to do something similar in the field of prose fiction when he began work on *Notre-Dame de Paris* in 1828, although he did not finish it until 1831.

Notre-Dame de Paris was not Hugo's first substantial work of prose fiction; at 18 he had written *Han d'Islande* (translated as *Hans of Iceland*) after being called upon to justify a boast that he could write a book in a week, and had published it—anonymously, at first—in 1821. He was eventually to rewrite and publish the novella he had drafted at sixteen, *Bug-Jargal*, as well. Both these pieces were, however, obvious finger-exercises by comparison with *Notre-Dame de Paris*, a far more adventurous endeavor whose publication had as profound an effect on the evolution of French prose fiction as *Hernani's* première had had on the the evolution of French theatre.

Although it can legitimately be described as a novel on the mundane grounds of its length, *Notre-Dame de Paris* is a key example of modern historical *romance*, in the now-obsolete sense of the word that continued to draw a crucial contrast between "romances" and "novels" as the Romantic Movement faded away and the novel acquired its modern form. Within this scheme, the essence of the novel—which had only just begun a long process of development in 1831—was supposed to be its scrupulous cultivation of naturalistic representation, thus enabling the reader to identify with the mundane experiences of the characters. The prose romance, by contrast—whose tradition was very well established before 1830—dealt with exceptional events and characters, whose endeavors and misfortunes were far more melodramatic; romances retained a more flamboyantly artificial mode of story-telling, in which an active narrator would address readers as if they were interested listeners.

Traditionally, romances had been set in a generalized "mythical past" whose settings were largely arbitrary and which often permitted supernatural intrusions, but Hugo's essential purpose was to modernize romance by transplanting it into a well-defined historical past, with a highly specific setting, from which the supernatural had been banished in actuality even though it still held enormous influence in common belief. All of the elements of the text were established with this end in mind; the book's original title was *Notre-Dame de Paris—1482*, specifying the date as well as the place of the action. That title is thrown into even sharper focus by the essay included in the novel which argues that "the book of architecture" was about to be replaced, in 1482, by "the book of printing" as the chief mode of cultural communication; implicit within this argument is that the ambition of *Notre-Dame de Paris* is to be nothing less than a modern Notre-Dame de Paris: a microcosm of Paris, and hence of civilization.

It is for this reason that the alternative title by which the novel is known in English, *The Hunchback of Notre Dame*, has a certain propriety. Although the deformed bell-ringer Quasimodo is one of a group of key characters, and owes his elevation to centrality to two classic Hollywood films—which set stern challenges for the make-up artists and the two star actors (Lon Chaney and Charles Laughton) charged with his representation—he is also explicitly established as a symbolic personification of the cathedral. Just as the actual Notre-Dame was a patchwork, replete with Gothic flourishes and gargoyles in spite of its embodiment of Christian ideals, so the cathedral of the printed book is equipped with a crude and misshapen appendage invested with a virtuous soul—a better representative of civilized values in his treatment of the exceedingly unfortunate Esmeralda, than his patron, Claude Frollo, or even his scatterbrained fellow-protégé, Pierre Gringoire.

Hugo had set out his manifesto for Romanticism in the preface to the unperformed play *Cromwell* (1827). There, far more elaborately than in the little essay featured in *Notre-Dame de Paris*, he had identified crucial phases in human history with distinctive artistic forms, culminating in the drama, and especially in the new kind of Romantic drama with which he was attempting to revolutionize a theatre steeped in Classicism. His suggestion in this preface that the dramatic artist should no longer attempt to repress the ugly from the beautiful and should make a concerted attempt to accommodate the sublime and the grotesque within his work is wholeheartedly exemplified in *Notre-Dame de Paris*. As the Romantic Movement faded away, though, Hugo became increasingly conscious of the fact that a new cultural phase was in birth, and that the prose romance was giving ground to the novel as a crucial form of cultural expression. Many years passed before he was to write his next full-length prose work, but when he did—working in exile, viewing his beloved Paris from afar—he set out to produce a very different work, which was very definitely a historical *novel*, even though it carefully retained the kind of philosophical grandiosity of which only the greatest novels are capable: *Les Misérables*.

   Les Misérables is one of the few French titles that defy any attempt at translation. To call it "The Poor," "The Wretched," or "The Unfortunate" would not begin to do justice to its compendious implications. Hugo began writing it in 1845, as an accompaniment to the intensification of his own political activism. He was elected a peer of France in that year—which served to intensify the scandal generated when the supposed paragon of marital virtue was caught *in flagrante delicto* with his mistress, Léonie d'Aunet. His marriage had cooled, and had been opened to other affections by mutual consent—partly due to the grand passion conceived by Hugo's close friend, the critic Charles-Augustin Sainte-Beuve, for Adèle—but they had been very discreet in keeping up appearances; the public exposure of his own flaw only made Hugo more fervently determined to explore the causes of sin, the censorious nature of society's response, and the possibility of personal redemption.

   Progress on the novel was interrupted in 1848, when the revolution that toppled Louis-Philippe encouraged Hugo to stand for the new National Assembly; he was elected to it as the deputy for Paris. Following his exile by Napoleon III he did not resume work on it immediately, but concentrated instead on the comprehensive account of French history contained in his epic poem *La Légende des Siècles*, published in 1859. He then decided that a return to prose fiction might be the best further means of expressing his anger and promoting his ideological antagonism, not merely to the new emperor but to moral dictatorship in general, and resumed work on *Les Misérables* in 1860; it was published in 1862.

   The name of the novel's central character, Jean Valjean, is intended to convey the impression that he is a modern Everyman, whose career exemplifies Rousseau's famous dictum that man, though "born free," is everywhere enchained by the meshes of an oppressive social order. Driven by desperation to steal a loaf of bread, Valjean finds his sentence serially augmented by the punitive zeal of the appalling Javert, necessitating his escape from penal servitude—but that turns out to be merely the beginning of a long and remarkably fervent pursuit, echoed by the history of France itself as it moves from Napoleon's final defeat at Waterloo to the July Revolution of 1830.

   It is entirely appropriate that the final phase of Valjean's redemption, which leads directly to his release from the furious attentions of Javert, takes place in the recently reconstructed sewers of Paris, in one of the most powerful and enduring scenes in literature. As in Leo Tolstoy's *War and Peace* or Fyodor Dostoyevsky's *Crime and Punishment*, the plot of *Les Misérables* is commissioned to carry the burden of a conscientious philosophical analysis, but it does not compromise its narrative verve in so doing; it remains immensely readable in spite of its length and depth.

   Les Misérables lives on in the twenty-first century, not merely as a monument to the progress of the nineteenth-century novel—and the novel's capacity to retain the best features of Romance—but as the basis of a popular musical drama, which broke box-office records during its London run and transferred successfully to Broadway. Such a translation may seem slightly absurd, but it was by no means inept or inappropriate. Hugo had observed that *Notre-Dame de Paris* had been a considerable inspiration to the writers of newspaper serials, who pioneered modern popular literature in the 1840s; not only had historical romance become by far the most important genre of serial fiction, but many authors of its key examples—most obviously Eugène Sue's *Les mystères de Paris* (1943; translated as *The Mysteries of Paris*)—had followed Hugo's example in making the city the real "central character" of their stories, dwelling lovingly on the detail and symbolic weight of its literary re-creation. Hugo was not ashamed to borrow some key features of serial fiction in *Les Misérables*—whose four parts were initially published at intervals—and carefully conserved a melodramatic quality that lent itself very well, not merely to adaptation for the stage, but to interpretation in the kind of lyric poetry—sentimental and bombastic at the same time—that is typical of the best modern musicals.

Hugo's awareness of the debt owed to him by the most prominent writers of serial fiction—Sue, Alexandre Dumas, Paul Féval, and Ponson du Terrail—became even more obvious when he reverted to the genre of *Notre-Dame de Paris*, deliberately setting out to write the *ultimate* modern historical romance in *L'homme qui rit* (1869), translated variously as *By Order of the King* and *The Man Who Laughs*.

Far more extensively than *Les Misérables*, *L'homme qui rit* adopts the discoveries made by the pioneers of popular fiction regarding the art and craft of keeping readers hooked. It immediately establishes an extraordinarily high pitch of dramatic tension, and exhibits some brilliant narrative flourishes. The *comprachicos* are a fabulous invention, and the prefatory description of their awful fate is a melodramatic *tour de force*. It is, however, also Hugo's most acidic political novel; the diplomatic removal of its critique of aristocratic privilege to England does not reduce its bite at all. It carefully preserves both his penchant for bold symbolic representation—in the key characters of the unnaturally long-lived Ursus (Bear), his pet wolf Homo (Humankind), and the compulsively-grinning Gwynplaine—and his intellectual flamboyance. The chapter in which Ursus, rightly suspected of unorthodoxy, is forced to defend his philosophical opinions against a tribunal of arrogant scholars, is a masterpiece of wordplay which retains its cleverness in spite of the difficulty of translation.

Although it is calculatedly lighter in substance and method than *Notre-Dame de Paris* or *Les Misérables*, *L'homme qui rit* completes an experimental set of sorts. Although some modern critics inevitably prefer his earnestly naturalistic late novels *Les travailleurs de la mer* (1866; translated as *Toilers of the Sea*) and *Quatrevingt-treize* (1874, translated as *Ninety-Three*) to *L'homme qui rit*, it is *L'homme qui rit* that forms the best complement to *Notre-Dame de Paris* and *Les Misérables* as an illustration of Hugo's development and accomplishment as a writer of prose fiction.

Hugo continued to write prolifically until disabled by a stroke in 1878. At his death in 1885, he was regarded one of the greatest writers of his century and a writer who had advanced the ambitions and possibilities of the novel. The examples set by the novels in this omnibus were highly influential, not merely as individual expressions of unique genius, but as a coherent and sequential exploration of the potential of prose fiction to leaven the essential naturalism of the novel with the finest seasonings of romance.

BRIAN STABLEFORD

Brian Stableford teaches fiction writing at the University of Reading, where he also served as a lecturer in philosophy of social science and the sociology of literature and the mass media. He is the author of more than seventy-five books, including fifty novels and short fiction collections and the definitive critical studies *Glorious Perversity: The Decline and Fall of Literary Decadence*, *Scientific Romance in Britain: 1890-1950*, and *The Sociology of Science Fiction*.

THE HUNCHBACK OF NOTRE-DAME

Contents

PREFACE

A FEW YEARS AGO, WHILE VISITING OR, RATHER, RUMMAGING ABOUT NOTRE-DAME, THE AUTHOR of this book found, in an obscure nook of one of the towers, the following word, engraved by hand upon the wall:—

’ANÁΓKH.

These Greek capitals, black with age, and quite deeply graven in the stone, with I know not what signs peculiar to Gothic caligraphy imprinted upon their forms and upon their attitudes, as though with the purpose of revealing that it had been a hand of the Middle Ages which had inscribed them there, and especially the fatal and melancholy meaning contained in them, struck the author deeply.

He questioned himself; he sought to divine who could have been that soul in torment which had not been willing to quit this world without leaving this stigma of crime or unhappiness upon the brow of the ancient church.

Afterwards, the wall was whitewashed or scraped down, I know not which, and the inscription disappeared. For it is thus that people have been in the habit of proceeding with the marvelous churches of the Middle Ages for the last two hundred years. Mutilations come to them from every quarter, from within as well as from without. The priest whitewashes them, the archdeacon scrapes them down; then the populace arrives and demolishes them.

Thus, with the exception of the fragile memory which the author of this book here consecrates to it, there remains to-day nothing whatever of the mysterious word engraved within the gloomy tower of Notre-Dame—nothing of the destiny which it so sadly summed up. The man who wrote that word upon the wall disappeared from the midst of the generations of man many centuries ago; the word, in its turn, has been effaced from the wall of the church; the church will, perhaps, itself soon disappear from the face of the earth.

It is upon this word that this book is founded.

MARCH, 1831

VOLUME I

Book First

Chapter I

The Grand Hall

THREE HUNDRED AND FORTY-EIGHT YEARS, SIX MONTHS, AND NINETEEN DAYS AGO TO-DAY, the Parisians awoke to the sound of all the bells in the triple circuit of the city, the university, and the town ringing a full peal.

The 6th of January, 1482, is not, however, a day of which history has preserved the memory. There was nothing notable in the event which thus set the bells and the bourgeois of Paris in a ferment from early morning. It was neither an assault by the Picards nor the Burgundians, nor a hunt led along in procession, nor a revolt of scholars in the town of Laas, nor an entry of "our much dread lord, monsieur the king," nor even a pretty hanging of male and female thieves by the courts of Paris. Neither was it the arrival, so frequent in the fifteenth century, of some plumed and bedizened embassy. It was barely two days since the last cavalcade of that nature, that of the Flemish ambassadors charged with concluding the marriage between the dauphin and Marguerite of Flanders, had made its entry into Paris, to the great annoyance of M. le Cardinal de Bourbon, who, for the sake of pleasing the king, had been obliged to assume an amiable mien toward this whole rustic rabble of Flemish burgomasters, and to regale them at his Hôtel de Bourbon, with a very "pretty morality, allegorical satire, and farce," while a driving rain drenched the magnificent tapestries at his door.

What put the "whole population of Paris in commotion," as Jehan de Troyes expresses it, on the 6th of January, was the double solemnity, united from time immemorial, of the Epiphany and the Feast of Fools.

On that day, there was to be a bonfire on the Place de Grève, a maypole at the Chapelle de Braque, and a mystery at the Palais de Justice. It had been cried, to the sound of the trumpet, the preceding evening at all the cross-roads, by the provost's men, clad in handsome, short, sleeveless coats of violet camelot, with large white crosses upon their breasts.

So the crowd of citizens, male and female, having closed their houses and shops, thronged from every direction, at early morn, toward some one of the three spots designated.

Each had made his choice; one, the bonfire; another, the maypole; another, the mystery play. It must be stated, in honor of the good sense of the loungers of Paris, that the greater part of this crowd directed their steps toward the bonfire, which was quite in season, or toward the mystery play, which was to be presented in the grand hall of the Palais de Justice (the courts of law), which was well roofed and walled; and that the curious left the poor, scantily flowered maypole to shiver all alone beneath the sky of January, in the cemetery of the Chapel of Braque.

The populace thronged the avenues of the law courts in particular, because they knew that the Flemish ambassadors, who had arrived two days previously, intended to be present at the representation of the mystery, and at the election of the Pope of the Fools, which was also to take place in the grand hall.

It was no easy matter on that day, to force one's way into that grand hall, although it was then reputed to be the largest covered enclosure in the world (it is true that Sauval had not yet measured the grand hall of the Château of Montargis). The palace place, encumbered with people, offered to the curious gazers at the windows the aspect of a sea; into which five or six streets, like so many mouths of rivers, discharged every moment fresh floods of heads. The waves of this crowd, augmented incessantly, dashed against the angles of the houses which projected here and there, like so many promontories, into the irregular basin of the place. In the center of the lofty Gothic façade of the palace, the grand staircase, incessantly ascended and descended by a double current, which, after parting on the intermediate landing-place, flowed in broad waves along its lateral slopes—the grand staircase, I say, trickled incessantly into the place, like a cascade into a lake. The cries, the laughter, the trampling of those thousands of feet, produced a great noise and a great clamor. From time to time, this noise and clamor redoubled; the current which drove the crowd toward the grand staircase flowed backwards, became troubled, formed whirlpools. This was produced by the buffet of an archer, or the horse of one of the provost's sergeants, which kicked to restore order; an admirable tradition which the provostship has bequeathed to the constablery, the constablery to the *maréchaussée*, the *maréchaussée* to our *gendarmeri* of Paris.

Thousands of good, calm, bourgeois faces thronged the windows, the doors, the dormer windows, the roofs, gazing at the palace, gazing at the populace, and asking nothing more; for many Parisians content themselves with the spectacle of the spectators, and a wall behind which something is going on becomes at once, for us, a very curious thing indeed.

If it could be granted to us, the men of 1830, to mingle in thought with those Parisians of the fifteenth century, and to enter with them, jostled, elbowed, pulled about, into that immense hall of the palace, which was so cramped on that 6th of January, 1482, the spectacle would not be devoid of either interest or charm, and we should have about us only things that were so old that they would seem new.

With the reader's consent, we will endeavor to retrace in thought, the impression which he would have experienced in company with us on crossing the threshold of that grand hall, in the midst of that tumultuous crowd in surcoats, short, sleeveless jackets, and doublets.

And, first of all, there is a buzzing in the ears, a dazzlement in the eyes. Above our heads is a double ogive vault, paneled with wood carving, painted azure, and sown with golden fleurs-de-lys; beneath our feet a pavement of black and white marble, alternating. A few paces distant, an enormous pillar, then another, then another; seven pillars in all, down the length of the hall, sustaining the spring of the arches of the double vault, in the center of its width. Around four of the pillars, stalls of merchants, all sparkling with glass and tinsel; around the last three, benches of oak, worn and polished by the trunk hose of the litigants, and the robes of the attorneys. Around the hall, along the lofty wall, between the doors, between the windows, between the pillars, the interminable row of all the kings of France, from Pharamond down: the lazy kings, with pendent arms and downcast eyes; the valiant and combative kings, with heads and arms raised boldly heavenward. Then in the long, pointed windows, glass of a thousand hues; at the wide entrances to the hall, rich doors, finely sculptured; and all, the vaults, pillars, walls, jambs, paneling, doors, statues, covered from top to bottom with a splendid blue and gold illumination, which, a trifle tarnished at the epoch when we behold it, had almost entirely disappeared beneath dust and spiders in the year of grace, 1549, when du Breul still admired it from tradition.

Let the reader picture to himself now, this immense, oblong hall, illuminated by the pallid light of a January day, invaded by a motley and noisy throng which drifts along the walls, and eddies round the seven pillars, and he will have a confused idea of the whole effect of the picture, whose curious details we shall make an effort to indicate with more precision.

It is certain, that if Ravaillac had not assassinated Henri IV, there would have been no documents in the trial of Ravaillac deposited in the clerk's office of the Palais de Justice, no accomplices interested in causing the said documents to disappear; hence, no incendiaries obliged, for lack of better means, to burn the clerk's office in order to burn the documents, and to burn the Palais de

Justice in order to burn the clerk's office; consequently, in short, no conflagration in 1618. The old Palais would be standing still, with its ancient grand hall; I should be able to say to the reader, "Go and look at it," and we should thus both escape the necessity—I of making, and he of reading, a description of it, such as it is. Which demonstrates a new truth: that great events have incalculable results.

It is true that it may be quite possible, in the first place, that Ravaillac had no accomplices; and in the second, that if he had any, they were in no way connected with the fire of 1618. Two other very plausible explanations exist: First, the great flaming star, a foot broad, and a cubit high, which fell from heaven, as everyone knows, upon the law courts, after midnight on the 7th of March; second, Théophile's quatrain—

> Sure, 'twas but a sorry game
> When at Paris, Dame Justice,
> Through having eaten too much spice,
> Set the palace all aflame.

Whatever may be thought of this triple explanation, political, physical, and poetical, of the burning of the law courts in 1618, the unfortunate fact of the fire is certain. Very little to-day remains, thanks to this catastrophe—thanks, above all, to the successive restorations which have completed what it spared—very little remains of that first dwelling of the kings of France—of that elder palace of the Louvre, already so old in the time of Philip the Handsome, that they sought there for the traces of the magnificent buildings erected by King Robert and described by Helgaldus. Nearly everything has disappeared. What has become of the chamber of the chancellery, where Saint Louis consummated his marriage? the garden where he administered justice, "clad in a coat of camelot, a surcoat of linsey-woolsey, without sleeves, and a sur-mantle of black sandal, as he lay upon the carpet with Joinville?" Where is the chamber of the Emperor Sigismond? and that of Charles IV? that of Jean the Landless? Where is the staircase, from which Charles VI promulgated his edict of pardon? the slab where Marcel cut the throats of Robert de Clermont and the Marshal of Champagne, in the presence of the dauphin? the wicket where the bulls of Pope Benedict were torn, and whence those who had brought them departed decked out, in derision, in copes and miters, and making an apology through all Paris? and the grand hall, with its gilding, its azure, its statues, its pointed arches, its pillars, its immense vault, all fretted with carvings? and the gilded chamber? and the stone lion, which stood at the door, with lowered head and tail between his legs, like the lions on the throne of Solomon, in the humiliated attitude which befits force in the presence of justice? and the beautiful doors? and the stained glass? and the chased ironwork, which drove Biscornette to despair? and the delicate woodwork of Hancy? What has time, what have men done with these marvels? What have they given us in return for all this Gallic history, for all this Gothic art? The heavy flattened arches of M. de Brosse, that awkward architect of the Saint-Gervais portal. So much for art; and, as for history, we have the gossiping reminiscences of the great pillar, still ringing with the tattle of the Patru.

It is not much. Let us return to the veritable grand hall of the veritable old palace. The two extremities of this gigantic parallelogram were occupied, the one by the famous marble table, so long, so broad, and so thick that, as the ancient land rolls—in a style that would have given Gargantua an appetite—say, "such a slice of marble as was never beheld in the world"; the other by the chapel where Louis XI had himself sculptured on his knees before the Virgin, and whither he caused to be brought, without heeding the two gaps thus made in the row of royal statues, the statues of Charlemagne and of Saint Louis, two saints whom he supposed to be great in favor in heaven, as kings of France. This chapel, quite new, having been built only six years, was entirely in that charming taste of delicate architecture, of marvelous sculpture, of fine and deep chasing, which marks with us the end of the Gothic era, and which is perpetuated to about the middle of the sixteenth century in the fairylike fancies of the Renaissance. The little open-work rose window, pierced above the portal, was, in particular, a masterpiece of lightness and grace; one would have pronounced it a star of lace.

In the middle of the hall, opposite the great door, a platform of gold brocade, placed against the wall, a special entrance to which had been effected through a window in the corridor of the gold chamber, had been erected for the Flemish emissaries and the other great personages invited to the presentation of the mystery play.

It was upon the marble table that the mystery was to be enacted, as usual. It had been arranged for the purpose, early in the morning; its rich slabs of marble, all scratched by the heels of law clerks, supported a cage of carpenter's work of considerable height, the upper surface of which, within view of the whole hall, was to serve as the theater, and whose interior, masked by tapestries, was to take the place of dressing-rooms for the personages of the piece. A ladder, naïvely placed on the outside, was to serve as means of communication between the dressing-room and the stage, and lend its rude rungs to entrances as well as to exits. There was no personage, however unexpected, no sudden change, no theatrical effect, which was not obliged to mount that ladder. Innocent and venerable infancy of art and contrivances!

Four of the bailiff of the palace's sergeants, perfunctory guardians of all the pleasures of the people, on days of festival as well as on days of execution, stood at the four corners of the marble table.

The piece was only to begin with the twelfth stroke of the great palace clock sounding midday. It was very late, no doubt, for a theatrical representation, but they had been obliged to fix the hour to suit the convenience of the ambassadors.

Now, this whole multitude had been waiting since morning. A goodly number of curious, good people had been shivering since daybreak before the grand staircase of the palace; some even affirmed that they had passed the night across the threshold of the great door, in order to make sure that they should be the first to pass in. The crowd grew more dense every moment, and, like water, which rises above its normal level, began to mount along the walls, to swell around the pillars, to spread out on the entablatures, on the cornices, on the window-sills, on all the salient points of the architecture, on all the reliefs of the sculpture. Hence, discomfort, impatience, weariness, the liberty of a day of cynicism and folly, the quarrels which break forth for all sorts of causes—a pointed elbow, an iron-shod shoe, the fatigue of long waiting—had already, long before the hour appointed for the arrival of the ambassadors, imparted a harsh and bitter accent to the clamor of these people who were shut in, fitted into each other, pressed, trampled upon, stifled. Nothing was to be heard but imprecations on the Flemish, the provost of the merchants, the Cardinal de Bourbon, the bailiff of the courts, Madame Marguerite of Austria, the sergeants with their rods, the cold, the heat, the bad weather, the Bishop of Paris, the Pope of the Fools, the pillars, the statues, that closed door, that open window; all to the vast amusement of a band of scholars and lackeys scattered through the mass, who mingled with all this discontent their teasing remarks, and their malicious suggestions, and pricked the general bad temper with a pin, so to speak.

Among the rest there was a group of those merry imps, who, after smashing the glass in a window, had seated themselves hardily on the entablature, and from that point dispatched their gaze and their railleries both within and without, upon the throng in the hall, and the throng upon the Place. It was easy to see, from their parodied gestures, their ringing laughter, the bantering appeals which they exchanged with their comrades, from one end of the hall to the other, that these young clerks did not share the weariness and fatigue of the rest of the spectators, and that they understood very well the art of extracting, for their own private diversion, from that which they had under their eyes, a spectacle which made them await the other with patience.

"Upon my soul, so it's you, 'Joannes Frollo de Molendino!' " cried one of them, to a sort of little, light-haired imp, with a well-favored and malign countenance, clinging to the acanthus leaves of a capital; "you are well named John of the Mill, for your two arms and your two legs have the air of four wings fluttering on the breeze. How long have you been here?"

"By the mercy of the devil," retorted Joannes Frollo, "these four hours and more; and I hope that they will be reckoned to my credit in purgatory. I heard the eight singers of the King of Sicily intone the first verse of seven o'clock mass in the Sainte-Chapelle."

"Fine singers!" replied the other, "with voices even more pointed than their caps! Before founding a mass for Monsieur Saint John, the king should have inquired whether Monsieur Saint John likes Latin droned out in a Provençal accent."

"He did it for the sake of employing those accursed singers of the King of Sicily!" cried an old woman sharply from among the crowd beneath the window. "I just put it to you! A thousand *livres parisi* for a mass! and out of the tax on sea fish in the markets of Paris, to boot!"

"Peace, old crone," said a tall, grave person, stopping up his nose on the side toward the fish-wife; "a mass had to be founded. Would you wish the king to fall ill again?"

"Bravely spoken, Sire Gilles Lecornu, master furrier of king's robes!" cried the little student, clinging to the capital.

A shout of laughter from all the students greeted the unlucky name of the poor furrier of the king's robes.

"Lecornu! Gilles Lecornu!" said some.

"*Cornutus et hirsutus*, horned and hairy," another went on.

"He! of course," continued the small imp on the capital, "What are they laughing at? An honorable man is Gilles Lecornu, brother of Master Jehan Lecornu, provost of the king's house, son of Master Mahiet Lecornu, first porter of the Bois de Vincennes—all bourgeois of Paris, all married, from father to son."

The gaiety redoubled. The big furrier, without uttering a word in reply, tried to escape all the eyes riveted upon him from all sides; but he perspired and panted in vain; like a wedge entering the wood, his efforts served only to bury still more deeply in the shoulders of his neighbors, his large, apoplectic face, purple with spite and rage.

At length one of these, as fat, short, and venerable as himself, came to his rescue.

"Abomination! scholars addressing a bourgeois in that fashion in my day would have been flogged with a fagot, which would have afterwards been used to burn them."

The whole band burst into laughter.

"Holà hé! who is scolding so? Who is that screech owl of evil fortune?"

"Hold, I know him" said one of them; " 'tis Master Andry Musnier."

"Because he is one of the four sworn booksellers of the university!" said the other.

"Everything goes by fours in that shop," cried a third; "the four nations, the four faculties, the four feasts, the four procurators, the four electors, the four booksellers."

"Well," began Jean Frollo once more, "we must play the devil with them."

"Musnier, we'll burn your books."

"Musnier, we'll beat your lackeys."

"Musnier, we'll kiss your wife."

"That fine, big Mademoiselle Oudarde."

"Who is as fresh and as gay as though she were a widow."

"Devil take you!" growled Master Andry Musnier.

"Master Andry," pursued Jean Jehan, still clinging to his capital, "hold your tongue, or I'll drop on your head!"

Master Andry raised his eyes, seemed to measure in an instant the height of the pillar, the weight of the scamp, mentally multiplied that weight by the square of the velocity, and remained silent.

Jehan, master of the field of battle, pursued triumphantly:

"That's what I'll do, even if I am the brother of an archdeacon!"

"Fine gentry are our people of the university, not to have caused our privileges to be respected on such a day as this! However, there is a maypole and a bonfire in the town; a mystery, Pope of the Fools, and Flemish ambassadors in the city; and, at the university, nothing!"

"Nevertheless, the Place Maubert is sufficiently large!" interposed one of the clerks established on the window-sill.

"Down with the rector, the electors, and the procurators!" cried Joannes.

"We must have a bonfire this evening in the Champ-Gaillard," went on the other, "made of Master Andry's books."

"And the desks of the scribes!" added his neighbor.

"And the beadles' wands!"

"And the spittoons of the deans!"

"And the cupboards of the procurators!"

"And the hutches of the electors!"

"And the stools of the rector!"

"Down with them!" put in little Jehan, as counterpoint; "down with Master Andry, the beadles and the scribes; the theologians, the doctors and the decretists; the procurators, the electors and the rector!"

"The end of the world has come!' muttered Master Andry, stopping up his ears.

"By the way, there's the rector! see, he is passing through the Place," cried one of those in the window.

Each rivaled his neighbor in his haste to turn toward the Place.

"Is it really our venerable rector, Master Thibaut?" demanded Jehan Frollo du Moulin, who, as he was clinging to one of the inner pillars, could not see what was going on outside.

"Yes, yes," replied all the others, "it is really he, Master Thibaut, the rector."

It was, in fact, the rector and all the dignitaries of the university, who were marching in procession in front of the embassy, and at that moment traversing the Place. The students crowded into the window, saluted them as they passed with sarcasms and ironical applause. The rector, who was walking at the head of his company, had to support the first broadside; it was severe.

"Good day, monsieur le recteur! Holà hé! good day there!"

"How does he manage to be here, the old gambler? Has he abandoned his dice?"

"How he trots along on his mule! her ears are not so long as his!"

"Holà hé! good day, monsieur le recteur Thibaut! *Tybalde aleator!* Old fool! old gambler!"

"God preserve you! Did you throw double six often last night?"

"Oh! what a decrepit face, livid and haggard and drawn with the love of gambling and of dice!"

"Where are you bound for in that fashion, Thibaut, *Tybalde ad dados,* with your back turned to the university, and trotting toward the town?"

"He is on his way, no doubt, to seek a lodging in the Rue Thibautodé?"[1] cried Jehan du M. Moulin.

The entire band repeated this quip in a voice of thunder, clapping their hands furiously.

"You are going to seek a lodging in the Rue Thibautodé, are you not, monsieur le recteur, gamester on the side of the devil?"

Then came the turns of the other dignitaries.

"Down with the beadles! down with the mace-bearers!"

"Tell me, Robin Poussepain, who is that yonder?"

"He is Gilbert de Suilly, *Gilbertus de Soliaco,* the chancellor of the College of Autun."

"Hold on, here's my shoe; you are better placed than I, fling it in his face."

---

1. *Thibaut au des*—Thibaut of the dice.

"Saturnalitias mittimus ecce nuces."

"Down with the six theologians, with their white surplices!"

"Are those the theologians? I thought they were the white geese given by Sainte-Geneviève to the city, for the fief of Roogny."

"Down with the doctors!"

"Down with the cardinal disputations, and quibblers!"

"My cap to you, Chancellor of Sainte-Geneviève! You have done me a wrong. 'Tis true; he gave my place in the nation of Normandy to little Ascanio Falzapada, who comes from the province of Bourges, since he is an Italian."

"That is an injustice," said all the scholars. "Down with the Chancellor of Sainte-Geneviève!"

"Ho hé! Master Joachim de Ladehors! Ho hé! Louis Dahuille! Ho hé Lambert Hoctement!"

"May the devil stifle the procurator of the German nation!"

"And the chaplains of the Sainte-Chapelle, with their gray *amices; cum tunices grisis!*"

"Seu de pellibus grisis fourratis!"

"Holà hé! Masters of Arts! All the beautiful black copes! all the fine red copes!"

"They make a fine tail for the rector."

"One would say that he was a Doge of Venice on his way to his bridal with the sea."

"Say, Jehan! here are the canons of Sainte-Geneviève!"

"To the deuce with the whole set of canons!"

"Abbé Claude Choart! Doctor Claude Choart! Are you in search of Marie la Giffarde?"

"She is in the Rue de Glatigny."

"She is making the bed of the king of the debauchees."

"She is paying her four deniers *quatuor denarios.*"

"Aut unum bombum."

"Would you like to have her pay you in the face?"

"Comrades! Master Simon Sanguin, the Elector of Picardy, with his wife on the crupper!"

"Post equitem sedet atra cura—behind the horseman sits black care."

"Courage, Master Simon!"

"Good day, Mister Elector!"

"Good night, Madame Electress!"

"How happy they are to see all that!" sighed Joannes de Molendino, still perched in the foliage of his capital.

Meanwhile, the sworn bookseller of the university, Master Andry Musnier, was inclining his ear to the furrier of the king's robes, Master Gilles Lecornu.

"I tell you, sir, that the end of the world has come. No one has ever beheld such outbreaks among the students! It is the accursed inventions of this century that are ruining everything—artilleries, bombards, and, above all, printing, that other German pest. No more manuscripts, no more books! printing will kill bookselling. It is the end of the world that is drawing nigh."

"I see that plainly, from the progress of velvet stuffs," said the fur-merchant.

At this moment, midday sounded.

"Ha!" exclaimed the entire crowd, in one voice.

The scholars held their peace. Then a great hurly-burly ensued; a vast movement of feet, hands, and heads; a general outbreak of coughs and handkerchiefs; each one arranged himself, assumed his post, raised himself up, and grouped himself. Then came a great silence; all necks remained outstretched, all mouths remained open, all glances were directed toward the marble table. Nothing made its appearance there. The bailiff's four sergeants were still there, stiff, motionless, as painted statues. All eyes turned to the estrade reserved for the Flemish envoys. The door remained closed, the platform empty. This crowd had been waiting since daybreak for three things: noonday, the embassy from Flanders, the mystery play. Noonday alone had arrived on time.

On this occasion, it was too much.

They waited one, two, three, five minutes, a quarter of an hour; nothing came. The dais remained empty, the theater dumb. In the meantime, wrath had succeeded to impatience. Irritated words circulated in a low tone, still, it is true. "The mystery! the mystery!" they murmured, in hollow voices. Heads began to ferment. A tempest, which was only rumbling in the distance as yet, was floating on the surface of this crowd. It was Jehan du Moulin who struck the first spark from it.

"The mystery, and to the devil with the Flemings!" he exclaimed at the full force of his lungs, twining like a serpent around his pillar.

The crowd clapped their hands.

"The mystery!" it repeated, "and may all the devils take Flanders!"

"We must have the mystery instantly," resumed the student; "or else, my advice is that we should hang the bailiff of the courts, by way of a morality and a comedy."

"Well said," cried the people, "and let us begin the hanging with his sergeants."

A grand acclamation followed. The four poor fellows began to turn pale, and to exchange glances. The crowd hurled itself toward them, and they already beheld the frail wooden railing, which separated them from it, giving way and bending before the pressure of the throng.

It was a critical moment.

"To the sack, to the sack!" rose the cry on all sides.

At that moment, the tapestry of the dressing-room, which we have described above, was raised, and afforded passage to a personage, the mere sight of whom suddenly stopped the crowd, and changed its wrath into curiosity as by enchantment.

"Silence! silence!"

The personage, but little reassured, and trembling in every limb, advanced to the edge of the marble table with a vast amount of bows, which, in proportion as he drew nearer, more and more resembled genuflections.

In the meanwhile, tranquility had gradually been restored. All that remained was that slight murmur which always rises above the silence of a crowd.

"Messieurs the bourgeois," said he, "and mesdemoiselles the bourgeoises, we shall have the honor of declaiming and representing, before his eminence, monsieur the cardinal, a very beautiful morality which has for its title, *The Good Judgment of Madame the Virgin Mary*. I am to play Jupiter. His eminence is, at this moment, escorting the very honorable embassy of the Duke of Austria; which is detained, at present, listening to the harangue of monsieur the rector of the university, at the gate Baudets. As soon as his illustrious eminence, the cardinal, arrives, we will begin."

It is certain, that nothing less than the intervention of Jupiter was required to save the four unfortunate sergeants of the bailiff of the courts. If we had the happiness of having invented this very veracious tale, and of being, in consequence, responsible for it before our Lady Criticism, it is not against us that the classic precept, *Nec deus intersit*, could be invoked. Moreover, the costume of Seigneur Jupiter, was very handsome, and contributed not a little toward calming the crowd, by attracting all its attention. Jupiter was clad in a coat of mail, covered with black velvet, with gilt nails; and had it not been for the rouge, and the huge red beard, each of which covered one-half of his face—had it not been for the roll of gilded cardboard, spangled, and all bristling with strips of tinsel, which he held in his hand, and in which the eyes of the initiated easily recognized thunderbolts—had not his feet been flesh-colored, and banded with ribbons in Greek fashion, he might have borne comparison, so far as the severity of his mien was concerned, with a Breton archer from the guard of Monsieur de Berry.

Chapter II

PIERRE GRINGOIRE

N EVERTHELESS, AS HE HARANGUED THEM, THE SATISFACTION AND ADMIRATION UNANIMOUSLY excited by his costume were dissipated by his words; and when he reached that untoward conclusion: "As soon as his illustrious eminence, the cardinal, arrives, we will begin," his voice was drowned in a thunder of hooting.

"Begin instantly! The mystery! the mystery immediately!" shrieked the people. And above all the voices, that of Johannes de Molendino was audible, piercing the uproar like the fife's derisive serenade: "Commence instantly!" yelped the scholar.

"Down with Jupiter and the Cardinal de Bourbon!" vociferated Robin Poussepain and the other clerks perched in the window.

"The morality this very instant!" repeated the crowd; "this very instant! the sack and the rope for the comedians, and the cardinal!"

Poor Jupiter, haggard, frightened, pale beneath his rouge, dropped his thunderbolt, took his cap in his hand; then he bowed and trembled and stammered: "His eminence—the ambassadors— Madame Marguerite of Flanders—." He did not know what to say. In truth, he was afraid of being hung.

Hung by the populace for waiting, hung by the cardinal for not having waited, he saw between the two dilemmas only an abyss; that is to say, a gallows.

Luckily, someone came to rescue him from his embarrassment, and assume the responsibility.

An individual who was standing beyond the railing, in the free space around the marble table, and whom no one had yet caught sight of, since his long, thin body was completely sheltered from every visual ray by the diameter of the pillar against which he was leaning; this individual, we say, tall, gaunt, pallid, blond, still young, although already wrinkled about the brow and cheeks, with brilliant eyes and a smiling mouth, clad in garments of black serge, worn and shining with age, approached the marble table, and made a sign to the poor sufferer. But the other was so confused that he did not see him. The newcomer advanced another step.

"Jupiter," said he, "my dear Jupiter!"

The other did not hear.

At last, the tall blond, driven out of patience, shrieked almost in his face—

"Michel Giborne!"

"Who calls me?" said Jupiter, as though awakened with a start.

"I," replied the person clad in black.

"Ah!" said Jupiter.

"Begin at once," went on the other. "Satisfy the populace; I undertake to appease the bailiff, who will appease monsieur the cardinal."

Jupiter breathed once more.

"Messeigneurs the bourgeois," he cried, at the top of his lungs to the crowd, which continued to hoot him, "we are going to begin at once."

"*Evoe Jupiter! Plaudite cives!* All hail, Jupiter! Applaud, citizens!" shouted the scholars.

"Noël! Noël! good, good," shouted the people.

The hand clapping was deafening, and Jupiter had already withdrawn under his tapestry, while the hall still trembled with acclamations.

In the meanwhile, the personage who had so magically turned the tempest into dead calm, as our old and dear Corneille puts it, had modestly retreated to the half-shadow of his pillar, and would, no doubt, have remained invisible there, motionless, and mute as before, had he not been plucked by the sleeve by two young women, who, standing in the front row of the spectators, had noticed his colloquy with Michel Giborne-Jupiter.

"Master," said one of them, making him a sign to approach.

"Hold your tongue, my dear Liénarde," said her neighbor, pretty, fresh, and very brave, in consequence of being dressed up in her best attire. "He is not a clerk, he is a layman; you must not say master to him, but messire."

"Messire," said Liénarde.

The stranger approached the railing.

"What would you have of me, damsels?" he asked, with alacrity.

"Oh! nothing," replied Liénarde, in great confusion; "it is my neighbor, Gisquette la Gencienne, who wishes to speak with you."

"Not so," replied Gisquette, blushing; "it was Liénarde who called you master; I only told her to say messire."

The two young girls dropped their eyes. The man, who asked nothing better than to enter into conversation, looked at them with a smile.

"So you have nothing to say to me, damsels?"

"Oh! nothing at all," replied Gisquette.

"Nothing," said Liénarde.

The tall, light-haired young man retreated a step; but the two curious maidens had no mind to let slip their prize.

"Messire," said Gisquette, with the impetuosity of an open sluice, or of a woman who has made up her mind, "do you know that soldier who is to play the part of Madame the Virgin in the mystery?"

"You mean the part of Jupiter?" replied the stranger.

"Hé! yes," said Liénarde, "isn't she stupid? So you know Jupiter?"

"Michel Giborne?" replied the unknown; "yes, madam."

"He has a fine beard!" said Liénarde.

"Will what they are about to say here be fine?" inquired Gisquette, timidly.

"Very fine, mademoiselle," replied the unknown, without the slightest hesitation.

"What is it to be?" said Liénarde.

"*The Good Judgment of Madame the Virgin*—a morality, if you please, damsel."

"Ah! that makes a difference," responded Liénarde.

A brief silence ensued—broken by the stranger.

"It is a perfectly new morality, and one which has never yet been played."

"Then it is not the same one," said Gisquette, "that was given two years ago, on the day of the entrance of monsieur the legate, and where three handsome maids played the parts—"

"Of sirens," said Liénarde.

"And all naked," added the young man.

Liénarde lowered her eyes modestly. Gisquette glanced at her and did the same. He continued, with a smile—

"It was a very pleasant thing to see. To-day it is a morality made expressly for Madame the Demoiselle of Flanders."

"Will they sing shepherd songs?" inquired Gisquette.

"Fie!" said the stranger, "in a morality? you must not confound styles. If it were a farce, well and good."

"That is a pity," resumed Gisquette. "That day, at the Ponceau Fountain, there were wild men and women, who fought and assumed many aspects, as they sang little motets and bergerettes."

"That which is suitable for a legate," returned the stranger, with a good deal of dryness, "is not suitable for a princess."

"And beside them," resumed Liénarde, "played many brass instruments, making great melodies."

"And for the refreshment of the passers-by," continued Gisquette, "the fountain spouted through three mouths, wine, milk, and hippocrass, of which everyone drank who wished."

"And a little below the Ponceau, at the Trinity," pursued Liénarde, "there was a passion performed, and without any speaking."

"How well I remember that!" exclaimed Gisquette; "God on the cross, and the two thieves on the right and the left."

Here the young gossips, growing warm at the memory of the entrance of monsieur the legate, both began to talk at once.

"And, further on, at the Painters' Gate, there were other personages, very richly clad."

"And at the fountain of Saint-Innocent, that huntsman, who was chasing a hind with great clamor of dogs and hunting-horns."

"And at the Paris slaughter-houses, stages, representing the fortress of Dieppe!"

"And when the legate passed, you remember, Gisquette? they made the assault, and the English all had their throats cut."

"And against the gate of the Châtelet, there were very fine personages!"

"And on the Port au Change, which was all draped above!"

"And when the legate passed, they let fly on the bridge more than two hundred sorts of birds; wasn't it beautiful, Liénarde?"

"It will be better to-day," finally resumed their interlocutor, who seemed to listen to them with impatience.

"Do you promise us that this mystery will be fine?" said Gisquette.

"Without doubt," he replied; then he added, with a certain emphasis—"I am the author of it, damsels."

"Truly?" said the young girls, quite taken aback.

"Truly!" replied the poet, bridling a little; "that is, to say, there are two of us; Jehan Marchand, who has sawed the planks and erected the framework of the theater and the woodwork; and I, who have made the piece. My name is Pierre Gringoire."

The author of the *Cid* could not have said "Pierre Corneille" with more pride.

Our readers have been able to observe, that a certain amount of time must have already elapsed from the moment when Jupiter had retired beneath the tapestry to the instant when the author of the new morality had thus abruptly revealed himself to the innocent admiration of Gisquette and Liénarde. Remarkable fact: that whole crowd, so tumultuous but a few moments before, now waited amiably on the word of the comedian; which proves the eternal truth, still experienced every day in our theaters, that the best means of making the public wait patiently is to assure them that one is about to begin instantly.

However, scholar Johannes had not fallen asleep.

"Holà hé!" he shouted suddenly, in the midst of the peaceable waiting which had followed the tumult. "Jupiter, Madame the Virgin, buffoons of the devil! are you jeering at us? The piece! the piece! commence or we will commence again!"

This was all that was needed.

The music of high and low instruments immediately became audible from the interior of the stage; the tapestry was raised; four personages, in motley attire and painted faces, emerged from it, climbed the steep ladder of the theater, and, arrived upon the upper platform, arranged themselves in a line before the public, whom they saluted with profound reverences; then the symphony ceased.

The mystery was about to begin.

The four personages, after having reaped a rich reward of applause for their reverences, began, in the midst of profound silence, a prologue, which we gladly spare the reader. Moreover, as happens in our own day, the public was more occupied with the costumes that the actors wore than with the rôles that they were enacting; and, in truth, they were right. All four were dressed in parti-colored robes of yellow and white, which were distinguished from each other only by the nature of the stuff; the first was of gold and silver brocade; the second, of silk; the third, of wool; the fourth, of linen. The first of these personages carried in his right hand a sword; the second, two golden keys; the third, a pair of scales; the fourth, a spade: and, in order to aid sluggish minds which would not have seen clearly through the transparency of these attributes, there was to be read, in large, black letters, on the hem of the robe of brocade, MY NAME IS NOBILITY; on the hem of the silken robe, MY NAME IS CLERGY; on the hem of the woolen robe, MY NAME IS MERCHANDISE; on the hem of the linen robe, MY NAME IS LABOR. The sex of the two male characters was briefly indicated to every judicious spectator, by their shorter robes, and by the cap which they wore on their heads; while the two female characters, less briefly clad, were covered with hoods.

Much ill-will would also have been required, not to comprehend, through the medium of the poetry of the prologue, that Labor was wedded to Merchandise, and Clergy to Nobility, and that the two happy couples possessed in common a magnificent golden dolphin, which they desired to adjudge to the fairest only. So they were roaming about the world seeking and searching for this beauty, and, after having successively rejected the Queen of Golconda, the Princess of Trebizonde, the daughter of the Grand Khan of Tartary, etc., Labor and Clergy, Nobility and Merchandise, had come to rest upon the marble table of the Palais de Justice, and to utter, in the presence of the honest audience, as many sentences and maxims as could then be dispensed at the Faculty of Arts, at examinations, sophisms, determinances, figures, and acts, where the masters took their degrees.

All this was, in fact, very fine.

Nevertheless, in that throng, upon which the four allegories vied with each other in pouring out floods of metaphors, there was no ear more attentive, no heart that palpitated more, not an eye was more haggard, no neck more outstretched, than the eye, the ear, the neck, and the heart of the author, of the poet, of that brave Pierre Gringoire, who had not been able to resist, a moment before, the joy of telling his name to two pretty girls. He had retreated a few paces from them, behind his pillar, and there he listened, looked, enjoyed. The amiable applause which had greeted the beginning of his prologue was still echoing in his bosom, and he was completely absorbed in that species of ecstatic contemplation with which an author beholds his ideas fall, one by one, from the mouth of the actor into the vast silence of the audience. Worthy Pierre Gringoire!

It pains us to say it, but this first ecstasy was speedily disturbed. Hardly had Gringoire raised this intoxicating cup of joy and triumph to his lips, when a drop of bitterness was mingled with it.

A tattered mendicant, who could not collect any coins, lost as he was in the midst of the crowd, and who had not probably found sufficient indemnity in the pockets of his neighbors, had hit upon the idea of perching himself upon some conspicuous point, in order to attract looks and alms. He had, accordingly, hoisted himself, during the first verses of the prologue, with the aid of the pillars of the reserve gallery, to the cornice which ran round the balustrade at its lower edge; and there he had seated himself, soliciting the attention and the pity of the multitude, with his rags and a hideous sore which covered his right arm. However, he uttered not a word.

The silence which he preserved allowed the prologue to proceed without hindrance, and no perceptible disorder would have ensued, if ill-luck had not willed that the scholar Joannes should catch sight, from the heights of his pillar, of the mendicant and his grimaces. A wild fit of laughter took possession of the young scamp, who, without caring that he was interrupting the spectacle, and disturbing the universal composure, shouted boldly—

"Look! see that sickly creature asking alms!"

Anyone who has thrown a stone into a frog pond, or fired a shot into a covey of birds, can

form an idea of the effect produced by these incongruous words, in the midst of the general attention. It made Gringoire shudder as though it had been an electric shock. The prologue stopped
short, and all heads turned tumultuously toward the beggar, who, far from being disconcerted by
this, saw, in this incident, a good opportunity for reaping his harvest, and who began to whine in a
doleful way, half closing his eyes the while—"Charity, please!"

"Well—upon my soul," resumed Joannes, "it's Clopin Trouillefou! Holà hé, my friend, did
your sore bother you on the leg, that you have transferred it to your arm?"

So saying, with the dexterity of a monkey, he flung a bit of silver into the gray felt hat which
the beggar held in his ailing arm. The mendicant received both the alms and the sarcasm without
wincing, and continued, in lamentable tones—"Charity, please!"

This episode considerably distracted the attention of the audience; and a goodly number of
spectators, among them Robin Poussepain, and all the clerks at their head, gaily applauded this eccentric duet, which the scholar, with his shrill voice, and the mendicant had just improvised in the
middle of the prologue.

Gringoire was highly displeased. On recovering from his first stupefaction, he bestirred himself to shout, to the four personages on the stage, "Go on! What the devil!—go on!"—without even
deigning to cast a glance of disdain upon the two interrupters.

At that moment, he felt someone pluck at the hem of his surtout; he turned round, and not
without ill-humor, and found considerable difficulty in smiling; but he was obliged to do so, nevertheless. It was the pretty arm of Gisquette la Gencienne, which, passed through the railing, was soliciting his attention in this manner.

"Monsieur," said the young girl, "are they going to continue?"

"Of course," replied Gringoire, a good deal shocked by the question.

"In that case, messire," she resumed, "would you have the courtesy to explain to me—"

"What they are about to say?" interrupted Gringoire. "Well, listen."

"No," said Gisquette, "but what they have said so far."

Gringoire started, like a man whose wound has been probed to the quick.

"A plague on the stupid and dull-witted little girl!" he muttered, between his teeth.

From that moment forth, Gisquette was nothing to him.

In the meantime, the actors had obeyed his injunction, and the public, seeing that they were
beginning to speak again, began once more to listen, not without having lost many beauties in the
sort of soldered joint which was formed between the two portions of the piece thus abruptly cut
short. Gringoire commented on it bitterly to himself. Nevertheless, tranquility was gradually restored, the scholar held his peace, the mendicant counted over some coins in his hat, and the piece
resumed the upper hand.

It was, in fact, a very fine work, and one which, as it seems to us, might be put to use to-day,
by the aid of a little rearrangement. The exposition, rather long and rather empty, that is to say, according to the rules, was simple; and Gringoire, in the candid sanctuary of his own conscience, admired its clearness. As the reader may surmise, the four allegorical personages were somewhat
weary with having traversed the three sections of the world, without having found suitable opportunity for getting rid of their golden dolphin. Thereupon a eulogy of the marvelous fish, with a
thousand delicate allusions to the young betrothed of Marguerite of Flanders, then sadly cloistered
in at Amboise, and without a suspicion that Labor and Clergy, Nobility and Merchandise had just
made the circuit of the world in his behalf. The said dauphin was then young, was handsome, was
stout, and, above all (magnificent origin of all royal virtues), he was the son of the Lion of France.
I declare that this bold metaphor is admirable, and that the natural history of the theater, on a day
of allegory and royal marriage songs, is not in the least startled by a dolphin who is the son of a
lion. It is precisely these rare and Pindaric mixtures which prove the poet's enthusiasm. Nevertheless, in order to play the part of critic also, the poet might have developed this beautiful idea in

something less than two hundred lines. It is true that the mystery was to last from noon until four o'clock, in accordance with the orders of monsieur the provost, and that it was necessary to say something. Besides, the people listened patiently.

All at once, in the very middle of a quarrel between Mademoiselle Merchandise and Madame Nobility, at the moment when Monsieur Labor was giving utterance to this wonderful line—

In forest ne'er was seen a more triumphant beast;

the door of the reserved gallery which had hitherto remained so inopportunely closed, opened still more inopportunely; and the ringing voice of the usher announced abruptly, "His eminence, Monseigneur the Cardinal de Bourbon."

Chapter III

MONSIEUR THE CARDINAL

POOR GRINGOIRE! THE DIN OF ALL THE GREAT DOUBLE PETARDS OF THE SAINT-JEAN, THE DIScharge of twenty arquebuses on supports, the detonation of that famous serpentine of the Tower of Billy, which, during the siege of Paris, on Sunday, the 26th of September, 1465, killed seven Burgundians at one blow, the explosion of all the powder stored at the gate of the Temple, would have rent his ears less rudely at that solemn and dramatic moment, than these few words, which fell from the lips of the usher, "His eminence, Monseigneur the Cardinal de Bourbon."

It is not that Pierre Gringoire either feared or disdained monsieur the cardinal. He had neither the weakness nor the audacity for that. A true eclectic, as it would be expressed nowadays, Gringoire was one of those firm and lofty, moderate and calm spirits, which always know how to bear themselves amid all circumstances (*stare in dimidio rerum*), and who are full of reason and of liberal philosophy, while still setting store by cardinals. A rare, precious, and never interrupted race of philosophers to whom wisdom, like another Ariadne, seems to have given a clew of thread which they have been walking along unwinding since the beginning of the world, through the labyrinth of human affairs. One finds them in all ages, ever the same; that is to say, always according to all times. And, without reckoning our Pierre Gringoire, who may represent them in the fifteenth century if we succeed in bestowing upon him the distinction which he deserves, it certainly was their spirit which animated Father du Breul, when he wrote, in the sixteenth, these naïvely sublime words, worthy of all centuries: "I am a Parisian by nation, and a Parrhisian in language, for *parrhisia* in Greek signifies liberty of speech; of which I have made use even toward messeigneurs the cardinals, uncle and brother to Monsieur the Prince de Conty, always with respect to their greatness, and without offending any one of their suite, which is much to say."

There was then neither hatred for the cardinal, nor disdain for his presence, in the disagreeable impression produced upon Pierre Gringoire. Quite the contrary; our poet had too much good sense and too threadbare a coat, not to attach particular importance to having the numerous allusions in his prologue, and, in particular, the glorification of the dauphin, son of the Lion of France, fall upon the most eminent ear. But it is not interest which predominates in the noble nature of poets. I suppose that the entity of the poet may be represented by the number ten; it is certain that a chemist on analyzing and pharmacopolizing it, as Rabelais says, would find it composed of one part interest to nine parts of self-esteem.

Now, at the moment when the door had opened to admit the cardinal, the nine parts of self-esteem in Gringoire, swollen and expanded by the breath of popular admiration, were in a state of prodigious augmentation, beneath which disappeared, as though stifled, that imperceptible molecule of which we have just remarked upon in the constitution of poets; a precious ingredient, by the way, a ballast of reality and humanity, without which they would not touch the earth. Gringoire enjoyed seeing, feeling, fingering, so to speak an entire assembly (of knaves, it is true, but what matters that?) stupefied, petrified, and as though asphyxiated in the presence of the incommensurable tirades which welled up every instant from all parts of his bridal song. I affirm that he shared the general beatitude, and that, quite the reverse of La Fontaine, who, at the presentation of his comedy of the *Florentine*, asked, "Who is the ill-bred lout who made that rhapsody?" Gringoire would gladly have inquired of his neighbor, "Whose masterpiece is this?"

The reader can now judge of the effect produced upon him by the abrupt and unseasonable arrival of the cardinal.

That which he had to fear was only too fully realized. The entrance of his eminence upset the audience. All heads turned toward the gallery. It was no longer possible to hear one's self. "The cardinal! The cardinal!" repeated all mouths. The unhappy prologue stopped short for the second time.

The cardinal halted for a moment on the threshold of the estrade. While he was sending a rather indifferent glance around the audience, the tumult redoubled. Each person wished to get a better view of him. Each man vied with the other in thrusting his head over his neighbor's shoulder.

He was, in fact, an exalted personage, the sight of whom was well worth any other comedy. Charles, Cardinal de Bourbon, Archbishop and Comte of Lyon, Primate of the Gauls, was allied both to Louis XI, through his brother, Pierre, Seigneur de Beaujeu, who had married the king's eldest daughter, and to Charles the Bold through his mother, Agnes of Burgundy. Now, the dominating trait, the peculiar and distinctive trait of the character of the Primate of the Gauls, was the spirit of the courtier, and devotion to the powers that be. The reader can form an idea of the numberless embarrassments which this double relationship had caused him, and of all the temporal reefs among which his spiritual bark had been forced to tack, in order not to suffer shipwreck on either Louis or Charles, that Scylla and that Charybdis which had devoured the Duc de Nemours and the Constable de Saint-Pol. Thanks to Heaven's mercy, he had made the voyage successfully, and had reached home without hindrance. But although he was in port, and precisely because he was in port, he never recalled without disquiet the varied haps of his political career, so long uneasy and laborious. Thus, he was in the habit of saying that the year 1476 had been "white and black" for him— meaning thereby, that in the course of that year he had lost his mother, the Duchesse de la Bourbonnais, and his cousin, the Duke of Burgundy, and that one grief had consoled him for the other.

Nevertheless, he was a fine man; he led a joyous cardinal's life, liked to enliven himself with the royal vintage of Challuau, did not hate Richarde la Garmoise and Thomasse la Saillarde, bestowed alms on pretty girls rather than on old women—and for all these reasons was very agreeable to the *populace* of Paris. He never went about otherwise than surrounded by a small court of bishops and abbés of high lineage, gallant, jovial, and given to carousing on occasion; and more than once the good and devout women of Saint Germain d'Auxerre, when passing at night beneath the brightly illuminated windows of Bourbon, had been scandalized to hear the same voices which had intoned vespers for them during the day caroling, to the clinking of glasses, the bacchic proverb of Benedict XII, that pope who had added a third crown to the tiara—*Bibamus papaliter*.

It was this justly acquired popularity, no doubt, which preserved him on his entrance from any bad reception at the hands of the mob, which had been so displeased but a moment before, and very little disposed to respect a cardinal on the very day when it was to elect a pope. But the Parisians cherish little rancor; and then, having forced the beginning of the play by their authority, the good bourgeois had got the upper hand of the cardinal, and this triumph was sufficient for them. Moreover, the Cardinal de Bourbon was a handsome man—he wore a fine scarlet robe, which he carried off very well—that is to say, he had all the women on his side, and, consequently, the best half of the audience. Assuredly, it would be injustice and bad taste to hoot a cardinal for having come late to the spectacle, when he is a handsome man, and when he wears his scarlet robe well.

He entered, then, bowed to those present with the hereditary smile of the great for the people, and directed his course slowly toward his scarlet velvet arm-chair, with the air of thinking of something quite different. His cortege—what we should nowadays call his staff—of bishops and abbés invaded the estrade in his train, not without causing redoubled tumult and curiosity among the audience. Each man vied with his neighbor in pointing them out and naming them, in seeing who should recognize at least one of them: this one, the Bishop of Marseilles (Alaudet, if my memory serves me right);—this one, the primicier of Saint-Denis;—this one, Robert de Lespinasse, Abbé of Saint-Germain des Prés, that libertine brother of a mistress of Louis XI; all with many errors and absurdities. As for the scholars, they swore. This was their day, their feast of fools, their saturnalia, the annual orgy of the corporation of law clerks and of the school. There was no turpitude which was not sacred on that day. And then there were gay gossips in the crowd—Simone Quatre-livres, Agnès la Gadine, and Rabine Piédebou. Was it not the least that one could do to swear at one's ease and revile the name of God a little, on so fine a day, in such good company as dignitaries of the church and loose women? So they did not abstain; and, in the midst of the uproar, there was a frightful concert of blasphemies and enormities of all the unbridled tongues, the tongues of clerks and students restrained during the rest of the year, by the fear of the hot iron of Saint Louis. Poor Saint Louis! how they set him at defiance in his own court of law! Each one of them selected from the newcomers on the platform, a black, gray, white, or violet cassock as his target. Joannes Frollo de Molendino, in his quality of brother to an archdeacon, boldly attacked the scarlet; he sang in deafening tones, with his impudent eyes fastened on the cardinal, *"Cappa repleta mero!"*

All these details which we here lay bare for the edification of the reader, were so covered by the general uproar, that they were lost in it before reaching the reserved platform; moreover, they would have moved the cardinal but little, so much a part of the customs were the liberties of that day. Moreover, he had another cause for solicitude, and his mien was wholly preoccupied with it, which entered the estrade the same time as himself; this was the embassy from Flanders.

Not that he was a profound politician, nor was he borrowing trouble about the possible consequences of the marriage of his cousin Marguerite de Bourgoyne to his cousin Charles, Dauphin de Vienne; nor as to how long the good understanding which had been patched up between the Duke of Austria and the King of France would last; nor how the King of England would take this disdain of his daughter. All that troubled him but little; and he gave a warm reception every evening to the wine of the royal vintage of Chaillot, without a suspicion that several flasks of that same wine (somewhat revised and corrected, it is true, by Doctor Coictier), cordially offered to Edward IV by Louis XI, would, some fine morning, rid Louis XI of Edward IV. "The much honored embassy of Monsieur the Duke of Austria," brought the cardinal none of these cares, but it troubled him in another direction. It was, in fact, somewhat hard, and we have already hinted at it on the second page of this book—for him, Charles de Bourbon, to be obliged to feast and receive cordially no one knows what bourgeois;—for him, a cardinal, to receive aldermen;—for him, a Frenchman, and a jolly companion, to receive Flemish beer-drinkers—and that in public! This was, certainly, one of the most irksome grimaces that he had ever executed for the good pleasure of the king.

So he turned toward the door, and with the best grace in the world (so well had he trained himself to it), when the usher announced, in a sonorous voice, "Messieurs the Envoys of Monsieur the Duke of Austria." It is useless to add that the whole hall did the same.

Then arrived, two by two, with a gravity which made a contrast in the midst of the frisky ecclesiastical escort of Charles de Bourbon, the eight and forty ambassadors of Maximilian of Austria, having at their head the reverend Father in God, Jehan, Abbot of Saint-Bertin, Chancellor of the Golden Fleece, and Jacques de Goy, Sieur Dauby, Grand Bailiff of Ghent. A deep silence settled over the assembly, accompanied by stifled laughter at the preposterous names and all the bourgeois designations which each of these personages transmitted with imperturbable gravity to the usher, who then tossed names and titles pell-mell and mutilated to the crowd below. There were Master Loys Roelof, alderman of the city of Louvain; Messire Clays d'Etuelde, alderman of Brussels; Messire Paul de Baeust, Sieur de Voirmizelle, President of Flanders; Master Jehan Coleghens, burgomaster of the city of Antwerp; Master George de la Moere, first alderman of the kuere of the city of Ghent; Master Gheldolf van der Hage, first alderman of the *parchons* of the said town; and the Sieur de Bierbecque, and Jehan Pinnock, and Jehan Dymaerzelle, etc., etc., etc.; bailiffs, aldermen, burgomasters; burgomasters, aldermen, bailiffs—all stiff, affectedly grave, formal, dressed out in velvet and damask, hooded with caps of black velvet, with great tufts of Cyprus gold thread; good Flemish heads, after all, severe and worthy faces, of the family which Rembrandt makes to stand out so strong and grave from the black background of his *Night Patrol*; personages all of whom bore, written on their brows, that Maximilian of Austria had done well in "trusting implicitly," as the manifest ran, "in their sense, valor, experience, loyalty, and good wisdom."

There was one exception, however. It was a subtle, intelligent, crafty-looking face, a sort of combined monkey and diplomat phiz, before whom the cardinal made three steps and a profound bow, and whose name, nevertheless, was only, "Guillaume Rym, counselor and pensioner of the City of Ghent."

Few persons were then aware who Guillaume Rym was. A rare genius who in a time of revolution would have made a brilliant appearance on the surface of events, but who in the fifteenth century was reduced to cavernous intrigues, and to "living in mines," as the Duc de Saint-Simon expresses it. Nevertheless, he was appreciated by the "miner" of Europe; he plotted familiarly with Louis XI, and often lent a hand to the king's secret jobs. All which things were quite unknown to that throng, who were amazed at the cardinal's politeness to that frail figure of a Flemish bailiff.

Chapter IV

MASTER JACQUES COPPENOLE

WHILE THE PENSIONER OF GHENT AND HIS EMINENCE WERE EXCHANGING VERY LOW BOWS AND a few words in voices still lower, a man of lofty stature, with a large face and broad shoulders, presented himself, in order to enter abreast with Guillaume Rym; one would have pronounced him a bull-dog by the side of a fox. His felt doublet and leather jerkin made a spot on the velvet and silk which surrounded him. Presuming that he was some groom who had stolen in, the usher stopped him.

"Hold, my friend, you cannot pass!"

The man in the leather jerkin shouldered him aside.

"What does this knave want with me?" said he, in stentorian tones, which rendered the entire hall attentive to this strange colloquy. "Don't you see that I am one of them?"

"Your name?" demanded the usher.

"Jacques Coppenole."

"Your titles?"

"Hosier at the sign of the 'Three Little Chains,' of Ghent."

The usher recoiled. One might bring one's self to announce aldermen and burgomasters, but a hosier was too much. The cardinal was on thorns. All the people were staring and listening. For two days his eminence had been exerting his utmost efforts to lick these Flemish bears into shape, and to render them a little more presentable to the public, and this freak was startling. But Guillaume Rym, with his polished smile, approached the usher.

"Announce Master Jacques Coppenole, clerk of the aldermen of the city of Ghent," he whispered, very low.

"Usher," interposed the cardinal, aloud, "announce Master Jacques Coppenole, clerk of the aldermen of the illustrious city of Ghent."

This was a mistake. Guillaume Rym alone might have conjured away the difficulty, but Coppenole had heard the cardinal.

"No, cross of God?" he exclaimed, in his voice of thunder, "Jacques Coppenole, hosier. Do you hear, usher? Nothing more, nothing less. Cross of God! hosier; that's fine enough. Monsieur the Archduke has more than once sought his *gant*[1] in my hose."

Laughter and applause burst forth. A jest is always understood in Paris, and, consequently, always applauded.

Let us add that Coppenole was of the people, and that the auditors which surrounded him were also of the people. Thus the communication between him and them had been prompt, electric, and, so to speak, on a level. The haughty air of the Flemish hosier, by humiliating the courtiers, had touched in all these plebeian souls that latent sentiment of dignity still vague and indistinct in the fifteenth century.

This hosier was an equal, who had just held his own before monsieur the cardinal. A very sweet reflection to poor fellows habituated to respect and obedience toward the underlings of the sergeants of the bailiff of Sainte-Geneviève, the cardinal's train-bearer.

Coppenole proudly saluted his eminence, who returned the salute of the all-powerful bourgeois feared by Louis XI. Then, while Guillaume Rym, a "sage and malicious man," as Philippe de Comines puts it, watched them both with a smile of raillery and superiority, each sought his place, the cardinal quite abashed and troubled, Coppenole tranquil and haughty, and thinking, no doubt, that his title of hosier was as good as any other, after all, and that Marie of Burgundy, mother to that Marguerite whom Coppenole was to-day bestowing in marriage, would have been less afraid of the cardinal than of the hosier; for it is not a cardinal who would have stirred up a revolt among the men of Ghent against the favorites of the daughter of Charles the Bold; it is not a cardinal who could have fortified the populace with a word against her tears and prayers, when the Maid of Flanders came to supplicate her people in their behalf, even at the very foot of the scaffold; while the hosier had only to raise his leather elbow, in order to cause to fall your two heads, most illustrious seigneurs, Guy d'Hymbercourt and Chancellor Guillaume Hugonet.

Nevertheless, all was over for the poor cardinal, and he was obliged to quaff to the dregs the bitter cup of being in such bad company.

The reader has, probably, not forgotten the impudent beggar who had been clinging fast to the fringes of the cardinal's gallery ever since the beginning of the prologue. The arrival of the illustrious guests had by no means caused him to relax his hold, and, while the prelates and ambassadors were packing themselves into the stalls—like genuine Flemish herrings—he settled himself at his ease, and boldly crossed his legs on the architrave. The insolence of this proceeding was extraordinary, yet no one noticed it at first, the attention of all being directed elsewhere. He, on his side, perceived nothing that was going on in the hall; he wagged his head with the unconcern of a Neapolitan, repeating from time to time, amid the clamor, as from a mechanical habit, "Charity, please!" And, assuredly, he was, out of all those present, the only one who had not deigned to turn his head at the altercation between Coppenole and the usher. Now, chance ordained that the master hosier of Ghent, with whom the people were already in lively sympathy, and upon whom all eyes

1. Got the first idea of a thing.

were riveted—should come and seat himself in the front row of the gallery, directly above the mendicant; and people were not a little amazed to see the Flemish ambassador, on concluding his inspection of the knave thus placed beneath his eyes, bestow a friendly tap on that ragged shoulder. The beggar turned round; there was surprise, recognition, a lighting up of the two countenances, and so forth; then, without paying the slightest heed in the world to the spectators, the hosier and the wretched being began to converse in a low tone, holding each other's hands, in the meantime, while the rags of Clopin Trouillefou, spread out upon the cloth of gold of the dais, produced the effect of a caterpillar on an orange.

The novelty of this singular scene excited such a murmur of mirth and gaiety in the hall, that the cardinal was not slow to perceive it; he half bent forward, and, as from the point where he was placed he could catch only an imperfect view of Trouillefou's ignominious doublet, he very naturally imagined that the mendicant was asking alms, and, disgusted with his audacity, he exclaimed: "Bailiff of the Courts, toss me that knave into the river!"

"Cross of God! monseigneur the cardinal," said Coppenole, without quitting Clopin's hand, "he's a friend of mine."

"Good! good!" shouted the populace. From that moment, Master Coppenole enjoyed in Paris as in Ghent, "great favor with the people; for men of that sort do enjoy it," says Philippe de Comines, "when they are thus disorderly."

The cardinal bit his lips. He bent toward his neighbor, the Abbé of Saint Geneviève, and said to him in a low tone—

"Fine ambassadors monsieur the archduke sends here, to announce to us Madame Marguerite!"

"Your eminence," replied the abbé, "wastes your politeness on these Flemish swine. *Margaritas ante porcos,* pearls before swine."

"Say rather," retorted the cardinal, with a smile, "*Porcos ante Margaritam,* swine before the pearl."

The whole little court in cassocks went into ecstacies over this play upon words. The cardinal felt a little relieved; he was quits with Coppenole, he also had had his jest applauded.

Now, will those of our readers who possess the power of generalizing an image or an idea, as the expression runs in the style of to-day, permit us to ask them if they have formed a very clear conception of the spectacle presented at this moment, upon which we have arrested their attention, by the vast parallelogram of the grand hall of the palace.

In the middle of the hall, backed against the western wall, a large and magnificent gallery draped with cloth of gold, into which enter in procession, through a small, arched door, grave personages, announced successively by the shrill voice of an usher. On the front benches were already a number of venerable figures, muffled in ermine, velvet, and scarlet. Around the dais—which remains silent and dignified—below, opposite, everywhere, a great crowd and a great murmur. Thousands of glances directed by the people on each face upon the dais, a thousand whispers over each name. Certainly, the spectacle is curious, and well deserves the attention of the spectators. But yonder, quite at the end, what is that sort of trestle work with four motley puppets upon it, and more below? Who is that man beside the trestle, with a black doublet and a pale face? Alas! my dear reader, it is Pierre Gringoire and his prologue.

We have all forgotten him completely.

This is precisely what he feared.

From the moment of the cardinal's entrance, Gringoire had never ceased to tremble for the safety of his prologue. At first he had enjoined the actors, who had stopped in suspense, to continue, and to raise their voices; then, perceiving that no one was listening, he had stopped them; and, during the entire quarter of an hour that the interruption lasted, he had not ceased to stamp, to flounce about, to appeal to Gisquette and Liénarde, and to urge his neighbors to the continuance of the prologue; all in vain. No one quitted the cardinal, the embassy, and the gallery—sole center of this vast circle of visual rays. We must also believe, and we say it with regret, that the prologue had begun slightly to weary the audience at the moment when his eminence had arrived, and created a diversion in so terrible a fashion. After all, on the gallery as well as on the marble table, the spectacle was the same: the conflict of Labor and Clergy, of Nobility and Merchandise. And many people preferred to see them alive, breathing, moving, elbowing each other in flesh and blood, in this Flemish embassy, in this Episcopal court, under the cardinal's robe, under Coppenole's jerkin, than painted, decked out, talking in verse, and, so to speak, stuffed beneath the yellow and white tunics in which Gringoire had so ridiculously clothed them.

Nevertheless, when our poet beheld quiet re-established to some extent, he devised a stratagem which might have redeemed all.

"Monsieur," he said, turning toward one of his neighbors, a fine, big man, with a patient face, "suppose we begin again."

"What?" said his neighbor.

"Hé! the Mystery," said Gringoire.

"As you like," returned his neighbor.

This semi-approbation sufficed for Gringoire, and, conducting his own affairs, he began to shout, confounding himself with the crowd as much as possible: "Begin the mystery again! begin again!"

"The devil!" said Joannes de Molendino, "what are they jabbering down yonder, at the end of the hall?" (for Gringoire was making noise enough for four.) "Say, comrades, isn't that mystery finished? They want to begin it all over again. That's not fair!"

"No, no!" shouted all the scholars. "Down with the mystery! Down with it!"

But Gringoire had multiplied himself, and only shouted the more vigorously: "Begin again! begin again!"

These clamors attracted the attention of the cardinal.

"Monsieur Bailiff of the Courts," said he to a tall, black man, placed a few paces from him, "are those knaves in a holy-water vessel, that they make such a hellish noise?"

The bailiff of the courts was a sort of amphibious magistrate, a sort of bat of the judicial order, related to both the rat and the bird, the judge and the soldier.

He approached his eminence, and not without a good deal of fear of the latter's displeasure, he awkwardly explained to him the seeming disrespect of the audience: that noonday had arrived before his eminence, and that the comedians had been forced to begin without waiting for his eminence.

The cardinal burst into a laugh.

"On my faith, the rector of the university ought to have done the same. What say you, Master Guillaume Rym?"

"Monseigneur," replied Guillaume Rym, "let us be content with having escaped half of the comedy. There is at least that much gained."

"Can these rascals continue their farce?" asked the bailiff.

"Continue, continue," said the cardinal, "it's all the same to me. I'll read my breviary in the meantime."

The bailiff advanced to the edge of the estrade, and cried, after having invoked silence by a wave of the hand—

"Bourgeois, rustics, and citizens, in order to satisfy those who wish the play to begin again, and those who wish it to end, his eminence orders that it be continued."

Both parties were forced to resign themselves. But the public and the author long cherished a grudge against the cardinal.

So the personages on the stage took up their parts, and Gringoire hoped that the rest of his work, at least, would be listened to. This hope was speedily dispelled like his other illusions; silence had indeed, been restored in the audience, after a fashion; but Gringoire had not observed that at the moment when the cardinal gave the order to continue, the gallery was far from full, and that after the Flemish envoys there had arrived new personages forming part of the *cortége*, whose names and ranks, shouted out in the midst of his dialogue by the intermittent cry of the usher, produced considerable ravages in it. Let the reader imagine the effect in the midst of a theatrical piece, of the yelping of an usher, flinging in between two rhymes, and often in the middle of a line, parentheses like the following—

"Master Jacques Charmolue, procurator to the king in the Ecclesiastical Courts!"

"Jehan de Harlay, equerry guardian of the office of chevalier of the night watch of the city of Paris!"

"Messire Galiot de Genoilhac, chevalier, seigneur de Brussac, master of the king's artillery!"

"Master Dreux-Raguier, surveyor of the woods and forests of the king our sovereign, in the land of France, Champagne and Brie!"

"Messire Louis de Graville, chevalier, councilor, and chamberlain of the king, admiral of France, keeper of the Forest of Vincennes!"

"Master Denis le Mercier, guardian of the house of the blind at Paris!" etc., etc., etc.

This was becoming unbearable.

This strange accompaniment, which rendered it difficult to follow the piece, made Gringoire all the more indignant because he could not conceal from himself the fact that the interest was continually increasing, and that all his work required was a chance of being heard.

It was, in fact, difficult to imagine a more ingenious and more dramatic composition. The four personages of the prologue were bewailing themselves in their mortal embarrassment, when Venus in person, (*vera incessa patuit dea*) presented herself to them, clad in a fine robe bearing the heraldic device of the ship of the city of Paris. She had come herself to claim the dolphin promised to the most beautiful. Jupiter, whose thunder could be heard rumbling in the dressing-room, supported her claim, and Venus was on the point of carrying it off—that is to say, without allegory, of marrying monsieur the dauphin, when a young child clad in white damask, and holding in her hand a daisy (a transparent personification of Mademoiselle Marguerite of Flanders) came to contest it with Venus.

Theatrical effect and change.

After a dispute, Venus, Marguerite, and the assistants agreed to submit to the good judgment of time holy Virgin. There was another good part, that of the king of Mesopotamia; but through so many interruptions, it was difficult to make out what end he served. All these persons had ascended by the ladder to the stage.

But all was over; none of these beauties had been felt nor understood. On the entrance of the cardinal, one would have said that an invisible magic thread had suddenly drawn all glances from the marble table to the gallery, from the southern to the western extremity of the hall. Nothing could disenchant the audience; all eyes remained fixed there, and the newcomers and their accursed names, and their faces, and their costumes, afforded a continual diversion. This was very distressing. With the exception of Gisquette and Liénarde, who turned round from time to time when Gringoire plucked them by the sleeve; with the exception of the big, patient neighbor, no one listened, no one looked at the poor, deserted morality full face. Gringoire saw only profiles.

With what bitterness did he behold his whole erection of glory and of poetry crumble away bit by bit! And to think that these people had been upon the point of instituting a revolt against the bailiff through impatience to hear his work! now that they had it they did not care for it. This same representation which had been begun amid so unanimous an acclamation! Eternal flood and ebb of popular favor! To think that they had been on the point of hanging the bailiff's sergeant! What would he not have given to be still at that hour of honey!

But the usher's brutal monologue came to an end; everyone had arrived, and Gringoire breathed freely once more; the actors continued bravely. But Master Coppenole, the hosier, must needs rise of a sudden, and Gringoire was forced to listen to him deliver, amid universal attention, the following abominable harangue.

"Messieurs the bourgeois and squires of Paris, I don't know, cross of God! what we are doing here. I certainly do see yonder in the corner on that stage, some people who appear to be fighting. I don't know whether that is what you call a "mystery," but it is not amusing; they quarrel with their tongues and nothing more. I have been waiting for the first blow this quarter of an hour; nothing comes; they are cowards who only scratch each other with insults. You ought to send for the fighters of London or Rotterdam; and, I can tell you! you would have had blows of the fist that could be heard in the Place; but these men excite our pity. They ought at least, to give us a moorish dance, or some other mummery! That is not what was told me; I was promised a feast of fools, with the election of a pope. We have our pope of fools at Ghent also; we're not behindhand in that, cross of God! But this is the way we manage it; we collect a crowd like this one here, then each person in turn passes his head through a hole, and makes a grimace at the rest; the one who makes the ugliest, is elected pope by general acclamation; that's the way it is. It is very diverting. Would you like to make your pope after the fashion of my country? At all events, it will be less wearisome than to listen to chatterers. If they wish to come and make their grimaces through the hole, they can join the game. What say you, Messieurs les bourgeois? You have here enough grotesque specimens of both sexes, to allow of laughing in Flemish fashion, and there are enough of us ugly in countenance to hope for a fine grinning match."

Gringoire would have liked to retort; stupefaction, rage, indignation, deprived him of words. Moreover, the suggestion of the popular hosier was received with such enthusiasm by these bourgeois who were flattered at being called "squires," that all resistance was useless. There was nothing to be done but to allow one's self to drift with the torrent. Gringoire hid his face between his two hands, not being so fortunate as to have a mantle with which to veil his head, like Agamemnon of Timantis.

Chapter V

QUASIMODO

IN THE TWINKLING OF AN EYE, ALL WAS READY TO EXECUTE COPPENOLE'S IDEA. BOURGEOIS, scholars and law clerks all set to work. The little chapel situated opposite the marble table was selected for the scene of the grinning match. A pane broken in the pretty rose window above the door, left free a circle of stone through which it was agreed that the competitors should thrust their heads. In order to reach it, it was only necessary to mount upon a couple of hogsheads, which had been produced from I know not where, and perched one upon the other, after a fashion. It was settled that each candidate, man or woman (for it was possible to choose a female pope), should, for the sake of leaving the impression of his grimace fresh and complete, cover his face and remain concealed in the chapel until the moment of his appearance. In less than an instant, the chapel was crowded with competitors, upon whom the door was then closed.

Coppenole, from his post, ordered all, directed all, arranged all. During the uproar, the cardinal, no less abashed than Gringoire, had retired with all his suite, under the pretext of business and vespers, without the crowd which his arrival had so deeply stirred being in the least moved by his departure. Guillaume Rym was the only one who noticed his eminence's discomfiture. The attention of the populace, like the sun, pursued its revolution; having set out from one end of the hall, and halted for a space in the middle, it had now reached the other end. The marble table, the brocaded gallery had each had their day; it was now the turn of the chapel of Louis XI. Henceforth, the field was open to all folly. There was no one there now, but the Flemings and the rabble.

The grimaces began. The first face which appeared at the aperture, with eyelids turned up to the reds, a mouth open like a maw, and a brow wrinkled like our hussar boots of the Empire, evoked such an inextinguishable peal of laughter that Homer would have taken all these louts for gods. Nevertheless, the grand hall was anything but Olympus, and Gringoire's poor Jupiter knew it better than anyone else. A second and third grimace followed, then another and another; and the laughter and transports of delight went on increasing. There was in this spectacle, a peculiar power of intoxication and fascination, of which it would be difficult to convey to the reader of our day and our salons any idea.

Let the reader picture to himself a series of visages presenting successively all geometrical forms, from the triangle to the trapezium, from the cone to the polyhedron; all human expressions, from wrath to lewdness; all ages, from the wrinkles of the newborn babe to the wrinkles of the aged and dying; all religious phantasmagories, from Faun to Beelzebub; all animal profiles, from the maw to the beak, from the jowl to the muzzle. Let the reader imagine all these grotesque figures of the Pont Neuf, those nightmares petrified beneath the hand of Germain Pilon, assuming life and breath, and coming in turn to stare you in the face with burning eyes; all the masks of the Carnival of Venice passing in succession before your glass—in a word, a human kaleidoscope.

The orgy grew more and more Flemish. Teniers could have given but a very imperfect idea of it. Let the reader picture to himself in bacchanal form, Salvator Rosa's battle. There were no longer either scholars or ambassadors or bourgeois or men or women; there was no longer any Clopin Trouillefou, nor Gilles Lecornu, nor Marie Quatrelivres, nor Robin Poussepain. All was universal license. The grand hall was no longer anything but a vast furnace of effrontry and joviality, where every mouth was a cry, every individual a posture; everything shouted and howled. The strange visages which came, in turn, to gnash their teeth in the rose window, were like so many brands cast into the brazier; and from the whole of this effervescing crowd, there escaped, as from a furnace, a sharp, piercing, stinging noise, hissing like the wings of a gnat.

"Ho hé! curse it!"

"Just look at that face!"

"It's not good for anything."

"Guillemette Maugerepuis, just look at that bull's muzzle; it only lacks the horns. It can't be your husband."

"Another!"

"Belly of the pope! what sort of a grimace is that?"

"Holà hé! that's cheating. One must show only one's face."

"That damned Perrette Callebotte! she's capable of that!"

"Good! Good!"

"I'm stifling!"

"There's a fellow whose ears won't go through!" Etc., etc.

But we must do justice to our friend Jehan. In the midst of this witches' sabbath, he was still to be seen on the top of his pillar, like the cabin-boy on the topmast. He floundered about with incredible fury. His mouth was wide open, and from it there escaped a cry which no one heard, not that it was covered by the general clamor, great as that was, but because it attained, no doubt, the limit of perceptible sharp sounds, the thousand vibrations of Sauveur, or the eight thousand of Biot.

As for Gringoire, the first moment of depression having passed, he had regained his composure. He had hardened himself against adversity.—"Continue!" he had said for the third time, to his comedians, speaking machines; then as he was marching with great strides in front of the marble table, a fancy seized him to go and appear in his turn at the aperture of the chapel, were it only for the pleasure of making a grimace at that ungrateful populace.—"But no, that would not be worthy of us; no, vengeance! let us combat until the end," he repeated to himself; "the power of poetry over people is great; I will bring them back. We shall see which will carry the day, grimaces or polite literature."

Alas! he had been left the sole spectator of his piece.

It was far worse than it had been a little while before. He no longer beheld anything but backs.

I am mistaken. The big, patient man, whom he had already consulted in a critical moment, had remained with his face turned toward the stage. As for Gisquette and Liénarde, they had deserted him long ago.

Gringoire was touched to the heart by the fidelity of his only spectator. He approached him and addressed him, shaking his arm slightly; for the good man was leaning on the balustrade and dozing a little.

"Monsieur," said Gringoire, "I thank you!"

"Monsieur," replied the big man with a yawn, "for what?"

"I see what wearies you," resumed the poet; " 'tis all this noise which prevents your hearing comfortably. But be at ease! your name shall descend to posterity! Your name, if you please?"

"Renauld Chateau, guardian of the seals of the Châtelet of Paris, at your service."

"Monsieur, you are the only representive of the muses here," said Gringoire.

"You are too kind, sir," said the guardian of the seals at the Châtelet.

"You are the only one," resumed Gringoire, "who has listened to the piece decorously. What do you think of it?"

"He! he!" replied the fat magistrate, half aroused, "it's tolerably jolly, that's a fact."

Gringoire was forced to content himself with this eulogy; for a thunder of applause, mingled with a prodigious acclamation, cut their conversation short. The Pope of the Fools had been elected.

"Noël! Noël! Noël!" shouted the people on all sides.

That was, in fact, a marvelous grimace which was beaming at that moment through the aperture in the rose window. After all the pentagonal, hexagonal, and whimsical faces, which had succeeded each other at that hole without realizing the ideal of the grotesque which their imaginations, excited by the orgy, had constructed, nothing less was needed to win their suffrages than the sublime grimace which had just dazzled the assembly. Master Coppenole himself applauded, and Clopin Trouillefou, who had been among the competitors (and God knows what intensity of ugliness his visage could attain), confessed himself conquered. We will do the same. We shall not try to give the reader an idea of that tetrahedral nose, that horseshoe mouth; that little left eye obstructed with a red, bushy, bristling eyebrow, while the right eye disappeared entirely beneath an enormous wart; of those teeth in disarray, broken here and there, like the embattled parapet of a fortress; of that callous lip, upon which one of these teeth encroached, like the tusk of an elephant; of that forked chin; and above all, of the expression spread over the whole; of that mixture of malice, amazement, and sadness. Let the reader dream of this whole, if he can.

The acclamation was unanimous; people rushed toward the chapel. They made the lucky Pope of the Fools come forth in triumph. But it was then that surprise and admiration attained their highest pitch; the grimace was his face.

Or rather, his whole person was a grimace. A huge head, bristling with red hair; between his shoulders an enormous hump, a counterpart perceptible in front; a system of thighs and legs so strangely astray that they could touch each other only at the knees, and, viewed from the front, resembled the crescents of two scythes joined by the handles; large feet, monstrous hands; and, with all this deformity, an indescribable and redoubtable air of vigor, agility, and courage—strange exception to the eternal rule which wills that force as well as beauty shall be the result of harmony. Such was the pope whom the fools had just chosen for themselves.

One would have pronounced him a giant who had been broken and badly put together again.

When this species of cyclops appeared on the threshold of the chapel, motionless, squat, and almost as broad as he was tall; *squared* on the *base,* as a great man says; with his doublet half red, half violet, sown with silver bells, and, above all, in the perfection of his ugliness, the populace recognized him on the instant, and shouted with one voice—

" 'Tis Quasimodo, the bellringer! 'tis Quasimodo, the hunchback of Notre-Dame! Quasimodo, the one-eyed! Quasimodo, the bandy-legged! Noël! Noël!"

It will be seen that the poor fellow had a choice of surnames.

"Let the women with child beware!" shouted the scholars.

"Or those who wish to be," resumed Joannes.

The women did, in fact, hide their faces.

"Oh! the horrible monkey!" said one of them.

"As wicked as he is ugly," retorted another.

"He's the devil," added a third.

"I have the misfortune to live near Notre-Dame; I hear him prowling round the eaves by night."

"With the cats."

"He's always on our roofs."

"He throws spells down our chimneys."

"The other evening, he came and made a grimace at me through my attic window. I thought that it was a man. Such a fright as I had!"

"I'm sure that he goes to the witches' sabbath. Once he left a broom on my leads."

"Oh! what a displeasing hunchback's face!"

"Oh! what an ill-favored soul!"

"Whew!"

The men, on the contrary, were delighted and applauded.

Quasimodo, the object of the tumult, still stood on the threshold of the chapel, somber and grave, and allowed them to admire him.

One scholar (Robin Poussepain, I think), came and laughed in his face, and too close. Quasimodo contented himself with taking him by the girdle, and hurling him ten paces off amid the crowd; all without uttering a word.

Master Coppenole, in amazement, approached him.

"Cross of God! Holy Father! you possess the handsomest ugliness that I have ever beheld in my life. You would deserve to be pope at Rome, as well as at Paris."

So saying, he placed his hand gaily on his shoulder. Quasimodo did not stir. Coppenole went on—

"You are a rogue with whom I have a fancy for carousing, were it to cost me a new dozen of twelve livres of Tours. How does it strike you?"

Quasimodo made no reply.

"Cross of God!" said the hosier, "are you deaf?"

He was, in truth, deaf.

Nevertheless, he began to grow impatient with Coppenole's behavior, and suddenly turned toward him with so formidable a gnashing of teeth, that the Flemish giant recoiled, like a bull-dog before a cat.

Then there was created around that strange personage, a circle of terror and respect, whose radius was at least fifteen geometrical feet. An old woman explained to Coppenole that Quasimodo was deaf.

"Deaf!" said the hosier, with his great Flemish laugh. "Cross of God! He's a perfect pope!"

"Hé! I recognize him," exclaimed Jehan, who had, at last, descended from his capital, in order to see Quasimodo at closer quarters, "he's the bellringer of my brother, the archdeacon. Good day, Quasimodo!"

"What a devil of a man!" said Robin Poussepain still all bruised with his fall. "He shows himself; he's a hunchback. He walks; he's bandy-legged. He looks at you; he's one-eyed. You speak to him; he's deaf. And what does this Polyphemus do with his tongue?"

"He speaks when he chooses," said the old woman; "he became deaf through ringing the bells. He is not dumb."

"That he lacks," remarks Jehan.

"And he has one eye too many," added Robin Poussepain.

"Not at all," said Jehan wisely. "A one-eyed man is far less complete than a blind man. He knows what he lacks."

In the meantime, all the beggars, all the lackeys, all the cut-purses, joined with the scholars, had gone in procession to seek, in the cupboard of the law clerks' company, the cardboard tiara, and the derisive robe of the Pope of the Fools. Quasimodo allowed them to array him in them without wincing, and with a sort of proud docility. Then they made him seat himself on a motley litter. Twelve officers of the fraternity of fools raised him on their shoulders; and a sort of bitter and disdainful joy lighted up the morose face of the cyclops, when he beheld beneath his deformed feet all those heads of handsome, straight, well-made men. Then the ragged and howling procession set out on its march, according to custom, around the inner galleries of the Courts, before making the circuit of the streets and squares.

Chapter VI

ESMERALDA

WE ARE DELIGHTED TO BE ABLE TO INFORM THE READER, THAT DURING THE WHOLE OF THIS scene, Gringoire and his piece had stood firm. His actors, spurred on by him, had not ceased to spout his comedy, and he had not ceased to listen to it. He had made up his mind about the tumult, and was determined to proceed to the end, not giving up the hope of a return of attention on the part of the public. This gleam of hope acquired fresh life, when he saw Quasimodo, Coppenole, and the deafening escort of the pope of the procession of fools quit the hall amid great uproar. The throng rushed eagerly after them. "Good," he said to himself, "there go all the mischief-makers." Unfortunately, all the mischief-makers constituted the entire audience. In the twinkling of an eye, the grand hall was empty.

To tell the truth, a few spectators still remained, some scattered, others in groups around the pillars, women, old men, or children, who had had enough of the uproar and tumult. Some scholars were still perched astride of the window-sills, engaged in gazing into the Place.

"Well," thought Gringoire, "here are still as many as are required to hear the end of my mystery. They are few in number, but it is a choice audience, a lettered audience."

An instant later, a symphony which had been intended to produce the greatest effect on the arrival of the Virgin, was lacking. Gringoire perceived that his music had been carried off by the procession of the Pope of the Fools. "Skip it," said he, stoically.

He approached a group of bourgeois, who seemed to him to be discussing his piece. This is the fragment of conversation which he caught—

"You know, Master Cheneteau, the Hôtel de Navarre, which belonged to Monsieur de Nemours?"

"Yes, opposite the Chapelle de Braque."

"Well, the treasury has just let it to Guillaume Alixandre, historian, for six livres, eight sols, parisian, a year."

"How rents are going up!"

"Come," said Gringoire to himself, with a sigh, "the others are listening."

"Comrades," suddenly shouted one of the young scamps from the window, "La Esmeralda! La Esmeralda in the Place!"

This word produced a magical effect. Everyone who was left in the hall flew to the windows, climbing the walls in order to see, and repeating, "La Esmeralda! La Esmeralda?" At the same time, a great sound of applause was heard from without.

"What's the meaning of this, of the Esmeralda?" said Gringoire, wringing his hands in despair. "Ah, good heavens! it seems to be the turn of the windows now."

He returned toward the marble table, and saw that the representation had been interrupted. It was precisely at the instant when Jupiter should have appeared with his thunder. But Jupiter was standing motionless at the foot of the stage.

"Michel Giborne!" cried the irritated poet, "what are you doing there? Is that your part? Come up!"

"Alas!" said Jupiter, "a scholar has just seized the ladder."

Gringoire looked. It was but too true. All communication between his plot and its solution was intercepted.

"The rascal," he murmured. "And why did he take that ladder?"

"In order to go and see the Esmeralda," replied Jupiter piteously. "He said, 'Come, here's a ladder that's of no use!' and he took it."

This was the last blow. Gringoire received it with resignation.

"May the devil fly away with you!" he said to the comedian, "and if I get my pay, you shall receive yours."

Then he beat a retreat, with drooping head, but the last in the field, like a general who has fought well.

And as he descended the winding stairs of the courts: "A fine rabble of asses and dolts these Parisians!" he muttered between his teeth; "they come to hear a mystery and don't listen to it at all! They are engrossed by everyone, by Clopin Trouillefou, by the cardinal, by Coppenole, by Quasimodo, by the devil! but by Madame the Virgin Mary, not at all. If I had known, I'd have given you Virgin Mary, you ninnies! And I! to come to see faces and behold only backs! to be a poet, and to reap the success of an apothecary! It is true that Homerus begged through the Greek towns, and that Naso died in exile among the Muscovites. But may the devil flay me if I understand what they mean with their Esmeralda! What is that word, in the first place?—'tis Egyptian!"

BOOK SECOND

Chapter I

FROM CHARYBDIS TO SCYLLA

N IGHT COMES ON EARLY IN JANUARY. THE STREETS WERE ALREADY DARK WHEN GRINGOIRE IS-
sued forth from the Courts. This gloom pleased him; he was in haste to reach some obscure
and deserted alley, in order there to meditate at his ease, and in order that the philosopher might
place the first dressing upon the wound of the poet. Philosophy, moreover, was his sole refuge, for
he did not know where he was to lodge for the night. After the brilliant failure of his first theatrical venture, he dared not return to the lodging which he occupied in the Rue Grenier-sur-l'Eau, opposite to the Port-au-Foin, having depended upon receiving from monsieur the provost for his
epithalamium, the wherewithal to pay Master Guillaume Doulx-Sire, farmer of the taxes on cloven-
footed animals in Paris, the rent which he owed him, that is to say, twelve sols parisian; twelve times
the value of all that he possessed in the world, including his trunk-hose, his shirt, and his cap. After
reflecting a moment, temporarily sheltered beneath the little wicket of the prison of the treasurer
of the Sainte-Chappelle, as to the shelter which he would select for the night, having all the pavements of Paris to choose from, he remembered to have noticed the week previously in the Rue de
la Savaterie, at the door of a councilor of the parliament, a stepping stone for mounting a mule, and
to have said to himself that that stone would furnish, on occasion, a very excellent pillow for a mendicant or a poet. He thanked Providence for having sent this happy idea to him; but, as he was
preparing to cross the Place, in order to reach the tortuous labyrinth of the city, where meander all
those old sister streets, the Rues de la Barillerie, de la Vielle-Draperie, de la Savaterie, de la Juiverie, etc., still extant to-day, with their nine-story houses, he saw the procession of the Pope of the
Fools, which was also emerging from the court-house, and rushing across the courtyard, with great
cries, a great flashing of torches, and the music which belonged to him, Gringoire. This sight revived the pain of his self-love; he fled. In the bitterness of his dramatic misadventure, everything
which reminded him of the festival of that day irritated his wound and made it bleed.

He was on the point of turning to the Pont Saint-Michel; children were running about here and
there with fire lances and rockets.

"Pest on firework candles!" said Gringoire; and he fell back on the Pont au Change. To the
house at the head of the bridge there had been affixed three small banners, representing the king,
the dauphin, and Marguerite of Flanders, and six little pennons on which were portrayed the Duke
of Austria, the Cardinal de Bourbon, M. de Beaujeu, and Madame Jeanne de France, and Monsieur
the Bastard of Bourbon, and I know not whom else; all being illuminated with torches. The rabble
were admiring.

"Happy painter, Jehan Fourbault!" said Gringoire with a deep sigh; and he turned his back
upon the bannerets and pennons. A street opened before him; he thought it so dark and deserted
that he hoped to there escape from all the rumors as well as from all the gleams of the festival. At
the end of a few moments his foot came in contact with an obstacle; he stumbled and fell. It was the
May truss, which the clerks of the clerks' law court had deposited that morning at the door of a
president of the parliament, in honor of the solemnity of the day. Gringoire bore this new disaster

heroically; he picked himself up, and reached the water's edge. After leaving behind him the civic Tournelle[1] and the criminal tower, and skirted the great walls of the king's garden, on that unpaved strand where the mud reached to his ankles, he reached the western point of the city, and considered for some time the islet of the Passeur-aux-Vaches, which has disappeared beneath the bronze horse of the Pont Neuf. The islet appeared to him in the shadow like a black mass, beyond the narrow strip of whitish water which separated him from it. One could divine by the ray of a tiny light the sort of hut in the form of a beehive where the ferryman of cows took refuge at night.

"Happy ferryman!" thought Gringoire; "you do not dream of glory, and you do not make marriage songs! What matters it to you, if kings and Duchesses of Burgundy marry? You know no other daisies (*marguerites*) than those which your April greensward gives your cows to browse upon; while I, a poet, am hooted, and shiver, and owe twelve sous, and the soles of my shoes are so transparent, that they might serve as glasses for your lantern! Thanks, ferryman, your cabin rests my eyes, and makes me forget Paris!"

He was roused from his almost lyric ecstacy, by a big double Saint-Jean cracker, which suddenly went off from the happy cabin. It was the cow ferryman, who was taking his part in the rejoicings of the day, and letting off fireworks.

This cracker made Gringoire's skin bristle up all over.

"Accursed festival!" he exclaimed, "wilt thou pursue me everywhere? Oh! good God! even to the ferryman's!"

Then he looked at the Seine at his feet, and a horrible temptation took possession of him:

"Oh!" said he, "I would gladly drown myself, were the water not so cold!"

Then a desperate resolution occurred to him. It was, since he could not escape from the Pope of the Fools, from Jehan Fourbault's bannerets, from May trusses, from squibs and crackers, to go to the Place de Grève.

"At least," he said to himself, "I shall there have a firebrand of joy wherewith to warm myself, and I can sup on some crumbs of the three great armorial bearings of royal sugar which have been erected on the public refreshment-stall of the city."

Chapter II

THE PLACE DE GRÈVE

THERE REMAINS TO-DAY BUT A VERY IMPERCEPTIBLE VESTIGE OF THE PLACE DE GRÈVE, SUCH AS it existed then; it consists in the charming little turret, which occupies the angle north of the Place, and which, already enshrouded in the ignoble plaster which fills with paste the delicate lines of its sculpture, would soon have disappeared, perhaps submerged by that flood of new houses which so rapidly devours all the ancient façades of Paris.

The persons who, like ourselves, never cross the Place de Grève without casting a glance of pity and sympathy on that poor turret strangled between two hovels of the time of Louis XV, can easily reconstruct in their minds the aggregate of edifices to which it belonged, and find again entire in it the ancient Gothic place of the fifteenth century.

It was then, as it is to-day, an irregular trapezoid, bordered on one side by the quay, and on the other three by a series of lofty, narrow, and gloomy houses. By day, one could admire the variety

1. A chamber of the ancient parliament of Paris.

of its edifices, all sculptured in stone or wood, and already presenting complete specimens of the different domestic architectures of the Middle Ages, running back from the fifteenth to the eleventh century, from the casement which had begun to dethrone the arch, to the Roman semi-circle, which had been supplanted by the ogive, and which still occupies, below it, the first story of that ancient house de la Tour Roland, at the corner of the Place upon the Seine, on the side of the street with the Tannerie. At night, one could distinguish nothing of all that mass of buildings, except the black indentation of the roofs, unrolling their chain of acute angles round the place; for one of the radical differences between the cities of that time, and the cities of the present day, lay in the façades which looked upon the places and streets, and which were then gables. For the last two centuries the houses have been turned round.

In the center of the eastern side of the Place, rose a heavy and hybrid construction, formed of three buildings placed in juxtaposition. It was called by three names which explain its history, its destination, and its architecture: "The House of the Dauphin," because Charles V, when Dauphin, had inhabited it; "The Marchandise," because it had served as town-hall; and "The Pillared House" (*domus ad piloria*), because of a series of large pillars which sustained the three stories. The city found there all that is required for a city like Paris; a chapel in which to pray to God; a *plaidoyer*, or pleading room, in which to hold hearings, and to repel, at need, the King's people; and under the roof, an *arsenac* full of artillery. For the bourgeois of Paris were aware that it is not sufficient to pray in every conjuncture, and to plead for the franchises of the city, and they had always in reserve, in the garret of the town-hall, a few good rusty arquebuses. The Grève had then that sinister aspect which it preserves to-day from the execrable ideas which it awakens, and from the somber town-hall of Dominique Bocador, which has replaced the Pillared House. It must be admitted that a permanent gibbet and a pillory, "a justice and a ladder," as they were called in that day, erected side by side in the center of the pavement, contributed not a little to cause eyes to be turned away from that fatal place, where so many beings full of life and health have agonized; where, fifty years later, that fever of Saint Vallier was destined to have its birth, that terror of the scaffold, the most monstrous of all maladies because it comes not from God, but from man.

It is a consoling idea (let us remark in passing), to think that the death penalty, which three hundred years ago still encumbered with its iron wheels, its stone gibbets, and all its paraphernalia of torture, permanent and riveted to the pavement, the Grève, the Halles, the Place Dauphine, the Cross du Trahoir, the Marché aux Pourceaux, that hideous Montfaucon, the barrier des Sergents, the Place aux Chats, the Porte Saint-Denis, Champeaux, the Porte Baudets, the Porte Saint Jacques, without reckoning the innumerable ladders of the provosts, the bishop of the chapters, of the abbots, of the priors, who had the decree of life and death—without reckoning the judicial drownings in the river Seine; it is consoling to-day, after having lost successively all the pieces of its armor, its luxury of torment, its penalty of imagination and fancy, its torture for which it reconstructed every five years a leather bed at the Grand Châtelet, that ancient suzerain of feudal society almost expunged from our laws and our cities, hunted from code to code, chased from place to place, has no longer, in our immense Paris, any more than a dishonored corner of the Grève—than a miserable guillotine, furtive, uneasy, shameful, which seems always afraid of being caught in the act, so quickly does it disappear after having dealt its blow.

Chapter III

KISSES FOR BLOWS

WHEN PIERRE GRINGOIRE ARRIVED ON THE PLACE DE GRÈVE, HE WAS PARALYZED. HE HAD DI-
rected his course across the Pont aux Meuniers, in order to avoid the rabble on the Pont au
Change, and the pennons of Jehan Fourbault; but the wheels of all the bishop's mills had splashed
him as he passed, and his doublet was drenched; it seemed to him besides, that the failure of his
piece had rendered him still more sensible to cold than usual. Hence he made haste to draw near the
bonfire, which was burning magnificently in the middle of the Place. But a considerable crowd
formed a circle around it.

"Accursed Parisians!" he said to himself (for Gringoire, like a true dramatic poet, was subject to monologues) "there they are obstructing my fire! Nevertheless, I am greatly in need of a
chimney corner; my shoes drink in the water, and all those cursed mills wept upon me! That
devil of a Bishop of Paris, with his mills! I'd just like to know what use a bishop can make of a
mill! Does he expect to become a miller instead of a bishop? If only my malediction is needed
for that, I bestow it upon him! and his cathedral, and his mills! Just see if those boobies will put
themselves out! Move aside! I'd like to know what they are doing there! They are warming
themselves, much pleasure may it give them! They are watching a hundred fagots burn; a fine
spectacle!"

On looking more closely, he perceived that the circle was much larger than was required simply for the purpose of getting warm at the king's fire, and that this concourse of people had not
been attracted solely by the beauty of the hundred fagots which were burning.

In a vast space left free between the crowd and the fire, a young girl was dancing.

Whether this young girl was a human being, a fairy, or an angel, is what Gringoire, skeptical
philosopher and ironical poet that he was, could not decide at the first moment, so fascinated was
he by this dazzling vision.

She was not tall, though she seemed so, so boldly did her slender form dart about. She was
swarthy of complexion, but one divined that, by day, her skin must possess that beautiful golden
tone of the Andalusians and the Roman women. Her little foot, too, was Andalusian, for it was both
pinched and at ease in its graceful shoe. She danced, she turned, she whirled rapidly about on an old
Persian rug, spread negligently under her feet; and each time that her radiant face passed before
you, as she whirled, her great black eyes darted a flash of lightning at you.

All around her, all glances were riveted, all mouths open; and, in fact, when she danced thus,
to the humming of the Basque tambourine, which her two pure, rounded arms raised above her
head, slender, frail and vivacious as a wasp, with her corsage of gold without a fold, her variegated
gown puffing out, her bare shoulders, her delicate limbs, which her petticoat revealed at times, her
black hair, her eyes of flame, she was a supernatural creature.

"In truth," said Gringoire to himself, "she is a salamander, she is a nymph, she is a goddess,
she is a bacchante of the Menelean Mount!"

At that moment, one of the salamander's braids of hair became unfastened, and a piece of yellow copper which was attached to it, rolled to the ground.

"Hé, no!" said he, "she is a gypsy!"

All illusions had disappeared.

She began her dance once more; she took from the ground two swords, whose points she rested
against her brow, and which she made to turn in one direction, while she turned in the other; it was

a purely gypsy effect. But, disenchanted though Gringoire was, the whole effect of this picture was not without its charm and its magic; the bonfire illuminated, with a red flaring light, which trembled, all alive, over the circle of faces in the crowd, on the brow of the young girl, and at the background of the Place cast a pallid reflection, on one side upon the ancient, black, and wrinkled façade of the House of Pillars, on the other, upon the old stone gibbet.

Among the thousands of visages which that light tinged with scarlet, there was one which seemed, even more than all the others, absorbed in contemplation of the dancer. It was the face of a man, austere, calm, and somber. This man, whose costume was concealed by the crowd which surrounded him, did not appear to be more than five and thirty years of age; nevertheless, he was bald; he had merely a few tufts of thin, gray hair on his temples; his broad, high forehead had begun to be furrowed with wrinkles, but his deep-set eyes sparkled with extraordinary youthfulness, an ardent life, a profound passion. He kept them fixed incessantly on the gypsy, and, while the giddy young girl of sixteen danced and whirled, for the pleasure of all, his reverie seemed to become more and more somber. From time to time, a smile and a sigh met upon his lips, but the smile was more melancholy than the sigh.

The young girl, stopped at length, breathless, and the people applauded her lovingly.

"Djali!" said the gypsy.

Then Gringoire saw come up to her, a pretty little white goat, alert, wide-awake, glossy, with gilded horns, gilded hoofs, and gilded collar, which he had not hitherto perceived, and which had remained lying curled up on one corner of the carpet watching his mistress dance.

"Djali!" said the dancer, "it is your turn."

And, seating herself, she gracefully presented her tambourine to the goat.

"Djali," she continued, "what month is this?"

The goat lifted its forefoot, and struck one blow upon the tambourine. It was the first month in the year, in fact.

"Djali," pursued the young girl, turning her tambourine round, "what day of the month is this?"

Djali raised his little gilt hoof, and struck six blows on the tambourine.

"Djali," pursued the Egyptian, with still another movement of the tambourine, "what hour of the day is it?"

Djali struck seven blows. At that moment, the clock of the Pillar House rang out seven.

The people were amazed.

"There's sorcery at the bottom of it," said a sinister voice in the crowd. It was that of the bald man, who never removed his eyes from the gypsy.

She shuddered and turned round; but applause broke forth and drowned the morose exclamation.

It even effaced it so completely from her mind, that she continued to question her goat.

"Djali, what does Master Guichard Grand-Remy, captain of the pistoliers of the town do, at the procession of Candlemas?"

Djali reared himself on his hindlegs, and began to bleat, marching along with so much dainty gravity, that the entire circle of spectators burst into a laugh at this parody of the interested devoutness of the captain of pistoliers.

"Djali," resumed the young girl, emboldened by her growing success, "how preaches Master Jacques Charmolue, procurator to the king in the ecclesiastical court?"

The goat seated himself on his hind quarters, and began to bleat, waving his forefeet in so strange a manner, that, with the exception of the bad French, and worse Latin, Jacques Charmolue was there complete—gesture, accent, and attitude.

And the crowd applauded louder than ever.

"Sacrilege! profanation!" resumed the voice of the bald man.

The gypsy turned round once more.

"Ah!" said she, " 'tis that villainous man!" Then, thrusting her under lip out beyond the upper, she made a little pout, which appeared to be familiar to her, executed a pirouette on her heel, and set about collecting in her tambourine the gifts of the multitude.

Big blanks, little blanks, targes[1] and eagle liards showered into it.

All at once, she passed in front of Gringoire. Gringoire put his hand so recklessly into his pocket that she halted. "The devil!" said the poet, finding at the bottom of his pocket the reality, that is, to say, a void. In the meantime, the pretty girl stood there, gazing at him with her big eyes, and holding out her tambourine to him and waiting. Gringoire broke into a violent perspiration.

If he had all Peru in his pocket, he would certainly have given it to the dancer; but Gringoire had not Peru, and, moreover, America had not yet been discovered.

Happily, an unexpected incident came to his rescue.

"Will you take yourself off, you Egyptian grasshopper?" cried a sharp voice, which proceeded from the darkest corner of the Place.

The young girl turned round in affright. It was no longer the voice of the bald man; it was the voice of a woman, bigoted and malicious.

However, this cry, which alarmed the gypsy, delighted a troop of children who were prowling about there.

"It is the recluse of the Tour-Roland," they exclaimed, with wild laughter, "it is the sacked nun who is scolding! Hasn't she supped? Let's carry her the remains of the city refreshments!"

All rushed toward the Pillar House.

In the meanwhile, Gringoire had taken advantage of the dancer's embarrassment, to disappear. The children's shouts had reminded him that he, also, had not supped, so he ran to the public buffet. But the little rascals had better legs than he; when he arrived, they had stripped the table. There remained not so much as a miserable *camichon* at five sous the pound. Nothing remained upon the wall but slender fleurs-de-lys, mingled with rose bushes, painted in 1434 by Mathieu Biterne. It was a meager supper.

It is an unpleasant thing to go to bed without supper, it is a still less pleasant thing not to sup and not to know where one is to sleep. That was Gringoire's condition. No supper, no shelter; he saw himself pressed on all sides by necessity, and he found necessity very crabbed. He had long ago discovered the truth, that Jupiter created men during a fit of misanthropy, and that during a wise man's whole life, his destiny holds his philosophy in a state of siege. As for himself, he had never seen the blockade so complete; he heard his stomach sounding a parley, and he considered it very much out of place that evil destiny should capture his philosophy by famine.

This melancholy reverie was absorbing him more and more, when a song, quaint but full of sweetness, suddenly tore him from it. It was the young gypsy who was singing.

Her voice was like her dancing, like her beauty. It was indefinable and charming; something pure and sonorous, aerial, winged, so to speak. There were continual outbursts, melodies, unexpected cadences, then simple phrases strewn with aerial and hissing notes; then floods of scales which would have put a nightingale to rout, but in which harmony was always present; then soft modulations of octaves which rose and fell, like the bosom of the young singer. Her beautiful face followed, with singular mobility, all the caprices of her song, from the wildest inspiration to the chastest dignity. One would have pronounced her now a mad creature, now a queen.

The words which she sang were in a tongue unknown to Gringoire, and which seemed to him to be unknown to herself, so little relation did the expression which she imparted to her song bear to the sense of the words. Thus, these four lines, in her mouth, were madly gay—

1. A blank: an old French coin.

> *Un cofre de gran riqueza*
> *Hallaron dentro un pilar,*
> *Dentro del, nuevas banderas*
> *Con figuras de espantar.*[1]

And an instant afterwards, at the accents which she imparted to this stanza—

> *Alarabes de cavallo*
> *Sin poderse menear,*
> *Con espadas, y los cuellos,*
> *Ballestas de buen echar,*

Gringoire felt the tears start to his eyes. Nevertheless, her song breathed joy, most of all, and she seemed to sing like a bird, from serenity and heedlessness.

The gypsy's song had disturbed Gringoire's reverie as the swan disturbs the water. He listened in a sort of rapture, and forgetfulness of everything. It was the first moment in the course of many hours when he did not feel that he suffered.

The moment was brief.

The same woman's voice, which had interrupted the gypsy's dance, interrupted her song.

"Will you hold your tongue, you cricket of hell?" it cried, still from the same obscure corner of the place.

The poor "cricket" stopped short. Gringoire covered up his ears.

"Oh!" he exclaimed, "accursed saw with missing teeth, which comes to break the lyre!"

Meanwhile, the other spectators murmured like himself; "To the devil with the sacked nun!" said some of them. And the old invisible kill-joy might have had occasion to repent of her aggressions against the gypsy had their attention not been diverted at this moment by the procession of the Pope of the Fools, which, after having traversed many streets and squares, debouched on the Place de Grève, with all its torches and all its uproar.

This procession, which our readers have seen set out from the Palais de Justice, had organized on the way, and had been recruited by all the knaves, idle thieves, and unemployed vagabonds in Paris; so that it presented a very respectable aspect when it arrived at the Grève.

First came Egypt. The Duke of Egypt headed it, on horseback, with his counts on foot holding his bridle and stirrups for him; behind them, the male and female Egyptians, pell-mell, with their little children crying on their shoulders; all—duke, counts, and populace—in rags and tatters. Then came the Kingdom of Argot; that is to say, all the thieves of France, arranged according to the order of their dignity; the minor people walking first. Thus defiled by fours, with the divers insignia of their grades, in that strange faculty, most of them lame, some cripples, others one-armed, shop clerks, pilgrims, *hubins,* bootblacks, thimble-riggers, street arabs, beggars, the blear-eyed beggars, thieves, the weakly, vagabonds, merchants, sham soldiers, goldsmiths, passed masters of pickpockets, isolated thieves. A catalogue that would weary Homer. In the center of the conclave of the passed masters of pickpockets, one had some difficulty in distinguishing the King of Argot, the grand coësre, so called, crouching in a little cart drawn by two big dogs. After the kingdom of the Argotiers, came the Empire of Galilee. Guillaume Rousseau, Emperor of the Empire of Galilee, marched majestically in his robe of purple, spotted with wine, preceded by buffoons wrestling and

1. A coffer to great richness
   In a pillar's heart they found,
   Within it lay new banners,
   With figures to astound.

executing military dances; surrounded by his macebearers, his pickpockets and clerks of the chamber of accounts. Last of all came the corporation of law clerks, with its maypoles crowned with flowers, its black robes, its music worthy of the orgy, and its large candles of yellow wax. In the center of this crowd, the grand officers of the Brotherhood of Fools bore on their shoulders a litter more loaded down with candles than the reliquary of Sainte-Geneviève in time of pest; and on this litter shone resplendent, with crosier, cope, and miter, the new Pope of the Fools, the bellringer of Notre-Dame, Quasimodo the hunchback.

Each section of this grotesque procession had its own music. The Egyptians made their drums and African tambourines resound. The slang men, not a very musical race, still clung to the goat's horn trumpet and the Gothic rubebbe of the twelfth century. The Empire of Galilee was not much more advanced; among its music one could hardly distinguish some miserable rebec, from the infancy of the art, still imprisoned in the *ré-la-mi*. But it was around the Pope of the Fools that all the musical riches of the epoch were displayed in a magnificent discord. It was nothing but soprano rebecs, counter-tenor rebecs, and tenor rebecs, not to reckon the flutes and brass instruments. Alas! our readers will remember that this was Gringoire's orchestra.

It is difficult to convey an idea of the degree of proud and blissful expansion to which the sad and hideous visage of Quasimodo had attained during the transit from the Palais de Justice, to the Place de Grève. It was the first enjoyment of self-love that he had ever experienced. Down to that day, he had known only humiliation, disdain for his condition, disgust for his person. Hence, deaf though he was, he enjoyed, like a veritable pope, the acclamations of that throng, which he hated because he felt that he was hated by it. What mattered it that his people consisted of a pack of fools, cripples, thieves, and beggars? it was still a people and he was its sovereign. And he accepted seriously all this ironical applause, all this derisive respect, with which the crowd mingled, it must be admitted, a good deal of very real fear. For the hunchback was robust; for the bandy-legged fellow was agile; for the deaf man was malicious: three qualities which temper ridicule.

We are far from believing, however, that the new Pope of the Fools understood both the sentiments which he felt and the sentiments which he inspired. The spirit which was lodged in this failure of a body had, necessarily, something incomplete and deaf about it. Thus, what he felt at the moment was to him, absolutely vague, indistinct, and confused. Only joy made itself felt, only pride dominated. Around that somber and unhappy face, there hung a radiance.

It was, then, not without surprise and alarm, that at the very moment when Quasimodo was passing the Pillar House, in that semi-intoxicated state, a man was seen to dart from the crowd, and to tear from his hands, with a gesture of anger, his crosier of gilded wood, the emblem of his mock popeship.

This man, this rash individual, was the man with the bald brow, who, a moment earlier, standing with the gypsy's group had chilled the poor girl with his words of menace and of hatred. He was dressed in an eccleslastical costume. At the moment when he stood forth from the crowd, Gringoire, who had not noticed him up to that time, recognized him: "Hold!" he said, with an exclamation of astonishment. "Eh! 'tis my master in Hermes, Dom Claude Frollo, the archdeacon! What the devil does he want of that old one-eyed fellow? He'll get himself devoured!"

A cry of terror arose, in fact. The formidable Quasimodo had hurled himself from the litter, and the women turned aside their eyes in order not to see him tear the archdeacon asunder.

He made one bound as far as the priest, looked at him, and fell upon his knees.

The priest tore off his tiara, broke his crozier, and rent his tinsel cope.

Quasimodo remained on his knees, with head bent and hands clasped. Then there was established between them a strange dialogue of signs and gestures, for neither of them spoke. The priest, erect on his feet, irritated, threatening, imperious; Quasimodo, prostrate, humble, suppliant. And, nevertheless, it is certain that Quasimodo could have crushed the priest with his thumb.

At length the archdeacon, giving Quasimodo's powerful shoulder a rough shake, made him a sign to rise and follow him.

Quasimodo rose.

Then the Brotherhood of Fools, their first stupor having passed off, wished to defend their pope, so abruptly dethroned. The Egyptians, the men of slang, and all the fraternity of law clerks, gathered howling round the priest.

Quasimodo placed himself in front of the priest, set in play the muscles of his athletic fists, and glared upon the assailants with the snarl of an angry tiger.

The priest resumed his somber gravity, made a sign to Quasimodo, and retired in silence.

Quasimodo walked in front of him, scattering the crowd as he passed.

When they had traversed the populace and the Place, the cloud of curious and idle were minded to follow them. Quasimodo then constituted himself the rearguard, and followed the archdeacon, walking backwards, squat, surly, monstrous, bristling, gathering up his limbs, licking his boar's tusks, growling like a wild beast, and imparting to the crowd immense vibrations, with a look or a gesture.

Both were allowed to plunge into a dark and narrow street, where no one dared to venture after them; so thoroughly did the mere chimera of Quasimodo gnashing his teeth bar the entrance.

"Here's a marvelous thing," said Gringoire; "but where the deuce shall I find some supper?"

Chapter IV

THE INCONVENIENCES OF FOLLOWING A PRETTY WOMAN THROUGH THE STREETS IN THE EVENING

GRINGOIRE SET OUT TO FOLLOW THE GYPSY AT ALL HAZARDS. HE HAD SEEN HER, ACCOMPANIED by her goat, take to the Rue de la Coutellerie; he took the Rue de la Coutellerie.

"Why not?" he said to himself.

Gringoire, a practical philosopher of the streets of Paris, had noticed that nothing is more propitious to reverie than following a pretty woman without knowing whither she is going. There was in this voluntary abdication of his free will, in this fancy submitting itself to another fancy, which suspects it not, a mixture of fantastic independence and blind obedience, something indescribable, intermediate between slavery and liberty, which pleased Gringoire—a spirit essentially compound, undecided, and complex, holding the extremities of all extremes, incessantly suspended between all human propensities, and neutralizing one by the other. He was fond of comparing himself to Mahomet's coffin, attracted in two different directions by two loadstones, and hesitating eternally between the heights and the depths, between the vault and the pavement, between fall and ascent, between zenith and nadir.

If Gringoire had lived in our day, what a fine middle course he would hold between classicism and romanticism!

But he was not sufficiently primitive to live three hundred years, and 'tis a pity. His absence is a void which is but too sensibly felt to-day.

Moreover, for the purpose of thus following passers-by (and especially female passers-by) in the streets, which Gringoire was fond of doing, there is no better disposition than ignorance of where one is going to sleep.

So he walked along, very thoughtfully, behind the young girl, who hastened her pace and made her goat trot as she saw the bourgeois returning home and the taverns—the only shops which had been open that day—closing.

"After all," he half thought to himself, "she must lodge somewhere; gypsies have kindly hearts. Who knows?—"

And in the points of suspense which he placed after this reticence in his mind, there lay I know not what flattering ideas.

Meanwhile, from time to time, as he passed the last groups of bourgeois closing their doors, he caught some scraps of their conversation, which broke the thread of his pleasant hypotheses.

Now it was two old men accosting each other.

"Do you know that it is cold, Master Thibaut Fernicle?" (Gringoire had been aware of this since the beginning of the winter.)

"Yes, indeed, Master Boniface Disome! Are we going to have a winter such as we had three years ago, in '80, when wood cost eight sous the measure?"

"Bah! that's nothing, Master Thibaut, compared with the winter of 1407, when it froze from St. Martin's Day until Candlemas! and so cold that the pen of the registrar of the parliament froze every three words, in the Grand Chamber! which interrupted the registration of justice."

Further on there were two female neighbors at their windows, holding candles, which the fog caused to sputter.

"Has your husband told you about the mishap, Mademoiselle la Boudraque?"

"No. What is it, Mademoiselle Turquant?"

"The horse of M. Gilles Godin, the notary at the Châtelet, took fright at the Flemings and their procession, and overturned Master Philippe Avrillot, lay monk of the Célestins."

"Really?"

"Actually."

"A bourgeois horse! 'tis rather too much! If it had been a cavalry horse, well and good!"

And the windows were closed. But Gringoire had lost the thread of his ideas, nevertheless.

Fortunately, he speedily found it again, and he knotted it together without difficulty, thanks to the gypsy, thanks to Djali, who still walked in front of him; two fine, delicate, and charming creatures, whose tiny feet, beautiful forms, and graceful manners he was engaged in admiring, almost confusing them in his contemplation; believing them to be both young girls, from their intelligence and good friendship; regarding them both as goats—so far as the lightness, agility, and dexterity of their walk were concerned.

But the streets were becoming blacker and more deserted every moment. The curfew had sounded long ago, and it was only at rare intervals now that they encountered a passer-by in the street, or a light in the windows. Gringoire had become involved, in his pursuit of the gypsy, in that inextricable labyrinth of alleys, squares, and closed courts which surround the ancient sepulcher of the Saints-Innocents, and which resembles a ball of thread tangled by a cat. "Here are streets which possess but little logic!" said Gringoire, lost in the thousands of circuits which returned upon themselves incessantly, but where the young girl pursued a road which seemed familiar to her, without hesitation and with a step which became ever more rapid. As for him, he would have been utterly ignorant of his situation had he not espied, in passing, at the turn of a street, the octagonal mass of the pillory of the fish markets, the open-work summit of which threw its black, fretted outlines clearly upon a window which was still lighted in the Rue Verdelet.

The young girl's attention had been attracted to him for the last few moments; she had repeatedly turned her head toward him with uneasiness; she had even once come to a standstill, and taking advantage of a ray of light which escaped from a half-open bakery to survey him intently, from head to foot, then, having cast this glance, Gringoire had seen her make that little pout which he had already noticed, after which she passed on.

This little pout had furnished Gringoire with food for thought. There was certainly both disdain and mockery in that graceful grimace. So he dropped his head, began to count the paving-stones, and to follow the young girl at a little greater distance, when, at the turn of a street, which had caused him to lose sight of her, he heard her utter a piercing cry.

He hastened his steps.

The street was full of shadows. Nevertheless, a twist of tow soaked in oil, which burned in a cage at the feet of the Holy Virgin at the street corner, permitted Gringoire to make out the gypsy struggling in the arms of two men, who were endeavoring to stifle her cries. The poor little goat, in great alarm, lowered his horns and bleated.

"Help! gentlemen of the watch!" shouted Gringoire, and advanced bravely. One of the men who held the young girl turned toward him. It was the formidable visage of Quasimodo.

Gringoire did not take to flight, but neither did he advance another step.

Quasimodo came up to him, tossed him four paces away on the pavement with a backward turn of the hand, and plunged rapidly into the gloom, bearing the young girl folded across one arm like a silken scarf. His companion followed him, and the poor goat ran after them all, bleating plaintively.

"Murder! murder!" shrieked the unhappy gypsy.

"Halt, rascals, and yield me that wench!" suddenly shouted in a voice of thunder, a cavalier who appeared suddenly from a neighboring square.

It was a captain of the king's archers, armed from head to foot, with his sword in his hand.

He tore the gypsy from the arms of the dazed Quasimodo, threw her across his saddle, and at the moment when the terrible hunchback, recovering from his surprise, rushed upon him to regain his prey, fifteen or sixteen archers, who followed their captain closely, made their appearance, with their two-edged swords in their fists. It was a squad of the king's police, which was making the rounds, by order of Messire Robert d'Estouteville, guard of the provostship of Paris.

Quasimodo was surrounded, seized, garroted; he roared, he foamed at the mouth, he bit; and had it been broad daylight, there is no doubt that his face alone, rendered more hideous by wrath, would have put the entire squad to flight. But by night he was deprived of his most formidable weapon, his ugliness.

His companion had disappeared during the struggle.

The gypsy gracefully raised herself upright upon the officer's saddle, placed both hands upon the young man's shoulders, and gazed fixedly at him for several seconds, as though enchanted with his good looks and with the aid which he had just rendered her. Then breaking silence first, she said to him, making her sweet voice still sweeter than usual—

"What is your name, monsieur le gendarme?"

"Captain Phœbus de Châteaupers, at your service, my beauty!" replied the officer, drawing himself up.

"Thanks," said she.

And while Captain Phœbus was turning up his moustache in Burgundian fashion, she slipped from the horse, like an arrow falling to earth, and fled!

A flash of lightning would have vanished less quickly.

"Nombrill of the Pope!" said the captain, causing Quasimodo's straps to be drawn tighter, "I should have preferred to keep the wench."

"What would you have, captain?" said one gendarme. "The warbler has fled, and the bat remains."

Chapter V

RESULT OF THE DANGERS

G RINGOIRE, THOROUGHLY STUNNED BY HIS FALL, REMAINED ON THE PAVEMENT IN FRONT OF THE Holy Virgin at the street corner. Little by little, he regained his senses; at first, for several minutes, he was floating in a sort of half-somnolent reverie, which was not without its charm, in which aeriel figures of the gypsy and her goat were coupled with Quasimodo's heavy fist. This state lasted but a short time. A decidedly vivid sensation of cold in the part of his body which was in contact with the pavement, suddenly aroused him and caused his spirit to return to the surface.

"Whence comes this chill?" he said abruptly, to himself. He then perceived that he was lying half in the middle of the gutter.

"That devil of a hunchbacked cyclops!" he muttered between his teeth; and he tried to rise. But he was too much dazed and bruised; he was forced to remain where he was. Moreover, his hand was tolerably free; he stopped up his nose and resigned himself.

"The mud of Paris," he said to himself—for decidedly he thought that he was sure that the gutter would prove his refuge for the night; and what can one do in a refuge, except dream?—"the mud of Paris is particularly stinking; it must contain a great deal of volatile and nitric salts. That, moreover, is the opinion of Master Nicolas Flamel, and of the alchemists—"

The word *alchemists* suddenly suggested to his mind the idea of Archdeacon Claude Frollo. He recalled the violent scene which he had just witnessed in part; that the gypsy was struggling with two men, that Quasimodo had a companion; and the morose and haughty face of the archdeacon passed confusedly through his memory. "That would be strange!" he said to himself. And on that fact and that basis he began to construct a fantastic edifice of hypothesis, that card-castle of philosophers; then, suddenly returning once more to reality, "Come! I'm freezing!" he ejaculated.

The place was, in fact, becoming less and less tenable. Each molecule of the gutter bore away a molecule of heat radiating from Gringoire's loins, and the equilibrium between the temperature of his body and the temperature of the brook, began to be established in rough fashion.

Quite a different annoyance suddenly assailed him. A group of children, those little barefooted savages who have always roamed the pavements of Paris under the eternal name of *gamins*, and who, when we were also children ourselves, threw stones at all of us in the afternoon, when we came out of school, because our trousers were not torn—a swarm of these young scamps rushed toward the square where Gringoire lay, with shouts and laughter which seemed to pay but little heed to the sleep of the neighbors. They were dragging after them some sort of hideous sack; and the noise of their wooden shoes alone would have roused the dead. Gringoire who was not quite dead yet, half raised himself.

"Ohé, Hennequin Dandéche! Ohé, Jehan Pincebourde!" they shouted in deafening tones, "old Eustache Moubon, the merchant at the corner, has just died. We've got his straw pallet, we're going to have a bonfire out of it. It's the turn of the Flemish to-day!"

And behold, they flung the pallet directly upon Gringoire, beside whom they had arrived, without spying him. At the same time, one of them took a handful of straw and set off to light it at the wick of the good Virgin.

"S'death!" growled Gringoire, "am I going to be too warm now?"

It was a critical moment. He was caught between fire and water; he made a superhuman effort, the effort of a counterfeiter of money who is on the point of being boiled, and who seeks to escape. He rose to his feet, flung aside the straw pallet upon the street urchins, and fled.

"Holy Virgin!" shrieked the children; " 'tis the merchant's ghost!"

And they fled in their turn.

The straw mattress remained master of the field. Bellefôret, Father Le Juge, and Corrozet affirm that it was picked up on the morrow, with great pomp, by the clergy of the quarter, and borne to the treasury of the church of Saint Opportune, where the sacristan, even as late as 1789, earned a tolerably handsome revenue out of the great miracle of the Statue of the Virgin at the corner of the Rue Mauconseil, which had, by its mere presence, on the memorable night between the sixth and 7th of January, 1482, exorcised the defunct Eustache Moubon, who, in order to play a trick on the devil, had at his death maliciously concealed his soul in his straw pallet.

Chapter VI

The Broken Jug

AFTER HAVING RUN FOR SOME TIME AT THE TOP OF HIS SPEED, WITHOUT KNOWING WHITHER, knocking his head against many a street corner, leaping many a gutter, traversing many an alley, many a court, many a square, seeking flight and passage through all the meanderings of the ancient passages of the Halles, exploring in his panic terror what the fine Latin of the maps calls *tota via, cheminum et viaria*, our poet suddenly halted for lack of breath in the first place, and in the second, because he had been collared, after a fashion, by a dilemma which had just occurred to his mind. "It strikes me, Master Pierre Gringoire," he said to himself, placing his finger to his brow, "that you are running like a madman. The little scamps are no less afraid of you than you are of them. It strikes me, I say, that you heard the clatter of their wooden shoes fleeing southward, while you were fleeing northward. Now, one of two things, either they have taken flight, and the pallet, which they must have forgotten in their terror, is precisely that hospitable bed in search of which you have been running ever since morning, and which madame the Virgin miraculously sends you, in order to recompense you for having made a morality in her honor, accompanied by triumphs and mummeries; or the children have not taken flight, and in that case they have put the brand to the pallet, and that is precisely the good fire which you need to cheer, dry, and warm you. In either case, good fire or good bed, that straw pallet is a gift from heaven. The blessed Virgin Marie who stands at the corner of the Rue Mauconseil, could only have made Eustache Moubon die for that express purpose; and it is folly on your part to flee thus zigzag, like a Picard before a Frenchman, leaving behind you what you seek before you; and you are a fool!"

Then he retraced his steps, and feeling his way and searching, with his nose to the wind and his ears on the alert, he tried to find the blessed pallet again, but in vain. There was nothing to be found but intersections of houses, closed courts, and crossings of streets, in the midst of which he hesitated and doubted incessantly, being more perplexed and entangled in this medley of streets than he would have been even in the labyrinth of the Hôtel des Tournelles. At length he lost patience, and exclaimed solemnly: "Cursed be cross-roads! 'tis the devil who has made them in the shape of his pitchfork!"

This exclamation afforded him a little solace, and a sort of reddish reflection which he caught sight of at that moment, at the extremity of a long and narrow lane, completed the elevation of his moral tone. "God be praised!" said he, "There it is yonder! There is my pallet burning." And comparing himself to the pilot who suffers shipwreck by night, *"Salve,"* he added piously, *"salve, maris stella!"*

Did he address this fragment of litany to the Holy Virgin, or to the pallet? We are utterly unable to say.

He had taken but a few steps in the long street, which sloped downwards, was unpaved, and more and more muddy and steep, when he noticed a very singular thing. It was not deserted; here and there along its extent crawled certain vague and formless masses, all directing their course toward the light which flickered at the end of the street, like those heavy insects which drag along by night, from blade to blade of grass, toward the shepherd's fire.

Nothing renders one so adventurous as not being able to feel the place where one's pocket is situated. Gringoire continued to advance, and had soon joined that one of the forms which dragged along most indolently, behind the others. On drawing near, he perceived that it was nothing else than a wretched legless cripple in a bowl, who was hopping along on his two hands like a wounded field-spider which has but two legs left. At the moment when he passed close to this species of spider with a human countenance, it raised toward him a lamentable voice: *"La buona mancia, signor! la buona mancia!"*[1]

"Deuce take you," said Gringoire, "and me with you, if I know what you mean!"

And he passed on.

He overtook another of these itinerant masses, and examined it. It was an impotent man, both halt and crippled, and halt and crippled to such a degree that the complicated system of crutches and wooden legs which sustained him, gave him the air of a mason's scaffolding on the march. Gringoire, who liked noble and classical comparisons, compared him in thought to the living tripod of Vulcan.

This living tripod saluted him as he passed, but stopping his hat on a level with Gringoire's chin, like a shaving dish, while he shouted in the latter's ears: *"Señor cabellero, para comprar un pedaso de pan!"*[2]

"It appears," said Gringoire, "that this one can also talk; but 'tis a rude language, and he is more fortunate than I if he understands it." Then, smiting his brow, in a sudden transition of ideas: "By the way, what the deuce did they mean this morning with their *Esmeralda?*"

He was minded to augment his pace, but for the third time something barred his way. This something or, rather, someone was a blind man, a little blind fellow with a bearded, Jewish face, who, rowing away in the space about him with a stick, and towed by a large dog, droned through his nose with a Hungarian accent: *"Facitote caritatem!"*

"Well, now," said Gringoire, "here's one at last who speaks a Christian tongue. I must have a very charitable aspect, since they ask alms of me in the present lean condition of my purse. My friend," and he turned toward the blind man, "I sold my last shirt last week; that is to say, since you understand only the language of Cicero: *Vendidi hebdomade nuper transita meam ultimam chemisam.*"

That said, he turned his back upon the blind man, and pursued his way. But the blind man began to increase his stride at the same time; and, behold! the cripple and the legless man, in his bowl, came up on their side in great haste, and with great clamor of bowl and crutches, upon the pavement. Then all three, jostling each other at poor Gringoire's heels, began to sing their song to him—

"Caritatem!" chanted the blind man.

"La buona mancia!" chanted the cripple in the bowl.

And the lame man took up the musical phrase by repeating: *"Un pedaso de pan!"*

Gringoire stopped up his ears. "Oh, tower of Babel!" he exclaimed.

He set out to run. The blind man ran! The lame man ran! The cripple in the bowl ran!

---

1. Alms.

2. Give me the means to buy a bit of bread, sir.

And then, in proportion as he plunged deeper into the street, cripples in bowls, blind men and lame men, swarmed about him, and men with one arm, and with one eye, and the leprous with their sores, some emerging from little streets adjacent, some from the air-holes of cellars, howling, bellowing, yelping, all limping and halting, all flinging themselves toward the light, and humped up in the mire, like snails after a shower.

Gringoire, still followed by his three persecutors, and not knowing very well what was to become of him, marched along in terror among them, turning out for the lame, stepping over the cripples in bowls, with his feet imbedded in that anthill of lame men, like the English captain who got caught in the quicksand of a swarm of crabs.

The idea occurred to him of making an effort to retrace his steps. But it was too late. This whole legion had closed in behind him, and his three beggars held him fast. So he proceeded, impelled both by this irresistible flood, by fear, and by a vertigo which converted all this into a sort of horrible dream.

At last he reached the end of the street. It opened upon an immense place, where a thousand scattered lights flickered in the confused mists of night. Gringoire flew thither, hoping to escape, by the swiftness of his legs, from the three infirm specters who had clutched him.

"Onde vas, hombre?" (Where are you going, my man?) cried the cripple, flinging away his crutches, and running after him with the best legs that ever traced a geometrical step upon the pavements of Paris.

In the meantime the legless man, erect upon his feet, crowned Gringoire with his heavy iron bowl, and the blind man glared in his face with flaming eyes!

"Where am I?" said the terrified poet.

"In the Court of Miracles," replied a fourth specter, who had accosted them.

"Upon my soul," resumed Gringoire, "I certainly do behold the blind who see, and the lame who walk, but where is the Savior?"

They replied by a burst of sinister laughter.

The poor poet cast his eyes about him. It was, in truth, that redoubtable Cour des Miracles, whither an honest man had never penetrated at such an hour; the magic circle where the officers of the Châtelet and the sergeants of the provostship, who ventured thither, disappeared in morsels; a city of thieves, a hideous wart on the face of Paris; a sewer, from which escaped every morning, and whither returned every night to crouch, that stream of vices, of mendicancy and vagabondage which always overflows in the streets of capitals; a monstrous hive, to which returned at nightfall, with their booty, all the drones of the social order; a lying hospital where the bohemian, the disfrocked monk, the ruined scholar, the ne'er-do-wells of all nations, Spaniards, Italians, Germans— of all religions, Jews, Christians, Mahometans, idolaters, covered with painted sores, beggars by day, were transformed by night into brigands; an immense dressing-room, in a word, where, at that epoch, the actors of that eternal comedy, which theft, prostitution, and murder play upon the pavements of Paris, dressed and undressed.

It was a vast place, irregular and badly paved, like all the squares of Paris at that date. Fires, around which swarmed strange groups, blazed here and there. Everyone was going, coming, and shouting. Shrill laughter was to be heard, the wailing of children, the voices of women. The hands and heads of this throng, black against the luminous background, outlined against it a thousand eccentric gestures. At times, upon the ground, where trembled the light of the fires, mingled with large, indefinite shadows, one could behold a dog passing, which resembled a man, a man who resembled a dog. The limits of races and species seemed effaced in this city, as in a pandemonium. Men, women, beasts, age, sex, health, maladies, all seemed to be in common among these people; all went together, they mingled, confounded, superposed; each one there participated in all.

The poor and flickering flames of the fire permitted Gringoire to distinguish, amid his trouble, all around the immense place, a hideous frame of ancient houses, whose wormeaten, shriveled, stunted façades, each pierced with one or two lighted attic windows, seemed to him, in the darkness, like enormous heads of old women, ranged in a circle, monstrous and crabbed, winking as they looked on at the Witches' Sabbath.

It was like a new world, unknown, unheard of, misshapen, creeping, swarming, fantastic.

Gringoire, more and more terrified, clutched by the three beggars as by three pairs of tongs, dazed by a throng of other faces which frothed and yelped around him, unhappy Gringoire endeavored to summon his presence of mind, in order to recall whether it was a Saturday. But his efforts were vain; the thread of his memory and of his thought was broken; and, doubting everything, wavering between what he saw and what he felt, he put to himself this unanswerable question—

"If I exist, does this exist? if this exists, do I exist?"

At that moment, a distinct cry arose in the buzzing throng which surrounded him, "Let's take him to the king! let's take him to the king!"

"Holy Virgin!" murmured Gringoire, "the king here must be a ram?"

"To the king! to the king!" repeated all voices.

They dragged him off. Each vied with the other in laying his claws upon him. But the three beggars did not loose their hold and tore him from the rest, howling, "He belongs to us?"

The poet's already sickly doublet yielded its last sigh in this struggle.

While traversing the horrible place, his vertigo vanished. After taking a few steps, the sentiment of reality returned to him. He began to become accustomed to the atmosphere of the place. At the first moment there had arisen from his poet's head, or, simply and prosaically, from his empty stomach, a mist, a vapor, so to speak, which, spreading between objects and himself, permitted him to catch a glimpse of them only in the incoherent fog of nightmare—in those shadows of dreams which distort every outline, agglomerating objects into unwieldy groups, dilating things into chimeras, and men into phantoms. Little by little, this hallucination was succeeded by a less bewildered and exaggerating view. Reality made its way to the light around him, struck his eyes, struck his feet, and demolished, bit by bit, all that frightful poetry with which he had, at first, believed himself to be surrounded. He was forced to perceive that he was not walking in the Styx, but in mud, that he was elbowed not by demons, but by thieves; that it was not his soul which was in question, but his life (since he lacked that precious conciliator, which places itself so effectually between the bandit and the honest man—a purse). In short, on examining the orgy more closely, and with more coolness, he fell from the witches' sabbath to the dram-shop.

The Cour des Miracles was, in fact, merely a dram-shop; but a brigand's dram-shop, reddened quite as much with blood as with wine.

The spectacle which presented itself to his eyes, when his ragged escort finally deposited him at the end of his trip, was not fitted to bear him back to poetry, even to the poetry of hell. It was more than ever the prosaic and brutal reality of the tavern. Were we not in the fifteenth century, we would say that Gringoire had descended from Michael Angelo to Callot.

Around a great fire which burned on a large, circular flagstone, the flames of which had heated red-hot the legs of a tripod, which was empty for the moment, some wormeaten tables were placed, here and there, haphazard, no lackey of a geometrical turn having deigned to adjust their parallelism, or to see to it that they did not make too unusual angles. Upon these tables gleamed several dripping pots of wine and beer, and round these pots were grouped many bacchic visages, purple with the fire and the wine. There was a man with a huge belly and a jovial face, noisily kissing a woman of the town, thickset and brawny. There was a sort of sham soldier, a "naquois," as the slang expression runs, who was whistling as he undid the bandages from his fictitious wound, and removing the numbness from his sound and vigorous knee, which had been swathed since morning in a thousand ligatures. On the other hand, there was a wretched fellow, preparing with celandine and beef's blood, his "leg of God," for the next day. Two tables further on, a palmer, with his pilgrim's costume complete, was practicing the lament of the Holy Queen, not forgetting the drone and the nasal drawl. Further on, a young scamp was taking a lesson in epilepsy from an old pretender, who was instructing him in the art of foaming at the mouth, by chewing a morsel of soap. Beside him, a man with the dropsy was getting rid of his swelling, and making four or five female thieves, who were disputing at the same table, over a child who had been stolen that evening, hold their noses. All circumstances which, two centuries later, "seemed so ridiculous to the court," as Sauval says, "that they served as a pastime to the king, and as an introduction to the royal ballet of Night, divided into four parts and danced on the theater of the Petit-Bourbon." "Never," adds an eye witness of 1653, "have the sudden metamorphoses of the Court of Miracles been more happily presented. Benserade prepared us for it by some very gallant verses."

Loud laughter everywhere, and obscene songs. Each one held his own course, carping and swearing, without listening to his neighbor. Pots clinked, and quarrels sprang up at the shock of the pots, and the broken pots made rents in the rags.

A big dog, seated on his tail, gazed at the fire. Some children were mingled in this orgy. The stolen child wept and cried. Another, a big boy four years of age, seated with legs dangling, upon a bench that was too high for him, before a table that reached to his chin, and uttering not a word. A third, gravely spreading out upon the table with his finger, the melted tallow which dripped from a candle. Last of all, a little fellow crouching in the mud, almost lost in a cauldron, which he was scraping with a tile, and from which he was evoking a sound that would have made Stradivarius swoon.

Near the fire was a hogshead, and on the hogshead a beggar. This was the king on his throne.

The three who had Gringoire in their clutches led him in front of this hogshead, and the entire bacchanal rout fell silent for a moment, with the exception of the cauldron inhabited by the child.

Gringoire dared neither breathe nor raise his eyes.

"Hombre, quita tu somberro!" said one of the three knaves, in whose grasp he was, and, before he had comprehended the meaning, the other had snatched his hat—a wretched headgear, it is true, but still good on a sunny day or when there was but little rain. Gringoire sighed.

Meanwhile the king addressed him, from the summit of his cask—

"Who is this rogue?"

Gringoire shuddered. That voice, although accentuated by menace, recalled to him another voice, which, that very morning, had dealt the deathblow to his mystery, by drawling, nasally, in the midst of the audience, "Charity, please!" He raised his head. It was indeed Clopin Trouillefou.

Clopin Trouillefou, arrayed in his royal insignia, wore neither one rag more nor one rag less. The sore upon his arm had already disappeared. He held in his hand one of those whips made of thongs of white leather, which police sergeants then used to repress the crowd, and which were called *boullayes*. On his head he wore a sort of headgear, bound round and closed at the top. But it was difficult to make out whether it was a child's cap or a king's crown, the two things bore so strong a resemblance to each other.

Meanwhile Gringoire, without knowing why, had regained some hope, on recognizing in the King of the Cour des Miracles his accursed mendicant of the Grand Hall.

"Master," stammered he; "monseigneur—sire—how ought I to address you?" he said at length, having reached the culminating point of his crescendo, and knowing neither how to mount higher, nor to descend again.

"Monseigneur, his majesty, or comrade, call me what you please. But make haste. What have you to say in your own defense?"

"In your own defense?" thought Gringoire, "that displeases me." He resumed, stuttering, "I am he, who this morning—"

"By the devil's claws!" interrupted Clopin, "your name, knave, and nothing more. Listen. You are in the presence of three powerful sovereigns: myself, Clopin Trouillefou, King of Thunes, successor to the Grand Coësre, supreme suzerain of the Realm of Argot; Mathias Hunyadi Spicali, Duke of Egypt and of Bohemia, the old yellow fellow whom you see yonder, with a dish clout round his head; Guillaume Rousseau, Emperor of Galilee, that fat fellow who is not listening to us but caressing a wench. We are your judges. You have entered the Kingdom of Argot, without being an *argotier*; you have violated the privileges of our city. You must be punished unless you are a *capon*, a *franc-mitou* or a *rifodé*; that is to say, in the slang of honest folks—a thief, a beggar, or a vagabond. Are you anything of that sort? Justify yourself; announce your titles."

"Alas!" said Gringoire, "I have not that honor. I am the author—"

"That is sufficient," resumed Trouillefou, without permitting him to finish. "You are going to be hanged. 'Tis a very simple matter, gentlemen and honest bourgeois! as you treat our people in your abode, so we treat you in ours! The law which you apply to vagabonds, vagabonds apply to you. 'Tis your fault if it is harsh. One really must behold the grimace of an honest man above the hempen collar now and then; that renders the thing honorable. Come, friend, divide your rags gaily among these damsels. I am going to have you hanged to amuse the vagabonds, and you are to give them your purse to drink your health. If you have any mummery to go through with, there's a very good God the Father in that mortar yonder, in stone, which we stole from Saint-Pierre aux Bœufs. You have four minutes in which to fling your soul at his head."

The harangue was formidable.

"Well said, upon my soul! Clopin Trouillefou preaches like the Holy Father the Pope!" exclaimed the Emperor of Galilee, smashing his pot in order to prop up his table.

"Messeigneurs, emperors, and kings," said Gringoire coolly (for I know not how, firmness had returned to him, and he spoke with resolution), "don't think of such a thing; my name is Pierre Gringoire. I am the poet whose morality was presented this morning in the grand hall of the Courts."

"Ah! so it was you, master!" said Clopin. "I was there, *par la tête Dieu!* Well! comrade, is that any reason, because you bored us to death this morning, that you should not be hung this evening?"

"I shall find difficulty in getting out of it," said Gringoire to himself. Nevertheless, he made one more effort: "I don't see why poets are not classed with vagabonds," said he. "Vagabond, Aesopus certainly was; Homerus was a beggar; Mercurius was a thief—"

Clopin interrupted him: "I believe that you are trying to blarney us with your jargon. Zounds! let yourself be hung, and don't kick up such a row over it!"

"Pardon me, monseigneur, the King of Thunes," replied Gringoire, disputing the ground foot by foot. "It is worth trouble—One moment!—Listen to me—You are not going to condemn me without having heard me"—

His unlucky voice was, in fact, drowned in the uproar which rose around him. The little boy scraped away at his cauldron with more spirit than ever; and, to crown all, an old woman had just placed on the tripod a frying-pan of grease, which hissed away on the fire with a noise similar to the cry of a troop of children in pursuit of a masker.

In the meantime, Clopin Trouillefou appeared to hold a momentary conference with the Duke of Egypt, and the Emperor of Galilee, who was completely drunk. Then he shouted shrilly: "Silence!" and, as the cauldron and the frying-pan did not heed him, and continued their duet, he jumped down from his hogshead, gave a kick to the boiler, which rolled ten paces away bearing the child with it, a kick to the frying-pan, which upset in the fire with all its grease, and gravely remounted his throne, without troubling himself about the stifled tears of the child, or the grumbling of the old woman, whose supper was wasting away in a fine white flame.

Trouillefou made a sign, and the duke, the emperor, and the passed masters of pickpockets, and the isolated robbers, came and ranged themselves around him in a horseshoe, of which Gringoire, still roughly held by the body, formed the center. It was a semi-circle of rags, tatters, tinsel, pitchforks, axes, legs staggering with intoxication, huge, bare arms, faces sordid, dull, and stupid. In the midst of this Round Table of beggary, Clopin Trouillefou—as the doge of this senate, as the king of this peerage, as the pope of this conclave—dominated; first by virtue of the height of his hogshead, and next by virtue of an indescribable, haughty, fierce, and formidable air, which caused his eyes to flash, and corrected in his savage profile the bestial type of the race of vagabonds. One would have pronounced him a boar amid a herd of swine.

"Listen," said he to Gringoire, fondling his misshapen chin with his horny hand; "I don't see why you should not be hung. It is true that it appears to be repugnant to you; and it is very natural, for you bourgeois are not accustomed to it. You form for yourselves a great idea of the thing. After all, we don't wish you any harm. Here is a means of extricating yourself from your predicament for the moment. Will you become one of us?"

The reader can judge of the effect which this proposition produced upon Gringoire, who beheld life slipping away from him, and who was beginning to lose his hold upon it. He clutched at it again with energy.

"Certainly I will, and right heartily," said he.

"Do you consent," resumed Clopin, "to enroll yourself among the people of the knife?"

"Of the knife, precisely," responded Gringoire.

"You recognize yourself as a member of the free bourgeoisie?"[1] added the King of Thunes.

"Of the free bourgeoisie."

"Subject of the Kingdom of Argot?"

"Of the Kingdom of Argot."[2]

"A vagabond?"

"A vagabond."

"In your soul?"

"In my soul."

"I must call your attention to the fact," continued the king, "that you will be hung all the same."

"The devil!" said the poet.

"Only," continued Clopin imperturbably, "you will be hung later on, with more ceremony, at the expense of the good city of Paris, on a handsome stone gibbet, and by honest men. That is a consolation."

"Just so," responded Gringoire.

"There are other advantages. In your quality of a high-toned sharper, you will not have to pay the taxes on mud, or the poor, or lanterns, to which the bourgeois of Paris are subject."

"So be it," said the poet. "I agree. I am a vagabond, a thief, a sharper, a man of the knife, anything you please; and I am all that already, monsieur, King of Thunes, for I am a philosopher; *et omnia in philosophia, omnes in philosopho continentur*—all things are contained in philosophy, all men in the philosopher, as you know."

The King of Thunes scowled.

"What do you take me for, my friend? What Hungarian Jew patter are you jabbering at us? I don't know Hebrew. One isn't a Jew because one is a bandit. I don't even steal any longer. I'm above that; I kill. Cut-throat, yes; cut-purse, no."

Gringoire tried to slip in some excuse between these curt words, which wrath rendered more and more jerky.

"I ask your pardon, monseigneur. It is not Hebrew; 'tis Latin."

1. A high-toned sharper.

2. Thieves.

"I tell you," resumed Clopin angrily, "that I'm not a Jew, and that I'll have you hung, belly of the synagogue, like that little shop-keeper of Judea, who is by your side, and whom I entertain strong hopes of seeing nailed to a counter one of these days, like the counterfeit coin that he is!"

So saying, he pointed his finger at the little, bearded Hungarian Jew who had accosted Gringoire with his *facitote caritatem,* and who, understanding no other language beheld with surprise the King of Thunes's ill-humor overflow upon him.

At length Monsieur Clopin calmed down.

"So you will be a vagabond, you knave?" he said to our poet.

"Of course," replied the poet.

"Willing is not all," said the surly Clopin; "good-will doesn't put one onion the more into the soup, and 'tis good for nothing except to go to Paradise with; now, Paradise and the thieves' band are two different things. In order to be received among the thieves, you must prove that you are good for something, and for that purpose, you must search the manikin."

"I'll search anything you like," said Gringoire.

Clopin made a sign. Several thieves detached themselves from the circle, and returned a moment later. They brought two thick posts, terminated at their lower extremities in spreading timber supports, which made them stand readily upon the ground; to the upper extremity of the two posts they fitted a cross-beam, and the whole constituted a very pretty portable gibbet, which Gringoire had the satisfaction of beholding rise before him, in a twinkling. Nothing was lacking, not even the rope, which swung gracefully over the cross-beam.

"What are they going to do?" Gringoire asked himself with some uneasiness. A sound of bells, which he heard at that moment, put an end to his anxiety; it was a stuffed manikin, which the vagabonds were suspending by the neck from the rope, a sort of scarecrow dressed in red, and so hung with mule-bells and larger bells, that one might have tricked out thirty Castilian mules with them. These thousand tiny bells quivered for some time with the vibration of the rope, then gradually died away, and finally became silent when the manikin had been brought into a state of immobility by that law of the pendulum which has dethroned the water clock and the hour-glass.

Then Clopin, pointing out to Gringoire a rickety old stool placed beneath the manikin—

"Climb up there."

"Death of the devil!" objected Gringoire; "I shall break my neck. Your stool limps like one of Martial's distiches; it has one hexameter leg and one pentameter leg."

"Climb!" repeated Clopin.

Gringoire mounted the stool, and succeeded, not without some oscillations of head and arms, in regaining his center of gravity.

"Now," went on the King of Thunes, "twist your right foot round your left leg, and rise on the tip of your left foot."

"Monseigneur," said Gringoire, "so you absolutely insist on my breaking some one of my limbs?"

Clopin tossed his head.

"Hark ye, my friend, you talk too much. Here's the gist of the matter in two words: you are to rise on tiptoe, as I tell you; in that way you will be able to reach the pocket of the manikin, you will rummage it, you will pull out the purse that is there—and if you do all this without our hearing the sound of a bell, all is well: you shall be a vagabond. All we shall then have to do, will be to thrash you soundly for the space of a week."

"*Ventre-Dieu!* I will be careful," said Gringoire. "And suppose I do make the bells sound?"

"Then you will be hanged. Do you understand?"

"I don't understand at all," replied Gringoire.

"Listen, once more. You are to search the manikin, and take away its purse; if a single bell stirs during the operation, you will be hung. Do you understand that?"

"Good," said Gringoire; "I understand that. And then?"

"If you succeed in removing the purse without our hearing the bells, you are a vagabond, and you will be thrashed for eight consecutive days. You understand now, no doubt?"

"No, monseigneur; I no longer understand. Where is the advantage to me? hanged in one case, cudgeled in the other?"

"And a vagabond," resumed Clopin, "and a vagabond; is that nothing? It is for your interest that we should beat you, in order to harden you to blows."

"Many thanks," replied the poet.

"Come, make haste," said the king, stamping upon his cask, which resounded like a huge drum! "Search the manikin, and let there be an end to this! I warn you for the last time, that if I hear a single bell, you will take the place of the manikin."

The band of thieves applauded Clopin's words, and arranged themselves in a circle round the gibbet, with a laugh so pitiless that Gringoire perceived that he amused them too much not to have everything to fear from them. No hope was left for him, accordingly, unless it were the slight chance of succeeding in the formidable operation which was imposed upon him; he decided to risk it, but it was not without first having addressed a fervent prayer to the manikin he was about to plunder, and who would have been easier to move to pity than the vagabonds. These myriad bells, with their little copper tongues, seemed to him like the mouths of so many asps, open and ready to sting and to hiss.

"Oh!" he said, in a very low voice, "is it possible that my life depends on the slightest vibration of the least of these bells? Oh!" he added, with clasped hands, "bells, do not ring, hand-bells do not clang, mule-bells do not quiver!"

He made one more attempt upon Trouillefou.

"And if there should come a gust of wind?"

"You will be hanged," replied the other, without hesitation.

Perceiving that no respite, nor reprieve, nor subterfuge was possible, he bravely decided upon his course of action; he wound his right foot round his left leg, raised himself on his left foot, and stretched out his arm: but at the moment when his hand touched the manikin, his body, which was now supported upon one leg only, wavered on the stool which had but three; he made an involuntary effort to support himself by the manikin, lost his balance, and fell heavily to the ground, deafened by the fatal vibration of the thousand bells of the manikin, which, yielding to the impulse imparted by his hand, described first a rotary motion, and then swayed majestically between the two posts.

"Malediction!" he cried as he fell, and remained as though dead, with his face to the earth.

Meanwhile, he heard the dreadful peal above his head, the diabolical laughter of the vagabonds, and the voice of Trouillefou saying—

"Pick me up that knave, and hang him without ceremony."

He rose. They had already detached the manikin to make room for him.

The thieves made him mount the stool, Clopin came to him, passed the rope about his neck, and, tapping him on the shoulder—

"Adieu, my friend. You can't escape now, even if you digested with the pope's guts."

The word "Mercy!" died away upon Gringoire's lips. He cast his eyes about him; but there was no hope: all were laughing.

"Bellevigne de l'Ètoile," said the King of Thunes to an enormous vagabond, who stepped out from the ranks, "climb upon the cross-beam."

Bellevigne de l'Ètoile nimbly mounted the transverse beam, and in another minute, Gringoire, on raising his eyes, beheld him, with terror, seated upon the beam above his head.

"Now," resumed Clopin Trouillefou, "as soon as I clap my hands, you, Andry the Red, will fling the stool to the ground with a blow of your knee; you, François Chante-Prune, will cling to the feet of the rascal; and you, Bellevigne, will fling yourself on his shoulders; and all three at once, do you hear?"

Gringoire shuddered.

"Are you ready?" said Clopin Trouillefou to the three thieves, who held themselves in readiness to fall upon Gringoire. A moment of horrible suspense ensued for the poor victim, during which Clopin tranquilly thrust into the fire with the tip of his foot, some bits of vine shoots which the flame had not caught. "Are you ready?" he repeated, and opened his hands to clap. One second more and all would have been over.

But he paused, as though struck by a sudden thought.

"One moment!" said he; "I forgot! It is our custom not to hang a man without inquiring whether there is any woman who wants him. Comrade, this is your last resource. You must wed either a female vagabond or the noose."

This law of the vagabonds, singular as it may strike the reader, remains to-day written out at length, in ancient English legislation. (See *Burington's Observations*.)

Gringoire breathed again. This was the second time that he had returned to life within an hour. So he did not dare to trust to it too implicitly.

"Holà!" cried Clopin, mounted once more upon his cask, "holà! women, females, is there among you, from the sorceress to her cat, a wench who wants this rascal? Holà, Colette la Charonne! Elisabeth Trouvain! Simone Jodouyne! Marie Piédebou! Thonne la Longue! Bérarde Fanouel! Michelle Genaille! Claude Ronge-oreille! Mathurine Girorou!—Holà! Isabeau-la-Thierrye! Come and see! A man for nothing! Who wants him?"

Gringoire, no doubt, was not very appetizing in this miserable condition. The female vagabonds did not seem to be much affected by the proposition. The unhappy wretch heard them answer: "No! no! hang him; there'll be the more fun for us all!"

Nevertheless, three emerged from the throng and came to smell of him. The first was a big wench, with a square face. She examined the philosopher's deplorable doublet attentively. His garment was worn, and more full of holes than a stove for roasting chestnuts. The girl made a wry face. "Old rag!" she muttered, and addressing Gringoire, "Let's see your cloak!" "I have lost it," replied Gringoire. "Your hat?" "They took it away from me." "Your shoes?" "They have hardly any soles left." "Your purse?" "Alas!" stammered Gringoire, "I have not even a sou." "Let them hang you, then, and say 'Thank you!'" retorted the vagabond wench, turning her back on him.

The second—old, black, wrinkled, hideous, with an ugliness conspicuous even in the Cour des Miracles, trotted round Gringoire. He almost trembled lest she should want him. But she mumbled between her teeth, "He's too thin," and went off.

The third was a young girl, quite fresh, and not too ugly. "Save me!" said the poor fellow to her, in a low tone. She gazed at him for a moment with an air of pity, then dropped her eyes, made a plait in her petticoat, and remained in indecision. He followed all these movements with his eyes; it was the last gleam of hope. "No," said the young girl, at length, "no! Guillaume Longuejoue would beat me." She retreated into the crowd.

"You are unlucky, comrade," said Clopin.

Then rising to his feet, upon his hogshead. "No one wants him," he exclaimed, imitating the accent of an auctioneer, to the great delight of all; "no one wants him? once, twice, three times!" and, turning toward the gibbet with a sign of his hand, "Gone!"

Bellevigne de l'Ètoile, Andry the Red, François Chante-Prune, stepped up to Gringoire.

At that moment a cry arose among the thieves: *"La Esmeralda! La Esmeralda!"*

Gringoire shuddered, and turned toward the side whence the clamor proceeded.

The crowd opened, and gave passage to a pure and dazzling form.

It was the gypsy.

"La Esmeralda!" said Gringoire, stupefied in the midst of his emotions, by the abrupt manner in which that magic word knotted together all his reminiscences of the day.

This rare creature seemed, even in the Cour des Miracles, to exercise her sway of charm and beauty. The vagabonds, male and female, ranged themselves gently along her path, and their brutal faces beamed beneath her glance.

She approached the victim with her light step. Her pretty Djali followed her. Gringoire was more dead than alive. She examined him for a moment in silence.

"You are going to hang this man?" she said gravely, to Clopin.

"Yes, sister," replied the King of Thunes, "unless you will take him for your husband."

She made her pretty little pout with her under lip.

"I'll take him," said she.

Gringoire firmly believed that he had been in a dream ever since morning, and that this was the continuation of it.

The change was, in fact, violent, though a gratifying one.

They undid the noose, and made the poet step down from the stool. His emotion was so lively that he was obliged to sit down.

The Duke of Egypt brought an earthenware crock, without uttering a word. The gypsy offered it to Gringoire: "Fling it on the ground," said she.

The crock broke into four pieces.

"Brother," then said the Duke of Egypt, laying his hands upon their foreheads, "she is your wife; sister, he is your husband for four years. Go."

Chapter VII

A BRIDAL NIGHT

A FEW MOMENTS LATER OUR POET FOUND HIMSELF IN A TINY ARCHED CHAMBER, VERY COSY, VERY warm, seated at a table which appeared to ask nothing better than to make some loans from a larder hanging nearby, having a good bed in prospect, and alone with a pretty girl. The adventure smacked of enchantment. He.began seriously to take himself for a personage in a fairy tale; he cast his eyes about him from time to time, as though to see if the chariot of fire, harnessed to two-winged chimeras, which alone could have so rapidly transported him from Tartarus to Paradise, were still there. At times, also, he fixed his eyes obstinately upon the holes in his doublet, in order to cling to reality, and not lose the ground from under his feet completely. His reason, tossed about in imaginary space, now hung only by this thread.

The young girl did not appear to pay any attention to him; she went and came, displaced a stool, talked to her goat, and indulged in a pout now and then. At last she came and seated herself near the table, and Gringoire was able to scrutinize her at his ease.

You have been a child, reader, and you would, perhaps, be very happy to be one still. It is quite certain that you have not, more than once (and for my part, I have passed whole days, the best employed of my life, at it) followed from thicket to thicket, by the side of running water, on a sunny day, a beautiful green or blue dragon-fly, breaking its flight in abrupt angles, and kissing the tips of all the branches. You recollect with what amorous curiosity your thought and your gaze were riveted upon this little whirlwind, hissing and humming with wings of purple and azure, in the midst of which floated an imperceptible body, veiled by the very rapidity of its movement. The aerial being which was dimly outlined amid this quivering of wings, appeared to you chimerical, imaginary, impossible to touch, impossible to see. But when, at length, the dragon-fly alighted on the tip of a reed, and, holding your breath the while, you were able to examine the long, gauze wings, the long enamel robe, the two globes of crystal, what astonishment you felt, and what fear lest you should again behold the form disappear into a shade, and the creature into a chimera! Recall these impressions, and you will readily appreciate what Gringoire felt on contemplating, beneath her visible and palpable form, that Esmeralda of whom, up to that time, he had only caught a glimpse, amidst a whirlwind of dance, song, and tumult.

Sinking deeper and deeper into his reverie: "So this," he said to himself, following her vaguely with his eyes, "is *la Esmeralda!* a celestial creature! a street dancer! so much, and so little! 'Twas she who dealt the death-blow to my mystery this morning, 'tis she who saves my life this evening! My evil genius! My good angel! A pretty woman, on my word! and who must needs love me madly to have taken me in that fashion. By the way," said he, rising suddenly, with that sentiment of the true which formed the foundation of his character and his philosophy, "I don't know very well how it happens, but I am her husband!"

With this idea in his head and in his eyes, he stepped up to the young girl in a manner so military and so gallant that she drew back.

"What do you want of me?" said she.

"Can you ask me, adorable Esmeralda?" replied Gringoire, with so passionate an accent that he was himself astonished at it on hearing himself speak.

The gypsy opened her great eyes. "I don't know what you mean."

"What!" resumed Gringoire, growing warmer and warmer, and supposing that, after all, he had to deal merely with a virtue of the Cour des Miracles; "am I not thine, sweet friend, art thou not mine?"

And, quite ingenuously, he clasped her waist.

The gypsy's corsage slipped through his hands like the skin of an eel. She bounded from one end of the tiny room to the other, stooped down, and raised herself again, with a little poniard in her hand, before Gringoire had even had time to see whence the poniard came; proud and angry, with swelling lips and inflated nostrils, her cheeks as red as an api apple,[1] and her eyes darting lightnings. At the same time, the white goat placed itself in front of her, and presented to Gringoire a hostile front, bristling with two pretty horns, gilded and very sharp. All this took place in the twinkling of an eye.

The dragon-fly had turned into a wasp, and asked nothing better than to sting.

Our philosopher was speechless, and turned his astonished eyes from the goat to the young girl. "Holy Virgin!" he said at last, when surprise permitted him to speak, "here are two hearty dames!"

The gypsy broke the silence on her side.

"You must be a very bold knave!"

"Pardon, mademoiselle," said Gringoire, with a smile. "But why did you take me for your husband?"

"Should I have allowed you to be hanged?"

"So," said the poet, somewhat disappointed in his amorous hopes. "You had no other idea in marrying me than to save me from the gibbet?"

"And what other idea did you suppose that I had?"

Gringoire bit his lips. "Come," said he, "I am not yet so triumphant in Cupido, as I thought. But then, what was the good of breaking that poor jug?"

Meanwhile Esmeralda's dagger and the goat's horns were still upon the defensive.

---

1. A small dessert apple, bright red on one side and greenish-white on the other.

"Mademoiselle Esmeralda," said the poet, "let us come to terms. I am not a clerk of the court, and I shall not go to law with you for thus carrying a dagger in Paris, in the teeth of the ordinances and prohibitions of M. the Provost. Nevertheless, you are not ignorant of the fact that Noël Lescrivain was condemned, a week ago, to pay ten Parisian sous, for having carried a cutlass. But this is no affair of mine, and I will come to the point. I swear to you, upon my share of Paradise, not to approach you without your leave and permission, but do give me some supper."

The truth is, Gringoire was, like M. Despreaux, "not very voluptuous." He did not belong to that chevalier and musketeer species, who take young girls by assault. In the matter of love, as in all other affairs, he willingly assented to temporizing and adjusting terms; and a good supper, and an amiable tête-à-tête appeared to him, especially when he was hungry, an excellent interlude between the prologue and the catastrophe of a love adventure.

The gypsy did not reply. She made her disdainful little grimace, drew up her head like a bird, then burst out laughing, and the tiny poniard disappeared as it had come, without Gringoire being able to see where the wasp concealed its sting.

A moment later, there stood upon the table a loaf of rye bread, a slice of bacon, some wrinkled apples and a jug of beer. Gringoire began to eat eagerly. One would have said, to hear the furious clashing of his iron fork and his earthenware plate, that all his love had turned to appetite.

The young girl seated opposite him, watched him in silence, visibly preoccupied with another thought, at which she smiled from time to time, while her soft hand caressed the intelligent head of the goat, gently pressed between her knees.

A candle of yellow wax illuminated this scene of voracity and reverie.

Meanwhile, the first cravings of his stomach having been stilled, Gringoire felt some false shame at perceiving that nothing remained but one apple.

"You do not eat, Mademoiselle Esmeralda?"

She replied by a negative sign of the head, and her pensive glance fixed itself upon the vault of the ceiling.

"What the deuce is she thinking of?" thought Gringoire, staring at what she was gazing at; " 'tis impossible that it can be that stone dwarf carved in the keystone of that arch, which thus absorbs her attention. What the deuce! I can bear the comparison!"

He raised his voice, "Mademoiselle!"

She seemed not to hear him.

He repeated, still more loudly, "Mademoiselle Esmeralda!"

Trouble wasted. The young girl's mind was elsewhere, and Gringoire's voice had not the power to recall it. Fortunately, the goat interfered. She began to pull her mistress gently by the sleeve.

"What dost thou want, Djali?" said the gypsy, hastily, as though suddenly awakened.

"She is hungry," said Gringoire, charmed to enter into conversation. Esmeralda began to crumble some bread, which Djali ate gracefully from the hollow of her hand.

Moreover, Gringoire did not give her time to resume her reverie. He hazarded a delicate question.

"So you don't want me for your husband?"

The young girl looked at him intently, and said, "No."

"For your lover?" went on Gringoire.

She pouted, and replied, "No."

"For your friend?" pursued Gringoire.

She gazed fixedly at him again, and said, after a momentary reflection, "Perhaps."

This "perhaps," so dear to philosophers, emboldened Gringoire.

"Do you know what friendship is?" he asked.

"Yes," replied the gypsy; "it is to be brother and sister; two souls which touch without mingling, two fingers on one hand."

"And love?" pursued Gringoire.

"Oh! love!" said she, and her voice trembled, and her eye beamed. "That is to be two and to be but one. A man and a woman mingled into one angel. It is heaven."

The street dancer had a beauty as she spoke thus, that struck Gringoire singularly, and seemed to him in perfect keeping with the almost oriental exaltation of her words. Her pure, red lips half smiled; her serene and candid brow became troubled, at intervals, under her thoughts, like a mirror under the breath; and from beneath her long, drooping, black eyelashes, there escaped a sort of ineffable light, which gave to her profile that ideal serenity which Raphael found at the mystic point of intersection of virginity, maternity, and divinity.

Nevertheless, Gringoire continued—

"What must one be then, in order to please you?"

"A man."

"And I—" said he, "what, then, am I?"

"A man has a hemlet on his head, a sword in his hand, and golden spurs on his heels."

"Good," said Gringoire, "without a horse, no man. Do you love anyone?"

"As a lover?—"

"Yes."

She remained thoughtful for a moment, then said with a peculiar expression: "That I shall know soon."

"Why not this evening?" resumed the poet tenderly. "Why not me?"

She cast a grave glance upon him and said—

"I can never love a man who cannot protect me."

Gringoire colored, and took the hint. It was evident that the young girl was alluding to the slight assistance which he had rendered her in the critical situation in which she had found herself two hours previously. This memory, effaced by his own adventures of the evening, now recurred to him. He smote his brow.

"By the way, mademoiselle, I ought to have begun there. Pardon my foolish absence of mind. How did you contrive to escape from the claws of Quasimodo?"

This question made the gypsy shudder.

"Oh! the horrible hunchback," said she, hiding her face in her hands. And she shuddered as though with violent cold.

"Horrible, in truth," said Gringoire, who clung to his idea; "but how did you manage to escape him?"

La Esmeralda smiled, sighed, and remained silent.

"Do you know why he followed you?" began Gringoire again, seeking to return to his question by a circuitous route.

"I don't know," said the young girl, and she added hastily, "But you were following me also, why were you following me?"

"In good faith," responded Gringoire, "I don't know either."

Silence ensued. Gringoire slashed the table with his knife. The young girl smiled and seemed to be gazing through the wall at something. All at once she began to sing in a barely articulate voice—

> *Quando las pintadas aves,*
> *Mudas estan, y la tierra—*[1]

She broke off abruptly, and began to caress Djali.

"That's a pretty animal of yours," said Gringoire.

1. When the gay-plumaged birds grow weary, and the earth—

"She is my sister," she answered.

"Why are you called *la Esmeralda?*" asked the poet.

"I do not know."

"But why?"

She drew from her bosom a sort of little oblong bag, suspended from her neck by a string of adrézarach beads. This bag exhaled a strong odor of camphor. It was covered with green silk, and bore in its center a large piece of green glass, in imitation of an emerald.

"Perhaps it is because of this," said she.

Gringoire was on the point of taking the bag in his hand. She drew back.

"Don't touch it! It is an amulet. You would injure the charm, or the charm would injure you."

The poet's curiosity was more and more aroused.

"Who gave it to you?"

She laid one finger on her mouth and concealed the amulet in her bosom. He tried a few more questions, but she hardly replied.

"What is the meaning of the words, *la Esmeralda?*"

"I don't know," said she.

"To what language do they belong?"

"They are Egyptian, I think."

"I suspected as much," said Gringoire, "you are not a native of France?"

"I don't know."

"Are your parents alive?"

She began to sing, to an ancient air—

> *Mon père est oiseau,*
> *Ma mère est oiselle.*
> *Je passe l'eau sans nacelle,*
> *Je passe l'eau sans bateau,*
> *Ma mère est oiselle,*
> *Mon père est oiseau.*[1]

"Good," said Gringoire. "At what age did you come to France?"

"When I was very young."

"And when to Paris?"

"Last year. At the moment when we were entering the papal gate I saw a reed warbler flit through the air, that was at the end of August; I said, it will be a hard winter."

"So it was," said Gringoire, delighted at this beginning of a conversation. "I passed it in blowing my fingers. So you have the gift of prophecy?"

She retired into her laconics again.

"No."

"Is that man whom you call the Duke of Egypt, the chief of your tribe?"

"Yes."

"But it was he who married us," remarked the poet timidly.

She made her customary pretty grimace.

"I don't even know your name."

"My name? If you want it, here it is—Pierre Gringoire."

"I know a prettier one," said she.

---

1. My father is a bird, my mother is a bird. I cross the water without a barque, I cross the water without a boat. My mother is a bird, my father is a bird.

"Naughty girl!" retorted the poet. "Never mind, you shall not provoke me. Wait, perhaps you will love me more when you know me better; and then, you have told me your story with so much confidence, that I owe you a little of mine. You must know, then, that my name is Pierre Gringoire, and that I am a son of the farmer of the notary's office of Gonesse. My father was hung by the Burgundians, and my mother disemboweled by the Picards, at the siege of Paris, twenty years ago. At six years of age, therefore, I was an orphan, without a sole to my foot except the pavements of Paris. I do not know how I passed the interval from six to sixteen. A fruit dealer gave me a plum here, a baker flung me a crust there; in the evening I got myself taken up by the watch, who threw me into prison, and there I found a bundle of straw. All this did not prevent my growing up and growing thin, as you see. In the winter I warmed myself in the sun, under the porch of the Hôtel de Sens, and I thought it very ridiculous that the fire on Saint John's Day was reserved for the dog days. At sixteen, I wished to choose a calling. I tried all in succession. I became a soldier; but I was not brave enough. I became a monk; but I was not sufficiently devout; and then I'm a bad hand at drinking. In despair, I became an apprentice of the woodcutters, but I was not strong enough; I had more of an inclination to become a schoolmaster; 'tis true that I did not know how to read, but that's no reason. I perceived at the end of a certain time, that I lacked something in every direction; and seeing that I was good for nothing, of my own free will I became a poet and rhymester. That is a trade which one can always adopt when one is a vagabond, and it's better than stealing, as some young brigands of my acquaintance advised me to do. One day I met by luck, Dom Claude Frollo, the reverend archdeacon of Notre-Dame. He took an interest in me, and it is to him that I to-day owe it that I am a veritable man of letters, who knows Latin from the *de Officiis* of Cicero to the mortuology of the Celestine Fathers, and a barbarian neither in scholastics, nor in politics, nor in rhythmics, that sophism of sophisms. I am the author of the Mystery which was presented to-day with great triumph and a great concourse of populace, in the grand hall of the Palais de Justice. I have also made a book which will contain six hundred pages, on the wonderful comet of 1465, which sent one man mad. I have enjoyed still other successes. Being somewhat of an artillery carpenter, I lent a hand to Jean Mangue's great bombard, which burst, as you know, on the day when it was tested, on the Pont de Charenton, and killed four and twenty curious spectators. You see that I am not a bad match in marriage. I know a great many sorts of very engaging tricks, which I will teach your goat; for example, to mimic the Bishop of Paris, that cursed Pharisee whose mill wheels splash passers-by the whole length of the Pont aux Meuniers. And then my mystery will bring me in a great deal of coined money, if they will only pay me. And finally, I am at your orders, I and my wits, and my science and my letters, ready to live with you, damsel, as it shall please you, chastely or joyously; husband and wife, if you see fit; brother and sister, if you think that better."

Gringoire ceased, awaiting the effect of his harangue on the young girl. Her eyes were fixed on the ground.

"*Phœbus,*" she said in a low voice. Then, turning toward the poet, "*Phœbus*—what does that mean?"

Gringoire, without exactly understanding what the connection could be between his address and this question, was not sorry to display his erudition. Assuming an air of importance, he replied—

"It is a Latin word which means *sun*."

"Sun!" she repeated.

"It is the name of a handsome archer, who was a god," added Gringoire.

"A god!" repeated the gypsy, and there was something pensive and passionate in her tone.

At that moment, one of her bracelets became unfastened and fell. Gringoire stooped quickly to pick it up; when he straightened up, the young girl and the goat had disappeared. He heard the sound of a bolt. It was a little door, communicating, no doubt, with a neighboring cell, which was being fastened on the outside.

"Has she left me a bed, at least?" said our philosopher.

He made the tour of his cell. There was no piece of furniture adapted to sleeping purposes, except a tolerably long wooden coffer; and its cover was carved, to boot; which afforded Gringoire, when he stretched himself out upon it, a sensation somewhat similar to that which Micromégas would feel if he were to lie down on the Alps.

"Come!" said he, adjusting himself as well as possible, "I must resign myself. But here's a strange nuptial night. 'Tis a pity. There was something innocent and antediluvian about that broken crock, which quite pleased me."

BOOK THIRD

Chapter I

NOTRE-DAME

THE CHURCH OF NOTRE-DAME DE PARIS IS STILL NO DOUBT, A MAJESTIC AND SUBLIME EDIFICE. But, beautiful as it has been preserved in growing old, it is difficult not to sigh, not to wax indignant, before the numberless degradations and mutilations which time and men have both caused the venerable monument to suffer, without respect for Charlemagne, who laid its first stone, or for Philip Augustus, who laid the last.

On the face of this aged queen of our cathedrals, by the side of a wrinkle, one always finds a scar. *Tempus edax, homo edacior*;[1] which I should be glad to translate thus: time is blind, man is stupid.

If we had leisure to examine with the reader, one by one, the divers traces of destruction imprinted upon the old church, time's share would be the least, the share of men the most, especially *the men of art*, since there have been individuals who assumed the title of architects during the last two centuries.

And, in the first place, to cite only a few leading examples, there certainly are few finer architectural pages than this façade, where, successively and at once, the three portals hollowed out in an arch; the broidered and dentated cordon of the eight and twenty royal niches; the immense central rose window, flanked by its two lateral windows, like a priest by his deacon and subdeacon; the frail and lofty gallery of trefoil arcades, which supports a heavy platform above its fine, slender columns; and lastly, the two black and massive towers with their slate penthouses, harmonious parts of a magnificent whole, superposed in five gigantic stories;—develop themselves before the eye, in a mass and without confusion, with their innumerable details of statuary, carving, and sculpture, joined powerfully to the tranquil grandeur of the whole; a vast symphony in stone, so to speak; the colossal work of one man and one people, all together one and complex, like the Iliads and the Romanceros, whose sister it is; prodigious product of the grouping together of all the forces of an epoch, where, upon each stone, one sees the fancy of the workman disciplined by the genius of the artist start forth in a hundred fashions; a sort of human creation, in a word, powerful and fecund as the divine creation of which it seems to have stolen the double character—variety, eternity.

1. Time is a devourer; man, more so.

And what we here say of the façade must be said of the entire church; and what we say of the cathedral church of Paris, must be said of all the churches of Christendom in the Middle Ages. All things are in place in that art, self-created, logical, and well proportioned. To measure the great toe of the foot is to measure the giant.

Let us return to the façade of Notre-Dame, as it still appears to us, when we go piously to admire the grave and puissant cathedral, which inspires terror, so its chronicles assert: *quoe mole sua terrorem incutit spectantibus.*

Three important things are to-day lacking in that façade: in the first place, the staircase of eleven steps which formerly raised it above the soil; next, the lower series of statues which occupied the niches of the three portals; and lastly the upper series, of the twenty-eight most ancient kings of France, which garnished the gallery of the first story, beginning with Childebert, and ending with Philip Augustus, holding in his hand "the imperial apple."

Time has caused the staircase to disappear, by raising the soil of the city with a slow and irresistible progress; but, while thus causing the eleven steps which added to the majestic height of the edifice, to be devoured, one by one, by the rising tide of the pavements of Paris—time has bestowed upon the church perhaps more than it has taken away, for it is time which has spread over the façade that somber hue of the centuries which makes the old age of monuments the period of their beauty.

But who has thrown down the two rows of statues? who has left the niches empty? who has cut, in the very middle of the central portal, that new and bastard arch? who has dared to frame therein that commonplace and heavy door of carved wood, à la Louis XV, beside the arabesques of Biscornette? The men, the architects, the artists of our day.

And if we enter the interior of the edifice, who has overthrown that colossus of Saint Christopher, proverbial for magnitude among statues, as the grand hall of the Palais de Justice was among halls, as the spire of Strasbourg among spires? And those myriads of statues, which peopled all the spaces between the columns of the nave and the choir, kneeling, standing, equestrian, men, women, children, kings, bishops, gendarmes, in stone, in marble, in gold, in silver, in copper, in wax even— who has brutally swept them away? It is not time.

And who substituted for the ancient Gothic altar, splendidly encumbered with shrines and reliquaries, that heavy marble sarcophagus, with angels' heads and clouds, which seems a specimen pillaged from the Val-de-Grâce or the Invalides? Who stupidly sealed that heavy anachronism of stone in the Carlovingian pavement of Hercandus? Was it not Louis XIV, fulfilling the request of Louis XIII?

And who put the cold, white panes in the place of those windows, "high in color," which caused the astonished eyes of our fathers to hesitate between the rose of the grand portal and the arches of the apse? And what would a sub-chanter of the sixteenth century say, on beholding the beautiful yellow wash, with which our archiepiscopal vandals have desmeared their cathedral? He would remember that it was the color with which the hangman smeared "accursed" edifices; he would recall the Hôtel du Petit-Bourbon, all smeared thus, on account of the constable's treason. "Yellow, after all, of so good a quality," said Sauval, "and so well recommended, that more than a century has not yet caused it to lose its color." He would think that the sacred place had become infamous, and would flee.

And if we ascend the cathedral, without mentioning a thousand barbarisms of every sort— what has become of that charming little bell tower, which rested upon the point of intersection of the cross-roofs, and which, no less frail and no less bold than its neighbor (also destroyed), the spire of the Sainte-Chapelle, buried itself in the sky, farther forward than the towers, slender, pointed, sonorous, carved in open work. An architect of good taste amputated it (1787), and considered it sufficient to mask the wound with that large, leaden plaster, which resembles a pot cover.

'Tis thus that the marvelous art of the Middle Ages has been treated in nearly every country, especially in France. One can distinguish on its ruins three sorts of lesions, all three of which cut into it at different depths; first, time, which has insensibly notched its surface here and there, and' gnawed it everywhere; next, political and religious revolution, which, blind and wrathful by nature, have flung themselves tumultuously upon it, torn its rich garment of carving and sculpture, burst its rose windows, broken its necklace of arabesques and tiny figures, torn out its statues, sometimes because of their miters, sometimes because of their crowns; lastly, fashions, even more grotesque and foolish, which, since the anarchical and splendid deviations of the Renaissance, have followed each other in the necessary decadence of architecture. Fashions have wrought more harm than revolutions. They have cut to the quick; they have attacked the very bone and framework of art; they have cut, slashed, disorganized, killed the edifice, in form as in the symbol, in its consistency as well as in its beauty. And then they have made it over; a presumption of which neither time nor revolutions at least have been guilty. They have audaciously adjusted, in the name of "good taste," upon the wounds of Gothic architecture, their miserable gewgaws of a day, their ribbons of marble, their pompons of metal, a veritable leprosy of egg-shaped ornaments, volutes, whorls, draperies, garlands, fringes, stone flames, bronze clouds, pudgy cupids, chubby-cheeked cherubim, which begin to devour the face of art in the oratory of Catherine de Medicis, and cause it to expire, two centuries later, tortured and grimacing, in the boudoir of the Dubarry.

Thus, to sum up the points which we have just indicated, three sorts of ravages to-day disfigure Gothic architecture. Wrinkles and warts on the epidermis; this is the work of time. Deeds of violence, brutalities, contusions, fractures; this is the work of the revolutions from Luther to Mirabeau. Mutilations, amputations, dislocation of the joints, *restorations*; this is the Greek, Roman, and barbarian work of professors according to Vitruvius and Vignole. This magnificent art produced by the Vandals has been slain by the academies. The centuries, the revolutions, which at least devastate with impartiality and grandeur, have been joined by a cloud of school architects, licensed, sworn, and bound by oath; defacing with the discernment and choice of bad taste, substituting the *chicorées* of Louis XV for the Gothic lace, for the greater glory of the Parthenon. It is the kick of the ass at the dying lion. It is the old oak crowning itself, and which, to heap the measure full, is stung, bitten, and gnawed by caterpillars.

How far it is from the epoch when Robert Cenalis, comparing Notre-Dame de Paris to the famous temple of Diana at Ephesus, *so much lauded by the ancient pagans,* which Erostatus *has* immortalized, found the Gallic temple "more excellent in length, breadth, height, and structure."

Notre Dame is not, moreover, what can be called a complete, definite, classified monument. It is no longer a Romanesque church; nor is it a Gothic church. This edifice is not a type. Notre-Dame de Paris has not, like the Abbey of Tournus, the grave and massive frame, the large and round vault, the glacial bareness, the majestic simplicity of the edifices which have the rounded arch for their progenitor. It is not, like the Cathedral of Bourges, the magnificent, light, multiform, tufted, bristling efflorescent product of the pointed arch. Impossible to class it in that ancient family of somber, mysterious churches, low and crushed as it were by the round arch, almost Egyptian, with the exception of the ceiling; all hieroglyphics, all sacerdotal, all symbolical, more loaded in their ornaments, with lozenges and zigzags, than with flowers, with flowers than with animals, with animals than with men; the work of the architect less than of the bishop; first transformation of art, all impressed with theocratic and military discipline, taking root in the Lower Empire, and stopping with the time of William the Conqueror. Impossible to place our Cathedral in that other family of lofty, aerial churches, rich in painted windows and sculpture; pointed in form; bold in attitude; communal and bourgeois as political symbols; free, capricious, lawless, as a work of art; second transformation of architecture, no longer hieroglyphic, immovable and sacerdotal, but artistic, progressive, and popular, which begins at the return from the crusades, and ends with Louis IX. Notre-Dame de Paris is not of pure Romanesque, like the first; nor of pure Arabian race, like the second.

It is an edifice of the transition period. The Saxon architect completed the erection of the first pillars of the nave, when the pointed arch, which dates from the Crusade, arrived and placed itself as a conqueror upon the large Romanesque capitals which should support only round arches. The pointed arch, mistress since that time, constructed the rest of the church. Nevertheless, timid and inexperienced at the start, it sweeps out, grows larger, restrains itself, and dares no longer dart upwards in spires and lancet windows, as it did later on, in so many marvelous cathedrals. One would say that it were conscious of the vicinity of the heavy Romanesque pillars.

However, these edifices of the transition from the Romanesque to the Gothic, are no less precious for study than the pure types. They express a shade of the art which would be lost without them. It is the graft of the pointed upon the round arch.

Notre-Dame de Paris is, in particular, a curious specimen of this variety. Each face, each stone of the venerable monument, is a page not only of the history of the country, but of the history of science and art as well. Thus, in order to indicate here only the principal details, while the little Red Door almost attains to the limits of the Gothic delicacy of the fifteenth century, the pillars of the nave, by their size and weight, go back to the Carlovingian Abbey of Saint-Germain des Prés. One would suppose that six centuries separated these pillars from that door. There is no one, not even the hermetics, who does not find in the symbols of the grand portal a satisfactory compendium of their science, of which the Church of Saint-Jacques de la Boucherie was so complete a hieroglyph. Thus, the Roman abbey, the philosophers' church, the Gothic art, Saxon art, the heavy, round pillar, which recalls Gregory VII, the hermetic symbolism, with which Nicolas Flamel played the prelude to Luther, papal unity, schism, Saint-Germain des Prés, Saint-Jacques de la Boucherie—all are mingled, combined, amalgamated in Notre-Dame. This central mother church is, among the ancient churches of Paris, a sort of chimera; it has the head of one, the limbs of another, the haunches of another, something of all.

We repeat it, these hybrid constructions are not the least interesting for the artist, for the antiquarian, for the historian. They make one feel to what a degree architecture is a primitive thing, by demonstrating (what is also demonstrated by the cyclopean vestiges, the pyramids of Egypt, the gigantic Hindu pagodas) that the greatest products of architecture are less the works of individuals than of society; rather the offspring of a nation's effort, than the inspired flash of a man of genius; the deposit left by a whole people; the heaps accumulated by centuries; the residue of successive evaporations of human society—in a word, species of formations. Each wave of time contributes its alluvium, each race deposits its layer on the monument, each individual brings his stone. Thus do the beavers, thus do the bees, thus do men. The great symbol of architecture, Babel, is a hive.

Great edifices, like great mountains, are the work of centuries. Art often undergoes a transformation while they are pending, *pendent opera interrupta*; they proceed quietly in accordance with the transformed art. The new art takes the monument where it finds it, encrusts itself there, assimilates it to itself, develops it according to its fancy, and finishes it if it can. The thing is accomplished without trouble, without effort, without reaction—following a natural and tranquil law. It is a graft which shoots up, a sap which circulates, a vegetation which starts forth anew. Certainly there is matter here for many large volumes, and often the universal history of humanity in the successive engrafting of many arts at many levels, upon the same monument. The man, the artist, the individual, is effaced in these great masses, which lack the name of their author; human intelligence is there summed up and totalized. Time is the architect, the nation is the builder.

Not to consider here anything except the Christian architecture of Europe, that younger sister of the great masonries of the Orient, it appears to the eyes as an immense formation divided into three well-defined zones, which are superposed, the one upon the other: the Romanesque zone, the Gothic zone, the zone of the Renaissance, which we would gladly call the Greco-Roman zone. The Roman layer, which is the most ancient and deepest, is occupied by the round arch, which reappears, supported by the Greek column, in the modern and upper layer of the Renaissance. The pointed arch is found between the two. The edifices which belong exclusively to any one of these three layers are perfectly distinct, uniform, and complete. There is the Abbey of Jumiéges, there is the Cathedral of Reims, there is the Sainte-Croix of Orléans. But the three zones mingle and amalgamate along the edges, like the colors in the solar spectrum. Hence, complex monuments, edifices of gradation and transition. One is Roman at the base, Gothic in the middle, Greco-Roman at the top. It is because it was six hundred years in building. This variety is rare. The donjon keep of d'Etampes is a specimen of it. But monuments of two formations are more frequent. There is Notre-Dame de Paris, a pointed-arch edifice, which is imbedded by its pillars in that Roman zone, in which are plunged the portal of Saint-Denis, and the nave of Saint-Germain des Prés. There is the charming, half-Gothic chapter-house of Bocherville, where the Roman layer extends halfway up. There is the cathedral of Rouen, which would be entirely Gothic if it did not bathe the tip of its central spire in the zone of the Renaissance.

However, all these shades, all these differences, do not affect the surfaces of edifices only. It is art which has changed its skin. The very constitution of the Christian church is not attacked by it. There is always the same internal woodwork, the same logical arrangement of parts. Whatever may be the carved and embroidered envelope of a cathedral, one always finds beneath it—in the state of a germ, and of a rudiment at the least—the Roman basilica. It is eternally developed upon the soil according to the same law. There are, invariably, two naves, which intersect in a cross, and whose upper portion, rounded into an apse, forms the choir; there are always the side aisles, for interior processions, for chapels—a sort of lateral walks or promenades where the principal nave discharges itself through the spaces between the pillars. That settled, the number of chapels, doors, bell towers, and pinnacles are modified to infinity, according to the fancy of the century, the people, and art. The service of religion once assured and provided for, architecture does what she pleases. Statues, stained glass, rose windows, arabesques, denticulations, capitals, bas-reliefs—she combines all these imaginings according to the arrangement which best suits her. Hence, the prodigious exterior variety of these edifices, at whose foundation dwells so much order and unity. The trunk of a tree is immovable; the foliage is capricious.

Chapter II

A BIRD'S-EYE VIEW OF PARIS

WE HAVE JUST ATTEMPTED TO RESTORE, FOR THE READER'S BENEFIT, THAT ADMIRABLE CHURCH of Notre-Dame de Paris. We have briefly pointed out the greater part of the beauties which it possessed in the fifteenth century, and which it lacks to-day; but we have omitted the principal thing—the view of Paris which was then to be obtained from the summits of its towers.

That was, in fact—when, after having long groped one's way up the dark spiral which perpendicularly pierces the thick wall of the belfries, one emerged, at last abruptly, upon one of the lofty platforms inundated with light and air—that was, in fact, a fine picture which spread out, on all sides at once, before the eye; a spectacle *sui generis*, of which those of our readers who have had the good fortune to see a Gothic city entire, complete, homogeneous—a few of which still remain, Nuremberg in Bavaria and Vittoria in Spain—can readily form an idea; or even smaller specimens, provided that they are well preserved—Vitré in Brittany, Nordhausen in Prussia.

The Paris of three hundred and fifty years ago—the Paris of the fifteenth century—was already a gigantic city. We Parisians generally make a mistake as to the ground which we think that we have gained, since Paris has not increased much over one-third since the time of Louis XI. It has certainly lost more in beauty than it has gained in size.

Paris had its birth, as the reader knows, in that old island of the City which has the form of a cradle. The strand of that island was its first boundary wall, the Seine its first moat. Paris remained for many centuries in its island state, with two bridges, one on the north, the other on the south; and two bridge heads, which were at the same time its gates and its fortresses—the Grand-Châtelet on the right bank, the Petit-Châtelet on the left. Then, from the date of the kings of the first race, Paris, being too cribbed and confined in its island, and unable to return thither, crossed the water. Then, beyond the Grand, beyond the Petit-Châtelet, a first circle of walls and towers began to infringe upon the country on the two sides of the Seine. Some vestiges of this ancient enclosure still remained in the last century; to-day, only the memory of it is left, and here and there a tradition, the Baudets or Baudoyer gate, *Porta Bagauda*.

Little by little, the tide of houses, always thrust from the heart of the city outwards, overflows, devours, wears away, and effaces this wall. Philip Augustus makes a new dike for it. He imprisons Paris in a circular chain of great towers, both lofty and solid. For the period of more than a century, the houses press upon each other, accumulate, and raise their level in this basin, like water in a reservoir. They begin to deepen; they pile story upon story; they mount upon each other; they gush forth at the top, like all laterally compressed growth, and there is a rivalry as to which shall thrust its head above its neighbors, for the sake of getting a little air. The street grows narrower and deeper, every space is overwhelmed and disappears. The houses finally leap the wall of Philip Augustus, and scatter joyfully over the plain, without order, and all askew, like runaways. There they plant themselves squarely, cut themselves gardens from the fields, and take their ease. Beginning with 1367, the city spreads to such an extent into the suburbs, that a new wall becomes necessary, particularly on the right bank; Charles V builds it. But a city like Paris is perpetually growing. It is only such cities that become capitals. They are funnels, into which all the geographical, political, moral, and intellectual water-sheds of a country, all the natural slopes of a people, pour; wells of civilization, so to speak, and also sewers, where commerce, industry, intelligence, population—all that is sap, all that is life, all that is the soul of a nation, filters and amasses unceasingly, drop by drop, century by century.

So Charles V's wall suffered the fate of that of Philip Augustus. At the end of the fifteenth century, the Faubourg strides across it, passes beyond it, and runs farther. In the sixteenth, it seems to retreat visibly, and to bury itself deeper and deeper in the old city, so thick had the new city already become outside of it. Thus, beginning with the fifteenth century, where our story finds us, Paris had already outgrown the three concentric circles of walls which, from the time of Julian the Apostate, existed, so to speak, in germ in the Grand-Châtelet and the Petit-Châtelet. The mighty city had cracked, in succession, its four enclosures of walls, like a child grown too large for his garments of last year. Under Louis XI, this sea of houses was seen to be pierced at intervals by several groups of ruined towers, from the ancient wall, like the summits of hills in an inundation—like archipelagos of the old Paris submerged beneath the new.

Since that time Paris has undergone yet another transformation, unfortunately for our eyes; but it has passed only one more wall, that of Louis XV, that miserable wall of mud and spittle, worthy of the king who built it, worthy of the poet who sung it—

Le mur murant Paris rend Paris murmurant.[1]

In the fifteenth century, Paris was still divided into three wholly distinct and separate towns, each having its own physiognomy, its own specialty, its manners, customs, privileges, and history:

1. The wall walling Paris makes Paris murmur.

the City, the University, the Town. The City, which occupied the island, was the most ancient, the smallest, and the mother of the other two, crowded in between them like (may we be pardoned the comparison) a little old woman between two large and handsome maidens. The University covered the left bank of the Seine, from the Tournelle to the Tour de Nesle, points which correspond in the Paris of to-day, the one to the wine market, the other to the mint. Its wall included a large part of that plain where Julian had built his hot baths. The hill of Sainte-Geneviève was enclosed in it. The culminating point of this sweep of walls was the Papal gate, that is to say, near the present site of the Pantheon. The Town, which was the largest of the three fragments of Paris, held the right bank. Its quay, broken or interrupted in many places, ran along the Seine, from the Tour de Billy to the Tour du Bois; that is to say, from the place where the granary stands to-day, to the present site of the Tuileries. These four points, where the Seine intersected the wall of the capital, the Tournelle and the Tour de Nesle on the right, the Tour de Billy and the Tour du Bois on the left, were called pre-eminently, *the four towers of Paris*. The Town encroached still more extensively upon the fields than the University. The culminating point of the Town wall (that of Charles V) was at the gates of Saint-Denis and Saint-Martin, whose situation has not been changed.

As we have just said, each of these three great divisions of Paris was a town, but too special a town to be complete, a city which could not get along without the other two. Hence, three entirely distinct aspects: churches abounded in the City; palaces, in the Town; and colleges, in the University. Neglecting here the originalities, of secondary importance in old Paris, and the capricious regulations regarding the public highways, we will say, from a general point of view, taking only masses and the whole group, in this chaos of communal jurisdictions, that the island belonged to the bishop, the right bank to the provost of the merchants, the left bank to the Rector; over all ruled the provost of Paris, a royal not a municipal official. The City had Notre-Dame; the Town, the Louvre and the Hôtel de Ville; the University, the Sorbonne. The Town had the markets (Halles); the city, the Hospital; the University, the Pré-aux-Clercs. Offenses committed by the scholars on the left bank were tried in the law courts on the island, and were punished on the right bank at Montfaucon; unless the rector, feeling the university to be strong and the king weak, intervened; for it was the students' privilege to be hanged on their own grounds.

The greater part of these privileges, it may be noted in passing, and there were some even better than the above, had been extorted from the kings by revolts and mutinies. It is the course of things from time immemorial; the king only lets go when the people tear away. There is an old charter which puts the matter naïvely: *àpropos* of fidelity: *Civibus fidelitas in reges, quoe tamen aliquoties seditionibus interrupta, multa peperit privilegia.*

In the fifteenth century, the Seine bathed five islands within the walls of Paris: Louviers island, where there were then trees, and where there is no longer anything but wood; l'île aux Vaches, and l'île Notre-Dame, both deserted, with the exception of one house, both fiefs of the bishop—in the seventeenth century, a single island was formed out of these two, which was built upon and named l'île Saint-Louis—, lastly the City, and at its point, the little islet of the cow tender, which was afterwards engulfed beneath the platform of the Pont-Neuf. The City then had five bridges: three on the right, the Pont Notre-Dame, and the Pont au Change, of stone, the Pont aux Meuniers, of wood; two on the left, the Petit Pont, of stone, the Pont Saint-Michel, of wood; all loaded with houses.

The University had six gates, built by Philip Augustus; there were, beginning with la Tournelle, the Porte Saint-Victor, the Porte Bordelle, the Porte Papale, the Porte Saint-Jacques, the Porte Saint-Michel, the Porte Saint-Germain. The Town had six gates, built by Charles V; beginning with the Tour de Billy they were: the Porte Saint-Antoine, the Porte du Temple, the Porte Saint-Martin, the Porte Saint-Denis, the Porte Montmartre, the Porte Saint-Honoré. All these gates were strong, and also handsome, which does not detract from strength. A large, deep moat, with a brisk current during the high water of winter, bathed the base of the wall round Paris; the Seine furnished the water. At night, the gates were shut, the river was barred at both ends of the city with huge iron chains, and Paris slept tranquilly.

From a bird's-eye view, these three burgs, the City, the Town, and the University, each presented to the eye an inextricable skein of eccentrically tangled streets. Nevertheless, at first sight, one recognized the fact that these three fragments formed but one body. One immediately perceived three long parallel streets, unbroken, undisturbed, traversing, almost in a straight line, all three cities, from one end to the other; from North to South, perpendicularly, to the Seine, which bound them together, mingled them, infused them in each other, poured and transfused the people incessantly, from one to the other, and made one out of the three. The first of these streets ran from the Porte Saint-Martin: it was called the Rue Saint-Jacques in the University, Rue de la Juiverie in the City, Rue Saint-Martin in the Town; it crossed the water twice, under the name of the Petit Pont and the Pont Notre-Dame. The second, which was called the Rue de la Harpe on the left bank, Rue de la Barillerié in the island, Rue Saint-Denis on the right bank, Pont Saint-Michel on one arm of the Seine, Pont au Change on the other, ran from the Porte Saint-Michel in the University, to the Porte Saint-Denis in the Town. However, under all these names, there were but two streets, parent streets, generating streets—the two arteries of Paris. All the other veins of the triple city either derived their supply from them or emptied into them.

Independently of these two principal streets, piercing Paris diametrically in its whole breadth, from side to side, common to the entire capital, the City and the University had also each its own great special street, which ran lengthwise by them, parallel to the Seine, cutting, as it passed, at right angles, the two arterial thoroughfares. Thus, in the Town, one descended in a straight line from the Porte Saint-Antoine to the Porte Saint-Honoré; in the University from the Porte Saint-Victor to the Porte Saint-Germain. These two great thoroughfares intersected by the two first, formed the canvas upon which reposed, knotted and crowded together on every hand, the labyrinthine network of the streets of Paris. In the incomprehensible plan of these streets, one distinguished likewise, on looking attentively, two clusters of great streets, like magnified sheaves of grain, one in the University, the other in the Town, which spread out gradually from the bridges to the gates.

Some traces of this geometrical plan still exist to-day.

Now, what aspect did this whole present, when, as viewed from the summit of the towers of Notre-Dame, in 1482? That we shall try to describe.

For the spectator who arrived, panting, upon that pinnacle, it was first a dazzling confusing view of roofs, chimneys, streets, bridges, places, spires, bell towers. Everything struck your eye at once: the carved gable, the pointed roof, the turrets suspended at the angles of the walls; the stone pyramids of the eleventh century, the slate obelisks of the fifteenth; the round, bare tower of the donjon keep; the square and fretted tower of the church; the great and the little, the massive and the aerial. The eye was, for a long time, wholly lost in this labyrinth, where there was nothing which did not possess its originality, its reason, its genius, its beauty—nothing which did not proceed from art; beginning with the smallest house, with its painted and carved front, with external beams, elliptical door, with projecting stories, to the royal Louvre, which then had a colonnade of towers. But these are the principal masses which were then to be distinguished when the eye began to accustom itself to this tumult of edifices.

In the first place, the City—"The island of the City," as Sauval says, who, in spite of his confused medley, sometimes has such happy turns of expression—"the island of the city is made like a great ship, stuck in the mud and run aground in the current, near the center of the Seine."

We have just explained that, in the fifteenth century, this ship was anchored to the two banks of the river by five bridges. This form of a ship had also struck the heraldic scribes; for it is from that, and not from the siege by the Normans, that the ship which blazons the old shield of Paris, comes, according to Favyn and Pasquier. For him who understands how to decipher them, armorial bearings are algebra, armorial bearings have a tongue. The whole history of the second half of the Middle Ages is written in armorial bearings—the first half is in the symbolism of the Roman churches. They are the hieroglyphics of feudalism, succeeding those of theocracy.

Thus the City first presented itself to the eye, with its stern to the east, and its prow to the west. Turning toward the prow, one had before one an innumerable flock of ancient roofs, over which arched broadly the lead-covered apse of the Sainte-Chapelle, like an elephant's haunches loaded with its tower. Only here, this tower was the most audacious, the most open, the most ornamented spire of cabinet-maker's work that ever let the sky peep through its cone of lace. In front of Notre-Dame, and very near at hand, three streets opened into the cathedral square—a fine square, lined with ancient houses. Over the south side of this place bent the wrinkled and sullen façade of the Hôtel Dieu, and its roof, which seemed covered with warts and pustules. Then, on the right and the left, to east and west, within that wall of the City, which was yet so contracted, rose the bell towers of its one and twenty churches, of every date, of every form, of every size, from the low and wormeaten belfry of Saint-Denis du Pas (*Carcer Glaucini*) to the slender needles of Saint-Pierre aux Bœufs and Saint-Landry.

Behind Notre-Dame, the cloister and its Gothic galleries spread out toward the north; on the south, the half-Roman palace of the bishop; on the east, the desert point of the Terrain. In this throng of houses the eye also distinguished, by the lofty open-work miters of stone which then crowned the roof itself, even the most elevated windows of the palace, the hôtel given by the city, under Charles VI, to Juvénal des Ursins; a little farther on, the pitch-covered sheds of the Palus Market; in still another quarter the new apse of Saint-Germain le Vieux, lengthened in 1458, with a bit of the Rue aux Febves; and then, in places, a square crowded with people; a pillory, erected at the corner of a street; a fine fragment of the pavement of Philip Augustus, a magnificent flagging, grooved for the horses' feet, in the middle of the road, and so badly replaced in the sixteenth century by the miserable cobblestones, called the *pavement of the League*; a deserted back courtyard, with one of those diaphanous staircase turrets, such as were erected in the fifteenth century, one of which is still to be seen in the Rue des Bourdonnais. Lastly, at the right of the Sainte-Chapelle, toward the west, the Palais de Justice rested its group of towers at the edge of the water. The thickets of the king's gardens, which covered the western point of the City, masked the Island du Passeur. As for the water, from the summit of the towers of Notre-Dame one hardly saw it, on either side of the City; the Seine was hidden by bridges, the bridges by houses.

And when the glance passed these bridges, whose roofs were visibly green, rendered moldy before their time by the vapors from the water, if it was directed to the left, toward the University, the first edifice which struck it was a large, low sheaf of towers, the Petit-Châtelet, whose yawning gate devoured the end of the Petit-Pont. Then, if your view ran along the bank, from east to west, from the Tournelle to the Tour de Nesle, there was a long cordon of houses, with carved beams, stained-glass windows, each story projecting over that beneath it, an interminable zigzag of bourgeois gables, frequently interrupted by the mouth of a street, and from time to time also by the front or angle of a huge stone mansion, planted at its ease, with courts and gardens, wings and detached buildings, amid this populace of crowded and narrow houses, like a grand gentleman among a throng of rustics. There were five or six of these mansions on the quay, from the house of Lorraine, which shared with the Bernardins the grand enclosure adjoining the Tournelle, to the Hôtel de Nesle, whose principal tower ended Paris, and whose pointed roofs were in a position, during three months of the year, to encroach, with their black triangles, upon the scarlet disk of the setting sun.

This side of the Seine was, however, the least mercantile of the two. Students furnished more of a crowd and more noise there than artisans, and there was not, properly speaking, any quay, except from the Pont Saint-Michel to the Tour de Nesle. The rest of the bank of the Seine was now a naked strand, the same as beyond the Bernardins; again, a throng of houses, standing with their feet in the water, as between the two bridges.

There was a great uproar of laundresses; they screamed, and talked, and sang from morning till night along the beach, and beat a great deal of linen there, just as in our day. This is not the least of the gaieties of Paris.

The University presented a dense mass to the eye. From one end to the other, it was homogeneous and compact. The thousand roofs, dense, angular, clinging to each other, composed, nearly all, of the same geometrical element, offered, when viewed from above, the aspect of a crystallization of the same substance.

The capricious ravine of streets did not cut this block of houses into too disproportionate slices. The forty-two colleges were scattered about in a fairly equal manner, and there were some everywhere. The amusingly varied crests of these beautiful edifices were the product of the same art as the simple roofs which they overshot, and were, actually, only a multiplication of the square or the cube of the same geometrical figure. Hence they complicated the whole effect, without disturbing it; completed, without overloading it. Geometry is harmony. Some fine mansions here and there made magnificent outlines against the picturesque attics of the left bank. The house of Nevers, the house of Rome, the house of Reims, which have disappeared; the Hôtel de Cluny, which still exists, for the consolation of the artist, and whose tower was so stupidly deprived of its crown a few years ago. Close to Cluny, that Roman palace, with fine round arches, were once the hot baths of Julian. There were a great many abbeys, of a beauty more devout, of a grandeur more solemn than the mansions, but not less beautiful, not less grand. Those which first caught the eye were the Bernardins, with their three bell towers; Sainte-Geneviève, whose square tower, which still exists, makes us regret the rest; the Sorbonne, half college, half monastery, of which so admirable a nave survives; the fine quadrilateral cloister of the Mathurins; its neighbor, the cloister of Saint-Benoît, within whose walls they have had time to cobble up a theater, between the seventh and eighth editions of this book; the Cordeliers, with their three enormous adjacent gables; the Augustins, whose graceful spire formed, after the Tour de Nesle, the second denticulation on this side of Paris, starting from the west. The colleges, which are, in fact, the intermediate ring between the cloister and the world, hold the middle position in the monumental series between the hôtels and the abbeys, with a severity full of elegance, sculpture less giddy than the palaces, an architecture less severe than the convents. Unfortunately, hardly anything remains of these monuments, where Gothic art combined with so just a balance, richness and economy. The churches (and they were numerous and splendid in the University, and they were graded there also in all the ages of architecture, from the round arches of Saint-Julian to the pointed arches of Saint-Séverin), the churches dominated the whole; and, like one harmony more in this mass of harmonies, they pierced in quick succession the multiple open work of the gables with slashed spires, with open-work bell towers, with slender pinnacles, whose line was also only a magnificent exaggeration of the acute angle of the roofs.

The ground of the University was hilly; Mount Sainte-Geneviève formed an enormous mound to the south; and it was a sight to see from the summit of Notre-Dame how that throng of narrow and tortuous streets (to-day the Latin Quarter), those bunches of houses which, spread out in every direction from the top of this eminence, precipitated themselves in disorder, and almost perpendicularly down its flanks, nearly to the water's edge, having the air, some of falling, others of clambering up again, and all of holding to one another. A continual flux of a thousand black points which passed each other on the pavements made everything move before the eyes; it was the populace seen thus from aloft and afar.

Lastly, in the intervals of these roofs, of these spires, of these accidents of numberless edifices, which bent and writhed, and jagged in so eccentric a manner the extreme line of the University, one caught a glimpse, here and there, of a great expanse of moss-grown wall, a thick, round tower, a crenellated city gate, shadowing forth the fortress; it was the wall of Philip Augustus. Beyond, the fields gleamed green; beyond, fled the roads, along which were scattered a few more suburban houses, which became more infrequent as they became more distant. Some of these faubourgs were important: there were, first, starting from la Tournelle, the Bourg Saint-Victor, with its one arch bridge over the Bièvre, its abbey where one could read the epitaph of Louis le Gros, *epitaphium Ludovici Grossi*, and its church with an octagonal spire, flanked with four little bell towers of the eleventh century (a similar one can be seen at Étampes; it is not yet destroyed); next, the Bourg Saint-Marceau, which already had three churches and one convent; then, leaving the mill of the Gobelins and its four white walls on the left, there was the Faubourg Saint-Jacques with the beautiful carved cross in its square; the church of Saint-Jacques du Haut-Pas, which was then Gothic, pointed, charming; Saint-Magloire, a fine nave of the fourteenth century, which Napoleon turned into a hayloft; Notre-Dame des Champs, where there were Byzantine mosaics; lastly, after having left behind, full in the country, the Monastery des Chartreux, a rich edifice contemporary with the Palais de Justice, with its little garden divided into compartments, and the haunted ruins of Vauvert, the eye fell, to the west, upon the three Roman spires of Saint-Germain des Prés. The Bourg Saint-Germain, already a large community, formed fifteen or twenty streets in the rear; the pointed bell tower of Saint-Sulpice marked one corner of the town. Close beside it one descried the quadrilateral enclosure of the fair of Saint-Germain, where the market is situated to-day; then the abbot's pillory, a pretty little round tower, well capped with a leaden cone; the brickyard was further on, and the Rue du Four, which led to the common bakehouse, and the mill on its hillock, and the lazar house, a tiny house, isolated and half seen.

But that which attracted the eye most of all, and fixed it for a long time on that point, was the abbey itself. It is certain that this monastery, which had a grand air, both as a church and as a seignory; that abbatial palace, where the bishops of Paris counted themselves happy if they could pass the night; that refectory, upon which the architect had bestowed the air, the beauty, and the rose window of a cathedral; that elegant chapel of the Virgin; that monumental dormitory; those vast gardens; that portcullis; that drawbridge; that envelope of battlements which notched to the eye the verdure of the surrounding meadows; those courtyards, where gleamed men at arms, intermingled with golden copes;—the whole grouped and clustered about three lofty spires, with round arches, well planted upon a Gothic apse, made a magnificent figure against the horizon.

When, at length, after having contemplated the University for a long time, you turned toward the right bank, toward the Town, the character of the spectacle was abruptly altered. The Town, in fact much larger than the University, was also less of a unit. At the first glance, one saw that it was divided into many masses, singularly distinct. First, to the eastward, in that part of the town which still takes its name from the marsh where Camulogènes entangled Cæsar, was a pile of palaces. The block extended to the very water's edge. Four almost contiguous hôtels, Jouy, Sens, Barbeau, the house of the Queen, mirrored their slate peaks, broken with slender turrets, in the Seine.

These four edifices filled the space from the Rue des Nonaindières, to the abbey of the Celestins, whose spire gracefully relieved their line of gables and battlements. A few miserable, greenish hovels, hanging over the water in front of these sumptuous hôtels, did not prevent one from seeing the fine angles of their façades, their large, square windows with stone mullions, their pointed porches overloaded with statues, the vivid outlines of their walls, always clear cut, and all those charming accidents of architecture, which cause Gothic art to have the air of beginning its combinations afresh with every monument.

Behind these palaces, extended in all directions, now broken, fenced in, battlemented like a citadel, now veiled by great trees like a Carthusian convent, the immense and multiform enclosure of that miraculous Hôtel de Saint-Pol, where the King of France possessed the means of lodging superbly two and twenty princes of the rank of the dauphin and the Duke of Burgundy, with their domestics and their suites, without counting the great lords, and the emperor when he came to view Paris, and the lions, who had their separate hôtel at the royal hôtel. Let us say here that a prince's apartment was then composed of never less than eleven large rooms, from the chamber of state to the oratory, not to mention the galleries, baths, vapor-baths, and other "superfluous places," with which each apartment was provided; not to mention the private gardens for each of the king's guests; not to mention the kitchens, the cellars, the domestic offices, the general refectories of the house, the poultry-yards, where there were twenty-two general laboratories, from the bake-houses to the wine-cellars; games of a thousand sorts, malls, tennis, and riding at the ring; aviaries, fish-ponds, menageries, stables, barns, libraries, arsenals and foundries. This was what a king's palace, a Louvre, a Hôtel de Saint-Pol was then. A city within a city.

From the tower where we are placed, the Hôtel Saint-Pol, almost half-hidden by the four great houses of which we have just spoken, was still very considerable and very marvelous to see. One could there distinguish, very well, though cleverly united with the principal building by long galleries, decked with painted glass and slender columns, the three hôtels which Charles V had amalgamated with his palace: the Hôtel du Petit-Muce, with the airy balustrade, which formed a graceful border to its roof; the Hôtel of the Abbe de Saint-Maur, having the vanity of a stronghold, a great tower, machicolations, loopholes, iron gratings, and over the large Saxon door, the armorial bearings of the abbé, between the two mortises of the drawbridge; the Hôtel of the Comte d' Ètampes, whose donjon keep, ruined at its summit, was rounded and notched like a cock's comb; here and there, three or four ancient oaks, forming a tuft together like enormous cauliflowers; gambols of swans, in the clear water of the fish-ponds, all in folds of light and shade; many courtyards of which one beheld picturesque bits; the Hôtel of the Lions, with its low, pointed arches on short, Saxon pillars, its iron gratings and its perpetual roar; shooting up above the whole, the scale-ornamented spire of the Ave-Maria; on the left, the house of the Provost of Paris, flanked by four small towers, delicately grooved, in the middle; at the extremity, the Hôtel Saint-Pol, properly speaking, with its multiplied façades, its successive enrichments from the time of Charles V, the hybrid excrescences, with which the fancy of the architects had loaded it during the last two centuries, with all the apses of its chapels, all the gables of its galleries, a thousand weathercocks for the four winds, and its two lofty contiguous towers, whose conical roof, surrounded by battlements at its base, looked like those pointed caps which have their edges turned up.

Continuing to mount the stories of this amphitheater of palaces spread out afar upon the ground, after crossing a deep ravine hollowed out of the roofs in the Town, which marked the passage of the Rue Saint-Antoine, the eye reached the house of Angoulême, a vast construction of many epochs, where there were perfectly new and very white parts, which melted no better into the whole than a red patch on a blue doublet. Nevertheless, the remarkably pointed and lofty roof of the modern palace, bristling with carved eaves, covered with sheets of lead, where coiled a thousand fantastic arabesques of sparkling encrustations of gilded bronze, that roof, so curiously damascened, darted upwards gracefully from the midst of the brown ruins of the ancient edifice; whose huge and ancient towers, rounded by age like casks, sinking together with old age, and rending themselves from top to bottom, resembled great bellies unbuttoned. Behind rose the forest of spires of the Palais des Tournelles. Not a view in the world, either at Chambord or at the Alhambra, is more magic, more aerial, more enchanting, than that thicket of spires, tiny bell towers, chimneys, weather-vanes, winding staircases, lanterns through which the daylight makes its way, which seem cut out at a blow, pavilions, spindle-shaped turrets, or, as they were then called, *tournelles*, all differing in form, in height, and attitude. One would have pronounced it a gigantic stone chess-board.

To the right of the Tournelles, that truss of enormous towers, black as ink, running into each other and tied, as it were, by a circular moat; that donjon keep, much more pierced with loopholes than with windows; that drawbridge, always raised; that portcullis, always lowered—is the Bastille. Those sorts of black beaks which project from between the battlements, and which you take from a distance to be eave spouts, are cannons.

Beneath them, at the foot of the formidable edifice, behold the Porte Sainte-Antoine, buried between its two towers.

Beyond the Tournelles, as far as the wall of Charles V, spread out, with rich compartments of verdure and of flowers, a velvet carpet of cultivated land and royal parks, in the midst of which one recognized, by its labyrinth of trees and alleys, the famous Dædalus garden which Louis XI had given to Coictier. The doctor's observatory rose above the labyrinth like a great isolated column, with a tiny house for a capital. Terrible astrologies took place in that laboratory.

There to-day is the Place Royale.

As we have just said, the quarter of the palace, of which we have just endeavored to give the reader some idea by indicating only the chief points, filled the angle which Charles V's wall made with the Seine on the east. The center of the Town was occupied by a pile of houses for the populace. It was there, in fact, that the three bridges disgorged upon the right bank, and bridges lead to the building of houses rather than palaces. That congregation of bourgeois habitations, pressed together like the cells in a hive, had a beauty of its own. It is with the roofs of a capital as with the waves of the sea—they are grand. First the streets, crossed and entangled, forming a hundred amusing figures in the block; around the market-place, it was like a star with a thousand rays.

The Rues Saint-Denis and Saint-Martin, with their innumerable ramifications, rose one after the other, like trees intertwining their branches; and then the tortuous lines, the Rues de la Plâtrerie, de la Verrerie, de la Tixeranderie, etc., meandered over all. There were also fine edifices which pierced the petrified undulations of that sea of gables. At the head of the Pont aux Changeurs, behind which one beheld the Seine foaming beneath the wheels of the Pont aux Meuniers, there was the Châlelet, no longer a Roman tower, as under Julian the Apostate, but a feudal tower of the thirteenth century, and of a stone so hard that the pickax could not break away so much as the thickness of the fist in a space of three hours; there was the rich square bell tower of Saint-Jacques de la Boucherie, with its angles all frothing with carvings, already admirable, although it was not finished in the fifteenth century. (It lacked, in particular, the four monsters, which, still perched to-day on the corners of its roof, have the air of so many sphinxes who are propounding to new Paris the riddle of the ancient Paris. Rault, the sculptor, only placed them in position in 1526, and received twenty francs for his pains.) There was the Maison-aux-Piliers, the Pillar House, opening upon that Place de Grève of which we have given the reader some idea; there was Saint-Gervais, which a front "in good taste" has since spoiled; Saint-Méry, whose ancient pointed arches were still almost round arches; Saint-Jean, whose magnificent spire was proverbial; there were twenty other monuments, which did not disdain to bury their wonders in that chaos of black, deep, narrow streets. Add the crosses of carved stone, more lavishly scattered through the squares than even the gibbets; the cemetery of the Innocents, whose architectural wall could be seen in the distance above the roofs; the pillory of the Markets, whose top was visible between two chimneys of the Rue de la Cossonnerie; the ladder of the Croix-du-Trahoir, in its square always black with people; the circular buildings of the wheat mart; the fragments of Philip Augustus's ancient wall, which could be made out here and there, drowned among the houses, its towers gnawed by ivy, its gates in ruins, with crumbling and deformed stretches of wall; the quay with its thousand shops, and its bloody knacker's yards; the Seine encumbered with boats, from the Port au Foin to For-l'Evêque, and you will have a confused picture of what the central trapezium of the Town was like in 1482.

With these two quarters, one of hôtels, the other of houses, the third feature of aspect presented by the city was a long zone of abbeys, which bordered it in nearly the whole of its circumference, from the rising to the setting sun, and, behind the circle of fortifications which hemmed in Paris, formed a second interior enclosure of convents and chapels. Thus, immediately adjoining the park des Tournelles, between the Rue Saint-Antoine and the Vielle Rue du Temple, there stood Sainte-Catherine, with its immense cultivated lands, which were terminated only by the wall of Paris. Between the old and the new Rue du Temple, there was the Temple, a sinister group of towers, lofty, erect, and isolated in the middle of a vast, battlemented enclosure. Between the Rue Neuve-du-Temple and the Rue Saint-Martin, there was the Abbey of Saint-Martin, in the midst of its gardens, a superb fortified church, whose girdle of towers, whose diadem of bell towers, yielded in force and splendor only to Saint-Germain des Prés. Between the Rue Saint-Martin and the Rue Saint-Denis, spread the enclosure of the Trinité.

Lastly, between the Rue Saint-Denis, and the Rue Montorgueil, stood the Filles-Dieu. On one side, the rotting roofs and unpaved enclosure of the Cour des Miracles could be descried. It was the sole profane ring which was linked to that devout chain of convents.

Finally, the fourth compartment, which stretched itself out in the agglomeration of the roofs on the right bank, and which occupied the western angle of the enclosure, and the banks of the river down stream, was a fresh cluster of palaces and hôtels pressed close about the base of the Louvre. The old Louvre of Philip Augustus, that immense edifice whose great tower rallied about it three and twenty chief towers, not to reckon the lesser towers, seemed from a distance to be enshrined in the Gothic roofs of the Hôtel d'Alençon, and the Petit-Bourbon. This hydra of towers, giant guardian of Paris, with its four and twenty heads, always erect, with its monstrous haunches, loaded or scaled with slates, and all streaming with metallic reflections, terminated with wonderful effect the configuration of the Town toward the west.

Thus an immense block, which the Romans called *iusula*, or island, of bourgeois houses, flanked on the right and the left by two blocks of palaces, crowned, the one by the Louvre, the other by the Tournelles, bordered on the north by a long girdle of abbeys and cultivated enclosures, all amalgamated and melted together in one view; upon these thousands of edifices, whose tiled and slated roofs outlined upon each other so many fantastic chains, the bell towers, tattooed, fluted, and ornamented with twisted bands, of the four and forty churches on the right bank; myriads of cross streets; for boundary on one side, an enclosure of lofty walls with square towers (that of the University had round towers); on the other, the Seine, cut by bridges, and bearing on its bosom a multitude of boats; behold the Town of Paris in the fifteenth century.

Beyond the walls, several suburban villages pressed close about the gates, but less numerous and more scattered than those of the University. Behind the Bastille there were twenty hovels clustered round the curious sculptures of the Croix-Faubin and the flying buttresses of the Abbey of Saint-Antoine des Champs; then Popincourt, lost amid wheat fields; then la Courtille, a merry village of wine-shops; the hamlet of Saint-Laurent with its church whose bell tower, from afar, seemed to add itself to the pointed towers of the Porte Saint-Martin; the Faubourg Saint-Denis, with the vast enclosure of Saint-Ladre; beyond the Montmartre Gate, the Grange-Batelière, encircled with white walls; behind it, with its chalky slopes, Montmartre, which had then almost as many churches as windmills, and which has kept only the windmills, for society no longer demands anything but bread for the body. Lastly, beyond the Louvre, the Faubourg Saint-Honoré, already considerable at that time, could be seen stretching away into the fields, and Petit-Bretagne gleaming green, and the Marché aux Pourceaux spreading abroad, in whose center swelled the horrible apparatus used for boiling counterfeiters. Between la Courtille and Saint-Laurent, your eye had already noticed, on the summit of an eminence crouching amid desert plains, a sort of edifice which resembled from a distance a ruined colonnade, mounted upon a basement with its foundation laid bare. This was neither a Parthenon, nor a temple of the Olympian Jupiter. It was Montfaucon.

Now, if the enumeration of so many edifices, summary as we have endeavored to make it, has not shattered in the reader's mind the general image of old Paris, as we have constructed it, we will recapitulate it in a few words. In the center, the island of the City, resembling as to form an enormous tortoise, and throwing out its bridges with tiles for scales, like legs from beneath its gray shell of roofs. On the left, the monolithic trapezium, firm, dense, bristling, of the University; on the right, the vast semi-circle of the Town, much more intermixed with gardens and monuments. The three blocks, city, university, and town, marbled with innumerable streets. Across all, the Seine, "foster-mother Seine," as says Father Du Breul, blocked with islands, bridges, and boats. All about an immense plain, patched with a thousand sorts of cultivated plots, sown with fine villages. On the left, Issy, Vanvres, Vaugirarde, Montrouge, Gentilly, with its round tower and its square tower, etc.; on the right, twenty others, from Conflans to Ville-l'Evêque. On the horizon, a border of hills arranged in a circle like the rim of the basin. Finally, far away to the east, Vincennes, and its seven quadrangular towers, to the south, Bicêtre and its pointed turrets; to the north, Saint-Denis and its spire; to the west, Saint Cloud and its donjon keep. Such was the Paris which the ravens, who lived in 1482, beheld from the summits of the towers of Notre-Dame.

Nevertheless, Voltaire said of this city, that "before Louis XIV, it possessed but four fine monuments": the dome of the Sorbonne, the Val-de-Grâce, the modern Louvre, and I know not what the fourth was—the Luxembourg, perhaps. Fortunately, Voltaire was the author of *Candide* in spite of this, and in spite of this, he is, among all the men who have followed each other in the long series of humanity, the one who has best possessed the diabolical laugh. Moreover, this proves that one can be a fine genius, and yet understand nothing of an art to which one does not belong. Did not Molière imagine that he was doing Raphael and Michael Angelo a very great honor, by calling them "those Mignards of their age?"

Let us return to Paris and to the fifteenth century.

It was not then merely a handsome city; it was a homogeneous city, an architectural and historical product of the Middle Ages, a chronicle in stone. It was a city formed of two layers only; the Romanesque layer and the Gothic layer; for the Roman layer had disappeared long before, with the exception of the Hot Baths of Julian, where it still pierced through the thick crust of the Middle Ages. As for the Celtic layer, no specimens were any longer to be found, even when sinking wells.

Fifty years later, when the Renaissance began to mingle with this unity which was so severe and yet so varied, the dazzling luxury of its fantasies and systems, its debasements of Roman round arches, Greek columns, and Gothic bases, its sculpture which was so tender and so ideal, its peculiar taste for arabesques and acanthus leaves, its architectural paganism, contemporary with Luther, Paris, was perhaps, still more beautiful, although less harmonious to the eye, and to the thought.

But this splendid moment lasted only for a short time; the Renaissance was not impartial; it did not content itself with building, it wished to destroy; it is true that it required the room. Thus Gothic Paris was complete only for a moment. Saint-Jacques de la Boucherie had barely been completed when the demolition of the old Louvre was begun.

After that, the great city became more disfigured every day. Gothic Paris, beneath which Roman Paris was effaced, was effaced in its turn; but can anyone say what Paris has replaced it?

There is the Paris of Catherine de Medicis at the Tuileries;—the Paris of Henri II, at the Hôtel de Ville, two edifices still in fine taste;—the Paris of Henri IV, at the Place Royale: façades of brick with stone corners, and slated roofs, tricolored houses;—the Paris of Louis XIII, at the Val-de-Grâce: a crushed and squat architecture, with vaults like basket-handles, and something indescribably pot-bellied in the column, and thickset in the dome;—the Paris of Louis XIV, in the Invalides: grand, rich, gilded, cold;—the Paris of Louis XV, in Saint-Sulpice: volutes, knots of ribbon, clouds, vermicelli and chiccory leaves, all in stone;—the Paris of Louis XVI, in the Pantheon: Saint Peter of Rome, badly copied (the edifice is awkwardly heaped together, which has not amended its lines);—the Paris of the Republic, in the School of Medicine: a poor Greek and Roman taste, which resembles the Coliseum or the Parthenon as the constitution of the year III, resembles the laws of Minos—it is called in architecture, "the Messidor" taste;—the Paris of Napoleon in the Place Vendôme: this one is sublime, a column of bronze made of cannons;—the Paris of the Restoration, at the Bourse: a very white colonnade supporting a very smooth frieze; the whole is square and cost twenty millions.

To each of these characteristic monuments there is attached by a similarity of taste, fashion, and attitude, a certain number of houses scattered about in different quarters and which the eyes of the connoisseur easily distinguishes and furnishes with a date. When one knows how to look, one finds the spirit of a century, and the physiognomy of a king, even in the knocker on a door.

The Paris of the present day has then, no general physiognomy. It is a collection of specimens of many centuries, and the finest have disappeared. The capital grows only in houses, and what houses! At the rate at which Paris is now proceeding, it will renew itself every fifty years.

Thus the historical significance of its architecture is being effaced every day. Monuments are becoming rarer and rarer, and one seems to see them gradually engulfed, by the flood of houses. Our fathers had a Paris of stone; our sons will have one of plaster.

So far as the modern monuments of new Paris are concerned, we would gladly be excused from mentioning them. It is not that we do not admire them as they deserve. The Sainte-Geneviève of M. Soufflot is certainly the finest Savoy cake that has ever been made in stone. The Palace of the Legion of Honor is also a very distinguished bit of pastry. The dome of the wheat market is an English jockey cap, on a grand scale. The towers of Saint-Sulpice are two huge clarinets, and the form is as good as any other; the telegraph, contorted and grimacing, forms an admirable accident upon their roofs. Saint-Roch has a door which, for magnificence, is comparable only to that of Saint-Thomas d'Aquin. It has, also, a crucifixion in high relief, in a cellar, with a sun of gilded wood. These things are fairly marvelous. The lantern of the labyrinth of the Jardin des Plantes is also very ingenious.

As for the Palace of the Bourse, which is Greek as to its colonnade, Roman in the round arches of its doors and windows, of the Renaissance by virtue of its flattened vault, it is indubitably a very correct and very pure monument; the proof is that it is crowned with an attic, such as was never seen in Athens, a beautiful, straight line, gracefully broken here and there by stovepipes. Let us add that if it is according to rule that the architecture of a building should be adapted to its purpose in such a manner that this purpose shall be immediately apparent from the mere aspect of the building, one cannot be too much amazed at a structure which might be indifferently—the palace of a king, a chamber of communes, a town-hall, a college, a riding-school, an academy, a warehouse, a court-house, a museum, a barracks, a sepulcher, a temple, or a theater. However, it is an Exchange. An edifice ought to be, moreover, suitable to the climate. This one is evidently constructed expressly for our cold and rainy skies. It has a roof almost as flat as roofs in the East, which involves sweeping the roof in winter, when it snows; and of course roofs are made to be swept. As for its purpose, of which we just spoke, it fulfills it to a marvel; it is a bourse in France as it would have been a temple in Greece. It is true that the architect was at a good deal of trouble to conceal the clock face, which would have destroyed the purity of the fine lines of the façade; but, on the other hand, we have that colonnade which circles round the edifice and under which, on days of high religious ceremony, the theories of the stock-brokers and the courtiers of commerce can be developed so majestically.

These are very superb structures. Let us add a quantity of fine, amusing, and varied streets, like the Rue de Rivoli, and I do not despair of Paris presenting to the eye, when viewed from a balloon, that richness of line, that opulence of detail, that diversity of aspect, that grandiose something in the simple, and unexpected in the beautiful, which characterizes a checker-board.

However, admirable as the Paris of to-day may seem to you, reconstruct the Paris of the fifteenth century, call it up before you in thought; look at the sky athwart that surprising forest of spires, towers, and belfries; spread out in the center of the city, tear away at the point of the islands, fold at the arches of the bridges, the Seine, with its broad green and yellow expanses, more variable than the skin of a serpent; project clearly against an azure horizon the Gothic profile of this ancient Paris. Make its contour float in a winter's mist which clings to its numerous chimneys; drown it in profound night and watch the odd play of lights and shadows in that somber labyrinth of edifices; cast upon it a ray of light which shall vaguely outline it and cause to emerge from the fog the great heads of the towers; or take that black silhouette again, enliven with shadow the thousand acute angles of the spires and gables, and make it start out more toothed than a shark's jaw against a copper-colored western sky—and then compare.

And if you wish to receive of the ancient city an impression with which the modern one can no longer furnish you, climb—on the morning of some grand festival, beneath the rising sun of Easter or of Pentecost—climb upon some elevated point, whence you command the entire capital;

and be present at the wakening of the chimes. Behold, at a signal given from heaven, for it is the sun which gives it, all those churches quiver simultaneously. First come scattered strokes, running from one church to another, as when musicians give warning that they are about to begin. Then, all at once, behold!—for it seems at times, as though the ear also possessed a sight of its own—behold, rising from each bell tower, something like a column of sound, a cloud of harmony. First, the vibration of each bell mounts straight upwards, pure and, so to speak, isolated from the others, into the splendid morning sky; then, little by little, as they swell they melt together, mingle, are lost in each other, and amalgamate in a magnificent concert. It is no longer anything but a mass of sonorous vibrations incessantly sent forth from the numerous belfries; floats, undulates, bounds, whirls over the city, and prolongs far beyond the horizon the deafening circle of its oscillations.

Nevertheless, this sea of harmony is not a chaos; great and profound as it is, it has not lost its transparency; you behold the windings of each group of notes which escapes from the belfries. You can follow the dialogue, by turns grave and shrill, of the treble and the bass; you can see the octaves leap from one tower to another; you watch them spring forth, winged, light, and whistling, from the silver bell, to fall, broken and limping from the bell of wood; you admire in their midst the rich gamut which incessantly ascends and reascends the seven bells of Saint-Eustache; you see light and rapid notes running across it, executing three or four luminous zigzags, and vanishing like flashes of lightning. Yonder is the Abbey of Saint-Martin, a shrill, cracked singer; here the gruff and gloomy voice of the Bastille; at the other end, the great tower of the Louvre, with its bass. The royal chime of the palace scatters on all sides, and without relaxation, resplendent trills, upon which fall, at regular intervals, the heavy strokes from the belfry of Notre-Dame, which makes them sparkle like the anvil under the hammer. At intervals you behold the passage of sounds of all forms which come from the triple peal of Saint-Germaine des Prés. Then, again, from time to time, this mass of sublime noises opens and gives passage to the beats of the Ave Maria, which bursts forth and sparkles like an aigrette of stars. Below, in the very depths of the concert, you confusedly distinguish the interior chanting of the churches, which exhales through the vibrating pores of their vaulted roofs.

Assuredly, this is an opera which it is worth the trouble of listening to. Ordinarily, the noise which escapes from Paris by day is the city speaking; by night, it is the city breathing; in this case, it is the city singing. Lend an ear, then, to this concert of bell towers; spread over all the murmur of half a million men, the eternal plaint of the river, the infinite breathings of the wind, the grave and distant quartette of the four forests arranged upon the hills, on the horizon, like immense stacks of organ pipes; extinguish, as in a half shade, all that is too hoarse and too shrill about the central chime, and say whether you know anything in the world more rich and joyful, more golden, more dazzling, than this tumult of bells and chimes;—than this furnace of music—than these ten thousand brazen voices chanting simultaneously in the flutes of stone, three hundred feet high—than this city which is no longer anything but an orchestra—than this symphony which produces the noise of a tempest.

BOOK FOURTH

Chapter I

GOOD SOULS

S IXTEEN YEARS PREVIOUS TO THE EPOCH WHEN THIS STORY TAKES PLACE, ONE FINE MORNING, ON Quasimodo Sunday, a living creature had been deposited, after mass, in the church of Notre-Dame, on the wooden bed securely fixed in the vestibule on the left, opposite that great image of Saint Christopher, which the figure of Messire Antoine des Essarts, chevalier, carved in stone, had been gazing at on his knees since 1413, when they took it into their heads to overthrow the saint and the faithful follower. Upon this bed of wood it was customary to expose foundlings for public charity. Whoever cared to take them did so. In front of the wooden bed was a copper basin for alms.

The sort of living being which lay upon that plank on the morning of Quasimodo, in the year of the Lord, 1467, appeared to excite to a high degree, the curiosity of the numerous group which had congregated about the wooden bed. The group was formed for the most part of the fair sex. Hardly anyone was there except old women.

In the first row, and among those who were most bent over the bed, four were noticeable, who, from their gray *cagoule,* a sort of cassock, were recognizable as attached to some devout sisterhood. I do not see why history has not transmitted to posterity the names of these four discreet and venerable damsels. They were Agnès la Herme, Jehanne de la Tarme, Henriette la Gaultière, Gauchère la Violette, all four widows, all four dames of the Chapel Étienne Haudry, who had quitted their house with the permission of their mistress, and in conformity with the statutes of Pierre d'Ailly, in order to come and hear the sermon.

However, if these good Haudriettes were, for the moment, complying with the statutes of Pierre d'Ailly, they certainly violated with joy those of Michel de Brache, and the Cardinal of Pisa, which so inhumanly enjoined silence upon them.

"What is this, sister?" said Agnès to Gauchère, gazing at the little creature exposed, which was screaming and writhing on the wooden bed, terrified by so many glances.

"What is to become of us," said Jehanne, "if that is the way children are made now?"

"I'm not learned in the matter of children," resumed Agnès, "but it must be a sin to look at this one."

" 'Tis not a child, Agnès."

" 'Tis an abortion of a monkey," remarked Gauchère.

" 'Tis a miracle," interposed Henriette la Gaultière.

"Then," remarked Agnès, "it is the third since the Sunday of the *Lætare:* for, in less than a week, we had the miracle of the mocker of pilgrims divinely punished by Notre-Dame d'Aubervilliers, and that was the second miracle within a month."

"This pretended foundling is a real monster of abomination," resumed Jehanne.

"He yells loud enough to deafen a chanter," continued Gauchère. "Hold your tongue, you little howler!"

"To think that Monsieur of Reims sent this enormity to Monsieur of Paris," added la Gaultière, clasping her hands.

"I imagine," said Agnès la Herme, "that it is a beast, an animal—the fruit of a Jew and a sow; something not Christian, in short, which ought to be thrown into the fire or into the water."

"I really hope," resumed la Gaultière, "that nobody will apply for it."

"Ah, good heavens!" exclaimed Agnès; "those poor nurses yonder in the foundling asylum, which forms the lower end of the lane as you go to the river, just beside Monseigneur the bishop! what if this little monster were to be carried to them to suckle? I'd rather give suck to a vampire."

"How innocent that poor la Herme is!" resumed Jehanne; "don't you see, sister, that this little monster is at least four years old, and that he would have less appetite for your breast than for a turnspit."

The "little monster" we should find it difficult ourselves to describe him otherwise, was, in fact, not a newborn child. It was a very angular and very lively little mass, imprisoned in its linen sack, stamped with the cipher of Messire Guillaume Chartier, then bishop of Paris, with a head projecting. That head was deformed enough; one beheld only a forest of red hair, one eye, a mouth, and teeth. The eye wept, the mouth cried, and the teeth seemed to ask only to be allowed to bite. The whole struggled in the sack, to the great consternation of the crowd, which increased and was renewed incessantly around it.

Dame Aloïse de Gondelaurier, a rich and noble woman, who held by the hand a pretty girl about five or six years of age, and dragged a long veil about, suspended to the golden horn of her headdress, halted as she passed the wooden bed, and gazed for a moment at the wretched creature, while her charming little daughter, Fleur-de-Lys de Gondelaurier, spelled out with her tiny, pretty finger, the permanent inscription attached to the wooden bed: "Foundlings."

"Really," said the dame, turning away in disgust, "I thought that they only exposed children here."

She turned her back, throwing into the basin a silver florin, which rang among the liards, and made the poor goodwives of the chapel of Ètienne Haudry open their eyes.

A moment later, the grave and learned Robert Mistricolle, the king's protonotary, passed, with an enormous missal under one arm and his wife on the other (Demoiselle Guillemette la Mairesse), having thus by his side his two regulators—spiritual and temporal.

"Foundling!" he said, after examining the object; "found, apparently, on the banks of the River Phlegethon."

"One can only see one eye," observed Demoiselle Guillemette; "there is a wart on the other."

"It's not a wart," returned Master Robert Mistricolle, "it is an egg which contains another demon exactly similar, who bears another little egg which contains another devil, and so on."

"How do you know that?" asked Guillemette la Mairesse.

"I know it pertinently," replied the protonotary.

"Monsieur le protonotare," asked Gauchère, "what do you prognosticate of this pretended foundling?"

"The greatest misfortunes," replied Mistricolle.

"Ah! good heavens!" said an old woman among the spectators, "and that besides our having had a considerable pestilence last year, and that they say that the English are going to disembark in a company at Harfleur."

"Perhaps that will prevent the queen from coming to Paris in the month of September," interposed another; "trade is so bad already."

"My opinion is," exclaimed Jehanne de la Tarme, "that it would be better for the louts of Paris, if this little magician were put to bed on a fagot than on a plank."

"A fine, flaming fagot," added the old woman.

"It would be more prudent," said Mistricolle.

For several minutes, a young priest had been listening to the reasoning of the Haudriettes and the sentences of the notary. He had a severe face, with a large brow, a profound glance. He thrust the crowd silently aside, scrutinized the "little magician," and stretched out his hand upon him. It was high time, for all the devotees were already licking their chops over the "fine, flaming fagot."

"I adopt this child," said the priest.

He took it in his cassock and carried it off. The spectators followed him with frightened glances. A moment later, he had disappeared through the "Red Door," which then led from the church to the cloister.

When the first surprise was over, Jehanne de la Tarme bent down to the ear of la Gaultière—

"I told you so, sister—that young clerk, Monsieur Claude Frollo, is a sorcerer."

Chapter II

CLAUDE FROLLO

IN FACT, CLAUDE FROLLO WAS NO COMMON PERSON.

He belonged to one of those middle-class families which were called indifferently, in the impertinent language of the last century, the high bourgeoise or the petty nobility. This family had inherited from the brothers Paclet the fief of Tirechappe, which was dependent upon the Bishop of Paris, and whose twenty-one houses had been in the thirteenth century the object of so many suits before the official. As possessor of this fief, Claude Frollo was one of the twenty-seven seigneurs keeping claim to a manor in fee in Paris and its suburbs; and for a long time, his name was to be seen inscribed in this quality, between the Hôtel de Tancarville, belonging to Master François Le Rez, and the college of Tours, in the records deposited at Saint Martin des Champs.

Claude Frollo had been destined from infancy, by his parents, to the ecclesiastical profession. He had been taught to read in Latin; he had been trained to keep his eyes on the ground and to speak low. While still a child, his father had cloistered him in the college of Torchi in the University. There it was that he had grown up, on the missal and the lexicon.

Moreover, he was a sad, grave, serious child, who studied ardently, and learned quickly; he never uttered a loud cry in recreation hour, mixed but little in the bacchanals of the Rue du Fouarre, did not know what it was to *dare alapas et capillos laniare*, and had cut no figure in that revolt of 1463, which the annalists register gravely, under the title of "The sixth trouble of the University." He seldom rallied the poor students of Montaigu on the *cappettes* from which they derived their name, or the bursars of the college of Dormans on their shaved tonsure, and their surtout particolored of bluish-green, blue, and violet cloth, *azurini coloris et bruni*, as says the charter of the Cardinal des Quatre-Couronnes.

On the other hand, he was assiduous at the great and the small schools of the Rue Saint Jean de Beauvais. The first pupil whom the Abbé de Saint Pierre de Val, at the moment of beginning his reading on canon law, always perceived, glued to a pillar of the school Saint-Vendregesile, opposite his rostrum, was Claude Frollo, armed with his horn ink-bottle, biting his pen, scribbling on his threadbare knee, and, in winter, blowing on his fingers. The first auditor whom Messire Miles d'Isliers, doctor in decretals, saw arrive every Monday morning, all breathless, at the opening of the gates of the school of the Chef-Saint-Denis, was Claude Frollo. Thus, at sixteen years of age, the young clerk might have held his own, in mystical theology, against a father of the church; in canonical theology, against a father of the councils; in scholastic theology, against a doctor of Sorbonne.

Theology conquered, he had plunged into decretals. From the "Master of Sentences," he had passed to the "Capitularies of Charlemagne"; and he had devoured in succession, in his appetite for science, decretals upon decretals, those of Theodore, Bishop of Hispalus; those of Bouchard, Bishop of Worms; those of Yves, Bishop of Chartres; next the decretal of Gratian, which succeeded the capitularies of Charlemagne; then the collection of Gregory IX; then the Epistle of *Superspecula*, of Honorius III. He rendered clear and familiar to himself that vast and tumultuous period of civil law and canon law in conflict and at strife with each other, in the chaos of the Middle Ages—a period which Bishop Theodore opens in 618, and which Pope Gregory closes in 1227.

Decretals digested, he flung himself upon medicine, on the liberal arts. He studied the science of herbs, the science of unguents; he became an expert in fevers and in contusions, in sprains abcesses. Jacques d' Espars would have received him as a physician; Richard Hellain, as a surgeon. He also passed through all the degrees of licentiate, master, and doctor of arts. He studied the languages, Latin, Greek, Hebrew, a triple sanctuary then very little frequented. His was a veritable fever for acquiring and hoarding, in the matter of science. At the age of eighteen, he had made his way through the four faculties; it seemed to the young man that life had but one sole object: learning.

It was toward this epoch, that the excessive heat of the summer of 1466 caused that grand outburst of the plague which carried off more than forty thousand souls in the vicomty of Paris, and among others, as Jean de Troyes states, "Master Arnoul, astrologer to the king, who was a very fine man, both wise and pleasant." The rumor spread in the University that the Rue Tirechappe was especially devastated by the malady. It was there that Claude's parents resided, in the midst of their fief. The young scholar rushed in great alarm to the paternal mansion. When he entered it, he found that both father and mother had died on the preceding day. A very young brother of his, who was in swaddling clothes, was still alive and crying abandoned in his cradle. This was all that remained to Claude of his family; the young man took the child under his arm and went off in a pensive mood. Up to that moment, he had lived only in science; he now began to live in life.

This catastrophe was a crisis in Claude's existence. Orphaned, the eldest, head of the family at the age of nineteen, he felt himself rudely recalled from the reveries of school to the realities of this world. Then, moved with pity, he was seized with passion and devotion toward that child, his brother; a sweet and strange thing was a human affection to him, who had hitherto loved his books alone.

This affection developed to a singular point; in a soul so new, it was like a first love. Separated since infancy from his parents, whom he had hardly known; cloistered and immured, as it were, in his books; eager above all things to study and to learn; exclusively attentive up to that time, to his intelligence which broadened in science, to his imagination, which expanded in letters—the poor scholar had not yet had time to feel the place of his heart.

This young brother, without mother or father, this little child which had fallen abruptly from heaven into his arms, made a new man of him. He perceived that there was something else in the world besides the speculations of the Sorbonne, and the verses of Homer; that man needed affections; that life without tenderness and without love was only a set of dry, shrieking, and rending wheels. Only, he imagined, for he was at the age when illusions are as yet replaced only by illusions, that the affections of blood and family were the sole ones necessary, and that a little brother to love sufficed to fill an entire existence.

He threw himself, therefore, into the love for his little Jehan with the passion of a character already profound, ardent, concentrated; that poor frail creature, pretty, fair-haired, rosy, and curly— that orphan with another orphan for his only support, touched him to the bottom of his heart; and grave thinker as he was, he set to meditating upon Jehan with an infinite compassion. He kept watch and ward over him as over something very fragile, and very worthy of care. He was more than a brother to the child; he became a mother to him.

Little Jehan had lost his mother while he was still at the breast; Claude gave him to a nurse. Besides the fief of Tirechappe, he had inherited from his father the fief of Moulin, which was a dependency of the square tower of Gentilly; it was a mill on a hill, near the château of Winchestre (Bicêtre). There was a miller's wife there who was nursing a fine child; it was not far from the university, and Claude carried the little Jehan to her in his own arms.

From that time forth, feeling that he had a burden to bear, he took life very seriously. The thought of his little brother became not only his recreation, but the object of his studies. He resolved to consecrate himself entirely to a future for which he was responsible in the sight of God, and never to have any other wife, any other child than the happiness and fortune of his brother. Therefore, he attached himself more closely than ever to the clerical profession. His merits, his learning, his quality of immediate vassal of the Bishop of Paris, threw the doors of the church wide open to him. At the age of twenty, by special dispensation of the Holy See, he was a priest, and served as the youngest of the chaplains of Notre-Dame the altar which is called, because of the late mass which is said there, *altare pigrorum*.

There, plunged more deeply than ever in his dear books, which he quitted only to run for an hour to the fief of Moulin, this mixture of learning and austerity, so rare at his age, had promptly acquired for him the respect and admiration of the monastery. From the cloister, his reputation as a learned man had passed to the people, among whom it had changed a little, a frequent occurrence at that time, into reputation as a sorcerer.

It was at the moment when he was returning, on Quasimodo day, from saying his mass at the Altar of the Lazy, which was by the side of the door leading to the nave on the right, near the image of the Virgin, that his attention had been attracted by the group of old women chattering around the bed for foundlings.

Then it was that he approached the unhappy little creature, which was so hated and so menaced. That distress, that deformity, that abandonment, the thought of his young brother, the idea which suddenly occurred to him, that if he were to die, his dear little Jehan might also be flung miserably on the plank for foundlings—all this had gone to his heart simultaneously; a great pity had moved in him, and he had carried off the child.

When he removed the child from the sack, he found it greatly deformed, in very sooth. The poor little wretch had a wart on his left eye, his head placed directly on his shoulders, his spinal column was crooked, his breast-bone prominent, and his legs bowed; but he appeared to be lively; and although it was impossible to say in what language he lisped, his cry indicated considerable force and health. Claude's compassion increased at the sight of this ugliness; and he made a vow in his heart to rear the child for the love of his brother, in order that, whatever might be the future faults of the little Jehan, he should have beside him that charity done for his sake. It was a sort of investment of good works, which he was effecting in the name of his young brother; it was a stock of good works which he wished to amass in advance for him, in case the little rogue should some day find himself short of that coin, the only sort which is received at the toll-bar of paradise.

He baptized his adopted child, and gave him the name of Quasimodo, either because he desired thereby to mark the day, when he had found him, or because he wished to designate by that name to what a degree the poor little creature was incomplete, and hardly sketched out. In fact, Quasimodo, blind, hunchbacked, knock-kneed, was only an "almost."

Chapter III

IMMANIS PECORIS CUSTOS, IMMANIOR IPSE

NOW, IN 1482, QUASIMODO HAD GROWN UP. HE HAD BECOME A FEW YEARS PREVIOUSLY THE BELL-ringer of Notre-Dame, thanks to his father by adoption, Claude Frollo—who had become archdeacon of Josas, thanks to his suzerain, Messire Louis de Beaumont—who had become Bishop of Paris, at the death of Guillaume Chartier in 1472, thanks to his patron, Olivier Le Daim, barber to Louis XI, king by the grace of God.

So Quasimodo was the ringer of the chimes of Notre-Dame.

In the course of time there had been formed a certain peculiarly intimate bond which united the ringer to the church. Separated forever from the world, by the double fatality of his unknown birth and his natural deformity, imprisoned from his infancy in that impassable double circle, the poor wretch had grown used to seeing nothing in this world beyond the religious walls which had received him under their shadow. Notre-Dame had been to him successively, as he grew up and developed, the egg, the nest, the house, the country, the universe.

There was certainly a sort of mysterious and pre-existing harmony between this creature and this church. When, still a little fellow, he had dragged himself tortuously and by jerks beneath the shadows of its vaults, he seemed, with his human face and his bestial limbs, the natural reptile of that humid and somber pavement, upon which the shadow of the Romanesque capitals cast so many strange forms.

Later on, the first time that he caught hold, mechanically, of the ropes to the towers, and hung suspended from them, and set the bell to clanging, it produced upon his adopted father, Claude, the effect of a child whose tongue is unloosed and who begins to speak.

It is thus that, little by little, developing always in sympathy with the cathedral, living there, sleeping there, hardly ever leaving it, subject every hour to the mysterious impress, he came to resemble it, he encrusted himself in it, so to speak, and became an integral part of it. His salient angles fitted into the retreating angles of the cathedral (if we may be allowed this figure of speech), and he seemed not only its inhabitant but more than that, its natural tenant. One might almost say that he had assumed its form, as the snail takes on the form of its shell. It was his dwelling, his hole, his envelope. There existed between him and the old church so profound an instinctive sympathy, so many magnetic affinities, so many material affinities, that he adhered to it somewhat as a tortoise adheres to its shell. The rough and wrinkled cathedral was his shell.

It is useless to warn the reader not to take literally all the similes which we are obliged to employ here to express the singular, symmetrical, direct, almost consubstantial union of a man and an edifice. It is equally unnecessary to state to what a degree that whole cathedral was familiar to him, after so long and so intimate a cohabitation. That dwelling was peculiar to him. It had no depths to which Quasimodo had not penetrated, no height which he had not scaled. He often climbed many stones up the front, aided solely by the uneven points of the carving. The towers, on whose exterior surface he was frequently seen clambering, like a lizard gliding along a perpendicular wall, those two gigantic twins, so lofty, so menacing, so formidable, possessed for him neither vertigo, nor terror, nor shocks of amazement.

To see them so gentle under his hand, so easy to scale, one would have said that he had tamed them. By dint of leaping, climbing, gamboling amid the abysses of the gigantic cathedral he had become, in some sort, a monkey and a goat, like the Calabrian child who swims before he walks, and plays with the sea while still a babe.

Moreover, it was not his body alone which seemed fashioned after the Cathedral, but his mind also. In what condition was that mind? What bent had it contracted, what form had it assumed beneath that knotted envelope, in that savage life? This it would be hard to determine. Quasimodo had been born one-eyed, hunchbacked, lame. It was with great difficulty, and by dint of great patience that Claude Frollo had succeeded in teaching him to talk. But a fatality was attached to the poor foundling. Bellringer of Notre-Dame at the age of fourteen, a new infirmity had come to complete his misfortunes: the bells had broken the drums of his ears; he had become deaf. The only gate which nature had left wide open for him had been abruptly closed, and forever.

In closing, it had cut off the only ray of joy and of light which still made its way into the soul of Quasimodo. His soul fell into profound night. The wretched being's misery became as incurable and as complete as his deformity. Let us add that his deafness rendered him to some extent dumb. For, in order not to make others laugh, the very moment that he found himself to be deaf, he resolved upon a silence which he only broke when he was alone. He voluntarily tied that tongue which Claude Frollo had taken so much pains to unloose. Hence, it came about, that when necessity constrained him to speak, his tongue was torpid, awkward, and like a door whose hinges have grown rusty.

If now we were to try to penetrate to the soul of Quasimodo through that thick, hard rind; if we could sound the depths of that badly constructed organism; if it were granted to us to look with a torch behind those non-transparent organs to explore the shadowy interior of that opaque creature, to elucidate his obscure corners, his absurd no-thoroughfares, and suddenly to cast a vivid light upon the soul enchained at the extremity of that cave, we should, no doubt, find the unhappy Psyche in some poor, cramped, and ricketty attitude, like those prisoners beneath the Leads of Venice, who grew old bent double in a stone box which was both too low and too short for them.

It is certain that the mind becomes atrophied in a defective body. Quasimodo was barely conscious of a soul cast in his own image, moving blindly within him. The impressions of objects underwent a considerable refraction before reaching his mind. His brain was a peculiar medium; the ideas which passed through it issued forth completely distorted. The reflection which resulted from this refraction was, necessarily, divergent and perverted.

Hence a thousand optical illusions, a thousand aberrations of judgment, a thousand deviations, in which his thought strayed, now mad, now idiotic.

The first effect of this fatal organization was to trouble the glance which he cast upon things. He received hardly any immediate perception of them. The external world seemed much farther away to him than it does to us.

The second effect of his misfortune was to render him malicious.

He was malicious, in fact, because he was savage; he was savage because he was ugly. There was logic in his nature, as there is in ours.

His strength, so extraordinarily developed, was a cause of still greater malevolence: *"Malus puer robustus,"* says Hobbes.

This justice must, however be rendered to him. Malevolence was not, perhaps, innate in him. From his very first steps among men, he had felt himself, later on he had seen himself, spewed out, blasted, rejected. Human words were, for him, always a raillery or a malediction. As he grew up, he had found nothing but hatred around him. He had caught the general malevolence. He had picked up the weapon with which he had been wounded.

After all, he turned his face toward men only with reluctance; his cathedral was sufficient for him. It was peopled with marble figures—kings, saints, bishops—who at least did not burst out laughing in his face, and who gazed upon him only with tranquility and kindliness. The other statues, those of the monsters and demons, cherished no hatred for him, Quasimodo. He resembled them too much for that. They seemed rather, to be scoffing at other men. The saints were his friends, and blessed him; the monsters were his friends and guarded him. So he held long communion with them. He sometimes passed whole hours crouching before one of these statues, in solitary conversation with it. If anyone came, he fled like a lover surprised in his serenade.

And the cathedral was not only society for him, but the universe, and all nature beside. He dreamed of no other hedgerows than the painted windows, always in flower; no other shade than that of the foliage of stone which spread out, loaded with birds, in the tufts of the Saxon capitals; of no other mountains than the colossal towers of the church; of no other ocean than Paris, roaring at their bases.

What he loved above all else in the maternal edifice, that which aroused his soul, and made it open its poor wings, which it kept so miserably folded in its cavern, that which sometimes rendered him even happy, was the bells. He loved them, fondled them, talked to them, understood them. From the chime in the spire, over the intersection of the aisles and nave, to the great bell of the front, he cherished a tenderness for them all. The central spire and the two towers were to him as three great cages, whose birds, reared by himself, sang for him alone. Yet it was these very bells which had made him deaf; but mothers often love best that child which has caused them the most suffering.

It is true that their voice was the only one which he could still hear. On this score, the big bell was his beloved. It was she whom he preferred out of all that family of noisy girls which bustled above him, on festival days. This bell was named Marie. She was alone in the southern tower, with her sister Jacqueline, a bell of lesser size, shut up in a smaller cage beside hers. This Jacqueline was so called from the name of the wife of Jean Montagu, who had given it to the church, which had not prevented his going and figuring without his head at Montfaucon. In the second tower there were six other bells, and, finally, six smaller ones inhabited the belfry over the crossing, with the wooden bell, which rang only between after dinner on Good Friday and the morning of the day before Easter. So Quasimodo had fifteen bells in his seraglio; but big Marie was his favorite.

No idea can be formed of his delight on days when the grand peal was sounded. At the moment when the archdeacon dismissed him, and said, "Go!" he mounted the spiral staircase of the clock tower faster than anyone else could have descended it. He entered perfectly breathless into the aerial chamber of the great bell; he gazed at her a moment, devoutly and lovingly; then he gently addressed her and patted her with his hand, like a good horse, which is about to set out on a long journey. He pitied her for the trouble that she was about to suffer. After these first caresses, he shouted to his assistants, placed in the lower story of the tower, to begin. They grasped the ropes, the wheel creaked, the enormous capsule of metal started slowly into motion. Quasimodo followed it with his glance and trembled. The first shock of the clapper and the brazen wall made the framework upon which it was mounted quiver. Quasimodo vibrated with the bell.

"Vah!" he cried, with a senseless burst of laughter. However, the movement of the bass was accelerated, and, in proportion as it described a wider angle, Quasimodo's eye opened also more and more widely, phosphoric and flaming. At length the grand peal began; the whole tower trembled; woodwork, leads, cut stones, all groaned at once, from the piles of the foundation to the trefoils of its summit. Then Quasimodo boiled and frothed; he went and came; he trembled from head to foot with the tower. The bell, furious, running riot, presented to the two walls of the tower alternately its brazen throat, whence escaped that tempestuous breath, which is audible leagues away. Quasimodo stationed himself in front of this open throat; he crouched and rose with the oscillations of the bell, breathed in this overwhelming breath, gazed by turns at the deep place, which swarmed with people, two hundred feet below him, and at that enormous, brazen tongue which came, second after second, to howl in his ear.

It was the only speech which he understood, the only sound which broke for him the universal silence. He swelled out in it as a bird does in the sun. All of a sudden, the frenzy of the bell seized upon him; his look became extraordinary; he lay in wait for the great bell as it passed, as a spider lies in wait for a fly, and flung himself abruptly upon it, with might and main. Then, suspended above the abyss, borne to and fro by the formidable swinging of the bell, he seized the brazen monster by the ear-laps, pressed it between both knees, spurred it on with his heels, and redoubled the fury of the peal with the whole shock and weight of his body. Meanwhile, the tower trembled; he shrieked and gnashed his teeth, his red hair rose erect, his breast heaving like a bellows, his eye flashed flames, the monstrous bell neighed, panting, beneath him; and then it was no longer the great bell of Notre-Dame nor Quasimodo: it was a dream, a whirlwind, a tempest, dizziness mounted astride of noise; a spirit clinging to a flying crupper, a strange centaur, half man, half bell; a sort of horrible Astolphus, borne away upon a prodigious hippogriff of living bronze.

The presence of this extraordinary being caused, as it were, a breath of life to circulate throughout the entire cathedral. It seemed as though there escaped from him, at least according to the growing superstitions of the crowd, a mysterious emanation which animated all the stones of Notre-Dame, and made the deep bowels of the ancient church to palpitate. It sufficed for people to know that he was there, to make them believe that they beheld the thousand statues of the galleries and the fronts in motion. And the cathedral did indeed seem a docile and obedient creature beneath his hand; it waited on his will to raise its great voice; it was possessed and filled with Quasimodo, as with a familiar spirit. One would have said that he made the immense edifice breathe. He was everywhere about it; in fact, he multiplied himself on all points of the structure. Now one perceived with affright at the very top of one of the towers, a fantastic dwarf climbing, writhing, crawling on all fours, descending outside above the abyss, leaping from projection to projection, and going to ransack the belly of some sculptured gorgon; it was Quasimodo dislodging the crows. Again, in some obscure corner of the church one came in contact with a sort of living chimera, crouching and scowling; it was Quasimodo engaged in thought. Sometimes one caught sight, upon a bell tower, of an enormous head and a bundle of disordered limbs swinging furiously at the end of a rope; it was Quasimodo ringing vespers or the Angelus. Often at night a hideous form was seen wandering along the frail balustrade of carved lacework, which crowns the towers and borders the circumference of the apse; again it was the hunchback of Notre-Dame. Then, said the women of the neighborhood, the whole church took on something fantastic, supernatural, horrible; eyes and mouths were opened, here and there; one heard the dogs, the monsters, and the gargoyles of stone, which keep watch night and day, with outstretched neck and open jaws, around the monstrous cathedral, barking. And, if it was a Christmas Eve, while the great bell, which seemed to emit the death-rattle, summoned the faithful to the midnight mass, such an air was spread over the somber façade that one would have declared that the grand portal was devouring the throng, and that the rose window was watching it. And all this came from Quasimodo. Egypt would have taken him for the god of this temple; the Middle Ages believed him to be its demon: he was in fact its soul.

To such an extent was this disease that for those who know that Quasimodo has existed, Notre-Dame is to-day deserted, inanimate, dead. One feels that something has disappeared from it. That immense body is empty; it is a skeleton; the spirit has quitted it, one sees its place and that is all. It is like a skull which still has holes for the eyes, but no longer sight.

Chapter IV

THE DOG AND HIS MASTER

NEVERTHELESS, THERE WAS ONE HUMAN CREATURE WHOM QUASIMODO EXCEPTED FROM HIS MAL-ice and from his hatred for others, and whom he loved even more, perhaps, than his cathedral: this was Claude Frollo.

The matter was simple; Claude Frollo had taken him in, had adopted him, had nourished him, had reared him. When a little lad, it was between Claude Frollo's legs that he was accustomed to seek refuge, when the dogs and the children barked after him. Claude Frollo had taught him to talk, to read, to write. Claude Frollo had finally made him the bellringer. Now, to give the big bell in marriage to Quasimodo was to give Juliet to Romeo.

Hence Quasimodo's gratitude was profound, passionate, boundless; and although the visage of his adopted father was often clouded or severe, although his speech was habitually curt, harsh, imperious, that gratitude never wavered for a single moment. The archdeacon had in Quasimodo the most submissive slave, the most docile lackey, the most vigilant of dogs. When the poor bell-ringer became deaf, there had been established between him and Claude Frollo, a language of signs, mysterious and understood by themselves alone. In this manner the archdeacon was the sole human being with whom Quasimodo had preserved communication. He was in sympathy with but two things in this world: Notre-Dame and Claude Frollo.

There is nothing which can be compared with the empire of the archdeacon over the bell-ringer; with the attachment of the bellringer for the archdeacon. A sign from Claude and the idea of giving him pleasure would have sufficed to make Quasimodo hurl himself headlong from the summit of Notre-Dame. It was a remarkable thing—all that physical strength which had reached in Quasimodo such an extraordinary development, and which was placed by him blindly at the dis-position of another. There was in it, no doubt, filial devotion, domestic attachment; there was also the fascination of one spirit by another spirit. It was a poor, awkward, and clumsy organization, which stood with lowered head and supplicating eyes before a lofty and profound, a powerful and superior intellect. Lastly, and above all, it was gratitude. Gratitude so pushed to its extremest limit, that we do not know to what to compare it. This virtue is not one of those of which the finest ex-amples are to be met with among men. We will say then, that Quasimodo loved the archdeacon as never a dog, never a horse, never an elephant loved his master.

Chapter V

MORE ABOUT CLAUDE FROLLO

IN 1482, QUASIMODO WAS ABOUT TWENTY YEARS OF AGE; CLAUDE FROLLO, ABOUT THIRTY-SIX. ONE had grown up, the other had grown old.

Claude Frollo was no longer the simple scholar of the college of Torchi, the tender protector of a little child, the young and dreamy philosopher who knew many things and was ignorant of many. He was a priest, austere, grave, morose; one charged with souls; monsieur the archdeacon of

Josas, the bishop's second acolyte, having charge of the two deaneries of Montlhéry, and Château-fort, and one hundred and seventy-four country curacies. He was an imposing and somber person-age, before whom the choir boys in alb and in jacket trembled, as well as the machicots, and the brothers of Saint-Augustine and the matutinal clerks of Notre-Dame, when he passed slowly be-neath the lofty arches of the choir, majestic, thoughtful, with arms folded and his head so bent upon his breast that all one saw of his face was his large, bald brow.

Dom Claude Frollo had, however, abandoned neither science nor the education of his young brother, those two occupations of his life. But as time went on, some bitterness had been mingled with these things which were so sweet. In the long run, says Paul Diacre, the best lard turns rancid. Little Jehan Frollo, surnamed (*du Moulin*) "of the Mill" because of the place where he had been reared, had not grown up in the direction which Claude would have liked to impose upon him. The big brother counted upon a pious, docile, learned, and honorable pupil. But the little brother, like those young trees which deceive the gardener's hopes and turn obstinately to the quarter whence they receive sun and air, the little brother did not grow and did not multiply, but only put forth fine bushy and luxuriant branches on the side of laziness, ignorance, and debauchery. He was a regular devil, and a very disorderly one, who made Dom Claude scowl; but very droll and very subtle, which made the big brother smile.

Claude had confided him to that same college of Torchi where he had passed his early years in study and meditation; and it was a grief to him that this sanctuary, formerly edified by the name of Frollo, should to-day be scandalized by it. He sometimes preached Jehan very long and severe sermons, which the latter intrepidly endured. After all, the young scapegrace had a good heart, as can be seen in all comedies. But the sermon over, he none the less tranquilly resumed his course of seditions and enormities. Now it was a *béjaune* or yellow beak (as they called the new arrivals at the university), whom he had been mauling by way of welcome; a precious tradition which has been carefully preserved to our own day. Again, he had set in movement a band of scholars, who had flung themselves upon a wine-shop in classic fashion, *quasi classico excitati*, had then beaten the tavern-keeper "with offensive cudgels," and joyously pillaged the tavern, even to smashing in the hogsheads of wine in the cellar. And then it was a fine report in Latin, which the sub-monitor of Torchi carried piteously to Dom Claude with this dolorous marginal comment—*Rixa; prima causa vinum optimum potatum*. Finally, it was said, a thing quite horrible in a boy of sixteen, that his de-bauchery often extended as far as the Rue de Glatigny.

Claude, saddened and discouraged in his human affections, by all this, had flung himself ea-gerly into the arms of learning, that sister which, at least does not laugh in your face, and which al-ways pays you, though in money that is sometimes a little hollow, for the attention which you have paid to her. Hence, he became more and more learned, and, at the same time, as a natural conse-quence, more and more rigid as a priest, more and more sad as a man. There are for each of us sev-eral parallelisms between our intelligence, our habits, and our character, which develop without a break, and break only in the great disturbances of life.

As Claude Frollo had passed through nearly the entire circle of human learning—positive, ex-terior, and permissible—since his youth, he was obliged, unless he came to a halt, *ubi defuit orbis*, to proceed further and seek other aliments for the insatiable activity of his intelligence. The antique symbol of the serpent biting its tail is, above all, applicable to science. It would appear that Claude Frollo had experienced this. Many grave persons affirm that, after having exhausted the *fas* of human learning, he had dared to penetrate into the *nefas*. He had, they said, tasted in succession all the apples of the tree of knowledge, and, whether from hunger or disgust, had ended by tasting the forbidden fruit. He had taken his place by turns, as the reader has seen, in the conferences of the theologians in Sorbonne—in the assemblies of the doctors of art, after the manner of Saint-Hilaire—in the disputes of the decretalists, after the manner of Saint-Martin—in the congregations of physicians at the holy water font of Notre-Dame, *ad cupam Nostræ-Dominæ*. All the dishes permitted and approved, which those four great kitchens called the four faculties could elaborate and serve to the understanding, he had devoured, and had been satiated with them before his hunger was appeased. Then he had penetrated further, lower, beneath all that finished, material, limited knowledge; he had, perhaps, risked his soul, and had seated himself in the cavern at that mysterious table of the alchemists, of the astrologers, of the hermetics, of which Averroès, Gillaume de Paris, and Nicolas Flamel hold the end in the Middle Ages; and which extends in the East, by the light of the seven-branched candlestick, to Solomon, Pythagoras, and Zoroaster.

That is, at least, what was supposed, whether rightly or not.

It is certain that the archdeacon often visited the cemetery of the Saints-Innocents, where, it is true, his father and mother had been buried, with other victims of the plague of 1466; but that he appeared far less devout before the cross of their grave than before the strange figures with which the tomb of Nicolas Flamel and Claude Pernelle, erected just beside it, was loaded.

It is certain that he had frequently been seen to pass along the Rue des Lombards, and furtively enter a little house which formed the corner of the Rue des Ecrivans and the Rue Marivault. It was the house which Nicolas Flamel had built, where he had died about 1417, and which, constantly deserted since that time, had already begun to fall in ruins—so greatly had the hermetics and the alchemists of all countries wasted away the walls, merely by carving their names upon them. Some neighbors even affirm that they had once seen, through an air-hole, Archdeacon Claude excavating, turning over, digging up the earth in the two cellars, whose supports had been daubed with numberless couplets and hieroglyphics by Nicolas Flamel himself. It was supposed that Flamel had buried the philosopher's stone in the cellar; and the alchemists, for the space of two centuries, from Magistri to Father Pacifique, never ceased to worry the soil until the house, so cruelly ransacked and turned over, ended by falling into dust beneath their feet.

Again, it is certain that the archdeacon had been seized with a singular passion for the symbolical door of Notre-Dame, that page of a conjuring book written in stone, by Bishop Guillaume de Paris, who has, no doubt, been damned for having affixed so infernal a frontispiece to the sacred poem chanted by the rest of the edifice. Archdeacon Claude had the credit also of having fathomed the mystery of the colossus of Saint Christopher, and of that lofty, enigmatical statue which then stood at the entrance of the vestibule, and which the people, in derision, called "Monsieur Legris." But, what everyone might have noticed was the interminable hours which he often employed, seated upon the parapet of the area in front of the church, in contemplating the sculptures of the front; examining now the foolish virgins with their lamps reversed, now the wise virgins with their lamps upright; again, calculating the angle of vision of that raven which belongs to the left front, and which is looking at a mysterious point inside the church, where is concealed the philosopher's stone, if it be not in the cellar of Nicolas Flamel.

It was, let us remark in passing, a singular fate for the Church of Notre-Dame at that epoch to be so beloved, in two different degrees, and with so much devotion, by two beings so dissimilar as Claude and Quasimodo. Beloved by one, a sort of instinctive and savage half-man, for its beauty, for its stature, for the harmonies which emanated from its magnificent ensemble; beloved by the other, a learned and passionate imagination, for its myth, for the sense which it contains, for the symbolism scattered beneath the sculptures of its front—like the first text underneath the second in a palimpsest—in a word, for the enigma which it is eternally propounding to the understanding.

Furthermore, it is certain that the archdeacon had established himself in that one of the two towers which looks upon the Grève, just beside the frame for the bells, a very secret little cell, into which no one, not even the bishop, entered without his leave, it was said. This tiny cell had formerly been made almost at the summit of the tower, among the ravens' nests, by Bishop Hugo de Besançon who had wrought sorcery there in his day. What that cell contained, no one knew; but from the strand of the Terrain, at night, there was often seen to appear, disappear, and reappear at brief and regular intervals, at a little dormer window opening upon the back of the tower, a certain red, intermittent, singular light which seemed to follow the panting breaths of a bellows, and to proceed from a flame, rather than from a light. In the darkness, at that height, it produced a singular effect; and the goodwives said: "There's the archdeacon blowing! hell is sparkling up yonder!"

There were no great proofs of sorcery in that, after all, but there was still enough smoke to warrant a surmise of fire, and the archdeacon bore a tolerably formidable reputation. We ought to mention however, that the sciences of Egypt, that necromancy and magic, even the whitest, even the most innocent, had no more envenomed enemy, no more pitiless denunciator before the gentlemen of the officiality of Notre-Dame. Whether this was sincere horror, or the game played by the thief who shouts, "stop thief!" at all events, it did not prevent the archdeacon from being considered by the learned heads of the chapter, as a soul who had ventured into the vestibule of hell, who was lost in the caves of the cabal, groping amid the shadows of the occult sciences. Neither were the people deceived thereby; with anyone who possessed any sagacity, Quasimodo passed for the demon; Claude Frollo, for the sorcerer. It was evident that the bellringer was to serve the archdeacon for a given time, at the end of which he would carry away the latter's soul, by way of payment. Thus the archdeacon, in spite of the excessive austerity of his life, was in bad odor among all pious souls; and there was no devout nose so inexperienced that it could not smell him out to be a magician.

And if, as he grew older, abysses had formed in his science, they had also formed in his heart. That at least, is what one had grounds for believing on scrutinizing that face upon which the soul was only seen to shine through a somber cloud. Whence that large, bald brow? that head forever bent? that breast always heaving with sighs? What secret thought caused his mouth to smile with so much bitterness, at the same moment that his scowling brows approached each other like two bulls on the point of fighting? Why was what hair he had left already gray? What was that internal fire which sometimes broke forth in his glance, to such a degree that his eye resembled a hole pierced in the wall of a furnace?

These symptoms of a violent moral preoccupation, had acquired an especially high degree of intensity at the epoch when this story takes place. More than once a choir-boy had fled in terror at finding him alone in the church, so strange and dazzling was his look. More than once, in the choir, at the hour of the offices, his neighbor in the stalls had heard him mingle with the plain song, *ad omnem tonum*, unintelligible parentheses. More than once the laundress of the Terrain charged "with washing the chapter" had observed, not without affright, the marks of nails and clenched fingers on the surplice of monsieur the archdeacon of Josas.

However, he redoubled his severity, and had never been more exemplary. By profession as well as by character, he had always held himself aloof from women; he seemed to hate them more than ever. The mere rustling of a silken petticoat caused his hood to fall over his eyes. Upon this score he was so jealous of austerity and reserve, that when the Dame de Beaujeu, the king's daughter, came to visit the cloister of Notre-Dame, in the month of December, 1481, he gravely opposed her entrance, reminding the bishop of the statute of the Black Book, dating from the vigil of Saint-Barthélemy, 1334, which interdicts access to the cloister to "any woman whatever, old or young, mistress or maid." Upon which the bishop had been constrained to recite to him the ordinance of Legate Odo, which excepts certain great dames, *aliquoe magnates mulieres, quoe sine scandalo vitari non possunt*. And again the archdeacon had protested, objecting that the ordinance of the legate, which dated back to 1207, was anterior by a hundred and twenty-seven years to the Black Book, and consequently was abrogated in fact by it. And he had refused to appear before the princess.

It was also noticed that his horror for Bohemian women and gypsies had seemed to redouble for some time past. He had petitioned the bishop for an edict which expressly forbade the Bohemian women to come and dance and beat their tambourines on the place of the Parvis; and for about the same length of time, he had been ransacking the moldy placards of the officiality, in order to collect the cases of sorcerers and witches condemned to fire or the rope, for complicity in crimes with rams, sows, or goats.

Chapter VI

UNPOPULARITY

THE ARCHDEACON AND THE BELLRINGER, AS WE HAVE ALREADY SAID, WERE BUT LITTLE LOVED by the populace great and small, in the vicinity of the cathedral. When Claude and Quasimodo went out together, which frequently happened, and when they were seen traversing in company, the valet behind the master, the cold, narrow, and gloomy streets of the block of Notre-Dame, more than one evil word, more than one ironical quaver, more than one insulting jest greeted them on their way, unless Claude Frollo, which was rarely the case, walked with head upright and raised, showing his severe and almost august brow to the dumbfounded jeerers.

Both were in their quarter like "the poets" of whom Régnier speaks—

All sorts of persons run after poets,
As warblers fly shrieking after owls.

Sometimes a mischievous child risked his skin and bones for the ineffable pleasure of driving a pin into Quasimodo's hump. Again, a young girl, more bold and saucy than was fitting, brushed the priest's black robe, singing in his face the sardonic ditty, "*niche, niche,* the devil is caught." Sometimes a group of squalid old crones, squatting in a file under the shadow of the steps to a porch, scolded noisily as the archdeacon and the bellringer passed, and tossed them this encouraging welcome, with a curse: "Hum! there's a fellow whose soul is made like the other one's body!" Or a band of schoolboys and street urchins, playing hop-scotch, rose in a body and saluted him classically, with some cry in Latin: "*Eia! eia! Claudius cum claudo!*"

But the insult generally passed unnoticed both by the priest and the bellringer. Quasimodo was too deaf to hear all these gracious things, and Claude was too dreamy.

BOOK FIFTH

Chapter I

ABBAS BEATI MARTINI

DOM CLAUDE'S FAME HAD SPREAD FAR AND WIDE. IT PROCURED FOR HIM, AT ABOUT THE EPOCH when he refused to see Madame de Beaujeu, a visit which he long remembered.

It was in the evening. He had just retired, after the office, to his canon's cell in the cloister of Notre-Dame. This cell, with the exception, possibly, of some glass phials, relegated to a corner, and filled with a decidedly equivocal powder, which strongly resembled the alchemist's "powder of projection," presented nothing strange or mysterious. There were, indeed, here and there, some inscriptions on the walls, but they were pure sentences of learning and piety, extracted from good authors. The archdeacon had just seated himself, by the light of a three-jetted copper lamp, before a vast coffer crammed with manuscripts. He had rested his elbow upon the open volume of Honorius d'Autun, *De predestinatione et libero arbitrio,* and he was turning over, in deep meditation, the leaves of a printed folio which he had just brought, the sole product of the press which his cell contained. In the midst of his reverie there came a knock at his door. "Who's there?" cried the learned man, in the gracious tone of a famished dog, disturbed over his bone.

A voice without replied, "Your friend, Jacques Coictier." He went to open the door.

It was, in fact, the king's physician; a person about fifty years of age, whose harsh physiognomy was modified only by a crafty eye. Another man accompanied him. Both wore long slate-colored robes, furred with minever, girded and closed, with caps of the same stuff and hue. Their hands were concealed by their sleeves, their feet by their robes, their eyes by their caps.

"God help me, messieurs!" said the archdeacon, showing them in; "I was not expecting distinguished visitors at such an hour." And while speaking in this courteous fashion he cast an uneasy and scrutinizing glance from the physician to his companion.

" 'Tis never too late to come and pay a visit to so considerable a learned man as Dom Claude Frollo de Tirechappe," replied Doctor Coictier, whose Franche-Comté accent made all his phrases drag along with the majesty of a train-robe.

There then ensued between the physician and the archdeacon one of those congratulatory prologues which, in accordance with custom, at that epoch preceded all conversations between learned men, and which did not prevent them from detesting each other in the most cordial manner in the world. However, it is the same nowadays; every wise man's mouth complimenting another wise man is a vase of honeyed gall.

Claude Frollo's felicitations to Jacques Coictier bore reference principally to the temporal advantages which the worthy physician had found means to extract, in the course of his much envied career, from each malady of the king, an operation of alchemy much better and more certain than the pursuit of the philosopher's stone.

"In truth, Monsieur le Docteur Coictier, I felt great joy on learning of the bishopric given your nephew, my reverend seigneur Pierre Versé. Is he not Bishop of Amiens?"

"Yes, monsieur Archdeacon; it is a grace and mercy of God."

"Do you know that you made a great figure on Christmas Day at the head of your company of the chamber of accounts, Monsieur President?"

"Vice-President, Dom Claude. Alas! nothing more."

"How is your superb house in the Rue Saint-André des Arcs coming on? 'Tis a Louvre. I love greatly the apricot-tree which is carved on the door, with this play of words: 'A L'ABRI-COTIER— Sheltered from reefs.' "

"Alas! Master Claude, all that masonry costeth me dear. In proportion as the house is erected, I am ruined."

"Ho! have you not your revenues from the jail, and the bailiwick of the Palais, and the rents of all the houses, sheds, stalls, and booths of the enclosure? 'Tis a fine breast to suck."

"My castellany of Poissy has brought me in nothing this year."

"But your tolls of Triel, of Saint-James, of Saint-Germain-en-Laye are always good."

"Six score livres, and not even Parisian livres at that."

"You have your office of counselor to the king. That is fixed."

"Yes, brother Claude; but that accursed seigneury of Poligny, which people make so much noise about, is worth not sixty gold crowns, year out and year in."

In the compliments which Dom Claude addressed to Jacques Coictier, there was that sardonical, biting, and covertly mocking accent, and the sad cruel smile of a superior and unhappy man who toys for a moment, by way of distraction, with the dense prosperity of a vulgar man. The other did not perceive it.

"Upon my soul," said Claude at length, pressing his hand, "I am glad to see you and in such good health."

"Thanks, Master Claude."

"By the way," exclaimed Dom Claude, "how is your royal patient?"

"He payeth not sufficiently his physician," replied the doctor, casting a side glance at his companion.

"Think you so, Gossip Coictier," said the latter.

These words, uttered in a tone of surprise and reproach, drew upon this unknown personage the attention of the archdeacon which, to tell the truth, had not been diverted from him a single moment since the stranger had set foot across the threshold of his cell. It had even required all the thousand reasons which he had for handling tenderly Doctor Jacques Coictier, the all-powerful physician of King Louis XI, to induce him to receive the latter thus accompanied. Hence, there was nothing very cordial in his manner when Jacques Coictier said to him—

"By the way, Dom Claude, I bring you a colleague who has desired to see you on account of your reputation."

"Monsieur belongs to science?" asked the archdeacon, fixing his piercing eye upon Coictier's companion. He found beneath the brows of the stranger a glance no less piercing or less distrustful than his own.

He was, so far as the feeble light of the lamp permitted one to judge, an old man about sixty years of age and of medium stature, who appeared somewhat sickly and broken in health. His profile, although of a very ordinary outline, had something powerful and severe about it; his eyes sparkled beneath a very deep superciliary arch, like a light in the depths of a cave; and beneath his cap which was well drawn down and fell upon his nose, one recognized the broad expanse of a brow of genius.

He took it upon himself to reply to the archdeacon's question—

"Reverend master," he said in a grave tone, "your renown has reached my ears, and I wish to consult you. I am but a poor provincial gentleman, who removeth his shoes before entering the dwellings of the learned. You must know my name. I am called Gossip Tourangeau."

"Strange name for a gentleman," said the archdeacon to himself.

Nevertheless, he had a feeling that he was in the presence of a strong and earnest character. The instinct of his own lofty intellect made him recognize an intellect no less lofty under Gossip Tourangeau's furred cap, and as he gazed at the solemn face, the ironical smile which Jacques Coictier's presence called forth on his gloomy face, gradually disappeared as twilight fades on the horizon of night.

Stern and silent, he had resumed his seat in his great arm-chair; his elbow rested as usual, on the table, and his brow on his hand. After a few moments of reflection, he motioned his visitors to be seated, and, turning to Gossip Tourangeau he said—

"You come to consult me, master, and upon what science?"

"Your reverence," replied Tourangeau, "I am ill, very ill. You are said to be great Æsculapius, and I am come to ask your advice in medicine."

"Medicine!" said the archdeacon, tossing his head. He seemed to meditate for a moment, and then resumed: "Gossip Tourangeau, since that is your name, turn your head, you will find my reply already written on the wall."

Gossip Tourangeau obeyed, and read this inscription engraved above his head:

"*MEDICINE IS THE DAUGHTER OF DREAMS.*—JAMBLIQUE."

Meanwhile, Doctor Jacques Coictier had heard his companion's question with a displeasure which Dom Claude's response had but redoubled. He bent down to the ear of Gossip Tourangeau, and said to him, softly enough not to be heard by the archdeacon: "I warned you that he was mad. You insisted on seeing him."

" 'Tis very possible that he is right, madman as he is, Doctor Jacques," replied his comrade in the same low tone, and with a bitter smile.

"As you please," replied Coictier dryly. Then, addressing the archdeacon: "You are clever at your trade, Dom Claude, and you are no more at a loss over Hippocrates than a monkey is over a nut. Medicine a dream! I suspect that the pharmacopolists and the master physicians would insist upon stoning you if they were here. So you deny the influence of philters upon the blood, and unguents on the skin! You deny that eternal pharmacy of flowers and metals, which is called the world, made expressly for that eternal invalid called man!"

"I deny," said Dom Claude coldly, "neither pharmacy nor the invalid. I reject the physician."

"Then it is not true," resumed Coictier hotly, "that gout is an internal eruption; that a wound caused by artillery is to be cured by the application of a young mouse roasted; that young blood, properly injected, restores youth to aged veins; it is not true that two and two make four, and that emprostathonos follows opistathonos."

The archdeacon replied without perturbation: "There are certain things of which I think in a certain fashion."

Coictier became crimson with anger.

"There, there, my good Coictier, let us not get angry," said Gossip Tourangeau. "Monsieur the archdeacon is our friend."

Coictier calmed down, muttering in a low tone—

"After all, he's mad."

"*Pasque-dieu*, Master Claude," resumed Gossip Tourangeau, after a silence, "You embarrass me greatly. I had two things to consult you upon, one touching my health and the other touching my star."

"Monsieur," returned the archdeacon, "if that be your motive, you would have done as well not to put yourself out of breath climbing my staircase. I do not believe in Medicine. I do not believe in Astrology."

"Indeed!" said the man, with surprise.

Coictier gave a forced laugh.

"You see that he is mad," he said, in a low tone, to Gossip Tourangeau. "He does not believe in astrology."

"The idea of imagining," pursued Dom Claude, "that every ray of a star is a thread which is fastened to the head of a man!"

"And what then, do you believe in?" exclaimed Gossip Tourangeau.

The archdeacon hesitated for a moment, then he allowed a gloomy smile to escape, which seemed to give the lie to his response: *Credo in Deum.*

"*Dominum nostrum,*" added Gossip Tourangeau, making the sign of the cross.

"Amen," said Coictier.

"Reverend master," resumed Tourangeau, "I am charmed in soul to see you in such a religious frame of mind. But have you reached the point, great savant as you are, of no longer believing in science?"

"No," said the archdeacon, grasping the arm of Gossip Tourangeau, and a ray of enthusiasm lighted up his gloomy eyes, "no, I do not reject science. I have not crawled so long, flat on my belly, with my nails in the earth, through the innumerable ramifications of its caverns, without perceiving far in front of me, at the end of the obscure gallery, a light, a flame, a something, the reflection, no doubt, of the dazzling central laboratory where the patient and the wise have found out God."

"And in short," interrupted Tourangeau, "what do you hold to be true and certain?"

"Alchemy."

Coictier exclaimed, "Pardieu, Dom Claude, alchemy has its use, no doubt, but why blaspheme medicine and astrology?"

"Naught is your science of man, naught is your science of the stars," said the archdeacon, commandingly.

"That's driving Epidaurus and Chaldea very fast," replied the physician with a grin.

"Listen, Messire Jacques. This is said in good faith. I am not the king's physician, and his majesty has not given me the Garden of Dædalus in which to observe the constellations. Don't get angry, but listen to me. What truth have you deduced, I will not say from medicine, which is too foolish a thing, but from astrology? Cite to me the virtues of the vertical boustrophedon, the treasures of the number ziruph and those of the number zephirod!"

"Will you deny," said Coictier, "the sympathetic force of the collar-bone, and the cabalistics which are derived from it?"

"An error, Messire Jacques! None of your formulas end in reality. Alchemy on the other hand has its discoveries. Will you contest results like this? Ice confined beneath the earth for a thousand years is transformed into rock crystals. Lead is the ancestor of all metals. For gold is not a metal, gold is light. Lead requires only four periods of two hundred years each, to pass in succession from the state of lead, to the state of red arsenic, from red arsenic to tin, from tin to silver. Are not these facts? But to believe in the collar-bone, in the full line and in the stars, is as ridiculous as to believe with the inhabitants of Grand-Cathay that the golden oriole turns into a mole, and that grains of wheat turn into fish of the carp species."

"I have studied hermetic science!" exclaimed Coictier, "and I affirm—"

The fiery archdeacon did not allow him to finish: "And I have studied medicine, astrology, and hermetics. Here alone is the truth." (As he spoke thus, he took from the top of the coffer a phial filled with the powder which we have mentioned above), "here alone is light! Hippocrates is a dream; Urania is a dream; Hermes, a thought. Gold is the sun; to make gold is to be God. Herein lies the one and only science. I have sounded the depths of medicine and astrology, I tell you! Naught, nothingness! The human body, shadows! the planets, shadows!"

And he fell back in his arm-chair in a commanding and inspired attitude. Gossip Touraugeau watched him in silence. Coictier tried to grin, shrugged his shoulders imperceptibly, and repeated in a low voice—

"A madman!"

"And," said Tourangeau suddenly, "the wondrous result—have you attained it, have you made gold?"

"If I had made it," replied the archdeacon, articulating his words slowly, like a man who is reflecting, "the king of France would be named Claude and not Louis."

The stranger frowned.

"What am I saying?" resumed Dom Claude, with a smile of disdain. "What would the throne of France be to me when I could rebuild the empire of the Orient?"

"Very good!" said the stranger.

"Oh, the poor fool!" murmured Coictier.

The archdeacon went on, appearing to reply now only to his thoughts—

"But no, I am still crawling; I am scratching my face and knees against the pebbles of the subterranean pathway. I catch a glimpse, I do not contemplate! I do not read, I spell out!"

"And when you know how to read!" demanded the stranger, "will you make gold?"

"Who doubts it?" said the archdeacon.

"In that case Our Lady knows that I am greatly in need of money, and I should much desire to read in your books. Tell me, reverend master, is your science inimical or displeasing to Our Lady?"

"Whose archdeacon I am?" Dom Claude contented himself with replying, with tranquil hauteur.

"That is true, my master. Well! will it please you to initiate me? Let me spell with you."

Claude assumed the majestic and pontifical attitude of a Samuel.

"Old man, it requires longer years than remain to you, to undertake this voyage across mysterious things. Your head is very gray! One comes forth from the cavern only with white hair, but only those with dark hair enter it. Science alone knows well how to hollow, wither, and dry up human faces; she needs not to have old age bring her faces already furrowed. Nevertheless, if the desire possesses you of putting yourself under discipline at your age, and of deciphering the formidable alphabet of the sages, come to me; 'tis well, I will make the effort. I will not tell you, poor old man, to go and visit the sepulchral chambers of the pyramids, of which ancient Herodotus speaks, nor the brick tower of Babylon, nor the immense white marble sanctuary of the Indian temple of Eklinga. I, no more than yourself, have seen the Chaldean masonry works constructed according to the sacred form of the Sikra, nor the temple of Solomon, which is destroyed, nor the stone doors of the sepulcher of the kings of Israel, which are broken. We will content ourselves with the fragments of the book of Hermes which we have here. I will explain to you the statue of Saint Christopher, the symbol of the sower, and that of the two angels which are on the front of the Sainte-Chapelle, and one of which holds in his hands a vase, the other, a cloud—"

Here Jacques Coictier, who had been unhorsed by the archdeacon's impetuous replies, regained his saddle, and interrupted him with the triumphant tone of one learned man correcting another—"*Erras amice Claudi*. The symbol is not the number. You take Orpheus for Hermes."

" 'Tis you who are in error," replied the archdeacon, gravely. "Dædalus is the base; Orpheus is the wall; Hermes is the edifice—that is all. You shall come when you will," he continued, turning to Tourangeau, "I will show you the little parcels of gold which remained at the bottom of Nicolas Flamel's alembic, and you shall compare them with the gold of Guillaume de Paris. I will teach you the secret virtues of the Greek word, *peristera*. But, first of all, I will make you read, one after the other, the marble letters of the alphabet, the granite pages of the book. We shall go to the portal of Bishop Guillaume and of Saint-Jean le Rond at the Sainte-Chapelle, then to the house of Nicolas Flamel, Rue Marivault, to his tomb, which is at the Saints-Innocents, to his two hospitals, Rue de Montmorency. I will make you read the hieroglyphics which cover the four great iron cramps on the portal of the hospital Saint-Gervais, and of the Rue de la Ferronnerie. We will spell out in company, also, the façade of Saint-Côme, of Sainte-Geneviève-des-Ardents, of Saint Martin, of Saint-Jacques de la Boucherie—."

For a long time, Gossip Tourangeau, intelligent as was his glance, had appeared not to understand Dom Claude. He interrupted.

"*Pasque-dieu!* what are your books, then?"

"Here is one of them," said the archdeacon.

And opening the window of his cell he pointed out with his finger the immense church of Notre-Dame, which, outlining against the starry sky the black silhouette of its two towers, its stone flanks, its monstrous haunches, seemed an enormous two-headed sphinx, seated in the middle of the city.

The archdeacon gazed at the gigantic edifice for some time in silence, then extending his right hand, with a sigh, toward the printed book which lay open on the table, and his left toward Notre-Dame, and turning a sad glance from the book to the church—"Alas," he said, "this will kill that."

Coictier, who had eagerly approached the book, could not repress an exclamation. "Hé, but now, what is there so formidable in this: 'GLOSSA IN EPISTOLAS D. PAULI, *Norimbergæ, Antonius Koburger,* 1474.' This is not new. 'Tis a book of Pierre Lombard, the Master of Sentences. Is it because it is printed?"

"You have said it," replied Claude, who seemed absorbed in a profound meditation, and stood resting, his forefinger bent backward on the folio which had come from the famous press of Nuremberg. Then he added these mysterious words: "Alas! alas! small things come at the end of great things; a tooth triumphs over a mass. The Nile rat kills the crocodile, the swordfish kills the whale, the book will kill the edifice."

The curfew of the cloister sounded at the moment when Master Jacques was repeating to his companion in low tones, his eternal refrain, *"He is mad!"* To which his companion this time replied, "I believe that he is."

It was the hour when no stranger could remain in the cloister. The two visitors withdrew. "Master," said Gossip Tourangeau, as he took leave of the archdeacon, "I love wise men and great minds, and I hold you in singular esteem. Come to-morrow to the Palace des Tournelles, and inquire for the Abbé de Sainte-Martin, of Tours."

The archdeacon returned to his chamber dumbfounded, comprehending at last who Gossip Tourangeau was, and recalling that passage of the register of Sainte-Martin, of Tours:—*Abbas beati Martini,* SCILICET REX FRANCIÆ, *est canonicus de consuetudine et habet parvam proebendam quam habet sanctus Venantius, et debet sedere in sede thesaurarii.*

It is asserted that after that epoch the archdeacon had frequent conferences with Louis XI, when his majesty came to Paris, and that Dom Claude's influence quite overshadowed that of Olivier le Daim and Jacques Coictier, who, as was his habit, rudely took the king to task on that account.

Chapter II

THIS WILL KILL THAT

OUR LADY READERS WILL PARDON US IF WE PAUSE FOR A MOMENT TO SEEK WHAT COULD HAVE been the thought concealed beneath those enigmatic words of the archdeacon: "This will kill that. The book will kill the edifice."

To our mind, this thought had two faces. In the first place, it was a priestly thought. It was the affright of the priest in the presence of a new agent, the printing press. It was the terror and dazzled amazement of the men of the sanctuary, in the presence of the luminous press of Gutenberg. It was the pulpit and the manuscript taking the alarm at the printed word: something similar to the stupor of a sparrow which should behold the angel Legion unfold his six million wings. It was the cry of the prophet who already hears emancipated humanity roaring and swarming; who beholds in the future, intelligence sapping faith, opinion dethroning belief, the world shaking off Rome. It was the prognostication of the philosopher who sees human thought, volatilized by the press, evaporating from the theocratic recipient. It was the terror of the soldier who examines the brazen battering-ram, and says:—"The tower will crumble." It signified that one power was about to succeed another power. It meant, "The press will kill the church."

But underlying this thought, the first and most simple one, no doubt, there was in our opinion another, newer one, a corollary of the first, less easy to perceive and more easy to contest, a view as philosophical and belonging no longer to the priest alone but to the savant and the artist. It was a presentiment that human thought, in changing its form, was about to change its mode of expression; that the dominant idea of each generation would no longer be written with the same matter, and in the same manner; that the book of stone, so solid and so durable, was about to make way for the book of paper, more solid and still more durable. In this connection the archdeacon's vague formula had a second sense. It meant, "Printing will kill architecture."

In fact, from the origin of things down to the fifteenth century of the Christian era, inclusive, architecture is the great book of humanity, the principal expression of man in his different stages of development, either as a force or as an intelligence.

When the memory of the first races felt itself overloaded, when the mass of reminiscences of the human race became so heavy and so confused that speech naked and flying, ran the risk of losing them on the way, men transcribed them on the soil in a manner which was at once the most visible, most durable, and most natural. They sealed each tradition beneath a monument.

The first monuments were simple masses of rock, "which the iron had not touched," as Moses says. Architecture began like all writing. It was first an alphabet. Men planted a stone upright, it was a letter, and each letter was a hieroglyph, and upon each hieroglyph rested a group of ideas, like the capital on the column. This is what the earliest races did everywhere, at the same moment, on the surface of the entire world. We find the "standing stones" of the Celts in Asian Siberia; in the pampas of America.

Later on, they made words; they placed stone upon stone, they coupled those syllables of granite, and attempted some combinations. The Celtic dolmen and cromlech, the Etruscan tumulus, the Hebrew galgal, are words. Some, especially the tumulus, are proper names. Sometimes even, when men had a great deal of stone, and a vast plain, they wrote a phrase. The immense pile of Karnac is a complete sentence.

At last they made books. Traditions had brought forth symbols, beneath which they disappeared like the trunk of a tree beneath its foliage; all these symbols in which humanity placed faith continued to grow, to multiply, to intersect, to become more and more complicated; the first monuments no longer sufficed to contain them, they were overflowing in every part; these monuments hardly expressed now the primitive tradition, simple like themselves, naked and prone upon the earth. The symbol felt the need of expansion in the edifice. Then architecture was developed in proportion with human thought; it became a giant with a thousand heads and a thousand arms, and fixed all this floating symbolism in an eternal, visible, palpable form. While Dædalus, who is force, measured; while Orpheus, who is intelligence, sang;—the pillar, which is a letter; the arcade, which is a syllable; the pyramid, which is a word—all set in movement at once by a law of geometry and by a law of poetry, grouped themselves, combined, amalgamated, descended, ascended, placed themselves side by side on the soil, ranged themselves in stories in the sky, until they had written under the dictation of the general idea of an epoch, those marvelous books which were also marvelous edifices: the Pagoda of Eklinga, the Rhamseion of Egypt, the Temple of Solomon.

The generating idea, the word, was not only at the foundation of all these edifices, but also in the form. The temple of Solomon, for example, was not alone the binding of the holy book; it was the holy book itself. On each one of its concentric walls, the priests could read the word translated and manifested to the eye, and thus they followed its transformations from sanctuary to sanctuary, until they seized it in its last tabernacle, under its most concrete form, which still belonged to architecture: the arch. Thus the word was enclosed in an edifice, but its image was upon its envelope, like the human form on the coffin of a mummy.

And not only the form of edifices, but the sites selected for them, revealed the thought which they represented, according as the symbol to be expressed was graceful or grave. Greece crowned her mountains with a temple harmonious to the eye; India disemboweled hers, to chisel therein those monstrous subterranean pagodas, borne up by gigantic rows of granite elephants.

Thus, during the first six thousand years of the world, from the most immemorial pagoda of Hindustan, to the cathedral of Cologne, architecture was the great handwriting of the human race. And this is so true, that not only every religious symbol, but every human thought, has its page and its monument in that immense book.

All civilization begins in theocracy and ends in democracy. This law of liberty following unity is written in architecture. For, let us insist upon this point, masonry must not be thought to be powerful only in erecting the temple and in expressing the myth and sacerdotal symbolism; in inscribing in hieroglyphs upon its pages of stone the mysterious tables of the law. If it were thus—as there comes in all human society a moment when the sacred symbol is worn out and becomes obliterated under freedom of thought, when man escapes from the priest, when the excrescence of philosophies and systems devour the face of religion—architecture could not reproduce this new state of human thought; its leaves, so crowded on the face, would be empty on the back; its work would be mutilated; its book would he incomplete. But no.

Let us take as an example the Middle Ages, where we see more clearly because it is nearer to us. During its first period, while theocracy is organizing Europe, while the Vatican is rallying and reclassing about itself the elements of a Rome made from the Rome which lies in ruins around the Capitol, while Christianity is seeking all the stages of society amid the rubbish of anterior civilization, and rebuilding with its ruins a new hierarchic universe, the keystone to whose vault is the priest—one first hears a dull echo from that chaos, and then, little by little, one sees, arising from beneath the breath of Christianity, from beneath the hand of the barbarians, from the fragments of the dead Greek and Roman architectures, that mysterious Romanesque architecture, sister of the theocratic masonry of Egypt and of India, inalterable emblem of pure catholicism, unchangeable hieroglyph of the papal unity. All the thought of that day is written, in fact, in this somber, Romanesque style. One feels everywhere in it authority, unity, the impenetrable, the absolute, Gregory VII; always the priest, never the man; everywhere caste, never the people.

But the Crusades arrive. They are a great popular movement, and every great popular movement, whatever may be its cause and object, always sets free the spirit of liberty from its final precipitate. New things spring into life every day. Here opens the stormy period of the Jacqueries, Pragueries, and Leagues. Authority wavers, unity is divided. Feudalism demands to share with theocracy, while awaiting the inevitable arrival of the people, who will assume the part of the lion: *Quia nominor leo*. Seignory pierces through sacerdotalism; the commonality, through seignory. The face of Europe is changed. Well! the face of architecture is changed also. Like civilization, it has turned a page, and the new spirit of the time finds her ready to write at its dictation. It returns from the crusades with the pointed arch, like the nations with liberty.

Then, while Rome is undergoing gradual dismemberment, Romanesque architecture dies. The hieroglyph deserts the cathedral, and betakes itself to blazoning the donjon keep, in order to lend prestige to feudalism. The cathedral itself, that edifice formerly so dogmatic, invaded henceforth by the bourgeoisie, by the community, by liberty, escapes the priest and falls into the power of the artist. The artist builds it after his own fashion. Farewell to mystery, myth, law. Fancy and caprice, welcome. Provided the priest has his basilica and his altar, he has nothing to say. The four walls belong to the artist. The architectural book belongs no longer to the priest, to religion, to Rome; it is the property of poetry, of imagination, of the people. Hence the rapid and innumerable transformations of that architecture which owns but three centuries, so striking after the stagnant immobility of the Romanesque architecture, which owns six or seven. Nevertheless, art marches on with giant strides. Popular genius amid originality accomplish the task which the bishops formerly fulfilled. Each race writes its line upon the book, as it passes; it erases the ancient Romanesque hieroglyphs on the frontispieces of cathedrals, and at the most one only sees dogma cropping out here and there, beneath the new symbol which it has deposited. The popular drapery hardly permits the religious skeleton to be suspected. One cannot even form an idea of the liberties which the architects then take, even toward the Church. There are capitals knitted of nuns and monks, shamelessly coupled, as on the hall of chimney pieces in the Palais de Justice, in Paris. There is Noah's adventure carved to the last detail, as under the great portal of Bourges. There is a bacchanalian monk, with ass's ears and glass in hand, laughing in the face of a whole community, as on the lavatory of the Abbey of Bocherville. There exists at that epoch, for thought written in stone, a privilege exactly comparable to our present liberty of the press. It is the liberty of architecture.

This liberty goes very far. Sometimes a portal, a façade, an entire church, presents a symbolical sense absolutely foreign to worship, or even hostile to the Church. In the thirteenth century, Guillaume de Paris, and Nicolas Flamel, in the fifteenth, wrote such seditious pages. Saint-Jacques de la Boucherie was a whole church of the opposition.

Thought was then free only in this manner; hence it never wrote itself out completely except on the books called edifices. Thought, under the form of edifice, could have beheld itself burned in the public square by the hands of the executioner, in its manuscript form, if it had been sufficiently imprudent to risk itself thus; thought, as the door of a church, would have been a spectator of the punishment of thought as a book. Having thus only this resource, masonry, in order to make its way to the light, flung itself upon it from all quarters. Hence the immense quantity of cathedrals which have covered Europe—a number so prodigious that one can hardly believe it even after having verified it. All the material forces, all the intellectual forces of society converged toward the same point: architecture. In this manner, under the pretext of building churches to God, art was developed in its magnificent proportions.

Then whoever was born a poet became an architect. Genius, scattered in the masses, repressed in every quarter under feudalism as under a *testudo* of brazen bucklers, finding no issue except in the direction of architecture—gushed forth through that art, and its Iliads assumed the form of cathedrals. All other arts obeyed, and placed themselves under the discipline of architecture. They were the workmen of the great work. The architect, the poet, the master, summed up in his person the sculpture which carved his façades, painting which illuminated his windows, music which set his bells to pealing, and breathed into his organs. There was nothing down to poor poetry—properly speaking, that which persisted in vegetating in manuscripts—which was not forced, in order to make something of itself, to come and frame itself in the edifice in the shape of a hymn or of prose; the same part, after all, which the tragedies of Æschylus had played in the sacerdotal festivals of Greece; Genesis, in the temple of Solomon.

Thus, down to the time of Gutenberg, architecture is the principal writing, the universal writing. In that granite book, begun by the Orient, continued by Greek and Roman antiquity, the Middle Ages wrote the last page. Moreover, this phenomenon of an architecture of the people following an architecture of caste, which we have just been observing in the Middle Ages, is reproduced with every analogous movement in the human intelligence at the other great epochs of history. Thus, in order to enunciate here only summarily, a law which it would require volumes to develop: in the high Orient, the cradle of primitive times, after Hindu architecture came Phœnician architecture, that opulent mother of Arabian architecture; in antiquity, after Egyptian architecture, of which Etruscan style and cyclopean monuments are but one variety, came Greek architecture (of which the Roman style is only a continuation), surcharged with the Carthaginian dome; in modern times, after Romanesque architecture came Gothic architecture. And by separating these three series into their component parts, we shall find in the three eldest sisters, Hindu architecture, Egyptian architecture, Romanesque architecture, the same symbol; that is to say, theocracy, caste, unity, dogma, myth, God: and for the three younger sisters, Phœnician architecture, Greek architecture, Gothic architecture, whatever, nevertheless, may be the diversity of form inherent in their nature, the same signification also; that is to say, liberty, the people, man.

In the Hindu, Egyptian, or Romanesque architecture, one feels the priest, nothing but the priest, whether he calls himself Brahmin, Magian, or Pope. It is not the same in the architectures of the people. They are richer and less sacred. In the Phœnician, one feels the merchant; in the Greek, the republican; in the Gothic, the citizen.

The general characteristics of all theocratic architecture are immutability, horror of progress, the preservation of traditional lines, the consecration of the primitive types, the constant bending of all the forms of men and of nature to the incomprehensible caprices of the symbol. These are dark books, which the initiated alone understand how to decipher. Moreover, every form, every deformity even, has there a sense which renders it inviolable. Do not ask of Hindu, Egyptian, Romanesque masonry to reform their design, or to improve their statuary. Every attempt at perfecting is an impiety to them. In these architectures it seems as though the rigidity of the dogma had spread over the stone like a sort of second petrifaction. The general characteristics of popular masonry, on the contrary, are progress, originality, opulence, perpetual movement. They are already sufficiently detached from religion to think of their beauty, to take care of it, to correct without relaxation their parure of statues or arabesques. They are of the age. They have something human, which they mingle incessantly with the divine symbol under which they still produce. Hence, edifices comprehensible to every soul, to every intelligence, to every imagination, symbolical still, but as easy to understand as nature. Between theocratic architecture and this there is the difference that lies between a sacred language and a vulgar language, between hieroglyphics and art, between Solomon and Phidias.

If the reader will sum up what we have hitherto briefly, very briefly, indicated, neglecting a thousand proofs and also a thousand objections of detail, he will be led to this: that architecture was, down to the fifteenth century, the chief register of humanity; that in that interval not a thought which is in any degree complicated made its appearance in the world, which has not been worked into an edifice; that every popular idea, and every religious law, has had its monumental records; that the human race has, in short, had no important thought which it has not written in stone. And why? Because every thought, either philosophical or religious, is interested in perpetuating itself; because the idea which has moved one generation wishes to move others also, and leave a trace. Now, what a precarious immortality is that of the manuscript! How much more solid, durable, unyielding, is a book of stone! In order to destroy the written word, a torch and a Turk are sufficient. To demolish the constructed word, a social revolution, a terrestrial revolution are required. The barbarians passed over the Coliseum; the deluge, perhaps, passed over the Pyramids.

In the fifteenth century everything changes.

Human thought discovers a mode of perpetuating itself, not only more durable and more resisting than architecture, but still more simple and easy. Architecture is dethroned. Gutenberg's letters of lead are about to supersede Orpheus's letters of stone.

The book is about to kill the edifice.

The invention of printing is the greatest event in history. It is the mother of revolution. It is the mode of expression of humanity which is totally renewed; it is human thought stripping off one form and donning another; it is the complete and definitive change of skin of that symbolical serpent which since the days of Adam has represented intelligence.

In its printed form, thought is more imperishable than ever; it is volatile, irresistible, indestructible. It is mingled with the air. In the days of architecture it made a mountain of itself, and took powerful possession of a century and a place. Now it converts itself into a flock of birds, scatters itself to the four winds, and occupies all points of air and space at once.

We repeat, who does not perceive that in this form it is far more indelible? It was solid, it has become alive. It passes from duration in time to immortality. One can demolish a mass; how can one extirpate ubiquity? If a flood comes, the mountains will have long disappeared beneath the waves, while the birds will still be flying about; and if a single ark floats on the surface of the cataclysm, they will alight upon it, will float with it, will be present with it at the ebbing of the waters; and the new world which emerges from this chaos will behold, on its awakening, the thought of the world which has been submerged soaring above it, winged and living.

And when one observes that this mode of expression is not only the most conservative, but also the most simple, the most convenient, the most practicable for all; when one reflects that it does not drag after it bulky baggage, and does not set in motion a heavy apparatus; when one compares thought forced, in order to transform itself into an edifice, to put in motion four or five other arts and tons of gold, a whole mountain of stones, a whole forest of timber-work, a whole nation of workmen; when one compares it to the thought which becomes a book, and for which a little paper, a little ink, and a pen suffice—how can one be surprised that human intelligence should have quitted architecture for printing? Cut the primitive bed of a river abruptly with a canal hollowed out below its level, and the river will desert its bed.

Behold how, beginning with the discovery of printing, architecture withers away little by little, becomes lifeless and bare. How one feels the water sinking, the sap departing, the thought of the times and of the people withdrawing from it! The chill is almost imperceptible in the fifteenth century; the press is, as yet, too weak, and, at the most, draws from powerful architecture a superabundance of life. But practically beginning with the sixteenth century, the malady of architecture is visible; it is no longer the expression of society; it becomes classic art in a miserable manner; from being Gallic, European, indigenous, it becomes Greek and Roman; from being true and modern, it becomes pseudo-classic. It is this decadence which is called the Renaissance. A magnificent decadence, however, for the ancient Gothic genius, that sun which sets behind the gigantic press of Mayence, still penetrates for a while longer with its rays that whole hybrid pile of Latin arcades and Corinthian columns.

It is that setting sun which we mistake for the dawn.

Nevertheless, from the moment when architecture is no longer anything but an art like any other; as soon as it is no longer the total art, the sovereign art, the tyrant art—it has no longer the power to retain the other arts. So they emancipate themselves, break the yoke of the architect, and take themselves off, each one in its own direction. Each one of them gains by this divorce. Isolation aggrandizes everything. Sculpture becomes statuary, the image trade becomes painting, the canon becomes music. One would pronounce it an empire dismembered at the death of its Alexander, and whose provinces become kingdoms.

Hence Raphael, Michael Angelo, Jean Goujon, Palestrina, those splendors of the dazzling sixteenth century.

Thought emancipates itself in all directions at the same time as the arts. The arch-heretics of the Middle Ages had already made large incisions into Catholicism. The sixteenth century breaks religious unity. Before the invention of printing, reform would have been merely a schism; printing converted it into a revolution. Take away the press; heresy is enervated. Whether it be Providence or Fate, Gutenburg is the precursor of Luther.

Nevertheless, when the sun of the Middle Ages is completely set, when the Gothic genius is forever extinct upon the horizon, architecture grows dim, loses its color, becomes more and more effaced. The printed book, the gnawing worm of the edifice, sucks and devours it. It becomes bare, denuded of its foliage, and grows visibly emaciated. It is petty, it is poor, it is nothing. It no longer expresses anything, not even the memory of the art of another time. Reduced to itself, abandoned by the other arts, because human thought is abandoning it, it summons bunglers in place of artists. Glass replaces the painted windows. The stone-cutter succeeds the sculptor. Farewell all sap, all originality, all life, all intelligence. It drags along, a lamentable workshop mendicant, from copy to copy. Michael Angelo, who, no doubt, felt even in the sixteenth century that it was dying, had a last idea, an idea of despair. That Titan of art piled the Pantheon on the Parthenon, and made Saint-Peter's at Rome. A great work, which deserved to remain unique, the last originality of architecture, the signature of a giant artist at the bottom of the colossal register of stone which was closed forever. With Michael Angelo dead, what does this miserable architecture, which survived itself in the state of a specter, do? It takes Saint-Peter in Rome, copies it and parodies it. It is a mania. It is a pity. Each century has its Saint-Peter's of Rome; in the seventeenth century, the Val-de-Grâce; in the eighteenth, Sainte-Geneviève. Each country has its Saint-Peter's of Rome. London has one; Petersburg has another; Paris has two or three. The insignificant testament, the last dotage of a decrepit grand art falling back into infancy before it dies.

If, in place of the characteristic monuments which we have just described, we examine the general aspect of art from the sixteenth to the eighteenth century, we notice the same phenomena of decay and phthisis. Beginning with François II, the architectural form of the edifice effaces itself more and more, and allows the geometrical form, like the bony structure of an emaciated invalid, to become prominent. The fine lines of art give way to the cold and inexorable lines of geometry. An edifice is no longer an edifice; it is a polyhedron. Meanwhile, architecture is tormented in her struggles to conceal this nudity. Look at the Greek pediment inscribed upon the Roman pediment, and vice versa. It is still the Pantheon on the Parthenon: Saint-Peter's of Rome. Here are the brick houses of Henri IV, with their stone corners; the Place Royale, the Place Dauphine. Here are the churches of Louis XIII, heavy, squat, thickset, crowded together, loaded with a dome like a hump. Here is the Mazarin architecture, the wretched Italian pasticcio of the Four Nations. Here are the palaces of Louis XIV, long barracks for courtiers, stiff, cold, tiresome. Here, finally, is Louis XV, with chiccory leaves and vermicelli, and all the warts, and all the fungi, which disfigure that decrepit, toothless, and coquettish old architecture. From François II to Louis XV, the evil has increased in geometrical progression. Art has no longer anything but skin upon its bones. It is miserably perishing.

Meanwhile what becomes of printing? All the life which is leaving architecture comes to it. In proportion as architecture ebbs, printing swells and grows. That capital of forces which human thought had been expending in edifices, it henceforth expends in books. Thus, from the sixteenth century onward, the press, raised to the level of decaying architecture, contends with it and kills it. In the seventeenth century it is already sufficiently the sovereign, sufficiently triumphant, sufficiently established in its victory, to give to the world the feast of a great literary century. In the eighteenth, having reposed for a long time at the Court of Louis XIV, it seizes again the old sword of Luther, puts it into the hand of Voltaire, and rushes impetuously to the attack of that ancient Europe, whose architectural expression it has already killed. At the moment when the eighteenth century comes to an end, it has destroyed everything. In the nineteenth, it begins to reconstruct.

Now, we ask, which of the three arts has really represented human thought for the last three centuries? which translates it? which expresses not only its literary and scholastic vagaries, but its vast, profound, universal movement? which constantly superposes itself, without a break, without a gap, upon the human race, which walks a monster with a thousand legs?—Architecture or printing?

It is printing. Let the reader make no mistake; architecture is dead; irretrievably slain by the printed book—slain because it endures for a shorter time—slain because it costs more. Every cathedral represents millions. Let the reader now imagine what an investment of funds it would require to rewrite the architectural book; to cause thousands of edifices to swarm once more upon the soil; to return to those epochs when the throng of monuments was such, according to the statement of an eye witness, "that one would have said that the world in shaking itself, had cast off its old garments in order to cover itself with a white vesture of churches." *Erat enim ut si mundus, ipse excutiendo semet, rejecta vetustate, candidam ecclesiarum vestem indueret.* (GLABER RADOLPHUS.)

A book is so soon made, costs so little, and can go so far! How can it surprise us that all human thought flows in this channel? This does not mean that architecture will not still have a fine monument, an isolated masterpiece, here and there. We may still have from time to time, under the reign of printing, a column made I suppose, by a whole army from melted cannon, as we had under the reign of architecture, Iliads and Romanceros, Mahabâhrata, and Nibelungen Lieds, made by a whole people, with rhapsodies piled up and melted together. The great accident of an architect of genius may happen in the twentieth century, like that of Dante in the thirteenth. But architecture will no longer be the social art, the collective art, the dominating art. The grand poem, the grand edifice, the grand work of humanity will no longer be built: it will be printed.

And henceforth, if architecture should arise again accidentally, it will no longer be mistress. It will be subservient to the law of literature, which formerly received the law from it. The respective positions of the two arts will be inverted. It is certain that in architectural epochs, the poems, rare it is true, resemble the monuments. In India, Vyasa is branching, strange, impenetrable as a pagoda. In Egyptian Orient, poetry has like the edifices, grandeur and tranquility of line; in antique Greece, beauty, serenity, calm; in Christian Europe, the Catholic majesty, the popular naïvete, the rich and luxuriant vegetation of an epoch of renewal. The Bible resembles the Pyramids; the Iliad, the Parthenon; Homer, Phidias. Dante in the thirteenth century is the last Romanesque church; Shakespeare in the sixteenth, the last Gothic cathedral.

Thus, to sum up what we have hitherto said, in a fashion which is necessarily incomplete and mutilated, the human race has two books, two registers, two testaments: masonry and printing; the Bible of stone and the Bible of paper. No doubt, when one contemplates these two Bibles, laid so broadly open in the centuries, it is permissible to regret the visible majesty of the writing of granite, those gigantic alphabets formulated in colonnades, in pylons, in obelisks, those sorts of human mountains which cover the world and the past, from the pyramid to the bell tower, from Cheops to Strasburg. The past must be reread upon these pages of marble. This book, written by architecture, must be admired and perused incessantly; but the grandeur of the edifice which printing erects in its turn must not be denied.

That edifice is colossal. Some compiler of statistics has calculated, that if all the volumes which have issued from the press since Gutenberg's day were to be piled one upon another, they would fill the space between the earth and the moon; but it is not that sort of grandeur of which we wished to speak. Nevertheless, when one tries to collect in one's mind a comprehensive image of the total products of printing down to our own days, does not that total appear to us like an immense construction, resting upon the entire world, at which humanity toils without relaxation, and whose monstrous crest is lost in the profound mists of the future? It is the anthill of intelligence. It is the hive whither come all imaginations, those golden bees, with their honey.

The edifice has a thousand stories. Here and there one beholds on its staircases the gloomy caverns of science which pierce its interior. Everywhere upon its surface, art causes its arabesques, rosettes, and laces to thrive luxuriantly before the eyes. There, every individual work, however capricious and isolated it may seem, has its place and its projection. Harmony results from the whole. From the cathedral of Shakespeare to the mosque of Byron, a thousand tiny bell towers are piled pell-mell above this metropolis of universal thought. At its base are written some ancient titles of humanity which architecture had not registered. To the left of the entrance has been fixed the ancient bas-relief, in white marble, of Homer; to the right, the polyglot Bible rears its seven heads. The hydra of the Romancero and some other hybrid forms, the Vedas and the Nibelungen bristle further on.

Nevertheless, the prodigious edifice still remains incomplete. The press, that giant machine, which incessantly pumps all the intellectual sap of society, belches forth without pause fresh materials for its work. The whole human race is on the scaffoldings. Each mind is a mason. The humblest fills his hole, or places his stone. Rétif dè le Bretonne brings his hod of plaster. Every day a new course rises. Independently of the original and individual contribution of each writer, there are collective contingents. The eighteenth century gives the *Encyclopedia*, the revolution gives the *Moniteur*. Assuredly, it is a construction which increases and piles up in endless spirals; there also are confusion of tongues, incessant activity, indefatigable labor, eager competition of all humanity, refuge promised to intelligence, a new Flood against an overflow of barbarians. It is the second tower of Babel of the human race.

BOOK SIXTH

Chapter I

AN IMPARTIAL GLANCE AT THE ANCIENT MAGISTRACY

A VERY HAPPY PERSONAGE IN THE YEAR OF GRACE 1482, WAS THE NOBLE GENTLEMAN ROBERT d'Estouteville, chevalier, Sieur de Beyne, Baron d'Ivry and Saint Andry en la Marche, counselor and chamberlain to the king, and guard of the provostship of Paris. It was already nearly seventeen years since he had received from the king, on November 7, 1465, the comet year, that fine charge of the provostship of Paris, which was reputed rather a seigneury than an office. *Dignitas*, says Joannes Lœmnœus, *quoe cum non exigua potestate politiam concernente, atque proerogativis multis et juribus conjuncta est.* A marvelous thing in '82 was a gentleman bearing the king's commission, and whose letters of institution ran back to the epoch of the marriage of the natural daughter of Louis XI with Monsieur the Bastard of Bourbon.

The same day on which Robert d'Estouteville took the place of Jacques de Villiers in the provostship of Paris, Master Jehan Dauvet replaced Messire Helye de Thorrettes in the first presidency of the Court of Parliament, Jehan Jouvenel des Ursins supplanted Pierre de Morvilliers in the office of chancellor of France, Regnault des Dormans ousted Pierre Puy from the charge of master of requests in ordinary of the king's household. Now, upon how many heads had the presidency, the chancellorship, the mastership passed since Robert d'Estouteville had held the provostship of Paris. It had been "granted to him for safekeeping," as the letters patent said; and certainly he kept it well. He had clung to it, he had incorporated himself with it, he had so identified himself with it that he had escaped that fury for change which possessed Louis XI, a tormenting and industrious king, whose policy it was to maintain the elasticity of his power by frequent appointments and revocations. More than this; the brave chevalier had obtained the reversion of the office for his son, and for two years already, the name of the noble man Jacques d'Estouteville, equerry, had figured beside his at the head of the register of the salary list of the provostship of Paris. A rare and notable favor indeed! It is true that Robert d'Estouteville was a good soldier, that he had loyally raised his pennon against "the league of public good," and that he had presented to the queen a very marvelous stag in confectionery on the day of her entrance to Paris in 14. . . . Moreover, he possessed the good friendship of Messire Tristan l'Hermite, provost of the marshals of the king's household. Hence a very sweet and pleasant existence was that of Messire Robert. In the first place, very good wages, to which were attached, and from which hung, like extra bunches of grapes on his vine, the revenues of the civil and criminal registries of the provostship, plus the civil and criminal revenues of the tribunals of Embas of the Châtelet, without reckoning some little toll from the bridges of Mantes and of Corbeil, and the profits on the craft of Shagreen-makers of Paris, on the corders of firewood and the measurers of salt. Add to this the pleasure of displaying himself in rides about the city, and of making his fine military costume, which you may still admire sculptured on his tomb in the abbey of Valmont in Normandy, and his morion, all embossed at Montlhéry, stand out a contrast against the parti-colored red and tawny robes of the aldermen and police. And then, was it nothing to wield absolute supremacy over the sergeants of the police, the porter and watch of the Châtelet, the two auditors of the Châtelet, *auditores castelleti*, the sixteen commissioners of the sixteen quarters, the jailer of the Châtelet, the four enfeoffed sergeants, the hundred and twenty mounted sergeants, with maces, the chevalier of the watch with his watch, his sub-watch, his counter-watch and his rear-watch? Was it nothing to exercise high and low justice, the right to interrogate, to hang and to draw, without reckoning petty jurisdiction in the first resort (*in prima instantia*, as the charters say), on that viscomty of Paris, so nobly appanaged with seven noble bailiwicks? Can anything sweeter be imagined than rendering judgments and decisions, as Messire Robert d'Estouteville daily did in the Grand Châtelet, under the large and flattened arches of Philip Augustus? and going, as he was wont to do every evening, to that charming house situated in the Rue Galilèe, in the enclosure of the royal palace, which he held in right of his wife, Madame Ambroise de Loré, to repose after the fatigue of having sent some poor wretch to pass the night in "that little cell of the Rue de Escorcherie, which the provosts and aldermen of Paris used to make their prison; the same being eleven feet long, seven feet and four inches wide, and eleven feet high?"

And not only had Messire Robert d'Estouteville his special court as provost and vicomte of Paris; but in addition he had a share, both for eye and tooth, in the grand court of the king. There was no head in the least elevated which had not passed through his hands before it came to the headsman. It was he who went to seek M. de Nemours at the Bastille Saint-Antoine, in order to conduct him to the Halles; and to conduct to the Grève M. de Saint-Pol, who clamored and resisted, to the great joy of the provost, who did not love monsieur the constable.

Here, assuredly, is more than sufficient to render a life happy and illustrious, and to deserve some day a notable page in that interesting history of the provosts of Paris, where one learns that Oudard de Villeneuve had a house in the Rue des Boucheries, that Guillaume de Hangest purchased the great and the little Savoy, that Guillaume Thiboust gave the nuns of Sainte-Geneviève his houses in the Rue Clopin, that Hugues Aubriot lived in the Hôtel du Porc-Epic, and other domestic facts.

Nevertheless, with so many reasons for taking life patiently and joyously, Messire Robert d'Estouteville woke up on the morning of the 7th of January, 1482, in a very surly and peevish mood. Whence came this ill temper? He could not have told himself. Was it because the sky was gray? or was the buckle of his old belt of Montlhéry badly fastened, so that it confined his provostal portliness too closely? had he beheld ribald fellows, marching in bands of four, beneath his window, and setting him at defiance, in doublets but no shirts, hats without crowns, with wallet and bottle at their side? Was it a vague presentiment of the three hundred and seventy livres, sixteen sous, eight farthings, which the future King Charles VII was to cut off from the provostship in the following year? The reader can take his choice; we, for our part, are much inclined to believe that he was in a bad humor, simply because he was in a bad humor.

Moreover, it was the day after a festival, a tiresome day for everyone, and above all for the magistrate who is charged with sweeping away all the filth, properly and figuratively speaking, which a festival day produces in Paris. And then he had to hold a sitting at the Grand Châtelet. Now, we have noticed that judges in general so arrange matters that their day of audience shall also be their day of bad humor, so that they may always have someone upon whom to vent it conveniently, in the name of the king, law, and justice.

However, the audience had begun without him. His lieutenants, civil, criminal, and private, were doing his work, according to usage; and from eight o'clock in the morning, some scores of bourgeois and bourgeoises, heaped and crowded into an obscure corner of the audience chamber of Embas du Châtelet, between a stout oaken barrier and the wall, had been gazing blissfully at the varied and cheerful spectacle of civil and criminal justice dispensed by Master Florian Barbedienne, auditor of the Châtelet, lieutenant of monsieur the provost, in a somewhat confused and utterly haphazard manner.

The hall was small, low, vaulted. A table studded with fleurs-de-lys stood at one end, with a large arm-chair of carved oak, which belonged to the provost and was empty, and a stool on the left for the auditor, Master Florian. Below sat the clerk of the court, scribbling; opposite was the populace; and in front of the door, and in front of the table were many sergeants of the provostship in sleeveless jackets of violet camlet, with white crosses. Two sergeants of the Parloir-aux-Bourgeois, clothed in their jackets of Toussaint, half red, half blue, were posted as sentinels before a low, closed door, which was visible at the extremity of the hall, behind the table. A single pointed window, narrowly encased in the thick wall, illuminated with a pale ray of January sun two grotesque figures—the capricious demon of stone carved as a tail-piece in the keystone of the vaulted ceiling, and the judge seated at the end of the hall on the fleurs-de-lys.

Imagine, in fact, at the provost's table, leaning upon his elbows between two bundles of documents of cases, with his foot on the train of his robe of plain brown cloth, his face buried in his hood of white lamb's skin, of which his brows seemed to be of a piece, red, crabbed, winking, bearing majestically the load of fat on his cheeks which met under his chin, Master Florian Barbedienne, auditor of the Châtelet.

Now, the auditor was deaf. A slight defect in an auditor. Master Florian delivered judgment, none the less, without appeal and very suitably. It is certainly quite sufficient for a judge to have the air of listening; and the venerable auditor fulfilled this condition, the sole one in justice, all the better because his attention could not be distracted by any noise.

Moreover, he had in the audience, a pitiless censor of his deeds and gestures, in the person of our friend Jehan Frollo du Moulin, that little student of yesterday, that "stroller," whom one was sure of encountering all over Paris, anywhere except before the rostrums of the professors.

"Stay," he said in a low tone to his companion, Robin Poussepain, who was grinning at his side, while he was making his comments on the scenes which were being unfolded before his eyes, "yonder is Jehanneton du Buisson. The beautiful daughter of the lazy dog at the Marché-Neuf!—Upon my soul, he is condemning her, the old rascal! he has no more eyes than ears. Fifteen sous, four farthings, parisian, for having worn two rosaries! 'Tis somewhat dear. *Lex duri carminis.* Who's that? Robin Chief-de-Ville, hauberk-maker. For having been passed and received master of the said trade! That's his entrance money. He! two gentlemen among these knaves! Aiglet de Soins, Hutin de Mailly. Two equerries, *Corpus Christi!* Ah! they have been playing at dice. When shall I see our rector here? A hundred livres parisian, fine to the king! That Barbedienne strikes like a deaf man— as he is! I'll be my brother the archdeacon, if that keeps me from gaming; gaming by day, gaming by night, living at play, dying at play, and gaming away my soul after my shirt. Holy Virgin, what damsels! One after the other, my lambs. Ambroise Lécuyère, Isabeau la Paynette, Bérarde Gironin! I know them all, by Heavens! A fine! a fine! That's what will teach you to wear gilded girdles! ten sous parisis! you coquettes! Oh! the old snout of a judge! deaf and imbecile! Oh! Florian the dolt! Oh! Barbedienne the blockhead! There he is at the table! He's eating the plaintiff, he's eating the suits, he eats, he chews, he crams, he fills himself. Fines, lost goods, taxes, expenses, loyal charges, salaries, damages, and interests, gehenna, prison, and jail, and fetters with expenses are Christmas spice cake and marchpanes of Saint-John to him! Look at him, the pig!—Come! Good! Another amorous woman! Thibaud-la-Thibaude, neither more nor less! For having come from the Rue Glatigny! What fellow is this? Gieffroy Mabonne, gendarme bearing the crossbow. He has cursed the name of the Father. A fine for la Thibaude! A fine for Gieffroy! A fine for them both! The deaf old fool! he must have mixed up the two cases! Ten to one that he makes the wench pay for the oath and the gendarme for the amour! Attention, Robin Poussepain! What are they going to bring in? Here are many sergeants! By Jupiter! all the bloodhounds of the pack are there. It must be the great beast of the hunt—a wild boar. And 'tis one, Robin, 'tis one. And a fine one too! *Hercle!* 'tis our prince of yesterday, our Pope of the Fools, our bellringer, our one-eyed man, our hunchback, our grimace! 'Tis Quasimodo!"—

It was he indeed.

It was Quasimodo, bound, encircled, roped, pinioned, and under good guard. The squad of policemen who surrounded him was assisted by the chevalier of the watch in person, wearing the arms of France embroidered on his breast, and the arms of the city on his back. There was nothing, however, about Quasimodo, except his deformity, which could justify the display of halberds and arquebuses; he was gloomy, silent, and tranquil. Only now and then did his single eye cast a sly and wrathful glance upon the bonds with which he was loaded.

He cast the same glance about him, but it was so dull and sleepy that the women only pointed him out to each other in derision.

Meanwhile Master Florian, the auditor, turned over attentively the document in the complaint entered against Quasimodo, which the clerk handed him, and, having thus glanced at it, appeared to reflect for a moment. Thanks to this precaution, which he always was careful to take at the moment when on the point of beginning an examination, he knew beforehand the names, titles, and misdeeds of the accused, made cut and dried responses to questions foreseen, and succeeded in extricating himself from all the windings of the interrogation without allowing his deafness to be too apparent. The written charges were to him what the dog is to the blind man. If his deafness did happen to betray him here and there, by some incoherent apostrophe or some unintelligible question, it passed for profundity with some, and for imbecility with others. In neither case did the honor of the magistracy sustain any injury; for it is far better that a judge should be reputed imbecile or profound than deaf. Hence he took great care to conceal his deafness from the eyes of all, and he generally succeeded so well that he had reached the point of deluding himself, which is, by the way, easier than is supposed. All hunchbacks walk with their heads held high, all stutterers harangue, all deaf people speak low. As for him, he believed, at the most, that his ear was a little refractory. It was the sole concession which he made on this point to public opinion, in his moments of frankness and examination of his conscience.

Having, then, thoroughly ruminated Quasimodo's affair, he threw back his head and half closed his eyes, for the sake of more majesty and impartiality, so that, at that moment, he was both deaf and blind. A double condition, without which no judge is perfect. It was in this magisterial attitude that he began the examination.

"Your name?"

Now this was a case which had not been "provided for by law," where a deaf man should be obliged to question a deaf man.

Quasimodo, whom nothing warned that a question had been addressed to him, continued to stare intently at the judge, and made no reply. The judge, being deaf, and being in no way warned of the deafness of the accused, thought that the latter had answered, as all accused do in general, and therefore he pursued, with his mechanical and stupid self-possession—

"Very well. And your age?"

Again Quasimodo made no reply to this question. The judge supposed that it had been replied to, and continued—

"Now, your profession?"

Still the same silence. The spectators had begun, meanwhile, to whisper together, and to exchange glances.

"That will do," went on the imperturbable auditor, when he supposed that the accused had finished his third reply. "You are accused before us, *primo*, of nocturnal disturbance; *secundo*, of a dishonorable act of violence upon the person of a foolish woman, *in proejudicium meretricis*; *tertio*, of rebellion and disloyalty toward the archers of the police of our lord, the king. Explain yourself upon all these points.—Clerk, have you written down what the prisoner has said thus far?"

At this unlucky question, a burst of laughter rose from the clerk's table caught by the audience, so violent, so wild, so contagious, so universal, that the two deaf men were forced to perceive it. Quasimodo turned round, shrugging his hump with disdain, while Master Florian, equally astonished, and supposing that the laughter of the spectators had been provoked by some irreverent reply from the accused, rendered visible to him by that shrug of the shoulders, apostrophized him indignantly—

"You have uttered a reply, knave, which deserves the halter. Do you know to whom you are speaking?"

This sally was not fitted to arrest the explosion of general merriment. It struck all as so whimsical, and so ridiculous, that the wild laughter even attacked the sergeants of the Parloir-aux-Bourgeois, a sort of pikemen, whose stupidity was part of their uniform. Quasimodo alone preserved his seriousness, for the good reason that he understood nothing of what was going on around him. The judge, more and more irritated, thought it his duty to continue in the same tone, hoping thereby to strike the accused with a terror which should react upon the audience, and bring it back to respect.

"So this is as much as to say, perverse and thieving knave that you are, that you permit yourself to be lacking in respect toward the Auditor of the Châtelet, to the magistrate committed to the popular police of Paris, charged with searching out crimes, delinquencies, and evil conduct; with controlling all trades, and interdicting monopoly; with maintaining the pavements; with debarring the hucksters of chickens, poultry, and water-fowl; of superintending the measuring of fagots and other sorts of wood; of purging the city of mud, and the air of contagious maladies; in a word, with attending continually to public affairs, without wages or hope of salary! Do you know that I am called Florian Barbedienne, actual lieutenant to monsieur the provost, and, moreover, commissioner, inquisitor, *controller*, and examiner, with equal power in provostship, bailiwick, preservation, and inferior court of judicature?—"

There is no reason why a deaf man talking to a deaf man should stop. God knows where and when Master Florian would have landed, when thus launched at full speed in lofty eloquence, if the low door at the extreme end of the room had not suddenly opened, and given entrance to the provost in person.

At his entrance Master Florian did not stop short, but, making a half-turn on his heels, and aiming at the provost the harangue with which he had been withering Quasimodo a moment before—

"Monseigneur," said he, "I demand such penalty as you shall deem fitting against the prisoner here present, for grave and aggravated offense against the court."

And he seated himself, utterly breathless, wiping away the great drops of sweat which fell from his brow and drenched, like tears, the parchments spread out before him. Messire Robert d'Estouteville frowned and made a gesture so imperious and significant to Quasimodo, that the deaf man in some measure understood it.

The provost addressed him with severity, "What have you done that you have been brought hither, knave?"

The poor fellow, supposing that the provost was asking his name, broke the silence which he habitually preserved, and replied, in a harsh and guttural voice, "Quasimodo."

The reply matched the question so little that the wild laugh began to circulate once more, and Messire Robert exclaimed, red with wrath—

"Are you mocking me also, you arrant knave?"

"Bellringer of Notre-Dame," replied Quasimodo, supposing that what was required of him was to explain to the judge who he was.

"Bellringer!" interpolated the provost, who had waked up early enough to be in a sufficiently bad temper, as we have said, not to require to have his fury inflamed by such strange responses. "Bellringer! I'll play you a chime of rods on your back through the squares of Paris! Do you hear, knave?"

"If it is my age that you wish to know," said Quasimodo, "I think that I shall be twenty at Saint Martin's day."

This was too much; the provost could no longer restrain himself.

"Ah! you are scoffing at the provostship, wretch! Messieurs the sergeants of the mace, you will take me this knave to the pillory of the Grève, you will flog him, and turn him for an hour. He shall pay me for it, *tête Dieu!* And I order that the present judgment shall be cried, with the assistance of four sworn trumpeters, in the seven castellanies of the viscomty of Paris."

The clerk set to work incontinently to draw up the account of the sentence.

"*Ventre Dieu!* 'tis well adjudged!" cried the little scholar, Jehan Frollo du Moulin, from his corner.

The provost turned and fixed his flashing eyes once more on Quasimodo. "I believe the knave said '*Ventre Dieu!*' Clerk, add twelve deniers Parisian for the oath, and let the vestry of Saint Eustache have the half of it; I have a particular devotion for Saint Eustache."

In a few minutes the sentence was drawn up. Its tenor was simple and brief. The customs of the provostship and the viscomty had not yet been worked over by President Thibaut Baillet, and by Roger Barmne, the king's advocate; they had not been obstructed, at that time, by that lofty hedge of quibbles and procedures, which the two jurisconsults planted there at the beginning of the sixteenth century. All was clear, expeditious, explicit. One went straight to the point then, and at the end of every path there was immediately visible, without thickets and without turnings, the wheel, the gibbet, or the pillory. One at least knew whither one was going.

The clerk presented the sentence to the provost, who affixed his seal to it, and departed to pursue his round of the audience hall, in a frame of mind which seemed destined to fill all the jails in Paris that day. Jehan Frollo and Robin Poussepain laughed in their sleeves. Quasimodo gazed on the whole with an indifferent and astonished air.

However, at the moment when Master Florian Barbedienne was reading the sentence in his turn, before signing it, the clerk felt himself moved with pity for the poor wretch of a prisoner, and, in the hope of obtaining some mitigation of the penalty, he approached as near the auditor's ear as possible, and said, pointing to Quasimodo, "That man is deaf."

He hoped that this community of infirmity would awaken Master Florian's interest in behalf of the condemned man. But, in the first place, we have already observed that Master Florian did not care to have his deafness noticed. In the next place, he was so hard of hearing that he did not catch a single word of what the clerk said to him; nevertheless, he wished to have the appearance of hearing, and replied, "Ah! ah! that is different; I did not know that. An hour more of the pillory, in that case."

And he signed the sentence thus modified.

" 'Tis well done," said Robin Poussepain, who cherished a grudge against Quasimodo. "That will teach him to handle people roughly."

Chapter II

THE RAT-HOLE

THE READER MUST PERMIT US TO TAKE HIM BACK TO THE PLACE DE GRÈVE, WHICH WE QUITTED yesterday with Gringoire, in order to follow la Esmeralda.

It is ten o'clock in the morning; everything is indicative of the day after a festival. The pavement is covered with rubbish; ribbons, rags, feathers from tufts of plumes, drops of wax from the torches, crumbs of the public feast. A goodly number of bourgeois are "sauntering," as we say, here and there, turning over with their feet the extinct brands of the bonfire, going into raptures in front of the Pillar House, over the memory of the fine hangings of the day before, and to-day staring at the nails that secured them a last pleasure. The venders of cider and beer are rolling their barrels among the groups. Some busy passers-by come and go. The merchants converse and call to each other from the thresholds of their shops. The festival, the ambassadors, Coppenole, the Pope of the Fools, are in all mouths; they vie with each other, each trying to criticize it best and laugh the most. And, meanwhile, four mounted sergeants, who have just posted themselves at the four sides of the pillory, have already concentrated around themselves a goodly proportion of the populace scattered on the Place, who condemn themselves to immobility and fatigue in the hope of a small execution.

If the reader, after having contemplated this lively and noisy scene which is being enacted in all parts of the Place, will now transfer his gaze toward that ancient demi-Gothic, demi-Romanesque house of the Tour-Roland, which forms the corner on the quay to the west, he will observe, at the angle of the façade, a large public breviary, with rich illuminations, protected from the rain by a little penthouse, and from thieves by a small grating, which, however, permits of the leaves being turned. Beside this breviary is a narrow, arched window, closed by two iron bars in the form of a cross, and looking on the square; the only opening which admits a small quantity of light and air to a little cell without a door, constructed on the ground floor, in the thickness of the walls of the old house, and filled with a peace all the more profound, with a silence all the more gloomy, because a public place, the most populous and most noisy in Paris swarms and shrieks around it.

This little cell had been celebrated in Paris for nearly three centuries, ever since Madame Rolande de la Tour-Roland, in mourning for her father who died in the Crusades, had caused it to be hollowed out in the wall of her own house, in order to immure herself there forever, keeping of all her palace only this lodging whose door was walled up, and whose window stood open, winter and summer, giving all the rest to the poor and to God. The afflicted damsel had, in fact, waited twenty years for death in this premature tomb, praying night and day for the soul of her father, sleeping in ashes, without even a stone for a pillow, clothed in a black sack, and subsisting on the bread and water which the compassion of the passers-by led them to deposit on the ledge of her window, thus receiving charity after having bestowed it. At her death, at the moment when she was passing to the other sepulcher, she had bequeathed this one in perpetuity to afflicted women, mothers, widows, or maidens, who should wish to pray much for others or for themselves, and who should desire to inter themselves alive in a great grief or a great penance. The poor of her day had made her a fine funeral, with tears and benedictions; but, to their great regret, the pious maid had not been canonized, for lack of influence. Those among them who were a little inclined to impiety, had hoped that the matter might be accomplished in Paradise more easily than at Rome, and had frankly besought God, instead of the pope, in behalf of the deceased. The majority had contented themselves with holding the memory of Rolande sacred, and converting her rags into relics. The city, on its side, had founded in honor of the demoiselle, a public breviary, which had been fastened near the window of the cell, in order that passers-by might halt there from time to time, were it only to pray; that prayer might remind them of alms, and that the poor recluses, heiresses of Madame Rolande's vault, might not die outright of hunger and forgetfulness.

Moreover, this sort of tomb was not so very rare a thing in the cities of the Middle Ages. One often encountered in the most frequented street, in the most crowded and noisy market, in the very middle, under the feet of the horses, under the wheels of the carts, as it were, a cellar, a well, a tiny walled and grated cabin, at the bottom of which a human being prayed night and day, voluntarily devoted to some eternal lamentation, to some great expiation. And all the reflections which that strange spectacle would awaken in us to-day; that horrible cell, a sort of intermediary link between a house and the tomb, the cemetery and the city; that living being cut off from the human community, and thenceforth reckoned among the dead; that lamp consuming its last drop of oil in the darkness; that remnant of life flickering in the grave; that breath, that voice, that eternal prayer in a box of stone; that face forever turned toward the other world; that eye already illuminated with another sun; that ear pressed to the walls of a tomb; that soul a prisoner in that body; that body a prisoner in that dungeon cell, and beneath that double envelope of flesh and granite, the murmur of that soul in pain;—nothing of all this was perceived by the crowd.

The piety of that age, not very subtle nor much given to reasoning, did not see so many facets in an act of religion. It took the thing in the block, honored, venerated, hallowed the sacrifice at need, but did not analyze the sufferings, and felt but moderate pity for them. It brought some pittance to the miserable penitent from time to time, looked through the hole to see whether he were still living, forgot his name, hardly knew how many years ago he had begun to die, and to the stranger, who questioned them about the living skeleton who was perishing in that cellar, the neighbors replied simply, "It is the recluse."

Everything was then viewed without metaphysics, without exaggeration, without magnifying glass, with the naked eye. The microscope had not yet been invented, either for things of matter or for things of the mind.

Moreover, although people were but little surprised by it, the examples of this sort of cloistration in the hearts of cities were in truth frequent, as we have just said. There were in Paris a considerable number of these cells, for praying to God and doing penance; they were nearly all occupied. It is true that the clergy did not like to have them empty, since that implied lukewarmness in believers, and that lepers were put into them when there were no penitents on hand. Besides the cell on the Grève, there was one at Montfaucon, one at the Charnier des Innocents, another I hardly know where—at the Clichon House, I think; others still at many spots where traces of them are found in traditions, in default of memorials. The University had also its own. On Mount Sainte-Geneviève a sort of Job of the Middle Ages, for the space of thirty years, chanted the seven penitential psalms on a dunghill at the bottom of a cistern, beginning anew when he had finished, singing loudest at night, *magna voce per umbras,* and to-day, the antiquary fancies that he hears his voice as he enters the Rue du Puits-qui-parle—the street of the "Speaking Well."

To confine ourselves to the cell in the Tour-Roland, we must say that it had never lacked recluses. After the death of Madame Roland, it had stood vacant for a year or two, though rarely. Many women had come thither to mourn, until their death, for relatives, lovers, faults. Parisian malice, which thrusts its finger into everything, even into things which concern it the least, affirmed that it had beheld but few widows there.

In accordance with the fashion of the epoch, a Latin inscription on the wall indicated to the learned passer-by the pious purpose of this cell. The custom was retained until the middle of the sixteenth century of explaining an edifice by a brief device inscribed above the door. Thus, one still reads in France, above the wicket of the prison in the seignorial mansion of Tourville, *Sileto et spera*; in Ireland, beneath the armorial bearings which surmount the grand door to Fortescue Castle, *Forte scutum, salus ducum*; in England, over the principal entrance to the hospitable mansion of the Earls Cowper: *Tuum est*. At that time every edifice was a thought.

As there was no door to the walled cell of the Tour-Roland, these two words had been carved in large Roman capitals over the window—

TU, ORA.

And this caused the people, whose good sense does not perceive so much refinement in things, and likes to translate *Ludovico Magno* by *Porte Saint-Denis,* to give to this dark, gloomy, damp cavity, the name of "The Rat-Hole." An explanation less sublime, perhaps, than the other; but, on the other hand, more picturesque.

Chapter III

HISTORY OF A LEAVENED CAKE OF MAIZE

A T THE EPOCH OF THIS HISTORY, THE CELL IN THE TOUR-ROLAND WAS OCCUPIED. IF THE READER desires to know by whom, he has only to lend an ear to the conversation of three worthy gossips, who, at the moment when we have directed his attention to the Rat-Hole, were directing their steps toward the same spot, coming up along the water's edge from the Châtelet, toward the Grève.

Two of these women were dressed like good bourgeoises of Paris. Their fine white ruffs; their petticoats of linsey-woolsey, striped red and blue; their white knitted stockings, with clocks embroidered in colors, well drawn upon their legs; the square-toed shoes of tawny leather with black soles, and, above all, their headgear, that sort of tinsel horn, loaded down with ribbons and laces, which the women of Champagne still wear, in company with the grenadiers of the imperial guard of Russia, announced that they belonged to that class of wealthy merchant's wives which holds the middle ground between what the lackeys call a woman and what they term a lady. They wore neither rings nor gold crosses, and it was easy to see that, in their case, this did not proceed from poverty, but simply from fear of being fined. Their companion was attired in very much the same manner; but there was that indescribable something about her dress and bearing which suggested the wife of a provincial notary. One could see, by the way in which her girdle rose above her hips, that she had not been long in Paris. Add to this a plaited tucker, knots of ribbon on her shoes—and that the stripes of her petticoat ran horizontally instead of vertically, and a thousand other enormities which shocked good taste.

The two first walked with that step peculiar to Parisian ladies, showing Paris to women from the country. The provincial held by the hand a big boy, who held in his a large, flat cake.

We regret to be obliged to add, that, owing to the rigor of the season, he was using his tongue as a handkerchief.

The child was making them drag him along, *non passibus oequis,* as Virgil says, and stumbling at every moment, to the great indignation of his mother. It is true that he was looking at his cake more than at the pavement. Some serious motive, no doubt, prevented his biting it (the cake), for he contented himself with gazing tenderly at it. But the mother should have rather taken charge of the cake. It was cruel to make a Tantalus of the chubby-cheeked boy.

Meanwhile, the three demoiselles (for the name of *dames* was then reserved for noble women) were all talking at once.

"Let us make haste, Demoiselle Mahiette," said the youngest of the three, who was also the largest, to the provincial, "I greatly fear that we shall arrive too late; they told us at the Châtelet that they were going to take him directly to the pillory."

"Ah, bah! what are you saying, Demoiselle Oudarde Musnier?" interposed the other Parisienne. "There are two hours yet to the pillory. We have time enough. Have you ever seen anyone pilloried, my dear Mahiette?"

"Yes," said the provincial, "at Reims."

"Ah, bah! What is your pillory at Reims? A miserable cage into which only peasants are turned. A great affair, truly!"

"Only peasants!" said Mahiette, "at the cloth market in Reims! We have seen very fine criminals there, who have killed their father and mother! Peasants! For what do you take us, Gervaise?"

It is certain that the provincial was on the point of taking offense, for the honor of her pillory. Fortunately, that discreet demoiselle, Oudarde Musnier, turned the conversation in time.

"By the way, Demoiselle Mahiette, what say you to our Flemish Ambassadors? Have you as fine ones at Reims?"

"I admit," replied Mahiette, "that it is only in Paris that such Flemings can be seen."

"Did you see among the embassy, that big ambassador who is a hosier?" asked Oudarde.

"Yes," said Mahiette. "He has the eye of a Saturn."

"And the big fellow whose face resembles a bare belly?" resumed Gervaise. "And the little one, with small eyes framed in red eyelids, pared down and slashed up like a thistle head?"

" 'Tis their horses that are worth seeing," said Oudarde, "caparisoned as they are after the fashion of their country!"

"Ah my dear," interrupted provincial Mahiette, assuming in her turn an air of superiority, "what would you say then, if you had seen in '61, at the consecration at Reims, eighteen years ago, the horses of the princes and of the king's company? Housings and caparisons of all sorts; some of damask cloth, of fine cloth of gold, furred with sables; others of velvet, furred with ermine; others all embellished with goldsmith's work and large bells of gold and silver! And what money that had cost! And what handsome boy pages rode upon them!"

"That," replied Oudarde dryly, "does not prevent the Flemings having very fine horses, and having had a superb supper yesterday with monsieur, the provost of the merchants, at the Hôtel-de-Ville, where they were served with comfits and hippocras, and spices, and other singularities."

"What are you saying, neighbor!" exclaimed Gervaise. "It was with monsieur the cardinal, at the Petit Bourbon that they supped."

"Not at all. At the Hôtel-de-Ville."

"Yes, indeed. At the Petit Bourbon!"

"It was at the Hôtel-de-Ville," retorted Oudarde sharply, "and Dr. Scourable addressed them a harangue in Latin, which pleased them greatly. My husband, who is sworn bookseller told me so."

"It was at the Petit Bourbon," replied Gervaise, with no less spirit, "and this is what monsieur the cardinal's procurator presented to them: twelve double quarts of hippocras, white, claret, and red; twenty-four boxes of double Lyons marchpane, gilded; as many torches, worth two livres a piece; and six demi-queues[1] of Beaune wine, white and claret, the best that could be found. I have it from my husband, who is a cinquantenier,[2] at the Parloir-aux-Bourgeois, and who was this morning comparing the Flemish ambassadors with those of Prester John and the Emperor of Trebizond, who came from Mesopotamia to Paris, under the last king, and who wore rings in their ears."

"So true is it that they supped at the Hôtel-de-Ville," replied Oudarde, but little affected by this catalogue, "that such a triumph of viands and comfits has never been seen."

"I tell you that they were served by Le Sec, sergeant of the city, at the Hôtel du Petit-Bourbon, and that that is where you are mistaken."

"At the Hôtel-de-Ville, I tell you!"

"At the Petit-Bourbon, my dear! and they had illuminated with magic glasses the word *Hope*, which is written on the grand portal."

"At the Hôtel-de-Ville! At the Hôtel-de-Ville! And Husson-le-Voir played the flute!"

"I tell you, no!"

"I tell you, yes!"

"I say, no!"

Plump and worthy Oudarde was preparing to retort, and the quarrel might, perhaps, have proceeded to a pulling of caps, had not Mahiette suddenly exclaimed—"Look at those people assembled yonder at the end of the bridge! There is something in their midst that they are looking at!"

---

1. A cask that holds a hogshead and a half.

2. A captain of fifty men.

"In sooth," said Gervaise, "I hear the sounds of a tambourine. I believe 'tis the little Esmeralda, who plays her mummeries with her goat. Eh, be quick, Mahiette! redouble your pace and drag along your boy. You are come hither to visit the curiosities of Paris. You saw the Flemings yesterday; you must see the gypsy to-day."

"The gypsy!" said Mahiette, suddenly retracing her steps, and clasping her son's arm forcibly. "God preserve me from it! She would steal my child from me! Come, Eustache!"

And she set out on a run along the quay toward the Grève, until she had left the bridge far behind her. In the meanwhile, the child whom she was dragging after her fell upon his knees; she halted breathless. Oudarde and Gervaise rejoined her.

"That gypsy steal your child from you!" said Gervaise. "That's a singular freak of yours!"

Mahiette shook her head with a pensive air.

"The singular point is," observed Oudarde, "that *la sachette* has the same idea about the Egyptian woman."

"What is *la sachette?*" asked Mahiette.

"Hé!" said Oudarde, "Sister Gudule."

"And who is Sister Gudule?" persisted Mahiette.

"You are certainly ignorant of all but your Reims, not to know that!" replied Oudarde. " 'Tis the recluse of the Rat-Hole."

"What!" demanded Mahiette, "that poor woman to whom we are carrying this cake?"

Oudarde nodded affirmatively.

"Precisely. You will see her presently at her window on the Grève. She has the same opinion as yourself of these vagabonds of Egypt, who play the tambourine and tell fortunes to the public. No one knows whence comes her horror of the gypsies and Egyptians. But you, Mahiette—why do you run so at the mere sight of them?"

"Oh!" said Mahiette, seizing her child's round head in both hands, "I don't want that to happen to me which happened to Paquette la Chantefleurie."

"Oh! you must tell us that story, my good Mahiette," said Gervaise, taking her arm.

"Gladly," replied Mahiette; "but you must be ignorant of all but your Paris not to know that! I will tell you then (but 'tis not necessary for us to halt that I may tell you the tale), that Paquette la Chantefleurie was a pretty maid of eighteen when I was one myself, that is to say, eighteen years ago, and 'tis her own fault if she is not to-day, like me, a good, plump, fresh mother of six and thirty, with a husband and a son. However, after the age of fourteen, it was too late! Well, she was the daughter of Guybertant, minstrel of the barges at Reims, the same who had played before King Charles VII, at his coronation, when he descended our river Vesle from Sillery to Muison, when Madame the Maid of Orleans was also in the boat. The old father died when Paquette was still a mere child; she had then no one but her mother, the sister of M. Pradon, master-brazier and coppersmith in Paris, Rue Parin-Garlin, who died last year. You see she was of good family. The mother was a good simple woman, unfortunately, and she taught Paquette nothing but a bit of embroidery and toy-making which did not prevent the little one from growing very large and remaining very poor. They both dwelt at Reims, on the river front, Rue de Folle-Peine. Mark this: For I believe it was this which brought misfortune to Paquette. In '61, the year of the coronation of our King Louis XI whom God preserve! Paquette was so gay and so pretty that she was called everywhere by no other name than *la Chantefleurie*—blossoming song. Poor girl! She had handsome teeth, she was fond of laughing and displaying them. Now, a maid who loves to laugh is on the road to weeping; handsome teeth ruin handsome eyes. So she was la Chantefleurie. She and her mother earned a precarious living; they had been very destitute since the death of the minstrel; their embroidery did not bring them in more than six farthings a week, which does not amount to quite two eagle liards. Where were the days when Father Guybertant had earned twelve sous parisian, in a single coronation, with a song? One winter (it was in that same year of '61), when the two women had neither fagots nor firewood, it was very cold, which gave la Chantefleurie such a fine color that the men called her Paquette![1] and many called her Pâquerette![2] and she was ruined.—Eustache, just let me see you bite that cake if you dare!—We immediately perceived that she was ruined, one Sunday when she came to church with a gold cross about her neck. At fourteen years of age! do you see? First it was the young Vicomte de Cormontreuil, who has his bell tower three leagues distant from Reims; then Messire Henri de Triancourt, equerry to the King; then less than that, Chiart de Beaulion, sergeant-at-arms; then, still descending, Guery Aubergeon, carver to the King; then, Macé de Frépus, barber to monsieur the dauphin; then, Thévenin le Moine, King's cook; then, the men growing continually younger and less noble, she fell to Guillaume Racine, minstrel of the hurdy-gurdy and to Thierry de Mer, lamplighter. Then, poor Chantefleurie, she belonged to every-one: she had reached the last sou of her gold piece. What shall I say to you, my demoiselles? At the coronation, in the same year, '61, 'twas she who made the bed of the king of the debauchees! In the same year!"

Mahiette sighed, and wiped away a tear which trickled from her eyes.

"This is no very extraordinary history," said Gervaise, "and in the whole of it I see nothing of any Egyptian women or children."

"Patience!" resumed Mahiette, "you will see one child.—In '66, 'twill be sixteen years ago this month, at Sainte-Paule's day, Paquette was brought to bed of a little girl. The unhappy creature! it was a great joy to her; she had long wished for a child. Her mother, good woman, who had never known what to do except to shut her eyes, her mother was dead. Paquette had no longer anyone to love in the world or anyone to love her. La Chantefleurie had been a poor creature during the five years since her fall. She was alone, alone in this life, fingers were pointed at her, she was hooted at in the streets, beaten by the sergeants, jeered at by the little boys in rags. And then, twenty had ar-rived: and twenty is an old age for amorous women. Folly began to bring her in no more than her trade of embroidery in former days; for every wrinkle that came, a crown fled; winter became hard to her once more, wood became rare again in her brazier, and bread in her cupboard. She could no longer work because, in becoming voluptuous, she had grown lazy; and she suffered much more be-cause, in growing lazy, she had become voluptuous. At least, that is the way in which monsieur the cure of Saint-Remy explains why these women are colder and hungrier than other poor women, when they are old."

"Yes," remarked Gervaise, "but the gypsies?"

"One moment, Gervaise!" said Oudarde, whose attention was less impatient. "What would be left for the end if all were in the beginning? Continue, Mahiette, I entreat you. That poor Chante-fleurie!"

Mahiette went on.

"So she was very sad, very miserable, and furrowed her cheeks with tears. But in the midst of her shame, her folly, her debauchery, it seemed to her that she should be less wild, less shameful, less dissipated, if there were something or someone in the world whom she could love, and who could love her. It was necessary that it should be a child, because only a child could be sufficiently innocent for that. She had recognized this fact after having tried to love a thief, the only man who wanted her; but after a short time, she perceived that the thief despised her. Those women of love require either a lover or a child to fill their hearts. Otherwise, they are very unhappy. As she could not have a lover, she turned wholly toward a desire for a child, and as she had not ceased to be pious, she made her constant prayer to the good God for it. So the good God took pity on her, and gave her a little daughter. I will not speak to you of her joy; it was a fury of tears, and caresses, and kisses.

1. Ox-eye daisy.

2. Easter daisy.

She nursed her child herself, made swaddling-bands for it out of her coverlet, the only one which she had on her bed, and no longer felt either cold or hunger. She became beautiful once more, in consequence of it. An old maid makes a young mother. Gallantry claimed her once more; men came to see la Chantefleurie; she found customers again for her merchandise, and out of all these horrors she made baby clothes, caps and bibs, bodices with shoulder-straps of lace, and tiny bonnets of satin, without even thinking of buying herself another coverlet.—Master Eustache, I have already told you not to eat that cake.—It is certain that little Agnès, that was the child's name, a baptismal name, for it was a long time since la Chantefleurie had had any surname—it is certain that that little one was more swathed in ribbons and embroideries than a dauphiness of Dauphiny! Among other things, she had a pair of little shoes, the like of which King Louis XI certainly never had! Her mother had stitched and embroidered them herself; she had lavished on them all the delicacies of her art of embroideress, and all the embellishments of a robe for the good Virgin. They certainly were the two prettiest little pink shoes that could be seen. They were no longer than my thumb, and one had to see the child's little feet come out of them, in order to believe that they had been able to get into them. 'Tis true that those little feet were so small, so pretty, so rosy! rosier than the satin of the shoes! When you have children, Oudarde, you will find that there is nothing prettier than those little hands and feet."

"I ask no better," said Oudarde with a sigh, "but I am waiting until it shall suit the good pleasure of M. Andry Musnier."

"However, Paquette's child had more that was pretty about it besides its feet. I saw her when she was only four months old; she was a love! She had eyes larger than her mouth, and the most charming black hair, which already curled. She would have been a magnificent brunette at the age of sixteen! Her mother became more crazy over her every day. She kissed her, caressed her, tickled her, washed her, decked her out, devoured her! She lost her head over her, she thanked God for her. Her pretty, little rosy feet above all were an endless source of wonderment, they were a delirium of joy! She was always pressing her lips to them, and she could never recover from her amazement at their smallness. She put them into the tiny shoes, took them out, admired them, marveled at them, looked at the light through them, was curious to see them try to walk on her bed, and would gladly have passed her life on her knees, putting on and taking off the shoes from those feet, as though they had been those of an Infant Jesus."

"The tale is fair and good," said Gervaise in a low tone; "but where do gypsies come into all that?"

"Here," replied Mahiette. "One day there arrived in Reims a very queer sort of people. They were beggars and vagabonds who were roaming over the country, led by their duke and their counts. They were browned by exposure to the sun, they had closely curling hair, and silver rings in their ears. The women were still uglier than the men. They had blacker faces, which were always uncovered, a miserable frock on their bodies, an old cloth woven of cords bound upon their shoulder, and their hair hanging like the tail of a horse. The children who scrambled between their legs would have frightened as many monkeys. A band of excommunicates. All these persons came direct from lower Egypt to Reims through Poland. The Pope had confessed them, it was said, and had prescribed to them as penance to roam through the world for seven years, without sleeping in a bed; and so they were called penancers, and smelt horribly. It appears that they had formerly been Saracens, which was why they believed in Jupiter, and claimed ten livres of Tournay from all archbishops, bishops, and mitered abbots with croziers. A bull from the Pope empowered them to do that. They came to Reims to tell fortunes in the name of the King of Algiers, and the Emperor of Germany. You can readily imagine that no more was needed to cause the entrance to the town to be forbidden them. Then the whole band camped with good grace outside the gate of Braine, on that hill where stands a mill, beside the cavities of the ancient chalk pits. And everybody in Reims vied with his neighbor in going to see them. They looked at your hand, and told you marvelous prophecies;

they were equal to predicting to Judas that he would become Pope. Nevertheless, ugly rumors were in circulation in regard to them; about children stolen, purses cut, and human flesh devoured. The wise people said to the foolish: "Don't go there!" and then went themselves on the sly. It was an infatuation. The fact is, that they said things fit to astonish a cardinal. Mothers triumphed greatly over their little ones after the Egyptians had read in their hands all sorts of marvels written in pagan and in Turkish. One had an emperor; another, a pope; another, a captain. Poor Chantefleurie was seized with curiosity; she wished to know about herself, and whether her pretty little Agnès would not become some day Empress of Armenia, or something else. So she carried her to the Egyptians; and the Egyptian women fell to admiring the child, and to caressing it, and to kissing it with their black mouths, and to marvelling over its little hand, alas! to the great joy of the mother. They were especially enthusiastic over her pretty feet and shoes. The child was not yet a year old. She already lisped a little, laughed at her mother like a little mad thing, was plump and quite round, and possessed a thousand charming little gestures of the angels of paradise.

"She was very much frightened by the Egyptians, and wept. But her mother kissed her more warmly and went away enchanted with the good fortune which the soothsayers had foretold for her Agnès. She was to be a beauty, virtuous, a queen. So she returned to her attic in the Rue Folle-Peine, very proud of bearing with her a queen. The next day she took advantage of a moment when the child was asleep on her bed (for they always slept together), gently left the door a little way open, and ran to tell a neighbor in the Rue de la Séchesserie, that the day would come when her daughter Agnès would be served at table by the King of England and the Archduke of Ethiopia, and a hundred other marvels. On her return, hearing no cries on the staircase, she said to herself: 'Good! the child is still asleep!' She found her door wider open than she had left it, but she entered, poor mother, and ran to the bed.—The child was no longer there, the place was empty. Nothing remained of the child, but one of her pretty little shoes. She flew out of the room, dashed down the stairs, and began to beat her head against the wall, crying: 'My child! who has my child? Who has taken my child?' The street was deserted, the house isolated; no one could tell her anything about it. She went about the town, searched all the streets, ran hither and thither the whole day long, wild, beside herself, terrible, snuffing at doors and windows like a wild beast which has lost its young. She was breathless, disheveled, frightful to see, and there was a fire in her eyes which dried her tears. She stopped the passers-by and cried: 'My daughter! my daughter! my pretty little daughter! If anyone will give me back my daughter, I will be his servant, the servant of his dog, and he shall eat my heart if he will.' She met M. le Curé of Saint-Remy, and said to him: 'Monsieur, I will till the earth with my finger-nails, but give me back my child!' It was heartrending, Oudarde; and I saw a very hard man, Master Ponce Lacabre, the procurator, weep. Ah! poor mother! In the evening she returned home. During her absence, a neighbor had seen two gypsies ascend up to it with a bundle in their arms, then descend again, after closing the door. After their departure, something like the cries of a child were heard in Paquette's room. The mother, burst into shrieks of laughter, ascended the stairs as though on wings, and entered.—A frightful thing to tell, Oudarde! Instead of her pretty little Agnès, so rosy and so fresh, who was a gift of the good God, a sort of hideous little monster, lame, one-eyed, deformed, was crawling and squalling over the floor. She hid her eyes in horror. 'Oh!' said she, 'have the witches transformed my daughter into this horrible animal?' They hastened to carry away the little club-foot; he would have driven her mad. It was the monstrous child of some gypsy woman, who had given herself to the devil. He appeared to be about four years old, and talked a language which was no human tongue; there were words in it which were impossible. La Chantefleurie flung herself upon the little shoe, all that remained to her of all that she loved. She remained so long motionless over it, mute, and without breath, that they thought she was dead. Suddenly she trembled all over, covered her relic with furious kisses, and burst out sobbing as though her heart were broken. I assure you that we were all weeping also. She said: 'Oh, my little daughter! my pretty little daughter! where art thou?'—and it wrung your very heart. I weep still when I think of it. Our children are the marrow of our bones, you see.—My poor Eustache! thou art so fair!—If you only knew how nice he is! yesterday he said to me: 'I want to be a gendarme, that I do.' Oh! my Eustache! if I were to lose thee!—All at once la Chantefleurie rose, and set out to run through Reims, screaming: 'To the gypsies' camp! to the gypsies' camp! Police, to burn the witches!' The gypsies were gone. It was pitch dark. They could not be followed. On the morrow, two leagues from Reims, on a heath between Gueux and Tilloy, the remains of a large fire were found, some ribbons which had belonged to Paquette's child, drops of blood, and the dung of a ram. The night just past had been a Saturday. There was no longer any doubt that the Egyptians had held their Sabbath on that heath, and that they had devoured the child in company with Beelzebub, as the practice is among the Mahometans. When la Chantefleurie learned these horrible things, she did not weep, she moved her lips as though to speak, but could not. On the morrow, her hair was gray. On the second day, she had disappeared."

" 'Tis in truth, a frightful tale," said Oudarde, "and one which would make even a Burgundian weep."

"I am no longer surprised," added Gervaise, "that fear of the gypsies should spur you on so sharply."

"And you did all the better," resumed Oudarde, "to flee with your Eustache just now, since these also are gypsies from Poland."

"No," said Gervais, " 'tis said that they come from Spain and Catalonia."

"Catalonia? 'tis possible," replied Oudarde. "Pologne, Catalogne, Valogne, I always confound those three provinces. One thing is certain, that they are gypsies."

"Who certainly," added Gervaise, "have teeth long enough to eat little children. I should not be surprised if la Sméralda ate a little of them also, though she pretends to be dainty. Her white goat knows tricks that are too malicious for there not to be some impiety underneath it all."

Mahiette walked on in silence. She was absorbed in that reverie which is, in some sort, the continuation of a mournful tale, and which ends only after having communicated the emotion, from vibration to vibration, even to the very last fibers of the heart. Nevertheless, Gervaise addressed her, "And did they ever learn what became of la Chantefleurie?" Mahiette made no reply. Gervaise repeated her question, and shook her arm, calling her by name. Mahiette appeared to awaken from her thoughts.

"What became of la Chantefleurie?" she said, repeating mechanically the words whose impression was still fresh in her ear; then, making an effort to recall her attention to the meaning of her words, "Ah!" she continued briskly, "no one ever found out."

She added, after a pause—

"Some said that she had been seen to quit Reims at nightfall by the Fléchembault gate; others, at daybreak, by the old Basée gate. A poor man found her gold cross hanging on the stone cross in the field where the fair is held. It was that ornament which had wrought her ruin, in '61. It was a gift from the handsome Vicomte de Cormontreuil, her first lover. Paquette had never been willing to part with it, wretched as she had been. She had clung to it as to life itself. So, when we saw that cross abandoned, we all thought that she was dead. Nevertheless, there were people of the Cabaret les Vantes, who said that they had seen her pass along the road to Paris, walking on the pebbles with her bare feet. But, in that case, she must have gone out through the Porte de Vesle, and all this does not agree. Or, to speak more truly, I believe that she actually did depart by the Porte de Vesle, but departed from this world."

"I do not understand you," said Gervaise.

"La Vesle," replied Mahiette, with a melancholy smile, "is the river."

"Poor Chantefleurie!" said Oudarde, with a shiver—"drowned!"

"Drowned!" resumed Mahiette; "who could have told good Father Guybertant, when he passed under the bridge of Tingueux with the current, singing in his barge, that one day his dear little Paquette would also pass beneath that bridge, but without song or boat."

"And the little shoe?" asked Gervaise.

"Disappeared with the mother," replied Mahiette.

"Poor little shoe!" said Oudarde.

Oudarde, a big and tender woman, would have been well pleased to sigh in company with Mahiette. But Gervaise, more curious, had not finished her questions.

"And the monster?" she said suddenly, to Mahiette.

"What monster?" inquired the latter.

"The little gypsy monster left by the sorceresses in Chantefleurie's chamber, in exchange for her daughter. What did you do with it? I hope you drowned it also."

"No," replied Mahiette.

"What? You burned it then? In sooth, that is more just. A witch child!"

"Neither the one nor the other, Gervaise. Monseigneur the archbishop interested himself in the child of Egypt, exorcised it, blessed it, removed the devil carefully from its body, and sent it to Paris, to be exposed on the wooden bed at Notre-Dame, as a foundling."

"Those bishops!" grumbled Gervaise, "because they are learned, they do nothing like any-body else. I just put it to you, Oudarde, the idea of placing the devil among the foundlings! For that little monster was assuredly the devil. Well, Mahiette, what did they do with it in Paris? I am quite sure that no charitable person wanted it."

"I do not know," replied the Rémoise; " 'twas just at that time that my husband bought the of-fice of notary, at Beru, two leagues from the town, and we were no longer occupied with that story; besides, in front of Beru, stand the two hills of Cernay, which hide the towers of the cathedral in Reims from view."

While chatting thus, the three worthy bourgeoises had arrived at the Place de Grève. In their absorption, they had passed the public breviary of the Tour-Roland without stopping, and took their way mechanically toward the pillory around which the throng was growing more dense with every moment. It is probable that the spectacle which at that moment attracted all looks in that di-rection, would have made them forget completely the Rat-Hole, and the halt which they intended to make there, if big Eustache, six years of age, whom Mahiette was dragging along by the hand, had not abruptly recalled the object to them: "Mother," said he, as though some instinct warned him that the Rat-Hole was behind him, "can I eat the cake now?"

If Eustache had been more adroit, that is to say, less greedy, he would have continued to wait, and would only have hazarded that simple question, "Mother, can I eat the cake, now?" on their re-turn to the University, to Master Andry Musnier's, Rue Madame la Valence, when he had the two arms of the Seine and the five bridges of the city between the Rat-Hole and the cake.

This question, highly imprudent at the moment when Eustache put it, aroused Mahiette's attention.

"By the way," she exclaimed, "we are forgetting the recluse! Show me the Rat-Hole, that I may carry her her cake."

"Immediately," said Oudarde, " 'tis a charity."

But this did not suit Eustache.

"Stop! my cake!" said he, rubbing both ears alternately with his shoulders, which, in such cases, is the supreme sign of discontent.

The three women retraced their steps, and, on arriving in the vicinity of the Tour-Roland, Oudarde said to the other two—

"We must not all three gaze into the hole at once, for fear of alarming the recluse. Do you two pretend to read the *Dominus* in the breviary, while I thrust my nose into the aperture; the recluse knows me a little. I will give you warning when you can approach."

She proceeded alone to the window. At the moment when she looked in, a profound pity was depicted on all her features, and her frank, gay visage altered its expression and color as abruptly as though it had passed from a ray of sunlight to a ray of moonlight; her eye became humid; her mouth contracted, like that of a person on the point of weeping. A moment later, she laid her finger on her lips, and made a sign to Mahiette to draw near and look.

Mahiette, much touched, stepped up in silence, on tiptoe, as though approaching the bedside of a dying person.

It was, in fact, a melancholy spectacle which presented itself to the eyes of the two women, as they gazed through the grating of the Rat-Hole, neither stirring nor breathing.

The cell was small, broader than it was long, with an arched ceiling, and viewed from within, it bore a considerable resemblance to the interior of a huge bishop's miter. On the bare flagstones which formed the floor, in one corner, a woman was sitting, or rather, crouching. Her chin rested on her knees, which her crossed arms pressed forcibly to her breast. Thus doubled up, clad in a brown sack, which enveloped her entirely in large folds, her long, gray hair pulled over in front, falling over her face and along her legs nearly to her feet, she presented, at the first glance, only a strange form outlined against the dark background of the cell, a sort of dusky triangle, which the ray of daylight falling through the opening, cut roughly into two shades, the one somber, the other illuminated. It was one of those specters, half light, half shadow, such as one beholds in dreams and in the extraordinary work of Goya, pale, motionless, sinister, crouching over a tomb, or leaning against the grating of a prison cell.

It was neither a woman, nor a man, nor a living being, nor a definite form; it was a figure, a sort of vision, in which the real and the fantastic intersected each other, like darkness and day. It was with difficulty that one distinguished, beneath her hair which spread to the ground, a gaunt and severe profile; her dress barely allowed the extremity of a bare foot to escape, which contracted on the hard, cold pavement. The little of human form of which one caught a sight beneath this envelope of mourning, caused a shudder.

That figure, which one might have supposed to be riveted to the flagstones, appeared to possess neither movement, nor thought, nor breath. Lying, in January, in that thin, linen sack, lying on a granite floor, without fire, in the gloom of a cell whose oblique air-hole allowed only the cold breeze, but never the sun, to enter from without, she did not appear to suffer or even to think. One would have said that she had turned to stone with the cell, ice with the season. Her hands were clasped, her eyes fixed. At first sight one took her for a specter; at the second, for a statue.

Nevertheless, at intervals, her blue lips half opened to admit a breath, and trembled, but as dead and as mechanical as the leaves which the wind sweeps aside.

Nevertheless, from her dull eyes there escaped a look, an ineffable look, a profound, lugubrious, imperturbable look, incessantly fixed upon a corner of the cell which could not be seen from without; a gaze which seemed to fix all the somber thoughts of that soul in distress upon some mysterious object.

Such was the creature who had received, from her habitation, the name of the "recluse"; and, from her garment, the name of "the sacked nun."

The three women, for Gervaise had rejoined Mahiette and Oudarde, gazed through the window. Their heads intercepted the feeble light in the cell, without the wretched being whom they thus deprived of it seeming to pay any attention to them. "Do not let us trouble her," said Oudarde, in a low voice, "she is in her ecstasy; she is praying."

Meanwhile, Mahiette was gazing with ever-increasing anxiety at that wan, withered, disheveled head, and her eyes filled with tears. "This is very singular," she murmured.

She thrust her head through the bars, and succeeded in casting a glance at the corner where the gaze of the unhappy woman was immovably riveted.

When she withdrew her head from the window, her countenance was inundated with tears.

"What do you call that woman?" she asked Oudarde.

Oudarde replied—

"We call her Sister Gudule."

"And I," returned Mahiette, "call her Paquette la Chantefleurie."

Then, laying her finger on her lips, she motioned to the astounded Oudarde to thrust her head through the window and look.

Oudarde looked and beheld, in the corner where the eyes of the recluse were fixed in that somber ecstasy, a tiny shoe of pink satin, embroidered with a thousand fanciful designs in gold and silver.

Gervaise looked after Oudarde, and then the three women, gazing upon the unhappy mother, began to weep.

But neither their looks nor their tears disturbed the recluse. Her hands remained clasped; her lips mute; her eyes fixed; and that little shoe, thus gazed at, broke the heart of anyone who knew her history.

The three women had not yet uttered a single word; they dared not speak, even in a low voice. This deep silence, this deep grief, this profound oblivion in which everything had disappeared except one thing, produced upon them the effect of the grand altar at Christmas or Easter. They remained silent, they meditated, they were ready to kneel. It seemed to them that they were ready to enter a church on the day of Tenebræ.

At length Gervaise, the most curious of the three, and consequently the least sensitive, tried to make the recluse speak: "Sister! Sister Gudule!"

She repeated this call three times, raising her voice each time. The recluse did not move; not a word, not a glance, not a sigh, not a sign of life.

Oudarde, in her turn, in a sweeter, more caressing voice—"Sister!" said she, "Sister Sainte-Gudule!"

The same silence; the same immobility.

"A singular woman!" exclaimed Gervaise, "and one not to be moved by a catapult!"

"Perchance she is deaf," said Oudarde.

"Perhaps she is blind," added Gervaise.

"Dead, perchance," returned Mahiette.

It is certain that if the soul had not already quitted this inert, sluggish, lethargic body, it had at least retreated and concealed itself in depths whither the perceptions of the exterior organs no longer penetrated.

"Then we must leave the cake on the window," said Oudarde; "some scamp will take it. What shall we do to rouse her?"

Eustache, who, up to that moment had been diverted by a little carriage drawn by a large dog, which had just passed, suddenly perceived that his three conductresses were gazing at something through the window, and, curiosity taking possession of him in his turn, he climbed upon a stone post, elevated himself on tiptoe, and applied his fat, red face to the opening, shouting, "Mother, let me see too!"

At the sound of this clear, fresh, ringing child's voice, the recluse trembled; she turned her head with the sharp, abrupt movement of a steel spring, her long, fleshless hands cast aside the hair from her brow, and she fixed upon the child, bitter, astonished, desperate eyes. This glance was but a lightning flash.

"Oh my God!" she suddenly exclaimed, hiding her head on her knees, and it seemed as though her hoarse voice tore her chest as it passed from it, "do not show me those of others!"

"Good day, madam," said the child, gravely.

Nevertheless, this shock had, so to speak, awakened the recluse. A long shiver traversed her frame from head to foot; her teeth chattered; she half raised her head and said, pressing her elbows against her hips, and clasping her feet in her hands as though to warm them—

"Oh, how cold it is!"

"Poor woman!" said Oudarde, with great compassion, "would you like a little fire?"

She shook her head in token of refusal.

"Well," resumed Oudarde, presenting her with a flagon; "here is some hippocras which will warm you; drink it."

Again she shook her head, looked at Oudarde fixedly and replied, "Water."

Oudarde persisted—"No, sister, that is no beverage for January. You must drink a little hippocras and eat this leavened cake of maize, which we have baked for you."

She refused the cake which Mahiette offered to her, and said, "Black bread."

"Come," said Gervaise, seized in her turn with an impulse of charity, and unfastening her woolen cloak, "here is a cloak which is a little warmer than yours."

She refused the cloak as she had refused the flagon and the cake, and replied, "A sack."

"But," resumed the good Oudarde, "you must have perceived to some extent, that yesterday was a festival."

"I do perceive it," said the recluse; " 'tis two days now since I have had any water in my crock."

She added, after a silence, " 'Tis a festival, I am forgotten. People do well. Why should the world think of me, when I do not think of it? Cold charcoal makes cold ashes."

And as though fatigued with having said so much, she dropped her head on her knees again. The simple and charitable Oudarde, who fancied that she understood from her last words that she was complaining of the cold, replied innocently, "Then you would like a little fire?"

"Fire!" said the sacked nun, with a strange accent; "and will you also make a little for the poor little one who has been beneath the sod for these fifteen years?"

Every limb was trembling, her voice quivered, her eyes flashed, she had raised herself upon her knees; suddenly she extended her thin, white hand toward the child, who was regarding her with a look of astonishment. "Take away that child!" she cried. "The Egyptian woman is about to pass by."

Then she fell face downward on the earth, and her forehead struck the stone, with the sound of one stone against another stone. The three women thought her dead. A moment later, however, she moved, and they beheld her drag herself, on her knees and elbows, to the corner where the little shoe was. Then they dared not look; they no longer saw her; but they heard a thousand kisses and a thousand sighs, mingled with heartrending cries, and dull blows like those of a head in contact with a wall. Then, after one of these blows, so violent that all three of them staggered, they heard no more.

"Can she have killed herself?" said Gervaise, venturing to pass her head through the air-hole. "Sister! Sister Gudule!"

"Sister Gudule!" repeated Oudarde.

"Ah! good heavens! she no longer moves!" resumed Gervaise; "is she dead? Gudule! Gudule!"

Mahiette, choked to such a point that she could not speak, made an effort. "Wait," said she. Then bending toward the window, "Paquette!" she said, "Paquette la Chantefleurie!"

A child who innocently blows upon the badly ignited fuse of a bomb, and makes it explode in his face, is no more terrified than was Mahiette at the effect of that name, abruptly launched into the cell of Sister Gudule.

The recluse trembled all over, rose erect on her bare feet, and leaped at the window with eyes so glaring that Mahiette and Oudarde, and the other woman and the child recoiled even to the parapet of the quay.

Meanwhile, the sinister face of the recluse appeared pressed to the grating of the air-hole. "Oh! oh!" she cried, with an appalling laugh; " 'tis the Egyptian who is calling me!"

At that moment, a scene which was passing at the pillory caught her wild eye. Her brow contracted with horror, she stretched her two skeleton arms from her cell, and shrieked in a voice which resembled a death-rattle, "So 'tis thou once more, daughter of Egypt! 'Tis thou who callest me, stealer of children! Well! Be thou accursed! accursed! accursed! accursed!"

Chapter IV

A Tear for a Drop of Water

THESE WORDS WERE, SO TO SPEAK, THE POINT OF UNION OF TWO SCENES, WHICH HAD, UP TO that time, been developed in parallel lines at the same moment, each on its particular theater; one, that which the reader has just perused, in the Rat-Hole; the other, which he is about to read, on the ladder of the pillory. The first had for witnesses only the three women with whom the reader has just made acquaintance; the second had for spectators all the public which we have seen above, collecting on the Place de Grève, around the pillory and the gibbet.

That crowd which the four sergeants posted at nine o'clock in the morning at the four corners of the pillory had inspired with the hope of some sort of an execution, no doubt, not a hanging, but a whipping, a cropping of ears, something, in short—that crowd had increased so rapidly that the four policemen, too closely besieged, had had occasion to "press" it, as the expression then ran, more than once, by sound blows of their whips, and the haunches of their horses.

This populace, disciplined to waiting for public executions, did not manifest very much impatience. It amused itself with watching the pillory, a very simple sort of monument, composed of a cube of masonry about six feet high and hollow in the interior. A very steep staircase, of unhewn stone, which was called by distinction "the ladder," led to the upper platform, upon which was visible a horizontal wheel of solid oak. The victim was bound upon this wheel, on his knees, with his hands behind his back. A wooden shaft, which set in motion a capstan concealed in the interior of the little edifice, imparted a rotatory motion to the wheel, which always maintained its horizontal position, and in this manner presented the face of the condemned man to all quarters of the square in succession. This was what was called "turning" a criminal.

As the reader perceives, the pillory of the Grève was far from presenting all the recreations of the pillory of the Halles. Nothing architectural, nothing monumental. No roof to the iron cross, no octagonal lantern, no frail, slender columns spreading out on the edge of the roof into capitals of acanthus leaves and flowers, no waterspouts of chimeras and monsters, on carved woodwork, no fine sculpture, deeply sunk in the stone.

They were forced to content themselves with those four stretches of rubble work, backed with sandstone, and a wretched stone gibbet, meager and bare, on one side.

The entertainment would have been but a poor one for lovers of Gothic architecture. It is true that nothing was ever less curious on the score of architecture than the worthy gapers of the Middle Ages, and that they cared very little for the beauty of a pillory.

The victim finally arrived, bound to the tail of a cart, and when he had been hoisted upon the platform, where he could be seen from all points of the Place, bound with cords and straps upon the wheel of the pillory, a prodigious hoot, mingled with laughter and acclamations, burst forth upon the Place. They had recognized Quasimodo.

It was he, in fact. The change was singular. Pilloried on the very place where, on the day before, he had been saluted, acclaimed, and proclaimed Pope and Prince of Fools, in the cortège of the Duke of Egypt, the King of Thunes, and the Emperor of Galilee! One thing is certain, and that is, that there was not a soul in the crowd, not even himself, though in turn triumphant and the sufferer, who set forth this combination clearly in his thought. Gringoire and his philosophy were missing at this spectacle.

Soon Michel Noiret, sworn trumpeter to the king, our lord, imposed silence on the louts, and proclaimed the sentence, in accordance with the order and command of monsieur the provost. Then he withdrew behind the cart, with his men in livery surcoats.

Quasimodo, impassible, did not wince. All resistance had been rendered impossible to him by what was then called, in the style of the criminal chancellery, "the vehemence and firmness of the bonds" which means that the thongs and chains probably cut into his flesh; moreover, it is a tradition of jail and wardens, which has not been lost, and which the handcuffs still preciously preserve among us, a civilized, gentle, humane people (the galleys and the guillotine in parentheses).

He had allowed himself to be led, pushed, carried, lifted, bound, and bound again. Nothing was to be seen upon his countenance but the astonishment of a savage or an idiot. He was known to be deaf; one might have pronounced him to be blind.

They placed him on his knees on the circular plank; he made no resistance. They removed his shirt and doublet as far as his girdle; he allowed them to have their way. They entangled him under a fresh system of thongs and buckles; he allowed them to bind and buckle him. Only from time to time he snorted noisily, like a calf whose head is hanging and bumping over the edge of a butcher's cart.

"The dolt," said Jehan Frollo of the Mill, to his friend Robin Poussepain (for the two students had followed the culprit, as was to have been expected), "he understands no more than a cockchafer shut up in a box!"

There was wild laughter among the crowd when they beheld Quasimodo's hump, his camel's breast, his callous and hairy shoulders laid bare. During this gaiety, a man in the livery of the city, short of stature and robust of mien, mounted the platform and placed himself near the victim. His name speedily circulated among the spectators. It was Master Pierrat Torterue, official torturer to the Châtelet.

He began by depositing on an angle of the pillory a black hour-glass, the upper lobe of which was filled with red sand, which it allowed to glide into the lower receptacle; then he removed his parti-colored surtout, and there became visible, suspended from his right hand, a thin and tapering whip of long, white, shining, knotted, plaited thongs, armed with metal nails. With his left hand, he negligently folded back his shirt around his right arm, to the very armpit.

In the meantime, Jehan Frollo, elevating his curly blonde head above the crowd (he had mounted upon the shoulders of Robin Poussepain for the purpose), shouted: "Come and look, gentle ladies and men! they are going to peremptorily flagellate Master Quasimodo, the bellringer of my brother, monsieur the archdeacon of Josas, a knave of oriental architecture, who has a back like a dome, and legs like twisted columns!"

And the crowd burst into a laugh, especially the boys and young girls.

At length the torturer stamped his foot. The wheel began to turn. Quasimodo wavered beneath his bonds. The amazement which was suddenly depicted upon his deformed face caused the bursts of laughter to redouble around him.

All at once, at the moment when the wheel in its revolution presented to Master Pierrat, the humped back of Quasimodo, Master Pierrat raised his arm; the fine thongs whistled sharply through the air, like a handful of adders, and fell with fury upon the wretch's shoulders.

Quasimodo leaped as though awakened with a start. He began to understand. He writhed in his bonds; a violent contraction of surprise and pain distorted the muscles of his face, but he uttered not a single sigh. He merely turned his head backward, to the right, then to the left, balancing it as a bull does who has been stung in the flanks by a gadfly.

A second blow followed the first, then a third, and another and another, and still others. The wheel did not cease to turn, nor the blows to rain down.

Soon the blood burst forth, and could be seen trickling in a thousand threads down the hunchback's black shoulders; and the slender thongs, in their rotatory motion which rent the air, sprinkled drops of it upon the crowd.

Quasimodo had resumed, to all appearance, his first imperturbability. He had at first tried, in a quiet way and without much outward movement, to break his bonds. His eye had been seen to light up, his muscles to stiffen, his members to concentrate their force, and the straps to stretch. The effort was powerful, prodigious, desperate; but the provost's seasoned bonds resisted. They cracked, and that was all. Quasimodo fell back exhausted. Amazement gave way, on his features, to a sentiment of profound and bitter discouragement. He closed his single eye, allowed his head to droop upon his breast, and feigned death.

From that moment forth, he stirred no more. Nothing could force a movement from him. Neither his blood, which did not cease to flow, nor the blows which redoubled in fury, nor the wrath of the torturer, who grew excited himself and intoxicated with the execution, nor the sound of the horrible thongs, more sharp and whistling than the claws of scorpions.

At length a bailiff from the Châtelet clad in black, mounted on a black horse, who had been stationed beside the ladder since the beginning of the execution, extended his ebony wand toward the hour-glass. The torturer stopped. The wheel stopped. Quasimodo's eye opened slowly.

The scourging was finished. Two lackeys of the official torturer bathed the bleeding shoulders of the patient, anointed them with some unguent which immediately closed all the wounds, and threw upon his back a sort of yellow vestment, in cut like a chasuble. In the meanwhile, Pierrat Torterue allowed the thongs, red and gorged with blood, to drip upon the pavement.

All was not over for Quasimodo. He had still to undergo that hour of pillory which Master Florian Barbedienne had so judiciously added to the sentence of Messire Robert d'Estouteville; all to the greater glory of the old physiological and psychological play upon words of Jean de Cumène, *Surdus absurdus:* a deaf man is absurd.

So the hour-glass was turned over once more, and they left the hunchback fastened to the plank, in order that justice might be accomplished to the very end.

The populace, especially in the Middle Ages, is in society what the child is in the family. As long as it remains in its state of primitive ignorance, of moral and intellectual minority, it can be said of it as of the child—

> *'Tis the pitiless age.*

We have already shown that Quasimodo was generally hated, for more than one good reason, it is true. There was hardly a spectator in that crowd who had not or who did not believe that he had reason to complain of the malevolent hunchback of Notre-Dame. The joy at seeing him appear thus in the pillory had been universal; and the harsh punishment which he had just suffered, and the pitiful condition in which it had left him, far from softening the populace had rendered its hatred more malicious by arming it with a touch of mirth.

Hence, the "public prosecution" satisfied, as the bigwigs of the law still express it in their jargon, the turn came of a thousand private vengeances. Here, as in the Grand Hall, the women rendered themselves particularly prominent. All cherished some rancor against him, some for his malice, others for his ugliness. The latter were the most furious.

"Oh! mask of Antichrist!" said one.

"Rider on a broom handle!" cried another.

"What a fine tragic grimace," howled a third, "and who would make him Pope of the Fools if to-day were yesterday?"

" 'Tis well," struck in an old woman. "This is the grimace of the pillory. When shall we have that of the gibbet?"

"When will you be coiffed with your big bell a hundred feet under ground, cursed bellringer?"

"But 'tis the devil who rings the Angelus!"

"Oh! the deaf man! the one-eyed creature! the hunchback! the monster!"

"A face to make a woman miscarry better than all the drugs and medicines!"

And the two scholars, Jehan du Moulin, and Robin Poussepain, sang at the top of their lungs, the ancient refrain—

"Une hart
Pour le pendard!
Un fagot
Pour le magot!"[1]

A thousand other insults rained down upon him, and hoots and imprecations, and laughter, and now and then, stones.

Quasimodo was deaf but his sight was clear, and the public fury was no less energetically depicted on their visages than in their words. Moreover, the blows from the stones explained the bursts of laughter.

At first he held his ground. But little by little that patience which had borne up under the lash of the torturer, yielded and gave way before all these stings of insects. The bull of the Asturias who has been but little moved by the attacks of the picador grows irritated with the dogs and banderilleras.

He first cast around a slow glance of hatred upon the crowd. But bound as he was, his glance was powerless to drive away those flies which were stinging his wound. Then he moved in his bonds, and his furious exertions made the ancient wheel of the pillory shriek on its axle. All this only increased the derision and hooting.

Then the wretched man, unable to break his collar, like that of a chained wild beast, became tranquil once more; only at intervals a sigh of rage heaved the hollows of his chest. There was neither shame nor redness on his face. He was too far from the state of society, and too near the state of nature to know what shame was. Moreover, with such a degree of deformity, is infamy a thing that can be felt? But wrath, hatred, despair, slowly lowered over that hideous visage a cloud which grew ever more and more somber, ever more and more charged with electricity, which burst forth in a thousand lightning flashes from the eye of the cyclops.

Nevertheless, that cloud cleared away for a moment, at the passage of a mule which traversed the crowd, bearing a priest. As far away as he could see that mule and that priest, the poor victim's visage grew gentler. The fury which had contracted it was followed by a strange smile full of ineffable sweetness, gentleness, and tenderness. In proportion as the priest approached, that smile became more clear, more distinct, more radiant. It was like the arrival of a Savior, which the unhappy man was greeting. But as soon as the mule was near enough to the pillory to allow of its rider recognizing the victim, the priest dropped his eyes, beat a hasty retreat, spurred on rigorously, as though in haste to rid himself of humiliating appeals, and not at all desirous of being saluted and recognized by a poor fellow in such a predicament.

This priest was Archdeacon Dom Claude Frollo.

The cloud descended more blackly than ever upon Quasimodo's brow. The smile was still mingled with it for a time, but was bitter, discouraged, profoundly sad.

Time passed on. He had been there at least an hour and a half, lacerated, maltreated, mocked incessantly, and almost stoned.

All at once he moved again in his chains with redoubled despair, which made the whole framework that bore him tremble, and, breaking the silence which he had obstinately preserved hitherto, he cried in a hoarse and furious voice, which resembled a bark rather than a human cry, and which was drowned in the noise of the hoots:—"Drink!"

This exclamation of distress, far from exciting compassion, only added amusement to the good Parisian populace who surrounded the ladder, and who, it must be confessed, taken in the mass and as a multitude, was then no less cruel and brutal than that horrible tribe of robbers among whom we have already conducted the reader, and which was simply the lower stratum of the populace.

1. A rope for the gallows bird! A fagot for the ape.

Not a voice was raised around the unhappy victim, except to jeer at his thirst. It is certain that at that moment he was more grotesque and repulsive than pitiable, with his face purple and dripping, his eye wild, his mouth foaming with rage and pain, and his tongue lolling half out. It must also be stated that if a charitable soul of a bourgeois or bourgeoise, in the rabble, had attempted to carry a glass of water to that wretched creature in torment, there reigned around the infamous steps of the pillory such a prejudice of shame and ignominy, that it would have sufficed to repulse the good Samaritan.

At the expiration of a few moments, Quasimodo cast a desperate glance upon the crowd, and repeated in a voice still more heartrending:—"Drink!"

And all began to laugh.

"Drink this!" cried Robin Poussepain, throwing in his face a sponge which had been soaked in the gutter. "There, you deaf villain, I'm your debtor."

A woman hurled a stone at his head—

"That will teach you to wake us up at night with your peal of a damned soul."

"Hé, good, my son!" howled a cripple, making an effort to reach him with his crutch, "will you cast any more spells on us from the top of the towers of Notre-Dame?"

"Here's a drinking cup!" chimed in a man, flinging a broken jug at his breast. " 'Twas you that made my wife, simply because she passed near you, give birth to a child with two heads!"

"And my cat bring forth a kitten with six paws!" yelped an old crone, launching a brick at him.

"Drink!" repeated Quasimodo panting, and for the third time.

At that moment he beheld the crowd give way. A young girl, fantastically dressed, emerged from the throng. She was accompanied by a little white goat with gilded horns, and carried a tambourine in her hand.

Quasimodo's eyes sparkled. It was the gypsy whom he had attempted to carry off on the preceding night, a misdeed for which he was dimly conscious that he was being punished at that very moment; which was not in the least the case, since he was being chastised only for the misfortune of being deaf, and of having been judged by a deaf man. He doubted not that she had come to wreak her vengeance also, and to deal her blow like the rest.

He beheld her, in fact, mount the ladder rapidly. Wrath and spite suffocate him. He would have liked to make the pillory crumble into ruins, and if the lightning of his eye could have dealt death, the gypsy would have been reduced to powder before she reached the platform.

She approached, without uttering a syllable, the victim who writhed in a vain effort to escape her, and detaching a gourd from her girdle, she raised it gently to the parched lips of the miserable man.

Then, from that eye which had been, up to that moment, so dry and burning, a big tear was seen to fall, and roll slowly down that deformed visage so long contracted with despair. It was the first, in all probability, that the unfortunate man had ever shed.

Meanwhile, he had forgotten to drink. The gypsy made her little pout, from impatience, and pressed the spout to the tusked mouth of Quasimodo, with a smile.

He drank with deep drafts. His thirst was burning.

When he had finished, the wretch protruded his black lips, no doubt, with the object of kissing the beautiful hand which had just succored him. But the young girl, who was, perhaps, somewhat distrustful, and who remembered the violent attempt of the night, withdrew her hand with the frightened gesture of a child who is afraid of being bitten by a beast.

Then the poor deaf man fixed on her a look full of reproach and inexpressible sadness.

It would have been a touching spectacle anywhere—this beautiful, fresh, pure, and charming girl, who was at the same time so weak, thus hastening to the relief of so much misery, deformity, and malevolence. On the pillory, the spectacle was sublime.

The very populace were captivated by it, and began to clap their hands, crying—

"Noël! Noël!"

It was at that moment that the recluse caught sight, from the window of her hole, of the gypsy on the pillory, and hurled at her her sinister imprecation—

"Accursed be thou, daughter of Egypt! Accursed! accursed!"

Chapter V

END OF THE STORY OF THE CAKE

L A ESMERALDA TURNED PALE AND DESCENDED FROM THE PILLORY, STAGGERING AS SHE WENT. The voice of the recluse still pursued her—

"Descend! descend! Thief of Egypt! thou shalt ascend it once more!"

"The sacked nun is in one of her tantrums," muttered the populace; and that was the end of it. For that sort of woman was feared; which rendered them sacred. People did not then willingly attack one who prayed day and night.

The hour had arrived for removing Quasimodo. He was unbound, the crowd dispersed.

Near the Grand Pont, Mahiette, who was returning with her two companions, suddenly halted—

"By the way, Eustache! what did you do with that cake?"

"Mother," said the child, "while you were talking with that lady in the bole, a big dog took a bite of my cake, and then I bit it also."

"What, sir, did you eat the whole of it?" she went on.

"Mother, it was the dog. I told him, but he would not listen to me. Then I bit into it, also."

" 'Tis a terrible child!" said the mother, smiling and scolding at one and the same time. "Do you see, Oudarde? He already eats all the fruit from the cherry-tree in our orchard of Charlerange. So his grandfather says that be will be a captain. Just let me catch you at it again, Master Eustache. Come along, you greedy fellow!"

VOLUME II

Book Seventh

Chapter I

The Danger of Confiding One's Secret to a Goat

MANY WEEKS HAD ELAPSED.

The first of March had arrived. The sun, which Dubartas, that classic ancestor of periphrase, had not yet dubbed the "Grand-duke of Candles," was none the less radiant and joyous on that account. It was one of those spring days which possesses so much sweetness and beauty, that all Paris turns out into the squares and promenades and celebrates them as though they were Sundays. In those days of brilliancy, warmth, and serenity, there is a certain hour above all others, when the façade of Notre-Dame should be admired. It is the moment when the sun, already declining toward the west, looks the cathedral almost full in the face. Its rays, growing more and more horizontal, withdraw slowly from the pavement of the square, and mount up the perpendicular façade, whose thousand bosses in high relief they cause to start out from the shadows, while the great central rose window flames like the eye of a cyclops, inflamed with the reflections of the forge.

This was the hour.

Opposite the lofty cathedral, reddened by the setting sun, on the stone balcony built above the porch of a rich Gothic house, which formed the angle of the square and the Rue du Parvis, several young girls were laughing and chatting with every sort of grace and mirth. From the length of the veil which fell from their pointed coif, twined with pearls, to their heels, from the fineness of the embroidered chemisette which covered their shoulders and allowed a glimpse, according to the pleasing custom of the time, of the swell of their fair virgin bosoms, from the opulence of their under-petticoats still more precious than their overdress (marvelous refinement), from the gauze, the silk, the velvet, with which all this was composed, and, above all, from the whiteness of their hands, which certified to their leisure and idleness, it was easy to divine they were noble and wealthy heiresses. They were, in fact, Demoiselle Fleur-de-Lys de Gondelaurier and her companions, Diane de Christeuil, Amelotte de Montmichel, Colombe de Gaillefontaine, and the little de Champchevrier maiden; all damsels of good birth, assembled at that moment at the house of the dame widow de Gondelaurier, on account of Monseigneur de Beaujeu and Madame his wife, who were to come to Paris in the month of April, there to choose maids of honor for the Dauphiness Marguerite, who was to be received in Picardy from the hands of the Flemings. Now, all the squires for twenty leagues around were intriguing for this favor for their daughters, and a goodly number of the latter had been already brought or sent to Paris. These four maidens had been confided to the discreet and venerable charge of Madame Aloïse de Gondelaurier, widow of a former commander of the king's crossbowmen, who had retired with her only daughter to her house in the Place du Parvis, Notre-Dame, in Paris.

The balcony on which these young girls stood opened from a chamber richly tapestried in fawn-colored Flanders leather, stamped with golden foliage. The beams, which cut the ceiling in parallel lines, diverted the eye with a thousand eccentric painted and gilded carvings. Splendid enamels gleamed here and there on carved chests; a boar's head in faïence crowned a magnificent dresser, whose two shelves announced that the mistress of the house was the wife or widow of a knight banneret. At the end of the room, by the side of a lofty chimney blazoned with arms from top to bottom, in a rich red velvet arm-chair, sat Dame de Gondelaurier, whose five and fifty years were written upon her garments no less distinctly than upon her face.

Beside her stood a young man of imposing mien, although partaking somewhat of vanity and bravado—one of those handsome fellows whom all women agree to admire, although grave men learned in physiognomy shrug their shoulders at them. This young man wore the garb of a captain of the king's unattached archers, which bears far too much resemblance to the costume of Jupiter, which the reader has already been enabled to admire in the first book of this history, for us to inflict upon him a second description.

The demoiselles were seated, a part in the chamber, a part in the balcony, some on square cushions of Utrecht velvet with golden corners, others on stools of oak carved in flowers and figures. Each of them held on her knee a section of a great needlework tapestry, on which they were working in company, while one end of it lay upon the rush mat which covered the floor.

They were chatting together in that whispering tone and with the half-stifled laughs peculiar to an assembly of young girls in whose midst there is a young man. The young man whose presence served to set in play all these feminine self-conceits, appeared to pay very little heed to the matter, and, while these pretty damsels were vying with one another to attract his attention, he seemed to be chiefly absorbed in polishing the buckle of his sword belt with his doeskin glove.

From time to time, the old lady addressed him in a very low tone, and he replied as well as he was able, with a sort of awkward and constrained politeness.

From the smiles and significant gestures of Dame Aloïse, from the glances which she threw toward her daughter, Fleur-de-Lys, as she spoke low to the captain, it was easy to see that there was here a question of some betrothal concluded, some marriage near at hand no doubt, between the young man and Fleur-de-Lys. From the embarrassed coldness of the officer, it was easy to see that on his side, at least, love had no longer any part in the matter. His whole air was expressive of constraint and weariness, which our lieutenants of the garrison would to-day translate admirably as, "What a beastly bore!"

The poor dame, very much infatuated with her daughter, like any other silly mother, did not perceive the officer's lack of enthusiasm, and strove in low tones to call his attention to the infinite grace with which Fleur-de-Lys used her needle or wound her skein.

"Come, little cousin," she said to him, plucking him by the sleeve, in order to speak in his ear, "Look at her, do! see her stoop."

"Yes, truly," replied the young man, and fell back into his glacial and absent-minded silence.

A moment later, he was obliged to bend down again, and Dame Aloïse said to him—

"Have you ever beheld a more gay and charming face than that of your betrothed? Can one be more white and blonde? are not her hands perfect? and that neck—does it not assume all the curves of the swan in ravishing fashion? How I envy you at times! and how happy you are to be a man, naughty libertine that you are! Is not my Fleur-de-Lys adorably beautiful, and are you not desperately in love with her?"

"Of course," he replied, still thinking of something else.

"But do say something," said Madame Aloïse, suddenly giving his shoulder a push; "you have grown very timid."

We can assure our readers that timidity was neither the captain's virtue nor his defect. But he made an effort to do what was demanded of him.

"Fair cousin," he said, approaching Fleur-de-Lys, "what is the subject of this tapestry work which you are fashioning?"

"Fair cousin," responded Fleur-de-Lys, in an offended tone, "I have already told you three times. 'Tis the grotto of Neptune."

It was evident that Fleur-de-Lys saw much more clearly than her mother through the captain's cold and absent-minded manner. He felt the necessity of making some conversation.

"And for whom is this Neptunerie destined?"

"For the Abbey of Saint-Antoine des Champs," answered Fleur-de-Lys, without raising her eyes.

The captain took up a corner of the tapestry.

"Who, my fair cousin, is this big gendarme, who is puffing out his cheeks to their full extent and blowing a trumpet?"

" 'Tis Triton," she replied.

There was a rather pettish intonation in Fleur-de-Lys's laconic words. The young man understood that it was indispensable that he should whisper something in her ear, a commonplace, a gallant compliment, no matter what. Accordingly he bent down, but he could find nothing in his imagination more tender and personal than this—

"Why does your mother always wear that surcoat with armorial designs, like our grandmothers of the time of Charles VII? Tell her, fair cousin, that 'tis no longer the fashion, and that the hinge (*gond*) and the laurel (*laurier*) embroidered on her robe give her the air of a walking mantle-piece. In truth, people no longer sit thus on their banners, I assure you."

Fleur-de-Lys raised her beautiful eyes, full of reproach, "Is that all of which you can assure me?" she said, in a low voice.

In the meantime, Dame Aloïse, delighted to see them thus bending toward each other and whispering, said as she toyed with the clasps of her prayer-book—

"Touching picture of love!"

The captain, more and more embarrassed, fell back upon the subject of the tapestry—" 'Tis, in sooth, a charming work!" he exclaimed.

Whereupon Colombe de Gaillefontaine, another beautiful blonde, with a white skin, dressed to the neck in blue damask, ventured a timid remark which she addressed to Fleur-de-Lys, in the hope that the handsome captain would reply to it, "My dear Gondelaurier, have you seen the tapestries of the Hôtel de la Roche-Guyon?"

"Is not that the hôtel in which is enclosed the garden of the Lingère du Louvre?" asked Diane de Christeuil with a laugh; for she had handsome teeth, and consequently laughed on every occasion.

"And where there is that big, old tower of the ancient wall of Paris," added Amelotte de Montmichel, a pretty fresh and curly-headed brunette, who had a habit of sighing just as the other laughed, without knowing why.

"My dear Colombe," interpolated Dame Aloïse, "do you not mean the hôtel which belonged to Monsieur de Bacqueville, in the reign of King Charles VI? there are indeed many superb high warp tapestries there."

"Charles VI! Charles VI!" muttered the young captain, twirling his moustache. "Good heavens! what old things the good dame does remember!"

Madame de Gondelaurier continued, "Fine tapestries, in truth. A work so esteemed that it passes as unrivaled."

At that moment Bérangère de Champchevrier, a slender little maid of seven years, who was peering into the square through the trefoils of the balcony, exclaimed, "Oh! look, fair Godmother Fleur-de-Lys, at that pretty dancer who is dancing on the pavement and playing the tambourine in the midst of the loutish bourgeois!"

The sonorous vibration of a tambourine was, in fact, audible.

"Some gypsy from Bohemia," said Fleur-de-Lys, turning carelessly toward the square.

"Look! look!" exclaimed her lively companions; and they all ran to the edge of the balcony, while Fleur-de-Lys, rendered thoughtful by the coldness of her betrothed, followed them slowly, and the latter, relieved by this incident, which put an end to an embarrassing conversation, retreated to the farther end of the room, with the satisfied air of a soldier released from duty. Nevertheless, the fair Fleur-de-Lys's was a charming and noble service, and such it had formerly appeared to him; but the captain had gradually become *blasé*; the prospect of a speedy marriage cooled him more every day. Moreover, he was of a fickle disposition, and, must we say it, rather vulgar in taste. Although of very noble birth, he had contracted in his official harness more than one habit of the common trooper. The tavern and its accompaniments pleased him. He was only at his ease amid gross language, military gallantries, facile beauties, and successes yet more easy. He had, nevertheless, received from his family some education and some politeness of manner; but he had been thrown on the world too young, he had been in garrison at too early an age, and every day the polish of a gentleman became more and more effaced by the rough friction of his gendarme's cross-belt. While still continuing to visit her from time to time, from a remnant of common respect, he felt doubly embarrassed with Fleur-de-Lys; in the first place, because, in consequence of having scattered his love in all sorts of places, he had reserved very little for her; in the next place, because, amid so many stiff, formal, and decent ladies, he was in constant fear lest his mouth, habituated to oaths, should suddenly take the bit in its teeth, and break out into the language of the tavern. The effect can be imagined!

Moreover, all this was mingled in him, with great pretentions to elegance, toilet, and a fine appearance. Let the reader reconcile these things as best he can. I am simply the historian.

He had remained, therefore, for several minutes, leaning in silence against the carved jamb of the chimney, and thinking or not thinking, when Fleur-de-Lys suddenly turned and addressed him. After all, the poor young girl was pouting against the dictates of her heart.

"Fair cousin, did you not speak to us of a little Bohemian whom you saved a couple of months ago, while making the patrol with the watch at night, from the hands of a dozen robbers?"

"I believe so, fair cousin," said the captain.

"Well," she resumed, "perchance 'tis that same gypsy girl who is dancing yonder, on the church square. Come and see if you recognize her, fair Cousin Phœbus."

A secret desire for reconciliation was apparent in this gentle invitation which she gave him to approach her, and in the care which she took to call him by name. Captain Phœbus de Châteaupers (for it is he whom the reader has had before his eyes since the beginning of this chapter) slowly approached the balcony. "Stay," said Fleur-de-Lys, laying her hand tenderly on Phœbus's arm; "look at that little girl yonder, dancing in that circle. Is she your Bohemian?"

Phœbus looked, and said—

"Yes, I recognize her by her goat."

"Oh! in fact, what a pretty little goat!" said Amelotte, clasping her hands in admiration.

"Are his horns of real gold?" inquired Bérangère.

Without moving from her arm-chair, Dame Aloïse interposed, "Is she not one of those gypsy girls who arrived last year by the Gibard gate?"

"Madame my mother," said Fleur-de-Lys gently, "that gate is now called the Porte d'Enfer."

Mademoiselle de Gondelaurier knew how her mother's antiquated mode of speech shocked the captain. In fact, he began to sneer, and muttered between his teeth: "Porte Gibard! Porte Gibard! 'Tis enough to make King Charles VI pass by."

"Godmother!" exclaimed Bérangère, whose eyes, incessantly in motion, had suddenly been raised to the summit of the towers of Notre-Dame, "who is that black man up yonder?"

All the young girls raised their eyes. A man was, in truth, leaning on the balustrade which surmounted the northern tower, looking on the Grève. He was a priest. His costume could be plainly discerned, and his face resting on both his hands. But he stirred no more than if he had been a statue. His eyes, intently fixed, gazed into the Place.

It was something like the immobility of a bird of prey, who has just discovered a nest of sparrows, and is gazing at it.

" 'Tis monsieur the archdeacon of Josas," said Fleur-de-Lys.

"You have good eyes if you can recognize him from here," said the Gaillefontaine.

"How he is staring at the little dancer!" went on Diane de Christeuil.

"Let the gypsy beware!" said Fleur-de-Lys, "for he loves not Egypt."

" 'Tis a great shame for that man to look upon her thus," added Amelotte de Montmichel, "for she dances delightfully."

"Fair cousin Phœbus," said Fleur-de-Lys suddenly, "Since you know this little gypsy, make her a sign to come up here. It will amuse us."

"Oh, yes!" exclaimed all the young girls, clapping their hands.

"Why! 'tis not worthwhile," replied Phœbus. "She has forgotten me, no doubt, and I know not so much as her name. Nevertheless, as you wish it, young ladies, I will make the trial." And leaning over the balustrade of the balcony, he began to shout, "Little one!"

The dancer was not beating her tambourine at the moment. She turned her head toward the point whence this call proceeded, her brilliant eyes rested on Phœbus, and she stopped short.

"Little one!" repeated the captain; and he beckoned her to approach.

The young girl looked at him again, then she blushed as though a flame had mounted into her cheeks, and, taking her tambourine under her arm, she made her way through the astonished spectators toward the door of the house where Phœbus was calling her, with slow, tottering steps, and with the troubled look of a bird which is yielding to the fascination of a serpent.

A moment later, the tapestry portière was raised, and the gypsy appeared on the threshold of the chamber, blushing, confused, breathless, her large eyes drooping, and not daring to advance another step.

Bérangère clapped her hands.

Meanwhile, the dancer remained motionless upon the threshold. Her appearance had produced a singular effect upon these young girls. It is certain that a vague and indistinct desire to please the handsome officer animated them all, that his splendid uniform was the target of all their coquetries, and that from the moment he presented himself, there existed among them a secret, suppressed rivalry, which they hardly acknowledged even to themselves, but which broke forth, none the less, every instant, in their gestures and remarks. Nevertheless, as they were all very nearly equal in beauty, they contended with equal arms, and each could hope for the victory. The arrival of the gypsy suddenly destroyed this equilibrium. Her beauty was so rare, that, at the moment when she appeared at the entrance of the apartment, it seemed as though she diffused a sort of light which was peculiar to herself. In that narrow chamber, surrounded by that somber frame of hangings and woodwork, she was incomparably more beautiful and more radiant than on the public square. She was like a torch which has suddenly been brought from broad daylight into the dark. The noble damsels were dazzled by her in spite of themselves. Each one felt herself, in some sort, wounded in her beauty. Hence, their battle front (may we be allowed the expression) was immediately altered, although they exchanged not a single word. But they understood each other perfectly. Women's instincts comprehend and respond to each other more quickly than the intelligences of men. An enemy had just arrived; all felt it—all rallied together. One drop of wine is sufficient to tinge a glass of water red; to diffuse a certain degree of ill temper throughout a whole assembly of pretty women, the arrival of a prettier woman suffices, especially when there is but one man present.

Hence the welcome accorded to the gypsy was marvelously glacial. They surveyed her from head to foot, then exchanged glances, and all was said; they understood each other. Meanwhile, the young girl was waiting to be spoken to, in such emotion that she dared not raise her eyelids.

The captain was the first to break the silence. "Upon my word," said he, in his tone of intrepid fatuity, "here is a charming creature! What think you of her, fair cousin?"

This remark, which a more delicate admirer would have uttered in a lower tone, at least was not of a nature to dissipate the feminine jealousies which were on the alert before the gypsy.

Fleur-de-Lys replied to the captain with a bland affectation of disdain—"Not bad."

The others whispered.

At length, Madame Aloïse, who was not the less jealous because she was so for her daughter, addressed the dancer—

"Approach, little one."

"Approach, little one!" repeated, with comical dignity, little Bérangère, who would have reached about as high as her hips.

The gypsy advanced toward the noble dame.

"Fair child," said Phœbus, with emphasis, taking several steps toward her, "I do not know whether I have the supreme honor of being recognized by you."

She interrupted him, with a smile and a look full of infinite sweetness—

"Oh! yes," said she.

"She has a good memory," remarked Fleur-de-Lys.

"Come, now," resumed Phœbus, "you escaped nimbly the other evening. Did I frighten you!"

"Oh! no," said the gypsy.

There was in the intonation of that "Oh! no," uttered after that "Oh! yes," an ineffable something which wounded Fleur-de-Lys.

"You left me in your stead, my beauty," pursued the captain, whose tongue was unloosed when speaking to a girl out of the street, "a crabbed knave, one-eyed and hunchbacked, the bishop's bell-ringer, I believe. I have been told that by birth he is the bastard of an archdeacon and a devil. He has a pleasant name: he is called *Quatre-Temps* (Ember Days), *Pâques-Fleuries* (Palm Sunday), *Mardi-Gras* (Shrove Tuesday), I know not what! The name of some festival when the bells are pealed! So he took the liberty of carrying you off, as though you were made for beadles! 'Tis too much. What the devil did that screech-owl want with you? Hey, tell me!"

"I do not know," she replied.

"The inconceivable impudence! A bellringer carrying off a wench, like a vicomte! a lout poaching on the game of gentlemen! that is a rare piece of assurance. However, he paid dearly for it. Master Pierrat Torterue is the harshest groom that ever curried a knave; and I can tell you, if it will be agreeable to you, that your bellringer's hide got a thorough dressing at his hands."

"Poor man!" said the gypsy, in whom these words revived the memory of the pillory.

The captain burst out laughing.

"Corne-de-boeuf! here's pity as well placed as a feather in a pig's tail! May I have as big a belly as a pope, if—"

He stopped short. "Pardon me, ladies; I believe that I was on the point of saying something foolish."

"Fie, sir!" said la Gaillefontaine.

"He talks to that creature in her own tongue!" added Fleur-de-Lys, in a low tone, her irritation increasing every moment. This irritation was not diminished when she beheld the captain, enchanted with the gypsy, and, most of all, with himself, execute a pirouette on his heel, repeating with coarse, naïve, and soldierly gallantry—

"A handsome wench, upon my soul!"

"Rather savagely dressed," said Diane de Christeuil, laughing to show her fine teeth.

This remark was a flash of light to the others. Not being able to impugn her beauty, they attacked her costume.

"That is true," said la Montmichel; "what makes you run about the streets thus, without guimpe or ruff?"

"That petticoat is so short that it makes one tremble," added la Gaillefontaine.

"My dear," continued Fleur-de-Lys, with decided sharpness, "You will get yourself taken up by the sumptuary police for your gilded girdle."

"Little one, little one," resumed la Christeuil, with an implacable smile, "if you were to put respectable sleeves upon your arms they would get less sunburned."

It was, in truth, a spectacle worthy of a more intelligent spectator than Phœbus, to see how these beautiful maidens, with their envenomed and angry tongues, wound, serpent-like, and glided and writhed around the street dancer. They were cruel and graceful; they searched and rummaged maliciously in her poor and silly toilet of spangles and tinsel. There was no end to their laughter, irony, and humiliation. Sarcasms rained down upon the gypsy, and haughty condescension and malevolent looks. One would have thought they were young Roman dames thrusting golden pins into the breast of a beautiful slave. One would have pronounced them elegant grayhounds, circling, with inflated nostrils, round a poor woodland fawn, whom the glance of their master forbade them to devour.

After all, what was a miserable dancer on the public squares in the presence of these high-born maidens? They seemed to take no heed of her presence, and talked of her aloud, to her face, as of something unclean, abject, and yet, at the same time, passably pretty.

The gypsy was not insensible to these pin-pricks. From time to time a flush of shame, a flash of anger inflamed her eyes or her cheeks; with disdain she made that little grimace with which the reader is already familiar, but she remained motionless; she fixed on Phœbus a sad, sweet, resigned look. There was also happiness and tenderness in that gaze. One would have said that she endured for fear of being expelled.

Phœbus laughed, and took the gypsy's part with a mixture of impertinence and pity.

"Let them talk, little one!" he repeated, jingling his golden spurs. "No doubt your toilet is a little extravagant and wild, but what difference does that make with such a charming damsel as yourself?"

"Good gracious!" exclaimed the blonde Gaillefontaine, drawing up her swan-like throat, with a bitter smile. "I see that messieurs the archers of the king's police easily take fire at the handsome eyes of gypsies!"

"Why not?" said Phœbus.

At this reply uttered carelessly by the captain, like a stray stone, whose fall one does not even watch, Colombe began to laugh, as well as Diane, Amelotte, and Fleur-de-Lys, into whose eyes at the same time a tear started.

The gypsy, who had dropped her eyes on the floor at the words of Colombe de Gaillefontaine, raised them beaming with joy and pride and fixed them once more on Phœbus. She was very beautiful at that moment.

The old dame, who was watching this scene, felt offended, without understanding why.

"Holy Virgin!" she suddenly exclaimed, "what is it moving about my legs? Ah! the villainous beast!"

It was the goat, who had just arrived, in search of his mistress, and who, in dashing toward the latter, had begun by entangling his horns in the pile of stuffs which the noble dame's garments heaped up on her feet when she was seated.

This created a diversion. The gypsy disentangled his horns without uttering a word.

"Oh! here's the little goat with golden hoofs!" exclaimed Bérangère, dancing with joy.

The gypsy crouched down on her knees and leaned her cheek against the fondling head of the goat. One would have said that she was asking pardon for having quitted it thus.

Meanwhile, Diane had bent down to Colombe's ear.

"Ah! good heavens! why did not I think of that sooner? 'Tis the gypsy with the goat. They say she is a sorceress, and that her goat executes very miraculous tricks."

"Well!" said Colombe, "the goat must now amuse us in its turn, and perform a miracle for us."

Diane and Colombe eagerly addressed the gypsy.

"Little one, make your goat perform a miracle."

"I do not know what you mean," replied the dancer.

"A miracle, a piece of magic, a bit of sorcery, in short."

"I do not understand." And she fell to caressing the pretty animal, repeating, "Djali! Djali!"

At that moment Fleur-de-Lys noticed a little bag of embroidered leather suspended from the neck of the goat—

"What is that?" she asked of the gypsy.

The gypsy raised her large eyes upon her and replied gravely—

"That is my secret."

"I should really like to know what your secret is," thought Fleur-de-Lys.

Meanwhile, the good dame had risen angrily—"Come now, gypsy, if neither you nor your goat can dance for us, what are you doing here?"

The gypsy walked slowly toward the door, without making any reply. But the nearer she approached it, the more her pace slackened. An irresistible magnet seemed to hold her. Suddenly she turned her eyes, wet with tears, toward Phœbus, and halted.

"True God!" exclaimed the captain, "that's not the way to depart. Come back and dance something for us. By the way, my sweet love, what is your name?"

"La Esmeralda," said the dancer, never taking her eyes from him.

At this strange name, a burst of wild laughter broke from the young girls.

"Here's a terrible name for a young lady," said Diane.

"You see well enough," retorted Amelotte, "that she is an enchantress."

"My dear," exclaimed Dame Aloïse solemnly, "your parents did not commit the sin of giving you that name at the baptismal font."

In the meantime, several minutes previously, Bérangère had coaxed the goat into a corner of the room with a marchpane cake, without anyone having noticed her. In an instant they had become good friends. The curious child had detached the bag from the goat's neck, had opened it, and had emptied out its contents on the rush matting; it was an alphabet, each letter of which was separately inscribed on a tiny block of boxwood. Hardly had these playthings been spread out on the matting, when the child, with surprise, beheld the goat (one of whose "miracles" this was no doubt), draw out certain letters with its golden hoof, and arrange them, with gentle pushes, in a certain order. In a moment they constituted a word, which the goat seemed to have been trained to write, so little hesitation did it show in forming it, and Bérangère suddenly exclaimed, clasping her hands in admiration—

"Godmother Fleur-de-Lys, see what the goat has just done!"

Fleur-de-Lys ran up and trembled. The letters arranged upon the floor formed this word—

PHŒBUS

"Was it the goat who wrote that?" she inquired in a changed voice.

"Yes, godmother," replied Bérangère.

It was impossible to doubt it; the child did not know how to write.

"This is the secret!" thought Fleur-de-Lys.

Meanwhile, at the child's exclamation, all had hastened up, the mother, the young girls, the gypsy, and the officer.

The gypsy beheld the piece of folly which the goat had committed. She turned red, then pale, and began to tremble like a culprit before the captain, who gazed at her with a smile of satisfaction and amazement.

"Phœbus!" whispered the young girls, stupefied: " 'tis the captain's name!"

"You have a marvelous memory!" said Fleur-de-Lys, to the petrified gypsy. Then, bursting into sobs:—"Oh!" she stammered mournfully, hiding her face in both her beautiful hands, "she is a magician!" And she heard another and a still more bitter voice at the bottom of her heart, saying—"She is a rival!"

She fell fainting.

"My daughter! my daughter!" cried the terrified mother. "Begone, you gypsy of hell!"

In a twinkling, la Esmeralda gathered up the unlucky letters, made a sign to Djali, and went out through one door, while Fleur-de-Lys was being carried out through the other.

Captain Phœbus, on being left alone, hesitated for a moment between the two doors, then he followed the gypsy.

Chapter II

A PRIEST AND A PHILOSOPHER ARE TWO DIFFERENT THINGS

THE PRIEST WHOM THE YOUNG GIRLS HAD OBSERVED AT THE TOP OF THE NORTH TOWER, LEANING over the Place and so attentive to the dance of the gypsy, was, in fact, Archdeacon Claude Frollo.

Our readers have not forgotten the mysterious cell which the archdeacon had reserved for himself in that tower. (I do not know, by the way be it said, whether it be not the same, the interior of which can be seen to-day through a little square window, opening to the east at the height of a man above the platform from which the towers spring; a bare and dilapidated den, whose badly plastered walls are ornamented here and there, at the present day, with some wretched yellow engravings representing the façades of cathedrals. I presume that this hole is jointly inhabited by bats and spiders, and that, consequently, it wages a double war of extermination on the flies).

Every day, an hour before sunset, the archdeacon ascended the staircase to the tower, and shut himself up in this cell, where he sometimes passed whole nights. That day, at the moment when, standing before the low door of his retreat, he was fitting into the lock the complicated little key which he always carried about him in the purse suspended to his side, a sound of tambourine and castanets had reached his ear. These sounds came from the Place du Parvis. The cell, as we have already said, had only one window opening upon the rear of the church. Claude Frollo had hastily withdrawn the key, and an instant later, he was on the top of the tower, in the gloomy and pensive attitude in which the maidens had seen him.

There he stood, grave, motionless, absorbed in one look and one thought. All Paris lay at his feet, with the thousand spires of its edifices and its circular horizon of gentle hills—with its river winding under its bridges, and its people moving to and fro through its streets—with the clouds of its smoke—with the mountainous chain of its roofs which presses Notre-Dame in its doubled folds; but out of all the city, the archdeacon gazed at one corner only of the pavement, the Place du Parvis; in all that throng at but one figure—the gypsy.

It would have been difficult to say what was the nature of this look, and whence proceeded the flame that flashed from it. It was a fixed gaze, which was, nevertheless, full of trouble and tumult. And, from the profound immobility of his whole body, barely agitated at intervals by an involuntary shiver, as a tree is moved by the wind; from the stiffness of his elbows, more marble than the balustrade on which they leaned; or the sight of the petrified smile which contracted his face—one would have said that nothing living was left about Claude Frollo except his eyes.

The gypsy was dancing; she was twirling her tambourine on the tip of her finger, and tossing it into the air as she danced Provençal sarabands; agile, light, joyous, and unconscious of the formidable gaze which descended perpendicularly upon her head.

The crowd was swarming around her; from time to time, a man accoutred in red and yellow made them form into a circle, and then returned, seated himself on a chair a few paces from the dancer, and took the goat's head on his knees. This man seemed to be the gypsy's companion. Claude Frollo could not distinguish his features from his elevated post.

From the moment when the archdeacon caught sight of this stranger, his attention seemed divided between him and the dancer, and his face became more and more gloomy. All at once he rose upright, and a quiver ran through his whole body: "Who is that man?" he muttered between his teeth: "I have always seen her alone before!"

Then he plunged down beneath the tortuous vault of the spiral staircase, and once more descended. As he passed the door of the bell chamber, which was ajar, be saw something which struck him; he beheld Quasimodo, who, leaning through an opening of one of those slate penthouses which resemble enormous blinds, appeared also to be gazing at the Place. He was engaged in so profound a contemplation, that he did not notice the passage of his adopted father. His savage eye had a singular expression; it was a charmed, tender look. "This is strange!" murmured Claude. "Is it the gypsy at whom he is thus gazing?" He continued his descent. At the end of a few minutes, the anxious archdeacon entered upon the Place from the door at the base of the tower.

"What has become of the gypsy girl?" he said, mingling with the group of spectators which the sound of the tambourine had collected.

"I know not," replied one of his neighbors, "I think that she has gone to make some of her fandangoes in the house opposite, whither they have called her."

In the place of the gypsy, on the carpet, whose arabesques had seemed to vanish but a moment previously by the capricious figures of her dance, the archdeacon no longer beheld anyone but the red and yellow man, who, in order to earn a few testers in his turn, was walking round the circle, with his elbows on his hips, his head thrown back, his face red, his neck outstretched, with a chair between his teeth. To the chair he had fastened a cat, which a neighbor had lent, and which was spitting in great affright.

"Notre-Dame!" exclaimed the archdeacon, at the moment when the juggler, perspiring heavily, passed in front of him with his pyramid of chair and his cat, "What is Master Pierre Gringoire doing here?"

The harsh voice of the archdeacon threw the poor fellow into such a commotion that he lost his equilibrium, together with his whole edifice, and the chair and the cat tumbled pell-mell upon the heads of the spectators, in the midst of inextinguishable hootings.

It is probable that Master Pierre Gringoire (for it was indeed he) would have had a sorry account to settle with the neighbor who owned the cat, and all the bruised and scratched faces which surrounded him, if he had not hastened to profit by the tumult to take refuge in the church, whither Claude Frollo had made him a sign to follow him.

The cathedral was already dark and deserted; the side-aisles were full of shadows, and the lamps of the chapels began to shine out like stars, so black had the vaulted ceiling become. Only the great rose window of the façade, whose thousand colors were steeped in a ray of horizontal sunlight, glittered in the gloom like a mass of diamonds, and threw its dazzling reflection to the other end of the nave.

When they had advanced a few paces, Dom Claude placed his back against a pillar, and gazed intently at Gringoire. The gaze was not the one which Gringoire feared, ashamed as he was of having been caught by a grave and learned person in the costume of a buffoon. There was nothing mocking or ironical in the priest's glance, it was serious, tranquil, piercing. The archdeacon was the first to break the silence.

"Come now, Master Pierre. You are to explain many things to me. And first of all, how comes it that you have not been seen for two months, and that now one finds you in the public squares, in a fine equipment in truth! Motley red and yellow, like a Caudebec apple?"

"Messire," said Gringoire, piteously, "it is, in fact, an amazing accoutrement. You see me no more comfortable in it than a cat coiffed with a calabash. 'Tis very ill done, I am conscious, to expose messieurs the sergeants of the watch to the liability of cudgeling beneath this cassock the humerus of a Pythagorean philosopher. But what would you have, my reverend master? 'tis the fault of my ancient jerkin, which abandoned me in cowardly wise, at the beginning of the winter, under the pretext that it was falling into tatters, and that it required repose in the basket of a rag-picker. What is one to do? Civilization has not yet arrived at the point where one can go stark naked, as ancient Diogenes wished. Add that a very cold wind was blowing, and 'tis not in the month of January that one can successfully attempt to make humanity take this new step. This garment presented itself, I took it, and I left my ancient black smock, which, for a hermetic like myself, was far from being hermetically closed. Behold me then, in the garments of a stage-player, like Saint Genest. What would you have? 'tis an eclipse. Apollo himself tended the flocks of Admetus."

" 'Tis a fine profession that you are engaged in!" replied the archdeacon.

"I agree, my master, that 'tis better to philosophize and poetize, to blow the flame in the furnace, or to receive it from heaven, than to carry cats on a shield. So, when you addressed me, I was as foolish as an ass before a turnspit. But what would you have, messire? One must eat every day, and the finest Alexandrine verses are not worth a bit of Brie cheese. Now, I made for Madame Marguerite of Flanders, that famous epithalamium, as you know, and the city will not pay me, under the pretext that it was not excellent; as though one could give a tragedy of Sophocles for four crowns! Hence, I was on the point of dying with hunger. Happily, I found that I was rather strong in the jaw; so I said to this jaw—perform some feats of strength and of equilibrium: nourish thyself. *Ale te ipsam.* A pack of beggars who have become my good friends, have taught me twenty sorts of herculean feats, and now I give to my teeth every evening the bread which they have earned during the day by the sweat of my brow. After all, *concedo,* I grant that it is a sad employment for my intellectual faculties, and that man is not made to pass his life in beating the tambourine and biting chairs. But, reverend master, it is not sufficient to pass one's life, one must earn the means for life."

Dom Claude listened in silence. All at once his deep-set eye assumed so sagacious and penetrating an expression, that Gringoire felt himself, so to speak, searched to the bottom of the soul by that glance.

"Very good, Master Pierre; but how comes it that you are now in company with that gypsy dancer?"

"In faith!" said Gringoire, " 'tis because she is my wife and I am her husband."

The priest's gloomy eyes flashed into flame.

"Have you done that, you wretch!" he cried, seizing Gringoire's arm with fury; "have you been so abandoned by God as to raise your hand against that girl?"

"On my chance of paradise, monseigneur," replied Gringoire, trembling in every limb, "I swear to you that I have never touched her, if that is what disturbs you."

"Then why do you talk of husband and wife?" said the priest.

Gringoire made haste to relate to him as succinctly as possible, all that the reader already knows, his adventure in the Court of Miracles and the broken-crock marriage. It appeared, moreover, that this marriage had led to no results whatever, and that each evening the gypsy girl cheated him of his nuptial right as on the first day. " 'Tis a mortification," he said in conclusion, "but that is because I have had the misfortune to wed a virgin."

"What do you mean?" demanded the archdeacon, who had been gradually appeased by this recital.

" 'Tis very difficult to explain," replied the poet. "It is a superstition. My wife is, according to what an old thief, who is called among us the Duke of Egypt, has told me, a foundling or a lost child, which is the same thing. She wears on her neck an amulet which, it is affirmed, will cause her to meet her parents some day, but which will lose its virtue if the young girl loses hers. Hence it follows that both of us remain very virtuous."

"So," resumed Claude, whose brow cleared more and more, "you believe, Master Pierre, that this creature has not been approached by any man?"

"What would you have a man do, Dom Claude, as against a superstition? She has got that in her head. I assuredly esteem as a rarity this nunlike prudery which is preserved untamed amid those Bohemian girls who are so easily brought into subjection. But she has three things to protect her: the Duke of Egypt, who has taken her under his safeguard, reckoning, perchance, on selling her to some gay abbé; all his tribe, who hold her in singular veneration, like a Notre-Dame; and a certain tiny poignard, which the buxom dame always wears about her, in some nook, in spite of the ordinances of the provost, and which one causes to fly out into her hands by squeezing her waist. 'Tis a proud wasp, I can tell you!"

The archdeacon pressed Gringoire with questions.

La Esmeralda, in the judgment of Gringoire, was an inoffensive and charming creature, pretty, with the exception of a pout which was peculiar to her; a naïve and passionate damsel, ignorant of everything and enthusiastic about everything; not yet aware of the difference between a man and a woman, even in her dreams; made like that; wild especially over dancing, noise, the open air; a sort of woman bee, with invisible wings on her feet, and living in a whirlwind. She owed this nature to the wandering life which she had always led. Gringoire had succeeded in learning that, while a mere child, she had traversed Spain and Catalonia, even to Sicily; he believed that she had even been taken by the caravan of Zingari, of which she formed a part, to the kingdom of Algiers, a country situated in Achaia, which country adjoins, on one side Albania and Greece; on the other, the Sicilian Sea, which is the road to Constantinople. The Bohemians, said Gringoire, were vassals of the King of Algiers, in his quality of chief of the White Moors. One thing is certain, that la Esmeralda had come to France while still very young, by way of Hungary. From all these countries the young girl had brought back fragments of queer jargons, songs, and strange ideas, which made her language as motley as her costume, half Parisian, half African. However, the people of the quarters which she frequented loved her for her gaiety, her daintiness, her lively manners, her dances, and her songs. She believed herself to be hated, in all the city, by but two persons, of whom she often spoke in terror: the sacked nun of the Tour-Roland, a villainous recluse who cherished some secret grudge against these gypsies, and who cursed the poor dancer every time that the latter passed before her window; and a priest, who never met her without casting at her looks and words which frightened her.

The mention of this last circumstance disturbed the archdeacon greatly, though Gringoire paid no attention to his perturbation; to such an extent had two months sufficed to cause the heedless poet to forget the singular details of the evening on which he had met the gypsy, and the presence of the archdeacon in it all. Otherwise, the little dancer feared nothing; she did not tell fortunes, which protected her against those trials for magic which were so frequently instituted against gypsy women. And then, Gringoire held the position of her brother, if not of her husband. After all, the philosopher endured this sort of platonic marriage very patiently. It meant a shelter and bread at least. Every morning, he set out from the lair of the thieves, generally with the gypsy; he helped her make her collections of targes and little blanks in the squares; each evening he returned to the same roof with her, allowed her to bolt herself into her little chamber, and slept the sleep of the just. A very sweet existence, taking it all in all, he said, and well adapted to reverie. And then, on his soul and conscience, the philosopher was not very sure that he was madly in love with the gypsy. He loved her goat almost as dearly. It was a charming animal, gentle, intelligent, clever; a learned goat. Nothing was more common in the Middle Ages than these learned animals, which amazed people greatly, and often led their instructors to the stake. But the witchcraft of the goat with the golden hoofs was a very innocent species of magic. Gringoire explained them to the archdeacon, whom these details seemed to interest deeply. In the majority of cases, it was sufficient to present the tambourine to the goat in such or such a manner, in order to obtain from him the trick desired. He had been trained to this by the gypsy, who possessed, in these delicate arts, so rare a talent that two months had sufficed to teach the goat to write, with movable letters, the word "Phœbus."

" 'Phœbus!' " said the priest; "why 'Phœbus'?"

"I know not," replied Gringoire. "Perhaps it is a word which she believes to be endowed with some magic and secret virtue. She often repeats it in a low tone when she thinks that she is alone."

"Are you sure," persisted Claude, with his penetrating glance, "that it is only a word and not a name?"

"The name of whom?" said the poet.

"How should I know?" said the priest.

"This is what I imagine, messire. These Bohemians are something like Guebrs, and adore the sun. Hence, Phœbus."

"That does not seem so clear to me as to you, Master Pierre."

"After all, that does not concern me. Let her mumble her Phœbus at her pleasure. One thing is certain, that Djali loves me almost as much as he does her."

"Who is Djali?"

"The goat."

The archdeacon dropped his chin into his hand, and appeared to reflect for a moment. All at once he turned abruptly to Gringoire once more.

"And do you swear to me that you have not touched her?"

"Whom?" said Gringoire; "the goat?"

"No, that woman."

"My wife? I swear to you that I have not."

"You are often alone with her?"

"A good hour every evening."

Dom Claude frowned.

"Oh! oh! *Solus cum sola non cogitabuntur orare Pater Noster.*"

"Upon my soul, I could say the *Pater,* and the *Ave Maria,* and the *Credo in Deum patrem omnipotentem* without her paying any more attention to me than a chicken to a church."

"Swear to me, by the body of your mother," repeated the archdeacon violently, "that you have not touched that creature with even the tip of your finger."

"I will also swear it by the head of my father, for the two things have more affinity between them. But, my reverend master, permit me a question in my turn."

"Speak, sir."

"What concern is it of yours?"

The archdeacon's pale face became as crimson as the cheek of a young girl. He remained for a moment without answering; then, with visible embarrassment—

"Listen, Master Pierre Gringoire. You are not yet damned, so far as I know. I take an interest in you, and wish you well. Now the least contact with that Egyptian of the demon would make you the vassal of Satan. You know that 'tis always the body which ruins the soul. Woe to you if you approach that woman! That is all."

"I tried once," said Gringoire, scratching his ear; "it was the first day: but I got stung."

"You were so audacious, Master Pierre?" and the priest's brow clouded over again.

"On another occasion," continued the poet, with a smile, "I peeped through the keyhole, before going to bed, and I beheld the most delicious dame in her shift that ever made a bed creak under her bare foot."

"Go to the devil!" cried the priest, with a terrible look; and, giving the amazed Gringoire a push on the shoulders, he plunged, with long strides, under the gloomiest arcades of the cathedral.

Chapter III

THE BELLS

AFTER THE MORNING IN THE PILLORY, THE NEIGHBORS OF NOTRE-DAME THOUGHT THEY NOTICED that Quasimodo's ardor for ringing had grown cool. Formerly, there had been peals for every occasion, long morning serenades, which lasted from prime to compline; peals from the belfry for a high mass, rich scales drawn over the smaller bells for a wedding, for a christening, and mingling in the air like a rich embroidery of all sorts of charming sounds. The old church, all vibrating and sonorous, was in a perpetual joy of bells. One was constantly conscious of the presence of a spirit of noise and caprice, who sang through all those mouths of brass. Now that spirit seemed to have departed; the cathedral seemed gloomy, and gladly remained silent; festivals and funerals had the simple peal, dry and bare, demanded by the ritual, nothing more. Of the double noise which constitutes a church, the organ within, the bell without, the organ alone remained. One would have said that there was no longer a musician in the belfry. Quasimodo was always there, nevertheless; what, then, had happened to him? Was it that the shame and despair of the pillory still lingered in the bottom of his heart, that the lashes of his tormentor's whip reverberated unendingly in his soul, and that the sadness of such treatment had wholly extinguished in him even his passion for the bells? or was it that Marie had a rival in the heart of the bellringer of Notre-Dame, and that the great bell and her fourteen sisters were neglected for something more amiable and more beautiful?

It chanced that, in the year of grace 1482, Annunciation Day fell on Tuesday, the 25th of March. That day the air was so pure and light that Quasimodo felt some returning affection for his bells. He therefore ascended the northern tower while the beadle below was opening wide the doors of the church, which were then enormous panels of stout wood, covered with leather, bordered with nails of gilded iron, and framed in carvings "very artistically elaborated."

On arriving in the lofty bell chamber, Quasimodo gazed for some time at the six bells and shook his head sadly, as though groaning over some foreign element which had interposed itself in his heart between them and him. But when he had set them to swinging, when he felt that cluster of bells moving under his hand, when he saw, for he did not hear it, the palpitating octave ascend and descend that sonorous scale, like a bird hopping from branch to branch; when the demon Music, that demon who shakes a sparkling bundle of strette, trills and arpeggios, had taken possession of the poor deaf man, he became happy once more, he forgot everything, and his heart expanding, made his face beam.

He went and came, he beat his hands together, he ran from rope to rope, he animated the six singers with voice and gesture, like the leader of an orchestra who is urging on intelligent musicians.

"Go on," said he, "go on, go on, Gabrielle, pour out all thy noise into the Place, 'tis a festival to-day. No laziness, Thibauld; thou art relaxing; go on, go on, then, art thou rusted, thou sluggard? That is well! quick! quick! let not thy clapper be seen! Make them all deaf like me. That's it, Thibauld, bravely done! Guillaume! Guillaume! thou art the largest, and Pasquier is the smallest, and Pasquier does best. Let us wager that those who hear him will understand him better than they understand thee. Good! good! my Gabrielle, stoutly, more stoutly! Eh! what are you doing up aloft there, you two Moineaux (sparrows)? I do not see you making the least little shred of noise. What is the meaning of those beaks of copper which seem to be gaping when they should sing? Come, work now, 'tis the Feast of the Annunciation. The sun is fine, the chime must be fine also. Poor Guillaume! thou art all out of breath, my big fellow!"

He was wholly absorbed in spurring on his bells, all six of which vied with each other in leaping and shaking their shining haunches, like a noisy team of Spanish mules, pricked on here and there by the apostrophes of the muleteer.

All at once, on letting his glance fall between the large slate scales which cover the perpendicular wall of the bell tower at a certain height, he beheld on the square a young girl, fantastically dressed, stop, spread out on the ground a carpet, on which a small goat took up its post, and a group of spectators collect around her. This sight suddenly changed the course of his ideas, and congealed his enthusiasm as a breath of air congeals melted rosin. He halted, turned his back to the bells, and crouched down behind the projecting roof of slate, fixing upon the dancer that dreamy, sweet, and tender look which had already astonished the archdeacon on one occasion. Meanwhile, the forgotten bells died away abruptly and all together, to the great disappointment of the lovers of bell ringing, who were listening in good faith to the peal from above the Pont du Change, and who went away dumbfounded, like a dog who has been offered a bone and given a stone.

Chapter IV

'ANÁΓKH

IT CHANCED THAT UPON A FINE MORNING IN THIS SAME MONTH OF MARCH, I THINK IT WAS ON SATurday the 29th, Saint Eustache's day, our young friend the student, Jehan Frollo du Moulin, perceived, as he was dressing himself, that his breeches, which contained his purse, gave out no metallic ring. "Poor purse," he said, drawing it from his fob, "what! not the smallest parisis! how cruelly the dice, beer-pots, and Venus have depleted thee! How empty, wrinkled, limp, thou art! Thou resemblest the throat of a fury! I ask you, Messer Cicero, and Messer Seneca, copies of whom, all dog's-eared, I behold scattered on the floor, what profits it me to know, better than any governor of the mint, or any Jew on the Pont aux Changeurs, that a golden crown stamped with a crown is worth thirty-five unzains of twenty-five sous, and eight deniers parisis apiece, and that a crown stamped with a crescent is worth thirty-six unzains of twenty-six sous, six deniers tournois apiece, if I have not a single wretched black liard to risk on the double-six! Oh! Consul Cicero! this is no calamity from which one extricates one's self with periphrases, *quemadmodum,* and *verum enim vero!*"

He dressed himself sadly. An idea had occurred to him as he laced his boots, but he rejected it at first; nevertheless, it returned, and he put on his waistcoat wrong side out, an evident sign of violent internal combat. At last he dashed his cap roughly on the floor, and exclaimed: "So much the worse! Let come of it what may. I am going to my brother! I shall catch a sermon, but I shall catch a crown."

Then be hastily donned his long jacket with furred half-sleeves, picked up his cap, and went out like a man driven to desperation.

He descended the Rue de la Harpe toward the City. As he passed the Rue de la Huchette, the odor of those admirable spits, which were incessantly turning, tickled his olfactory apparatus, and he bestowed a loving glance toward the Cyclopean roast, which one day drew from the Franciscan friar, Calatagirone, this pathetic exclamation: *Veramente, queste rotisserie sono cosa stupenda!*[1] But Jehan had not the wherewithal to buy a breakfast, and he plunged, with a profound sigh, under the gateway of the Petit-Châtelet, that enormous double trefoil of massive towers which guarded the entrance to the City.

1. Truly, these roastings are a stupendous thing!

He did not even take the trouble to cast a stone in passing, as was the usage, at the miserable statue of that Périnet Leclerc who had delivered up the Paris of Charles VI to the English, a crime which his effigy, its face battered with stones and soiled with mud, expiated for three centuries at the corner of the Rue de la Harpe and the Rue de Buci, as in an eternal pillory.

The Petit-Pont traversed, the Rue Neuve-Sainte-Geneviève crossed, Jehan de Molendino found himself in front of Notre-Dame. Then indecision seized upon him once more, and he paced for several minutes round the statue of M. Legris, repeating to himself with anguish: "The sermon is sure, the crown is doubtful."

He stopped a beadle who emerged from the cloister—"Where is monsieur the archdeacon of Josas?"

"I believe that he is in his secret cell in the tower," said the beadle; "I should advise you not to disturb him there, unless you come from someone like the pope or monsieur the king."

Jehan clapped his hands.

"*Bédiable*! here's a magnificent chance to see the famous sorcery cell!"

This reflection having brought him to a decision, he plunged resolutely into the small black doorway, and began the ascent of the spiral of Saint-Gilles, which leads to the upper stories of the tower. "I am going to see," he said to himself on the way. "By the ravens of the Holy Virgin! it must needs be a curious thing, that cell which my reverend brother hides so secretly! 'Tis said that he lights up the kitchens of hell there, and that he cooks the philosopher's stone there over a hot fire. *Bédieu!* I care no more for the philosopher's stone than for a pebble, and I would rather find over his furnace an omelette of Easter eggs and bacon, than the biggest philosopher's stone in the world."

On arriving at the gallery of slender columns, he took breath for a moment, and swore against the interminable staircase by I know not how many million cartloads of devils; then he resumed his ascent through the narrow door of the north tower, now closed to the public. Several moments after passing the bell chamber, he came upon a little landing-place, built in a lateral niche, and under the vault of a low, pointed door, whose enormous lock and strong iron bars he was enabled to see through a loophole pierced in the opposite circular wall of the staircase. Persons desirous of visiting this door at the present day will recognize it by this inscription engraved in white letters on the black wall:

J'ADORE CORALIE, 1823. SIGNÉ UGÈNE.

"Signé" stands in the text.

"Ugh!" said the scholar; " 'tis here, no doubt."

The key was in the lock, the door was very close to him; he gave it a gentle push and thrust his head through the opening.

The reader cannot have failed to turn over the admirable works of Rembrandt, that Shakespeare of painting. Amid so many marvelous engravings, there is one etching in particular, which is supposed to represent Doctor Faust, and which it is impossible to contemplate without being dazzled. It represents a gloomy cell; in the center is a table loaded with hideous objects; skulls, spheres, alembics, compasses, hieroglyphic parchments. The doctor is before this table clad in his large coat and covered to the very eyebrows with his furred cap. He is visible only to his waist. He has half risen from his immense arm-chair, his clenched fists rest on the table, and he is gazing with curiosity and terror at a large luminous circle, formed of magic letters, which gleams from the wall beyond, like the solar spectrum in a dark chamber. This cabalistic sun seems to tremble before the eye, and fills the wan cell with its mysterious radiance. It is horrible and it is beautiful.

Something very similar to Faust's cell presented itself to Jehan's view, when he ventured his head through the half-open door. It also was a gloomy and sparsely lighted retreat. There also stood a large arm-chair and a large table, compasses, alembics, skeletons of animals suspended from the ceiling, a globe rolling on the floor, hippocephali mingled promiscuously with drinking cups, in which quivered leaves of gold, skulls placed upon vellum checkered with figures and characters, huge manuscripts piled up wide open, without mercy on the cracking corners of the parchment; in short, all the rubbish of science, and everywhere on this confusion dust and spiders' webs; but there was no circle of luminous letters, no doctor in an ecstasy contemplating the flaming vision, as the eagle gazes upon the sun.

Nevertheless, the cell was not deserted. A man was seated in the arm-chair, and bending over the table. Jehan, to whom his back was turned, could see only his shoulders and the back of his skull; but he had no difficulty in recognizing that bald head, which nature had provided with an eternal tonsure, as though desirous of marking, by this external symbol, the archdeacon's irresistible clerical vocation.

Jehan accordingly recognized his brother; but the door had been opened so softly, that nothing warned Dom Claude of his presence. The inquisitive scholar took advantage of this circumstance to examine the cell for a few moments at his leisure. A large furnace, which he had not at first observed, stood to the left of the arm-chair, beneath the window. The ray of light which penetrated through this aperture made its way through a spider's circular web, which tastefully inscribed its delicate rose in the arch of the window, and in the center of which the insect architect hung motionless, like the hub of this wheel of lace. Upon the furnace were accumulated in disorder, all sorts of vases, earthenware bottles, glass retorts, and mattresses of charcoal. Jehan observed, with a sigh, that there was no frying-pan. "How cold the kitchen utensils are!" he said to himself.

In fact, there was no fire in the furnace, and it seemed as though none had been lighted for a long time. A glass mask, which Jehan noticed among the utensils of alchemy, and which served no doubt, to protect the archdeacon's face when he was working over some substance to be dreaded, lay in one corner covered with dust and apparently forgotten. Beside it lay a pair of bellows no less dusty, the upper side of which bore this inscription encrusted in copper letters:

SPIRA SPERA.

Other inscriptions were written, in accordance with the fashion of the hermetics, in great numbers on the walls; some traced with ink, others engraved with a metal point. There were, moreover, Gothic letters, Hebrew letters, Greek letters, and Roman letters, pell-mell; the inscriptions overflowed at haphazard, on top of each other, the more recent effacing the more ancient, and all entangled with each other, like the branches in a thicket, like pikes in an affray. It was, in fact, a strangely confused mingling of all human philosophies, all reveries, all human wisdom. Here and there one shone out from among the rest like a banner among lance heads. Generally, it was a brief Greek or Roman device, such as the Middle Ages knew so well how to formulate.—*Unde? Inde?*—*Homo homini monstrum*—*Astra, castra, nomen, numen.*—Μέγα βιβλίον, μέγα χαχόν.—*Sapere aude. Fiat ubi vult*—etc.; sometimes a word devoid of all apparent sense, 'Αναγχοφαγία, which possibly contained a bitter allusion to the régime of the cloister; sometimes a simple maxim of clerical discipline formulated in a regular hexameter: *Coelestem dominum terrestrem dicite domnum.* There was also Hebrew jargon, of which Jehan, who as yet knew but little Greek, understood nothing; and all were traversed in every direction by stars, by figures of men or animals, and by intersecting triangles; and this contributed not a little to make the scrawled wall of the cell resemble a sheet of paper over which a monkey had drawn back and forth a pen filled with ink.

The whole chamber, moreover, presented a general aspect of abandonment and dilapidation; and the bad state of the utensils induced the supposition that their owner had long been distracted from his labors by other preoccupations.

Meanwhile, this master, bent over a vast manuscript, ornamented with fantastical illustrations, appeared to be tormented by an idea which incessantly mingled with his meditations. That at least was Jehan's idea, when he heard him exclaim, with the thoughtful breaks of a dreamer thinking aloud—

"Yes, Manou said it, and Zoroaster taught it! the sun is born from fire, the moon from the sun; fire is the soul of the universe; its elementary atoms pour forth and flow incessantly upon the world through infinite channels! At the point where these currents intersect each other in the heavens, they produce light; at their points of intersection on earth, they produce gold. Light, gold; the same thing! From fire to the concrete state. The difference between the visible and the palpable, between the fluid and the solid in the same substance, between water and ice, nothing more. These are no dreams; it is the general law of nature. But what is one to do in order to extract from science the secret of this general law? What! this light which inundates my hand is gold! These same atoms dilated in accordance with a certain law need only be condensed in accordance with another law. How is it to be done? Some have fancied by burying a ray of sunlight, Averroës—yes, 'tis Averroës—Averroës buried one under the first pillar on the left of the sanctuary of the Koran, in the great Mahometan mosque of Cordova; but the vault cannot be opened for the purpose of ascertaining whether the operation has succeeded, until after the lapse of eight thousand years."

"The devil!" said Jehan, to himself, " 'tis a long while to wait for a crown!"

"Others have thought," continued the dreamy archdeacon, "that it would be better worthwhile to operate upon a ray of Sirius. But 'tis exceeding hard to obtain this ray pure, because of the simultaneous presence of other stars whose rays mingle with it. Flamel esteemed it more simple to operate upon terrestrial fire. Flamel! there's predestination in the name! *Flamma!* yes, fire. All lies there. The diamond is contained in the carbon, gold is in the fire. But how to extract it? Magistri affirms that there are certain feminine names, which possess a charm so sweet and mysterious, that it suffices to pronounce them during the operation. Let us read what Manon says on the matter: 'Where women are honored, the divinities are rejoiced; where they are despised, it is useless to pray to God. The mouth of a woman is constantly pure; it is a running water, it is a ray of sunlight. The name of a woman should be agreeable, sweet, fanciful; it should end in long vowels, and resemble words of benediction.' Yes, the sage is right; in truth, Maria, Sophia, la Esmeral—Damnation! always that thought!"

And he closed the book violently.

He passed his hand over his brow, as though to brush away the idea which assailed him; then he took from the table a nail and a small hammer, whose handle was curiously painted with cabalistic letters.

"For some time," he said with a bitter smile, "I have failed in all my experiments! one fixed idea possesses me, and sears my brain like fire. I have not even been able to discover the secret of Cassiodorus, whose lamp burned without wick and without oil. A simple matter, nevertheless—"

"The deuce!" muttered Jehan in his beard.

"Hence," continued the priest, "one wretched thought is sufficient to render a man weak and beside himself! Oh! how Claude Pernelle would laugh at me. She who could not turn Nicolas Flamel aside, for one moment, from his pursuit of the great work! What! I hold in my hand the magic hammer of Zéchiélé! at every blow dealt by the formidable rabbi, from the depths of his cell, upon this nail, that one of his enemies whom he had condemned, were he a thousand leagues away, was buried a cubit deep in the earth which swallowed him. The King of France himself, in consequence of once having inconsiderately knocked at the door of the thermaturgist, sank to the knees through the pavement of his own Paris. This took place three centuries ago. Well! I possess the hammer and the nail, and in my hands they are utensils no more formidable than a club in the hands of a maker of edge tools. And yet all that is required is to find the magic word which Zéchiélé pronounced when he struck his nail."

"What nonsense!" thought Jehan.

"Let us see, let us try!" resumed the archdeacon briskly. "Were I to succeed, I should behold the blue spark flash from the head of the nail. Emen-Hétan! Emen-Hétan! That's not it. Sigéani! Sigéani! May this nail open the tomb to anyone who bears the name of Phœbus! A curse upon it! Always and eternally the same idea!"

And he flung away the hammer in a rage. Then he sank down so deeply on the arm-chair and the table, that Jehan lost him from view behind the great pile of manuscripts. For the space of several minutes, all that he saw was his fist convulsively clenched on a book. Suddenly, Dom Claude sprang up, seized a compass and engraved in silence upon the wall in capital letters, this Greek word

'ANÁΓKH

"My brother is mad," said Jehan to himself; "it would have been far more simple to write *Fatum*, everyone is not obliged to know Greek."

The archdeacon returned and seated himself in his arm-chair, and placed his head on both his hands, as a sick man does, whose head is heavy and burning.

The student watched his brother with surprise. He did not know, he who wore his heart on his sleeve, he who observed only the good old law of Nature in the world, he who allowed his passions to follow their inclinations, and in whom the lake of great emotions was always dry, so freely did he let it off each day by fresh drains—he did not know with what fury the sea of human passions ferments and boils when all egress is denied to it, how it accumulates, how it swells, how it overflows, how it hollows out the heart; how it breaks in inward sobs, and dull convulsions, until it has rent its dikes and burst its bed. The austere and glacial envelope of Claude Frollo, that cold surface of steep and inaccessible virtue, had always deceived Jehan. The merry scholar had never dreamed that there was boiling lava, furious and profound, beneath the snowy brow of Ætna.

We do not know whether he suddenly became conscious of these things; but, giddy as he was, he understood that he had seen what he ought not to have seen, that he had just surprised the soul of his elder brother in one of its most secret altitudes, and that Claude must not be allowed to know it. Seeing that the archdeacon had fallen back into his former immobility, he withdrew his head very softly, and made some noise with his feet outside the door, like a person who has just arrived and is giving warning of his approach.

"Enter!" cried the archdeacon, from the interior of his cell; "I was expecting you. I left the door unlocked expressly; enter Master Jacques!"

The scholar entered boldly. The archdeacon, who was very much embarrassed by such a visit in such a place, trembled in his arm-chair. "What! 'tis you, Jehan?"

" 'Tis a J, all the same," said the scholar, with his ruddy, merry, and audacious face.

Dom Claude's visage had resumed its severe expression.

"What are you come for?"

"Brother," replied the scholar, making an effort to assume a decent, pitiful, and modest mien, and twirling his cap in his hands with an innocent air; "I am come to ask of you—"

"What?"

"A little lecture on morality, of which I stand greatly in need," Jehan did not dare to add aloud—"and a little money of which I am in still greater need." This last member of his phrase remained unuttered.

"Monsieur," said the archdeacon, in a cold tone, "I am greatly displeased with you."

"Alas!" sighed the scholar.

Dom Claude made his arm-chair describe a quarter circle, and gazed intently at Jehan.

"I am very glad to see you."

This was a formidable exordium. Jehan braced himself for a rough encounter.

"Jehan, complaints are brought me about you every day. What affray was that in which you bruised with a cudgel a little vicomte, Albert de Ramonchamp?"

"Oh!" said Jehan, "a vast thing that! A malicious page amused himself by splashing the scholars, by making his horse gallop through the mire!"

"Who," pursued the archdeacon, "is that Mahiet Fargel, whose gown you have torn? *Tunicam dechiraverunt*, saith the complaint."

"Ah bah! a wretched cap of a Montaigu! Isn't that it?"

"The complaint says *tunicam* and not *cappettam*. Do you know Latin?"

Jehan did not reply.

"Yes," pursued the priest shaking his head, "That is the state of learning and letters at the present day. The Latin tongue is hardly understood, Syriac is unknown, Greek so odious that 'tis accounted no ignorance in the most learned to skip a Greek word without reading it, and to say, '*Græcum est non legitur.*'"

The scholar raised his eyes boldly. "Monsieur my brother, doth it please you that I shall explain in good French vernacular that Greek word which is written yonder on the wall?"

"What word?"

"'*ANÁΓΚΗ*."

A slight flush spread over the cheeks of the priest with their high bones, like the puff of smoke which announces on the outside the secret commotions of a volcano. The student hardly noticed it.

"Well, Jehan," stammered the elder brother with an effort, "What is the meaning of yonder word?"

"FATE."

Dom Claude turned pale again, and the scholar pursued carelessly.

"And that word below it, graved by the same hand, 'Aváγνεία, signifies 'impurity.' You see that people do know their Greek."

And the archdeacon remained silent. This Greek lesson had rendered him thoughtful.

Master Jehan, who possessed all the artful ways of a spoiled child, judged that the moment was a favorable one in which to risk his request. Accordingly, he assumed an extremely soft tone and began—

"My good brother, do you hate me to such a degree as to look savagely upon me because of a few mischievous cuffs and blows distributed in a fair war to a pack of lads and brats, *quibusdam marmosetis?* You see, good Brother Claude, that people know their Latin."

But all this caressing hypocrisy did not have its usual effect on the severe elder brother. Cerberus did not bite at the honey cake. The archdeacon's brow did not lose a single wrinkle.

"What are you driving at?" he said dryly.

"Well, in point of fact, this!" replied Jehan bravely, "I stand in need of money."

At this audacious declaration, the archdeacon's visage assumed a thoroughly pedagogical and paternal expression.

"You know, Monsieur Jehan, that our fief of Tirechappe, putting the direct taxes and the rents of the nine and twenty houses in a block, yields only nine and thirty livres, eleven sous, six deniers, Parisian. It is one half more than in the time of the brothers Paclet, but it is not much."

"I need money," said Jehan stoically.

"You know that the official has decided that our twenty-one houses should he moved full into the fief of the Bishopric, and that we could redeem this homage only by paying the reverend bishop two marks of silver gilt of the price of six livres parisis. Now, these two marks I have not yet been able to get together. You know it."

"I know that I stand in need of money," repeated Jehan for the third time.

"And what are you going to do with it?"

This question caused a flash of hope to gleam before Jehan's eyes. He resumed his dainty, caressing air.

"Stay, dear Brother Claude, I should not come to you, with any evil motive. There is no intention of cutting a dash in the taverns with your unzains, and of strutting about the streets of Paris in a caparison of gold brocade, with a lackey, *cum meo laquasio*. No, brother, 'tis for a good work."

"What good work?" demanded Claude, somewhat surprised.

"Two of my friends wish to purchase an outfit for the infant of a poor Haudriette widow. It is a charity. It will cost three florins, and I should like to contribute to it."

"What are names of your two friends?"

"Pierre l'Assommeur and Baptiste Croque-Oison."[1]

"Hum," said the archdeacon; "those are names as fit for a good work as a catapult for the chief altar."

It is certain that Jehan had made a very bad choice of names for his two friends. He realized it too late.

"And then," pursued the sagacious Claude, "what sort of an infant's outfit is it that is to cost three florins, and that for the child of a Haudriette? Since when have the Haudriette widows taken to having babes in swaddling-clothes?"

Jehan broke the ice once more.

"Eh, well! yes! I need money in order to go and see Isabeau la Thierrye to-night; in the Val-d' Amour!"

"Impure wretch!" exclaimed the priest.

" Ἀναγνεία!" said Jehan.

This quotation, which the scholar borrowed with malice, perchance, from the wall of the cell, produced a singular effect on the archdeacon. He bit his lips and his wrath was drowned in a crimson flush.

"Begone," he said to Jehan. "I am expecting someone."

The scholar made one more effort.

"Brother Claude, give me at least one little parisis to buy something to eat."

"How far have you gone in the Decretals of Gratian?" demanded Dom Claude.

"I have lost my copy-books."

"Where are you in your Latin humanities?"

"My copy of Horace has been stolen."

"Where are you in Aristotle?"

"I' faith! brother what father of the church is it, who says that the errors of heretics have always had for their lurking place the thickets of Aristotle's metaphysics? A plague on Aristotle! I care not to tear my religion on his metaphysics."

"Young man," resumed the archdeacon, "at the king's last entry, there was a young gentleman, named Philippe de Comines, who wore embroidered on the housings of his horse this device, upon which I counsel you to meditate: *Qui non laborat, non manducet.*"

The scholar remained silent for a moment, with his finger in his ear, his eyes on the ground, and a discomfited mien.

All at once he turned round to Claude with the agile quickness of a wagtail.

"So, my good brother, you refuse me a sou parisis, wherewith to buy a crust at a baker's shop?"

"*Qui non laborat, non manducet.*"

At this response of the inflexible archdeacon, Jehan hid his head in his hands, like a woman sobbing, and exclaimed with an expression of despair: "Ὀτοτοτοτοτοῖ."

"What is the meaning of this, sir?" demanded Claude, surprised at this freak.

"What indeed!" said the scholar; and he lifted to Claude his impudent eyes into which he had just thrust his fists in order to communicate to them the redness of tears; " 'tis Greek! 'tis an anapaest of Æschylus which expresses grief perfectly."

---

1. Peter the Slaughterer and Baptist Crack-Gosling.

And here he burst into a laugh so droll and violent that it made the archdeacon smile. It was Claude's fault, in fact: why had he so spoiled that child?

"Oh! good Brother Claude," resumed Jehan, emboldened by this smile, "look at my worn out boots. Is there a cothurnus in the world more tragic than these boots, whose soles are hanging out their tongues?"

The archdeacon promptly returned to his original severity.

"I will send you some new boots, but no money."

"Only a poor little parisis, brother," continued the suppliant Jehan. "I will learn Gratian by heart, I will believe firmly in God, I will be a regular Pythagoras of science and virtue. But one little parisis, in mercy! Would you have famine bite me with its jaws which are gaping in front of me, blacker, deeper, and more noisome than a Tartarus or the nose of a monk?"

Dom Claude shook his wrinkled head: *"Qui non laborat—"*

Jehan did not allow him to finish.

"Well," he exclaimed, "to the devil then! Long live joy! I will live in the tavern, I will fight, I will break pots and I will go and see the wenches." And thereupon, he hurled his cap at the wall, and snapped his fingers like castanets.

The archdeacon surveyed him with a gloomy air.

"Jehan, you have no soul."

"In that case, according to Epicurius, I lack a something made of another something which has no name."

"Jehan, you must think seriously of amending your ways."

"Oh, come now," cried the student, gazing in turn at his brother and the alembics on the furnace, "everything is preposterous here, both ideas and bottles!"

"Jehan, you are on a very slippery downward road. Do you know whither you are going?"

"To the wine-shop," said Jehan.

"The wine-shop leads to the pillory."

" 'Tis as good a lantern as any other, and perchance with that one, Diogenes would have found his man."

"The pillory leads to the gallows."

"The gallows is a balance which has a man at one end and the whole earth at the other. 'Tis fine to be the man."

"The gallows leads to hell."

" 'Tis a big fire."

"Jehan, Jehan, the end will be bad."

"The beginning will have been good."

At that moment, the sound of a footstep was heard on the staircase.

"Silence!" said the archdeacon, laying his finger on his mouth, "here is Master Jacques. Listen, Jehan," he added, in a low voice; "have a care never to speak of what you shall have seen or heard here. Hide yourself quickly under the furnace, and do not breathe."

The scholar concealed himself; just then a happy idea occurred to him.

"By the way, Brother Claude, a florin for not breathing."

"Silence! I promise."

"You must give it to me."

"Take it, then!" said the archdeacon angrily, flinging his purse at him.

Jehan darted under the furnace again, and the door opened.

Chapter V

THE TWO MEN CLOTHED IN BLACK

T HE PERSONAGE WHO ENTERED WORE A BLACK GOWN AND A GLOOMY MIEN. THE FIRST POINT which struck the eye of our Jehan (who, as the reader will readily surmise, had ensconced himself in his nook in such a manner as to enable him to see and hear everything at his good pleasure) was the perfect sadness of the garments and the visage of this newcomer. There was, nevertheless, some sweetness diffused over that face, but it was the sweetness of a cat or a judge, an affected, treacherous sweetness. He was very gray and wrinkled, and not far from his sixtieth year, his eyes blinked, his eyebrows were white, his lip pendulous, and his hands large. When Jehan saw that it was only this, that is to say, no doubt a physician or a magistrate, and that this man had a nose very far from his mouth, a sign of stupidity, he nestled down in his hole, in despair at being obliged to pass an indefinite time in such an uncomfortable attitude, and in such bad company.

The archdeacon, in the meantime, had not even risen to receive this personage. He had made the latter a sign to seat himself on a stool near the door, and, after several moments of a silence which appeared to be a continuation of a preceding meditation, he said to him in a rather patronizing way, "Good day, Master Jacques."

"Greeting, master," replied the man in black.

There was in the two ways in which "Master Jacques" was pronounced on the one hand, and the "master" by preeminence on the other, the difference between monseigneur and monsieur, between *domine* and *domne*. It was evidently the meeting of a teacher and a disciple.

"Well!" resumed the archdeacon, after a fresh silence which Master Jacques took good care not to disturb, "how are you succeeding?"

"Alas! master," said the other, with a sad smile, "I am still seeking the stone. Plenty of ashes. But not a spark of gold."

Dom Claude made a gesture of impatience. "I am not talking to you of that, Master Jacques Charmolue, but of the trial of your magician. Is it not Marc Cenaine that you call him? the butler of the Court of Accounts? Does he confess his witchcraft? Have you been successful with the torture?"

"Alas! no," replied Master Jacques, still with his sad smile; "we have not that consolation. That man is a stone; we might have him boiled in the Marché aux Pourceaux, before he would say anything. Nevertheless, we are sparing nothing for the sake of getting at the truth; he is already thoroughly dislocated, we are applying all the herbs of Saint John's day; as saith the old comedian Plautus—

> *'Advorsum stimulos, laminas, crucesque, compedesque,*
> *Nervos, catenas, carceres, numellas, pedicas, boias.'*

Nothing answers; that man is terrible. I am at my wit's end over him."

"You have found nothing new in his house?"

"I' faith, yes," said Master Jacques, fumbling in his pouch; "this parchment. There are words in it which we cannot comprehend. The criminal advocate, Monsieur Philippe Lheulier, nevertheless, knows a little Hebrew, which he learned in that matter of the Jews of the Rue Kantersten, at Brussels."

So saying, Master Jacques unrolled a parchment. "Give it here," said the archdeacon. And casting his eyes upon this writing: "Pure magic, Master Jacques!" he exclaimed. " 'Emen-Hétan!' 'Tis the cry of the vampires when they arrive at the witches' sabbath. *Per ipsum, et cum ipso, et in ipso!* 'Tis the command which chains the devil in hell. *Hax, pax, max!* that refers to medicine. A formula against the bite of mad dogs. Master Jacques! you are procurator to the king in the Ecclesiastical Courts: this parchment is abominable."

"We will put the man to the torture once more. Here again," added Master Jacques, fumbling afresh in his pouch, "is something that we have found at Marc Cenaine's house."

It was a vessel belonging to the same family as those which covered Dom Claude's furnace.

"Ah!" said the archdeacon, "a crucible for alchemy."

"I will confess to you," continued Master Jacques, with his timid and awkward smile, "that I have tried it over the furnace, but I have succeeded no better than with my own."

The archdeacon began an examination of the vessel. "What has he engraved on his crucible? *Och! och!* the word which expels fleas! That Marc Cenaine is an ignoramus! I verily believe that you will never make gold with this! 'Tis good to set in your bedroom in summer and that is all!"

"Since we are talking about errors," said the king's procurator, "I have just been studying the figures on the portal below before ascending hither; is your reverence quite sure that the opening of the work of physics is there portrayed on the side toward the Hôtel-Dieu, and that among the seven nude figures which stand at the feet of Notre-Dame, that which has wings on his heels is Mercurius?"

"Yes," replied the priest; " 'tis Augustin Nypho who writes it, that Italian doctor who had a bearded demon who acquainted him with all things. However, we will descend, and I will explain it to you with the text before us."

"Thanks, master," said Charmolue, bowing to the earth. "By the way, I was on the point of forgetting. When doth it please you that I shall apprehend the little sorceress?"

"What sorceress?"

"That gypsy girl you know, who comes every day to dance on the church square, in spite of the official's prohibition! She hath a demoniac goat with horns of the devil, which reads, which writes, which knows mathematics like Picatrix, and which would suffice to hang all Bohemia. The prosecution is all ready; 'twill soon be finished, I assure you! A pretty creature, on my soul, that dancer! The handsomest black eyes! Two Egyptian carbuncles! When shall we begin?"

The archdeacon was excessively pale.

"I will tell you that hereafter," he stammered, in a voice that was barely articulate; then he resumed with an effort, "Busy yourself with Marc Cenaine."

"Be at ease," said Charmolue with a smile; "I'll buckle him down again for you on the leather bed when I get home. But 'tis a devil of a man; he wearies even Pierrat Torterue himself, who hath hands larger than my own. As that good Plautus saith—

'Nudus vinctus, centum pondo, es quando pendes per pedes.'

The torture of the wheel and axle! 'Tis the most effectual! He shall taste it!"

Dom Claude seemed absorbed in gloomy abstraction. He turned to Charmolue—

"Master Pierrat—Master Jacques, I mean, busy yourself with Marc Cenaine."

"Yes, yes, Dom Claude. Poor man! he will have suffered like Mummol. What an idea to go to the witches' sabbath! a butler of the Court of Accounts, who ought to know Charlemagne's text; *Stryga vel masca!*—In the matter of the little girl—Smelarda, as they call her—I will await your orders. Ah! as we pass through the portal, you will explain to me also the meaning of the gardener painted in relief, which one sees as one enters the church. Is it not the Sower? Hé! master, of what are you thinking, pray?"

Dom Claude, buried in his own thoughts, no longer listened to him. Charmolue, following the direction of his glance, perceived that it was fixed mechanically on the great spider's web which draped the window. At that moment, a bewildered fly which was seeking the March sun, flung itself through the net and became entangled there. On the agitation of his web, the enormous spider made an abrupt move from his central cell, then with one bound, rushed upon the fly, which he folded together with his fore antennae, while his hideous proboscis dug into the victim's head. "Poor fly!" said the king's procurator in the ecclesiastical court; and he raised his hand to save it. The archdeacon, as though roused with a start, withheld his arm with convulsive violence.

"Master Jacques," he cried, "let fate take its course!"

The procurator wheeled round in affright; it seemed to him that pincers of iron had clutched his arm. The priest's eye was staring, wild, flaming, and remained riveted on the horrible little group of the spider and the fly.

"Oh, yes!" continued the priest, in a voice which seemed to proceed from the depths of his being, "behold here a symbol of all. She flies, she is joyous, she is just born; she seeks the spring, the open air, liberty: oh, yes! but let her come in contact with the fatal network, and the spider issues from it, the hideous spider! Poor dancer! poor, predestined fly! Let things take their course, Master Jacques, 'tis fate! Alas! Claude, thou art the spider! Claude, thou art the fly also! Thou wert flying toward learning, light, the sun. Thou hadst no other care than to reach the open air, the full daylight of eternal truth; but in precipitating thyself toward the dazzling window which opens upon the other world—upon the world of brightness, intelligence, and science—blind fly! senseless, learned man! thou hast not perceived that subtle spider's web, stretched by destiny betwixt the light and thee—thou hast flung thyself headlong into it, and now thou art struggling with head broken and mangled wings between the iron antennae of fate! Master Jacques! Master Jacques! let the spider work its will!"

"I assure you," said Charmolue, who was gazing at him without comprehending him, "that I will not touch it. But release my arm, master, for pity's sake! You have a hand like a pair of pincers."

The archdeacon did not hear him. "Oh, madman!" he went on, without removing his gaze from the window. "And even couldst thou have broken through that formidable web, with thy gnat's wings, thou believest that thou couldst have reached the light? Alas! that pane of glass which is further on, that transparent obstacle, that wall of crystal, harder than brass, which separates all philosophies from the truth, how wouldst thou have overcome it? Oh, vanity of science! how many wise men come flying from afar, to dash their heads against thee! How many systems vainly fling themselves buzzing against that eternal pane!"

He became silent. These last ideas, which had gradually led him back from himself to science, appeared to have calmed him. Jacques Charmolue recalled him wholly to a sense of reality by addressing to him this question: "Come, now, master, when will you come to aid me in making gold? I am impatient to succeed."

The archdeacon shook his head, with a bitter smile. "Master Jacques read Michel Psellus' *Dialogus de Energia et Operatione Doemonum*. What we are doing is not wholly innocent."

"Speak lower, master! I have my suspicions of it," said Jacques Charmolue. "But one must practice a bit of hermetic science when one is only procurator of the king in the ecclesiastical court, at thirty crowns tournois a year. Only speak low."

At that moment the sound of jaws in the act of mastication, which proceeded from beneath the furnace, struck Charmolue's uneasy ear.

"What's that?" he inquired.

It was the scholar, who, ill at ease, and greatly bored in his hiding-place, had succeeded in discovering there a stale crust and a triangle of moldy cheese, and had set to devouring the whole without ceremony, by way of consolation and breakfast. As he was very hungry, he made a great deal of noise, and he accented each mouthful strongly, which startled and alarmed the procurator.

" 'Tis a cat of mine," said the archdeacon, quickly, "who is regaling herself under there with a mouse."

This explanation satisfied Charmolue.

"In fact, master," he replied, with a respectful smile, "all great philosophers have their familiar animal. You know what Servius saith: *'Nullus enim locus sine genio est*—for there is no place that hath not its spirit.' "

But Dom Claude, who stood in terror of some new freak on the part of Jehan, reminded his worthy disciple that they had some figures on the façade to study together, and the two quitted the cell, to the accompaniment of a great "ouf!" from the scholar, who began to seriously fear that his knee would acquire the imprint of his chin.

Chapter VI

The Effect Which Seven Oaths in the Open Air Can Produce

"*TE DEUM LAUDAMUS!*" EXCLAIMED MASTER JEHAN, CREEPING OUT FROM HIS HOLE, "THE SCREECH-owls have departed. Och! och! Hax! pax! max! fleas! mad dogs! the devil! I have had enough of their conversation! My head is humming like a bell tower. And moldy cheese to boot! Come on! Let us descend, take the big brother's purse and convert all these coins into bottles!"

He cast a glance of tenderness and admiration into the interior of the precious pouch, readjusted his toilet, rubbed up his boots, dusted his poor half sleeves, all gray with ashes, whistled an air, indulged in a sportive pirouette, looked about to see whether there were not something more in the cell to take, gathered up here and there on the furnace some amulet in glass which might serve to bestow, in the guise of a trinket, on Isabeau la Thierrye, finally pushed open the door which his brother had left unfastened, as a last indulgence, and which he, in his turn, left open as a last piece of malice, and descended the circular staircase, skipping like a bird.

In the midst of the gloom of the spiral staircase, he elbowed something which drew aside with a growl; he took it for granted that it was Quasimodo, and it struck him as so droll that he descended the remainder of the staircase holding his sides with laughter. On emerging upon the Place, he laughed yet more heartily.

He stamped his foot when he found himself on the ground once again. "Oh!" said he, "good and honorable pavement of Paris, cursed staircase, fit to put the angels of Jacob's ladder out of breath! What was I thinking of to thrust myself into that stone gimlet which pierces the sky; all for the sake of eating bearded cheese, and looking at the bell towers of Paris through a hole in the wall!"

He advanced a few paces, and caught sight of the two screech-owls, that is to say, Dom Claude and Master Jacques Charmolue, absorbed in contemplation before a carving on the façade. He approached them on tiptoe, and heard the archdeacon say in a low tone to Charmolue: " 'Twas Guillaume de Paris who caused a Job to be carved upon this stone of the hue of lapis-lazuli, gilded on the edges. Job represents the philosopher's stone, which must also be tried and martyrized in order to become perfect, as saith Raymond Lulle: *Sub conservatione formoe specificoe salva anima.*"

"That makes no difference to me," said Jehan, " 'tis I who have the purse."

At that moment he heard a powerful and sonorous voice articulate behind him a formidable series of oaths. "*Sang Dieu! Ventre-Dieu! Bédieu! Corps de Dieu! Nombril de Belzébuth! Nom d'un pape! Corne et tonnerre.*"

"Upon my soul!" exclaimed Jehan, "that can only be my friend, Captain Phœbus!"

This name of Phœbus reached the ears of the archdeacon at the moment when he was explaining to the king's procurator the dragon which is hiding its tail in a bath, from which issue smoke and the head of a king. Dom Claude started, interrupted himself and, to the great amazement of Charmolue, turned round and beheld his brother Jehan accosting a tall officer at the door of the Gondelaurier mansion.

It was, in fact, Captain Phœbus de Châteaupers. He was backed up against a corner of the house of his betrothed and swearing like a heathen.

"By my faith! Captain Phœbus," said Jehan, taking him by the hand, "you are cursing with admirable vigor."

"Horns and thunder!" replied the captain.

"Horns and thunder yourself!" replied the student. "Come now, fair captain, whence comes this overflow of fine words?"

"Pardon me, good comrade Jehan," exclaimed Phœbus, shaking his hand, "a horse going at a gallop cannot halt short. Now, I was swearing at a hard gallop. I have just been with those prudes, and when I come forth, I always find my throat full of curses, I must spit them out or strangle, *ventre et tonnerre!*"

"Will you come and drink?" asked the scholar.

This proposition calmed the captain.

"I'm willing, but I have no money."

"But I have!"

"Bah! let's see it!"

Jehan spread out the purse before the captain's eyes, with dignity and simplicity. Meanwhile, the archdeacon, who had abandoned the dumbfounded Charmolue where he stood, had approached them and halted a few paces distant, watching them without their noticing him, so deeply were they absorbed in contemplation of the purse.

Phœbus exclaimed: "A purse in your pocket, Jehan! 'tis the moon in a bucket of water, one sees it there but 'tis not there. There is nothing but its shadow. Pardieu! let us wager that these are pebbles!"

Jehan replied coldly: "Here are the pebbles wherewith I pave my fob!"

And without adding another word, he emptied the purse on a neighboring post, with the air of a Roman saving his country.

"True God!" muttered Phœbus, "targes, big-blanks, little blanks, mailles, every two worth one of Tournay, farthings of Paris, real eagle liards! 'Tis dazzling!"

Jehan remained dignified and immovable. Several liards had rolled into the mud; the captain in his enthusiasm stooped to pick them up. Jehan restrained him.

"Fye, Captain Phœbus de Châteaupers!"

Phœbus counted the coins, and turning toward Jehan with solemnity, "Do you know, Jehan, that there are three and twenty sous parisis! whom have you plundered to-night, in the Street Cut-Weazand?"

Jehan flung back his blonde and curly head, and said, half-closing his eyes disdainfully—

"We have a brother who is an archdeacon and a fool."

"*Corne de Dieu!*" exclaimed Phœbus, "the worthy man!"

"Let us go and drink," said Jehan.

"Where shall we go?" said Phœbus; " 'To Eve's Apple.' "

"No, captain, to 'Ancient Science.' An old woman sawing a basket handle; 'tis a rebus, and I like that."

"A plague on rebuses, Jehan! the wine is better at 'Eve's Apple'; and then, beside the door there is a vine in the sun which cheers me while I am drinking."

"Well! here goes for Eve and her apple," said the student, and taking Phœbus's arm. "By the way, my dear captain, you just mentioned the Rue Coupe-Gueule.[1] That is a very bad form of speech; people are no longer so barbarous. They say, Coupe-Gorge."[2]

The two friends set out toward "Eve's Apple." It is unnecessary to mention that they had first gathered up the money, and that the archdeacon followed them.

The archdeacon followed them, gloomy and haggard. Was this the Phœbus whose accursed name had been mingled with all his thoughts ever since his interview with Gringoire? He did not know it, but it was at least a Phœbus, and that magic name sufficed to make the archdeacon follow the two heedless comrades with the stealthy tread of a wolf, listening to their words and observing their slightest gestures with anxious attention. Moreover, nothing was easier than to hear everything they said, as they talked loudly, not in the least concerned that the passers-by were taken into their confidence. They talked of duels, wenches, wine pots, and folly.

At the turning of a street, the sound of a tambourine reached them from a neighboring square. Dom Claude heard the officer say to the scholar—

"Thunder! Let us hasten our steps!"

"Why, Phœbus?"

"I'm afraid lest the Bohemian should see me."

"What Bohemian?"

"The little girl with the goat."

"La Smeralda?"

"That's it, Jehan. I always forget her devil of a name. Let us make haste, she will recognize me. I don't want to have that girl accost me in the street."

"Do you know her, Phœbus?"

Here the archdeacon saw Phœbus sneer, bend down to Jehan's ear, and say a few words to him in a low voice; then Phœbus burst into a laugh, and shook his head with a triumphant air.

"Truly?" said Jehan.

"Upon my soul!" said Phœbus.

"This evening?"

"This evening."

"Are you sure that she will come?"

"Are you a fool, Jehan? Does one doubt such things?"

"Captain Phœbus, you are a happy gendarme!"

The archdeacon heard the whole of this conversation. His teeth chattered; a visible shiver ran through his whole body. He halted for a moment, leaned against a post like a drunken man, then followed the two merry knaves.

At the moment when he overtook them once more, they had changed their conversation. He heard them singing at the top of their lungs the ancient refrain—

> Les enfants des Petits-Carreaux
> Se font pendre comme des veaux.[3]

1. Cut-Weazand Street.

2. Cut-Throat Street.

3. The children of the Petits Carreaux let themselves be hung like calves.

Chapter VII

THE MYSTERIOUS MONK

THE ILLUSTRIOUS WINE-SHOP OF "EVE'S APPLE" WAS SITUATED IN THE UNIVERSITY, AT THE COR-ner of the Rue de la Rondelle and the Rue de la Bâtonnier. It was a very spacious and very low hall on the ground floor, with a vaulted ceiling whose central spring rested upon a huge pillar of wood painted yellow; tables everywhere, shining pewter jugs hanging on the walls, always a large number of drinkers, a plenty of wenches, a window on the street, a vine at the door, and over the door a flaring piece of sheet-iron, painted with an apple and a woman, rusted by the rain and turning with the wind on an iron pin. This species of weather-vane which looked upon the pavement was the signboard.

Night was falling; the square was dark; the wine-shop, full of candles, flamed afar like a forge in the gloom; the noise of glasses and feasting, of oaths and quarrels, which escaped through the broken panes, was audible. Through the mist which the warmth of the room spread over the window in front, a hundred confused figures could be seen swarming, and from time to time a burst of noisy laughter broke forth from it. The passers-by who were going about their business, slipped past this tumultuous window without glancing at it. Only at intervals did some little ragged boy raise himself on tiptoe as far as the ledge, and hurl into the drinking-shop, that ancient, jeering hoot, with which drunken men were then pursued: "Aux Houls, saouls, saouls, saouls!"

Nevertheless, one man paced imperturbably back and forth in front of the tavern, gazing at it incessantly, and going no further from it than a pikeman from his sentry-box. He was enveloped in a mantle to his very nose. This mantle he had just purchased of the old-clothes man, in the vicinity of the "Eve's Apple," no doubt to protect himself from the cold of the March evening, possibly also, to conceal his costume. From time to time he paused in front of the dim window with its leaden lattice, listened, looked, and stamped his foot.

At length the door of the dram-shop opened. This was what he appeared to be waiting for. Two boon companions came forth. The ray of light which escaped from the door crimsoned for a moment their jovial faces.

The man in the mantle went and stationed himself on the watch under a porch on the other side of the street.

"*Corne et tonnerre!*" said one of the comrades. "Seven o'clock is on the point of striking. 'Tis the hour of my appointed meeting."

"I tell you," repeated his companion, with a thick tongue, "that I don't live in the Rue des Mauvaises Paroles, *indignus qui inter mala verba habitat*. I have a lodging in the Rue Jean-Pain-Mollet, *in vico Johannis Pain-Mollet*. You are more horned than a unicorn if you assert the contrary. Everyone knows that he who once mounts astride a bear is never after afraid; but you have a nose turned to dainties like Saint-Jacques of the hospital."

"Jehan, my friend, you are drunk," said the other.

The other replied staggering, "It pleases you to say so, Phœbus; but it hath been proved that Plato had the profile of a hound."

The reader has, no doubt, already recognized our two brave friends, the captain and the scholar. It appears that the man who was lying in wait for them had also recognized them, for he slowly followed all the zigzags that the scholar caused the captain to make, who being a more hardened drinker had retained all his self-possession. By listening to them attentively, the man in the mantle could catch in its entirety the following interesting conversation—

"*Corbacque!* Do try to walk straight, master bachelor; you know that I must leave you. Here it is seven o'clock. I have an appointment with a woman."

"Leave me then! I see stars and lances of fire. You are like the Chateau de Dampmartin, which is bursting with laughter."

"By the warts of my grandmother, Jehan, you are raving with too much rabidness. By the way, Jehan, have you any money left?"

"Monsieur Rector, there is no mistake; the little butcher's shop, *parva boucheria.*"

"Jehan! my friend Jehan! You know that I made an appointment with that little girl at the end of the Pont Saint-Michel, and I can only take her to the Falourdel's, the old crone of the bridge, and that I must pay for a chamber. The old witch with a white moustache would not trust me. Jehan! for pity's sake! Have we drunk up the whole of the curé's purse? Have you not a single parisis left?"

"The consciousness of having spent the other hours well is a just and savory condiment for the table."

"Belly and guts! a truce to your whimsical nonsense! Tell me, Jehan of the devil! have you any money left? Give it to me, *bédieu!* or I will search you, were you as leprous as Job, and as scabby as Cæsar!"

"Monsieur, the Rue Galiache is a street which hath at one end the Rue de la Verrerie, and at the other the Rue de la Tixeranderie."

"Well, yes! my good friend Jehan, my poor comrade, the Rue Galiache is good, very good. But in the name of heaven collect your wits. I must have a sou parisis, and the appointment is for seven o'clock."

"Silence for the rondo, and attention to the refrain—

> *"Quand les rats mangeront les cas,*
> *Le roi sera seigneur d'Arras;*
> *Quand la mer, qui est grande et lée*
> *Sera à la Saint-Jean gelée,*
> *On verra, par-dessus la glace,*
> *Sortir ceux d'Arras de leur place."*[1]

"Well, scholar of Antichrist, may you be strangled with the entrails of your mother!" exclaimed Phœbus, and he gave the drunken scholar a rough push; the latter slipped against the wall, and slid flabbily to the pavement of Philip Augustus. A remnant of fraternal pity, which never abandons the heart of a drinker, prompted Phœbus to roll Jehan with his foot upon one of those pillows of the poor, which Providence keeps in readiness at the corner of all the street posts of Paris, and which the rich blight with the name of "a rubbish-heap." The captain adjusted Jehan's head upon an inclined plane of cabbage-stumps, and on the very instant, the scholar fell to snoring in a magnificent bass. Meanwhile, all malice was not extinguished in the captain's heart. "So much the worse if the devil's cart picks you up on its passage!" he said to the poor, sleeping clerk; and he strode off.

The man in the mantle, who had not ceased to follow him, halted for a moment before the prostrate scholar, as though agitated by indecision; then, uttering a profound sigh, he also strode off in pursuit of the captain.

We, like them, will leave Jehan to slumber beneath the open sky, and will follow them also, if it pleases the reader.

On emerging into the Rue Saint-André-des-Arcs, Captain Phœbus perceived that someone

---

1. When the rats eat the cats, the king will be lord of Arras; when the sea which is great and wide, is frozen over at St. John's tide, men will see across the ice, those who dwell in Arras quit their place.

was following him. On glancing sideways by chance, he perceived a sort of shadow crawling after him along the walls. He halted, it halted; he resumed his march, it resumed its march. This disturbed him not overmuch. "Ah, bah!" he said to himself, "I have not a sou."

He paused in front of the College d'Autun. It was at this college that he had sketched out what he called his studies, and, through a scholar's teasing habit which still lingered in him, he never passed the façade without inflicting on the statue of Cardinal Pierre Bertrand, sculptured to the right of the portal, the affront of which Priapus complains so bitterly in the satire of Horace, *Olim truncus eram ficulnus*. He had done this with so much unrelenting animosity that the inscription, *Eduensis episcopus*, had become almost effaced. Therefore, he halted before the statue according to his wont. The street was utterly deserted. At the moment when he was coolly retying his shoulder knots, with his nose in the air, he saw the shadow approaching him with slow steps, so slow that he had ample time to observe that this shadow wore a cloak and a hat. On arriving near him, it halted and remained more motionless than the statue of Cardinal Bertrand. Meanwhile, it riveted upon Phœbus two intent eyes, full of that vague light which issues in the night time from the pupils of a cat.

The captain was brave, and would have cared very little for a highwayman, with a rapier in his hand. But this walking statue, this petrified man, froze his blood. There were then in circulation, strange stories of a surly monk, a nocturnal prowler about the streets of Paris, and they recurred confusedly to his memory. He remained for several minutes in stupefaction, and finally broke the silence with a forced laugh.

"Monsieur, if you are a robber, as I hope you are, you produce upon me the effect of a heron attacking a nutshell. I am the son of a ruined family, my dear fellow. Try your hand nearby here. In the chapel of this college there is some wood of the true cross set in silver."

The hand of the shadow emerged from beneath its mantle and descended upon the arm of Phœbus with the grip of an eagle's talon; at the same time the shadow spoke—

"Captain Phœbus de Châteaupers!"

What, the devil!" said Phœbus, "you know my name!"

"I know not your name alone," continued the man in the mantle, with his sepulchral voice. "You have a *rendezvous* this evening."

"Yes," replied Phœbus in amazement.

"At seven o'clock."

"In a quarter of an hour."

"At la Falourdel's."

"Precisely."

"The lewd hag of the Pont Saint-Michel."

"Of Saint Michel the archangel, as the Pater Noster saith."

"Impious wretch!" muttered the specter. "With a woman?"

"*Confiteor*—I confess—."

"Who is called—?"

"La Smeralda," said Phœbus, gaily. All his heedlessness had gradually returned.

At this name, the shadow's grasp shook the arm of Phœbus in a fury.

"Captain Phœbus de Châteaupers, thou liest!"

Anyone who could have beheld at that moment the captain's inflamed countenance, his leap backwards, so violent that he disengaged himself from the grip which held him, the proud air with which he clapped his hand on his sword-hilt, and, in the presence of this wrath the gloomy immobility of the man in the cloak—anyone who could have beheld this would have been frightened. There was in it a touch of the combat of Don Juan and the statue.

"Christ and Satan!" exclaimed the captain. "That is a word which rarely strikes the ear of a Châteaupers! Thou wilt not dare repeat it."

"Thou liest!" said the shadow coldly.

The captain gnashed his teeth. Surly monk, phantom, superstitions—he had forgotten all at that moment. He no longer beheld anything but a man, and an insult.

"Ah! this is well!" he stammered, in a voice stifled with rage. He drew his sword, then stammering, for anger as well as fear makes a man tremble:—"Here! On the spot! Come on! Swords! Swords! Blood on the pavement!"

But the other never stirred. When he beheld his adversary on guard and ready to parry—

"Captain Phœbus," he said, and his tone vibrated with bitterness, "you forget your appointment."

The rages of men like Phœbus are milk-soups, whose ebullition is calmed by a drop of cold water. This simple remark caused the sword which glittered in the captain's hand to be lowered.

"Captain," pursued the man, "to-morrow, the day after to-morrow, a month hence, ten years hence, you will find me ready to cut your throat; but go first to your rendezvous."

"In sooth," said Phœbus, as though seeking to capitulate with himself, "these are two charming things to be encountered in a rendezvous—a sword and a wench; but I do not see why I should miss the one for the sake of the other, when I can have both."

He replaced his sword in its scabbard.

"Go to your rendezvous," said the man.

"Monsieur," replied Phœbus with some embarrassment, "many thanks for your courtesy. In fact, there will be ample time to-morrow for us to chop up father Adam's doublet into slashes and buttonholes. I am obliged to you for allowing me to pass one more agreeable quarter of an hour. I certainly did hope to put you in the gutter, and still arrive in time for the fair one, especially as it has a better appearance to make the women wait a little in such cases. But you strike me as having the air of a gallant man, and it is safer to defer our affair until to-morrow. So I will betake myself to my rendezvous; it is for seven o'clock, as you know." Here Phœbus scratched his ear. "Ah. *Corne Dieu!* I had forgotten! I haven't a sou to discharge the price of the garret, and the old crone will insist on being paid in advance. She distrusts me."

"Here is the wherewithal to pay."

Phœbus felt the stranger's cold hand slip into his a large piece of money. He could not refrain from taking the money and pressing the hand.

"*Vrai Dieu!*" he exclaimed, "you are a good fellow!"

"One condition," said the man. "Prove to me that I have been wrong and that you were speaking the truth. Hide me in some corner whence I can see whether this woman is really the one whose name you uttered."

"Oh!" replied Phœbus, " 'tis all one to me. We will take the Sainte-Marthe chamber; you can look at your ease from the kennel hard by."

"Come then," said the shadow.

"At your service," said the captain, "I know not whether you are Messer Diavolus in person; but let us be good friends for this evening; to-morrow I will repay you all my debts, both of purse and sword."

They set out again at a rapid pace. At the expiration of a few minutes, the sound of the river announced to them that they were on the Pont Saint-Michel, then loaded with houses.

"I will first show you the way," said Phœbus to his companion, "I will then go in search of the fair one who is awaiting me near the Petit-Châtelet."

His companion made no reply; he had not uttered a word since they had been walking side by side. Phœbus halted before a low door, and knocked roughly; a light made its appearance through the cracks of the door.

"Who is there?" cried a toothless voice.

"*Corps-Dieu! Tête-Dieu! Ventre-Dieu!*" replied the captain.

The door opened instantly, and allowed the newcomers to see an old woman and an old lamp, both of which trembled. The old woman was bent double, clad in tatters, with a shaking head, pierced with two small eyes, and coiffed with a dish clout; wrinkled everywhere, on hands and face and neck; her lips retreated under her gums, and about her mouth she had tufts of white hairs which gave her the whiskered look of a cat.

The interior of the den was no less dilapitated than she; there were chalk walls, blackened beams in the ceiling, a dismantled chimney-piece, spiders' webs in all the corners, in the middle a staggering herd of tables and lame stools, a dirty child among the ashes, and at the back a staircase, or rather, a wooden ladder, which ended in a trapdoor in the ceiling.

On entering this lair, Phœbus's mysterious companion raised his mantle to his very eyes. Meanwhile, the captain, swearing like a Saracen, hastened to "make the sun shine in a crown" as saith our admirable Régnier.

"The Sainte-Marthe chamber," said he.

The old woman addressed him as monseigneur, and shut up the crown in a drawer. It was the coin which the man in the black mantle had given to Phœbus. While her back was turned, the bushy-headed and ragged little boy who was playing in the ashes, adroitly approached the drawer, abstracted the crown, and put in its place a dry leaf which he had plucked from a fagot.

The old crone made a sign to the two gentlemen, as she called them, to follow her, and mounted the ladder in advance of them. On arriving at the upper story, she set her lamp on a coffer, and, Phœbus, like a frequent visitor of the house, opened a door which opened on a dark hole. "Enter here, my dear fellow," he said to his companion. The man in the mantle obeyed without a word in reply, the door closed upon him; he heard Phœbus bolt it, and a moment later descend the stairs again with the aged hag. The light had disappeared.

Chapter VIII

THE UTILITY OF WINDOWS WHICH OPEN ON THE RIVER

CLAUDE FROLLO (FOR WE PRESUME THAT THE READER, MORE INTELLIGENT THAN PHŒBUS, HAS seen in this whole adventure no other surly monk than the archdeacon), Claude Frollo groped about for several moments in the dark lair into which the captain had bolted him. It was one of those nooks which architects sometimes reserve at the point of junction between the roof and the supporting wall. A vertical section of this kennel, as Phœbus had so justly styled it, would have made a triangle. Moreover, there was neither window nor air-hole, and the slope of the roof prevented one from standing upright. Accordingly, Claude crouched down in the dust, and the plaster which cracked beneath him; his head was on fire; rummaging around him with his hands, he found on the floor a bit of broken glass, which he pressed to his brow, and whose coolness afforded him some relief.

What was taking place at that moment in the gloomy soul of the archdeacon? God and himself could alone know.

In what order was he arranging in his mind la Esmeralda, Phœbus, Jacques Charmolue, his young brother so beloved, yet abandoned by him in the mire, his archdeacon's cassock, his reputation perhaps dragged to la Falourdel's, all these adventures, all these images? I cannot say. But it is certain that these ideas formed in his mind a horrible group.

He had been waiting a quarter of an hour; it seemed to him that he had grown a century older. All at once he heard the creaking of the boards of the stairway; someone was ascending. The trapdoor opened once more; a light reappeared. There was a tolerably large crack in the wormeaten door of his den; he put his face to it. In this manner he could see all that went on in the adjoining room. The cat-faced old crone was the first to emerge from the trapdoor, lamp in hand; then Phœbus, twirling his moustache, then a third person, that beautiful and graceful figure, la Esmeralda. The priest beheld her rise from below like a dazzling apparition. Claude trembled, a cloud spread over his eyes, his pulses beat violently, everything rustled and whirled around him; he no longer saw nor heard anything.

When he recovered himself, Phœbus and Esmeralda were alone seated on the wooden coffer beside the lamp which made these two youthful figures and a miserable pallet at the end of the attic stand out plainly before the archdeacon's eyes.

Beside the pallet was a window, whose panes broken like a spider's web upon which rain has fallen, allowed a view, through its rent meshes, of a corner of the sky, and the moon lying far away on an eiderdown bed of soft clouds.

The young girl was blushing, confused, palpitating. Her long, drooping lashes shaded her crimson cheeks. The officer, to whom she dared not lift her eyes, was radiant. Mechanically, and with a charmingly unconscious gesture, she traced with the tip of her finger incoherent lines on the bench, and watched her finger. Her foot was not visible. The little goat was nestling upon it.

The captain was very gallantly clad; he had tufts of embroidery at his neck and wrists; a great elegance at that day.

It was not without difficulty that Dom Claude managed to hear what they were saying, through the humming of the blood, which was boiling in his temples.

(A conversation between lovers is a very commonplace affair. It is a perpetual "I love you." A musical phrase which is very insipid and very bald for indifferent listeners, when it is not ornamented with some *fioriture*; but Claude was not an indifferent listener.)

"Oh!" said the young girl, without raising her eyes, "do not despise me, monseigneur Phœbus. I feel that what I am doing is not right."

"Despise you, my pretty child!" replied the officer with an air of superior and distinguished gallantry, "despise you, *tête-Dieu!* and why?"

"For having followed you!"

"On that point, my beauty, we don't agree. I ought not to despise you, but to hate you."

The young girl looked at him in affright: "Hate me! what have I done?"

"For having required so much urging."

"Alas!" said she, " 'tis because I am breaking a vow. I shall not find my parents! The amulet will lose its virtue. But what matters it? What need have I of father or mother now?"

So saying, she fixed upon the captain her great black eyes, moist with joy and tenderness.

"Devil take me if I understand you!" exclaimed Phœbus.

La Esmeralda remained silent for a moment, then a tear dropped from her eyes, a sigh from her lips, and she said—"Oh! monseigneur, I love you."

Such a perfume of chastity, such a charm of virtue surrounded the young girl, that Phœbus did not feel completely at his ease beside her. But this remark emboldened him: "You love me!" he said with rapture, and he threw his arm round the gypsy's waist. He had only been waiting for this opportunity.

The priest saw it, and tested with the tip of his finger the point of a poniard which he wore concealed in his breast.

"Phœbus," continued the Bohemian, gently releasing her waist from the captain's tenacious hands, "You are good, you are generous, you are handsome; you saved me, me who am only a poor child lost in Bohemia. I had long been dreaming of an officer who should save my life. 'Twas of you that I was dreaming, before I knew you, my Phœbus; the officer of my dream had a beautiful uniform like yours, a grand look, a sword; your name is Phœbus; 'tis a beautiful name. I love your name; I love your sword. Draw your sword, Phœbus, that I may see it."

"Child!" said the captain, and he unsheathed his sword with a smile.

The gypsy looked at the hilt, the blade; examined the cipher on the guard with adorable curiosity, and kissed the sword, saying—

"You are the sword of a brave man. I love my captain."

Phœbus again profited by the opportunity to impress upon her beautiful bent neck a kiss which made the young girl straighten herself up as scarlet as a poppy. The priest gnashed his teeth over it in the dark.

"Phœbus," resumed the gypsy, "let me talk to you. Pray walk a little, that I may see you at full height, and that I may hear your spurs jingle. How handsome you are!"

The captain rose to please her, chiding her with a smile of satisfaction—

"What a child you are! By the way, my charmer, have you seen me in my archer's ceremonial doublet?"

"Alas! no," she replied.

"It is very handsome!"

Phœbus returned and seated himself beside her, but much closer than before.

"Listen, my dear—"

The gypsy gave him several little taps with her pretty hand on his mouth, with a childish mirth and grace and gaiety.

"No, no, I will not listen to you. Do you love me? I want you to tell me whether you love me."

"Do I love thee, angel of my life!" exclaimed the captain, half kneeling. "My body, my blood, my soul, all are thine; all are for thee. I love thee, and I have never loved anyone but thee."

The captain had repeated this phrase so many times, in many similar conjunctures, that he delivered it all in one breath, without committing a single mistake. At this passionate declaration, the gypsy raised to the dirty ceiling which served for the skies a glance full of angelic happiness.

"Oh!" she murmured, "this is the moment when one should die!"

Phœbus found "the moment" favorable for robbing her of another kiss, which went to torture the unhappy archdeacon in his nook. "Die!" exclaimed the amorous captain, "What are you saying, my lovely angel? 'Tis a time for living, or Jupiter is only a scamp! Die at the beginning of so sweet a thing! *Corne-de-boeuf*, what a jest! It is not that. Listen, my dear Similar, Esmenarda—Pardon! you have so prodigiously Saracen a name that I never can get it straight. 'Tis a thicket which stops me short."

"Good heavens!" said the poor girl, "and I thought my name pretty because of its singularity! But since it displeases you, I would that I were called Goton."

"Ah! do not weep for such a trifle, my graceful maid! 'tis a name to which one must get accustomed, that is all. When I once know it by heart, all will go smoothly. Listen then, my dear Similar; I adore you passionately. I love you so that 'tis simply miraculous. I know a girl who is bursting with rage over it—"

The jealous girl interrupted him: "Who?"

"What matters that to us?" said Phœbus; "do you love me?"

"Oh!"—said she.

"Well! that is all. You shall see how I love you also. May the great devil Neptunus spear me if I do not make you the happiest woman in the world. We will have a pretty little house somewhere. I will make my archers parade before your windows. They are all mounted, and set at defiance those of Captain Mignon. There are *voulgiers*, *cranequiniers* and hand *couleveiniers*.[1] I will take you to the great sights of the Parisians at the store-house of Rully. Eighty thousand armed men, thirty thousand white harnesses, short coats or coats of mail; the sixty-seven banners of the trades; the standards of the parliaments, of the chamber of accounts, of the treasury of the generals, of the aides of the mint; a devilish fine array, in short! I will conduct you to see the lions of the Hôtel du Roi, which are wild beasts. All women love that."

1. Varieties of the crossbow.

For several moments the young girl, absorbed in her charming thoughts, was dreaming to the sound of his voice, without listening to the sense of his words.

"Oh! how happy you will be!" continued the captain, and at the same time he gently unbuckled the gypsy's girdle.

"What are you doing?" she said quickly. This "act of violence" had roused her from her reverie.

"Nothing," replied Phœbus, "I was only saying that you must abandon all this garb of folly, and the street corner when you are with me."

"When I am with you, Phœbus!" said the young girl tenderly.

She became pensive and silent once more.

The captain, emboldened by her gentleness, clasped her waist without resistance; then began softly to unlace the poor child's corsage, and disarranged her tucker to such an extent that the panting priest beheld the gypsy's beautiful shoulder emerge from the gauze, as round and brown as the moon rising through the mists of the horizon.

The young girl allowed Phœbus to have his way. She did not appear to perceive it. The eye of the bold captain flashed.

Suddenly she turned toward him—

"Phœbus," she said, with an expression of infinite love, "instruct me in thy religion."

"My religion!" exclaimed the captain, bursting with laughter, "I instruct you in my religion! *Corne et tonnerre!* What do you want with my religion?"

"In order that we may be married," she replied.

The captain's face assumed an expression of mingled surprise and disdain, of carelessness and libertine passion.

"Ah, bah!" said he, "do people marry?"

The Bohemian turned pale, and her head drooped sadly on her breast.

"My beautiful love," resumed Phœbus, tenderly, "what nonsense is this? A great thing is marriage, truly! one is none the less loving for not having spit Latin into a priest's shop!"

While speaking thus in his softest voice, he approached extremely near the gypsy; his caressing hands resumed their place around her supple and delicate waist, his eye flashed more and more, and everything announced that Monsieur Phœbus was on the verge of one of those moments when Jupiter himself commits so many follies that Homer is obliged to summon a cloud to his rescue.

But Dom Claude saw everything. The door was made of thoroughly rotten cask staves, which left large apertures for the passage of his hawklike gaze. This brown-skinned, broad-shouldered priest, hitherto condemned to the austere virginity of the cloister, was quivering and boiling in the presence of this night scene of love and voluptuousness. This young and beautiful girl given over in disarray to the ardent young man, made melted lead flow in his veins; his eyes darted with sensual jealousy beneath all those loosened pins. Anyone who could, at that moment, have seen the face of the unhappy man glued to the wormeaten bars, would have thought that he beheld the face of a tiger glaring from the depths of a cage at some jackal devouring a gazelle. His eye shone like a candle through the cracks of the door.

All at once, Phœbus, with a rapid gesture, removed the gypsy's gorgerette. The poor child, who had remained pale and dreamy, awoke with a start; she recoiled hastily from the enterprising officer, and, casting a glance at her bare neck and shoulders, red, confused, mute with shame, she crossed her two beautiful arms on her breast to conceal it. Had it not been for the flame which burned in her cheeks, at the sight of her so silent and motionless, one would have declared her a statue of Modesty. Her eyes were lowered.

But the captain's gesture had revealed the mysterious amulet which she wore about her neck.

"What is that?" he said, seizing this pretext to approach once more the beautiful creature whom he had just alarmed.

"Don't touch it!" she replied, quickly, " 'tis my guardian. It will make me find my family again, if I remain worthy to do so. Oh, leave me, monsieur le capitaine! My mother! My poor mother! My mother! Where art thou? Come to my rescue! Have pity, Monsieur Phœbus, give me back my gorgerette!"

Phœbus retreated and said in a cold tone—

"Oh, mademoiselle! I see plainly that you do not love me!"

"I do not love him!" exclaimed the unhappy child, and at the same time she clung to the captain, whom she drew to a seat beside her. "I do not love thee, my Phœbus? What art thou saying, wicked man, to break my heart? Oh, take me! take all! do what you will with me, I am thine. What matters to me the amulet! What matters to me my mother! 'Tis thou who art my mother since I love thee! Phœbus, my beloved Phœbus, dost thou see me? 'Tis I. Look at me; 'tis the little one whom thou wilt surely not repulse, who comes, who comes herself to seek thee. My soul, my life, my body, my person, all is one thing—which is thine, my captain. Well, no! We will not marry, since that displeases thee; and then, what am I? a miserable girl of the gutters; whilst thou, my Phœbus, art a gentleman. A fine thing, truly! A dancer wed an officer! I was mad. No, Phœbus, no; I will be thy mistress, thy amusement, thy pleasure, when thou wilt; a girl who shall belong to thee. I was only made for that, soiled, despised, dishonored, but what matters it?—beloved. I shall be the proudest and the most joyous of women. And when I grow old or ugly, Phœbus, when I am no longer good to love you, you will suffer me to serve you still. Others will embroider scarfs for you; 'tis I, the servant, who will care for them. You will let me polish your spurs, brush your doublet, dust your riding-boots. You will have that pity, will you not, Phœbus? Meanwhile, take me! here, Phœbus, all this belongs to thee, only love me! We gypsies need only air and love."

So saying, she threw her arms round the officer's neck; she looked up at him, supplicatingly, with a beautiful smile, and all in tears. Her delicate neck rubbed against his cloth doublet with its rough embroideries. She writhed on her knees, her beautiful body half naked. The intoxicated captain pressed his ardent lips to those lovely African shoulders. The young girl, her eyes bent on the ceiling, as she leaned backwards, quivered, all palpitating, beneath this kiss.

All at once, above Phœbus's head she beheld another head; a green, livid, convulsed face, with the look of a lost soul; near this face was a hand grasping a poniard. It was the face and hand of the priest; he had broken the door and he was there. Phœbus could not see him. The young girl remained motionless, frozen with terror, dumb, beneath that terrible apparition, like a dove which should raise its head at the moment when the hawk is gazing into her nest with its round eyes.

She could not even utter a cry. She saw the poniard descend upon Phœbus, and rise again, reeking.

"Maledictions!" said the captain, and fell.

She fainted.

At the moment when her eyes closed, when all feeling vanished in her, she thought that she felt a touch of fire imprinted upon her lips, a kiss more burning than the red-hot iron of the executioner.

When she recovered her senses, she was surrounded by soldiers of the watch, they were carrying away the captain, bathed in his blood, the priest had disappeared; the window at the back of the room which opened on the river was wide open; they picked up a cloak which they supposed to belong to the officer, and she heard them saying around her—

" 'Tis a sorceress, who has stabbed a captain."

BOOK EIGHTH

Chapter I

THE CROWN CHANGED INTO A DRY LEAF

G RINGOIRE AND THE ENTIRE COURT OF MIRACLES WERE SUFFERING MORTAL ANXIETY. FOR A whole month they had not known what had become of la Esmeralda, which greatly pained the Duke of Egypt and his friends the vagabonds, nor what had become of the goat, which redoubled Gringoire's grief. One evening the gypsy had disappeared, and since that time had given no signs of life. All search had proved fruitless. Some tormenting bootblacks had told Gringoire about meeting her that same evening near the Pont Saint-Michel, going off with an officer; but this husband, after the fashion of Bohemia, was an incredulous philosopher, and besides, he, better than anyone else, knew to what a point his wife was virginal. He had been able to form a judgment as to the unconquerable modesty resulting from the combined virtues of the amulet and the gypsy, and he had mathematically calculated the resistance of that chastity to the second power. Accordingly, he was at ease on that score.

Still he could not understand this disappearance. It was a profound sorrow. He would have grown thin over it, had that been possible. He had forgotten everything, even his literary tastes, even his great work, *De figuris regularibus et irregularibus,* which it was his intention to have printed with the first money which he should procure (for he had raved over printing, ever since he had seen the "Didascalon" of Hugues de Saint Victor, printed with the celebrated characters of Vindelin de Spire).

One day, as he was passing sadly before the criminal Tournelle, he perceived a considerable crowd at one of the gates of the Palais de Justice.

"What is this?" he inquired of a young man who was coming out.

"I know not, sir," replied the young man. " 'Tis said that they are trying a woman who hath assassinated a gendarme. It appears that there is sorcery at the bottom of it, the archbishop and the official have intervened in the case, and my brother, who is the archdeacon of Josas, can think of nothing else. Now, I wished to speak with him, but I have not been able to reach him because of the throng, which vexes me greatly, as I stand in need of money."

"Alas! sir," said Gringoire, "I would that I could lend you some, but my breeches are worn to holes, and 'tis not crowns which have done it."

He dared not tell the young man that he was acquainted with his brother the archdeacon, to whom he had not returned after the scene in the church; a negligence which embarrassed him.

The scholar went his way, and Gringoire set out to follow the crowd which was mounting the staircase of the great chamber. In his opinion, there was nothing like the spectacle of a criminal process for dissipating melancholy, so exhilaratingly stupid are judges as a rule. The populace which he had joined walked and elbowed in silence. After a slow and tiresome march through a long, gloomy corridor, which wound through the court-house like the intestinal canal of the ancient edifice, he arrived near a low door, opening upon a hall which his lofty stature permitted him to survey with a glance over the waving heads of the rabble.

The hall was vast and gloomy, which latter fact made it appear still more spacious. The day was declining; the long, pointed windows permitted only a pale ray of light to enter, which was extinguished before it reached the vaulted ceiling, an enormous trellis-work of sculptured beams, whose thousand figures seemed to move confusedly in the shadows, many candles were already lighted here and there on tables, and beaming on the heads of clerks buried in masses of documents. The anterior portion of the hall was occupied by the crowd; on the right and left were magistrates and tables; at the end, upon a platform, a number of judges, whose rear rank sank into the shadows, sinister and motionless faces. The walls were sown with innumerable fleurs-de-lys. A large figure of Christ might be vaguely descried above the judges, and everywhere there were pikes and halberds, upon whose points the reflection of the candles placed tips of fire.

"Monsieur," Gringoire inquired of one of his neighbors, "who are all those persons ranged yonder, like prelates in council?"

"Monsieur," replied the neighbor, "those on the right are the counselors of the grand chamber; those on the left, the councilors of inquiry; the masters in black gowns, the messires in red."

"Who is that big red fellow, yonder above them, who is sweating?" pursued Gringoire.

"It is monsieur the president."

"And those sheep behind him?" continued Gringoire, who as we have seen, did not love the magistracy, which arose, possibly, from the grudge which he cherished against the Palais de Justice since his dramatic misadventure.

"They are messieurs the masters of requests of the king's household."

"And that boar in front of him?"

"He is monsieur the clerk of the Court of Parliament."

"And that crocodile on the right?"

"Master Philippe Lheulier, advocate extraordinary of the king."

"And that big, black tom-cat on the left?"

"Master Jacques Charmolue, procurator of the king in the Ecclesiastical Court, with the gentlemen of the officialty."

"Come now, monsieur, said Gringoire, "pray what are all those fine fellows doing yonder?"

"They are judging."

"Judging whom? I do not see the accused."

" 'Tis a woman, sir. You cannot see her. She has her back turned to us, and she is hidden from us by the crowd. Stay, yonder she is, where you see a group of partisans."

"Who is the woman?" asked Gringoire. "Do you know her name?"

"No, monsieur, I have but just arrived. I merely assume that there is some sorcery about it, since the official is present at the trial."

"Come!" said our philosopher, "we are going to see all these magistrates devour human flesh. 'Tis as good a spectacle as any other."

"Monsieur," remarked his neighbor, "think you not, that Master Jacques Charmolue has a very sweet air?"

"Hum!" replied Gringoire. "I distrust a sweetness which hath pinched nostrils and thin lips."

Here the bystanders imposed silence upon the two chatterers. They were listening to an important deposition.

"Messeigneurs," said an old woman in the middle of the hall, whose form was so concealed beneath her garments that one would have pronounced her a walking heap of rags; "Messeigneurs, the thing is as true as that I am la Falourdel, established these forty years at the Pont Saint Michel, and paying regularly my rents, lord's dues, and quit rents; at the gate opposite the house of Tassin-Caillart, the dyer, which is on the side up the river—a poor old woman now, but a pretty maid in former days, my lords. Someone said to me lately, 'La Falourdel, don't use your spinning-wheel too much in the evening; the devil is fond of combing the distaffs of old women with his horns. 'Tis certain that the surly monk who was round about the temple last year, now prowls in the City. Take care, la Falourdel, that he doth not knock at your door.' One evening I was spinning on my wheel, there comes a knock at my door; I ask who it is. They swear. I open. Two men enter. A man in black and a handsome officer. Of the black man nothing could be seen but his eyes, two coals of fire. All the rest was hat and cloak. They say to me—'The Sainte-Marthe chamber.'—'Tis my upper chamber, my lords, my cleanest. They give me a crown. I put the crown in my drawer, and I say: 'This shall go to buy tripe at the slaughter-house of la Gloriette to-morrow.' We go upstairs. On arriving at the upper chamber, and while my back is turned, the black man disappears. That dazed me a bit. The officer, who was as handsome as a great lord, goes downstairs again with me. He goes out. In about the time it takes to spin a quarter of a handful of flax, he returns with a beautiful young girl, a doll who would have shone like the sun had she been coiffed. She had with her a goat; a big billy-goat, whether black or white, I no longer remember. That set me to thinking. The girl does not concern me, but the goat! I love not those beasts, they have a beard and horns. They are so like a man. And then, they smack of the witches, sabbath. However, I say nothing. I had the crown. That is right, is it not, Monsieur Judge? I show the captain and the wench to the upper chamber, and I leave them alone; that is to say, with the goat. I go down and set to spinning again—I must inform you that my house has a ground floor and story above. I know not why I fell to thinking of the surly monk whom the goat had put into my head again, and then the beautiful girl was rather strangely decked out. All at once, I hear a cry upstairs, and something falls on the floor and the window opens. I run to mine which is beneath it, and I behold a black mass pass before my eyes and fall into the water. It was a phantom clad like a priest. It was a moonlight night. I saw him quite plainly. He was swimming in the direction of the city. Then, all of a tremble, I call the watch. The gentlemen of the police enter, and not knowing just at the first moment what the matter was, and being merry, they beat me. I explain to them. We go upstairs, and what do we find? my poor chamber all blood, the captain stretched out at full length with a dagger in his neck, the girl pretending to be dead, and the goat all in a fright. 'Pretty work!' I say, 'I shall have to wash that floor for more than a fortnight. It will have to be scraped; it will be a terrible job.' They carried off the officer, poor young man, and the wench with her bosom all bare. But wait, the worst is that on the next day, when I wanted to take the crown to buy tripe, I found a dead leaf in its place."

The old woman ceased. A murmur of horror ran through the audience.

"That phantom, that goat—all smacks of magic," said one of Gringoire's neighbors.

"And that dry leaf!" added another.

"No doubt about it," joined in a third, "she is a witch who has dealings with the surly monk, for the purpose of plundering officers."

Gringoire himself was not disinclined to regard this as altogether alarming and probable.

"Goody Falourdel," said the president majestically, "have you nothing more to communicate to the court?"

"No, monseigneur," replied the crone, "except that the report has described my house as a hovel and stinking; which is an outrageous fashion of speaking. The houses on the bridge are not imposing, because there are such multitudes of people; but, nevertheless, the butchers continue to dwell there, who are wealthy folk, and married to very proper and handsome women."

The magistrate who had reminded Gringoire of a crocodile rose—

"Silence!" said he. "I pray the gentlemen not to lose sight of the fact that a dagger was found on the person of the accused. Goody Falourdel, have you brought that leaf into which the crown which the demon gave you was transformed?

"Yes, monseigneur," she replied; "I found it again. Here it is."

A bailiff handed the dead leaf to the crocodile, who made a doleful shake of the head, and passed it on to the president, who gave it to the procurator of the king in the ecclesiastical court, and thus it made the circuit of the hall.

"It is a birch leaf," said Master Jacques Charmolue. "A fresh proof of magic."

A counselor took up the word.

"Witness, two men went upstairs together in your house: the black man, whom you first saw disappear and afterwards swimming in the Seine, with his priestly garments, and the officer. Which of the two handed you the crown?"

The old woman pondered for a moment and then said—

"The officer."

A murmur ran through the crowd.

"Ah!" thought Gringoire, "this makes some doubt in my mind."

But Master Philippe Lheulier, advocate extraordinary to the king, interposed once more.

"I will recall to these gentlemen, that in the deposition taken at his bedside, the assassinated officer, while declaring that he had a vague idea when the black man accosted him that the latter might be the surly monk, added that the phantom had pressed him eagerly to go and make acquaintance with the accused; and upon his, the captain's, remarking that he had no money, he had given him the crown which the said officer paid to la Falourdel. Hence, that crown is the money of hell."

This conclusive observation appeared to dissipate all the doubts of Gringoire and the other skeptics in the audience.

"You have the documents, gentlemen," added the king's advocate, as he took his seat; "you can consult the testimony of Phœbus de Châteaupers."

At that name, the accused sprang up, her head rose above the throng. Gringoire with horror, recognized la Esmeralda.

She was pale; her tresses, formerly so gracefully braided and spangled with sequins, hung in disorder; her lips were blue, her hollow eyes were terrible. Alas!

"Phœbus!" she said, in bewilderment; "where is he? O messeigneurs! before you kill me, tell me, for pity sake, whether he still lives?"

"Hold your tongue, woman," replied the president, "that is no affair of ours."

"Oh! for mercy's sake, tell me if he is alive!" she repeated, clasping her beautiful emaciated hands; and the sound of her chains in contact with her dress, was heard.

"Well!" said the king's advocate roughly, "he is dying. Are you satisfied?"

The unhappy girl fell back on her criminal's seat, speechless, tearless, white as a wax figure.

The president bent down to a man at his feet, who wore a gold cap and a black gown, a chain on his neck and a wand in his hand.

"Bailiff, bring in the second accused."

All eyes turned toward a small door, which opened, and, to the great agitation of Gringoire, gave passage to a pretty goat with horns and hoofs of gold. The elegant beast halted for a moment on the threshold, stretching out its neck as though, perched on the summit of a rock, it had before its eyes an immense horizon. Suddenly it caught sight of the gypsy girl, and leaping over the table and the head of a clerk, in two bounds it was at her knees; then it rolled gracefully on its mistress's feet, soliciting a word or a caress; but the accused remained motionless, and poor Djali himself obtained not a glance.

"Eh, why—'tis my villainous beast," said old Falourdel, "I recognize the two perfectly!"

Jacques Charmolue interfered.

"If the gentlemen please, we will proceed to the examination of the goat." He was, in fact, the second criminal. Nothing more simple in those days than a suit of sorcery instituted against an animal. We find, among others in the accounts of the provost's office for 1466, a curious detail concerning the expenses of the trial of Gillet-Soulart and his sow, "executed for their demerits," at Corbeil. Everything is there, the cost of the pens in which to place the sow, the five hundred bundles of brushwood purchased at the port of Morsant, the three pints of wine and the bread, the last repast of the victim fraternally shared by the executioner, down to the eleven days of guard and food for the sow, at eight deniers parisis each. Sometimes, they went even further than animals. The capitularies of Charlemagne and of Louis le Débonnaire impose severe penalties on fiery phantoms which presume to appear in the air.

Meanwhile the procurator had exclaimed: "If the demon which possesses this goat, and which has resisted all exorcisms, persists in its deeds of witchcraft, if it alarms the court with them, we warn it that we shall be forced to put in requisition against it the gallows or the stake."

Gringoire broke out into a cold perspiration. Charmolue took from the table the gypsy's tambourine, and presenting it to the goat, in a certain manner, asked the latter—

"What o'clock is it?"

The goat looked at it with an intelligent eye, raised its gilded hoof, and struck seven blows.

It was, in fact, seven o'clock. A movement of terror ran through the crowd.

Gringoire could not endure it.

"He is destroying himself!" he cried aloud; "You see well that he does not know what he is doing."

"Silence among the louts at the end of the hall!" said the bailiff sharply.

Jacques Charmolue, by the aid of the same maneuvers of the tambourine, made the goat perform many other tricks connected with the date of the day, the month of the year, etc., which the reader has already witnessed. And, by virtue of an optical illusion peculiar to judicial proceedings, these same spectators who had, probably, more than once applauded in the public square Djali's innocent magic were terrified by it beneath the roof of the Palais de Justice. The goat was undoubtedly the devil.

It was far worse when the procurator of the king, having emptied upon a floor a certain bag filled with movable letters, which Djali wore round his neck, they beheld the goat extract with his hoof from the scattered alphabet the fatal name of *Phœbus*. The witchcraft of which the captain had been the victim appeared irresistibly demonstrated, and in the eyes of all, the gypsy, that ravishing dancer, who had so often dazzled the passers-by with her grace, was no longer anything but a frightful vampire.

However, she betrayed no sign of life; neither Djali's graceful evolutions, nor the menaces of the court, nor the suppressed imprecations of the spectators any longer reached her mind.

In order to arouse her, a police officer was obliged to shake her unmercifully, and the president had to raise his voice—

"Girl, you are of the Bohemian race, addicted to deeds of witchcraft. You, in complicity with the bewitched goat implicated in this suit, during the night of the 29th of March last, murdered and stabbed, in concert with the powers of darkness, by the aid of charms and underhand practices, a captain of the king's arches of the watch, Phœbus de Châteaupers. Do you persist in denying it?"

"Horror!" exclaimed the young girl, hiding her face in her hands. "My Phœbus! Oh, this is hell!"

"Do you persist in your denial?" demanded the president coldly.

"Do I deny it?" she said with terrible accents; and she rose with flashing eyes.

The president continued squarely—

"Then how do you explain the facts laid to your charge?"

She replied in a broken voice—

"I have already told you. I do not know. 'Twas a priest, a priest whom I do not know; an infernal priest who pursues me!"

"That is it," retorted the judge; "the surly monk."

"Oh, gentlemen! have mercy! I am but a poor girl—"

"Of Egypt," said the judge.

Master Jacques Charmolue interposed sweetly—

"In view of the sad obstinacy of the accused, I demand the application of the torture."

"Granted," said the president.

The unhappy girl quivered in every limb. But she rose at the command of the men with partisans, and walked with a tolerably firm step, preceded by Charmolue and the priests of the official-ity, between two rows of halberds, toward a medium-sized door which suddenly opened and closed again behind her, and which produced upon the grief-stricken Gringoire the effect of a horrible mouth which had just devoured her.

When she disappeared, they heard a plaintive bleating; it was the little goat mourning.

The sitting of the court was suspended. A counselor having remarked that the gentlemen were fatigued, and that it would be a long time to wait until the torture was at an end, the president replied that a magistrate must know how to sacrifice himself to his duty.

"What an annoying and vexatious hussy," said an aged judge, "to get herself put to the ques-tion when one has not supped!"

Chapter II

CONTINUATION OF THE CROWN WHICH WAS CHANGED INTO A DRY LEAF

AFTER ASCENDING AND DESCENDING SEVERAL STEPS IN THE CORRIDORS, WHICH WERE SO DARK that they were lighted by lamps at midday, la Esmeralda, still surrounded by her lugubrious escort, was thrust by the police into a gloomy chamber. This chamber, circular in form, occupied the ground floor of one of those great towers, which, even in our own century, still pierce through the layer of modern edifices with which modern Paris has covered ancient Paris. There were no windows to this cellar; no other opening than the entrance, which was low, and closed by an enor-mous iron door. Nevertheless, light was not lacking; a furnace had been constructed in the thick-ness of the wall; a large fire was lighted there, which filled the vault with its crimson reflections and deprived a miserable candle, which stood in one corner, of all radiance. The iron grating which served to close the oven, being raised at that moment, allowed only a view at the mouth of the flam-ing vent-hole in the dark wall, the lower extremity of its bars, like a row of black and pointed teeth, set flat apart; which made the furnace resemble one of those mouths of dragons which spout forth flames in ancient legends. By the light which escaped from it, the prisoner beheld, all about the room, frightful instruments whose use she did not understand. In the center lay a leather mattress, placed almost flat upon the ground, over which hung a strap provided with a buckle, attached to a brass ring in the mouth of a flat-nosed monster carved in the keystone of the vault. Tongs, pincers, large plowshares, filled the interior of the furnace, and glowed in a confused heap on the coals. The sanguine light of the furnace illuminated in the chamber only a confused mass of horrible things.

This Tartarus was called simply, The Question Chamber.

On the bed, in a negligent attitude, sat Pierrat Torterue, the official torturer. His underlings, two gnomes with square faces, leather aprons, and linen breeches, were moving the iron instru-ments on the coals.

In vain did the poor girl summon up her courage; on entering this chamber she was stricken with horror.

The sergeants of the bailiff of the courts drew up in line on one side, the priests of the offi-ciality on the other. A clerk, inkhorn, and a table were in one corner.

Master Jacques Charmolue approached the gypsy with a very sweet smile.

"My dear child," said he, "do you still persist in your denial?"

"Yes," she replied, in a dying voice.

"In that case," replied Charmolue, "it will be very painful for us to have to question you more urgently than we should like. Pray take the trouble to seat yourself on this bed. Master Pierrat, make room for mademoiselle, and close the door."

Pierrat rose with a growl.

"If I shut the door," he muttered, "my fire will go out."

"Well, my dear fellow," replied Charmolue, "leave it open then."

Meanwhile, la Esmeralda had remained standing. That leather bed on which so many unhappy wretches had writhed, frightened her. Terror chilled the very marrow of her bones; she stood there bewildered and stupefied. At a sign from Charmolue, the two assistants took her and placed her in a sitting posture on the bed. They did her no harm; but when these men touched her, when that leather touched her, she felt all her blood retreat to her heart. She cast a frightened look around the chamber. It seemed to her as though she beheld advancing from all quarters toward her, with the intention of crawling up her body and biting and pinching her, all those hideous implements of torture, which as compared to the instruments of all sorts she had hitherto seen, were like what bats, centipedes, and spiders are among insects and birds.

"Where is the physician?" asked Charmolue.

"Here," replied a black gown whom she had not before noticed.

She shuddered.

"Mademoiselle," resumed the caressing voice of the procurator of the ecclesiastical court, "for the third time, do you persist in denying the deeds of which you are accused?"

This time she could only make a sign with her head.

"You persist?" said Jacques Charmolue. "Then it grieves me deeply, but I must fulfill my office."

"Monsieur le Procureur du Roi," said Pierrat abruptly, "How shall we begin?"

Charmolue hesitated for a moment with the ambiguous grimace of a poet in search of a rhyme. "With the boot," he said at last.

The unfortunate girl felt herself so utterly abandoned by God and men, that her head fell upon her breast like an inert thing which has no power in itself.

The tormentor and the physician approached her simultaneously. At the same time, the two assistants began to fumble among their hideous arsenal.

At the clanking of their frightful irons, the unhappy child quivered like a dead frog which is being galvanized. "Oh!" she murmured, so low that no one heard her; "oh, my Phœbus!" Then she fell back once more into her immobility and her marble silence. This spectacle would have rent any other heart than those of her judges. One would have pronounced her a poor sinful soul, being tortured by Satan beneath the scarlet wicket of hell. The miserable body which that frightful swarm of saws, wheels, and racks were about to clasp in their clutches, the being who was about to be manipulated by the harsh hands of executioners and pincers, was that gentle, white, fragile creature, a poor grain of millet which human justice was handing over to the terrible mills of torture to grind.

Meanwhile, the callous hands of Pierrat Torterue's assistants had bared that charming leg, that tiny foot, which had so often amazed the passers-by with their delicacy and beauty, in the squares of Paris.

" 'Tis a shame!" muttered the tormentor, glancing at these graceful and delicate forms.

Had the archdeacon been present, he certainly would have recalled at that moment his symbol of the spider and the fly. Soon the unfortunate girl, through a mist which spread before her eyes, beheld the boot approach; she soon beheld her foot encased between iron plates disappear in the frightful apparatus. Then terror restored her strength.

"Take that off!" she cried angrily; and drawing herself up, with her hair all disheveled: "Mercy!"

She darted from the bed to fling herself at the feet of the king's procurator, but her leg was fast in the heavy block of oak and iron, and she sank down upon the boot, more crushed than a bee with a lump of lead on its wing.

At a sign from Charmolue, she was replaced on the bed, and two coarse hands adjusted to her delicate waist the strap which hung from the ceiling.

"For the last time, do you confess the facts in the case?" demanded Charmolue, with his imperturbable benignity.

"I am innocent."

"Then, mademoiselle, how do you explain the circumstance laid to your charge?"

"Alas, monseigneur, I do not know."

"So you deny them?"

"All!"

"Proceed," said Charmolue to Pierrat.

Pierrat turned the handle of the screw-jack, the boot was contracted, and the unhappy girl uttered one of those horrible cries which have no orthography in any human language.

"Stop!" said Charmolue to Pierrat. "Do you confess?" he said to the gypsy.

"All!" cried the wretched girl. "I confess! I confess! Mercy!"

She had not calculated her strength when she faced the torture. Poor child, whose life up to that time had been so joyous, so pleasant, so sweet, the first pain had conquered her!

"Humanity forces me to tell you," remarked the king's procurator, "that in confessing, it is death that you must expect."

"I certainly hope so!" said she. And she fell back upon the leather bed, dying, doubled up, allowing herself to hang suspended from the strap buckled round her waist.

"Come, fair one, hold up a little," said Master Pierrat, raising her. "You have the air of the lamb of the Golden Fleece which hangs from Monsieur de Bourgogne's neck."

Jacques Charmolue raised his voice—

"Clerk, write. Young Bohemian maid, you confess your participation in the feasts, witches' sabbaths, and witchcrafts of hell, with ghosts, hags, and vampires? Answer."

"Yes," she said, so low that her words were lost in her breathing.

"You confess to having seen the ram which Beelzebub causes to appear in the clouds to call together the witches' sabbath, and which is beheld by sorcerers alone?"

"Yes."

"You confess to having adored the heads of Bophomet, those abominable idols of the Templars?"

"Yes."

"To having had habitual dealings with the devil under the form of a goat familiar, joined with you in the suit?"

"Yes."

"Lastly, you avow and confess to having, with the aid of the demon, and of the phantom vulgarly known as the surly monk, on the night of the 29th of March last, murdered and assassinated a captain named Phœbus de Châteaupers?"

She raised her large, staring eyes to the magistrate, and replied, as though mechanically, without convulsion or agitation—

"Yes."

It was evident that everything within her was broken.

"Write, clerk," said Charmolue. And, addressing the torturers, "Release the prisoner, and take her back to the court."

When the prisoner had been "unbooted," the procurator of the ecclesiastical court examined her foot, which was still swollen with pain. "Come," said he, "there's no great harm done. You shrieked in good season. You could still dance, my beauty!"

Then he turned to his acolytes of the officiality—

"Behold justice enlightened at last! This is a solace, gentlemen! Mademoiselle will bear us witness that we have acted with all possible gentleness."

Chapter III

END OF THE CROWN WHICH WAS TURNED INTO A DRY LEAF

WHEN SHE RE-ENTERED THE AUDIENCE HALL, PALE AND LIMPING, SHE WAS RECEIVED WITH A general murmur of pleasure. On the part of the audience there was the feeling of impatience gratified which one experiences at the theater at the end of the last entr'acte of the comedy, when the curtain rises and the conclusion is about to begin. On the part of the judges, it was the hope of getting their suppers sooner.

The little goat also bleated with joy. He tried to run toward his mistress, but they had tied him to the bench.

Night was fully set in. The candles, whose number had not been increased, cast so little light, that the walls of the hall could not be seen. The shadows there enveloped all objects in a sort of mist. A few apathetic faces of judges alone could be dimly discerned. Opposite them, at the extremity of the long hall, they could see a vaguely white point standing out against the somber background. This was the accused.

She had dragged herself to her place. When Charmolue had installed himself in a magisterial manner in his own, he seated himself, then rose and said, without exhibiting too much self-complacency at his success—"The accused has confessed all."

"Bohemian girl," the president continued, "have you avowed all your deeds of magic, prostitution, and assassination on Phœbus de Châteaupers?"

Her heart contracted. She was heard to sob amid the darkness. "Anything you like," she replied feebly, "but kill me quickly!"

"Monsieur, procurator of the king in the ecclesiastical courts," said the president, "the chamber is ready to hear you in your charge."

Master Charmolue exhibited an alarming notebook, and began to read, with many gestures and the exaggerated accentuation of the pleader, an oration in Latin, wherein all the proofs of the suit were piled up in Ciceronian periphrases, flanked with quotations from Plautus, his favorite comic author. We regret that we are not able to offer to our readers this remarkable piece. The orator pronounced it with marvelous action. Before he had finished the exordium, the perspiration was starting from his brow, and his eyes from his head.

All at once, in the middle of a fine period, he interrupted himself, and his glance, ordinarily so gentle and even stupid, became menacing.

"Gentlemen," he exclaimed (this time in French, for it was not in his copy-book), "Satan is so mixed up in this affair, that here he is present at our debates, and making sport of their majesty. Behold!"

So saying, he pointed to the little goat, who, on seeing Charmolue gesticulating, had, in point of fact, thought it appropriate to do the same, and had seated himself on his haunches, reproducing to the best of his ability, with his forepaws and his bearded head the pathetic pantomine of the king's procurator in the ecclesiastical court. This was, if the reader remembers, one of his prettiest accomplishments. This incident, this last proof, produced a great effect. The goat's hoofs were tied, and the king's procurator resumed the thread of his eloquence.

It was very long, but the peroration was admirable. Here is the concluding phrase; let the reader add the hoarse voice and the breathless gestures of Master Charmolue—

"Ideo, domni, coram stryga demonstrata, crimine patente, intentione criminis existente, in nomine sanctoe ecclesioe Nostrœ-Dominœ Parisiensis quoe est in saisina habendi omnimodam altam et bassam

justitiam in illa hac intemerata Civitatis insula, tenore proesentium declaremus nos requirere, primo, ali-
quamdam pecuniariam indemnitatem; secundo, amendationem honorabilem ante portalium maximum
Nostrœ-Dominœ, ecclesioe cathedralis; tertio, sententiam in virtute cujus ista styrga cum sua capella, seu
in trivio vulgariter dicto la Grève, *seu in insula exeunte in fluvio Secanœ, juxta pointam juardini regalis,*
executatoe sint!"

He put on his cap again and seated himself.

"Eheu!" sighed the broken-hearted Gringoire, *"bassa latinitas*—bastard latin!"

Another man in a black gown rose near the accused; he was her lawyer. The judges, who were fasting, began to grumble.

"Advocate, be brief," said the president.

"Monsieur the President," replied the advocate, "since the defendant has confessed the crime, I have only one word to say to these gentlemen. Here is a text from the Salic law; 'If a witch hath eaten a man, and if she be convicted of it, she shall pay a fine of eight thousand deniers, which amount to two hundred sous of gold.' May it please the chamber to condemn my client to the fine?"

"An abrogated text," said the advocate extraordinary of the king.

"Nego, I deny it," replied the advocate.

"Put it to the vote!" said one of the councilors; "the crime is manifest, and it is late."

They proceeded to take a vote without leaving the room. The judges signified their assent without giving their reasons, they were in a hurry. Their capped heads were seen uncovering one after the other, in the gloom, at the lugubrious question addressed to them by the president in a low voice. The poor accused had the appearance of looking at them, but her troubled eye no longer saw.

Then the clerk began to write; then he handed a long parchment to the president.

Then the unhappy girl heard the people moving, the pikes clashing, and a freezing voice saying to her—

"Bohemian wench, on the day when it shall seem good to our lord the king, at the hour of noon, you will be taken in a tumbrel, in your shift, with bare feet, and a rope about your neck, before the grand portal of Notre-Dame, and you will there make an apology with a wax torch of the weight of two pounds in your hand, and thence you will be conducted to the Place de Grève, where you will be hanged and strangled on the town gibbet; and likewise your goat; and you will pay to the official three lions of gold, in reparation of the crimes by you committed and by you confessed, of sorcery and magic, debauchery and murder, upon the person of the Sieur Phœbus de Châteaupers. May God have mercy on your soul!"

"Oh! 'tis a dream!" she murmured; and she felt rough hands bearing her away.

Chapter IV

LASCIATE OGNI SPERANZA—LEAVE ALL HOPE BEHIND, YE WHO ENTER HERE

IN THE MIDDLE AGES, WHEN AN EDIFICE WAS COMPLETE, THERE WAS ALMOST AS MUCH OF IT IN THE earth as above it. Unless built upon piles, like Notre-Dame, a palace, a fortress, a church, had always a double bottom. In cathedrals, it was, in some sort, another subterranean cathedral, low, dark, mysterious, blind, and mute, under the upper nave which was overflowing with light and reverberating with organs and bells day and night. Sometimes it was a sepulcher. In palaces, in fortresses, it was a prison, sometimes a sepulcher also, sometimes both together. These mighty buildings, whose mode of formation and *vegetation* we have elsewhere explained, had not simply *foundations*, but, so to speak, roots which ran branching through the soil in chambers, galleries, and staircases, like the construction above. Thus churches, palaces, fortresses, had the earth halfway up their bodies. The cellars of an edifice formed another edifice, into which one descended instead of ascending, and which extended its subterranean grounds under the external piles of the monument, like those forests and mountains which are reversed in the mirror-like waters of a lake, beneath the forests and mountains of the banks.

At the fortress of Saint-Antoine, at the Palais de Justice of Paris, at the Louvre, these subterranean edifices were prisons. The stories of these prisons, as they sank into the soil, grew constantly narrower and more gloomy. They were so many zones, where the shades of horror were graduated. Dante could never imagine anything better for his hell. These tunnels of cells usually terminated in a sack of a lowest dungeon, with a vat-like bottom, where Dante placed Satan, where society placed those condemned to death. A miserable human existence, once interred there; farewell light, air, life, *ogni speranza*—every hope; it only came forth to the scaffold or the stake. Sometimes it rotted there; human justice called this *forgetting*. Between men and himself, the condemned man felt a pile of stones and jailers weighing down upon his head; and the entire prison, the massive bastille was nothing more than an enormous, complicated lock, which barred him off from the rest of the world.

It was in a sloping cavity of this description, in the *oubliettes* excavated by Saint-Louis, in the *inpace* of the Tournelle, that la Esmeralda had been placed on being condemned to death, through fear of her escape, no doubt, with the colossal court-house over her head. Poor fly, who could not have lifted even one of its blocks of stone!

Assuredly, Providence and society had been equally unjust; such an excess of unhappiness and of torture was not necessary to break so frail a creature.

There she lay, lost in the shadows, buried, hidden, immured. Anyone who could have beheld her in this state, after having seen her laugh and dance in the sun, would have shuddered. Cold as night, cold as death, not a breath of air in her tresses, not a human sound in her ear, no longer a ray of light in her eyes; snapped in twain, crushed with chains, crouching beside a jug and a loaf, on a little straw, in a pool of water, which was formed under her by the sweating of the prison walls; without motion, almost without breath, she had no longer the power to suffer; Phœbus, the sun, midday, the open air, the streets of Paris, the dances with applause, the sweet babblings of love with the officer; then the priest, the old crone, the poignard, the blood, the torture, the gibbet; all this did, indeed, pass before her mind, sometimes as a charming and golden vision, sometimes as a hideous nightmare; but it was no longer anything but a vague and horrible struggle, lost in the gloom, or distant music played up above ground, and which was no longer audible at the depth where the unhappy girl had fallen.

Since she had been there, she had neither waked nor slept. In that misfortune, in that cell, she could no longer distinguish her waking hours from slumber, dreams from reality, any more than day from night. All this was mixed, broken, floating, disseminated confusedly in her thought. She no longer felt, she no longer knew, she no longer thought; at the most, she only dreamed. Never had a living creature been thrust more deeply into nothingness.

Thus benumbed, frozen, petrified, she had barely noticed on two or three occasions, the sound of a trapdoor opening somewhere above her, without even permitting the passage of a little light, and through which a hand had tossed her a bit of black bread. Nevertheless, this periodical visit of the jailer was the sole communication which was left her with mankind.

A single thing still mechanically occupied her ear; above her head, the dampness was filtering through the moldy stones of the vault, and a drop of water dropped from them at regular intervals. She listened stupidly to the noise made by this drop of water as it fell into the pool beside her.

This drop of water falling from time to time into that pool, was the only movement which still went on around her, the only clock which marked the time, the only noise which reached her of all the noise made on the surface of the earth.

To tell the whole, however, she also felt, from time to time, in that cesspool of mire and darkness, something cold passing over her foot or her arm, and she shuddered.

How long had she been there? She did not know. She had a recollection of a sentence of death pronounced somewhere, against someone, then of having been herself carried away, and of waking up in darkness and silence, chilled to the heart. She had dragged herself along on her hands. Then iron rings that cut her ankles, and chains had rattled. She had recognized the fact that all around her was wall, that below her there was a pavement covered with moisture and a truss of straw; but neither lamp nor air-hole. Then she had seated herself on that straw and, sometimes, for the sake of changing her attitude, on the last stone step in her dungeon.

For a while she had tried to count the black minutes measured off for her by the drop of water; but that melancholy labor of an ailing brain had broken off of itself in her head, and had left her in stupor.

At length, one day, or one night (for midnight and midday were of the same color in that sepulcher), she heard above her a louder noise than was usually made by the turnkey when he brought her bread and jug of water. She raised her head, and beheld a ray of reddish light passing through the crevices in the sort of trapdoor contrived in the roof of the *inpace*.

At the same time, the heavy lock creaked, the trap grated on its rusty hinges, turned, and she beheld a lantern, a hand, and the lower portions of the bodies of two men, the door being too low to admit of her seeing their heads. The light pained her so acutely that she shut her eyes.

When she opened them again the door was closed, the lantern was deposited on one of the steps of the staircase; a man alone stood before her. A monk's black cloak fell to his feet, a cowl of the same color concealed his face. Nothing was visible of his person, neither face nor hands. It was a long, black shroud standing erect, and beneath which something could be felt moving. She gazed fixedly for several minutes at this sort of specter. But neither he nor she spoke. One would have pronounced them two statues confronting each other. Two things only seemed alive in that cavern; the wick of the lantern, which sputtered on account of the dampness of the atmosphere, and the drop of water from the roof, which cut this irregular sputtering with its monotonous splash, and made the light of the lantern quiver in concentric waves on the oily water of the pool.

At last the prisoner broke the silence.

"Who are you?"

"A priest."

The words, the accent, the sound of his voice made her tremble.

The priest continued, in a hollow voice—

"Are you prepared?"

"For what?"

"To die."

"Oh!" said she, "will it be soon?"

"To-morrow."

Her head, which had been raised with joy, fell back upon her breast.

" 'Tis very far away yet!" she murmured; "why could they not have done it to-day?"

"Then you are very unhappy?" asked the priest, after a silence.

"I am very cold," she replied.

She took her feet in her hands, a gesture habitual with unhappy wretches who are cold, as we have already seen in the case of the recluse of the Tour-Roland, and her teeth chattered.

The priest appeared to cast his eyes around the dungeon from beneath his cowl.

"Without light! without fire! in the water! it is horrible!"

"Yes," she replied, with the bewildered air which unhappiness had given her. "The day belongs to everyone, why do they give me only night?"

"Do you know," resumed the priest, after a fresh silence, "why you are here?"

"I thought I knew once," she said, passing her thin fingers over her eyelids, as though to aid her memory, "but I know no longer."

All at once she began to weep like a child.

"I should like to get away from here, sir. I am cold, I am afraid, and there are creatures which crawl over my body."

"Well, follow me."

So saying, the priest took her arm. The unhappy girl was frozen to her very soul. Yet that hand produced an impression of cold upon her.

"Oh!" she murmured, " 'tis the icy hand of death. Who are you?"

The priest threw back his cowl; she looked. It was the sinister visage which had so long pursued her; that demon's head which had appeared at la Falourdel's, above the head of her adored Phœbus; that eye which she last had seen glittering beside a dagger.

This apparition, always so fatal for her, and which had thus driven her on from misfortune to misfortune, even to torture, roused her from her stupor. It seemed to her that the sort of veil which had lain thick upon her memory was rent away. All the details of her melancholy adventure, from the nocturnal scene at la Falourdel's to her condemnation to the Tournelle, recurred to her memory, no longer vague and confused as heretofore, but distinct, harsh, clear, palpitating, terrible. These souvenirs, half effaced and almost obliterated by excess of suffering, were revived by the somber figure which stood before her, as the approach of fire causes letters traced upon white paper with invisible ink, to start out perfectly fresh. It seemed to her that all the wounds of her heart opened and bled simultaneously.

"Hah!" she cried, with her hands on her eyes, and a convulsive trembling, " 'tis the priest!"

Then she dropped her arms in discouragement, and remained seated, with lowered head, eyes fixed on the ground, mute and still trembling.

The priest gazed at her with the eye of a hawk which has long been soaring in a circle from the heights of heaven over a poor lark cowering in the wheat, and has long been silently contracting the formidable circles of his flight, and has suddenly swooped down upon his prey like a flash of lightning, and holds it panting in his talons.

She began to murmur in a low voice—

"Finish! finish! the last blow!" and she drew her head down in terror between her shoulders, like the lamb awaiting the blow of the butcher's ax.

"So I inspire you with horror?" he said at length.

She made no reply.

"Do I inspire you with horror?" he repeated.

Her lips contracted, as though with a smile.

"Yes," said she, "the headsman scoffs at the condemned. Here he has been pursuing me, threatening me, terrifying me for months! Had it not been for him, my God, how happy I should have been! It was he who cast me into this abyss! Oh heavens! it was he who killed him! my Phœbus!"

Here, bursting into sobs, and raising her eyes to the priest—

"Oh! wretch, who are you? What have I done to you? Do you then, hate me so? Alas! what have you against me?"

"I love thee!" cried the priest.

Her tears suddenly ceased, she gazed at him with the look of an idiot. He had fallen on his knees and was devouring her with eyes of flame.

"Dost thou understand? I love thee!" he cried again.

"What love!" said the unhappy girl with a shudder.

He resumed—

"The love of a damned soul."

Both remained silent for several minutes, crushed beneath the weight of their emotions; he maddened, she stupefied.

"Listen," said the priest at last, and a singular calm had come over him; "you shall know all I am about to tell you that which I have hitherto hardly dared to say to myself, when furtively interrogating my conscience at those deep hours of the night when it is so dark that it seems as though God no longer saw us. Listen. Before I knew you, young girl, I was happy."

"So was I!" she sighed feebly.

"Do not interrupt me. Yes, I was happy, at least I believed myself to be so. I was pure, my soul was filled with limpid light. No head was raised more proudly and more radiantly than mine. Priests consulted me on chastity; doctors, on doctrines. Yes, science was all in all to me; it was a sister to me, and a sister sufficed. Not but that with age other ideas came to me. More than once my flesh had been moved as a woman's form passed by. That force of sex and blood which, in the madness of youth, I had imagined that I had stifled forever had, more than once, convulsively raised the chain of iron vows which bind me, a miserable wretch, to the cold stones of the altar. But fasting, prayer, study, the mortifications of the cloister, rendered my soul mistress of my body once more, and then I avoided women. Moreover, I had but to open a book, and all the impure mists of my brain vanished before the splendors of science. In a few moments, I felt the gross things of earth flee far away, and I found myself once more calm, quieted, and serene, in the presence of the tranquil radiance of eternal truth. As long as the demon sent to attack me only vague shadows of women who passed occasionally before my eyes in church, in the streets, in the fields, and who hardly recurred to my dreams, I easily vanquished him. Alas! if the victory has not remained with me, it is the fault of God, who has not created man and the demon of equal force. Listen. One day—"

Here the priest paused, and the prisoner heard sighs of anguish break from his breast with a sound of the death-rattle.

He resumed—

"One day I was leaning on the window of my cell. What book was I reading then? Oh! all that is a whirlwind in my head. I was reading. The window opened upon a Square. I heard a sound of tambourine and music. Annoyed at being thus disturbed in my reverie, I glanced into the Square. What I beheld, others saw beside myself, and yet it was not a spectacle made for human eyes. There, in the middle of the pavement—it was midday, the sun was shining brightly—a creature was dancing. A creature so beautiful that God would have preferred her to the Virgin and have chosen her for his mother and have wished to be born of her if she had been in existence when he was made man! Her eyes were black and splendid; in the midst of her black locks, some hairs through which the sun shone glistened like threads of gold. Her feet disappeared in their movements like the spokes of a rapidly turning wheel. Around her head, in her black tresses, there were disks of metal, which glittered in the sun, and formed a coronet of stars on her brow. Her dress thick set with spangles, blue, and dotted with a thousand sparks, gleamed like a summer night. Her brown, supple arms twined and untwined around her waist, like two scarfs. The form of her body was surprisingly beautiful. Oh! what a resplendent figure stood out, like something luminous even in the sunlight! Alas, young girl, it was thou! Surprised, intoxicated, charmed, I allowed myself to gaze upon thee. I looked so long that I suddenly shuddered with terror; I felt that fate was seizing hold of me."

The priest paused for a moment, overcome with emotion. Then he continued—

"Already half fascinated, I tried to cling fast to something and hold myself back from falling. I recalled the snares which Satan had already set for me. The creature before my eyes possessed that superhuman beauty which can come only from heaven or hell. It was no simple girl made with a little of our earth, and dimly lighted within by the vacillating ray of a woman's soul. It was an angel!

but of shadows and flame, and not of light. At the moment when I was meditating thus, I beheld beside you a goat, a beast of witches, which smiled as it gazed at me. The midday sun gave him golden horns. Then I perceived the snare of the demon, and I no longer doubted that you had come from hell and that you had come thence for my perdition. I believed it."

Here the priest looked the prisoner full in the face, and added, coldly—

"I believe it still. Nevertheless, the charm operated little by little; your dancing whirled through my brain; I felt the mysterious spell working within me. All that should have awakened was lulled to sleep; and like those who die in the snow, I felt pleasure in allowing this sleep to draw on. All at once, you began to sing. What could I do, unhappy wretch? Your song was still more charming than your dancing. I tried to flee. Impossible. I was nailed, rooted to the spot. It seemed to me that the marble of the pavement had risen to my knees. I was forced to remain until the end. My feet were like ice, my head was on fire. At last you took pity on me, you ceased to sing, you disappeared. The reflection of the dazzling vision, the reverberation of the enchanting music disappeared by degrees from my eyes and my ears. Then I fell back into the embrasure of the window, more rigid, more feeble than a statue torn from its base. The vesper bell roused me. I drew myself up; I fled; but alas! something within me had fallen never to rise again, something had come upon me from which I could not flee."

He made another pause and went on—

"Yes, dating from that day, there was within me a man whom I did not know. I tried to make use of all my remedies. The cloister, the altar, work, books—follies! Oh, how hollow does science sound when one in despair dashes against it a head full of passions! Do you know, young girl, what I saw thenceforth between my book and me? You, your shade, the image of the luminous apparition which had one day crossed the space before me. But this image had no longer the same color; it was somber, funereal, gloomy as the black circle which long pursues the vision of the imprudent man who has gazed intently at the sun.

"Unable to rid myself of it, since I heard your song humming ever in my head, beheld your feet dancing always on my breviary, felt even at night, in my dreams, your form in contact with my own, I desired to see you again, to touch you, to know who you were, to see whether I should really find you like the ideal image which I had retained of you, to shatter my dream, perchance, with reality. At all events, I hoped that a new impression would efface the first, and the first had become insupportable. I sought you. I saw you once more. Calamity! When I had seen you twice, I wanted to see you a thousand times, I wanted to see you always. Then—how stop myself on that slope of hell?—then I no longer belonged to myself. The other end of the thread which the demon had attached to my wings he had fastened to his foot. I became vagrant and wandering like yourself. I waited for you under porches, I stood on the lookout for you at the street corners, I watched for you from the summit of my tower. Every evening I returned to myself more charmed, more despairing, more bewitched, more lost!

"I had learned who you were; an Egyptian, Bohemian, gypsy, zingara. How could I doubt the magic? Listen. I hoped that a trial would free me from the charm. A witch enchanted Bruno d'Ast; he had her burned, and was cured. I knew it. I wanted to try the remedy. First I tried to have you forbidden the square in front of Notre-Dame, hoping to forget you if you returned no more. You paid no heed to it. You returned. Then the idea of abducting you occurred to me. One night I made the attempt. There were two of us. We already had you in our power, when that miserable officer came up. He delivered you. Thus did he begin your unhappiness, mine, and his own. Finally, no longer knowing what to do, and what was to become of me, I denounced you to the official.

"I thought that I should be cured like Bruno d'Ast. I also had a confused idea that a trial would deliver you into my hands; that, as a prisoner I should hold you, I should have you; that there you could not escape from me; that you had already possessed me a sufficiently long time to give me the right to possess you in my turn. When one does wrong, one must do it thoroughly. 'Tis madness to halt midway in the monstrous! The extreme of crime has its deliriums of joy. A priest and a witch can mingle in delight upon the truss of straw in a dungeon!

"Accordingly, I denounced you. It was then that I terrified you when we met. The plot which I was weaving against you, the storm which I was heaping up above your head, burst from me in threats and lightning glances. Still, I hesitated. My project had its terrible sides which made me shrink back.

"Perhaps I might have renounced it; perhaps my hideous thought would have withered in my brain, without bearing fruit. I thought that it would always depend upon me to follow up or discontinue this prosecution. But every evil thought is inexorable, and insists on becoming a deed; but where I believed myself to be all powerful, fate was more powerful than I. Alas! 'tis fate which has seized you and delivered you to the terrible wheels of the machine which I had constructed doubly. Listen. I am nearing the end.

"One day—again the sun was shining brilliantly—I behold man pass me uttering your name and laughing, who carries sensuality in his eyes. Damnation! I followed him; you know the rest."

He ceased.

The young girl could find but one word:

"Oh, my Phœbus!"

"Not that name!" said the priest, grasping her arm violently. "Utter not that name! Oh! miserable wretches that we are, 'tis that name which has ruined us! or, rather we have ruined each other by the inexplicable play of fate! you are suffering, are you not? you are cold; the night makes you blind, the dungeon envelops you; but perhaps you still have some light in the bottom of your soul, were it only your childish love for that empty man who played with your heart, while I bear the dungeon within me; within me there is winter, ice, despair; I have night in my soul.

"Do you know what I have suffered? I was present at your trial. I was seated on the official's bench. Yes, under one of the priests' cowls, there were the contortions of the damned. When you were brought in, I was there; when you were questioned, I was there.—Den of wolves!—It was my crime, it was my gallows that I beheld being slowly reared over your head. I was there for every witness, every proof, every plea; I could count each of your steps in the painful path; I was still there when that ferocious beast—oh! I had not foreseen torture! Listen. I followed you to that chamber of anguish. I beheld you stripped and handled, half naked, by the infamous hands of the tormentor. I beheld your foot, that foot which I would have given an empire to kiss and die, that foot, beneath which to have had my head crushed I should have felt such rapture—I beheld it encased in that horrible boot, which converts the limbs of a living being into one bloody clod. Oh, wretch! while I looked on at that, I held beneath my shroud a dagger, with which I lacerated my breast. When you uttered that cry, I plunged it into my flesh; at a second cry, it would have entered my heart. Look! I believe that it still bleeds."

He opened his cassock. His breast was in fact, mangled as by the claw of a tiger, and on his side he had a large and badly healed wound.

The prisoner recoiled with horror.

"Oh!" said the priest, "young girl, have pity upon me! You think yourself unhappy; alas! alas! you know not what unhappiness is. Oh! to love a woman! to be a priest! to be hated! to love with all the fury of one's soul; to feel that one would give for the least of her smiles, one's blood, one's vitals, one's fame, one's salvation, one's immortality and eternity, this life and the other; to regret that one is not a king, emperor, archangel, God, in order that one might place a greater slave beneath her feet; to clasp her night and day in one's dreams and one's thoughts, and to behold her in love with the trappings of a soldier! and to have nothing to offer her but a priest's dirty cassock, which will inspire her with fear and disgust! To be present with one's jealousy and one's rage, while she lavishes on a miserable, blustering imbecile, treasures of love and beauty! To behold that body whose form burns you, that bosom which possesses so much sweetness, that flesh palpitate and blush beneath the kisses of another! Oh heaven! to love her foot, her arm, her shoulder, to think of her blue veins, of her brown skin, until one writhes for whole nights together on the pavement of one's cell, and to behold all those caresses which one has dreamed of, end in torture! To have succeeded only in stretching her upon the leather bed! Oh! these are the veritable pincers, reddened in the fires of hell. Oh! blessed is he who is sawn between two planks, or torn in pieces by four horses! Do you know what that torture is, which is imposed upon you for long nights by your burning arteries, your bursting heart, your breaking head, your teeth-gnawed hands; mad tormentors which turn you incessantly, as upon a red-hot gridiron, to a thought of love, of jealousy, and of despair! Young girl, mercy! a truce for a moment! a few ashes on these live coals! Wipe away, I beseech you, the perspiration which trickles in great drops from my brow! Child! torture me with one hand, but caress me with the other! Have pity, young girl! Have pity upon me!"

The priest writhed on the wet pavement, beating his head against the corners of the stone steps. The young girl gazed at him, and listened to him.

When he ceased, exhausted and panting, she repeated in a low voice—

"Oh my Phœbus!"

The priest dragged himself toward her on his knees.

"I beseech you," he cried, "if you have any heart, do not repulse me! Oh! I love you! I am a wretch! When you utter that name, unhappy girl, it is as though you crushed all the fibers of my heart between your teeth. Mercy! If you come from hell I will go thither with you. I have done everything to that end. The hell where you are, shall be paradise; the sight of you is more charming than that of God! Oh! speak! you will have none of me? I should have thought the mountains would be shaken in their foundations on the day when a woman would repulse such a love. Oh! if you only would! Oh! how happy we might be. We would flee—I would help you to flee—we would go somewhere, we would seek that spot on earth, where the sun is brightest, the sky the bluest, where the trees are most luxuriant. We would love each other, we would pour our two souls into each other, and we would have a thirst for ourselves which we would quench in common and incessantly at that fountain of inexhaustible love."

She interrupted with a terrible and thrilling laugh.

"Look, father, you have blood on your fingers!"

The priest remained for several moments as though petrified, with his eyes fixed upon his hand.

"Well, yes!" he resumed at last, with strange gentleness, "insult me, scoff at me, overwhelm me with scorn! but come, come. Let us make haste. It is to be to-morrow, I tell you. The gibbet on the Grève, you know it? it stands always ready. It is horrible! to see you ride in that tumbrel! Oh! mercy! Until now I have never felt the power of my love for you.—Oh! follow me. You shall take your time to love me after I have saved you. You shall hate me as long as you will. But come. To-morrow! to-morrow! the gallows! your execution! Oh! save yourself! spare me!"

He seized her arm, he was beside himself, he tried to drag her away.

She fixed her eye intently on him.

"What has become of my Phœbus?"

"Ah!" said the priest, releasing her arm, "you are pitiless."

"What has become of Phœbus?" she repeated coldly.

"He is dead!" cried the priest.

"Dead!" said she, still icy and motionless; "then why do you talk to me of living?"

He was not listening to her.

"Oh! yes," said he, as though speaking to himself, "he certainly must be dead. The blade pierced deeply. I believe I touched his heart with the point. Oh! my very soul was at the end of the dagger!"

The young girl flung herself upon him like a raging tigress, and pushed him upon the steps of the staircase with supernatural force.

"Begone, monster! Begone, assassin! Leave me to die! May the blood of both of us make an eternal stain upon your brow! Be thine, priest! Never! never! Nothing shall unite us! not hell itself! Go, accursed man! never!"

The priest had stumbled on the stairs. He silently disentangled his feet from the folds of his robe, picked up his lantern again, and slowly began the ascent of the steps which led to the door; he opened the door and passed through it.

All at once, the young girl beheld his head reappear; it wore a frightful expression, and he cried, hoarse with rage and despair—

"I tell you he is dead!"

She fell face downwards upon the floor, and there was no longer any sound audible in the cell than the sob of the drop of water which made the pool palpitate amid the darkness.

Chapter V

THE MOTHER

I DO NOT BELIEVE THAT THERE IS ANYTHING SWEETER IN THE WORLD THAN THE IDEAS WHICH awake in a mother's heart at the sight of her child's tiny shoe; especially if it is a shoe for festivals, for Sunday, for baptism, the shoe embroidered to the very sole, a shoe in which the infant has not yet taken a step. That shoe has so much grace and daintiness, it is so impossible for it to walk, that it seems to the mother as though she saw her child. She smiles upon it, she kisses it, she talks to it; she asks herself whether there can actually be a foot so tiny; and if the child be absent, the pretty shoe suffices to place the sweet and fragile creature before her eyes. She thinks she sees it, she does see it, complete, living, joyous, with its delicate hands, its round head, its pure lips, its serene eyes whose white is blue. If it is in winter, it is yonder, crawling on the carpet, it is laboriously climbing upon an ottoman, and the mother trembles lest it should approach the fire. If it is summer time, it crawls about the yard, in the garden, plucks up the grass between the paving-stones, gazes innocently at the big dogs, the big horses, without fear, plays with the shells, with the flowers, and makes the gardener grumble because he finds sand in the flower-beds and earth in the paths. Everything laughs, and shines and plays around it, like it, even the breath of air and the ray of sun which vie with each other in disporting among the silky ringlets of its hair. The shoe shows all this to the mother, and makes her heart melt as fire melts wax.

But when the child is lost, these thousand images of joy, of charms, of tenderness, which throng around the little shoe, become so many horrible things. The pretty broidered shoe is no longer anything but an instrument of torture which eternally crushes the heart of the mother. It is always the same fiber which vibrates, the tenderest and most sensitive; but instead of an angel caressing it, it is a demon who is wrenching at it.

One May morning, when the sun was rising on one of those dark blue skies against which Garofolo loves to place his Descents from the Cross, the recluse of the Tour-Roland heard a sound of wheels, of horses and irons in the Place de Grève. She was somewhat aroused by it, knotted her hair upon her ears in order to deafen herself, and resumed her contemplation, on her knees, of the inanimate object which she had adored for fifteen years. This little shoe was the universe to her, as we have already said. Her thought was shut up in it, and was destined never more to quit it except at death. The somber cave of the Tour-Roland alone knew how many bitter imprecations, touching complaints, prayers and sobs she had wafted to heaven in connection with that charming bauble of rose-colored satin. Never was more despair bestowed upon a prettier and more graceful thing.

It seemed as though her grief were breaking forth more violently than usual; and she could be heard outside lamenting in a loud and monotonous voice which rent the heart.

"Oh my daughter!" she said, "my daughter, my poor, dear little child, so I shall never see thee more! It is over! It always seems to me that it happened yesterday! My God! my God! it would have been better not to give her to me than to take her away so soon. Did you not know that our children are part of ourselves, and that a mother who has lost her child no longer believes in God? Ah! wretch that I am to have gone out that day! Lord! Lord! to have taken her from me thus; you could never have looked at me with her, when I was joyously warming her at my fire, when she laughed as she suckled, when I made her tiny feet creep up my breast to my lips? Oh! if you had looked at that, my God, you would have taken pity on my joy; you would not have taken from me the only love which lingered in my heart! Was I then, Lord, so miserable a creature, that you could not look at me before condemning me?—Alas! Alas! here is the shoe; where is the foot? where is the rest? Where is the child? My daughter! my daughter! what did they do with thee? Lord, give her back to me. My knees have been worn for fifteen years in praying to thee, my God! Is not that enough? Give her back to me one day, one hour, one minute; one minute, Lord! and then cast me to the demon for all eternity! Oh! if I only knew where the skirt of your garment trails, I would cling to it with both hands, and you would be obliged to give me back my child! Have you no pity on her pretty little shoe? Could you condemn a poor mother to this torture for fifteen years? Good Virgin! good Virgin of heaven! my infant Jesus has been taken from me, has been stolen from me; they devoured her on a heath, they drank her blood, they cracked her bones! Good Virgin, have pity upon me. My daughter, I want my daughter! What is it to me that she is in paradise? I do not want your angel, I want my child! I am a lioness, I want my whelp. Oh! I will writhe on the earth, I will break the stones with my forehead, and I will damn myself, and I will curse you, Lord, if you keep my child from me! you see plainly that my arms are all bitten, Lord! Has the good God no mercy?— Oh! give me only salt and black bread, only let me have my daughter to warm me like a sun! Alas! Lord my God. Alas! Lord my God, I am only a vile sinner; but my daughter made me pious. I was full of religion for the love of her, and I beheld you through her smile as through an opening into heaven. Oh! if I could only once, just once more, a single time, put this shoe on her pretty little pink foot, I would die blessing you, good Virgin. Ah! fifteen years! she will be grown up now!— Unhappy child! what! it is really true then I shall never see her more, not even in heaven, for I shall not go there myself. Oh! what misery to think that here is her shoe, and that that is all!"

The unhappy woman flung herself upon that shoe; her consolation and her despair for so many years, and her vitals were rent with sobs as on the first day; because, for a mother who has lost her child, it is always the first day. That grief never grows old. The mourning garments may grow white and threadbare, the heart remains dark.

At that moment, the fresh and joyous cries of children passed in front of the cell. Every time that children crossed her vision or struck her ear, the poor mother flung herself into the darkest corner of her sepulcher, and one would have said, that she sought to plunge her head into the stone in order not to hear them. This time, on the contrary, she drew herself upright with a start, and listened eagerly. One of the little boys had just said—

"They are going to hang a gypsy to-day."

With the abrupt leap of that spider which we have seen fling itself upon a fly at the trembling of its web, she rushed to her air-hole, which opened as the reader knows, on the Place de Grève. A ladder had, in fact, been raised up against the permanent gibbet, and the hangman's assistant was busying himself with adjusting the chains which had been rusted by the rain. There were some people standing about.

The laughing group of children was already far away. The sacked nun sought with her eyes some passer-by whom she might question. All at once, beside her cell, she perceived a priest making a pretext of reading the public breviary, but who was much less occupied with the "lectern of latticed iron," than with the gallows, toward which he cast a fierce and gloomy glance from time to time. She recognized monsieur the archdeacon of Josas, a holy man.

"Father," she inquired, "whom are they about to hang yonder?"

The priest looked at her and made no reply; she repeated her question. Then he said—

"I know not."

"Some children said that it was a gypsy," went on the recluse.

"I believe so," said the priest.

Then Paquette la Chantefleurie burst into hyena-like laughter.

"Sister," said the archdeacon, "do you then hate the gypsies heartily?"

"Do I hate them!" exclaimed the recluse, "they are vampires, stealers of children! They devoured my little daughter, my child, my only child! I have no longer any heart, they devoured it!"

She was frightful. The priest looked at her coldly.

"There is one in particular whom I hate, and whom I have cursed," she resumed; "it is a young one, of the age which my daughter would be if her mother had not eaten my daughter. Every time that that young viper passes in front of my cell, she sets my blood in a ferment."

"Well, sister, rejoice," said the priest, icy as a sepulchral statue; "that is the one whom you are about to see die."

His head fell upon his bosom and he moved slowly away.

The recluse writhed her arms with joy.

"I predicted it for her, that she would ascend thither! Thanks, priest!" she cried.

And she began to pace up and down with long strides before the grating of her window, her hair disheveled, her eyes flashing, with her shoulder striking against the wall, with the wild air of a female wolf in a cage, who has long been famished, and who feels the hour for her repast drawing near.

Chapter VI

THREE HUMAN HEARTS DIFFERENTLY CONSTRUCTED

PHŒBUS WAS NOT DEAD, HOWEVER. MEN OF THAT STAMP DIE HARD. WHEN MASTER PHILIPPE Lheulier, advocate extraordinary of the king, had said to poor Esmeralda; "He is dying," it was an error or a jest. When the archdeacon had repeated to the condemned girl; "He is dead," the fact is that he knew nothing about it, but that he believed it, that he counted on it, that he did not doubt it, that he devoutly hoped it. It would have been too hard for him to give favorable news of his rival to the woman whom he loved. Any man would have done the same in his place.

It was not that Phœbus's wound had not been serious, but it had not been as much so as the archdeacon believed. The physician, to whom the soldiers of the watch had carried him at the first moment, had feared for his life during the space of a week, and had even told him so in Latin. But youth had gained the upper hand; and, as frequently happens, in spite of prognostications and diagnoses, nature had amused herself by saving the sick man under the physician's very nose. It was while he was still lying on the leech's pallet that he had submitted to the interrogations of Philippe Lheulier and the official inquisitors, which had annoyed him greatly. Hence, one fine morning, feeling himself better, he had left his golden spurs with the leech as payment, and had slipped away.

This had not, however, interfered with the progress of the affair. Justice, at that epoch, troubled itself very little about the clearness and definiteness of a criminal suit. Provided that the accused was hung, that was all that was necessary. Now the judge had plenty of proofs against la Esmeralda. They had supposed Phœbus to be dead, and that was the end of the matter.

Phœbus, on his side, had not fled far. He had simply rejoined his company in garrison at Queue-en-Brie, in the Isle-de-France, a few stages from Paris.

After all, it did not please him in the least to appear in this suit. He had a vague feeling that he should play a ridiculous figure in it. On the whole, he did not know what to think of the whole affair. Superstitious, and not given to devoutness, like every soldier who is only a soldier, when he came to question himself about this adventure, he did not feel assured as to the goat, as to the singular fashion in which he had met la Esmeralda, as to the no less strange manner in which she had allowed him to divine her love, as to her character as a gypsy, and lastly, as to the surly monk. He perceived in all these incidents much more magic than love, probably a sorceress, perhaps the devil; a comedy, in short, or to speak in the language of that day, a very disagreeable mystery, in which he played a very awkward part, the *rôle* of blows and derision. The captain was quite put out of countenance about it; he experienced that sort of shame which our la Fontaine has so admirably defined—

Ashamed as a fox who has been caught by a fowl.

Moreover, he hoped that the affair would not get noised abroad, that his name would hardly be pronounced in it, and that in any case it would not go beyond the courts of the Tournelle. In this he was not mistaken, there was then no *Gazette des Tribunaux*; and as not a week passed which had not its counterfeiter to boil, or its witch to hang, or its heretic to burn, at some one of the innumerable justices of Paris, people were so accustomed to seeing in all the squares the ancient feudal Themis, bare armed, with sleeves stripped up, performing her duty at the gibbets, the ladders, and the pillories, that they hardly paid any heed to it. Fashionable society of that day hardly knew the name of the victim who passed by at the corner of the street, and it was the populace at the most who regaled themselves with this coarse fare. An execution was an habitual incident of the public highways, like the braising-pan of the baker or the slaughter-house of the knacker. The executioner was only a sort of butcher of a little deeper dye than the rest.

Hence Phœbus's mind was soon at ease on the score of the enchantress Esmeralda, or Similar, as he called her, concerning the blow from the dagger of the Bohemian or of the surly monk (it mattered little which to him), and as to the issue of the trial. But as soon as his heart was vacant in that direction, Fleur-de-Lys returned to it. Captain Phœbus's heart, like the physics of that day, abhorred a vacuum.

Queue-en-Brie was a very insipid place to stay at then, a village of farriers, and cow-girls with chapped hands, a long line of poor dwellings and thatched cottages, which borders the grand road on both sides for half a league; a tail (queue), in short, as its name imports.

Fleur-de-Lys was his last passion but one, a pretty girl, a charming dowry; accordingly, one fine morning, quite cured, and assuming that, after the lapse of two months, the Bohemian affair must be completely finished and forgotten, the amorous cavalier arrived on a prancing horse at the door of the Gondelaurier mansion.

He paid no attention to a tolerably numerous rabble which had assembled in the Place du Parvis, before the portal of Notre-Dame; he remembered that it was the month of May; he supposed that it was some procession, some Pentecost, some festival, hitched his horse to the ring at the door, and gaily ascended the stairs to his beautiful betrothed.

She was alone with her mother.

The scene of the witch, her goat, her cursed alphabet, and Phœbus's long absences, still weighed on Fleur-de-Lys's heart. Nevertheless, when she beheld her captain enter, she thought him so handsome, his doublet so new, his baldrick so shining, and his air so impassioned, that she blushed with pleasure. The noble damsel herself was more charming than ever. Her magnificent blond hair was plaited in a ravishing manner, she was dressed entirely in that sky blue which becomes fair people so well, a bit of coquetry which she had learned from Colombe, and her eyes were swimming in that languor of love which becomes them still better.

Phœbus, who had seen nothing in the line of beauty, since he left the village maids of Queue-en-Brie, was intoxicated with Fleur-de-Lys, which imparted to our officer so eager and gallant an air, that his peace was immediately made. Madame de Gondelaurier herself, still maternally seated in her big arm-chair, had not the heart to scold him. As for Fleur-de-Lys's reproaches, they expired in tender cooings.

The young girl was seated near the window still embroidering her grotto of Neptune. The captain was leaning over the back of her chair, and she was addressing her caressing reproaches to him in a low voice.

"What has become of you these two long months, wicked man?"

"I swear to you," replied Phœbus, somewhat embarrassed by the question, "that you are beautiful enough to set an archbishop to dreaming."

She could not repress a smile.

"Good, good, sir. Let my beauty alone and answer my question. A fine beauty, in sooth!"

"Well, my dear cousin, I was recalled to the garrison."

"And where is that, if you please? and why did not you come to say farewell?"

"At Queue-en-Brie."

Phœbus was delighted with the first question, which helped him to avoid the second.

"But that is quite close by, monsieur. Why did you not come to see me a single time?"

Here Phœbus was rather seriously embarrassed.

"Because—the service—and then, charming cousin, I have been ill."

"Ill!" she repeated in alarm.

"Yes, wounded!"

"Wounded!"

She poor child was completely upset.

"Oh! do not be frightened at that," said Phœbus, carelessly, "it was nothing. A quarrel, a sword cut; what is that to you?"

"What is that to me?" exclaimed Fleur-de-Lys, raising her beautiful eyes filled with tears. "Oh! you do not say what you think when you speak thus. What sword cut was that? I wish to know all."

"Well, my dear fair one, I had a falling out with Mahè Fédy, you know? the lieutenant of Saint-Germain-en-Laye, and we ripped open a few inches of skin for each other. That is all."

The mendacious captain was perfectly well aware that an affair of honor always makes a man stand well in the eyes of a woman. In fact, Fleur-de-Lys looked him full in the face, all agitated with fear, pleasure, and admiration. Still, she was not completely reassured.

"Provided that you are wholly cured, my Phœbus!" said she. "I do not know your Mahè Fédy, but he is a villainous man. And whence arose this quarrel?"

Here Phœbus, whose imagination was endowed with but mediocre power of creation, began to find himself in a quandary as to a means of extricating himself for his prowess.

"Oh! how do I know?—a mere nothing, a horse, a remark! Fair cousin," he exclaimed, for the sake of changing the conversation, "what noise is this in the Cathedral Square?"

He approached the window.

"Oh! *Mon Dieu,* fair cousin, how many people there are on the Place!"

"I know not," said Fleur-de-Lys; "it appears that a witch is to do penance this morning before the church, and thereafter to be hung."

The captain was so thoroughly persuaded that la Esmeralda's affair was concluded, that he was but little disturbed by Fleur-de-Lys's words. Still, he asked her one or two questions.

"What is the name of this witch?"

"I do not know," she replied.

"And what is she said to have done?"

She shrugged her white shoulders.

"I know not."

"Oh, *mon Dieu Jésus!*" said her mother; "there are so many witches nowadays that I dare say they burn them without knowing their names. One might as well seek the name of every cloud in the sky. After all, one may be tranquil. The good God keeps his register." Here the venerable dame rose and came to the window. "Good Lord! you are right, Phœbus," said she. "The rabble is indeed great. There are people on all the roofs, blessed be God! Do you know, Phœbus, this reminds me of my best days. The entrance of King Charles VII, when, also, there were many people. I no longer remember in what year that was. When I speak of this to you, it produces upon you the effect—does it not?—the effect of something very old, and upon me of something very young. Oh! the crowd was far finer than at the present day. They even stood upon the machicolations of the Porte Sainte-Antoine. The king had the queen on a pillion, and after their highnesses came all the ladies mounted behind all the lords. I remember that they laughed loudly, because beside Amanyon de Garlande, who was very short of stature, there rode the Sire Matefelon, a chevalier of gigantic size, who had killed heaps of English. It was very fine. A procession of all the gentlemen of France, with their oriflammes waving red before the eye. There were some with pennons and some with banners. How can I tell? the Sire de Calan with a pennon; Jean de Châteaumorant with a banner; the Sire de Courcy with a banner, and a more ample one than any of the others except the Duc de Bourbon. Alas! 'tis a sad thing to think that all that has existed and exists no longer!"

The two lovers were not listening to the venerable dowager. Phœbus had returned and was leaning on the back of his betrothed's chair, a charming post whence his libertine glance plunged into all the openings of Fleur-de-Lys's gorget. This gorget gaped so conveniently, and allowed him to see so many exquisite things and to divine so many more, that Phœbus, dazzled by this skin with its gleams of satin, said to himself, "How can anyone love anything but a fair skin?"

Both were silent. The young girl raised sweet, enraptured eyes to him from time to time, and their hair mingled in a ray of spring sunshine.

"Phœbus," said Fleur-de-Lys suddenly, in a low voice, "we are to be married three months hence; swear to me that you have never loved any other woman than myself."

"I swear it, fair angel!" replied Phœbus, and his passionate glances aided the sincere tone of his voice in convincing Fleur-de-Lys.

Meanwhile, the good mother, charmed to see the betrothed pair on terms of such perfect understanding, had just quitted the apartment to attend to some domestic matter; Phœbus observed it, and this so emboldened the adventurous captain that very strange ideas mounted to his brain. Fleur-de-Lys loved him, he was her betrothed; she was alone with him; his former taste for her had reawakened, not with all its freshness but with all its ardor; after all, there is no great harm in tasting one's wheat while it is still in the blade; I do not know whether these ideas passed through his mind, but one thing is certain, that Fleur-de-Lys was suddenly alarmed by the expression of his glance. She looked round and saw that her mother was no longer there.

"Good heavens!" said she, blushing and uneasy, "how very warm I am?"

"I think, in fact," replied Phœbus, "that it cannot be far from midday. The sun is troublesome. We need only lower the curtains."

"No, no," exclaimed the poor little thing, "on the contrary, I need air."

And like a fawn who feels the breath of the pack of hounds, she rose, ran to the window, opened it, and rushed upon the balcony.

Phœbus, much discomfited, followed her.

The Place du Parvis Notre-Dame, upon which the balcony looked, as the reader knows, presented at that moment a singular and sinister spectacle which caused the fright of the timid Fleur-de-Lys to change its nature.

An immense crowd, which overflowed into all the neighboring streets, encumbered the Place, properly speaking. The little wall, breast high, which surrounded the Place, would not have sufficed to keep it free had it not been lined with a thick hedge of sergeants and hackbuteers, culverines in hand. Thanks to this thicket of pikes and arquebuses, the Parvis was empty. Its entrance was guarded by a force of halberdiers with the armorial bearings of the bishop. The large doors of the church were closed, and formed a contrast with the innumerable windows on the Place, which, open to their very gables, allowed a view of thousands of heads heaped up almost like the piles of bullets in a park of artillery.

The surface of this rabble was dingy, dirty, earthy. The spectacle which it was expecting was evidently one of the sort which possess the privilege of bringing out and calling together the vilest among the populace. Nothing is so hideous as the noise which was made by that swarm of yellow caps and dirty heads. In that throng there were more laughs than cries, more women than men.

From time to time, a sharp and vibrating voice pierced the general clamor.

"Ohé! Mahiet Baliffre! Is she to be hung yonder?"

"Fool! 'tis here that she is to make her apology in her shift! the good God is going to cough Latin in her face! That is always done here, at midday. If 'tis the gallows that you wish, go to the Grève."

"I will go there, afterwards."

"Tell me, la Boucanbry? Is it true that she has refused a confessor?"

"It appears so, la Bechaigne."

"You see what a pagan she is!"

" 'Tis the custom, monsieur. The bailiff of the courts is bound to deliver the malefactor ready judged for execution, if he be a layman, to the provost of Paris; if a clerk, to the official of the bishopric."

"Thank you, sir."

"Oh, God!" said Fleur-de-Lys, "the poor creature!"

This thought filled with sadness the glance which she cast upon the populace. The captain, much more occupied with her than with that pack of the rabble, was amorously rumpling her girdle behind. She turned round, entreating and smiling.

"Please let me alone, Phœbus! If my mother were to return, she would see your hand!"

At that moment, midday rang slowly out from the clock of Notre-Dame. A murmur of satisfaction broke out in the crowd. The last vibration of the twelfth stroke had hardly died away when all heads surged like the waves beneath a squall, and an immense shout went up from the pavement, the windows, and the roofs—

"There she is!"

Fleur-de-Lys pressed her hands to her eyes, that she might not see.

"Charming girl," said Phœbus, "do you wish to withdraw?"

"No," she replied; and she opened through curiosity, the eyes which she had closed through fear.

A tumbrel drawn by a stout Norman horse, and all surrounded by cavalry in violet livery with white crosses, had just debouched upon the Place through the Rue Saint-Pierre-aux-Bœufs. The sergeants of the watch were clearing a passage for it through the crowd, by stout blows from their clubs. Beside the cart rode several officers of justice and police, recognizable by their black costume and their awkwardness in the saddle. Master Jacques Charmolue paraded at their head.

In the fatal cart sat a young girl with her arms tied behind her back, and with no priest beside her. She was in her shift; her long black hair (the fashion then was to cut it off only at the foot of the gallows) fell in disorder upon her half-bared throat and shoulders.

Athwart that waving hair, more glossy than the plumage of a raven, a thick, rough, gray rope was visible, twisted and knotted, chafing her delicate collar-bones and twining round the charming neck of the poor girl, like an earthworm round a flower. Beneath that rope glittered a tiny amulet ornamented with bits of green glass, which had been left to her no doubt, because nothing is refused to those who are about to die. The spectators in the windows could see in the bottom of the cart her naked legs which she strove to hide beneath her, as by a final feminine instinct. At her feet lay a little goat, bound. The condemned girl held together with her teeth her imperfectly fastened shift. One would have said that she suffered still more in her misery from being thus exposed almost naked to the eyes of all. Alas! modesty is not made for such shocks.

"Jesus!" said Fleur-de-Lys hastily to the captain. "Look fair cousin, 'tis that wretched Bohemian with the goat."

So saying, she turned to Phœbus. His eyes were fixed on the tumbrel. He was very pale.

"What Bohemian with the goat?" he stammered.

"What!" resumed Fleur-de-Lys, "do you not remember?"

Phœbus interrupted her.

"I do not know what you mean."

He made a step to re-enter the room, but Fleur-de-Lys, whose jealousy, previously so vividly aroused by this same gypsy, had just been reawakened, Fleur-de-Lys gave him a look full of penetration and distrust. She vaguely recalled at that moment having heard of a captain mixed up in the trial of that witch.

"What is the matter with you?" she said to Phœbus, "one would say, that this woman had disturbed you."

Phœbus forced a sneer—

"Me! Not the least in the world! Ah! yes, certainly!"

"Remain, then!" she continued imperiously, "and let us see the end."

The unlucky captain was obliged to remain. He was somewhat reassured by the fact that the condemned girl never removed her eyes from the bottom of the cart. It was but too surely la Esmeralda. In this last stage of opprobrium and misfortune, she was still beautiful; her great black eyes appeared still larger, because of the emaciation of her cheeks; her pale profile was pure and sublime. She resembled what she had been, in the same degree that a virgin by Masaccio, resembles a virgin of Raphael—weaker, thinner, more delicate.

Moreover, there was nothing in her which was not shaken in some sort, and which with the exception of her modesty, she did not let go at will, so profoundly had she been broken by stupor and despair. Her body bounded at every jolt of the tumbrel like a dead or broken thing; her gaze was dull and imbecile. A tear was still visible in her eyes, but motionless and frozen, so to speak.

Meanwhile, the lugubrious cavalcade has traversed the crowd amid cries of joy and curious attitudes. But as a faithful historian, we must state that on beholding her so beautiful, so depressed, many were moved with pity, even among the hardest of them.

The tumbrel had entered the Parvis.

It halted before the central portal. The escort ranged themselves in line on both sides. The crowd became silent, and, in the midst of this silence full of anxiety and solemnity, the two leaves of the grand door swung back, as of themselves, on their hinges, which gave a creak like the sound of a fife. Then there became visible in all its length, the deep, gloomy church, hung in black, sparely lighted with a few candles gleaming afar off on the principal altar, opened in the midst of the Place which was dazzling with light, like the mouth of a cavern. At the very extremity, in the gloom of the apse, a gigantic silver cross was visible against a black drapery which hung from the vault to the pavement. The whole nave was deserted. But a few heads of priests could be seen moving confusedly in the distant choir stalls, and, at the moment when the great door opened, there escaped from the church a loud, solemn, and monotonous chanting, which cast over the head of the condemned girl, in gusts, fragments of melancholy psalms—

"Non timebo millia populi circumdantis me: exsurge, Domine; salvum me fac, Deus!
"Salvum me fac, Deus, quoniam intraverunt aquae usque ad animam meam.
"Infixus sum in limo profundi; et non est substantia."

At the same time, another voice, separate from the choir, intoned upon the steps of the chief altar, this melancholy offertory—

"Qui verbum meum audit, et credit ei qui misit me, habet vitam oeternam et in judicium non venit; sed transit a morte im vitam."[1]

This chant, which a few old men buried in the gloom sang from afar over that beautiful creature, full of youth and life, caressed by the warm air of spring, inundated with sunlight, was the mass for the dead.

The people listened devoutly.

The unhappy girl seemed to lose her sight and her consciousness in the obscure interior of the church. Her white lips moved as though in prayer, and the headsman's assistant who approached to assist her to alight from the cart, heard her repeating this word in a low tone—"Phœbus."

They untied her hands, made her alight, accompanied by her goat, which had also been unbound, and which bleated with joy at finding itself free: and they made her walk barefoot on the hard pavement to the foot of the steps leading to the door. The rope about her neck trailed behind her. One would have said it was a serpent following her.

Then the chanting in the church ceased. A great golden cross and a row of wax candles began to move through the gloom. The halberds of the motley beadles clanked; and, a few moments later, a long procession of priests in chasubles, and deacons in dalmatics, marched gravely toward the condemned girl, as they drawled their song, spread out before her view and that of the crowd. But her glance rested on the one who marched at the head, immediately after the cross-bearer.

"Oh!" she said in a low voice, and with a shudder, " 'tis he again! the priest!"

It was in fact, the archdeacon. On his left he had the sub-chanter, on his right, the chanter, armed with his official wand. He advanced with head thrown back, his eyes fixed and wide open, intoning in a strong voice—

"De ventre inferi clamavi, et exaudisti vocem meam.
"Et projecisti me in profundum in corde maris, et flumen circumdedit me."[2]

At the moment when he made his appearance in the full daylight beneath the lofty arched portal, enveloped in an ample cope of silver barred with a black cross, he was so pale that more than

1. "He that heareth my word and believeth on Him that sent me, hath eternal life, and hath not come into condemnation; but is passed from death to life."

2. "Out of the belly of hell cried I, and thou heardest my voice. For thou hadst cast me into the deep in the midst of seas, and the floods compassed me about."

one person in the crowd thought that one of the marble bishops who knelt on the sepulchral stones of the choir had risen and was come to receive upon the brink of the tomb, the woman who was about to die.

She, no less pale, no less like a statue, had hardly noticed that they had placed in her hand a heavy, lighted candle of yellow wax; she had not heard the yelping voice of the clerk reading the fatal contents of the apology; when they told her to respond with *Amen,* she responded *Amen.* She only recovered life and force when she beheld the priest make a sign to her guards to withdraw, and himself advance alone toward her.

Then she felt her blood boil in her head, and a remnant of indignation flashed up in that soul already benumbed and cold.

The archdeacon approached her slowly; even in that extremity, she beheld him cast an eye sparkling with sensuality, jealousy, and desire, over her exposed form. Then he said aloud—

"Young girl, have you asked God's pardon for your faults and shortcomings?"

He bent down to her ear, and added (the spectators supposed that he was receiving her last confession): "Will you have me? I can still save you!"

She looked intently at him: "Begone, demon, or I will denounce you!"

He gave vent to a horrible smile: "You will not be believed. You will only add a scandal to a crime. Reply quickly! Will you have me?"

"What have you done with my Phœbus?"

"He is dead!" said the priest.

At that moment the wretched archdeacon raised his head mechanically and beheld at the other end of the Place, in the balcony of the Gondelaurier mansion, the captain standing beside Fleur-de-Lys. He staggered, passed his hand across his eyes, looked again, muttered a curse, and all his features were violently contorted.

"Well, die then!" he hissed between his teeth. "No one shall have you." Then, raising his hand over the gypsy, he exclaimed in a funereal voice:—"*I nunc, anima anceps, et sit tibi Deus misericors!*"[1]

This was the dread formula with which it was the custom to conclude these gloomy ceremonies. It was the signal agreed upon between the priest and the executioner.

The crowd knelt.

"*Kyrie eleison,*"[2] said the priests, who had remained beneath the arch of the portal.

"*Kyrie eleison,*" repeated the throng in that murmur which runs over all heads, like the waves of a troubled sea.

"*Amen,*" said the archdeacon.

He turned his back on the condemned girl, his head sank upon his breast once more, he crossed his hands and rejoined his escort of priests, and a moment later he was seen to disappear, with the cross, the candles, and the copes, beneath the misty arches of the cathedral, and his sonorous voice was extinguished by degrees in the choir, as he chanted this verse of despair—

"Omnes gurgites tui et fluctus tui super me transierunt."[3]

At the same time, the intermittent clash of the iron butts of the beadles' halberds, gradually dying away among the columns of the nave, produced the effect of a clock hammer striking the last hour of the condemned.

The doors of Notre-Dame remained open, allowing a view of the empty desolate church, draped in mourning, without candles, and without voices.

1. "Go now, soul, trembling in the balance, and God have mercy upon thee."

2. "Lord have mercy upon us."

3. "All thy waves and thy billows have gone over me."

The condemned girl remained motionless in her place, waiting to be disposed of. One of the sergeants of police was obliged to notify Master Charmolue of the fact, as the latter, during this entire scene, had been engaged in studying the bas-relief of the grand portal which represents, according to some, the sacrifice of Abraham; according to others, the philosopher's alchemical operation: the sun being figured forth by the angel; the fire, by the fagot; the artisan, by Abraham.

There was considerable difficulty in drawing him away from that contemplation, but at length he turned round; and, at a signal which he gave, two men clad in yellow, the executioner's assistants, approached the gypsy to bind her hands once more.

The unhappy creature, at the moment of mounting once again the fatal cart, and proceeding to her last halting-place, was seized, possibly, with some poignant clinging to life. She raised her dry, red eyes to heaven, to the sun, to the silvery clouds, cut here and there by a blue trapezium or triangle; then she lowered them to objects around her, to the earth, the throng, the houses; all at once, while the yellow man was binding her elbows, she uttered a terrible cry, a cry of joy. Yonder, on that balcony, at the corner of the Place, she had just caught sight of him, of her friend, her lord, Phœbus, the other apparition of her life!

The judge had lied! the priest had lied! it was certainly he, she could not doubt it; he was there, handsome, alive, dressed in his brilliant uniform, his plume on his head, his sword by his side!

"Phœbus!" she cried, "my Phœbus!"

And she tried to stretch toward him arms trembling with love and rapture, but they were bound.

Then she saw the captain frown, a beautiful young girl who was leaning against him gazed at him with disdainful lips and irritated eyes; then Phœbus uttered some words which did not reach her, and both disappeared precipitately behind the window opening upon the balcony, which closed after them.

"Phœbus!" she cried wildly, "can it be you believe it?"

A monstrous thought had just presented itself to her. She remembered that she had been condemned to death for murder committed on the person of Phœbus de Châteaupers.

She had borne up until that moment. But this last blow was too harsh. She fell lifeless on the pavement.

"Come," said Charmolue, "carry her to the cart, and make an end of it."

No one had yet observed in the gallery of the statues of the kings, carved directly above the arches of the portal, a strange spectator, who had, up to that time, observed everything with such impassiveness, with a neck so strained, a visage so hideous that, in his motley accoutrement of red and violet, he might have been taken for one of those stone monsters through whose mouths the long gutters of the cathedral have discharged their waters for six hundred years. This spectator had missed nothing that had taken place since midday in front of the portal of Notre-Dame. And at the very beginning he had securely fastened to one of the small columns a large knotted rope, one end of which trailed on the flight of steps below. This being done, he began to look on tranquilly, whistling from time to time when a blackbird flitted past.

Suddenly, at the moment when the superintendent's assistants were preparing to execute Charmolue's phlegmatic order, he threw his leg over the balustrade of the gallery, seized the rope with his feet, his knees and his hands; then he was seen to glide down the façade, as a drop of rain slips down a window-pane, rush to the two executioners with the swiftness of a cat which has fallen from a roof, knock them down with two enormous fists, pick up the gypsy with one hand, as a child would her doll, and dash back into the church with a single bound, lifting the young girl above his head and crying in a formidable voice—

"Sanctuary!"

This was done with such rapidity, that had it taken place at night, the whole of it could have been seen in the space of a single flash of lightning.

"Sanctuary! Sanctuary!" repeated the crowd; and the clapping of ten thousand hands made Quasimodo's single eye sparkle with joy and pride.

This shock restored the condemned girl to her senses. She raised her eyelids, looked at Quasimodo, then closed them again suddenly, as though terrified by her deliverer.

Charmolue was stupefied, as well as the executioners and the entire escort. In fact, within the bounds of Notre-Dame, the condemned girl could not be touched. The cathedral was a place of refuge. All temporal jurisdiction expired upon its threshold.

Quasimodo had halted beneath the great portal, his huge feet seemed as solid on the pavement of the church as the heavy Roman pillars. His great, bushy head sat low between his shoulders, like the heads of lions, who also have a mane and no neck. He held the young girl, who was quivering all over, suspended from his horny hands like a white drapery; but he carried her with as much care as though he feared to break her or blight her. One would have said that he felt that she was a delicate, exquisite, precious thing, made for other hands than his. There were moments when he looked as if not daring to touch her, even with his breath. Then, all at once, he would press her forcibly in his arms, against his angular bosom, like his own possession, his treasure, as the mother of that child would have done. His gnome's eye, fastened upon her, inundated her with tenderness, sadness, and pity, and was suddenly raised filled with lightnings. Then the women laughed and wept, the crowd stamped with enthusiasm, for, at that moment Quasimodo had a beauty of his own. He was handsome; he, that orphan, that foundling, that outcast, he felt himself august and strong, he gazed in the face of that society from which he was banished, and in which he had so powerfully intervened, of that human justice from which he had wrenched its prey, of all those tigers whose jaws were forced to remain empty, of those policemen, those judges, those executioners, of all that force of the king which he, the meanest of creatures, had just broken, with the force of God.

And then, it was touching to behold this protection which had fallen from a being so hideous upon a being so unhappy, a creature condemned to death saved by Quasimodo. They were two extremes of natural and social wretchedness, coming into contact and aiding each other.

Meanwhile, after several moments of triumph, Quasimodo had plunged abruptly into the church with his burden. The populace, fond of all prowess, sought him with their eyes, beneath the gloomy nave, regretting that he had so speedily disappeared from their acclamations. All at once, he was seen to reappear at one of the extremities of the gallery of the kings of France; he traversed it, running like a madman, raising his conquest high in his arms and shouting: "Sanctuary!" The crowd broke forth into fresh applause. The gallery passed, he plunged once more into the interior of the church. A moment later, he reappeared upon the upper platform, with the gypsy still in his arms, still running madly, still crying, "Sanctuary!" and the throng applauded. Finally, he made his appearance for the third time upon the summit of the tower where hung the great bell; from that point he seemed to be showing to the entire city the girl whom he had saved, and his voice of thunder, that voice which was so rarely heard, and which he never heard himself, repeated thrice with frenzy, even to the clouds: "Sanctuary! Sanctuary! Sanctuary!"

"Noël! Noël!" shouted the populace in its turn; and that immense acclamation flew to astonish the crowd assembled at the Grève on the other bank, and the recluse who was still waiting with her eyes riveted on the gibbet.

BOOK NINTH

Chapter I

DELIRIUM

CLAUDE FROLLO WAS NO LONGER IN NOTRE-DAME WHEN HIS ADOPTED SON SO ABRUPTLY CUT THE fatal web in which the archdeacon and the gypsy were entangled. On returning to the sacristy he had torn off his alb, cope, and stole, had flung all into the hands of the stupefied beadle, had made his escape through the private door of the cloister, had ordered a boatman of the Terrain to transport him to the left bank of the Seine, and had plunged into the hilly streets of the University, not knowing whither he was going, encountering at every step groups of men and women who were hurrying joyously toward the Pont Saint-Michel, in the hope of still arriving in time to see the witch hung there—pale, wild, more troubled, more blind and more fierce than a night bird let loose and pursued by a troop of children in broad daylight. He no longer knew where he was, what he thought, or whether he were dreaming. He went forward, walking, running, taking any street at haphazard, making no choice, only urged ever onward away from the Grève, the horrible Grève, which he felt confusedly, to be behind him.

In this manner he skirted Mount Sainte-Geneviève, and finally emerged from the town by the Porte Saint-Victor. He continued his flight as long as he could see, when he turned round, the turreted enclosure of the University, and the rare houses of the suburb; but, when, at length, a rise of ground had completely concealed from him that odious Paris, when he could believe himself to be a hundred leagues distant from it, in the fields, in the desert, he halted, and it seemed to him that he breathed more freely.

Then frightful ideas thronged his mind. Once more he could see clearly into his soul, and he shuddered. He thought of that unhappy girl who had destroyed him, and whom he had destroyed. He cast a haggard eye over the double, tortuous way which fate had caused their two destinies to pursue up to their point of intersection, where it had dashed them against each other without mercy. He meditated on the folly of eternal vows, on the vanity of chastity, of science, of religion, of virtue, on the uselessness of God. He plunged to his heart's content in evil thoughts, and in proportion as he sank deeper, he felt a Satanic laugh burst forth within him.

And as he thus sifted his soul to the bottom, when he perceived how large a space nature had prepared there for the passions, he sneered still more bitterly. He stirred up in the depths of his heart all his hatred, all his malevolence; and, with the cold glance of a physician who examines a patient, he recognized the fact that this malevolence was nothing but vitiated love; that love, that source of every virtue in man, turned to horrible things in the heart of a priest, and that a man constituted like himself, in making himself a priest, made himself a demon. Then he laughed frightfully, and suddenly became pale again, when he considered the most sinister side of his fatal passion, of that corrosive, venomous malignant, implacable love, which had ended only in the gibbet for one of them and in hell for the other; condemnation for her, damnation for him.

And then his laughter came again, when he reflected that Phœbus was alive; that after all, the captain lived, was gay and happy, had handsomer doublets than ever, and a new mistress whom he was conducting to see the old one hanged. His sneer redoubled its bitterness when he reflected that out of the living beings whose death he had desired, the gypsy, the only creature whom he did not hate, was the only one who had not escaped him.

Then from the captain, his thought passed to the people, and there came to him a jealousy of an unprecedented sort. He reflected that the people also, the entire populace, had had before their eyes the woman whom he loved exposed almost naked. He writhed his arms with agony as he thought that the woman whose form, caught by him alone in the darkness would have been supreme happiness, had been delivered up in broad daylight at full noonday, to a whole people, clad as for a night of voluptuousness. He wept with rage over all these mysteries of love, profaned, soiled, laid bare, withered forever. He wept with rage as he pictured to himself how many impure looks had been gratified at the sight of that badly fastened shift, and that this beautiful girl, this virgin lily, this cup of modesty and delight, to which he would have dared to place his lips only trembling, had just been transformed into a sort of public bowl, whereat the vilest populace of Paris, thieves, beggars, lackeys, had come to quaff in common an audacious, impure, and depraved pleasure.

And when he sought to picture to himself the happiness which he might have found upon earth, if she had not been a gypsy, and if he had not been a priest, if Phœbus had not existed and if she had loved him; when he pictured to himself that a life of serenity and love would have been possible to him also, even to him; that there were at that very moment, here and there upon the earth, happy couples spending the hours in sweet converse beneath orange-trees, on the banks of brooks, in the presence of a setting sun, of a starry night; and that if God had so willed, he might have formed with her one of those blessed couples—his heart melted in tenderness and despair.

Oh! she! still she! It was this fixed idea which returned incessantly, which tortured him, which ate into his brain, and rent his vitals. He did not regret, he did not repent; all that he had done he was ready to do again; he preferred to behold her in the hands of the executioner rather than in the arms of the captain. But he suffered; he suffered so that at intervals he tore out handfuls of his hair to see whether it were not turning white.

Among other moments there came one, when it occurred to him that it was perhaps the very minute when the hideous chain which he had seen that morning, was pressing its iron noose closer about that frail and graceful neck. This thought caused the perspiration to start from every pore.

There was another moment when, while laughing diabolically at himself, he represented to himself la Esmeralda as he had seen her on that first day, lively, careless, joyous, gaily attired, dancing, winged, harmonious, and la Esmeralda of the last day, in her scanty shift, with a rope about her neck, mounting slowly with her bare feet, the angular ladder of the gallows; he figured to himself this double picture in such a manner that he gave vent to a terrible cry.

While this hurricane of despair overturned, broke, tore up, bent, uprooted everything in his soul, he gazed at nature around him. At his feet, some chickens were searching the thickets and pecking, enameled beetles ran about in the sun; overhead, some groups of dappled gray clouds were floating across the blue sky; on the horizon, the spire of the Abbey Saint-Victor pierced the ridge of the hill with its slate obelisk; and the miller of the Copeaue hillock was whistling as he watched the laborious wings of his mill turning. All this active, organized, tranquil life, recurring around him under a thousand forms, hurt him. He resumed his flight.

He sped thus across the fields until evening. This flight from nature, life, himself, man, God, everything, lasted all day long. Sometimes he flung himself face downward on the earth, and tore up the young blades of wheat with his nails. Sometimes he halted in the deserted street of a village, and his thoughts were so intolerable that he grasped his head in both hands and tried to tear it from his shoulders in order to dash it upon the pavement.

Toward the hour of sunset, he examined himself again, and found himself nearly mad. The tempest which had raged within him ever since the instant when he had lost the hope and the will to save the gypsy—that tempest had not left in his conscience a single healthy idea, a single thought which maintained its upright position. His reason lay there almost entirely destroyed. There remained but two distinct images in his mind, la Esmeralda and the gallows; all the rest was blank. Those two images united, presented to him a frightful group; and the more he concentrated what attention and thought was left to him, the more he beheld them grow, in accordance with a fantastic progression, the one in grace, in charm, in beauty, in light, the other in deformity and horror; so that at last la Esmeralda appeared to him like a star, the gibbet like an enormous, fleshless arm.

One remarkable fact is, that during the whole of this torture, the idea of dying did not seriously occur to him. The wretch was made so. He clung to life. Perhaps he really saw hell beyond it.

Meanwhile, the day continued to decline. The living being which still existed in him reflected vaguely on retracing its steps. He believed himself to be far away from Paris; on taking his bearings, he perceived that he had only circled the enclosure of the University. The spire of Saint-Sulpice, and the three lofty needles of Saint Germain-des-Prés, rose above the horizon on his right. He turned his steps in that direction. When he heard the brisk challenge of the men-at-arms of the abbey, around the crenelated, circumscribing wall of Saint-Germain, he turned aside, took a path which presented itself between the abbey and the lazar-house of the bourg, and at the expiration of a few minutes found himself on the verge of the Pré-aux-Clercs. This meadow was celebrated by reason of the brawls which went on there night and day; it was the *hydra* of the poor monks of Saint-Germain: *quod monachis Sancti-Germaini pratensis hydra fuit, clericis nova semper dissidiorum capita suscitantibus.* The archdeacon was afraid of meeting someone there, he feared every human countenance; he had just avoided the University and the Bourg Saint-Germain; he wished to re-enter the streets as late as possible. He skirted the Pré-aux-Clercs, took the deserted path which separated it from the Dieu-Neuf, and at last reached the water's edge. There Dom Claude found a boatman, who, for a few farthings in Parisian coinage, rowed him up the Seine as far as the point of the city, and landed him on that tongue of abandoned land where the reader has already beheld Gringoire dreaming, and which was prolonged beyond the king's gardens, parallel to the Ile du Passeur-aux-Vaches.

The monotonous rocking of the boat and the ripple of the water had, in some sort, quieted the unhappy Claude. When the boatman had taken his departure, he remained standing stupidly on the strand, staring straight before him and perceiving objects only through magnifying oscillations which rendered everything a sort of phantasmagoria to him. The fatigue of a great grief not infrequently produces this effect on the mind.

The sun had set behind the lofty Tour-de-Nesle. It was the twilight hour. The sky was white, the water of the river was white. Between these two white expanses, the left bank of the Seine, on which his eyes were fixed, projected its gloomy mass and, rendered ever thinner and thinner by perspective, it plunged into the gloom of the horizon like a black spire. It was loaded with houses, of which only the obscure outline could be distinguished, sharply brought out in shadows against the light background of the sky and the water. Here and there windows began to gleam, like the holes in a brazier. That immense black obelisk thus isolated between the two white expanses of the sky and the river, which was very broad at this point, produced upon Dom Claude a singular effect, comparable to that which would be experienced by a man who, reclining on his back at the foot of the tower of Strasbourg, should gaze at the enormous spire plunging into the shadows of the twilight above his head. Only, in this case, it was Claude who was erect and the obelisk which was lying down; but, as the river, reflecting the sky, prolonged the abyss below him, the immense promontory seemed to be as boldly launched into space as any cathedral spire; and the impression was the same. This impression had even one stronger and more profound point about it, that it was indeed the tower of Strasbourg, but the tower of Strasbourg two leagues in height; something unheard of, gigantic, immeasurable; an edifice such as no human eye has ever seen; a tower of Babel. The chimneys of the houses, the battlements of the walls, the faceted gables of the roofs, the spire of the Augustines, the tower of Nesle, all these projections which broke the profile of the colossal obelisk added to the illusion by displaying in eccentric fashion to the eye the indentations of a luxuriant and fantastic sculpture.

Claude, in the state of hallucination in which he found himself, believed that he saw, that he saw with his actual eyes, the bell tower of hell; the thousand lights scattered over the whole height of the terrible tower seemed to him so many porches of the immense interior furnace; the voices and noises which escaped from it seemed so many shrieks, so many death groans. Then he became alarmed, he put his hands on his ears that he might no longer hear, turned his back that he might no longer see, and fled from the frightful vision with hasty strides.

But the vision was in himself.

When he re-entered the streets, the passers-by elbowing each other by the light of the shop-fronts, produced upon him the effect of a constant going and coming of specters about him. There were strange noises in his ears; extraordinary fancies disturbed his brain. He saw neither houses, nor pavements, nor chariots, nor men and women, but a chaos of indeterminate objects whose edges melted into each other. At the corner of the Rue de la Barillerie, there was a grocer's shop whose porch was garnished all about, according to immemorial custom, with hoops of tin from which hung a circle of wooden candles, which came in contact with each other in the wind, and rattled like castanets. He thought he heard a cluster of skeletons at Montfaucon clashing together in the gloom.

"Oh!" he muttered, "the night breeze dashes them against each other, and mingles the noise of their chains with the rattle of their bones! Perhaps she is there among them!"

In his state of frenzy, he knew not whither he was going. After a few strides he found himself on the Pont Saint-Michel. There was a light in the window of a ground-floor room; he approached. Through a cracked window he beheld a mean chamber which recalled some confused memory to his mind. In that room, badly lighted by a meager lamp, there was a fresh, light-haired young man, with a merry face, who amid loud bursts of laughter was embracing a very audaciously attired young girl; and near the lamp sat an old crone spinning and singing in a quavering voice. As the young man did not laugh constantly, fragments of the old woman's ditty reached the priest; it was something unintelligible yet frightful—

> *Grève, aboie, Grève, grouille!*
> *File, file, ma quenouille,*
> *File sa corde au bourreau,*
> *Qui siffle dans le préau,*
> *Grève, aboie, Grève, grouille!*
>
> *La belle corde de chanvre!*
> *Semez d'Issy jusqu'á Vanvre*
> *Du chanvre et non pas du blé.*
> *Le voleur n'a pas volé*
> *La belle corde de chanvre.*
>
> *Grève, grouille, Grève, aboie!*
> *Pour voir la fille de joie,*
> *Prendre au gibet chassieux,*
> *Les fenêtres sont des yeux.*
> *Grève, grouille, Grève, aboie!*[1]

1. Bark, Grève, grumble, Grève! Spin, spin, my distaff, spin her rope for the hangman, who is whistling in the meadow. What a beautiful hempen rope! Sow hemp, not wheat, from Issy to Vanvre. The thief hath not stolen the beautiful hempen rope. Grumble, Grève, bark, Grève! To see the dissolute wench hang on the blear-eyed gibbet, windows are eyes.

Thereupon the young man laughed and caressed the wench. The crone was la Falourdel; the girl was a courtesan; the young man was his brother Jehan.

He continued to gaze. That spectacle was as good as any other.

He saw Jehan go to a window at the end of the room, open it, cast a glance on the quay, where in the distance blazed a thousand lighted casements, and he heard him say as he closed the sash—

" 'Pon my soul! How dark it is; the people are lighting their candles, and the good God his stars."

Then Jehan came back to the hag, smashed a bottle standing on the table, exclaiming—

"Already empty, cor-boeuf! and I have no more money! Isabeau, my dear, I shall not be satisfied with Jupiter until he has changed your two white nipples into two black bottles, where I may suck wine of Beaune day and night."

This fine pleasantry made the courtesan laugh, and Jehan left the room.

Dom Claude had barely time to fling himself on the ground in order that he might not be met, stared in the face and recognized by his brother. Luckily, the street was dark, and the scholar was tipsy. Nevertheless, he caught sight of the archdeacon prone upon the earth in the mud.

"Oh! oh!" said he; "here's a fellow who has been leading a jolly life, to-day."

He stirred up Dom Claude with his foot, and the latter held his breath.

"Dead drunk," resumed Jehan. "Come, he's full. A regular leech detached from a hogshead. He's bald," he added, bending down, " 'tis an old man! *Fortunate senex!*"

Then Dom Claude heard him retreat, saying—

" 'Tis all the same, reason is a fine thing, and my brother the archdeacon is very happy in that he is wise and has money."

Then the archdeacon rose to his feet, and ran without halting, toward Notre-Dame, whose enormous towers he beheld rising above the houses through the gloom.

At the instant when he arrived, panting, on the Place du Parvis, he shrank back and dared not raise his eyes to the fatal edifice.

"Oh!" he said, in a low voice, "is it really true that such a thing took place here, to-day, this very morning?"

Still, he ventured to glance at the church. The front was somber; the sky behind was glittering with stars. The crescent of the moon, in her flight upward from the horizon, had paused at the moment, on the summit of the right hand tower, and seemed to have perched itself, like a luminous bird, on the edge of the balustrade, cut out in black trefoils.

The cloister door was shut; but the archdeacon always carried with him the key of the tower in which his laboratory was situated. He made use of it to enter the church.

In the church he found the gloom and silence of a cavern. By the deep shadows which fell in broad sheets from all directions, he recognized the fact that the hangings for the ceremony of the morning had not yet been removed. The great silver cross shone from the depths of the gloom, powdered with some sparkling points, like the milky way of that sepulchral night. The long windows of the choir showed the upper extremities of their arches above the black draperies, and their painted panes, traversed by a ray of moonlight had no longer any hues but the doubtful colors of night, a sort of violet, white and blue, whose tint is found only on the faces of the dead. The archdeacon, on perceiving these wan spots all around the choir, thought he beheld the miters of damned bishops. He shut his eyes, and when he opened them again, he thought they were a circle of pale visages gazing at him.

He started to flee across the church. Then it seemed to him that the church also was shaking, moving, becoming endued with animation, that it was alive; that each of the great columns was turning into an enormous paw, which was beating the earth with its big stone spatula, and that the gigantic cathedral was no longer anything but a sort of prodigious elephant, which was breathing and marching with its pillars for feet, its two towers for trunks and the immense black cloth for its housings.

This fever or madness had reached such a degree of intensity that the external world was no longer anything more for the unhappy man than a sort of Apocalypse—visible, palpable, terrible.

For one moment, he was relieved. As he plunged into the side aisles, he perceived a reddish light behind a cluster of pillars. He ran toward it as to a star. It was the poor lamp which lighted the public breviary of Notre-Dame night and day, beneath its iron grating. He flung himself eagerly upon the holy book in the hope of finding some consolation, or some encouragement there. The book lay open at this passage of Job, over which his staring eye glanced—

"And a spirit passed before my face, and I heard a small voice, and the hair of my flesh stood up."

On reading these gloomy words, he felt that which a blind man feels when he feels himself pricked by the staff which he has picked up. His knees gave way beneath him, and he sank upon the pavement, thinking of her who had died that day. He felt so many monstrous vapors pass and discharge themselves in his brain, that it seemed to him that his head had become one of the chimneys of hell.

It would appear that he remained a long time in this attitude, no longer thinking, overwhelmed and passive beneath the hand of the demon. At length some strength returned to him; it occurred to him to take refuge in his tower beside his faithful Quasimodo. He rose; and, as he was afraid, he took the lamp from the breviary to light his way. It was a sacrilege; but he had got beyond heeding such a trifle now.

He slowly climbed the stairs of the towers, filled with a secret fright which must have been communicated to the rare passers-by in the Place du Parvis by the mysterious light of his lamp, mounting so late from loophole to loophole of the bell tower.

All at once, he felt a freshness on his face, and found himself at the door of the highest gallery. The air was cold; the sky was filled with hurrying clouds, whose large, white flakes drifted one upon another like the breaking up of river ice after the winter. The crescent of the moon, stranded in the midst of the clouds, seemed a celestial vessel caught in the ice-cakes of the air.

He lowered his gaze, and contemplated for a moment, through the railing of slender columns which unites the two towers, far away, through a gauze of mists and smoke, the silent throng of the roofs of Paris, pointed, innumerable, crowded and small like the waves of a tranquil sea on a summer night.

The moon cast a feeble ray, which imparted to earth and heaven an ashy hue.

At that moment the clock raised its shrill, cracked voice. Midnight rang out. The priest thought of midday; twelve o'clock had come back again.

"Oh!" he said in a very low tone, "she must be cold now."

All at once, a gust of wind extinguished his lamp, and almost at the same instant, he beheld a shade, a whiteness, a form, a woman, appear from the opposite angle of the tower. He started. Beside this woman was a little goat, which mingled its bleat with the last bleat of the clock.

He had strength enough to look. It was she.

She was pale, she was gloomy. Her hair fell over her shoulders as in the morning; but there was no longer a rope on her neck, her hands were no longer bound; she was free, she was dead.

She was dressed in white and had a white veil on her head.

She came toward him, slowly, with her gaze fixed on the sky. The supernatural goat followed her. He felt as though made of stone and too heavy to flee. At every step which she took in advance, he took one backwards, and that was all. In this way he retreated once more beneath the gloomy arch of the stairway. He was chilled by the thought that she might enter there also; had she done so, he would have died of terror.

She did arrive, in fact, in front of the door to the stairway, and paused there for several minutes, stared intently into the darkness, but without appearing to see the priest, and passed on. She seemed taller to him than when she had been alive; he saw the moon through her white robe; he heard her breath.

When she had passed on, he began to descend the staircase again, with the slowness which he had observed in the specter, believing himself to be a specter too, haggard, with hair on end, his extinguished lamp still in his hand; and as he descended the spiral steps, he distinctly heard in his ear a voice laughing and repeating—

"A spirit passed before my face, and I heard a small voice, and the hair of my flesh stood up."

Chapter II

HUNCHBACKED, ONE-EYED, LAME

EVERY CITY DURING THE MIDDLE AGES, AND EVERY CITY IN FRANCE DOWN TO THE TIME OF LOUIS XII had its places of asylum. These sanctuaries, in the midst of the deluge of penal and barbarous jurisdictions which inundated the city, were a species of islands which rose above the level of human justice. Every criminal who landed there was safe. There were in every suburb almost as many places of asylum as gallows. It was the abuse of impunity by the side of the abuse of punishment; two bad things which strove to correct each other. The palaces of the king, the hôtels of the princes, and especially churches, possessed the right of asylum. Sometimes a whole city which stood in need of being repeopled was temporarily created a place of refuge. Louis XI made all Paris a refuge in 1467.

His foot once within the asylum, the criminal was sacred; but he must beware of leaving it; one step outside the sanctuary, and he fell back into the flood. The wheel, the gibbet, the strappado, kept good guard around the place of refuge, and lay in watch incessantly for their prey, like sharks around a vessel. Hence, condemned men were to be seen whose hair had grown white in a cloister, on the steps of a palace, in the enclosure of an abbey, beneath the porch of a church; in this manner the asylum was a prison as much as any other. It sometimes happened that a solemn decree of parliament violated the asylum and restored the condemned man to the executioner; but this was of rare occurrence. Parliaments were afraid of the bishops, and when there was friction between these two robes, the gown had but a poor chance against the cassock. Sometimes, however, as in the affair of the assassins of Petit-Jean, the headsman of Paris, and in that of Emery Rousseau, the murderer of Jean Valleret, justice overleaped the church and passed on to the execution of its sentences; but unless by virtue of a decree of Parliament, woe to him who violated a place of asylum with armed force! The reader knows the manner of death of Robert de Clermont, Marshal of France, and of Jean de Châlons, Marshal of Champagne; and yet the question was only of a certain Perrin Marc, the clerk of a money-changer, a miserable assassin; but the two marshals had broken the doors of St. Méry. Therein lay the enormity.

Such respect was cherished for places of refuge that, according to tradition, animals even felt it at times. Aymoire relates that a stag, being chased by Dagobert, having taken refuge near the tomb of Saint-Denis, the pack of hounds stopped short and barked.

Churches generally had a small apartment prepared for the reception of supplicants. In 1407, Nicolas Flamel caused to be built on the vaults of Saint-Jacques de la Boucherie, a chamber which cost him four livres six sous, sixteen farthings, parisis.

At Notre-Dame it was a tiny cell situated on the roof of the side aisle, beneath the flying buttresses, precisely at the spot where the wife of the present janitor of the towers has made for herself a garden, which is to the hanging gardens of Babylon what a lettuce is to a palm-tree, what a porter's wife is to a Semiramis.

It was here that Quasimodo had deposited la Esmeralda, after his wild and triumphant course. As long as that course lasted, the young girl had been unable to recover her senses, half unconscious, half awake, no longer feeling anything, except that she was mounting through the air, floating in it, flying in it, that something was raising her above the earth. From time to time she heard the loud laughter, the noisy voice of Quasimodo in her ear; she half opened her eyes; then below her she confusedly beheld Paris checkered with its thousand roofs of slate and tiles, like a red and blue mosaic, above her head the frightful and joyous face of Quasimodo. Then her eyelids drooped again; she thought that all was over, that they had executed her during her swoon, and that the misshapen spirit which had presided over her destiny, had laid hold of her and was bearing her away. She dared not look at him, and she surrendered herself to her fate.

But when the bellringer, disheveled and panting, had deposited her in the cell of refuge, when she felt his huge hands gently detaching the cord which bruised her arms, she felt that sort of shock which awakens with a start the passengers of a vessel which runs aground in the middle of a dark night. Her thoughts awoke also, and returned to her one by one. She saw that she was in Notre-Dame; she remembered having been torn from the hands of the executioner; that Phœbus was alive, that Phœbus loved her no longer; and as these two ideas, one of which shed so much bitterness over the other, presented themselves simultaneously to the poor condemned girl; she turned to Quasimodo, who was standing in front of her, and who terrified her; she said to him—

"Why have you saved me?"

He gazed at her with anxiety, as though seeking to divine what she was saying to him. She repeated her question. Then he gave her a profoundly sorrowful glance and fled.

She was astonished.

A few moments later he returned, bearing a package which he cast at her feet. It was clothing which some charitable women had left on the threshold of the church for her.

Then she dropped her eyes upon herself and saw that she was almost naked, and blushed. Life had returned.

Quasimodo appeared to experience something of this modesty. He covered his eyes with his large hand and retired once more, but slowly.

She made haste to dress herself. The robe was a white one with a white veil—the garb of a novice of the Hôtel-Dieu.

She had barely finished when she beheld Quasimodo returning. He carried a basket under one arm and a mattress under the other. In the basket there was a bottle, bread, and some provisions. He set the basket on the floor and said, "Eat!" He spread the mattress on the flagging and said, "Sleep."

It was his own repast, it was his own bed, which the bellringer had gone in search of.

The gypsy raised her eyes to thank him, but she could not articulate a word. She dropped her head with a quiver of terror.

Then he said to her—

"I frighten you. I am very ugly, am I not? Do not look at me; only listen to me. During the day you will remain here; at night you can walk all over the church. But do not leave the church either by day or by night. You would be lost. They would kill you, and I should die."

She was touched and raised her head to answer him. He had disappeared. She found herself alone once more, meditating upon the singular words of this almost monstrous being, and struck by the sound of his voice, which was so hoarse yet so gentle.

Then she examined her cell. It was a chamber about six feet square, with a small window and a door on the slightly sloping plane of the roof formed of flat stones. Many gutters with the figures of animals seemed to be bending down around her, and stretching their necks in order to stare at her through the window. Over the edge of her roof she perceived the tops of thousands of chimneys which caused the smoke of all the fires in Paris to rise beneath her eyes. A sad sight for the poor gypsy, a foundling, condemned to death, an unhappy creature, without country, without family, without a hearthstone.

At the moment when the thought of her isolation thus appeared to her more poignant than ever, she felt a bearded and hairy head glide between her hands, upon her knees. She started (everything alarmed her now) and looked. It was the poor goat, the agile Djali, which had made its escape after her, at the moment when Quasimodo had put to flight Charmolue's brigade, and which had been lavishing caresses on her feet for nearly an hour past, without being able to win a glance. The gypsy covered him with kisses.

"Oh! Djali!" she said, "how I have forgotten thee! And so thou still thinkest of me! Oh! thou art not an ingrate!"

At the same time, as though an invisible hand had lifted the weight which had repressed her tears in her heart for so long, she began to weep, and, in proportion as her tears flowed, she felt all that was most acrid and bitter in her grief depart with them.

Evening came, she thought the night so beautiful that she made the circuit of the elevated gallery which surrounds the church. It afforded her some relief, so calm did the earth appear when viewed from that height.

Chapter III

DEAF

ON THE FOLLOWING MORNING, SHE PERCEIVED ON AWAKING, THAT SHE HAD BEEN ASLEEP. THIS singular thing astonished her. She had been so long unaccustomed to sleep! A joyous ray of the rising sun entered through her window and touched her face. At the same time with the sun, she beheld at that window an object which frightened her, the unfortunate face of Quasimodo. She involuntarily closed her eyes again, but in vain; she fancied that she still saw through the rosy lids that gnome's mask, one-eyed and gap-toothed. Then, while she still kept her eyes closed, she heard a rough voice saying, very gently—

"Be not afraid. I am your friend. I came to watch you sleep. It does not hurt you if I come to see you sleep, does it? What difference does it make to you if I am here when your eyes are closed! Now I am going. Stay, I have placed myself behind the wall. You can open your eyes again."

There was something more plaintive than these words, and that was the accent in which they were uttered. The gypsy, much touched, opened her eyes. He was, in fact, no longer at the window. She approached the opening, and beheld the poor hunchback crouching in an angle of the wall, in a sad and resigned attitude. She made an effort to surmount the repugnance with which he inspired her. "Come," she said to him gently. From the movement of the gypsy's lips, Quasimodo thought that she was driving him away; then he rose and retired limping, slowly, with drooping head, without even daring to raise to the young girl his gaze full of despair. "Do come," she cried, but he continued to retreat. Then she darted from her cell, ran to him, and grasped his arm. On feeling her touch him, Quasimodo trembled in every limb. He raised his suppliant eye, and seeing that she was leading him back to her quarters, his whole face beamed with joy and tenderness. She tried to make him enter the cell; but he persisted in remaining on the threshold. "No, no," said he; "the owl enters not the nest of the lark."

Then she crouched down gracefully on her couch, with her goat asleep at her feet. Both remained motionless for several moments, considering in silence, she so much grace, he so much ugliness. Every moment she discovered some fresh deformity in Quasimodo. Her glance traveled from his knock knees to his humped back, from his humped back to his only eye. She could not comprehend the existence of a being so awkwardly fashioned. Yet there was so much sadness and so much gentleness spread over all this, that she began to become reconciled to it.

He was the first to break the silence. "So you were telling me to return?"

She made an affirmative sign of the head, and said, "Yes."

He understood the motion of the head. "Alas!" he said, as though hesitating whether to finish, "I am—I am deaf."

"Poor man!" exclaimed the Bohemian, with an expression of kindly pity.

He began to smile sadly.

"You think that that was all that I lacked, do you not? Yes, I am deaf, that is the way I am made. 'Tis horrible, is it not? You are so beautiful!"

There lay in the accents of the wretched man so profound a consciousness of his misery, that she had not the strength to say a word. Besides, he would not have heard her. He went on—

"Never have I seen my ugliness as at the present moment. When I compare myself to you, I feel a very great pity for myself, poor unhappy monster that I am! Tell me, I must look to you like a beast. You, you are a ray of sunshine, a drop of dew, the song of a bird! I am something frightful, neither man nor animal, I know not what, harder, more trampled underfoot, and more unshapely than a pebble stone!"

Then he began to laugh, and that laugh was the most heartbreaking thing in the world. He continued—

"Yes, I am deaf; but you shall talk to me by gestures, by signs. I have a master who talks with me in that way. And then, I shall very soon know your wish from the movement of your lips, from your look."

"Well!" she interposed with a smile, "tell me why you saved me."

He watched her attentively while she was speaking.

"I understand," he replied. "You ask me why I saved you. You have forgotten a wretch who tried to abduct you one night, a wretch to whom you rendered succor on the following day on their infamous pillory. A drop of water and a little pity—that is more than I can repay with my life. You have forgotten that wretch; but he remembers it."

She listened to him with profound tenderness. A tear swam in the eye of the bellringer, but did not fall. He seemed to make it a sort of point of honor to retain it.

"Listen," he resumed, when he was no longer afraid that the tear would escape; "our towers here are very high, a man who should fall from them would be dead before touching the pavement; when it shall please you to have me fall, you will not have to utter even a word, a glance will suffice."

Then he rose. Unhappy as was the Bohemian, this eccentric being still aroused some compassion in her. She made him a sign to remain.

"No, no," said he; "I must not remain too long. I am not at my ease. It is out of pity that you do not turn away your eyes. I shall go to some place where I can see you without your seeing me: it will be better so."

He drew from his pocket a little metal whistle.

"Here," said he, "when you have need of me, when you wish me to come, when you will not feel too much horror at the sight of me, use this whistle. I can hear this sound."

He laid the whistle on the floor and fled.

Chapter IV

EARTHENWARE AND CRYSTAL

DAY FOLLOWED DAY. CALM GRADUALLY RETURNED TO THE SOUL OF LA ESMERALDA. EXCESS OF grief, like excess of joy is a violent thing which lasts but a short time. The heart of man cannot remain long in one extremity. The gypsy had suffered so much, that nothing was left her but astonishment. With security, hope had returned to her. She was outside the pale of society, outside the pale of life, but she had a vague feeling that it might not be impossible to return to it. She was like a dead person, who should hold in reserve the key to her tomb.

She felt the terrible images which had so long persecuted her, gradually departing. All the hideous phantoms, Pierrat Torterue, Jacques Charmolue, were effaced from her mind, all, even the priest.

And then, Phœbus was alive; she was sure of it, she had seen him. To her the fact of Phœbus being alive was everything. After the series of fatal shocks which had overturned everything within her, she had found but one thing intact in her soul, one sentiment—her love for the captain. Love is like a tree; it sprouts forth of itself, sends its roots out deeply through our whole being, and often continues to flourish greenly over a heart in ruins.

And the inexplicable point about it is that the more blind is this passion, the more tenacious it is. It is never more solid than when it has no reason in it.

La Esmeralda did not think of the captain without bitterness, no doubt. No doubt it was terrible that he also should have been deceived; that he should have believed that impossible thing, that he could have conceived of a stab dealt by her who would have given a thousand lives for him. But, after all, she must not be too angry with him for it; had she not confessed her crime? had she not yielded, weak woman that she was, to torture? The fault was entirely hers. She should have allowed her finger-nails to be torn out rather than such a word to be wrenched from her. In short, if she could but see Phœbus once more, for a single minute, only one word would be required, one look, in order to undeceive him, to bring him back. She did not doubt it. She was astonished also at many singular things, at the accident of Phœbus's presence on the day of the penance, at the young girl with whom he had been. She was his sister, no doubt. An unreasonable explanation, but she contented herself with it, because she needed to believe that Phœbus still loved her, and loved her alone. Had he not sworn it to her? What more was needed, simple and credulous as she was? And then, in this matter, were not appearances much more against her than against him? Accordingly, she waited. She hoped.

Let us add that the church, that vast church, which surrounded her on every side, which guarded her, which saved her, was itself a sovereign tranquilizer. The solemn lines of that architecture, the religious attitude of all the objects which surrounded the young girl, the serene and pious thoughts which emanated, so to speak, from all the pores of that stone, acted upon her without her being aware of it. The edifice had also sounds fraught with such benediction and such majesty, that they soothed this ailing soul. The monotonous chanting of the celebrants, the responses of the people to the priest, sometimes inarticulate, sometimes thunderous, the harmonious trembling of the painted windows, the organ, bursting forth like a hundred trumpets, the three belfries, humming like hives of huge bees, that whole orchestra on which bounded a gigantic scale, ascending, descending incessantly from the voice of a throng to that of one bell, dulled her memory, her imagination, her grief. The bells, in particular, lulled her. It was something like a powerful magnetism which those vast instruments shed over her in great waves.

Thus every sunrise found her more calm, breathing better, less pale. In proportion as her inward wounds closed, her grace and beauty blossomed once more on her countenance, but more thoughtful, more reposeful. Her former character also returned to her, somewhat even of her gaiety, her pretty pout, her love for her goat, her love for singing, her modesty. She took care to dress herself in the morning in the corner of her cell for fear some inhabitants of the neighboring attics might see her through the window.

When the thought of Phœbus left her time, the gypsy sometimes thought of Quasimodo. He was the sole bond, the sole connection, the sole communication which remained to her with men, with the living. Unfortunate girl! she was more outside the world than Quasimodo. She understood not in the least the strange friend whom chance had given her. She often reproached herself for not feeling a gratitude which should close her eyes, but decidedly, she could not accustom herself to the poor bellringer. He was too ugly.

She had left the whistle which he had given her lying on the ground. This did not prevent Quasimodo from making his appearance from time to time during the first few days. She did her best not to turn aside with too much repugnance when he came to bring her her basket of provisions or her jug of water, but he always perceived the slightest movement of this sort, and then he withdrew sadly.

Once he came at the moment when she was caressing Djali. He stood pensively for several minutes before this graceful group of the goat and the gypsy; at last he said, shaking his heavy and ill-formed head—

"My misfortune is that I still resemble a man too much. I should like to be wholly a beast like that goat."

She gazed at him in amazement.

He replied to the glance—

"Oh! I well know why," and he went away.

On another occasion he presented himself at the door of the cell (which he never entered) at the moment when la Esmeralda was singing an old Spanish ballad, the words of which she did not understand, but which had lingered in her ear because the gypsy women had lulled her to sleep with it when she was a little child. At the sight of that villainous form which made its appearance so abruptly in the middle of her song, the young girl paused with an involuntary gesture of alarm. The unhappy bellringer fell upon his knees on the threshold, and clasped his large, misshapen hands with a suppliant air. "Oh!" he said, sorrowfully, "continue, I implore you, and do not drive me away." She did not wish to pain him, and resumed her lay, trembling all over. By degrees, however, her terror disappeared, and she yielded herself wholly to the slow and melancholy air which she was singing. He remained on his knees with hands clasped, as in prayer, attentive, hardly breathing, his gaze riveted upon the gypsy's brilliant eyes.

On another occasion, he came to her with an awkward and timid air. "Listen," he said, with an effort; "I have something to say to you." She made him a sign that she was listening. Then he began to sigh, half opened his lips, appeared for a moment to be on the point of speaking, then he looked at her again, shook his head, and withdrew slowly, with his brow in his hand, leaving the gypsy stupefied.

Among the grotesque personages sculptured on the wall, there was one to whom he was particularly attached, and with which he often seemed to exchange fraternal glances. Once the gypsy heard him saying to it—

"Oh! why am not I of stone, like you!"

At last, one morning, la Esmeralda had advanced to the edge of the roof, and was looking into the Place over the pointed roof of Saint-Jean le Rond. Quasimodo was standing behind her. He had placed himself in that position in order to spare the young girl, as far as possible, the displeasure of seeing him. All at once the gypsy started, a tear and a flash of joy gleamed simultaneously in her eyes, she knelt on the brink of the roof and extended her arms toward the Place with anguish, exclaiming: "Phœbus! come! come! a word, a single word in the name of heaven! Phœbus! Phœbus!" Her voice, her face, her gesture, her whole person bore the heartrending expression of a shipwrecked man who is making a signal of distress to the joyous vessel which is passing afar off in a ray of sunlight on the horizon.

Quasimodo leaned over the Place, and saw that the object of this tender and agonizing prayer was a young man, a captain, a handsome cavalier all glittering with arms and decorations, prancing across the end of the Place, and saluting with his plume a beautiful lady who was smiling at him from her balcony. However, the officer did not hear the unhappy girl calling him; he was too far away.

But the poor deaf man heard. A profound sigh heaved his breast; he turned round; his heart was swollen with all the tears which he was swallowing; his convulsively-clenched fists struck against his head, and when he withdrew them there was a bunch of red hair in each hand.

The gypsy paid no heed to him. He said in a low voice as he gnashed his teeth—

"Damnation! That is what one should be like! 'Tis only necessary to be handsome on the outside!"

Meanwhile, she remained kneeling, and cried with extraordinary agitation—

"Oh! there he is alighting from his horse! He is about to enter that house!—Phœbus!—He does not hear me! Phœbus!—How wicked that woman is to speak to him at the same time with me! Phœbus! Phœbus!"

The deaf man gazed at her. He understood this pantomime. The poor bellringer's eye filled with tears, but he let none fall. All at once he pulled her gently by the border of her sleeve. She turned round. He had assumed a tranquil air; he said to her—

"Would you like to have me bring him to you?"

She uttered a cry of joy.

"Oh! go! hasten! run! quick! that captain! that captain! bring him to me! I will love you for it!"

She clasped his knees. He could not refrain from shaking his head sadly.

"I will bring him to you," he said, in a weak voice. Then he turned his head and plunged down the staircase with great strides, stifling with sobs.

When he reached the Place, he no longer saw anything except the handsome horse hitched at the door of the Gondelaurier house; the captain had just entered there.

He raised his eyes to the roof of the church. La Esmeralda was there in the same spot, in the same attitude. He made her a sad sign with his head; then he planted his back against one of the stone posts of the Gondelaurier porch, determined to wait until the captain should come forth.

In the Gondelaurier house it was one of those gala days which precede a wedding. Quasimodo beheld many people enter, but no one come out. He cast a glance toward the roof from time to time; the gypsy did not stir any more than himself. A groom came and unhitched the horse and led it to the stable of the house.

The entire day passed thus, Quasimodo at his post, la Esmeralda on the roof, Phœbus, no doubt, at the feet of Fleur-de-Lys.

At length night came, a moonless night, a dark night. Quasimodo fixed his gaze in vain upon la Esmeralda; soon she was no more than a whiteness amid the twilight; then nothing. All was effaced, all was black.

Quasimodo beheld the front windows from top to bottom of the Gondelaurier mansion illuminated; he saw the other casements in the Place lighted one by one, he also saw them extinguished to the very last, for he remained the whole evening at his post. The officer did not come forth. When the last passers-by had returned home, when the windows of all the other houses were extinguished, Quasimodo was left entirely alone, entirely in the dark. There were at that time no lamps in the square before Notre-Dame.

Meanwhile, the windows of the Gondelaurier mansion remained lighted, even after midnight.

Quasimodo, motionless and attentive, beheld a throng of lively, dancing shadows pass athwart the many-colored painted panes. Had he not been deaf, he would have heard more and more distinctly, in proportion as the noise of sleeping Paris died away, a sound of feasting, laughter, and music in the Gondelaurier mansion.

Toward one o'clock in the morning, the guests began to take their leave. Quasimodo, shrouded in darkness watched them all pass out through the porch illuminated with torches. None of them was the captain.

He was filled with sad thoughts; at times he looked upwards into the air, like a person who is weary of waiting. Great black clouds, heavy, torn, split, hung like crape hammocks beneath the starry dome of night. One would have pronounced them spiders' webs of the vault of heaven.

In one of these moments he suddenly beheld the long window on the balcony, whose stone balustrade projected above his head, open mysteriously. The frail glass door gave passage to two persons, and closed noiselessly behind them; it was a man and a woman.

It was not without difficulty that Quasimodo succeeded in recognizing in the man the handsome captain, in the woman the young lady whom he had seen welcome the officer in the morning from that very balcony. The place was perfectly dark, and a double crimson curtain which had fallen across the door the very moment it closed again, allowed no light to reach the balcony from the apartment.

The young man and the young girl, so far as our deaf man could judge, without hearing a single one of their words, appeared to abandon themselves to a very tender tête-à-tête. The young girl seemed to have allowed the officer to make a girdle for her of his arm, and gently repulsed a kiss.

Quasimodo looked on from below at this scene which was all the more pleasing to witness because it was not meant to be seen. He contemplated with bitterness that beauty, that happiness. After all, nature was not dumb in the poor fellow, and his human sensibility, all maliciously contorted as it was, quivered no less than any other. He thought of the miserable portion which Providence had allotted to him; that woman and the pleasure of love, would pass forever before his eyes, and that he should never do anything but behold the felicity of others. But that which rent his heart most in this sight, that which mingled indignation with his anger, was the thought of what the gypsy would suffer could she behold it. It is true that the night was very dark, that la Esmeralda, if she had remained at her post (and he had no doubt of this), was very far away, and that it was all that he himself could do to distinguish the lovers on the balcony. This consoled him.

Meanwhile, their conversation grew more and more animated. The young lady appeared to be entreating the officer to ask nothing more of her. Of all this Quasimodo could distinguish only the beautiful clasped hands, the smiles mingled with tears, the young girl's glances directed to the stars, the eyes of the captain lowered ardently upon her.

Fortunately, for the young girl was beginning to resist but feebly, the door of the balcony suddenly opened once more and an old dame appeared; the beauty seemed confused, the officer assumed an air of displeasure, and all three withdrew.

A moment later, a horse was champing his bit under the porch, and the brilliant officer, enveloped in his night cloak, passed rapidly before Quasimodo.

The bellringer allowed him to turn the corner of the street, then he ran after him with his ape-like agility, shouting: "Hey there! captain!"

The captain halted.

"What wants this knave with me?" he said, catching sight through the gloom of that hipshot form which ran limping after him.

Meanwhile, Quasimodo had caught up with him, and had boldly grasped his horse's bridle: "Follow me, captain; there is one here who desires to speak with you!"

"Cornemahom!" grumbled Phœbus, "here's a villainous, ruffled bird which I fancy I have seen somewhere. Holà! master, will you let my horse's bridle alone?"

"Captain," replied the deaf man, "do you not ask me who it is?"

"I tell you to release my horse," retorted Phœbus, impatiently. "What means the knave by clinging to the bridle of my steed? Do you take my horse for a gallows?"

Quasimodo, far from releasing the bridle, prepared to force him to retrace his steps. Unable to comprehend the captain's resistance, he hastened to say to him—

"Come, captain, 'tis a woman who is waiting for you." He added with an effort: "A woman who loves you."

"A rare rascal!" said the captain, "who thinks me obliged to go to all the women who love me! or who say they do. And what if, by chance, she should resemble you, you face of a screech-owl? Tell the woman who has sent you that I am about to marry, and that she may go to the devil!"

"Listen," exclaimed Quasimodo, thinking to overcome his hesitation with a word, "come, monseigneur! 'tis the gypsy whom you know!"

This word did, indeed, produce a great effect on Phœbus, but not of the kind which the deaf man expected. It will be remembered that our gallant officer had retired with Fleur-de-Lys several moments before Quasimodo had rescued the condemned girl from the hands of Charmolue. Afterwards, in all his visits to the Gondelaurier mansion he had taken care not to mention that woman, the memory of whom was, after all, painful to him; and on her side, Fleur-de-Lys had not deemed it politic to tell him that the gypsy was alive. Hence Phœbus believed poor "Similar" to be dead, and that a month or two had elapsed since her death. Let us add that for the last few moments the captain had been reflecting on the profound darkness of the night, the supernatural ugliness, the sepulchral voice of the strange messenger; that it was past midnight; that the street was deserted, as on the evening when the surly monk had accosted him; and that his horse snorted as it looked at Quasimodo.

"The gypsy!" he exclaimed, almost frightened. "Look here, do you come from the other world?"

And he laid his hand on the hilt of his dagger.

"Quick, quick," said the deaf man, endeavoring to drag the horse along; "this way!"

Phœbus dealt him a vigorous kick in the breast.

Quasimodo's eye flashed. He made a motion to fling himself on the captain. Then he drew himself up stiffly and said—

"Oh! how happy you are to have some one who loves you!"

He emphasized the words "some one," and loosing the horse's bridle—

"Begone!"

Phœbus spurred on in all haste, swearing. Quasimodo watched him disappear in the shades of the street.

"Oh!" said the poor deaf man, in a very low voice; "to refuse that!"

He re-entered Notre-Dame, lighted his lamp and climbed to the tower again. The gypsy was still in the same place, as he had supposed.

She flew to meet him as far off as she could see him.

"Alone!" she cried, clasping her beautiful hands sorrowfully.

"I could not find him," said Quasimodo coldly.

"You should have waited all night," she said angrily.

He saw her gesture of wrath, and understood the reproach.

"I will lie in wait for him better another time," he said, dropping his head.

"Begone!" she said to him.

He left her. She was displeased with him. He preferred to have her abuse him rather than to have afflicted her. He had kept all the pain to himself.

From that day forth, the gypsy no longer saw him. He ceased to come to her cell. At the most she occasionally caught a glimpse at the summit of the towers, of the bellringer's face turned sadly to her. But as soon as she perceived him, he disappeared.

We must admit that she was not much grieved by this voluntary absence on the part of the poor hunchback. At the bottom of her heart she was grateful to him for it. Moreover, Quasimodo did not deceive himself on this point.

She no longer saw him, but she felt the presence of a good genius about her. Her provisions were replenished by an invisible hand during her slumbers. One morning she found a cage of birds on her window. There was a piece of sculpture above her window which frightened her. She had shown this more than once in Quasimodo's presence. One morning, for all these things happened at night, she no longer saw it, it had been broken. The person who had climbed up to that carving must have risked his life.

Sometimes, in the evening, she heard a voice, concealed beneath the wind screen of the bell tower, singing a sad, strange song, as though to lull her to sleep. The lines were unrhymed, such as a deaf person can make.

> *Ne regarde pas la figure,*
> *Jeune fille, regarde le coeur.*
> *Le coeur d'un beau jeune homme est souvent difforme.*
> *Il y a des coeurs où l' amour ne se conserve pas.*

> *Jeune fille, le sapin n'est pas beau,*
> *N'est pas beau comme le peuplier,*
> *Mais il garde son feuillage l'hiver.*

> *Hélas! à quoi bon dire cela?*
> *Ce qui n'est pas beau a tort d'être;*
> *La beauté n'aime que la beauté,*
> *Avril tourne le dos á Janvier.*

> *La beauté est parfaite,*
> *La beauté peut tout,*
> *La beauté est la seule chose qui n'existe pàs a demi.*

> *Le corbeau ne vole que le jour,*
> *Le hibou ne vole que la nuit,*
> *Le cygne vole la nuit et le jour.*[1]

One morning, on awaking, she saw on her window two vases filled with flowers. One was a very beautiful and very brilliant but cracked vase of glass. It had allowed the water with which it had been filled to escape, and the flowers which it contained were withered. The other was an earthenware pot, coarse and common, but which had preserved all its water, and its flowers remained fresh and crimson.

I know not whether it was done intentionally, but la Esmeralda took the faded nosegay and wore it all day long upon her breast.

---

1. Look not at the face, young girl, look at the heart. The heart of a handsome young man is often deformed. There are hearts in which love does not keep. Young girl, the pine is not beautiful; it is not beautiful like the poplar, but it keeps its foliage in winter. Alas! What is the use of saying that? That which is not beautiful has no right to exist; beauty loves only beauty; April turns her back on January. Beauty is perfect, beauty can do all things, beauty is the only thing which does not exist by halves. The raven flies only by day, the owl flies only by night, the swan flies by day and by night.

That day she did not hear the voice singing in the tower.

She troubled herself very little about it. She passed her days in caressing Djali, in watching the door of the Gondelaurier house, in talking to herself about Phœbus, and in crumbling up her bread for the swallows.

She had entirely ceased to see or hear Quasimodo. The poor bellringer seemed to have disappeared from the church. One night, nevertheless, when she was not asleep, but was thinking of her handsome captain, she heard something breathing near her cell. She rose in alarm, and saw by the light of the moon, a shapeless mass lying across her door on the outside. It was Quasimodo asleep there upon the stones.

Chapter V

THE KEY TO THE RED DOOR

IN THE MEANTIME, PUBLIC RUMOR HAD INFORMED THE ARCHDEACON OF THE MIRACULOUS MANNER in which the gypsy had been saved. When he learned it, he knew not what his sensations were. He had reconciled himself to la Esmeralda's death. In that matter he was tranquil; he had reached the bottom of personal suffering. The human heart (Dom Claude had meditated upon these matters) can contain only a certain quantity of despair. When the sponge is saturated, the sea may pass over it without causing a single drop more to enter it.

Now, with la Esmeralda dead, the sponge was soaked, all was at an end on this earth for Dom Claude. But to feel that she was alive, and Phœbus also, meant that tortures, shocks, alternatives, life, were beginning again. And Claude was weary of all this.

When he heard this news, he shut himself in his cell in the cloister. He appeared neither at the meetings of the chapter nor at the services. He closed his door against all, even against the bishop. He remained thus immured for several weeks. He was believed to be ill. And so he was, in fact.

What did he do while thus shut up? With what thoughts was the unfortunate man contending? Was he giving final battle to his formidable passion? Was he concocting a final plan of death for her and of perdition for himself?

His Jehan, his cherished brother, his spoiled child, came once to his door, knocked, swore, entreated, gave his name half a score of times. Claude did not open.

He passed whole days with his face close to the panes of his window. From that window, situated in the cloister, he could see la Esmeralda's chamber. He often saw herself with her goat, sometimes with Quasimodo. He remarked the little attentions of the ugly deaf man, his obedience, his delicate and submissive ways with the gypsy. He recalled, for he had a good memory, and memory is the tormentor of the jealous, he recalled the singular look of the bellringer, bent on the dancer upon a certain evening. He asked himself what motive could have impelled Quasimodo to save her. He was the witness of a thousand little scenes between the gypsy and the deaf man, the pantomime of which, viewed from afar and commented on by his passion, appeared very tender to him. He distrusted the capriciousness of women. Then he felt a jealousy which be could never have believed possible awakening within him, a jealousy which made him redden with shame and indignation: "One might condone the captain, but this one!" This thought upset him.

His nights were frightful. As soon as he learned that the gypsy was alive, the cold ideas of specter and tomb which had persecuted him for a whole day vanished, and the flesh returned to goad him. He turned and twisted on his couch at the thought that the dark-skinned maiden was so near him.

Every night his delirious imagination represented la Esmeralda to him in all the attitudes which had caused his blood to boil most. He beheld her outstretched upon the poniarded captain, her eyes closed, her beautiful bare throat covered with Phœbus's blood, at that moment of bliss when the archdeacon had imprinted on her pale lips that kiss whose burn the unhappy girl, though half dead, had felt. He beheld her again, stripped by the savage hands of the torturers, allowing them to bare and to enclose in the boot with its iron screw, her tiny foot, her delicate rounded leg, her white and supple knee. Again he beheld that ivory knee which alone remained outside of Torterue's horrible apparatus. Lastly, he pictured the young girl in her shift, with the rope about her neck, shoulders bare, feet bare, almost nude, as he had seen her on that last day. These images of voluptuousness made him clench his fists, and a shiver run along his spine.

One night, among others, they heated so cruelly his virgin and priestly blood, that he bit his pillow, leaped from his bed, flung on a surplice over his shirt, and left his cell, lamp in hand, half naked, wild, his eyes aflame.

He knew where to find the key to the red door, which connected the cloister with the church, and he always had about him, as the reader knows, the key of the staircase leading to the towers.

Chapter VI

CONTINUATION OF THE KEY TO THE RED DOOR

THAT NIGHT, LA ESMERALDA HAD FALLEN ASLEEP IN HER CELL, FULL OF OBLIVION, OF HOPE, AND of sweet thoughts. She had already been asleep for some time, dreaming as always, of Phœbus, when it seemed to her that she heard a noise near her. She slept lightly and uneasily, the sleep of a bird; a mere nothing waked her. She opened her eyes. The night was very dark. Nevertheless, she saw a figure gazing at her through the window; a lamp lighted up this apparition. The moment that the figure saw that la Esmeralda had perceived it, it blew out the lamp. But the young girl had had time to catch a glimpse of it; her eyes closed again with terror.

"Oh!" she said in a faint voice, "the priest!"

All her past unhappiness came back to her like a flash of lightning. She fell back on her bed, chilled.

A moment later she felt a touch along her body which made her shudder so that she straightened herself up in a sitting posture, wide awake and furious.

The priest had just slipped in beside her. He encircled her with both arms.

She tried to scream and could not.

"Begone, monster! begone assassin!" she said, in a voice which was low and trembling with wrath and terror.

"Mercy! mercy!" murmured the priest, pressing his lips to her shoulder.

She seized his bald head by its remnant of hair and tried to thrust aside his kisses as though they had been bites.

"Mercy!" repeated the unfortunate man. "If you but knew what my love for you is! 'Tis fire, melted lead, a thousand daggers in my heart."

She stopped his two arms with superhuman force.

"Let me go," she said, "or I will spit in your face!"

He released her. "Vilify me, strike me, be malicious! Do what you will! But have mercy! love me!"

Then she struck him with the fury of a child. She made her beautiful hands stiff to bruise his face. "Begone, demon!"

"Love me! love me! pity!" cried the poor priest returning her blows with caresses.

All at once she felt him stronger than herself.

"There must be an end to this!" he said, gnashing his teeth.

She was conquered, palpitating in his arms, and in his power. She felt a wanton hand straying over her. She made a last effort, and began to cry: "Help! Help! A vampire! a vampire!"

Nothing came. Djali alone was awake and bleating with anguish.

"Hush!" said the panting priest.

All at once, as she struggled and crawled on the floor, the gypsy's hand came in contact with something cold and metallic—it was Quasimodo's whistle. She seized it with a convulsive hope, raised it to her lips and blew with all the strength that she had left. The whistle gave a clear, piercing sound.

"What is that?" said the priest.

Almost at the same instant he felt himself raised by a vigorous arm. The cell was dark; he could not distinguish clearly who it was that held him thus; but he heard teeth chattering with rage, and there was just sufficient light scattered among the gloom to allow him to see above his head the blade of a large knife.

The priest fancied that he perceived the form of Quasimodo. He assumed that it could be no one but he. He remembered to have stumbled, as he entered, over a bundle which was stretched across the door on the outside. But, as the newcomer did not utter a word, he knew not what to think. He flung himself on the arm which held the knife, crying: "Quasimodo!" He forgot, at that moment of distress, that Quasimodo was deaf.

In a twinkling, the priest was overthrown and a leaden knee rested on his breast.

From the angular imprint of that knee he recognized Quasimodo; but what was to be done? how could he make the other recognize him? the darkness rendered the deaf man blind.

He was lost. The young girl, pitiless as an enraged tigress, did not intervene to save him. The knife was approaching his head; the moment was critical. All at once, his adversary seemed stricken with hesitation.

"No blood on her!" he said in a dull voice.

It was, in fact, Quasimodo's voice.

Then the priest felt a large hand dragging him feet first out of the cell; it was there that he was to die. Fortunately for him, the moon had risen a few moments before.

When they had passed through the door of the cell, its pale rays fell upon the priest's countenance. Quasimodo looked him full in the face, a trembling seized him, and he released the priest and shrank back.

The gypsy, who had advanced to the threshold of her cell, beheld with surprise their roles abruptly changed. It was now the priest who menaced, Quasimodo who was the suppliant.

The priest, who was overwhelming the deaf man with gestures of wrath and reproach, made the latter a violent sign to retire.

The deaf man dropped his head, then he came and knelt at the gypsy's door—"Monseigneur," he said, in a grave and resigned voice, "you shall do all that you please afterwards, but kill me first."

So saying, he presented his knife to the priest. The priest, beside himself, was about to seize it. But the young girl was quicker than he; she wrenched the knife from Quasimodo's hands and burst into a frantic laugh—"Approach," she said to the priest.

She held the blade high. The priest remained undecided. She would certainly have struck him.

Then she added with a pitiless expression, well aware that she was about to pierce the priest's heart with thousands of red-hot irons—

"Ah! I know that Phœbus is not dead!"

The priest overturned Quasimodo on the floor with a kick, and, quivering with rage, darted back under the vault of the staircase.

When he was gone, Quasimodo picked up the whistle which had just saved the gypsy.

"It was getting rusty," he said, as he handed it back to her; then he left her alone.

The young girl, deeply agitated by this violent scene, fell back exhausted on her bed, and began to sob and weep. Her horizon was becoming gloomy once more.

The priest had groped his way back to his cell.

It was settled. Dom Claude was jealous of Quasimodo!

He repeated with a thoughtful air his fatal words: "No one shall have her."

BOOK TENTH

Chapter I

GRINGOIRE HAS MANY GOOD IDEAS IN SUCCESSION. —RUE DES BERNARDINS

AS SOON AS PIERRE GRINGOIRE HAD SEEN HOW THIS WHOLE AFFAIR WAS TURNING, AND THAT there would decidedly be the rope, hanging, and other disagreeable things for the principal personages in this comedy, he had not cared to identify himself with the matter further. The outcasts with whom he had remained, reflecting that, after all, it was the best company in Paris—the outcasts had continued to interest themselves in behalf of the gypsy. He had thought it very simple on the part of people who had, like herself, nothing else in prospect but Charmolue and Torterue, and who, unlike himself, did not gallop through the regions of imagination between the wings of Pegasus. From their remarks, he had learned that his wife of the broken crock had taken refuge in Notre-Dame, and he was very glad of it. But he felt no temptation to go and see her there. He meditated occasionally on the little goat, and that was all. Moreover, he was busy executing feats of strength during the day for his living, and at night he was engaged in composing a memorial against the Bishop of Paris, for he remembered having been drenched by the wheels of his mills, and he cherished a grudge against him for it. He also occupied himself with annotating the fine work of Baudry-le-Rouge, Bishop of Noyon and Tournay, *De Cupa Petrarum*, which had given him a violent passion for architecture, an inclination which had replaced in his heart his passion for hermeticism, of which it was, moreover, only a natural corollary, since there is an intimate relation between hermeticism and masonry. Gringoire had passed from the love of an idea to the love of the form of that idea.

One day he had halted near Saint Germain-l'Auxerrois, at the corner of a mansion called "For-l'Evêque" (the Bishop's Tribunal), which stood opposite another called "For-le-Roi" (the King's Tribunal). At this For-l'Evêque, there was a charming chapel of the fourteenth century, whose apse was on the street. Gringoire was devoutly examining its exterior sculptures. He was in one of those moments of egotistical, exclusive, supreme, enjoyment when the artist beholds nothing in the world but art, and the world in art. All at once he feels a hand laid gravely on his shoulder. He turns round. It was his old friend, his former master, monsieur the archdeacon.

He was stupefied. It was a long time since he had seen the archdeacon, and Dom Claude was one of those solemn and impassioned men, a meeting with whom always upsets the equilibrium of a skeptical philosopher.

The archdeacon maintained silence for several minutes, during which Gringoire had time to observe him. He found Dom Claude greatly changed; pale as a winter's morning, with hollow eyes, and hair almost white. The priest broke the silence at length, by saying, in a tranquil but glacial tone—

"How do you do, Master Pierre?"

"My health?" replied Gringoire. "Eh! eh! one can say both one thing and another on that score. Still, it is good, on the whole. I take not too much of anything. You know, master, that the secret of keeping well, according to Hippocrates; *id est: cibi, potus, somni, venus, omnia moderata sint.*"

"So you have no care, Master Pierre?" resumed the archdeacon, gazing intently at Gringoire.

"None, i' faith!"

"And what are you doing now?"

"You see, master. I am examining the chiseling of these stones, and the manner in which yonder bas-relief is thrown out."

The priest began to smile with that bitter smile which raises only one corner of the mouth.

"And that amuses you?"

" 'Tis paradise!" exclaimed Gringoire. And leaning over the sculptures with the fascinated air of a demonstrator of living phenomena: "Do you not think, for instance, that yon metamorphosis in bas-relief is executed with much adroitness, delicacy and patience? Observe that slender column. Around what capital have you seen foliage more tender and better caressed by the chisel. Here are three raised bosses of Jean Maillevin. They are not the finest works of this great master. Nevertheless, the naïvete, the sweetness of the faces, the gaiety of the attitudes and draperies, and that inexplicable charm which is mingled with all the defects, render the little figures very diverting and delicate, perchance, even too much so. You think that it is not diverting?"

"Yes, certainly!" said the priest.

"And if you were to see the interior of the chapel!" resumed the poet, with his garrulous enthusiasm. "Carvings everywhere. 'Tis as thickly clustered as the head of a cabbage! The apse is of a very devout, and so peculiar a fashion that I have never beheld anything like it elsewhere!"

Dom Claude interrupted him—

"You are happy, then?"

Gringoire replied warmly—

"On my honor, yes! First I loved women, then animals. Now I love stones. They are quite as amusing as women and animals, and less treacherous."

The priest laid his hand on his brow. It was his habitual gesture.

"Really?"

"Stay!" said Gringoire, "one has one's pleasures!" He took the arm of the priest, who let him have his way, and made him enter the staircase turret of For-l'Evêque. "Here is a staircase! every time that I see it I am happy. It is of the simplest and rarest manner of steps in Paris. All the steps are beveled underneath. Its beauty and simplicity consist in the interspacing of both, being a foot or more wide, which are interlaced, interlocked, fitted together, enchained enchased, interlined one upon another, and bite into each other in a manner that is truly firm and graceful."

"And you desire nothing?"

"No."

"And you regret nothing?"

"Neither regret nor desire. I have arranged my mode of life."

"What men arrange," said Claude, "things disarrange."

"I am a Pyrrhonian philosopher," replied Gringoire, "and I hold all things in equilibrium."

"And how do you earn your living?"

"I still make epics and tragedies now and then; but that which brings me in most is the industry with which you are acquainted, master; carrying pyramids of chairs in my teeth."

"The trade is but a rough one for a philosopher."

" 'Tis still equilibrium," said Gringoire. "When one has an idea, one encounters it in everything."

"I know that," replied the archdeacon.

After a silence, the priest resumed—

"You are, nevertheless, tolerably poor?"

"Poor, yes; unhappy, no."

At that moment, a trampling of horses was heard, and our two interlocutors beheld defiling at the end of the street, a company of the king's unattached archers, their lances borne high, an officer at their head. The cavalcade was brilliant, and its march resounded on the pavement.

"How you gaze at that officer!" said Gringoire, to the archdeacon.

"Because I think I recognize him."

"What do you call him?"

"I think," said Claude, "that his name is Phœbus de Châteaupers."

"Phœbus! A curious name! There is also a Phœbus, Comte de Foix. I remember having known a wench who swore only by the name of Phœbus."

"Come away from here," said the priest. "I have something to say to you."

From the moment of that troop's passing, some agitation had pierced through the archdeacon's glacial envelope. He walked on. Gringoire followed him, being accustomed to obey him, like all who had once approached that man so full of ascendency. They reached in silence the Rue des Bernardins, which was nearly deserted. Here Dom Claude paused.

"What have you to say to me, master?" Gringoire asked him.

"Do you not think that the dress of those cavaliers whom we have just seen is far handsomer than yours and mine?"

Gringoire tossed his head.

"I' faith! I love better my red and yellow jerkin, than those scales of iron and steel. A fine pleasure to produce, when you walk, the same noise as the Quay of Old Iron, in an earthquake!"

"So, Gringoire, you have never cherished envy for those handsome fellows in their military doublets?"

"Envy for what, monsieur the archdeacon? their strength, their armor, their discipline? Better philosophy and independence in rags. I prefer to be the head of a fly rather than the tail of a lion."

"That is singular," said the priest dreamily. "Yet a handsome uniform is a beautiful thing."

Gringoire, perceiving that he was in a pensive mood, quitted him to go and admire the porch of a neighboring house. He came back clapping his hands.

"If you were less engrossed with the fine clothes of men of war, monsieur the archdeacon, I would entreat you to come and see this door. I have always said that the house of the Sieur Aubry had the most superb entrance in the world."

"Pierre Gringoire," said the archdeacon, "What have you done with that little gypsy dancer?"

"La Esmeralda? You change the conversation very abruptly."

"Was she not your wife?"

"Yes, by virtue of a broken crock. We were to have four years of it. By the way," added Gringoire, looking at the archdeacon in a half bantering way, "are you still thinking of her?"

"And you think of her no longer?"

"Very little. I have so many things. Good heavens, how pretty that little goat was!"

"Had she not saved your life?"

" 'Tis true, pardieu!"

"Well, what has become of her? What have you done with her?"

"I cannot tell you. I believe that they have hanged her."

"You believe so?"

"I am not sure. When I saw that they wanted to hang people, I retired from the game."

"That is all you know of it?"

"Wait a bit. I was told that she had taken refuge in Notre-Dame, and that she was safe there, and I am delighted to hear it, and I have not been able to discover whether the goat was saved with her, and that is all I know."

"I will tell you more," cried Dom Claude; and his voice, hitherto low, slow, and almost indistinct, turned to thunder. "She has in fact, taken refuge in Notre-Dame. But in three days justice will reclaim her, and she will be hanged on the Grève. There is a decree of parliament."

"That's annoying," said Gringoire.

The priest, in an instant, became cold and calm again.

"And who the devil," resumed the poet, "has amused himself with soliciting a decree of reintegration? Why couldn't they leave parliament in peace? What harm does it do if a poor girl takes shelter under the flying buttresses of Notre-Dame, beside the swallows' nests?"

"There are satans in this world," remarked the archdeacon.

" 'Tis devilish badly done," observed Gringoire.

The archdeacon resumed after a silence—

"So, she saved your life?"

"Among my good friends the outcasts. A little more or a little less and I should have been hanged. They would have been sorry for it to-day."

"Would not you like to do something for her?"

"I ask nothing better, Dom Claude; but what if I entangle myself in some villainous affair?"

"What matters it?"

"Bah! what matters it? You are good, master, that you are! I have two great works already begun."

The priest smote his brow. In spite of the calm which he affected, a violent gesture betrayed his internal convulsions from time to time.

"How is she to be saved?"

Gringoire said to him; "Master, I will reply to you; *Il padelt*, which means in Turkish, 'God is our hope.' "

"How is she to be saved?" repeated Claude dreamily.

Gringoire smote his brow in his turn.

"Listen, master. I have imagination; I will devise expedients for you. What if one were to ask her pardon from the king?"

"Of Louis XI! A pardon!"

"Why not?"

"To take the tiger's bone from him!"

Gringoire began to seek fresh expedients.

"Well, stay! Shall I address to the midwives a request accompanied by the declaration that the girl is with child!"

This made the priest's hollow eye flash.

"With child! knave! do you know anything of this?"

Gringoire was alarmed by his air. He hastened to say, "Oh, no, not I! Our marriage was a real *forismaritagium*. I stayed outside. But one might obtain a respite, all the same."

"Madness! Infamy! Hold your tongue!"

"You do wrong to get angry," muttered Gringoire. "One obtains a respite; that does no harm to anyone, and allows the midwives, who are poor women, to earn forty deniers parisis."

The priest was not listening to him!

"But she must leave that place, nevertheless!" he murmured, "the decree is to be executed within three days. Moreover, there will be no decree; that Quasimodo! Women have very depraved tastes!" He raised his voice: "Master Pierre, I have reflected well; there is but one means of safety for her."

"What? I see none myself."

"Listen, Master Pierre, remember that you owe your life to her. I will tell you my idea frankly. The church is watched night and day; only those are allowed to come out, who have been seen to enter. Hence you can enter. You will come. I will lead you to her. You will change clothes with her. She will take your doublet; you will take her petticoat."

"So far, it goes well," remarked the philosopher, "and then?"

"And then? she will go forth in your garments; you will remain with hers. You will be hanged, perhaps, but she will be saved."

Gringoire scratched his ear, with a very serious air. "Stay!" said he, "that is an idea which would never have occurred to me unaided."

At Dom Claude's proposition, the open and benign face of the poet had abruptly clouded over, like a smiling Italian landscape, when an unlucky squall comes up and dashes a cloud across the sun.

"Well! Gringoire, what say you to the means?"

"I say, master, that I shall not be hanged, perchance, but that I shall be hanged indubitably."

"That concerns us not."

"The deuce!" said Gringoire.

"She has saved your life. 'Tis a debt that you are discharging."

"There are a great many others which I do not discharge."

"Master Pierre, it is absolutely necessary."

The archdeacon spoke imperiously.

"Listen, Dom Claude," replied the poet in utter consternation. "You cling to that idea, and you are wrong. I do not see why I should get myself hanged in someone else's place."

"What have you, then, which attaches you so strongly to life?"

"Oh! a thousand reasons!"

"What reasons, if you please?"

"What? The air, the sky, the morning, the evening, the moonlight, my good friends the thieves, our jeers with the old hags of go-betweens, the fine architecture of Paris to study, three great books to make, one of them being against the bishops and his mills; and how can I tell all? Anaxagoras said that he was in the world to admire the sun. And then, from morning till night, I have the happiness of passing all my days with a man of genius, who is myself, which is very agreeable."

"A head fit for a mule bell!" muttered the archdeacon. "Oh! tell me who preserved for you that life which you render so charming to yourself? To whom do you owe it that you breathe that air, behold that sky, and can still amuse your lark's mind with your whimsical nonsense and madness? Where would you be, had it not been for her? Do you then desire that she through whom you are alive, should die? that she should die, that beautiful, sweet, adorable creature, who is necessary to the light of the world and more divine than God, while you, half wise, and half fool, a vain sketch of something, a sort of vegetable, which thinks that it walks, and thinks that it thinks, you will continue to live with the life which you have stolen from her, as useless as a candle in broad daylight? Come, have a little pity, Gringoire; be generous in your turn; it was she who set the example."

The priest was vehement. Gringoire listened to him at first with an undecided air, then he became touched, and wound up with a grimace which made his pallid face resemble that of a newborn infant with an attack of the colic.

"You are pathetic!" said he, wiping away a tear. "Well! I will think about it. That's a queer idea of yours.—After all," he continued after a pause, "who knows? perhaps they will not hang me. He who becomes betrothed does not always marry. When they find me in that little lodging so grotesquely muffled in petticoat and coif, perchance they will burst with laughter. And then, if they do hang me—well! the halter is as good a death as any. 'Tis a death worthy of a sage who has wavered all his life; a death which is neither flesh nor fish, like the mind of a veritable skeptic; a death all stamped with Pyrrhonism and hesitation, which holds the middle station betwixt heaven and earth, which leaves you in suspense. 'Tis a philosopher's death, and I was destined thereto, perchance. It is magnificent to die as one has lived."

The priest interrupted him: "Is it agreed?"

"What is death, after all?" pursued Gringoire with exaltation. "A disagreeable moment, a toll-gate, the passage of little to nothingness. Someone having asked Cercidas, the Megalopolitan, if he were willing to die: 'Why not?' he replied; 'for after my death I shall see those great men, Pythagoras among the philosophers, Hecatæus among historians, Homer among poets, Olympus among musicians.' "

The archdeacon gave him his hand: "It is settled, then? You will come to-morrow?"

This gesture recalled Gringoire to reality.

"Ah! i' faith no!" he said in the tone of a man just waking up. "Be hanged! 'tis too absurd. I will not."

"Farewell, then!" and the archdeacon added between his teeth: "I'll find you again!"

"I do not want that devil of a man to find me," thought Gringoire; and he ran after Dom Claude. "Stay, monsieur the archdeacon, no ill-feeling between old friends! You take an interest in that girl, my wife, I mean, and 'tis well. You have devised a scheme to get her out of Notre-Dame, but your way is extremely disagreeable to me, Gringoire. If I had only another one myself! I beg to say that a luminous inspiration has just occurred to me. If I possessed an expedient for extricating her from a dilemma, without compromising my own neck to the extent of a single running knot, what would you say to it? Will not that suffice you? Is it absolutely necessary that I should be hanged, in order that you may be content?"

The priest tore out the buttons of his cassock with impatience: "Stream of words! What is your plan?"

"Yes," resumed Gringoire, talking to himself and touching his nose with his forefinger in sign of meditation—"that's it!—The thieves are brave fellows!—The tribe of Egypt love her!—They will rise at the first word!—Nothing easier!—A sudden stroke.—Under cover of the disorder, they will easily carry her off!—Beginning to-morrow evening. They will ask nothing better."

"The plan! speak," cried the archdeacon shaking him.

Gringoire turned majestically toward him: "Leave me! You see that I am composing." He meditated for a few moments more, then began to clap his hands over his thought, crying: "Admirable! success is sure!"

"The plan!" repeated Claude in wrath.

Gringoire was radiant.

"Come, that I may tell you that very softly. 'Tis a truly gallant counter-plot, which will extricate us all from the matter. Pardieu, it must be admitted that I am no fool."

He broke off.

"Oh, by the way! is the little goat with the wench?"

"Yes. The devil take you!"

"They would have hanged it also, would they not?"

"What is that to me?"

"Yes, they would have hanged it. They hanged a sow last month. The headsman loveth that; he eats the beast afterwards. Take my pretty Djali! Poor little lamb!"

"Malediction!" exclaimed Dom Claude. "You are the executioner. What means of safety have you found, knave? Must your idea be extracted with the forceps?"

"Very fine, master, this is it."

Gringoire bent his head to the archdeacon's head and spoke to him in a very low voice, casting an uneasy glance the while from one end to the other of the street, though no one was passing. When he had finished, Dom Claude took his hand and said coldly: " 'Tis well. Farewell until tomorrow."

"Until to-morrow," repeated Gringoire. And, while the archdeacon was disappearing in one direction, he set off in the other, saying to himself in a low voice: "Here's a grand affair, Monsieur Pierre Gringoire. Never mind! 'Tis not written that because one is of small account one should take fright at a great enterprise. Bitou carried a great bull on his shoulders; the water-wagtails, the warblers, and the buntings traverse the ocean."

Chapter II

TURN VAGABOND

ON RE-ENTERING THE CLOISTER, THE ARCHDEACON FOUND AT THE DOOR OF HIS CELL HIS BROTHER Jehan du Moulin, who was waiting for him, and who had beguiled the tedium of waiting by drawing on the wall with a bit of charcoal, a profile of his elder brother, enriched with a monstrous nose.

Dom Claude hardly looked at his brother; his thoughts were elsewhere. That merry scamp's face whose beaming had so often restored serenity to the priest's somber physiognomy, was now powerless to melt the gloom which grew more dense every day over that corrupted, mephitic, and stagnant soul.

"Brother," said Jehan timidly, "I am come to see you."

The archdeacon did not even raise his eyes.

"What then?"

"Brother," resumed the hypocrite, "you are so good to me, and you give me such wise counsels that I always return to you."

"What next?"

"Alas! brother, you were perfectly right when you said to me—'Jehan! Jehan! *cessat doctorum doctrina, discipulorum disciplina.* Jehan, be wise, Jehan, be learned, Jehan, pass not the night outside of the college without lawful occasion and due leave of the master. Cudgel not the Picards: *noli, Joannes, verberare Picardos.* Rot not like an unlettered ass, *quasi asinus illitteratus,* on the straw seats of the school. Jehan, allow yourself to be punished at the discretion of the master. Jehan go every evening to chapel, and sing there an anthem with verse and orison to Madame the glorious Virgin Mary.'—Alas! what excellent advice was that!"

"And then?"

"Brother, you behold a culprit, a criminal, a wretch, a libertine, a man of enormities! My dear brother, Jehan hath made of your counsels straw and dung to trample underfoot. I have been well chastised for it, and God is extraordinarily just. As long as I had money, I feasted, I lead a mad and joyous life. Oh! how ugly and crabbed behind is debauch which is so charming in front! Now I have no longer a blank; I have sold my napery, my shirt and my towels; no more merry life! The beautiful candle is extinguished and I have henceforth, only a wretched tallow dip which smokes in my nose. The wenches jeer at me. I drink water. I am overwhelmed with remorse and with creditors."

"The rest?" said the archdeacon.

"Alas! my very dear brother, I should like to settle down to a better life. I come to you full of contrition, I am penitent. I make my confession. I beat my breast violently. You are quite right in wishing that I should some day become a licentiate and sub-monitor in the college of Torchi. At the present moment I feel a magnificent vocation for that profession. But I have no more ink and I must buy some; I have no more paper, I have no more books, and I must buy some. For this purpose, I am greatly in need of a little money, and I come to you, brother, with my heart full of contrition."

"Is that all?"

"Yes," said the scholar. "A little money."

"I have none."

Then the scholar said, with an air which was both grave and resolute: "Well, brother, I am sorry to be obliged to tell you that very fine offers and propositions are being made to me in another quarter. You will not give me any money? No. In that case I shall become a professional vagabond."

As he uttered these monstrous words, he assumed the mien of Ajax, expecting to see the lightnings descend upon his head.

The archdeacon said coldly to him—

"Become a vagabond."

Jehan made him a deep bow, and descended the cloister stairs, whistling.

At the moment when he was passing through the courtyard of the cloister, beneath his brother's window, he heard that window open, raised his eyes and beheld the archdeacon's severe head emerge.

"Go to the devil!" said Dom Claude; "here is the last money which you will get from me!"

At the same time, the priest flung Jehan a purse, which gave the scholar a big bump on the forehead, and with which Jehan retreated, both vexed and content, like a dog who had been stoned with marrow bones.

Chapter III

LONG LIVE MIRTH

THE READER HAS PROBABLY NOT FORGOTTEN THAT A PART OF THE COUR DE MIRACLES WAS ENclosed by the ancient wall which surrounded the city, a goodly number of whose towers had begun, even at that epoch, to fall to ruin. One of these towers had been converted into a pleasure resort by the vagabonds. There was a drain-shop in the underground story, and the rest in the upper stories. This was the most lively, and consequently the most hideous, point of the whole outcast den. It was a sort of monstrous hive, which buzzed there night and day. At night, when the remainder of the beggar horde slept, when there was no longer a window lighted in the dingy façades of the Place, when not a cry was any longer to be heard proceeding from those innumerable families, those anthills of thieves, of wenches, and stolen or bastard children, the merry tower was still recognizable by the noise which it made, by the scarlet light which, flashing simultaneously from the air-holes, the windows, the fissures in the cracked walls, escaped, so to speak, from its every pore.

The cellar then, was the dram-shop. The descent to it was through a low door and by a staircase as steep as a classic Alexandrine. Over the door, by way of a sign there hung a marvelous daub, representing new sous and dead chickens, with this pun below: *Aux sonneurs pour les trépassés*—The wringers for the dead.

One evening when the curfew was sounding from all the belfries in Paris, the sergeants of the watch might have observed, had it been granted to them to enter the formidable Court of Miracles, that more tumult than usual was in progress in the vagabonds' tavern, that more drinking was being done, and louder swearing. Outside in the Place, there were many groups conversing in low tones, as when some great plan is being framed, and here and there a knave crouching down engaged in sharpening a villainous iron blade on a paving-stone.

Meanwhile, in the tavern itself, wine and gaming offered such a powerful diversion to the ideas which occupied the vagabonds' lair that evening, that it would have been difficult to divine from the remarks of the drinkers, what was the matter in hand. They merely wore a gayer air than was their wont, and some weapon could be seen glittering between the legs of each of them—a sickle, an ax, a big two-edged sword or the hook of an old hackbut.

The room, circular in form, was very spacious; but the tables were so thickly set and the drinkers so numerous, that all that the tavern contained, men, women, benches, beer-jugs, all that were drinking, all that were sleeping, all that were playing, the well, the lame, seemed piled up pell-mell, with as much order and harmony as a heap of oyster shells. There were a few tallow dips lighted on the tables; but the real luminary of this tavern, that which played the part in this dram-shop of the chandelier of an opera house, was the fire. This cellar was so damp that the fire was never allowed to go out, even in midsummer; an immense chimney with a sculptured mantel, all bristling with heavy iron andirons and cooking utensils, with one of those huge fires of mixed wood and peat which at night, in village streets make the reflection of forge windows stand out so red on the opposite walls. A big dog gravely seated in the ashes was turning a spit loaded with meat before the coals.

Great as was the confusion, after the first glance one could distinguish in that multitude, three principal groups which thronged around three personages already known to the reader. One of these personages, fantastically accoutred in many an oriental rag, was Mathias Hungadi Spicali, Duke of Egypt and Bohemia. The knave was seated on a table with his legs crossed, and in a loud voice was bestowing his knowledge of magic, both black and white, on many a gaping face which surrounded him. Another rabble pressed close around our old friend, the valiant King of Thunes, armed to the teeth. Clopin Trouillefou, with a very serious air and in a low voice, was regulating the distribution of an enormous cask of arms, which stood wide open in front of him and from whence poured out in profusion, axes, swords, bassinets, coats of mail, broadswords, lance-heads, arrows, and viretons,[1] like apples and grapes from a horn of plenty. Everyone took something from the cask, one a morion, another a long, straight sword, another a dagger with a cross-shaped hilt. The very children were arming themselves, and there were even cripples in bowls who, in armor and cuirass, made their way between the legs of the drinkers like great beetles.

Finally, a third audience, the most noisy, the most jovial, and the most numerous, encumbered benches and tables, in the midst of which harangued and swore a flute-like voice, which escaped from beneath a heavy armor, complete from casque to spurs. The individual who had thus screwed a whole outfit upon his body, was so hidden by his warlike accoutrements that nothing was to be seen of his person save an impertinent, red, snub nose, a rosy mouth, and bold eyes. His belt was full of daggers and poniards, a huge sword on his hip, a rusted crossbow at his left, and a vast jug of wine in front of him, without reckoning on his right, a fat wench with her bosom uncovered. All mouths around him were laughing, cursing, and drinking.

Add twenty secondary groups, the waiters, male and female, running with jugs on their heads,

1. An arrow with a pyramidal head of iron and copper spiral wings, by which a rotatory motion was communicated.

gamblers squatting over taws, merelles,[1] dice, vachettes, the ardent game of tringlet, quarrels in one corner, kisses in another, and the reader will have some idea of this whole picture, over which flickered the light of a great, flaming fire, which made a thousand huge and grotesque shadows dance over the walls of the drinking shop.

As for the noise, it was like the inside of a bell at full peal.

The dripping-pan, where crackled a rain of grease, filled with its continual sputtering the intervals of these thousand dialogues, which intermingled from one end of the apartment to the other.

In the midst of this uproar, at the extremity of the tavern, on the bench inside the chimney, sat a philosopher meditating with his feet in the ashes and his eyes on the brands. It was Pierre Gringoire.

"Be quick! make haste, arm yourselves! we set out on the march in an hour!" said Clopin Trouillefou to his thieves.

A wench was humming—

> *Bonsoir mon père et ma mère,*
> *Les derniers couvrent le feu*[2]

Two card players were disputing—

"Knave!" cried the reddest faced of the two, shaking his fist at the other; "I'll mark you with the club. You can take the place of Mistigri in the pack of cards of monseigneur the king."

"Ugh!" roared a Norman, recognizable by his nasal accent; "we are packed in here like the saints of Caillouville!"

"My sons," the Duke of Egypt was saying to his audience, in a falsetto voice, "sorceresses in France go to the witches' sabbath without broomsticks, or grease, or steed, merely by means of some magic words. The witches of Italy always have a buck waiting for them at their door. All are bound to go out through the chimney."

The voice of the young scamp armed from head to foot, dominated the uproar.

"Hurrah! hurrah!" he was shouting. "My first day in armor! Outcast! I am an outcast. Give me something to drink. My friends, my name is Jehan Frollo du Moulin, and I am a gentleman. My opinion is that if God were a *gendarme*, he would turn robber. Brothers, we are about to set out on a fine expedition. Lay siege to the church, burst in the doors, drag out the beautiful girl, save her from the judges, save her from the priests, dismantle the cloister, burn the bishop in his palace—all this we will do in less time than it takes for a burgomaster to eat a spoonful of soup. Our cause is just, we will plunder Notre-Dame and that will be the end of it. We will hang Quasimodo. Do you know Quasimodo, ladies? Have you seen him make himself breathless on the big bell on a grand Pentecost festival! *Corne du Père!* 'tis very fine! One would say he was a devil mounted on a man. Listen to me, my friends; I am a vagabond to the bottom of my heart, I am a member of the slang thief gang in my soul, I was born an independent thief. I have been rich, and I have devoured all my property. My mother wanted to make an officer of me; my father, a sub-deacon; my aunt, a councilor of inquests; my grandmother, prothonotary to the king; my great-aunt, a treasurer of the short robe—and I have made myself an outcast. I said this to my father, who spit his curse in my face; to my mother, who set to weeping and chattering, poor old lady, like yonder fagot on the andirons. Long live mirth! I am a real Bicêtre. Waitress, my dear, more wine. I have still the where-

---

1. A game played on a checker-board containing three concentric sets of squares, with small stones. The game consisted in getting three stones in a row.

2. Good night, father and mother, the last cover up the fire.

withal to pay. I want no more Surène wine. It distresses my throat. I'd as lief, *corboeuf!* gargle my throat with a basket."

Meanwhile, the rabble applauded with shouts of laughter; and seeing that the tumult was increasing around him, the scholar cried—

"Oh! what a fine noise! *Populi debacchantis populosa debacchatio!*" Then he began to sing, his eye swimming in ecstasy, in the tone of a canon intoning vespers, "*Quoe cantica! quoe organa! quoe cantilenoe! quoe melodioe hic sine fine decantantur! Sonant melliflua hymnorum organa, suavissima angelorum melodia, cantica canticorum mira!*" He broke off: "Tavern-keeper of the devil, give me some supper!"

There was a moment of partial silence, during which the sharp voice of the Duke of Egypt rose, as he gave instructions to his Bohemians.

"The weasel is called Adrune; the fox, Blue-foot, or the Racer of the Woods; the wolf, Grayfoot, or Gold-foot; the bear the Old Man, or Grandfather. The cap of a gnome confers invisibility, and causes one to behold invisible things. Every toad that is baptized must be clad in red or black velvet, a bell on its neck, a bell on its feet. The godfather holds its head, the godmother its hinder parts. 'Tis the demon Sidragasum who hath the power to make wenches dance stark naked."

"By the mass!" interrupted Jehan, "I should like to be the demon Sidragasum."

Meanwhile, the vagabonds continued to arm themselves and whisper at the other end of the dram-shop.

"That poor Esmeralda!" said a Bohemian. "She is our sister. She must be taken away from there."

"Is she still at Notre-Dame?" went on a merchant with the appearance of a Jew.

"Yes, pardieu!"

"Well! comrades!" exclaimed the merchant, "to Notre-Dame! So much the better, since there are in the chapel of Saints Féréol and Ferrution two statues, the one of John the Baptist, the other of Saint-Antoine, of solid gold, weighing together seven marks of gold and fifteen estellins; and the pedestals are of silver-gilt, of seventeen marks, five ounces. I know that; I am a goldsmith."

Here they served Jehan with his supper. As he threw himself back on the bosom of the wench beside him, he exclaimed—

"By Saint Voult-de-Lucques, whom people call Saint Goguelu, I am perfectly happy. I have before me a fool who gazes at me with the smooth face of an archduke. Here is one on my left whose teeth are so long that they hide his chin. And then, I am like the Marshal de Gié at the siege of Pontoise, I have my right resting on a hillock. *Ventre-Mahom!* Comrade! you have the air of a merchant of tennis-balls; and you come and sit yourself beside me! I am a nobleman, my friend! Trade is incompatible with nobility. Get out of that! Holà hé! You others, don't fight! What, Baptiste Croque-Oison, you who have such a fine nose are going to risk it against the big fists of that lout! Fool! *Non cuiquam datum est habere nasum*—not everyone is favored with a nose. You are really divine, Jacqueline Ronge-Oreille! 'tis a pity that you have no hair! Holà! my name is Jehan Frollo, and my brother is an archdeacon. May the devil fly off with him! All that I tell you is the truth. In turning vagabond, I have gladly renounced the half of a house situated in paradise, which my brother had promised me. *Dimidiam domum in paradiso.* I quote the text. I have a fief in the Rue Tirechappe, and all the women are in love with me, as true as Saint Èloy was an excellent goldsmith, and that the five trades of the good city of Paris are the tanners, the tawers, the makers of cross-belts, the purse-makers, and the sweaters, and that Saint Laurent was burned with eggshells. I swear to you, comrades.

> "*Que je ne beuvrai de piment,*
> *Devant un an, si je cy ment.*[1]

---

1. That I will drink no spiced and honeyed wine for a year, if I am lying now.

" 'Tis moonlight, my charmer; see yonder through the window how the wind is tearing the clouds to tatters! Even thus will I do to your gorget.—Wenches, wipe the children's noses and snuff the candles.—Christ and Mahom! What am I eating here, Jupiter? Ohé! inn-keeper! the hair which is not on the heads of your hussies one finds in your omelettes. Old woman! I like bald omelettes. May the devil confound you!—A fine hostelry of Beelzebub, where the hussies comb their heads with the forks!

"Et je n'ai moi,
Par la sang-Dieu!
Ni foi, ni loi,
Ni feu, ni lieu,
Ni roi,
Ni Dieu."[1]

In the meantime, Clopin Trouillefou had finished the distribution of arms. He approached Gringoire, who appeared to be plunged in a profound reverie, with his feet on an andiron.

"Friend Pierre," said the King of Thunes, "what the devil are you thinking about?"

Gringoire turned to him with a melancholy smile.

"I love the fire, my dear lord. Not for the trivial reason that fire warms the feet or cooks our soup, but because it has sparks. Sometimes I pass whole hours in watching the sparks. I discover a thousand things in those stars which are sprinkled over the black background of the hearth. Those stars are also worlds."

"Thunder, if I understand you!" said the outcast. "Do you know what o'clock it is?"

"I do not know," replied Gringoire.

Clopin approached the Duke of Egypt.

"Comrade Mathias, the time we have chosen is not a good one. King Louis XI is said to be in Paris."

"Another reason for snatching our sister from his claws," replied the old Bohemian.

"You speak like a man, Mathias," said the King of Thunes. "Moreover, we will act promptly. No resistance is to be feared in the church. The canons are hares, and we are in force. The people of the parliament will be well balked to-morrow when they come to seek her! Guts of the pope! I don't want them to hang the pretty girl!"

Clopin quitted the dram-shop.

Meanwhile, Jehan was shouting in a hoarse voice:

"I eat, I drink, I am drunk, I am Jupiter! Eh! Pierre, the Slaughterer, if you look at me like that again, I'll fillip the dust off your nose for you."

Gringoire, torn from his meditations, began to watch the wild and noisy scene which surrounded him, muttering between his teeth: *"Luxuriosa res vinum et tumultuosa ebrietas.* Alas! what good reason I have not to drink, and how excellently spoke Saint-Benoit: *'Vinum apostatare facit etiam sapientes!'* "

At that moment, Clopin returned and shouted in a voice of thunder: "Midnight!"

At this word, which produced the effect of the call to boot and saddle on a regiment at a halt, all the outcasts, men, women, children, rushed in a mass from the tavern, with great noise of arms and old iron implements.

The moon was obscured.

The Cour des Miracles was entirely dark. There was not a single light. One could make out there a throng of men and women conversing in low tones. They could be heard buzzing, and a gleam of all sorts of weapons was visible in the darkness. Clopin mounted a large stone.

---

1. And by the blood of God, I have neither faith nor law, nor fire nor dwelling-place, nor king nor God.

"To your ranks, Argot!" he cried. "Fall into line, Egypt! Form ranks, Galilee!"

A movement began in the darkness. The immense multitude appeared to form in a column. After a few minutes, the King of Thunes raised his voice once more—

"Now, silence to march through Paris! The password is, 'Little sword in pocket!' The torches will not be lighted till we reach Notre-Dame! Forward, march!"

Ten minutes later, the cavaliers of the watch fled in terror before a long procession of black and silent men which was descending toward the Pont au Change, through the tortuous streets which pierce the close-built neighborhood of the markets in every direction.

Chapter IV

AN AWKWARD FRIEND

THAT NIGHT, QUASIMODO DID NOT SLEEP. HE HAD JUST MADE HIS LAST ROUND OF THE CHURCH. He had not noticed, that at the moment when he was closing the doors, the archdeacon had passed close to him and betrayed some displeasure on seeing him bolting and barring with care the enormous iron locks which gave to their large leaves the solidity of a wall. Dom Claude's air was even more preoccupied than usual. Moreover, since the nocturnal adventure in the cell, he had constantly abused Quasimodo, but in vain did he ill treat, and even beat him occasionally, nothing disturbed the submission, patience, the devoted resignation of the faithful bellringer. He endured everything on the part of the archdeacon, insults, threats, blows, without murmuring a complaint. At the most, he gazed uneasily after Dom Claude when the latter ascended the staircase of the tower; but the archdeacon had abstained from presenting himself again before the gypsy's eyes.

On that night, accordingly, Quasimodo, after having cast a glance at his poor bells which he so neglected now, Jacqueline, Marie, and Thibauld, mounted to the summit of the Northern tower, and there setting his dark lantern, well closed, upon the leads, he began to gaze at Paris. The night, as we have already said, was very dark. Paris which, so to speak was not lighted at that epoch, presented to the eye a confused collection of black masses, cut here and there by the whitish curve of the Seine. Quasimodo no longer saw any light with the exception of one window in a distant edifice, whose vague and somber profile was outlined well above the roofs, in the direction of the Porte Sainte-Antoine. There also, there was someone awake.

As the only eye of the bellringer peered into that horizon of mist and night, he felt within him an inexpressible uneasiness. For several days he had been upon his guard. He had perceived men of sinister mien, who never took their eyes from the young girl's asylum, prowling constantly about the church. He fancied that some plot might be in process of formation against the unhappy refugee. He imagined that there existed a popular hatred against her, as against himself, and that it was very possible that something might happen soon. Hence he remained upon his tower on the watch, "dreaming in his dream-place," as Rabelais says, with his eye directed alternately on the cell and on Paris, keeping faithful guard, like a good dog, with a thousand suspicions in his mind.

All at once, while he was scrutinizing the great city with that eye which nature, by a sort of compensation, had made so piercing that it could almost supply the other organs which Quasimodo lacked, it seemed to him that there was something singular about the Quay de la Vieille-Pelleterie, that there was a movement at that point, that the line of the parapet, standing out blackly against the whiteness of the water was not straight and tranquil, like that of the other quays, but that it undulated to the eye, like the waves of a river, or like the heads of a crowd in motion.

This struck him as strange. He redoubled his attention. The movement seemed to be advancing toward the City. There was no light. It lasted for some time on the quay; then it gradually ceased, as though that which was passing were entering the interior of the island; then it stopped altogether, and the line of the quay became straight and motionless again.

At the moment when Quasimodo was lost in conjectures, it seemed to him that the movement had reappeared in the Rue du Parvis, which is prolonged into the city perpendicularly to the façade of Notre-Dame. At length, dense as was the darkness, he beheld the head of a column debouch from that street, and in an instant a crowd—of which nothing could be distinguished in the gloom except that it was a crowd—spread over the Place.

This spectacle had a terror of its own. It is probable that this singular procession, which seemed so desirous of concealing itself under profound darkness, maintained a silence no less profound. Nevertheless, some noise must have escaped it, were it only a trampling. But this noise did not even reach our deaf man, and this great multitude, of which he saw hardly anything, and of which he heard nothing, though it was marching and moving so near him, produced upon him the effect of a rabble of dead men, mute, impalpable, lost in a smoke. It seemed to him, that he beheld advancing toward him a fog of men, and that he saw shadows moving in the shadow.

Then his fears returned to him, the idea of an attempt against the gypsy presented itself once more to his mind. He was conscious, in a confused way, that a violent crisis was approaching. At that critical moment he took counsel with himself, with better and prompter reasoning than one would have expected from so badly organized a brain. Ought he to awaken the gypsy? to make her escape? Whither? The streets were invested, the church backed on the river. No boat, no issue!— There was but one thing to be done; to allow himself to be killed on the threshold of Notre-Dame, to resist at least until succor arrived, if it should arrive, and not to trouble la Esmeralda's sleep. This resolution once taken, he set to examining the enemy with more tranquility.

The throng seemed to increase every moment in the church square. Only, he presumed that it must be making very little noise, since the windows on the Place remained closed. All at once, a flame flashed up, and in an instant seven or eight lighted torches passed over the heads of the crowd, shaking their tufts of flame in the deep shade. Quasimodo then beheld distinctly surging in the Parvis a frightful herd of men and women in rags, armed with scythes, pikes, billhooks and partisans, whose thousand points glittered. Here and there black pitchforks formed horns to the hideous faces. He vaguely recalled this populace, and thought that he recognized all the heads who had saluted him as Pope of the Fools some months previously. One man who held a torch in one hand and a club in the other, mounted a stone post and seemed to be haranguing them. At the same time the strange army executed several evolutions, as though it were taking up its post around the church. Quasimodo picked up his lantern and descended to the platform between the towers, in order to get a nearer view, and to spy out a means of defense.

Clopin Trouillefou, on arriving in front of the lofty portal of Notre-Dame had, in fact, ranged his troops in order of battle. Although he expected no resistance, he wished, like a prudent general, to preserve an order which would permit him to face, at need, a sudden attack of the watch or the police. He had accordingly stationed his brigade in such a manner that, viewed from above and from a distance, one would have pronounced it the Roman triangle of the battle of Ecnomus, the boar's head of Alexander or the famous wedge of Gustavus Adolphus. The base of this triangle rested on the back of the Place in such a manner as to bar the entrance of the Rue du Parvis; one of its sides faced Hôtel-Dieu, the other the Rue Saint-Pierre-aux-Bœufs. Clopin Trouillefou had placed himself at the apex with the Duke of Egypt, our friend Jehan, and the most daring of the scavengers.

An enterprise like that which the vagabonds were now undertaking against Notre-Dame was not a very rare thing in the cities of the Middle Ages. What we now call the "police" did not exist then. In populous cities, especially in capitals, there existed no single, central, regulating power.

Feudalism had constructed these great communities in a singular manner. A city was an assembly of a thousand seigneuries, which divided it into compartments of all shapes and sizes. Hence, a thousand conflicting establishments of police; that is to say, no police at all. In Paris, for example, independently of the hundred and forty-one lords who laid claim to a manor, there were five and twenty who laid claim to a manor and to administering justice, from the Bishop of Paris, who had five hundred streets, to the Prior of Notre-Dame des Champs, who had four. All these feudal justices recognized the suzerain authority of the king only in name. All possessed the right of control over the roads. All were at home. Louis XI, that indefatigable worker, who so largely began the demolition of the feudal edifice, continued by Richelieu and Louis XIV for the profit of royalty, and finished by Mirabeau for the benefit of the people—Louis XI had certainly made an effort to break this network of seignories which covered Paris, by throwing violently across them all two or three troops of general police. Thus, in 1465, an order to the inhabitants to light candles in their windows at nightfall, and to shut up their dogs under penalty of death; in the same year, an order to close the streets in the evening with iron chains, and a prohibition to wear daggers or weapons of offense in the streets at night. But in a very short time, all these efforts at communal legislation fell into abeyance. The bourgeois permitted the wind to blow out their candles in the windows, and their dogs to stray; the iron chains were stretched only in a state of siege; the prohibition to wear daggers wrought no other changes than from the name of the Rue Coupe-Gueule to the name of the Rue Coupe-Gorge[1] which is an evident progress. The old scaffolding of feudal jurisdictions remained standing; an immense aggregation of bailiwicks and seignories crossing each other all over the city, interfering with each other, entangled in one another, enmeshing each other, trespassing on each other; a useless thicket of watches, sub-watches and counter-watches, over which, with armed force, passed brigandage, rapine, and sedition. Hence, in this disorder, deeds of violence on the part of the populace directed against a palace, a hôtel, or house in the most thickly populated quarters, were not unheard-of occurrences. In the majority of such cases, the neighbors did not meddle with the matter unless the pillaging extended to themselves. They stopped up their ears to the musket shots, closed their shutters, barricaded their doors, allowed the matter to be concluded with or without the watch, and the next day it was said in Paris, "Etienne Barbette was broken open last night. The Marshal de Clermont was seized last night, etc." Hence, not only the royal habitations, the Louvre, the Palace, the Bastille, the Tournelles, but simply seignorial residences, the Petit-Bourbon, the Hôtel de Sens, the Hôtel d' Angoulême, etc., had battlements on their walls, and machicolations over their doors. Churches were guarded by their sanctity. Some, among the number Notre-Dame, were fortified. The Abbey of Saint-German-des-Prés was castellated like a baronial mansion, and more brass expended about it in bombards than in bells. Its fortress was still to be seen in 1610. To-day, barely its church remains.

Let us return to Notre-Dame.

When the first arrangements were completed, and we must say, to the honor of vagabond discipline, that Clopin's orders were executed in silence, and with admirable precision, the worthy chief of the band, mounted on the parapet of the church square, and raised his hoarse and surly voice, turning toward Notre-Dame, and brandishing his torch whose light, tossed by the wind, and veiled every moment by its own smoke, made the reddish façade of the church appear and disappear before the eye.

"To you, Louis de Beaumont, bishop of Paris, counselor in the Court of Parliament, I, Clopin Trouillefou, king of Thunes, grand Coësre, prince of Argot, bishop of fools, I say: Our sister, falsely condemned for magic, hath taken refuge in your church, you owe her asylum and safety. Now the Court of Parliament wishes to seize her once more there, and you consent to it; so that she would be hanged to-morrow in the Grève, if God and the outcasts were not here. If your church is

1. Cut-throat.

sacred, so is our sister; if our sister is not sacred, neither is your church. That is why we call upon you to return the girl if you wish to save your church, or we will take possession of the girl again and pillage the church, which will be a good thing. In token of which I here plant my banner, and may God preserve you, bishop of Paris,"

Quasimodo could not, unfortunately, hear these words uttered with a sort of somber and savage majesty. A vagabond presented his banner to Clopin, who planted it solemnly between two paving-stones. It was a pitchfork from whose points hung a bleeding quarter of carrion meat.

That done, the King of Thunes turned round and cast his eyes over his army, a fierce multitude whose glances flashed almost equally with their pikes. After a momentary pause—

"Forward, my sons!" he cried; "to work, locksmiths!"

Thirty bold men, square shouldered, and with pick-lock faces, stepped from the ranks, with hammers, pincers, and bars of iron on their shoulders. They betook themselves to the principal door of the church, ascended the steps, and were soon to be seen squatting under the arch, working at the door with pincers and levers; a throng of vagabonds followed them to help or look on. The eleven steps before the portal were covered with them.

But the door stood firm. "The devil! 'tis hard and obstinate!" said one. "It is old, and its gristles have become bony," said another. "Courage, comrades!" resumed Clopin. "I wager my head against a dipper that you will have opened the door, rescued the girl, and despoiled the chief altar before a single beadle is awake. Stay! I think I hear the lock breaking up."

Clopin was interrupted by a frightful uproar which resounded behind him at that moment. He wheeled round. An enormous beam had just fallen from above; it had crushed a dozen vagabonds on the pavement with the sound of a cannon, breaking in addition, legs here and there in the crowd of beggars, who sprang aside with cries of terror. In a twinkling, the narrow precincts of the church parvis were cleared. The locksmiths, although protected by the deep vaults of the portal, abandoned the door and Clopin himself retired to a respectful distance from the church.

"I had a narrow escape!" cried Jehan. "I felt the wind, of it, tête-de-boeuf! but Pierre the Slaughterer is slaughtered!"

It is impossible to describe the astonishment mingled with fright which fell upon the ruffians in company with this beam.

They remained for several minutes with their eyes in the air, more dismayed by that piece of wood than by the king's twenty thousand archers.

"Satan!" muttered the Duke of Egypt, "this smacks of magic!"

" 'Tis the moon which threw this log at us," said Andry the Red.

"Call the moon the friend of the Virgin, after that!" went on Francois Chanteprune.

"A thousand popes!" exclaimed Clopin, "you are all fools!" But he did not know how to explain the fall of the beam.

Meanwhile, nothing could be distinguished on the façade, to whose summit the light of the torches did not reach. The heavy beam lay in the middle of the enclosure, and groans were heard from the poor wretches who had received its first shock, and who had been almost cut in twain, on the angle of the stone steps.

The King of Thunes, his first amazement passed, finally found an explanation which appeared plausible to his companions.

"Throat of God! are the canons defending themselves? To the sack, then! to the sack!"

"To the sack!" repeated the rabble, with a furious hurrah. A discharge of crossbows and hackbuts against the front of the church followed.

At this detonation, the peaceable inhabitants of the surrounding houses woke up; many windows were seen to open, and nightcaps and hands holding candles appeared at the casements.

"Fire at the windows," shouted Clopin. The windows were immediately closed, and the poor bourgeois, who had hardly had time to cast a frightened glance on this scene of gleams and tumult, returned, perspiring with fear to their wives, asking themselves whether the witches' sabbath was now being held in the parvis of Notre-Dame, or whether there was an assault of Burgundians, as in '64. Then the husbands thought of theft; the wives, of rape; and all trembled.

"To the sack!" repeated the thieves' crew; but they dared not approach. They stared at the beam, they stared at the church. The beam did not stir, the edifice preserved its calm and deserted air; but something chilled the outcasts.

"To work, locksmiths!" shouted Trouillefou. "Let the door be forced!"

No one took a step.

"Beard and belly!" said Clopin, "here be men afraid of a beam."

An old locksmith addressed him:—

"Captain, 'tis not the beam which bothers us, 'tis the door, which is all covered with iron bars. Our pincers are powerless against it."

"What more do you want to break it in?" demanded Clopin.

"Ah! we ought to have a battering-ram."

The King of Thunes ran boldly to the formidable beam, and placed his foot upon it: "Here is one!" he exclaimed; " 'tis the canons who send it to you." And, making a mocking salute in the direction of the church, "Thanks, canons!"

This piece of bravado produced its effects—the spell of the beam was broken. The vagabonds recovered their courage; soon the heavy joist, raised like a feather by two hundred vigorous arms, was flung with fury against the great door which they had tried to batter down. At the sight of that long beam, in the half-light which the infrequent torches of the brigands spread over the Place, thus borne by that crowd of men who dashed it at a run against the church, one would have thought that he beheld a monstrous beast with a thousand feet attacking with lowered head the giant of stone.

At the shock of the beam, the half metallic door sounded like an immense drum; it was not burst in, but the whole cathedral trembled, and the deepest cavities of the edifice were heard to echo.

At the same moment, a shower of large stones began to fall from the top of the façade on the assailants.

"The devil!" cried Jehan, "are the towers shaking their balustrades down on our heads?"

But the impulse had been given, the King of Thunes had set the example. Evidently, the bishop was defending himself, and they only battered the door with the more rage, in spite of the stones which cracked skulls right and left.

It was remarkable that all these stones fell one by one; but they followed each other closely. The thieves always felt two at a time, one on their legs and one on their heads. There were few which did not deal their blow, and a large layer of dead and wounded lay bleeding and panting beneath the feet of the assailants who, now grown furious, replaced each other without intermission. The long beam continued to belabor the door, at regular intervals, like the clapper of a bell, the stones to rain down, the door to groan.

The reader has no doubt divined that this unexpected resistance which had exasperated the outcasts came from Quasimodo.

Chance had, unfortunately, favored the brave deaf man.

When he had descended to the platform between the towers, his ideas were all in confusion. He had run up and down along the gallery for several minutes like a madman, surveying from above, the compact mass of vagabonds ready to hurl itself on the church, demanding the safety of the gypsy from the devil or from God. The thought had occurred to him of ascending to the southern belfry and sounding the alarm, but before he could have set the bell in motion, before Marie's voice could have uttered a single clamor, was there not time to burst in the door of the church ten times over? It was precisely the moment when the locksmiths were advancing upon it with their tools. What was to be done?

All at once, he remembered that some masons had been at work all day repairing the wall, the timber-work, and the roof of the south tower. This was a flash of light. The wall was of stone, the roof of lead, the timber-work of wood. (That prodigious timber-work, so dense that it was called "the forest.")

Quasimodo hastened to that tower. The lower chambers were, in fact, full of materials. There were piles of rough blocks of stone, sheets of lead in rolls, bundles of laths, heavy beams already notched with the saw, heaps of plaster.

Time was pressing. The pikes and hammers were at work below. With a strength which the sense of danger increased tenfold, he seized one of the beams—the longest and heaviest; he pushed it out through a loophole, then, grasping it again outside of the tower, he made it slide along the angle of the balustrade which surrounds the platform, and let it fly into the abyss. The enormous timber, during that fall of a hundred and sixty feet, scraping the wall, breaking the carvings, turned many times on its center, like the arm of a windmill flying off alone through space. At last it reached the ground, the horrible cry arose, and the black beam, as it rebounded from the pavement, resembled a serpent leaping.

Quasimodo beheld the outcasts scatter at the fall of the beam, like ashes at the breath of a child. He took advantage of their fright, and while they were fixing a superstitious glance on the club which had fallen from heaven, and while they were putting out the eyes of the stone saints on the front with a discharge of arrows and buck-shot, Quasimodo was silently piling up plaster, stones, and rough blocks of stone, even the sacks of tools belonging to the masons, on the edge of the balustrade from which the beam had already been hurled.

Thus, as soon as they began to batter the grand door, the shower of rough blocks of stone began to fall, and it seemed to them that the church itself was being demolished over their heads.

Anyone who could have beheld Quasimodo at that moment would have been frightened. Independently of the projectiles which he had piled upon the balustrade, he had collected a heap of stones on the platform itself. As fast as the blocks on the exterior edge were exhausted, he drew on the heap. Then he stooped and rose, stooped and rose again with incredible activity. His huge gnome's head bent over the balustrade, then an enormous stone fell, then another, then another. From time to time, he followed a fine stone with his eye, and when it did good execution, he said, "Hum!"

Meanwhile, the beggars did not grow discouraged. The thick door on which they were venting their fury had already trembled more than twenty times beneath the weight of their oaken battering-ram, multiplied by the strength of a hundred men. The panels cracked, the carved work flew into splinters, the hinges, at every blow, leaped from their pins, the planks yawned, the wood crumbled to powder, ground between the iron sheathing. Fortunately for Quasimodo, there was more iron than wood.

Nevertheless, he felt that the great door was yielding. Although he did not hear it, every blow of the ram reverberated simultaneously in the vaults of the church and within it. From above he beheld the vagabonds, filled with triumph and rage, shaking their fists at the gloomy façade; and both on the gypsy's account and his own he envied the wings of the owls which flitted away above his head in flocks.

His shower of stone blocks was not sufficient to repel the assailants.

At this moment of anguish, he noticed, a little lower down than the balustrade whence he was crushing the thieves, two long stone gutters which discharged immediately over the great door; the internal orifice of these gutters terminated on the pavement of the platform. An idea occurred to him; he ran in search of a fagot in his bellringer's den, placed on this fagot a great many bundles of laths, and many rolls of lead, munitions which he had not employed so far, and having arranged this pile in front of the hole to the two gutters, he set it on fire with his lantern.

During this time, since the stones no longer fell, the outcasts ceased to gaze into the air. The bandits, panting like a pack of hounds who are forcing a boar into his lair, pressed tumultuously round the great door, all disfigured by the battering-ram, but still standing. They were waiting with a quiver for the great blow which should split it open. They vied with each other in pressing as close as possible, in order to dash among the first, when it should open, into that opulent cathedral, a vast reservoir where the wealth of three centuries had been piled up. They reminded each other with roars of exultation and greedy lust, of the beautiful silver crosses, the fine copes of brocade, the beautiful tombs of silver gilt, the great magnificences of the choir, the dazzling festivals, the Christ-masses sparkling with torches, the Easters sparkling with sunshine—all those splendid solemneties wherein chandeliers, ciboriums, tabernacles, and reliquaries, studded the altars with a crust of gold and diamonds. Certainly, at that fine moment, thieves and pseudo sufferers, doctors in stealing, and vagabonds, were thinking much less of delivering the gypsy than of pillaging Notre-Dame. We could even easily believe that for a goodly number among them la Esmeralda was only a pretext, if thieves needed pretexts.

All at once, at the moment when they were grouping themselves round the ram for a last ef-fort, each one holding his breath and stiffening his muscles in order to communicate all his force to the decisive blow, a howl more frightful still than that which had burst forth and expired beneath the beam, rose among them. Those who did not cry out, those who were still alive, looked. Two streams of melted lead were falling from the summit of the edifice into the thickest of the rabble. That sea of men had just sunk down beneath the boiling metal, which had made, at the two points where it fell, two black and smoking holes in the crowd, such as hot water would make in snow. Dying men, half consumed and groaning with anguish, could be seen writhing there. Around these two principal streams there were drops of that horrible rain, which scattered over the assailants and entered their skulls like gimlets of fire. It was a heavy fire which overwhelmed these wretches with a thousand hailstones.

The outcry was heartrending. They fled pell-mell, hurling the beam upon the bodies, the bold-est as well as the most timid, and the parvis was cleared a second time.

All eyes were raised to the top of the church. They beheld there an extraordinary sight. On the crest of the highest gallery, higher than the central rose window, there was a great flame rising be-tween the two towers with whirlwinds of sparks, a vast, disordered, and furious flame, a tongue of which was borne into the smoke by the wind, from time to time. Below that fire, below the gloomy balustrade with its trefoils showing darkly against its glare, two spouts with monster throats were vomiting forth unceasingly that burning rain, whose silvery stream stood out against the shadows of the lower façade. As they approached the earth, these two jets of liquid lead spread out in sheaves, like water springing from the thousand holes of a watering-pot. Above the flame, the enormous tow-ers, two sides of each of which were visible in sharp outline, the one wholly black, the other wholly red, seemed still more vast with all the immensity of the shadow which they cast even to the sky.

Their innumerable sculptures of demons and dragons assumed a lugubrious aspect. The rest-less light of the flame made them move to the eye. There were griffins which had the air of laugh-ing, gargoyles which one fancied one heard yelping, salamanders which puffed at the fire, tarasques[1] which sneezed in the smoke. And among the monsters thus roused from their sleep of stone by this flame, by this noise, there was one who walked about, and who was seen, from time to time, to pass across the glowing face of the pile, like a bat in front of a candle.

Without doubt, this strange beacon light would awaken far away, the woodcutter of the hills of Bicêtre, terrified to behold the gigantic shadow of the towers of Notre-Dame quivering over his heaths.

A terrified silence ensued among the outcasts, during which nothing was heard, but the cries

1. The representation of a monstrous animal solemnly drawn about in Tarascon and other French towns.

of alarm of the canons shut up in their cloister, and more uneasy than horses in a burning stable, the furtive sound of windows hastily opened and still more hastily closed, the internal hurly-burly of the houses and of the Hôtel-Dieu, the wind in the flame, the last death-rattle of the dying, and the continued crackling of the rain of lead upon the pavement.

In the meanwhile, the principal vagabonds had retired beneath the porch of the Gondelaurier mansion, and were holding a council of war.

The Duke of Egypt, seated on a stone post, contemplated the phantasmagorical bonfire, glowing at a height of two hundred feet in the air, with religious terror. Clopin Trouillefou bit his huge fists with rage.

"Impossible to get in!" he muttered between his teeth.

"An old, enchanted church!" grumbled the aged Bohemian, Mathias Hungadi Spicali.

"By the Pope's whiskers!" went on a sham soldier, who had once been in service, "here are church gutters spitting melted lead at you better than the machicolations of Lectoure."

"Do you see that demon passing and repassing in front of the fire?" exclaimed the Duke of Egypt.

"Pardieu, 'tis that damned bellringer, 'tis Quasimodo," said Clopin.

The Bohemian tossed his head. "I tell you, that 'tis the spirit Sabnac, the grand marquis, the demon of fortifications. He has the form of an armed soldier, the head of a lion. Sometimes he rides a hideous horse. He changes men into stones, of which he builds towers. He commands fifty legions. 'Tis he indeed; I recognize him. Sometimes he is clad in a handsome golden robe, figured after the Turkish fashion."

"Where is Bellevigne de l' Étoile?" demanded Clopin.

"He is dead."

Andry the Red laughed in an idiotic way: "Notre-Dame is making work for the hospital," said he.

"Is there, then, no way of forcing this door," exclaimed the King of Thunes, stamping his foot.

The Duke of Egypt pointed sadly to the two streams of boiling lead which did not cease to streak the black facade, like two long distaffs of phosphorus.

"Churches have been known to defend themselves thus all by themselves," he remarked with a sigh. "Saint-Sophia at Constantinople, forty years ago, hurled to the earth three times in succession, the crescent of Mahom, by shaking her domes, which are her heads. Guillaume de Paris, who built this one was a magician."

"Must we then retreat in pitiful fashion, like highwaymen?" said Clopin. "Must we leave our sister here, whom those hooded wolves will hang to-morrow."

"And the sacristy, where there are wagon-loads of gold!" added a vagabond, whose name, we regret to say, we do not know.

"Beard of Mahom!" cried Trouillefou.

"Let us make another trial," resumed the vagabond.

Mathias Hungadi shook his head.

"We shall never get in by the door. We must find the defect in the armor of the old fairy; a hole, a false postern, some joint or other."

"Who will go with me?" said Clopin. "I shall go at it again. By the way, where is the little scholar Jehan, who is so encased in iron?"

"He is dead, no doubt," someone replied; "we no longer hear his laugh."

The King of Thunes frowned: "So much the worse. There was a brave heart under that iron-mongery. And Master Pierre Gringoire?"

"Captain Clopin," said Andry the Red, "he slipped away before we reached the Pont-aux-Changeurs."

Clopin stamped his foot. "*Gueule-Dieu!* 'twas he who pushed us on hither, and he has deserted us in the very middle of the job! Cowardly chatterer, with a slipper for a helmet!"

"Captain Clopin," said Andry the Red, who was gazing down Rue du Parvis, "yonder is the little scholar."

"Praised be Pluto!" said Clopin. "But what the devil is he dragging after him?"

It was, in fact, Jehan, who was running as fast as his heavy outfit of a Paladin, and a long ladder which trailed on the pavement, would permit, more breathless than an ant harnessed to a blade of grass twenty times longer than itself.

"Victory! *Te Deum!*" cried the scholar. "Here is the ladder of the longshoremen of Port Saint-Landry."

Clopin approached him.

"Child, what do you mean to do, *corne-dieu!* with this ladder?"

"I have it," replied Jehan, panting. "I knew where it was under the shed of the lieutenant's house. There's a wench there whom I know, who thinks me as handsome as Cupido. I made use of her to get the ladder, and I have the ladder, *Pasque-Mahom!* The poor girl came to open the door to me in her shift."

"Yes," said Clopin, "but what are you going to do with that ladder?"

Jehan gazed at him with a malicious, knowing look, and cracked his fingers like castanets. At that moment he was sublime. On his head he wore one of those overloaded helmets of the fifteenth century, which frightened the enemy with their fanciful crests. His bristled with ten iron beaks, so that Jehan could have disputed with Nestor's Homeric vessel the redoubtable title of $\delta\epsilon\chi\dot{\epsilon}\mu\lambda\delta$.

"What do I mean to do with it, august king of Thunes? Do you see that row of statues which have such idiotic expressions, yonder, above the three portals?"

"Yes. Well?"

" 'Tis the gallery of the kings of France."

"What is that to me?" said Clopin.

"Wait! At the end of that gallery there is a door which is never fastened otherwise than with a latch, and with this ladder I ascend, and I am in the church."

"Child let me be the first to ascend."

"No, comrade, the ladder is mine. Come, you shall be the second."

"May Beelzebub strangle you!" said surly Clopin, "I won't be second to anybody."

"Then find a ladder, Clopin!"

Jehan set out on a run across the Place, dragging his ladder and shouting: "Follow me, lads!"

In an instant the ladder was raised, and propped against the balustrade of the lower gallery, above one of the lateral doors. The throng of vagabonds, uttering loud acclamations, crowded to its foot to ascend. But Jehan maintained his right, and was the first to set foot on the rungs. The passage was tolerably long. The gallery of the kings of France is to-day about sixty feet above the pavement. The eleven steps of the flight before the door, made it still higher. Jehan mounted slowly, a good deal incommoded by his heavy armor, holding his crossbow in one hand, and clinging to a rung with the other. When he reached the middle of the ladder, he cast a melancholy glance at the poor dead outcasts, with which the steps were strewn. "Alas!" said he, "here is a heap of bodies worthy of the fifth book of the Iliad!" Then he continued his ascent. The vagabonds followed him. There was one on every rung. At the sight of this line of cuirassed backs, undulating as they rose through the gloom, one would have pronounced it a serpent with steel scales, which was raising itself erect in front of the church. Jehan who formed the head, and who was whistling, completed the illusion.

The scholar finally reached the balcony of the gallery, and climbed over it nimbly, to the applause of the whole vagabond tribe. Thus master of the citadel, he uttered a shout of joy, and suddenly halted, petrified. He had just caught sight of Quasimodo concealed in the dark, with flashing eye, behind one of the statues of the kings.

Before a second assailant could gain a foothold on the gallery, the formidable hunchback leaped to the head of the ladder, without uttering a word, seized the ends of the two uprights with his powerful hands, raised them, pushed them out from the wall, balanced the long and pliant ladder, loaded with vagabonds from top to bottom for a moment, in the midst of shrieks of anguish, then suddenly, with superhuman force, hurled this cluster of men backward into the Place. There was a moment when even the most resolute trembled. The ladder, launched backwards, remained erect and standing for an instant, and seemed to hesitate, then wavered, then suddenly, describing a frightful arc of a circle eighty feet in radius, crashed upon the pavement with its load of ruffians, more rapidly than a drawbridge when its chains break. There arose an immense imprecation, then all was still, and a few mutilated wretches were seen, crawling over the heap of dead.

A sound of wrath and grief followed the first cries of triumph among the besiegers. Quasimodo, impassive, with both elbows propped on the balustrade, looked on. He had the air of an old, bushy-headed king at his window.

As for Jehan Frollo, he was in a critical position. He found himself in the gallery with the formidable bellringer, alone, separated from his companions by a vertical wall eighty feet high. While Quasimodo was dealing with the ladder, the scholar had run to the postern which he believed to be open. It was not. The deaf man had closed it behind him when he entered the gallery. Jehan had then concealed himself behind a stone king, not daring to breathe, and fixing upon the monstrous hunchback a frightened gaze, like the man, who, when courting the wife of the guardian of a menagerie, went one evening to a love rendezvous, mistook the wall which he was to climb, and suddenly found himself face to face with a white bear.

For the first few moments, the deaf man paid no heed to him; but at last he turned his head, and suddenly straightened up. He had just caught sight of the scholar.

Jehan prepared himself for a rough shock, but the deaf man remained motionless; only he had turned toward the scholar and was looking at him.

"Ho! ho!" said Jehan, "what do you mean by staring at me with that solitary and melancholy eye?"

As he spoke thus, the young scamp stealthily adjusted his crossbow.

"Quasimodo!" he cried, "I am going to change your surname: you shall be called the blind man."

The shot sped. The feathered vireton whizzed and entered the hunchback's left arm. Quasimodo appeared no more moved by it than by a scratch to King Pharamond. He laid his hand on the arrow, tore it from his arm, and tranquilly broke it across his big knee; then he let the two pieces drop on the floor, rather than threw them down. But Jehan had no opportunity to fire a second time. The arrow broken, Quasimodo breathing heavily, bounded like a grasshopper, and he fell upon the scholar, whose armor was flattened against the wall by the blow.

Then in that gloom, wherein wavered the light of the torches, a terrible thing was seen.

Quasimodo had grasped with his left hand the two arms of Jehan, who did not offer any resistance, so thoroughly did he feel that he was lost. With his right hand, the deaf man detached one by one, in silence, with sinister slowness, all the pieces of his armor, the sword, the daggers, the helmet, the cuirass, the leg pieces. One would have said that it was a monkey taking the shell from a nut. Quasimodo flung the scholar's iron shell at his feet, piece by piece.

When the scholar beheld himself disarmed, stripped, weak, and naked in those terrible hands, he made no attempt to speak to the deaf man, but began to laugh audaciously in his face, and to sing with his intrepid heedlessness of a child of sixteen, the then popular ditty:—

> *Elle est bien habillée,*
> *La ville de Cambrai;*
> *Marafin l'a pillée. . . .*[1]

1. The city of Cambrai is well dressed. Marafin plundered it.

He did not finish. Quasimodo was seen on the parapet of the gallery, holding the scholar by the feet with one hand, and whirling him over the abyss like a sling; then a sound like that of a bony structure in contact with a wall was heard, and something was seen to fall which halted a third of the way down in its fall, on a projection in the architecture. It was a dead body which remained hanging there, bent double, its loins broken, its skull empty.

A cry of horror rose among the vagabonds.

"Vengeance!" shouted Clopin. "To the sack!" replied the multitude. "Assault! assault!"

There came a tremendous howl, in which were mingled all tongues, all dialects, all accents. The death of the poor scholar imparted a furious ardor to that crowd. It was seized with shame, and the wrath of having been held so long in check before a church by a hunchback. Rage found ladders, multiplied the torches, and, at the expiration of a few minutes, Quasimodo, in despair, beheld that terrible ant heap mount on all sides to the assault of Notre-Dame. Those who had no ladders had knotted ropes; those who had no ropes climbed by the projections of the carvings. They hung from each other's rags. There were no means of resisting that rising tide of frightful faces; rage made these fierce countenances ruddy; their clayey brows were dripping with sweat; their eyes darted lightnings; all these grimaces, all these horrors laid siege to Quasimodo. One would have said that some other church had dispatched to the assault of Notre-Dame its gorgons, its dogs, its drées, its demons, its most fantastic sculptures. It was like a layer of living monsters on the stone monsters of the façade.

Meanwhile, the Place was studded with a thousand torches. This scene of confusion, till now hid in darkness, was suddenly flooded with light. The parvis was resplendent, and cast a radiance on the sky; the bonfire lighted on the lofty platform was still burning, and illuminated the city far away. The enormous silhouette of the two towers, projected afar on the roofs of Paris, and formed a large notch of black in this light. The city seemed to be aroused. Alarm bells wailed in the distance. The vagabonds howled, panted, swore, climbed; and Quasimodo, powerless against so many enemies, shuddering for the gypsy, beholding the furious faces approaching ever nearer and nearer to his gallery, entreated heaven for a miracle, and wrung his arms in despair.

Chapter V

THE RETREAT IN WHICH MONSIEUR LOUIS OF FRANCE SAYS HIS PRAYERS

THE READER HAS NOT, PERHAPS, FORGOTTEN THAT ONE MOMENT BEFORE CATCHING SIGHT OF the nocturnal band of vagabonds, Quasimodo, as he inspected Paris from the heights of his bell tower, perceived only one light burning, which gleamed like a star from a window on the topmost story of a lofty edifice beside the Porte Saint-Antoine. This edifice was the Bastille. That star was the candle of Louis XI.

King Louis XI had, in fact, been two days in Paris. He was to take his departure on the next day but one for his citadel of Montilz-les-Tours. He made but seldom and brief appearance in his good city of Paris, since there he did not feel about him enough pitfalls, gibbets, and Scotch archers.

He had come, that day, to sleep at the Bastille. The great chamber five toises[1] square, which he had at the Louvre, with its huge chimney-piece loaded with twelve great beasts and thirteen great

---

1. Approximately six feet and five inches.

prophets, and his grand bed, eleven feet by twelve, pleased him but little. He felt himself lost amid all this grandeur. This good bourgeois king preferred the Bastille with a tiny chamber and couch. And then, the Bastille was stronger than the Louvre.

This little chamber, which the king reserved for himself in the famous state prison, was also tolerably spacious and occupied the topmost story of a turret rising from the donjon keep. It was circular in form, carpeted with mats of shining straw, ceiled with beams, enriched with fleurs-de-lys of gilded metal with interjoists in color; wainscoted with rich woods sown with rosettes of white metal, and with others painted a fine, bright green, made of orpiment and fine indigo.

There was only one window, a long pointed casement, latticed with brass wire and bars of iron, further darkened by fine colored panes with the arms of the king and of the queen, each pane being worth two and twenty sols.

There was but one entrance, a modern door, with a flat arch, garnished with a piece of tapestry on the inside, and on the outside by one of those porches of Irish wood, frail edifices of cabinet-work curiously wrought, numbers of which were still to be seen in old houses a hundred and fifty years ago. "Although they disfigure and embarrass the places," says Sauvel in despair, "our old people are still unwilling to get rid of them, and keep them in spite of everybody."

In this chamber, nothing was to be found of what furnishes ordinary apartments, neither benches, nor trestles, nor forms, nor common stools in the form of a chest, nor fine stools sustained by pillars and counter-pillars, at four sols a piece. Only one easy arm-chair, very magnificent, was to be seen; the wood was painted with roses on a red ground, the seat was of ruby Cordovan leather, ornamented with long silken fringes, and studded with a thousand golden nails. The loneliness of this chair made it apparent that only one person had a right to sit down in this apartment. Beside the chair, and quite close to the window, there was a table covered with a cloth with a pattern of birds. On this table stood an inkhorn spotted with ink, some parchments, several pens, and a large goblet of chased silver. A little further on was a brazier, a praying stool in crimson velvet, relieved with small bosses of gold. Finally, at the extreme end of the room, a simple bed of scarlet and yellow damask, without either tinsel or lace; having only an ordinary fringe. This bed, famous for having borne the sleep or the sleeplessness of Louis XI, was still to be seen two hundred years ago, at the house of a councilor of state, where it was seen by old Madame Pilou, celebrated in *Cyrus* under the name *Arricidie* and of *la Morale Vivante*.

Such was the chamber which was called "the retreat where Monsieur Louis de France says his prayers."

At the moment when we have introduced the reader into it, this retreat was very dark. The curfew bell had sounded an hour before; night was come, and there was only one flickering wax candle set on the table to light five persons variously grouped in the chamber.

The first on which the light fell was a seigneur superbly clad in breeches and jerkin of scarlet striped with silver, and a loose coat with half sleeves of cloth of gold with black figures. This splendid costume, on which the light played, seemed glazed with flame on every fold. The man who wore it had his armorial bearings embroidered on his breast in vivid colors; a chevron accompanied by a deer passant. The shield was flanked, on the right by an olive branch, on the left by a deer's antlers. This man wore in his girdle a rich dagger whose hilt, of silver gilt, was chased in the form of a helmet, and surmounted by a count's coronet. He had a forbidding air, a proud mien, and a head held high. At the first glance one read arrogance on his visage; at the second, craft.

He was standing bareheaded, a long roll of parchment in his hand, behind the arm-chair in which was seated, his body ungracefully doubled up, his knees crossed, his elbow on the table, a very badly accoutred personage. Let the reader imagine in fact, on the rich seat of Cordova leather, two crooked knees, two thin thighs, poorly clad in black worsted tricot, a body enveloped in a cloak of fustian, with fur trimming of which more leather than hair was visible; lastly, to crown all, a greasy old hat of the worst sort of black cloth, bordered with a circular string of leaden figures.

This, in company with a dirty skull-cap, which hardly allowed a hair to escape, was all that distinguished the seated personage. He held his head so bent upon his breast, that nothing was to be seen of his face thus thrown into shadow, except the tip of his nose, upon which fell a ray of light, and which must have been long. From the thinness of his wrinkled hand, one divined that he was an old man. It was Louis XI.

At some distance behind them, two men dressed in garments of Flemish style were conversing, who were not sufficiently lost in the shadow to prevent anyone who had been present at the performance of Gringoire's mystery from recognizing in them two of the principal Flemish envoys, Guillaume Rym, the sagacious pensioner of Ghent, and Jacques Coppenole, the popular hosier. The reader will remember that these men were mixed up in the secret politics of Louis XI.

Finally, quite at the end of the room, near the door, in the dark, stood, motionless as a statue, a vigorous man with thickset limbs, a military harness, with a surcoat of armorial bearings, whose square face pierced with staring eyes, slit with an immense mouth, his ears concealed by two large screens of flat hair, had something about it both of the dog and the tiger.

All were uncovered except the king.

The gentleman who stood near the king was reading him a sort of long memorial to which his majesty seemed to be listening attentively. The two Flemings were whispering together.

"Cross of God!" grumbled Coppenole, "I am tired of standing; is there no chair here?"

Rym replied by a negative gesture, accompanied by a discreet smile.

"Croix-Dieu!" resumed Coppenole, thoroughly unhappy at being obliged to lower his voice thus, "I should like to sit down on the floor, with my legs crossed, like a hosier, as I do in my shop."

"Take good care that you do not, Master Jacques."

"Ouais! Master Guillaume! can one only remain here on his feet?"

"Or on his knees," said Rym.

At that moment the king's voice was uplifted. They held their peace.

"Fifty sols for the robes of our valets, and twelve livres for the mantles of the clerks of our crown! That's it! Pour out gold by the ton! Are you mad, Olivier?"

As he spoke thus, the old man raised his head. The golden shells of the collar of Saint-Michael could be seen gleaming on his neck. The candle fully illuminated his gaunt and morose profile. He tore the papers from the other's hand.

"You are ruining us!" he cried, casting his hollow eyes over the scroll. "What is all this? What need have we of so prodigious a household? Two chaplains at ten livres a month each, and a chapel clerk at one hundred sols! A valet-de-chambre at ninety livres a year. Four head cooks at six score livres a year each! A spit-cook, an herb-cook, a sauce-cook, a butler, two sumpter-horse lackeys, at ten livres a month each! Two scullions at eight livres! A groom of the stables and his two aids at four and twenty livres a month! A porter, a pastry-cook, a baker, two carters, each sixty livres a year! And the farrier six score livres! And the master of the chamber of our funds, twelve hundred livres! And the comptroller five hundred. And how do I know what else? 'Tis ruinous. The wages of our servants are putting France to the pillage! All the ingots of the Louvre will melt before such a fire of expenses! We shall have to sell our plate! And next year, if God and our Lady (here he raised his hat) lend us life, we shall drink our potions from a pewter pot!"

So saying, he cast a glance at the silver goblet which gleamed upon the table. He coughed and continued—

"Master Olivier, the princes who reign over great lordships, like kings and emperors, should not allow sumptuousness in their houses; for the fire spreads thence through the province. Hence, Master Olivier, consider this said once for all. Our expenditure increases every year. The thing displease us. How, *pasque-Dieu!* when in '79 it did not exceed six and thirty thousand livres, did it attain in '80, forty-three thousand six hundred and nineteen livres? I have the figures in my head. In

'81, sixty-six thousand six hundred and eighty livres, and this year, by the faith of my body, it will reach eighty thousand livres! Doubled in four years! Monstrous!"

He paused breathless, then resumed energetically—

"I behold around me only people who fatten on my leanness! you suck crowns from me at every pore!"

All remained silent. This was one of those fits of wrath which are allowed to take their course. He continued—

" 'Tis like that request in Latin from the gentlemen of France, that we should re-establish what they call the grand charges of the Crown! Charges in very deed! Charges which crush! Ah! gentlemen! you say that we are not a king to reign *dapifero nullo, buticulario nullo!* We will let you see, *pasque-Dieu!* whether we are not a king!"

Here he smiled, in the consciousness of his power; this softened his bad humor, and he turned toward the Flemings—

"Do you see, Gossip Guillaume? the grand warden of the keys, the grand butler, the grand chamberlain, the grand seneschal are not worth the smallest valet. Remember this, Gossip Coppenole. They serve no purpose, as they stand thus useless round the king; they produce upon me the effect of the four Evangelists who surround the face of the big clock of the palace, and which Philippe Brille has just set in order afresh. They are gilt, but they do not indicate the hour, and the hands can get on without them."

He remained in thought for a moment, then added, shaking his aged head—

"Ho! ho! by our Lady, I am not Philippe Brille, and I shall not gild the great vassals anew. Continue, Olivier."

The person whom he designated by this name, took the papers into his hands again, and began to read aloud—

"To Adam Tenon, clerk of the warden of the seals of the provostship of Paris; for the silver, making, and engraving of said seals, which have been made new because the others preceding, by reason of their antiquity and their worn condition, could no longer be successfully used, twelve livres parisis.

"To Guillaume Frère, the sum of four livres, four sols parisis, for his trouble and salary, for having nourished and fed the doves in the two dove-cots of the Hôtel des Tournelles, during the months of January, February, and March of this year; and for this he hath given seven sextiers of barley.

"To a gray friar for confessing a criminal, four sols parisis."

The king listened in silence. From time to time he coughed; then he raised the goblet to his lips and drank a draft with a grimace.

"During this year there have been made by the ordinance of justice, to the sound of the trumpet, through the squares of Paris, fifty-six proclamations. Account to be regulated.

"For having searched and ransacked in certain places, in Paris as well as elsewhere, for money said to be there concealed; but nothing hath been found: forty-five livres parisis."

"Bury a crown to unearth a soul!" said the king.

". . . For having set in the Hôtel des Tournelles six panes of white glass in the place where the iron cage is, thirteen sols; for having made and delivered by command of the king, on the day of the musters, four shields with the escutcheons of the said seigneur, encircled with garlands of roses all about, six livres; for two new sleeves to the king's old doublet, twenty sols; for a box of grease to grease the boots of the king, fifteen deniers; a stable newly made to lodge the king's black pigs, thirty livres parisis; many partitions, planks, and trapdoors, for the safekeeping of the lions at Saint-Paul, twenty-two livres."

"These be dear beasts," said Louis XI. "It matters not; it is a fine magnificence in a king. There is a great red lion whom I love for his pleasant ways. Have you seen him, Master Guillaume?

Princes must have these terrific animals; for we kings must have lions for our dogs and tigers for our cats. The great befits a crown. In the days of the pagans of Jupiter, when the people offered the temples a hundred oxen and a hundred sheep, the emperors gave a hundred lions and a hundred eagles. This was wild and very fine. The kings of France have always had roarings round their throne. Nevertheless, people must do me this justice, that I spend still less money on it than they did, and that I possess a greater modesty of lions, bears, elephants, and leopards.—Go on, Master Olivier. We wished to say thus much to our Flemish friends."

Guillaume Rym bowed low, while Coppenole, with his surly mien, had the air of one of the bears of which his majesty was speaking. The king paid no heed. He had just dipped his lips into the goblet, and he spat out the beverage, saying: "Foh! what a disagreeable potion!" The man who was reading continued:—

"For feeding a rascally footpad, locked up these six months in the little cell of the flayer, until it should be determined what to do with him, six livres, four sols."

"What's that?" interrupted the king; "feed what ought to be hanged! *Pasque-Dieu!* I will give not a sou more for that nourishment. Olivier, come to an understanding about the matter with Monsieur d'Estouteville, and prepare me this very evening the wedding of the gallant and the gallows. Resume."

Olivier made a mark with his thumb against the article of the "rascally foot soldier," and passed on.

"To Henriet Cousin, master executor of the high works of justice in Paris, the sum of sixty sols parisis, to him assessed and ordained by monseigneur the provost of Paris, for having bought, by order of the said sieur the provost, a great broad sword, serving to execute and decapitate persons who are by justice condemned for their demerits, and he hath caused the same to be garnished with a sheath and with all things thereto appertaining; and hath likewise caused to be repointed and set in order the old sword, which had become broken and notched in executing justice on Messire Louis de Luxembourg, as will more fully appear . . ."

The king interrupted: "That suffices. I allow the sum with great good-will. Those are expenses which I do not begrudge. I have never regretted that money. Continue."

"For having made over a great cage . . ."

"Ah!" said the king, grasping the arms of his chair in both hands, "I knew well that I came hither to this Bastille for some purpose. Hold, Master Olivier; I desire to see that cage myself. You shall read me the cost while I am examining it. Messieurs Flemings, come and see this, 'tis curious."

Then he rose, leaned on the arm of his interlocutor, made a sign to the sort of mute who stood before the door to precede him, to the two Flemings to follow him, and quitted the room.

The royal company was recruited, at the door of the retreat, by men of arms, all loaded down with iron, and by slender pages bearing flambeaux. It marched for some time through the interior of the gloomy donjon, pierced with staircases and corridors even in the very thickness of the walls. The captain of the Bastille marched at their head, and caused the wickets to be opened before the bent and aged king, who coughed as he walked.

At each wicket, all heads were obliged to stoop, except that of the old man bent double with age. "Hum," said he between his gums, for he had no longer any teeth, "we are already quite prepared for the door of the sepulcher. For a low door, a bent passer."

At length, after having passed a final wicket, so loaded with locks that a quarter of an hour was required to open it, they entered a vast and lofty vaulted hall, in the center of which they could distinguish by the light of the torches, a huge cubic mass of masonry, iron, and wood. The interior was hollow. It was one of those famous cages of prisoners of state, which were called "the little daughters of the king." In its walls there were two or three little windows so closely trellised with stout iron bars, that the glass was not visible. The door was a large flat slab of stone, as on tombs; the sort of door which serves for entrance only. Only here, the occupant was alive.

The king began to walk slowly round the little edifice, examining it carefully, while Master Olivier, who followed him, read aloud the note.

"For having made a great cage of wood of solid beams, timbers and wall-plates, measuring nine feet in length by eight in breadth, and of the height of seven feet between the partitions, smoothed and clamped with great bolts of iron, which has been placed in a chamber situated in one of the towers of the Bastille Saint-Antoine, in which cage is placed and detained, by command of the king our lord, a prisoner who formerly inhabited an old, decrepit, and ruined cage. There have been employed in making the said new cage, ninety-six horizontal beams, and fifty-two upright joists, ten wall-plates three toises long; there have been occupied nineteen carpenters to hew, work, and fit all the said wood in the courtyard of the Bastille during twenty days."

"Very fine heart of oak," said the king, striking the woodwork with his fist.

"There have been used in this cage," continued the other, "two hundred and twenty great bolts of iron, of nine feet, and of eight, the rest of medium length, with the rowels, caps and counter-bands appertaining to the said bolts; weighing, the said iron in all, three thousand, seven hundred and thirty-five pounds; beside eight great squares of iron, serving to attach the said cage in place with clamps and nails weighing in all two hundred and eighteen pounds, not reckoning the iron of the trellises for the windows of the chamber wherein the cage hath been placed, the bars of iron for the door of the cage and other things."

" 'Tis a great deal of iron," said the king, "to contain the light of a spirit."

"The whole amounts to three hundred and seventeen livres, five sols, seven deniers."

"Pasque-Dieu!" exclaimed the king.

At this oath, which was the favorite of Louis XI, someone seemed to awaken in the interior of the cage; the sound of chains was heard, grating on the floor, and a feeble voice, which seemed to issue from the tomb was uplifted. "Sire! sire! mercy!" The one who spoke thus could not be seen.

"Three hundred and seventeen livres, five sols, seven deniers," repeated Louis XI.

The lamentable voice which had proceeded from the cage had frozen all present, even Master Olivier himself. The king alone wore the air of not having heard. At his order, Master Olivier resumed his reading, and his majesty coldly continued his inspection of the cage.

"In addition to this there hath been paid to a mason who hath made the holes wherein to place the gratings of the windows, and the floor of the chamber where the cage is, because that floor could not support this cage by reason of its weight, twenty-seven livres fourteen sols parisis."

The voice began to moan again.

"Mercy, sire! I swear to you that 'twas Monsieur the Cardinal d'Angers and not I, who was guilty of treason."

"The mason is bold!" said the king. "Continue, Olivier."

Olivier continued—

"To a joiner for window frames, bedstead, hollow stool, and other things, twenty livres, two sols parisis."

The voice also continued.

"Alas, sire! will you not listen to me? I protest to you that 'twas not I who wrote the matter to Monseigneur de Guyenne, but Monsieur le Cardinal Balue."

"The joiner is dear," quoth the king. "Is that all?"

"No, sire. To a glazier, for the windows of the said chamber, forty-six sols, eight deniers parisis."

"Have mercy, sire! Is it not enough to have given all my goods to my judges, my plate to Monsieur de Torcy, my library to Master Pierre Doriolle, my tapestry to the governor of the Roussillon? I am innocent. I have been shivering in an iron cage for fourteen years. Have mercy, sire! You will find your reward in heaven."

"Master Olivier," said the king, "the total?"

"Three hundred sixty-seven livres, eight sols, three deniers parisis."

"Notre-Dame!" cried the king. "This is an outrageous cage!"

He tore the book from Master Olivier's hands, and set to reckoning it himself upon his fingers, examining the paper and the cage alternately. Meanwhile, the prisoner could be heard sobbing. This was lugubrious in the darkness, and their faces turned pale as they looked at each other.

"Fourteen years, sire! Fourteen years now! since the month of April, 1469. In the name of the Holy Mother of God, sire, listen to me! During all this time you have enjoyed the heat of the sun. Shall I, frail creature, never more behold the day? Mercy, sire! Be pitiful! Clemency is a fine, royal virtue, which turns aside the currents of wrath. Does your majesty believe that in the hour of death it will be a great cause of content for a king never to have left any offense unpunished? Besides, sire, I did not betray your majesty, 'twas Monsieur d'Angers; and I have on my foot a very heavy chain, and a great ball of iron at the end, much heavier than it should be in reason. Eh! sire! Have pity on me!"

"Olivier," cried the king, throwing back his head, "I observe that they charge me twenty sols a hogshead for plaster, while it is worth but twelve. You will refer back this account."

He turned his back on the cage, and set out to leave the room. The miserable prisoner divined from the removal of the torches and the noise, that the king was taking his departure.

"Sire! sire!" he cried in despair.

The door closed again. He no longer saw anything, and heard only the hoarse voice of the turnkey, singing in his ears this ditty—

> Maître Jean Balue,
> A perdu la vue
> De ses évêchés.
> Monsieur de Verdun.
> N'en a plus pas un;
> Tous sont dépêchés.[1]

The king reascended in silence to his retreat, and his suite followed him, terrified by the last groans of the condemned man. All at once his majesty turned to the Governor of the Bastille—

"By the way," said he, "was there not someone in that cage?"

"Pardieu, yes sire!" replied the governor, astounded by the question.

"And who was it?"

"Monsieur the Bishop of Verdun."

The king knew this better than anyone else. But it was a mania of his.

"Ah!" said he, with the innocent air of thinking of it for the first time, "Guillaume de Harancourt, the friend of Monsieur the Cardinal Balue. A good devil of a bishop!"

At the expiration of a few moments, the door of the retreat had opened again, then closed upon the five personages whom the reader has seen at the beginning of this chapter, and who resumed their places, their whispered conversations, and their attitudes.

During the king's absence, several dispatches had been placed on his table, and he broke the seals himself. Then he began to read them promptly, one after the other, made a sign to Master Olivier who appeared to exercise the office of minister, to take a pen, and without communicating to him the contents of the dispatches, he began to dictate in a low voice, the replies which the latter wrote, on his knees, in an inconvenient attitude before the table.

Guillaume Rym was on the watch.

---

1. Master Jean Balue has lost sight of his bishoprics. Monsieur of Verdun has no longer one; all have been killed off.

The king spoke so low that the Flemings heard nothing of his dictation, except some isolated and rather unintelligible scraps, such as—

"To maintain the fertile places by commerce, and the sterile by manufactures. . . . —To show the English lords our four bombards, London, Brabant, Bourg-en-Bresse, Saint-Omer. . . . —Artillery is the cause of war being made more judiciously now. . . . —To Monsieur de Bressuire, our friend. . . . —Armies cannot be maintained without tribute, etc."

Once he raised his voice—

"*Pasque Dieu!* Monsieur the King of Sicily seals his letters with yellow wax, like a king of France. Perhaps we are in the wrong to permit him so to do. My fair cousin of Burgundy granted no armorial bearings with a field of gules. The grandeur of houses is assured by the integrity of prerogatives. Note this, friend Olivier."

Again—

"Oh! oh!" said he, "What a long message! What doth our brother the emperor claim?" And running his eye over the missive and breaking his reading with interjection: "Surely! the Germans are so great and powerful, that it is hardly credible—But let us not forget the old proverb: 'The finest county is Flanders; the finest duchy, Milan; the finest kingdom, France.' Is it not so, Messieurs Flemings?"

This time Coppenole bowed in company with Guillaume Rym. The hosier's patriotism was tickled.

The last dispatch made Louis XI frown.

"What is this?" he said, "Complaints and fault finding against our garrisons in Picardy! Olivier, write with diligence to M. the Marshal de Rouault:—That discipline is relaxed. That the gendarmes of the unattached troops, the feudal nobles, the free archers, and the Swiss inflict infinite evils on the rustics.—That the military, not content with what they find in the houses of the rustics, constrain them with violent blows of cudgel or of lash to go and get wine, spices, and other unreasonable things in the town.—That monsieur the king knows this. That we undertake to guard our people against inconveniences, larcenies and pillage.—That such is our will, by our Lady!—That in addition, it suits us not that any fiddler, barber, or any soldier varlet should be clad like a prince, in velvet, cloth of silk, and rings of gold.—That these vanities are hateful to God.—That we, who are gentlemen, content ourselves with a doublet of cloth at sixteen sols the ell, of Paris.—That messieurs the camp-followers can very well come down to that, also.—Command and ordain.—To Monsieur de Rouault, our friend.—Good."

He dictated this letter aloud, in a firm tone, and in jerks. At the moment when he finished it, the door opened and gave passage to a new personage, who precipitated himself into the chamber, crying in affright—

"Sire! sire! there is a sedition of the populace in Paris!"

Louis XI's grave face contracted; but all that was visible of his emotion passed away like a flash of lightning. He controlled himself and said with tranquil severity—

"Gossip Jacques, you enter very abruptly!"

"Sire! sire! there is a revolt!" repeated Gossip Jacques breathlessly.

The king, who had risen, grasped him roughly by the arm, and said in his ear, in such a manner as to be heard by him alone, with concentrated rage and a sidelong glance at the Flemings—

"Hold your tongue! or speak low!"

The newcomer understood, and began in a low tone to give a very terrified account, to which the king listened calmly, while Guillaume Rym called Coppenole's attention to the face and dress of the new arrival, to his furred cowl (*caputia fourrata*), his short cape (*epitogia curta*), his robe of black velvet, which bespoke a president of the court of accounts.

Hardly had this personage given the king some explanations, when Louis XI exclaimed, bursting into a laugh—

"In truth? Speak aloud, Gossip Coictier! What call is there for you to talk so low? Our Lady knoweth that we conceal nothing from our good friends the Flemings."

"But sire. . . ."

"Speak loud!"

Gossip Coictier was struck dumb with surprise.

"So," resumed the king—"speak sir—there is a commotion among the louts in our good city of Paris?"

"Yes, sire."

"And which is moving you say, against monsieur the bailiff of the Palais-de-Justice?"

"So it appears," said the gossip, who still stammered, utterly astounded by the abrupt and inexplicable change which had just taken place in the king's thoughts.

Louis XI continued: "Where did the watch meet the rabble?"

"Marching from the Grand Truanderie, toward the Pont-aux-Changeurs. I met it myself as I was on my way hither to obey your majesty's commands. I heard some of them shouting: 'Down with the bailiff of the palace!' "

"And what complaints have they against the bailiff?"

"Ah!" said Gossip Jacques, "because he is their lord."

"Really?"

"Yes, sire. They are knaves from the Cour des Miracles. They have been complaining this long while, of the bailiff, whose vassals they are. They do not wish to recognize him either as judge or as voyer?"[1]

"Yes, certainly!" retorted the king with a smile of satisfaction which he strove in vain to disguise.

"In all their petitions to the Parliament, they claim to have but two masters. Your majesty and their God, who is the devil, I believe."

"Eh! eh!" said the king.

He rubbed his hands, he laughed with that inward mirth which makes the countenance beam; he was unable to dissimulate his joy, although he endeavored at moments to compose himself. No one understood it in the least, not even Master Olivier. He remained silent for a moment, with a thoughtful but contented air.

"Are they in force?" he suddenly inquired.

"Yes, assuredly, sire," replied Gossip Jacques.

"How many?"

"Six thousand at the least."

The king could not refrain from saying: "Good!" he went on—

"Are they armed?"

"With scythes, pikes, hackbuts, pickaxes. All sorts of very violent weapons."

The king did not appear in the least disturbed by this list. Jacques considered it his duty to add—

"If your majesty does not send prompt succor to the bailiff, he is lost."

"We will send," said the king with an air of false seriousness. "It is well. Assuredly we will send. Monsieur the bailiff is our friend. Six thousand! They are desperate scamps! Their audacity is marvelous, and we are greatly enraged at it. But we have only a few people about us to-night. To-morrow morning will be time enough."

Gossip Jacques exclaimed, "Instantly, sire! there will be time to sack the bailiwick a score of times, to violate the seignory, to hang the bailiff. For God's sake, sire! send before to-morrow morning."

1. One in charge of the highways.

The king looked him full in the face. "I have told you to-morrow morning."

It was one of those looks to which one does not reply.

After a silence, Louis XI raised his voice once more—

"You should know that, Gossip Jacques. What was—" He corrected himself. "What is the bailiff's feudal jurisdiction?"

"Sire, the bailiff of the palace has the Rue Calendre as far as the Rue de l'Herberie, the Place Saint-Michel, and the localities vulgarly known as the Mureaux, situated near the church of Notre-Dame des Champs (here Louis XI raised the brim of his hat), which hôtels number thirteen, plus the Cour des Miracles, plus the Maladerie, called the Banlieue, plus the whole highway which begins at that Maladerie and ends at the Porte Sainte-Jacques. Of these divers places he is voyer, high, middle, and low, justiciary, full seigneur."

"Bless me!" said the king, scratching his left ear with his right hand, "that makes a goodly bit of my city! Ah! monsieur the bailiff was king of all that."

This time he did not correct himself. He continued dreamily, and as though speaking to himself—

"Very fine, monsieur the bailiff! You had there between your teeth a pretty slice of our Paris."

All at once he broke out explosively, "*Pasque-Dieu!* What people are those who claim to be voyers, justiciaries, lords and masters in our domains? who have their toll-gates at the end of every field? their gallows and their hangman at every cross-road among our people? So that as the Greek believed that he had as many gods as there were fountains, and the Persian as many as he beheld stars, the Frenchman counts as many kings as he sees gibbets! Pardieu! 'tis an evil thing, and the confusion of it displeases me. I should greatly like to know whether it be the mercy of God that there should be in Paris any other lord than the king, any other judge than our parliament, any other emperor than ourselves in this empire! By the faith of my soul! the day must certainly come when there shall exist in France but one king, one lord, one judge, one headsman, as there is in paradise but one God!"

He lifted his cap again, and continued, still dreamily, with the air and accent of a hunter who is cheering on his pack of hounds: "Good, my people! bravely done! break these false lords! do your duty! at them! have at them! pillage them! take them! sack them! . . . Ah! you want to be kings, messeigneurs? On, my people on!"

Here he interrupted himself abruptly, bit his lips as though to take back his thought which had already half escaped, bent his piercing eyes in turn on each of the five persons who surrounded him, and suddenly grasping his hat with both hands and staring full at it, he said to it: "Oh! I would burn you if you knew what there was in my head."

Then casting about him once more the cautious and uneasy glance of the fox re-entering his hole—

"No matter! we will succor monsieur the bailiff. Unfortunately, we have but few troops here at the present moment, against so great a populace. We must wait until to-morrow. The order will be transmitted to the City and everyone who is caught will be immediately hung."

"By the way, sire," said Gossip Coictier, "I had forgotten that in the first agitation, the watch have seized two laggards of the band. If your majesty desires to see these men, they are here."

"If I desire to see them!" cried the king. "What! *Pasque-Dieu!* You forget a thing like that! Run quick, you, Olivier! Go, seek them!"

Master Olivier quitted the room and returned a moment later with the two prisoners, surrounded by archers of the guard. The first had a coarse, idiotic, drunken and astonished face. He was clothed in rags, and walked with one knee bent and dragging his leg. The second had a pallid and smiling countenance, with which the reader is already acquainted.

The king surveyed them for a moment without uttering a word, then addressing the first one abruptly—

"What's your name?"

"Gieffroy Pincebourde."

"Your trade."

"Outcast."

"What were you going to do in this damnable sedition?"

The outcast stared at the king, and swung his arms with a stupid air.

He had one of those awkwardly shaped heads where intelligence is about as much at its ease as a light beneath an extinguisher.

"I know not," said he. "They went, I went."

"Were you not going to outrageously attack and pillage your lord, the bailiff of the palace?"

"I know that they were going to take something from someone. That is all."

A soldier pointed out to the king a billhook which he had seized on the person of the vagabond.

"Do you recognize this weapon?" demanded the king.

"Yes; 'tis my billhook; I am a vine-dresser."

"And do you recognize this man as your companion?" added Louis XI, pointing to the other prisoner.

"No, I do not know him."

"That will do," said the king, making a sign with his finger to the silent personage who stood motionless beside the door, to whom we have already called the reader's attention.

"Gossip Tristan, here is a man for you."

Tristan l'Hermite bowed. He gave an order in a low voice to two archers, who led away the poor vagabond.

In the meantime, the king had approached the second prisoner, who was perspiring in great drops: "Your name?"

"Sire, Pierre Gringoire."

"Your trade?"

"Philosopher, sire."

"How do you permit yourself, knave, to go and besiege our friend, monsieur the bailiff of the palace, and what have you to say concerning this popular agitation?"

"Sire, I had nothing to do with it."

"Come, now! you wanton wretch, were not you apprehended by the watch in that bad company?"

"No, sire, there is a mistake. 'Tis a fatality. I make tragedies. Sire, I entreat your majesty to listen to me. I am a poet. 'Tis the melancholy way of men of my profession to roam the streets by night. I was passing there. It was mere chance. I was unjustly arrested; I am innocent of this civil tempest. Your majesty sees that the vagabond did not recognize me. I conjure your majesty—"

"Hold your tongue!" said the king, between two swallows of his ptisan. "You split our head!"

Tristan l'Hermite advanced and pointing to Gringoire—

"Sire, can this one be hanged also?"

This was the first word that he had uttered.

"Phew!" replied the king, "I see no objection."

"I see a great many!" said Gringoire.

At that moment, our philosopher was greener than an olive. He perceived from the king's cold and indifferent mien that there was no other resource than something very pathetic, and he flung himself at the feet of Louis XI, exclaiming, with gestures of despair:—

"Sire! will your majesty deign to hear me. Sire! break not in thunder over so small a thing as myself. God's great lightning doth not bombard a lettuce. Sire, you are an august and very puissant monarch; have pity on a poor man who is honest, and who would find it more difficult to stir up a revolt than a cake of ice would to give out a spark! Very gracious sire, kindness is the virtue of a lion and a king. Alas! rigor only frightens minds; the impetuous gusts of the north wind do not make the traveler lay aside his cloak; the sun, bestowing his rays little by little, warms him in such ways that it will make him strip to his shirt. Sire, you are the sun. I protest to you, my sovereign lord and master, that I am not an outcast, thief, and disorderly fellow. Revolt and brigandage belong not to the outfit of Apollo. I am not the man to fling myself into those clouds which break out into seditious clamor. I am your majesty's faithful vassal. That same jealousy which a husband cherisheth for the honor of his wife, the resentment which the son hath for the love of his father, a good vassal should feel for the glory of his king; he should pine away for the zeal of this house, for the aggrandizement of his service. Every other passion which should transport him would be but madness. These, sire, are my maxims of state: then do not judge me to be a seditious and thieving rascal because my garment is worn at the elbows. If you will grant me mercy, sire, I will wear it out on the knees in praying to God for you night and morning! Alas! I am not extremely rich, 'tis true. I am even rather poor. But not vicious on that account. It is not my fault. Everyone knoweth that great wealth is not to be drawn from literature, and that those who are best posted in good books do not always have a great fire in winter. The advocate's trade taketh all the grain, and leaveth only straw to the other scientific professions. There are forty very excellent proverbs anent the hole-ridden cloak of the philosopher. Oh, sire! clemency is the only light which can enlighten the interior of so great a soul. Clemency beareth the torch before all the other virtues. Without it they are but blind men groping after God in the dark. Compassion, which is the same thing as clemency, causeth the love of subjects, which is the most powerful bodyguard to a prince. What matters it to your majesty, who dazzles all faces, if there is one poor man more on earth, a poor innocent philosopher spluttering amid the shadows of calamity, with an empty pocket which resounds against his hollow belly? Moreover, sire, I am a man of letters. Great kings make a pearl for their crowns by protecting letters. Hercules did not disdain the title of Musagetes. Mathias Corvin favored Jean de Monroyal, the ornament of mathematics. Now, 'tis an ill way to protect letters to hang men of letters. What a stain on Alexander if he had hung Aristoteles! This act would not be a little patch on the face of his reputation to embellish it, but a very malignant ulcer to disfigure it. Sire! I made a very proper epithalamium for Mademoiselle of Flanders and Monseigneur the very august Dauphin. That is not a firebrand of rebellion. Your majesty sees that I am not a scribbler of no reputation, that I have studied excellently well, and that I possess much natural eloquence. Have mercy upon me, sire! In so doing you will perform a gallant deed to our Lady, and I swear to you that I am greatly terrified at the idea of being hanged!"

So saying, the unhappy Gringoire kissed the king's slippers, and Guillaume Rym said to Coppenole in a low tone: "He doth well to drag himself on the earth. Kings are like the Jupiter of Crete, they have ears only in their feet." And without troubling himself about the Jupiter of Crete, the hosier replied with a heavy smile, and his eyes fixed on Gringoire: "Oh! that's it exactly! I seem to hear Chancellor Hugonet craving mercy of me."

When Gringoire paused at last, quite out of breath, he raised his head tremblingly toward the king, who was engaged in scratching a spot on the knee of his breeches with his finger-nail; then his majesty began to drink from the goblet of ptisan. But he uttered not a word, and this silence tortured Gringoire. At last the king looked at him. "Here is a terrible bawler!" said, he. Then, turning to Tristan l'Hermite, "Bah! let him go!"

Gringoire fell backwards, quite thunderstruck with joy.

"At liberty!" growled Tristan. "Doth not your majesty wish to have him detained a little while in a cage?"

"Gossip," retorted Louis XI, "think you that 'tis for birds of this feather that we cause to be made cages at three hundred and sixty-seven livres, eight sous, three deniers apiece? Release him at once, the wanton (Louis XI was fond of this word which formed, with *Pasque-Dieu*, the foundation of his joviality), and put him out with a buffet."

"Ugh!" cried Gringoire, "what a great king is here!"

And for fear of a counter order, he rushed toward the door, which Tristan opened for him with a very bad grace. The soldiers left the room with him, pushing him before them with stout thwacks, which Gringoire bore like a true stoical philosopher.

The king's good humor since the revolt against the bailiff had been announced to him, made itself apparent in every way. This unwonted clemency was no small sign of it. Tristan l'Hermite in his corner wore the surly look of a dog who has had a bone snatched away from him.

Meanwhile, the king thrummed gaily with his fingers on the arm of his chair, the March of Pont-Audemer. He was a dissembling prince, but one who understood far better how to hide his troubles than his joys. These external manifestations of joy at any good news sometimes proceeded to very great lengths; thus, on the death, of Charles the Bold, to the point of vowing silver balustrades to Saint Martin of Tours; on his advent to the throne, so far as forgetting to order his father's obsequies.

"Hé! sire!" suddenly exclaimed Jacques Coictier, "what has become of the acute attack of illness for which your majesty had me summoned?"

"Oh!" said the king, "I really suffer greatly, my gossip. There is a hissing in my ear and fiery rakes rack my chest."

Coictier took the king's hand, and begun to feel of his pulse with a knowing air.

"Look, Coppenole," said Rym, in a low voice. "Behold him between Coictier and Tristan. They are his whole court. A physician for himself, a headsman for others."

As he felt the king's pulse, Coictier assumed an air of greater and greater alarm. Louis XI watched him with some anxiety. Coictier grew visibly more gloomy. The brave man had no other farm than the king's bad health. He speculated on it to the best of his ability.

"Oh! oh!" he murmured at length, "this is serious indeed."

"Is it not?" said the king, uneasily.

"*Pulsus creber, anhelans, crepitans, irregularis,*" continued the leech.

"*Pasque-Dieu!*"

"This may carry off its man in less than three days."

"Our Lady!" exclaimed the king. "And the remedy, gossip?"

"I am meditating upon that, sire."

He made Louis XI put out his tongue, shook his head, made a grimace, and in the very midst of these affectations—

"Pardieu, sire," he suddenly said, "I must tell you that there is a receivership of the royal prerogatives vacant, and that I have a nephew."

"I give the receivership to your nephew, Gossip Jacques," replied the king; "but draw this fire from my breast."

"Since your majesty is so clement," replied the leech, "you will not refuse to aid me a little in building my house, Rue Saint-André-des-Arcs."

"Heugh!" said the king.

"I am at the end of my finances," pursued the doctor; "and it would really be a pity that the house should not have a roof; not on account of the house, which is simple and thoroughly bourgeois, but because of the paintings of Jehan Fourbault, which adorn its wainscoting. There is a Diana flying in the air, but so excellent, so tender, so delicate, of so ingenuous an action, her hair so well coiffed and adorned with a crescent, her flesh so white, that she leads into temptation those who regard her too curiously. There is also a Ceres. She is another very fair divinity. She is seated on sheaves of wheat and crowned with a gallant garland of wheat ears interlaced with salsify and other flowers. Never were seen more amorous eyes, more rounded limbs, a nobler air, or a more gracefully flowing skirt. She is one of the most innocent and most perfect beauties whom the brush has ever produced."

"Executioner!" grumbled Louis XI, "what are you driving at?"

"I must have a roof for these paintings, sire, and, although 'tis but a small matter, I have no more money."

"How much doth your roof cost?"

"Why a roof of copper, embellished and gilt, two thousand livres at the most."

"Ah, assassin!" cried the king, "He never draws out one of my teeth which is not a diamond."

"Am I to have my roof?" said Coictier.

"Yes; and go to the devil, but cure me."

Jacques Coictier bowed low and said—

"Sire, it is a repellent which will save you. We will apply to your loins the great defensive composed of cerate, Armenian bole, white of egg, oil, and vinegar. You will continue your ptisan and we will answer for your majesty."

A burning candle does not attract one gnat alone. Master Olivier, perceiving the king to be in a liberal mood, and judging the moment to be propitious, approached in his turn. "Sire—"

"What is it now?" said Louis XI.

"Sire, your majesty knoweth that Simon Radin is dead?"

"Well?"

"He was councilor to the king in the matter of the courts of the treasury."

"Well?"

"Sire, his place is vacant."

As he spoke thus, Master Olivier's haughty face quitted its arrogant expression for a lowly one. It is the only change which ever takes place in a courtier's visage. The king looked him well in the face and said in a dry tone—"I understand."

He resumed—

"Master Olivier, the Marshal de Boucicaut was wont to say, 'There's no master save the king, there are no fishes save in the sea.' I see that you agree with Monsieur de Boucicaut. Now listen to this; we have a good memory. In '68 we made you valet of our chamber: in '69, guardian of the fortress of the bridge of Saint-Cloud, at a hundred livres of Tournay in wages (you wanted them of Paris). In November, '73, by letters given to Gergeole, we instituted you keeper of the Wood of Vincennes, in the place of Gilbert Acle, equerry; in '75, gruyer[1] of the forest of Rouvray-lez-Saint-Cloud, in the place of Jacques le Maire; in '78, we graciously settled on you, by letters patent sealed doubly with green wax, an income of ten livres parisis, for you and your wife, on the Place of the Merchants, situated at the School Saint-Germain; in '79, we made you gruyer of the forest of Senart, in place of that poor Jehan Daiz; then captain of the Château of Loches; then governor of Saint-Quentin; then captain of the bridge of Meulan, of which you cause yourself to be called comte. Out of the five sols fine paid by every barber who shaves on a festival day, there are three sols for you and we have the rest. We have been good enough to change your name of Le Mauvais (The Evil), which resembled your face too closely. In '76, we granted you, to the great displeasure of our nobility, armorial bearings of a thousand colors, which give you the breast of a peacock. Pasque-Dieu! Are not you surfeited? Is not the draft of fishes sufficiently fine and miraculous? Are you not afraid that one salmon more will make your boat sink? Pride will be your ruin, gossip. Ruin and disgrace always press hard on the heels of pride. Consider this and hold your tongue."

These words, uttered with severity, made Master Olivier's face revert to its insolence.

"Good!" he muttered, almost aloud, " 'tis easy to see that the king is ill to-day; he giveth all to the leech."

Louis XI far from being irritated by this petulant insult, resumed with some gentleness, "Stay, I was forgetting that I made you my ambassador to Madame Marie, at Ghent. Yes, gentlemen,"

---

1. A lord having a right on the woods of his vassals.

added the king turning to the Flemings, "this man hath been an ambassador. There, my gossip," he pursued, addressing Master Olivier, "let us not get angry; we are old friends. 'Tis very late. We have terminated our labors. Shave me."

Our readers have not, without doubt, waited until the present moment to recognize in Master Olivier that terrible Figaro whom Providence, the great maker of dramas, mingled so artistically in the long and bloody comedy of the reign of Louis XI. We will not here undertake to develop that singular figure. This barber of the king had three names. At court he was politely called Olivier le Daim (the Deer); among the people Olivier the Devil. His real name was Olivier le Mauvais.

Accordingly, Olivier le Mauvais remained motionless, sulking at the king, and glancing askance at Jacques Coictier.

"Yes, yes, the physician!" he said between his teeth.

"Ah, yes, the physician!" retorted Louis XI, with singular good humor; "the physician has more credit than you. 'Tis very simple; he has taken hold upon us by the whole body, and you hold us only by the chin. Come, my poor barber, all will come right. What would you say and what would become of your office if I were a king like Chilpéric, whose gesture consisted in holding his beard in one hand? Come, gossip mine, fulfill your office, shave me. Go get what you need therefore."

Olivier perceiving that the king had made up his mind to laugh, and that there was no way of even annoying him, went off grumbling to execute his orders.

The king rose, approached the window, and suddenly opening it with extraordinary agitation—

"Oh! yes!" he exclaimed, clapping his hands, "yonder is a redness in the sky over the City. 'Tis the bailiff burning. It can be nothing else but that. Ah! my good people! here you are aiding me at last in tearing down the rights of lordship!"

Then turning toward the Flemings: "Come, look at this, gentlemen. Is it not a fire which gloweth yonder?"

The two men of Ghent drew near.

"A great fire," said Guillaume Rym.

"Oh!" exclaimed Coppenole, whose eyes suddenly flashed, "that reminds me of the burning of the house of the Seigneur d'Hymbercourt. There must be a goodly revolt yonder."

"You think so, Master Coppenole?" And Louis XI's glance was almost as joyous as that of the hosier. "Will it not be difficult to resist?"

"Cross of God! Sire! Your majesty will damage many companies of men of war thereon."

"Ah! I! 'tis different," returned the king. "If I willed."

The hosier replied hardily—

"If this revolt be what I suppose, sire, you might will in vain."

"Gossip," said Louis XI, "with the two companies of my unattached troops and one discharge of a serpentine, short work is made of a populace of louts."

The hosier, in spite of the signs made to him by Guillaume Rym, appeared determined to hold his own against the king.

"Sire, the Swiss were also louts. Monsieur the Duke of Burgundy was a great gentleman, and he turned up his nose at that rabble rout. At the battle of Grandson, sire, he cried: 'Men of the cannon! Fire on the villains!' and he swore by Saint-George. But Advoyer Scharnachtal hurled himself on the handsome duke with his battle-club and his people, and when the glittering Burgundian army came in contact with these peasants in bull hides, it flew in pieces like a pane of glass at the blow of a pebble. Many lords were then slain by low-born knaves; and Monsieur de Château-Guyon, the greatest seigneur in Burgundy, was found dead, with his gray horse, in a little marsh meadow."

"Friend," returned the king, "you are speaking of a battle. The question here is of a mutiny. And I will gain the upper hand of it as soon as it shall please me to frown."

The other replied indifferently—

"That may be, sire; in that case, 'tis because the people's hour hath not yet come."

Guillaume Rym considered it incumbent on him to intervene—

"Master Coppenole, you are speaking to a puissant king."

"I know it," replied the hosier, gravely.

"Let him speak, Monsieur Rym, my friend," said the king; "I love this frankness of speech. My father, Charles the Seventh, was accustomed to say that the truth was ailing; I thought her dead, and that she had found no confessor. Master Coppenole undeceiveth me."

Then, laying his hand familiarly on Coppenole's shoulder—

"You were saying, Master Jacques?"

"I say, sire, that you may possibly be in the right, that the hour of the people may not yet have come with you."

Louis XI gazed at him with his penetrating eye—

"And when will that hour come, master?"

"You will hear it strike."

"On what clock, if you please?"

Coppenole, with his tranquil and rustic countenance, made the king approach the window.

"Listen, sire! There is here a donjon keep, a belfry, cannons, bourgeois, soldiers, when the belfry shall hum, when the cannons shall roar, when the donjon shall fall in ruins amid great noise, when bourgeois and soldiers shall howl and slay each other, the hour will strike."

Louis's face grew somber and dreamy. He remained silent for a moment, then he gently patted with his hand the thick wall of the donjon, as one strokes the haunches of a steed.

"Oh! no!" said he. "You will not crumble so easily, will you, my good Bastille?"

And turning with an abrupt gesture toward the sturdy Fleming—

"Have you never seen a revolt, Master Jacques?"

"I have made them," said the hosier.

"How do you set to work to make a revolt?" said the king.

"Ah!" replied Coppenole, " 'tis not very difficult. There are a hundred ways. In the first place, there must be discontent in the city. The thing is not uncommon. And then, the character of the inhabitants. Those of Ghent are easy to stir into revolt. They always love the prince's son; the prince, never. Well! One morning, I will suppose, someone enters my shop, and says to me: 'Father Coppenole, there is this and there is that, the Demoiselle of Flanders wishes to save her ministers, the grand bailiff is doubling the impost on shagreen, or something else'—what you will. I leave my work as it stands, I come out of my hosier's stall, and I shout: 'To the sack?' There is always some smashed cask at hand. I mount it, and I say aloud, in the first words that occur to me, what I have on my heart; and when one is of the people, sire, one always has something on the heart. Then people troop up, they shout, they ring the alarm bell, they arm the louts with what they take from the soldiers, the market people join in, and they set out. And it will always be thus, so long as there are lords in the seignories, bourgeois in the bourgs, and peasants in the country."

"And against whom do you thus rebel?" inquired the king; "against your bailiffs? against your lords?"

"Sometimes; that depends. Against the duke, also, sometimes."

Louis XI returned and seated himself, saying, with a smile—

"Ah! here they have only got as far as the bailiffs."

At that instant Olivier le Daim returned. He was followed by two pages, who bore the king's toilet articles; but what struck Louis XI was that he was also accompanied by the provost of Paris and the chevalier of the watch, who appeared to be in consternation. The spiteful barber also wore an air of consternation, which was one of contentment beneath, however. It was he who spoke first.

"Sire, I ask your majesty's pardon for the calamitous news which I bring."

The king turned quickly and grazed the mat on the floor with the feet of his chair—

"What does this mean?"

"Sire," resumed Olivier le Daim, with the malicious air of a man who rejoices that he is about to deal a violent blow, " 'tis not against the bailiff of the courts that this popular sedition is directed."

"Against whom, then?"

"Against you, sire?"

The aged king rose erect and straight as a young man—

"Explain yourself, Olivier! And guard your head well, gossip; for I swear to you by the cross of Saint-Lô that, if you lie to us at this hour, the sword which severed the head of Monsieur de Luxembourg is not so notched that it cannot yet sever yours!"

The oath was formidable; Louis XI had only sworn twice in the course of his life by the cross of Saint-Lô.

Olivier opened his mouth to reply.

"Sire—"

"On your knees!" interrupted the king violently. "Tristan, have an eye to this man."

Olivier knelt down and said coldly—

"Sire, a sorceress was condemned to death by your court of parliament. She took refuge in Notre-Dame. The people are trying to take her from thence by main force. Monsieur the provost and monsieur the chevalier of the watch, who have just come from the riot, are here to give me the lie if this is not the truth. The populace is besieging Notre-Dame."

"Yes, indeed!" said the king in a low voice, all pale and trembling with wrath. "Notre-Dame! They lay siege to our Lady, my good mistress in her cathedral!—Rise, Olivier. You are right. I give you Simon Radin's charge. You are right. 'Tis I whom they are attacking. The witch is under the protection of this church, the church is under my protection. And I thought that they were acting against the bailiff! 'Tis against myself!"

Then, rendered young by fury, he began to walk up and down with long strides. He no longer laughed, he was terrible, he went and came; the fox was changed into a hyena. He seemed suffocated to such a degree that he could not speak; his lips moved, and his fleshless fists were clenched. All at once he raised his head, his hollow eye appeared full of light, and his voice burst forth like a clarion: "Down with them, Tristan! A heavy hand for these rascals! Go, Tristan, my friend! slay! slay!"

This eruption having passed, he returned to his seat, and said with cold and concentrated wrath—

"Here, Tristan! There are here with us in the Bastille the fifty lances of the Vicomte de Gif, which makes three hundred horse: you will take them. There is also the company of our unattached archers of Monsieur de Châteaupers: you will take it. You are provost of the marshals; you have the men of your provostship: you will take them. At the Hôtel Saint-Pol you will find forty archers of monsieur the dauphin's new guard: you will take them. And, with all these, you will hasten to Notre-Dame. Ah! messieurs, louts of Paris, do you fling yourselves thus against the crown of France, the sanctity of Notre-Dame, and the peace of this commonwealth! Exterminate, Tristan! exterminate! and let not a single one escape, except it be for Montfaucon."

Tristan bowed. " 'Tis well, sire."

He added, after a silence, "And what shall I do with the sorceress?"

This question caused the king to meditate.

"Ah!" said he, "the sorceress! Monsieur d'Estouteville, what did the people wish to do with her?"

"Sire," replied the provost of Paris, "I imagine that since the populace has come to tear her from her asylum in Notre-Dame, 'tis because that impunity wounds them, and they desire to hang her."

The king appeared to reflect deeply: then, addressing Tristan l'Hermite, "Well! gossip, exterminate the people and hang the sorceress."

"That's it," said Rym in a low tone to Coppenole, "punish the people for willing a thing, and then do what they wish."

"Enough, sire," replied Tristan. "If the sorceress is still in Notre-Dame, must she be seized in spite of the sanctuary?"

"*Pasque-Dieu!* the sanctuary!" said the king, scratching his ear. "But the woman must be hung, nevertheless."

Here, as though seized with a sudden idea, he flung himself on his knees before his chair, took off his hat, placed it on the seat, and gazing devoutly at one of the leaden amulets which loaded it down, "Oh!" said he, with clasped hands, "our Lady of Paris, my gracious patroness, pardon me. I will only do it this once. This criminal must be punished. I assure you, madame the virgin, my good mistress, that she is a sorceress who is not worthy of your amiable protection. You know, madame, that many very pious princes have overstepped the privileges of the churches for the glory of God and the necessities of the State. Saint Hugues, bishop of England, permitted King Edward to hang a witch in his church. Saint-Louis of France, my master, transgressed, with the same object, the church of Monsieur Saint-Paul; and Monsieur Alphonse, son of the king of Jerusalem, the very church of the Holy Sepulcher. Pardon me, then, for this once. Our Lady of Paris, I will never do so again, and I will give you a fine statue of silver, like the one which I gave last year to Our Lady of Écouys. So be it."

He made the sign of the cross, rose, donned his hat once more, and said to Tristan—

"Be diligent, gossip. Take Monsieur Châteaupers with you. You will cause the tocsin to be sounded. You will crush the populace. You will seize the witch. 'Tis said. And I mean the business of the execution to be done by you. You will render me an account of it. Come, Olivier, I shall not go to bed this night. Shave me."

Tristan l'Hermite bowed and departed. Then the king, dismissing Rym and Coppenole with a gesture—

"God guard you, messieurs, my good friends the Flemings. Go, take a little repose. The night advances, and we are nearer the morning than the evening."

Both retired and gained their apartments under the guidance of the captain of the Bastille. Coppenole said to Guillaume Rym—

"Hum! I have had enough of that coughing king! I have seen Charles of Burgundy drunk, and he was less malignant than Louis XI when ailing."

"Master Jacques," replied Rym, " 'tis because wine renders kings less cruel than does barley water."

Chapter VI

LITTLE SWORD IN POCKET

ON EMERGING FROM THE BASTILLE, GRINGOIRE DESCENDED THE RUE SAINT-ANTOINE WITH THE swiftness of a runaway horse. On arriving at the Baudoyer gate, he walked straight to the stone cross which rose in the middle of that place, as though he were able to distinguish in the darkness the figure of a man clad and cloaked in black, who was seated on the steps of the cross.

"Is it you, master?" said Gringoire.

The personage in black rose.

"Death and passion! You make me boil, Gringoire. The man on the tower of Saint-Gervais has just cried half-past one o'clock in the morning."

"Oh," retorted Gringoire, " 'tis no fault of mine, but of the watch and the king. I have just had a narrow escape. I always just miss being hung. 'Tis my predestination."

"You lack everything," said the other. "But come quickly. Have you the password?"

"Fancy, master, I have seen the king. I come from him. He wears fustian breeches. 'Tis an adventure."

"Oh! distaff of words! what is your adventure to me! Have you the password of the outcasts?"

"I have it. Be at ease. 'Little sword in pocket.' "

"Good. Otherwise, we could not make our way as far as the church. The outcasts bar the streets. Fortunately, it appears that they have encountered resistance. We may still arrive in time."

"Yes, master, but how are we to get into Notre-Dame?"

"I have the key to the tower."

"And how are we to get out again?"

"Behind the cloister there is a little door which opens on the Terrain and the water. I have taken the key to it, and I moored a boat there this morning."

"I have had a beautiful escape from being hung!" Gringoire repeated.

"Eh, quick! come!" said the other.

Both descended toward the city with long strides.

Chapter VII

CHÂTEAUPERS TO THE RESCUE

THE READER WILL, PERHAPS, RECALL THE CRITICAL SITUATION IN WHICH WE LEFT QUASIMODO. The brave deaf man, assailed on all sides, had lost, if not all courage, at least all hope of saving, not himself (he was not thinking of himself), but the gypsy. He ran distractedly along the gallery. Notre-Dame was on the point of being taken by storm by the outcasts. All at once, a great galloping of horses filled the neighboring streets, and, with a long file of torches and a thick column of cavaliers, with free reins and lances in rest, these furious sounds debouched on the Place like a hurricane—

"France! France! cut down the louts! Châteaupers to the rescue! Provostship! Provostship!"

The frightened vagabonds wheeled round.

Quasimodo who did not hear, saw the naked swords, the torches, the irons of the pikes, all that cavalry, at the head of which he recognized Captain Phœbus; he beheld the confusion of the outcasts, the terror of some, the disturbance among the bravest of them, and from this unexpected succor he recovered so much strength, that he hurled from the church the first assailants who were already climbing into the gallery.

It was, in fact, the king's troops who had arrived.

The vagabonds behaved bravely. They defended themselves like desperate men. Caught on the flank, by the Rue Saint-Pierre-aux-Bœufs, and in the rear through the Rue du Parvis, driven to bay against Notre-Dame, which they still assailed and Quasimodo defended, at the same time besiegers and besieged, they were in the singular situation in which Comte Henri Harcourt, *Taurinum obsessor idem et obsessus,* as his epitaph says, found himself later on, at the famous siege of Turin, in 1640, between Prince Thomas of Savoy, whom he was besieging, and the Marquis de Leganez, who was blockading him.

The battle was frightful. There was a dog's tooth for wolf's flesh, as P. Mathieu says. The king's cavaliers, in whose midst Phœbus de Châteaupers bore himself valiantly, gave no quarter, and the slash of the sword disposed of those who escaped the thrust of the lance. The outcasts, badly armed, foamed and bit with rage. Men, women, children, hurled themselves on the cruppers and the breasts of the horses, and hung there like cats, with teeth, finger-nails and toe-nails. Others struck the archers' in the face with their torches. Others thrust iron hooks into the necks of the cavaliers and dragged them down. They slashed in pieces those who fell.

One was noticed who had a large, glittering scythe, and who, for a long time, mowed the legs of the horses. He was frightful. He was singing a ditty, with a nasal intonation, he swung and drew back his scythe incessantly. At every blow he traced around him a great circle of severed limbs. He advanced thus into the very thickest of the cavalry, with the tranquil slowness, the lolling of the head and the regular breathing of a harvester attacking a field of wheat. It was Clopin Trouillefou. A shot from an arquebus laid him low.

In the meantime, windows had been opened again. The neighbors hearing the war cries of the king's troops, had mingled in the affray, and bullets rained upon the outcasts from every story. The Parvis was filled with a thick smoke, which the musketry streaked with flame. Through it one could confusedly distinguish the front of Notre-Dame, and the decrepit Hôtel-Dieu with some wan invalids gazing down from the heights of its roof all checkered with dormer windows.

At length the vagabonds gave way. Weariness, the lack of good weapons, the fright of this surprise, the musketry from the windows, the valiant attack of the king's troops, all overwhelmed them. They forced the line of assailants, and fled in every direction, leaving the Parvis encumbered with dead.

When Quasimodo, who had not ceased to fight for a moment, beheld this rout, he fell on his knees and raised his hands to heaven; then, intoxicated with joy, he ran, he ascended with the swiftness of a bird to that cell, the approaches to which he had so intrepidly defended. He had but one thought now; it was to kneel before her whom he had just saved for the second time.

When he entered the cell, he found it empty.

BOOK ELEVENTH

Chapter I

THE LITTLE SHOE

LA ESMERALDA WAS SLEEPING AT THE MOMENT WHEN THE OUTCASTS ASSAILED THE CHURCH. Soon the ever-increasing uproar around the edifice, and the uneasy bleating of her goat which had been awakened, had roused her from her slumbers. She had sat up, she had listened, she had looked; then, terrified by the light and noise, she had rushed from her cell to see. The aspect of the Place, the vision which was moving in it, the disorder of that nocturnal assault, that hideous crowd, leaping like a cloud of frogs, half seen in the gloom, the croaking of that hoarse multitude, those few red torches running and crossing each other in the darkness like the meteors which streak the misty surfaces of marshes, this whole scene produced upon her the effect of a mysterious battle between the phantoms of the witches' sabbath and the stone monsters of the church. Imbued from her very infancy with the superstitions of the Bohemian tribe, her first thought was that she had caught the strange beings peculiar to the night, in their deeds of witchcraft. Then she ran in terror to cower in her cell, asking of her pallet some less terrible nightmare.

But little by little the first vapors of terror had been dissipated; from the constantly increasing noise, and from many other signs of reality, she felt herself besieged not by specters, but by human beings. Then her fear, though it did not increase, changed its character. She had dreamed of the possibility of a popular mutiny to tear her from her asylum. The idea of once more recovering life, hope, Phœbus, who was ever present in her future, the extreme helplessness of her condition, flight cut off, no support, her abandonment, her isolation—these thoughts and a thousand others overwhelmed her. She fell upon her knees, with her head on her bed, her hands clasped over her head, full of anxiety and tremors, and, although a gypsy, an idolater, and a pagan, she began to entreat with sobs, mercy from the good Christian God, and to pray to our Lady, her hostess. For even if one believes in nothing, there are moments in life when one is always of the religion of the temple which is nearest at hand.

She remained thus prostrate for a very long time, trembling in truth, more than praying, chilled by the ever-closer breath of that furious multitude, understanding nothing of this outburst, ignorant of what was being plotted, what was being done, what they wanted, but foreseeing a terrible issue.

In the midst of this anguish, she heard someone walking near her. She turned round. Two men, one of whom carried a lantern, had just entered her cell. She uttered a feeble cry.

"Fear nothing," said a voice which was not unknown to her, "it is I."

"Who are you?" she asked.

"Pierre Gringoire."

This name reassured her. She raised her eyes once more, and recognized the poet in very fact. But there stood beside him a black figure veiled from head to foot, which struck her by its silence.

"Oh!" continued Gringoire in a tone of reproach, "Djali recognized me before you!"

The little goat had not, in fact, waited for Gringoire to announce his name. No sooner had he entered than it rubbed itself gently against his knees, covering the poet with caresses and with white hairs, for it was shedding its hair. Gringoire returned the caresses.

"Who is this with you?" said the gypsy, in a low voice.

"Be at ease," replied Gringoire. " 'Tis one of my friends."

Then the philosopher setting his lantern on the ground, crouched upon the stones, and exclaimed enthusiastically, as he pressed Djali in his arms—

"Oh! 'tis a graceful beast, more considerable no doubt, for it's neatness than for its size, but ingenious, subtle, and lettered as a grammarian! Let us see, my Djali, hast thou forgotten any of thy pretty tricks? How does Master Jacques Charmolue? . . ."

The man in black did not allow him to finish. He approached Gringoire and shook him roughly by the shoulder. Gringoire rose.

" 'Tis true," said he: "I forgot that we are in haste. But that is no reason master, for getting furious with people in this manner. My dear and lovely child, your life is in danger, and Djali's also. They want to hang you again. We are your friends, and we have come to save you. Follow us."

"Is it true?" she exclaimed in dismay.

"Yes, perfectly true. Come quickly!"

"I am willing," she stammered. "But why does not your friend speak?"

"Ah!" said Gringoire, " 'tis because his father and mother were fantastic people who made him of a taciturn temperament."

She was obliged to content herself with this explanation. Gringoire took her by the hand; his companion picked up the lantern and walked on in front. Fear stunned the young girl. She allowed herself to be led away. The goat followed them, frisking, so joyous at seeing Gringoire again that it made him stumble every moment by thrusting its horns between his legs.

"Such is life," said the philosopher, every time that he came near falling down; " 'tis often our best friends who cause us to be overthrown."

They rapidly descended the staircase of the towers, crossed the church, full of shadows and solitude, and all reverberating with uproar, which formed a frightful contrast, and emerged into the courtyard of the cloister by the red door. The cloister was deserted; the canons had fled to the bishop's palace in order to pray together; the courtyard was empty, a few frightened lackeys were crouching in dark corners. They directed their steps toward the door which opened from this court upon the Terrain. The man in black opened it with a key which he had about him. Our readers are aware that the Terrain was a tongue of land enclosed by walls on the side of the City and belonging to the chapter of Notre-Dame, which terminated the island on the east, behind the church. They found this enclosure perfectly deserted. There was here less tumult in the air. The roar of the outcasts' assault reached them more confusedly and less clamorously. The fresh breeze which follows the current of a stream, rustled the leaves of the only tree planted on the point of the Terrain, with a noise that was already perceptible. But they were still very close to danger. The nearest edifices to them were the bishop's palace and the church. It was plainly evident that there was great internal commotion in the bishop's palace. Its shadowy mass was all furrowed with lights which flitted from window to window; as, when one has just burned paper, there remains a somber edifice of ashes in which bright sparks run a thousand eccentric courses. Beside them, the enormous towers of Notre-Dame, thus viewed from behind, with the long nave above which they rise cut out in black against the red and vast light which filled the Parvis, resembled two gigantic andirons of some cyclopean fire-grate.

What was to be seen of Paris on all sides wavered before the eye in a gloom mingled with light. Rembrandt has such backgrounds to his pictures.

The man with the lantern walked straight to the point of the Terrain. There, at the very brink of the water, stood the wormeaten remains of a fence of posts latticed with laths, whereon a low vine spread out a few thin branches like the fingers of an outspread hand. Behind, in the shadow cast by this trellis, a little boat lay concealed. The man made a sign to Gringoire and his companion to enter. The goat followed them. The man was the last to step in. Then he cut the boat's moorings, pushed it from the shore with a long boat-hook, and, seizing two oars, seated himself in the bow, rowing with all his might toward midstream. The Seine is very rapid at this point, and he had a good deal of trouble in leaving the point of the island.

Gringoire's first care on entering the boat was to place the goat on his knees. He took a position in the stern; and the young girl, whom the stranger inspired with an indefinable uneasiness, seated herself close to the poet.

When our philosopher felt the boat sway, he clapped his hands and kissed Djali between the horns.

"Oh!" said he, "now we are safe, all four of us."

He added with the air of a profound thinker, "One is indebted sometimes to fortune, sometimes to ruse, for the happy issue of great enterprises."

The boat made its way slowly toward the right shore. The young girl watched the unknown man with secret terror. He had carefully turned off the light of his dark lantern. A glimpse could be caught of him in the obscurity, in the bow of the boat, like a specter. His cowl, which was still lowered, formed a sort of mask; and every time that he spread his arms, upon which hung large black sleeves, as he rowed, one would have said they were two huge bat's wings. Moreover, he had not yet uttered a word or breathed a syllable. No other noise was heard in the boat than the splashing of the oars, mingled with the rippling of the water along her sides.

"On my soul!" exclaimed Gringoire suddenly, "we are as cheerful and joyous as young owls! We preserve the silence of Pythagoreans or fishes! *Pasque-Dieu!* my friends, I should greatly like to have someone speak to me. The human voice is music to the human ear. 'Tis not I who say that, but Didymus of Alexandria, and they are illustrious words. Assuredly, Didymus of Alexandria is no mediocre philosopher.—One word, my lovely child! say but one word to me, I entreat you. By the way, you had a droll and peculiar little pout; do you still make it? Do you know, my dear, that parliament hath full jurisdiction over all places of asylum, and that you were running a great risk in your little chamber at Notre-Dame? Alas! the little bird trochylus maketh its nest in the jaws of the crocodile.—Master, here is the moon reappearing. If only they do not perceive us. We are doing a laudable thing in saving mademoiselle, and yet we should be hung by order of the king if we were caught. Alas! human actions are taken by two handles. That is branded with disgrace in one which is crowned in another. He admires Cicero who blames Catiline. Is it not so, master? What say you to this philosophy? I possess philosophy by instinct, by nature, *ut apes geometriam.*—Come! no one answers me. What unpleasant moods you two are in! I must do all the talking alone. That is what we call a monologue in tragedy.—*Pasque-Dieu!* I must inform you that I have just seen the king, Louis XI, and that I have caught this oath from him—*Pasque-Dieu!* They are still making a hearty howl in the city.—'Tis a villainous, malicious old king. He is all swathed in furs. He still owes me the money for my epithalamium, and he came within a nick of hanging me this evening, which would have been very inconvenient to me.—He is niggardly toward men of merit. He ought to read the four books of Salvien of Cologne, *Adversus Avaritiam.* In truth! 'Tis a paltry king in his ways with men of letters, and one who commits very barbarous cruelties. He is a sponge, to soak money raised from the people. His saving is like the spleen which swelleth with the leanness of all the other members. Hence complaints against the hardness of the times become murmurs against the prince. Under this gentle and pious sire, the gallows crack with the hung, the blocks rot with blood, the prisons burst like over full bellies. This king hath one hand which grasps, and one which hangs. He is the procurator of Dame Tax and Monsieur Gibbet. The great are despoiled of their dignities, and the little incessantly overwhelmed with fresh oppressions. He is an exorbitant prince. I love not this monarch. And you, master?"

The man in black let the garrulous poet chatter on. He continued to struggle against the violent and narrow current, which separates the prow of the City and the stem of the island of Notre-Dame, which we call to-day the Isle St. Louis.

"By the way, master!" continued Gringoire suddenly. "At the moment when we arrived on the Parvis, through the enraged outcasts, did your reverence observe that poor little devil whose skull your deaf man was just cracking on the railing of the gallery of the kings? I am near sighted and I could not recognize him. Do you know who he could be?"

The stranger answered not a word. But he suddenly ceased rowing, his arms fell as though broken, his head sank on his breast, and la Esmeralda heard him sigh convulsively. She shuddered. She had heard such sighs before.

The boat, abandoned to itself, floated for several minutes with the stream. But the man in black finally recovered himself, seized the oars once more and began to row against the current. He doubled the point of the Isle of Notre-Dame, and made for the landing-place of the Port au Foin.

"Ah!" said Gringoire, "yonder is the Barbeau mansion.—Stay, master, look: that group of black roofs which make such singular angles yonder, above that heap of black, fibrous grimy, dirty clouds, where the moon is completely crushed and spread out like the yolk of an egg whose shell is broken.— 'Tis a fine mansion. There is a chapel crowned with a small vault full of very well carved enrichments. Above, you can see the bell tower, very delicately pierced. There is also a pleasant garden, which consists of a pond, an aviary, an echo, a mall, a labyrinth, a house for wild beasts, and a quantity of leafy alleys very agreeable to Venus. There is also a rascal of a tree which is called 'the lewd,' because it favored the pleasures of a famous princess and a constable of France, who was a gallant and a wit.—Alas! we poor philosophers are to a constable as a plot of cabbages or a radish bed to the garden of the Louvre. What matters it, after all? human life, for the great as well as for us, is a mixture of good and evil. Pain is always by the side of joy, the spondee by the dactyl.—Master, I must relate to you the history of the Barbeau mansion. It ends in tragic fashion. It was in 1319, in the reign of Philippe V, the longest reign of the kings of France. The moral of the story is that the temptations of the flesh are pernicious and malignant. Let us not rest our glance too long on our neighbor's wife, however gratified our senses may be by her beauty. Fornication is a very libertine thought. Adultery is a prying into the pleasures of others—Ohé! the noise yonder is redoubling!"

The tumult around Notre-Dame was, in fact, increasing. They listened. Cries of victory were heard with tolerable distinctness. All at once, a hundred torches, the light of which glittered upon the helmets of men at arms, spread over the church at all heights, on the towers, on the galleries, on the flying buttresses. These torches seemed to be in search of something; and soon distant clamors reached the fugitives distinctly:—"The gypsy! the sorceress! death to the gypsy!"

The unhappy girl dropped her head upon her hands, and the unknown began to row furiously toward the shore. Meanwhile our philosopher reflected. He clasped the goat in his arms, and gently drew away from the gypsy, who pressed closer and closer to him, as though to the only asylum which remained to her.

It is certain that Gringoire was enduring cruel perplexity. He was thinking that the goat also, "according to existing law," would be hung if recaptured; which would be a great pity, poor Djali! that he had thus two condemned creatures attached to him; that his companion asked no better than to take charge of the gypsy. A violent combat began between his thoughts, in which, like the Jupiter of the Iliad, he weighed in turn the gypsy and the goat; and he looked at them alternately with eyes moist with tears, saying between his teeth: "But I cannot save you both!"

A shock informed them that the boat had reached the land at last. The uproar still filled the city. The unknown rose, approached the gypsy, and endeavored to take her arm to assist her to alight. She repulsed him and clung to the sleeve of Gringoire, who, in his turn, absorbed in the goat, almost repulsed her. Then she sprang alone from the boat. She was so troubled that she did not know what she did or whither she was going. Thus she remained for a moment, stunned, watching the water flow past; when she gradually returned to her senses, she found herself alone on the wharf with the unknown. It appears that Gringoire had taken advantage of the moment of debarcation to slip away with the goat into the block of houses of the Rue Grenier-sur-l'Eau.

The poor gypsy shivered when she beheld herself alone with this man. She tried to speak, to cry out, to call Gringoire; her tongue was dumb in her mouth, and no sound left her lips. All at once she felt the stranger's hand on hers. It was a strong, cold hand. Her teeth chattered, she turned paler than the ray of moonlight which illuminated her. The man spoke not a word. He began to ascend toward the Place de Grève, holding her by the hand.

At that moment, she had a vague feeling that destiny is an irresistible force. She had no more resistance left in her, she allowed herself to be dragged along, running while he walked. At this spot the quay ascended. But it seemed to her as though she were descending a slope.

She gazed about her on all sides. Not a single passer-by. The quay was absolutely deserted. She heard no sound, she felt no people moving save in the tumultuous and glowing city, from which she was separated only by an arm of the Seine, and whence her name reached her, mingled with cries of "Death!" The rest of Paris was spread around her in great blocks of shadows.

Meanwhile, the stranger continued to drag her along with the same silence and the same rapidity. She had no recollection of any of the places where she was walking. As she passed before a lighted window, she made an effort, drew up suddenly, and cried out, "Help!"

The bourgeois who was standing at the window opened it, appeared there in his shirt with his lamp, stared at the quay with a stupid air, uttered some words which she did not understand, and closed his shutter again. It was her last gleam of hope extinguished.

The man in black did not utter a syllable; he held her firmly, and set out again at a quicker pace. She no longer resisted, but followed him, completely broken.

From time to time she called together a little strength, and said, in a voice broken by the unevenness of the pavement and the breathlessness of their flight, "Who are you? Who are you?" He made no reply.

They arrived thus, still keeping along the quay, at a tolerably spacious square. It was the Grève. In the middle, a sort of black, erect cross was visible; it was the gallows. She recognized all this, and saw where she was.

The man halted, turned toward her and raised his cowl.

"Oh!" she stammered, almost petrified, "I knew well that it was he again!"

It was the priest. He looked like the ghost of himself; that is an effect of the moonlight, it seems as though one beheld only the specters of things in that light.

"Listen!" he said to her; and she shuddered at the sound of that fatal voice which she had not heard for a long time. He continued speaking with those brief and panting jerks, which betoken deep internal convulsions. "Listen! we are here. I am going to speak to you. This is the Grève. This is an extreme point. Destiny gives us to one another. I am going to decide as to your life; you will decide as to my soul. Here is a place, here is a night beyond which one sees nothing. Then listen to me. I am going to tell you. . . . In the first place, speak not to me of your Phœbus. (As he spoke thus he paced to and fro, like a man who cannot remain in one place, and dragged her after him.) Do not speak to me of him. Do you see? If you utter that name, I know not what I shall do, but it will be terrible."

Then, like a body which recovers its center of gravity, he became motionless once more, but his words betrayed no less agitation. His voice grew lower and lower.

"Do not turn your head aside thus. Listen to me. It is a serious matter. In the first place, here is what has happened.—All this will not be laughed at. I swear it to you.—What was I saying? Remind me! Oh!—There is a decree of Parliament which gives you back to the scaffold. I have just rescued you from their hands. But they are pursuing you. Look!"

He extended his arm toward the City. The search seemed, in fact, to be still in progress there. The uproar drew nearer; the tower of the lieutenant's house, situated opposite the Grève, was full of clamors and light, and soldiers could be seen running on the opposite quay with torches and these cries, "The gypsy! Where is the gypsy! Death! Death!"

"You see that they are in pursuit of you, and that I am not lying to you. I love you.—Do not open your mouth; refrain from speaking to me rather, if it be only to tell me that you hate me. I have made up my mind not to hear that again.—I have just saved you.—Let me finish first. I can save you wholly. I have prepared everything. It is yours at will. If you wish, I can do it."

He broke off violently. "No, that is not what I should say!"

As he went with hurried step and made her hurry also, for he did not release her, he walked straight to the gallows, and pointed to it with his finger—

"Choose between us two," he said, coldly.

She tore herself from his hands and fell at the foot of the gibbet, embracing that funereal support, then she half turned her beautiful head, and looked at the priest over her shoulder. One would have said that she was a Holy Virgin at the foot of the cross. The priest remained motionless, his finger still raised toward the gibbet, preserving his attitude like a statue.

At length the gypsy said to him—

"It causes me less horror than you do."

Then he allowed his arm to sink slowly, and gazed at the pavement in profound dejection.

"If these stones could speak," he murmured, "yes, they would say that a very unhappy man stands here."

He went on. The young girl, kneeling before the gallows, enveloped in her long flowing hair, let him speak on without interruption. He now had a gentle and plaintive accent which contrasted sadly with the haughty harshness of his features.

"I love you. Oh! how true that is! So nothing comes of that fire which burns my heart! Alas! young girl, night and day—yes, night and day I tell you—it is torture. Oh! I suffer too much, my poor child. 'Tis a thing deserving of compassion, I assure you. You see that I speak gently to you. I really wish that you should no longer cherish this horror of me.—After all, if a man loves a woman, 'tis not his fault!—Oh, my God!—What! So you will never pardon me? You will always hate me? All is over then. It is that which renders me evil, do you see? and horrible to myself.—You will not even look at me! You are thinking of something else, perchance, while I stand here and talk to you, shuddering on the brink of eternity for both of us! Above all things, do not speak to me of the officer!—I would cast myself at your knees, I would kiss not your feet, but the earth which is under your feet; I would sob like a child, I would tear from my breast not words, but my very heart and vitals, to tell you that I love you;—all would be useless, all!—And yet you have nothing in your heart but what is tender and merciful. You are radiant with the most beautiful mildness; you are wholly sweet, good, pitiful, and charming. Alas! You cherish no ill-will for anyone but me alone! Oh! what a fatality!"

He hid his face in his hands. The young girl heard him weeping. It was for the first time. Thus erect and shaken by sobs, he was more miserable and more suppliant than when on his knees. He wept thus for a considerable time.

"Come!" he said, these first tears passed, "I have no more words. I had, however, thought well as to what you would say. Now I tremble and shiver and break down at the decisive moment, I feel conscious of something supreme enveloping us, and I stammer. Oh! I shall fall upon the pavement if you do not take pity on me, pity on yourself. Do not condemn us both. If you only knew how much I love you! What a heart is mine! Oh! what desertion of all virtue! What desperate abandonment of myself! A doctor, I mock at science; a gentleman, I tarnish my own name; a priest, I make of the missal a pillow of sensuality, I spit in the face of my God! all this for thee, enchantress! to be more worthy of thy hell! And you will not have the apostate! Oh! let me tell you all! more still, something more horrible, oh! yet more horrible! . . ."

As he uttered these last words, his air became utterly distracted. He was silent for a moment, and resumed, as though speaking to himself, and in a strong voice—

"Cain, what hast thou done with thy brother?"

There was another silence, and he went on:—

"What have I done with him, Lord? I received him, I reared him, I nourished him, I loved him, I idolized him, and I have slain him! Yes, Lord, they have just dashed his head before my eyes on the stone of thine house, and it is because of me, because of this woman, because of her."

His eye was wild. His voice grew ever weaker; he repeated many times, yet, mechanically, at tolerably long intervals, like a bell prolonging its last vibration: "Because of her.—Because of her."

Then his tongue no longer articulated any perceptible sound; but his lips still moved. All at once he sank together, like something crumbling, and lay motionless on the earth, with his head on his knees.

A touch from the young girl, as she drew her foot from under him, brought him to himself. He passed his hand slowly over his hollow cheeks, and gazed for several moments at his fingers, which were wet, "What!" he murmured, "I have wept!"

And turning suddenly to the gypsy with unspeakable anguish—

"Alas! you have looked coldly on at my tears! Child, do you know that those tears are of lava? Is it indeed true? Nothing touches when it comes from the man whom one does not love. If you were to see me die, you would laugh. Oh! I do not wish to see you die! One word! A single word of pardon! Say not that you love me, say only that you will do it; that will suffice; I will save you. If not—oh! the hour is passing. I entreat you by all that is sacred, do not wait until I shall have turned to stone again, like that gibbet which also claims you! Reflect that I hold the destinies of both of us in my hand, that I am mad—it is terrible—that I may let all go to destruction, and that there is beneath us a bottomless abyss, unhappy girl, whither my fall will follow yours to all eternity! One word of kindness! Say one word! only one word!"

She opened her mouth to answer him. He flung himself on his knees to receive with adoration the word, possibly a tender one, which was on the point of issuing from her lips. She said to him, "You are an assassin!"

The priest clasped her in his arms with fury, and began to laugh with an abominable laugh.

"Well, yes, an assassin!" he said, "and I will have you. You will not have me for your slave, you shall have me for your master. I will have you! I have a den, whither I will drag you. You will follow me, you will be obliged to follow me, or I will deliver you up! You must die, my beauty, or be mine! belong to the priest! belong to the apostate! belong to the assassin! this very night, do you hear? Come! joy; kiss me, mad girl! The tomb or my bed!"

His eyes sparkled with impurity and rage. His lewd lips reddened the young girl's neck. She struggled in his arms. He covered her with furious kisses.

"Do not bite me, monster!" she cried. "Oh! the foul, odious monk! leave me! I will tear out thy ugly gray hair and fling it in thy face by the handful!"

He reddened, turned pale, then released her and gazed at her with a gloomy air. She thought herself victorious, and continued—

"I tell you that I belong to my Phœbus, that 'tis Phœbus whom I love, that 'tis Phœbus who is handsome! you are old, priest! you are ugly! Begone!"

He gave vent to a horrible cry, like the wretch to whom a hot iron is applied. "Die, then!" he said, gnashing his teeth. She saw his terrible look and tried to fly. He caught her once more, he shook her, he flung her on the ground, and walked with rapid strides toward the corner of the Tour-Roland, dragging her after him along the pavement by her beautiful hands.

On arriving there, he turned to her—

"For the last time, will you be mine?"

She replied with emphasis—

"No."

Then he cried in a loud voice—

"Gudule! Gudule! here is the gypsy! take your vengeance!"

The young girl felt herself seized suddenly by the elbow. She looked. A fleshless arm was stretched from an opening in the wall, and held her like a hand of iron.

"Hold her well," said the priest; " 'tis the gypsy escaped. Release her not. I will go in search of the sergeants. You shall see her hanged."

A guttural laugh replied from the interior of the wall to these bloody words:—"Hah! hah! hah!"—The gypsy watched the priest retire in the direction of the Pont Notre-Dame. A cavalcade was heard in that direction.

The young girl had recognized the spiteful recluse. Panting with terror, she tried to disengage herself. She writhed, she made many starts of agony and despair, but the other held her with incredible strength. The lean and bony fingers which bruised her, clenched on her flesh and met around it. One would have said that this hand was riveted to her arm. It was more than a chain, more than a fetter, more than a ring of iron, it was a living pair of pincers endowed with intelligence, which emerged from the wall.

She fell back against the wall exhausted, and then the fear of death took possession of her. She thought of the beauty of life, of youth, of the view of heaven, the aspects of nature, of her love for Phœbus, of all that was vanishing and all that was approaching, of the priest who was denouncing her, of the headsman who was to come, of the gallows which was there. Then she felt terror mount to the very roots of her hair and she heard the mocking laugh of the recluse, saying to her in a very low tone: "Hah! hah! hah! you are going to be hanged!"

She turned a dying look toward the window, and she beheld the fierce face of the sacked nun through the bars.

"What have I done to you?" she said, almost lifeless.

The recluse did not reply, but began to mumble with a singsong irritated, mocking intonation: "Daughter of Egypt! daughter of Egypt! daughter of Egypt!"

The unhappy Esmeralda dropped her head beneath her flowing hair, comprehending that it was no human being she had to deal with.

All at once the recluse exclaimed, as though the gypsy's question had taken all this time to reach her brain—

" 'What have you done to me?' you say! Ah! what have you done to me, gypsy! Well! listen.— I had a child! you see! I had a child! a child, I tell you!—a pretty little girl!—my Agnès!" she went on wildly, kissing something in the dark.—"Well! do you see, daughter of Egypt? they took my child from me; they stole my child; they ate my child. That is what you have done to me."

The young girl replied like a lamb—

"Alas! perchance I was not born then!"

"Oh! yes!" returned the recluse, "you must have been born. You were among them. She would be the same age as you! so!—I have been here fifteen years; fifteen years have I suffered; fifteen years have I prayed; fifteen years have I beat my head against these four walls—I tell you that 'twas the gypsies who stole her from me, do you hear that? and who ate her with their teeth.—Have you a heart? imagine a child playing, a child sucking; a child sleeping. It is so innocent a thing!—Well! that, that is what they took from me, what they killed. The good God knows it well! To-day, it is my turn; I am going to eat the gypsy.—Oh! I would bite you well, if the bars did not prevent me! My head is too large!—Poor little one! while she was asleep! And if they woke her up when they took her, in vain she might cry; I was not there!—Ah! gypsy mothers, you devoured my child! come see your own."

Then she began to laugh or to gnash her teeth, for the two things resembled each other in that furious face. The day was beginning to dawn. An ashy gleam dimly lighted this scene, and the gallows grew more and more distinct in the square. On the other side, in the direction of the bridge of Notre-Dame, the poor condemned girl fancied that she heard the sound of cavalry approaching.

"Madam," she cried, clasping her hands and falling on her knees, disheveled, distracted, mad with fright; "madam! have pity! They are coming. I have done nothing to you. Would you wish to see me die in this horrible fashion before your very eyes? You are pitiful, I am sure. It is too frightful. Let me make my escape. Release me! Mercy. I do not wish to die like that!"

"Give me back my child!" said the recluse.

"Mercy! Mercy!"

"Give me back my child!"

"Release me, in the name of heaven!"

"Give me back my child!"

Again the young girl fell; exhausted, broken, and having already the glassy eye of a person in the grave.

"Alas!" she faltered, "you seek your child, I seek my parents."

"Give me back my little Agnès!" pursued Gudule. "You do not know where she is? Then die!—I will tell you. I was a woman of the town, I had a child, they took my child. It was the gypsies. You see plainly that you must die. When your mother, the gypsy, comes to reclaim you, I shall say to her: 'Mother, look at that gibbet!'—Or, give me back my child. Do you know where she is, my little daughter? Stay! I will show you. Here is her shoe, all that is left me of her. Do you know where its mate is? If you know, tell me, and if it is only at the other end of the world, I will crawl to it on my knees."

As she spoke thus, with her other arm extended through the window, she showed the gypsy the little embroidered shoe. It was already light enough to distinguish its shape and its colors.

"Let me see that shoe," said the gypsy, quivering. "God! God!"

And at the same time, with her hand which was at liberty, she quickly opened the little bag ornamented with green glass, which she wore about her neck.

"Go on, go on!" grumbled Gudule, "search your demon's amulet!"

All at once, she stopped short, trembled in every limb, and cried in a voice which proceeded from the very depths of her being: "My daughter!"

The gypsy had just drawn from the bag a little shoe absolutely similar to the other. To this little shoe was attached a parchment on which was inscribed this charm—

QUAND LE PAREIL RETROUVERAS
TA MÈRE TE TENDRAS LES BRAS.[1]

Quicker than a flash of lightning, the recluse had laid the two shoes together, had read the parchment and had put close to the bars of the window her face beaming with celestial joy as she cried—

"My daughter! my daughter!"

"My mother!" said the gypsy.

Here we are unequal to the task of depicting the scene.

The wall and the iron bars were between them. "Oh! the wall!" cried the recluse. "Oh! to see her and not to embrace her! Your hand! your hand!"

The young girl passed her arm through the opening; the recluse threw herself on that hand, pressed her lips to it and there remained, buried in that kiss, giving no other sign of life than a sob which heaved her breast from time to time. In the meanwhile, she wept in torrents, in silence, in the dark, like a rain at night. The poor mother poured out in floods upon that adored hand the dark and deep well of tears, which lay within her, and into which her grief had filtered, drop by drop, for fifteen years.

All at once she rose, flung aside her long gray hair from her brow, and without uttering a word, began to shake the bars of her cage cell, with both hands, more furiously than a lioness. The bars held firm. Then she went to seek in the corner of her cell a huge paving stone, which served her as a pillow, and launched it against them with such violence that one of the bars broke, emitting thousands of sparks. A second blow completely shattered the old iron cross which barricaded the window. Then with her two hands, she finished breaking and removing the rusted stumps of the bars. There are moments when woman's hands possess superhuman strength.

A passage broken, less than a minute was required for her to seize her daughter by the middle of her body, and draw her into her cell. "Come let me draw you out of the abyss," she murmured.

When her daughter was inside the cell, she laid her gently on the ground, then raised her up again, and bearing her in her arms as though she were still only her little Agnès, she walked to and fro in her little room, intoxicated, frantic, joyous, crying out, singing, kissing her daughter, talking to her, bursting into laughter, melting into tears, all at once and with vehemence.

"My daughter! my daughter!" she said. "I have my daughter! here she is! The good God has given her back to me! Ha you! come all of you! Is there anyone there to see that I have my daughter? Lord Jesus, how beautiful she is! You have made me wait fifteen years, my good God, but it was in order to give her back to me beautiful.—Then the gypsies did not eat her! Who said so? My little daughter! my little daughter! Kiss me. Those good gypsies! I love the gypsies!—It is really you! That was what made my heart leap every time that you passed by. And I took that for hatred! Forgive me, my Agnès, forgive me. You thought me very malicious, did you not? I love you. Have you still the little mark on your neck? Let us see. She still has it. Oh! you are beautiful! It was I who

1. When thou shalt find its mate, thy mother will stretch out her arms to thee.

gave you those big eyes, mademoiselle. Kiss me. I love you. It is nothing to me that other mothers have children; I scorn them now. They have only to come and see. Here is mine. See her neck, her eyes, her hair, her hands. Find me anything as beautiful as that! Oh! I promise you she will have lovers, that she will! I have wept for fifteen years. All my beauty has departed and has fallen to her. Kiss me."

She addressed to her a thousand other extravagant remarks, whose accent constituted their sole beauty, disarranged the poor girl's garments even to the point of making her blush, smoothed her silky hair with her hand, kissed her foot, her knee, her brow, her eyes, was in raptures over everything. The young girl let her have her way, repeating at intervals and very low and with infinite tenderness, "My mother!"

"Do you see, my little girl," resumed the recluse, interspersing her words with kisses, "I shall love you dearly? We will go away from here. We are going to be very happy. I have inherited something in Reims, in our country. You know Reims? Ah! no, you do not know it; you were too small! If you only knew how pretty you were at the age of four months! Tiny feet that people came even from Epernay, which is seven leagues away, to see! We shall have a field, a house. I will put you to sleep in my bed. My God! my God! who would believe this? I have my daughter!"

"Oh, my mother!" said the young girl, at length finding strength to speak in her emotion, "the gypsy woman told me so. There was a good gypsy of our band who died last year, and who always cared for me like a nurse. It was she who placed this little bag about my neck. She always said to me: 'Little one, guard this jewel well! 'Tis a treasure. It will cause thee to find thy mother once again. Thou wearest thy mother about thy neck.'—The gypsy predicted it!"

The sacked nun again pressed her daughter in her arms.

"Come, let me kiss you! You say that prettily. When we are in the country, we will place these little shoes on an infant Jesus in the church. We certainly owe that to the good, holy Virgin. What a pretty voice you have! When you spoke to me just now, it was music! Ah! my Lord God! I have found my child again! But is this story credible? Nothing will kill one—or I should have died of joy."

And then she began to clap her hands again and to laugh and to cry out: "We are going to be so happy!"

At that moment, the cell resounded with the clang of arms and a galloping of horses which seemed to be coming from the Pont Notre-Dame, and advancing farther and farther along the quay. The gypsy threw herself with anguish into the arms of the sacked nun.

"Save me! save me! mother! they are coming!"

"Oh, heaven! what are you saying? I had forgotten! They are in pursuit of you! What have you done?"

"I know not," replied the unhappy child; "but I am condemned to die."

"To die!" said Gudule, staggering as though struck by lightning; "to die!" she repeated slowly, gazing at her daughter with staring eyes.

"Yes, mother," replied the frightened young girl, "they want to kill me. They are coming to seize me. That gallows is for me! Save me! save me! They are coming! Save me!"

The recluse remained for several moments motionless and petrified, then she moved her head in sign of doubt, and suddenly giving vent to a burst of laughter, but with that terrible laugh which had come back to her—

"Ho! ho! no! 'tis a dream of which you are telling me. Ah, yes! I lost her, that lasted fifteen years, and then I found her again, and that lasted a minute! And they would take her from me again! And now, when she is beautiful, when she is grown up, when she speaks to me, when she loves me; it is now that they would come to devour her, before my very eyes, and I her mother! Oh! no! these things are not possible. The good God does not permit such things as that."

Here the cavalcade appeared to halt, and a voice was heard to say in the distance—

"This way, Messire Tristan! The priest says that we shall find her at the Rat-Hole." The noise of the horses began again.

The recluse sprang to her feet with a shriek of despair.

"Fly! fly! my child! All comes back to me. You are right. It is your death! Horror! Maledictions! Fly!"

She thrust her head through the window, and withdrew it again hastily.

"Remain," she said, in a low, curt, and lugubrious tone, as she pressed the hand of the gypsy, who was more dead than alive. "Remain! Do not breathe! There are soldiers everywhere. You cannot get out. It is too light."

Her eyes were dry and burning. She remained silent for a moment; but she paced the cell hurriedly, and halted now and then to pluck out handfuls of her gray hairs, which she afterwards tore with her teeth.

Suddenly she said: "They draw near. I will speak with them. Hide yourself in this corner. They will not see you. I will tell them that you have made your escape. That I released you, i' faith!"

She set her daughter (down for she was still carrying her), in one corner of the cell which was not visible from without. She made her crouch down, arranged her carefully so that neither foot nor hand projected from the shadow, untied her black hair which she spread over her white robe to conceal it, placed in front of her her jug and her paving stone, the only articles of furniture which she possessed, imagining that this jug and stone would hide her. And when this was finished she became more tranquil, and knelt down to pray. The day, which was only dawning, still left many shadows in the Rat-Hole.

At that moment, the voice of the priest, that infernal voice, passed very close to the cell, crying—

"This way, Captain Phœbus de Châteaupers."

At that name, at that voice, la Esmeralda, crouching in her corner, made a movement.

"Do not stir!" said Gudule.

She had barely finished when a tumult of men, swords, and horses halted around the cell. The mother rose quickly and went to post herself before her window, in order to stop it up. She beheld a large troop of armed men, both horse and foot, drawn up on the Grève.

The commander dismounted, and came toward her.

"Old woman!" said this man, who had an atrocious face, "we are in search of a witch to hang her; we were told that you had her."

The poor mother assumed as indifferent an air as she could, and replied—

"I know not what you mean."

The other resumed, "Tête Dieu! What was it that frightened archdeacon said? Where is he?"

"Monseigneur," said a soldier, "he has disappeared."

"Come, now, old madwoman," began the commander again, "do not lie. A sorceress was given in charge to you. What have you done with her?"

The recluse did not wish to deny all, for fear of awakening suspicion, and replied in a sincere and surly tone—

"If you are speaking of a big young girl who was put into my hands a while ago, I will tell you that she bit me, and that I released her. There! Leave me in peace."

The commander made a grimace of disappointment.

"Don't lie to me, old specter!" said he. "My name is Tristan l'Hermite, and I am the king's gossip. Tristan the Hermit, do you hear?" He added, as he glanced at the Place de Grève around him, " 'Tis a name which has an echo here."

"You might be Satan the Hermit," replied Gudule, who was regaining hope, "but I should have nothing else to say to you, and I should never be afraid of you."

"Tête-Dieu," said Tristan, "here is a crone! Ah! So the witch girl hath fled! And in which direction did she go?"

Gudule replied in a careless tone—

"Through the Rue du Mouton, I believe."

Tristan turned his head and made a sign to his troop to prepare to set out on the march again. The recluse breathed freely once more.

"Monseigneur," suddenly said an archer, "ask the old elf why the bars of her window are broken in this manner."

This question brought anguish again to the heart of the miserable mother. Nevertheless, she did not lose all presence of mind.

"They have always been thus," she stammered.

"Bah!" retorted the archer, "only yesterday they still formed a fine black cross, which inspired devotion."

Tristan cast a sidelong glance at the recluse.

"I think the old dame is getting confused!"

The unfortunate woman felt that all depended on her self-possession, and, although with death in her soul, she began to grin. Mothers possess such strength.

"Bah!" said she, "the man is drunk. 'Tis more than a year since the tail of a stone cart dashed against my window and broke in the grating. And how I cursed the carter, too."

" 'Tis true," said another archer, "I was there."

Always and everywhere people are to be found who have seen everything. This unexpected testimony from the archer re-encouraged the recluse, whom this interrogatory was forcing to cross an abyss on the edge of a knife. But she was condemned to a perpetual alternative of hope and alarm.

"If it was a cart which did it," retorted the first soldier, "the stumps of the bars should be thrust inwards, while they actually are pushed outwards."

"Hé! hé!" said Tristan to the soldier, "you have the nose of an inquisitor of the Châtelet. Reply to what he says, old woman."

"Good heavens!" she exclaimed, driven to bay, and in a voice that was full of tears in despite of her efforts, "I swear to you, monseigneur, that 'twas a cart which broke those bars. You hear the man who saw it. And then, what has that to do with your gypsy?"

"Hum!" growled Tristan.

"The devil!" went on the soldier, flattered by the provost's praise, "these fractures of the iron are perfectly fresh."

Tristan tossed his head. She turned pale.

"How long ago, say you, did the cart do it?"

"A month, a fortnight, perhaps, monseigneur, I know not."

"She first said more than a year," observed the soldier.

"That is suspicious," said the provost.

"Monseigneur!" she cried, still pressed against the opening, and trembling lest suspicion should lead them to thrust their heads through and look into her cell; "monseigneur, I swear to you that 'twas a cart which broke this grating. I swear it to you by the angels of paradise. If it was not a cart, may I be eternally damned, and I reject God!"

"You put a great deal of heat into that oath," said Tristan, with his inquisitorial glance.

The poor woman felt her assurance vanishing more and more. She had reached the point of blundering, and she comprehended with terror that she was saying what she ought not to have said.

Here another soldier came up, crying—

"Monsieur, the old hag lies. The sorceress did not flee through the Rue de Mouton. The street chain has remained stretched all night, and the chain guard has seen no one pass."

Tristan, whose face became more sinister with every moment, addressed the recluse—

"What have you to say to that?"

She tried to make head against this new incident—

"That I do not know, monseigneur; that I may have been mistaken. I believe, in fact, that she crossed the water."

"That is in the opposite direction," said the provost, "and it is not very likely that she would wish to re-enter the city, where she was being pursued. You are lying, old woman."

"And then," added the first soldier, "there is no boat either on this side of the stream or on the other."

"She swam across," replied the recluse, defending her ground foot by foot.

"Do women swim?" said the soldier.

"*Tête Dieu!* old woman! You are lying!" repeated Tristan angrily. "I have a good mind to abandon that sorceress and take you. A quarter of an hour of torture will, perchance, draw the truth from your throat. Come! You are to follow us."

She seized on these words with avidity.

"As you please, monseigneur. Do it. Do it. Torture. I am willing. Take me away. Quick, quick! let us set out at once!—During that time," she said to herself, "my daughter will make her escape."

" 'S death!" said the provost, "what an appetite for the rack! I understand not this madwoman at all."

An old, gray-haired sergeant of the guard stepped out of the ranks, and addressing the provost—

"Mad in sooth, monseigneur. If she released the gypsy, it was not her fault, for she loves not the gypsies. I have been of the watch these fifteen years, and I hear her every evening cursing the Bohemian women with endless imprecations. If the one of whom we are in pursuit is, as I suppose, the little dancer with the goat, she detests that one above all the rest."

Gudule made an effort and said—

"That one above all."

The unanimous testimony of the men of the watch confirmed the old sergeant's words to the provost. Tristan l'Hermite, in despair at extracting anything from the recluse, turned his back on her, and with unspeakable anxiety she beheld him direct his course slowly toward his horse.

"Come!" he said, between his teeth, "March on! let us set out again on the quest. I shall not sleep until that gypsy is hanged."

But he still hesitated for some time before mounting his horse. Gudule palpitated between life and death, as she beheld him cast about the Place that uneasy look of a hunting dog which instinctively feels that the lair of the beast is close to him, and is loath to go away. At length he shook his head and leaped into his saddle. Gudule's horribly compressed heart now dilated, and she said in a low voice, as she cast a glance at her daughter, whom she had not ventured to look at while they were there, "Saved!"

The poor child had remained all this time in her corner, without breathing, without moving, with the idea of death before her. She had lost nothing of the scene between Gudule and Tristan, and the anguish of her mother had found its echo in her heart. She had heard all the successive snappings of the thread by which she hung suspended over the gulf; twenty times she had fancied that she saw it break, and at last she began to breathe again and to feel her foot on firm ground. At that moment she heard a voice saying to the provost: "*Corboeuf!* Monsieur le Prevôt, 'tis no affair of mine, a man of arms, to hang witches. The rabble of the populace is suppressed. I leave you to attend to the matter alone. You will allow me to rejoin my company, who are waiting for their captain."

The voice was that of Phœbus de Châteaupers; that which took place within her was ineffable. He was there, her friend, her protector, her support, her refuge, her Phœbus. She rose, and before her mother could prevent her, she had rushed to the window, crying—

"Phœbus! aid me, my Phœbus!"

Phœbus was no longer there. He had just turned the corner of the Rue de la Coutellerie at a gallop. But Tristan had not yet taken his departure.

The recluse rushed upon her daughter with a roar of agony. She dragged her violently back, digging her nails into her neck. A tigress mother does not stand on trifles. But it was too late. Tristan had seen.

"Hé! hé!" he exclaimed with a laugh which laid bare all his teeth and made his face resemble the muzzle of a wolf, "two mice in the trap!"

"I suspected as much," said the soldier.

Tristan clapped him on the shoulder—

"You are a good cat! Come!" he added, "where is Henriet Cousin?"

A man who had neither the garments nor the air of a soldier, stepped from the ranks. He wore a costume half gray, half brown, flat hair, leather sleeves, and carried a bundle of ropes in his huge hand. This man always attended Tristan, who always attended Louis XI.

"Friend," said Tristan l'Hermite, "I presume that this is the sorceress of whom we are in search. You will hang me this one. Have you your ladder?"

"There is one yonder, under the shed of the Pillar-House," replied the man. "Is it on this justice that the thing is to be done?" he added, pointing to the stone gibbet.

"Yes."

"Ho, hé!" continued the man with a huge laugh, which was still more brutal than that of the provost, "we shall not have far to go."

"Make haste!" said Tristan, "you shall laugh afterwards."

In the meantime, the recluse had not uttered another word since Tristan had seen her daughter and all hope was lost. She had flung the poor gypsy, half dead, into the corner of the cellar, and had placed herself once more at the window with both hands resting on the angle of the sill like two claws. In this attitude she was seen to cast upon all those soldiers her glance which had become wild and frantic once more. At the moment when Henriet Cousin approached her cell, she showed him so savage a face that he shrank back.

"Monseigneur," he said, returning to the provost, "which am I to take?"

"The young one."

"So much the better, for the old one seemeth difficult."

"Poor little dancer with the goat!" said the old sergeant of the watch.

Henriet Cousin approached the window again. The mother's eyes made his own droop. He said with a good deal of timidity—

"Madam"—

She interrupted him in a very low but furious voice—

"What do you ask?"

"It is not you," he said, "it is the other."

"What other?"

"The young one."

She began to shake her head, crying—

"There is no one! there is no one! there is no one!"

"Yes, there is!" retorted the hangman, "and you know it well. Let me take the young one. I have no wish to harm you."

She said, with a strange sneer—

"Ah! so you have no wish to harm me!"

"Let me have the other, madam; 'tis monsieur the provost who wills it."

She repeated with a look of madness—

"There is no one here."

"I tell you that there is!" replied the executioner. "We have all seen that there are two of you."

"Look then!" said the recluse, with a sneer. "Thrust your head through the window."

The executioner observed the mother's finger-nails and dared not.

"Make haste!" shouted Tristan, who had just ranged his troops in a circle round the Rat-Hole, and who sat on his horse beside the gallows.

Henriet returned once more to the provost in great embarrassment. He had flung his rope on the ground, and was twisting his hat between his hands with an awkward air.

"Monseigneur," he asked, "where am I to enter?"

"By the door."

"There is none."

"By the window."

" 'Tis too small."

"Make it larger," said Tristan angrily. "Have you not pickaxes?"

The mother still looked on steadfastly from the depths of her cavern. She no longer hoped for anything, she no longer knew what she wished, except that she did not wish them to take her daughter.

Henriet Cousin went in search of the chest of tools for the night man, under the shed of the Pillar-House. He drew from it also the double ladder, which he immediately set up against the gallows. Five or six of the provost's men armed themselves with picks and crowbars, and Tristan betook himself, in company with them, toward the window.

"Old woman," said the provost, in a severe tone, "deliver up to us that girl quietly."

She looked at him like one who does not understand.

"Tête Dieu!" continued Tristan, "why do you try to prevent this sorceress being hung as it pleases the king?"

The wretched woman began to laugh in her wild way.

"Why? She is my daughter."

The tone in which she pronounced these words made even Henriet Cousin shudder.

"I am sorry for that," said the provost, "but it is the king's good pleasure."

She cried, redoubling her terrible laugh—

"What is your king to me? I tell you that she is my daughter!"

"Pierce the wall," said Tristan.

In order to make a sufficiently wide opening, it sufficed to dislodge one course of stone below the window. When the mother heard the picks and crowbars mining her fortress, she uttered a terrible cry; then she began to stride about her cell with frightful swiftness, a wild beasts' habit which her cage had imparted to her. She no longer said anything, but her eyes flamed. The soldiers were chilled to the very soul.

All at once she seized her paving stone, laughed, and hurled it with both fists upon the workmen. The stone, badly flung (for her hands trembled), touched no one, and fell short under the feet of Tristan's horse. She gnashed her teeth.

In the meantime, although the sun had not yet risen, it was broad daylight; a beautiful rose color enlivened the ancient, decayed chimneys of the Pillar-House. It was the hour when the earliest windows of the great city open joyously on the roofs. Some workmen, a few fruit-sellers on their way to the markets on their asses, began to traverse the Grève; they halted for a moment before this group of soldiers clustered round the Rat-Hole, stared at it with an air of astonishment and passed on.

The recluse had gone and seated herself by her daughter, covering her with her body, in front of her, with staring eyes, listening to the poor child, who did not stir, but who kept murmuring in a low voice, these words only, "Phœbus! Phœbus!" In proportion as the work of the demolishers seemed to advance, the mother mechanically retreated, and pressed the young girl closer and closer to the wall. All at once, the recluse beheld the stone (for she was standing guard and never took her eyes from it), move, and she heard Tristan's voice encouraging the workers. Then she aroused from the depression into which she had fallen during the last few moments, cried out, and as she spoke, her voice now rent the ear like a saw, then stammered as though all kind of maledictions were pressing to her lips to burst forth at once.

"Ho! ho! ho! Why this is terrible! You are ruffians! Are you really going to take my daughter? Oh! the cowards! Oh! the hangman lackeys! the wretched, blackguard assassins! Help! help! fire! Will they take my child from me like this? Who is it then who is called the good God?"

Then, addressing Tristan, foaming at the mouth, with wild eyes, all bristling and on all fours like a female panther—

"Draw near and take my daughter! Do not you understand that this woman tells you that she is my daughter? Do you know what it is to have a child? Eh! lynx, have you never lain with your female? have you never had a cub? and if you have little ones, when they howl have you nothing in your vitals that moves?"

"Throw down the stone," said Tristan; "it no longer holds."

The crowbars raised the heavy course. It was, as we have said, the mother's last bulwark.

She threw herself upon it, she tried to hold it back; she scratched the stone with her nails, but the massive block, set in movement by six men, escaped her and glided gently to the ground along the iron levers.

The mother, perceiving an entrance effected, fell down in front of the opening, barricading the breach with her body, beating the pavement with her head, and shrieking with a voice rendered so hoarse by fatigue that it was hardly audible—

"Help! fire! fire!"

"Now take the wench," said Tristan, still impassive.

The mother gazed at the soldiers in such formidable fashion that they were more inclined to retreat than to advance.

"Come, now," repeated the provost. "Here you, Henriet Cousin!"

No one took a step.

The provost swore—

"*Tête de Christ!* my men of war! afraid of a woman!"

"Monseigneur," said Rennet, "do you call that a woman?"

"She has the mane of a lion," said another.

"Come!" repeated the provost, "the gap is wide enough. Enter three abreast, as at the breach of Pontoise. Let us make an end of it, death of Mahom! I will make two pieces of the first man who draws back!"

Placed between the provost and the mother, both threatening, the soldiers hesitated for a moment, then took their resolution, and advanced toward the Rat-Hole.

When the recluse saw this, she rose abruptly on her knees, flung aside her hair from her face, then let her thin flayed hands fall by her side. Then great tears fell, one by one, from her eyes; they flowed down her cheeks through a furrow, like a torrent through a bed which it has hollowed for itself.

At the same time she began to speak, but in a voice so supplicating, so gentle, so submissive, so heartrending, that more than one old convict-warder around Tristan who must have devoured human flesh wiped his eyes.

"Messeigneurs! messieurs the sergeants, one word. There is one thing which I must say to you. She is my daughter, do you see? my dear little daughter whom I had lost! Listen. It is quite a history. Consider that I knew the sergeants very well. They were always good to me in the days when the little boys threw stones at me, because I led a life of pleasure. Do you see? You will leave me my child when you know! I was a poor woman of the town. It was the Bohemians who stole her from me. And I kept her shoe for fifteen years. Stay, here it is. That was the kind of foot which she had. At Reims! La Chantefleurie! Rue Folle-Peine! Perchance, you knew about that. It was I. In your youth, then, there was a merry time, when one passed good hours. You will take pity on me, will you not, gentlemen? The gypsies stole her from me; they hid her from me for fifteen years. I thought her dead. Fancy, my good friends, believed her to be dead. I have passed fifteen years here, in this cellar, without a fire in winter. It is hard. The poor, dear little shoe! I have cried so much that the good God has heard me. This night he has given my daughter back to me. It is a miracle of the good God. She was not dead. You will not take her from me, I am sure. If it were myself, I would say nothing; but she, a child of sixteen! Leave her time to see the sun! What has she done to you? nothing at all. Nor have I. If you did but know that she is all I have, that I am old, that she is a blessing which the Holy Virgin has sent to me! And then, you are all so good! You did not know that she was my daughter; but now you do know it. Oh! I love her! Monsieur, the grand provost. I would prefer a stab in my own vitals to a scratch on her finger! You have the air of such a good lord! What I have told you explains the matter, does it not? Oh! if you have had a mother, monsiegneur! you are the captain, leave me my child! Consider that I pray you on my knees, as one prays to Jesus Christ! I ask nothing of anyone; I am from Reims, gentlemen; I own a little field inherited from my uncle, Mahiet Pradon. I am no beggar. I wish nothing, but I do want my child! oh! I want to keep my child! The good God, who is the master, has not given her back to me for nothing! The king! you say the king! It would not cause him much pleasure to have my little daughter killed! And then, the king is good! she is my daughter! she is my own daughter! She belongs not to the king! she is not yours! I want to go away! we want to go away! and when two women pass, one a mother and the other a daughter, one lets them go! Let us pass! we belong in Reims. Oh! you are very good, messieurs the sergeants, I love you all. You will not take my dear little one, it is impossible! It is utterly impossible, is it not? My child, my child!"

We will not try to give an idea of her gestures, her tone, of the tears which she swallowed as she spoke, of the hands which she clasped and then wrung, of the heart-breaking smiles, of the swimming glances, of the groans, the sighs, the miserable and affecting cries which she mingled with her disordered, wild, and incoherent words. When she became silent Tristan l'Hermite frowned, but it was to conceal a tear which welled up in his tiger's eye. He conquered this weakness, however, and said in a curt tone—

"The king wills it."

Then he bent down to the ear of Henriet Cousin, and said to him in a very low tone—

"Make an end of it quickly!" Possibly, the redoubtable provost felt his heart also failing him.

The executioner and the sergeants entered the cell. The mother offered no resistance, only she dragged herself toward her daughter and threw herself bodily upon her.

The gypsy beheld the soldiers approach. The horror of death reanimated her—

"Mother!" she shrieked, in a tone of indescribable distress, "Mother! they are coming! defend me!"

"Yes, my love, I am defending you!" replied the mother, in a dying voice; and clasping her closely in her arms, she covered her with kisses. The two lying thus on the earth, the mother upon the daughter, presented a spectacle worthy of pity.

Henriet Cousin grasped the young girl by the middle of her body, beneath her beautiful shoulders. When she felt that hand, she cried, "Heuh!" and fainted. The executioner who was shedding large tears upon her, drop by drop, was about to bear her away in his arms. He tried to detach the mother, who had, so to speak, knotted her hands around her daughter's waist; but she clung so strongly to her child, that it was impossible to separate them. Then Henriet Cousin dragged the young girl outside the cell, and the mother after her. The mother's eyes were also closed.

At that moment, the sun rose, and there was already on the Place a fairly numerous assembly of people who looked on from a distance at what was being thus dragged along the pavement to the gibbet. For that was Provost Tristan's way at executions. He had a passion for preventing the approach of the curious.

There was no one at the windows. Only at a distance, at the summit of that one of the towers of Notre-Dame which commands the Grève, two men outlined in black against the light morning sky, and who seemed to be looking on, were visible.

Henriet Cousin paused at the foot of the fatal ladder, with that which he was dragging, and, barely breathing, with so much pity did the thing inspire him, he passed the rope around the lovely neck of the young girl. The unfortunate child felt the horrible touch of the hemp. She raised her eyelids, and saw the fleshless arm of the stone gallows extended above her head. Then she shook herself and shrieked in a loud and heartrending voice: "No! no! I will not!" Her mother, whose head was buried and concealed in her daughter's garments, said not a word; only her whole body could be seen to quiver, and she was heard to redouble her kisses on her child. The executioner took advantage of this moment to hastily loose the arms with which she clasped the condemned girl. Either through exhaustion or despair, she let him have his way. Then he took the young girl on his shoulder, from which the charming creature hung, gracefully bent over his large head. Then he set his foot on the ladder in order to ascend.

At that moment, the mother who was crouching on the pavement, opened her eyes wide. Without uttering a cry, she raised herself erect with a terrible expression; then she flung herself upon the hand of the executioner, like a beast on its prey, and bit it. It was done like a flash of lightning. The headsman howled with pain. Those nearby rushed up. With difficulty they withdrew his bleeding hand from the mother's teeth. She preserved a profound silence. They thrust her back with much brutality, and noticed that her head fell heavily on the pavement. They raised her, she fell back again. She was dead.

The executioner, who had not loosed his hold on the young girl, began to ascend the ladder once more.

Chapter II

THE BEAUTIFUL CREATURE CLAD IN WHITE (DANTE)

WHEN QUASIMODO SAW THAT THE CELL WAS EMPTY, THAT THE GYPSY WAS NO LONGER THERE, that while he had been defending her she had been abducted, he grasped his hair with both hands and stamped with surprise and pain; then he set out to run through the entire church seeking his Bohemian, howling strange cries to all the corners of the walls, strewing his red hair on the pavement. It was just at the moment when the king's archers were making their victorious entrance into Notre-Dame, also in search of the gypsy. Quasimodo, poor, deaf fellow, aided them in their fatal intentions, without suspecting it; he thought that the outcasts were the gypsy's enemies. He himself conducted Tristan l'Hermite to all possible hiding-places, opened to him the secret doors, the double bottoms of the altars, the rear sacristries. If the unfortunate girl had still been there, it would have been he himself who would have delivered her up.

When the fatigue of finding nothing had disheartened Tristan, who was not easily discouraged, Quasimodo continued the search alone. He made the tour of the church twenty times, length and breadth, up and down, ascending and descending, running, calling, shouting, peeping, rummaging, ransacking, thrusting his head into every hole, pushing a torch under every vault, despairing, mad. A male who has lost his female is no more roaring nor more haggard.

At last when he was sure, perfectly sure that she was no longer there, that all was at an end, that she had been snatched from him, he slowly mounted the staircase to the towers, that staircase which he had ascended with so much eagerness and triumph on the day when he had saved her. He passed those same places once more with drooping head, voiceless, tearless, almost breathless. The church was again deserted, and had fallen back into its silence. The archers had quitted it to track the sorceress in the city. Quasimodo, left alone in that vast Notre-Dame, so besieged and tumultuous but a short time before, once more betook himself to the cell where the gypsy had slept for so many weeks under his guardianship.

As he approached it, he fancied that he might, perhaps, find her there. When, at the turn of the gallery which opens on the roof of the side aisles, he perceived the tiny cell with its little window and its little door crouching beneath a great flying buttress like a bird's nest under a branch, the poor man's heart failed him, and he leaned against a pillar to keep from falling. He imagined that she might have returned thither, that some good genius had, no doubt, brought her back, that this chamber was too tranquil, too safe, too charming for her not to be there, and he dared not take another step for fear of destroying his illusion. "Yes," he said to himself, "perchance she is sleeping, or praying. I must not disturb her."

At length he summoned up courage, advanced on tiptoe, looked, entered. Empty. The cell was still empty. The unhappy deaf man walked slowly round it, lifted the bed and looked beneath it, as though she might be concealed between the pavement and the mattress, then he shook his head and remained stupefied. All at once, he crushed his torch under his foot, and, without uttering a word, without giving vent to a sigh, he flung himself at full speed, head foremost against the wall, and fell fainting on the floor.

When he recovered his senses, he threw himself on the bed and rolling about, he kissed frantically the place where the young girl had slept and which was still warm; he remained there for several moments as motionless as though he were about to expire; then he rose, dripping with perspiration, panting, mad, and began to beat his head against the wall with the frightful regularity of the clapper of his bells, and the resolution of a man determined to kill himself. At length he fell a second time, exhausted; he dragged himself on his knees outside the cell, and crouched down facing the door, in an attitude of astonishment.

He remained thus for more than an hour without making a movement, with his eye fixed on the deserted cell, more gloomy, and more pensive than a mother seated between an empty cradle and a full coffin. He uttered not a word; only at long intervals, a sob heaved his body violently, but it was a tearless sob, like summer lightning which makes no noise.

It appears to have been then, that, seeking at the bottom of his lonely thoughts for the unexpected abductor of the gypsy, he thought of the archdeacon. He remembered that Dom Claude alone possessed a key to the staircase leading to the cell; he recalled his nocturnal attempts on the young girl, in the first of which he, Quasimodo, had assisted, the second of which he had prevented. He recalled a thousand details, and soon he no longer doubted that the archdeacon had taken the gypsy. Nevertheless, such was his respect for the priest, such his gratitude, his devotion, his love for this man had taken such deep root in his heart, that they resisted, even at this moment, the talons of jealousy and despair.

He reflected that the archdeacon had done this thing, and the wrath of blood and death which it would have evoked in him against any other person, turned in the poor deaf man, from the moment when Claude Frollo was in question, into an increase of grief and sorrow.

At the moment when his thought was thus fixed upon the priest, while the daybreak was whitening the flying buttresses, he perceived on the highest story of Notre-Dame, at the angle formed by the external balustrade as it makes the turn of the chancel, a figure walking. This figure was coming toward him. He recognized it. It was the archdeacon.

Claude was walking with a slow, grave step. He did not look before him as he walked, he was directing his course toward the northern tower, but his face was turned aside toward the right bank of the Seine, and he held his head high, as though trying to see something over the roofs. The owl often assumes this oblique attitude. It flies toward one point and looks toward another. In this manner the priest passed above Quasimodo without seeing him.

The deaf man, who had been petrified by this sudden apparition, beheld him disappear through the door of the staircase to the north tower. The reader is aware that this is the tower from which the Hôtel-de-Ville is visible. Quasimodo rose and followed the archdeacon.

Quasimodo ascended the tower staircase for the sake of ascending it, for the sake of seeing why the priest was ascending it. Moreover, the poor bellringer did not know what he (Quasimodo) should do, what he should say, what he wished. He was full of fury and full of fear. The archdeacon and the gypsy had come into conflict in his heart.

When he reached the summit of the tower, before emerging from the shadow of the staircase and stepping upon the platform, he cautiously examined the position of the priest. The priest's back was turned to him. There is an open-work balustrade which surrounds the platform of the bell tower. The priest, whose eyes looked down upon the town, was resting his breast on that one of the four sides of the balustrades which looks upon the Pont Notre-Dame.

Quasimodo, advancing with the tread of a wolf behind him, went to see what he was gazing at thus.

The priest's attention was so absorbed elsewhere that he did not hear the deaf man walking behind him.

Paris is a magnificent and charming spectacle, and especially at that day, viewed from the top of the towers of Notre-Dame, in the fresh light of a summer dawn. The day might have been in July. The sky was perfectly serene. Some tardy stars were fading away at various points, and there was a very brilliant one in the east, in the brightest part of the heavens. The sun was about to appear; Paris was beginning to move. A very white and very pure light brought out vividly to the eye all the outlines that its thousands of houses present to the east. The giant shadow of the towers leaped from roof to roof, from one end of the great city to the other. There were several quarters from which were already heard voices and noisy sounds. Here the stroke of a bell, there the stroke of a hammer, beyond, the complicated clatter of a cart in motion.

Already several columns of smoke were being belched forth from the chimneys scattered over the whole surface of roofs, as through the fissures of an immense sulfurous crater. The river, which ruffles its waters against the arches of so many bridges, against the points of so many islands, was wavering with silvery folds. Around the city, outside the ramparts, sight was lost in a great circle of fleecy vapors through which one confusedly distinguished the indefinite line of the plains, and the graceful swell of the heights. All sorts of floating sounds were dispersed over this half-awakened city. Toward the east, the morning breeze chased a few soft white bits of wool torn from the misty fleece of the hills.

In the Parvis, some good women, who had their milk jugs in their hands, were pointing out to each other, with astonishment, the singular dilapidation of the great door of Notre-Dame, and the two solidified streams of lead in the crevices of the stone. This was all that remained of the tempest of the night. The bonfire lighted between the towers by Quasimodo had died out. Tristan had already cleared up the Place, and had the dead thrown into the Seine. Kings like Louis XI are careful to clean the pavement quickly after a massacre.

Outside the balustrade of the tower, directly under the point where the priest had paused, there was one of those fantastically carved stone gutters with which Gothic edifices bristle, and, in a crevice of that gutter, two pretty wallflowers in blossom, shaken out and vivified, as it were, by the breath of air, made frolicsome salutations to each other. Above the towers, on high, far away in the depths of the sky, the cries of little birds were heard.

But the priest was not listening to, was not looking at, anything of all this. He was one of the men for whom there are no mornings, no birds, no flowers. In that immense horizon, which assumed so many aspects about him, his contemplation was concentrated on a single point.

Quasimodo was burning to ask him what he had done with the gypsy; but the archdeacon seemed to be out of the world at that moment. He was evidently in one of those violent moments of life when one would not feel the earth crumble. He remained motionless and silent, with his eyes steadily fixed on a certain point; and there was something so terrible about this silence and immobility that the savage bellringer shuddered before it and dared not come in contact with it. Only, and this was also one way of interrogating the archdeacon, he followed the direction of his vision, and in this way the glance of the unhappy deaf man fell upon the Place de Grève.

Thus he saw what the priest was looking at. The ladder was erected near the permanent gallows. There were some people and many soldiers in the Place. A man was dragging a white thing, from which hung something black, along the pavement. This man halted at the foot of the gallows.

Here something took place which Quasimodo could not see very clearly. It was not because his only eye had not preserved its long range, but there was a group of soldiers which prevented his seeing everything. Moreover, at that moment the sun appeared, and such a flood of light overflowed the horizon that one would have said that all the points in Paris, spires, chimneys, gables, had simultaneously taken fire.

Meanwhile, the man began to mount the ladder. Then Quasimodo saw him again distinctly. He was carrying a woman on his shoulder, a young girl dressed in white; that young girl had a noose about her neck. Quasimodo recognized her.

It was she.

The man reached the top of the ladder. There he arranged the noose. Here the priest, in order to see the better, knelt upon the balustrade.

All at once the man kicked away the ladder abruptly, and Quasimodo, who had not breathed for several moments, beheld the unhappy child dangling at the end of the rope two fathoms above the pavement, with the man squatting on her shoulders. The rope made several gyrations on itself, and Quasimodo beheld horrible convulsions run along the gypsy's body. The priest, on his side, with outstretched neck and eyes starting from his head, contemplated this horrible group of the man and the young girl—the spider and the fly.

At the moment when it was most horrible, the laugh of a demon, a laugh which one can only give vent to when one is no longer human, burst forth on the priest's livid face.

Quasimodo did not hear that laugh, but he saw it.

The bellringer retreated several paces behind the archdeacon, and suddenly hurling himself upon him with fury, with his huge hands he pushed him by the back over into the abyss over which Dom Claude was leaning.

The priest shrieked: "Damnation!" and fell.

The spout, above which he had stood, arrested him in his fall. He clung to it with desperate hands, and, at the moment when he opened his mouth to utter a second cry, he beheld the formidable and avenging face of Quasimodo thrust over the edge of the balustrade above his head.

Then he was silent.

The abyss was there below him. A fall of more than two hundred feet and the pavement.

In this terrible situation, the archdeacon said not a word, uttered not a groan. He merely writhed upon the spout, with incredible efforts to climb up again; but his hands had no hold on the granite, his feet slid along the blackened wall without catching fast. People who have ascended the towers of Notre-Dame know that there is a swell of the stone immediately beneath the balustrade. It was on this retreating angle that miserable archdeacon exhausted himself. He had not to deal with a perpendicular wall, but with one which sloped away beneath him.

Quasimodo had but to stretch out his hand in order to draw him from the gulf; but he did not even look at him. He was looking at the Grève. He was looking at the gallows. He was looking at the gypsy.

The deaf man was leaning, with his elbows on the balustrade, at the spot where the archdeacon had been a moment before, and there, never detaching his gaze from the only object which existed for him in the world at that moment, he remained motionless and mute, like a man struck by lightning, and a long stream of tears flowed in silence from that eye which, up to that time, had never shed but one tear.

Meanwhile, the archdeacon was panting. His bald brow was dripping with perspiration, his nails were bleeding against the stones, his knees were flayed by the wall.

He heard his cassock, which was caught on the spout, crack and rip at every jerk that he gave it. To complete his misfortune, this spout ended in a leaden pipe which bent under the weight of his body. The archdeacon felt this pipe slowly giving way. The miserable man said to himself that, when his hands should be worn out with fatigue, when his cassock should tear asunder, when the lead should give way, he would be obliged to fall, and terror seized upon his very vitals. Now and then he glanced wildly at a sort of narrow shelf formed, ten feet lower down, by projections of the sculpture, and he prayed heaven, from the depths of his distressed soul, that he might be allowed to finish his life, were it to last two centuries, on that space two feet square. Once, he glanced below him into the Place, into the abyss; the head which he raised again had its eyes closed and its hair standing erect.

There was something frightful in the silence of these two men. While the archdeacon agonized in this terrible fashion a few feet below him, Quasimodo wept and gazed at the Grève.

The archdeacon, seeing that all his exertions served only to weaken the fragile support which remained to him, decided to remain quiet. There he hung, embracing the gutter, hardly breathing, no longer stirring, making no longer any other movements than that mechanical convulsion of the stomach, which one experiences in dreams when one fancies himself falling. His fixed eyes were wide open with a stare. He lost ground little by little, nevertheless, his fingers slipped along the spout; he became more and more conscious of the feebleness of his arms and the weight of his body. The curve of the lead which sustained him inclined more and more each instant toward the abyss.

He beheld below him, a frightful thing, the roof of Saint-Jean le Rond, as small as a card folded in two. He gazed at the impressive carvings, one by one, of the tower, suspended like himself over the precipice, but without terror for themselves or pity for him. All was stone around him; before his eyes, gaping monsters; below, quite at the bottom, in the Place, the pavement; above his head, Quasimodo weeping.

In the Parvis there were several groups of curious good people, who were tranquilly seeking to divine who the madman could be who was amusing himself in so strange a manner. The priest heard them saying, for their voices reached him, clear and shrill: "Why, he will break his neck!"

Quasimodo wept.

At last the archdeacon, foaming with rage and despair, understood that all was in vain. Nevertheless, he collected all the strength which remained to him for a final effort. He stiffened himself upon the spout, pushed against the wall with both his knees, clung to a crevice in the stones with his hands, and succeeded in climbing back with one foot, perhaps; but this effort made the leaden beak on which he rested bend abruptly. His cassock burst open at the same time. Then, feeling everything give way beneath him, with nothing but his stiffened and failing hands to support him, the unfortunate man closed his eyes and let go of the spout. He fell.

Quasimodo watched him fall.

A fall from such a height is seldom perpendicular. The archdeacon, launched into space, fell at first head foremost, with outspread hands; then he whirled over and over many times; the wind blew him upon the roof of a house, where the unfortunate man began to break up. Nevertheless, he was not dead when he reached there. The bellringer saw him still endeavor to cling to a gable with his nails; but the surface sloped too much, and he had no more strength. He slid rapidly along the roof like a loosened tile, and dashed upon the pavement. There he no longer moved.

Then Quasimodo raised his eyes to the gypsy, whose body he beheld hanging from the gibbet, quivering far away beneath her white robe with the last shudderings of anguish, then he dropped them on the archdeacon, stretched out at the base of the tower, and no longer retaining the human form, and he said, with a sob which heaved his deep chest—

"Oh! all that I have ever loved!"

Chapter III

THE MARRIAGE OF PHŒBUS

TOWARD EVENING ON THAT DAY, WHEN THE JUDICIARY OFFICERS OF THE BISHOP CAME TO PICK up from the pavement of the Parvis the dislocated corpse of the archdeacon, Quasimodo had disappeared.

A great many rumors were in circulation with regard to this adventure. No one doubted but that the day had come when, in accordance with their compact, Quasimodo, that is to say, the devil, was to carry off Claude Frollo, that is to say, the sorcerer. It was presumed that he had broken the body when taking the soul, like monkeys who break the shell to get at the nut.

This is why the archdeacon was not interred in consecrated earth.

Louis XI died a year later, in the month of August, 1483.

As for Pierre Gringoire, he succeeded in saving the goat, and he won success in tragedy. It appears that, after having tasted astrology, philosophy, architecture, hermetics—all vanities, he returned to tragedy, vainest pursuit of all. This is what he called "coming to a tragic end." This is what is to be read, on the subject of his dramatic triumphs, in 1483, in the accounts of the *Ordinary*: "To Jehan Marchand and Pierre Gringoire, carpenter and composer, who have made and composed the mystery made at the Châtelet of Paris, at the entry of Monsieur the Legate, and have ordered the personages, clothed and dressed the same, as in the said mystery was required; and likewise, for having made the scaffoldings thereto necessary; and for this deed—one hundred livres."

Phœbus de Châteaupers also came to a tragic end. He married.

Chapter IV

THE MARRIAGE OF QUASIMODO

WE HAVE JUST SAID THAT QUASIMODO DISAPPEARED FROM NOTRE-DAME ON THE DAY OF THE gypsy's and of the archdeacon's death. He was not seen again, in fact; no one knew what had become of him.

During the night which followed the execution of la Esmeralda, the night men had detached her body from the gibbet, and had carried it, according to custom, to the cellar of Montfaucon.

Montfaucon was, as Sauval says, "the most ancient and the most superb gibbet in the kingdom." Between the faubourgs of the Temple and Saint Martin, about a hundred and sixty toises from the walls of Paris, a few bow shots from La Courtille, there was to be seen on the crest of a gentle, almost imperceptible eminence, but sufficiently elevated to be seen for several leagues round about, an edifice of strange form, bearing considerable resemblance to a Celtic cromlech, and where also human sacrifices were offered.

Let the reader picture to himself, crowning a limestone hillock, an oblong mass of masonry fifteen feet in height, thirty wide, forty long, with a gate, an external railing and a platform; on this platform sixteen enormous pillars of rough hewn stone, thirty feet in height, arranged in a colonnade round three of the four sides of the mass which support them, bound together at their summits by heavy beams, whence hung chains at intervals; on all these chains, skeletons; in the vicinity, on the plain, a stone cross and two gibbets of secondary importance, which seemed to have sprung up as shoots around the central gallows; above all this, in the sky, a perpetual flock of crows; that was Montfaucon.

At the end of the fifteenth century, the formidable gibbet which dated from 1328, was already very much dilapidated; the beams were wormeaten, the chains rusted, the pillars green with mold; the layers of hewn stone were all cracked at their joints, and grass was growing on that platform which no feet touched. The monument made a horrible profile against the sky; especially at night when there was a little moonlight on those white skulls, or when the breeze of evening brushed the chains and the skeletons, and swayed all these in the darkness. The presence of this gibbet sufficed to render gloomy all the surrounding places.

The mass of masonry which served as foundation to the odious edifice was hollow. A huge cellar had been constructed there, closed by an old iron grating, which was out of order, into which were cast not only the human remains, which were taken from the chains of Montfaucon, but also the bodies of all the unfortunates executed on the other permanent gibbets of Paris. To that deep charnel-house, where so many human remains and so many crimes have rotted in company, many great ones of this world, many innocent people, have contributed their bones, from Enguerrand de Marigni, the first victim, and a just man, to Admiral de Coligni, who was its last, and who was also a just man.

As for the mysterious disappearance of Quasimodo, this is all that we have been able to discover.

About eighteen months or two years after the events which terminate this story, when search was made in that cavern for the body of Olivier le Daim, who had been hanged two days previously, and to whom Charles VIII had granted the favor of being buried in Saint Laurent, in better company, they found among all those hideous carcasses two skeletons, one of which held the other in its embrace. One of these skeletons, which was that of a woman, still had a few strips of a garment which had once been white, and around her neck was to be seen a string of adrézarach beads with a little silk bag ornamented with green glass, which was open and empty. These objects were of so little value that the executioner had probably not cared for them. The other, which held this one in a close embrace, was the skeleton of a man. It was noticed that his spinal column was crooked, his head seated on his shoulder-blades, and that one leg was shorter than the other. Moreover, there was no fracture of the vertebrae at the nape of the neck, and it was evident that he had not been hanged. Hence, the man to whom it had belonged had come thither and had died there. When they tried to detach the skeleton which he held in his embrace, he fell to dust.

LES MISÉRABLES

CONTENTS

Volume III—Marius

PREFACE

SO LONG AS THERE SHALL EXIST, BY VIRTUE OF LAW AND CUSTOM, DECREES OF DAMNATION PRO-
nounced by society, artificially creating hells amid the civilization of earth, and adding the element of human fate to divine destiny; so long as the three great problems of the century—the
degradation of man through pauperism, the corruption of woman through hunger, the crippling of
children through lack of light—are unsolved; so long as social asphyxia is possible in any part of
the world—in other words, and with a still wider significance, so long as ignorance and poverty
exist on earth, books of the nature of Les Miserables cannot fail to be of use.

HAUTEVILLE HOUSE, 1862

Volume I

Fantine

BOOK FIRST

A JUST MAN

Chapter I

M. MYRIEL

IN 1815, M. CHARLES-FRANÇOIS-BIENVENU MYRIEL WAS BISHOP OF D——. HE WAS AN OLD MAN OF about seventy-five years of age; he had occupied the see of D—— since 1806.

Although this detail has no connection whatever with the real substance of what we are about to relate, it will not be superfluous, if merely for the sake of exactness in all points, to mention here the various rumors and remarks which had been in circulation about him from the very moment when he arrived in the diocese. True or false, that which is said of men often occupies as important a place in their lives, and above all, in their destinies, as that which they do. M. Myriel was the son of a councilor of the Parliament of Aix; hence he belonged to the nobility of the bar. It was said that his father, destining him to be the heir of his own post, had married him at a very early age, eighteen or twenty, in accordance with a custom which is rather widely prevalent in parliamentary families. In spite of this marriage, however, it was said that Charles Myriel created a great deal of talk. He was well formed, though rather short in stature, elegant, graceful, intelligent; the whole of the first portion of his life had been devoted to the world and to gallantry.

The Revolution came; events succeeded each other with precipitation; the parliamentary families, decimated, pursued, hunted down, were dispersed. M. Charles Myriel emigrated to Italy at the very beginning of the Revolution. There his wife died of a malady of the chest, from which she had long suffered. He had no children. What took place next in the fate of M. Myriel? The ruin of the French society of the olden days, the fall of his own family, the tragic spectacles of '93, which were, perhaps, even more alarming to the emigrants who viewed them from a distance, with the magnifying powers of terror—did these cause the ideas of renunciation and solitude to germinate in him? Was he, in the midst of these distractions, these affections which absorbed his life, suddenly smitten with one of those mysterious and terrible blows which sometimes overwhelm, by striking to his heart, a man whom public catastrophes would not shake, by striking at his existence and his fortune? No one could have told: all that was known was, that when he returned from Italy he was a priest.

In 1804, M. Myriel was the Curé of B—— [Brignolles] He was already advanced in years, and lived in a very retired manner.

About the epoch of the coronation, some petty affair connected with his curacy—just what, is not precisely known—took him to Paris. Among other powerful persons to whom he went to solicit aid for his parishioners was M. le Cardinal Fesch. One day, when the Emperor had come to visit his uncle, the worthy Curé, who was waiting in the anteroom, found himself present when his Majesty passed. Napoleon, on finding himself observed with a certain curiosity by this old man, turned round and said abruptly:

"Who is this good man who is staring at me?"

"Sire," said M. Myriel, "you are looking at a good man, and I at a great man. Each of us can profit by it."

That very evening, the Emperor asked the Cardinal the name of the Curé, and some time afterwards M. Myriel was utterly astonished to learn that he had been appointed Bishop of D——.

What truth was there, after all, in the stories which were invented as to the early portion of M. Myriel's life? No one knew. Very few families had been acquainted with the Myriel family before the Revolution.

M. Myriel had to undergo the fate of every newcomer in a little town, where there are many mouths which talk, and very few heads which think. He was obliged to undergo it although he was a bishop, and because he was a bishop. But after all, the rumors with which his name was connected were rumors only—noise, sayings, words; less than words—*palabres,* as the energetic language of the South expresses it.

However that may be, after nine years of episcopal power and of residence in D——, all the stories and subjects of conversation which engross petty towns and petty people at the outset had fallen into profound oblivion. No one would have dared to mention them; no one would have dared to recall them.

M. Myriel had arrived at D—— accompanied by an elderly spinster, Mademoiselle Baptistine, who was his sister, and ten years his junior.

Their only domestic was a female servant of the same age as Mademoiselle Baptistine, and named Madame Magloire, who, after having been *the servant of M. le Curé,* now assumed the double title of maid to Mademoiselle and housekeeper to Monseigneur.

Mademoiselle Baptistine was a long, pale, thin, gentle creature; she realized the ideal expressed by the word "respectable"; for it seems that a woman must needs be a mother in order to be venerable. She had never been pretty; her whole life, which had been nothing but a succession of holy deeds, had finally conferred upon her a sort of pallor and transparency; and as she advanced in years she had acquired what may be called the beauty of goodness. What had been leanness in her youth had become transparency in her maturity; and this diaphaneity allowed the angel to be seen. She was a soul rather than a virgin. Her person seemed made of a shadow; there was hardly sufficient body to provide for sex; a little matter enclosing a light; large eyes forever drooping;—a mere pretext for a soul's remaining on the earth.

Madame Magloire was a little, fat, white old woman, corpulent and bustling; always out of breath—in the first place, because of her activity, and in the next, because of her asthma.

On his arrival, M. Myriel was installed in the episcopal palace with the honors required by the Imperial decrees, which class a bishop immediately after a major-general. The mayor and the president paid the first call on him, and he, in turn, paid the first call on the general and the prefect.

The installation over, the town waited to see its bishop at work.

Chapter II

M. MYRIEL BECOMES M. WELCOME

THE EPISCOPAL PALACE OF D—— ADJOINS THE HOSPITAL.

The episcopal palace was a huge and beautiful house, built of stone at the beginning of the last century by M. Henri Puget, Doctor of Theology of the Faculty of Paris, Abbé of Simore, who had been Bishop of D—— in 1712. This palace was a genuine seignorial residence. Everything about it had a grand air—the apartments of the Bishop, the drawing-rooms, the chambers, the principal courtyard, which was very large, with walks encircling it under arcades in the old Florentine fashion, and gardens planted with magnificent trees. In the dining-room, a long and superb gallery which was situated on the ground floor and opened on the gardens, M. Henri Puget had entertained in state, on July 29, 1714, My Lords Charles Brûlart de Genlis, archbishop; Prince d'Embrun; Antoine de Mesgrigny, the capuchin, Bishop of Grasse; Philippe de Vendôme, Grand Prior of France, Abbé of Saint Honoré de Lérins; François de Berton de Crillon, bishop, Baron de Vence; César de Sabran de Forcalquier, bishop, Seignor of Glandève; and Jean Soanen, Priest of the Oratory, preacher in ordinary to the king, bishop, Seignor of Senez. The portraits of these seven reverend personages decorated this apartment; and this memorable date, the 29th of July, 1714, was there engraved in letters of gold on a table of white marble.

The hospital was a low and narrow building of a single story, with a small garden.

Three days after his arrival, the Bishop visited the hospital. The visit ended, he had the director requested to be so good as to come to his house.

"Monsieur the director of the hospital," said he to him, "how many sick people have you at the present moment?"

"Twenty-six, Monseigneur."

"That was the number which I counted," said the Bishop.

"The beds," pursued the director, "are very much crowded against each other."

"That is what I observed."

"The halls are nothing but rooms, and it is with difficulty that the air can be changed in them."

"So it seems to me."

"And then, when there is a ray of sun, the garden is very small for the convalescents."

"That was what I said to myself."

"In case of epidemics—we have had the typhus fever this year; we had the sweating sickness two years ago, and a hundred patients at times—we know not what to do."

"That is the thought which occurred to me."

"What would you have, Monseigneur?" said the director. "One must resign one's self."

This conversation took place in the gallery dining-room on the ground floor.

The Bishop remained silent for a moment; then he turned abruptly to the director of the hospital.

"Monsieur," said he, "how many beds do you think this hall alone would hold?"

"Monseigneur's dining-room?" exclaimed the stupefied director.

The Bishop cast a glance round the apartment, and seemed to be taking measures and calculations with his eyes.

"It would hold full twenty beds," said he, as though speaking to himself. Then, raising his voice:

"Hold, Monsieur the director of the hospital, I will tell you something. There is evidently a mistake here. There are thirty-six of you, in five or six small rooms. There are three of us here, and we have room for sixty. There is some mistake, I tell you; you have my house, and I have yours. Give me back my house; you are at home here."

On the following day the thirty-six patients were installed in the Bishop's palace, and the Bishop was settled in the hospital.

M. Myriel had no property, his family having been ruined by the Revolution. His sister was in receipt of a yearly income of five hundred francs, which sufficed for her personal wants at the vicarage. M. Myriel received from the State, in his quality of bishop, a salary of fifteen thousand francs. On the very day when he took up his abode in the hospital, M. Myriel settled on the disposition of this sum once for all, in the following manner. We transcribe here a note made by his own hand:

NOTE ON THE REGULATION OF MY HOUSEHOLD EXPENSES.

For the little seminary	1,500	livres
Society of the mission	100	"
For the Lazarists of Montdidier.	100	"
Seminary for foreign missions in Paris	200	"
Congregation of the Holy Spirit.	150	"
Religious establishments of the Holy Land	100	"
Charitable maternity societies	300	"
Extra, for that of Arles	50	"
Work for the amelioration of prisons	400	"
Work for the relief and delivery of prisoners	500	"
To liberate fathers of families incarcerated for debt	1,000	"
Addition to the salary of the poor teachers of the diocese	2,000	"
Public granary of the Hautes-Alpes	100	"
Congregation of the ladies of D——, of Manosque, and of		
Sisteron, for the gratuitous instruction of poor girls	1,500	"
For the poor	6,000	"
My personal expenses	1,000	"
Total	15,000	"

M. Myriel made no change in this arrangement during the entire period that he occupied the see of D——. As has been seen, he called it *regulating his household expenses.*

This arrangement was accepted with absolute submission by Mademoiselle Baptistine. This holy woman regarded Monseigneur of D—— as at one and the same time her brother and her bishop, her friend according to the flesh and her superior according to the Church. She simply loved and venerated him. When he spoke, she bowed; when he acted, she yielded her adherence. Their only servant, Madame Magloire, grumbled a little. It will be observed that Monsieur the Bishop had reserved for himself only one thousand livres, which, added to the pension of Mademoiselle Baptistine, made fifteen hundred francs a year. On these fifteen hundred francs these two old women and the old man subsisted.

And when a village curate came to D——, the Bishop still found means to entertain him, thanks to the severe economy of Madame Magloire, and to the intelligent administration of Mademoiselle Baptistine.

One day, after he had been in D—— about three months, the Bishop said:

"And still I am quite cramped with it all!"

"I should think so!" exclaimed Madame Magloire. "Monseigneur has not even claimed the allowance which the department owes him for the expense of his carriage in town, and for his journeys about the diocese. It was customary for bishops in former days."

"Hold!" cried the Bishop, "you are quite right, Madame Magloire."

And he made his demand.

Some time afterwards the General Council took this demand under consideration, and voted him an annual sum of three thousand francs, under this heading: *Allowance to M. the Bishop for expenses of carriage, expenses of posting, and expenses of pastoral visits.*

This provoked a great outcry among the local burgesses; and a senator of the Empire, a former member of the Council of the Five Hundred which favored the 18 Brumaire, and who was provided with a magnificent senatorial office in the vicinity of the town of D——, wrote to M. Bigot de Préameneu, the minister of public worship, a very angry and confidential note on the subject, from which we extract these authentic lines:

"Expenses of carriage? What can be done with it in a town of less than four thousand inhabitants? Expenses of journeys? What is the use of these trips, in the first place? Next, how can the posting be accomplished in these mountainous parts? There are no roads. No one travels otherwise than on horseback. Even the bridge between Durance and Château-Arnoux can barely support ox-teams. These priests are all thus, greedy and avaricious. This man played the good priest when he first came. Now he does like the rest; he must have a carriage and a posting-chaise, he must have luxuries, like the bishops of the olden days. Oh, all this priesthood! Things will not go well, M. le Comte, until the Emperor has freed us from these black-capped rascals. Down with the Pope! [Matters were getting embroiled with Rome.] For my part, I am for Cæsar alone." Etc., etc.

On the other hand, this affair afforded great delight to Madame Magloire. "Good," said she to Mademoiselle Baptistine; "Monseigneur began with other people, but he has had to wind up with himself, after all. He has regulated all his charities. Now here are three thousand francs for us! At last!"

That same evening the Bishop wrote out and handed to his sister a memorandum conceived in the following terms:

EXPENSES OF CARRIAGE AND CIRCUIT.

For furnishing meat soup to the patients in the hospital	1,500	livres
For the maternity charitable society of Aix	250	"
For the maternity charitable society of Draguignan	250	"
For foundlings	500	"
For orphans	500	"
Total	3,000	"

Such was M. Myriel's budget.

As for the chance episcopal perquisites, the fees for marriage bans, dispensations, private baptisms, sermons, benedictions, of churches or chapels, marriages, etc., the Bishop levied them on the wealthy with all the more asperity, since he bestowed them on the needy.

After a time, offerings of money flowed in. Those who had and those who lacked knocked at M. Myriel's door—the latter in search of the alms which the former came to deposit. In less than a year the Bishop had become the treasurer of all benevolence and the cashier of all those in distress. Considerable sums of money passed through his hands; but nothing could induce him to make any change whatever in his mode of life, or add anything superfluous to his bare necessities.

Far from it. As there is always more wretchedness below than there is brotherhood above, all was given away, so to speak, before it was received. It was like water on dry soil; no matter how much money he received, he never had any. Then he stripped himself.

The usage being that bishops shall announce their baptismal names at the head of their charges and their pastoral letters, the poor people of the countryside had selected, with a sort of affectionate instinct, among the names and prenomens of their bishop, that which had a meaning for them; and they never called him anything except Monseigneur Bienvenu [Welcome]. We will follow their example, and will also call him thus when we have occasion to name him. Moreover, this appellation pleased him.

"I like that name," said he. "Bienvenu makes up for the Monseigneur."

We do not claim that the portrait herewith presented is probable; we confine ourselves to stating that it resembles the original.

Chapter III

A Hard Bishopric for a Good Bishop

THE BISHOP DID NOT OMIT HIS PASTORAL VISITS BECAUSE HE HAD CONVERTED HIS CARRIAGE INTO alms. The diocese of D—— is a fatiguing one. There are very few plains and a great many mountains; hardly any roads, as we have just seen; thirty-two curacies, forty-one vicarships, and two hundred and eighty-five auxiliary chapels. To visit all these is quite a task. The Bishop managed to do it. He went on foot when it was in the neighborhood, in a tilted spring-cart when it was on the plain, and on a donkey in the mountains. The two old women accompanied him. When the trip was too hard for them, he went alone.

One day he arrived at Senez, which is an ancient episcopal city. He was mounted on an ass. His purse, which was very dry at that moment, did not permit him any other equipage. The mayor of the town came to receive him at the gate of the town, and watched him dismount from his ass, with scandalized eyes. Some of the citizens were laughing around him. "Monsieur the Mayor," said the Bishop, "and Messieurs Citizens, I perceive that I shock you. You think it very arrogant in a poor priest to ride an animal which was used by Jesus Christ. I have done so from necessity, I assure you, and not from vanity."

In the course of these trips he was kind and indulgent, and talked rather than preached. He never went far in search of his arguments and his examples. He quoted to the inhabitants of one district the example of a neighboring district. In the cantons where they were harsh to the poor, he said: "Look at the people of Briançon! They have conferred on the poor, on widows and orphans, the right to have their meadows mown three days in advance of everyone else. They rebuild their houses for them gratuitously when they are ruined. Therefore it is a country which is blessed by God. For a whole century, there has not been a single murderer among them."

In villages which were greedy for profit and harvest, he said: "Look at the people of Embrun! If, at the harvest season, the father of a family has his son away on service in the army, and his daughters at service in the town, and if he is ill and incapacitated, the curé recommends him to the prayers of the congregation; and on Sunday, after the mass, all the inhabitants of the village—men, women, and children—go to the poor man's field and do his harvesting for him, and carry his straw and his grain to his granary." To families divided by questions of money and inheritance he said: "Look at the mountaineers of Devolny, a country so wild that the nightingale is not heard there once in fifty years. Well, when the father of a family dies, the boys go off to seek their fortunes, leaving the property to the girls, so that they may find husbands." To the cantons which had a taste for lawsuits, and where the farmers ruined themselves in stamped paper, he said: "Look at those good peasants in the valley of Queyras! There are three thousand souls of them. Mon Dieu! it is like a little republic. Neither judge nor bailiff is known there. The mayor does everything. He allots the imposts, taxes each person conscientiously, judges quarrels for nothing, divides inheritances without charge, pronounces sentences gratuitously; and he is obeyed, because he is a just man among simple men." To villages where he found no schoolmaster, he quoted once more the people of Queyras: "Do you know how they manage?" he said. "Since a little country of a dozen or fifteen hearths cannot always support a teacher, they have schoolmasters who are paid by the whole valley, who make the round of the villages, spending a week in this one, ten days in that, and instruct them. These teachers go to the fairs. I have seen them there. They are to be recognized by the quill pens which they wear in the cord of their hat. Those who teach reading only have one pen; those who teach reading and reckoning have two pens; those who teach reading, reckoning, and Latin have three pens. But what a disgrace to be ignorant! Do like the people of Queyras!"

Thus he discoursed gravely and paternally; in default of examples, he invented parables, going directly to the point, with few phrases and many images, which characteristic formed the real eloquence of Jesus Christ. And being convinced himself, he was persuasive.

Chapter IV

Works Corresponding to Words

HIS CONVERSATION WAS GAY AND AFFABLE. HE PUT HIMSELF ON a LEVEL WITH THE TWO OLD women who had passed their lives beside him. When he laughed, it was the laugh of a schoolboy. Madame Magloire liked to call him Your Grace [*Votre Grandeur*]. One day he rose from his arm-chair, and went to his library in search of a book. This book was on one of the upper shelves. As the bishop was rather short of stature, he could not reach it. "Madame Magloire," said he, "fetch me a chair. My greatness [*grandeur*] does not reach as far as that shelf."

One of his distant relatives, Madame la Comtesse de Lô, rarely allowed an opportunity to escape of enumerating, in his presence, what she designated as "the expectations" of her three sons. She had numerous relatives, who were very old and near to death, and of whom her sons were the natural heirs. The youngest of the three was to receive from a grand-aunt a good hundred thousand livres of income; the second was the heir by entail to the title of the Duke, his uncle; the eldest was to succeed to the peerage of his grandfather. The Bishop was accustomed to listen in silence to these innocent and pardonable maternal boasts. On one occasion, however, he appeared to be more thoughtful than usual, while Madame de Lô was relating once again the details of all these inheritances and all these "expectations." She interrupted herself impatiently: "Mon Dieu, cousin! What are you thinking about?" "I am thinking," replied the Bishop, "of a singular remark, which is to be found, I believe, in St. Augustine—'Place your hopes in the man from whom you do not inherit.' "

At another time, on receiving a notification of the decease of a gentleman of the countryside, wherein not only the dignities of the dead man, but also the feudal and noble qualifications of all his relatives, spread over an entire page: "What a stout back Death has!" he exclaimed. "What a strange burden of titles is cheerfully imposed on him, and how much wit must men have, in order thus to press the tomb into the service of vanity!"

He was gifted, on occasion, with a gentle raillery, which almost always concealed a serious meaning. In the course of one Lent, a youthful vicar came to D——, and preached in the cathedral. He was tolerably eloquent. The subject of his sermon was charity. He urged the rich to give to the poor, in order to avoid hell, which he depicted in the most frightful manner of which he was capable, and to win paradise, which he represented as charming and desirable. Among the audience there was a wealthy retired merchant, who was somewhat of a usurer, named M. Géborand, who had amassed two millions in the manufacture of coarse cloth, serges, and woolen galloons. Never in his whole life had M. Géborand bestowed alms on any poor wretch. After the delivery of that sermon, it was observed that he gave a sou every Sunday to the poor old beggar-women at the door of the cathedral. There were six of them to share it. One day the Bishop caught sight of him in the act of bestowing this charity, and said to his sister, with a smile, "There is M. Géborand purchasing paradise for a sou."

When it was a question of charity, he was not to be rebuffed even by a refusal, and on such occasions he gave utterance to remarks which induced reflection. Once he was begging for the poor in a drawing-room of the town; there was present the Marquis de Champtercier, a wealthy and avaricious old man, who contrived to be, at one and the same time, an ultra-royalist and an ultra-Voltairian. This variety of man has actually existed. When the Bishop came to him, he touched his arm, *"You must give me something, M. le Marquis."* The Marquis turned round and answered dryly, *"I have poor people of my own, Monseigneur."* *"Give them to me,"* replied the Bishop.

One day he preached the following sermon in the cathedral:

"My very dear brethren, my good friends, there are thirteen hundred and twenty thousand peasants' dwellings in France which have but three openings; eighteen hundred and seventeen thousand hovels which have but two openings, the door and one window; and three hundred and forty-six thousand cabins besides which have but one opening, the door. And this arises from a thing which is called the tax on doors and windows. Just put poor families, old women and little children, in those buildings, and behold the fevers and maladies which result! Alas! God gives air to men; the law sells it to them. I do not blame the law, but I bless God. In the department of the Isère, in the Var, in the two departments of the Alpes, the Hautes, and the Basses, the peasants have not even wheelbarrows; they transport their manure on the backs of men; they have no candles, and they burn resinous sticks, and bits of rope dipped in pitch. That is the state of affairs throughout the whole of the hilly country of Dauphiné. They make bread for six months at one time; they bake it with dried cow-dung. In the winter they break this bread up with an ax, and they soak it for twenty-four hours, in order to render it eatable. My brethren, have pity! behold the suffering on all sides of you!"

Born a Provençal, he easily familiarized himself with the dialect of the south. He said, *"En bé! moussu, sés sagé?"* as in lower Languedoc; *"Onté anaras passa?"* as in the Basses-Alpes; *"Puerte un bouen moutu embe un bouen fromage grase,"* as in upper Dauphiné. This pleased the people extremely, and contributed not a little to win him access to all spirits. He was perfectly at home in the thatched cottage and in the mountains. He understood how to say the grandest things in the most vulgar of idioms. As he spoke all tongues, he entered into all hearts.

Moreover, he was the same toward people of the world and toward the lower classes. He condemned nothing in haste and without taking circumstances into account. He said, "Examine the road over which the fault has passed."

Being, as he described himself with a smile, an *ex-sinner,* he had none of the asperities of austerity, and he professed, with a good deal of distinctness, and without the frown of the ferociously virtuous, a doctrine which may be summed up as follows:

"Man has upon him his flesh, which is at once his burden and his temptation. He drags it with him and yields to it. He must watch it, cheek it, repress it, and obey it only at the last extremity. There may be some fault even in this obedience; but the fault thus committed is venial; it is a fall, but a fall on the knees which may terminate in prayer.

"To be a saint is the exception; to be an upright man is the rule. Err, fall, sin if you will, but be upright.

"The least possible sin is the law of man. No sin at all is the dream of the angel. All which is terrestrial is subject to sin. Sin is a gravitation."

When he saw everyone exclaiming very loudly, and growing angry very quickly, "Oh! oh!" he said, with a smile; "to all appearance, this is a great crime which all the world commits. These are hypocrisies which have taken fright, and are in haste to make protest and to put themselves under shelter."

He was indulgent toward women and poor people, on whom the burden of human society rest. He said, "The faults of women, of children, of the feeble, the indigent, and the ignorant, are the fault of the husbands, the fathers, the masters, the strong, the rich, and the wise."

He said, moreover, "Teach those who are ignorant as many things as possible; society is culpable, in that it does not afford instruction gratis; it is responsible for the night which it produces. This soul is full of shadow; sin is therein committed. The guilty one is not the person who has committed the sin, but the person who has created the shadow."

It will be perceived that he had a peculiar manner of his own of judging things: I suspect that he obtained it from the Gospel.

One day he heard a criminal case, which was in preparation and on the point of trial, discussed in a drawing-room. A wretched man, being at the end of his resources, had coined counterfeit money, out of love for a woman, and for the child which he had had by her. Counterfeiting was still punishable with death at that epoch. The woman had been arrested in the act of passing the first false piece made by the man. She was held, but there were no proofs except against her. She alone could accuse her lover, and destroy him by her confession. She denied; they insisted. She persisted in her denial. Thereupon an idea occurred to the attorney for the crown. He invented an infidelity on the part of the lover, and succeeded, by means of fragments of letters cunningly presented, in persuading the unfortunate woman that she had a rival, and that the man was deceiving her. Thereupon, exasperated by jealousy, she denounced her lover, confessed all, proved all.

The man was ruined. He was shortly to be tried at Aix with his accomplice. They were relating the matter, and each one was expressing enthusiasm over the cleverness of the magistrate. By bringing jealousy into play, he had caused the truth to burst forth in wrath, he had educed the justice of revenge. The Bishop listened to all this in silence. When they had finished, he inquired—

"Where are this man and woman to be tried?"

"At the Court of Assizes."

He went on, "And where will the advocate of the crown be tried?"

A tragic event occurred at D——. A man was condemned to death for murder. He was a wretched fellow, not exactly educated, not exactly ignorant, who had been a mountebank at fairs, and a writer for the public. The town took a great interest in the trial. On the eve of the day fixed for the execution of the condemned man, the chaplain of the prison fell ill. A priest was needed to attend the criminal in his last moments. They sent for the curé. It seems that he refused to come, saying, "That is no affair of mine. I have nothing to do with that unpleasant task, and with that mountebank: I, too, am ill; and besides, it is not my place." This reply was reported to the Bishop, who said, *"Monsieur le Curé is right: it is not his place; it is mine."*

He went instantly to the prison, descended to the cell of the "mountebank," called him by name, took him by the hand, and spoke to him. He passed the entire day with him, forgetful of food and sleep, praying to God for the soul of the condemned man, and praying the condemned man for his own. He told him the best truths, which are also the most simple. He was father, brother, friend; he was bishop only to bless. He taught him everything, encouraged and consoled him. The man was on the point of dying in despair. Death was an abyss to him. As he stood trembling on its mournful brink, he recoiled with horror. He was not sufficiently ignorant to be absolutely indifferent. His condemnation, which had been a profound shock, had, in a manner, broken through, here and there, that wall which separates us from the mystery of things, and which we call life. He gazed incessantly beyond this world through these fatal breaches, and beheld only darkness. The Bishop made him see light.

On the following day, when they came to fetch the unhappy wretch, the Bishop was still there. He followed him, and exhibited himself to the eyes of the crowd in his purple camail and with his episcopal cross upon his neck, side by side with the criminal bound with cords.

He mounted the tumbril with him, he mounted the scaffold with him. The sufferer, who had been so gloomy and cast down on the preceding day, was radiant. He felt that his soul was reconciled, and he hoped in God. The Bishop embraced him, and at the moment when the knife was about to fall, he said to him: "God raises from the dead him whom man slays; he whom his brothers have rejected finds his Father once more. Pray, believe, enter into life: the Father is there."

When he descended from the scaffold, there was something in his look which made the people draw aside to let him pass. They did not know which was most worthy of admiration, his pallor or his serenity. On his return to the humble dwelling, which he designated, with a smile, as *his palace*, he said to his sister, *"I have just officiated pontifically."*

Since the most sublime things are often those which are the least understood, there were people in the town who said, when commenting on this conduct of the Bishop, *"It is affectation."*

This, however, was a remark which was confined to the drawing-rooms. The populace, which perceives no jest in holy deeds, was touched, and admired him.

As for the Bishop, it was a shock to him to have beheld the guillotine, and it was a long time before he recovered from it.

In fact, when the scaffold is there, all erected and prepared, it has something about it which produces hallucination. One may feel a certain indifference to the death penalty, one may refrain from pronouncing upon it, from saying yes or no, so long as one has not seen a guillotine with one's own eyes: but if one encounters one of them, the shock is violent; one is forced to decide, and to take part for or against. Some admire it, like de Maistre; others execrate it, like Beccaria. The guillotine is the concretion of the law; it is called *vindicte*; it is not neutral, and it does not permit you to remain neutral. He who sees it shivers with the most mysterious of shivers. All social problems erect their interrogation point around this chopping-knife. The scaffold is a vision. The scaffold is not a piece of carpentry; the scaffold is not a machine; the scaffold is not an inert bit of mechanism constructed of wood, iron, and cords.

It seems as though it were a being, possessed of I know not what somber initiative; one would say that this piece of carpenter's work saw, that this machine heard, that this mechanism understood, that this wood, this iron, and these cords were possessed of will. In the frightful meditation into which its presence casts the soul the scaffold appears in terrible guise, and as though taking part in what is going on. The scaffold is the accomplice of the executioner; it devours, it eats flesh, it drinks blood; the scaffold is a sort of monster fabricated by the judge and the carpenter, a specter which seems to live with a horrible vitality composed of all the death which it has inflicted.

Therefore, the impression was terrible and profound; on the day following the execution, and on many succeeding days, the Bishop appeared to be crushed. The almost violent serenity of the funereal moment had disappeared; the phantom of social justice tormented him. He, who generally returned from all his deeds with a radiant satisfaction, seemed to be reproaching himself. At times he talked to himself, and stammered lugubrious monologues in a low voice. This is one which his sister overheard one evening and preserved: "I did not think that it was so monstrous. It is wrong to become absorbed in the divine law to such a degree as not to perceive human law. Death belongs to God alone. By what right do men touch that unknown thing?"

In course of time these impressions weakened and probably vanished. Nevertheless, it was observed that the Bishop thenceforth avoided passing the place of execution.

M. Myriel could be summoned at any hour to the bedside of the sick and dying. He did not ignore the fact that therein lay his greatest duty and his greatest labor. Widowed and orphaned families had no need to summon him; he came of his own accord. He understood how to sit down and hold his peace for long hours beside the man who had lost the wife of his love, of the mother who had lost her child. As he knew the moment for silence, he knew also the moment for speech. Oh, admirable consoler! He sought not to efface sorrow by forgetfulness, but to magnify and dignify it by hope. He said:

"Have a care of the manner in which you turn toward the dead. Think not of that which perishes. Gaze steadily. You will perceive the living light of your well-beloved dead in the depths of heaven." He knew that faith is wholesome. He sought to counsel and calm the despairing man, by pointing out to him the resigned man, and to transform the grief which gazes upon a grave by showing him the grief which fixes its gaze upon a star.

Chapter V

MONSEIGNEUR BIENVENU MADE HIS CASSOCKS LAST TOO LONG

THE PRIVATE LIFE OF M. MYRIEL WAS FILLED WITH THE SAME THOUGHTS AS HIS PUBLIC LIFE. THE voluntary poverty in which the Bishop of D—— lived, would have been a solemn and charming sight for anyone who could have viewed it close at hand.

Like all old men, and like the majority of thinkers, he slept little. This brief slumber was profound. In the morning he meditated for an hour, then he said his mass, either at the cathedral or in his own house. His mass said, he broke his fast on rye bread dipped in the milk of his own cows. Then he set to work.

A Bishop is a very busy man: he must every day receive the secretary of the bishopric, who is generally a canon, and nearly every day his vicars-general. He has congregations to reprove, privileges to grant, a whole ecclesiastical library to examine—prayer-books, diocesan catechisms, books of hours, etc.—charges to write, sermons to authorize, curés and mayors to reconcile, a clerical correspondence, an administrative correspondence; on one side the State, on the other the Holy See; and a thousand matters of business.

What time was left to him, after these thousand details of business, and his offices and his breviary, he bestowed first on the necessitous, the sick, and the afflicted; the time which was left to him from the afflicted, the sick, and the necessitous, he devoted to work. Sometimes he dug in his garden; again, he read or wrote. He had but one word for both these kinds of toil; he called them *gardening*. "The mind is a garden," said he.

Towards midday, when the weather was fine, he went forth and took a stroll in the country or in town, often entering lowly dwellings. He was seen walking alone, buried in his own thoughts, his eyes cast down, supporting himself on his long cane, clad in his wadded purple garment of silk, which was very warm, wearing purple stockings inside his coarse shoes, and surmounted by a flat hat which allowed three golden tassels of large bullion to droop from its three points.

It was a perfect festival wherever he appeared. One would have said that his presence had something warming and luminous about it. The children and the old people came out to the doorsteps for the Bishop as for the sun. He bestowed his blessing, and they blessed him. They pointed out his house to anyone who was in need of anything.

Here and there he halted, accosted the little boys and girls, and smiled upon the mothers. He visited the poor so long as he had any money; when he no longer had any, he visited the rich.

As he made his cassocks last a long while, and did not wish to have it noticed, he never went out in the town without his wadded purple cloak. This inconvenienced him somewhat in summer.

On his return, he dined. The dinner resembled his breakfast.

At half-past eight in the evening he supped with his sister, Madame Magloire standing behind them and serving them at table. Nothing could be more frugal than this repast. If, however, the Bishop had one of his curés to supper, Madame Magloire took advantage of the opportunity to serve Monseigneur with some excellent fish from the lake, or with some fine game from the mountains. Every curé furnished the pretext for a good meal: the Bishop did not interfere. With that exception, his ordinary diet consisted only of vegetables boiled in water, and oil soup. Thus it was said in the town, *When the Bishop does not indulge in the cheer of a curé, he indulges in the cheer of a trappist.*

After supper he conversed for half an hour with Mademoiselle Baptistine and Madame Magloire; then he retired to his own room and set to writing, sometimes on loose sheets, and again on the margin of some folio. He was a man of letters and rather learned. He left behind him five or six very curious manuscripts; among others, a dissertation on this verse in Genesis, *In the beginning, the spirit of God floated upon the waters.* With this verse he compares three texts: the Arabic verse which says, *The winds of God blew;* Flavius Josephus, who says, *A wind from above was precipitated upon the earth;* and finally, the Chaldaic paraphrase of Onkelos, which renders it, *A wind coming from God blew upon the face of the waters.* In another dissertation, he examines the theological works of Hugo, Bishop of Ptolemaïs, great-granduncle to the writer of this book, and he establishes the fact, that to this bishop must be attributed the divers little works published during the last century, under the pseudonym of Barleycourt.

Sometimes, in the midst of his reading, no matter what the book might be which he had in his hand, he would suddenly fall into a profound meditation, whence he only emerged to write a few lines on the pages of the volume itself. These lines have often no connection whatever with the book which contains them. We now have under our eyes a note written by him on the margin of a quarto entitled, *Correspondence of Lord Germain with Generals Clinton, Cornwallis, and the Admirals on the American station. Versailles, Poinçot, bookseller; and Paris, Pissot, bookseller, Quai des Augustins.*

Here is the note:—

Oh, you who are!

Ecclesiastes calls you the All-powerful; the Maccabees call you the Creator; the Epistle to the Ephesians calls you Liberty; Baruch calls you Immensity; the Psalms call you Wisdom and Truth; John calls you Light; the Books of Kings call you Lord; Exodus calls you Providence; Leviticus, Sanctity; Esdras, Justice; the creation calls you God; man calls you Father; but Solomon calls you Compassion, and that is the most beautiful of all your names.

Toward nine o'clock in the evening the two women retired and betook themselves to their chambers on the first floor, leaving him alone until morning on the ground floor.

It is necessary that we should, in this place, give an exact idea of the dwelling of the Bishop of D——.

Chapter VI

WHO GUARDED HIS HOUSE FOR HIM

THE HOUSE IN WHICH HE LIVED CONSISTED, AS WE HAVE SAID, OF A GROUND FLOOR, AND ONE story above; three rooms on the ground floor, three chambers on the first, and an attic above. Behind the house was a garden, a quarter of an acre in extent. The two women occupied the first floor; the Bishop was lodged below. The first room, opening on the street, served him as dining-room, the second was his bedroom, and the third his oratory. There was no exit possible from this oratory, except by passing through the bedroom, nor from the bedroom, without passing through the dining-room. At the end of the suite, in the oratory, there was a detached alcove with a bed, for use in cases of hospitality. The Bishop offered this bed to country curates whom business or the requirements of their parishes brought to D——.

The pharmacy of the hospital, a small building which had been added to the house, and abutted on the garden, had been transformed into a kitchen and cellar. In addition to this, there was in the garden a stable, which had formerly been the kitchen of the hospital, and in which the Bishop kept two cows. No matter what the quantity of milk they gave, he invariably sent half of it every morning to the sick people in the hospital. *"I am paying my tithes,"* he said.

His bedroom was tolerably large, and rather difficult to warm in bad weather. As wood is extremely dear at D——, he hit upon the idea of having a compartment of boards constructed in the cow-shed. Here he passed his evenings during seasons of severe cold: he called it his *winter salon.*

In this winter salon, as in the dining-room, there was no other furniture than a square table in white wood, and four straw-seated chairs. In addition to this the dining-room was ornamented with an antique sideboard, painted pink, in water-colors. Out of a similar sideboard, properly draped with white napery and imitation lace, the Bishop had constructed the altar which decorated his oratory.

His wealthy penitents and the sainted women of D—— had more than once assessed themselves to raise the money for a new altar for Monseigneur's oratory; on each occasion he had taken the money and had given it to the poor. "The most beautiful of altars," he said, "is the soul of an unhappy creature consoled and thanking God."

In his oratory there were two straw prie-Dieu, and there was an arm-chair, also in straw, in his bedroom. When, by chance, he received seven or eight persons at one time, the prefect, or the general, or the staff of the regiment in garrison, or several pupils from the little seminary, the chairs had to be fetched from the winter salon in the stable, the prie-Dieu from the oratory, and the arm-chair from the bedroom: in this way as many as eleven chairs could be collected for the visitors. A room was dismantled for each new guest.

It sometimes happened that there were twelve in the party; the Bishop then relieved the embarrassment of the situation by standing in front of the chimney if it was winter, or by strolling in the garden if it was summer.

There was still another chair in the detached alcove, but the straw was half gone from it, and it had but three legs, so that it was of service only when propped against the wall. Mademoiselle Baptistine had also in her own room a very large easy-chair of wood, which had formerly been gilded, and which was covered with flowered pekin; but they had been obliged to hoist this bergère up to the first story through the window, as the staircase was too narrow; it could not, therefore, be reckoned among the possibilities in the way of furniture.

Mademoiselle Baptistine's ambition had been to be able to purchase a set of drawing-room furniture in yellow Utrecht velvet, stamped with a rose pattern, and with mahogany in swan's-neck style, with a sofa. But this would have cost five hundred francs at least, and in view of the fact that she had only been able to lay by forty-two francs and ten sous for this purpose in the course of five years, she had ended by renouncing the idea. However, who is there who has attained his ideal?

Nothing is more easy to present to the imagination than the Bishop's bedchamber. A glazed door opened on the garden; opposite this was the bed—a hospital bed of iron, with a canopy of green serge; in the shadow of the bed, behind a curtain, were the utensils of the toilet, which still betrayed the elegant habits of the man of the world: there were two doors, one near the chimney, opening into the oratory; the other near the bookcase, opening into the dining-room. The bookcase was a large cupboard with glass doors filled with books; the chimney was of wood painted to represent marble, and habitually without fire. In the chimney stood a pair of firedogs of iron, ornamented above with two garlanded vases, and flutings which had formerly been silvered with silver leaf, which was a sort of episcopal luxury; above the chimney-piece hung a crucifix of copper, with the silver worn off, fixed on a background of threadbare black velvet in a wooden frame from which the gilding had fallen; near the glass door a large table with an inkstand, loaded with a confusion of papers and with huge volumes; before the table an arm-chair of straw; in front of the bed a prie-Dieu, borrowed from the oratory.

Two portraits in oval frames were fastened to the wall on each side of the bed. Small gilt inscriptions on the plain surface of the cloth at the side of these figures indicated that the portraits represented, one the Abbé of Chaliot, bishop of Saint Claude; the other, the Abbé Tourteau, vicar-general of Agde, abbé of Grand-Champ, order of Cîteaux, diocese of Chartres. When the Bishop succeeded to this apartment, after the hospital patients, he had found these portraits there, and had left them. They were priests, and probably donors—two reasons for respecting them. All that he knew about these two persons was, that they had been appointed by the king, the one to his bishopric, the other to his benefice, on the same day, the 27th of April, 1785. Madame Magloire having taken the pictures down to dust, the Bishop had discovered these particulars written in whitish ink on a little square of paper, yellowed by time, and attached to the back of the portrait of the Abbé of Grand-Champ with four wafers.

At his window he had an antique curtain of a coarse woolen stuff, which finally became so old, that, in order to avoid the expense of a new one, Madame Magloire was forced to take a large seam in the very middle of it. This seam took the form of a cross. The Bishop often called attention to it: "How delightful that is!" he said.

All the rooms in the house, without exception, those on the ground floor as well as those on the first floor, were whitewashed, which is a fashion in barracks and hospitals.

However, in their latter years, Madame Magloire discovered beneath the paper which had been washed over, paintings ornamenting the apartment of Mademoiselle Baptistine, as we shall see further on. Before becoming a hospital, this house had been the ancient parliament house of the Bourgeois. Hence this decoration. The chambers were paved in red bricks, which were washed every week, with straw mats in front of all the beds. Altogether, this dwelling, which was attended to by the two women, was exquisitely clean from top to bottom. This was the sole luxury which the Bishop permitted. He said, *"That takes nothing from the poor."*

It must be confessed, however, that he still retained from his former possessions six silver knives and forks and a soup-ladle, which Madame Magloire contemplated every day with delight, as they glistened splendidly upon the coarse linen cloth. And since we are now painting the Bishop of D—— as he was in reality, we must add that he had said more than once, "I find it difficult to renounce eating from silver dishes."

To this silverware must be added two large candlesticks of massive silver, which he had inherited from a great-aunt. These candlesticks held two wax candles, and usually figured on the Bishop's chimney-piece. When he had anyone to dinner, Madame Magloire lighted the two candles and set the candlesticks on the table.

In the Bishop's own chamber, at the head of his bed, there was a small cupboard, in which Madame Magloire locked up the six silver knives and forks, and the big spoon every night. But it is necessary to add, that the key was never removed.

The garden, which had been rather spoiled by the ugly buildings which we have mentioned, was composed of four alleys in cross-form, radiating from a tank. Another walk made the circuit of the garden, and skirted the white wall which enclosed it. These alleys left behind them four square plots rimmed with box. In three of these Madame Magloire cultivated vegetables; in the fourth, the Bishop had planted some flowers; here and there stood a few fruit-trees. Madame Magloire had once remarked, with a sort of gentle malice: "Monseigneur, you who turn everything to account have, nevertheless, one useless plot. It would be better to grow salads there than bouquets." "Madame Magloire," retorted the Bishop, "you are mistaken. The beautiful is as useful as the useful." He added after a pause, "More so, perhaps."

This plot, consisting of three or four beds, occupied the Bishop almost as much as did his books. He liked to pass an hour or two there, trimming, hoeing, and making holes here and there in the earth, into which he dropped seeds. He was not as hostile to insects as a gardener could have wished to see him. Moreover, he made no pretensions to botany; he ignored groups and consistency; he made not the slightest effort to decide between Tournefort and the natural method; he took part neither with the buds against the cotyledons, nor with Jussieu against Linnæus. He did not study plants; he loved flowers. He respected learned men greatly; he respected the ignorant still more; and, without ever failing in these two respects, he watered his flower-beds every summer evening with a tin watering-pot painted green.

The house had not a single door which could be locked. The door of the dining-room, which, as we have said, opened directly on the cathedral square, had formerly been ornamented with locks and bolts like the door of a prison. The Bishop had had all this ironwork removed, and this door was never fastened, either by night or by day, with anything except the latch. All that the first passer-by had to do at any hour, was to give it a push. At first, the two women had been very much tried by this door which was never fastened, but Monsieur de D—— had said to them, "Have bolts put on your rooms, if that will please you." They had ended by sharing his confidence, or by at least acting as though they shared it. Madame Magloire alone had frights from time to time. As for the Bishop, his thought can be found explained, or at least indicated, in the three lines which he wrote on the margin of a Bible, "This is the shade of difference: the door of the physician should never be shut, the door of the priest should always be open."

On another book, entitled *Philosophy of the Medical Science*, he had written this other note: "Am not I a physician like them? I also have my patients, and then, too, I have some whom I call my unfortunates."

Again he wrote: "Do not inquire the name of him who asks a shelter of you. The very man who is embarrassed by his name is the one who needs shelter."

It chanced that a worthy curé, I know not whether it was the curé of Couloubroux or the curé of Pompierry, took it into his head to ask him one day, probably at the instigation of Madame Magloire, whether Monsieur was sure that he was not committing an indiscretion, to a certain extent, in leaving his door unfastened day and night, at the mercy of anyone who should choose to enter, and whether, in short, he did not fear lest some misfortune might occur in a house so little guarded. The Bishop touched his shoulder, with gentle gravity, and said to him, *"Nisi Dominus custodierit domum, in vanum vigilant qui custodiunt eam," Unless the Lord guard the house, in vain do they watch who guard it.*

Then he spoke of something else.

He was fond of saying, "There is a bravery of the priest as well as the bravery of a colonel of dragoons—only," he added, "ours must be tranquil."

Chapter VII

CRAVATTE

IT IS HERE THAT A FACT FALLS NATURALLY INTO PLACE, WHICH WE MUST NOT OMIT, BECAUSE IT IS one of the sort which show us best what sort of a man the Bishop of D—— was.

After the destruction of the band of Gaspard Bès, who had infested the gorges of Ollioules, one of his lieutenants, Cravatte, took refuge in the mountains. He concealed himself for some time with his bandits, the remnant of Gaspard Bès's troop, in the county of Nice; then he made his way to Piédmont, and suddenly reappeared in France, in the vicinity of Barcelonette. He was first seen at Jauziers, then at Tuiles. He hid himself in the caverns of the Joug-de-l'Aigle, and thence he descended towards the hamlets and villages through the ravines of Ubaye and Ubayette.

He even pushed as far as Embrun, entered the cathedral one night, and despoiled the sacristy. His highway robberies laid waste the countryside. The gendarmes were set on his track, but in vain.

He always escaped; sometimes he resisted by main force. He was a bold wretch. In the midst of all this terror the Bishop arrived. He was making his circuit to Chastelar. The mayor came to meet him, and urged him to retrace his steps. Cravatte was in possession of the mountains as far as Arche, and beyond; there was danger even with an escort; it merely exposed three or four unfortunate gendarmes to no purpose.

"Therefore," said the Bishop, "I intend to go without escort."

"You do not really mean that, Monseigneur!" exclaimed the mayor.

"I do mean it so thoroughly that I absolutely refuse any gendarmes, and shall set out in an hour."

"Set out?"

"Set out."

"Alone?"

"Alone."

"Monseigneur, you will not do that!"

"There exists, yonder in the mountains," said the Bishop, "a tiny community no bigger than that, which I have not seen for three years. They are my good friends, those gentle and honest shepherds. They own one goat out of every thirty that they tend. They make very pretty woolen cords of various colors, and they play the mountain airs on little flutes with six holes. They need to be told of the good God now and then. What would they say to a bishop who was afraid? What would they say if I did not go?"

"But the brigands, Monseigneur?"

"Hold," said the Bishop, "I must think of that. You are right. I may meet them. They, too, need to be told of the good God."

"But, Monseigneur, there is a band of them! A flock of wolves!"

"Monsieur le maire, it may be that it is of this very flock of wolves that Jesus has constituted me the shepherd. Who knows the ways of Providence?"

"They will rob you, Monseigneur."

"I have nothing."

"They will kill you."

"An old goodman of a priest, who passes along mumbling his prayers? Bah! To what purpose?"

"Oh, mon Dieu! what if you should meet them!"

"I should beg alms of them for my poor."

"Do not go, Monseigneur. In the name of Heaven! You are risking your life!"

"Monsieur le maire," said the Bishop, "is that really all? I am not in the world to guard my own life, but to guard souls."

They had to allow him to do as he pleased. He set out, accompanied only by a child who offered to serve as a guide. His obstinacy was bruited about the countryside, and caused great consternation.

He would take neither his sister nor Madame Magloire. He traversed the mountain on muleback, encountered no one, and arrived safe and sound at the residence of his "good friends," the shepherds. He remained there for a fortnight, preaching, administering the sacrament, teaching, exhorting. When the time of his departure approached, he resolved to chant a *Te Deum* pontifically. He mentioned it to the curé. But what was to be done? There were no episcopal ornaments. They could only place at his disposal a wretched village sacristy, with a few ancient chasubles of threadbare damask adorned with imitation lace.

"Bah!" said the Bishop. "Let us announce our *Te Deum* from the pulpit, nevertheless, Monsieur le Curé. Things will arrange themselves."

They instituted a search in the churches of the neighborhood. All the magnificence of these humble parishes combined would not have sufficed to clothe the chorister of a cathedral properly.

While they were thus embarrassed, a large chest was brought and deposited in the presbytery for the Bishop, by two unknown horsemen, who departed on the instant. The chest was opened; it contained a cope of cloth of gold, a miter ornamented with diamonds, an archbishop's cross, a magnificent crosier—all the pontifical vestments which had been stolen a month previously from the treasury of Notre-Dame d'Embrun. In the chest was a paper, on which these words were written, *"From Cravatte to Monseigneur Bienvenu."*

"Did not I say that things would come right of themselves?" said the Bishop. Then he added, with a smile, "'To him who contents himself with the surplice of a curate, God sends the cope of an archbishop."

"Monseigneur," murmured the curé, throwing back his head with a smile. "God—or the Devil."

The Bishop looked steadily at the curé, and repeated with authority, "God!"

When he returned to Chastelar, the people came out to stare at him as at a curiosity, all along the road. At the priest's house in Chastelar he rejoined Mademoiselle Baptistine and Madame Magloire, who were waiting for him, and he said to his sister: "Well! was I in the right? The poor priest went to his poor mountaineers with empty hands, and he returns from them with his hands full. I set out bearing only my faith in God; I have brought back the treasure of a cathedral."

That evening, before he went to bed, he said again: "Let us never fear robbers nor murderers. Those are dangers from without, petty dangers. Let us fear ourselves. Prejudices are the real robbers; vices are the real murderers. The great dangers lie within ourselves. What matters it what threatens our head or our purse! Let us think only of that which threatens our soul."

Then, turning to his sister: "Sister, never a precaution on the part of the priest, against his fellow-man. That which his fellow does, God permits. Let us confine ourselves to prayer, when we think that a danger is approaching us. Let us pray, not for ourselves, but that our brother may not fall into sin on our account."

However, such incidents were rare in his life. We relate those of which we know; but generally he passed his life in doing the same things at the same moment. One month of his year resembled one hour of his day.

As to what became of "the treasure" of the cathedral of Embrun, we should be embarrassed by any inquiry in that direction. It consisted of very handsome things, very tempting things, and things which were very well adapted to be stolen for the benefit of the unfortunate. Stolen they had already been elsewhere. Half of the adventure was completed; it only remained to impart a new direction to the theft, and to cause it to take a short trip in the direction of the poor. However, we make no assertions on this point. Only, a rather obscure note was found among the Bishop's papers, which may bear some relation to this matter, and which is couched in these terms, *"The question is, to decide whether this should be turned over to the cathedral or to the hospital."*

Chapter VIII

PHILOSOPHY AFTER DRINKING

THE SENATOR ABOVE MENTIONED WAS A CLEVER MAN, WHO HAD MADE HIS OWN WAY, HEEDLESS of those things which present obstacles, and which are called conscience, sworn faith, justice, duty: he had marched straight to his goal, without once flinching in the line of his advancement and his interest. He was an old attorney, softened by success; not a bad man by any means, who rendered all the small services in his power to his sons, his sons-in-law, his relations, and even to his friends, having wisely seized upon, in life, good sides, good opportunities, good windfalls. Everything else seemed to him very stupid. He was intelligent, and just sufficiently educated to think himself a disciple of Epicurus; while he was, in reality, only a product of Pigault-Lebrun. He laughed willingly and pleasantly over infinite and eternal things, and at the "crotchets of that good old fellow the Bishop." He even sometimes laughed at him with an amiable authority in the presence of M. Myriel himself, who listened to him.

On some semi-official occasion or other, I do not recollect what, Count ———, [this senator], and M. Myriel were to dine with the prefect. At dessert, the senator, who was slightly exhilarated, though still perfectly dignified, exclaimed:

"Egad, Bishop, let's have a discussion. It is hard for a senator and a bishop to look at each other without winking. We are two augurs. I am going to make a confession to you. I have a philosophy of my own."

"And you are right," replied the Bishop. "As one makes one's philosophy, so one lies on it. You are on the bed of purple, Senator."

The senator was encouraged, and went on:

"Let us be good fellows."

"Good devils even," said the Bishop.

"I declare to you," continued the senator, "that the Marquis d'Argens, Pyrrhon, Hobbes, and M. Naigeon are no rascals. I have all the philosophers in my library gilded on the edges."

"Like yourself, Count," interposed the Bishop.

The senator resumed:

"I hate Diderot; he is an ideologist, a declaimer, and a revolutionist, a believer in God at bottom, and more bigoted than Voltaire. Voltaire made sport of Needham, and he was wrong, for Needham's eels prove that God is useless. A drop of vinegar in a spoonful of flour paste supplies the *fiat lux*. Suppose the drop to be larger and the spoonful bigger; you have the world. Man is the eel. Then what is the good of the Eternal Father? The Jehovah hypothesis tires me, Bishop. It is good for nothing but to produce shallow people, whose reasoning is hollow. Down with that great All, which torments me! Hurrah for Zero which leaves me in peace! Between you and me, and in order to empty my sack, and make confession to my pastor, as it behooves me to do, I will admit to you that I have good sense. I am not enthusiastic over your Jesus, who preaches renunciation and sacrifice to the last extremity. 'Tis the counsel of an avaricious man to beggars. Renunciation; why? Sacrifice; to what end? I do not see one wolf immolating himself for the happiness of another wolf. Let us stick to nature, then. We are at the top; let us have a superior philosophy. What is the advantage of being at the top, if one sees no further than the end of other people's noses? Let us live merrily. Life is all. That man has another future elsewhere, on high, below, anywhere, I don't believe; not one single word of it. Ah! sacrifice and renunciation are recommended to me; I must take heed to everything I do; I must cudgel my brains over good and evil, over the just and the unjust, over the *fas* and the *nefas*. Why? Because I shall have to render an account of my actions. When? After death. What a fine dream! After my death it will be a very clever person who can catch me. Have a handful of dust seized by a shadow-hand, if you can. Let us tell the truth, we who are initiated, and who have raised the veil of Isis: there is no such thing as either good or evil; there is vegetation. Let us seek the real. Let us get to the bottom of it. Let us go into it thoroughly. What the deuce! let us go to the bottom of it! We must scent out the truth; dig in the earth for it, and seize it. Then it gives you exquisite joys. Then you grow strong, and you laugh. I am square on the bottom, I am. Immortality, Bishop, is a chance, a waiting for dead men's shoes. Ah! what a charming promise! trust to it, if you like! What a fine lot Adam has! We are souls, and we shall be angels, with blue wings on our shoulder-blades. Do come to my assistance: is it not Tertullian who says that the blessed shall travel from star to star? Very well. We shall be the grasshoppers of the stars. And then, besides, we shall see God. Ta, ta, ta! What twaddle all these paradises are! God is a nonsensical monster. I would not say that in the *Moniteur*, egad! but I may whisper it among friends. *Inter pocula*. To sacrifice the world to paradise is to let slip the prey for the shadow. Be the dupe of the infinite! I'm not such a fool. I am a nought. I call myself Monsieur le Comte Nought, senator. Did I exist before my birth? No. Shall I exist after death? No. What am I? A little dust collected in an organism. What am I to do on this earth? The choice rests with me: suffer or enjoy. Whither will suffering lead me? To nothingness; but I shall have suffered. Whither will enjoyment lead me? To nothingness; but I shall have enjoyed myself. My choice is made. One must eat or be eaten. I shall eat. It is better to be the tooth than the grass. Such is my wisdom. After which, go whither I push thee, the gravedigger is there; the Pantheon for some of us: all falls into the great hole. End. *Finis*. Total liquidation. This is the vanishing-point. Death is death, believe me. I laugh at the idea of there being anyone who has anything to tell me on that subject. Fables of nurses; bugaboo for children; Jehovah for men. No; our to-morrow is the night. Beyond the tomb there is nothing but equal nothingness. You have been Sardanapalus, you have been Vincent de Paul—it makes no difference. That is the truth. Then live your life, above all things. Make use of your *I* while you have it. In truth, Bishop, I tell you that I have a philosophy of my own, and I have my philosophers. I don't let myself be taken in with that nonsense. Of course, there must be something for those who are down— for the barefooted beggars, knife-grinders, and miserable wretches. Legends, chimeras, the soul, immortality, paradise, the stars, are provided for them to swallow. They gobble it down. They spread it on their dry bread. He who has nothing else has the good God. That is the least he can have. I oppose no objection to that; but I reserve Monsieur Naigeon for myself. The good God is good for the populace."

The Bishop clapped his hands.

"That's talking!" he exclaimed. "What an excellent and really marvelous thing is this materialism! Not everyone who wants it can have it. Ah! when one does have it, one is no longer a dupe, one does not stupidly allow one's self to be exiled like Cato, nor stoned like Stephen, nor burned alive like Jeanne d'Arc. Those who have succeeded in procuring this admirable materialism have the joy of feeling themselves irresponsible, and of thinking that they can devour everything without uneasiness—places, sinecures, dignities, power, whether well or ill acquired, lucrative recantations, useful treacheries, savory capitulations of conscience—and that they shall enter the tomb with their digestion accomplished. How agreeable that is! I do not say that with reference to you, Senator. Nevertheless, it is impossible for me to refrain from congratulating you. You great lords have, so you say, a philosophy of your own, and for yourselves, which is exquisite, refined, accessible to the rich alone, good for all sauces, and which seasons the voluptuousness of life admirably. This philosophy has been extracted from the depths, and unearthed by special seekers. But you are good-natured princes, and you do not think it a bad thing that belief in the good God should constitute the philosophy of the people, very much as the goose stuffed with chestnuts is the truffled turkey of the poor."

Chapter IX

THE BROTHER AS DEPICTED BY THE SISTER

IN ORDER TO FURNISH AN IDEA OF THE PRIVATE ESTABLISHMENT OF THE BISHOP OF D——, AND OF the manner in which those two sainted women subordinated their actions, their thoughts, their feminine instincts even, which are easily alarmed, to the habits and purposes of the Bishop, without his even taking the trouble of speaking in order to explain them, we cannot do better than transcribe in this place a letter from Mademoiselle Baptistine to Madame the Vicomtesse de Boischevron, the friend of her childhood. This letter is in our possession.

D——, Dec. 16, 18——.

MY GOOD MADAM: Not a day passes without our speaking of you. It is our established custom; but there is another reason besides. Just imagine, while washing and dusting the ceilings and walls, Madam Magloire has made some discoveries; now our two chambers hung with antique paper whitewashed over, would not discredit a chateau in the style of yours. Madam Magloire has pulled off all the paper. There were things beneath. My drawing-room, which contains no furniture, and which we use for spreading out the linen after washing, is fifteen feet in height, eighteen square, with a ceiling which was formerly painted and gilded, and with beams, as in yours. This was covered with a cloth while this was the hospital. And the woodwork was of the era of our grandmothers. But my room is the one you ought to see. Madam Magloire has discovered, under at least ten thicknesses of paper pasted on top, some paintings which without being good are very tolerable. The subject is Telemachus being knighted by Minerva in some gardens, the name of which escapes me. In short, where the Roman ladies repaired on one single night. What shall I say to you? I have Romans, and Roman ladies [here occurs an illegible word], and the whole train. Madam Magloire has cleaned it all off; this summer she is going to have some small injuries repaired, and the whole revarnished, and my chamber will be a regular museum. She has also found in a corner of the attic two wooden pier-tables of ancient fashion. They asked us two crowns of six francs each to regild them, but it is much better to give the money to the poor; and they are very ugly besides, and I should much prefer a round table of mahogany.

I am always very happy. My brother is so good. He gives all he has to the poor and sick. We are very much cramped. The country is trying in the winter, and we really must do something for those who are in need. We are almost comfortably lighted and warmed. You see that these are great treats.

My brother has ways of his own. When he talks, he says that a bishop ought to be so. Just imagine! the door of our house is never fastened. Whoever chooses to enter finds himself at once in my brother's room. He fears nothing, even at night. That is his sort of bravery, he says.

He does not wish me or Madame Magloire feel any fear for him. He exposes himself to all sorts of dangers, and he does not like to have us even seem to notice it. One must know how to understand him.

He goes out in the rain, he walks in the water, he travels in winter. He fears neither suspicious roads nor dangerous encounters, nor night.

Last year he went quite alone into a country of robbers. He would not take us. He was absent for a fortnight. On his return nothing had happened to him; he was thought to be dead, but was perfectly well, and said, "This is the way I have been robbed!" And then he opened a trunk full of jewels, all the jewels of the cathedral of Embrun, which the thieves had given him.

When he returned on that occasion, I could not refrain from scolding him a little, taking care, however, not to speak except when the carriage was making a noise, so that no one might hear me.

At first I used to say to myself, "There are no dangers which will stop him; he is terrible." Now I have ended by getting used to it. I make a sign to Madam Magloire that she is not to oppose him. He risks himself as he sees fit. I carry off Madam Magloire, I enter my chamber, I pray for him and fall asleep. I am at ease, because I know that if anything were to happen to him, it would be the end of me. I should go to the good God with my brother and my bishop. It has cost Madam Magloire more trouble than it did me to accustom herself to what she terms his imprudences. But now the habit has been acquired. We pray together, we tremble together, and we fall asleep. If the devil were to enter this house, he would be allowed to do so. After all, what is there for us to fear in this house? There is always someone with us who is stronger than we. The devil may pass through it, but the good God dwells here.

This suffices me. My brother has no longer any need of saying a word to me. I understand him without his speaking, and we abandon ourselves to the care of Providence. That is the way one has to do with a man who possesses grandeur of soul.

I have interrogated my brother with regard to the information which you desire on the subject of the Faux family. You are aware that he knows everything, and that he has memories, because he is still a very good royalist. They really are a very ancient Norman family of the generalship of Caen. Five hundred years ago there was a Raoul de Faux, a Jean de Faux, and a Thomas de Faux, who were gentlemen, and one of whom was a seigneur de Rochefort. The last was Guy-Étienne-Alexandre, and was commander of a regiment, and something in the light horse of Bretagne. His daughter, Marie-Louise, married Adrien-Charles de Gramont, son of the Duke Louis de Gramont, peer of France, colonel of the French guards, and lieutenant-general of the army. It is written Faux, Fauq, and Faoucq.

Good Madame, recommend us to the prayers of your sainted relative, Monsieur the Cardinal. As for your dear Sylvanie, she has done well in not wasting the few moments which she passes with you in writing to me. She is well, works as you would wish, and loves me. That is all that I desire. The souvenir which she sent through you reached me safely, and it makes me very happy. My health is not so very bad, and yet I grow thinner everyday. Farewell; my paper is at an end, and this forces me to leave you. A thousand good wishes.

BAPTISTINE

P.S. Your grandnephew is charming. Do you know that he will soon be five years old? Yesterday he saw someone riding by on horseback who had on knee-caps, and he said, "What has he got on his knees?" He is a charming child! His little brother is dragging an old broom about the room, like a carriage, and saying, "Hu!"

As will be perceived from this letter, these two women understood how to mold themselves to the Bishop's ways with that special feminine genius which comprehends the man better than he comprehends himself. The Bishop of D——, in spite of the gentle and candid air which never deserted him, sometimes did things that were grand, bold, and magnificent, without seeming to have even a suspicion of the fact. They trembled, but they let him alone. Sometimes Madame Magloire essayed a remonstrance in advance, but never at the time, nor afterwards. They never interfered with him by so much as a word or a sign, in any action once entered upon. At certain moments, without his having occasion to mention it, when he was not even conscious of it himself in all probability, so perfect was his simplicity, they vaguely felt that he was acting as a bishop; then they were nothing more than two shadows in the house. They served him passively; and if obedience consisted in disappearing, they disappeared. They understood, with an admirable delicacy of instinct, that certain cares may be put under constraint. Thus, even when believing him to be in peril, they understood, I will not say his thought, but his nature, to such a degree that they no longer watched over him. They confided him to God.

Moreover, Baptistine said, as we have just read, that her brother's end would prove her own. Madame Magloire did not say this, but she knew it.

Chapter X

THE BISHOP IN THE PRESENCE OF AN UNKNOWN LIGHT

AT AN EPOCH A LITTLE LATER THAN THE DATE OF THE LETTER CITED IN THE PRECEDING PAGES, he did a thing which, if the whole town was to be believed, was even more hazardous than his trip across the mountains infested with bandits.

In the country near D—— a man lived quite alone. This man, we will state at once, was a former member of the Convention. His name was G——.

Member of the Convention, G—— was mentioned with a sort of horror in the little world of D——. A member of the Convention—can you imagine such a thing? That existed from the time when people called each other *thou,* and when they said "citizen." This man was almost a monster. He had not voted for the death of the king, but almost. He was a quasi-regicide. He had been a terrible man. How did it happen that such a man had not been brought before a provost's court, on the return of the legitimate princes? They need not have cut off his head, if you please; clemency must be exercised, agreed; but a good banishment for life. An example, in short, etc. Besides, he was an atheist, like all the rest of those people. Gossip of the geese about the vulture.

Was G—— a vulture after all? Yes; if he were to be judged by the element of ferocity in this solitude of his. As he had not voted for the death of the king, he had not been included in the decrees of exile, and had been able to remain·in France.

He dwelt at a distance of three-quarters of an hour from the city, far from any hamlet, far from any road, in some hidden turn of a very wild valley, no one knew exactly where. He had there, it was said, a sort of field, a hole, a lair. There were no neighbors, not even passers-by. Since he had dwelt in that valley, the path which led thither had disappeared under a growth of grass. The locality was spoken of as though it had been the dwelling of a hangman.

Nevertheless, the Bishop meditated on the subject, and from time to time he gazed at the horizon at a point where a clump of trees marked the valley of the former member of the Convention, and he said, "There is a soul yonder which is lonely."

And he added, deep in his own mind, "I owe him a visit."

But, let us avow it, this idea, which seemed natural at the first blush, appeared to him after a moment's reflection, as strange, impossible, and almost repulsive. For, at bottom, he shared the general impression, and the old member of the Convention inspired him, without his being clearly conscious of the fact himself, with that sentiment which borders on hate, and which is so well expressed by the word estrangement.

Still, should the scab of the sheep cause the shepherd to recoil? No. But what a sheep!

The good Bishop was perplexed. Sometimes he set out in that direction; then he returned.

Finally, the rumor one day spread through the town that a sort of young shepherd, who served the member of the Convention in his hovel, had come in quest of a doctor; that the old wretch was dying, that paralysis was gaining on him, and that he would not live over the night.—"Thank God!" some added.

The Bishop took his staff, put on his cloak, on account of his too threadbare cassock, as we have mentioned, and because of the evening breeze which was sure to rise soon, and set out.

The sun was setting, and had almost touched the horizon when the Bishop arrived at the ex-communicated spot. With a certain beating of the heart, he recognized the fact that he was near the lair. He strode over a ditch, leaped a hedge, made his way through a fence of dead boughs, entered a neglected paddock, took a few steps with a good deal of boldness, and suddenly, at the extremity of the waste land, and behind lofty brambles, he caught sight of the cavern.

It was a very low hut, poor, small, and clean, with a vine nailed against the outside.

Near the door, in an old wheel-chair, the arm-chair of the peasants, there was a white-haired man, smiling at the sun.

Near the seated man stood a young boy, the shepherd lad. He was offering the old man a jar of milk.

While the Bishop was watching him, the old man spoke: "Thank you," he said, "I need nothing." And his smile quitted the sun to rest upon the child.

The Bishop stepped forward. At the sound which he made in walking, the old man turned his head, and his face expressed the sum total of the surprise which a man can still feel after a long life.

"This is the first time since I have been here," said he, "that anyone has entered here. Who are you, sir?"

The Bishop answered:

"My name is Bienvenu Myriel."

"Bienvenu Myriel? I have heard that name. Are you the man whom the people call Monseigneur Welcome?"

"I am."

The old man resumed with a half-smile:

"In that case, you are my bishop?"

"Something of that sort."

"Enter, sir."

The member of the Convention extended his hand to the Bishop, but the Bishop did not take it. The Bishop confined himself to the remark:

"I am pleased to see that I have been misinformed. You certainly do not seem to me to be ill."

"Monsieur," replied the old man, "I am going to recover."

He paused, and then said:

"I shall die three hours hence."

Then he continued:

"I am something of a doctor; I know in what fashion the last hour draws on. Yesterday, only my feet were cold; to-day, the chill has ascended to my knees; now I feel it mounting to my waist; when it reaches the heart, I shall stop. The sun is beautiful, is it not? I had myself wheeled out here to take a last look at things. You can talk to me; it does not fatigue me. You have done well to come and look at a man who is on the point of death. It is well that there should be witnesses at that moment. One has one's caprices; I should have liked to last until the dawn, but I know that I shall hardly live three hours. It will be night then. What does it matter, after all? Dying is a simple affair. One has no need of the light for that. So be it. I shall die by starlight."

The old man turned to the shepherd lad:

"Go to thy bed; thou wert awake all last night; thou art tired."

The child entered the hut.

The old man followed him with his eyes, and added, as though speaking to himself:

"I shall die while he sleeps. The two slumbers may be good neighbors."

The Bishop was not touched as it seems that he should have been. He did not think he discerned God in this manner of dying; let us say the whole, for these petty contradictions of great hearts must be indicated like the rest: he, who on occasion, was so fond of laughing at "His Grace," was rather shocked at not being addressed as Monseigneur, and he was almost tempted to retort "citizen." He was assailed by a fancy for peevish familiarity, common enough to doctors and priests, but which was not habitual with him. This man, after all, this member of the Convention, this representative of the people, had been one of the powerful ones of the earth; for the first time in his life, probably, the Bishop felt in a mood to be severe.

Meanwhile, the member of the Convention had been surveying him with a modest cordiality, in which one could have distinguished, possibly, that humility which is so fitting when one is on the verge of returning to dust.

The Bishop, on his side, although he generally restrained his curiosity, which, in his opinion, bordered on a fault, could not refrain from examining the member of the Convention with an attention which, as it did not have its course in sympathy, would have served his conscience as a matter of reproach, in connection with any other man. A member of the Convention produced on him somewhat the effect of being outside the pale of the law, even of the law of charity. G——, calm, his body almost upright, his voice vibrating, was one of those octogenarians who form the subject of astonishment to the physiologist. The Revolution had many of these men, proportioned to the epoch. In this old man one was conscious of a man put to the proof. Though so near to his end, he preserved all the gestures of health. In his clear glance, in his firm tone, in the robust movement of his shoulders, there was something calculated to disconcert death. Azrael, the Mohammedan angel of the sepulcher, would have turned back, and thought that he had mistaken the door. G—— seemed to be dying because he willed it so. There was freedom in his agony. His legs alone were motionless. It was there that the shadows held him fast. His feet were cold and dead, but his head survived with all the power of life, and seemed full of light. G——, at this solemn moment, resembled the king in that tale of the Orient who was flesh above and marble below.

There was a stone there. The Bishop sat down. The exordium was abrupt.

"I congratulate you," said he, in the tone which one uses for a reprimand. "You did not vote for the death of the king, after all."

The old member of the Convention did not appear to notice the bitter meaning underlying the words "after all." He replied. The smile had quite disappeared from his face.

"Do not congratulate me too much, sir. I did vote for the death of the tyrant."

It was the tone of austerity answering the tone of severity.

"What do you mean to say?" resumed the Bishop.

"I mean to say that man has a tyrant—ignorance. I voted for the death of that tyrant. That tyrant engendered royalty, which is authority falsely understood, while science is authority rightly understood. Man should be governed only by science."

"And conscience," added the Bishop.

"It is the same thing. Conscience is the quantity of innate science which we have within us."

Monseigneur Bienvenu listened in some astonishment to this language, which was very new to him.

The member of the Convention resumed:

"So far as Louis XVI was concerned, I said 'no.' I did not think that I had the right to kill a man; but I felt it my duty to exterminate evil. I voted the end of the tyrant, that is to say, the end of prostitution for woman, the end of slavery for man, the end of night for the child. In voting for the Republic, I voted for that. I voted for fraternity, concord, the dawn. I have aided in the overthrow of prejudices and errors. The crumbling away of prejudices and errors causes light. We have caused the fall of the old world, and the old world, that vase of miseries, has become, through its upsetting upon the human race, an urn of joy."

"Mixed joy," said the Bishop.

"You may say troubled joy, and to-day, after that fatal return of the past, which is called 1814, joy which has disappeared! Alas! The work was incomplete, I admit: we demolished the ancient régime in deeds; we were not able to suppress it entirely in ideas. To destroy abuses is not sufficient; customs must be modified. The mill is there no longer; the wind is still there."

"You have demolished. It may be of use to demolish, but I distrust a demolition complicated with wrath."

"Right has its wrath, Bishop; and the wrath of right is an element of progress. In any case, and in spite of whatever may be said, the French Revolution is the most important step of the human race since the advent of Christ. Incomplete, it may be, but sublime. It set free all the unknown social quantities; it softened spirits, it calmed, appeased, enlightened; it caused the waves of civilization to flow over the earth. It was a good thing. The French Revolution is the consecration of humanity."

The Bishop could not refrain from murmuring:

"Yes? '93!"

The member of the Convention straightened himself up in his chair with an almost lugubrious solemnity, and exclaimed, so far as a dying man is capable of exclamation:

"Ah, there you go; '93! I was expecting that word. A cloud had been forming for the space of fifteen hundred years; at the end of fifteen hundred years it burst. You are putting the thunderbolt on its trial."

The Bishop felt, without, perhaps, confessing it, that something within him had suffered extinction. Nevertheless, he put a good face on the matter. He replied:

"The judge speaks in the name of justice; the priest speaks in the name of pity, which is nothing but a more lofty justice. A thunderbolt should commit no error." And he added, regarding the member of the Convention steadily the while, "Louis XVII?"

The conventionary stretched forth his hand and grasped the Bishop's arm.

"Louis XVII! let us see. For whom do you mourn? is it for the innocent child? very good; in that case I mourn with you. Is it for the royal child? I demand time for reflection. To me, the brother of Cartouche, an innocent child who was hung up by the armpits in the Place de Grève, until death ensued, for the sole crime of having been the brother of Cartouche, is no less painful than the grandson of Louis XV, an innocent child, martyred in the tower of the Temple, for the sole crime of having been the grandson of Louis XV."

"Monsieur," said the Bishop, "I like not this conjunction of names."

"Cartouche? Louis XV? To which of the two do you object?"

A momentary silence ensued. The Bishop almost regretted having come, and yet he felt vaguely and strangely shaken.

The conventionary resumed:

"Ah, Monsieur Priest, you love not the crudities of the true. Christ loved them. He seized a rod and cleared out the Temple. His scourge full of lightnings was a harsh speaker of truths. When he cried, '*Sinite parvulos,*' he made no distinction between the little children. It would not have embarrassed him to bring together the Dauphin of Barabbas and the Dauphin of Herod. Innocence, Monsieur, is its own crown. Innocence has no need to be a highness. It is as august in rags as in fleurs-de-lys."

"That is true," said the Bishop in a low voice.

"I persist," continued the conventionary G———. "You have mentioned Louis XVII to me. Let us come to an understanding. Shall we weep for all the innocent, all martyrs, all children, the lowly as well as the exalted? I agree to that. But in that case, as I have told you, we must go back further than '93, and our tears must begin before Louis XVII. I will weep with you over the children of kings, provided that you will weep with me over the children of the people."

"I weep for all," said the Bishop.

"Equally!" exclaimed conventionary G———; "and if the balance must incline, let it be on the side of the people. They have been suffering longer."

Another silence ensued. The conventionary was the first to break it. He raised himself on one elbow, took a bit of his cheek between his thumb and his forefinger, as one does mechanically when one interrogates and judges, and appealed to the Bishop with a gaze full of all the forces of the death-agony. It was almost an explosion.

"Yes, sir, the people have been suffering a long while. And hold! that is not all, either; why have you just questioned me and talked to me about Louis XVII? I know you not. Ever since I have been in these parts I have dwelt in this enclosure alone, never setting foot outside, and seeing no one but that child who helps me. Your name has reached me in a confused manner, it is true, and very badly pronounced, I must admit; but that signifies nothing: clever men have so many ways of imposing on that honest goodman, the people. By the way, I did not hear the sound of your carriage; you have left it yonder, behind the coppice at the fork of the roads, no doubt. I do not know you, I tell you. You have told me that you are the Bishop; but that affords me no information as to your moral personality. In short, I repeat my question. Who are you? You are a bishop; that is to say, a prince of the church, one of those gilded men with heraldic bearings and revenues, who have vast prebends—the bishopric of D—— fifteen thousand francs settled income, ten thousand in perquisites; total, twenty-five thousand francs—who have kitchens, who have liveries, who make good cheer, who eat moor-hens on Friday, who strut about, a lackey before, a lackey behind, in a gala coach, and who have palaces, and who roll in their carriages in the name of Jesus Christ who went barefoot! You are a prelate—revenues, palace, horses, servants, good table, all the sensualities of life; you have this like the rest, and like the rest, you enjoy it; it is well, but this says either too much or too little; this does not enlighten me upon the intrinsic and essential value of the man who comes with the probable intention of bringing wisdom to me. To whom do I speak? Who are you?"

The Bishop hung his head and replied, "*Vermis sum*—I am a worm."

"A worm of the earth in a carriage?" growled the conventionary.

It was the conventionary's turn to be arrogant, and the Bishop's to be humble.

The Bishop resumed mildly:

"So be it, sir. But explain to me how my carriage, which is a few paces off behind the trees yonder, how my good table and the moor-hens which I eat on Friday, how my twenty-five thousand francs income, how my palace and my lackeys prove that clemency is not a duty, and that '93 was not inexorable."

The conventionary passed his hand across his brow, as though to sweep away a cloud.

"Before replying to you," he said, "I beseech you to pardon me. I have just committed a wrong, sir. You are at my house, you are my guest, I owe you courtesy. You discuss my ideas, and it becomes me to confine myself to combating your arguments. Your riches and your pleasures are advantages which I hold over you in the debate; but good taste dictates that I shall not make use of them. I promise you to make no use of them in the future."

"I thank you," said the Bishop.

G—— resumed:

"Let us return to the explanation which you have asked of me. Where were we? What were you saying to me? That '93 was inexorable?"

"Inexorable; yes," said the Bishop. "What think you of Marat clapping his hands at the guillotine?"

"What think you of Bossuet chanting the *Te Deum* over the dragonnades?"

The retort was a harsh one, but it attained its mark with the directness of a point of steel. The Bishop quivered under it; no reply occurred to him; but he was offended by this mode of alluding to Bossuet. The best of minds will have their fetiches, and they sometimes feel vaguely wounded by the want of respect of logic.

The conventionary began to pant; the asthma of the agony which is mingled with the last breaths interrupted his voice; still, there was a perfect lucidity of soul in his eyes. He went on:

"Let me say a few words more in this and that direction; I am willing. Apart from the Revolution, which, taken as a whole, is an immense human affirmation, '93 is, alas! a rejoinder. You think it inexorable, sir; but what of the whole monarchy, sir? Carrier is a bandit; but what name do you give to Montrevel? Fouquier-Tainville is a rascal; but what is your opinion as to Lamoignon-Bâville? Maillard is terrible; but Saulx-Tavannes, if you please? Duchêne senior is ferocious; but what epithet will you allow me for the elder Letellier? Jourdan-Coupe-Tête is a monster; but not so great a one as M. the Marquis de Louvois. Sir, sir, I am sorry for Marie Antoinette, archduchess and queen; but I am also sorry for that poor Huguenot woman, who, in 1685, under Louis the Great, sir, while with a nursing infant, was bound, naked to the waist, to a stake, and the child kept at a distance; her breast swelled with milk and her heart with anguish; the little one, hungry and pale, beheld that breast and cried and agonized; the executioner said to the woman, a mother and a nurse, 'Abjure!' giving her her choice between the death of her infant and the death of her conscience. What say you to that torture of Tantalus as applied to a mother? Bear this well in mind, sir: the French Revolution had its reasons for existence; its wrath will be absolved by the future; its result is the world made better. From its most terrible blows there comes forth a caress for the human race. I abridge, I stop, I have too much the advantage; moreover, I am dying."

And ceasing to gaze at the Bishop, the conventionary concluded his thoughts in these tranquil words:

"Yes, the brutalities of progress are called revolutions. When they are over, this fact is recognized—that the human race has been treated harshly, but that it has progressed."

The conventionary doubted not that he had successively conquered all the inmost entrenchments of the Bishop. One remained, however, and from this entrenchment, the last resource of Monseigneur Bienvenu's resistance, came forth this reply, wherein appeared nearly all the harshness of the beginning:

"Progress should believe in God. Good cannot have an impious servitor. He who is an atheist is but a bad leader for the human race."

The former representative of the people made no reply. He was seized with a fit of trembling. He looked towards heaven, and in his glance a tear gathered slowly. When the eyelid was full, the tear trickled down his livid cheek, and he said, almost in a stammer, quite low, and to himself, while his eyes were plunged in the depths:

"O thou! O ideal! Thou alone existest!"

The Bishop experienced an indescribable shock.

After a pause, the old man raised a finger heavenward and said:

"The infinite is. He is there. If the infinite had no person, person would be without limit; it would not be infinite; in other words, it would not exist. There is, then, an *I*. That *I* of the infinite is God."

The dying man had pronounced these last words in a loud voice, and with the shiver of ecstasy, as though he beheld someone. When he had spoken, his eyes closed. The effort had exhausted him. It was evident that he had just lived through in a moment the few hours which had been left to him. That which he had said brought him nearer to him who is in death. The supreme moment was approaching.

The Bishop understood this; time pressed; it was as a priest that he had come: from extreme coldness he had passed by degrees to extreme emotion; he gazed at those closed eyes, he took that wrinkled, aged and ice-cold hand in his, and bent over the dying man.

"This hour is the hour of God. Do you not think that it would be regrettable if we had met in vain?"

The conventionary opened his eyes again. A gravity mingled with gloom was imprinted on his countenance.

"Bishop," said he, with a slowness which probably arose more from his dignity of soul than from the failing of his strength, "I have passed my life in meditation, study, and contemplation. I was sixty years of age when my country called me and commanded me to concern myself with its affairs. I obeyed. Abuses existed, I combated them; tyrannies existed, I destroyed them; rights and principles existed, I proclaimed and confessed them. Our territory was invaded, I defended it; France was menaced, I offered my breast. I was not rich; I am poor. I have been one of the masters of the state; the vaults of the treasury were encumbered with specie to such a degree that we were forced to shore up the walls, which were on the point of bursting beneath the weight of gold and silver; I dined in Dead Tree Street, at twenty-two sous. I have succored the oppressed, I have comforted the suffering. I tore the cloth from the altar, it is true; but it was to bind up the wounds of my country. I have always upheld the march forward of the human race, forward towards the light, and I have sometimes resisted progress without pity. I have, when the occasion offered, protected my own adversaries, men of your profession. And there is at Peteghem, in Flanders, at the very spot where the Merovingian kings had their summer palace, a convent of Urbanists, the Abbey of Sainte Claire en Beaulieu, which I saved in 1793. I have done my duty according to my powers, and all the good that I was able. After which I was hunted down, pursued, persecuted, blackened, jeered at, scorned, cursed, proscribed. For many years past: I with my white hair have been conscious that many people think they have the right to despise me; to the poor ignorant masses I present the visage of one damned. And I accept this isolation of hatred, without hating anyone myself. Now I am eighty-six years old; I am on the point of death. What is it that you have come to ask of me?"

"*Your blessing,*" said the Bishop.

And he knelt down.

When the Bishop raised his head again, the face of the conventionary had become august. He had just expired.

The Bishop returned home, deeply absorbed in thoughts which cannot be known to us. He passed the whole night in prayer. On the following morning some bold and curious persons attempted to speak to him about member of the Convention G——; he contented himself with pointing heavenward.

From that moment he redoubled his tenderness and brotherly feeling toward all children and sufferers.

Any allusion to "that old wretch of a G——" caused him to fall into a singular preoccupation. No one could say that the passage of that soul before his, and the reflection of that grand conscience upon his, did not count for something in his approach to perfection.

This "pastoral visit" naturally furnished an occasion for a murmur of comment in all the little local coteries.

"Was the bedside of such a dying man as that the proper place for a bishop? There was evidently no conversion to be expected. All those revolutionists are backsliders. Then why go there? What was there to be seen there? He must have been very curious indeed to see a soul carried off by the devil."

One day a dowager of the impertinent variety who thinks herself spiritual, addressed this sally to him, "Monseigneur, people are inquiring when Your Greatness will receive the red cap!"— "Oh! oh! that's a coarse color," replied the Bishop. "It is lucky that those who despise it in a cap revere it in a hat."

Chapter XI

A RESTRICTION

WE SHOULD INCUR A GREAT RISK OF DECEIVING OURSELVES, WERE WE TO CONCLUDE FROM THIS that Monseigneur Welcome was "a philosophical bishop," or a "patriotic curé." His meeting, which may almost be designated as his union, with conventionary G——, left behind it in his mind a sort of astonishment, which rendered him still more gentle. That is all.

Although Monseigneur Bienvenu was far from being a politician, this is, perhaps, the place to indicate very briefly what his attitude was in the events of that epoch, supposing that Monseigneur Bienvenu ever dreamed of having an attitude.

Let us, then, go back a few years.

Some time after the elevation of M. Myriel to the episcopate, the Emperor had made him a baron of the Empire, in company with many other bishops. The arrest of the Pope took place, as everyone knows, on the night of the 5th to the 6th of July, 1809; on this occasion, M. Myriel was summoned by Napoleon to the synod of the bishops of France and Italy convened at Paris. This synod was held at Notre-Dame, and assembled for the first time on the 15th of June, 1811, under the presidency of Cardinal Fesch. M. Myriel was one of the ninety-five bishops who attended it. But he was present only at one sitting and at three or four private conferences. Bishop of a mountain diocese, living so very close to nature, in rusticity and deprivation, it appeared that he imported among these eminent personages, ideas which altered the temperature of the assembly. He very soon returned to D——. He was interrogated as to this speedy return, and he replied: *"I embarrassed them. The outside air penetrated to them through me. I produced on them the effect of an open door."*

On another occasion he said, *"What would you have? Those gentlemen are princes. I am only a poor peasant bishop."*

The fact is that he displeased them. Among other strange things, it is said that he chanced to remark one evening, when he found himself at the house of one of his most notable colleagues: "What beautiful clocks! What beautiful carpets! What beautiful liveries! They must be a great trouble. I would not have all those superfluities, crying incessantly in my ears: 'There are people who are hungry! There are people who are cold! There are poor people! There are poor people!' "

Let us remark, by the way, that the hatred of luxury is not an intelligent hatred. This hatred would involve the hatred of the arts. Nevertheless, in churchmen, luxury is wrong, except in connection with representations and ceremonies. It seems to reveal habits which have very little that is charitable about them. An opulent priest is a contradiction. The priest must keep close to the poor. Now, can one come in contact incessantly night and day with all this distress, all these misfortunes, and this poverty, without having about one's own person a little of that misery, like the dust of labor? Is it possible to imagine a man near a brazier who is not warm? Can one imagine a workman who is working near a furnace, and who has neither a singed hair, nor blackened nails, nor a drop of sweat, nor a speck of ashes on his face? The first proof of charity in the priest, in the bishop especially, is poverty.

This is, no doubt, what the Bishop of D—— thought.

It must not be supposed, however, that he shared what we call the "ideas of the century" on certain delicate points. He took very little part in the theological quarrels of the moment, and maintained silence on questions in which Church and State were implicated; but if he had been strongly pressed, it seems that he would have been found to be an ultramontane rather than a gallican. Since we are making a portrait, and since we do not wish to conceal anything, we are forced to add that he was glacial towards Napoleon in his decline. Beginning with 1813, he gave in his adherence to or applauded all hostile manifestations. He refused to see him, as he passed through on his return from the island of Elba, and he abstained from ordering public prayers for the Emperor in his diocese during the Hundred Days.

Besides his sister, Mademoiselle Baptistine, he had two brothers, one a general, the other a prefect. He wrote to both with tolerable frequency. He was harsh for a time toward the former, because, holding a command in Provence at the epoch of the disembarkation at Cannes, the general had put himself at the head of twelve hundred men and had pursued the Emperor as though the latter had been a person whom one is desirous of allowing to escape. His correspondence with the other brother, the ex-prefect, a fine, worthy man who lived in retirement at Paris, Rue Cassette, remained more affectionate.

Thus Monseigneur Bienvenu also had his hour of party spirit, his hour of bitterness, his cloud. The shadow of the passions of the moment traversed this grand and gentle spirit occupied with eternal things. Certainly, such a man would have done well not to entertain any political opinions. Let there be no mistake as to our meaning: we are not confounding what is called "political opinions" with the grand aspiration for progress, with the sublime faith, patriotic, democratic, humane, which in our day should be the very foundation of every generous intellect. Without going deeply into questions which are only indirectly connected with the subject of this book, we will simply say this: It would have been well if Monseigneur Bienvenu had not been a royalist, and if his glance had never been, for a single instant, turned away from that serene contemplation in which is distinctly discernible, above the fictions and the hatreds of this world, above the stormy vicissitudes of human things, the beaming of those three pure radiances, truth, justice, and charity.

While admitting that it was not for a political office that God created Monseigneur Welcome, we should have understood and admired his protest in the name of right and liberty, his proud opposition, his just but perilous resistance to the all-powerful Napoleon. But that which pleases us in people who are rising pleases us less in the case of people who are falling. We only love the fray so long as there is danger, and in any case, the combatants of the first hour have alone the right to be the exterminators of the last. He who has not been a stubborn accuser in prosperity should hold his peace in the face of ruin. The denunciator of success is the only legitimate executioner of the fall. As for us, when Providence intervenes and strikes, we let it work. 1812 commenced to disarm us. In 1813 the cowardly breach of silence of that taciturn legislative body, emboldened by catastrophe, possessed only traits which aroused indignation. And it was a crime to applaud, in 1814, in the presence of those marshals who betrayed; in the presence of that senate which passed from one dunghill to another, insulting after having deified; in the presence of that idolatry which was loosing its footing and spitting on its idol—it was a duty to turn aside the head. In 1815, when the supreme disasters filled the air, when France was seized with a shiver at their sinister approach, when Waterloo could be dimly discerned opening before Napoleon, the mournful acclamation of the army and the people to the condemned of destiny had nothing laughable in it, and, after making all allowance for the despot, a heart like that of the Bishop of D—— ought not perhaps to have failed to recognize the august and touching features presented by the embrace of a great nation and a great man on the brink of the abyss.

With this exception, he was in all things just, true, equitable, intelligent, humble and dignified, beneficent and kindly, which is only another sort of benevolence. He was a priest, a sage, and a man. It must be admitted, that even in the political views with which we have just reproached him, and which we are disposed to judge almost with severity, he was tolerant and easy, more so, perhaps, than we who are speaking here. The porter of the town-hall had been placed there by the Emperor. He was an old non-commissioned officer of the old guard, a member of the Legion of Honor at Austerlitz, as much of a Bonapartist as the eagle. This poor fellow occasionally let slip inconsiderate remarks, which the law then stigmatized as *seditious speeches*. After the imperial profile disappeared from the Legion of Honor, he never dressed himself in his regimentals, as he said, so that he should not be obliged to wear his cross. He had himself devoutly removed the imperial effigy from the cross which Napoleon had given him; this made a hole, and he would not put anything in its place. *"I will die,"* he said, *"rather than wear the three frogs upon my heart!"* He liked to scoff aloud at Louis XVIII. *"The gouty old creature in English gaiters!"* he said; *"let him take himself off to Prussia with that queue of his."* He was happy to combine in the same imprecation the two things which he most detested, Prussia and England. He did it so often that he lost his place. There he was, turned out of the house, with his wife and children, and without bread. The Bishop sent for him, reproved him gently, and appointed him beadle in the cathedral.

In the course of nine years Monseigneur Bienvenu had, by dint of holy deeds and gentle manners, filled the town of D—— with a sort of tender and filial reverence. Even his conduct toward Napoleon had been accepted and tacitly pardoned, as it were, by the people, the good and weakly flock who adored their emperor, but loved their bishop.

Chapter XII

THE SOLITUDE OF MONSEIGNEUR WELCOME

A BISHOP IS ALMOST ALWAYS SURROUNDED BY A FULL SQUADRON OF LITTLE ABBÉS, JUST AS A GENeral is by a covey of young officers. This is what that charming Saint François de Sales calls somewhere "les prêtres blancs-becs," callow priests. Every career has its aspirants, who form a train for those who have attained eminence in it. There is no power which has not its dependents. There is no fortune which has not its court. The seekers of the future eddy around the splendid present. Every metropolis has its staff of officials. Every bishop who possesses the least influence has about him his patrol of cherubim from the seminary, which goes the round, and maintains good order in the episcopal palace, and mounts guard over monseigneur's smile. To please a bishop is equivalent to getting one's foot in the stirrup for a sub-diaconate. It is necessary to walk one's path discreetly; the apostleship does not disdain the canonship.

Just as there are bigwigs elsewhere, there are big miters in the Church. These are the bishops who stand well at court, who are rich, well endowed, skillful, accepted by the world, who know how to pray, no doubt, but who know also how to beg, who feel little scruple at making a whole diocese dance attendance in their person, who are connecting links between the sacristy and diplomacy, who are abbés rather than priests, prelates rather than bishops. Happy those who approach them! Being persons of influence, they create a shower about them, upon the assiduous and the favored, and upon all the young men who understand the art of pleasing, of large parishes, prebends, archidiaconates, chaplaincies, and cathedral posts, while awaiting episcopal honors. As they advance themselves, they cause their satellites to progress also; it is a whole solar system on the march. Their radiance casts a gleam of purple over their suite. Their prosperity is crumbled up behind the scenes, into nice little promotions. The larger the diocese of the patron, the fatter the curacy for the favorite. And then, there is Rome. A bishop who understands how to become an archbishop, an archbishop who knows how to become a cardinal, carries you with him as conclavist; you enter a court of papal jurisdiction, you receive the pallium, and behold! you are an auditor, then a papal chamberlain, then monsignor, and from a Grace to an Eminence is only a step, and between the Eminence and the Holiness there is but the smoke of a ballot. Every skull-cap may dream of the tiara. The priest is nowadays the only man who can become a king in a regular manner; and what a king! the supreme king. Then what a nursery of aspirations is a seminary! How many blushing choristers, how many youthful abbés bear on their heads Perrette's pot of milk! Who knows how easy it is for ambition to call itself vocation? in good faith, perchance, and deceiving itself, devotee that it is.

Monseigneur Bienvenu, poor, humble, retiring, was not accounted among the big miters. This was plain from the complete absence of young priests about him. We have seen that he "did not take" in Paris. Not a single future dreamed of engrafting itself on this solitary old man. Not a single sprouting ambition committed the folly of putting forth its foliage in his shadow. His canons and grand-vicars were good old men, rather vulgar like himself, walled up like him in this diocese, without exit to a cardinalship, and who resembled their bishop, with this difference, that they were finished and he was completed. The impossibility of growing great under Monseigneur Bienvenu was so well understood, that no sooner had the young men whom he ordained left the seminary than they got themselves recommended to the archbishops of Aix or of Auch, and went off in a great hurry. For, in short, we repeat it, men wish to be pushed. A saint who dwells in a paroxysm of abnegation is a dangerous neighbor; he might communicate to you, by contagion, an incurable poverty, an anchylosis of the joints, which are useful in advancement, and in short, more renunciation than you desire; and this infectious virtue is avoided. Hence the isolation of Monseigneur Bienvenu. We live in the midst of a gloomy society. Success; that is the lesson which falls drop by drop from the slope of corruption.

Be it said in passing, that success is a very hideous thing. Its false resemblance to merit deceives men. For the masses, success has almost the same profile as supremacy. Success, that Menæchmus of talent, has one dupe—history. Juvenal and Tacitus alone grumble at it. In our day, a philosophy which is almost official has entered into its service, wears the livery of success, and performs the service of its antechamber. Succeed: theory. Prosperity argues capacity. Win in the lottery, and behold! you are a clever man. He who triumphs is venerated. Be born with a silver spoon in your mouth! everything lies in that. Be lucky, and you will have all the rest; be happy, and people will think you great. Outside of five or six immense exceptions, which compose the splendor of a century, contemporary admiration is nothing but short-sightedness. Gilding is gold. It does no harm to be the first arrival by pure chance, so long as you do arrive. The common herd is an old Narcissus who adores himself, and who applauds the vulgar herd. That enormous ability by virtue of which one is Moses, Æschylus, Dante, Michael Angelo, or Napoleon, the multitude awards on the spot, and by acclamation, to whomsoever attains his object, in whatsoever it may consist. Let a notary transfigure himself into a deputy; let a false Corneille compose *Tiridate*; let a eunuch come to possess a harem; let a military Prudhomme accidentally win the decisive battle of an epoch; let an apothecary invent cardboard shoe-soles for the army of the Sambre-and-Meuse, and construct for himself, out of this cardboard, sold as leather, four hundred thousand francs of income; let a pork-packer espouse usury, and cause it to bring forth seven or eight millions, of which he is the father and of which it is the mother; let a preacher become a bishop by force of his nasal drawl; let the steward of a fine family be so rich on retiring from service that he is made minister of finances— and men call that Genius, just as they call the face of Mousqueton *Beauty*, and the mien of Claude *Majesty*. With the constellations of space they confound the stars of the abyss which are made in the soft mire of the puddle by the feet of ducks.

Chapter XIII

WHAT HE BELIEVED

WE ARE NOT OBLIGED TO SOUND THE BISHOP OF D—— ON THE SCORE OF ORTHODOXY. IN THE presence of such a soul we feel ourselves in no mood but respect. The conscience of the just man should be accepted on his word. Moreover, certain natures being given, we admit the possible development of all beauties of human virtue in a belief that differs from our own.

What did he think of this dogma, or of that mystery? These secrets of the inner tribunal of the conscience are known only to the tomb, where souls enter naked. The point on which we are certain is, that the difficulties of faith never resolved themselves into hypocrisy in his case. No decay is possible to the diamond. He believed to the extent of his powers. *"Credo in Patrem,"* he often exclaimed. Moreover, he drew from good works that amount of satisfaction which suffices to the conscience, and which whispers to a man, "Thou art with God!"

The point which we consider it our duty to note is, that outside of and beyond his faith, as it were, the Bishop possessed an excess of love. In was in that quarter, *quia multum amavit*—because he loved much—that he was regarded as vulnerable by "serious men," "grave persons" and "reasonable people"; favorite locutions of our sad world where egotism takes its word of command from pedantry. What was this excess of love? It was a serene benevolence which overflowed men, as we have already pointed out, and which, on occasion, extended even to things. He lived without disdain. He was indulgent towards God's creation. Every man, even the best, has within him a thoughtless harshness which he reserves for animals. The Bishop of D—— had none of that harshness, which is peculiar to many priests, nevertheless. He did not go as far as the Brahmin, but he seemed to have weighed this saying of Ecclesiastes: "Who knoweth whither the soul of the animal goeth?" Hideousness of aspect, deformity of instinct, troubled him not, and did not arouse his indignation. He was touched, almost softened by them. It seemed as though he went thoughtfully away to seek beyond the bounds of life which is apparent, the cause, the explanation, or the excuse for them. He seemed at times to be asking God to commute these penalties. He examined without wrath, and with the eye of a linguist who is deciphering a palimpsest, that portion of chaos which still exists in nature. This reverie sometimes caused him to utter odd sayings. One morning he was in his garden, and thought himself alone, but his sister was walking behind him, unseen by him: suddenly he paused and gazed at something on the ground; it was a large, black, hairy, frightful spider. His sister heard him say:

"Poor beast! It is not its fault!"

Why not mention these almost divinely childish sayings of kindness? Puerile they may be; but these sublime puerilities were peculiar to Saint Francis d'Assisi and of Marcus Aurelius. One day he sprained his ankle in his effort to avoid stepping on an ant. Thus lived this just man. Sometimes he fell asleep in his garden, and then there was nothing more venerable possible.

Monseigneur Bienvenu had formerly been, if the stories anent his youth, and even in regard to his manhood, were to be believed, a passionate, and, possibly, a violent man. His universal suavity was less an instinct of nature than the result of a grand conviction which had filtered into his heart through the medium of life, and had trickled there slowly, thought by thought; for, in a character, as in a·rock, there may exist apertures made by drops of water. These hollows are uneffaceable; these formations are indestructible.

In 1815, as we think we have already said, he reached his seventy-fifth birthday, but he did not appear to be more than sixty. He was not tall; he was rather plump; and, in order to combat this tendency, he was fond of taking long strolls on foot: his step was firm, and his form was but slightly bent, a detail from which we do not pretend to draw any conclusion. Gregory XVI, at the age of eighty, held himself erect and smiling, which did not prevent him from being a bad bishop. Monseigneur Welcome had what the people term a "fine head," but so amiable was he that they forgot that it was fine.

When he conversed with that infantile gaiety which was one of his charms, and of which we have already spoken, people felt at their ease with him, and joy seemed to radiate from his whole person. His fresh and ruddy complexion, his very white teeth, all of which he had preserved, and which were displayed by his smile, gave him that open and easy air which causes the remark to be made of a man, "He's a good fellow"; and of an old man, "He is a fine man." That, it will be recalled, was the effect which he produced upon Napoleon. On the first encounter, and to one who saw him for the first time, he was nothing, in fact, but a fine man. But if one remained near him for a few hours, and beheld him in the least degree pensive, the fine man became gradually transfigured, and took on some imposing quality, I know not what; his broad and serious brow, rendered august by his white locks, became august also by virtue of meditation; majesty radiated from his goodness, though his goodness ceased not to be radiant; one experienced something of the emotion which one would feel on beholding a smiling angel slowly unfold his wings, without ceasing to smile. Respect, an unutterable respect, penetrated you by degrees and mounted to your heart, and one felt that one had before him one of those strong, thoroughly tried, and indulgent souls where thought is so grand that it can no longer be anything but gentle.

As we have seen, prayer, the celebration of the offices of religion, alms-giving, the consolation of the afflicted, the cultivation of a bit of land, fraternity, frugality, hospitality, renunciation, confidence, study, work, filled every day of his life. *Filled* is exactly the word; certainly the Bishop's day was quite full to the brim, of good words and good deeds. Nevertheless, it was not complete if cold or rainy weather prevented his passing an hour or two in his garden before going to bed, and after the two women had retired. It seemed to be a sort of rite with him, to prepare himself for slumber by meditation in the presence of the grand spectacles of the nocturnal heavens. Sometimes, if the two old women were not asleep, they heard him pacing slowly along the walks at a very advanced hour of the night. He was there alone, communing with himself, peaceful, adoring, comparing the serenity of his heart with the serenity of the ether, moved amid the darkness by the visible splendor of the constellations and the invisible splendor of God, opening his heart to the thoughts which fall from the Unknown. At such moments, while he offered his heart at the hour when nocturnal flowers offer their perfume, illuminated like a lamp amid the starry night, as he poured himself out in ecstasy in the midst of the universal radiance of creation, he could not have told himself, probably, what was passing in his spirit; he felt something take its flight from him, and something descend into him. Mysterious exchange of the abysses of the soul with the abysses of the universe!

He thought of the grandeur and presence of God; of the future eternity, that strange mystery; of the eternity past, a mystery still more strange; of all the infinities, which pierced their way into all his senses, beneath his eyes; and, without seeking to comprehend the incomprehensible, he gazed upon it. He did not study God; he was dazzled by him. He considered those magnificent conjunctions of atoms, which communicate aspects to matter, reveal forces by verifying them, create individualities in unity, proportions in extent, the innumerable in the infinite, and, through light, produce beauty. These conjunctions are formed and dissolved incessantly; hence life and death.

He seated himself on a wooden bench, with his back against a decrepit vine; he gazed at the stars, past the puny and stunted silhouettes of his fruit-trees. This quarter of an acre, so poorly planted, so encumbered with mean buildings and sheds, was dear to him, and satisfied his wants.

What more was needed by this old man, who divided the leisure of his life, where there was so little leisure, between gardening in the daytime and contemplation at night? Was not this narrow enclosure, with the heavens for a ceiling, sufficient to enable him to adore God in his most divine works, in turn? Does not this comprehend all, in fact? and what is there left to desire beyond it? A little garden in which to walk, and immensity in which to dream. At one's feet that which can be cultivated and plucked; over head that which one can study and meditate upon: some flowers on earth, and all the stars in the sky.

Chapter XIV

WHAT HE THOUGHT

ONE LAST WORD.

    Since this sort of details might, particularly at the present moment, and to use an expression now in fashion, give to the Bishop of D—— a certain "pantheistical" physiognomy, and induce the belief, either to his credit or his discredit, that he entertained one of those personal philosophies which are peculiar to our century, which sometimes spring up in solitary spirits, and there take on a form and grow until they usurp the place of religion, we insist upon it, that not one of those persons who knew Monseigneur Welcome would have thought himself authorized to think anything of the sort. That which enlightened this man was his heart. His wisdom was made of the light which comes from there.

No systems; many works. Abstruse speculations contain vertigo; no, there is nothing to indicate that he risked his mind in apocalypses. The apostle may be daring, but the bishop must be timid. He would probably have felt a scruple at sounding too far in advance certain problems which are, in a manner, reserved for terrible great minds. There is a sacred horror beneath the porches of the enigma; those gloomy openings stand yawning there, but something tells you, you, a passer-by in life, that you must not enter. Woe to him who penetrates thither!

Geniuses in the impenetrable depths of abstraction and pure speculation, situated, so to speak, above all dogmas, propose their ideas to God. Their prayer audaciously offers discussion. Their adoration interrogates. This is direct religion, which is full of anxiety and responsibility for him who attempts its steep cliffs.

Human meditation has no limits. At its own risk and peril, it analyzes and digs deep into its own bedazzlement. One might almost say, that by a sort of splendid reaction, it with it dazzles nature; the mysterious world which surrounds us renders back what it has received; it is probable that the contemplators are contemplated. However that may be, there are on earth men who—are they men?—perceive distinctly at the verge of the horizons of reverie the heights of the absolute, and who have the terrible vision of the infinite mountain. Monseigneur Welcome was not one of these men; Monseigneur Welcome was not a genius. He would have feared those sublimities whence some very great men even, like Swedenborg and Pascal, have slipped into insanity. Certainly, these powerful reveries have their moral utility, and by these arduous paths one approaches to ideal perfection. As for him, he took the path which shortens—the Gospel's.

He did not attempt to impart to his chasuble the folds of Elijah's mantle; he projected no ray of future upon the dark groundswell of events; he did not seek to condense in flame the light of things; he had nothing of the prophet and nothing of the magician about him. This humble soul loved, and that was all.

That he carried prayer to the pitch of a superhuman aspiration is probable: but one can no more pray too much than one can love too much; and if it is a heresy to pray beyond the texts, Saint Theresa and Saint Jerome would be heretics.

He inclined toward all that groans and all that expiates. The universe appeared to him like an immense malady; everywhere he felt fever, everywhere he heard the sound of suffering, and, without seeking to solve the enigma, he strove to dress the wound. The terrible spectacle of created things developed tenderness in him; he was occupied only in finding for himself, and in inspiring others with the best way to compassionate and relieve. That which exists was for this good and rare priest a permanent subject of sadness which sought consolation.

There are men who toil at extracting gold; he toiled at the extraction of pity. Universal misery was his mine. The sadness which reigned everywhere was but an excuse for unfailing kindness. *Love each other*; he declared this to be complete, desired nothing further, and that was the whole of his doctrine. One day, that man who believed himself to be a "philosopher," the senator who has already been alluded to, said to the Bishop: "Just survey the spectacle of the world: all war against all; the strongest has the most wit. Your *love each other* is nonsense."—*"Well,"* replied Monseigneur Welcome, without contesting the point, *"if it is nonsense, the soul should shut itself up in it, as the pearl in the oyster."* Thus he shut himself up, he lived there, he was absolutely satisfied with it, leaving on one side the prodigious questions which attract and terrify, the fathomless perspectives of abstraction, the precipices of metaphysics—all those profundities which converge, for the apostle in God, for the atheist in nothingness; destiny, good and evil, the way of being against being, the conscience of man, the thoughtful somnambulism of the animal, the transformation in death, the recapitulation of existences which the tomb contains, the incomprehensible grafting of successive loves on the persistent *I*, the essence, the substance, the Nile, and the Ens, the soul, nature, liberty, necessity; perpendicular problems, sinister obscurities, where lean the gigantic archangels of the human mind; formidable abysses, which Lucretius, Manou, Saint Paul, Dante, contemplate with eyes flashing lightning, which seems by its steady gaze on the infinite to cause stars to blaze forth there.

Monseigneur Bienvenu was simply a man who took note of the exterior of mysterious questions without scrutinizing them, and without troubling his own mind with them, and who cherished in his own soul a grave respect for darkness.

BOOK SECOND

THE FALL

Chapter I

THE EVENING OF A DAY OF WALKING

EARLY IN THE MONTH OF OCTOBER, 1815, ABOUT AN HOUR BEFORE SUNSET, A MAN WHO WAS TRAVeling on foot entered the little town of D——. The few inhabitants who were at their windows or on their thresholds at the moment stared at this traveler with a sort of uneasiness. It was difficult to encounter a wayfarer of more wretched appearance. He was a man of medium stature, thickset and robust, in the prime of life. He might have been forty-six or forty-eight years old. A cap with a drooping leather visor partly concealed his face, burned and tanned by sun and wind, and dripping with perspiration. His shirt of coarse yellow linen, fastened at the neck by a small silver anchor, permitted a view of his hairy breast: he had a cravat twisted into a string; trousers of blue drilling, worn and threadbare, white on one knee and torn on the other; an old gray, tattered blouse, patched on one of the elbows with a bit of green cloth sewed on with twine; a tightly packed soldier's knapsack, well buckled and perfectly new, on his back; an enormous, knotty stick in his hand; iron-shod shoes on his stockingless feet; a shaved head and a long beard.

The sweat, the heat, the journey on foot, the dust, added I know not what sordid quality to this dilapidated whole. His hair was closely cut, yet bristling, for it had begun to grow a little, and did not seem to have been cut for some time.

No one knew him. He was evidently only a chance passer-by. Whence came he? From the south; from the seashore, perhaps, for he made his entrance into D—— by the same street which, seven months previously, had witnessed the passage of the Emperor Napoleon on his way from Cannes to Paris. This man must have been walking all day. He seemed very much fatigued. Some women of the ancient market town which is situated below the city had seen him pause beneath the trees of the boulevard Gassendi, and drink at the fountain which stands at the end of the promenade. He must have been very thirsty: for the children who followed him saw him stop again for a drink, two hundred paces further on, at the fountain in the market-place.

On arriving at the corner of the Rue Poichevert, he turned to the left, and directed his steps toward the town-hall. He entered, then came out a quarter of an hour later. A gendarme was seated near the door, on the stone bench which General Drouot had mounted on the 4th of March to read to the frightened throng of the inhabitants of D—— the proclamation of the Gulf Juan. The man pulled off his cap and humbly saluted the gendarme.

The gendarme, without replying to his salute, stared attentively at him, followed him for a while with his eyes, and then entered the town-hall.

There then existed at D—— a fine inn at the sign of the *Cross of Colbas*. This inn had for a landlord a certain Jacquin Labarre, a man of consideration in the town on account of his relationship to another Labarre, who kept the inn of the *Three Dauphins* in Grenoble, and had served in the Guides. At the time of the Emperor's landing, many rumors had circulated throughout the country with regard to this inn of the *Three Dauphins*. It was said that General Bertrand, disguised as a carter, had made frequent trips thither in the month of January, and that he had distributed crosses of honor to the soldiers and handfuls of gold to the citizens. The truth is, that when the Emperor entered Grenoble he had refused to install himself at the hôtel of the prefecture; he had thanked the mayor, saying, *"I am going to the house of a brave man of my acquaintance"*; and he had betaken himself to the *Three Dauphins*. This glory of the Labarre of the *Three Dauphins* was reflected upon the Labarre of the *Cross of Colbas*, at a distance of five-and-twenty leagues. It was said of him in the town, *"That is the cousin of the man of Grenoble."*

The man bent his steps toward this inn, which was the best in the countryside. He entered the kitchen, which opened on a level with the street. All the stoves were lighted; a huge fire blazed gaily in the fireplace. The host, who was also the chief cook, was going from one stew-pan to another, very busily superintending an excellent dinner designed for the wagoners, whose loud talking, conversation, and laughter were audible from an adjoining apartment. Anyone who has traveled knows that there is no one who indulges in better cheer than wagoners. A fat marmot, flanked by white partridges and heather-cocks, was turning on a long spit before the fire; on the stove, two huge carps from Lake Lauzet and a trout from Lake Alloz were cooking.

The host, hearing the door open and seeing a newcomer enter, said, without raising his eyes from his stoves:

"What do you wish, sir?"

"Food and lodging," said the man.

"Nothing easier," replied the host. At that moment he turned his head, took in the traveler's appearance with a single glance, and added, "By paying for it."

The man drew a large leather purse from the pocket of his blouse, and answered, "I have money."

"In that case, we are at your service," said the host.

The man put his purse back in his pocket, removed his knapsack from his back, put it on the ground near the door, retained his stick in his hand, and seated himself on a low stool close to the fire. D—— is in the mountains. The evenings are cold there in October.

But as the host went back and forth, he scrutinized the traveler.

"Will dinner be ready soon?" said the man.

"Immediately," replied the landlord.

While the newcomer was warming himself before the fire, with his back turned, the worthy host, Jacquin Labarre, drew a pencil from his pocket, then tore off the corner of an old newspaper which was lying on a small table near the window. On the white margin he wrote a line or two, folded it without sealing, and then intrusted this scrap of paper to a child who seemed to serve him in the capacity both of scullion and lackey. The landlord whispered a word in the scullion's ear, and the child set off on a run in the direction of the town-hall.

The traveler saw nothing of all this.

Once more he inquired, "Will dinner be ready soon?"

"Immediately," responded the host.

The child returned. He brought back the paper. The host unfolded it eagerly, like a person who is expecting a reply. He seemed to read it attentively, then tossed his head, and remained thoughtful for a moment. Then he took a step in the direction of the traveler, who appeared to be immersed in reflections which were not very serene.

"I cannot receive you, sir," said he.

The man half rose.

"What! Are you afraid that I will not pay you? Do you want me to pay you in advance? I have money, I tell you."

"It is not that."

"What then?"

"You have money—"

"Yes," said the man.

"And I," said the host, "have no room."

The man resumed tranquilly, "Put me in the stable."

"I cannot."

"Why?"

"The horses take up all the space."

"Very well!" retorted the man; "a corner of the loft then, a truss of straw. We will see about that after dinner."

"I cannot give you any dinner."

This declaration, made in a measured but firm tone, struck the stranger as grave. He rose.

"Ah! bah! But I am dying of hunger. I have been walking since sunrise. I have traveled twelve leagues. I pay. I wish to eat."

"I have nothing," said the landlord.

The man burst out laughing, and turned toward the fireplace and the stoves: "Nothing! and all that?"

"All that is engaged."

"By whom?"

"By messieurs the wagoners."

"How many are there of them?"

"Twelve."

"There is enough food there for twenty."

"They have engaged the whole of it and paid for it in advance."

The man seated himself again, and said, without raising his voice, "I am at an inn; I am hungry, and I shall remain."

Then the host bent down to his ear, and said in a tone which made him start, "Go away!"

At that moment the traveler was bending forward and thrusting some brands into the fire with the iron-shod tip of his staff; he turned quickly round, and as he opened his mouth to reply, the host gazed steadily at him and added, still in a low voice: "Stop! there's enough of that sort of talk. Do you want me to tell you your name? Your name is Jean Valjean. Now do you want me to tell you who you are? When I saw you come in I suspected something; I sent to the town-hall, and this is the reply that was sent to me. Can you read?"

So saying, he held out to the stranger, fully unfolded, the paper which had just traveled from the inn to the town-hall, and from the town-hall to the inn. The man cast a glance upon it. The landlord resumed after a pause.

"I am in the habit of being polite to everyone. Go away!"

The man dropped his head, picked up the knapsack which he had deposited on the ground, and took his departure.

He chose the principal street. He walked straight on at a venture, keeping close to the houses like a sad and humiliated man. He did not turn round a single time. Had he done so, he would have seen the host of the *Cross of Colbas* standing on his threshold, surrounded by all the guests of his inn, and all the passers-by in the street, talking vivaciously, and pointing him out with his finger; and, from the glances of terror and distrust cast by the group, he might have divined that his arrival would speedily become an event for the whole town.

He saw nothing of all this. People who are crushed do not look behind them. They know but too well the evil fate which follows them.

Thus he proceeded for some time, walking on without ceasing, traversing at random streets of which he knew nothing, forgetful of his fatigue, as is often the case when a man is sad. All at once he felt the pangs of hunger sharply. Night was drawing near. He glanced about him, to see whether he could not discover some shelter.

The fine hostelry was closed to him; he was seeking some very humble public-house, some hovel, however lowly.

Just then a light flashed up at the end of the streets; a pine branch suspended from a cross-beam of iron was outlined against the white sky of the twilight. He proceeded thither.

It proved to be, in fact, a public-house. The public-house which is in the Rue de Chaffaut.

The wayfarer halted for a moment, and peeped through the window into the interior of the low-studded room of the public-house, illuminated by a small lamp on a table and by a large fire on the hearth. Some men were engaged in drinking there. The landlord was warming himself. An iron pot, suspended from a crane, bubbled over the flame.

The entrance to this public-house, which is also a sort of an inn, is by two doors. One opens on the street, the other upon a small yard filled with manure. The traveler dare not enter by the street door. He slipped into the yard, halted again, then raised the latch timidly and opened the door.

"Who goes there?" said the master.

"Someone who wants supper and bed."

"Good. We furnish supper and bed here."

He entered. All the men who were drinking turned round. The lamp illuminated him on one side, the firelight on the other. They examined him for some time while he was taking off his knapsack.

The host said to him, "There is the fire. The supper is cooking in the pot. Come and warm yourself, comrade."

He approached and seated himself near the hearth. He stretched out his feet, which were exhausted with fatigue, to the fire; a fine odor was emitted by the pot. All that could be distinguished of his face, beneath his cap, which was well pulled down, assumed a vague appearance of comfort, mingled with that other poignant aspect which habitual suffering bestows.

It was, moreover, a firm, energetic, and melancholy profile. This physiognomy was strangely composed; it began by seeming humble, and ended by seeming severe. The eye shone beneath its lashes like a fire beneath brushwood.

One of the men seated at the table, however, was a fishmonger who, before entering the public-house of the Rue de Chaffaut, had been to stable his horse at Labarre's. It chanced that he had that very morning encountered this unprepossessing stranger on the road between Bras d'Asse and—I have forgotten the name. I think it was Escoublon. Now, when he met him, the man, who then seemed already extremely weary, had requested him to take him on his crupper; to which the fishmonger had made no reply except by redoubling his gait. This fishmonger had been a member half an hour previously of the group which surrounded Jacquin Labarre, and had himself related his disagreeable encounter of the morning to the people at the *Cross of Colbas*. From where he sat he made an imperceptible sign to the tavern-keeper. The tavern-keeper went to him. They exchanged a few words in a low tone. The man had again become absorbed in his reflections.

The tavern-keeper returned to the fireplace, laid his hand abruptly on the shoulder of the man, and said to him:

"You are going to get out of here."

The stranger turned round and replied gently, "Ah! You know?—"

"Yes."

"I was sent away from the other inn."

"And you are to be turned out of this one."

"Where would you have me go?"

"Elsewhere."

The man took his stick and his knapsack and departed.

As he went out, some children who had followed him from the *Cross of Colbas*, and who seemed to be lying in wait for him, threw stones at him. He retraced his steps in anger, and threatened them with his stick: the children dispersed like a flock of birds.

He passed before the prison. At the door hung an iron chain attached to a bell. He rang.

The wicket opened.

"Turnkey," said he, removing his cap politely, "will you have the kindness to admit me, and give me a lodging for the night?"

A voice replied:

"The prison is not an inn. Get yourself arrested, and you will be admitted."

The wicket closed again.

He entered a little street in which there were many gardens. Some of them are enclosed only by hedges, which lends a cheerful aspect to the street. In the midst of these gardens and hedges he caught sight of a small house of a single story, the window of which was lighted up. He peered through the pane as he had done at the public-house. Within was a large whitewashed room, with a bed draped in printed cotton stuff, and a cradle in one corner, a few wooden chairs, and a double-barreled gun hanging on the wall. A table was spread in the center of the room. A copper lamp illuminated the table-cloth of coarse white linen, the pewter jug shining like silver, and filled with wine, and the brown, smoking soup-tureen. At this table sat a man of about forty, with a merry and open countenance, who was dandling a little child on his knees. Close by a very young woman was nursing another child. The father was laughing, the child was laughing, the mother was smiling.

The stranger paused a moment in reverie before this tender and calming spectacle. What was taking place within him? He alone could have told. It is probable that he thought that this joyous house would be hospitable, and that, in a place where he beheld so much happiness, he would find perhaps a little pity.

He tapped on the pane with a very small and feeble knock.

They did not hear him.

He tapped again.

He heard the woman say, "It seems to me, husband, that someone is knocking."

"No," replied the husband.

He tapped a third time.

The husband rose, took the lamp, and went to the door, which he opened.

He was a man of lofty stature, half peasant, half artisan. He wore a huge leather apron, which reached to his left shoulder, and which a hammer, a red handkerchief, a powder-horn, and all sorts of objects which were upheld by the girdle, as in a pocket, caused to bulge out. He carried his head thrown backwards; his shirt, widely opened and turned back, displayed his bull neck, white and bare. He had thick eyelashes, enormous black whiskers, prominent eyes, the lower part of his face like a snout; and besides all this, that air of being on his own ground, which is indescribable.

"Pardon me, sir," said the wayfarer. "Could you, in consideration of payment, give me a plate of soup and a corner of that shed yonder in the garden, in which to sleep? Tell me; can you? For money?"

"Who are you?" demanded the master of the house.

The man replied: "I have just come from Puy-Moisson. I have walked all day long. I have traveled twelve leagues. Can you?—if I pay?"

"I would not refuse," said the peasant, "to lodge any respectable man who would pay me. But why do you not go to the inn?"

"There is no room."

"Bah! Impossible. This is neither a fair nor a market day. Have you been to Labarre?"

"Yes."

"Well?"

The traveler replied with embarrassment: "I do not know. He did not receive me."

"Have you been to What's-his-name's, in the Rue Chaffaut?"

The stranger's embarrassment increased; he stammered, "He did not receive me either."

The peasant's countenance assumed an expression of distrust; he surveyed the newcomer from head to feet, and suddenly exclaimed, with a sort of shudder:

"Are you the man?—"

He cast a fresh glance upon the stranger, took three steps backwards, placed the lamp on the table, and took his gun down from the wall.

Meanwhile, at the words, *Are you the man?* the woman had risen, had clasped her two children in her arms, and had taken refuge precipitately behind her husband, staring in terror at the stranger, with her bosom uncovered, and with frightened eyes, as she murmured in a low tone, *"Tso-maraude."*

All this took place in less time than it requires to picture it to one's self. After having scrutinized the man for several moments, as one scrutinizes a viper, the master of the house returned to the door and said:

"Clear out!"

"For pity's sake, a glass of water," said the man.

"A shot from my gun!" said the peasant.

Then he closed the door violently, and the man heard him shoot two large bolts. A moment later, the window-shutter was closed, and the sound of a bar of iron which was placed against it was audible outside.

Night continued to fall. A cold wind from the Alps was blowing. By the light of the expiring day the stranger perceived, in one of the gardens which bordered the street, a sort of hut, which seemed to him to be built of sods. He climbed over the wooden fence resolutely, and found himself in the garden. He approached the hut; its door consisted of a very low and narrow aperture, and it resembled those buildings which road-laborers construct for themselves along the roads. He thought without doubt, that it was, in fact, the dwelling of a road-laborer; he was suffering from cold and hunger, but this was, at least, a shelter from the cold. This sort of dwelling is not usually occupied at night. He threw himself flat on his face, and crawled into the hut. It was warm there, and he found a tolerably good bed of straw. He lay, for a moment, stretched out on this bed, without the power to make a movement, so fatigued was he. Then, as the knapsack on his back was in his way, and as it furnished, moreover, a pillow ready to his hand, he set about unbuckling one of the straps. At that moment, a ferocious growl became audible. He raised his eyes. The head of an enormous dog was outlined in the darkness at the entrance of the hut.

It was a dog's kennel.

He was himself vigorous and formidable; he armed himself with his staff, made a shield of his knapsack, and made his way out of the kennel in the best way he could, not without enlarging the rents in his rags.

He left the garden in the same manner, but backwards, being obliged, in order to keep the dog respectful, to have recourse to that maneuver with his stick, which masters in that sort of fencing designate as *la rose couverte*.

When he had, not without difficulty, repassed the fence, and found himself once more in the street, alone, without refuge, without shelter, without a roof over his head, chased even from that bed of straw and from that miserable kennel, he dropped rather than seated himself on a stone, and it appears that a passer-by heard him exclaim, "I am not even a dog!"

He soon rose again and resumed his march. He went out of the town, hoping to find some tree or hay-stack in the fields which would afford him shelter.

He walked thus for some time, with his head still drooping. When he felt himself far from every human habitation, he raised his eyes and gazed searchingly about him. He was in a field. Before him was one of those low hills covered with close-cut stubble, which, after the harvest, resemble shaved heads.

The horizon was perfectly black. This was not alone the obscurity of night; it was caused by very low-hanging clouds which seemed to rest upon the hill itself, and which were mounting and filling the whole sky. Meanwhile, as the moon was about to rise, and as there was still floating in the zenith a remnant of the brightness of twilight, these clouds formed at the summit of the sky a sort of whitish arch, whence a gleam of light fell upon the earth.

The earth was thus better lighted than the sky, which produces a particularly sinister effect, and the hill, whose contour was poor and mean, was outlined vague and wan against the gloomy horizon. The whole effect was hideous, petty, lugubrious, and narrow.

There was nothing in the field or on the hill except a deformed tree, which writhed and shivered a few paces distant from the wayfarer.

This man was evidently very far from having those delicate habits of intelligence and spirit which render one sensible to the mysterious aspects of things; nevertheless, there was something in that sky, in that hill, in that plain, in that tree, which was so profoundly desolate, that after a moment of immobility and reverie he turned back abruptly. There are instants when nature seems hostile.

He retraced his steps; the gates of D—— were closed. D——, which had sustained sieges during the wars of religion, was still surrounded in 1815 by ancient walls flanked by square towers which have been demolished since. He passed through a breach and entered the town again.

It might have been eight o'clock in the evening. As he was not acquainted with the streets, he recommenced his walk at random.

In this way he came to the prefecture, then to the seminary. As he passed through the Cathedral Square, he shook his fist at the church.

At the corner of this square there is a printing establishment. It is there that the proclamations of the Emperor and of the Imperial Guard to the army, brought from the Island of Elba and dictated by Napoleon himself, were printed for the first time.

Worn out with fatigue, and no longer entertaining any hope, he lay down on a stone bench which stands at the doorway of this printing office.

At that moment an old woman came out of the church. She saw the man stretched out in the shadow. "What are you doing there, my friend?" said she.

He answered harshly and angrily: "As you see, my good woman, I am sleeping." The good woman, who was well worthy the name, in fact, was the Marquise de R——.

"On this bench?" she went on.

"I have had a mattress of wood for nineteen years," said the man; "to-day I have a mattress of stone."

"You have been a soldier?"

"Yes, my good woman, a soldier."

"Why do you not go to the inn?"

"Because I have no money."

"Alas!" said Madame de R——, "I have only four sous in my purse."

"Give it to me all the same."

The man took the four sous. Madame de R—— continued: "You cannot obtain lodgings in an inn for so small a sum. But have you tried? It is impossible for you to pass the night thus. You are cold and hungry, no doubt. Someone might have given you a lodging out of charity."

"I have knocked at all doors."

"Well?"

"I have been driven away everywhere."

The "good woman" touched the man's arm, and pointed out to him on the other side of the street a small, low house, which stood beside the Bishop's palace.

"You have knocked at all doors?"

"Yes."

"Have you knocked at that one?"

"No."

"Knock there."

Chapter II

PRUDENCE COUNSELED TO WISDOM

THAT EVENING, THE BISHOP OF D——, AFTER HIS PROMENADE THROUGH THE TOWN, REMAINED shut up rather late in his room. He was busy over a great work on *Duties*, which was never completed, unfortunately. He was carefully compiling everything that the Fathers and the doctors have said on this important subject. His book was divided into two parts: firstly, the duties of all; secondly, the duties of each individual, according to the class to which he belongs. The duties of all are the great duties. There are four of these. Saint Matthew points them out: duties toward God (*Matt.* vi.); duties toward one's self (*Matt.* v. 29, 30); duties toward one's neighbor (*Matt.* vii. 12);

duties toward animals (*Matt.* vi. 20, 25). As for the other duties the Bishop found them pointed out and prescribed elsewhere: to sovereigns and subjects, in the Epistle to the Romans; to magistrates, to wives, to mothers, to young men, by Saint Peter; to husbands, fathers, children and servants, in the Epistle to the Ephesians; to the faithful, in the Epistle to the Hebrews; to virgins, in the Epistle to the Corinthians. Out of all these precepts he was laboriously constructing a harmonious whole, which he desired to present to souls.

At eight o'clock he was still at work, writing with a good deal of inconvenience upon little squares of paper, with a big book open on his knees, when Madame Magloire entered, according to her wont, to get the silverware from the cupboard near his bed. A moment later, the Bishop, knowing that the table was set, and that his sister was probably waiting for him, shut his book, rose from his table, and entered the dining-room.

The dining-room was an oblong apartment, with a fireplace, which had a door opening on the street (as we have said), and a window opening on the garden.

Madame Magloire was, in fact, just putting the last touches to the table.

As she performed this service, she was conversing with Mademoiselle Baptistine.

A lamp stood on the table; the table was near the fireplace. A wood fire was burning there.

One can easily picture to one's self these two women, both of whom were over sixty years of age. Madame Magloire small, plump, vivacious; Mademoiselle Baptistine gentle, slender, frail, somewhat taller than her brother, dressed in a gown of puce-colored silk, of the fashion of 1806, which she had purchased at that date in Paris, and which had lasted ever since. To borrow vulgar phrases, which possess the merit of giving utterance in a single word to an idea which a whole page would hardly suffice to express, Madame Magloire had the air of a *peasant,* and Mademoiselle Baptistine that of a *lady.* Madame Magloire wore a white quilted cap, a gold Jeannette cross on a velvet ribbon upon her neck, the only bit of feminine jewelry that there was in the house, a very white fichu puffing out from a gown of coarse black woolen stuff, with large, short sleeves, an apron of cotton cloth in red and green checks, knotted round the waist with a green ribbon, with a stomacher of the same attached by two pins at the upper corners, coarse shoes on her feet, and yellow stockings, like the women of Marseilles. Mademoiselle Baptistine's gown was cut on the patterns of 1806, with a short waist, a narrow, sheath-like skirt, puffed sleeves, with flaps and buttons. She concealed her gray hair under a frizzed wig known as the *baby* wig. Madame Magloire had an intelligent, vivacious, and kindly air; the two corners of her mouth unequally raised, and her upper lip, which was larger than the lower, imparted to her a rather crabbed and imperious look. So long as Monseigneur held his peace, she talked to him resolutely with a mixture of respect and freedom; but as soon as Monseigneur began to speak, as we have seen, she obeyed passively like her mistress. Mademoiselle Baptistine did not even speak. She confined herself to obeying and pleasing him. She had never been pretty, even when she was young; she had large, blue, prominent eyes, and a long arched nose; but her whole visage, her whole person, breathed forth an ineffable goodness, as we stated in the beginning. She had always been predestined to gentleness; but faith, charity, hope, those three virtues which mildly warm the soul, had gradually elevated that gentleness to sanctity. Nature had made her a lamb, religion had made her an angel. Poor sainted virgin! Sweet memory which has vanished!

Mademoiselle Baptistine has so often narrated what passed at the episcopal residence that evening, that there are many people now living who still recall the most minute details.

At the moment when the Bishop entered, Madame Magloire was talking with considerable vivacity. She was haranguing Mademoiselle Baptistine on a subject which was familiar to her and to which the Bishop was also accustomed. The question concerned the lock upon the entrance door.

It appears that while procuring some provisions for supper, Madame Magloire had heard things in divers places. People had spoken of a prowler of evil appearance; a suspicious vagabond had arrived who must be somewhere about the town, and those who should take it into their heads to return home late that night might be subjected to unpleasant encounters. The police was very badly organized, moreover, because there was no love lost between the Prefect and the Mayor, who sought to injure each other by making things happen. It behooved wise people to play the part of their own police, and to guard themselves well, and care must be taken to duly close, bar and barricade their houses, and to *fasten the doors well.*

Madame Magloire emphasized these last words; but the Bishop had just come from his room, where it was rather cold. He seated himself in front of the fire, and warmed himself, and then fell to thinking of other things. He did not take up the remark dropped with design by Madame Magloire. She repeated it. Then Mademoiselle Baptistine, desirous of satisfying Madame Magloire without displeasing her brother, ventured to say timidly:

"Did you hear what Madame Magloire is saying, brother?"

"I have heard something of it in a vague way," replied the Bishop. Then half-turning in his chair, placing his hands on his knees, and raising toward the old servant woman his cordial face, which so easily grew joyous, and which was illuminated from below by the firelight—"Come, what is the matter? What is the matter? Are we in any great danger?"

Then Madame Magloire began the whole story afresh, exaggerating it a little without being aware of the fact. It appeared that a Bohemian, a barefooted vagabond, a sort of dangerous mendicant, was at that moment in the town. He had presented himself at Jacquin Labarre's to obtain lodgings, but the latter had not been willing to take him in. He had been seen to arrive by the way of the boulevard Gassendi and roam about the streets in the gloaming. A gallows-bird with a terrible face.

"Really!" said the Bishop.

This willingness to interrogate encouraged Madame Magloire; it seemed to her to indicate that the Bishop was on the point of becoming alarmed; she pursued triumphantly:

"Yes, Monseigneur. That is how it is. There will be some sort of catastrophe in this town tonight. Everyone says so. And withal, the police is so badly regulated" (a useful repetition). "The idea of living in a mountainous country, and not even having lights in the streets at night! One goes out. Black as ovens, indeed! And I say, Monseigneur, and Mademoiselle there says with me—"

"I," interrupted his sister, "say nothing. What my brother does is well done."

Madame Magloire continued as though there had been no protest:

"We say that this house is not safe at all; that if Monseigneur will permit, I will go and tell Paulin Musebois, the locksmith, to come and replace the ancient locks on the doors; we have them, and it is only the work of a moment; for I say that nothing is more terrible than a door which can be opened from the outside with a latch by the first passer-by; and I say that we need bolts, Monseigneur, if only for this night; moreover, Monseigneur has the habit of always saying 'come in'; and besides, even in the middle of the night, O mon Dieu! there is no need to ask permission."

At that moment there came a tolerably violent knock on the door.

"Come in," said the Bishop.

Chapter III

THE HEROISM OF PASSIVE OBEDIENCE

THE DOOR OPENED.

It opened wide with a rapid movement, as though someone had given it an energetic and resolute push.

A man entered.

We already know the man. It was the wayfarer whom we have seen wandering about in search of shelter.

He entered, advanced a step, and halted, leaving the door open behind him. He had his knapsack on his shoulders, his cudgel in his hand, a rough, audacious, weary, and violent expression in his eyes. The fire on the hearth lighted him up. He was hideous. It was a sinister apparition.

Madame Magloire had not even the strength to utter a cry. She trembled, and stood with her mouth wide open.

Mademoiselle Baptistine turned round, beheld the man entering, and half started up in terror; then, turning her head by degrees toward the fireplace again, she began to observe her brother, and her face became once more profoundly calm and serene.

The Bishop fixed a tranquil eye on the man.

As he opened his mouth, doubtless to ask the newcomer what he desired, the man rested both hands on his staff, directed his gaze in turn at the old man and the two women, and without waiting for the Bishop to speak, he said, in a loud voice:

"See here. My name is Jean Valjean. I am a convict from the galleys. I have passed nineteen years in the galleys. I was liberated four days ago, and am on my way to Pontarlier, which is my destination. I have been walking for four days since I left Toulon. I have traveled a dozen leagues today on foot. This evening, when I arrived in these parts, I went to an inn, and they turned me out, because of my yellow passport, which I had shown at the town-hall. I had to do it. I went to an inn. They said to me, 'Be off,' at both places. No one would take me. I went to the prison; the jailer would not admit me. I went into a dog's kennel; the dog bit me and chased me off, as though he had been a man. One would have said that he knew who I was. I went into the fields, intending to sleep in the open air, beneath the stars. There were no stars. I thought it was going to rain, and I re-entered the town, to seek the recess of a doorway. Yonder, in the square, I meant to sleep on a stone bench. A good woman pointed out your house to me, and said to me, 'Knock there!' I have knocked. What is this place? Do you keep an inn? I have money—savings. One hundred and nine francs fifteen sous, which I earned in the galleys by my labor, in the course of nineteen years. I will pay. What is that to me? I have money. I am very weary; twelve leagues on foot; I am very hungry. Are you willing that I should remain?"

"Madame Magloire," said the Bishop, "you will set another place."

The man advanced three paces, and approached the lamp which was on the table. "Stop," he resumed, as though he had not quite understood; "that's not it. Did you hear? I am a galley-slave; a convict. I come from the galleys." He drew from his pocket a large sheet of yellow paper, which he unfolded. "Here's my passport. Yellow, as you see. This serves to expel me from every place where I go. Will you read it? I know how to read. I learned in the galleys. There is a school there for those who choose to learn. Hold, this is what they put on this passport: 'Jean Valjean, discharged convict, native of'—that is nothing to you—'has been nineteen years in the galleys: five years for house-breaking and burglary; fourteen years for having attempted to escape on four occasions. He is a very dangerous man.' There! Everyone has cast me out. Are you willing to receive me? Is this an inn? Will you give me something to eat and a bed? Have you a stable?"

"Madame Magloire," said the Bishop, "you will put white sheets on the bed in the alcove." We have already explained the character of the two women's obedience.

Madame Magloire retired to execute these orders.

The Bishop turned to the man.

"Sit down, sir, and warm yourself. We are going to sup in a few moments, and your bed will be prepared while you are supping."

At this point the man suddenly comprehended. The expression of his face, up to that time somber and harsh, bore the imprint of stupefaction, of doubt, of joy, and became extraordinary. He began stammering like a crazy man:

"Really? What! You will keep me? You do not drive me forth? A convict! You call me *sir!* You do not address me as *thou?* 'Get out of here, you dog!' is what people always say to me. I felt sure that you would expel me, so I told you at once who I am. Oh, what a good woman that was who directed me hither! I am going to sup! A bed with a mattress and sheets, like the rest of the world! a bed! It is nineteen years since I have slept in a bed! You actually do not want me to go! You are good people. Besides, I have money. I will pay well. Pardon me, monsieur the inn-keeper, but what is your name? I will pay anything you ask. You are a fine man. You are an inn-keeper, are you not?"

"I am," replied the Bishop, "a priest who lives here."

"A priest!" said the man. "Oh, what a fine priest! Then you are not going to demand any money of me? You are the curé, are you not? the curé of this big church? Well! I am a fool, truly! I had not perceived your skull-cap."

As he spoke, he deposited his knapsack and his cudgel in a corner, replaced his passport in his pocket, and seated himself. Mademoiselle Baptistine gazed mildly at him. He continued:

"You are humane, Monsieur le Curé; you have not scorned me. A good priest is a very good thing. Then you do not require me to pay?"

"No," said the Bishop; "keep your money. How much have you? Did you not tell me one hundred and nine francs?"

"And fifteen sous," added the man.

"One hundred and nine francs fifteen sous. And how long did it take you to earn that?"

"Nineteen years."

"Nineteen years!"

The Bishop sighed deeply.

The man continued: "I have still the whole of my money. In four days I have spent only twenty-five sous, which I earned by helping unload some wagons at Grasse. Since you are an abbé, I will tell you that we had a chaplain in the galleys. And one day I saw a bishop there. Monseigneur is what they call him. He was the Bishop of Majore at Marseilles. He is the curé who rules over the other curés, you understand. Pardon me, I say that very badly; but it is such a far-off thing to me! You understand what we are! He said mass in the middle of the galleys, on an altar. He had a pointed thing, made of gold, on his head; it glittered in the bright light of midday. We were all ranged in lines on the three sides, with cannons with lighted matches facing us. We could not see very well. He spoke; but he was too far off, and we did not hear. That is what a bishop is like."

While he was speaking, the Bishop had gone and shut the door, which had remained wide open.

Madame Magloire returned. She brought a silver fork and spoon, which she placed on the table.

"Madame Magloire," said the Bishop, "place those things as near the fire as possible." And turning to his guest: "The night wind is harsh on the Alps. You must be cold, sir."

Each time that he uttered the word *sir,* in his voice which was so gently grave and polished, the man's face lighted up. *Monsieur* to a convict is like a glass of water to one of the shipwrecked of the *Medusa*. Ignominy thirsts for consideration.

"This lamp gives a very bad light," said the Bishop.

Madame Magloire understood him, and went to get the two silver candlesticks from the chimney-piece in Monseigneur's bedchamber, and placed them, lighted, on the table.

"Monsieur le Curé," said the man, "you are good; you do not despise me. You receive me into your house. You light your candles for me. Yet I have not concealed from you whence I come and that I am an unfortunate man."

The Bishop, who was sitting close to him, gently touched his hand. "You could not help telling me who you were. This is not my house; it is the house of Jesus Christ. This door does not demand of him who enters whether he has a name, but whether he has a grief. You suffer, you are hungry and thirsty; you are welcome. And do not thank me; do not say that I receive you in my house. No one is at home here, except the man who needs a refuge. I say to you, who are passing by, that you are much more at home here than I am myself. Everything here is yours. What need have I to know your name? Besides, before you told me, you had one which I knew."

The man opened his eyes in astonishment.

"Really? You knew what I was called?"

"Yes," replied the Bishop, "you are called my brother."

"Stop, Monsieur le Curé!" exclaimed the man. "I was very hungry when I entered here; but you are so good, that I no longer know what has happened to me."

The Bishop looked at him, and said—

"You have suffered much?"

"Oh, the red coat, the ball on the ankle, a plank to sleep on, heat, cold, toil, the convicts, the thrashings, the double chain for nothing, the cell for one word; even sick and in bed, still the chain! Dogs, dogs are happier! Nineteen years! I am forty-six. Now, there is the yellow passport. That is what it is like."

"Yes," resumed the Bishop, "you have come from a very sad place. Listen. There will be more joy in heaven over the tear-bathed face of a repentant sinner than over the white robes of a hundred just men. If you emerge from that sad place with thoughts of hatred and of wrath against mankind, you are deserving of pity; if you emerge with thoughts of good-will and of peace, you are more worthy than any one of us."

In the meantime, Madame Magloire had served supper: soup, made with water, oil, bread, and salt; a little bacon, a bit of mutton, figs, a fresh cheese, and a large loaf of rye bread. She had, of her own accord, added to the Bishop's ordinary fare a bottle of his old Mauves wine.

The Bishop's face at once assumed that expression of gaiety which is peculiar to hospitable natures. "To table!" he cried vivaciously. As was his custom when a stranger supped with him, he made the man sit on his right. Mademoiselle Baptistine, perfectly peaceable and natural, took her seat at his left.

The Bishop asked a blessing; then helped the soup himself, according to his custom. The man began to eat with avidity.

All at once the Bishop said: "It strikes me there is something missing on this table."

Madame Magloire had, in fact, only placed the three sets of forks and spoons which were absolutely necessary. Now, it was the usage of the house, when the Bishop had anyone to supper, to lay out the whole six sets of silver on the table-cloth—an innocent ostentation. This graceful semblance of luxury was a kind of child's play, which was full of charm in that gentle and severe household, which raised poverty into dignity.

Madame Magloire understood the remark, went out without saying a word, and a moment later the three sets of silver forks and spoons demanded by the Bishop were glittering upon the cloth, symmetrically arranged before the three persons seated at the table.

Chapter IV

DETAILS CONCERNING THE CHEESE-DAIRIES OF PONTARLIER

NOW, IN ORDER TO CONVEY AN IDEA OF WHAT PASSED AT THAT TABLE, WE CANNOT DO BETTER than to transcribe here a passage from one of Mademoiselle Baptistine's letters to Madame Boischevron, wherein the conversation between the convict and the Bishop is described with ingenuous minuteness.

". . . This man paid no attention to anyone. He ate with the voracity of a starving man. However, after supper he said:

" 'Monsieur le Curé of the good God, all this is far too good for me; but I must say that the carters who would not allow me to eat with them keep a better table than you do.'

"Between ourselves, the remark rather shocked me. My brother replied:

" 'They are more fatigued than I.'

" 'No,' returned the man, 'they have more money. You are poor; I see that plainly. You cannot be even a curate. Are you really a curé? Ah, if the good God were but just, you certainly ought to be a curé!'

" 'The good God is more than just,' said my brother.

"A moment later he added:

" 'Monsieur Jean Valjean, is it to Pontarlier that you are going?'

" 'With my road marked out for me.'

"I think that is what the man said. Then he went on:

" 'I must be on my way by daybreak to-morrow. Traveling is hard. If the nights are cold, the days are hot.'

" 'You are going to a good country,' said my brother. 'During the Revolution my family was ruined. I took refuge in Franche-Comté at first, and there I lived for some time by the toil of my hands. My will was good. I found plenty to occupy me. One has only to choose. There are paper mills, tanneries, distilleries, oil factories, watch factories on a large scale, steel mills, copper works, twenty iron foundries at least, four of which, situated at Lods, at Châtillon, at Audincourt, and at Beure, are tolerably large.'

"I think I am not mistaken in saying that those are the names which my brother mentioned. Then he interrupted himself and addressed me:

" 'Have we not some relatives in those parts, my dear sister?'

"I replied—

" 'We did have some; among others, M. de Lucenet, who was captain of the gates at Pontarlier under the old régime.'

" 'Yes,' resumed my brother; 'but in '93, one had no longer any relatives, one had only one's arms. I worked. They have, in the country of Pontarlier, whither you are going, Monsieur Valjean, a truly patriarchal and truly charming industry, my sister. It is their cheese-dairies, which they call *fruitières*.'

"Then my brother, while urging the man to eat, explained to him, with great minuteness, what these *fruitières* of Pontarlier were; that they were divided into two classes: the *big barns*, which belong to the rich, and where there are forty or fifty cows, which produce from seven to eight thousand cheeses each summer, and the *associated fruitières*, which belong to the poor; these are the peasants of mid-mountain, who hold their cows in common, and share the proceeds. 'They engage the services of a cheese-maker, whom they call the *grurin*; the *grurin* receives the milk of the associates three times a day, and marks the quantity on a double tally. It is toward the end of April that the work of the cheese-dairies begins; it is toward the middle of June that the cheese-makers drive their cows to the mountains.'

"The man recovered his animation as he ate. My brother made him drink that good Mauves wine, which he does not drink himself, because he says that wine is expensive. My brother imparted all these details with that easy gaiety of his with which you are acquainted, interspersing his words with graceful attentions to me. He recurred frequently to that comfortable trade of *grurin*, as though he wished the man to understand, without advising him directly and harshly, that this would afford him a refuge. One thing struck me. This man was what I have told you. Well, neither during supper, nor during the entire evening, did my brother utter a single word, with the exception of a few words about Jesus when he entered, which could remind the man of what he was, nor of what my brother was. To all appearances, it was an occasion for preaching him a little sermon, and of impressing the Bishop on the convict, so that a mark of the passage might remain behind. This might have appeared to anyone else who had this unfortunate man in his hands to afford a chance to nourish his soul as well as his body, and to bestow upon him some reproach, seasoned with moralizing and advice, or a little commiseration, with an exhortation to conduct himself better in the future. My brother did not even ask him from what country he came, nor what was his history. For in his history there is a fault, and my brother seemed to avoid everything which could remind him of it. To such a point did he carry it, that at one time, when my brother was speaking of the mountaineers of Pontarlier, *who exercise a gentle labor near heaven, and who,* he added, *are happy because they are innocent,* he stopped short, fearing lest in this remark there might have escaped him something which might wound the man. By dint of reflection, I think I have comprehended what was passing in my brother's heart. He was thinking, no doubt, that this man, whose name is Jean Valjean, had his misfortune only too vividly present in his mind; that the best thing was to divert him from it, and to make him believe, if only momentarily, that he was a person like any other, by treating him just in his ordinary way. Is not this, indeed, to understand charity well? Is there not, dear Madame, something truly evangelical in this delicacy which abstains from sermon, from moralizing, from allusions? and is it not the truest pity, when a man has a sore point, not to touch it at all? It has seemed to me that this might have been my brother's private thought. In any case, what I can say is that, if he entertained all these ideas, he gave no sign of them; from beginning to end, even to me he was the same as he is every evening, and he supped with this Jean Valjean with the same air and in the same manner in which he would have supped with M. Gédéon le Prévost, or with the curate of the parish.

"Toward the end, when he had reached the figs, there came a knock at the door. It was Mother Gerbaud, with her little one in her arms. My brother kissed the child on the brow, and borrowed fifteen sous which I had about me to give to Mother Gerbaud. The man was not paying much heed to anything then. He was no longer talking, and he seemed very much fatigued. After poor old Gerbaud had taken her departure, my brother said grace; then he turned to the man and said to him, 'You must be in great need of your bed.' Madame Magloire cleared the table very promptly. I understood that we must retire, in order to allow this traveler to go to sleep, and we both went upstairs. Nevertheless, I sent Madame Magloire down a moment later, to carry to the man's bed a goat skin from the Black Forest, which was in my room. The nights are frigid, and that keeps one warm. It is a pity that this skin is old; all the hair is falling out. My brother bought it while he was in Germany, at Tottlingen, near the sources of the Danube, as well as the little ivory-handled knife which I use at table.

"Madame Magloire returned immediately. We said our prayers in the drawing-room, where we hang up the linen, and then we each retired to our own chambers, without saying a word to each other."

Chapter V

TRANQUILITY

AFTER BIDDING HIS SISTER GOOD NIGHT, MONSEIGNEUR BIENVENU TOOK ONE OF THE TWO SILVER candlesticks from the table, handed the other to his guest, and said to him—

"Monsieur, I will conduct you to your room."

The man followed him.

As might have been observed from what has been said above, the house was so arranged that in order to pass into the oratory where the alcove was situated, or to get out of it, it was necessary to traverse the Bishop's bedroom.

At the moment when he was crossing this apartment, Madame Magloire was putting away the silverware in the cupboard near the head of the bed. This was her last care every evening before she went to bed.

The Bishop installed his guest in the alcove. A fresh white bed had been prepared there. The man set the candle down on a small table.

"Well," said the Bishop, "may you pass a good night. To-morrow morning, before you set out, you shall drink a cup of warm milk from our cows."

"Thanks, Monsieur l'Abbé," said the man.

Hardly had he pronounced these words full of peace, when all of a sudden, and without transition, he made a strange movement, which would have frozen the two sainted women with horror, had they witnessed it. Even at this day it is difficult for us to explain what inspired him at that moment. Did he intend to convey a warning or to throw out a menace? Was he simply obeying a sort of instinctive impulse which was obscure even to himself? He turned abruptly to the old man, folded his arms, and bending upon his host a savage gaze, he exclaimed in a hoarse voice:

"Ah! really! You lodge me in your house, close to yourself, like this?"

He broke off, and added with a laugh in which there lurked something monstrous:

"Have you really reflected well? How do you know that I have not been an assassin?"

The Bishop replied:

"That is the concern of the good God."

Then gravely, and moving his lips like one who is praying or talking to himself, he raised two fingers of his right hand and bestowed his benediction on the man, who did not bow, and without turning his head or looking behind him, he returned to his bedroom.

When the alcove was in use, a large serge curtain drawn from wall to wall concealed the altar. The Bishop knelt before this curtain as he passed and said a brief prayer. A moment later he was in his garden, walking, meditating, contemplating, his heart and soul wholly absorbed in those grand and mysterious things which God shows at night to the eyes which remain open.

As for the man, he was actually so fatigued that he did not even profit by the nice white sheets. Snuffing out his candle with his nostrils after the manner of convicts, he dropped, all dressed as he was, upon the bed, where he immediately fell into a profound sleep.

Midnight struck as the Bishop returned from his garden to his apartment.

A few minutes later all were asleep in the little house.

Chapter VI

JEAN VALJEAN

T OWARD THE MIDDLE OF THE NIGHT, JEAN VALJEAN WOKE.

Jean Valjean came from a poor peasant family of Brie. He had not learned to read in his childhood. When he reached man's estate, he became a tree-pruner at Faverolles. His mother was named Jeanne Mathieu; his father was called Jean Valjean or Vlajean, probably a sobriquet, and a contraction of *violà Jean*, "here's Jean."

Jean Valjean was of that thoughtful but not gloomy disposition which constitutes the peculiarity of affectionate natures. On the whole, however, there was something decidedly sluggish and insignificant about Jean Valjean, in appearance, at least. He had lost his father and mother at a very early age. His mother had died of a milk fever, which had not been properly attended to. His father, a tree-pruner, like himself, had been killed by a fall from a tree. All that remained to Jean Valjean was a sister older than himself—a widow with seven children, boys and girls. This sister had brought up Jean Valjean, and so long as she had a husband she lodged and fed her young brother.

The husband died. The eldest of the seven children was eight years old. The youngest, one.

Jean Valjean had just attained his twenty-fifth year. He took the father's place, and, in his turn, supported the sister who had brought him up. This was done simply as a duty and even a little churlishly on the part of Jean Valjean. Thus his youth had been spent in rude and ill-paid toil. He had never known a "kind woman friend" in his native parts. He had not had the time to fall in love.

He returned at night weary, and ate his broth without uttering a word. His sister, mother Jeanne, often took the best part of his repast from his bowl while he was eating—a bit of meat, a slice of bacon, the heart of the cabbage—to give to one of her children. As he went on eating, with his head bent over the table and almost into his soup, his long hair falling about his bowl and concealing his eyes, he had the air of perceiving nothing and allowing it. There was at Faverolles, not far from the Valjean thatched cottage, on the other side of the lane, a farmer's wife named Marie-Claude; the Valjean children, habitually famished, sometimes went to borrow from Marie-Claude a pint of milk, in their mother's name, which they drank behind a hedge or in some alley corner, snatching the jug from each other so hastily that the little girls spilled it on their aprons and down their necks. If their mother had known of this marauding, she would have punished the delinquents severely. Jean Valjean gruffly and grumblingly paid Marie-Claude for the pint of milk behind their mother's back, and the children were not punished.

In pruning season he earned eighteen sous a day; then he hired out as a hay-maker, as laborer, as neat-herd on a farm, as a drudge. He did whatever he could. His sister worked also, but what could she do with seven little children? It was a sad group enveloped in misery, which was being gradually annihilated. A very hard winter came. Jean had no work. The family had no bread. No bread literally. Seven children!

One Sunday evening, Maubert Isabeau, the baker on the Church Square at Faverolles, was preparing to go to bed, when he heard a violent blow on the grated front of his shop. He arrived in time to see an arm passed through a hole made by a blow from a fist, through the grating and the glass. The arm seized a loaf of bread and carried it off. Isabeau ran out in haste; the robber fled at the full speed of his legs. Isabeau ran after him and stopped him. The thief had flung away the loaf, but his arm was still bleeding. It was Jean Valjean.

This took place in 1795. Jean Valjean was taken before the tribunals of the time for theft and breaking and entering an inhabited house at night. He had a gun which he used better than anyone else in the world, he was a bit of a poacher, and this injured his case. There exists a legitimate prejudice against poachers. The poacher, like the smuggler, smacks too strongly of the brigand. Nevertheless, we will remark cursorily, there is still an abyss between these races of men and the hideous assassin of the towns. The poacher lives in the forest, the smuggler lives in the mountains or on the sea. The cities make ferocious men because they make corrupt men. The mountain, the sea, the forest, make savage men; they develop the fierce side, but often without destroying the humane side.

Jean Valjean was pronounced guilty. The terms of the Code were explicit. There occur formidable hours in our civilization; there are moments when the penal laws decree a shipwreck. What an ominous minute is that in which society draws back and consummates the irreparable abandonment of a sentient being! Jean Valjean was condemned to five years in the galleys.

On the 22d of April, 1796, the victory of Montenotte, won by the general-in-chief of the army of Italy, whom the message of the Directory to the Five Hundred, of the 2d of Floréal, year IV, calls Buona-Parte, was announced in Paris; on that same day a great gang of galley-slaves was put in chains at Bicêtre. Jean Valjean formed a part of that gang. An old turnkey of the prison, who is now nearly eighty years old, still recalls perfectly that unfortunate wretch who was chained to the end of the fourth line, in the north angle of the courtyard. He was seated on the ground like the others. He did not seem to comprehend his position, except that it was horrible. It is probable that he, also, was disentangling from amid the vague ideas of a poor man, ignorant of everything, something excessive. While the bolt of his iron collar was being riveted behind his head with heavy blows from the hammer, he wept, his tears stifled him, they impeded his speech; he only managed to say from time to time, "I was a tree-pruner at Faverolles." Then still sobbing, he raised his right hand and lowered it gradually seven times, as though he were touching in succession seven heads of unequal heights, and from this gesture it was divined that the thing which he had done, whatever it was, he had done for the sake of clothing and nourishing seven little children.

He set out for Toulon. He arrived there, after a journey of twenty-seven days, on a cart, with a chain on his neck. At Toulon he was clothed in the red cassock. All that had constituted his life, even to his name, was effaced; he was no longer even Jean Valjean; he was number 24,601. What became of his sister? What became of the seven children? Who troubled himself about that? What becomes of the handful of leaves from the young tree which is sawed off at the root?

It is always the same story. These poor living beings, these creatures of God, henceforth without support, without guide, without refuge, wandered away at random—who even knows?—each in his own direction perhaps, and little by little buried themselves in that cold mist which engulfs solitary destinies; gloomy shades, into which disappear in succession so many unlucky heads, in the somber march of the human race. They quitted the country. The clock-tower of what had been their village forgot them; the boundary line of what had been their field forgot them; after a few years' residence in the galleys, Jean Valjean himself forgot them. In that heart, where there had been a wound, there was a scar. That is all. Only once, during all the time which he spent at Toulon, did he hear his sister mentioned. This happened, I think, toward the end of the fourth year of his captivity. I know not through what channels the news reached him. Someone who had known them in their own country had seen his sister. She was in Paris. She lived in a poor street near Saint-Sulpice, in the Rue du Gindre. She had with her only one child, a little boy, the youngest. Where were the other six? Perhaps she did not know herself. Every morning she went to a printing office, No. 3 Rue du Sabot, where she was a folder and stitcher. She was obliged to be there at six o'clock in the morning—long before daylight in winter. In the same building with the printing office there was a school, and to this school she took her little boy, who was seven years old. But as she entered the printing office at six, and the school only opened at seven, the child had to wait in the courtyard, for the school to open, for an hour—one hour of a winter night in the open air! They would not allow the child to come into the printing office, because he was in the way, they said. When the workmen passed in the morning, they beheld this poor little being seated on the pavement, overcome with drowsiness, and often fast asleep in the shadow, crouched down and doubled up over his basket. When it rained, an old woman, the portress, took pity on him; she took him into her den, where there was a pallet, a spinning-wheel, and two wooden chairs, and the little one slumbered in a corner, pressing himself close to the cat that he might suffer less from cold. At seven o'clock the school opened, and he entered. That is what was told to Jean Valjean.

They talked to him about it for one day; it was a moment, a flash, as though a window had suddenly been opened upon the destiny of those beings whom he had loved; then all closed again. He heard nothing more forever. Nothing from them ever reached him again; he never beheld them; he never met them again; and in the continuation of this mournful history they will not be met with anymore.

Toward the end of this fourth year Jean Valjean's turn to escape arrived. His comrades assisted him, as is the custom in that sad place. He escaped. He wandered for two days in the fields at liberty, if being at liberty is to be hunted, to turn the head every instant, to quake at the slightest noise, to be afraid of everything—of a smoking roof, of a passing man, of a barking dog, of a galloping horse, of a striking clock, of the day because one can see, of the night because one cannot see, of the highway, of the path, of a bush, of sleep. On the evening of the second day he was captured. He had neither eaten nor slept for thirty-six hours. The maritime tribunal condemned him, for this crime, to a prolongation of his term for three years, which made eight years. In the sixth year his turn to escape occurred again; he availed himself of it, but could not accomplish his flight fully. He was missing at roll-call. The cannon were fired, and at night the patrol found him hidden under the keel of a vessel in process of construction; he resisted the galley guards who seized him. Escape and rebellion. This case, provided for by a special code, was punished by an addition of five years, two of them in the double chain. Thirteen years. In the tenth year his turn came round again; he again profited by it; he succeeded no better. Three years for this fresh attempt. Sixteen years. Finally, I think it was during his thirteenth year, he made a last attempt, and only succeeded in getting retaken at the end of four hours of absence. Three years for those four hours. Nineteen years. In October, 1815, he was released; he had entered there in 1796, for having broken a pane of glass and taken a loaf of bread.

Room for a brief parenthesis. This is the second time, during his studies on the penal question and damnation by law, that the author of this book has come across the theft of a loaf of bread as the point of departure for the disaster of a destiny. Claude Gueux had stolen a loaf; Jean Valjean had stolen a loaf. English statistics prove the fact that four thefts out of five in London have hunger for their immediate cause.

Jean Valjean had entered the galleys sobbing and shuddering; he emerged impassive. He had entered in despair; he emerged gloomy.

What had taken place in that soul?

Chapter VII

THE INTERIOR OF DESPAIR

LET US TRY TO SAY IT.
It is necessary that society should look at these things, because it is itself which creates them.

He was, as we have said, an ignorant man, but he was not a fool. The light of nature was ignited in him. Unhappiness, which also possesses a clearness of vision of its own, augmented the small amount of daylight which existed in this mind. Beneath the cudgel, beneath the chain, in the cell, in hardship, beneath the burning sun of the galleys, upon the plank bed of the convict, he withdrew into his own consciousness and meditated.

He constituted himself the tribunal.

He began by putting himself on trial.

He recognized the fact that he was not an innocent man unjustly punished. He admitted that he had committed an extreme and blameworthy act; that that loaf of bread would probably not have been refused to him had he asked for it; that, in any case, it would have been better to wait until he could get it through compassion or through work; that it is not an unanswerable argument to say, "Can one wait when one is hungry?" That, in the first place, it is very rare for anyone to die of hunger, literally; and next, that, fortunately or unfortunately, man is so constituted that he can suffer long and much, both morally and physically, without dying; that it is therefore necessary to have patience; that that would even have been better for those poor little children; that it had been an act of madness for him, a miserable, unfortunate wretch, to take society at large violently by the collar, and to imagine that one can escape from misery through theft; that that is in any case a poor door through which to escape from misery through which infamy enters; in short, that he was in the wrong.

Then he asked himself—

Whether he had been the only one in fault in his fatal history. Whether it was not a serious thing, that he, a laborer, out of work, that he, an industrious man, should have lacked bread. And whether, the fault once committed and confessed, the chastisement had not been ferocious and disproportioned. Whether there had not been more abuse on the part of the law, in respect to the penalty, than there had been on the part of the culprit in respect to his fault. Whether there had not been an excess of weights in one balance of the scale, in the one which contains expiation. Whether the over-weight of the penalty was not equivalent to the annihilation of the crime, and did not result in reversing the situation, of replacing the fault of the delinquent by the fault of the repression, of converting the guilty man into the victim, and the debtor into the creditor, and of ranging the law definitely on the side of the man who had violated it.

Whether this penalty, complicated by successive aggravations for attempts at escape, had not ended in becoming a sort of outrage perpetrated by the stronger upon the feebler, a crime of society against the individual, a crime which was being committed afresh every day, a crime which had lasted nineteen years.

He asked himself whether human society could have the right to force its members to suffer equally in one case for its own unreasonable lack of foresight, and in the other case for its pitiless foresight; and to seize a poor man forever between a defect and an excess, a default of work and an excess of punishment.

Whether it was not outrageous for society to treat thus precisely those of its members who were the least well endowed in the division of goods made by chance, and consequently the most deserving of consideration.

These questions put and answered, he judged society and condemned it.

He condemned it to his hatred.

He made it responsible for the fate which he was suffering, and he said to himself that it might be that one day he should not hesitate to call it to account. He declared to himself that there was no equilibrium between the harm which he had caused and the harm which was being done to him; he finally arrived at the conclusion that his punishment was not, in truth, unjust, but that it most assuredly was iniquitous.

Anger may be both foolish and absurd; one can be irritated wrongfully; one is exasperated only when there is some show of right on one's side at bottom. Jean Valjean felt himself exasperated.

And besides, human society had done him nothing but harm; he had never seen anything of it save that angry face which it calls Justice, and which it shows to those whom it strikes. Men had only touched him to bruise him. Every contact with them had been a blow. Never, since his infancy, since the days of his mother, of his sister, had he ever encountered a friendly word and a kindly glance. From suffering to suffering, he had gradually arrived at the conviction that life is a war; and that in this war he was the conquered. He had no other weapon than his hate. He resolved to whet it in the galleys and to bear it away with him when he departed.

There was at Toulon a school for the convicts, kept by the Ignorantin friars, where the most necessary branches were taught to those of the unfortunate men who had a mind for them. He was of the number who had a mind. He went to school at the age of forty, and learned to read, to write, to cipher. He felt that to fortify his intelligence was to fortify his hate. In certain cases, education and enlightenment can serve to eke out evil.

This is a sad thing to say; after having judged society, which had caused his unhappiness, he judged Providence, which had made society, and he condemned it also.

Thus during nineteen years of torture and slavery, this soul mounted and at the same time fell. Light entered it on one side, and darkness on the other.

Jean Valjean had not, as we have seen, an evil nature. He was still good when he arrived at the galleys. He there condemned society, and felt that he was becoming wicked; he there condemned Providence, and was conscious that he was becoming impious.

It is difficult not to indulge in meditation at this point.

Does human nature thus change utterly and from top to bottom? Can the man created good by God be rendered wicked by man? Can the soul be completely made over by fate, and become evil, fate being evil? Can the heart become misshapen and contract incurable deformities and infirmities under the oppression of a disproportionate unhappiness, as the vertebral column beneath too low a vault? Is there not in every human soul, was there not in the soul of Jean Valjean in particular, a first spark, a divine element, incorruptible in this world, immortal in the other, which good can develop, fan, ignite, and make to glow with splendor, and which evil can never wholly extinguish?

Grave and obscure questions, to the last of which every physiologist would probably have responded no, and that without hesitation, had he beheld at Toulon, during the hours of repose, which were for Jean Valjean hours of reverie, this gloomy galley-slave, seated with folded arms upon the bar of some capstan, with the end of his chain thrust into his pocket to prevent its dragging, serious, silent, and thoughtful, a pariah of the laws which regarded the man with wrath, condemned by civilization, and regarding heaven with severity.

Certainly—and we make no attempt to dissimulate the fact—the observing physiologist would have beheld an irremediable misery; he would, perchance, have pitied this sick man, of the law's making; but he would not have even essayed any treatment; he would have turned aside his gaze from the caverns of which he would have caught a glimpse within this soul, and, like Dante at the portals of hell, he would have effaced from this existence the word which the finger of God has, nevertheless, inscribed upon the brow of every man—hope.

Was this state of his soul, which we have attempted to analyze, as perfectly clear to Jean Valjean as we have tried to render it for those who read us? Did Jean Valjean distinctly perceive, after their formation, and had he seen distinctly during the process of their formation, all the elements of which his moral misery was composed? Had this rough and unlettered man gathered a perfectly clear perception of the succession of ideas through which he had, by degrees, mounted and descended to the lugubrious aspects which had, for so many years, formed the inner horizon of his spirit? Was he conscious of all that passed within him, and of all that was working there? That is something which we do not presume to state; it is something which we do not even believe. There was too much ignorance in Jean Valjean, even after his misfortune, to prevent much vagueness from still lingering there. At times he did not rightly know himself what he felt. Jean Valjean was in the shadows; he suffered in the shadows; he hated in the shadows; one might have said that he hated in advance of himself. He dwelt habitually in this shadow, feeling his way like a blind man and a dreamer. Only, at intervals, there suddenly came to him, from without and from within, an access of wrath, a surcharge of suffering, a livid and rapid flash which illuminated his whole soul, and caused to appear abruptly all around him, in front, behind, amid the gleams of a frightful light, the hideous precipices and the somber perspective of his destiny.

The flash passed, the night closed in again; and where was he? He no longer knew. The peculiarity of pains of this nature, in which that which is pitiless—that is to say, that which is brutalizing—predominates, is to transform a man, little by little, by a sort of stupid transfiguration, into a wild beast; sometimes into a ferocious beast.

Jean Valjean's successive and obstinate attempts at escape would alone suffice to prove this strange working of the law upon the human soul. Jean Valjean would have renewed these attempts, utterly useless and foolish as they were, as often as the opportunity had presented itself, without reflecting for an instant on the result, nor on the experiences which he had already gone through. He escaped impetuously, like the wolf who finds his cage open. Instinct said to him, "Flee!" Reason would have said, "Remain!" But in the presence of so violent a temptation, reason vanished; nothing remained but instinct. The beast alone acted. When he was recaptured, the fresh severities inflicted on him only served to render him still more wild.

One detail, which we must not omit, is that he possessed a physical strength which was not approached by a single one of the denizens of the galleys. At work, at paying out a cable or winding up a capstan, Jean Valjean was worth four men. He sometimes lifted and sustained enormous weights on his back; and when the occasion demanded it, he replaced that implement which is called a jack-screw, and was formerly called *orgueil* [pride], whence, we may remark in passing, is derived the name of the Rue Montorgueil, near the Halles [Fishmarket] in Paris. His comrades had nicknamed him Jean the Jack-screw. Once, when they were repairing the balcony of the town-hall at Toulon, one of those admirable caryatids of Puget, which support the balcony, became loosened, and was on the point of falling. Jean Valjean, who was present, supported the caryatid with his shoulder, and gave the workmen time to arrive.

His suppleness even exceeded his strength. Certain convicts who were forever dreaming of escape, ended by making a veritable science of force and skill combined. It is the science of muscles. An entire system of mysterious statics is daily practiced by prisoners, men who are forever envious of the flies and birds. To climb a vertical surface, and to find points of support where hardly a projection was visible, was play to Jean Valjean. An angle of the wall being given, with the tension of his back and his legs, with his elbows and his heels fitted into the unevenness of the stone, he raised himself as if by magic to the third story. He sometimes mounted thus even to the roof of the galley prison.

He spoke but little. He laughed not at all. An excessive emotion was required to wring from him, once or twice a year, that lugubrious laugh of the convict, which is like the echo of the laugh of a demon. To all appearance, he seemed to be occupied in the constant contemplation of something terrible.

He was absorbed, in fact.

Athwart the unhealthy perceptions of an incomplete nature and a crushed intelligence, he was confusedly conscious that some monstrous thing was resting on him. In that obscure and wan shadow within which he crawled, each time that he turned his neck and essayed to raise his glance, he perceived with terror, mingled with rage, a sort of frightful accumulation of things, collecting and mounting above him, beyond the range of his vision—laws, prejudices, men, and deeds—whose outlines escaped him, whose mass terrified him, and which was nothing else than that prodigious pyramid which we call civilization. He distinguished, here and there in that swarming and formless mass, now near him, now afar off and on inaccessible table-lands, some group, some detail, vividly illuminated; here the galley-sergeant and his cudgel; there the gendarme and his sword; yonder the mitered archbishop; away at the top, like a sort of sun, the Emperor, crowned and dazzling. It seemed to him that these distant splendors, far from dissipating his night, rendered it more funereal and more black. All this—laws, prejudices, deeds, men, things—went and came above him, over his head, in accordance with the complicated and mysterious movement which God imparts to civilization, walking over him and crushing him with I know not what peacefulness in its cruelty and inexorability in its indifference. Souls which have fallen to the bottom of all possible misfortune, unhappy men lost in the lowest of those limbos at which no one any longer looks, the reproved of the law, feel the whole weight of this human society, so formidable for him who is without, so frightful for him who is beneath, resting upon their heads.

In this situation Jean Valjean meditated; and what could be the nature of his meditation?

If the grain of millet beneath the millstone had thoughts, it would, doubtless, think that same thing which Jean Valjean thought.

All these things, realities full of specters, phantasmagories full of realities, had eventually created for him a sort of interior state which is almost indescribable.

At times, amid his convict toil, he paused. He fell to thinking. His reason, at one and the same time riper and more troubled than of yore, rose in revolt. Everything which had happened to him seemed to him absurd; everything that surrounded him seemed to him impossible. He said to himself, "It is a dream." He gazed at the galley-sergeant standing a few paces from him; the galley-sergeant seemed a phantom to him. All of a sudden the phantom dealt him a blow with his cudgel.

Visible nature hardly existed for him. It would almost be true to say that there existed for Jean Valjean neither sun, nor fine summer days, nor radiant sky, nor fresh April dawns. I know not what vent-hole daylight habitually illumined his soul.

To sum up, in conclusion, that which can be summed up and translated into positive results in all that we have just pointed out, we will confine ourselves to the statement that, in the course of nineteen years, Jean Valjean, the inoffensive tree-pruner of Faverolles, the formidable convict of Toulon, had become capable, thanks to the manner in which the galleys had molded him, of two sorts of evil action: firstly, of evil action which was rapid, unpremeditated, dashing, entirely instinctive, in the nature of reprisals for the evil which he had undergone; secondly, of evil action which was serious, grave, consciously argued out and premeditated, with the false ideas which such a misfortune can furnish. His deliberate deeds passed through three successive phases, which natures of a certain stamp can alone traverse—reasoning, will, perseverance. He had for moving causes his habitual wrath, bitterness of soul, a profound sense of indignities suffered, the reaction even against the good, the innocent, and the just, if there are any such. The point of departure, like the point of arrival, for all his thoughts, was hatred of human law; that hatred which, if it be not arrested in its development by some providential incident, becomes, within a given time, the hatred of society, then the hatred of the human race, then the hatred of creation, and which manifests itself by a vague, incessant, and brutal desire to do harm to some living being, no matter whom. It will be perceived that it was not without reason that Jean Valjean's passport described him as *a very dangerous man.*

From year to year this soul had dried away slowly, but with fatal sureness. When the heart is dry, the eye is dry. On his departure from the galleys it had been nineteen years since he had shed a tear.

Chapter VIII

BILLOWS AND SHADOWS

A MAN OVERBOARD!
What matters it? The vessel does not halt. The wind blows. That somber ship has a path which it is forced to pursue. It passes on.

The man disappears, then reappears; he plunges, he rises again to the surface; he calls, he stretches out his arms; he is not heard. The vessel, trembling under the hurricane, is wholly absorbed in its own workings; the passengers and sailors do not even see the drowning man; his miserable head is but a speck amid the immensity of the waves. He gives vent to desperate cries from out of the depths. What a specter is that retreating sail! He gazes and gazes at it frantically. It retreats, it grows dim, it diminishes in size. He was there but just now, he was one of the crew, he went and came along the deck with the rest, he had his part of breath and of sunlight, he was a living man. Now, what has taken place? He has slipped, he has fallen; all is at an end.

He is in the tremendous sea. Underfoot he has nothing but what flees and crumbles. The billows, torn and lashed by the wind, encompass him hideously; the tossings of the abyss bear him away; all the tongues of water dash over his head; a populace of waves spits upon him; confused openings half devour him; every time that he sinks, he catches glimpses of precipices filled with night; frightful and unknown vegetations seize him, knot about his feet, draw him to them; he is conscious that he is becoming an abyss, that he forms part of the foam; the waves toss him from one to another; he drinks in the bitterness; the cowardly ocean attacks him furiously, to drown him; the enormity plays with his agony. It seems as though all that water were hate.

Nevertheless, he struggles.

He tries to defend himself; he tries to sustain himself; he makes an effort; he swims. He, his petty strength all exhausted instantly, combats the inexhaustible.

Where, then, is the ship? Yonder. Barely visible in the pale shadows of the horizon.

The wind blows in gusts, all the foam overwhelms him. He raises his eyes, and beholds only the lividness of the clouds. He witnesses, amid his death-pangs, the immense madness of the sea. He is tortured by this madness; he hears noises strange to man, which seem to come from beyond the limits of the earth, and from one knows not what frightful region beyond.

There are birds in the clouds, just as there are angels above human distresses; but what can they do for him? They sing and fly and float, and he, he rattles in the death-agony.

He feels himself buried in those two infinities, the ocean and the sky, at one and the same time: the one is a tomb; the other is a shroud.

Night descends; he has been swimming for hours; his strength is exhausted; that ship, that distant thing in which there were men, has vanished; he is alone in the formidable twilight gulf; he sinks, he stiffens himself, he twists himself; he feels under him the monstrous billows of the invisible; he shouts.

There are no more men. Where is God?

He shouts. Help! Help! He still shouts on.

Nothing on the horizon; nothing in heaven.

He implores the expanse, the waves, the seaweed, the reef; they are deaf. He beseeches the tempest; the imperturbable tempest obeys only the infinite.

Around him darkness, fog, solitude, the stormy and non-sentient tumult, the undefined curling of those wild waters. In him horror and fatigue. Beneath him the depths. Not a point of support. He thinks of the gloomy adventures of the corpse in the limitless shadow. The bottomless cold paralyzes him. His hands contract convulsively; they close, and grasp nothingness. Winds, clouds, whirlwinds, gusts, useless stars! What is to be done? The desperate man gives up; he is weary, he chooses the alternative of death; he resists not; he lets himself go; he abandons his grip; and then he tosses forevermore in the lugubrious dreary depths of engulfment.

Oh, implacable march of human societies! Oh, losses of men and of souls on the way! Ocean into which falls all that the law lets slip! Disastrous absence of help! Oh, moral death!

The sea is the inexorable social night into which the penal laws fling their condemned. The sea is the immensity of wretchedness.

The soul, going down stream in this gulf, may become a corpse. Who shall resuscitate it?

Chapter IX

New Troubles

WHEN THE HOUR CAME FOR HIM TO TAKE HIS DEPARTURE FROM THE GALLEYS, WHEN JEAN VAL-jean heard in his ear the strange words, *Thou art free!* the moment seemed improbable and unprecedented; a ray of vivid light, a ray of the true light of the living, suddenly penetrated within him. But it was not long before this ray paled. Jean Valjean had been dazzled by the idea of liberty. He had believed in a new life. He very speedily perceived what sort of liberty it is to which a yellow passport is provided.

And this was encompassed with much bitterness. He had calculated that his earnings, during his sojourn in the galleys, ought to amount to a hundred and seventy-one francs. It is but just to add that he had forgotten to include in his calculations the forced repose of Sundays and festival days during nineteen years, which entailed a diminution of about eighty francs. At all events, his hoard had been reduced by various local levies to the sum of one hundred and nine francs fifteen sous, which had been counted out to him on his departure.

He had understood nothing of this, and had thought himself wronged. Let us say the word—robbed.

On the day following his liberation, he saw, at Grasse, in front of an orange-flower distillery, some men engaged in unloading bales. He offered his services. Business was pressing; they were accepted. He set to work. He was intelligent, robust, adroit; he did his best; the master seemed pleased. While he was at work, a gendarme passed, observed him, and demanded his papers. It was necessary to show him the yellow passport. That done, Jean Valjean resumed his labor. A little while before he had questioned one of the workmen as to the amount which they earned each day at this occupation; he had been told *thirty sous*. When evening arrived, as he was forced to set out again on the following day, he presented himself to the owner of the distillery and requested to be paid. The owner did not utter a word, but handed him fifteen sous. He objected. He was told, *"That is enough for thee."* He persisted. The master looked him straight between the eyes, and said to him, *"Beware of the prison."*

There, again, he considered that he had been robbed.

Society, the State, by diminishing his hoard, had robbed him wholesale. Now it was the individual who was robbing him at retail.

Liberation is not deliverance. One gets free from the galleys, but not from the sentence.

That is what happened to him at Grasse. We have seen in what manner he was received at D——.

Chapter X

THE MAN AROUSED

AS THE CATHEDRAL CLOCK STRUCK TWO IN THE MORNING, JEAN VALJEAN AWOKE.
What woke him was that his bed was too good. It was nearly twenty years since he had slept in a bed, and, although he had not undressed, the sensation was too novel not to disturb his slumbers.

He had slept more than four hours. His fatigue had passed away. He was accustomed not to devote many hours to repose.

He opened his eyes and stared into the gloom which surrounded him; then he closed them again, with the intention of going to sleep once more.

When many varied sensations have agitated the day, when various matters preoccupy the mind, one falls asleep once, but not a second time. Sleep comes more easily than it returns. This is what happened to Jean Valjean. He could not get to sleep again, and he fell to thinking.

He was at one of those moments when the thoughts which one has in one's mind are troubled. There was a sort of dark confusion in his brain. His memories of the olden time and of the immediate present floated there pell-mell and mingled confusedly, losing their proper forms, becoming disproportionately large, then suddenly disappearing, as in a muddy and perturbed pool. Many thoughts occurred to him; but there was one which kept constantly presenting itself afresh, and which drove away all the others. We will mention this thought at once: he had observed the six sets of silver forks and spoons and the ladle which Madame Magloire had placed on the table.

Those six sets of silver haunted him.—They were there.—A few paces distant.—Just as he was traversing the adjoining room to reach the one in which he then was, the old servant-woman had been in the act of placing them in a little cupboard near the head of the bed.—He had taken careful note of this cupboard.—On the right, as you entered from the dining-room.—They were solid.—And old silver.—From the ladle one could get at least two hundred francs.—Double what he had earned in nineteen years.—It is true that he would have earned more if "the administration had not robbed him."

His mind wavered for a whole hour in fluctuations with which there was certainly mingled some struggle. Three o'clock struck. He opened his eyes again, drew himself up abruptly into a sitting posture, stretched out his arm and felt of his knapsack, which he had thrown down on a corner of the alcove; then he hung his legs over the edge of the bed, and placed his feet on the floor, and thus found himself, almost without knowing it, seated on his bed.

He remained for a time thoughtfully in this attitude, which would have been suggestive of something sinister for anyone who had seen him thus in the dark, the only person awake in that house where all were sleeping. All of a sudden he stooped down, removed his shoes and placed them softly on the mat beside the bed; then he resumed his thoughtful attitude, and became motionless once more.

Throughout this hideous meditation, the thoughts which we have above indicated moved incessantly through his brain; entered, withdrew, re-entered, and in a manner oppressed him; and then he thought, also, without knowing why, and with the mechanical persistence of reverie, of a convict named Brevet, whom he had known in the galleys, and whose trousers had been upheld by a single suspender of knitted cotton. The checkered pattern of that suspender recurred incessantly to his mind.

He remained in this situation, and would have so remained indefinitely, even until daybreak, had not the clock struck one—the half or quarter hour. It seemed to him that that stroke said to him, "Come on!"

He rose to his feet, hesitated still another moment, and listened; all was quiet in the house; then he walked straight ahead, with short steps, to the window, of which he caught a glimpse. The night was not very dark; there was a full moon, across which coursed large clouds, driven by the wind. This created, outdoors, alternate shadow and gleams of light, eclipses, then bright openings of the clouds; and indoors a sort of twilight. This twilight, sufficient to enable a person to see his way, intermittent on account of the clouds, resembled the sort of livid light which falls through an air-hole in a cellar, before which the passers-by come and go. On arriving at the window, Jean Valjean examined it. It had no grating; it opened in the garden and was fastened, according to the fashion of the country, only by a small pin. He opened it; but as a rush of cold and piercing air penetrated the room abruptly, he closed it again immediately. He scrutinized the garden with that attentive gaze which studies rather than looks. The garden was enclosed by a tolerably low white wall, easy to climb. Far away, at the extremity, he perceived tops of trees, spaced at regular intervals, which indicated that the wall separated the garden from an avenue or lane planted with trees.

Having taken this survey, he executed a movement like that of a man who has made up his mind, strode to his alcove, grasped his knapsack, opened it, fumbled in it, pulled out of it something which he placed on the bed, put his shoes into one of his pockets, shut the whole thing up again, threw the knapsack on his shoulders, put on his cap, drew the visor down over his eyes, felt for his cudgel, went and placed it in the angle of the window; then returned to the bed, and resolutely seized the object which he had deposited there. It resembled a short bar of iron, pointed like a pike at one end. It would have been difficult to distinguish in that darkness for what employment that bit of iron could have been designed. Perhaps it was a lever; possibly it was a club.

In the daytime it would have been possible to recognize it as nothing more than a miner's candlestick. Convicts were, at that period, sometimes employed in quarrying stone from the lofty hills which environ Toulon, and it was not rare for them to have miners' tools at their command. These miners' candlesticks are of massive iron, terminated at the lower extremity by a point, by means of which they are stuck into the rock.

He took the candlestick in his right hand; holding his breath and trying to deaden the sound of his tread, he directed his steps to the door of the adjoining room, occupied by the Bishop, as we already know.

On arriving at this door, he found it ajar. The Bishop had not closed it.

Chapter XI

WHAT HE DOES

JEAN VALJEAN LISTENED. NOT A SOUND.

He gave the door a push.

He pushed it gently with the tip of his finger, lightly, with the furtive and uneasy gentleness of a cat which is desirous of entering.

The door yielded to this pressure, and made an imperceptible and silent movement, which enlarged the opening a little.

He waited a moment; then gave the door a second and a bolder push.

It continued to yield in silence. The opening was now large enough to allow him to pass. But near the door there stood a little table, which formed an embarrassing angle with it, and barred the entrance.

Jean Valjean recognized the difficulty. It was necessary, at any cost, to enlarge the aperture still further.

He decided on his course of action, and gave the door a third push, more energetic than the two preceding. This time a badly oiled hinge suddenly emitted amid the silence a hoarse and prolonged cry.

Jean Valjean shuddered. The noise of the hinge rang in his ears with something of the piercing and formidable sound of the trump of the Day of Judgment.

In the fantastic exaggerations of the first moment he almost imagined that that hinge had just become animated, and had suddenly assumed a terrible life, and that it was barking like a dog to arouse everyone, and warn and to wake those who were asleep. He halted, shuddering, bewildered, and fell back from the tips of his toes upon his heels. He heard the arteries in his temples beating like two forge hammers, and it seemed to him that his breath issued from his breast with the roar of the wind issuing from a cavern. It seemed impossible to him that the horrible clamor of that irritated hinge should not have disturbed the entire household, like the shock of an earthquake; the door, pushed by him, had taken the alarm, and had shouted; the old man would rise at once; the two old women would shriek out, people would come to their assistance; in less than a quarter of an hour the town would be in an uproar, and the gendarmerie on hand. For a moment he thought himself lost.

He remained where he was, petrified like the statue of salt, not daring to make a movement. Several minutes elapsed. The door had fallen wide open. He ventured to peep into the next room. Nothing had stirred there. He lent an ear. Nothing was moving in the house. The noise made by the rusty hinge had not awakened anyone.

This first danger was past; but there still reigned a frightful tumult within him. Nevertheless, he did not retreat. Even when he had thought himself lost, he had not drawn back. His only thought now was to finish as soon as possible. He took a step and entered the room.

This room was in a state of perfect calm. Here and there vague and confused forms were distinguishable, which in the daylight were papers scattered on a table, open folios, volumes piled upon a stool, an arm-chair heaped with clothing, a prie-Dieu, and which at that hour were only shadowy corners and whitish spots. Jean Valjean advanced with precaution, taking care not to knock against the furniture. He could hear, at the extremity of the room, the even and tranquil breathing of the sleeping Bishop.

He suddenly came to a halt. He was near the bed. He had arrived there sooner than he had thought for.

Nature sometimes mingles her effects and her spectacles with our actions with somber and intelligent appropriateness, as though she desired to make us reflect. For the last half-hour a large cloud had covered the heavens. At the moment when Jean Valjean paused in front of the bed, this cloud parted, as though on purpose, and a ray of light, traversing the long window, suddenly illuminated the Bishop's pale face. He was sleeping peacefully. He lay in his bed almost completely dressed, on account of the cold of the Basses-Alpes, in a garment of brown wool, which covered his arms to the wrists. His head was thrown back on the pillow, in the careless attitude of repose; his hand, adorned with the pastoral ring, and whence had fallen so many good deeds and so many holy actions, was hanging over the edge of the bed. His whole face was illumined with a vague expression of satisfaction, of hope, and of felicity. It was more than a smile, and almost a radiance. He bore upon his brow the indescribable reflection of a light which was invisible. The soul of the just contemplates in sleep a mysterious heaven.

A reflection of that heaven rested on the Bishop.

It was, at the same time, a luminous transparency, for that heaven was within him. That heaven was his conscience.

At the moment when the ray of moonlight superposed itself, so to speak, upon that inward radiance, the sleeping Bishop seemed as in a glory. It remained, however, gentle and veiled in an ineffable half-light. That moon in the sky, that slumbering nature, that garden without a quiver, that
house which was so calm, the hour, the moment, the silence, added some solemn and unspeakable
quality to the venerable repose of this man, and enveloped in a sort of serene and majestic aureole
that white hair, those closed eyes, that face in which all was hope and all was confidence, that head
of an old man, and that slumber of an infant.

There was something almost divine in this man, who was thus august, without being himself
aware of it.

Jean Valjean was in the shadow, and stood motionless, with his iron candlestick in his hand,
frightened by this luminous old man. Never had he beheld anything like this. This confidence terrified him. The moral world has no grander spectacle than this: a troubled and uneasy conscience,
which has arrived on the brink of an evil action, contemplating the slumber of the just.

That slumber in that isolation, and with a neighbor like himself, had about it something sublime, of which he was vaguely but imperiously conscious.

No one could have told what was passing within him, not even himself. In order to attempt to
form an idea of it, it is necessary to think of the most violent of things in the presence of the most
gentle. Even on his visage it would have been impossible to distinguish anything with certainty. It
was a sort of haggard astonishment. He gazed at it, and that was all. But what was his thought? It
would have been impossible to divine it. What was evident was, that he was touched and astounded.
But what was the nature of this emotion?

His eye never quitted the old man. The only thing which was clearly to be inferred from his
attitude and his physiognomy was a strange indecision. One would have said that he was hesitating
between the two abysses—the one in which one loses one's self and that in which one saves one's
self. He seemed prepared to crush that skull or to kiss that hand.

At the expiration of a few minutes his left arm rose slowly toward his brow, and he took off
his cap; then his arm fell back with the same deliberation, and Jean Valjean fell to meditating once
more, his cap in his left hand, his club in his right hand, his hair bristling all over his savage head.

The Bishop continued to sleep in profound peace beneath that terrifying gaze.

The gleam of the moon rendered confusedly visible the crucifix over the chimney-piece,
which seemed to be extending its arms to both of them, with a benediction for one and pardon for
the other.

Suddenly Jean Valjean replaced his cap on his brow; then stepped rapidly past the bed, without glancing at the Bishop, straight to the cupboard, which he saw near the head; he raised his iron
candlestick as though to force the lock; the key was there; he opened it; the first thing which presented itself to him was the basket of silverware; he seized it, traversed the chamber with long
strides, without taking any precautions and without troubling himself about the noise, gained the
door, re-entered the oratory, opened the window, seized his cudgel, bestrode the window-sill of the
ground floor, put the silver into his knapsack, threw away the basket, crossed the garden, leaped
over the wall like a tiger, and fled.

Chapter XII

THE BISHOP WORKS

•

THE NEXT MORNING AT SUNRISE MONSEIGNEUR BIENVENU WAS STROLLING IN HIS GARDEN. Madame Magloire ran up to him in utter consternation.

"Monseigneur, Monseigneur!" she exclaimed, "does your Grace know where the basket of silver is?"

"Yes," replied the Bishop.

"Jesus the Lord be blessed!" she resumed; "I did not know what had become of it."

The Bishop had just picked up the basket in a flower-bed. He presented it to Madame Magloire. "Here it is."

"Well!" said she. "Nothing in it! And the silver?"

"Ah," returned the Bishop, "so it is the silver which troubles you? I don't know where it is."

"Great, good God! It is stolen! That man who was here last night has stolen it."

In a twinkling, with all the vivacity of an alert old woman, Madame Magloire had rushed to the oratory, entered the alcove, and returned to the Bishop. The Bishop had just bent down, and was sighing as he examined a plant of cochlearia des Guillons, which the basket had broken as it fell across the bed. He rose up at Madame Magloire's cry.

"Monseigneur, the man is gone! The silver has been stolen!"

As she uttered this exclamation, her eyes fell upon a corner of the garden, where traces of the wall having been scaled were visible. The coping of the wall had been torn away.

"Stay! yonder is the way he went. He jumped over into Cochefilet Lane. Ah, the abomination! He has stolen our silver!"

The Bishop remained silent for a moment; then he raised his grave eyes, and said gently to Madame Magloire:

"And, in the first place, was that silver ours?"

Madame Magloire was speechless. Another silence ensued; then the Bishop went on:

"Madame Magloire, I have for a long time detained that silver wrongfully. It belonged to the poor. Who was that man? A poor man, evidently."

"Alas! Jesus!" returned Madame Magloire. "It is not for my sake, nor for Mademoiselle's. It makes no difference to us. But it is for the sake of Monseigneur. What is Monseigneur to eat with now?"

The Bishop gazed at her with an air of amazement.

"Ah, come! Are there no such things as pewter forks and spoons?"

Madame Magloire shrugged her shoulders.

"Pewter has an odor."

"Iron forks and spoons, then."

Madame Magloire made an expressive grimace.

"Iron has a taste."

"Very well," said the Bishop; "wooden ones then."

A few moments later he was breakfasting at the very table at which Jean Valjean had sat on the previous evening. As he ate his breakfast, Monseigneur Welcome remarked gaily to his sister, who said nothing, and to Madame Magloire, who was grumbling under her breath, that one really does not need either fork or spoon, even of wood, in order to dip a bit of bread in a cup of milk.

"A pretty idea, truly," said Madame Magloire to herself, as she went and came, "to take in a man like that! and to lodge him close to one's self! And how fortunate that he did nothing but steal! Ah, mon Dieu! it makes one shudder to think of it!"

As the brother and sister were about to rise from the table, there came a knock at the door.

"Come in," said the Bishop.

The door opened. A singular and violent group made its appearance on the threshold. Three men were holding a fourth man by the collar. The three men were gendarmes; the other was Jean Valjean.

A brigadier of gendarmes, who seemed to be in command of the group, was standing near the door. He entered and advanced to the Bishop, making a military salute.

"Monseigneur—" said he.

At this word, Jean Valjean, who was dejected and seemed overwhelmed, raised his head with an air of stupefaction.

"Monseigneur!" he murmured. "So he is not the curé?"

"Silence!" said the gendarme. "He is Monseigneur the Bishop."

In the meantime, Monseigneur Bienvenu had advanced as quickly as his great age permitted.

"Ah! here you are!" he exclaimed, looking at Jean Valjean. "I am glad to see you. Well, but how is this? I gave you the candlesticks too, which are of silver like the rest, and for which you can certainly get two hundred francs. Why did you not carry them away with your forks and spoons?"

Jean Valjean opened his eyes wide, and stared at the venerable Bishop with an expression which no human tongue can render any account of.

"Monseigneur," said the brigadier of gendarmes, "so what this man said is true, then? We came across him. He was walking like a man who is running away. We stopped him to look into the matter. He had this silver—"

"And he told you," interposed the Bishop, with a smile, "that it had been given to him by a kind old fellow of a priest with whom he had passed the night? I see how the matter stands. And you have brought him back here? It is a mistake."

"In that case," replied the brigadier, "we can let him go?"

"Certainly," replied the Bishop.

The gendarmes released Jean Valjean, who recoiled.

"Is it true that I am to be released?" he said, in an almost inarticulate voice, and as though he were talking in his sleep.

"Yes, thou art released; dost thou not understand?" said one of the gendarmes.

"My friend," resumed the Bishop, "before you go, here are your candlesticks. Take them."

He stepped to the chimney-piece, took the two silver candlesticks, and brought them to Jean Valjean. The two women looked on without uttering a word, without a gesture, without a look which could disconcert the Bishop.

Jean Valjean was trembling in every limb. He took the two candlesticks mechanically, and with a bewildered air.

"Now," said the Bishop, "go in peace. By the way, when you return, my friend, it is not necessary to pass through the garden. You can always enter and depart through the street door. It is never fastened with anything but a latch, either by day or by night."

Then, turning to the gendarmes:

"You may retire, gentlemen."

The gendarmes retired.

Jean Valjean was like a man on the point of fainting.

The Bishop drew near to him, and said in a low voice:

"Do not forget, never forget, that you have promised to use this money in becoming an honest man."

Jean Valjean, who had no recollection of ever having promised anything, remained speechless. The Bishop had emphasized the words when he uttered them. He resumed with solemnity:

"Jean Valjean, my brother, you no longer belong to evil, but to good. It is your soul that I buy from you; I withdraw it from black thoughts and the spirit of perdition, and I give it to God."

Chapter XIII

LITTLE GERVAIS

JEAN VALJEAN LEFT THE TOWN AS THOUGH HE WERE FLEEING FROM IT. HE SET OUT AT A VERY HASTY pace through the fields, taking whatever roads and paths presented themselves to him, without perceiving that he was incessantly retracing his steps. He wandered thus the whole morning, without having eaten anything and without feeling hungry. He was the prey of a throng of novel sensations. He was conscious of a sort of rage; he did not know against whom it was directed. He could not have told whether he was touched or humiliated. There came over him at moments a strange emotion which he resisted and to which he opposed the hardness acquired during the last twenty years of his life. This state of mind fatigued him. He perceived with dismay that the sort of frightful calm which the injustice of his misfortune had conferred upon him was giving way within him. He asked himself what would replace this. At times he would have actually preferred to be in prison with the gendarmes, and that things should not have happened in this way; it would have agitated him less. Although the season was tolerably far advanced, there were still a few late flowers in the hedge-rows here and there, whose odor as he passed through them in his march recalled to him memories of his childhood. These memories were almost intolerable to him, it was so long since they had recurred to him.

Unutterable thoughts assembled within him in this manner all day long.

As the sun declined to its setting, casting long shadows athwart the soil from every pebble, Jean Valjean sat down behind a bush upon a large ruddy plain, which was absolutely deserted. There was nothing on the horizon except the Alps. Not even the spire of a distant village. Jean Valjean might have been three leagues distant from D——. A path which intersected the plain passed a few paces from the bush.

In the middle of this meditation, which would have contributed not a little to render his rags terrifying to anyone who might have encountered him, a joyous sound became audible.

He turned his head and saw a little Savoyard, about ten years of age, coming up the path and singing, his hurdy-gurdy on his hip, and his marmot-box on his back,

One of those gay and gentle children, who go from land to land affording a view of their knees through the holes in their trousers.

Without stopping his song, the lad halted in his march from time to time, and played at knuckle-bones with some coins which he had in his hand—his whole fortune, probably.

Among this money there was one forty-sou piece.

The child halted beside the bush, without perceiving Jean Valjean, and tossed up his handful of sous, which, up to that time, he had caught with a good deal of adroitness on the back of his hand.

This time the forty-sou piece escaped him, and went rolling toward the brushwood until it reached Jean Valjean.

Jean Valjean set his foot upon it.

In the meantime, the child had looked after his coin and had caught sight of him.

He showed no astonishment, but walked straight up to the man.

The spot was absolutely solitary. As far as the eye could see there was not a person on the plain or on the path. The only sound was the tiny, feeble cries of a flock of birds of passage, which was traversing the heavens at an immense height. The child was standing with his back to the sun, which cast threads of gold in his hair and empurpled with its blood-red gleam the savage face of Jean Valjean.

"Sir," said the little Savoyard, with that childish confidence which is composed of ignorance and innocence, "my money."

"What is your name?" said Jean Valjean.

"Little Gervais, sir."

"Go away," said Jean Valjean.

"Sir," resumed the child, "give me back my money."

Jean Valjean dropped his head, and made no reply.

The child began again, "My money, sir."

Jean Valjean's eyes remained fixed on the earth.

"My piece of money!" cried the child, "my white piece! my silver!"

It seemed as though Jean Valjean did not hear him. The child grasped him by the collar of his blouse and shook him. At the same time he made an effort to displace the big iron-shod shoe which rested on his treasure.

"I want my piece of money! my piece of forty sous!"

The child wept. Jean Valjean raised his head. He still remained seated. His eyes were troubled. He gazed at the child in a sort of amazement, then he stretched out his hand toward his cudgel and cried in a terrible voice, "Who's there?"

"I, sir," replied the child. "Little Gervais! I! Give me back my forty sous, if you please! Take your foot away, sir, if you please!"

Then irritated, though he was so small, and becoming almost menacing:

"Come now, will you take your foot away? Take your foot away, or we'll see!"

"Ah! It's still you!" said Jean Valjean, and rising abruptly to his feet, his foot still resting on the silver piece, he added:

"Will you take yourself off!"

The frightened child looked at him, then began to tremble from head to foot, and after a few moments of stupor he set out, running at the top of his speed, without daring to turn his neck or to utter a cry.

Nevertheless, lack of breath forced him to halt after a certain distance, and Jean Valjean heard him sobbing, in the midst of his own reverie.

At the end of a few moments the child had disappeared.

The sun had set.

The shadows were descending around Jean Valjean. He had eaten nothing all day; it is probable that he was feverish.

He had remained standing and had not changed his attitude after the child's flight. The breath heaved his chest at long and irregular intervals. His gaze, fixed ten or twelve paces in front of him, seemed to be scrutinizing with profound attention the shape of an ancient fragment of blue earthenware which had fallen in the grass. All at once he shivered; he had just begun to feel the chill of evening.

He settled his cap more firmly on his brow, sought mechanically to cross and button his blouse, advanced a step, and stopped to pick up his cudgel.

At that moment he caught sight of the forty-sou piece, which his foot had half ground into the earth, and which was shining among the pebbles. It was as though he had received a galvanic shock.

"What is this?" he muttered between his teeth. He recoiled three paces, then halted, without being able to detach his gaze from the spot which his foot had trodden but an instant before, as though the thing which lay glittering there in the gloom had been an open eye riveted upon him.

At the expiration of a few moments he darted convulsively towards the silver coin, seized it, and straightened himself up again and began to gaze afar off over the plain, at the same time casting his eyes towards all points of the horizon, as he stood there erect and shivering, like a terrified wild animal which is seeking refuge.

He saw nothing. Night was falling, the plain was cold and vague, great banks of violet haze were rising in the gleam of the twilight.

He said, "Ah!" and set out rapidly in the direction in which the child had disappeared. After about thirty paces he paused, looked about him and saw nothing.

Then he shouted with all his might:

"Little Gervais! Little Gervais!"

He paused and waited.

There was no reply.

The landscape was gloomy and deserted. He was encompassed by space. There was nothing around him but an obscurity in which his gaze was lost, and a silence which engulfed his voice.

An icy north wind was blowing, and imparted to things around him a sort of lugubrious life. The bushes shook their thin little arms with incredible fury. One would have said that they were threatening and pursuing someone.

He set out on his march again, then he began to run; and from time to time he halted and shouted into that solitude, with a voice which was the most formidable and the most disconsolate that it was possible to hear, "Little Gervais! Little Gervais!"

Assuredly, if the child had heard him, he would have been alarmed and would have taken good care not to show himself. But the child was no doubt already far away.

He encountered a priest on horseback. He stepped up to him and said:

"Monsieur le Curé, have you seen a child pass?"

"No," said the priest.

"One named Little Gervais?"

"I have seen no one."

He drew two five-franc pieces from his money-bag and handed them to the priest.

"Monsieur le Curé, this is for your poor people. Monsieur le Curé, he was a little lad, about ten years old, with a marmot, I think, and a hurdy-gurdy. One of those Savoyards, you know?"

"I have not seen him."

"Little Gervais? There are no villages here? Can you tell me?"

"If he is like what you say, my friend, he is a little stranger. Such persons pass through these parts. We know nothing of them."

Jean Valjean seized two more coins of five francs each with violence, and gave them to the priest.

"For your poor," he said.

Then he added, wildly:

"Monsieur l'Abbé, have me arrested. I am a thief."

The priest put spurs to his horse and fled in haste, much alarmed.

Jean Valjean set out on a run, in the direction which he had first taken.

In this way he traversed a tolerably long distance, gazing, calling, shouting, but he met no one. Two or three times he ran across the plain toward something which conveyed to him the effect of a human being reclining or crouching down; it turned out to be nothing but brushwood or rocks nearly on a level with the earth. At length, at a spot where three paths intersected each other, he stopped. The moon had risen. He sent his gaze into the distance and shouted for the last time, "Little Gervais! Little Gervais! Little Gervais!" His shout died away in the mist, without even awakening an echo. He murmured yet once more, "Little Gervais!" but in a feeble and almost inarticulate voice. It was his last effort; his legs gave way abruptly under him, as though an invisible power had suddenly overwhelmed him with the weight of his evil conscience; he fell exhausted, on a large stone, his fists clenched in his hair and his face on his knees, and he cried, "I am a wretch!"

Then his heart burst, and he began to cry. It was the first time that he had wept in nineteen years.

When Jean Valjean left the Bishop's house, he was, as we have seen, quite thrown out of everything that had been his thought hitherto. He could not yield to the evidence of what was going on within him. He hardened himself against the angelic action and the gentle words of the old man. "You have promised me to become an honest man. I buy your soul. I take it away from the spirit of perversity; I give it to the good God."

This recurred to his mind unceasingly. To this celestial kindness he opposed pride, which is the fortress of evil within us. He was indistinctly conscious that the pardon of this priest was the greatest assault and the most formidable attack which had moved him yet; that his obduracy was finally settled if he resisted this clemency; that if he yielded, he should be obliged to renounce that hatred with which the actions of other men had filled his soul through so many years, and which pleased him; that this time it was necessary to conquer or to be conquered; and that a struggle, a colossal and final struggle, had been begun between his viciousness and the goodness of that man.

In the presence of these lights, he proceeded like a man who is intoxicated. As he walked thus with haggard eyes, did he have a distinct perception of what might result to him from his adventure at D——? Did he understand all those mysterious murmurs which warn or importune the spirit at certain moments of life? Did a voice whisper in his ear that he had just passed the solemn hour of his destiny; that there no longer remained a middle course for him; that if he were not henceforth the best of men, he would be the worst; that it behooved him now, so to speak, to mount higher than the Bishop, or fall lower than the convict; that if he wished to become good, he must become an angel; that if he wished to remain evil, he must become a monster?

Here, again, some questions must be put, which we have already put to ourselves elsewhere: did he catch some shadow of all this in his thought, in a confused way? Misfortune certainly, as we have said, does form the education of the intelligence; nevertheless, it is doubtful whether Jean Valjean was in a condition to disentangle all that we have here indicated. If these ideas occurred to him, he but caught glimpses of, rather than saw them, and they only succeeded in throwing him into an unutterable and almost painful state of emotion. On emerging from that black and deformed thing which is called the galleys, the Bishop had hurt his soul, as too vivid a light would have hurt his eyes on emerging from the dark. The future life, the possible life which offered itself to him henceforth, all pure and radiant, filled him with tremors and anxiety. He no longer knew where he really was. Like an owl, who should suddenly see the sun rise, the convict had been dazzled and blinded, as it were, by virtue.

That which was certain, that which he did not doubt, was that he was no longer the same man, that everything about him was changed, that it was no longer in his power to make it as though the Bishop had not spoken to him and had not touched him.

In this state of mind he had encountered little Gervais, and had robbed him of his forty sous. Why? He certainly could not have explained it; was this the last effect and the supreme effort, as it were, of the evil thoughts which he had brought away from the galleys—a remnant of impulse, a result of what is called in statics, *acquired force?* It was that, and it was also, perhaps, even less than that. Let us say it simply, it was not he who stole; it was not the man; it was the beast, who, by habit and instinct, had simply placed its foot upon that money, while the intelligence was struggling amid so many novel and hitherto unheard-of thoughts besetting it.

When intelligence reawakened and beheld that action of the brute, Jean Valjean recoiled with anguish and uttered a cry of terror.

It was because—strange phenomenon, and one which was possible only in the situation in which he found himself—in stealing the money from that child, he had done a thing of which he was no longer capable.

However that may be, this last evil action had a decisive effect on him; it abruptly traversed that chaos which he bore in his mind, and dispersed it, placed on one side the thick obscurity, and on the other the light, and acted on his soul, in the state in which it then was, as certain chemical reagents act upon a troubled mixture by precipitating one element and clarifying the other.

First of all, even before examining himself and reflecting, all bewildered, like one who seeks to save himself, he tried to find the child in order to return his money to him; then, when he recognized the fact that this was impossible, he halted in despair. At the moment when he exclaimed "I am a wretch!" he had just perceived what he was, and he was already separated from himself to such a degree, that he seemed to himself to be no longer anything more than a phantom, and as if he had, there before him, in flesh and blood, the hideous galley-convict, Jean Valjean, cudgel in hand, his blouse on his hips, his knapsack filled with stolen objects on his back, with his resolute and gloomy visage, with his thoughts filled with abominable projects.

Excess of unhappiness had, as we have remarked, made him in some sort a visionary. This, then, was in the nature of a vision. He actually saw that Jean Valjean, that sinister face, before him. He had almost reached the point of asking himself who that man was, and he was horrified by him.

His brain was going through one of those violent and yet perfectly calm moments in which reverie is so profound that it absorbs reality. One no longer beholds the object which one has before one, and one sees, as though apart from one's self, the figures which one has in one's own mind.

Thus he contemplated himself, so to speak, face to face, and at the same time, athwart this hallucination, he perceived in a mysterious depth a sort of light which he at first took for a torch. On scrutinizing this light which appeared to his conscience with more attention, he recognized the fact that it possessed a human form and that this torch was the Bishop.

His conscience weighed in turn these two men thus placed before it—the Bishop and Jean Valjean. Nothing less than the first was required to soften the second. By one of those singular effects, which are peculiar to this sort of ecstasies, in proportion as his reverie continued, as the Bishop grew great and resplendent in his eyes, so did Jean Valjean grow less and vanish. After a certain time he was no longer anything more than a shade. All at once he disappeared. The Bishop alone remained; he filled the whole soul of this wretched man with a magnificent radiance.

Jean Valjean wept for a long time. He wept burning tears, he sobbed with more weakness than a woman, with more fright than a child.

As he wept, daylight penetrated more and more clearly into his soul; an extraordinary light; a light at once ravishing and terrible. His past life, his first fault, his long expiation, his external brutishness, his internal hardness, his dismissal to liberty, rejoicing in manifold plans of vengeance, what had happened to him at the Bishop's, the last thing that he had done, that theft of forty sous from a child, a crime all the more cowardly and all the more monstrous since it had come after the Bishop's pardon—all this recurred to his mind and appeared clearly to him, but with a clearness which he had never hitherto witnessed. He examined his life, and it seemed horrible to him; his soul, and it seemed frightful to him. In the meantime a gentle light rested over this life and this soul. It seemed to him that he beheld Satan by the light of Paradise.

How many hours did he weep thus? What did he do after he had wept? Whither did he go? No one ever knew. The only thing which seems to be authenticated is that that same night the carrier who served Grenoble at that epoch, and who arrived at D—— about three o'clock in the morning, saw, as he traversed the street in which the Bishop's residence was situated, a man in the attitude of prayer, kneeling on the pavement in the shadow, in front of the door of Monseigneur Welcome.

BOOK THIRD

IN THE YEAR 1817

Chapter I

THE YEAR 1817

1817 IS THE YEAR WHICH LOUIS XVIII, WITH A CERTAIN ROYAL ASSURANCE WHICH WAS NOT WANTING in pride, entitled the twenty-second of his reign. It is the year in which M. Bruguière de Sorsum was celebrated. All the hairdressers' shops, hoping for powder and the return of the royal bird, were besmeared with azure and decked with fleurs-de-lys. It was the candid time at which Count Lynch sat every Sunday as church-warden in the church-warden's pew of Saint-Germain-des-Prés, in his costume of a peer of France, with his red ribbon and his long nose and the majesty of profile peculiar to a man who has performed a brilliant action. The brilliant action performed by M. Lynch was this: being mayor of Bordeaux, on the 12th of March, 1814, he had surrendered the city a little too promptly to M. the Duke d'Angoulême. Hence his peerage. In 1817 fashion swallowed up little boys of from four to six years of age in vast caps of morocco leather with ear-tabs resembling Esquimaux miters. The French army was dressed in white, after the mode of the Austrian; the regiments were called legions; instead of numbers they bore the names of departments; Napoleon was at St. Helena; and since England refused him green cloth, he was having his old coats turned. In 1817 Pelligrini sang; Mademoiselle Bigottini danced; Potier reigned; Odry did not yet exist. Madame Saqui had succeeded to Forioso. There were still Prussians in France. M. Delalot was a personage. Legitimacy had just asserted itself by cutting off the hand, then the head, of Pleignier, of Carbonneau, and of Tolleron. The Prince de Talleyrand, grand chamberlain, and the Abbé Louis, appointed minister of finance, laughed as they looked at each other, with the laugh of the two augurs; both of them had celebrated, on the 14th of July, 1790, the mass of federation in the Champ de Mars; Talleyrand had said it as bishop, Louis had served it in the capacity of deacon. In 1817, in the side-alleys of this same Champ de Mars, two great cylinders of wood might have been seen lying in the rain, rotting amid the grass, painted blue, with traces of eagles and bees, from which the gilding was falling. These were the columns which two years before had upheld the Emperor's platform in the Champ de Mai. They were blackened here and there with the scorches of the bivouac of Austrians encamped near Gros-Caillou. Two or three of these columns had disappeared in these bivouac fires, and had warmed the large hands of the Imperial troops. The Field of May had this remarkable point: that it had been held in the month of June and in the Field of March (Mars). In this year, 1817, two things were popular: the Voltaire-Touquet and the snuff-box à la Charter. The most recent Parisian sensation was the crime of Dautun, who had thrown his brother's head into the fountain of the Flower-Market.

They had begun to feel anxious at the Naval Department, on account of the lack of news from that fatal frigate, *The Medusa*, which was destined to cover Chaumareix with infamy and Géricault with glory. Colonel Selves was going to Egypt to become Soliman-Pasha. The palace of Thermes, in the Rue de La Harpe, served as a shop for a cooper. On the platform of the octagonal tower of the Hôtel de Cluny, the little shed of boards, which had served as an observatory to Messier, the naval astronomer under Louis XVI, was still to be seen. The Duchesse de Duras read to three or four friends her unpublished *Ourika*, in her boudoir furnished by X. in sky-blue satin. The N's were scratched off the Louvre. The bridge of Austerlitz had abdicated, and was entitled the bridge of the King's Garden [du Jardin du Roi], a double enigma, which disguised the bridge of Austerlitz and the Jardin des Plantes at one stroke. Louis XVIII, much preoccupied while annotating Horace with the corner of his finger-nail, heroes who have become emperors, and makers of wooden shoes who have become dauphins, had two anxieties—Napoleon and Mathurin Bruneau. The French Academy had given for its prize subject, *The Happiness procured through Study*. M. Bellart was officially eloquent. In his shadow could be seen germinating that future advocate-general of Broë, dedicated to the sarcasms of Paul-Louis Courier. There was a false Chateaubriand, named Marchangy, in the interim, until there should be a false Marchangy, named d'Arlincourt. *Claire d'Albe* and *Malek-Adel* were masterpieces; Madame Cottin was proclaimed the chief writer of the epoch. The Institute had the academician, Napoleon Bonaparte, stricken from its list of members. A royal ordinance erected Angoulême into a naval school; for the Duc d'Angoulême, being lord high admiral, it was evident that the city of Angoulême had all the qualities of a seaport; otherwise the monarchical principle would have received a wound. In the Council of Ministers the question was agitated whether vignettes representing slack-rope performances, which adorned Franconi's advertising posters, and which attracted throngs of street urchins, should be tolerated. M. Paër, the author of *Agnese*, a good sort of fellow, with a square face and a wart on his cheek, directed the little private concerts of the Marquise de Sasenaye, in the Rue Ville l'Évêque. All the young girls were singing the *Hermit of Saint-Avelle*, with words by Edmond Géraud. *The Yellow Dwarf* was transferred into *Mirror*. The Café Lemblin stood up for the Emperor, against the Café Valois, which upheld the Bourbons. The Duc de Berri, already surveyed from the shadow by Louvel, had just been married to a princess of Sicily. Madame de Staël had died a year previously. The bodyguard hissed Mademoiselle Mars. The grand newspapers were all very small. Their form was restricted, but their liberty was great. The *Constitutionnel* was constitutional. *La Minerve* called Chateaubriand *Chateaubriant*. That *t* made the good middle-class people laugh heartily at the expense of the great writer. In journals which sold themselves, prostituted journalists, insulted the exiles of 1815. David had no longer any talent, Arnault had no longer any wit, Carnot was no longer honest, Soult had won no battles; it is true that Napoleon had no longer any genius. No one is ignorant of the fact that letters sent to an exile by post very rarely reached him, as the police made it their religious duty to intercept them. This is no new fact; Descartes complained of it in his exile. Now David, having, in a Belgian publication, shown some displeasure at not receiving letters which had been written to him, it struck the royalist journals as amusing; and they derided the prescribed man well on this occasion. What separated two men more than an abyss was to say, the *regicides*, or to say the *voters*; to say the *enemies*, or to say the *allies*; to say *Napoleon*, or to say *Buonaparte*. All sensible people were agreed that the era of revolution had been closed forever by King Louis XVIII, surnamed "The Immortal Author of the Charter." On the platform of the Pont-Neuf, the word *Redivivus* was carved on the pedestal that awaited the statue of Henry IV. M. Piet, in the Rue Thérèse, No. 4, was making the rough draft of his privy assembly to consolidate the monarchy. The leaders of the Right said at grave conjunctures, "We must write to Bacot." MM. Canuel, O'Mahoney, and De Chappedelaine were preparing the sketch, to some extent with Monsieur's approval, of what was to become later on "The Conspiracy of the Bord de l'Eau"—of the waterside. L'Épingle Noire was already plotting in his own quarter. Delaverderie was conferring with Trogoff. M. Decazes, who was liberal to a degree, reigned. Chateaubriand stood every morning at his window at No. 27 Rue Saint-Dominique, clad in footed trousers, and slippers, with a madras kerchief knotted over his gray hair, with his eyes fixed on a mirror, a complete set of dentist's instruments spread out before him, cleaning his teeth, which were charming, while he dictated *The Monarchy according to the Char-*

ter to M. Pilorge, his secretary. Criticism, assuming an authoritative tone, preferred Lafon to Talma. M. de Féletz signed himself A.; M. Hoffmann signed himself Z. Charles Nodier wrote *Thérèse Aubert*. Divorce was abolished. Lyceums called themselves colleges. The collegians, decorated on the collar with a golden fleur-de-lys, fought each other *apropos* of the King of Rome. The counter-police of the château had denounced to her Royal Highness Madame, the portrait, everywhere exhibited, of M. the Duc d'Orléans, who made a better appearance in his uniform of a colonel-general of hussars than M. the Duc de Berri, in his uniform of colonel-general of dragoons—a serious inconvenience. The city of Paris was having the dome of the Invalides regilded at its own expense. Serious men asked themselves what M. de Trinquelague would do on such or such an occasion; M. Clausel de Montals differed on divers points from M. Clausel de Coussergues; M. de Salaberry was not satisfied. The comedian Picard, who belonged to the Academy, which the comedian Molière had not been able to do, had *The Two Philiberts* played at the Odéon, upon whose pediment the removal of the letters still allowed THEATRE OF THE EMPRESS to be plainly read. People took part for or against Cugnet de Montarlot. Fabvier was factious; Bavoux was revolutionary. The Liberal, Pélicier, published an edition of Voltaire, with the following title: *Works of Voltaire*, of the French Academy. "That will attract purchasers," said the ingenious editor. The general opinion was that M. Charles Loyson would be the genius of the century; envy was beginning to gnaw at him—a sign of glory; and this verse was composed on him:

> *Even when Loyson steals, one feels that he has paws.*

As Cardinal Fesch refused to resign, M. de Pins, Archbishop of Amasie, administered the diocese of Lyons. The quarrel over the valley of Dappes was begun between Switzerland and France by a memoir from Captain, afterwards General, Dufour. Saint-Simon, ignored, was erecting his sublime dream. There was a celebrated Fourier at the Academy of Science, whom posterity has forgotten; and in some garret an obscure Fourier, whom the future will recall. Lord Byron was beginning to make his mark; a note to a poem by Millevoye introduced him to France in these terms: *a certain Lord Baron*. David d'Angers was trying to work in marble. The Abbé Caron was speaking in terms of praise, to a private gathering of seminarists in the blind-alley of Feuillantines, of an unknown priest, named Félicité-Robert, who, at a latter date, became Lamennais. A thing which smoked and clattered on the Seine with the noise of a swimming dog went and came beneath the windows of the Tuileries, from the Pont Royal to the Pont Louis XV; it was a piece of mechanism which was not good for much; a sort of plaything, the idle dream of a dream-ridden inventor; a utopia—a steamboat. The Parisians stared indifferently at this useless thing. M. de Vaublanc, the reformer of the Institute by a coup d'état, the distinguished author of numerous academicians, ordinances, and batches of members, after having created them, could not succeed in becoming one himself. The Faubourg Saint-Germain and the pavilion de Marsan wished to have M. Delaveau for prefect of police, on account of his piety. Dupuytren and Récamier entered into a quarrel in the amphitheater of the School of Medicine, and threatened each other with their fists on the subject of the divinity of Jesus Christ. Cuvier, with one eye on Genesis and the other on nature, tried to please bigoted reaction by reconciling fossils with texts and by making mastodons flatter Moses.

M. François de Neufchâteau, the praiseworthy cultivator of the memory of Parmentier, made a thousand efforts to have *pomme de terre* [potato] pronounced *parmentière*, and succeeded therein not at all. The Abbé Grégoire, ex-bishop, ex-conventionary, ex-senator, had passed, in the royalist polemics, to the state of "Infamous Grégoire." The locution of which we have made use—*passed to the state of*—has been condemned as a neologism by M. Royer Collard. Under the third arch of the Pont de Jéna, the new stone with which, the two years previously, the mining aperture made by Blücher to blow up the bridge had been stopped up, was still recognizable on account of its whiteness. Justice summoned to its bar a man who, on seeing the Comte d'Artois enter Notre-Dame, had said aloud: *"Sapristi! I regret the time when I saw Bonaparte and Talma enter the Bel Sauvage, arm in arm."* A seditious utterance. Six months in prison. Traitors showed themselves unbuttoned; men who had gone over to the enemy on the eve of battle made no secret of their recompense, and strutted immodestly in the light of day, in the cynicism of riches and dignities; deserters from Ligny and Quatre-Bras, in the brazenness of their well-paid turpitude, exhibited their devotion to the monarchy in the most barefaced manner.

This is what floats up confusedly, pell-mell, for the year 1817, and is now forgotten. History neglects nearly all these particulars, and cannot do otherwise; the infinity would overwhelm it. Nevertheless, these details, which are wrongly called trivial—there are no trivial facts in humanity, nor little leaves in vegetation—are useful. It is of the physiognomy of the years that the physiognomy of the centuries is composed. In this year of 1817 four young Parisians arranged "a fine farce."

Chapter II

A DOUBLE QUARTETTE

THESE PARISIANS CAME, ONE FROM TOULOUSE, ANOTHER FROM LIMOGES, THE THIRD FROM CAhors, and the fourth from Montauban; but they were students; and when one says student, one says Parisian: to study in Paris is to be born in Paris.

These young men were insignificant; everyone has seen such faces; four specimens of humanity taken at random; neither good nor bad, neither wise nor ignorant, neither geniuses nor fools; handsome, with that charming April which is called twenty years. They were four Oscars; for, at that epoch, Arthurs did not yet exist. *Burn for him the perfumes of Araby!* exclaimed romance. *Oscar advances. Oscar, I shall behold him!* People had just emerged from Ossian; elegance was Scandinavian and Caledonian; the pure English style was only to prevail later, and the first of the Arthurs, Wellington, had but just won the battle of Waterloo.

These Oscars bore the names, one of Felix Tholomyès, of Toulouse; the second, Listolier, of Cahors; the next, Fameuil, of Limoges; the last, Blachevelle, of Montauban. Naturally, each of them had his mistress. Blachevelle loved Favourite, so named because she had been in England; Listolier adored Dahlia, who had taken for her nickname the name of a flower; Fameuil idolized Zéphine, an abridgment of Joséphine; Tholomyès had Fantine, called the Blonde, because of her beautiful, sunny hair.

Favourite, Dahlia, Zéphine, and Fantine were four ravishing young women, perfumed and radiant, still a little like working-women, and not yet entirely divorced from their needles; somewhat disturbed by intrigues, but still retaining on their faces something of the serenity of toil, and in their souls that flower of honesty which survives the first fall in woman. One of the four was called the young, because she was the youngest of them, and one was called the old; the old one was twenty-three. Not to conceal anything, the three first were more experienced, more heedless, and more emancipated into the tumult of life than Fantine the Blonde, who was still in her first illusions.

Dahlia, Zéphine, and especially Favourite, could not have said as much. There had already been more than one episode in their romance, though hardly begun; and the lover who had borne the name of Adolph in the first chapter had turned out to be Alphonse in the second, and Gustave in the third. Poverty and coquetry are two fatal counselors; one scolds and the other flatters, and the beautiful daughters of the people have both of them whispering in their ear, each on its own side.

These badly guarded souls listen. Hence the falls which they accomplish, and the stones which are thrown at them. They are overwhelmed with splendor of all that is immaculate and inaccessible. Alas! what if the Jungfrau were hungry?

Favourite having been in England, was admired by Dahlia and Zéphine. She had had an establishment of her own very early in life. Her father was an old unmarried professor of mathematics, a brutal man and a braggart, who went out to give lessons in spite of his age. This professor, when he was a young man, had one day seen a chambermaid's gown catch on a fender; he had fallen in love in consequence of this accident. The result had been Favourite. She met her father from time to time, and he bowed to her. One morning an old woman, with the air of a devotee, had entered her apartments, and had said to her, "You do not know me, Mademoiselle?" "No." "I am your mother." Then the old woman opened the sideboard, and ate and drank, had a mattress which she owned brought in, and installed herself. This cross and pious old mother never spoke to Favourite, remained hours without uttering a word, breakfasted, dined, and supped for four, and went down to the porter's quarters for company, where she spoke ill of her daughter.

It was having rosy nails that were too pretty which had drawn Dahlia to Listolier, to others perhaps, to idleness. How could she make such nails work? She who wishes to remain virtuous must not have pity on her hands. As for Zéphine, she had conquered Fameuil by her roguish and caressing little way of saying "Yes, sir."

The young men were comrades; the young girls were friends. Such loves are always accompanied by such friendships.

Goodness and philosophy are two distinct things; the proof of this is that, after making all due allowances for these little irregular households, Favourite, Zéphine, and Dahlia were philosophical young women, while Fantine was a good girl.

Good! someone will exclaim; and Tholomyès? Solomon would reply that love forms a part of wisdom. We will confine ourselves to saying that the love of Fantine was a first love, a sole love, a faithful love.

She alone, of all the four, was not called "thou" by a single one of them.

Fantine was one of those beings who blossom, so to speak, from the dregs of the people. Though she had emerged from the most unfathomable depths of social shadow, she bore on her brow the sign of the anonymous and the unknown. She was born at M. sur M. Of what parents? Who can say? She had never known father or mother. She was called Fantine. Why Fantine? She had never borne any other name. At the epoch of her birth the Directory still existed. She had no family name; she had no family; no baptismal name; the Church no longer existed. She bore the name which pleased the first random passer-by, who had encountered her, when a very small child, running bare-legged in the street. She received the name as she received the water from the clouds upon her brow when it rained. She was called little Fantine. No one knew more than that. This human creature had entered life in just this way. At the age of ten, Fantine quitted the town and went to service with some farmers in the neighborhood. At fifteen she came to Paris "to seek her fortune." Fantine was beautiful, and remained pure as long as she could. She was a lovely blonde, with fine teeth. She had gold and pearls for her dowry; but her gold was on her head, and her pearls were in her mouth.

She worked for her living; then, still for the sake of her living—for the heart, also, has its hunger—she loved.

She loved Tholomyès.

An amour for him; passion for her. The streets of the Latin Quarter, filled with throngs of students and grisettes, saw the beginning of their dream. Fantine had long evaded Tholomyès in the mazes of the hill of the Pantheon, where so many adventurers twine and untwine, but in such a way as constantly to encounter him again. There is a way of avoiding which resembles seeking. In short, the eclogue took place.

Blachevelle, Listolier, and Fameuil formed a sort of group of which Tholomyès was the head. It was he who possessed the wit.

Tholomyès was the antique old student; he was rich; he had an income of four thousand francs; four thousand francs! a splendid scandal on Mount Sainte-Geneviève. Tholomyès was a fast man of thirty, and badly preserved. He was wrinkled and toothless, and he had the beginning of a bald spot, of which he himself said with sadness, *the skull at thirty, the knee at forty*. His digestion was mediocre, and he had been attacked by a watering in one eye. But in proportion as his youth disappeared, gaiety was kindled; he replaced his teeth with buffooneries, his hair with mirth, his health with irony, his weeping eye laughed incessantly. He was dilapidated but still in flower. His youth, which was packing up for departure long before its time, beat a retreat in good order, bursting with laughter, and no one saw anything but fire. He had had a piece rejected at the Vaudeville. He made a few verses now and then. In addition to this he doubted everything to the last degree, which is a vast force in the eyes of the weak. Being thus ironical and bald, he was the leader. *Iron* is an English word. Is it possible that irony is derived from it?

One day Tholomyès took the three others aside, with the gesture of an oracle, and said to them:

"Fantine, Dahlia, Zéphine, and Favourite have been teasing us for nearly a year to give them a surprise. We have promised them solemnly that we would. They are forever talking about it to us, to me in particular, just as the old women in Naples cry to Saint Januarius, *'Faccia gialluta, fa o miracolo,* Yellow face, perform thy miracle,' so our beauties say to me incessantly, 'Tholomyès, when will you bring forth your surprise?' At the same time our parents keep writing to us. Pressure on both sides. The moment has arrived, it seems to me; let us discuss the question."

Thereupon, Tholomyès lowered his voice and articulated something so mirthful, that a vast and enthusiastic grin broke out upon the four mouths simultaneously, and Blachevelle exclaimed, "That is an idea."

A smoky tap-room presented itself; they entered, and the remainder of their confidential colloquy was lost in shadow.

The result of these shades was a dazzling pleasure party which took place on the following Sunday, the four young men inviting the four young girls.

Chapter III

FOUR AND FOUR

IT IS HARD NOWADAYS TO PICTURE TO ONE'S SELF WHAT A PLEASURE-TRIP OF STUDENTS AND grisettes to the country was like, forty-five years ago. The suburbs of Paris are no longer the same; the physiognomy of what may be called circumparisian life has changed completely in the last half-century; where there was the cuckoo, there is the railway car; where there was a tender-boat, there is now the steamboat; people speak of Fécamp nowadays as they spoke of Saint-Cloud in those days. The Paris of 1862 is a city which has France for its outskirts.

The four couples conscientiously went through with all the country follies possible at that time. The vacation was beginning, and it was a warm, bright, summer day. On the preceding day, Favourite, the only one who knew how to write, had written the following to Tholomyès in the name of the four: "It is a good hour to emerge from happiness." That is why they rose at five o'clock in the morning. Then they went to Saint-Cloud by the coach, looked at the dry cascade and exclaimed, "This must be very beautiful when there is water!" They breakfasted at the *Tête-Noir*, where Castaing had not yet been; they treated themselves to a game of ring-throwing under the quincunx of trees of the grand fountain; they ascended Diogenes's lantern, they gambled for macaroons at the roulette establishment of the Pont de Sèvres, picked bouquets at Puteaux, bought reed-pipes at Neuilly, ate apple tarts everywhere, and were perfectly happy.

The young girls rustled and chatted like warblers escaped from their cage. It was a perfect delirium. From time to time they bestowed little taps on the young men. Matutinal intoxication of life! adorable years! the wings of the dragonfly quiver. Oh, whoever you may be, do you not remember? Have you rambled through the brushwood, holding aside the branches, on account of the charming head which is coming on behind you? Have you slid, laughing, down a slope all wet with rain, with a beloved woman holding your hand, and crying, "Ah, my new boots! what a state they are in!"

Let us say at once that that merry obstacle, a shower, was lacking in the case of this good-humored party, although Favourite had said as they set out, with a magisterial and maternal tone, *"The slugs are crawling in the paths—a sign of rain, children."*

All four were madly pretty. A good old classic poet, then famous, a good fellow who had an Éléonore, M. le Chevalier de Labouisse, as he strolled that day beneath the chestnut-trees of Saint-Cloud, saw them pass about ten o'clock in the morning, and exclaimed, "There is one too many of them," as he thought of the Graces. Favourite, Blachevelle's friend, the one aged three-and-twenty, the old one, ran on in front under the great green boughs, jumped the ditches, stalked distractedly over bushes, and presided over this merry-making with the spirit of a young female faun. Zéphine and Dahlia, whom chance had made beautiful in such a way that they set each off when they were together, and completed each other, never left each other, more from an instinct of coquetry than from friendship, and clinging to each other, they assumed English poses; the first *keepsakes* had just made their appearance, melancholy was dawning for women, as later on, Byronism dawned for men; and the hair of the tender sex began to droop dolefully. Zéphine and Dahlia had their hair dressed in rolls. Listolier and Fameuil, who were engaged in discussing their professors, explained to Fantine the difference that existed between M. Delvincourt and M. Blondeau.

Blachevelle seemed to have been created expressly to carry Favourite's single-bordered, imitation India shawl of Ternaux's manufacture, on his arm on Sundays.

Tholomyès followed, dominating the group. He was very gay, but one felt the force of government in him; there was dictation in his joviality; his principal ornament was a pair of trousers of elephant-leg pattern of nankeen, with straps of braided copper wire; he carried a stout rattan worth two hundred francs in his hand, and, as he treated himself to everything, a strange thing called a cigar in his mouth. Nothing was sacred to him; he smoked.

"That Tholomyès is astounding!" said the others, with veneration. "What trousers! What energy!"

As for Fantine, she was a joy to behold. Her splendid teeth had evidently received an office from God—laughter. She preferred to carry her little hat of sewed straw, with its long white strings, in her hand rather than on her head. Her thick blond hair, which was inclined to wave, and which easily uncoiled, and which it was necessary to fasten up incessantly, seemed made for the flight of Galatea under the willows. Her rosy lips babbled enchantingly. The corners of her mouth voluptuously turned up, as in the antique masks of Erigone, had an air of encouraging the audacious; but her long, shadowy lashes drooped discreetly over the jollity of the lower part of the face as though to call a halt. There was something indescribably harmonious and striking about her entire dress. She wore a gown of mauve barège, little reddish brown buskins, whose ribbons traced an X on her fine, white, open-worked stockings, and that sort of muslin spencer, a Marseilles invention, whose name, *canezou*, a corruption of the words *quinze août*, pronounced after the fashion of the Canebière, signifies fine weather, heat, and midday. The three others, less timid, as we have already said, wore low-necked dresses without disguise, which in summer, beneath flower-adorned hats, are very graceful and enticing; but by the side of these audacious outfits, blond Fantine's *cane-ʒou*, with its transparencies, its indiscretion, and its reticence, concealing and displaying at one and the same time, seemed an alluring godsend of decency, and the famous Court of Love, presided over by the Vicomtesse de Cette, with the sea-green eyes, would, perhaps, have awarded the prize for coquetry to this *caneʒou*, in the contest for the prize of modesty. The most ingenious is, at times, the wisest. This does happen.

Brilliant of face, delicate of profile, with eyes of a deep blue, heavy lids, feet arched and small, wrists and ankles admirably formed, a white skin which, here and there allowed the azure branching of the veins to be seen, joy, a cheek that was young and fresh, the robust throat of the Juno of Ægina, a strong and supple nape of the neck, shoulders modeled as though by Coustou, with a voluptuous dimple in the middle, visible through the muslin; a gaiety cooled by dreaminess; sculptural and exquisite—such was Fantine; and beneath these feminine adornments and these ribbons one could divine a statue, and in that statue a soul.

Fantine was beautiful, without being too conscious of it. Those rare dreamers, mysterious priests of the beautiful who silently confront everything with perfection, would have caught a glimpse in this little working-woman, through the transparency of her Parisian grace, of the ancient sacred euphony. This daughter of the shadows was thoroughbred. She was beautiful in the two ways—style and rhythm. Style is the form of the ideal; rhythm is its movement.

We have said that Fantine was joy; she was also modesty.

To an observer who studied her attentively, that which breathed from her athwart all the intoxication of her age, the season, and her love affair, was an invincible expression of reserve and modesty. She remained a little astonished. This chaste astonishment is the shade of difference which separates Psyche from Venus. Fantine had the long, white, fine fingers of the vestal virgin who stirs the ashes of the sacred fire with a golden pin. Although she would have refused nothing to Tholomyès, as we shall have more than ample opportunity to see, her face in repose was supremely virginal; a sort of serious and almost austere dignity suddenly overwhelmed her at certain times, and there was nothing more singular and disturbing than to see gaiety become so suddenly extinct there, and meditation succeed to cheerfulness without any transition state. This sudden and sometimes severely accentuated gravity resembled the disdain of a goddess. Her brow, her nose, her chin, presented that equilibrium of outline which is quite distinct from equilibrium of proportion, and from which harmony of countenance results; in the very characteristic interval which separates the base of the nose from the upper lip, she had that imperceptible and charming fold, a mysterious sign of chastity, which makes Barberousse fall in love with a Diana found in the treasures of Iconia.

Love is a fault; so be it. Fantine was innocence floating high over fault.

Chapter IV

THOLOMYÈS IS SO MERRY THAT HE SINGS A SPANISH DITTY

THAT DAY WAS COMPOSED OF DAWN, FROM ONE END TO THE OTHER. ALL NATURE SEEMED TO BE having a holiday, and to be laughing. The flower-beds of Saint-Cloud perfumed the air; the breath of the Seine rustled the leaves vaguely; the branches gesticulated in the wind, bees pillaged the jasmines; a whole bohemia of butterflies swooped down upon the yarrow, the clover, and the sterile oats; in the august park of the King of France there was a pack of vagabonds, the birds.

The four merry couples, mingled with the sun, the fields, the flowers, the trees, were resplendent.

And in this community of Paradise, talking, singing, running, dancing, chasing butterflies, plucking convolvulus, wetting their pink, open-work stockings in the tall grass, fresh, wild, without malice, all received, to some extent, the kisses of all, with the exception of Fantine, who was hedged about with that vague resistance of hers composed of dreaminess and wildness, and who was in love. "You always have a queer look about you," said Favourite to her.

Such things are joys. These passages of happy couples are a profound appeal to life and nature, and make a caress and light spring forth from everything. There was once a fairy who created the fields and forests expressly for those in love—in that eternal hedge-school of lovers, which is forever beginning anew, and which will last as long as there are hedges and scholars. Hence the popularity of spring among thinkers. The patrician and the knife-grinder, the duke and the peer, the limb of the law, the courtiers and townspeople, as they used to say in olden times, all are subjects of this fairy. They laugh and hunt, and there is in the air the brilliance of an apotheosis—what a transfiguration effected by love! Notaries' clerks are gods. And the little cries, the pursuits through the grass, the waists embraced on the fly, those jargons which are melodies, those adorations which burst forth in the manner of pronouncing a syllable, those cherries torn from one mouth by another—all this blazes forth and takes its place among the celestial glories. Beautiful women waste themselves sweetly. They think that this will never come to an end. Philosophers, poets, painters, observe these ecstasies and know not what to make of it, so greatly are they dazzled by it. The departure for Cythera! exclaims Watteau; Lancret, the painter of plebeians, contemplates his bourgeois, who have flitted away into the azure sky; Diderot stretches out his arms to all these love idyls, and d'Urfé mingles druids with them.

After breakfast the four couples went to what was then called the King's Square to see a newly arrived plant from India, whose name escapes our memory at this moment, and which, at that epoch, was attracting all Paris to Saint-Cloud. It was an odd and charming shrub with a long stem, whose numerous branches, bristling and leafless and as fine as threads, were covered with a million tiny white rosettes; this gave the shrub the air of a head of hair studded with flowers. There was always an admiring crowd about it.

After viewing the shrub, Tholomyès exclaimed, "I offer you asses!" and having agreed upon a price with the owner of the asses, they returned by way of Vanvres and Issy. At Issy an incident occurred. The truly national park, at that time owned by Bourguin the contractor, happened to be wide open. They passed the gates, visited the manikin anchorite in his grotto, tried the mysterious little effects of the famous cabinet of mirrors, the wanton trap worthy of a satyr become a millionaire or of Turcaret metamorphosed into a Priapus. They had stoutly shaken the swing attached to the two chestnut-trees celebrated by the Abbé de Bernis. As he swung these beauties, one after the other, producing folds in the fluttering skirts which Greuze would have found to his taste, amid peals of laughter, the Toulousan Tholomyès, who was somewhat of a Spaniard, Toulouse being the cousin of Tolosa, sang, to a melancholy chant, the old ballad *gallega*, probably inspired by some lovely maid dashing in full flight upon a rope between two trees:

> "*Soy de Badajoz,*   "*Badajoz is my home,*
> *Amor me llama,*   *And Love is my name;*
> *Toda mi alma,*   *To my eyes in flame,*
> *Es en mi ojos,*   *All my soul doth come;*
> *Porque enseñas,*   *For instruction meet*
> *A tuas piernas.*   *I receive at thy feet.*"

Fantine alone refused to swing.

"I don't like to have people put on airs like that," muttered Favourite, with a good deal of acrimony.

After leaving the asses there was a fresh delight; they crossed the Seine in a boat, and proceeding from Passy on foot they reached the barrier of l'Étoile. They had been up since five o'clock that morning, as the reader will remember; but *bah! there is no such thing as fatigue on Sunday,* said Favourite; *on Sunday fatigue does not work.*

About three o'clock the four couples, frightened at their happiness, were sliding down the Russian mountains, a singular edifice which then occupied the heights of Beaujon, and whose undulating line was visible above the trees of the Champs-Élysées.

From time to time Favourite exclaimed:

"And the surprise? I claim the surprise."

"Patience," replied Tholomyès.

Chapter V

At Bombarda's

THE RUSSIAN MOUNTAINS HAVING BEEN EXHAUSTED, THEY BEGAN TO THINK ABOUT DINNER; AND the radiant party of eight, somewhat weary at last, became stranded in Bombarda's public-house, a branch establishment which had been set up in the Champs-Élysées by that famous restaurant-keeper, Bombarda, whose sign could then be seen in the Rue de Rivoli, near Delorme Alley.

A large but ugly room, with an alcove and a bed at the end (they had been obliged to put up with this accommodation in view of the Sunday crowd); two windows whence they could survey beyond the elms, the quay, and the river; a magnificent August sunlight lightly touching the panes; two tables; upon one of them a triumphant mountain of bouquets, mingled with the hats of men and of women; at the other the four couples seated round a merry confusion of platters, dishes, glasses, and bottles; jugs of beer mingled with flasks of wine; very little order on the table, some disorder beneath it;

> *"They made beneath the table*
> *A noise, a clatter of the feet that was abominable,"*

says Molière.

This was the state which the shepherd idyl, begun at five o'clock in the morning, had reached at half-past four in the afternoon. The sun was setting; their appetites were satisfied.

The Champs-Élysées, filled with sunshine and with people, were nothing but light and dust, the two things of which glory is composed. The horses of Marly, those neighing marbles, were prancing in a cloud of gold. Carriages were going and coming. A squadron of magnificent body-guards, with their clarions at their head, were descending the Avenue de Neuilly; the white flag, showing faintly rosy in the setting sun, floated over the dome of the Tuileries. The Place de la Concorde, which had become the Place Louis XV once more, was choked with happy promenaders. Many wore the silver fleur-de-lys suspended from the white-watered ribbon, which had not yet wholly disappeared from buttonholes in the year 1817. Here and there choruses of little girls threw to the winds, amid the passers-by, who formed into circles and applauded, the then celebrated Bourbon air, which was destined to strike the Hundred Days with lightning, and which had for its refrain:

> *"Rendez-nous notre père de Gand,*
> *Rendez-nous notre père."*

> *"Give us back our father from Ghent,*
> *Give us back our father."*

Groups of dwellers in the suburbs, in Sunday array, sometimes even decorated with the fleur-de-lys, like the bourgeois, scattered over the large square and the Marigny square, were playing at rings and revolving on the wooden horses; others were engaged in drinking; some journeyman printers had on paper caps; their laughter was audible. Everything was radiant. It was a time of undisputed peace and profound royalist security; it was the epoch when a special and private report of Chief of Police Anglès to the King, on the subject of the suburbs of Paris, terminated with these lines:

"Taking all things into consideration, Sire, there is nothing to be feared from these people. They are as heedless and as indolent as cats. The populace is restless in the provinces; it is not in Paris. These are very pretty men, Sire. It would take all of two of them to make one of your grenadiers. There is nothing to be feared on the part of the populace of Paris the capital. It is remarkable that the stature of this population should have diminished in the last fifty years; and the populace of the suburbs is still more puny than at the time of the Revolution. It is not dangerous. In short, it is an amiable rabble."

Prefects of the police do not deem it possible that a cat can transform itself into a lion; that does happen, however, and in that lies the miracle wrought by the populace of Paris. Moreover, the cat so despised by Count Anglès possessed the esteem of the republics of old. In their eyes it was liberty incarnate; and as though to serve as pendant to the Minerva Aptera of the Piræus, there stood on the public square in Corinth the colossal bronze figure of a cat. The ingenuous police of the Restoration beheld the populace of Paris in too "rose-colored" a light; it is not so much of "an amiable rabble" as it is thought. The Parisian is to the Frenchman what the Athenian was to the Greek: no one sleeps more soundly than he, no one is more frankly frivolous and lazy than he, no one can better assume the air of forgetfulness; let him not be trusted, nevertheless; he is ready for any sort of cool deed; but when there is glory at the end of it, he is worthy of admiration in every sort of fury. Give him a pike, he will produce the 10th of August; give him a gun, you will have Austerlitz. He is Napoleon's stay, and Danton's resource. Is it a question of country, he enlists; is it a question of liberty, he tears up the pavements. Beware! his hair, filled with wrath, is epic; his blouse drapes itself like the folds of a chlamys. Take care! he will make of the first Rue Grenétat which comes to hand Caudine Forks. When the hour strikes, this man of the faubourgs will grow in stature; this little man will arise, and his gaze will be terrible, and his breath will become a tempest, and there will issue forth from that slender chest enough wind to disarrange the folds of the Alps. It is, thanks to the suburban man of Paris, that the Revolution, mixed with arms, conquers Europe. He sings; it is his delight. Proportion his song to his nature, and you will see! As long as he has for refrain nothing but *la Carmagnole,* he only overthrows Louis XVI; make him sing the *Marseillaise,* and he will free the world.

This note jotted down on the margin of Anglès's report, we will return to our four couples. The dinner, as we have said, was drawing to its close.

Chapter VI

A CHAPTER IN WHICH THEY ADORE EACH OTHER

CHAT AT TABLE, THE CHAT OF LOVE; IT IS AS IMPOSSIBLE TO REPRODUCE ONE AS THE OTHER; THE chat of love is a cloud; the chat at table is smoke.

Fameuil and Dahlia were humming. Tholomyès was drinking. Zéphine was laughing, Fantine smiling, Listolier blowing a wooden trumpet which he had purchased at Saint-Cloud.

Favourite gazed tenderly at Blachevelle and said:

"Blachevelle, I adore you."

This called forth a question from Blachevelle:

"What would you do, Favourite, if I were to cease to love you?"

"I!" cried Favourite. "Ah! Do not say that even in jest! If you were to cease to love me, I would spring after you, I would scratch you, I should rend you, I would throw you into the water, I would have you arrested."

Blachevelle smiled with the voluptuous self-conceit of a man who is tickled in his self-love. Favourite resumed:

"Yes, I would scream to the police! Ah! I should not restrain myself, not at all! Rabble!"

Blachevelle threw himself back in his chair, in an ecstasy, and closed both eyes proudly.

Dahlia, as she ate, said in a low voice to Favourite, amid the uproar:

"So you really idolize him deeply, that Blachevelle of yours?"

"I? I detest him," replied Favourite in the same tone, seizing her fork again. "He is avaricious. I love the little fellow opposite me in my house. He is very nice, that young man; do you know him? One can see that he is an actor by profession. I love actors. As soon as he comes in, his mother says to him: 'Ah! mon Dieu! my peace of mind is gone. There he goes with his shouting. But, my dear, you are splitting my head!' So he goes up to rat-ridden garrets, to black holes, as high as he can mount, and there he sets to singing, declaiming, how do I know what? so that he can be heard downstairs! He earns twenty sous a day at an attorney's by penning quibbles. He is the son of a former precentor of Saint-Jacques-du-Haut-Pas. Ah! he is very nice. He idolizes me so, that one day when he saw me making batter for some pancakes, he said to me: 'Mamselle, make your gloves into fritters, and I will eat them.' It is only artists who can say such things as that. Ah! he is very nice. I am in a fair way to go out of my head over that little fellow. Never mind; I tell Blachevelle that I adore him—how I lie! Hey! How I do lie!"

Favourite paused, and then went on:

"I am sad, you see, Dahlia. It has done nothing but rain all summer; the wind irritates me; the wind does not abate. Blachevelle is very stingy; there are hardly any green peas in the market; one does not know what to eat. I have the spleen, as the English say, butter is so dear! and then you see it is horrible, here we are dining in a room with a bed in it, and that disgusts me with life."

Chapter VII

THE WISDOM OF THOLOMYÈS

IN THE MEANTIME, WHILE SOME SANG, THE REST TALKED TOGETHER TUMULTUOUSLY ALL AT ONCE; it was no longer anything but noise. Tholomyès intervened.

"Let us not talk at random nor too fast," he exclaimed. "Let us reflect, if we wish to be brilliant. Too much improvisation empties the mind in a stupid way. Running beer gathers no froth. No haste, gentlemen. Let us mingle majesty with the feast. Let us eat with meditation; let us make haste slowly. Let us not hurry. Consider the springtime; if it makes haste, it is done for; that is to say, it gets frozen. Excess of zeal ruins peach-trees and apricot-trees. Excess of zeal kills the grace and the mirth of good dinners. No zeal, gentlemen! Grimod de la Reynière agrees with Talleyrand."

A hollow sound of rebellion rumbled through the group.

"Leave us in peace, Tholomyès," said Blachevelle.

"Down with the tyrant!" said Fameuil.

"Bombarda, Bombance, and Bambochel!" cried Listolier.

"Sunday exists," resumed Fameuil.

"We are sober," added Listolier.

"Tholomyès," remarked Blachevelle, "contemplate my calmness [*mon calme*]."

"You are the Marquis of that," retorted Tholomyès.

This mediocre play upon words produced the effect of a stone in a pool. The Marquis de Montcalm was at that time a celebrated royalist. All the frogs held their peace.

"Friends," cried Tholomyès, with the accent of a man who had recovered his empire, "come to yourselves. This pun which has fallen from the skies must not be received with too much stupor. Everything which falls in that way is not necessarily worthy of enthusiasm and respect. The pun is the dung of the mind which soars. The jest falls, no matter where; and the mind after producing a piece of stupidity plunges into the azure depths. A whitish speck flattened against the rock does not prevent the condor from soaring aloft. Far be it from me to insult the pun! I honor it in proportion to its merits; nothing more. All the most august, the most sublime, the most charming of humanity, and perhaps outside of humanity, have made puns. Jesus Christ made a pun on St. Peter, Moses on Isaac, Æschylus on Polynices, Cleopatra on Octavius. And observe that Cleopatra's pun preceded the battle of Actium, and that had it not been for it, no one would have remembered the city of Toryne, a Greek name which signifies a ladle. That once conceded, I return to my exhortation. I repeat, brothers, I repeat, no zeal, no hubbub, no excess; even in witticisms, gaiety, jollities, or plays on words. Listen to me. I have the prudence of Amphiaraüs and the baldness of Cæsar. There must be a limit, even to rebuses. *Est modus in rebus.*

"There must be a limit, even to dinners. You are fond of apple turnovers, ladies; do not indulge in them to excess. Even in the matter of turnovers, good sense and art are requisite. Gluttony chastises the glutton, *Gula punit Gulax*. Indigestion is charged by the good God with preaching morality to stomachs. And remember this: each one of our passions, even love, has a stomach which must not be filled too full. In all things the word *finis* must be written in good season; self-control must be exercised when the matter becomes urgent; the bolt must be drawn on appetite; one must set one's own fantasy to the violin, and carry one's self to the post. The sage is the man who knows how, at a given moment, to effect his own arrest. Have some confidence in me, for I have succeeded to some extent in my study of the law, according to the verdict of my examinations, for I know the difference between the question put and the question pending, for I have sustained a thesis in Latin upon the manner in which torture was administered at Rome at the epoch when Munatius Demens was quaestor of the Parricide; because I am going to be a doctor, apparently it does not follow that it is absolutely necessary that I should be an imbecile. I recommend you to moderation in your desires. It is true that my name is Félix Tholomyès; I speak well. Happy is he who, when the hour strikes, takes a heroic resolve, and abdicates like Sylla or Origenes."

Favourite listened with profound attention.

"Félix," said she, "what a pretty word! I love that name. It is Latin; it means prosper."

Tholomyès went on:

"Quirites, gentlemen, caballeros, my friends. Do you wish never to feel the prick, to do without the nuptial bed, and to brave love? Nothing more simple. Here is the receipt: lemonade, excessive exercise, hard labor; work yourself to death, drag blocks, sleep not, hold vigil, gorge yourself with nitrous beverages, and potions of nymphaeas; drink emulsions of poppies and agnus castus; season this with a strict diet, starve yourself, and add thereto cold baths, girdles of herbs, the application of a plate of lead, lotions made with the subacetate of lead, and fomentations of oxycrat."

"I prefer a woman," said Listolier.

"Woman," resumed Tholomyès; "distrust her. Woe to him who yields himself to the unstable heart of woman! Woman is perfidious and disingenuous. She detests the serpent from professional jealousy. The serpent is the shop over the way."

"Tholomyès!" cried Blachevelle, "you are drunk!"

"Pardieu," said Tholomyès.

"Then be gay," resumed Blachevelle.

"I agree to that," responded Tholomyès.

And, refilling his glass, he rose.

"Glory to wine! *Nunc te, Bacche, canam!* Pardon me, ladies; that is Spanish. And the proof of it, señoras, is this: like people, like cask. The arrobe of Castile contains sixteen liters; the cantaro of Alicante, twelve; the almude of the Canaries, twenty-five; the cuartin of the Balearic Isles, twenty-six; the boot of Tzar Peter, thirty. Long live that Tzar who was great, and long live his boot, which was still greater! Ladies, take the advice of a friend; make a mistake in your neighbor if you see fit. The property of love is to err. A love affair is not made to crouch down and brutalize itself like an English serving-maid who has calluses on her knees from scrubbing. It is not made for that; it errs gaily, our gentle love. It has been said, error is human; I say, error is love. Ladies, I idolize you all. O Zéphine, O Joséphine! face more than irregular, you would be charming were you not all askew. You have the air of a pretty face upon which someone has sat down by mistake. As for Favourite, O nymphs and muses! one day when Blachevelle was crossing the gutter in the Rue Guérin-Boisseau, he spied a beautiful girl with white stockings well drawn up, which displayed her legs. This prologue pleased him, and Blachevelle fell in love. The one he loved was Favourite. O Favourite, thou hast Ionian lips. There was a Greek painter named Euphorion, who was surnamed the painter of the lips. That Greek alone would have been worthy to paint thy mouth. Listen! before thee, there was never a creature worthy of the name. Thou wert made to receive the apple like Venus, or to eat it like Eve; beauty begins with thee. I have just referred to Eve; it is thou who hast created her. Thou deservest the letters-patent of the beautiful woman. O Favourite, I cease to address you as 'thou,' because I pass from poetry to prose. You were speaking of my name a little while ago. That touched me; but let us, whoever we may be, distrust names. They may delude us. I am called Félix, and I am not happy. Words are liars. Let us not blindly accept the indications which they afford us. It would be a mistake to write to Liège for corks, and to Pau for gloves. Miss Dahlia, were I in your place, I would call myself Rosa. A flower should smell sweet, and woman should have wit. I say nothing of Fantine; she is a dreamer, a musing, thoughtful, pensive person; she is a phantom possessed of the form of a nymph and the modesty of a nun, who has strayed into the life of a grisette, but who takes refuge in illusions, and who sings and prays and gazes into the azure without very well knowing what she sees or what she is doing, and who, with her eyes fixed on heaven, wanders in a garden where there are more birds than are in existence. O Fantine, know this: I, Tholomyès, I am all illusion; but she does not even hear me, that blond maid of Chimeras! as for the rest, everything about her is freshness, suavity, youth, sweet morning light. O Fantine, maid worthy of being called Marguerite or Pearl, you are a woman from the beauteous Orient. Ladies, a second piece of advice: do not marry; marriage is a graft; it takes well or ill; avoid that risk. But bah! what am I saying? I am wasting my words. Girls are incurable on the subject of marriage, and all that we wise men can say will not prevent the waistcoat-makers and the shoe-stitchers from dreaming of husbands studded with diamonds. Well, so be it; but, my beauties, remember this, you eat too much sugar. You have but one fault, O woman, and that is nibbling sugar. O nibbling sex, your pretty little white teeth adore sugar. Now, heed me well, sugar is a salt. All salts are withering. Sugar is the most desiccating of all salts; it sucks the liquids of the blood through the veins; hence the coagulation, and then the solidification of the blood; hence tubercles in the lungs, hence death. That is why diabetes borders on consumption. Then, do not crunch sugar, and you will live. I turn to the men: gentlemen, make conquest, rob each other of your well-beloved without remorse. Chassez across. In love there are no friends. Everywhere where there is a pretty woman hostility is open. No quarter, war to the death! a pretty woman is a *casus belli*; a pretty woman is flagrant misdemeanor. All the invasions of history have been determined by petticoats. Woman is man's right. Romulus carried off the Sabines; William carried off the Saxon women; Cæsar carried off the Roman women. The man who is not loved soars like a vulture over the mistresses of other men; and for my own part, to all those unfortunate men who are widowers, I throw the sublime proclamation of Bonaparte to the army of Italy: 'Soldiers, you are in need of everything; the enemy has it.' "

Tholomyès paused.

"Take breath, Tholomyès," said Blachevelle.

At the same moment Blachevelle, supported by Listolier and Fameuil, struck up to a plaintive air, one of those studio songs composed of the first words which come to hand, rhymed richly and not at all, as destitute of sense as the gesture of the tree and the sound of the wind, which have their birth in the vapor of pipes, and are dissipated and take their flight with them. This is the couplet by which the group replied to Tholomyès's harangue:

> "*The father turkey-cocks so grave*
> *Some money to an agent gave,*
> *That master good Clermont-Tonnerre*
> *Might be made pope on Saint John's day fair.*
> *But this good Clermont could not be*
> *Made pope, because no priest was he;*
> *And then their agent, whose wrath burned,*
> *With all their money back returned.*"

This was not calculated to calm Tholomyès's improvisation; he emptied his glass, filled, refilled it, and began again:

"Down with wisdom! Forget all that I have said. Let us be neither prudes nor prudent men nor prudhommes. I propose a toast to mirth; be merry. Let us complete our course of law by folly and eating! Indigestion and the digest. Let Justinian be the male, and Feasting, the female! Joy in the depths! Live, O creation! The world is a great diamond. I am happy. The birds are astonishing. What a festival everywhere! The nightingale is a gratuitous Elleviou. Summer, I salute thee! O Luxembourg! O Georgics of the Rue Madame and of the Allée de l'Observatoire! O pensive infantry soldiers! O all those charming nurses who, while they guard the children, amuse themselves!

The pampas of America would please me if I had not the arcades of the Odéon. My soul flits away into the virgin forests and to the savannas. All is beautiful. The flies buzz in the sun. The sun has sneezed out the humming bird. Embrace me, Fantine!"

He made a mistake and embraced Favourite.

Chapter VIII

The Death of a Horse

THE DINNERS ARE BETTER AT ÉDON'S THAN AT BOMBARDA'S," EXCLAIMED ZÉPHINE.
"I prefer Bombarda to Édon," declared Blachevelle. "There is more luxury. It is more Asiatic. Look at the room downstairs; there are mirrors [*glaces*] on the walls."

"I prefer them [*glaces*, ices] on my plate," said Favourite.

Blachevelle persisted:

"Look at the knives. The handles are of silver at Bombarda's and of bone at Édon's. Now, silver is more valuable than bone."

"Except for those who have a silver chin," observed Tholomyès.

He was looking at the dome of the Invalides, which was visible from Bombarda's windows.

A pause ensued.

"Tholomyès," exclaimed Fameuil, "Listolier and I were having a discussion just now."

"A discussion is a good thing," replied Tholomyès; "a quarrel is better."

"We were disputing about philosophy."

"Well?"

"Which do you prefer, Descartes or Spinoza?"

"Désaugiers," said Tholomyès.

This decree pronounced, he took a drink, and went on:

"I consent to live. All is not at an end on earth since we can still talk nonsense. For that I return thanks to the immortal gods. We lie. One lies, but one laughs. One affirms, but one doubts. The unexpected bursts forth from the syllogism. That is fine. There are still human beings here below who know how to open and close the surprise box of the paradox merrily. This, ladies, which you are drinking with so tranquil an air is Madeira wine, you must know, from the vineyard of Coural das Freiras, which is three hundred and seventeen fathoms above the level of the sea. Attention while you drink! three hundred and seventeen fathoms! and Monsieur Bombarda, the magnificent eating-house keeper, gives you those three hundred and seventeen fathoms for four francs and fifty centimes."

Again Fameuil interrupted him:

"Tholomyès, your opinions fix the law. Who is your favorite author?"

"Ber—"

"Quin?"

"No; Choux."

And Tholomyès continued:

"Honor to Bombarda! He would equal Munophis of Elephanta if he could but get me an Indian dancing-girl, and Thygelion of Chæronea if he could bring me a Greek courtesan; for, oh, ladies! there were Bombardas in Greece and in Egypt. Apuleius tells us of them. Alas! always the same, and nothing new; nothing more unpublished by the creator in creation! *Nil sub sole novum,* says Solomon; *amor omnibus idem,* says Virgil; and Carabine mounts with Carabin into the bark at Saint-Cloud, as Aspasia embarked with Pericles upon the fleet at Samos. One last word. Do you know what Aspasia was, ladies? Although she lived at an epoch when women had, as yet, no soul, she was a soul; a soul of a rosy and purple hue, more ardent hued than fire, fresher than the dawn. Aspasia was a creature in whom the two extremes of womanhood met; she was the goddess prostitute; Socrates plus Manon Lescaut. Aspasia was created in case a mistress should be needed for Prometheus."

Tholomyès, once started, would have found some difficulty in stopping, had not a horse fallen down upon the quay just at that moment. The shock caused the cart and the orator to come to a dead halt. It was a Beauceron mare, old and thin, and one fit for the knacker, which was dragging a very heavy cart. On arriving in front of Bombarda's, the worn-out, exhausted beast had refused to proceed any further. This incident attracted a crowd. Hardly had the cursing and indignant carter had time to utter with proper energy the sacramental word, *Mâtin* (the jade), backed up with a pitiless cut of the whip, when the jade fell, never to rise again. On hearing the hubbub made by the passers-by, Tholomyès's merry auditors turned their heads, and Tholomyès took advantage of the opportunity to bring his allocution to a close with this melancholy strophe:

> *"Elle était de ce monde ou coucous et carrosses*
> *Ont le même destin;*
> *Et, rosse, elle a vecu ce que vivant les rosses,*
> *L'espace d'un mâtin!"*[1]

"Poor horse!" sighed Fantine.

And Dahlia exclaimed:

"There is Fantine on the point of crying over horses. How can one be such a pitiful fool as that!"

At that moment Favourite, folding her arms and throwing her head back, looked resolutely at Tholomyès and said:

"Come, now! the surprise?"

"Exactly. The moment has arrived," replied Tholomyès. "Gentlemen, the hour for giving these ladies a surprise has struck. Wait for us a moment, ladies."

"It begins with a kiss," said Blachevelle.

"On the brow," added Tholomyès.

Each gravely bestowed a kiss on his mistress's brow; then all four filed out through the door, with their fingers on their lips.

Favourite clapped her hands on their departure.

"It is beginning to be amusing already," said she.

"Don't be too long," murmured Fantine; "we are waiting for you."

---

1. She belonged to that circle where cuckoos and carriages share the same fate; and a jade herself, she lived, as jades live, for the space of a morning (or jade).

Chapter IX

A MERRY END TO MIRTH

WHEN THE YOUNG GIRLS WERE LEFT ALONE, THEY LEANED TWO BY TWO ON THE WINDOW-sills, chatting, craning out their heads, and talking from one window to the other.

They saw the young men emerge from the Café Bombarda arm in arm. The latter turned round, made signs to them, smiled, and disappeared in that dusty Sunday throng which makes a weekly invasion into the Champs-Élysées.

"Don't be long!" cried Fantine.

"What are they going to bring us?" said Zéphine.

"It will certainly be something pretty," said Dahlia.

"For my part," said Favourite, "I want it to be of gold."

Their attention was soon distracted by the movements on the shore of the lake, which they could see through the branches of the large trees, and which diverted them greatly.

It was the hour for the departure of the mail-coaches and diligences. Nearly all the stage-coaches for the south and west passed through the Champs-Élysées. The majority followed the quay and went through the Passy Barrier. From moment to moment, some huge vehicle, painted yellow and black, heavily loaded, noisily harnessed, rendered shapeless by trunks, tarpaulins, and valises, full of heads which immediately disappeared, rushed through the crowd with all the sparks of a forge, with dust for smoke, and an air of fury, grinding the pavements, changing all the paving-stones into steels. This uproar delighted the young girls. Favourite exclaimed:

"What a row! One would say that it was a pile of chains flying away."

It chanced that one of these vehicles, which they could only see with difficulty through the thick elms, halted for a moment, then set out again at a gallop. This surprised Fantine.

"That's odd!" said she. "I thought the diligence never stopped."

Favourite shrugged her shoulders.

"This Fantine is surprising. I am coming to take a look at her out of curiosity. She is dazzled by the simplest things. Suppose a case: I am a traveler; I say to the diligence, 'I will go on in advance; you shall pick me up on the quay as you pass.' The diligence passes, sees me, halts, and takes me. That is done every day. You do not know life, my dear."

In this manner a certain time elapsed. All at once Favourite made a movement, like a person who is just waking up.

"Well," said she, "and the surprise?"

"Yes, by the way," joined in Dahlia, "the famous surprise?"

"They are a very long time about it!" said Fantine.

As Fantine concluded this sigh, the waiter who had served them at dinner entered. He held in his hand something which resembled a letter.

"What is that?" demanded Favourite.

The waiter replied:

"It is a paper that those gentlemen left for these ladies."

"Why did you not bring it at once?"

"Because," said the waiter, "the gentlemen ordered me not to deliver it to the ladies for an hour."

Favourite snatched the paper from the waiter's hand. It was, in fact, a letter.

"Stop!" said she; "there is no address; but this is what is written on it":

"This is the Surprise."

She tore the letter open hastily, opened it, and read [she knew how to read]:

"O Our Beloved—You must know that we have parents. Parents—you do not know much about such things. They are called fathers and mothers by the civil code, which is puerile and honest. Now, these parents groan, these old folks implore us, these good men and these good women call us prodigal sons; they desire our return, and offer to kill calves for us. Being virtuous, we obey them. At the hour when you read this, five fiery horses will be bearing us to our papas and mammas. We are pulling up our stakes, as Bossuet says. We are going; we are gone. We flee in the arms of Laffitte and on the wings of Caillard. The Toulouse diligence tears us from the abyss, and the abyss is you, O our little beauties! We return to society, to duty, to respectability, at full trot, at the rate of three leagues an hour. It is necessary for the good of the country that we should be, like all the rest of the world, prefects, fathers of families, rural police, and councilors of state. Venerate us. We are sacrificing ourselves. Mourn for us in haste, and replace us with speed. If this letter lacerates you, do the same by it. Adieu.

"For the space of nearly two years we have made you happy. We bear you no grudge for that.

"Signed:　　　Blachevelle

Famueil

Listolier

Félix Tholomyès

"*Postscriptum*. The dinner is paid for."

The four young women looked at each other.
Favourite was the first to break the silence.
"Well!" she exclaimed, "it's a very pretty farce, all the same."
"It is very droll," said Zéphine.
"That must have been Blachevelle's idea," resumed Favourite. "It makes me in love with him. No sooner is he gone than he is loved. This is an adventure, indeed."
"No," said Dahlia; "it was one of Tholomyès's ideas. That is evident."
"In that case," retorted Favourite, "death to Blachevelle, and long live Tholomyès!"
"Long live Tholomyès!" exclaimed Dahlia and Zéphine.
And they burst out laughing.
Fantine laughed with the rest.
An hour later, when she had returned to her room, she wept. It was her first love affair, as we have said; she had given herself to this Tholomyès as to a husband, and the poor girl had a child.

BOOK FOURTH

TO CONFIDE IS SOMETIMES TO DELIVER INTO A PERSON'S POWER

Chapter I

ONE MOTHER MEETS ANOTHER MOTHER

THERE WAS, AT MONTFERMEIL, NEAR PARIS, DURING THE FIRST QUARTER OF THIS CENTURY, A SORT of cook-shop which no longer exists. This cook-shop was kept by some people named Thénardier, husband and wife. It was situated in Boulanger Lane. Over the door there was a board nailed flat against the wall. Upon this board was painted something which resembled a man carrying another man on his back, the latter wearing the big gilt epaulettes of a general, with large silver stars; red spots represented blood; the rest of the picture consisted of smoke, and probably represented a battle. Below ran this inscription: AT THE SIGN OF SERGEANT OF WATERLOO (*Au Sergent de Waterloo*).

Nothing is more common than a cart or a truck at the door of a hostelry. Nevertheless, the vehicle, or, to speak more accurately, the fragment of a vehicle, which encumbered the street in front of the cook-shop of the *Sergeant of Waterloo*, one evening in the spring of 1818, would certainly have attracted, by its mass, the attention of any painter who had passed that way.

It was the fore-carriage of one of those trucks which are used in wooded tracts of country, and which serve to transport thick planks and the trunks of trees. This fore-carriage was composed of a massive iron axle-tree with a pivot, into which was fitted a heavy shaft, and which was supported by two huge wheels. The whole thing was compact, overwhelming, and misshapen. It seemed like the gun-carriage of an enormous cannon. The ruts of the road had bestowed on the wheels, the fellies, the hub, the axle, and the shaft, a layer of mud, a hideous yellowish daubing hue, tolerably like that with which people are fond of ornamenting cathedrals. The wood was disappearing under mud, and the iron beneath rust. Under the axle-tree hung, like drapery, a huge chain, worthy of some Goliath of a convict. This chain suggested, not the beams, which it was its office to transport, but the mastodons and mammoths which it might have served to harness; it had the air of the galleys, but of cyclopean and superhuman galleys, and it seemed to have been detached from some monster. Homer would have bound Polyphemus with it, and Shakespeare, Caliban.

Why was that fore-carriage of a truck in that place in the street? In the first place, to encumber the street; next, in order that it might finish the process of rusting. There is a throng of institutions in the old social order, which one comes across in this fashion as one walks about outdoors, and which have no other reasons for existence than the above.

The center of the chain swung very near the ground in the middle, and in the loop, as in the rope of a swing, there were seated and grouped, on that particular evening, in exquisite interlacement, two little girls; one about two years and a half old, the other, eighteen months; the younger in the arms of the other. A handkerchief, cleverly knotted about them, prevented their falling out.

A mother had caught sight of that frightful chain, and had said, "Come! there's a plaything for my children."

The two children, who were dressed prettily and with some elegance, were radiant with pleasure; one would have said that they were two roses amid old iron; their eyes were a triumph; their fresh cheeks were full of laughter. One had chestnut hair; the other, brown. Their innocent faces were two delighted surprises; a blossoming shrub which grew near wafted to the passers-by perfumes which seemed to emanate from them; the child of eighteen months displayed her pretty little bare stomach with the chaste indecency of childhood. Above and around these two delicate heads, all made of happiness and steeped in light, the gigantic fore-carriage, black with rust, almost terrible, all entangled in curves and wild angles, rose in a vault, like the entrance of a cavern. A few paces apart, crouching down upon the threshold of the hostelry, the mother, not a very prepossessing woman, by the way, though touching at that moment, was swinging the two children by means of a long cord, watching them carefully, for fear of accidents, with that animal and celestial expression which is peculiar to maternity. At every backward and forward swing the hideous links emitted a strident sound, which resembled a cry of rage; the little girls were in ecstasies; the setting sun mingled in this joy, and nothing could be more charming than this caprice of chance which had made of a chain of Titans the swing of cherubim.

As she rocked her little ones, the mother hummed in a discordant voice a romance then celebrated:

> *"It must be, said a warrior."*

Her song, and the contemplation of her daughters, prevented her hearing and seeing what was going on in the street.

In the meantime, someone had approached her, as she was beginning the first couplet of the romance, and suddenly she heard a voice saying very near her ear:

"You have two beautiful children there, Madame."

> *"To the fair and tender Imogene—"*

replied the mother, continuing her romance; then she turned her head.

A woman stood before her, a few paces distant. This woman also had a child, which she carried in her arms.

She was carrying, in addition, a large carpet-bag, which seemed very heavy.

This woman's child was one of the most divine creatures that it is possible to behold. It was a girl, two or three years of age. She could have entered into competition with the two other little ones, so far as the coquetry of her dress was concerned; she wore a cap of fine linen, ribbons on her bodice, and Valenciennes lace on her cap. The folds of her skirt were raised so as to permit a view of her white, firm, and dimpled leg. She was admirably rosy and healthy. The little beauty inspired a desire to take a bite from the apples of her cheeks. Of her eyes nothing could be known, except that they must be very large, and that they had magnificent lashes. She was asleep.

She slept with that slumber of absolute confidence peculiar to her age. The arms of mothers are made of tenderness; in them children sleep profoundly.

As for the mother, her appearance was sad and poverty-stricken. She was dressed like a working-woman who is inclined to turn into a peasant again. She was young. Was she handsome? Perhaps; but in that attire it was not apparent. Her hair, a golden lock of which had escaped, seemed very thick, but was severely concealed beneath an ugly, tight, close, nunlike cap, tied under the chin. A smile displays beautiful teeth when one has them; but she did not smile. Her eyes did not seem to have been dry for a very long time. She was pale; she had a very weary and rather sickly appearance. She gazed upon her daughter asleep in her arms with the air peculiar to a mother who has nursed her own child. A large blue handkerchief, such as the Invalides use, was folded into a fichu, and concealed her figure clumsily. Her hands were sunburned and all dotted with freckles, her forefinger was hardened and lacerated with the needle; she wore a cloak of coarse brown woolen stuff, a linen gown, and coarse shoes. It was Fantine.

It was Fantine, but difficult to recognize. Nevertheless, on scrutinizing her attentively, it was evident that she still retained her beauty. A melancholy fold, which resembled the beginning of irony, wrinkled her right cheek. As for her toilette, that aerial toilette of muslin and ribbons, which seemed made of mirth, of folly, and of music, full of bells, and perfumed with lilacs, had vanished like that beautiful and dazzling hoar-frost which is mistaken for diamonds in the sunlight; it melts and leaves the branch quite black.

Ten months had elapsed since the "pretty farce."

What had taken place during those ten months? It can be divined.

After abandonment, straightened circumstances. Fantine had immediately lost sight of Favourite, Zéphine, and Dahlia; the bond once broken on the side of the men, it was loosed between the women; they would have been greatly astonished had anyone told them a fortnight later, that they had been friends; there no longer existed any reason for such a thing. Fantine had remained alone. The father of her child gone—alas! such ruptures are irrevocable—she found herself absolutely isolated, minus the habit of work and plus the taste for pleasure. Drawn away by her *liaison* with Tholomyès to disdain the pretty trade which she knew, she had neglected to keep her market open; it was now closed to her. She had no resource. Fantine barely knew how to read, and did not know how to write; in her childhood she had only been taught to sign her name; she had a public letter-writer indite an epistle to Tholomyès, then a second, then a third. Tholomyès replied to none of them. Fantine heard the gossips say, as they looked at her child: "Who takes those children seriously! One only shrugs one's shoulders over such children!" Then she thought of Tholomyès, who had shrugged his shoulders over his child, and who did not take that innocent being seriously; and her heart grew gloomy toward that man. But what was she to do? She no longer knew to whom to apply. She had committed a fault, but the foundation of her nature, as will be remembered, was modesty and virtue. She was vaguely conscious that she was on the verge of falling into distress, and of gliding into a worse state. Courage was necessary; she possessed it, and held herself firm. The idea of returning to her native town of M. sur M. occurred to her. There, someone might possibly know her and give her work; yes, but it would be necessary to conceal her fault. In a confused way she perceived the necessity of a separation which would be more painful than the first one. Her heart contracted, but she took her resolution. Fantine, as we shall see, had the fierce bravery of life. She had already valiantly renounced finery, had dressed herself in linen, and had put all her silks, all her ornaments, all her ribbons, and all her laces on her daughter, the only vanity which was left to her, and a holy one it was. She sold all that she had, which produced for her two hundred francs; her little debts paid, she had only about eighty francs left. At the age of twenty-two, on a beautiful spring morning, she quitted Paris, bearing her child on her back. Anyone who had seen these two pass would have had pity on them. This woman had, in all the world, nothing but her child, and the child had, in all the world, no one but this woman. Fantine had nursed her child, and this had tired her chest, and she coughed a little.

We shall have no further occasion to speak of M. Félix Tholomyès. Let us confine ourselves to saying, that, twenty years later, under King Louis Philippe, he was a great provincial lawyer, wealthy and influential, a wise elector, and a very severe juryman; he was still a man of pleasure.

Toward the middle of the day, after having, from time to time, for the sake of resting herself, traveled, for three or four sous a league, in what was then known as the *Petites Voitures des Environs de Paris*, the "little suburban coach service," Fantine found herself at Montfermeil, in the alley Boulanger.

As she passed the Thénardier hostelry, the two little girls, blissful in the monster swing, had dazzled her in a manner, and she had halted in front of that vision of joy.

Charms exist. These two little girls were a charm to this mother.

She gazed at them in much emotion. The presence of angels is an announcement of Paradise. She thought that, above this inn, she beheld the mysterious HERE of Providence. These two little creatures were evidently happy. She gazed at them, she admired them, in such emotion that at the moment when their mother was recovering her breath between two couplets of her song, she could not refrain from addressing to her the remark which we have just read:

"You have two pretty children, Madame."

The most ferocious creatures are disarmed by caresses bestowed on their young.

The mother raised her head and thanked her, and bade the wayfarer sit down on the bench at the door, she herself being seated on the threshold. The two women began to chat.

"My name is Madame Thénardier," said the mother of the two little girls. "We keep this inn."

Then, her mind still running on her romance, she resumed, humming between her teeth:

> *"It must be so; I am a knight,*
> *And I am off to Palestine."*

This Madame Thénardier was a sandy-complexioned woman, thin and angular—the type of the soldier's wife in all its unpleasantness; and what was odd, with a languishing air, which she owed to her perusal of romances. She was a simpering, but masculine creature. Old romances produce that effect when rubbed against the imagination of cook-shop woman. She was still young; she was barely thirty. If this crouching woman had stood upright, her lofty stature and her frame of a per-ambulating colossus suitable for fairs, might have frightened the traveler at the outset, troubled her confidence, and disturbed what caused what we have to relate to vanish. A person who is seated in-stead of standing erect—destinies hang upon such a thing as that.

The traveler told her story, with slight modifications.

That she was a working-woman; that her husband was dead; that her work in Paris had failed her, and that she was on her way to seek it elsewhere, in her own native parts; that she had left Paris that morning, on foot; that, as she was carrying her child, and felt fatigued, she had got into the Villemomble coach when she met it; that from Villemomble she had come to Montfermeil on foot; that the little one had walked a little, but not much, because she was so young, and that she had been obliged to take her up, and the jewel had fallen asleep.

At this word she bestowed on her daughter a passionate kiss, which woke her. The child opened her eyes, great blue eyes like her mother's, and looked at—what? Nothing; with that seri-ous and sometimes severe air of little children, which is a mystery of their luminous innocence in the presence of our twilight of virtue. One would say that they feel themselves to be angels, and that they know us to be men. Then the child began to laugh; and although the mother held fast to her, she slipped to the ground with the unconquerable energy of a little being which wished to run. All at once she caught sight of the two others in the swing, stopped short, and put out her tongue, in sign of admiration.

Mother Thénardier released her daughters, made them descend from the swing, and said:

"Now amuse yourselves, all three of you."

Children become acquainted quickly at that age, and at the expiration of a minute the little Thénardiers were playing with the newcomer at making holes in the ground, which was an im-mense pleasure.

The newcomer was very gay; the goodness of the mother is written in the gaiety of the child; she had seized a scrap of wood which served her for a shovel, and energetically dug a cavity big enough for a fly. The gravedigger's business becomes a subject for laughter when performed by a child.

The two women pursued their chat.

"What is your little one's name?"

"Cosette."

For Cosette, read Euphrasie. The child's name was Euphrasie. But out of Euphrasie the mother had made Cosette by that sweet and graceful instinct of mothers and of the populace which changes Josepha into Pepita, and Françoise into Sillette. It is a sort of derivative which disarranges and disconcerts the whole science of etymologists. We have known a grandmother who succeeded in turning Theodore into Gnon.

"How old is she?"

"She is going on three."

"That is the age of my eldest."

In the meantime, the three little girls were grouped in an attitude of profound anxiety and blissfulness; an event had happened; a big worm had emerged from the ground, and they were afraid; and they were in ecstasies over it.

Their radiant brows touched each other; one would have said that there were three heads in one aureole.

"How easily children get acquainted at once!" exclaimed Mother Thénardier; "one would swear that they were three sisters!"

This remark was probably the spark which the other mother had been waiting for. She seized the Thénardier's hand, looked at her fixedly, and said:

"Will you keep my child for me?"

The Thénardier made one of those movements of surprise which signify neither assent nor refusal.

Cosette's mother continued:

"You see, I cannot take my daughter to the country. My work will not permit it. With a child one can find no situation. People are ridiculous in the country. It was the good God who caused me to pass your inn. When I caught sight of your little ones, so pretty, so clean, and so happy, it overwhelmed me. I said: 'Here is a good mother. That is just the thing; that will make three sisters.' And then, it will not be long before I return. Will you keep my child for me?"

"I must see about it," replied the Thénardier.

"I will give you six francs a month."

Here a man's voice called from the depths of the cook-shop:

"Not for less than seven francs. And six months paid in advance."

"Six times seven makes forty-two," said the Thénardier.

"I will give it," said the mother.

"And fifteen francs in addition for preliminary expenses," added the man's voice.

"Total, fifty-seven francs," said Madame Thénardier. And she hummed vaguely, with these figures:

"It must be, said a warrior."

"I will pay it," said the mother. "I have eighty francs. I shall have enough left to reach the country, by traveling on foot. I shall earn money there, and as soon as I have a little, I will return for my darling."

The man's voice resumed:

"The little one has an outfit?"

"That is my husband," said the Thénardier.

"Of course she has an outfit, the poor treasure.—I understood perfectly that it was your husband.—And a beautiful outfit, too! a senseless outfit, everything by the dozen, and silk gowns like a lady. It is here, in my carpet-bag."

"You must hand it over," struck in the man's voice again.

"Of course I shall give it to you," said the mother. "It would be very queer if I were to leave my daughter quite naked!"

The master's face appeared.

"That's good," said he.

The bargain was concluded. The mother passed the night at the inn, gave up her money and left her child, fastened her carpet-bag once more, now reduced in volume by the removal of the outfit, and light henceforth, and set out on the following morning, intending to return soon. People arrange such departures tranquilly; but they are despairs!

A neighbor of the Thénardiers met this mother as she was setting out, and came back with the remark:

"I have just seen a woman crying in the street so that it was enough to rend your heart."

When Cosette's mother had taken her departure, the man said to the woman:

"That will serve to pay my note for one hundred and ten francs which falls due to-morrow; I lacked fifty francs. Do you know that I should have had a bailiff and a protest after me? You played the mouse-trap nicely with your young ones."

"Without suspecting it," said the woman.

Chapter II

FIRST SKETCH OF TWO UNPREPOSSESSING FIGURES

THE MOUSE WHICH HAD BEEN CAUGHT WAS A PITIFUL SPECIMEN; BUT THE CAT REJOICES EVEN over a lean mouse.

Who were these Thénardiers?

Let us say a word or two of them now. We will complete the sketch later on.

These beings belonged to that bastard class composed of coarse people who have been successful, and of intelligent people who have descended in the scale, which is between the class called "middle" and the class denominated as "inferior," and which combines some of the defects of the second with nearly all the vices of the first, without possessing the generous impulse of the workingman nor the honest order of the bourgeois.

They were of those dwarfed natures which, if a dull fire chances to warm them up, easily become monstrous. There was in the woman a substratum of the brute, and in the man the material for a blackguard. Both were susceptible, in the highest degree, of the sort of hideous progress which is accomplished in the direction of evil. There exist crab-like souls which are continually retreating toward the darkness, retrograding in life rather than advancing, employing experience to augment their deformity, growing incessantly worse, and becoming more and more impregnated with an ever-augmenting blackness. This man and woman possessed such souls.

Thénardier, in particular, was troublesome for a physiognomist. One can only look at some men to distrust them; for one feels that they are dark in both directions. They are uneasy in the rear and threatening in front. There is something of the unknown about them. One can no more answer for what they have done than for what they will do. The shadow which they bear in their glance denounces them. From merely hearing them utter a word or seeing them make a gesture, one obtains a glimpse of somber secrets in their past and of somber mysteries in their future.

This Thénardier, if he himself was to be believed, had been a soldier—a sergeant, he said. He had probably been through the campaign of 1815, and had even conducted himself with tolerable valor, it would seem. We shall see later on how much truth there was in this. The sign of his hostelry was in allusion to one of his feats of arms. He had painted it himself; for he knew how to do a little of everything, and badly.

It was at the epoch when the ancient classical romance which, after having been *Clélie*, was no longer anything but *Lodoïska*, still noble, but ever more and more vulgar, having fallen from Mademoiselle de Scudéri to Madame Bournon-Malarme, and from Madame de Lafayette to Madame Barthélemy-Hadot, was setting the loving hearts of the portresses of Paris aflame, and even ravaging the suburbs to some extent. Madame Thénardier was just intelligent enough to read this sort of books. She lived on them. In them she drowned what brains she possessed. This had given her, when very young, and even a little later, a sort of pensive attitude towards her husband, a scamp of a certain depth, a ruffian lettered to the extent of the grammar, coarse and fine at one and the same time, but, so far as sentimentalism was concerned, given to the perusal of Pigault-Lebrun, and "in what concerns the sex," as he said in his jargon—a downright, unmitigated lout. His wife was twelve or fifteen years younger than he was. Later on, when her hair, arranged in a romantically drooping fashion, began to grow gray, when the Magæra began to be developed from the Pamela, the female Thénardier was nothing but a coarse, vicious woman, who had dabbled in stupid romances. Now, one cannot read nonsense with impunity. The result was that her eldest daughter was named Éponine; as for the younger, the poor little thing came near being called Gulnare; I know not to what diversion, effected by a romance of Ducray-Dumenil, she owed the fact that she merely bore the name of Azelma.

However, we will remark by the way, everything was not ridiculous and superficial in that curious epoch to which we are alluding, and which may be designated as the anarchy of baptismal names. By the side of this romantic element which we have just indicated there is the social symptom. It is not rare for the neatherd's boy nowadays to bear the name of Arthur, Alfred, or Alphonse, and for the vicomte—if there are still any vicomtes—to be called Thomas, Pierre, or Jacques. This displacement, which places the "elegant" name on the plebeian and the rustic name on the aristocrat, is nothing else than an eddy of equality. The irresistible penetration of the new inspiration is there as everywhere else. Beneath this apparent discord there is a great and a profound thing—the French Revolution.

Chapter III

THE LARK

IT IS NOT ALL IN ALL SUFFICIENT TO BE WICKED IN ORDER TO PROSPER. THE COOK-SHOP WAS IN A bad way.

Thanks to the traveler's fifty-seven francs, Thénardier had been able to avoid a protest and to honor his signature. On the following month they were again in need of money. The woman took Cosette's outfit to Paris, and pawned it at the pawnbroker's for sixty francs. As soon as that sum was spent, the Thénardiers grew accustomed to look on the little girl merely as a child whom they were caring for out of charity; and they treated her accordingly. As she had no longer any clothes, they dressed her in the cast-off petticoats and chemises of the Thénardier brats; that is to say, in rags. They fed her on what all the rest had left—a little better than the dog, a little worse than the cat. Moreover, the cat and the dog were her habitual table-companions; Cosette ate with them under the table, from a wooden bowl similar to theirs.

The mother, who had established herself, as we shall see later on, at M. sur M., wrote, or, more correctly, caused to be written, a letter every month, that she might have news of her child. The Thénardiers replied invariably, "Cosette is doing wonderfully well."

At the expiration of the first six months the mother sent seven francs for the seventh month, and continued her remittances with tolerable regularity from month to month. The year was not completed when Thénardier said: "A fine favor she is doing us, in sooth! What does she expect us to do with her seven francs?" and he wrote to demand twelve francs. The mother, whom they had persuaded into the belief that her child was happy, "and was coming on well," submitted, and forwarded the twelve francs.

Certain natures cannot love on the one hand without hating on the other. Mother Thénardier loved her two daughters passionately, which caused her to hate the stranger.

It is sad to think that the love of a mother can possess villainous aspects. Little as was the space occupied by Cosette, it seemed to her as though it were taken from her own, and that that little child diminished the air which her daughters breathed. This woman, like many women of her sort, had a load of caresses and a burden of blows and injuries to dispense each day. If she had not had Cosette, it is certain that her daughters, idolized as they were, would have received the whole of it; but the stranger did them the service to divert the blows to herself. Her daughters received nothing but caresses. Cosette could not make a motion which did not draw down upon her head a heavy shower of violent blows and unmerited chastisement. The sweet, feeble being, who should not have understood anything of this world or of God, incessantly punished, scolded, ill-used, beaten, and seeing beside her two little creatures like herself, who lived in a ray of dawn!

Madame Thénardier was vicious with Cosette. Éponine and Azelma were vicious. Children at that age are only copies of their mother. The size is smaller; that is all.

A year passed; then another.

People in the village said:

"Those Thénardiers are good people. They are not rich, and yet they are bringing up a poor child who was abandoned on their hands!"

They thought that Cosette's mother had forgotten her.

In the meanwhile, Thénardier, having learned, it is impossible to say by what obscure means, that the child was probably a bastard, and that the mother could not acknowledge it, exacted fifteen francs a month, saying that "the creature" was growing and "eating," and threatening to send her away. "Let her not bother me," he exclaimed, "or I'll fire her brat right into the middle of her secrets. I must have an increase." The mother paid the fifteen francs.

From year to year the child grew, and so did her wretchedness.

As long as Cosette was little, she was the scape-goat of the two other children; as soon as she began to develop a little, that is to say, before she was even five years old, she became the servant of the household.

Five years old! the reader will say; that is not probable. Alas! it is true. Social suffering begins at all ages. Have we not recently seen the trial of a man named Dumollard, an orphan turned bandit, who, from the age of five, as the official documents state, being alone in the world, "worked for his living and stole"?

Cosette was made to run on errands, to sweep the rooms, the courtyard, the street, to wash the dishes, to even carry burdens. The Thénardiers considered themselves all the more authorized to behave in this manner, since the mother, who was still at M. sur M. had become irregular in her payments. Some months she was in arrears.

If this mother had returned to Montfermeil at the end of these three years, she would not have recognized her child. Cosette, so pretty and rosy on her arrival in that house, was now thin and pale. She had an indescribably uneasy look. "The sly creature," said the Thénardiers.

Injustice had made her peevish, and misery had made her ugly. Nothing remained to her except her beautiful eyes, which inspired pain, because, large as they were, it seemed as though one beheld in them a still larger amount of sadness.

It was a heart-breaking thing to see this poor child, not yet six years old, shivering in the winter in her old rags of linen, full of holes, sweeping the street before daylight, with an enormous broom in her tiny red hands, and a tear in her great eyes.

She was called the *Lark* in the neighborhood. The populace, who are fond of these figures of speech, had taken a fancy to bestow this name on this trembling, frightened, and shivering little creature, no bigger than a bird, who was awake every morning before anyone else in the house or the village, and was always in the street or the fields before daybreak.

Only the little lark never sang.

BOOK FIFTH

THE DESCENT

Chapter I

THE HISTORY OF A PROGRESS IN BLACK GLASS TRINKETS

AND IN THE MEANTIME, WHAT HAD BECOME OF THAT MOTHER WHO, ACCORDING TO THE PEOPLE at Montfermeil, seemed to have abandoned her child? Where was she? What was she doing?

After leaving her little Cosette with the Thénardiers, she had continued her journey, and had reached M. sur M.

This, it will be remembered, was in 1818.

Fantine had quitted her province ten years before. M. sur M. had changed its aspect. While Fantine had been slowly descending from wretchedness to wretchedness, her native town had prospered.

About two years previously one of those industrial facts which are the grand events of small districts had taken place.

This detail is important, and we regard it as useful to develop it at length; we should almost say, to underline it.

From time immemorial, M. sur M. had had for its special industry the imitation of English jet and the black glass trinkets of Germany. This industry had always vegetated, on account of the high price of the raw material, which reacted on the manufacture. At the moment when Fantine returned to M. sur M., an unheard-of transformation had taken place in the production of "black goods." Toward the close of 1815 a man, a stranger, had established himself in the town, and had been inspired with the idea of substituting, in this manufacture, gum-lac for resin, and, for bracelets in particular, slides of sheet-iron simply laid together, for slides of soldered sheet-iron.

This very small change had effected a revolution.

This very small change had, in fact, prodigiously reduced the cost of the raw material, which had rendered it possible in the first place, to raise the price of manufacture, a benefit to the country; in the second place, to improve the workmanship, an advantage to the consumer; in the third place, to sell at a lower price, while trebling the profit, which was a benefit to the manufacturer.

Thus three results ensued from one idea.

In less than three years the inventor of this process had become rich, which is good, and had made everyone about him rich, which is better. He was a stranger in the Department. Of his origin, nothing was known; of the beginning of his career, very little. It was rumored that he had come to town with very little money, a few hundred francs at the most.

It was from this slender capital, enlisted in the service of an ingenious idea, developed by method and thought, that he had drawn his own fortune, and the fortune of the whole countryside.

On his arrival at M. sur M. he had only the garments, the appearance, and the language of a workingman.

It appears that on the very day when he made his obscure entry into the little town of M. sur M., just at nightfall, on a December evening, knapsack on back and thorn club in hand, a large fire had broken out in the town-hall. This man had rushed into the flames and had saved, at the risk of his own life, two children who belonged to the captain of the gendarmerie; this is why they had forgotten to ask him for his passport. Afterwards they had learned his name. He was called Father Madeleine.

Chapter II

MADELEINE

H E WAS A MAN ABOUT FIFTY YEARS OF AGE, WHO HAD A PREOCCUPIED AIR, AND WHO WAS GOOD. That was all that could be said about him.

Thanks to the rapid progress of the industry which he had so admirably reconstructed, M. sur M. had become a rather important center of trade. Spain, which consumes a good deal of black jet, made enormous purchases there each year. M. sur M. almost rivaled London and Berlin in this branch of commerce. Father Madeleine's profits were such, that at the end of the second year he was able to erect a large factory, in which there were two vast workrooms, one for the men, and the other for women. Anyone who was hungry could present himself there, and was sure of finding employment and bread. Father Madeleine required of the men good-will, of the women pure morals, and of all, probity. He had separated the work-rooms in order to separate the sexes, and so that the women and girls might remain discreet. On this point he was inflexible. It was the only thing in which he was in a manner intolerant. He was all the more firmly set on this severity, since M. sur M., being a garrison town, opportunities for corruption abounded. However, his coming had been a boon, and his presence was a godsend. Before Father Madeleine's arrival, everything had languished in the country; now everything lived with a healthy life of toil. A strong circulation warmed everything and penetrated everywhere. Slack seasons and wretchedness were unknown. There was no pocket so obscure that it had not a little money in it; no dwelling so lowly that there was not some little joy within it.

Father Madeleine gave employment to everyone. He exacted but one thing: Be an honest man. Be an honest woman.

As we have said, in the midst of this activity of which he was the cause and the pivot, Father Madeleine made his fortune; but a singular thing in a simple man of business, it did not seem as though that were his chief care. He appeared to be thinking much of others, and little of himself.

In 1820 he was known to have a sum of six hundred and thirty thousand francs lodged in his name with Laffitte; but before reserving these six hundred and thirty thousand francs, he had spent more than a million for the town and its poor.

The hospital was badly endowed; he founded six beds there. M. sur M. is divided into the upper and the lower town. The lower town, in which he lived, had but one school, a miserable hovel, which was falling to ruin: he constructed two, one for girls, the other for boys. He allotted a salary from his own funds to the two instructors, a salary twice as large as their meager official salary, and one day he said to someone who expressed surprise, "The two prime functionaries of the state are the nurse and the schoolmaster." He created at his own expense an infant school, a thing then almost unknown in France, and a fund for aiding old and infirm workmen. As his factory was a center, a new quarter, in which there were a good many indigent families, rose rapidly around him; he established there a free dispensary.

At first, when they watched his beginnings, the good souls said, "He's a jolly fellow who means to get rich." When they saw him enriching the country before he enriched himself, the good souls said, "He is an ambitious man." This seemed all the more probable since the man was religious, and even practiced his religion to a certain degree, a thing which was very favorably viewed at that epoch. He went regularly to low mass every Sunday. The local deputy, who nosed out all rivalry everywhere, soon began to grow uneasy over this religion. This deputy had been a member of the legislative body of the Empire, and shared the religious ideas of a father of the Oratoire, known under the name of Fouché, Duc d'Otrante, whose creature and friend he had been. He indulged in gentle raillery at God with closed doors. But when he beheld the wealthy manufacturer Madeleine going to low mass at seven o'clock, he perceived in him a possible candidate, and resolved to outdo him; he took a Jesuit confessor, and went to high mass and to vespers. Ambition was at that time, in the direct acceptation of the word, a race to the steeple. The poor profited by this terror as well as the good God, for the honorable deputy also founded two beds in the hospital, which made twelve.

Nevertheless, in 1819 a rumor one morning circulated through the town to the effect that, on the representations of the prefect and in consideration of the services rendered by him to the country, Father Madeleine was to be appointed by the King, mayor of M. sur M. Those who had pronounced this newcomer to be "an ambitious fellow," seized with delight on this opportunity which all men desire, to exclaim, "There! what did we say!" All M. sur M. was in an uproar. The rumor was well founded. Several days later the appointment appeared in the *Moniteur*. On the following day Father Madeleine refused.

In this same year of 1819 the products of the new process invented by Madeleine figured in the industrial exhibition; when the jury made their report, the King appointed the inventor a chevalier of the Legion of Honor. A fresh excitement in the little town. Well, so it was the cross that he wanted! Father Madeleine refused the cross.

Decidedly, this man was an enigma. The good souls got out of their predicament by saying, "After all, he is some sort of an adventurer."

We have seen that the country owed much to him; the poor owed him everything; he was so useful and he was so gentle that people had been obliged to honor and respect him. His workmen, in particular, adored him, and he endured this adoration with a sort of melancholy gravity. When he was known to be rich, "people in society" bowed to him, and he received invitations in the town; he was called, in town, Monsieur Madeleine; his workmen and the children continued to call him Father Madeleine, and that was what was most adapted to make him smile. In proportion as he mounted, throve, invitations rained down upon him. "Society" claimed him for its own. The prim little drawing-rooms on M. sur M., which, of course, had at first been closed to the artisan, opened both leaves of their folding-doors to the millionaire. They made a thousand advances to him. He refused.

This time the good gossips had no trouble. "He is an ignorant man, of no education. No one knows where he came from. He would not know how to behave in society. It has not been absolutely proved that he knows how to read."

When they saw him making money, they said, "He is a man of business." When they saw him scattering his money about, they said, "He is an ambitious man." When he was seen to decline honors, they said, "He is an adventurer." When they saw him repulse society, they said, "He is a brute."

In 1820, five years after his arrival in M. sur M., the services which he had rendered to the district were so dazzling, the opinion of the whole country round about was so unanimous, that the King again appointed him mayor of the town. He again declined; but the prefect resisted his refusal, all the notabilities of the place came to implore him, the people in the street besought him; the urging was so vigorous that he ended by accepting. It was noticed that the thing which seemed chiefly to bring him to a decision was the almost irritated apostrophe addressed to him by an old woman of the people, who called to him from her threshold, in an angry way: *"A good mayor is a useful thing. Is he drawing back before the good which he can do?"*

This was the third phase of his ascent. Father Madeleine had become Monsieur Madeleine. Monsieur Madeleine became Monsieur le Maire.

Chapter III

SUMS DEPOSITED WITH LAFFITTE

O N THE OTHER HAND, HE REMAINED AS SIMPLE AS ON THE FIRST DAY. HE HAD GRAY HAIR, A SErious eye, the sunburned complexion of a laborer, the thoughtful visage of a philosopher. He habitually wore a hat with a wide brim, and a long coat of coarse cloth, buttoned to the chin. He fulfilled his duties as mayor; but, with that exception, he lived in solitude. He spoke to but few people. He avoided polite attentions; he escaped quickly; he smiled to relieve himself of the necessity of talking; he gave, in order to get rid of the necessity for smiling. The women said of him, "What a good-natured bear!" His pleasure consisted in strolling in the fields.

He always took his meals alone, with an open book before him, which he read. He had a well-selected little library. He loved books; books are cold but safe friends. In proportion as leisure came to him with fortune, he seemed to take advantage of it to cultivate his mind. It had been observed that, ever since his arrival at M. sur M., his language had grown more polished, more choice, and more gentle with every passing year. He liked to carry a gun with him on his strolls, but he rarely made use of it. When he did happen to do so, his shooting was something so infallible as to inspire terror. He never killed an inoffensive animal. He never shot at a little bird.

Although he was no longer young, it was thought that he was still prodigiously strong. He offered his assistance to anyone who was in need of it, lifted a horse, released a wheel clogged in the mud, or stopped a runaway bull by the horns. He always had his pockets full of money when he went out; but they were empty on his return. When he passed through a village, the ragged brats ran joyously after him, and surrounded him like a swarm of gnats.

It was thought that he must, in the past, have lived a country life, since he knew all sorts of useful secrets, which he taught to the peasants. He taught them how to destroy scurf on wheat, by sprinkling it and the granary and inundating the cracks in the floor with a solution of common salt; and how to chase away weevils by hanging up orviot in bloom everywhere, on the walls and the ceilings, among the grass and in the houses.

He had "recipes" for exterminating from a field, blight, tares, foxtail, and all parasitic growths which destroy the wheat. He defended a rabbit warren against rats, simply by the odor of a guinea-pig which he placed in it.

One day he saw some country people busily engaged in pulling up nettles; he examined the plants, which were uprooted and already dried, and said: "They are dead. Nevertheless, it would be a good thing to know how to make use of them. When the nettle is young, the leaf makes an excellent vegetable; when it is older, it has filaments and fibers like hemp and flax. Nettle cloth is as good as linen cloth. Chopped up, nettles are good for poultry; pounded, they are good for horned cattle. The seed of the nettle, mixed with fodder, gives gloss to the hair of animals; the root, mixed with salt, produces a beautiful yellow coloring-matter. Moreover, it is an excellent hay, which can be cut twice. And what is required for the nettle? A little soil, no care, no culture. Only the seed falls as it is ripe, and it is difficult to collect it. That is all. With the exercise of a little care, the nettle could be made useful; it is neglected and it becomes hurtful. It is exterminated. How many men resemble the nettle!" He added, after a pause: "Remember this, my friends: there are no such things as bad plants or bad men. There are only bad cultivators."

The children loved him because he knew how to make charming little trifles of straw and cocoanuts.

When he saw the door of a church hung in black, he entered: he sought out funerals as other men seek christenings. Widowhood and the grief of others attracted him, because of his great gentleness; he mingled with the friends clad in mourning, with families dressed in black, with the priests groaning around a coffin. He seemed to like to give to his thoughts for text these funereal psalmodies filled with the vision of the other world. With his eyes fixed on heaven, he listened with a sort of aspiration towards all the mysteries of the infinite, those sad voices which sing on the verge of the obscure abyss of death.

He performed a multitude of good actions, concealing his agency in them as a man conceals himself because of evil actions. He penetrated houses privately, at night; he ascended staircases furtively. A poor wretch on returning to his attic would find that his door had been opened, sometimes even forced, during his absence. The poor man made a clamor over it: some malefactor had been there! He entered, and the first thing he beheld was a piece of gold lying forgotten on some piece of furniture. The "malefactor" who had been there was Father Madeleine.

He was affable and sad. The people said: "There is a rich man who has not a haughty air. There is a happy man who has not a contented air."

Some people maintained that he was a mysterious person, and that no one ever entered his chamber, which was a regular anchorite's cell, furnished with winged hour-glasses and enlivened by cross-bones and skulls of dead men! This was much talked of, so that one of the elegant and malicious young women of M. sur M. came to him one day, and asked: "Monsieur le Maire, pray show us your chamber. It is said to be a grotto." He smiled, and introduced them instantly into this "grotto." They were well punished for their curiosity. The room was very simply furnished in mahogany, which was rather ugly, like all furniture of that sort, and hung with paper worth twelve sous. They could see nothing remarkable about it, except two candlesticks of antique pattern which stood on the chimney-piece and appeared to be silver, "for they were hall-marked," an observation full of the type of wit of petty towns.

Nevertheless, people continued to say that no one ever got into the room, and that it was a hermit's cave, a mysterious retreat, a hole, a tomb.

It was also whispered about that he had "immense" sums deposited with Laffitte, with this peculiar feature, that they were always at his immediate disposal, so that, it was added, M. Madeleine could make his appearance at Laffitte's any morning, sign a receipt, and carry off his two or three millions in ten minutes. In reality, "these two or three millions" were reducible, as we have said, to six hundred and thirty or forty thousand francs.

Chapter IV

M. MADELEINE IN MOURNING

AT THE BEGINNING OF 1820 THE NEWSPAPERS ANNOUNCED THE DEATH OF M. MYRIEL, BISHOP OF D——, surnamed "Monseigneur Bienvenu," who had died in the odor of sanctity at the age of eighty-two.

The Bishop of D—— —to supply here a detail which the papers omitted—had been blind for many years before his death, and content to be blind, as his sister was beside him.

Let us remark by the way, that to be blind and to be loved, is, in fact, one of the most strangely exquisite forms of happiness upon this earth, where nothing is complete. To have continually at one's side a woman, a daughter, a sister, a charming being, who is there because you need her and because she cannot do without you; to know that we are indispensable to a person who is necessary to us; to be able to incessantly measure one's affection by the amount of her presence which she bestows on us, and to say to ourselves, "Since she consecrates the whole of her time to me, it is because I possess the whole of her heart"; to behold her thought in lieu of her face; to be able to verify the fidelity of one being amid the eclipse of the world; to regard the rustle of a gown as the sound of wings; to hear her come and go, retire, speak, return, sing, and to think that one is the center of these steps, of this speech; to manifest at each instant one's personal attraction; to feel one's self all the more powerful because of one's infirmity; to become in one's obscurity, and through one's obscurity, the star around which this angel gravitates—few felicities equal this. The supreme happiness of life consists in the conviction that one is loved; loved for one's own sake—let us say rather, loved in spite of one's self; this conviction the blind man possesses. To be served in this distress is to be caressed. Does he lack anything? No. One does not lose the light when one has love. And what love! A love wholly constituted of virtue! There is no blindness where there is certainty. Soul seeks soul, gropingly, and finds it. And this soul, found and tested, is a woman. A hand sustains you; it is hers: a mouth lightly touches your brow; it is her mouth: you hear a breath very near you; it is hers. To have everything of her, from her worship to her pity, never to be left, to have that sweet weakness aiding you, to lean upon that immovable reed, to touch Providence with one's hands, and to be able to take it in one's arms—God made tangible—what bliss! The heart, that obscure, celestial flower, undergoes a mysterious blossoming. One would not exchange that shadow for all brightness! The angel soul is there, uninterruptedly there; if she departs, it is but to return again; she vanishes like a dream, and reappears like reality. One feels warmth approaching, and behold! she is there. One overflows with serenity, with gaiety, with ecstasy; one is a radiance amid the night. And there are a thousand little cares. Nothings, which are enormous in that void. The most ineffable accents of the feminine voice employed to lull you, and supplying the vanished universe to you. One is caressed with the soul. One sees nothing, but one feels that one is adored. It is a paradise of shadows.

It was from this paradise that Monseigneur Welcome had passed to the other.

The announcement of his death was reprinted by the local journal of M. sur M. On the following day, M. Madeleine appeared clad wholly in black, and with crape on his hat.

This mourning was noticed in the town, and commented on. It seemed to throw a light on M. Madeleine's origin. It was concluded that some relationship existed between him and the venerable Bishop. *"He has gone into mourning for the Bishop of D——,"* said the drawing-rooms; this raised M. Madeleine's credit greatly, and procured for him, instantly and at one blow, a certain consideration in the noble world of M. sur M. The microscopic Faubourg Saint-Germain of the place meditated raising the quarantine against M. Madeleine, the probable relative of a bishop. M. Madeleine perceived the advancement which he had obtained, by the more numerous courtesies of the old women and the more plentiful smiles of the young ones. One evening, a ruler in that petty great world, who was curious by right of seniority, ventured to ask him, "M. le Maire is doubtless a cousin of the late Bishop of D——?"

He said, "No, Madame."

"But," resumed the dowager, "you are wearing mourning for him."

He replied, "It is because I was a servant in his family in my youth."

Another thing which was remarked, was, that every time that he encountered in the town a young Savoyard who was roaming about the country and seeking chimneys to sweep, the mayor had him summoned, inquired his name, and gave him money. The little Savoyards told each other about it: a great many of them passed that way.

Chapter V

VAGUE FLASHES ON THE HORIZON

LITTLE BY LITTLE, AND IN THE COURSE OF TIME, ALL THIS OPPOSITION SUBSIDED. THERE HAD AT first been exercised against M. Madeleine, in virtue of a sort of law which all those who rise must submit to, blackenings and calumnies; then they grew to be nothing more than ill-nature, then merely malicious remarks, then even this entirely disappeared; respect became complete, unanimous, cordial, and towards 1821 the moment arrived when the word "Monsieur le Maire" was pronounced at M. sur M. with almost the same accent as "Monseigneur the Bishop" had been pronounced in D—— in 1815. People came from a distance of ten leagues around to consult M. Madeleine. He put an end to differences, he prevented lawsuits, he reconciled enemies. Everyone took him for the judge, and with good reason. It seemed as though he had for a soul the book of the natural law. It was like an epidemic of veneration, which in the course of six or seven years gradually took possession of the whole district.

One single man in the town, in the arrondissement, absolutely escaped this contagion, and, whatever Father Madeleine did, remained his opponent as though a sort of incorruptible and imperturbable instinct kept him on the alert and uneasy. It seems, in fact, as though there existed in certain men a veritable bestial instinct, though pure and upright, like all instincts, which creates antipathies and sympathies, which fatally separates one nature from another nature, which does not hesitate, which feels no disquiet, which does not hold its peace, and which never belies itself, clear in its obscurity, infallible, imperious, intractable, stubborn to all counsels of the intelligence and to all the dissolvents of reason, and which, in whatever manner destinies are arranged, secretly warns the man-dog of the presence of the man-cat, and the man-fox of the presence of the man-lion.

It frequently happened that when M. Madeleine was passing along a street, calm, affectionate, surrounded by the blessings of all, a man of lofty stature, clad in an iron-gray frock-coat armed with a heavy cane, and wearing a battered hat, turned round abruptly behind him, and followed him with his eyes until he disappeared, with folded arms and a slow shake of the head, and his upper lip raised in company with his lower to his nose, a sort of significant grimace which might be translated by: "What is that man, after all? I certainly have seen him somewhere. In any case, I am not his dupe."

This person, grave with a gravity which was almost menacing, was one of those men who, even when only seen by a rapid glimpse, arrest the spectator's attention.

His name was Javert, and he belonged to the police.

At M. sur M. he exercised the unpleasant but useful functions of an inspector. He had not seen Madeleine's beginnings. Javert owed the post which he occupied to the protection of M. Chabouil-let, the secretary of the Minister of State, Comte Anglès, then prefect of police at Paris. When Javert arrived at M. sur M. the fortune of the great manufacturer was already made, and Father Madeleine had become Monsieur Madeleine.

Certain police officers have a peculiar physiognomy, which is complicated with an air of base-ness mingled with an air of authority. Javert possessed this physiognomy minus the baseness.

It is our conviction that if souls were visible to the eyes, we should be able to see distinctly that strange thing that each one individual of the human race corresponds to some one of the species of the animal creation; and we could easily recognize this truth, hardly perceived by the thinker, that from the oyster to the eagle, from the pig to the tiger, all animals exist in man, and that each one of them is in a man. Sometimes even several of them at a time.

Animals are nothing else than the figures of our virtues and our vices, straying before our eyes, the visible phantoms of our souls. God shows them to us in order to induce us to reflect. Only since animals are mere shadows, God has not made them capable of education in the full sense of the word; what is the use? On the contrary, our souls being realities and having a goal which is ap-propriate to them, God has bestowed on them intelligence; that is to say, the possibility of educa-tion. Social education, when well done, can always draw from a soul, of whatever sort it may be, the utility which it contains.

This, be it said, is of course from the restricted point of view of the terrestrial life which is ap-parent, and without prejudging the profound question of the anterior or ulterior personality of the beings which are not man. The visible *I* in nowise authorizes the thinker to deny the latent *I*. Hav-ing made this reservation, let us pass on.

Now, if the reader will admit, for a moment, with us, that in every man there is one of the an-imal species of creation, it will be easy for us to say what there was in Police Officer Javert.

The peasants of Asturias are convinced that in every litter of wolves there is one dog, which is killed by the mother because, otherwise, as he grew up, he would devour the other little ones.

Give to this dog-son of a wolf a human face, and the result will be Javert.

Javert had been born in prison, of a fortune-teller, whose husband was in the galleys. As he grew up, he thought that he was outside the pale of society, and he despaired of ever re-entering it. He observed that society unpardoningly excludes two classes of men—those who attack it and those who guard it; he had no choice except between these two classes; at the same time, he was con-scious of an indescribable foundation of rigidity, regularity, and probity, complicated with an inex-pressible hatred for the race of bohemians whence he was sprung. He entered the police; he succeeded there. At forty years of age he was an inspector.

During his youth he had been employed in the convict establishments of the South.

Before proceeding further, let us come to an understanding as to the words, "human face," which we have just applied to Javert.

The human face of Javert consisted of a flat nose, with two deep nostrils, toward which enor-mous whiskers ascended on his cheeks. One felt ill at ease when he saw these two forests and these two caverns for the first time. When Javert laughed—and his laugh was rare and terrible—his thin lips parted and revealed to view not only his teeth, but his gums, and around his nose there formed a flattened and savage fold, as on the muzzle of a wild beast. Javert, serious, was a watchdog; when he laughed, he was a tiger. As for the rest, he had very little skull and a great deal of jaw; his hair concealed his forehead and fell over his eyebrows; between his eyes there was a permanent, central frown, like an imprint of wrath; his gaze was obscure; his mouth pursed up and terrible; his air that of ferocious command.

This man was composed of two very simple and two very good sentiments, comparatively; but he rendered them almost bad, by dint of exaggerating them—respect for authority, hatred of rebellion; and in his eyes, murder, robbery, all crimes, are only forms of rebellion. He enveloped in a blind and profound faith everyone who had a function in the state, from the prime minister to the rural policeman. He covered with scorn, aversion, and disgust everyone who had once crossed the legal threshold of evil. He was absolute, and admitted no exceptions. On the one hand, he said, "The functionary can make no mistake; the magistrate is never in the wrong." On the other hand, he said, "These men are irremediably lost. Nothing good can come from them." He fully shared the opinion of those extreme minds which attribute to human law I know not what power of making, or, if the reader will have it so, of authenticating, demons, and who place a Styx at the base of society. He was stoical, serious, austere; a melancholy dreamer, humble and haughty, like fanatics. His glance was like a gimlet, cold and piercing. His whole life hung on these two words: watchfulness and supervision. He had introduced a straight line into what is the most crooked thing in the world; he possessed the conscience of his usefulness, the religion of his functions, and he was a spy as other men are priests. Woe to the man who fell into his hands! He would have arrested his own father, if the latter had escaped from the galleys, and would have denounced his mother, if she had broken her ban. And he would have done it with that sort of inward satisfaction which is conferred by virtue. And, withal, a life of privation, isolation, abnegation, chastity, with never a diversion. It was implacable duty; the police understood, as the Spartans understood Sparta, a pitiless lying in wait, a ferocious honesty, a marble informer, Brutus in Vidocq.

Javert's whole person was expressive of the man who spies and who withdraws himself from observation. The mystical school of Joseph de Maistre, which at that epoch seasoned with lofty cosmogony those things which were called the ultra newspapers, would not have failed to declare that Javert was a symbol. His brow was not visible; it disappeared beneath his hat: his eyes were not visible, since they were lost under his eyebrows: his chin was not visible, for it was plunged in his cravat: his hands were not visible; they were drawn up in his sleeves: and his cane was not visible; he carried it under his coat. But when the occasion presented itself, there was suddenly seen to emerge from all this shadow, as from an ambuscade, a narrow and angular forehead, a baleful glance, a threatening chin, enormous hands, and a monstrous cudgel.

In his leisure moments, which were far from frequent, he read, although he hated books; this caused him to be not wholly illiterate. This could be recognized by some emphasis in his speech.

As we have said, he had no vices. When he was pleased with himself, he permitted himself a pinch of snuff. Therein lay his connection with humanity.

The reader will have no difficulty in understanding that Javert was the terror of that whole class which the annual statistics of the Ministry of Justice designates under the rubric, Vagrants. The name of Javert routed them by its mere utterance; the face of Javert petrified them at sight.

Such was this formidable man.

Javert was like an eye constantly fixed on M. Madeleine. An eye full of suspicion and conjecture. M. Madeleine had finally perceived the fact; but it seemed to be of no importance to him. He did not even put a question to Javert; he neither sought nor avoided him; he bore that embarrassing and almost oppressive gaze without appearing to notice it. He treated Javert with ease and courtesy, as he did all the rest of the world.

It was divined, from some words which escaped Javert, that he had secretly investigated, with that curiosity which belongs to the race, and into which there enters as much instinct as will, all the anterior traces which Father Madeleine might have left elsewhere. He seemed to know, and he sometimes said in covert words, that someone had gleaned certain information in a certain district about a family which had disappeared. Once he chanced to say, as he was talking to himself, "I think I have him!" Then he remained pensive for three days, and uttered not a word. It seemed that the thread which he thought he held had broken.

Moreover, and this furnishes the necessary corrective for the too absolute sense which certain words might present, there can be nothing really infallible in a human creature, and the peculiarity of instinct is that it can become confused, thrown off the track, and defeated. Otherwise, it would be superior to intelligence, and the beast would be found to be provided with a better light than man.

Javert was evidently somewhat disconcerted by the perfect naturalness and tranquility of M. Madeleine.

One day, nevertheless, his strange manner appeared to produce an impression on M. Madeleine. It was on the following occasion.

Chapter VI

FATHER FAUCHELEVENT

ONE MORNING M. MADELEINE WAS PASSING THROUGH AN UNPAVED ALLEY OF M. SUR M.; HE HEARD a noise, and saw a group some distance away. He approached. An old man named Father Fauchelevent had just fallen beneath his cart, his horse having tumbled down.

This Fauchelevent was one of the few enemies whom M. Madeleine had at that time. When Madeleine arrived in the neighborhood, Fauchelevent, an ex-notary and a peasant who was almost educated, had a business which was beginning to be in a bad way. Fauchelevent had seen this simple workman grow rich, while he, a lawyer, was being ruined. This had filled him with jealousy, and he had done all he could, on every occasion, to injure Madeleine. Then bankruptcy had come; and as the old man had nothing left but a cart and a horse, and neither family nor children, he had turned carter.

The horse had two broken legs and could not rise. The old man was caught in the wheels. The fall had been so unlucky that the whole weight of the vehicle rested on his breast. The cart was quite heavily laden. Father Fauchelevent was rattling in the throat in the most lamentable manner. They had tried, but in vain, to drag him out. An unmethodical effort, aid awkwardly given, a wrong shake, might kill him. It was impossible to disengage him otherwise than by lifting the vehicle off of him. Javert, who had come up at the moment of the accident, had sent for a jack-screw.

M. Madeleine arrived. People stood aside respectfully.

"Help!" cried old Fauchelevent. "Who will be good and save the old man?"

M. Madeleine turned toward those present:

"Is there a jack-screw to be had?"

"One has been sent for," answered the peasant.

"How long will it take to get it!"

"They have gone for the nearest, to Flachot's place, where there is a farrier; but it makes no difference; it will take a good quarter of an hour."

"A quarter of an hour!" exclaimed Madeleine.

It had rained on the preceding night; the soil was soaked. The cart was sinking deeper into the earth every moment, and crushing the old carter's breast more and more. It was evident that his ribs would be broken in five minutes more.

"It is impossible to wait another quarter of an hour," said Madeleine to the peasants, who were staring at him.

"We must!"

"But it will be too late then! Don't you see that the cart is sinking?"

"Well!"

"Listen," resumed Madeleine; "there is still room enough under the cart to allow a man to crawl beneath it and raise it with his back. Only half a minute, and the poor man can be taken out. Is there anyone here who has stout loins and heart? There are five louis d'or to be earned!"

Not a man in the group stirred.

"Ten louis," said Madeleine.

The persons present dropped their eyes. One of them muttered: "A man would need to be devilish strong. And then he runs the risk of getting crushed!"

"Come," began Madeleine again, "twenty louis."

The same silence.

"It is not the will which is lacking," said a voice.

M. Madeleine turned round, and recognized Javert. He had not noticed him on his arrival.

Javert went on:

"It is strength. One would have to be a terrible man to do such a thing as lift a cart like that on his back."

Then, gazing fixedly at M. Madeleine, he went on, emphasizing every word that he uttered: "Monsieur Madeleine, I have never known but one man capable of doing what you ask."

Madeleine shuddered.

Javert added, with an air of indifference, but without removing his eyes from Madeleine: "He was a convict."

"Ah!" said Madeleine.

"In the galleys at Toulon."

Madeleine turned pale.

Meanwhile, the cart continued to sink slowly. Father Fauchelevent rattled in the throat, and shrieked:

"I am strangling! My ribs are breaking! a screw! something! Ah!"

Madeleine glanced about him.

"Is there, then, no one who wishes to earn twenty louis and save the life of this poor old man?"

No one stirred. Javert resumed:

"I have never known but one man who could take the place of a screw, and he was that convict."

"Ah! It is crushing me!" cried the old man.

Madeleine raised his head, met Javert's falcon eye still fixed upon him, looked at the motionless peasants, and smiled sadly. Then, without saying a word, he fell on his knees, and before the crowd had even had time to utter a cry, he was underneath the vehicle.

A terrible moment of expectation and silence ensued.

They beheld Madeleine, almost flat on his stomach beneath that terrible weight, make two vain efforts to bring his knees and his elbows together. They shouted to him, "Father Madeleine, come out!" Old Fauchelevent himself said to him, "Monsieur Madeleine, go away! You see that I am fated to die! Leave me! You will get yourself crushed also!" Madeleine made no reply.

All the spectators were panting. The wheels had continued to sink, and it had become almost impossible for Madeleine to make his way from under the vehicle.

Suddenly the enormous mass was seen to quiver, the cart rose slowly, the wheels half emerged from the ruts. They heard a stifled voice crying, "Make haste! Help!" It was Madeleine, who had just made a final effort.

They rushed forwards. The devotion of a single man had given force and courage to all. The cart was raised by twenty arms. Old Fauchelevent was saved.

Madeleine rose. He was pale, though dripping with perspiration. His clothes were torn and covered with mud. All wept. The old man kissed his knees and called him the good God. As for him, he bore upon his countenance an indescribable expression of happy and celestial suffering, and he fixed his tranquil eye on Javert, who was still staring at him.

Chapter VII

FAUCHELEVENT BECOMES A GARDENER IN PARIS

F AUCHELEVENT HAD DISLOCATED HIS KNEEPAN IN HIS FALL. FATHER MADELEINE HAD HIM CON-
veyed to an infirmary which he had established for his workmen in the factory building itself,
and which was served by two sisters of charity. On the following morning the old man found a
thousand-franc bank-note on his nightstand, with these words in Father Madeleine's writing: *"I purchase your horse and cart."* The cart was broken, and the horse was dead. Fauchelevent recovered, but
his knee remained stiff. M. Madeleine, on the recommendation of the sisters of charity and of his
priest, got the good man a place as gardener in a female convent in the Rue Saint-Antoine in Paris.

Some time afterwards, M. Madeleine was appointed mayor. The first time that Javert beheld
M. Madeleine clothed in the scarf which gave him authority over the town, he felt the sort of shudder which a watchdog might experience on smelling a wolf in his master's clothes. From that time
forth he avoided him as much as he possibly could. When the requirements of the service imperatively demanded it, and he could not do otherwise than meet the mayor, he addressed him with profound respect.

This prosperity created at M. sur M. by Father Madeleine had, besides the visible signs which
we have mentioned, another symptom which was none the less significant for not being visible.
This never deceives. When the population suffers, when work is lacking, when there is no commerce, the tax-payer resists imposts through penury, he exhausts and oversteps his respite, and the
state expends a great deal of money in the charges for compelling and collection. When work is
abundant, when the country is rich and happy, the taxes are paid easily and cost the state nothing.
It may be said, that there is one infallible thermometer of the public misery and riches—the cost of
collecting the taxes. In the course of seven years the expense of collecting the taxes had diminished
three-fourths in the arrondissement of M. sur M., and this led to this arrondissement being frequently cited from all the rest by M. de Villèle, then Minister of Finance.

Such was the condition of the country when Fantine returned thither. No one remembered
her. Fortunately, the door of M. Madeleine's factory was like the face of a friend. She presented
herself there, and was admitted to the women's workroom. The trade was entirely new to Fantine;
she could not be very skillful at it, and she therefore earned but little by her day's work; but it was
sufficient; the problem was solved; she was earning her living.

Chapter VIII

MADAME VICTURNIEN EXPENDS THIRTY FRANCS ON MORALITY

W HEN FANTINE SAW THAT SHE WAS MAKING HER LIVING, SHE FELT JOYFUL FOR A MOMENT. TO
live honestly by her own labor, what mercy from heaven! The taste for work had really returned to her. She bought a looking-glass, took pleasure in surveying in it her youth, her beautiful
hair, her fine teeth; she forgot many things; she thought only of Cosette and of the possible future,
and was almost happy. She hired a little room and furnished on credit on the strength of her future

work—a lingering trace of her improvident ways. As she was not able to say that she was married, she took good care, as we have seen, not to mention her little girl.

At first, as the reader has seen, she paid the Thénardiers promptly. As she only knew how to sign her name, she was obliged to write through a public letter-writer.

She wrote often, and this was noticed. It began to be said in an undertone, in the women's workroom, that Fantine "wrote letters" and that "she had ways about her."

There is no one for spying on people's actions like those who are not concerned in them. Why does that gentleman never come except at nightfall? Why does Mr. So-and-So never hang his key on its nail on Tuesday? Why does he always take the narrow streets? Why does Madame always descend from her hackney-coach before reaching her house? Why does she send out to purchase six sheets of note paper, when she has a "whole stationer's shop full of it?" etc. There exist beings who, for the sake of obtaining the key to these enigmas, which are, moreover, of no consequence whatever to them, spend more money, waste more time, take more trouble, than would be required for ten good actions, and that gratuitously, for their own pleasure, without receiving any other payment for their curiosity than curiosity. They will follow up such and such a man or woman for whole days; they will do sentry duty for hours at a time on the corners of the streets, under alley-way doors at night, in cold and rain; they will bribe errand-porters, they will make the drivers of hackney-coaches and lackeys tipsy, buy a waiting-maid, suborn a porter. Why? For no reason. A pure passion for seeing, knowing, and penetrating into things. A pure itch for talking. And often these secrets once known, these mysteries made public, these enigmas illuminated by the light of day, bring on catastrophes, duels, failures, the ruin of families, and broken lives, to the great joy of those who have "found out everything," without any interest in the matter, and by pure instinct. A sad thing.

Certain persons are malicious solely through a necessity for talking. Their conversation, the chat of the drawing-room, gossip of the anteroom, is like those chimneys which consume wood rapidly; they need a great amount of combustibles; and their combustibles are furnished by their neighbors.

So Fantine was watched.

In addition, many a one was jealous of her golden hair and of her white teeth.

It was remarked that in the workroom she often turned aside, in the midst of the rest, to wipe away a tear. These were the moments when she was thinking of her child; perhaps, also, of the man whom she had loved.

Breaking the gloomy bonds of the past is a mournful task.

It was observed that she wrote twice a month at least, and that she paid the carriage on the letter. They managed to obtain the address: *Monsieur, Monsieur Thénardier, inn-keeper at Montfermeil.* The public writer, a good old man who could not fill his stomach with red wine without emptying his pocket of secrets, was made to talk in the wine-shop. In short, it was discovered that Fantine had a child. "She must be a pretty sort of a woman." An old gossip was found, who made the trip to Montfermeil, talked to the Thénardiers, and said on her return: "For my five-and-thirty francs I have freed my mind. I have seen the child."

The gossip who did this thing was a gorgon named Madame Victurnien, the guardian and door-keeper of everyone's virtue. Madame Victurnien was fifty-six, and re-enforced the mask of ugliness with the mask of age. A quavering voice, a whimsical mind. This old dame had once been young—astonishing fact! In her youth, in '93, she had married a monk who had fled from his cloister in a red cap, and passed from the Bernardines to the Jacobins. She was dry, rough, peevish, sharp, captious, almost venomous; all this in memory of her monk, whose widow she was, and who had ruled over her masterfully and bent her to his will. She was a nettle in which the rustle of the cassock was visible. At the Restoration she had turned bigot, and that with so much energy that the priests had forgiven her her monk. She had a small property, which she bequeathed with much ostentation to a religious community. She was in high favor at the episcopal palace of Arras. So this Madame Victurnien went to Montfermeil, and returned with the remark, "I have seen the child."

All this took time. Fantine had been at the factory for more than a year, when, one morning, the superintendent of the workroom handed her fifty francs from the mayor, told her that she was no longer employed in the shop, and requested her, in the mayor's name, to leave the neighborhood.

This was the very month when the Thénardiers, after having demanded twelve francs instead of six, had just exacted fifteen francs instead of twelve.

Fantine was overwhelmed. She could not leave the neighborhood; she was in debt for her rent and furniture. Fifty francs was not sufficient to cancel this debt. She stammered a few supplicating words. The superintendent ordered her to leave the shop on the instant. Besides, Fantine was only a moderately good workwoman. Overcome with shame, even more than with despair, she quitted the shop, and returned to her room. So her fault was now known to everyone.

She no longer felt strong enough to say a word. She was advised to see the mayor; she did not dare. The mayor had given her fifty francs because he was good, and had dismissed her because he was just. She bowed before the decision.

Chapter IX

MADAME VICTURNIEN'S SUCCESS

So THE MONK'S WIDOW WAS GOOD FOR SOMETHING.

But M. Madeleine had heard nothing of all this. Life is full of just such combinations of events. M. Madeleine was in the habit of almost never entering the women's workroom.

At the head of this room he had placed an elderly spinster, whom the priest had provided for him, and he had full confidence in this superintendent—a truly respectable person, firm, equitable, upright, full of the charity which consists in giving, but not having in the same degree that charity which consists in understanding and in forgiving. M. Madeleine relied wholly on her. The best men are often obliged to delegate their authority. It was with this full power, and the conviction that she was doing right, that the superintendent had instituted the suit, judged, condemned, and executed Fantine.

As regards the fifty francs, she had given them from a fund which M. Madeleine had intrusted to her for charitable purposes, and for giving assistance to the workwomen, and of which she rendered no account.

Fantine tried to obtain a situation as a servant in the neighborhood; she went from house to house. No one would have her. She could not leave town. The second-hand dealer, to whom she was in debt for her furniture—and what furniture!—said to her, "If you leave, I will have you arrested as a thief." The householder, whom she owed for her rent, said to her, "You are young and pretty; you can pay." She divided the fifty francs between the landlord and the furniture-dealer, returned to the latter three-quarters of his goods, kept only necessaries, and found herself without work, without a trade, with nothing but her bed, and still about fifty francs in debt.

She began to make coarse shirts for soldiers of the garrison, and earned twelve sous a day. Her daughter cost her ten. It was at this point that she began to pay the Thénardiers irregularly.

However, the old woman who lighted her candle for her when she returned at night, taught her the art of living in misery. Back of living on little, there is the living on nothing. These are the two chambers; the first is dark, the second is black.

Fantine learned how to live without fire entirely in the winter; how to give up a bird which eats a half a farthing's worth of millet every two days; how to make a coverlet of one's petticoat, and a petticoat of one's coverlet; how to save one's candle, by taking one's meals by the light of the opposite window. No one knows all that certain feeble creatures, who have grown old in privation and honesty, can get out of a sou. It ends by being a talent. Fantine acquired this sublime talent, and regained a little courage.

At this epoch she said to a neighbor, "Bah! I say to myself, by only sleeping five hours, and working all the rest of the time at my sewing, I shall always manage to nearly earn my bread. And, then, when one is sad, one eats less. Well, sufferings, uneasiness, a little bread on one hand, trouble on the other—all this will support me."

It would have been a great happiness to have her little girl with her in this distress. She thought of having her come. But what then! Make her share her own destitution! And then, she was in debt to the Thénardiers! How could she pay them? And the journey! How pay for that?

The old woman who had given her lessons in what may be called the life of indigence, was a sainted spinster named Marguerite, who was pious with a true piety, poor and charitable toward the poor, and even toward the rich, knowing how to write just sufficiently to sign herself Marguerite, and believing in God, which is science.

There are many such virtuous people in this lower world; someday they will be in the world above. This life has a morrow.

At first, Fantine had been so ashamed that she had not dared to go out.

When she was in the street, she divined that people turned round behind her, and pointed at her; everyone stared at her, and no one greeted her; the cold and bitter scorn of the passers-by penetrated her very flesh and soul like a north wind.

It seems as though an unfortunate woman were utterly bare beneath the sarcasm and the curiosity of all in small towns. In Paris, at least, no one knows you, and this obscurity is a garment. Oh! how she would have liked to betake herself to Paris! Impossible!

She was obliged to accustom herself to disrepute, as she had accustomed herself to indigence. Gradually she decided on her course. At the expiration of two or three months she shook off her shame, and began to go about as though there were nothing the matter. "It is all the same to me," she said.

She went and came, bearing her head well up, with a bitter smile, and was conscious that she was becoming brazen-faced.

Madame Victurnien sometimes saw her passing, from her window, noticed the distress of "that creature" who, "thanks to her," had been "put back in her proper place," and congratulated herself. The happiness of the evil-minded is black.

Excess of toil wore out Fantine, and the little dry cough which troubled her increased. She sometimes said to her neighbor, Marguerite, "Just feel how hot my hands are!"

Nevertheless, when she combed her beautiful hair in the morning with an old broken comb, and it flowed about her like floss silk, she experienced a moment of happy coquetry.

Chapter X

RESULT OF THE SUCCESS

SHE HAD BEEN DISMISSED TOWARD THE END OF THE WINTER; THE SUMMER PASSED, BUT WINTER came again. Short days, less work. Winter: no warmth, no light, no noonday, the evening joining on to the morning, fogs, twilight; the window is gray; it is impossible to see clearly at it. The sky is but a vent-hole. The whole day is a cavern. The sun has the air of a beggar. A frightful season! Winter changes the water of heaven and the heart of man into a stone. Her creditors harrassed her.

Fantine earned too little. Her debts had increased. The Thénardiers, who were not promptly paid, wrote to her constantly letters whose contents drove her to despair, and whose carriage ruined her. One day they wrote to her that her little Cosette was entirely naked in that cold weather, that she needed a woolen skirt, and that her mother must send at least ten francs for this. She received the letter, and crushed it in her hands all day long. That evening she went into a barber's shop at the corner of the street, and pulled out her comb. Her admirable golden hair fell to her knees.

"What splendid hair!" exclaimed the barber.

"How much will you give me for it?" said she.

"Ten francs."

"Cut it off."

She purchased a knitted petticoat and sent it to the Thénardiers. This petticoat made the Thénardiers furious. It was the money that they wanted. They gave the petticoat to Éponine. The poor Lark continued to shiver.

Fantine thought: "My child is no longer cold. I have clothed her with my hair." She put on little round caps which concealed her shorn head, and in which she was still pretty.

Dark thoughts held possession of Fantine's heart.

When she saw that she could no longer dress her hair, she began to hate everyone about her. She had long shared the universal veneration for Father Madeleine; yet, by dint of repeating to herself that it was he who had discharged her, that he was the cause of her unhappiness, she came to hate him also, and most of all. When she passed the factory in working hours, when the workpeople were at the door, she affected to laugh and sing.

An old workwoman who once saw her laughing and singing in this fashion said, "There's a girl who will come to a bad end."

She took a lover, the first who offered, a man whom she did not love, out of bravado and with rage in her heart. He was a miserable scamp, a sort of mendicant musician, a lazy beggar, who beat her, and who abandoned her as she had taken him, in disgust.

She adored her child.

The lower she descended, the darker everything grew about her, the more radiant shone that little angel at the bottom of her heart. She said, "When I get rich, I will have my Cosette with me"; and she laughed. Her cough did not leave her, and she had sweats on her back.

One day she received from the Thénardiers a letter couched in the following terms: "Cosette is ill with a malady which is going the rounds of the neighborhood. A miliary fever, they call it. Expensive drugs are required. This is ruining us, and we can no longer pay for them. If you do not send us forty francs before the week is out, the little one will be dead."

She burst out laughing, and said to her old neighbor: "Ah! they are good! Forty francs! the idea! That makes two napoleons! Where do they think I am to get them? These peasants are stupid, truly."

Nevertheless she went to a dormer window in the staircase and read the letter once more. Then she descended the stairs and emerged, running and leaping and still laughing.

Someone met her and said to her, "What makes you so gay?"

She replied: "A fine piece of stupidity that some country people have written to me. They demand forty francs of me. So much for you, you peasants!"

As she crossed the square, she saw a great many people collected around a carriage of eccentric shape, upon the top of which stood a man dressed in red, who was holding forth. He was a quack dentist on his rounds, who was offering to the public full sets of teeth, opiates, powders, and elixirs.

Fantine mingled in the group, and began to laugh with the rest at the harangue, which contained slang for the populace and jargon for respectable people. The tooth-puller spied the lovely, laughing girl, and suddenly exclaimed: "You have beautiful teeth, you girl there, who are laughing; if you want to sell me your palettes, I will give you a gold napoleon apiece for them."

"What are my palettes?" asked Fantine.

"The palettes," replied the dental professor, "are the front teeth, the two upper ones."

"How horrible!" exclaimed Fantine.

"Two napoleons!" grumbled a toothless old woman who was present. "Here's a lucky girl!"

Fantine fled and stopped her ears that she might not hear the hoarse voice of the man shouting to her: "Reflect, my beauty! two napoleons; they may prove of service. If your heart bids you, come this evening to the inn of the *Tillac d'Argent*; you will find me there."

Fantine returned home. She was furious, and related the occurrence to her good neighbor Marguerite: "Can you understand such a thing? Is he not an abominable man? How can they allow such people to go about the country! Pull out my two front teeth! Why, I should be horrible! My hair will grow again, but my teeth! Ah! what a monster of a man! I should prefer to throw myself head first on the pavement from the fifth story! He told me that he should be at the *Tillac d'Argent* this evening."

"And what did he offer?" asked Marguerite.

"Two napoleons."

"That makes forty francs."

"Yes," said Fantine; "that makes forty francs."

She remained thoughtful, and began her work. At the expiration of a quarter of an hour she left her sewing and went to read the Thénardiers's letter once more on the staircase.

On her return, she said to Marguerite, who was at work beside her:

"What is a miliary fever? Do you know?"

"Yes," answered the old spinster; "it is a disease."

"Does it require many drugs?"

"Oh! terrible drugs."

"How does one get it?"

"It is a malady that one gets without knowing how."

"Then it attacks children?"

"Children in particular."

"Do people die of it?"

"They may," said Marguerite.

Fantine left the room and went to read her letter once more on the staircase.

That evening she went out, and was seen to turn her steps in the direction of the Rue de Paris, where the inns are situated.

The next morning, when Marguerite entered Fantine's room before daylight—for they always worked together, and in this manner used only one candle for the two—she found Fantine seated on her bed, pale and frozen. She had not lain down. Her cap had fallen on her knees. Her candle had burned all night, and was almost entirely consumed. Marguerite halted on the threshold, petrified at this tremendous wastefulness, and exclaimed:

"Lord! the candle is all burned out! Something has happened."

Then she looked at Fantine, who turned toward her her head bereft of its hair.

Fantine had grown ten years older since the preceding night.

"Jesus!" said Marguerite, "what is the matter with you, Fantine?"

"Nothing," replied Fantine. "Quite the contrary. My child will not die of that frightful malady, for lack of succor. I am content."

So saying, she pointed out to the spinster two napoleons which were glittering on the table.

"Ah! Jesus God!" cried Marguerite. "Why, it is a fortune! Where did you get those louis d'or?"

"I got them," replied Fantine.

At the same time she smiled. The candle illuminated her countenance. It was a bloody smile. A reddish saliva soiled the corners of her lips, and she had a black hole in her mouth.

The two teeth had been extracted.

She sent the forty francs to Montfermeil.

After all it was a ruse of the Thénardiers to obtain money. Cosette was not ill.

Fantine threw her mirror out of the window. She had long since quitted her cell on the second floor for an attic with only a latch to fasten it, next the roof; one of those attics whose extremity forms an angle with the floor, and knocks you on the head every instant. The poor occupant can reach the end of his chamber as he can the end of his destiny, only by bending over more and more.

She had no longer a bed; a rag which she called her coverlet, a mattress on the floor, and a seatless chair still remained. A little rosebush which she had, had dried up, forgotten, in one corner. In the other corner was a butter-pot to hold water, which froze in winter, and in which the various levels of the water remained long marked by these circles of ice. She had lost her shame; she lost her coquetry. A final sign. She went out, with dirty caps. Whether from lack of time or from indifference, she no longer mended her linen. As the heels wore out, she dragged her stockings down into her shoes. This was evident from the perpendicular wrinkles. She patched her bodice which was old and worn out, with scraps of calico which tore at the slightest movement. The people to whom she was indebted made "scenes" and gave her no peace. She found them in the street, she found them again on her staircase. She passed many a night weeping and thinking. Her eyes were very bright, and she felt a steady pain in her shoulder toward the top of the left shoulder-blade. She coughed a great deal. She deeply hated Father Madeleine, but made no complaint. She sewed seventeen hours a day; but a contractor for the work of prisons, who made the prisoners work at a discount, suddenly made prices fall, which reduced the daily earnings of working-women to nine sous. Seventeen hours of toil, and nine sous a day! Her creditors were more pitiless than ever. The second-hand dealer, who had taken back nearly all his furniture, said to her incessantly, "When will you pay me, you hussy?" What did they want of her, good God! She felt that she was being hunted, and something of the wild beast developed in her. About the same time, Thénardier wrote to her that he had waited with decidedly too much amiability and that he must have a hundred francs at once; otherwise he would turn little Cosette out of doors, convalescent as she was from her heavy illness, into the cold and the streets, and that she might do what she liked with herself, and die if she chose. "A hundred francs," thought Fantine. "But in what trade can one earn a hundred sous a day?"

"Come!" said she, "let us sell what is left."

The unfortunate girl became a woman of the town.

Chapter XI

CHRISTUS NOS LIBERAVIT

WHAT IS THIS HISTORY OF FANTINE? IT IS SOCIETY PURCHASING A SLAVE.
From whom? From misery.

From hunger, cold, isolation, destitution. A dolorous bargain. A soul for a morsel of bread. Misery offers; society accepts.

The sacred law of Jesus Christ governs our civilization, but it does not, as yet, permeate it; it is said that slavery has disappeared from European civilization. This is a mistake. It still exists; but it weighs only upon the woman, and it is called prostitution.

It weighs upon the woman, that is to say, upon grace, weakness, beauty, maternity. This is not one of the least of man's disgraces.

At the point in this melancholy drama which we have now reached, nothing is left to Fantine of that which she had formerly been.

She has become marble in becoming mire. Whoever touches her feels cold. She passes; she endures you; she ignores you; she is the severe and dishonored figure. Life and the social order have said their last word for her. All has happened to her that will happen to her. She has felt everything, borne everything, experienced everything, suffered everything, lost everything, mourned everything. She is resigned, with that resignation which resembles indifference, as death resembles sleep. She no longer avoids anything. Let all the clouds fall upon her, and all the ocean sweep over her! What matters it to her? She is a sponge that is soaked.

At least, she believes it to be so; but it is an error to imagine that fate can be exhausted, and that one has reached the bottom of anything whatever.

Alas! What are all these fates, driven on pell-mell? Whither are they going? Why are they thus?

He who knows that sees the whole of the shadow.

He is alone. His name is God.

Chapter XII

M. BAMATABOIS'S INACTIVITY

THERE IS, IN ALL SMALL TOWNS, AND THERE WAS AT M. SUR M. IN PARTICULAR, A CLASS OF YOUNG men who nibble away an income of fifteen hundred francs with the same air with which their prototypes devour two hundred thousand francs a year in Paris. These are beings of the great neuter species: impotent men, parasites, cyphers, who have a little land, a little folly, a little wit; who would be rustics in a drawing-room, and who think themselves gentlemen in the dram-shop; who say, "My fields, my peasants, my woods"; who hiss actresses at the theater to prove that they are persons of taste; quarrel with the officers of the garrison to prove that they are men of war; hunt, smoke, yawn, drink, smell of tobacco, play billiards, stare at travelers as they descend from the diligence, live at the café, dine at the inn, have a dog which eats the bones under the table, and a mistress who eats the dishes on the table; who stick at a sou, exaggerate the fashions, admire tragedy, despise women, wear out their old boots, copy London through Paris, and Paris through the medium of Pont-à-Mousson, grow old as dullards, never work, serve no use, and do no great harm.

M. Félix Tholomyès, had he remained in his own province and never beheld Paris, would have been one of these men.

If they were richer, one would say, "They are dandies"; if they were poorer, one would say, "They are idlers." They are simply men without employment. Among these unemployed there are bores, the bored, dreamers, and some knaves.

At that period a dandy was composed of a tall collar, a big cravat, a watch with trinkets, three vests of different colors, worn one on top of the other—the red and blue inside; of a short-waisted olive coat, with a codfish tail, a double row of silver buttons set close to each other and running up to the shoulder; and a pair of trousers of a lighter shade of olive, ornamented on the two seams with an indefinite, but always uneven, number of lines, varying from one to eleven—a limit which was never exceeded. Add to this, high shoes with little irons on the heels, a tall hat with a narrow brim, hair worn in a tuft, an enormous cane, and conversation set off by puns of Potier. Over all, spurs and a mustache. At that epoch mustaches indicated the bourgeois, and spurs the pedestrian.

The provincial dandy wore the longest of spurs and the fiercest of mustaches.

It was the period of the conflict of the republics of South America with the King of Spain, of Bolivar against Morillo. Narrow-brimmed hats were royalist, and were called *morillos*; liberals wore hats with wide brims, which were called *bolivars*.

Eight or ten months, then, after that which is related in the preceding pages, towards the first of January, 1823, on a snowy evening, one of these dandies, one of these unemployed, a "right thinker," for he wore a morillo, and was, moreover, warmly enveloped in one of those large cloaks which completed the fashionable costume in cold weather, was amusing himself by tormenting a creature who was prowling about in a ball-dress, with neck uncovered and flowers in her hair, in front of the officers' café. This dandy was smoking, for he was decidedly fashionable.

Each time that the woman passed in front of him, he bestowed on her, together with a puff from his cigar, some apostrophe which he considered witty and mirthful, such as, "How ugly you are!—Will you get out of my sight?—You have no teeth!" etc., etc. This gentleman was known as M. Bamatabois. The woman, a melancholy, decorated specter which went and came through the snow, made him no reply, did not even glance at him, and nevertheless continued her promenade in silence, and with a somber regularity, which brought her every five minutes within reach of this sarcasm, like the condemned soldier who returns under the rods. The small effect which he produced no doubt piqued the lounger; and taking advantage of a moment when her back was turned, he crept up behind her with the gait of a wolf, and stifling his laugh, bent down, picked up a handful of snow from the pavement, and thrust it abruptly into her back, between her bare shoulders. The woman uttered a roar, whirled round, gave a leap like a panther, and hurled herself upon the man, burying her nails in his face, with the most frightful words which could fall from the guard-room into the gutter. These insults, poured forth in a voice roughened by brandy, did, indeed, proceed in hideous wise from a mouth which lacked its two front teeth. It was Fantine.

At the noise thus produced, the officers ran out in throngs from the café, passers-by collected, and a large and merry circle, hooting and applauding, was formed around this whirlwind composed of two beings, whom there was some difficulty in recognizing as a man and a woman: the man struggling, his hat on the ground; the woman striking out with feet and fists, bareheaded, howling, minus hair and teeth, livid with wrath, horrible.

Suddenly a man of lofty stature emerged vivaciously from the crowd, seized the woman by her satin bodice, which was covered with mud, and said to her, "Follow me!"

The woman raised her head; her furious voice suddenly died away. Her eyes were glassy; she turned pale instead of livid, and she trembled with a quiver of terror. She had recognized Javert.

The dandy took advantage of the incident to make his escape.

Chapter XIII

THE SOLUTION OF SOME QUESTIONS CONNECTED WITH THE MUNICIPAL POLICE

JAVERT THRUST ASIDE THE SPECTATORS, BROKE THE CIRCLE, AND SET OUT WITH LONG STRIDES toward the police station, which is situated at the extremity of the square, dragging the wretched woman after him. She yielded mechanically. Neither he nor she uttered a word. The cloud of spectators followed, jesting, in a paroxysm of delight. Supreme misery an occasion for obscenity.

On arriving at the police station, which was a low room, warmed by a stove, with a glazed and grated door opening on the street, and guarded by a detachment, Javert opened the door, entered with Fantine, and shut the door behind him, to the great disappointment of the curious, who raised themselves on tiptoe, and craned their necks in front of the thick glass of the station-house, in their effort to see. Curiosity is a sort of gluttony. To see is to devour.

On entering, Fantine fell down in a corner, motionless and mute, crouching down like a terrified dog.

The sergeant of the guard brought a lighted candle to the table. Javert seated himself, drew a sheet of stamped paper from his pocket, and began to write.

This class of women is consigned by our laws entirely to the discretion of the police. The latter do what they please, punish them, as seems good to them, and confiscate at their will those two sorry things which they entitle their industry and their liberty. Javert was impassive; his grave face betrayed no emotion whatever. Nevertheless, he was seriously and deeply preoccupied. It was one of those moments when he was exercising without control, but subject to all the scruples of a severe conscience, his redoubtable discretionary power. At that moment he was conscious that his police agent's stool was a tribunal. He was entering judgment. He judged and condemned. He summoned all the ideas which could possibly exist in his mind, around the great thing which he was doing. The more he examined the deed of this woman, the more shocked he felt. It was evident that he had just witnessed the commission of a crime. He had just beheld, yonder, in the street, society, in the person of a freeholder and an elector, insulted and attacked by a creature who was outside all pales. A prostitute had made an attempt on the life of a citizen. He had seen that, he, Javert. He wrote in silence.

When he had finished he signed the paper, folded it, and said to the sergeant of the guard, as he handed it to him, "Take three men and conduct this creature to jail."

Then, turning to Fantine, "You are to have six months of it." The unhappy woman shuddered.

"Six months! six months of prison!" she exclaimed. "Six months in which to earn seven sous a day! But what will become of Cosette? My daughter! my daughter! But I still owe the Thénardiers over a hundred francs; do you know that, Monsieur Inspector?"

She dragged herself across the damp floor, among the muddy boots of all those men, without rising, with clasped hands, and taking great strides on her knees.

"Monsieur Javert," said she, "I beseech your mercy. I assure you that I was not in the wrong. If you had seen the beginning, you would have seen. I swear to you by the good God that I was not to blame! That gentleman, the bourgeois, whom I do not know, put snow in my back. Has anyone the right to put snow down our backs when we are walking along peaceably, and doing no harm to anyone? I am rather ill, as you see. And then, he had been saying impertinent things to me for a long time: 'You are ugly! you have no teeth!' I know well that I have no longer those teeth. I did nothing; I said to myself, 'The gentleman is amusing himself.' I was honest with him; I did not speak to him. It was at that moment that he put the snow down my back. Monsieur Javert, good Monsieur Inspector! is there not some person here who saw it and can tell you that this is quite true? Perhaps I did wrong to get angry. You know that one is not master of one's self at the first moment. One gives way to vivacity; and then, when someone puts something cold down your back just when you are not expecting it! I did wrong to spoil that gentleman's hat. Why did he go away? I would ask his pardon. Oh, my God! It makes no difference to me whether I ask his pardon. Do me the favor to-day, for this once, Monsieur Javert. Hold! you do not know that in prison one can earn only seven sous a day; it is not the government's fault, but seven sous is one's earnings; and just fancy, I must pay one hundred francs, or my little girl will be sent to me. Oh, my God! I cannot have her with me. What I do is so vile! Oh, my Cosette! Oh, my little angel of the Holy Virgin! what will become of her, poor creature? I will tell you: it is the Thénardiers, inn-keepers, peasants; and such people are unreasonable. They want money. Don't put me in prison! You see, there is a little girl who will be turned out into the street, to get along as best she may, in the very heart of the winter; and you must have pity on such a being, my good Monsieur Javert. If she were older, she might earn her living; but it cannot be done at that age. I am not a bad woman at bottom. It is not cowardliness and gluttony that have made me what I am. If I have drunk brandy, it was out of misery. I do not love it; but it benumbs the senses. When I was happy, it was only necessary to glance into my clos-ets, and it would have been evident that I was not a coquettish and untidy woman. I had linen, a great deal of linen. Have pity on me, Monsieur Javert!"

She spoke thus, rent in twain, shaken with sobs, blinded with tears, her neck bare, wringing her hands, and coughing with a dry, short cough, stammering softly with a voice of agony. Great sorrow is a divine and terrible ray, which transfigures the unhappy. At that moment Fantine had become beautiful once more. From time to time she paused, and tenderly kissed the police agent's coat. She would have softened a heart of granite; but a heart of wood cannot be softened.

"Come!" said Javert, "I have heard you out. Have you entirely finished? You will get six months. Now march! The Eternal Father in person could do nothing more."

At these solemn words, *"the Eternal Father in person could do nothing more,"* she understood that her fate was sealed. She sank down, murmuring, "Mercy!"

Javert turned his back.

The soldiers seized her by the arms.

A few moments earlier a man had entered, but no one had paid any heed to him. He shut the door, leaned his back against it, and listened to Fantine's despairing supplications.

At the instant when the soldiers laid their hands upon the unfortunate woman, who would not rise, he emerged from the shadow, and said:

"One moment, if you please."

Javert raised his eyes and recognized M. Madeleine. He removed his hat, and, saluting him with a sort of aggrieved awkwardness:

"Excuse me, Mr. Mayor—"

The words "Mr. Mayor" produced a curious effect upon Fantine. She rose to her feet with one bound, like a specter springing from the earth, thrust aside the soldiers with both arms, walked straight up to M. Madeleine before anyone could prevent her, and gazing intently at him, with a bewildered air, she cried:

"Ah! so it is you who are M. le Maire!"

Then she burst into a laugh, and spit in his face.

M. Madeleine wiped his face, and said:

"Inspector Javert, set this woman at liberty."

Javert felt that he was on the verge of going mad. He experienced at that moment, blow upon blow and almost simultaneously, the most violent emotions which he had ever undergone in all his life. To see a woman of the town spit in the mayor's face was a thing so monstrous that, in his most daring flights of fancy, he would have regarded it as a sacrilege to believe it possible. On the other hand, at the very bottom of his thought, he made a hideous comparison as to what this woman was, and as to what this mayor might be; and then he, with horror, caught a glimpse of I know not what simple explanation of this prodigious attack. But when he beheld that mayor, that magistrate, calmly wipe his face and say, *"Set this woman at liberty,"* he underwent a sort of intoxication of amazement; thought and word failed him equally; the sum total of possible astonishment had been exceeded in his case. He remained mute.

The words had produced no less strange an effect on Fantine. She raised her bare arm, and clung to the damper of the stove, like a person who is reeling. Nevertheless, she glanced about her, and began to speak in a low voice, as though talking to herself:

"At liberty! I am to be allowed to go! I am not to go to prison for six months! Who said that? It is not possible that anyone could have said that. I did not hear aright. It cannot have been that monster of a mayor! Was it you, my good Monsieur Javert, who said that I was to be set free? Oh, see here! I will tell you about it, and you will let me go. That monster of a mayor, that old black-guard of a mayor, is the cause of all. Just imagine, Monsieur Javert, he turned me out! all because of a pack of rascally women, who gossip in the workroom. If that is not a horror, what is? To dismiss a poor girl who is doing her work honestly! Then I could no longer earn enough, and all this misery followed. In the first place, there is one improvement which these gentlemen of the police ought to make, and that is, to prevent prison contractors from wronging poor people. I will explain it to you, you see: you are earning twelve sous at shirt-making, the price falls to nine sous; and it is not enough to live on. Then one has to become whatever one can. As for me, I had my little Cosette, and I was actually forced to become a bad woman. Now you understand how it is that that black-guard of a mayor caused all the mischief. After that I stamped on that gentleman's hat in front of the officers' café; but he had spoiled my whole dress with snow. We women have but one silk dress for evening wear. You see that I did not do wrong deliberately—truly, Monsieur Javert; and every-where I behold women who are far more wicked than I, and who are much happier. O Monsieur Javert! it was you who gave orders that I am to be set free, was it not? Make inquiries, speak to my landlord; I am paying my rent now; they will tell you that I am perfectly honest. Ah! my God! I beg your pardon; I have unintentionally touched the damper of the stove, and it has made it smoke."

M. Madeleine listened to her with profound attention. While she was speaking, he fumbled in his waistcoat, drew out his purse and opened it. It was empty. He put it back in his pocket. He said to Fantine, "How much did you say that you owed?"

Fantine, who was looking at Javert only, turned towards him:

"Was I speaking to you?"

Then, addressing the soldiers:

"Say, you fellows, did you see how I spit in his face? Ah! you old wretch of a mayor, you came here to frighten me, but I'm not afraid of you. I am afraid of Monsieur Javert. I am afraid of my good Monsieur Javert!"

So saying, she turned to the inspector again:

"And yet, you see, Mr. Inspector, it is necessary to be just. I understand that you are just, Mr. Inspector; in fact, it is perfectly simple: a man amuses himself by putting snow down a woman's back, and that makes the officers laugh; one must divert themselves in some way; and we—well, we are here for them to amuse themselves with, of course! And then, you, you come; you are cer-tainly obliged to preserve order, you lead off the woman who is in the wrong; but on reflection, since you are a good man, you say that I am to be set at liberty; it is for the sake of the little one, for six months in prison would prevent my supporting my child. 'Only, don't do it again, you hussy!' Oh! I won't do it again, Monsieur Javert! They may do whatever they please to me now; I will not stir. But to-day, you see, I cried because it hurt me. I was not expecting that snow from the gentle-man at all; and then, as I told you, I am not well; I have a cough; I seem to have a burning ball in my stomach, and the doctor tells me, 'Take care of yourself.' Here, feel, give me your hand; don't be afraid—it is here."

She no longer wept, her voice was caressing; she placed Javert's coarse hand on her delicate, white throat and looked smilingly at him.

All at once she rapidly adjusted her disordered garments, dropped the folds of her skirt, which had been pushed up as she dragged herself along, almost to the height of her knee, and stepped toward the door, saying to the soldiers in a low voice, and with a friendly nod:

"Children, Monsieur l'Inspecteur has said that I am to be released, and I am going."

She laid her hand on the latch of the door. One step more and she would be in the street.

Javert up to that moment had remained erect, motionless, with his eyes fixed on the ground, cast athwart this scene like some displaced statue, which is waiting to be put away somewhere.

The sound of the latch roused him. He raised his head with an expression of sovereign authority, an expression all the more alarming in proportion as the authority rests on a low level, ferocious in the wild beast, atrocious in the man of no estate.

"Sergeant!" he cried, "don't you see that that jade is walking off! Who bade you let her go?"

"I," said Madeleine.

Fantine trembled at the sound of Javert's voice, and let go of the latch as a thief relinquishes the article which he has stolen. At the sound of Madeleine's voice she turned around, and from that moment forth she uttered no word, nor dared so much as to breathe freely, but her glance strayed from Madeleine to Javert, and from Javert to Madeleine in turn, according to which was speaking.

It was evident that Javert must have been exasperated beyond measure before he would permit himself to apostrophize the sergeant as he had done, after the mayor's suggestion that Fantine should be set at liberty. Had he reached the point of forgetting the mayor's presence? Had he finally declared to himself that it was impossible that any "authority" should have given such an order, and that the mayor must certainly have said one thing by mistake for another, without intending it? Or, in view of the enormities of which he had been a witness for the past two hours, did he say to himself, that it was necessary to recur to supreme resolutions, that it was indispensable that the small should be made great, that the police spy should transform himself into a magistrate, that the policeman should become a dispenser of justice, and that, in this prodigious extremity, order, law, morality, government, society in its entirety, was personified in him, Javert?

However that may be, when M. Madeleine uttered that word, *I,* as we have just heard, Police Inspector Javert was seen to turn toward the mayor, pale, cold, with blue lips, and a look of despair, his whole body agitated by an imperceptible quiver and an unprecedented occurrence, and say to him, with downcast eyes but a firm voice:

"Mr. Mayor, that cannot be."

"Why not?" said M. Madeleine.

"This miserable woman has insulted a citizen."

"Inspector Javert," replied the mayor, in a calm and conciliating tone, "listen. You are an honest man, and I feel no hesitation in explaining matters to you. Here is the true state of the case: I was passing through the square just as you were leading this woman away; there were still groups of people standing about, and I made inquiries, and learned everything; it was the townsman who was in the wrong and who should have been arrested by properly conducted police."

Javert retorted:

"This wretch has just insulted Monsieur le Maire."

"That concerns me," said M. Madeleine. "My own insult belongs to me, I think. I can do what I please about it."

"I beg Monsieur le Maire's pardon. The insult is not to him, but to the law."

"Inspector Javert," replied M. Madeleine, "the highest law is conscience. I have heard this woman; I know what I am doing."

"And I, Mr. Mayor, do not know what I see."

"Then content yourself with obeying."

"I am obeying my duty. My duty demands that this woman shall serve six months in prison."

M. Madeleine replied gently:

"Heed this well; she will not serve a single day."

At this decisive word, Javert ventured to fix a searching look on the mayor and to say, but in a tone of voice that was still profoundly respectful:

"I am sorry to oppose Monsieur le Maire; it is for the first time in my life, but he will permit me to remark that I am within the bounds of my authority. I confine myself, since Monsieur le Maire desires it, to the question of the gentleman. I was present. This woman flung herself on Monsieur Bamatabois, who is an elector and the proprietor of that handsome house with a balcony, which forms the corner of the esplanade, three stories high and entirely of cut stone. Such things as there are in the world! In any case, Monsieur le Maire, this is a question of police regulations in the streets, and concerns me, and I shall detain this woman Fantine."

Then M. Madeleine folded his arms, and said in a severe voice which no one in the town had heard hitherto:

"The matter to which you refer is one connected with the municipal police. According to the terms of articles nine, eleven, fifteen, and sixty-six of the code of criminal examination, I am the judge. I order that this woman shall be set at liberty."

Javert ventured to make a final effort.

"But, Mr. Mayor—"

"I refer you to article eighty-one of the law of the 13th of December, 1799, in regard to arbitrary detention."

"Monsieur le Maire, permit me—"

"Not another word."

"But—"

"Leave the room," said M. Madeleine.

Javert received the blow erect, full in the face, in his breast, like a Russian soldier. He bowed to the very earth before the mayor and left the room.

Fantine stood aside from the door and stared at him in amazement as he passed.

Nevertheless, she also was the prey to a strange confusion. She had just seen herself a subject of dispute between two opposing powers. She had seen two men who held in their hands her liberty, her life, her soul, her child, in combat before her very eyes; one of these men was drawing her toward darkness, the other was leading her back toward the light. In this conflict, viewed through the exaggerations of terror, these two men had appeared to her like two giants; the one spoke like her demon, the other like her good angel. The angel had conquered the demon, and, strange to say, that which made her shudder from head to foot was the fact that this angel, this liberator, was the very man whom she abhorred, that mayor whom she had so long regarded as the author of all her woes, that Madeleine! And at the very moment when she had insulted him in so hideous a fashion, he had saved her! Had she, then, been mistaken? Must she change her whole soul? She did not know; she trembled. She listened in bewilderment, she looked on in affright, and at every word uttered by M. Madeleine she felt the frightful shades of hatred crumble and melt within her, and something warm and ineffable, indescribable, which was both joy, confidence and love, dawn in her heart.

When Javert had taken his departure, M. Madeleine turned to her and said to her in a deliberate voice, like a serious man who does not wish to weep and who finds some difficulty in speaking:

"I have heard you. I knew nothing about what you have mentioned. I believe that it is true, and I feel that it is true. I was even ignorant of the fact that you had left my shop. Why did you not apply to me? But here; I will pay your debts, I will send for your child, or you shall go to her. You shall live here, in Paris, or where you please. I undertake the care of your child and yourself. You shall not work any longer if you do not like. I will give all the money you require. You shall be honest and happy once more. And listen! I declare to you that if all is as you say—and I do not doubt it— you have never ceased to be virtuous and holy in the sight of God. Oh! poor woman."

This was more than Fantine could bear. To have Cosette! To leave this life of infamy. To live free, rich, happy, respectable with Cosette; to see all these realities of paradise blossom of a sudden in the midst of her misery. She stared stupidly at this man who was talking to her, and could only give vent to two or three sobs, "Oh! Oh! Oh!"

Her limbs gave way beneath her, she knelt in front of M. Madeleine, and before he could prevent her he felt her grasp his hand and press her lips to it.

Then she fainted.

BOOK SIXTH

JAVERT

Chapter I

THE BEGINNING OF REPOSE

M. MADELEINE HAD FANTINE REMOVED TO THAT INFIRMARY WHICH HE HAD ESTABLISHED IN HIS OWN house. He confided her to the sisters, who put her to bed. A burning fever had come on. She passed a part of the night in delirium and raving. At length, however, she fell asleep.

On the morrow, towards midday, Fantine awoke. She heard someone breathing close to her bed; she drew aside the curtain and saw M. Madeleine standing there and looking at something over her head. His gaze was full of pity, anguish, and supplication. She followed its direction, and saw that it was fixed on a crucifix which was nailed to the wall.

Thenceforth, M. Madeleine was transfigured in Fantine's eyes. He seemed to her to be clothed in light. He was absorbed in a sort of prayer. She gazed at him for a long time without daring to interrupt him. At last she said timidly:

"What are you doing?"

M. Madeleine had been there for an hour. He had been waiting for Fantine to awake. He took her hand, felt of her pulse, and replied:

"How do you feel?"

"Well, I have slept," she replied; "I think that I am better. It is nothing."

He answered, responding to the first question which she had put to him as though he had but just heard it:

"I was praying to the martyr there on high."

And he added in his own mind, "For the martyr here below."

M. Madeleine had passed the night and the morning in making inquiries. He knew all now. He knew Fantine's history in all its heartrending details. He went on:

"You have suffered much, poor mother. Oh! do not complain; you now have the dowry of the elect. It is thus that men are transformed into angels. It is not their fault they do not know how to go to work otherwise. You see, this hell from which you have just emerged is the first form of heaven. It was necessary to begin there."

He sighed deeply. But she smiled on him with that sublime smile in which two teeth were lacking.

That same night, Javert wrote a letter. The next morning he posted it himself at the office of M. sur M. It was addressed to Paris, and the superscription ran: *To Monsieur Chabouillet, Secretary of Monsieur le Préfet of Police.* As the affair in the station-house had been bruited about, the post-mistress and some other persons who saw the letter before it was sent off, and who recognized Javert's handwriting on the cover, thought that he was sending in his resignation.

M. Madeleine made haste to write to the Thénardiers. Fantine owed them one hundred and twenty francs. He sent them three hundred francs, telling them to pay themselves from that sum, and to fetch the child instantly to M. sur M., where her sick mother required her presence.

This dazzled Thénardier. "The devil!" said the man to his wife; "don't let's allow the child to go. This lark is going to turn into a milch cow. I see through it. Some ninny has taken a fancy to the mother."

He replied with a very well drawn-up bill for five hundred and some odd francs. In this memorandum two indisputable items figured up over three hundred francs—one for the doctor, the other for the apothecary who had attended and physicked Éponine and Azelma through two long illnesses. Cosette, as we have already said, had not been ill. It was only a question of a trifling substitution of names. At the foot of the memorandum, Thénardier wrote, *Received on account, three hundred francs.*

M. Madeleine immediately sent three hundred francs more, and wrote, "Make haste to bring Cosette."

"Christi!" said Thénardier, "let's not give up the child."

In the meantime, Fantine did not recover. She still remained in the infirmary.

The sisters had at first only received and nursed "that woman" with repugnance. Those who have seen the bas-reliefs of Rheims will recall the inflation of the lower lip of the wise virgins as they survey the foolish virgins. The ancient scorn of the vestals for the ambubajae is one of the most profound instincts of feminine dignity; the sisters felt it with the double force contributed by religion. But in a few days Fantine disarmed them. She said all kinds of humble and gentle things, and the mother in her provoked tenderness. One day the sisters heard her say amid her fever: "I have been a sinner; but when I have my child beside me, it will be a sign that God has pardoned me. While I was leading a bad life, I should not have liked to have my Cosette with me; I could not have borne her sad, astonished eyes. It was for her sake that I did evil, and that is why God pardons me. I shall feel the benediction of the good God when Cosette is here. I shall gaze at her; it will do me good to see that innocent creature. She knows nothing at all. She is an angel, you see, my sisters. At that age the wings have not fallen off."

M. Madeleine went to see her twice a day, and each time she asked him:

"Shall I see my Cosette soon?"

He answered:

"To-morrow, perhaps. She may arrive at any moment. I am expecting her."

And the mother's pale face grew radiant.

"Oh!" she said, "how happy I am going to be!"

We have just said that she did not recover her health. On the contrary, her condition seemed to become more grave from week to week. That handful of snow applied to her bare skin between her shoulder-blades had brought about a sudden suppression of perspiration, as a consequence of which the malady which had been smoldering within her for many years was violently developed at last. At that time people were beginning to follow the fine Laënnec's fine suggestions in the study and treatment of chest maladies. The doctor sounded Fantine's chest and shook his head.

M. Madeleine said to the doctor:

"Well?"

"Has she not a child which she desires to see?" said the doctor.

"Yes."

"Well! Make haste and get it here."

M. Madeleine shuddered.

Fantine inquired:

"What did the doctor say?"

M. Madeleine forced himself to smile.

"He said that your child was to be brought speedily. That that would restore your health."

"Oh!" she rejoined, "he is right! But what do those Thénardiers mean by keeping my Cosette from me! Oh! she is coming. At last I behold happiness close beside me!"

In the meantime, Thénardier did not "let go of the child," and gave a hundred insufficient reasons for it. Cosette was not quite well enough to take a journey in the winter. And then, there still remained some petty but pressing debts in the neighborhood, and they were collecting the bills for them, etc., etc.

"I shall send someone to fetch Cosette!" said Father Madeleine. "If necessary, I will go myself."

He wrote the following letter to Fantine's dictation, and made her sign it:

MONSIEUR THÉNARDIER—You will deliver Cosette to this person. You will be paid for all the little things. I have the honor to salute you with respect.

FANTINE

In the meantime a serious incident occurred. Carve as we will the mysterious block of which our life is made, the black vein of destiny constantly reappears in it.

Chapter II

HOW JEAN MAY BECOME CHAMP

ONE MORNING M. MADELEINE WAS IN HIS STUDY, OCCUPIED IN ARRANGING IN ADVANCE SOME pressing matters connected with the mayor's office, in case he should decide to take the trip to Montfermeil, when he was informed that Police Inspector Javert was desirous of speaking with him. Madeleine could not refrain from a disagreeable impression on hearing this name. Javert had avoided him more than ever since the affair of the police-station, and M. Madeleine had not seen him.

"Admit him," he said.

Javert entered.

M. Madeleine had retained his seat near the fire, pen in hand, his eyes fixed on the docket which he was turning over and annotating, and which contained the trials of the commission on highways for the infraction of police regulations. He did not disturb himself on Javert's account. He could not help thinking of poor Fantine, and it suited him to be glacial in his manner.

Javert bestowed a respectful salute on the mayor, whose back was turned to him. The mayor did not look at him, but went on annotating this docket.

Javert advanced two or three paces into the study, and halted, without breaking the silence.

If any physiognomist who had been familiar with Javert, and who had made a lengthy study of this savage in the service of civilization, this singular composite of the Roman, the Spartan, the monk, and the corporal, this spy who was incapable of a lie, this unspotted police agent—if any physiognomist had known his secret and long-cherished aversion for M. Madeleine, his conflict with the mayor on the subject of Fantine, and had examined Javert at that moment, he would have said to himself, "What has taken place?" It was evident to anyone acquainted with that clear, upright, sincere, honest, austere, and ferocious conscience, that Javert had but just gone through some great interior struggle. Javert had nothing in his soul which he had not also in his countenance. Like violent people in general, he was subject to abrupt changes of opinion. His physiognomy had never been more peculiar and startling. On entering he bowed to M. Madeleine with a look in which there was neither rancor, anger, nor distrust; he halted a few paces in the rear of the mayor's arm-chair, and there he stood, perfectly erect, in an attitude almost of discipline, with the cold, ingenuous roughness of a man who has never been gentle and who has always been patient; he waited without uttering a word, without making a movement, in genuine humility and tranquil resignation, calm, serious, hat in hand, with eyes cast down, and an expression which was halfway between that of a soldier in the presence of his officer and a criminal in the presence of his judge, until it should please the mayor to turn round. All the sentiments as well as all the memories which one might have attributed to him had disappeared. That face, as impenetrable and simple as granite, no longer bore any trace of anything but a melancholy depression. His whole person breathed lowliness and firmness and an indescribable courageous despondency.

At last the mayor laid down his pen and turned half round.

"Well! What is it? what is the matter, Javert?"

Javert remained silent for an instant as though collecting his ideas, then raised his voice with a sort of sad solemnity, which did not, however, preclude simplicity.

"This is the matter, Mr. Mayor; a culpable act has been committed."

"What act?"

"An inferior agent of the authorities has failed in respect, and in the gravest manner, toward a magistrate. I have come to bring the fact to your knowledge, as it is my duty to do."

"Who is the agent?" asked M. Madeleine.

"I," said Javert.

"You?"

"I."

"And who is the magistrate who has reason to complain of the agent?"

"You, Mr. Mayor."

M. Madeleine sat erect in his arm-chair. Javert went on, with a severe air and his eyes still cast down.

"Mr. Mayor, I have come to request you to instigate the authorities to dismiss me."

M. Madeleine opened his mouth in amazement. Javert interrupted him:

"You will say that I might have handed in my resignation, but that does not suffice. Handing in one's resignation is honorable. I have failed in my duty; I ought to be punished; I must be turned out."

And after a pause he added:

"Mr. Mayor, you were severe with me the other day, and unjustly. Be so to-day, with justice."

"Come, now! Why?" exclaimed M. Madeleine. "What nonsense is this? What is the meaning of this? What culpable act have you been guilty of toward me? What have you done to me? What are your wrongs with regard to me? You accuse yourself; you wish to be superseded—"

"Turned out," said Javert.

"Turned out; so it be, then. That is well. I do not understand."

"You shall understand, Mr. Mayor."

Javert sighed from the very bottom of his chest, and resumed, still coldly and sadly:

"Mr. Mayor, six weeks ago, in consequence of the scene over that woman, I was furious, and I informed against you."

"Informed against me!"

"At the Prefecture of Police in Paris."

M. Madeleine, who was not in the habit of laughing much oftener than Javert himself, burst out laughing now:

"As a mayor who had encroached on the province of the police?"

"As an ex-convict."

The mayor turned livid.

Javert, who had not raised his eyes, went on:

"I thought it was so. I had had an idea for a long time; a resemblance; inquiries which you had caused to be made at Faverolles; the strength of your loins; the adventure with old Fauchelevent; your skill in marksmanship; your leg, which you drag a little—I hardly know what all—absurdities! But, at all events, I took you for a certain Jean Valjean."

"A certain— What did you say the name was?"

"Jean Valjean. He was a convict whom I was in the habit of seeing twenty years ago, when I was adjutant-guard of convicts at Toulon. On leaving the galleys, this Jean Valjean, as it appears, robbed a bishop; then he committed another theft, accompanied with violence, on a public highway on the person of a little Savoyard. He disappeared eight years ago, no one knows how, and he has been sought, I fancied. In short, I did this thing! Wrath impelled me; I denounced you at the Prefecture!"

M. Madeleine, who had taken up the docket again several moments before this, resumed with an air of perfect indifference:

"And what reply did you receive?"

"That I was mad."

"Well?"

"Well, they were right."

"It is lucky that you recognize the fact."

"I am forced to do so, since the real Jean Valjean has been found."

The sheet of paper which M. Madeleine was holding dropped from his hand; he raised his head, gazed fixedly at Javert, and said with his indescribable accent:

"Ah!"

Javert continued:

"This is the way it is, Mr. Mayor. It seems that there was in the neighborhood near Ailly-le-Haut-Clocher an old fellow who was called Father Champmathieu. He was a very wretched creature. No one paid any attention to him. No one knows what such people subsist on. Lately, last autumn, Father Champmathieu was arrested for the theft of some cider apples from— Well, no matter, a theft had been committed, a wall scaled, branches of trees broken. My Champmathieu was arrested. He still had the branch of apple-tree in his hand. The scamp is locked up. Up to this point it was merely an affair of a misdemeanor. But here is where Providence intervened.

"The jail being in a bad condition, the examining magistrate finds it convenient to transfer Champmathieu to Arras, where the departmental prison is situated. In this prison at Arras there is an ex-convict named Brevet, who is detained for I know not what, and who has been appointed turnkey of the house, because of good behavior. Mr. Mayor, no sooner had Champmathieu arrived than Brevet exclaims: 'Eh! Why, I know that man! He is a *fagot!*[1] Take a good look at me, my good man!

1. An ex-convict.

You are Jean Valjean!' 'Jean Valjean! who's Jean Valjean?' Champmathieu feigns astonishment. 'Don't play the innocent dodge,' says Brevet. 'You are Jean Valjean! You have been in the galleys of Toulon; it was twenty years ago; we were there together.' Champmathieu denies it. Parbleu! You understand. The case is investigated. The thing was well ventilated for me. This is what they discovered: This Champmathieu had been, thirty years ago, a pruner of trees in various localities, notably at Faverolles. There all trace of him was lost. A long time afterwards he was seen again in Auvergne; then in Paris, where he is said to have been a wheelwright, and to have had a daughter, who was a laundress; but that has not been proved. Now, before going to the galleys for theft, what was Jean Valjean? A pruner of trees. Where? At Faverolles. Another fact. This Valjean's Christian name was Jean, and his mother's surname was Mathieu. What more natural to suppose than that, on emerging from the galleys, he should have taken his mother's name for the purpose of concealing himself, and have called himself Jean Mathieu? He goes to Auvergne. The local pronunciation turns *Jean* into *Chan*—he is called Chan Mathieu. Our man offers no opposition, and behold him transformed into Champmathieu. You follow me, do you not? Inquiries were made at Faverolles. The family of Jean Valjean is no longer there. It is not known where they have gone. You know that among those classes a family often disappears. Search was made, and nothing was found. When such people are not mud, they are dust. And then, as the beginning of the story dates thirty years back, there is no longer anyone at Faverolles who knew Jean Valjean. Inquiries were made at Toulon. Besides Brevet, there are only two convicts in existence who have seen Jean Valjean; they are Cochepaille and Chenildieu, and are sentenced for life. They are taken from the galleys and confronted with the pretended Champmathieu. They do not hesitate; he is Jean Valjean for them as well as for Brevet. The same age—he is fifty-four—the same height, the same air, the same man; in short, it is he. It was precisely at this moment that I forwarded my denunciation to the Prefecture in Paris. I was told that I had lost my reason, and that Jean Valjean is at Arras, in the power of the authorities. You can imagine whether this surprised me, when I thought that I had that same Jean Valjean here. I write to the examining judge; he sends for me; Champmathieu is conducted to me—"

"Well?" interposed M. Madeleine.

Javert replied, his face incorruptible, and as melancholy as ever:

"Mr. Mayor, the truth is the truth. I am sorry; but that man is Jean Valjean. I recognized him also."

M. Madeleine resumed in a very low voice:

"You are sure?"

Javert began to laugh, with that mournful laugh which comes from profound conviction.

"O! Sure!"

He stood there thoughtfully for a moment, mechanically taking pinches of powdered wood for blotting ink from the wooden bowl which stood on the table, and he added:

"And even now that I have seen the real Jean Valjean, I do not see how I could have thought otherwise. I beg your pardon, Mr. Mayor."

Javert, as he addressed these grave and supplicating words to the man, who six weeks before had humiliated him in the presence of the whole station-house, and bade him "leave the room"— Javert, that haughty man, was unconsciously full of simplicity and dignity—M. Madeleine made no other reply to his prayer than the abrupt question:

"And what does this man say?"

"Ah! Indeed, Mr. Mayor, it's a bad business. If he is Jean Valjean, he has his previous conviction against him. To climb a wall, to break a branch, to purloin apples, is a mischievous trick in a child; for a man it is a misdemeanor; for a convict it is a crime. Robbing and housebreaking—it is all there. It is no longer a question of correctional police; it is a matter for the Court of Assizes. It is no longer a matter of a few days in prison; it is the galleys for life. And then, there is the affair with the little Savoyard, who will return, I hope. The deuce! there is plenty to dispute in the matter, is there not? Yes, for anyone but Jean Valjean. But Jean Valjean is a sly dog. That is the way I recognized him. Any other man would have felt that things were getting hot for him; he would struggle, he would cry out—the kettle sings before the fire; he would not be Jean Valjean, *et cetera*. But he has not the appearance of understanding; he says, 'I am Champmathieu, and I won't depart from that!' He has an astonished air, he pretends to be stupid; it is far better. Oh! the rogue is clever! But it makes no difference. The proofs are there. He has been recognized by four persons; the old scamp will be condemned. The case has been taken to the Assizes at Arras. I shall go there to give my testimony. I have been summoned."

M. Madeleine had turned to his desk again, and taken up his docket, and was turning over the leaves tranquilly, reading and writing by turns, like a busy man. He turned to Javert:

"That will do, Javert. In truth, all these details interest me but little. We are wasting our time, and we have pressing business on hand. Javert, you will betake yourself at once to the house of the woman Buseaupied, who sells herbs at the corner of the Rue Saint-Saulve. You will tell her that she must enter her complaint against carter Pierre Chesnelong. The man is a brute, who came near crushing this woman and her child. He must be punished. You will then go to M. Charcellay, Rue Montre-de-Champigny. He complained that there is a gutter on the adjoining house which discharges rainwater on his premises, and is undermining the foundations of his house. After that, you will verify the infractions of police regulations which have been reported to me in the Rue Guibourg, at Widow Doris's, and Rue du Garraud-Blanc, at Madame Renée le Bossé's, and you will prepare documents. But I am giving you a great deal of work. Are you not to be absent? Did you not tell me that you were going to Arras on that matter in a week or ten days?"

"Sooner than that, Mr. Mayor."

"On what day, then?"

"Why, I thought that I had said to Monsieur le Maire that the case was to be tried to-morrow, and that I am to set out by diligence to-night."

M. Madeleine made an imperceptible movement.

"And how long will the case last?"

"One day, at the most. The judgment will be pronounced to-morrow evening at latest. But I shall not wait for the sentence, which is certain; I shall return here as soon as my deposition has been taken."

"That is well," said M. Madeleine.

And he dismissed Javert with a wave of the hand.

Javert did not withdraw.

"Excuse me, Mr. Mayor," said he.

"What is it now?" demanded M. Madeleine.

"Mr. Mayor, there is still something of which I must remind you."

"What is it?"

"That I must be dismissed."

M. Madeleine rose.

"Javert, you are a man of honor, and I esteem you. You exaggerate your fault. Moreover, this is an offense which concerns me. Javert, you deserve promotion instead of degradation. I wish you to retain your post."

Javert gazed at M. Madeleine with his candid eyes, in whose depths his not very enlightened but pure and rigid conscience seemed visible, and said in a tranquil voice:

"Mr. Mayor, I cannot grant you that."

"I repeat," replied M. Madeleine, "that the matter concerns me."

But Javert, heeding his own thought only, continued:

"So far as exaggeration is concerned, I am not exaggerating. This is the way I reason: I have suspected you unjustly. That is nothing. It is our right to cherish suspicion, although suspicion directed above ourselves is an abuse. But without proofs, in a fit of rage, with the object of wreaking my vengeance, I have denounced you as a convict, you, a respectable man, a mayor, a magistrate! That is serious, very serious. I have insulted authority in your person, I, an agent of the authorities! If one of my subordinates had done what I have done, I should have declared him unworthy of the service, and have expelled him. Well? Stop, Mr. Mayor; one word more. I have often been severe in the course of my life toward others. That is just. I have done well. Now, if I were not severe toward myself, all the justice that I have done would become injustice. Ought I to spare myself more than others? No! What! I should be good for nothing but to chastise others, and not myself! Why, I should be a blackguard! Those who say, 'That blackguard of a Javert!' would be in the right. Mr. Mayor, I do not desire that you should treat me kindly; your kindness roused sufficient bad blood in me when it was directed to others. I want none of it for myself. The kindness which consists in upholding a woman of the town against a citizen, the police agent against the mayor, the man who is down against the man who is up in the world, is what I call false kindness. That is the sort of kindness which disorganizes society. Good God! it is very easy to be kind; the difficulty lies in being just. Come! if you had been what I thought you, I should not have been kind to you, not I! You would have seen! Mr. Mayor, I must treat myself as I would treat any other man. When I have subdued malefactors, when I have proceeded with vigor against rascals, I have often said to myself, 'If you flinch, if ever I catch you in fault, you may rest at your ease!' I have flinched, I have caught myself in a fault. So much the worse! Come, discharged, cashiered, expelled! That is well. I have arms. I will till the soil; it makes no difference to me. Mr. Mayor, the good of the service demands an example. I simply require the discharge of Inspector Javert."

All this was uttered in a proud, humble, despairing, yet convinced tone, which lent indescribable grandeur to this singular, honest man.

"We shall see," said M. Madeleine.

And he offered him his hand.

Javert recoiled, and said in a wild voice:

"Excuse me, Mr. Mayor, but this must not be. A mayor does not offer his hand to a police spy."

He added between his teeth:

"A police spy, yes; from the moment when I have misused the police, I am no more than a police spy."

Then he bowed profoundly, and directed his steps toward the door.

There he wheeled round, and with eyes still downcast:

"Mr. Mayor," he said, "I shall continue to serve until I am superseded."

He withdrew. M. Madeleine remained thoughtfully listening to the firm, sure step, which died away on the pavement of the corridor.

BOOK SEVENTH

THE CHAMPMATHIEU AFFAIR

Chapter I

SISTER SIMPLICE

THE INCIDENTS THE READER IS ABOUT TO PERUSE WERE NOT ALL KNOWN AT M. SUR M. BUT THE small portion of them which became known left such a memory in that town that a serious gap would exist in this book if we did not narrate them in their most minute details. Among these details the reader will encounter two or three improbable circumstances, which we preserve out of respect for the truth.

On the afternoon following the visit of Javert, M. Madeleine went to see Fantine according to his wont.

Before entering Fantine's room, he had Sister Simplice summoned.

The two nuns who performed the services of nurse in the infirmary, Lazariste ladies, like all sisters of charity, bore the names of Sister Perpétue and Sister Simplice.

Sister Perpétue was an ordinary villager, a sister of charity in a coarse style, who had entered the service of God as one enters any other service. She was a nun as other women are cooks. This type is not so very rare. The monastic orders gladly accept this heavy peasant earthenware, which is easily fashioned into a Capuchin or an Ursuline. These rustics are utilized for the rough work of devotion. The transition from a drover to a Carmelite is not in the least violent; the one turns into the other without much effort; the fund of ignorance common to the village and the cloister is a preparation ready at hand, and places the boor at once on the same footing as the monk: a little more amplitude in the smock, and it becomes a frock. Sister Perpétue was a robust nun from Marines near Pontoise, who chattered her patois, droned, grumbled, sugared the potion according to the bigotry or the hypocrisy of the invalid, treated her patients abruptly, roughly, was crabbed with the dying, almost flung God in their faces, stoned their death-agony with prayers mumbled in a rage; was bold, honest, and ruddy.

Sister Simplice was white, with a waxen pallor. Beside Sister Perpétue, she was the taper beside the candle. Vincent de Paul has divinely traced the features of the Sister of Charity in these admirable words, in which he mingles as much freedom as servitude: "They shall have for their convent only the house of the sick; for cell only a hired room; for chapel only their parish church; for cloister only the streets of the town and the wards of the hospitals; for enclosure only obedience; for gratings only the fear of God; for veil only modesty." This ideal was realized in the living person of Sister Simplice: she had never been young, and it seemed as though she would never grow old. No one could have told Sister Simplice's age. She was a person—we dare not say a woman—who was gentle, austere, well-bred, cold, and who had never lied. She was so gentle that she appeared fragile; but she was more solid than granite. She touched the unhappy with fingers that were charmingly pure and fine. There was, so to speak, silence in her speech; she said just what was necessary, and she possessed a tone of voice which would have equally edified a confessional or enchanted a drawing-room. This delicacy accommodated itself to the serge gown, finding in this harsh contact a continual reminder of heaven and of God. Let us emphasize one detail. Never to have lied, never to have said, for any interest whatever, even in indifference, any single thing which was not the truth, the sacred truth, was Sister Simplice's distinctive trait; it was the accent of her virtue. She was almost renowned in the congregation for this imperturbable veracity. The Abbé Sicard speaks of Sister Simplice in a letter to the deaf-mute Massieu. However pure and sincere we may be, we all bear upon our candor the crack of the little, innocent lie. She did not. Little lie, innocent lie—does such a thing exist? To lie is the absolute form of evil. To lie a little is not possible: he who lies, lies the whole lie. To lie is the very face of the demon. Satan has two names; he is called Satan and Lying. That is what she thought; and as she thought, so she did. The result was the whiteness which we have mentioned—a whiteness which covered even her lips and her eyes with radiance. Her smile was white, her glance was white. There was not a single spider's web, not a grain of dust, on the glass window of that conscience. On entering the order of Saint Vincent de Paul, she had taken the name of Simplice by special choice. Simplice of Sicily, as we know, is the saint who preferred to allow both her breasts to be torn off rather than to say that she had been born at Segesta when she had been born at Syracuse—a lie which would have saved her. This patron saint suited this soul.

Sister Simplice, on her entrance into the order, had had two faults which she had gradually corrected: she had a taste for dainties, and she liked to receive letters. She never read anything but a book of prayers printed in Latin, in coarse type. She did not understand Latin, but she understood the book.

This pious woman had conceived an affection for Fantine, probably feeling a latent virtue there, and she had devoted herself almost exclusively to her care.

M. Madeleine took Sister Simplice apart and recommended Fantine to her in a singular tone, which the sister recalled later on.

On leaving the sister, he approached Fantine.

Fantine awaited M. Madeleine's appearance every day as one awaits a ray of warmth and joy. She said to the sisters, "I only live when Monsieur le Maire is here."

She had a great deal of fever that day. As soon as she saw M. Madeleine she asked him:

"And Cosette?"

He replied with a smile:

"Soon."

M. Madeleine was the same as usual with Fantine. Only he remained an hour instead of half an hour, to Fantine's great delight. He urged everyone repeatedly not to allow the invalid to want for anything. It was noticed that there was a moment when his countenance became very somber. But this was explained when it became known that the doctor had bent down to his ear and said to him, "She is losing ground fast."

Then he returned to the town-hall, and the clerk observed him attentively examining a road map of France which hung in his study. He wrote a few figures on a bit of paper with a pencil.

Chapter II

THE PERSPICACITY OF MASTER SCAUFFLAIRE

FROM THE TOWN-HALL HE BETOOK HIMSELF TO THE EXTREMITY OF THE TOWN, TO A FLEMING named Master Scaufflaer, French Scaufflaire, who let out "horses and cabriolets as desired."

In order to reach this Scaufflaire, the shortest way was to take the little-frequented street in which was situated the parsonage of the parish in which M. Madeleine resided. The curé was, it was said, a worthy, respectable, and sensible man. At the moment when M. Madeleine arrived in front of the parsonage there was but one passer-by in the street, and this person noticed this: After the mayor had passed the priest's house he halted, stood motionless, then turned about, and retraced his steps to the door of the parsonage, which had an iron knocker. He laid his hand quickly on the knocker and lifted it; then he paused again and stopped short, as though in thought, and after the lapse of a few seconds, instead of allowing the knocker to fall abruptly, he placed it gently, and resumed his way with a sort of haste which had not been apparent previously.

M. Madeleine found Master Scaufflaire at home, engaged in stitching a harness over.

"Master Scaufflaire," he inquired, "have you a good horse?"

"Mr. Mayor," said the Fleming, "all my horses are good. What do you mean by a good horse?"

"I mean a horse which can travel twenty leagues in a day."

"The deuce!" said the Fleming. "Twenty leagues!"

"Yes."

"Hitched to a cabriolet?"

"Yes."

"And how long can he rest at the end of his journey?"

"He must be able to set out again on the next day if necessary."

"To traverse the same road?"

"Yes."

"The deuce! the deuce! And it is twenty leagues?"

M. Madeleine drew from his pocket the paper on which he had pencilled some figures. He showed it to the Fleming. The figures were 5, 6, 8½.

"You see," he said, "total, nineteen and a half; as well say twenty leagues."

"Mr. Mayor," returned the Fleming, "I have just what you want. My little white horse—you may have seen him pass occasionally; he is a small beast from Lower Boulonnais. He is full of fire. They wanted to make a saddle-horse of him at first. Bah! He reared, he kicked, he laid everybody flat on the ground. He was thought to be vicious, and no one knew what to do with him. I bought him. I harnessed him to a carriage. That is what he wanted, sir; he is as gentle as a girl; he goes like the wind. Ah! indeed he must not be mounted. It does not suit his ideas to be a saddle-horse. Everyone has his ambition. 'Draw? Yes. Carry? No.' We must suppose that is what he said to himself."

"And he will accomplish the trip?"

"Your twenty leagues all at a full trot, and in less than eight hours. But here are the conditions."

"State them."

"In the first place, you will give him half an hour's breathing spell midway of the road; he will eat; and someone must be by while he is eating to prevent the stable boy of the inn from stealing his oats; for I have noticed that in inns the oats are more often drunk by the stable men than eaten by the horses."

"Someone will be by."

"In the second place—is the cabriolet for Monsieur le Maire?"

"Yes."

"Does Monsieur le Maire know how to drive?"

"Yes."

"Well, Monsieur le Maire will travel alone and without baggage, in order not to overload the horse?"

"Agreed."

"But as Monsieur le Maire will have no one with him, he will be obliged to take the trouble himself of seeing that the oats are not stolen."

"That is understood."

"I am to have thirty francs a day. The days of rest to be paid for also—not a farthing less; and the beast's food to be at Monsieur le Maire's expense."

M. Madeleine drew three napoleons from his purse and laid them on the table.

"Here is the pay for two days in advance."

"Fourthly, for such a journey a cabriolet would be too heavy, and would fatigue the horse. Monsieur le Maire must consent to travel in a little tilbury that I own."

"I consent to that."

"It is light, but it has no cover."

"That makes no difference to me."

"Has Monsieur le Maire reflected that we are in the middle of winter?"

M. Madeleine did not reply. The Fleming resumed:

"That it is very cold?"

M. Madeleine preserved silence.

Master Scaufflaire continued:

"That it may rain?"

M. Madeleine raised his head and said:

"The tilbury and the horse will be in front of my door to-morrow morning at half-past four o'clock."

"Of course, Monsieur le Maire," replied Scaufflaire; then, scratching a speck in the wood of the table with his thumb-nail, he resumed with that careless air which the Flemings understand so well how to mingle with their shrewdness:

"But this is what I am thinking of now: Monsieur le Maire has not told me where he is going. Where is Monsieur le Maire going?"

He had been thinking of nothing else since the beginning of the conversation, but he did not know why he had not dared to put the question.

"Are your horse's forelegs good?" said M. Madeleine.

"Yes, Monsieur le Maire. You must hold him in a little when going downhill. Are there many descends between here and the place whither you are going?"

"Do not forget to be at my door at precisely half-past four o'clock to-morrow morning," replied M. Madeleine; and he took his departure.

The Fleming remained "utterly stupid," as he himself said some time afterwards.

The mayor had been gone two or three minutes when the door opened again: it was the mayor once more.

He still wore the same impassive and preoccupied air.

"Monsieur Scaufflaire," said he, "at what sum do you estimate the value of the horse and tilbury which you are to let to me—the one bearing the other?"

"The one dragging the other, Monsieur le Maire," said the Fleming, with a broad smile.

"So be it. Well?"

"Does Monsieur le Maire wish to purchase them of me?"

"No; but I wish to guarantee you in any case. You shall give me back the sum at my return. At what value do you estimate your horse and cabriolet?"

"Five hundred francs, Monsieur le Maire."

"Here it is."

M. Madeleine laid a bank-bill on the table, then left the room; and this time he did not return.

Master Scaufflaire experienced a frightful regret that he had not said a thousand francs. Besides, the horse and tilbury together were worth but a hundred crowns.

The Fleming called his wife, and related the affair to her. "Where the devil could Monsieur le Maire be going?" They held counsel together. "He is going to Paris," said the wife. "I don't believe it," said the husband.

M. Madeleine had forgotten the paper with the figures on it, and it lay on the chimney-piece. The Fleming picked it up and studied it. "Five, six, eight and a half? That must designate the posting relays." He turned to his wife:

"I have found out."

"What?"

"It is five leagues from here to Hesdin, six from Hesdin to Saint-Pol, eight and a half from Saint-Pol to Arras. He is going to Arras."

Meanwhile, M. Madeleine had returned home. He had taken the longest way to return from Master Scaufflaire's, as though the parsonage door had been a temptation for him, and he had wished to avoid it. He ascended to his room, and there he shut himself up, which was a very simple act, since he liked to go to bed early. Nevertheless, the portress of the factory, who was, at the same time, M. Madeleine's only servant, noticed that the latter's light was extinguished at half-past eight, and she mentioned it to the cashier when he came home, adding:

"Is Monsieur le Maire ill? I thought he had a rather singular air."

This cashier occupied a room situated directly under M. Madeleine's chamber. He paid no heed to the portress's words, but went to bed and to sleep. Toward midnight he woke up with a start; in his sleep he had heard a noise above his head. He listened; it was a footstep pacing back and forth, as though someone were walking in the room above him. He listened more attentively, and recognized M. Madeleine's step. This struck him as strange; usually, there was no noise in M. Madeleine's chamber until he rose in the morning. A moment later the cashier heard a noise which resembled that of a cupboard being opened, and then shut again; then a piece of furniture was disarranged; then a pause ensued; then the step began again. The cashier sat up in bed, quite awake now, and staring; and through his window-panes he saw the reddish gleam of a lighted window reflected on the opposite wall; from the direction of the rays, it could only come from the window of M. Madeleine's chamber. The reflection wavered, as though it came rather from a fire which had been lighted than from a candle. The shadow of the window-frame was not shown, which indicated that the window was wide open. The fact that this window was open in such cold weather was surprising. The cashier fell asleep again. An hour or two later he waked again. The same step was still passing slowly and regularly back and forth overhead.

The reflection was still visible on the wall, but now it was pale and peaceful, like the reflection of a lamp or of a candle. The window was still open.

This is what had taken place in M. Madeleine's room.

Chapter III

A Tempest in a Skull

The reader has, no doubt, already divined that M. Madeleine is no other than Jean Valjean.

We have already gazed into the depths of this conscience; the moment has now come when we must take another look into it. We do so not without emotion and trepidation. There is nothing more terrible in existence than this sort of contemplation. The eye of the spirit can nowhere find more dazzling brilliance and more shadow than in man; it can fix itself on no other thing which is more formidable, more complicated, more mysterious, and more infinite. There is a spectacle more grand than the sea; it is heaven: there is a spectacle more grand than heaven; it is the inmost recesses of the soul.

To make the poem of the human conscience, were it only with reference to a single man, were it only in connection with the basest of men, would be to blend all epics into one superior and definitive epic. Conscience is the chaos of chimeras, of lusts, and of temptations; the furnace of dreams; the lair of ideas of which we are ashamed; it is the pandemonium of sophisms; it is the battlefield of the passions. Penetrate, at certain hours, past the livid face of a human being who is engaged in reflection, and look behind, gaze into that soul, gaze into that obscurity. There, beneath that external silence, battles of giants, like those recorded in Homer, are in progress; skirmishes of dragons and hydras and swarms of phantoms, as in Milton; visionary circles, as in Dante. What a solemn thing is this infinity which every man bears within him, and which he measures with despair against the caprices of his brain and the actions of his life!

Alighieri one day met with a sinister-looking door, before which he hesitated. Here is one before us, upon whose threshold we hesitate. Let us enter, nevertheless.

We have but little to add to what the reader already knows of what had happened to Jean Valjean after the adventure with Little Gervais. From that moment forth he was, as we have seen, a totally different man. What the Bishop had wished to make of him, that he carried out. It was more than a transformation; it was a transfiguration.

He succeeded in disappearing, sold the Bishop's silver, reserving only the candlesticks as a souvenir, crept from town to town, traversed France, came to M. sur M., conceived the idea which we have mentioned, accomplished what we have related, succeeded in rendering himself safe from seizure and inaccessible, and, thenceforth, established at M. sur M., happy in feeling his conscience saddened by the past and the first half of his existence belied by the last, he lived in peace, reassured and hopeful, having henceforth only two thoughts—to conceal his name and to sanctify his life; to escape men and to return to God.

These two thoughts were so closely intertwined in his mind that they formed but a single one there; both were equally absorbing and imperative and ruled his slightest actions. In general, they conspired to regulate the conduct of his life; they turned him toward the gloom; they rendered him kindly and simple; they counseled him to the same things. Sometimes, however, they conflicted. In that case, as the reader will remember, the man whom all the country of M. sur M. called M. Madeleine did not hesitate to sacrifice the first to the second—his security to his virtue. Thus, in spite of all his reserve and all his prudence, he had preserved the Bishop's candlesticks, worn mourning for him, summoned and interrogated all the little Savoyards who passed that way, collected information regarding the families at Faverolles, and saved old Fauchelevent's life, despite the disquieting insinuations of Javert. It seemed, as we have already remarked, as though he thought, following the example of all those who have been wise, holy, and just, that his first duty was not toward himself.

At the same time, it must be confessed, nothing just like this had yet presented itself.

Never had the two ideas which governed the unhappy man whose sufferings we are narrating, engaged in so serious a struggle. He understood this confusedly but profoundly at the very first words pronounced by Javert, when the latter entered his study. At the moment when that name, which he had buried beneath so many layers, was so strangely articulated, he was struck with stupor, and as though intoxicated with the sinister eccentricity of his destiny; and through this stupor he felt that shudder which precedes great shocks. He bent like an oak at the approach of a storm, like a soldier at the approach of an assault. He felt shadows filled with thunders and lightnings descending upon his head. As he listened to Javert, the first thought which occurred to him was to go, to run and denounce himself, to take that Champmathieu out of prison and place himself there; this was as painful and as poignant as an incision in the living flesh. Then it passed away, and he said to himself, "We will see! We will see!" He repressed this first, generous instinct, and recoiled before heroism.

It would be beautiful, no doubt, after the Bishop's holy words, after so many years of repentance and abnegation, in the midst of a penitence admirably begun, if this man had not flinched for an instant, even in the presence of so terrible a conjecture, but had continued to walk with the same step toward this yawning precipice, at the bottom of which lay heaven; that would have been beautiful; but it was not thus. We must render an account of the things which went on in this soul, and we can only tell what there was there. He was carried away, at first, by the instinct of self-preservation; he rallied all his ideas in haste, stifled his emotions, took into consideration Javert's presence, that great danger, postponed all decision with the firmness of terror, shook off thought as to what he had to do, and resumed his calmness as a warrior picks up his buckler.

He remained in this state during the rest of the day, a whirlwind within, a profound tranquility without. He took no "preservative measures," as they may be called. Everything was still confused, and jostling together in his brain. His trouble was so great that he could not perceive the form of a single idea distinctly, and he could have told nothing about himself, except that he had received a great blow.

He repaired to Fantine's bed of suffering, as usual, and prolonged his visit, through a kindly instinct, telling himself that he must behave thus, and recommend her well to the sisters, in case he should be obliged to be absent himself. He had a vague feeling that he might be obliged to go to Arras; and without having the least in the world made up his mind to this trip, he said to himself that being, as he was, beyond the shadow of any suspicion, there could be nothing out of the way in being a witness to what was to take place, and he engaged the tilbury from Scaufflaire in order to be prepared in any event.

He dined with a good deal of appetite.

On returning to his room, he communed with himself.

He examined the situation, and found it unprecedented; so unprecedented that in the midst of his reverie he rose from his chair, moved by some inexplicable impulse of anxiety, and bolted his door. He feared lest something more should enter. He was barricading himself against possibilities.

A moment later he extinguished his light; it embarrassed him.

It seemed to him as though he might be seen.

By whom?

Alas! That on which he desired to close the door had already entered; that which he desired to blind was staring him in the face—his conscience.

His conscience; that is to say, God.

Nevertheless, he deluded himself at first; he had a feeling of security and of solitude; the bolt once drawn, he thought himself impregnable; the candle extinguished, he felt himself invisible.

Then he took possession of himself: he set his elbows on the table, leaned his head on his hand, and began to meditate in the dark.

"Where do I stand? Am not I dreaming? What have I heard? Is it really true that I have seen that Javert, and that he spoke to me in that manner? Who can that Champmathieu be? So he resembles me! Is it possible? When I reflect that yesterday I was so tranquil, and so far from suspecting anything! What was I doing yesterday at this hour? What is there in this incident? What will the end be? What is to be done?"

This was the torment in which he found himself. His brain had lost its power of retaining ideas; they passed like waves, and he clutched his brow in both hands to arrest them.

Nothing but anguish extricated itself from this tumult which overwhelmed his will and his reason, and from which he sought to draw proof and resolution.

His head was burning. He went to the window and threw it wide open. There were no stars in the sky. He returned and seated himself at the table.

The first hour passed in this manner.

Gradually, however, vague outlines began to take form and to fix themselves in his meditation, and he was able to catch a glimpse with precision of the reality—not the whole situation, but some of the details. He began by recognizing the fact that, critical and extraordinary as was this situation, he was completely master of it.

This only caused an increase of his stupor.

Independently of the severe and religious aim which he had assigned to his actions, all that he had made up to that day had been nothing but a hole in which to bury his name. That which he had always feared most of all in his hours of self-communion, during his sleepless nights, was to ever hear that name pronounced; he had said to himself that that would be the end of all things for him; that on the day when that name made its reappearance it would cause his new life to vanish from about him, and—who knows?—perhaps even his new soul within him, also. He shuddered at the very thought that this was possible. Assuredly, if anyone had said to him at such moments that the hour would come when that name would ring in his ears, when the hideous words, Jean Valjean, would suddenly emerge from the darkness and rise in front of him, when that formidable light, capable of dissipating the mystery in which he had enveloped himself, would suddenly blaze forth above his head, and that that name would not menace him, that that light would but produce an obscurity more dense, that this rent veil would but increase the mystery, that this earthquake would solidify his edifice, that this prodigious incident would have no other result, so far as he was concerned, if so it seemed good to him, than that of rendering his existence at once clearer and more impenetrable, and that, out of his confrontation with the phantom of Jean Valjean, the good and worthy citizen Monsieur Madeleine would emerge more honored, more peaceful, and more respected than ever—if anyone had told him that, he would have tossed his head and regarded the words as those of a madman. Well, all this was precisely what had just come to pass; all that accumulation of impossibilities was a fact, and God had permitted these wild fancies to become real things!

His reverie continued to grow clearer. He came more and more to an understanding of his position.

It seemed to him that he had but just waked up from some inexplicable dream, and that he found himself slipping down a declivity in the middle of the night, erect, shivering, holding back all in vain, on the very brink of the abyss. He distinctly perceived in the darkness a stranger, a man unknown to him, whom destiny had mistaken for him, and whom she was thrusting into the gulf in his stead; in order that the gulf might close once more, it was necessary that someone, himself or that other man, should fall into it: he had only let things take their course.

The light became complete, and he acknowledged this to himself: That his place was empty in the galleys; that do what he would, it was still awaiting him; that the theft from little Gervais had led him back to it; that this vacant place would await him, and draw him on until he filled it; that this was inevitable and fatal; and then he said to himself, "that, at this moment, he had a substitute; that it appeared that a certain Champmathieu had that ill luck, and that, as regards himself, being present in the galleys in the person of that Champmathieu, present in society under the name of M. Madeleine, he had nothing more to fear, provided that he did not prevent men from sealing over the head of that Champmathieu this stone of infamy which, like the stone of the sepulcher, falls once, never to rise again."

All this was so strange and so violent, that there suddenly took place in him that indescribable movement, which no man feels more than two or three times in the course of his life, a sort of convulsion of the conscience which stirs up all that there is doubtful in the heart, which is composed of irony, of joy, and of despair, and which may be called an outburst of inward laughter.

He hastily relighted his candle.

"Well, what then?" he said to himself; "what am I afraid of? What is there in all that for me to think about? I am safe; all is over. I had but one partly open door through which my past might invade my life, and behold that door is walled up forever! That Javert, who has been annoying me so long; that terrible instinct which seemed to have divined me, which had divined me—good God! and which followed me everywhere; that frightful hunting-dog, always making a point at me, is thrown off the scent, engaged elsewhere, absolutely turned from the trail: henceforth he is satisfied; he will leave me in peace; he has his Jean Valjean. Who knows? it is even probable that he will wish to leave town! And all this has been brought about without any aid from me, and I count for nothing in it! Ah! but where is the misfortune in this? Upon my honor, people would think, to see me, that some catastrophe had happened to me! After all, if it does bring harm to someone, that is not my fault in the least: it is Providence which has done it all; it is because it wishes it so to be, evidently. Have I the right to disarrange what it has arranged? What do I ask now? Why should I meddle? It does not concern me; what! I am not satisfied: but what more do I want? The goal to which I have aspired for so many years, the dream of my nights, the object of my prayers to Heaven— security—I have now attained; it is God who wills it; I can do nothing against the will of God, and why does God will it? In order that I may continue what I have begun, that I may do good, that I may one day be a grand and encouraging example, that it may be said at last, that a little happiness has been attached to the penance which I have undergone, and to that virtue to which I have returned. Really, I do not understand why I was afraid, a little while ago, to enter the house of that good curé, and to ask his advice; this is evidently what he would have said to me: It is settled; let things take their course; let the good God do as he likes!"

Thus did he address himself in the depths of his own conscience, bending over what may be called his own abyss; he rose from his chair, and began to pace the room: "Come," said he, "let us think no more about it; my resolve is taken!" but he felt no joy.

Quite the reverse.

One can no more prevent thought from recurring to an idea than one can the sea from returning to the shore: the sailor calls it the tide; the guilty man calls it remorse; God upheaves the soul as he does the ocean.

After the expiration of a few moments, do what he would, he resumed the gloomy dialogue in which it was he who spoke and he who listened, saying that which he would have preferred to ignore, and listened to that which he would have preferred not to hear, yielding to that mysterious power which said to him: "Think!" as it said to another condemned man, two thousand years ago, "March on!"

Before proceeding further, and in order to make ourselves fully understood, let us insist upon one necessary observation.

It is certain that people do talk to themselves; there is no living being who has not done it. It may even be said that the word is never a more magnificent mystery than when it goes from thought to conscience within a man, and when it returns from conscience to thought; it is in this sense only that the words so often employed in this chapter, *he said, he exclaimed,* must be understood; one speaks to one's self, talks to one's self, exclaims to one's self without breaking the external silence; there is a great tumult; everything about us talks except the mouth. The realities of the soul are none the less realities because they are not visible and palpable.

So he asked himself where he stood. He interrogated himself upon that "settled resolve." He confessed to himself that all that he had just arranged in his mind was monstrous, that "to let things take their course, to let the good God do as he liked," was simply horrible; to allow this error of fate and of men to be carried out, not to hinder it, to lend himself to it through his silence, to do nothing, in short, was to do everything! that this was hypocritical baseness in the last degree! that it was a base, cowardly, sneaking, abject, hideous crime!

For the first time in eight years, the wretched man had just tasted the bitter savor of an evil thought and of an evil action.

He spit it out with disgust.

He continued to question himself. He asked himself severely what he had meant by this, "My object is attained!" He declared to himself that his life really had an object; but what object? To conceal his name? To deceive the police? Was it for so petty a thing that he had done all that he had done? Had he not another and a grand object, which was the true one—to save, not his person, but his soul; to become honest and good once more; to be a just man? Was it not that above all, that alone, which he had always desired, which the Bishop had enjoined upon him—to shut the door on his past? But he was not shutting it! great God! he was reopening it by committing an infamous action! He was becoming a thief once more, and the most odious of thieves! He was robbing another of his existence, his life, his peace, his place in the sunshine. He was becoming an assassin. He was murdering, morally murdering, a wretched man. He was inflicting on him that frightful living death, that death beneath the open sky, which is called the galleys. On the other hand, to surrender himself to save that man, struck down with so melancholy an error, to resume his own name, to become once more, out of duty, the convict Jean Valjean, that was, in truth, to achieve his resurrection, and to close forever that hell whence he had just emerged; to fall back there in appearance was to escape from it in reality. This must be done! He had done nothing if he did not do all this; his whole life was useless; all his penitence was wasted. There was no longer any need of saying, "What is the use?" He felt that the Bishop was there, that the Bishop was present all the more because he was dead, that the Bishop was gazing fixedly at him, that henceforth Mayor Madeleine, with all his virtues, would be abominable to him, and that the convict Jean Valjean would be pure and admirable in his sight; that men beheld his mask, but that the Bishop saw his face; that men saw his life, but that the Bishop beheld his conscience. So he must go to Arras, deliver the false Jean Valjean, and denounce the real one. Alas! that was the greatest of sacrifices, the most poignant of victories, the last step to take; but it must be done. Sad fate! he would enter into sanctity only in the eyes of God when he returned to infamy in the eyes of men.

"Well," said he, "let us decide upon this; let us do our duty; let us save this man." He uttered these words aloud, without perceiving that he was speaking aloud.

He took his books, verified them, and put them in order. He flung in the fire a bundle of bills which he had against petty and embarrassed tradesmen. He wrote and sealed a letter, and on the envelope it might have been read, had there been anyone in his chamber at the moment, *To Monsieur Laffitte, Banker, Rue d'Artois, Paris.* He drew from his secretary a pocket-book which contained several bank-notes and the passport of which he had made use that same year when he went to the elections.

Anyone who had seen him during the execution of these various acts, into which there entered such grave thought, would have had no suspicion of what was going on within him. Only occasionally did his lips move; at other times he raised his head and fixed his gaze upon some point of the wall, as though there existed at that point something which he wished to elucidate or interrogate.

When he had finished the letter to M. Laffitte, he put it into his pocket, together with the pocket-book, and began his walk once more.

His reverie had not swerved from its course. He continued to see his duty clearly, written in luminous letters, which flamed before his eyes and changed its place as he altered the direction of his glance:

"Go! Tell your name! Denounce yourself!"

In the same way he beheld, as though they had passed before him in visible forms, the two ideas which had, up to that time, formed the double rule of his soul—the concealment of his name, the sanctification of his life. For the first time they appeared to him as absolutely distinct, and he perceived the distance which separated them. He recognized the fact that one of these ideas was, necessarily, good, while the other might become bad; that the first was self-devotion, and that the other was personality; that the one said, *my neighbor,* and that the other said, *myself;* that one emanated from the light, and the other from darkness.

They were antagonistic. He saw them in conflict. In proportion as he meditated, they grew before the eyes of his spirit. They had now attained colossal statures, and it seemed to him that he beheld within himself, in that infinity of which we were recently speaking, in the midst of the darkness and the lights, a goddess and a giant contending.

He was filled with terror; but it seemed to him that the good thought was getting the upper hand.

He felt that he was on the brink of the second decisive crisis of his conscience and of his destiny; that the Bishop had marked the first phase of his new life, and that Champmathieu marked the second. After the grand crisis, the grand test.

But the fever, allayed for an instant, gradually resumed possession of him. A thousand thoughts traversed his mind, but they continued to fortify him in his resolution.

One moment he said to himself that he was, perhaps, taking the matter too keenly; that, after all, this Champmathieu was not interesting, and that he had actually been guilty of theft.

He answered himself: "If this man has, indeed, stolen a few apples, that means a month in prison. It is a long way from that to the galleys. And who knows? Did he steal? Has it been proved? The name of Jean Valjean overwhelms him, and seems to dispense with proofs. Do not the attorneys for the Crown always proceed in this manner? He is supposed to be a thief because he is known to be a convict."

In another instant the thought had occurred to him that, when he denounced himself, the heroism of his deed might, perhaps, be taken into consideration, and his honest life for the last seven years, and what he had done for the district, and that they would have mercy on him.

But this supposition vanished very quickly, and he smiled bitterly as he remembered that the theft of the forty sous from little Gervais put him in the position of a man guilty of a second offense after conviction, that this affair would certainly come up, and, according to the precise terms of the law, would render him liable to penal servitude for life.

He turned aside from all illusions, detached himself more and more from earth, and sought strength and consolation elsewhere. He told himself that he must do his duty; that perhaps he should not be more unhappy after doing his duty than after having avoided it; that if he *allowed things to take their own course,* if he remained at M. sur M., his consideration, his good name, his good works, the deference and veneration paid to him, his charity, his wealth, his popularity, his virtue, would be seasoned with a crime. And what would be the taste of all these holy things when bound up with this hideous thing? while, if he accomplished his sacrifice, a celestial idea would be mingled with the galleys, the post, the iron necklet, the green cap, unceasing toil, and pitiless shame.

At length he told himself that it must be so, that his destiny was thus allotted, that he had not authority to alter the arrangements made on high, that, in any case, he must make his choice: virtue without and abomination within, or holiness within and infamy without.

The stirring up of these lugubrious ideas did not cause his courage to fail, but his brain grew weary. He began to think of other things, of indifferent matters, in spite of himself.

The veins in his temples throbbed violently; he still paced to and fro; midnight sounded first from the parish church, then from the town-hall; he counted the twelve strokes of the two clocks, and compared the sounds of the two bells; he recalled in this connection the fact that, a few days previously, he had seen in an ironmonger's shop an ancient clock for sale, upon which was written the name, *Antoine-Albin de Romainville.*

He was cold; he lighted a small fire; it did not occur to him to close the window.

In the meantime he had relapsed into his stupor; he was obliged to make a tolerably vigorous effort to recall what had been the subject of his thoughts before midnight had struck; he finally succeeded in doing this.

"Ah! yes," he said to himself, "I had resolved to inform against myself."

And then, all of a sudden, he thought of Fantine.

"Hold!" said he, "and what about that poor woman?"

Here a fresh crisis declared itself.

Fantine, by appearing thus abruptly in his reverie, produced the effect of an unexpected ray of light; it seemed to him as though everything about him were undergoing a change of aspect: he exclaimed:

"Ah! but I have hitherto considered no one but myself; it is proper for me to hold my tongue or to denounce myself, to conceal my person or to save my soul, to be a despicable and respected magistrate, or an infamous and venerable convict; it is I, it is always I and nothing but I: but, good God! all this is egotism; these are diverse forms of egotism, but it is egotism all the same. What if I were to think a little about others? The highest holiness is to think of others; come, let us examine the matter. The *I* excepted, the *I* effaced, the *I* forgotten, what would be the result of all this? What if I denounce myself? I am arrested; this Champmathieu is released; I am put back in the galleys; that is well—and what then? What is going on here? Ah! here is a country, a town, here are factories, an industry, workers, both men and women, aged grandsires, children, poor people! All this I have created; all these I provide with their living; everywhere where there is a smoking chimney, it is I who have placed the brand on the hearth and meat in the pot; I have created ease, circulation, credit; before me there was nothing; I have elevated, vivified, informed with life, fecundated, stimulated, enriched the whole countryside; lacking me, the soul is lacking; I take myself off, everything dies: and this woman, who has suffered so much, who possesses so many merits in spite of her fall; the cause of all whose misery I have unwittingly been! And that child whom I meant to go in search of, whom I have promised to her mother; do I not also owe something to this woman, in reparation for the evil which I have done her? If I disappear, what happens? The mother dies; the child becomes what it can; that is what will take place, if I denounce myself. If I do not denounce myself? come, let us see how it will be if I do not denounce myself."

After putting this question to himself, he paused; he seemed to undergo a momentary hesitation and trepidation; but it did not last long, and he answered himself calmly:

"Well, this man is going to the galleys; it is true, but what the deuce! he has stolen! There is no use in my saying that he has not been guilty of theft, for he has! I remain here; I go on: in ten years I shall have made ten millions; I scatter them over the country; I have nothing of my own; what is that to me? It is not for myself that I am doing it; the prosperity of all goes on augmenting; industries are aroused and animated; factories and shops are multiplied; families, a hundred families, a thousand families, are happy; the district becomes populated; villages spring up where there were only farms before; farms rise where there was nothing; wretchedness disappears, and with wretchedness debauchery, prostitution, theft, murder; all vices disappear, all crimes: and this poor mother rears her child; and behold a whole country rich and honest! Ah! I was a fool! I was absurd! what was that I was saying about denouncing myself? I really must pay attention and not be precipitate about anything. What! because it would have pleased me to play the grand and generous; this is melodrama, after all; because I should have thought of no one but myself, the idea! for the sake of saving from a punishment, a trifle exaggerated, perhaps, but just at bottom, no one knows whom, a thief, a good-for-nothing, evidently, a whole countryside must perish! a poor woman must die in the hospital! a poor little girl must die in the street! like dogs; ah, this is abominable! And without the mother even having seen her child once more, almost without the child's having known her mother; and all that for the sake of an old wretch of an apple-thief who, most assuredly, has deserved the galleys for something else, if not for that; fine scruples, indeed, which save a guilty man and sacrifice the innocent, which save an old vagabond who has only a few years to live at most, and who will not be more unhappy in the galleys than in his hovel, and which sacrifice a whole population, mothers, wives, children. This poor little Cosette who has no one in the world but me, and who is, no doubt, blue with cold at this moment in the den of those Thénardiers; those peoples are rascals; and I was going to neglect my duty toward all these poor creatures; and I was going off to denounce myself; and I was about to commit that unspeakable folly! Let us put it at the worst: suppose that there is a wrong action on my part in this, and that my conscience will reproach me for it some day, to accept, for the good of others, these reproaches which weigh only on myself; this evil action which compromises my soul alone; in that lies self-sacrifice; in that alone there is virtue."

He rose and resumed his march; this time, he seemed to be content.

Diamonds are found only in the dark places of the earth; truths are found only in the depths of thought. It seemed to him, that, after having descended into these depths, after having long groped among the darkest of these shadows, he had at last found one of these diamonds, one of these truths, and that he now held it in his hand, and he was dazzled as he gazed upon it.

"Yes," he thought, "this is right; I am on the right road; I have the solution; I must end by holding fast to something; my resolve is taken; let things take their course; let us no longer vacillate; let us no longer hang back; this is for the interest of all, not for my own; I am Madeleine, and Madeleine I remain. Woe to the man who is Jean Valjean! I am no longer he; I do not know that man; I no longer know anything; it turns out that someone is Jean Valjean at the present moment; let him look out for himself; that does not concern me; it is a fatal name which was floating abroad in the night; if it halts and descends on a head, so much the worse for that head."

He looked into the little mirror which hung above his chimney-piece, and said:

"Hold! it has relieved me to come to a decision; I am quite another man now."

He proceeded a few paces further, then he stopped short.

"Come!" he said, "I must not flinch before any of the consequences of the resolution which I have once adopted; there are still threads which attach me to that Jean Valjean; they must be broken; in this very room there are objects which would betray me, dumb things which would bear witness against me; it is settled; all these things must disappear."

He fumbled in his pocket, drew out his purse, opened it, and took out a small key; he inserted the key in a lock whose aperture could hardly be seen, so hidden was it in the most somber tones of the design which covered the wall-paper; a secret receptacle opened, a sort of false cupboard constructed in the angle between the wall and the chimney-piece; in this hiding-place there were some rags—a blue linen blouse, an old pair of trousers, an old knapsack, and a huge thorn cudgel shod with iron at both ends. Those who had seen Jean Valjean at the epoch when he passed through D—— in October, 1815, could easily have recognized all the pieces of this miserable outfit.

He had preserved them as he had preserved the silver candlesticks, in order to remind himself continually of his starting-point, but he had concealed all that came from the galleys, and he had allowed the candlesticks which came from the Bishop to be seen.

He cast a furtive glance toward the door, as though he feared that it would open in spite of the bolt which fastened it; then, with a quick and abrupt movement, he took the whole in his arms at once, without bestowing so much as a glance on the things which he had so religiously and so perilously preserved for so many years, and flung them all, rags, cudgel, knapsack, into the fire.

He closed the false cupboard again, and with redoubled precautions, henceforth unnecessary, since it was now empty, he concealed the door behind a heavy piece of furniture, which he pushed in front of it.

After the lapse of a few seconds, the room and the opposite wall were lighted up with a fierce, red, tremulous glow. Everything was on fire; the thorn cudgel snapped and threw out sparks to the middle of the chamber.

As the knapsack was consumed, together with the hideous rags which it contained, it revealed something which sparkled in the ashes. By bending over, one could have readily recognized a coin—no doubt the forty-sou piece stolen from the little Savoyard.

He did not look at the fire, but paced back and forth with the same step.

All at once his eye fell on the two silver candlesticks, which shone vaguely on the chimney-piece, through the glow.

"Hold!" he thought; "the whole of Jean Valjean is still in them. They must be destroyed also."

He seized the two candlesticks.

There was still fire enough to allow of their being put out of shape, and converted into a sort of unrecognizable bar of metal.

He bent over the hearth and warmed himself for a moment. He felt a sense of real comfort. "How good warmth is!" said he.

He stirred the live coals with one of the candlesticks.

A minute more, and they were both in the fire.

At that moment it seemed to him that he heard a voice within him shouting: "Jean Valjean! Jean Valjean!"

His hair rose upright: he became like a man who is listening to some terrible thing.

"Yes, that's it! finish!" said the voice. "Complete what you are about! Destroy these candlesticks! Annihilate this souvenir! Forget the Bishop! Forget everything! Destroy this Champmathieu, do! That is right! Applaud yourself! So it is settled, resolved, fixed, agreed: here is an old man who does not know what is wanted of him, who has, perhaps, done nothing, an innocent man, whose whole misfortune lies in your name, upon whom your name weighs like a crime, who is about to be taken for you, who will be condemned, who will finish his days in abjectness and horror. That is good! Be an honest man yourself; remain Monsieur le Maire; remain honorable and honored; enrich the town; nourish the indigent; rear the orphan; live happy, virtuous, and admired; and, during this time, while you are here in the midst of joy and light, there will be a man who will wear your red blouse, who will bear your name in ignominy, and who will drag your chain in the galleys. Yes, it is well arranged thus. Ah, wretch!"

The perspiration streamed from his brow. He fixed a haggard eye on the candlesticks. But that within him which had spoken had not finished. The voice continued:

"Jean Valjean, there will be around you many voices, which will make a great noise, which will talk very loud, and which will bless you, and only one which no one will hear, and which will curse you in the dark. Well! listen, infamous man! All those benedictions will fall back before they reach heaven, and only the malediction will ascend to God."

This voice, feeble at first, and which had proceeded from the most obscure depths of his conscience, had gradually become startling and formidable, and he now heard it in his very ear. It seemed to him that it had detached itself from him, and that it was now speaking outside of him. He thought that he heard the last words so distinctly, that he glanced around the room in a sort of terror.

"Is there anyone here?" he demanded aloud, in utter bewilderment.

Then he resumed, with a laugh which resembled that of an idiot:

"How stupid I am! There can be no one!"

There was someone; but the person who was there was of those whom the human eye cannot see.

He placed the candlesticks on the chimney-piece.

Then he resumed his monotonous and lugubrious tramp, which troubled the dreams of the sleeping man beneath him, and awoke him with a start.

This tramping to and fro soothed and at the same time intoxicated him. It sometimes seems, on supreme occasions, as though people moved about for the purpose of asking advice of everything that they may encounter by change of place. After the lapse of a few minutes he no longer knew his position.

He now recoiled in equal terror before both the resolutions at which he had arrived in turn. The two ideas which counseled him appeared to him equally fatal. What a fatality! What conjunction that that Champmathieu should have been taken for him; to be overwhelmed by precisely the means which Providence seemed to have employed, at first, to strengthen his position!

There was a moment when he reflected on the future. Denounce himself, great God! Deliver himself up! With immense despair he faced all that he should be obliged to leave, all that he should be obliged to take up once more. He should have to bid farewell to that existence which was so good, so pure, so radiant, to the respect of all, to honor, to liberty. He should never more stroll in the fields; he should never more hear the birds sing in the month of May; he should never more bestow alms on the little children; he should never more experience the sweetness of having glances of gratitude and love fixed upon him; he should quit that house which he had built, that little chamber! Everything seemed charming to him at that moment. Never again should he read those books; never more should he write on that little table of white wood; his old portress, the only servant whom he kept, would never more bring him his coffee in the morning. Great God! instead of that, the convict gang, the iron necklet, the red waistcoat, the chain on his ankle, fatigue, the cell, the camp bed all those horrors which he knew so well! At his age, after having been what he was! If he were only young again! but to be addressed in his old age as "thou" by anyone who pleased; to be searched by the convict guard; to receive the galley-sergeant's cudgelings; to wear iron-bound shoes on his bare feet; to have to stretch out his leg night and morning to the hammer of the roundsman who visits the gang; to submit to the curiosity of strangers, who would be told: "That man yonder is the famous Jean Valjean, who was mayor of M. sur M."; and at night, dripping with perspiration, overwhelmed with lassitude, their green caps drawn over their eyes, to remount, two by two, the ladder staircase of the galleys beneath the sergeant's whip. Oh, what misery! Can destiny, then, be as malicious as an intelligent being, and become as monstrous as the human heart?

And do what he would, he always fell back upon the heartrending dilemma which lay at the foundation of his reverie: "Should he remain in paradise and become a demon? Should he return to hell and become an angel?"

What was to be done? Great God! what was to be done?

The torment from which he had escaped with so much difficulty was unchained afresh within him. His ideas began to grow confused once more; they assumed a kind of stupefied and mechanical quality which is peculiar to despair. The name of Romainville recurred incessantly to his mind, with the two verses of a song which he had heard in the past. He thought that Romainville was a little grove near Paris, where young lovers go to pluck lilacs in the month of April.

He wavered outwardly as well as inwardly. He walked like a little child who is permitted to toddle alone.

At intervals, as he combated his lassitude, he made an effort to recover the mastery of his mind. He tried to put to himself, for the last time, and definitely, the problem over which he had, in a manner, fallen prostrate with fatigue: Ought he to denounce himself? Ought he to hold his peace? He could not manage to see anything distinctly. The vague aspects of all the courses of reasoning which had been sketched out by his meditations quivered and vanished, one after the other, into smoke. He only felt that, to whatever course of action he made up his mind, something in him must die, and that of necessity, and without his being able to escape the fact; that he was entering a sepulcher on the right hand as much as on the left; that he was passing through a death-agony—the agony of his happiness, or the agony of his virtue.

Alas! all his resolution had again taken possession of him. He was no further advanced than at the beginning.

Thus did this unhappy soul struggle in its anguish. Eighteen hundred years before this unfortunate man, the mysterious Being in whom are summed up all the sanctities and all the sufferings of humanity had also long thrust aside with his hand, while the olive-trees quivered in the wild wind of the infinite, the terrible cup which appeared to Him dripping with darkness and overflowing with shadows in the depths all studded with stars.

Chapter IV

FORMS ASSUMED BY SUFFERING DURING SLEEP

THREE O'CLOCK IN THE MORNING HAD JUST STRUCK, AND HE HAD BEEN WALKING THUS FOR FIVE hours, almost uninterruptedly, when he at length allowed himself to drop into his chair.

There he fell asleep and had a dream.

This dream, like the majority of dreams, bore no relation to the situation, except by its painful and heartrending character, but it made an impression on him. This nightmare struck him so forcibly that he wrote it down later on. It is one of the papers in his own handwriting which he has bequeathed to us. We think that we have here reproduced the thing in strict accordance with the text.

Of whatever nature this dream may be, the history of this night would be incomplete if we were to omit it: it is the gloomy adventure of an ailing soul.

Here it is. On the envelope we find this line inscribed, "The Dream I had that Night."

"I was in a plain; a vast, gloomy plain, where there was no grass. It did not seem to me to be daylight nor yet night.

"I was walking with my brother, the brother of my childish years, the brother of whom, I must say, I never think, and whom I now hardly remember.

"We were conversing and we met some passers-by. We were talking of a neighbor of ours in former days, who had always worked with her window open from the time when she came to live on the street. As we talked we felt cold because of that open window.

"There were no trees in the plain. We saw a man passing close to us. He was entirely nude, of the hue of ashes, and mounted on a horse which was earth color. The man had no hair; we could see his skull and the veins on it. In his hand he held a switch which was as supple as a vine-shoot and as heavy as iron. This horseman passed and said nothing to us.

"My brother said to me, 'Let us take to the hollow road.'

"There existed a hollow way wherein one saw neither a single shrub nor a spear of moss. Everything was dirt-colored, even the sky. After proceeding a few paces, I received no reply when I spoke: I perceived that my brother was no longer with me.

"I entered a village which I spied. I reflected that it must be Romainville. (Why Romainville?)[1]

1. This parenthesis is due to Jean Valjean.

"The first street that I entered was deserted. I entered a second street. Behind the angle formed by the two streets, a man was standing erect against the wall. I said to this man:

" 'What country is this? Where am I?' The man made no reply. I saw the door of a house open, and I entered.

"The first chamber was deserted. I entered the second. Behind the door of this chamber a man was standing erect against the wall. I inquired of this man, 'Whose house is this? Where am I?' The man replied not.

"The house had a garden. I quitted the house and entered the garden. The garden was deserted. Behind the first tree I found a man standing upright. I said to this man, 'What garden is this? Where am I?' The man did not answer.

"I strolled into the village, and perceived that it was a town. All the streets were deserted, all the doors were open. Not a single living being was passing in the streets, walking through the chambers, or strolling in the gardens. But behind each angle of the walls, behind each door, behind each tree, stood a silent man. Only one was to be seen at a time. These men watched me pass.

"I left the town and began to ramble about the fields.

"After the lapse of some time I turned back and saw a great crowd coming up behind me. I recognized all the men whom I had seen in that town. They had strange heads. They did not seem to be in a hurry, yet they walked faster than I did. They made no noise as they walked. In an instant this crowd had overtaken and surrounded me. The faces of these men were earthen in hue.

"Then the first one whom I had seen and questioned on entering the town said to me:

" 'Whither are you going! Do you not know that you have been dead this long time?'

"I opened my mouth to reply, and I perceived that there was no one near me."

He woke. He was icy cold. A wind which was chill like the breeze of dawn was rattling the leaves of the window, which had been left open on their hinges. The fire was out. The candle was nearing its end. It was still black night.

He rose, he went to the window. There were no stars in the sky even yet.

From his window the yard of the house and the street were visible. A sharp, harsh noise, which made him drop his eyes, resounded from the earth.

Below him he perceived two red stars, whose rays lengthened and shortened in a singular manner through the darkness.

As his thoughts were still half immersed in the mists of sleep, "Hold!" said he, "there are no stars in the sky. They are on earth now."

But this confusion vanished; a second sound similar to the first roused him thoroughly; he looked and recognized the fact that these two stars were the lanterns of a carriage. By the light which they cast he was able to distinguish the form of this vehicle. It was a tilbury harnessed to a small white horse. The noise which he had heard was the trampling of the horse's hoofs on the pavement.

"What vehicle is this?" he said to himself. "Who is coming here so early in the morning?"

At that moment there came a light tap on the door of his chamber.

He shuddered from head to foot, and cried in a terrible voice:

"Who is there?"

Someone said:

"I, Monsieur le Maire."

He recognized the voice of the old woman who was his portress.

"Well!" he replied, "what is it?"

"Monsieur le Maire, it is just five o'clock in the morning."

"What is that to me?"

"The cabriolet is here, Monsieur le Maire."

"What cabriolet?"

"The tilbury."

"What tilbury?"

"Did not Monsieur le Maire order a tilbury?"

"No," said he.

"The coachman says that he has come for Monsieur le Maire."

"What coachman?"

"M. Scaufflaire's coachman."

"M. Scaufflaire?"

That name sent a shudder over him, as though a flash of lightning had passed in front of his face.

"Ah! yes," he resumed; "M. Scaufflaire!"

If the old woman could have seen him at that moment, she would have been frightened.

A tolerably long silence ensued. He examined the flame of the candle with a stupid air, and from around the wick he took some of the burning wax, which he rolled between his fingers. The old woman waited for him. She even ventured to uplift her voice once more:

"What am I to say, Monsieur le Maire?"

"Say that it is well, and that I am coming down."

Chapter V

HINDRANCES

THE POSTING SERVICE FROM ARRAS TO M. SUR M. WAS STILL OPERATED AT THIS PERIOD BY SMALL mail-wagons of the time of the Empire. These mail-wagons were two-wheeled cabriolets, upholstered inside with fawn-colored leather, hung on springs, and having but two seats, one for the postboy, the other for the traveler. The wheels were armed with those long, offensive axles which keep other vehicles at a distance, and which may still be seen on the road in Germany. The dispatch box, an immense oblong coffer, was placed behind the vehicle and formed a part of it. This coffer was painted black, and the cabriolet yellow.

These vehicles, which have no counterparts nowadays, had something distorted and hunchbacked about them; and when one saw them passing in the distance, and climbing up some road to the horizon, they resembled the insects which are called, I think, termites, and which, though with but little corselet, drag a great train behind them. But they traveled at a very rapid rate. The postwagon which set out from Arras at one o'clock every night, after the mail from Paris had passed, arrived at M. sur M. a little before five o'clock in the morning.

That night the wagon which was descending to M. sur M. by the Hesdin road, collided at the corner of a street, just as it was entering the town, with a little tilbury harnessed to a white horse, which was going in the opposite direction, and in which there was but one person, a man enveloped in a mantle. The wheel of the tilbury received quite a violent shock. The postman shouted to the man to stop, but the traveler paid no heed and pursued his road at full gallop.

"That man is in a devilish hurry!" said the postman.

The man thus hastening on was the one whom we have just seen struggling in convulsions which are certainly deserving of pity.

Whither was he going? He could not have told. Why was he hastening? He did not know. He was driving at random, straight ahead. Whither? To Arras, no doubt; but he might have been going elsewhere as well. At times he was conscious of it, and he shuddered. He plunged into the night as into a gulf. Something urged him forward; something drew him on. No one could have told what was taking place within him; everyone will understand it. What man is there who has not entered, at least once in his life, into that obscure cavern of the unknown?

However, he had resolved on nothing, decided nothing, formed no plan, done nothing. None of the actions of his conscience had been decisive. He was, more than ever, as he had been at the first moment.

Why was he going to Arras?

He repeated what he had already said to himself when he had hired Scaufflaire's cabriolet: that, whatever the result was to be, there was no reason why he should not see with his own eyes, and judge of matters for himself; that this was even prudent; that he must know what took place; that no decision could be arrived at without having observed and scrutinized; that one made mountains out of everything from a distance; that, at any rate, when he should have seen that Champmathieu, some wretch, his conscience would probably be greatly relieved to allow him to go to the galleys in his stead; that Javert would indeed be there; and that Brevet, that Chenildieu, that Cochepaille, old convicts who had known him; but they certainly would not recognize him;—bah! what an idea! that Javert was a hundred leagues from suspecting the truth; that all conjectures and all suppositions were fixed on Champmathieu, and that there is nothing so headstrong as suppositions and conjectures; that accordingly there was no danger.

That it was, no doubt, a dark moment, but that he should emerge from it; that, after all, he held his destiny, however bad it might be, in his own hand; that he was master of it. He clung to this thought.

At bottom, to tell the whole truth, he would have preferred not to go to Arras.

Nevertheless, he was going thither.

As he meditated, he whipped up his horse, which was proceeding at that fine, regular, and even trot which accomplishes two leagues and a half an hour.

In proportion as the cabriolet advanced, he felt something within him draw back.

At daybreak he was in the open country; the town of M. sur M. lay far behind him. He watched the horizon grow white; he stared at all the chilly figures of a winter's dawn as they passed before his eyes, but without seeing them. The morning has its specters as well as the evening. He did not see them; but without his being aware of it, and by means of a sort of penetration which was almost physical, these black silhouettes of trees and of hills added some gloomy and sinister quality to the violent state of his soul.

Each time that he passed one of those isolated dwellings which sometimes border on the highway, he said to himself, "And yet there are people there within who are sleeping!"

The trot of the horse, the bells on the harness, the wheels on the road, produced a gentle, monotonous noise. These things are charming when one is joyous, and lugubrious when one is sad.

It was broad daylight when he arrived at Hesdin. He halted in front of the inn, to allow the horse a breathing spell, and to have him given some oats.

The horse belonged, as Scaufflaire had said, to that small race of the Boulonnais, which has too much head, too much belly, and not enough neck and shoulders, but which has a broad chest, a large crupper, thin, fine legs, and solid hoofs—a homely, but a robust and healthy race. The excellent beast had traveled five leagues in two hours, and had not a drop of sweat on his loins.

He did not get out of the tilbury. The stableman who brought the oats suddenly bent down and examined the left wheel.

"Are you going far in this condition?" said the man.

He replied, with an air of not having roused himself from his reverie:

"Why?"

"Have you come from a great distance?" went on the man.

"Five leagues."

"Ah!"

"Why do you say, 'Ah'?"

The man bent down once more, was silent for a moment, with his eyes fixed on the wheel; then he rose erect and said:

"Because, though this wheel has traveled five leagues, it certainly will not travel another quarter of a league."

He sprang out of the tilbury.

"What is that you say, my friend?"

"I say that it is a miracle that you should have traveled five leagues without you and your horse rolling into some ditch on the highway. Just see here!"

The wheel really had suffered serious damage. The shock administered by the mail-wagon had split two spokes and strained the hub, so that the nut no longer held firm.

"My friend," he said to the stableman, "is there a wheelwright here?"

"Certainly, sir."

"Do me the service to go and fetch him."

"He is only a step from here. Hey! Master Bourgaillard!"

Master Bourgaillard, the wheelwright, was standing on his own threshold. He came, examined the wheel, and made a grimace like a surgeon when the latter thinks a limb is broken.

"Can you repair this wheel immediately?"

"Yes, sir."

"When can I set out again?"

"To-morrow."

"To-morrow!"

"There is a long day's work on it. Are you in a hurry, sir?"

"In a very great hurry. I must set out again in an hour at the latest."

"Impossible, sir."

"I will pay whatever you ask."

"Impossible."

"Well, in two hours, then."

"Impossible to-day. Two new spokes and a hub must be made. Monsieur will not be able to start before to-morrow morning."

"The matter cannot wait until to-morrow. What if you were to replace this wheel instead of repairing it?"

"How so?"

"You are a wheelwright?"

"Certainly, sir."

"Have you not a wheel that you can sell me? Then I could start again at once."

"A spare wheel?"

"Yes."

"I have no wheel on hand that would fit your cabriolet. Two wheels make a pair. Two wheels cannot be put together haphazard."

"In that case, sell me a pair of wheels."

"Not all wheels fit all axles, sir."

"Try, nevertheless."

"It is useless, sir. I have nothing to sell but cart-wheels. We are but a poor country here."

"Have you a cabriolet that you can let me have?"

The wheelwright had seen at the first glance that the tilbury was a hired vehicle. He shrugged his shoulders.

"You treat the cabriolets that people let you so well! If I had one, I would not let it to you!"

"Well, sell it to me, then."

"I have none."

"What! not even a spring-cart? I am not hard to please, as you see."

"We live in a poor country. There is, in truth," added the wheelwright, "an old calash under the shed yonder, which belongs to a bourgeois of the town, who gave it to me to take care of, and who only uses it on the thirty-sixth of the month—never, that is to say. I might let that to you, for what matters it to me? But the bourgeois must not see it pass—and then, it is a calash; it would require two horses."

"I will take two post-horses."

"Where is Monsieur going?"

"To Arras."

"And Monsieur wishes to reach there to-day?"

"Yes, of course."

"By taking two post-horses?"

"Why not?"

"Does it make any difference whether Monsieur arrives at four o'clock to-morrow morning?"

"Certainly not."

"There is one thing to be said about that, you see, by taking post-horses—Monsieur has his passport?"

"Yes."

"Well, by taking post-horses, Monsieur cannot reach Arras before to-morrow. We are on a cross-road. The relays are badly served, the horses are in the fields. The season for plowing is just beginning; heavy teams are required, and horses are seized upon everywhere, from the post as well as elsewhere. Monsieur will have to wait three or four hours at the least at every relay. And, then, they drive at a walk. There are many hills to ascend."

"Come then, I will go on horseback. Unharness the cabriolet. Someone can surely sell me a saddle in the neighborhood."

"Without doubt. But will this horse bear the saddle?"

"That is true; you remind me of that; he will not bear it."

"Then—"

"But I can surely hire a horse in the village?"

"A horse to travel to Arras at one stretch?"

"Yes."

"That would require such a horse as does not exist in these parts. You would have to buy it to begin with, because no one knows you. But you will not find one for sale nor to let, for five hundred francs, or for a thousand."

"What am I to do?"

"The best thing is to let me repair the wheel like an honest man, and set out on your journey to-morrow."

"To-morrow will be too late."

"The deuce!"

"Is there not a mail-wagon which runs to Arras? When will it pass?"

"To-night. Both the posts pass at night; the one going as well as the one coming."

"What! It will take you a day to mend this wheel?"

"A day, and a good long one."

"If you set two men to work?"

"If I set ten men to work."

"What if the spokes were to be tied together with ropes?"

"That could be done with the spokes, not with the hub; and the felly is in a bad state, too."

"Is there anyone in this village who lets out teams?"

"No."

"Is there another wheelwright?"

The stableman and the wheelwright replied in concert, with a toss of the head:

"No."

He felt an immense joy.

It was evident that Providence was intervening. That it was it who had broken the wheel of the tilbury and who was stopping him on the road. He had not yielded to this sort of first summons; he had just made every possible effort to continue the journey; he had loyally and scrupulously exhausted all means; he had been deterred neither by the season, nor fatigue, nor by the expense; he had nothing with which to reproach himself. If he went no further, that was no fault of his. It did not concern him further. It was no longer his fault. It was not the act of his own conscience, but the act of Providence.

He breathed again. He breathed freely and to the full extent of his lungs for the first time since Javert's visit. It seemed to him that the hand of iron which had held his heart in its grasp for the last twenty hours had just released him.

It seemed to him that God was for him now, and was manifesting Himself.

He said himself that he had done all he could, and that now he had nothing to do but retrace his steps quietly.

If his conversation with the wheelwright had taken place in a chamber of the inn, it would have had no witnesses, no one would have heard him, things would have rested there, and it is probable that we should not have had to relate any of the occurrences which the reader is about to peruse; but this conversation had taken place in the street. Any colloquy in the street inevitably attracts a crowd. There are always people who ask nothing better than to become spectators. While he was questioning the wheelwright, some people who were passing back and forth halted around them. After listening for a few minutes, a young lad, to whom no one had paid any heed, detached himself from the group and ran off.

At the moment when the traveler, after the inward deliberation which we have just described, resolved to retrace his steps, this child returned. He was accompanied by an old woman.

"Monsieur," said the woman, "my boy tells me that you wish to hire a cabriolet."

These simple words uttered by an old woman led by a child made the perspiration trickle down his limbs. He thought that he beheld the hand which had relaxed its grasp reappear in the darkness behind him, ready to seize him once more.

He answered:

"Yes, my good woman; I am in search of a cabriolet which I can hire."

And he hastened to add:

"But there is none in the place."

"Certainly there is," said the old woman.

"Where?" interpolated the wheelwright.

"At my house," replied the old woman.

He shuddered. The fatal hand had grasped him again.

The old woman really had in her shed a sort of basket spring-cart. The wheelwright and the stable-man, in despair at the prospect of the traveler escaping their clutches, interfered.

"It was a frightful old trap; it rests flat on the axle; it is an actual fact that the seats were suspended inside it by leather thongs; the rain came into it; the wheels were rusted and eaten with moisture; it would not go much further than the tilbury; a regular ramshackle old stage-wagon; the gentleman would make a great mistake if he trusted himself to it," etc., etc.

All this was true; but this trap, this ramshackle old vehicle, this thing, whatever it was, ran on its two wheels and could go to Arras.

He paid what was asked, left the tilbury with the wheelwright to be repaired, intending to re-claim it on his return, had the white horse put to the cart, climbed into it, and resumed the road which he had been traveling since morning.

At the moment when the cart moved off, he admitted that he had felt, a moment previously, a certain joy in the thought that he should not go whither he was now proceeding. He examined this joy with a sort of wrath, and found it absurd. Why should he feel joy at turning back? After all, he was taking this trip of his own free will. No one was forcing him to it.

And assuredly nothing would happen except what he should choose.

As he left Hesdin, he heard a voice shouting to him: "Stop! Stop!" He halted the cart with a vigorous movement which contained a feverish and convulsive element resembling hope.

It was the old woman's little boy.

"Monsieur," said the latter, "it was I who got the cart for you."

"Well?"

"You have not given me anything."

He who gave to all so readily thought this demand exorbitant and almost odious.

"Ah! it's you, you scamp?" said he; "you shall have nothing."

He whipped up his horse and set off at full speed.

He had lost a great deal of time at Hesdin. He wanted to make it good. The little horse was courageous, and pulled for two; but it was the month of February, there had been rain; the roads were bad. And then, it was no longer the tilbury. The cart was very heavy, and in addition, there were many ascents.

He took nearly four hours to go from Hesdin to Saint-Pol, four hours for five leagues.

At Saint-Pol he had the horse unharnessed at the first inn he came to and led to the stable; as he had promised ScAufflaire, he stood beside the manger while the horse was eating; he thought of sad and confusing things.

The inn-keeper's wife came to the stable.

"Does not Monsieur wish to breakfast?"

"Come, that is true; I even have a good appetite."

He followed the woman, who had a rosy, cheerful face; she led him to the public-room where there were tables covered with waxed cloth.

"Make haste!" said he; "I must start again; I am in a hurry."

A big Flemish servant-maid placed his knife and fork in all haste; he looked at the girl with a sensation of comfort.

"That is what ailed me," he thought; "I had not breakfasted."

His breakfast was served; he seized the bread, took a mouthful, and then slowly replaced it on the table, and did not touch it again.

A carter was eating at another table; he said to this man:

"Why is their bread so bitter here?"

The carter was a German and did not understand him.

He returned to the stable and remained near the horse.

An hour later he had quitted Saint-Pol and was directing his course toward Tinques, which is only five leagues from Arras.

What did he do during this journey? Of what was he thinking? As in the morning, he watched the trees, the thatched roofs, the tilled fields pass by, and the way in which the landscape, broken at every turn of the road, vanished; this is a sort of contemplation which sometimes suffices to the soul, and almost relieves it from thought. What is more melancholy and more profound than to see a thousand objects for the first and the last time? To travel is to be born and to die at every instant; perhaps, in the vaguest region of his mind, he did make comparisons between the shifting horizon and our human existence: all the things of life are perpetually fleeing before us; the dark and bright intervals are intermingled; after a dazzling moment, an eclipse; we look, we hasten, we stretch out our hands to grasp what is passing; each event is a turn in the road, and, all at once, we are old; we feel a shock; all is black; we distinguish an obscure door; the gloomy horse of life, which has been drawing us halts, and we see a veiled and unknown person unharnessing amid the shadows.

Twilight was falling when the children who were coming out of school beheld this traveler enter Tinques; it is true that the days were still short; he did not halt at Tinques; as he emerged from the village, a laborer, who was mending the road with stones, raised his head and said to him:

"That horse is very much fatigued."

The poor beast was, in fact, going at a walk.

"Are you going to Arras?" added the road-mender.

"Yes."

"If you go on at that rate, you will not arrive very early."

He stopped his horse, and asked the laborer:

"How far is it from here to Arras?"

"Nearly seven good leagues."

"How is that? the posting guide only says five leagues and a quarter."

"Ah!" returned the road-mender, "so you don't know that the road is under repair? You will find it barred a quarter of an hour further on; there is no way to proceed further."

"Really?"

"You will take the road on the left, leading to Carency; you will cross the river; when you reach Camblin, you will turn to the right; that is the road to Mont-Saint-Éloy which leads to Arras."

"But it is night, and I shall lose my way."

"You do not belong in these parts?"

"No."

"And, besides, it is all cross-roads; stop! sir," resumed the road-mender; "shall I give you a piece of advice? your horse is tired; return to Tinques; there is a good inn there; sleep there; you can reach Arras to-morrow."

"I must be there this evening."

"That is different; but go to the inn all the same, and get an extra horse; the stable-boy will guide you through the cross-roads."

He followed the road-mender's advice, retraced his steps, and, half an hour later, he passed the same spot again, but this time at full speed, with a good horse to aid; a stable-boy, who called himself a postilion, was seated on the shaft of the cariole.

Still, he felt that he had lost time.

Night had fully come.

They turned into the cross-road; the way became frightfully bad; the cart lurched from one rut to the other; he said to the postilion:

"Keep at a trot, and you shall have a double fee."

In one of the jolts, the whiffle-tree broke.

"There's the whiffle-tree broken, sir," said the postilion; "I don't know how to harness my horse now; this road is very bad at night; if you wish to return and sleep at Tinques, we could be in Arras early to-morrow morning."

He replied, "Have you a bit of rope and a knife?"

"Yes, sir."

He cut a branch from a tree and made a whiffle-tree of it.

This caused another loss of twenty minutes; but they set out again at a gallop.

The plain was gloomy; low-hanging, black, crisp fogs crept over the hills and wrenched themselves away like smoke: there were whitish gleams in the clouds; a strong breeze which blew in from the sea produced a sound in all quarters of the horizon, as of someone moving furniture; everything that could be seen assumed attitudes of terror. How many things shiver beneath these vast breaths of the night!

He was stiff with cold; he had eaten nothing since the night before; he vaguely recalled his other nocturnal trip in the vast plain in the neighborhood of D——, eight years previously, and it seemed but yesterday.

The hour struck from a distant tower; he asked the boy:

"What time is it?"

"Seven o'clock, sir; we shall reach Arras at eight; we have but three leagues still to go."

At that moment, he for the first time indulged in this reflection, thinking it odd the while that it had not occurred to him sooner: that all this trouble which he was taking was, perhaps, useless; that he did not know so much as the hour of the trial; that he should, at least, have informed himself of that; that he was foolish to go thus straight ahead without knowing whether he would be of any service or not; then he sketched out some calculations in his mind: that, ordinarily, the sittings of the Court of Assizes began at nine o'clock in the morning; that it could not be a long affair; that the theft of the apples would be very brief; that there would then remain only a question of identity, four or five depositions, and very little for the lawyers to say; that he should arrive after all was over.

The postilion whipped up the horses; they had crossed the river and left Mont-Saint-Éloy behind them.

The night grew more profound.

Chapter VI

SISTER SIMPLICE PUT TO THE PROOF

BUT AT THAT MOMENT FANTINE WAS JOYOUS.

She had passed a very bad night; her cough was frightful; her fever had doubled in intensity; she had had dreams: in the morning, when the doctor paid his visit, she was delirious; he assumed an alarmed look, and ordered that he should be informed as soon as M. Madeleine arrived.

All the morning she was melancholy, said but little, and laid plaits in her sheets, murmuring the while, in a low voice, calculations which seemed to be calculations of distances. Her eyes were hollow and staring. They seemed almost extinguished at intervals, then lighted up again and shone like stars. It seems as though, at the approach of a certain dark hour, the light of heaven fills those who are quitting the light of earth.

Each time that Sister Simplice asked her how she felt, she replied invariably, "Well. I should like to see M. Madeleine."

Some months before this, at the moment when Fantine had just lost her last modesty, her last shame, and her last joy, she was the shadow of herself; now she was the specter of herself. Physical suffering had completed the work of moral suffering. This creature of five-and-twenty had a wrinkled brow, flabby cheeks, pinched nostrils, teeth from which the gums had receded, a leaden complexion, a bony neck, prominent shoulder-blades, frail limbs, a clayey skin, and her golden hair was growing out sprinkled with gray. Alas! how illness improvises old age!

At midday the physician returned, gave some directions, inquired whether the mayor had made his appearance at the infirmary, and shook his head.

M. Madeleine usually came to see the invalid at three o'clock. As exactness is kindness, he was exact.

About half-past two, Fantine began to be restless. In the course of twenty minutes, she asked the nun more than ten times, "What time is it, sister?"

Three o'clock struck. At the third stroke, Fantine sat up in bed; she who could, in general, hardly turn over, joined her yellow, fleshless hands in a sort of convulsive clasp, and the nun heard her utter one of those profound sighs which seem to throw off dejection. Then Fantine turned and looked at the door.

No one entered; the door did not open.

She remained thus for a quarter of an hour, her eyes riveted on the door, motionless and apparently holding her breath. The sister dared not speak to her. The clock struck a quarter past three. Fantine fell back on her pillow.

She said nothing, but began to plait the sheets once more.

Half an hour passed, then an hour, no one came; every time the clock struck, Fantine started up and looked toward the door, then fell back again.

Her thought was clearly perceptible, but she uttered no name, she made no complaint, she blamed no one. But she coughed in a melancholy way. One would have said that something dark was descending upon her. She was livid and her lips were blue. She smiled now and then.

Five o'clock struck. Then the sister heard her say, very low and gently, "He is wrong not to come to-day, since I am going away to-morrow."

Sister Simplice herself was surprised at M. Madeleine's delay.

In the meantime, Fantine was staring at the tester of her bed. She seemed to be endeavoring to recall something. All at once she began to sing in a voice as feeble as a breath. The nun listened. This is what Fantine was singing:

> *"Lovely things we will buy*
> *As we stroll the faubourgs through.*
> *Roses are pink, corn-flowers are blue,*
> *I love my love, corn-flowers are blue.*

"Yestere'en the Virgin Mary came near my stove, in a broidered mantle clad, and said to me, 'Here, hide 'neath my veil the child whom you one day begged from me. Haste to the city, buy linen, buy a needle, buy thread.'

> *"Lovely things we will buy*
> *As we stroll the faubourgs through.*

"Dear Holy Virgin, beside my stove I have set a cradle with ribbons decked. God may give me his loveliest star; I prefer the child thou hast granted me. 'Madame, what shall I do with this linen fine?'—'Make of it clothes for thy newborn babe.'

> *"Roses are pink and corn-flowers are blue,*
> *I love my love, and corn-flowers are blue.*

" 'Wash this linen.'—'Where?'—'In the stream. Make of it, soiling not, spoiling not, a petticoat fair with its bodice fine, which I will embroider and fill with flowers.'—'Madame, the child is no longer here; what is to be done?'—'Then make of it a winding-sheet in which to bury me.'

> *"Lovely things we will buy*
> *As we stroll the faubourgs through,*
> *Roses are pink, corn-flowers are blue,*
> *I love my love, corn-flowers are blue."*

This song was an old cradle romance with which she had, in former days, lulled her little Cosette to sleep, and which had never recurred to her mind in all the five years during which she had been parted from her child. She sang it in so sad a voice, and to so sweet an air, that it was enough to make anyone, even a nun, weep. The sister, accustomed as she was to austerities, felt a tear spring to her eyes.

The clock struck six. Fantine did not seem to hear it. She no longer seemed to pay attention to anything about her.

Sister Simplice sent a serving-maid to inquire of the portress of the factory, whether the mayor had returned, and if he would not come to the infirmary soon. The girl returned in a few minutes.

Fantine was still motionless and seemed absorbed in her own thoughts.

The servant informed Sister Simplice in a very low tone, that the mayor had set out that morning before six o'clock, in a little tilbury harnessed to a white horse, cold as the weather was; that he had gone alone, without even a driver; that no one knew what road he had taken; that people said he had been seen to turn into the road to Arras; that others asserted that they had met him on the road to Paris. That when he went away he had been very gentle, as usual, and that he had merely told the portress not to expect him that night.

While the two women were whispering together, with their backs turned to Fantine's bed, the sister interrogating, the servant conjecturing, Fantine, with the feverish vivacity of certain organic maladies, which unite the free movements of health with the frightful emaciation of death, had raised herself to her knees in bed, with her shriveled hands resting on the bolster, and her head thrust through the opening of the curtains, and was listening. All at once she cried:

"You are speaking of M. Madeleine! Why are you talking so low? What is he doing? Why does he not come?"

Her voice was so abrupt and hoarse that the two women thought they heard the voice of a man; they wheeled round in affright.

"Answer me!" cried Fantine.

The servant stammered:

"The portress told me that he could not come to-day."

"Be calm, my child," said the sister; "lie down again."

Fantine, without changing her attitude, continued in a loud voice, and with an accent that was both imperious and heartrending:

"He cannot come? Why not? You know the reason. You are whispering it to each other there. I want to know it."

The servant-maid hastened to say in the nun's ear, "Say that he is busy with the city council."

Sister Simplice blushed faintly, for it was a lie that the maid had proposed to her.

On the other hand, it seemed to her that the mere communication of the truth to the invalid would, without doubt, deal her a terrible blow, and that this was a serious matter in Fantine's present state. Her flush did not last long; the sister raised her calm, sad eyes to Fantine, and said, "Monsieur le Maire has gone away."

Fantine raised herself and crouched on her heels in the bed; her eyes sparkled; indescribable joy beamed from that melancholy face.

"Gone!" she cried; "he has gone to get Cosette."

Then she raised her arms to heaven, and her white face became ineffable; her lips moved; she was praying in a low voice.

When her prayer was finished, "Sister," she said, "I am willing to lie down again; I will do anything you wish; I was naughty just now; I beg your pardon for having spoken so loud; it is very wrong to talk loudly; I know that well, my good sister, but, you see, I am very happy: the good God is good; M. Madeleine is good; just think! he has gone to Montfermeil to get my little Cosette."

She lay down again, with the nun's assistance, helped the nun to arrange her pillow, and kissed the little silver cross which she wore on her neck, and which Sister Simplice had given her.

"My child," said the sister, "try to rest now, and do not talk anymore."

Fantine took the sister's hand in her moist hands, and the latter was pained to feel that perspiration.

"He set out this morning for Paris; in fact, he need not even go through Paris; Montfermeil is a little to the left as you come thence. Do you remember how he said to me yesterday, when I spoke to him of Cosette, *Soon, soon?* He wants to give me a surprise, you know! he made me sign a letter so that she could be taken from the Thénardiers; they cannot say anything, can they? they will give back Cosette, for they have been paid; the authorities will not allow them to keep the child since they have received their pay. Do not make signs to me that I must not talk, sister! I am extremely happy; I am doing well; I am not ill at all anymore; I am going to see Cosette again; I am even quite hungry; it is nearly five years since I saw her last; you cannot imagine how much attached one gets to children, and then, she will be so pretty; you will see! If you only knew what pretty little rosy fingers she had! In the first place, she will have very beautiful hands; she had ridiculous hands when she was only a year old; like this! she must be a big girl now; she is seven years old; she is quite a young lady; I call her Cosette, but her name is really Euphrasie. Stop! this morning I was looking at the dust on the chimney-piece, and I had a sort of idea come across me, like that, that I should see Cosette again soon. Mon Dieu! how wrong it is not to see one's children for years! One ought to reflect that life is not eternal. Oh, how good M. le Maire is to go! it is very cold! it is true; he had on his cloak, at least? he will be here to-morrow, will he not? to-morrow will be a festival day; to-morrow morning, sister, you must remind me to put on my little cap that has lace on it. What a place that Montfermeil is! I took that journey on foot once; it was very long for me, but the diligences go very quickly! he will be here to-morrow with Cosette: how far is it from here to Montfermeil?"

The sister, who had no idea of distances, replied, "Oh, I think that he will be here to-morrow."

"To-morrow! to-morrow!" said Fantine, "I shall see Cosette to-morrow! you see, good sister of the good God, that I am no longer ill; I am mad; I could dance if anyone wished it."

A person who had seen her a quarter of an hour previously would not have understood the change; she was all rosy now; she spoke in a lively and natural voice; her whole face was one smile; now and then she talked, she laughed softly; the joy of a mother is almost infantile.

"Well," resumed the nun, "now that you are happy, mind me, and do not talk anymore."

Fantine laid her head on her pillow and said in a low voice: "Yes, lie down again; be good, for you are going to have your child; Sister Simplice is right; everyone here is right."

And then, without stirring, without even moving her head, she began to stare all about her with wide-open eyes and a joyous air, and she said nothing more.

The sister drew the curtains together again, hoping that she would fall into a doze. Between seven and eight o'clock the doctor came; not hearing any sound, he thought Fantine was asleep, entered softly, and approached the bed on tiptoe; he opened the curtains a little, and, by the light of the taper, he saw Fantine's big eyes gazing at him.

She said to him, "She will be allowed to sleep beside me in a little bed, will she not, sir?"

The doctor thought that she was delirious. She added:

"See! there is just room."

The doctor took Sister Simplice aside, and she explained matters to him; that M. Madeleine was absent for a day or two, and that in their doubt they had not thought it well to undeceive the invalid, who believed that the mayor had gone to Montfermeil; that it was possible, after all, that her guess was correct: the doctor approved.

He returned to Fantine's bed, and she went on:

"You see, when she wakes up in the morning, I shall be able to say good morning to her, poor kitten, and when I cannot sleep at night, I can hear her asleep; her little gentle breathing will do me good."

"Give me your hand," said the doctor.

She stretched out her arm, and exclaimed with a laugh:

"Ah, hold! in truth, you did not know it; I am cured; Cosette will arrive to-morrow."

The doctor was surprised; she was better; the pressure on her chest had decreased; her pulse had regained its strength; a sort of life had suddenly supervened and reanimated this poor, worn-out creature.

"Doctor," she went on, "did the sister tell you that M. le Maire has gone to get that mite of a child?"

The doctor recommended silence, and that all painful emotions should be avoided; he prescribed an infusion of pure chinchona, and, in case the fever should increase again during the night, a calming potion. As he took his departure, he said to the sister:

"She is doing better; if good luck willed that the mayor should actually arrive to-morrow with the child, who knows? there are crises so astounding; great joy has been known to arrest maladies; I know well that this is an organic disease, and in an advanced state, but all those things are such mysteries: we may be able to save her."

Chapter VII

THE TRAVELER ON HIS ARRIVAL TAKES PRECAUTIONS FOR DEPARTURE

IT WAS NEARLY EIGHT O'CLOCK IN THE EVENING WHEN THE CART, WHICH WE LEFT ON THE ROAD, entered the porte-cochère of the Hôtel de la Poste in Arras; the man whom we have been following up to this moment alighted from it, responded with an abstracted air to the attentions of the people of the inn, sent back the extra horse, and with his own hands led the little white horse to the stable; then he opened the door of a billiard-room which was situated on the ground floor, sat down there, and leaned his elbows on a table; he had taken fourteen hours for the journey which he had counted on making in six; he did himself the justice to acknowledge that it was not his fault, but at bottom, he was not sorry.

The landlady of the hôtel entered.

"Does Monsieur wish a bed? Does Monsieur require supper?"

He made a sign of the head in the negative.

"The stableman says that Monsieur's horse is extremely fatigued."

Here he broke his silence.

"Will not the horse be in a condition to set out again to-morrow morning?"

"Oh, Monsieur! he must rest for two days at least."

He inquired:

"Is not the posting-station located here?"

"Yes, sir."

The hostess conducted him to the office; he showed his passport, and inquired whether there was any way of returning that same night to M. sur M. by the mail-wagon; the seat beside the post-boy chanced to be vacant; he engaged it and paid for it. "Monsieur," said the clerk, "do not fail to be here ready to start at precisely one o'clock in the morning."

This done, he left the hôtel and began to wander about the town.

He was not acquainted with Arras; the streets were dark, and he walked on at random; but he seemed bent upon not asking the way of the passers-by. He crossed the little river Crinchon, and found himself in a labyrinth of narrow alleys where he lost his way. A citizen was passing along with a lantern. After some hesitation, he decided to apply to this man, not without having first glanced behind and in front of him, as though he feared lest someone should hear the question which he was about to put.

"Monsieur," said he, "where is the court-house, if you please."

"You do not belong in town, sir?" replied the bourgeois, who was an oldish man; "well, follow me. I happen to be going in the direction of the court-house, that is to say, in the direction of the hôtel of the prefecture; for the court-house is undergoing repairs just at this moment, and the courts are holding their sittings provisionally in the prefecture."

"Is it there that the Assizes are held?" he asked.

"Certainly, sir; you see, the prefecture of to-day was the bishop's palace before the Revolution. M. de Conzié, who was bishop in '82, built a grand hall there. It is in this grand hall that the court is held."

On the way, the bourgeois said to him:

"If Monsieur desires to witness a case, it is rather late. The sittings generally close at six o'clock."

When they arrived on the grand square, however, the man pointed out to him four long windows all lighted up, in the front of a vast and gloomy building.

"Upon my word, sir, you are in luck; you have arrived in season. Do you see those four windows? That is the Court of Assizes. There is light there, so they are not through. The matter must have been greatly protracted, and they are holding an evening session. Do you take an interest in this affair? Is it a criminal case? Are you a witness?"

He replied:

"I have not come on any business; I only wish to speak to one of the lawyers."

"That is different," said the bourgeois. "Stop, sir; here is the door where the sentry stands. You have only to ascend the grand staircase."

He conformed to the bourgeois's directions, and a few minutes later he was in a hall containing many people, and where groups, intermingled with lawyers in their gowns, were whispering together here and there.

It is always a heart-breaking thing to see these congregations of men robed in black, murmuring together in low voices, on the threshold of the halls of justice. It is rare that charity and pity are the outcome of these words. Condemnations pronounced in advance are more likely to be the result. All these groups seem to the passing and thoughtful observer so many somber hives where buzzing spirits construct in concert all sorts of dark edifices.

This spacious hall, illuminated by a single lamp, was the old hall of the episcopal palace, and served as the large hall of the palace of justice. A double-leaved door, which was closed at that moment, separated it from the large apartment where the court was sitting.

The obscurity was such that he did not fear to accost the first lawyer whom he met.

"What stage have they reached, sir?" he asked.

"It is finished," said the lawyer.

"Finished!"

This word was repeated in such accents that the lawyer turned round.

"Excuse me sir; perhaps you are a relative?"

"No; I know no one here. Has judgment been pronounced?"

"Of course. Nothing else was possible."

"To penal servitude?"

"For life."

He continued, in a voice so weak that it was barely audible:

"Then his identity was established?"

"What identity?" replied the lawyer. "There was no identity to be established. The matter was very simple. The woman had murdered her child; the infanticide was proved; the jury threw out the question of premeditation, and she was condemned for life."

"So it was a woman?" said he.

"Why, certainly. The Limosin woman. Of what are you speaking?"

"Nothing. But since it is all over, how comes it that the hall is still lighted?"

"For another case, which was begun about two hours ago."

"What other case?"

"Oh! this one is a clear case also. It is about a sort of blackguard; a man arrested for a second offense; a convict who has been guilty of theft. I don't know his name exactly. There's a bandit's phiz for you! I'd send him to the galleys on the strength of his face alone."

"Is there any way of getting into the court-room, sir?" said he.

"I really think that there is not. There is a great crowd. However, the hearing has been suspended. Some people have gone out, and when the hearing is resumed, you might make an effort."

"Where is the entrance?"

"Through yonder large door."

The lawyer left him. In the course of a few moments he had experienced, almost simultaneously, almost intermingled with each other, all possible emotions. The words of this indifferent spectator had, in turn, pierced his heart like needles of ice and like blades of fire. When he saw that nothing was settled, he breathed freely once more; but he could not have told whether what he felt was pain or pleasure.

He drew near to many groups and listened to what they were saying. The docket of the session was very heavy; the president had appointed for the same day two short and simple cases. They had begun with the infanticide, and now they had reached the convict, the old offender, the "return horse." This man had stolen apples, but that did not appear to be entirely proved; what had been proved was, that he had already been in the galleys at Toulon. It was that which lent a bad aspect to his case. However, the man's examination and the depositions of the witnesses had been completed, but the lawyer's plea, and the speech of the public prosecutor were still to come; it could not be finished before midnight. The man would probably be condemned; the attorney-general was very clever, and never *missed* his culprits; he was a brilliant fellow who wrote verses.

An usher stood at the door communicating with the hall of the Assizes. He inquired of this usher:

"Will the door be opened soon, sir?"

"It will not be opened at all," replied the usher.

"What! It will not be opened when the hearing is resumed? Is not the hearing suspended?"

"The hearing has just been begun again," replied the usher, "but the door will not be opened again."

"Why?"

"Because the hall is full."

"What! There is not room for one more?"

"Not another one. The door is closed. No one can enter now."

The usher added after a pause: "There are, to tell the truth, two or three extra places behind Monsieur le Président, but Monsieur le Président only admits public functionaries to them."

So saying, the usher turned his back.

He retired with bowed head, traversed the antechamber, and slowly descended the stairs, as though hesitating at every step. It is probable that he was holding counsel with himself. The violent conflict which had been going on within him since the preceding evening was not yet ended; and every moment he encountered some new phase of it. On reaching the landing-place, he leaned his back against the balusters and folded his arms. All at once he opened his coat, drew out his pocket-book, took from it a pencil, tore out a leaf, and upon that leaf he wrote rapidly, by the light of the street-lantern this line: *M. Madeleine, Mayor of M. sur M.*; then he ascended the stairs once more with great strides, made his way through the crowd, walked straight up to the usher, handed him the paper, and said in an authoritative manner:

"Take this to Monsieur le Président."

The usher took the paper, cast a glance upon it, and obeyed.

Chapter VIII

AN ENTRANCE BY FAVOR

ALTHOUGH HE DID NOT SUSPECT THE FACT, THE MAYOR OF M. SUR M. ENJOYED A SORT OF celebrity. For the space of seven years his reputation for virtue had filled the whole of Bas Boulonnais; it had eventually passed the confines of a small district and had been spread abroad through two or three neighboring departments. Besides the service which he had rendered to the chief town by resuscitating the black jet industry, there was not one out of the hundred and forty communes of the arrondissement of M. sur M. which was not indebted to him for some benefit. He had even at need contrived to aid and multiply the industries of other arrondissements. It was thus that he had, when occasion offered, supported with his credit and his funds the linen factory at Boulogne, the flax-spinning industry at Frévent, and the hydraulic manufacture of cloth at Boubers-sur-Canche. Everywhere the name of M. Madeleine was pronounced with veneration. Arras and Douai envied the happy little town of M. sur M. its mayor.

The Councilor of the Royal Court of Douai, who was presiding over this session of the Assizes at Arras, was acquainted, in common with the rest of the world, with this name which was so profoundly and universally honored. When the usher, discreetly opening the door which connected the council-chamber with the court-room, bent over the back of the President's arm-chair and handed him the paper on which was inscribed the line which we have just perused, adding: *"The gentleman desires to be present at the trial,"* the President, with a quick and deferential movement, seized a pen and wrote a few words at the bottom of the paper and returned it to the usher, saying, "Admit him."

The unhappy man whose history we are relating had remained near the door of the hall, in the same place and the same attitude in which the usher had left him. In the midst of his reverie he heard someone saying to him, "Will Monsieur do me the honor to follow me?" It was the same usher who had turned his back upon him but a moment previously, and who was now bowing to the earth before him. At the same time, the usher handed him the paper. He unfolded it, and as he chanced to be near the light, he could read it.

"The President of the Court of Assizes presents his respects to M. Madeleine."

He crushed the paper in his hand as though those words contained for him a strange and bitter aftertaste.

He followed the usher.

A few minutes later he found himself alone in a sort of wainscoted cabinet of severe aspect, lighted by two wax candles, placed upon a table with a green cloth. The last words of the usher who had just quitted him still rang in his ears: "Monsieur, you are now in the council-chamber; you have only to turn the copper handle of yonder door, and you will find yourself in the court-room, behind the President's chair." These words were mingled in his thoughts with a vague memory of narrow corridors and dark staircases which he had recently traversed.

The usher had left him alone. The supreme moment had arrived. He sought to collect his faculties, but could not. It is chiefly at the moment when there is the greatest need for attaching them to the painful realities of life, that the threads of thought snap within the brain. He was in the very place where the judges deliberated and condemned. With stupid tranquility he surveyed this peaceful and terrible apartment, where so many lives had been broken, which was soon to ring with his name, and which his fate was at that moment traversing. He stared at the wall, then he looked at himself, wondering that it should be that chamber and that it should be he.

He had eaten nothing for four-and-twenty hours; he was worn out by the jolts of the cart, but he was not conscious of it. It seemed to him that he felt nothing.

He approached a black frame which was suspended on the wall, and which contained, under glass, an ancient autograph letter of Jean Nicolas Pache, mayor of Paris and minister, and dated, through an error, no doubt, the *9th of June,* of the year II, and in which Pache forwarded to the commune the list of ministers and deputies held in arrest by them. Any spectator who had chanced to see him at that moment, and who had watched him, would have imagined, doubtless, that this letter struck him as very curious, for he did not take his eyes from it, and he read it two or three times. He read it without paying any attention to it, and unconsciously. He was thinking of Fantine and Cosette.

As he dreamed, he turned round, and his eyes fell upon the brass knob of the door which separated him from the Court of Assizes. He had almost forgotten that door. His glance, calm at first, paused there, remained fixed on that brass handle, then grew terrified, and little by little became impregnated with fear. Beads of perspiration burst forth among his hair and trickled down upon his temples.

At a certain moment he made that indescribable gesture of a sort of authority mingled with rebellion, which is intended to convey, and which does so well convey, *"Pardieu! who compels me to this?"* Then he wheeled briskly round, caught sight of the door through which he had entered in front of him, went to it, opened it, and passed out. He was no longer in that chamber; he was outside in a corridor, a long, narrow corridor, broken by steps and gratings, making all sorts of angles, lighted here and there by lanterns similar to the night taper of invalids, the corridor through which he had approached. He breathed, he listened; not a sound in front, not a sound behind him, and he fled as though pursued.

When he had turned many angles in this corridor, he still listened. The same silence reigned, and there was the same darkness around him. He was out of breath; he staggered; he leaned against the wall. The stone was cold; the perspiration lay ice-cold on his brow; he straightened himself up with a shiver.

Then, there alone in the darkness, trembling with cold and with something else, too, perchance, he meditated.

He had meditated all night long; he had meditated all the day: he heard within him but one voice, which said, "Alas!"

A quarter of an hour passed thus. At length he bowed his head, sighed with agony, dropped his arms, and retraced his steps. He walked slowly, and as though crushed. It seemed as though someone had overtaken him in his flight and was leading him back.

He re-entered the council-chamber. The first thing he caught sight of was the knob of the door. This knob, which was round and of polished brass, shone like a terrible star for him. He gazed at it as a lamb might gaze into the eye of a tiger.

He could not take his eyes from it. From time to time he advanced a step and approached the door.

Had he listened, he would have heard the sound of the adjoining hall like a sort of confused murmur; but he did not listen, and he did not hear.

Suddenly, without himself knowing how it happened, he found himself near the door; he grasped the knob convulsively; the door opened.

He was in the court-room.

Chapter IX

A PLACE WHERE CONVICTIONS ARE IN PROCESS OF FORMATION

HE ADVANCED A PACE, CLOSED THE DOOR MECHANICALLY BEHIND HIM, AND REMAINED STANDing, contemplating what he saw.

It was a vast and badly lighted apartment, now full of uproar, now full of silence, where all the apparatus of a criminal case, with its petty and mournful gravity in the midst of the throng, was in process of development.

At the one end of the hall, the one where he was, were judges, with abstracted air, in threadbare robes, who were gnawing their nails or closing their eyelids; at the other end, a ragged crowd; lawyers in all sorts of attitudes; soldiers with hard but honest faces; ancient, spotted woodwork, a dirty ceiling, tables covered with serge that was yellow rather than green; doors blackened by handmarks; tap-room lamps which emitted more smoke than light, suspended from nails in the wainscot; on the tables candles in brass candlesticks; darkness, ugliness, sadness; and from all this there was disengaged an austere and august impression, for one there felt that grand human thing which is called the law, and that grand divine thing which is called justice.

No one in all that throng paid any attention to him; all glances were directed toward a single point, a wooden bench placed against a small door, in the stretch of wall on the President's left; on this bench, illuminated by several candles, sat a man between two gendarmes.

This man was *the* man.

He did not seek him; he saw him; his eyes went thither naturally, as though they had known beforehand where that figure was.

He thought he was looking at himself, grown old; not absolutely the same in face, of course, but exactly similar in attitude and aspect, with his bristling hair, with that wild and uneasy eye, with that blouse, just as it was on the day when he entered D——, full of hatred, concealing his soul in that hideous mass of frightful thoughts which he had spent nineteen years in collecting on the floor of the prison.

He said to himself with a shudder, "Good God! shall I become like that again?"

This creature seemed to be at least sixty; there was something indescribably coarse, stupid, and frightened about him.

At the sound made by the opening door, people had drawn aside to make way for him; the President had turned his head, and, understanding that the personage who had just entered was the mayor of M. sur M., he had bowed to him; the attorney-general, who had seen M. Madeleine at M. sur M., whither the duties of his office had called him more than once, recognized him and saluted him also: he had hardly perceived it; he was the victim of a sort of hallucination; he was watching.

Judges, clerks, gendarmes, a throng of cruelly curious heads, all these he had already beheld once, in days gone by, twenty-seven years before; he had encountered those fatal things once more; there they were; they moved; they existed; it was no longer an effort of his memory, a mirage of his thought; they were real gendarmes and real judges, a real crowd, and real men of flesh and blood: it was all over; he beheld the monstrous aspects of his past reappear and live once more around him, with all that there is formidable in reality.

All this was yawning before him.

He was horrified by it; he shut his eyes, and exclaimed in the deepest recesses of his soul, "Never!"

And by a tragic play of destiny which made all his ideas tremble, and rendered him nearly mad, it was another self of his that was there! all called that man who was being tried Jean Valjean.

Under his very eyes, unheard-of vision, he had a sort of representation of the most horrible moment of his life, enacted by his specter.

Everything was there; the apparatus was the same, the hour of the night, the faces of the judges, of soldiers, and of spectators; all were the same, only above the President's head there hung a crucifix, something which the courts had lacked at the time of his condemnation: God had been absent when he had been judged.

There was a chair behind him; he dropped into it, terrified at the thought that he might be seen; when he was seated, he took advantage of a pile of cardboard boxes, which stood on the judge's desk, to conceal his face from the whole room; he could now see without being seen; he had fully regained consciousness of the reality of things; gradually he recovered; he attained that phase of composure where it is possible to listen.

M. Bamatabois was one of the jurors.

He looked for Javert, but did not see him; the seat of the witnesses was hidden from him by the clerk's table, and then, as we have just said, the hall was sparely lighted.

At the moment of this entrance, the defendant's lawyer had just finished his plea.

The attention of all was excited to the highest pitch; the affair had lasted for three hours: for three hours that crowd had been watching a strange man, a miserable specimen of humanity, either profoundly stupid or profoundly subtle, gradually bending beneath the weight of a terrible likeness. This man, as the reader already knows, was a vagabond who had been found in a field carrying a branch laden with ripe apples, broken in the orchard of a neighbor, called the Pierron orchard. Who was this man? an examination had been made; witnesses had been heard, and they were unanimous; light had abounded throughout the entire debate; the accusation said: "We have in our grasp not only a marauder, a stealer of fruit; we have here, in our hands, a bandit, an old offender who has broken his ban, an ex-convict, a miscreant of the most dangerous description, a malefactor named Jean Valjean, whom justice has long been in search of, and who, eight years ago, on emerging from the galleys at Toulon, committed a highway robbery, accompanied by violence, on the person of a child, a Savoyard named Little Gervais; a crime provided for by article 383 of the Penal Code, the right to try him for which we reserve hereafter, when his identity shall have been judicially established. He has just committed a fresh theft; it is a case of a second offense; condemn him for the fresh deed; later on he will be judged for the old crime." In the face of this accusation, in the face of the unanimity of the witnesses, the accused appeared to be astonished more than anything else; he made signs and gestures which were meant to convey No, or else he stared at the ceiling: he spoke with difficulty, replied with embarrassment, but his whole person, from head to foot, was a denial; he was an idiot in the presence of all these minds ranged in order of battle around him, and like a stranger in the midst of this society which was seizing fast upon him; nevertheless, it was a question of the most menacing future for him; the likeness increased every moment, and the entire crowd surveyed, with more anxiety than he did himself, that sentence freighted with calamity, which descended ever closer over his head; there was even a glimpse of a possibility afforded; besides the galleys, a possible death penalty, in case his identity were established, and the affair of Little Gervais were to end thereafter in condemnation. Who was this man? what was the nature of his apathy? was it imbecility or craft? Did he understand too well, or did he not understand at all? these were questions which divided the crowd, and seemed to divide the jury; there was something both terrible and puzzling in this case: the drama was not only melancholy; it was also obscure.

The counsel for the defense had spoken tolerably well, in that provincial tongue which has long constituted the eloquence of the bar, and which was formerly employed by all advocates, at Paris as well as at Romorantin or at Montbrison, and which to-day, having become classic, is no longer spoken except by the official orators of magistracy, to whom it is suited on account of its grave sonorousness and its majestic stride; a tongue in which a husband is called *a consort*, and a woman *a spouse*; Paris, *the center of art and civilization*; the king, *the monarch*; Monseigneur the Bishop, *a sainted pontiff*; the district-attorney, *the eloquent interpreter of public prosecution*; the arguments, *the accents which we have just listened to*; the age of Louis XIV, *the grand age*; a theater, *the temple of Melpomene*; the reigning family, *the august blood of our kings*; a concert, *a musical solemnity*; the General Commandant of the province, *the illustrious warrior, who, etc.*; the pupils in the seminary, *these tender levities*; errors imputed to newspapers, *the imposture which distills its venom through the columns of those organs*; etc. The lawyer had, accordingly, begun with an explanation as to the theft of the apples—an awkward matter couched in fine style; but Bénigne Bossuet himself was obliged to allude to a chicken in the midst of a funeral oration, and he extricated himself from the situation in stately fashion. The lawyer established the fact that the theft of the apples had not been circumstantially proved. His client, whom he, in his character of counsel, persisted in calling Champmathieu, had not been seen scaling that wall nor breaking that branch by anyone. He had been taken with that branch (which the lawyer preferred to call a *bough*) in his possession; but he said that he had found it broken off and lying on the ground, and had picked it up. Where was there any proof to the contrary? No doubt that branch had been broken off and concealed after the scaling of the wall, then thrown away by the alarmed marauder; there was no doubt that there had been a thief in the case. But what proof was there that that thief had been Champmathieu? One thing only. His character as an ex-convict. The lawyer did not deny that that character appeared to be, unhappily, well attested; the accused had resided at Faverolles; the accused had exercised the calling of a tree-pruner there; the name of Champmathieu might well have had its origin in Jean Mathieu; all that was true—in short, four witnesses recognize Champmathieu, positively and without hesitation, as that convict, Jean Valjean; to these signs, to this testimony, the counsel could oppose nothing but the denial of his client, the denial of an interested party; but supposing that he was the convict Jean Valjean, did that prove that he was the thief of the apples? that was a presumption at the most, not a proof. The prisoner, it was true, and his counsel, "in good faith," was obliged to admit it, had adopted "a bad system of defense." He obstinately denied everything, the theft and his character of convict. An admission upon this last point would certainly have been better, and would have won for him the indulgence of his judges; the counsel had advised him to do this; but the accused had obstinately refused, thinking, no doubt, that he would save everything by admitting nothing. It was an error; but ought not the paucity of this intelligence to be taken into consideration? This man was visibly stupid. Long-continued wretchedness in the galleys, long misery outside the galleys, had brutalized him, etc. He defended himself badly; was that a reason for condemning him? As for the affair with Little Gervais, the counsel need not discuss it; it did not enter into the case. The lawyer wound up by beseeching the jury and the court, if the identity of Jean Valjean appeared to them to be evident, to apply to him the police penalties which are provided for a criminal who has broken his ban, and not the frightful chastisement which descends upon the convict guilty of a second offense.

The district-attorney answered the counsel for the defense. He was violent and florid, as district-attorneys usually are.

He congratulated the counsel for the defense on his "loyalty," and skillfully took advantage of this loyalty. He reached the accused through all the concessions made by his lawyer. The advocate had seemed to admit that the prisoner was Jean Valjean. He took note of this. So this man was Jean

Valjean. This point had been conceded to the accusation and could no longer be disputed. Here, by means of a clever autonomasia which went back to the sources and causes of crime, the district-attorney thundered against the immorality of the romantic school, then dawning under the name of *the Satanic school,* which had been bestowed upon it by the critics of the *Quotidienne* and the *Oriflamme*; he attributed, not without some probability, to the influence of this perverse literature the crime of Champmathieu, or rather, to speak more correctly, of Jean Valjean. Having exhausted these considerations, he passed on to Jean Valjean himself. Who was this Jean Valjean? Description of Jean Valjean: a monster spewed forth, etc. The model for this sort of description is contained in the tale of Théramène, which is not useful to tragedy, but which every day renders great services to judicial eloquence. The audience and the jury "shuddered." The description finished, the district-attorney resumed with an oratorical turn calculated to raise the enthusiasm of the journal of the prefecture to the highest pitch on the following day: And it is such a man, etc., etc., etc., vagabond, beggar, without means of existence, etc., etc., inured by his past life to culpable deeds, and but little reformed by his sojourn in the galleys, as was proved by the crime committed against Little Gervais, etc., etc.; it is such a man, caught upon the highway in the very act of theft, a few paces from a wall that had been scaled, still holding in his hand the object stolen, who denies the crime, the theft, the climbing the wall; denies everything; denies even his own identity! In addition to a hundred other proofs, to which we will not recur, four witnesses recognize him—Javert, the upright inspector of police; Javert, and three of his former companions in infamy, the convicts Brevet, Chenildieu, and Cochepaille. What does he offer in opposition to this overwhelming unanimity? His denial. What obduracy! You will do justice, gentlemen of the jury, etc., etc. While the district-attorney was speaking, the accused listened to him open-mouthed, with a sort of amazement in which some admiration was assuredly blended. He was evidently surprised that a man could talk like that. From time to time, at those "energetic" moments of the prosecutor's speech, when eloquence which cannot contain itself overflows in a flood of withering epithets and envelops the accused like a storm, he moved his head slowly from right to left and from left to right in the sort of mute and melancholy protest with which he had contented himself since the beginning of the argument. Two or three times the spectators who were nearest to him heard him say in a low voice, "That is what comes of not having asked M. Baloup." The district-attorney directed the attention of the jury to this stupid attitude, evidently deliberate, which denoted not imbecility, but craft, skill, a habit of deceiving justice, and which set forth in all its nakedness the "profound perversity" of this man. He ended by making his reserves on the affair of Little Gervais and demanding a severe sentence.

At that time, as the reader will remember, it was penal servitude for life.

The counsel for the defense rose, began by complimenting Monsieur l'Avocat-General on his "admirable speech," then replied as best he could; but he weakened; the ground was evidently slipping away from under his feet.

Chapter X

THE SYSTEM OF DENIALS

THE MOMENT FOR CLOSING THE DEBATE HAD ARRIVED. THE PRESIDENT HAD THE ACCUSED STAND up, and addressed to him the customary question, "Have you anything to add to your defense?"

The man did not appear to understand, as he stood there, twisting in his hands a terrible cap which he had.

The President repeated the question.

This time the man heard it. He seemed to understand. He made a motion like a man who is just waking up, cast his eyes about him, stared at the audience, the gendarmes, his counsel, the jury, the court, laid his monstrous fist on the rim of woodwork in front of his bench, took another look, and all at once, fixing his glance upon the district-attorney, he began to speak. It was like an eruption. It seemed, from the manner in which the words escaped from his mouth—incoherent, impetuous, pell-mell, tumbling over each other—as though they were all pressing forward to issue forth at once. He said:

"This is what I have to say. That I have been a wheelwright in Paris, and that it was with Monsieur Baloup. It is a hard trade. In the wheelwright's trade one works always in the open air, in courtyards, under sheds when the masters are good, never in closed workshops, because space is required, you see. In winter one gets so cold that one beats one's arms together to warm one's self; but the masters don't like it; they say it wastes time. Handling iron when there is ice between the paving-stones is hard work. That wears a man out quickly. One is old while he is still quite young in that trade. At forty a man is done for. I was fifty-three. I was in a bad state. And then, workmen are so mean! When a man is no longer young, they call him nothing but an old bird, old beast! I was not earning more than thirty sous a day. They paid me as little as possible. The masters took advantage of my age—and then I had my daughter, who was a laundress at the river. She earned a little, also. It sufficed for us two. She had trouble, also; all day long up to her waist in a tub, in rain, in snow. When the wind cuts your face, when it freezes, it is all the same; you must still wash. There are people who have not much linen, and wait until late; if you do not wash, you lose your custom. The planks are badly joined, and water drops on you from everywhere; you have your petticoats all damp above and below. That penetrates. She has also worked at the laundry of the Enfants-Rouges, where the water comes through faucets. You are not in the tub there; you wash at the faucet in front of you, and rinse in a basin behind you. As it is enclosed, you are not so cold; but there is that hot steam, which is terrible, and which ruins your eyes. She came home at seven o'clock in the evening, and went to bed at once, she was so tired. Her husband beat her. She is dead. We have not been very happy. She was a good girl, who did not go to the ball, and who was very peaceable. I remember one Shrove-Tuesday when she went to bed at eight o'clock. There, I am telling the truth; you have only to ask. Ah, yes! how stupid I am! Paris is a gulf. Who knows Father Champmathieu there? But M. Baloup does, I tell you. Go see at M. Baloup's; and after all, I don't know what is wanted of me."

The man ceased speaking, and remained standing. He had said these things in a loud, rapid, hoarse voice, with a sort of irritated and savage ingenuousness. Once he paused to salute someone in the crowd. The sort of affirmations which he seemed to fling out before him at random came like hiccoughs, and to each he added the gesture of a wood-cutter who is splitting wood. When he had finished, the audience burst into a laugh. He stared at the public, and, perceiving that they were laughing, and not understanding why, he began to laugh himself.

It was inauspicious.

The President, an attentive and benevolent man, raised his voice.

He reminded "the gentlemen of the jury" that "the sieur Baloup, formerly a master-wheelwright, with whom the accused stated that he had served, had been summoned in vain. He had become bankrupt, and was not to be found." Then turning to the accused, he enjoined him to listen to what he was about to say, and added: "You are in a position where reflection is necessary. The gravest presumptions rest upon you, and may induce vital results. Prisoner, in your own interests, I summon you for the last time to explain yourself clearly on two points. In the first place, did you or did you not climb the wall of the Pierron orchard, break the branch, and steal the apples; that is to say, commit the crime of breaking in and theft? In the second place, are you the discharged convict, Jean Valjean—yes or no?"

The prisoner shook his head with a capable air, like a man who has thoroughly understood, and who knows what answer he is going to make. He opened his mouth, turned toward the President, and said:

"In the first place—"

Then he stared at his cap, stared at the ceiling, and held his peace.

"Prisoner," said the district-attorney, in a severe voice, "pay attention. You are not answering anything that has been asked of you. Your embarrassment condemns you. It is evident that your name is not Champmathieu; that you are the convict, Jean Valjean, concealed first under the name of Jean Mathieu, which was the name of his mother; that you went to Auvergne; that you were born at Faverolles, where you were a pruner of trees. It is evident that you have been guilty of entering, and of the theft of ripe apples from the Pierron orchard. The gentlemen of the jury will form their own opinion."

The prisoner had finally resumed his seat; he arose abruptly when the district-attorney had finished, and exclaimed:

"You are very wicked; that you are! This what I wanted to say; I could not find words for it at first. I have stolen nothing. I am a man who does not have something to eat every day. I was coming from Ailly; I was walking through the country after a shower, which had made the whole country yellow: even the ponds were overflowed, and nothing sprang from the sand anymore but the little blades of grass at the wayside. I found a broken branch with apples on the ground; I picked up the branch without knowing that it would get me into trouble. I have been in prison, and they have been dragging me about for the last three months; more than that I cannot say; people talk against me, they tell me, 'Answer!' The gendarme, who is a good fellow, nudges my elbow, and says to me in a low voice, 'Come, answer!' I don't know how to explain; I have no education; I am a poor man; that is where they wrong me, because they do not see this. I have not stolen; I picked up from the ground things that were lying there. You say, Jean Valjean, Jean Mathieu! I don't know those persons; they are villagers. I worked for M. Baloup, Boulevard de l'Hôpital; my name is Champmathieu. You are very clever to tell me where I was born; I don't know myself: it's not everybody who has a house in which to come into the world; that would be too convenient. I think that my father and mother were people who strolled along the highways; I know nothing different. When I was a child, they called me *young fellow*; now they call me *old fellow*; those are my baptismal names; take that as you like. I have been in Auvergne; I have been at Faverolles. Pardi. Well! can't a man have been in Auvergne, or at Faverolles, without having been in the galleys? I tell you that I have not stolen, and that I am Father Champmathieu; I have been with M. Baloup; I have had a settled residence. You worry me with your nonsense, there! Why is everybody pursuing me so furiously?"

The district-attorney had remained standing; he addressed the President:

"Monsieur le Président, in view of the confused but exceedingly clever denials of the prisoner, who would like to pass himself off as an idiot, but who will not succeed in so doing—we shall attend to that—we demand that it shall please you and that it shall please the court to summon once more into this place the convicts Brevet, Cochepaille, and Chenildieu, and Police-Inspector Javert, and question them for the last time as to the identity of the prisoner with the convict Jean Valjean."

"I would remind the district-attorney," said the President, "that Police-Inspector Javert, recalled by his duties to the capital of a neighboring arrondissement, left the court-room and the town as soon as he had made his deposition; we have accorded him permission, with the consent of the district-attorney and of the counsel for the prisoner."

"That is true, Mr. President," responded the district-attorney. "In the absence of sieur Javert, I think it my duty to remind the gentlemen of the jury of what he said here a few hours ago. Javert is an estimable man, who does honor by his rigorous and strict probity to inferior but important functions. These are the terms of his deposition: 'I do not even stand in need of circumstantial proofs and moral presumptions to give the lie to the prisoner's denial. I recognize him perfectly. The name of this man is not Champmathieu; he is an ex-convict named Jean Valjean, and is very vicious and much to be feared. It is only with extreme regret that he was released at the expiration of his term. He underwent nineteen years of penal servitude for theft. He made five or six attempts to escape. Besides the theft from Little Gervais, and from the Pierron orchard, I suspect him of a theft committed in the house of his Grace the late Bishop of D———. I often saw him at the time when I was adjutant of the galley-guard at the prison in Toulon. I repeat that I recognize him perfectly.' "

This extremely precise statement appeared to produce a vivid impression on the public and on the jury. The district-attorney concluded by insisting, that in default of Javert, the three witnesses Brevet, Chenildieu, and Cochepaille should be heard once more and solemnly interrogated.

The President transmitted the order to an usher, and, a moment later, the door of the witnesses' room opened. The usher, accompanied by a gendarme ready to lend him armed assistance, introduced the convict Brevet. The audience was in suspense; and all breasts heaved as though they had contained but one soul.

The ex-convict Brevet wore the black and gray waistcoat of the central prisons. Brevet was a person sixty years of age, who had a sort of business man's face, and the air of a rascal. The two sometimes go together. In prison, whither fresh misdeeds had led him, he had become something in the nature of a turnkey. He was a man of whom his superiors said, "He tries to make himself of use." The chaplains bore good testimony as to his religious habits. It must not be forgotten that this passed under the Restoration.

"Brevet," said the President, "you have undergone an ignominious sentence, and you cannot take an oath."

Brevet dropped his eyes.

"Nevertheless," continued the President, "even in the man whom the law has degraded, there may remain, when the divine mercy permits it, a sentiment of honor and of equity. It is to this sentiment that I appeal at this decisive hour. If it still exists in you—and I hope it does—reflect before replying to me: consider on the one hand, this man, whom a word from you may ruin; on the other hand, justice, which a word from you may enlighten. The instant is solemn; there is still time to retract if you think you have been mistaken. Rise, prisoner. Brevet, take a good look at the accused, recall your souvenirs, and tell us on your soul and conscience, if you persist in recognizing this man as your former companion in the galleys, Jean Valjean?"

Brevet looked at the prisoner, then turned toward the court.

"Yes, Mr. President, I was the first to recognize him, and I stick to it; that man is Jean Valjean, who entered at Toulon in 1796, and left in 1815. I left a year later. He has the air of a brute now; but it must be because age has brutalized him; he was sly at the galleys: I recognize him positively."

"Take your seat," said the President. "Prisoner, remain standing."

Chenildieu was brought in, a prisoner for life, as was indicated by his red cassock and his green cap. He was serving out his sentence at the galleys of Toulon, whence he had been brought for this case. He was a small man of about fifty, brisk, wrinkled, frail, yellow, brazen-faced, feverish, who had a sort of sickly feebleness about all his limbs and his whole person, and an immense force in his glance. His companions in the galleys had nicknamed him *I-deny-God* (*Je-nie Dieu*, Chenildieu).

The President addressed him in nearly the same words which he had used to Brevet. At the moment when he reminded him of his infamy which deprived him of the right to take an oath, Chenildieu raised his head and looked the crowd in the face. The President invited him to reflection, and asked him as he had asked Brevet, if he persisted in recognition of the prisoner.

Chenildieu burst out laughing.

"Pardieu, as if I didn't recognize him! We were attached to the same chain for five years. So you are sulking, old fellow?"

"Go take your seat," said the President.

The usher brought in Cochepaille. He was another convict for life, who had come from the galleys, and was dressed in red, like Chenildieu, was a peasant from Lourdes, and a half-bear of the Pyrenees. He had guarded the flocks among the mountains, and from a shepherd he had slipped into a brigand. Cochepaille was no less savage and seemed even more stupid than the prisoner. He was one of those wretched men whom nature has sketched out for wild beasts, and on whom society puts the finishing touches as convicts in the galleys.

The President tried to touch him with some grave and pathetic words, and asked him, as he had asked the other two, if he persisted, without hesitation or trouble, in recognizing the man who was standing before him.

"He is Jean Valjean," said Cochepaille. "He was even called Jean-the-Screw, because he was so strong."

Each of these affirmations from these three men, evidently sincere and in good faith, had raised in the audience a murmur of bad augury for the prisoner—a murmur which increased and lasted longer each time that a fresh declaration was added to the proceeding.

The prisoner had listened to them, with that astounded face which was, according to the accusation, his principal means of defense; at the first, the gendarmes, his neighbors, had heard him mutter between his teeth: "Ah well, he's a nice one!" after the second, he said, a little louder, with an air that was almost that of satisfaction, "Good!" at the third, he cried, "Famous!"

The President addressed him:

"Have you heard, prisoner? what have you to say?"

He replied:

"I say, 'Famous!' "

An uproar broke out among the audience, and was communicated to the jury; it was evident that the man was lost.

"Ushers," said the President, "enforce silence! I am going to sum up the arguments."

At that moment there was a movement just beside the President; a voice was heard crying:

"Brevet! Chenildieu! Cochepaille! look here!"

All who heard that voice were chilled, so lamentable and terrible was it; all eyes were turned to the point whence it had proceeded. A man, placed among the privileged spectators who were seated behind the court, had just risen, had pushed open the half-door which separated the tribunal from the audience, and was standing in the middle of the hall; the President, the district-attorney, M. Bamatabois, twenty persons, recognized him, and exclaimed in concert:

"M. Madeleine!"

Chapter XI

CHAMPMATHIEU MORE AND MORE ASTONISHED

IT WAS HE, IN FACT. THE CLERK'S LAMP ILLUMINED HIS COUNTENANCE. HE HELD HIS HAT IN HIS hand; there was no disorder in his clothing; his coat was carefully buttoned; he was very pale, and he trembled slightly; his hair, which had still been gray on his arrival in Arras, was now entirely white: it had turned white during the hour he had sat there.

All heads were raised; the sensation was indescribable; there was a momentary hesitation in the audience, the voice had been so heartrending; the man who stood there appeared so calm that they did not understand at first. They asked themselves whether he had indeed uttered that cry; they could not believe that that tranquil man had been the one to give that terrible outcry.

This indecision only lasted a few seconds. Even before the President and the district-attorney could utter a word, before the ushers and the gendarmes could make a gesture, the man whom all still called, at that moment, M. Madeleine, had advanced toward the witnesses Cochepaille, Brevet, and Chenildieu.

"Do you not recognize me?" said he.

All three remained speechless, and indicated by a sign of the head that they did not know him. Cochepaille, who was intimidated, made a military salute. M. Madeleine turned toward the jury and the court, and said in a gentle voice:

"Gentlemen of the jury, order the prisoner to be released! Mr. President, have me arrested. He is not the man whom you are in search of; it is I: I am Jean Valjean."

Not a mouth breathed; the first commotion of astonishment had been followed by a silence like that of the grave; those within the hall experienced that sort of religious terror which seizes the masses when something grand has been done.

In the meantime, the face of the President was stamped with sympathy and sadness; he had exchanged a rapid sign with the district-attorney and a few low-toned words with the assistant judges; he addressed the public, and asked in accents which all understood:

"Is there a physician present?"

The district-attorney took the word:

"Gentlemen of the jury, the very strange and unexpected incident which disturbs the audience inspires us, like yourselves, only with a sentiment which it is unnecessary for us to express. You all know, by reputation at least, the honorable M. Madeleine, mayor of M. sur M.; if there is a physician in the audience, we join the President in requesting him to attend to M. Madeleine, and to conduct him to his home."

M. Madeleine did not allow the district-attorney to finish; he interrupted him in accents full of suavity and authority. These are the words which he uttered; here they are literally, as they were written down, immediately after the trial, by one of the witnesses to this scene, and as they now ring in the ears of those who heard them nearly forty years ago:

"I thank you, Mr. District-Attorney, but I am not mad; you shall see; you were on the point of committing a great error; release this man! I am fulfilling a duty; I am that miserable criminal. I am the only one here who sees the matter clearly, and I am telling you the truth. God, who is on high, looks down on what I am doing at this moment, and that suffices. You can take me, for here I am: but I have done my best; I concealed myself under another name; I have become rich; I have become a mayor; I have tried to re-enter the ranks of the honest. It seems that that is not to be done. In short, there are many things which I cannot tell. I will not narrate the story of my life to you; you will hear it one of these days. I robbed Monseigneur the Bishop, it is true; it is true that I robbed Little Gervais; they were right in telling you that Jean Valjean was a very vicious wretch. Perhaps it was not altogether his fault. Listen, honorable judges! a man who has been so greatly humbled as I have has neither any remonstrances to make to Providence, nor any advice to give to society; but, you see, the infamy from which I have tried to escape is an injurious thing; the galleys make the convict what he is; reflect upon that, if you please. Before going to the galleys, I was a poor peasant, with very little intelligence, a sort of idiot; the galleys wrought a change in me. I was stupid; I became vicious: I was a block of wood; I became a firebrand. Later on, indulgence and kindness saved me, as severity had ruined me. But, pardon me, you cannot understand what I am saying. You will find at my house, among the ashes in the fireplace, the forty-sou piece which I stole, seven years ago, from Little Gervais. I have nothing further to add; take me. Good God! the district-attorney shakes his head; you say, 'M. Madeleine has gone mad!' you do not believe me! that is distressing. Do not, at least, condemn this man! What! these men do not recognize me! I wish Javert were here; he would recognize me."

Nothing can reproduce the somber and kindly melancholy of tone which accompanied these words.

He turned to the three convicts, and said:

"Well, I recognize you; do you remember, Brevet?——"

He paused, hesitated for an instant, and said:

"Do you remember the knitted suspenders with a checked pattern which you wore in the galleys?"

Brevet gave a start of surprise, and surveyed him from head to foot with a frightened air. He continued:

"Chenildieu, you who conferred on yourself the name of 'Je-nie-Dieu,' your whole right shoulder bears a deep burn, because you one day laid your shoulder against the chafing-dish full of coals, in order to efface the three letters T. F. P., which are still visible, nevertheless; answer, is this true?"

"It is true," said Chenildieu.

He addressed himself to Cochepaille:

"Cochepaille, you have, near the bend in your left arm, a date stamped in blue letters with burned powder; the date is that of the landing of the Emperor at Cannes, March 1, 1815; pull up your sleeve!"

Cochepaille pushed up his sleeve; all eyes were focused on him and on his bare arm.

A gendarme held a light close to it; there was the date.

The unhappy man turned to the spectators and the judges with a smile which still rends the hearts of all who saw it whenever they think of it. It was a smile of triumph; it was also a smile of despair.

"You see plainly," he said, "that I am Jean Valjean."

In that chamber there were no longer either judges, accusers, nor gendarmes; there was nothing but staring eyes and sympathizing hearts. No one recalled any longer the part that each might be called upon to play; the district-attorney forgot he was there for the purpose of prosecuting, the President that he was there to preside, the counsel for the defense that he was there to defend. It was a striking circumstance that no question was put, that no authority intervened. The peculiarity of sublime spectacles is, that they capture all souls and turn witnesses into spectators. No one, probably, could have explained what he felt; no one, probably, said to himself that he was witnessing the splendid outburst of a grand light: all felt themselves inwardly dazzled.

It was evident that they had Jean Valjean before their eyes. That was clear. The appearance of this man had sufficed to suffuse with light that matter which had been so obscure but a moment previously, without any further explanation; the whole crowd, as by a sort of electric revelation, understood instantly and at a single glance the simple and magnificent history of a man who was delivering himself up so that another man might not be condemned in his stead. The details, the hesitations, little possible oppositions, were swallowed up in that vast and luminous fact.

It was an impression which vanished speedily, but which was irresistible at the moment.

"I do not wish to disturb the court further," resumed Jean Valjean. "I shall withdraw, since you do not arrest me. I have many things to do. The district-attorney knows who I am; he knows whither I am going; he can have me arrested when he likes."

He directed his steps toward the door. Not a voice was raised, not an arm extended to hinder him. All stood aside. At that moment there was about him that divine something which causes multitudes to stand aside and make way for a man. He traversed the crowd slowly. It was never known who opened the door, but it is certain that he found the door open when he reached it. On arriving there he turned round and said:

"I am at your command, Mr. District-Attorney."

Then he addressed the audience:

"All of you, all who are present—consider me worthy of pity, do you not? Good God! When

I think of what I was on the point of doing, I consider that I am to be envied. Nevertheless, I should have preferred not to have had this occur."

He withdrew, and the door closed behind him as it had opened, for those who do certain sovereign things are always sure of being served by someone in the crowd.

Less than an hour after this, the verdict of the jury freed the said Champmathieu from all accusations; and Champmathieu, being at once released, went off in a state of stupefaction, thinking that all men were fools, and comprehending nothing of this vision.

BOOK EIGHTH

A COUNTER-BLOW

Chapter I

IN WHAT MIRROR M. MADELEINE CONTEMPLATES HIS HAIR

THE DAY HAD BEGUN TO DAWN. FANTINE HAD PASSED A SLEEPLESS AND FEVERISH NIGHT, FILLED with happy visions; at daybreak she fell asleep. Sister Simplice, who had been watching with her, availed herself of this slumber to go and prepare a new potion of chinchona. The worthy sister had been in the laboratory of the infirmary but a few moments, bending over her drugs and phials, and scrutinizing things very closely, on account of the dimness which the half-light of dawn spreads over all objects. Suddenly she raised her head and uttered a faint shriek. M. Madeleine stood before her; he had just entered silently.

"Is it you, Mr. Mayor?" she exclaimed.

He replied in a low voice:

"How is that poor woman?"

"Not so bad just now; but we have been very uneasy."

She explained to him what had passed: that Fantine had been very ill the day before, and that she was better now, because she thought that the mayor had gone to Montfermeil to get her child. The sister dared not question the mayor; but she perceived plainly from his air that he had not come from there.

"All that is good," said he; "you were right not to undeceive her."

"Yes," responded the sister; "but now, Mr. Mayor, she will see you and will not see her child. What shall we say to her?"

He reflected for a moment.

"God will inspire us," said he.

"But we cannot tell a lie," murmured the sister, half-aloud.

It was broad daylight in the room. The light fell full on M. Madeleine's face. The sister chanced to raise her eyes to it.

"Good God, sir!" she exclaimed; "what has happened to you? Your hair is perfectly white!"

"White!" said he.

Sister Simplice had no mirror. She rummaged in a drawer, and pulled out the little glass which the doctor of the infirmary used to see whether a patient was dead and whether he no longer breathed. M. Madeleine took the mirror, looked at his hair, and said:

"Well!"

He uttered the word indifferently, and as though his mind were on something else.

The sister felt chilled by something strange of which she caught a glimpse in all this.

He inquired:

"Can I see her?"

"Is not Monsieur le Maire going to have her child brought back to her?" said the sister, hardly venturing to put the question.

"Of course; but it will take two or three days at least."

"If she were not to see Monsieur le Maire until that time," went on the sister, timidly, "she would not know that Monsieur le Maire had returned, and it would be easy to inspire her with patience; and when the child arrived, she would naturally think Monsieur le Maire had just come with the child. We should not have to enact a lie."

M. Madeleine seemed to reflect for a few moments; then he said with his calm gravity:

"No, sister, I must see her. I may, perhaps, be in haste."

The nun did not appear to notice this word "perhaps," which communicated an obscure and singular sense to the words of the mayor's speech. She replied, lowering her eyes and her voice respectfully:

"In that case, she is asleep; but Monsieur le Maire may enter."

He made some remarks about a door which shut badly, and the noise of which might awaken the sick woman; then he entered Fantine's chamber, approached the bed, and drew aside the curtains. She was asleep. Her breath issued from her breast with that tragic sound which is peculiar to those maladies, and which breaks the hearts of mothers when they are watching through the night beside their sleeping child who is condemned to death. But this painful respiration hardly troubled a sort of ineffable serenity which overspread her countenance, and which transfigured her in her sleep. Her pallor had become whiteness; her cheeks were crimson; her long golden lashes, the only beauty of her youth and her virginity which remained to her, palpitated, though they remained closed and drooping. Her whole person was trembling with an indescribable unfolding of wings, all ready to open wide and bear her away, which could be felt as they rustled, though they could not be seen. To see her thus, one would never have dreamed that she was an invalid whose life was almost despaired of. She resembled rather something on the point of soaring away than something on the point of dying.

The branch trembles when a hand approaches it to pluck a flower, and seems to both withdraw and to offer itself at one and the same time. The human body has something of this tremor when the instant arrives in which the mysterious fingers of Death are about to pluck the soul.

M. Madeleine remained for some time motionless beside that bed, gazing in turn upon the sick woman and the crucifix, as he had done two months before, on the day when he had come for the first time to see her in that asylum. They were both still there in the same attitude—she sleeping, he praying; only now, after the lapse of two months, her hair was gray and his was white.

The sister had not entered with him. He stood beside the bed, with his finger on his lips, as though there were someone in the chamber whom he must enjoin to silence.

She opened her eyes, saw him, and said quietly, with a smile:

"And Cosette?"

Chapter II

FANTINE HAPPY

S HE MADE NO MOVEMENT OF EITHER SURPRISE OR OF JOY; SHE WAS JOY ITSELF. THAT SIMPLE QUES-
tion, "And Cosette?" was put with so profound a faith, with so much certainty, with such a complete absence of disquiet and of doubt, that he found not a word of reply. She continued:

"I knew that you were there. I was asleep, but I saw you. I have seen you for a long, long time.
I have been following you with my eyes all night long. You were in a glory, and you had around
you all sorts of celestial forms."

He raised his glance to the crucifix.

"But," she resumed, "tell me where Cosette is. Why did not you place her on my bed against
the moment of my waking?"

He made some mechanical reply which he was never afterwards able to recall.

Fortunately, the doctor had been warned, and he now made his appearance. He came to the aid
of M. Madeleine.

"Calm yourself, my child," said the doctor; "your child is here."

Fantine's eyes beamed and filled her whole face with light. She clasped her hands with an expression which contained all that is possible to prayer in the way of violence and tenderness.

"Oh!" she exclaimed, "bring her to me!"

Touching illusion of a mother! Cosette was, for her, still the little child who is carried.

"Not yet," said the doctor, "not just now. You still have some fever. The sight of your child
would agitate you and do you harm. You must be cured first."

She interrupted him impetuously:

"But I am cured! Oh, I tell you that I am cured! What an ass that doctor is! The idea! I want to
see my child!"

"You see," said the doctor, "how excited you become. So long as you are in this state I shall
oppose your having your child. It is not enough to see her; it is necessary that you should live for
her. When you are reasonable, I will bring her to you myself."

The poor mother bowed her head.

"I beg your pardon, doctor, I really beg your pardon. Formerly I should never have spoken as
I have just done; so many misfortunes have happened to me, that I sometimes do not know what I
am saying. I understand you; you fear the emotion. I will wait as long as you like, but I swear to you
that it would not have harmed me to see my daughter. I have been seeing her; I have not taken my
eyes from her since yesterday evening. Do you know? If she were brought to me now, I should talk
to her very gently. That is all. Is it not quite natural that I should desire to see my daughter, who
has been brought to me expressly from Montfermeil? I am not angry. I know well that I am about
to be happy. All night long I have seen white things, and persons who smiled at me. When Monsieur le Docteur pleases, he shall bring me Cosette. I have no longer any fever; I am well. I am perfectly conscious that there is nothing the matter with me anymore; but I am going to behave as
though I were ill, and not stir, to please these ladies here. When it is seen that I am very calm, they
will say, 'She must have her child.' "

M. Madeleine was sitting on a chair beside the bed. She turned toward him; she was making a
visible effort to be calm and "very good," as she expressed it in the feebleness of illness which resembles infancy, in order that, seeing her so peaceable, they might make no difficulty about bringing
Cosette to her. But while she controlled herself she could not refrain from questioning M. Madeleine.

"Did you have a pleasant trip, Monsieur le Maire? Oh! how good you were to go and get her for me! Only tell me how she is. Did she stand the journey well? Alas! she will not recognize me. She must have forgotten me by this time, poor darling! Children have no memories. They are like birds. A child sees one thing to-day and another thing to-morrow, and thinks of nothing any longer. And did she have white linen? Did those Thénardiers keep her clean? How have they fed her? Oh! if you only knew how I have suffered, putting such questions as that to myself during all the time of my wretchedness. Now, it is all past. I am happy. Oh, how I should like to see her! Do you think her pretty, Monsieur le Maire? Is not my daughter beautiful? You must have been very cold in that diligence! Could she not be brought for just one little instant? She might be taken away directly afterwards. Tell me; you are the master; it could be so if you chose!"

He took her hand. "Cosette is beautiful," he said, "Cosette is well. You shall see her soon; but calm yourself; you are talking with too much vivacity, and you are throwing your arms out from under the clothes, and that makes you cough."

In fact, fits of coughing interrupted Fantine at nearly every word.

Fantine did not murmur; she feared that she had injured by her too passionate lamentations the confidence which she was desirous of inspiring, and she began to talk of indifferent things.

"Montfermeil is quite pretty, is it not? People go there on pleasure parties in summer. Are the Thénardiers prosperous? There are not many travelers in their parts. That inn of theirs is a sort of a cook-shop."

M. Madeleine was still holding her hand, and gazing at her with anxiety; it was evident that he had come to tell her things before which his mind now hesitated. The doctor, having finished his visit, retired. Sister Simplice remained alone with them.

But in the midst of this pause Fantine exclaimed:

"I hear her! mon Dieu, I hear her!"

She stretched out her arm to enjoin silence about her, held her breath, and began to listen with rapture.

There was a child playing in the yard—the child of the portress or of some workwoman. It was one of those accidents which are always occurring, and which seem to form a part of the mysterious stage-setting of mournful scenes. The child—a little girl—was going and coming, running to warm herself, laughing, singing at the top of her voice. Alas! in what are the plays of children not intermingled. It was this little girl whom Fantine heard singing.

"Oh!" she resumed, "it is my Cosette! I recognize her voice."

The child retreated as it had come; the voice died away. Fantine listened for a while longer, then her face clouded over, and M. Madeleine heard her say, in a low voice: "How wicked that doctor is not to allow me to see my daughter! That man has an evil countenance, that he has."

But the smiling background of her thoughts came to the front again. She continued to talk to herself, with her head resting on the pillow: "How happy we are going to be! We shall have a little garden the very first thing; M. Madeleine has promised it to me. My daughter will play in the garden. She must know her letters by this time. I will make her spell. She will run over the grass after butterflies. I will watch her. Then she will take her first communion. Ah! when will she take her first communion?"

She began to reckon on her fingers.

"One, two, three, four—she is seven years old. In five years she will have a white veil, and open-work stockings; she will look like a little woman. O my good sister, you do not know how foolish I become when I think of my daughter's first communion!"

She began to laugh.

He had released Fantine's hand. He listened to her words as one listens to the sighing of the breeze, with his eyes on the ground, his mind absorbed in reflection which had no bottom. All at once she ceased speaking, and this caused him to raise his head mechanically. Fantine had become terrible.

She no longer spoke, she no longer breathed; she had raised herself to a sitting posture, her thin shoulder emerged from her chemise; her face, which had been radiant but a moment before, was ghastly, and she seemed to have fixed her eyes, rendered large with terror, on something alarming at the other extremity of the room.

"Good God!" he exclaimed; "what ails you, Fantine?"

She made no reply; she did not remove her eyes from the object which she seemed to see. She removed one hand from his arm, and with the other made him a sign to look behind him.

He turned, and beheld Javert.

Chapter III

JAVERT SATISFIED

THIS IS WHAT HAD TAKEN PLACE.
The half-hour after midnight had just struck when M. Madeleine quitted the Hall of Assizes in Arras. He regained his inn just in time to set out again by the mail-wagon, in which he had engaged his place. A little before six o'clock in the morning he had arrived at M. sur M., and his first care had been to post a letter to M. Laffitte, then to enter the infirmary and see Fantine.

However, he had hardly quitted the audience hall of the Court of Assizes, when the district-attorney, recovering from his first shock, had taken the word to deplore the mad deed of the honorable mayor of M. sur M., to declare that his convictions had not been in the least modified by that curious incident, which would be explained thereafter, and to demand, in the meantime, the condemnation of that Champmathieu, who was evidently the real Jean Valjean. The district-attorney's persistence was visibly at variance with the sentiments of everyone, of the public, of the court, and of the jury. The counsel for the defense had some difficulty in refuting this harangue and in establishing that, in consequence of the revelations of M. Madeleine, that is to say, of the real Jean Valjean, the aspect of the matter had been thoroughly altered, and that the jury had before their eyes now only an innocent man. Thence the lawyer had drawn some epiphonemas, not very fresh, unfortunately, upon judicial errors, etc., etc.; the President, in his summing up, had joined the counsel for the defense, and in a few minutes the jury had thrown Champmathieu out of the case.

Nevertheless, the district-attorney was bent on having a Jean Valjean; and as he had no longer Champmathieu, he took Madeleine.

Immediately after Champmathieu had been set at liberty, the district-attorney shut himself up with the President. They conferred "as to the necessity of seizing the person of M. le Maire of M. sur M." This phrase, in which there was a great deal of *of*, is the district-attorney's, written with his own hand, on the minutes of his report to the attorney-general. His first emotion having passed off, the President did not offer many objections. Justice must, after all, take its course. And then, when all was said, although the President was a kindly and a tolerably intelligent man, he was, at the same time, a devoted and almost an ardent royalist, and he had been shocked to hear the Mayor of M. sur M. say the *Emperor*, and not *Bonaparte*, when alluding to the landing at Cannes.

The order for his arrest was accordingly dispatched. The district-attorney forwarded it to M. sur M. by a special messenger, at full speed, and entrusted its execution to Police Inspector Javert.

The reader knows that Javert had returned to M. sur M. immediately after having given his deposition.

Javert was just getting out of bed when the messenger handed him the order of arrest and the command to produce the prisoner.

The messenger himself was a very clever member of the police, who, in two words, informed Javert of what had taken place at Arras. The order of arrest, signed by the district-attorney was couched in these words: "Inspector Javert will apprehend the body of the Sieur Madeleine, mayor of M. sur M., who, in this day's session of the court, was recognized as the liberated convict, Jean Valjean."

Anyone who did not know Javert, and who had chanced to see him at the moment when he penetrated the antechamber of the infirmary, could have divined nothing of what had taken place, and would have thought his air the most ordinary in the world. He was cool, calm, grave, his gray hair was perfectly smooth upon his temples, and he had just mounted the stairs with his habitual deliberation. Anyone who was thoroughly acquainted with him, and who had examined him attentively at the moment, would have shuddered. The buckle of his leather stock was under his left ear instead of at the nape of his neck. This betrayed unwonted agitation.

Javert was a complete character, who never had a wrinkle in his duty or in his uniform; methodical with malefactors, rigid with the buttons of his coat.

That he should have set the buckle of his stock awry, it was indispensable that there should have taken place in him one of those emotions which may be designated as internal earthquakes.

He had come in a simple way, had made a requisition on the neighboring post for a corporal and four soldiers, had left the soldiers in the courtyard, had had Fantine's room pointed out to him by the portress, who was utterly unsuspicious, accustomed as she was to seeing armed men inquiring for the mayor.

On arriving at Fantine's chamber, Javert turned the handle, pushed the door open with the gentleness of a sick-nurse or a police spy, and entered.

Properly speaking, he did not enter. He stood erect in the half-open door, his hat on his head and his left hand thrust into his coat, which was buttoned up to the chin. In the bend of his elbow the leaden head of his enormous cane, which was hidden behind him, could be seen.

Thus he remained for nearly a minute, without his presence being perceived. All at once Fantine raised her eyes, saw him, and made M. Madeleine turn round.

The instant that Madeleine's glance encountered Javert's glance, Javert, without stirring, without moving from his post, without approaching , became terrible. No human sentiment can be as terrible as joy.

It was the visage of a demon who has just found his damned soul.

The satisfaction of at last getting hold of Jean Valjean caused all that was in his soul to appear in his countenance. The depths having been stirred up, mounted to the surface. The humiliation of having, in some slight degree, lost the scent, and of having indulged, for a few moments, in an error with regard to Champmathieu, was effaced by pride at having so well and accurately divined in the first place, and of having for so long cherished a just instinct. Javert's content shone forth in his sovereign attitude. The deformity of triumph overspread that narrow brow. All the demonstrations of horror which a satisfied face can afford were there.

Javert was in heaven at that moment. Without putting the thing clearly to himself, but with a confused intuition of the necessity of his presence and of his success, he, Javert, personified justice, light, and truth in their celestial function of crushing out evil. Behind him and around him, at an infinite distance, he had authority, reason, the case judged, the legal conscience, the public prosecution, all the stars; he was protecting order, he was causing the law to yield up its thunders, he was avenging society, he was lending a helping hand to the absolute, he was standing erect in the midst of a glory. There existed in his victory a remnant of defiance and of combat. Erect, haughty, brilliant, he flaunted abroad in open day the superhuman bestiality of a ferocious archangel. The terrible shadow of the action which he was accomplishing caused the vague flash of the social sword to be visible in his clenched fist; happy and indignant, he held his heel upon crime, vice, rebellion, perdition, hell; he was radiant, he exterminated, he smiled, and there was an incontestable grandeur in this monstrous Saint Michael.

Javert, though frightful, had nothing ignoble about him.

Probity, sincerity, candor, conviction, the sense of duty, are things which may become hideous when wrongly directed; but which, even when hideous, remain grand: their majesty, the majesty peculiar to the human conscience, clings to them in the midst of horror; they are virtues which have one vice—error. The honest, pitiless joy of a fanatic in the full flood of his atrocity preserves a certain lugubriously venerable radiance. Without himself suspecting the fact, Javert in his formidable happiness was to be pitied, as is every ignorant man who triumphs. Nothing could be so poignant and so terrible as this face, wherein was displayed all that may be designated as the evil of the good.

Chapter IV

Authority Reasserts Its Rights

FANTINE HAD NOT SEEN JAVERT SINCE THE DAY ON WHICH THE MAYOR HAD TORN HER FROM THE man. Her ailing brain comprehended nothing, but the only thing which she did not doubt was that he had come to get her. She could not endure that terrible face; she felt her life quitting her; she hid her face in both hands, and shrieked in her anguish:

"Monsieur Madeleine, save me!"

Jean Valjean—we shall henceforth not speak of him otherwise—had risen. He said to Fantine in the gentlest and calmest of voices:

"Be at ease; it is not for you that he is come."

Then he addressed Javert, and said:

"I know what you want."

Javert replied:

"Be quick about it!"

There lay in the inflection of voice which accompanied these words something indescribably fierce and frenzied. Javert did not say, "Be quick about it!" he said "Bequiabouit."

No orthography can do justice to the accent with which it was uttered: it was no longer a human word; it was a roar.

He did not proceed according to his custom, he did not enter into the matter, he exhibited no warrant of arrest. In his eyes, Jean Valjean was a sort of mysterious combatant, who was not to be laid hands upon, a wrestler in the dark whom he had had in his grasp for the last five years, without being able to throw him. This arrest was not a beginning, but an end. He confined himself to saying, "Be quick about it!"

As he spoke thus, he did not advance a single step; he hurled at Jean Valjean a glance which he threw out like a grappling-hook, and with which he was accustomed to draw wretches violently to him.

It was this glance which Fantine had felt penetrating to the very marrow of her bones two months previously.

At Javert's exclamation, Fantine opened her eyes once more. But the mayor was there; what had she to fear?

Javert advanced to the middle of the room, and cried:

"See here now! Art thou coming?"

The unhappy woman glanced about her. No one was present excepting the nun and the mayor. To whom could that abject use of "thou" be addressed? To her only. She shuddered.

Then she beheld a most unprecedented thing, a thing so unprecedented that nothing equal to it had appeared to her even in the blackest deliriums of fever.

She beheld Javert, the police spy, seize the mayor by the collar; she saw the mayor bow his head. It seemed to her that the world was coming to an end.

Javert had, in fact, grasped Jean Valjean by the collar.

"Monsieur le Maire!" shrieked Fantine.

Javert burst out laughing with that frightful laugh which displayed all his gums.

"There is no longer any Monsieur le Maire here!"

Jean Valjean made no attempt to disengage the hand which grasped the collar of his coat. He said:

"Javert—"

Javert interrupted him: "Call me Mr. Inspector."

"Monsieur," said Jean Valjean, "I should like to say a word to you in private."

"Aloud! Say it aloud!" replied Javert; "people are in the habit of talking aloud to me."

Jean Valjean went on in a lower tone:

"I have a request to make of you—"

"I tell you to speak loud."

"But you alone should hear it—"

"What difference does that make to me? I shall not listen."

Jean Valjean turned toward him and said very rapidly and in a very low voice:

"Grant me three days' grace! three days in which to go and fetch the child of this unhappy woman. I will pay whatever is necessary. You shall accompany me if you choose."

"You are making sport of me!" cried Javert. "Come now, I did not think you such a fool! You ask me to give you three days in which to run away! You say that it is for the purpose of fetching that creature's child! Ah! Ah! That's good! That's really capital!"

Fantine was seized with a fit of trembling.

"My child!" she cried, "to go and fetch my child! She is not here, then! Answer me, sister; where is Cosette? I want my child! Monsieur Madeleine! Monsieur le Maire!"

Javert stamped his foot.

"And now there's the other one! Will you hold your tongue, you hussy? It's a pretty sort of a place where convicts are magistrates, and where women of the town are cared for like countesses! Ah! But we are going to change all that; it is high time!"

He stared intently at Fantine, and added, once more taking into his grasp Jean Valjean's cravat, shirt and collar:

"I tell you that there is no Monsieur Madeleine and that there is no Monsieur le Maire. There is a thief, a brigand, a convict named Jean Valjean! And I have him in my grasp! That's what there is!"

Fantine raised herself in bed with a bound, supporting herself on her stiffened arms and on both hands: she gazed at Jean Valjean, she gazed at Javert, she gazed at the nun, she opened her mouth as though to speak; a rattle proceeded from the depths of her throat, her teeth chattered; she stretched out her arms in her agony, opening her hands convulsively, and fumbling about her like a drowning person; then suddenly fell back on her pillow.

Her head struck the head-board of the bed and fell forwards on her breast, with gaping mouth and staring, sightless eyes.

She was dead.

Jean Valjean laid his hand upon the detaining hand of Javert, and opened it as he would have opened the hand of a baby; then he said to Javert:

"You have murdered that woman."

"Let's have an end of this!" shouted Javert, in a fury; "I am not here to listen to argument. Let us economize all that; the guard is below; march on instantly, or you'll get the thumb-screws!"

In the corner of the room stood an old iron bedstead, which was in a decidedly decrepit state, and which served the sisters as a camp-bed when they were watching with the sick. Jean Valjean stepped up to this bed, in a twinkling wrenched off the head-piece, which was already in a dilapidated condition, an easy matter to muscles like his, grasped the principal rod like a bludgeon, and glanced at Javert. Javert retreated towards the door. Jean Valjean, armed with his bar of iron, walked slowly up to Fantine's couch. When he arrived there he turned and said to Javert, in a voice that was barely audible:

"I advise you not to disturb me at this moment."

One thing is certain, and that is, that Javert trembled.

It did occur to him to summon the guard, but Jean Valjean might avail himself of that moment to effect his escape; so he remained, grasped his cane by the small end, and leaned against the door-post, without removing his eyes from Jean Valjean.

Jean Valjean rested his elbow on the knob at the head of the bed, and his brow on his hand, and began to contemplate the motionless body of Fantine, which lay extended there. He remained thus, mute, absorbed, evidently with no further thought of anything connected with this life. Upon his face and in his attitude there was nothing but inexpressible pity. After a few moments of this meditation he bent towards Fantine, and spoke to her in a low voice.

What did he say to her? What could this man, who was reproved, say to that woman, who was dead? What words were those? No one on earth heard them. Did the dead woman hear them? There are some touching illusions which are, perhaps, sublime realities. The point as to which there exists no doubt is, that Sister Simplice, the sole witness of the incident, often said that at the moment that Jean Valjean whispered in Fantine's ear, she distinctly beheld an ineffable smile dawn on those pale lips, and in those dim eyes, filled with the amazement of the tomb.

Jean Valjean took Fantine's head in both his hands, and arranged it on the pillow as a mother might have done for her child; then he tied the string of her chemise, and smoothed her hair back under her cap. That done, he closed her eyes.

Fantine's face seemed strangely illuminated at that moment.

Death, that signifies entrance into the great light.

Fantine's hand was hanging over the side of the bed. Jean Valjean knelt down before that hand, lifted it gently, and kissed it.

Then he rose, and turned to Javert.

"Now," said he, "I am at your disposal."

Chapter V

A SUITABLE TOMB

JAVERT DEPOSITED JEAN VALJEAN IN THE CITY PRISON.

The arrest of M. Madeleine occasioned a sensation, or rather, an extraordinary commotion in M. sur M. We are sorry that we cannot conceal the fact, that at the single word, "He was a convict," nearly everyone deserted him. In less than two hours all the good that he had done had been forgotten, and he was nothing but a "convict from the galleys." It is just to add that the details of what had taken place at Arras were not yet known. All day long conversations like the following were to be heard in all quarters of the town:

"You don't know? He was a liberated convict!" "Who?" "The mayor." "Bah! M. Madeleine?" "Yes." "Really?" "His name was not Madeleine at all; he had a frightful name, Béjean, Bojean, Boujean." "Ah! Good God!" "He has been arrested." "Arrested!" "In prison, in the city prison, while waiting to be transferred." "Until he is transferred!" "He is to be transferred!" "Where is he to be taken?" "He will be tried at the Assizes for a highway robbery which he committed long ago." "Well! I suspected as much. That man was too good, too perfect, too affected. He refused the cross; he bestowed sous on all the little scamps he came across. I always thought there was some evil history back of all that."

The "drawing-rooms" particularly abounded in remarks of this nature.

One old lady, a subscriber to the *Drapeau Blanc,* made the following remark, the depth of which it is impossible to fathom:

"I am not sorry. It will be a lesson to the Bonapartists!"

It was thus that the phantom which had been called M. Madeleine vanished from M. sur M. Only three or four persons in all the town remained faithful to his memory. The old portress who had served him was among the number.

On the evening of that day the worthy old woman was sitting in her lodge, still in a thorough fright, and absorbed in sad reflections. The factory had been closed all day, the carriage gate was bolted, the street was deserted. There was no one in the house but the two nuns, Sister Perpétue and Sister Simplice, who were watching beside the body of Fantine.

Towards the hour when M. Madeleine was accustomed to return home, the good portress rose mechanically, took from a drawer the key of M. Madeleine's chamber, and the flat candlestick which he used every evening to go up to his quarters; then she hung the key on the nail whence he was accustomed to take it, and set the candlestick on one side, as though she was expecting him. Then she sat down again on her chair, and became absorbed in thought once more. The poor, good old woman had done all this without being conscious of it.

It was only at the expiration of two hours that she roused herself from her reverie, and exclaimed, "Hold! My good God Jesus! And I hung his key on the nail!"

At that moment the small window in the lodge opened, a hand passed through, seized the key and the candlestick, and lighted the taper at the candle which was burning there.

The portress raised her eyes, and stood there with gaping mouth, and a shriek which she confined to her throat.

She knew that hand, that arm, the sleeve of that coat.

It was M. Madeleine.

It was several seconds before she could speak; she had a *seizure,* as she said herself, when she related the adventure afterwards.

"Good God, Monsieur le Maire," she cried at last, "I thought you were—"

She stopped; the conclusion of her sentence would have been lacking in respect toward the beginning. Jean Valjean was still Monsieur le Maire to her.

He finished her thought.

"In prison," said he. "I was there; I broke a bar of one of the windows; I let myself drop from the top of a roof, and here I am. I am going up to my room; go and find Sister Simplice for me. She is with that poor woman, no doubt."

The old woman obeyed in all haste.

He gave her no orders; he was quite sure that she would guard him better than he should guard himself.

No one ever found out how he had managed to get into the courtyard without opening the big gates. He had, and always carried about him, a pass-key which opened a little side-door; but he must have been searched, and his latch-key must have been taken from him. This point was never explained.

He ascended the staircase leading to his chamber. On arriving at the top, he left his candle on the top step of his stairs, opened his door with very little noise, went and closed his window and his shutters by feeling, then returned for his candle and re-entered his room.

It was a useful precaution; it will be recollected that his window could be seen from the street.

He cast a glance about him, at his table, at his chair, at his bed which had not been disturbed for three days. No trace of the disorder of the night before last remained. The portress had "done up" his room; only she had picked out of the ashes and placed neatly on the table the two iron ends of the cudgel and the forty-sou piece which had been blackened by the fire.

He took a sheet of paper, on which he wrote: "These are the two tips of my iron-shod cudgel and the forty-sou piece stolen from Little Gervais, which I mentioned at the Court of Assizes," and he arranged this piece of paper, the bits of iron, and the coin in such a way that they were the first things to be seen on entering the room. From a cupboard he pulled out one of his old shirts, which he tore in pieces. In the strips of linen thus prepared he wrapped the two silver candlesticks. He betrayed neither haste nor agitation; and while he was wrapping up the Bishop's candlesticks, he nibbled at a piece of black bread. It was probably the prison-bread which he had carried with him in his flight.

This was proved by the crumbs which were found on the floor of the room when the authorities made an examination later on.

There came two taps at the door.

"Come in," said he.

It was Sister Simplice.

She was pale; her eyes were red; the candle which she carried trembled in her hand. The peculiar feature of the violences of destiny is, that however polished or cool we may be, they wring human nature from our very bowels, and force it to reappear on the surface. The emotions of that day had turned the nun into a woman once more. She had wept, and she was trembling.

Jean Valjean had just finished writing a few lines on a paper, which he handed to the nun, saying, "Sister, you will give this to Monsieur le Curé."

The paper was not folded. She cast a glance upon it.

"You can read it," said he.

She read:

"I beg Monsieur le Curé to keep an eye on all that I leave behind me. He will be so good as to pay out of it the expenses of my trial, and of the funeral of the woman who died yesterday. The rest is for the poor."

The sister tried to speak, but she only managed to stammer a few inarticulate sounds. She succeeded in saying, however:

"Does not Monsieur le Maire desire to take a last look at that poor, unhappy woman?"

"No," said he; "I am pursued; it would only end in their arresting me in that room, and that would disturb her."

He had hardly finished when a loud noise became audible on the staircase. They heard a tumult of ascending footsteps, and the old portress saying in her loudest and most piercing tones:

"My good sir, I swear to you by the good God, that not a soul has entered this house all day, nor all the evening, and that I have not even left the door."

A man responded:

"But there is a light in that room, nevertheless."

They recognized Javert's voice.

The chamber was so arranged that the door in opening masked the corner of the wall on the right. Jean Valjean blew out the light and placed himself in this angle.

Sister Simplice fell on her knees near the table.

The door opened.

Javert entered.

The whispers of many men and the protestations of the portress were audible in the corridor.

The nun did not raise her eyes. She was praying.

The candle was on the chimney-piece, and gave but very little light.

Javert caught sight of the nun and halted in amazement.

It will be remembered that the fundamental point in Javert, his element, the very air he breathed, was veneration for all authority. This was impregnable, and admitted of neither objection nor restriction. In his eyes, of course, the ecclesiastical authority was the chief of all; he was religious, superficial and correct on this point as on all others. In his eyes, a priest was a mind, who never makes a mistake; a nun was a creature who never sins; they were souls walled in from this world, with a single door which never opened except to allow the truth to pass through.

On perceiving the sister, his first movement was to retire.

But there was also another duty which bound him and impelled him imperiously in the opposite direction. His second movement was to remain and to venture on at least one question.

This was Sister Simplice, who had never told a lie in her life. Javert knew it, and held her in special veneration in consequence.

"Sister," said he, "are you alone in this room?"

A terrible moment ensued, during which the poor portress felt as though she should faint.

The sister raised her eyes and answered:

"Yes."

"Then," resumed Javert, "you will excuse me if I persist; it is my duty; you have not seen a certain person—a man—this evening? He has escaped; we are in search of him—that Jean Valjean; you have not seen him?"

The sister replied:

"No."

She lied. She had lied twice in succession, one after the other, without hesitation, promptly, as a person does when sacrificing herself.

"Pardon me," said Javert, and he retired with a deep bow.

O sainted maid! you left this world many years ago; you have rejoined your sisters, the virgins, and your brothers, the angels, in the light; may this lie be counted to your credit in paradise!

The sister's affirmation was for Javert so decisive a thing that he did not even observe the singularity of that candle which had but just been extinguished, and which was still smoking on the table.

An hour later, a man, marching amid trees and mists, was rapidly departing from M. sur M. in the direction of Paris. That man was Jean Valjean. It has been established by the testimony of two or three carters who met him, that he was carrying a bundle; that he was dressed in a blouse. Where had he obtained that blouse? No one ever found out. But an aged workman had died in the infirmary of the factory a few days before, leaving behind him nothing but his blouse. Perhaps that was the one.

One last word about Fantine.

We all have a mother—the earth. Fantine was given back to that mother.

The curé thought that he was doing right, and perhaps he really was, in reserving as much money as possible from what Jean Valjean had left for the poor. Who was concerned, after all? A convict and a woman of the town. That is why he had a very simple funeral for Fantine, and reduced it to that strictly necessary form known as the pauper's grave.

So Fantine was buried in the free corner of the cemetery which belongs to anybody and everybody, and where the poor are lost. Fortunately, God knows where to find the soul again. Fantine was laid in the shade, among the first bones that came to hand; she was subjected to the promiscuousness of ashes. She was thrown into the public grave. Her grave resembled her bed.

VOLUME II

COSETTE

Book First

Waterloo

Chapter I

What is Met with on the Way from Nivelles

LAST YEAR (1861), ON A BEAUTIFUL MAY MORNING, A TRAVELER, THE PERSON WHO IS TELLING this story, was coming from Nivelles, and directing his course toward La Hulpe. He was on foot. He was pursuing a broad paved road, which undulated between two rows of trees, over the hills which succeed each other, raise the road and let it fall again, and produce something in the nature of enormous waves.

He had passed Lillois and Bois-Seigneur-Isaac. In the west he perceived the slate-roofed tower of Braine-l'Alleud, which has the form of a reversed vase. He had just left behind a wood upon an eminence; and at the angle of the cross-road, by the side of a sort of moldy gibbet bearing the inscription *Ancient Barrier No. 4*, a public-house, bearing on its front this sign: *At the Four Winds* (Aux Quatre Vents). *Échabeau, Private Café.*

A quarter of a league further on, he arrived at the bottom of a little valley, where there is water which passes beneath an arch made through the embankment of the road. The clump of sparsely planted but very green trees, which fills the valley on one side of the road, is dispersed over the meadows on the other, and disappears gracefully and as in disorder in the direction of Braine-l'Alleud.

On the right, close to the road, was an inn, with a four-wheeled cart at the door, a large bundle of hop-poles, a plow, a heap of dried brushwood near a flourishing hedge, lime smoking in a square hole, and a ladder suspended along an old penthouse with straw partitions. A young girl was weeding in a field, where a huge yellow poster, probably of some outside spectacle, such as a parish festival, was fluttering in the wind. At one corner of the inn, beside a pool in which a flotilla of ducks was navigating, a badly paved path plunged into the bushes. The wayfarer struck into this.

After traversing a hundred paces, skirting a wall of the fifteenth century, surmounted by a pointed gable, with bricks set in contrast, he found himself before a large door of arched stone, with a rectilinear impost, in the somber style of Louis XIV, flanked by two flat medallions. A severe façade rose above this door; a wall, perpendicular to the façade, almost touched the door, and flanked it with an abrupt right angle. In the meadow before the door lay three harrows, through which, in disorder, grew all the flowers of May. The door was closed. The two decrepit leaves which barred it were ornamented with an old rusty knocker.

The sun was charming; the branches had that soft shivering of May, which seems to proceed rather from the nests than from the wind. A brave little bird, probably a lover, was caroling in a distracted manner in a large tree.

The wayfarer bent over and examined a rather large circular excavation, resembling the hollow of a sphere, in the stone on the left, at the foot of the pier of the door.

At this moment the leaves of the door parted, and a peasant woman emerged.

She saw the wayfarer, and perceived what he was looking at.

"It was a French cannon-ball which made that," she said to him. And she added:

"That which you see there, higher up in the door, near a nail, is the hole of a big iron bullet as large as an egg. The bullet did not pierce the wood."

"What is the name of this place?" inquired the wayfarer.

"Hougomont," said the peasant woman.

The traveler straightened himself up. He walked on a few paces, and went off to look over the tops of the hedges. On the horizon, through the trees, he perceived a sort of little elevation, and on this elevation something which at that distance resembled a lion.

He was on the battlefield of Waterloo.

Chapter II

HOUGOMONT

HOUGOMONT—THIS WAS A FUNEREAL SPOT, THE BEGINNING OF THE OBSTACLE, THE FIRST RE-sistance, which that great wood-cutter of Europe, called Napoleon, encountered at Waterloo, the first knot under the blows of his ax.

It was a château; it is no longer anything but a farm. For the antiquary, Hougomont is *Hugomons.* This manor was built by Hugo, Sire of Somerel, the same who endowed the sixth chaplaincy of the Abbey of Villiers.

The traveler pushed open the door, elbowed an ancient calash under the porch, and entered the courtyard.

The first thing which struck him in this paddock was a door of the sixteenth century, which here simulates an arcade, everything else having fallen prostrate around it. A monumental aspect often has its birth in ruin. In a wall near the arcade opens another arched door, of the time of Henry IV, permitting a glimpse of the trees of an orchard; beside this door, a manure-hole, some pickaxes, some shovels, some carts, an old well, with its flagstone and its iron reel, a chicken jumping, and a turkey spreading its tail, a chapel surmounted by a small bell tower, a blossoming pear-tree trained in espalier against the wall of the chapel—behold the court, the conquest of which was one of Napoleon's dreams. This corner of earth, could he but have seized it, would, perhaps, have given him the world likewise. Chickens are scattering its dust abroad with their beaks. A growl is audible; it is a huge dog, who shows his teeth and replaces the English.

The English behaved admirably there. Cooke's four companies of guards there held out for seven hours against the fury of an army.

Hougomont viewed on the map, as a geometrical plan, comprising buildings and enclosures, presents a sort of irregular rectangle, one angle of which is nicked out. It is this angle which contains the southern door, guarded by this wall, which commands it only a gun's length away. Hougomont has two doors—the southern door, that of the château; and the northern door, belonging to the farm. Napoleon sent his brother Jérôme against Hougomont; the divisions of Foy, Guilleminot, and Bachelu hurled themselves against it; nearly the entire corps of Reille was employed against it, and miscarried; Kellermann's balls were exhausted on this heroic section of wall. Bauduin's brigade was not strong enough to force Hougomont on the north, and the brigade of Soye could not do more than effect the beginning of a breach on the south, but without taking it.

The farm buildings border the courtyard on the south. A bit of the north door, broken by the

French, hangs suspended to the wall. It consists of four planks nailed to two cross-beams, on which the scars of the attack are visible.

The northern door, which was beaten in by the French, and which has had a piece applied to it to replace the panel suspended on the wall stands half-open at the bottom of the paddock; it is cut squarely in the wall, built of stone below, of brick above, which closes in the courtyard on the north. It is a simple door for carts, such as exist in all farms, with the two large leaves made of rustic planks: beyond lie the meadows. The dispute over this entrance was furious. For a long time, all sorts of imprints of bloody hands were visible on the door-posts. It was there that Bauduin was killed.

The storm of the combat still lingers in this courtyard; its horror is visible there; the confusion of the fray was petrified there; it lives and it dies there; it was only yesterday. The walls are in the death-agony, the stones fall; the breaches cry aloud; the holes are wounds; the drooping, quivering trees seem to be making an effort to flee.

This courtyard was more built up in 1815 than it is to-day. Buildings which have since been pulled down, then formed redans and angles.

The English barricaded themselves there; the French made their way in, but could not stand their ground. Beside the chapel, one wing of the château, the only ruin now remaining of the manor of Hougomont, rises in a crumbling state—disemboweled, one might say. The château served for a dungeon, the chapel for a block-house. There men exterminated each other. The French, fired on from every point—from behind the walls, from the summits of the garrets, from the depths of the cellars, through all the casements, through all the air-holes, through every crack in the stones—fetched fagots and set fire to walls and men; the reply to the grape-shot was a conflagration.

In the ruined wing, through windows garnished with bars of iron, the dismantled chambers of the main building of brick are visible; the English guards were in ambush in these rooms; the spiral of the staircase, cracked from the ground floor to the very roof, appears like the inside of a broken shell. The staircase has two stories; the English, besieged on the staircase, and massed on its upper steps, had cut off the lower steps. These consisted of large slabs of blue stone, which form a heap among the nettles. Half a score of steps still cling to the wall; on the first is cut the figure of a trident. These inaccessible steps are solid in their niches. All the rest resembles a jaw which has been denuded of its teeth. There are two old trees there: one is dead; the other is wounded at its base, and is clothed with verdure in April. Since 1815 it has taken to growing through the staircase.

A massacre took place in the chapel. The interior, which has recovered its calm, is singular. The mass has not been said there since the carnage. Nevertheless, the altar has been left there—an altar of unpolished wood, placed against a background of roughhewn stone. Four whitewashed walls, a door opposite the altar, two small arched windows; over the door a large wooden crucifix, below the crucifix a square air-hole stopped up with a bundle of hay; on the ground, in one corner, an old window-frame with the glass all broken to pieces—such is the chapel. Near the altar there is nailed up a wooden statue of Saint Anne, of the fifteenth century; the head of the infant Jesus has been carried off by a large ball. The French, who were masters of the chapel for a moment, and were then dislodged, set fire to it. The flames filled this building; it was a perfect furnace; the door was burned, the floor was burned, the wooden Christ was not burned. The fire preyed upon his feet, of which only the blackened stumps are now to be seen; then it stopped—a miracle, according to the assertion of the people of the neighborhood. The infant Jesus, decapitated, was less fortunate than the Christ.

The walls are covered with inscriptions. Near the feet of Christ this name is to be read: *Henquinez*. Then these others: *Conde de Rio Maior Marques y Marquesa de Almagro (Habana)*. There are French names with exclamation points—a sign of wrath. The wall was freshly whitewashed in 1849. The nations insulted each other there.

It was at the door of this chapel that the corpse was picked up which held an ax in its hand; this corpse was Sub-Lieutenant Legros.

On emerging from the chapel, a well is visible on the left. There are two in this courtyard. One inquires, Why is there no bucket and pulley to this? It is because water is no longer drawn there. Why is water not drawn there? Because it is full of skeletons.

The last person who drew water from the well was named Guillaume van Kylsom. He was a peasant who lived at Hougomont, and was gardener there. On the 18th of June, 1815, his family fled and concealed themselves in the woods.

The forest surrounding the Abbey of Villiers sheltered these unfortunate people who had been scattered abroad, for many days and nights. There are at this day certain traces recognizable, such as old boles of burned trees, which mark the site of these poor bivouacs trembling in the depths of the thickets.

Guillaume van Kylsom remained at Hougomont, "to guard the château," and concealed himself in the cellar. The English discovered him there. They tore him from his hiding-place, and the combatants forced this frightened man to serve them, by administering blows with the flats of their swords. They were thirsty; this Guillaume brought them water. It was from this well that he drew it. Many drank there their last draft. This well where drank so many of the dead was destined to die itself.

After the engagement, they were in haste to bury the dead bodies. Death has a fashion of harassing victory, and she causes the pest to follow glory. The typhus is a concomitant of triumph. This well was deep, and it was turned into a sepulcher. Three hundred dead bodies were cast into it. With too much haste perhaps. Were they all dead? Legend says they were not. It seems that on the night succeeding the interment, feeble voices were heard calling from the well.

This well is isolated in the middle of the courtyard. Three walls, part stone, part brick, and simulating a small, square tower, and folded like the leaves of a screen, surround it on all sides. The fourth side is open. It is there that the water was drawn. The wall at the bottom has a sort of shapeless loophole, possibly the hole made by a shell. This little tower had a platform, of which only the beams remain. The iron supports of the well on the right form a cross. On leaning over, the eye is lost in a deep cylinder of brick which is filled with a heaped-up mass of shadows. The base of the walls all about the well is concealed in a growth of nettles.

This well has not in front of it that large blue slab which forms the table for all wells in Belgium. The slab has here been replaced by a cross-beam, against which lean five or six shapeless fragments of knotty and petrified wood which resemble huge bones. There is no longer either pail, chain, or pulley; but there is still the stone basin which served the overflow. The rainwater collects there, and from time to time a bird of the neighboring forests comes thither to drink, and then flies away. One house in this ruin, the farm-house, is still inhabited. The door of this house opens on the courtyard. Upon this door, beside a pretty Gothic lock-plate, there is an iron handle with trefoils placed slanting. At the moment when the Hanoverian lieutenant, Wilda, grasped this handle in order to take refuge in the farm, a French sapper hewed off his hand with an ax.

The family who occupy the house had for their grandfather Guillaume van Kylsom, the old gardener, dead long since. A woman with gray hair said to us: "I was there. I was three years old. My sister, who was older, was terrified and wept. They carried us off to the woods. I went there in my mother's arms. We glued our ears to the earth to hear. I imitated the cannon, and went *boum! boum!*"

A door opening from the courtyard on the left led into the orchard, so we were told. The orchard is terrible.

It is in three parts; one might almost say, in three acts. The first part is a garden, the second is an orchard, the third is a wood. These three parts have a common enclosure: on the side of the entrance, the buildings of the château and the farm; on the left, a hedge; on the right, a wall; and at the end, a wall. The wall on the right is of brick, the wall at the bottom is of stone. One enters the garden first. It slopes downwards, is planted with gooseberry bushes, choked with a wild growth of vegetation, and terminated by a monumental terrace of cut stone, with balustrade with a double curve.

It was a seignorial garden in the first French style which preceded Le Nôtre; to-day it is ruins and briars. The pilasters are surmounted by globes which resemble cannon-balls of stone. Forty-three balusters can still be counted on their sockets; the rest lie prostrate in the grass. Almost all bear scratches of bullets. One broken baluster is placed on the pediment like a fractured leg.

It was in this garden, further down than the orchard, that six light-infantry men of the 1st, having made their way thither, and being unable to escape, hunted down and caught like bears in their dens, accepted the combat with two Hanoverian companies, one of which was armed with carbines. The Hanoverians lined this balustrade and fired from above. The infantry men, replying from below, six against two hundred, intrepid and with no shelter save the currant-bushes, took a quarter of an hour to die.

One mounts a few steps and passes from the garden into the orchard, properly speaking. There, within the limits of those few square fathoms, fifteen hundred men fell in less than an hour. The wall seems ready to renew the combat. Thirty-eight loopholes, pierced by the English at irregular heights, are there still. In front of the sixth are placed two English tombs of granite. There are loopholes only in the south wall, as the principal attack came from that quarter. The wall is hidden on the outside by a tall hedge; the French came up, thinking that they had to deal only with a hedge, crossed it, and found the wall both an obstacle and an ambuscade, with the English Guards behind it, the thirty-eight loopholes firing at once a shower of grape-shot and balls, and Soye's brigade was broken against it. Thus Waterloo began.

Nevertheless, the orchard was taken. As they had no ladders, the French scaled it with their nails. They fought hand to hand amid the trees. All this grass has been soaked in blood. A battalion of Nassau, seven hundred strong, was overwhelmed there. The outside of the wall, against which Kellermann's two batteries were trained, is gnawed by grape-shot.

This orchard is sentient, like others, in the month of May. It has its buttercups and its daisies; the grass is tall there; the cart-horses browse there; cords of hair, on which linen is drying, traverse the spaces between the trees and force the passer-by to bend his head; one walks over this uncultivated land, and one's foot dives into mole-holes. In the middle of the grass one observes an uprooted tree-bole which lies there all verdant. Major Blackmann leaned against it to die. Beneath a great tree in the neighborhood fell the German general, Duplat, descended from a French family which fled on the revocation of the Edict of Nantes. An aged and falling apple-tree leans far over to one side, its wound dressed with a bandage of straw and of clayey loam. Nearly all the apple-trees are falling with age. There is not one which has not had its bullet or its biscayan. The skeletons of dead trees abound in this orchard. Crows fly through their branches, and at the end of it is a wood full of violets.

Bauduin, killed, Foy wounded, conflagration, massacre, carnage, a rivulet formed of English blood, French blood, German blood mingled in fury, a well crammed with corpses, the regiment of Nassau and the regiment of Brunswick destroyed, Duplat killed, Blackmann killed, the English Guards mutilated, twenty French battalions, besides the forty from Reille's corps, decimated, three thousand men in that hovel of Hougomont alone cut down, slashed to pieces, shot, burned, with their throats cut—and all this so that a peasant can say to-day to the traveler: *Monsieur, give me three francs, and if you like, I will explain to you the affair of Waterloo!*

Chapter III

THE EIGHTEENTH OF JUNE, 1815

LET US TURN BACK—THAT IS ONE OF THE STORY-TELLER'S RIGHTS—AND PUT OURSELVES ONCE more in the year 1815, and even a little earlier than the epoch when the action narrated in the first part of this book took place.

If it had not rained in the night between the 17th and the 18th of June, 1815, the fate of Europe would have been different. A few drops of water, more or less, decided the downfall of Napoleon. All that Providence required in order to make Waterloo the end of Austerlitz was a little more rain, and a cloud traversing the sky out of season sufficed to make a world crumble.

The battle of Waterloo could not be begun until half-past eleven o'clock, and that gave Blücher time to come up. Why? Because the ground was wet. The artillery had to wait until it became a little firmer before they could maneuver.

Napoleon was an artillery officer, and felt the effects of this. The foundation of this wonderful captain was the man who, in the report to the Directory on Aboukir, said: *Such a one of our balls killed six men.* All his plans of battle were arranged for projectiles. The key to his victory was to make the artillery converge on one point. He treated the strategy of the hostile general like a citadel, and made a breach in it. He overwhelmed the weak point with grape-shot; he joined and dissolved battles with cannon. There was something of the sharpshooter in his genius. To beat in squares, to pulverize regiments, to break lines, to crush and disperse masses—for him everything lay in this, to strike, strike, strike incessantly—and he intrusted this task to the cannon-ball. A redoubtable method, and one which, united with genius, rendered this gloomy athlete of the pugilism of war invincible for the space of fifteen years.

On the 18th of June, 1815, he relied all the more on his artillery, because he had numbers on his side. Wellington had only one hundred and fifty-nine mouths of fire; Napoleon had two hundred and forty.

Suppose the soil dry, and the artillery capable of moving, the action would have begun at six o'clock in the morning. The battle would have been won and ended at two o'clock, three hours before the change of fortune in favor of the Prussians. What amount of blame attaches to Napoleon for the loss of this battle? Is the shipwreck due to the pilot?

Was it the evident physical decline of Napoleon that complicated this epoch by an inward diminution of force? Had the twenty years of war worn out the blade as it had worn the scabbard, the soul as well as the body? Did the veteran make himself disastrously felt in the leader? In a word, was this genius, as many historians of note have thought, suffering from an eclipse? Did he go into a frenzy in order to disguise his weakened powers from himself? Did he begin to waver under the delusion of a breath of adventure? Had he become—a grave matter in a general—unconscious of peril? Is there an age, in this class of material great men, who may be called the giants of action, when genius grows short-sighted? Old age has no hold on the geniuses of the ideal; for the Dantes and Michael Angelos to grow old is to grow in greatness; is it to grow less for the Hannibals and the Bonapartes? Had Napoleon lost the direct sense of victory? Had he reached the point where he could no longer recognize the reef, could no longer divine the snare, no longer discern the crumbling brink of abysses? Had he lost his power of scenting out catastrophes? He who had in former days known all the roads to triumph, and who, from the summit of his chariot of lightning, pointed them out with a sovereign finger, had he now reached that state of sinister amazement when he could lead his tumultuous legions harnessed to it, to the precipice? Was he seized at the age of forty-six with a supreme madness? Was that titanic charioteer of destiny no longer anything more than an immense dare-devil?

We do not think so.

His plan of battle was, by the confession of all, a masterpiece. To go straight to the center of the Allies' line, to make a breach in the enemy, to cut them in two, to drive the British half back on Hal, and the Prussian half on Tongres, to make two shattered fragments of Wellington and Blücher, to carry Mont-Saint-Jean, to seize Brussels, to hurl the German into the Rhine, and the Englishman into the sea. All this was contained in that battle, according to Napoleon. Afterwards people would see.

Of course, we do not here pretend to furnish a history of the battle of Waterloo; one of the scenes of the foundation of the story which we are relating is connected with this battle, but this history is not our subject; this history, moreover, has been finished, and finished in a masterly manner, from one point of view by Napoleon, and from another point of view by a whole pleiad of historians.

As for us, we leave the historians at loggerheads; we are but a distant witness, a passer-by on the plain, a seeker bending over that soil all made of human flesh, taking appearances for realities, perchance; we have no right to oppose, in the name of science, a collection of facts which contain illusions, no doubt; we possess neither military practice nor strategic ability which authorize a system; in our opinion, a chain of accidents dominated the two leaders at Waterloo; and when it becomes a question of destiny, that mysterious culprit, we judge like that ingenious judge, the populace.

Chapter IV

A

THOSE PERSONS WHO WISH TO GAIN A CLEAR IDEA OF THE BATTLE OF WATERLOO HAVE ONLY TO place, mentally, on the ground, a capital A. The left limb of the A is the road to Nivelles, the right limb is the road to Genappe, the tie of the A is the hollow road to Ohain from Braine-l'Alleud. The top of the A is Mont-Saint-Jean, where Wellington is; the lower left tip is Hougomont, where Reille is stationed with Jérôme Bonaparte; the right tip is the Belle-Alliance, where Napoleon was. At the center of this chord is the precise point where the final word of the battle was pronounced. It was there that the lion has been placed, the involuntary symbol of the supreme heroism of the Imperial Guard.

The triangle included in the top of the A, between the two limbs and the tie, is the plateau of Mont-Saint-Jean. The dispute over this plateau constituted the whole battle. The wings of the two armies extended to the right and left of the two roads to Genappe and Nivelles; d'Erlon facing Picton, Reille facing Hill.

Behind the tip of the A, behind the plateau of Mont-Saint-Jean, is the forest of Soignes.

As for the plain itself, let the reader picture to himself a vast undulating sweep of ground; each rise commands the next rise, and all the undulations mount towards Mont-Saint-Jean, and there end in the forest.

Two hostile troops on a field of battle are two wrestlers. It is a question of seizing the opponent round the waist. The one seeks to trip up the other. They clutch at everything; a bush is a point of support; an angle of the wall offers them a rest to the shoulder; for the lack of a hovel under whose cover they can draw up, a regiment yields its ground; an unevenness in the ground, a chance turn in the landscape, a cross-path encountered at the right moment, a grove, a ravine, can stay the heel of that colossus which is called an army, and prevent its retreat. He who quits the field is beaten; hence the necessity devolving on the responsible leader, of examining the most insignificant clump of trees, and of studying deeply the slightest relief in the ground.

The two generals had attentively studied the plain of Mont-Saint-Jean, now called the plain of Waterloo. In the preceding year, Wellington, with the sagacity of foresight, had examined it as the possible seat of a great battle. Upon this spot, and for this duel, on the 18th of June, Wellington had the good post, Napoleon the bad post. The English army was stationed above, the French army below.

It is almost superfluous here to sketch the appearance of Napoleon on horseback, glass in hand, upon the heights of Rossomme, at daybreak, on June 18, 1815. All the world has seen him before we can show him. That calm profile under the little three-cornered hat of the school of Brienne, that green uniform, the white revers concealing the star of the Legion of Honor, his great-coat hiding his epaulets, the corner of red ribbon peeping from beneath his vest, his leather trousers, the white horse with the saddle-cloth of purple velvet bearing on the corners crowned N's and eagles, Hessian boots over silk stockings, silver spurs, the sword of Marengo—that whole figure of the last of the Cæsars is present to all imaginations, saluted with acclamations by some, severely regarded by others.

That figure stood for a long time wholly in the light; this arose from a certain legendary dimness evolved by the majority of heroes, and which always veils the truth for a longer or shorter time; but to-day history and daylight have arrived.

That light called history is pitiless; it possesses this peculiar and divine quality, that, pure light as it is, and precisely because it is wholly light, it often casts a shadow in places where people had hitherto beheld rays; from the same man it constructs two different phantoms, and the one attacks the other and executes justice on it, and the shadows of the despot contend with the brilliancy of the leader. Hence arises a truer measure in the definitive judgments of nations. Babylon violated lessens Alexander, Rome enchained lessens Cæsar, Jerusalem murdered lessens Titus, tyranny follows the tyrant. It is a misfortune for a man to leave behind him the night which bears his form.

Chapter V

THE QUID OBSCURUM OF BATTLES

EVERYONE IS ACQUAINTED WITH THE FIRST PHASE OF THIS BATTLE; A BEGINNING WHICH WAS troubled, uncertain, hesitating, menacing to both armies, but still more so for the English than for the French.

It had rained all night, the earth had been cut up by the downpour, the water had accumulated here and there in the hollows of the plain as if in casks; at some points the gear of the artillery carriages was buried up to the axles, the circingles of the horses were dripping with liquid mud. If the wheat and rye trampled down by this cohort of transports on the march had not filled in the ruts and strewn a litter beneath the wheels, all movement, particularly in the valleys, in the direction of Papelotte would have been impossible.

The affair began late. Napoleon, as we have already explained, was in the habit of keeping all his artillery well in hand, like a pistol, aiming it now at one point, now at another, of the battle; and it had been his wish to wait until the horse batteries could move and gallop freely. In order to do that it was necessary that the sun should come out and dry the soil. But the sun did not make its appearance. It was no longer the rendezvous of Austerlitz. When the first cannon was fired, the English general, Colville, looked at his watch, and noted that it was thirty-five minutes past eleven.

The action was begun furiously, with more fury, perhaps, than the Emperor would have wished, by the left wing of the French resting on Hougomont. At the same time Napoleon attacked the center by hurling Quiot's brigade on La Haie-Sainte, and Ney pushed forward the right wing of the French against the left wing of the English, which rested on Papelotte.

The attack on Hougomont was something of a feint; the plan was to draw Wellington thither, and to make him swerve to the left. This plan would have succeeded if the four companies of the English Guards and the brave Belgians of Perponcher's division had not held the position solidly, and Wellington, instead of massing his troops there, could confine himself to dispatching thither, as reinforcements, only four more companies of guards and one battalion from Brunswick.

The attack of the right wing of the French on Papelotte was calculated, in fact, to overthrow the English left, to cut off the road to Brussels, to bar the passage against possible Prussians, to force Mont-Saint-Jean, to turn Wellington back on Hougomont, thence on Braine-l'Alleud, thence on Hal; nothing easier. With the exception of a few incidents this attack succeeded Papelotte was taken; La Haie-Sainte was carried.

A detail to be noted. There was in the English infantry, particularly in Kempt's brigade, a great many raw recruits. These young soldiers were valiant in the presence of our redoubtable infantry; their inexperience extricated them intrepidly from the dilemma; they performed particularly excellent service as skirmishers: the soldier skirmisher, left somewhat to himself, becomes, so to speak, his own general. These recruits displayed some of the French ingenuity and fury. This novice of an infantry had dash. This displeased Wellington.

After the taking of La Haie-Sainte the battle wavered.

There is in this day an obscure interval, from midday to four o'clock; the middle portion of this battle is almost indistinct, and participates in the somberness of the hand-to-hand conflict. Twilight reigns over it. We perceive vast fluctuations in that fog, a dizzy mirage, paraphernalia of war almost unknown to-day, pendant colbacks, floating saber-taches, cross-belts, cartridge-boxes for grenades, hussar dolmans, red boots with a thousand wrinkles, heavy shakos garlanded with torsades, the almost black infantry of Brunswick mingled with the scarlet infantry of England, the English soldiers with great, white circular pads on the slopes of their shoulders for epaulets, the Hanoverian light-horse with their oblong casques of leather, with brass hands and red horse-tails, the Scotch with their bare knees and plaids, the great white gaiters of our grenadiers; pictures, not strategic lines—what Salvator Rosa requires, not what is suited to the needs of Gribeauval.

A certain amount of tempest is always mingled with a battle. *Quid obscurum, quid divinum.* Each historian traces, to some extent, the particular feature which pleases him amid this pell-mell. Whatever may be the combinations of the generals, the shock of armed masses has an incalculable ebb. During the action the plans of the two leaders enter into each other and become mutually thrown out of shape. Such a point of the field of battle devours more combatants than such another, just as more or less spongy soils soak up more or less quickly the water which is poured on them. It becomes necessary to pour out more soldiers than one would like; a series of expenditures which are the unforeseen. The line of battle waves and undulates like a thread, the trails of blood gush illogically, the fronts of the armies waver, the regiments form capes and gulfs as they enter and withdraw; all these reefs are continually moving in front of each other. Where the infantry stood the artillery arrives, the cavalry rushes in where the artillery was, the battalions are like smoke. There was something there; seek it. It has disappeared; the open spots change place, the somber folds advance and retreat, a sort of wind from the sepulcher pushes forward, hurls back, distends, and disperses these tragic multitudes. What is a fray? an oscillation? The immobility of a mathematical plan expresses a minute, not a day. In order to depict a battle, there is required one of those powerful painters who have chaos in their brushes. Rembrandt is better than Vandermeulen; Vandermeulen, exact at noon, lies at three o'clock. Geometry is deceptive; the hurricane alone is trustworthy. That is what confers on Folard the right to contradict Polybius. Let us add, that there is a certain instant when the battle degenerates into a combat, becomes specialized, and disperses into innumerable detailed feats, which, to borrow the expression of Napoleon himself, "belong rather to the biography of the regiments than to the history of the army." The historian has, in this case, the evident right to sum up the whole. He cannot do more than seize the principal outlines of the struggle, and it is not given to any one narrator, however conscientious he may be, to fix, absolutely, the form of that horrible cloud which is called a battle.

This, which is true of all great armed encounters, is particularly applicable to Waterloo.

Nevertheless, at a certain moment in the afternoon the battle came to a point.

Chapter VI

FOUR O'CLOCK IN THE AFTERNOON

TOWARD FOUR O'CLOCK THE CONDITION OF THE ENGLISH ARMY WAS SERIOUS. THE PRINCE OF Orange was in command of the center, Hill of the right wing, Picton of the left wing. The Prince of Orange, desperate and intrepid, shouted to the Hollando-Belgians: "Nassau! Brunswick! Never retreat!" Hill, having been weakened, had come up to the support of Wellington; Picton was dead. At the very moment when the English had captured from the French the flag of the 105th of the line, the French had killed the English general, Picton, with a bullet through the head. The battle had, for Wellington, two bases of action, Hougomont and La Haie-Sainte; Hougomont still held out, but was on fire; La Haie-Sainte was taken. Of the German battalion which defended it, only forty-two men survived; all the officers, except five, were either dead or captured. Three thousand combatants had been massacred in that barn. A sergeant of the English Guards, the foremost boxer in England, reputed invulnerable by his companions, had been killed there by a little French drummer-boy. Baring had been dislodged, Alten put to the sword. Many flags had been lost, one from Alten's division, and one from the battalion of Lunenburg, carried by a prince of the house of Deux-Ponts. The Scotch Grays no longer existed; Ponsonby's great dragoons had been hacked to pieces. That valiant cavalry had bent beneath the lancers of Bro and beneath the cuirassiers of Travers; out of twelve hundred horses, six hundred remained; out of three lieutenant-colonels, two lay on the earth—Hamilton wounded, Mater slain. Ponsonby had fallen, riddled by seven lance-thrusts. Gordon was dead. Marsh was dead. Two divisions, the fifth and the sixth, had been annihilated.

Hougomont injured, La Haie-Sainte taken, there now existed but one rallying-point, the center. That point still held firm. Wellington reinforced it. He summoned thither Hill, who was at Merle-Braine; he summoned Chassé, who was at Braine-l'Alleud.

The center of the English army, rather concave, very dense, and very compact, was strongly posted. It occupied the plateau of Mont-Saint-Jean, having behind it the village, and in front of it the slope, which was tolerably steep then. It rested on that stout stone dwelling which at that time belonged to the domain of Nivelles, and which marks the intersection of the roads—a pile of the sixteenth century, and so robust that the cannon-balls rebounded from it without injuring it. All about the plateau the English had cut the hedges here and there, made embrasures in the hawthorntrees, thrust the throat of a cannon between two branches, embattled the shrubs. There artillery was ambushed in the brushwood. This punic labor, incontestably authorized by war, which permits traps, was so well done, that Haxo, who had been dispatched by the Emperor at nine o'clock in the morning to reconnoiter the enemy's batteries, had discovered nothing of it, and had returned and reported to Napoleon that there were no obstacles except the two barricades which barred the road to Nivelles and to Genappe. It was at the season when the grain is tall; on the edge of the plateau a battalion of Kempt's brigade, the 95th, armed with carabines, was concealed in the tall wheat.

Thus assured and buttressed, the center of the Anglo-Dutch army was well posted. The peril of this position lay in the forest of Soignes, then adjoining the field of battle, and intersected by the ponds of Groenendael and Boitsfort. An army could not retreat thither without dissolving; the regiments would have broken up immediately there. The artillery would have been lost among the morasses. The retreat, according to many a man versed in the art—though it is disputed by others—would have been a disorganized flight.

To this center, Wellington added one of Chassé's brigades taken from the right wing, and one of Wincke's brigades taken from the left wing, plus Clinton's division. To his English, to the regiments of Halkett, to the brigades of Mitchell, to the guards of Maitland, he gave as reinforcements and aids, the infantry of Brunswick, Nassau's contingent, Kielmansegg's Hanoverians, and Ompteda's Germans. This placed twenty-six battalions under his hand. *The right wing*, as Charras says, *was thrown back on the center*. An enormous battery was masked by sacks of earth at the spot where there now stands what is called the "Museum of Waterloo." Besides this, Wellington had, behind a rise in the ground, Somerset's Dragoon Guards, fourteen hundred horse strong. It was the remaining half of the justly celebrated English cavalry. Ponsonby destroyed, Somerset remained.

The battery, which, if completed, would have been almost a redoubt, was ranged behind a very low garden wall, backed up with a coating of bags of sand and a large slope of earth. This work was not finished; there had been no time to make a palisade for it.

Wellington, uneasy but impassive, was on horseback, and there remained the whole day in the same attitude, a little in advance of the old mill of Mont-Saint-Jean, which is still in existence, beneath an elm, which an Englishman, an enthusiastic vandal, purchased later on for two hundred francs, cut down, and carried off. Wellington was coldly heroic. The bullets rained about him. His aide-de-camp, Gordon, fell at his side. Lord Hill, pointing to a shell which had burst, said to him: "My lord, what are your orders in case you are killed?" "To do like me," replied Wellington. To Clinton he said laconically, "To hold this spot to the last man." The day was evidently turning out ill. Wellington shouted to his old companions of Talavera, of Vittoria, of Salamanca: "Boys, can retreat be thought of? Think of old England!"

Toward four o'clock, the English line drew back. Suddenly nothing was visible on the crest of the plateau except the artillery and the sharpshooters; the rest had disappeared: the regiments, dislodged by the shells and the French bullets, retreated into the bottom, now intersected by the back road of the farm of Mont-Saint-Jean; a retrograde movement took place, the English front hid itself, Wellington drew back. "The beginning of retreat!" cried Napoleon.

Chapter VII

NAPOLEON IN A GOOD HUMOR

THE EMPEROR, THOUGH ILL AND DISCOMMODED ON HORSEBACK BY A LOCAL TROUBLE, HAD never been in a better humor than on that day. His impenetrability had been smiling ever since the morning. On the 18th of June, that profound soul masked by marble beamed blindly. The man who had been gloomy at Austerlitz was gay at Waterloo. The greatest favorites of destiny make mistakes. Our joys are composed of shadow. The supreme smile is God's alone.

Ridet Cæsar, Pompeius flebit, said the legionaries of the Fulminatrix Legion. Pompey was not destined to weep on that occasion, but it is certain that Cæsar laughed. While exploring on horseback at one o'clock on the preceding night, in storm and rain, in company with Bertrand, the communes in the neighborhood of Rossomme, satisfied at the sight of the long line of the English camp-fires illuminating the whole horizon from Frischemont to Braine-l'Alleud, it had seemed to him that fate, to whom he had assigned a day on the field of Waterloo, was exact to the appointment; he stopped his horse, and remained for some time motionless, gazing at the lightning and listening to the thunder; and this fatalist was heard to cast into the darkness this mysterious saying, "We are in accord." Napoleon was mistaken. They were no longer in accord.

He took not a moment for sleep; every instant of that night was marked by a joy for him. He traversed the line of the principal outposts, halting here and there to talk to the sentinels. At half-past two, near the wood of Hougomont, he heard the tread of a column on the march; he thought at the moment that it was a retreat on the part of Wellington. He said: "It is the rear-guard of the English getting under way for the purpose of decamping. I will take prisoners the six thousand English who have just arrived at Ostend." He conversed expansively; he regained the animation which he had shown at his landing on the 1st of March, when he pointed out to the Grand-Marshal the enthusiastic peasant of the Gulf Juan, and cried, "Well, Bertrand, here is a reinforcement already!" On the night of the 17th to the 18th of June he rallied Wellington. "That little Englishman needs a lesson," said Napoleon. The rain redoubled in violence; the thunder rolled while the Emperor was speaking.

At half-past three o'clock in the morning, he lost one illusion; officers who had been dispatched to reconnoiter announced to him that the enemy was not making any movement. Nothing was stirring; not a bivouac-fire had been extinguished; the English army was asleep. The silence on earth was profound; the only noise was in the heavens. At four o'clock, a peasant was brought in to him by the scouts; this peasant had served as guide to a brigade of English cavalry, probably Vivian's brigade, which was on its way to take up a position in the village of Ohain, at the extreme left. At five o'clock, two Belgian deserters reported to him that they had just quitted their regiment, and that the English army was ready for battle. "So much the better!" exclaimed Napoleon. "I prefer to overthrow them rather than to drive them back."

In the morning he dismounted in the mud on the slope which forms an angle with the Plancenoit road, had a kitchen table and a peasant's chair brought to him from the farm of Rossomme, seated himself, with a truss of straw for a carpet, and spread out on the table the chart of the battlefield, saying to Soult as he did so, "A pretty checker-board."

In consequence of the rains during the night, the transports of provisions, embedded in the soft roads, had not been able to arrive by morning; the soldiers had had no sleep; they were wet and fasting. This did not prevent Napoleon from exclaiming cheerfully to Ney, "We have ninety chances out of a hundred." At eight o'clock the Emperor's breakfast was brought to him. He invited many generals to it. During breakfast, it was said that Wellington had been to a ball two nights before, in Brussels, at the Duchess of Richmond's; and Soult, a rough man of war, with a face of an archbishop, said, "The ball takes place to-day." The Emperor jested with Ney, who said, "Wellington will not be so simple as to wait for your Majesty." That was his way, however. "He was fond of jesting," says Fleury de Chaboulon. "A merry humor was at the foundation of his character," says Gourgaud. "He abounded in pleasantries, which were more peculiar than witty," says Benjamin Constant. These gaieties of a giant are worthy of insistence. It was he who called his grenadiers "his grumblers"; he pinched their ears; he pulled their mustaches. "The Emperor did nothing but play pranks on us," is the remark of one of them. During the mysterious trip from the island of Elba to France, on the 27th of February, on the open sea, the French brig of war, *Le Zéphyr*, having encountered the brig *L'Inconstant*, on which Napoleon was concealed, and having asked the news of Napoleon from *L'Inconstant*, the Emperor, who still wore in his hat the white and amaranthine cockade sown with bees, which he had adopted at the isle of Elba, laughingly seized the speaking-trumpet, and answered for himself, "The Emperor is well." A man who laughs like that is on familiar terms with events. Napoleon indulged in many fits of this laughter during the breakfast at Waterloo. After breakfast he meditated for a quarter of an hour; then two generals seated themselves on the truss of straw, pen in hand and their paper on their knees, and the Emperor dictated to them the order of battle.

At nine o'clock, at the instant when the French army, ranged in echelons and set in motion in five columns, had deployed—the divisions in two lines, the artillery between the brigades, the music at their head; as they beat the march, with rolls on the drums and the blasts of trumpets, mighty, vast, joyous, a sea of casques, of sabers, and of bayonets on the horizon, the Emperor was touched, and twice exclaimed, "Magnificent! Magnificent!"

Between nine o'clock and half-past ten the whole army, incredible as it may appear, had taken up its position and ranged itself in six lines, forming, to repeat the Emperor's expression, "the figure of six V's." A few moments after the formation of the battle-array, in the midst of that profound silence, like that which heralds the beginning of a storm, which precedes engagements, the Emperor tapped Haxo on the shoulder, as he beheld the three batteries of twelve-pounders, detached by his orders from the corps of Erlon, Reille, and Lobau, and destined to begin the action by taking Mont-Saint-Jean, which was situated at the intersection of the Nivelles and the Genappe roads, and said to him, "There are four-and-twenty handsome maids, General."

Sure of the issue, he encouraged with a smile, as they passed before him, the company of sappers of the first corps, which he had appointed to barricade Mont-Saint-Jean as soon as the village should be carried. All this serenity had been traversed by but a single word of haughty pity; perceiving on his left, at a spot where there now stands a large tomb, those admirable Scotch Grays, with their superb horses, massing themselves, he said, "It is a pity."

Then he mounted his horse, advanced beyond Rossomme, and selected for his post of observation a contracted elevation of turf to the right of the road from Genappe to Brussels, which was his second station during the battle. The third station, the one adopted at seven o'clock in the evening, between La Belle-Alliance and La Haie-Sainte, is formidable; it is a rather elevated knoll, which still exists, and behind which the guard was massed on a slope of the plain. Around this knoll the balls rebounded from the pavements of the road, up to Napoleon himself. As at Brienne, he had over his head the shriek of the bullets and of the heavy artillery. Moldy cannon-balls, old sword-blades, and shapeless projectiles, eaten up with rust, were picked up at the spot where his horse's feet stood. *Scabra rubigine.* A few years ago, a shell of sixty pounds, still charged, and with its fuse broken off level with the bomb, was unearthed. It was at this last post that the Emperor said to his guide, Lacoste, a hostile and terrified peasant, who was attached to the saddle of a hussar, and who turned round at every discharge of canister and tried to hide behind Napoleon: "Fool, it is shameful! You'll get yourself killed with a ball in the back." He who writes these lines has himself found, in the friable soil of this knoll, on turning over the sand, the remains of the neck of a bomb, disintegrated, by the oxidization of six-and-forty years, and old fragments of iron which parted like elder-twigs between the fingers.

Everyone is aware that the variously inclined undulations of the plains, where the engagement between Napoleon and Wellington took place, are no longer what they were on June 18, 1815. By taking from this mournful field the wherewithal to make a monument to it, its real relief has been taken away, and history, disconcerted, no longer finds her bearings there. It has been disfigured for the sake of glorifying it. Wellington, when he beheld Waterloo once more, two years later, exclaimed, "They have altered my field of battle!" Where the great pyramid of earth, surmounted by the lion, rises to-day, there was a hillock which descended in an easy slope toward the Nivelles road, but which was almost an escarpment on the side of the highway to Genappe. The elevation of this escarpment can still be measured by the height of the two knolls of the two great sepulchers which enclose the road from Genappe to Brussels: one, the English tomb, is on the left; the other, the German tomb, is on the right. There is no French tomb. The whole of that plain is a sepulcher for France. Thanks to the thousands upon thousands of cartloads of earth employed in the hillock one hundred and fifty feet in height and half a mile in circumference, the plateau of Mont-Saint-Jean is now accessible by an easy slope. On the day of battle, particularly on the side of La Haie-Sainte, it was abrupt and difficult of approach. The slope there is so steep that the English cannon could not see the farm, situated in the bottom of the valley, which was the center of the combat. On the 18th of June, 1815, the rains had still further increased this acclivity, the mud complicated the problem of the ascent, and the men not only slipped back, but stuck fast in the mire. Along the crest of the plateau ran a sort of trench whose presence it was impossible for the distant observer to divine.

What was this trench? Let us explain. Braine-l'Alleud is a Belgian village; Ohain is another. These villages, both of them concealed in curves of the landscape, are connected by a road about a league and a half in length, which traverses the plain along its undulating level, and often enters and buries itself in the hills like a furrow, which makes a ravine of this road in some places. In 1815, as at the present day, this road cut the crest of the plateau of Mont-Saint-Jean between the two highways from Genappe and Nivelles; only, it is now on a level with the plain; it was then a hollow way. Its two slopes have been appropriated for the monumental hillock. This road was, and still is, a trench throughout the greater portion of its course; a hollow trench, sometimes a dozen feet in depth, and whose banks, being too steep, crumbled away here and there, particularly in winter, under driving rains. Accidents happened here. The road was so narrow at the Braine-l'Alleud entrance that a passer-by was crushed by a cart, as is proved by a stone cross which stands near the cemetery, and which gives the name of the dead, *Monsieur Bernard Debrye, Merchant of Brussels,* and the date of the accident, *February, 1637.* It was so deep on the table-land of Mont-Saint-Jean that a peasant, Mathieu Nicaise, was crushed there, in 1783, by a slide from the slope, as is stated on another stone cross, the top of which has disappeared in the process of clearing the ground, but whose overturned pedestal is still visible on the grassy slope to the left of the highway between La Haie-Sainte and the farm of Mont-Saint-Jean.

On the day of battle, this hollow road whose existence was in no way indicated, bordering the crest of Mont-Saint-Jean, a trench at the summit of the escarpment, a rut concealed in the soil, was invisible; that is to say, terrible.

Chapter VIII

THE EMPEROR PUTS A QUESTION TO THE GUIDE LACOSTE

S O, ON THE MORNING OF WATERLOO, NAPOLEON WAS CONTENT.
He was right; the plan of battle conceived by him was, as we have seen, really admirable.

The battle once begun, its very various changes—the resistance of Hougomont; the tenacity of La Haie-Sainte; the killing of Bauduin; the disabling of Foy; the unexpected wall against which Soye's brigade was shattered; Guilleminot's fatal heedlessness when he had neither petard nor powder sacks; the miring of the batteries; the fifteen unescorted pieces overwhelmed in a hollow way by Uxbridge; the small effect of the bombs falling in the English lines, and there embedding themselves in the rain-soaked soil, and only succeeding in producing volcanoes of mud, so that the canister was turned into a splash; the uselessness of Piré's demonstration on Braine-l'Alleud; all that cavalry, fifteen squadrons, almost exterminated; the right wing of the English badly alarmed, the left wing badly cut into; Ney's strange mistake in massing, instead of echelonning the four divisions of the first corps; men delivered over to grape-shot, arranged in ranks twenty-seven deep and with a frontage of two hundred; the frightful holes made in these masses by the cannon-balls; attacking columns disorganized; the side-battery suddenly unmasked on their flank; Bourgeois, Donzelot, and Durutte compromised; Quiot repulsed; Lieutenant Vieux, that Hercules graduated at the Polytechnic School, wounded at the moment when he was beating in with an ax the door of La Haie-Sainte under the downright fire of the English barricade which barred the angle of the road from Genappe to Brussels; Marcognet's division caught between the infantry and the cavalry, shot down at the very muzzle of the guns amid the grain by Best and Pack, put to the sword by Ponsonby; his battery of seven pieces spiked; the Prince of Saxe-Weimar holding and guarding, in spite of the Comte d'Erlon, both Frischemont and Smohain; the flag of the 105th taken, the flag of the 45th captured; that black Prussian hussar stopped by runners of the flying column of three hundred light cavalry on the scout between Wavre and Plancenoit; the alarming things that had been said by prisoners; Grouchy's delay; fifteen hundred men killed in the orchard of Hougomont in less than an hour; eighteen hundred men overthrown in a still shorter time about La Haie-Sainte—all these stormy incidents passing like the clouds of battle before Napoleon, had hardly troubled his gaze and had not overshadowed that face of imperial certainty. Napoleon was accustomed to gaze steadily at war; he never added up the heartrending details, cipher by cipher; ciphers mattered little to him, provided that they furnished the total, victory; he was not alarmed if the beginnings did go astray, since he thought himself the master and the possessor at the end; he knew how to wait, supposing himself to be out of the question, and he treated destiny as his equal: he seemed to say to fate, Thou wilt not dare.

Composed half of light and half of shadow, Napoleon thought himself protected in good and tolerated in evil. He had, or thought that he had, a connivance, one might almost say a complicity, of events in his favor, which was equivalent to the invulnerability of antiquity.

Nevertheless, when one has Bérésina, Leipzig, and Fontainebleau behind one, it seems as though one might distrust Waterloo. A mysterious frown becomes perceptible in the depths of the heavens.

At the moment when Wellington retreated, Napoleon shuddered. He suddenly beheld the table-land of Mont-Saint-Jean cleared, and the van of the English army disappear. It was rallying, but hiding itself. The Emperor half rose in his stirrups. The lightning of victory flashed from his eyes.

Wellington, driven into a corner at the forest of Soignes and destroyed—that was the definitive conquest of England by France; it was Crécy, Poitiers, Malplaquet, and Ramillies avenged. The man of Marengo was wiping out Azincourt.

So the Emperor, meditating on this terrible turn of fortune, swept his glass for the last time over all the points of the field of battle. His guard, standing behind him with grounded arms, watched him from below with a sort of religion. He pondered; he examined the slopes, noted the declivities, scrutinized the clumps of trees, the square of rye, the path; he seemed to be counting each bush. He gazed with some intentness at the English barricades of the two highways—two large, abatis of trees, that on the road to Genappe above La Haie-Sainte, armed with two cannon, the only ones out of all the English artillery which commanded the extremity of the field of battle, and that on the road to Nivelles where gleamed the Dutch bayonets of Chassé's brigade. Near this barricade he observed the old chapel of Saint Nicholas, painted white, which stands at the angle of the cross-road near Braine-l'Alleud; he bent down and spoke in a low voice to the guide Lacoste. The guide made a negative sign with his head, which was probably perfidious.

The Emperor straightened himself up and fell to thinking.

Wellington had drawn back.

All that remained to do was to complete this retreat by crushing him.

Napoleon turning round abruptly, dispatched an express at full speed to Paris to announce that the battle was won.

Napoleon was one of those geniuses from whom thunder darts.

He had just found his clap of thunder.

He gave orders to Milhaud's cuirassiers to carry the table-land of Mont-Saint-Jean.

Chapter IX

THE UNEXPECTED

THERE WERE THREE THOUSAND FIVE HUNDRED OF THEM. THEY FORMED A FRONT A QUARTER OF a league in extent. They were giant men, on colossal horses. There were six-and-twenty squadrons of them; and they had behind them to support them Lefebvre-Desnouettes's division— the one hundred and six picked gendarmes, the light cavalry of the Guard, eleven hundred and ninety-seven men, and the lancers of the guard of eight hundred and eighty lances. They wore casques without horse-tails, and cuirasses of beaten iron, with horse-pistols in their holsters, and long saber-swords. That morning the whole army had admired them, when, at nine o'clock, with braying of trumpets and all the music playing "Let us watch o'er the Safety of the Empire," they had come in a solid column, with one of their batteries on their flank, another in their center, and deployed in two ranks between the roads to Genappe and Frischemont, and taken up their position for battle in that powerful second line, so cleverly arranged by Napoleon, which, having on its extreme left Kellermann's cuirassiers and on its extreme right Milhaud's cuirassiers, had, so to speak, two wings of iron.

Aide-de-camp Bernard carried them the Emperor's orders. Ney drew his sword and placed himself at their head. The enormous squadrons were set in motion.

Then a formidable spectacle was seen.

All their cavalry, with upraised swords, standards and trumpets flung to the breeze, formed in columns by divisions, descended, by a simultaneous movement and like one man, with the precision of a brazen battering-ram which is affecting a breach, the hill of La Belle Alliance, plunged into the terrible depths in which so many men had already fallen, disappeared there in the smoke, then emerging from that shadow, reappeared on the other side of the valley, still compact and in close ranks, mounting at a full trot, through a storm of grape-shot which burst upon them, the terrible muddy slope of the table-land of Mont-Saint-Jean. They ascended, grave, threatening, imperturbable; in the intervals between the musketry and the artillery, their colossal trampling was audible. Being two divisions, there were two columns of them; Wathier's division held the right, Delort's division was on the left. It seemed as though two immense adders of steel were to be seen crawling toward the crest of the table-land. It traversed the battle like a prodigy.

Nothing like it had been seen since the taking of the great redoubt of the Moskowa by the heavy cavalry; Murat was lacking here, but Ney was again present. It seemed as though that mass had become a monster and had but one soul. Each column undulated and swelled like the ring of a polyp. They could be seen through a vast cloud of smoke which was rent here and there. A confusion of helmets, of cries, of sabers, a stormy heaving of the cruppers of horses amid the cannons and the flourish of trumpets, a terrible and disciplined tumult; over all, the cuirasses like the scales on the hydra.

These narrations seemed to belong to another age. Something parallel to this vision appeared, no doubt, in the ancient Orphic epics, which told of the centaurs, the old hippanthropes, those Titans with human heads and equestrian chests who scaled Olympus at a gallop, horrible, invulnerable, sublime—gods and beasts.

Odd numerical coincidence—twenty-six battalions rode to meet twenty-six battalions. Behind the crest of the plateau, in the shadow of the masked battery, the English infantry, formed into thirteen squares, two battalions to the square, in two lines, with seven in the first line, six in the second, the stocks of their guns to their shoulders, taking aim at that which was on the point of appearing, waited, calm, mute, motionless. They did not see the cuirassiers, and the cuirassiers did not see them. They listened to the rise of this flood of men. They heard the swelling noise of three thousand horse, the alternate and symmetrical tramp of their hoofs at full trot, the jingling of the cuirasses, the clang of the sabers, and a sort of grand and savage breathing. There ensued a most terrible silence; then, all at once, a long file of uplifted arms, brandishing sabers, appeared above the crest, and casques, trumpets, and standards, and three thousand heads with gray mustaches, shouting, "Vive l'Empereur!" All this cavalry debouched on the plateau, and it was like the appearance of an earthquake.

All at once, a tragic incident; on the English left, on our right, the head of the column of cuirassiers reared up with a frightful clamor. On arriving at the culminating point of the crest, ungovernable, utterly given over to fury and their course of extermination of the squares and cannon, the cuirassiers had just caught sight of a trench—a trench between them and the English. It was the hollow road of Ohain.

It was a terrible moment. The ravine was there, unexpected, yawning, directly under the horses' feet, two fathoms deep between its double slopes; the second file pushed the first into it, and the third pushed on the second; the horses reared and fell backward, landed on their haunches, slid down, all four feet in the air, crushing and overwhelming the riders; and there being no means of retreat—the whole column being no longer anything more than a projectile—the force which had been acquired to crush the English crushed the French; the inexorable ravine could only yield when filled; horses and riders rolled there pell-mell, grinding each other, forming but one mass of flesh in this gulf: when this trench was full of living men, the rest marched over them and passed on. Almost a third of Dubois's brigade fell into that abyss.

This began the loss of the battle.

A local tradition, which evidently exaggerates matters, says that two thousand horses and fifteen hundred men were buried in the hollow road of Ohain. This figure probably comprises all the other corpses which were flung into this ravine the day after the combat.

Let us note in passing that it was Dubois's sorely tried brigade which, an hour previously, making a charge to one side, had captured the flag of the Lunenburg battalion.

Napoleon, before giving the order for this charge of Milhaud's cuirassiers, had scrutinized the ground, but had not been able to see that hollow road, which did not even form a wrinkle on the surface of the plateau. Warned, nevertheless, and put on the alert by the little white chapel which marks its angle of juncture with the Nivelles highway, he had probably put a question as to the possibility of an obstacle, to the guide Lacoste. The guide had answered No. We might almost affirm that Napoleon's catastrophe originated in that sign of a peasant's head.

Other fatalities were destined to arise.

Was it possible that Napoleon should have won that battle? We answer No. Why? Because of Wellington? Because of Blücher? No. Because of God.

Bonaparte victor at Waterloo; that does not come within the law of the nineteenth century. Another series of facts was in preparation, in which there was no longer any room for Napoleon. The ill-will of events had declared itself long before.

It was time that this vast man should fall.

The excessive weight of this man in human destiny disturbed the balance. This individual alone counted for more than a universal group. These plethoras of all human vitality concentrated in a single head; the world mounting to the brain of one man—this would be mortal to civilization were it to last. The moment had arrived for the incorruptible and supreme equity to alter its plan. Probably the principles and the elements, on which the regular gravitations of the moral, as of the material, world depend, had complained. Smoking blood, over-filled cemeteries, mothers in tears—these are formidable pleaders. When the earth is suffering from too heavy a burden, there are mysterious groanings of the shades, to which the abyss lends an ear.

Napoleon had been denounced in the infinite, and his fall had been decided on.

He embarrassed God.

Waterloo is not a battle; it is a change of front on the part of the Universe.

Chapter X

THE PLATEAU OF MONT-SAINT-JEAN

THE BATTERY WAS UNMASKED AT THE SAME MOMENT WITH THE RAVINE.
Sixty cannons and the thirteen squares darted lightning point-blank on the cuirassiers. The intrepid General Delort made the military salute to the English battery.

The whole of the flying artillery of the English had re-entered the squares at a gallop. The cuirassiers had not had even the time for a halt. The disaster of the hollow road had decimated, but not discouraged them. They belonged to that class of men who, when diminished in number, increase in courage.

Wathier's column alone had suffered in the disaster; Delort's column, which Ney had deflected to the left, as though he had a presentiment of an ambush, had arrived whole.

The cuirassiers hurled themselves on the English squares.

At full speed, with bridles loose, swords in their teeth, pistols in fist—such was the attack.

There are moments in battles in which the soul hardens the man until the soldier is changed into a statue, and when all this flesh turns into granite. The English battalions, desperately assaulted, did not stir.

Then it was terrible.

All the faces of the English squares were attacked at once. A frenzied whirl enveloped them. That cold infantry remained impassive. The first rank knelt and received the cuirassiers on their bayonets, the second ranks shot them down; behind the second rank the cannoneers charged their guns, the front of the square parted, permitted the passage of an eruption of grape-shot, and closed again. The cuirassiers replied by crushing them. Their great horses reared, strode across the ranks, leaped over the bayonets and fell, gigantic, in the midst of these four living wells. The cannon-balls plowed furrows in these cuirassiers; the cuirassiers made breaches in the squares. Files of men disappeared, ground to dust under the horses. The bayonets plunged into the bellies of these centaurs; hence a hideousness of wounds which has probably never been seen anywhere else. The squares, wasted by this mad cavalry, closed up their ranks without flinching. Inexhaustible in the matter of grape-shot, they created explosions in their assailants' midst. The form of this combat was monstrous. These squares were no longer battalions, they were craters; those cuirassiers were no longer cavalry, they were a tempest. Each square was a volcano attacked by a cloud; lava contended with lightning.

The square on the extreme right, the most exposed of all, being in the air, was almost annihilated at the very first shock. It was formed of the 75th regiment of Highlanders. The bagpipe-player in the center dropped his melancholy eyes, filled with the reflections of the forests and the lakes, in profound inattention, while men were being exterminated around him, and seated on a drum, with his pibroch under his arm, played the Highland airs. These Scotchmen died thinking of Ben Lothian, as did the Greeks recalling Argos. The sword of a cuirassier, which hewed down the bagpipes and the arm which bore it, put an end to the song by killing the singer.

The cuirassiers, relatively few in number, and still further diminished by the catastrophe of the ravine, had almost the whole English army against them, but they multiplied themselves so that each man of them was equal to ten. Nevertheless, some Hanoverian battalions yielded. Wellington perceived it, and thought of his cavalry. Had Napoleon at that same moment thought of his infantry, he would have won the battle. This forgetfulness was his great and fatal mistake.

All at once, the cuirassiers, who had been the assailants, found themselves assailed. The English cavalry was at their back. Before them two squares, behind them Somerset; Somerset meant fourteen hundred dragoons of the guard. On the right, Somerset had Dornberg with the German light-horse, and on his left, Trip with the Belgian carabineers; the cuirassiers attacked on the flank and in front, before and in the rear, by infantry and cavalry, had to face all sides. What mattered it to them? They were a whirlwind. Their valor was something indescribable.

In addition to this, they had behind them the battery, which was still thundering. It was necessary that it should be so, or they could never have been wounded in the back. One of their cuirasses, pierced on the shoulder by a ball from a biscayan, is in the collection of the Waterloo Museum.

For such Frenchmen nothing less than such Englishmen was needed. It was no longer a hand-to-hand conflict; it was a shadow, a fury, a dizzy transport of souls and courage, a hurricane of lightning swords. In an instant the fourteen hundred dragoon guards numbered only eight hundred. Fuller, their lieutenant-colonel, fell dead. Ney rushed up with the lancers and Lefebvre-Desnouettes's light-horse. The plateau of Mont-Saint-Jean was captured, recaptured, captured again. The cuirassiers quitted the cavalry to return to the infantry; or, to put it more exactly, the whole of that formidable rout collared each other without releasing the other. The squares still held firm.

There were a dozen assaults. Ney had four horses killed under him. Half the cuirassiers remained on the plateau. This conflict lasted two hours.

The English army was profoundly shaken. There is no doubt that, had they not been enfeebled in their first shock by the disaster of the hollow road, the cuirassiers would have overwhelmed the center and decided the victory. This extraordinary cavalry petrified Clinton, who had seen Talavera and Badajoz. Wellington, three-quarters vanquished, admired heroically. He said in an undertone, "Sublime!"

The cuirassiers annihilated seven squares out of thirteen, took or spiked sixty pieces of ordnance, and captured from the English regiments six flags, which three cuirassiers and three chasseurs of the Guard bore to the Emperor, in front of the farm of La Belle Alliance.

Wellington's situation had grown worse. This strange battle was like a duel between two raging, wounded men, each of whom, still fighting and still resisting, is expending all his blood.

Which of the two will be the first to fall?

The conflict on the plateau continued.

What had become of the cuirassiers? No one could have told. One thing is certain, that on the day after the battle, a cuirassier and his horse were found dead among the woodwork of the scales for vehicles at Mont-Saint-Jean, at the very point where the four roads from Nivelles, Genappe, La Hulpe, and Brussels meet and intersect each other. This horseman had pierced the English lines. One of the men who picked up the body still lives at Mont-Saint-Jean. His name is Dehaze. He was eighteen years old at that time.

Wellington felt that he was yielding. The crisis was at hand.

The cuirassiers had not succeeded, since the center was not broken through. As everyone was in possession of the plateau, no one held it, and in fact it remained, to a great extent, with the English. Wellington held the village and the culminating plain; Ney had only the crest and the slope. They seemed rooted in that fatal soil on both sides.

But the weakening of the English seemed irremediable. The bleeding of that army was horrible. Kempt, on the left wing, demanded reinforcements. "There are none," replied Wellington; "he must let himself be killed!" Almost at that same moment, a singular coincidence which paints the exhaustion of the two armies, Ney demanded infantry from Napoleon, and Napoleon exclaimed, "Infantry! Where does he expect me to get it? Does he think I can make it?"

Nevertheless, the English army was in the worse case of the two. The furious onsets of those great squadrons with cuirasses of iron and breasts of steel had ground the infantry to nothing. A few men clustered round a flag marked the post of a regiment; such and such a battalion was commanded only by a captain or a lieutenant; Alten's division, already so roughly handled at La Haie-Sainte, was almost destroyed; the intrepid Belgians of Van Kluze's brigade strewed the rye-fields all along the Nivelles road; hardly anything was left of those Dutch grenadiers, who, intermingled with Spaniards in our ranks in 1811, fought against Wellington; and who, in 1815, rallied to the English standard, fought against Napoleon. The loss in officers was considerable. Lord Uxbridge, who had his leg buried on the following day, had his knee shattered. If, on the French side, in that tussle of the cuirassiers, Delort, l'Héritier, Colbert, Dnop, Travers, and Blancard were disabled, on the side of the English there was Alten wounded, Barne wounded, Delancey killed, Van Meeren killed, Ompteda killed, the whole of Wellington's staff decimated, and England had the worse of it in that bloody scale. The second regiment of foot-guards had lost five lieutenant-colonels, four captains, and three ensigns; the first battalion of the 30th infantry had lost 24 officers and 1,200 soldiers; the 79th Highlanders had lost 24 officers wounded, 18 officers killed, 450 soldiers killed. The Hanoverian hussars of Cumberland, a whole regiment, with Colonel Hacke at its head, who was destined to be tried later on and cashiered, had turned bridle in the presence of the fray, and had fled to the forest of Soignes, sowing defeat all the way to Brussels. The transports, ammunition-wagons, the baggage-wagons, the wagons filled with wounded, on perceiving that the French were gaining ground and approaching the forest, rushed headlong thither. The Dutch, mowed down by the French cavalry, cried, "Alarm!" From Vert-Coucou to Groentendael, for a distance of nearly two leagues in the direction of Brussels, according to the testimony of eye witnesses who are still alive, the roads were encumbered with fugitives. This panic was such that it attacked the Prince de Condé at Mechlin, and Louis XVIII at Ghent. With the exception of the feeble reserve echelonned behind the ambulance established at the farm of Mont-Saint-Jean, and of Vivian's and Vandeleur's brigades, which flanked the left wing, Wellington had no cavalry left. A number of batteries lay unhorsed. These facts are attested by Siborne; and Pringle, exaggerating the disaster, goes so far as to say that the Anglo-Dutch army was reduced to thirty-four thousand men. The Iron Duke remained calm, but his lips blanched. Vincent, the Austrian commissioner, Alava, the Spanish commissioner, who were present at the battle in the English staff, thought the Duke lost. At five o'clock Wellington drew out his watch, and he was heard to murmur these sinister words, "Blücher, or night!"

It was at about that moment that a distant line of bayonets gleamed on the heights in the direction of Frischemont.

Here comes the change of face in this giant drama.

Chapter XI

A BAD GUIDE TO NAPOLEON; A GOOD GUIDE TO BÜLOW

THE PAINFUL SURPRISE OF NAPOLEON IS WELL KNOWN. GROUCHY HOPED FOR, BLÜCHER ARRIVing. Death instead of life.

Fate has these turns; the throne of the world was expected; it was Saint Helena that was seen.

If the little shepherd who served as guide to Bülow, Blücher's lieutenant, had advised him to debouch from the forest above Frischemont, instead of below Plancenoit, the form of the nineteenth century might, perhaps, have been different. Napoleon would have won the battle of Waterloo. By any other route than that below Plancenoit, the Prussian army would have come out upon a ravine impassable for artillery, and Bülow would not have arrived.

Now the Prussian general, Muffling, declares that one hour's delay, and Blücher would not have found Wellington on his feet. "The battle was lost."

It was time that Bülow should arrive, as will be seen. He had, moreover, been very much delayed. He had bivouacked at Dion-le-Mont, and had set out at daybreak; but the roads were impassable, and his divisions stuck fast in the mire. The ruts were up to the hubs of the cannons. Moreover, he had been obliged to pass the Dyle on the narrow bridge of Wavre; the street leading to the bridge had been fired by the French, so the caissons and ammunition-wagons could not pass between two rows of burning houses, and had been obliged to wait until the conflagration was extinguished. It was midday before Bülow's vanguard had been able to reach Chapelle-Saint-Lambert.

Had the action been begun two hours earlier, it would have been over at four o'clock, and Blücher would have fallen on the battle won by Napoleon. Such are these immense risks proportioned to an infinite which we cannot comprehend.

The Emperor had been the first, as early as midday, to descry with his field-glass, on the extreme horizon, something which had attracted his attention. He had said, "I see yonder a cloud, which seems to me to be troops." Then he asked the Duc de Dalmatie, "Soult, what do you see in the direction of Chapelle-Saint-Lambert?" The marshal, leveling his glass, answered, "Four or five thousand men, Sire; evidently Grouchy." But it remained motionless in the mist. All the glasses of the staff had studied "the cloud" pointed out by the Emperor. Some said: "It is trees." The truth is, that the cloud did not move. The Emperor detached Domon's division of light cavalry to reconnoiter in that quarter.

Bülow had not moved, in fact. His vanguard was very feeble, and could accomplish nothing.

He was obliged to wait for the body of the army corps, and he had received orders to concentrate his forces before entering into line; but at five o'clock, perceiving Wellington's peril, Blücher ordered Bülow to attack, and uttered these remarkable words: "We must give air to the English army."

A little later, the divisions of Losthin, Hiller, Hacke, and Ryssel deployed before Lobau's corps, the cavalry of Prince William of Prussia debouched from the forest of Paris, Plancenoit was in flames, and the Prussian cannon-balls began to rain even upon the ranks of the guard in reserve behind Napoleon.

Chapter XII

THE GUARD

EVERYONE KNOWS THE REST—THE ERUPTION OF A THIRD ARMY; THE BATTLE BROKEN TO PIECES; eighty-six months of fire thundering simultaneously; Pirch the first coming up with Bülow; Zieten's cavalry led by Blücher in person, the French driven back; Marcognet swept from the plateau of Ohain; Durutte dislodged from Papelotte; Donzelot and Quiot retreating; Lobau caught on the flank; a fresh battle precipitating itself on our dismantled regiments at nightfall; the whole English line resuming the offensive and thrust forward; the gigantic breach made in the French army; the English grape-shot and the Prussian grape-shot aiding each other; the extermination; disaster in front; disaster on the flank; the Guard entering the line in the midst of this terrible crumbling of all things.

Conscious that they were about to die, they shouted, "Vive l'Empereur!" History records nothing more touching than that agony bursting forth in acclamations.

The sky had been overcast all day long. All of a sudden, at that very moment—it was eight o'clock in the evening—the clouds on the horizon parted, and allowed the grand and sinister glow of the setting sun to pass through, athwart the elms on the Nivelles road. They had seen it rise at Austerlitz.

Each battalion of the Guard was commanded by a general for this final catastrophe. Friant, Michel, Roguet, Harlet, Mallet, Poret de Morvan, were there. When the tall caps of the grenadiers of the Guard, with their large plaques bearing the eagle appeared, symmetrical, in line, tranquil, in the midst of that combat, the enemy felt a respect for France; they thought they beheld twenty victories entering the field of battle, with wings outspread, and those who were the conquerors, believing themselves to be vanquished, retreated; but Wellington shouted, "Up, Guards, and aim straight!" The red regiment of English Guards, lying flat behind the hedges, sprang up, a cloud of grape-shot riddled the tricolored flag and whistled round our eagles; all hurled themselves forwards, and the final carnage began. In the darkness, the Imperial Guard felt the army losing ground around it, and in the vast shock of the rout it heard the desperate flight which had taken the place of the "Vive l'Empereur!" and, with flight behind it, it continued to advance, more crushed, losing more men at every step that it took. There were none who hesitated, no timid men in its ranks. The soldier in that troop was as much of a hero as the general. Not a man was missing in that suicide.

Ney, bewildered, great with all the grandeur of accepted death, offered himself to all blows in that tempest. He had his fifth horse killed under him there. Perspiring, his eyes aflame, foaming at the mouth, with uniform unbuttoned, one of his epaulets half cut off by a sword-stroke from a horse guard, his plaque with the great eagle dented by a bullet; bleeding, bemired, magnificent, a broken sword in his hand, he said, "Come and see how a Marshal of France dies on the field of battle!" But in vain; he did not die. He was haggard and angry. At Drouet d'Erlon he hurled this question, "Are you not going to get yourself killed?" In the midst of all that artillery engaged in crushing a handful of men, he shouted: "So there is nothing for me! Oh! I should like to have all these English bullets enter my bowels!" Unhappy man, thou wert reserved for French bullets!

Chapter XIII

THE CATASTROPHE

THE ROUT BEHIND THE GUARD WAS MELANCHOLY.
The army yielded suddenly on all sides at once—Hougomont, La Haie-Sainte, Papelotte, Plancenoit. The cry, "Treachery!" was followed by a cry of "Save yourselves who can!" An army which is disbanding is like a thaw. All yields, splits, cracks, floats, rolls, falls, jostles, hastens, is precipitated. The disintegration is unprecedented. Ney borrows a horse, leaps upon it, and without hat, cravat, or sword, places himself across the Brussels road, stopping both English and French. He strives to detain the army, he recalls it to its duty, he insults it, he clings to the rout. He is overwhelmed. The soldiers fly from him, shouting, "Long live Marshal Ney!" Two of Durutte's regiments go and come in affright as though tossed back and forth between the swords of the Uhlans and the fusillade of the brigades of Kempt, Best, Pack, and Rylandt; the worst of hand-to-hand conflicts is the defeat; friends kill each other in order to escape; squadrons and battalions break and disperse against each other, like the tremendous foam of battle. Lobau at one extremity, and Reille at the other, are drawn into the tide. In vain does Napoleon erect walls from what is left to him of his Guard; in vain does he expend in a last effort his last serviceable squadrons. Quiot retreats before Vivian, Kellermann before Vandeleur, Lobau before Bülow, Morand before Pirch, Domon and Subervic before Prince William of Prussia; Guyot, who led the Emperor's squadrons to the charge, falls beneath the feet of the English dragoons. Napoleon gallops past the line of fugitives, harangues, urges, threatens, entreats them. All the mouths which in the morning had shouted, "Long live the Emperor!" remain gaping; they hardly recognize him. The Prussian cavalry, newly arrived, dashes forwards, flies, hews, slashes, kills, exterminates. Horses lash out, the cannons flee; the soldiers of the artillery-train unharness the caissons and use the horses to make their escape; transports overturned, with all four wheels in the air, clog the road and occasion massacres. Men are crushed, trampled down, others walk over the dead and the living. Arms are lost. A dizzy multitude fills the roads, the paths, the bridges, the plains, the hills, the valleys, the woods, encumbered by this invasion of forty thousand men. Shouts, despair, knapsacks and guns flung among the rye, passages forced at the point of the sword, no more comrades, no more officers, no more generals, an inexpressible terror. Zieten putting France to the sword at its leisure. Lions converted into goats. Such was the flight.

At Genappe, an effort was made to wheel about, to present a battle front, to draw up in line. Lobau rallied three hundred men. The entrance to the village was barricaded, but at the first volley of Prussian canister, all took to flight again, and Lobau was taken. That volley of grape-shot can be seen to-day imprinted on the ancient gable of a brick building on the right of the road at a few minutes' distance before you enter Genappe. The Prussians threw themselves into Genappe, furious, no doubt, that they were not more entirely the conquerors. The pursuit was stupendous. Blücher ordered extermination. Roguet had set the lugubrious example of threatening with death any French grenadier who should bring him a Prussian prisoner. Blücher outdid Roguet. Duhesme, the general of the Young Guard, hemmed in at the doorway of an inn at Genappe, surrendered his sword to a hussar of death, who took the sword and slew the prisoner. The victory was completed by the assassination of the vanquished. Let us inflict punishment, since we are history: old Blücher disgraced himself. This ferocity put the finishing touch to the disaster. The desperate route traversed Genappe, traversed Quatre-Bras, traversed Gosselies, traversed Frasnes, traversed Charleroi, traversed Thuin, and only halted at the frontier. Alas! and who, then, was fleeing in that manner? The Grand Army.

This vertigo, this terror, this downfall into ruin of the loftiest bravery which ever astounded history—is that causeless? No. The shadow of an enormous right is projected athwart Waterloo. It is the day of destiny. The force which is mightier than man produced that day. Hence the terrified wrinkle of those brows; hence all those great souls surrendering their swords. Those who had conquered Europe have fallen prone on the earth, with nothing left to say nor to do, feeling the present shadow of a terrible presence. *Hoc erat in fatis.* That day the perspective of the human race underwent a change. Waterloo is the hinge of the nineteenth century. The disappearance of the great man was necessary to the advent of the great century. Someone, a person to whom one replies not, took the responsibility on himself. The panic of heroes can be explained. In the battle of Waterloo there is something more than a cloud, there is something of the meteor. God has passed by.

At nightfall, in a meadow near Genappe, Bernard and Bertrand seized by the skirt of his coat and detained a man, haggard, pensive, sinister, gloomy, who, dragged to that point by the current of the rout, had just dismounted, had passed the bridle of his horse over his arm, and with wild eye was returning alone to Waterloo. It was Napoleon, the immense somnambulist of this dream which had crumbled, essaying once more to advance.

Chapter XIV

THE LAST SQUARE

S EVERAL SQUARES OF THE GUARD, MOTIONLESS AMID THIS STREAM OF THE DEFEAT, AS ROCKS IN running water, held their own until night. Night came, death also; they awaited that double shadow, and, invincible, allowed themselves to be enveloped therein. Each regiment, isolated from the rest, and having no bond with the army, now shattered in every part, died alone. They had taken up position for this final action, some on the heights of Rossomme, others on the plain of Mont-Saint-Jean. There, abandoned, vanquished, terrible, those gloomy squares endured their death-throes in formidable fashion. Ulm, Wagram, Jena, Friedland, died with them.

At twilight, toward nine o'clock in the evening, one of them was left at the foot of the plateau of Mont-Saint-Jean. In that fatal valley, at the foot of that declivity which the cuirassiers had ascended, now inundated by the masses of the English, under the converging fires of the victorious hostile cavalry, under a frightful density of projectiles, this square fought on. It was commanded by an obscure officer named Cambronne. At each discharge, the square diminished and replied. It replied to the grape-shot with a fusillade, continually contracting its four walls. The fugitives pausing breathless for a moment in the distance, listened in the darkness to that gloomy and ever-decreasing thunder.

When this legion had been reduced to a handful, when nothing was left of their flag but a rag, when their guns, the bullets all gone, were no longer anything but clubs, when the heap of corpses was larger than the group of survivors, there reigned among the conquerors, around those men dying so sublimely, a sort of sacred terror, and the English artillery, taking breath, became silent. This furnished a sort of respite. These combatants had around them something in the nature of a swarm of specters, silhouettes of men on horseback, the black profiles of cannon, the white sky viewed through wheels and gun-carriages, the colossal death's-head, which the heroes saw constantly through the smoke, in the depths of the battle, advanced upon them and gazed at them. Through the shades of twilight they could hear the pieces being loaded; the matches all lighted, like the eyes of tigers at night, formed a circle round their heads; all the lint-stocks of the English batteries approached the cannons, and then, with emotion, holding the supreme moment suspended above these men, an English general, Colville according to some, Maitland according to others, shouted to them, "Surrender, brave Frenchmen!" Cambronne replied, "————."

Chapter XV

CAMBRONNE

IF ANY FRENCH READER OBJECT TO HAVING HIS SUSCEPTIBILITIES OFFENDED, ONE WOULD HAVE TO refrain from repeating in his presence what is perhaps the finest reply that a Frenchman ever made. This would enjoin us from consigning something sublime to History.

At our own risk and peril, let us violate this injunction.

Now, then, among those giants there was one Titan—Cambronne.

To make that reply and then perish, what could be grander? For being willing to die is the same as to die; and it was not this man's fault if he survived after he was shot.

The winner of the battle of Waterloo was not Napoleon, who was put to flight; nor Wellington, giving way at four o'clock, in despair at five; nor Blücher, who took no part in the engagement. The winner of Waterloo was Cambronne.

To thunder forth such a reply at the lightning-flash that kills you is to conquer!

Thus to answer the Catastrophe, thus to speak to Fate, to give this pedestal to the future lion, to hurl such a challenge to the midnight rainstorm, to the treacherous wall of Hougomont, to the sunken road of Ohain, to Grouchy's delay, to Blücher's arrival, to be Irony itself in the tomb, to act so as to stand upright though fallen, to drown in two syllables the European coalition, to offer kings privies which the Caesars once knew, to make the lowest of words the most lofty by entwining with it the glory of France, insolently to end Waterloo with Mardigras, to finish Leonidas with Rabelais, to set the crown on this victory by a word impossible to speak, to lose the field and preserve history, to have the laugh on your side after such a carnage—this is immense!

It was an insult such as a thunder-cloud might hurl! It reaches the grandeur of Æschylus!

Cambronne's reply produces the effect of a violent break. 'Tis like the breaking of a heart under a weight of scorn. 'Tis the overflow of agony bursting forth. Who conquered? Wellington? No! Had it not been for Blücher, he was lost. Was it Blücher? No! If Wellington had not begun, Blücher could not have finished. This Cambronne, this man spending his last hour, this unknown soldier, this infinitesimal of war, realizes that here is a falsehood, a falsehood in a catastrophe, and so doubly agonizing; and at the moment when his rage is bursting forth because of it, he is offered this mockery—life! How could he restrain himself? Yonder are all the kings of Europe, the generals flushed with victory, the Jupiters darting thunderbolts; they have a hundred thousand victorious soldiers, and back of the hundred thousand a million; their cannon stand with yawning mouths, the match is lighted; they grind down under their heels the Imperial Guards and the grand army; they have just crushed Napoleon, and only Cambronne remains—only this earthworm is left to protest. He will protest. Then he seeks for the appropriate word as one seeks for a sword. His mouth froths, and the froth is the word. In face of this mean and mighty victory, in face of this victory which counts none victorious, this desperate soldier stands erect. He grants its overwhelming immensity, but he establishes its triviality; and he does more than spit upon it. Borne down by numbers, by superior force, by brute matter, he finds in his soul an expression: *"Excrément!"* We repeat it—to use that word, to do thus, to invent such an expression, is to be the conqueror!

The spirit of mighty days at that portentous moment made its descent on that unknown man. Cambronne invents the word for Waterloo, as Rouget invents the "Marseillaise," under the visitation of a breath from on high. An emanation from the divine whirlwind leaps forth and comes sweeping over these men, and they shake, and one of them sings the song supreme, and the other utters the frightful cry.

This challenge of titanic scorn Cambronne hurls not only at Europe in the name of the Empire—that would be a trifle: he hurls it at the past in the name of the Revolution. It is heard, and Cambronne is recognized as possessed by the ancient spirit of the Titans. Danton seems to be speaking! Kléber seems to be bellowing!

At that word from Cambronne, the English voice responded, "Fire!" The batteries flamed, the hill trembled, from all those brazen mouths belched a last terrible gush of grape-shot; a vast volume of smoke, vaguely white in the light of the rising moon, rolled out, and when the smoke dispersed, there was no longer anything there. That formidable remnant had been annihilated; the Guard was dead. The four walls of the living redoubt lay prone, and hardly was there discernible, here and there, even a quiver in the bodies; it was thus that the French legions, greater than the Roman legions, expired on Mont-Saint-Jean, on the soil watered with rain and blood, amid the gloomy grain, on the spot where nowadays Joseph, who drives the post-wagon from Nivelles, passes whistling, and cheerfully whipping up his horse at four o'clock in the morning.

Chapter XVI

QUOT LIBRAS IN DUCE?

THE BATTLE OF WATERLOO IS AN ENIGMA. IT IS AS OBSCURE TO THOSE WHO WON IT AS TO THOSE who lost it. For Napoleon it was a panic; Blücher sees nothing in it but fire; Wellington understands nothing in regard to it. Look at the reports. The bulletins are confused, the commentaries involved. Some stammer, others lisp. Jomini divides the battle of Waterloo into four moments; Muffling cuts it up into three changes; Charras alone, though we hold another judgment than his on some points, seized with his haughty glance the characteristic outlines of that catastrophe of human genius in conflict with divine chance. All the other historians suffer from being somewhat dazzled, and in this dazzled state they fumble about. It was a day of lightning brilliancy; in fact, a crumbling of the military monarchy which, to the vast stupefaction of kings, drew all the kingdoms after it— the fall of force, the defeat of war.

In this event, stamped with superhuman necessity, the part played by men amounts to nothing.

If we take Waterloo from Wellington and Blücher, do we thereby deprive England and Germany of anything? No. Neither that illustrious England nor that august Germany enter into the problem of Waterloo. Thank Heaven, nations are great, independently of the lugubrious feats of the sword. Neither England, nor Germany, nor France is contained in a scabbard. At this epoch when Waterloo is only a clashing of swords, above Blücher, Germany has Schiller; above Wellington, England has Byron. A vast dawn of ideas is the peculiarity of our century, and in that aurora England and Germany have a magnificent radiance. They are majestic because they think. The elevation of level which they contribute to civilization is intrinsic with them; it proceeds from themselves and not from an accident. The aggrandizement which they have brought to the nineteenth century has not Waterloo as its source. It is only barbarous peoples who undergo rapid growth after a victory. That is the temporary vanity of torrents swelled by a storm. Civilized people, especially in our day, are neither elevated nor abased by the good or bad fortune of a captain. Their specific gravity in the human species results from something more than a combat. Their honor, thank God! their dignity, their intelligence, their genius, are not numbers which those gamblers, heroes and conquerors, can put in the lottery of battles. Often a battle is lost and progress is conquered. There is less glory and more liberty. The drum holds its peace; reason takes the word. It is a game in which he who loses wins. Let us, therefore, speak of Waterloo coldly from both sides. Let us render to chance that which is due to chance, and to God that which is due to God. What is Waterloo? A victory? No. The winning number in the lottery.

The quine[1] won by Europe, paid by France.

It was not worthwhile to place a lion there.

Waterloo, moreover, is the strangest encounter in history. Napoleon and Wellington. They are not enemies; they are opposites. Never did God, who is fond of antitheses, make a more striking contrast, a more extraordinary comparison. On one side, precision, foresight, geometry, prudence, an assured retreat, reserves spared, with an obstinate coolness, an imperturbable method, strategy, which takes advantage of the ground, tactics, which preserve the equilibrium of battalions, carnage, executed according to rule, war regulated, watch in hand, nothing voluntarily left to chance, the ancient classic courage, absolute regularity; on the other, intuition, divination, military oddity, superhuman instinct, a flaming glance, an indescribable something which gazes like an eagle, and which strikes like the lightning, a prodigious art in disdainful impetuosity, all the mysteries of a profound soul, associated with destiny; the stream, the plain, the forest, the hill, summoned, and in a manner, forced to obey, the despot going even so far as to tyrannize over the field of battle; faith in a star mingled with strategic science, elevating but perturbing it. Wellington was the Barême of war; Napoleon was its Michael Angelo; and on this occasion, genius was vanquished by calculation. On both sides someone was awaited. It was the exact calculator who succeeded. Napoleon was waiting for Grouchy; he did not come. Wellington expected Blücher; he came.

Wellington is classic war taking its revenge. Bonaparte, at his dawning, had encountered him in Italy, and beaten him superbly. The old owl had fled before the young vulture. The old tactics had been not only struck as by lightning, but disgraced. Who was that Corsican of six-and-twenty? What signified that splendid ignoramus, who, with everything against him, nothing in his favor, without provisions, without ammunition, without cannon, without shoes, almost without an army, with a mere handful of men against masses, hurled himself on Europe combined, and absurdly won victories in the impossible? Whence had issued that fulminating convict, who almost without taking breath, and with the same set of combatants in hand, pulverized, one after the other, the five armies of the emperor of Germany, upsetting Beaulieu on Alvinzi, Wurmser on Beaulieu, Mélas on Wurmser, Mack on Mélas? Who was this novice in war with the effrontery of a luminary? The academical military school excommunicated him, and as it lost its footing; hence, the implacable rancor of the old Cæsarism against the new; of the regular sword against the flaming sword; and of the exchequer against genius. On the 18th of June, 1815, that rancor had the last word. and beneath Lodi, Montebello, Montenotte, Mantua, Arcola, it wrote: Waterloo. A triumph of the mediocres

---

1. Five winning numbers in a lottery.

which is sweet to the majority. Destiny consented to this irony. In his decline, Napoleon found Wurmser, the younger, again in front of him.

In fact, to get Wurmser, it sufficed to blanch the hair of Wellington.

Waterloo is a battle of the first order, won by a captain of the second.

That which must be admired in the battle of Waterloo, is England; the English firmness, the English resolution, the English blood; the superb thing about England there, no offense to her, was herself. It was not her captain; it was her army.

Wellington, oddly ungrateful, declares in a letter to Lord Bathurst, that his army, the army which fought on the 18th of June, 1815, was a "detestable army." What does that somber intermingling of bones buried beneath the furrows of Waterloo think of that?

England has been too modest in the matter of Wellington. To make Wellington so great is to belittle England. Wellington is nothing but a hero like many another. Those Scotch Grays, those Horse Guards, those regiments of Maitland and of Mitchell, that infantry of Pack and Kempt, that cavalry of Ponsonby and Somerset, those Highlanders playing the pibroch under the shower of grape-shot, those battalions of Rylandt, those utterly raw recruits, who hardly knew how to handle a musket holding their own against Essling's and Rivoli's old troops—that is what was grand. Wellington was tenacious; in that lay his merit, and we are not seeking to lessen it: but the least of his foot-soldiers and of his cavalry would have been as solid as he. The iron soldier is worth as much as the Iron Duke. As for us, all our glorification goes to the English soldier, to the English army, to the English people. If trophy there be, it is to England that the trophy is due. The column of Waterloo would be more just, if, instead of the figure of a man, it bore on high the statue of a people.

But this great England will be angry at what we are saying here. She still cherishes, after her own 1688 and our 1789, the feudal illusion. She believes in heredity and hierarchy. This people, surpassed by none in power and glory, regards itself as a nation, and not as a people. And as a people, it willingly subordinates itself and takes a lord for its head. As a workman, it allows itself to be disdained; as a soldier, it allows itself to be flogged.

It will be remembered, that at the battle of Inkermann a sergeant who had, it appears, saved the army, could not be mentioned by Lord Raglan, as the English military hierarchy does not permit any hero below the grade of an officer to be mentioned in the reports.

That which we admire above all, in an encounter of the nature of Waterloo, is the marvelous cleverness of chance. A nocturnal rain, the wall of Hougomont, the hollow road of Ohain, Grouchy deaf to the cannon, Napoleon's guide deceiving him, Bülow's guide enlightening him—the whole of this cataclysm is wonderfully conducted.

On the whole, let us say it plainly, it was more of a massacre than of a battle at Waterloo.

Of all pitched battles, Waterloo is the one which has the smallest front for such a number of combatants. Napoleon, three-quarters of a league; Wellington, half a league; seventy-two thousand combatants on each side. From this denseness the carnage arose.

The following calculation has been made, and the following proportion established: Loss of men: at Austerlitz, French, fourteen per cent; Russians, thirty per cent; Austrians, forty-four per cent. At Wagram, French, thirteen per cent; Austrians, fourteen. At the Moskowa, French, thirty-seven per cent; Russians, forty-four. At Bautzen, French, thirteen per cent; Russians and Prussians, fourteen. At Waterloo, French, fifty-six per cent; the Allies, thirty-one. Total for Waterloo, forty-one per cent; one hundred and forty-four thousand combatants; sixty thousand dead.

To-day, the field of Waterloo has the calm which belongs to the earth, the impassive support of man, and it resembles all plains.

At night, moreover, a sort of visionary mist arises from it; and if a traveler strolls there, if he listens, if he watches, if he dreams like Virgil in the fatal plains of Philippi, the hallucination of the catastrophe takes possession of him. The frightful 18th of June lives again; the false monumental hillock disappears, the lion vanishes in air, the battlefield resumes its reality, lines of infantry un-dulate over the plain, furious gallops traverse the horizon; the frightened dreamer beholds the flash of sabers, the gleam of bayonets, the flare of bombs, the tremendous interchange of thunders; he hears, as it were, the death-rattle in the depths of a tomb, the vague clamor of the battle phantom; those shadows are grenadiers, those lights are cuirassiers; that skeleton Napoleon, that other skele-ton is Wellington; all this no longer exists, and yet it clashes together and combats still; and the ravines are empurpled, and the trees quiver, and there is fury even in the clouds and in the shadows; all those terrible heights, Hougomont, Mont-Saint-Jean, Frischemont, Papelotte, Plancenoit, ap-pear confusedly crowned with whirlwinds of specters engaged in exterminating each other.

Chapter XVII

IS WATERLOO TO BE CONSIDERED GOOD?

THERE EXISTS A VERY RESPECTABLE LIBERAL SCHOOL WHICH DOES NOT HATE WATERLOO. WE DO not belong to it. To us, Waterloo is but the stupefied date of liberty. That such an eagle should emerge from such an egg is certainly unexpected.

If one places one's self at the culminating point of view of the question, Waterloo is inten-tionally a counter-revolutionary victory. It is Europe against France; it is Petersburg, Berlin, and Vienna against Paris; it is the *status quo* against the initiative; it is the 14th of July, 1789, attacked through the 20th of March, 1815; it is the monarchies clearing the decks in opposition to the in-domitable French rioting. The final extinction of that vast people which had been in eruption for twenty-six years—such was the dream. The solidarity of the Brunswicks, the Nassaus, the Ro-manoffs, the Hohenzollerns, the Hapsburgs with the Bourbons. Waterloo bears divine right on its crupper. It is true, that the Empire having been despotic, the kingdom by the natural reaction of things, was forced to be liberal, and that a constitutional order was the unwilling result of Water-loo, to the great regret of the conquerors. It is because revolution cannot be really conquered, and that being providential and absolutely fatal, it is always cropping up afresh: before Waterloo, in Bonaparte overthrowing the old thrones; after Waterloo, in Louis XVIII granting and conforming to the charter. Bonaparte places a postilion on the throne of Naples, and a sergeant on the throne of Sweden, employing inequality to demonstrate equality; Louis XVIII at Saint-Ouen countersigns the declaration of the rights of man. If you wish to gain an idea of what revolution is, call it Progress; and if you wish to acquire an idea of the nature of progress, call it To-morrow. To-morrow fulfills its work irresistibly, and it is already fulfilling it to-day. It always reaches its goal strangely. It employs Wellington to make of Foy, who was only a soldier, an orator. Foy falls at Hougomont and rises again in the tribune. Thus does progress proceed. There is no such thing as a bad tool for that workman. It does not become disconcerted, but adjusts to its divine work the man who has bestridden the Alps, and the good old tottering invalid of Father Élysée. It makes use of the gouty man as well as of the conqueror; of the conqueror without, of the gouty man within. Wa-terloo, by cutting short the demolition of European thrones by the sword, had no other effect than to cause the revolutionary work to be continued in another direction. The slashers have finished; it was the turn of the thinkers. The century that Waterloo was intended to arrest has pursued its march. That sinister victory was vanquished by liberty.

In short, and incontestably, that which triumphed at Waterloo; that which smiled in Welling-ton's rear; that which brought him all the marshals' staffs of Europe, including, it is said, the staff of a marshal of France; that which joyously trundled the barrows full of bones to erect the knoll of the lion; that which triumphantly inscribed on that pedestal the date "*June* 18, 1815"; that which encouraged Blücher, as he put the flying army to the sword; that which, from the heights of the plateau of Mont-Saint-Jean, hovered over France as over its prey, was the counter-revolution. It was the counter-revolution which murmured that infamous word "dismemberment." On arriving in Paris, it beheld the crater close at hand; it felt those ashes which scorched its feet, and it changed its mind; it returned to the stammer of a charter.

Let us behold in Waterloo only that which is in Waterloo. Of intentional liberty there is none. The counter-revolution was involuntarily liberal, in the same manner as, by a corresponding phenomenon, Napoleon was involuntarily revolutionary. On the 18th of June, 1815, the mounted Robespierre was hurled from his saddle.

Chapter XVIII

A RECRUDESCENCE OF DIVINE RIGHT

END OF THE DICTATORSHIP. A WHOLE EUROPEAN SYSTEM CRUMBLED AWAY.
The Empire sank into a gloom which resembled that of the Roman world as it expired. Again we behold the abyss, as in the days of the barbarians; only the barbarism of 1815, which must be called by its pet name of the counter-revolution, was not long breathed, soon fell to panting, and halted short. The Empire was bewept—let us acknowledge the fact—and bewept by heroic eyes. If glory lies in the sword converted into a scepter, the Empire had been glory in person. It had diffused over the earth all the light which tyranny can give—a somber light. We will say more; an obscure light. Compared to the true daylight, it is night. This disappearance of night produces the effect of an eclipse.

Louis XVIII re-entered Paris. The circling dances of the 8th of July effaced the enthusiasms of the 20th of March. The Corsican became the antithesis of the Bearnese. The flag on the dome of the Tuileries was white. The exile reigned. Hartwell's pine table took its place in front of the fleur-de-lys-strewn throne of Louis XIV. Bouvines and Fontenoy were mentioned as though they had taken place on the preceding day, Austerlitz having become antiquated. The altar and the throne fraternized majestically. One of the most undisputed forms of the health of society in the nineteenth century was established over France, and over the continent. Europe adopted the white cockade. Trestaillon was celebrated. The device *non pluribus impar* reappeared on the stone rays representing a sun upon the front of the barracks on the Quai d'Orsay. Where there had been an Imperial Guard, there was now a red house. The Arc du Carrousel, all laden with badly borne victories, thrown out of its element among these novelties, a little ashamed, it may be, of Marengo and Arcola, extricated itself from its predicament with the statue of the Duc d'Angoulême. The cemetery of the Madeleine, a terrible pauper's grave in 1793, was covered with jasper and marble, since the bones of Louis XVI and Marie Antoinette lay in that dust.

In the moat of Vincennes a sepulchral shaft sprang from the earth, recalling the fact that the Duc d'Enghien had perished in the very month when Napoleon was crowned. Pope Pius VII, who had performed the coronation very near this death, tranquilly bestowed his blessing on the fall as he had bestowed it on the elevation. At Schoenbrunn there was a little shadow, aged four, whom it was seditious to call the King of Rome. And these things took place, and the kings resumed their thrones, and the master of Europe was put in a cage, and the old régime became the new regime, and all the shadows and all the light of the earth changed place, because, on the afternoon of a certain summer's day, a shepherd said to a Prussian in the forest, "Go this way, and not that!"

This 1815 was a sort of lugubrious April. Ancient unhealthy and poisonous realities were covered with new appearances. A lie wedded 1789; the right divine was masked under a charter; fictions became constitutional; prejudices, superstitions, and mental reservations, with Article 14 in the heart, were varnished over with liberalism. It was the serpent's change of skin.

Man had been rendered both greater and smaller by Napoleon. Under this reign of splendid matter, the ideal had received the strange name of ideology! It is a grave imprudence in a great man to turn the future into derision. The populace, however, that food for cannon which is so fond of the cannoneer, sought him with its glance. Where is he? What is he doing? "Napoleon is dead," said a passer-by to a veteran of Marengo and Waterloo. "He dead!" cried the soldier; "you don't know him." Imagination distrusted this man, even when overthrown. The depths of Europe were full of darkness after Waterloo. Something enormous remained long empty through Napoleon's disappearance.

The kings placed themselves in this void. Ancient Europe profited by it to undertake reforms. There was a Holy Alliance; *Belle-Alliance*, Beautiful Alliance, the fatal field of Waterloo had said in advance.

In presence and in face of that antique Europe reconstructed, the features of a new France were sketched out. The future, which the Emperor had rallied, made its entry. On its brow it bore the star, Liberty. The glowing eyes of all young generations were turned on it. Singular fact! people were, at one and the same time, in love with the future, Liberty, and the past, Napoleon. Defeat had rendered the vanquished greater. Bonaparte fallen seemed more lofty than Napoleon erect. Those who had triumphed were alarmed. England had him guarded by Hudson Lowe, and France had him watched by Montchenu. His folded arms became a source of uneasiness to thrones. Alexander called him "my sleeplessness." This terror was the result of the quantity of revolution which was contained in him. That is what explains and excuses Bonapartist liberalism. This phantom caused the old world to tremble. The kings reigned, but ill at their ease, with the rock of Saint Helena on the horizon.

While Napoleon was passing through the death struggle at Longwood, the sixty thousand men who had fallen on the field of Waterloo were quietly rotting, and something of their peace was shed abroad over the world. The Congress of Vienna made the treaties in 1815, and Europe called this the Restoration.

This is what Waterloo was.

But what matters it to the Infinite? all that tempest, all that cloud, that war, then that peace? All that darkness did not trouble for a moment the light of that immense Eye before which a grub skipping from one blade of grass to another equals the eagle soaring from belfry to belfry on the towers of Notre-Dame.

Chapter XIX

THE BATTLEFIELD AT NIGHT

LET US RETURN—IT IS A NECESSITY IN THIS BOOK—TO THAT FATAL BATTLEFIELD. On the 18th of June the moon was full. Its light favored Blücher's ferocious pursuit, betrayed the traces of the fugitives, delivered up that disastrous mass to the eager Prussian cavalry, and aided the massacre. Such tragic favors of the night do occur sometimes during catastrophes.

After the last cannon-shot had been fired, the plain of Mont-Saint-Jean remained deserted.

The English occupied the encampment of the French; it is the usual sign of victory to sleep in the bed of the vanquished. They established their bivouac beyond Rossomme. The Prussians, let loose on the retreating rout, pushed forward. Wellington went to the village of Waterloo to draw up his report to Lord Bathurst.

If ever the *sic vos non vobis* was applicable, it certainly is to that village of Waterloo. Waterloo took no part, and lay half a league from the scene of action. Mont-Saint-Jean was cannonaded, Hougomont was burned, La Haie-Sainte was taken by assault, Papelotte was burned, Plancenoit was burned, La Belle-Alliance beheld the embrace of the two conquerors; these names are hardly known, and Waterloo, which worked not in the battle, bears off all the honor.

We are not of the number of those who flatter war; when the occasion presents itself, we tell the truth about it. War has frightful beauties which we have not concealed; it has also, we acknowledge, some hideous features. One of the most surprising is the prompt stripping of the bodies of the dead after the victory. The dawn which follows a battle always rises on naked corpses.

Who does this? Who thus soils the triumph? What hideous, furtive hand is that which is slipped into the pocket of victory? What pickpockets are they who ply their trade in the rear of glory? Some philosophers—Voltaire among the number—affirm that it is precisely those persons have made the glory. It is the same men, they say; there is no relief corps; those who are erect pillage those who are prone on the earth. The hero of the day is the vampire of the night. One has assuredly the right, after all, to strip a corpse a bit when one is the author of that corpse. For our own part, we do not think so; it seems to us impossible that the same hand should pluck laurels and purloin the shoes from a dead man.

One thing is certain, which is, that generally after conquerors follow thieves. But let us leave the soldier, especially the contemporary soldier, out of the question.

Every army has a rear-guard, and it is that which must be blamed. Bat-like creatures, half brigands and lackeys; all the sorts of vespertillos that that twilight called war engenders; wearers of uniforms, who take no part in the fighting; pretended invalids; formidable limpers; interloping sutlers, trotting along in little carts, sometimes accompanied by their wives, and stealing things which they sell again; beggars offering themselves as guides to officers; soldiers' servants; marauders; armies on the march in days gone by—we are not speaking of the present—dragged all this behind them, so that in the special language they are called "stragglers." No army, no nation, was responsible for those beings; they spoke Italian and followed the Germans, then spoke French and followed the English. It was by one of these wretches, a Spanish straggler who spoke French, that the Marquis of Fervacques, deceived by his Picard jargon, and taking him for one of our own men, was traitorously slain and robbed on the battlefield itself, in the course of the night which followed the victory of Cerisoles. The rascal sprang from this marauding. The detestable maxim, *Live on the enemy!* produced this leprosy, which a strict discipline alone could heal. There are reputations which are deceptive; one does not always know why certain generals, great in other directions, have been so popular. Turenne was adored by his soldiers because he tolerated pillage; evil permitted constitutes part of goodness. Turenne was so good that he allowed the Palatinate to be delivered over to fire and blood. The marauders in the train of an army were more or less in number, according as the chief was more or less severe. Hoche and Marceau had no stragglers; Wellington had few, and we do him the justice to mention it.

Nevertheless, on the night from the 18th to the 19th of June, the dead were robbed. Wellington was rigid; he gave orders that anyone caught in the act should be shot; but rapine is tenacious. The marauders stole in one corner of the battlefield while others were being shot in another.

The moon was sinister over this plain.

Toward midnight, a man was prowling about, or rather, climbing in the direction of the hollow road of Ohain. To all appearance he was one of those whom we have just described—neither

English nor French, neither peasant nor soldier, less a man than a ghoul attracted by the scent of the dead bodies, having theft for his victory, and come to rifle Waterloo. He was clad in a blouse that was something like a great coat; he was uneasy and audacious; he walked forwards and gazed behind him. Who was this man? The night probably knew more of him than the day. He had no sack, but evidently he had large pockets under his coat. From time to time he halted, scrutinized the plain around him as though to see whether he were observed, bent over abruptly, disturbed something silent and motionless on the ground, then rose and fled. His sliding motion, his attitudes, his mysterious and rapid gestures, caused him to resemble those twilight larvae which haunt ruins, and which ancient Norman legends call the Alleurs.

Certain nocturnal wading birds produce these silhouettes among the marshes.

A glance capable of piercing all that mist deeply would have perceived at some distance a sort of little sutler's wagon with a fluted wicker hood, harnessed to a famished nag which was cropping the grass across its bit as it halted, hidden, as it were, behind the hovel which adjoins the highway to Nivelles, at the angle of the road from Mont-Saint-Jean to Braine-l'Alleud; and in the wagon, a sort of woman seated on coffers and packages. Perhaps there was some connection between that wagon and that prowler.

The darkness was serene. Not a cloud in the zenith. What matters it if the earth be red! the moon remains white; these are the indifferences of the sky. In the fields, branches of trees broken by grape-shot, but not fallen, upheld by their bark, swayed gently in the breeze of night. A breath, almost a respiration, moved the shrubbery. Quivers which resembled the departure of souls ran through the grass.

In the distance the coming and going of patrols and the general rounds of the English camp were audible.

Hougomont and La Haie-Sainte continued to burn, forming, one in the west, the other in the east, two great flames which were joined by the cordon of bivouac fires of the English, like a necklace of rubies with two carbuncles at the extremities, as they extended in an immense semi-circle over the hills along the horizon.

We have described the catastrophe of the road of Ohain. The heart is terrified at the thought of what that death must have been to so many brave men.

If there is anything terrible, if there exists a reality which surpasses dreams, it is this: to live, to see the sun; to be in full possession of virile force; to possess health and joy; to laugh valiantly; to rush toward a glory which one sees dazzling in front of one; to feel in one's breast lungs which breathe, a heart which beats, a will which reasons; to speak, think, hope, love; to have a mother, to have a wife, to have children; to have the light—and all at once, in the space of a shout, in less than a minute, to sink into an abyss; to fall, to roll, to crush, to be crushed; to see ears of wheat, flowers, leaves, branches; not to be able to catch hold of anything; to feel one's sword useless, men beneath one, horses on top of one; to struggle in vain, since one's bones have been broken by some kick in the darkness; to feel a heel which makes one's eyes start from their sockets; to bite horses' shoes in one's rage; to stifle, to yell, to writhe; to be beneath, and to say to one's self, "But just a little while ago I was a living man!"

There, where that lamentable disaster had uttered its death-rattle, all was silence now. The edges of the hollow road were encumbered with horses and riders, inextricably heaped up. Terrible entanglement! There was no longer any slope, for the corpses had leveled the road with the plain, and reached the brim like a well-filled bushel of barley. A heap of dead bodies in the upper part, a river of blood in the lower part—such was that road on the evening of the 18th of June, 1815. The blood ran even to the Nivelles highway, and there overflowed in a large pool in front of the abatis of trees which barred the way, at a spot which is still pointed out.

It will be remembered that it was at the opposite point, in the direction of the Genappe road, that the destruction of the cuirassiers had taken place. The thickness of the layer of bodies was proportioned to the depth of the hollow road. Toward the middle, at the point where it became level, where Delort's division had passed, the layer of corpses was thinner.

The nocturnal prowler whom we have just shown to the reader was going in that direction. He was searching that vast tomb. He gazed about. He passed the dead in some sort of hideous review. He walked with his feet in the blood.

All at once he paused.

A few paces in front of him, in the hollow road, at the point where the pile of dead came to an end, an open hand, illumined by the moon, projected from beneath that heap of men. That hand had on its finger something sparkling, which was a ring of gold.

The man bent over, remained in a crouching attitude for a moment, and when he rose there was no longer a ring on the hand.

He did not precisely rise; he remained in a stooping and frightened attitude, with his back turned to the heap of dead, scanning the horizon on his knees, with the whole upper portion of his body supported on his two forefingers, which rested on the earth, and his head peering above the edge of the hollow road. The jackal's four paws suit some actions.

Then coming to a decision, he rose to his feet.

At that moment, he gave a terrible start. He felt someone clutch him from behind.

He wheeled round; it was the open hand, which had closed, and had seized the skirt of his coat.

An honest man would have been terrified; this man burst into a laugh.

"Come," said he, "it's only a dead body. I prefer a spook to a gendarme."

But the hand weakened and released him. Effort is quickly exhausted in the grave.

"Well now," said the prowler, "is that dead fellow alive? Let's see."

He bent down again, fumbled among the heap, pushed aside everything that was in his way, seized the hand, grasped the arm, freed the head, pulled out the body, and a few moments later he was dragging the lifeless, or at least the unconscious, man, through the shadows of hollow road. He was a cuirassier, an officer, and even an officer of considerable rank; a large gold epaulet peeped from beneath the cuirass; this officer no longer possessed a helmet. A furious sword-cut had scarred his face, where nothing was discernible but blood.

However, he did not appear to have any broken limbs, and, by some happy chance, if that word is permissible here, the dead had been vaulted above him in such a manner as to preserve him from being crushed. His eyes were still closed.

On his cuirass he wore the silver cross of the Legion of Honor.

The prowler tore off this cross, which disappeared into one of the gulfs which he had beneath his great-coat.

Then he felt of the officer's fob, discovered a watch there, and took possession of it. Next he searched his waistcoat, found a purse and pocketed it.

When he had arrived at this stage of succor which he was administering to this dying man, the officer opened his eyes.

"Thanks," he said feebly.

The abruptness of the movements of the man who was manipulating him, the freshness of the night, the air which he could inhale freely, had roused him from his lethargy.

The prowler made no reply. He raised his head. A sound of footsteps was audible in the plain; some patrol was probably approaching.

The officer murmured, for the death-agony was still in his voice:

"Who won the battle?"

"The English," answered the prowler.

The officer went on:

"Look in my pockets; you will find a watch and a purse. Take them."

It was already done.

The prowler executed the required feint, and said:

"There is nothing there."

"I have been robbed," said the officer; "I am sorry for that. You should have had them."

The steps of the patrol became more and more distinct.

"Someone is coming," said the prowler, with the movement of a man who is taking his departure.

The officer raised his arm feebly, and detained him.

"You have saved my life. Who are you?"

The prowler answered rapidly, and in a low voice:

"Like yourself, I belonged to the French army. I must leave you. If they were to catch me, they would shoot me. I have saved your life. Now get out of the scrape yourself."

"What is your rank?"

"Sergeant."

"What is your name?"

"Thénardier."

"I shall not forget that name," said the officer; "and do you remember mine. My name is Pontmercy."

BOOK SECOND

THE SHIP *ORION*

Chapter I

NUMBER 24,601 BECOMES NUMBER 9,430

JEAN VALJEAN HAD BEEN RECAPTURED.

The reader will be grateful to us if we pass rapidly over the sad details. We will confine ourselve to transcribing two paragraphs published by the journals of that day, a few months after the surprising events which had taken place at M. sur M.

These articles are rather summary. It must be remembered, that at that epoch the *Gazette des Tribunaux* was not yet in existence.

We borrow the first from the *Drapeau Blanc*. It bears the date of July 25, 1823.

An arrondissement of the Pas de Calais has just been the theater of an event quite out of the ordinary course. A man, who was a stranger in the Department, and who bore the name of M. Madeleine, had, thanks to the new methods, resuscitated some years ago an ancient local industry, the manufacture of jet and of black glass trinkets. He had made his fortune in the business, and that of the arrondissement as well, we will admit. He had been appointed mayor, in recognition of his services. The police discovered that M. Madeleine was no other than an ex-convict who had broken his ban, condemned in 1796 for theft, and named Jean Valjean. Jean Valjean has been recommitted to prison. It appears that previous to his arrest he had succeeded in withdrawing from the hands of M. Laffitte, a sum of over half a million which he had lodged there, and which he had, moreover, and by perfectly legitimate means, acquired in his business. No one has been able to discover where Jean Valjean has concealed this money since his return to prison at Toulon.

The second article, which enters a little more into detail, is an extract from the *Journal de Paris*, of the same date.

A former convict, who had been liberated, named Jean Valjean, has just appeared before the Court of Assizes of the Var, under circumstances calculated to attract attention. This wretch had succeeded in escaping the vigilance of the police, he had changed his name, and had succeeded in getting himself appointed mayor of one of our small northern towns; in this town he had established a considerable commerce. He has at last been unmasked and arrested, thanks to the indefatigable zeal of the public prosecutor. He had for his concubine a woman of the town, who died of a shock at the moment of his arrest. This scoundrel, who is endowed with Herculean strength, found means to escape; but three or four days after his flight the police laid their hands on him once more, in Paris itself, at the very moment when he was entering one of those little vehicles which run between the capital and the village of Montfermeil (Seine-et-Oise). He is said to have profited by this interval of three or four days of liberty, to withdraw a considerable sum deposited by him with one of our leading bankers. This sum has been estimated at six or seven hundred thousand francs. If the indictment is to be trusted, he has hidden it in some place known to himself alone, and it has not been possible to lay hands on it. However that may be, the said Jean Valjean has just been brought before the Assizes of the Department of the Var as accused of highway robbery accompanied with violence, about eight years ago, on the person of one of those honest children who, as the patriarch of Ferney has said, in immortal verse,

> . . . *Arrive from Savoy every year,*
> *And who, with gentle hands, do clear*
> *Those long canals choked up with soot.*

This bandit refused to defend himself. It was proved by the skillful and eloquent representative of the public prosecutor, that the theft was committed in complicity with others, and that Jean Valjean was a member of a band of robbers in the south. Jean Valjean was pronounced guilty and was condemned to the death penalty in consequence. This criminal refused to lodge an appeal. The king, in his inexhaustible clemency, has deigned to commute his penalty to that of penal servitude for life. Jean Valjean was immediately taken to the prison at Toulon.

The reader has not forgotten that Jean Valjean had religious habits at M. sur M. Some papers, among others the *Constitutional*, presented this commutation as a triumph of the priestly party. Jean Valjean changed his number in the galleys. He was called 9,430.

However, and we will mention it at once in order that we may not be obliged to recur to the subject, the prosperity of M. sur M. vanished with M. Madeleine; all that he had foreseen during his night of fever and hesitation was realized; lacking him, there actually was *a soul lacking*. After this fall, there took place at M. sur M. that egotistical division of great existences which have fallen, that fatal dismemberment of flourishing things which is accomplished every day, obscurely, in the human community, and which history has noted only once, because it occurred after the death of Alexander. Lieutenants are crowned kings; superintendents improvise manufacturers out of themselves. Envious rivalries arose. M. Madeleine's vast workshops were shut; his buildings fell to ruin, his workmen were scattered. Some of them quitted the country, others abandoned the trade. Thenceforth, everything was done on a small scale, instead of on a grand scale; for lucre instead of the general good. There was no longer a center; everywhere there was competition and animosity. M. Madeleine had reigned over all and directed all. No sooner had he fallen, than each pulled things to himself; the spirit of combat succeeded to the spirit of organization, bitterness to cordiality, hatred of one another to the benevolence of the founder toward all; the threads which M. Madeleine had set were tangled and broken, the methods were adulterated, the products were debased, confidence was killed; the market diminished, for lack of orders; salaries were reduced, the workshops stood still, bankruptcy arrived. And then there was nothing more for the poor. All had vanished.

The state itself perceived that someone had been crushed somewhere. Less than four years after the judgment of the Court of Assizes establishing the identity of Jean Valjean and M. Madeleine, for the benefit of the galleys, the cost of collecting taxes had doubled in the arrondissement of M. sur M.; and M. de Villèle called attention to the fact in the rostrum, in the month of February, 1827.

Chapter II

IN WHICH THE READER WILL PERUSE TWO VERSES, WHICH ARE OF THE DEVIL'S COMPOSITION, POSSIBLY

BEFORE PROCEEDING FURTHER, IT WILL BE TO THE PURPOSE TO NARRATE IN SOME DETAIL, A SINgular occurrence which took place at about the same epoch, in Montfermeil, and which is not lacking in coincidence with certain conjectures of the indictment.

There exists in the region of Montfermeil a very ancient superstition, which is all the more curious and all the more precious, because a popular superstition in the vicinity of Paris is like an aloe in Siberia. We are among those who respect everything which is in the nature of a rare plant. Here, then, is the superstition of Montfermeil: it is thought that the devil, from time immemorial, has selected the forest as a hiding-place for his treasures. Goodwives affirm that it is no rarity to encounter at nightfall, in secluded nooks of the forest, a black man with the air of a carter or a wood-chopper, wearing wooden shoes, clad in trousers and a blouse of linen, and recognizable by the fact, that, instead of a cap or hat, he has two immense horns on his head. This ought, in fact, to render him recognizable. This man is habitually engaged in digging a hole. There are three ways of profiting by such an encounter. The first is to approach the man and speak to him. Then it is seen that the man is simply a peasant, that he appears black because it is nightfall; that he is not digging any hole whatever, but is cutting grass for his cows, and that what had been taken for horns is nothing but a dung-fork which he is carrying on his back, and whose teeth, thanks to the perspective of evening, seemed to spring from his head. The man returns home and dies within the week. The second way is to watch him, to wait until he has dug his hole, until he has filled it and has gone away; then to run with great speed to the trench, to open it once more, and to seize the "treasure" which the black man has necessarily placed there. In this case one dies within the month. Finally, the last method is not to speak to the black man, not to look at him, and to flee at the best speed of one's legs. One then dies within the year.

As all three methods are attended with their special inconveniences, the second, which at all events, presents some advantages, among others that of possessing a treasure, if only for a month, is the one most generally adopted. So bold men, who are tempted by every chance, have quite frequently, as we are assured, opened the holes excavated by the black man, and tried to rob the devil. The success of the operation appears to be but moderate. At least, if the tradition is to be believed, and in particular the two enigmatical lines in barbarous Latin, which an evil Norman monk, a bit of a sorcerer, named Tryphon has left on this subject. This Tryphon is buried at the Abbey of Saint-Georges de Bocherville, near Rouen, and toads spawn on his grave.

Accordingly, enormous efforts are made. Such trenches are ordinarily extremely deep; a man sweats, digs, toils all night—for it must be done at night; he wets his shirt, burns out his candle, breaks his mattock, and when he arrives at the bottom of the hole, when he lays his hand on the "treasure," what does he find? What is the devil's treasure? A sou, sometimes a crown-piece, a stone, a skeleton, a bleeding body, sometimes a specter folded in four like a sheet of paper in a portfolio, sometimes nothing. This is what Tryphon's verses seem to announce to the indiscreet and curious:

> *"Fodit, et in fossa thesauros condit opaca,*
> *As, nummas, lapides, cadaver, simulacra, nihilque."*

It seems that in our day there is sometimes found a powder-horn with bullets, sometimes an old pack of cards greasy and worn, which has evidently served the devil. Tryphon does not record these two finds, since Tryphon lived in the twelfth century, and since the devil does not appear to have had the wit to invent powder before Roger Bacon's time, and cards before the time of Charles VI.

Moreover, if one plays at cards, one is sure to lose all that one possesses! and as for the powder in the horn, it possesses the property of making your gun burst in your face.

Now, a very short time after the epoch when it seemed to the prosecuting attorney that the liberated convict Jean Valjean during his flight of several days had been prowling around Montfermeil, it was remarked in that village that a certain old road-laborer, named Boulatruelle, had "peculiar ways" in the forest. People thereabouts thought they knew that this Boulatruelle had been in the galleys. He was subjected to certain police supervision, and, as he could find work nowhere, the administration employed him at reduced rates as a road-mender on the cross-road from Gagny to Lagny.

This Boulatruelle was a man who was viewed with disfavor by the inhabitants of the district as too respectful, too humble, too prompt in removing his cap to everyone, and trembling and smiling in the presence of the gendarmes—probably affiliated to robber bands, they said; suspected of lying in ambush at verge of copses at nightfall. The only thing in his favor was that he was a drunkard.

This is what people thought they had noticed:

Of late, Boulatruelle had taken to quitting his task of stone-breaking and care of the road at a very early hour, and to betaking himself to the forest with his pickax. He was encountered toward evening in the most deserted clearings, in the wildest thickets; and he had the appearance of being in search of something, and sometimes he was digging holes. The goodwives who passed took him at first for Beelzebub; then they recognized Boulatruelle, and were not in the least reassured thereby. These encounters seemed to cause Boulatruelle a lively displeasure. It was evident that he sought to hide, and that there was some mystery in what he was doing.

It was said in the village: "It is clear that the devil has appeared. Boulatruelle has seen him, and is on the search. In sooth, he is cunning enough to pocket Lucifer's hoard."

The Voltairians added, "Will Boulatruelle catch the devil, or will the devil catch Boulatruelle?" The old women made a great many signs of the cross.

In the meantime, Boulatruelle's maneuvers in the forest ceased; and he resumed his regular occupation of road-mending; and people gossiped of something else.

Some persons, however, were still curious, surmising that in all this there was probably no fabulous treasure of the legends, but some fine windfall of a more serious and palpable sort than the devil's bank-bills, and that the road-mender had half discovered the secret. The most "puzzled" were the schoolmaster and Thénardier, the proprietor of the tavern, who was everybody's friend, and had not disdained to ally himself with Boulatruelle.

"He has been in the galleys," said Thénardier. "Eh! Good God! no one knows who has been there or will be there."

One evening the schoolmaster affirmed that in former times the law would have instituted an inquiry as to what Boulatruelle did in the forest, and that the latter would have been forced to speak, and that he would have been put to the torture in case of need, and that Boulatruelle would not have resisted the water test, for example. "Let us put him to the wine test," said Thénardier.

They made an effort, and got the old road-mender to drinking. Boulatruelle drank an enormous amount, but said very little. He combined with admirable art, and in masterly proportions, the thirst of a gormandizer with the discretion of a judge. Nevertheless, by dint of returning to the charge and of comparing and putting together the few obscure words which he did allow to escape him, this is what Thénardier and the schoolmaster imagined that they had made out:

One morning, when Boulatruelle was on his way to his work, at daybreak, he had been surprised to see, at a nook of the forest, in the underbrush, a shovel and a pickax, *concealed, as one might say.*

However, he might have supposed that they were probably the shovel and pick of Father Six-Fours, the water-carrier, and would have thought no more about it. But, on the evening of that day, he saw, without being seen himself, as he was hidden by a large tree, "a person who did not belong in those parts, and whom he, Boulatruelle, knew well," directing his steps toward the densest part of the wood. Translation by Thénardier: *A comrade of the galleys.* Boulatruelle obstinately refused to reveal his name. This person carried a package—something square, like a large box or a small trunk. Surprise on the part of Boulatruelle. However, it was only after the expiration of seven or eight minutes that the idea of following that "person" had occurred to him. But it was too late; the person was already in the thicket, night had descended, and Boulatruelle had not been able to catch up with him. Then he had adopted the course of watching for him at the edge of the woods. "It was moonlight." Two or three hours later, Boulatruelle had seen this person emerge from the brushwood, carrying no longer the coffer, but a shovel and pick. Boulatruelle had allowed the person to pass, and had not dreamed of accosting him, because he said to himself that the other man was three times as strong as he was, and armed with a pickax, and that he would probably knock him over the head on recognizing him, and on perceiving that he was recognized. Touching effusion of two old comrades on meeting again. But the shovel and pick had served as a ray of light to Boulatruelle; he had hastened to the thicket in the morning, and had found neither shovel nor pick. From this he had drawn the inference that this person, once in the forest, had dug a hole with his pick, buried the coffer, and reclosed the hole with his shovel. Now, the coffer was too small to contain a body; therefore it contained money. Hence his researches. Boulatruelle had explored, sounded, searched the entire forest and the thicket, and had dug wherever the earth appeared to him to have been recently turned up. In vain.

He had "ferreted out" nothing. No one in Montfermeil thought anymore about it. There were only a few brave gossips, who said, "You may be certain that the mender on the Gagny road did not take all that trouble for nothing; he was sure that the devil had come."

Chapter III

THE ANKLE-CHAIN MUST HAVE UNDERGONE A CERTAIN PREPARATORY MANIPULATION TO BE THUS BROKEN WITH A BLOW FROM A HAMMER

TOWARD THE END OF OCTOBER, IN THAT SAME YEAR, 1823, THE INHABITANTS OF TOULON BEHELD the entry into their port, after heavy weather, and for the purpose of repairing some damages, of the ship *Orion*, which was employed later at Brest as a school-ship, and which then formed a part of the Mediterranean squadron.

This vessel, battered as it was—for the sea had handled it roughly—produced a fine effect as it entered the roads. It flew some colors which procured for it the regulation salute of eleven guns, which it returned, shot for shot; total, twenty-two. It has been calculated that what with salvos, royal and military politenesses, courteous exchanges of uproar, signals of etiquette, formalities of roadsteads and citadels, sunrises and sunsets, saluted everyday by all fortresses and all ships of war, openings and closings of ports, etc., the civilized world, discharged all over the earth, in the course of four-and-twenty hours, one hundred and fifty thousand useless shots. At six francs the shot, that comes to nine hundred thousand francs a day, three hundred millions a year, which vanish in smoke. This is a mere detail. All this time the poor were dying of hunger.

The year 1823 was what the Restoration called "the epoch of the Spanish war."

This war contained many events in one, and a quantity of peculiarities. A grand family affair for the house of Bourbon; the branch of France succoring and protecting the branch of Madrid, that is to say, performing an act devolving on the elder; an apparent return to our national traditions, complicated by servitude and by subjection to the cabinets of the North; M. le Duc d'Angoulême, surnamed by the liberal sheets *the hero of Andujar,* compressing in a triumphal attitude that was somewhat contradicted by his peaceable air, the ancient and very powerful terrorism of the Holy Office at variance with the chimerical terrorism of the liberals; the *sansculottes* resuscitated, to the great terror of dowagers, under the name of *descamisados*; monarchy opposing an obstacle to progress described as anarchy; the theories of '89 roughly interrupted in the sap; a European halt, called to the French idea, which was making the tour of the world; beside the son of France as generalissimo, the Prince de Carignan, afterwards Charles Albert, enrolling himself in that crusade of kings against people as a volunteer, with grenadier epaulets of red worsted; the soldiers of the Empire setting out on a fresh campaign, but aged, saddened, after eight years of repose, and under the white cockade; the tricolored standard waved abroad by a heroic handful of Frenchmen, as the white standard had been thirty years earlier at Coblentz; monks mingled with our troops; the spirit of liberty and of novelty brought to its senses by bayonets; principles slaughtered by cannonades; France undoing by her arms that which she had done by her mind; in addition to this, hostile leaders sold, soldiers hesitating, cities besieged by millions; no military perils, and yet possible explosions, as in every mine which is surprised and invaded; but little bloodshed, little honor won, shame for some, glory for no one. Such was this war, made by the princes descended from Louis XIV, and conducted by generals who had been under Napoleon. Its sad fate was to recall neither the grand war nor grand politics.

Some feats of arms were serious; the taking of the Trocadéro, among others, was a fine military action; but after all, we repeat, the trumpets of this war give back a cracked sound, the whole effect was suspicious; history approves of France for making a difficulty about accepting this false triumph. It seemed evident that certain Spanish officers charged with resistance yielded too easily;

the idea of corruption was connected with the victory; it appears as though generals and not battles had been won, and the conquering soldier returned humiliated. A debasing war, in short, in which the *Bank of France* could be read in the folds of the flag.

Soldiers of the war of 1808, on whom Saragossa had fallen in formidable ruin, frowned in 1823 at the easy surrender of citadels, and began to regret Palafox. It is the nature of France to prefer to have Rostopchine rather than Ballesteros in front of her.

From a still more serious point of view, and one which it is also proper to insist upon here, this war, which wounded the military spirit of France, enraged the democratic spirit. It was an enterprise of enthrallment. In that campaign, the object of the French soldier, the son of democracy, was the conquest of a yoke for others. A hideous contradiction. France is made to arouse the soul of nations, not to stifle it. All the revolutions of Europe since 1792 are the French Revolution: liberty darts rays from France. That is a solar fact. Blind is he who will not see! It was Bonaparte who said it.

The war of 1823, an outrage on the generous Spanish nation, was then, at the same time, an outrage on the French Revolution. It was France who committed this monstrous violence; by foul means, for, with the exception of wars of liberation, everything that armies do is by foul means. The words *passive obedience* indicate this. An army is a strange masterpiece of combination where force results from an enormous sum of impotence. Thus is war, made by humanity against humanity, despite humanity, explained.

As for the Bourbons, the war of 1823 was fatal to them. They took it for a success. They did not perceive the danger that lies in having an idea slain to order. They went astray, in their innocence, to such a degree that they introduced the immense enfeeblement of a crime into their establishment as an element of strength. The spirit of the ambush entered into their politics. 1830 had its germ in 1823. The Spanish campaign became in their counsels an argument for force and for adventures by right Divine. France, having re-established *el rey netto* in Spain, might well have re-established the absolute king at home. They fell into the alarming error of taking the obedience of the soldier for the consent of the nation. Such confidence is the ruin of thrones. It is not permitted to fall asleep, either in the shadow of a machineel-tree, nor in the shadow of an army.

Let us return to the ship *Orion.*

During the operations of the army commanded by the prince generalissimo, a squadron had been cruising in the Mediterranean. We have just stated that the *Orion* belonged to this fleet, and that accidents of the sea had brought it into port at Toulon.

The presence of a vessel of war in a port has something about it which attracts and engages a crowd. It is because it is great, and the crowd loves what is great.

A ship of the line is one of the most magnificent combinations of the genius of man with the powers of nature.

A ship of the line is composed, at the same time, of the heaviest and the lightest of possible matter, for it deals at one and the same time with three forms of substance—solid, liquid, and fluid—and it must do battle with all three. It has eleven claws of iron with which to seize the granite on the bottom of the sea, and more wings and more antennae than winged insects, to catch the wind in the clouds. Its breath pours out through its hundred and twenty cannons as through enormous trumpets, and replies proudly to the thunder. The ocean seeks to lead it astray in the alarming sameness of its billows, but the vessel has its soul, its compass, which counsels it and always shows it the north. In the blackest nights, its lanterns supply the place of the stars. Thus, against the wind, it has its cordage and its canvas; against the water, wood; against the rocks, its iron, brass, and lead; against the shadows, its light; against immensity, a needle.

If one wishes to form an idea of all those gigantic proportions which, taken as a whole, constitute the ship of the line, one has only to enter one of the six-story covered construction stocks, in the ports of Brest or Toulon. The vessels in process of construction are under a bell-glass there, as it were. This colossal beam is a yard; that great column of wood which stretches out on the earth as far as the eye can reach is the main-mast. Taking it from its root in the stocks to its tip in the clouds, it is sixty fathoms long, and its diameter at its base is three feet. The English main-mast rises to a height of two hundred and seventeen feet above the waterline. The navy of our fathers employed cables, ours employs chains. The simple pile of chains on a ship of a hundred guns is four feet high, twenty feet in breadth, and eight feet in depth. And how much wood is required to make this ship? Three thousand cubic meters. It is a floating forest.

And moreover, let this be borne in mind, it is only a question here of the military vessel of forty years ago, of the simple sailing-vessel; steam, then in its infancy, has since added new miracles to that prodigy which is called a war vessel. At the present time, for example, the mixed vessel with a screw is a surprising machine, propelled by three thousand square meters of canvas and by an engine of two thousand five hundred horse-power.

Not to mention these new marvels, the ancient vessel of Christopher Columbus and of De Ruyter is one of the masterpieces of man. It is as inexhaustible in force as is the Infinite in gales; it stores up the wind in its sails, it is precise in the immense vagueness of the billows, it floats, and it reigns.

There comes an hour, nevertheless, when the gale breaks that sixty-foot yard like a straw, when the wind bends that mast four hundred feet tall, when that anchor, which weighs tens of thousands, is twisted in the jaws of the waves like a fisherman's hook in the jaws of a pike, when those monstrous cannons utter plaintive and futile roars, which the hurricane bears forth into the void and into night, when all that power and all that majesty are engulfed in a power and majesty which are superior.

Every time that immense force is displayed to culminate in an immense feebleness it affords men food for thought. Hence in the ports curious people abound around these marvelous machines of war and of navigation, without being able to explain perfectly to themselves why.

Every day, accordingly, from morning until night, the quays, sluices, and the jetties of the port of Toulon were covered with a multitude of idlers and loungers, as they say in Paris, whose business consisted in staring at the *Orion*.

The *Orion* was a ship that had been ailing for a long time; in the course of its previous cruises thick layers of barnacles had collected on its keel to such a degree as to deprive it of half its speed; it had gone into the dry dock the year before this, in order to have the barnacles scraped off, then it had put to sea again; but this cleaning had affected the bolts of the keel: in the neighborhood of the Balearic Isles the sides had been strained and had opened; and, as the plating in those days was not of sheet iron, the vessel had sprung a leak. A violent equinoctial gale had come up, which had first staved in a grating and a porthole on the larboard side, and damaged the foretop-gallant-shrouds; in consequence of these injuries, the *Orion* had run back to Toulon.

It anchored near the Arsenal; it was fully equipped, and repairs were begun. The hull had received no damage on the starboard, but some of the planks had been unnailed here and there, according to custom, to permit of air entering the hold.

One morning the crowd which was gazing at it witnessed an accident.

The crew was busy bending the sails; the topman, who had to take the upper corner of the main-top-sail on the starboard, lost his balance; he was seen to waver; the multitude thronging the Arsenal quay uttered a cry; the man's head overbalanced his body; the man fell around the yard, with his hands outstretched towards the abyss; on his way he seized the foot-rope, first with one hand, then with the other, and remained hanging from it: the sea lay below him at a dizzy depth; the shock of his fall had imparted to the foot-rope a violent swinging motion; the man swayed back and forth at the end of that rope, like a stone in a sling.

It was incurring a frightful risk to go to his assistance; not one of the sailors, all fishermen of the coast, recently levied for the service, dared to attempt it. In the meantime, the unfortunate topman was losing his strength; his anguish could not be discerned on his face, but his exhaustion was visible in every limb; his arms were contracted in horrible twitchings; every effort which he made to reascend served but to augment the oscillations of the foot-rope; he did not shout, for fear of exhausting his strength. All were awaiting the minute when he should release his hold on the rope, and, from instant to instant, heads were turned aside that his fall might not be seen. There are moments when a bit of rope, a pole, the branch of a tree, is life itself, and it is a terrible thing to see a living being detach himself from it and fall like a ripe fruit.

All at once, a man was seen climbing into the rigging with the agility of a tiger-cat; this man was dressed in red; he was a convict; he wore a green cap; he was a life convict. On arriving on a level with the top, a gust of wind carried away his cap, and allowed a perfectly white head to be seen: he was not a young man.

A convict employed on board with a detachment from the galleys had, in fact, at the very first instant, hastened to the officer of the watch, and, in the midst of the consternation and the hesitation of the crew, while all the sailors were trembling and drawing back, he had asked the officer's permission to risk his life to save the topman; at an affirmative sign from the officer he had broken the chain riveted to his ankle with one blow of a hammer, then he had caught up a rope, and had dashed into the rigging: no one noticed, at the instant, with what ease that chain had been broken; it was only later on that the incident was recalled.

In a twinkling he was on the yard; he paused for a few seconds and appeared to be measuring it with his eye; these seconds, during which the breeze swayed the topman at the extremity of a thread, seemed centuries to those who were looking on. At last, the convict raised his eyes to heaven and advanced a step: the crowd drew a long breath. He was seen to run out along the yard: on arriving at the point, he fastened the rope which he had brought to it, and allowed the other end to hang down, then he began to descend the rope, hand over hand, and then—and the anguish was indescribable—instead of one man suspended over the gulf, there were two.

One would have said it was a spider coming to seize a fly, only here the spider brought life, not death. Ten thousand glances were fastened on this group; not a cry, not a word; the same tremor contracted every brow; all mouths held their breath, as though they feared to add the slightest puff to the wind which was swaying the two unfortunate men.

In the meantime, the convict had succeeded in lowering himself to a position near the sailor. It was high time; one minute more, and the exhausted and despairing man would have allowed himself to fall into the abyss. The convict had moored him securely with the cord to which he clung with one hand, while he was working with the other. At last, he was seen to climb back on the yard, and to drag the sailor up after him; he held him there a moment to allow him to recover his strength, then he grasped him in his arms and carried him, walking on the yard himself to the cap, and from there to the main-top, where he left him in the hands of his comrades.

At that moment the crowd broke into applause: old convict-sergeants among them wept, and women embraced each other on the quay, and all voices were heard to cry with a sort of tender rage, "Pardon for that man!"

He, in the meantime, had immediately begun to make his descent to rejoin his detachment. In order to reach them the more speedily, he dropped into the rigging, and ran along one of the lower yards; all eyes were following him. At a certain moment fear assailed them; whether it was that he was fatigued, or that his head turned, they thought they saw him hesitate and stagger. All at once the crowd uttered a loud shout: the convict had fallen into the sea.

The fall was perilous. The frigate *Algésiras* was anchored alongside the *Orion*, and the poor convict had fallen between the two vessels: it was to be feared that he would slip under one or the other of them. Four men flung themselves hastily into a boat; the crowd cheered them on; anxiety again took possession of all souls; the man had not risen to the surface; he had disappeared in the sea without leaving a ripple, as though he had fallen into a cask of oil: they sounded, they dived. In vain. The search was continued until the evening: they did not even find the body.

On the following day the Toulon newspaper printed these lines:

"Nov. 17, 1823. Yesterday, a convict belonging to the detachment on board of the *Orion*, on his return from rendering assistance to a sailor, fell into the sea and was drowned. The body has not yet been found; it is supposed that it is entangled among the piles of the Arsenal point: this man was committed under the number 9,430, and his name was Jean Valjean."

BOOK THIRD

ACCOMPLISHMENT OF THE PROMISE MADE TO THE DEAD WOMAN

Chapter I

THE WATER QUESTION AT MONTFERMEIL

MONTFERMEIL IS SITUATED BETWEEN LIVRY AND CHELLES, ON THE SOUTHERN EDGE OF THAT lofty table-land which separates the Ourcq from the Marne. At the present day it is a tolerably large town, ornamented all the year through with plaster villas, and on Sundays with beaming bourgeois. In 1823 there were at Montfermeil neither so many white houses nor so many well-satisfied citizens: it was only a village in the forest. Some pleasure-houses of the last century were to be met with there, to be sure, which were recognizable by their grand air, their balconies in twisted iron, and their long windows, whose tiny panes cast all sorts of varying shades of green on the white of the closed shutters; but Montfermeil was none the less a village. Retired cloth-merchants and rusticating attorneys had not discovered it as yet; it was a peaceful and charming place, which was not on the road to anywhere: there people lived, and cheaply, that peasant rustic life which is so bounteous and so easy; only, water was rare there, on account of the elevation of the plateau.

It was necessary to fetch it from a considerable distance; the end of the village towards Gagny drew its water from the magnificent ponds which exist in the woods there. The other end, which surrounds the church and which lies in the direction of Chelles, found drinking-water only at a little spring halfway down the slope, near the road to Chelles, about a quarter of an hour from Montfermeil.

Thus each household found it hard work to keep supplied with water. The large houses, the aristocracy, of which the Thénardier tavern formed a part, paid half a farthing a bucketful to a man who made a business of it, and who earned about eight sous a day in his enterprise of supplying Montfermeil with water; but this good man only worked until seven o'clock in the evening in summer, and five in winter; and night once come and the shutters on the ground floor once closed, he who had no water to drink went to fetch it for himself or did without it.

This constituted the terror of the poor creature whom the reader has probably not forgotten—little Cosette. It will be remembered that Cosette was useful to the Thénardiers in two ways: they made the mother pay them, and they made the child serve them. So when the mother ceased to pay altogether, the reason for which we have read in preceding chapters, the Thénardiers kept Cosette. She took the place of a servant in their house. In this capacity she it was who ran to fetch water when it was required. So the child, who was greatly terrified at the idea of going to the spring at night, took great care that water should never be lacking in the house.

Christmas of the year 1823 was particularly brilliant at Montfermeil. The beginning of the winter had been mild; there had been neither snow nor frost up to that time. Some mountebanks from Paris had obtained permission of the mayor to erect their booths in the principal street of the village, and a band of itinerant merchants, under protection of the same tolerance, had constructed their stalls on the Church Square, and even extended them into Boulanger Alley, where, as the reader will perhaps remember, the Thénardiers' hostelry was situated. These people filled the inns and drinking-shops, and communicated to that tranquil little district a noisy and joyous life. In order to play the part of a faithful historian, we ought even to add that, among the curiosities displayed in the square, there was a menagerie, in which frightful clowns, clad in rags and coming no one knew whence, exhibited to the peasants of Montfermeil in 1823 one of those horrible Brazilian vultures, such as our Royal Museum did not possess until 1845, and which have a tricolored cockade for an eye. I believe that naturalists call this bird Caracara Polyborus; it belongs to the order of the Apicides, and to the family of the vultures. Some good old Bonapartist soldiers, who had retired to the village, went to see this creature with great devotion. The mountebanks gave out that the tricolored cockade was a unique phenomenon made by God expressly for their menagerie.

On Christmas Eve itself, a number of men, carters, and peddlers, were seated at table, drinking and smoking around four or five candles in the public-room of Thénardier's hostelry. This room resembled all drinking-shop rooms—tables, pewter jugs, bottles, drinkers, smokers; but little light and a great deal of noise. The date of the year 1823 was indicated, nevertheless, by two objects which were then fashionable in the bourgeois class: to wit, a kaleidoscope and a lamp of ribbed tin. The female Thénardier was attending to the supper, which was roasting in front of a clear fire; her husband was drinking with his customers and talking politics.

Besides political conversations which had for their principal subjects the Spanish war and M. le Duc d'Angoulême, strictly local parentheses, like the following, were audible amid the uproar:

"About Nanterre and Suresnes the vines have flourished greatly. When ten pieces were reckoned on there have been twelve. They have yielded a great deal of juice under the press." "But the grapes cannot be ripe?" "In those parts the grapes should not be ripe; the wine turns oily as soon as spring comes." "Then it is very thin wine?" "There are wines poorer even than these. The grapes must be gathered while green." Etc.

Or a miller would call out:

"Are we responsible for what is in the sacks? We find in them a quantity of small seed which we cannot sift out, and which we are obliged to send through the mill-stones; there are tares, fennel, vetches, hempseed, fox-tail, and a host of other weeds, not to mention pebbles, which abound in certain wheat, especially in Breton wheat. I am not fond of grinding Breton wheat, anymore than long-sawyers like to saw beams with nails in them. You can judge of the bad dust that makes in grinding. And then people complain of the flour. They are in the wrong. The flour is no fault of ours."

In a space between two windows a mower, who was seated at table with a landed proprietor who was fixing on a price for some meadow work to be performed in the spring, was saying:

"It does no harm to have the grass wet. It cuts better. Dew is a good thing, sir. It makes no difference with that grass. Your grass is young and very hard to cut still. It's terribly tender. It yields before the iron." Etc.

Cosette was in her usual place, seated on the cross-bar of the kitchen table near the chimney. She was in rags; her bare feet were thrust into wooden shoes, and by the firelight she was engaged in knitting woolen stockings destined for the young Thénardiers. A very young kitten was playing about among the chairs. Laughter and chatter were audible in the adjoining room, from two fresh children's voices: it was Éponine and Azelma.

In the chimney-corner a cat-o'-nine-tails was hanging on a nail.

At intervals the cry of a very young child, which was somewhere in the house, rang through the noise of the dram-shop. It was a little boy who had been born to the Thénardiers during one of the preceding winters—"she did not know why," she said, "the result of the cold"—and who was a little more than three years old. The mother had nursed him, but she did not love him. When the persistent clamor of the brat became too annoying, "Your son is squalling," Thénardier would say; "do go and see what he wants." "Bah!" the mother would reply, "he bothers me." And the neglected child continued to shriek in the dark.

Chapter II

Two Complete Portraits

SO FAR IN THIS BOOK THE THÉNARDIERS HAVE BEEN VIEWED ONLY IN PROFILE; THE MOMENT HAS arrived for making the circuit of this couple, and considering it under all its aspects.

Thénardier had just passed his fiftieth birthday; Madame Thénardier was approaching her forties, which is equivalent to fifty in a woman; so that there existed a balance of age between husband and wife.

Our readers have possibly preserved some recollection of this Thénardier woman, ever since her first appearance—tall, blond, red, fat, angular, square, enormous, and agile; she belonged, as we have said, to the race of those colossal wild women, who contort themselves at fairs with paving-stones hanging from their hair. She did everything about the house—made the beds, did the washing, the cooking, and everything else. Cosette was her only servant; a mouse in the service of an elephant. Everything trembled at the sound of her voice—window panes, furniture, and people. Her big face, dotted with red blotches, presented the appearance of a skimmer. She had a beard. She was an ideal market-porter dressed in woman's clothes. She swore splendidly; she boasted of being able to crack a nut with one blow of her fist. Except for the romances which she had read, and which made the affected lady peep through the ogress at times, in a very queer way, the idea would never have occurred to anyone to say of her, "That is a woman." This Thénardier female was like the product of a wench engrafted on a fishwife. When one heard her speak, one said, "That is a gendarme"; when one saw her drink, one said, "That is a carter"; when one saw her handle Cosette, one said, "That is the hangman." One of her teeth projected when her face was in repose.

Thénardier was a small, thin, pale, angular, bony, feeble man, who had a sickly air and who was wonderfully healthy. His cunning began here; he smiled habitually, by way of precaution, and was almost polite to everybody, even to the beggar to whom he refused half a farthing. He had the glance of a pole-cat and the bearing of a man of letters. He greatly resembled the portraits of the Abbé Delille. His coquetry consisted in drinking with the carters. No one had ever succeeded in rendering him drunk. He smoked a big pipe. He wore a blouse, and under his blouse an old black coat. He made pretensions to literature and to materialism. There were certain names which he often pronounced to support whatever things he might be saying—Voltaire, Raynal, Parny, and, singularly enough, Saint Augustine. He declared that he had "a system." In addition, he was a great swindler. A *filousophe* [philosophe], a scientific thief. The species does exist. It will be remembered that he pretended to have served in the army; he was in the habit of relating with exuberance, how, being a sergeant in the 6th or the 9th light something or other, at Waterloo, he had alone, and in the presence of a squadron of death-dealing hussars, covered with his body and saved from death, in the midst of the grape-shot, "a general, who had been dangerously wounded." Thence arose for his wall the flaring sign, and for his inn the name which it bore in the neighborhood, of "the cabaret of the Sergeant of Waterloo." He was a liberal, a classic, and a Bonapartist. He had subscribed for the Champ d'Asile. It was said in the village that he had studied for the priesthood.

We believe that he had simply studied in Holland for an inn-keeper. This rascal of composite order was, in all probability, some Fleming from Lille, in Flanders, a Frenchman in Paris, a Belgian at Brussels, being comfortably astride of both frontiers. As for his prowess at Waterloo, the reader is already acquainted with that. It will be perceived that he exaggerated it a trifle. Ebb and flow, wandering, adventure, was the leven of his existence; a tattered conscience entails a fragmentary life, and, apparently at the stormy epoch of June 18, 1815, Thénardier belonged to that variety of marauding sutlers of which we have spoken, beating about the country, selling to some, stealing from others, and traveling like a family man, with wife and children, in a rickety cart, in the rear of troops on the march, with an instinct for always attaching himself to the victorious army. This campaign ended, and having, as he said, "some quibus," he had come to Montfermeil and set up an inn there.

This *quibus,* composed of purses and watches, of gold rings and silver crosses, gathered in harvest-time in furrows sown with corpses, did not amount to a large total, and did not carry this sutler turned eating-house-keeper very far.

Thénardier had that peculiar rectilinear something about his gestures which, accompanied by an oath, recalls the barracks, and by a sign of the cross, the seminary. He was a fine talker. He allowed it to be thought that he was an educated man. Nevertheless, the schoolmaster had noticed that he pronounced improperly.

He composed the travelers' tariff card in a superior manner, but practiced eyes sometimes spied out orthographical errors in it. Thénardier was cunning, greedy, slothful, and clever. He did not disdain his servants, which caused his wife to dispense with them. This giantess was jealous. It seemed to her that that thin and yellow little man must be an object coveted by all.

Thénardier, who was, above all, an astute and well-balanced man, was a scamp of a temperate sort. This is the worst species; hypocrisy enters into it.

It is not that Thénardier was not, on occasion, capable of wrath to quite the same degree as his wife; but this was very rare, and at such times, since he was enraged with the human race in general, as he bore within him a deep furnace of hatred. And since he was one of those people who are continually avenging their wrongs, who accuse everything that passes before them of everything which has befallen them, and who are always ready to cast upon the first person who comes to hand, as a legitimate grievance, the sum total of the deceptions, the bankruptcies, and the calamities of their lives—when all this leaven was stirred up in him and boiled forth from his mouth and eyes, he was terrible. Woe to the person who came under his wrath at such a time!

In addition to his other qualities, Thénardier was attentive and penetrating, silent or talkative, according to circumstances, and always highly intelligent. He had something of the look of sailors, who are accustomed to screw up their eyes to gaze through marine glasses. Thénardier was a statesman.

Every newcomer who entered the tavern said, on catching sight of Madame Thénardier, "There is the master of the house." A mistake. She was not even the mistress. The husband was both master and mistress. She worked; he created. He directed everything by a sort of invisible and constant magnetic action. A word was sufficient for him, sometimes a sign; the mastodon obeyed. Thénardier was a sort of special and sovereign being in Madame Thénardier's eyes, though she did not thoroughly realize it. She was possessed of virtues after her own kind; if she had ever had a disagreement as to any detail with "Monsieur Thénardier"—which was an inadmissible hypothesis, by the way—she would not have blamed her husband in public on any subject whatever. She would never have committed "before strangers" that mistake so often committed by women, and which is called in parliamentary language, "exposing the crown." Although their concord had only evil as its result, there was contemplation in Madame Thénardier's submission to her husband. That mountain of noise and of flesh moved under the little finger of that frail despot. Viewed on its dwarfed and grotesque side, this was that grand and universal thing, the adoration of mind by matter; for certain ugly features have a cause in the very depths of eternal beauty. There was an unknown quantity about Thénardier; hence the absolute empire of the man over that woman. At certain moments she beheld him like a lighted candle; at others she felt him like a claw.

This woman was a formidable creature who loved no one except her children, and who did not fear anyone except her husband. She was a mother because she was mammiferous. But her maternity stopped short with her daughters, and, as we shall see, did not extend to boys. The man had but one thought—how to enrich himself.

He did not succeed in this. A theater worthy of this great talent was lacking. Thénardier was ruining himself at Montfermeil, if ruin is possible to zero; in Switzerland or in the Pyrenees this penniless scamp would have become a millionaire; but an inn-keeper must browse where fate has hitched him.

It will be understood that the word *inn-keeper* is here employed in a restricted sense, and does not extend to an entire class.

In this same year, 1823, Thénardier was burdened with about fifteen hundred francs' worth of petty debts, and this rendered him anxious.

Whatever may have been the obstinate injustice of destiny in this case, Thénardier was one of those men who understand best, with the most profundity and in the most modern fashion, that thing which is a virtue among barbarous peoples and an object of merchandise among civilized peoples—hospitality. Besides, he was an admirable poacher, and quoted for his skill in shooting. He had a certain cold and tranquil laugh, which was particularly dangerous.

His theories as a landlord sometimes burst forth in lightning flashes. He had professional aphorisms, which he inserted into his wife's mind. "The duty of the inn-keeper," he said to her one day, violently, and in a low voice, "is to sell to the first comer, stews, repose, light, fire, dirty sheets, a servant, lice, and a smile; to stop passers-by, to empty small purses, and to honestly lighten heavy ones; to shelter traveling families respectfully: to shave the man, to pluck the woman, to pick the child clean; to quote the window open, the window shut, the chimney-corner, the arm-chair, the chair, the ottoman, the stool, the feather-bed, the mattress and the truss of straw; to know how much the shadow uses up the mirror, and to put a price on it; and, by five hundred thousand devils, to make the traveler pay for everything, even for the flies which his dog eats!"

This man and this woman were ruse and rage wedded—a hideous and terrible team.

While the husband pondered and combined, Madame Thénardier thought not of absent creditors, took no heed of yesterday nor of to-morrow, and lived in a fit of anger, all in a minute.

Such were these two beings. Cosette was between them, subjected to their double pressure, like a creature who is at the same time being ground up in a mill and pulled to pieces with pincers. The man and the woman each had a different method: Cosette was overwhelmed with blows—this was the woman's; she went barefooted in winter—that was the man's doing.

Cosette ran up stairs and down, washed, swept, rubbed, dusted, ran, fluttered about, panted, moved heavy articles, and weak as she was, did the coarse work. There was no mercy for her; a fierce mistress and venomous master. The Thénardier hostelry was like a spider's web, in which Cosette had been caught, and where she lay trembling. The ideal of oppression was realized by this sinister household. It was something like the fly serving the spiders.

The poor child passively held her peace.

What takes place within these souls when they have but just quitted God, find themselves thus, at the very dawn of life, very small and in the midst of men all naked!

Chapter III

MEN MUST HAVE WINE, AND HORSES MUST HAVE WATER

FOUR NEW TRAVELERS HAD ARRIVED.

Cosette was meditating sadly; for, although she was only eight years old, she had already suffered so much that she reflected with the lugubrious air of an old woman. Her eye was black in consequence of a blow from Madame Thénardier's fist, which caused the latter to remark from time to time, "How ugly she is with her fist-blow on her eye!"

Cosette was thinking that it was dark, very dark, that the pitchers and caraffes in the chambers of the travelers who had arrived must have been filled and that there was no more water in the cistern.

She was somewhat reassured because no one in the Thénardier establishment drank much water. Thirsty people were never lacking there; but their thirst was of the sort which applies to the jug rather than to the pitcher. Anyone who had asked for a glass of water among all those glasses of wine would have appeared a savage to all these men. But there came a moment when the child trembled; Madame Thénardier raised the cover of a stew-pan which was boiling on the stove, then seized a glass and briskly approached the cistern. She turned the faucet; the child had raised her head and was following all the woman's movements. A thin stream of water trickled from the faucet, and half filled the glass. "Well," said she, "there is no more water!" A momentary silence ensued. The child did not breathe.

"Bah!" resumed Madame Thénardier, examining the half-filled glass, "this will be enough."

Cosette applied herself to her work once more, but for a quarter of an hour she felt her heart leaping in her bosom like a big snowflake.

She counted the minutes that passed in this manner, and wished it were the next morning.

From time to time one of the drinkers looked into the street, and exclaimed, "It's as black as an oven!" or, "One must needs be a cat to go about the streets without a lantern at this hour!" And Cosette trembled.

All at once one of the peddlers who lodged in the hostelry entered, and said in a harsh voice:

"My horse has not been watered."

"Yes, it has," said Madame Thénardier.

"I tell you that it has not," retorted the peddler.

Cosette had emerged from under the table.

"Oh, yes, sir!" said she, "the horse has had a drink; he drank out of a bucket, a whole bucketful, and it was I who took the water to him, and I spoke to him."

It was not true; Cosette lied.

"There's a brat as big as my fist who tells lies as big as the house," exclaimed the peddler. "I tell you that he has not been watered, you little jade! He has a way of blowing when he has had no water, which I know well."

Cosette persisted, and added in a voice rendered hoarse with anguish, and which was hardly audible:

"And he drank heartily."

"Come," said the peddler, in a rage, "this won't do at all, let my horse be watered, and let that be the end of it!"

Cosette crept under the table again.

"In truth, that is fair!" said Madame Thénardier, "if the beast has not been watered, it must be."

Then glancing about her:

"Well, now! Where's that other beast?"

She bent down and discovered Cosette cowering at the other end of the table, almost under the drinkers' feet.

"Are you coming?" shrieked Madame Thénardier.

Cosette crawled out of the sort of hole in which she had hidden herself. The Thénardier resumed:

"Mademoiselle Dog-lack-name, go and water that horse."

"But, Madame," said Cosette, feebly, "there is no water."

The Thénardier threw the street door wide open:

"Well, go and get some, then!"

Cosette dropped her head, and went for an empty bucket which stood near the chimney-corner.

This bucket was bigger than she was, and the child could have set down in it at her ease.

The Thénardier returned to her stove, and tasted what was in the stew-pan, with a wooden spoon, grumbling the while:

"There's plenty in the spring. There never was such a malicious creature as that. I think I should have done better to strain my onions."

Then she rummaged in a drawer which contained sous, pepper, and shallots.

"See here, Mam'selle Toad," she added, "on your way back, you will get a big loaf from the baker. Here's a fifteen-sou piece."

Cosette had a little pocket on one side of her apron; she took the coin without saying a word, and put it in that pocket.

Then she stood motionless, bucket in hand, the open door before her. She seemed to be waiting for someone to come to her rescue.

"Get along with you!" screamed the Thénardier.

Cosette went out. The door closed behind her.

Chapter IV

ENTRANCE ON THE SCENE OF A DOLL

THE LINE OF OPEN-AIR BOOTHS STARTING AT THE CHURCH, EXTENDED, AS THE READER WILL RE-member, as far as the hostelry of the Thénardiers. These booths were all illuminated, because the citizens would soon pass on their way to the midnight mass, with candles burning in paper funnels, which, as the schoolmaster, then seated at the table at the Thénardiers' observed, produced "a magical effect." In compensation, not a star was visible in the sky.

The last of these stalls, established precisely opposite the Thénardiers' door, was a toy-shop all glittering with tinsel, glass, and magnificent objects of tin. In the first row, and far forwards, the merchant had placed on a background of white napkins, an immense doll, nearly two feet high, who was dressed in a robe of pink crepe, with gold wheat-ears on her head, which had real hair and enamel eyes. All that day, this marvel had been displayed to the wonderment of all passers-by under ten years of age, without a mother being found in Montfermeil sufficiently rich or sufficiently extravagant to give it to her child. Éponine and Azelma had passed hours in contemplating it, and Cosette herself had ventured to cast a glance at it, on the sly, it is true.

At the moment when Cosette emerged, bucket in hand, melancholy and overcome as she was, she could not refrain from lifting her eyes to that wonderful doll, towards *the lady,* as she called it. The poor child paused in amazement. She had not yet beheld that doll close to. The whole shop seemed a palace to her: the doll was not a doll; it was a vision. It was joy, splendor, riches, happiness, which appeared in a sort of chimerical halo to that unhappy little being so profoundly engulfed in gloomy and chilly misery. With the sad and innocent sagacity of childhood, Cosette measured the abyss which separated her from that doll. She said to herself that one must be a queen, or at least a princess, to have a "thing" like that. She gazed at that beautiful pink dress, that beautiful smooth hair, and she thought, "How happy that doll must be!" She could not take her eyes from that fantastic stall. The more she looked, the more dazzled she grew. She thought she was gazing at paradise. There were other dolls behind the large one, which seemed to her to be fairies and genii. The merchant, who was pacing back and forth in front of his shop, produced on her somewhat the effect of being the Eternal Father.

In this adoration she forgot everything, even the errand with which she was charged.

All at once the Thénardier's coarse voice recalled her to reality: "What, you silly jade! you have not gone? Wait! I'll give it to you! I want to know what you are doing there! Get along, you little monster!"

The Thénardier had cast a glance into the street, and had caught sight of Cosette in her ecstasy.

Cosette fled, dragging her pail, and taking the longest strides of which she was capable.

Chapter V

THE LITTLE ONE ALL ALONE

AS THE THÉNARDIER HOSTELRY WAS IN THAT PART OF THE VILLAGE WHICH IS NEAR THE CHURCH, it was to the spring in the forest in the direction of Chelles that Cosette was obliged to go for her water.

She did not glance at the display of a single other merchant. So long as she was in Boulanger Lane and in the neighborhood of the church, the lighted stalls illuminated the road; but soon the last light from the last stall vanished. The poor child found herself in the dark. She plunged into it. Only, as a certain emotion overcame her, she made as much motion as possible with the handle of the bucket as she walked along. This made a noise which afforded her company.

The further she went, the denser the darkness became. There was no one in the streets. However, she did encounter a woman, who turned around on seeing her, and stood still, muttering between her teeth: "Where can that child be going? Is it a werewolf child?" Then the woman recognized Cosette. "Well," said she, "it's the Lark!"

In this manner Cosette traversed the labyrinth of tortuous and deserted streets which terminate in the village of Montfermeil on the side of Chelles. So long as she had the houses or even the walls only on both sides of her path, she proceeded with tolerable boldness. From time to time she caught the flicker of a candle through the crack of a shutter—this was light and life; there were people there, and it reassured her. But in proportion as she advanced, her pace slackened mechanically, as it were. When she had passed the corner of the last house, Cosette paused. It had been hard to advance further than the last stall; it became impossible to proceed further than the last house. She set her bucket on the ground, thrust her hand into her hair, and began slowly to scratch her head—a gesture peculiar to children when terrified and undecided what to do. It was no longer Montfermeil; it was the open fields. Black and desert space was before her. She gazed in despair at that darkness, where there was no longer anyone, where there were beasts, where there were specters, possibly. She took a good look, and heard the beasts walking on the grass, and she distinctly saw specters moving in the trees. Then she seized her bucket again; fear had lent her audacity. "Bah!" said she; "I will tell him that there was no more water!" And she resolutely re-entered Montfermeil.

Hardly had she gone a hundred paces when she paused and began to scratch her head again. Now it was the Thénardier who appeared to her, with her hideous, hyena mouth, and wrath flashing in her eyes. The child cast a melancholy glance before her and behind her. What was she to do? What was to become of her? Where was she to go? In front of her was the specter of the Thénardier; behind her all the phantoms of the night and of the forest. It was before the Thénardier that she recoiled. She resumed her path to the spring, and began to run. She emerged from the village, she entered the forest at a run, no longer looking at or listening to anything. She only paused in her course when her breath failed her; but she did not halt in her advance. She went straight before her in desperation.

As she ran she felt like crying.

The nocturnal quivering of the forest surrounded her completely.

She no longer thought, she no longer saw. The immensity of night was facing this tiny creature. On the one hand, all shadow; on the other, an atom.

It was only seven or eight minutes' walk from the edge of the woods to the spring. Cosette knew the way, through having gone over it many times in daylight. Strange to say, she did not get lost. A remnant of instinct guided her vaguely. But she did not turn her eyes either to right or to left, for fear of seeing things in the branches and in the brushwood. In this manner she reached the spring.

It was a narrow, natural basin, hollowed out by the water in a clayey soil, about two feet deep, surrounded with moss and with those tall, crimped grasses which are called Henry IV's frills, and paved with several large stones. A brook ran out of it, with a tranquil little noise.

Cosette did not take time to breathe. It was very dark, but she was in the habit of coming to this spring. She felt with her left hand in the dark for a young oak which leaned over the spring, and which usually served to support her, found one of its branches, clung to it, bent down, and plunged the bucket in the water. She was in a state of such violent excitement that her strength was trebled. While thus bent over, she did not notice that the pocket of her apron had emptied itself into the spring. The fifteen-sou piece fell into the water. Cosette neither saw nor heard it fall. She drew out the bucket nearly full, and set it on the grass.

That done, she perceived that she was worn out with fatigue. She would have liked to set out again at once, but the effort required to fill the bucket had been such that she found it impossible to take a step. She was forced to sit down. She dropped on the grass, and remained crouching there.

She shut her eyes; then she opened them again, without knowing why, but because she could not do otherwise. The agitated water in the bucket beside her was describing circles which resembled tin serpents.

Overhead the sky was covered with vast black clouds, which were like masses of smoke. The tragic mask of shadow seemed to bend vaguely over the child.

Jupiter was setting in the depths.

The child stared with bewildered eyes at this great star, with which she was unfamiliar, and which terrified her. The planet was, in fact, very near the horizon and was traversing a dense layer of mist which imparted to it a horrible ruddy hue. The mist, gloomily empurpled, magnified the star. One would have called it a luminous wound.

A cold wind was blowing from the plain. The forest was dark, not a leaf was moving; there were none of the vague, fresh gleams of summertide. Great boughs uplifted themselves in frightful wise. Slender and misshapen bushes whistled in the clearings. The tall grasses undulated like eels under the north wind. The nettles seemed to twist long arms furnished with claws in search of prey. Some bits of dry heather, tossed by the breeze, flew rapidly by, and had the air of fleeing in terror before something which was coming after. On all sides there were lugubrious stretches.

The darkness was bewildering. Man requires light. Whoever buries himself in the opposite of day feels his heart contract. When the eye sees black, the heart sees trouble. In an eclipse in the night, in the sooty opacity, there is anxiety even for the stoutest of hearts. No one walks alone in the forest at night without trembling. Shadows and trees—two formidable densities. A chimerical reality appears in the indistinct depths. The inconceivable is outlined a few paces distant from you with a spectral clearness. One beholds floating, either in space or in one's own brain, one knows not what vague and intangible thing, like the dreams of sleeping flowers. There are fierce attitudes on the horizon. One inhales the effluvia of the great black void. One is afraid to glance behind him, yet desirous of doing so. The cavities of night, things grown haggard, taciturn profiles which vanish when one advances, obscure dishevelments, irritated tufts, livid pools, the lugubrious reflected in the funereal, the sepulchral immensity of silence, unknown but possible beings, bendings of mysterious branches, alarming torsos of trees, long handfuls of quivering plants—against all this one has no protection. There is no hardihood which does not shudder and which does not feel the vicinity of anguish. One is conscious of something hideous, as though one's soul were becoming amalgamated with the darkness. This penetration of the shadows is indescribably sinister in the case of a child.

Forests are apocalypses, and the beating of the wings of a tiny soul produces a sound of agony beneath their monstrous vault.

Without understanding her sensations, Cosette was conscious that she was seized upon by that black enormity of nature; it was no longer terror alone which was gaining possession of her; it was something more terrible even than terror; she shivered. There are no words to express the strangeness of that shiver which chilled her to the very bottom of her heart; her eye grew wild; she thought she felt that she should not be able to refrain from returning there at the same hour on the morrow.

Then, by a sort of instinct, she began to count aloud, one, two, three, four, and so on up to ten, in order to escape from that singular state which she did not understand, but which terrified her, and, when she had finished, she began again; this restored her to a true perception of the things about her. Her hands, which she had wet in drawing the water, felt cold; she rose; her terror, a natural and unconquerable terror, had returned: she had but one thought now—to flee at full speed through the forest, across the fields to the houses, to the windows, to the lighted candles. Her glance fell upon the water which stood before her; such was the fright which the Thénardier inspired in her, that she dared not flee without that bucket of water: she seized the handle with both hands; she could hardly lift the pail.

In this manner she advanced a dozen paces, but the bucket was full; it was heavy; she was forced to set it on the ground once more. She took breath for an instant, then lifted the handle of the bucket again, and resumed her march, proceeding a little further this time, but again she was obliged to pause. After some seconds of repose she set out again. She walked bent forward, with drooping head, like an old woman; the weight of the bucket strained and stiffened her thin arms. The iron handle completed the benumbing and freezing of her wet and tiny hands; she was forced to halt from time to time, and each time that she did so, the cold water which splashed from the pail fell on her bare legs. This took place in the depths of a forest, at night, in winter, far from all human sight; she was a child of eight: no one but God saw that sad thing at the moment.

And her mother, no doubt, alas!

For there are things that make the dead open their eyes in their graves.

She panted with a sort of painful rattle; sobs contracted her throat, but she dared not weep, so afraid was she of the Thénardier, even at a distance: it was her custom to imagine the Thénardier always present.

However, she could not make much headway in that manner, and she went on very slowly. In spite of diminishing the length of her stops, and of walking as long as possible between them, she reflected with anguish that it would take her more than an hour to return to Montfermeil in this manner, and that the Thénardier would beat her. This anguish was mingled with her terror at being alone in the woods at night; she was worn out with fatigue, and had not yet emerged from the forest. On arriving near an old chestnut-tree with which she was acquainted, made a last halt, longer than the rest, in order that she might get well rested; then she summoned up all her strength, picked up her bucket again, and courageously resumed her march, but the poor little desperate creature could not refrain from crying, "O my God! my God!"

At that moment she suddenly became conscious that her bucket no longer weighed anything at all: a hand, which seemed to her enormous, had just seized the handle, and lifted it vigorously. She raised her head. A large black form, straight and erect, was walking beside her through the darkness; it was a man who had come up behind her, and whose approach she had not heard. This man, without uttering a word, had seized the handle of the bucket which she was carrying.

There are instincts for all the encounters of life.

The child was not afraid.

Chapter VI

WHICH POSSIBLY PROVES BOULATRUELLE'S INTELLIGENCE

O N THE AFTERNOON OF THAT SAME CHRISTMAS DAY, 1823, A MAN HAD WALKED FOR RATHER A long time in the most deserted part of the Boulevard de l'Hôpital in Paris. This man had the air of a person who is seeking lodgings, and he seemed to halt, by preference, at the most modest houses on that dilapidated border of the faubourg Saint-Marceau.

We shall see further on that this man had, in fact, hired a chamber in that isolated quarter.

This man, in his attire, as in all his person, realized the type of what may be called the well-bred mendicant—extreme wretchedness combined with extreme cleanliness. This is a very rare mixture which inspires intelligent hearts with that double respect which one feels for the man who is very poor, and for the man who is very worthy. He wore a very old and very well brushed round hat; a coarse coat, worn perfectly threadbare, of an ochre yellow, a color that was not in the least eccentric at that epoch; a large waistcoat with pockets of a venerable cut; black breeches, worn gray at the knee, stockings of black worsted; and thick shoes with copper buckles. He would have been pronounced a preceptor in some good family, returned from the emigration. He would have been taken for more than sixty years of age, from his perfectly white hair, his wrinkled brow, his livid lips, and his countenance, where everything breathed depression and weariness of life. Judging from his firm tread, from the singular vigor which stamped all his movements, he would have been hardly been thought fifty. The wrinkles on his brow were well placed, and would have disposed in his favor anyone who observed him attentively. His lip contracted with a strange fold which seemed severe, and which was humble. There was in the depth of his glance an indescribable melancholy serenity. In his left hand he carried a little bundle tied up in a handkerchief; in his right he leaned on a sort of a cudgel, cut from some hedge. This stick had been carefully trimmed, and had an air that was not too threatening; the most had been made of its knots, and it had received a coral-like head, made from red wax: it was a cudgel, and it seemed to be a cane.

There are but few passers-by on that boulevard, particularly in the winter. The man seemed to avoid them rather than to seek them, but this without any affectation.

At that epoch, King Louis XVIII went nearly every day to Choisy-le-Roi: it was one of his favorite excursions. Toward two o'clock, almost invariably, the royal carriage and cavalcade was seen to pass at full speed along the Boulevard de l'Hôpital.

This served in lieu of a watch or clock to the poor women of the quarter who said, "It is two o'clock; there *he* is returning to the Tuileries."

And some rushed forward, and others drew up in line, for a passing king always creates a tumult; besides, the appearance and disappearance of Louis XVIII produced a certain effect in the streets of Paris. It was rapid but majestic. This impotent king had a taste for a fast gallop; as he was not able to walk, he wished to run: that cripple would gladly have had himself drawn by the lightning. He passed, pacific and severe, in the midst of naked swords. His massive couch, all covered with gilding, with great branches of lilies painted on the panels, thundered noisily along. There was hardly time to cast a glance upon it. In the rear angle on the right there was visible on tufted cushions of white satin a large, firm, and ruddy face, a brow freshly powdered *à l'oiseau royal*, a proud, hard, crafty eye, the smile of an educated man, two great epaulets with bullion fringe floating over a bourgeois coat, the Golden Fleece, the cross of Saint Louis, the cross of the Legion of Honor, the silver plaque of the Saint-Esprit, a huge belly, and a wide blue ribbon. it was the king. Outside of Paris, he held his hat decked with white ostrich plumes on his knees enwrapped in high English gaiters; when he re-entered the city, he put on his hat and saluted rarely; he stared coldly at the people, and they returned it in kind. When he appeared for the first time in the Saint-Marceau quarter, the whole success which he produced is contained in this remark of an inhabitant of the faubourg to his comrade, "That big fellow yonder is the government."

This infallible passage of the king at the same hour was, therefore, the daily event of the Boulevard de l'Hôpital.

The promenader in the yellow coat evidently did not belong in the quarter, and probably did not belong in Paris, for he was ignorant as to this detail. When, at two o'clock, the royal carriage, surrounded by a squadron of the bodyguard all covered with silver lace, debouched on the boulevard, after having made the turn of the Salpêtriére, he appeared surprised and almost alarmed. There was no one but himself in this cross-lane. He drew up hastily behind the corner of the wall of an enclosure, though this did not prevent M. le Duc de Havré from spying him out.

M. le Duc de Havré, as captain of the guard on duty that day, was seated in the carriage, opposite the king. He said to his Majesty, "Yonder is an evil-looking man." Members of the police, who were clearing the king's route, took equal note of him: one of them received an order to follow him. But the man plunged into the deserted little streets of the faubourg, and as twilight was beginning to fall, the agent lost trace of him, as is stated in a report addressed that same evening to M. le Comte d'Anglés, Minister of State, Prefect of Police.

When the man in the yellow coat had thrown the agent off his track, he redoubled his pace, not without turning round many a time to assure himself that he was not being followed. At a quarter-past four, that is to say, when night was fully come, he passed in front of the theater of the Porte Saint-Martin, where *The Two Convicts* was being played that day. This poster, illuminated by the theater lanterns, struck him; for, although he was walking rapidly, he halted to read it. An instant later he was in the blind-alley of La Planchette, and he entered the *Plat d'Étain* [the Pewter Platter], where the office of the coach for Lagny was then situated. This coach set out at half-past four. The horses were harnessed, and the travelers, summoned by the coachman, were hastily climbing the lofty iron ladder of the vehicle.

The man inquired:

"Have you a place?"

"Only one—beside me on the box," said the coachman.

"I will take it."

"Climb up."

Nevertheless, before setting out, the coachman cast a glance at the traveler's shabby dress, at the diminutive size of his bundle, and made him pay his fare.

"Are you going as far as Lagny?" demanded the coachman.

"Yes," said the man.

The traveler paid to Lagny.

They started. When they had passed the barrier, the coachman tried to enter into conversation, but the traveler only replied in monosyllables. The coachman took to whistling and swearing at his horses.

The coachman wrapped himself up in his cloak. It was cold. The man did not appear to be thinking of that. Thus they passed Gournay and Neuilly-sur-Marne.

Towards six o'clock in the evening they reached Chelles. The coachman drew up in front of the carters' inn installed in the ancient buildings of the Royal Abbey, to give his horses a breathing spell.

"I get down here," said the man.

He took his bundle and his cudgel and jumped down from the vehicle.

An instant later he had disappeared.

He did not enter the inn.

When the coach set out for Lagny a few minutes later, it did not encounter him in the principal street of Chelles.

The coachman turned to the inside travelers.

"There," said he, "is a man who does not belong here, for I do not know him. He had not the air of owning a sou, but he does not consider money; he pays to Lagny, and he goes only as far as Chelles. It is night; all the houses are shut; he does not enter the inn, and he is not to be found. So he has dived through the earth."

The man had not plunged into the earth, but he had gone with great strides through the dark, down the principal street of Chelles, then he had turned to the right before reaching the church, into the cross-road leading to Montfermeil, like a person who was acquainted with the country and had been there before.

He followed this road rapidly. At the spot where it is intersected by the ancient tree-bordered road which runs from Gagny to Lagny, he heard people coming. He concealed himself precipitately in a ditch, and there waited until the passers-by were at a distance. The precaution was nearly superfluous, however; for, as we have already said, it was a very dark December night. Not more than two or three stars were visible in the sky.

It is at this point that the ascent of the hill begins. The man did not return to the road to Montfermeil; he struck across the fields to the right, and entered the forest with long strides.

Once in the forest he slackened his pace, and began a careful examination of all the trees, advancing, step by step, as though seeking and following a mysterious road known to himself alone. There came a moment when he appeared to lose himself, and he paused in indecision. At last he arrived, by dint of feeling his way inch by inch, at a clearing where there was a great heap of whitish stones. He stepped up briskly to these stones, and examined them attentively through the mists of night, as though he were passing them in review. A large tree, covered with those excrescences which are the warts of vegetation, stood a few paces distant from the pile of stones. He went up to this tree and passed his hand over the bark of the trunk, as though seeking to recognize and count all the warts.

Opposite this tree, which was an ash, there was a chestnut-tree, suffering from a peeling of the bark, to which a band of zinc had been nailed by way of dressing. He raised himself on tiptoe and touched this band of zinc.

Then he trod about for awhile on the ground comprised in the space between the tree and the heap of stones, like a person who is trying to assure himself that the soil has not recently been disturbed.

That done, he took his bearings, and resumed his march through the forest.

It was the man who had just met Cosette.

As he walked through the thicket in the direction of Montfermeil, he had spied that tiny shadow moving with a groan, depositing a burden on the ground, then taking it up and setting out again. He drew near, and perceived that it was a very young child, laden with an enormous bucket of water. Then he approached the child, and silently grasped the handle of the bucket.

Chapter VII

COSETTE SIDE BY SIDE WITH THE STRANGER IN THE DARK

COSETTE, AS WE HAVE SAID, WAS NOT FRIGHTENED.

The man accosted her. He spoke in a voice that was grave and almost bass.

"My child, what you are carrying is very heavy for you."

Cosette raised her head, and replied:

"Yes, sir."

"Give it to me," said the man; "I will carry it for you."

Cosette let go of the bucket-handle. The man walked along beside her.

"It really is very heavy," he muttered between his teeth. Then he added:

"How old are you, little one?"

"Eight, sir."

"And have you come from far like this?"

"From the spring in the forest."

"Are you going far?"

"A good quarter of an hour's walk from here."

The man said nothing for a moment; then he remarked abruptly:

"So you have no mother?"

"I don't know," answered the child.

Before the man had time to speak again, she added:

"I don't think so. Other people have mothers. I have none."

And after a silence she went on:

"I think that I never had any."

The man halted; he set the bucket on the ground, bent down and placed both hands on the child's shoulders, making an effort to look at her and to see her face in the dark.

Cosette's thin and sickly face was vaguely outlined by the livid light in the sky.

"What is your name?" said the man.

"Cosette."

The man seemed to have received an electric shock. He looked at her once more; then he removed his hands from Cosette's shoulders, seized the bucket, and set out again.

After a moment he inquired:

"Where do you live, little one?"

"At Montfermeil, if you know where that is."

"That is where we are going?"

"Yes, sir."

He paused; then began again:

"Who sent you at such an hour to get water in the forest?"

"It was Madame Thénardier."

The man resumed, in a voice which he strove to render indifferent, but in which there was, nevertheless, a singular tremor:

"What does your Madame Thénardier do?"

"She is my mistress," said the child. "She keeps the inn."

"The inn?" said the man. "Well, I am going to lodge there to-night. Show me the way."

"We are on the way there," said the child.

The man walked tolerably fast. Cosette followed him without difficulty. She no longer felt any fatigue. From time to time she raised her eyes toward the man, with a sort of tranquility and an indescribable confidence. She had never been taught to turn to Providence and to pray; nevertheless, she felt within her something which resembled hope and joy, and which mounted toward heaven.

Several minutes elapsed. The man resumed:

"Is there no servant in Madame Thénardier's house?"

"No, sir."

"Are you alone there?"

"Yes, sir."

Another pause ensued. Cosette lifted up her voice:

"That is to say, there are two little girls."

"What little girls?"

"Ponine and Zelma."

This was the way the child simplified the romantic names so dear to the female Thénardier.

"Who are Ponine and Zelma?"

"They are Madame Thénardier's young ladies; her daughters, as you would say."

"And what do those girls do?"

"Oh!" said the child, "they have beautiful dolls; things with gold in them, all full of affairs. They play; they amuse themselves."

"All day long?"

"Yes, sir."

"And you?"

"I? I work."

"All day long?"

The child raised her great eyes, in which hung a tear, which was not visible because of the darkness, and replied gently:

"Yes, sir."

After an interval of silence she went on:

"Sometimes, when I have finished my work and they let me, I amuse myself, too."

"How do you amuse yourself?"

"In the best way I can. They let me alone; but I have not many playthings. Ponine and Zelma will not let me play with their dolls. I have only a little lead sword, no longer than that."

The child held up her tiny finger.

"And it will not cut?"

"Yes, sir," said the child; "it cuts salad and the heads of flies."

They reached the village. Cosette guided the stranger through the streets. They passed the bake-shop, but Cosette did not think of the bread which she had been ordered to fetch. The man had ceased to ply her with questions, and now preserved a gloomy silence.

When they had left the church behind them, the man, on perceiving all the open-air booths, asked Cosette:

"So there is a fair going on here?"

"No, sir; it is Christmas."

As they approached the tavern, Cosette timidly touched his arm:

"Monsieur?"

"What, my child?"

"We are quite near the house."

"Well?"

"Will you let me take my bucket now?"

"Why?"

"If Madame sees that someone has carried it for me, she will beat me."

The man handed her the bucket. An instant later they were at the tavern door.

Chapter VIII

THE UNPLEASANTNESS OF RECEIVING INTO ONE'S HOUSE A POOR MAN WHO MAY BE A RICH MAN

COSETTE COULD NOT REFRAIN FROM CASTING A SIDELONG GLANCE AT THE BIG DOLL, WHICH was still displayed at the toy-merchant's; then she knocked. The door opened. The Thénardier appeared with a candle in her hand.

"Ah! so it's you, you little wretch! good mercy, but you've taken your time! The hussy has been amusing herself!"

"Madame," said Cosette, trembling all over, "here's a gentleman who wants a lodging."

The Thénardier speedily replaced her gruff air by her amiable grimace, a change of aspect common to tavern-keepers, and eagerly sought the newcomer with her eyes.

"This is the gentleman?" said she.

"Yes, Madame," replied the man, raising his hand to his hat.

Wealthy travelers are not so polite. This gesture, and an inspection of the stranger's costume and baggage, which the Thénardier passed in review with one glance, caused the amiable grimace to vanish, and the gruff mien to reappear. She resumed dryly:

"Enter, my good man."

The "good man" entered. The Thénardier cast a second glance at him, paid particular attention to his frock-coat, which was absolutely threadbare, and to his hat, which was a little battered, and, tossing her head, wrinkling her nose, and screwing up her eyes, she consulted her husband, who was still drinking with the carters. The husband replied by that imperceptible movement of the forefinger, which, backed up by an inflation of the lips, signifies in such cases: A regular beggar. Thereupon, the Thénardier exclaimed:

"Ah! see here, my good man; I am very sorry, but I have no room left."

"Put me where you like," said the man; "in the attic, in the stable. I will pay as though I occupied a room."

"Forty sous."

"Forty sous; agreed."

"Very well, then!"

"Forty sous!" said a carter, in a low tone, to the Thénardier woman; "why, the charge is only twenty sous!"

"It is forty in his case," retorted the Thénardier, in the same tone. "I don't lodge poor folks for less."

"That's true," added her husband, gently; "it ruins a house to have such people in it."

In the meantime, the man, laying his bundle and his cudgel on a bench, had seated himself at a table, on which Cosette made haste to place a bottle of wine and a glass. The merchant who had demanded the bucket of water took it to his horse himself. Cosette resumed her place under the kitchen table, and her knitting.

The man, who had barely moistened his lips in the wine which he had poured out for himself, observed the child with peculiar attention.

Cosette was ugly. If she had been happy, she might have been pretty. We have already given a sketch of that somber little figure. Cosette was thin and pale; she was nearly eight years old, but she seemed to be hardly six. Her large eyes, sunken in a sort of shadow, were almost put out with weeping. The corners of her mouth had that curve of habitual anguish which is seen in condemned persons and desperately sick people. Her hands were, as her mother had divined, "ruined with chilblains." The fire which illuminated her at that moment, brought into relief all the angles of her bones, and rendered her thinness frightfully apparent. As she was always shivering, she had acquired the habit of pressing her knees one against the other. Her entire clothing was but a rag which would have inspired pity in summer, and which inspired horror in winter. All she had on was hole-ridden linen, not a scrap of woolen. Her skin was visible here and there, and everywhere black and blue spots could be descried, which marked the places where the Thénardier woman had touched her. Her naked legs were thin and red. The hollows in her neck were enough to make one weep. This child's whole person, her mien, her attitude, the sound of her voice, the intervals which she allowed to elapse between one word and the next, her glance, her silence, her slightest gesture, expressed and betrayed one sole idea—fear.

Fear was diffused all over her; she was covered with it, so to speak; fear drew her elbows close to her hips, withdrew her heels under her petticoat, made her occupy as little space as possible, allowed her only the breath that was absolutely necessary, and had become what might be called the habit of her body, admitting of no possible variation except an increase. In the depths of her eyes there was an astonished nook where terror lurked.

Her fear was such, that on her arrival, wet as she was, Cosette did not dare to approach the fire and dry herself, but sat silently down to her work again.

The expression in the glance of that child of eight years was habitually so gloomy, and at times so tragic, that it seemed at certain moments as though she were on the verge of becoming an idiot or a demon.

As we have stated, she had never known what it is to pray; she had never set foot in a church. "Have I the time?" said the Thénardier.

The man in the yellow coat never took his eyes from Cosette.

All at once, the Thénardier exclaimed:

"By the way, where's that bread?"

Cosette, according to her custom whenever the Thénardier uplifted her voice, emerged with great haste from beneath the table.

She had completely forgotten the bread. She had recourse to the expedient of children who live in a constant state of fear. She lied.

"Madame, the baker's shop was shut."

"You should have knocked."

"I did knock, Madame."

"Well?"

"He did not open the door."

"I'll find out to-morrow whether that is true," said the Thénardier; "and if you are telling me a lie, I'll lead you a pretty dance. In the meantime, give me back my fifteen-sou piece."

Cosette plunged her hand into the pocket of her apron, and turned green. The fifteen-sou piece was not there.

"Ah, come now," said Madame Thénardier, "did you hear me?"

Cosette turned her pocket inside out; there was nothing in it. What could have become of that money? The unhappy little creature could not find a word to say. She was petrified.

"Have you lost that fifteen-sou piece?" screamed the Thénardier, hoarsely, "or do you want to rob me of it?"

At the same time, she stretched out her arm toward the cat-o'-nine-tails which hung on a nail in the chimney-corner.

This formidable gesture restored to Cosette sufficient strength to shriek:

"Mercy, Madame, Madame! I will not do so any more!"

The Thénardier took down the whip.

In the meantime, the man in the yellow coat had been fumbling in the fob of his waistcoat, without anyone having noticed his movements. Besides, the other travelers were drinking or playing cards, and were not paying attention to anything.

Cosette contracted herself into a ball, with anguish, within the angle of the chimney, endeavoring to gather up and conceal her poor half-nude limbs. The Thénardier raised her arm.

"Pardon me, Madame," said the man, "but just now I caught sight of something which had fallen from this little one's apron pocket, and rolled aside. Perhaps this is it."

At the same time he bent down and seemed to be searching on the floor for a moment.

"Exactly; here it is," he went on, straightening himself up.

And he held out a silver coin to the Thénardier.

"Yes, that's it," said she.

It was not it, for it was a twenty-sou piece; but the Thénardier found it to her advantage. She put the coin in her pocket, and confined herself to casting a fierce glance at the child, accompanied with the remark, "Don't let this ever happen again!"

Cosette returned to what the Thénardier called "her kennel," and her large eyes, which were riveted on the traveler, began to take on an expression such as they had never worn before. Thus far it was only an innocent amazement, but a sort of stupefied confidence was mingled with it.

"By the way, would you like some supper?" the Thénardier inquired of the traveler.

He made no reply. He appeared to be absorbed in thought.

"What sort of a man is that?" she muttered between her teeth. "He's some frightfully poor wretch. He hasn't a sou to pay for a supper. Will he even pay me for his lodging? It's very lucky, all the same, that it did not occur to him to steal the money that was on the floor."

In the meantime, a door had opened, and Éponine and Azelma entered.

They were two really pretty little girls, more bourgeois than peasant in looks, and very charming; the one with shining chestnut tresses, the other with long black braids hanging down her back, both vivacious, neat, plump, rosy, and healthy, and a delight to the eye. They were warmly clad, but with so much maternal art that the thickness of the stuffs did not detract from the coquetry of arrangement. There was a hint of winter, though the springtime was not wholly effaced. Light emanated from these two little beings. Besides this, they were on the throne. In their toilettes, in their gaiety, in the noise which they made, there was sovereignty. When they entered, the Thénardier said to them in a grumbling tone which was full of adoration, "Ah! there you are, you children!"

Then drawing them, one after the other to her knees, smoothing their hair, tying their ribbons afresh, and then releasing them with that gentle manner of shaking off which is peculiar to mothers, she exclaimed, "What frights they are!"

They went and seated themselves in the chimney-corner. They had a doll, which they turned over and over on their knees with all sorts of joyous chatter. From time to time Cosette raised her eyes from her knitting, and watched their play with a melancholy air.

Éponine and Azelma did not look at Cosette. She was the same as a dog to them. These three little girls did not yet reckon up four-and-twenty years between them, but they already represented the whole society of man; envy on the one side, disdain on the other.

The doll of the Thénardier sisters was very much faded, very old, and much broken; but it seemed none the less admirable to Cosette, who had never had a doll in her life, *a real doll,* to make use of the expression which all children will understand.

All at once, the Thénardier, who had been going back and forth in the room, perceived that Cosette's mind was distracted, and that, instead of working, she was paying attention to the little ones at their play.

"Ah! I've caught you at it!" she cried. "So that's the way you work! I'll make you work to the tune of the whip; that I will."

The stranger turned to the Thénardier, without quitting his chair.

"Bah, Madame," he said, with an almost timid air, "let her play!"

Such a wish expressed by a traveler who had eaten a slice of mutton and had drunk a couple of bottles of wine with his supper, and who had not the air of being frightfully poor, would have been equivalent to an order. But that a man with such a hat should permit himself such a desire, and that a man with such a coat should permit himself to have a will, was something which Madame Thénardier did not intend to tolerate. She retorted with acrimony:

"She must work, since she eats. I don't feed her to do nothing."

"What is she making?" went on the stranger, in a gentle voice which contrasted strangely with his beggarly garments and his porter's shoulders.

The Thénardier deigned to reply:

"Stockings, if you please. Stockings for my little girls, who have none, so to speak, and who are absolutely barefoot just now."

The man looked at Cosette's poor little red feet, and continued:

"When will she have finished this pair of stockings?"

"She has at least three or four good days' work on them still, the lazy creature!"

"And how much will that pair of stockings be worth when she has finished them?"

The Thénardier cast a glance of disdain on him.

"Thirty sous at least."

"Will you sell them for five francs?" went on the man.

"Good heavens!" exclaimed a carter who was listening, with a loud laugh; "five francs! the deuce, I should think so! five balls!"

Thénardier thought it time to strike in.

"Yes, sir; if such is your fancy, you will be allowed to have that pair of stockings for five francs. We can refuse nothing to travelers."

"You must pay on the spot," said the Thénardier, in her curt and peremptory fashion.

"I will buy that pair of stockings," replied the man, "and," he added, drawing a five-franc piece from his pocket, and laying it on the table, "I will pay for them."

Then he turned to Cosette.

"Now I own your work; play, my child."

The carter was so much touched by the five-franc piece, that he abandoned his glass and hastened up.

"But it's true!" he cried, examining it. "A real hind-wheel! and not counterfeit!"

Thénardier approached and silently put the coin in his pocket.

The Thénardier had no reply to make. She bit her lips, and her face assumed an expression of hatred.

In the meantime, Cosette was trembling. She ventured to ask:

"Is it true, Madame? May I play?"

"Play!" said the Thénardier, in a terrible voice.

"Thanks, Madame," said Cosette.

And while her mouth thanked the Thénardier, her whole little soul thanked the traveler.

Thénardier had resumed his drinking; his wife whispered in his ear:—

"Who can this yellow man be?"

"I have seen millionaires with coats like that," replied Thénardier, in a sovereign manner.

Cosette had dropped her knitting, but had not left her seat. Cosette always moved as little as possible. She picked up some old rags and her little lead sword from a box behind her.

Éponine and Azelma paid no attention to what was going on. They had just executed a very important operation; they had just got hold of the cat. They had thrown their doll on the ground, and Éponine, who was the elder, was swathing the little cat, in spite of its mewing and its contortions, in a quantity of clothes and red and blue scraps. While performing this serious and difficult work she was saying to her sister in that sweet and adorable language of children, whose grace, like the splendor of the butterfly's wing, vanishes when one essays to fix it fast.

"You see, sister, this doll is more amusing than the other. She twists, she cries, she is warm. See, sister, let us play with her. She shall be my little girl. I will be a lady. I will come to see you, and you shall look at her. Gradually, you will perceive her whiskers, and that will surprise you. And then you will see her ears, and then you will see her tail, and it will amaze you. And you will say to me, 'Ah! Mon Dieu!' and I will say to you: 'Yes, Madame, it is my little girl. Little girls are made like that just at present.'"

Azelma listened admiringly to Éponine.

In the meantime, the drinkers had begun to sing an obscene song, and to laugh at it until the ceiling shook. Thénardier accompanied and encouraged them.

As birds make nests out of everything, so children make a doll out of anything which comes to hand. While Éponine and Azelma were bundling up the cat, Cosette, on her side, had dressed up her sword. That done, she laid it in her arms, and sang to it softly, to lull it to sleep.

The doll is one of the most imperious needs and, at the same time, one of the most charming instincts of feminine childhood. To care for, to clothe, to deck, to dress, to undress, to redress, to teach, scold a little, to rock, to dandle, to lull to sleep, to imagine that something is someone—therein lies the whole woman's future. While dreaming and chattering, making tiny outfits, and baby clothes, while sewing little gowns, and corsages and bodices, the child grows into a young girl, the young girl into a big girl, the big girl into a woman. The first child is the continuation of the last doll.

A little girl without a doll is almost as unhappy, and quite as impossible, as a woman without children.

So Cosette had made herself a doll out of the sword.

Madame Thénardier approached *the yellow man*; "My husband is right," she thought; "perhaps it is M. Laffitte; there are such queer rich men!"

She came and set her elbows on the table.

"Monsieur," said she. At this word, *Monsieur*, the man turned; up to that time, the Thénardier had addressed him only as *brave homme* or *bonhomme*.

"You see, sir," she pursued, assuming a sweetish air that was even more repulsive to behold than her fierce mien, "I am willing that the child should play; I do not oppose it, but it is good for once, because you are generous. You see, she has nothing; she must needs work."

"Then this child is not yours?" demanded the man.

"Oh! mon Dieu! no, sir! she is a little beggar whom we have taken in through charity; a sort of imbecile child. She must have water on the brain; she has a large head, as you see. We do what we can for her, for we are not rich; we have written in vain to her native place, and have received no reply these six months. It must be that her mother is dead."

"Ah!" said the man, and fell into his reverie once more.

"Her mother didn't amount to much," added the Thénardier; "she abandoned her child."

During the whole of this conversation Cosette, as though warned by some instinct that she was under discussion, had not taken her eyes from the Thénardier's face; she listened vaguely; she caught a few words here and there.

Meanwhile, the drinkers, all three-quarters intoxicated, were repeating their unclean refrain with redoubled gaiety; it was a highly spiced and wanton song, in which the Virgin and the infant Jesus were introduced. The Thénardier went off to take part in the shouts of laughter. Cosette, from her post under the table, gazed at the fire, which was reflected from her fixed eyes. She had begun to rock the sort of baby which she had made, and, as she rocked it, she sang in a low voice, "My mother is dead! my mother is dead! my mother is dead!"

On being urged afresh by the hostess, the yellow man, "the millionaire," consented at last to take supper.

"What does Monsieur wish?"

"Bread and cheese," said the man.

"Decidedly, he is a beggar" thought Madame Thénardier.

The drunken men were still singing their song, and the child under the table was singing hers.

All at once, Cosette paused; she had just turned round and caught sight of the little Thénardiers' doll, which they had abandoned for the cat and had left on the floor a few paces from the kitchen table.

Then she dropped the swaddled sword, which only half met her needs, and cast her eyes slowly round the room. Madame Thénardier was whispering to her husband and counting over some money; Ponine and Zelma were playing with the cat; the travelers were eating or drinking or singing; not a glance was fixed on her. She had not a moment to lose; she crept out from under the table on her hands and knees, made sure once more that no one was watching her; then she slipped quickly up to the doll and seized it. An instant later, she was in her place again, seated motionless, and only turned so as to cast a shadow on the doll which she held in her arms. The happiness of playing with a doll was so rare for her that it contained all the violence of voluptuousness.

No one had seen her, except the traveler, who was slowly devouring his meager supper.

This joy lasted about a quarter of an hour.

But with all the precautions that Cosette had taken she did not perceive that one of the doll's legs stuck out and that the fire on the hearth lighted it up very vividly. That pink and shining foot, projecting from the shadow, suddenly struck the eye of Azelma, who said to Éponine, "Look! sister."

The two little girls paused in stupefaction; Cosette had dared to take their doll!

Éponine rose, and, without releasing the cat, she ran to her mother, and began to tug at her skirt.

"Let me alone!" said her mother; "what do you want?"

"Mother," said the child, "look there!"

And she pointed to Cosette.

Cosette, absorbed in the ecstasies of possession, no longer saw or heard anything.

Madame Thénardier's countenance assumed that peculiar expression which is composed of the terrible mingled with the trifles of life, and which has caused this style of woman to be named *megaeras*.

On this occasion, wounded pride exasperated her wrath still further. Cosette had overstepped all bounds; Cosette had laid violent hands on the doll belonging to "these young ladies." A czarina who should see a muzhik trying on her imperial son's blue ribbon would wear no other face.

She shrieked in a voice rendered hoarse with indignation:

"Cosette!"

Cosette started as though the earth had trembled beneath her; she turned round.

"Cosette!" repeated the Thénardier.

Cosette took the doll and laid it gently on the floor with a sort of veneration mingled with despair; then, without taking her eyes from it, she clasped her hands, and, what is terrible to relate of a child of that age, she wrung them; then—not one of the emotions of the day, neither the trip to the forest, nor the weight of the bucket of water, nor the loss of the money, nor the sight of the whip, nor even the sad words which she had heard Madame Thénardier utter had been able to wring this from her—she wept; she burst out sobbing.

Meanwhile, the traveler had risen to his feet.

"What is the matter?" he said to the Thénardier.

"Don't you see?" said the Thénardier, pointing to the *corpus delicti* which lay at Cosette's feet.

"Well, what of it?" resumed the man.

"That beggar," replied the Thénardier, "has permitted herself to touch the children's doll!"

"All this noise for that!" said the man; "well, what if she did play with that doll?"

"She touched it with her dirty hands!" pursued the Thénardier, "with her frightful hands!"

Here Cosette redoubled her sobs.

"Will you stop your noise?" screamed the Thénardier.

The man went straight to the street door, opened it, and stepped out.

As soon as he had gone, the Thénardier profited by his absence to give Cosette a hearty kick under the table, which made the child utter loud cries.

The door opened again, the man reappeared; he carried in both hands the fabulous doll which we have mentioned, and which all the village brats had been staring at ever since the morning, and he set it upright in front of Cosette, saying:

"Here; this is for you."

It must be supposed that in the course of the hour and more which he had spent there he had taken confused notice through his reverie of that toy-shop, lighted up by fire-pots and candles so splendidly that it was visible like an illumination through the window of the drinking-shop.

Cosette raised her eyes; she gazed at the man approaching her with that doll as she might have gazed at the sun; she heard the unprecedented words, "It is for you"; she stared at him; she stared at the doll; then she slowly retreated, and hid herself at the extreme end, under the table in a corner of the wall.

She no longer cried; she no longer wept; she had the appearance of no longer daring to breathe.

The Thénardier, Éponine, and Azelma were like statues also; the very drinkers had paused; a solemn silence reigned through the whole room.

Madame Thénardier, petrified and mute, recommenced her conjectures: "Who is that old fellow? Is he a poor man? Is he a millionaire? Perhaps he is both; that is to say, a thief."

The face of the male Thénardier presented that expressive fold which accentuates the human countenance whenever the dominant instinct appears there in all its bestial force. The tavern-keeper stared alternately at the doll and at the traveler; he seemed to be scenting out the man, as he would have scented out a bag of money. This did not last longer than the space of a flash of lightning. He stepped up to his wife and said to her in a low voice:

"That machine costs at least thirty francs. No nonsense. Down on your belly before that man!"

Gross natures have this in common with *naïve* natures, that they possess no transition state.

"Well, Cosette," said the Thénardier, in a voice that strove to be sweet, and which was composed of the bitter honey of malicious women, "aren't you going to take your doll?"

Cosette ventured to emerge from her hole.

"The gentleman has given you a doll, my little Cosette," said Thénardier, with a caressing air. "Take it; it is yours."

Cosette gazed at the marvelous doll in a sort of terror. Her face was still flooded with tears, but her eyes began to fill, like the sky at daybreak, with strange beams of joy. What she felt at that moment was a little like what she would have felt if she had been abruptly told, "Little one, you are the Queen of France."

It seemed to her that if she touched that doll, lightning would dart from it.

This was true, up to a certain point, for she said to herself that the Thénardier would scold and beat her.

Nevertheless, the attraction carried the day. She ended by drawing near and murmuring timidly as she turned toward Madame Thénardier:

"May I, Madame?"

No words can render that air, at once despairing, terrified, and ecstatic.

"Pardi!" cried the Thénardier, "it is yours. The gentleman has given it to you."

"Truly, sir?" said Cosette. "Is it true? Is the 'lady' mine?"

The stranger's eyes seemed to be full of tears. He appeared to have reached that point of emotion where a man does not speak for fear lest he should weep. He nodded to Cosette, and placed the "lady's" hand in her tiny hand.

Cosette hastily withdrew her hand, as though that of the "lady" scorched her, and began to stare at the floor. We are forced to add that at that moment she stuck out her tongue immoderately. All at once she wheeled round and seized the doll in a transport.

"I shall call her Catherine," she said.

It was an odd moment when Cosette's rags met and clasped the ribbons and fresh pink muslins of the doll.

"Madame," she resumed, "may I put her on a chair?"

"Yes, my child," replied the Thénardier.

It was now the turn of Éponine and Azelma to gaze at Cosette with envy.

Cosette placed Catherine on a chair, then seated herself on the floor in front of her, and remained motionless, without uttering a word, in an attitude of contemplation.

"Play, Cosette," said the stranger.

"Oh! I am playing," returned the child.

This stranger, this unknown individual, who had the air of a visit which Providence was making on Cosette, was the person whom the Thénardier hated worse than anyone in the world at that moment. However, it was necessary to control herself. Habituated as she was to dissimulation through endeavoring to copy her husband in all his actions, these emotions were more than she could endure. She made haste to send her daughters to bed, then she asked the man's *permission* to send Cosette off also; "for she has worked hard all day," she added with a maternal air. Cosette went off to bed, carrying Catherine in her arms.

From time to time the Thénardier went to the other end of the room where her husband was, to *relieve her soul*, as she said. She exchanged with her husband words which were all the more furious because she dared not utter them aloud.

"Old beast! What has he got in his belly, to come and upset us in this manner! To want that little monster to play! to give away forty-franc dolls to a jade that I would sell for forty sous, so I would! A little more and he will be saying *your Majesty* to her, as though to the Duchess de Berry! Is there any sense in it? Is he mad, then, that mysterious old fellow?"

"Why! it is perfectly simple," replied Thénardier, "if that amuses him! It amuses you to have the little one work; it amuses him to have her play. He's all right. A traveler can do what he pleases when he pays for it. If the old fellow is a philanthropist, what is that to you? If he is an imbecile, it does not concern you. What are you worrying for, so long as he has money?"

The language of a master, and the reasoning of an inn-keeper, neither of which admitted of any reply.

The man had placed his elbows on the table, and resumed his thoughtful attitude. All the other travelers, both peddlers and carters, had withdrawn a little, and had ceased singing. They were staring at him from a distance, with a sort of respectful awe. This poorly dressed man, who drew "hind-wheels" from his pocket with so much ease, and who lavished gigantic dolls on dirty little brats in wooden shoes, was certainly a magnificent fellow, and one to be feared.

Many hours passed. The midnight mass was over, the chimes had ceased, the drinkers had taken their departure, the drinking-shop was closed, the public-room was deserted, the fire extinct, the stranger still remained in the same place and the same attitude. From time to time he changed the elbow on which he leaned. That was all; but he had not said a word since Cosette had left the room.

The Thénardiers alone, out of politeness and curiosity, had remained in the room.

"Is he going to pass the night in that fashion?" grumbled the Thénardier. When two o'clock in the morning struck, she declared herself vanquished, and said to her husband, "I'm going to bed. Do as you like." Her husband seated himself at a table in the corner, lighted a candle, and began to read the *Courrier Français*.

A good hour passed thus. The worthy inn-keeper had perused the *Courrier Français* at least three times, from the date of the number to the printer's name. The stranger did not stir.

Thénardier fidgeted, coughed, spit, blew his nose, and creaked his chair. Not a movement on the man's part. "Is he asleep?" thought Thénardier. The man was not asleep, but nothing could arouse him.

At last Thénardier took off his cap, stepped gently up to him, and ventured to say:

"Is not Monsieur going to his repose?"

Not going to bed would have seemed to him excessive and familiar. *To repose* smacked of luxury and respect. These words possess the mysterious and admirable property of swelling the bill on the following day. A chamber where one *sleeps* costs twenty sous; a chamber in which one *reposes* costs twenty francs.

"Well!" said the stranger, "you are right. Where is your stable?"

"Sir!" exclaimed Thénardier, with a smile, "I will conduct you, sir."

He took the candle; the man picked up his bundle and cudgel, and Thénardier conducted him to a chamber on the first floor, which was of rare splendor, all furnished in mahogany, with a low bedstead, curtained with red calico.

"What is this?" said the traveler.

"It is really our bridal chamber," said the tavern-keeper. "My wife and I occupy another. This is only entered three or four times a year."

"I should have liked the stable quite as well," said the man, abruptly.

Thénardier pretended not to hear this unamiable remark.

He lighted two perfectly fresh wax candles which figured on the chimney-piece. A very good fire was flickering on the hearth.

On the chimney-piece, under a glass globe, stood a woman's headdress in silver wire and orange flowers.

"And what is this?" resumed the stranger.

"That, sir," said Thénardier, "is my wife's wedding bonnet."

The traveler surveyed the object with a glance which seemed to say, "There really was a time, then, when that monster was a maiden?"

Thénardier lied, however. When he had leased this paltry building for the purpose of converting it into a tavern, he had found this chamber decorated in just this manner, and had purchased the furniture and obtained the orange flowers at second hand, with the idea that this would cast a graceful shadow on "his spouse," and would result in what the English call respectability for his house.

When the traveler turned round, the host had disappeared. Thénardier had withdrawn discreetly, without venturing to wish him a good night, as he did not wish to treat with disrespectful cordiality a man whom he proposed to fleece royally the following morning.

The inn-keeper retired to his room. His wife was in bed, but she was not asleep. When she heard her husband's step she turned over and said to him:

"Do you know, I'm going to turn Cosette out of doors to-morrow."

Thénardier replied coldly:

"How you do go on!"

They exchanged no further words, and a few moments later their candle was extinguished.

As for the traveler, he had deposited his cudgel and his bundle in a corner. The landlord once gone, he threw himself into an arm-chair and remained for some time buried in thought. Then he removed his shoes, took one of the two candles, blew out the other, opened the door, and quitted the room, gazing about him like a person who is in search of something. He traversed a corridor and came upon a staircase. There he heard a very faint and gentle sound like the breathing of a child. He followed this sound, and came to a sort of triangular recess built under the staircase, or rather formed by the staircase itself. This recess was nothing else than the space under the steps. There, in the midst of all sorts of old papers and potsherds, among dust and spiders' webs, was a bed—if one can call by the name of bed a straw pallet so full of holes as to display the straw, and a coverlet so tattered as to show the pallet. No sheets. This was placed on the floor.

In this bed Cosette was sleeping.

The man approached and gazed down upon her.

Cosette was in a profound sleep; she was fully dressed. In the winter she did not undress, in order that she might not be so cold.

Against her breast was pressed the doll, whose large eyes, wide open, glittered in the dark. From time to time she gave vent to a deep sigh as though she were on the point of waking, and she strained the doll almost convulsively in her arms. Beside her bed there was only one of her wooden shoes.

A door which stood open near Cosette's pallet permitted a view of a rather large, dark room. The stranger stepped into it. At the further extremity, through a glass door, he saw two small, very white beds. They belonged to Éponine and Azelma. Behind these beds, and half-hidden, stood an uncurtained wicker cradle, in which the little boy who had cried all the evening lay asleep.

The stranger conjectured that this chamber connected with that of the Thénardier pair. He was on the point of retreating when his eye fell upon the fireplace—one of those vast tavern chimneys where there is always so little fire when there is any fire at all, and which are so cold to look at. There was no fire in this one, there was not even ashes; but there was something which attracted the stranger's gaze, nevertheless. It was two tiny children's shoes, coquettish in shape and unequal in size. The traveler recalled the graceful and immemorial custom in accordance with which children place their shoes in the chimney on Christmas Eve, there to await in the darkness some sparkling gift from their good fairy. Éponine and Azelma had taken care not to omit this, and each of them had set one of her shoes on the hearth.

The traveler bent over them.

The fairy, that is to say, their mother, had already paid her visit, and in each he saw a brand-new and shining ten-sou piece.

The man straightened himself up, and was on the point of withdrawing, when far in, in the darkest corner of the hearth, he caught sight of another object. He looked at it, and recognized a wooden shoe, a frightful shoe of the coarsest description, half dilapidated and all covered with ashes and dried mud. It was Cosette's sabot. Cosette, with that touching trust of childhood, which can always be deceived yet never discouraged, had placed her shoe on the hearth-stone also.

Hope in a child who has never known anything but despair is a sweet and touching thing.

There was nothing in this wooden shoe.

The stranger fumbled in his waistcoat, bent over and placed a louis d'or in Cosette's shoe.

Then he regained his own chamber with the stealthy tread of a wolf.

Chapter IX

THÉNARDIER AT HIS MANEUVERS

ON THE FOLLOWING MORNING, TWO HOURS AT LEAST BEFORE DAYBREAK, THÉNARDIER, SEATED beside a candle in the public-room of the tavern, pen in hand, was making out the bill for the traveler with the yellow coat.

His wife, standing beside him, and half bent over him, was following him with her eyes. They exchanged not a word. On the one hand, there was profound meditation, on the other, the religious admiration with which one watches the birth and development of a marvel of the human mind. A noise was audible in the house; it was the Lark sweeping the stairs.

After the lapse of a good quarter of an hour, and some erasures, Thénardier produced the following masterpiece:

BILL OF THE GENTLEMAN IN NO. 1.

Supper	3	francs.
Chamber	10	"
Candle	5	"
Fire	4	"
Service	1	"
Total	23	francs.

Service was written *servisse.*

"Twenty-three francs!" cried the woman, with an enthusiasm which was mingled with some hesitation.

Like all great artists, Thénardier was dissatisfied.

"Peuh!" he exclaimed.

It was the accent of Castlereagh auditing France's bill at the Congress of Vienna.

"Monsieur Thénardier, you are right; he certainly owes that," murmured the wife, who was thinking of the doll bestowed on Cosette in the presence of her daughters. "It is just, but it is too much. He will not pay it."

Thénardier laughed coldly, as usual, and said:

"He will pay."

This laugh was the supreme assertion of certainty and authority. That which was asserted in this manner must needs be so. His wife did not insist.

She set about arranging the table; her husband paced the room. A moment later he added:

"I owe full fifteen hundred francs!"

He went and seated himself in the chimney-corner, meditating, with his feet among the warm ashes.

"Ah! by the way," resumed his wife, "you don't forget that I'm going to turn Cosette out of doors to-day? The monster! She breaks my heart with that doll of hers! I'd rather marry Louis XVIII than keep her another day in the house!"

Thénardier lighted his pipe, and replied between two puffs:

"You will hand that bill to the man."

Then he went out.

Hardly had he left the room when the traveler entered.

Thénardier instantly reappeared behind him and remained motionless in the half-open door, visible only to his wife.

The yellow man carried his bundle and his cudgel in his hand.

"Up so early?" said Madame Thénardier; "is Monsieur leaving us already?"

As she spoke thus, she was twisting the bill about in her hands with an embarrassed air, and making creases in it with her nails. Her hard face presented a shade which was not habitual with it— timidity and scruples.

To present such a bill to a man who had so completely the air "of a poor wretch" seemed difficult to her.

The traveler appeared to be preoccupied and absent-minded. He replied:

"Yes, Madame, I am going."

"So Monsieur has no business in Montfermeil?"

"No, I was passing through. That is all. What do I owe you, Madame?" he added.

The Thénardier silently handed him the folded bill.

The man unfolded the paper and glanced at it; but his thoughts were evidently elsewhere.

"Madame," he resumed, "is business good here in Montfermeil?"

"So so, Monsieur," replied the Thénardier, stupefied at not witnessing another sort of explosion.

She continued, in a dreary and lamentable tone:

"Oh! Monsieur, times are so hard! and then, we have so few bourgeois in the neighborhood! All the people are poor, you see. If we had not, now and then, some rich and generous travelers like Monsieur, we should not get along at all. We have so many expenses. Just see, that child is costing us our very eyes."

"What child?"

"Why, the little one, you know! Cosette—the Lark, as she is called hereabouts!"

"Ah!" said the man.

She went on:

"How stupid these peasants are with their nicknames! She has more the air of a bat than of a lark. You see, sir, we do not ask charity, and we cannot bestow it. We earn nothing and we have to pay out a great deal. The license, the imposts, the door and window tax, the hundredths! Monsieur is aware that the government demands a terrible deal of money. And then, I have my daughters. I have no need to bring up other people's children."

The man resumed, in that voice which he strove to render indifferent, and in which there lingered a tremor:

"What if one were to rid you of her?"

"Who? Cosette?"

"Yes."

The landlady's red and violent face brightened up hideously.

"Ah! sir, my dear sir, take her, keep her, lead her off, carry her away, sugar her, stuff her with truffles, drink her, eat her, and the blessings of the good holy Virgin and of all the saints of paradise be upon you!"

"Agreed."

"Really! You will take her away?"

"I will take her away."

"Immediately?"

"Immediately. Call the child."

"Cosette!" screamed the Thénardier.

"In the meantime," pursued the man, "I will pay you what I owe you. How much is it?"

He cast a glance on the bill, and could not restrain a start of surprise:

"Twenty-three francs!"

He looked at the landlady, and repeated:

"Twenty-three francs?"

There was in the enunciation of these words, thus repeated, an accent between an exclamation and an interrogation point.

The Thénardier had had time to prepare herself for the shock. She replied, with assurance:

"Good gracious, yes, sir, it is twenty-three francs."

The stranger laid five five-franc pieces on the table.

"Go and get the child," said he.

At that moment Thénardier advanced to the middle of the room, and said:

"Monsieur owes twenty-six sous."

"Twenty-six sous!" exclaimed his wife.

"Twenty sous for the chamber," resumed Thénardier, coldly, "and six sous for his supper. As for the child, I must discuss that matter a little with the gentleman. Leave us, wife."

Madame Thénardier was dazzled as with the shock caused by unexpected lightning flashes of talent. She was conscious that a great actor was making his entrance on the stage, uttered not a word in reply, and left the room.

As soon as they were alone, Thénardier offered the traveler a chair. The traveler seated himself; Thénardier remained standing, and his face assumed a singular expression of good-fellowship and simplicity.

"Sir," said he, "what I have to say to you is this, that I adore that child."

The stranger gazed intently at him.

"What child?"

Thénardier continued:

"How strange it is, one grows attached. What money is that? Take back your hundred-sou piece. I adore the child."

"Whom do you mean?" demanded the stranger.

"Eh! our little Cosette! Are you not intending to take her away from us? Well, I speak frankly; as true as you are an honest man, I will not consent to it. I shall miss that child. I saw her first when she was a tiny thing. It is true that she costs us money; it is true that she has her faults; it is true that we are not rich; it is true that I have paid out over four hundred francs for drugs for just one of her illnesses! But one must do something for the good God's sake. She has neither father nor mother. I have brought her up. I have bread enough for her and for myself. In truth, I think a great deal of that child. You understand, one conceives an affection for a person; I am a good sort of a beast, I am; I do not reason; I love that little girl; my wife is quick-tempered, but she loves her also. You see, she is just the same as our own child. I want to keep her to babble about the house."

The stranger kept his eye intently fixed on Thénardier. The latter continued:

"Excuse me, sir, but one does not give away one's child to a passer-by, like that. I am right, am

I not? Still, I don't say—you are rich; you have the air of a very good man—if it were for her happiness. But one must find out that. You understand: suppose that I were to let her go and to sacrifice myself, I should like to know what becomes of her; I should not wish to lose sight of her; I should like to know with whom she is living, so that I could go to see her from time to time; so that she may know that her good foster-father is alive, that he is watching over her. In short, there are things which are not possible. I do not even know your name. If you were to take her away, I should say: 'Well, and the Lark, what has become of her?' One must, at least, see some petty scrap of paper, some trifle in the way of a passport, you know!"

The stranger, still surveying him with that gaze which penetrates, as the saying goes, to the very depths of the conscience, replied in a grave, firm voice:

"Monsieur Thénardier, one does not require a passport to travel five leagues from Paris. If I take Cosette away, I shall take her away, and that is the end of the matter. You will not know my name, you will not know my residence, you will not know where she is; and my intention is that she shall never set eyes on you again so long as she lives. I break the thread which binds her foot, and she departs. Does that suit you? Yes or no?"

Since geniuses, like demons, recognize the presence of a superior God by certain signs, Thénardier comprehended that he had to deal with a very strong person. It was like an intuition; he comprehended it with his clear and sagacious promptitude. While drinking with the carters, smoking, and singing coarse songs on the preceding evening, he had devoted the whole of the time to observing the stranger, watching him like a cat, and studying him like a mathematician. He had watched him, both on his own account, for the pleasure of the thing, and through instinct, and had spied upon him as though he had been paid for so doing. Not a movement, not a gesture, on the part of the man in the yellow great-coat had escaped him. Even before the stranger had so clearly manifested his interest in Cosette, Thénardier had divined his purpose. He had caught the old man's deep glances returning constantly to the child. Who was this man? Why this interest? Why this hideous costume, when he had so much money in his purse? Questions which he put to himself without being able to solve them, and which irritated him. He had pondered it all night long. He could not be Cosette's father. Was he her grandfather? Then why not make himself known at once? When one has a right, one asserts it. This man evidently had no right over Cosette. What was it, then? Thénardier lost himself in conjectures. He caught glimpses of everything, but he saw nothing. Be that as it may, on entering into conversation with the man, sure that there was some secret in the case, that the latter had some interest in remaining in the shadow, he felt himself strong; when he perceived from the stranger's clear and firm retort, that this mysterious personage was mysterious in so simple a way, he became conscious that he was weak. He had expected nothing of the sort. His conjectures were put to the rout. He rallied his ideas. He weighed everything in the space of a second. Thénardier was one of those men who take in a situation at a glance. He decided that the moment had arrived for proceeding straightforward, and quickly at that. He did as great leaders do at the decisive moment, which they know that they alone recognize; he abruptly unmasked his batteries.

"Sir," said he, "I am in need of fifteen hundred francs."

The stranger took from his side pocket an old pocket-book of black leather, opened it, drew out three bank-bills, which he laid on the table. Then he placed his large thumb on the notes and said to the inn-keeper:

"Go and fetch Cosette."

While this was taking place, what had Cosette been doing?

On waking up, Cosette had run to get her shoe. In it she had found the gold piece. It was not a Napoleon; it was one of those perfectly new twenty-franc pieces of the Restoration, on whose effigy the little Prussian queue had replaced the laurel wreath. Cosette was dazzled. Her destiny began to intoxicate her. She did not know what a gold piece was; she had never seen one; she hid it quickly in her pocket, as though she had stolen it. Still, she felt that it really was hers; she guessed whence her gift had come, but the joy which she experienced was full of fear. She was happy; above all she was stupefied. Such magnificent and beautiful things did not appear real. The doll frightened her, the gold piece frightened her. She trembled vaguely in the presence of this magnificence. The stranger alone did not frighten her. On the contrary, he reassured her. Ever since the preceding evening, amid all her amazement, even in her sleep, she had been thinking in her little childish mind of that man who seemed to be so poor and so sad, and who was so rich and so kind. Everything had changed for her since she had met that good man in the forest. Cosette, less happy than the most insignificant swallow of heaven, had never known what it was to take refuge under a mother's shadow and under a wing. For the last five years, that is to say, as far back as her memory ran, the poor child had shivered and trembled. She had always been exposed completely naked to the sharp wind of adversity; now it seemed to her she was clothed. Formerly her soul had seemed cold, now it was warm. Cosette was no longer afraid of the Thénardier. She was no longer alone; there was someone there.

She hastily set about her regular morning duties. That louis, which she had about her, in the very apron pocket whence the fifteen-sou piece had fallen on the night before, distracted her thoughts. She dared not touch it, but she spent five minutes in gazing at it, with her tongue hanging out, if the truth must be told. As she swept the staircase, she paused, remained standing there motionless, forgetful of her broom and of the entire universe, occupied in gazing at that star which was blazing at the bottom of her pocket.

It was during one of these periods of contemplation that the Thénardier joined her. She had gone in search of Cosette at her husband's orders. What was quite unprecedented, she neither struck her nor said an insulting word to her.

"Cosette," she said, almost gently, "come immediately."

An instant later Cosette entered the public-room.

The stranger took up the bundle which he had brought and untied it. This bundle contained a little woolen gown, an apron, a fustian bodice, a kerchief, a petticoat, woolen stockings, shoes—a complete outfit for a girl of seven years. All was black.

"My child," said the man, "take these, and go and dress yourself quickly."

Daylight was appearing when those of the inhabitants of Montfermeil who had begun to open their doors beheld a poorly clad old man leading a little girl dressed in mourning, and carrying a pink doll in her arms, pass along the road to Paris. They were going in the direction of Livry.

It was our man and Cosette.

No one knew the man; as Cosette was no longer in rags, many did not recognize her. Cosette was going away. With whom? She did not know. Whither? She knew not. All that she understood was that she was leaving the Thénardier tavern behind her. No one had thought of bidding her farewell, nor had she thought of taking leave of anyone. She was leaving that hated and hating house.

Poor, gentle creature, whose heart had been repressed up to that hour!

Cosette walked along gravely, with her large eyes wide open, and gazing at the sky. She had put her louis in the pocket of her new apron. From time to time, she bent down and glanced at it; then she looked at the good man. She felt something as though she were beside the good God.

Chapter X

HE WHO SEEKS TO BETTER HIMSELF MAY
RENDER HIS SITUATION WORSE

MADAME THÉNARDIER HAD ALLOWED HER HUSBAND TO HAVE HIS OWN WAY, AS WAS HER WONT. She had expected great results. When the man and Cosette had taken their departure, Thénardier allowed a full quarter of an hour to elapse; then he took her aside and showed her the fifteen hundred francs.

"Is that all?" said she.

It was the first time since they had set up housekeeping that she had dared to criticize one of the master's acts.

The blow told.

"You are right, in sooth," said he; "I am a fool. Give me my hat."

He folded up the three bank-bills, thrust them into his pocket, and ran out in all haste; but he made a mistake and turned to the right first. Some neighbors, of whom he made inquiries, put him on the track again; the Lark and the man had been seen going in the direction of Livry. He followed these hints, walking with great strides, and talking to himself the while:

"That man is evidently a million dressed in yellow, and I am an animal. First he gave twenty sous, then five francs, then fifty francs, then fifteen hundred francs, all with equal readiness. He would have given fifteen thousand francs. But I shall overtake him."

And then, that bundle of clothes prepared beforehand for the child; all that was singular; many mysteries lay concealed under it. One does not let mysteries out of one's hand when one has once grasped them. The secrets of the wealthy are sponges of gold; one must know how to subject them to pressure. All these thoughts whirled through his brain. "I am an animal," said he.

When one leaves Montfermeil and reaches the turn which the road takes that runs to Livry, it can be seen stretching out before one to a great distance across the plateau. On arriving there, he calculated that he ought to be able to see the old man and the child. He looked as far as his vision reached, and saw nothing. He made fresh inquiries, but he had wasted time. Some passers-by informed him that the man and child of whom he was in search had gone toward the forest in the direction of Gagny. He hastened in that direction.

They were far in advance of him; but a child walks slowly, and he walked fast; and then, he was well acquainted with the country.

All at once he paused and dealt himself a blow on his forehead like a man who has forgotten some essential point and who is ready to retrace his steps.

"I ought to have taken my gun," said he to himself.

Thénardier was one of those double natures which sometimes pass through our midst without our being aware of the fact, and who disappear without our finding them out, because destiny has only exhibited one side of them. It is the fate of many men to live thus half submerged. In a calm and even situation, Thénardier possessed all that is required to make—we will not say to be—what people have agreed to call an honest trader, a good bourgeois. At the same time certain circumstances being given, certain shocks arriving to bring his under-nature to the surface, he had all the requisites for a blackguard. He was a shop-keeper in whom there was some taint of the monster. Satan must have occasionally crouched down in some corner of the hovel in which Thénardier dwelt, and have fallen a-dreaming in the presence of this hideous masterpiece.

After a momentary hesitation:

"Bah!" he thought; "they will have time to make their escape."

And he pursued his road, walking rapidly straight ahead, and with almost an air of certainty, with the sagacity of a fox scenting a covey of partridges.

In truth, when he had passed the ponds and had traversed in an oblique direction the large clearing which lies on the right of the Avenue de Bellevue, and reached that turf alley which nearly makes the circuit of the hill, and covers the arch of the ancient aqueduct of the Abbey of Chelles, he caught sight, over the top of the brushwood, of the hat on which he had already erected so many conjectures; it was that man's hat. The brushwood was not high. Thénardier recognized the fact that the man and Cosette were sitting there. The child could not be seen on account of her small size, but the head of her doll was visible.

Thénardier was not mistaken. The man was sitting there, and letting Cosette get somewhat rested. The inn-keeper walked round the brushwood and presented himself abruptly to the eyes of those whom he was in search of.

"Pardon, excuse me, sir," he said, quite breathless, "but here are your fifteen hundred francs."

So saying, he handed the stranger the three bank-bills.

The man raised his eyes.

"What is the meaning of this?"

Thénardier replied respectfully:

"It means, sir, that I shall take back Cosette."

Cosette shuddered, and pressed close to the old man.

He replied, gazing to the very bottom of Thénardier's eyes the while, and enunciating every syllable distinctly:

"You are go-ing to take back Co-sette?"

"Yes, sir, I am. I will tell you; I have considered the matter. In fact, I have not the right to give her to you. I am an honest man, you see; this child does not belong to me; she belongs to her mother. It was her mother who confided her to me; I can only resign her to her mother. You will say to me, 'But her mother is dead.' Good; in that case I can only give the child up to the person who shall bring me a writing, signed by her mother, to the effect that I am to hand the child over to the person therein mentioned; that is clear."

The man, without making any reply, fumbled in his pocket, and Thénardier beheld the pocket-book of bank-bills make its appearance once more.

The tavern-keeper shivered with joy.

"Good!" thought he; "let us hold firm; he is going to bribe me!"

Before opening the pocket-book, the traveler cast a glance about him: the spot was absolutely deserted; there was not a soul either in the woods or in the valley. The man opened his pocket-book once more and drew from it, not the handful of bills which Thénardier expected, but a simple little paper, which he unfolded and presented fully open to the inn-keeper, saying:

"You are right; read!"

Thénardier took the paper and read:

"M. SUR M., March 25, 1823

"MONSIEUR THÉNARDIER—You will deliver Cosette to this person. You will be paid for all the little things. I have the honor to salute you with respect,

FANTINE"

"You know that signature?" resumed the man.

It certainly was Fantine's signature; Thénardier recognized it.

There was no reply to make; he experienced two violent vexations, the vexation of renouncing the bribery which he had hoped for, and the vexation of being beaten; the man added:

"You may keep this paper as your receipt."

Thénardier retreated in tolerably good order.

"This signature is fairly well imitated," he growled between his teeth; "however, let it go!"

Then he essayed a desperate effort.

"It is well, sir," he said, "since you are the person, but I must be paid for all those little things. A great deal is owing to me."

The man rose to his feet, filliping the dust from his threadbare sleeve:

"Monsieur Thénardier, in January last, the mother reckoned that she owed you one hundred and twenty francs. In February, you sent her a bill of five hundred francs; you received three hundred francs at the end of February, and three hundred francs at the beginning of March. Since then nine months have elapsed, at fifteen francs a month, the price agreed upon, which makes one hundred and thirty-five francs. You had received one hundred francs too much; that makes thirty-five still owing you. I have just given you fifteen hundred francs."

Thénardier's sensations were those of the wolf at the moment when he feels himself nipped and seized by the steel jaw of the trap.

"Who is this devil of a man?" he thought.

He did what the wolf does: he shook himself. Audacity had succeeded with him once.

"Monsieur-I-don't-know-your-name," he said resolutely, and this time casting aside all respectful ceremony, "I shall take back Cosette if you do not give me a thousand crowns."

The stranger said tranquilly:

"Come, Cosette."

He took Cosette by his left hand, and with his right he picked up his cudgel, which was lying on the ground.

Thénardier noted the enormous size of the cudgel and the solitude of the spot.

The man plunged into the forest with the child, leaving the inn-keeper motionless and speechless.

While they were walking away, Thénardier scrutinized his huge shoulders, which were a little rounded, and his great fists.

Then, bringing his eyes back to his own person, they fell upon his feeble arms and his thin hands. "I really must have been exceedingly stupid not to have thought to bring my gun," he said to himself, "since I was going hunting!"

However, the inn-keeper did not give up.

"I want to know where he is going," said he, and he set out to follow them at a distance. Two things were left on his hands, an irony in the shape of the paper signed *Fantine*, and a consolation, the fifteen hundred francs.

The man led Cosette off in the direction of Livry and Bondy. He walked slowly, with drooping head, in an attitude of reflection and sadness. The winter had thinned out the forest, so that Thénardier did not lose them from sight, although he kept at a good distance. The man turned round from time to time, and looked to see if he was being followed. All at once he caught sight of Thénardier. He plunged suddenly into the brushwood with Cosette, where they could both hide themselves. "The deuce!" said Thénardier, and he redoubled his pace.

The thickness of the undergrowth forced him to draw nearer to them. When the man had reached the densest part of the thicket, he wheeled round. It was in vain that Thénardier sought to conceal himself in the branches; he could not prevent the man seeing him. The man cast upon him an uneasy glance, then elevated his head and continued his course. The inn-keeper set out again in pursuit. Thus they continued for two or three hundred paces. All at once the man turned round once more; he saw the inn-keeper. This time he gazed at him with so somber an air that Thénardier decided that it was "useless" to proceed further. Thénardier retraced his steps.

Chapter XI

NUMBER 9,430 REAPPEARS, AND COSETTE WINS IT IN THE LOTTERY

JEAN VALJEAN WAS NOT DEAD.

When he fell into the sea, or rather, when he threw himself into it, he was not ironed, as we have seen. He swam under water until he reached a vessel at anchor, to which a boat was moored. He found means of hiding himself in this boat until night. At night he swam off again, and reached the shore a little way from Cape Brun. There, as he did not lack money, he procured clothing. A small country-house in the neighborhood of Balaguier was at that time the dressing-room of escaped convicts—a lucrative specialty. Then Jean Valjean, like all the sorry fugitives who are seeking to evade the vigilance of the law and social fatality, pursued an obscure and undulating itinerary. He found his first refuge at Pradeaux, near Beausset. Then he directed his course toward Grand-Villard, near Briançon, in the Hautes-Alpes. It was a fumbling and uneasy flight—a mole's track, whose branchings are untraceable. Later on, some trace of his passage into Ain, in the territory of Civrieux, was discovered; in the Pyrenees, at Accons; at the spot called Grange-de-Doumec, near the market of Chavailles, and in the environs of Perigueux at Brunies, canton of La Chapelle-Gonaguet. He reached Paris. We have just seen him at Montfermeil.

His first care on arriving in Paris had been to buy mourning clothes for a little girl of from seven to eight years of age; then to procure a lodging. That done, he had betaken himself to Montfermeil. It will be remembered that already, during his preceding escape, he had made a mysterious trip thither, or somewhere in that neighborhood, of which the law had gathered an inkling.

However, he was thought to be dead, and this still further increased the obscurity which had gathered about him. At Paris, one of the journals which chronicled the fact fell into his hands. He felt reassured and almost at peace, as though he had really been dead.

On the evening of the day when Jean Valjean rescued Cosette from the claws of the Thénardiers, he returned to Paris. He re-entered it at nightfall, with the child, by way of the Barrier Monceaux. There he entered a cabriolet, which took him to the esplanade of the Observatoire. There he got out, paid the coachman, took Cosette by the hand, and together they directed their steps through the darkness—through the deserted streets which adjoin the Ourcine and the Glacière, toward the Boulevard de l'Hôpital.

The day had been strange and filled with emotions for Cosette. They had eaten some bread and cheese purchased in isolated taverns, behind hedges; they had changed carriages frequently; they had traveled short distances on foot. She made no complaint, but she was weary, and Jean Valjean perceived it by the way she dragged more and more on his hand as she walked. He took her on his back. Cosette, without letting go of Catherine, laid her head on Jean Valjean's shoulder, and there fell asleep.

BOOK FOURTH

THE GORBEAU HOVEL

Chapter I

MASTER GORBEAU

FORTY YEARS AGO, A RAMBLER WHO HAD VENTURED INTO THAT UNKNOWN COUNTRY OF THE Salpêtrière, and who had mounted to the Barrière d'Italie by way of the boulevard, reached a point where it might be said that Paris disappeared. It was no longer solitude, for there were passers-by; it was not the country, for there were houses and streets; it was not the city, for the streets had ruts like highways, and the grass grew in them; it was not a village, the houses were too lofty. What was it, then? It was an inhabited spot where there was no one; it was a desert place where there was someone; it was a boulevard of the great city, a street of Paris; more wild at night than the forest, more gloomy by day than a cemetery.

It was the old quarter of the Marché-aux-Chevaux.

The rambler, if he risked himself outside the four decrepit walls of this Marché-aux-Chevaux; if he consented even to pass beyond the Rue du Petit-Banquier, after leaving on his right a garden protected by high walls; then a field in which tan-bark mills rose like gigantic beaver huts; then an enclosure encumbered with timber, with a heap of stumps, sawdust, and shavings, on which stood a large dog, barking; then a long, low, utterly dilapidated wall, with a little black door in mourning, laden with mosses, which were covered with flowers in the spring; then, in the most deserted spot, a frightful and decrepit building, on which ran the inscription in large letters: POST NO BILLS— this daring rambler would have reached little known latitudes at the corner of the Rue des Vignes-Saint-Marcel. There, near a factory, and between two garden walls, there could be seen, at that epoch, a mean building, which, at the first glance, seemed as small as a thatched hovel, and which was, in reality, as large as a cathedral. It presented its side and gable to the public road; hence its apparent diminutiveness. Nearly the whole of the house was hidden. Only the door and one window could be seen.

This hovel was only one story high.

The first detail that struck the observer was, that the door could never have been anything but the door of a hovel, while the window, if it had been carved out of dressed stone instead of being in rough masonry, might have been the lattice of a lordly mansion.

The door was nothing but a collection of wormeaten planks roughly bound together by crossbeams which resembled roughly hewn logs. It opened directly on a steep staircase of lofty steps, muddy, chalky, plaster-stained, dusty steps, of the same width as itself, which could be seen from the street, running straight up like a ladder and disappearing in the darkness between two walls. The top of the shapeless bay into which this door shut was masked by a narrow scantling in the center of which a triangular hole had been sawed, which served both as wicket and air-hole when the door was closed. On the inside of the door the figures 52 had been traced with a couple of strokes of a brush dipped in ink, and above the scantling the same hand had daubed the number 50, so that one hesitated. Where was one? Above the door it said, "Number 50"; the inside replied, "no, Number 52." No one knows what dust-colored figures were suspended like draperies from the triangular opening.

The window was large, sufficiently elevated, garnished with Venetian blinds, and with a frame in large square panes; only these large panes were suffering from various wounds, which were both concealed and betrayed by an ingenious paper bandage. And the blinds, dislocated and unpasted, threatened passers-by rather than screened the occupants. The horizontal slats were missing here and there and had been naïvely replaced with boards nailed on perpendicularly; so that what began as a blind ended as a shutter. This door with an unclean, and this window with an honest though dilapidated air, thus beheld on the same house, produced the effect of two incomplete beggars walking side by side, with different miens beneath the same rags, the one having always been a mendicant, and the other having once been a gentleman.

The staircase led to a very vast edifice which resembled a shed which had been converted into a house. This edifice had, for its intestinal tube, a long corridor, on which opened to right and left sorts of compartments of varied dimensions which were inhabitable under stress of circumstances, and rather more like stalls than cells. These chambers received their light from the vague waste grounds in the neighborhood.

All this was dark, disagreeable, wan, melancholy, sepulchral; traversed according as the crevices lay in the roof or in the door, by cold rays or by icy winds. An interesting and picturesque peculiarity of this sort of dwelling is the enormous size of the spiders.

To the left of the entrance door, on the boulevard side, at about the height of a man from the ground, a small window which had been walled up formed a square niche full of stones which the children had thrown there as they passed by.

A portion of this building has recently been demolished. From what still remains of it one can form a judgment as to what it was in former days. As a whole, it was not over a hundred years old. A hundred years is youth in a church and age in a house. It seems as though man's lodging partook of his ephemeral character, and God's house of his eternity.

The postmen called the house Number 50-52; but it was known in the neighborhood as the Gorbeau house.

Let us explain whence this appellation was derived.

Collectors of petty details, who become herbalists of anecdotes, and prick slippery dates into their memories with a pin, know that there was in Paris, during the last century, about 1770, two attorneys at the Châtelet named, one Corbeau (Raven), the other Renard (Fox). The two names had been forestalled by La Fontaine. The opportunity was too fine for the lawyers; they made the most of it. A parody was immediately put in circulation in the galleries of the court-house, in verses that limped a little:

> *Maître Corbeau, sur un dossier perché,*
> *Tenait dans son bec une saisie exécutoire;*
> *Maître Renard, par l'odeur alléché,*
> *Lui fit à peu près cette histoire:*
> *Hé! bonjour. Etc.*[1]

The two honest practitioners, embarrassed by the jests, and finding the bearing of their heads interfered with by the shouts of laughter which followed them, resolved to get rid of their names, and hit upon the expedient of applying to the king.

---

1. Lawyer Corbeau, perched on a docket, held in his beak a writ of execution; Lawyer Renard, attracted by the smell, addressed him nearly as follows, etc.

Their petition was presented to Louis XV on the same day when the Papal Nuncio, on the one hand, and the Cardinal de la Roche-Aymon on the other, both devoutly kneeling, were each engaged in putting on, in his Majesty's presence, a slipper on the bare feet of Madame du Barry, who had just got out of bed. The king, who was laughing, continued to laugh, passed gaily from the two bishops to the two lawyers, and bestowed on these limbs of the law their former names, or nearly so. By the king's command, Maître Corbeau was permitted to add a tail to his initial letter and to call himself Gorbeau. Maître Renard was less lucky; all he obtained was leave to place a P in front of his R, and to call himself Prenard; so that the second name bore almost as much resemblance as the first.

Now, according to local tradition, this Maître Gorbeau had been the proprietor of the building numbered 50-52 on the Boulevard de l'Hôpital. He was even the author of the monumental window.

Hence the edifice bore the name of the Gorbeau house.

Opposite this house, among the trees of the boulevard, rose a great elm which was three-quarters dead; almost directly facing it opens the Rue de la Barrière des Gobelins, a street then without houses, unpaved, planted with unhealthy trees, which was green or muddy according to the season, and which ended squarely in the exterior wall of Paris. An odor of copperas issued in puffs from the roofs of the neighboring factory.

The barrier was close at hand. In 1823 the city wall was still in existence.

This barrier itself evoked gloomy fancies in the mind. It was the road to Bicêtre. It was through it that, under the Empire and the Restoration, prisoners condemned to death re-entered Paris on the day of their execution. It was there, that, about 1829, was committed that mysterious assassination, called "The assassination of the Fontainebleau barrier," whose authors justice was never able to discover; a melancholy problem which has never been elucidated, a frightful enigma which has never been unriddled. Take a few steps, and you come upon that fatal Rue Croulebarbe, where Ulbach stabbed the goat-girl of Ivry to the sound of thunder, as in the melodramas. A few paces more, and you arrive at the abominable pollarded elms of the Barrière Saint-Jacques, that expedient of the philanthropist to conceal the scaffold, that miserable and shameful Place de Grève of a shop-keeping and bourgeois society, which recoiled before the death penalty, neither daring to abolish it with grandeur, nor to uphold it with authority.

Leaving aside this Place Saint-Jacques, which was, as it were, predestined, and which has always been horrible, probably the most mournful spot on that mournful boulevard, seven-and-thirty years ago, was the spot which even to-day is so unattractive, where stood the building Number 50-52.

Bourgeois houses only began to spring up there twenty-five years later. The place was unpleasant. In addition to the gloomy thoughts which assailed one there, one was conscious of being between the Salpêtrière, a glimpse of whose dome could be seen, and Bicêtre, whose outskirts one was fairly touching, that is to say, between the madness of women and the madness of men. As far as the eye could see, one could perceive nothing but the abattoirs, the city wall, and the fronts of a few factories, resembling barracks or monasteries; everywhere about stood hovels, rubbish, ancient walls blackened like cerecloths, new white walls like winding-sheets; everywhere parallel rows of trees, buildings erected on a line, flat constructions, long, cold rows, and the melancholy sadness of right angles. Not an unevenness of the ground, not a caprice in the architecture, not a fold. The *ensemble* was glacial, regular, hideous. Nothing oppresses the heart like symmetry. It is because symmetry is ennui, and ennui is at the very foundation of grief. Despair yawns. Something more terrible than a hell where one suffers may be imagined, and that is a hell where one is bored. If such a hell existed, that bit of the Boulevard de l'Hôpital might have formed the entrance to it.

Nevertheless, at nightfall, at the moment when the daylight is vanishing, especially in winter, at the hour when the twilight breeze tears from the elms their last russet leaves, when the darkness is deep and starless, or when the moon and the wind are making openings in the clouds and losing themselves in the shadows, this boulevard suddenly becomes frightful. The black lines sink inwards and are lost in the shades, like morsels of the infinite. The passer-by cannot refrain from recalling the innumerable traditions of the place which are connected with the gibbet. The solitude of this spot, where so many crimes have been committed, had something terrible about it. One almost had a presentiment of meeting with traps in that darkness; all the confused forms of the darkness seemed suspicious, and the long, hollow square, of which one caught a glimpse between each tree, seemed graves: by day it was ugly; in the evening melancholy; by night it was sinister.

In summer, at twilight, one saw, here and there, a few old women seated at the foot of the elm, on benches moldy with rain. These good old women were fond of begging.

However, this quarter, which had a superannuated rather than an antique air, was tending even then to transformation. Even at that time anyone who was desirous of seeing it had to make haste. Each day some detail of the whole effect was disappearing. For the last twenty years the station of the Orleans railway has stood beside the old faubourg and distracted it, as it does to-day. Wherever it is placed on the borders of a capital, a railway station is the death of a suburb and the birth of a city. It seems as though, around these great centers of the movements of a people, the earth, full of germs, trembled and yawned, to engulf the ancient dwellings of men and to allow new ones to spring forth, at the rattle of these powerful machines, at the breath of these monstrous horses of civilization which devour coal and vomit fire. The old houses crumble and new ones rise.

Since the Orleans railway has invaded the region of the Salpêtrière, the ancient, narrow streets which adjoin the moats Saint-Victor and the Jardin des Plantes tremble, as they are violently traversed three or four times each day by those currents of coach fiacres and omnibuses which, in a given time, crowd back the houses to the right and the left; for there are things which are odd when said that are rigorously exact; and just as it is true to say that in large cities the sun makes the southern fronts of houses to vegetate and grow, it is certain that the frequent passage of vehicles enlarges streets. The symptoms of a new life are evident. In this old provincial quarter, in the wildest nooks, the pavement shows itself, the sidewalks begin to crawl and to grow longer, even where there are as yet no pedestrians. One morning—a memorable morning in July, 1845—black pots of bitumen were seen smoking there; on that day it might be said that civilization had arrived in the Rue de l'Ourcine, and that Paris had entered the suburb of Saint-Marceau.

Chapter II

A NEST FOR OWL AND A WARBLER

IT WAS IN FRONT OF THIS GORBEAU HOUSE THAT JEAN VALJEAN HALTED. LIKE WILD BIRDS, HE HAD chosen this desert place to construct his nest.

He fumbled in his waistcoat pocket, drew out a sort of a pass-key, opened the door, entered, closed it again carefully, and ascended the staircase, still carrying Cosette.

At the top of the stairs he drew from his pocket another key, with which he opened another door. The chamber which he entered, and which he closed again instantly, was a kind of moderately spacious attic, furnished with a mattress laid on the floor, a table, and several chairs; a stove in which a fire was burning, and whose embers were visible, stood in one corner. A lantern on the boulevard cast a vague light into this poor room. At the extreme end there was a dressing-room with a folding bed; Jean Valjean carried the child to this bed and laid her down there without waking her.

He struck a match and lighted a candle. All this was prepared beforehand on the table, and, as he had done on the previous evening, he began to scrutinize Cosette's face with a gaze full of ecstasy, in which the expression of kindness and tenderness almost amounted to aberration. The little girl, with that tranquil confidence which belongs only to extreme strength and extreme weakness, had fallen asleep without knowing with whom she was, and continued to sleep without knowing where she was.

Jean Valjean bent down and kissed that child's hand.

Nine months before he had kissed the hand of the mother, who had also just fallen asleep.

The same sad, piercing, religious sentiment filled his heart.

He knelt beside Cosette's bed.

It was broad daylight, and the child still slept. A wan ray of the December sun penetrated the window of the attic and lay upon the ceiling in long threads of light and shade. All at once a heavily laden carrier's cart, which was passing along the boulevard, shook the frail bed, like a clap of thunder, and made it quiver from top to bottom.

"Yes, Madame!" cried Cosette, waking with a start, "here I am! here I am!"

And she sprang out of bed, her eyes still half shut with the heaviness of sleep, extending her arms toward the corner of the wall.

"Ah! mon Dieu, my broom!" said she.

She opened her eyes wide now, and beheld the smiling countenance of Jean Valjean.

"Ah! so it is true!" said the child. "Good morning, Monsieur."

Children accept joy and happiness instantly and familiarly, being themselves by nature joy and happiness.

Cosette caught sight of Catherine at the foot of her bed, and took possession of her, and, as she played, she put a hundred questions to Jean Valjean. Where was she? Was Paris very large? Was Madame Thénardier very far away? Was she to go back? etc., etc. All at once she exclaimed, "How pretty it is here!"

It was a frightful hole, but she felt free.

"Must I sweep?" she resumed at last.

"Play!" said Jean Valjean.

The day passed thus. Cosette, without troubling herself to understand anything, was inexpressibly happy with that doll and that kind man.

Chapter III

Two Misfortunes Make One Piece of Good Fortune

ON THE FOLLOWING MORNING, AT DAYBREAK, JEAN VALJEAN WAS STILL BY COSETTE'S BEDSIDE; he watched there motionless, waiting for her to wake.

Some new thing had come into his soul.

Jean Valjean had never loved anything; for twenty-five years he had been alone in the world. He had never been father, lover, husband, friend. In the prison he had been vicious, gloomy, chaste, ignorant, and shy. The heart of that ex-convict was full of virginity. His sister and his sister's children had left him only a vague and far-off memory which had finally almost completely vanished; he had made every effort to find them, and not having been able to find them, he had forgotten them. Human nature is made thus; the other tender emotions of his youth, if he had ever had any, had fallen into an abyss.

When he saw Cosette, when he had taken possession of her, carried her off, and delivered her, he felt his heart moved within him.

All the passion and affection within him awoke, and rushed toward that child. He approached the bed, where she lay sleeping, and trembled with joy. He suffered all the pangs of a mother, and he knew not what it meant; for that great and singular movement of a heart which begins to love is a very obscure and a very sweet thing.

Poor old man, with a perfectly new heart!

Only, as he was five-and-fifty, and Cosette eight years of age, all that might have been love in the whole course of his life flowed together into a sort of ineffable light.

It was the second white apparition which he had encountered. The Bishop had caused the dawn of virtue to rise on his horizon; Cosette caused the dawn of love to rise.

The early days passed in this dazzled state.

Cosette, on her side, had also, unknown to herself, become another being, poor little thing! She was so little when her mother left her, that she no longer remembered her. Like all children, who resemble young shoots of the vine, which cling to everything, she had tried to love; she had not succeeded. All had repulsed her—the Thénardiers, their children, other children. She had loved the dog, and he had died, after which nothing and nobody would have anything to do with her. It is a sad thing to say, and we have already intimated it, that, at eight years of age, her heart was cold. It was not her fault; it was not the faculty of loving that she lacked; alas! it was the possibility. Thus, from the very first day, all her sentient and thinking powers loved this kind man. She felt that which she had never felt before—a sensation of expansion.

The man no longer produced on her the effect of being old or poor; she thought Jean Valjean handsome, just as she thought the hovel pretty.

These are the effects of the dawn, of childhood, of joy. The novelty of the earth and of life counts for something here. Nothing is so charming as the coloring reflection of happiness on a garret. We all have in our past a delightful garret.

Nature, a difference of fifty years, had set a profound gulf between Jean Valjean and Cosette; destiny filled in this gulf. Destiny suddenly united and wedded with its irresistible power these two uprooted existences, differing in age, alike in sorrow. One, in fact, completed the other. Cosette's instinct sought a father, as Jean Valjean's instinct sought a child. To meet was to find each other. At the mysterious moment when their hands touched, they were welded together. When these two souls perceived each other, they recognized each other as necessary to each other, and embraced each other closely.

Taking the words in their most comprehensive and absolute sense, we may say that, separated from everyone by the walls of the tomb, Jean Valjean was the widower, and Cosette was the orphan: this situation caused Jean Valjean to become Cosette's father after a celestial fashion.

And in truth, the mysterious impression produced on Cosette in the depths of the forest of Chelles by the hand of Jean Valjean grasping hers in the dark was not an illusion, but a reality. The entrance of that man into the destiny of that child had been the advent of God.

Moreover, Jean Valjean had chosen his refuge well. There he seemed perfectly secure.

The chamber with a dressing-room, which he occupied with Cosette, was the one whose window opened on the boulevard. This being the only window in the house, no neighbors' glances were to be feared from across the way or at the side.

The ground floor of Number 50-52, a sort of dilapidated penthouse, served as a wagon-house for market-gardeners, and no communication existed between it and the first story. It was separated by the flooring, which had neither traps nor stairs, and which formed the diaphragm of the building, as it were. The first story contained, as we have said, numerous chambers and several attics, only one of which was occupied by the old woman who took charge of Jean Valjean's housekeeping; all the rest was uninhabited.

It was this old woman, ornamented with the name of the *principal lodger,* and in reality intrusted with the functions of portress, who had let him the lodging on Christmas Eve. He had represented himself to her as a gentleman of means who had been ruined by Spanish bonds, who was coming there to live with his little daughter. He had paid her six months in advance, and had commissioned the old woman to furnish the chamber and dressing-room, as we have seen. It was this good woman who had lighted the fire in the stove, and prepared everything on the evening of their arrival.

Week followed week; these two beings led a happy life in that hovel.

Cosette laughed, chattered, and sang from daybreak. Children have their morning song as well as birds.

It sometimes happened that Jean Valjean clasped her tiny red hand, all cracked with chilblains, and kissed it. The poor child, who was used to being beaten, did not know the meaning of this, and ran away in confusion.

At times she became serious and stared at her little black gown. Cosette was no longer in rags; she was in mourning. She had emerged from misery, and she was entering into life.

Jean Valjean had undertaken to teach her to read. Sometimes, as he made the child spell, he remembered that it was with the idea of doing evil that he had learned to read in prison. This idea had ended in teaching a child to read. Then the ex-convict smiled with the pensive smile of the angels.

He felt in it a premeditation from on high, the will of someone who was not man, and he became absorbed in reverie. Good thoughts have their abysses as well as evil ones.

To teach Cosette to read, and to let her play, this constituted nearly the whole of Jean Valjean's existence. And then he talked of her mother, and he made her pray.

She called him *father,* and knew no other name for him.

He passed hours in watching her dressing and undressing her doll, and in listening to her prattle. Life, henceforth, appeared to him to be full of interest; men seemed to him good and just; he no longer reproached anyone in thought; he saw no reason why he should not live to be a very old man, now that this child loved him. He saw a whole future stretching out before him, illuminated by Cosette as by a charming light. The best of us are not exempt from egotistical thoughts. At times, he reflected with a sort of joy that she would be ugly.

This is only a personal opinion; but, to utter our whole thought, at the point where Jean Valjean had arrived when he began to love Cosette, it is by no means clear to us that he did not need this encouragement in order that he might persevere in well-doing. He had just viewed the malice of men and the misery of society under a new aspect—incomplete aspects, which unfortunately only exhibited one side of the truth, the fate of woman as summed up in Fantine, and public authority as personified in Javert. He had returned to prison, this time for having done right; he had quaffed fresh bitterness; disgust and lassitude were overpowering him; even the memory of the Bishop probably suffered a temporary eclipse, though sure to reappear later on luminous and triumphant; but, after all, that sacred memory was growing dim. Who knows whether Jean Valjean had not been on the eve of growing discouraged and of falling once more? He loved and grew strong again. Alas! he walked with no less indecision than Cosette. He protected her, and she strengthened him. Thanks to him, she could walk through life; thanks to her, he could continue in virtue. He was that child's stay, and she was his prop. Oh, unfathomable and divine mystery of the balances of destiny!

Chapter IV

The Remarks of the Principal Tenant

Jean Valjean was prudent enough never to go out by day. Every evening, at twilight, he walked for an hour or two, sometimes alone, often with Cosette, seeking the most deserted side alleys of the boulevard, and entering churches at nightfall. He liked to go to Saint-Médard, which is the nearest church. When he did not take Cosette with him, she remained with the old woman; but the child's delight was to go out with the good man. She preferred an hour with him to all her rapturous *tête-à-têtes* with Catherine. He held her hand as they walked, and said sweet things to her.

It turned out that Cosette was a very gay little person.

The old woman attended to the housekeeping and cooking and went to market.

They lived soberly, always having a little fire, but like people in very moderate circumstances. Jean Valjean had made no alterations in the furniture as it was the first day; he had merely had the glass door leading to Cosette's dressing-room replaced by a solid door.

He still wore his yellow coat, his black breeches, and his old hat. In the street, he was taken for a poor man. It sometimes happened that kind-hearted women turned back to bestow a sou on him. Jean Valjean accepted the sou with a deep bow. It also happened occasionally that he encountered some poor wretch asking alms; then he looked behind him to make sure that no one was observing him, stealthily approached the unfortunate man, put a piece of money into his hand, often a silver coin, and walked rapidly away. This had its disadvantages. He began to be known in the neighborhood under the name of *the beggar who gives alms.*

The old *principal lodger,* a cross-looking creature, who was thoroughly permeated, so far as her neighbors were concerned, with the inquisitiveness peculiar to envious persons, scrutinized Jean Valjean a great deal, without his suspecting the fact. She was a little deaf, which rendered her talkative. There remained to her from her past, two teeth—one above, the other below—which she was continually knocking against each other. She had questioned Cosette, who had not been able to tell her anything, since she knew nothing herself except that she had come from Montfermeil. One morning, this spy saw Jean Valjean, with an air which struck the old gossip as peculiar, entering one of the uninhabited compartments of the hovel. She followed him with the step of an old cat, and was able to observe him without being seen, through a crack in the door, which was directly opposite him. Jean Valjean had his back turned toward this door, by way of greater security, no doubt. The old woman saw him fumble in his pocket and draw thence a case, scissors, and thread; then he began to rip the lining of one of the skirts of his coat, and from the opening he took a bit of yellowish paper, which he unfolded. The old woman recognized, with terror, the fact that it was a bank-bill for a thousand francs. It was the second or third only that she had seen in the course of her existence. She fled in alarm.

A moment later, Jean Valjean accosted her, and asked her to go and get this thousand-franc bill changed for him, adding that it was his quarterly income, which he had received the day before. "Where?" thought the old woman. "He did not go out until six o'clock in the evening, and the government bank certainly is not open at that hour." The old woman went to get the bill changed, and mentioned her surmises. That thousand-franc note, commented on and multiplied, produced a vast amount of terrified discussion among the gossips of the Rue des Vignes Saint-Marcel.

A few days later, it chanced that Jean Valjean was sawing some wood, in his shirt-sleeves, in the corridor. The old woman was in the chamber, putting things in order. She was alone. Cosette was occupied in admiring the wood as it was sawed. The old woman caught sight of the coat hanging on a nail, and examined it. The lining had been sewed up again. The good woman felt of it carefully, and thought she observed in the skirts and revers thicknesses of paper. More thousand-franc bank-bills, no doubt!

She also noticed that there were all sorts of things in the pockets. Not only the needles, thread, and scissors which she had seen, but a big pocket-book, a very large knife, and—a suspicious circumstance—several wigs of various colors. Each pocket of this coat had the air of being in a manner provided against unexpected accidents.

Thus the inhabitants of the house reached the last days of winter.

Chapter V

A FIVE-FRANC PIECE FALLS ON THE GROUND AND PRODUCES A TUMULT

NEAR SAINT-MÉDARD'S CHURCH THERE WAS A POOR MAN WHO WAS IN THE HABIT OF CROUCHing on the brink of a public well which had been condemned, and on whom Jean Valjean was fond of bestowing charity. He never passed this man without giving him a few sous. Sometimes he spoke to him. Those who envied this mendicant said that he belonged to the police. He was an ex-beadle of seventy-five, who was constantly mumbling his prayers.

One evening, as Jean Valjean was passing by, when he had not Cosette with him, he saw the beggar in his usual place, beneath the lantern which had just been lighted. The man seemed engaged in prayer, according to his custom, and was much bent over. Jean Valjean stepped up to him and placed his customary alms in his hand. The mendicant raised his eyes suddenly, stared intently at Jean Valjean, then dropped his head quickly. This movement was like a flash of lightning. Jean Valjean was seized with a shudder. It seemed to him that he had just caught sight, by the light of the street-lantern, not of the placid and beaming visage of the old beadle, but of a well-known and startling face. He experienced the same impression that one would have on finding one's self, all of a sudden, face to face, in the dark, with a tiger. He recoiled, terrified, petrified, daring neither to breathe, to speak, to remain, nor to flee, staring at the beggar who had dropped his head which was enveloped in a rag, and no longer appeared to know that he was there. At this strange moment, an instinct—possibly the mysterious instinct of self-preservation—restrained Jean Valjean from uttering a word. The beggar had the same figure, the same rags, the same appearance as he had every day. "Bah!" said Jean Valjean, "I am mad! I am dreaming! Impossible!" And he returned profoundly troubled.

He hardly dared to confess, even to himself, that the face which he thought he had seen was the face of Javert.

That night, on thinking the matter over, he regretted not having questioned the man, in order to force him to raise his head a second time.

On the following day, at nightfall, he went back. The beggar was at his post. "Good day, my good man," said Jean Valjean, resolutely, handing him a sou. The beggar raised his head, and replied in a whining voice, "Thanks, my good sir." It was unmistakably the ex-beadle.

Jean Valjean felt completely reassured. He began to laugh. "How the deuce could I have thought that I saw Javert there?" he thought. "Am I going to lose my eyesight now?" And he thought no more about it.

A few days afterwards—it might have been at eight o'clock in the evening—he was in his room, and engaged in making Cosette spell aloud, when he heard the house door open and then shut again. This struck him as singular. The old woman, who was the only inhabitant of the house except himself, always went to bed at nightfall, so that she might not burn out her candles. Jean Valjean made a sign to Cosette to be quiet. He heard someone ascending the stairs. It might possibly be the old woman, who might have fallen ill and have been out to the apothecary's. Jean Valjean listened.

The step was heavy, and sounded like that of a man; but the old woman wore stout shoes, and there is nothing which so strongly resembles the step of a man as that of an old woman. Nevertheless, Jean Valjean blew out his candle.

He had sent Cosette to bed, saying to her in a low voice, "Get into bed very softly"; and as he kissed her brow, the steps paused.

Jean Valjean remained silent, motionless, with his back toward the door, seated on the chair from which he had not stirred, and holding his breath in the dark.

After the expiration of a rather long interval, he turned round, as he heard nothing more, and, as he raised his eyes toward the door of his chamber, he saw a light through the keyhole. This light formed a sort of sinister star in the blackness of the door and the wall. There was evidently someone there, who was holding a candle in his hand and listening.

Several minutes elapsed thus, and the light retreated. But he heard no sound of footsteps, which seemed to indicate that the person who had been listening at the door had removed his shoes.

Jean Valjean threw himself, all dressed as he was, on his bed, and could not close his eyes all night.

At daybreak, just as he was falling into a doze through fatigue, he was awakened by the creaking of a door which opened on some attic at the end of the corridor, then he heard the same masculine footstep which had ascended the stairs on the preceding evening. The step was approaching. He sprang off the bed and applied his eye to the keyhole, which was tolerably large, hoping to see the person who had made his way by night into the house and had listened at his door, as he passed. It was a man, in fact, who passed, this time without pausing, in front of Jean Valjean's chamber. The corridor was too dark to allow of the person's face being distinguished; but when the man reached the staircase, a ray of light from without made it stand out like a silhouette, and Jean Valjean had a complete view of his back. The man was of lofty stature, clad in a long frock coat, with a cudgel under his arm. The formidable neck and shoulders belonged to Javert.

Jean Valjean might have attempted to catch another glimpse of him through his window opening on the boulevard, but he would have been obliged to open the window: he dared not.

It was evident that this man had entered with a key, and like himself. Who had given him that key? What was the meaning of this?

When the old woman came to do the work, at seven o'clock in the morning, Jean Valjean cast a penetrating glance on her, but he did not question her. The good woman appeared as usual.

As she swept up she remarked to him:

"Possibly Monsieur may have heard someone come in last night?"

At that age, and on that boulevard, eight o'clock in the evening was the dead of the night.

"That is true, by the way," he replied, in the most natural tone possible. "Who was it?"

"It was a new lodger who has come into the house," said the old woman.

"And what is his name?"

"I don't know exactly; Dumont, or Daumont, or some name of that sort."

"And who is this Monsieur Dumont?"

The old woman gazed at him with her little polecat eyes, and answered:

"A gentleman of property, like yourself."

Perhaps she had no ulterior meaning. Jean Valjean thought he perceived one.

When the old woman had taken her departure, he did up a hundred francs which he had in a cupboard, into a roll, and put it in his pocket. In spite of all the precautions which he took in this operation so that he might not be heard rattling silver, a hundred-sou piece escaped from his hands and rolled noisily on the floor.

When darkness came on, he descended and carefully scrutinized both sides of the boulevard. He saw no one. The boulevard appeared to be absolutely deserted. It is true that a person can conceal himself behind trees.

He went upstairs again.

"Come," he said to Cosette.

He took her by the hand, and they both went out.

BOOK FIFTH

FOR A BLACK HUNT, A MUTE PACK

Chapter I

THE ZIGZAGS OF STRATEGY

AN OBSERVATION HERE BECOMES NECESSARY, IN VIEW OF THE PAGES WHICH THE READER IS ABOUT to peruse, and of others which will be met with further on.

The author of this book, who regrets the necessity of mentioning himself, has been absent from Paris for many years. Paris has been transformed since he quitted it. A new city has arisen, which is, after a fashion, unknown to him. There is no need for him to say that he loves Paris: Paris is his mind's natal city. In consequence of demolitions and reconstructions, the Paris of his youth, that Paris which he bore away religiously in his memory, is now a Paris of days gone by. He must be permitted to speak of that Paris as though it still existed. It is possible that when the author conducts his readers to a spot and says, "In such a street there stands such and such a house," neither street nor house will any longer exist in that locality. Readers may verify the facts, if they care to take the trouble. For his own part, he is unacquainted with the new Paris, and he writes with the old Paris before his eyes in an illusion which is precious to him. It is a delight to him to dream that there still lingers behind him something of that which he beheld when he was in his own country, and that all has not vanished. So long as you go and come in your native land, you imagine that those streets are a matter of indifference to you; that those windows, those roofs, and those doors are nothing to you; that those walls are strangers to you; that those trees are merely the first encountered haphazard; that those houses, which you do not enter, are useless to you; that the pavements which you tread are merely stones. Later on, when you are no longer there, you perceive that the streets are dear to you; that you miss those roofs, those doors; and that those walls are necessary to you, those trees are well beloved by you; that you entered those houses which you never entered, every day, and that you have left a part of your heart, of your blood, of your soul, in those pavements. All those places which you no longer behold, which you may never behold again, perchance, and whose memory you have cherished, take on a melancholy charm, recur to your mind with the melancholy of an apparition, make the holy land visible to you, and are, so to speak, the very form of France, and you love them; and you call them up as they are, as they were, and you persist in this, and you will submit to no change: for you are attached to the figure of your fatherland as to the face of your mother.

May we, then, be permitted to speak of the past in the present? That said, we beg the reader to take note of it, and we continue.

Jean Valjean instantly quitted the boulevard and plunged into the streets, taking the most intricate lines which he could devise, returning on his track at times, to make sure that he was not being followed.

This maneuver is peculiar to the hunted stag. On soil where an imprint of the track may be left, this maneuver possesses, among other advantages, that of deceiving the huntsmen and the dogs, by throwing them on the wrong scent. In venery this is called *false reimbushment*.

The moon was full that night. Jean Valjean was not sorry for this. The moon, still very close to the horizon, cast great masses of light and shadow in the streets. Jean Valjean could glide along close to the houses on the dark side, and yet keep watch of the light side. He did not, perhaps, take sufficiently into consideration the fact that the dark side escaped him. Still, in the deserted lanes which lie near the Rue Poliveau, he thought he felt certain that no one was following him.

Cosette walked on without asking any questions. The sufferings of the first six years of her life had instilled something passive into her nature. Moreover—and this is a remark to which we shall frequently have occasion to recur—she had grown used, without being herself aware of it, to the peculiarities of this good man and to the freaks of destiny. And then she was with him, and she felt safe.

Jean Valjean knew no more where he was going than did Cosette. He trusted in God, as she trusted in him. It seemed as though he also were clinging to the hand of someone greater than himself; he thought he felt a being leading him, though invisible. However, he had no settled idea, no plan, no project. He was not even absolutely sure that it was Javert, and then it might have been Javert, without Javert knowing that he was Jean Valjean. Was not he disguised? Was not he believed to be dead? Still, queer things had been going on for several days. He wanted no more of them. He was determined not to return to the Gorbeau house. Like the wild animal chased from its lair, he was seeking a hole in which he might hide until he could find one where he might dwell.

Jean Valjean described many and varied labyrinths in the Mouffetard quarter, which was already asleep, as though the discipline of the Middle Ages and the yoke of the curfew still existed; he combined in various manners, with cunning strategy, the Rue Censier and the Rue Copeau, the Rue du Battoir-Saint-Victor and the Rue du Puits l'Ermite. There are lodging-houses in this locality, but he did not even enter one, finding nothing which suited him. He had no doubt that if anyone had chanced to be upon his track, they would have lost it.

As eleven o'clock struck from Saint-Étienne-du-Mont, he was traversing the Rue de Pontoise, in front of the office of the commissary of police, situated at No. 14. A few moments later, the instinct of which we have spoken above made him turn round. At that moment he saw distinctly, thanks to the commissary's lantern, which betrayed them, three men who were following him closely, pass, one after the other, under that lantern, on the dark side of the street. One of the three entered the alley leading to the commissary's house. The one who marched at their head struck him as decidedly suspicious.

"Come, child," he said to Cosette; and he made haste to quit the Rue Pontoise.

He took a circuit, turned into the Passage des Patriarches, which was closed on account of the hour, strode along the Rue de l'Épée-de-Bois and the Rue de l'Arbalète, and plunged into the Rue des Postes.

At that time there was a square formed by the intersection of streets, where the College Rollin stands to-day, and where the Rue Neuve-Sainte-Geneviève turns off.

It is understood, of course, that the Rue Neuve-Sainte-Geneviève is an old street, and that a posting-chaise does not pass through the Rue des Postes once in ten years. In the thirteenth century this Rue des Postes was inhabited by potters, and its real name is Rue des Pots.

The moon cast a livid light into this open space. Jean Valjean went into ambush in a doorway, calculating that if the men were still following him, he could not fail to get a good look at them, as they traversed this illuminated space.

In point of fact, three minutes had not elapsed when the men made their appearance. There were four of them now. All were tall, dressed in long, brown coats, with round hats, and huge cudgels in their hands. Their great stature and their vast fists rendered them no less alarming than did their sinister stride through the darkness. One would have pronounced them four specters disguised as bourgeois.

They halted in the middle of the space and formed a group, like men in consultation. They had an air of indecision. The one who appeared to be their leader turned round and pointed hastily with his right hand in the direction which Jean Valjean had taken; another seemed to indicate the contrary direction with considerable obstinacy. At the moment when the first man wheeled round, the moon fell full in his face. Jean Valjean recognized Javert perfectly.

Chapter II

IT IS LUCKY THAT THE PONT D'AUSTERLITZ BEARS CARRIAGES

UNCERTAINTY WAS AT AN END FOR JEAN VALJEAN: FORTUNATELY IT STILL LASTED FOR THE MEN. He took advantage of their hesitation. It was time lost for them, but gained for him. He slipped from under the gate where he had concealed himself, and went down the Rue des Postes, toward the region of the Jardin des Plantes. Cosette was beginning to be tired. He took her in his arms and carried her. There were no passers-by, and the street-lanterns had not been lighted on account of there being a moon.

He redoubled his pace.

In a few strides he had reached the Goblet potteries, on the front of which the moonlight rendered distinctly legible the ancient inscription:

> *De Goblet fils c'est ici la fabrique;*
> *Venez choisir des cruches et des broos,*
> *Des pots à fleurs, des tuyaux, de la brique.*
> *À tout venant le Cœur vend des Carreaux.*[1]

He left behind him the Rue de la Clef, then the Fountain Saint-Victor, skirted the Jardin des Plantes by the lower streets, and reached the quay. There he turned round. The quay was deserted. The streets were deserted. There was no one behind him. He drew a long breath.

He gained the Pont d'Austerlitz.

---

1. This is the factory of Goblet Junior:
   Come choose your jugs and crocks,
   Flower-pots, pipes, bricks.
   The Heart sells Diamonds to every comer.

Tolls were still collected there at that epoch.

He presented himself at the toll office and handed over a sou.

"It is two sous," said the old soldier in charge of the bridge. "You are carrying a child who can walk. Pay for two."

He paid, vexed that his passage should have aroused remark. Every flight should be an imperceptible slipping away.

A heavy cart was crossing the Seine at the same time as himself, and on its way, like him, to the right bank. This was of use to him. He could traverse the bridge in the shadow of the cart.

Toward the middle of the bridge, Cosette, whose feet were benumbed, wanted to walk. He set her on the ground and took her hand again.

The bridge once crossed, he perceived some timber-yards on his right. He directed his course thither. In order to reach them, it was necessary to risk himself in a tolerably large unsheltered and illuminated space. He did not hesitate. Those who were on his track had evidently lost the scent, and Jean Valjean believed himself to be out of danger. Hunted, yes; followed, no.

A little street, the Rue du Chemin-Vert-Saint-Antoine, opened out between two timber-yards enclosed in walls. This street was dark and narrow and seemed made expressly for him. Before entering it he cast a glance behind him.

From the point where he stood he could see the whole extent of the Pont d'Austerlitz.

Four shadows were just entering on the bridge.

These shadows had their backs turned to the Jardin des Plantes and were on their way to the right bank.

These four shadows were the four men.

Jean Valjean shuddered like the wild beast which is recaptured.

One hope remained to him; it was, that the men had not, perhaps, stepped on the bridge, and had not caught sight of him while he was crossing the large illuminated space, holding Cosette by the hand.

In that case, by plunging into the little street before him, he might escape, if he could reach the timber-yards, the marshes, the market-gardens, the uninhabited ground which was not built upon.

It seemed to him that he might commit himself to that silent little street. He entered it.

Chapter III

To Wit, the Plan of Paris in 1727

THREE HUNDRED PACES FURTHER ON, HE ARRIVED AT A POINT WHERE THE STREET FORKED. IT separated into two streets, which ran in a slanting line, one to the right, and the other to the left.

Jean Valjean had before him what resembled the two branches of a Y. Which should he choose? He did not hesitate, but took the one on the right.

Why?

Because that to the left ran toward a suburb, that is to say, toward inhabited regions, and the right branch toward the open country, that is to say, toward deserted regions.

However, they no longer walked very fast. Cosette's pace retarded Jean Valjean's.

He took her up and carried her again. Cosette laid her head on the shoulder of the good man and said not a word.

He turned round from time to time and looked behind him. He took care to keep always on the dark side of the street. The street was straight in his rear. The first two or three times that he turned round he saw nothing; the silence was profound, and he continued his march somewhat reassured. All at once, on turning round, he thought he perceived in the portion of the street which he had just passed through, far off in the obscurity, something which was moving.

He rushed forward precipitately rather than walked, hoping to find some side-street, to make his escape through it, and thus to break his scent once more.

He arrived at a wall.

This wall, however, did not absolutely prevent further progress; it was a wall which bordered a transverse street, in which the one he had taken ended.

Here again, he was obliged to come to a decision; should he go to the right or to the left.

He glanced to the right. The fragmentary lane was prolonged between buildings which were either sheds or barns, then ended at a blind-alley. The extremity of the cul-de-sac was distinctly visible—a lofty white wall.

He glanced to the left. On that side the lane was open, and about two hundred paces further on, ran into a street of which it was the affluent. On that side lay safety.

At the moment when Jean Valjean was meditating a turn to the left, in an effort to reach the street which he saw at the end of the lane, he perceived a sort of motionless, black statue at the corner of the lane and the street toward which he was on the point of directing his steps.

It was someone, a man, who had evidently just been posted there, and who was barring the passage and waiting.

Jean Valjean recoiled.

The point of Paris where Jean Valjean found himself, situated between the Faubourg Saint-Antoine and la Râpée, is one of those which recent improvements have transformed from top to bottom—resulting in disfigurement according to some, and in a transfiguration according to others. The market-gardens, the timber-yards, and the old buildings have been effaced. To-day, there are brand-new, wide streets, arenas, circuses, hippodromes, railway stations, and a prison, Mazas, there; progress, as the reader sees, with its antidote.

Half a century ago, in that ordinary, popular tongue, which is all compounded of traditions, which persists in calling the Institut *les Quatre-Nations*, and the Opera-Comique *Feydeau*, the precise spot whither Jean Valjean had arrived was called *le Petit Picpus*. The Porte Saint-Jacques, the Porte Paris, the Barrière des Sergents, the Porcherons, la Galiote, les Célestins, les Capucins, le Mail, la Bourbe, l'Arbre de Cracovie, la Petite-Pologne—these are the names of old Paris which survive amid the new. The memory of the populace hovers over these relics of the past.

Le Petit-Picpus, which, moreover, hardly ever had any existence, and never was more than the outline of a quarter, had nearly the monkish aspect of a Spanish town. The roads were not much paved; the streets were not much built up. With the exception of the two or three streets, of which we shall presently speak, all was wall and solitude there. Not a shop, not a vehicle, hardly a candle lighted here and there in the windows; all lights extinguished after ten o'clock. Gardens, convents, timber-yards, marshes; occasional lowly dwellings and great walls as high as the houses.

Such was this quarter in the last century. The Revolution snubbed it soundly. The republican government demolished and cut through it. Rubbish shoots were established there. Thirty years ago, this quarter was disappearing under the erasing process of new buildings. To-day, it has been utterly blotted out. The Petit-Picpus, of which no existing plan has preserved a trace, is indicated with sufficient clearness in the plan of 1727, published at Paris by Denis Thierry, Rue Saint-Jacques, opposite the Rue du Plâtre; and at Lyons, by Jean Girin, Rue Mercière, at the sign of Prudence. Petit-Picpus had, as we have just mentioned, a Y of streets, formed by the Rue du Chemin-Vert-Saint-Antoine, which spread out in two branches, taking on the left the name of Little Picpus Street, and on the right the name of the Rue Polonceau. The two limbs of the Y were connected at the apex as by a bar; this bar was called Rue Droit-Mur. The Rue Polonceau ended there; Rue Petit-Picpus passed on, and ascended toward the Lenoir market. A person coming from the Seine reached the extremity of the Rue Polonceau, and had on his right the Rue Droit-Mur, turning abruptly at a right angle, in front of him the wall of that street, and on his right a truncated prolongation of the Rue Droit-Mur, which had no issue and was called the Cul-de-Sac Genrot.

It was here that Jean Valjean stood.

As we have just said, on catching sight of that black silhouette standing on guard at the angle of the Rue Droit-Mur and the Rue Petit-Picpus, he recoiled. There could be no doubt of it. That phantom was lying in wait for him.

What was he to do?

The time for retreating was passed. That which he had perceived in movement an instant before, in the distant darkness, was Javert and his squad without a doubt. Javert was probably already at the commencement of the street at whose end Jean Valjean stood. Javert, to all appearances, was acquainted with this little labyrinth, and had taken his precautions by sending one of his men to guard the exit. These surmises, which so closely resembled proofs, whirled suddenly, like a handful of dust caught up by an unexpected gust of wind, through Jean Valjean's mournful brain. He examined the Cul-de-Sac Genrot; there he was cut off. He examined the Rue Petit-Picpus; there stood a sentinel. He saw that black form standing out in relief against the white pavement, illuminated by the moon; to advance was to fall into this man's hands; to retreat was to fling himself into Javert's arms. Jean Valjean felt himself caught, as in a net, which was slowly contracting; he gazed heavenward in despair.

Chapter IV

THE GROPINGS OF FLIGHT

IN ORDER TO UNDERSTAND WHAT FOLLOWS, IT IS REQUISITE TO FORM AN EXACT IDEA OF THE Droit-Mur lane, and, in particular, of the angle which one leaves on the left when one emerges from the Rue Polonceau into this lane. Droit-Mur lane was almost entirely bordered on the right, as far as the Rue Petit-Picpus, by houses of mean aspect; on the left by a solitary building of severe outlines, composed of numerous parts which grew gradually higher by a story or two as they approached the Rue Petit-Picpus side; so that this building, which was very lofty on the Rue Petit-Picpus side, was tolerably low on the side adjoining the Rue Polonceau. There, at the angle of which we have spoken, it descended to such a degree that it consisted of merely a wall. This wall did not abut directly on the street; it formed a deeply retreating niche, concealed by its two corners from two observers who might have been, one in the Rue Polonceau, the other in the Rue Droit-Mur.

Beginning with these angles of the niche, the wall extended along the Rue Polonceau as far as a house which bore the number 49, and along the Rue Droit-Mur, where the fragment was much shorter, as far as the gloomy building which we have mentioned and whose gable it intersected, thus forming another retreating angle in the street. This gable was somber of aspect; only one window was visible, or, to speak more correctly, two shutters covered with a sheet of zinc and kept constantly closed.

The state of the places of which we are here giving a description is rigorously exact, and will certainly awaken a very precise memory in the mind of old inhabitants of the quarter.

The niche was entirely filled by a thing which resembled a colossal and wretched door; it was a vast, formless assemblage of perpendicular planks, the upper ones being broader than the lower, bound together by long transverse strips of iron. At one side there was a carriage gate of the ordinary dimensions, and which had evidently not been cut more than fifty years previously.

A linden-tree showed its crest above the niche, and the wall was covered with ivy on the side of the Rue Polonceau.

In the imminent peril in which Jean Valjean found himself, this somber building had about it a solitary and uninhabited look which tempted him. He ran his eyes rapidly over it; he said to himself, that if he could contrive to get inside it, he might save himself. First he conceived an idea, then a hope.

In the central portion of the front of this building, on the Rue Droit-Mur side, there were at all the windows of the different stories ancient cistern pipes of lead. The various branches of the pipes which led from one central pipe to all these little basins sketched out a sort of tree on the front. These ramifications of pipes with their hundred elbows imitated those old leafless vine-stocks which writhe over the fronts of old farm-houses.

This odd espalier, with its branches of lead and iron, was the first thing that struck Jean Valjean. He seated Cosette with her back against a stone post, with an injunction to be silent, and ran to the spot where the conduit touched the pavement. Perhaps there was some way of climbing up by it and entering the house. But the pipe was dilapidated and past service, and hardly hung to its fastenings. Moreover, all the windows of this silent dwelling were grated with heavy iron bars, even the attic windows in the roof. And then, the moon fell full upon that façade, and the man who was watching at the corner of the street would have seen Jean Valjean in the act of climbing. And finally, what was to be done with Cosette? How was she to be drawn up to the top of a three-story house?

He gave up all idea of climbing by means of the drain-pipe, and crawled along the wall to get back into the Rue Polonceau.

When he reached the slant of the wall where he had left Cosette, he noticed that no one could see him there. As we have just explained, he was concealed from all eyes, no matter from which direction they were approaching; besides this, he was in the shadow. Finally, there were two doors; perhaps they might be forced. The wall above which he saw the linden-tree and the ivy evidently abutted on a garden where he could, at least, hide himself, although there were as yet no leaves on the trees, and spend the remainder of the night.

Time was passing; he must act quickly.

He felt over the carriage door, and immediately recognized the fact that it was impracticable outside and in.

He approached the other door with more hope; it was frightfully decrepit; its very immensity rendered it less solid; the planks were rotten; the iron bands—there were only three of them—were rusted. It seemed as though it might be possible to pierce this wormeaten barrier.

On examining it he found that the door was not a door; it had neither hinges, cross-bars, lock, nor fissure in the middle; the iron bands traversed it from side to side without any break. Through the crevices in the planks he caught a view of unhewn slabs and blocks of stone roughly cemented together, which passers-by might still have seen there ten years ago. He was forced to acknowledge with consternation that this apparent door was simply the wooden decoration of a building against which it was placed. It was easy to tear off a plank; but then, one found one's self face to face with a wall.

Chapter V

WHICH WOULD BE IMPOSSIBLE WITH GAS LANTERNS

AT THAT MOMENT A HEAVY AND MEASURED SOUND BEGAN TO BE AUDIBLE AT SOME DISTANCE. Jean Valjean risked a glance round the corner of the street. Seven or eight soldiers, drawn up in a platoon, had just debouched into the Rue Polonceau. He saw the gleam of their bayonets. They were advancing toward him; these soldiers, at whose head he distinguished Javert's tall figure, advanced slowly and cautiously. They halted frequently; it was plain that they were searching all the nooks of the walls and all the embrasures of the doors and alleys.

This was some patrol that Javert had encountered—there could be no mistake as to this surmise—and whose aid he had demanded.

Javert's two acolytes were marching in their ranks.

At the rate at which they were marching, and in consideration of the halts which they were making, it would take them about a quarter of an hour to reach the spot where Jean Valjean stood. It was a frightful moment. A few minutes only separated Jean Valjean from that terrible precipice which yawned before him for the third time. And the galleys now meant not only the galleys, but Cosette lost to him forever; that is to say, a life resembling the interior of a tomb.

There was but one thing which was possible.

Jean Valjean had this peculiarity, that he carried, as one might say, two beggar's pouches: in one he kept his saintly thoughts; in the other the redoubtable talents of a convict. He rummaged in the one or the other, according to circumstances.

Among his other resources, thanks to his numerous escapes from the prison at Toulon, he was, as it will be remembered, a past master in the incredible art of crawling up without ladder or climbing-irons, by sheer muscular force, by leaning on the nape of his neck, his shoulders, his hips, and his knees, by helping himself on the rare projections of the stone, in the right angle of a wall, as high as the sixth story, if need be; an art which has rendered so celebrated and so alarming that corner of the wall of the Conciergerie of Paris by which Battemolle, condemned to death, made his escape twenty years ago.

Jean Valjean measured with his eyes the wall above which he spied the linden; it was about eighteen feet in height. The angle which it formed with the gable of the large building was filled, at its lower extremity, by a mass of masonry of a triangular shape, probably intended to preserve that too convenient corner from the rubbish of those dirty creatures called the passers-by. This practice of filling up corners of the wall is much in use in Paris.

This mass was about five feet in height; the space above the summit of this mass which it was necessary to climb was not more than fourteen feet.

The wall was surmounted by a flat stone without a coping.

Cosette was the difficulty, for she did not know how to climb a wall. Should he abandon her? Jean Valjean did not once think of that. It was impossible to carry her. A man's whole strength is required to successfully carry out these singular ascents. The least burden would disturb his center of gravity and pull him downwards.

A rope would have been required; Jean Valjean had none. Where was he to get a rope at midnight, in the Rue Polonceau? Certainly, if Jean Valjean had had a kingdom, he would have given it for a rope at that moment.

All extreme situations have their lightning flashes which sometimes dazzle, sometimes illuminate us.

Jean Valjean's despairing glance fell on the street-lantern-post of the blind-alley Genrot.

At that epoch there were no gas-jets in the streets of Paris. At nightfall lanterns placed at regular distances were lighted; they were ascended and descended by means of a rope, which traversed the street from side to side, and was adjusted in a groove of the post. The pulley over which this rope ran was fastened underneath the lantern in a little iron box, the key to which was kept by the lamp-lighter, and the rope itself was protected by a metal case.

Jean Valjean, with the energy of a supreme struggle, crossed the street at one bound, entered the blind-alley, broke the latch of the little box with the point of his knife, and an instant later he was beside Cosette once more. He had a rope. These gloomy inventors of expedients work rapidly when they are fighting against fatality.

We have already explained that the lanterns had not been lighted that night. The lantern in the Cul-de-Sac Genrot was thus naturally extinct, like the rest; and one could pass directly under it without even noticing that it was no longer in its place.

Nevertheless, the hour, the place, the darkness, Jean Valjean's absorption, his singular gestures, his goings and comings, all had begun to render Cosette uneasy. Any other child than she would have given vent to loud shrieks long before. She contented herself with plucking Jean Valjean by the skirt of his coat. They could hear the sound of the patrol's approach ever more and more distinctly.

"Father," said she, in a very low voice, "I am afraid. Who is coming yonder?"

"Hush!" replied the unhappy man; "it is Madame Thénardier."

Cosette shuddered. He added:

"Say nothing. Don't interfere with me. If you cry out, if you weep, the Thénardier is lying in wait for you. She is coming to take you back."

Then, without haste, but without making a useless movement, with firm and curt precision, the more remarkable at a moment when the patrol and Javert might come upon him at any moment, he undid his cravat, passed it round Cosette's body under the armpits, taking care that it should not hurt the child, fastened this cravat to one end of the rope, by means of that knot which seafaring men call a "swallow knot," took the other end of the rope in his teeth, pulled off his shoes and stockings, which he threw over the wall, stepped upon the mass of masonry, and began to raise himself in the angle of the wall and the gable with as much solidity and certainty as though he had the rounds of a ladder under his feet and elbows. Half a minute had not elapsed when he was resting on his knees on the wall.

Cosette gazed at him in stupid amazement, without uttering a word. Jean Valjean's injunction, and the name of Madame Thénardier, had chilled her blood.

All at once she heard Jean Valjean's voice crying to her, though in a very low tone:

"Put your back against the wall."

She obeyed.

"Don't say a word, and don't be alarmed," went on Jean Valjean.

And she felt herself lifted from the ground.

Before she had time to recover herself, she was on the top of the wall.

Jean Valjean grasped her, put her on his back, took her two tiny hands in his large left hand, lay down flat on his stomach and crawled along on top of the wall as far as the cant. As he had guessed, there stood a building whose roof started from the top of the wooden barricade and descended to within a very short distance of the ground, with a gentle slope which grazed the linden-tree. A lucky circumstance, for the wall was much higher on this side than on the street side. Jean Valjean could only see the ground at a great depth below him.

He had just reached the slope of the roof, and had not yet left the crest of the wall, when a violent uproar announced the arrival of the patrol. The thundering voice of Javert was audible:

"Search the blind-alley! The Rue Droit-Mur is guarded! so is the Rue Petit-Picpus. I'll answer for it that he is in the blind-alley."

The soldiers rushed into the Genrot alley.

Jean Valjean allowed himself to slide down the roof, still holding fast to Cosette, reached the linden-tree, and leaped to the ground. Whether from terror or courage, Cosette had not breathed a sound, though her hands were a little abraded.

Chapter VI

THE BEGINNING OF AN ENIGMA

JEAN VALJEAN FOUND HIMSELF IN A SORT OF GARDEN WHICH WAS VERY VAST AND OF SINGULAR ASpect; one of those melancholy gardens which seem made to be looked at in winter and at night. This garden was oblong in shape, with an alley of large poplars at the further end, tolerably tall forest trees in the corners, and an unshaded space in the center, where could be seen a very large, solitary tree, then several fruit-trees, gnarled and bristling like bushes, beds of vegetables, a melon patch, whose glass frames sparkled in the moonlight, and an old well. Here and there stood stone benches which seemed black with moss. The alleys were bordered with gloomy and very erect little shrubs. The grass had half taken possession of them, and a green mold covered the rest.

Jean Valjean had beside him the building whose roof had served him as a means of descent, a pile of fagots, and, behind the fagots, directly against the wall, a stone statue, whose mutilated face was no longer anything more than a shapeless mask which loomed vaguely through the gloom.

The building was a sort of ruin, where dismantled chambers were distinguishable, one of which, much encumbered, seemed to serve as a shed.

The large building of the Rue Droit-Mur, which had a wing on the Rue Petit-Picpus, turned two façades, at right angles, toward this garden. These interior façades were even more tragic than the exterior. All the windows were grated. Not a gleam of light was visible at any one of them. The upper story had scuttles like prisons. One of those façades cast its shadow on the other, which fell over the garden like an immense black pall.

No other house was visible. The bottom of the garden was lost in mist and darkness. Nevertheless, walls could be confusedly made out, which intersected as though there were more cultivated land beyond, and the low roofs of the Rue Polonceau.

Nothing more wild and solitary than this garden could be imagined. There was no one in it, which was quite natural in view of the hour; but it did not seem as though this spot were made for anyone to walk in, even in broad daylight.

Jean Valjean's first care had been to get hold of his shoes and put them on again, then to step under the shed with Cosette. A man who is fleeing never thinks himself sufficiently hidden. The child, whose thoughts were still on the Thénardier, shared his instinct for withdrawing from sight as much as possible.

Cosette trembled and pressed close to him. They heard the tumultuous noise of the patrol searching the blind-alley and the streets; the blows of their gun-stocks against the stones; Javert's appeals to the police spies whom he had posted, and his imprecations mingled with words which could not be distinguished.

At the expiration of a quarter of an hour it seemed as though that species of stormy roar were becoming more distant. Jean Valjean held his breath.

He had laid his hand lightly on Cosette's mouth.

However, the solitude in which he stood was so strangely calm, that this frightful uproar, close and furious as it was, did not disturb him by so much as the shadow of a misgiving. It seemed as though those walls had been built of the deaf stones of which the Scriptures speak.

All at once, in the midst of this profound calm, a fresh sound arose; a sound as celestial, divine, ineffable, ravishing, as the other had been horrible. It was a hymn which issued from the gloom, a dazzling burst of prayer and harmony in the obscure and alarming silence of the night; women's voices, but voices composed at one and the same time of the pure accents of virgins and the innocent accents of children—voices which are not of the earth, and which resemble those that the newborn infant still hears, and which the dying man hears already. This song proceeded from the gloomy edifice which towered above the garden. At the moment when the hubbub of demons retreated, one would have said that a choir of angels was approaching through the gloom.

Cosette and Jean Valjean fell on their knees.

They knew not what it was, they knew not where they were; but both of them, the man and the child, the penitent and the innocent, felt that they must kneel.

These voices had this strange characteristic, that they did not prevent the building from seeming to be deserted. It was a supernatural chant in an uninhabited house.

While these voices were singing, Jean Valjean thought of nothing. He no longer beheld the night; he beheld a blue sky. It seemed to him that he felt those wings which we all have within us, unfolding.

The song died away. It may have lasted a long time. Jean Valjean could not have told. Hours of ecstasy are never more than a moment.

All fell silent again. There was no longer anything in the street; there was nothing in the garden. That which had menaced, that which had reassured him—all had vanished. The breeze swayed a few dry weeds on the crest of the wall, and they gave out a faint, sweet, melancholy sound.

Chapter VII

CONTINUATION OF THE ENIGMA

THE NIGHT WIND HAD RISEN, WHICH INDICATED THAT IT MUST BE BETWEEN ONE AND TWO o'clock in the morning. Poor Cosette said nothing. As she had seated herself beside him and leaned her head against him, Jean Valjean had fancied that she was asleep. He bent down and looked at her. Cosette's eyes were wide open, and her thoughtful air pained Jean Valjean.

She was still trembling.

"Are you sleepy?" said Jean Valjean.

"I am very cold," she replied.

A moment later she resumed:

"Is she still there?"

"Who?" said Jean Valjean.

"Madame Thénardier."

Jean Valjean had already forgotten the means which he had employed to make Cosette keep silent.

"Ah!" said he, "she is gone. You need fear nothing further."

The child sighed as though a load had been lifted from her breast.

The ground was damp, the shed open on all sides, the breeze grew more keen every instant. The good man took off his coat and wrapped it round Cosette.

"Are you less cold now?" said he.

"Oh, yes, father."

"Well, wait for me a moment. I will soon be back."

He quitted the ruin and crept along the large building, seeking a better shelter. He came across doors, but they were closed. There were bars at all the windows of the ground floor.

Just after he had turned the inner angle of the edifice, he observed that he was coming to some arched windows, where he perceived a light. He stood on tiptoe and peeped through one of these windows. They all opened on a tolerably vast hall, paved with large flagstones, cut up by arcades and pillars, where only a tiny light and great shadows were visible. The light came from a taper which was burning in one corner. The apartment was deserted, and nothing was stirring in it. Nevertheless, by dint of gazing intently he thought he perceived on the ground something which appeared to be covered with a winding-sheet, and which resembled a human form. This form was lying face downward, flat on the pavement, with the arms extended in the form of a cross, in the immobility of death. One would have said, judging from a sort of serpent which undulated over the floor, that this sinister form had a rope round its neck.

The whole chamber was bathed in that mist of places which are sparely illuminated, which adds to horror.

Jean Valjean often said afterwards, that, although many funereal specters had crossed his path in life, he had never beheld anything more blood-curdling and terrible than that enigmatical form accomplishing some inexplicable mystery in that gloomy place, and beheld thus at night. It was alarming to suppose that that thing was perhaps dead; and still more alarming to think that it was perhaps alive.

He had the courage to plaster his face to the glass, and to watch whether the thing would move. In spite of his remaining thus what seemed to him a very long time, the outstretched form made no movement. All at once he felt himself overpowered by an inexpressible terror, and he fled. He began to run toward the shed, not daring to look behind him. It seemed to him, that if he turned his head, he should see that form following him with great strides and waving its arms.

He reached the ruin all out of breath. His knees were giving way beneath him; the perspiration was pouring from him.

Where was he? Who could ever have imagined anything like that sort of sepulcher in the midst of Paris! What was this strange house? An edifice full of nocturnal mystery, calling to souls through the darkness with the voice of angels, and when they came, offering them abruptly that terrible vision; promising to open the radiant portals of heaven, and then opening the horrible gates of the tomb! And it actually was an edifice, a house, which bore a number on the street! It was not a dream! He had to touch the stones to convince himself that such was the fact.

Cold, anxiety, uneasiness, the emotions of the night, had given him a genuine fever, and all these ideas were clashing together in his brain.

He stepped up to Cosette. She was asleep.

Chapter VIII

THE ENIGMA BECOMES DOUBLY MYSTERIOUS

THE CHILD HAD LAID HER HEAD ON A STONE AND FALLEN ASLEEP.

He sat down beside her and began to think. Little by little, as he gazed at her, he grew calm and regained possession of his freedom of mind.

He clearly perceived this truth, the foundation of his life henceforth, that so long as she was there, so long as he had her near him, he should need nothing except for her, he should fear nothing except for her. He was not even conscious that he was very cold, since he had taken off his coat to cover her.

Nevertheless, athwart this reverie into which he had fallen, he had heard for some time a peculiar noise. It was like the tinkling of a bell. This sound proceeded from the garden. It could be heard distinctly though faintly. It resembled the faint, vague music produced by the bells of cattle at night in the pastures.

This noise made Jean Valjean turn round.

He looked and saw that there was someone in the garden.

A being resembling a man was walking amid the bell-glasses of the melon beds, rising, stooping, halting, with regular movements, as though he were dragging or spreading out something on the ground. This person appeared to limp.

Jean Valjean shuddered with the continual tremor of the unhappy. For them everything is hostile and suspicious. They distrust the day because it enables people to see them, and the night because it aids in surprising them. A little while before he had shivered because the garden was deserted, and now he shivered because there was someone there.

He fell back from chimerical terrors to real terrors. He said to himself that Javert and the spies had, perhaps, not taken their departure; that they had, no doubt, left people on the watch in the street; that if this man should discover him in the garden, he would cry out for help against thieves and deliver him up. He took the sleeping Cosette gently in his arms and carried her behind a heap of old furniture, which was out of use, in the most remote corner of the shed. Cosette did not stir.

From that point he scrutinized the appearance of the being in the melon patch. The strange thing about it was, that the sound of the bell followed each of this man's movements. When the man approached, the sound approached; when the man retreated, the sound retreated; if he made any hasty gesture, a tremulo accompanied the gesture; when he halted, the sound ceased. It appeared evident that the bell was attached to that man; but what could that signify? Who was this man who had a bell suspended about him like a ram or an ox?

As he put these questions to himself, he touched Cosette's hands. They were icy cold.

"Ah! good God!" he cried.

He spoke to her in a low voice:

"Cosette!"

She did not open her eyes.

He shook her vigorously.

She did not wake.

"Is she dead?" he said to himself, and sprang to his feet, quivering from head to foot.

The most frightful thoughts rushed pell-mell through his mind. There are moments when hideous surmises assail us like a cohort of furies, and violently force the partitions of our brains.

When those we love are in question, our prudence invents every sort of madness. He remembered that sleep in the open air on a cold night may be fatal.

Cosette was pale, and had fallen at full length on the ground at his feet, without a movement.

He listened to her breathing: she still breathed, but with a respiration which seemed to him weak and on the point of extinction.

How was he to warm her back to life? How was he to rouse her? All that was not connected with this vanished from his thoughts. He rushed wildly from the ruin.

It was absolutely necessary that Cosette should be in bed and beside a fire in less than a quarter of an hour.

Chapter IX

THE MAN WITH THE BELL

HE WALKED STRAIGHT UP TO THE MAN WHOM HE SAW IN THE GARDEN. HE HAD TAKEN IN HIS hand the roll of silver which was in the pocket of his waistcoat.

The man's head was bent down, and he did not see him approaching. In a few strides Jean Valjean stood beside him.

Jean Valjean accosted him with the cry:

"One hundred francs!"

The man gave a start and raised his eyes.

"You can earn a hundred francs," went on Jean Valjean, "if you will grant me shelter for this night."

The moon shone full upon Jean Valjean's terrified countenance.

"What! so it is you, Father Madeleine!" said the man.

That name, thus pronounced, at that obscure hour, in that unknown spot, by that strange man, made Jean Valjean start back.

He had expected anything but that. The person who thus addressed him was a bent and lame old man, dressed almost like a peasant, who wore on his left knee a leather knee-cap, whence hung a moderately large bell. His face, which was in the shadow, was not distinguishable.

However, the good man had removed his cap, and exclaimed, trembling all over:

"Ah, good God! How come you here, Father Madeleine? Where did you enter? Dieu-Jésus! Did you fall from heaven? There is no trouble about that: if ever you do fall, it will be from there. And what a state you are in! You have no cravat; you have no hat; you have no coat! Do you know, you would have frightened anyone who did not know you? No coat! Lord God! Are the saints going mad nowadays? But how did you get in here?"

His words tumbled over each other. The good man talked with a rustic volubility, in which there was nothing alarming. All this was uttered with a mixture of stupefaction and *naïve* kindliness.

"Who are you? and what house is this?" demanded Jean Valjean.

"Ah! pardieu, this is too much!" exclaimed the old man. "I am the person for whom you got the place here, and this house is the one where you had me placed. What! You don't recognize me?"

"No," said Jean Valjean; "and how happens it that you know me?"

"You saved my life," said the man.

He turned. A ray of moonlight outlined his profile, and Jean Valjean recognized old Fauchelevent.

"Ah!" said Jean Valjean, "so it is you? Yes, I recollect you."

"That is very lucky," said the old man, in a reproachful tone.

"And what are you doing here?" resumed Jean Valjean.

"Why, I am covering my melons, of course!"

In fact, at the moment when Jean Valjean accosted him, old Fauchelevent held in his hand the end of a straw mat which he was occupied in spreading over the melon bed. During the hour or thereabouts that he had been in the garden he had already spread out a number of them. It was this operation which had caused him to execute the peculiar movements observed from the shed by Jean Valjean.

He continued:

"I said to myself, 'The moon is bright: it is going to freeze. What if I were to put my melons into their great-coats?' And," he added, looking at Jean Valjean with a broad smile—"pardieu! you ought to have done the same! But how do you come here?"

Jean Valjean, finding himself known to this man, at least only under the name of Madeleine, thenceforth advanced only with caution. He multiplied his questions. Strange to say, their rôles seemed to be reversed. It was he, the intruder, who interrogated.

"And what is this bell which you wear on your knee?"

"This," replied Fauchelevent, "is so that I may be avoided."

"What! so that you may be avoided?"

Old Fauchelevent winked with an indescribable air.

"Ah, goodness! there are only women in this house—many young girls. It appears that I should be a dangerous person to meet. The bell gives them warning. When I come, they go."

"What house is this?"

"Come, you know well enough."

"But I do not."

"Not when you got me the place here as gardener?"

"Answer me as though I knew nothing."

"Well, then, this is the Petit-Picpus convent."

Memories recurred to Jean Valjean. Chance, that is to say, Providence, had cast him into precisely that convent in the Quartier Saint-Antoine where old Fauchelevent, crippled by the fall from his cart, had been admitted on his recommendation two years previously. He repeated, as though talking to himself:

"The Petit-Picpus convent."

"Exactly," returned old Fauchelevent. "But to come to the point, how the deuce did you manage to get in here, you, Father Madeleine? No matter if you are a saint; you are a man as well, and no man enters here."

"You certainly are here."

"There is no one but me."

"Still," said Jean Valjean, "I must stay here."

"Ah, good God!" cried Fauchelevent.

Jean Valjean drew near to the old man, and said to him in a grave voice:

"Father Fauchelevent, I saved your life."

"I was the first to recall it," returned Fauchelevent.

"Well, you can do to-day for me that which I did for you in the olden days."

Fauchelevent took in his aged, trembling, and wrinkled hands Jean Valjean's two robust hands, and stood for several minutes as though incapable of speaking. At length he exclaimed:

"Oh! that would be a blessing from the good God, if I could make you some little return for that! Save your life! Monsieur le Maire, dispose of the old man!"

A wonderful joy had transfigured this old man. His countenance seemed to emit a ray of light.

"What do you wish me to do?" he resumed.

"That I will explain to you. You have a chamber?"

"I have an isolated hovel yonder, behind the ruins of the old convent, in a corner which no one ever looks into. There are three rooms in it."

The hut was, in fact, so well hidden behind the ruins, and so cleverly arranged to prevent it being seen, that Jean Valjean had not perceived it.

"Good," said Jean Valjean. "Now I am going to ask two things of you."

"What are they, Mr. Mayor?"

"In the first place, you are not to tell anyone what you know about me. In the second, you are not to try to find out anything more."

"As you please. I know that you can do nothing that is not honest, that you have always been a man after the good God's heart. And then, moreover, you it was who placed me here. That concerns you. I am at your service."

"That is settled then. Now, come with me. We will go and get the child."

"Ah!" said Fauchelevent, "so there is a child?"

He added not a word further, and followed Jean Valjean as a dog follows his master.

Less than half an hour afterwards Cosette, who had grown rosy again before the flame of a good fire, was lying asleep in the old gardener's bed. Jean Valjean had put on his cravat and coat once more; his hat, which he had flung over the wall, had been found and picked up. While Jean Valjean was putting on his coat, Fauchelevent had removed the bell and knee-cap, which now hung on a nail beside a vintage basket that adorned the wall. The two men were warming themselves with their elbows resting on a table upon which Fauchelevent had placed a bit of cheese, black bread, a bottle of wine, and two glasses, and the old man was saying to Jean Valjean, as he laid his hand on the latter's knee: "Ah! Father Madeleine! You did not recognize me immediately; you save people's lives, and then you forget them! That is bad! But they remember you! You are an ingrate!"

Chapter X

WHICH EXPLAINS HOW JAVERT GOT ON THE SCENT

T HE EVENTS OF WHICH WE HAVE JUST BEHELD THE REVERSE SIDE, SO TO SPEAK, HAD COME ABOUT in the simplest possible manner.

When Jean Valjean, on the evening of the very day when Javert had arrested him beside Fantine's death-bed, had escaped from the town jail of M. sur M., the police had supposed that he had betaken himself to Paris. Paris is a maelstrom where everything is lost, and everything disappears in this belly of the world, as in the belly of the sea. No forest hides a man as does that crowd. Fugitives of every sort know this. They go to Paris as to an abyss; there are gulfs which save. The police know it also, and it is in Paris that they seek what they have lost elsewhere. There they sought the ex-mayor of M. sur M. Javert was summoned to Paris to throw light on their researches. Javert had, in fact, rendered powerful assistance in the recapture of Jean Valjean. Javert's zeal and intelligence on that occasion had been remarked by M. Chabouillet, secretary of the Prefecture under Comte Anglès. M. Chabouillet, who had, moreover, already been Javert's patron, had the inspector of M. sur M. attached to the police force of Paris. There Javert rendered himself useful in divers and, though the word may seem strange for such services, honorable manners.

He no longer thought of Jean Valjean—the wolf of to-day causes these dogs who are always on the chase to forget the wolf of yesterday—when, in December, 1823, he read a newspaper, he who never read newspapers; but Javert, a monarchical man, had a desire to know the particulars of the triumphal entry of the "Prince Generalissimo" into Bayonne. Just as he was finishing the article, which interested him, a name, the name of Jean Valjean, attracted his attention at the bottom of a page. The paper announced that the convict Jean Valjean was dead, and published the fact in such formal terms that Javert did not doubt it. He confined himself to the remark, "That's a good entry." Then he threw aside the paper, and thought no more about it.

Some time afterwards, it chanced that a police report was transmitted from the prefecture of the Seine-et-Oise to the prefecture of police in Paris, concerning the abduction of a child, which had taken place, under peculiar circumstances, as it was said, in the commune of Montfermeil. A little girl of seven or eight years of age, the report said, who had been intrusted by her mother to an inn-keeper of that neighborhood, had been stolen by a stranger; this child answered to the name of Cosette, and was the daughter of a girl named Fantine, who had died in the hospital, it was not known where or when.

This report came under Javert's eye and set him to thinking.

The name of Fantine was well known to him. He remembered that Jean Valjean had made him, Javert, burst into laughter, by asking him for a respite of three days, for the purpose of going to fetch that creature's child. He recalled the fact that Jean Valjean had been arrested in Paris at the very moment when he was stepping into the coach for Montfermeil. Some signs had made him suspect at the time that this was the second occasion of his entering that coach, and that he had already, on the previous day, made an excursion to the neighborhood of that village, for he had not been seen in the village itself. What had he been intending to do in that region of Montfermeil? It could not even be surmised. Javert understood it now. Fantine's daughter was there. Jean Valjean was going there in search of her. And now this child had been stolen by a stranger! Who could that stranger be? Could it be Jean Valjean? But Jean Valjean was dead. Javert, without saying anything to anybody, took the coach from the *Pewter Platter,* Cul-de-Sac de la Planchette, and made a trip to Montfermeil.

He expected to find a great deal of light on the subject there; he found a great deal of obscurity.

For the first few days the Thénardiers had chattered in their rage. The disappearance of the Lark had created a sensation in the village. He immediately obtained numerous versions of the story, which ended in the abduction of a child. Hence the police report. But their first vexation having passed off, Thénardier, with his wonderful instinct, had very quickly comprehended that it is never advisable to stir up the prosecutor of the Crown, and that his complaints with regard to the *abduction* of Cosette would have as their first result to fix upon himself, and upon many dark affairs which he had on hand, the glittering eye of justice. The last thing that owls desire is to have a candle brought to them. And in the first place, how explain the fifteen hundred francs which he had received? He turned squarely round, put a gag on his wife's mouth, and feigned astonishment when the *stolen child* was mentioned to him. He understood nothing about it; no doubt he had grumbled for a while at having that dear little creature "taken from him" so hastily; he should have liked to keep her two or three days longer, out of tenderness; but her "grandfather" had come for her in the most natural way in the world. He added the "grandfather," which produced a good effect. This was the story that Javert hit upon when he arrived at Montfermeil. The grandfather caused Jean Valjean to vanish.

Nevertheless, Javert dropped a few questions, like plummets, into Thénardier's history. "Who was that grandfather? and what was his name?" Thénardier replied with simplicity: "He is a wealthy farmer. I saw his passport. I think his name was M. Guillaume Lambert."

Lambert is a respectable and extremely reassuring name. Thereupon Javert returned to Paris.

"Jean Valjean is certainly dead," said he, "and I am a ninny."

He had again begun to forget this history, when, in the course of March, 1824, he heard of a singular personage who dwelt in the parish of Saint-Médard and who had been surnamed "the mendicant who gives alms." This person, the story ran, was a man of means, whose name no one knew exactly, and who lived alone with a little girl of eight years, who knew nothing about herself, save that she had come from Montfermeil. Montfermeil! that name was always coming up, and it made Javert prick up his ears. An old beggar police spy, an ex-beadle, to whom this person had given alms, added a few more details. This gentleman of property was very shy—never coming out except in the evening, speaking to no one, except, occasionally to the poor, and never allowing anyone to approach him. He wore a horrible old yellow frock-coat, which was worth many millions, being all wadded with bank-bills. This piqued Javert's curiosity in a decided manner. In order to get a close look at this fantastic gentleman without alarming him, he borrowed the beadle's outfit for a day, and the place where the old spy was in the habit of crouching every evening, whining orisons through his nose, and playing the spy under cover of prayer.

"The suspected individual" did indeed approach Javert thus disguised, and bestow alms on him. At that moment Javert raised his head, and the shock which Jean Valjean received on recognizing Javert was equal to the one received by Javert when he thought he recognized Jean Valjean.

However, the darkness might have misled him; Jean Valjean's death was official; Javert cherished very grave doubts; and when in doubt, Javert, the man of scruples, never laid a finger on anyone's collar.

He followed his man to the Gorbeau house, and got "the old woman" to talking, which was no difficult matter. The old woman confirmed the fact regarding the coat lined with millions, and narrated to him the episode of the thousand-franc bill. She had seen it! She had handled it! Javert hired a room; that evening he installed himself in it. He came and listened at the mysterious lodger's door, hoping to catch the sound of his voice, but Jean Valjean saw his candle through the key-hole, and foiled the spy by keeping silent.

On the following day Jean Valjean decamped; but the noise made by the fall of the five-franc piece was noticed by the old woman, who, hearing the rattling of coin, suspected that he might be intending to leave, and made haste to warn Javert. At night, when Jean Valjean came out, Javert was waiting for him behind the trees of the boulevard with two men.

Javert had demanded assistance at the Prefecture, but he had not mentioned the name of the individual whom he hoped to seize; that was his secret, and he had kept it for three reasons: in the first place, because the slightest indiscretion might put Jean Valjean on the alert; next, because, to lay hands on an ex-convict who had made his escape and was reputed dead, on a criminal whom justice had formerly classed forever as *among malefactors of the most dangerous sort*, was a magnificent success which the old members of the Parisian police would assuredly not leave to a newcomer like Javert, and he was afraid of being deprived of his convict; and lastly, because Javert, being an artist, had a taste for the unforeseen. He hated those well-heralded successes which are talked of long in advance and have had the bloom brushed off. He preferred to elaborate his masterpieces in the dark and to unveil them suddenly at the last.

Javert had followed Jean Valjean from tree to tree, then from corner to corner of the street, and had not lost sight of him for a single instant; even at the moments when Jean Valjean believed himself to be the most secure Javert's eye had been on him. Why had not Javert arrested Jean Valjean? Because he was still in doubt.

It must be remembered that at that epoch the police was not precisely at its ease; the free press embarrassed it; several arbitrary arrests, denounced by the newspapers, had echoed even as far as the Chambers, and had rendered the Prefecture timid. Interference with individual liberty was a grave matter. The police agents were afraid of making a mistake; the prefect laid the blame on them; a mistake meant dismissal. The reader can imagine the effect which this brief paragraph, reproduced by twenty newspapers, would have caused in Paris: "Yesterday, an aged grandfather, with white hair, a respectable and well-to-do gentleman, who was walking with his grandchild, aged eight, was arrested and conducted to the agency of the Prefecture as an escaped convict!"

Let us repeat in addition that Javert had scruples of his own; injunctions of his conscience were added to the injunctions of the prefect. He was really in doubt.

Jean Valjean turned his back on him and walked in the dark.

Sadness, uneasiness, anxiety, depression, this fresh misfortune of being forced to flee by night, to seek a chance refuge in Paris for Cosette and himself, the necessity of regulating his pace to the pace of the child—all this, without his being aware of it, had altered Jean Valjean's walk, and impressed on his bearing such senility, that the police themselves, incarnate in the person of Javert, might, and did in fact, make a mistake. The impossibility of approaching too close, his costume of an *émigré* preceptor, the declaration of Thénardier which made a grandfather of him, and, finally, the belief in his death in prison, added still further to the uncertainty which gathered thick in Javert's mind.

For an instant it occurred to him to make an abrupt demand for his papers; but if the man was not Jean Valjean, and if this man was not a good, honest old fellow living on his income, he was probably some merry blade deeply and cunningly implicated in the obscure web of Parisian misdeeds, some chief of a dangerous band, who gave alms to conceal his other talents, which was an old dodge. He had trusty fellows, accomplices' retreats in case of emergencies, in which he would, no doubt, take refuge. All these turns which he was making through the streets seemed to indicate that he was not a simple and honest man. To arrest him too hastily would be "to kill the hen that laid the golden eggs." Where was the inconvenience in waiting? Javert was very sure that he would not escape.

Thus he proceeded in a tolerably perplexed state of mind, putting to himself a hundred questions about this enigmatical personage.

It was only quite late in the Rue de Pontoise, that, thanks to the brilliant light thrown from a dram-shop, he decidedly recognized Jean Valjean.

There are in this world two beings who give a profound start—the mother who recovers her child and the tiger who recovers his prey. Javert gave that profound start.

As soon as he had positively recognized Jean Valjean, the formidable convict, he perceived that there were only three of them, and he asked for reinforcements at the police station of the Rue de Pontoise. One puts on gloves before grasping a thorn cudgel.

This delay and the halt at the Carrefour Rollin to consult with his agents came near causing him to lose the trail. He speedily divined, however, that Jean Valjean would want to put the river between his pursuers and himself. He bent his head and reflected like a bloodhound who puts his nose to the ground to make sure that he is on the right scent. Javert, with his powerful rectitude of instinct, went straight to the bridge of Austerlitz. A word with the toll-keeper furnished him with the information which he required: "Have you seen a man with a little girl?" "I made him pay two sous," replied the toll-keeper. Javert reached the bridge in season to see Jean Valjean traverse the small illuminated spot on the other side of the water, leading Cosette by the hand. He saw him enter the Rue du Chemin-Vert-Saint-Antoine; he remembered the Cul-de-Sac Genrot arranged there like a trap, and of the sole exit of the Rue Droit-Mur into the Rue Petit-Picpus. *He made sure of his back burrows,* as huntsmen say; he hastily dispatched one of his agents, by a roundabout way, to guard that issue. A patrol which was returning to the Arsenal post having passed him, he made a requisition on it, and caused it to accompany him. In such games soldiers are aces. Moreover, the principle is, that in order to get the best of a wild boar, one must employ the science of venery and plenty of dogs. These combinations having been effected, feeling that Jean Valjean was caught between the blind-alley Genrot on the right, his agent on the left, and himself, Javert, in the rear, he took a pinch of snuff.

Then he began the game. He experienced one ecstatic and infernal moment; he allowed his man to go on ahead, knowing that he had him safe, but desirous of postponing the moment of arrest as long as possible, happy at the thought that he was taken and yet at seeing him free, gloating over him with his gaze, with that voluptuousness of the spider which allows the fly to flutter, and of the cat which lets the mouse run. Claws and talons possess a monstrous sensuality—the obscure movements of the creature imprisoned in their pincers. What a delight this strangling is!

Javert was enjoying himself. The meshes of his net were stoutly knotted. He was sure of success; all he had to do now was to close his hand.

Accompanied as he was, the very idea of resistance was impossible, however vigorous, energetic, and desperate Jean Valjean might be.

Javert advanced slowly, sounding, searching on his way all the nooks of the street like so many pockets of thieves.

When he reached the center of the web he found the fly no longer there.

His exasperation can be imagined.

He interrogated his sentinel of the Rues Droit-Mur and Petit-Picpus; that agent, who had remained imperturbably at his post, had not seen the man pass.

It sometimes happens that a stag is lost head and horns; that is to say, he escapes although he has the pack on his very heels, and then the oldest huntsmen know not what to say. Duvivier, Ligniville, and Desprez halt short. In a discomfiture of this sort, Artonge exclaims, "It was not a stag, but a sorcerer." Javert would have liked to utter the same cry.

His disappointment bordered for a moment on despair and rage.

It is certain that Napoleon made mistakes during the war with Russia, that Alexander committed blunders in the war in India, that Cæsar made mistakes in the war in Africa, that Cyrus was at fault in the war in Scythia, and that Javert blundered in this campaign against Jean Valjean. He was wrong, perhaps, in hesitating in his recognition of the ex-convict. The first glance should have sufficed him. He was wrong in not arresting him purely and simply in the old building; he was wrong in not arresting him when he positively recognized him in the Rue de Pontoise. He was wrong in taking counsel with his auxiliaries in the full light of the moon in the Carrefour Rollin. Advice is certainly useful; it is a good thing to know and to interrogate those of the dogs who deserve confidence; but the hunter cannot be too cautious when he is chasing uneasy animals like the wolf and the convict. Javert, by taking too much thought as to how he should set the bloodhounds of the pack on the trail, alarmed the beast by giving him wind of the dart, and so made him run. Above all, he was wrong in that after he had picked up the scent again on the bridge of Austerlitz, he played that formidable and puerile game of keeping such a man at the end of a thread. He thought himself stronger than he was, and believed that he could play at the game of the mouse and the lion. At the same time, he reckoned himself as too weak, when he judged it necessary to obtain reinforcement. Fatal precaution, waste of precious time! Javert committed all these blunders, and none the less was one of the cleverest and most correct spies that ever existed. He was, in the full force of the term, what is called in venery a *knowing dog.* But what is there that is perfect?

Great strategists have their eclipses.

The greatest follies are often composed, like the largest ropes, of a multitude of strands. Take the cable thread by thread, take all the petty determining motives separately, and you can break them one after the other, and you say, "That is all there is of it!" Braid them, twist them together; the result is enormous: it is Attila hesitating between Marcian on the east and Valentinian on the west; it is Hannibal tarrying at Capua; it is Danton falling asleep at Arcis-sur-Aube.

However that may be, even at the moment when he saw that Jean Valjean had escaped him, Javert did not lose his head. Sure that the convict who had broken his ban could not be far off, he established sentinels, he organized traps and ambuscades, and beat the quarter all that night. The first thing he saw was the disorder in the street-lantern whose rope had been cut. A precious sign which, however, led him astray, since it caused him to turn all his researches in the direction of the Cul-de-Sac Genrot. In this blind-alley there were tolerably low walls which abutted on gardens whose bounds adjoined the immense stretches of waste land. Jean Valjean evidently must have fled in that direction. The fact is, that had he penetrated a little further in the Cul-de-Sac Genrot, he would probably have done so and have been lost. Javert explored these gardens and these waste stretches as though he had been hunting for a needle.

At daybreak he left two intelligent men on the outlook, and returned to the Prefecture of Police, as much ashamed as a police spy who had been captured by a robber might have been.

BOOK SIXTH

LE PETIT-PICPUS

Chapter I

NUMBER 62 RUE PETIT-PICPUS

NOTHING, HALF A CENTURY AGO, MORE RESEMBLED EVERY OTHER CARRIAGE GATE THAN THE carriage gate of Number 62 Rue Petit-Picpus. This entrance, which usually stood ajar in the most inviting fashion, permitted a view of two things, neither of which have anything very funereal about them—a courtyard surrounded by walls hung with vines, and the face of a lounging porter. Above the wall, at the bottom of the court, tall trees were visible. When a ray of sunlight enlivened the courtyard, when a glass of wine cheered up the porter, it was difficult to pass Number 62 Little Picpus Street without carrying away a smiling impression of it. Nevertheless, it was a somber place of which one had had a glimpse.

The threshold smiled; the house prayed and wept.

If one succeeded in passing the porter, which was not easy—which was even nearly impossible for everyone, for there was an *open sesame!* which it was necessary to know—if, the porter once passed, one entered a little vestibule on the right, on which opened a staircase shut in between two walls and so narrow that only one person could ascend it at a time, if one did not allow one's self to be alarmed by a daubing of canary yellow, with a dado of chocolate which clothed this staircase, if one ventured to ascend it, one crossed a first landing, then a second, and arrived on the first story at a corridor where the yellow wash and the chocolate-hued plinth pursued one with a peaceable persistency. Staircase and corridor were lighted by two beautiful windows. The corridor took a turn and became dark. If one doubled this cape, one arrived a few paces further on, in front of a door which was all the more mysterious because it was not fastened. If one opened it, one found one's self in a little chamber about six feet square, tiled, well-scrubbed, clean, cold, and hung with nankin paper with green flowers, at fifteen sous the roll. A white, dull light fell from a large window, with tiny panes, on the left, which usurped the whole width of the room. One gazed about, but saw no one; one listened, one heard neither a footstep nor a human murmur. The walls were bare, the chamber was not furnished; there was not even a chair.

One looked again, and beheld on the wall facing the door a quadrangular hole, about a foot square, with a grating of interlacing iron bars, black, knotted, solid, which formed squares—I had almost said meshes—of less than an inch and a half in diagonal length. The little green flowers of the nankin paper ran in a calm and orderly manner to those iron bars, without being startled or thrown into confusion by their funereal contact. Supposing that a living being had been so wonderfully thin as to essay an entrance or an exit through the square hole, this grating would have prevented it. It did not allow the passage of the body, but it did allow the passage of the eyes; that is to say, of the mind. This seems to have occurred to them, for it had been re-enforced by a sheet of tin inserted in the wall a little in the rear, and pierced with a thousand holes more microscopic than the holes of a strainer. At the bottom of this plate, an aperture had been pierced exactly similar to the orifice of a letter-box. A bit of tape attached to a bell-wire hung at the right of the grated opening.

If the tape was pulled, a bell rang, and one heard a voice very near at hand, which made one start.

"Who is there?" the voice demanded.

It was a woman's voice, a gentle voice, so gentle that it was mournful.

Here, again, there was a magical word which it was necessary to know. If one did not know it, the voice ceased, the wall became silent once more, as though the terrified obscurity of the sepulcher had been on the other side of it.

If one knew the password, the voice resumed, "Enter on the right."

One then perceived on the right, facing the window, a glass door surmounted by a frame glazed and painted gray. On raising the latch and crossing the threshold, one experienced precisely the same impression as when one enters at the theater into a grated *baignoire*, before the grating is lowered and the chandelier is lighted. One was, in fact, in a sort of theater-box, narrow, furnished with two old chairs, and a much-frayed straw matting, sparely illuminated by the vague light from the glass door; a regular box, with its front just of a height to lean upon, bearing a tablet of black wood. This box was grated, only the grating of it was not of gilded wood, as at the opera; it was a monstrous lattice of iron bars, hideously interlaced and riveted to the wall by enormous fastenings which resembled clenched fists.

The first minutes passed; when one's eyes began to grow used to this cellar-like half-twilight, one tried to pass the grating, but got no further than six inches beyond it. There he encountered a barrier of black shutters, re-enforced and fortified with transverse beams of wood painted a gingerbread yellow. These shutters were divided into long, narrow slats, and they masked the entire length of the grating. They were always closed. At the expiration of a few moments one heard a voice proceeding from behind these shutters, and saying:

"I am here. What do you wish with me?"

It was a beloved, sometimes an adored, voice. No one was visible. Hardly the sound of a breath was audible. It seemed as though it were a spirit which had been evoked, that was speaking to you across the walls of the tomb.

If one chanced to be within certain prescribed and very rare conditions, the slat of one of the shutters opened opposite you; the evoked spirit became an apparition. Behind the grating, behind the shutter, one perceived so far as the grating permitted sight, a head, of which only the mouth and the chin were visible; the rest was covered with a black veil. One caught a glimpse of a black guimpe, and a form that was barely defined, covered with a black shroud. That head spoke with you, but did not look at you and never smiled at you.

The light which came from behind you was adjusted in such a manner that you saw her in the white, and she saw you in the black. This light was symbolical.

Nevertheless, your eyes plunged eagerly through that opening which was made in that place shut off from all glances. A profound vagueness enveloped that form clad in mourning. Your eyes searched that vagueness, and sought to make out the surroundings of the apparition. At the expiration of a very short time you discovered that you could see nothing. What you beheld was night, emptiness, shadows, a wintry mist mingled with a vapor from the tomb, a sort of terrible peace, a silence from which you could gather nothing, not even sighs, a gloom in which you could distinguish nothing, not even phantoms.

What you beheld was the interior of a cloister.

It was the interior of that severe and gloomy edifice which was called the Convent of the Bernardines of the Perpetual Adoration. The box in which you stood was the parlor. The first voice which had addressed you was that of the portress, who always sat motionless and silent, on the other side of the wall, near the square opening, screened by the iron grating and the plate with its thousand holes, as by a double visor. The obscurity which bathed the grated box arose from the fact that the parlor, which had a window on the side of the world, had none on the side of the convent. Profane eyes must see nothing of that sacred place.

Nevertheless, there was something beyond that shadow; there was a light; there was life in the midst of that death. Although this was the most strictly walled of all convents, we shall endeavor to make our way into it, and to take the reader in, and to say, without transgressing the proper bounds, things which story-tellers have never seen, and have, therefore, never described.

Chapter II

THE OBEDIENCE OF MARTIN VERGA

THIS CONVENT, WHICH IN 1824 HAD ALREADY EXISTED FOR MANY A LONG YEAR IN THE RUE PETIT-Picpus, was a community of Bernardines of the obedience of Martin Verga.

These Bernardines were attached, in consequence, not to Clairvaux, like the Bernardine monks, but to Cîteaux, like the Benedictine monks. In other words, they were the subjects, not of Saint Bernard, but of Saint Benoît.

Anyone who has turned over old folios to any extent knows that Martin Verga founded in 1425 a congregation of Bernardines-Benedictines, with Salamanca for the head of the order, and Alcala as the branch establishment.

This congregation had sent out branches throughout all the Catholic countries of Europe.

There is nothing unusual in the Latin Church in these grafts of one order on another. To mention only a single order of Saint-Benoît, which is here in question: there are attached to this order, without counting the obedience of Martin Verga, four congregations—two in Italy, Mont-Cassin and Sainte-Justine of Padua; two in France, Cluny and Saint-Maur; and nine orders—Vallombrosa, Granmont, the Célestins, the Camaldules, the Carthusians, the Humiliés, the Olivateurs, the Silvestrins, and lastly, Cîteaux; for Cîteaux itself, a trunk for other orders, is only an offshoot of Saint-Benoît. Cîteaux dates from Saint Robert, Abbé de Molesme, in the diocese of Langres, in 1098. Now it was in 529 that the devil, having retired to the desert of Subiaco—he was old—had he turned hermit?—was chased from the ancient temple of Apollo, where he dwelt, by Saint-Benoît, then aged seventeen.

After the rule of the Carmelites, who go barefoot, wear a bit of willow on their throats, and never sit down, the harshest rule is that of the Bernardines-Benedictines of Martin Verga. They are clothed in black, with a guimpe, which, in accordance with the express command of Saint-Benoît, mounts to the chin. A robe of serge with large sleeves, a large woolen veil, the guimpe which mounts to the chin cut square on the breast, the band which descends over their brow to their eyes—this is their dress. All is black except the band, which is white. The novices wear the same habit, but all in white. The professed nuns also wear a rosary at their side.

The Bernardines-Benedictines of Martin Verga practice the Perpetual Adoration, like the Benedictines called Ladies of the Holy Sacrament, who, at the beginning of this century, had two houses in Paris—one at the Temple, the other in the Rue Neuve-Sainte-Geneviève. However, the

Bernardines-Benedictines of the Petit-Picpus, of whom we are speaking, were a totally different order from the Ladies of the Holy Sacrament, cloistered in the Rue Neuve-Sainte-Geneviève and at the Temple. There were numerous differences in their rule; there were some in their costume. The Bernardines-Benedictines of the Petit-Picpus wore the black guimpe, and the Benedictines of the Holy Sacrament and of the Rue Neuve-Sainte-Geneviève wore a white one, and had, besides, on their breasts, a Holy Sacrament about three inches long, in silver gilt or gilded copper. The nuns of the Petit-Picpus did not wear this Holy Sacrament. The Perpetual Adoration, which was common to the house of the Petit-Picpus and to the house of the Temple, leaves those two orders perfectly distinct. Their only resemblance lies in this practice of the Ladies of the Holy Sacrament and the Bernardines of Martin Verga, just as there existed a similarity in the study and the glorification of all the mysteries relating to the infancy, the life, and death of Jesus Christ and the Virgin, between the two orders, which were, nevertheless, widely separated, and on occasion even hostile. The Oratory of Italy, established at Florence by Philip de Neri, and the Oratory of France, established by Pierre de Bérulle. The Oratory of France claimed the precedence, since Philip de Neri was only a saint, while Bérulle was a cardinal.

Let us return to the harsh Spanish rule of Martin Verga.

The Bernardines-Benedictines of this obedience fast all the year round, abstain from meat, fast in Lent and on many other days which are peculiar to them, rise from their first sleep, from one to three o'clock in the morning, to read their breviary and chant matins, sleep in all seasons between serge sheets and on straw, make no use of the bath, never light a fire, scourge themselves every Friday, observe the rule of silence, speak to each other only during the recreation hours, which are very brief, and wear drugget chemises for six months in the year, from September 14th, which is the Exaltation of the Holy Cross, until Easter. These six months are a modification: the rule says all the year, but this drugget chemise, intolerable in the heat of summer, produced fevers and nervous spasms. The use of it had to be restricted. Even with this palliation, when the nuns put on this chemise on the 14th of September, they suffer from fever for three or four days. Obedience, poverty, chastity, perseverance in their seclusion—these are their vows, which the rule greatly aggravates.

The prioress is elected for three years by the mothers, who are called *mères vocales* because they have a voice in the chapter. A prioress can only be re-elected twice, which fixes the longest possible reign of a prioress at nine years.

They never see the officiating priest, who is always hidden from them by a serge curtain nine feet in height. During the sermon, when the preacher is in the chapel, they drop their veils over their faces. They must always speak low, walk with their eyes on the ground and their heads bowed. One man only is allowed to enter the convent—the archbishop of the diocese.

There is really one other—the gardener. But he is always an old man, and, in order that he may always be alone in the garden, and that the nuns may be warned to avoid him, a bell is attached to his knee.

Their submission to the prioress is absolute and passive. It is the canonical subjection in the full force of its abnegation. As at the voice of Christ, *ut voci Christi*, at a gesture, at the first sign, *ad nutum, ad primum signum*, immediately, with cheerfulness, with perseverance, with a certain blind obedience, *prompte, hilariter, perseveranter et caeca quadam obedientia*, as the file in the hand of the workman, *quasi limam in manibus fabri*, without power to read or to write without express permission, *legere vel scribere non addiscerit sine expressa superioris licentia*.

Each one of them in turn makes what they call *reparation*. The reparation is the prayer for all the sins, for all the faults, for all the dissensions, for all the violations, for all the iniquities, for all the crimes committed on earth. For the space of twelve consecutive hours, from four o'clock in the afternoon till four o'clock in the morning, or from four o'clock in the morning until four o'clock in the afternoon, the sister who is making *reparation* remains on her knees on the stone before the Holy Sacrament, with hands clasped, a rope around her neck. When her fatigue becomes unendurable, she prostrates herself flat on her face against the earth, with her arms outstretched in the form of a cross; this is her only re-lief. In this attitude she prays for all the guilty in the universe. This is great to sublimity.

As this act is performed in front of a post on which burns a candle, it is called without distinc-tion, *to make reparation* or *to be at the post*. The nuns even prefer, out of humility, this last expres-sion, which contains an idea of torture and abasement.

To make reparation is a function in which the whole soul is absorbed. The sister at the post would not turn round were a thunderbolt to fall directly behind her.

Besides this, there is always a sister kneeling before the Holy Sacrament. This station lasts an hour. They relieve each other like soldiers on guard. This is the Perpetual Adoration.

The prioresses and the mothers almost always bear names stamped with peculiar solemnity, re-calling, not the saints and martyrs, but moments in the life of Jesus Christ: as Mother Nativity, Mother Conception, Mother Presentation, Mother Passion. But the names of saints are not interdicted.

When one sees them, one never sees anything but their mouths.

All their teeth are yellow. No tooth-brush ever entered that convent. Brushing one's teeth is at the top of a ladder at whose bottom is the loss of one's soul.

They never say *my*. They possess nothing of their own, and they must not attach themselves to anything. They call everything *our*; thus: our veil, our chaplet; if they were speaking of their chemise, they would say *our chemise*. Sometimes they grow attached to some petty object—to a book of hours, a relic, a medal that has been blessed. As soon as they become aware that they are growing attached to this object, they must give it up. They recall the words of Saint Thérèse, to whom a great lady said, as she was on the point of entering her order, "Permit me, mother, to send for a Bible to which I am greatly attached." "Ah, you are attached to something! In that case, do not enter our order!"

Every person whatever is forbidden to shut herself up, to have *a place of her own, a chamber*. They live with their cells open. When they meet, one says, "Blessed and adored be the most Holy Sacrament of the altar!" The other responds, "Forever." The same ceremony when one taps at the other's door. Hardly has she touched the door when a soft voice on the other side is heard to say hastily, "Forever!" Like all practices, this becomes mechanical by force of habit; and one sometimes says *forever* before the other has had time to say the rather long sentence, "Praised and adored be the most Holy Sacrament of the altar."

Among the Visitandines the one who enters says; "Ave Maria," and the one whose cell is en-tered says, "Gratia plena." It is their way of saying good day, which is in fact full of grace.

At each hour of the day three supplementary strokes sound from the church bell of the convent. At this signal prioress, vocal mothers, professed nuns, lay-sisters, novices, postulants, interrupt what they are saying, what they are doing, or what they are thinking, and all say in unison if it is five o'clock, for instance, "At five o'clock and at all hours praised and adored be the most Holy Sacrament of the altar!" If it is eight o'clock, "At eight o'clock and at all hours!" and so on, according to the hour.

This custom, the object of which is to break the thread of thought and to lead it back con-stantly to God, exists in many communities; the formula alone varies. Thus at The Infant Jesus they say, "At this hour and at every hour may the love of Jesus kindle my heart!" The Bernardines-Benedictines of Martin Verga, cloistered fifty years ago at Petit-Picpus, chant the offices to a solemn psalmody, a pure Gregorian chant, and always with full voice during the whole course of the office. Everywhere in the missal where an asterisk occurs they pause, and say in a low voice, "Jesus-Marie-Joseph." For the office of the dead they adopt a tone so low that the voices of women can hardly descend to such a depth. The effect produced is striking and tragic.

The nuns of the Petit-Picpus had made a vault under their grand altar for the burial of their community. *The Government*, as they say, does not permit this vault to receive coffins, so they leave the convent when they die. This is an affliction to them, and causes them consternation as an in-fraction of the rules.

They had obtained a mediocre consolation at best—permission to be interred at a special hour and in a special corner in the ancient Vaugirard cemetery, which was made of land which had formerly belonged to their community.

On Fridays the nuns hear high mass, vespers, and all the offices, as on Sunday. They scrupulously observe in addition all the little festivals unknown to people of the world, of which the Church of France was so prodigal in the olden days, and of which it is still prodigal in Spain and Italy. Their stations in the chapel are interminable. As for the number and duration of their prayers we can convey no better idea of them than by quoting the ingenuous remark of one of them: "The prayers of the postulants are frightful, the prayers of the novices are still worse, and the prayers of the professed nuns are still worse."

Once a week the chapter assembles: the prioress presides; the vocal mothers assist. Each sister kneels in turn on the stones, and confesses aloud, in the presence of all, the faults and sins which she has committed during the week. The vocal mothers consult after each confession and inflict the penance aloud.

Beside this confession in a loud tone, for which all faults in the least serious are reserved, they have for their venial offenses what they call the *coulpe*. *To make one's coulpe* means to prostrate one's self flat on one's face during the office in front of the prioress until the latter, who is never called anything but *our mother*, notifies the culprit by a slight tap of her foot against the wood of her stall that she can rise. The *coulpe* or *peccavi*, is made for a very small matter—a broken glass, a torn veil, an involuntary delay of a few seconds at an office, a false note in church, etc.; this suffices, and the *coulpe* is made. The *coulpe* is entirely spontaneous; it is the culpable person herself (the word is etymologically in its place here) who judges herself and inflicts it on herself. On festival days and Sundays four mother precentors intone the offices before a large reading-desk with four places. One day one of the mother precentors intoned a psalm beginning with *Ecce,* and instead of *Ecce* she uttered aloud the three notes *do si sol*; for this piece of absent-mindedness she underwent a *coulpe* which lasted during the whole service: what rendered the fault enormous was the fact that the chapter had laughed.

When a nun is summoned to the parlor, even were it the prioress herself, she drops her veil, as will be remembered, so that only her mouth is visible.

The prioress alone can hold communication with strangers. The others can see only their immediate family, and that very rarely. If, by chance, an outsider presents herself to see a nun, or one whom she has known and loved in the outer world, a regular series of negotiations is required. If it is a woman, the authorization may sometimes be granted; the nun comes, and they talk to her through the shutters, which are opened only for a mother or sister. It is unnecessary to say that permission is always refused to men.

Such is the rule of Saint-Benoît, aggravated by Martin Verga.

These nuns are not gay, rosy, and fresh, as the daughters of other orders often are. They are pale and grave. Between 1825 and 1830 three of them went mad.

Chapter III

AUSTERITIES

ONE IS A POSTULANT FOR TWO YEARS AT LEAST, OFTEN FOR FOUR; A NOVICE FOR FOUR. IT IS rare that the definitive vows can be pronounced earlier than the age of twenty-three or twenty-four years. The Bernardines-Benedictines of Martin Verga do not admit widows to their order.

In their cells, they deliver themselves up to many unknown macerations, of which they must never speak.

On the day when a novice makes her profession, she is dressed in her handsomest attire, she is crowned with white roses, her hair is brushed until it shines, and curled. Then she prostrates herself; a great black veil is thrown over her, and the office for the dead is sung. Then the nuns separate into two files; one file passes close to her, saying in plaintive accents, "Our sister is dead"; and the other file responds in a voice of ecstasy, "Our sister is alive in Jesus Christ!"

At the epoch when this story takes place, a boarding-school was attached to the convent—a boarding-school for young girls of noble and mostly wealthy families, among whom could be remarked Mademoiselle de Saint-Aulaire and de Bélissen, and an English girl bearing the illustrious Catholic name of Talbot. These young girls, reared by these nuns between four walls, grew up with a horror of the world and of the age. One of them said to us one day, "The sight of the street pavement made me shudder from head to foot." They were dressed in blue, with a white cap and a Holy Spirit of silver gilt or of copper on their breast. On certain grand festival days, particularly Saint Martha's day, they were permitted, as a high favor and a supreme happiness, to dress themselves as nuns and to carry out the offices and practice of Saint-Benoît for a whole day. In the early days the nuns were in the habit of lending them their black garments. This seemed profane, and the prioress forbade it. Only the novices were permitted to lend. It is remarkable that these performances, tolerated and encouraged, no doubt, in the convent out of a secret spirit of proselytism and in order to give these children a foretaste of the holy habit, were a genuine happiness and a real recreation for the scholars. They simply amused themselves with it. *It was new; it gave them a change.* Candid reasons of childhood, which do not, however, succeed in making us worldlings comprehend the felicity of holding a holy water sprinkler in one's hand and standing for hours together singing hard enough for four in front of a reading-desk.

The pupils conformed, with the exception of the austerities, to all the practices of the convent. There was a certain young woman who entered the world, and who after many years of married life had not succeeded in breaking herself of the habit of saying in great haste whenever anyone knocked at her door, "forever!" Like the nuns, the pupils saw their relatives only in the parlor. Their very mothers did not obtain permission to embrace them. The following illustrates to what a degree severity on that point was carried. One day a young girl received a visit from her mother, who was accompanied by a little sister three years of age. The young girl wept, for she wished greatly to embrace her sister. Impossible. She begged that, at least, the child might be permitted to pass her little hand through the bars so that she could kiss it. This was almost indignantly refused.

Chapter IV

GAIETIES

NONE THE LESS, THESE YOUNG GIRLS FILLED THIS GRAVE HOUSE WITH CHARMING SOUVENIRS. At certain hours childhood sparkled in that cloister. The recreation hour struck. A door swung on its hinges. The birds said, "Good; here come the children!" An eruption of youth inundated that garden intersected with a cross like a shroud. Radiant faces, white foreheads, innocent eyes full of merry light, all sorts of auroras, were scattered about amid these shadows. After the psalmodies, the bells, the peals, and knells and offices, the sound of these little girls burst forth on a sudden more sweetly than the noise of bees. The hive of joy was opened, and each one brought her honey. They played, they called to each other, they formed into groups, they ran about; pretty little white teeth chattered in the corners; the veils superintended the laughs from a distance, shades kept watch of the sunbeams, but what mattered it? Still they beamed and laughed. Those four lugubrious walls had their moment of dazzling brilliancy. They looked on, vaguely blanched with the reflection of so much joy at this sweet swarming of the hives. It was like a shower of roses falling athwart this house of mourning. The young girls frolicked beneath the eyes of the nuns; the gaze of impeccability does not embarrass innocence. Thanks to these children, there was, among so many austere hours, one hour of ingenuousness. The little ones skipped about; the elder ones danced. In this cloister play was mingled with heaven. Nothing is so delightful and so august as all these fresh, expanding young souls. Homer would have come thither to laugh with Perrault; and there was in that black garden, youth, health, noise, cries, giddiness, pleasure, happiness enough to smooth out the wrinkles of all their ancestresses, those of the epic as well as those of the fairy-tale, those of the throne as well as those of the thatched cottage from Hecuba to la Mère-Grand.

In that house more than anywhere else, perhaps, arise those children's sayings which are so graceful and which evoke a smile that is full of thoughtfulness. It was between those four gloomy walls that a child of five years exclaimed one day: "Mother! one of the big girls has just told me that I have only nine years and ten months longer to remain here. What happiness!"

It was here, too, that this memorable dialogue took place:

"*A Vocal Mother.* Why are you weeping, my child?

The child (aged six). I told Alix that I knew my French history. She says that I do not know it, but I do.

Alix, the big girl (aged nine). No; she does not know it.

The Mother. How is that, my child?

Alix. She told me to open the book at random and to ask her any question in the book, and she would answer it.

"Well?"

"She did not answer it."

"Let us see about it. What did you ask her?"

"I opened the book at random, as she proposed, and I put the first question that I came across."

"And what was the question?"

"It was, 'What happened after that?' "

It was there that that profound remark was made anent a rather greedy parakeet which belonged to a lady boarder:

"How well bred! it eats the top of the slice of bread and butter just like a person!"

It was on one of the flagstones of this cloister that there was once picked up a confession which had been written out in advance, in order that she might not forget it, by a sinner of seven years:

"Father, I accuse myself of having been avaricious.

"Father, I accuse myself of having been an adulteress.

"Father, I accuse myself of having raised my eyes to the gentlemen."

It was on one of the turf benches of this garden that a rosy mouth six years of age improvised the following tale, which was listened to by blue eyes aged four and five years:

"There were three little cocks who owned a country where there were a great many flowers. They plucked the flowers and put them in their pockets. After that they plucked the leaves and put them in their playthings. There was a wolf in that country; there was a great deal of forest; and the wolf was in the forest; and he ate the little cocks."

And this other poem:

"There came a blow with a stick.

"It was Punchinello who bestowed it on the cat.

"It was not good for her; it hurt her.

"Then a lady put Punchinello in prison."

It was there that a little abandoned child, a foundling whom the convent was bringing up out of charity, uttered this sweet and heart-breaking saying. She heard the others talking of their mothers, and she murmured in her corner:

"As for me, my mother was not there when I was born!"

There was a stout portress who could always be seen hurrying through the corridors with her bunch of keys, and whose name was Sister Agatha. The *big big girls*—those over ten years of age—called her *Agathocles.*

The refectory, a large apartment of an oblong square form, which received no light except through a vaulted cloister on a level with the garden, was dark and damp, and, as the children say, full of beasts. All the places round about furnished their contingent of insects.

Each of its four corners had received, in the language of the pupils, a special and expressive name. There was Spider corner, Caterpillar corner, Wood-louse corner, and Cricket corner.

Cricket corner was near the kitchen and was highly esteemed. It was not so cold there as elsewhere. From the refectory the names had passed to the boarding-school, and there served as in the old College Mazarin to distinguish four nations. Every pupil belonged to one of these four nations according to the corner of the refectory in which she sat at meals. One day Monseigneur the Archbishop while making his pastoral visit saw a pretty little rosy girl with beautiful golden hair enter the class-room through which he was passing.

He inquired of another pupil, a charming brunette with rosy cheeks, who stood near him:

"Who is that?"

"She is a spider, Monseigneur."

"Bah! And that one yonder?"

"She is a cricket."

"And that one?"

"She is a caterpillar."

"Really! and yourself?"

"I am a wood-louse, Monseigneur."

Every house of this sort has its own peculiarities. At the beginning of this century Écouen was one of those strict and graceful places where young girls pass their childhood in a shadow that is almost august. At Écouen, in order to take rank in the procession of the Holy Sacrament, a distinction was made between virgins and florists. There were also the "dais" and the "censors"—the first who held the cords of the dais, and the others who carried incense before the Holy Sacrament. The flowers belonged by right to the florists. Four "virgins" walked in advance. On the morning of that great day it was no rare thing to hear the question put in the dormitory, "Who is a virgin?"

Madame Campan used to quote this saying of a "little one" of seven years, to a "big girl" of sixteen, who took the head of the procession, while she, the little one, remained at the rear, "You are a virgin, but I am not."

Chapter V

DISTRACTIONS

ABOVE THE DOOR OF THE REFECTORY THIS PRAYER, WHICH WAS CALLED THE *WHITE PATERNOS-ter*, and which possessed the property of bearing people straight to paradise, was inscribed in large black letters:

"Little white Paternoster, which God made, which God said, which God placed in paradise. In the evening, when I went to bed, I found three angels sitting on my bed, one at the foot, two at the head, the good Virgin Mary in the middle, who told me to lie down without hesitation. The good God is my father, the good Virgin is my mother, the three apostles are my brothers, the three virgins are my sisters. The shirt in which God was born envelopes my body; Saint Margaret's cross is written on my breast. Madame the Virgin was walking through the meadows, weeping for God, when she met M. Saint John. 'Monsieur Saint John, whence come you?' 'I come from *Ave Salus.*' 'You have not seen the good God; where is he?' 'He is on the tree of the Cross, his feet hanging, his hands nailed, a little cap of white thorns on his head.' Whoever shall say this thrice at eventide, thrice in the morning, shall win paradise at the last."

In 1827 this characteristic orison had disappeared from the wall under a triple coating of daubing paint. At the present time it is finally disappearing from the memories of several who were young girls then, and who are old women now.

A large crucifix fastened to the wall completed the decoration of this refectory, whose only door, as we think we have mentioned, opened on the garden. Two narrow tables, each flanked by two wooden benches, formed two long parallel lines from one end to the other of the refectory. The walls were white, the tables were black; these two mourning colors constitute the only variety in convents. The meals were plain, and the food of the children themselves severe. A single dish of meat and vegetables combined, or salt fish—such was their luxury. This meager fare, which was reserved for the pupils alone, was, nevertheless, an exception. The children ate in silence, under the eye of the mother whose turn it was, who, if a fly took a notion to fly or to hum against the rule, opened and shut a wooden book from time to time. This silence was seasoned with the lives of the saints, read aloud from a little pulpit with a desk, which was situated at the foot of the crucifix. The reader was one of the big girls, in weekly turn. At regular distances, on the bare tables, there were large, varnished bowls, in which the pupils washed their own silver cups and knives and forks, and into which they sometimes threw some scrap of tough meat or spoiled fish; this was punished. These bowls were called *ronds d'eau.* The child who broke the silence "made a cross with her tongue." Where? On the ground. She licked the pavement. The dust, that end of all joys, was charged with the chastisement of those poor little rose-leaves which had been guilty of chirping.

There was in the convent a book which has never been printed except as a *unique copy*, and which it is forbidden to read. It is the rule of Saint-Benoît. An arcanum which no profane eye must penetrate. *Nemo regulas, seu constitutiones nostras, externis communicabit.*

The pupils one day succeeded in getting possession of this book, and set to reading it with avidity, a reading which was often interrupted by the fear of being caught, which caused them to close the volume precipitately.

From the great danger thus incurred they derived but a very moderate amount of pleasure. The most "interesting thing" they found were some unintelligible pages about the sins of young boys.

They played in an alley of the garden bordered with a few shabby fruit-trees. In spite of the extreme surveillance and the severity of the punishments administered, when the wind had shaken the trees, they sometimes succeeded in picking up a green apple or a spoiled apricot or an inhabited pear on the sly. I will now cede the privilege of speech to a letter which lies before me, a letter written five-and-twenty years ago by an old pupil, now Madame la Duchesse de ——— one of the most elegant women in Paris. I quote literally: "One hides one's pear or one's apple as best one may. When one goes upstairs to put the veil on the bed before supper, one stuffs them under one's pillow and at night one eats them in bed, and when one cannot do that, one eats them in the closet." That was one of their greatest luxuries.

Once—it was at the epoch of the visit from the archbishop to the convent—one of the young girls, Mademoiselle Bouchard, who was connected with the Montmorency family, laid a wager that she would ask for a day's leave of absence—an enormity in so austere a community. The wager was accepted, but not one of those who bet believed that she would do it. When the moment came, as the archbishop was passing in front of the pupils, Mademoiselle Bouchard, to the indescribable terror of her companions, stepped out of the ranks, and said, "Monseigneur, a day's leave of absence." Mademoiselle Bouchard was tall, blooming, with the prettiest little rosy face in the world. M. de Quélen smiled and said; "What, my dear child, a day's leave of absence! Three days if you like. I grant you three days." The prioress could do nothing; the archbishop had spoken. Horror of the convent, but joy of the pupil. The effect may be imagined.

This stern cloister was not so well walled off, however, but that the life of the passions of the outside world, drama, and even romance, did not make their way in. To prove this, we will confine ourselves to recording here and to briefly mentioning a real and incontestable fact, which, however, bears no reference in itself to, and is not connected by any thread whatever with the story which we are relating. We mention the fact for the sake of completing the physiognomy of the convent in the reader's mind.

About this time there was in the convent a mysterious person who was not a nun, who was treated with great respect, and who was addressed as *Madame Albertine*. Nothing was known about her, save that she was mad, and that in the world she passed for dead. Beneath this history it was said there lay the arrangements of fortune necessary for a great marriage.

This woman, hardly thirty years of age, of dark complexion and tolerably pretty, had a vague look in her large black eyes. Could she see? There was some doubt about this. She glided rather than walked, she never spoke; it was not quite known whether she breathed. Her nostrils were livid and pinched as after yielding up their last sigh. To touch her hand was like touching snow. She possessed a strange spectral grace. Wherever she entered, people felt cold. One day a sister, on seeing her pass, said to another sister, "She passes for a dead woman." "Perhaps she is one," replied the other.

A hundred tales were told of Madame Albertine. This arose from the eternal curiosity of the pupils. In the chapel there was a gallery called *L'Oeil de Boeuf*. It was in this gallery, which had only a circular bay, an *oeil de bouef*, that Madame Albertine listened to the offices. She always occupied it alone because this gallery, being on the level of the first story, the preacher or the officiating priest could be seen, which was interdicted to the nuns. One day the pulpit was occupied by a young priest of high rank, M. Le Duc de Rohan, peer of France, officer of the Red Musketeers in 1815, when he was Prince de Léon, and who died afterward, in 1830, as cardinal and Archbishop of Besançon. It was the first time that M. de Rohan had preached at the Petit-Picpus convent. Madame Albertine usually preserved perfect calmness and complete immobility during the sermons and services. That day, as soon as she caught sight of M. de Rohan, she half rose, and said, in a loud voice, amid the silence of the chapel, "Ah! Auguste!" The whole community turned their heads in amazement, the preacher raised his eyes, but Madame Albertine had relapsed into her immobility. A breath from the outer world, a flash of life, had passed for an instant across that cold and lifeless face and had then vanished, and the mad woman had become a corpse again.

Those two words, however, had set everyone in the convent who had the privilege of speech, to chattering. How many things were contained in that "Ah! Auguste!" what revelations! M. de

Rohan's name really was Auguste. It was evident that Madame Albertine belonged to the very highest society, since she knew M. de Rohan, and that her own rank there was of the highest, since she spoke thus familiarly of so great a lord, and that there existed between them some connection, of relationship, perhaps, but a very close one in any case, since she knew his "pet name."

Two very severe duchesses, Mesdames de Choiseul and de Sérent, often visited the community, whither they penetrated, no doubt, in virtue of the privilege *Magnates mulieres,* and caused great consternation in the boarding-school. When these two old ladies passed by, all the poor young girls trembled and dropped their eyes.

Moreover, M. de Rohan, quite unknown to himself, was an object of attention to the school-girls. At that epoch he had just been made, while waiting for the episcopate, vicar-general of the Archbishop of Paris. It was one of his habits to come tolerably often to celebrate the offices in the chapel of the nuns of the Petit-Picpus. Not one of the young recluses could see him, because of the serge curtain, but he had a sweet and rather shrill voice, which they had come to know and to distinguish. He had been a mousquetaire, and then, he was said to be very coquettish, that his handsome brown hair was very well dressed in a roll around his head, and that he had a broad girdle of magnificent moire, and that his black cassock was of the most elegant cut in the world. He held a great place in all these imaginations of sixteen years.

Not a sound from without made its way into the convent. But there was one year when the sound of a flute penetrated thither. This was an event, and the girls who were at school there at the time still recall it.

It was a flute which was played in the neighborhood. This flute always played the same air, an air which is very far away nowadays—"My Zétulbé, come reign o'er my soul"—and it was heard two or three times a day. The young girls passed hours in listening to it, the vocal mothers were upset by it, brains were busy, punishments descended in showers. This lasted for several months. The girls were all more or less in love with the unknown musician. Each one dreamed that she was Zétulbé. The sound of the flute proceeded from the direction of the Rue Droit-Mur; and they would have given anything, compromised everything, attempted anything for the sake of seeing, of catching a glance, if only for a second, of the "young man" who played that flute so deliciously, and who, no doubt, played on all these souls at the same time. There were some who made their escape by a back door, and ascended to the third story on the Rue Droit-Mur side, in order to attempt to catch a glimpse through the gaps. Impossible! One even went so far as to thrust her arm through the grating, and to wave her white handkerchief. Two were still bolder. They found means to climb on a roof, and risked their lives there, and succeeded at last in seeing "the young man." He was an old *émigré* gentleman, blind and penniless, who was playing his flute in his attic, in order to pass the time.

Chapter VI

THE LITTLE CONVENT

IN THIS ENCLOSURE OF THE PETIT-PICPUS THERE WERE THREE PERFECTLY DISTINCT BUILDINGS—the Great Convent, inhabited by the nuns, the Boarding-school, where the scholars were lodged; and lastly, what was called the Little Convent. It was a building with a garden, in which lived all sorts of aged nuns of various orders, the relics of cloisters destroyed in the Revolution; a reunion of all the black, gray, and white medleys of all communities and all possible varieties; what might be called, if such a coupling of words is permissible, a sort of harlequin convent.

When the Empire was established, all these poor old dispersed and exiled women had been accorded permission to come and take shelter under the wings of the Bernardines-Benedictines. The government paid them a small pension, the ladies of the Petit-Picpus received them cordially. It was a singular pell-mell. Each followed her own rule. Sometimes the pupils of the boarding-school were allowed, as a great recreation, to pay them a visit; the result is, that all those young memories have retained among other souvenirs that of Mother Sainte-Bazile, Mother Sainte-Scolastique, and Mother Jacob.

One of these refugees found herself almost at home. She was a nun of Sainte-Aure, the only one of her order who had survived. The ancient convent of the ladies of Sainte-Aure occupied, at the beginning of the eighteenth century, this very house of the Petit-Picpus, which belonged later to the Benedictines of Martin Verga. This holy woman, too poor to wear the magnificent habit of her order, which was a white robe with a scarlet scapulary, had piously put it on a little manikin, which she exhibited with complacency and which she bequeathed to the house at her death. In 1824, only one nun of this order remained; to-day, there remains only a doll.

In addition to these worthy mothers, some old society women had obtained permission of the prioress, like Madame Albertine, to retire into the Little Convent. Among the number were Madame Beaufort d'Hautpoul and Marquise Dufresne. Another was never known in the convent except by the formidable noise which she made when she blew her nose. The pupils called her Madame Vacarmini (hubbub).

About 1820 or 1821, Madame de Genlis, who was at that time editing a little periodical publication called *l'Intrépide,* asked to be allowed to enter the convent of the Petit-Picpus as lady resident. The Duc d'Orléans recommended her. Uproar in the hive; the vocal mothers were all in a flutter; Madame de Genlis had made romances. But she declared that she was the first to detest them, and then, she had reached her fierce stage of devotion. With the aid of God, and of the Prince, she entered. She departed at the end of six or eight months, alleging as a reason, that there was no shade in the garden. The nuns were delighted. Although very old, she still played the harp, and did it very well.

When she went away she left her mark in her cell. Madame de Genlis was superstitious and a Latinist. These two words furnish a tolerably good profile of her. A few years ago, there were still to be seen, pasted in the inside of a little cupboard in her cell in which she locked up her silverware and her jewels, these five lines in Latin, written with her own hand in red ink on yellow paper, and which, in her opinion, possessed the property of frightening away robbers:

> *Imparibus meritis pendent tria corpora ramis:*
> *Dismas et Gesmas, media est divina potestas;*
> *Alta petit Dismas, infelix, infima, Gesmas;*
> *Nos et res nostras conservet summa potestas.*
> *Hos versus dicas, ne tu furto tua perdas.*[1]

These verses in sixth century Latin raise the question whether the two thieves of Calvary were named, as is commonly believed, Dismas and Gestas, or Dismas and Gesmas. This orthography might have confounded the pretensions put forward in the last century by the Vicomte de Gestas, of a descent from the wicked thief. However, the useful virtue attached to these verses forms an article of faith in the order of the Hospitallers.

The church of the house, constructed in such a manner as to separate the Great Convent from

---

1. On the boughs hang three bodies of unequal merits: Dismas and Gesmas, between is the divine power. Dismas seeks the heights, Gesmas, unhappy man, the lowest regions; the highest power will preserve us and our effects. If you repeat this verse, you will not lose your things by theft.

the Boarding-school like a veritable entrenchment, was, of course, common to the Boarding-school, the Great Convent, and the Little Convent. The public was even admitted by a sort of lazaretto entrance on the street. But all was so arranged, that none of the inhabitants of the cloister could see a face from the outside world. Suppose a church whose choir is grasped in a gigantic hand, and folded in such a manner as to form, not, as in ordinary churches, a prolongation behind the altar, but a sort of hall, or obscure cellar, to the right of the officiating priest; suppose this hall to be shut off by a curtain seven feet in height, of which we have already spoken; in the shadow of that curtain, pile up on wooden stalls the nuns in the choir on the left, the schoolgirls on the right, the lay-sisters and the novices at the bottom, and you will have some idea of the nuns of the Petit-Picpus assisting at divine service. That cavern, which was called the choir, communicated with the cloister by a lobby. The church was lighted from the garden. When the nuns were present at services where their rule enjoined silence, the public was warned of their presence only by the folding seats of the stalls noisily rising and falling.

Chapter VII

SOME SILHOUETTES OF THIS DARKNESS

DURING THE SIX YEARS WHICH SEPARATE 1819 FROM 1825, THE PRIORESS OF THE PETIT-PICPUS WAS Mademoiselle de Blemeur, whose name, in religion, was Mother Innocente. She came of the family of Marguerite de Blemeur, author of *Lives of the Saints of the Order of Saint-Benoît*. She had been re-elected. She was a woman about sixty years of age, short, thick, "singing like a cracked pot," says the letter which we have already quoted; an excellent woman, moreover, and the only merry one in the whole convent, and for that reason adored. She was learned, erudite, wise, competent, curiously proficient in history, crammed with Latin, stuffed with Greek, full of Hebrew, and more of a Benedictine monk than a Benedictine nun.

The sub prioress was an old Spanish nun, Mother Cineres, who was almost blind.

The most esteemed among the vocal mothers were Mother Sainte-Honorine; the treasurer, Mother Sainte-Gertrude, the chief mistress of the novices; Mother-Saint-Ange, the assistant mistress; Mother Annonciation, the sacristan; Mother Saint-Augustin, the nurse, the only one in the convent who was malicious; then Mother Sainte-Mechtilde (Mademoiselle Gauvain), very young and with a beautiful voice; Mother des Anges (Mademoiselle Drouet), who had been in the convent of the Filles-Dieu, and in the convent du Trésor, between Gisors and Magny; Mother Saint-Joseph (Mademoiselle de Cogolludo), Mother Sainte-Adélaide (Mademoiselle d'Auverney), Mother Miséricorde (Mademoiselle de Cifuentes, who could not resist austerities), Mother Compassion (Mademoiselle de la Miltière, received at the age of sixty, in defiance of the rule, and very wealthy); Mother Providence (Mademoiselle de Laudinière), Mother Présentation (Mademoiselle de Siguenza), who was prioress in 1847; and finally, Mother Sainte-Céligne (sister of the sculptor Ceracchi), who went mad; Mother Sainte-Chantal (Mademoiselle de Suzon), who went mad.

There was also, among the prettiest of them, a charming girl of three-and-twenty, who was from the Isle de Bourbon, a descendant of the Chevalier Roze, whose name had been Mademoiselle Roze, and who was called Mother Assumption.

Mother Sainte-Mechtilde, intrusted with the singing and the choir, was fond of making use of the pupils in this quarter. She usually took a complete scale of them, that is to say, seven, from ten to sixteen years of age, inclusive, of assorted voices and sizes, whom she made sing standing, drawn up in a line, side by side, according to age, from the smallest to the largest. This presented to the eye, something in the nature of a reed-pipe of young girls, a sort of living Pan-pipe made of angels.

Those of the lay-sisters whom the scholars loved most were Sister Euphrasie, Sister Sainte-Marguérite, Sister Sainte-Marthe, who was in her dotage, and Sister Sainte-Michel, whose long nose made them laugh.

All these women were gentle with the children. The nuns were severe only toward themselves. No fire was lighted except in the school, and the food was choice compared to that in the convent. Moreover, they lavished a thousand cares on their scholars. Only, when a child passed near a nun and addressed her, the nun never replied.

This rule of silence had had this effect, that throughout the whole convent, speech had been withdrawn from human creatures, and bestowed on inanimate objects. Now it was the church-bell which spoke, now it was the gardener's bell. A very sonorous bell, placed beside the portress, and which was audible throughout the house, indicated by its varied peals, which formed a sort of acoustic telegraph, all the actions of material life which were to be performed, and summoned to the parlor, in case of need, such or such an inhabitant of the house. Each person and each thing had its own peal. The prioress had one and one, the sub-prioress one and two. Six-five announced lessons, so that the pupils never said "to go to lessons," but "to go to six-five." Four-four was Madame de Genlis's signal. It was very often heard. "C'est le diable a quatre"—it's the very deuce—said the uncharitable. Ten-nine strokes announced a great event. It was the opening of *the door of seclusion*, a frightful sheet of iron bristling with bolts, which only turned on its hinges in the presence of the archbishop.

With the exception of the archbishop and the gardener, no man entered the convent, as we have already said. The schoolgirls saw two others: one, the chaplain, the Abbé Banés, old and ugly, whom they were permitted to contemplate in the choir, through a grating; the other the drawing-master, M. Ansiaux, whom the letter, of which we have perused a few lines, calls *M. Anciot*, and describes as *a frightful old hunchback*.

It will be seen that all these men were carefully chosen.

Such was this curious house.

Chapter VIII

Post Corda Lapides

AFTER HAVING SKETCHED ITS MORAL FACE, IT WILL NOT PROVE UNPROFITABLE TO POINT OUT, in a few words, its material configuration. The reader already has some idea of it.

The convent of the Petit-Picpus-Sainte-Antoine filled almost the whole of the vast trapezium which resulted from the intersection of the Rue Polonceau, the Rue Droit-Mur, the Rue Petit-Picpus, and the unused lane, called Rue Aumarais on old plans. These four streets surrounded this trapezium like a moat. The convent was composed of several buildings and a garden. The principal building, taken in its entirety, was a juxtaposition of hybrid constructions which, viewed from a bird's-eye view, outlined, with considerable exactness, a gibbet laid flat on the ground. The main arm of the gibbet occupied the whole of the fragment of the Rue Droit-Mur comprised between the Rue Petit-Picpus and the Rue Polonceau; the lesser arm was a lofty, gray, severe grated façade which faced the Rue Petit-Picpus; the carriage entrance No. 62 marked its extremity. Toward the center of this façade was a low, arched door, whitened with dust and ashes, where the spiders wove their webs, and which was open only for an hour or two on Sundays, and on rare occasions, when the coffin of a nun left the convent. This was the public entrance of the church. The elbow of the gibbet was a square hall which was used as the servants' hall, and which the nuns called *the buttery.* In the main arm were the cells of the mothers, the sisters, and the novices. In the lesser arm lay the kitchens, the refectory, backed up by the cloisters and the church. Between the door No. 62 and the corner of the closed lane Aumarais, was the school, which was not visible from without. The remainder of the trapezium formed the garden, which was much lower than the level of the Rue Polonceau, which caused the walls to be very much higher on the inside than on the outside. The garden, which was slightly arched, had in its center, on the summit of a hillock, a fine pointed and conical fir-tree, whence ran, as from the peaked boss of a shield, four grand alleys, and, ranged by twos in between the branchings of these, eight small ones, so that, if the enclosure had been circular, the geometrical plan of the alleys would have resembled a cross superposed on a wheel. As the alleys all ended in the very irregular walls of the garden, they were of unequal length. They were bordered with currant-bushes. At the bottom, an alley of tall poplars ran from the ruins of the old convent, which was at the angle of the Rue Droit-Mur to the house of the Little Convent, which was at the angle of the Aumarais lane. In front of the Little Convent was what was called the little garden. To this whole, let the reader add a courtyard, all sorts of varied angles formed by the interior buildings, prison walls, the long black line of roofs which bordered the other side of the Rue Polonceau for its sole perspective and neighborhood, and he will be able to form for himself a complete image of what the house of the Bernardines of the Petit-Picpus was forty years ago. This holy house had been built on the precise site of a famous tennis-ground of the fourteenth to the sixteenth century, which was called the "tennis-ground of the eleven thousand devils."

All these streets, moreover, were more ancient than Paris. These names, Droit-Mur and Aumarais are very ancient; the streets which bear them are very much more ancient still. Aumarais Lane was called Maugout Lane; the Rue Droit-Mur was called the Rue des Églantiers, for God opened flowers before man cut stones.

Chapter IX

A CENTURY UNDER A GUIMPE

SINCE WE ARE ENGAGED IN GIVING DETAILS AS TO WHAT THE CONVENT OF THE PETIT-PICPUS WAS in former times, and since we have ventured to open a window on that discreet retreat, the reader will permit us one other little digression, utterly foreign to this book, but characteristic and useful, since it shows that the cloister even has its original figures.

In the Little Convent there was a centenarian who came from the Abbey of Fontevrault. She had even been in society before the Revolution. She talked a great deal of M. de Miromesnil, Keeper of the Seals under Louis XVI and of a Presidentess Duplat, with whom she had been very intimate. It was her pleasure and her vanity to drag in these names on every pretext. She told wonders of the Abbey of Fontevrault—that it was like a city, and that there were streets in the monastery.

She talked with a Picard accent which amused the pupils. Every year, she solemnly renewed her vows, and at the moment of taking the oath, she said to the priest, "Monseigneur Saint-François gave it to Monseigneur Saint-Julien, Monseigneur Saint-Julien gave it to Monseigneur Saint-Eusebius, Monseigneur Saint-Eusebius gave it to Monseigneur Saint-Procopius, etc., etc.; and thus

I give it to you, father." And the schoolgirls would begin to laugh, not in their sleeves, but under their veils; charming little stifled laughs which made the vocal mothers frown.

On another occasion, the centenarian was telling stories. She said that *in her youth the Bernardine monks were every whit as good as the mousquetaires.* It was a century which spoke through her, but it was the eighteenth century. She told about the custom of the four wines, which existed before the Revolution in Champagne and Bourgogne. When a great personage, a marshal of France, a prince, a duke, and a peer traversed a town in Burgundy or Champagne, the city fathers came out to harangue him and presented him with four silver gondolas into which they had poured four different sorts of wine. On the first goblet this inscription could be read, *monkey wine*; on the second, *lion wine*; on the third, *sheep wine*; on the fourth, *hog wine*. These four legends express the four stages descended by the drunkard; the first, intoxication, which enlivens; the second, that which irritates; the third, that which dulls; and the fourth, that which brutalizes.

In a cupboard, under lock and key, she kept a mysterious object of which she thought a great deal. The rule of Fontevrault did not forbid this. She would not show this object to anyone. She shut herself up, which her rule allowed her to do, and hid herself, every time that she desired to contemplate it. If she heard a footstep in the corridor, she closed the cupboard again as hastily as it was possible with her aged hands. As soon as it was mentioned to her, she became silent, she who was so fond of talking. The most curious were baffled by her silence and the most tenacious by her obstinacy. Thus it furnished a subject of comment for all those who were unoccupied or bored in the convent. What could that treasure of the centenarian be, which was so precious and so secret? Some holy book, no doubt? Some unique chaplet? Some authentic relic? They lost themselves in conjectures. When the poor old woman died, they rushed to her cupboard more hastily than was fitting, perhaps, and opened it. They found the object beneath a triple linen cloth, like some consecrated paten. It was a Faenza platter representing little Loves flitting away pursued by apothecary lads armed with enormous syringes. The chase abounds in grimaces and in comical postures. One of the charming little Loves is already fairly spitted. He is resisting, fluttering his tiny wings, and still making an effort to fly, but the dancer is laughing with a satanical air. Moral: Love conquered by the colic. This platter, which is very curious, and which had, possibly, the honor of furnishing Molière with an idea, was still in existence in September, 1845; it was for sale by a bric-à-brac merchant in the Boulevard Beaumarchais.

This good old woman would not receive any visits from outside *because,* said she, the *parlor is too gloomy.*

Chapter X

ORIGIN OF THE PERPETUAL ADORATION

Howbver, THIS ALMOST SEPULCHRAL PARLOR, OF WHICH WE HAVE SOUGHT TO CONVEY AN IDEA, is a purely local trait which is not reproduced with the same severity in other convents. At the convent of the Rue du Temple, in particular, which belonged, in truth, to another order, the black shutters were replaced by brown curtains, and the parlor itself was a salon with a polished wood floor, whose windows were draped in white muslin curtains and whose walls admitted all sorts of frames, a portrait of a Benedictine nun with unveiled face, painted bouquets, and even the head of a Turk.

It is in that garden of the Temple convent, that stood that famous chestnut-tree which was renowned as the finest and the largest in France, and which bore the reputation among the good people of the eighteenth century of being *the father of all the chestnut-trees of the realm.*

As we have said, this convent of the Temple was occupied by Benedictines of the Perpetual Adoration, Benedictines quite different from those who depended on Cîteaux. This order of the Perpetual Adoration is not very ancient and does not go back more than two hundred years. In 1649 the holy sacrament was profaned on two occasions a few days apart, in two churches in Paris, at Saint-Sulpice and at Saint-Jean en Grève, a rare and frightful sacrilege which set the whole town in an uproar. M. the Prior and Vicar-General of Saint-Germain des Prés ordered a solemn procession of all his clergy, in which the Pope's Nuncio officiated. But this expiation did not satisfy two sainted women, Madame Courtin, Marquise de Boucs, and the Comtesse de Châteauvieux. This outrage committed on "the most holy sacrament of the altar," though but temporary, would not depart from these holy souls, and it seemed to them that it could only be extenuated by a "Perpetual Adoration" in some female monastery. Both of them, one in 1652, the other in 1653, made donations of notable sums to Mother Catherine de Bar, called of the Holy Sacrament, a Benedictine nun, for the purpose of founding, to this pious end, a monastery of the order of Saint-Benoît; the first permission for this foundation was given to Mother Catherine de Bar by M. de Metz, Abbé of Saint-Germain, "on condition that no woman could be received unless she contributed three hundred livres income, which amounts to six thousand livres, to the principal." After the Abbé of Saint-Germain, the king accorded letters-patent; and all the rest, abbatial charter, and royal letters, was confirmed in 1654 by the Chamber of Accounts and the Parliament.

Such is the origin and the legal consecration of the establishment of the Benedictines of the Perpetual Adoration of the Holy Sacrament at Paris. Their first convent was "a new building" in the Rue Cassette, out of the contributions of Mesdames de Boucs and de Châteauvieux.

This order, as it will be seen, was not to be confounded with the Benedictine nuns of Cîteaux. It mounted back to the Abbé of Saint-Germain des Prés, in the same manner that the ladies of the Sacred Heart go back to the general of the Jesuits, and the sisters of charity to the general of the Lazarists.

It was also totally different from the Bernardines of the Petit-Picpus, whose interior we have just shown. In 1657, Pope Alexander VII had authorized, by a special brief, the Bernardines of the Rue Petit-Picpus, to practice the Perpetual Adoration like the Benedictine nuns of the Holy Sacrament. But the two orders remained distinct none the less.

Chapter XI

END OF THE PETIT-PICPUS

AT THE BEGINNING OF THE RESTORATION, THE CONVENT OF THE PETIT-PICPUS WAS IN ITS DECAY; this forms a part of the general death of the order, which, after the eighteenth century, has been disappearing like all the religious orders. Contemplation is, like prayer, one of humanity's needs; but, like everything which the Revolution touched, it will be transformed, and from being hostile to social progress, it will become favorable to it.

The house of the Petit-Picpus was becoming rapidly depopulated. In 1840, the Little Convent had disappeared, the school had disappeared. There were no longer any old women, nor young girls; the first were dead, the latter had taken their departure. *Volaverunt.*

The rule of the Perpetual Adoration is so rigid in its nature that it alarms, vocations recoil be-

fore it, the order receives no recruits. In 1845, it still obtained lay-sisters here and there. But of professed nuns, none at all. Forty years ago, the nuns numbered nearly a hundred; fifteen years ago
there were not more than twenty-eight of them. How many are there to-day? In 1847, the prioress
was young, a sign that the circle of choice was restricted. She was not forty years old. In proportion as the number diminishes, the fatigue increases, the service of each becomes more painful; the
moment could then be seen drawing near when there would be but a dozen bent and aching shoulders to bear the heavy rule of Saint-Benoît. The burden is implacable, and remains the same for the
few as for the many. It weighs down, it crushes. Thus they die. At the period when the author of
this book still lived in Paris, two died. One was twenty-five years old, the other twenty-three. This
latter can say, like Julia Alpinula: *"Hic jaceo. Vixi annos viginti et tres."* It is in consequence of this
decay that the convent gave up the education of girls.

   We have not felt able to pass before this extraordinary house without entering it, and without
introducing the minds which accompany us, and which are listening to our tale, to the profit of
some, perchance, of the melancholy history of Jean Valjean. We have penetrated into this community, full of those old practices which seem so novel to-day. It is the closed garden, *hortus conclusus.*
We have spoken of this singular place in detail, but with respect, in so far, at least, as detail and respect are compatible. We do not understand all, but we insult nothing. We are equally far removed
from the hosanna of Joseph de Maistre, who wound up by anointing the executioner, and from the
sneer of Voltaire, who even goes so far as to ridicule the cross.

   An illogical act on Voltaire's part, we may remark, by the way; for Voltaire would have defended Jesus as he defended Calas; and even for those who deny superhuman incarnations, what
does the crucifix represent? The assassinated sage.

   In this nineteenth century, the religious idea is undergoing a crisis. People are unlearning certain things, and they do well, provided that, while unlearning them they learn this: There is no vacuum in the human heart. Certain demolitions take place, and it is well that they do, but on condition
that they are followed by reconstructions.

   In the meantime, let us study things which are no more. It is necessary to know them, if only
for the purpose of avoiding them. The counterfeits of the past assume false names, and gladly call
themselves the future. This specter, this past, is given to falsifying its own passport. Let us inform
ourselves of the trap. Let us be on our guard. The past has a visage, superstition, and a mask,
hypocrisy. Let us denounce the visage and let us tear off the mask.

   As for convents, they present a complex problem—a question of civilization, which condemns
them; a question of liberty, which protects them.

BOOK SEVENTH

PARENTHESIS

Chapter I

THE CONVENT AS AN ABSTRACT IDEA

THIS BOOK IS A DRAMA, WHOSE LEADING PERSONAGE IS THE INFINITE. Man is the second.

Such being the case, and a convent having happened to be on our road, it has been our duty to enter it. Why? Because the convent, which is common to the Orient as well as to the Occident, to antiquity as well as to modern times, to paganism, to Buddhism, to Mahometanism, as well as to Christianity, is one of the optical apparatuses applied by man to the Infinite.

This is not the place for enlarging disproportionately on certain ideas; nevertheless, while absolutely maintaining our reserves, our restrictions, and even our indignations, we must say that every time we encounter man in the Infinite, either well or ill understood, we feel ourselves overpowered with respect. There is, in the synagogue, in the mosque, in the pagoda, in the wigwam, a hideous side which we execrate, and a sublime side, which we adore. What a contemplation for the mind, and what endless food for thought, is the reverberation of God upon the human wall!

Chapter II

THE CONVENT AS AN HISTORICAL FACT

FROM THE POINT OF VIEW OF HISTORY, OF REASON, AND OF TRUTH, MONASTICISM IS CONDEMNED. Monasteries, when they abound in a nation, are clogs in its circulation, cumbrous establishments, centers of idleness where centers of labor should exist. Monastic communities are to the great social community what the mistletoe is to the oak, what the wart is to the human body. Their prosperity and their fatness mean the impoverishment of the country. The monastic regime, good at the beginning of civilization, useful in the reduction of the brutal by the spiritual, is bad when peoples have reached their manhood. Moreover, when it becomes relaxed, and when it enters into its period of disorder, it becomes bad for the very reasons which rendered it salutary in its period of purity, because it still continues to set the example.

Claustration has had its day. Cloisters, useful in the early education of modern civilization, have embarrassed its growth, and are injurious to its development. So far as institution and formation with relation to man are concerned, monasteries, which were good in the tenth century, questionable in the fifteenth, are detestable in the nineteenth. The leprosy of monasticism has gnawed nearly to a skeleton two wonderful nations, Italy and Spain; the one the light, the other the splendor of Europe for centuries; and, at the present day, these two illustrious peoples are but just beginning to convalesce, thanks to the healthy and vigorous hygiene of 1789 alone.

The convent—the ancient female convent in particular, such as it still presents itself on the threshold of this century, in Italy, in Austria, in Spain—is one of the most somber concretions of the Middle Ages. The cloister, that cloister, is the point of intersection of horrors. The Catholic cloister, properly speaking, is wholly filled with the black radiance of death.

The Spanish convent is the most funereal of all. There rise, in obscurity, beneath vaults filled with gloom, beneath domes vague with shadow, massive altars of Babel, as high as cathedrals; there immense white crucifixes hang from chains in the dark; there are extended, all nude on the ebony, great Christs of ivory; more than bleeding—bloody; hideous and magnificent, with their elbows displaying the bones, their knee-pans showing their integuments, their wounds showing their flesh, crowned with silver thorns, nailed with nails of gold, with blood drops of rubies on their brows, and diamond tears in their eyes. The diamonds and rubies seem wet, and make veiled beings in the shadow below weep, their sides bruised with the hair shirt and their iron-tipped scourges, their breasts crushed with wicker hurdles, their knees excoriated with prayer; women who think themselves wives, specters who think themselves seraphim. Do these women think? No. Have they any will? No. Do they love? No. Do they live? No. Their nerves have turned to bone; their bones have turned to stone. Their veil is of woven night. Their breath under their veil resembles the indescribably tragic respiration of death. The abbess, a specter, sanctifies them and terrifies them. The immaculate one is there, and very fierce. Such are the ancient monasteries of Spain. Liars of terrible devotion, caverns of virgins, ferocious places.

Catholic Spain is more Roman than Rome herself. The Spanish convent was, above all others, the Catholic convent. There was a flavor of the Orient about it. The archbishop, the kislar-aga of heaven, locked up and kept watch over this seraglio of souls reserved for God. The nun was the odalisque, the priest was the eunuch. The fervent were chosen in dreams and possessed Christ. At night, the beautiful, nude young man descended from the cross and became the ecstasy of the cloistered one. Lofty walls guarded the mystic sultana, who had the crucified for her sultan, from all living distraction. A glance on the outer world was infidelity. The *in pace* replaced the leather sack. That which was cast into the sea in the East was thrown into the ground in the West. In both quarters, women wrung their hands; the waves for the first, the grave for the last; here the drowned, there the buried. Monstrous parallel.

To-day the upholders of the past, unable to deny these things, have adopted the expedient of smiling at them. There has come into fashion a strange and easy manner of suppressing the revelations of history, of invalidating the commentaries of philosophy, of eliding all embarrassing facts and all gloomy questions. *A matter for declamations,* say the clever. Declamations, repeat the foolish. Jean-Jacques a declaimer; Diderot a declaimer; Voltaire on Calas, Labarre, and Sirven, declaimers. I know not who has recently discovered, that Tacitus was a declaimer, that Nero was a victim, and that pity is decidedly due to "that poor Holofernes."

Facts, however, are awkward things to disconcert, and they are obstinate. The author of this book has seen, with his own eyes, eight leagues distant from Brussels—there are relics of the Middle Ages there which are attainable for everybody—at the Abbey of Villers, the hole of the oubliettes, in the middle of the field which was formerly the courtyard of the cloister, and, on the banks of the Thil, four stone dungeons, half under ground, half under the water. They were *in pace*. Each of these dungeons has the remains of an iron door, a vault, and a grated opening which, on the outside, is two feet above the level of the river, and on the inside, six feet above the level of the ground. Four feet of river flow past along the outside wall. The ground is always soaked. The occupant of the *in pace* had this wet soil for his bed. In one of these dungeons, there is a fragment of an iron necklet riveted to the wall; in another, there can be seen a square box made of four slabs of granite, too short for a person to lie down in, too low for him to stand upright in. A human being was put inside, with a coverlid of stone on top. This exists. It can be seen. It can be touched. These *in pace*, these dungeons, these iron hinges, these necklets, that lofty peephole on a level with the river's current, that box of stone closed with a lid of granite like a tomb, with this difference, that the dead man here was a living being, that soil which is but mud, that vault hole, those oozing walls—what declaimers!

Chapter III

ON WHAT CONDITIONS ONE CAN RESPECT THE PAST

MONASTICISM, SUCH AS IT EXISTED IN SPAIN, AND SUCH AS IT STILL EXISTS IN THIBET, IS A SORT of phthisis for civilization. It stops life short. It simply depopulates. Claustration, castration. It has been the scourge of Europe. Add to this the violence so often done to the conscience, the forced vocations, feudalism bolstered up by the cloister, the right of the first-born pouring the excess of the family into monasticism, the ferocities of which we have just spoken, the *in pace*, the closed mouths, the walled-up brains, so many unfortunate minds placed in the dungeon of eternal vows, the taking of the habit, the interment of living souls. Add individual tortures to national degradations, and, whoever you may be, you will shudder before the frock and the veil—those two winding-sheets of human devising. Nevertheless, at certain points and in certain places, in spite of philosophy, in spite of progress, the spirit of the cloister persists in the midst of the nineteenth century, and a singular ascetic recrudescence is, at this moment, astonishing the civilized world. The obstinacy of antiquated institutions in perpetuating themselves resembles the stubbornness of the rancid perfume which should claim our hair, the pretensions of the spoiled fish which should persist in being eaten, the persecution of the child's garment which should insist on clothing the man, the tenderness of corpses which should return to embrace the living.

"Ingrates!" says the garment, "I protected you in inclement weather. Why will you have nothing to do with me?" "I have just come from the deep sea," says the fish. "I have been a rose," says the perfume. "I have loved you," says the corpse. "I have civilized you," says the convent.

To this there is but one reply: "In former days."

To dream of the indefinite prolongation of defunct things, and of the government of men by embalming, to restore dogmas in a bad condition, to regild shrines, to patch up cloisters, to rebless reliquaries, to refurnish superstitions, to revictual fanaticisms, to put new handles on holy water brushes and militarism, to reconstitute monasticism and militarism, to believe in the salvation of society by the multiplication of parasites, to force the past on the present—this seems strange. Still, there are theorists who hold such theories. These theorists, who are in other respects people of intelligence, have a very simple process; they apply to the past a glazing which they call social order, divine right, morality, family, the respect of elders, antique authority, sacred tradition, legitimacy, religion; and they go about shouting, "Look! take this, honest people." This logic was known to the ancients. The soothsayers practice it. They rubbed a black heifer over with chalk, and said, "She is white, *Bos cretatus.*"

As for us, we respect the past here and there, and we spare it, above all, provided that it consents to be dead. If it insists on being alive, we attack it, and we try to kill it.

Superstitions, bigotries, affected devotion, prejudices, those forms, all forms as they are, are tenacious of life; they have teeth and nails in their smoke, and they must be clasped close, body to body, and war must be made on them, and that without truce; for it is one of the fatalities of humanity to be condemned to eternal combat with phantoms. It is difficult to seize darkness by the throat, and to hurl it to the earth.

A convent in France, in the broad daylight of the nineteenth century, is a college of owls facing the light. A cloister, caught in the very act of asceticism, in the very heart of the city of '89 and of 1830 and of 1848, Rome blossoming out in Paris, is an anachronism. In ordinary times, in order to dissolve an anachronism and to cause it to vanish, one has only to make it spell out the date. But we are not in ordinary times.

Let us fight.

Let us fight, but let us make a distinction. The peculiar property of truth is never to commit excesses. What need has it of exaggeration? There is that which it is necessary to destroy, and there is that which it is simply necessary to elucidate and examine. What a force is kindly and serious examination! Let us not apply a flame where only a light is required.

So, given the nineteenth century, we are opposed, as a general proposition, and among all peoples, in Asia as well as in Europe, in India as well as in Turkey, to ascetic claustration. Whoever says cloister, says marsh. Their putrescence is evident, their stagnation is unhealthy, their fermentation infects people with fever, and etiolates them; their multiplication becomes a plague of Egypt. We cannot think without affright of those lands where fakirs, bonzes, santons, Greek monks, marabouts, talapoins, and dervishes multiply even like swarms of vermin.

This said, the religious question remains. This question has certain mysterious, almost formidable sides; may we be permitted to look at it fixedly.

Chapter IV

THE CONVENT FROM THE POINT OF VIEW OF PRINCIPLES

MEN UNITE THEMSELVES AND DWELL IN COMMUNITIES. BY VIRTUE OF WHAT RIGHT? BY VIRTUE of the right of association.

They shut themselves up at home. By virtue of what right? By virtue of the right which every man has to open or shut his door.

They do not come forth. By virtue of what right? By virtue of the right to go and come, which implies the right to remain at home.

There, at home, what do they do?

They speak in low tones; they drop their eyes; they toil. They renounce the world, towns, sensualities, pleasures, vanities, pride, interests. They are clothed in coarse woolen or coarse linen. Not one of them possesses in his own right anything whatever. On entering there, each one who was rich makes himself poor. What he has, he gives to all. He who was what is called noble, a gentleman and a lord, is the equal of him who was a peasant. The cell is identical for all. All undergo the same tonsure, wear the same frock, eat the same black bread, sleep on the same straw, die on the same ashes. The same sack on their backs, the same rope around their loins. If the decision has been to go barefoot, all go barefoot. There may be a prince among them; that prince is the same shadow as the rest. No titles. Even family names have disappeared. They bear only first names. All are bowed beneath the equality of baptismal names. They have dissolved the carnal family, and constituted in their community a spiritual family. They have no other relatives than all men. They succor the poor, they care for the sick. They elect those whom they obey. They call each other "my brother."

You stop me and exclaim, "But that is the ideal convent!"

It is sufficient that it may be the possible convent, that I should take notice of it.

Thence it results that, in the preceding book, I have spoken of a convent with respectful accents. The Middle Ages cast aside, Asia cast aside, the historical and political question held in reserve, from the purely philosophical point of view, outside the requirements of militant policy, on condition that the monastery shall be absolutely a voluntary matter and shall contain only consenting parties, I shall always consider a cloistered community with a certain attentive, and, in some respects, a deferential gravity.

Wherever there is a community, there is a commune; where there is a commune, there is right. The monastery is the product of the formula: Equality, Fraternity. Oh! how grand is liberty! And what a splendid transfiguration! Liberty suffices to transform the monastery into a republic.

Let us continue.

But these men, or these women who are behind these four walls. They dress themselves in coarse woolen, they are equals, they call each other brothers, that is well; but they do something else?

Yes.

What?

They gaze on the darkness, they kneel, and they clasp their hands.

What does this signify?

Chapter V

PRAYER

THEY PRAY.

To whom?

To God.

To pray to God—what is the meaning of these words?

Is there an infinite beyond us? Is that infinite there, inherent, permanent; necessarily substantial, since it is infinite; and because, if it lacked matter it would be bounded; necessarily intelligent, since it is infinite, and because, if it lacked intelligence, it would end there? Does this infinite awaken in us the idea of essence, while we can attribute to ourselves only the idea of existence? In other terms, is it not the absolute, of which we are only the relative?

At the same time that there is an infinite without us, is there not an infinite within us? Are not these two infinities (what an alarming plural!) superposed, the one upon the other? Is not this second infinite, so to speak, subjacent to the first? Is it not the latter's mirror, reflection, echo, an abyss which is concentric with another abyss? Is this second infinity intelligent also? Does it think? Does it love? Does it will? If these two infinities are intelligent, each of them has a will principle, and there is an *I* in the upper infinity as there is an *I* in the lower infinity. The *I* below is the soul; the *I* on high is God.

To place the infinity here below in contact, by the medium of thought, with the infinity on high, is called praying.

Let us take nothing from the human mind; to suppress is bad. We must reform and transform. Certain faculties in man are directed towards the Unknown; thought, reverie, prayer. The Unknown is an ocean. What is conscience? It is the compass of the Unknown. Thought, reverie, prayer—these are great and mysterious radiations. Let us respect them. Whither go these majestic irradiations of the soul? Into the shadow; that is to say, to the light.

The grandeur of democracy is to disown nothing and to deny nothing of humanity. Close to the right of the man, beside it at the least, there exists the right of the soul.

To crush fanaticism and to venerate the infinite, such is the law. Let us not confine ourselves to prostrating ourselves before the tree of creation, and to the contemplation of its branches full of stars. We have a duty to labor over the human soul, to defend the mystery against the miracle, to adore the incomprehensible and reject the absurd, to admit, as an inexplicable fact, only what is necessary, to purify belief, to remove superstitions from above religion; to clear God of caterpillars.

Chapter VI

The Absolute Goodness of Prayer

WITH REGARD TO THE MODES OF PRAYER, ALL ARE GOOD, PROVIDED THAT THEY ARE SINCERE. Turn your book upside down and be in the infinite.

There is, as we know, a philosophy which denies the infinite. There is also a philosophy, pathologically classified, which denies the sun; this philosophy is called blindness.

To erect a sense which we lack into a source of truth, is a fine blind man's self-sufficiency.

The curious thing is the haughty, superior, and compassionate airs which this groping philosophy assumes toward the philosophy which beholds God. One fancies he hears a mole crying, "I pity them with their sun!"

There are, as we know, powerful and illustrious atheists. At bottom, led back to the truth by their very force, they are not absolutely sure that they are atheists; it is with them only a question of definition, and in any case, if they do not believe in God, being great minds, they prove God.

We salute them as philosophers, while inexorably denouncing their philosophy.

Let us go on.

The remarkable thing about it is, also, their facility in paying themselves off with words. A metaphysical school of the North, impregnated to some extent with fog, has fancied that it has worked a revolution in human understanding by replacing the word Force with the word Will.

To say: "the plant wills," instead of: "the plant grows": this would be fecund in results, indeed, if we were to add: "the universe wills." Why? Because it would come to this: the plant wills, therefore it has an *I*; the universe wills, therefore it has a God.

As for us, who, however, in contradistinction to this school, reject nothing *a priori*, a will in the plant, accepted by this school, appears to us more difficult to admit than a will in the universe denied by it.

To deny the will of the infinite, that is to say, God, is impossible on any other conditions than a denial of the infinite. We have demonstrated this.

The negation of the infinite leads straight to nihilism. Everything becomes "a mental conception."

With nihilism, no discussion is possible; for the nihilist logic doubts the existence of its interlocutor, and is not quite sure that it exists itself.

From its point of view, it is possible that it may be for itself, only "a mental conception."

Only, it does not perceive that all which it has denied it admits in the lump, simply by the utterance of the word, mind.

In short, no way is open to the thought by a philosophy which makes all end in the monosyllable, No.

To No there is only one reply, Yes.

Nihilism has no point.

There is no such thing as nothingness. Zero does not exist. Everything is something. Nothing is nothing.

Man lives by affirmation even more than by bread.

Even to see and to show does not suffice. Philosophy should be an energy; it should have for effort and effect to ameliorate the condition of man. Socrates should enter into Adam and produce Marcus Aurelius; in other words, the man of wisdom should be made to emerge from the man of felicity. Eden should be changed into a Lyceum. Science should be a cordial. To enjoy— what a sad aim, and what a paltry ambition! The brute enjoys. To offer thought to the thirst of men, to give them all as an elixir the notion of God, to make conscience and science fraternize in them, to render them just by this mysterious confrontation; such is the function of real philosophy. Morality is a blossoming out of truths. Contemplation leads to action. The absolute should be practicable. It is necessary that the ideal should be breathable, drinkable, and eatable to the human mind. It is the ideal which has the right to say: *Take, this is my body, this is my blood.* Wisdom is a holy communion. It is on this condition that it ceases to be a sterile love of science and becomes the one and sovereign mode of human rallying, and that philosophy herself is promoted to religion.

Philosophy should not be a corbel erected on mystery to gaze upon it at its ease, without any other result than that of being convenient to curiosity.

For our part, adjourning the development of our thought to another occasion, we will confine ourselves to saying that we neither understand man as a point of departure nor progress as an end, without those two forces which are their two motors: faith and love.

Progress is the goal, the ideal is the type.

What is this ideal? It is God.

Ideal, absolute, perfection, infinity: identical words.

Chapter VII

PRECAUTIONS TO BE OBSERVED IN BLAME

HISTORY AND PHILOSOPHY HAVE ETERNAL DUTIES, WHICH ARE, AT THE SAME TIME, SIMPLE DUties; to combat Caiphas the High-priest, Draco the Lawgiver, Trimalcion the Legislator, Tiberius the Emperor; this is clear, direct, and limpid, and offers no obscurity.

But the right to live apart, even with its inconveniences and its abuses, insists on being stated and taken into account. Cenobitism is a human problem.

When one speaks of convents, those abodes of error, but of innocence, of aberration but of good-will, of ignorance but of devotion, of torture but of martyrdom, it always becomes necessary to say either yes or no.

A convent is a contradiction. Its object, salvation; its means thereto, sacrifice. The convent is supreme egoism having for its result supreme abnegation.

To abdicate with the object of reigning seems to be the device of monasticism.

In the cloister, one suffers in order to enjoy. One draws a bill of exchange on death. One discounts in terrestrial gloom celestial light. In the cloister, hell is accepted in advance as a post obit on paradise.

The taking of the veil or the frock is a suicide paid for with eternity.

It does not seem to us, that on such a subject mockery is permissible. All about it is serious, the good as well as the bad.

The just man frowns, but never smiles with a malicious sneer. We understand wrath, but not malice.

Chapter VIII

FAITH, LAW

A FEW WORDS MORE.
     We blame the church when she is saturated with intrigues, we despise the spiritual which is harsh toward the temporal; but we everywhere honor the thoughtful man.

We salute the man who kneels.

A faith; this is a necessity for man. Woe to him who believes nothing.

One is not unoccupied because one is absorbed. There is visible labor and invisible labor.

To contemplate is to labor, to think is to act.

Folded arms toil, clasped hands work. A gaze fixed on heaven is a work.

Thales remained motionless for four years. He founded philosophy.

In our opinion, cenobites are not lazy men, and recluses are not idlers.

To meditate on the Shadow is a serious thing.

Without invalidating anything that we have just said, we believe that a perpetual memory of the tomb is proper for the living. On this point, the priest and the philosopher agree. *We must die.* The Abbé de la Trappe replies to Horace.

To mingle with one's life a certain presence of the sepulcher—this is the law of the sage; and it is the law of the ascetic. In this respect, the ascetic and the sage converge. There is a material growth; we admit it. There is a moral grandeur; we hold to that. Thoughtless and vivacious spirits say:

"What is the good of those motionless figures on the side of mystery? What purpose do they serve? What do they do?"

Alas! In the presence of the darkness which environs us, and which awaits us, in our ignorance of what the immense dispersion will make of us, we reply: "There is probably no work more divine than that performed by these souls." And we add: "There is probably no work which is more useful."

There certainly must be some who pray constantly for those who never pray at all.

In our opinion the whole question lies in the amount of thought that is mingled with prayer.

Leibnitz praying is grand, Voltaire adoring is fine. *Deo erexit Voltaire.*

We are for religion as against religions.

We are of the number who believe in the wretchedness of orisons, and the sublimity of prayer.

Moreover, at this minute which we are now traversing—a minute which will not, fortunately, leave its impress on the nineteenth century—at this hour, when so many men have low brows and souls but little elevated, among so many mortals whose morality consists in enjoyment, and who are busied with the brief and misshapen things of matter, whoever exiles himself seems worthy of veneration to us.

The monastery is a renunciation. Sacrifice wrongly directed is still sacrifice. To mistake a grave error for a duty has a grandeur of its own.

Taken by itself, and ideally, and in order to examine the truth on all sides until all aspects have been impartially exhausted, the monastery, the female convent in particular—for in our century it is woman who suffers the most, and in this exile of the cloister there is something of protestation—the female convent has incontestably a certain majesty.

This cloistered existence which is so austere, so depressing, a few of whose features we have just traced, is not life, for it is not liberty; it is not the tomb, for it is not plenitude; it is the strange place whence one beholds, as from the crest of a lofty mountain, on one side the abyss where we are, on the other, the abyss whither we shall go; it is the narrow and misty frontier separating two worlds, illuminated and obscured by both at the same time, where the ray of life which has become enfeebled is mingled with the vague ray of death; it is the half obscurity of the tomb.

We, who do not believe what these women believe, but who, like them, live by faith—we have never been able to think without a sort of tender and religious terror, without a sort of pity, that is full of envy, of those devoted, trembling and trusting creatures, of these humble and august souls who dare to dwell on the very brink of the mystery, waiting between the world which is closed and heaven which is not yet open, turned toward the light which one cannot see, possessing the sole happiness of thinking that they know where it is, aspiring toward the gulf, and the unknown, their eyes fixed motionless on the darkness, kneeling, bewildered, stupefied, shuddering, half lifted, at times, by the deep breaths of eternity.

BOOK EIGHTH

CEMETERIES TAKE THAT WHICH IS COMMITTED THEM

Chapter I

WHICH TREATS OF THE MANNER OF ENTERING A CONVENT

IT WAS INTO THIS HOUSE THAT JEAN VALJEAN HAD, AS FAUCHELEVENT EXPRESSED IT, "FALLEN FROM the sky."

He had scaled the wall of the garden which formed the angle of the Rue Polonceau. That hymn of the angels which he had heard in the middle of the night, was the nuns chanting matins; that hall, of which he had caught a glimpse in the gloom, was the chapel. That phantom which he had seen stretched on the ground was the sister who was making reparation; that bell, the sound of which had so strangely surprised him, was the gardener's bell attached to the knee of Father Fauchelevent.

Cosette once put to bed, Jean Valjean and Fauchelevent had, as we have already seen, supped on a glass of wine and a bit of cheese before a good, crackling fire; then, the only bed in the hut being occupied by Cosette, each threw himself on a truss of straw.

Before he shut his eyes, Jean Valjean said: "I must remain here henceforth." This remark trotted through Fauchelevent's head all night long.

To tell the truth, neither of them slept.

Jean Valjean, feeling that he was discovered and that Javert was on his scent, understood that he and Cosette were lost if they returned to Paris. Then the new storm which had just burst upon him had stranded him in this cloister. Jean Valjean had, henceforth, but one thought—to remain there. Now, for an unfortunate man in his position, this convent was both the safest and the most dangerous of places; the most dangerous, because, as no men might enter there, if he were discovered, it was a flagrant offense, and Jean Valjean would find but one step intervening between the convent and prison; the safest, because, if he could manage to get himself accepted there and remain there, who would ever seek him in such a place? To dwell in an impossible place was safety.

On his side, Fauchelevent was cudgeling his brains. He began by declaring to himself that he understood nothing of the matter. How had M. Madeleine got there, when the walls were what they were? Cloister walls are not to be stepped over. How did he get there with a child? One cannot scale a perpendicular wall with a child in one's arms. Who was that child? Where did they both come from? Since Fauchelevent had lived in the convent, he had heard nothing of M. sur M., and he knew nothing of what had taken place there. Father Madeleine had an air which discouraged questions; and besides, Fauchelevent said to himself: "One does not question a saint." M. Madeleine had preserved all his prestige in Fauchelevent's eyes. Only, from some words which Jean Valjean had let fall, the gardener thought he could draw the inference that M. Madeleine had probably become bankrupt through the hard times, and that he was pursued by his creditors; or that he had compromised himself in some political affair, and was in hiding; which last did not displease Fauchelevent, who, like many of our peasants of the North, had an old fund of Bonapartism about him. While in hiding, M. Madeleine had selected the convent as a refuge, and it was quite simple that he should wish to remain there. But the inexplicable point, to which Fauchelevent returned constantly and over which he wearied his brain, was that M. Madeleine should be there, and that he should have that little girl with him. Fauchelevent saw them, touched them, spoke to them, and still did not believe it possible. The incomprehensible had just made its entrance into Fauchelevent's hut. Fauchelevent groped about amid conjectures, and could see nothing clearly but this: "M. Madeleine saved my life." This certainty alone was sufficient and decided his course. He said to himself: "It is my turn now." He added in his conscience: "M. Madeleine did not stop to deliberate when it was a question of thrusting himself under the cart for the purpose of dragging me out." He made up his mind to save M. Madeleine.

Nevertheless, he put many questions to himself and made himself divers replies: "After what he did for me, would I save him if he were a thief? Just the same. If he were an assassin, would I save him? Just the same. Since he is a saint, shall I save him? Just the same."

But what a problem it was to manage to have him remain in the convent! Fauchelevent did not recoil in the face of this almost chimerical undertaking; this poor peasant of Picardy without any other ladder than his self-devotion, his good-will, and a little of that old rustic cunning, on this occasion enlisted in the service of a generous enterprise, undertook to scale the difficulties of the cloister, and the steep escarpments of the rule of Saint-Benoît. Father Fauchelevent was an old man who had been an egoist all his life, and who, toward the end of his days, halt, infirm, with no interest left to him in the world, found it sweet to be grateful, and perceiving a generous action to be performed, flung himself upon it like a man, who at the moment when he is dying, should find close to his hand a glass of good wine which he had never tasted, and should swallow it with avidity. We may add, that the air which he had breathed for many years in this convent had destroyed all personality in him, and had ended by rendering a good action of some kind absolutely necessary to him.

So he took his resolve: to devote himself to M. Madeleine.

We have just called him a *poor peasant of Picardy*. That description is just, but incomplete. At the point of this story which we have now reached, a little of Father Fauchelevent's physiology becomes useful. He was a peasant, but he had been a notary, which added trickery to his cunning, and penetration to his ingenuousness. Having, through various causes, failed in his business, he had descended to the calling of a carter and a laborer. But, in spite of oaths and lashings, which horses seem to require, something of the notary had lingered in him. He had some natural wit; he talked good grammar; he conversed, which is a rare thing in a village; and the other peasants said of him: "He talks almost like a gentleman with a hat." Fauchelevent belonged, in fact, to that species, which the impertinent and flippant vocabulary of the last century qualified as *demi-bourgeois, demi-lout,* and which the metaphors showered by the château upon the thatched cottage ticketed in the pigeon-hole of the plebeian: *rather rustic, rather citified; pepper and salt.* Fauchelevent, though sorely tried and harshly used by fate, worn out, a sort of poor, threadbare old soul, was, nevertheless, an impulsive man, and extremely spontaneous in his actions; a precious quality which prevents one from ever being wicked. His defects and his vices, for he had some, were all superficial; in short, his physiognomy was of the kind which succeeds with an observer. His aged face had none of those disagreeable wrinkles at the top of the forehead, which signify malice or stupidity.

At daybreak, Father Fauchelevent opened his eyes, after having done an enormous deal of thinking, and beheld M. Madeleine seated on his truss of straw, and watching Cosette's slumbers. Fauchelevent sat up and said:

"Now that you are here, how are you going to contrive to enter?"

This remark summed up the situation and aroused Jean Valjean from his reverie.

The two men took counsel together.

"In the first place," said Fauchelevent, "you will begin by not setting foot outside of this chamber, either you or the child. One step in the garden and we are done for."

"That is true."

"Monsieur Madeleine," resumed Fauchelevent, "you have arrived at a very auspicious moment, I mean to say a very inauspicious moment; one of the ladies is very ill. This will prevent them from looking much in our direction. It seems that she is dying. The prayers of the forty hours are being said. The whole community is in confusion. That occupies them. The one who is on the point of departure is a saint. In fact, we are all saints here; all the difference between them and me is that they say 'our cell,' and that I say 'my cabin.' The prayers for the dying are to be said, and then the prayers for the dead. We shall be at peace here for to-day; but I will not answer for to-morrow."

"Still," observed Jean Valjean, "this cottage is in the niche of the wall, it is hidden by a sort of ruin, there are trees, it is not visible from the convent."

"And I add that the nuns never come near it."

"Well?" said Jean Valjean.

The interrogation mark which accentuated this "well" signified: "it seems to me that one may remain concealed here?" It was to this interrogation point that Fauchelevent responded:

"There are the little girls."

"What little girls?" asked Jean Valjean.

Just as Fauchelevent opened his mouth to explain the words which he had uttered, a bell emitted one stroke.

"The nun is dead," said he. "There is the knell."

And he made a sign to Jean Valjean to listen.

The bell struck a second time.

"It is the knell, Monsieur Madeleine. The bell will continue to strike once a minute for twenty-four hours, until the body is taken from the church.—You see, they play. At recreation hours it suffices to have a ball roll aside, to send them all hither, in spite of prohibitions, to hunt and rummage for it all about here. Those cherubs are devils."

"Who?" asked Jean Valjean.

"The little girls. You would be very quickly discovered. They would shriek: 'Oh! a man!' There is no danger to-day. There will be no recreation hour. The day will be entirely devoted to prayers. You hear the bell. As I told you, a stroke each minute. It is the death knell."

"I understand, Father Fauchelevent. There are pupils."

And Jean Valjean thought to himself:

"Here is Cosette's education already provided."

Fauchelevent exclaimed:

"Pardine! There are little girls indeed! And they would bawl around you! And they would rush off! To be a man here is to have the plague. You see how they fasten a bell to my paw as though I were a wild beast."

Jean Valjean fell into more and more profound thought.—"This convent would be our salvation," he murmured.

Then he raised his voice:

"Yes, the difficulty is to remain here."

"No," said Fauchelevent, "the difficulty is to get out."

Jean Valjean felt the blood rush back to his heart.

"To get out!"

"Yes, Monsieur Madeleine. In order to return here it is first necessary to get out."

And after waiting until another stroke of the knell had sounded, Fauchelevent went on:

"You must not be found here in this fashion. Whence come you? For me, you fall from heaven, because I know you; but the nuns require one to enter by the door."

All at once they heard a rather complicated pealing from another bell.

"Ah!" said Fauchelevent, "they are ringing up the vocal mothers. They are going to the chapter. They always hold a chapter when anyone dies. She died at daybreak. People generally do die at daybreak. But cannot you get out by the way in which you entered? Come, I do not ask for the sake of questioning you, but how did you get in?"

Jean Valjean turned pale; the very thought of descending again into that terrible street made him shudder. You make your way out of a forest filled with tigers, and once out of it, imagine a friendly counsel that shall advise you to return thither! Jean Valjean pictured to himself the whole police force still engaged in swarming in that quarter, agents on the watch, sentinels everywhere, frightful fists extended toward his collar, Javert at the corner of the intersection of the streets perhaps.

"Impossible!" said he. "Father Fauchelevent, say that I fell from the sky."

"But I believe it, I believe it," retorted Fauchelevent. "You have no need to tell me that. The good God must have taken you in his hand for the purpose of getting a good look at you close to, and then dropped you. Only, he meant to place you in a man's convent; he made a mistake. Come, there goes another peal, that is to order the porter to go and inform the municipality that the deaddoctor is to come here and view a corpse. All that is the ceremony of dying. These good ladies are not at all fond of that visit. A doctor is a man who does not believe in anything. He lifts the veil. Sometimes he lifts something else too. How quickly they have had the doctor summoned this time! What is the matter? Your little one is still asleep. What is her name?"

"Cosette."

"She is your daughter? You are her grandfather, that is?"

"Yes."

"It will be easy enough for her to get out of here. I have my service door which opens on the courtyard. I knock. The porter opens; I have my vintage basket on my back, the child is in it, I go out. Father Fauchelevent goes out with his basket—that is perfectly natural. You will tell the child to keep very quiet. She will be under the cover. I will leave her for whatever time is required with a good old friend, a fruit-seller whom I know in the Rue Chemin-Vert, who is deaf, and who has a little bed. I will shout in the fruit-seller's ear, that she is a niece of mine, and that she is to keep her for me until to-morrow. Then the little one will re-enter with you; for I will contrive to have you re-enter. It must be done. But how will you manage to get out?"

Jean Valjean shook his head.

"No one must see me, the whole point lies there, Father Fauchelevent. Find some means of getting me out in a basket, under cover, like Cosette."

Fauchelevent scratched the lobe of his ear with the middle finger of his left hand, a sign of serious embarrassment.

A third peal created a diversion.

"That is the dead-doctor taking his departure," said Fauchelevent. "He has taken a look and said: 'She is dead, that is well.' When the doctor has signed the passport for paradise, the undertaker's company sends a coffin. If it is a mother, the mothers lay her out; if she is a sister, the sisters lay her out. After which, I nail her up. That forms a part of my gardener's duty. A gardener is a bit of a gravedigger. She is placed in a lower hall of the church which communicates with the street, and into which no man may enter save the doctor of the dead. I don't count the undertaker's men and myself as men. It is in that hall that I nail up the coffin. The undertaker's men come and get it, and whip up, coachman! that's the way one goes to heaven. They fetch a box with nothing in it, they take it away again with something in it. That's what a burial is like. *De profundis.*"

A horizontal ray of sunshine lightly touched the face of the sleeping Cosette, who lay with her mouth vaguely open, and had the air of an angel drinking in the light. Jean Valjean had fallen to gazing at her. He was no longer listening to Fauchelevent.

That one is not listened to is no reason for preserving silence. The good old gardener went on tranquilly with his babble:

"The grave is dug in the Vaugirard cemetery. They declare that they are going to suppress that Vaugirard cemetery. It is an ancient cemetery which is outside the regulations, which has no uniform, and which is going to retire. It is a shame, for it is convenient. I have a friend there, Father Mestienne, the gravedigger. The nuns here possess one privilege, it is to be taken to that cemetery at nightfall. There is a special permission from the Prefecture on their behalf. But how many events have happened since yesterday! Mother Crucifixion is dead, and Father Madeleine—"

"Is buried," said Jean Valjean, smiling sadly.

Fauchelevent caught the word.

"Goodness! if you were here for good, it would be a real burial."

A fourth peal burst out. Fauchelevent hastily detached the belled knee-cap from its nail and buckled it on his knee again.

"This time it is for me. The Mother Prioress wants me. Good, now I am pricking myself on the tongue of my buckle. Monsieur Madeleine, don't stir from here, and wait for me. Something new has come up. If you are hungry, there is wine, bread, and cheese."

And he hastened out of the hut, crying: "Coming! coming!"

Jean Valjean watched him hurrying across the garden as fast as his crooked leg would permit, casting a sidelong glance by the way on his melon patch.

Less than ten minutes later, Father Fauchelevent, whose bell put the nuns in his road to flight, tapped gently at a door, and a gentle voice replied: *"Forever! Forever!"* that is to say: *"Enter."*

The door was the one leading to the parlor reserved for seeing the gardener on business. This parlor adjoined the chapter hall. The prioress, seated on the only chair in the parlor, was waiting for Fauchelevent.

Chapter II

FAUCHELEVENT IN THE PRESENCE OF A DIFFICULTY

I T IS THE PECULIARITY OF CERTAIN PERSONS AND CERTAIN PROFESSIONS, NOTABLY PRIESTS AND nuns, to wear a grave and agitated air on critical occasions. At the moment when Fauchelevent entered, this double form of preoccupation was imprinted on the countenance of the prioress, who was that wise and charming Mademoiselle de Blemeur, Mother Innocente, who was ordinarily cheerful.

The gardener made a timid bow, and remained at the door of the cell. The prioress, who was telling her beads, raised her eyes and said:

"Ah! it is you, Father Fauvent."

This abbreviation had been adopted in the convent.

Fauchelevent bowed again.

"Father Fauvent, I have sent for you."

"Here I am, reverend Mother."

"I have something to say to you."

"And so have I," said Fauchelevent with a boldness which caused him inward terror, "I have something to say to the very reverend Mother."

The prioress stared at him.

"Ah! you have a communication to make to me."

"A request."

"Very well, speak."

Goodman Fauchelevent, the ex-notary, belonged to the category of peasants who have assurance. A certain clever ignorance constitutes a force; you do not distrust it, and you are caught by it. Fauchelevent had been a success during the something more than two years which he had passed in the convent. Always solitary and busied about his gardening, he had nothing else to do than to indulge his curiosity. As he was at a distance from all those veiled women passing to and fro, he saw before him only an agitation of shadows. By dint of attention and sharpness he had succeeded in clothing all those phantoms with flesh, and those corpses were alive for him. He was like a deaf man whose sight grows keener, and like a blind man whose hearing becomes more acute. He had applied himself to riddling out the significance of the different peals, and he had succeeded, so that this taciturn and enigmatical cloister possessed no secrets for him; the sphinx babbled all her secrets in his ear. Fauchelevent knew all and concealed all; that constituted his art. The whole convent thought him stupid. A great merit in religion. The vocal mothers made much of Fauchelevent. He was a curious mute. He inspired confidence. Moreover, he was regular, and never went out except for well-demonstrated requirements of the orchard and vegetable garden. This discretion of conduct had inured to his credit. None the less, he had set two men to chattering: the porter, in the convent, and he knew the singularities of their parlor, and the gravedigger, at the cemetery, and he was acquainted with the peculiarities of their sepulture; in this way, he possessed a double light on the subject of these nuns, one as to their life, the other as to their death. But he did not abuse his knowledge. The congregation thought a great deal of him. Old, lame, blind to everything, probably a little deaf into the bargain—what qualities! They would have found it difficult to replace him.

The good man, with the assurance of a person who feels that he is appreciated, entered into a rather diffuse and very deep rustic harangue to the reverend prioress. He talked a long time about his age, his infirmities, the surcharge of years counting double for him henceforth, of the increasing demands of his work, of the great size of the garden, of nights which must be passed, like the last, for instance, when he had been obliged to put straw mats over the melon beds, because of the moon, and he wound up as follows: "That he had a brother"—(the prioress made a movement)—"a brother no longer young"—(a second movement on the part of the prioress, but one expressive of reassurance)—"that, if he might be permitted, this brother would come and live with him and help him, that he was an excellent gardener, that the community would receive from him good service, better than his own; that, otherwise, if his brother were not admitted, as he, the elder, felt that his health was broken and that he was insufficient for the work, he should be obliged, greatly to his regret, to go away; and that his brother had a little daughter whom he would bring with him, who might be reared for God in the house, and who might, who knows, become a nun someday."

When he had finished speaking, the prioress stayed the slipping of her rosary between her fingers, and said to him:

"Could you procure a stout iron bar between now and this evening?"

"For what purpose?"

"To serve as a lever."

"Yes, reverend Mother," replied Fauchelevent.

The prioress, without adding a word, rose and entered the adjoining room, which was the hall of the chapter, and where the vocal mothers were probably assembled. Fauchelevent was left alone.

Chapter III

MOTHER INNOCENTE

ABOUT A QUARTER OF AN HOUR ELAPSED. THE PRIORESS RETURNED AND SEATED HERSELF ONCE more on her chair.

The two interlocutors seemed preoccupied. We will present a stenographic report of the dialogue which then ensued, to the best of our ability.

"Father Fauvent!"

"Reverend Mother!"

"Do you know the chapel?"

"I have a little cage there, where I hear the mass and the offices."

"And you have been in the choir in pursuance of your duties?"

"Two or three times."

"There is a stone to be raised."

"Heavy?"

"The slab of the pavement which is at the side of the altar."

"The slab which closes the vault?"

"Yes."

"It would be a good thing to have two men for it."

"Mother Ascension, who is as strong as a man, will help you."

"A woman is never a man."

"We have only a woman here to help you. Each one does what he can. Because Dom Mabillon gives four hundred and seventeen epistles of Saint Bernard, while Merlonus Horstius only gives three hundred and sixty-seven, I do not despise Merlonus Horstius."

"Neither do I."

"Merit consists in working according to one's strength. A cloister is not a dock-yard."

"And a woman is not a man. But my brother is the strong one, though!"

"And can you get a lever?"

"That is the only sort of key that fits that sort of door."

"There is a ring in the stone."

"I will put the lever through it."

"And the stone is so arranged that it swings on a pivot."

"That is good, reverend Mother. I will open the vault."

"And the four Mother Precentors will help you."

"And when the vault is open?"

"It must be closed again."

"Will that be all?"

"No."

"Give me your orders, very reverend Mother."

"Fauvent, we have confidence in you."

"I am here to do anything you wish."

"And to hold your peace about everything."

"Yes, reverend Mother."

"When the vault is open—"

"I will close it again."

"But before that—"

"What, reverend Mother?"

"Something must be lowered into it."

A silence ensued. The prioress, after a pout of the under lip which resembled hesitation, broke it.

"Father Fauvent!"

"Reverend Mother!"

"You know that a mother died this morning?"

"No."

"Did you not hear the bell?"

"Nothing can be heard at the bottom of the garden."

"Really?"

"I can hardly distinguish my own signal."

"She died at daybreak."

"And then, the wind is not blowing in my direction this morning."

"It was Mother Crucifixion. A blessed woman."

The prioress paused, moved her lips, as though in mental prayer, and resumed:

"Three years ago, Madame de Béthune, a Jansenist, turned orthodox, merely from having seen Mother Crucifixion at prayer."

"Ah! yes, now I hear the knell, reverend Mother."

"The mothers have taken her to the dead-room, which opens on the church."

"I know."

"No other man than you can or must enter that chamber. See to that. A fine sight it would be, to see a man enter the dead-room!"

"More often!"

"Hey?"

"More often!"

"What do you say?"

"I say more often."

"More often than what?"

"Reverend Mother, I did not say more often than what, I said more often."

"I don't understand you. Why do you say more often?"

"In order to speak like you, reverend Mother."

"But I did not say 'more often.' "

At that moment, nine o'clock struck.

"At nine o'clock in the morning and at all hours, praised and adored be the most Holy Sacrament of the altar," said the prioress.

"Amen," said Fauchelevent.

The clock struck opportunely. It cut "more often" short. It is probable, that had it not been for this, the prioress and Fauchelevent would never have unraveled that skein.

Fauchelevent mopped his forehead.

The prioress indulged in another little inward murmur, probably sacred, then raised her voice: "In her lifetime, Mother Crucifixion made converts; after her death, she will perform miracles."

"She will!" replied Father Fauchelevent, falling into step, and striving not to flinch again.

"Father Fauvent, the community has been blessed in Mother Crucifixion. No doubt, it is not granted to everyone to die, like Cardinal de Bérulle, while saying the holy mass, and to breathe forth their souls to God, while pronouncing these words: *Hanc igitur oblationem*. But without attaining to such happiness, Mother Crucifixion's death was very precious. She retained her consciousness to the very last moment. She spoke to us, then she spoke to the angels. She gave us her last commands. If you had a little more faith, and if you could have been in her cell, she would have cured your leg merely by touching it. She smiled. We felt that she was regaining her life in God. There was something of paradise in that death."

Fauchelevent thought that it was an orison which she was finishing.

"Amen," said he.

"Father Fauvent, what the dead wish must be done."

The prioress told off several beads of her chaplet. Fauchelevent held his peace.

She went on:

"I have consulted upon this point many ecclesiastics laboring in Our Lord, who occupy themselves in the exercises of the clerical life, and who bear wonderful fruit."

"Reverend Mother, you can hear the knell much better here than in the garden."

"Besides, she is more than a dead woman, she is a saint."

"Like yourself, reverend Mother."

"She slept in her coffin for twenty years, by express permission of our Holy Father, Pius VII—"

"The one who crowned the Emp—Buonaparte."

For a clever man like Fauchelevent, this allusion was an awkward one. Fortunately, the prioress, completely absorbed in her own thoughts, did not hear it. She continued:

"Father Fauvent?"

"Reverend Mother?"

"Saint Didorus, Archbishop of Cappadocia, desired that this single word might be inscribed on his tomb: *Acarus*, which signifies, a worm of the earth; this was done. Is this true?"

"Yes, reverend Mother."

"The blessed Mezzocane, Abbot of Aquila, wished to be buried beneath the gallows; this was done."

"That is true."

"Saint Terentius, Bishop of Port, where the mouth of the Tiber empties into the sea, requested that on his tomb might be engraved the sign which was placed on the graves of parricides, in the hope that passers-by would spit on his tomb. This was done. The dead must be obeyed."

"So be it."

"The body of Bernard Guidonis, born in France near Roche-Abeille, was, as he had ordered, and in spite of the king of Castile, borne to the church of the Dominicans in Limoges, although Bernard Guidonis was Bishop of Tuy in Spain. Can the contrary be affirmed?"

"For that matter, no, reverend Mother."

"The fact is attested by Plantavit de la Fosse."

Several beads of the chaplet were told off, still in silence. The prioress resumed:

"Father Fauvent, Mother Crucifixion will be interred in the coffin in which she has slept for the last twenty years."

"That is just."

"It is a continuation of her slumber."

"So I shall have to nail up that coffin?"

"Yes."

"And we are to reject the undertaker's coffin?"

"Precisely."

"I am at the orders of the very reverend community."

"The four Mother Precentors will assist you."

"In nailing up the coffin? I do not need them."

"No. In lowering the coffin."

"Where?"

"Into the vault."

"What vault?"

"Under the altar."

Fauchelevent started.

"The vault under the altar?"

"Under the altar."

"But—"

"You will have an iron bar."

"Yes, but—"

"You will raise the stone with the bar by means of the ring."

"But—"

"The dead must be obeyed. To be buried in the vault under the altar of the chapel, not to go to profane earth; to remain there in death where she prayed while living; such was the last wish of Mother Crucifixion. She asked it of us; that is to say, commanded us."

"But it is forbidden."

"Forbidden by men, enjoined by God."

"What if it became known?"

"We have confidence in you."

"Oh! I am a stone in your walls."

"The chapter assembled. The vocal mothers, whom I have just consulted again, and who are now deliberating, have decided that Mother Crucifixion shall be buried, according to her wish, in her own coffin, under our altar. Think, Father Fauvent, if she were to work miracles here! What a glory of God for the community! And miracles issue from tombs."

"But, reverend Mother, if the agent of the sanitary commission—"

"Saint Benoît II, in the matter of sepulture, resisted Constantine Pogonatus."

"But the commissary of police—"

"Chonodemaire, one of the seven German kings who entered among the Gauls under the Empire of Constantius, expressly recognized the right of nuns to be buried in religion, that is to say, beneath the altar."

"But the inspector from the Prefecture—"

"The world is nothing in the presence of the cross. Martin, the eleventh general of the Carthusians, gave to his order this device: *Stat crux dum volvitur orbis*."

"Amen," said Fauchelevent, who imperturbably extricated himself in this manner from the dilemma, whenever he heard Latin.

Any audience suffices for a person who has held his peace too long. On the day when the rhetorician Gymnastoras left his prison, bearing in his body many dilemmas and numerous syllogisms which had struck in, he halted in front of the first tree which he came to, harangued it and made very great efforts to convince it. The prioress, who was usually subjected to the barrier of silence, and whose reservoir was overfull, rose and exclaimed with the loquacity of a dam which has broken away:

"I have on my right Benoît and on my left Bernard. Who was Bernard? The first abbot of Clairvaux. Fontaines in Burgundy is a country that is blest because it gave him birth. His father was named Técelin, and his mother Alèthe. He began at Cîteaux, to end in Clairvaux; he was ordained abbot by the Bishop of Châlon-sur-Saône, Guillaume de Champeaux; he had seven hundred novices, and founded a hundred and sixty monasteries; he overthrew Abeilard at the council of Sens in 1140, and Pierre de Bruys and Henry his disciple, and another sort of erring spirits who were called the Apostolics; he confounded Arnauld de Brescia, darted lightning at the monk Raoul, the murderer of the Jews, dominated the council of Reims in 1148, caused the condemnation of Gilbert de Poréa, Bishop of Poitiers, caused the condemnation of Éon de l'Étoile, arranged the disputes of princes, enlightened King Louis the Young, advised Pope Eugene III, regulated the Temple, preached the crusade, performed two hundred and fifty miracles during his lifetime, and as many as thirty-nine in one day. Who was Benoît? He was the patriarch of Mont-Cassin; he was the second founder of the Sainteté Claustrale, he was the Basil of the West. His order has produced forty popes, two hundred cardinals, fifty patriarchs, sixteen hundred archbishops, four thousand six hundred bishops, four emperors, twelve empresses, forty-six kings, forty-one queens, three thousand six hundred canonized saints, and has been in existence for fourteen hundred years. On one side Saint Bernard, on the other the agent of the sanitary department! On one side Saint Benoît, on the other the inspector of public ways! The state, the road commissioners, the public undertaker, regulations, the administration, what do we know of all that? There is not a chance passer-by who would not be indignant to see how we are treated. We have not even the right to give our dust to Jesus Christ! Your sanitary department is a revolutionary invention, God subordinated to the commissary of police; such is the age. Silence, Fauvent!"

Fauchelevent was but ill at ease under this shower bath. The prioress continued:

"No one doubts the right of the monastery to sepulture. Only fanatics and those in error deny it. We live in times of terrible confusion. We do not know that which it is necessary to know, and we know that which we should ignore. We are ignorant and impious. In this age there exist people who do not distinguish between the very great Saint Bernard and the Saint Bernard denominated of the poor Catholics, a certain good ecclesiastic who lived in the thirteenth century. Others are so blasphemous as to compare the scaffold of Louis XVI to the cross of Jesus Christ. Louis XVI was merely a king. Let us beware of God! There is no longer just nor unjust. The name of Voltaire is known, but not the name of César de Bus. Nevertheless, César de Bus is a man of blessed memory, and Voltaire one of unblessed memory. The last archbishop, the Cardinal de Périgord, did not even know that Charles de Gondren succeeded to Berulle, and François Bourgoin to Gondren, and Jean-François Senault to Bourgoin, and Father Sainte-Marthe to Jean-François Senault. The name of Father Coton is known, not because he was one of the three who urged the foundation of the Oratorie, but because he furnished Henri IV, the Huguenot king, with the material for an oath. That which pleases people of the world in Saint François de Sales, is that he cheated at play. And then, religion is attacked. Why? Because there have been bad priests, because Sagittaire, Bishop of Gap, was the brother of Salone, Bishop of Embrun, and because both of them followed Mommol. What has that to do with the question? Does that prevent Martin de Tours from being a saint, and giving half of his cloak to a beggar? They persecute the saints. They shut their eyes to the truth. Darkness is the rule. The most ferocious beasts are beasts which are blind. No one thinks of hell as a reality. Oh! how wicked people are! By order of the king signifies to-day, by order of the revolution. One no longer knows what is due to the living or to the dead. A holy death is prohibited. Burial is a civil matter. This is horrible. Saint Leo II wrote two special letters, one to Pierre Notaire, the other to the king of the Visigoths, for the purpose of combating and rejecting, in questions touching the dead, the authority of the exarch and the supremacy of the Emperor. Gauthier, Bishop of Châlons, held his own in this matter against Otho, Duke of Burgundy. The ancient magistracy agreed with him. In former times we had voices in the chapter, even on matters of the day. The Abbot of Cîteaux, the general of the order, was councilor by right of birth to the parliament of Burgundy. We do what we please with our dead. Is not the body of Saint Benoît himself in France, in the abbey of Fleury, called Saint Benoît-sur-Loire, although he died in Italy at Mont-Cassin, on Saturday, the 21st of the month of March, of the year 543? All this is incontestable. I abhor psalmsingers, I hate priors, I execrate heretics, but I should detest yet more anyone who should maintain the contrary. One has only to read Arnoul Wion, Gabriel Bucelin, Trithemus, Maurolics, and Dom Luc d'Achery."

The prioress took breath, then turned to Fauchelevent.

"Is it settled, Father Fauvent?"

"It is settled, reverend Mother."

"We may depend on you?"

"I will obey."

"That is well."

"I am entirely devoted to the convent."

"That is understood. You will close the coffin. The sisters will carry it to the chapel. The office for the dead will then be said. Then we shall return to the cloister. Between eleven o'clock and midnight, you will come with your iron bar. All will be done in the most profound secrecy. There will be in the chapel only the four Mother Precentors, Mother Ascension and yourself."

"And the sister at the post?"

"She will not turn round."

"But she will hear."

"She will not listen. Besides, what the cloister knows the world learns not."

A pause ensued. The prioress went on:

"You will remove your bell. It is not necessary that the sister at the post should perceive your presence."

"Reverend Mother?"

"What, Father Fauvent?"

"Has the doctor for the dead paid his visit?"

"He will pay it at four o'clock to-day. The peal which orders the doctor for the dead to be summoned has already been rung. But you do not understand any of the peals?"

"I pay no attention to any but my own."

"That is well, Father Fauvent."

"Reverend Mother, a lever at least six feet long will be required."

"Where will you obtain it?"

"Where gratings are not lacking, iron bars are not lacking. I have my heap of old iron at the bottom of the garden."

"About three-quarters of an hour before midnight; do not forget."

"Reverend Mother?"

"What?"

"If you were ever to have any other jobs of this sort, my brother is the strong man for you. A perfect Turk!"

"You will do it as speedily as possible."

"I cannot work very fast. I am infirm; that is why I require an assistant. I limp."

"To limp is no sin, and perhaps it is a blessing. The Emperor Henry II, who combated Antipope Gregory and re-established Benoît VIII, has two surnames, the Saint and the Lame."

"Two surtouts are a good thing," murmured Fauchelevent, who really was a little hard of hearing.

"Now that I think of it, Father Fauvent, let us give a whole hour to it. That is not too much. Be near the principal altar, with your iron bar, at eleven o'clock. The office begins at midnight. Everything must have been completed a good quarter of an hour before that."

"I will do anything to prove my zeal toward the community. These are my orders. I am to nail up the coffin. At eleven o'clock exactly, I am to be in the chapel. The Mother Precentors will be there. Mother Ascension will be there. Two men would be better. However, never mind! I shall have my lever. We will open the vault, we will lower the coffin, and we will close the vault again. After which, there will be no trace of anything. The government will have no suspicion. Thus all has been arranged, reverend Mother?"

"No!"

"What else remains?"

"The empty coffin remains."

This produced a pause. Fauchelevent meditated. The prioress meditated.

"What is to be done with that coffin, Father Fauvent?"

"It will be given to the earth."

"Empty?"

Another silence. Fauchelevent made, with his left hand, that sort of a gesture which dismisses a troublesome subject.

"Reverend Mother, I am the one who is to nail up the coffin in the basement of the church, and no one can enter there but myself, and I will cover the coffin with the pall."

"Yes, but the bearers, when they place it in the hearse and lower it into the grave, will be sure to feel that there is nothing in it."

"Ah! the de——!" exclaimed Fauchelevent.

The prioress began to make the sign of the cross, and looked fixedly at the gardener. The *vil* stuck fast in his throat.

He made haste to improvise an expedient to make her forget the oath.

"I will put earth in the coffin, reverend Mother. That will produce the effect of a corpse."

"You are right. Earth, that is the same thing as man. So you will manage the empty coffin?"

"I will make that my special business."

The prioress's face, up to that moment troubled and clouded, grew serene once more. She made the sign of a superior dismissing an inferior to him. Fauchelevent went toward the door. As he was on the point of passing out, the prioress raised her voice gently:

"I am pleased with you, Father Fauvent; bring your brother to me to-morrow, after the burial, and tell him to fetch his daughter."

Chapter IV

IN WHICH JEAN VALJEAN HAS QUITE THE AIR OF HAVING READ AUSTIN CASTILLEJO

THE STRIDES OF A LAME MAN ARE LIKE THE OGLING GLANCES OF A ONE-EYED MAN; THEY DO NOT reach their goal very promptly. Moreover, Fauchelevent was in a dilemma. He took nearly a quarter of an hour to return to his cottage in the garden. Cosette had waked up. Jean Valjean had placed her near the fire. At the moment when Fauchelevent entered, Jean Valjean was pointing out to her the vintner's basket on the wall, and saying to her, "Listen attentively to me, my little Cosette. We must go away from this house, but we shall return to it, and we shall be very happy here. The good man who lives here is going to carry you off on his back in that. You will wait for me at a lady's house. I shall come to fetch you. Obey, and say nothing, above all things, unless you want Madame Thénardier to get you again!"

Cosette nodded gravely.

Jean Valjean turned round at the noise made by Fauchelevent opening the door.

"Well?"

"Everything is arranged, and nothing is," said Fauchelevent. "I have permission to bring you in; but before bringing you in you must be got out. That's where the difficulty lies. It is easy enough with the child."

"You will carry her out?"

"And she will hold her tongue?"

"I answer for that."

"But you, Father Madeleine?"

And, after a silence, fraught with anxiety, Fauchelevent exclaimed:

"Why, get out as you came in!"

Jean Valjean, as in the first instance, contented himself with saying, "Impossible."

Fauchelevent grumbled, more to himself than to Jean Valjean:

"There is another thing which bothers me. I have said that I would put earth in it. When I come to think it over, the earth instead of the corpse will not seem like the real thing, it won't do, it will get displaced, it will move about. The men will bear it. You understand, Father Madeleine, the government will notice it."

Jean Valjean stared him straight in the eye and thought that he was raving.

Fauchelevent went on:

"How the de——uce are you going to get out? It must all be done by to-morrow morning. It is to-morrow that I am to bring you in. The prioress expects you."

Then he explained to Jean Valjean that this was his recompense for a service which he, Fauchelevent, was to render to the community. That it fell among his duties to take part in their burials, that he nailed up the coffins and helped the gravedigger at the cemetery. That the nun who had died that morning had requested to be buried in the coffin which had served her for a bed, and interred in the vault under the altar of the chapel. That the police regulations forbade this, but that she was one of those dead to whom nothing is refused. That the prioress and the vocal mothers intended to fulfill the wish of the deceased. That it was so much the worse for the government. That he, Fauchelevent, was to nail up the coffin in the cell, raise the stone in the chapel, and lower the corpse into the vault. And that, by way of thanks, the prioress was to admit his brother to the house as a gardener, and his niece as a pupil. That his brother was M. Madeleine, and that his niece was

Cosette. That the prioress had told him to bring his brother on the following evening, after the counterfeit interment in the cemetery. But that he could not bring M. Madeleine in from the outside if M. Madeleine was not outside. That that was the first problem. And then, that there was another: the empty coffin.

"What is that empty coffin?" asked Jean Valjean.

Fauchelevent replied:

"The coffin of the administration."

"What coffin? What administration?"

"A nun dies. The municipal doctor comes and says, 'A nun has died.' The government sends a coffin. The next day it sends a hearse and undertaker's men to get the coffin and carry it to the cemetery. The undertaker's men will come and lift the coffin; there will be nothing in it."

"Put something in it."

"A corpse? I have none."

"No."

"What then?"

"A living person."

"What person?"

"Me!" said Jean Valjean.

Fauchelevent, who was seated, sprang up as though a bomb had burst under his chair.

"You!"

"Why not?"

Jean Valjean gave way to one of those rare smiles which lighted up his face like a flash from heaven in the winter.

"You know, Fauchelevent, what you have said: 'Mother Crucifixion is dead,' and I add: 'and Father Madeleine is buried.'"

"Ah! good, you can laugh, you are not speaking seriously."

"Very seriously, I must get out of this place."

"Certainly."

"I have told you to find a basket, and a cover for me also."

"Well?"

"The basket will be of pine, and the cover a black cloth."

"In the first place, it will be a white cloth. Nuns are buried in white."

"Let it be a white cloth, then."

"You are not like other men, Father Madeleine."

To behold such devices, which are nothing else than the savage and daring inventions of the galleys, spring forth from the peaceable things which surrounded him, and mingle with what he called the "petty course of life in the convent," caused Fauchelevent as much amazement as a gull fishing in the gutter of the Rue Saint-Denis would inspire in a passer-by.

Jean Valjean went on:

"The problem is to get out of here without being seen. This offers the means. But give me some information, in the first place. How is it managed? Where is this coffin?"

"The empty one?"

"Yes."

"Downstairs, in what is called the dead-room. It stands on two trestles, under the pall."

"How long is the coffin?"

"Six feet."

"What is this dead-room?"

"It is a chamber on the ground floor which has a grated window opening on the garden, which is closed on the outside by a shutter, and two doors; one leads into the convent, the other into the church."

"What church?"

"The church in the street, the church which anyone can enter."

"Have you the keys to those two doors?"

"No; I have the key to the door which communicates with the convent; the porter has the key to the door which communicates with the church."

"When does the porter open that door?"

"Only to allow the undertaker's men to enter, when they come to get the coffin. When the coffin has been taken out, the door is closed again."

"Who nails up the coffin?"

"I do."

"Who spreads the pall over it?"

"I do."

"Are you alone?"

"Not another man, except the police doctor, can enter the dead-room. That is even written on the wall."

"Could you hide me in that room to-night when everyone is asleep?"

"No. But I could hide you in a small, dark nook which opens on the dead-room, where I keep my tools to use for burials, and of which I have the key."

"At what time will the hearse come for the coffin to-morrow?"

"About three o'clock in the afternoon. The burial will take place at the Vaugirard cemetery a little before nightfall. It is not very near."

"I will remain concealed in your tool-closet all night and all the morning. And how about food? I shall be hungry."

"I will bring you something."

"You can come and nail me up in the coffin at two o'clock."

Fauchelevent recoiled and cracked his finger-joints.

"But that is impossible!"

"Bah! Impossible to take a hammer and drive some nails in a plank?"

What seemed unprecedented to Fauchelevent was, we repeat, a simple matter to Jean Valjean. Jean Valjean had been in worse straits than this. Any man who has been a prisoner understands how to contract himself to fit the diameter of the escape. The prisoner is subject to flight as the sick man is subject to a crisis which saves or kills him. An escape is a cure. What does not a man undergo for the sake of a cure? To have himself nailed up in a case and carried off like a bale of goods, to live for a long time in a box, to find air where there is none, to economize his breath for hours, to know how to stifle without dying—this was one of Jean Valjean's gloomy talents.

Moreover, a coffin containing a living being—that convict's expedient—is also an imperial expedient. If we are to credit the monk Austin Castillejo, this was the means employed by Charles the Fifth, desirous of seeing the Plombes for the last time after his abdication.

He had her brought into and carried out of the monastery of Saint-Yuste in this manner.

Fauchelevent, who had recovered himself a little, exclaimed:

"But how will you manage to breathe?"

"I will breathe."

"In that box! The mere thought of it suffocates me."

"You surely must have a gimlet, you will make a few holes here and there, around my mouth, and you will nail the top plank on loosely."

"Good! And what if you should happen to cough or to sneeze?"

"A man who is making his escape does not cough or sneeze."

And Jean Valjean added:

"Father Fauchelevent, we must come to a decision: I must either be caught here, or accept this escape through the hearse."

Everyone has noticed the taste which cats have for pausing and lounging between the two leaves of a half-shut door. Who is there who has not said to a cat, "Do come in!" There are men who, when an incident stands half-open before them, have the same tendency to halt in indecision between two resolutions, at the risk of getting crushed through the abrupt closing of the adventure by fate. The over-prudent, cats as they are, and because they are cats, sometimes incur more danger than the audacious. Fauchelevent was of this hesitating nature. But Jean Valjean's coolness prevailed over him in spite of himself. He grumbled:

"Well, since there is no other means."

Jean Valjean resumed:

"The only thing which troubles me is what will take place at the cemetery."

"That is the very point that is not troublesome," exclaimed Fauchelevent. "If you are sure of coming out of the coffin all right, I am sure of getting you out of the grave. The gravedigger is a drunkard, and a friend of mine. He is Father Mestienne. An old fellow of the old school. The gravedigger puts the corpses in the grave, and I put the gravedigger in my pocket. I will tell you what will take place. They will arrive a little before dusk, three-quarters of an hour before the gates of the cemetery are closed. The hearse will drive directly up to the grave. I shall follow; that is my business. I shall have a hammer, a chisel, and some pincers in my pocket. The hearse halts, the undertaker's men knot a rope around your coffin and lower you down. The priest says the prayers, makes the sign of the cross, sprinkles the holy water, and takes his departure. I am left alone with Father Mestienne. He is my friend, I tell you. One of two things will happen, he will either be sober, or he will not be sober. If he is not drunk, I shall say to him: 'Come and drink a bout while the *Bon Coing* [the Good Quince] is open.' I carry him off, I get him drunk—it does not take long to make Father Mestienne drunk, he always has the beginning of it about him—I lay him under the table, I take his card, so that I can get into the cemetery again, and I return without him. Then you have no longer anyone but me to deal with. If he is drunk, I shall say to him: 'Be off; I will do your work for you.' Off he goes, and I drag you out of the hole."

Jean Valjean held out his hand, and Fauchelevent precipitated himself upon it with the touching effusion of a peasant.

"That is settled, Father Fauchelevent. All will go well."

"Provided nothing goes wrong," thought Fauchelevent. "In that case, it would be terrible."

Chapter V

IT IS NOT NECESSARY TO BE DRUNK IN ORDER TO BE IMMORTAL

ON THE FOLLOWING DAY, AS THE SUN WAS DECLINING, THE VERY RARE PASSERS-BY ON THE Boulevard du Maine pulled off their hats to an old-fashioned hearse, ornamented with skulls, cross-bones, and tears. This hearse contained a coffin covered with a white cloth over which spread a large black cross, like a huge corpse with drooping arms. A mourning-coach, in which could be seen a priest in his surplice, and a choir boy in his red cap, followed. Two undertaker's men in gray uniforms trimmed with black walked on the right and the left of the hearse. Behind it came an old man in the garments of a laborer, who limped along. The procession was going in the direction of the Vaugirard cemetery.

The handle of a hammer, the blade of a cold chisel, and the antennae of a pair of pincers were visible, protruding from the man's pocket.

The Vaugirard cemetery formed an exception among the cemeteries of Paris. It had its peculiar usages, just as it had its carriage entrance and its house door, which old people in the quarter, who clung tenaciously to ancient words, still called the *porte cavalière* and the *porte piétonne*. The Bernardines-Benedictines of the Rue Petit-Picpus had obtained permission, as we have already stated, to be buried there in a corner apart, and at night, the plot of land having formerly belonged to their community. The gravediggers being thus bound to service in the evening in summer and at night in winter, in this cemetery, they were subjected to a special discipline. The gates of the Paris cemeteries closed, at that epoch, at sundown, and this being a municipal regulation, the Vaugirard cemetery was bound by it like the rest. The carriage gate and the house door were two contiguous grated gates, adjoining a pavilion built by the architect Perronet, and inhabited by the door-keeper of the cemetery. These gates, therefore, swung inexorably on their hinges at the instant when the sun disappeared behind the dome of the Invalides. If any gravedigger were delayed after that moment in the cemetery, there was but one way for him to get out—his gravedigger's card furnished by the department of public funerals. A sort of letter-box was constructed in the porter's window. The gravedigger dropped his card into this box, the porter heard it fall, pulled the rope, and the small door opened. If the man had not his card, he mentioned his name, the porter, who was sometimes in bed and asleep, rose, came out and identified the man, and opened the gate with his key; the gravedigger stepped out, but had to pay a fine of fifteen francs.

This cemetery, with its peculiarities outside the regulations, embarrassed the symmetry of the administration. It was suppressed a little later than 1830. The cemetery of Mont-Parnasse, called the Eastern cemetery, succeeded to it, and inherited that famous dram-shop next to the Vaugirard cemetery, which was surmounted by a quince painted on a board, and which formed an angle, one side on the drinkers' tables, and the other on the tombs, with this sign: *Au Bon Coing*.

The Vaugirard cemetery was what may be called a faded cemetery. It was falling into disuse. Dampness was invading it, the flowers were deserting it. The bourgeois did not care much about being buried in the Vaugirard; it hinted at poverty. Père-Lachaise if you please! to be buried in Père-Lachaise is equivalent to having furniture of mahogany. It is recognized as elegant. The Vaugirard cemetery was a venerable enclosure, planted like an old-fashioned French garden. Straight alleys, box, thuya-trees, holly, ancient tombs beneath aged cypress-trees, and very tall grass. In the evening it was tragic there. There were very lugubrious lines about it.

The sun had not yet set, when the hearse with the white pall and the black cross entered the avenue of the Vaugirard cemetery. The lame man who followed it was no other than Fauchelevent.

The interment of Mother Crucifixion in the vault under the altar, the exit of Cosette, the introduction of Jean Valjean to the dead-room—all had been executed without difficulty, and there had been no hitch.

Let us remark in passing, that the burial of Mother Crucifixion under the altar of the convent is a perfectly venial offense in our sight. It is one of the faults which resemble a duty. The nuns had committed it, not only without difficulty, but even with the applause of their own consciences. In the cloister, what is called the "government" is only an intermeddling with authority, an interference which is always questionable. In the first place, the rule; as for the code, we shall see. Make as many laws as you please, men; but keep them for yourselves. The tribute to Cæsar is never anything but the remnants of the tribute to God. A prince is nothing in the presence of a principle.

Fauchelevent limped along behind the hearse in a very contented frame of mind. His twin plots, the one with the nuns, the one for the convent, the other against it, the other with M. Madeleine, had succeeded, to all appearance. Jean Valjean's composure was one of those powerful tranquilities which are contagious. Fauchelevent no longer felt doubtful as to his success.

What remained to be done was a mere nothing. Within the last two years, he had made good

Father Mestienne, a chubby-cheeked person, drunk at least ten times. He played with Father Mestienne. He did what he liked with him. He made him dance according to his whim. Mestienne's head adjusted itself to the cap of Fauchelevent's will. Fauchelevent's confidence was perfect.

At the moment when the convoy entered the avenue leading to the cemetery, Fauchelevent glanced cheerfully at the hearse, and said half-aloud, as he rubbed his big hands:

"Here's a fine farce!"

All at once the hearse halted; it had reached the gate. The permission for interment must be exhibited. The undertaker's man addressed himself to the porter of the cemetery. During this colloquy, which always is productive of a delay of from one to two minutes, someone, a stranger, came and placed himself behind the hearse, beside Fauchelevent. He was a sort of laboring man, who wore a waistcoat with large pockets and carried a mattock under his arm.

Fauchelevent surveyed this stranger.

"Who are you?" he demanded.

The man replied:

"The gravedigger."

If a man could survive the blow of a cannon-ball full in the breast, he would make the same face that Fauchelevent made.

"The gravedigger?"

"Yes."

"You?"

"I."

"Father Mestienne is the gravedigger."

"He was."

"What! He was?"

"He is dead."

Fauchelevent had expected anything but this, that a gravedigger could die. It is true, nevertheless, that gravediggers do die themselves. By dint of excavating graves for other people, one hollows out one's own.

Fauchelevent stood there with his mouth wide open. He had hardly the strength to stammer:

"But it is not possible!"

"It is so."

"But," he persisted feebly, "Father Mestienne is the gravedigger."

"After Napoleon, Louis XVIII. After Mestienne, Gribier. Peasant, my name is Gribier."

Fauchelevent, who was deadly pale, stared at this Gribier.

He was a tall, thin, livid, utterly funereal man. He had the air of an unsuccessful doctor who had turned gravedigger.

Fauchelevent burst out laughing.

"Ah!" said he, "what queer things do happen! Father Mestienne is dead, but long live little Father Lenoir! Do you know who little Father Lenoir is? He is a jug of red wine. It is a jug of Surêne, morbigou! of real Paris Surêne? Ah! So old Mestienne is dead! I am sorry for it; he was a jolly fellow. But you are a jolly fellow, too. Are you not, comrade? We'll go and have a drink together presently."

The man replied:

"I have been a student. I passed my fourth examination. I never drink."

The hearse had set out again, and was rolling up the grand alley of the cemetery.

Fauchelevent had slackened his pace. He limped more out of anxiety than from infirmity.

The gravedigger walked on in front of him.

Fauchelevent passed the unexpected Gribier once more in review.

He was one of those men who, though very young, have the air of age, and who, though slender, are extremely strong.

"Comrade!" cried Fauchelevent.

The man turned round.

"I am the convent gravedigger."

"My colleague," said the man.

Fauchelevent, who was illiterate but very sharp, understood that he had to deal with a formidable species of man, with a fine talker. He muttered:

"So Father Mestienne is dead."

The man replied:

"Completely. The good God consulted his notebook which shows when the time is up. It was Father Mestienne's turn. Father Mestienne died."

Fauchelevent repeated mechanically: "The good God—"

"The good God," said the man authoritatively. "According to the philosophers, the Eternal Father; according to the Jacobins, the Supreme Being."

"Shall we not make each other's acquaintance?" stammered Fauchelevent.

"It is made. You are a peasant, I am a Parisian."

"People do not know each other until they have drunk together. He who empties his glass empties his heart. You must come and have a drink with me. Such a thing cannot be refused."

"Business first."

Fauchelevent thought: "I am lost."

They were only a few turns of the wheel distant from the small alley leading to the nuns' corner.

The gravedigger resumed:

"Peasant, I have seven small children who must be fed. As they must eat, I cannot drink."

And he added, with the satisfaction of a serious man who is turning a phrase well:

"Their hunger is the enemy of my thirst."

The hearse skirted a clump of cypress-trees, quitted the grand alley, turned into a narrow one, entered the waste land, and plunged into a thicket. This indicated the immediate proximity of the place of sepulture. Fauchelevent slackened his pace, but he could not detain the hearse. Fortunately, the soil, which was light and wet with the winter rains, clogged the wheels and retarded its speed.

He approached the gravedigger.

"They have such a nice little Argenteuil wine," murmured Fauchelevent.

"Villager," retorted the man, "I ought not be a gravedigger. My father was a porter at the Prytaneum [Town-Hall]. He destined me for literature. But he had reverses. He had losses on 'change. I was obliged to renounce the profession of author. But I am still a public writer."

"So you are not a gravedigger, then?" returned Fauchelevent, clutching at this branch, feeble as it was.

"The one does not hinder the other. I cumulate."

Fauchelevent did not understand this last word.

"Come have a drink," said he.

Here a remark becomes necessary. Fauchelevent, whatever his anguish, offered a drink, but he did not explain himself on one point; who was to pay? Generally, Fauchelevent offered and Father Mestienne paid. An offer of a drink was the evident result of the novel situation created by the new gravedigger, and it was necessary to make this offer, but the old gardener left the proverbial quarter of an hour named after Rabelais in the dark, and that not unintentionally. As for himself, Fauchelevent did not wish to pay, troubled as he was.

The gravedigger went on with a superior smile:

"One must eat. I have accepted Father Mestienne's reversion. One gets to be a philosopher when one has nearly completed his classes. To the labor of the hand I join the labor of the arm. I have my scrivener's stall in the market of the Rue de Sèvres. You know? the Umbrella Market. All the cooks of the Red Cross apply to me. I scribble their declarations of love to the raw soldiers. In the morning I write love letters; in the evening I dig graves. Such is life, rustic."

The hearse was still advancing. Fauchelevent, uneasy to the last degree, was gazing about him on all sides. Great drops of perspiration trickled down from his brow.

"But," continued the gravedigger, "a man cannot serve two mistresses. I must choose between the pen and the mattock. The mattock is ruining my hand."

The hearse halted.

The choir boy alighted from the mourning-coach, then the priest.

One of the small front wheels of the hearse had run up a little on a pile of earth, beyond which an open grave was visible.

"What a farce this is!" repeated Fauchelevent in consternation.

Chapter VI

BETWEEN FOUR PLANKS

WHO WAS IN THE COFFIN? THE READER KNOWS. JEAN VALJEAN.
Jean Valjean had arranged things so that he could exist there, and he could almost breathe.

It is a strange thing to what a degree security of conscience confers security of the rest. Every combination thought out by Jean Valjean had been progressing, and progressing favorably, since the preceding day. He, like Fauchelevent, counted on Father Mestienne. He had no doubt as to the end. Never was there a more critical situation, never more complete composure.

The four planks of the coffin breathe out a kind of terrible peace. It seemed as though something of the repose of the dead entered into Jean Valjean's tranquility.

From the depths of that coffin he had been able to follow, and he had followed, all the phases of the terrible drama which he was playing with death.

Shortly after Fauchelevent had finished nailing on the upper plank, Jean Valjean had felt himself carried out, then driven off. He knew, from the diminution in the jolting, when they left the pavements and reached the earth road. He had divined, from a dull noise, that they were crossing the bridge of Austerlitz. At the first halt, he had understood that they were entering the cemetery; at the second halt, he said to himself:

"Here is the grave."

Suddenly, he felt hands seize the coffin, then a harsh grating against the planks; he explained it to himself as the rope which was being fastened round the casket in order to lower it into the cavity.

Then he experienced a giddiness.

The undertaker's man and the gravedigger had probably allowed the coffin to lose its balance, and had lowered the head before the foot. He recovered himself fully when he felt himself horizontal and motionless. He had just touched the bottom.

He had a certain sensation of cold.

A voice rose above him, glacial and solemn. He heard Latin words, which he did not understand, pass over him, so slowly that he was able to catch them one by one:

"*Qui dormiunt in terrae pulvere, evigilabunt; alii in vitam aeternam, et alii in opprobrium, ut videant semper.*"

A child's voice said:

"*De profundis.*"

The grave voice began again:

"*Requiem aeternam dona ei, Domine.*"

The child's voice responded:

"*Et lux perpetua luceat ei.*"

He heard something like the gentle patter of several drops of rain on the plank which covered him. It was probably the holy water.

He thought: "This will be over soon now. Patience for a little while longer. The priest will take his departure. Fauchelevent will take Mestienne off to drink. I shall be left. Then Fauchelevent will return alone, and I shall get out. That will be the work of a good hour."

The grave voice resumed:

"*Requiescat in pace.*"

And the child's voice said:

"*Amen.*"

Jean Valjean strained his ears, and heard something like retreating footsteps.

"There, they are going now," thought he. "I am alone."

All at once, he heard over his head a sound which seemed to him to be a clap of thunder.

It was a shovelful of earth falling on the coffin.

A second shovelful fell.

One of the holes through which he breathed had just been stopped up.

A third shovelful of earth fell.

Then a fourth.

There are things which are too strong for the strongest man. Jean Valjean lost consciousness.

Chapter VII

IN WHICH WILL BE FOUND THE ORIGIN OF THE SAYING: DON'T LOSE THE CARD

THIS IS WHAT HAD TAKEN PLACE ABOVE THE COFFIN IN WHICH LAY JEAN VALJEAN.

When the hearse had driven off, when the priest and the choir boy had entered the carriage again and taken their departure, Fauchelevent, who had not taken his eyes from the gravedigger, saw the latter bend over and grasp his shovel, which was sticking upright in the heap of dirt.

Then Fauchelevent took a supreme resolve.

He placed himself between the grave and the gravedigger, crossed his arms and said:

"I am the one to pay!"

The gravedigger stared at him in amazement, and replied:

"What's that, peasant?"

Fauchelevent repeated:

"I am the one who pays!"

"What?"

"For the wine."

"What wine?"

"That Argenteuil wine."

"Where is the Argenteuil?"

"At the *Bon Coing.*"

"Go to the devil!" said the gravedigger.

And he flung a shovelful of earth on the coffin.

The coffin gave back a hollow sound. Fauchelevent felt himself stagger and on the point of falling headlong into the grave himself. He shouted in a voice in which the strangling sound of the death-rattle began to mingle:

"Comrade! Before the *Bon Coing* is shut!"

The gravedigger took some more earth on his shovel. Fauchelevent continued:

"I will pay."

And he seized the man's arm.

"Listen to me, comrade. I am the convent gravedigger, I have come to help you. It is a business which can be performed at night. Let us begin, then, by going for a drink."

And as he spoke, and clung to this desperate insistence, this melancholy reflection occurred to him: "And if he drinks, will he get drunk?"

"Provincial," said the man, "if you positively insist upon it, I consent. We will drink. After work, never before."

And he flourished his shovel briskly. Fauchelevent held him back.

"It is Argenteuil wine, at six."

"Oh, come," said the gravedigger, "you are a bellringer. Ding dong, ding dong, that's all you know how to say. Go hang yourself."

And he threw in a second shovelful.

Fauchelevent had reached a point where he no longer knew what he was saying.

"Come along and drink," he cried, "since it is I who pay the bill."

"When we have put the child to bed," said the gravedigger.

He flung in a third shovelful.

Then he thrust his shovel into the earth and added:

"It's cold to-night, you see, and the corpse would shriek out after us if we were to plant her there without a coverlet."

At that moment, as he loaded his shovel, the gravedigger bent over, and the pocket of his waistcoat gaped.

Fauchelevent's wild gaze fell mechanically into that pocket, and there it stopped.

The sun was not yet hidden behind the horizon; there was still light enough to enable him to distinguish something white at the bottom of that yawning pocket.

The sum total of lightning that the eye of a Picard peasant can contain, traversed Fauchelevent's pupils. An idea had just occurred to him.

He thrust his hand into the pocket from behind, without the gravedigger, who was wholly absorbed in his shovelful of earth, observing it, and pulled out the white object which lay at the bottom of it.

The man sent a fourth shovelful tumbling into the grave.

Just as he turned round to get the fifth, Fauchelevent looked calmly at him and said:

"By the way, you new man, have you your card?"

The gravedigger paused.

"What card?"

"The sun is on the point of setting."

"That's good, it is going to put on its nightcap."

"The gate of the cemetery will close immediately."

"Well, what then?"

"Have you your card?"

"Ah! my card?" said the gravedigger.

And he fumbled in his pocket.

Having searched one pocket, he proceeded to search the other. He passed on to his fobs, explored the first, returned to the second.

"Why, no," said he, "I have not my card. I must have forgotten it."

"Fifteen francs fine," said Fauchelevent.

The gravedigger turned green. Green is the pallor of livid people.

"Ah! Jésus-mon-Dieu-bancroche-á-bas-la-lune!"[1] he exclaimed. "Fifteen francs fine!"

"Three pieces of a hundred sous," said Fauchelevent.

The gravedigger dropped his shovel.

Fauchelevent's turn had come.

"Ah, come now, conscript," said Fauchelevent, "none of this despair. There is no question of committing suicide and benefiting the grave. Fifteen francs is fifteen francs, and besides, you may not be able to pay it. I am an old hand, you are a new one. I know all the ropes and the devices. I will give you some friendly advice. One thing is clear, the sun is on the point of setting, it is touching the dome now, the cemetery will be closed in five minutes more."

"That is true," replied the man.

"Five minutes more and you will not have time to fill the grave, it is as hollow as the devil, this grave, and to reach the gate in season to pass it before it is shut."

"That is true."

"In that case, a fine of fifteen francs."

"Fifteen francs."

"But you have time. Where do you live?"

"A couple of steps from the barrier, a quarter of an hour from here. No. 87 Rue de Vaugirard."

"You have just time to get out by taking to your heels at your best speed."

"That is exactly so."

"Once outside the gate, you gallop home, you get your card, you return, the cemetery porter admits you. As you have your card, there will be nothing to pay. And you will bury your corpse. I'll watch it for you in the meantime, so that it shall not run away."

"I am indebted to you for my life, peasant."

"Decamp!" said Fauchelevent.

The gravedigger, overwhelmed with gratitude, shook his hand and set off on a run.

When the man had disappeared in the thicket, Fauchelevent listened until he heard his footsteps die away in the distance, then he leaned over the grave, and said in a low tone:

"Father Madeleine!"

There was no reply.

Fauchelevent was seized with a shudder. He tumbled rather than climbed into the grave, flung himself on the head of the coffin and cried:

"Are you there?"

Silence in the coffin.

Fauchelevent, hardly able to draw his breath for trembling, seized his cold chisel and his hammer, and pried up the coffin lid.

Jean Valjean's face appeared in the twilight; it was pale and his eyes were closed.

Fauchelevent's hair rose upright on his head, he sprang to his feet, then fell back against the side of the grave, ready to swoon on the coffin. He stared at Jean Valjean.

Jean Valjean lay there pallid and motionless.

Fauchelevent murmured in a voice as faint as a sigh:

"He is dead!"

1. Jesus-my-God-bandy-leg—down with the moon!

And, drawing himself up, and folding his arms with such violence that his clenched fists came in contact with his shoulders, he cried:

"And this is the way I save his life!"

Then the poor man fell to sobbing. He soliloquized the while, for it is an error to suppose that the soliloquy is unnatural. Powerful emotion often talks aloud.

"It is Father Mestienne's fault. Why did that fool die? What need was there for him to give up the ghost at the very moment when no one was expecting it? It is he who has killed M. Madeleine. Father Madeleine! He is in the coffin. It is quite handy. All is over. Now, is there any sense in these things? Ah! my God! he is dead! Well! and his little girl, what am I to do with her? What will the fruit-seller say? The idea of its being possible for a man like that to die like this! When I think how he put himself under that cart! Father Madeleine! Father Madeleine! Pardine! He was suffocated, I said so. He wouldn't believe me. Well! Here's a pretty trick to play! He is dead, that good man, the very best man out of all the good God's good folks! And his little girl! Ah! In the first place, I won't go back there myself. I shall stay here. After having done such a thing as that! What's the use of being two old men, if we are two old fools! But, in the first place, how did he manage to enter the convent? That was the beginning of it all. One should not do such things. Father Madeleine! Father Madeleine! Madeleine! Monsieur Madeleine! Monsieur le Maire! He does not hear me. Now get out of this scrape if you can!"

And he tore his hair.

A grating sound became audible through the trees in the distance. It was the cemetery gate closing.

Fauchelevent bent over Jean Valjean, and all at once he bounded back and recoiled so far as the limits of a grave permit.

Jean Valjean's eyes were open and gazing at him.

To see a corpse is alarming, to behold a resurrection is almost as much so. Fauchelevent became like stone, pale, haggard, overwhelmed by all these excesses of emotion, not knowing whether he had to do with a living man or a dead one, and staring at Jean Valjean, who was gazing at him.

"I fell asleep," said Jean Valjean.

And he raised himself to a sitting posture.

Fauchelevent fell on his knees.

"Just, good Virgin! How you frightened me!"

Then he sprang to his feet and cried:

"Thanks, Father Madeleine!"

Jean Valjean had merely fainted. The fresh air had revived him.

Joy is the ebb of terror. Fauchelevent found almost as much difficulty in recovering himself as Jean Valjean had.

"So you are not dead! Oh! How wise you are! I called you so much that you came back. When I saw your eyes shut, I said: 'Good! there he is, stifled,' I should have gone raving mad, mad enough for a strait jacket. They would have put me in Bicêtre. What do you suppose I should have done if you had been dead? And your little girl? There's that fruit-seller—she would never have understood it! The child is thrust into your arms, and then—the grandfather is dead! What a story! good saints of paradise, what a tale! Ah! you are alive, that's the best of it!"

"I am cold," said Jean Valjean.

This remark recalled Fauchelevent thoroughly to reality, and there was pressing need of it. The souls of these two men were troubled even when they had recovered themselves, although they did not realize it, and there was about them something uncanny, which was the sinister bewilderment inspired by the place.

"Let us get out of here quickly," exclaimed Fauchelevent.

He fumbled in his pocket, and pulled out a gourd with which he had provided himself.

"But first, take a drop," said he.

The flask finished what the fresh air had begun, Jean Valjean swallowed a mouthful of brandy, and regained full possession of his faculties.

He got out of the coffin, and helped Fauchelevent to nail on the lid again.

Three minutes later they were out of the grave.

Moreover, Fauchelevent was perfectly composed. He took his time. The cemetery was closed. The arrival of the gravedigger Gribier was not to be apprehended. That "conscript" was at home busily engaged in looking for his card, and at some difficulty in finding it in his lodgings, since it was in Fauchelevent's pocket. Without a card, he could not get back into the cemetery.

Fauchelevent took the shovel, and Jean Valjean the pickax, and together they buried the empty coffin.

When the grave was full, Fauchelevent said to Jean Valjean:

"Let us go. I will keep the shovel; do you carry off the mattock."

Night was falling.

Jean Valjean experienced some difficulty in moving and in walking. He had stiffened himself in that coffin, and had become a little like a corpse. The rigidity of death had seized upon him between those four planks. He had, in a manner, to thaw out, from the tomb.

"You are benumbed," said Fauchelevent. "It is a pity that I have a game leg, for otherwise we might step out briskly."

"Bah!" replied Jean Valjean, "four paces will put life into my legs once more."

They set off by the alleys through which the hearse had passed. On arriving before the closed gate and the porter's pavilion Fauchelevent, who held the gravedigger's card in his hand, dropped it into the box, the porter pulled the rope, the gate opened, and they went out.

"How well everything is going!" said Fauchelevent; "what a capital idea that was of yours, Father Madeleine!"

They passed the Vaugirard barrier in the simplest manner in the world. In the neighborhood of the cemetery, a shovel and pick are equal to two passports.

The Rue Vaugirard was deserted.

"Father Madeleine," said Fauchelevent as they went along, and raising his eyes to the houses, "Your eyes are better than mine. Show me No. 87."

"Here it is," said Jean Valjean.

"There is no one in the street," said Fauchelevent. "Give me your mattock and wait a couple of minutes for me."

Fauchelevent entered No. 87, ascended to the very top, guided by the instinct which always leads the poor man to the garret, and knocked in the dark, at the door of an attic.

A voice replied: "Come in."

It was Gribier's voice.

Fauchelevent opened the door. The gravedigger's dwelling was, like all such wretched habitations, an unfurnished and encumbered garret. A packing-case—a coffin, perhaps—took the place of a commode, a butter-pot served for a drinking-fountain, a straw mattress served for a bed, the floor served instead of tables and chairs. In a corner, on a tattered fragment which had been a piece of an old carpet, a thin woman and a number of children were piled in a heap. The whole of this poverty-stricken interior bore traces of having been overturned. One would have said that there had been an earthquake "for one." The covers were displaced, the rags scattered about, the jug broken, the mother had been crying, the children had probably been beaten; traces of a vigorous and ill-tempered search. It was plain that the gravedigger had made a desperate search for his card, and had made everybody in the garret, from the jug to his wife, responsible for its loss. He wore an air of desperation.

But Fauchelevent was in too great a hurry to terminate this adventure to take any notice of this sad side of his success.

He entered and said:

"I have brought you back your shovel and pick."

Gribier gazed at him in stupefaction.

"Is it you, peasant?"

"And to-morrow morning you will find your card with the porter of the cemetery."

And he laid the shovel and mattock on the floor.

"What is the meaning of this?" demanded Gribier.

"The meaning of it is, that you dropped your card out of your pocket, that I found it on the ground after you were gone, that I have buried the corpse, that I have filled the grave, that I have done your work, that the porter will return your card to you, and that you will not have to pay fifteen francs. There you have it, conscript."

"Thanks, villager!" exclaimed Gribier, radiant. "The next time I will pay for the drinks."

Chapter VIII

A Successful Interrogatory

AN HOUR LATER, IN THE DARKNESS OF NIGHT, TWO MEN AND A CHILD PRESENTED THEMSELVES at No. 62 Rue Petit-Picpus. The elder of the men lifted the knocker and rapped.

They were Fauchelevent, Jean Valjean, and Cosette.

The two old men had gone to fetch Cosette from the fruiterer's in the Rue du Chemin-Vert, where Fauchelevent had deposited her on the preceding day. Cosette had passed these twenty-four hours trembling silently and understanding nothing. She trembled to such a degree that she wept. She had neither eaten nor slept. The worthy fruit-seller had plied her with a hundred questions, without obtaining any other reply than a melancholy and unvarying gaze. Cosette had betrayed nothing of what she had seen and heard during the last two days. She divined that they were passing through a crisis. She was deeply conscious that it was necessary to "be good." Who has not experienced the sovereign power of those two words, pronounced with a certain accent in the ear of a terrified little being: *Say nothing!* Fear is mute. Moreover, no one guards a secret like a child.

But when, at the expiration of these lugubrious twenty-four hours, she beheld Jean Valjean again, she gave vent to such a cry of joy, that any thoughtful person who had chanced to hear that cry, would have guessed that it issued from an abyss.

Fauchelevent belonged to the convent and knew the passwords. All the doors opened.

Thus was solved the double and alarming problem of how to get out and how to get in.

The porter, who had received his instructions, opened the little servant's door which connected the courtyard with the garden, and which could still be seen from the street twenty years ago, in the wall at the bottom of the court, which faced the carriage entrance.

The porter admitted all three of them through this door, and from that point they reached the inner, reserved parlor where Fauchelevent, on the preceding day, had received his orders from the prioress.

The prioress, rosary in hand, was waiting for them. A vocal mother, with her veil lowered, stood beside her.

A discreet candle lighted, one might almost say, made a show of lighting the parlor.

The prioress passed Jean Valjean in review. There is nothing which examines like a downcast eye.

Then she questioned him:

"You are the brother?"

"Yes, reverend Mother," replied Fauchelevent.

"What is your name?"

Fauchelevent replied:

"Ultime Fauchelevent."

He really had had a brother named Ultime, who was dead.

"Where do you come from?"

Fauchelevent replied:

"From Picquigny, near Amiens."

"What is your age?"

Fauchelevent replied:

"Fifty."

"What is your profession?"

Fauchelevent replied:

"Gardener."

"Are you a good Christian?"

Fauchelevent replied:

"Everyone is in the family."

"Is this your little girl?"

Fauchelevent replied:

"Yes, reverend Mother."

"You are her father?"

Fauchelevent replied:

"Her grandfather."

The vocal mother said to the prioress in a low voice:

"He answers well."

Jean Valjean had not uttered a single word.

The prioress looked attentively at Cosette, and said half-aloud to the vocal mother:

"She will grow up ugly."

The two mothers consulted for a few moments in very low tones in the corner of the parlor, then the prioress turned round and said:

"Father Fauvent, you will get another knee-cap with a bell. Two will be required now."

On the following day, therefore, two bells were audible in the garden, and the nuns could not resist the temptation to raise the corner of their veils. At the extreme end of the garden, under the trees, two men, Fauvent and another man, were visible as they dug side by side. An enormous event. Their silence was broken to the extent of saying to each other: "He is an assistant gardener."

The vocal mothers added: "He is a brother of Father Fauvent."

Jean Valjean was, in fact, regularly installed; he had his belled knee-cap; henceforth he was official. His name was Ultime Fauchelevent.

The most powerful determining cause of his admission had been the prioress's observation upon Cosette: "She will grow up ugly."

The prioress, that pronounced prognosticator, immediately took a fancy to Cosette and gave her a place in the school as a charity pupil.

There is nothing that is not strictly logical about this.

It is in vain that mirrors are banished from the convent, women are conscious of their faces; now, girls who are conscious of their beauty do not easily become nuns; the vocation being voluntary in inverse proportion to their good looks, more is to be hoped from the ugly than from the pretty. Hence a lively taste for plain girls.

The whole of this adventure increased the importance of good, old Fauchelevent; he won a triple success; in the eyes of Jean Valjean, whom he had saved and sheltered; in those of gravedigger Gribier, who said to himself: "He spared me that fine"; with the convent, which, being enabled, thanks to him, to retain the coffin of Mother Crucifixion under the altar, eluded Cæsar and satisfied God. There was a coffin containing a body in the Petit-Picpus, and a coffin without a body in the Vaugirard cemetery, public order had no doubt been deeply disturbed thereby, but no one was aware of it.

As for the convent, its gratitude to Fauchelevent was very great. Fauchelevent became the best of servitors and the most precious of gardeners. Upon the occasion of the archbishop's next visit, the prioress recounted the affair to his Grace, making something of a confession at the same time, and yet boasting of her deed. On leaving the convent, the archbishop mentioned it with approval, and in a whisper to M. de Latil, Monsieur's confessor, afterwards Archbishop of Reims and Cardinal. This admiration for Fauchelevent became widespread, for it made its way to Rome. We have seen a note addressed by the then reigning Pope, Leo XII, to one of his relatives, a Monsignor in the Nuncio's establishment in Paris, and bearing, like himself, the name of Della Genga; it contained these lines: "It appears that there is in a convent in Paris an excellent gardener, who is also a holy man, named Fauvent." Nothing of this triumph reached Fauchelevent in his hut; he went on grafting, weeding, and covering up his melon beds, without in the least suspecting his excellences and his sanctity. Neither did he suspect his glory, anymore than a Durham or Surrey bull whose portrait is published in the *London Illustrated News,* with this inscription: "Bull which carried off the prize at the Cattle Show."

Chapter IX

CLOISTERED

COSETTE CONTINUED TO HOLD HER TONGUE IN THE CONVENT.
It was quite natural that Cosette should think herself Jean Valjean's daughter. Moreover, as she knew nothing, she could say nothing, and then, she would not have said anything in any case. As we have just observed, nothing trains children to silence like unhappiness. Cosette had suffered so much, that she feared everything, even to speak or to breathe. A single word had so often brought down an avalanche upon her. She had hardly begun to regain her confidence since she had been with Jean Valjean. She speedily became accustomed to the convent. Only she regretted Catherine, but she dared not say so. Once, however, she did say to Jean Valjean: "Father, if I had known, I would have brought her away with me."

Cosette had been obliged, on becoming a scholar in the convent, to don the garb of the pupils of the house. Jean Valjean succeeded in getting them to restore to him the garments which she laid aside. This was the same mourning suit which he had made her put on when she had quitted the Thénardiers' inn. It was not very threadbare even now. Jean Valjean locked up these garments, plus the stockings and the shoes, with a quantity of camphor and all the aromatics in which convents abound, in a little valise which he found means of procuring. He set this valise on a chair near his bed, and he always carried the key about his person. "Father," Cosette asked him one day, "what is there in that box which smells so good?"

Father Fauchelevent received other recompense for his good action, in addition to the glory which we just mentioned, and of which he knew nothing; in the first place it made him happy; next, he had much less work, since it was shared. Lastly, as he was very fond of snuff, he found the presence of M. Madeleine an advantage, in that he used three times as much as he had done previously, and that in an infinitely more luxurious manner, seeing that M. Madeleine paid for it.

The nuns did not adopt the name of Ultime; they called Jean Valjean *the other Fauvent*.

If these holy women had possessed anything of Javert's glance, they would eventually have noticed that when there was any errand to be done outside in the behalf of the garden, it was always the elder Fauchelevent, the old, the infirm, the lame man, who went, and never the other; but whether it is that eyes constantly fixed on God know not how to spy, or whether they were, by preference, occupied in keeping watch on each other, they paid no heed to this.

Moreover, it was well for Jean Valjean that he kept close and did not stir out. Javert watched the quarter for more than a month.

This convent was for Jean Valjean like an island surrounded by gulfs. Henceforth, those four walls constituted his world. He saw enough of the sky there to enable him to preserve his serenity, and Cosette enough to remain happy.

A very sweet life began for him.

He inhabited the old hut at the end of the garden, in company with Fauchelevent. This hovel, built of old rubbish, which was still in existence in 1845, was composed, as the reader already knows, of three chambers, all of which were utterly bare and had nothing beyond the walls. The principal one had been given up, by force, for Jean Valjean had opposed it in vain, to M. Madeleine, by Father Fauchelevent. The walls of this chamber had for ornament, in addition to the two nails whereon to hang the knee-cap and the basket, a royalist bank-note of '93, applied to the wall over the chimney-piece, and of which the following is an exact facsimile:

This specimen of Vendean paper money had been nailed to the wall by the preceding gardener, an old Chouan, who had died in the convent, and whose place Fauchelevent had taken.

Jean Valjean worked in the garden every day and made himself very useful. He had formerly been a pruner of trees, and he gladly found himself a gardener once more. It will be remembered that he knew all sorts of secrets and receipts for agriculture. He turned these to advantage. Almost all the trees in the orchard were ungrafted, and wild. He budded them and made them produce excellent fruit.

Cosette had permission to pass an hour with him every day. As the sisters were melancholy and he was kind, the child made comparisons and adored him. At the appointed hour, she flew to the hut. When she entered the lowly cabin, she filled it with paradise. Jean Valjean blossomed out and felt his happiness increase with the happiness which he afforded Cosette. The joy which we inspire has this charming property, that, far from growing meager, like all reflections, it returns to us more radiant than ever. At recreation hours, Jean Valjean watched her running and playing in the distance, and he distinguished her laugh from that of the rest.

For Cosette laughed now.

Cosette's face had even undergone a change, to a certain extent. The gloom had disappeared from it. A smile is the same as sunshine; it banishes winter from the human countenance.

Recreation over, when Cosette went into the house again, Jean Valjean gazed at the windows of her class-room, and at night he rose to look at the windows of her dormitory.

God has his own ways, moreover; the convent contributed, like Cosette, to uphold and complete the Bishop's work in Jean Valjean. It is certain that virtue adjoins pride on one side. A bridge built by the devil exists there. Jean Valjean had been, unconsciously, perhaps, tolerably near that side and that bridge, when Providence cast his lot in the convent of the Petit-Picpus; so long as he had compared himself only to the Bishop, he had regarded himself as unworthy and had remained humble; but for sometime past he had been comparing himself to men in general, and pride was beginning to spring up. Who knows? He might have ended by returning very gradually to hatred.

The convent stopped him on that downward path.

This was the second place of captivity which he had seen. In his youth, in what had been for him the beginning of his life, and later on, quite recently again, he had beheld another—a frightful place, a terrible place, whose severities had always appeared to him the iniquity of justice, and the crime of the law. Now, after the galleys, he saw the cloister; and when he meditated how he had formed a part of the galleys, and that he now, so to speak, was a spectator of the cloister, he confronted the two in his own mind with anxiety.

Sometimes he crossed his arms and leaned on his hoe, and slowly descended the endless spirals of reverie.

He recalled his former companions: how wretched they were; they rose at dawn, and toiled until night; hardly were they permitted to sleep; they lay on camp beds, where nothing was tolerated but mattresses two inches thick, in rooms which were heated only in the very harshest months of the year; they were clothed in frightful red blouses; they were allowed, as a great favor, linen trousers in the hottest weather, and a woolen carter's blouse on their backs when it was very cold; they drank no wine, and ate no meat, except when they went on "fatigue duty." They lived nameless, designated only by numbers, and converted, after a manner, into ciphers themselves, with downcast eyes, with lowered voices, with shorn heads, beneath the cudgel and in disgrace.

Then his mind reverted to the beings whom he had under his eyes.

These beings also lived with shorn heads, with downcast eyes, with lowered voices, not in disgrace, but amid the scoffs of the world, not with their backs bruised with the cudgel, but with their shoulders lacerated with their discipline. Their names, also, had vanished from among men; they no longer existed except under austere appellations. They never ate meat and they never drank wine; they often remained until evening without food; they were attired, not in a red blouse, but in a black shroud, of woolen, which was heavy in summer and thin in winter, without the power to add or subtract anything from it; without having even, according to the season, the resource of the linen garment or the woolen cloak; and for six months in the year they wore serge chemises which gave them fever. They dwelt, not in rooms warmed only during rigorous cold, but in cells where no fire was ever lighted; they slept, not on mattresses two inches thick, but on straw. And finally, they were not even allowed their sleep; every night, after a day of toil, they were obliged, in the weariness of their first slumber, at the moment when they were falling sound asleep and beginning to get warm, to rouse themselves, to rise and to go and pray in an ice-cold and gloomy chapel, with their knees on the stones.

On certain days each of these beings in turn had to remain for twelve successive hours in a kneeling posture, or prostrate, with face upon the pavement, and arms outstretched in the form of a cross.

The others were men; these were women.

What had those men done? They had stolen, violated, pillaged, murdered, assassinated. They were bandits, counterfeiters, poisoners, incendiaries, murderers, parricides. What had these women done? They had done nothing whatever.

On the one hand, highway robbery, fraud, deceit, violence, sensuality, homicide, all sorts of sacrilege, every variety of crime; on the other, one thing only, innocence.

Perfect innocence, almost caught up into heaven in a mysterious assumption, attached to the earth by virtue, already possessing something of heaven through holiness.

On the one hand, confidences over crimes, which are exchanged in whispers; on the other, the confession of faults made aloud. And what crimes! And what faults!

On the one hand, miasms; on the other, an ineffable perfume. On the one hand, a moral pest, guarded from sight, penned up under the range of cannon, and literally devouring its plague-stricken victims; on the other, the chaste flame of all souls on the same hearth. There, darkness; here, the shadow; but a shadow filled with gleams of light, and of gleams full of radiance.

Two strongholds of slavery; but in the first, deliverance possible, a legal limit always in sight, and then, escape. In the second, perpetuity; the sole hope, at the distant extremity of the future, that faint light of liberty which men call death.

In the first, men are bound only with chains; in the other, chained by faith.

What flowed from the first? An immense curse, the gnashing of teeth, hatred, desperate viciousness, a cry of rage against human society, a sarcasm against heaven.

What results flowed from the second? Blessings and love.

And in these two places, so similar yet so unlike, these two species of beings who were so very unlike, were undergoing the same work, expiation.

Jean Valjean understood thoroughly the expiation of the former; that personal expiation, the expiation for one's self. But he did not understand that of these last, that of creatures without reproach and without stain, and he trembled as he asked himself: The expiation of what? What expiation?

A voice within his conscience replied: "The most divine of human generosities, the expiation for others."

Here all personal theory is withheld; we are only the narrator; we place ourselves at Jean Valjean's point of view, and we translate his impressions.

Before his eyes he had the sublime summit of abnegation, the highest possible pitch of virtue; the innocence which pardons men their faults, and which expiates in their stead; servitude submitted to, torture accepted, punishment claimed by souls which have not sinned, for the sake of sparing it to souls which have fallen; the love of humanity swallowed up in the love of God, but even there preserving its distinct and mediatorial character; sweet and feeble beings possessing the misery of those who are punished and the smile of those who are recompensed.

And he remembered that he had dared to murmur!

Often, in the middle of the night, he rose to listen to the grateful song of those innocent creatures weighed down with severities, and the blood ran cold in his veins at the thought that those who were justly chastised raised their voices heavenward only in blasphemy, and that he, wretch that he was, had shaken his fist at God.

There was one striking thing which caused him to meditate deeply, like a warning whisper from Providence itself: the scaling of that wall, the passing of those barriers, the adventure accepted even at the risk of death, the painful and difficult ascent, all those efforts even, which he had made to escape from that other place of expiation, he had made in order to gain entrance into this one. Was this a symbol of his destiny? This house was a prison likewise and bore a melancholy resemblance to that other one whence he had fled, and yet he had never conceived an idea of anything similar.

Again he beheld gratings, bolts, iron bars—to guard whom? Angels.

These lofty walls which he had seen around tigers, he now beheld once more around lambs.

This was a place of expiation, and not of punishment; and yet, it was still more austere, more gloomy, and more pitiless than the other.

These virgins were even more heavily burdened than the convicts. A cold, harsh wind, that wind which had chilled his youth, traversed the barred and padlocked grating of the vultures; a still harsher and more biting breeze blew in the cage of these doves.

Why?

When he thought on these things, all that was within him was lost in amazement before this mystery of sublimity.

In these meditations, his pride vanished. He scrutinized his own heart in all manner of ways; he felt his pettiness, and many a time he wept. All that had entered into his life for the last six months had led him back toward the Bishop's holy injunctions; Cosette through love, the convent through humility.

Sometimes at eventide, in the twilight, at an hour when the garden was deserted, he could be seen on his knees in the middle of the walk which skirted the chapel, in front of the window through which he had gazed on the night of his arrival, and turned toward the spot where, as he knew, the sister was making reparation, prostrated in prayer. Thus he prayed as he knelt before the sister.

It seemed as though he dared not kneel directly before God.

Everything that surrounded him, that peaceful garden, those fragrant flowers, those children who uttered joyous cries, those grave and simple women, that silent cloister, slowly permeated him, and little by little, his soul became compounded of silence like the cloister, of perfume like the flowers, of simplicity like the women, of joy like the children. And then he reflected that these had been two houses of God which had received him in succession at two critical moments in his life: the first, when all doors were closed and when human society rejected him; the second, at a moment when human society had again set out in pursuit of him, and when the galleys were again yawning; and that, had it not been for the first, he should have relapsed into crime, and had it not been for the second, into torment.

His whole heart melted in gratitude, and he loved more and more.

Many years passed in this manner; Cosette was growing up.

Volume III

Marius

BOOK FIRST

PARIS STUDIED IN ITS ATOM

Chapter I

PARVULUS

PARIS HAS A CHILD, AND THE FOREST HAS A BIRD; THE BIRD IS CALLED THE SPARROW; THE child is called the gamin.

Couple these two ideas which contain, the one all the furnace, the other all the dawn; strike these two sparks together, Paris, childhood; there leaps out from them a little being. *Homuncio*, Plautus would say.

This little being is joyous. He has not food every day, and he goes to the play every evening, if he sees good. He has no shirt on his body, no shoes on his feet, no roof over his head; he is like the flies of heaven, who have none of these things. He is from seven to thirteen years of age, he lives in bands, roams the streets, lodges in the open air, wears an old pair of trousers of his father's, which descend below his heels, an old hat of some other father, which descends below his ears, a single suspender of yellow listing; he runs, lies in wait, rummages about, wastes time, blackens pipes, swears like a convict, haunts the wine-shop, knows thieves, calls gay women *thou*, talks slang, sings obscene songs, and has no evil in his heart. This is because he has in his heart a pearl, innocence; and pearls are not to be dissolved in mud. So long as man is in his childhood, God wills that he shall be innocent.

If one were to ask that enormous city: "What is this?" she would reply: "It is my little one."

Chapter II

SOME OF HIS PARTICULAR CHARACTERISTICS

THE GAMIN—THE STREET ARAB—OF PARIS IS THE DWARF OF THE GIANT.

Let us not exaggerate, this cherub of the gutter sometimes has a shirt, but, in that case, he owns but one; he sometimes has shoes, but then they have no soles; he sometimes has a lodging, and he loves it, for he finds his mother there; but he prefers the street, because there he finds liberty. He has his own games, his own bits of mischief, whose foundation consists of hatred for the bourgeois; his peculiar metaphors: to be dead is *to eat dandelions by the root*; his own occupations, calling hackney-coaches, letting down carriage-steps, establishing means of transit between the two sides of a street in heavy rains, which he calls *making the bridge of arts*, crying discourses pronounced by the authorities in favor of the French people, cleaning out the cracks in the pavement;

he has his own coinage, which is composed of all the little morsels of worked copper which are found on the public streets. This curious money, which receives the name of *loques*—rags—has an invariable and well-regulated currency in this little Bohemia of children.

Lastly, he has his own fauna, which he observes attentively in the corners; the lady-bird, the death's-head plant-louse, the daddy-long-legs, "the devil," a black insect, which menaces by twisting about its tail armed with two horns. He has his fabulous monster, which has scales under its belly, but is not a lizard, which has pustules on its back, but is not a toad, which inhabits the nooks of old lime-kilns and wells that have run dry, which is black, hairy, sticky, which crawls sometimes slowly, sometimes rapidly, which has no cry, but which has a look, and is so terrible that no one has ever beheld it; he calls this monster "the deaf thing." The search for these "deaf things" among the stones is a joy of formidable nature. Another pleasure consists in suddenly prying up a paving-stone, and taking a look at the wood-lice. Each region of Paris is celebrated for the interesting treasures which are to be found there. There are ear-wigs in the timber-yards of the Ursulines, there are millipedes in the Pantheon, there are tadpoles in the ditches of the Champs-de-Mars.

As far as sayings are concerned, this child has as many of them as Talleyrand. He is no less cynical, but he is more honest. He is endowed with a certain indescribable, unexpected joviality; he upsets the composure of the shop-keeper with his wild laughter. He ranges boldly from high comedy to farce.

A funeral passes by. Among those who accompany the dead there is a doctor. "Hey there!" shouts some street Arab, "how long has it been customary for doctors to carry home their own work?"

Another is in a crowd. A grave man, adorned with spectacles and trinkets, turns round indignantly: "You good-for-nothing, you have seized my wife's waist!"—"I, sir? Search me!"

Chapter III

HE IS AGREEABLE

IN THE EVENING, THANKS TO A FEW SOUS, WHICH HE ALWAYS FINDS MEANS TO PROCURE, THE *HOmuncio* enters a theater. On crossing that magic threshold, he becomes transfigured; he was the street Arab, he becomes the titi. Theaters are a sort of ship turned upside down with the keel in the air. It is in that keel that the titi huddle together. The titi is to the gamin what the moth is to the larva; the same being endowed with wings and soaring. It suffices for him to be there, with his radiance of happiness, with his power of enthusiasm and joy, with his hand-clapping, which resembles a clapping of wings, to confer on that narrow, dark, fetid, sordid, unhealthy, hideous, abominable keel, the name of Paradise.

Bestow on an individual the useless and deprive him of the necessary, and you have the gamin.

The gamin is not devoid of literary intuition. His tendency, and we say it with the proper amount of regret, would not constitute classic taste. He is not very academic by nature. Thus, to give an example, the popularity of Mademoiselle Mars among that little audience of stormy children was seasoned with a touch of irony. The gamin called her *Mademoiselle Muche*—"hide yourself."

This being bawls and scoffs and ridicules and fights, has rags like a baby and tatters like a philosopher, fishes in the sewer, hunts in the cesspool, extracts mirth from foulness, whips up the squares with his wit, grins and bites, whistles and sings, shouts and shrieks, tempers Alleluia with Matanturlurette, chants every rhythm from the De Profundis to the Jack-pudding, finds without seeking, knows what he is ignorant of, is a Spartan to the point of thieving, is mad to wisdom, is lyrical to filth, would crouch down on Olympus, wallows in the dunghill and emerges from it covered with stars. The gamin of Paris is Rabelais in this youth.

He is not content with his trousers unless they have a watch-pocket.

He is not easily astonished, he is still less easily terrified, he makes songs on superstitions, he takes the wind out of exaggerations, he twits mysteries, he thrusts out his tongue at ghosts, he takes the poetry out of stilted things, he introduces caricature into epic extravaganzas. It is not that he is prosaic; far from that; but he replaces the solemn vision by the farcical phantasmagoria. If Adamastor were to appear to him, the street Arab would say: "Hi there! The bugaboo!"

Chapter IV

He May be of Use

PARIS BEGINS WITH THE LOUNGER AND ENDS WITH THE STREET ARAB, TWO BEINGS OF WHICH NO other city is capable; the passive acceptance, which contents itself with gazing, and the inexhaustible initiative; Prudhomme and Fouillou. Paris alone has this in its natural history. The whole of the monarchy is contained in the lounger; the whole of anarchy in the gamin.

This pale child of the Parisian faubourgs lives and develops, makes connections, "grows supple" in suffering, in the presence of social realities and of human things, a thoughtful witness. He thinks himself heedless; and he is not. He looks and is on the verge of laughter; he is on the verge of something else also. Whoever you may be, if your name is Prejudice, Abuse, Ignorance, Oppression, Iniquity, Despotism, Injustice, Fanaticism, Tyranny, beware of the gaping gamin.

The little fellow will grow up.

Of what clay is he made? Of the first mud that comes to hand. A handful of dirt, a breath, and behold Adam. It suffices for a God to pass by. A God has always passed over the street Arab. Fortune labors at this tiny being. By the word "fortune" we mean chance, to some extent. That pigmy kneaded out of common earth, ignorant, unlettered, giddy, vulgar, low. Will that become an Ionian or a Bœotian? Wait, *currit rota,* the spirit of Paris, that demon which creates the children of chance and the men of destiny, reversing the process of the Latin potter, makes of a jug an amphora.

Chapter V

His Frontiers

THE GAMIN LOVES THE CITY, HE ALSO LOVES SOLITUDE, SINCE HE HAS SOMETHING OF THE SAGE in him. *Urbis amator,* like Fuscus; *ruris amator,* like Flaccus.

To roam thoughtfully about, that is to say, to lounge, is a fine employment of time in the eyes of the philosopher; particularly in that rather illegitimate species of campaign, which is tolerably ugly but odd and composed of two natures, which surrounds certain great cities, notably Paris. To study the suburbs is to study the amphibious animal. End of the trees, beginning of the roofs; end of the grass, beginning of the pavements; end of the furrows, beginning of the shops; end of the wheel-ruts, beginning of the passions; end of the divine murmur, beginning of the human uproar; hence an extraordinary interest.

Hence, in these not very attractive places, indelibly stamped by the passing stroller with the epithet: *melancholy,* the apparently objectless promenades of the dreamer.

He who writes these lines has long been a prowler about the barriers of Paris, and it is for him a source of profound souvenirs. That close-shaven turf, those pebbly paths, that chalk, those pools, those harsh monotonies of waste and fallow lands, the plants of early market-garden suddenly springing into sight in a bottom, that mixture of the savage and the citizen, those vast desert nooks where the garrison drums practice noisily, and produce a sort of lisping of battle, those hermits by day and cut-throats by night, that clumsy mill which turns in the wind, the hoisting-wheels of the quarries, the tea-gardens at the corners of the cemeteries; the mysterious charm of great, somber walls squarely intersecting immense, vague stretches of land inundated with sunshine and full of butterflies—all this attracted him.

There is hardly anyone on earth who is not acquainted with those singular spots, the Glacière, the Cunette, the hideous wall of Grenelle all speckled with balls, Mont-Parnasse, the Fosse-aux-Loups, Aubiers on the bank of the Marne, Mont-Souris, the Tombe-Issoire, the Pierre-Plate de Châtillon, where there is an old, exhausted quarry which no longer serves any purpose except to raise mushrooms, and which is closed, on a level with the ground, by a trapdoor of rotten planks. The campagna of Rome is one idea, the banlieue of Paris is another; to behold nothing but fields, houses, or trees in what a stretch of country offers us, is to remain on the surface; all aspects of things are thoughts of God. The spot where a plain effects its junction with a city is always stamped with a certain piercing melancholy. Nature and humanity both appeal to you at the same time there. Local originalities there make their appearance.

Anyone who, like ourselves, has wandered about in these solitudes contiguous to our faubourgs, which may be designated as the limbos of Paris, has seen here and there, in the most desert spot, at the most unexpected moment, behind a meager hedge, or in the corner of a lugubrious wall, children grouped tumultuously, fetid, muddy, dusty, ragged, disheveled, playing hide-and-seek, and crowned with corn-flowers. All of them are little ones who have made their escape from poor families. The outer boulevard is their breathing space; the suburbs belong to them. There they are eternally playing truant. There they innocently sing their repertory of dirty songs. There they are, or rather, there they exist, far from every eye, in the sweet light of May or June, kneeling round a hole in the ground, snapping marbles with their thumbs, quarreling over half-farthings, irresponsible, volatile, free and happy; and, no sooner do they catch sight of you than they recollect that they have an industry, and that they must earn their living, and they offer to sell you an old woolen stocking filled with cockchafers, or a bunch of lilacs. These encounters with strange children are one of the charming and at the same time poignant graces of the environs of Paris.

Sometimes there are little girls among the throng of boys—are they their sisters?—who are almost young maidens, thin, feverish, with sunburned hands, covered with freckles, crowned with poppies and ears of rye, gay, haggard, barefooted. They can be seen devouring cherries among the wheat. In the evening they can be heard laughing. These groups, warmly illuminated by the full glow of midday, or indistinctly seen in the twilight, occupy the thoughtful man for a very long time, and these visions mingle with his dreams.

Paris, center, banlieue, circumference; this constitutes all the earth to those children. They never venture beyond this. They can no more escape from the Parisian atmosphere than fish can escape from the water. For them, nothing exists two leagues beyond the barriers: Ivry, Gentilly, Arcueil, Belleville, Aubervilliers, Menilmontant, Choisy-le-Roi, Billancourt, Meudon, Issy, Vanvre, Sèvres, Puteaux, Neuilly, Gennevilliers, Colombes, Romainville, Chatou, Asnières, Bougival, Nanterre, Enghien, Noisy-le-Sec, Nogent, Gournay, Drancy, Gonesse; the universe ends there.

Chapter VI

A BIT OF HISTORY

At THE EPOCH, NEARLY CONTEMPORARY BY THE WAY, WHEN THE ACTION OF THIS BOOK TAKES place, there was not, as there is to-day, a policeman at the corner of every street (a benefit which there is no time to discuss here); stray children abounded in Paris. The statistics give an average of two hundred and sixty homeless children picked up annually at that period, by the police patrols, in unenclosed lands, in houses in process of construction, and under the arches of the bridges. One of these nests, which has become famous, produced "the swallows of the bridge of Arcola." This is, moreover, the most disastrous of social symptoms. All crimes of the man begin in the vagabondage of the child.

Let us make an exception in favor of Paris, nevertheless. In a relative measure, and in spite of the souvenir which we have just recalled, the exception is just. While in any other great city the vagabond child is a lost man, while nearly everywhere the child left to itself is, in some sort, sacrificed and abandoned to a kind of fatal immersion in the public vices which devour in him honesty and conscience, the street boy of Paris, we insist on this point, however defaced and injured on the surface, is almost intact on the interior. It is a magnificent thing to put on record, and one which shines forth in the splendid probity of our popular revolutions, that a certain incorruptibility results from the idea which exists in the air of Paris, as salt exists in the water of the ocean. To breathe Paris preserves the soul.

What we have just said takes away nothing of the anguish of heart which one experiences every time that one meets one of these children around whom one fancies that he beholds floating the threads of a broken family. In the civilization of the present day, incomplete as it still is, it is not a very abnormal thing to behold these fractured families pouring themselves out into the darkness, not knowing clearly what has become of their children, and allowing their own entrails to fall on the public highway. Hence these obscure destinies. This is called, for this sad thing has given rise to an expression, "to be cast on the pavements of Paris."

Let it be said by the way, that this abandonment of children was not discouraged by the ancient monarchy. A little of Egypt and Bohemia in the lower regions suited the upper spheres, and compassed the aims of the powerful. The hatred of instruction for the children of the people was a dogma. What is the use of "half-lights"? Such was the countersign. Now, the erring child is the corollary of the ignorant child.

Besides this, the monarchy sometimes was in need of children, and in that case it skimmed the streets.

Under Louis XIV, not to go any further back, the king rightly desired to create a fleet. The idea was a good one. But let us consider the means. There can be no fleet, if, beside the sailing ship, that plaything of the winds, and for the purpose of towing it, in case of necessity, there is not the vessel which goes where it pleases, either by means of oars or of steam; the galleys were then to the marine what steamers are to-day. Therefore, galleys were necessary; but the galley is moved only by the galley-slave; hence, galley-slaves were required. Colbert had the commissioners of provinces and the parliaments make as many convicts as possible. The magistracy showed a great deal of complaisance in the matter. A man kept his hat on in the presence of a procession—it was a Huguenot attitude; he was sent to the galleys. A child was encountered in the streets; provided that he was fifteen years of age and did not know where he was to sleep, he was sent to the galleys. Grand reign; grand century.

Under Louis XV children disappeared in Paris; the police carried them off, for what mysterious purpose no one knew. People whispered with terror monstrous conjectures as to the king's baths of purple. Barbier speaks ingenuously of these things. It sometimes happened that the exempts of the guard, when they ran short of children, took those who had fathers. The fathers, in despair, attacked the exempts. In that case, the parliament intervened and had someone hung. Who? The exempts? No, the fathers.

Chapter VII

THE GAMIN SHOULD HAVE HIS PLACE IN THE CLASSIFICATIONS OF INDIA

THE BODY OF STREET ARABS IN PARIS ALMOST CONSTITUTES A CASTE. ONE MIGHT ALMOST SAY: Not everyone who wishes to belong to it can do so.

This word *gamin* was printed for the first time, and reached popular speech through the literary tongue, in 1834. It is in a little work entitled *Claude Gueux* that this word made its appearance. The horror was lively. The word passed into circulation.

The elements which constitute the consideration of the gamins for each other are very various. We have known and associated with one who was greatly respected and vastly admired because he had seen a man fall from the top of the tower of Notre-Dame; another, because he had succeeded in making his way into the rear courtyard where the statues of the dome of the Invalides had been temporarily deposited, and had "prigged" some lead from them; a third, because he had seen a diligence tip over; still another, because he "knew" a soldier who came near putting out the eye of a citizen.

This explains that famous exclamation of a Parisian gamin, a profound epiphonema, which the vulgar herd laughs at without comprehending—*Dieu de Dieu! What ill-luck I do have! to think that I have never yet seen anybody tumble from a fifth-story window!* (*I have* pronounced *I'ave*, and *fifth* pronounced *fift'*.)

Surely, this saying of a peasant is a fine one: "Father So-and-So, your wife has died of her malady; why did you not send for the doctor?" "What would you have, sir, we poor folks *die of ourselves*." But if the peasant's whole passivity lies in this saying, the whole of the free-thinking anarchy of the brat of the faubourgs is, assuredly, contained in this other saying. A man condemned to death is listening to his confessor in the tumbrel. The child of Paris exclaims: "He is talking to his black cap! Oh, the sneak!"

A certain audacity on matters of religion sets off the gamin. To be strong-minded is an important item.

To be present at executions constitutes a duty. He shows himself at the guillotine, and he laughs. He calls it by all sorts of pet names: The End of the Soup, The Growler, The Mother in the Blue (the sky), The Last Mouthful, etc., etc. In order not to lose anything of the affair, he scales the walls, he hoists himself to balconies, he ascends trees, he suspends himself to gratings, he clings fast to chimneys. The gamin is born a tiler as he is born a mariner. A roof inspires him with no more fear than a mast. There is no festival which comes up to an execution on the Place de Grève. Samson and the Abbé Montès are the truly popular names. They hoot at the victim in order to encourage him. They sometimes admire him. Lacenaire, when a gamin, on seeing the hideous Dautun die bravely, uttered these words which contain a future: "I was jealous of him."

In the brotherhood of gamins Voltaire is not known, but Papavoine is. "Politicians" are confused with assassins in the same legend. They have a tradition as to everybody's last garment. It is known that Tolleron had a fireman's cap, Avril an otter cap, Losvel a round hat, that old Delaporte was bald and bare-headed, that Castaing was all ruddy and very handsome, that Bories had a romantic small beard, that Jean Martin kept on his suspenders, that Lecouffé and his mother quarreled. "Don't reproach each other for your basket," shouted a gamin to them. Another, in order to get a look at Debacker as he passed, and being too small in the crowd, caught sight of the lantern on the quay and climbed it. A gendarme stationed opposite frowned. "Let me climb up, m'sieu le gendarme," said the gamin. And, to soften the heart of the authorities, he added: "I will not fall." "I don't care if you do," retorted the gendarme.

In the brotherhood of gamins, a memorable accident counts for a great deal. One reaches the height of consideration if one chances to cut one's self very deeply, "to the very bone."

The fist is no mediocre element of respect. One of the things that the gamin is fondest of saying is: "I am fine and strong, come now!" To be left-handed renders you very enviable. A squint is highly esteemed.

Chapter VIII

IN WHICH THE READER WILL FIND A CHARMING SAYING OF THE LAST KING

IN SUMMER, HE METAMORPHOSES HIMSELF INTO A FROG; AND IN THE EVENING, WHEN NIGHT IS falling, in front of the bridges of Austerlitz and Jena, from the tops of coal wagons, and the washerwomen's boats, he hurls himself headlong into the Seine, and into all possible infractions of the laws of modesty and of the police. Nevertheless the police keep an eye on him, and the result is a highly dramatic situation which once gave rise to a fraternal and memorable cry; that cry which was celebrated about 1830, is a strategic warning from gamin to gamin; it scans like a verse from Homer, with a notation as inexpressible as the eleusiac chant of the Panathenæa, and in it one encounters again the ancient Evohe. Here it is: "Ohé, Titi, ohéée! Here comes the bobby, here comes the p'lice, pick up your duds and be off, through the sewer with you!"

Sometimes this gnat—that is what he calls himself—knows how to read; sometimes he knows how to write; he always knows how to daub. He does not hesitate to acquire, by no one knows what mysterious mutual instruction, all the talents which can be of use to the public; from 1815 to 1830, he imitated the cry of the turkey; from 1830 to 1848, he scrawled pears on the walls. One summer evening, when Louis Philippe was returning home on foot, he saw a little fellow, no higher than his knee, perspiring and climbing up to draw a gigantic pear in charcoal on one of the pillars of the gate of Neuilly; the King, with that good-nature which came to him from Henry IV, helped the gamin, finished the pear, and gave the child a louis, saying: "The pear is on that also."[1] The gamin loves uproar. A certain state of violence pleases him. He execrates "the curés." One day, in the Rue de l'Université, one of these scamps was putting his thumb to his nose at the carriage gate of No. 69. "Why are you doing that at the gate?" a passer-by asked. The boy replied: "There is a curé there." It was there, in fact, that the Papal Nuncio lived.

Nevertheless, whatever may be the Voltairianism of the small gamin, if the occasion to become

1. Louis XVIII is represented in comic pictures of that day as having a pear-shaped head.

a chorister presents itself, it is quite possible that he will accept, and in that case he serves the mass civilly. There are two things to which he plays Tantalus, and which he always desires without ever attaining them: to overthrow the government, and to get his trousers sewed up again.

The gamin in his perfect state possesses all the policemen of Paris, and can always put the name to the face of anyone which he chances to meet. He can tell them off on the tips of his fingers. He studies their habits, and he has special notes on each one of them. He reads the souls of the police like an open book. He will tell you fluently and without flinching: "Such an one is a *traitor*; such another is very *malicious*; such another is *great*; such another is *ridiculous*." (All these words: traitor, malicious, great, ridiculous, have a particular meaning in his mouth.) That one imagines that he owns the Pont-Neuf, and he prevents *people* from walking on the cornice outside the parapet; that other has a mania for pulling *person's* ears; etc., etc.

Chapter IX

THE OLD SOUL OF GAUL

THERE WAS SOMETHING OF THAT BOY IN POQUELIN, THE SON OF THE FISH-MARKET; BEAUMARchais had something of it. Gaminerie is a shade of the Gallic spirit. Mingled with good sense, it sometimes adds force to the latter, as alcohol does to wine. Sometimes it is a defect. Homer repeats himself eternally, granted; one may say that Voltaire plays the gamin. Camille Desmoulins was a native of the faubourgs. Championnet, who treated miracles brutally, rose from the pavements of Paris; he had, when a small lad, inundated the porticos of Saint-Jean de Beauvais, and of Saint-Étienne du Mont; he had addressed the shrine of Sainte-Geneviève familiarly to give orders to the phial of Saint Januarius.

The gamin of Paris is respectful, ironical, and insolent. He has villainous teeth, because he is badly fed and his stomach suffers, and handsome eyes because he has wit. If Jehovah himself were present, he would go hopping up the steps of paradise on one foot. He is strong on boxing. All beliefs are possible to him. He plays in the gutter, and straightens himself up with a revolt; his effrontery persists even in the presence of grape-shot; he was a scapegrace, he is a hero; like the little Theban, he shakes the skin from the lion; Barra the drummer-boy was a gamin of Paris; he shouts: "Forward!" as the horse of Scripture says "Vah!" and in a moment he has passed from the small brat to the giant.

This child of the puddle is also the child of the ideal. Measure that spread of wings which reaches from Molière to Barra.

To sum up the whole, and in one word, the gamin is a being who amuses himself, because he is unhappy.

Chapter X

Ecce Paris, Ecce Homo

To sum it all up once more, the Paris gamin of to-day, like the *Graeculus* of Rome in days gone by, is the infant populace with the wrinkle of the old world on his brow.

The gamin is a grace to the nation, and at the same time a disease; a disease which must be cured, how? By light.

Light renders healthy.

Light kindles.

All generous social irradiations spring from science, letters, arts, education. Make men, make men. Give them light that they may warm you. Sooner or later the splendid question of universal education will present itself with the irresistible authority of the absolute truth; and then, those who govern under the superintendence of the French idea will have to make this choice; the children of France or the gamins of Paris; flames in the light or will-o'-the-wisps in the gloom.

The gamin expresses Paris, and Paris expresses the world.

For Paris is a total. Paris is the ceiling of the human race. The whole of this prodigious city is a foreshortening of dead manners and living manners. He who sees Paris thinks he sees the bottom of all history with heaven and constellations in the intervals. Paris has a capital, the Town-Hall, a Parthenon, Notre-Dame, a Mount Aventine, the Faubourg Saint-Antoine, an Asinarium, the Sorbonne, a Pantheon, the Pantheon, a Via Sacra, the Boulevard des Italiens, a temple of the winds, opinion; and it replaces the Gemoniæ by ridicule. Its *majo* is called "faraud," its Transteverin is the man of the faubourgs, its *hammal* is the market-porter, its lazzarone is the pègre, its cockney is the native of Ghent. Everything that exists elsewhere exists at Paris. The fishwoman of Dumarsais can retort on the herb-seller of Euripides, the discobols Vejanus lives again in the Forioso, the tightrope dancer. Therapontigonus Miles could walk arm in arm with Vadeboncœur the grenadier, Damasippus the second-hand dealer would be happy among bric-à-brac merchants, Vincennes could grasp Socrates in its fist as just as Agora could imprison Diderot, Grimod de la Reynière discovered larded roast beef, as Curtillus invented roast hedgehog, we see the trapeze which figures in Plautus reappear under the vault of the Arc de l'Etoile, the sword-eater of Pœcilus encountered by Apuleius is a sword-swallower on the Pont-Neuf, the nephew of Rameau and Curculio the parasite make a pair, Ergasilus could get himself presented to Cambacères by d'Aigrefeuille; the four dandies of Rome: Alcesimarchus, Phœdromus, Diabolus, and Argyrippus, descend from Courtille in Labatut's posting-chaise; Aulus Gellius would halt no longer in front of Congrio than would Charles Nodier in front of Punchinello; Marto is not a tigress, but Pardalisca was not a dragon; Pantolabus the wag jeers in the Café Anglais at Nomentanus the fast liver, Hermogenus is a tenor in the Champs-Élysées, and round him, Thracius the beggar, clad like Bobèche, takes up a collection; the bore who stops you by the button of your coat in the Tuileries makes you repeat after a lapse of two thousand years Thesprion's apostrophe: *Quis properantem me prehendit pallio?* The wine on Surène is a parody of the wine of Alba, the red border of Desaugiers forms a balance to the great cutting of Balatro, Père-Lachaise exhales beneath nocturnal rains same gleams as the Esquiliæ, and the grave of the poor bought for five years, is certainly the equivalent of the slave's hived coffin.

Seek something that Paris has not. The vat of Trophonius contains nothing that is not in Mesmer's tub; Ergaphilas lives again in Cagliostro; the Brahmin Vâsaphantâ become incarnate in the Comte de Saint-Germain; the cemetery of Saint-Médard works quite as good miracles as the Mosque of Oumoumié at Damascus.

Paris has an Aesop-Mayeux, and a Canidia, Mademoiselle Lenormand. It is terrified, like Delphos at the fulgurating realities of the vision; it makes tables turn as Dodona did tripods. It places the grisette on the throne, as Rome placed the courtesan there; and, taking it altogether, if Louis XV is worse than Claudian, Madame Dubarry is better than Messalina. Paris combines in an unprecedented type, which has existed and which we have elbowed, Grecian nudity, the Hebraic ulcer, and the Gascon pun. It mingles Diogenes, Job, and Jack-pudding, dresses up a specter in old numbers of the *Constitutionnel*, and makes Chodruc Duclos.

Although Plutarch says: *the tyrant never grows old*, Rome, under Sylla as under Domitian, re-signed itself and willingly put water in its wine. The Tiber was a Lethe, if the rather doctrinary eu-logium made of it by Varus Vibiscus is to be credited: *Contra Gracchos Tiberim habemus, Bibere Tiberim, id est seditionem oblivisci*. Paris drinks a million liters of water a day, but that does not pre-vent it from occasionally beating the general alarm and ringing the tocsin.

With that exception, Paris is amiable. It accepts everything royally; it is not too particular about its Venus; its Callipyge is Hottentot; provided that it is made to laugh, it condones; ugliness cheers it, deformity provokes it to laughter, vice diverts it; be eccentric and you may be an eccen-tric; even hypocrisy, that supreme cynicism, does not disgust it; it is so literary that it does not hold its nose before Basile, and is no more scandalized by the prayer of Tartuffe than Horace was re-pelled by the "hiccup" of Priapus. No trait of the universal face is lacking in the profile of Paris. The bal Mabile is not the polymnia dance of the Janiculum, but the dealer in ladies' wearing apparel there devours the lorette with her eyes, exactly as the procuress Staphyla lay in wait for the virgin Planesium. The Barrière du Combat is not the Coliseum, but people are as ferocious there as though Cæsar were looking on. The Syrian hostess has more grace than Mother Saguet, but, if Vir-gil haunted the Roman wine-shop, David d'Angers, Balzac and Charlet have sat at the tables of Parisian taverns. Paris reigns. Geniuses flash forth there, the red tails prosper there. Adonaï passes on his chariot with its twelve wheels of thunder and lightning; Silenus makes his entry there on his ass. For Silenus read Ramponneau.

Paris is the synonym of Cosmos, Paris is Athens, Sybaris, Jerusalem, Pantin. All civilizations are there in an abridged form, all barbarisms also. Paris would greatly regret it if it had not a guillotine.

A little of the Place de Grève is a good thing. What would all that eternal festival be without this seasoning? Our laws are wisely provided, and thanks to them, this blade drips on this Shrove Tuesday.

Chapter XI

TO SCOFF, TO REIGN

THERE IS NO LIMIT TO PARIS. NO CITY HAS HAD THAT DOMINATION WHICH SOMETIMES DERIDES those whom it subjugates. To please you, O Athenians! exclaimed Alexander. Paris makes more than the law, it makes the fashion; Paris sets more than the fashion, it sets the routine. Paris may be stupid, if it sees fit; it sometimes allows itself this luxury; then the universe is stupid in com-pany with it; then Paris awakes, rubs its eyes, says: "How stupid I am!" and bursts out laughing in the face of the human race. What a marvel is such a city! it is a strange thing that this grandioseness and this burlesque should be amicable neighbors, that all this majesty should not be thrown into dis-order by all this parody, and that the same mouth can to-day blow into the trump of the Judgment

Day, and to-morrow into the reed-flute! Paris has a sovereign joviality. Its gaiety is of the thunder and its farce holds a scepter.

Its tempest sometimes proceeds from a grimace. Its explosions, its days, its masterpieces, its prodigies, its epics, go forth to the bounds of the universe, and so also do its cock-and-bull stories. Its laugh is the mouth of a volcano which spatters the whole earth. Its jests are sparks. It imposes its caricatures as well as its ideal on people; the highest monuments of human civilization accept its ironies and lend their eternity to its mischievous pranks. It is superb; it has a prodigious 14th of July, which delivers the globe; it forces all nations to take the oath of tennis; its night of the 4th of August dissolves in three hours a thousand years of feudalism; it makes of its logic the muscle of unanimous will; it multiplies itself under all sorts of forms of the sublime; it fills with its light Washington, Kosciusko, Bolivar, Bozzaris, Riego, Bem, Manin, Lopez, John Brown, Garibaldi; it is everywhere where the future is being lighted up, at Boston in 1779, at the Isle de Léon in 1820, at Pesth in 1848, at Palermo in 1860, it whispers the mighty countersign: Liberty, in the ear of the American abolitionists grouped about the boat at Harper's Ferry, and in the ear of the patriots of Ancona assembled in the shadow, to the Archi before the Gozzi inn on the seashore; it creates Canaris; it creates Quiroga; it creates Pisacane; it irradiates the great on earth; it was while proceeding whither its breath urge them, that Byron perished at Missolonghi, and that Mazet died at Barcelona; it is the tribune under the feet of Mirabeau, and a crater under the feet of Robespierre; its books, its theater, its art, its science, its literature, its philosophy, are the manuals of the human race; it has Pascal, Régnier, Corneille, Descartes, Jean-Jacques: Voltaire for all moments, Molière for all centuries; it makes its language to be talked by the universal mouth, and that language becomes the word; it constructs in all minds the idea of progress, the liberating dogmas which it forges are for the generations trusty friends, and it is with the soul of its thinkers and its poets that all heroes of all nations have been made since 1789; this does not prevent vagabondism, and that enormous genius which is called Paris, while transfiguring the world by its light, sketches in charcoal Bouginier's nose on the wall of the temple of Theseus and writes *Credeville the thief* on the Pyramids.

Paris is always showing its teeth; when it is not scolding it is laughing.

Such is Paris. The smoke of its roofs forms the ideas of the universe. A heap of mud and stone, if you will, but, above all, a moral being. It is more than great, it is immense. Why? Because it is daring.

To dare; that is the price of progress.

All sublime conquests are, more or less, the prizes of daring. In order that the Revolution should take place, it does not suffice that Montesquieu should foresee it, that Diderot should preach it, that Beaumarchais should announce it, that Condorcet should calculate it, that Arouet should prepare it, that Rousseau should premeditate it; it is necessary that Danton should dare it.

The cry: *Audacity!* is a *Fiat lux*. It is necessary, for the sake of the forward march of the human race, that there should be proud lessons of courage permanently on the heights. Daring deeds dazzle history and are one of man's great sources of light. The dawn dares when it rises. To attempt, to brave, to persist, to persevere, to be faithful to one's self, to grasp fate bodily, to astound catastrophe by the small amount of fear that it occasions us, now to affront unjust power, again to insult drunken victory, to hold one's position, to stand one's ground; that is the example which nations need, that is the light which electrifies them. The same formidable lightning proceeds from the torch of Prometheus to Cambronne's short pipe.

Chapter XII

THE FUTURE LATENT IN THE PEOPLE

As FOR THE PARISIAN POPULACE, EVEN WHEN A MAN GROWN, IT IS ALWAYS THE STREET ARAB; TO paint the child is to paint the city; and it is for that reason that we have studied this eagle in this arrant sparrow. It is in the faubourgs, above all, we maintain, that the Parisian race appears; there is the pure blood; there is the true physiognomy; there this people toils and suffers, and suffering and toil are the two faces of man. There exist there immense numbers of unknown beings, among whom swarm types of the strangest, from the porter of la Râpée to the knacker of Montfaucon. *Fex urbis*, exclaims Cicero; *mob*, adds Burke indignantly; rabble, multitude, populace. These are words and quickly uttered. But so be it. What does it matter? What is it to me if they do go barefoot! They do not know how to read; so much the worse. Would you abandon them for that? Would you turn their distress into a malediction? Cannot the light penetrate these masses? Let us return to that cry: Light! and let us obstinately persist therein! Light! Light! Who knows whether these opacities will not become transparent? Are not revolutions transfigurations? Come, philosophers, teach, enlighten, light up, think aloud, speak aloud, hasten joyously to the great sun, fraternize with the public place, announce the good news, spend your alphabets lavishly, proclaim rights, sing the Marseillaises, sow enthusiasms, tear green boughs from the oaks. Make a whirlwind of the idea. This crowd may be rendered sublime. Let us learn how to make use of that vast conflagration of principles and virtues, which sparkles, bursts forth and quivers at certain hours. These bare feet, these bare arms, these rags, these ignorances, these abjectnesses, these darknesses, may be employed in the conquest of the ideal. Gaze past the people, and you will perceive truth. Let that vile sand which you trample underfoot be cast into the furnace, let it melt and seethe there, it will become a splendid crystal, and it is thanks to it that Galileo and Newton will discover stars.

Chapter XIII

LITTLE GAVROCHE

EIGHT OR NINE YEARS AFTER THE EVENTS NARRATED IN THE SECOND PART OF THIS STORY, PEOple noticed on the Boulevard du Temple, and in the regions of the Château-d'Eau, a little boy eleven or twelve years of age, who would have realized with tolerable accuracy that ideal of the gamin sketched out above, if, with the laugh of his age on his lips, he had not had a heart absolutely somber and empty. This child was well muffled up in a pair of man's trousers, but he did not get them from his father, and a woman's chemise, but he did not get it from his mother. Some people or other had clothed him in rags out of charity. Still, he had a father and a mother. But his father did not think of him, and his mother did not love him.

He was one of those children most deserving of pity, among all, one of those who have father and mother, and who are orphans nevertheless.

This child never felt so well as when he was in the street. The pavements were less hard to him than his mother's heart.

His parents had dispatched him into life with a kick.

He simply took flight.

He was a boisterous, pallid, nimble, wide-awake, jeering, lad, with a vivacious but sickly air. He went and came, sang, played at hopscotch, scraped the gutters, stole a little, but, like cats and sparrows, gaily laughed when he was called a rogue, and got angry when called a thief. He had no shelter, no bread, no fire, no love; but he was merry because he was free.

When these poor creatures grow to be men, the millstones of the social order meet them and crush them, but so long as they are children, they escape because of their smallness. The tiniest hole saves them.

Nevertheless, abandoned as this child was, it sometimes happened, every two or three months, that he said, "Come, I'll go and see mamma!" Then he quitted the boulevard, the Cirque, the Porte Saint-Martin, descended to the quays, crossed the bridges, reached the suburbs, arrived at the Salpêtrière, and came to a halt, where? Precisely at that double number 50-52 with which the reader is acquainted—at the Gorbeau hovel.

At that epoch, the hovel 50-52 generally deserted and eternally decorated with the placard: "Chambers to let," chanced to be, a rare thing, inhabited by numerous individuals who, however, as is always the case in Paris, had no connection with each other. All belonged to that indigent class which begins to separate from the lowest of petty bourgeoisie in straitened circumstances, and which extends from misery to misery into the lowest depths of society down to those two beings in whom all the material things of civilization end, the sewer-man who sweeps up the mud, and the rag-picker who collects scraps.

The "principal lodger" of Jean Valjean's day was dead and had been replaced by another exactly like her. I know not what philosopher has said: "Old women are never lacking."

This new old woman was named Madame Bourgon, and had nothing remarkable about her life except a dynasty of three parakeets, who had reigned in succession over her soul.

The most miserable of those who inhabited the hovel were a family of four persons, consisting of father, mother, and two daughters, already well grown, all four of whom were lodged in the same attic, one of the cells which we have already mentioned.

At first sight, this family presented no very special feature except its extreme destitution; the father, when he hired the chamber, had stated that his name was Jondrette. Some time after his moving in, which had borne a singular resemblance to *the entrance of nothing at all*, to borrow the memorable expression of the principal tenant, this Jondrette had said to the woman, who, like her predecessor, was at the same time portress and stair-sweeper: "Mother So-and-So, if anyone should chance to come and inquire for a Pole or an Italian, or even a Spaniard, perchance, it is I."

This family was that of the merry barefoot boy. He arrived there and found distress, and, what is still sadder, no smile; a cold hearth and cold hearts. When he entered, he was asked: "Whence come you?" He replied: "From the street." When he went away, they asked him: "Whither are you going?" He replied: "Into the streets." His mother said to him: "What did you come here for?"

This child lived, in this absence of affection, like the pale plants which spring up in cellars. It did not cause him suffering, and he blamed no one. He did not know exactly how a father and mother should be.

Nevertheless, his mother loved his sisters.

We have forgotten to mention, that on the Boulevard du Temple this child was called Little Gavroche. Why was he called Little Gavroche?

Probably because his father's name was Jondrette.

It seems to be the instinct of certain wretched families to break the thread.

The chamber which the Jondrettes inhabited in the Gorbeau hovel was the last at the end of the corridor. The cell next to it was occupied by a very poor young man who was called M. Marius.

Let us explain who this M. Marius was.

BOOK SECOND

THE GREAT BOURGEOIS

Chapter I

NINETY YEARS AND THIRTY-TWO TEETH

IN THE RUE BOUCHERAT, RUE DE NORMANDIE, AND THE RUE DE SAINTONGE THERE STILL EXIST A few ancient inhabitants who have preserved the memory of a worthy man named M. Gillenormand, and who mention him with complaisance. This good man was old when they were young. This silhouette has not yet entirely disappeared—for those who regard with melancholy that vague swarm of shadows which is called the past—from the labyrinth of streets in the vicinity of the Temple to which, under Louis XIV, the names of all the provinces of France were appended exactly as in our day, the streets of the new Tivoli quarter have received the names of all the capitals of Europe; a progression, by the way, in which progress is visible.

M. Gillenormand, who was as much alive as possible in 1831, was one of those men who had become curiosities to be viewed, simply because they have lived a long time, and who are strange because they formerly resembled everybody, and now resemble nobody. He was a peculiar old man, and in very truth, a man of another age, the real, complete and rather haughty bourgeois of the eighteenth century, who wore his good, old bourgeoisie with the air with which marquises wear their marquisates. He was over ninety years of age, his walk was erect, he talked loudly, saw clearly, drank neat, ate, slept, and snored. He had all thirty-two of his teeth. He only wore spectacles when he read. He was of an amorous disposition, but declared that, for the last ten years, he had wholly and decidedly renounced women. He could no longer please, he said; he did not add: "I am too old," but: "I am too poor." He said: "If I were not ruined—Héée!" All he had left, in fact, was an income of about fifteen thousand francs. His dream was to come into an inheritance and to have a hundred thousand livres income for mistresses. He did not belong, as the reader will perceive, to that puny variety of octogenaries who, like M. de Voltaire, have been dying all their life; his was no longevity of a cracked pot; this jovial old man had always had good health. He was superficial, rapid, easily angered. He flew into a passion at everything, generally quite contrary to all reason. When contradicted, he raised his cane; he beat people as he had done in the great century. He had a daughter over fifty years of age, and unmarried, whom he chastised severely with his tongue, when in a rage, and whom he would have liked to whip. She seemed to him to be eight years old. He boxed his servants' ears soundly, and said: "Ah! carogne!" One of his oaths was: "By the pantoufloche of the pantouflochade!" He had singular freaks of tranquility; he had himself shaved every day by a barber who had been mad and who detested him, being jealous of M. Gillenormand on account of his wife, a pretty and coquettish barberess. M. Gillenormand admired his own discernment in all things, and declared that he was extremely sagacious; here is one of his sayings: "I have, in truth, some penetration; I am able to say when a flea bites me, from what woman it came."

The words which he uttered the most frequently were: *the sensible man*, and *nature*. He did not give to this last word the grand acceptation which our epoch has accorded to it, but he made it enter, after his own fashion, into his little chimney-corner satires: "Nature," he said, "in order that civilization may have a little of everything, gives it even specimens of its amusing barbarism. Europe possesses specimens of Asia and Africa on a small scale. The cat is a drawing-room tiger, the lizard is a pocket crocodile. The dancers at the opera are pink female savages. They do not eat men, they crunch them; or, magicians that they are, they transform them into oysters and swallow them. The Caribbeans leave only the bones, they leave only the shell. Such are our morals. We do not devour, we gnaw; we do not exterminate, we claw."

Chapter II

LIKE MASTER, LIKE HOUSE

HE LIVED IN THE MARAIS, RUE DES FILLES-DU-CALVAIRE, NO. 6. HE OWNED THE HOUSE. THIS house has since been demolished and rebuilt, and the number has probably been changed in those revolutions of numeration which the streets of Paris undergo. He occupied an ancient and vast apartment on the first floor, between street and gardens, furnished to the very ceilings with great Gobelins and Beauvais tapestries representing pastoral scenes; the subjects of the ceilings and the panels were repeated in miniature on the arm-chairs. He enveloped his bed in a vast, nine-leaved screen of Coromandel lacquer. Long, full curtains hung from the windows, and formed great, broken folds that were very magnificent. The garden situated immediately under his windows was attached to that one of them which formed the angle, by means of a staircase twelve or fifteen steps long, which the old gentleman ascended and descended with great agility. In addition to a library adjoining his chamber, he had a boudoir of which he thought a great deal, a gallant and elegant retreat, with magnificent hangings of straw, with a pattern of flowers and fleurs-de-lys made on the galleys of Louis XIV and ordered of his convicts by M. de Vivonne for his mistress. M. Gillenormand had inherited it from a grim maternal great-aunt, who had died a centenarian. He had had two wives. His manners were something between those of the courtier, which he had never been, and the lawyer, which he might have been. He was gay, and caressing when he had a mind. In his youth he had been one of those men who are always deceived by their wives and never by their mistresses, because they are, at the same time, the most sullen of husbands and the most charming of lovers in existence. He was a connoisseur of painting. He had in his chamber a marvelous portrait of no one knows whom, painted by Jordaens, executed with great dashes of the brush, with millions of details, in a confused and haphazard manner. M. Gillenormand's attire was not the habit of Louis XIV nor yet that of Louis XVI; it was that of the Incroyables of the Directory. He had thought himself young up to that period and had followed the fashions. His coat was of light-weight cloth with voluminous revers, a long swallow-tail and large steel buttons. With this he wore knee-breeches and buckle shoes. He always thrust his hands into his fobs. He said authoritatively: "The French Revolution is a heap of blackguards."

Chapter III

LUC-ESPRIT

AT THE AGE OF SIXTEEN, ONE EVENING AT THE OPERA, HE HAD HAD THE HONOR TO BE STARED at through opera-glasses by two beauties at the same time—ripe and celebrated beauties then, and sung by Voltaire, the Camargo and the Sallé. Caught between two fires, he had beaten a heroic retreat toward a little dancer, a young girl named Nahenry, who was sixteen like himself, obscure as a cat, and with whom he was in love. He abounded in memories. He was accustomed to exclaim: "How pretty she was—that Guimard-Guimardini-Guimardinette, the last time I saw her at Longchamps, her hair curled in sustained sentiments, with her come-and-see of turquoises, her gown of the color of persons newly arrived, and her little agitation muff!" He had worn in his young manhood a waistcoat of Nain-Londrin, which he was fond of talking about effusively. "I was dressed like a Turk of the Levant Levantin," said he. Madame de Boufflers, having seen him by chance when he was twenty, had described him as "a charming fool." He was horrified by all the names which he saw in politics and in power, regarding them as vulgar and bourgeois. He read the journals, the *newspapers, the gazettes* as he said, stifling outbursts of laughter the while. "Oh!" he said, "what people these are! Corbière! Humann! Casimir Périer! There's a minister for you! I can imagine this in a journal: 'M. Gillenormand, minister!' that would be a farce. Well! They are so stupid that it would pass"; he merrily called everything by its name, whether decent or indecent, and did not restrain himself in the least before ladies. He uttered coarse speeches, obscenities, and filth with a certain tranquility and lack of astonishment which was elegant. It was in keeping with the unceremoniousness of his century. It is to be noted that the age of periphrase in verse was the age of crudities in prose. His godfather had predicted that he would turn out a man of genius, and had bestowed on him these two significant names: Luc-Esprit.

Chapter IV

A CENTENARIAN ASPIRANT

HE HAD TAKEN PRIZES IN HIS BOYHOOD AT THE COLLEGE OF MOULINS, WHERE HE WAS BORN, AND he had been crowned by the hand of the Duc de Nivernais, whom he called the Duc de Nevers. Neither the Convention, nor the death of Louis XVI, nor the Napoleon, nor the return of the Bourbons, nor anything else had been able to efface the memory of this crowning. *The Duc de Nevers* was, in his eyes, the great figure of the century. "What a charming grand seigneur," he said, "and what a fine air he had with his blue ribbon!"

In the eyes of M. Gillenormand, Catherine the Second had made reparation for the crime of the partition of Poland by purchasing, for three thousand roubles, the secret of the elixir of gold, from Bestucheff. He grew animated on this subject: "The elixir of gold," he exclaimed, "the yellow dye of Bestucheff, General Lamotte's drops, in the eighteenth century—this was the great remedy for the catastrophes of love, the panacea against Venus, at one louis the half-ounce phial. Louis XV sent two hundred phials of it to the Pope." He would have been greatly irritated and thrown off his balance, had anyone told him that the elixir of gold is nothing but the perchloride of iron. M. Gillenormand adored the Bourbons, and had a horror of 1789; he was forever narrating in what manner he had saved himself during the Terror, and how he had been obliged to display a vast deal of gaiety and cleverness in order to escape having his head cut off. If any young man ventured to pronounce an eulogium on the Republic in his presence, he turned purple and grew so angry that he was on the point of swooning. He sometimes alluded to his ninety years, and said: "I hope that I shall not see ninety-three twice." On these occasions, he hinted to people that he meant to live to be a hundred.

Chapter V

BASQUE AND NICOLETTE

HE HAD THEORIES. HERE IS ONE OF THEM: "WHEN A MAN IS PASSIONATELY FOND OF WOMEN, AND when he has himself a wife for whom he cares but little, who is homely, cross, legitimate, with plenty of rights, perched on the code, and jealous at need, there is but one way of extricating himself from the quandry and of procuring peace, and that is to let his wife control the purse-strings. This abdication sets him free. Then his wife busies herself, grows passionately fond of handling coin, gets her fingers covered with verdigris in the process, undertakes the education of half-share tenants and the training of farmers, convokes lawyers, presides over notaries, harangues scriveners, visits limbs of the law, follows lawsuits, draws up leases, dictates contracts, feels herself the sovereign, sells, buys, regulates, promises and compromises, binds fast and annuls, yields, concedes and retrocedes, arranges, disarranges, hoards, lavishes; she commits follies, a supreme and personal delight, and that consoles her. While her husband disdains her, she has the satisfaction of ruining her husband." This theory M. Gillenormand had himself applied, and it had become his history. His wife—the second one—had administered his fortune in such a manner that, one fine day, when M. Gillenormand found himself a widower, there remained to him just sufficient to live on, by sinking nearly the whole of it in an annuity of fifteen thousand francs, three-quarters of which would expire with him. He had not hesitated on this point, not being anxious to leave a property behind him. Besides, he had noticed that patrimonies are subject to adventures, and, for instance, become *national property*; he had been present at the avatars of consolidated three per cents, and he had no great faith in the Great Book of the Public Debt. "All that's the Rue Quincampois!" he said. His house in the Rue Filles-du-Clavaire belonged to him, as we have already stated. He had two servants, "a male and a female." When a servant entered his establishment, M. Gillenormand rebaptized him. He bestowed on the men the name of their province: Nîmois, Comtois, Poitevin, Picard. His last valet was a big, foundered, short-winded fellow of fifty-five, who was incapable of running twenty paces; but, as he had been born at Bayonne, M. Gillenormand called him *Basque*. All the female servants in his house were called Nicolette (even the Magnon, of whom we shall hear more farther on). One day, a haughty cook, a cordon bleu, of the lofty race of porters, presented herself. "How much wages do you want a month?" asked M. Gillenormand. "Thirty francs." "What is your name?" "Olympie." "You shall have fifty francs, and you shall be called Nicolette."

Chapter VI

IN WHICH MAGNON AND HER TWO CHILDREN ARE SEEN

WITH M. GILLENORMAND, SORROW WAS CONVERTED INTO WRATH; HE WAS FURIOUS AT BEING in despair. He had all sorts of prejudices and took all sorts of liberties. One of the facts of which his exterior relief and his internal satisfaction was composed, was, as we have just hinted, that he had remained a brisk spark, and that he passed energetically for such. This he called having "royal renown." This royal renown sometimes drew down upon him singular windfalls. One day, there was brought to him in a basket, as though it had been a basket of oysters, a stout, newly born boy, who was yelling like the deuce, and duly wrapped in swaddling-clothes, which a servant-maid, dismissed six months previously, attributed to him. M. Gillenormand had, at that time, fully completed his eighty-fourth year. Indignation and uproar in the establishment. And whom did that bold hussy think she could persuade to believe that? What audacity! What an abominable calumny! M. Gillenormand himself was not at all enraged. He gazed at the brat with the amiable smile of a good man who is flattered by the calumny, and said in an aside: "Well, what now? What's the matter? You are finely taken aback, and really, you are excessively ignorant. M. le Duc d'Angoulême, the bastard of his Majesty Charles IX, married a silly jade of fifteen when he was eighty-five; M. Virginal, Marquis d'Alluye, brother to the Cardinal de Sourdis, Archbishop of Bordeaux, had, at the age of eighty-three, by the maid of Madame la Presidente Jacquin, a son, a real child of love, who became a Chevalier of Malta and a counselor of state; one of the great men of this century, the Abbé Tabaraud, is the son of a man of eighty-seven. There is nothing out of the ordinary in these things. And then, the Bible! Upon that I declare that this little gentleman is none of mine. Let him be taken care of. It is not his fault." This manner of procedure was good-tempered. The woman, whose name was Magnon, sent him another parcel in the following year. It was a boy again. Thereupon, M. Gillenormand capitulated. He sent the two brats back to their mother, promising to pay eighty francs a month for their maintenance, on the condition that the said mother would not do so anymore. He added: "I insist upon it that the mother shall treat them well. I shall go to see them from time to time." And this he did. He had had a brother who was a priest, and who had been rector of the Academy of Poitiers for three-and-thirty years, and had died at seventy-nine. "I lost him young," said he. This brother, of whom but little memory remains, was a peaceable miser, who, being a priest, thought himself bound to bestow alms on the poor whom he met, but he never gave them anything except bad or demonetized sous, thereby discovering a means of going to hell by way of paradise. As for M. Gillenormand the elder, he never haggled over his alms-giving, but gave gladly and nobly. He was kindly, abrupt, charitable, and if he had been rich, his turn of mind would have been magnificent. He desired that all which concerned him should be done in a grand manner, even his rogueries. One day, having been cheated by a business man in a matter of inheritance, in a gross and apparent manner, he uttered this solemn exclamation: "That was indecently done! I am really ashamed of this pilfering. Everything has degenerated in this century, even the rascals. Morbleu! this is not the way to rob a man of my standing. I am robbed as though in a forest, but badly robbed. *Silvae sint consule dignae!*" He had had two wives, as we have already mentioned; by the first he had had a daughter, who had remained unmarried, and by the second another daughter, who had died at about the age of thirty, who had wedded, through love, or chance, or otherwise, a soldier of fortune who had served in the armies of the Republic and of the Empire, who had won the cross at Austerlitz and had been made colonel at Waterloo. *"He is the disgrace of my family,"* said the old bourgeois. He took an immense amount of snuff, and had a particularly graceful manner of plucking at his lace ruffle with the back of one hand. He believed very little in God.

Chapter VII

Rule: Receive No One Except in the Evening

Such was M. Luc-esprit Gillenormand, who had not lost his hair—which was gray rather than white—and which was always dressed in "dog's ears." To sum up, he was venerable in spite of all this.

He had something of the eighteenth century about him; frivolous and great.

In 1814 and during the early years of the Restoration, M. Gillenormand, who was still young—he was only seventy-four—lived in the Faubourg Saint Germain, Rue Servandoni, near Saint-Sulpice. He had only retired to the Marais when he quitted society, long after attaining the age of eighty.

And, on abandoning society, he had immured himself in his habits. The principal one, and that which was invariable, was to keep his door absolutely closed during the day, and never to receive anyone whatever except in the evening. He dined at five o'clock, and after that his door was open. That had been the fashion of his century, and he would not swerve from it. "The day is vulgar," said he, "and deserves only a closed shutter. Fashionable people only light up their minds when the zenith lights up its stars." And he barricaded himself against everyone, even had it been the king himself. This was the antiquated elegance of his day.

Chapter VIII

Two Do Not Make a Pair

We have just spoken of M. Gillenormand's two daughters. They had come into the world ten years apart. In their youth they had borne very little resemblance to each other, either in character or countenance, and had also been as little like sisters to each other as possible. The youngest had a charming soul, which turned toward all that belongs to the light, was occupied with flowers, with verses, with music, which fluttered away into glorious space, enthusiastic, ethereal, and was wedded from her very youth, in ideal, to a vague and heroic figure. The elder had also her chimera; she spied in the azure some very wealthy purveyor, a contractor, a splendidly stupid husband, a million made man, or even a prefect; the receptions of the Prefecture, an usher in the antechamber with a chain on his neck, official balls, the harangues of the town-hall, to be "Madame la Préfète"—all this had created a whirlwind in her imagination. Thus the two sisters strayed, each in her own dream, at the epoch when they were young girls. Both had wings, the one like an angel, the other like a goose.

No ambition is ever fully realized, here below at least. No paradise becomes terrestrial in our day. The younger wedded the man of her dreams, but she died. The elder did not marry at all.

At the moment when she makes her entrance into this history which we are relating, she was an antique virtue, an incombustible prude, with one of the sharpest noses, and one of the most obtuse minds that it is possible to see. A characteristic detail; outside of her immediate family, no one had ever known her first name. She was called *Mademoiselle Gillenormand, the elder.*

In the matter of *cant*, Mademoiselle Gillenormand could have given points to a miss. Her modesty was carried to the other extreme of blackness. She cherished a frightful memory of her life; one day, a man had beheld her garter.

Age had only served to accentuate this pitiless modesty. Her guimpe was never sufficiently opaque, and never ascended sufficiently high. She multiplied clasps and pins where no one would have dreamed of looking. The peculiarity of prudery is to place all the more sentinels in proportion as the fortress is the less menaced.

Nevertheless, let him who can explain these antique mysteries of innocence, she allowed an officer of the Lancers, her grandnephew, named Théodule, to embrace her without displeasure.

In spite of this favored Lancer, the label: *Prude*, under which we have classed her, suited her to absolute perfection. Mademoiselle Gillenormand was a sort of twilight soul. Prudery is a demi-virtue and a demi-vice.

To prudery she added bigotry, a well-assorted lining. She belonged to the society of the Virgin, wore a white veil on certain festivals, mumbled special orisons, revered "the holy blood," venerated "the sacred heart," remained for hours in contemplation before a rococo-jesuit altar in a chapel which was inaccessible to the rank and file of the faithful, and there allowed her soul to soar among little clouds of marble, and through great rays of gilded wood.

She had a chapel friend, an ancient virgin like herself, named Mademoiselle Vaubois, who was a positive blockhead, and beside whom Mademoiselle Gillenormand had the pleasure of being an eagle. Beyond the Agnus Dei and Ave Maria, Mademoiselle Vaubois had no knowledge of anything except of the different ways of making preserves. Mademoiselle Vaubois, perfect in her style, was the ermine of stupidity without a single spot of intelligence.

Let us say it plainly, Mademoiselle Gillenormand had gained rather than lost as she grew older. This is the case with passive natures. She had never been malicious, which is relative kindness; and then, years wear away the angles, and the softening which comes with time had come to her. She was melancholy with an obscure sadness of which she did not herself know the secret. There breathed from her whole person the stupor of a life that was finished, and which had never had a beginning.

She kept house for her father. M. Gillenormand had his daughter near him, as we have seen that Monseigneur Bienvenu had his sister with him. These households comprised of an old man and an old spinster are not rare, and always have the touching aspect of two weaknesses leaning on each other for support.

There was also in this house, between this elderly spinster and this old man, a child, a little boy, who was always trembling and mute in the presence of M. Gillenormand. M. Gillenormand never addressed this child except in a severe voice, and sometimes, with uplifted cane: "Here, sir! rascal, scoundrel, come here!—Answer me, you scamp! Just let me see you, you good-for-nothing!" etc., etc. He idolized him.

This was his grandson. We shall meet with this child again later on.

BOOK THIRD

THE GRANDFATHER AND THE GRANDSON

Chapter I

AN ANCIENT SALON

WHEN M. GILLENORMAND LIVED IN THE RUE SERVANDONI, HE HAD FREQUENTED MANY VERY good and very aristocratic salons. Although a bourgeois, M. Gillenormand was received in society. As he had a double measure of wit, in the first place, that which was born with him, and secondly, that which was attributed to him, he was even sought out and made much of. He never went anywhere except on condition of being the chief person there. There are people who will have influence at any price, and who will have other people busy themselves over them; when they cannot be oracles, they turn wags. M. Gillenormand was not of this nature; his domination in the royalist salons which he frequented cost his self-respect nothing. He was an oracle everywhere. It had happened to him to hold his own against M. de Bonald, and even against M. Bengy-Puy-Vallée.

About 1817, he invariably passed two afternoons a week in a house in his own neighborhood, in the Rue Férou, with Madame la Baronne de T., a worthy and respectable person, whose husband had been Ambassador of France to Berlin under Louis XVI. Baron de T., who, during his lifetime, had gone very passionately into ecstasies and magnetic visions, had died bankrupt, during the emigration, leaving, as his entire fortune, some very curious Memoirs about Mesmer and his tub, in ten manuscript volumes, bound in red morocco and gilded on the edges. Madame de T. had not published the memoirs, out of pride, and maintained herself on a meager income which had survived no one knew how.

Madame de T. lived far from the court; "a very mixed society," as she said, in a noble isolation, proud and poor. A few friends assembled twice a week about her widowed hearth, and these constituted a purely royalist salon. They sipped tea there, and uttered groans or cries of horror at the century, the charter, the Bonapartists, the prostitution of the blue ribbon, or the Jacobinism of Louis XVIII, according as the wind veered toward elegy or dithyrambs; and they spoke in low tones of the hopes which were presented by Monsieur, afterwards Charles X.

The songs of the fishwomen, in which Napoleon was called *Nicolas,* were received there with transports of joy. Duchesses, the most delicate and charming women in the world, went into ecstasies over couplets like the following, addressed to "the federates":

> *Refoncez dans vos culottes*
> *Le bout d' chemis' qui vous pend.*
> *Qu'on n' dis' pas qu' les patriotes*
> *Ont arboré l' drapeau blanc?*[1]

---

1. Tuck into your trousers the shirt-tail that is hanging out. Let it not be said that patriots have hoisted the white flag.

There they amused themselves with puns which were considered terrible, with innocent plays upon words which they supposed to be venomous, with quatrains, with distiches even; thus, upon the Dessolles ministry, a moderate cabinet, of which MM. Decazes and Deserre were members:

> *Pour raffermir le trone ébranlé sur sa base,*
> *Il faut changer de sol, et de serre et de case.*[1]

Or they drew up a list of the chamber of peers, "an abominably Jacobin chamber," and from this list they combined alliances of names, in such a manner as to form, for example, phrases like the following: *Damas. Sabran. Gouvion-Saint-Cyr.*—All this was done merrily. In that society, they parodied the Revolution. They used I know not what desires to give point to the same wrath in inverse sense. They sang their little *Ça ira:*

> *Ah! ça ira ça ira ça ira!*
> *Les Bonapartistes à la lanterne!*

Songs are like the guillotine; they chop away indifferently, to-day this head, to-morrow that. It is only a variation.

In the Fualdès affair, which belongs to this epoch, 1816, they took part for Bastide and Jausion, because Fualdès was "a Buonapartist." They designated the liberals as *friends and brothers*; this constituted the most deadly insult.

Like certain church towers, Madame de T.'s salon had two cocks. One of them was M. Gillenormand, the other was Comte de Lamothe-Valois, of whom it was whispered about, with a sort of respect: "Do you know? That is the Lamothe of the affair of the necklace." These singular amnesties do occur in parties.

Let us add the following: in the bourgeoisie, honored situations decay through too easy relations; one must beware whom one admits; in the same way that there is a loss of caloric in the vicinity of those who are cold, there is a diminution of consideration in the approach of despised persons. The ancient society of the upper classes held themselves above this law, as above every other. Marigny, the brother of the Pompadour, had his entry with M. le Prince de Soubise. In spite of? No, because. Du Barry, the godfather of the Vaubernier, was very welcome at the house of M. le Maréchal de Richelieu. This society is Olympus. Mercury and the Prince de Guémenée are at home there. A thief is admitted there, provided he be a god.

The Comte de Lamothe, who, in 1815, was an old man seventy-five years of age, had nothing remarkable about him except his silent and sententious air, his cold and angular face, his perfectly polished manners, his coat buttoned up to his cravat, and his long legs always crossed in long, flabby trousers of the hue of burnt sienna. His face was the same color as his trousers.

This M. de Lamothe was "held in consideration" in this salon on account of his "celebrity," and, strange to say, though true, because of his name of Valois.

As for M. Gillenormand, his consideration was of absolutely first-rate quality. He had, in spite of his levity, and without its interfering in any way with his dignity, a certain manner about him which was imposing, dignified, honest, and lofty, in a bourgeois fashion; and his great age added to it. One is not a century with impunity. The years finally produce around a head, a venerable dishevelment.

In addition to this, he said things which had the genuine sparkle of the old rock. Thus, when the King of Prussia, after having restored Louis XVIII, came to pay the latter a visit under the name

---

1. In order to re-establish the shaken throne firmly on its base, soil (Dessolles), greenhouse and house (Decazas) must be changed.

of the Count de Ruppin, he was received by the descendant of Louis XIV somewhat as though he had been the Marquis de Brandebourg, and with the most delicate impertinence. M. Gillenormand approved: "All kings who are not the King of France," said he, "are provincial kings." One day, the following question was put and the following answer returned in his presence: "To what was the editor of the *Courrier Français* condemned?" "To be suspended." "*Sus* is superfluous," observed M. Gillenormand.[1] Remarks of this nature found a situation.

At the Te Deum on the anniversary of the return of the Bourbons, he said, on seeing M. de Talleyrand pass by: "There goes his Excellency the Evil One."

M. Gillenormand was always accompanied by his daughter, that tall mademoiselle, who was over forty and looked fifty, and by a handsome little boy of seven years, white, rosy, fresh, with happy and trusting eyes, who never appeared in that salon without hearing voices murmur around him: "How handsome he is! What a pity! Poor child!" This child was the one of whom we dropped a word a while ago. He was called "poor child," because he had for a father "a brigand of the Loire."

This brigand of the Loire was M. Gillenormand's son-in-law, who has already been mentioned, and whom M. Gillenormand called "the disgrace of his family."

Chapter II

ONE OF THE RED SPECTERS OF THAT EPOCH

ANYONE WHO HAD CHANCED TO PASS THROUGH THE LITTLE TOWN OF VERNON AT THIS EPOCH, and who had happened to walk across that fine monumental bridge, which will soon be succeeded, let us hope, by some hideous iron cable bridge, might have observed, had he dropped his eyes over the parapet, a man about fifty years of age wearing a leather cap, and trousers and a waistcoat of coarse gray cloth, to which something yellow which had been a red ribbon, was sewn, shod with wooden sabots, tanned by the sun, his face nearly black and his hair nearly white, a large scar on his forehead which ran down upon his cheek, bowed, bent, prematurely aged, who walked nearly every day, hoe and sickle in hand, in one of those compartments surrounded by walls which abut on the bridge, and border the left bank of the Seine like a chain of terraces, charming enclosures full of flowers of which one could say, were they much larger: "these are gardens," and were they a little smaller: "these are bouquets." All these enclosures abut upon the river at one end, and on a house at the other. The man in the waistcoat and the wooden shoes of whom we have just spoken, inhabited the smallest of these enclosures and the most humble of these houses about 1817. He lived there alone and solitary, silently and poorly, with a woman who was neither young nor old, neither homely nor pretty, neither a peasant nor a bourgeoise, who served him. The plot of earth which he called his garden was celebrated in the town for the beauty of the flowers which he cultivated there. These flowers were his occupation.

By dint of labor, of perseverance, of attention, and of buckets of water, he had succeeded in creating after the Creator, and he had invented certain tulips and certain dahlias which seemed to have been forgotten by nature. He was ingenious; he had forestalled Soulange Bodin in the formation of little clumps of earth of heath mold, for the cultivation of rare and precious shrubs from America and China. He was in his alleys from the break of day, in summer, planting, cutting, hoe-

1. *Suspendu*, suspended; *pendu*, hung.

ing, watering, walking amid his flowers with an air of kindness, sadness, and sweetness, sometimes standing motionless and thoughtful for hours, listening to the song of a bird in the trees, the babble of a child in a house, or with his eyes fixed on a drop of dew at the tip of a spear of grass, of which the sun made a carbuncle. His table was very plain, and he drank more milk than wine. A child could make him give way, and his servant scolded him. He was so timid that he seemed shy, he rarely went out, and he saw no one but the poor people who tapped at his pane and his curé, the Abbé Mabeuf, a good old man. Nevertheless, if the inhabitants of the town, or strangers, or any chance comers, curious to see his tulips, rang at his little cottage, he opened his door with a smile. He was the "brigand of the Loire."

Anyone who had, at the same time, read military memoirs, biographies, the *Moniteur,* and the bulletins of the grand army, would have been struck by a name which occurs there with tolerable frequency, the name of Georges Pontmercy. When very young, this Georges Pontmercy had been a soldier in Saintonge's regiment. The Revolution broke out. Saintonge's regiment formed a part of the army of the Rhine; for the old regiments of the monarchy preserved their names of provinces even after the fall of the monarchy, and were only divided into brigades in 1794. Pontmercy fought at Spire, at Worms, at Neustadt, at Turkheim, at Alzey, at Mayence, where he was one of the two hundred who formed Houchard's rear-guard. It was the twelfth to hold its ground against the corps of the Prince of Hesse, behind the old rampart of Andernach, and only rejoined the main body of the army when the enemy's cannon had opened a breach from the cord of the parapet to the foot of the glacis. He was under Kléber at Marchiennes and at the battle of Mont-Palissel, where a ball from a biscaien broke his arm. Then he passed to the frontier of Italy, and was one of the thirty grenadiers who defended the Col de Tende with Joubert. Joubert was appointed its adjutant-general, and Pontmercy sub-lieutenant. Pontmercy was by Berthier's side in the midst of the grape-shot of that day at Lodi which caused Bonaparte to say: "Berthier has been cannoneer, cavalier, and grenadier." He beheld his old general, Joubert, fall at Novi, at the moment when, with uplifted saber, he was shouting: "Forward!" Having been embarked with his company in the exigencies of the campaign, on board a pinnace which was proceeding from Genoa to some obscure port on the coast, he fell into a wasps'-nest of seven or eight English vessels. The Genoese commander wanted to throw his cannon into the sea, to hide the soldiers between decks, and to slip along in the dark as a merchant vessel. Pontmercy had the colors hoisted to the peak, and sailed proudly past under the guns of the British frigates. Twenty leagues further on, his audacity having increased, he attacked with his pinnace, and captured a large English transport which was carrying troops to Sicily, and which was so loaded down with men and horses that the vessel was sunk to the level of the sea. In 1805 he was in that Malher division which took Günzberg from the Archduke Ferdinand. At Weltingen he received into his arms, beneath a storm of bullets, Colonel Maupetit, mortally wounded at the head of the 9th Dragoons. He distinguished himself at Austerlitz in that admirable march in echelons effected under the enemy's fire. When the cavalry of the Imperial Russian Guard crushed a battalion of the 4th of the line, Pontmercy was one of those who took their revenge and overthrew the Guard. The Emperor gave him the cross. Pontmercy saw Wurmser at Mantua, Mélas, and Alexandria, Mack at Ulm, made prisoners in succession. He formed a part of the eighth corps of the grand army which Mortier commanded, and which captured Hamburg. Then he was transferred to the 55th of the line, which was the old regiment of Flanders. At Eylau he was in the cemetery where, for the space of two hours, the heroic Captain Louis Hugo, the uncle of the author of this book, sustained alone with his company of eighty-three men every effort of the hostile army. Pontmercy was one of the three who emerged alive from that cemetery. He was at Friedland. Then he saw Moscow. Then La Bérésina, then Lutzen, Bautzen, Dresden, Wachau, Leipzig, and the defiles of Gelenhausen; then Montmirail, Château-Thierry, Craon, the banks of the Marne, the banks of the Aisne, and the redoubtable position of Laon. At Arnay-Le-Duc, being then a captain, he put ten Cossacks to the sword, and saved, not his general, but his corporal. He was well slashed up on this occasion, and twenty-seven splinters were extracted from his left arm alone. Eight days before the capitulation of Paris he had just exchanged with a comrade and entered the cavalry. He had what was called under the old regime, *the double hand,* that is to say, an equal aptitude for handling the saber or the musket as a soldier, or a squadron or a battalion as an officer. It is from this aptitude, perfected by a military education, which certain special branches of the service arise, the dragoons, for example, who are both cavalry-men and infantry at one and the same time. He accompanied Napoleon to the Island of Elba. At Waterloo, he was chief of a squadron of cuirassiers, in Dubois's brigade. It was he who captured the standard of the Lunenburg battalion. He came and cast the flag at the Emperor's feet. He was covered with blood. While tearing down the banner he had received a sword-cut across his face. The Emperor, greatly pleased, shouted to him: "You are a colonel, you are a baron, you are an officer of the Legion of Honor!" Pontmercy replied: "Sire, I thank you for my widow." An hour later, he fell in the ravine of Ohain. Now, who was this Georges Pontmercy? He was this same "brigand of the Loire."

We have already seen something of his history. After Waterloo, Pontmercy, who had been pulled out of the hollow road of Ohain, as it will be remembered, had succeeded in joining the army, and had dragged himself from ambulance to ambulance as far as the cantonments of the Loire.

The Restoration had placed him on half-pay, then had sent him into residence, that is to say, under surveillance, at Vernon. King Louis XVIII, regarding all that which had taken place during the Hundred Days as not having occurred at all, did not recognize his quality as an officer of the Legion of Honor, nor his grade of colonel, nor his title of baron. He, on his side, neglected no occasion of signing himself "Colonel Baron Pontmercy." He had only an old blue coat, and he never went out without fastening to it his rosette as an officer of the Legion of Honor. The Attorney for the Crown had him warned that the authorities would prosecute him for "illegal" wearing of this decoration. When this notice was conveyed to him through an officious intermediary, Pontmercy retorted with a bitter smile: "I do not know whether I no longer understand French, or whether you no longer speak it; but the fact is that I do not understand." Then he went out for eight successive days with his rosette. They dared not interfere with him. Two or three times the Minister of War and the general in command of the department wrote to him with the following address: *"À Monsieur le Commandant Pontmercy."* He sent back the letters with the seals unbroken. At the same moment, Napoleon at Saint Helena was treating in the same fashion the missives of Sir Hudson Lowe addressed to *General Bonaparte.* Pontmercy had ended, may we be pardoned the expression, by having in his mouth the same saliva as his Emperor.

In the same way, there were at Rome Carthaginian prisoners who refused to salute Flaminius, and who had a little of Hannibal's spirit.

One day he encountered the district-attorney in one of the streets of Vernon, stepped up to him, and said: "Mr. Crown Attorney, am I permitted to wear my scar?"

He had nothing save his meager half-pay as chief of squadron. He had hired the smallest house which he could find at Vernon. He lived there alone, we have just seen how. Under the Empire, between two wars, he had found time to marry Mademoiselle Gillenormand. The old bourgeois, thoroughly indignant at bottom, had given his consent with a sigh, saying: "The greatest families are forced into it." In 1815, Madame Pontmercy, an admirable woman in every sense, by the way, lofty in sentiment and rare, and worthy of her husband, died, leaving a child. This child had been the colonel's joy in his solitude; but the grandfather had imperatively claimed his grandson, declaring that if the child were not given to him he would disinherit him. The father had yielded in the little one's interest, and had transferred his love to flowers.

Moreover, he had renounced everything, and neither stirred up mischief nor conspired. He shared his thoughts between the innocent things which he was then doing and the great things which he had done. He passed his time in expecting a pink or in recalling Austerlitz.

M. Gillenormand kept up no relations with his son-in-law. The colonel was "a bandit" to him. M. Gillenormand never mentioned the colonel, except when he occasionally made mocking allusions to "his Baronship." It had been expressly agreed that Pontmercy should never attempt to see his son nor to speak to him, under penalty of having the latter handed over to him disowned and disinherited. For the Gillenormands, Pontmercy was a man afflicted with the plague. They intended to bring up the child in their own way. Perhaps the colonel was wrong to accept these conditions, but he submitted to them, thinking that he was doing right and sacrificing no one but himself.

The inheritance of Father Gillenormand did not amount to much; but the inheritance of Mademoiselle Gillenormand the elder was considerable. This aunt, who had remained unmarried, was very rich on the maternal side, and her sister's son was her natural heir. The boy, whose name was Marius, knew that he had a father, but nothing more. No one opened his mouth to him about it. Nevertheless, in the society into which his grandfather took him, whispers, innuendoes, and winks, had eventually enlightened the little boy's mind; he had finally understood something of the case, and as he naturally took in the ideas and opinions which were, so to speak, the air he breathed, by a sort of infiltration and slow penetration, he gradually came to think of his father only with shame and with a pain at his heart.

While he was growing up in this fashion, the colonel slipped away every two or three months, came to Paris on the sly, like a criminal breaking his ban, and went and posted himself at Saint-Sulpice, at the hour when Aunt Gillenormand led Marius to the mass. There, trembling lest the aunt should turn round, concealed behind a pillar, motionless, not daring to breathe, he gazed at his child. The scarred veteran was afraid of that old spinster.

From this had arisen his connection with the curé of Vernon, M. l'Abbé Mabeuf.

That worthy priest was the brother of a warden of Saint-Sulpice, who had often observed this man gazing at his child, and the scar on his cheek, and the large tears in his eyes. That man, who had so manly an air, yet who was weeping like a woman, had struck the warden. That face had clung to his mind. One day, having gone to Vernon to see his brother, he had encountered Colonel Pontmercy on the bridge, and had recognized the man of Saint-Sulpice. The warden had mentioned the circumstance to the curé, and both had paid the colonel a visit, on some pretext or other. This visit led to others. The colonel, who had been extremely reserved at first, ended by opening his heart, and the curé and the warden finally came to know the whole history, and how Pontmercy was sacrificing his happiness to his child's future. This caused the curé to regard him with veneration and tenderness, and the colonel, on his side, became fond of the curé. And moreover, when both are sincere and good, no men so penetrate each other, and so amalgamate with each other, as an old priest and an old soldier. At bottom, the man is the same. The one has devoted his life to his country here below, the other to his country on high; that is the only difference.

Twice a year, on the 1st of January and on St. George's day, Marius wrote duty letters to his father, which were dictated by his aunt, and which one would have pronounced to be copied from some formula; this was all that M. Gillenormand tolerated; and the father answered them with very tender letters which the grandfather thrust into his pocket unread.

Chapter III

REQUIESCANT

MADAME DE T.'S SALON WAS ALL THAT MARIUS PONTMERCY KNEW OF THE WORLD. IT WAS THE only opening through which he could get a glimpse of life. This opening was somber, and more cold than warmth, more night than day, came to him through this skylight. This child, who had been all joy and light on entering this strange world, soon became melancholy, and, what is still more contrary to his age, grave. Surrounded by all those singular and imposing personages, he gazed about him with serious amazement. Everything conspired to increase this astonishment in him. There were in Madame de T.'s salon some very noble ladies named Mathan, Noé, Lévis—which was pronounced Lévi—Cambis, pronounced Cambyse. These antique visages and these Biblical names mingled in the child's mind with the Old Testament which he was learning by heart, and when they were all there, seated in a circle around a dying fire, sparely lighted by a lamp shaded with green, with their severe profiles, their gray or white hair, their long gowns of another age, whose lugubrious colors could not be distinguished, dropping, at rare intervals, words which were both majestic and severe, little Marius stared at them with frightened eyes, in the conviction that he beheld not women, but patriarchs and magi, not real beings, but phantoms.

With these phantoms, priests were sometimes mingled, frequenters of this ancient salon, and some gentlemen; the Marquis de Sass——, private secretary to Madame de Berry, the Vicomte de Val——, who published, under the pseudonym of *Charles-Antoine*, monorhymed odes, the Prince de Beauff——, who, though very young, had a gray head and a pretty and witty wife, whose very low-necked toilettes of scarlet velvet with gold torsades alarmed these shadows, the Marquis de C—— d'E——, the man in all France who best understood "proportioned politeness," the Comte d'Am——, the kindly man with the amiable chin, and the Chévalier de Port-de-Guy, a pillar of the library of the Louvre, called the King's cabinet. M. de Port-de-Guy, bald, and rather aged than old, was wont to relate that in 1793, at the age of sixteen, he had been put in the galleys as refractory and chained with an octogenarian, the Bishop of Mirepoix, also refractory, but as a priest, while he was so in the capacity of a soldier. This was at Toulon. Their business was to go at night and gather up on the scaffold the heads and bodies of the persons who had been guillotined during the day; they bore away on their backs these dripping corpses, and their red galley-slave blouses had a clot of blood at the back of the neck, which was dry in the morning and wet at night. These tragic tales abounded in Madame de T.'s salon, and by dint of cursing Marat, they applauded Trestaillon. Some deputies of the undiscoverable variety played their whist there; M. Thibord du Chalard, M. Lemarchant de Gomi-court, and the celebrated scoffer of the right, M. Cornet-Dincourt. The bailiff de Ferrette, with his short breeches and his thin legs, sometimes traversed this salon on his way to M. de Talleyrand. He had been M. le Comte d'Artois's companion in pleasures and unlike Aristotle crouching under Cam-paspe, he had made the Guimard crawl on all fours, and in that way he had exhibited to the ages a philosopher avenged by a bailiff. As for the priests, there was the Abbé Halma, the same to whom M. Larose, his collaborator on *la Foudre*, said: "Bah! Who is there who is not fifty years old? a few green-horns perhaps?" The Abbé Letourneur, preacher to the King, the Abbé Frayssinous, who was not, as yet, either count, or bishop, or minister, or peer, and who wore an old cassock whose buttons were missing, and the Abbé Keravenant, Curé of Saint-Germain-des-Prés; also the Pope's Nuncio, then Monsignor Macchi, Archbishop of Nisibi, later on Cardinal, remarkable for his long, pensive nose, and another Monsignor, entitled thus: Abbate Palmieri, domestic prelate, one of the seven participant prothonotaries of the Holy See, Canon of the illustrious Liberian basilica, Advocate of the saints,

Postulatore dei Santi, which refers to matters of canonization, and signifies very nearly: Master of Requests of the section of Paradise. Lastly, two cardinals, M. de la Luzerne, and M. de Cl—— T——. The Cardinal of Luzerne was a writer and was destined to have, a few years later, the honor of signing in the *Conservateur* articles side by side with Chateaubriand; M. de Cl—— T—— was Archbishop of Toul——, and often made trips to Paris, to his nephew, the Marquis de T——, who was Minister of Marine and War. The Cardinal of Cl—— T—— was a merry little man, who displayed his red stockings beneath his tucked-up cassock; his specialty was a hatred of the Encyclopedia, and his desperate play at billiards, and persons who, at that epoch, passed through the Rue M—— on summer evenings, where the Hôtel de Cl—— T—— then stood, halted to listen to the shock of the balls and the piercing voice of the Cardinal shouting to his conclavist, Monseigneur Cotiret, Bishop *in partibus* of Caryste: "Mark, Abbé, I make a cannon." The Cardinal de Cl—— T—— had been brought to Madame de T.'s by his most intimate friend, M. de Roquelaure, former Bishop of Senlis, and one of the Forty. M. de Roquelaure was notable for his lofty figure and his assiduity at the Academy; through the glass door of the neighboring hall of the library where the French Academy then held its meetings, the curious could, on every Tuesday, contemplate the Ex-Bishop of Senlis, usually standing erect, freshly powdered, in violet hose, with his back turned to the door, apparently for the purpose of allowing a better view of his little collar. All these ecclesiastics, though for the most part as much courtiers as churchmen, added to the gravity of the T. salon, whose seigniorial aspect was accentuated by five peers of France, the Marquis de Vib——, the Marquis de Tal——, the Marquis de Herb——, the Vicomte Damb——, and the Duc de Val——. This Duc de Val——, although Prince de Mon——, that is to say, a reigning prince abroad, had so high an idea of France and its peerage, that he viewed everything through their medium. It was he who said: "The Cardinals are the peers of France of Rome; the lords are the peers of France of England." Moreover, as it is indispensable that the Revolution should be everywhere in this century, this feudal salon was, as we have said, dominated by a bourgeois. M. Gillenormand reigned there.

There lay the essence and quintessence of the Parisian white society. There reputations, even royalist reputations, were held in quarantine. There is always a trace of anarchy in renown. Chateaubriand, had he entered there, would have produced the effect of Père Duchêne. Some of the scoffed-at did, nevertheless, penetrate thither on sufferance. Comte Beug—— was received there, subject to correction.

The "noble" salons of the present day no longer resemble those salons. The Faubourg Saint-Germain reeks of the fagot even now. The royalists of to-day are demagogues, let us record it to their credit.

At Madame de T.'s the society was superior, taste was exquisite and haughty, under the cover of a great show of politeness. Manners there admitted of all sorts of involuntary refinements which were the old régime itself, buried but still alive. Some of these habits, especially in the matter of language, seem eccentric. Persons but superficially acquainted with them would have taken for provincial that which was only antique. A woman was called *Madame la Génerale. Madame la Colonelle* was not entirely disused. The charming Madame de Léon, in memory, no doubt, of the Duchesses de Longueville and de Chevreuse, preferred this appellation to her title of Princesse. The Marquise de Créquy was also called *Madame la Colonelle.*

It was this little high society which invented at the Tuileries the refinement of speaking to the King in private as *the King,* in the third person, and never as *your Majesty,* the designation of *your Majesty* having been "soiled by the usurper."

Men and deeds were brought to judgment there. They jeered at the age, which released them from the necessity of understanding it. They abetted each other in amazement. They communicated to each other that modicum of light which they possessed. Methuselah bestowed information on Epimenides. The deaf man made the blind man acquainted with the course of things. They declared that the time which had elasped since Coblentz had not existed. In the same manner that

Louis XVIII was by the grace of God, in the five-and-twentieth year of his reign, the emigrants were, by rights, in the five-and-twentieth year of their adolescence.

All was harmonious; nothing was too much alive; speech hardly amounted to a breath; the newspapers, agreeing with the salons, seemed a papyrus. There were some young people, but they were rather dead. The liveries in the antechamber were antiquated. These utterly obsolete personages were served by domestics of the same stamp.

They all had the air of having lived a long time ago, and of obstinately resisting the sepulcher. Nearly the whole dictionary consisted of *Conserver, Conservation, Conservateur; to be in good odor*—that was the point. There are, in fact, aromatics in the opinions of these venerable groups, and their ideas smelled of it. It was a mummified society. The masters were embalmed, the servants were stuffed with straw.

A worthy old marquise, an *emigrée* and ruined, who had but a solitary maid, continued to say: "My people."

What did they do in Madame de T.'s salon? They were ultra.

To be ultra; this word, although what it represents may not have disappeared, has no longer any meaning at the present day. Let us explain it.

To be ultra is to go beyond. It is to attack the scepter in the name of the throne, and the miter in the name of the altar; it is to ill-treat the thing which one is dragging, it is to kick over the traces; it is to cavil at the fagot on the score of the amount of cooking received by heretics; it is to reproach the idol with its small amount of idolatry; it is to insult through excess of respect; it is to discover that the Pope is not sufficiently papish, that the King is not sufficiently royal, and that the night has too much light; it is to be discontented with alabaster, with snow, with the swan and the lily in the name of whiteness; it is to be a partisan of things to the point of becoming their enemy; it is to be so strongly for, as to be against.

The ultra spirit especially characterizes the first phase of the Restoration.

Nothing in history resembles that quarter of an hour which begins in 1814 and terminates about 1820, with the advent of M. de Villèle, the practical man of the Right. These six years were an extraordinary moment; at one and the same time brilliant and gloomy, smiling and somber, illuminated as by the radiance of dawn and entirely covered, at the same time, with the shadows of the great catastrophes which still filled the horizon and were slowly sinking into the past. There existed in that light and that shadow, a complete little new and old world, comic and sad, juvenile and senile, which was rubbing its eyes; nothing resembles an awakening like a return; a group which regarded France with ill-temper, and which France regarded with irony; good old owls of marquises by the streetful, who had returned, and of ghosts, the "former" subjects of amazement at everything, brave and noble gentlemen who smiled at being in France but wept also, delighted to behold their country once more, in despair at not finding their monarchy; the nobility of the Crusades treating the nobility of the Empire, that is to say, the nobility of the sword, with scorn; historic races who had lost the sense of history; the sons of the companions of Charlemagne disdaining the companions of Napoleon. The swords, as we have just remarked, returned the insult; the sword of Fontenoy was laughable and nothing but a scrap of rusty iron; the sword of Marengo was odious and was only a saber. Former days did not recognize Yesterday. People no longer had the feeling for what was grand. There was someone who called Bonaparte Scapin. This society no longer exists. Nothing of it, we repeat, exists to-day. When we select from it some one figure at random, and attempt to make it live again in thought, it seems as strange to us as the world before the Deluge. It is because it, too, as a matter of fact, has been engulfed in a deluge. It has disappeared beneath two Revolutions. What billows are ideas! How quickly they cover all that it is their mission to destroy and to bury, and how promptly they create frightful gulfs!

Such was the physiognomy of the salons of those distant and candid times when M. Martainville had more wit than Voltaire.

These salons had a literature and politics of their own. They believed in Fiévée. M. Agier laid down the law in them. They commentated M. Colnet, the old bookseller and publicist of the Quay Malaquais. Napoleon was to them thoroughly the Corsican Ogre. Later on the introduction into history of M. le Marquis de Bonaparte, Lieutenant-General of the King's armies, was a concession to the spirit of the age.

These salons did not long preserve their purity. Beginning with 1818, doctrinarians began to spring up in them, a disturbing shade. Their way was to be royalists and to excuse themselves for being so. Where the ultras were very proud, the doctrinarians were rather ashamed. They had wit; they had silence; their political dogma was suitably impregnated with arrogance; they should have succeeded. They indulged, and usefully too, in excesses in the matter of white neckties and tightly buttoned coats. The mistake or the misfortune of the doctrinarian party was to create aged youth. They assumed the poses of wise men. They dreamed of engrafting a temperate power on the absolute and excessive principle. They opposed, and sometimes with rare intelligence, conservative liberalism to the liberalism which demolishes. They were heard to say: "Thanks for royalism! It has rendered more than one service. It has brought back tradition, worship, religion, respect. It is faithful, brave, chivalric, loving, devoted. It has mingled, though with regret, the secular grandeurs of the monarchy with the new grandeurs of the nation. Its mistake is not to understand the Revolution, the Empire, glory, liberty, young ideas, young generations, the age. But this mistake which it makes with regard to us—have we not sometimes been guilty of it toward them? The Revolution, whose heirs we are, ought to be intelligent on all points. To attack royalism is a misconstruction of liberalism. What an error! And what blindness! Revolutionary France is wanting in respect toward historic France, that is to say, toward its mother, that is to say, toward itself. After the 5th of September, the nobility of the monarchy is treated as the nobility of the Empire was treated after the 8th of July. They were unjust to the eagle, we are unjust to the fleur-de-lys. It seems that we must always have something to proscribe! Does it serve any purpose to ungild the crown of Louis XIV, to scrape the coat-of-arms of Henry IV? We scoff at M. de Vaublanc for erasing the N's from the bridge of Jena! What was it that he did? What are we doing? Bouvines belongs to us as well as Marengo. The fleurs-de-lys are ours as well as the N's. That is our patrimony. To what purpose shall we diminish it? We must not deny our country in the past any more than in the present. Why not accept the whole of history? Why not love the whole of France?"

It is thus that the doctrinarians criticized and protected royalism, which was displeased at criticism and furious at protection.

The ultras marked the first epoch of royalism, congregation characterized the second. Skill follows ardor. Let us confine ourselves here to this sketch.

In the course of this narrative, the author of this book has encountered in his path this curious moment of contemporary history; he has been forced to cast a passing glance upon it, and to trace once more some of the singular features of this society which is unknown to-day. But he does it rapidly and without any bitter or derisive idea. Souvenirs both respectful and affectionate, for they touch his mother, attach him to this past. Moreover, let us remark, this same petty world had a grandeur of its own. One may smile at it, but one can neither despise nor hate it. It was the France of former days.

Marius Pontmercy pursued some studies, as all children do. When he emerged from the hands of Aunt Gillenormand, his grandfather confided him to a worthy professor of the most purely classic innocence. This young soul which was expanding passed from a prude to a vulgar pedant.

Marius went through his years of college, then he entered the law school. He was a royalist, fanatical and severe. He did not love his grandfather much, as the latter's gaiety and cynicism repelled him, and his feelings toward his father were gloomy.

He was, on the whole, a cold and ardent, noble, generous, proud, religious, enthusiastic lad; dignified to harshness, pure to shyness.

Chapter IV

End of the Brigand

THE CONCLUSION OF MARIUS'S CLASSICAL STUDIES COINCIDED WITH M. GILLENORMAND'S DE-parture from society. The old man bade farewell to the Faubourg Saint-Germain and to Madame de T.'s salon, and established himself in the Marais, in his house of the Rue des Filles-du-Calvaire. There he had for servants, in addition to the porter, that chambermaid, Nicolette, who had succeeded to Magnon, and that short-breathed and pursy Basque, who have been mentioned above.

In 1827, Marius had just attained his seventeenth year. One evening on his return home, he saw his grandfather holding a letter in his hand.

"Marius," said M. Gillenormand, "you will set out for Vernon to-morrow."

"Why?" said Marius.

"To see your father."

Marius was seized with a trembling fit. He had thought of everything except this—that he should one day be called upon to see his father. Nothing could be more unexpected, more surpris-ing, and, let us admit it, more disagreeable to him. It was forcing estrangement into reconciliation. It was not an affliction, but it was an unpleasant duty.

Marius, in addition to his motives of political antipathy, was convinced that his father, *the slasher*, as M. Gillenormand called him on his amiable days, did not love him; this was evident, since he had abandoned him to others. Feeling that he was not beloved, he did not love. "Nothing is more simple," he said to himself.

He was so astounded that he did not question M. Gillenormand. The grandfather resumed:

"It appears that he is ill. He demands your presence."

And after a pause, he added:

"Set out to-morrow morning. I think there is a coach which leaves the Cour des Fontaines at six o'clock, and which arrives in the evening. Take it. He says that here is haste."

Then he crushed the letter in his hand and thrust it into his pocket. Marius might have set out that very evening and have been with his father on the following morning. A diligence from the Rue du Bouloi took the trip to Rouen by night at that date, and passed through Vernon. Neither Marius nor M. Gillenormand thought of making inquiries about it.

The next day, at twilight, Marius reached Vernon. People were just beginning to light their candles. He asked the first person whom he met for "M. Pontmercy's house." For in his own mind, he agreed with the Restoration, and like it, did not recognize his father's claim to the title of either colonel or baron.

The house was pointed out to him. He rang; a woman with a little lamp in her hand opened the door.

"M. Pontmercy?" said Marius.

The woman remained motionless.

"Is this his house?" demanded Marius.

The woman nodded affirmatively.

"Can I speak with him?"

The woman shook her head.

"But I am his son!" persisted Marius. "He is expecting me."

"He no longer expects you," said the woman.

Then he perceived that she was weeping.

She pointed to the door of a room on the ground floor; he entered.

In that room, which was lighted by a tallow candle standing on the chimney-piece, there were three men, one standing erect, another kneeling, and one lying at full length, on the floor in his shirt. The one on the floor was the colonel.

The other two were the doctor, and the priest, who was engaged in prayer.

The colonel had been attacked by brain fever three days previously. As he had a foreboding of evil at the very beginning of his illness, he had written to M. Gillenormand to demand his son. The malady had grown worse. On the very evening of Marius's arrival at Vernon, the colonel had had an attack of delirium; he had risen from his bed, in spite of the servant's efforts to prevent him, crying: "My son is not coming! I shall go to meet him!" Then he ran out of his room and fell prostrate on the floor of the antechamber. He had just expired.

The doctor had been summoned, and the curé. The doctor had arrived too late. The son had also arrived too late.

By the dim light of the candle, a large tear could be distinguished on the pale and prostrate colonel's cheek, where it had trickled from his dead eye. The eye was extinguished, but the tear was not yet dry. That tear was his son's delay.

Marius gazed upon that man whom he beheld for the first time, on that venerable and manly face, on those open eyes which saw not, on those white locks, those robust limbs, on which, here and there, brown lines, marking sword-thrusts, and a sort of red stars, which indicated bullet-holes, were visible. He contemplated that gigantic scar which stamped heroism on that countenance upon which God had imprinted goodness. He reflected that this man was his father, and that this man was dead, and a chill ran over him.

The sorrow which he felt was the sorrow which he would have felt in the presence of any other man whom he had chanced to behold stretched out in death.

Anguish, poignant anguish, was in that chamber. The servant-woman was lamenting in a corner, the curé was praying, and his sobs were audible, the doctor was wiping his eyes; the corpse itself was weeping.

The doctor, the priest, and the woman gazed at Marius in the midst of their affliction without uttering a word; he was the stranger there. Marius, who was far too little affected, felt ashamed and embarrassed at his own attitude; he held his hat in his hand; and he dropped it on the floor, in order to produce the impression that grief had deprived him of the strength to hold it.

At the same time, he experienced remorse, and he despised himself for behaving in this manner. But was it his fault? He did not love his father. Why should he!

The colonel had left nothing. The sale of his furniture barely paid the expenses of his burial.

The servant found a scrap of paper, which she handed to Marius. It contained the following, in the colonel's handwriting:

"*For my son.*—The Emperor made me a Baron on the battlefield of Waterloo. Since the Restoration disputes my right to this title which I purchased with my blood, my son shall take it and bear it. That he will be worthy of it is a matter of course." Below, the colonel had added: "At that same battle of Waterloo, a sergeant saved my life. The man's name was Thénardier. I think that he has recently been keeping a little inn, in a village in the neighborhood of Paris, at Chelles or Montfermeil. If my son meets him, he will do all the good he can to Thénardier."

Marius took this paper and preserved it, not out of duty to his father, but because of that vague respect for death which is always imperious in the heart of man.

Nothing remained of the colonel. M. Gillenormand had his sword and uniform sold to an old-clothes dealer. The neighbors devastated the garden and pillaged the rare flowers. The other plants turned to nettles and weeds, and died.

Marius remained only forty-eight hours at Vernon. After the interment he returned to Paris, and applied himself again to his law studies, with no more thought of his father than if the latter had never lived. In two days the colonel was buried, and in three forgotten.

Marius wore crape on his hat. That was all.

Chapter V

THE UTILITY OF GOING TO MASS, IN ORDER TO BECOME A REVOLUTIONIST

MARIUS HAD PRESERVED THE RELIGIOUS HABITS OF HIS CHILDHOOD. ONE SUNDAY, WHEN HE went to hear mass at Saint-Sulpice, at that same chapel of the Virgin whither his aunt had led him when a small lad, he placed himself behind a pillar, being more absent-minded and thoughtful than usual on that occasion, and knelt down, without paying any special heed, upon a chair of Utrecht velvet, on the back of which was inscribed this name: *Monsieur Mabeuf, warden.* Mass had hardly begun when an old man presented himself and said to Marius:

"This is my place, sir."

Marius stepped aside promptly, and the old man took possession of his chair.

The mass concluded, Marius still stood thoughtfully a few paces distant; the old man approached him again and said:

"I beg your pardon, sir, for having disturbed you awhile ago, and for again disturbing you at this moment; you must have thought me intrusive, and I will explain myself."

"There is no need of that, sir," said Marius.

"Yes!" went on the old man, "I do not wish you to have a bad opinion of me. You see, I am attached to this place. It seems to me that the mass is better from here. Why? I will tell you. It is from this place, that I have watched a poor, brave father come regularly, every two or three months, for the last ten years, since he had no other opportunity and no other way of seeing his child, because he was prevented by family arrangements. He came at the hour when he knew that his son would be brought to mass. The little one never suspected that his father was there. Perhaps he did not even know that he had a father, poor innocent! The father kept behind a pillar, so that he might not be seen. He gazed at his child and he wept. He adored that little fellow, poor man! I could see that. This spot has become sanctified in my sight, and I have contracted a habit of coming hither to listen to the mass. I prefer it to the stall to which I have a right, in my capacity of warden. I knew that unhappy gentleman a little, too. He had a father-in-law, a wealthy aunt, relatives, I don't know exactly what all, who threatened to disinherit the child if he, the father, saw him. He sacrificed himself in order that his son might be rich and happy someday. He was separated from him because of political opinions. Certainly, I approve of political opinions, but there are people who do not know where to stop. Mon Dieu! a man is not a monster because he was at Waterloo; a father is not separated from his child for such a reason as that. He was one of Bonaparte's colonels. He is dead, I believe. He lived at Vernon, where I have a brother who is a curé, and his name was something like Pontmarie or Montpercy. He had a fine sword-cut, on my honor."

"Pontmercy," suggested Marius, turning pale.

"Precisely, Pontmercy. Did you know him?"

"Sir," said Marius, "he was my father."

The old warden clasped his hands and exclaimed:

"Ah! you are the child! Yes, that's true, he must be a man by this time. Well! poor child, you may say that you had a father who loved you dearly!"

Marius offered his arm to the old man and conducted him to his lodgings.

On the following day, he said to M. Gillenormand:

"I have arranged a hunting-party with some friends. Will you permit me to be absent for three days?"

"Four!" replied his grandfather. "Go and amuse yourself."

And he said to his daughter in a low tone, and with a wink, "Some love affair!"

Chapter VI

THE CONSEQUENCES OF HAVING MET A WARDEN

WHERE IT WAS THAT MARIUS WENT WILL BE DISCLOSED A LITTLE FURTHER ON. Marius was absent for three days, then he returned to Paris, went straight to the library of the law-school and asked for the files of the *Moniteur*.

He read the *Moniteur*, he read all the histories of the Republic and the Empire, the *Memorial de Sainte-Hélène*, all the memoirs, all the newspapers, the bulletins, the proclamations; he devoured everything. The first time that he came across his father's name in the bulletins of the grand army, he had a fever for a week. He went to see the generals under whom Georges Pontmercy had served, among others, Comte H. Church-warden Mabeuf, whom he went to see again, told him about the life at Vernon, the colonel's retreat, his flowers, his solitude. Marius came to a full knowledge of that rare, sweet, and sublime man, that species of lion-lamb who had been his father.

In the meanwhile, occupied as he was with this study which absorbed all his moments as well as his thoughts, he hardly saw the Gillenormands at all. He made his appearance at meals; then they searched for him, and he was not to be found. Father Gillenormand smiled. "Bah! bah! He is just of the age for the girls!" Sometimes the old man added: "The deuce! I thought it was only an affair of gallantry. It seems that it is an affair of passion!"

It was a passion, in fact. Marius was on the high road to adoring his father.

At the same time, his ideas underwent an extraordinary change. The phases of this change were numerous and successive. As this is the history of many minds of our day, we think it will prove useful to follow these phases step by step and to indicate them all.

That history upon which he had just cast his eyes appalled him.

The first effect was to dazzle him.

Up to that time, the Republic, the Empire, had been to him only monstrous words. The Republic, a guillotine in the twilight; the Empire, a sword in the night. He had just taken a look at it, and where he had expected to find only a chaos of shadows, he had beheld, with a sort of unprecedented surprise, mingled with fear and joy, stars sparkling, Mirabeau, Vergniaud, Saint-Just, Robespierre, Camille, Desmoulins, Danton, and a sun arise, Napoleon. He did not know where he stood. He recoiled, blinded by the brilliant lights. Little by little, when his astonishment had passed off, he grew accustomed to this radiance, he contemplated these deeds without dizziness, he examined these personages without terror; the Revolution and the Empire presented themselves luminously, in perspective, before his mind's eye; he beheld each of these groups of events and of men summed up in two tremendous facts: the Republic in the sovereignty of civil right restored to the masses, the

Empire in the sovereignty of the French idea imposed on Europe; he beheld the grand figure of the people emerge from the Revolution, and the grand figure of France spring forth from the Empire. He asserted in his conscience, that all this had been good. What his dazzled state neglected in this, his first far too synthetic estimation, we do not think it necessary to point out here. It is the state of a mind on the march that we are recording. Progress is not accomplished in one stage. That stated, once for all, in connection with what precedes as well as with what is to follow, we continue.

He then perceived that, up to that moment, he had comprehended his country no more than he had comprehended his father. He had not known either the one or the other, and a sort of voluntary night had obscured his eyes. Now he saw, and on the one hand he admired, while on the other he adored.

He was filled with regret and remorse, and he reflected in despair that all he had in his soul could now be said only to the tomb. Oh! if his father had still been in existence, if he had still had him, if God, in his compassion and his goodness, had permitted his father to be still among the living, how he would have run, how he would have precipitated himself, how he would have cried to his father: "Father! Here I am! It is I! I have the same heart as thou! I am thy son!" How he would have embraced that white head, bathed his hair in tears, gazed upon his scar, pressed his hands, adored his garment, kissed his feet! Oh! Why had his father died so early, before his time, before the justice, the love of his son had come to him? Marius had a continual sob in his heart, which said to him every moment: "Alas!" At the same time, he became more truly serious, more truly grave, more sure of his thought and his faith. At each instant, gleams of the true came to complete his reason. An inward growth seemed to be in progress within him. He was conscious of a sort of natural enlargement, which gave him two things that were new to him—his father and his country.

As everything opens when one has a key, so he explained to himself that which he had hated, he penetrated that which he had abhorred; henceforth he plainly perceived the providential, divine and human sense of the great things which he had been taught to detest, and of the great men whom he had been instructed to curse. When he reflected on his former opinions, which were but those of yesterday, and which, nevertheless, seemed to him already so very ancient, he grew indignant, yet he smiled.

From the rehabilitation of his father, he naturally passed to the rehabilitation of Napoleon.

But the latter, we will confess, was not effected without labor.

From his infancy, he had been imbued with the judgments of the party of 1814, on Bonaparte. Now, all the prejudices of the Restoration, all its interests, all its instincts tended to disfigure Napoleon. It execrated him even more than it did Robespierre. It had very cleverly turned to sufficiently good account the fatigue of the nation, and the hatred of mothers. Bonaparte had become an almost fabulous monster, and in order to paint him to the imagination of the people, which, as we lately pointed out, resembles the imagination of children, the party of 1814 made him appear under all sorts of terrifying masks in succession, from that which is terrible though it remains grandiose to that which is terrible and becomes grotesque, from Tiberius to the bugaboo. Thus, in speaking of Bonaparte, one was free to sob or to puff up with laughter, provided that hatred lay at the bottom. Marius had never entertained—about *that man*, as he was called—any other ideas in his mind. They had combined with the tenacity which existed in his nature. There was in him a headstrong little man who hated Napoleon.

On reading history, on studying him, especially in the documents and materials for history, the veil which concealed Napoleon from the eyes of Marius was gradually rent. He caught a glimpse of something immense, and he suspected that he had been deceived up to that moment, on the score of Bonaparte as about all the rest; each day he saw more distinctly; and he set about mounting, slowly, step by step, almost regretfully in the beginning, then with intoxication and as though attracted by an irresistible fascination, first the somber steps, then the vaguely illuminated steps, at last the luminous and splendid steps of enthusiasm.

One night, he was alone in his little chamber near the roof. His candle was burning; he was reading, with his elbows resting on his table close to the open window. All sorts of reveries reached him from space, and mingled with his thoughts. What a spectacle is the night! One hears dull sounds, without knowing whence they proceed; one beholds Jupiter, which is twelve hundred times larger than the earth, glowing like a firebrand, the azure is black, the stars shine; it is formidable.

He was perusing the bulletins of the grand army, those heroic strophes penned on the field of battle; there, at intervals, he beheld his father's name, always the name of the Emperor; the whole of that great Empire presented itself to him; he felt a flood swelling and rising within him; it seemed to him at moments that his father passed close to him like a breath, and whispered in his ear; he gradually got into a singular state; he thought that he heard drums, cannon, trumpets, the measured tread of battalions, the dull and distant gallop of the cavalry; from time to time, his eyes were raised heavenward, and gazed upon the colossal constellations as they gleamed in the measureless depths of space, then they fell upon his book once more, and there they beheld other colossal things moving confusedly. His heart contracted within him. He was in a transport, trembling, panting. All at once, without himself knowing what was in him, and what impulse he was obeying, he sprang to his feet, stretched both arms out of the window, gazed intently into the gloom, the silence, the infinite darkness, the eternal immensity, and exclaimed: "Long live the Emperor!"

From that moment forth, all was over; the Ogre of Corsica—the usurper—the tyrant—the monster who was the lover of his own sisters—the actor who took lessons of Talma—the poisoner of Jaffa—the tiger—Buonaparte—all this vanished, and gave place in his mind to a vague and brilliant radiance in which shone, at an inaccessible height, the pale marble phantom of Cæsar. The Emperor had been for his father only the well-beloved captain whom one admires, for whom one sacrifices one's self; he was something more to Marius. He was the predestined constructor of the French group, succeeding the Roman group in the domination of the universe. He was a prodigious architect, of a destruction, the continuer of Charlemagne, of Louis XI, of Henry IV, of Richelieu, of Louis XIV, and of the Committee of Public Safety, having his spots, no doubt, his faults, his crimes even, being a man, that is to say; but august in his faults, brilliant in his spots, powerful in his crime.

He was the predestined man, who had forced all nations to say: "The great nation!" He was better than that, he was the very incarnation of France, conquering Europe by the sword which he grasped, and the world by the light which he shed. Marius saw in Bonaparte the dazzling specter which will always rise upon the frontier, and which will guard the future. Despot but dictator; a despot resulting from a republic and summing up a revolution. Napoleon became for him the man-people as Jesus Christ is the man-God.

It will be perceived, that like all new converts to a religion, his conversion intoxicated him, he hurled himself headlong into adhesion and he went too far. His nature was so constructed; once on the downward slope, it was almost impossible for him to put on the drag. Fanaticism for the sword took possession of him, and complicated in his mind his enthusiasm for the idea. He did not perceive that, along with genius, and pell-mell, he was admitting force, that is to say, that he was installing in two compartments of his idolatry, on the one hand that which is divine, on the other that which is brutal. In many respects, he had set about deceiving himself otherwise. He admitted everything. There is a way of encountering error while on one's way to the truth. He had a violent sort of good faith which took everything in the lump. In the new path which he had entered on, in judging the mistakes of the old régime, as in measuring the glory of Napoleon, he neglected the attenuating circumstances.

At all events, a tremendous step had been taken. Where he had formerly beheld the fall of the monarchy, he now saw the advent of France. His orientation had changed. What had been his East became the West. He had turned squarely round.

All these revolutions were accomplished within him, without his family obtaining an inkling of the case.

When, during this mysterious labor, he had entirely shed his old Bourbon and ultra skin, when he had cast off the aristocrat, the Jacobite and the royalist, when he had become thoroughly a revolutionist, profoundly democratic and republican, he went to an engraver on the Quai des Orfévres and ordered a hundred cards bearing this name: *Le Baron Marius Pontmercy.*

This was only the strictly logical consequence of the change which had taken place in him, a change in which everything gravitated round his father.

Only, as he did not know anyone and could not sow his cards with any porter, he put them in his pocket.

By another natural consequence, in proportion as he drew nearer to his father, to the latter's memory, and to the things for which the colonel had fought five-and-twenty years before, he receded from his grandfather. We have long ago said, that M. Gillenormand's temper did not please him. There already existed between them all the dissonances of the grave young man and the frivolous old man. The gaiety of Géronte shocks and exasperates the melancholy of Werther. So long as the same political opinions and the same ideas had been common to them both, Marius had met M. Gillenormand there as on a bridge. When the bridge fell, an abyss was formed. And then, over and above all, Marius experienced unutterable impulses to revolt, when he reflected that it was M. Gillenormand who had, from stupid motives, torn him ruthlessly from the colonel, thus depriving the father of the child, and the child of the father.

By dint of pity for his father, Marius had nearly arrived at aversion for his grandfather.

Nothing of this sort, however, was betrayed on the exterior, as we have already said. Only he grew colder and colder; laconic at meals, and rare in the house. When his aunt scolded him for it, he was very gentle and alleged his studies, his lectures, the examinations, etc., as a pretext. His grandfather never departed from his infallible diagnosis: "In love! I know all about it."

From time to time Marius absented himself.

"Where is it that he goes off like this?" said his aunt.

On one of these trips, which were always very brief, he went to Montfermeil, in order to obey the injunction which his father had left him, and he sought the old sergeant to Waterloo, the innkeeper Thénardier. Thénardier had failed, the inn was closed, and no one knew what had become of him. Marius was away from the house for four days on this quest.

"He is getting decidedly wild," said his grandfather.

They thought they had noticed that he wore something on his breast, under his shirt, which was attached to his neck by a black ribbon.

Chapter VII

SOME PETTICOAT

WE HAVE MENTIONED A LANCER. He was a great-grandnephew of M. Gillenormand, on the paternal side, who led a garrison life, outside the family and far from the domestic hearth. Lieutenant Théodule Gillenormand fulfilled all the conditions required to make what is called a fine officer. He had "a lady's waist," a victorious manner of trailing his sword and of twirling his mustache in a hook. He visited Paris very rarely, and so rarely that Marius had never seen him. The cousins knew each other only by name. We think we have said that Théodule was the favorite of Aunt Gillenormand, who preferred him because she did not see him. Not seeing people permits one to attribute to them all possible perfections.

One morning, Mademoiselle Gillenormand the elder returned to her apartment as much disturbed as her placidity was capable of allowing. Marius had just asked his grandfather's permission to take a little trip, adding that he meant to set out that very evening. "Go!" had been his grandfather's reply, and M. Gillenormand had added in an aside, as he raised his eyebrows to the top of his forehead: "Here he is passing the night out again." Mademoiselle Gillenormand had ascended to her chamber greatly puzzled, and on the staircase had dropped this exclamation: "This is too much!"—and this interrogation: "But where is it that he goes?" She spied some adventure of the heart, more or less illicit, a woman in the shadow, a rendezvous, a mystery, and she would not have been sorry to thrust her spectacles into the affair. Tasting a mystery resembles getting the first flavor of a scandal; sainted souls do not detest this. There is some curiosity about scandal in the secret compartments of bigotry.

So she was the prey of a vague appetite for learning a history.

In order to get rid of this curiosity which agitated her a little beyond her wont, she took refuge in her talents, and set about scalloping, with one layer of cotton after another, one of those embroideries of the Empire and the Restoration, in which there are numerous cart-wheels. The work was clumsy, the worker cross. She had been seated at this for several hours when the door opened. Mademoiselle Gillenormand raised her nose; Lieutenant Théodule stood before her, making the regulation salute. She uttered a cry of delight. One may be old, one may be a prude, one may be pious, one may be an aunt, but it is always agreeable to see a lancer enter one's chamber.

"You here, Théodule!" she exclaimed.

"On my way through town, aunt."

"Embrace me."

"Here goes!" said Théodule.

And he kissed her. Aunt Gillenormand went to her writing-desk and opened it.

"You will remain with us a week at least?"

"I leave this very evening, aunt."

"It is not possible!"

"Mathematically!"

"Remain, my little Théodule, I beseech you."

"My heart says 'yes,' but my orders say 'no.' The matter is simple. They are changing our garrison; we have been at Melun, we are being transferred to Gaillon. It is necessary to pass through Paris in order to get from the old post to the new one. I said: 'I am going to see my aunt.' "

"Here is something for your trouble."

And she put ten louis into his hand.

"For my pleasure, you mean to say, my dear aunt."

Théodule kissed her again, and she experienced the joy of having some of the skin scratched from her neck by the braidings on his uniform.

"Are you making the journey on horseback, with your regiment?" she asked him.

"No, aunt. I wanted to see you. I have special permission. My servant is taking my horse; I am traveling by diligence. And, by the way, I want to ask you something."

"What is it?"

"Is my cousin Marius Pontmercy traveling so, too?"

"How do you know that?" said his aunt, suddenly pricked to the quick with a lively curiosity.

"On my arrival, I went to the diligence to engage my seat in the coupé."

"Well?"

"A traveler had already come to engage a seat in the imperial. I saw his name on the card."

"What name?"

"Marius Pontmercy."

"The wicked fellow!" exclaimed his aunt. "Ah! your cousin is not a steady lad like yourself. To think that he is to pass the night in a diligence!"

"Just as I am going to do."

"But you—it is your duty; in his case, it is wildness."

"Bosh!" said Théodule.

Here an event occurred to Mademoiselle Gillenormand the elder—an idea struck her. If she had been a man, she would have slapped her brow. She apostrophized Théodule:

"Are you aware whether your cousin knows you?"

"No. I have seen him; but he has never deigned to notice me."

"So you are going to travel together?"

"He in the imperial, I in the coupé."

"Where does this diligence run?"

"To Andelys."

"Then that is where Marius is going?"

"Unless, like myself, he should stop on the way. I get down at Vernon, in order to take the branch coach for Gaillon. I know nothing of Marius's plan of travel."

"Marius! what an ugly name! what possessed them to name him Marius! While you, at least, are called Théodule."

"I would rather be called Alfred," said the officer.

"Listen, Théodule."

"I am listening, aunt."

"Pay attention."

"I am paying attention."

"You understand?"

"Yes."

"Well, Marius absents himself."

"Eh! eh!"

"He travels."

"Ah! ah!"

"He spends the night out."

"Oh! oh!"

"We should like to know what there is behind all this."

Théodule replied with the composure of a man of bronze:

"Some petticoat or other."

And with that inward laugh which denotes certainty, he added:

"A lass."

"That is evident," exclaimed his aunt, who thought she heard M. Gillenormand speaking, and who felt her conviction become irresistible at that word *fillette*, accentuated in almost the very same fashion by the granduncle and the grandnephew. She resumed:

"Do us a favor. Follow Marius a little. He does not know you, it will be easy. Since a lass there is, try to get a sight of her. You must write us the tale. It will amuse his grandfather."

Théodule had no excessive taste for this sort of spying; but he was much touched by the ten louis, and he thought he saw a chance for a possible sequel. He accepted the commission and said: "As you please, aunt."

And he added in an aside, to himself: "Here I am a duenna."

Mademoiselle Gillenormand embraced him.

"You are not the man to play such pranks, Théodule. You obey discipline, you are the slave of orders, you are a man of scruples and duty, and you would not quit your family to go and see a creature."

The lancer made the pleased grimace of Cartouche when praised for his probity.

Marius, on the evening following this dialogue, mounted the diligence without suspecting that he was watched. As for the watcher, the first thing he did was to fall asleep. His slumber was complete and conscientious. Argus snored all night long.

At daybreak, the conductor of the diligence shouted: "Vernon! relay of Vernon! Travelers for Vernon!" And Lieutenant Théodule woke.

"Good," he growled, still half asleep, "this is where I get out."

Then, as his memory cleared by degrees, the effect of waking, he recalled his aunt, the ten louis, and the account which he had undertaken to render of the deeds and proceedings of Marius. This set him to laughing.

"Perhaps he is no longer in the coach," he thought, as he rebuttoned the waistcoat of his undress uniform. "He may have stopped at Poissy; he may have stopped at Triel; if he did not get out at Meulan, he may have got out at Mantes, unless he got out at Rolleboise, or if he did not go on as far as Pacy, with the choice of turning to the left at Évreux, or to the right at Laroche-Guyon. Run after him, aunty. What the devil am I to write to that good old soul?"

At that moment, a pair of black trousers descending from the imperial, made its appearance at the window of the coupé.

"Can that be Marius?" said the lieutenant.

It was Marius.

A little peasant girl, all entangled with the horses and the postilions at the end of the vehicle, was offering flowers to the travelers. "Give your ladies flowers!" she cried.

Marius approached her and purchased the finest flowers in her flat basket.

"Come now," said Théodule, leaping down from the coupé, "this piques my curiosity. Who the deuce is he going to carry those flowers to? She must be a splendidly handsome woman for so fine a bouquet. I want to see her."

And no longer in pursuance of orders, but from personal curiosity, like dogs who hunt on their own account, he set out to follow Marius.

Marius paid no attention to Théodule. Elegant women descended from the diligence; he did not glance at them. He seemed to see nothing around him.

"He is pretty deeply in love!" thought Théodule.

Marius directed his steps toward the church.

"Capital," said Théodule to himself. "Rendezvous seasoned with a bit of mass are the best sort. Nothing is so exquisite as an ogle which passes over the good God's head."

On arriving at the church, Marius did not enter it, but skirted the apse. He disappeared behind one of the angles of the apse.

"The rendezvous is appointed outside," said Théodule. "Let's have a look at the lass."

And he advanced on the tips of his boots toward the corner which Marius had turned.

On arriving there, he halted in amazement.

Marius, with his forehead clasped in his hands, was kneeling upon the grass on a grave. He had strewn his bouquet there. At the extremity of the grave, on a little swelling which marked the head, there stood a cross of black wood with this name in white letters: COLONEL BARON PONTMERCY. Marius's sobs were audible.

The "lass" was a grave.

Chapter VIII

MARBLE AGAINST GRANITE

I T WAS HITHER THAT MARIUS HAD COME ON THE FIRST OCCASION OF HIS ABSENTING HIMSELF FROM Paris. It was hither that he had come every time that M. Gillenormand had said: "He is sleeping out."

Lieutenant Théodule was absolutely put out of countenance by this unexpected encounter with a sepulcher; he experienced a singular and disagreeable sensation which he was incapable of analyzing, and which was composed of respect for the tomb, mingled with respect for the colonel. He retreated, leaving Marius alone in the cemetery, and there was discipline in this retreat. Death appeared to him with large epaulets, and he almost made the military salute to him. Not knowing what to write to his aunt, he decided not to write at all; and it is probable that nothing would have resulted from the discovery made by Théodule as to the love affairs of Marius, if, by one of those mysterious arrangements which are so frequent in chance, the scene at Vernon had not had an almost immediate counter-shock at Paris.

Marius returned from Vernon on the third day, in the middle of the morning, descended at his grandfather's door, and, wearied by the two nights spent in the diligence, and feeling the need of repairing his loss of sleep by an hour at the swimming-school, he mounted rapidly to his chamber, took merely time enough to throw off his traveling-coat, and the black ribbon which he wore round his neck, and went off to the bath.

M. Gillenormand, who had risen betimes like all old men in good health, had heard his entrance, and had made haste to climb, as quickly as his old legs permitted, the stairs to the upper story where Marius lived, in order to embrace him, and to question him while so doing, and to find out where he had been.

But the youth had taken less time to descend than the old man had to ascend, and when Father Gillenormand entered the attic, Marius was no longer there.

The bed had not been disturbed, and on the bed lay, outspread, but not defiantly, the great-coat and the black ribbon.

"I like this better," said M. Gillenormand.

And a moment later, he made his entrance into the salon, where Mademoiselle Gillenormand was already seated, busily embroidering her cart-wheels.

The entrance was a triumphant one.

M. Gillenormand held in one hand the great-coat, and in the other the neck-ribbon, and exclaimed:

"Victory! We are about to penetrate the mystery! We are going to learn the most minute details; we are going to lay our finger on the debaucheries of our sly friend! Here we have the romance itself. I have the portrait!"

In fact, a case of black shagreen, resembling a medallion portrait, was suspended from the ribbon.

The old man took this case and gazed at it for some time without opening it, with that air of enjoyment, rapture, and wrath, with which a poor hungry fellow beholds an admirable dinner which is not for him, pass under his very nose.

"For this evidently is a portrait. I know all about such things. That is worn tenderly on the heart. How stupid they are! Some abominable fright that will make us shudder, probably! Young men have such bad taste nowadays!"

"Let us see, father," said the old spinster.

The case opened by the pressure of a spring. They found in it nothing but a carefully folded paper.

"*From the same to the same,*" said M. Gillenormand, bursting with laughter. "I know what it is. A billet-doux."

"Ah! let us read it!" said the aunt.

And she put on her spectacles. They unfolded the paper and read as follows:

"*For my son.*—The Emperor made me a Baron on the battlefield of Waterloo. Since the Restoration disputes my right to this title which I purchased with my blood, my son shall take it and bear it. That he will be worthy of it is a matter of course."

The feelings of father and daughter cannot be described. They felt chilled as by the breath of a death's-head. They did not exchange a word.

Only, M. Gillenormand said in a low voice and as though speaking to himself:

"It is the slasher's handwriting."

The aunt examined the paper, turned it about in all directions, then put it back in its case.

At the same moment, a little oblong packet, enveloped in blue paper, fell from one of the pockets of the great-coat. Mademoiselle Gillenormand picked it up and unfolded the blue paper.

It contained Marius's hundred cards. She handed one of them to M. Gillenormand, who read: *Le Baron Marius Pontmercy.*

The old man rang the bell. Nicolette came. M. Gillenormand took the ribbon, the case, and the coat, flung them all on the floor in the middle of the room, and said:

"Carry those duds away."

A full hour passed in the most profound silence. The old man and the old spinster had seated themselves with their backs to each other, and were thinking, each on his own account, the same things, in all probability.

At the expiration of this hour, Aunt Gillenormand said:

"A pretty state of things!"

A few moments later, Marius made his appearance. He entered. Even before he had crossed the threshold, he saw his grandfather holding one of his own cards in his hand, and on catching sight of him, the latter exclaimed with his air of bourgeois and grinning superiority which was something crushing:

"Well! well! well! well! well! so you are a baron now. I present you my compliments. What is the meaning of this?"

Marius reddened slightly and replied:

"It means that I am the son of my father."

M. Gillenormand ceased to laugh, and said harshly:

"I am your father."

"My father," retorted Marius, with downcast eyes and a severe air, "was a humble and heroic man, who served the Republic and France gloriously, who was great in the greatest history that men have ever made, who lived in the bivouac for a quarter of a century, beneath grape-shot and bullets, in snow and mud by day, beneath rain at night, who captured two flags, who received twenty wounds, who died forgotten and abandoned, and who never committed but one mistake, which was to love too fondly two ingrates, his country and myself."

This was more than M. Gillenormand could bear to hear. At the word *republic*, he rose, or, to speak more correctly, he sprang to his feet. Every word that Marius had just uttered produced on the visage of the old royalist the effect of the puffs of air from a forge upon a blazing brand. From a dull hue he had turned red, from red, purple, and from purple, flame-colored.

"Marius!" he cried. "Abominable child! I do not know what your father was! I do not wish to know! I know nothing about that, and I do not know him! But what I do know is, that there never was anything but scoundrels among those men! They were all rascals, assassins, red-caps, thieves! I say all! I say all! I know not one! I say all! Do you hear me, Marius! See here, you are no more a baron than my slipper is! They were all bandits in the service of Robespierre! All who served B-u-o-naparté were brigands! They were all traitors who betrayed, betrayed, betrayed their legitimate king! All cowards who fled before the Prussians and the English at Waterloo! That is what I do know! Whether monsieur your father comes in that category, I do not know! I am sorry for it, so much the worse, your humble servant!"

In his turn, it was Marius who was the firebrand and M. Gillenormand who was the bellows. Marius quivered in every limb, he did not know what would happen next, his brain was on fire. He was the priest who beholds all his sacred wafers cast to the winds, the fakir who beholds a passer-by spit upon his idol. It could not be that such things had been uttered in his presence. What was he to do? His father had just been trampled underfoot and stamped upon in his presence, but by whom? By his grandfather. How was he to avenge the one without outraging the other? It was impossible for him to insult his grandfather and it was equally impossible for him to leave his father unavenged. On the one hand was a sacred grave, on the other hoary locks.

He stood there for several moments, staggering as though intoxicated, with all this whirlwind dashing through his head; then he raised his eyes, gazed fixedly at his grandfather, and cried in a voice of thunder:

"Down with the Bourbons, and that great hog of a Louis XVIII!"

Louis XVIII had been dead for four years; but it was all the same to him.

The old man, who had been crimson, turned whiter than his hair. He wheeled round toward a bust of M. le Duc de Berry, which stood on the chimney-piece, and made a profound bow, with a sort of peculiar majesty. Then he paced twice, slowly and in silence, from the fireplace to the window and from the window to the fireplace, traversing the whole length of the room, and making the polished floor creak as though he had been a stone statue walking.

On his second turn, he bent over his daughter, who was watching this encounter with the stupefied air of an antiquated lamb, and said to her with a smile that was almost calm: "A baron like this gentleman, and a bourgeois like myself cannot remain under the same roof."

And drawing himself up, all at once, pallid, trembling, terrible, with his brow rendered more lofty by the terrible radiance of wrath, he extended his arm toward Marius and shouted to him:

"Be off!"

Marius left the house.

On the following day, M. Gillenormand said to his daughter:

"You will send sixty pistoles every six months to that blood-drinker, and you will never mention his name to me."

Having an immense reserve fund of wrath to get rid of, and not knowing what to do with it, he continued to address his daughter as *you* instead of *thou* for the next three months.

Marius, on his side, had gone forth in indignation. There was one circumstance which, it must be admitted, aggravated his exasperation. There are always petty fatalities of the sort which complicate domestic dramas. They augment the grievances in such cases, although, in reality, the wrongs are not increased by them. While carrying Marius's "duds" precipitately to his chamber, at his grandfather's command, Nicolette had, inadvertently, let fall, probably, on the attic staircase, which was dark, that medallion of black shagreen which contained the paper penned by the colonel. Neither paper nor case could afterwards be found. Marius was convinced that "Monsieur Gillenormand"—from that day forth he never alluded to him otherwise—had flung "his father's testament" in the fire. He knew by heart the few lines which the colonel had written, and, consequently, nothing was lost. But the paper, the writing, that sacred relic—all that was his very heart. What had been done with it?

Marius had taken his departure without saying whither he was going, and without knowing where, with thirty francs, his watch, and a few clothes in a hand-bag. He had entered a hackney-coach, had engaged it by the hour, and had directed his course at haphazard toward the Latin Quarter.

What was to become of Marius?

BOOK FOURTH

THE FRIENDS OF THE A B C

Chapter I

A GROUP WHICH BARELY MISSED BECOMING HISTORIC

A T THAT EPOCH, WHICH WAS, TO ALL APPEARANCES INDIFFERENT, A CERTAIN REVOLUTIONARY
quiver was vaguely current. Breaths which had started forth from the depths of '89 and '93
were in the air. Youth was on the point, may the reader pardon us the word, of molting. People were
undergoing a transformation, almost without being conscious of it, through the movement of the
age. The needle which moves round the compass also moves in souls. Each person was taking that
step in advance which he was bound to take. The royalists were becoming liberals, liberals were
turning democrats. It was a flood tide complicated with a thousand ebb movements; the peculiarity
of ebbs is to create intermixtures; hence the combination of very singular ideas; people adored both
Napoleon and liberty. We are making history here. These were the mirages of that period. Opinions traverse phases. Voltairian royalism, a quaint variety, had a no less singular sequel, Bonapartist
liberalism.

Other groups of minds were more serious. In that direction, they sounded principles, they attached themselves to the right. They grew enthusiastic for the absolute, they caught glimpses of infinite realizations; the absolute, by its very rigidity, urges spirits toward the sky and causes them to
float in illimitable space. There is nothing like dogma for bringing forth dreams. And there is nothing like dreams for engendering the future. Utopia to-day, flesh and blood to-morrow.

These advanced opinions had a double foundation. A beginning of mystery menaced "the established order of things," which was suspicious and underhand. A sign which was revolutionary
to the highest degree. The second thoughts of power meet the second thoughts of the populace in
the mine. The incubation of insurrections gives the retort to the premeditation of *coups d'état.*

There did not, as yet, exist in France, any of those vast underlying organizations, like the German *tugendbund* and Italian Carbonarism; but here and there, there were dark underminings, which
were in process of throwing off shoots. The Cougourde was being outlined at Aix; there existed at
Paris, among other affiliations of that nature, the society of the Friends of the A B C.

What were these Friends of the A B C? A society which had for its object apparently the education of children, in reality the elevation of man.

They declared themselves the Friends of the A B C—the *Abaissé*—the debased—that is to
say, the people. They wished to elevate the people. It was a pun which we should do wrong to smile
at. Puns are sometimes serious factors in politics; witness the *Castratus ad castra*, which made a general of the army of Narses; witness: *Barbari et Barberini*; witness: *Tu es Petrus et super hanc petram*,
etc., etc.

The Friends of the A B C were not numerous, it was a secret society in the state of embryo,
we might almost say a coterie, if coteries ended in heroes. They assembled in Paris in two localities, near the fish-market, in a wine-shop called *Corinthe*, of which more will be heard later on, and

near the Pantheon in a little café in the Rue Saint-Michel called the *Café Musain*, now torn down; the first of these meeting-places was close to the workingman, the second to the students.

The assemblies of the Friends of the A B C were usually held in a back room of the Café Musain.

This hall, which was tolerably remote from the café, with which it was connected by an extremely long corridor, had two windows and an exit with a private stairway on the little Rue des Grès. There they smoked and drank, and gambled and laughed. There they conversed in very loud tones about everything, and in whispers of other things. An old map of France under the Republic was nailed to the wall—a sign quite sufficient to excite the suspicion of a police agent.

The greater part of the Friends of the A B C were students, who were on cordial terms with the working classes. Here are the names of the principal ones. They belong, in a certain measure, to history: Enjolras, Combeferre, Jean Prouvaire, Feuilly, Courfeyrac, Bahorel, Lesgle or Laigle, Joly, Grantaire.

These young men formed a sort of family, through the bond of friendship. All, with the exception of Laigle, were from the South.

This was a remarkable group. It vanished in the invisible depths which lie behind us. At the point of this drama which we have now reached, it will not perhaps be superfluous to throw a ray of light upon these youthful heads, before the reader beholds them plunging into the shadow of a tragic adventure.

Enjolras, whose name we have mentioned first of all—the reader shall see why later on—was an only son and wealthy.

Enjolras was a charming young man, who was capable of being terrible. He was angelically handsome. He was a savage Antinous. One would have said, to see the pensive thoughtfulness of his glance, that he had already, in some previous state of existence, traversed the revolutionary apocalypse. He possessed the tradition of it as though he had been a witness. He was acquainted with all the minute details of the great affair. A pontifical and warlike nature, a singular thing in a youth. He was an officiating priest and a man of war; from the immediate point of view, a soldier of the democracy; above the contemporary movement, the priest of the ideal. His eyes were deep, his lids a little red, his lower lip was thick and easily became disdainful, his brow was lofty. A great deal of brow in a face is like a great deal of horizon in a view. Like certain young men at the beginning of this century and the end of the last, who became illustrious at an early age, he was endowed with excessive youth, and was as rosy as a young girl, although subject to hours of pallor. Already a man, he still seemed a child. His two-and-twenty years appeared to be but seventeen; he was serious, it did not seem as though he were aware there was on earth a thing called woman. He had but one passion—the right; but one thought—to overthrow the obstacle. On Mount Aventine, he would have been Gracchus; in the Convention, he would have been Saint-Just. He hardly saw the roses, he ignored spring, he did not hear the caroling of the birds; the bare throat of Evadne would have moved him no more than it would have moved Aristogeiton; he, like Harmodius, thought flowers good for nothing except to conceal the sword. He was severe in his enjoyments. He chastely dropped his eyes before everything which was not the Republic. He was the marble lover of liberty. His speech was harshly inspired, and had the thrill of a hymn. He was subject to unexpected outbursts of soul. Woe to the love-affair which should have risked itself beside him! If any grisette of the Place Cambrai or the Rue Saint-Jean de Beauvais, seeing that face of a youth escaped from college, that page's mien, those long, golden lashes, those blue eyes, that hair billowing in the wind, those rosy cheeks, those fresh lips, those exquisite teeth, had conceived an appetite for that complete aurora, and had tried her beauty on Enjolras, an astounding and terrible glance would have promptly shown her the abyss, and would have taught her not to confound the mighty cherub of Ezekiel with the gallant Cherubino of Beaumarchais.

By the side of Enjolras, who represented the logic of the Revolution, Combeferre represented

its philosophy. Between the logic of the Revolution and its philosophy there exists this difference—
that its logic may end in war, whereas its philosophy can end only in peace. Combeferre comple-
mented and rectified Enjolras. He was less lofty, but broader. He desired to pour into all minds the
extensive principles of general ideas: he said: "Revolution, but civilization"; and around the mountain peak he opened out a vast view of the blue sky. The Revolution was more adapted for breathing with Combeferre than with Enjolras. Enjolras expressed its divine right, and Combeferre its
natural right. The first attached himself to Robespierre; the second confined himself to Condorcet.
Combeferre lived the life of all the rest of the world more than did Enjolras. If it had been granted
to these two young men to attain to history, the one would have been the just, the other the wise
man. Enjolras was the more virile, Combeferre the more humane. *Homo* and *vir,* that was the exact
effect of their different shades. Combeferre was as gentle as Enjolras was severe, through natural
whiteness. He loved the word *citizen,* but he preferred the word *man.* He would gladly have said:
Hombre, like the Spanish. He read everything, went to the theaters, attended the courses of public
lecturers, learned the polarization of light from Arago, grew enthusiastic over a lesson in which Ge-
offrey Sainte-Hilaire explained the double function of the external carotid artery, and the internal,
the one which makes the face, and the one which makes the brain; he kept up with what was going
on, followed science step by step, compared Saint-Simon with Fourier, deciphered hieroglyphics,
broke the pebble which he found and reasoned on geology, drew from memory a silkworm moth,
pointed out the faulty French in the Dictionary of the Academy, studied Puységur and Deleuze, affirmed nothing, not even miracles; denied nothing, not even ghosts; turned over the files of the
Moniteur, reflected. He declared that the future lies in the hand of the schoolmaster, and busied himself with educational questions. He desired that society should labor without relaxation at the elevation of the moral and intellectual level, at coining science, at putting ideas into circulation, at
increasing the mind in youthful persons, and he feared lest the present poverty of method, the pal-
triness from a literary point of view confined to two or three centuries called classic, the tyrannical
dogmatism of official pedants, scholastic prejudices and routines should end by converting our colleges into artificial oyster beds. He was learned, a purist, exact, a graduate of the Polytechnic, a
close student, and at the same time, thoughtful "even to chimeras," so his friends said. He believed
in all dreams, railroads, the suppression of suffering in chirurgical operations, the fixing of images
in the dark chamber, the electric telegraph, the steering of balloons. Moreover, he was not much
alarmed by the citadels erected against the human mind in every direction, by superstition, despotism, and prejudice. He was one of those who think that science will eventually turn the position.
Enjolras was a chief, Combeferre was a guide. One would have liked to fight under the one and to
march behind the other. It is not that Combeferre was not capable of fighting, he did not refuse a
hand-to-hand combat with the obstacle, and to attack it by main force and explosively; but it suited
him better to bring the human race into accord with its destiny gradually, by means of education,
the inculcation of axioms, the promulgation of positive laws; and, between two lights, his preference was rather for illumination than for conflagration. A conflagration can create an aurora, no
doubt, but why not await the dawn? A volcano illuminates, but daybreak furnishes a still better illumination. Possibly, Combeferre preferred the whiteness of the beautiful to the blaze of the sublime. A light troubled by smoke, progress purchased at the expense of violence, only half satisfied
this tender and serious spirit. The headlong precipitation of a people into the truth, a '93, terrified
him; nevertheless, stagnation was still more repulsive to him, in it he detected putrefaction and
death; on the whole, he preferred scum to miasma, and he preferred the torrent to the cesspool, and
the falls of Niagara to the lake of Montfaucon. In short, he desired neither halt nor haste. While his
tumultuous friends, captivated by the absolute, adored and invoked splendid revolutionary adventures, Combeferre was inclined to let progress, good progress, take its own course; he may have
been cold, but he was pure; methodical, but irreproachable; phlegmatic, but imperturbable. Combeferre would have knelt and clasped his hands to enable the future to arrive in all its candor, and that

nothing might disturb the immense and virtuous evolution of the races. *The good must be innocent,* he repeated incessantly. And in fact, if the grandeur of the Revolution consists in keeping the dazzling ideal fixedly in view, and of soaring thither athwart the lightnings, with fire and blood in its talons, the beauty of progress lies in being spotless; and there exists between Washington, who represents the one, and Danton, who incarnates the other, that difference which separates the swan from the angel with the wings of an eagle.

Jean Prouvaire was a still softer shade than Combeferre. His name was Jehan, owing to that petty momentary freak which mingled with the powerful and profound movement whence sprang the very essential study of the Middle Ages. Jean Prouvaire was in love; he cultivated a pot of flowers, played on the flute, made verses, loved the people, pitied woman, wept over the child, confounded God and the future in the same confidence, and blamed the Revolution for having caused the fall of a royal head, that of André Chénier. His voice was ordinarily delicate, but suddenly grew manly. He was learned even to erudition, and almost an Orientalist. Above all, he was good; and, a very simple thing to those who know how nearly goodness borders on grandeur, in the matter of poetry, he preferred the immense. He knew Italian, Latin, Greek, and Hebrew; and these served him only for the perusal of four poets: Dante, Juvenal, Æschylus, and Isaiah. In French, he preferred Corneille to Racine, and Agrippa d'Aubigné to Corneille. He loved to saunter through fields of wild oats and corn-flowers, and busied himself with clouds nearly as much as with events. His mind had two attitudes, one on the side toward man, the other on that toward God; he studied or he contemplated. All day long, he buried himself in social questions, salary, capital, credit, marriage, religion, liberty of thought, education, penal servitude, poverty, association, property, production and sharing, the enigma of this lower world which covers the human anthill with darkness; and at night, he gazed upon the planets, those enormous beings. Like Enjolras, he was wealthy and an only son. He spoke softly, bowed his head, lowered his eyes, smiled with embarrassment, dressed badly, had an awkward air, blushed at a mere nothing, and was very timid. Yet he was intrepid.

Feuilly was a workingman, a fan-maker, orphaned both of father and mother, who earned with difficulty three francs a day, and had but one thought, to deliver the world. He had one other preoccupation, to educate himself; he called this also, delivering himself. He had taught himself to read and write; everything that he knew, he had learned by himself. Feuilly had a generous heart. The range of his embrace was immense. This orphan had adopted the peoples. As his mother had failed him, he meditated on his country. He brooded with the profound divination of the man of the people, over what we now call the *idea of the nationality,* had learned history with the express object of raging with full knowledge of the case. In this club of young Utopians, occupied chiefly with France, he represented the outside world. He had for his specialty Greece, Poland, Hungary, Roumania, Italy. He uttered these names incessantly, appropriately and inappropriately, with the tenacity of right. The violations of Turkey on Greece and Thessaly, of Russia on Warsaw, of Austria on Venice, enraged him. Above all things, the great violence of 1772 aroused him. There is no more sovereign eloquence than the true in indignation; he was eloquent with that eloquence. He was inexhaustible on that infamous date of 1772, on the subject of that noble and valiant race suppressed by treason, and that three-sided crime, on that monstrous ambush, the prototype and pattern of all those horrible suppressions of states, which, since that time, have struck many a noble nation, and have annulled their certificate of birth, so to speak. All contemporary social crimes have their origin in the partition of Poland. The partition of Poland is a theorem of which all present political outrages are the corollaries. There has not been a despot, nor a traitor for nearly a century back, who has not signed, approved, counter-signed, and copied, *ne variatur,* the partition of Poland. When the record of modern treasons was examined, that was the first thing which made its appearance. The congress of Vienna consulted that crime before consummating its own. 1772 sounded the onset; 1815 was the death of the game. Such was Feuilly's habitual text. This poor workingman had constituted himself the tutor of Justice, and she recompensed him by rendering him great. The fact is, that there is eternity in right. Warsaw can no more be Tartar than Venice can be Teuton. Kings lose their pains and their honor in the attempt to make them so. Sooner or later, the submerged part floats to the surface and reappears. Greece becomes Greece again, Italy is once more Italy. The protest of right against the deed persists forever. The theft of a nation cannot be allowed by prescription. These lofty deeds of rascality have no future. A nation cannot have its mark extracted like a pocket handkerchief.

Courfeyrac had a father who was called M. de Courfeyrac. One of the false ideas of the bourgeoisie under the Restoration as regards aristocracy and the nobility was to believe in the particle. The particle, as everyone knows, possesses no significance. But the bourgeois of the epoch of *la Minerve* estimated so highly that poor *de,* that they thought themselves bound to abdicate it. M. de Chauvelin had himself called M. Chauvelin; M. de Caumartin, M. Caumartin; M. de Constant de Robecque, Benjamin Constant; M. de Lafayette, M. Lafayette. Courfeyrac had not wished to remain behind the rest, and called himself plain Courfeyrac.

We might almost, so far as Courfeyrac is concerned, stop here, and confine ourselves to saying with regard to what remains: "For Courfeyrac, see Tholomyès."

Courfeyrac had, in fact, that animation of youth which may be called the *beauté du diable* of the mind. Later on, this disappears like the playfulness of the kitten, and all this grace ends, with the bourgeois, on two legs, and with the tomcat, on four paws.

This sort of wit is transmitted from generation to generation of the successive levies of youth who traverse the schools, who pass it from hand to hand, *quasi cursores,* and is almost always exactly the same; so that, as we have just pointed out, anyone who had listened to Courfeyrac in 1828 would have thought he heard Tholomyès in 1817. Only, Courfeyrac was an honorable fellow. Beneath the apparent similarities of the exterior mind, the difference between him and Tholomyès was very great. The latent man which existed in the two was totally different in the first from what it was in the second. There was in Tholomyès a district attorney, and in Courfeyrac a paladin.

Enjolras was the chief, Combeferre was the guide, Courfeyrac was the center. The others gave more light, he shed more warmth; the truth is, that he possessed all the qualities of a center, roundness and radiance.

Bahorel had figured in the bloody tumult of June, 1822, on the occasion of the burial of young Lallemand.

Bahorel was a good-natured mortal, who kept bad company, brave, a spendthrift, prodigal, and to the verge of generosity, talkative, and at times eloquent, bold to the verge of effrontery; the best fellow possible; he had daring waistcoats, and scarlet opinions; a wholesale blusterer, that is to say, loving nothing so much as a quarrel, unless it were an uprising; and nothing so much as an uprising, unless it were a revolution; always ready to smash a window-pane, then to tear up the pavement, then to demolish a government, just to see the effect of it; a student in his eleventh year. He had nosed about the law but did not practice it. He had taken for his device: "Never a lawyer," and for his armorial bearings a nightstand in which was visible a square cap. Every time that he passed the law-school, which rarely happened, he buttoned up his frock-coat—the paletot had not yet been invented—and took hygienic precautions. Of the school porter he said: "What a fine old man!" and of the dean, M. Delvincourt: "What a monument!" In his lectures he spied subjects for ballads, and in his professors occasions for caricature. He wasted a tolerably large allowance, something like three thousand francs a year, in doing nothing.

He had peasant parents whom he had contrived to imbue with respect for their son.

He said of them: "They are peasants and not bourgeois; that is the reason they are intelligent."

Bahorel, a man of caprice, was scattered over numerous cafés; the others had habits, he had none. He sauntered. To stray is human. To saunter is Parisian. In reality, he had a penetrating mind and was more of a thinker than appeared to view.

He served as a connecting link between the Friends of the A B C and other still unorganized groups, which were destined to take form later on.

In this conclave of young heads, there was one bald member.

The Marquis d'Avaray, whom Louis XVIII made a duke for having assisted him to enter a hackney-coach on the day when he emigrated, was wont to relate, that in 1814, on his return to France, as the King was disembarking at Calais, a man handed him a petition.

"What is your request?" said the King.

"Sire, a post-office."

"What is your name?"

"L'Aigle."

The King frowned, glanced at the signature of the petition and beheld the name written thus: LESGLE. This non-Bonoparte orthography touched the King and he began to smile. "Sire," resumed the man with the petition, "I had for ancestor a keeper of the hounds surnamed Lesgueules. This surname furnished my name. I am called Lesgueules, by contraction Lesgle, and by corruption l'Aigle." This caused the King to smile broadly. Later on he gave the man the posting office of Meaux, either intentionally or accidentally.

The bald member of the group was the son of this Lesgle, or Légle, and he signed himself, Légle [de Meaux]. As an abbreviation, his companions called him Bossuet.

Bossuet was a gay but unlucky fellow. His specialty was not to succeed in anything. As an offset, he laughed at everything. At five-and-twenty he was bald. His father had ended by owning a house and a field; but he, the son, had made haste to lose that house and field in a bad speculation. He had nothing left. He possessed knowledge and wit, but all he did miscarried. Everything failed him and everybody deceived him; what he was building tumbled down on top of him. If he were splitting wood, he cut off a finger. If he had a mistress, he speedily discovered that he had a friend also. Some misfortune happened to him every moment, hence his joviality. He said: "I live under falling tiles." He was not easily astonished, because, for him, an accident was what he had foreseen, he took his bad luck serenely, and smiled at the teasing of fate, like a person who is listening to pleasantries. He was poor, but his fund of good humor was inexhaustible. He soon reached his last sou, never his last burst of laughter. When adversity entered his doors, he saluted this old acquaintance cordially, he tapped all catastrophes on the stomach; he was familiar with fatality to the point of calling it by its nickname: "Good day, Guignon," he said to it.

These persecutions of fate had rendered him inventive. He was full of resources. He had no money, but he found means, when it seemed good to him, to indulge in "unbridled extravagance." One night, he went so far as to eat a "hundred francs" in a supper with a wench, which inspired him to make this memorable remark in the midst of the orgy: "Pull off my boots, you five-louis jade."

Bossuet was slowly directing his steps toward the profession of a lawyer; he was pursuing his law studies after the manner of Bahorel. Bossuet had not much domicile, sometimes none at all. He lodged now with one, now with another, most often with Joly. Joly was studying medicine. He was two years younger than Bossuet.

Joly was the "malade imaginaire" junior. What he had won in medicine was to be more of an invalid than a doctor. At three-and-twenty he thought himself a valetudinarian, and passed his life in inspecting his tongue in the mirror. He affirmed that man becomes magnetic like a needle, and in his chamber he placed his bed with its head to the south, and the foot to the north, so that, at night, the circulation of his blood might not be interfered with by the great electric current of the globe. During thunderstorms, he felt his pulse. Otherwise, he was the gayest of them all. All these young, maniacal, puny, merry incoherences lived in harmony together, and the result was an eccentric and agreeable being whom his comrades, who were prodigal of winged consonants, called Jolllly. "You may fly away on the four L's," Jean Prouvaire said to him.[1]

1. L'Aile, wing.

Joly had a trick of touching his nose with the tip of his cane, which is an indication of a sagacious mind.

All these young men who differed so greatly, and who, on the whole, can only be discussed seriously, held the same religion: Progress.

All were the direct sons of the French Revolution. The most giddy of them became solemn when they pronounced that date: '89. Their fathers in the flesh had been, either royalists, doctrinaires, it matters not what; this confusion anterior to themselves, who were young, did not concern them at all; the pure blood of principle ran in their veins. They attached themselves, without intermediate shades, to incorruptible right and absolute duty.

Affiliated and initiated, they sketched out the ideal underground.

Among all these glowing hearts and thoroughly convinced minds, there was one skeptic. How came he there? By juxtaposition. This skeptic's name was Grantaire, and he was in the habit of signing himself with this rebus: R. Grantaire was a man who took good care not to believe in anything. Moreover, he was one of the students who had learned the most during their course at Paris; he knew that the best coffee was to be had at the Café Lemblin, and the best billiards at the Café Voltaire, that good cakes and lasses were to be found at the Ermitage, on the Boulevard du Maine, spatchcocked chickens at Mother Sauget's, excellent matelotes at the Barrière de la Cunette, and a certain thin white wine at the Barrière du Compat. He knew the best place for everything; in addition, boxing and foot-fencing and some dances; and he was a thorough single-stick player. He was a tremendous drinker to boot. He was inordinately homely: the prettiest boot-stitcher of that day, Irma Boissy, enraged with his homeliness, pronounced sentence on him as follows: "Grantaire is impossible"; but Grantaire's fatuity was not to be disconcerted. He stared tenderly and fixedly at all women, with the air of saying to them all: "If I only chose!" and of trying to make his comrades believe that he was in general demand.

All those words: rights of the people, rights of man, the social contract, the French Revolution, the Republic, democracy, humanity, civilization, religion, progress, came very near to signifying nothing whatever to Grantaire. He smiled at them. Skepticism, that caries of the intelligence, had not left him a single whole idea. He lived with irony. This was his axiom: "There is but one certainty, my full glass." He sneered at all devotion in all parties, the father as well as the brother, Robespierre junior as well as Loizerolles. "They are greatly in advance to be dead," he exclaimed. He said of the crucifix: "There is a gibbet which has been a success." A rover, a gambler, a libertine, often drunk, he displeased these young dreamers by humming incessantly: "J'aimons les filles, et j'aimons le bon vin." Air: Vive Henri IV.

However, this skeptic had one fanaticism. This fanaticism was neither a dogma, nor an idea, nor an art, nor a science; it was a man: Enjolras. Grantaire admired, loved, and venerated Enjolras. To whom did this anarchical scoffer unite himself in this phalanx of absolute minds? To the most absolute. In what manner had Enjolras subjugated him? By his ideas? No. By his character. A phenomenon which is often observable. A skeptic who adheres to a believer is as simple as the law of complementary colors. That which we lack attracts us. No one loves the light like the blind man. The dwarf adores the drum-major. The toad always has his eyes fixed on heaven. Why? In order to watch the bird in its flight. Grantaire, in whom writhed doubt, loved to watch faith soar in Enjolras. He had need of Enjolras. That chaste, healthy, firm, upright, hard, candid nature charmed him, without his being clearly aware of it, and without the idea of explaining it to himself having occurred to him. He admired his opposite by instinct. His soft, yielding, dislocated, sickly, shapeless ideas attached themselves to Enjolras as to a spinal column. His moral backbone leaned on that firmness. Grantaire in the presence of Enjolras became someone once more. He was, himself, moreover, composed of two elements, which were, to all appearance, incompatible. He was ironical and cordial. His indifference loved. His mind could get along without belief, but his heart could not get along without friendship. A profound contradiction; for an affection is a conviction. His nature was thus constituted. There are men who seem to be born to be the reverse, the obverse, the wrong side. They are Pollux, Patrocles, Nisus, Eudamidas, Ephestion, Pechmeja. They only exist on condition that they are backed up with another man; their name is a sequel, and is only written preceded by the conjunction *and*; and their existence is not their own; it is the other side of an existence which is not theirs. Grantaire was one of these men. He was the obverse of Enjolras.

One might almost say that affinities begin with the letters of the alphabet. In the series O and P are inseparable. You can, at will, pronounce O and P or Orestes and Pylades.

Grantaire, Enjolras's true satellite, inhabited this circle of young men; he lived there, he took no pleasure anywhere but there; he followed them everywhere. His joy was to see these forms go and come through the fumes of wine. They tolerated him on account of his good humor.

Enjolras, the believer, disdained this skeptic; and, a sober man himself, scorned this drunkard. He accorded him a little lofty pity. Grantaire was an unaccepted Pylades. Always harshly treated by Enjolras, roughly repulsed, rejected yet ever returning to the charge, he said of Enjolras: "What fine marble!"

Chapter II

BLONDEAU'S FUNERAL ORATION BY BOSSUET

ON A CERTAIN AFTERNOON, WHICH HAD, AS WILL BE SEEN HEREAFTER, SOME COINCIDENCE WITH the events heretofore related, Laigle de Meaux was to be seen leaning in a sensual manner against the doorpost of the Café Musain. He had the air of a caryatid on a vacation; he carried nothing but his reverie, however. He was staring at the Place Saint-Michel. To lean one's back against a thing is equivalent to lying down while standing erect, which attitude is not hated by thinkers. Laigle de Meaux was pondering, without melancholy, over a little misadventure which had befallen him two days previously at the law-school, and which had modified his personal plans for the future, plans which were rather indistinct in any case.

Reverie does not prevent a cab from passing by, nor the dreamer from taking note of that cab. Laigle de Meaux, whose eyes were straying about in a sort of diffuse lounging, perceived, athwart his somnambulism, a two-wheeled vehicle proceeding through the place, at a foot pace and apparently in indecision. For whom was this cabriolet? Why was it driving at a walk? Laigle took a survey. In it, beside the coachman, sat a young man, and in front of the young man lay a rather bulky hand-bag. The bag displayed to passers-by the following name inscribed in large black letters on a card which was sewn to the stuff: MARIUS PONTMERCY.

This name caused Laigle to change his attitude. He drew himself up and hurled this apostrophe at the young man in the cabriolet:

"Monsieur Marius Pontmercy!"

The cabriolet thus addressed came to a halt.

The young man, who also seemed deeply buried in thought, raised his eyes:

"Hey?" said he.

"You are M. Marius Pontmercy?"

"Certainly."

"I was looking for you," resumed Laigle de Meaux.

"How so?" demanded Marius; for it was he: in fact, he had just quitted his grandfather's, and had before him a face which he now beheld for the first time. "I do not know you."

"Neither do I know you," responded Laigle.

Marius thought he had encountered a wag, the beginning of a mystification in the open street. He was not in a very good humor at the moment. He frowned. Laigle de Meaux went on imperturbably:

"You were not at the school day before yesterday."

"That is possible."

"That is certain."

"You are a student?" demanded Marius.

"Yes, sir. Like yourself. Day before yesterday, I entered the school, by chance. You know, one does have such freaks sometimes. The professor was just calling the roll. You are not unaware that they are very ridiculous on such occasions. At the third call, unanswered, your name is erased from the list. Sixty francs in the gulf."

Marius began to listen.

"It was Blondeau who was making the call. You know Blondeau, he has a very pointed and very malicious nose, and he delights to scent out the absent. He slyly began with the letter P. I was not listening, not being compromised by that letter. The call was not going badly. No erasures; the universe was present. Blondeau was grieved. I said to myself: 'Blondeau, my love, you will not get the very smallest sort of an execution to-day.' All at once Blondeau calls, 'Marius Pontmercy!' No one answers. Blondeau, filled with hope, repeats more loudly: 'Marius Pontmercy!' And he takes his pen. Monsieur, I have bowels of compassion. I said to myself hastily: 'Here's a brave fellow who is going to get scratched out. Attention. Here is a veritable mortal who is not exact. He's not a good student. Here is none of your heavy-sides, a student who studies, a greenhorn pedant, strong on letters, theology, science, and sapience, one of those dull wits cut by the square; a pin by profession. He is an honorable idler who lounges, who practices country jaunts, who cultivates the grisette, who pays court to the fair sex, who is at this very moment, perhaps, with my mistress. Let us save him. Death to Blondeau!' At that moment, Blondeau dipped his pen in, all black with erasures in the ink, cast his yellow eyes round the audience room, and repeated for the third time: 'Marius Pontmercy!' I replied: 'Present!' This is why you were not crossed off."

"Monsieur!—" said Marius.

"And why I was," added Laigle de Meaux.

"I do not understand you," said Marius.

Laigle resumed:

"Nothing is more simple. I was close to the desk to reply, and close to the door for the purpose of flight. The professor gazed at me with a certain intensity. All of a sudden, Blondeau, who must be the malicious nose alluded to by Boileau, skipped to the letter L. L is my letter. I am from Meaux, and my name is Lesgle."

"L'Aigle!" interrupted Marius, "what a fine name!"

"Monsieur, Blondeau came to this fine name, and called: 'Laigle!' I reply: 'Present!' Then Blondeau gazes at me, with the gentleness of a tiger, and says to me: 'If you are Pontmercy, you are not Laigle.' A phrase which has a disobliging air for you, but which was lugubrious only for me. That said, he crossed me off."

Marius exclaimed:

"I am mortified, sir—"

"First of all," interposed Laigle, "I demand permission to embalm Blondeau in a few phrases of deeply felt eulogium. I will assume that he is dead. There will be no great change required in his gauntness, in his pallor, in his coldness, and in his smell. And I say: '*Erudimini qui judicatis terram.* Here lies Blondeau, Blondeau the Nose, Blondeau Nasica, the ox of discipline, *bos disciplinae*, the bloodhound of the password, the angel of the roll-call, who was upright, square, exact, rigid, honest, and hideous. God crossed him off as he crossed me off.'"

Marius resumed:

"I am very sorry—"

"Young man," said Laigle de Meaux, "let this serve you as a lesson. In future, be exact."

"I really beg you a thousand pardons."

"Do not expose your neighbor to the danger of having his name erased again."

"I am extremely sorry—"

Laigle burst out laughing.

"And I am delighted. I was on the brink of becoming a lawyer. This erasure saves me. I renounce the triumphs of the bar. I shall not defend the widow, and I shall not attack the orphan. No more toga, no more stage. Here is my erasure all ready for me. It is to you that I am indebted for it, Monsieur Pontmercy. I intend to pay a solemn call of thanks upon you. Where do you live?"

"In this cab," said Marius.

"A sign of opulence," retorted Laigle calmly. "I congratulate you. You have there a rent of nine thousand francs per annum."

At that moment, Courfeyrac emerged from the café.

Marius smiled sadly.

"I have paid this rent for the last two hours, and I aspire to get rid of it; but, there is a sort of history attached to it, and I don't know where to go."

"Come to my place, sir," said Courfeyrac.

"I have the priority," observed Laigle, "but I have no home."

"Hold your tongue, Bossuet," said Courfeyrac.

"Bossuet," said Marius, "but I thought that your name was Laigle."

"De Meaux," replied Laigle; "by metaphor, Bossuet."

Courfeyrac entered the cab.

"Coachman," said he, "Hôtel de la Porte-Saint-Jacques."

And that very evening, Marius found himself installed in a chamber of the Hôtel de la Porte-Saint-Jacques side by side with Courfeyrac.

Chapter III

MARIUS'S ASTONISHMENTS

IN A FEW DAYS, MARIUS HAD BECOME COURFEYRAC'S FRIEND. YOUTH IS THE SEASON FOR PROMPT welding and the rapid healing of scars. Marius breathed freely in Courfeyrac's society, a decidedly new thing for him. Courfeyrac put no questions to him. He did not even think of such a thing. At that age, faces disclose everything on the spot. Words are superfluous. There are young men of whom it can be said that their countenances chatter. One looks at them and one knows them.

One morning, however, Courfeyrac abruptly addressed this interrogation to him:

"By the way, have you any political opinions?"

"The idea!" said Marius, almost affronted by the question.

"What are you?"

"A democrat-Bonapartist."

"The gray hue of a reassured rat," said Courfeyrac.

On the following day, Courfeyrac introduced Marius at the Café Musain. Then he whispered in his ear, with a smile: "I must give you your entry to the revolution." And he led him to the hall of the Friends of the A B C. He presented him to the other comrades, saying this simple word which Marius did not understand: "A pupil."

Marius had fallen into a wasps'-nest of wits. However, although he was silent and grave, he was, none the less, both winged and armed.

Marius, up to that time solitary and inclined to soliloquy, and to asides, both by habit and by taste, was a little fluttered by this covey of young men around him. All these various initiatives solicited his attention at once, and pulled him about. The tumultuous movements of these minds at liberty and at work set his ideas in a whirl. Sometimes, in his trouble, they fled so far from him, that he had difficulty in recovering them. He heard them talk of philosophy, of literature, of art, of history, of religion, in unexpected fashion. He caught glimpses of strange aspects; and, as he did not place them in proper perspective, he was not altogether sure that it was not chaos that he grasped. On abandoning his grandfather's opinions for the opinions of his father, he had supposed himself fixed; he now suspected, with uneasiness, and without daring to avow it to himself, that he was not. The angle at which he saw everything began to be displaced anew. A certain oscillation set all the horizons of his brains in motion. An odd internal upsetting. He almost suffered from it.

It seemed as though there were no "consecrated things" for those young men. Marius heard singular propositions on every sort of subject, which embarrassed his still timid mind.

A theater poster presented itself, adorned with the title of a tragedy from the ancient repertory called classic: "Down with tragedy dear to the bourgeois!" cried Bahorel. And Marius heard Combeferre reply:

"You are wrong, Bahorel. The bourgeoisie loves tragedy, and the bourgeoisie must be left at peace on that score. Bewigged tragedy has a reason for its existence, and I am not one of those who, by order of Æschylus, contest its right to existence. There are rough outlines in nature; there are, in creation, ready-made parodies; a beak which is not a beak, wings which are not wings, gills which are not gills, paws which are not paws, a cry of pain which arouses a desire to laugh, there is the duck. Now, since poultry exists by the side of the bird, I do not see why classic tragedy should not exist in the face of antique tragedy."

Or chance decreed that Marius should traverse Rue Jean-Jacques Rousseau between Enjolras and Courfeyrac.

Courfeyrac took his arm:

"Pay attention. This is the Rue Plâtrière, now called Rue Jean-Jacques Rousseau, on account of a singular household which lived in it sixty years ago. This consisted of Jean-Jacques and Thérèse. From time to time, little beings were born there. Thérèse gave birth to them, Jean-Jacques represented them as foundlings."

And Enjolras addressed Courfeyrac roughly:

"Silence in the presence of Jean-Jacques! I admire that man. He denied his own children, that may be; but he adopted the people."

Not one of these young men articulated the word: The Emperor. Jean Prouvaire alone sometimes said Napoleon; all the others said "Bonaparte." Enjolras pronounced it "Buonaparte."

Marius was vaguely surprised. *Initium sapientiae.*

Chapter IV

THE BACK ROOM OF THE CAFÉ MUSAIN

ONE OF THE CONVERSATIONS AMONG THE YOUNG MEN, AT WHICH MARIUS WAS PRESENT AND IN which he sometimes joined, was a veritable shock to his mind.

This took place in the back room of the Café Musain. Nearly all the Friends of the Λ B C had convened that evening. The argand lamp was solemnly lighted. They talked of one thing and another, without passion and with noise. With the exception of Enjolras and Marius, who held their peace, all were haranguing rather at haphazard. Conversations between comrades sometimes are subject to these peaceable tumults. It was a game and an uproar as much as a conversation. They tossed words to each other and caught them up in turn. They were chattering in all quarters.

No woman was admitted to this back room, except Louison, the dish-washer of the café, who passed through it from time to time, to go to her washing in the "lavatory."

Grantaire, thoroughly drunk, was deafening the corner of which he had taken possession, reasoning and contradicting at the top of his lungs, and shouting:

"I am thirsty. Mortals, I am dreaming: that the tun of Heidelberg has an attack of apoplexy, and that I am one of the dozen leeches which will be applied to it. I want a drink. I desire to forget life. Life is a hideous invention of I know not whom. It lasts no time at all, and is worth nothing. One breaks one's neck in living. Life is a theater set in which there are but few practicable entrances. Happiness is an antique reliquary painted on one side only. Ecclesiastes says: 'All is vanity.' I agree with that good man, who never existed, perhaps. Zero not wishing to go stark naked, clothed himself in vanity. O vanity! The patching up of everything with big words! a kitchen is a laboratory, a dancer is a professor, an acrobat is a gymnast, a boxer is a pugilist, an apothecary is a chemist, a wigmaker is an artist, a hodman is an architect, a jockey is a sportsman, a wood-louse is a pterigybranche. Vanity has a right and a wrong side; the right side is stupid, it is the negro with his glass beads; the wrong side is foolish, it is the philosopher with his rags. I weep over the one and I laugh over the other. What are called honors and dignities, and even dignity and honor, are generally of pinchbeck. Kings make playthings of human pride. Caligula made a horse a consul; Charles II made a knight of a sirloin. Wrap yourself up now, then, between Consul Incitatus and Baronet Roastbeef. As for the intrinsic value of people, it is no longer respectable in the least. Listen to the panegyric which neighbor makes of neighbor. White on white is ferocious; if the lily could speak, what a setting down it would give the dove! A bigoted woman prating of a devout woman is more venomous than the asp and the cobra. It is a shame that I am ignorant, otherwise I would quote to you a mass of things; but I know nothing. For instance, I have always been witty; when I was a pupil of Gros, instead of daubing wretched little pictures, I passed my time in pilfering apples; rapin[1] is the masculine of rapine. So much for myself; as for the rest of you, you are worth no more than I am. I scoff at your perfections, excellencies, and qualities. Every good quality tends toward a defect; economy borders on avarice, the generous man is next door to the prodigal, the brave man rubs elbows with the braggart; he who says very pious says a trifle bigoted; there are just as many vices in virtue as there are holes in Diogenes's cloak. Whom do you admire, the slain or the slayer, Cæsar or Brutus? Generally men are in favor of the slayer. Long live Brutus, he has slain! There lies the virtue. Virtue, granted, but madness also. There are queer spots on those great men. The Brutus who killed Cæsar was in love with the statue of a little boy. This statue was from the hand of the Greek sculp-

1. The slang term for a painter's assistant.

tor Strongylion, who also carved that figure of an Amazon known as the Beautiful Leg, Eucnemos, which Nero carried with him in his travels. This Strongylion left but two statues which placed Nero and Brutus in accord. Brutus was in love with the one, Nero with the other. All history is nothing but wearisome repetition. One century is the plagiarist of the other. The battle of Marengo copies the battle of Pydna; the Tolbiac of Clovis and the Austerlitz of Napoleon are as like each other as two drops of water. I don't attach much importance to victory. Nothing is so stupid as to conquer; true glory lies in convincing. But try to prove something! If you are content with success, what mediocrity, and with conquering, what wretchedness! Alas, vanity and cowardice everywhere. Everything obeys success, even grammar. *Si volet usus,* says Horace. Therefore I disdain the human race. Shall we descend to the party at all? Do you wish me to begin admiring the peoples? what people, if you please? Shall it be Greece? The Athenians, those Parisians of days gone by, slew Phocion, as we might say Coligny, and fawned upon tyrants to such an extent that Anacephorus said of Pisistratus: "His urine attracts the bees." The most prominent man in Greece for fifty years was that grammarian Philetas, who was so small and so thin that he was obliged to load his shoes with lead in order not to be blown away by the wind. There stood on the great square in Corinth a statue carved by Silanion and catalogued by Pliny; this statue represented Episthates. What did Episthates do? He invented a trip. That sums up Greece and glory. Let us pass on to others. Shall I admire England? Shall I admire France? France? Why? Because of Paris? I have just told you my opinion of Athens. England? Why? Because of London? I hate Carthage. And then, London, the metropolis of luxury, is the headquarters of wretchedness. There are a hundred deaths a year of hunger in the parish of Charing-Cross alone. Such is Albion. I add, as the climax, that I have seen an Englishwoman dancing in a wreath of roses and blue spectacles. A fig then for England! If I do not admire John Bull, shall I admire Brother Jonathan? I have but little taste for that slaveholding brother. Take away *Time is money,* what remains of England? Take away *Cotton is king,* what remains of America? Germany is the lymph, Italy is the bile. Shall we go into ecstasies over Russia? Voltaire admired it. He also admired China. I admit that Russia has its beauties, among others, a stout despotism; but I pity the despots. Their health is delicate. A decapitated Alexis, a poignarded Peter, a strangled Paul, another Paul crushed flat with kicks, divers Ivans strangled, with their throats cut, numerous Nicholases and Basils poisoned, all this indicates that the palace of the Emperors of Russia is in a condition of flagrant insalubrity. All civilized peoples offer this detail to the admiration of the thinker; war; now, war, civilized war, exhausts and sums up all the forms of ruffianism, from the brigandage of the Trabuceros in the gorges of Mont Jaxa to the marauding of the Comanche Indians in the Doubtful Pass. 'Bah!' you will say to me, 'but Europe is certainly better than Asia?' I admit that Asia is a farce; but I do not precisely see what you find to laugh at in the Grand Lama, you peoples of the west, who have mingled with your fashions and your elegances all the complicated filth of majesty, from the dirty chemise of Queen Isabella to the chamber-chair of the Dauphin. Gentlemen of the human race, I tell you, not a bit of it! It is at Brussels that the most beer is consumed, at Stockholm the most brandy, at Madrid the most chocolate, at Amsterdam the most gin, at London the most wine, at Constantinople the most coffee, at Paris the most absinthe; there are all the useful notions. Paris carries the day, in short. In Paris, even the rag-pickers are sybarites; Diogenes would have loved to be a rag-picker of the Place Maubert better than to be a philosopher at the Piræus. Learn this in addition; the wine-shops of the rag-pickers are called *bibines*; the most celebrated are the *Saucepan* and *The Slaughter-House.* Hence, tea-gardens, goguettes, caboulots, bouibuis, mastroquets, bastringues, manezingues, bibines of the rag-pickers, caravanseries of the caliphs, I certify to you, I am a voluptuary, I eat at Richard's at forty sous a head, I must have Persian carpets to roll naked Cleopatra in! Where is Cleopatra? Ah! So it is you, Louison. Good day."

Thus did Grantaire, more than intoxicated, launch into speech, catching at the dish-washer in her passage, from his corner in the back room of the Café Musain.

Bossuet, extending his hand toward him, tried to impose silence on him, and Grantaire began again worse than ever:

"Aigle de Meaux, down with your paws. You produce on me no effect with your gesture of Hippocrates refusing Artaxerxes's bric-à-brac. I excuse you from the task of soothing me. Moreover, I am sad. What do you wish me to say to you? Man is evil, man is deformed; the butterfly is a success, man is a failure. God made a mistake with that animal. A crowd offers a choice of ugliness. The first comer is a wretch. *Femme*—woman—rhymes with *infâme*—infamous. Yes, I have the spleen, complicated with melancholy, with homesickness, plus hypochondria, and I am vexed and I rage, and I yawn, and I am bored, and I am tired to death, and I am stupid! Let God go to the devil!"

"Silence then, capital R!" resumed Bossuet, who was discussing a point of law behind the scenes, and who was plunged more than waist high in a phrase of judicial slang, of which this is the conclusion:

"—And as for me, although I am hardly a legist, and at the most, an amateur attorney, I maintain this: that, in accordance with the terms of the customs of Normandy, at Saint-Michel, and for each year, an equivalent must be paid to the profit of the lord of the manor, saving the rights of others, and by all and several, the proprietors as well as those seized with inheritance, and that, for all emphyteuses, leases, freeholds, contracts of domain, mortgages—"

"Echo, plaintive nymph," hummed Grantaire.

Near Grantaire, an almost silent table, a sheet of paper, an inkstand and a pen between two glasses of brandy, announced that a vaudeville was being sketched out.

This great affair was being discussed in a low voice, and the two heads at work touched each other: "Let us begin by finding names. When one has the names, one finds the subject."

"That is true. Dictate. I will write."

"Monsieur Dorimon."

"An independent gentleman?"

"Of course."

"His daughter, Célestine."

"——tine. What next?"

"Colonel Sainval."

"Sainval is stale. I should say Valsin."

Beside the vaudeville aspirants, another group, which was also taking advantage of the uproar to talk low, was discussing a duel. An old fellow of thirty was counseling a young one of eighteen, and explaining to him what sort of an adversary he had to deal with.

"The deuce! Look out for yourself. He is a fine swordsman. His play is neat. He has the attack, no wasted feints, wrist, dash, lightning, a just parade, mathematical parries, *bigre!* and he is left-handed."

In the angle opposite Grantaire, Joly and Bahorel were playing dominoes, and talking of love.

"You are in luck, that you are," Joly was saying. "You have a mistress who is always laughing."

"That is a fault of hers," returned Bahorel. "One's mistress does wrong to laugh. That encourages one to deceive her. To see her gay removes your remorse; if you see her sad, your conscience pricks you."

"Ingrate! a woman who laughs is such a good thing! And you never quarrel!"

"That is because of the treaty which we have made. On forming our little Holy Alliance we assigned ourselves each our frontier, which we never cross. What is situated on the side of winter belongs to Vaud, on the side of the wind to Gex. Hence the peace."

"Peace is happiness digesting."

"And you, Jollly, where do you stand in your entanglement with Mamselle—you know whom I mean."

"She sulks at me with cruel patience."

"Yet you are a lover to soften the heart with gauntness."

"Alas!"

"In your place, I would let her alone."

"That is easy enough to say."

"And to do. Is not her name Musichetta?"

"Yes. Ah! my poor Bahorel, she is a superb girl, very literary, with tiny feet, little hands, she dresses well, and is white and dimpled, with the eyes of a fortune-teller. I am wild over her."

"My dear fellow, then in order to please her, you must be elegant, and produce effects with your knees. Buy a good pair of trousers of double-milled cloth at Staub's. That will assist."

"At what price?" shouted Grantaire.

The third corner was delivered up to a poetical discussion. Pagan mythology was giving battle to Christian mythology. The question was about Olympus, whose part was taken by Jean Prouvaire, out of pure romanticism.

Jean Prouvaire was timid only in repose. Once excited, he burst forth, a sort of mirth accentuated his enthusiasm, and he was at once both laughing and lyric.

"Let us not insult the gods," said he. "The gods may not have taken their departure. Jupiter does not impress me as dead. The gods are dreams, you say. Well, even in nature, such as it is to-day, after the flight of these dreams, we still find all the grand old pagan myths. Such and such a mountain with the profile of a citadel, like the Vignemale, for example, is still to me the headdress of Cybele; it has not been proved to me that Pan does not come at night to breathe into the hollow trunks of the willows, stopping up the holes in turn with his fingers, and I have always believed that Io had something to do with the cascade of Pissevache."

In the last corner, they were talking politics. The Charter which had been granted was getting roughly handled. Combeferre was upholding it weakly. Courfeyrac was energetically making a breach in it. On the table lay an unfortunate copy of the famous Touquet Charter. Courfeyrac had seized it, and was brandishing it, mingling with his arguments the rattling of this sheet of paper.

"In the first place, I won't have any kings; if it were only from an economical point of view, I don't want any; a king is a parasite. One does not have kings gratis. Listen to this: the dearness of kings. At the death of François I, the national debt of France amounted to an income of thirty thousand livres; at the death of Louis XIV it was two milliards, six hundred millions, at twenty-eight livres the mark, which was equivalent in 1760, according to Desmarets, to four milliards, five hundred millions, which would to-day be equivalent to twelve milliards. In the second place, and no offense to Combeferre, a charter granted is but a poor expedient of civilization. To save the transition, to soften the passage, to deaden the shock, to cause the nation to pass insensibly from the monarchy to democracy by the practice of constitutional fictions—what detestable reasons all those are! No! no! let us never enlighten the people with false daylight. Principles dwindle and pale in your constitutional cellar. No illegitimacy, no compromise, no grant from the king to the people. In all such grants there is an Article 14. By the side of the hand which gives there is the claw which snatches back. I refuse your charter point-blank. A charter is a mask; the lie lurks beneath it. A people which accepts a charter abdicates. The law is only the law when entire. No! no charter!"

It was winter; a couple of fagots were crackling in the fireplace. This was tempting, and Courfeyrac could not resist. He crumpled the poor Touquet Charter in his fist, and flung it in the fire. The paper flashed up. Combeferre watched the masterpiece of Louis XVIII burn philosophically, and contented himself with saying:

"The charter metamorphosed into flame."

And sarcasms, sallies, jests, that French thing which is called *entrain*, and that English thing which is called humor, good and bad taste, good and bad reasons, all the wild pyrotechnics of dialogue, mounting together and crossing from all points of the room, produced a sort of merry bombardment over their heads.

Chapter V

ENLARGEMENT OF HORIZON

THE SHOCKS OF YOUTHFUL MINDS AMONG THEMSELVES HAVE THIS ADMIRABLE PROPERTY, THAT one can never foresee the spark, nor divine the lightning flash. What will dart out presently? No one knows. The burst of laughter starts from a tender feeling.

At the moment of jest, the serious makes its entry. Impulses depend on the first chance word. The spirit of each is sovereign, jest suffices to open the field to the unexpected. These are conversations with abrupt turns, in which the perspective changes suddenly. Chance is the stage-manager of such conversations.

A severe thought, starting oddly from a clash of words, suddenly traversed the conflict of quips in which Grantaire, Bahorel, Prouvaire, Bossuet, Combeferre, and Courfeyrac were confusedly fencing.

How does a phrase crop up in a dialogue? Whence comes it that it suddenly impresses itself on the attention of those who hear it? We have just said, that no one knows anything about it. In the midst of the uproar, Bossuet all at once terminated some apostrophe to Combeferre, with this date:

"June 18th, 1815: Waterloo."

At this name of Waterloo, Marius, who was leaning his elbows on a table, beside a glass of water, removed his wrist from beneath his chin, and began to gaze fixedly at the audience.

"Pardieu!" exclaimed Courfeyrac ("Parbleu" was falling into disuse at this period), "that number 18 is strange and strikes me. It is Bonaparte's fatal number. Place Louis in front and Brumaire behind, you have the whole destiny of the man, with this significant peculiarity, that the end treads close on the heels of the commencement."

Enjolras, who had remained mute up to that point, broke the silence and addressed this remark to Combeferre:

"You mean to say, the crime and the expiation."

This word *crime* overpassed the measure of what Marius, who was already greatly agitated by the abrupt evocation of Waterloo, could accept.

He rose, walked slowly to the map of France spread out on the wall, and at whose base an island was visible in a separate compartment, laid his finger on this compartment and said:

"Corsica, a little island which has rendered France very great."

This was like a breath of icy air. All ceased talking. They felt that something was on the point of occurring.

Bahorel, replying to Bossuet, was just assuming an attitude of the torso to which he was addicted. He gave it up to listen.

Enjolras, whose blue eye was not fixed on anyone, and who seemed to be gazing at space, replied, without glancing at Marius:

"France needs no Corsica to be great. France is great because she is France. *Quia nomina leo.*"

Marius felt no desire to retreat; he turned toward Enjolras, and his voice burst forth with a vibration which came from a quiver of his very being:

"God forbid that I should diminish France! But amalgamating Napoleon with her is not diminishing her. Come! let us argue the question. I am a newcomer among you, but I will confess that you amaze me. Where do we stand? Who are we? Who are you? Who am I? Let us come to an explanation about the Emperor. I hear you say *Buonaparte*, accenting the *u* like the royalists. I warn you that my grandfather does better still; he says *Buonaparté*. I thought you were young men. Where, then, is your enthusiasm? And what are you doing with it? Whom do you admire, if you do not admire the Emperor? And what more do you want? If you will have none of that great man, what great men would you like? He had everything. He was complete. He had in his brain the sum of human faculties. He made codes like Justinian, he dictated like Cæsar, his conversation was mingled with the lightning flash of Pascal, with the thunderclap of Tacitus, he made history and he wrote it, his bulletins are Iliads, he combined the cipher of Newton with the metaphor of Mahomet, he left behind him in the East words as great as the pyramids, at Tilsit he taught Emperors majesty, at the Academy of Sciences he replied to Laplace, in the Council of State be held his own against Merlin, he gave a soul to the geometry of the first, and to the chicanery of the last, he was a legist with the attorneys and sidereal with the astronomers; like Cromwell blowing out one of two candles, he went to the Temple to bargain for a curtain tassel; he saw everything; he knew everything; which did not prevent him from laughing good-naturedly beside the cradle of his little child; and all at once, frightened Europe lent an ear, armies put themselves in motion, parks of artillery rumbled, pontoons stretched over the rivers, clouds of cavalry galloped in the storm, cries, trumpets, a trembling of thrones in every direction, the frontiers of kingdoms oscillated on the map, the sound of a superhuman sword was heard, as it was drawn from its sheath; they beheld him, him, rise erect on the horizon with a blazing brand in his hand, and a glow in his eyes, unfolding amid the thunder, his two wings, the grand army and the old guard, and he was the archangel of war!"

All held their peace, and Enjolras bowed his head. Silence always produces somewhat the effect of acquiescence, of the enemy being driven to the wall. Marius continued with increased enthusiasm, and almost without pausing for breath:

"Let us be just, my friends! What a splendid destiny for a nation to be the Empire of such an Emperor, when that nation is France and when it adds its own genius to the genius of that man! To appear and to reign, to march and to triumph, to have for halting-places all capitals, to take his grenadiers and to make kings of them, to decree the falls of dynasties, and to transfigure Europe at the pace of a charge; to make you feel that when you threaten you lay your hand on the hilt of the sword of God; to follow in a single man, Hannibal, Cæsar, Charlemagne; to be the people of someone who mingles with your dawns the startling announcement of a battle won, to have the cannon of the Invalides to rouse you in the morning, to hurl into abysses of light prodigious words which flame forever, Marengo, Arcola, Austerlitz, Jena, Wagram! To cause constellations of victories to flash forth at each instant from the zenith of the centuries, to make the French Empire a pendant to the Roman Empire, to be the great nation and to give birth to the grand army, to make its legions fly forth over all the earth, as a mountain sends out its eagles on all sides to conquer, to dominate, to strike with lightning, to be in Europe a sort of nation gilded through glory, to sound athwart the centuries a trumpet-blast of Titans, to conquer the world twice, by conquest and by dazzling, that is sublime; and what greater thing is there?"

"To be free," said Combeferre.

Marius lowered his head in his turn; that cold and simple word had traversed his epic effusion like a blade of steel, and he felt it vanishing within him. When he raised his eyes, Combeferre was no longer there. Probably satisfied with his reply to the apotheosis, he had just taken his departure, and all, with the exception of Enjolras, had followed him. The room had been emptied. Enjolras, left alone with Marius, was gazing gravely at him. Marius, however, having rallied his ideas to some extent, did not consider himself beaten; there lingered in him a trace of inward fermentation which was on the point, no doubt, of translating itself into syllogisms arrayed against Enjolras, when all of a sudden, they heard someone singing on the stairs as he went. It was Combeferre, and this is what he was singing:

"Si César m'avait donné
La gloire et la guerre,
Et qu'il me fallait quitter
L'amour de ma mère,
Je dirais au grand César:
Reprends ton sceptre et ton char,
J'aime mieux ma mère, ô gué!
J'aime mieux ma mère!"[1]

The wild and tender accents with which Combeferre sang communicated to this couplet a sort of strange grandeur. Marius, thoughtfully, and with his eyes diked on the ceiling, repeated almost mechanically: "My mother?—"

At that moment, he felt Enjolras's hand on his shoulder.

"Citizen," said Enjolras to him, "my mother is the Republic."

Chapter VI

RES ANGUSTA

THAT EVENING LEFT MARIUS PROFOUNDLY SHAKEN, AND WITH A MELANCHOLY SHADOW IN HIS soul. He felt what the earth may possibly feel, at the moment when it is torn open with the iron, in order that grain may be deposited within it; it feels only the wound; the quiver of the germ and the joy of the fruit only arrive later.

Marius was gloomy. He had but just acquired a faith; must he then reject it already? He affirmed to himself that he would not. He declared to himself that he would not doubt, and he began to doubt in spite of himself. To stand between two religions, from one of which you have not as yet emerged, and another into which you have not yet entered, is intolerable; and twilight is pleasing only to bat-like souls. Marius was clear-eyed, and he required the true light. The half-lights of doubt pained him. Whatever may have been his desire to remain where he was, he could not halt there, he was irresistibly constrained to continue, to advance, to examine, to think, to march further. Whither would this lead him? He feared, after having taken so many steps which had brought him nearer to his father, to now take a step which should estrange him from that father. His discomfort was augmented by all the reflections which occurred to him. An escarpment rose around him. He was in accord neither with his grandfather nor with his friends; daring in the eyes of the one, he was behind the times in the eyes of the others; and he recognized the fact that he was doubly isolated, on the side of age and on the side of youth. He ceased to go to the Café Musain.

In the troubled state of his conscience, he no longer thought of certain serious sides of existence. The realities of life do not allow themselves to be forgotten. They soon elbowed him abruptly.

One morning, the proprietor of the hôtel entered Marius's room and said to him:

"Monsieur Courfeyrac answered for you."

---

1. If Cæsar had given me glory and war, and I were obliged to quit my mother's love, I would say to great Cæsar, "Take back thy scepter and thy chariot; I prefer the love of my mother."

"Yes."

"But I must have my money."

"Request Courfeyrac to come and talk with me," said Marius.

Courfeyrac having made his appearance, the host left them. Marius then told him what it had not before occurred to him to relate, that he was the same as alone in the world, and had no relatives.

"What is to become of you?" said Courfeyrac.

"I do not know in the least," replied Marius.

"What are you going to do?"

"I do not know."

"Have you any money?"

"Fifteen francs."

"Do you want me to lend you some?"

"Never."

"Have you clothes?"

"Here is what I have."

"Have you trinkets?"

"A watch."

"Silver?"

"Gold; here it is."

"I know a clothes-dealer who will take your frock-coat and a pair of trousers."

"That is good."

"You will then have only a pair of trousers, a waistcoat, a hat and a coat."

"And my boots."

"What! you will not go barefoot? What opulence!"

"That will be enough."

"I know a watchmaker who will buy your watch."

"That is good."

"No; it is not good. What will you do after that?"

"Whatever is necessary. Anything honest, that is to say."

"Do you know English?"

"No."

"Do you know German?"

"No."

"So much the worse."

"Why?"

"Because one of my friends, a publisher, is getting up a sort of an encyclopedia, for which you might have translated English or German articles. It is badly paid work, but one can live by it."

"I will learn English and German."

"And in the meanwhile?"

"In the meanwhile I will live on my clothes and my watch."

The clothes-dealer was sent for. He paid twenty francs for the cast-off garments. They went to the watchmaker's. He bought the watch for forty-five francs.

"That is not bad," said Marius to Courfeyrac, on their return to the hôtel, "with my fifteen francs, that makes eighty."

"And the hôtel bill?" observed Courfeyrac.

"Hello, I had forgotten that," said Marius.

The landlord presented his bill, which had to be paid on the spot. It amounted to seventy francs.

"I have ten francs left," said Marius.

"The deuce," exclaimed Courfeyrac, "you will eat up five francs while you are learning English, and five while learning German. That will be swallowing a tongue very fast, or a hundred sous very slowly."

In the meantime Aunt Gillenormand, a rather good-hearted person at bottom in difficulties, had finally hunted up Marius's abode.

One morning, on his return from the law-school, Marius found a letter from his aunt, and the *sixty pistoles,* that is to say, six hundred francs in gold, in a sealed box.

Marius sent back the thirty louis to his aunt, with a respectful letter, in which he stated that he had sufficient means of subsistence and that he should be able thenceforth to supply all his needs. At that moment, he had three francs left.

His aunt did not inform his grandfather of this refusal, for fear of exasperating him. Besides, had he not said: "Let me never hear the name of that blood-drinker again!"

Marius left the Hôtel de la Porte Saint-Jacques, as he did not wish to run in debt there.

BOOK FIFTH

THE EXCELLENCE OF MISFORTUNE

Chapter I

MARIUS INDIGENT

LIFE BECAME HARD FOR MARIUS. IT WAS NOTHING TO EAT HIS CLOTHES AND HIS WATCH. HE ATE of that terrible, inexpressible thing that is called *de la vache enragé*; that is to say, he endured great hardships and privations. A terrible thing it is, containing days without bread, nights without sleep, evenings without a candle, a hearth without a fire, weeks without work, a future without hope, a coat out at the elbows, an old hat which evokes the laughter of young girls, a door which one finds locked on one at night because one's rent is not paid, the insolence of the porter and the cook-shop man, the sneers of neighbors, humiliations, dignity trampled on, work of whatever nature accepted, disgusts, bitterness, despondency. Marius learned how all this is eaten, and how such are often the only things which one has to devour. At that moment of his existence when a man needs his pride, because he needs love, he felt that he was jeered at because he was badly dressed, and ridiculous because he was poor. At the age when youth swells the heart with imperial pride, he dropped his eyes more than once on his dilapidated boots, and he knew the unjust shame and the poignant blushes of wretchedness. Admirable and terrible trial from which the feeble emerge base, from which the strong emerge sublime. A crucible into which destiny casts a man, whenever it desires a scoundrel or a demi-god.

For many great deeds are performed in petty combats. There are instances of bravery ignored and obstinate, which defend themselves step by step in that fatal onslaught of necessities and turpitudes. Noble and mysterious triumphs which no eye beholds, which are requited with no renown, which are saluted with no trumpet-blast. Life, misfortune, isolation, abandonment, poverty, are the fields of battle which have their heroes; obscure heroes, who are, sometimes, grander than the heroes who win renown.

Firm and rare natures are thus created; misery, almost always a step-mother, is sometimes a mother; destitution gives birth to might of soul and spirit; distress is the nurse of pride; unhappiness is a good milk for the magnanimous.

There came a moment in Marius's life, when he swept his own landing, when he bought his sou's worth of Brie cheese at the fruiterer's, when he waited until twilight had fallen to slip into the baker's and purchase a loaf, which he carried off furtively to his attic as though he had stolen it. Sometimes there could be seen gliding into the butcher's shop on the corner, in the midst of the bantering cooks who elbowed him, an awkward young man, carrying big books under his arm, who had a timid yet angry air, who, on entering, removed his hat from a brow whereon stood drops of perspiration, made a profound bow to the butcher's astonished wife, asked for a mutton cutlet, paid six or seven sous for it, wrapped it up in a paper, put it under his arm, between two books, and went away. It was Marius. On this cutlet, which he cooked for himself, he lived for three days.

On the first day he ate the meat, on the second he ate the fat, on the third he gnawed the bone. Aunt Gillenormand made repeated attempts, and sent him the sixty pistoles several times. Marius returned them on every occasion, saying that he needed nothing.

He was still in mourning for his father when the revolution which we have just described was effected within him. From that time forth, he had not put off his black garments. But his garments were quitting him. The day came when he had no longer a coat. The trousers would go next. What was to be done? Courfeyrac, to whom he had, on his side, done some good turns, gave him an old coat. For thirty sous, Marius got it turned by some porter or other, and it was a new coat. But this coat was green. Then Marius ceased to go out until after nightfall. This made his coat black. As he wished always to appear in mourning, he clothed himself with the night.

In spite of all this, he got admitted to practice as a lawyer. He was supposed to live in Courfeyrac's room, which was decent, and where a certain number of law-books backed up and completed by several dilapidated volumes of romance, passed as the library required by the regulations. He had his letters addressed to Courfeyrac's quarters.

When Marius became a lawyer, he informed his grandfather of the fact in a letter which was cold but full of submission and respect. M. Gillenormand trembled as he took the letter, read it, tore it in four pieces, and threw it into the waste-basket. Two or three days later, Mademoiselle Gillenormand heard her father, who was alone in his room, talking aloud to himself. He always did this whenever he was greatly agitated. She listened, and the old man was saying: "If you were not a fool, you would know that one cannot be a baron and a lawyer at the same time."

Chapter II

MARIUS POOR

IT IS THE SAME WITH WRETCHEDNESS AS WITH EVERYTHING ELSE. IT ENDS BY BECOMING BEARABLE. It finally assumes a form, and adjusts itself. One vegetates, that is to say, one develops in a certain meager fashion, which is, however, sufficient for life. This is the mode in which the existence of Marius Pontmercy was arranged:

He had passed the worst straits; the narrow pass was opening out a little in front of him. By dint of toil, perseverance, courage, and will, he had managed to draw from his work about seven hundred francs a year. He had learned German and English; thanks to Courfeyrac, who had put him in communication with his friend the publisher, Marius filled the modest post of utility man in the literature of the publishing house. He drew up prospectuses, translated newspapers, annotated editions, compiled biographies, etc.; net product, year in and year out, seven hundred francs. He lived on it. How? Not so badly. We will explain.

Marius occupied in the Gorbeau house, for an annual sum of thirty francs, a den minus a fireplace, called a cabinet, which contained only the most indispensable articles of furniture. This furniture belonged to him. He gave three francs a month to the old *principal tenant* to come and sweep his hole, and to bring him a little hot water every morning, a fresh egg, and a penny roll. He breakfasted on this egg and roll. His breakfast varied in cost from two to four sous, according as eggs were dear or cheap. At six o'clock in the evening he descended the Rue Saint-Jacques to dine at Rousseau's, opposite Basset's, the stamp-dealer's, on the corner of the Rue des Mathurins. He ate no soup. He took a six-sou plate of meat, a half-portion of vegetables for three sous, and a three-sou dessert. For three sous he got as much bread as he wished. As for wine, he drank water. When he paid at the desk where Madam Rousseau, at that period still plump and rosy majestically presided, he gave a sou to the waiter, and Madam Rousseau gave him a smile. Then he went away. For sixteen sous he had a smile and a dinner.

This Restaurant Rousseau, where so few bottles and so many water carafes were emptied, was a calming potion rather than a restaurant. It no longer exists. The proprietor had a fine nickname: he was called *Rousseau the Aquatic.*

Thus, breakfast four sous, dinner sixteen sous; his food cost him twenty sous a day; which made three hundred and sixty-five francs a year. Add the thirty francs for rent, and the thirty-six francs to the old woman, plus a few trifling expenses; for four hundred and fifty francs, Marius was fed, lodged, and waited on. His clothing cost him a hundred francs, his linen fifty francs, his washing fifty francs; the whole did not exceed six hundred and fifty francs. He was rich. He sometimes lent ten francs to a friend. Courfeyrac had once been able to borrow sixty francs of him. As far as fire was concerned, as Marius had no fireplace, he had "simplified matters."

Marius always had two complete suits of clothes, the one old, "for every day"; the other, brand new for special occasions. Both were black. He had but three shirts, one on his person, the second in the commode, and the third in the washerwoman's hands. He renewed them as they wore out. They were always ragged, which caused him to button his coat to the chin.

It had required years for Marius to attain to this flourishing condition. Hard years; difficult, some of them to traverse, others to climb. Marius had not failed for a single day. He had endured everything in the way of destitution; he had done everything except contract debts. He did himself the justice to say that he had never owed anyone a sou. A debt was, to him, the beginning of slavery. He even said to himself, that a creditor is worse than a master; for the master possesses only your person, a creditor possesses your dignity and can administer to it a box on the ear. Rather than borrow, he went without food. He had passed many a day fasting. Feeling that all extremes meet, and that, if one is not on one's guard, lowered fortunes may lead to baseness of soul, he kept a jealous watch on his pride. Such and such a formality or action, which, in any other situation would have appeared merely a deference to him, now seemed insipidity, and he nerved himself against it. His face wore a sort of severe flush. He was timid even to rudeness.

During all these trials he had felt himself encouraged and even uplifted, at times, by a secret force that he possessed within himself. The soul aids the body, and at certain moments, raises it. It is the only bird which bears up its own cage.

Besides his father's name, another name was graven in Marius's heart, the name of Thénardier. Marius, with his grave and enthusiastic nature, surrounded with a sort of aureole the man to whom, in his thoughts, he owed his father's life—that intrepid sergeant who had saved the colonel amid the bullets and the cannon-balls of Waterloo. He never separated the memory of this man from the memory of his father, and he associated them in his veneration. It was a sort of worship in two steps, with the grand altar for the colonel and the lesser one for Thénardier. What redoubled the tenderness of his gratitude toward Thénardier, was the idea of the distress into which he knew that Thénardier had fallen, and which had engulfed the latter. Marius had learned at Montfermeil of the ruin and bankruptcy of the unfortunate inn-keeper. Since that time, he had made unheard-of efforts to find traces of him and to reach him in that dark abyss of misery in which Thénardier had disappeared. Marius had beaten the whole country; he had gone to Chelles, to Bondy, to Gourney, to Nogent, to Lagny. He had persisted for three years, expending in these explorations the little money which he had laid by. No one had been able to give him any news of Thénardier: he was supposed to have gone abroad. His creditors had also sought him, with less love than Marius, but with as much assiduity, and had not been able to lay their hands on him. Marius blamed himself, and was almost angry with himself for his lack of success in his researches. It was the only debt left him by the colonel, and Marius made it a matter of honor to pay it. "What," he thought, "when my father lay dying on the field of battle, did Thénardier contrive to find him amid the smoke and the grape-shot, and bear him off on his shoulders, and yet he owed him nothing, and I, who owe so much to Thénardier, cannot join him in this shadow where he is lying in the pangs of death, and in my turn bring him back from death to life! Oh! I will find him!" To find Thénardier, in fact, Marius would have given one of his arms, to rescue him from his misery, he would have sacrificed all his blood. To see Thénardier, to render Thénardier some service, to say to him: "You do not know me; well, I do know you! Here I am. Dispose of me!" This was Marius's sweetest and most magnificent dream.

Chapter III

MARIUS GROWN UP

AT THIS EPOCH, MARIUS WAS TWENTY YEARS OF AGE. IT WAS THREE YEARS SINCE HE HAD LEFT his grandfather. Both parties had remained on the same terms, without attempting to approach each other, and without seeking to see each other. Besides, what was the use of seeing each other? Marius was the brass vase, while Father Gillenormand was the iron pot.

We admit that Marius was mistaken as to his grandfather's heart. He had imagined that M. Gillenormand had never loved him, and that that crusty, harsh, and smiling old fellow who cursed, shouted, and stormed and brandished his cane, cherished for him, at the most, only that affection, which is at once slight and severe, of the dotards of comedy. Marius was in error. There are fathers who do not love their children; there exists no grandfather who does not adore his grandson. At bottom, as we have said, M. Gillenormand idolized Marius. He idolized him after his own fashion, with an accompaniment of snappishness and boxes on the ear; but, this child once gone, he felt a black void in his heart; he would allow no one to mention the child to him, and all the while secretly regretted that he was so well obeyed. At first, he hoped that this Buonapartist, this Jacobin, this terrorist, this Septembrist, would return. But the weeks passed by, years passed; to M. Gillenormand's great despair, the "blood-drinker" did not make his appearance. "I could not do otherwise than turn him out," said the grandfather to himself, and he asked himself: "If the thing were to do over again, would I do it?" His pride instantly answered "yes," but his aged head, which he shook in silence, replied sadly "no." He had his hours of depression. He missed Marius. Old men need affection as they need the sun. It is warmth. Strong as his nature was, the absence of Marius had wrought some change in him. Nothing in the world could have induced him to take a step toward "that rogue";

but he suffered. He never inquired about him, but he thought of him incessantly. He lived in the Marais in a more and more retired manner; he was still merry and violent as of old, but his merriment had a convulsive harshness, and his violences always terminated in a sort of gentle and gloomy dejection. He sometimes said: "Oh! if he only would return, what a good box on the ear I would give him!"

As for his aunt, she thought too little to love much; Marius was no longer for her much more than a vague black form; and she eventually came to occupy herself with him much less than with the cat or the parakeet which she probably had. What augmented Father Gillenormand's secret suffering was, that he locked it all up within his breast, and did not allow its existence to be divined. His sorrow was like those recently invented furnaces which consume their own smoke. It sometimes happened that officious busybodies spoke to him of Marius, and asked him: "What is your grandson doing?" "What has become of him?" The old bourgeois replied with a sigh, that he was a sad case, and giving a fillip to his cuff, if he wished to appear gay: "Monsieur le Baron de Pontmercy is practicing pettifogging in some corner or other."

While the old man regretted, Marius applauded himself. As is the case with all good-hearted people, misfortune had eradicated his bitterness. He only thought of M. Gillenormand in an amiable light, but he had set his mind on not receiving anything more from the man who *had been unkind to his father*. This was the mitigated translation of his first indignation. Moreover, he was happy at having suffered, and at suffering still. It was for his father's sake. The hardness of his life satisfied and pleased him. He said to himself with a sort of joy that—*it was certainly the least he could do*; that it was an expiation;—that, had it not been for that, he would have been punished in some other way and later on for his impious indifference toward his father, and such a father! that it would not have been just that his father should have all the suffering, and he none of it; and, that, in any case, what were his toils and his destitution compared with the colonel's heroic life? that, in short, the only way for him to approach his father and resemble him, was to be brave in the face of indigence, as the other had been valiant before the enemy; and that that was, no doubt, what the colonel had meant to imply by the words: "He will be worthy of it." Words which Marius continued to wear, not on his breast, since the colonel's writing had disappeared, but in his heart.

And then, on the day when his grandfather had turned him out of doors, he had been only a child, now he was a man. He felt it. Misery, we repeat, had been good for him. Poverty in youth, when it succeeds, has this magnificent property about it, that it turns the whole will toward effort, and the whole soul toward aspiration. Poverty instantly lays material life bare and renders it hideous; hence inexpressible bounds toward the ideal life. The wealthy young man has a hundred coarse and brilliant distractions, horse races, hunting, dogs, tobacco, gaming, good repasts, and all the rest of it; occupations for the baser side of the soul, at the expense of the loftier and more delicate sides. The poor young man wins his bread with difficulty; he eats; when he has eaten, he has nothing more but meditation. He goes to the spectacles which God furnishes gratis; he gazes at the sky, space, the stars, flowers, children, the humanity among which he is suffering, the creation amid which he beams. He gazes so much on humanity that he perceives its soul, he gazes upon creation to such an extent that he beholds God. He dreams, he feels himself great; he dreams on, and feels himself tender. From the egotism of the man who suffers he passes to the compassion of the man who meditates. An admirable sentiment breaks forth in him, forgetfulness of self and pity for all. As he thinks of the innumerable enjoyments which nature offers, gives, and lavishes to souls which stand open, and refuses to souls that are closed, he comes to pity, he the millionnaire of the mind, the millionnaire of money. All hatred departs from his heart, in proportion as light penetrates his spirit. And is he unhappy? No. The misery of a young man is never miserable. The first young lad who comes to hand, however poor he may be, with his strength, his health, his rapid walk, his brilliant eyes, his warmly circulating blood, his black hair, his red lips, his white teeth, his pure breath, will always arouse the envy of an aged emperor. And then, every morning, he sets himself afresh to the task of earning his bread; and while his hands earn his bread, his dorsal column gains pride, his brain gathers ideas. His task finished, he returns to ineffable ecstasies, to contemplation, to joys; he beholds his feet set in afflictions, in obstacles, on the pavement, in the nettles, sometimes in the mire; his head in the light. He is firm, serene, gentle, peaceful, attentive, serious, content with little, kindly; and he thanks God for having bestowed on him those two forms of riches which many a rich man lacks: work, which makes him free; and thought, which makes him dignified.

This is what had happened with Marius. To tell the truth, he inclined a little too much to the side of contemplation. From the day when he had succeeded in earning his living with some approach to certainty, he had stopped, thinking it good to be poor, and retrenching time from his work to give to thought; that is to say, he sometimes passed entire days in meditation, absorbed, engulfed, like a visionary, in the mute voluptuousness of ecstasy and inward radiance. He had thus propounded the problem of his life: to toil as little as possible at material labor, in order to toil as much as possible at the labor which is impalpable; in other words, to bestow a few hours on real life, and to cast the rest to the infinite. As he believed that he lacked nothing, he did not perceive that contemplation, thus understood, ends by becoming one of the forms of idleness; that he was contenting himself with conquering the first necessities of life, and that he was resting from his labors too soon.

It was evident that, for this energetic and enthusiastic nature, this could only be a transitory state, and that, at the first shock against the inevitable complications of destiny, Marius would awaken.

In the meantime, although he was a lawyer, and whatever Father Gillenormand thought about the matter, he was not practicing, he was not even pettifogging. Meditation had turned him aside from pleading. To haunt attorneys, to follow the court, to hunt up cases—what a bore! Why should he do it? He saw no reason for changing the manner of gaining his livelihood! The obscure and ill-paid publishing establishment had come to mean for him a sure source of work which did not involve too much labor, as we have explained, and which sufficed for his wants.

One of the publishers for whom he worked, M. Magimel, I think, offered to take him into his own house, to lodge him well, to furnish him with regular occupation, and to give him fifteen hundred francs a year. To be well lodged! Fifteen hundred francs! No doubt. But renounce his liberty! Be on fixed wages! A sort of hired man of letters! According to Marius's opinion, if he accepted, his position would become both better and worse at the same time, he acquired comfort, and lost his dignity; it was a fine and complete unhappiness converted into a repulsive and ridiculous state of torture: something like the case of a blind man who should recover the sight of one eye. He refused.

Marius dwelt in solitude. Owing to his taste for remaining outside of everything, and through having been too much alarmed, he had not entered decidedly into the group presided over by Enjolras. They had remained good friends; they were ready to assist each other on occasion in every possible way; but nothing more. Marius had two friends: one young, Courfeyrac; and one old, M. Mabeuf. He inclined more to the old man. In the first place, he owed to him the revolution which had taken place within him; to him he was indebted for having known and loved his father. "He operated on me for a cataract," he said.

The churchwarden had certainly played a decisive part.

It was not, however, that M. Mabeuf had been anything but the calm and impassive agent of Providence in this connection. He had enlightened Marius by chance and without being aware of the fact, as does a candle which someone brings; he had been the candle and not the someone.

As for Marius's inward political revolution, M. Mabeuf was totally incapable of comprehending it, of willing or of directing it.

As we shall see M. Mabeuf again, later on, a few words will not be superfluous.

Chapter IV

M. MABEUF

ON THE DAY WHEN M. MABEUF SAID TO MARIUS: "CERTAINLY I APPROVE OF POLITICAL OPINIONS," he expressed the real state of his mind. All political opinions were matters of indifference to him, and he approved them all, without distinction, provided they left him in peace, as the Greeks called the furies "the beautiful, the good, the charming," the Eumenides. M. Mabeuf's political opinion consisted in a passionate love for plants, and, above all, for books. Like all the rest of the world, he possessed the termination in *ist*, without which no one could exist at that time, but he was neither a royalist, a Bonapartist, a chartist, an Orleanist, nor an anarchist; he was a *bouquinist*, a collector of old books. He did not understand how men could busy themselves with hating each other because of silly stuff like the charter, democracy, legitimacy, monarchy, the republic, etc., when there were in the world all sorts of mosses, grasses, and shrubs which they might be looking at, and heaps of folios, and even of 32mos, which they might turn over. He took good care not to become useless; having books did not prevent his reading, being a botanist did not prevent his being a gardener. When he made Pontmercy's acquaintance, this sympathy had existed between the colonel and himself—that what the colonel did for flowers, he did for fruits. M. Mabeuf had succeeded in producing seedling pears as savory as the pears of St. Germain; it is from one of his combinations, apparently, that the October Mirabelle, now celebrated and no less perfumed than the summer Mirabelle, owes its origin. He went to mass rather from gentleness than from piety, and because, as he loved the faces of men, but hated their noise, he found them assembled and silent only in church. Feeling that he must be something in the State, he had chosen the career of warden. However, he had never succeeded in loving any woman as much as a tulip bulb, nor any man as much as an Elzevir. He had long passed sixty, when, one day, someone asked him: "Have you never been married?" "I have forgotten," said he. When it sometimes happened to him—and to whom does it not happen?—to say: "Oh! if I were only rich!" it was not when ogling a pretty girl, as was the case with Father Gillenormand, but when contemplating an old book. He lived alone with an old housekeeper. He was somewhat gouty, and when he was asleep, his aged fingers, stiffened with rheumatism, lay crooked up in the folds of his sheets. He had composed and published a *Flora of the Environs of Cauteretz*, with colored plates, a work which enjoyed a tolerable measure of esteem and which sold well. People rang his bell, in the Rue Mésières, two or three times a day, to ask for it. He drew as much as two thousand francs a year from it; this constituted nearly the whole of his fortune. Although poor, he had had the talent to form for himself, by dint of patience, privations, and time, a precious collection of rare copies of every sort. He never went out without a book under his arm, and he often returned with two. The sole decoration of the four rooms on the ground floor, which composed his lodgings, consisted of framed herbariums, and engravings of the old masters. The sight of a sword or a gun chilled his blood. He had never approached a cannon in his life, even at the Invalides. He had a passable stomach, a brother who was a curé, perfectly white hair, no teeth, either in his mouth or his mind, a trembling in every limb, a Picard accent, an infantile laugh, the air of an old sheep, and he was easily frightened. Add to this, that he had no other friendship, no other acquaintance among the living, than an old bookseller of the Porte-Saint-Jacques, named Royal. His dream was to naturalize indigo in France.

His servant was also a sort of innocent. The poor good old woman was a spinster. Sultan, her cat, which might have mewed Allegri's miserere in the Sistine Chapel, had filled her heart and sufficed for the quantity of passion which existed in her. None of her dreams had ever proceeded as far as man. She had never been able to get further than her cat. Like him, she had a mustache. Her glory consisted in her caps, which were always white. She passed her time, on Sundays, after mass, in counting over the linen in her chest, and in spreading out on her bed the dresses in the piece which she bought and never had made up. She knew how to read. M. Mabeuf had nicknamed her Mother Plutarque.

M. Mabeuf had taken a fancy to Marius, because Marius, being young and gentle, warmed his age without startling his timidity. Youth combined with gentleness produces on old people the effect of the sun without wind. When Marius was saturated with military glory, with gunpowder, with marches and countermarches, and with all those prodigious battles in which his father had given and received such tremendous blows of the sword, he went to see M. Mabeuf, and M. Mabeuf talked to him of his hero from the point of view of flowers.

His brother the curé died about 1830, and almost immediately, as when the night is drawing on, the whole horizon grew dark for M. Mabeuf. A notary's failure deprived him of the sum of ten thousand francs, which was all that he possessed in his brother's right and his own. The Revolution of July brought a crisis to publishing. In a period of embarrassment, the first thing which does not sell is a *Flora*. The *Flora of the Environs of Cauteret₃* stopped short. Weeks passed by without a single purchaser. Sometimes M. Mabeuf started at the sound of the bell. "Monsieur," said Mother Plutarque sadly, "it is the water-carrier." In short, one day, M. Mabeuf quitted the Rue Mésières, abdicated the functions of warden, gave up Saint-Sulpice, sold not a part of his books, but of his prints—that to which he was the least attached—and installed himself in a little house on the Rue Montparnasse, where, however, he remained but one quarter for two reasons: in the first place, the ground floor and the garden cost three hundred francs, and he dared not spend more than two hundred francs on his rent; in the second, being near Fatou's shooting-gallery, he could hear the pistol-shots; which was intolerable to him.

He carried off his *Flora*, his copper-plates, his herbariums, his portfolios, and his books, and established himself near the Salpêtrière, in a sort of thatched cottage of the village of Austerlitz, where, for fifty crowns a year, he got three rooms and a garden enclosed by a hedge, and containing a well. He took advantage of this removal to sell off nearly all his furniture. On the day of his entrance into his new quarters, he was very gay, and drove the nails on which his engravings and herbariums were to hang, with his own hands, dug in his garden the rest of the day, and at night, perceiving that Mother Plutarque had a melancholy air, and was very thoughtful, he tapped her on the shoulder and said to her with a smile: "We have the indigo!"

Only two visitors, the bookseller of the Porte-Saint-Jacques and Marius, were admitted to view the thatched cottage at Austerlitz, a brawling name which was, to tell the truth, extremely disagreeable to him.

However, as we have just pointed out, brains which are absorbed in some bit of wisdom, or folly, or, as it often happens, in both at once, are but slowly accessible to the things of actual life. Their own destiny is a far-off thing to them. There results from such concentration a passivity, which, if it were the outcome of reasoning, would resemble philosophy. One declines, descends, trickles away, even crumbles away, and yet is hardly conscious of it one's self. It always ends, it is true, in an awakening, but the awakening is tardy. In the meantime, it seems as though we held ourselves neutral in the game which is going on between our happiness and our unhappiness. We are the stake, and we look on at the game with indifference.

It is thus that, athwart the cloud which formed about him, when all his hopes were extinguished one after the other, M. Mabeuf remained rather puerilely, but profoundly serene. His habits of mind had the regular swing of a pendulum. Once mounted on an illusion, he went for a very long time, even after the illusion had disappeared. A clock does not stop short at the precise moment when the key is lost.

M. Mabeuf had his innocent pleasures. These pleasures were inexpensive and unexpected; the merest chance furnished them. One day, Mother Plutarque was reading a romance in one corner of the room. She was reading aloud, finding that she understood better thus. To read aloud is to assure one's self of what one is reading. There are people who read very loud, and who have the appearance of giving themselves their word of honor as to what they are perusing.

It was with this sort of energy that Mother Plutarque was reading the romance which she had in hand. M. Mabeuf heard her without listening to her.

In the course of her reading, Mother Plutarque came to this phrase. It was a question of an officer of dragoons and a beauty:

"—The beauty pouted, and the dragoon—"

Here she interrupted herself to wipe her glasses.

"Buddha and the Dragon," struck in M. Mabeuf in a low voice. "Yes, it is true that there was a dragon, which, from the depths of its cave, spouted flame through his maw and set the heavens on fire. Many stars had already been consumed by this monster, which, besides, had the claws of a tiger. Buddha went into its den and succeeded in converting the dragon. That is a good book that you are reading, Mother Plutarque. There is no more beautiful legend in existence."

And M. Mabeuf fell into a delicious reverie.

Chapter V

POVERTY A GOOD NEIGHBOR FOR MISERY

MARIUS LIKED THIS CANDID OLD MAN WHO SAW HIMSELF GRADUALLY FALLING INTO THE clutches of indigence, and who came to feel astonishment, little by little, without, however, being made melancholy by it. Marius met Courfeyrac and sought out M. Mabeuf. Very rarely, however; twice a month at most.

Marius's pleasure consisted in taking long walks alone on the outer boulevards, or in the Champs-de-Mars, or in the least frequented alleys of the Luxembourg. He often spent half a day in gazing at a market garden, the beds of lettuce, the chickens on the dung-heap, the horse turning the water-wheel. The passers-by stared at him in surprise, and some of them thought his attire suspicious and his mien sinister. He was only a poor young man dreaming in an objectless way.

It was during one of his strolls that he had hit upon the Gorbeau house, and, tempted by its isolation and its cheapness, had taken up his abode there. He was known there only under the name of M. Marius.

Some of his father's old generals or old comrades had invited him to go and see them, when they learned about him. Marius had not refused their invitations. They afforded opportunities of talking about his father. Thus he went from time to time, to Comte Pajol, to General Bellavesne, to General Fririon, to the Invalides. There was music and dancing there. On such evenings, Marius put on his new coat. But he never went to these evening parties or balls except on days when it was freezing cold, because he could not afford a carriage, and he did not wish to arrive with boots otherwise than like mirrors.

He said sometimes, but without bitterness: "Men are so made that in a drawing-room you may be soiled everywhere except on your shoes. In order to insure a good reception there, only one irreproachable thing is asked of you; your conscience? No, your boots."

All passions except those of the heart are dissipated by reverie. Marius's political fevers vanished thus. The Revolution of 1830 assisted in the process, by satisfying and calming him. He remained the same, setting aside his fits of wrath. He still held the same opinions. Only, they had been tempered. To speak accurately, he had no longer any opinions, he had sympathies. To what party did he belong? To the party of humanity. Out of humanity he chose France; out of the Nation he chose the people; out of the people he chose the woman. It was to that point above all, that his pity was directed. Now he preferred an idea to a deed, a poet to a hero, and he admired a book like Job more than an event like Marengo. And then, when, after a day spent in meditation, he returned in the evening through the boulevards, and caught a glimpse through the branches of the trees of the fathomless space beyond, the nameless gleams, the abyss, the shadow, the mystery, all that which is only human seemed very petty indeed to him.

He thought that he had, and he really had, in fact, arrived at the truth of life and of human philosophy, and he had ended by gazing at nothing but heaven, the only thing which Truth can perceive from the bottom of her well.

This did not prevent him from multiplying his plans, his combinations, his scaffoldings, his projects for the future. In this state of reverie, an eye which could have cast a glance into Marius's interior would have been dazzled with the purity of that soul. In fact, had it been given to our eyes of the flesh to gaze into the consciences of others, we should be able to judge a man much more surely according to what he dreams, than according to what he thinks. There is will in thought, there is none in dreams. Reverie, which is utterly spontaneous, takes and keeps, even in the gigantic and the ideal, the form of our spirit. Nothing proceeds more directly and more sincerely from the very depth of our soul, than our unpremeditated and boundless aspirations toward the splendors of destiny. In these aspirations, much more than in deliberate, rational coordinated ideas, is the real character of a man to be found. Our chimeras are the things which the most resemble us. Each one of us dreams of the unknown and the impossible in accordance with his nature.

Toward the middle of this year 1831, the old woman who waited on Marius told him that his neighbors, the wretched Jondrette family, had been turned out of doors. Marius, who passed nearly the whole of his days out of the house, hardly knew that he had any neighbors.

"Why are they turned out?" he asked.

"Because they do not pay their rent; they owe for two quarters."

"How much is it?"

"Twenty francs," said the old woman.

Marius had thirty francs saved up in a drawer.

"Here," he said to the old woman, "take these twenty-five francs. Pay for the poor people and give them five francs, and do not tell them that it was I."

Chapter VI

THE SUBSTITUTE

IT CHANCED THAT THE REGIMENT TO WHICH LIEUTENANT THÉODULE BELONGED CAME TO PERform garrison duty in Paris. This inspired Aunt Gillenormand with a second idea. She had, on the first occasion, hit upon the plan of having Marius spied upon by Théodule; now she plotted to have Théodule take Marius's place.

At all events and in case the grandfather should feel the vague need of a young face in the house—these rays of dawn are sometimes sweet to ruin—it was expedient to find another Marius. "Take it as a simple erratum," she thought, "such as one sees in books. For Marius, read Théodule."

A grandnephew is almost the same as a grandson; in default of a lawyer one takes a lancer.

One morning, when M. Gillenormand was about to read something in the *Quotidienne*, his daughter entered and said to him in her sweetest voice; for the question concerned her favorite:

"Father, Théodule is coming to present his respects to you this morning."

"Who's Théodule?"

"Your grandnephew."

"Ah!" said the grandfather.

Then he went back to his reading, thought no more of his grandnephew, who was merely some Théodule or other, and soon flew into a rage, which almost always happened when he read. The "sheet" which he held, although royalist, of course, announced for the following day, without any softening phrases, one of these little events which were of daily occurrence at that date in Paris: "That the students of the schools of law and medicine were to assemble on the Place du Panthéon, at midday—to deliberate." The discussion concerned one of the questions of the moment, the artillery of the National Guard, and a conflict between the Minister of War and "the citizen's militia," on the subject of the cannon parked in the courtyard of the Louvre. The students were to "deliberate" over this. It did not take much more than this to swell M. Gillenormand's rage.

He thought of Marius, who was a student, and who would probably go with the rest, to "deliberate, at midday, on the Place du Panthéon."

As he was indulging in this painful dream, Lieutenant Théodule entered clad in plain clothes as a bourgeois, which was clever of him, and was discreetly introduced by Mademoiselle Gillenormand. The lancer had reasoned as follows: "The old druid has not sunk all his money in a life pension. It is well to disguise one's self as a civilian from time to time."

Mademoiselle Gillenormand said aloud to her father:

"Théodule, your grandnephew."

And in a low voice, to the lieutenant:

"Approve of everything."

And she withdrew.

The lieutenant, who was but little accustomed to such venerable encounters, stammered with some timidity: "Good day, uncle"—and made a salute composed of the involuntary and mechanical outline of the military salute finished off as a bourgeois salute.

"Ah! so it's you; that is well, sit down," said the old gentleman,

That said, he totally forgot the lancer.

Théodule seated himself, and M. Gillenormand rose.

M. Gillenormand began to pace back and forth, his hands in his pockets, talking aloud, and twitching, with his irritated old fingers, at the two watches which he wore in his two fobs.

"That pack of brats! they convene on the Place du Panthéon! by my life! urchins who were with their nurses but yesterday! If one were to squeeze their noses, milk would burst out. And they deliberate to-morrow, at midday. What are we coming to? What are we coming to? It is clear that we are making for the abyss. That is what the *descamisados* have brought us to! To deliberate on the citizen artillery! To go and jabber in the open air over the jibes of the National Guard! And with whom are they to meet there? Just see whither Jacobinism leads. I will bet anything you like, a million against a counter, that there will be no one there but returned convicts and released galley-slaves. The Republicans and the galley-slaves—they form but one nose and one handkerchief. Carnot used to say: 'Where would you have me go, traitor?' Fouché replied: 'Wherever you please, imbecile!' That's what the Republicans are like."

"That is true," said Théodule.

M. Gillenormand half turned his head, saw Théodule, and went on:

"When one reflects that that scoundrel was so vile as to turn carbonaro! Why did you leave my house? To go and become a Republican! Pssst! In the first place, the people want none of your republic, they have common sense, they know well that there always have been kings, and that there always will be; they know well that the people are only the people, after all, they make sport of it, of your republic—do you understand, idiot? Is it not a horrible caprice? To fall in love with Père Duchesne, to make sheep's-eyes at the guillotine, to sing romances, and play on the guitar under the balcony of '93—it's enough to make one spit on all these young fellows, such fools are they! They are all alike. Not one escapes. It suffices for them to breathe the air which blows through the street to lose their senses. The nineteenth century is poison. The first scamp that happens along lets his beard grow like a goat's, thinks himself a real scoundrel, and abandons his old relatives. He's a Republican, he's a romantic. What does that mean, romantic? Do me the favor to tell me what it is. All possible follies. A year ago, they ran to *Hernani*. Now, I just ask you, *Hernani!* antitheses! abominations which are not even written in French! And then, they have cannons in the courtyard of the Louvre. Such are the rascalities of this age!"

"You are right, uncle," said Théodule.

M. Gillenormand resumed:

"Cannons in the courtyard of the Museum! For what purpose? Do you want to fire grape-shot at the Apollo Belvedere? What have those cartridges to do with the Venus de Medici? Oh! the young men of the present day are all blackguards! What a petty creature is their Benjamin Constant! And those who are not rascals are simpletons! They do all they can to make themselves ugly, they are badly dressed, they are afraid of women, in the presence of petticoats they have a mendicant air which sets the girls into fits of laughter; on my word of honor, one would say the poor creatures were ashamed of love. They are deformed, and they complete themselves by being stupid; they repeat the puns of Tiercelin and Potier, they have sack coats, stablemen's waistcoats, shirts of coarse linen, trousers of coarse cloth, boots of coarse leather, and their rigmarole resembles their plumage. One might make use of their jargon to put new soles on their old shoes. And all this awkward batch of brats has political opinions, if you please. Political opinions should be strictly forbidden. They fabricate systems, they recast society, they demolish the monarchy, they fling all laws to the earth, they put the attic in the cellar's place and my porter in the place of the King, they turn Europe topsy-turvy, they reconstruct the world, and all their love affairs consist in staring slyly at the ankles of the laundresses as these women climb into their carts. Ah! Marius! Ah! you blackguard! to go and vociferate on the public place! to discuss, to debate, to take measures! They call that measures, just God! Disorder humbles itself and becomes silly. I have seen chaos, I now see a mess. Students deliberating on the National Guard—such a thing could not be seen among the Ogibewas nor the Cadodaches! Savages who go naked, with their noddles dressed like a shuttlecock, with a club in their paws, are less of brutes than those bachelors of arts! The four-penny monkeys! And they set up for judges! Those creatures deliberate and ratiocinate! The end of the world is come! This is plainly the end of this miserable terraqueous globe! A final hiccough was required, and France has emitted it. Deliberate, my rascals! Such things will happen so long as they go and read the newspapers under the arcades of the Odéon. That costs them a sou, and their good sense, and their intelligence, and their heart and their soul, and their wits. They emerge thence, and decamp from their families. All newspapers are pests; all, even the *Drapeau Blanc!* At bottom, Martainville was a Jacobin. Ah! just Heaven! you may boast of having driven your grandfather to despair, that you may!"

"That is evident," said Théodule.

And profiting by the fact that M. Gillenormand was taking breath, the lancer added in a magisterial manner:

"There should be no other newspaper than the *Moniteur,* and no other book than the *Annuaire Militaire.*"

M. Gillenormand continued:

"It is like their Sieyès! A regicide ending in a senator; for that is the way they always end. They give themselves a scar with the address of *thou* as citizens, in order to get themselves called, eventually, *Monsieur le Comte*. Monsieur le Comte as big as my arm, assassins of September. The philosopher Sieyès! I will do myself the justice to say, that I have never had any better opinion of the philosophies of all those philosophers, than of the spectacles of the grimacer of Tivoli! One day I saw the Senators cross the Quai Malplaquet in mantles of violet velvet sown with bees, with hats à la Henri IV. They were hideous. One would have pronounced them monkeys from the tiger's court. Citizens, I declare to you, that your progress is madness, that your humanity is a dream, that your revolution is a crime, that your republic is a monster, that your young and virgin France comes from the brothel, and I maintain it against all, whoever you may be, whether journalists, economists, legists, or even were you better judges of liberty, of equality, and fraternity than the knife of the guillotine! And that I announce to you, my fine fellows!"

"Parbleu!" cried the lieutenant, "that is wonderfully true."

M. Gillenormand paused in a gesture which he had begun, wheeled round, stared Lancer Théodule intently in the eyes, and said to him:

"You are a fool."

Book Sixth

The Conjunction of Two Stars

Chapter I

The Sobriquet: Mode of Formation of Family Names

MARIUS WAS, AT THIS EPOCH, A HANDSOME YOUNG MAN, OF MEDIUM STATURE, WITH THICK AND intensely black hair, a lofty and intelligent brow, well-opened and passionate nostrils, an air of calmness and sincerity, and with something indescribably proud, thoughtful, and innocent over his whole countenance. His profile, all of whose lines were rounded, without thereby losing their firmness, had a certain Germanic sweetness, which has made its way into the French physiognomy by way of Alsace and Lorraine, and that complete absence of angles which rendered the Sicambres so easily recognizable among the Romans, and which distinguishes the leonine from the aquiline race. He was at that period of life when the mind of men who think is composed, in nearly equal parts, of depth and ingenuousness. A grave situation being given, he had all that is required to be stupid: one more turn of the key, and he might be sublime. His manners were reserved, cold, polished, not very genial. As his mouth was charming, his lips the reddest, and his teeth the whitest in the world, his smile corrected the severity of his face, as a whole. At certain moments, that pure brow and that voluptuous smile presented a singular contrast. His eyes were small, but his glance was large.

At the period of his most abject misery, he had observed that young girls turned round when he passed by, and he fled or hid, with death in his soul. He thought that they were staring at him because of his old clothes, and that they were laughing at them; the fact is, that they stared at him because of his grace, and that they dreamed of him.

This mute misunderstanding between him and the pretty passers-by had made him shy. He chose none of them for the excellent reason that he fled from all of them. He lived thus indefinitely—stupidly, as Courfeyrac said.

Courfeyrac also said to him: "Do not aspire to be venerable" [they called each other *thou*; it is the tendency of youthful friendships to slip into this mode of address]. "Let me give you a piece of advice, my dear fellow. Don't read so many books, and look a little more at the lasses. The jades have some good points about them, O Marius! By dint of fleeing and blushing, you will become brutalized."

On other occasions, Courfeyrac encountered him and said: "Good morning, Monsieur l'Abbé!"

When Courfeyrac had addressed to him some remark of this nature, Marius avoided women, both young and old, more than ever for a week to come, and he avoided Courfeyrac to boot.

Nevertheless, there existed in all the immensity of creation, two women whom Marius did not flee, and to whom he paid no attention whatever. In truth, he would have been very much amazed if he had been informed that they were women. One was the bearded old woman who swept out his chamber, and caused Courfeyrac to say: "Seeing that his servant woman wears his beard, Marius does not wear his own beard." The other was a sort of little girl whom he saw very often, and whom he never looked at.

For more than a year, Marius had noticed in one of the walks of the Luxembourg, the one which skirts the parapet of the Pépinière, a man and a very young girl, who were almost always seated side by side on the same bench, at the most solitary end of the alley, on the Rue de l'Ouest side. Every time that that chance which meddles with the strolls of persons whose gaze is turned inwards, led Marius to that walk—and it was nearly every day—he found this couple there. The man appeared to be about sixty years of age; he seemed sad and serious; his whole person presented the robust and weary aspect peculiar to military men who have retired from the service. If he had worn a decoration, Marius would have said: "He is an ex-officer." He had a kindly but unapproachable air, and he never let his glance linger on the eyes of anyone. He wore blue trousers, a blue frock-coat and a broad-brimmed hat, which always appeared to be new, a black cravat, a quaker shirt, that is to say, it was dazzlingly white, but of coarse linen. A grisette who passed near him one day, said: "Here's a very tidy widower." His hair was very white.

The first time that the young girl who accompanied him came and seated herself on the bench which they seemed to have adopted, she was a sort of child thirteen or fourteen years of age, so thin as to be almost homely, awkward, insignificant, and with a possible promise of handsome eyes. Only, they were always raised with a sort of displeasing assurance. Her dress was both aged and childish, like the dress of the scholars in a convent; it consisted of a badly cut gown of black merino. They had the air of being father and daughter.

Marius scanned this old man, who was not yet aged, and this little girl, who was not yet a person, for a few days, and thereafter paid no attention to them. They, on their side, did not appear even to see him. They conversed together with a peaceful and indifferent air. The girl chattered incessantly and merrily. The old man talked but little, and, at times, he fixed on her eyes overflowing with an ineffable paternity.

Marius had acquired the mechanical habit of strolling in that walk. He invariably found them there.

This is the way things went:

Marius liked to arrive by the end of the alley which was furthest from their bench; he walked the whole length of the alley, passed in front of them, then returned to the extremity whence he had come, and began again. This he did five or six times in the course of his promenade, and the promenade was taken five or six times a week, without its having occurred to him or to these people to exchange a greeting. That personage, and that young girl, although they appeared—and perhaps because they appeared—to shun all glances, had, naturally, caused some attention on the part of the five or six students who strolled along the Pépinière from time to time; the studious after their lectures, the others after their game of billiards. Courfeyrac, who was among the last, had observed them several times, but, finding the girl homely, he had speedily and carefully kept out of the way. He had fled, discharging at them a sobriquet, like a Parthian dart. Impressed solely with the child's gown and the old man's hair, he had dubbed the daughter Mademoiselle Lanoire, and the father, Monsieur Leblanc, so that, as no one knew them under any other title, this nickname became a law in the default of any other name. The students said: "Ah! Monsieur Leblanc is on his bench." And Marius, like the rest, had found it convenient to call this unknown gentleman Monsieur Leblanc.

We shall follow their example, and we shall say M. Leblanc, in order to facilitate this tale.

So Marius saw them nearly every day, at the same hour, during the first year. He found the man to his taste, but the girl insipid.

Chapter II

Lux Facta Est

DURING THE SECOND YEAR, PRECISELY AT THE POINT IN THIS HISTORY WHICH THE READER HAS now reached, it chanced that this habit of the Luxembourg was interrupted, without Marius himself being quite aware why, and nearly six months elapsed, during which he did not set foot in the alley. One day, at last, he returned thither once more; it was a serene summer morning, and Marius was in joyous mood, as one is when the weather is fine. It seemed to him that he had in his heart all the songs of the birds that he was listening to, and all the bits of blue sky of which he caught glimpses through the leaves of the trees.

He went straight to "his alley," and when he reached the end of it he perceived, still on the same bench, that well-known couple. Only, when he approached, it certainly was the same man; but it seemed to him that it was no longer the same girl. The person whom he now beheld was a tall and beautiful creature, possessed of all the most charming lines of a woman at the precise moment when they are still combined with all the most ingenuous graces of the child; a pure and fugitive moment, which can be expressed only by these two words—"fifteen years." She had wonderful brown hair, shaded with threads of gold, a brow that seemed made of marble, cheeks that seemed made of rose-leaf, a pale flush, an agitated whiteness, an exquisite mouth, whence smiles darted like sunbeams, and words like music, a head such as Raphael would have given to Mary, set upon a neck that Jean Goujon would have attributed to a Venus. And, in order that nothing might be lacking to this bewitching face, her nose was not handsome—it was pretty; neither straight nor curved, neither Italian nor Greek; it was the Parisian nose, that is to say, spiritual, delicate, irregular, pure—which drives painters to despair, and charms poets.

When Marius passed near her, he could not see her eyes, which were constantly lowered. He saw only her long chestnut lashes, permeated with shadow and modesty.

This did not prevent the beautiful child from smiling as she listened to what the white-haired old man was saying to her, and nothing could be more fascinating than that fresh smile, combined with those drooping eyes.

For a moment, Marius thought that she was another daughter of the same man, a sister of the former, no doubt. But when the invariable habit of his stroll brought him, for the second time, near the bench, and he had examined her attentively, he recognized her as the same. In six months the little girl had become a young maiden; that was all. Nothing is more frequent than this phenomenon. There is a moment when girls blossom out in the twinkling of an eye, and become roses all at once. One left them children but yesterday; to-day, one finds them disquieting to the feelings.

This child had not only grown, she had become idealized. As three days in April suffice to cover certain trees with flowers, six months had sufficed to clothe her with beauty. Her April had arrived.

One sometimes sees people, who, poor and mean, seem to wake up, pass suddenly from indigence to luxury, indulge in expenditures of all sorts, and become dazzling, prodigal, magnificent, all of a sudden. That is the result of having pocketed an income; a note fell due yesterday. The young girl had received her quarterly income.

And then, she was no longer the schoolgirl with her felt hat, her merino gown, her scholar's shoes, and red hands; taste had come to her with beauty; she was a well-dressed person, clad with a sort of rich and simple elegance, and without affectation. She wore a dress of black damask, a cape of the same material, and bonnet of white crape. Her white gloves displayed the delicacy of the hand which toyed with the carved, Chinese ivory handle of a parasol, and her silken shoe outlined the smallness of her foot. When one passed near her, her whole toilette exhaled a youthful and penetrating perfume.

As for the man, he was the same as usual.

The second time that Marius approached her, the young girl raised her eyelids; her eyes were of a deep, celestial blue, but in that veiled azure, there was, as yet, nothing but the glance of a child. She looked at Marius indifferently, as she would have stared at the brat running beneath the sycamores, or the marble vase which cast a shadow on the bench, and Marius, on his side, continued his promenade, and thought about something else.

He passed near the bench where the young girl sat, five or six times, but without even turning his eyes in her direction.

On the following days, he returned, as was his wont, to the Luxembourg; as usual, he found there "the father and daughter"; but he paid no further attention to them. He thought no more about the girl now that she was beautiful, than he had when she was homely. He passed very near the bench where she sat, because such was his habit.

Chapter III

EFFECT OF THE SPRING

ONE DAY, THE AIR WAS WARM, THE LUXEMBOURG WAS INUNDATED WITH LIGHT AND SHADE, THE sky was as pure as though the angels had washed it that morning, the sparrows were giving vent to little twitters in the depths of the chestnut-trees. Marius had thrown open his whole soul to nature, he was not thinking of anything, he simply lived and breathed, he passed near the bench, the young girl raised her eyes to him, the two glances met.

What was there in the young girl's glance on this occasion? Marius could not have told. There was nothing and there was everything. It was a strange flash.

She dropped her eyes, and he pursued his way.

What he had just seen was no longer the ingenuous and simple eye of a child; it was a mysterious gulf which had half opened, then abruptly closed again.

There comes a day when the young girl glances in this manner. Woe to him who chances to be there!

That first gaze of a soul which does not, as yet, know itself, is like the dawn in the sky. It is the awakening of something radiant and strange. Nothing can give any idea of the dangerous charm of that unexpected gleam, which flashes suddenly and vaguely forth from adorable shadows, and which is composed of all the innocence of the present, and of all the passion of the future. It is a sort of undecided tenderness which reveals itself by chance, and which waits. It is a snare which the innocent maiden sets unknown to herself, and in which she captures hearts without either wishing or knowing it. It is a virgin looking like a woman.

It is rare that a profound reverie does not spring from that glance, where it falls. All purities and all candors meet in that celestial and fatal gleam which, more than all the best-planned tender glances of coquettes, possesses the magic power of causing the sudden blossoming, in the depths of the soul, of that somber flower, impregnated with perfume and with poison, which is called love.

That evening, on his return to his garret, Marius cast his eyes over his garments, and perceived, for the first time, that he had been so slovenly, indecorous, and inconceivably stupid as to go for his walk in the Luxembourg with his "everyday clothes," that is to say, with a hat battered near the band, coarse carter's boots, black trousers which showed white at the knees, and a black coat which was pale at the elbows.

Chapter IV

BEGINNING OF A GREAT MALADY

ON THE FOLLOWING DAY, AT THE ACCUSTOMED HOUR, MARIUS DREW FROM HIS WARDROBE HIS new coat, his new trousers, his new hat, and his new boots; he clothed himself in this complete panoply, put on his gloves, a tremendous luxury, and set off for the Luxembourg.

On the way thither, he encountered Courfeyrac, and pretended not to see him. Courfeyrac, on his return home, said to his friends:

"I have just met Marius's new hat and new coat, with Marius inside them. He was going to pass an examination, no doubt. He looked utterly stupid."

On arriving at the Luxembourg, Marius made the tour of the fountain basin, and stared at the swans; then he remained for a long time in contemplation before a statue whose head was perfectly black with mold, and one of whose hips was missing. Near the basin there was a bourgeois forty years of age, with a prominent stomach, who was holding by the hand a little urchin of five, and saying to him: "Shun excess, my son, keep at an equal distance from despotism and from anarchy." Marius listened to this bourgeois. Then he made the circuit of the basin once more. At last he directed his course toward "his alley," slowly, and as if with regret. One would have said that he was both forced to go there and withheld from doing so. He did not perceive it himself, and thought that he was doing as he always did.

On turning into the walk, he saw M. Leblanc and the young girl at the other end, "on their bench." He buttoned his coat up to the very top, pulled it down on his body so that there might be no wrinkles, examined, with a certain complaisance, the lustrous gleams of his trousers, and marched on the bench. This march savored of an attack, and certainly of a desire for conquest. So I say that he marched on the bench, as I should say: "Hannibal marched on Rome."

However, all his movements were purely mechanical, and he had interrupted none of the habitual preoccupations of his mind and labors. At that moment, he was thinking that the *Manuel du Baccalauréat* was a stupid book, and that it must have been drawn up by rare idiots, to allow of three tragedies of Racine and only one comedy of Molière being analyzed therein as masterpieces of the human mind. There was a piercing whistling going on in his ears. As he approached the bench, he held fast to the folds in his coat, and fixed his eyes on the young girl. It seemed to him that she filled the entire extremity of the alley with a vague blue light.

In proportion as he drew near, his pace slackened more and more. On arriving at some little distance from the bench, and long before he had reached the end of the walk, he halted, and could not explain to himself why he retraced his steps. He did not even say to himself that he would not go as far as the end. It was only with difficulty that the young girl could have perceived him in the distance and noted his fine appearance in his new clothes. Nevertheless, he held himself very erect, in case anyone should be looking at him from behind.

He attained the opposite end, then came back, and this time he approached a little nearer to the bench. He even got to within three intervals of trees, but there he felt an indescribable impossibility of proceeding further, and he hesitated. He thought he saw the young girl's face bending toward him. But he exerted a manly and violent effort, subdued his hesitation, and walked straight ahead. A few seconds later, he rushed in front of the bench, erect and firm, reddening to the very ears, without daring to cast a glance either to the right or to the left, with his hand thrust into his coat like a statesman. At the moment when he passed—under the cannon of the place—he felt his heart beat wildly. As on the preceding day, she wore her damask gown and her crape bonnet. He heard an ineffable voice, which must have been "her voice." She was talking tranquilly. She was very pretty. He felt it, although he made no attempt to see her. "She could not, however," he thought, "help feeling esteem and consideration for me, if she only knew that I am the veritable author of the dissertation on Marcos Obrégon de la Ronde, which M. François de Neufchâteau put, as though it were his own, at the head of his edition of *Gil Blas*." He went beyond the bench as far as the extremity of the walk, which was very near, then turned on his heel and passed once more in front of the lovely girl. This time, he was very pale. Moreover, all his emotions were disagreeable. As he went further from the bench and the young girl, and while his back was turned to her, he fancied that she was gazing after him, and that made him stumble.

He did not attempt to approach the bench again; he halted near the middle of the walk, and there, a thing which he never did, he sat down, and reflecting in the most profoundly indistinct depths of his spirit, that after all, it was hard that persons whose white bonnet and black gown he admired should be absolutely insensible to his splendid trousers and his new coat.

At the expiration of a quarter of an hour, he rose, as though he were on the point of again beginning his march toward that bench which was surrounded by an aureole. But he remained standing there, motionless. For the first time in fifteen months, he said to himself that that gentleman who sat there every day with his daughter, had, on his side, noticed him, and probably considered his assiduity singular.

For the first time, also, he was conscious of some irreverence in designating that stranger, even in his secret thoughts, by the sobriquet of M. Leblanc.

He stood thus for several minutes, with drooping head, tracing figures in the sand, with the cane which he held in his hand.

Then he turned abruptly in the direction opposite to the bench, to M. Leblanc and his daughter, and went home.

That day he forgot to dine. At eight o'clock in the evening he perceived this fact, and as it was too late to go down to the Rue Saint-Jacques, he said: "Never mind!" and ate a bit of bread.

He did not go to bed until he had brushed his coat and folded it up with great care.

Chapter V

DIVERS CLAPS OF THUNDER FALL ON MA'AM BOUGON

On the following day, Ma'am Bougon, as Courfeyrac styled the old portress-principal-tenant, housekeeper of the Gorbeau hovel, Ma'am Bougon, whose name was, in reality, Madame Burgon, as we have found out, but this iconoclast, Courfeyrac, respected nothing—Ma'am Bougon observed, with stupefaction, that M. Marius was going out again in his new coat.

He went to the Luxembourg again, but he did not proceed further than his bench midway of the alley. He seated himself there, as on the preceding day, surveying from a distance, and clearly making out, the white bonnet, the black dress, and above all, that blue light. He did not stir from it, and only went home when the gates of the Luxembourg closed. He did not see M. Leblanc and his daughter retire. He concluded that they had quitted the garden by the gate on the Rue de l'Ouest. Later on, several weeks afterwards, when he came to think it over, he could never recall where he had dined that evening.

On the following day, which was the third, Ma'am Bougon was thunderstruck. Marius went out in his new coat. "Three days in succession!" she exclaimed.

She tried to follow him, but Marius walked briskly, and with immense strides; it was a hippopotamus undertaking the pursuit of a chamois. She lost sight of him in two minutes, and returned breathless, three-quarters choked with asthma, and furious. "If there is any sense," she growled, "in putting on one's best clothes every day, and making people run like this!"

Marius betook himself to the Luxembourg.

The young girl was there with M. Leblanc. Marius approached as near as he could, pretending to be busy reading a book, but he halted afar off, then returned and seated himself on his bench, where he spent four hours in watching the house-sparrows who were skipping about the walk, and who produced on him the impression that they were making sport of him.

A fortnight passed thus. Marius went to the Luxembourg no longer for the sake of strolling there, but to seat himself always in the same spot, and that without knowing why. Once arrived there, he did not stir. He put on his new coat every morning, for the purpose of not showing himself, and he began all over again on the morrow.

She was decidedly a marvelous beauty. The only remark approaching a criticism, that could be made, was, that the contradiction between her gaze, which was melancholy, and her smile, which was merry, gave a rather wild effect to her face, which sometimes caused this sweet countenance to become strange without ceasing to be charming.

Chapter VI

TAKEN PRISONER

On one of the last days of the second week, Marius was seated on his bench, as usual, holding in his hand an open book, of which he had not turned a page for the last two hours. All at once, he started. An event was taking place at the other extremity of the walk. Leblanc and his daughter had just left their seat, and the daughter had taken her father's arm, and both were advancing slowly, toward the middle of the alley where Marius was. Marius closed his book, then opened it again, then forced himself to read; he trembled; the aureole was coming straight toward him. "Ah! good Heavens!" thought he, "I shall not have time to strike an attitude." Still the white-haired man and the girl advanced. It seemed to him that this lasted for a century, and that it was but a second. "What are they coming in this direction for?" he asked himself. "What! She will pass here? Her feet will tread this sand, this walk, two paces from me?" He was utterly upset, he would have liked to be very handsome, he would have liked to own the cross. He heard the soft and meas-ured sound of their approaching footsteps. He imagined that M. Leblanc was darting angry glances at him. "Is that gentleman going to address me?" he thought to himself. He dropped his head; when he raised it again, they were very near him. The young girl passed, and as she passed, she glanced at him. She gazed steadily at him, with a pensive sweetness which thrilled Marius from head to foot. It seemed to him that she was reproaching him for having allowed so long a time to elapse without coming as far as her, and that she was saying to him: "I am coming myself." Marius was dazzled by those eyes fraught with rays and abysses.

He felt his brain on fire. She had come to him, what joy! And then, how she had looked at him! She appeared to him more beautiful than he had ever seen her yet. Beautiful with a beauty which was wholly feminine and angelic, with a complete beauty which would have made Petrarch sing and Dante kneel. It seemed to him that he was floating free in the azure heavens. At the same time, he was horribly vexed because there was dust on his boots.

He thought he felt sure that she had looked at his boots too.

He followed her with his eyes, until she disappeared. Then he started up and walked about the Luxembourg garden like a madman. It is probable that, at times, he laughed to himself and talked aloud. He was so dreamy when he came near the children's nurses, that each one of them thought him in love with her.

He quitted the Luxembourg, hoping to find her again in the street.

He encountered Courfeyrac under the arcades of the Odéon, and said to him: "Come and dine with me." They went off to Rousseau's and spent six francs. Marius ate like an ogre. He gave the waiter six sous. At dessert, he said to Courfeyrac: "Have you read the paper? What a fine discourse Audry de Puyraveau delivered!"

He was desperately in love.

After dinner, he said to Courfeyrac: "I will treat you to the play." They went to the Porte-Sainte-Martin to see Frédérick in *l'Auberge des Adrets*. Marius was enormously amused.

At the same time, he had a redoubled attack of shyness. On emerging from the theater, he re-fused to look at the garter of a modiste who was stepping across a gutter, and Courfeyrac, who said: "I should like to put that woman in my collection," almost horrified him.

Courfeyrac invited him to breakfast at the Café Voltaire on the following morning. Marius went thither, and ate even more than on the preceding evening. He was very thoughtful and very merry. One would have said that he was taking advantage of every occasion to laugh uproariously. He tenderly embraced some man or other from the provinces, who was presented to him. A circle of students formed round the table, and they spoke of the nonsense paid for by the State which was uttered from the rostrum in the Sorbonne, then the conversation fell upon the faults and omissions in Guicherat's dictionaries and grammars. Marius interrupted the discussion to exclaim: "But it is very agreeable, all the same to have the cross!"

"That's queer!" whispered Courfeyrac to Jean Prouvaire.

"No," responded Prouvaire "that's serious."

It was serious; in fact, Marius had reached that first violent and charming hour with which grand passions begin.

A glance had wrought all this.

When the mine is charged, when the conflagration is ready, nothing is more simple. A glance is a spark.

It was all over with him. Marius loved a woman. His fate was entering the unknown.

The glance of women resembles certain combinations of wheels, which are tranquil in appearance yet formidable. You pass close to them every day, peaceably and with impunity, and without a suspicion of anything. A moment arrives when you forget that the thing is there. You go and come, dream, speak, laugh. All at once you feel yourself clutched; all is over. The wheels hold you fast, the glance has ensnared you. It has caught you, no matter where or how, by some portion of your thought which was fluttering loose, by some distraction which had attacked you. You are lost. The whole of you passes into it. A chain of mysterious forces takes possession of you. You struggle in vain; no more human succor is possible. You go on falling from gearing to gearing, from agony to agony, from torture to torture, you, your mind, your fortune, your future, your soul; and, according to whether you are in the power of a wicked creature, or of a noble heart, you will not escape from this terrifying machine otherwise than disfigured with shame, or transfigured by passion.

Chapter VII

ADVENTURES OF THE LETTER U DELIVERED OVER TO CONJECTURES

ISOLATION, DETACHMENT FROM EVERYTHING, PRIDE, INDEPENDENCE, THE TASTE OF NATURE, THE absence of daily and material activity, the life within himself, the secret conflicts of chastity, a benevolent ecstasy toward all creation, had prepared Marius for this possession which is called passion. His worship of his father had gradually become a religion, and, like all religions, it had retreated to the depths of his soul. Something was required in the foreground. Love came.

A full month elapsed, during which Marius went every day to the Luxembourg. When the hour arrived, nothing could hold him back.—"He is on duty," said Courfeyrac. Marius lived in a state of delight. It is certain that the young girl did look at him.

He had finally grown bold, and approached the bench. Still, he did not pass in front of it anymore, in obedience to the instinct of timidity and to the instinct of prudence common to lovers. He considered it better not to attract "the attention of the father." He combined his stations behind the trees and the pedestals of the statues with a profound diplomacy, so that he might be seen as much as possible by the young girl and as little as possible by the old gentleman. Sometimes, he remained motionless by the half-hour together in the shade of a Leonidas or a Spartacus, holding in his hand a book, above which his eyes, gently raised, sought the beautiful girl, and she, on her side, turned her charming profile toward him with a vague smile. While conversing in the most natural and tranquil manner in the world with the white-haired man, she bent upon Marius all the reveries of a virginal and passionate eye. Ancient and time-honored maneuver which Eve understood from the very first day of the world, and which every woman understands from the very first day of her life! her mouth replied to one, and her glance replied to another.

It must be supposed, that M. Leblanc finally noticed something, for often, when Marius arrived, he rose and began to walk about. He had abandoned their accustomed place and had adopted the bench by the Gladiator, near the other end of the walk, as though with the object of seeing whether Marius would pursue them thither. Marius did not understand, and committed this error. "The father" began to grow inexact, and no longer brought "his daughter" every day. Sometimes, he came alone. Then Marius did not stay. Another blunder.

Marius paid no heed to these symptoms. From the phase of timidity, he had passed, by a natural and fatal progress, to the phase of blindness. His love increased. He dreamed of it every night. And then, an unexpected bliss had happened to him, oil on the fire, a redoubling of the shadows over his eyes. One evening, at dusk, he had found, on the bench which "M. Leblanc and his daughter" had just quitted, a handkerchief, a very simple handkerchief, without embroidery, but white, and fine, and which seemed to him to exhale ineffable perfume. He seized it with rapture. This handkerchief was marked with the letters U. F. Marius knew nothing about this beautiful child— neither her family name, her Christian name, nor her abode; these two letters were the first thing of her that he had gained possession of, adorable initials, upon which he immediately began to construct his scaffolding. U was evidently the Christian name. "Ursule!" he thought, "what a delicious name!" He kissed the handkerchief, drank it in, placed it on his heart, on his flesh, during the day, and at night, laid it beneath his lips that he might fall asleep on it.

"I feel that her whole soul lies within it!" he exclaimed.

This handkerchief belonged to the old gentleman, who had simply let it fall from his pocket.

In the days which followed the finding of this treasure, he only displayed himself at the Luxembourg in the act of kissing the handkerchief and laying it on his heart. The beautiful child understood nothing of all this, and signified it to him by imperceptible signs.

"O modesty!" said Marius.

Chapter VIII

THE VETERANS THEMSELVES CAN BE HAPPY

SINCE WE HAVE PRONOUNCED THE WORD MODESTY, AND SINCE WE CONCEAL NOTHING, WE OUGHT to say that once, nevertheless, in spite of his ecstasies, "his Ursule" caused him very serious grief. It was on one of the days when she persuaded M. Leblanc to leave the bench and stroll along the walk. A brisk May breeze was blowing, which swayed the crests of the plantain-trees. The father and daughter, arm in arm, had just passed Marius's bench. Marius had risen to his feet behind them, and was following them with his eyes, as was fitting in the desperate situation of his soul.

All at once, a gust of wind, more merry than the rest, and probably charged with performing the affairs of Springtime, swept down from the nursery, flung itself on the alley, enveloped the young girl in a delicious shiver, worthy of Virgil's nymphs, and the fawns of Theocritus, and lifted her dress, the robe more sacred than that of Isis, almost to the height of her garter. A leg of exquisite shape appeared. Marius saw it. He was exasperated and furious.

The young girl had hastily thrust down her dress, with a divinely troubled motion, but he was none the less angry for all that. He was alone in the alley, it is true. But there might have been someone there. And what if there had been someone there! Can anyone comprehend such a thing? What she had just done is horrible!—Alas! the poor child had done nothing; there had been but one culprit, the wind; but Marius, in whom quivered the Bartholo who exists in Cherubin, was determined to be vexed, and was jealous of his own shadow. It is thus, in fact, that the harsh and capricious jealousy of the flesh awakens in the human heart, and takes possession of it, even without any right. Moreover, setting aside even that jealousy, the sight of that charming leg had contained nothing agreeable for him; the white stocking of the first woman he chanced to meet would have afforded him more pleasure.

When "his Ursule," after having reached the end of the walk, retraced her steps with M.

Leblanc, and passed in front of the bench on which Marius had seated himself once more, Marius darted a sullen and ferocious glance at her. The young girl gave way to that slight straightening up with a backward movement, accompanied by a raising of the eyelids, which signifies: "Well, what is the matter?"

This was "their first quarrel."

Marius had hardly made this scene at her with his eyes, when someone crossed the walk. It was a veteran, very much bent, extremely wrinkled, and pale, in a uniform of the Louis XV pattern, bearing on his breast the little oval plaque of red cloth, with the crossed swords, the soldier's cross of Saint-Louis, and adorned, in addition, with a coat-sleeve, which had no arm within it, with a silver chin and a wooden leg. Marius thought he perceived that this man had an extremely well satisfied air. It even struck him that the aged cynic, as he hobbled along past him, addressed to him a very fraternal and very merry wink, as though some chance had created an understanding between them, and as though they had shared some piece of good luck together. What did that relic of Mars mean by being so contented? What had passed between that wooden leg and the other? Marius reached a paroxysm of jealousy.—"Perhaps he was there!" he said to himself; "perhaps he saw!"— And he felt a desire to exterminate the veteran.

With the aid of time, all points grow dull. Marius's wrath against "Ursule," just and legitimate as it was, passed off. He finally pardoned her; but this cost him a great effort; he sulked for three days.

Nevertheless, in spite of all this, and because of all this, his passion augmented and grew to madness.

Chapter IX

ECLIPSE

THE READER HAS JUST SEEN HOW MARIUS DISCOVERED, OR THOUGHT THAT HE DISCOVERED, THAT *She* was named Ursule.

Appetite grows with loving. To know that her name was Ursule was a great deal; it was very little. In three or four weeks, Marius had devoured this bliss. He wanted another. He wanted to know where she lived.

He had committed his first blunder, by falling into the ambush of the bench by the Gladiator. He had committed a second, by not remaining at the Luxembourg when M. Leblanc, came thither alone. He now committed a third, and an immense one. He followed "Ursule."

She lived in the Rue de l'Ouest, in the most unfrequented spot, in a new, three-story house, of modest appearance.

From that moment forth, Marius added to his happiness of seeing her at the Luxembourg the happiness of following her home.

His hunger was increasing. He knew her first name, at least, a charming name, a genuine woman's name; he knew where she lived; he wanted to know who she was.

One evening, after he had followed them to their dwelling, and had seen them disappear through the carriage gate, he entered in their train and said boldly to the porter:

"Is that the gentleman who lives on the first floor, who has just come in?"

"No," replied the porter. "He is the gentleman on the third floor."

Another step gained. This success emboldened Marius.

"On the front?" he asked.

"Parbleu!" said the porter, "the house is only built on the street."

"And what is that gentleman's business?" began Marius again.

"He is a gentleman of property, sir. A very kind man who does good to the unfortunate, though not rich himself."

"What is his name?" resumed Marius.

The porter raised his head and said:

"Are you a police spy, sir?"

Marius went off quite abashed, but delighted. He was getting on.

"Good," thought he, "I know that her name is Ursule, that she is the daughter of a gentleman who lives on his income, and that she lives there, on the third floor, in the Rue de l'Ouest."

On the following day, M. Leblanc and his daughter made only a very brief stay in the Luxembourg; they went away while it was still broad daylight. Marius followed them to the Rue de l'Ouest, as he had taken up the habit of doing. On arriving at the carriage entrance, M. Leblanc made his daughter pass in first, then paused, before crossing the threshold, and stared intently at Marius.

On the next day they did not come to the Luxembourg. Marius waited for them all day in vain.

At nightfall, he went to the Rue de l'Ouest, and saw a light in the windows of the third story. He walked about beneath the windows until the light was extinguished.

The next day, no one at the Luxembourg. Marius waited all day, then went and did sentinel duty under their windows. This carried him on to ten o'clock in the evening.

His dinner took care of itself. Fever nourishes the sick man, and love the lover.

He spent a week in this manner. M. Leblanc no longer appeared at the Luxembourg.

Marius indulged in melancholy conjectures; he dared not watch the porte cochère during the day; he contented himself with going at night to gaze upon the red light of the windows. At times he saw shadows flit across them, and his heart began to beat.

On the eighth day, when he arrived under the windows, there was no light in them.

"Hello!" he said, "the lamp is not lighted yet. But it is dark. Can they have gone out?" He waited until ten o'clock. Until midnight. Until one in the morning. Not a light appeared in the windows of the third story, and no one entered the house.

He went away in a very gloomy frame of mind.

On the morrow—for he only existed from morrow to morrow, there was, so to speak, no to-day for him—on the morrow, he found no one at the Luxembourg; he had expected this. At dusk, he went to the house.

No light in the windows; the shades were drawn; the third floor was totally dark.

Marius rapped at the porte cochère, entered, and said to the porter:

"The gentleman on the third floor?"

"Has moved away," replied the porter.

Marius reeled and said feebly:

"How long ago?"

"Yesterday."

"Where is he living now?"

"I don't know anything about it."

"So he has not left his new address?"

"No."

And the porter, raising his eyes, recognized Marius.

"Come! So it's you!" said he; "but you are decidedly a spy then?"

BOOK SEVENTH

PATRON MINETTE

Chapter I

MINES AND MINERS

H UMAN SOCIETIES ALL HAVE WHAT IS CALLED IN THEATRICAL PARLANCE, *A THIRD LOWER FLOOR*. The social soil is everywhere undermined, sometimes for good, sometimes for evil. These works are superposed one upon the other. There are superior mines and inferior mines. There is a top and a bottom in this obscure sub-soil, which sometimes gives way beneath civilization, and which our indifference and heedlessness trample underfoot. The Encyclopedia, in the last century, was a mine that was almost open to the sky. The shades, those somber hatchers of primitive Christianity, only awaited an opportunity to bring about an explosion under the Cæsars and to inundate the human race with light. For in the sacred shadows there lies latent light. Volcanoes are full of a shadow that is capable of flashing forth. Every form begins by being night. The catacombs, in which the first mass was said, were not alone the cellar of Rome, there were the vaults of the world.

Beneath the social construction, that complicated marvel of a structure, there are excavations of all sorts. There is the religious mine, the philosophical mine, the economic mine, the revolutionary mine. Such and such a pickax with the idea, such a pick with ciphers. Such another with wrath. People hail and answer each other from one catacomb to another. Utopias travel about underground, in the pipes. There they branch out in every direction. They sometimes meet, and fraternize there. Jean-Jacques lends his pick to Diogenes, who lends him his lantern. Sometimes they enter into combat there. Calvin seizes Socinius by the hair. But nothing arrests nor interrupts the tension of all these energies toward the goal, and the vast, simultaneous activity, which goes and comes, mounts, descends, and mounts again in these obscurities, and which immense unknown swarming slowly transforms the top and the bottom and the inside and the outside. Society hardly even suspects this digging which leaves its surface intact and changes its bowels. There are as many different subterranean stages as there are varying works, as there are extractions. What emerges from these deep excavations? The future.

The deeper one goes, the more mysterious are the toilers. The work is good, up to a degree which the social philosophies are able to recognize; beyond that degree it is doubtful and mixed; lower down, it becomes terrible. At a certain depth, the excavations are no longer penetrable by the spirit of civilization, the limit breathable by man has been passed; a beginning of monsters is possible.

The descending scale is a strange one; and each one of the rungs of this ladder corresponds to a stage where philosophy can find foothold, and where one encounters one of these workmen, sometimes divine, sometimes misshapen. Below John Huss, there is Luther; below Luther, there is Descartes; below Descartes, there is Voltaire; below Voltaire, there is Condorcet; below Condorcet, there is Robespierre; below Robespierre, there is Marat; below Marat, there is Babeuf. And so it goes on. Lower down, confusedly, at the limit which separates the indistinct from the invisible, one perceives other gloomy men, who perhaps do not exist as yet. The men of yesterday are specters; those of to-morrow are forms. The eye of the spirit distinguishes them but obscurely. The embryonic work of the future is one of the visions of philosophy.

A world in limbo, in the state of fetus, what an unheard-of specter!

Saint-Simon, Owen, Fourier, are there also, in lateral galleries.

Surely, although a divine and invisible chain unknown to themselves, binds together all these subterranean pioneers who, almost always, think themselves isolated, and who are not so, their works vary greatly, and the light of some contrasts with the blaze of others. The first are paradisiacal, the last are tragic. Nevertheless, whatever may be the contrast, all these toilers, from the highest to the most nocturnal, from the wisest to the most foolish, possess one likeness, and this is it: disinterestedness. Marat forgets himself like Jesus. They throw themselves on one side, they omit themselves, they think not of themselves. They have a glance, and that glance seeks the absolute. The first has the whole heavens in his eyes; the last, enigmatical though he may be, has still, beneath his eyelids, the pale beam of the infinite. Venerate the man, whoever he may be, who has this sign— the starry eye.

The shadowy eye is the other sign.

With it, evil commences. Reflect and tremble in the presence of anyone who has no glance at all. The social order has its black miners.

There is a point where depth is tantamount to burial, and where light becomes extinct.

Below all these mines which we have just mentioned, below all these galleries, below this whole immense, subterranean, venous system of progress and utopia, much further on in the earth, much lower than Marat, lower than Babeuf, lower, much lower, and without any connection with the upper levels, there lies the last mine. A formidable spot. This is what we have designated as the *le troisième dessous*. It is the grave of shadows. It is the cellar of the blind. *Inferi*.

This communicates with the abyss.

Chapter II

THE LOWEST DEPTHS

THERE DISINTERESTEDNESS VANISHES. THE DEMON IS VAGUELY OUTLINED; EACH ONE IS FOR HIMself. The *I* in the eyes howls, seeks, fumbles, and gnaws. The social Ugolino is in this gulf.

The wild specters who roam in this grave, almost beasts, almost phantoms, are not occupied with universal progress; they are ignorant both of the idea and of the word; they take no thought for anything but the satisfaction of their individual desires. They are almost unconscious, and there exists within them a sort of terrible obliteration. They have two mothers, both step-mothers, ignorance and misery. They have a guide, necessity; and for all forms of satisfaction, appetite. They are brutally voracious, that is to say, ferocious, not after the fashion of the tyrant, but after the fashion of the tiger. From suffering these specters pass to crime; fatal affiliation, dizzy creation, logic of darkness. That which crawls in the social third lower level is no longer complaint stifled by the absolute; it is the protest of matter. Man there becomes a dragon. To be hungry, to be thirsty—that is the point of departure; to be Satan—that is the point reached. From that vault Lacenaire emerges.

We have just seen, in Book Fourth, one of the compartments of the upper mine, of the great political, revolutionary, and philosophical excavation. There, as we have just said, all is pure, noble, dignified, honest. There, assuredly, one might be misled; but error is worthy of veneration there, so thoroughly does it imply heroism. The work there effected, taken as a whole, has a name: Progress.

The moment has now come when we must take a look at other depths, hideous depths. There exists beneath society, we insist upon this point, and there will exist, until that day when ignorance shall be dissipated, the great cavern of evil.

This cavern is below all, and is the foe of all. It is hatred, without exception. This cavern knows no philosophers; its dagger has never cut a pen. Its blackness has no connection with the sublime blackness of the inkstand. Never have the fingers of night which contract beneath this stifling ceiling, turned the leaves of a book nor unfolded a newspaper. Babeuf is a speculator to Cartouche; Marat is an aristocrat to Schinderhannes. This cavern has for its object the destruction of everything.

Of everything. Including the upper superior mines, which it execrates. It not only undermines, in its hideous swarming, the actual social order; it undermines philosophy, it undermines human thought, it undermines civilization, it undermines revolution, it undermines progress. Its name is simply theft, prostitution, murder, assassination. It is darkness, and it desires chaos. Its vault is formed of ignorance.

All the others, those above it, have but one object—to suppress it. It is to this point that philosophy and progress tend, with all their organs simultaneously, by their amelioration of the real, as well as by their contemplation of the absolute. Destroy the cavern Ignorance and you destroy the lair Crime.

Let us condense, in a few words, a part of what we have just written. The only social peril is darkness.

Humanity is identity. All men are made of the same clay. There is no difference, here below, at least, in predestination. The same shadow in front, the same flesh in the present, the same ashes afterwards. But ignorance, mingled with the human paste, blackens it. This incurable blackness takes possession of the interior of a man and is there converted into evil.

Chapter III

BABET, GUEULEMER, CLAQUESOUS, AND MONTPARNASSE

A QUARTETTE OF RUFFIANS, CLAQUESOUS, GUEULEMER, BABET, AND MONTPARNASSE GOVERNED the third lower floor of Paris, from 1830 to 1835.

Gueulemer was a Hercules of no defined position. For his lair he had the sewer of the Arche-Marion. He was six feet high, his pectoral muscles were of marble, his biceps of brass, his breath was that of a cavern, his torso that of a colossus, his head that of a bird. One thought one beheld the Farnese Hercules clad in duck trousers and a cotton velvet waistcoat. Gueulemer, built after this sculptural fashion, might have subdued monsters; he had found it more expeditious to be one. A low brow, large temples, less than forty years of age, but with crow's-feet, harsh, short hair, cheeks like a brush, a beard like that of a wild boar; the reader can see the man before him. His muscles called for work, his stupidity would have none of it. He was a great, idle force. He was an assassin through coolness. He was thought to be a creole. He had, probably, somewhat to do with Marshal Brune, having been a porter at Avignon in 1815. After this stage, he had turned ruffian.

The diaphaneity of Babet contrasted with the grossness of Gueulemer. Babet was thin and learned. He was transparent but impenetrable. Daylight was visible through his bones, but nothing through his eyes. He declared that he was a chemist. He had been a jack of all trades. He had played in vaudeville at Saint-Mihiel. He was a man of purpose, a fine talker, who underlined his smiles and accentuated his gestures. His occupation consisted in selling, in the open air, plaster busts and portraits of "the head of the State." In addition to this, he extracted teeth. He had exhibited phenomena at fairs, and he had owned a booth with a trumpet and this poster: "Babet, Dental Artist, Member of the Academies, makes physical experiments on metals and metalloids, extracts teeth, undertakes stumps abandoned by his brother practitioners. Price: one tooth, one franc, fifty centimes; two teeth, two francs; three teeth, two francs, fifty. Take advantage of this opportunity." This *Take advantage of this opportunity* meant: Have as many teeth extracted as possible. He had been married and had had children. He did not know what had become of his wife and children. He had lost them as one loses his handkerchief. Babet read the papers, a striking exception in the world to which he belonged. One day, at the period when he had his family with him in his booth on wheels, he had read in the *Messager,* that a woman had just given birth to a child, who was doing well, and had a calf's muzzle, and he exclaimed: "There's a fortune! my wife has not the wit to present me with a child like that!"

Later on he had abandoned everything, in order to "undertake Paris." This was his expression.

Who was Claquesous? He was night. He waited until the sky was daubed with black, before he showed himself. At nightfall he emerged from the hole whither he returned before daylight. Where was this hole? No one knew. He only addressed his accomplices in the most absolute darkness, and with his back turned to them. Was his name Claquesous? Certainly not. If a candle was brought, he put on a mask. He was a ventriloquist. Babet said: "Claquesous is a nocturne for two voices." Claquesous was vague, terrible, and a roamer. No one was sure whether he had a name, Claquesous being a sobriquet; none was sure that he had a voice, as his stomach spoke more frequently than his voice; no one was sure that he had a face, as he was never seen without his mask. He disappeared as though he had vanished into thin air; when he appeared, it was as though he sprang from the earth.

A lugubrious being was Montparnasse. Montparnasse was a child; less than twenty years of age, with a handsome face, lips like cherries, charming black hair, the brilliant light of springtime in his eyes; he had all vices and aspired to all crimes.

The digestion of evil aroused in him an appetite for worse. It was the street boy turned pickpocket, and a pickpocket turned garroter. He was genteel, effeminate, graceful, robust, sluggish, ferocious. The rim of his hat was curled up on the left side, in order to make room for a tuft of hair, after the style of 1829. He lived by robbery with violence. His coat was of the best cut, but threadbare. Montparnasse was a fashion-plate in misery and given to the commission of murders. The cause of all this youth's crimes was the desire to be well dressed. The first grisette who had said to him: "You are handsome!" had cast the stain of darkness into his heart, and had made a Cain of this Abel. Finding that he was handsome, he desired to be elegant: now, the height of elegance is idleness; idleness in a poor man means crime. Few prowlers were so dreaded as Montparnasse. At eighteen, he had already numerous corpses in his past. More than one passer-by lay with outstretched arms in the presence of this wretch, with his face in a pool of blood. Curled, pomaded, with laced waist, the hips of a woman, the bust of a Prussian officer, the murmur of admiration from the boulevard wenches surrounding him, his cravat knowingly tied, a bludgeon in his pocket, a flower in his buttonhole; such was this dandy of the sepulcher.

Chapter IV

COMPOSITION OF THE TROUPE

THESE FOUR RUFFIANS FORMED A SORT OF PROTEUS, WINDING LIKE A SERPENT AMONG THE PO-lice, and striving to escape Vidocq's indiscreet glances "under divers forms, tree, flame, fountain," lending each other their names and their traps, hiding in their own shadows, boxes with secret compartments and refuges for each other, stripping off their personalities, as one removes his false nose at a masked ball, sometimes simplifying matters to the point of consisting of but one individual, sometimes multiplying themselves to such a point that Coco-Latour himself took them for a whole throng.

These four men were not four men; they were a sort of mysterious robber with four heads, operating on a grand scale on Paris; they were that monstrous polyp of evil, which inhabits the crypt of society.

Thanks to their ramifications, and to the network underlying their relations, Babet, Gueulemer, Claquesous, and Montparnasse were charged with the general enterprise of the ambushes of the department of the Seine. The inventors of ideas of that nature, men with nocturnal imaginations, applied to them to have their ideas executed. They furnished the canvas to the four rascals, and the latter undertook the preparation of the scenery. They labored at the stage setting. They were always in a condition to lend a force proportioned and suitable to all crimes which demanded a lift of the shoulder, and which were sufficiently lucrative. When a crime was in quest of arms, they under-let their accomplices. They kept a troupe of actors of the shadows at the disposition of all underground tragedies.

They were in the habit of assembling at nightfall, the hour when they woke up, on the plains which adjoin the Salpêtrière. There they held their conferences. They had twelve black hours before them; they regulated their employment accordingly.

Patron-Minette—such was the name which was bestowed in the subterranean circulation on the association of these four men. In the fantastic, ancient, popular parlance, which is vanishing day by day, *Patron-Minette* signifies the morning, the same as *entre chien et loup*—between dog and wolf—signifies the evening. This appellation, *Patron-Minette,* was probably derived from the hour at which their work ended, the dawn being the vanishing moment for phantoms and for the separation of ruffians. These four men were known under this title. When the President of the Assizes visited Lacenaire in his prison, and questioned him concerning a misdeed which Lacenaire denied, "Who did it?" demanded the President. Lacenaire made this response, enigmatical so far as the magistrate was concerned, but clear to the police: "Perhaps it was Patron-Minette."

A piece can sometimes be divined on the enunciation of the personages; in the same manner a band can almost be judged from the list of ruffians composing it. Here are the appellations to which the principal members of Patron-Minette answered—for the names have survived in special memoirs.

Panchaud, alias Printanier, alias Bigrenaille.

Brujon. [There was a Brujon dynasty; we cannot refrain from interpolating this word.]

Boulatruelle, the road-mender already introduced.

Laveuve.

Finistère.

Homère-Hogu, a negro.

Mardisoir. (Tuesday evening.)

Dépêche. (Make haste.)

Fauntleroy, alias Bouquetière (the Flower Girl).

Glorieux, a discharged convict.

Barrecarrosse (Stop-carriage), called Monsieur Dupont.

L'Esplanade-du-Sud.

Poussagrive.

Carmagnolet.

Kruideniers, called Bizarro.

Mangedentelle. (Lace-eater.)

Les-pieds-en-l'Air. (Feet in the air.)

Demi-Liard, called Deux-Milliards.

Etc., etc.

We pass over some, and not the worst of them. These names have faces attached. They do not express merely beings, but species. Each one of these names corresponds to a variety of those misshapen fungi from the under side of civilization.

Those beings, who were not very lavish with their countenances, were not among the men whom one sees passing along the streets. Fatigued by the wild nights which they passed, they went off by day to sleep, sometimes in the lime-kilns, sometimes in the abandoned quarries of Montmatre or Montrouge, sometimes in the sewers. They ran to earth.

What became of these men? They still exist. They have always existed. Horace speaks of them: *Ambubaiarum collegia, pharmacopolae, mendici, mimae*; and so long as society remains what it is, they will remain what they are. Beneath the obscure roof of their cavern, they are continually born again from the social ooze. They return, specters, but always identical; only, they no longer bear the same names and they are no longer in the same skins. The individuals extirpated, the tribe subsists.

They always have the same faculties. From the vagrant to the tramp, the race is maintained in its purity. They divine purses in pockets, they scent out watches in fobs. Gold and silver possess an odor for them. There exist ingenuous bourgeois, of whom it might be said, that they have a "stealable" air. These men patiently pursue these bourgeois. They experience the quivers of a spider at the passage of a stranger or of a man from the country.

These men are terrible, when one encounters them, or catches a glimpse of them, toward midnight, on a deserted boulevard. They do not seem to be men, but forms composed of living mists; one would say that they habitually constitute one mass with the shadows, that they are in no wise distinct from them, that they possess no other soul than the darkness, and that it is only momentarily and for the purpose of living for a few minutes a monstrous life, that they have separated from the night.

What is necessary to cause these specters to vanish? Light. Light in floods. Not a single bat can resist the dawn. Light up society from below.

BOOK EIGHTH

THE WICKED POOR MAN

Chapter I

MARIUS, WHILE SEEKING A GIRL IN A BONNET, ENCOUNTERS A MAN IN A CAP

SUMMER PASSED, THEN THE AUTUMN; WINTER CAME. NEITHER M. LEBLANC NOR THE YOUNG GIRL had again set foot in the Luxembourg garden. Thenceforth, Marius had but one thought—to gaze once more on that sweet and adorable face. He sought constantly, he sought everywhere; he found nothing. He was no longer Marius, the enthusiastic dreamer, the firm, resolute, ardent man, the bold defier of fate, the brain which erected future on future, the young spirit encumbered with plans, with projects, with pride, with ideas and wishes; he was a lost dog. He fell into a black melancholy. All was over. Work disgusted him, walking tired him. Vast nature, formerly so filled with forms, lights, voices, counsels, perspectives, horizons, teachings, now lay empty before him. It seemed to him that everything had disappeared.

He thought incessantly, for he could not do otherwise; but he no longer took pleasure in his thoughts. To everything that they proposed to him in a whisper, he replied in his darkness: "What is the use?"

He heaped a hundred reproaches on himself. "Why did I follow her? I was so happy at the mere sight of her! She looked at me; was not that immense? She had the air of loving me. Was not that everything? I wished to have, what? There was nothing after that. I have been absurd. It is my own fault," etc., etc. Courfeyrac, to whom he confided nothing—it was his nature—but who made some little guess at everything—that was his nature—had begun by congratulating him on being in love, though he was amazed at it; then, seeing Marius fall into this melancholy state, he ended by saying to him: "I see that you have been simply an animal. Here, come to the Chaumière."

Once, having confidence in a fine September sun, Marius had allowed himself to be taken to the ball at Sceaux by Courfeyrac, Bossuet, and Grantaire, hoping, what a dream! that he might, perhaps, find her there. Of course he did not see the one he sought.—"But this is the place, all the same, where all lost women are found," grumbled Grantaire in an aside. Marius left his friends at the ball and returned home on foot, alone, through the night, weary, feverish, with sad and troubled eyes, stunned by the noise and dust of the merry wagons filled with singing creatures on their way home from the feast, which passed close to him, as he, in his discouragement, breathed in the acrid scent of the walnut-trees, along the road, in order to refresh his head.

He took to living more and more alone, utterly overwhelmed, wholly given up to his inward anguish, going and coming in his pain like the wolf in the trap, seeking the absent one everywhere, stupefied by love.

On another occasion, he had an encounter which produced on him a singular effect. He met, in the narrow streets in the vicinity of the Boulevard des Invalides, a man dressed like a working-man and wearing a cap with a long visor, which allowed a glimpse of locks of very white hair. Marius was struck with the beauty of this white hair, and scrutinized the man, who was walking slowly and as though absorbed in painful meditation. Strange to say, he thought that he recognized M. Leblanc. The hair was the same, also the profile, so far as the cap permitted a view of it, the mien identical, only more depressed. But why these workingman's clothes? What was the meaning of this? What signified that disguise? Marius was greatly astonished. When he recovered himself, his first impulse was to follow the man; who knows whether he did not hold at last the clue which he was seeking? In any case, he must see the man near at hand, and clear up the mystery. But the idea occurred to him too late, the man was no longer there. He had turned into some little side street, and Marius could not find him. This encounter occupied his mind for three days and then was effaced. "After all," he said to himself, "it was probably only a resemblance."

Chapter II

TREASURE TROVE

MARIUS HAD NOT LEFT THE GORBEAU HOUSE. HE PAID NO ATTENTION TO ANYONE THERE. At that epoch, to tell the truth, there were no other inhabitants in the house, except himself and those Jondrettes whose rent he had once paid, without, moreover, ever having spoken to either father, mother, or daughters. The other lodgers had moved away or had died, or had been turned out in default of payment.

One day during that winter, the sun had shown itself a little in the afternoon, but it was the 2d of February, that ancient Candlemas day whose treacherous sun, the precursor of a six weeks' cold spell, inspired Mathieu Laensberg with these two lines, which have with justice remained classic:

> Qu'il luise ou qu'il luiserne,
> L'ours rentre dans en sa caverne.[1]

Marius had just emerged from his: night was falling. It was the hour for his dinner; for he had been obliged to take to dining again, alas! oh, infirmities of ideal passions!

He had just crossed his threshold, where Ma'am Bougon was sweeping at the moment, as she uttered this memorable monologue:

"What is there that is cheap now? Everything is dear. There is nothing in the world that is cheap except trouble; you can get that for nothing, the trouble of the world!"

Marius slowly ascended the boulevard toward the barrier, in order to reach the Rue Saint-Jacques. He was walking along with drooping head.

All at once, he felt someone elbow him in the dusk; he wheeled round, and saw two young girls clad in rags, the one tall and slim, the other a little shorter, who were passing rapidly, all out of breath, in terror, and with the appearance of fleeing; they had been coming to meet him, had not seen him, and had jostled him as they passed. Through the twilight, Marius could distinguish their livid faces, their wild heads, their disheveled hair, their hideous bonnets, their ragged petticoats, and their bare feet. They were talking as they ran. The taller said in a very low voice:

"The bobbies have come. They came near nabbing me at the half-circle." The other answered: "I saw them. I bolted, bolted, bolted!"

1. Whether the sun shines brightly or dim, the bear returrns to his cave.

Through this repulsive slang, Marius understood that gendarmes or the police had come near apprehending these two children, and that the latter had escaped.

They plunged among the trees of the boulevard behind him, and there created, for a few minutes, in the gloom, a sort of vague white spot, then disappeared.

Marius had halted for a moment.

He was about to pursue his way, when his eye lighted on a little grayish package lying on the ground at his feet. He stooped and picked it up. It was a sort of envelope which appeared to contain papers.

"Good," he said to himself, "those unhappy girls dropped it."

He retraced his steps, he called, he did not find them; he reflected that they must already be far away, put the package in his pocket, and went off to dine.

On the way, he saw in an alley of the Rue Mouffetard, a child's coffin, covered with a black cloth, resting on three chairs, and illuminated by a candle. The two girls of the twilight recurred to his mind.

"Poor mothers!" he thought. "There is one thing sadder than to see one's children die; it is to see them leading an evil life."

Then those shadows which had varied his melancholy vanished from his thoughts, and he fell back once more into his habitual preoccupations. He fell to thinking once more of his six months of love and happiness in the open air and the broad daylight, beneath the beautiful trees of Luxembourg.

"How gloomy my life has become!" he said to himself. "Young girls are always appearing to me, only formerly they were angels and now they are ghouls."

Chapter III

QUADRIFRONS

THAT EVENING, AS HE WAS UNDRESSING PREPARATORY TO GOING TO BED, HIS HAND CAME IN CONtact, in the pocket of his coat, with the packet which he had picked up on the boulevard. He had forgotten it. He thought that it would be well to open it, and that this package might possibly contain the address of the young girls, if it really belonged to them, and, in any case, the information necessary to a restitution to the person who had lost it.

He opened the envelope.

It was not sealed and contained four letters, also unsealed.

They bore addresses.

All four exhaled a horrible odor of tobacco.

The first was addressed: *"To Madame, Madame la Marquise de Grucheray, the place opposite the Chamber of Deputies, No.——"*

Marius said to himself, that he should probably find in it the information which he sought, and that, moreover, the letter being open, it was probable that it could be read without impropriety.

It was conceived as follows:

MADAME LA MARQUISE—The virtue of clemency and piety is that which most closely unites sosiety. Turn your christian spirit and cast a look of compassion on this unfortunate Spanish victim of loyalty and attachment to the sacred cause of legitimacy, who has given with his blood, consecrated his fortune, evverything, to defend that cause, and to-day finds himself in the greatest missery. He doubts not that your honorable person will grant succor to preserve an existence exteremely painful for a military man of education and honor full of wounds, counts in advance on the humanity which animates you and on the interest which Madame la Marquise bears to a nation so unfortunate. Their prayer will not be in vain, and their gratitude will preserve theirs charming souvenir.

My respectful sentiments, with which I have the honor to be

Madame,

DON ALVARÈS, Spanish Captain
of Cavalry, a royalist who has
take refuge in France, who
finds himself on travells for
his country, and the resources
are lacking him to continue his travells

No address was joined to the signature. Marius hoped to find the address in the second letter, whose superscription read: *À Madame, Madame la Comtesse de Montvernet, Rue Cassette, No. 9*. This is what Marius read in it:

MADAME LA COMTESSE—It is an unhappy mother of a family of six children the last of which is only eight months old. I sick since my last confinement, abandoned by my husband five months ago, haveing no resources in the world the most frightful indigance.

In the hope of Madame la Comtesse, she has the honor to be, Madame, with profound respect,

MISTRESS BALIZARD

Marius turned to the third letter, which was a petition like the preceding; he read:

Monsieur PABOURGEOT, Elector, wholesale stocking merchant,
Rue Saint-Denis on the corner of the Rue aux Fers

I permit myself to address you this letter to beg you to grant me the pretious favor of your simpaties and to interest yourself in a man of letters who has just sent a drama to the Théâtre-Français. The subject is historical, and the action takes place in Auvergne in the time of the Empire; the style, I think, is natural, laconic, and may have some merit. There are couplets to be sung in four places. The comic, the serious, the unexpected, are mingled in a variety of characters, and a tinge of romanticism lightly spread through all the intrigue which proceeds misteriously, and ends, after striking altarations, in the midst of many beautiful strokes of brilliant scenes.

My principal object is to satisfi the desire which progressively animates the man of our century, that is to say, the fashion, that capritious and bizarre weathervane which changes at almost every new wind.

In spite of these qualities I have reason to fear that jealousy, the egotism of priviliged authors, may obtain my exclusion from the theater, for I am not ignorant of the mortificateons with which newcomers are treated.

Monsiuer Pabourgeot, your just reputation as an enlightened protector of men of litters emboldens me to send you my daughter who will explain our indigant situation to you, lacking bread and fire in this wynter season. When I say to you that I beg you to accept the dedication of my drama which I desire to make to you and of all those that I shall make, is to prove to you how great is my ambition to have the honor of sheltering myself under your protection, and of adorning my writings with your name. If you deign to honor me with the most modest offering, I shall immediately occupy myself in making a piesse of verse to pay you my tribute of gratitude. Which I shall endeavor to render this piesse as perfect as possible, will be sent to you before it is inserted at the beginning of the drama and delivered on the stage.

To Monsieur

and Madame PABOURGEOT,

My most respectful complements,

GENFLOT, man of letters

P.S. Even if it is only forty sous.

Excuse me for sending my daughter and not presenting myself, but sad motives connected with the toilet do not permit me, alas! to go out.

Finally, Marius opened the fourth letter. The address ran: *To the benevolent Gentleman of the church of Saint-Jacques-du-haut-Pas*. It contained the following lines:

BENEVOLENT MAN—If you deign to accompany my daughter, you will behold a misserable calamity, and I will show you my certificates.

At the aspect of these writings your generous soul will be moved with a sentiment of obvious benevolence, for true philosophers always feel lively emotions.

Admit, compassionate man, that it is necessary to suffer the most cruel need, and that it is very painful, for the sake of obtaining a little relief, to get one's self attested by the authorities as though one were not free to suffer and to die of inanition while waiting to have our misery relieved. Destinies are very fatal for several and too prodigal or too protecting for others.

I await your presence or your offering, if you deign to make one, and I beseech you to accept the respectful sentiments with which I have the honor to be,

truly magnanimous man,

your very humble

and very obedient servant,

P. FABANTOU, dramatic artist

After perusing these four letters, Marius did not find himself much further advanced than before. In the first place, not one of the signers gave his address.

Then, they seemed to come from four different individuals, Don Alvèras, Mistress Balizard, the poet Genflot, and dramatic artist Fabantou; but the singular thing about these letters was, that all four were written by the same hand.

What conclusion was to be drawn from this, except that they all came from the same person?

Moreover, and this rendered the conjecture all the more probable, the coarse and yellow paper was the same in all four, the odor of tobacco was the same, and, although an attempt had been made to vary the style, the same orthographical faults were reproduced with the greatest tranquility, and the man of letters Genflot was no more exempt from them than the Spanish captain.

It was waste of trouble to try to solve this petty mystery. Had it not been a chance find, it would have borne the air of a mystification. Marius was too melancholy to take even a chance pleasantry well, and to lend himself to a game which the pavement of the street seemed desirous of playing with him. It seemed to him that he was playing the part of the blind man in blind man's buff between the four letters, and that they were making sport of him.

Nothing, however, indicated that these letters belonged to the two young girls whom Marius had met on the boulevard. After all, they were evidently papers of no value. Marius replaced them in their envelope, flung the whole into a corner and went to bed. About seven o'clock in the morning, he had just risen and breakfasted, and was trying to settle down to work, when there came a soft knock at his door.

As he owned nothing, he never locked his door, unless occasionally, though very rarely, when he was engaged in some pressing work. Even when absent he left his key in the lock. "You will be robbed," said Ma'am Bougon. "Of what?" said Marius. The truth is, however, that he had, one day, been robbed of an old pair of boots, to the great triumph of Ma'am Bougon.

There came a second knock, as gentle as the first.

"Come in," said Marius.

The door opened.

"What do you want, Ma'am Bougon?" asked Marius, without raising his eyes from the books and manuscripts on his table.

A voice which did not belong to Ma'am Bougon replied:

"Excuse me, sir—"

It was a dull, broken, hoarse, strangled voice, the voice of an old man, roughened with brandy and liquor.

Marius turned round hastily, and beheld a young girl.

Chapter IV

A ROSE IN MISERY

A VERY YOUNG GIRL WAS STANDING IN THE HALF-OPEN DOOR. THE DORMER WINDOW OF THE garret, through which the light fell, was precisely opposite the door, and illuminated the figure with a wan light. She was a frail, emaciated, slender creature; there was nothing but a chemise and a petticoat upon that chilled and shivering nakedness. Her girdle was a string, her head ribbon a string, her pointed shoulders emerged from her chemise, a blond and lymphatic pallor, earth-colored collar-bones, red hands, a half-open and degraded mouth, missing teeth, dull, bold, base eyes; she had the form of a young girl who has missed her youth, and the look of a corrupt old woman; fifty years mingled with fifteen; one of those beings which are both feeble and horrible, and which cause those to shudder whom they do not cause to weep.

Marius had risen, and was staring in a sort of stupor at this being, who was almost like the forms of the shadows which traverse dreams.

The most heart-breaking thing of all was, that this young girl had not come into the world to be homely. In her early childhood she must even have been pretty. The grace of her age was still struggling against the hideous, premature decrepitude of debauchery and poverty. The remains of beauty were dying away in that face of sixteen, like the pale sunlight which is extinguished under hideous clouds at dawn on a winter's day.

That face was not wholly unknown to Marius. He thought he remembered having seen it somewhere.

"What do you wish, Mademoiselle?" he asked.

The young girl replied in her voice of a drunken convict:

"Here is a letter for you, Monsieur Marius."

She called Marius by his name; he could not doubt that he was the person whom she wanted; but who was this girl? How did she know his name?

Without waiting for him to tell her to advance, she entered. She entered resolutely, staring, with a sort of assurance that made the heart bleed, at the whole room and the unmade bed. Her feet were bare. Large holes in her petticoat permitted glimpses of her long legs and her thin knees. She was shivering.

She held a letter in her hand, which she presented to Marius.

Marius, as he opened the letter, noticed that the enormous wafer which sealed it was still moist. The message could not have come from a distance. He read:

MY AMIABLE NEIGHBOR, YOUNG MAN—I have learned of your goodness to me, that you paid my rent six months ago. I bless you, young man. My eldest daughter will tell you that we have been without a morsel of bread for two days, four persons and my spouse ill. If I am not deseaved in my opinion, I think I may hope that your generous heart will melt at this statement and the desire will subjugate you to be propitious to me by daigning to lavish on me a slight favor.

I am with the distinguished consideration which is due to the benefactors of humanity—

JONDRETTE

P.S. My eldest daughter will await your orders, dear Monsieur Marius.

This letter, coming in the very midst of the mysterious adventure which had occupied Marius's thoughts ever since the preceding evening, was like a candle in a cellar. All was suddenly illuminated.

This letter came from the same place as the other four. There was the same writing, the same style, the same orthography, the same paper, the same odor of tobacco.

There were five missives, five histories, five signatures, and a single signer. The Spanish Captain Don Alvarès, the unhappy Mistress Balizard, the dramatic poet Genflot, the old comedian Fabantou, were all four named Jondrette, if, indeed, Jondrette himself were named Jondrette.

Marius had lived in the house for a tolerably long time, and he had had, as we have said, but very rare occasion to see, to even catch a glimpse of, his extremely mean neighbors. His mind was elsewhere, and where the mind is, there the eyes are also. He had been obliged more than once to pass the Jondrettes in the corridor or on the stairs; but they were mere forms to him; he had paid so little heed to them, that, on the preceding evening, he had jostled the Jondrette girls on the boulevard, without recognizing them, for it had evidently been they, and it was with great difficulty that the one who had just entered his room had awakened in him, in spite of disgust and pity, a vague recollection of having met her elsewhere.

Now he saw everything clearly. He understood that his neighbor Jondrette, in his distress, exercised the industry of speculating on the charity of benevolent persons, that he procured addresses, and that he wrote under feigned names to people whom he judged to be wealthy and compassionate, letters which his daughters delivered at their risk and peril, for this father had come to such a pass, that he risked his daughters; he was playing a game with fate, and he used them as the stake. Marius understood that probably, judging from their flight on the evening before, from their breathless condition, from their terror and from the words of slang which he had overheard, these unfortunate creatures were plying some inexplicably sad profession, and that the result of the whole was, in the midst of human society, as it is now constituted, two miserable beings who were neither girls nor women, a species of impure and innocent monsters produced by misery.

Sad creatures, without name, or sex, or age, to whom neither good nor evil were any longer possible, and who, on emerging from childhood, have already nothing in this world, neither liberty, nor virtue, nor responsibility. Souls which blossomed out yesterday, and are faded to-day, like those flowers let fall in the streets, which are soiled with every sort of mire, while waiting for some wheel to crush them. Nevertheless, while Marius bent a pained and astonished gaze on her, the young girl was wandering back and forth in the garret with the audacity of a specter. She kicked about, without troubling herself as to her nakedness. Occasionally, her chemise, which was untied and torn, fell almost to her waist. She moved the chairs about, she disarranged the toilet articles which stood on the commode, she handled Marius's clothes, she rummaged about to see what there was in the corners.

"Hullo!" said she, "you have a mirror!"

And she hummed scraps of vaudevilles, as though she had been alone, frolicsome refrains which her hoarse and guttural voice rendered lugubrious.

An indescribable constraint, weariness, and humiliation were perceptible beneath this hardihood. Effrontery is a disgrace.

Nothing could be more melancholy than to see her sport about the room, and, so to speak, flit with the movements of a bird which is frightened by the daylight, or which has broken its wing. One felt that under other conditions of education and destiny, the gay and over-free mien of this young girl might have turned out sweet and charming. Never, even among animals, does the creature born to be a dove change into an osprey. That is only to be seen among men.

Marius reflected, and allowed her to have her way.

She approached the table.

"Ah!" said she, "books!"

A flash pierced her glassy eye. She resumed, and her accent expressed the happiness which she felt in boasting of something, to which no human creature is insensible:

"I know how to read, I do!"

She eagerly seized a book which lay open on the table, and read with tolerable fluency:

"—General Bauduin received orders to take the château of Hougomont which stands in the middle of the plain of Waterloo, with five battalions of his brigade."

She paused.

"Ah! Waterloo! I know about that. It was a battle long ago. My father was there. My father has served in the armies. We are fine Bonapartists in our house, that we are! Waterloo was against the English."

She laid down the book, caught up a pen, and exclaimed:

"And I know how to write, too!"

She dipped her pen in the ink, and turning to Marius:

"Do you want to see? Look here, I'm going to write a word to show you."

And before he had time to answer, she wrote on a sheet of white paper, which lay in the middle of the table: "The bobbies are here."

Then throwing down the pen:

"There are no faults of orthography. You can look. We have received an education, my sister and I. We have not always been as we are now. We were not made—"

Here she paused, fixed her dull eyes on Marius, and burst out laughing, saying, with an intonation which contained every form of anguish, stifled by every form of cynicism:

"Bah!"

And she began to hum these words to a gay air:

"J'ai faim, mon père.	*"I am hungry, father.*
Pas de fricot.	*I have no food.*
J'ai froid, ma mère.	*I am cold, mother.*
Pas de tricot.	*I have no clothes.*
Grelotte,	*Shiver,*
Lolotte!	*Lolotte!*
Sanglote,	*Sob,*
Jacquot!"	*Jacquot!"*

She had hardly finished this couplet, when she exclaimed:

"Do you ever go the play, Monsieur Marius? I do. I have a little brother who is a friend of the artists, and who gives me tickets sometimes. But I don't like the benches in the galleries. One is cramped and uncomfortable there. There are rough people there sometimes; and people who smell bad."

Then she scrutinized Marius, assumed a singular air and said:

"Do you know, Mr. Marius, that you are a very handsome fellow?"

And at the same moment the same idea occurred to them both, and made her smile and him blush. She stepped up to him, and laid her hand on his shoulder: "You pay no heed to me, but I know you, Mr. Marius. I meet you here on the staircase, and then I often see you going to a person named Father Mabeuf who lives in the direction of Austerlitz, sometimes when I have been strolling in that quarter. It is very becoming to you to have your hair tumbled thus."

She tried to render her voice soft, but only succeeded in making it very deep. A portion of her words was lost in the transit from her larynx to her lips, as though on a piano where some notes are missing.

Marius had retreated gently.

"Mademoiselle," said he, with his cool gravity, "I have here a package which belongs to you, I think. Permit me to return it to you."

And he held out the envelope containing the four letters.

She clapped her hands and exclaimed:

"We have been looking everywhere for that!"

Then she eagerly seized the package, and opened the envelope, saying as she did so:

"Dieu de Dieu! how my sister and I have hunted! And it was you who found it! On the boulevard, was it not? It must have been on the boulevard? You see, we let it fall when we were running. It was that brat of a sister of mine who was so stupid. When we got home, we could not find it anywhere. As we did not wish to be beaten, as that is useless, as that is entirely useless, as that is absolutely useless, we said that we had carried the letters to the proper persons, and that they had said to us: 'Nix.' So here they are, those poor letters! And how did you find out that they belonged to me? Ah! yes, the writing. So it was you that we jostled as we passed last night. We couldn't see. I said to my sister: 'Is it a gentleman?' My sister said to me: 'I think it is a gentleman.'"

In the meanwhile, she had unfolded the petition addressed to "the benevolent gentleman of the church of Saint-Jacques-du-Haut-Pas."

"Here!" said she, "this is for that old fellow who goes to mass. By the way, this is his hour. I'll go and carry it to him. Perhaps he will give us something to breakfast on."

Then she began to laugh again, and added:

"Do you know what it will mean if we get a breakfast to-day? It will mean that we shall have had our breakfast of the day before yesterday, our breakfast of yesterday, our dinner of to-day, and all that at once, and this morning. Come! Parbleu! if you are not satisfied, dogs, burst!"

This reminded Marius of the wretched girl's errand to himself. He fumbled in his waistcoat pocket, and found nothing there.

The young girl went on, and seemed to have no consciousness of Marius's presence.

"I often go off in the evening. Sometimes I don't come home again. Last winter, before we came here, we lived under the arches of the bridges. We huddled together to keep from freezing. My little sister cried. How melancholy the water is! When I thought of drowning myself, I said to myself: 'No, it's too cold.' I go out alone, whenever I choose, I sometimes sleep in the ditches. Do you know, at night, when I walk along the boulevard, I see the trees like forks, I see houses, all black and as big as Notre-Dame, I fancy that the white walls are the river, I say to myself: 'Why, there's water there!' The stars are like the lamps in illuminations, one would say that they smoked and that the wind blew them out, I am bewildered, as though horses were breathing in my ears; although it is night, I hear hand-organs and spinning-machines, and I don't know what all. I think people are flinging stones at me, I flee without knowing whither, everything whirls and whirls. You feel very queer when you have had no food."

And then she stared at him with a bewildered air.

By dint of searching and ransacking his pockets, Marius had finally collected five francs sixteen sous. This was all he owned in the world for the moment. "At all events," he thought, "there is my dinner for to-day, and to-morrow we will see." He kept the sixteen sous, and handed the five francs to the young girl.

She seized the coin.

"Good!" said she, "the sun is shining!"

And, as though the sun had possessed the property of melting the avalanches of slang in her brain, she went on:

"Five francs! the shiner! a monarch! in this hole! Ain't this fine! You're a jolly thief! I'm your humble servant! Bravo for the good fellows! Two days' wine! and meat! and stew! we'll have a royal feast! and a good fill!"

She pulled her chemise up on her shoulders, made a low bow to Marius, then a familiar sign with her hand, and went toward the door, saying:

"Good morning, sir. It's all right. I'll go and find my old man."

As she passed, she caught sight of a dry crust of bread on the commode, which was molding there amid the dust; she flung herself upon it and bit into it, muttering:

"That's good! it's hard! it breaks my teeth!"

Then she departed.

Chapter V

A PROVIDENTIAL PEEPHOLE

MARIUS HAD LIVED FOR FIVE YEARS IN POVERTY, IN DESTITUTION, EVEN IN DISTRESS, BUT HE now perceived that he had not known real misery. True misery he had but just had a view of. It was its specter which had just passed before his eyes. In fact, he who has only beheld the misery of man has seen nothing; the misery of woman is what he must see; he who has seen only the misery of woman has seen nothing; he must see the misery of the child.

When a man has reached his last extremity, he has reached his last resources at the same time. Woe to the defenseless beings who surround him! Work, wages, bread, fire, courage, good-will, all fail him simultaneously. The light of day seems extinguished without, the moral light within; in these shadows man encounters the feebleness of the woman and the child, and bends them violently to ignominy.

Then all horrors become possible. Despair is surrounded with fragile partitions which all open on either vice or crime.

Health, youth, honor, all the shy delicacies of the young body, the heart, virginity, modesty, that epidermis of the soul, are manipulated in sinister wise by that fumbling which seeks resources, which encounters opprobrium, and which accomodates itself to it. Fathers, mothers, children, brothers, sisters, men, women, daughters, adhere and become incorporated, almost like a mineral formation, in that dusky promiscuousness of sexes, relationships, ages, infamies, and innocences. They crouch, back to back, in a sort of hut of fate. They exchange woe-begone glances. Oh, the unfortunate wretches! How pale they are! How cold they are! It seems as though they dwelt in a planet much further from the sun than ours.

This young girl was to Marius a sort of messenger from the realm of sad shadows. She revealed to him a hideous side of the night.

Marius almost reproached himself for the preoccupations of reverie and passion which had prevented his bestowing a glance on his neighbors up to that day. The payment of their rent had been a mechanical movement, which anyone would have yielded to; but he, Marius, should have done better than that. What! only a wall separated him from those abandoned beings who lived gropingly in the dark outside the pale of the rest of the world, he was elbow to elbow with them, he was, in some sort, the last link of the human race which they touched, he heard them live, or rather, rattle in the death-agony beside him, and he paid no heed to them! Every day, every instant, he heard them walking on the other side of the wall, he heard them go, and come, and speak, and he did not even lend an ear! And groans lay in those words, and he did not even listen to them, his thoughts were elsewhere, given up to dreams, to impossible radiances, to loves in the air, to follies; and all the while, human creatures, his brothers in Jesus Christ, his brothers in the people, were agonizing in vain beside him! He even formed a part of their misfortune, and he aggravated it. For if they had had another neighbor who was less chimerical and more attentive, any ordinary and charitable man, evidently their indigence would have been noticed, their signals of distress would have been perceived, and they would have been taken hold of and rescued! They appeared very corrupt and very depraved, no doubt, very vile, very odious even; but those who fall without becoming degraded are rare; besides, there is a point, where the unfortunate and the infamous unite and are confounded in a single word, a fatal word, *the miserable*; whose fault is this? And then should not the charity be all the more profound, in proportion as the fall is great?

While reading himself this moral lesson, for there were occasions on which Marius, like all truly honest hearts, was his own pedagogue and scolded himself more than he deserved, he stared at the wall which separated him from the Jondrettes, as though he were able to make his gaze, full of pity, penetrate that partition and warm these wretched people. The wall was a thin layer of plaster upheld by lathes and beams, and, as the reader had just learned, it allowed the sound of voices and words to be clearly distinguished. Only a man as dreamy as Marius could have failed to perceive this long before. There was no paper pasted on the wall, either on the side of the Jondrettes or on that of Marius; the coarse construction was visible in its nakedness. Marius examined the partition, almost unconsciously; sometimes reverie examines, observes, and scrutinizes as thought would. All at once he sprang up; he had just perceived, near the top, close to the ceiling, a triangular hole, which resulted from the space between three lathes. The plaster which should have filled this cavity was missing, and by mounting on the commode, a view could be had through this aperture into the Jondrettes' attic. Commiseration has, and should have, its curiosity. This aperture formed a sort of peephole. It is permissible to gaze at misfortune like a traitor in order to succor it.

"Let us get some little idea of what these people are like," thought Marius, "and in what condition they are."

He climbed upon the commode, put his eye to the crevice, and looked.

Chapter VI

THE WILD MAN IN HIS LAIR

CITIES, LIKE FORESTS, HAVE THEIR CAVERNS IN WHICH ALL THE MOST WICKED AND FORMIDABLE creatures which they contain conceal themselves. Only, in cities, that which thus conceals itself is ferocious, unclean, and petty, that is to say, ugly; in forests, that which conceals itself is ferocious, savage, and grand, that is to say, beautiful. Taking one lair with another, the beast's is preferable to the man's. Caverns are better than hovels.

What Marius now beheld was a hovel.

Marius was poor, and his chamber was poverty-stricken, but as his poverty was noble, his garret was neat. The den upon which his eye now rested was abject, dirty, fetid, pestiferous, mean, sordid. The only furniture consisted of a straw chair, an infirm table, some old bits of crockery, and in two of the corners, two indescribable pallets; all the light was furnishd by a dormer window of four panes, draped with spiders' webs. Through this aperture there penetrated just enough light to make the face of a man appear like the face of a phantom. The walls had a leprous aspect, and were covered with seams and scars, like a visage disfigured by some horrible malady; a repulsive moisture exuded from them. Obscene sketches roughly sketched with charcoal could be distinguished upon them.

The chamber which Marius occupied had a dilapidated brick pavement; this one was neither tiled nor planked; its inhabitants stepped directly on the antique plaster of the hovel, which had grown black under the long-continued pressure of feet. Upon this uneven floor, where the dirt seemed to be fairly encrusted, and which possessed but one virginity, that of the broom, were capriciously grouped constellations of old shoes, socks, and repulsive rags; however, this room had a fireplace; so it was let for forty francs a year. There was every sort of thing in that fireplace, a brazier, a pot, broken boards, rags suspended from nails, a bird-cage, ashes, and even a little fire. Two brands were smoldering there in a melancholy way.

One thing which added still more to the horrors of this garret was, that it was large. It had projections and angles and black holes, the lower sides of roofs, bays, and promontories. Hence horrible, unfathomable nooks where it seemed as though spiders as big as one's fist, wood-lice as large as one's foot, and perhaps even—who knows?—some monstrous human beings, must be hiding.

One of the pallets was near the door, the other near the window. One end of each touched the fireplace and faced Marius. In a corner near the aperture through which Marius was gazing, a colored engraving in a black frame was suspended to a nail on the wall, and at its bottom, in large letters, was the inscription; THE DREAM. This represented a sleeping woman, and a child, also asleep, the child on the woman's lap, an eagle in a cloud, with a crown in his beak, and the woman thrusting the crown away from the child's head, without awaking the latter; in the background, Napoleon in a glory, leaning on a very blue column with a yellow capital ornamented with this inscription;

MARINGO

AUSTERLITS

IENA

WAGRAMME

ELOT.

Beneath this frame, a sort of wooden panel, which was no longer than it was broad, stood on the ground and rested in a sloping attitude against the wall. It had the appearance of a picture with its face turned to the wall, of a frame probably showing a daub on the other side, of some pier-glass detached from a wall and lying forgotten there while waiting to be rehung.

Near the table, upon which Marius descried a pen, ink, and paper, sat a man about sixty years of age, small, thin, livid, haggard, with a cunning, cruel, and uneasy air; a hideous scoundrel.

If Lavater had studied this visage, he would have found the vulture mingled with the attorney there, the bird of prey and the pettifogger rendering each other mutually hideous and complementing each other; the pettifogger making the bird of prey ignoble, the bird of prey making the pettifogger horrible.

This man had a long gray beard. He was clad in a woman's chemise, which allowed his hairy breast and his bare arms, bristling with gray hair, to be seen. Beneath this chemise, muddy trousers and boots through which his toes projected were visible.

He had a pipe in his mouth and was smoking. There was no bread in the hovel, but there was still tobacco.

He was writing probably some more letters like those which Marius had read.

On the corner of the table lay an ancient, dilapidated, reddish volume, and the size, which was the antique 12mo of reading-rooms, betrayed a romance. On the cover sprawled the following title, printed in large capitals: GOD; THE KING; HONOR AND THE LADIES; BY DUCRAY DU-MINIL, 1814.

As the man wrote, he talked aloud, and Marius heard his words:

"The idea that there is no equality, even when you are dead! Just look at Pere Lachaise! The great, those who are rich, are up above, in the acacia alley, which is paved. They can reach it in a carriage. The little people, the poor, the unhappy, well, what of them? they are put down below, where the mud is up to your knees, in the damp places. They are put there so that they will decay the sooner! You cannot go to see them without sinking into the earth."

He paused, smote the table with his fist, and added, as he ground his teeth:

"Oh! I could eat the whole world!"

A big woman, who might be forty years of age, or a hundred, was crouching near the fireplace on her bare heels.

She, too, was clad only in a chemise and a knitted petticoat patched with bits of old cloth. A coarse linen apron concealed the half of her petticoat. Although this woman was doubled up and bent together, it could be seen that she was of very lofty stature. She was a sort of giant, beside her husband. She had hideous hair, of a reddish blond which was turning gray, and which she thrust back from time to time, with her enormous shining hands, with their flat nails.

Beside her, on the floor, wide open, lay a book of the same form as the other, and probably a volume of the same romance.

On one of the pallets, Marius caught a glimpse of a sort of tall pale young girl, who sat there half naked and with pendant feet, and who did not seem to be listening or seeing or living.

No doubt the younger sister of the one who had come to his room.

She seemed to be eleven or twelve years of age. On closer scrutiny it was evident that she really was fourteen. She was the child who had said, on the boulevard the evening before: "I bolted, bolted, bolted!"

She was of that puny sort which remains backward for a long time, then suddenly starts up rapidly. It is indigence which produces these melancholy human plants. These creatures have neither childhood nor youth. At fifteen years of age they appear to be twelve, at sixteen they seem twenty. To-day a little girl, to-morrow a woman. One might say that they stride through life, in order to get through with it the more speedily.

At this moment, this being had the air of a child.

Moreover, no trace of work was revealed in that dwelling; no handicraft, no spinning-wheel, not a tool. In one corner lay some ironmongery of dubious aspect. It was the dull listlessness which follows despair and precedes the death-agony.

Marius gazed for a while at this gloomy interior, more terrifying than the interior of a tomb, for the human soul could be felt fluttering there, and life was palpitating there. The garret, the cellar, the lowly ditch where certain indigent wretches crawl at the very bottom of the social edifice, is not exactly the sepulcher, but only its antechamber; but, as the wealthy display their greatest magnificence at the entrance of their palaces, it seems that death, which stands directly side by side with them, places its greatest miseries in that vestibule.

The man held his peace, the woman spoke no word, the young girl did not even seem to breathe. The scratching of the pen on the paper was audible.

The man grumbled, without pausing in his writing: "Canaille! canaille! everybody is canaille!"

This variation to Solomon's exclamation elicited a sigh from the woman.

"Calm yourself, my little friend," she said. "Don't hurt yourself, my dear. You are too good to write to all those people, husband."

Bodies press close to each other in misery, as in cold, but hearts draw apart. This woman must have loved this man, to all appearance, judging from the amount of love within her; but probably, in the daily and reciprocal reproaches of the horrible distress which weighed on the whole group, this had become extinct. There no longer existed in her anything more than the ashes of affection for her husband. Nevertheless, caressing appellations had survived, as is often the case. She called him: *My dear, my little friend, my good man,* etc., with her mouth while her heart was silent.

The man resumed his writing.

Chapter VII

STRATEGY AND TACTICS

MARIUS, WITH A LOAD UPON HIS BREAST, WAS ON THE POINT OF DESCENDING FROM THE SPECIES of observatory which he had improvised, when a sound attracted his attention and caused him to remain at his post.

The door of the attic had just burst open abruptly. The eldest girl made her appearance on the threshold. On her feet, she had large, coarse, men's shoes, bespattered with mud, which had splashed even to her red ankles, and she was wrapped in an old mantle which hung in tatters. Marius had not seen it on her an hour previously, but she had probably deposited it at his door, in order that she might inspire the more pity, and had picked it up again on emerging. She entered, pushed the door to behind her, paused to take breath, for she was completely breathless, then exclaimed with an expression of triumph and joy:

"He is coming!"

The father turned his eyes toward her, the woman turned her head, the little sister did not stir.

"Who?" demanded her father.

"The gentleman!"

"The philanthropist?"

"Yes."

"From the church of Saint-Jacques?"

"Yes."

"That old fellow?"

"Yes."

"And he is coming?"

"He is following me."

"You are sure?"

"I am sure."

"There, truly, he is coming?"

"He is coming in a fiacre."

"In a fiacre. He is Rothschild."

The father rose.

"How are you sure? If he is coming in a fiacre, how is it that you arrive before him? You gave him our address at least? Did you tell him that it was the last door at the end of the corridor, on the right? If he only does not make a mistake? So you found him at the church? Did he read my letter? What did he say to you?"

"Ta, ta, ta," said the girl, "how you do gallop on, my good man! See here: I entered the church, he was in his usual place, I made him a reverence, and I handed him the letter; he read it and said to me: 'Where do you live, my child?' I said: 'Monsieur, I will show you.' He said to me: 'No, give me your address, my daughter has some purchases to make, I will take a carriage and reach your house at the same time that you do.' I gave him the address. When I mentioned the house, he seemed surprised and hesitated for an instant, then he said: 'Never mind, I will come.' When the mass was finished, I watched him leave the church with his daughter, and I saw them enter a carriage. I certainly did tell him the last door in the corridor, on the right."

"And what makes you think that he will come?"

"I have just seen the fiacre turn into the Rue Petit-Banquier. That is what made me run so."

"How do you know that it was the same fiacre?"

"Because I took notice of the number, so there!"

"What was the number?"

"440."

"Good, you are a clever girl."

The girl stared boldly at her father, and showing the shoes which she had on her feet:

"A clever girl, possibly; but I tell you I won't put these shoes on again, and that I won't, for the sake of my health, in the first place, and for the sake of cleanliness, in the next. I don't know anything more irritating than shoes that squelch, and go *ghi, ghi, ghi,* the whole time. I prefer to go barefoot."

"You are right," said her father, in a sweet tone which contrasted with the young girl's rudeness, "but then, you will not be allowed to enter churches, for poor people must have shoes to do that. One cannot go barefoot to the good God," he added bitterly.

Then, returning to the subject which absorbed him:

"So you are sure that he will come?"

"He is following on my heels," said she.

The man started up. A sort of illumination appeared on his countenance.

"Wife!" he exclaimed, "you hear. Here is the philanthropist. Extinguish the fire."

The stupefied mother did not stir.

The father, with the agility of an acrobat, seized a broken-nosed jug which stood on the chimney, and flung the water on the brands.

Then, addressing his eldest daughter:

"Here you! Pull the straw off that chair!"

His daughter did not understand.

He seized the chair, and with one kick he rendered it seatless. His leg passed through it.

As he withdrew his leg, he asked his daughter:

"Is it cold?"

"Very cold. It is snowing."

The father turned toward the younger girl who sat on the bed near the window, and shouted to her in a thundering voice:

"Quick! get off that bed, you lazy thing! will you never do anything! break a pane of glass!"

The little girl jumped off the bed with a shiver.

"Break a pane!" he repeated.

The child stood still in bewilderment.

"Do you hear me?" repeated her father, "I tell you to break a pane!"

The child, with a sort of terrified obedience, rose on tiptoe, and struck a pane with her fist. The glass broke and fell with a loud clatter.

"Good," said the father.

He was grave and abrupt. His glance swept rapidly over all the crannies of the garret. One would have said that he was a general making the final preparation at the moment when the battle is on the point of beginning.

The mother, who had not said a word so far, now rose and demanded in a dull, slow, languid voice, whence her words seemed to emerge in a congealed state:

"What do you mean to do, my dear?"

"Get into bed," replied the man.

His intonation admitted of no deliberation. The mother obeyed, and threw herself heavily on one of the pallets.

In the meantime, a sob became audible in one corner.

"What's that?" cried the father.

The younger daughter exhibited her bleeding fist, without quitting the corner in which she was cowering. She had wounded herself while breaking the window; she went off, near her mother's pallet and wept silently.

It was now the mother's turn to start up and exclaim:

"Just see there! What follies you commit! She has cut herself breaking that pane for you!"

"So much the better!" said the man. "I foresaw that."

"What? So much the better?" retorted his wife.

"Peace!" replied the father, "I suppress the liberty of the press."

Then tearing the woman's chemise which he was wearing, he made a strip of cloth with which he hastily swathed the little girl's bleeding wrist.

That done, his eye fell with a satisfied expression on his torn chemise.

"And the chemise too," said he, "this has a good appearance."

An icy breeze whistled through the window and entered the room. The outer mist penetrated thither and diffused itself like a whitish sheet of wadding vaguely spread by invisible fingers. Through the broken pane the snow could be seen falling. The snow promised by the Candlemas sun of the preceding day had actually come.

The father cast a glance about him as though to make sure that he had forgotten nothing. He seized an old shovel and spread ashes over the wet brands in such a manner as to entirely conceal them.

Then drawing himself up and leaning against the chimney-piece:

"Now," said he, "we can receive the philanthropist."

Chapter VIII

THE RAY OF LIGHT IN THE HOVEL

THE BIG GIRL APPROACHED AND LAID HER HAND IN HER FATHER'S.

"Feel how cold I am," said she.

"Bah!" replied the father, "I am much colder than that."

The mother exclaimed impetuously:

"You always have something better than anyone else, so you do! even bad things."

"Down with you!" said the man.

The mother, being eyed after a certain fashion, held her tongue.

Silence reigned for a moment in the hovel. The elder girl was removing the mud from the bottom of her mantle, with a careless air; her younger sister continued to sob; the mother had taken the latter's head between her hands, and was covering it with kisses, whispering to her the while:

"My treasure, I entreat you, it is nothing of consequence, don't cry, you will anger your father."

"No!" exclaimed the father, "quite the contrary! sob! sob! that's right."

Then turning to the elder:

"There now! He is not coming! What if he were not to come! I shall have extinguished my fire, wrecked my chair, torn my shirt, and broken my pane all for nothing."

"And wounded the child!" murmured the mother.

"Do you know," went on the father, "that it's beastly cold in this devil's garret! What if that man should not come! Oh! See there, you! He makes us wait! He says to himself: 'Well! they will wait for me! That's what they're there for.' Oh! how I hate them, and with what joy, jubilation, enthusiasm, and satisfaction I could strangle all those rich folks! all those rich folks! These men who pretend to be charitable, who put on airs, who go to mass, who make presents to the priesthood, *preachy, preachy,* in their skull-caps, and who think themselves above us, and who come for the purpose of humiliating us, and to bring us 'clothes,' as they say! old duds that are not worth four sous! And bread! That's not what I want, pack of rascals that they are, it's money! Ah! money! Never! Because they say that we would go off and drink it up, and that we are drunkards and idlers! And they! What are they, then, and what have they been in their time! Thieves! They never could have become rich otherwise! Oh! Society ought to be grasped by the four corners of the cloth and tossed into the air, all of it! It would all be smashed, very likely, but at least, no one would have anything, and there would be that much gained! But what is that blockhead of a benevolent gentleman doing? Will he come? Perhaps the animal has forgotten the address! I'll bet that that old beast—"

At that moment there came a light tap at the door, the man rushed to it and opened it, exclaiming, amid profound bows and smiles of adoration:

"Enter, sir! Deign to enter, most respected benefactor, and your charming young lady, also."

A man of ripe age and a young girl made their appearance on the threshold of the attic.

Marius had not quitted his post. His feelings for the moment surpassed the powers of the human tongue.

It was She!

Whoever has loved knows all the radiant meanings contained in those three letters of that word: She.

It was certainly she. Marius could hardly distinguish her through the luminous vapor which had suddenly spread before his eyes. It was that sweet, absent being, that star which had beamed upon him for six months; it was those eyes, that brow, that mouth, that lovely vanished face which had created night by its departure. The vision had been eclipsed, now it reappeared.

It reappeared in that gloom, in that garret, in that misshapen attic, in all that horror.

Marius shuddered in dismay. What! It was she! The palpitations of his heart troubled his sight. He felt that he was on the brink of bursting into tears! What! He beheld her again at last, after having sought her so long! It seemed to him that he had lost his soul, and that he had just found it again.

She was the same as ever, only a little pale; her delicate face was framed in a bonnet of violet velvet, her figure was concealed beneath a pelisse of black satin. Beneath her long dress, a glimpse could be caught of her tiny foot shod in a silken boot.

She was still accompanied by M. Leblanc.

She had taken a few steps into the room, and had deposited a tolerably bulky parcel on the table.

The eldest Jondrette girl had retired behind the door, and was staring with somber eyes at that velvet bonnet, that silk mantle, and that charming, happy face.

Chapter IX

JONDRETTE COMES NEAR WEEPING

THE HOVEL WAS SO DARK, THAT PEOPLE COMING FROM WITHOUT FELT ON ENTERING IT THE EF-fect produced on entering a cellar. The two newcomers advanced, therefore, with a certain hesitation, being hardly able to distinguish the vague forms surrounding them, while they could be clearly seen and scrutinized by the eyes of the inhabitants of the garret, who were accustomed to this twilight.

M. Leblanc approached, with his sad but kindly look, and said to Jondrette the father:

"Monsieur, in this package you will find some new clothes and some woolen stockings and blankets."

"Our angelic benefactor overwhelms us," said Jondrette, bowing to the very earth.

Then, bending down to the ear of his eldest daughter, while the two visitors were engaged in examining this lamentable interior, he added in a low and rapid voice:

"Hey? What did I say? Duds! No money! They are all alike! By the way, how was the letter to that old blockhead signed?"

"Fabantou," replied the girl.

"The dramatic artist, good!"

It was lucky for Jondrette, that this had occurred to him, for at the very moment, M. Leblanc turned to him, and said to him with the air of a person who is seeking to recall a name:

"I see that you are greatly to be pitied, Monsieur—"

"Fabantou," replied Jondrette quickly.

"Monsieur Fabantou, yes, that is it. I remember."

"Dramatic artist, sir, and one who has had some success."

Here Jondrette evidently judged the moment propitious for capturing the "philanthropist." He exclaimed with an accent which smacked at the same time of the vainglory of the mountebank at fairs, and the humility of the mendicant on the highway:

"A pupil of Talma! Sir! I am a pupil of Talma! Fortune formerly smiled on me—Alas! Now it is misfortune's turn. You see, my benefactor, no bread, no fire. My poor babes have no fire! My only chair has no seat! A broken pane! And in such weather! My spouse in bed! Ill!"

"Poor woman!" said M. Leblanc.

"My child wounded!" added Jondrette.

The child, diverted by the arrival of the strangers, had fallen to contemplating "the young lady," and had ceased to sob.

"Cry! bawl!" said Jondrette to her in a low voice.

At the same time he pinched her sore hand. All this was done with the talent of a juggler.

The little girl gave vent to loud shrieks.

The adorable young girl, whom Marius, in his heart, called "his Ursule," approached her hastily.

"Poor, dear child!" said she.

"You see, my beautiful young lady," pursued Jondrette, "her bleeding wrist! It came through an accident while working at a machine to earn six sous a day. It may be necessary to cut off her arm."

"Really?" said the old gentleman, in alarm.

The little girl, taking this seriously, fell to sobbing more violently than ever.

"Alas! yes, my benefactor!" replied the father.

For several minutes, Jondrette had been scrutinizing "the benefactor" in a singular fashion. As he spoke, he seemed to be examining the other attentively, as though seeking to summon up his recollections. All at once, profiting by a moment when the newcomers were questioning the child with interest as to her injured hand, he passed near his wife, who lay in her bed with a stupid and dejected air, and said to her in a rapid but very low tone:

"Take a look at that man!"

Then, turning to M. Leblanc, and continuing his lamentations:

"You see, sir! All the clothing that I have is my wife's chemise! And all torn at that! In the depths of winter! I can't go out for lack of a coat. If I had a coat of any sort, I would go and see Mademoiselle Mars, who knows me and is very fond of me. Does she not still reside in the Rue de la Tour-des-Dames? Do you know, sir? We played together in the provinces. I shared her laurels. Célimène would come to my succor, sir! Elmire would bestow alms on Bélisaire! But no, nothing! And not a sou in the house! My wife ill, and not a sou! My daughter dangerously injured, not a sou! My wife suffers from fits of suffocation. It comes from her age, and besides, her nervous system is affected. She ought to have assistance, and my daughter also! But the doctor! But the apothecary! How am I to pay them? I would kneel to a penny, sir! Such is the condition to which the arts are reduced. And do you know, my charming young lady, and you, my generous protector, do you know, you who breathe forth virtue and goodness, and who perfume that church where my daughter sees you every day when she says her prayers?—For I have brought up my children religiously, sir. I did not want them to take to the theater. Ah! the hussies! If I catch them tripping! I do not jest, that I don't! I read them lessons on honor, on morality, on virtue! Ask them! They have got to walk straight. They are none of your unhappy wretches who begin by having no family, and end by espousing the public. One is Mamselle Nobody, and one becomes Madame Everybody. Deuce take it! None of that in the Fabantou family! I mean to bring them up virtuously, and they shall be honest, and nice, and believe in God, by the sacred name! Well, sir, my worthy sir, do you know what is going to happen to-morrow? To-morrow is the fourth day of February, the fatal day, the last day of grace allowed me by my landlord; if by this evening I have not paid my rent, to-morrow my oldest daughter, my spouse with her fever, my child with her wound—we shall all four be turned out of here and thrown into the street, on the boulevard, without shelter, in the rain, in the snow. There, sir. I owe for four quarters—a whole year! that is to say, sixty francs."

Jondrette lied. Four quarters would have amounted to only forty francs, and he could not owe four, because six months had not elapsed since Marius had paid for two.

M. Leblanc drew five francs from his pocket and threw them on the table.

Jondrette found time to mutter in the ear of his eldest daughter:

"The scoundrel! What does he think I can do with his five francs? That won't pay me for my chair and pane of glass! That's what comes of incurring expenses!"

In the meanwhile, M. Leblanc had removed the large brown great-coat which he wore over his blue coat, and had thrown it over the back of the chair.

"Monsieur Fabantou," he said, "these five francs are all that I have about me, but I shall now take my daughter home, and I will return this evening—it is this evening that you must pay, is it not?"

Jondrette's face lighted up with a strange expression. He replied vivaciously:

"Yes, respected sir. At eight o'clock, I must be at my landlord's."

"I will be here at six, and I will fetch you the sixty francs."

"My benefactor!" exclaimed Jondrette, overwhelmed. And he added, in a low tone: "Take a good look at him, wife!"

M. Leblanc had taken the arm of the young girl, once more, and had turned toward the door.

"Farewell until this evening, my friends!" said he.

"Six o'clock?" said Jondrette.

"Six o'clock precisely."

At that moment, the over-coat lying on the chair caught the eye of the elder Jondrette girl.

"You are forgetting your coat, sir," said she.

Jondrette darted an annihilating look at his daughter, accompanied by a formidable shrug of the shoulders.

M. Leblanc turned back and said, with a smile:

"I have not forgotten it, I am leaving it."

"O my protector!" said Jondrette, "my august benefactor, I melt into tears! Permit me to accompany you to your carriage."

"If you come out," answered M. Leblanc, "put on this coat. It really is very cold."

Jondrette did not need to be told twice. He hastily donned the brown great-coat. And all three went out, Jondrette preceding the two strangers.

Chapter X

TARIFF OF LICENSED CABS: TWO FRANCS AN HOUR

MARIUS HAD LOST NOTHING OF THIS ENTIRE SCENE, AND YET, IN REALITY, HAD SEEN NOTHING. His eyes had remained fixed on the young girl, his heart had, so to speak, seized her and wholly enveloped her from the moment of her very first step in that garret. During her entire stay there, he had lived that life of ecstasy which suspends material perceptions and precipitates the whole soul on a single point. He contemplated, not that girl, but that light which wore a satin pelisse and a velvet bonnet. The star Sirius might have entered the room, and he would not have been any more dazzled.

While the young girl was engaged in opening the package, unfolding the clothing and the blankets, questioning the sick mother kindly, and the little injured girl tenderly, he watched her every movement, he sought to catch her words. He knew her eyes, her brow, her beauty, her form, her walk, he did not know the sound of her voice. He had once fancied that he had caught a few words at the Luxembourg, but he was not absolutely sure of the fact. He would have given ten years of his life to hear it, in order that he might bear away in his soul a little of that music. But everything was drowned in the lamentable exclamations and trumpet bursts of Jondrette. This added a touch of genuine wrath to Marius's ecstasy. He devoured her with his eyes. He could not believe that it really was that divine creature whom he saw in the midst of those vile creatures in that monstrous lair. It seemed to him that he beheld a humming-bird in the midst of toads.

When she took her departure, he had but one thought, to follow her, to cling to her trace, not to quit her until he learned where she lived, not to lose her again, at least, after having so miraculously rediscovered her. He leaped down from the commode, and seized his hat. As he laid his hand on the lock of the door, and was on the point of opening it, a sudden reflection caused him to pause. The corridor was long, the staircase steep, Jondrette was talkative, M. Leblanc had, no doubt, not yet regained his carriage; if, on turning round in the corridor, or on the staircase, he were to catch sight of him, Marius, in that house, he would, evidently, take the alarm, and find means to escape from him again, and this time it would be final. What was he to do? Should he wait a little? But while he was waiting, the carriage might drive off. Marius was perplexed. At last he accepted the risk and quitted his room.

There was no one in the corridor. He hastened to the stairs. There was no one on the staircase. He descended in all haste, and reached the boulevard in time to see a fiacre turning the corner of the Rue du Petit-Banquier, on its way back to Paris.

Marius rushed headlong in that direction. On arriving at the angle of the boulevard, he caught sight of the fiacre again, rapidly descending the Rue Mouffetard; the carriage was already a long way off, and there was no means of overtaking it; what! run after it? Impossible; and besides, the people in the carriage would assuredly notice an individual running at full speed in pursuit of a fiacre, and the father would recognize him. At that moment, wonderful and unprecedented good luck, Marius perceived an empty cab passing along the boulevard. There was but one thing to be done, to jump into this cab and follow the fiacre. That was sure, efficacious, and free from danger.

Marius made the driver a sign to halt, and called to him:

"By the hour?"

Marius wore no cravat, he had on his working-coat, which was destitute of buttons, his shirt was torn along one of the plaits on the bosom.

The driver halted, winked, and held out his left hand to Marius, rubbing his forefinger gently with his thumb.

"What is it?" said Marius.

"Pay in advance," said the coachman.

Marius recollected that he had but sixteen sous about him.

"How much?" he demanded.

"Forty sous."

"I will pay on my return."

The driver's only reply was to whistle the air of La Palisse and to whip up his horse.

Marius stared at the retreating cabriolet with a bewildered air. For the lack of four-and-twenty sous, he was losing his joy, his happiness, his love! He had seen, and he was becoming blind again. He reflected bitterly, and it must be confessed, with profound regret, on the five francs which he had bestowed, that very morning, on that miserable girl. If he had had those five francs, he would have been saved, he would have been born again, he would have emerged from the limbo and darkness, he would have made his escape from isolation and spleen, from his widowed state; he might have re-knotted the black thread of his destiny to that beautiful golden thread, which had just floated before his eyes and had broken at the same instant, once more! He returned to his hovel in despair.

He might have told himself that M. Leblanc had promised to return in the evening, and that all he had to do was to set about the matter more skillfully, so that he might follow him on that occasion; but, in his contemplation, it is doubtful whether he had heard this.

As he was on the point of mounting the staircase, he perceived, on the other side of the boulevard, near the deserted wall skirting the Rue de la Barrière-des-Gobelins, Jondrette, wrapped in the "philanthropist's" great-coat, engaged in conversation with one of those men of disquieting aspect who have been dubbed by common consent, *prowlers of the barriers*; people of equivocal face, of suspicious monologues, who present the air of having evil minds, and who generally sleep in the daytime, which suggests the supposition that they work by night.

These two men, standing there motionless and in conversation, in the snow which was falling in whirlwinds, formed a group that a policeman would surely have observed, but which Marius hardly noticed.

Still, in spite of his mournful preoccupation, he could not refrain from saying to himself that this prowler of the barriers with whom Jondrette was talking, resembled a certain Panchaud, alias Printanier, alias Bigrenaille, whom Courfeyrac had once pointed out to him as a very dangerous nocturnal roamer. This man's name the reader has learned in the preceding book. This Panchaud, alias Printanier, alias Bigrenaille, figured later on, in many criminal trials, and became a notorious rascal. He was at that time only a famous rascal. To-day he exists in the state of tradition among ruffians and assassins. He was at the head of a school toward the end of the last reign. And in the evening, at nightfall, at the hour when groups form and talk in whispers, he was discussed at La Force in the Fosse-aux-Lions. One might even, in that prison, precisely at the spot where the sewer which served the unprecedented escape, in broad daylight, of thirty prisoners, in 1843, passes under the culvert, read his name, PANCHAUD, audaciously carved by his own hand on the wall of the sewer, during one of his attempts at flight. In 1832, the police already had their eye on him, but he had not as yet made a serious beginning.

Chapter XI

OFFERS OF SERVICE FROM MISERY TO WRETCHEDNESS

MARIUS ASCENDED THE STAIRS OF THE HOVEL WITH SLOW STEPS; AT THE MOMENT WHEN HE WAS about to re-enter his cell, he caught sight of the elder Jondrette girl following him through the corridor. The very sight of this girl was odious to him; it was she who had his five francs, it was too late to demand them back, the cab was no longer there, the fiacre was far away. Moreover, she would not have given them back. As for questioning her about the residence of the persons who had just been there, that was useless; it was evident that she did not know, since the letter signed Fabantou had been addressed "to the benevolent gentleman of the church of Saint-Jacques-du-Haut-Pas."

Marius entered his room and pushed the door to after him.

It did not close; he turned round and beheld a hand which held the door half-open.

"What is it?" he asked, "who is there?"

It was the Jondrette girl.

"Is it you?" resumed Marius almost harshly, "still you! What do you want with me?"

She appeared to be thoughtful and did not look at him. She no longer had the air of assurance which had characterized her that morning. She did not enter, but held back in the darkness of the corridor, where Marius could see her through the half-open door.

"Come now? will you answer," cried Marius, "What do you want with me?"

She raised her dull eyes, in which a sort of gleam seemed to flicker vaguely, and said:

"Monsieur Marius, you look sad. What is the matter with you?"

"With me!" said Marius.

"Yes, you."

"There is nothing the matter with me."

"Yes, there is!"

"No."

"I tell you there is!"

"Let me alone!"

Marius gave the door another push, but she retained her hold on it.

"Stop," said she, "you are in the wrong. Although you are not rich, you were kind this morning. Be so again now. You gave me something to eat, now tell me what ails you. You are grieved, that is plain. I do not want you to be grieved. What can be done for it? Can I be of any service? Employ me. I do not ask for your secrets, you need not tell them to me, but I may be of use, nevertheless. I may be able to help you, since I help my father. When it is necessary to carry letters, to go to houses, to inquire from door to door, to find out an address, to follow anyone, I am of service. Well, you may assuredly tell me what is the matter with you, and I will go and speak to the persons; sometimes it is enough if someone speaks to the persons, that suffices to let them understand matters, and everything comes right. Make use of me."

An idea flashed across Marius's mind. What branch does one disdain when one feels that one is falling?

He drew near to the Jondrette girl.

"Listen—" he said to her.

She interrupted him with a gleam of joy in her eyes.

"Oh yes, do call me *thou!* I like that better."

"Well," he resumed, "thou hast brought hither that old gentleman and his daughter!"

"Yes."

"Dost thou know their address?"

"No."

"Find it for me."

The Jondrette's dull eyes had grown joyous, and they now became gloomy.

"Is that what you want?" she demanded.

"Yes."

"Do you know them?"

"No."

"That is to say," she resumed quickly, "you do not know her, but you wish to know her."

This *them* which had turned into *her* had something indescribably significant and bitter about it.

"Well, can you do it?" said Marius.

"You shall have the beautiful lady's address."

There was still a shade in the words "the beautiful lady" which troubled Marius. He resumed: "Never mind, after all, the address of the father and daughter. Their address, indeed!"

She gazed fixedly at him.

"What will you give me?"

"Anything you like."

"Anything I like?"

"Yes."

"You shall have the address."

She dropped her head; then, with a brusque movement, she pulled to the door, which closed behind her.

Marius found himself alone.

He dropped into a chair, with his head and both elbows on his bed, absorbed in thoughts which he could not grasp, and as though a prey to vertigo. All that had taken place since the morning, the appearance of the angel, her disappearance, what that creature had just said to him, a gleam of hope floating in an immense despair—this was what filled his brain confusedly.

All at once he was violently aroused from his reverie.

He heard the shrill, hard voice of Jondrette utter these words, which were fraught with a strange interest for him:

"I tell you that I am sure of it, and that I recognized him."

Of whom was Jondrette speaking? Whom had he recognized? M. Leblanc? The father of "his Ursule"? What! Did Jondrette know him? Was Marius about to obtain in this abrupt and unexpected fashion all the information without which his life was so dark to him? Was he about to learn at last who it was that he loved, who that young girl was? Who her father was? Was the dense shadow which enwrapped them on the point of being dispelled? Was the veil about to be rent? Ah! Heavens!

He bounded rather than climbed upon his commode, and resumed his post near the little peep-hole in the partition wall.

Again he beheld the interior of Jondrette's hovel.

Chapter XII

THE USE MADE OF M. LEBLANC'S FIVE-FRANC PIECE

NOTHING IN THE ASPECT OF THE FAMILY WAS ALTERED, EXCEPT THAT THE WIFE AND DAUGHTERS had levied on the package and put on woolen stockings and jackets. Two new blankets were thrown across the two beds.

Jondrette had evidently just returned. He still had the breathlessness of out of doors. His daughters were seated on the floor near the fireplace, the elder engaged in dressing the younger's wounded hand. His wife had sunk back on the bed near the fireplace, with a face indicative of astonishment. Jondrette was pacing up and down the garret with long strides. His eyes were extraordinary.

The woman, who seemed timid and overwhelmed with stupor in the presence of her husband, turned to say:

"What, really? You are sure?"

"Sure! Eight years have passed! But I recognize him! Ah? I recognize him! I knew him at once! What! Didn't it force itself on you?"

"No."

"But I told you: 'Pay attention!' Why, it is his figure, it is his face, only older—there are people who do not grow old, I don't know how they manage it—it is the very sound of his voice. He is better dressed, that is all! Ah! you mysterious old devil, I've got you, that I have!"

He paused, and said to his daughters:

"Get out of here, you!—It's queer that it didn't strike you!"

They arose to obey.

The mother stammered:

"With her injured hand."

"The air will do it good," said Jondrette. "Be off."

It was plain that this man was of the sort to whom no one offers to reply. The two girls departed.

At the moment when they were about to pass through the door, the father detained the elder by the arm, and said to her with a peculiar accent:

"You will be here at five o'clock precisely. Both of you. I shall need you."

Marius redoubled his attention.

On being left alone with his wife, Jondrette began to pace the room again, and made the tour of it two or three times in silence. Then he spent several minutes in tucking the lower part of the woman's chemise which he wore into his trousers.

All at once, he turned to the female Jondrette, folded his arms and exclaimed:

"And would you like to have me tell you something? The young lady—"

"Well, what?" retorted his wife, "the young lady?"

Marius could not doubt that it was really she of whom they were speaking. He listened with ardent anxiety. His whole life was in his ears.

But Jondrette had bent over and spoke to his wife in a whisper. Then he straightened himself up and concluded aloud:

"It is she!"

"That one?" said his wife.

"That very one," said the husband.

No expression can reproduce the significance of the mother's words. Surprise, rage, hate, wrath, were mingled and combined in one monstrous intonation. The pronunciation of a few words, the name, no doubt, which her husband had whispered in her ear, had sufficed to rouse this huge, somnolent woman, and from being repulsive she became terrible.

"It is not possible!" she cried. "When I think that my daughters are going barefoot, and have not a gown to their backs! What! A satin pelisse, a velvet bonnet, boots, and everything; more than two hundred francs' worth of clothes! so that one would think she was a lady! No, you are mistaken! Why, in the first place, the other was hideous, and this one is not so bad-looking! She really is not bad-looking! It can't be she!"

"I tell you that it is she. You will see."

At this absolute assertion, the Jondrette woman raised her large, red, blonde face and stared at the ceiling with a horrible expression. At that moment, she seemed to Marius even more to be feared than her husband. She was a sow with the look of a tigress.

"What!" she resumed, "that horrible, beautiful young lady, who gazed at my daughters with an air of pity—she is that beggar brat! Oh! I should like to kick her stomach in for her!"

She sprang off of the bed, and remained standing for a moment, her hair in disorder, her nostrils dilating, her mouth half-open, her fists clenched and drawn back. Then she fell back on the bed once more. The man paced to and fro and paid no attention to his female.

After a silence lasting several minutes, he approached the female Jondrette, and halted in front of her, with folded arms, as he had done a moment before:

"And shall I tell you another thing?"

"What is it?" she asked.

He answered in a low, curt voice:

"My fortune is made."

The woman stared at him with the look that signifies: "Is the person who is addressing me on the point of going mad?"

He went on:

"Thunder! It was not so very long ago that I was a parishioner of the parish of die-of-hunger-if-you-have-a-fire,-die-of-cold-if-you-have-bread! I have had enough of misery! my share and other people's share! I am not joking any longer, I don't find it comic anymore, I've had enough of puns, good God! no more farces, Eternal Father! I want to eat till I am full, I want to drink my filll to gormandize! to sleep! to do nothing! I want to have my turn, so I do, come now! before I die! I want to be a bit of a millionnaire!"

He took a turn round the hovel, and added:

"Like other people."

"What do you mean by that?" asked the woman.

He shook his head, winked, screwed up one eye, and raised his voice like a medical professor who is about to make a demonstration:

"What do I mean by that? Listen!"

"Hush!" muttered the woman, "not so loud! These are matters which must not be overheard."

"Bah! Who's here? Our neighbor? I saw him go out a little while ago. Besides, he doesn't listen, the big booby. And I tell you that I saw him go out."

Nevertheless, by a sort of instinct, Jondrette lowered his voice, although not sufficiently to prevent Marius hearing his words. One favorable circumstance, which enabled Marius not to lose a word of this conversation was the falling snow which deadened the sound of vehicles on the boulevard.

This is what Marius heard:

"Listen carefully. The Crœsus is caught, or as good as caught! That's all settled already. Everything is arranged. I have seen some people. He will come here this evening at six o'clock. To bring sixty francs, the rascal! Did you notice how I played that game on him, my sixty francs, my landlord, my fourth of February? I don't even owe for one quarter! Isn't he a fool! So he will come at six o'clock! That's the hour when our neighbor goes to his dinner. Mother Burgon is off washing dishes in the city. There's not a soul in the house. The neighbor never comes home until eleven o'clock. The children shall stand on watch. You shall help us. He will give in."

"And what if he does not give in?" demanded his wife.

Jondrette made a sinister gesture, and said:

"We'll fix him."

And he burst out laughing.

This was the first time Marius had seen him laugh. The laugh was cold and sweet, and provoked a shudder.

Jondrette opened a cupboard near the fireplace, and drew from it an old cap, which he placed on his head, after brushing it with his sleeve.

"Now," said he, "I'm going out. I have some more people that I must see. Good ones. You'll see how well the whole thing will work. I shall be away as short a time as possible, it's a fine stroke of business, do you look after the house."

And with both fists thrust into the pockets of his trousers, he stood for a moment in thought, then exclaimed:

"Do you know, it's mighty lucky, by the way, that he didn't recognize me! If he had recognized me on his side, he would not have come back again. He would have slipped through our fingers! It was my beard that saved us! my romantic beard! my pretty little romantic beard!"

And again he broke into a laugh.

He stepped to the window. The snow was still falling, and streaking the gray of the sky.

"What beastly weather!" said he.

Then lapping his over-coat across his breast:

"This rind is too large for me. Never mind," he added, "he did a devilish good thing in leaving it for me, the old scoundrel! If it hadn't been for that, I couldn't have gone out, and everything would have gone wrong! What small points things hang on, any way!"

And pulling his cap down over his eyes, he quitted the room.

He had barely had time to take half a dozen steps from the door, when the door opened again, and his savage but intelligent face made its appearance once more in the opening.

"I came near forgetting," said he. "You are to have a brazier of charcoal ready."

And he flung into his wife's apron the five-franc piece which the "philanthropist" had left with him.

"A brazier of charcoal?" asked his wife.

"Yes."

"How many bushels?"

"Two good ones."

"That will come to thirty sous. With the rest I will buy something for dinner."

"The devil, no."

"Why?"

"Don't go and spend the hundred-sou piece."

"Why?"

"Because I shall have to buy something, too."

"What?"

"Something."

"How much shall you need?"

"Whereabouts in the neighborhood is there an ironmonger's shop?"

"Rue Mouffetard."

"Ah! yes, at the corner of a street; I can see the shop."

"But tell me how much you will need for what you have to purchase?"

"Fifty sous—three francs."

"There won't be much left for dinner."

"Eating is not the point to-day. There's something better to be done."

"That's enough, my jewel."

At this word from his wife, Jondrette closed the door again, and this time, Marius heard his step die away in the corridor of the hovel, and descend the staircase rapidly.

At that moment, one o'clock struck from the church of Saint-Médard.

Chapter XIII

Solus Cum Solo, in Loco Remoto, non Cogitabuntur Orare Pater Noster

MARIUS, DREAMER AS HE WAS, WAS, AS WE HAVE SAID, FIRM AND ENERGETIC BY NATURE. HIS habits of solitary meditation, while they had developed in him sympathy and compassion, had, perhaps, diminished the faculty for irritation, but had left intact the power of waxing indignant; he had the kindliness of a brahmin, and the severity of a judge; he took pity upon a toad, but he crushed a viper. Now, it was into a hole of vipers that his glance had just been directed, it was a nest of monsters that he had beneath his eyes.

"These wretches must be stamped upon," said he.

Not one of the enigmas which he had hoped to see solved had been elucidated; on the contrary, all of them had been rendered more dense, if anything; he knew nothing more about the beautiful maiden of the Luxembourg and the man whom he called M. Leblanc, except that Jondrette was acquainted with them. Athwart the mysterious words which had been uttered, the only thing of which he caught a distinct glimpse was the fact that an ambush was in course of preparation, a dark but terrible trap; that both of them were incurring great danger, she probably, her father certainly; that they must be saved; that the hideous plots of the Jondrettes must be thwarted, and the web of these spiders broken.

He scanned the female Jondrette for a moment. She had pulled an old sheet-iron stove from a corner, and she was rummaging among the old heap of iron.

He descended from the commode as softly as possible, taking care not to make the least noise. Amid his terror as to what was in preparation, and in the horror with which the Jondrettes had inspired him, he experienced a sort of joy at the idea that it might be granted to him perhaps to render a service to the one whom he loved.

But how was it to be done? How warn the persons threatened? He did not know their address. They had reappeared for an instant before his eyes, and had then plunged back again into the immense depths of Paris. Should he wait for M. Leblanc at the door that evening at six o'clock, at the moment of his arrival, and warn him of the trap? But Jondrette and his men would see him on the watch, the spot was lonely, they were stronger than he, they would devise means to seize him or to get him away, and the man whom Marius was anxious to save would be lost. One o'clock had just struck, the trap was to be sprung at six. Marius had five hours before him.

There was but one thing to be done.

He put on his decent coat, knotted a silk handkerchief round his neck, took his hat, and went out, without making any more noise than if he had been treading on moss with bare feet.

Moreover, the Jondrette woman continued to rummage among her old iron.

Once outside of the house, he made for the Rue du Petit-Banquier.

He had almost reached the middle of this street, near a very low wall which a man can easily step over at certain points, and which abuts on a waste space, and was walking slowly, in consequence of his preoccupied condition, and the snow deadened the sound of his steps; all at once he heard voices talking very close by. He turned his head, the street was deserted, there was not a soul in it, it was broad daylight, and yet he distinctly heard voices.

It occurred to him to glance over the wall which he was skirting.

There, in fact, sat two men, flat on the snow, with their backs against the wall, talking together in subdued tones.

These two persons were strangers to him; one was a bearded man in a blouse, and the other a long-haired individual in rags. The bearded man had on a fez, the other's head was bare, and the snow had lodged in his hair.

By thrusting his head over the wall, Marius could hear their remarks.

The hairy one jogged the other man's elbow and said:

"—With the assistance of Patron-Minette, it can't fail."

"Do you think so?" said the bearded man.

And the long-haired one began again:

"It's as good as a warrant for each one, of five hundred balls, and the worst that can happen is five years, six years, ten years at the most!"

The other replied with some hesitation, and shivering beneath his fez:

"That's a real thing. You can't go against such things."

"I tell you that the affair can't go wrong," resumed the long-haired man. "Father What's-his-name's team will be already harnessed."

Then they began to discuss a melodrama that they had seen on the preceding evening at the Gaîté Theatre.

Marius went his way.

It seemed to him that the mysterious words of these men, so strangely hidden behind that wall, and crouching in the snow, could not but bear some relation to Jondrette's abominable projects. That must be *the affair.*

He directed his course toward the faubourg Saint-Marceau and asked at the first shop he came to where he could find a commissary of police.

He was directed to Rue de Pontoise, No. 14.

Thither Marius betook himself.

As he passed a baker's shop, he bought a two-penny roll, and ate it, foreseeing that he should not dine.

On the way, he rendered justice to Providence. He reflected that he had not given his five francs to the Jondrette girl in the morning, he would have followed M. Leblanc's fiacre, and consequently have remained ignorant of everything, and that there would have been no obstacle to the trap of the Jondrettes, and that M. Leblanc would have been lost, and his daughter with him, no doubt.

Chapter XIV

IN WHICH A POLICE AGENT BESTOWS TWO FISTFULS ON A LAWYER

ON ARRIVING AT NO. 14, RUE DE PONTOISE, HE ASCENDED TO tHE FIRST FLOOR AND INQUIRED FOR the commissary of police.

"The commissary of police is not here," said a clerk; "but there is an inspector who takes his place. Would you like to speak to him? Are you in haste?"

"Yes," said Marius.

The clerk introduced him into the commissary's office. There stood a tall man behind a grating, leaning against a stove, and holding up with both hands the tails of a vast top-coat, with three collars. His face was square, with a thin, firm mouth, thick, gray, and very ferocious whiskers, and a look that was enough to turn your pockets inside out. Of that glance it might have been well said, not that it penetrated, but that it searched.

This man's air was not much less ferocious nor less terrible than Jondrette's; the dog is, at times, no less terrible to meet than the wolf.

"What do you want?" he said to Marius, without adding "monsieur."

"Is this Monsieur le Commissaire de Police?"

"He is absent. I am here in his stead."

"The matter is very private."

"Then speak."

"And great haste is required."

"Then speak quick."

This calm, abrupt man was both terrifying and reassuring at one and the same time. He inspired fear and confidence. Marius related the adventure to him: That a person with whom he was not acquainted otherwise than by sight, was to be inveigled into a trap that very evening; that, as he occupied the room adjoining the den, he, Marius Pontmercy, a lawyer, had heard the whole plot through the partition; that the wretch who had planned the trap was a certain Jondrette; that there would be accomplices, probably some prowlers of the barriers, among others a certain Panchaud, alias Printanier, alias Bigrenaille; that Jondrette's daughters were to lie in wait; that there was no way of warning the threatened man, since he did not even know his name; and that, finally, all this was to be carried out at six o'clock that evening, at the most deserted point of the Boulevard de l'Hôpital, in house No. 50-52.

At the sound of this number, the inspector raised his head, and said coldly:

"So it is in the room at the end of the corridor?"

"Precisely," answered Marius, and he added: "Are you acquainted with that house?"

The inspector remained silent for a moment, then replied, as he warmed the heel of his boot at the door of the stove:

"Apparently."

He went on, muttering between his teeth, and not addressing Marius so much as his cravat:

"Patron-Minette must have had a hand in this."

This word struck Marius.

"Patron-Minette," said he, "I did hear that word pronounced, in fact."

And he repeated to the inspector the dialogue between the long-haired man and the bearded man in the snow behind the wall of the Rue du Petit-Banquier.

The inspector muttered:

"The long-haired man must be Brujon, and the bearded one Demi-Liard, alias Deux-Milliards."

He had dropped his eyelids again, and became absorbed in thought.

"As for Father What's-his-name, I think I recognize him. Here, I've burned my coat. They always have too much fire in these cursed stoves. Number 50-52. Former property of Gorbeau."

Then he glanced at Marius.

"You saw only that bearded and that long-haired man?"

"And Panchaud."

"You didn't see a little imp of a dandy prowling about the premises?"

"No."

"Nor a big lump of matter, resembling an elephant in the Jardin des Plantes?"

"No."

"Nor a scamp with the air of an old red tail?"

"No."

"As for the fourth, no one sees him, not even his adjutants, clerks, and employees. It is not surprising that you did not see him."

"No. Who are all those persons?" asked Marius.

The inspector answered:

"Besides, this is not the time for them."

He relapsed into silence, then resumed:

"50-52. I know that barrack. Impossible to conceal ourselves inside it without the artists seeing us, and then they will get off simply by countermanding the vaudeville. They are so modest! An audience embarrasses them. None of that, none of that. I want to hear them sing and make them dance."

This monologue concluded, he turned to Marius, and demanded, gazing at him intently the while:

"Are you afraid?"

"Of what?" said Marius.

"Of these men?"

"No more than yourself!" retorted Marius rudely, who had begun to notice that this police agent had not yet said "monsieur" to him.

The inspector stared still more intently at Marius, and continued with sententious solemnity:

"There, you speak like a brave man, and like an honest man. Courage does not fear crime, and honesty does not fear authority."

Marius interrupted him:

"That is well, but what do you intend to do?"

The inspector contented himself with the remark:

"The lodgers have pass-keys with which to get in at night. You must have one."

"Yes," said Marius.

"Have you it about you?"

"Yes."

"Give it to me," said the inspector.

Marius took his key from his waistcoat pocket, handed it to the inspector and added:

"If you will take my advice, you will come in force."

The inspector cast on Marius such a glance as Voltaire might have bestowed on a provincial academician who had suggested a rhyme to him; with one movement he plunged his hands, which were enormous, into the two immense pockets of his top-coat, and pulled out two small steel pistols, of the sort called "knock-me-downs." Then he presented them to Marius, saying rapidly, in a curt tone:

"Take these. Go home. Hide in your chamber, so that you may be supposed to have gone out. They are loaded. Each one carries two balls. You will keep watch; there is a hole in the wall, as you have informed me. These men will come. Leave them to their own devices for a time. When you think matters have reached a crisis, and that it is time to put a stop to them, fire a shot. Not too soon. The rest concerns me. A shot into the ceiling, the air, no matter where. Above all things, not too soon. Wait until they begin to put their project into execution; you are a lawyer; you know the proper point."

Marius took the pistols and put them in the side pocket of his coat.

"That makes a lump that can be seen," said the inspector. "Put them in your trousers pocket."

Marius hid the pistols in his trousers pockets.

"Now," pursued the inspector, "there is not a minute more to be lost by anyone. What time is it? Half-past two. Seven o'clock is the hour?"

"Six o'clock," answered Marius.

"I have plenty of time," said the inspector, "but no more than enough. Don't forget anything that I have said to you. Bang. A pistol shot."

"Rest easy," said Marius.

And as Marius laid his hand on the handle of the door on his way out, the inspector called to him:

"By the way, if you have occasion for my services between now and then, come or send here. You will ask for Inspector Javert."

Chapter XV

JONDRETTE MAKES HIS PURCHASES

A FEW MOMENTS LATER, ABOUT THREE O'CLOCK, COURFEYRAC CHANCED TO BE PASSING ALONG the Rue Mouffetard in company with Bossuet. The snow had redoubled in violence, and filled the air. Bossuet was just saying to Courfeyrac:

"One would say, to see all these snowflakes fall, that there was a plague of white butterflies in heaven." All at once, Bossuet caught sight of Marius coming up the street toward the barrier with a peculiar air.

"Hold!" said Bossuet. "There's Marius."

"I saw him," said Courfeyrac. "Don't let's speak to him."

"Why?"

"He is busy."

"With what?"

"Don't you see his air?"

"What air?"

"He has the air of a man who is following someone."

"That's true," said Bossuet.

"Just see the eyes he is making!" said Courfeyrac.

"But who the deuce is he following?"

"Some fine, flowery bonneted wench! He's in love."

"But," observed Bossuet, "I don't see any wench nor any flowery bonnet in the street. There's not a woman round."

Courfeyrac took a survey, and exclaimed:

"He's following a man!"

A man, in fact, wearing a gray cap, and whose gray beard could be distinguished, although they only saw his back, was walking along about twenty paces in advance of Marius.

This man was dressed in a great-coat which was perfectly new and too large for him, and in a frightful pair of trousers all hanging in rags and black with mud.

Bossuet burst out laughing.

"Who is that man?"

"He?" retorted Courfeyrac, "He's a poet. Poets are very fond of wearing the trousers of dealers in rabbit skins and the over-coats of peers of France."

"Let's see where Marius will go," said Bossuet; "let's see where the man is going, let's follow them, hey?"

"Bossuet!" exclaimed Courfeyrac, "eagle of Meaux! You are a prodigious brute. Follow a man who is following another man, indeed!"

They retraced their steps.

Marius had, in fact, seen Jondrette passing along the Rue Mouffetard, and was spying on his proceedings.

Jondrette walked straight ahead, without a suspicion that he was already held by a glance.

He quitted the Rue Mouffetard, and Marius saw him enter one of the most terrible hovels in the Rue Gracieuse; he remained there about a quarter of an hour, then returned to the Rue Mouffetard. He halted at an ironmonger's shop, which then stood at the corner of the Rue Pierre-Lombard, and a few minutes later, Marius saw him emerge from the shop, holding in his hand a huge cold chisel with a white wood handle, which he concealed beneath his great-coat. At the top of the Rue Petit-Gentilly, he turned to the left and proceeded rapidly to the Rue du Petit-Banquier. The day was declining; the snow, which had ceased for a moment, had just begun again. Marius posted himself on the watch at the very corner of the Rue du Petit-Banquier, which was deserted, as usual, and did not follow Jondrette into it. It was lucky that he did so, for, on arriving in the vicinity of the wall where Marius had heard the long-haired man and the bearded man conversing, Jondrette turned round, made sure that no one was following him, did not see him, then sprang across the wall and disappeared.

The waste land bordered by this wall communicated with the backyard of an ex-livery stable-keeper of bad repute, who had failed and who still kept a few old single-seated berlins under his sheds.

Marius thought that it would be wise to profit by Jondrette's absence to return home; moreover, it was growing late; every evening, Ma'am Burgon when she set out for her dish-washing in town, had a habit of locking the door, which was always closed at dusk. Marius had given his key to the inspector of police; it was important, therefore, that he should make haste.

Evening had arrived, night had almost closed in; on the horizon and in the immensity of space, there remained but one spot still illuminated by the sun, and that was the moon.

It was rising in a ruddy glow behind the low dome of Salpêtrière.

Marius returned to No. 50-52 with great strides. The door was still open when he arrived. He mounted the stairs on tiptoe and glided along the wall of the corridor to his chamber. This corridor, as the reader will remember, was bordered on both sides by attics, all of which were, for the moment, empty and to let. Ma'am Burgon was in the habit of leaving all the doors open. As he passed one of these attics, Marius thought he perceived in the uninhabited cell the motionless heads of four men, vaguely lighted up by a remnant of daylight, falling through a dormer window. Marius made no attempt to see, not wishing to be seen himself. He succeeded in reaching his chamber without being seen and without making any noise. It was high time. A moment later he heard Ma'am Burgon take her departure, locking the door of the house behind her.

Chapter XVI

IN WHICH WILL BE FOUND THE WORDS TO AN ENGLISH AIR WHICH WAS IN FASHION IN 1832

MARIUS SEATED HIMSELF ON HIS BED. IT MIGHT HAVE BEEN HALF-PAST FIVE O'CLOCK. ONLY HALF an hour separated him from what was about to happen. He heard the beating of his arteries as one hears the ticking of a watch in the dark. He thought of the double march which was going on at that moment in the dark—crime advancing on one side, justice coming up on the other. He was not afraid, but he could not think without a shudder of what was about to take place. As is the case with all those who are suddenly assailed by an unforeseen adventure, the entire day produced upon him the effect of a dream, and, in order to persuade himself that he was not the prey of a nightmare, he had to feel the cold barrels of the steel pistols in his trousers pockets.

It was no longer snowing; the moon disengaged itself more and more clearly from the mist, and its light, mingled with the white reflection of the snow which had fallen, communicated to the chamber a sort of twilight aspect.

There was a light in the Jondrette den. Marius saw the hole in the wall shining with a reddish glow which seemed bloody to him.

It was true that the light could not be produced by a candle. However, there was not a sound in the Jondrette quarters, not a soul was moving there, not a soul speaking, not a breath; the silence was glacial and profound, and had it not been for that light, he might have thought himself next door to a sepulcher.

Marius softly removed his boots and pushed them under his bed.

Several minutes elapsed. Marius heard the lower door turn on its hinges; a heavy step mounted the staircase, and hastened along the corridor; the latch of the hovel was noisily lifted; it was Jondrette returning.

Instantly, several voices arose. The whole family was in the garret. Only, it had been silent in the master's absence, like wolf whelps in the absence of the wolf.

"It's I," said he.

"Good evening, daddy," yelped the girls.

"Well?" said the mother.

"All's going first-rate," responded Jondrette, "but my feet are beastly cold. Good! You have dressed up. You have done well! You must inspire confidence."

"All ready to go out."

"Don't forget what I told you? You will do everything sure?"

"Rest easy."

"Because—" said Jondrette. And he left the phrase unfinished.

Marius heard him lay something heavy on the table, probably the chisel which he had purchased.

"By the way," said Jondrette, "have you been eating here?"

"Yes," said the mother. "I got three large potatoes and some salt. I took advantage of the fire to cook them."

"Good," returned Jondrette. "To-morrow I will take you out to dine with me. We will have a duck and fixings. You shall dine like Charles the Tenth; all is going well!"

Then he added:

"The mouse-trap is open. The cats are there."

He lowered his voice still further, and said:

"Put this in the fire."

Marius heard a sound of charcoal being knocked with the tongs or some iron utensil, and Jondrette continued:

"Have you greased the hinges of the door so that they will not squeak?"

"Yes," replied the mother.

"What time is it?"

"Nearly six. The half-hour struck from Saint-Médard a while ago."

"The devil!" ejaculated Jondrette; "the children must go and watch. Come you, do you listen here."

A whispering ensued.

Jondrette's voice became audible again:

"Has old Burgon left?"

"Yes," said the mother.

"Are you sure that there is no one in our neighbor's room?"

"He has not been in all day, and you know very well that this is his dinner hour."

"You are sure?"

"Sure."

"All the same," said Jondrette, "there's no harm in going to see whether he is there. Here, my girl, take the candle and go there."

Marius fell on his hands and knees and crawled silently under his bed.

Hardly had he concealed himself, when he perceived a light through the crack of his door.

"P'pa," cried a voice, "he is not in here."

He recognized the voice of the eldest daughter.

"Did you go in?" demanded her father.

"No," replied the girl, "but as his key is in the door, he must be out."

The father exclaimed:

"Go in, nevertheless."

The door opened, and Marius saw the tall Jondrette come in with a candle in her hand. She was as she had been in the morning, only still more repulsive in this light.

She walked straight up to the bed. Marius endured an indescribable moment of anxiety; but near the bed there was a mirror nailed to the wall, and it was thither that she was directing her steps. She raised herself on tiptoe and looked at herself in it. In the neighboring room, the sound of iron articles being moved was audible.

She smoothed her hair with the palm of her hand, and smiled into the mirror, humming with her cracked and sepulchral voice:

> *"Nos amours ont duré toute une semaine,*
> *Mais que du bonheur les instants sont courts!*
> *S'adorer huit jours, c' était bien la peine!*
> *Le temps des amours devait durer toujours!*
> *Devrait durer toujours! devrait durer toujours!"*[1]

In the meantime, Marius trembled. It seemed impossible to him that she should not hear his breathing.

She stepped to the window and looked out with the half-foolish way she had.

---

1. Our love has lasted a whole week, but how short are the instants of happiness! To adore each other for eight days was hardly worth the while! The time of love should last forever.

"How ugly Paris is when it has put on a white chemise!" said she.

She returned to the mirror and began again to put on airs before it, scrutinizing herself full-face and three-quarters face in turn.

"Well!" cried her father, "what are you about there?"

"I am looking under the bed and the furniture," she replied, continuing to arrange her hair; "there's no one here."

"Booby!" yelled her father. "Come here this minute! And don't waste any time about it!"

"Coming! Coming!" said she. "One has no time for anything in this hovel!"

She hummed:

> *"Vous me quittez pour aller à la gloire;*
> *Mon triste cœur suivra partout."*[1]

She cast a parting glance in the mirror and went out, shutting the door behind her.

A moment more, and Marius heard the sound of the two young girls' bare feet in the corridor, and Jondrette's voice shouting to them:

"Pay strict heed! One on the side of the barrier, the other at the corner of the Rue du Petit-Banquier. Don't lose sight for a moment of the door of this house, and the moment you see anything, rush here on the instant! as hard as you can go! You have a key to get in."

The eldest girl grumbled:

"The idea of standing watch in the snow barefoot!"

"To-morrow you shall have some dainty little green silk boots!" said the father.

They ran downstairs, and a few seconds later the shock of the outer door as it banged to announced that they were outside.

There now remained in the house only Marius, the Jondrettes and probably, also, the mysterious persons of whom Marius had caught a glimpse in the twilight, behind the door of the unused attic.

Chapter XVII

THE USE MADE OF MARIUS'S FIVE-FRANC PIECE

MARIUS DECIDED THAT THE MOMENT HAD NOW ARRIVED WHEN HE MUST RESUME HIS POST AT his observatory. In a twinkling, and with the agility of his age, he had reached the hole in the partition.

He looked.

The interior of the Jondrette apartment presented a curious aspect, and Marius found an explanation of the singular light which he had noticed. A candle was burning in a candlestick covered with verdigris, but that was not what really lighted the chamber. The hovel was completely illuminated, as it were, by the reflection from a rather large sheet-iron brazier standing in the fireplace, and filled with burning charcoal, the brazier prepared by the Jondrette woman that morning. The charcoal was glowing hot, and the brazier was red; a blue flame flickered over it, and helped him to make out the form of the chisel purchased by Jondrette in the Rue Pierre-Lombard, where it had been thrust into the brazier to heat. In one corner, near the door, and as though prepared for some

1. You leave me to go to the glory; my sad heart will follow you everywhere.

definite use, two heaps were visible, which appeared to be, the one a heap of old iron, the other a heap of ropes. All this would have caused the mind of a person who knew nothing of what was in preparation, to waver between a very sinister and a very simple idea. The lair thus lighted up more resembled a forge than a mouth of hell, but Jondrette, in this light, had rather the air of a demon than of a smith.

The heat of the brazier was so great, that the candle on the table was melting on the side next the chafing-dish, and was drooping over. An old dark-lantern of copper, worthy of Diogenes turned Cartouche, stood on the chimney-piece.

The brazier, placed in the fireplace itself, beside the nearly extinct brands, sent its vapors up the chimney, and gave out no odor.

The moon, entering through the four panes of the window, cast its whiteness into the crimson and flaming garret; and to the poetic spirit of Marius, who was dreamy even in the moment of action, it was like a thought of heaven mingled with the misshapen reveries of earth.

A breath of air which made its way in through the open pane, helped to dissipate the smell of the charcoal and to conceal the presence of the brazier.

The Jondrette lair was, if the reader recalls what we have said of the Gorbeau building, admirably chosen to serve as the theater of a violent and somber deed, and as the envelope for a crime. It was the most retired chamber in the most isolated house on the most deserted boulevard in Paris. If the system of ambush and traps had not already existed, they would have been invented there.

The whole thickness of a house and a multitude of uninhabited rooms separated this den from the boulevard, and the only window that existed opened on waste lands enclosed with walls and palisades.

Jondrette had lighted his pipe, seated himself on the seatless chair, and was engaged in smoking. His wife was talking to him in a low tone.

If Marius had been Courfeyrac, that is to say, one of those men who laugh on every occasion in life, he would have burst with laughter when his gaze fell on the Jondrette woman. She had on a black bonnet with plumes not unlike the hats of the heralds-at-arms at the coronation of Charles X, an immense tartan shawl over her knitted petticoat, and the man's shoes which her daughter had scorned in the morning. It was this toilette which had extracted from Jondrette the exclamation: "Good! You have dressed up. You have done well. You must inspire confidence!"

As for Jondrette, he had not taken off the new surtout, which was too large for him, and which M. Leblanc had given him, and his costume continued to present that contrast of coat and trousers which constituted the ideal of a poet in Courfeyrac's eyes.

All at once, Jondrette lifted up his voice:

"By the way! Now that I think of it. In this weather, he will come in a carriage. Light the lantern, take it and go downstairs. You will stand behind the lower door. The very moment that you hear the carriage stop, you will open the door, instantly, he will come up, you will light the staircase and the corridor, and when he enters here, you will go downstairs again as speedily as possible, you will pay the coachman, and dismiss the fiacre."

"And the money?" inquired the woman.

Jondrette fumbled in his trousers pocket and handed her five francs.

"What's this?" she exclaimed.

Jondrette replied with dignity:

"That is the monarch which our neighbor gave us this morning."

And he added:

"Do you know what? Two chairs will be needed here."

"What for?"

"To sit on."

Marius felt a cold chill pass through his limbs at hearing this mild answer from Jondrette.

"Pardieu! I'll go and get one of our neighbor's."

And with a rapid movement, she opened the door of the den, and went out into the corridor.

Marius absolutely had not the time to descend from the commode, reach his bed, and conceal himself beneath it.

"Take the candle," cried Jondrette.

"No," said she, "it would embarrass me, I have the two chairs to carry. There is moonlight."

Marius heard Mother Jondrette's heavy hand fumbling at his lock in the dark. The door opened. He remained nailed to the spot with the shock and with horror.

The Jondrette entered.

The dormer window permitted the entrance of a ray of moonlight between two blocks of shadow. One of these blocks of shadow entirely covered the wall against which Marius was leaning, so that he disappeared within it.

Mother Jondrette raised her eyes, did not see Marius, took the two chairs, the only ones which Marius possessed, and went away, letting the door fall heavily to behind her.

She re-entered the lair.

"Here are the two chairs."

"And here is the lantern. Go down as quick as you can."

She hastily obeyed, and Jondrette was left alone.

He placed the two chairs on opposite sides of the table, turned the chisel in the brazier, set in front of the fireplace an old screen which masked the chafing-dish, then went to the corner where lay the pile of rope, and bent down as though to examine something. Marius then recognized the fact, that what he had taken for a shapeless mass was a very well-made rope-ladder, with wooden rungs and two hooks with which to attach it.

This ladder, and some large tools, veritable masses of iron, which were mingled with the old iron piled up behind the door, had not been in the Jondrette hovel in the morning, and had evidently been brought thither in the afternoon, during Marius's absence.

"Those are the utensils of an edge-tool maker," thought Marius.

Had Marius been a little more learned in this line, he would have recognized in what he took for the engines of an edge-tool maker, certain instruments which will force a lock or pick a lock, and others which will cut or slice, the two families of tools which burglars call *cadets* and *fauchants*.

The fireplace and the two chairs were exactly opposite Marius. The brazier being concealed, the only light in the room was now furnished by the candle; the smallest bit of crockery on the table or on the chimney-piece cast a large shadow. There was something indescribably calm, threatening, and hideous about this chamber. One felt that there existed in it the anticipation of something terrible.

Jondrette had allowed his pipe to go out, a serious sign of preoccupation, and had again seated himself. The candle brought out the fierce and the fine angles of his countenance. He indulged in scowls and in abrupt unfoldings of the right hand, as though he were responding to the last counsels of a somber inward monologue. In the course of one of these dark replies which he was making to himself, he pulled the table drawer rapidly toward him, took out a long kitchen knife which was concealed there, and tried the edge of its blade on his nail. That done, he put the knife back in the drawer and shut it.

Marius, on his side, grasped the pistol in his right pocket, drew it out and cocked it.

The pistol emitted a sharp, clear click, as he cocked it.

Jondrette started, half rose, listened a moment, then began to laugh and said:

"What a fool I am! It's the partition cracking!"

Marius kept the pistol in his hand.

Chapter XVIII

MARIUS'S TWO CHAIRS FORM A VIS-À-VIS

SUDDENLY, THE DISTANT AND MELANCHOLY VIBRATION OF A CLOCK SHOOK THE PANES. SIX o'clock was striking from Saint-Médard.

Jondrette marked off each stroke with a toss of his head. When the sixth had struck, he snuffed the candle with his fingers.

Then he began to pace up and down the room, listened at the corridor, walked on again, then listened once more.

"Provided only that he comes!" he muttered, then he returned to his chair.

He had hardly reseated himself when the door opened.

Mother Jondrette had opened it, and now remained in the corridor making a horrible, amiable grimace, which one of the holes of the dark-lantern illuminated from below.

"Enter, sir," she said.

"Enter, my benefactor," repeated Jondrette, rising hastily.

M. Leblanc made his appearance.

He wore an air of serenity which rendered him singularly venerable.

He laid four louis on the table.

"Monsieur Fabantou," said he, "this is for your rent and your most pressing necessities. We will attend to the rest hereafter."

"May God requite it to you, my generous benefactor!" said Jondrette.

And rapidly approaching his wife:

"Dismiss the carriage!"

She slipped out while her husband was lavishing salutes and offering M. Leblanc a chair. An instant later she returned and whispered in his ear:

" 'Tis done."

The snow, which had not ceased falling since the morning, was so deep that the arrival of the fiacre had not been audible, and they did not now hear its departure.

Meanwhile, M. Leblanc had seated himself.

Jondrette had taken possession of the other chair, facing M. Leblanc.

Now, in order to form an idea of the scene which is to follow, let the reader picture to himself in his own mind, a cold night, the solitudes of the Salpêtrière covered with snow and white as winding-sheets in the moonlight, the taper-like lights of the street-lanterns which shone redly here and there along those tragic boulevards, and the long rows of black elms, not a passer-by for perhaps a quarter of a league around, the Gorbeau hovel, at its highest pitch of silence, of horror, and of darkness; in that building, in the midst of those solitudes, in the midst of that darkness, the vast Jondrette garret lighted by a single candle, and in that den two men seated at a table, M. Leblanc tranquil, Jondrette smiling and alarming, the Jondrette woman, the female wolf, in one corner, and, behind the partition, Marius, invisible, erect, not losing a word, not missing a single movement, his eye on the watch, and pistol in hand.

However, Marius experienced only an emotion of horror, but no fear. He clasped the stock of the pistol firmly and felt reassured. "I shall be able to stop that wretch whenever I please," he thought.

He felt that the police were there somewhere in ambuscade, waiting for the signal agreed upon and ready to stretch out their arm.

Moreover, he was in hopes, that this violent encounter between Jondrette and M. Leblanc would cast some light on all the things which he was interested in learning.

Chapter XIX

OCCUPYING ONE'S SELF WITH OBSCURE DEPTHS

HARDLY WAS M. LEBLANC SEATED, WHEN HE TURNED HIS EYES TOWARD THE PALLETS, WHICH were empty.

"How is the poor little wounded girl?" he inquired.

"Bad," replied Jondrette with a heart-broken and grateful smile, "very bad, my worthy sir. Her elder sister has taken her to the Bourbe to have her hurt dressed. You will see them presently; they will be back immediately."

"Madame Fabantou seems to me to be better," went on M. Leblanc, casting his eyes on the eccentric costume of the Jondrette woman, as she stood between him and the door, as though already guarding the exit, and gazed at him in an attitude of menace and almost of combat.

"She is dying," said Jondrette. "But what do you expect, sir! She has so much courage, that woman has! She's not a woman, she's an ox."

The Jondrette, touched by this compliment, deprecated it with the affected airs of a flattered monster.

"You are always too good to me, Monsieur Jondrette!"

"Jondrette!" said M. Leblanc, "I thought your name was Fabantou?"

"Fabantou, alias Jondrette!" replied the husband hurriedly. "An artistic sobriquet!"

And launching at his wife a shrug of the shoulders which M. Leblanc did not catch, he continued with an emphatic and caressing inflection of voice:

"Ah! we have had a happy life together, this poor darling and I! What would there be left for us if we had not that? We are so wretched, my respectable sir! We have arms, but there is no work! We have the will, no work! I don't know how the government arranges that, but, on my word of honor, sir, I am not Jacobin, sir, I am not a bousingot.[1] I don't wish them any evil, but if I were the ministers, on my most sacred word, things would be different. Here, for instance, I wanted to have my girls taught the trade of paper box makers. You will say to me: 'What! a trade?' Yes! A trade! A simple trade! A bread-winner! What a fall, my benefactor! What a degradation, when one has been what we have been! Alas! There is nothing left to us of our days of prosperity! One thing only, a picture, of which I think a great deal, but which I am willing to part with, for I must live! Item, one must live!"

While Jondrette thus talked, with an apparent incoherence which detracted nothing from the thoughtful and sagacious expression of his physiognomy, Marius raised his eyes, and perceived at the other end of the room a person whom he had not seen before. A man had just entered, so softly that the door had not been heard to turn on its hinges. This man wore a violet knitted vest, which was old, worn, spotted, cut and gaping at every fold, wide trousers of cotton velvet, wooden shoes on his feet, no shirt, had his neck bare, his bare arms tattooed, and his face smeared with black. He had seated himself in silence on the nearest bed, and, as he was behind Jondrette, he could only be indistinctly seen.

That sort of magnetic instinct which turns aside the gaze, caused M. Leblanc to turn round almost at the same moment as Marius. He could not refrain from a gesture of surprise which did not escape Jondrette.

"Ah! I see!" exclaimed Jondrette, buttoning up his coat with an air of complaisance, "you are looking at your over-coat? It fits me! My faith, but it fits me!"

1. A democrat.

"Who is that man?" said M. Leblanc.

"Him?" ejaculated Jondrette, "he's a neighbor of mine. Don't pay any attention to him."

The neighbor was a singular-looking individual. However, manufactories of chemical products abound in the Faubourg Saint-Marceau. Many of the workmen might have black faces. Besides this, M. Leblanc's whole person was expressive of candid and intrepid confidence.

He went on:

"Excuse me; what were you saying, M. Fabantou?"

"I was telling you, sir, and dear protector," replied Jondrette, placing his elbows on the table and contemplating M. Leblanc with steady and tender eyes, not unlike the eyes of the boa-constrictor, "I was telling you, that I have a picture to sell."

A slight sound came from the door. A second man had just entered and seated himself on the bed, behind Jondrette.

Like the first, his arms were bare, and he had a mask of ink or lampblack.

Although this man had, literally, glided into the room, he had not been able to prevent M. Leblanc catching sight of him.

"Don't mind them," said Jondrette, "they are people who belong in the house. So I was saying, that there remains in my possession a valuable picture. But stop, sir, take a look at it."

He rose, went to the wall at the foot of which stood the panel which we have already mentioned, and turned it round, still leaving it supported against the wall. It really was something which resembled a picture, and which the candle illuminated, somewhat. Marius could make nothing out of it, as Jondrette stood between the picture and him; he only saw a coarse daub, and a sort of principal personage colored with the harsh crudity of foreign canvasses and screen paintings.

"What is that?" asked M. Leblanc.

Jondrette exclaimed:

"A painting by a master, a picture of great value, my benefactor! I am as much attached to it as I am to my two daughters; it recalls souvenirs to me! But I have told you, and I will not take it back, that I am so wretched that I will part with it."

Either by chance, or because he had begun to feel a dawning uneasiness, M. Leblanc's glance returned to the bottom of the room as he examined the picture.

There were now four men, three seated on the bed, one standing near the door-post, all four with bare arms and motionless, with faces smeared with black. One of those on the bed was leaning against the wall, with closed eyes, and it might have been supposed that he was asleep. He was old; his white hair contrasting with his blackened face produced a horrible effect. The other two seemed to be young; one wore a beard, the other wore his hair long. None of them had on shoes; those who did not wear socks were barefooted.

Jondrette noticed that M. Leblanc's eye was fixed on these men.

"They are friends. They are neighbors," said he. "Their faces are black because they work in charcoal. They are chimney-builders. Don't trouble yourself about them, my benefactor, but buy my picture. Have pity on my misery. I will not ask you much for it. How much do you think it is worth?"

"Well," said M. Leblanc, looking Jondrette full in the eye, and with the manner of a man who is on his guard, "it is some signboard for a tavern, and is worth about three francs."

Jondrette replied sweetly:

"Have you your pocket-book with you? I should be satisfied with a thousand crowns."

M. Leblanc sprang up, placed his back against the wall, and cast a rapid glance around the room. He had Jondrette on his left, on the side next the window, and the Jondrette woman and the four men on his right, on the side next the door. The four men did not stir, and did not even seem to be looking on.

Jondrette had again begun to speak in a plaintive tone, with so vague an eye, and so lamentable an intonation, that M. Leblanc might have supposed that what he had before him was a man who had simply gone mad with misery.

"If you do not buy my picture, my dear benefactor," said Jondrette, "I shall be left without resources; there will be nothing left for me but to throw myself into the river. When I think that I wanted to have my two girls taught the middle-class paper-box trade, the making of boxes for New Year's gifts! Well! A table with a board at the end to keep the glasses from falling off is required, then a special stove is needed, a pot with three compartments for the different degrees of strength of the paste, according as it is to be used for wood, paper, or stuff, a paring-knife to cut the cardboard, a mold to adjust it, a hammer to nail the steels, pincers, how the devil do I know what all? And all that in order to earn four sous a day! And you have to work fourteen hours a day! And each box passes through the workwoman's hands thirteen times! And you can't wet the paper! And you mustn't spot anything! And you must keep the paste hot! The devil, I tell you! Four sous a day! How do you suppose a man is to live?"

As he spoke, Jondrette did not look at M. Leblanc, who was observing him. M. Leblanc's eye was fixed on Jondrette, and Jondrette's eye was fixed on the door. Marius's eager attention was transferred from one to the other. M. Leblanc seemed to be asking himself: "Is this man an idiot?" Jondrette repeated two or three distinct times, with all manner of varying inflections of the whining and supplicating order: "There is nothing left for me but to throw myself into the river! I went down three steps at the side of the bridge of Austerlitz the other day for that purpose."

All at once his dull eyes lighted up with a hideous flash; the little man drew himself up and became terrible, took a step toward M. Leblanc and cried in a voice of thunder: "That has nothing to do with the question! Do you know me?"

Chapter XX

THE TRAP

THE DOOR OF THE GARRET HAD JUST OPENED ABRUPTLY, AND ALLOWED A VIEW OF THREE MEN clad in blue linen blouses, and masked with masks of black paper. The first was thin, and had a long, iron-tipped cudgel; the second, who was a sort of colossus, carried, by the middle of the handle, with the blade downward, a butcher's pole-ax for slaughtering cattle. The third, a man with thick-set shoulders, not so slender as the first, held in his hand an enormous key stolen from the door of some prison.

It appeared that the arrival of these men was what Jondrette had been waiting for. A rapid dialogue ensued between him and the man with the cudgel, the thin one.

"Is everything ready?" said Jondrette.

"Yes," replied the thin man.

"Where is Montparnasse?"

"The young principal actor stopped to chat with your girl."

"Which?"

"The eldest."

"Is there a carriage at the door?"

"Yes."

"Is the team harnessed?"

"Yes."

"With two good horses?"

"Excellent."

"Is it waiting where I ordered?"

"Yes."

"Good," said Jondrette.

M. Leblanc was very pale. He was scrutinizing everything around him in the den, like a man who understands what he has fallen into, and his head, directed in turn toward all the heads which surrounded him, moved on his neck with an astonished and attentive slowness, but there was nothing in his air which resembled fear. He had improvised an entrenchment out of the table; and the man, who but an instant previously, had borne merely the appearance of a kindly old man, had suddenly become a sort of athlete, and placed his robust fist on the back of his chair, with a formidable and surprising gesture.

This old man, who was so firm and so brave in the presence of such a danger, seemed to possess one of those natures which are as courageous as they are kind, both easily and simply. The father of a woman whom we love is never a stranger to us. Marius felt proud of that unknown man.

Three of the men, of whom Jondrette had said: "They are chimney-builders," had armed themselves from the pile of old iron, one with a heavy pair of shears, the second with weighing-tongs, the third with a hammer, and had placed themselves across the entrance without uttering a syllable. The old man had remained on the bed, and had merely opened his eyes. The Jondrette woman had seated herself beside him.

Marius decided that in a few seconds more the moment for intervention would arrive, and he raised his right hand toward the ceiling, in the direction of the corridor, in readiness to discharge his pistol.

Jondrette having terminated his colloquy with the man with the cudgel, turned once more to M. Leblanc, and repeated his question, accompanying it with that low, repressed, and terrible laugh which was peculiar to him:

"So you don't recognize me?"

M. Leblanc looked him full in the face, and replied:

"No."

Then Jondrette advanced to the table. He leaned across the candle, crossing his arms, putting his angular and ferocious jaw close to M. Leblanc's calm face, and advancing as far as possible without forcing M. Leblanc to retreat, and, in this posture of a wild beast who is about to bite, he exclaimed:

"My name is not Fabantou, my name is not Jondrette, my name is Thénardier! I am the inn-keeper of Montfermeil! Do you understand? Thénardier! Now do you know me?"

An almost imperceptible flush crossed M. Leblanc's brow, and he replied with a voice which neither trembled nor rose above its ordinary level, with his accustomed placidity:

"No more than before."

Marius did not hear this reply. Anyone who had seen him at that moment through the darkness, would have perceived that he was haggard, stupid, thunder-struck. At the moment when Jondrette said: "My name is Thénardier," Marius had trembled in every limb, and had leaned against the wall, as though he felt the cold of a steel blade through his heart. Then his right arm, all ready to discharge the signal shot, dropped slowly, and at the moment when Jondrette repeated, "Thénardier, do you understand?" Marius's faltering fingers had come near letting the pistol fall. Jondrette, by revealing his identity, had not moved M. Leblanc, but he had quite upset Marius. That name of Thénardier, with which M. Leblanc did not seem to be acquainted, Marius knew well. Let the reader recall what that name meant to him! That name he had worn on his heart, inscribed in his father's testament! He bore it at the bottom of his mind, in the depths of his memory, in that sacred injunction: "A certain Thénardier saved my life. If my son encounters him, he will do him all the good that lies in his power." That name, it will be remembered, was one of the pieties of his soul; he mingled it with the name of his father in his worship. What! This man was that Thénardier, that inn-keeper of Montfermeil whom he had so long and so vainly sought! He had found him at last, and how! His father's savior was a ruffian! That man, to whose service Marius was burning to devote himself, was a monster! That liberator of Colonel Pontmercy was on the point of committing a crime whose scope Marius did not, as yet, clearly comprehend, but which resembled an assassination! And against whom, great God! what a fatality! What a bitter mockery of fate! His father had commanded him from the depths of his coffin to do all the good in his power to this Thénardier, and for four years Marius had cherished no other thought than to acquit this debt of his father's, and at the moment when he was on the eve of having a brigand seized in the very act of crime by justice, destiny cried to him: "This is Thénardier!" He could at last repay this man for his father's life, saved amid a hail-storm of grape-shot on the heroic field of Waterloo, and repay it with the scaffold! He had sworn to himself that if ever he found that Thénardier, he would address him only by throwing himself at his feet; and now he actually had found him, but it was only to deliver him over to the executioner! His father said to him: "Succor Thénardier!" And he replied to that adored and sainted voice by crushing Thénardier! He was about to offer to his father in his grave the spectacle of that man who had torn him from death at the peril of his own life, executed on the Place Saint-Jacques through the means of his son, of that Marius to whom he had entrusted that man by his will! And what a mockery to have so long worn on his breast his father's last commands, written in his own hand, only to act in so horribly contrary a sense! But, on the other hand, now look on that trap and not prevent it! Condemn the victim and to spare the assassin! Could one be held to any gratitude toward so miserable a wretch? All the ideas which Marius had cherished for the last four years were pierced through and through, as it were, by this unforeseen blow.

He shuddered. Everything depended on him. Unknown to themselves, he held in his hand all those beings who were moving about there before his eyes. If he fired his pistol, M. Leblanc was saved, and Thénardier lost; if he did not fire, M. Leblanc would be sacrificed, and, who knows? Thénardier would escape. Should he dash down the one or allow the other to fall? Remorse awaited him in either case.

What was he to do? What should he choose? Be false to the most imperious souvenirs, to all those solemn vows to himself, to the most sacred duty, to the most venerated text! Should he ignore his father's testament, or allow the perpetration of a crime! On the one hand, it seemed to him that he heard "his Ursule" supplicating for her father, and on the other, the colonel commending Thénardier to his care. He felt that he was going mad. His knees gave way beneath him. And he had not even the time for deliberation, so great was the fury with which the scene before his eyes was hastening to its catastrophe. It was like a whirlwind of which he had thought himself the master, and which was now sweeping him away. He was on the verge of swooning.

In the meantime, Thénardier, whom we shall henceforth call by no other name, was pacing up and down in front of the table in a sort of frenzy and wild triumph.

He seized the candle in his fist, and set it on the chimney-piece with so violent a bang that the wick came near being extinguished, and the tallow bespattered the wall.

Then he turned to M. Leblanc, with a horrible look, and spit out these words:

"Done for! Smoked brown! Cooked! Spitchcocked!"

And again he began to march back and forth, in full eruption.

"Ah!" he cried, "so I've found you again at last, Mister philanthropist! Mister threadbare millionnaire! Mister giver of dolls! you old ninny! Ah! so you don't recognize me! No, it wasn't you who came to Montfermeil, to my inn, eight years ago, on Christmas Eve, 1823! It wasn't you who carried off that Fantine's child from me! The Lark! It wasn't you who had a yellow great-coat! No! Nor a package of duds in your hand, as you had this morning here! Say, wife, it seems to be his mania to carry packets of woolen stockings into houses! Old charity monger, get out with you! Are you a hosier, Mister millionnaire? You give away your stock in trade to the poor, holy man! What bosh! merry-andrew! Ah! and you don't recognize me? Well, I recognize you, that I do! I recognized you the very moment you poked your snout in here. Ah! you'll find out presently, that it isn't all roses to thrust yourself in that fashion into the people's houses, under the pretext that they are taverns, in wretched clothes, with the air of a poor man, to whom one would give a sou, to deceive persons, to play the generous, to take away their means of livelihood, and to make threats in the woods, and you can't call things quits because afterwards, when people are ruined, you bring a coat that is too large, and two miserable hospital blankets, you old blackguard, you child-stealer!"

He paused, and seemed to be talking to himself for a moment. One would have said that his wrath had fallen into some hole, like the Rhone; then, as though he were concluding aloud the things which he had been saying to himself in a whisper, he smote the table with his fist, and shouted:

"And with his goody-goody air!"

And, apostrophizing M. Leblanc:

"Parbleu! You made game of me in the past! You are the cause of all my misfortunes! For fifteen hundred francs you got a girl whom I had, and who certainly belonged to rich people, and who had already brought in a great deal of money, and from whom I might have extracted enough to live on all my life! A girl who would have made up to me for everything that I lost in that vile cook-shop, where there was nothing but one continual row, and where, like a fool, I ate up my last farthing! Oh! I wish all the wine folks drank in my house had been poison to those who drank it! Well, never mind! Say, now! You must have thought me ridiculous when you went off with the Lark! You had your cudgel in the forest. You were the stronger. Revenge. I'm the one to hold the trumps to-day! You're in a sorry case, my good fellow! Oh, but I can laugh! Really, I laugh! Didn't he fall into the trap! I told him that I was an actor, that my name was Fabantou, that I had played comedy with Mamselle Mars, with Mamselle Muche, that my landlord insisted on being paid to-morrow, the 4th of February, and he didn't even notice that the 8th of January, and not the 4th of February is the time when the quarter runs out! Absurd idiot! And the four miserable Philippes which he has brought me! Scoundrel! He hadn't the heart even to go as high as a hundred francs! And how he swallowed my platitudes! That did amuse me. I said to myself: 'Blockhead! Come, I've got you! I lick your paws this morning, but I'll gnaw your heart this evening!' "

Thénardier paused. He was out of breath. His little, narrow chest panted like a forge bellows. His eyes were full of the ignoble happiness of a feeble, cruel, and cowardly creature, which finds that it can, at last, harass what it has feared, and insult what it has flattered, the joy of a dwarf who should be able to set his heel on the head of Goliath, the joy of a jackal which is beginning to rend a sick bull, so nearly dead that he can no longer defend himself, but sufficiently alive to suffer still.

M. Leblanc did not interrupt him, but said to him when he paused:

"I do not know what you mean to say. You are mistaken in me. I am a very poor man, and anything but a millionaire. I do not know you. You are mistaking me for some other person."

"Ah!" roared Thénardier hoarsely, "a pretty lie! You stick to that pleasantry, do you! You're floundering, my old buck! Ah! You don't remember! You don't see who I am?"

"Excuse me, sir," said M. Leblanc with a politeness of accent, which at that moment seemed peculiarly strange and powerful, "I see that you are a villain!"

Who has not remarked the fact that odious creatures possess a susceptibility of their own, that monsters are ticklish! At this word "villain," the female Thénardier sprang from the bed, Thénardier grasped his chair as though he were about to crush it in his hands. "Don't you stir!" he shouted to his wife; and, turning to M. Leblanc:

"Villain! Yes, I know that you call us that, you rich gentlemen! Stop! it's true that I became bankrupt, that I am in hiding, that I have no bread, that I have not a single sou, that I am a villain! It's three days since I have had anything to eat, so I'm a villain! Ah! you folks warm your feet, you have Sakoski boots, you have wadded great-coats, like archbishops, you lodge on the first floor in houses that have porters, you eat truffles, you eat asparagus at forty francs the bunch in the month of January, and green peas, you gorge yourselves, and when you want to know whether it is cold, you look in the papers to see what the engineer Chevalier's thermometer says about it. We, it is we who are thermometers. We don't need to go out and look on the quay at the corner of the Tour de l'Horloge, to find out the number of degrees of cold; we feel our blood congealing in our veins, and the ice forming round our hearts, and we say: 'There is no God!' And you come to our caverns, yes, our caverns, for the purpose of calling us villains! But we'll devour you! But we'll devour you, poor little things! Just see here, Mister millionnaire: I have been a solid man, I have held a license, I have been an elector, I am a bourgeois, that I am! And it's quite possible that you are not!"

Here Thénardier took a step toward the men who stood near the door, and added with a shudder:

"When I think that he has dared to come here and talk to me like a cobbler!"

Then addressing M. Leblanc with a fresh outburst of frenzy:

"And listen to this also, Mister philanthropist! I'm not a suspicious character, not a bit of it! I'm not a man whose name nobody knows, and who comes and abducts children from houses! I'm an old French soldier, I ought to have been decorated! I was at Waterloo, so I was! And in the battle I saved a general called the Comte of I don't know what. He told me his name, but his beastly voice was so weak that I didn't hear. All I caught was Merci [thanks]. I'd rather have had his name than his thanks. That would have helped me to find him again. The picture that you see here, and which was painted by David at Bruqueselles—do you know what it represents? It represents me. David wished to immortalize that feat of prowess. I have that general on my back, and I am carrying him through the grape-shot. There's the history of it! That general never did a single thing for me; he was no better than the rest! But none the less, I saved his life at the risk of my own, and I have the certificate of the fact in my pocket! I am a soldier of Waterloo, by all the furies! And now that I have had the goodness to tell you all this, let's have an end of it. I want money, I want a deal of money, I must have an enormous lot of money, or I'll exterminate you, by the thunder of the good God!"

Marius had regained some measure of control over his anguish, and was listening. The last possibility of doubt had just vanished. It certainly was the Thénardier of the will. Marius shuddered at that reproach of ingratitude directed against his father, and which he was on the point of so fatally justifying. His perplexity was redoubled.

Moreover, there was in all those words of Thénardier, in his accent, in his gesture, in his glance which darted flames at every word, there was, in this explosion of an evil nature disclosing everything, in that mixture of braggadocio and abjectness, of pride and pettiness, of rage and folly, in that chaos of real griefs and false sentiments, in that immodesty of a malicious man tasting the voluptuous delights of violence, in that shameless nudity of a repulsive soul, in that conflagration of all sufferings combined with all hatreds, something which was as hideous as evil, and as heartrending as the truth.

The picture of the master, the painting by David which he had proposed that M. Leblanc should purchase, was nothing else, as the reader has divined, than the sign of his tavern painted, as it will be remembered, by himself, the only relic which he had preserved from his shipwreck at Montfermeil.

As he had ceased to intercept Marius's visual ray, Marius could examine this thing, and in the daub, he actually did recognize a battle, a background of smoke, and a man carrying another man. It was the group composed of Pontmercy and Thénardier; the sergeant the rescuer, the colonel rescued. Marius was like a drunken man; this picture restored his father to life, in some sort; it was no longer the signboard of the wine-shop at Montfermeil, it was a resurrection; a tomb had yawned, a phantom had risen there. Marius heard his heart beating in his temples, he had the cannon of Waterloo in his ears, his bleeding father, vaguely depicted on that sinister panel terrified him, and it seemed to him that the misshapen specter was gazing intently at him.

When Thénardier had recovered his breath, he turned his bloodshot eyes on M. Leblanc, and said to him in a low, curt voice:

"What have you to say before we put the handcuffs on you?"

M. Leblanc held his peace.

In the midst of this silence, a cracked voice launched this lugubrious sarcasm from the corridor:

"If there's any wood to be split, I'm there!"

It was the man with the ax, who was growing merry.

At the same moment, an enormous, bristling, and clayey face made its appearance at the door, with a hideous laugh which exhibited not teeth, but fangs.

It was the face of the man with the butcher's ax.

"Why have you taken off your mask?" cried Thénardier in a rage.

"For fun," retorted the man.

For the last few minutes M. Leblanc had appeared to be watching and following all the movements of Thénardier, who, blinded and dazzled by his own rage, was stalking to and fro in the den with full confidence that the door was guarded, and of holding an unarmed man fast, he being armed himself, of being nine against one, supposing that the female Thénardier counted for but one man.

During his address to the man with the pole-ax, he had turned his back to M. Leblanc.

M. Leblanc seized this moment, overturned the chair with his foot and the table with his fist, and with one bound, with prodigious agility, before Thénardier had time to turn round, he had reached the window. To open it, to scale the frame, to bestride it, was the work of a second only. He was half out when six robust fists seized him and dragged him back energetically into the hovel. These were the three "chimney-builders," who had flung themselves upon him. At the same time the Thénardier woman had wound her hands in his hair.

At the trampling which ensued, the other ruffians rushed up from the corridor. The old man on the bed, who seemed under the influence of wine, descended from the pallet and came reeling up, with a stone-breaker's hammer in his hand.

One of the "chimney-builders," whose smirched face was lighted up by the candle, and in whom Marius recognized, in spite of his daubing, Panchaud, alias Printanier, alias Bigrenaille, lifted above M. Leblanc's head a sort of bludgeon made of two balls of lead, at the two ends of a bar of iron.

Marius could not resist this sight. "My father," he thought, "forgive me!"

And his finger sought the trigger of his pistol.

The shot was on the point of being discharged when Thénardier's voice shouted:

"Don't harm him!"

This desperate attempt of the victim, far from exasperating Thénardier, had calmed him. There existed in him two men, the ferocious man and the adroit man. Up to that moment, in the excess of his triumph in the presence of the prey which had been brought down, and which did not stir, the ferocious man had prevailed; when the victim struggled and tried to resist, the adroit man reappeared and took the upper hand.

"Don't hurt him!" he repeated, and without suspecting it, his first success was to arrest the pistol in the act of being discharged, and to paralyze Marius, in whose opinion the urgency of the case disappeared, and who, in the face of this new phase, saw no inconvenience in waiting a while longer.

Who knows whether some chance would not arise which would deliver him from the horrible alternative of allowing Ursule's father to perish, or of destroying the colonel's savior?

A herculean struggle had begun. With one blow full in the chest, M. Leblanc had sent the old man tumbling, rolling in the middle of the room, then with two backward sweeps of his hand he had overthrown two more assailants, and he held one under each of his knees; the wretches were rattling in the throat beneath this pressure as under a granite millstone; but the other four had seized the formidable old man by both arms, and the back of his neck, and were holding him doubled up over the two "chimney-builders" on the floor.

Thus, the master of some and mastered by the rest, crushing those beneath him and stifling under those on top of him, endeavoring in vain to shake off all the efforts which were heaped upon him, M. Leblanc disappeared under the horrible group of ruffians like the wild boar beneath a howling pile of dogs and hounds.

They succeeded in overthrowing him upon the bed nearest the window, and there they held him in awe. The Thénardier woman had not released her clutch on his hair.

"Don't you mix yourself up in this affair," said Thénardier. "You'll tear your shawl."

The Thénardier obeyed, as the female wolf obeys the male wolf, with a growl.

"Now," said Thénardier, "search him, you other fellows!"

M. Leblanc seemed to have renounced the idea of resistance.

They searched him.

He had nothing on his person except a leather purse containing six francs, and his handkerchief.

Thénardier put the handkerchief into his own pocket.

"What! No pocket-book?" he demanded.

"No, nor watch," replied one of the "chimney-builders."

"Never mind," murmured the masked man who carried the big key, in the voice of a ventriloquist, "he's a tough old fellow."

Thénardier went to the corner near the door, picked up a bundle of ropes and threw them at the men.

"Tie him to the leg of the bed," said he.

And, catching sight of the old man who had been stretched across the room by the blow from M. Leblanc's fist, and who made no movement, he added:

"Is Boulatruelle dead?"

"No," replied Bigrenaille, "he's drunk."

"Sweep him into a corner," said Thénardier.

Two of the "chimney-builders" pushed the drunken man into the corner near the heap of old iron with their feet.

"Babet," said Thénardier in a low tone to the man with the cudgel, "why did you bring so many; they were not needed."

"What can you do?" replied the man with the cudgel, "they all wanted to be in it. This is a bad season. There's no business going on."

The pallet on which M. Leblanc had been thrown was a sort of hospital bed, elevated on four coarse wooden legs, roughly hewn.

M. Leblanc let them take their own course.

The ruffians bound him securely, in an upright attitude, with his feet on the ground at the head of the bed, the end which was most remote from the window, and nearest to the fireplace.

When the last knot had been tied, Thénardier took a chair and seated himself almost facing M. Leblanc.

Thénardier no longer looked like himself; in the course of a few moments, his face had passed from unbridled violence to tranquil and cunning sweetness.

Marius found it difficult to recognize in that polished smile of a man in official life, the almost bestial mouth which had been foaming but a moment before; he gazed with amazement on that fantastic and alarming metamorphosis, and he felt as a man might feel who should behold a tiger converted into a lawyer.

"Monsieur—" said Thénardier.

And dismissing with a gesture the ruffians who still kept their hands on M. Leblanc:

"Stand off a little, and let me have a talk with the gentleman."

All retired toward the door.

He went on:

"Monsieur, you did wrong to try to jump out of the window. You might have broken your leg. Now, if you will permit me, we will converse quietly. In the first place, I must communicate to you an observation which I have made, which is, that you have not uttered the faintest cry."

Thénardier was right, this detail was correct, although it had escaped Marius in his agitation. M. Leblanc had barely pronounced a few words, without raising his voice, and even during his struggle with the six ruffians near the window, he had preserved the most profound and singular silence.

Thénardier continued:

"Mon Dieu! You might have shouted 'stop thief' a bit, and I should not have thought it improper. 'Murder!' That, too, is said occasionally, and, so far as I am concerned, I should not have taken it in bad part. It is very natural that you should make a little row when you find yourself with persons who don't inspire you with sufficient confidence. You might have done that, and no one would have troubled you on that account. You would not even have been gagged. And I will tell you why. This room is very private. That's its only recommendation, but it has that in its favor. You might fire off a mortar and it would produce about as much noise at the nearest police station as the snores of a drunken man. Here a cannon would make a *boum*, and the thunder would make a *pouf*. It's a handy lodging. But, in short, you did not shout, and it is better so. I present you my compliments, and I will tell you the conclusion that I draw from that fact: My dear sir, when a man shouts, who comes? The police. And after the police? Justice. Well! You have not made an outcry; that is because you don't care to have the police and the courts come in any more than we do. It is because—I have long suspected it—you have some interest in hiding something. On our side we have the same interest. So we can come to an understanding."

As he spoke thus, it seemed as though Thénardier, who kept his eyes fixed on M. Leblanc, were trying to plunge the sharp points which darted from the pupils into the very conscience of his prisoner. Moreover, his language, which was stamped with a sort of moderated, subdued insolence and crafty insolence, was reserved and almost choice, and in that rascal, who had been nothing but a robber a short time previously, one now felt "the man who had studied for the priesthood."

The silence preserved by the prisoner, that precaution which had been carried to the point of forgetting all anxiety for his own life, that resistance opposed to the first impulse of nature, which is to utter a cry, all this, it must be confessed, now that his attention had been called to it, troubled Marius, and affected him with painful astonishment.

Thénardier's well-grounded observation still further obscured for Marius the dense mystery which enveloped that grave and singular person on whom Courfeyrac had bestowed the sobriquet of Monsieur Leblanc.

But whoever he was, bound with ropes, surrounded with executioners, half plunged, so to speak, in a grave which was closing in upon him to the extent of a degree with every moment that passed, in the presence of Thénardier's wrath, as in the presence of his sweetness, this man remained impassive; and Marius could not refrain from admiring at such a moment the superbly melancholy visage.

Here, evidently, was a soul which was inaccessible to terror, and which did not know the meaning of despair. Here was one of those men who command amazement in desperate circumstances. Extreme as was the crisis, inevitable as was the catastrophe, there was nothing here of the agony of the drowning man, who opens his horror-filled eyes under the water.

Thénardier rose in an unpretending manner, went to the fireplace, shoved aside the screen, which he leaned against the neighboring pallet, and thus unmasked the brazier full of glowing coals, in which the prisoner could plainly see the chisel white-hot and spotted here and there with tiny scarlet stars.

Then Thénardier returned to his seat beside M. Leblanc.

"I continue," said he. "We can come to an understanding. Let us arrange this matter in an amicable way. I was wrong to lose my temper just now, I don't know what I was thinking of, I went a great deal too far, I said extravagant things. For example, because you are a millionnaire, I told you that I exacted money, a lot of money, a deal of money. That would not be reasonable. Mon Dieu, in spite of your riches, you have expenses of your own—who has not? I don't want to ruin you, I am not a greedy fellow, after all. I am not one of those people, who, because they have the advantage of the position, profit by the fact to make themselves ridiculous. Why, I'm taking things into consideration and making a sacrifice on my side. I only want two hundred thousand francs."

M. Leblanc uttered not a word.

Thénardier went on:

"You see that I put not a little water in my wine; I'm very moderate. I don't know the state of your fortune, but I do know that you don't stick at money, and a benevolent man like yourself can certainly give two hundred thousand francs to the father of a family who is out of luck. Certainly, you are reasonable, too; you haven't imagined that I should take all the trouble I have to-day and organized this affair this evening, which has been labor well bestowed, in the opinion of these gentlemen, merely to wind up by asking you for enough to go and drink red wine at fifteen sous and eat veal at Desnoyers. Two hundred thousand francs—it's surely worth all that. This trifle once out of your pocket, I guarantee you that that's the end of the matter, and that you have no further demands to fear. You will say to me: 'But I haven't two hundred thousand francs about me.' Oh! I'm not extortionate. I don't demand that. I only ask one thing of you. Have the goodness to write what I am about to dictate to you."

Here Thénardier paused; then he added, emphasizing his words, and casting a smile in the direction of the brazier:

"I warn you that I shall not admit that you don't know how to write."

A grand inquisitor might have envied that smile.

Thénardier pushed the table close to M. Leblanc, and took an inkstand, a pen, and a sheet of paper from the drawer which he left half-open, and in which gleamed the long blade of the knife.

He placed the sheet of paper before M. Leblanc.

"Write," said he.

The prisoner spoke at last.

"How do you expect me to write? I am bound."

"That's true, excuse me!" ejaculated Thénardier, "you are quite right."

And turning to Bigrenaille:

"Untie the gentleman's right arm."

Panchaud, alias Printanier, alias Bigrenaille, executed Thénardier's order.

When the prisoner's right arm was free, Thénardier dipped the pen in the ink and presented it to him.

"Understand thoroughly, sir, that you are in our power, at our discretion, that no human power can get you out of this, and that we shall be really grieved if we are forced to proceed to disagreeable extremities. I know neither your name, nor your address, but I warn you, that you will remain bound until the person charged with carrying the letter which you are about to write shall have returned. Now, be so good as to write."

"What?" demanded the prisoner.

"I will dictate."

M. Leblanc took the pen.

Thénardier began to dictate:

"My daughter—"

The prisoner shuddered, and raised his eyes to Thénardier.

"Put down 'My dear daughter'—" said Thénardier.

M. Leblanc obeyed.

Thénardier continued:

"Come instantly—"

He paused:

"You address her as *thou*, do you not?"

"Who?" asked M. Leblanc.

"Parbleu!" cried Thénardier, "the little one, the Lark."

M. Leblanc replied without the slightest apparent emotion:

"I do not know what you mean."

"Go on, nevertheless," ejaculated Thénardier, and he continued to dictate:

"Come immediately, I am in absolute need of thee. The person who will deliver this note to thee is instructed to conduct thee to me. I am waiting for thee. Come with confidence."

M. Leblanc had written the whole of this.

Thénardier resumed:

"Ah! erase 'come with confidence'; that might lead her to suppose that everything was not as it should be, and that distrust is possible."

M. Leblanc erased the three words.

"Now," pursued Thénardier, "sign it. What's your name?"

The prisoner laid down the pen and demanded:

"For whom is this letter?"

"You know well," retorted Thénardier, "for the little one. I just told you so."

It was evident that Thénardier avoided naming the young girl in question. He said "the Lark," he said "the little one," but he did not pronounce her name—the precaution of a clever man guarding his secret from his accomplices. To mention the name was to deliver the whole "affair" into their hands, and to tell them more about it than there was any need of their knowing.

He went on:

"Sign. What is your name?"

"Urbain Fabre," said the prisoner.

Thénardier, with the movement of a cat, dashed his hand into his pocket and drew out the handkerchief which had been seized on M. Leblanc. He looked for the mark on it, and held it close to the candle.

"U. F. That's it. Urbain Fabre. Well, sign it U. F."

The prisoner signed.

"As two hands are required to fold the letter, give it to me, I will fold it."

That done, Thénardier resumed:

"Address it, 'Mademoiselle Fabre,' at your house. I know that you live a long distance from here, near Saint-Jacques-du-Haut-Pas, because you go to mass there every day, but I don't know in what street. I see that you understand your situation. As you have not lied about your name, you will not lie about your address. Write it yourself."

The prisoner paused thoughtfully for a moment, then he took the pen and wrote:

"Mademoiselle Fabre, at M. Urbain Fabre's, Rue Saint-Dominique-D'Enfer, No. 17."

Thénardier seized the letter with a sort of feverish convulsion.

"Wife!" he cried.

The Thénardier woman hastened to him.

"Here's the letter. You know what you have to do. There is a carriage at the door. Set out at once, and return ditto."

And addressing the man with the meat-ax:

"Since you have taken off your nose-screen, accompany the mistress. You will get up behind the fiacre. You know where you left the team?"

"Yes," said the man.

And depositing his ax in a corner, he followed Madame Thénardier.

As they set off, Thénardier thrust his head through the half-open door, and shouted into the corridor:

"Above all things, don't lose the letter! remember that you carry two hundred thousand francs with you!"

The Thénardier's hoarse voice replied:

"Be easy. I have it in my bosom."

A minute had not elapsed, when the sound of the cracking of a whip was heard, which rapidly retreated and died away.

"Good!" growled Thénardier. "They're going at a fine pace. At such a gallop, the bourgeoise will be back inside three-quarters of an hour."

He drew a chair close to the fireplace, folding his arms, and presenting his muddy boots to the brazier.

"My feet are cold!" said he.

Only five ruffians now remained in the den with Thénardier and the prisoner.

These men, through the black masks or paste which covered their faces, and made of them, at fear's pleasure, charcoal-burners, negroes, or demons, had a stupid and gloomy air, and it could be felt that they perpetrated a crime like a bit of work, tranquilly, without either wrath or mercy, with a sort of ennui. They were crowded together in one corner like brutes, and remained silent.

Thénardier warmed his feet.

The prisoner had relapsed into his taciturnity. A somber calm had succeeded to the wild uproar which had filled the garret but a few moments before.

The candle, on which a large "stranger" had formed, cast but a dim light in the immense hovel, the brazier had grown dull, and all those monstrous heads cast misshapen shadows on the walls and ceiling.

No sound was audible except the quiet breathing of the old drunken man, who was fast asleep.

Marius waited in a state of anxiety that was augmented by every trifle. The enigma was more impenetrable than ever.

Who was this "little one" whom Thénardier had called the Lark? Was she his "Ursule"? The prisoner had not seemed to be affected by that word, "the Lark," and had replied in the most natural manner in the world: "I do not know what you mean." On the other hand, the two letters U. F. were explained; they meant Urbain Fabre; and Ursule was no longer named Ursule. This was what Marius perceived most clearly of all.

A sort of horrible fascination held him nailed to his post, from which he was observing and commanding this whole scene. There he stood, almost incapable of movement or reflection, as though annihilated by the abominable things viewed at such close quarters. He waited, in the hope of some incident, no matter of what nature, since he could not collect his thoughts and did not know upon what course to decide.

"In any case," he said, "if she is the Lark, I shall see her, for the Thénardier woman is to bring her hither. That will be the end, and then I will give my life and my blood if necessary, but I will deliver her! Nothing shall stop me."

Nearly half an hour passed in this manner. Thénardier seemed to be absorbed in gloomy reflections, the prisoner did not stir. Still, Marius fancied that at intervals, and for the last few moments, he had heard a faint, dull noise in the direction of the prisoner.

All at once, Thénardier addressed the prisoner:

"By the way, Monsieur Fabre, I might as well say it to you at once."

These few words appeared to be the beginning of an explanation. Marius strained his ears. Thénardier continued:

"My wife will be back shortly, don't get impatient. I think that the Lark really is your daughter, and it seems to me quite natural that you should keep her. Only, listen to me a bit. My wife will go and hunt her up with your letter. I told my wife to dress herself in the way she did, so that your young lady might make no difficulty about following her. They will both enter the carriage with my comrade behind. Somewhere, outside the barrier, there is a trap harnessed to two very good horses. Your young lady will be taken to it. She will alight from the fiacre. My comrade will enter the other vehicle with her, and my wife will come back here to tell us: 'It's done.' As for the young lady, no harm will be done to her; the trap will conduct her to a place where she will be quiet, and just as soon as you have handed over to me those little two hundred thousand francs, she will be returned to you. If you have me arrested, my comrade will give a turn of his thumb to the Lark, that's all."

The prisoner uttered not a syllable. After a pause, Thénardier continued:

"It's very simple, as you see. There'll be no harm done unless you wish that there should be harm done. I'm telling you how things stand. I warn you so that you may be prepared."

He paused: the prisoner did not break the silence, and Thénardier resumed:

"As soon as my wife returns and says to me: 'The Lark is on the way,' we will release you, and you will be free to go and sleep at home. You see that our intentions are not evil."

Terrible images passed through Marius's mind. What! That young girl whom they were abducting was not to be brought back? One of those monsters was to bear her off into the darkness? Whither? And what if it were she!

It was clear that it was she. Marius felt his heart stop beating.

What was he to do? Discharge the pistol? Place all those scoundrels in the hands of justice? But the horrible man with the meat-ax would, none the less, be out of reach with the young girl, and Marius reflected on Thénardier's words, of which he perceived the bloody significance: "If you have me arrested, my comrade will give a turn of his thumb to the Lark."

Now, it was not alone by the colonel's testament, it was by his own love, it was by the peril of the one he loved, that he felt himself restrained.

This frightful situation, which had already lasted above half an hour, was changing its aspect every moment.

Marius had sufficient strength of mind to review in succession all the most heart-breaking conjectures, seeking hope and finding none.

The tumult of his thoughts contrasted with the funereal silence of the den.

In the midst of this silence, the door at the bottom of the staircase was heard to open and shut again.

The prisoner made a movement in his bonds.

"Here's the bourgeoise," said Thénardier.

He had hardly uttered the words, when the Thénardier woman did in fact rush hastily into the room, red, panting, breathless, with flaming eyes, and cried, as she smote her huge hands on her thighs simultaneously:

"False address!"

The ruffian who had gone with her made his appearance behind her and picked up his ax again.

She resumed:

"Nobody there! Rue Saint-Dominique, No. 17, no Monsieur Urbain Fabre! They know not what it means!"

She paused, choking, then went on:

"Monsieur Thénardier! That old fellow has duped you! You are too good, you see! If it had been me, I'd have chopped the beast in four quarters to begin with! And if he had acted ugly, I'd have boiled him alive! He would have been obliged to speak, and say where the girl is, and where he keeps his shiners! That's the way I should have managed matters! People are perfectly right when they say that men are a deal stupider than women! Nobody at No. 17. It's nothing but a big carriage gate! No Monsieur Fabre in the Rue Saint-Dominique! And after all that racing and fee to the coachman and all! I spoke to both the porter and the portress, a fine, stout woman, and they know nothing about him!"

Marius breathed freely once more.

She, Ursule or the Lark, he no longer knew what to call her, was safe.

While his exasperated wife vociferated, Thénardier had seated himself on the table.

For several minutes he uttered not a word, but swung his right foot, which hung down, and stared at the brazier with an air of savage reverie.

Finally, he said to the prisoner, with a slow and singularly ferocious tone:

"A false address? What did you expect to gain by that?"

"To gain time!" cried the prisoner in a thundering voice, and at the same instant he shook off his bonds; they were cut. The prisoner was only attached to the bed now by one leg.

Before the seven men had time to collect their senses and dash forward, he had bent down into the fireplace, had stretched out his hand to the brazier, and had then straightened himself up again, and now Thénardier, the female Thénardier, and the ruffians, huddled in amazement at the extremity of the hovel, stared at him in stupefaction, as almost free and in a formidable attitude, he brandished above his head the red-hot chisel, which emitted a threatening glow.

The judicial examination to which the ambush in the Gorbeau house eventually gave rise, established the fact that a large sou piece, cut and worked in a peculiar fashion, was found in the garret, when the police made their descent on it. This sou piece was one of those marvels of industry, which are engendered by the patience of the galleys in the shadows and for the shadows, marvels which are nothing else than instruments of escape. These hideous and delicate products of wonderful art are to jewelers' work what the metaphors of slang are to poetry. There are Benvenuto Cellinis in the galleys, just as there are Villons in language. The unhappy wretch who aspires to deliverance finds means sometimes without tools, sometimes with a common wooden-handled knife, to saw a sou into two thin plates, to hollow out these plates without affecting the coinage stamp, and to make a furrow on the edge of the sou in such a manner that the plates will adhere again. This can be screwed together and unscrewed at will; it is a box. In this box he hides a watch-spring, and this watch-spring, properly handled, cuts good-sized chains and bars of iron. The unfortunate convict is supposed to possess merely a sou; not at all, he possesses liberty. It was a large sou of this sort which, during the subsequent search of the police, was found under the bed near the window. They also found a tiny saw of blue steel which would fit the sou.

It is probable that the prisoner had this sou piece on his person at the moment when the ruffians searched him, that he contrived to conceal it in his hand, and that afterward, having his right hand free, he unscrewed it, and used it as a saw to cut the cords which fastened him, which would explain the faint noise and almost imperceptible movements which Marius had observed.

As he had not been able to bend down, for fear of betraying himself, he had not cut the bonds of his left leg.

The ruffians had recovered from their first surprise.

"Be easy," said Bigrenaille to Thénardier. "He still holds by one leg, and he can't get away. I'll answer for that. I tied that paw for him."

In the meanwhile, the prisoner had begun to speak:

"You are wretches, but my life is not worth the trouble of defending it. When you think that you can make me speak, that you can make me write what I do not choose to write, that you can make me say what I do not choose to say—"

He stripped up his left sleeve, and added:

"See here."

At the same moment, he extended his arm, and laid the glowing chisel which he held in his left hand by its wooden handle on his bare flesh.

The crackling of the burning flesh became audible, and the odor peculiar to chambers of torture filled the hovel.

Marius reeled in utter horror, the very ruffians shuddered, hardly a muscle of the old man's face contracted, and while the red-hot iron sank into the smoking wound, impassive and almost august, he fixed on Thénardier his beautiful glance, in which there was no hatred, and where suffering vanished in serene majesty.

With grand and lofty natures, the revolts of the flesh and the senses when subjected to physical suffering cause the soul to spring forth, and make it appear on the brow, just as rebellions among the soldiery force the captain to show himself.

"Wretches!" said he, "have no more fear of me than I have for you!"

And, tearing the chisel from the wound, he hurled it through the window, which had been left open; the horrible, glowing tool disappeared into the night, whirling as it flew, and fell far away on the snow.

The prisoner resumed:

"Do what you please with me." He was disarmed.

"Seize him!" said Thénardier.

Two of the ruffians laid their hands on his shoulder, and the masked man with the ventriloquist's voice took up his station in front of him, ready to smash his skull at the slightest movement.

At the same time, Marius heard below him, at the base of the partition, but so near that he could not see who was speaking, this colloquy conducted in a low tone:

"There is only one thing left to do."

"Cut his throat?"

"That's it."

It was the husband and wife taking counsel together.

Thénardier walked slowly toward the table, opened the drawer, and took out the knife. Marius fretted with the handle of his pistol. Unprecedented perplexity! For the last hour he had had two voices in his conscience, the one enjoining him to respect his father's testament, the other crying to him to rescue the prisoner. These two voices continued uninterruptedly that struggle which tormented him to agony. Up to that moment he had cherished a vague hope that he should find some means of reconciling these two duties, but nothing within the limits of possibility had presented itself.

However, the peril was urgent, the last bounds of delay had been reached; Thénardier was standing thoughtfully a few paces distant from the prisoner.

Marius cast a wild glance about him, the last mechanical resource of despair. All at once a shudder ran through him.

At his feet, on the table, a bright ray of light from the full moon illuminated and seemed to point out to him a sheet of paper. On this paper he read the following line written that very morning, in large letters, by the eldest of the Thénardier girls:

"THE BOBBIES ARE HERE."

An idea, a flash, crossed Marius's mind; this was the expedient of which he was in search, the solution of that frightful problem which was torturing him, of sparing the assassin and saving the victim.

He knelt down on his commode, stretched out his arm, seized the sheet of paper, softly detached a bit of plaster from the wall, wrapped the paper round it, and tossed the whole through the crevice into the middle of the den.

It was high time. Thénardier had conquered his last fears or his last scruples, and was advancing on the prisoner.

"Something is falling!" cried the Thénardier woman.

"What is it?" asked her husband.

The woman darted forward and picked up the bit of plaster. She handed it to her husband.

"Where did this come from?" demanded Thénardier.

"Pardie!" ejaculated his wife, "where do you suppose it came from? Through the window, of course."

"I saw it pass," said Bigrenaille.

Thénardier rapidly unfolded the paper and held it close to the candle.

"It's in Éponine's handwriting. The devil!"

He made a sign to his wife, who hastily drew near, and showed her the line written on the sheet of paper, then he added in a subdued voice:

"Quick! The ladder! Let's leave the bacon in the mouse-trap and decamp!"

"Without cutting that man's throat?" asked the Thénardier woman.

"We haven't the time."

"Through what?" resumed Bigrenaille.

"Through the window," replied Thénardier. "Since Ponine has thrown the stone through the window, it indicates that the house is not watched on that side."

The mask with the ventriloquist's voice deposited his huge key on the floor, raised both arms in the air, and opened and clenched his fists three times rapidly without uttering a word.

This was the signal like the signal for clearing the decks for action on board ship.

The ruffians who were holding the prisoner released him; in the twinkling of an eye the rope ladder was unrolled outside the window, and solidly fastened to the sill by the two iron hooks.

The prisoner paid no attention to what was going on around him. He seemed to be dreaming or praying.

As soon as the ladder was arranged, Thénardier cried:

"Come! the bourgeoise first!"

And he rushed headlong to the window.

But just as he was about to throw his leg over, Bigrenaille seized him roughly by the collar.

"Not much, come now, you old dog, after us!"

"After us!" yelled the ruffians.

"You are children," said Thénardier, "we are losing time. The police are on our heels."

"Well," said the ruffians, "let's draw lots to see who shall go down first."

Thénardier exclaimed:

"Are you mad! Are you crazy! What a pack of boobies! You want to waste time, do you? Draw lots, do you? By a wet finger, by a short straw! With written names! Thrown into a hat!—"

"Would you like my hat!" cried a voice on the threshold.

All wheeled round. It was Javert.

He had his hat in his hand, and was holding it out to them with a smile.

Chapter XXI

ONE SHOULD ALWAYS BEGIN BY ARRESTING THE VICTIMS

AT NIGHTFALL, JAVERT HAD POSTED HIS MEN AND HAD GONE INTO AMBUSH HIMSELF BETWEEN the trees of the Rue de la Barrière-des-Gobelins which faced the Gorbeau house, on the other side of the boulevard. He had begun operations by opening "his pockets," and dropping into it the two young girls who were charged with keeping a watch on the approaches to the den. But he had only "caged" Azelma. As for Éponine, she was not at her post, she had disappeared, and he had not been able to seize her. Then Javert had made a point and had bent his ear to waiting for the signal agreed upon. The comings and goings of the fiacres had greatly agitated him. At last, he had grown impatient, and, *sure that there was a nest there,* sure of being in "luck," having recognized many of the ruffians who had entered, he had finally decided to go upstairs without waiting for the pistol-shot.

It will be remembered that he had Marius's pass-key.

He had arrived just in the nick of time.

The terrified ruffians flung themselves on the arms which they had abandoned in all the corners at the moment of flight. In less than a second, these seven men, horrible to behold, had grouped themselves in an attitude of defense, one with his meat-ax, another with his key, another with his bludgeon, the rest with shears, pincers, and hammers. Thénardier had his knife in his fist. The Thénardier woman snatched up an enormous paving-stone which lay in the angle of the window and served her daughters as an ottoman.

Javert put on his hat again, and advanced a couple of paces into the room, with arms folded, his cane under one arm, his sword in its sheath.

"Halt there," said he. "You shall not go out by the window, you shall go through the door. It's less unhealthy. There are seven of you, there are fifteen of us. Don't let's fall to collaring each other like men of Auvergne."

Bigrenaille drew out a pistol which he had kept concealed under his blouse, and put it in Thénardier's hand, whispering in the latter's ear:

"It's Javert. I don't dare fire at that man. Do you dare?"

"Parbleu!" replied Thénardier.

"Well then, fire."

Thénardier took the pistol and aimed at Javert.

Javert, who was only three paces from him, stared intently at him and contented himself with saying:

"Come now, don't fire. You'll miss fire."

Thénardier pulled the trigger. The pistol missed fire.

"Didn't I tell you so!" ejaculated Javert.

Bigrenaille flung his bludgeon at Javert's feet.

"You're the emperor of the fiends! I surrender."

"And you?" Javert asked the rest of the ruffians.

They replied:

"So do we."

Javert began again calmly:

"That's right, that's good, I said so, you are nice fellows."

"I only ask one thing," said Bigrenaille, "and that is, that I may not be denied tobacco while I am in confinement."

"Granted," said Javert.

And turning round and calling behind him:

"Come in now!"

A squad of policemen, sword in hand, and agents armed with bludgeons and cudgels, rushed in at Javert's summons. They pinioned the ruffians.

This throng of men, sparely lighted by the single candle, filled the den with shadows.

"Handcuff them all!" shouted Javert.

"Come on!" cried a voice which was not the voice of a man, but of which no one would ever have said: "It is a woman's voice."

The Thénardier woman had entrenched herself in one of the angles of the window, and it was she who had just given vent to this roar.

The policemen and agents recoiled.

She had thrown off her shawl, but retained her bonnet; her husband, who was crouching behind her, was almost hidden under the discarded shawl, and she was shielding him with her body, as she elevated the paving-stone above her head with the gesture of a giantess on the point of hurling a rock.

"Beware!" she shouted.

All crowded back toward the corridor. A broad open space was cleared in the middle of the garret.

The Thénardier woman cast a glance at the ruffians who had allowed themselves to be pinioned, and muttered in hoarse and guttural accents:

"The cowards!"

Javert smiled, and advanced across the open space which the Thénardier was devouring with her eyes.

"Don't come near me," she cried, "or I'll crush you."

"What a grenadier!" ejaculated Javert; "you've got a beard like a man, mother, but I have claws like a woman."

And he continued to advance.

The Thénardier, disheveled and terrible, set her feet far apart, threw herself backwards, and hurled the paving-stone at Javert's head. Javert ducked, the stone passed over him, struck the wall behind, knocked off a huge piece of plastering, and, rebounding from angle to angle across the hovel, now luckily almost empty, rested at Javert's feet.

At the same moment, Javert reached the Thénardier couple. One of his big hands descended on the woman's shoulder; the other on the husband's head.

"The handcuffs!" he shouted.

The policemen trooped in in force, and in a few seconds Javert's order had been executed.

The Thénardier female, overwhelmed, stared at her pinioned hands, and at those of her husband, who had dropped to the floor, and exclaimed, weeping:

"My daughters!"

"They are in the jug," said Javert.

In the meanwhile, the agents had caught sight of the drunken man asleep behind the door, and were shaking him:

He awoke, stammering:

"Is it all over, Jondrette?"

"Yes," replied Javert.

The six pinioned ruffians were standing, and still preserved their spectral mien; all three besmeared with black, all three masked.

"Keep on your masks," said Javert.

And passing them in review with a glance of a Frederick II at a Potsdam parade, he said to the three "chimney-builders":

"Good day, Bigrenaille! good day, Brujon! good day, Deux-milliards!"

Then turning to the three masked men, he said to the man with the meat-ax:

"Good day, Gueulemer!"

And to the man with the cudgel:

"Good day, Babet!"

And to the ventriloquist:

"Your health, Claquesous."

At that moment, he caught sight of the ruffians' prisoner, who, ever since the entrance of the police, had not uttered a word, and had held his head down.

"Untie the gentleman!" said Javert, "and let no one go out!"

That said, he seated himself with sovereign dignity before the table, where the candle and the writing-materials still remained, drew a stamped paper from his pocket, and began to prepare his report.

When he had written the first lines, which are formulas that never vary, he raised his eyes:

"Let the gentleman whom these gentlemen bound step forward."

The policemen glanced around them.

"Well," said Javert, "where is he?"

The prisoner of the ruffians, M. Leblanc, M. Urbain Fabre, the father of Ursule or the Lark, had disappeared.

The door was guarded, but the window was not. As soon as he had found himself released from his bonds, and while Javert was drawing up his report, he had taken advantage of confusion, the crowd, the darkness, and of a moment when the general attention was diverted from him, to dash out of the window.

An agent sprang to the opening and looked out. He saw no one outside.

The rope ladder was still shaking.

"The devil!" ejaculated Javert between his teeth, "he must have been the most valuable of the lot."

Chapter XXII

THE LITTLE ONE WHO WAS CRYING IN VOLUME TWO

ON THE DAY FOLLOWING THAT ON WHICH THESE EVENTS TOOK PLACE IN THE HOUSE ON THE Boulevard de l'Hôpital, a child, who seemed to be coming from the direction of the bridge of Austerlitz, was ascending the side-alley on the right in the direction of the Barrière de Fontainebleau.

Night had fully come.

This lad was pale, thin, clad in rags, with linen trousers in the month of February, and was singing at the top of his voice.

At the corner of the Rue du Petit-Banquier, a bent old woman was rummaging in a heap of refuse by the light of a street-lantern; the child jostled her as he passed, then recoiled, exclaiming:

"Hello! And I took it for an enormous, enormous dog!"

He pronounced the word *enormous* the second time with a jeering swell of the voice which might be tolerably well represented by capitals: "an enormous, ENORMOUS dog."

The old woman straightened herself up in a fury.

"Nasty brat!" she grumbled. "If I hadn't been bending over, I know well where I would have planted my foot on you."

The boy was already far away.

"Kisss! kisss!" he cried. "After that, I don't think I was mistaken!"

The old woman, choking with indignation, now rose completely upright, and the red gleam of the lantern fully lighted up her livid face, all hollowed into angles and wrinkles, with crow's-feet meeting the corners of her mouth.

Her body was lost in the darkness, and only her head was visible. One would have pronounced her a mask of Decrepitude carved out by a light from the night.

The boy surveyed her.

"Madame," said he, "does not possess that style of beauty which pleases me."

He then pursued his road, and resumed his song:

> *"Le roi Coupdesabot*
> *S'en allait à la chasse,*
> *À la chasse aux corbeaux—"*

At the end of these three lines he paused. He had arrived in front of No. 50-52, and finding the door fastened, he began to assault it with resounding and heroic kicks, which betrayed rather the man's shoes that he was wearing than the child's feet which he owned.

In the meanwhile, the very old woman whom he had encountered at the corner of the Rue du Petit-Banquier hastened up behind him, uttering clamorous cries and indulging in lavish and exaggerated gestures.

"What's this? What's this? Lord God! He's battering the door down! He's knocking the house down."

The kicks continued.

The old woman strained her lungs.

"Is that the way buildings are treated nowadays?"

All at once she paused.

She had recognized the gamin.

"What! so it's that imp!"

"Why, it's the old lady," said the lad. "Good day, Burgonmuche. I have come to see my ancestors."

The old woman retorted with a composite grimace, and a wonderful improvisation of hatred taking advantage of feebleness and ugliness, which was, unfortunately, wasted in the dark:

"There's no one here."

"Bah!" retorted the boy, "where's my father?"

"At La Force."

"Come, now! And my mother?"

"At Saint-Lazare."

"Well! And my sisters?"

"At the Madelonettes."

The lad scratched his head behind his ear, stared at Ma'am Burgon, and said:

"Ah!"

Then he executed a pirouette on his heel; a moment later, the old woman, who had remained on the door-step, heard him singing in his clear, young voice, as he plunged under the black elm-trees, in the wintry wind:

> *"Le roi Coupdesabot*
> *S'en allait à la chasse,*
> *À la chasse aux corbeaux,*
> *Monté sur deux échasses.*
> *Quand on passait dessous,*
> *On lui payait deux sous."*[1]

---

1. King Bootkick went a-hunting after crows, mounted on two stilts. When one passed beneath them, one paid him two sous.

VOLUME IV

SAINT-DENIS
THE IDYL IN THE RUE PLUMET AND the EPIC IN THE RUE SAINT-DENIS

BOOK FIRST

A FEW PAGES OF HISTORY

Chapter I

WELL CUT

1831 AND 1832, THE TWO YEARS WHICH ARE IMMEDIATELY CONNECTED WITH THE REVOLUTION OF JULY, form one of the most peculiar and striking moments of history. These two years rise like two mountains midway between those which precede and those which follow them. They have a revolutionary grandeur. Precipices are to be distinguished there. The social masses, the very assizes of civilization, the solid group of superposed and adhering interests, the century-old profiles of the ancient French formation, appear and disappear in them every instant, athwart the storm clouds of systems, of passions, and of theories. These appearances and disappearances have been designated as movement and resistance. At intervals, truth, that daylight of the human soul, can be descried shining there.

This remarkable epoch is decidedly circumscribed and is beginning to be sufficiently distant from us to allow of our grasping the principal lines even at the present day.

We shall make the attempt.

The Restoration had been one of those intermediate phases, hard to define, in which there is fatigue, buzzing, murmurs, sleep, tumult, and which are nothing else than the arrival of a great nation at a halting-place.

These epochs are peculiar and mislead the politicians who desire to convert them to profit. In the beginning, the nation asks nothing but repose; it thirsts for but one thing, peace; it has but one ambition, to be small. Which is the translation of remaining tranquil. Of great events, great hazards, great adventures, great men, thank God, we have seen enough, we have them heaped higher than our heads. We would exchange Cæsar for Prusias, and Napoleon for the King of Yvetot. "What a good little king was he!" We have marched since daybreak, we have reached the evening of a long and toilsome day; we have made our first change with Mirabeau, the second with Robespierre, the third with Bonaparte; we are worn out. Each one demands a bed.

Devotion which is weary, heroism which has grown old, ambitions which are sated, fortunes which are made, seek, demand, implore, solicit, what? A shelter. They have it. They take possession of peace, of tranquility, of leisure; behold, they are content. But, at the same time certain facts arise, compel recognition, and knock at the door in their turn. These facts are the products of revolutions and wars, they are, they exist, they have the right to install themselves in society, and they do install themselves therein; and most of the time, facts are the stewards of the household and fouriers[1] who do nothing but prepare lodgings for principles.

This, then, is what appears to philosophical politicians:

At the same time that weary men demand repose, accomplished facts demand guarantees. Guarantees are the same to facts that repose is to men.

---

1. In olden times, fouriers were the officials who preceded the Court and allotted the lodgings.

This is what England demanded of the Stuarts after the Protector; this is what France demanded of the Bourbons after the Empire.

These guarantees are a necessity of the times. They must be accorded. Princes "grant" them, but in reality, it is the force of things which gives them. A profound truth, and one useful to know, which the Stuarts did not suspect in 1662, and which the Bourbons did not even obtain a glimpse of in 1814.

The predestined family, which returned to France when Napoleon fell, had the fatal simplicity to believe that it was itself which bestowed, and that what it had bestowed it could take back again; that the House of Bourbon possessed the right divine, that France possessed nothing, and that the political right conceded in the charter of Louis XVIII was merely a branch of the right divine, was detached by the House of Bourbon and graciously given to the people until such day as it should please the King to reassume it. Still, the House of Bourbon should have felt, from the displeasure created by the gift, that it did not come from it.

This house was churlish to the nineteenth century. It put on an ill-tempered look at every development of the nation. To make use of a trivial word, that is to say, of a popular and a true word, it looked glum. The people saw this.

It thought it possessed strength because the Empire had been carried away before it like a theatrical stage-setting. It did not perceive that it had, itself, been brought in in the same fashion. It did not perceive that it also lay in that hand which had removed Napoleon.

It thought that it had roots, because it was the past. It was mistaken; it formed a part of the past, but the whole past was France. The roots of French society were not fixed in the Bourbons, but in the nations. These obscure and lively roots constituted, not the right of a family, but the history of a people. They were everywhere, except under the throne.

The House of Bourbon was to France the illustrious and bleeding knot in her history, but was no longer the principal element of her destiny, and the necessary base of her politics. She could get along without the Bourbons; she had done without them for two-and-twenty years; there had been a break of continuity; they did not suspect the fact. And how should they have suspected it, they who fancied that Louis XVII reigned on the 9th of Thermidor, and that Louis XVIII was reigning at the battle of Marengo? Never, since the origin of history, had princes been so blind in the presence of facts and the portion of divine authority which facts contain and promulgate. Never had that pretension here below which is called the right of kings denied to such a point the right from on high.

A capital error which led this family to lay its hand once more on the guarantees "granted" in 1814, on the concessions, as it termed them. Sad. A sad thing! What it termed its concessions were our conquests; what it termed our encroachments were our rights.

When the hour seemed to it to have come, the Restoration, supposing itself victorious over Bonaparte and well-rooted in the country, that is to say, believing itself to be strong and deep, abruptly decided on its plan of action, and risked its stroke. One morning it drew itself up before the face of France, and, elevating its voice, it contested the collective title and the individual right of the nation to sovereignty, of the citizen to liberty. In other words, it denied to the nation that which made it a nation, and to the citizen that which made him a citizen.

This is the foundation of those famous acts which are called the ordinances of July. The Restoration fell.

It fell justly. But, we admit, it had not been absolutely hostile to all forms of progress. Great things had been accomplished, with it alongside.

Under the Restoration, the nation had grown accustomed to calm discussion, which had been lacking under the Republic, and to grandeur in peace, which had been wanting under the Empire. France free and strong had offered an encouraging spectacle to the other peoples of Europe. The Revolution had had the word under Robespierre; the cannon had had the word under Bonaparte; it was under Louis XVIII and Charles X that it was the turn of intelligence to have the word. The wind ceased, the torch was lighted once more. On the lofty heights, the pure light of mind could be seen flickering. A magnificent, useful, and charming spectacle. For a space of fifteen years, those great principles which are so old for the thinker, so new for the statesman, could be seen at work in perfect peace, on the public square; equality before the law, liberty of conscience, liberty of speech, liberty of the press, the accessibility of all aptitudes to all functions. Thus it proceeded until 1830. The Bourbons were an instrument of civilization which broke in the hands of Providence.

The fall of the Bourbons was full of grandeur, not on their side, but on the side of the nation. They quitted the throne with gravity, but without authority; their descent into the night was not one of those solemn disappearances which leave a somber emotion in history; it was neither the spectral calm of Charles I, nor the eagle scream of Napoleon. They departed, that is all. They laid down the crown, and retained no aureole. They were worthy, but they were not august. They lacked, in a certain measure, the majesty of their misfortune. Charles X during the voyage from Cherbourg, causing a round table to be cut over into a square table, appeared to be more anxious about imperilled etiquette than about the crumbling monarchy. This diminution saddened devoted men who loved their persons, and serious men who honored their race. The populace was admirable. The nation, attacked one morning with weapons, by a sort of royal insurrection, felt itself in the possession of so much force that it did not go into a rage. It defended itself, restrained itself, restored things to their places, the government to law, the Bourbons to exile, alas! and then halted! It took the old king Charles X from beneath that dais which had sheltered Louis XIV and set him gently on the ground. It touched the royal personages only with sadness and precaution. It was not one man, it was not a few men, it was France, France entire, France victorious and intoxicated with her victory, who seemed to be coming to herself, and who put into practice, before the eyes of the whole world, these grave words of Guillaume du Vair after the day of the Barricades:

"It is easy for those who are accustomed to skim the favors of the great, and to spring, like a bird from bough to bough, from an afflicted fortune to a flourishing one, to show themselves harsh toward their Prince in his adversity; but as for me, the fortune of my Kings and especially of my afflicted Kings, will always be venerable to me."

The Bourbons carried away with them respect, but not regret. As we have just stated, their misfortune was greater than they were. They faded out in the horizon.

The Revolution of July instantly had friends and enemies throughout the entire world. The first rushed toward her with joy and enthusiasm, the others turned away, each according to his nature. At the first blush, the princes of Europe, the owls of this dawn, shut their eyes, wounded and stupefied, and only opened them to threaten. A fright which can be comprehended, a wrath which can be pardoned. This strange revolution had hardly produced a shock; it had not even paid to vanquished royalty the honor of treating it as an enemy, and of shedding its blood. In the eyes of despotic governments, who are always interested in having liberty calumniate itself, the Revolution of July committed the fault of being formidable and of remaining gentle. Nothing, however, was attempted or plotted against it. The most discontented, the most irritated, the most trembling, saluted it; whatever our egotism and our rancor may be, a mysterious respect springs from events in which we are sensible of the collaboration of someone who is working above man.

The Revolution of July is the triumph of right overthrowing the fact. A thing which is full of splendor.

Right overthrowing the fact. Hence the brilliancy of the Revolution of 1830, hence, also, its mildness. Right triumphant has no need of being violent.

Right is the just and the true.

The property of right is to remain eternally beautiful and pure. The fact, even when most necessary to all appearances, even when most thoroughly accepted by contemporaries, if it exist only as a fact, and if it contain only too little of right, or none at all, is infallibly destined to become, in the course of time, deformed, impure, perhaps, even monstrous. If one desires to learn at one blow, to what degree of hideousness the fact can attain, viewed at the distance of centuries, let him look at Machiavelli. Machiavelli is not an evil genius, nor a demon, nor a miserable and cowardly writer; he is nothing but the fact. And he is not only the Italian fact; he is the European fact, the fact of the sixteenth century. He seems hideous, and so he is, in the presence of the moral idea of the nineteenth.

This conflict of right and fact has been going on ever since the origin of society. To terminate this duel, to amalgamate the pure idea with the human reality, to cause right to penetrate pacifically into the fact and the fact into right, that is the task of sages.

Chapter II

Badly Sewed

B UT THE TASK OF SAGES IS ONE THING, THE TASK OF CLEVER MEN IS ANOTHER. THE REVOLUTION of 1830 came to a sudden halt.

As soon as a revolution has made the coast, the skillful make haste to prepare the shipwreck.

The skillful in our century have conferred on themselves the title of Statesmen; so that this word, *statesmen*, has ended by becoming somewhat of a slang word. It must be borne in mind, in fact, that wherever there is nothing but skill, there is necessarily pettiness. To say "the skillful" amounts to saying "the mediocre."

In the same way, to say "statesmen" is sometimes equivalent to saying "traitors." If, then, we are to believe the skillful, revolutions like the Revolution of July are severed arteries; a prompt ligature is indispensable. The right, too grandly proclaimed, is shaken. Also, right once firmly fixed, the state must be strengthened. Liberty once assured, attention must be directed to power.

Here the sages are not, as yet, separated from the skillful, but they begin to be distrustful. Power, very good. But, in the first place, what is power? In the second, whence comes it? The skillful do not seem to hear the murmured objection, and they continue their maneuvers.

According to the politicians, who are ingenious in putting the mask of necessity on profitable fictions, the first requirement of a people after a revolution, when this people forms part of a monarchical continent, is to procure for itself a dynasty. In this way, say they, peace, that is to say, time to dress our wounds, and to repair the house, can be had after a revolution. The dynasty conceals the scaffolding and covers the ambulance. Now, it is not always easy to procure a dynasty.

If it is absolutely necessary, the first man of genius or even the first man of fortune who comes to hand suffices for the manufacture of a king. You have, in the first case, Napoleon; in the second, Iturbide.

But the first family that comes to hand does not suffice to make a dynasty. There is necessarily required a certain modicum of antiquity in a race, and the wrinkle of the centuries cannot be improvised.

If we place ourselves at the point of view of the "statesmen," after making all allowances, of course, after a revolution, what are the qualities of the king which result from it? He may be and it is useful for him to be a revolutionary; that is to say, a participant in his own person in that revolution, that he should have lent a hand to it, that he should have either compromised or distinguished himself therein, that he should have touched the ax or wielded the sword in it.

What are the qualities of a dynasty? It should be national; that is to say, revolutionary at a distance, not through acts committed, but by reason of ideas accepted. It should be composed of past and be historic; be composed of future and be sympathetic.

All this explains why the early revolutions contented themselves with finding a man, Cromwell or Napoleon; and why the second absolutely insisted on finding a family, the House of Brunswick or the House of Orleans.

Royal houses resemble those Indian fig-trees, each branch of which, bending over to the earth, takes root and becomes a fig-tree itself. Each branch may become a dynasty. On the sole condition that it shall bend down to the people.

Such is the theory of the skillful.

Here, then, lies the great art: to make a little render to success the sound of a catastrophe in order that those who profit by it may tremble from it also, to season with fear every step that is taken, to augment the curve of the transition to the point of retarding progress, to dull that aurora, to denounce and retrench the harshness of enthusiasm, to cut all angles and nails, to wad triumph, to muffle up right, to envelop the giant-people in flannel, and to put it to bed very speedily, to impose a diet on that excess of health, to put Hercules on the treatment of a convalescent, to dilute the event with the expedient, to offer to spirits thirsting for the ideal that nectar thinned out with a potion, to take one's precautions against too much success, to garnish the revolution with a shade.

1830 practiced this theory, already applied to England by 1688.

1830 is a revolution arrested midway. Half of progress, quasi-right. Now, logic knows not the "almost," absolutely as the sun knows not the candle.

Who arrests revolutions halfway? The bourgeoisie?

Why?

Because the bourgeoisie is interest which has reached satisfaction. Yesterday it was appetite, to-day it is plenitude, to-morrow it will be satiety.

The phenomenon of 1814 after Napoleon was reproduced in 1830 after Charles X.

The attempt has been made, and wrongly, to make a class of the bourgeoisie. The bourgeoisie is simply the contented portion of the people. The bourgeois is the man who now has time to sit down. A chair is not a caste.

But through a desire to sit down too soon, one may arrest the very march of the human race. This has often been the fault of the bourgeoisie.

One is not a class because one has committed a fault. Selfishness is not one of the divisions of the social order.

Moreover, we must be just to selfishness. The state to which that part of the nation which is called the bourgeoisie aspired after the shock of 1830 was not the inertia which is complicated with indifference and laziness, and which contains a little shame; it was not the slumber which presupposes a momentary forgetfulness accessible to dreams; it was the halt.

The halt is a word formed of a singular double and almost contradictory sense: a troop on the march, that is to say, movement; a stand, that is to say, repose.

The halt is the restoration of forces; it is repose armed and on the alert; it is the accomplished fact which posts sentinels and holds itself on its guard.

The halt presupposes the combat of yesterday and the combat of to-morrow.

It is the partition between 1830 and 1848.

What we here call combat may also be designated as progress.

The bourgeoisie then, as well as the statesmen, required a man who should express this word Halt. An Although-Because. A composite individuality, signifying revolution and signifying stability, in other terms, strengthening the present by the evident compatibility of the past with the future.

This man was "already found." His name was Louis Philippe d'Orleans.

The 221 made Louis Philippe King. Lafayette undertook the coronation.

He called it *the best of republics*. The town-hall of Paris took the place of the Cathedral of Rheims.

This substitution of a half-throne for a whole throne was "the work of 1830."

When the skillful had finished, the immense vice of their solution became apparent. All this had been accomplished outside the bounds of absolute right. Absolute right cried: "I protest!" then, terrible to say, it retired into the darkness.

Chapter III

LOUIS PHILIPPE

REVOLUTIONS HAVE A TERRIBLE ARM AND A HAPPY HAND, THEY STRIKE FIRMLY AND CHOOSE well. Even incomplete, even debased and abused and reduced to the state of a junior revolution like the Revolution of 1830, they nearly always retain sufficient providential lucidity to prevent them from falling amiss. Their eclipse is never an abdication.

Nevertheless, let us not boast too loudly; revolutions also may be deceived, and grave errors have been seen.

Let us return to 1830. 1830, in its deviation, had good luck. In the establishment which entitled itself order after the revolution had been cut short, the King amounted to more than royalty. Louis Philippe was a rare man.

The son of a father to whom history will accord certain attenuating circumstances, but also as worthy of esteem as that father had been of blame; possessing all private virtues and many public virtues; careful of his health, of his fortune, of his person, of his affairs, knowing the value of a minute and not always the value of a year; sober, serene, peaceable, patient; a good man and a good prince; sleeping with his wife, and having in his palace lackeys charged with the duty of showing the conjugal bed to the bourgeois, an ostentation of the regular sleeping-apartment which had become useful after the former illegitimate displays of the elder branch; knowing all the languages of Europe, and, what is more rare, all the languages of all interests, and speaking them; an admirable representative of the "middle class," but outstripping it, and in every way greater than it; possessing excellent sense, while appreciating the blood from which he had sprung, counting most of all on his intrinsic worth, and, on the question of his race, very particular, declaring himself Orleans and not Bourbon; thoroughly the first Prince of the Blood Royal while he was still only a Serene Highness, but a frank bourgeois from the day he became king; diffuse in public, concise in private; reputed, but not proved to be a miser; at bottom, one of those economists who are readily prodigal at their own fancy or duty; lettered, but not very sensitive to letters; a gentleman, but not a chevalier; simple, calm, and strong; adored by his family and his household; a fascinating talker, an undeceived statesman, inwardly cold, dominated by immediate interest, always governing at the shortest range, incapable of rancor and of gratitude, making use without mercy of superiority on mediocrity, clever in getting parliamentary majorities to put in the wrong those mysterious unanimities which mutter dully under thrones; unreserved, sometimes imprudent in his lack of reserve, but with marvelous address in that imprudence; fertile in expedients, in countenances, in masks; making France fear Europe and Europe France! Incontestably fond of his country, but preferring his family; assuming more domination than authority and more authority than dignity, a disposition which has this unfortunate property, that as it turns everything to success, it admits of ruse and does not absolutely repudiate baseness, but which has this valuable side, that it preserves politics from violent shocks, the state from fractures, and society from catastrophes; minute, correct, vigilant, attentive, sagacious, indefatigable; contradicting himself at times and giving himself the lie; bold against Austria at Ancona, obstinate against England in Spain, bombarding Antwerp, and paying off Pritchard; singing the Marseillaise with conviction, inaccessible to despondency, to lassitude, to the taste for the beautiful and the ideal, to daring generosity, to Utopia, to chimeras, to wrath, to vanity, to fear; possessing all the forms of personal intrepidity; a general at Valmy; a soldier at Jemappes; attacked eight times by regicides and always smiling; brave as a grenadier, courageous as a thinker; uneasy only in the face of the chances of a European shaking up, and unfitted for great political adventures; always ready to risk his life, never his work; disguising his will in influence, in order that he might be obeyed as an intelligence rather than as a king; endowed with observation and not with divination; not very attentive to minds, but knowing men, that is to say, requiring to see in order to judge; prompt and penetrating good sense, practical wisdom, easy speech, prodigious memory; drawing incessantly on this memory, his only point of resemblance with Cæsar, Alexander, and Napoleon; knowing deeds, facts, details, dates, proper names, ignorant of tendencies, passions, the diverse geniuses of the crowd, the interior aspirations, the hidden and obscure uprisings of souls, in a word, all that can be designated as the invisible currents of consciences; accepted by the surface, but little in accord with France lower down; extricating himself by dint of tact; governing too much and not enough; his own first minister; excellent at creating out of the pettiness of realities, an obstacle to the immensity of ideas; mingling a genuine creative faculty of civilization, of order and organization, an indescribable spirit of proceedings and chicanery, the founder and lawyer of a dynasty; having something of Charlemagne and something of an attorney; in short, a lofty and original figure, a prince who understood how to create authority in spite of the uneasiness of France, and power in spite of the jealousy of Europe. Louis Philippe will be classed among the eminent men of his century, and would be ranked among the most illustrious governors of history had he loved glory but a little, and if he had had the sentiment of what is great to the same degree as the feeling for what is useful.

Louis Philippe had been handsome, and in his old age he remained graceful; not always approved by the nation, he always was so by the masses; he pleased. He had that gift of charming. He lacked majesty; he wore no crown, although a king, and no white hair, although an old man; his manners belonged to the old régime and his habits to the new; a mixture of the noble and the bourgeois which suited 1830; Louis Philippe was transition reigning; he had preserved the ancient pronunciation and the ancient orthography which he placed at the service of opinions modern; he loved Poland and Hungary, but he wrote *les Polonois*, and he pronounced *les Hongrais*. He wore the uniform of the national guard, like Charles X, and the ribbon of the Legion of Honor, like Napoleon.

He went a little to chapel, not at all to the chase, never to the opera. Incorruptible by sacristans, by whippers-in, by ballet-dancers; this made a part of his bourgeois popularity. He had no heart. He went out with his umbrella under his arm, and this umbrella long formed a part of his aureole. He was a bit of a mason, a bit of a gardener, something of a doctor; he bled a postilion who had tumbled from his horse; Louis Philippe no more went about without his lancet, than did Henri IV without his poniard. The royalists jeered at this ridiculous king, the first who had ever shed blood with the object of healing.

For the grievances against Louis Philippe, there is one deduction to be made; there is that which accuses royalty, that which accuses the reign, that which accuses the King; three columns which all give different totals. Democratic right confiscated, progress becomes a matter of secondary interest, the protests of the street violently repressed, military execution of insurrections, the rising passed over by arms, the Rue Transnonain, the counsels of war, the absorption of the real country by the legal country, on half-shares with three hundred thousand privileged persons—these are the deeds of royalty; Belgium refused, Algeria too harshly conquered, and, as in the case of India by the English, with more barbarism than civilization, the breach of faith, to Abd-el-Kader, Blaye, Deutz bought, Pritchard paid—these are the doings of the reign; the policy which was more domestic than national was the doing of the King.

As will be seen, the proper deduction having been made, the King's charge is decreased.

This is his great fault; he was modest in the name of France.

Whence arises this fault?

We will state it.

Louis Philippe was rather too much of a paternal king; that incubation of a family with the object of founding a dynasty is afraid of everything and does not like to be disturbed; hence excessive timidity, which is displeasing to the people, who have the 14th of July in their civil and Austerlitz in their military tradition.

Moreover, if we deduct the public duties which require to be fulfilled first of all, that deep tenderness of Louis Philippe toward his family was deserved by the family. That domestic group was worthy of admiration. Virtues there dwelt side by side with talents. One of Louis Philippe's daughters, Marie d'Orléans, placed the name of her race among artists, as Charles d'Orléans had placed it among poets. She made of her soul a marble which she named Jeanne d'Arc. Two of Louis Philippe's daughters elicited from Metternich this eulogium: "They are young people such as are rarely seen, and princes such as are never seen."

This, without any dissimulation, and also without any exaggeration, is the truth about Louis Philippe.

To be Prince Equality, to bear in his own person the contradiction of the Restoration and the Revolution, to have that disquieting side of the revolutionary which becomes reassuring in governing power, therein lay the fortune of Louis Philippe in 1830; never was there a more complete adaptation of a man to an event; the one entered into the other, and the incarnation took place. Louis Philippe is 1830 made man. Moreover, he had in his favor that great recommendation to the throne, exile. He had been proscribed, a wanderer, poor. He had lived by his own labor. In Switzerland, this heir to the richest princely domains in France had sold an old horse in order to obtain bread. At Reichenau, he gave lessons in mathematics, while his sister Adelaide did wool work and sewed. These souvenirs connected with a king rendered the bourgeoisie enthusiastic. He had, with his own hands, demolished the iron cage of Mont-Saint-Michel, built by Louis XI and used by Louis XV. He was the companion of Dumouriez, he was the friend of Lafayette; he had belonged to the Jacobins' club; Mirabeau had slapped him on the shoulder; Danton had said to him: "Young man!" At the age of four-and-twenty, in '93, being then M. de Chartres, he had witnessed, from the depth of a box, the trial of Louis XVI, so well named *that poor tyrant*. The blind clairvoyance of the Revolution, breaking royalty in the King and the King with royalty, did so almost without noticing the man in the fierce crushing of the idea, the vast storm of the Assembly-Tribunal, the public wrath interrogating, Capet not knowing what to reply, the alarming, stupefied vacillation by that royal head beneath that somber breath, the relative innocence of all in that catastrophe, of those who condemned as well as of the man condemned—he had looked on those things, he had contemplated that giddiness; he had seen the centuries appear before the bar of the Assembly-Convention; he had beheld, behind Louis XVI, that unfortunate passer-by who was made responsible, the terrible culprit, the monarchy, rise through the shadows; and there had lingered in his soul the respectful fear of these immense justices of the populace, which are almost as impersonal as the justice of God.

The trace left in him by the Revolution was prodigious. Its memory was like a living imprint of those great years, minute by minute. One day, in the presence of a witness whom we are not permitted to doubt, he rectified from memory the whole of the letter A in the alphabetical list of the Constituent Assembly.

Louis Philippe was a king of the broad daylight. While he reigned the press was free, the tribune was free, conscience and speech were free. The laws of September are open to sight. Although fully aware of the gnawing power of light on privileges, he left his throne exposed to the light. History will do justice to him for this loyalty.

Louis Philippe, like all historical men who have passed from the scene, is to-day put on his trial by the human conscience. His case is, as yet, only in the lower court.

The hour when history speaks with its free and venerable accent, has not yet sounded for him; the moment has not come to pronounce a definite judgment on this king; the austere and illustrious historian Louis Blanc has himself recently softened his first verdict; Louis Philippe was elected by those two *almosts* which are called the 221 and 1830, that is to say, by a half-Parliament, and a half-revolution; and in any case, from the superior point of view where philosophy must place itself, we cannot judge him here, as the reader has seen above, except with certain reservations in the name of the absolute democratic principle; in the eyes of the absolute, outside these two rights, the right of man in the first place, the right of the people in the second, all is usurpation; but what we can say, even at the present day, that after making these reserves is, that to sum up the whole, and in whatever manner he is considered, Louis Philippe, taken in himself, and from the point of view of human goodness, will remain, to use the antique language of ancient history, one of the best princes who ever sat on a throne.

What is there against him? That throne. Take away Louis Philippe the king, there remains the man. And the man is good. He is good at times even to the point of being admirable. Often, in the midst of his gravest souvenirs, after a day of conflict with the whole diplomacy of the continent, he returned at night to his apartments, and there, exhausted with fatigue, overwhelmed with sleep, what did he do? He took a death sentence and passed the night in revising a criminal suit, considering it something to hold his own against Europe, but that it was a still greater matter to rescue a man from the executioner. He obstinately maintained his opinion against his keeper of the seals; he disputed the ground with the guillotine foot by foot against the crown attorneys, those *chatterers of the law*, as he called them. Sometimes the pile of sentences covered his table; he examined them all; it was anguish to him to abandon these miserable, condemned heads. One day, he said to the same witness to whom we have recently referred: "I won seven last night." During the early years of his reign, the death penalty was as good as abolished, and the erection of a scaffold was a violence committed against the King. The Grève having disappeared with the elder branch, a bourgeois place of execution was instituted under the name of the Barrière-Saint-Jacques; "practical men" felt the necessity of a quasi-legitimate guillotine; and this was one of the victories of Casimir Périer, who represented the narrow sides of the bourgeoisie, over Louis Philippe, who represented its liberal sides. Louis Philippe annotated Beccaria with his own hand. After the Fieschi machine, he exclaimed: "What a pity that I was not wounded! Then I might have pardoned!" On another occasion, alluding to the resistance offered by his ministry, he wrote in connection with a political criminal, who is one of the most generous figures of our day: "His pardon is granted; it only remains for me to obtain it." Louis Philippe was as gentle as Louis IX and as kindly as Henri IV.

Now, to our mind, in history, where kindness is the rarest of pearls, the man who is kindly almost takes precedence of the man who is great.

Louis Philippe having been severely judged by some, harshly, perhaps, by others, it is quite natural that a man, himself a phantom at the present day, who knew that king, should come and testify in his favor before history; this deposition, whatever else it may be, is evidently and above all things, entirely disinterested; an epitaph penned by a dead man is sincere; one shade may console another shade; the sharing of the same shadows confers the right to praise it; it is not greatly to be feared that it will ever be said of two tombs in exile: "This one flattered the other."

Chapter IV

CRACKS BENEATH THE FOUNDATION

AT THE MOMENT WHEN THE DRAMA WHICH WE ARE NARRATING IS ON THE POINT OF PENETRAT-
ing into the depths of one of the tragic clouds which envelop the beginning of Louis
Philippe's reign, it was necessary that there should be no equivoque, and it became requisite that
this book should offer some explanation with regard to this king.

Louis Philippe had entered into possession of his royal authority without violence, without
any direct action on his part, by virtue of a revolutionary change, evidently quite distinct from the
real aim of the Revolution, but in which he, the Duc d'Orléans, exercised no personal initiative. He
had been born a Prince, and he believed himself to have been elected King. He had not served this
mandate on himself; he had not taken it; it had been offered to him, and he had accepted it; convinced, wrongly, to be sure, but convinced nevertheless, that the offer was in accordance with right
and that the acceptance of it was in accordance with duty. Hence his possession was in good faith.
Now, we say it in good conscience, Louis Philippe being in possession in perfect good faith, and the
democracy being in good faith in its attack, the amount of terror discharged by the social conflicts
weighs neither on the King nor on the democracy. A clash of principles resembles a clash of elements. The ocean defends the water, the hurricane defends the air, the King defends Royalty, the
democracy defends the people; the relative, which is the monarchy, resists the absolute, which is the
republic; society bleeds in this conflict, but that which constitutes its suffering to-day will constitute
its safety later on; and, in any case, those who combat are not to be blamed; one of the two parties
is evidently mistaken; the right is not, like the Colossus of Rhodes, on two shores at once, with one
foot on the republic, and one in Royalty; it is indivisible, and all on one side; but those who are in
error are so sincerely; a blind man is no more a criminal than a Vendean is a ruffian. Let us, then,
impute to the fatality of things alone these formidable collisions. Whatever the nature of these tempests may be, human irresponsibility is mingled with them.

Let us complete this exposition.

The government of 1840 led a hard life immediately. Born yesterday, it was obliged to fight
to-day.

Hardly installed, it was already everywhere conscious of vague movements of traction on the
apparatus of July so recently laid, and so lacking in solidity.

Resistance was born on the morrow; perhaps even, it was born on the preceding evening.
From month to month the hostility increased, and from being concealed it became patent.

The Revolution of July, which gained but little acceptance outside of France by kings, had
been diversely interpreted in France, as we have said.

God delivers over to men his visible will in events, an obscure text written in a mysterious
tongue. Men immediately make translations of it; translations hasty, incorrect, full of errors, of
gaps, and of nonsense. Very few minds comprehend the divine language. The most sagacious, the
calmest, the most profound, decipher slowly, and when they arrive with their text, the task has long
been completed; there are already twenty translations on the public place. From each remaining
springs a party, and from each misinterpretation a faction; and each party thinks that it alone has the
true text, and each faction thinks that it possesses the light.

Power itself is often a faction.

There are, in revolutions, swimmers who go against the current; they are the old parties.

For the old parties who clung to heredity by the grace of God, think that revolutions, having sprung from the right to revolt, one has the right to revolt against them. Error. For in these revolutions, the one who revolts is not the people; it is the king. Revolution is precisely the contrary of revolt. Every revolution, being a normal outcome, contains within itself its legitimacy, which false revolutionists sometimes dishonor, but which remains even when soiled, which survives even when stained with blood.

Revolutions spring not from an accident, but from necessity. A revolution is a return from the fictitious to the real. It is because it must be that it is.

None the less did the old legitimist parties assail the Revolution of 1830 with all the vehemence which arises from false reasoning. Errors make excellent projectiles. They strike it cleverly in its vulnerable spot, in default of a cuirass, in its lack of logic; they attacked this revolution in its royalty. They shouted to it: "Revolution, why this king?" Factions are blind men who aim correctly.

This cry was uttered equally by the republicans. But coming from them, this cry was logical. What was blindness in the legitimists was clearness of vision in the democrats. 1830 had bankrupted the people. The enraged democracy reproached it with this.

Between the attack of the past and the attack of the future, the establishment of July struggled. It represented the minute at loggerheads on the one hand with the monarchical centuries, on the other hand with eternal right.

In addition, and beside all this, as it was no longer revolution and had become a monarchy, 1830 was obliged to take precedence of all Europe. To keep the peace, was an increase of complication. A harmony established contrary to sense is often more onerous than a war. From this secret conflict, always muzzled, but always growling, was born armed peace, that ruinous expedient of civilization which in the harness of the European cabinets is suspicious in itself. The Royalty of July reared up, in spite of the fact that it caught it in the harness of European cabinets. Metternich would gladly have put it in kicking-straps. Pushed on in France by progress, it pushed on the monarchies, those loiterers in Europe. After having been towed, it undertook to tow.

Meanwhile, within her, pauperism, the proletariat, salary, education, penal servitude, prostitution, the fate of the woman, wealth, misery, production, consumption, division, exchange, coin, credit, the rights of capital, the rights of labor—all these questions were multiplied above society, a terrible slope.

Outside of political parties properly so called, another movement became manifest. Philosophical fermentation replied to democratic fermentation. The elect felt troubled as well as the masses; in another manner, but quite as much.

Thinkers meditated, while the soil, that is to say, the people, traversed by revolutionary currents, trembled under them with indescribably vague epileptic shocks. These dreamers, some isolated, others united in families and almost in communion, turned over social questions in a pacific but profound manner; impassive miners, who tranquilly pushed their galleries into the depths of a volcano, hardly disturbed by the dull commotion and the furnaces of which they caught glimpses.

This tranquility was not the least beautiful spectacle of this agitated epoch.

These men left to political parties the question of rights, they occupied themselves with the question of happiness.

The well-being of man, that was what they wanted to extract from society.

They raised material questions, questions of agriculture, of industry, of commerce, almost to the dignity of a religion. In civilization, such as it has formed itself, a little by the command of God, a great deal by the agency of man, interests combine, unite, and amalgamate in a manner to form a veritable hard rock, in accordance with a dynamic law, patiently studied by economists, those geologists of politics. These men who grouped themselves under different appellations, but who may all be designated by the generic title of socialists, endeavored to pierce that rock and to cause it to spout forth the living waters of human felicity.

From the question of the scaffold to the question of war, their works embraced everything. To the rights of man, as proclaimed by the French Revolution, they added the rights of woman and the rights of the child.

The reader will not be surprised if, for various reasons, we do not here treat in a thorough manner, from the theoretical point of view, the questions raised by socialism. We confine ourselves to indicating them.

All the problems that the socialists proposed to themselves, cosmogonic visions, reverie and mysticism being cast aside, can be reduced to two principal problems.

First problem: To produce wealth.

Second problem: To share it.

The first problem contains the question of work.

The second contains the question of salary.

In the first problem the employment of forces is in question.

In the second, the distribution of enjoyment.

From the proper employment of forces results public power.

From a good distribution of enjoyments results individual happiness.

By a good distribution, not an equal but an equitable distribution must be understood.

From these two things combined, the public power without, individual happiness within, results social prosperity.

Social prosperity means the man happy, the citizen free, the nation great.

England solves the first of these two problems. She creates wealth admirably, she divides it badly. This solution which is complete on one side only leads her fatally to two extremes: monstrous opulence, monstrous wretchedness. All enjoyments for some, all privations for the rest, that is to say, for the people; privilege, exception, monopoly, feudalism, born from toil itself. A false and dangerous situation, which sates public power or private misery, which sets the roots of the State in the sufferings of the individual. A badly constituted grandeur in which are combined all the material elements and into which no moral element enters.

Communism and agrarian law think that they solve the second problem. They are mistaken. Their division kills production. Equal partition abolishes emulation; and consequently labor. It is a partition made by the butcher, which kills that which it divides. It is therefore impossible to pause over these pretended solutions. Slaying wealth is not the same thing as dividing it.

The two problems require to be solved together, to be well solved. The two problems must be combined and made but one.

Solve only the first of the two problems; you will be Venice, you will be England. You will have, like Venice, an artificial power, or, like England, a material power; you will be the wicked rich man. You will die by an act of violence, as Venice died, or by bankruptcy, as England will fall. And the world will allow to die and fall all that is merely selfishness, all that does not represent for the human race either a virtue or an idea.

It is well understood here, that by the words Venice, England, we designate not the peoples, but social structures; the oligarchies superposed on nations, and not the nations themselves. The nations always have our respect and our sympathy. Venice, as a people, will live again; England, the aristocracy, will fall, but England, the nation, is immortal. That said, we continue.

Solve the two problems, encourage the wealthy, and protect the poor, suppress misery, put an end to the unjust farming out of the feeble by the strong, put a bridle on the iniquitous jealousy of the man who is making his way against the man who has reached the goal, adjust, mathematically and fraternally, salary to labor, mingle gratuitous and compulsory education with the growth of childhood, and make of science the base of manliness, develop minds while keeping arms busy, be at one and the same time a powerful people and a family of happy men, render property democratic, not by abolishing it, but by making it universal, so that every citizen, without exception, may be a proprietor, an easier matter than is generally supposed; in two words, learn how to produce wealth and how to distribute it, and you will have at once moral and material greatness; and you will be worthy to call yourself France.

This is what socialism said outside and above a few sects which have gone astray; that is what it sought in facts, that is what it sketched out in minds.

Efforts worthy of admiration! Sacred attempts!

These doctrines, these theories, these resistances, the unforeseen necessity for the statesman to take philosophers into account, confused evidences of which we catch a glimpse, a new system of politics to be created, which shall be in accord with the old world without too much disaccord with the new revolutionary ideal, a situation in which it became necessary to use Lafayette to defend Polignac, the intuition of progress transparent beneath the revolt, the chambers and streets, the competitions to be brought into equilibrium around him, his faith in the Revolution, perhaps an eventual indefinable resignation born of the vague acceptance of a superior definitive right, his desire to remain of his race, his domestic spirit, his sincere respect for the people, his own honesty, preoccupied Louis Philippe almost painfully, and there were moments when, strong and courageous as he was, he was overwhelmed by the difficulties of being a king.

He felt under his feet a formidable disaggregation, which was not, nevertheless, a reduction to dust, France being more France than ever.

Piles of shadows covered the horizon. A strange shade, gradually drawing nearer, extended little by little over men, over things, over ideas; a shade which came from wraths and systems. Everything which had been hastily stifled was moving and fermenting. At times the conscience of the honest man resumed its breathing, so great was the discomfort of that air in which sophisms were intermingled with truths. Spirits trembled in the social anxiety like leaves at the approach of a storm. The electric tension was such that at certain instants, the first comer, a stranger, brought light. Then the twilight obscurity closed in again. At intervals, deep and dull mutterings allowed a judgment to be formed as to the quantity of thunder contained by the cloud.

Twenty months had barely elapsed since the Revolution of July, the year 1832 had opened with an aspect of something impending and threatening.

The distress of the people, the laborers without bread, the last Prince de Condé engulfed in the shadows, Brussels expelling the Nassaus as Paris did the Bourbons, Belgium offering herself to a French Prince and giving herself to an English Prince, the Russian hatred of Nicolas, behind us the demons of the South, Ferdinand in Spain, Miguel in Portugal, the earth quaking in Italy, Metternich extending his hand over Bologna, France treating Austria sharply at Ancona, at the North no one knew what sinister sound of the hammer nailing up Poland in her coffin, irritated glances watching France narrowly all over Europe, England, a suspected ally, ready to give a push to that which was tottering and to hurl herself on that which should fall, the peerage sheltering itself behind Beccaria to refuse four heads to the law, the fleurs-de-lys erased from the King's carriage, the cross torn from Notre-Dame, Lafayette lessened, Laffitte ruined, Benjamin Constant dead in indigence, Casimir Périer dead in the exhaustion of his power; political and social malady breaking out simultaneously in the two capitals of the kingdom, the one in the city of thought, the other in the city of toil; at Paris civil war, at Lyons servile war; in the two cities, the same glare of the furnace; a crater-like crimson on the brow of the people; the South rendered fanatic, the West troubled, the Duchesse de Berry in la Vendée, plots, conspiracies, risings, cholera, added the somber roar of tumult of events to the somber roar of ideas.

Chapter V

FACTS WHENCE HISTORY SPRINGS AND WHICH HISTORY IGNORES

TOWARD THE END OF APRIL, EVERYTHING HAD BECOME AGGRAVATED. THE FERMENTATION EN-
tered the boiling state. Ever since 1830, petty partial revolts had been going on here and there,
which were quickly suppressed, but ever bursting forth afresh, the sign of a vast underlying conflagration. Something terrible was in preparation. Glimpses could be caught of the features still indistinct and imperfectly lighted, of a possible revolution. France kept an eye on Paris; Paris kept an
eye on the Faubourg Saint-Antoine.

The Faubourg Saint-Antoine, which was in a dull glow, was beginning its ebullition.

The wine-shops of the Rue de Charonne were, although the union of the two epithets seems
singular when applied to wine-shops, grave and stormy.

The government was there purely and simply called in question. There people publicly discussed the *question of fighting or of keeping quiet.* There were back shops where workingmen were
made to swear that they would hasten into the street at the first cry of alarm, and "that they would
fight without counting the number of the enemy." This engagement once entered into, a man seated
in the corner of the wine-shop "assumed a sonorous tone," and said: "You understand! You have
sworn!"

Sometimes they went upstairs, to a private room on the first floor, and there scenes that were
almost masonic were enacted. They made the initiated take oaths *to render service to himself as well
as to the fathers of families.* That was the formula.

In the tap-rooms, "subversive" pamphlets were read. *They treated the government with contempt,* says a secret report of that time.

Words like the following could be heard there:

"I don't know the names of the leaders. We folks shall not know the day until two hours beforehand." One workman said: "There are three hundred of us, let each contribute ten sous, that
will make one hundred and fifty francs with which to procure powder and shot."

Another said: "I don't ask for six months, I don't ask for even two. In less than a fortnight we
shall be parallel with the government. With twenty-five thousand men we can face them." Another
said: "I don't sleep at night, because I make cartridges all night." From time to time, men "of bourgeois appearance, and in good coats" came and "caused embarrassment," and with the air of "command," shook hands with *the most important,* and then went away. They never stayed more than ten
minutes. Significant remarks were exchanged in a low tone: "The plot is ripe, the matter is
arranged." "It was murmured by all who were there," to borrow the very expression of one of
those who were present. The exaltation was such that one day, a workingman exclaimed, before the
whole wine-shop: "We have no arms!" One of his comrades replied: "The soldiers have!" thus par-
odying without being aware of the fact, Bonaparte's proclamation to the army in Italy: "When they
had anything of a more secret nature on hand," adds one report, "they did not communicate it to
each other." It is not easy to understand what they could conceal after what they said.

These reunions were sometimes periodical. At certain ones of them, there were never more
than eight or ten persons present, and they were always the same. In others, anyone entered who
wished, and the room was so full that they were forced to stand. Some went thither through enthusiasm and passion; others because it *was on their way to their work.* As during the Revolution, there
were patriotic women in some of these wine-shops who embraced newcomers.

Other expressive facts came to light.

A man would enter a shop, drink, and go his way with the remark: "Wine-merchant, the revolution will pay what is due to you."

Revolutionary agents were appointed in a wine-shop facing the Rue de Charonne. The balloting was carried on in their caps.

Workingmen met at the house of a fencing-master who gave lessons in the Rue de Cotte. There there was a trophy of arms formed of wooden broadswords, canes, clubs, and foils. One day, the buttons were removed from the foils.

A workman said: "There are twenty-five of us, but they don't count on me, because I am looked upon as a machine." Later on, that machine became Quenisset.

The indefinite things which were brewing gradually acquired a strange and indescribable notoriety. A woman sweeping off her doorsteps said to another woman: "For a long time, there has been a strong force busy making cartridges." In the open street, proclamation could be seen addressed to the National Guard in the departments. One of these proclamations was signed: *Burtot, wine-merchant*.

One day a man with his beard worn like a collar and with an Italian accent mounted a stone post at the door of a liquor-seller in the Marché Lenoir, and read aloud a singular document, which seemed to emanate from an occult power. Groups formed around him, and applauded.

The passages which touched the crowd most deeply were collected and noted down. "—Our doctrines are trammeled, our proclamations torn, our bill-stickers are spied upon and thrown into prison."—"The breakdown which has recently taken place in cottons has converted to us many mediums."—"The future of nations is being worked out in our obscure ranks."—"Here are the fixed terms: action or reaction, revolution or counter-revolution. For, at our epoch, we no longer believe either in inertia or in immobility. For the people against the people, that is the question. There is no other."—"On the day when we cease to suit you, break us, but up to that day, help us to march on." All this in broad daylight.

Other deeds, more audacious still, were suspicious in the eyes of the people by reason of their very audacity. On the 4th of April, 1832, a passer-by mounted the post on the corner which forms the angle of the Rue Sainte-Marguerite and shouted: "I am a Babouvist!" But beneath Babeuf, the people scented Gisquet.

Among other things, this man said:

"Down with property! The opposition of the left is cowardly and treacherous. When it wants to be on the right side, it preaches revolution, it is democratic in order to escape being beaten, and royalist so that it may not have to fight. The republicans are beasts with feathers. Distrust the republicans, citizens of the laboring classes."

"Silence, citizen spy!" cried an artisan.

This shout put an end to the discourse.

Mysterious incidents occurred.

At nightfall, a workingman encountered near the canal a "very well-dressed man," who said to him: "Whither are you bound, citizen?" "Sir," replied the workingman, "I have not the honor of your acquaintance." "I know you very well, however." And the man added: "Don't be alarmed, I am an agent of the committee. You are suspected of not being quite faithful. You know that if you reveal anything, there is an eye fixed on you." Then he shook hands with the workingman and went away, saying: "We shall meet again soon."

The police, who were on the alert, collected singular dialogues, not only in the wine-shops, but in the street.

"Get yourself received very soon," said a weaver to a cabinet-maker.

"Why?"

"There is going to be a shot to fire."

Two ragged pedestrians exchanged these remarkable replies, fraught with evident Jacquerie:

"Who governs us?"

"M. Philippe."

"No, it is the bourgeoisie."

The reader is mistaken if he thinks that we take the word *Jacquerie* in a bad sense. The Jacques were the poor.

On another occasion two men were heard to say to each other as they passed by: "We have a good plan of attack."

Only the following was caught of a private conversation between four men who were crouching in a ditch of the circle of the Barrière du Trône:

"Everything possible will be done to prevent his walking about Paris anymore."

Who was the *he?* Menacing obscurity.

"The principal leaders," as they said in the faubourg, held themselves apart. It was supposed that they met for consultation in a wine-shop near the point Saint-Eustache. A certain Aug——, chief of the Society aid for tailors, Rue Mondétour, had the reputation of serving as intermediary central between the leaders and the Faubourg Saint-Antoine.

Nevertheless, there was always a great deal of mystery about these leaders, and no certain fact can invalidate the singular arrogance of this reply made later on by a man accused before the Court of Peers:

"Who was your leader?"

"I knew of none and I recognized none."

There was nothing but words, transparent but vague; sometimes idle reports, rumors, hearsay. Other indications cropped up.

A carpenter, occupied in nailing boards to a fence around the ground on which a house was in process of construction, in the Rue de Reuilly, found on that plot the torn fragment of a letter on which were still legible the following lines:

The committee must take measures to prevent recruiting in the sections for the different societies.

And, as a postscript:

We have learned that there are guns in the Rue du Faubourg-Poissonnière, No. 5 [bis], to the number of five or six thousand, in the house of a gunsmith in that court. The section owns no arms.

What excited the carpenter and caused him to show this thing to his neighbors was the fact, that a few paces further on he picked up another paper, torn like the first, and still more significant, of which we reproduce a facsimile, because of the historical interest attaching to these strange documents:

Q	C	D	E	
				Learn this list by heart. After so doing you will tear it up. The men admitted will do the same when you have trans-mitted their orders to them. *Health and Fraternity,* *u og a' fe* *L.*

It was only later on that the persons who were in the secret of this find at the time, learned the significance of those four capital letters: *quinturions, centurions, decurions, éclaireurs* [scouts], and the sense of the letters: u og a' fe, which was a date, and meant April 15th, 1832. Under each capital letter were inscribed names followed by very characteristic notes. Thus: Q. *Bannerel*. 8 guns, 83 cartridges. A safe man.—C. *Boubière.* 1 pistol, 40 cartridges.—D. Rollet. 1 foil, 1 pistol, 1 pound of powder.—E. *Tessier.* 1 sword, 1 cartridge-box. Exact.—*Terreur.* 8 guns. Brave, etc.

Finally, this carpenter found, still in the same enclosure, a third paper on which was written in pencil, but very legibly, this sort of enigmatical list:

Unité: Blanchard: Arbre-Sec. 6.
Barra. Soize. Salle-au-Comte.
Kosciusko. Aubry the Butcher?
J. J. R.
Caius Gracchus.
Right of revision. Dufond. Four.
Fall of the Girondists. Derbac. Maubuée.
Washington. Pinson. 1 pistol, 86 cartridges.
Marseillaise.
Sovereignty of the people. Michel. Quincampoix. Sword.
Hoche.
Marceau. Plato. Arbre-Sec.
Warsaw. Tilly, crier of the *Populaire.*

The honest bourgeois into whose hands this list fell knew its significance. It appears that this list was the complete nomenclature of the sections of the fourth arondissement of the Society of the Rights of Man, with the names and dwellings of the chiefs of sections. To-day, when all these facts which were obscure are nothing more than history, we may publish them. It should be added, that the foundation of the Society of the Rights of Man seems to have been posterior to the date when this paper was found. Perhaps this was only a rough draft.

Still, according to all the remarks and the words, according to written notes, material facts begin to make their appearance.

In the Rue Popincourt, in the house of a dealer in bric-à-brac, there were seized seven sheets of gray paper, all folded alike lengthwise and in four; these sheets enclosed twenty-six squares of this same gray paper folded in the form of a cartridge, and a card, on which was written the following:

Saltpeter . . . . 12 ounces.
Sulfur . . . . 2 ounces.
Charcoal . . . . 2 ounces and a half.
Water . . . . 2 ounces.

The report of the seizure stated that the drawer exhaled a strong smell of powder.

A mason returning from his day's work, left behind him a little package on a bench near the bridge of Austerlitz. This package was taken to the police station. It was opened, and in it were found two printed dialogues, signed *Lahautière,* a song entitled: "Workmen, band together," and a tin box full of cartridges.

One artisan drinking with a comrade made the latter feel him to see how warm he was; the other man felt a pistol under his waistcoat.

In a ditch on the boulevard, between Père-Lachaise and the Barrière du Trône, at the most deserted spot, some children, while playing, discovered beneath a mass of shavings and refuse bits of wood, a bag containing a bullet-mold, a wooden punch for the preparation of cartridges, a wooden bowl, in which there were grains of hunting-powder, and a little cast-iron pot whose interior presented evident traces of melted lead.

Police agents, making their way suddenly and unexpectedly at five o'clock in the morning, into the dwelling of a certain Pardon, who was afterwards a member of the Barricade-Merry section and got himself killed in the insurrection of April, 1834, found him standing near his bed, and holding in his hand some cartridges which he was in the act of preparing.

Toward the hour when workingmen repose, two men were seen to meet between the Barrière Picpus and the Barrière Charenton in a little lane between two walls, near a wine-shop, in front of which there was a "Jeu de Siam."[1] One drew a pistol from beneath his blouse and handed it to the other. As he was handing it to him, he noticed that the perspiration of his chest had made the powder damp. He primed the pistol and added more powder to what was already in the pan. Then the two men parted.

A certain Gallais, afterwards killed in the Rue Beaubourg in the affair of April, boasted of having in his house seven hundred cartridges and twenty-four flints.

The government one day received a warning that arms and two hundred thousand cartridges had just been distributed in the faubourg. On the following week thirty thousand cartridges were distributed. The remarkable point about it was, that the police were not able to seize a single one.

An intercepted letter read: "The day is not far distant when, within four hours by the clock, eighty thousand patriots will be under arms."

All this fermentation was public, one might almost say tranquil. The approaching insurrection was preparing its storm calmly in the face of the government. No singularity was lacking to this still subterranean crisis, which was already perceptible. The bourgeois talked peaceably to the working-classes of what was in preparation. They said: "How is the rising coming along?" in the same tone in which they would have said: "How is your wife?"

A furniture-dealer, of the Rue Moreau, inquired: "Well, when are you going to make the attack?"

Another shop-keeper said:

"The attack will be made soon."

"I know it. A month ago, there were fifteen thousand of you, now there are twenty-five thousand." He offered his gun, and a neighbor offered a small pistol which he was willing to sell for seven francs.

Moreover, the revolutionary fever was growing. Not a point in Paris nor in France was exempt from it. The artery was beating everywhere. Like those membranes which arise from certain inflammations and form in the human body, the network of secret societies began to spread all over the country. From the associations of the Friends of the People, which was at the same time public and secret, sprang the Society of the Rights of Man, which also dated from one of the orders of the day: *Pluviôse, Year* 40 *of the republican era,* which was destined to survive even the mandate of the Court of Assizes which pronounced its dissolution, and which did not hesitate to bestow on its sections significant names like the following:

Pikes.

Tocsin.

Signal cannon.

Phrygian cap.

January 21.

The beggars.

The vagabonds.

Forward march.

Robespierre.

1. A game of ninepins, in which the ball is smaller than the other, so that it does not roll straight, but describes a curve on the ground.

Level.

Ça Ira.

The Society of the Rights of Man engendered the Society of Action. These were impatient individuals who broke away and hastened ahead. Other associations sought to recruit themselves from the great mother societies. The members of sections complained that they were torn asunder. Thus, the Gallic Society, and the committee of organization of the Municipalities. Thus the associations for the liberty of the press, for individual liberty, for the instruction of the people against indirect taxes. Then the Society of Equal Workingmen which was divided into three fractions, the levelers, the communists, the reformers. Then the Army of the Bastilles, a sort of cohort organized on a military footing, four men commanded by a corporal, ten by a sergeant, twenty by a sub-lieutenant, forty by a lieutenant; there were never more than five men who knew each other. Creation where precaution is combined with audacity and which seemed stamped with the genius of Venice.

The central committee, which was at the head, had two arms, the Society of Action, and the Army of the Bastilles.

A legitimist association, the Chevaliers of Fidelity, stirred about among these the republican affiliations. It was denounced and repudiated there.

The Parisian societies had ramifications in the principal cities, Lyons, Nantes, Lille, Marseilles, and each had its Society of the Rights of Man, the Charbonnière, and The Free Men. All had a revolutionary society which was called the Cougourde. We have already mentioned this word.

In Paris, the Faubourg Saint-Marceau kept up an equal buzzing with the Faubourg Saint-Antoine, and the schools were no less moved than the faubourgs. A café in the Rue Saint-Hyacinthe and the wine-shop of the *Seven Billiards*, Rue des Mathurins-Saint-Jacques, served as rallying points for the students. The Society of the Friends of the A B C affiliated to the Mutualists of Angers, and to the Cougourde of Aix, met, as we have seen, in the Café Musain. These same young men assembled also, as we have stated already, in a restaurant wine-shop of the Rue Mondé-tour which was called Corinthe. These meetings were secret. Others were as public as possible, and the reader can judge of their boldness from these fragments of an interrogatory undergone in one of the ulterior prosecutions: "Where was this meeting held?" "In the Rue de la Paix." "At whose house?" "In the street." "What sections were there?" "Only one." "Which?" "The Manuel section." "Who was its leader?" "I." "You are too young to have decided alone upon the bold course of attacking the government. Where did your instructions come from?" "From the central committee."

The army was mined at the same time as the population, as was proved subsequently by the operations of Béford, Luneville, and Épinard. They counted on the fifty-second regiment, on the fifth, on the eighth, on the thirty-seventh, and on the twentieth light cavalry. In Burgundy and in the southern towns they planted the liberty tree; that is to say, a pole surmounted by a red cap.

Such was the situation.

The Faubourg Saint-Antoine, more than any other group of the population, as we stated in the beginning, accentuated this situation and made it felt. That was the sore point. This old faubourg, peopled like an anthill, laborious, courageous, and angry as a hive of bees, was quivering with expectation and with the desire for a tumult. Everything was in a state of agitation there, without any interruption, however, of the regular work. It is impossible to convey an idea of this lively yet somber physiognomy. In this faubourg exists poignant distress hidden under attic roofs; there also exist rare and ardent minds. It is particularly in the matter of distress and intelligence that it is dangerous to have extremes meet.

The Faubourg Saint-Antoine had also other causes to tremble; for it received the counter-shock of commercial crises, of failures, strikes, slack seasons, all inherent to great political disturbances. In times of revolution misery is both cause and effect. The blow which it deals rebounds upon it. This population full of proud virtue, capable to the highest degree of latent heat, always ready to fly to arms, prompt to explode, irritated, deep, undermined, seemed to be only awaiting the fall of a spark. Whenever certain sparks float on the horizon, chased by the wind of events, it is impossible not to think of the Faubourg Saint-Antoine and of the formidable chance which has placed at the very gates of Paris that powder-house of suffering and ideas.

The wine-shops of the *Faubourg Antoiné,* which have been more than once drawn in the sketches which the reader has just perused, possess historical notoriety. In troublous times people grow intoxicated there more on words than on wine. A sort of prophetic spirit and an afflatus of the future circulates there, swelling hearts and enlarging souls. The cabarets of the Faubourg Saint-Antoine resemble those taverns of Mont Aventine erected on the cave of the Sibyl and communicating with the profound and sacred breath; taverns where the tables were almost tripods, and where was drunk what Ennius calls the *sibylline wine.*

The Faubourg Saint-Antoine is a reservoir of people. Revolutionary agitations create fissures there, through which trickles the popular sovereignty. This sovereignty may do evil; it can be mistaken like any other; but, even when led astray, it remains great. We may say of it as of the blind cyclops, *Ingens.*

In '93, according as the idea which was floating about was good or evil, according as it was the day of fanaticism or of enthusiasm, there leaped forth from the Faubourg Saint-Antoine now savage legions, now heroic bands.

Savage. Let us explain this word. When these bristling men, who in the early days of the revolutionary chaos, tattered, howling, wild, with uplifted bludgeon, pike on high, hurled themselves upon ancient Paris in an uproar, what did they want? They wanted an end to oppression, an end to tyranny, an end to the sword, work for men, instruction for the child, social sweetness for the woman, liberty, equality, fraternity, bread for all, the idea for all, the Edenizing of the world. Progress; and that holy, sweet, and good thing, progress, they claimed in terrible wise, driven to extremities as they were, half naked, club in fist, a roar in their mouths. They were savages, yes; but the savages of civilization.

They proclaimed right furiously; they were desirous, if only with fear and trembling, to force the human race to paradise. They seemed barbarians, and they were saviors. They demanded light with the mask of night.

Facing these men, who were ferocious, we admit, and terrifying, but ferocious and terrifying for good ends, there are other men, smiling, embroidered, gilded, beribboned, starred, in silk stockings, in white plumes, in yellow gloves, in varnished shoes, who, with their elbows on a velvet table, beside a marble chimney-piece, insist gently on demeanor and the preservation of the past, of the Middle Ages, of divine right, of fanaticism, of innocence, of slavery, of the death penalty, of war, glorifying in low tones and with politeness, the sword, the stake, and the scaffold. For our part, if we were forced to make a choice between the barbarians of civilization and the civilized men of barbarism, we should choose the barbarians.

But, thank Heaven, still another choice is possible. No perpendicular fall is necessary, in front any more than in the rear.

Neither despotism nor terrorism. We desire progress with a gentle slope.

God takes care of that. God's whole policy consists in rendering slopes less steep.

Chapter VI

ENJOLRAS AND HIS LIEUTENANTS

IT WAS ABOUT THIS EPOCH THAT ENJOLRAS, IN VIEW OF A POSSIBLE CATASTROPHE, INSTITUTED A kind of mysterious census.

All were present at a secret meeting at the Café Musain.

Enjolras said, mixing his words with a few half-enigmatical but significant metaphors:

"It is proper that we should know where we stand and on whom we may count. If combatants are required, they must be provided. It can do no harm to have something with which to strike. Passers-by always have more chance of being gored when there are bulls on the road than when there are none. Let us, therefore, reckon a little on the herd. How many of us are there? There is no question of postponing this task until to-morrow. Revolutionists should always be hurried; progress has no time to lose. Let us mistrust the unexpected. Let us not be caught unprepared. We must go over all the seams that we have made and see whether they hold fast. This business ought to be concluded to-day. Courfeyrac, you will see the polytechnic students. It is their day to go out. To-day is Wednesday. Feuilly, you will see those of the Glacière, will you not? Combeferre has promised me to go to Picpus. There is a perfect swarm and an excellent one there. Bahorel will visit the Estrapade. Prouvaire, the masons are growing lukewarm; you will bring us news from the lodge of the Rue de Grenelle-Saint-Honoré. Joly will go to Dupuytren's clinical lecture, and feel the pulse of the medical school. Bossuet will take a little turn in the court and talk with the young law licentiates. I will take charge of the Cougourde myself."

"That arranges everything," said Courfeyrac.

"No."

"What else is there?"

"A very important thing."

"What is that?" asked Courfeyrac.

"The Barrière du Maine," replied Enjolras.

Enjolras remained for a moment as though absorbed in reflection, then he resumed:

"At the Barrière du Maine there are marble-workers, painters, and journeymen in the studios of sculptors. They are an enthusiastic family, but liable to cool off. I don't know what has been the matter with them for some time past. They are thinking of something else. They are becoming extinguished. They pass their time playing dominos. There is urgent need that someone should go and talk with them a little, but with firmness. They meet at Richefeu's. They are to be found there between twelve and one o'clock. Those ashes must be fanned into a glow. For that errand I had counted on that abstracted Marius, who is a good fellow on the whole, but he no longer comes to us. I need someone for the Barrière du Maine. I have no one."

"What about me?" said Grantaire. "Here am I."

"You?"

"I."

"You indoctrinate republicans! you warm up hearts that have grown cold in the name of principle!"

"Why not?"

"Are you good for anything?"

"I have a vague ambition in that direction," said Grantaire.

"You do not believe in everything."

"I believe in you."

"Grantaire, will you do me a service?"

"Anything. I'll black your boots."

"Well, don't meddle with our affairs. Sleep yourself sober from your absinthe."

"You are an ingrate, Enjolras."

"You the man to go to the Barrière du Maine! You capable of it!"

"I am capable of descending the Rue de Grès, of crossing the Place Saint-Michel, of sloping through the Rue Monsieur-le-Prince, of taking the Rue de Vaugirard, of passing the Carmelites, of turning into the Rue d'Assas, of reaching the Rue du Cherche-Midi, of leaving behind me the Conseil de Guerre, of pacing the Rue des Vielles Tuileries, of striding across the boulevard, of following the Chaussée du Maine, of passing the barrier, and entering Richefeu's. I am capable of that. My shoes are capable of that."

"Do you know anything of those comrades who meet at Richefeu's?"

"Not much. We only address each other as *thou*."

"What will you say to them?"

"I will speak to them of Robespierre, pardi! Of Danton. Of principles."

"You?"

"I. But I don't receive justice. When I set about it, I am terrible. I have read Prudhomme, I know the Social Contract, I know my Constitution of the year Two by heart. 'The liberty of one citizen ends where the liberty of another citizen begins.' Do you take me for a brute? I have an old bank-bill of the Republic in my drawer. The Rights of Man, the sovereignty of the people, sapristi! I am even a bit of a Hébertist. I can talk the most superb twaddle for six hours by the clock, watch in hand."

"Be serious," said Enjolras.

"I am wild," replied Grantaire.

Enjolras meditated for a few moments, and made the gesture of a man who has taken a resolution.

"Grantaire," he said gravely, "I consent to try you. You shall go to the Barrière du Maine."

Grantaire lived in furnished lodgings very near the Café Musain. He went out, and five minutes later he returned. He had gone home to put on a Robespierre waistcoat.

"Red," said he as he entered, and he looked intently at Enjolras. Then, with the palm of his energetic hand, he laid the two scarlet points of the waistcoat across his breast.

And stepping up to Enjolras, he whispered in his ear:

"Be easy."

He jammed his hat on resolutely and departed.

A quarter of an hour later, the back room of the Café Musain was deserted. All the friends of the A B C were gone, each in his own direction, each to his own task. Enjolras, who had reserved the Cougourde of Aix for himself, was the last to leave.

Those members of the Cougourde of Aix who were in Paris then met on the plain of Issy, in one of the abandoned quarries which are so numerous in that side of Paris.

As Enjolras walked toward this place, he passed the whole situation in review in his own mind. The gravity of events was self-evident. When facts, the premonitory symptoms of latent social malady, move heavily, the slightest complication stops and entangles them. A phenomenon whence arises ruin and new births. Enjolras descried a luminous uplifting beneath the gloomy skirts of the future. Who knows? Perhaps the moment was at hand. The people were again taking possession of right, and what a fine spectacle! The revolution was again majestically taking possession of France and saying to the world: "The sequel to-morrow!" Enjolras was content. The furnace was being heated. He had at that moment a powder train of friends scattered all over Paris. He composed, in his own mind, with Combeferre's philosophical and penetrating eloquence,

Feuilly's cosmopolitan enthusiasm, Courfeyrac's dash, Bahorel's smile, Jean Prouvaire's melancholy, Joly's science, Bossuet's sarcasms, a sort of electric spark which took fire nearly everywhere at once. All hands to work. Surely, the result would answer to the effort. This was well. This made him think of Grantaire.

"Hold," said he to himself, "the Barrière du Maine will not take me far out of my way. What if I were to go on as far as Richefeu's? Let us have a look at what Grantaire is about, and see how he is getting on."

One o'clock was striking from the Vaugirard steeple when Enjolras reached the Richefeu smoking-room.

He pushed open the door, entered, folded his arms, letting the door fall to and strike his shoulders, and gazed at that room filled with tables, men, and smoke.

A voice broke forth from the mist of smoke, interrupted by another voice. It was Grantaire holding a dialogue with an adversary.

Grantaire was sitting opposite another figure, at a marble Saint-Anne table, strewn with grains of bran and dotted with dominos. He was hammering the table with his fist, and this is what Enjolras heard:

"Double-six."

"Fours."

"The pig! I have no more."

"You are dead. A two."

"Six."

"Three."

"One."

"It's my move."

"Four points."

"Not much."

"It's your turn."

"I have made an enormous mistake."

"You are doing well."

"Fifteen."

"Seven more."

"That makes me twenty-two." [Thoughtfully, "Twenty-two!"]

"You weren't expecting that double-six. If I had placed it at the beginning, the whole play would have been changed."

"A two again."

"One."

"One! Well, five."

"I haven't any."

"It was your play, I believe?"

"Yes."

"Blank."

"What luck he has! Ah! You are lucky! [Long reverie.] Two."

"One."

"Neither five nor one. That's bad for you."

"Domino."

"Plague take it!"

BOOK SECOND

ÉPONINE

Chapter I

THE LARK'S MEADOW

MARIUS HAD WITNESSED THE UNEXPECTED TERMINATION OF THE AMBUSH UPON WHOSE TRACK he had set Javert; but Javert had no sooner quitted the building, bearing off his prisoners in three hackney-coaches, than Marius also glided out of the house. It was only nine o'clock in the evening. Marius betook himself to Courfeyrac. Courfeyrac was no longer the imperturbable inhabitant of the Latin Quarter, he had gone to live in the Rue de la Verrerie "for political reasons"; this quarter was one where, at that epoch, insurrection liked to install itself. Marius said to Courfeyrac: "I have come to sleep with you." Courfeyrac dragged a mattress off his bed, which was furnished with two, spread it out on the floor, and said: "There."

At seven o'clock on the following morning, Marius returned to the hovel, paid the quarter's rent which he owed to Ma'am Bougon, had his books, his bed, his table, his commode, and his two chairs loaded on a hand-cart and went off without leaving his address, so that when Javert returned in the course of the morning, for the purpose of questioning Marius as to the events of the preceding evening, he found only Ma'am Bougon, who answered: "Moved away!"

Ma'am Bougon was convinced that Marius was to some extent an accomplice of the robbers who had been seized the night before. "Who would ever have said it?" she exclaimed to the portresses of the quarter, "a young man like that, who had the air of a girl!"

Marius had two reasons for this prompt change of residence. The first was, that he now had a horror of that house, where he had beheld, so close at hand, and in its most repulsive and most ferocious development, a social deformity which is, perhaps, even more terrible than the wicked rich man, the wicked poor man. The second was, that he did not wish to figure in the lawsuit which would insue in all probability, and be brought in to testify against Thénardier.

Javert thought that the young man, whose name he had forgotten, was afraid, and had fled, or perhaps, had not even returned home at the time of the ambush; he made some efforts to find him, however, but without success.

A month passed, then another. Marius was still with Courfeyrac. He had learned from a young licentiate in law, an habitual frequenter of the courts, that Thénardier was in close confinement. Every Monday, Marius had five francs handed in to the clerk's office of La Force for Thénardier.

As Marius had no longer any money, he borrowed the five francs from Courfeyrac. It was the first time in his life that he had ever borrowed money. These periodical five francs were a double riddle to Courfeyrac who lent and to Thénardier who received them. "To whom can they go?" thought Courfeyrac. "Whence can this come to me?" Thénardier asked himself.

Moreover, Marius was heart-broken. Everything had plunged through a trapdoor once more. He no longer saw anything before him; his life was again buried in mystery where he wandered fumblingly. He had for a moment beheld very close at hand, in that obscurity, the young girl whom he loved, the old man who seemed to be her father, those unknown beings, who were his only interest and his only hope in this world; and, at the very moment when he thought himself on the point of grasping them, a gust had swept all these shadows away. Not a spark of certainty and truth had been emitted even in the most terrible of collisions. No conjecture was possible. He no longer knew even the name that he thought he knew. It certainly was not Ursule. And the Lark was a nickname. And what was he to think of the old man? Was he actually in hiding from the police? The white-haired workman whom Marius had encountered in the vicinity of the Invalides recurred to his mind. It now seemed probable that that workingman and M. Leblanc were one and the same person. So he disguised himself? That man had his heroic and his equivocal sides. Why had he not called for help? Why had he fled? Was he, or was he not, the father of the young girl? Was he, in short, the man whom Thénardier thought that he recognized? Thénardier might have been mistaken. These formed so many insoluble problems. All this, it is true, detracted nothing from the angelic charms of the young girl of the Luxembourg. Heartrending distress; Marius bore a passion in his heart, and night over his eyes. He was thrust onward, he was drawn, and he could not stir. All had vanished, save love. Of love itself he had lost the instincts and the sudden illuminations. Ordinarily, this flame which burns us lights us also a little, and casts some useful gleams without. But Marius no longer even heard these mute counsels of passion. He never said to himself: "What if I were to go to such a place? What if I were to try such and such a thing?" The girl whom he could no longer call Ursule was evidently somewhere; nothing warned Marius in what direction he should seek her. His whole life was now summed up in two words; absolute uncertainty within an impenetrable fog. To see her once again; he still aspired to this, but he no longer expected it.

To crown all, his poverty had returned. He felt that icy breath close to him, on his heels. In the midst of his torments, and long before this, he had discontinued his work, and nothing is more dangerous than discontinued work; it is a habit which vanishes. A habit which is easy to get rid of, and difficult to take up again.

A certain amount of dreaming is good, like a narcotic in discreet doses. It lulls to sleep the fevers of the mind at labor, which are sometimes severe, and produces in the spirit a soft and fresh vapor which corrects the over-harsh contours of pure thought, fills in gaps here and there, binds together and rounds off the angles of the ideas. But too much dreaming sinks and drowns. Woe to the brain-worker who allows himself to fall entirely from thought into reverie! He thinks that he can reascend with equal ease, and he tells himself that, after all, it is the same thing. Error!

Thought is the toil of the intelligence, reverie is its voluptuousness. To replace thought with reverie is to confound a poison with a food.

Marius had begun in that way, as the reader will remember. Passion had supervened and had finished the work of precipitating him into chimeras without object or bottom. One no longer emerges from one's self except for the purpose of going off to dream. Idle production. Tumultuous and stagnant gulf. And, in proportion as labor diminishes, needs increase. This is a law. Man, in a state of reverie, is generally prodigal and slack; the unstrung mind cannot hold life within close bounds.

There is, in that mode of life, good mingled with evil, for if enervation is baleful, generosity is good and healthful. But the poor man who is generous and noble, and who does not work, is lost. Resources are exhausted, needs crop up.

Fatal declivity down which the most honest and the firmest as well as the most feeble and most vicious are drawn, and which ends in one of two holes, suicide or crime.

By dint of going outdoors to think, the day comes when one goes out to throw one's self in the water.

Excess of reverie breeds men like Escousse and Lebras.

Marius was descending this declivity at a slow pace, with his eyes fixed on the girl whom he no longer saw. What we have just written seems strange, and yet it is true. The memory of an absent being kindles in the darkness of the heart; the more it has disappeared, the more it beams; the gloomy and despairing soul sees this light on its horizon; the star of the inner night. She—that was Marius's whole thought. He meditated of nothing else; he was confusedly conscious that his old coat was becoming an impossible coat, and that his new coat was growing old, that his shirts were wearing out, that his hat was wearing out, that his boots were giving out, and he said to himself: "If I could but see her once again before I die!"

One sweet idea alone was left to him, that she had loved him, that her glance had told him so, that she did not know his name, but that she did know his soul, and that, wherever she was, however mysterious the place, she still loved him, perhaps. Who knows whether she were not thinking of him as he was thinking of her? Sometimes, in those inexplicable hours such as are experienced by every heart that loves, though he had no reasons for anything but sadness and yet felt an obscure quiver of joy, he said to himself: "It is her thoughts that are coming to me!" Then he added: "Perhaps my thoughts reach her also."

This illusion, at which he shook his head a moment later, was sufficient, nevertheless, to throw beams, which at times resembled hope, into his soul. From time to time, especially at that evening hour which is the most depressing to even the dreamy, he allowed the purest, the most impersonal, the most ideal of the reveries which filled his brain, to fall upon a notebook which contained nothing else. He called this "writing to her."

It must not be supposed that his reason was deranged. Quite the contrary. He had lost the faculty of working and of moving firmly toward any fixed goal, but he was endowed with more clear-sightedness and rectitude than ever. Marius surveyed by a calm and real, although peculiar light, what passed before his eyes, even the most indifferent deeds and men; he pronounced a just criticism on everything with a sort of honest dejection and candid disinterestedness. His judgment, which was almost wholly disassociated from hope, held itself aloof and soared on high.

In this state of mind nothing escaped him, nothing deceived him, and every moment he was discovering the foundation of life, of humanity, and of destiny. Happy, even in the midst of anguish, is he to whom God has given a soul worthy of love and of unhappiness! He who has not viewed the things of this world and the heart of man under this double light has seen nothing and knows nothing of the true.

The soul which loves and suffers is in a state of sublimity.

However, day followed day, and nothing new presented itself. It merely seemed to him, that the somber space which still remained to be traversed by him was growing shorter with every instant. He thought that he already distinctly perceived the brink of the bottomless abyss.

"What!" he repeated to himself, "shall I not see her again before then!"

When you have ascended the Rue Saint-Jacques, left the barrier on one side and followed the old inner boulevard for some distance, you reach the Rue de la Santé, then the Glacière, and, a little while before arriving at the little river of the Gobelins, you come to a sort of field which is the only spot in the long and monotonous chain of the boulevards of Paris, where Ruysdeel would be tempted to sit down.

There is something indescribable there which exhales grace, a green meadow traversed by tightly stretched lines, from which flutter rags drying in the wind, and an old market-gardener's house, built in the time of Louis XIII, with its great roof oddly pierced with dormer-windows, dilapidated palisades, a little water amid poplar-trees, women, voices, laughter; on the horizon the Panthéon, the pole of the Deaf-Mutes, the Val-de-Grâce, black, squat, fantastic, amusing, magnificent, and in the background, the severe square crests of the towers of Notre-Dame.

As the place is worth looking at, no one goes thither. Hardly one cart or wagoner passes in a quarter of an hour.

It chanced that Marius's solitary strolls led him to this plot of ground, near the water. That day, there was a rarity on the boulevard, a passer-by. Marius, vaguely impressed with the almost savage beauty of the place, asked this passer-by: "What is the name of this spot?"

The person replied: "It is the Lark's meadow."

And he added: "It was here that Ulbach killed the shepherdess of Ivry."

But after the word "Lark" Marius heard nothing more. These sudden congealments in the state of reverie, which a single word suffices to evoke, do occur. The entire thought is abruptly condensed around an idea, and it is no longer capable of perceiving anything else.

The Lark was the appellation which had replaced Ursule in the depths of Marius's melancholy.— "Stop," said he with a sort of unreasoning stupor peculiar to these mysterious asides, "this is her meadow. I shall know where she lives now."

It was absurd, but irresistible.

And every day he returned to that meadow of the Lark.

Chapter II

Embryonic Formation of Crimes in the Incubation of Prisons

Javert's triumph in the Gorbeau hovel seemed complete, but had not been so.

In the first place, and this constituted the principal anxiety, Javert had not taken the prisoner prisoner. The assassinated man who flees is more suspicious than the assassin, and it is probable that this personage, who had been so precious a capture for the ruffians, would be no less fine a prize for the authorities.

And then, Montparnasse had escaped Javert.

Another opportunity of laying hands on that "devil's dandy" must be waited for. Montparnasse had, in fact, encountered Éponine as she stood on the watch under the trees of the boulevard, and had led her off, preferring to play Nemorin with the daughter rather than Schinderhannes with the father. It was well that he did so. He was free. As for Éponine, Javert had caused her to be seized; a mediocre consolation. Éponine had joined Azelma at Les Madelonettes.

And finally, on the way from the Gorbeau house to La Force, one of the principal prisoners, Claquesous, had been lost. It was not known how this had been effected, the police agents and the sergeants "could not understand it at all." He had converted himself into vapor, he had slipped through the handcuffs, he had trickled through the crevices of the carriage, the fiacre was cracked, and he had fled; all that they were able to say was, that on arriving at the prison, there was no Claquesous. Either the fairies or the police had had a hand in it. Had Claquesous melted into the shadows like a snowflake in water? Had there been unavowed connivance of the police agents? Did this man belong to the double enigma of order and disorder? Was he concentric with infraction and repression? Had this sphinx his forepaws in crime and his hindpaws in authority? Javert did not accept such comminations, and would have bristled up against such compromises; but his squad included other inspectors besides himself, who were more initiated than he, perhaps, although they were his subordinates in the secrets of the Prefecture, and Claquesous had been such a villain that he might make a very good agent. It is an excellent thing for ruffianism and an admirable thing for the police to be on such intimate juggling terms with the night. These double-edged rascals do exist. However that may be, Claquesous had gone astray and was not found again. Javert appeared to be more irritated than amazed at this.

As for Marius, "that booby of a lawyer," who had probably become frightened, and whose name Javert had forgotten, Javert attached very little importance to him. Moreover, a lawyer can be hunted up at any time. But was he a lawyer after all?

The investigation had begun.

The magistrate had thought it advisable not to put one of these men of the band of Patron Minette in close confinement, in the hope that he would chatter. This man was Brujon, the long-haired man of the Rue du Petit-Banquier. He had been let loose in the Charlemagne courtyard, and the eyes of the watchers were fixed on him.

This name of Brujon is one of the souvenirs of La Force. In that hideous courtyard, called the court of the Bâtiment-Neuf (New Building), which the administration called the court Saint-Bernard, and which the robbers called the Fosse-aux-Lions (The Lions' Ditch), on that wall covered with scales and leprosy, which rose on the left to a level with the roofs, near an old door of rusty iron which led to the ancient chapel of the ducal residence of La Force, then turned in a dormitory for ruffians, there could still be seen, twelve years ago, a sort of fortress roughly carved in the stone with a nail, and beneath it this signature:

BRUJON, 1811.

The Brujon of 1811 was the father of the Brujon of 1832.

The latter, of whom the reader caught but a glimpse at the Gorbeau house, was a very cunning and very adroit young spark, with a bewildered and plaintive air. It was in consequence of this plaintive air that the magistrate had released him, thinking him more useful in the Charlemagne yard than in close confinement.

Robbers do not interrupt their profession because they are in the hands of justice. They do not let themselves be put out by such a trifle as that. To be in prison for one crime is no reason for not beginning on another crime. They are artists, who have one picture in the salon, and who toil, none the less, on a new work in their studios.

Brujon seemed to be stupefied by prison. He could sometimes be seen standing by the hour together in front of the sutler's window in the Charlemagne yard, staring like an idiot at the sordid list of prices which began with: *garlic, 62 centimes,* and ended with: *cigar, 5 centimes.* Or he passed his time in trembling, chattering his teeth, saying that he had a fever, and inquiring whether one of the eight-and-twenty beds in the fever ward was vacant.

All at once, toward the end of February, 1832, it was discovered that Brujon, that somnolent fellow, had had three different commissions executed by the errand-men of the establishment, not under his own name, but in the name of three of his comrades; and they had cost him in all fifty sous, an exorbitant outlay which attracted the attention of the prison corporal.

Inquiries were instituted, and on consulting the tariff of commissions posted in the convicts' parlor, it was learned that the fifty sous could be analyzed as follows: three commissions; one to the Panthéon, ten sous; one to Val-de-Grâce, fifteen sous; and one to the Barrière de Grenelle, twenty-five sous. This last was the dearest of the whole tariff. Now, at the Panthéon, at the Val-de-Grâce, and at the Barrière de Grenelle were situated the domiciles of the three very redoubtable prowlers of the barriers, Kruideniers, alias Bizarro, Glorieux, an ex-convict, and Barre-Carosse, upon whom the attention of the police was directed by this incident. It was thought that these men were members of Patron Minette; two of those leaders, Babet and Gueulemer had been captured. It was supposed that the messages, which had been addressed, not to houses, but to people who were waiting for them in the street, must have contained information with regard to some crime that had been plotted. They were in possession of other indications; they laid hand on the three prowlers, and supposed that they had circumvented some one or other of Brujon's machinations.

About a week after these measures had been taken, one night, as the superintendent of the watch, who had been inspecting the lower dormitory in the Bâtiment-Neuf, was about to drop his chestnut in the box—this was the means adopted to make sure that the watchmen performed their duties punctually; every hour a chestnut must be dropped into all the boxes nailed to the doors of the dormitories—a watchman looked through the peephole of the dormitory and beheld Brujon sitting on his bed and writing something by the light of the hall-lamp. The guardian entered, Brujon was put in a solitary cell for a month, but they were not able to seize what he had written. The police learned nothing further about it.

What is certain is, that on the following morning, a "postilion" was flung from the Charlemagne yard into the Lions' Ditch, over the five-story building which separated the two courtyards.

What prisoners call a "postilion" is a pallet of bread artistically molded, which is sent *into Ireland*, that is to say, over the roofs of a prison, from one courtyard to another. Etymology: over England; from one land to another; *into Ireland*. This little pellet falls in the yard. The man who picks it up opens it and finds in it a note addressed to some prisoner in that yard. If it is a prisoner who finds the treasure, he forwards the note to its destination; if it is a keeper, or one of the prisoners secretly sold who are called *sheep* in prisons and *foxes* in the galleys, the note is taken to the office and handed over to the police.

On this occasion, the postilion reached its address, although the person to whom it was addressed was, at that moment, in solitary confinement. This person was no other than Babet, one of the four heads of Patron Minette.

The postilion contained a roll of paper on which only these two lines were written:

"Babet. There is an affair in the Rue Plumet. A gate on a garden."

This is what Brujon had written the night before.

In spite of male and female searchers, Babet managed to pass the note on from La Force to the Salpêtrière, to a "good friend" whom he had and who was shut up there. This woman in turn transmitted the note to another woman of her acquaintance, a certain Magnon, who was strongly suspected by the police, though not yet arrested. This Magnon, whose name the reader has already seen, had relations with the Thénardier, which will be described in detail later on, and she could, by going to see Éponine, serve as a bridge between the Salpêtrière and Les Madelonettes.

It happened, that at precisely that moment, as proofs were wanting in the investigation directed against Thénardier in the matter of his daughters, Éponine and Azelma were released. When Éponine came out, Magnon, who was watching the gate of the Madelonettes, handed her Brujon's note to Babet, charging her to look into the matter.

Éponine went to the Rue Plumet, recognized the gate and the garden, observed the house, spied, lurked, and, a few days later, brought to Magnon, who delivers in the Rue Clocheperce, a biscuit, which Magnon transmitted to Babet's mistress in the Salpêtrière. A biscuit, in the shady symbolism of prisons, signifies: Nothing to be done.

So that in less than a week from that time, as Brujon and Babet met in the circle of La Force, the one on his way to the examination, the other on his way from it:

"Well?" asked Brujon, "the Rue P.?"

"Biscuit," replied Babet. Thus did the fetus of crime engendered by Brujon in La Force miscarry.

This miscarriage had its consequences, however, which were perfectly distinct from Brujon's program. The reader will see what they were.

Often when we think we are knotting one thread, we are tying quite another.

Chapter III

APPARITION TO FATHER MABEUF

MARIUS NO LONGER WENT TO SEE ANYONE, BUT HE SOMETIMES ENCOUNTERED FATHER MABEUF by chance.

While Marius was slowly descending those melancholy steps which may be called the cellar stairs, and which lead to places without light, where the happy can be heard walking overhead, M. Mabeuf was descending on his side.

The *Flora of Cauteretz* no longer sold at all. The experiments on indigo had not been success-ful in the little garden of Austerlitz, which had a bad exposure. M. Mabeuf could cultivate there only a few plants which love shade and dampness. Nevertheless, he did not become discouraged. He had obtained a corner in the Jardin des Plantes, with a good exposure, to make his trials with in-digo "at his own expense." For this purpose he had pawned his copperplates of the *Flora*. He had reduced his breakfast to two eggs, and he left one of these for his old servant, to whom he had paid no wages for the last fifteen months. And often his breakfast was his only meal. He no longer smiled with his infantile smile, he had grown morose and no longer received visitors. Marius did well not to dream of going thither. Sometimes, at the hour when M. Mabeuf was on his way to the Jardin des Plantes, the old man and the young man passed each other on the Boulevard de l'Hôpital. They did not speak, and only exchanged a melancholy sign of the head. A heart-breaking thing it is that there comes a moment when misery looses bonds! Two men who have been friends become two chance passers-by.

Royol the bookseller was dead. M. Mabeuf no longer knew his books, his garden, or his indigo: these were the three forms which happiness, pleasure, and hope had assumed for him. This sufficed him for his living. He said to himself: "When I shall have made my balls of blueing, I shall be rich, I will withdraw my copperplates from the pawn-shop, I will put my *Flora* in vogue again with trick-ery, plenty of money, and advertisements in the newspapers and I will buy, I know well where, a copy of Pierre de Médine's *Art de Naviguer,* with wood-cuts, edition of 1655." In the meantime, he toiled all day over his plot of indigo, and at night he returned home to water his garden, and to read his books. At that epoch, M. Mabeuf was nearly eighty years of age.

One evening he had a singular apparition.

He had returned home while it was still broad daylight. Mother Plutarque, whose health was declining, was ill and in bed. He had dined on a bone, on which a little meat lingered, and a bit of bread that he had found on the kitchen table, and had seated himself on an overturned stone post, which took the place of a bench in his garden.

Near this bench there rose, after the fashion in orchard-gardens, a sort of large chest, of beams and planks, much dilapidated, a rabbit-hutch on the ground floor, a fruit-closet on the first. There was nothing in the hutch, but there were a few apples in the fruit-closet—the remains of the win-ter's provision.

M. Mabeuf had set himself to turning over and reading, with the aid of his glasses, two books of which he was passionately fond and in which, a serious thing at his age, he was interested. His natural timidity rendered him accessible to the acceptance of superstitions in a certain degree. The first of these books was the famous treatise of President Delancre, *De l'Inconstance des Démons*; the other was a quarto by Mutor de la Rubaudière, *Sur les Diables de Vauvert et les Gobelins de la Bièvre.* This last-mentioned old volume interested him all the more, because his garden had been one of the spots haunted by goblins in former times. The twilight had begun to whiten what was on high and to blacken all below. As he read, over the top of the book which he held in his hand, Father Mabeuf was surveying his plants, and among others a magnificent rhododendron which was one of his consolations; four days of heat, wind, and sun without a drop of rain, had passed; the stalks were bending, the buds drooping, the leaves falling; all this needed water, the rhododendron was particularly sad. Father Mabeuf was one of those persons for whom plants have souls. The old man had toiled all day over his indigo plot, he was worn out with fatigue, but he rose, laid his books on the bench, and walked, all bent over and with tottering footsteps to the well, but when he had grasped the chain, he could not even draw it sufficiently to unhook it. Then he turned round and cast a glance of anguish toward heaven which was becoming studded with stars.

The evening had that serenity which overwhelms the troubles of man beneath an indescribably mournful and eternal joy. The night promised to be as arid as the day had been.

"Stars everywhere!" thought the old man; "not the tiniest cloud! Not a drop of water!"

And his head, which had been upraised for a moment, fell back upon his breast.

He raised it again, and once more looked at the sky, murmuring:

"A tear of dew! A little pity!"

He tried again to unhook the chain of the well, and could not.

At that moment, he heard a voice saying:

"Father Mabeuf, would you like to have me water your garden for you?"

At the same time, a noise as of a wild animal passing became audible in the hedge, and he beheld emerging from the shrubbery a sort of tall, slender girl, who drew herself up in front of him and stared boldly at him. She had less the air of a human being than of a form which had just blossomed forth from the twilight.

Before Father Mabeuf, who was easily terrified, and who was, as we have said, quick to take alarm, was able to reply by a single syllable, this being, whose movements had a sort of odd abruptness in the darkness, had unhooked the chain, plunged in and withdrawn the bucket, and filled the watering-pot, and the good man beheld this apparition, which had bare feet and a tattered petticoat, running about among the flower-beds distributing life around her. The sound of the watering-pot on the leaves filled Father Mabeuf's soul with ecstasy. It seemed to him that the rhododendron was happy now.

The first bucketful emptied, the girl drew a second, then a third. She watered the whole garden.

There was something about her, as she thus ran about among paths, where her outline appeared perfectly black, waving her angular arms, and with her fichu all in rags, that resembled a bat.

When she had finished, Father Mabeuf approached her with tears in his eyes, and laid his hand on her brow.

"God will bless you," said he, "you are an angel since you take care of the flowers."

"No," she replied. "I am the devil, but that's all the same to me."

The old man exclaimed, without either waiting for or hearing her response:

"What a pity that I am so unhappy and so poor, and that I can do nothing for you!"

"You can do something," said she.

"What?"

"Tell me where M. Marius lives."

The old man did not understand. "What Monsieur Marius?"

He raised his glassy eyes and seemed to be seeking something that had vanished.

"A young man who used to come here."

In the meantime, M. Mabeuf had searched his memory.

"Ah! yes—" he exclaimed. "I know what you mean. Wait! Monsieur Marius—the Baron Marius Pontmercy, parbleu! He lives—or rather, he no longer lives—ah well, I don't know."

As he spoke, he had bent over to train a branch of rhododendron, and he continued:

"Hold, I know now. He very often passes along the boulevard, and goes in the direction of the Glacière, Rue Croulebarbe. The meadow of the Lark. Go there. It is not hard to meet him."

When M. Mabeuf straightened himself up, there was no longer anyone there; the girl had disappeared.

He was decidedly terrified.

"Really," he thought, "if my garden had not been watered, I should think that she was a spirit."

An hour later, when he was in bed, it came back to him, and as he fell asleep, at that confused moment when thought, like that fabulous bird which changes itself into a fish in order to cross the sea, little by little assumes the form of a dream in order to traverse slumber, he said to himself in a bewildered way:

"In sooth, that greatly resembles what Rubaudière narrates of the goblins. Could it have been a goblin?"

Chapter IV

AN APPARITION TO MARIUS

SOME DAYS AFTER THIS VISIT OF A "SPIRIT" TO FARMER MABEUF, ONE MORNING—IT WAS ON A Monday, the day when Marius borrowed the hundred-sou piece from Courfeyrac for Thénardier—Marius had put this coin in his pocket, and before carrying it to the clerk's office, he had gone "to take a little stroll," in the hope that this would make him work on his return. It was always thus, however. As soon as he rose, he seated himself before a book and a sheet of paper in order to scribble some translation; his task at that epoch consisted in turning into French a celebrated quarrel between Germans, the Gans and Savigny controversy; he took Savigny, he took Gans, read four lines, tried to write one, could not, saw a star between him and his paper, and rose from his chair, saying: "I shall go out. That will put me in spirits."

And off he went to the Lark's meadow.

There he beheld more than ever the star, and less than ever Savigny and Gans.

He returned home, tried to take up his work again, and did not succeed; there was no means of re-knotting a single one of the threads which were broken in his brain; then he said to himself: "I will not go out to-morrow. It prevents my working." And he went out every day.

He lived in the Lark's meadow more than in Courfeyrac's lodgings. That was his real address: Boulevard de la Santé, at the seventh tree from the Rue Croulebarbe.

That morning he had quitted the seventh tree, and had seated himself on the parapet of the River des Gobelins. A cheerful sunlight penetrated the freshly unfolded and luminous leaves.

He was dreaming of "Her." And his meditation turning to a reproach, fell back upon himself; he reflected dolefully on his idleness, his paralysis of soul, which was gaining on him, and of that night which was growing more dense every moment before him, to such a point that he no longer even saw the sun.

Nevertheless, athwart this painful extrication of indistinct ideas which was not even a monologue, so feeble had action become in him, and he had no longer the force to care to despair, athwart this melancholy absorption, sensations from without did reach him. He heard behind him, beneath him, on both banks of the river, the laundresses of the Gobelins beating their linen, and above his head, the birds chattering and singing in the elm-trees. On the one hand, the sound of liberty, the careless happiness of the leisure which has wings; on the other, the sound of toil. What caused him to meditate deeply, and almost reflect, were two cheerful sounds.

All at once, in the midst of his dejected ecstasy, he heard a familiar voice saying:

"Come! Here he is!"

He raised his eyes, and recognized that wretched child who had come to him one morning, the elder of the Thénardier daughters, Éponine; he knew her name now. Strange to say, she had grown poorer and prettier, two steps which it had not seemed within her power to take. She had accomplished a double progress, toward the light and toward distress. She was barefooted and in rags, as on the day when she had so resolutely entered his chamber, only her rags were two months older now, the holes were larger, the tatters more sordid. It was the same harsh voice, the same brow dimmed and wrinkled with tan, the same free, wild, and vacillating glance. She had besides, more than formerly, in her face that indescribably terrified and lamentable something which sojourn in a prison adds to wretchedness.

She had bits of straw and hay in her hair, not like Ophelia through having gone mad from the contagion of Hamlet's madness, but because she had slept in the loft of some stable.

And in spite of it all, she was beautiful. What a star art thou, O youth!

In the meantime, she had halted in front of Marius with a trace of joy on her livid countenance, and something which resembled a smile.

She stood for several moments as though incapable of speech.

"So I have met you at last!" she said at length. "Father Mabeuf was right, it was on this boulevard! How I have hunted for you! If you only knew! Do you know? I have been in the jug. A fortnight! They let me out! seeing that there was nothing against me, and that, moreover, I had not reached years of discretion. I lack two months of it. Oh! how I have hunted for you! These six weeks! So you don't live down there anymore?"

"No," said Marius.

"Ah! I understand. Because of that affair. Those take-downs are disagreeable. You cleared out. Come now! Why do you wear old hats like this! A young man like you ought to have fine clothes. Do you know, Monsieur Marius, Father Mabeuf calls you Baron Marius, I don't know what. It isn't true that you are a baron? Barons are old fellows, they go to the Luxembourg, in front of the chateau, where there is the most sun, and they read the *Quotidienne* for a sou. I once carried a letter to a baron of that sort. He was over a hundred years old. Say, where do you live now?"

Marius made no reply.

"Ah!" she went on, "you have a hole in your shirt. I must sew it up for you."

She resumed with an expression which gradually clouded over:

"You don't seem glad to see me."

Marius held his peace; she remained silent for a moment, then exclaimed:

"But if I choose, nevertheless, I could force you to look glad!"

"What?" demanded Marius. "What do you mean?"

"Ah! you used to call me *thou*," she retorted.

"Well, then, what dost thou mean?"

She bit her lip; she seemed to hesitate, as though a prey to some sort of inward conflict. At last she appeared to come to a decision.

"So much the worse, I don't care. You have a melancholy air, I want you to be pleased. Only promise me that you will smile. I want to see you smile and hear you say: 'Ah, well, that's good.' Poor Mr. Marius! you know? You promised me that you would give me anything I like—"

"Yes! Only speak!"

She looked Marius full in the eye, and said:

"I have the address."

Marius turned pale. All the blood flowed back to his heart.

"What address?"

"The address that you asked me to get!"

She added, as though with an effort:

"The address—you know very well!"

"Yes!" stammered Marius.

"Of that young lady."

This word uttered, she sighed deeply.

Marius sprang from the parapet on which he had been sitting, and seized her hand distractedly.

"Oh! Well! lead me thither! Tell me! Ask of me anything you wish! Where is it?"

"Come with me," she responded. "I don't know the street or number very well; it is in quite the other direction from here, but I know the house well, I will take you to it."

She withdrew her hand and went on, in a tone which could have rent the heart of an observer, but which did not even graze Marius in his intoxicated and ecstatic state:

"Oh! how glad you are!"

A cloud swept across Marius's brow. He seized Éponine by the arm:

"Swear one thing to me!"

"Swear!" said she, "what does that mean? Come! You want me to swear?"

And she laughed.

"Your father! promise me, Éponine! Swear to me that you will not give this address to your father!"

She turned to him with a stupefied air.

"Éponine! How do you know that my name is Éponine?"

"Promise what I tell you!"

But she did not seem to hear him.

"That's nice! You have called me Éponine!"

Marius grasped both her arms at once.

"But answer me, in the name of Heaven! pay attention to what I am saying to you, swear to me that you will not tell your father this address that you know!"

"My father!" said she. "Ah yes, my father! Be at ease. He's in close confinement. Besides, what do I care for my father!"

"But you do not promise me!" exclaimed Marius.

"Let go of me!" she said, bursting into a laugh, "how you do shake me! Yes! Yes! I promise that! I swear that to you! What is that to me? I will not tell my father the address. There! Is that right? Is that it?"

"Nor to anyone?" said Marius.

"Nor to anyone."

"Now," resumed Marius, "take me there."

"Immediately?"

"Immediately."

"Come along. Ah! how pleased he is!" said she.

After a few steps she halted.

"You are following me too closely, Monsieur Marius. Let me go on ahead, and follow me so, without seeming to do it. A nice young man like you must not be seen with a woman like me."

No tongue can express all that lay in that word, *woman,* thus pronounced by that child.

She proceeded a dozen paces and then halted once more; Marius joined her. She addressed him sideways and without turning toward him:

"By the way, you know that you promised me something?"

Marius fumbled in his pocket. All that he owned in the world was the five francs intended for Thénardier the father. He took them and laid them in Éponine's hand.

She opened her fingers and let the coin fall to the ground, and gazed at him with a gloomy air.

"I don't want your money," said she.

BOOK THIRD

THE HOUSE IN THE RUE PLUMET

Chapter I

THE HOUSE WITH A SECRET

ABOUT THE MIDDLE OF THE LAST CENTURY, A CHIEF JUSTICE IN THE PARLIAMENT OF PARIS HAVing a mistress and concealing the fact, for at that period the grand seignors displayed their mistresses, and the bourgeois concealed them, had "a little house" built in the Faubourg Saint-Germain, in the deserted Rue Blomet, which is now called Rue Plumet, not far from the spot which was then designated as *Combat des Animaux*.

This house was composed of a single-storied pavilion; two rooms on the ground floor, two chambers on the first floor, a kitchen downstairs, a boudoir upstairs, an attic under the roof, the whole preceded by a garden with a large gate opening on the street. This garden was about an acre and a half in extent. This was all that could be seen by passers-by; but behind the pavilion there was a narrow courtyard, and at the end of the courtyard a low building consisting of two rooms and a cellar, a sort of preparation destined to conceal a child and nurse in case of need. This building communicated in the rear by a masked door which opened by a secret spring, with a long, narrow, paved winding corridor, open to the sky, hemmed in with two lofty walls, which, hidden with wonderful art, and lost as it were between garden enclosures and cultivated land, all of whose angles and detours it followed, ended in another door, also with a secret lock which opened a quarter of a league away, almost in another quarter, at the solitary extremity of the Rue du Babylone.

Through this the chief justice entered, so that even those who were spying on him and following him would merely have observed that the justice betook himself every day in a mysterious way somewhere, and would never have suspected that to go to the Rue de Babylone was to go to the Rue Blomet. Thanks to clever purchasers of land, the magistrate had been able to make a secret, sewer-like passage on his own property, and consequently, without interference. Later on, he had sold in little parcels, for gardens and market-gardens, the lots of ground adjoining the corridor, and the proprietors of these lots on both sides thought they had a party wall before their eyes, and did not even suspect the long, paved ribbon winding between two walls amid their flower-beds and their orchards. Only the birds beheld this curiosity. It is probable that the linnets and tomtits of the last century gossiped a great deal about the chief justice.

The pavilion, built of stone in the taste of Mansard, wainscoted and furnished in the Watteau style, rocaille on the inside, old-fashioned on the outside, walled in with a triple hedge of flowers, had something discreet, coquettish, and solemn about it, as befits a caprice of love and magistracy.

This house and corridor, which have now disappeared, were in existence fifteen years ago. In '93 a coppersmith had purchased the house with the idea of demolishing it, but had not been able to pay the price; the nation made him bankrupt. So that it was the house which demolished the coppersmith. After that, the house remained uninhabited, and fell slowly to ruin, as does every dwelling to which the presence of man does not communicate life. It had remained fitted with its old furniture, was always for sale or to let, and the ten or a dozen people who passed through the Rue Plumet were warned of the fact by a yellow and illegible bit of writing which had hung on the garden wall since 1819.

Toward the end of the Restoration, these same passers-by might have noticed that the bill had disappeared, and even that the shutters on the first floor were open. The house was occupied, in fact. The windows had short curtains, a sign that there was a woman about.

In the month of October, 1829, a man of a certain age had presented himself and had hired the house just as it stood, including, of course, the back building and the lane which ended in the Rue de Babylone. He had had the secret openings of the two doors to this passage repaired. The house, as we have just mentioned, was still very nearly furnished with the justice's old fitting; the new tenant had ordered some repairs, had added what was lacking here and there, had replaced the paving-stones in the yard, bricks in the floors, steps in the stairs, missing bits in the inlaid floors and the glass in the lattice windows, and had finally installed himself there with a young girl and an elderly maid-servant, without commotion, rather like a person who is slipping in than like a man who is entering his own house. The neighbors did not gossip about him, for the reason that there were no neighbors.

This unobtrusive tenant was Jean Valjean, the young girl was Cosette. The servant was a woman named Toussaint, whom Jean Valjean had saved from the hospital and from wretchedness, and who was elderly, a stammerer, and from the provinces, three qualities which had decided Jean Valjean to take her with him. He had hired the house under the name of M. Fauchelevent, independent gentleman. In all that has been related heretofore, the reader has, doubtless, been no less prompt than Thénardier to recognize Jean Valjean.

Why had Jean Valjean quitted the convent of the Petit-Picpus? What had happened?

Nothing had happened.

It will be remembered that Jean Valjean was happy in the convent, so happy that his conscience finally took the alarm. He saw Cosette every day, he felt paternity spring up and develop within him more and more, he brooded over the soul of that child, he said to himself that she was his, that nothing could take her from him, that this would last indefinitely, that she would certainly become a nun, being thereto gently incited every day, that thus the convent was henceforth the universe for her as it was for him, that he should grow old there, and that she would grow up there, that she would grow old there, and that he should die there; that, in short, delightful hope, no separation was possible. On reflecting upon this, he fell into perplexity. He interrogated himself. He asked himself if all that happiness were really his, if it were not composed of the happiness of another, of the happiness of that child which he, an old man, was confiscating and stealing; if that were not theft? He said to himself, that this child had a right to know life before renouncing it, that to deprive her in advance, and in some sort without consulting her, of all joys, under the pretext of saving her from all trials, to take advantage of her ignorance of her isolation, in order to make an artificial vocation germinate in her, was to rob a human creature of its nature and to lie to God. And who knows if, when she came to be aware of all this someday, and found herself a nun to her sorrow, Cosette would not come to hate him? A last, almost selfish thought, and less heroic than the rest, but which was intolerable to him. He resolved to quit the convent.

He resolved on this; he recognized with anguish, the fact that it was necessary. As for objections, there were none. Five years' sojourn between these four walls and of disappearance had necessarily destroyed or dispersed the elements of fear. He could return tranquilly among men. He had grown old, and all had undergone a change. Who would recognize him now? And then, to face the worst, there was danger only for himself, and he had no right to condemn Cosette to the cloister for the reason that he had been condemned to the galleys. Besides, what is danger in comparison with the right? Finally, nothing prevented his being prudent and taking his precautions.

As for Cosette's education, it was almost finished and complete.

His determination once taken, he awaited an opportunity. It was not long in presenting itself. Old Fauchelevent died.

Jean Valjean demanded an audience with the revered prioress and told her that, having come into a little inheritance at the death of his brother, which permitted him henceforth to live without working, he should leave the service of the convent and take his daughter with him; but that, as it was not just that Cosette, since she had not taken the vows, should have received her education gratuitously, he humbly begged the Reverend Prioress to see fit that he should offer to the community, as indemnity, for the five years which Cosette had spent there, the sum of five thousand francs.

It was thus that Jean Valjean quitted the convent of the Perpetual Adoration.

On leaving the convent, he took in his own arms the little valise the key to which he still wore on his person, and would permit no porter to touch it. This puzzled Cosette, because of the odor of embalming which proceeded from it.

Let us state at once, that this trunk never quitted him more. He always had it in his chamber. It was the first and only thing sometimes, that he carried off in his moving when he moved about. Cosette laughed at it, and called this valise *his inseparable*, saying: "I am jealous of it."

Nevertheless, Jean Valjean did not reappear in the open air without profound anxiety.

He discovered the house in the Rue Plumet, and hid himself from sight there. Henceforth, he was in the possession of the name: Ultime Fauchelevent.

At the same time he hired two other apartments in Paris, in order that he might attract less attention than if he were to remain always in the same quarter, and so that he could, at need, take himself off at the slightest disquietude which should assail him, and in short, so that he might not again be caught unprovided as on the night when he had so miraculously escaped from Javert. These two apartments were very pitiable, poor in appearance, and in two quarters which were far remote from each other, the one in the Rue de l'Ouest, the other in the Rue de l'Homme Armé.

He went from time to time, now to the Rue de l'Homme Armé, now to the Rue de l'Ouest, to pass a month or six weeks, without taking Toussaint. He had himself served by the porters, and gave himself out as a gentleman from the suburbs, living on his funds, and having a little temporary resting-place in town. This lofty virtue had three domiciles in Paris for the sake of escaping from the police.

Chapter II

JEAN VALJEAN AS A NATIONAL GUARD

HOWEVER, PROPERLY SPEAKING, HE LIVED IN THE RUE PLUMET, AND HE HAD ARRANGED HIS EXistence there in the following fashion:

Cosette and the servant occupied the pavilion; she had the big sleeping-room with the painted pier-glasses, the boudoir with the gilded fillets, the justice's drawing-room furnished with tapestries and vast arm-chairs; she had the garden. Jean Valjean had a canopied bed of antique damask in three colors and a beautiful Persian rug purchased in the Rue du Figuier-Saint-Paul at Mother Gaucher's, put into Cosette's chamber, and, in order to redeem the severity of these magnificent old things, he had amalgamated with this bric-à-brac all the gay and graceful little pieces of furniture suitable to young girls, an étagère, a bookcase filled with gilt-edged books, an inkstand, a blotting-book, paper, a work-table encrusted with mother of pearl, a silver-gilt dressing-case, a toilet service in Japanese porcelain. Long damask curtains with a red foundation and three colors, like those on the bed, hung at the windows of the first floor. On the ground floor, the curtains were of tapestry. All winter long, Cosette's little house was heated from top to bottom. Jean Valjean inhabited the sort of porter's lodge which was situated at the end of the back courtyard, with a mattress on a folding-bed, a white wood table, two straw chairs, an earthenware water-jug, a few old volumes on a shelf, his beloved valise in one corner, and never any fire. He dined with Cosette, and he had a loaf of black bread on the table for his own use.

When Toussaint came, he had said to her: "It is the young lady who is the mistress of this house."—"And you, monsieur?" Toussaint replied in amazement.—"I am a much better thing than the master, I am the father."

Cosette had been taught housekeeping in the convent, and she regulated their expenditure, which was very modest. Every day, Jean Valjean put his arm through Cosette's and took her for a walk. He led her to the Luxembourg, to the least frequented walk, and every Sunday he took her to mass at Saint-Jacques-du-Haut-Pas, because that was a long way off. As it was a very poor quarter, he bestowed alms largely there, and the poor people surrounded him in church, which had drawn down upon him Thénardier's epistle: "To the benevolent gentleman of the church of Saint-Jacques-du-Haut-Pas." He was fond of taking Cosette to visit the poor and the sick. No stranger ever entered the house in the Rue Plumet. Toussaint brought their provisions, and Jean Valjean went himself for water to a fountain nearby on the boulevard. Their wood and wine were put into a half-subterranean hollow lined with rock-work which lay near the Rue de Babylone and which had formerly served the chief justice as a grotto; for at the epoch of follies and "Little Houses" no love was without a grotto.

In the door opening on the Rue de Babylone, there was a box destined for the reception of letters and papers; only, as the three inhabitants of the pavilion in the Rue Plumet received neither papers nor letters, the entire usefulness of that box, formerly the go-between of a love affair, and the confidant of a love-lorn lawyer, was now limited to the tax-collector's notices, and the summons of the guard. For M. Fauchelevent, independent gentleman, belonged to the national guard; he had not been able to escape through the fine meshes of the census of 1831. The municipal information collected at that time had even reached the convent of the Petit-Picpus, a sort of impenetrable and holy cloud, whence Jean Valjean had emerged in venerable guise, and, consequently, worthy of mounting guard in the eyes of the town-hall.

Three or four times a year, Jean Valjean donned his uniform and mounted guard; he did this willingly, however; it was a correct disguise which mixed him with everyone, and yet left him solitary. Jean Valjean had just attained his sixtieth birthday, the age of legal exemption; but he did not appear to be over fifty; moreover, he had no desire to escape his sergeant-major nor to quibble with Comte de Lobau; he possessed no civil status, he was concealing his name, he was concealing his identity, so he concealed his age, he concealed everything; and, as we have just said, he willingly did his duty as a national guard; the sum of his ambition lay in resembling any other man who paid his taxes. This man had for his ideal, within, the angel, without, the bourgeois.

Let us note one detail, however; when Jean Valjean went out with Cosette, he dressed as the reader has already seen, and had the air of a retired officer. When he went out alone, which was generally at night, he was always dressed in a workingman's trousers and blouse, and wore a cap which concealed his face. Was this precaution or humility? Both. Cosette was accustomed to the enigmatical side of her destiny, and hardly noticed her father's peculiarities. As for Toussaint, she venerated Jean Valjean, and thought everything he did right.

One day, her butcher, who had caught a glimpse of Jean Valjean, said to her: "That's a queer fish." She replied: "He's a saint."

Neither Jean Valjean nor Cosette nor Toussaint ever entered or emerged except by the door on the Rue de Babylone. Unless seen through the garden gate it would have been difficult to guess that they lived in the Rue Plumet. That gate was always closed. Jean Valjean had left the garden uncultivated, in order not to attract attention.

In this, possibly, he made a mistake.

Chapter III

FOLIIS AC FRONDIBUS

THE GARDEN THUS LEFT TO ITSELF FOR MORE THAN HALF A CENTURY HAD BECOME EXTRAORDI-nary and charming. The passers-by of forty years ago halted to gaze at it, without a suspicion of the secrets which it hid in its fresh and verdant depths. More than one dreamer of that epoch often allowed his thoughts and his eyes to penetrate indiscreetly between the bars of that ancient, padlocked gate, twisted, tottering, fastened to two green and moss-covered pillars, and oddly crowned with a pediment of undecipherable arabesque.

There was a stone bench in one corner, one or two moldy statues, several lattices which had lost their nails with time, were rotting on the wall, and there were no walks nor turf; but there was enough grass everywhere. Gardening had taken its departure, and nature had returned. Weeds abounded, which was a great piece of luck for a poor corner of land. The festival of gilliflowers was something splendid. Nothing in this garden obstructed the sacred effort of things toward life, venerable growth reigned there among them. The trees had bent over toward the nettles, the plant had sprung upward, the branch had inclined, that which crawls on the earth had gone in search of that which expands in the air, that which floats on the wind had bent over toward that which trails in the moss; trunks, boughs, leaves, fibers, clusters, tendrils, shoots, spines, thorns, had mingled, crossed, married, confounded themselves in each other; vegetation in a deep and close embrace, had celebrated and accomplished there, under the well-pleased eye of the Creator, in that enclosure three hundred feet square, the holy mystery of fraternity, symbol of the human fraternity. This garden was no longer a garden, it was a colossal thicket, that is to say, something as impenetrable as a forest, as peopled as a city, quivering like a nest, somber like a cathedral, fragrant like a bouquet, solitary as a tomb, living as a throng.

In Floréal[1] this enormous thicket, free behind its gate and within its four walls, entered upon the secret labor of germination, quivered in the rising sun, almost like an animal which drinks in the breaths of cosmic love, and which feels the sap of April rising and boiling in its veins, and shakes to the wind its enormous wonderful green locks, sprinkled on the damp earth, on the de-faced statues, on the crumbling steps of the pavilion, and even on the pavement of the deserted street, flowers like stars, dew like pearls, fecundity, beauty, life, joy, perfumes. At midday, a thou-sand white butterflies took refuge there, and it was a divine spectacle to see that living summer snow whirling about there in flakes amid the shade. There, in those gay shadows of verdure, a throng of innocent voices spoke sweetly to the soul, and what the twittering forgot to say the hum-ming completed. In the evening, a dreamy vapor exhaled from the garden and enveloped it; a shroud of mist, a calm and celestial sadness covered it; the intoxicating perfume of the honey-suckles and convolvulus poured out from every part of it, like an exquisite and subtle poison; the last appeals of the woodpeckers and the wagtails were audible as they dozed among the branches; one felt the sacred intimacy of the birds and the trees; by day the wings rejoice the leaves, by night the leaves protect the wings.

In winter the thicket was black, dripping, bristling, shivering, and allowed some glimpse of the house. Instead of flowers on the branches and dew in the flowers, the long silvery tracks of the snails were visible on the cold, thick carpet of yellow leaves; but in any fashion, under any aspect, at all seasons, spring, winter, summer, autumn, this tiny enclosure breathed forth melancholy, con-

1. From April 19 to May 20.

templation, solitude, liberty, the absence of man, the presence of God; and the rusty old gate had the air of saying: "This garden belongs to me."

It was of no avail that the pavements of Paris were there on every side, the classic and splendid hôtels of the Rue de Varennes a couple of paces away, the dome of the Invalides close at hand, the Chamber of Deputies not far off; the carriages of the Rue de Bourgogne and of the Rue Saint-Dominique rumbled luxuriously, in vain, in the vicinity, in vain did the yellow, brown, white, and red omnibuses cross each other's course at the neighboring cross-roads; the Rue Plumet was the desert; and the death of the former proprietors, the revolution which had passed over it, the crumbling away of ancient fortunes, absence, forgetfulness, forty years of abandonment and widowhood, had sufficed to restore to this privileged spot ferns, mulleins, hemlock, yarrow, tall weeds, great crimped plants, with large leaves of pale green cloth, lizards, beetles, uneasy and rapid insects; to cause to spring forth from the depths of the earth and to reappear between these four walls a certain indescribable and savage grandeur; and for nature, which disconcerts the petty arrangements of man, and which sheds herself always thoroughly where she diffuses herself at all, in the ant as well as in the eagle, to blossom out in a petty little Parisian garden with as much rude force and majesty as in a virgin forest of the New World.

Nothing is small, in fact; anyone who is subject to the profound and penetrating influence of nature knows this. Although no absolute satisfaction is given to philosophy, either to circumscribe the cause or to limit the effect, the contemplator falls into those unfathomable ecstasies caused by these decompositions of force terminating in unity. Everything toils at everything.

Algebra is applied to the clouds; the radiation of the star profits the rose; no thinker would venture to affirm that the perfume of the hawthorn is useless to the constellations. Who, then, can calculate the course of a molecule? How do we know that the creation of worlds is not determined by the fall of grains of sand? Who knows the reciprocal ebb and flow of the infinitely great and the infinitely little, the reverberations of causes in the precipices of being, and the avalanches of creation? The tiniest worm is of importance; the great is little, the little is great; everything is balanced in necessity; alarming vision for the mind. There are marvelous relations between beings and things; in that inexhaustible whole, from the sun to the grub, nothing despises the other; all have need of each other. The light does not bear away terrestrial perfumes into the azure depths, without knowing what it is doing; the night distributes stellar essences to the sleeping flowers. All birds that fly have round their leg the thread of the infinite. Germination is complicated with the bursting forth of a meteor and with the peck of a swallow cracking its egg, and it places on one level the birth of an earthworm and the advent of Socrates. Where the telescope ends, the microscope begins. Which of the two possesses the larger field of vision? Choose. A bit of mold is a pleiad of flowers; a nebula is an anthill of stars. The same promiscuousness, and yet more unprecedented, exists between the things of the intelligence and the facts of substance. Elements and principles mingle, combine, wed, multiply, with each other, to such a point that the material and the moral world are brought eventually to the same clearness. The phenomenon is perpetually returning upon itself. In the vast cosmic exchanges the universal life goes and comes in unknown quantities, rolling entirely in the invisible mystery of effluvia, employing everything, not losing a single dream, not a single slumber, sowing an animalcule here, crumbling to bits a planet there, oscillating and winding, making of light a force and of thought an element, disseminated and invisible, dissolving all, except that geometrical point, the *I*; bringing everything back to the soul-atom; expanding everything in God, entangling all activity, from summit to base, in the obscurity of a dizzy mechanism, attaching the flight of an insect to the movement of the earth, subordinating, who knows? Were it only by the identity of the law, the evolution of the comet in the firmament to the whirling of the infusoria in the drop of water. A machine made of mind. Enormous gearing, the prime motor of which is the gnat, and whose final wheel is the zodiac.

Chapter IV

CHANGE OF GATE

IT SEEMED THAT THIS GARDEN, CREATED IN OLDEN DAYS TO CONCEAL WANTON MYSTERIES, HAD been transformed and become fitted to shelter chaste mysteries. There were no longer either arbors, or bowling greens, or tunnels, or grottos; there was a magnificent, disheveled obscurity falling like a veil over all. Paphos had been made over into Eden. It is impossible to say what element of repentance had rendered this retreat wholesome. This flower-girl now offered her blossom to the soul. This coquettish garden, formerly decidedly compromised, had returned to virginity and modesty. A justice assisted by a gardener, a good man who thought that he was a continuation of Lamoignon, and another good man who thought that he was a continuation of Lenôtre, had turned it about, cut, ruffled, decked, molded it to gallantry; nature had taken possession of it once more, had filled it with shade, and had arranged it for love.

There was, also, in this solitude, a heart which was quite ready. Love had only to show himself; he had here a temple composed of verdure, grass, moss, the sight of birds, tender shadows, agitated branches, and a soul made of sweetness, of faith, of candor, of hope, of aspiration, and of illusion.

Cosette had left the convent when she was still almost a child; she was a little more than fourteen, and she was at the "ungrateful age"; we have already said, that with the exception of her eyes, she was homely rather than pretty; she had no ungraceful feature, but she was awkward, thin, timid and bold at once, a grown-up little girl, in short.

Her education was finished, that is to say, she has been taught religion, and even and above all, devotion; then "history," that is to say the thing that bears that name in convents, geography, grammar, the participles, the kings of France, a little music, a little drawing, etc.; but in all other respects she was utterly ignorant, which is a great charm and a great peril. The soul of a young girl should not be left in the dark; later on, mirages that are too abrupt and too lively are formed there, as in a dark chamber. She should be gently and discreetly enlightened, rather with the reflection of realities than with their harsh and direct light. A useful and graciously austere half-light which dissipates puerile fears and obviates falls. There is nothing but the maternal instinct, that admirable intuition composed of the memories of the virgin and the experience of the woman, which knows how this half-light is to be created and of what it should consist.

Nothing supplies the place of this instinct. All the nuns in the world are not worth as much as one mother in the formation of a young girl's soul.

Cosette had had no mother. She had only had many mothers, in the plural.

As for Jean Valjean, he was, indeed, all tenderness, all solicitude; but he was only an old man and he knew nothing at all.

Now, in this work of education, in this grave matter of preparing a woman for life, what science is required to combat that vast ignorance which is called innocence!

Nothing prepares a young girl for passions like the convent. The convent turns the thoughts in the direction of the unknown. The heart, thus thrown back upon itself, works downward within itself, since it cannot overflow, and grows deep, since it cannot expand. Hence visions, suppositions, conjectures, outlines of romances, a desire for adventures, fantastic constructions, edifices built wholly in the inner obscurity of the mind, somber and secret abodes where the passions immediately find a lodgement as soon as the open gate permits them to enter. The convent is a compression which, in order to triumph over the human heart, should last during the whole life.

On quitting the convent, Cosette could have found nothing more sweet and more dangerous than the house in the Rue Plumet. It was the continuation of solitude with the beginning of liberty; a garden that was closed, but a nature that was acrid, rich, voluptuous, and fragrant; the same dreams as in the convent, but with glimpses of young men; a grating, but one that opened on the street.

Still, when she arrived there, we repeat, she was only a child. Jean Valjean gave this neglected garden over to her. "Do what you like with it," he said to her. This amused Cosette; she turned over all the clumps and all the stones, she hunted for "beasts"; she played in it, while awaiting the time when she would dream in it; she loved this garden for the insects that she found beneath her feet amid the grass, while awaiting the day when she would love it for the stars that she would see through the boughs above her head.

And then, she loved her father, that is to say, Jean Valjean, with all her soul, with an innocent filial passion which made the good man a beloved and charming companion to her. It will be remembered that M. Madeleine had been in the habit of reading a great deal. Jean Valjean had continued this practice; he had come to converse well; he possessed the secret riches and the eloquence of a true and humble mind which has spontaneously cultivated itself. He retained just enough sharpness to season his kindness; his mind was rough and his heart was soft. During their conversations in the Luxembourg, he gave her explanations of everything, drawing on what he had read, and also on what he had suffered. As she listened to him, Cosette's eyes wandered vaguely about.

This simple man sufficed for Cosette's thought, the same as the wild garden sufficed for her eyes. When she had had a good chase after the butterflies, she came panting up to him and said: "Ah! How I have run!" He kissed her brow.

Cosette adored the good man. She was always at his heels. Where Jean Valjean was, there happiness was. Jean Valjean lived neither in the pavilion nor the garden; she took greater pleasure in the paved back courtyard, than in the enclosure filled with flowers, and in his little lodge furnished with straw-seated chairs than in the great drawing-room hung with tapestry, against which stood tufted easy-chairs. Jean Valjean sometimes said to her, smiling at his happiness in being importuned: "Do go to your own quarters! Leave me alone a little!"

She gave him those charming and tender scoldings which are so graceful when they come from a daughter to her father.

"Father, I am very cold in your rooms; why don't you have a carpet here and a stove?"

"Dear child, there are so many people who are better than I and who have not even a roof over their heads."

"Then why is there a fire in my rooms, and everything that is needed?"

"Because you are a woman and a child."

"Bah! must men be cold and feel uncomfortable?"

"Certain men."

"That is good, I shall come here so often that you will be obliged to have a fire."

And again she said to him:

"Father, why do you eat horrible bread like that?"

"Because, my daughter."

"Well, if you eat it, I will eat it too."

Then, in order to prevent Cosette eating black bread, Jean Valjean ate white bread.

Cosette had but a confused recollection of her childhood. She prayed morning and evening for her mother whom she had never known. The Thénardiers had remained with her as two hideous figures in a dream. She remembered that she had gone "one day, at night" to fetch water in a forest. She thought that it had been very far from Paris. It seemed to her that she had begun to live in an abyss, and that it was Jean Valjean who had rescued her from it. Her childhood produced upon her the effect of a time when there had been nothing around her but millipedes, spiders, and serpents. When she meditated in the evening, before falling asleep, as she had not a very clear idea that she was Jean Valjean's daughter, and that he was her father, she fancied that the soul of her mother had passed into that good man and had come to dwell near her.

When he was seated, she leaned her cheek against his white hair, and dropped a silent tear, saying to herself: "Perhaps this man is my mother."

Cosette, although this is a strange statement to make, in the profound ignorance of a girl brought up in a convent—maternity being also absolutely unintelligible to virginity—had ended by fancying that she had had as little mother as possible. She did not even know her mother's name. Whenever she asked Jean Valjean, Jean Valjean remained silent. If she repeated her question, he responded with a smile. Once she insisted; the smile ended in a tear.

This silence on the part of Jean Valjean covered Fantine with darkness.

Was it prudence? Was it respect? Was it a fear that he should deliver this name to the hazards of another memory than his own?

So long as Cosette had been small, Jean Valjean had been willing to talk to her of her mother; when she became a young girl, it was impossible for him to do so. It seemed to him that he no longer dared. Was it because of Cosette? Was it because of Fantine? He felt a certain religious horror at letting that shadow enter Cosette's thought; and of placing a third in their destiny. The more sacred this shade was to him, the more did it seem that it was to be feared. He thought of Fantine, and felt himself overwhelmed with silence.

Through the darkness, he vaguely perceived something which appeared to have its finger on its lips. Had all the modesty which had been in Fantine, and which had violently quitted her during her lifetime, returned to rest upon her after her death, to watch in indignation over the peace of that dead woman, and in its shyness, to keep her in her grave? Was Jean Valjean unconsciously submitting to the pressure? We who believe in death, are not among the number who will reject this mysterious explanation.

Hence the impossibility of uttering, even for Cosette, that name of Fantine.

One day Cosette said to him:

"Father, I saw my mother in a dream last night. She had two big wings. My mother must have been almost a saint during her life."

"Through martyrdom," replied Jean Valjean.

However, Jean Valjean was happy.

When Cosette went out with him, she leaned on his arm, proud and happy, in the plenitude of her heart. Jean Valjean felt his heart melt within him with delight, at all these sparks of a tenderness so exclusive, so wholly satisfied with himself alone. The poor man trembled, inundated with angelic joy; he declared to himself ecstatically that this would last all their lives; he told himself that he really had not suffered sufficiently to merit so radiant a bliss, and he thanked God, in the depths of his soul, for having permitted him to be loved thus, he, a wretch, by that innocent being.

Chapter V

THE ROSE PERCEIVES THAT IT IS AN ENGINE OF WAR

ONE DAY, COSETTE CHANCED TO LOOK AT HERSELF IN HER MIRROR, AND SHE SAID TO HERSELF: "Really!" it seemed to her almost that she was pretty. This threw her in a singularly troubled state of mind. Up to that moment she had never thought of her face. She saw herself in her mirror, but she did not look at herself. And then, she had so often been told that she was homely; Jean Valjean alone said gently: "No indeed! no indeed!" At all events, Cosette had always thought herself homely, and had grown up in that belief with the easy resignation of childhood. And here, all at once, was her mirror saying to her, as Jean Valjean had said: "No indeed!" That night, she did not sleep. "What if I were pretty!" she thought. "How odd it would be if I were pretty!" And she recalled those of her companions whose beauty had produced a sensation in the convent, and she said to herself: "What! Am I to be like Mademoiselle So-and-So!"

The next morning she looked at herself again, not by accident this time, and she was assailed with doubts: "Where did I get such an idea?" said she; "no, I am ugly." She had not slept well, that was all, her eyes were sunken and she was pale. She had not felt very joyous on the preceding evening in the belief that she was beautiful, but it made her very sad not to be able to believe in it any longer. She did not look at herself again, and for more than a fortnight, she tried to dress her hair with her back turned to the mirror.

In the evening, after dinner, she generally embroidered in wool or did some convent needle-work in the drawing-room, and Jean Valjean read beside her. Once she raised her eyes from her work, and was rendered quite uneasy by the manner in which her father was gazing at her.

On another occasion, she was passing along the street, and it seemed to her that someone behind her, whom she did not see, said: "A pretty woman! but badly dressed." "Bah!" she thought, "he does not mean me. I am well dressed and ugly." She was then wearing a plush hat and her merino gown.

At last, one day when she was in the garden, she heard poor old Toussaint saying: "Do you notice how pretty Cosette is growing, sir?" Cosette did not hear her father's reply, but Toussaint's words caused a sort of commotion within her. She fled from the garden, ran up to her room, flew to the looking-glass—it was three months since she had looked at herself—and gave vent to a cry. She had just dazzled herself.

She was beautiful and lovely; she could not help agreeing with Toussaint and her mirror. Her figure was formed, her skin had grown white, her hair was lustrous, an unaccustomed splendor had been lighted in her blue eyes. The consciousness of her beauty burst upon her in an instant, like the sudden advent of daylight; other people noticed it also, Toussaint had said so, it was evidently she of whom the passer-by had spoken, there could no longer be any doubt of that; she descended to the garden again, thinking herself a queen, imagining that she heard the birds singing, though it was winter, seeing the sky gilded, the sun among the trees, flowers in the thickets, distracted, wild, in inexpressible delight.

Jean Valjean, on his side, experienced a deep and undefinable oppression at heart.

In fact, he had, for some time past, been contemplating with terror that beauty which seemed to grow more radiant every day on Cosette's sweet face. The dawn that was smiling for all was gloomy for him.

Cosette had been beautiful for a tolerably long time before she became aware of it herself. But, from the very first day, that unexpected light which was rising slowly and enveloping the whole of the young girl's person, wounded Jean Valjean's somber eye. He felt that it was a change in a happy life, a life so happy that he did not dare to move for fear of disarranging something. This man, who had passed through all manner of distresses, who was still all bleeding from the bruises of fate, who had been almost wicked and who had become almost a saint, who, after having dragged the chain of the galleys, was now dragging the invisible but heavy chain of indefinite misery, this man whom the law had not released from its grasp and who could be seized at any moment and brought back from the obscurity of his virtue to the broad daylight of public opprobrium, this man accepted all, excused all, pardoned all, and merely asked of Providence, of man, of the law, of society, of nature, of the world, one thing, that Cosette might love him!

That Cosette might continue to love him! That God would not prevent the heart of the child from coming to him, and from remaining with him! Beloved by Cosette, he felt that he was healed, rested, appeased, loaded with benefits, recompensed, crowned. Beloved by Cosette, it was well with him! He asked nothing more! Had anyone said to him: "Do you want anything better?" he would have answered: "No." God might have said to him: "Do you desire heaven?" and he would have replied: "I should lose by it."

Everything which could affect this situation, if only on the surface, made him shudder like the beginning of something new. He had never known very distinctly himself what the beauty of a woman means; but he understood, instinctively, that it was something terrible.

He gazed with terror on this beauty, which was blossoming out ever more triumphant and superb beside him, beneath his very eyes, on the innocent and formidable brow of that child, from the depths of her homeliness, of his old age, of his misery, of his reprobation.

He said to himself: "How beautiful she is! What is to become of me?"

There, moreover, lay the difference between his tenderness and the tenderness of a mother. What he beheld with anguish, a mother would have gazed upon with joy.

The first symptoms were not long in making their appearance.

On the very morrow of the day on which she had said to herself: "Decidedly I am beautiful!" Cosette began to pay attention to her toilet. She recalled the remark of that passer-by: "Pretty, but badly dressed," the breath of an oracle which had passed beside her and had vanished, after depositing in her heart one of the two germs which are destined, later on, to fill the whole life of woman, coquetry. Love is the other.

With faith in her beauty, the whole feminine soul expanded within her. She conceived a horror for her merinos, and shame for her plush hat. Her father had never refused her anything. She at once acquired the whole science of the bonnet, the gown, the mantle, the boot, the cuff, the stuff which is in fashion, the color which is becoming, that science which makes of the Parisian woman something so charming, so deep, and so dangerous. The words *heady woman* were invented for the Parisienne.

In less than a month, little Cosette, in that Thebaid of the Rue de Babylone was not only one of the prettiest, but one of the "best dressed" women in Paris, which means a great deal more.

She would have liked to encounter her "passer-by," to see what he would say, and to "teach him a lesson!" The truth is, that she was ravishing in every respect, and that she distinguished the difference between a bonnet from Gérard and one from Herbaut in the most marvelous way.

Jean Valjean watched these ravages with anxiety. He who felt that he could never do anything but crawl, walk at the most, beheld wings sprouting on Cosette.

Moreover, from the mere inspection of Cosette's toilet, a woman would have recognized the fact that she had no mother. Certain little proprieties, certain special conventionalities, were not observed by Cosette. A mother, for instance, would have told her that a young girl does not dress in damask.

The first day that Cosette went out in her black damask gown and mantle, and her white crape bonnet, she took Jean Valjean's arm, gay, radiant, rosy, proud, dazzling. "Father," she said, "how do you like me in this guise?" Jean Valjean replied in a voice which resembled the bitter voice of an envious man: "Charming!" He was the same as usual during their walk. On their return home, he asked Cosette:

"Won't you put on that other gown and bonnet again—you know the ones I mean?"

This took place in Cosette's chamber. Cosette turned toward the wardrobe where her cast-off schoolgirl's clothes were hanging.

"That disguise!" said she. "Father, what do you want me to do with it? Oh no, the idea! I shall never put on those horrors again. With that machine on my head, I have the air of Madame Maddog."

Jean Valjean heaved a deep sigh.

From that moment forth, he noticed that Cosette, who had always heretofore asked to remain at home, saying: "Father, I enjoy myself more here with you," now was always asking to go out. In fact, what is the use of having a handsome face and a delicious costume if one does not display them?

He also noticed that Cosette had no longer the same taste for the back garden. Now she preferred the garden, and did not dislike to promenade back and forth in front of the railed fence. Jean Valjean, who was shy, never set foot in the garden. He kept to his backyard, like a dog.

Cosette, in gaining the knowledge that she was beautiful, lost the grace of ignoring it. An exquisite grace, for beauty enhanced by ingenuousness is ineffable, and nothing is so adorable as a dazzling and innocent creature who walks along, holding in her hand the key to paradise without being conscious of it. But what she had lost in ingenuous grace, she gained in pensive and serious charm. Her whole person, permeated with the joy of youth, of innocence, and of beauty, breathed forth a splendid melancholy.

It was at this epoch that Marius, after the lapse of six months, saw her once more at the Luxembourg.

Chapter VI

THE BATTLE BEGUN

COSETTE IN HER SHADOW, LIKE MARIUS IN HIS, WAS ALL READY TO TAKE FIRE. DESTINY, WITH ITS mysterious and fatal patience, slowly drew together these two beings, all charged and all languishing with the stormy electricity of passion, these two souls which were laden with love as two clouds are laden with lightning, and which were bound to overflow and mingle in a look like the clouds in a flash of fire.

The glance has been so much abused in love romances that it has finally fallen into disrepute. One hardly dares to say, nowadays, that two beings fell in love because they looked at each other. That is the way people do fall in love, nevertheless, and the only way. The rest is nothing, but the rest comes afterwards. Nothing is more real than these great shocks which two souls convey to each other by the exchange of that spark.

At that particular hour when Cosette unconsciously darted that glance which troubled Marius, Marius had no suspicion that he had also launched a look which disturbed Cosette.

He caused her the same good and the same evil.

She had been in the habit of seeing him for a long time, and she had scrutinized him as girls scrutinize and see, while looking elsewhere. Marius still considered Cosette ugly, when she had already begun to think Marius handsome. But as he paid no attention to her, the young man was nothing to her.

Still, she could not refrain from saying to herself that he had beautiful hair, beautiful eyes, handsome teeth, a charming tone of voice when she heard him conversing with his comrades, that he held himself badly when he walked, if you like, but with a grace that was all his own, that he did not appear to be at all stupid, that his whole person was noble, gentle, simple, proud, and that, in short, though he seemed to be poor, yet his air was fine.

On the day when their eyes met at last, and said to each other those first, obscure, and ineffable things which the glance lisps, Cosette did not immediately understand. She returned thoughtfully to the house in the Rue de l'Ouest, where Jean Valjean, according to his custom, had come to spend six weeks. The next morning, on waking, she thought of that strange young man, so long indifferent and icy, who now seemed to pay attention to her, and it did not appear to her that this attention was the least in the world agreeable to her. She was, on the contrary, somewhat incensed at this handsome and disdainful individual. A substratum of war stirred within her. It struck her, and the idea caused her a wholly childish joy, that she was going to take her revenge at last.

Knowing that she was beautiful, she was thoroughly conscious, though in an indistinct fashion, that she possessed a weapon. Women play with their beauty as children do with a knife. They wound themselves.

The reader will recall Marius's hesitations, his palpitations, his terrors. He remained on his bench and did not approach. This vexed Cosette. One day, she said to Jean Valjean: "Father, let us stroll about a little in that direction." Seeing that Marius did not come to her, she went to him. In such cases, all women resemble Mahomet. And then, strange to say, the first symptom of true love in a young man is timidity; in a young girl it is boldness. This is surprising, and yet nothing is more simple. It is the two sexes tending to approach each other and assuming, each the other's qualities.

That day, Cosette's glance drove Marius beside himself, and Marius's glance set Cosette to trembling. Marius went away confident, and Cosette uneasy. From that day forth, they adored each other.

The first thing that Cosette felt was a confused and profound melancholy. It seemed to her that her soul had become black since the day before. She no longer recognized it. The whiteness of soul in young girls, which is composed of coldness and gaiety, resembles snow. It melts in love, which is its sun.

Cosette did not know what love was. She had never heard the word uttered in its terrestrial sense. On the books of profane music which entered the convent, *amour* (love) was replaced by *tambour* (drum) or *pandour*. This created enigmas which exercised the imaginations of the *big girls,* such as: *Ah, how delightful is the drum!* or, *Pity is not a pandour.* But Cosette had left the convent too early to have occupied herself much with the "drum." Therefore, she did not know what name to give to what she now felt. Is anyone the less ill because one does not know the name of one's malady?

She loved with all the more passion because she loved ignorantly. She did not know whether it was a good thing or a bad thing, useful or dangerous, eternal or temporary, allowable or prohibited; she loved. She would have been greatly astonished, had anyone said to her: "You do not sleep? But that is forbidden! You do not eat? Why, that is very bad! You have oppressions and palpitations of the heart! That must not be! You blush and turn pale, when a certain being clad in black appears at the end of a certain green walk? But that is abominable!" She would not have understood, and she would have replied: "What fault is there of mine in a matter in which I have no power and of which I know nothing?"

It turned out that the love which presented itself was exactly suited to the state of her soul. It was a sort of admiration at a distance, a mute contemplation, the deification of a stranger. It was the apparition of youth to youth, the dream of nights become a reality yet remaining a dream, the longed-for phantom realized and made flesh at last, but having as yet, neither name, nor fault, nor spot, nor exigence, nor defect; in a word, the distant lover who lingered in the ideal, a chimera with a form. Any nearer and more palpable meeting would have alarmed Cosette at this first stage, when she was still half immersed in the exaggerated mists of the cloister. She had all the fears of children and all the fears of nuns combined. The spirit of the convent, with which she had been permeated for the space of five years, was still in the process of slow evaporation from her person, and made everything tremble around her. In this situation he was not a lover, he was not even an admirer, he was a vision. She set herself to adoring Marius as something charming, luminous, and impossible.

As extreme innocence borders on extreme coquetry, she smiled at him with all frankness.

Every day, she looked forward to the hour for their walk with impatience, she found Marius there, she felt herself unspeakably happy, and thought in all sincerity that she was expressing her whole thought when she said to Jean Valjean:

"What a delicious garden that Luxembourg is!"

Marius and Cosette were in the dark as to one another. They did not address each other, they did not salute each other, they did not know each other; they saw each other; and like stars of heaven which are separated by millions of leagues, they lived by gazing at each other.

It was thus that Cosette gradually became a woman and developed, beautiful and loving, with a consciousness of her beauty, and in ignorance of her love. She was a coquette to boot through her ignorance.

<h1 style="text-align:center">Chapter VII</h1>

<h2 style="text-align:center">TO ONE SADNESS OPPOSE A SADNESS AND A HALF</h2>

ALL SITUATIONS HAVE THEIR INSTINCTS. OLD AND ETERNAL MOTHER NATURE WARNED JEAN VAL-jean in a dim way of the presence of Marius. Jean Valjean shuddered to the very bottom of his soul. Jean Valjean saw nothing, knew nothing, and yet he scanned with obstinate attention, the darkness in which he walked, as though he felt on one side of him something in process of construction, and on the other, something which was crumbling away. Marius, also warned, and, in accordance with the deep law of God, by that same Mother Nature, did all he could to keep out of sight of "the father." Nevertheless, it came to pass that Jean Valjean sometimes spied him. Marius's manners were no longer in the least natural. He exhibited ambiguous prudence and awkward daring. He no longer came quite close to them as formerly. He seated himself at a distance and pretended to be reading; why did he pretend that? Formerly he had come in his old coat, now he wore his new one every day; Jean Valjean was not sure that he did not have his hair curled, his eyes were very queer, he wore gloves; in short, Jean Valjean cordially detested this young man.

Cosette allowed nothing to be divined. Without knowing just what was the matter with her she was convinced that there was something in it, and that it must be concealed.

There was a coincidence between the taste for the toilet which had recently come to Cosette, and the habit of new clothes developed by that stranger which was very repugnant to Jean Valjean. It might be accidental, no doubt, certainly, but it was a menacing accident.

He never opened his mouth to Cosette about this stranger. One day, however, he could not refrain from so doing, and, with that vague despair which suddenly casts the lead into the depths of its despair, he said to her: "What a very pedantic air that young man has!"

Cosette, but a year before only an indifferent little girl, would have replied: "Why, no, he is charming." Ten years later, with the love of Marius in her heart, she would have answered: "A pedant, and insufferable to the sight! You are right!"—At the moment in life and the heart which she had then attained, she contented herself with replying, with supreme calmness: "That young man!"

As though she now beheld him for the first time in her life.

"How stupid I am!" thought Jean Valjean. "She had not noticed him. It is I who have pointed him out to her."

Oh, simplicity of the old! oh, the depth of children!

It is one of the laws of those fresh years of suffering and trouble, of those vivacious conflicts between a first love and the first obstacles, that the young girl does not allow herself to be caught in any trap whatever, and that the young man falls into every one. Jean Valjean had instituted an undeclared war against Marius, which Marius, with the sublime stupidity of his passion and his age, did not divine. Jean Valjean laid a host of ambushes for him; he changed his hour, he changed his bench, he forgot his handkerchief, he came alone to the Luxembourg; Marius dashed headlong into all these snares; and to all the interrogation marks planted by Jean Valjean in his pathway, he ingenuously answered "yes." But Cosette remained immured in her apparent unconcern and in her imperturbable tranquility, so that Jean Valjean arrived at the following conclusion: "That ninny is madly in love with Cosette, but Cosette does not even know that he exists."

None the less did he bear in his heart a mournful tremor. The minute when Cosette would love might strike at any moment. Does not everything begin with indifference?

Only once did Cosette make a mistake and alarm him. He rose from his seat to depart, after a stay of three hours, and she said: "What, already?"

Jean Valjean had not discontinued his trips to the Luxembourg, as he did not wish to do anything out of the way, and as, above all things, he feared to arouse Cosette; but during the hours which were so sweet to the lovers, while Cosette was sending her smile to the intoxicated Marius, who perceived nothing else now, and who now saw nothing in all the world but an adored and radiant face, Jean Valjean was fixing on Marius flashing and terrible eyes. He, who had finally come to believe himself incapable of a malevolent feeling, experienced moments when Marius was present, in which he thought he was becoming savage and ferocious once more, and he felt the old depths of his soul, which had formerly contained so much wrath, opening once more and rising up against that young man. It almost seemed to him that unknown craters were forming in his bosom.

What! he was there, that creature! What was he there for? He came creeping about, smelling out, examining, trying! He came, saying: "Hey! Why not?" He came to prowl about his, Jean Valjean's, life! to prowl about his happiness, with the purpose of seizing it and bearing it away!

Jean Valjean added: "Yes, that's it! What is he in search of? An adventure! What does he want? A love affair! A love affair! And I? What! I have been first, the most wretched of men, and then the most unhappy, and I have traversed sixty years of life on my knees, I have suffered everything that man can suffer, I have grown old without having been young, I have lived without a family, without relatives, without friends, without life, without children, I have left my blood on every stone, on every bramble, on every mile-post, along every wall, I have been gentle, though others have been hard to me, and kind, although others have been malicious, I have become an honest man once more, in spite of everything, I have repented of the evil that I have done and have forgiven the evil that has been done to me, and at the moment when I receive my recompense, at the moment when it is all over, at the moment when I am just touching the goal, at the moment when I have what I desire, it is well, it is good, I have paid, I have earned it, all this is to take flight, all this will vanish, and I shall lose Cosette, and I shall lose my life, my joy, my soul, because it has pleased a great booby to come and lounge at the Luxembourg."

Then his eyes were filled with a sad and extraordinary gleam.

It was no longer a man gazing at a man; it was no longer an enemy surveying an enemy. It was a dog scanning a thief.

The reader knows the rest. Marius pursued his senseless course. One day he followed Cosette to the Rue de l'Ouest. Another day he spoke to the porter. The porter, on his side, spoke, and said to Jean Valjean: "Monsieur, who is that curious young man who is asking for you?" On the morrow Jean Valjean bestowed on Marius that glance which Marius at last perceived. A week later, Jean Valjean had taken his departure. He swore to himself that he would never again set foot either in the Luxembourg or in the Rue de l'Ouest. He returned to the Rue Plumet.

Cosette did not complain, she said nothing, she asked no questions, she did not seek to learn his reasons; she had already reached the point where she was afraid of being divined, and of betraying herself. Jean Valjean had no experience of these miseries, the only miseries which are charming and the only ones with which he was not acquainted; the consequence was that he did not understand the grave significance of Cosette's silence.

He merely noticed that she had grown sad, and he grew gloomy. On his side and on hers, inexperience had joined issue.

Once he made a trial. He asked Cosette:

"Would you like to come to the Luxembourg?"

A ray illuminated Cosette's pale face.

"Yes," said she.

They went thither. Three months had elapsed. Marius no longer went there. Marius was not there.

On the following day, Jean Valjean asked Cosette again:

"Would you like to come to the Luxembourg?"

She replied, sadly and gently:

"No."

Jean Valjean was hurt by this sadness, and heart-broken at this gentleness.

What was going on in that mind which was so young and yet already so impenetrable? What was on its way there within? What was taking place in Cosette's soul? Sometimes, instead of going to bed, Jean Valjean remained seated on his pallet, with his head in his hands, and he passed whole nights asking himself: "What has Cosette in her mind?" and in thinking of the things that she might be thinking about.

Oh! at such moments, what mournful glances did he cast toward that cloister, that chaste peak, that abode of angels, that inaccessible glacier of virtue! How he contemplated, with despairing ecstasy, that convent garden, full of ignored flowers and cloistered virgins, where all perfumes and all souls mount straight to heaven! How he adored that Eden forever closed against him, whence he had voluntarily and madly emerged! How he regretted his abnegation and his folly in having brought Cosette back into the world, poor hero of sacrifice, seized and hurled to the earth by his very self-devotion! How he said to himself: "What have I done?"

However, nothing of all this was perceptible to Cosette. No ill-temper, no harshness. His face was always serene and kind. Jean Valjean's manners were more tender and more paternal than ever. If anything could have betrayed his lack of joy, it was his increased suavity.

On her side, Cosette languished. She suffered from the absence of Marius as she had rejoiced in his presence, peculiarly, without exactly being conscious of it. When Jean Valjean ceased to take her on their customary strolls, a feminine instinct murmured confusedly, at the bottom of her heart, that she must not seem to set store on the Luxembourg garden, and that if this proved to be a matter of indifference to her, her father would take her thither once more. But days, weeks, months, elapsed. Jean Valjean had tacitly accepted Cosette's tacit consent. She regretted it. It was too late. So Marius had disappeared; all was over. The day on which she returned to the Luxembourg, Marius was no longer there. What was to be done? Should she ever find him again? She felt an anguish at her heart, which nothing relieved, and which augmented every day; she no longer knew whether it was winter or summer, whether it was raining or shining, whether the birds were singing, whether it was the season for dahlias or daisies, whether the Luxembourg was more charming than the Tuileries, whether the linen which the laundress brought home was starched too much or not enough, whether Toussaint had done "her marketing" well or ill; and she remained dejected, absorbed, attentive to but a single thought, her eyes vague and staring, as when one gazes by night at a black and fathomless spot where an apparition has vanished.

However, she did not allow Jean Valjean to perceive anything of this, except her pallor.

She still wore her sweet face for him.

This pallor sufficed but too thoroughly to trouble Jean Valjean. Sometimes he asked her:

"What is the matter with you?"

She replied: "There is nothing the matter with me."

And after a silence, when she divined that he was sad also, she would add:

"And you, father—is there anything wrong with you?"

"With me? Nothing," said he.

These two beings who had loved each other so exclusively, and with so touching an affection, and who had lived so long for each other, now suffered side by side, each on the other's account; without acknowledging it to each other, without anger toward each other, and with a smile.

Chapter VIII

THE CHAIN-GANG

JEAN VALJEAN WAS THE MORE UNHAPPY OF THE TWO. YOUTH, EVEN IN ITS SORROWS, ALWAYS POSsesses its own peculiar radiance.

At times, Jean Valjean suffered so greatly that he became puerile. It is the property of grief to cause the childish side of man to reappear. He had an unconquerable conviction that Cosette was escaping from him. He would have liked to resist, to retain her, to arouse her enthusiasm by some external and brilliant matter. These ideas, puerile as we have just said, and at the same time senile, conveyed to him, by their very childishness, a tolerably just notion of the influence of gold lace on the imaginations of young girls. He once chanced to see a general on horseback, in full uniform, pass along the street, Comte Coutard, the commandant of Paris. He envied that gilded man; what happiness it would be, he said to himself, if he could put on that suit which was an incontestable thing; and if Cosette could behold him thus, she would be dazzled, and when he had Cosette on his arm and passed the gates of the Tuileries, the guard would present arms to him, and that would suffice for Cosette, and would dispel her idea of looking at young men.

An unforeseen shock was added to these sad reflections.

In the isolated life which they led, and since they had come to dwell in the Rue Plumet, they had contracted one habit. They sometimes took a pleasure trip to see the sun rise, a mild species of enjoyment which befits those who are entering life and those who are quitting it.

For those who love solitude, a walk in the early morning is equivalent to a stroll by night, with the cheerfulness of nature added. The streets are deserted and the birds are singing. Cosette, a bird herself, liked to rise early. These matutinal excursions were planned on the preceding evening. He proposed, and she agreed. It was arranged like a plot, they set out before daybreak, and these trips were so many small delights for Cosette. These innocent eccentricities please young people.

Jean Valjean's inclination led him, as we have seen, to the least frequented spots, to solitary nooks, to forgotten places. There then existed, in the vicinity of the barriers of Paris, a sort of poor meadows, which were almost confounded with the city, where grew in summer sickly grain, and which, in autumn, after the harvest had been gathered, presented the appearance, not of having been reaped, but peeled. Jean Valjean loved to haunt these fields. Cosette was not bored there. It meant solitude to him and liberty to her. There, she became a little girl once more, she could run and almost play; she took off her hat, laid it on Jean Valjean's knees, and gathered bunches of flowers. She gazed at the butterflies on the flowers, but did not catch them; gentleness and tenderness are born with love, and the young girl who cherishes within her breast a trembling and fragile ideal has mercy on the wing of a butterfly. She wove garlands of poppies, which she placed on her head, and which, crossed and penetrated with sunlight, glowing until they flamed, formed for her rosy face a crown of burning embers.

Even after their life had grown sad, they kept up their custom of early strolls.

One morning in October, therefore, tempted by the serene perfection of the autumn of 1831, they set out, and found themselves at break of day near the Barrière du Maine. It was not dawn, it was daybreak; a delightful and stern moment. A few constellations here and there in the deep, pale azure, the earth all black, the heavens all white, a quiver amid the blades of grass, everywhere the mysterious chill of twilight. A lark, which seemed mingled with the stars, was caroling at a prodigious height, and one would have declared that that hymn of pettiness calmed immensity. In the East, the Val-de-Grâce projected its dark mass on the clear horizon with the sharpness of steel; Venus dazzlingly brilliant was rising behind that dome and had the air of a soul making its escape from a gloomy edifice.

All was peace and silence; there was no one on the road; a few stray laborers, of whom they caught barely a glimpse, were on their way to their work along the side-paths.

Jean Valjean was sitting in a cross-walk on some planks deposited at the gate of a timber-yard. His face was turned toward the highway, his back toward the light; he had forgotten the sun which was on the point of rising; he had sunk into one of those profound absorptions in which the mind becomes concentrated, which imprison even the eye, and which are equivalent to four walls. There are meditations which may be called vertical; when one is at the bottom of them, time is required to return to earth. Jean Valjean had plunged into one of these reveries. He was thinking of Cosette, of the happiness that was possible if nothing came between him and her, of the light with which she filled his life, a light which was but the emanation of her soul. He was almost happy in his reverie. Cosette, who was standing beside him, was gazing at the clouds as they turned rosy.

All at once Cosette exclaimed: "Father, I should think someone was coming yonder." Jean Valjean raised his eyes.

Cosette was right. The causeway which leads to the ancient Barrière du Maine is a prolongation, as the reader knows, of the Rue de Sèvres, and is cut at right angles by the inner boulevard. At the elbow of the causeway and the boulevard, at the spot where it branches, they heard a noise which it was difficult to account for at that hour, and a sort of confused pile made its appearance. Some shapeless thing which was coming from the boulevard was turning into the road.

It grew larger, it seemed to move in an orderly manner, though it was bristling and quivering; it seemed to be a vehicle, but its load could not be distinctly made out. There were horses, wheels, shouts; whips were cracking. By degrees the outlines became fixed, although bathed in shadows. It was a vehicle, in fact, which had just turned from the boulevard into the highway, and which was directing its course toward the barrier near which sat Jean Valjean; a second, of the same aspect followed, then a third, then a fourth; seven chariots made their appearance in succession, the heads of the horses touching the rear of the wagon in front. Figures were moving on these vehicles, flashes were visible through the dusk as though there were naked swords there, a clanking became audible which resembled the rattling of chains, and as this something advanced, the sound of voices waxed louder, and it turned into a terrible thing such as emerges from the cave of dreams.

As it drew nearer, it assumed a form, and was outlined behind the trees with the pallid hue of an apparition; the mass grew white; the day, which was slowly dawning, cast a wan light on this swarming heap which was at once both sepulchral and living, the heads of the figures turned into the faces of corpses, and this is what it proved to be:

Seven wagons were driving in a file along the road. The first six were singularly constructed. They resembled coopers' drays; they consisted of long ladders placed on two wheels and forming barrows at their rear extremities. Each dray, or rather let us say, each ladder, was attached to four horses harnessed tandem. On these ladders strange clusters of men were being drawn. In the faint light, these men were to be divined rather than seen. Twenty-four on each vehicle, twelve on a side, back to back, facing the passers-by, their legs dangling in the air—this was the manner in which these men were traveling, and behind their backs they had something which clanked, and which was a chain, and on their necks something which shone, and which was an iron collar. Each man had his collar, but the chain was for all; so that if these four-and-twenty men had occasion to alight from the dray and walk, they were seized with a sort of inexorable unity, and were obliged to wind over the ground with the chain for a backbone, somewhat after the fashion of millipedes. In the back and front of each vehicle, two men armed with muskets stood erect, each holding one end of the chain under his foot. The iron necklets were square. The seventh vehicle, a huge rack-sided baggage wagon, without a hood, had four wheels and six horses, and carried a sonorous pile of iron boilers, cast-iron pots, braziers, and chains, among which were mingled several men who were pinioned and stretched at full length, and who seemed to be ill. This wagon, all lattice-work, was garnished with dilapidated hurdles which appeared to have served for former punishments. These vehicles kept to the middle of the road. On each side marched a double hedge of guards of infamous aspect, wearing three-cornered hats, like the soldiers under the Directory, shabby, covered with spots and holes, muffled in uniforms of veterans and the trousers of undertakers' men, half gray, half blue, which were almost hanging in rags, with red epaulets, yellow shoulder-belts, short sabers, muskets, and cudgels; they were a species of soldier-blackguards. These myrmidons seemed composed of the abjectness of the beggar and the authority of the executioner. The one who appeared to be their chief held a postilion's whip in his hand. All these details, blurred by the dimness of dawn, became more and more clearly outlined as the light increased. At the head and in the rear of the convoy rode mounted gendarmes, serious and with sword in fist.

This procession was so long that when the first vehicle reached the barrier, the last was barely debouching from the boulevard. A throng, sprung it is impossible to say whence, and formed in a twinkling, as is frequently the case in Paris, pressed forward from both sides of the road and looked on. In the neighboring lanes the shouts of people calling to each other and the wooden shoes of market-gardeners hastening up to gaze were audible.

The men massed upon the drays allowed themselves to be jolted along in silence. They were livid with the chill of morning. They all wore linen trousers, and their bare feet were thrust into wooden shoes. The rest of their costume was a fantasy of wretchedness. Their accoutrements were horribly incongruous; nothing is more funereal than the harlequin in rags. Battered felt hats, tarpaulin caps, hideous woolen nightcaps, and, side by side with a short blouse, a black coat broken at the elbow; many wore women's headgear, others had baskets on their heads; hairy breasts were visible, and through the rent in their garments tattooed designs could be descried; temples of Love, flaming hearts, Cupids, eruptions and unhealthy red blotches could also be seen. Two or three had a straw rope attached to the cross-bar of the dray, and suspended under them like a stirrup, which supported their feet. One of them held in his hand and raised to his mouth something which had the appearance of a black stone and which he seemed to be gnawing; it was bread which he was eating. There were no eyes there which were not either dry, dulled, or flaming with an evil light. The escort troop cursed, the men in chains did not utter a syllable; from time to time, the sound of a blow became audible as the cudgels descended on shoulder-blades or skulls; some of these men were yawning; their rags were terrible; their feet hung down, their shoulders oscillated, their heads clashed together, their fetters clanked, their eyes glared ferociously, their fists clenched or fell open inertly like the hands of corpses; in the rear of the convoy ran a band of children screaming with laughter.

This file of vehicles, whatever its nature was, was mournful. It was evident that to-morrow, that an hour hence, a pouring rain might descend, that it might be followed by another and another, and that their dilapidated garments would be drenched, that once soaked, these men would not get dry again, that once chilled, they would not again get warm, that their linen trousers would be glued to their bones by the downpour, that the water would fill their shoes, that no lashes from the whips would be able to prevent their jaws from chattering, that the chain would continue to bind them by the neck, that their legs would continue to dangle, and it was impossible not to shudder at the sight of these human beings thus bound and passive beneath the cold clouds of autumn, and delivered over to the rain, to the blast, to all the furies of the air, like trees and stones.

Blows from the cudgel were not omitted even in the case of the sick men, who lay there knotted with ropes and motionless on the seventh wagon, and who appeared to have been tossed there like sacks filled with misery.

Suddenly, the sun made its appearance; the immense light of the Orient burst forth, and one would have said that it had set fire to all those ferocious heads. Their tongues were unloosed; a conflagration of grins, oaths, and songs exploded. The broad horizontal sheet of light severed the file in two parts, illuminating heads and bodies, leaving feet and wheels in the obscurity. Thoughts made their appearance on these faces; it was a terrible moment; visible demons with their masks removed, fierce souls laid bare. Though lighted up, this wild throng remained in gloom. Some, who were gay, had in their mouths quills through which they blew vermin over the crowd, picking out the women; the dawn accentuated these lamentable profiles with the blackness of its shadows; there was not one of these creatures who was not deformed by reason of wretchedness; and the whole was so monstrous that one would have said that the sun's brilliancy had been changed into the glare of the lightning. The wagon-load which headed the line had struck up a song, and were shouting at the top of their voices with a haggard joviality, a pot-pourri by Desaugiers, then famous, called *The Vestal*; the trees shivered mournfully; in the cross-lanes, countenances of bourgeois listened in idiotic delight to these coarse strains droned by specters.

All sorts of distress met in this procession as in chaos; here were to be found the facial angles of every sort of beast, old men, youths, bald heads, gray beards, cynical monstrosities, sour resignation, savage grins, senseless attitudes, snouts surmounted by caps, heads like those of young girls with corkscrew curls on the temples, infantile visages, and by reason of that, horrible thin skeleton faces, to which death alone was lacking. On the first cart was a negro, who had been a slave, in all probability, and who could make a comparison of his chains. The frightful leveler from below, shame, had passed over these brows; at that degree of abasement, the last transformations were suffered by all in their extremest depths, and ignorance, converted into dullness, was the equal of intelligence converted into despair. There was no choice possible between these men who appeared to the eye as the flower of the mud. It was evident that the person who had had the ordering of that unclean procession had not classified them. These beings had been fettered and coupled pell-mell, in alphabetical disorder, probably, and loaded haphazard on those carts. Nevertheless, horrors, when grouped together, always end by evolving a result; all additions of wretched men give a sum total, each chain exhaled a common soul, and each dray-load had its own physiognomy. By the side of the one where they were singing, there was one where they were howling; a third where they were begging; one could be seen in which they were gnashing their teeth; another load menaced the spectators, another blasphemed God; the last was as silent as the tomb. Dante would have thought that he beheld his seven circles of hell on the march. The march of the damned to their tortures, performed in sinister wise, not on the formidable and flaming chariot of the Apocalypse, but, what was more mournful than that, on the gibbet cart.

One of the guards, who had a hook on the end of his cudgel, made a pretence from time to time, of stirring up this mass of human filth. An old woman in the crowd pointed them out to her little boy five years old, and said to him: "Rascal, let that be a warning to you!"

As the songs and blasphemies increased, the man who appeared to be the captain of the escort cracked his whip, and at that signal, a fearful dull and blind flogging, which produced the sound of hail, fell upon the seven dray-loads; many roared and foamed at the mouth; which redoubled the delight of the street urchins who had hastened up, a swarm of flies on these wounds.

Jean Valjean's eyes had assumed a frightful expression. They were no longer eyes; they were those deep and glassy objects which replace the glance in the case of certain wretched men, which seem unconscious of reality, and in which flames the reflection of terrors and of catastrophes. He was not looking at a spectacle, he was seeing a vision. He tried to rise, to flee, to make his escape; he could not move his feet. Sometimes, the things that you see seize upon you and hold you fast. He remained nailed to the spot, petrified, stupid, asking himself, athwart confused and inexpressible anguish, what this sepulchral persecution signified, and whence had come that pandemonium which was pursuing him. All at once, he raised his hand to his brow, a gesture habitual to those whose memory suddenly returns; he remembered that this was, in fact, the usual itinerary, that it was customary to make this detour in order to avoid all possibility of encountering royalty on the road to Fontainebleau, and that, five-and-thirty years before, he had himself passed through that barrier.

Cosette was no less terrified, but in a different way. She did not understand; what she beheld did not seem to her to be possible; at length she cried:

"Father! What are those men in those carts?"

Jean Valjean replied: "Convicts."

"Whither are they going?"

"To the galleys."

At that moment, the cudgeling, multiplied by a hundred hands, became zealous, blows with the flat of the sword were mingled with it, it was a perfect storm of whips and clubs; the convicts bent before it, a hideous obedience was evoked by the torture, and all held their peace, darting glances like chained wolves.

Cosette trembled in every limb; she resumed:

"Father, are they still men?"

"Sometimes," answered the unhappy man.

It was the chain-gang, in fact, which had set out before daybreak from Bicêtre, and had taken the road to Mans in order to avoid Fontainebleau, where the King then was. This caused the horrible journey to last three or four days longer; but torture may surely be prolonged with the object of sparing the royal personage a sight of it.

Jean Valjean returned home utterly overwhelmed. Such encounters are shocks, and the memory that they leave behind them resembles a thorough shaking up.

Nevertheless, Jean Valjean did not observe that, on his way back to the Rue de Babylone with Cosette, the latter was plying him with other questions on the subject of what they had just seen; perhaps he was too much absorbed in his own dejection to notice her words and reply to them. But when Cosette was leaving him in the evening, to betake herself to bed, he heard her say in a low voice, and as though talking to herself: "It seems to me, that if I were to find one of those men in my pathway, oh, my God, I should die merely from the sight of him close at hand."

Fortunately, chance ordained that on the morrow of that tragic day, there was some official solemnity apropos of I know not what—fêtes in Paris, a review in the Champ de Mars, jousts on the Seine, theatrical performances in the Champs-Élysées, fireworks at the Arc de l'Étoile, illuminations everywhere. Jean Valjean did violence to his habits, and took Cosette to see these rejoicings, for the purpose of diverting her from the memory of the day before, and of effacing, beneath the smiling tumult of all Paris, the abominable thing which had passed before her. The review with which the festival was spiced made the presence of uniforms perfectly natural; Jean Valjean donned his uniform of a national guard with the vague inward feeling of a man who is betaking himself to shelter. However, this trip seemed to attain its object. Cosette, who made it her law to please her father, and to whom, moreover, all spectacles were a novelty, accepted this diversion with the light and easy good grace of youth, and did not pout too disdainfully at that flutter of enjoyment called a public fête; so that Jean Valjean was able to believe that he had succeeded, and that no trace of that hideous vision remained.

Some days later, one morning, when the sun was shining brightly, and they were both on the steps leading to the garden, another infraction of the rules which Jean Valjean seemed to have imposed upon himself, and to the custom of remaining in her chamber which melancholy had caused Cosette to adopt, Cosette, in a wrapper, was standing erect in that negligent attire of early morning which envelops young girls in an adorable way and which produces the effect of a cloud drawn over a star; and, with her head bathed in light, rosy after a good sleep, submitting to the gentle glances of the tender old man, she was picking a daisy to pieces. Cosette did not know the delightful legend, *I love a little, passionately, etc.*—who was there who could have taught her? She was handling the flower instinctively, innocently, without a suspicion that to pluck a daisy apart is to do the same by a heart. If there were a fourth, and smiling Grace called Melancholy, she would have worn the air of that Grace. Jean Valjean was fascinated by the contemplation of those tiny fingers on that flower, and forgetful of everything in the radiance emitted by that child. A red-breast was warbling in the thicket, on one side. White cloudlets floated across the sky, so gaily, that one would have said that they had just been set at liberty. Cosette went on attentively tearing the leaves from her flower; she seemed to be thinking about something; but whatever it was, it must be something charming; all at once, she turned her head over her shoulder with the delicate languor of a swan, and said to Jean Valjean: "Father, what are the galleys like?"

BOOK FOURTH

SUCCOR FROM BELOW MAY TURN OUT TO BE SUCCOR FROM ON HIGH

Chapter I

A WOUND WITHOUT, HEALING WITHIN

THUS THEIR LIFE CLOUDED OVER BY DEGREES.

But one diversion, which had formerly been a happiness, remained to them, which was to carry bread to those who were hungry, and clothing to those who were cold. Cosette often accompanied Jean Valjean on these visits to the poor, on which they recovered some remnants of their former free intercourse; and sometimes, when the day had been a good one, and they had assisted many in distress, and cheered and warmed many little children, Cosette was rather merry in the evening. It was at this epoch that they paid their visit to the Jondrette den.

On the day following that visit, Jean Valjean made his appearance in the pavilion in the morning, calm as was his wont, but with a large wound on his left arm which was much inflamed, and very angry, which resembled a burn, and which he explained in some way or other. This wound resulted in his being detained in the house for a month with fever. He would not call in a doctor. When Cosette urged him "Call the dog-doctor," said he.

Cosette dressed the wound morning and evening with so divine an air and such angelic happiness at being of use to him, that Jean Valjean felt all his former joy returning, his fears and anxieties dissipating, and he gazed at Cosette, saying: "Oh! what a kindly wound! Oh! what a good misfortune!"

Cosette on perceiving that her father was ill, had deserted the pavilion and again taken a fancy to the little lodging and the back courtyard. She passed nearly all her days beside Jean Valjean and read to him the books which he desired. Generally, they were books of travel. Jean Valjean was undergoing a new birth; his happiness was reviving in these ineffable rays; the Luxembourg, the prowling young stranger, Cosette's coldness—all these clouds upon his soul were growing dim. He had reached the point where he said to himself: "I imagined all that. I am an old fool."

His happiness was so great that the horrible discovery of the Thénardiers made in the Jondrette hovel, unexpected as it was, had, after a fashion, glided over him unnoticed. He had succeeded in making his escape; all trace of him was lost—what more did he care for! he only thought of those wretched beings to pity them. "Here they are in prison, and henceforth they will be incapacitated for doing any harm," he thought, "but what a lamentable family in distress!"

As for the hideous vision of the Barrière du Maine, Cosette had not referred to it again.

Sister Sainte-Mechtilde had taught Cosette music in the convent; Cosette had the voice of a linnet with a soul, and sometimes, in the evening, in the wounded man's humble abode, she warbled melancholy songs which delighted Jean Valjean.

Spring came; the garden was so delightful at that season of the year, that Jean Valjean said to Cosette:

"You never go there; I want you to stroll in it."

"As you like, father," said Cosette.

And for the sake of obeying her father, she resumed her walks in the garden, generally alone, for, as we have mentioned, Jean Valjean, who was probably afraid of being seen through the fence, hardly ever went there.

Jean Valjean's wound had created a diversion.

When Cosette saw that her father was suffering less, that he was convalescing, and that he appeared to be happy, she experienced a contentment which she did not even perceive, so gently and naturally had it come. Then, it was in the month of March, the days were growing longer, the winter was departing, the winter always bears away with it a portion of our sadness; then came April, that daybreak of summer, fresh as dawn always is, gay like every childhood; a little inclined to weep at times like the newborn being that it is. In that month, nature has charming gleams which pass from the sky, from the trees, from the meadows and the flowers into the heart of man.

Cosette was still too young to escape the penetrating influence of that April joy which bore so strong a resemblance to herself. Insensibly, and without her suspecting the fact, the blackness departed from her spirit. In spring, sad souls grow light, as light falls into cellars at midday. Cosette was no longer sad. However, though this was so, she did not account for it to herself. In the morning, about ten o'clock, after breakfast, when she had succeeded in enticing her father into the garden for a quarter of an hour, and when she was pacing up and down in the sunlight in front of the steps, supporting his left arm for him, she did not perceive that she laughed every moment and that she was happy.

Jean Valjean, intoxicated, beheld her growing fresh and rosy once more.

"Oh! What a good wound!" he repeated in a whisper.

And he felt grateful to the Thénardiers.

His wound once healed, he resumed his solitary twilight strolls.

It is a mistake to suppose that a person can stroll alone in that fashion in the uninhabited regions of Paris without meeting with some adventure.

Chapter II

MOTHER PLUTARQUE FINDS NO DIFFICULTY IN EXPLAINING A PHENOMENON

ONE EVENING, LITTLE GAVROCHE HAD HAD NOTHING TO EAT; HE REMEMBERED THAT HE HAD NOT dined on the preceding day either; this was becoming tiresome. He resolved to make an effort to secure some supper. He strolled out beyond the Salpêtrière into deserted regions; that is where windfalls are to be found; where there is no one, one always finds something. He reached a settlement which appeared to him to be the village of Austerlitz.

In one of his preceding lounges he had noticed there an old garden haunted by an old man and an old woman, and in that garden, a passable apple-tree. Beside the apple-tree stood a sort of fruit-house, which was not securely fastened, and where one might contrive to get an apple. One apple is a supper; one apple is life. That which was Adam's ruin might prove Gavroche's salvation. The garden abutted on a solitary, unpaved lane, bordered with brushwood while awaiting the arrival of houses; the garden was separated from it by a hedge.

Gavroche directed his steps toward this garden; he found the lane, he recognized the apple-tree, he verified the fruit-house, he examined the hedge; a hedge means merely one stride. The day was declining, there was not even a cat in the lane, the hour was propitious. Gavroche began the operation of scaling the hedge, then suddenly paused. Someone was talking in the garden. Gavroche peeped through one of the breaks in the hedge.

A couple of paces distant, at the foot of the hedge on the other side, exactly at the point where the gap which he was meditating would have been made, there was a sort of recumbent stone which formed a bench, and on this bench was seated the old man of the garden, while the old woman was standing in front of him. The old woman was grumbling. Gavroche, who was not very discreet, listened.

"Monsieur Mabeuf!" said the old woman.

"Mabeuf!" thought Gavroche, "that name is a perfect farce."

The old man who was thus addressed, did not stir. The old woman repeated:

"Monsieur Mabeuf!"

The old man, without raising his eyes from the ground, made up his mind to answer:

"What is it, Mother Plutarque?"

"Mother Plutarque!" thought Gavroche, "another farcical name."

Mother Plutarque began again, and the old man was forced to accept the conversation:

"The landlord is not pleased."

"Why?"

"We owe three quarters rent."

"In three months, we shall owe him for four quarters."

"He says that he will turn you out to sleep."

"I will go."

"The green-grocer insists on being paid. She will no longer leave her fagots. What will you warm yourself with this winter? We shall have no wood."

"There is the sun."

"The butcher refuses to give credit; he will not let us have anymore meat."

"That is quite right. I do not digest meat well. It is too heavy."

"What shall we have for dinner?"

"Bread."

"The baker demands a settlement, and says, 'no money, no bread.' "

"That is well."

"What will you eat?"

"We have apples in the apple-room."

"But, Monsieur, we can't live like that without money."

"I have none."

The old woman went away, the old man remained alone. He fell into thought. Gavroche became thoughtful also. It was almost dark.

The first result of Gavroche's meditation was, that instead of scaling the hedge, he crouched down under it. The branches stood apart a little at the foot of the thicket.

"Come," exclaimed Gavroche mentally, "here's a nook!" and he curled up in it. His back was almost in contact with Father Mabeuf's bench. He could hear the octogenarian breathe.

Then, by way of dinner, he tried to sleep.

It was a cat-nap, with one eye open. While he dozed, Gavroche kept on the watch.

The twilight pallor of the sky blanched the earth, and the lane formed a livid line between two rows of dark bushes.

All at once, in this whitish band, two figures made their appearance. One was in front, the other some distance in the rear.

"There come two creatures," muttered Gavroche.

The first form seemed to be some elderly bourgeois, who was bent and thoughtful, dressed more than plainly, and who was walking slowly because of his age, and strolling about in the open evening air.

The second was straight, firm, slender. It regulated its pace by that of the first; but in the voluntary slowness of its gait, suppleness and agility were discernible. This figure had also something fierce and disquieting about it, the whole shape was that of what was then called *an elegant*; the hat was of good shape, the coat black, well cut, probably of fine cloth, and well fitted in at the waist. The head was held erect with a sort of robust grace, and beneath the hat the pale profile of a young man could be made out in the dim light. The profile had a rose in its mouth. This second form was well known to Gavroche; it was Montparnasse.

He could have told nothing about the other, except that he was a respectable old man.

Gavroche immediately began to take observations.

One of these two pedestrians evidently had a project connected with the other. Gavroche was well placed to watch the course of events. The bedroom had turned into a hiding-place at a very opportune moment.

Montparnasse on the hunt at such an hour, in such a place, betokened something threatening. Gavroche felt his gamin's heart moved with compassion for the old man.

What was he to do? Interfere? One weakness coming to the aid of another! It would be merely a laughing matter for Montparnasse. Gavroche did not shut his eyes to the fact that, the old man in the first place, and the child in the second, would make but two mouthfuls for that redoubtable ruffian eighteen years of age.

While Gavroche was deliberating, the attack took place, abruptly and hideously. The attack of the tiger on the wild ass, the attack of the spider on the fly. Montparnasse suddenly tossed away his rose, bounded upon the old man, seized him by the collar, grasped and clung to him, and Gavroche with difficulty restrained a scream. A moment later one of these men was underneath the other, groaning, struggling, with a knee of marble upon his breast. Only, it was not just what Gavroche had expected. The one who lay on the earth was Montparnasse; the one who was on top was the old man. All this took place a few paces distant from Gavroche.

The old man had received the shock, had returned it, and that in such a terrible fashion, that in a twinkling, the assailant and the assailed had exchanged rôles.

"Here's a hearty veteran!" thought Gavroche.

He could not refrain from clapping his hands. But it was applause wasted. It did not reach the combatants, absorbed and deafened as they were, each by the other, as their breath mingled in the struggle.

Silence ensued. Montparnasse ceased his struggles. Gavroche indulged in this aside: "Can he be dead!"

The good man had not uttered a word, nor given vent to a cry. He rose to his feet, and Gavroche heard him say to Montparnasse:

"Get up."

Montparnasse rose, but the good man held him fast. Montparnasse's attitude was the humiliated and furious attitude of the wolf who has been caught by a sheep.

Gavroche looked on and listened, making an effort to reinforce his eyes with his ears. He was enjoying himself immensely.

He was repaid for his conscientious anxiety in the character of a spectator. He was able to catch on the wing a dialogue which borrowed from the darkness an indescribably tragic accent. The good man questioned, Montparnasse replied.

"How old are you?"

"Nineteen."

"You are strong and healthy. Why do you not work?"

"It bores me."

"What is your trade?"

"An idler."

"Speak seriously. Can anything be done for you? What would you like to be?"

"A thief."

A pause ensued. The old man seemed absorbed in profound thought. He stood motionless, and did not relax his hold on Montparnasse.

Every moment the vigorous and agile young ruffian indulged in the twitchings of a wild beast caught in a snare. He gave a jerk, tried a crook of the knee, twisted his limbs desperately, and made efforts to escape.

The old man did not appear to notice it, and held both his arms with one hand, with the sovereign indifference of absolute force.

The old man's reverie lasted for some time, then, looking steadily at Montparnasse, he addressed to him in a gentle voice, in the midst of the darkness where they stood, a solemn harangue, of which Gavroche did not lose a single syllable:

"My child, you are entering, through indolence, on one of the most laborious of lives. Ah! You declare yourself to be an idler! prepare to toil. There is a certain formidable machine, have you seen it? It is the rolling-mill. You must be on your guard against it, it is crafty and ferocious; if it catches hold of the skirt of your coat, you will be drawn in bodily. That machine is laziness. Stop while there is yet time, and save yourself! Otherwise, it is all over with you; in a short time you will be among the gearing. Once entangled, hope for nothing more. Toil, lazybones! there is no more repose for you! The iron hand of implacable toil has seized you. You do not wish to earn your living, to have a task, to fulfill a duty! It bores you to be like other men? Well! You will be different. Labor is the law; he who rejects it will find ennui his torment. You do not wish to be a workingman, you will be a slave. Toil lets go of you on one side only to grasp you again on the other. You do not desire to be its friend, you shall be its negro slave. Ah! You would have none of the honest weariness of men, you shall have the sweat of the damned. Where others sing, you will rattle in your throat. You will see afar off, from below, other men at work; it will seem to you that they are resting. The laborer, the harvester, the sailor, the blacksmith, will appear to you in glory like the blessed spirits in paradise. What radiance surrounds the forge! To guide the plow, to bind the sheaves, is joy. The bark at liberty in the wind, what delight! Do you, lazy idler, delve, drag on, roll, march! Drag your halter. You are a beast of burden in the team of hell! Ah! To do nothing is your object. Well, not a week, not a day, not an hour shall you have free from oppression. You will be able to lift nothing without anguish. Every minute that passes will make your muscles crack. What is a feather to others will be a rock to you. The simplest things will become steep acclivities. Life will become monstrous all about you. To go, to come, to breathe, will be just so many terrible labors. Your lungs will produce on you the effect of weighing a hundred pounds. Whether you shall walk here rather than there, will become a problem that must be solved. Anyone who wants to go out simply gives his door a push, and there he is in the open air. If you wish to go out, you will be obliged to pierce your wall. What does everyone who wants to step into the street do? He goes downstairs; you will tear up your sheets, little by little you will make of them a rope, then you will climb out of your window, and you will suspend yourself by that thread over an abyss, and it will be night, amid storm, rain, and the hurricane, and if the rope is too short, but one way of descending will remain to you, to fall. To drop haphazard into the gulf, from an unknown height, on what? On what is beneath, on the unknown. Or you will crawl up a chimney-flue, at the risk of burning; or you will creep through a sewer-pipe, at the risk of drowning; I do not speak of the holes that you will be obliged to mask, of the stones which you will have to take up and replace twenty times a day, of the plaster that you will have to hide in your straw pallet. A lock presents itself; the bourgeois has in his pocket a key made by a locksmith. If you wish to pass out, you will be condemned to execute a terrible work of art; you will take a large sou, you will cut it in two plates; with what tools? You will have to invent them. That is your business. Then you will hollow out the interior of these plates, taking great care of the outside, and you will make on the edges a thread, so that they can be adjusted one upon the other like a box and its cover. The top and bottom thus screwed together, nothing will be suspected. To the overseers it will be only a sou; to you it will be a box. What will you put in this box? A small bit of steel. A watch-spring, in which you will have cut teeth, and which will form a saw. With this saw, as long as a pin, and concealed in a sou, you will cut the bolt of the lock, you will sever bolts, the padlock of your chain, and the bar at your window, and the fetter on your leg. This masterpiece finished, this prodigy accomplished, all these miracles of art, address, skill, and patience executed, what will be your recompense if it becomes known that you are the author? The dungeon. There is your future. What precipices are idleness and pleasure! Do you know that to do nothing is a melancholy resolution? To live in idleness on the property of society! to be useless, that is to say, pernicious! This leads straight to the depth of wretchedness. Woe to the man who desires to be parasite! He will become vermin! Ah! So it does not please you to work? Ah! You have but one thought, to drink well, to eat well, to sleep well. You will drink water, you will eat black bread, you will sleep on a plank with a fetter whose cold touch you will feel on your flesh all night long, riveted to your limbs. You will break those fetters, you will flee. That is well. You will crawl on your belly through the brushwood, and you will eat grass like the beasts of the forest. And you will be recaptured. And then you will pass years in a dungeon, riveted to a wall, groping for your jug that you may drink, gnawing at a horrible loaf of darkness which dogs would not touch, eating beans that the worms have eaten before you. You will be a wood-louse in a cellar. Ah! Have pity on yourself, you miserable young child, who were sucking at nurse less than twenty years ago, and who have, no doubt, a mother still alive! I conjure you, listen to me, I entreat you. You desire fine black cloth, varnished shoes, to have your hair curled and sweet-smelling oils on your locks, to please low women, to be handsome. You will be shaven clean, and you will wear a red blouse and wooden shoes. You want rings on your fingers, you will have an iron necklet on your neck. If you glance at a woman, you will receive a blow. And you will enter there at the age of twenty. And you will come out at fifty! You will enter young, rosy, fresh, with brilliant eyes, and all your white teeth, and your handsome, youthful hair; you will come out broken, bent, wrinkled, toothless, horrible, with white locks! Ah! my poor child, you are on the wrong road; idleness is counseling you badly; the hardest of all work is thieving. Believe me, do not undertake that painful profession of an idle man. It is not comfortable to become a rascal. It is less disagreeable to be an honest man. Now go, and ponder on what I have said to you. By the way, what did you want of me? My purse? Here it is."

And the old man, releasing Montparnasse, put his purse in the latter's hand; Montparnasse weighed it for a moment, after which he allowed it to slide gently into the back pocket of his coat, with the same mechanical precaution as though he had stolen it.

All this having been said and done, the good man turned his back and tranquilly resumed his stroll.

"The blockhead!" muttered Montparnasse.

Who was this good man? The reader has, no doubt, already divined.

Montparnasse watched him with amazement, as he disappeared in the dusk. This contemplation was fatal to him.

While the old man was walking away, Gavroche drew near.

Gavroche had assured himself, with a sidelong glance, that Father Mabeuf was still sitting on his bench, probably sound asleep. Then the gamin emerged from his thicket, and began to crawl after Montparnasse in the dark, as the latter stood there motionless. In this manner he came up to Montparnasse without being seen or heard, gently insinuated his hand into the back pocket of that frock-coat of fine black cloth, seized the purse, withdrew his hand, and having recourse once more to his crawling, he slipped away like an adder through the shadows. Montparnasse, who had no reason to be on his guard, and who was engaged in thought for the first time in his life, perceived nothing. When Gavroche had once more attained the point where Father Mabeuf was, he flung the purse over the hedge, and fled as fast as his legs would carry him.

The purse fell on Father Mabeuf's foot. This commotion roused him.

He bent over and picked up the purse.

He did not understand in the least, and opened it.

The purse had two compartments; in one of them there was some small change; in the other lay six napoleons.

M. Mabeuf, in great alarm, referred the matter to his housekeeper.

"That has fallen from heaven," said Mother Plutarque.

BOOK FIFTH

THE END OF WHICH DOES NOT RESEMBLE THE BEGINNING

Chapter I

SOLITUDE AND THE BARRACKS COMBINED

COSETTE'S GRIEF, WHICH HAD BEEN SO POIGNANT AND LIVELY FOUR OR FIVE MONTHS PREVIously, had, without her being conscious of the fact, entered upon its convalescence. Nature, spring, youth, love for her father, the gaiety of the birds and flowers, caused something almost resembling forgetfulness to filter gradually, drop by drop, into that soul, which was so virgin and so young. Was the fire wholly extinct there? Or was it merely that layers of ashes had formed? The truth is, that she hardly felt the painful and burning spot any longer.

One day she suddenly thought of Marius: "Why!" said she, "I no longer think of him."

That same week, she noticed a very handsome officer of lancers, with a wasp-like waist, a delicious uniform, the cheeks of a young girl, a sword under his arm, waxed mustaches, and a glazed schapka, passing the gate. Moreover, he had light hair, prominent blue eyes, a round face, was vain, insolent and good-looking; quite the reverse of Marius. He had a cigar in his mouth. Cosette thought that this officer doubtless belonged to the regiment in barracks in the Rue de Babylone.

On the following day, she saw him pass again. She took note of the hour.

From that time forth, was it chance? she saw him pass nearly every day.

The officer's comrades perceived that there was, in that "badly kept" garden, behind that malicious rococo fence, a very pretty creature, who was almost always there when the handsome lieutenant—who is not unknown to the reader, and whose name was Théodule Gillenormand—passed by.

"See here!" they said to him, "there's a little creature there who is making eyes at you, look."

"Have I the time," replied the lancer, "to look at all the girls who look at me?"

This was at the precise moment when Marius was descending heavily toward agony, and was saying: "If I could but see her before I die!"—Had his wish been realized, had he beheld Cosette at that moment gazing at the lancer, he would not have been able to utter a word, and he would have expired with grief.

Whose fault was it? No one's.

Marius possessed one of those temperaments which bury themselves in sorrow and there abide; Cosette was one of those persons who plunge into sorrow and emerge from it again.

Cosette was, moreover, passing through that dangerous period, the fatal phase of feminine reverie abandoned to itself, in which the isolated heart of a young girl resembles the tendrils of the vine which cling, as chance directs, to the capital of a marble column or to the post of a wine-shop. A rapid and decisive moment, critical for every orphan, be she poor or rich, for wealth does not prevent a bad choice; misalliances are made in very high circles, real misalliance is that of souls; and as many an unknown young man, without name, without birth, without fortune, is a marble column which bears up a temple of grand sentiments and grand ideas, so such and such a man of the world satisfied and opulent, who has polished boots and varnished words, if looked at not outside, but inside, a thing which is reserved for his wife, is nothing more than a block obscurely haunted by violent, unclean, and vinous passions; the post of a drinking-shop.

What did Cosette's soul contain? Passion calmed or lulled to sleep; something limpid, brilliant, troubled to a certain depth, and gloomy lower down. The image of the handsome officer was reflected in the surface. Did a souvenir linger in the depths?—Quite at the bottom?—Possibly. Cosette did not know.

A singular incident supervened.

Chapter II

COSETTE'S APPREHENSIONS

DURING THE FIRST FORTNIGHT IN APRIL, JEAN VALJEAN TOOK A JOURNEY. THIS, AS THE READER knows happened from time to time, at very long intervals. He remained absent a day or two days at the utmost. Where did he go? No one knew, not even Cosette. Once only, on the occasion of one of these departures, she had accompanied him in a hackney-coach as far as a little blind-alley at the corner of which she read: *Impasse de la Planchette*. There he alighted, and the coach took Cosette back to the Rue de Babylone. It was usually when money was lacking in the house that Jean Valjean took these little trips.

So Jean Valjean was absent. He had said: "I shall return in three days."

That evening, Cosette was alone in the drawing-room. In order to get rid of her ennui, she had opened her piano-organ, and had begun to sing, accompanying herself the while, the chorus from *Euryanthe:* "Hunters astray in the wood!" which is probably the most beautiful thing in all the sphere of music. When she had finished, she remained wrapped in thought.

All at once, it seemed to her that she heard the sound of footsteps in the garden.

It could not be her father, he was absent; it could not be Toussaint, she was in bed, and it was ten o'clock at night.

She stepped to the shutter of the drawing-room, which was closed, and laid her ear against it.

It seemed to her that it was the tread of a man, and that he was walking very softly.

She mounted rapidly to the first floor, to her own chamber, opened a small wicket in her shutter, and peeped into the garden. The moon was at the full. Everything could be seen as plainly as by day.

There was no one there.

She opened the window. The garden was absolutely calm, and all that was visible was that the street was deserted as usual.

Cosette thought that she had been mistaken. She thought that she had heard a noise. It was a hallucination produced by the melancholy and magnificent chorus of Weber, which lays open before the mind terrified depths, which trembles before the gaze like a dizzy forest, and in which one hears the crackling of dead branches beneath the uneasy tread of the huntsmen of whom one catches a glimpse through the twilight.

She thought no more about it.

Moreover, Cosette was not very timid by nature. There flowed in her veins some of the blood of the bohemian and the adventuress who runs barefoot. It will be remembered that she was more of a lark than a dove. There was a foundation of wildness and bravery in her.

On the following day, at an earlier hour, toward nightfall, she was strolling in the garden. In the midst of the confused thoughts which occupied her, she fancied that she caught for an instant a sound similar to that of the preceding evening, as though someone were walking beneath the trees in the dusk, and not very far from her; but she told herself that nothing so closely resembles a step on the grass as the friction of two branches which have moved from side to side, and she paid no heed to it. Besides, she could see nothing.

She emerged from "the thicket"; she had still to cross a small lawn to regain the steps.

The moon, which had just risen behind her, cast Cosette's shadow in front of her upon this lawn, as she came out from the shrubbery.

Cosette halted in alarm.

Beside her shadow, the moon outlined distinctly upon the turf another shadow, which was particularly startling and terrible, a shadow which had a round hat.

It was the shadow of a man, who must have been standing on the border of the clump of shrubbery, a few paces in the rear of Cosette.

She stood for a moment without the power to speak, or cry, or call, or stir, or turn her head.

Then she summoned up all her courage, and turned round resolutely.

There was no one there.

She glanced on the ground. The figure had disappeared.

She re-entered the thicket, searched the corners boldly, went as far as the gate, and found nothing.

She felt herself absolutely chilled with terror. Was this another hallucination? What! Two days in succession! One hallucination might pass, but two hallucinations? The disquieting point about it was, that the shadow had assuredly not been a phantom. Phantoms do not wear round hats.

On the following day Jean Valjean returned. Cosette told him what she thought she had heard and seen. She wanted to be reassured and to see her father shrug his shoulders and say to her: "You are a little goose."

Jean Valjean grew anxious.

"It cannot be anything," said he.

He left her under some pretext, and went into the garden, and she saw him examining the gate with great attention.

During the night she woke up: this time she was sure, and she distinctly heard someone walking close to the flight of steps beneath her window. She ran to her little wicket and opened it. In point of fact, there was a man in the garden, with a large club in his hand. Just as she was about to scream, the moon lighted up the man's profile. It was her father. She returned to her bed, saying to herself: "He is very uneasy!"

Jean Valjean passed that night and the two succeeding nights in the garden. Cosette saw him through the hole in her shutter.

On the third night, the moon was on the wane and had begun to rise later; at one o'clock in the morning, possibly, she heard a loud burst of laughter and her father's voice calling her:

"Cosette!"

She jumped out of bed, threw on her dressing-gown, and opened her window.

Her father was standing on the grass-plot below.

"I have waked you for the purpose of reassuring you," said he; "look, there is your shadow with the round hat."

And he pointed out to her on the turf a shadow cast by the moon, and which did, indeed, bear considerable resemblance to the specter of a man wearing a round hat. It was the shadow produced by a chimney-pipe of sheet iron, with a hood, which rose above a neighboring roof.

Cosette joined in his laughter, all her lugubrious suppositions were allayed, and the next morning, as she was at breakfast with her father, she made merry over the sinister garden haunted by the shadows of iron chimney-pots.

Jean Valjean became quite tranquil once more; as for Cosette, she did not pay much attention to the question whether the chimney-pot was really in the direction of the shadow which she had seen, or thought she had seen, and whether the moon had been in the same spot in the sky.

She did not question herself as to the peculiarity of a chimney-pot which is afraid of being caught in the act, and which retires when someone looks at its shadow, for the shadow had taken the alarm when Cosette had turned round, and Cosette had thought herself very sure of this. Cosette's serenity was fully restored. The proof appeared to her to be complete, and it quite vanished from her mind, whether there could possibly be anyone walking in the garden during the evening or at night.

A few days later, however, a fresh incident occurred.

Chapter III

ENRICHED WITH COMMENTARIES BY TOUSSAINT

IN THE GARDEN, NEAR THE RAILING ON THE STREET, THERE WAS A STONE BENCH, SCREENED FROM the eyes of the curious by a plantation of yoke-elms, but which could, in case of necessity, be reached by an arm from the outside, past the trees and the gate.

One evening during that same month of April, Jean Valjean had gone out; Cosette had seated herself on this bench after sundown. The breeze was blowing briskly in the trees, Cosette was meditating; an objectless sadness was taking possession of her little by little, that invincible sadness evoked by the evening, and which arises, perhaps, who knows, from the mystery of the tomb which is ajar at that hour.

Perhaps Fantine was within that shadow.

Cosette rose, slowly made the tour of the garden, walking on the grass drenched in dew, and saying to herself, through the species of melancholy somnambulism in which she was plunged: "Really, one needs wooden shoes for the garden at this hour. One takes cold."

She returned to the bench.

As she was about to resume her seat there, she observed on the spot which she had quitted, a tolerably large stone which had, evidently, not been there a moment before.

Cosette gazed at the stone, asking herself what it meant. All at once the idea occurred to her that the stone had not reached the bench all by itself, that someone had placed it there, that an arm had been thrust through the railing, and this idea appeared to alarm her. This time, the fear was genuine; the stone was there. No doubt was possible; she did not touch it, fled without glancing behind her, took refuge in the house, and immediately closed with shutter, bolt, and bar the door-like window opening on the flight of steps. She inquired of Toussaint:

"Has my father returned yet?"

"Not yet, Mademoiselle."

[We have already noted once for all the fact that Toussaint stuttered. May we be permitted to dispense with it for the future. The musical notation of an infirmity is repugnant to us.]

Jean Valjean, a thoughtful man, and given to nocturnal strolls, often returned quite late at night.

"Toussaint," went on Cosette, "are you careful to thoroughly barricade the shutters opening on the garden, at least with bars, in the evening, and to put the little iron things in the little rings that close them?"

"Oh! be easy on that score, Miss."

Toussaint did not fail in her duty, and Cosette was well aware of the fact, but she could not refrain from adding:

"It is so solitary here."

"So far as that is concerned," said Toussaint, "it is true. We might be assassinated before we had time to say *ouf!* And Monsieur does not sleep in the house, to boot. But fear nothing, Miss, I fasten the shutters up like prisons. Lone women! That is enough to make one shudder, I believe you! Just imagine, what if you were to see men enter your chamber at night and say: 'Hold your tongue!' and begin to cut your throat. It's not the dying so much; you die, for one must die, and that's all right; it's the abomination of feeling those people touch you. And then, their knives; they can't be able to cut well with them! Ah, good gracious!"

"Be quiet," said Cosette. "Fasten everything thoroughly."

Cosette, terrified by the melodrama improvised by Toussaint, and possibly, also, by the recollection of the apparitions of the past week, which recurred to her memory, dared not even say to her: "Go and look at the stone which has been placed on the bench!" for fear of opening the garden gate and allowing "the men" to enter. She saw that all the doors and windows were carefully fastened, made Toussaint go all over the house from garret to cellar, locked herself up in her own chamber, bolted her door, looked under her couch, went to bed and slept badly. All night long she saw that big stone, as large as a mountain and full of caverns.

At sunrise—the property of the rising sun is to make us laugh at all our terrors of the past night, and our laughter is in direct proportion to our terror which they have caused—at sunrise Cosette, when she woke, viewed her fright as a nightmare, and said to herself: "What have I been thinking of? It is like the footsteps that I thought I heard a week or two ago in the garden at night! It is like the shadow of the chimney-pot! Am I becoming a coward?" The sun, which was glowing through the crevices in her shutters, and turning the damask curtains crimson, reassured her to such an extent that everything vanished from her thoughts, even the stone.

"There was no more a stone on the bench than there was a man in a round hat in the garden; I dreamed about the stone, as I did all the rest."

She dressed herself, descended to the garden, ran to the bench, and broke out in a cold perspiration. The stone was there.

But this lasted only for a moment. That which is terror by night is curiosity by day.

"Bah!" said she, "come, let us see what it is."

She lifted the stone, which was tolerably large. Beneath it was something which resembled a letter. It was a white envelope. Cosette seized it. There was no address on one side, no seal on the other. Yet the envelope, though unsealed, was not empty. Papers could be seen inside.

Cosette examined it. It was no longer alarm, it was no longer curiosity; it was a beginning of anxiety.

Cosette drew from the envelope its contents, a little notebook of paper, each page of which was numbered and bore a few lines in a very fine and rather pretty handwriting, as Cosette thought.

Cosette looked for a name; there was none. To whom was this addressed? To her, probably, since a hand had deposited the packet on her bench. From whom did it come? An irresistible fascination took possession of her; she tried to turn away her eyes from the leaflets which were trembling in her hand, she gazed at the sky, the street, the acacias all bathed in light, the pigeons fluttering over a neighboring roof, and then her glance suddenly fell upon the manuscript, and she said to herself that she must know what it contained.

This is what she read.

Chapter IV

A Heart beneath a Stone

The reduction of the universe to a single being, the expansion of a single being even to God, that is love.

———————

Love is the salutation of the angels to the stars.

———————

How sad is the soul, when it is sad through love!

———————

What a void in the absence of the being who, by herself alone fills the world! Oh! how true it is that the beloved being becomes God. One could comprehend that God might be jealous of this had not God the Father of all evidently made creation for the soul, and the soul for love.

The glimpse of a smile beneath a white crape bonnet with a lilac curtain is sufficient to cause the soul to enter into the palace of dreams.

God is behind everything, but everything hides God. Things are black, creatures are opaque. To love a being is to render that being transparent.

Certain thoughts are prayers. There are moments when, whatever the attitude of the body may be, the soul is on its knees.

Parted lovers beguile absence by a thousand chimerical devices, which possess, however, a reality of their own. They are prevented from seeing each other, they cannot write to each other; they discover a multitude of mysterious means to correspond. They send each other the song of the birds, the perfume of the flowers, the smiles of children, the light of the sun, the sighings of the breeze, the rays of stars, all creation. And why not? All the works of God are made to serve love. Love is sufficiently potent to charge all nature with its messages.

> *Oh Spring! Thou art a letter that I write to her.*

The future belongs to hearts even more than it does to minds. Love, that is the only thing that can occupy and fill eternity. In the infinite, the inexhaustible is requisite.

Love participates of the soul itself. It is of the same nature. Like it, it is the divine spark; like it, it is incorruptible, indivisible, imperishable. It is a point of fire that exists within us, which is immortal and infinite, which nothing can confine, and which nothing can extinguish. We feel it burning even to the very marrow of our bones, and we see it beaming in the very depths of heaven.

Oh Love! Adorations! voluptuousness of two minds which understand each other, of two hearts which exchange with each other, of two glances which penetrate each other! You will come to me, will you not, bliss! strolls by twos in the solitudes! Blessed and radiant days! I have sometimes dreamed that from time to time hours detached themselves from the lives of the angels and came here below to traverse the destinies of men.

God can add nothing to the happiness of those who love, except to give them endless duration. After a life of love, an eternity of love is, in fact, an augmentation; but to increase in intensity even the ineffable felicity which love bestows on the soul even in this world, is impossible, even to God. God is the plenitude of heaven; love is the plenitude of man.

You look at a star for two reasons, because it is luminous, and because it is impenetrable. You have beside you a sweeter radiance and a greater mystery, woman.

All of us, whoever we may be, have our respirable beings. We lack air and we stifle. Then we die. To die for lack of love is horrible. Suffocation of the soul.

When love has fused and mingled two beings in a sacred and angelic unity, the secret of life has been discovered so far as they are concerned; they are no longer anything more than the two boundaries of the same destiny; they are no longer anything but the two wings of the same spirit. Love, soar.

On the day when a woman as she passes before you emits light as she walks, you are lost, you love. But one thing remains for you to do: to think of her so intently that she is constrained to think of you.

What love commences can be finished by God alone.

True love is in despair and is enchanted over a glove lost or a handkerchief found, and eternity is required for its devotion and its hopes. It is composed both of the infinitely great and the infinitely little.

If you are a stone, be adamant; if you are a plant, be the sensitive plant; if you are a man, be love.

Nothing suffices for love. We have happiness, we desire paradise; we possess paradise, we desire heaven.

Oh ye who love each other, all this is contained in love. Understand how to find it there. Love has contemplation as well as heaven, and more than heaven, it has voluptuousness.

"Does she still come to the Luxembourg?" "No, sir." "This is the church where she attends mass, is it not?" "She no longer comes here." "Does she still live in this house?" "She has moved away." "Where has she gone to dwell?" "She did not say."

What a melancholy thing not to know the address of one's soul!

Love has its childishness, other passions have their pettinesses. Shame on the passions which belittle man! Honor to the one which makes a child of him!

There is one strange thing, do you know it? I dwell in the night. There is a being who carried off my sky when she went away.

Oh! would that we were lying side by side in the same grave, hand in hand, and from time to time, in the darkness, gently caressing a finger—that would suffice for my eternity!

Ye who suffer because ye love, love yet more. To die of love, is to live in it.

Love. A somber and starry transfiguration is mingled with this torture. There is ecstasy in agony.

Oh joy of the birds! It is because they have nests that they sing.

Love is a celestial respiration of the air of paradise.

Deep hearts, sage minds, take life as God has made it; it is a long trial, an incomprehensible preparation for an unknown destiny. This destiny, the true one, begins for a man with the first step inside the tomb. Then something appears to him, and he begins to distinguish the definitive. The definitive, meditate upon that word. The living perceive the infinite; the definitive permits itself to be seen only by the dead. In the meanwhile, love and suffer, hope and contemplate. Woe, alas! to him who shall have loved only bodies, forms, appearances! Death will deprive him of all. Try to love souls, you will find them again.

I encountered in the street, a very poor young man who was in love. His hat was old, his coat was worn, his elbows were in holes; water trickled through his shoes, and the stars through his soul.

What a grand thing it is to be loved! What a far grander thing it is to love! The heart becomes heroic, by dint of passion. It is no longer composed of anything but what is pure; it no longer rests on anything that is not elevated and great. An unworthy thought can no more germinate in it, than a nettle on a glacier.

The serene and lofty soul, inaccessible to vulgar passions and emotions, dominating the clouds and the shades of this world, its follies, its lies, its hatreds, its vanities, its miseries, inhabits the blue of heaven, and no longer feels anything but profound and subterranean shocks of destiny, as the crests of mountains feel the shocks of earthquake.

If there did not exist someone who loved, the sun would become extinct.

Chapter V

COSETTE AFTER THE LETTER

AS COSETTE READ, SHE GRADUALLY FELL INTO THOUGHT. AT THE VERY MOMENT WHEN SHE raised her eyes from the last line of the notebook, the handsome officer passed triumphantly in front of the gate—it was his hour; Cosette thought him hideous.

She resumed her contemplation of the book. It was written in the most charming of chirography, thought Cosette; in the same hand, but with divers inks, sometimes very black, again whitish, as when ink has been added to the inkstand, and consequently on different days. It was, then, a mind which had unfolded itself there, sigh by sigh, irregularly, without order, without choice, without object, haphazard. Cosette had never read anything like it. This manuscript, in which she already perceived more light than obscurity, produced upon her the effect of a half-open sanctuary. Each one of these mysterious lines shone before her eyes and inundated her heart with a strange radiance. The education which she had received had always talked to her of the soul, and never of love, very much as one might talk of the firebrand and not of the flame. This manuscript of fifteen pages suddenly and sweetly revealed to her all of love, sorrow, destiny, life, eternity, the beginning, the end. It was as if a hand had opened and suddenly flung upon her a handful of rays of light. In these few lines she felt a passionate, ardent, generous, honest nature, a sacred will, an immense sorrow, and an immense despair, a suffering heart, an ecstasy fully expanded. What was this manuscript? A letter. A letter without name, without address, without date, without signature, pressing and disinterested, an enigma composed of truths, a message of love made to be brought by an angel and read by a virgin, an appointment made beyond the bounds of earth, the love-letter of a phantom to a shade. It was an absent one, tranquil and dejected, who seemed ready to take refuge in death and who sent to the absent love, his lady, the secret of fate, the key of life, love. This had been written with one foot in the grave and one finger in heaven. These lines, which had fallen one by one on the paper, were what might be called drops of soul.

Now, from whom could these pages come? Who could have penned them?

Cosette did not hesitate a moment. One man only.

He!

Day had dawned once more in her spirit; all had reappeared. She felt an unheard-of joy, and a profound anguish. It was he! he who had written! he was there! it was he whose arm had been thrust through that railing! While she was forgetful of him, he had found her again! But had she forgotten him? No, never! She was foolish to have thought so for a single moment. She had always loved him, always adored him. The fire had been smothered, and had smoldered for a time, but she saw all plainly now; it had but made headway, and now it had burst forth afresh, and had inflamed her whole being. This notebook was like a spark which had fallen from that other soul into hers. She felt the conflagration starting up once more.

She imbued herself thoroughly with every word of the manuscript: "Oh yes!" said she, "how perfectly I recognize all that! That is what I had already read in his eyes." As she was finishing it for the third time, Lieutenant Théodule passed the gate once more, and rattled his spurs upon the pavement. Cosette was forced to raise her eyes. She thought him insipid, silly, stupid, useless, foppish, displeasing, impertinent, and extremely ugly. The officer thought it his duty to smile at her.

She turned away as in shame and indignation. She would gladly have thrown something at his head.

She fled, re-entered the house, and shut herself up in her chamber to peruse the manuscript once more, to learn it by heart, and to dream. When she had thoroughly mastered it she kissed it and put it in her bosom.

All was over, Cosette had fallen back into deep, seraphic love. The abyss of Eden had yawned once more.

All day long, Cosette remained in a sort of bewilderment. She scarcely thought, her ideas were in the state of a tangled skein in her brain, she could not manage to conjecture anything, she hoped through a tremor, what? vague things. She dared make herself no promises, and she did not wish to refuse herself anything. Flashes of pallor passed over her countenance, and shivers ran through her frame. It seemed to her, at intervals, that she was entering the land of chimeras; she said to herself: "Is this reality?" Then she felt of the dear paper within her bosom under her gown, she pressed it to her heart, she felt its angles against her flesh; and if Jean Valjean had seen her at the moment, he would have shuddered in the presence of that luminous and unknown joy, which overflowed from beneath her eyelids.—"Oh yes!" she thought, "it is certainly he! This comes from him, and is for me!"

And she told herself that an intervention of the angels, a celestial chance, had given him back to her.

Oh transfiguration of love! Oh dreams! That celestial chance, that intervention of the angels, was a pellet of bread tossed by one thief to another thief, from the Charlemagne Courtyard to the Lion's Ditch, over the roofs of La Force.

Chapter VI

OLD PEOPLE ARE MADE TO GO OUT OPPORTUNELY

WHEN EVENING CAME, JEAN VALJEAN WENT OUT; COSETTE DRESSED HERSELF. SHE ARRANGED her hair in the most becoming manner, and she put on a dress whose bodice had received one snip of the scissors too much, and which, through this slope permitted a view of the beginning of her throat, and was, as young girls say, "a trifle indecent." It was not in the least indecent, but it was prettier than usual. She made her toilet thus without knowing why she did so.

Did she mean to go out? No.

Was she expecting a visitor? No.

At dusk, she went down to the garden. Toussaint was busy in her kitchen, which opened on the backyard.

She began to stroll about under the trees, thrusting aside the branches from time to time with her hand, because there were some which hung very low.

In this manner she reached the bench.

The stone was still there.

She sat down, and gently laid her white hand on this stone as though she wished to caress and thank it.

All at once, she experienced that indefinable impression which one undergoes, when there is someone standing behind one, even when she does not see the person.

She turned her head and rose to her feet.

It was he.

His head was bare. He appeared to have grown thin and pale. His black clothes were hardly discernible. The twilight threw a wan light on his fine brow, and covered his eyes in shadows. Beneath a veil of incomparable sweetness, he had something about him that suggested death and night. His face was illuminated by the light of the dying day, and by the thought of a soul that is taking flight.

He seemed to be not yet a ghost, and he was no longer a man.

He had flung away his hat in the thicket, a few paces distant.

Cosette, though ready to swoon, uttered no cry. She retreated slowly, for she felt herself attracted. He did not stir. By virtue of something ineffable and melancholy which enveloped him, she felt the look in his eyes which she could not see.

Cosette, in her retreat, encountered a tree and leaned against it. Had it not been for this tree, she would have fallen.

Then she heard his voice, that voice which she had really never heard, barely rising above the rustle of the leaves, and murmuring:

"Pardon me, here I am. My heart is full. I could not live on as I was living, and I have come. Have you read what I placed there on the bench? Do you recognize me at all? Have no fear of me. It is a long time, you remember the day, since you looked at me at the Luxembourg, near the Gladiator. And the day when you passed before me? It was on the 16th of June and the 2d of July. It is nearly a year ago. I have not seen you for a long time. I inquired of the woman who let the chairs, and she told me that she no longer saw you. You lived in the Rue de l'Ouest, on the third floor, in the front apartments of a new house—you see that I know! I followed you. What else was there for me to do? And then you disappeared. I thought I saw you pass once, while I was reading the newspapers under the arcade of the Odéon. I ran after you. But no. It was a person who had a bonnet like yours. At night, I came hither. Do not be afraid, no one sees me. I come to gaze upon your windows near at hand. I walk very softly, so that you may not hear, for you might be alarmed. The other evening I was behind you, you turned round, I fled. Once, I heard you singing. I was happy. Did it affect you, because I heard you singing through the shutters? That could not hurt you. No, it is not so? You see, you are my angel! Let me come sometimes; I think that I am going to die. If you only knew! I adore you. Forgive me, I speak to you, but I do not know what I am saying; I may have displeased you; have I displeased you?"

"O! my mother!" said she.

And she sank down as though on the point of death.

He grasped her, she fell, he took her in his arms, he pressed her close without knowing what he was doing. He supported her, though he was tottering himself. It was as though his brain were full of smoke; lightnings darted between his lips; his ideas vanished; it seemed to him that he was accomplishing some religious act, and that he was committing a profanation. Moreover, he had not the least passion for this lovely woman whose force he felt against his breast. He was beside himself with love.

She took his hand and laid it on her heart. He felt the paper there, he stammered:

"You love me, then?"

She replied in a voice so low that it was no longer anything more than a barely audible breath: "Hush! Thou knowest it!"

And she hid her blushing face on the breast of the superb and intoxicated young man.

He fell upon the bench, and she beside him. They had no words more. The stars were beginning to gleam. How did it come to pass that their lips met? How comes it to pass that the birds sing, that snow melts, that the rose unfolds, that May expands, that the dawn grows white behind the black trees on the shivering crest of the hills?

A kiss, and that was all.

Both started, and gazed into the darkness with sparkling eyes.

They felt neither the cool night, nor the cold stone, nor the damp earth, nor the wet grass; they looked at each other, and their hearts were full of thoughts. They had clasped hands unconsciously.

She did not ask him, she did not even wonder, how he had entered there, and how he had made his way into the garden. It seemed so simple to her that he should be there!

From time to time, Marius's knee touched Cosette's knee, and both shivered.

At intervals, Cosette stammered a word. Her soul fluttered on her lips like a drop of dew on a flower.

Little by little they began to talk to each other. Effusion followed silence, which is fullness. The night was serene and splendid overhead. These two beings, pure as spirits, told each other everything, their dreams, their intoxications, their ecstasies, their chimeras, their weaknesses, how they had adored each other from afar, how they had longed for each other, their despair when they had ceased to see each other. They confided to each other in an ideal intimacy, which nothing could augment, their most secret and most mysterious thoughts. They related to each other, with candid faith in their illusions, all that love, youth, and the remains of childhood which still lingered about them, suggested to their minds. Their two hearts poured themselves out into each other in such wise, that at the expiration of a quarter of an hour, it was the young man who had the young girl's soul, and the young girl who had the young man's soul. Each became permeated with the other, they were enchanted with each other, they dazzled each other.

When they had finished, when they had told each other everything, she laid her head on his shoulder and asked him:

"What is your name?"

"My name is Marius," said he. "And yours?"

"My name is Cosette."

BOOK SIXTH

LITTLE GAVROCHE

Chapter I

THE MALICIOUS PLAYFULNESS OF THE WIND

SINCE 1823, WHEN THE TAVERN OF MONTFERMEIL WAS ON THE WAY TO SHIPWRECK AND WAS BEING gradually engulfed, not in the abyss of a bankruptcy, but in the cesspool of petty debts, the Thénardier pair had had two other children; both males. That made five; two girls and three boys.

Madame Thénardier had got rid of the last two, while they were still young and very small, with remarkable luck.

Got rid of is the word. There was but a mere fragment of nature in that woman. A phenomenon, by the way, of which there is more than one example extant. Like the Maréchale de La Mothe-Houdancourt, the Thénardier was a mother to her daughters only. There her maternity ended. Her hatred of the human race began with her own sons. In the direction of her sons her evil disposition was uncompromising, and her heart had a lugubrious wall in that quarter. As the reader has seen, she detested the eldest; she cursed the other two. Why? Because. The most terrible of motives, the most unanswerable of retorts—Because. "I have no need of a litter of squalling brats," said this mother.

Let us explain how the Thénardiers had succeeded in getting rid of their last two children; and even in drawing profit from the operation.

The woman Magnon, who was mentioned a few pages further back, was the same one who had succeeded in making old Gillenormand support the two children which she had had. She lived on the Quai des Célestins, at the corner of this ancient street of the Petit-Musc which afforded her the opportunity of changing her evil repute into good odor. The reader will remember the great epidemic of croup which ravaged the river districts of the Seine in Paris thirty-five years ago, and of which science took advantage to make experiments on a grand scale as to the efficacy of inhalations of alum, so beneficially replaced at the present day by the external tincture of iodine. During this epidemic, the Magnon lost both her boys, who were still very young, one in the morning, the other in the evening of the same day. This was a blow. These children were precious to their mother; they represented eighty francs a month. These eighty francs were punctually paid in the name of M. Gillenormand, by collector of his rents, M. Barge, a retired tip-staff, in the Rue du Roi-de-Sicile. The children dead, the income was at an end. The Magnon sought an expedient. In that dark free-masonry of evil of which she formed a part, everything is known, all secrets are kept, and all lend mutual aid. Magnon needed two children; the Thénardiers had two. The same sex, the same age. A good arrangement for the one, a good investment for the other. The little Thénardiers became little Magnons. Magnon quitted the Quai des Célestins and went to live in the Rue Clocheperce. In Paris, the identity which binds an individual to himself is broken between one street and another.

The registry office being in no way warned, raised no objections, and the substitution was effected in the most simple manner in the world. Only, the Thénardier exacted for this loan of her children, ten francs a month, which Magnon promised to pay, and which she actually did pay. It is unnecessary to add that M. Gillenormand continued to perform his compact. He came to see the children every six months. He did not perceive the change. "Monsieur," Magnon said to him, "how much they resemble you!"

Thénardier, to whom avatars were easy, seized this occasion to become Jondrette. His two daughters and Gavroche had hardly had time to discover that they had two little brothers. When a certain degree of misery is reached, one is overpowered with a sort of spectral indifference, and one regards human beings as though they were specters. Your nearest relations are often no more for you than vague shadowy forms, barely outlined against a nebulous background of life and easily confounded again with the invisible.

On the evening of the day when she had handed over her two little ones to Magnon, with express intention of renouncing them forever, the Thénardier had felt, or had appeared to feel, a scruple. She said to her husband: "But this is abandoning our children!" Thénardier, masterful and phlegmatic, cauterized the scruple with this saying: "Jean Jacques Rousseau did even better!" From scruples, the mother proceeded to uneasiness: "But what if the police were to annoy us? Tell me, Monsieur Thénardier, is what we have done permissible?" Thénardier replied: "Everything is permissible. No one will see anything but true blue in it. Besides, no one has any interest in looking closely after children who have not a sou."

Magnon was a sort of fashionable woman in the sphere of crime. She was careful about her toilet. She shared her lodgings, which were furnished in an affected and wretched style, with a clever gallicized English thief. This English woman, who had become a naturalized Parisienne, recommended by very wealthy relations, intimately connected with the medals in the Library and Mademoiselle Mar's diamonds, became celebrated later on in judicial accounts. She was called *Mamselle Miss.*

The two little creatures who had fallen to Magnon had no reason to complain of their lot. Recommended by the eighty francs, they were well cared for, as is everything from which profit is derived; they were neither badly clothed, nor badly fed; they were treated almost like "little gentlemen"—better by their false mother than by their real one. Magnon played the lady, and talked no thieves' slang in their presence.

Thus passed several years. Thénardier augured well from the fact. One day, he chanced to say to Magnon as she handed him his monthly stipend of ten francs: "The father must give them some education."

All at once, these two poor children, who had up to that time been protected tolerably well, even by their evil fate, were abruptly hurled into life and forced to begin it for themselves.

A wholesale arrest of malefactors, like that in the Jondrette garret, necessarily complicated by investigations and subsequent incarcerations, is a veritable disaster for that hideous and occult counter-society which pursues its existence beneath public society; an adventure of this description entails all sorts of catastrophes in that somber world. The Thénardier catastrophe involved the catastrophe of Magnon.

One day, a short time after Magnon had handed to Éponine the note relating to the Rue Plumet, a sudden raid was made by the police in the Rue Clocheperce; Magnon was seized, as was also Mamselle Miss; and all the inhabitants of the house, which was of a suspicious character, were gathered into the net. While this was going on, the two little boys were playing in the backyard, and saw nothing of the raid. When they tried to enter the house again, they found the door fastened and the house empty. A cobbler opposite called them to him, and delivered to them a paper which "their mother" had left for them. On this paper there was an address: *M. Barge, collector of rents, Rue du Roi-de-Sicile, No.* 8. The proprietor of the stall said to them: "You cannot live here any longer. Go there. It is nearby. The first street on the left. Ask your way from this paper."

The children set out, the elder leading the younger, and holding in his hand the paper which was to guide them. It was cold, and his benumbed little fingers could not close very firmly, and they did not keep a very good hold on the paper. At the corner of the Rue Clocheperce, a gust of wind tore it from him, and as night was falling, the child was not able to find it again.

They began to wander aimlessly through the streets.

Chapter II

IN WHICH LITTLE GAVROCHE EXTRACTS PROFIT FROM NAPOLEON THE GREAT

SPRING IN PARIS IS OFTEN TRAVERSED BY HARSH AND PIERCING BREEZES WHICH DO NOT PRECISELY chill but freeze one; these north winds which sadden the most beautiful days produce exactly the effect of those puffs of cold air which enter a warm room through the cracks of a badly fitting door or window. It seems as though the gloomy door of winter had remained ajar, and as though the wind were pouring through it. In the spring of 1832, the epoch when the first great epidemic of this century broke out in Europe, these north gales were more harsh and piercing than ever. It was a door even more glacial than that of winter which was ajar. It was the door of the sepulcher. In these winds one felt the breath of the cholera.

From a meteorological point of view, these cold winds possessed this peculiarity, that they did not preclude a strong electric tension. Frequent storms, accompanied by thunder and lightning, burst forth at this epoch.

One evening, when these gales were blowing rudely, to such a degree that January seemed to have returned and that the bourgeois had resumed their cloaks, Little Gavroche, who was always shivering gaily under his rags, was standing as though in ecstasy before a wig-maker's shop in the vicinity of the Orme-Saint-Gervais. He was adorned with a woman's woolen shawl, picked up no one knows where, and which he had converted into a neck comforter. Little Gavroche appeared to be engaged in intent admiration of a wax bride, in a low-necked dress, and crowned with orange-flowers, who was revolving in the window, and displaying her smile to passers-by, between two argand lamps; but in reality, he was taking an observation of the shop, in order to discover whether he could not "prig" from the shop-front a cake of soap, which he would then proceed to sell for a sou to a "hair-dresser" in the suburbs. He had often managed to breakfast off of such a roll. He called his species of work, for which he possessed special aptitude, "shaving barbers."

While contemplating the bride, and eyeing the cake of soap, he muttered between his teeth: "Tuesday. It was not Tuesday. Was it Tuesday? Perhaps it was Tuesday. Yes, it was Tuesday."

No one has ever discovered to what this monologue referred.

Yes, perchance, this monologue had some connection with the last occasion on which he had dined, three days before, for it was now Friday.

The barber in his shop, which was warmed by a good stove, was shaving a customer and casting a glance from time to time at the enemy, that freezing and impudent street urchin both of whose hands were in his pockets, but whose mind was evidently unsheathed.

While Gavroche was scrutinizing the shop-window and the cakes of windsor soap, two children of unequal stature, very neatly dressed, and still smaller than himself, one apparently about seven years of age, the other five, timidly turned the handle and entered the shop, with a request for something or other, alms possibly, in a plaintive murmur which resembled a groan rather than a prayer. They both spoke at once, and their words were unintelligible because sobs broke the voice of the younger, and the teeth of the elder were chattering with the cold. The barber wheeled round with a furious look, and without abandoning his razor, thrust back the elder with his left hand and the younger with his knee, and slammed his door, saying: "The idea of coming in and freezing everybody for nothing!"

The two children resumed their march in tears. In the meantime, a cloud had risen; it had begun to rain.

Little Gavroche ran after them and accosted them:

"What's the matter with you, brats?"

"We don't know where we are to sleep," replied the elder.

"Is that all?" said Gavroche. "A great matter, truly. The idea of bawling about that. They must be greenies!"

And adopting, in addition to his superiority, which was rather bantering, an accent of tender authority and gentle patronage:

"Come along with me, young 'uns!"

"Yes, sir," said the elder.

And the two children followed him as they would have followed an archbishop. They had stopped crying.

Gavroche led them up the Rue Saint-Antoine in the direction of the Bastille.

As Gavroche walked along, he cast an indignant backward glance at the barber's shop.

"That fellow has no heart, the whiting," he muttered. "He's an Englishman."

A woman who caught sight of these three marching in a file, with Gavroche at their head, burst into noisy laughter. This laugh was wanting in respect toward the group.

"Good day, Mamselle Omnibus," said Gavroche to her.

An instant later, the wig-maker occurred to his mind once more, and he added:

"I am making a mistake in the beast; he's not a whiting, he's a serpent. Barber, I'll go and fetch a locksmith, and I'll have a bell hung to your tail."

This wig-maker had rendered him aggressive. As he strode over a gutter, he apostrophized a bearded portress who was worthy to meet Faust on the Brocken, and who had a broom in her hand.

"Madam," said he, "so you are going out with your horse?"

And thereupon, he spattered the polished boots of a pedestrian.

"You scamp!" shouted the furious pedestrian.

Gavroche elevated his nose above his shawl.

"Is Monsieur complaining?"

"Of you!" ejaculated the man.

"The office is closed," said Gavroche, "I do not receive anymore complaints."

In the meanwhile, as he went on up the street, he perceived a beggar-girl, thirteen or fourteen years old, and clad in so short a gown that her knees were visible, lying thoroughly chilled under a porte-cochère. The little girl was getting to be too old for such a thing. Growth does play these tricks. The petticoat becomes short at the moment when nudity becomes indecent.

"Poor girl!" said Gavroche. "She hasn't even trousers. Hold on, take this."

And unwinding all the comfortable woolen which he had around his neck, he flung it on the thin and purple shoulders of the beggar-girl, where the scarf became a shawl once more.

The child stared at him in astonishment, and received the shawl in silence. When a certain stage of distress has been reached in his misery, the poor man no longer groans over evil, no longer returns thanks for good.

That done: "Brrr!" said Gavroche, who was shivering more than Saint Martin, for the latter retained one half of his cloak.

At this *brrr!* the downpour of rain, redoubling its spite, became furious. The wicked skies punish good deeds.

"Ah, come now!" exclaimed Gavroche, "what's the meaning of this? It's reraining! Good Heavens, if it goes on like this, I shall stop my subscription."

And he set out on the march once more.

"It's all right," he resumed, casting a glance at the beggar-girl, as she coiled up under the shawl, "she's got a famous peel."

And looking up at the clouds he exclaimed:

"Caught!"

The two children followed close on his heels.

As they were passing one of these heavy grated lattices, which indicate a baker's shop, for bread is put behind bars like gold, Gavroche turned round:

"Ah, by the way, brats, have we dined?"

"Monsieur," replied the elder, "we have had nothing to eat since this morning."

"So you have neither father nor mother?" resumed Gavroche majestically.

"Excuse us, sir, we have a papa and a mamma, but we don't know where they are."

"Sometimes that's better than knowing where they are," said Gavroche, who was a thinker.

"We have been wandering about these two hours," continued the elder, "we have hunted for things at the corners of the streets, but we have found nothing."

"I know," ejaculated Gavroche, "it's the dogs who eat everything."

He went on, after a pause:

"Ah! we have lost our authors. We don't know what we have done with them. This should not be, gamins. It's stupid to let old people stray off like that. Come now! we must have a snooze all the same."

However, he asked them no questions. What was more simple than that they should have no dwelling-place!

The elder of the two children, who had almost entirely recovered the prompt heedlessness of childhood, uttered this exclamation:

"It's queer, all the same. Mamma told us that she would take us to get a blessed spray on Palm Sunday."

"Bosh," said Gavroche.

"Mamma," resumed the elder, "is a lady who lives with Mamselle Miss."

"Tanflûte!" retorted Gavroche.

Meanwhile he had halted, and for the last two minutes, he had been feeling and fumbling in all sorts of nooks which his rags contained.

At last he tossed his head with an air intended to be merely satisfied, but which was triumphant, in reality.

"Let us be calm, young 'uns. Here's supper for three."

And from one of his pockets he drew forth a sou.

Without allowing the two urchins time for amazement, he pushed both of them before him into the baker's shop, and flung his sou on the counter, crying:

"Boy! five centimes' worth of bread."

The baker, who was the proprietor in person, took up a loaf and a knife.

"In three pieces, my boy!" went on Gavroche.

And he added with dignity:

"There are three of us."

And seeing that the baker, after scrutinizing the three customers had taken down a black loaf, he thrust his finger far up his nose with an inhalation as imperious as though he had had a pinch of the great Frederick's snuff on the tip of his thumb, and hurled this indignant apostrophe full in the baker's face:

"Keksekça?"

Those of our readers who might be tempted to spy in this interpellation of Gavroche's to the baker a Russian or a Polish word, or one of those savage cries which the Yoways and the Botocudos hurl at each other from bank to bank of a river, athwart the solitudes, are warned that it is a word which they [our readers] utter every day, and which takes the place of the phrase: "Qu'est-ce que c'est que cela?" The baker understood perfectly, and replied:

"Well! It's bread, and very good bread of the second quality."

"You mean *larton brutal* [black bread]!" retorted Gavroche, calmly and coldly disdainful. "White bread, boy! white bread [*larton savonné*]! I'm standing treat."

The baker could not repress a smile, and as he cut the white bread, he surveyed them in a compassionate way which shocked Gavroche.

"Come, now, baker's boy!" said he, "what are you taking our measure like that for?"

All three of them placed end to end would have hardly made a measure.

When the bread was cut, the baker threw the sou into his drawer, and Gavroche said to the two children:

"Grub away."

The little boys stared at him in surprise.

Gavroche began to laugh.

"Ah! hullo, that's so! they don't understand yet, they're too small."

And he repeated:

"Eat away."

At the same time, he held out a piece of bread to each of them.

And thinking that the elder, who seemed to him the more worthy of his conversation, deserved some special encouragement and ought to be relieved from all hesitation to satisfy his appetite, he added, as be handed him the largest share:

"Ram that into your muzzle."

One piece was smaller than the others; he kept this for himself.

The poor children, including Gavroche, were famished. As they tore their bread apart in big mouthfuls, they blocked up the shop of the baker, who, now that they had paid their money, looked angrily at them.

"Let's go into the street again," said Gavroche.

They set off once more in the direction of the Bastille.

From time to time, as they passed the lighted shop-windows, the smallest halted to look at the time on a leaden watch which was suspended from his neck by a cord.

"Well, he is a very green 'un," said Gavroche.

Then, becoming thoughtful, he muttered between his teeth:

"All the same, if I had charge of the babes I'd lock 'em up better than that."

Just as they were finishing their morsel of bread, and had reached the angle of that gloomy Rue des Ballets, at the other end of which the low and threatening wicket of La Force was visible:

"Hullo, is that you, Gavroche?" said someone.

"Hullo, is that you, Montparnasse?" said Gavroche.

A man had just accosted the street urchin, and the man was no other than Montparnasse in disguise, with blue spectacles, but recognizable to Gavroche.

"The bow-wows!" went on Gavroche, "you've got a hide the color of a linseed plaster, and blue specs like a doctor. You're putting on style, 'pon my word!"

"Hush!" ejaculated Montparnasse, "not so loud."

And he drew Gavroche hastily out of range of the lighted shops.

The two little ones followed mechanically, holding each other by the hand.

When they were ensconced under the arch of a porte-cochère, sheltered from the rain and from all eyes:

"Do you know where I'm going?" demanded Montparnasse.

"To the Abbey of Ascend-with-Regret,"[1] replied Gavroche.

"Joker!"

And Montparnasse went on:

"I'm going to find Babet."

"Ah!" exclaimed Gavroche, "so her name is Babet."

Montparnasse lowered his voice:

"Not she, he."

"Ah! Babet."

"Yes, Babet."

"I thought he was buckled."

"He has undone the buckle," replied Montparnasse.

And he rapidly related to the gamin how, on the morning of that very day, Babet, having been transferred to La Conciergerie, had made his escape, by turning to the left instead of to the right in "the police office."

Gavroche expressed his admiration for this skill.

"What a dentist!" he cried.

Montparnasse added a few details as to Babet's flight, and ended with:

"Oh! That's not all."

Gavroche, as he listened, had seized a cane that Montparnasse held in his hand, and mechanically pulled at the upper part, and the blade of a dagger made its appearance.

"Ah!" he exclaimed, pushing the dagger back in haste, "you have brought along your gendarme disguised as a bourgeois."

Montparnasse winked.

"The deuce!" resumed Gavroche, "so you're going to have a bout with the bobbies?"

"You can't tell," replied Montparnasse with an indifferent air. "It's always a good thing to have a pin about one."

Gavroche persisted:

"What are you up to to-night?"

Again Montparnasse took a grave tone, and said, mouthing every syllable: "Things."

And abruptly changing the conversation:

"By the way!"

"What?"

"Something happened t'other day. Fancy. I meet a bourgeois. He makes me a present of a sermon and his purse. I put it in my pocket. A minute later, I feel in my pocket. There's nothing there."

"Except the sermon," said Gavroche.

"But you," went on Montparnasse, "where are you bound for now?"

Gavroche pointed to his two protégés, and said:

"I'm going to put these infants to bed."

"Whereabouts is the bed?"

"At my house."

"Where's your house?"

"At my house."

"So you have a lodging?"

"Yes, I have."

"And where is your lodging?"

"In the elephant," said Gavroche.

1. The scaffold.

Montparnasse, though not naturally inclined to astonishment, could not restrain an exclamation.

"In the elephant!"

"Well, yes, in the elephant!" retorted Gavroche. "Kekçaa?"

This is another word of the language which no one writes, and which everyone speaks. Kekçaa signifies: *Qu'est que c'est que cela a?* [What's the matter with that?]

The urchin's profound remark recalled Montparnasse to calmness and good sense. He appeared to return to better sentiments with regard to Gavroche's lodging.

"Of course," said he, "yes, the elephant. Is it comfortable there?"

"Very," said Gavroche. "It's really bully there. There ain't any drafts, as there are under the bridges."

"How do you get in?"

"Oh, I get in."

"So there is a hole?" demanded Montparnasse.

"Parbleu! I should say so. But you mustn't tell. It's between the forelegs. The bobbies haven't seen it."

"And you climb up? Yes, I understand."

"A turn of the hand, cric, crac, and it's all over, no one there."

After a pause, Gavroche added:

"I shall have a ladder for these children."

Montparnasse burst out laughing:

"Where the devil did you pick up those young 'uns?"

Gavroche replied with great simplicity:

"They are some brats that a wig-maker made me a present of."

Meanwhile, Montparnasse had fallen to thinking:

"You recognized me very readily," he muttered.

He took from his pocket two small objects which were nothing more than two quills wrapped in cotton, and thrust one up each of his nostrils. This gave him a different nose.

"That changes you," remarked Gavroche, "you are less homely so, you ought to keep them on all the time."

Montparnasse was a handsome fellow, but Gavroche was a tease.

"Seriously," demanded Montparnasse, "how do you like me so?"

The sound of his voice was different also. In a twinkling, Montparnasse had become unrecognizable.

"Oh! Do play Porrichinelle for us!" exclaimed Gavroche.

The two children, who had not been listening up to this point, being occupied themselves in thrusting their fingers up their noses, drew near at this name, and stared at Montparnasse with dawning joy and admiration.

Unfortunately, Montparnasse was troubled.

He laid his hand on Gavroche's shoulder, and said to him, emphasizing his words: "Listen to what I tell you, boy! if I were on the square with my dog, my knife, and my wife, and if you were to squander ten sous on me, I wouldn't refuse to work, but this isn't Shrove Tuesday."

This odd phrase produced a singular effect on the gamin. He wheeled round hastily, darted his little sparkling eyes about him with profound attention, and perceived a police sergeant standing with his back to them a few paces off. Gavroche allowed an: "Ah! good!" to escape him, but immediately suppressed it, and shaking Montparnasse's hand:

"Well, good evening," said he, "I'm going off to my elephant with my brats. Supposing that you should need me some night, you can come and hunt me up there. I lodge on the entresol. There is no porter. You will inquire for Monsieur Gavroche."

"Very good," said Montparnasse.

And they parted, Montparnasse betaking himself in the direction of the Grève, and Gavroche toward the Bastille. The little one of five, dragged along by his brother who was dragged by Gavroche, turned his head back several times to watch "Porrichinelle" as he went.

The ambiguous phrase by means of which Montparnasse had warned Gavroche of the presence of the policeman, contained no other talisman than the assonance *dig* repeated five or six times in different forms. This syllable, *dig,* uttered alone or artistically mingled with the words of a phrase, means: "Take care, we can no longer talk freely." There was besides, in Montparnasse's sentence, a literary beauty which was lost upon Gavroche, that is *mon dogue, ma dague et ma digue,* a slang expression of the Temple, which signifies my dog, my knife, and my wife, greatly in vogue among clowns and the red-tails in the great century when Molière wrote and Callot drew.

Twenty years ago, there was still to be seen in the southwest corner of the Place de la Bastille, near the basin of the canal, excavated in the ancient ditch of the fortress-prison, a singular monument, which has already been effaced from the memories of Parisians, and which deserved to leave some trace, for it was the idea of a "member of the Institute, the General-in-chief of the army of Egypt."

We say monument, although it was only a rough model. But this model itself, a marvelous sketch, the grandiose skeleton of an idea of Napoleon's, which successive gusts of wind have carried away and thrown, on each occasion, still further from us, had become historical and had acquired a certain definiteness which contrasted with its provisional aspect. It was an elephant forty feet high, constructed of timber and masonry, bearing on its back a tower which resembled a house, formerly painted green by some dauber, and now painted black by heaven, the wind, and time. In this deserted and unprotected corner of the place, the broad brow of the colossus, his trunk, his tusks, his tower, his enormous crupper, his four feet, like columns produced, at night, under the starry heavens, a surprising and terrible form. It was a sort of symbol of popular force. It was somber, mysterious, and immense. It was some mighty, visible phantom, one knew not what, standing erect beside the invisible specter of the Bastille.

Few strangers visited this edifice, no passer-by looked at it. It was falling into ruins; every season the plaster which detached itself from its sides formed hideous wounds upon it. "The aediles," as the expression ran in elegant dialect, had forgotten it ever since 1814. There it stood in its corner, melancholy, sick, crumbling, surrounded by a rotten palisade, soiled continually by drunken coachmen; cracks meandered athwart its belly, a lath projected from its tail, tall grass flourished between its legs; and, as the level of the place had been rising all around it for a space of thirty years, by that slow and continuous movement which insensibly elevates the soil of large towns, it stood in a hollow, and it looked as though the ground were giving way beneath it. It was unclean, despised, repulsive, and superb, ugly in the eyes of the bourgeois, melancholy in the eyes of the thinker. There was something about it of the dirt which is on the point of being swept out, and something of the majesty which is on the point of being decapitated. As we have said, at night, its aspect changed. Night is the real element of everything that is dark. As soon as twilight descended, the old elephant became transfigured; he assumed a tranquil and redoubtable appearance in the formidable serenity of the shadows. Being of the past, he belonged to night; and obscurity was in keeping with his grandeur.

This rough, squat, heavy, hard, austere, almost misshapen, but assuredly majestic monument, stamped with a sort of magnificent and savage gravity, has disappeared, and left to reign in peace, a sort of gigantic stove, ornamented with its pipe, which has replaced the somber fortress with its nine towers, very much as the bourgeoisie replaces the feudal classes. It is quite natural that a stove should be the symbol of an epoch in which a pot contains power. This epoch will pass away, people have already begun to understand that, if there can be force in a boiler, there can be no force except in the brain; in other words, that which leads and drags on the world, is not locomotives, but ideas. Harness locomotives to ideas—that is well done; but do not mistake the horse for the rider.

At all events, to return to the Place de la Bastille, the architect of this elephant succeeded in making a grand thing out of plaster; the architect of the stove has succeeded in making a pretty thing out of bronze.

This stove-pipe, which has been baptized by a sonorous name, and called the column of July, this monument of a revolution that miscarried, was still enveloped in 1832, in an immense shirt of woodwork, which we regret, for our part, and by a vast plank enclosure, which completed the task of isolating the elephant.

It was toward this corner of the place, dimly lighted by the reflection of a distant street lamp, that the gamin guided his two "brats."

The reader must permit us to interrupt ourselves here and to remind him that we are dealing with simple reality, and that twenty years ago, the tribunals were called upon to judge, under the charge of vagabondage, and mutilation of a public monument, a child who had been caught asleep in this very elephant of the Bastille. This fact noted, we proceed.

On arriving in the vicinity of the colossus, Gavroche comprehended the effect which the infinitely great might produce on the infinitely small, and said:

"Don't be scared, infants."

Then he entered through a gap in the fence into the elephant's enclosure and helped the young ones to clamber through the breach. The two children, somewhat frightened, followed Gavroche without uttering a word, and confided themselves to this little Providence in rags which had given them bread and had promised them a shelter.

There, extended along the fence, lay a ladder which by day served the laborers in the neighboring timber-yard. Gavroche raised it with remarkable vigor, and placed it against one of the elephant's forelegs. Near the point where the ladder ended, a sort of black hole in the belly of the colossus could be distinguished.

Gavroche pointed out the ladder and the hole to his guests, and said to them:

"Climb up and go in."

The two little boys exchanged terrified glances.

"You're afraid, brats!" exclaimed Gavroche.

And he added:

"You shall see!"

He clasped the rough leg of the elephant, and in a twinkling, without deigning to make use of the ladder, he had reached the aperture. He entered it as an adder slips through a crevice, and disappeared within, and an instant later, the two children saw his head, which looked pale, appear vaguely, on the edge of the shadowy hole, like a wan and whitish specter.

"Well!" he exclaimed, "climb up, young 'uns! You'll see how snug it is here! Come up, you!" he said to the elder, "I'll lend you a hand."

The little fellows nudged each other, the gamin frightened and inspired them with confidence at one and the same time, and then, it was raining very hard. The elder one undertook the risk. The younger, on seeing his brother climbing up, and himself left alone between the paws of this huge beast, felt greatly inclined to cry, but he did not dare.

The elder lad climbed, with uncertain steps, up the rungs of the ladder; Gavroche, in the meanwhile, encouraging him with exclamations like a fencing-master to his pupils, or a muleteer to his mules.

"Don't be afraid!—That's it!—Come on!—Put your feet there!—Give us your hand here!—Boldly!"

And when the child was within reach, he seized him suddenly and vigorously by the arm and pulled him toward him.

"Nabbed!" said he.

The brat had passed through the crack.

"Now," said Gavroche, "wait for me. Be so good as to take a seat, Monsieur."

And making his way out of the hole as he had entered it, he slipped down the elephant's leg with the agility of a monkey, landed on his feet in the grass, grasped the child of five round the body, and planted him fairly in the middle of the ladder, then he began to climb up behind him, shouting to the elder:

"I'm going to boost him, do you tug."

And in another instant, the small lad was pushed, dragged, pulled, thrust, stuffed into the hole, before he had time to recover himself, and Gavroche, entering behind him, and repulsing the ladder with a kick which sent it flat on the grass, began to clap his hands and to cry:

"Here we are! Long live General Lafayette!"

This explosion over, he added:

"Now, young 'uns, you are in my house."

Gavroche was at home, in fact.

Oh, unforeseen utility of the useless! Charity of great things! Goodness of giants! This huge monument, which had embodied an idea of the Emperor's had become the box of a street urchin. The brat had been accepted and sheltered by the colossus. The bourgeois decked out in their Sunday finery who passed the elephant of the Bastille, were fond of saying as they scanned it disdainfully with their prominent eyes: "What's the good of that?" It served to save from the cold, the frost, the hail, and rain, to shelter from the winds of winter, to preserve from slumber in the mud which produces fever, and from slumber in the snow which produces death, a little being who had no father, no mother, no bread, no clothes, no refuge. It served to receive the innocent whom society repulsed. It served to diminish public crime. It was a lair open to one against whom all doors were shut. It seemed as though the miserable old mastodon, invaded by vermin and oblivion, covered with warts, with mold, and ulcers, tottering, wormeaten, abandoned, condemned, a sort of mendicant colossus, asking alms in vain with a benevolent look in the midst of the cross-roads, had taken pity on that other mendicant, the poor pygmy, who roamed without shoes to his feet, without a roof over his head, blowing on his fingers, clad in rags, fed on rejected scraps. That was what the elephant of the Bastille was good for. This idea of Napoleon, disdained by men, had been taken back by God. That which had been merely illustrious, had become august. In order to realize his thought, the Emperor should have had porphyry, brass, iron, gold, marble; the old collection of planks, beams, and plaster sufficed for God. The Emperor had had the dream of a genius; in that Titanic elephant, armed, prodigious, with trunk uplifted, bearing its tower, and scattering on all sides its merry and vivifying waters, he wished to incarnate the people. God had done a grander thing with it, he had lodged a child there.

The hole through which Gavroche had entered was a breach which was hardly visible from the outside, being concealed, as we have stated, beneath the elephant's belly, and so narrow that it was only cats and homeless children who could pass through it.

"Let's begin," said Gavroche, "by telling the porter that we are not at home."

And plunging into the darkness with the assurance of a person who is well acquainted with his apartments, he took a plank and stopped up the aperture.

Again Gavroche plunged into the obscurity. The children heard the crackling of the match thrust into the phosphoric bottle. The chemical match was not yet in existence; at that epoch, the Fumade steel represented progress.

A sudden light made them blink; Gavroche had just managed to ignite one of those bits of cord dipped in resin which are called *cellar rats*. The *cellar rat*, which emitted more smoke than light, rendered the interior of the elephant confusedly visible.

Gavroche's two guests glanced about them, and the sensation which they experienced was something like that which one would feel if shut up in the great tun of Heidelberg, or, better still, like what Jonah must have felt in the biblical belly of the whale. An entire and gigantic skeleton appeared enveloping them. Above, a long brown beam, whence started at regular distances, massive, arching ribs, represented the vertebral column with its sides, stalactites of plaster depended from them like entrails, and vast spiders' webs stretching from side to side, formed dirty diaphragms. Here and there, in the corners, were visible large blackish spots which had the appearance of being alive, and which changed places rapidly with an abrupt and frightened movement.

Fragments which had fallen from the elephant's back into his belly had filled up the cavity, so that it was possible to walk upon it as on a floor.

The smaller child nestled up against his brother and whispered to him:

"It's black."

This remark drew an exclamation from Gavroche. The petrified air of the two brats rendered some shock necessary.

"What's that you're gabbling about there?" he exclaimed. "Are you scoffing at me? Are you turning up your noses? Do you want the Tuileries? Are you brutes? Come, say! I warn you that I don't belong to the regiment of simpletons. Ah, come now, are you brats from the Pope's establishment?"

A little roughness is good in cases of fear. It is reassuring. The two children drew close to Gavroche.

Gavroche, paternally touched by this confidence, passed from grave to gentle, and addressing the smaller:

"Stupid," said he, accenting the insulting word, with a caressing intonation, "it's outside that it is black. Outside it's raining, here it does not rain; outside it's cold, here there's not an atom of wind; outside there are heaps of people, here there's no one; outside there ain't even the moon, here there's my candle, confound it!"

The two children began to look upon the apartment with less terror; but Gavroche allowed them no more time for contemplation.

"Quick," said he.

And he pushed them toward what we are very glad to be able to call the end of the room.

There stood his bed.

Gavroche's bed was complete; that is to say, it had a mattress, a blanket, and an alcove with curtains.

The mattress was a straw mat, the blanket a rather large strip of gray woolen stuff, very warm and almost new. This is what the alcove consisted of:

Three rather long poles, thrust into and consolidated with the rubbish which formed the floor, that is to say, the belly of the elephant, two in front and one behind, and united by a rope at their summits, so as to form a pyramidal bundle. This cluster supported a trellis-work of brass wire which was simply placed upon it, but artistically applied, and held by fastenings of iron wire, so that it enveloped all three poles. A row of very heavy stones kept this network down to the floor so that nothing could pass under it. This grating was nothing else than a piece of the brass screens with which aviaries are covered in menageries. Gavroche's bed stood as in a cage, behind this net. The whole resembled an Esquimaux tent.

This trellis-work took the place of curtains.

Gavroche moved aside the stones which fastened the net down in front, and the two folds of the net which lapped over each other fell apart.

"Down on all fours, brats!" said Gavroche.

He made his guests enter the cage with great precaution, then he crawled in after them, pulled the stones together, and closed the opening hermetically again.

All three had stretched out on the mat. Gavroche still had the *cellar rat* in his hand.

"Now," said he, "go to sleep! I'm going to suppress the candelabra."

"Monsieur," the elder of the brothers asked Gavroche, pointing to the netting, "what's that for?"

"That," answered Gavroche gravely, "is for the rats. Go to sleep!"

Nevertheless, he felt obliged to add a few words of instruction for the benefit of these young creatures, and he continued:

"It's a thing from the Jardin des Plantes. It's used for fierce animals. There's a whole shopful of them there. All you've got to do is to climb over a wall, crawl through a window, and pass through a door. You can get as much as you want."

As he spoke, he wrapped the younger one up bodily in a fold of the blanket, and the little one murmured:

"Oh! how good that is! It's warm!"

Gavroche cast a pleased eye on the blanket.

"That's from the Jardin des Plantes, too," said he. "I took that from the monkeys."

And, pointing out to the eldest the mat on which he was lying, a very thick and admirably made mat, he added:

"That belonged to the giraffe."

After a pause he went on:

"The beasts had all these things. I took them away from them. It didn't trouble them. I told them: 'It's for the elephant.' "

He paused, and then resumed:

"You crawl over the walls and you don't care a straw for the government. So there now!"

The two children gazed with timid and stupefied respect on this intrepid and ingenious being, a vagabond like themselves, isolated like themselves, frail like themselves, who had something admirable and all-powerful about him, who seemed supernatural to them, and whose physiognomy was composed of all the grimaces of an old mountebank, mingled with the most ingenuous and charming smiles.

"Monsieur," ventured the elder timidly, "you are not afraid of the police, then?"

Gavroche contented himself with replying:

"Brat! Nobody says 'police,' they say 'bobbies.' "

The smaller had his eyes wide open, but he said nothing. As he was on the edge of the mat, the elder being in the middle, Gavroche tucked the blanket round him as a mother might have done, and heightened the mat under his head with old rags, in such a way as to form a pillow for the child. Then he turned to the elder:

"Hey? We're jolly comfortable here, ain't we?"

"Ah, yes!" replied the elder, gazing at Gavroche with the expression of a saved angel.

The two poor little children who had been soaked through, began to grow warm once more.

"Ah, by the way," continued Gavroche, "what were you bawling about?"

And pointing out the little one to his brother:

"A mite like that, I've nothing to say about, but the idea of a big fellow like you crying! It's idiotic; you looked like a calf."

"Gracious," replied the child, "we have no lodging."

"Bother!" retorted Gavroche, "you don't say 'lodgings,' you say 'crib.' "

"And then, we were afraid of being alone like that at night."

"You don't say 'night,' you say 'darkmans.' "

"Thank you, sir," said the child.

"Listen," went on Gavroche, "you must never bawl again over anything. I'll take care of you. You shall see what fun we'll have. In summer, we'll go to the Glacière with Navet, one of my pals, we'll bathe in the Gare, we'll run stark naked in front of the rafts on the bridge at Austerlitz—that makes the laundresses raging. They scream, they get mad, and if you only knew how ridiculous they are! We'll go and see the man-skeleton. And then I'll take you to the play. I'll take you to see Frédérick Lemaître. I have tickets, I know some of the actors, I even played in a piece once. There were a lot of us fellers, and we ran under a cloth, and that made the sea. I'll get you an engagement at my theater. We'll go to see the savages. They ain't real, those savages ain't. They wear pink tights that go all in wrinkles, and you can see where their elbows have been darned with white. Then, we'll go to the Opera. We'll get in with the hired applauders. The Opera claque is well managed. I wouldn't associate with the claque on the boulevard. At the Opera, just fancy! some of them pay twenty sous, but they're ninnies. They're called dishclouts. And then we'll go to see the guillotine work. I'll show you the executioner. He lives in the Rue des Marais. Monsieur Sanson. He has a letter-box at his door. Ah! we'll have famous fun!"

At that moment a drop of wax fell on Gavroche's finger, and recalled him to the realities of life.

"The deuce!" said he, "there's the wick giving out. Attention! I can't spend more than a sou a month on my lighting. When a body goes to bed, he must sleep. We haven't the time to read M. Paul de Kock's romances. And besides, the light might pass through the cracks of the porte-cochère, and all the bobbies need to do is to see it."

"And then," remarked the elder timidly—he alone dared talk to Gavroche, and reply to him, "a spark might fall in the straw, and we must look out and not burn the house down."

"People don't say 'burn the house down,' " remarked Gavroche, "they say 'blaze the crib.' "

The storm increased in violence, and the heavy downpour beat upon the back of the colossus amid claps of thunder. "You're taken in, rain!" said Gavroche. "It amuses me to hear the decanter run down the legs of the house. Winter is a stupid; it wastes its merchandise, it loses its labor, it can't wet us, and that makes it kick up a row, old water-carrier that it is."

This allusion to the thunder, all the consequences of which Gavroche, in his character of a philosopher of the nineteenth century, accepted, was followed by a broad flash of lightning, so dazzling that a hint of it entered the belly of the elephant through the crack. Almost at the same instant, the thunder rumbled with great fury. The two little creatures uttered a shriek, and started up so eagerly that the network came near being displaced, but Gavroche turned his bold face to them, and took advantage of the clap of thunder to burst into a laugh.

"Calm down, children. Don't topple over the edifice. That's fine, first-class thunder; all right. That's no slouch of a streak of lightning. Bravo for the good God! Deuce take it! It's almost as good as it is at the Ambigu."

That said, he restored order in the netting, pushed the two children gently down on the bed, pressed their knees, in order to stretch them out at full length, and exclaimed:

"Since the good God is lighting his candle, I can blow out mine. Now, babes, now, my young humans, you must shut your peepers. It's very bad not to sleep. It'll make you swallow the strainer, or, as they say in fashionable society, stink in the gullet. Wrap yourself up well in the hide! I'm going to put out the light. Are you ready?"

"Yes," murmured the elder, "I'm all right. I seem to have feathers under my head."

"People don't say 'head,' " cried Gavroche, "they say 'nut.' "

The two children nestled close to each other, Gavroche finished arranging them on the mat, drew the blanket up to their very ears, then repeated, for the third time, his injunction in the hieratical tongue:

"Shut your peepers!"

And he snuffed out his tiny light.

Hardly had the light been extinguished, when a peculiar trembling began to affect the netting under which the three children lay.

It consisted of a multitude of dull scratches which produced a metallic sound, as if claws and teeth were gnawing at the copper wire. This was accompanied by all sorts of little piercing cries.

The little five-year-old boy, on hearing this hubbub overhead, and chilled with terror, jogged his brother's elbow; but the elder brother had already shut his peepers, as Gavroche had ordered.

Then the little one, who could no longer control his terror, questioned Gavroche, but in a very low tone, and with bated breath:

"Sir?"

"Hey?" said Gavroche, who had just closed his eyes.

"What is that?"

"It's the rats," replied Gavroche.

And he laid his head down on the mat again.

The rats, in fact, who swarmed by thousands in the carcass of the elephant, and who were the living black spots which we have already mentioned, had been held in awe by the flame of the candle, so long as it had been lighted; but as soon as the cavern, which was the same as their city, had returned to darkness, scenting what the good story-teller Perrault calls "fresh meat," they had hurled themselves in throngs on Gavroche's tent, had climbed to the top of it, and had begun to bite the meshes as though seeking to pierce this new-fangled trap.

Still the little one could not sleep.

"Sir?" he began again.

"Hey?" said Gavroche.

"What are rats?"

"They are mice."

This explanation reassured the child a little. He had seen white mice in the course of his life, and he was not afraid of them. Nevertheless, he lifted up his voice once more.

"Sir?"

"Hey?" said Gavroche again.

"Why don't you have a cat?"

"I did have one," replied Gavroche, "I brought one here, but they ate her."

This second explanation undid the work of the first, and the little fellow began to tremble again.

The dialogue between him and Gavroche began again for the fourth time:

"Monsieur?"

"Hey?"

"Who was it that was eaten?"

"The cat."

"And who ate the cat?"

"The rats."

"The mice?"

"Yes, the rats."

The child, in consternation, dismayed at the thought of mice which ate cats, pursued:

"Sir, would those mice eat us?"

"Wouldn't they just!" ejaculated Gavroche.

The child's terror had reached its climax. But Gavroche added:

"Don't be afraid. They can't get in. And besides, I'm here! Here, catch hold of my hand. Hold your tongue and shut your peepers!"

At the same time Gavroche grasped the little fellow's hand across his brother. The child pressed the hand close to him, and felt reassured. Courage and strength have these mysterious ways of communicating themselves. Silence reigned round them once more, the sound of their voices had frightened off the rats; at the expiration of a few minutes, they came raging back, but in vain, the three little fellows were fast asleep and heard nothing more.

The hours of the night fled away. Darkness covered the vast Place de la Bastille. A wintry gale, which mingled with the rain, blew in gusts, the patrol searched all the doorways, alleys, enclosures, and obscure nooks, and in their search for nocturnal vagabonds, they passed in silence before the elephant; the monster, erect, motionless, staring open-eyed into the shadows, had the appearance of dreaming happily over his good deed; and sheltered from heaven and from men the three poor sleeping children.

In order to understand what is about to follow, the reader must remember, that, at that epoch, the Bastille guard-house was situated at the other end of the square, and that what took place in the vicinity of the elephant could neither be seen nor heard by the sentinel.

Toward the end of that hour which immediately precedes the dawn, a man turned from the Rue Saint-Antoine at a run, made the circuit of the enclosure of the column of July, and glided between the palings until he was underneath the belly of the elephant. If any light had illuminated that man, it might have been divined from the thorough manner in which he was soaked, that he had passed the night in the rain. Arrived beneath the elephant, he uttered a peculiar cry, which did not belong to any human tongue, and which a parakeet alone could have imitated. Twice he repeated this cry, of whose orthography the following barely conveys an idea:

"Kirikikiou!"

At the second cry, a clear, young, merry voice responded from the belly of the elephant: "Yes!"

Almost immediately, the plank which closed the hole was drawn aside, and gave passage to a child who descended the elephant's leg, and fell briskly near the man. It was Gavroche. The man was Montparnasse.

As for his cry of *Kirikikiou*—that was, doubtless, what the child had meant, when he said: "You will ask for Monsieur Gavroche."

On hearing it, he had waked with a start, had crawled out of his "alcove," pushing apart the netting a little, and carefully drawing it together again, then he had opened the trap, and descended.

The man and the child recognized each other silently amid the gloom: Montparnasse confined himself to the remark:

"We need you. Come, lend us a hand."

The lad asked for no further enlightenment.

"I'm with you," said he.

And both took their way toward the Rue Saint-Antoine, whence Montparnasse had emerged, winding rapidly through the long file of market-gardeners' carts which descend toward the markets at that hour.

The market-gardeners, crouching, half-asleep, in their wagons, amid the salads and vegetables, enveloped to their very eyes in their mufflers on account of the beating rain, did not even glance at these strange pedestrians.

Chapter III

THE VICISSITUDES OF FLIGHT

THIS IS WHAT HAD TAKEN PLACE THAT SAME NIGHT AT THE LA FORCE:

An escape had been planned between Babet, Brujon, Guelemer, and Thénardier, although Thénardier was in close confinement. Babet had arranged the matter for his own benefit, on the same day, as the reader has seen from Montparnasse's account to Gavroche. Montparnasse was to help them from outside.

Brujon, after having passed a month in the punishment cell, had had time, in the first place, to weave a rope, in the second, to mature a plan. In former times, those severe places where the discipline of the prison delivers the convict into his own hands, were composed of four stone walls, a stone ceiling, a flagged pavement, a camp bed, a grated window, and a door lined with iron, and were called *dungeons*; but the dungeon was judged to be too terrible; nowadays they are composed of an iron door, a grated window, a camp bed, a flagged pavement, four stone walls, and a stone ceiling, and are called *chambers of punishment*. A little light penetrates toward midday. The inconvenient point about these chambers which, as the reader sees, are not dungeons, is that they allow the persons who should be at work to think.

So Brujon meditated, and he emerged from the chamber of punishment with a rope. As he had the name of being very dangerous in the Charlemagne courtyard, he was placed in the New Building. The first thing he found in the New Building was Guelemer, the second was a nail; Guelemer, that is to say, crime; a nail, that is to say, liberty. Brujon, of whom it is high time that the reader should have a complete idea, was, with an appearance of delicate health and a profoundly premeditated languor, a polished, intelligent sprig, and a thief, who had a caressing glance, and an atrocious smile. His glance resulted from his will, and his smile from his nature. His first studies in his art had been directed to roofs. He had made great progress in the industry of the men who tear off lead, who plunder the roofs and despoil the gutters by the process called *double pickings*.

The circumstance which put the finishing touch on the moment peculiarly favorable for an attempt at escape, was that the roofers were relaying and rejointing, at that very moment, a portion of the slates on the prison. The Saint-Bernard courtyard was no longer absolutely isolated from the Charlemagne and the Saint-Louis courts. Up above there were scaffoldings and ladders; in other words, bridges and stairs in the direction of liberty.

The New Building, which was the most cracked and decrepit thing to be seen anywhere in the world, was the weak point in the prison. The walls were eaten by saltpeter to such an extent that the authorities had been obliged to line the vaults of the dormitories with a sheathing of wood, because stones were in the habit of becoming detached and falling on the prisoners in their beds. In spite of this antiquity, the authorities committed the error of confining in the New Building the most troublesome prisoners, of placing there "the hard cases," as they say in prison parlance.

The New Building contained four dormitories, one above the other, and a top story which was called the Bel-Air (Fine-Air). A large chimney-flue, probably from some ancient kitchen of the Dukes de la Force, started from the ground floor, traversed all four stories, cut the dormitories, where it figured as a flattened pillar, into two portions, and finally pierced the roof.

Guelemer and Brujon were in the same dormitory. They had been placed, by way of precaution, on the lower story. Chance ordained that the heads of their beds should rest against the chimney.

Thénardier was directly over their heads in the top story known as Fine-Air. The pedestrian who halts on the Rue Culture-Sainte-Catherine, after passing the barracks of the firemen, in front of the porte-cochère of the bathing establishment, beholds a yard full of flowers and shrubs in wooden boxes, at the extremity of which spreads out a little white rotunda with two wings, brightened up with green shutters, the bucolic dream of Jean Jacques.

Not more than ten years ago, there rose above that rotunda an enormous black, hideous, bare wall by which it was backed up.

This was the outer wall of La Force.

This wall, beside that rotunda, was Milton viewed through Berquin.

Lofty as it was, this wall was overtopped by a still blacker roof, which could be seen beyond. This was the roof of the New Building. There one could descry four dormer-windows, guarded with bars; they were the windows of the Fine-Air.

A chimney pierced the roof; this was the chimney which traversed the dormitories.

The Bel-Air, that top story of the New Building, was a sort of large hall, with a Mansard roof, guarded with triple gratings and double doors of sheet iron, which were studded with enormous bolts. When one entered from the north end, one had on one's left the four dormer-windows, on one's right, facing the windows, at regular intervals, four square, tolerably vast cages, separated by narrow passages, built of masonry to about the height of the elbow, and the rest, up to the roof, of iron bars.

Thénardier had been in solitary confinement in one of these cages since the night of the 3d of February. No one was ever able to discover how, and by what connivance, he succeeded in procuring, and secreting a bottle of wine, invented, so it is said, by Desrues, with which a narcotic is mixed, and which the band of the *Endormeurs,* or *Sleep-compellers,* rendered famous.

There are, in many prisons, treacherous employees, half-jailers, half-thieves, who assist in escapes, who sell to the police an unfaithful service, and who turn a penny whenever they can.

On that same night, then, when Little Gavroche picked up the two lost children, Brujon and Guelemer, who knew that Babet, who had escaped that morning, was waiting for them in the street as well as Montparnasse, rose softly, and with the nail which Brujon had found, began to pierce the chimney against which their beds stood. The rubbish fell on Brujon's bed, so that they were not heard. Showers mingled with thunder shook the doors on their hinges, and created in the prison a terrible and opportune uproar. Those of the prisoners who woke, pretended to fall asleep again, and left Guelemer and Brujon to their own devices. Brujon was adroit; Guelemer was vigorous. Before any sound had reached the watcher, who was sleeping in the grated cell which opened into the dormitory, the wall had been pierced, the chimney scaled, the iron grating which barred the upper orifice of the flue forced, and the two redoubtable ruffians were on the roof. The wind and rain redoubled, the roof was slippery.

"What a good night to leg it!" said Brujon.

An abyss six feet broad and eighty feet deep separated them from the surrounding wall. At the bottom of this abyss, they could see the musket of a sentinel gleaming through the gloom. They fastened one end of the rope which Brujon had spun in his dungeon to the stumps of the iron bars which they had just wrenched off, flung the other over the outer wall, crossed the abyss at one bound, clung to the coping of the wall, got astride of it, let themselves slip, one after the other, along the rope, upon a little roof which touches the bath-house, pulled their rope after them, jumped down into the courtyard of the bath-house, traversed it, pushed open the porter's wicket, beside which hung his rope, pulled this, opened the porte-cochère, and found themselves in the street.

Three-quarters of an hour had not elapsed since they had risen in bed in the dark, nail in hand, and their project in their heads.

A few moments later they had joined Babet and Montparnasse, who were prowling about the neighborhood.

They had broken their rope in pulling it after them, and a bit of it remained attached to the chimney on the roof. They had sustained no other damage, however, than that of scratching nearly all the skin off their hands.

That night, Thénardier was warned, without anyone being able to explain how, and was not asleep.

Toward one o'clock in the morning, the night being very dark, he saw two shadows pass along the roof, in the rain and squalls, in front of the dormer-window which was opposite his cage. One halted at the window, long enough to dart in a glance. This was Brujon.

Thénardier recognized him, and understood. This was enough.

Thénardier, rated as a burglar, and detained as a measure of precaution under the charge of organizing a nocturnal ambush, with armed force, was kept in sight. The sentry, who was relieved every two hours, marched up and down in front of his cage with loaded musket. The Fine-Air was lighted by a skylight. The prisoner had on his feet fetters weighing fifty pounds. Every day, at four o'clock in the afternoon, a jailer, escorted by two dogs—this was still in vogue at that time—entered his cage, deposited beside his bed a loaf of black bread, weighing two pounds, a jug of water, a bowl filled with rather thin bouillon, in which swam a few Mayagan beans, inspected his irons and tapped the bars. This man and his dogs made two visits during the night.

Thénardier had obtained permission to keep a sort of iron bolt which he used to spike his bread into a crack in the wall, "in order to preserve it from the rats," as he said. As Thénardier was kept in sight, no objection had been made to this spike. Still, it was remembered afterwards, that one of the jailers had said: "It would be better to let him have only a wooden spike."

At two o'clock in the morning, the sentinel, who was an old soldier, was relieved, and replaced by a conscript. A few moments later, the man with the dogs paid his visit, and went off without noticing anything, except, possibly, the excessive youth and "the rustic air" of the "raw recruit." Two hours afterwards, at four o'clock, when they came to relieve the conscript, he was found asleep on the floor, lying like a log near Thénardier's cage. As for Thénardier, he was no longer there. There was a hole in the ceiling of his cage, and, above it, another hole in the roof. One of the planks of his bed had been wrenched off, and probably carried away with him, as it was not found. They also seized in his cell a half-empty bottle which contained the remains of the stupefying wine with which the soldier had been drugged. The soldier's bayonet had disappeared.

At the moment when this discovery was made, it was assumed that Thénardier was out of reach. The truth is, that he was no longer in the New Building, but that he was still in great danger.

Thénardier, on reaching the roof of the New Building, had found the remains of Brujon's rope hanging to the bars of the upper trap of the chimney, but, as this broken fragment was much too short, he had not been able to escape by the outer wall, as Brujon and Guelemer had done.

When one turns from the Rue des Ballets into the Rue du Roi-de-Sicile, one almost immediately encounters a repulsive ruin. There stood on that spot, in the last century, a house of which only the back wall now remains, a regular wall of masonry, which rises to the height of the third story between the adjoining buildings. This ruin can be recognized by two large square windows which are still to be seen there; the middle one, that nearest the right gable, is barred with a worm-eaten beam adjusted like a prop. Through these windows there was formerly visible a lofty and lugubrious wall, which was a fragment of the outer wall of La Force.

The empty space on the street left by the demolished house is half-filled by a fence of rotten boards, shored up by five stone posts. In this recess lies concealed a little shanty which leans against the portion of the ruin which has remained standing. The fence has a gate, which, a few years ago, was fastened only by a latch.

It was the crest of this ruin that Thénardier had succeeded in reaching, a little after one o'clock in the morning.

How had he got there? That is what no one has ever been able to explain or understand. The lightning must, at the same time, have hindered and helped him. Had he made use of the ladders and scaffoldings of the slaters to get from roof to roof, from enclosure to enclosure, from compartment to compartment, to the buildings of the Charlemagne court, then to the buildings of the Saint-Louis court, to the outer wall, and thence to the hut on the Rue du Roi-de-Sicile? But in that itinerary there existed breaks which seemed to render it an impossibility. Had he placed the plank from his bed like a bridge from the roof of the Fine-Air to the outer wall, and crawled flat on his belly on the coping of the outer wall the whole distance round the prison as far as the hut? But the outer wall of La Force formed a crenellated and unequal line; it mounted and descended, it dropped at the firemen's barracks, it rose toward the bath-house, it was cut in twain by buildings, it was not even of the same height on the Hôtel Lamoignon as on the Rue Pavée; everywhere occurred falls and right angles; and then, the sentinels must have spied the dark form of the fugitive; hence, the route taken by Thénardier still remains rather inexplicable. In two manners, flight was impossible. Had Thénardier, spurred on by that thirst for liberty which changes precipices into ditches, iron bars into wattles of osier, a legless man into an athlete, a gouty man into a bird, stupidity into instinct, instinct into intelligence, and intelligence into genius, had Thénardier invented a third mode? No one has ever found out.

The marvels of escape cannot always be accounted for. The man who makes his escape, we repeat, is inspired; there is something of the star and of the lightning in the mysterious gleam of flight; the effort toward deliverance is no less surprising than the flight toward the sublime, and one says of the escaped thief: "How did he contrive to scale that wall?" in the same way that one says of Corneille: "Where did he find *the means of dying?*"

At all events, dripping with perspiration, drenched with rain, with his clothes hanging in ribbons, his hands flayed, his elbows bleeding, his knees torn, Thénardier had reached what children, in their figurative language, call *the edge* of the wall of the ruin, there he had stretched himself out at full length, and there his strength had failed him. A steep escarpment three stories high separated him from the pavement of the street.

The rope which he had was too short.

There he waited, pale, exhausted, desperate with all the despair which he had undergone, still hidden by the night, but telling himself that the day was on the point of dawning, alarmed at the idea of hearing the neighboring clock of Saint-Paul strike four within a few minutes, an hour when the sentinel was relieved and when the latter would be found asleep under the pierced roof, staring in horror at a terrible depth, at the light of the street-lanterns, the wet, black pavement, that pavement longed for yet frightful, which meant death, and which meant liberty.

He asked himself whether his three accomplices in flight had succeeded, if they had heard him, and if they would come to his assistance. He listened. With the exception of the patrol, no one had passed through the street since he had been there. Nearly the whole of the descent of the market-gardeners from Montreuil, from Charonne, from Vincennes, and from Bercy to the markets was accomplished through the Rue Saint-Antoine.

Four o'clock struck. Thénardier shuddered. A few moments later, that terrified and confused uproar which follows the discovery of an escape broke forth in the prison. The sound of doors opening and shutting, the creaking of gratings on their hinges, a tumult in the guard-house, the hoarse shouts of the turnkeys, the shock of musket-butts on the pavement of the courts, reached his ears. Lights ascended and descended past the grated windows of the dormitories, a torch ran along the ridge pole of the top story of the New Building, the firemen belonging in the barracks on the right had been summoned. Their helmets, which the torch lighted up in the rain, went and came along the roofs. At the same time, Thénardier perceived in the direction of the Bastille a wan whiteness lighting up the edge of the sky in doleful wise.

He was on top of a wall ten inches wide, stretched out under the heavy rain, with two gulfs to right and left, unable to stir, subject to the giddiness of a possible fall, and to the horror of a certain arrest, and his thoughts, like the pendulum of a clock, swung from one of these ideas to the other: "Dead if I fall, caught if I stay." In the midst of this anguish, he suddenly saw, the street being still dark, a man who was gliding along the walls and coming from the Rue Pavée, halt in the recess above which Thénardier was, as it were, suspended. Here this man was joined by a second who walked with the same caution, then by a third, then by a fourth. When these men were reunited, one of them lifted the latch of the gate in the fence, and all four entered the enclosure in which the shanty stood. They halted directly under Thénardier. These men had evidently chosen this vacant space in order that they might consult without being seen by the passers-by or by the sentinel who guards the wicket of La Force a few paces distant. It must be added, that the rain kept this sentinel blocked in his box. Thénardier, not being able to distinguish their visages, lent an ear to their words with the desperate attention of a wretch who feels himself lost.

Thénardier saw something resembling a gleam of hope flash before his eyes—these men conversed in slang.

The first said in a low but distinct voice:

"Let's cut. What are we up to here?"

The second replied: "It's raining hard enough to put out the very devil's fire. And the bobbies will be along instanter. There's a soldier on guard yonder. We shall get nabbed here."

These two words, *icigo* and *icicaille*, both of which mean *ici*, and which belong, the first to the slang of the barriers, the second to the slang of the Temple, were flashes of light for Thénardier. By the *icigo* he recognized Brujon, who was a prowler of the barriers, by the *icicaille* he knew Babet, who, among his other trades, had been an old-clothes broker at the Temple.

The antique slang of the great century is no longer spoken except in the Temple, and Babet was really the only person who spoke it in all its purity. Had it not been for the *icicaille*, Thénardier would not have recognized him, for he had entirely changed his voice.

In the meanwhile, the third man had intervened.

"There's no hurry yet, let's wait a bit. How do we know that he doesn't stand in need of us?"

By this, which was nothing but French, Thénardier recognized Montparnasse, who made it a point in his elegance to understand all slangs and to speak none of them.

As for the fourth, he held his peace, but his huge shoulders betrayed him. Thénardier did not hesitate. It was Guelemer.

Brujon replied almost impetuously, but still in a low tone:

"What are you jabbering about? The tavern-keeper hasn't managed to cut his stick. He don't tumble to the racket, that he don't! You have to be a pretty knowing cove to tear up your shirt, cut up your sheet to make a rope, punch holes in doors, get up false papers, make false keys, file your irons, hang out your cord, hide yourself, and disguise yourself! The old fellow hasn't managed to play it, he doesn't understand how to work the business."

Babet added, still in that classical slang which was spoken by Poulailler and Cartouche, and which is to the bold, new, highly colored and risky argot used by Brujon what the language of Racine is to the language of André Chenier:

"Your tavern-keeper must have been nabbed in the act. You have to be knowing. He's only a greenhorn. He must have let himself be taken in by a bobby, perhaps even by a sheep who played it on him as his pal. Listen, Montparnasse, do you hear those shouts in the prison? You have seen all those lights. He's recaptured, there! He'll get off with twenty years. I ain't afraid, I ain't a coward, but there ain't anything more to do, or otherwise they'd lead us a dance. Don't get mad, come with us, let's go drink a bottle of old wine together."

"One doesn't desert one's friends in a scrape," grumbled Montparnasse.

"I tell you he's nabbed!" retorted Brujon. "At the present moment, the inn-keeper ain't worth a ha'penny. We can't do nothing for him. Let's be off. Every minute I think a bobby has got me in his fist."

Montparnasse no longer offered more than a feeble resistance; the fact is, that these four men, with the fidelity of ruffians who never abandon each other, had prowled all night long about La Force, great as was their peril, in the hope of seeing Thénardier make his appearance on the top of some wall. But the night, which was really growing too fine—for the downpour was such as to render all the streets deserted—the cold which was overpowering them, their soaked garments, their hole-ridden shoes, the alarming noise which had just burst forth in the prison, the hours which had elapsed, the patrol which they had encountered, the hope which was vanishing, all urged them to beat a retreat. Montparnasse himself, who was, perhaps, almost Thénardier's son-in-law, yielded. A moment more, and they would be gone. Thénardier was panting on his wall like the shipwrecked sufferers of the *Méduse* on their raft when they beheld the vessel which had appeared in sight vanish on the horizon.

He dared not call to them; a cry might be heard and ruin everything. An idea occurred to him, a last idea, a flash of inspiration; he drew from his pocket the end of Brujon's rope, which he had detached from the chimney of the New Building, and flung it into the space enclosed by the fence.

This rope fell at their feet.

"A widow," said Babet.

"My tortouse!" said Brujon.

"The tavern-keeper is there," said Montparnasse.

They raised their eyes. Thénardier thrust out his head a very little.

"Quick!" said Montparnasse, "have you the other end of the rope, Brujon?"

"Yes."

"Knot the two pieces together, we'll fling him the rope, he can fasten it to the wall, and he'll have enough of it to get down with."

Thénardier ran the risk, and spoke:

"I am paralyzed with cold."

"We'll warm you up."

"I can't budge."

"Let yourself slide, we'll catch you."

"My hands are benumbed."

"Only fasten the rope to the wall."

"I can't."

"Then one of us must climb up," said Montparnasse.

"Three stories!" ejaculated Brujon.

An ancient plaster flue, which had served for a stove that had been used in the shanty in former times, ran along the wall and mounted almost to the very spot where they could see Thénardier. This flue, then much damaged and full of cracks, has since fallen, but the marks of it are still visible.

It was very narrow.

"One might get up by the help of that," said Montparnasse.

"By that flue?" exclaimed Babet, "a grown-up cove, never! it would take a brat."

"A brat must be got," resumed Brujon.

"Where are we to find a young 'un?" said Guelemer.

"Wait," said Montparnasse. "I've got the very article."

He opened the gate of the fence very softly, made sure that no one was passing along the street, stepped out cautiously, shut the gate behind him, and set off at a run in the direction of the Bastille.

Seven or eight minutes elapsed, eight thousand centuries to Thénardier, Babet, Brujon, and Guelemer did not open their lips; at last the gate opened once more, and Montparnasse appeared, breathless, and followed by Gavroche. The rain still rendered the street completely deserted.

Little Gavroche entered the enclosure and gazed at the forms of these ruffians with a tranquil air. The water was dripping from his hair. Guelemer addressed him:

"Are you a man, young 'un?"

Gavroche shrugged his shoulders, and replied:

"A young 'un like me's a man, and men like you are babes."

"The brat's tongue's well hung!" exclaimed Babet.

"The Paris brat ain't made of straw," added Brujon.

"What do you want?" asked Gavroche.

Montparnasse answered:

"Climb up that flue."

"With this rope," said Babet.

"And fasten it," continued Brujon.

"To the top of the wall," went on Babet.

"To the cross-bar of the window," added Brujon.

"And then?" said Gavroche.

"There!" said Guelemer.

The gamin examined the rope, the flue, the wall, the windows, and made that indescribable and disdainful noise with his lips which signifies:

"Is that all!"

"There's a man up there whom you are to save," resumed Montparnasse.

"Will you?" began Brujon again.

"Greenhorn!" replied the lad, as though the question appeared a most unprecedented one to him. And he took off his shoes.

Guelemer seized Gavroche by one arm, set him on the roof of the shanty, whose wormeaten planks bent beneath the urchin's weight, and handed him the rope which Brujon had knotted together during Montparnasse's absence. The gamin directed his steps toward the flue, which it was easy to enter, thanks to a large crack which touched the roof. At the moment when he was on the point of ascending, Thénardier, who saw life and safety approaching, bent over the edge of the wall; the first light of dawn struck white upon his brow dripping with sweat, upon his livid cheekbones, his sharp and savage nose, his bristling gray beard, and Gavroche recognized him.

"Hullo! it's my father! Oh! that won't hinder."

And taking the rope in his teeth, he resolutely began the ascent.

He reached the summit of the hut, bestrode the old wall as though it had been a horse, and knotted the rope firmly to the upper cross-bar of the window.

A moment later, Thénardier was in the street.

As soon as he touched the pavement, as soon as he found himself out of danger, he was no longer either weary, or chilled or trembling; the terrible things from which he had escaped vanished like smoke, all that strange and ferocious mind awoke once more, and stood erect and free, ready to march onward.

These were this man's first words:

"Now, whom are we to eat?"

It is useless to explain the sense of this frightfully transparent remark, which signifies both to kill, to assassinate, and to plunder. *To eat*, true sense: *to devour*.

"Let's get well into a corner," said Brujon. "Let's settle it in three words, and part at once. There was an affair that promised well in the Rue Plumet, a deserted street, an isolated house, an old rotten gate on a garden, and lone women."

"Well! why not?" demanded Thénardier.

"Your girl, Éponine, went to see about the matter," replied Babet.

"And she brought a biscuit to Magnon," added Guelemer. "Nothing to be made there."

"The girl's no fool," said Thénardier. "Still, it must be seen to."

"Yes, yes," said Brujon, "it must be looked up."

In the meanwhile, none of the men seemed to see Gavroche, who, during this colloquy, had seated himself on one of the fence-posts; he waited a few moments, thinking that perhaps his father would turn toward him, then he put on his shoes again, and said:

"Is that all? You don't want anymore, my men? Now you're out of your scrape. I'm off. I must go and get my brats out of bed."

And off he went.

The five men emerged, one after another, from the enclosure.

When Gavroche had disappeared at the corner of the Rue des Ballets, Babet took Thénardier aside.

"Did you take a good look at that young 'un?" he asked.

"What young 'un?"

"The one who climbed the wall and carried you the rope."

"Not particularly."

"Well, I don't know, but it strikes me that it was your son."

"Bah!" said Thénardier, "do you think so?"

BOOK SEVENTH

SLANG

Chapter I

ORIGIN

P IGRITIA IS A TERRIBLE WORD.

It engenders a whole world, *la pègre*, for which read *theft*, and a hell, *la pégrenne*, for which read *hunger*.

Thus, idleness is the mother.

She has a son, theft, and a daughter, hunger.

Where are we at this moment? In the land of slang.

What is slang? It is at one and the same time, a nation and a dialect; it is theft in its two kinds; people and language.

When, four-and-thirty years ago, the narrator of this grave and somber history introduced into a work written with the same aim as this a thief who talked argot, there arose amazement and clamor.—"What! How! Argot! Why, argot is horrible! It is the language of prisons, galleys, convicts, of everything that is most abominable in society!" etc., etc.

We have never understood this sort of objections.

Since that time, two powerful romancers, one of whom is a profound observer of the human heart, the other an intrepid friend of the people, Balzac and Eugène Sue, having represented their ruffians as talking their natural language, as the author of *The Last Day of a Condemned Man* did in 1828, the same objections have been raised. People repeated: "What do authors mean by that revolting dialect? Slang is odious! Slang makes one shudder!"

Who denies that? Of course it does.

When it is a question of probing a wound, a gulf, a society, since when has it been considered wrong to go too far? to go to the bottom? We have always thought that it was sometimes a courageous act, and, at least, a simple and useful deed, worthy of the sympathetic attention which duty accepted and fulfilled merits. Why should one not explore everything, and study everything? why should one halt on the way? The halt is a matter depending on the sounding-line, and not on the leadsman.

Certainly, too, it is neither an attractive nor an easy task to undertake an investigation into the lowest depths of the social order, where terra firma comes to an end and where mud begins, to rummage in those vague, murky waves, to follow up, to seize and to fling, still quivering, upon the pavement that abject dialect which is dripping with filth when thus brought to the light, that pustulous vocabulary each word of which seems an unclean ring from a monster of the mire and the shadows. Nothing is more lugubrious than the contemplation thus in its nudity, in the broad light of thought, of the horrible swarming of slang. It seems, in fact, to be a sort of horrible beast made for the night which has just been torn from its cesspool. One thinks one beholds a frightful, living, and bristling thicket which quivers, rustles, wavers, returns to shadow, threatens and glares. One word resembles a claw, another an extinguished and bleeding eye, such and such a phrase seems to move like the claw of a crab. All this is alive with the hideous vitality of things which have been organized out of disorganization.

Now, when has horror ever excluded study? Since when has malady banished medicine? Can one imagine a naturalist refusing to study the viper, the bat, the scorpion, the centipede, the tarantula, and one who would cast them back into their darkness, saying: "Oh! how ugly that is!" The thinker who should turn aside from slang would resemble a surgeon who should avert his face from an ulcer or a wart. He would be like a philologist refusing to examine a fact in language, a philosopher hesitating to scrutinize a fact in humanity. For, it must be stated to those who are ignorant of the case, that argot is both a literary phenomenon and a social result. What is slang, properly speaking? It is the language of wretchedness.

We may be stopped; the fact may be put to us in general terms, which is one way of attenuating it; we may be told, that all trades, professions, it may be added, all the accidents of the social hierarchy and all forms of intelligence, have their own slang. The merchant who says: "Montpellier not active, Marseilles fine quality," the broker on 'change who says: "Assets at end of current month," the gambler who says: *"Tiers et tout, refait de pique,"* the sheriff of the Norman Isles who says: "The holder in fee reverting to his landed estate cannot claim the fruits of that estate during the hereditary seizure of the real estate by the mortgagor," the playwright who says: "The piece was hissed," the comedian who says: "I've made a hit," the philosopher who says: "Phenomenal triplicity," the huntsman who says: *"Voileci allais, Voileci fuyant,"* the phrenologist who says: "Amativeness, combativeness, secretiveness," the infantry soldier who says: "My shooting-iron," the cavalry-man who says: "My turkey-cock," the fencing-master who says: "Tierce, quarte, break," the printer who says: "My shooting-stick and galley"—all, printer, fencing-master, cavalry dragoon, infantry-man, phrenologist, huntsman, philosopher, comedian, playwright, sheriff, gambler, stock-broker, and merchant, speak slang. The painter who says: "My grinder," the notary who says: "My Skip-the-Gutter," the hairdresser who says: "My mealyback," the cobbler who says: "My cub," talk slang. Strictly speaking, if one absolutely insists on the point, all the different fashions of saying the right and the left, the sailor's *port* and *starboard*, the scene-shifter's *court-side*, and *garden-side*, the beadle's *Gospel-side* and *Epistle-side*, are slang. There is the slang of the affected lady as well as of the *précieuses*. The Hôtel Rambouillet nearly adjoins the Cour des Miracles. There is a slang of duchesses, witness this phrase contained in a love-letter from a very great lady and a very pretty woman of the Restoration: "You will find in this gossip a fultitude of reasons why I should libertize." Diplomatic ciphers are slang; the pontifical chancellery by using 26 for Rome, *grkʒtntgʒyal* for dispatch, and *abfxustgrnogrkʒu tu XI* for the Duc de Modena, speaks slang. The physicians of the Middle Ages who, for carrot, radish, and turnip, said *Opoponach, perfroschinum, reptitalmus, dracatholicum, angelorum, postmegorum,* talked slang. The sugar-manufacturer who says: "Loaf, clarified, lumps, bastard, common, burned"—this honest manufacturer talks slang. A certain school of criticism twenty years ago, which used to say: "Half of the works of Shakespeare consists of plays upon words and puns"—talked slang. The poet, and the artist who, with profound understanding, would designate M. de Montmorency as "a bourgeois," if he were not a judge of verses and statues, speak slang. The classic Academician who calls flowers "Flora," fruits, "Pomona," the sea, "Neptune," love, "fires," beauty, "charms," a horse, "a courser," the white or tricolored cockade, "the rose of Bellona," the three-cornered hat, "Mars's triangle"—that classical Academician talks slang. Algebra, medicine, botany, have each their slang. The tongue which is employed on board ship, that wonderful language of the sea, which is so complete and so picturesque, which was spoken by Jean Bart, Duquesne, Suffren, and Duperré, which mingles with the whistling of the rigging, the sound of the speaking-trumpets, the shock of the boarding-irons, the roll of the sea, the wind, the gale, the cannon, is wholly a heroic and dazzling slang, which is to the fierce slang of the thieves what the lion is to the jackal.

No doubt. But say what we will, this manner of understanding the word *slang* is an extension which everyone will not admit. For our part, we reserve to the word its ancient and precise, circumscribed and determined significance, and we restrict slang to slang. The veritable slang and the slang that is pre-eminently slang, if the two words can be coupled thus, the slang immemorial which was a kingdom, is nothing else, we repeat, than the homely, uneasy, crafty, treacherous, venomous, cruel, equivocal, vile, profound, fatal tongue of wretchedness. There exists, at the extremity of all abasement and all misfortunes, a last misery which revolts and makes up its mind to enter into conflict with the whole mass of fortunate facts and reigning rights; a fearful conflict, where, now cunning, now violent, unhealthy and ferocious at one and the same time, it attacks the social order with pin-pricks through vice, and with club-blows through crime. To meet the needs of this conflict, wretchedness has invented a language of combat, which is slang.

To keep afloat and to rescue from oblivion, to hold above the gulf, were it but a fragment of some language which man has spoken and which would, otherwise, be lost, that is to say, one of the elements, good or bad, of which civilization is composed, or by which it is complicated, to extend the records of social observation; is to serve civilization itself. This service Plautus rendered, consciously or unconsciously, by making two Carthaginian soldiers talk Phœnician; that service Molière rendered, by making so many of his characters talk Levantine and all sorts of dialects. Here objections spring up afresh. Phœnician, very good! Levantine, quite right! Even dialect, let that pass! They are tongues which have belonged to nations or provinces; but slang! What is the use of preserving slang? What is the good of assisting slang "to survive"?

To this we reply in one word, only. Assuredly, if the tongue which a nation or a province has spoken is worthy of interest, the language which has been spoken by a misery is still more worthy of attention and study.

It is the language which has been spoken, in France, for example, for more than four centuries, not only by a misery, but by every possible human misery.

And then, we insist upon it, the study of social deformities and infirmities, and the task of pointing them out with a view to remedy, is not a business in which choice is permitted. The historian of manners and ideas has no less austere a mission than the historian of events. The latter has the surface of civilization, the conflicts of crowns, the births of princes, the marriages of kings, battles, assemblages, great public men, revolutions in the daylight, everything on the exterior; the other historian has the interior, the depths, the people who toil, suffer, wait, the oppressed woman, the agonizing child, the secret war between man and man, obscure ferocities, prejudices, plotted iniquities, the subterranean, the indistinct tremors of multitudes, the die-of-hunger, the counter-blows of the law, the secret evolution of souls, the go-barefoot, the bare-armed, the disinherited, the orphans, the unhappy, and the infamous, all the forms which roam through the darkness. He must descend with his heart full of charity, and severity at the same time, as a brother and as a judge, to those impenetrable casemates where crawl, pell-mell, those who bleed and those who deal the blow, those who weep and those who curse, those who fast and those who devour, those who endure evil and those who inflict it. Have these historians of hearts and souls duties at all inferior to the historians of external facts? Does anyone think that Alighieri has any fewer things to say than Machiavelli? Is the under side of civilization any less important than the upper side merely because it is deeper and more somber? Do we really know the mountain well when we are not acquainted with the cavern?

Let us say, moreover, parenthetically, that from a few words of what precedes a marked separation might be inferred between the two classes of historians which does not exist in our mind. No one is a good historian of the patent, visible, striking, and public life of peoples, if he is not, at the same time, in a certain measure, the historian of their deep and hidden life; and no one is a good historian of the interior unless he understands how, at need, to be the historian of the exterior also. The history of manners and ideas permeates the history of events, and this is true reciprocally. They constitute two different orders of facts which correspond to each other, which are always interlaced, and which often bring forth results. All the lineaments which Providence traces on the surface of a nation have their parallels, somber but distinct, in their depths, and all convulsions of the depths produce ebullitions on the surface. True history being a mixture of all things, the true historian mingles in everything.

Man is not a circle with a single center; he is an ellipse with a double focus. Facts form one of these, and ideas the other.

Slang is nothing but a dressing-room where the tongue having some bad action to perform, disguises itself. There it clothes itself in word-masks, in metaphor-rags. In this guise it becomes horrible.

One finds it difficult to recognize. Is it really the French tongue, the great human tongue? Behold it ready to step upon the stage and to retort upon crime, and prepared for all the employments of the repertory of evil. It no longer walks, it hobbles; it limps on the crutch of the Court of Miracles, a crutch metamorphosable into a club; it is called vagrancy; every sort of specter, its dressers, have painted its face, it crawls and rears, the double gait of the reptile. Henceforth, it is apt at all rôles, it is made suspicious by the counterfeiter, covered with verdigris by the forger, blacked by the soot of the incendiary; and the murderer applies its rouge.

When one listens, by the side of honest men, at the portals of society, one overhears the dialogues of those who are on the outside. One distinguishes questions and replies. One perceives, without understanding it, a hideous murmur, sounding almost like human accents, but more nearly resembling a howl than an articulate word. It is slang. The words are misshapen and stamped with an indescribable and fantastic bestiality. One thinks one hears hydras talking.

It is unintelligible in the dark. It gnashes and whispers, completing the gloom with mystery. It is black in misfortune, it is blacker still in crime; these two blacknesses amalgamated, compose slang. Obscurity in the atmosphere, obscurity in acts, obscurity in voices. Terrible, toad-like tongue which goes and comes, leaps, crawls, slobbers, and stirs about in monstrous wise in that immense gray fog composed of rain and night, of hunger, of vice, of falsehood, of injustice, of nudity, of suffocation, and of winter, the high noonday of the miserable.

Let us have compassion on the chastised. Alas! Who are we ourselves? Who am I who now address you? Who are you who are listening to me? And are you very sure that we have done nothing before we were born? The earth is not devoid of resemblance to a jail. Who knows whether man is not a recaptured offender against divine justice? Look closely at life. It is so made, that everywhere we feel the sense of punishment.

Are you what is called a happy man? Well! you are sad every day. Each day has its own great grief or its little care. Yesterday you were trembling for a health that is dear to you, to-day you fear for your own; to-morrow it will be anxiety about money, the day after to-morrow the diatribe of a slanderer, the day after that, the misfortune of some friend; then the prevailing weather, then something that has been broken or lost, then a pleasure with which your conscience and your vertebral column reproach you; again, the course of public affairs. This without reckoning in the pains of the heart. And so it goes on. One cloud is dispelled, another forms. There is hardly one day out of a hundred which is wholly joyous and sunny. And you belong to that small class who are happy! As for the rest of mankind, stagnating night rests upon them.

Thoughtful minds make but little use of the phrase: the fortunate and the unfortunate. In this world, evidently the vestibule of another, there are no fortunate.

The real human division is this: the luminous and the shady. To diminish the number of the shady, to augment the number of the luminous—that is the object. That is why we cry: Education! science! To teach reading, means to light the fire; every syllable spelled out sparkles.

However, he who says light does not, necessarily, say joy. People suffer in the light; excess burns. The flame is the enemy of the wing. To burn without ceasing to fly—therein lies the marvel of genius.

When you shall have learned to know, and to love, you will still suffer. The day is born in tears. The luminous weep, if only over those in darkness.

Chapter II

ROOTS

S LANG IS THE TONGUE OF THOSE WHO SIT IN DARKNESS.
    Thought is moved in its most somber depths, social philosophy is bidden to its most poignant meditations, in the presence of that enigmatic dialect at once so blighted and rebellious. Therein lies chastisement made visible. Every syllable has an air of being marked. The words of the vulgar tongue appear therein wrinkled and shriveled, as it were, beneath the hot iron of the executioner. Some seem to be still smoking. Such and such a phrase produces upon you the effect of the shoulder of a thief branded with the fleur-de-lys, which has suddenly been laid bare. Ideas almost refuse to be expressed in these substantives which are fugitives from justice. Metaphor is sometimes so shameless, that one feels that it has worn the iron neck-fetter.

Moreover, in spite of all this, and because of all this, this strange dialect has by rights, its own compartment in that great impartial case of pigeon-holes where there is room for the rusty farthing as well as for the gold medal, and which is called literature. Slang, whether the public admit the fact or not, has its syntax and its poetry. It is a language. Yes, by the deformity of certain terms, we recognize the fact that it was chewed by Mandrin, and by the splendor of certain metonymies, we feel that Villon spoke it.

That exquisite and celebrated verse—

> *Mais où sont les neiges d'antan?*
> *But where are the snows of years gone by?*

is a verse of slang. *Antan—ante annum*—is a word of Thunes slang, which signified the past year, and by extension, *formerly*. Thirty-five years ago, at the epoch of the departure of the great chain-gang, there could be read in one of the cells at Bicêtre, this maxim engraved with a nail on the wall by a king of Thunes condemned to the galleys: *Les dabs d'antan trimaient siempre pour la piorre du Coësre*. This means: *Kings in days gone by always went and had themselves anointed*. In the opinion of that king, anointment meant the galleys.

The word *décarade*, which expresses the departure of heavy vehicles at a gallop, is attributed to Villon, and it is worthy of him. This word, which strikes fire with all four of its feet, sums up in a masterly onomatopoeia the whole of La Fontaine's admirable verse:

> *Six forts chevaux tiraient un coche.*
> *Six stout horses drew a coach.*

From a purely literary point of view, few studies would prove more curious and fruitful than the study of slang. It is a whole language within a language, a sort of sickly excrescence, an unhealthy graft which has produced a vegetation, a parasite which has its roots in the old Gallic trunk, and whose sinister foliage crawls all over one side of the language. This is what may be called the first, the vulgar aspect of slang. But, for those who study the tongue as it should be studied, that is to say, as geologists study the earth, slang appears like a veritable alluvial deposit. According as one digs a longer or shorter distance into it, one finds in slang, below the old popular French, Provençal, Spanish, Italian, Levantine, that language of the Mediterranean ports, English and German, the Romance language in its three varieties, French, Italian, and Romance Romance, Latin, and finally

Basque and Celtic. A profound and unique formation. A subterranean edifice erected in common by all the miserable. Each accursed race has deposited its layer, each suffering has dropped its stone there, each heart has contributed its pebble. A throng of evil, base, or irritated souls, who have traversed life and have vanished into eternity, linger there almost entirely visible still beneath the form of some monstrous word.

Do you want Spanish? The old Gothic slang abounded in it. Here is *boffete*, a box on the ear, which is derived from *bofeton*; *vantane*, window (later on *vanterne*), which comes from *vantana*; *gat*, cat, which comes from *gato*; *acite*, oil, which comes from *aceyte*. Do you want Italian? Here is *spade*, sword, which comes from *spada*; *carvel*, boat, which comes from *caravella*. Do you want English? Here is *bichot*, which comes from *bishop*; *raille*, spy, which comes from *rascal*, *rascalion*; *pilche*, a case, which comes from *pilcher*, a sheath. Do you want German? Here is the *caleur*, the waiter, *kellner*; the *hers*, the master, *herzog* (duke). Do you want Latin? Here is *frangir*, to break, *frangere*; *affurer*, to steal, *fur*; *cadene*, chain, *catena*. There is one word which crops up in every language of the continent, with a sort of mysterious power and authority. It is the word *magnus*; the Scotchman makes of it his *mac*, which designates the chief of the clan; Mac-Farlane, Mac-Callumore, the great Farlane, the great Callumore; slang turns it into *meck* and later *le meg*, that is to say, God. Would you like Basque? Here is *gahisto*, the devil, which comes from *gaïztoa*, evil; *sorgabon*, good night, which comes from *gabon*, good evening. Do you want Celtic? Here is *blavin*, a handkerchief, which comes from *blavet*, gushing water; *ménesse*, a woman (in a bad sense), which comes from *meinec*, full of stones; *barant*, brook, from *baranton*, fountain; *goffeur*, locksmith, from *goff*, blacksmith; *guedouze*, death, which comes from *guenn-du*, black-white. Finally, would you like history? Slang calls crowns *les maltèses*, a souvenir of the coin in circulation on the galleys of Malta.

In addition to the philological origins just indicated, slang possesses other and still more natural roots, which spring, so to speak, from the mind of man itself.

In the first place, the direct creation of words. Therein lies the mystery of tongues. To paint with words, which contains figures one knows not how or why, is the primitive foundation of all human languages, what may be called their granite.

Slang abounds in words of this description, immediate words, words created instantaneously no one knows either where or by whom, without etymology, without analogies, without derivatives, solitary, barbarous, sometimes hideous words, which at times possess a singular power of expression and which live. The executioner, *le taule*; the forest, *le sabri*; fear, flight, *taf*; the lackey, *le larbin*; the mineral, the prefect, the minister, *pharos*; the devil, *le rabouin*. Nothing is stranger than these words which both mask and reveal. Some, *le rabouin*, for example, are at the same time grotesque and terrible, and produce on you the effect of a cyclopean grimace.

In the second place, metaphor. The peculiarity of a language which is desirous of saying all yet concealing all is that it is rich in figures. Metaphor is an enigma, wherein the thief who is plotting a stroke, the prisoner who is arranging an escape, take refuge. No idiom is more metaphorical than slang: *dévisser le coco* (to unscrew the nut), to twist the neck; *tortiller* (to wriggle), to eat; *être gerbé*, to be tried; *a rat*, a bread thief; *il lansquine*, it rains, a striking, ancient figure which partly bears its date about it, which assimilates long oblique lines of rain, with the dense and slanting pikes of the lancers, and which compresses into a single word the popular expression: it rains halberds. Sometimes, in proportion as slang progresses from the first epoch to the second, words pass from the primitive and savage sense to the metaphorical sense. The devil ceases to be *le rabouin*, and becomes *le boulanger* (the baker), who puts the bread into the oven. This is more witty, but less grand, something like Racine after Corneille, like Euripides after Æschylus. Certain slang phrases which participate in the two epochs and have at once the barbaric character and the metaphorical character resemble phantasmagories. *Les sorgueurs vont solliciter des gails à la lune*—the prowlers are going to steal horses by night—this passes before the mind like a group of specters. One knows not what one sees.

In the third place, the expedient. Slang lives on the language. It uses it in accordance with its fancy, it dips into it haphazard, and it often confines itself, when occasion arises, to alter it in a gross and summary fashion. Occasionally, with the ordinary words thus deformed and complicated with words of pure slang, picturesque phrases are formed, in which there can be felt the mixture of the two preceding elements, the direct creation and the metaphor: *le cab jaspine, je marronne que la roulotte de Pantin trime dans le sabri*, the dog is barking, I suspect that the diligence for Paris is passing through the woods. *Le dab est sinve, la dabuge est merloussière, la fée est bative*, the bourgeois is stupid, the bourgeoise is cunning, the daughter is pretty. Generally, to throw listeners off the track, slang confines itself to adding to all the words of the language without distinction, an ignoble tail, a termination in *aille*, in *orgue*, in *iergue*, or in *uche*. Thus: *Vousiergue trouvaille bonorgue ce gigot-muche?* Do you think that leg of mutton good? A phrase addressed by Cartouche to a turnkey in order to find out whether the sum offered for his escape suited him.

The termination in *mar* has been added recently.

Slang, being the dialect of corruption, quickly becomes corrupted itself. Besides this, as it is always seeking concealment, as soon as it feels that it is understood, it changes its form. Contrary to what happens with every other vegetation, every ray of light which falls upon it kills whatever it touches. Thus slang is in constant process of decomposition and recomposition; an obscure and rapid work which never pauses. It passes over more ground in ten years than a language in ten centuries. Thus *le larton* (bread) becomes *le lartif*; *le gail* (horse) becomes *le gaye*; *la fertanche* (straw) becomes *la fertille*; *le momignard* (brat), *le momacque*; *les fiques* (duds), *frusques*; *la chique* (the church), *l'égrugeoir*; *le colabre* (neck), *le colas*. The devil is at first, *gahisto*, then *le rabouin*, then *the baker*; the priest is a *ratichon*, then the boar (*le sanglier*); the dagger is *le vingt-deux* (twenty-two), then *le surin*, then *le lingre*; the police are *railles*, then *roussins*, then *rousses*, then *marchands de lacets* (dealers in stay-laces), then *coquers*, then *cognes*; the executioner is *le taule*, then *Charlot*, then *l'atigeur*, then *le becquillard*. In the seventeenth century, to fight was "to give each other snuff"; in the nineteenth it is "to chew each other's throats." There have been twenty different phrases between these two extremes. Cartouche's talk would have been Hebrew to Lacenaire. All the words of this language are perpetually engaged in flight like the men who utter them.

Still, from time to time, and in consequence of this very movement, the ancient slang crops up again and becomes new once more. It has its headquarters where it maintains its sway. The Temple preserved the slang of the seventeenth century; Bicêtre, when it was a prison, preserved the slang of Thunes. There one could hear the termination in *anche* of the old Thuneurs. *Boyanches-tu* (bois-tu), do you drink? But perpetual movement remains its law, nevertheless.

If the philosopher succeeds in fixing, for a moment, for purposes of observation, this language which is incessantly evaporating, he falls into doleful and useful meditation. No study is more efficacious and more fecund in instruction. There is not a metaphor, not an analogy, in slang, which does not contain a lesson. Among these men, to beat means to feign; one beats a malady; ruse is their strength.

For them, the idea of the man is not separated from the idea of darkness. The night is called *la sorgue*; man, *l'orgue*. Man is a derivative of the night.

They have taken up the practice of considering society in the light of an atmosphere which kills them, of a fatal force, and they speak of their liberty as one would speak of his health. A man under arrest is a *sick man*; one who is condemned is a *dead man*.

The most terrible thing for the prisoner within the four walls in which he is buried, is a sort of glacial chastity, and he calls the dungeon the *castus*. In that funereal place, life outside always presents itself under its most smiling aspect. The prisoner has irons on his feet; you think, perhaps, that his thought is that it is with the feet that one walks? No; he is thinking that it is with the feet that one dances; so, when he has succeeded in severing his fetters, his first idea is that now he can dance, and he calls the saw the *bastringue* (public-house ball).—A name is a center; profound assimilation.—The ruffian has two heads, one of which reasons out his actions and leads him all his life long, and the other which he has upon his shoulders on the day of his death; he calls the head which counsels him in crime *la sorbonne,* and the head which expiates it *la tronche.*—When a man has no longer anything but rags upon his body and vices in his heart, when he has arrived at that double moral and material degradation which the word blackguard characterizes in its two accepta- tions, he is ripe for crime; he is like a well-whetted knife; he has two cutting edges, his distress and his malice; so slang does not say a blackguard, it says *un réguisé.*—What are the galleys? A brazier of damnation, a hell. The convict calls himself a *fagot.*—And finally, what name do malefactors give to their prison? The *college.* A whole penitentiary system can be evolved from that word.

Does the reader wish to know where the majority of the songs of the galleys, those refrains called in the special vocabulary *lirlonfa,* have had their birth?

Let him listen to what follows:

There existed at the Châtelet in Paris a large and long cellar. This cellar was eight feet below the level of the Seine. It had neither windows nor air-holes, its only aperture was the door; men could enter there, air could not. This vault had for ceiling a vault of stone, and for floor ten inches of mud. It was flagged; but the pavement had rotted and cracked under the oozing of the water. Eight feet above the floor, a long and massive beam traversed this subterranean excavation from side to side; from this beam hung, at short distances apart, chains three feet long, and at the end of these chains there were rings for the neck. In this vault men who had been condemned to the gal- leys were incarcerated until the day of their departure for Toulon. They were thrust under this beam, where each one found his fetters swinging in the darkness and waiting for him.

The chains, those pendant arms, and the necklets, those open hands, caught the unhappy wretches by the throat. They were rivetted and left there. As the chain was too short, they could not lie down. They remained motionless in that cavern, in that night, beneath that beam, almost hang- ing, forced to unheard-of efforts to reach their bread, jug, or their vault overhead, mud even to mid-leg, filth flowing to their very calves, broken asunder with fatigue, with thighs and knees giv- ing way, clinging fast to the chain with their hands in order to obtain some rest, unable to sleep ex- cept when standing erect, and awakened every moment by the strangling of the collar; some woke no more. In order to eat, they pushed the bread, which was flung to them in the mud, along their leg with their heel until it reached their hand.

How long did they remain thus? One month, two months, six months sometimes; one stayed a year. It was the antechamber of the galleys. Men were put there for stealing a hare from the king. In this sepulcher-hell, what did they do? What man can do in a sepulcher, they went through the agonies of death, and what can man do in hell, they sang; for song lingers where there is no longer any hope. In the waters of Malta, when a galley was approaching, the song could be heard before the sound of the oars. Poor Survincent, the poacher, who had gone through the prison-cellar of the Châtelet, said: "It was the rhymes that kept me up." Uselessness of poetry. What is the good of rhyme?

It is in this cellar that nearly all the slang songs had their birth. It is from the dungeon of the Grand-Châtelet of Paris that comes the melancholy refrain of the Montgomery galley: *"Timaloumisaine, timaloumison."* The majority of these songs are melancholy; some are gay; one is tender:

> *Icicaille est la theatre*   *Here is the theater*
> *Du petit dardant.*   *Of the little archer (Cupid).*

Do what you will, you cannot annihilate that eternal relic in the heart of man, love.

In this world of dismal deeds, people keep their secrets. The secret is the thing above all oth- ers. The secret, in the eyes of these wretches, is unity which serves as a base of union. To betray a secret is to tear from each member of this fierce community something of his own personality. To inform against, in the energetic slang dialect, is called: "to eat the bit." As though the informer drew to himself a little of the substance of all and nourished himself on a bit of each one's flesh.

What does it signify to receive a box on the ear? Commonplace metaphor replies: "It is to see thirty-six candles." Here slang intervenes and takes it up: Candle, *camoufle*. Thereupon, the ordinary tongue gives *camouflet*[1] as the synonym for *soufflet*. Thus, by a sort of infiltration from below upwards, with the aid of metaphor, that incalculable, trajectory slang mounts from the cavern to the Academy; and Poulailler saying: "I light my *camoufle*," causes Voltaire to write: "Langleviel La Beaumelle deserves a hundred *camouflets*."

Researches in slang mean discoveries at every step. Study and investigation of this strange idiom lead to the mysterious point of intersection of regular society with society which is accursed.

The thief also has his food for cannon, stealable matter, you, I, whoever passes by; *le pantre*. (*Pan*, everybody.)

Slang is language turned convict.

That the thinking principle of man be thrust down ever so low, that it can be dragged and pinioned there by obscure tyrannies of fatality, that it can be bound by no one knows what fetters in that abyss, is sufficient to create consternation.

Oh, poor thought of miserable wretches!

Alas! will no one come to the succor of the human soul in that darkness? Is it her destiny there to await forever the mind, the liberator, the immense rider of Pegasi and hippo-griffs, the combatant of heroes of the dawn who shall descend from the azure between two wings, the radiant knight of the future? Will she forever summon in vain to her assistance the lance of light of the ideal? Is she condemned to hear the fearful approach of Evil through the density of the gulf, and to catch glimpses, nearer and nearer at hand, beneath the hideous water, of that dragon's head, that maw streaked with foam, and that writhing undulation of claws, swellings, and rings? Must it remain there, without a gleam of light, without hope, given over to that terrible approach, vaguely scented out by the monster, shuddering, disheveled, wringing its arms, forever chained to the rock of night, a somber Andromeda white and naked amid the shadows!

Chapter III

SLANG WHICH WEEPS AND SLANG WHICH LAUGHS

AS THE READER PERCEIVES, SLANG IN ITS ENTIRETY, SLANG OF FOUR HUNDRED YEARS AGO, LIKE the slang of to-day, is permeated with that somber, symbolical spirit which gives to all words a mien which is now mournful, now menacing. One feels in it the wild and ancient sadness of those vagrants of the Court of Miracles who played at cards with packs of their own, some of which have come down to us. The eight of clubs, for instance, represented a huge tree bearing eight enormous trefoil leaves, a sort of fantastic personification of the forest. At the foot of this tree a fire was burning, over which three hares were roasting a huntsman on a spit, and behind him, on another fire, hung a steaming pot, whence emerged the head of a dog. Nothing can be more melancholy than these reprisals in painting, by a pack of cards, in the presence of stakes for the roasting of smugglers and of the cauldron for the boiling of counterfeiters. The diverse forms assumed by thought

---

1. Smoke puffed in the face of a person asleep.

in the realm of slang, even song, even raillery, even menace, all partook of this powerless and dejected character. All the songs, the melodies of some of which have been collected, were humble and lamentable to the point of evoking tears. The *pègre* is always the poor *pègre*, and he is always the hare in hiding, the fugitive mouse, the flying bird. He hardly complains, he contents himself with sighing; one of his moans has come down to us: "I do not understand how God, the father of men, can torture his children and his grandchildren and hear them cry, without himself suffering torture." The wretch, whenever he has time to think, makes himself small before the low, and frail in the presence of society; he lies down flat on his face, he entreats, he appeals to the side of compassion; we feel that he is conscious of his guilt.

Toward the middle of the last century a change took place, prison songs and thieves' ritournelles assumed, so to speak, an insolent and jovial mien. The plaintive *maluré* was replaced by the *larifla*. We find in the eighteenth century, in nearly all the songs of the galleys and prisons, a diabolical and enigmatical gaiety. We hear this strident and lilting refrain which we should say had been lighted up by a phosphorescent gleam, and which seems to have been flung into the forest by a will-o'-the-wisp playing the fife:

> *Miralabi suslababo*
> *Mirliton ribonribette*
> *Surlababi mirlababo*
> *Mirliton ribonribo.*

This was sung in a cellar or in a nook of the forest while cutting a man's throat.

A serious symptom. In the eighteenth century, the ancient melancholy of the dejected classes vanishes. They began to laugh. They rally the *grand meg* and the *grand dab*. Given Louis XV they call the King of France "le Marquis de Pantin." And behold, they are almost gay. A sort of gleam proceeds from these miserable wretches, as though their consciences were not heavy within them anymore. These lamentable tribes of darkness have no longer merely the desperate audacity of actions, they possess the heedless audacity of mind. A sign that they are losing the sense of their criminality, and that they feel, even among thinkers and dreamers, some indefinable support which the latter themselves know not of. A sign that theft and pillage are beginning to filter into doctrines and sophisms, in such a way as to lose somewhat of their ugliness, while communicating much of it to sophisms and doctrines. A sign, in short, of some outbreak which is prodigious and near unless some diversion shall arise.

Let us pause a moment. Whom are we accusing here? Is it the eighteenth century? Is it philosophy? Certainly not. The work of the eighteenth century is healthy and good and wholesome. The encyclopedists, Diderot at their head; the physiocrates, Turgot at their head; the philosophers, Voltaire at their head; the Utopians, Rousseau at their head—these are four sacred legions. Humanity's immense advance toward the light is due to them. They are the four vanguards of the human race, marching toward the four cardinal points of progress. Diderot toward the beautiful, Turgot toward the useful, Voltaire toward the true, Rousseau toward the just. But by the side of and above the philosophers, there were the sophists, a venomous vegetation mingled with a healthy growth, hemlock in the virgin forest. While the executioner was burning the great books of the liberators of the century on the grand staircase of the court-house, writers now forgotten were publishing, with the King's sanction, no one knows what strangely disorganizing writings, which were eagerly read by the unfortunate. Some of these publications, odd to say, which were patronized by a prince, are to be found in the Secret Library. These facts, significant but unknown, were imperceptible on the surface. Sometimes, in the very obscurity of a fact lurks its danger. It is obscure because it is underhand. Of all these writers, the one who probably then excavated in the masses the most unhealthy gallery was Restif de La Bretonne.

This work, peculiar to the whole of Europe, effected more ravages in Germany than anywhere else. In Germany, during a given period, summed up by Schiller in his famous drama *The Robbers,* theft and pillage rose up in protest against property and labor, assimilated certain specious and false elementary ideas, which, though just in appearance, were absurd in reality, enveloped themselves in these ideas, disappeared within them, after a fashion, assumed an abstract name, passed into the state of theory, and in that shape circulated among the laborious, suffering, and honest masses, unknown even to the imprudent chemists who had prepared the mixture, unknown even to the masses who accepted it. Whenever a fact of this sort presents itself, the case is grave. Suffering engenders wrath; and while the prosperous classes blind themselves or fall asleep, which is the same thing as shutting one's eyes, the hatred of the unfortunate classes lights its torch at some aggrieved or ill-made spirit which dreams in a corner, and sets itself to the scrutiny of society. The scrutiny of hatred is a terrible thing.

Hence, if the ill-fortune of the times so wills it, those fearful commotions which were formerly called *jacqueries,* beside which purely political agitations are the merest child's play, which are no longer the conflict of the oppressed and the oppressor, but the revolt of discomfort against comfort. Then everything crumbles.

Jacqueries are earthquakes of the people.

It is this peril, possibly imminent toward the close of the eighteenth century, which the French Revolution, that immense act of probity, cut short.

The French Revolution, which is nothing else than the idea armed with the sword, rose erect, and, with the same abrupt movement, closed the door of ill and opened the door of good.

It put a stop to torture, promulgated the truth, expelled miasma, rendered the century healthy, crowned the populace.

It may be said of it that it created man a second time, by giving him a second soul, the right.

The nineteenth century has inherited and profited by its work, and to-day, the social catastrophe to which we lately alluded, is simply impossible. Blind is he who announces it! Foolish is he who fears it! Revolution is the vaccine of Jacquerie.

Thanks to the Revolution, social conditions have changed. Feudal and monarchical maladies no longer run in our blood. There is no more of the Middle Ages in our constitution. We no longer live in the days when terrible swarms within made eruptions, when one heard beneath his feet the obscure course of a dull rumble, when indescribable elevations from mole-like tunnels appeared on the surface of civilization, where the soil cracked open, where the roofs of caverns yawned, and where one suddenly beheld monstrous heads emerging from the earth.

The revolutionary sense is a moral sense. The sentiment of right, once developed, develops the sentiment of duty. The law of all is liberty, which ends where the liberty of others begins, according to Robespierre's admirable definition. Since '89, the whole people has been dilating into a sublime individual; there is not a poor man, who, possessing his right, has not his ray of sun; the die-of-hunger feels within him the honesty of France; the dignity of the citizen is an internal armor; he who is free is scrupulous; he who votes reigns. Hence incorruptibility; hence the miscarriage of unhealthy lusts; hence eyes heroically lowered before temptations. The revolutionary wholesomeness is such, that on a day of deliverance, a 14th of July, a 10th of August, there is no longer any populace. The first cry of the enlightened and increasing throngs is: death to thieves! Progress is an honest man; the ideal and the absolute do not filch pocket-handkerchiefs. By whom were the wagons containing the wealth of the Tuileries escorted in 1848? By the rag-pickers of the Faubourg Saint-Antoine. Rags mounted guard over the treasure. Virtue rendered these tatterdemalions resplendent. In those wagons in chests, hardly closed, and some, even, half-open, amid a hundred dazzling caskets, was that ancient crown of France, studded with diamonds, surmounted by the carbuncle of royalty, by the Regent diamond, which was worth thirty millions. Barefooted, they guarded that crown.

Hence, no more Jacquerie. I regret it for the sake of the skillful. The old fear has produced its last effects in that quarter; and henceforth it can no longer be employed in politics. The principal spring of the red specter is broken. Everyone knows it now. The scare-crow scares no longer. The birds take liberties with the manikin, foul creatures alight upon it, the bourgeois laugh at it.

Chapter IV

THE TWO DUTIES: TO WATCH AND TO HOPE

THIS BEING THE CASE, IS ALL SOCIAL DANGER DISPELLED? CERTAINLY NOT. THERE IS NO Jacquerie; society may rest assured on that point; blood will no longer rush to its head. But let society take heed to the manner in which it breathes. Apoplexy is no longer to be feared, but phthisis is there. Social phthisis is called misery.

One can perish from being undermined as well as from being struck by lightning.

Let us not weary of repeating, and sympathetic souls must not forget that this is the first of fraternal obligations, and selfish hearts must understand that the first of political necessities consists in thinking first of all of the disinherited and sorrowing throngs, in solacing, airing, enlightening, loving them, in enlarging their horizon to a magnificent extent, in lavishing upon them education in every form, in offering them the example of labor, never the example of idleness, in diminishing the individual burden by enlarging the notion of the universal aim, in setting a limit to poverty without setting a limit to wealth, in creating vast fields of public and popular activity, in having, like Briareus, a hundred hands to extend in all directions to the oppressed and the feeble, in employing the collective power for that grand duty of opening workshops for all arms, schools for all aptitudes, and laboratories for all degrees of intelligence, in augmenting salaries, diminishing trouble, balancing what should be and what is, that is to say, in proportioning enjoyment to effort and a glut to need; in a word, in evolving from the social apparatus more light and more comfort for the benefit of those who suffer and those who are ignorant.

And, let us say it, all this is but the beginning. The true question is this: labor cannot be a law without being a right.

We will not insist upon this point; this is not the proper place for that.

If nature calls itself Providence, society should call itself foresight.

Intellectual and moral growth is no less indispensable than material improvement. To know is a sacrament, to think is the prime necessity, truth is nourishment as well as grain. A reason which fasts from science and wisdom grows thin. Let us enter equal complaint against stomachs and minds which do not eat. If there is anything more heart-breaking than a body perishing for lack of bread, it is a soul which is dying from hunger for the light.

The whole of progress tends in the direction of solution. Someday we shall be amazed. As the human race mounts upward, the deep layers emerge naturally from the zone of distress. The obliteration of misery will be accomplished by a simple elevation of level.

We should do wrong were we to doubt this blessed consummation.

The past is very strong, it is true, at the present moment. It censures. This rejuvenation of a corpse is surprising. Behold, it is walking and advancing. It seems a victor; this dead body is a conqueror. He arrives with his legions, superstitions, with his sword, despotism, with his banner, ignorance; a while ago, he won ten battles. He advances, he threatens, he laughs, he is at our doors. Let us not despair, on our side. Let us sell the field on which Hannibal is encamped.

What have we to fear, we who believe?

No such thing as a back-flow of ideas exists any more than there exists a return of a river on its course.

But let those who do not desire a future reflect on this matter. When they say "no" to progress, it is not the future but themselves that they are condemning. They are giving themselves a sad malady; they are inoculating themselves with the past. There is but one way of rejecting To-morrow, and that is to die.

Now, no death, that of the body as late as possible, that of the soul never—this is what we desire.

Yes, the enigma will utter its word, the sphinx will speak, the problem will be solved.

Yes, the people, sketched out by the eighteenth century, will be finished by the nineteenth. He who doubts this is an idiot! The future blossoming, the near blossoming forth of universal well-being, is a divinely fatal phenomenon.

Immense combined propulsions direct human affairs and conduct them within a given time to a logical state, that is to say, to a state of equilibrium; that is to say, to equity. A force composed of earth and heaven results from humanity and governs it; this force is a worker of miracles; marvelous issues are no more difficult to it than extraordinary vicissitudes. Aided by science, which comes from one man, and by the event, which comes from another, it is not greatly alarmed by these contradictions in the attitude of problems, which seem impossibilities to the vulgar herd. It is no less skillful at causing a solution to spring forth from the reconciliation of ideas, than a lesson from the reconciliation of facts, and we may expect anything from that mysterious power of progress, which brought the Orient and the Occident face to face one fine day, in the depths of a sepulcher, and made the imaums converse with Bonaparte in the interior of the Great Pyramid.

In the meantime, let there be no halt, no hesitation, no pause in the grandiose onward march of minds. Social philosophy consists essentially in science and peace. Its object is, and its result must be, to dissolve wrath by the study of antagonisms. It examines, it scrutinizes, it analyzes; then it puts together once more, it proceeds by means of reduction, discarding all hatred.

More than once, a society has been seen to give way before the wind which is let loose upon mankind; history is full of the shipwrecks of nations and empires; manners, customs, laws, religions—and some fine day, that unknown force, the hurricane, passes by and bears them all away. The civilizations of India, of Chaldea, of Persia, of Syria, of Egypt, have disappeared one after the other. Why? We know not. What are the causes of these disasters? We do not know. Could these societies have been saved? Was it their fault? Did they persist in the fatal vice which destroyed them? What is the amount of suicide in these terrible deaths of a nation and a race? Questions to which there exists no reply. Darkness enwraps condemned civilizations. They sprung a leak, then they sank. We have nothing more to say; and it is with a sort of terror that we look on, at the bottom of that sea which is called the past, behind those colossal waves, at the shipwreck of those immense vessels, Babylon, Nineveh, Tarsus, Thebes, Rome, beneath the fearful gusts which emerge from all the mouths of the shadows. But shadows are there, and light is here. We are not acquainted with the maladies of these ancient civilizations, we do not know the infirmities of our own. Everywhere upon it we have the right of light, we contemplate its beauties, we lay bare its defects. Where it is ill, we probe; and the sickness once diagnosed, the study of the cause leads to the discovery of the remedy. Our civilization, the work of twenty centuries, is its law and its prodigy; it is worth the trouble of saving. It will be saved. It is already much to have solaced it; its enlightenment is yet another point. All the labors of modern social philosophies must converge toward this point. The thinker of to-day has a great duty—to auscultate civilization.

We repeat, that this auscultation brings encouragement; it is by this persistence in encouragement that we wish to conclude these pages, an austere interlude in a mournful drama. Beneath the social mortality, we feel human imperishableness. The globe does not perish, because it has these wounds, craters, eruptions, sulfur pits, here and there, nor because of a volcano which ejects its pus. The maladies of the people do not kill man.

And yet, anyone who follows the course of social clinics shakes his head at times. The strongest, the tenderest, the most logical have their hours of weakness.

Will the future arrive? It seems as though we might almost put this question, when we behold so much terrible darkness. Melancholy face-to-face encounter of selfish and wretched. On the part of the selfish, the prejudices, shadows of costly education, appetite increasing through intoxication, a giddiness of prosperity which dulls, a fear of suffering which, in some goes as far as an aversion for the suffering, an implacable satisfaction, the *I* so swollen that it bars the soul; on the side of the wretched covetousness, envy, hatred of seeing others enjoy, the profound impulses of the human beast toward assuaging its desires, hearts full of mist, sadness, need, fatality, impure and simple ignorance.

Shall we continue to raise our eyes to heaven? is the luminous point which we distinguish there one of those which vanish? The ideal is frightful to behold, thus lost in the depths, small, isolated, imperceptible, brilliant, but surrounded by those great, black menaces, monstrously heaped around it; yet no more in danger than a star in the maw of the clouds.

BOOK EIGHTH

ENCHANTMENTS AND DESOLATIONS

Chapter I

FULL LIGHT

THE READER HAS PROBABLY UNDERSTOOD THAT ÉPONINE, HAVING RECOGNIZED THROUGH THE gate, the inhabitant of that Rue Plumet whither Magnon had sent her, had begun by keeping the ruffians away from the Rue Plumet, and had then conducted Marius thither, and that, after many days spent in ecstasy before that gate, Marius, drawn on by that force which draws the iron to the magnet and a lover toward the stones of which is built the house of her whom he loves, had finally entered Cosette's garden as Romeo entered the garden of Juliet. This had even proved easier for him than for Romeo; Romeo was obliged to scale a wall, Marius had only to use a little force on one of the bars of the decrepit gate which vacillated in its rusty recess, after the fashion of old people's teeth. Marius was slender and readily passed through.

As there was never anyone in the street, and as Marius never entered the garden except at night, he ran no risk of being seen.

Beginning with that blessed and holy hour when a kiss betrothed these two souls, Marius was there every evening. If, at that period of her existence, Cosette had fallen in love with a man in the least unscrupulous or debauched, she would have been lost; for there are generous natures which yield themselves, and Cosette was one of them. One of woman's magnanimities is to yield. Love, at the height where it is absolute, is complicated with some indescribably celestial blindness of modesty. But what dangers you run, O noble souls! Often you give the heart, and we take the body. Your heart remains with you, you gaze upon it in the gloom with a shudder. Love has no middle course; it either ruins or it saves. All human destiny lies in this dilemma. This dilemma, ruin, or safety, is set forth no more inexorably by any fatality than by love. Love is life, if it is not death. Cradle; also coffin. The same sentiment says "yes" and "no" in the human heart. Of all the things that God has made, the human heart is the one which sheds the most light, alas! and the most darkness.

God willed that Cosette's love should encounter one of the loves which save.

Throughout the whole of the month of May of that year 1832, there were there, in every night, in that poor, neglected garden, beneath that thicket which grew thicker and more fragrant day by day, two beings composed of all chastity, all innocence, overflowing with all the felicity of heaven, nearer to the archangels than to mankind, pure, honest, intoxicated, radiant, who shone for each other amid the shadows. It seemed to Cosette that Marius had a crown, and to Marius that Cosette had a nimbus. They touched each other, they gazed at each other, they clasped each other's hands, they pressed close to each other; but there was a distance which they did not pass. Not that they respected it; they did not know of its existence. Marius was conscious of a barrier, Cosette's innocence; and Cosette of a support, Marius's loyalty. The first kiss had also been the last. Marius, since that time, had not gone further than to touch Cosette's hand, or her kerchief, or a lock of her hair, with his lips. For him, Cosette was a perfume and not a woman. He inhaled her. She refused nothing, and he asked nothing. Cosette was happy, and Marius was satisfied. They lived in this ecstatic state which can be described as the dazzling of one soul by another soul. It was the ineffable first embrace of two maiden souls in the ideal. Two swans meeting on the Jungfrau.

At that hour of love, an hour when voluptuousness is absolutely mute, beneath the omnipotence of ecstasy, Marius, the pure and seraphic Marius, would rather have gone to a woman of the town than have raised Cosette's robe to the height of her ankle. Once, in the moonlight, Cosette stooped to pick up something on the ground, her bodice fell apart and permitted a glimpse of the beginning of her throat. Marius turned away his eyes.

What took place between these two beings? Nothing. They adored each other.

At night, when they were there, that garden seemed a living and a sacred spot. All flowers unfolded around them and sent them incense; and they opened their souls and scattered them over the flowers. The wanton and vigorous vegetation quivered, full of strength and intoxication, around these two innocents, and they uttered words of love which set the trees to trembling.

What words were these? Breaths. Nothing more. These breaths sufficed to trouble and to touch all nature round about. Magic power which we should find it difficult to understand were we to read in a book these conversations which are made to be borne away and dispersed like smoke wreaths by the breeze beneath the leaves. Take from those murmurs of two lovers that melody which proceeds from the soul and which accompanies them like a lyre, and what remains is nothing more than a shade; you say: "What! is that all!" eh! yes, childish prattle, repetitions, laughter at nothing, nonsense, everything that is deepest and most sublime in the world! The only things which are worth the trouble of saying and hearing!

The man who has never heard, the man who has never uttered these absurdities, these paltry remarks, is an imbecile and a malicious fellow. Cosette said to Marius:

"Dost thou know?—"

[In all this and athwart this celestial maidenliness, and without either of them being able to say how it had come about, they had begun to call each other *thou*.]

"Dost thou know? My name is Euphrasie."

"Euphrasie? Why, no, thy name is Cosette."

"Oh! Cosette is a very ugly name that was given to me when I was a little thing. But my real name is Euphrasie. Dost thou like that name—Euphrasie?"

"Yes. But Cosette is not ugly."

"Do you like it better than Euphrasie?"

"Why, yes."

"Then I like it better too. Truly, it is pretty, Cosette. Call me Cosette."

And the smile that she added made of this dialogue an idyl worthy of a grove situated in heaven. On another occasion she gazed intently at him and exclaimed:

"Monsieur, you are handsome, you are good-looking, you are witty, you are not at all stupid, you are much more learned than I am, but I bid you defiance with this word: I love you!"

And Marius, in the very heavens, thought he heard a strain sung by a star.

Or she bestowed on him a gentle tap because he coughed, and she said to him:

"Don't cough, sir; I will not have people cough on my domain without my permission. It's very naughty to cough and to disturb me. I want you to be well, because, in the first place, if you were not well, I should be very unhappy. What should I do then?"

And this was simply divine.

Once Marius said to Cosette:

"Just imagine, I thought at one time that your name was Ursule."

This made both of them laugh the whole evening.

In the middle of another conversation, he chanced to exclaim:

"Oh! One day, at the Luxembourg, I had a good mind to finish breaking up a veteran!" But he stopped short, and went no further. He would have been obliged to speak to Cosette of her garter, and that was impossible. This bordered on a strange theme, the flesh, before which that immense and innocent love recoiled with a sort of sacred fright.

Marius pictured life with Cosette to himself like this, without anything else; to come every evening to the Rue Plumet, to displace the old and accommodating bar of the chief-justice's gate, to sit elbow to elbow on that bench, to gaze through the trees at the scintillation of the on-coming night, to fit a fold of the knee of his trousers into the ample fall of Cosette's gown, to caress her thumb-nail, to call her *thou*, to smell of the same flower, one after the other, forever, indefinitely. During this time, clouds passed above their heads. Every time that the wind blows it bears with it more of the dreams of men than of the clouds of heaven.

This chaste, almost shy love was not devoid of gallantry, by any means. To pay compliments to the woman whom a man loves is the first method of bestowing caresses, and he is half audacious who tries it. A compliment is something like a kiss through a veil. Voluptuousness mingles there with its sweet tiny point, while it hides itself. The heart draws back before voluptuousness only to love the more. Marius's blandishments, all saturated with fancy, were, so to speak, of azure hue. The birds when they fly up yonder, in the direction of the angels, must hear such words. There were mingled with them, nevertheless, life, humanity, all the positiveness of which Marius was capable. It was what is said in the bower, a prelude to what will be said in the chamber; a lyrical effusion, strophe and sonnet intermingled, pleasing hyperboles of cooing, all the refinements of adoration arranged in a bouquet and exhaling a celestial perfume, an ineffable twitter of heart to heart.

"Oh!" murmured Marius, "how beautiful you are! I dare not look at you. It is all over with me when I contemplate you. You are a grace. I know not what is the matter with me. The hem of your gown, when the tip of your shoe peeps from beneath, upsets me. And then, what an enchanted gleam when you open your thought even but a little! You talk astonishingly good sense. It seems to me at times that you are a dream. Speak, I listen, I admire. Oh Cosette! how strange it is and how charming! I am really beside myself. You are adorable, Mademoiselle. I study your feet with the microscope and your soul with the telescope."

And Cosette answered:

"I have been loving a little more all the time that has passed since this morning."

Questions and replies took care of themselves in this dialogue, which always turned with mutual consent upon love, as the little pith figures always turn on their peg.

Cosette's whole person was ingenuousness, ingenuity, transparency, whiteness, candor, radiance. It might have been said of Cosette that she was clear. She produced on those who saw her the sensation of April and dawn. There was dew in her eyes. Cosette was a condensation of the auroral light in the form of a woman.

It was quite simple that Marius should admire her, since he adored her. But the truth is that this little schoolgirl, fresh from the convent, talked with exquisite penetration and uttered, at times, all sorts of true and delicate sayings. Her prattle was conversation. She never made a mistake about anything, and she saw things justly. The woman feels and speaks with the tender instinct of the heart, which is infallible.

No one understands so well as a woman, how to say things that are, at once, both sweet and deep. Sweetness and depth, they are the whole of woman; in them lies the whole of heaven.

In this full felicity, tears welled up to their eyes every instant. A crushed lady-bug, a feather fallen from a nest, a branch of hawthorn broken, aroused their pity, and their ecstasy, sweetly mingled with melancholy, seemed to ask nothing better than to weep. The most sovereign symptom of love is a tenderness that is, at times, almost unbearable.

And, in addition to this—all these contradictions are the lightning play of love—they were fond of laughing, they laughed readily and with a delicious freedom, and so familiarly that they sometimes presented the air of two boys.

Still, though unknown to hearts intoxicated with purity, nature is always present and will not be forgotten. She is there with her brutal and sublime object; and however great may be the innocence of souls, one feels in the most modest private interview, the adorable and mysterious shade which separates a couple of lovers from a pair of friends.

They idolized each other.

The permanent and the immutable are persistent. People live, they smile, they laugh, they make little grimaces with the tips of their lips, they interlace their fingers, they call each other *thou*, and that does not prevent eternity.

Two lovers hide themselves in the evening, in the twilight, in the invisible, with the birds, with the roses; they fascinate each other in the darkness with their hearts which they throw into their eyes, they murmur, they whisper, and in the meantime, immense librations of the planets fill the infinite universe.

Chapter II

THE BEWILDERMENT OF PERFECT HAPPINESS

THEY EXISTED VAGUELY, FRIGHTENED AT THEIR HAPPINESS. THEY DID NOT NOTICE THE CHOLERA which decimated Paris precisely during that very month. They had confided in each other as far as possible, but this had not extended much further than their names. Marius had told Cosette that he was an orphan, that his name was Marius Pontmercy, that he was a lawyer, that he lived by writing things for publishers, that his father had been a colonel, that the latter had been a hero, and that he, Marius, was on bad terms with his grandfather who was rich. He had also hinted at being a baron, but this had produced no effect on Cosette. She did not know the meaning of the word. Marius was Marius. On her side, she had confided to him that she had been brought up at the Petit-Picpus convent, that her mother, like his own, was dead, that her father's name was M. Fauchelevent, that he was very good, that he gave a great deal to the poor, but that he was poor himself, and that he denied himself everything though he denied her nothing.

Strange to say, in the sort of symphony in which Marius had lived since he had been in the habit of seeing Cosette, the past, even the most recent past, had become so confused and distant to him, that what Cosette told him satisfied him completely. It did not even occur to him to tell her about the nocturnal adventure in the hovel, about Thénardier, about the burn, and about the strange attitude and singular flight of her father. Marius had momentarily forgotten all this; in the evening he did not even know that there had been a morning, what he had done, where he had breakfasted, nor who had spoken to him; he had songs in his ears which rendered him deaf to every other thought; he only existed at the hours when he saw Cosette. Then, as he was in heaven, it was quite natural that he should forget earth. Both bore languidly the indefinable burden of immaterial pleasures. Thus lived these somnambulists who are called lovers.

Alas! Who is there who has not felt all these things? Why does there come an hour when one emerges from this azure, and why does life go on afterwards?

Loving almost takes the place of thinking. Love is an ardent forgetfulness of all the rest. Then ask logic of passion if you will. There is no more absolute logical sequence in the human heart than there is a perfect geometrical figure in the celestial mechanism. For Cosette and Marius nothing existed except Marius and Cosette. The universe around them had fallen into a hole. They lived in a golden minute. There was nothing before them, nothing behind. It hardly occurred to Marius that Cosette had a father. His brain was dazzled and obliterated. Of what did these lovers talk then? We have seen, of the flowers, and the swallows, the setting sun and the rising moon, and all sorts of important things. They had told each other everything except everything. The everything of lovers is nothing. But the father, the realities, that lair, the ruffians, that adventure, to what purpose? And was he very sure that this nightmare had actually existed? They were two, and they adored each other, and beyond that there was nothing. Nothing else existed. It is probable that this vanishing of hell in our rear is inherent to the arrival of paradise. Have we beheld demons? Are there any? Have we trembled? Have we suffered? We no longer know. A rosy cloud hangs over it.

So these two beings lived in this manner, high aloft, with all that improbability which is in nature; neither at the nadir nor at the zenith, between man and seraphim, above the mire, below the ether, in the clouds; hardly flesh and blood, soul and ecstasy from head to foot; already too sublime to walk the earth, still too heavily charged with humanity to disappear in the blue, suspended like atoms which are waiting to be precipitated; apparently beyond the bounds of destiny; ignorant of that rut; yesterday, to-day, to-morrow; amazed, rapturous, floating, soaring; at times so light that they could take their flight out into the infinite; almost prepared to soar away to all eternity. They slept wide-awake, thus sweetly lulled. Oh! splendid lethargy of the real overwhelmed by the ideal.

Sometimes, beautiful as Cosette was, Marius shut his eyes in her presence. The best way to look at the soul is through closed eyes.

Marius and Cosette never asked themselves whither this was to lead them. They considered that they had already arrived. It is a strange claim on man's part to wish that love should lead to something.

Chapter III

THE BEGINNING OF SHADOW

J EAN VALJEAN SUSPECTED NOTHING.
  Cosette, who was rather less dreamy than Marius, was gay, and that sufficed for Jean Valjean's happiness. The thoughts which Cosette cherished, her tender preoccupations, Marius's image which filled her heart, took away nothing from the incomparable purity of her beautiful, chaste, and smiling brow. She was at the age when the virgin bears her love as the angel his lily. So Jean Valjean was at ease. And then, when two lovers have come to an understanding, things always go well; the third party who might disturb their love is kept in a state of perfect blindness by a restricted number of precautions which are always the same in the case of all lovers. Thus, Cosette never objected to any of Jean Valjean's proposals. Did she want to take a walk? "Yes, dear little father." Did she want to stay at home? Very good. Did he wish to pass the evening with Cosette? She was delighted. As he always went to bed at ten o'clock, Marius did not come to the garden on such occasions until after that hour, when, from the street, he heard Cosette open the long glass door on the veranda. Of course, no one ever met Marius in the daytime. Jean Valjean never even dreamed any longer that Marius was in existence. Only once, one morning, he chanced to say to Cosette: "Why, you have whitewash on your back!" On the previous evening, Marius, in a transport, had pushed Cosette against the wall.

Old Toussaint, who retired early, thought of nothing but her sleep, and was as ignorant of the whole matter as Jean Valjean.

Marius never set foot in the house. When he was with Cosette, they hid themselves in a recess near the steps, in order that they might neither be seen nor heard from the street, and there they sat, frequently contenting themselves, by way of conversation, with pressing each other's hand twenty times a minute as they gazed at the branches of the trees. At such times, a thunderbolt might have fallen thirty paces from them, and they would not have noticed it, so deeply was the reverie of the one absorbed and sunk in the reverie of the other.

Limpid purity. Hours wholly white; almost all alike. This sort of love is a recollection of lily petals and the plumage of the dove.

The whole extent of the garden lay between them and the street. Every time that Marius entered and left, he carefully adjusted the bar of the gate in such a manner that no displacement was visible.

He usually went away about midnight, and returned to Courfeyrac's lodgings. Courfeyrac said to Bahorel:

"Would you believe it? Marius comes home nowadays at one o'clock in the morning."

Bahorel replied:

"What do you expect? There's always a petard in a seminary fellow."

At times, Courfeyrac folded his arms, assumed a serious air, and said to Marius:

"You are getting irregular in your habits, young man."

Courfeyrac, being a practical man, did not take in good part this reflection of an invisible paradise upon Marius; he was not much in the habit of concealed passions; it made him impatient, and now and then he called upon Marius to come back to reality.

One morning, he threw him this admonition:

"My dear fellow, you produce upon me the effect of being located in the moon, the realm of dreams, the province of illusions, capital, soap-bubble. Come, be a good boy, what's her name?"

But nothing could induce Marius "to talk." They might have torn out his nails before one of the two sacred syllables of which that ineffable name, Cosette, was composed. True love is as luminous as the dawn, and as silent as the tomb. Only, Courfeyrac saw this change in Marius, that his taciturnity was of the beaming order.

During this sweet month of May, Marius and Cosette learned to know these immense delights. To dispute and to say *you* for *thou*, simply that they might say *thou* the better afterwards. To talk at great length with very minute details, of persons in whom they took not the slightest interest in the world; another proof that in that ravishing opera called love, the libretto counts for almost nothing;

For Marius, to listen to Cosette discussing finery;

For Cosette, to listen to Marius talk in politics;

To listen, knee pressed to knee, to the carriages rolling along the Rue de Babylone;

To gaze upon the same planet in space, or at the same glowworm gleaming in the grass;

To hold their peace together; a still greater delight than conversation;

Etc., etc.

In the meantime, divers complications were approaching.

One evening, Marius was on his way to the rendezvous, by way of the Boulevard des Invalides. He habitually walked with drooping head. As he was on the point of turning the corner of the Rue Plumet, he heard someone quite close to him say:

"Good evening, Monsieur Marius."

He raised his head and recognized Éponine.

This produced a singular effect upon him. He had not thought of that girl a single time since the day when she had conducted him to the Rue Plumet, he had not seen her again, and she had gone completely out of his mind. He had no reasons for anything but gratitude toward her, he owed her his happiness, and yet, it was embarrassing to him to meet her.

It is an error to think that passion, when it is pure and happy, leads man to a state of perfection; it simply leads him, as we have noted, to a state of oblivion. In this situation, man forgets to be bad, but he also forgets to be good. Gratitude, duty, matters essential and important to be remembered, vanish. At any other time, Marius would have behaved quite differently to Éponine. Absorbed in Cosette, he had not even clearly put it to himself that this Éponine was named Éponine Thénardier, and that she bore the name inscribed in his father's will, that name, for which, but a few months before, he would have so ardently sacrificed himself. We show Marius as he was. His father himself was fading out of his soul to some extent, under the splendor of his love.

He replied with some embarrassment:

"Ah! so it's you, Éponine?"

"Why do you call me *you?* Have I done anything to you?"

"No," he answered.

Certainly, he had nothing against her. Far from it. Only, he felt that he could not do otherwise, now that he used *thou* to Cosette, than say *you* to Éponine.

As he remained silent, she exclaimed:

"Say—"

Then she paused. It seemed as though words failed that creature formerly so heedless and so bold. She tried to smile and could not. Then she resumed:

"Well?"

Then she paused again, and remained with downcast eyes.

"Good evening, Mr. Marius," said she suddenly and abruptly; and away she went.

Chapter IV

A Cab Runs in English and Barks in Slang

THE FOLLOWING DAY WAS THE 3D OF JUNE, 1832, A DATE WHICH IT IS NECESSARY TO INDICATE ON account of the grave events which at that epoch hung on the horizon of Paris in the state of lightning-charged clouds. Marius, at nightfall, was pursuing the same road as on the preceding evening, with the same thoughts of delight in his heart when he caught sight of Éponine approaching, through the trees of the boulevard. Two days in succession—this was too much. He turned hastily aside, quitted the boulevard, changed his course and went to the Rue Plumet through the Rue Monsieur.

This caused Éponine to follow him to the Rue Plumet, a thing which she had not yet done. Up to that time, she had contented herself with watching him on his passage along the boulevard without ever seeking to encounter him. It was only on the evening before that she had attempted to address him.

So Éponine followed him, without his suspecting the fact. She saw him displace the bar and slip into the garden.

She approached the railing, felt of the bars one after the other, and readily recognized the one which Marius had moved.

She murmured in a low voice and in gloomy accents:

"None of that, Lisette!"

She seated herself on the underpinning of the railing, close beside the bar, as though she were guarding it. It was precisely at the point where the railing touched the neighboring wall. There was a dim nook there, in which Éponine was entirely concealed.

She remained thus for more than an hour, without stirring and without breathing, a prey to her thoughts.

Toward ten o'clock in the evening, one of the two or three persons who passed through the Rue Plumet, an old, belated bourgeois who was making haste to escape from this deserted spot of evil repute, as he skirted the garden railings and reached the angle which it made with the wall, heard a dull and threatening voice saying:

"I'm no longer surprised that he comes here every evening."

The passer-by cast a glance around him, saw no one, dared not peer into the black niche, and was greatly alarmed. He redoubled his pace.

This passer-by had reason to make haste, for a very few instants later, six men, who were marching separately and at some distance from each other, along the wall, and who might have been taken for a gray patrol, entered the Rue Plumet.

The first to arrive at the garden railing halted, and waited for the others; a second later, all six were reunited.

These men began to talk in a low voice.

"This is the place," said one of them.

"Is there a *cab* [dog] in the garden?" asked another.

"I don't know. In any case, I have fetched a ball that we'll make him eat."

"Have you some putty to break the pane with?"

"Yes."

"The railing is old," interpolated a fifth, who had the voice of a ventriloquist.

"So much the better," said the second who had spoken. "It won't screech under the saw, and it won't be hard to cut."

The sixth, who had not yet opened his lips, now began to inspect the gate, as Éponine had done an hour earlier, grasping each bar in succession, and shaking them cautiously.

Thus he came to the bar which Marius had loosened. As he was on the point of grasping this bar, a hand emerged abruptly from the darkness, fell upon his arm; he felt himself vigorously thrust aside by a push in the middle of his breast, and a hoarse voice said to him, but not loudly:

"There's a dog."

At the same moment, he perceived a pale girl standing before him.

The man underwent that shock which the unexpected always brings. He bristled up in hideous wise; nothing is so formidable to behold as ferocious beasts who are uneasy; their terrified air evokes terror.

He recoiled and stammered:

"What jade is this?"

"Your daughter."

It was, in fact, Éponine, who had addressed Thénardier.

At the apparition of Éponine, the other five, that is to say, Claquesous, Guelemer, Babet, Brujon, and Montparnasse had noiselessly drawn near, without precipitation, without uttering a word, with the sinister slowness peculiar to these men of the night.

Some indescribable but hideous tools were visible in their hands. Guelemer held one of those pairs of curved pincers which prowlers call *fanchons*.

"Ah, see here, what are you about there? What do you want with us? Are you crazy?" exclaimed Thénardier, as loudly as one can exclaim and still speak low; "what have you come here to hinder our work for?"

Éponine burst out laughing, and threw herself on his neck.

"I am here, little father, because I am here. Isn't a person allowed to sit on the stones nowadays? It's you who ought not to be here. What have you come here for, since it's a biscuit? I told Magnon so. There's nothing to be done here. But embrace me, my good little father! It's a long time since I've seen you! So you're out?"

Thénardier tried to disentangle himself from Éponine's arms, and grumbled:

"That's good. You've embraced me. Yes, I'm out. I'm not in. Now, get away with you."

But Éponine did not release her hold, and redoubled her caresses.

"But how did you manage it, little pa? You must have been very clever to get out of that. Tell me about it! And my mother? Where is mother? Tell me about mamma."

Thénardier replied:

"She's well. I don't know, let me alone, and be off, I tell you."

"I won't go, so there now," pouted Éponine like a spoiled child; "you send me off, and it's four months since I saw you, and I've hardly had time to kiss you."

And she caught her father round the neck again.

"Come, now, this is stupid!" said Babet.

"Make haste!" said Guelemer, "the cops may pass."

The ventriloquist's voice repeated his distich:

"*Nous n' sommes pas le jour de l'an,*   "*This isn't New Year's day,*
  A bécoter papa, maman."   *To peck at pa and ma.*"

Éponine turned to the five ruffians.

"Why, it's Monsieur Brujon. Good day, Monsieur Babet. Good day, Monsieur Claquesous. Don't you know me, Monsieur Guelemer? How goes it, Montparnasse?"

"Yes, they know you!" ejaculated Thénardier. "But good day, good evening, sheer off! leave us alone!"

"It's the hour for foxes, not for chickens," said Montparnasse.

"You see the job we have on hand here," added Babet.

Éponine caught Montparnasse's hand.

"Take care," said he, "you'll cut yourself, I've a knife open."

"My little Montparnasse," responded Éponine very gently, "you must have confidence in people. I am the daughter of my father, perhaps. Monsieur Babet, Monsieur Guelemer, I'm the person who was charged to investigate this matter."

It is remarkable that Éponine did not talk slang. That frightful tongue had become impossible to her since she had known Marius.

She pressed in her hand, small, bony, and feeble as that of a skeleton, Guelemer's huge, coarse fingers, and continued:

"You know well that I'm no fool. Ordinarily, I am believed. I have rendered you service on various occasions. Well, I have made inquiries; you will expose yourselves to no purpose, you see. I swear to you that there is nothing in this house."

"There are lone women," said Guelemer.

"No, the persons have moved away."

"The candles haven't, anyway!" ejaculated Babet.

And he pointed out to Éponine, across the tops of the trees, a light which was wandering about in the mansard roof of the pavilion. It was Toussaint, who had stayed up to spread out some linen to dry.

Éponine made a final effort.

"Well," said she, "they're very poor folks, and it's a hovel where there isn't a sou."

"Go to the devil!" cried Thénardier. "When we've turned the house upside down and put the cellar at the top and the attic below, we'll tell you what there is inside, and whether it's francs or sous or half-farthings."

And he pushed her aside with the intention of entering.

"My good friend, Mr. Montparnasse," said Éponine, "I entreat you, you are a good fellow, don't enter."

"Take care, you'll cut yourself," replied Montparnasse.

Thénardier resumed in his decided tone:

"Decamp, my girl, and leave men to their own affairs!"

Éponine released Montparnasse's hand, which she had grasped again, and said:

"So you mean to enter this house?"

"Rather!" grinned the ventriloquist.

Then she set her back against the gate, faced the six ruffians who were armed to the teeth, and to whom the night lent the visages of demons, and said in a firm, low voice:

"Well, I don't mean that you shall."

They halted in amazement. The ventriloquist, however, finished his grin. She went on:

"Friends! Listen well. This is not what you want. Now I'm talking. In the first place, if you enter this garden, if you lay a hand on this gate, I'll scream, I'll beat on the door, I'll rouse everybody, I'll have the whole six of you seized, I'll call the police."

"She'd do it, too," said Thénardier in a low tone to Brujon and the ventriloquist.

She shook her head and added:

"Beginning with my father!"

Thénardier stepped nearer.

"Not so close, my good man!" said she.

He retreated, growling between his teeth:

"Why, what's the matter with her?"

And he added:

"Bitch!"

She began to laugh in a terrible way:

"As you like, but you shall not enter here. I'm not the daughter of a dog, since I'm the daughter of a wolf. There are six of you, what matters that to me? You are men. Well, I'm a woman. You don't frighten me. I tell you that you shan't enter this house, because it doesn't suit me. If you approach, I'll bark. I told you, I'm the dog, and I don't care a straw for you. Go your way, you bore me! Go where you please, but don't come here, I forbid it! You can use your knives, I'll use kicks; it's all the same to me, come on!"

She advanced a pace nearer the ruffians, she was terrible, she burst out laughing:

"Pardine! I'm not afraid. I shall be hungry this summer, and I shall be cold this winter. Aren't they ridiculous, these ninnies of men, to think they can scare a girl! What! Scare? Oh, yes, much! Because you have finical poppets of mistresses who hide under the bed when you put on a big voice, forsooth! I ain't afraid of anything, that I ain't!"

She fastened her intent gaze upon Thénardier and said:

"Not even of you, father!"

Then she continued, as she cast her blood-shot, specter-like eyes upon the ruffians in turn:

"What do I care if I'm picked up to-morrow morning on the pavement of the Rue Plumet, killed by the blows of my father's club, or whether I'm found a year from now in the nets at Saint-Cloud or the Isle of Swans in the midst of rotten old corks and drowned dogs?"

She was forced to pause; she was seized by a dry cough, her breath came from her weak and narrow chest like the death-rattle.

She resumed:

"I have only to cry out, and people will come, and then slap, bang! There are six of you; I represent the whole world."

Thénardier made a movement toward her.

"Don't approach!" she cried.

He halted, and said gently:

"Well, no; I won't approach, but don't speak so loud. So you intend to hinder us in our work, my daughter? But we must earn our living all the same. Have you no longer any kind feeling for your father?"

"You bother me," said Éponine.

"But we must live, we must eat—"

"Burst!"

So saying, she seated herself on the underpinning of the fence and hummed:

> "Mon bras si dodu,   "My arm so plump,
> Ma jambe bien faite,   My leg well formed,
> Et le temps perdu."   And time wasted."

She had set her elbow on her knee and her chin in her hand, and she swung her foot with an air of indifference. Her tattered gown permitted a view of her thin shoulder-blades. The neighboring street-lantern illuminated her profile and her attitude. Nothing more resolute and more surprising could be seen.

The six rascals, speechless and gloomy at being held in check by a girl, retreated beneath the shadow cast by the lantern, and held counsel with furious and humiliated shrugs.

In the meantime she stared at them with a stern but peaceful air.

"There's something the matter with her," said Babet. "A reason. Is she in love with the dog? It's a shame to miss this, anyway. Two women, an old fellow who lodges in the backyard, and curtains that ain't so bad at the windows. The old cove must be a Jew. I think the job's a good one."

"Well, go in, then, the rest of you," exclaimed Montparnasse. "Do the job. I'll stay here with the girl, and if she fails us—"

He flashed the knife, which he held open in his hand, in the light of the lantern.

Thénardier said not a word, and seemed ready for whatever the rest pleased.

Brujon, who was somewhat of an oracle, and who had, as the reader knows, "put up the job," had not as yet spoken. He seemed thoughtful. He had the reputation of not sticking at anything, and it was known that he had plundered a police post simply out of bravado. Besides this he made verses and songs, which gave him great authority.

Babet interrogated him:

"You say nothing, Brujon?"

Brujon remained silent an instant longer, then he shook his head in various ways, and finally concluded to speak:

"See here; this morning I came across two sparrows fighting, this evening I jostled a woman who was quarreling. All that's bad. Let's quit."

They went away.

As they went, Montparnasse muttered:

"Never mind! if they had wanted, I'd have cut her throat."

Babet responded:

"I wouldn't. I don't hit a lady."

At the corner of the street they halted and exchanged the following enigmatical dialogue in a low tone:

"Where shall we go to sleep to-night?"

"Under Pantin [Paris]."

"Have you the key to the gate, Thénardier?"

"Pardi."

Éponine, who never took her eyes off of them, saw them retreat by the road by which they had come. She rose and began to creep after them along the walls and the houses. She followed them thus as far as the boulevard.

There they parted, and she saw these six men plunge into the gloom, where they appeared to melt away.

Chapter V

THINGS OF THE NIGHT

AFTER THE DEPARTURE OF THE RUFFIANS, THE RUE PLUMET RESUMED ITS TRANQUIL, NOCTURNAL aspect. That which had just taken place in this street would not have astonished a forest. The lofty trees, the copses, the heaths, the branches rudely interlaced, the tall grass, exist in a somber manner; the savage swarming there catches glimpses of sudden apparitions of the invisible; that which is below man distinguishes, through the mists, that which is beyond man; and the things of which we living beings are ignorant there meet face to face in the night. Nature, bristling and wild, takes alarm at certain approaches in which she fancies that she feels the supernatural. The forces of the gloom know each other, and are strangely balanced by each other. Teeth and claws fear what they cannot grasp. Blood-drinking bestiality, voracious appetites, hunger in search of prey, the armed instincts of nails and jaws which have for source and aim the belly, glare and smell out uneasily the impassive spectral forms straying beneath a shroud, erect in its vague and shuddering robe, and which seem to them to live with a dead and terrible life. These brutalities, which are only matter, entertain a confused fear of having to deal with the immense obscurity condensed into an unknown being. A black figure barring the way stops the wild beast short. That which emerges from the cemetery intimidates and disconcerts that which emerges from the cave; the ferocious fear the sinister; wolves recoil when they encounter a ghoul.

Chapter VI

MARIUS BECOMES PRACTICAL ONCE MORE TO THE EXTENT OF GIVING COSETTE HIS ADDRESS

WHILE THIS SORT OF A DOG WITH A HUMAN FACE WAS MOUNTING GUARD OVER THE GATE, AND while the six ruffians were yielding to a girl, Marius was by Cosette's side.

Never had the sky been more studded with stars and more charming, the trees more trembling, the odor of the grass more penetrating; never had the birds fallen asleep among the leaves with a sweeter noise; never had all the harmonies of universal serenity responded more thoroughly to the inward music of love; never had Marius been more captivated, more happy, more ecstatic.

But he had found Cosette sad; Cosette had been weeping. Her eyes were red.

This was the first cloud in that wonderful dream.

Marius's first word had been: "What is the matter?"

And she had replied: "This."

Then she had seated herself on the bench near the steps, and while he tremblingly took his place beside her, she had continued:

"My father told me this morning to hold myself in readiness, because he has business, and we may go away from here."

Marius shivered from head to foot.

When one is at the end of one's life, to die means to go away; when one is at the beginning of it, to go away means to die.

For the last six weeks, Marius had little by little, slowly, by degrees, taken possession of Cosette each day. As we have already explained, in the case of first love, the soul is taken long before the body; later on, one takes the body long before the soul; sometimes one does not take the soul at all; the Faublas and the Prudhommes add: "Because there is none"; but the sarcasm is, fortunately, a blasphemy. So Marius possessed Cosette, as spirits possess, but he enveloped her with all his soul, and seized her jealously with incredible conviction. He possessed her smile, her breath, her perfume, the profound radiance of her blue eyes, the sweetness of her skin when he touched her hand, the charming mark which she had on her neck, all her thoughts. Therefore, he possessed all Cosette's dreams.

He incessantly gazed at, and he sometimes touched lightly with his breath, the short locks on the nape of her neck, and he declared to himself that there was not one of those short hairs which did not belong to him, Marius. He gazed upon and adored the things that she wore, her knot of ribbon, her gloves, her sleeves, her shoes, her cuffs, as sacred objects of which he was the master. He dreamed that he was the lord of those pretty shell combs which she wore in her hair, and he even said to himself, in confused and suppressed stammerings of voluptuousness which did not make their way to the light, that there was not a ribbon of her gown, not a mesh in her stockings, not a fold in her bodice, which was not his. Beside Cosette he felt himself beside his own property, his own thing, his own despot and his slave. It seemed as though they had so intermingled their souls, that it would have been impossible to tell them apart had they wished to take them back again.— "This is mine." "No, it is mine." "I assure you that you are mistaken. This is my property." "What you are taking as your own is myself."—Marius was something that made a part of Cosette, and Cosette was something which made a part of Marius. Marius felt Cosette within him. To have Cosette, to possess Cosette, this, to him, was not to be distinguished from breathing. It was in the midst of this faith, of this intoxication, of this virgin possession, unprecedented and absolute, of this sovereignty, that these words: "We are going away," fell suddenly, at a blow, and that the harsh voice of reality cried to him: "Cosette is not yours!"

Marius awoke. For six weeks Marius had been living, as we have said, outside of life; those words, *going away!* caused him to re-enter it harshly.

He found not a word to say. Cosette merely felt that his hand was very cold. She said to him in her turn: "What is the matter?"

He replied in so low a tone that Cosette hardly heard him:

"I did not understand what you said."

She began again:

"This morning my father told me to settle all my little affairs and to hold myself in readiness, that he would give me his linen to put in a trunk, that he was obliged to go on a journey, that we were to go away, that it is necessary to have a large trunk for me and a small one for him, and that all is to be ready in a week from now, and that we might go to England."

"But this is outrageous!" exclaimed Marius.

It is certain, that, at that moment, no abuse of power, no violence, not one of the abominations of the worst tyrants, no action of Busiris, of Tiberius, or of Henry VIII, could have equaled this in atrocity, in the opinion of Marius; M. Fauchelevent taking his daughter off to England because he had business there.

He demanded in a weak voice:

"And when do you start?"

"He did not say when."

"And when shall you return?"

"He did not say when."

Marius rose and said coldly:

"Cosette, shall you go?"

Cosette turned toward him her beautiful eyes, all filled with anguish, and replied in a sort of bewilderment:

"Where?"

"To England. Shall you go?"

"Why do you say *you* to me?"

"I ask you whether you will go?"

"What do you expect me to do?" she said, clasping her hands.

"So, you will go?"

"If my father goes."

"So, you will go?"

Cosette took Marius's hand, and pressed it without replying.

"Very well," said Marius, "then I will go elsewhere."

Cosette felt rather than understood the meaning of these words. She turned so pale that her face shone white through the gloom. She stammered:

"What do you mean?"

Marius looked at her, then raised his eyes to heaven, and answered: "Nothing."

When his eyes fell again, he saw Cosette smiling at him. The smile of a woman whom one loves possesses a visible radiance, even at night.

"How silly we are! Marius, I have an idea."

"What is it?"

"If we go away, do you go too! I will tell you where! Come and join me wherever I am."

Marius was now a thoroughly roused man. He had fallen back into reality. He cried to Cosette:

"Go away with you! Are you mad? Why, I should have to have money, and I have none! Go to England? But I am in debt now, I owe, I don't know how much, more than ten louis to Courfeyrac, one of my friends with whom you are not acquainted! I have an old hat which is not worth three francs, I have a coat which lacks buttons in front, my shirt is all ragged, my elbows are torn, my boots let in the water; for the last six weeks I have not thought about it, and I have not told you about it. You only see me at night, and you give me your love; if you were to see me in the daytime, you would give me a sou! Go to England! Eh! I haven't enough to pay for a passport!"

He threw himself against a tree which was close at hand, erect, his brow pressed close to the bark, feeling neither the wood which flayed his skin, nor the fever which was throbbing in his temples, and there he stood motionless, on the point of falling, like the statue of despair.

He remained a long time thus. One could remain for eternity in such abysses. At last he turned round. He heard behind him a faint stifled noise, which was sweet yet sad.

It was Cosette sobbing.

She had been weeping for more than two hours beside Marius as he meditated.

He came to her, fell at her knees, and slowly prostrating himself, he took the tip of her foot which peeped out from beneath her robe, and kissed it.

She let him have his way in silence. There are moments when a woman accepts, like a somber and resigned goddess, the religion of love.

"Do not weep," he said.

She murmured:

"Not when I may be going away, and you cannot come!"

He went on:

"Do you love me?"

She replied, sobbing, by that word from paradise which is never more charming than amid tears:

"I adore you!"

He continued in a tone which was an indescribable caress:

"Do not weep. Tell me, will you do this for me, and cease to weep?"

"Do you love me?" said she.

He took her hand.

"Cosette, I have never given my word of honor to anyone, because my word of honor terrifies me. I feel that my father is by my side. Well, I give you my most sacred word of honor, that if you go away I shall die."

In the tone with which he uttered these words there lay a melancholy so solemn and so tranquil, that Cosette trembled. She felt that chill which is produced by a true and gloomy thing as it passes by. The shock made her cease weeping.

"Now, listen," said he, "do not expect me to-morrow."

"Why?"

"Do not expect me until the day after to-morrow."

"Oh! Why?"

"You will see."

"A day without seeing you! But that is impossible!"

"Let us sacrifice one day in order to gain our whole lives, perhaps."

And Marius added in a low tone and in an aside:

"He is a man who never changes his habits, and he has never received anyone except in the evening."

"Of what man are you speaking?" asked Cosette.

"I? I said nothing."

"What do you hope, then?"

"Wait until the day after to-morrow."

"You wish it?"

"Yes, Cosette."

She took his head in both her hands, raising herself on tiptoe in order to be on a level with him, and tried to read his hope in his eyes.

Marius resumed:

"Now that I think of it, you ought to know my address: something might happen, one never knows; I live with that friend named Courfeyrac, Rue de la Verrerie, No. 16."

He searched in his pocket, pulled out his penknife, and with the blade he wrote on the plaster of the wall:

"*16 Rue de la Verrerie.*"

In the meantime, Cosette had begun to gaze into his eyes once more.

"Tell me your thought, Marius; you have some idea. Tell it to me. Oh! tell me, so that I may pass a pleasant night."

"This is my idea: that it is impossible that God should mean to part us. Wait; expect me the day after to-morrow."

"What shall I do until then?" said Cosette. "You are outside, you go, and come! How happy men are! I shall remain entirely alone! Oh! How sad I shall be! What is it that you are going to do to-morrow evening? tell me."

"I am going to try something."

"Then I will pray to God and I will think of you here, so that you may be successful. I will question you no further, since you do not wish it. You are my master. I shall pass the evening to-morrow in singing that music from *Euryanthe* that you love, and that you came one evening to listen to, outside my shutters. But day after to-morrow you will come early. I shall expect you at dusk, at nine o'clock precisely, I warn you. Mon Dieu! how sad it is that the days are so long! On the stroke of nine, do you understand, I shall be in the garden."

"And I also."

And without having uttered it, moved by the same thought, impelled by those electric currents which place lovers in continual communication, both being intoxicated with delight even in their sorrow, they fell into each other's arms, without perceiving that their lips met while their uplifted eyes, overflowing with rapture and full of tears, gazed upon the stars.

When Marius went forth, the street was deserted. This was the moment when Éponine was following the ruffians to the boulevard.

While Marius had been dreaming with his head pressed to the tree, an idea had crossed his mind; an idea, alas! that he himself judged to be senseless and impossible. He had come to a desperate decision.

Chapter VII

THE OLD HEART AND THE YOUNG HEART IN THE
PRESENCE OF EACH OTHER

AT THAT EPOCH, FATHER GILLENORMAND WAS WELL PAST HIS NINETY-FIRST BIRTHDAY. HE STILL lived with Mademoiselle Gillenormand in the Rue des Filles-du-Calvaire, No. 6, in the old house which he owned. He was, as the reader will remember, one of those antique old men who await death perfectly erect, whom age bears down without bending, and whom even sorrow cannot curve.

Still, his daughter had been saying for some time: "My father is sinking." He no longer boxed the maids' ears; he no longer thumped the landing-place so vigorously with his cane when Basque was slow in opening the door. The Revolution of July had exasperated him for the space of barely six months. He had viewed, almost tranquilly, that coupling of words, in the *Moniteur:* M. Humblot-Conté, peer of France. The fact is, that the old man was deeply dejected. He did not bend, he did not yield; this was no more a characteristic of his physical than of his moral nature, but he felt himself giving way internally. For four years he had been waiting for Marius, with his foot firmly planted, that is the exact word, in the conviction that that good-for-nothing young scamp would ring at his door some day or other; now he had reached the point, where, at certain gloomy hours he said to himself, that if Marius made him wait much longer—It was not death that was insupportable to him; it was the idea that perhaps he should never see Marius again. The idea of never seeing Marius again had never entered his brain until that day; now the thought began to recur to him, and it chilled him. Absence, as is always the case in genuine and natural sentiments, had only served to augment the grandfather's love for the ungrateful child, who had gone off like a flash. It is during December nights, when the cold stands at ten degrees, that one thinks oftenest of the son.

M. Gillenormand was, or thought himself, above all things, incapable of taking a single step, he—the grandfather, toward his grandson; "I would die rather," he said to himself. He did not consider himself as the least to blame; but he thought of Marius only with profound tenderness, and the mute despair of an elderly, kindly old man who is about to vanish in the dark.

He began to lose his teeth, which added to his sadness.

M. Gillenormand, without however acknowledging it to himself, for it would have rendered him furious and ashamed, had never loved a mistress as he loved Marius.

He had had placed in his chamber, opposite the head of his bed, so that it should be the first thing on which his eyes fell on waking, an old portrait of his other daughter, who was dead, Madame Pontmercy, a portrait which had been taken when she was eighteen. He gazed incessantly at that portrait. One day, he happened to say, as he gazed upon it:

"I think the likeness is strong."

"To my sister?" inquired Mademoiselle Gillenormand. "Yes, certainly."

The old man added:

"And to him also."

Once as he sat with his knees pressed together, and his eyes almost closed, in a despondent attitude, his daughter ventured to say to him:

"Father, are you as angry with him as ever?"

She paused, not daring to proceed further.

"With whom?" he demanded.

"With that poor Marius."

He raised his aged head, laid his withered and emaciated fist on the table, and exclaimed in his most irritated and vibrating tone:

"Poor Marius, do you say! That gentleman is a knave, a wretched scoundrel, a vain little ingrate, a heartless, soulless, haughty, and wicked man!"

And he turned away so that his daughter might not see the tear that stood in his eye.

Three days later he broke a silence which had lasted four hours, to say to his daughter pointblank:

"I had the honor to ask Mademoiselle Gillenormand never to mention him to me."

Aunt Gillenormand renounced every effort, and pronounced this acute diagnosis: "My father never cared very much for my sister after her folly. It is clear that he detests Marius."

"After her folly" meant: "after she had married the colonel."

However, as the reader has been able to conjecture, Mademoiselle Gillenormand had failed in her attempt to substitute her favorite, the officer of lancers, for Marius. The substitute, Théodule, had not been a success. M. Gillenormand had not accepted the *quid pro quo*. A vacancy in the heart does not accommodate itself to a stop-gap. Théodule, on his side, though he scented the inheritance, was disgusted at the task of pleasing. The good man bored the lancer; and the lancer shocked the good man. Lieutenant Théodule was gay, no doubt, but a chatter-box, frivolous, but vulgar; a high liver, but a frequenter of bad company; he had mistresses, it is true, and he had a great deal to say about them, it is true also; but he talked badly. All his good qualities had a defect. M. Gillenormand was worn out with hearing him tell about the love affairs that he had in the vicinity of the barracks in the Rue de Babylone. And then, Lieutenant Gillenormand sometimes came in his uniform, with the tricolored cockade. This rendered him downright intolerable. Finally, Father Gillenormand had said to his daughter: "I've had enough of that Théodule. I haven't much taste for warriors in time of peace. Receive him if you choose. I don't know but I prefer slashers to fellows that drag their swords. The clash of blades in battle is less dismal, after all, than the clank of the scabbard on the pavement. And then, throwing out your chest like a bully and lacing yourself like a girl, with stays under your cuirass, is doubly ridiculous. When one is a veritable man, one holds equally aloof from swagger and from affected airs. He is neither a blusterer nor a finnicky-hearted man. Keep your Théodule for yourself."

It was in vain that his daughter said to him: "But he is your grandnephew, nevertheless"—it turned out that M. Gillenormand who was a grandfather to the very finger-tips, was not in the least a granduncle.

In fact, as he had good sense, and as he had compared the two, Théodule had only served to make him regret Marius all the more.

One evening—it was the 24th of June, which did not prevent Father Gillenormand having a rousing fire on the hearth—he had dismissed his daughter, who was sewing in a neighboring apartment. He was alone in his chamber, amid its pastoral scenes, with his feet propped on the andirons, half enveloped in his huge screen of coromandel lacquer, with its nine leaves, with his elbow resting on a table where burned two candles under a green shade, engulfed in his tapestry arm-chair, and in his hand a book which he was not reading. He was dressed, according to his wont, like an *incroyable*, and resembled an antique portrait by Garat. This would have made people run after him in the street, had not his daughter covered him up, whenever he went out, in a vast bishop's wadded cloak, which concealed his attire. At home, he never wore a dressing-gown, except when he rose and retired. "It gives one a look of age," said he.

Father Gillenormand was thinking of Marius lovingly and bitterly; and, as usual, bitterness predominated. His tenderness once soured always ended by boiling and turning to indignation. He had reached the point where a man tries to make up his mind and to accept that which rends his heart. He was explaining to himself that there was no longer any reason why Marius should return, that if he intended to return, he should have done it long ago, that he must renounce the idea. He was trying to accustom himself to the thought that all was over, and that he should die without having beheld "that gentleman" again. But his whole nature revolted; his aged paternity would not consent to this. "Well!" said he—this was his doleful refrain—"he will not return!" His bald head had fallen upon his breast, and he fixed a melancholy and irritated gaze upon the ashes on his hearth.

In the very midst of his reverie, his old servant Basque entered, and inquired:

"Can Monsieur receive M. Marius?"

The old man sat up erect, pallid, and like a corpse which rises under the influence of a galvanic shock. All his blood had retreated to his heart. He stammered:

"M. Marius what?"

"I don't know," replied Basque, intimidated and put out of countenance by his master's air; "I have not seen him. Nicolette came in and said to me: 'There's a young man here; say that it is M. Marius.'"

Father Gillenormand stammered in a low voice:

"Show him in."

And he remained in the same attitude, with shaking head, and his eyes fixed on the door. It opened once more. A young man entered. It was Marius.

Marius halted at the door, as though waiting to be bidden to enter.

His almost squalid attire was not perceptible in the obscurity caused by the shade. Nothing could be seen but his calm, grave, but strangely sad face.

It was several minutes before Father Gillenormand, dulled with amazement and joy, could see anything except a brightness as when one is in the presence of an apparition. He was on the point of swooning; he saw Marius through a dazzling light. It certainly was he, it certainly was Marius.

At last! After the lapse of four years! He grasped him entire, so to speak, in a single glance. He found him noble, handsome, distinguished, well-grown, a complete man, with a suitable mien and a charming air. He felt a desire to open his arms, to call him, to fling himself forward; his heart melted with rapture, affectionate words swelled and overflowed his breast; at length all his tenderness came to the light and reached his lips, and, by a contrast which constituted the very foundation of his nature, what came forth was harshness. He said abruptly:

"What have you come here for?"

Marius replied with embarrassment:

"Monsieur—"

M. Gillenormand would have liked to have Marius throw himself into his arms. He was displeased with Marius and with himself. He was conscious that he was brusque, and that Marius was cold. It caused the good man unendurable and irritating anxiety to feel so tender and forlorn within, and only to be able to be hard outside. Bitterness returned. He interrupted Marius in a peevish tone:

"Then why did you come?"

That "then" signified: *If you do not come to embrace me.* Marius looked at his grandfather, whose pallor gave him a face of marble.

"Monsieur—"

"Have you come to beg my pardon? Do you acknowledge your faults?"

He thought he was putting Marius on the right road, and that "the child" would yield. Marius shivered; it was the denial of his father that was required of him; he dropped his eyes and replied:

"No, sir."

"Then," exclaimed the old man impetuously, with a grief that was poignant and full of wrath, "what do you want of me?"

Marius clasped his hands, advanced a step, and said in a feeble and trembling voice:

"Sir, have pity on me."

These words touched M. Gillenormand; uttered a little sooner, they would have rendered him tender, but they came too late. The grandfather rose; he supported himself with both hands on his cane; his lips were white, his brow wavered, but his lofty form towered above Marius as he bowed.

"Pity on you, sir! It is youth demanding pity of the old man of ninety-one! You are entering into life, I am leaving it; you go to the play, to balls, to the café, to the billiard-hall; you have wit, you please the women, you are a handsome fellow; as for me, I spit on my brands in the heart of summer; you are rich with the only riches that are really such, I possess all the poverty of age; infirmity, isolation! You have your thirty-two teeth, a good digestion, bright eyes, strength, appetite, health, gaiety, a forest of black hair; I have no longer even white hair, I have lost my teeth, I am losing my legs, I am losing my memory; there are three names of streets that I confound incessantly, the Rue Charlot, the Rue du Chaume, and the Rue Saint-Claude, that is what I have come to; you have before you the whole future, full of sunshine, and I am beginning to lose my sight, so far am I advancing into the night; you are in love, that is a matter of course, I am beloved by no one in all the world; and you ask pity of me! Parbleu! Molière forgot that. If that is the way you jest at the court-house, Messieurs the lawyers, I sincerely compliment you. You are droll."

And the octogenarian went on in a grave and angry voice:

"Come, now, what do you want of me?"

"Sir," said Marius, "I know that my presence is displeasing to you, but I have come merely to ask one thing of you, and then I shall go away immediately."

"You are a fool!" said the old man. "Who said that you were to go away?"

This was the translation of the tender words which lay at the bottom of his heart:

"Ask my pardon! Throw yourself on my neck!"

M. Gillenormand felt that Marius would leave him in a few moments, that his harsh reception had repelled the lad, that his hardness was driving him away; he said all this to himself, and it augmented his grief; and as his grief was straightway converted into wrath, it increased his harshness. He would have liked to have Marius understand, and Marius did not understand, which made the good man furious.

He began again:

"What! you deserted me, your grandfather, you left my house to go no one knows whither, you drove your aunt to despair, you went off, it is easily guessed, to lead a bachelor life; it's more convenient, to play the dandy, to come in at all hours, to amuse yourself; you have given me no signs of life, you have contracted debts without even telling me to pay them, you have become a smasher of windows and a blusterer, and, at the end of four years, you come to me, and that is all that you have to say to me!"

This violent fashion of driving a grandson to tenderness was productive only of silence on the part of Marius. M. Gillenormand folded his arms; a gesture which with him was peculiarly imperious, and apostrophized Marius bitterly:

"Let us make an end of this. You have come to ask something of me, you say? Well, what? What is it? Speak!"

"Sir," said Marius, with the look of a man who feels that he is falling over a precipice, "I have come to ask your permission to marry."

M. Gillenormand rang the bell. Basque opened the door halfway.

"Call my daughter."

A second later, the door was opened once more, Mademoiselle Gillenormand did not enter, but showed herself; Marius was standing, mute, with pendant arms and the face of a criminal; M. Gillenormand was pacing back and forth in the room. He turned to his daughter and said to her:

"Nothing. It is Monsieur Marius. Say good day to him. Monsieur wishes to marry. That's all. Go away."

The curt, hoarse sound of the old man's voice announced a strange degree of excitement. The aunt gazed at Marius with a frightened air, hardly appeared to recognize him, did not allow a gesture or a syllable to escape her, and disappeared at her father's breath more swiftly than a straw before the hurricane.

In the meantime, Father Gillenormand had returned and placed his back against the chimney-piece once more.

"You marry! At one-and-twenty! You have arranged that! You have only a permission to ask! a formality. Sit down, sir. Well, you have had a revolution since I had the honor to see you last. The Jacobins got the upper hand. You must have been delighted. Are you not a Republican since you are a Baron? You can make that agree. The Republic makes a good sauce for the barony. Are you one of those decorated by July? Have you taken the Louvre at all, sir? Quite near here, in the Rue Saint-Antoine, opposite the Rue des Nonaindières, there is a cannon-ball encrusted in the wall of the third story of a house with this inscription: 'July 28th, 1830.' Go take a look at that. It produces a good effect. Ah! those friends of yours do very pretty things. By the way, aren't they erecting a fountain in the place of the monument of M. le Duc de Berry? So you want to marry? Whom? Can one inquire without indiscretion?"

He paused, and, before Marius had time to answer, he added violently:

"Come now, you have a profession? A fortune made? How much do you earn at your trade of lawyer?"

"Nothing," said Marius, with a sort of firmness and resolution that was almost fierce.

"Nothing? Then all that you have to live upon is the twelve hundred livres that I allow you?"

Marius did not reply. M. Gillenormand continued:

"Then I understand the girl is rich?"

"As rich as I am."

"What! No dowry?"

"No."

"Expectations?"

"I think not."

"Utterly naked! What's the father?"

"I don't know."

"And what's her name?"

"Mademoiselle Fauchelevent."

"Fauchewhat?"

"Fauchelevent."

"Pttt!" ejaculated the old gentleman.

"Sir!" exclaimed Marius.

M. Gillenormand interrupted him with the tone of a man who is speaking to himself:

"That's right, one-and-twenty years of age, no profession, twelve hundred livres a year, Madame la Baronne de Pontmercy will go and purchase a couple of sous' worth of parsley from the fruiterer."

"Sir," repeated Marius, in the despair at the last hope, which was vanishing, "I entreat you! I conjure you in the name of Heaven, with clasped hands, sir, I throw myself at your feet, permit me to marry her!"

The old man burst into a shout of strident and mournful laughter, coughing and laughing at the same time.

"Ah! ah! ah! You said to yourself: 'Pardine! I'll go hunt up that old blockhead, that absurd numskull! What a shame that I'm not twenty-five! How I'd treat him to a nice respectful summons! How nicely I'd get along without him! It's nothing to me, I'd say to him: "You're only too happy to see me, you old idiot, I want to marry, I desire to wed Mamselle No-matter-whom, daughter of Monsieur No-matter-what, I have no shoes, she has no chemise, that just suits; I want to throw my career, my future, my youth, my life to the dogs; I wish to take a plunge into wretchedness with a woman around my neck, that's an idea, and you must consent to it!" and the old fossil will consent.'

Go, my lad, do as you like, attach your paving-stone, marry your Pousselevent, your Coupelevent—Never, sir, never!"

"Father—"

"Never!"

At the tone in which that "never" was uttered, Marius lost all hope. He traversed the chamber with slow steps, with bowed head, tottering and more like a dying man than like one merely taking his departure. M. Gillenormand followed him with his eyes, and at the moment when the door opened, and Marius was on the point of going out, he advanced four paces, with the senile vivacity of impetuous and spoiled old gentlemen, seized Marius by the collar, brought him back energetically into the room, flung him into an arm-chair and said to him:

"Tell me all about it!"

It was that single word "father" which had effected this revolution.

Marius stared at him in bewilderment. M. Gillenormand's mobile face was no longer expressive of anything but rough and ineffable good-nature. The grandsire had given way before the grandfather.

"Come, see here, speak, tell me about your love affairs, jabber, tell me everything! Sapristi! how stupid young folks are!"

"Father—" repeated Marius.

The old man's entire countenance lighted up with indescribable radiance.

"Yes, that's right, call me father, and you'll see!"

There was now something so kind, so gentle, so open-hearted, and so paternal in this brusqueness, that Marius, in the sudden transition from discouragement to hope, was stunned and intoxicated by it, as it were. He was seated near the table, the light from the candles brought out the dilapidation of his costume, which Father Gillenormand regarded with amazement.

"Well, father—" said Marius.

"Ah, by the way," interrupted M. Gillenormand, "you really have not a penny then? You are dressed like a pickpocket."

He rummaged in a drawer, drew forth a purse, which he laid on the table: "Here are a hundred louis, buy yourself a hat."

"Father," pursued Marius, "my good father, if you only knew! I love her. You cannot imagine it; the first time I saw her was at the Luxembourg, she came there; in the beginning, I did not pay much heed to her, and then, I don't know how it came about, I fell in love with her. Oh! how unhappy that made me! Now, at last, I see her every day, at her own home, her father does not know it, just fancy, they are going away, it is in the garden that we meet, in the evening, her father means to take her to England, then I said to myself: 'I'll go and see my grandfather and tell him all about the affair. I should go mad first, I should die, I should fall ill, I should throw myself into the water. I absolutely must marry her, since I should go mad otherwise.' This is the whole truth, and I do not think that I have omitted anything. She lives in a garden with an iron fence, in the Rue Plumet. It is in the neighborhood of the Invalides."

Father Gillenormand had seated himself, with a beaming countenance, beside Marius. As he listened to him and drank in the sound of his voice, he enjoyed at the same time a protracted pinch of snuff. At the words "Rue Plumet" he interrupted his inhalation and allowed the remainder of his snuff to fall upon his knees.

"The Rue Plumet, the Rue Plumet, did you say?—Let us see!—Are there not barracks in that vicinity?—Why, yes, that's it. Your cousin Théodule has spoken to me about it. The lancer, the officer. A gay girl, my good friend, a gay girl!—Pardieu, yes, the Rue Plumet. It is what used to be called the Rue Blomet.—It all comes back to me now. I have heard of that little girl of the iron railing in the Rue Plumet. In a garden, a Pamela. Your taste is not bad. She is said to be a very tidy creature. Between ourselves, I think that simpleton of a lancer has been courting her a bit. I don't know where he did it. However, that's not to the purpose. Besides, he is not to be believed. He brags, Marius! I think it quite proper that a young man like you should be in love. It's the right thing at your age. I like you better as a lover than as a Jacobin. I like you better in love with a petticoat, sapristi! with twenty petticoats, than with M. de Robespierre. For my part, I will do myself the justice to say, that in the line of *sans-culottes*, I have never loved anyone but women. Pretty girls are pretty girls, the deuce! There's no objection to that. As for the little one, she receives you without her father's knowledge. That's in the established order of things. I have had adventures of that same sort myself. More than one. Do you know what is done then? One does not take the matter ferociously; one does not precipitate himself into the tragic; one does not make one's mind to marriage and M. le Maire with his scarf. One simply behaves like a fellow of spirit. One shows good sense. Slip along, mortals; don't marry. You come and look up your grandfather, who is a good-natured fellow at bottom, and who always has a few rolls of louis in an old drawer; you say to him: 'See here, grandfather.' And the grandfather says: 'That's a simple matter. Youth must amuse itself, and old age must wear out. I have been young, you will be old. Come, my boy, you shall pass it on to your grandson. Here are two hundred pistoles. Amuse yourself, deuce take it!' Nothing better! That's the way the affair should be treated. You don't marry, but that does no harm. You understand me?"

Marius, petrified and incapable of uttering a syllable, made a sign with his head that he did not.

The old man burst out laughing, winked his aged eye, gave him a slap on the knee, stared him full in the face with a mysterious and beaming air, and said to him, with the tenderest of shrugs of the shoulder:

"Booby! make her your mistress."

Marius turned pale. He had understood nothing of what his grandfather had just said. This twaddle about the Rue Blomet, Pamela, the barracks, the lancer, had passed before Marius like a dissolving view. Nothing of all that could bear any reference to Cosette, who was a lily. The good man was wandering in his mind. But this wandering terminated in words which Marius did understand, and which were a mortal insult to Cosette. Those words, "make her your mistress," entered the heart of the strict young man like a sword.

He rose, picked up his hat which lay on the floor, and walked to the door with a firm, assured step. There he turned round, bowed deeply to his grandfather, raised his head erect again, and said:

"Five years ago you insulted my father; to-day you have insulted my wife. I ask nothing more of you, sir. Farewell."

Father Gillenormand, utterly confounded, opened his mouth, extended his arms, tried to rise, and before he could utter a word, the door closed once more, and Marius had disappeared.

The old man remained for several minutes motionless and as though struck by lightning, without the power to speak or breathe, as though a clenched fist grasped his throat. At last he tore himself from his arm-chair, ran, so far as a man can run at ninety-one, to the door, opened it, and cried:

"Help! Help!"

His daughter made her appearance, then the domestics. He began again, with a pitiful rattle: "Run after him! Bring him back! What have I done to him? He is mad! He is going away! Ah! my God! Ah! my God! This time he will not come back!"

He went to the window which looked out on the street, threw it open with his aged and palsied hands, leaned out more than halfway, while Basque and Nicolette held him behind, and shouted:

"Marius! Marius! Marius! Marius!"

But Marius could no longer hear him, for at that moment he was turning the corner of the Rue Saint-Louis.

The octogenarian raised his hands to his temples two or three times with an expression of anguish, recoiled tottering, and fell back into an arm-chair, pulseless, voiceless, tearless, with quivering head and lips which moved with a stupid air, with nothing in his eyes and nothing any longer in his heart except a gloomy and profound something which resembled night.

Book Ninth

Whither are They Going?

Chapter I

Jean Valjean

THAT SAME DAY, TOWARD FOUR O'CLOCK IN THE AFTERNOON, JEAN VALJEAN WAS SITTING ALONE on the back side of one of the most solitary slopes in the Champ-de-Mars. Either from prudence, or from a desire to meditate, or simply in consequence of one of those insensible changes of habit which gradually introduce themselves into the existence of everyone, he now rarely went out with Cosette. He had on his workman's waistcoat, and trousers of gray linen; and his long-visored cap concealed his countenance.

He was calm and happy now beside Cosette; that which had, for a time, alarmed and troubled him had been dissipated; but for the last week or two, anxieties of another nature had come up. One day, while walking on the boulevard, he had caught sight of Thénardier; thanks to his disguise, Thénardier had not recognized him; but since that day, Jean Valjean had seen him repeatedly, and he was now certain that Thénardier was prowling about in their neighborhood.

This had been sufficient to make him come to a decision.

Moreover, Paris was not tranquil: political troubles presented this inconvenient feature, for anyone who had anything to conceal in his life, that the police had grown very uneasy and very suspicious, and that while seeking to ferret out a man like Pépin or Morey, they might very readily discover a man like Jean Valjean.

Jean Valjean had made up his mind to quit Paris, and even France, and go over to England.

He had warned Cosette. He wished to set out before the end of the week.

He had seated himself on the slope in the Champ-de-Mars, turning over all sorts of thoughts in his mind—Thénardier, the police, the journey, and the difficulty of procuring a passport.

He was troubled from all these points of view.

Last of all, an inexplicable circumstance which had just attracted his attention, and from which he had not yet recovered, had added to his state of alarm.

On the morning of that very day, when he alone of the household was stirring, while strolling in the garden before Cosette's shutters were open, he had suddenly perceived on the wall, the following line, engraved, probably with a nail:

16 Rue de la Verrerie.

This was perfectly fresh, the grooves in the ancient black mortar were white, a tuft of nettles at the foot of the wall was powdered with the fine, fresh plaster.

This had probably been written on the preceding night.

What was this? A signal for others? A warning for himself?

In any case, it was evident that the garden had been violated, and that strangers had made their way into it.

He recalled the odd incidents which had already alarmed the household.

His mind was now filling in this canvas.

He took good care not to speak to Cosette of the line written on the wall, for fear of alarming her.

In the midst of his preoccupations, he perceived, from a shadow cast by the sun, that someone had halted on the crest of the slope immediately behind him.

He was on the point of turning round, when a paper folded in four, fell upon his knees as though a hand had dropped it over his head.

He took the paper, unfolded it, and read these words written in large characters, with a pencil:

"MOVE AWAY FROM YOUR HOUSE."

Jean Valjean sprang hastily to his feet; there was no one on the slope; he gazed all around him and perceived a creature larger than a child, not so large as a man, clad in a gray blouse and trousers of dust-colored cotton velvet, who was jumping over the parapet and who slipped into the moat of the Champ-de-Mars.

Jean Valjean returned home at once, in a very thoughtful mood.

Chapter II

MARIUS

MARIUS HAD LEFT M. GILLENORMAND IN DESPAIR. HE HAD ENTERED THE HOUSE WITH VERY LIT-
tle hope, and quitted it with immense despair.

However, and those who have observed the depths of the human heart will understand this, the officer, the lancer, the ninny, Cousin Théodule, had left no trace in his mind. Not the slightest. The dramatic poet might, apparently, expect some complications from this revelation made point-blank by the grandfather to the grandson. But what the drama would gain thereby, truth would lose. Marius was at an age when one believes nothing in the line of evil; later on comes the age when one believes everything. Suspicions are nothing else than wrinkles. Early youth has none of them. That which overwhelmed Othello glides innocuous over Candide. Suspect Cosette! There are hosts of crimes which Marius could sooner have committed.

He began to wander about the streets, the resource of those who suffer. He thought of nothing, so far as he could afterwards remember. At two o'clock in the morning he returned to Courfeyrac's quarters and flung himself, without undressing, on his mattress. The sun was shining brightly when he sank into that frightful leaden slumber which permits ideas to go and come in the brain. When he awoke, he saw Courfeyrac, Enjolras, Feuilly, and Combeferre standing in the room with their hats on and all ready to go out.

Courfeyrac said to him:

"Are you coming to General Lamarque's funeral?"

It seemed to him that Courfeyrac was speaking Chinese.

He went out some time after them. He put in his pocket the pistols which Javert had given him at the time of the adventure on the 3d of February, and which had remained in his hands. These pistols were still loaded. It would be difficult to say what vague thought he had in his mind when he took them with him.

All day long he prowled about, without knowing where he was going; it rained at times, he did not perceive it; for his dinner he purchased a penny roll at a baker's, put it in his pocket and forgot it. It appears that he took a bath in the Seine without being aware of it. There are moments when a man has a furnace within his skull. Marius was passing through one of those moments. He no longer hoped for anything; this step he had taken since the preceding evening. He waited for night with feverish impatience, he had but one idea clearly before his mind;—this was, that at nine o'clock he should see Cosette. This last happiness now constituted his whole future; after that, gloom. At intervals, as he roamed through the most deserted boulevards, it seemed to him that he heard strange noises in Paris. He thrust his head out of his reverie and said: "Is there fighting on hand?"

At nightfall, at nine o'clock precisely, as he had promised Cosette, he was in the Rue Plumet. When he approached the grating he forgot everything. It was forty-eight hours since he had seen Cosette; he was about to behold her once more; every other thought was effaced, and he felt only a profound and unheard-of joy. Those minutes in which one lives centuries always have this sovereign and wonderful property, that at the moment when they are passing they fill the heart completely.

Marius displaced the bar, and rushed headlong into the garden. Cosette was not at the spot where she ordinarily waited for him. He traversed the thicket, and approached the recess near the flight of steps: "She is waiting for me there," said he. Cosette was not there. He raised his eyes, and saw that the shutters of the house were closed. He made the tour of the garden, the garden was deserted. Then he returned to the house, and, rendered senseless by love, intoxicated, terrified, exasperated with grief and uneasiness, like a master who returns home at an evil hour, he tapped on the shutters. He knocked and knocked again, at the risk of seeing the window open, and her father's gloomy face make its appearance, and demand: "What do you want?" This was nothing in comparison with what he dimly caught a glimpse of. When he had rapped, he lifted up his voice and called Cosette.—"Cosette!" he cried; "Cosette!" he repeated imperiously. There was no reply. All was over. No one in the garden; no one in the house.

Marius fixed his despairing eyes on that dismal house, which was as black and as silent as a tomb and far more empty. He gazed at the stone seat on which he had passed so many adorable hours with Cosette. Then he seated himself on the flight of steps, his heart filled with sweetness and resolution, he blessed his love in the depths of his thought, and he said to himself that, since Cosette was gone, all that there was left for him was to die.

All at once he heard a voice which seemed to proceed from the street, and which was calling to him through the trees:

"Mr. Marius!"

He started to his feet.

"Hey?" said he.

"Mr. Marius, are you there?"

"Yes."

"Mr. Marius," went on the voice, "your friends are waiting for you at the barricade of the Rue de la Chanvrerie."

This voice was not wholly unfamiliar to him. It resembled the hoarse, rough voice of Éponine. Marius hastened to the gate, thrust aside the movable bar, passed his head through the aperture, and saw someone who appeared to him to be a young man, disappearing at a run into the gloom.

Chapter III

M. Mabeuf

J EAN VALJEAN'S PURSE WAS OF NO USE TO M. MABEUF. M. MABEUF, IN HIS VENERABLE, INFANTILE austerity, had not accepted the gift of the stars; he had not admitted that a star could coin itself into louis d'or. He had not divined that what had fallen from heaven had come from Gavroche. He had taken the purse to the police commissioner of the quarter, as a lost article placed by the finder at the disposal of claimants. The purse was actually lost. It is unnecessary to say that no one claimed it, and that it did not succor M. Mabeuf.

Moreover, M. Mabeuf had continued his downward course.

His experiments on indigo had been no more successful in the Jardin des Plantes than in his garden at Austerlitz. The year before he had owed his housekeeper's wages; now, as we have seen, he owed three quarters of his rent. The pawn-shop had sold the plates of his *Flora* after the expiration of thirteen months. Some coppersmith had made stew-pans of them. His copper plates gone, and being unable to complete even the incomplete copies of his *Flora* which were in his possession, he had disposed of the text, at a miserable price, as waste paper, to a second-hand bookseller. Nothing now remained to him of his life's work. He set to work to eat up the money for these copies. When he saw that this wretched resource was becoming exhausted, he gave up his garden and allowed it to run to waste. Before this, a long time before, he had given up his two eggs and the morsel of beef which he ate from time to time. He dined on bread and potatoes. He had sold the last of his furniture, then all duplicates of his bedding, his clothing and his blankets, then his herbariums and prints; but he still retained his most precious books, many of which were of the greatest rarity, among others, *Les Quadrins Historiques de la Bible,* edition of 1560; *La Concordance des Bibles,* by Pierre de Besse; *Les Marguerites de la Marguerite,* of Jean de La Haye, with a dedication to the Queen of Navarre; the book *de la Charge et Dignité de l'Ambassadeur,* by the Sieur de Villiers Hotman; a *Florilegium Rabbinicum* of 1644; a *Tibullus* of 1567, with this magnificent inscription: *Venetiis, in aedibus Manutianis*; and lastly, a Diogenes Laertius, printed at Lyons in 1644, which contained the famous variant of the manuscript 411, thirteenth century, of the Vatican, and those of the two manuscripts of Venice, 393 and 394, consulted with such fruitful results by Henri Estienne, and all the passages in Doric dialect which are only found in the celebrated manuscript of the twelfth century belonging to the Naples Library. M. Mabeuf never had any fire in his chamber, and went to bed at sundown, in order not to consume any candles. It seemed as though he had no longer any neighbors: people avoided him when he went out; he perceived the fact. The wretchedness of a child interests a mother, the wretchedness of a young man interests a young girl, the wretchedness of an old man interests no one. It is, of all distresses, the coldest. Still, Father Mabeuf had not entirely lost his childlike serenity. His eyes acquired some vivacity when they rested on his books, and he smiled when he gazed at the Diogenes Laertius, which was a unique copy. His bookcase with glass doors was the only piece of furniture which he had kept beyond what was strictly indispensable.

One day, Mother Plutarque said to him:

"I have no money to buy any dinner."

What she called dinner was a loaf of bread and four or five potatoes.

"On credit?" suggested M. Mabeuf.

"You know well that people refuse me."

M. Mabeuf opened his bookcase, took a long look at all his books, one after another, as a father obliged to decimate his children would gaze upon them before making a choice, then seized one hastily, put it in under his arm and went out. He returned two hours later, without anything under his arm, laid thirty sous on the table, and said:

"You will get something for dinner."

From that moment forth, Mother Plutarque saw a somber veil, which was never more lifted, descend over the old man's candid face.

On the following day, on the day after, and on the day after that, it had to be done again.

M. Mabeuf went out with a book and returned with a coin. As the second-hand dealers perceived that he was forced to sell, they purchased of him for twenty sous, that for which he had paid twenty francs, sometimes at those very shops. Volume by volume, the whole library went the same road. He said at times: "But I am eighty"; as though he cherished some secret hope that he should arrive at the end of his days before reaching the end of his books. His melancholy increased. Once, however, he had a pleasure. He had gone out with a Robert Estienne, which he had sold for thirty-five sous under the Quai Malaquais, and he returned with an Aldus which he had bought for forty sous in the Rue des Grès.—"I owe five sous," he said, beaming on Mother Plutarque. That day he had no dinner.

He belonged to the Horticultural Society. His destitution became known there. The president of the society came to see him, promised to speak to the Minister of Agriculture and Commerce about him, and did so.—"Why, what!" exclaimed the Minister, "I should think so! An old savant! a botanist! an inoffensive man! Something must be done for him!" On the following day, M. Mabeuf received an invitation to dine with the Minister. Trembling with joy, he showed the letter to Mother Plutarque. "We are saved!" said he. On the day appointed, he went to the Minister's house. He perceived that his ragged cravat, his long, square coat, and his waxed shoes astonished the ushers. No one spoke to him, not even the Minister. About ten o'clock in the evening, while he was still waiting for a word, he heard the Minister's wife, a beautiful woman in a low-necked gown whom he had not ventured to approach, inquire: "Who is that old gentleman?" He returned home on foot at midnight, in a driving rainstorm. He had sold an Elzevir to pay for a carriage in which to go thither.

He had acquired the habit of reading a few pages in his Diogenes Laertius every night, before he went to bed. He knew enough Greek to enjoy the peculiarities of the text which he owned. He had now no other enjoyment. Several weeks passed. All at once, Mother Plutarque fell ill. There is one thing sadder than having no money with which to buy bread at the baker's, and that is having no money to purchase drugs at the apothecary's. One evening, the doctor had ordered a very expensive potion. And the malady was growing worse; a nurse was required. M. Mabeuf opened his bookcase; there was nothing there. The last volume had taken its departure. All that was left to him was Diogenes Laertius. He put this unique copy under his arm, and went out. It was the 4th of June, 1832; he went to the Porte Saint-Jacques, to Royal's successor, and returned with one hundred francs. He laid the pile of five-franc pieces on the old serving-woman's nightstand, and returned to his chamber without saying a word.

On the following morning, at dawn, he seated himself on the overturned post in his garden, and he could be seen over the top of the hedge, sitting the whole morning motionless, with drooping head, his eyes vaguely fixed on the withered flower-beds. It rained at intervals; the old man did not seem to perceive the fact.

In the afternoon, extraordinary noises broke out in Paris. They resembled shots and the clamors of a multitude.

Father Mabeuf raised his head. He saw a gardener passing, and inquired:

"What is it?"

The gardener, spade on back, replied in the most unconcerned tone:

"It is the riots."

"What riots?"

"Yes, they are fighting."

"Why are they fighting?"

"Ah, good Heavens!" ejaculated the gardener.

"In what direction?" went on M. Mabeuf.

"In the neighborhood of the Arsenal."

Father Mabeuf went to his room, took his hat, mechanically sought for a book to place under his arm, found none, said: "Ah! truly!" and went off with a bewildered air.

BOOK TENTH

THE 5TH OF JUNE, 1832

Chapter I

THE SURFACE OF THE QUESTION

O F WHAT IS REVOLT COMPOSED? OF NOTHING AND OF EVERYTHING. OF AN ELECTRICITY DISEN-gaged, little by little, of a flame suddenly darting forth, of a wandering force, of a passing breath. This breath encounters heads which speak, brains which dream, souls which suffer, passions which burn, wretchedness which howls, and bears them away.

Whither?

At random. Athwart the state, the laws, athwart prosperity and the insolence of others.

Irritated convictions, embittered enthusiasms, agitated indignations, instincts of war which have been repressed, youthful courage which has been exalted, generous blindness; curiosity, the taste for change, the thirst for the unexpected, the sentiment which causes one to take pleasure in reading the posters for the new play, and love, the prompter's whistle, at the theater; the vague hatreds, rancors, disappointments, every vanity which thinks that destiny has bankrupted it; discomfort, empty dreams, ambitious that are hedged about, whoever hopes for a downfall, some outcome, in short, at the very bottom, the rabble, that mud which catches fire—such are the elements of revolt. That which is grandest and that which is basest; the beings who prowl outside of all bounds, awaiting an occasion, bohemians, vagrants, vagabonds of the cross-roads, those who sleep at night in a desert of houses with no other roof than the cold clouds of heaven, those who, each day, demand their bread from chance and not from toil, the unknown of poverty and nothingness, the bare-armed, the barefooted, belong to revolt. Whoever cherishes in his soul a secret revolt against any deed whatever on the part of the state, of life or of fate, is ripe for riot, and, as soon as it makes its appearance, he begins to quiver, and to feel himself borne away with the whirlwind.

Revolt is a sort of waterspout in the social atmosphere which forms suddenly in certain conditions of temperature, and which, as it eddies about, mounts, descends, thunders, tears, razes, crushes, demolishes, uproots, bearing with it great natures and small, the strong man and the feeble mind, the tree trunk and the stalk of straw. Woe to him whom it bears away as well as to him whom it strikes! It breaks the one against the other.

It communicates to those whom it seizes an indescribable and extraordinary power. It fills the first-comer with the force of events; it converts everything into projectiles. It makes a cannon-ball of a rough stone, and a general of a porter.

If we are to believe certain oracles of crafty political views, a little revolt is desirable from the point of view of power. System: revolt strengthens those governments which it does not overthrow. It puts the army to the test; it consecrates the bourgeoisie, it draws out the muscles of the police; it demonstrates the force of the social framework. It is an exercise in gymnastics; it is almost hygiene. Power is in better health after a revolt, as a man is after a good rubbing down.

Revolt, thirty years ago, was regarded from still other points of view.

There is for everything a theory, which proclaims itself "good sense"; Philintus against Alcestis; mediation offered between the false and the true; explanation, admonition, rather haughty extenuation which, because it is mingled with blame and excuse, thinks itself wisdom, and is often only pedantry. A whole political school called "the golden mean" has been the outcome of this. As between cold water and hot water, it is the lukewarm water party. This school with its false depth, all on the surface, which dissects effects without going back to first causes, chides from its height of a demi-science, the agitation of the public square.

If we listen to this school, "The riots which complicated the affair of 1830 deprived that great event of a portion of its purity. The Revolution of July had been a fine popular gale, abruptly followed by blue sky. They made the cloudy sky reappear. They caused that revolution, at first so remarkable for its unanimity, to degenerate into a quarrel. In the Revolution of July, as in all progress accomplished by fits and starts, there had been secret fractures; these riots rendered them perceptible. It might have been said: 'Ah! this is broken.' After the Revolution of July, one was sensible only of deliverance; after the riots, one was conscious of a catastrophe.

"All revolt closes the shops, depresses the funds, throws the Exchange into consternation, suspends commerce, clogs business, precipitates failures; no more money, private fortunes rendered uneasy, public credit shaken, industry disconcerted, capital withdrawing, work at a discount, fear everywhere; counter-shocks in every town. Hence gulfs. It has been calculated that the first day of a riot costs France twenty millions, the second day forty, the third sixty, a three days' uprising costs one hundred and twenty millions, that is to say, if only the financial result be taken into consideration, it is equivalent to a disaster, a shipwreck or a lost battle, which should annihilate a fleet of sixty ships of the line.

"No doubt, historically, uprisings have their beauty; the war of the pavements is no less grandiose, and no less pathetic, than the war of thickets: in the one there is the soul of forests, in the other the heart of cities; the one has Jean Chouan, the other has a Jeanne. Revolts have illuminated with a red glare all the most original points of the Parisian character, generosity, devotion, stormy gaiety, students proving that bravery forms part of intelligence, the National Guard invincible, bivouacs of shopkeepers, fortresses of street urchins, contempt of death on the part of passers-by. Schools and legions clashed together. After all, between the combatants, there was only a difference of age; the race is the same; it is the same stoical men who died at the age of twenty for their ideas, at forty for their families. The army, always a sad thing in civil wars, opposed prudence to audacity. Uprisings, while proving popular intrepidity, also educated the courage of the bourgeois.

"This is well. But is all this worth the bloodshed? And to the bloodshed add the future darkness, progress compromised, uneasiness among the best men, honest liberals in despair, foreign absolutism happy in these wounds dealt to revolution by its own hand, the vanquished of 1830 triumphing and saying: 'We told you so!' Add Paris enlarged, possibly, but France most assuredly diminished. Add, for all must needs be told, the massacres which have too often dishonored the victory of order grown ferocious over liberty gone mad. To sum up all, uprisings have been disastrous."

Thus speaks that approximation to wisdom with which the bourgeoisie, that approximation to the people, so willingly contents itself.

For our parts, we reject this word *uprisings* as too large, and consequently as too convenient. We make a distinction between one popular movement and another popular movement. We do not inquire whether an uprising costs as much as a battle. Why a battle, in the first place? Here the question of war comes up. Is war less of a scourge than an uprising is of a calamity? And then, are all uprisings calamities? And what if the revolt of July did cost a hundred and twenty millions? The establishment of Philip V in Spain cost France two milliards. Even at the same price, we should prefer the 14th of July. However, we reject these figures, which appear to be reasons and which are only words. An uprising being given, we examine it by itself. In all that is said by the doctrinarian objection above presented, there is no question of anything but effect, we seek the cause.

We will be explicit.

Chapter II

THE ROOT OF THE MATTER

THERE IS SUCH A THING AS AN UPRISING, AND THERE IS SUCH A THING AS INSURRECTION; THESE are two separate phases of wrath; one is in the wrong, the other is in the right. In democratic states, the only ones which are founded on justice, it sometimes happens that the fraction usurps; then the whole rises and the necessary claim of its rights may proceed as far as resort to arms. In all questions which result from collective sovereignty, the war of the whole against the fraction is insurrection; the attack of the fraction against the whole is revolt; according as the Tuileries contain a king or the Convention, they are justly or unjustly attacked. The same cannon, pointed against the populace, is wrong on the 10th of August, and right on the 14th of Vendémiaire. Alike in appearance, fundamentally different in reality; the Swiss defend the false, Bonaparte defends the true. That which universal suffrage has effected in its liberty and in its sovereignty cannot be undone by the street. It is the same in things pertaining purely to civilization; the instinct of the masses, clearsighted to-day, may be troubled to-morrow. The same fury legitimate when directed against Terray and absurd when directed against Turgot. The destruction of machines, the pillage of warehouses, the breaking of rails, the demolition of docks, the false routes of multitudes, the refusal by the people of justice to progress, Ramus assassinated by students, Rousseau driven out of Switzerland and stoned—that is revolt. Israel against Moses, Athens against Phocian, Rome against Cicero—that is an uprising; Paris against the Bastille—that is insurrection. The soldiers against Alexander, the sailors against Christopher Columbus—this is the same revolt; impious revolt; why? Because Alexander is doing for Asia with the sword that which Christopher Columbus is doing for America with the compass; Alexander, like Columbus, is finding a world. These gifts of a world to civilization are such augmentations of light, that all resistance in that case, is culpable. Sometimes the populace counterfeits fidelity to itself. The masses are traitors to the people. Is there, for example, anything stranger than that long and bloody protest of dealers in contraband salt, a legitimate chronic revolt, which, at the decisive moment, on the day of salvation, at the very hour of popular victory, espouses the throne, turns into *chouannerie*, and, from having been an insurrection against, becomes an uprising for, somber masterpieces of ignorance! the contraband salt-dealer escapes the royal gibbets, and with a rope's end round his neck, mounts the white cockade. "Death to the salt duties," brings forth, "Long live the King!" The assassins of Saint-Barthélemy, the cut-throats of September, the manslaughterers of Avignon, the assassins of Coligny, the assassins of Madam Lamballe, the assassins of Brune, Miquelets, Verdets, Cadenettes, the companions of Jéhu, the chevaliers of Brassard—behold an uprising. La Vendée is a grand, catholic uprising. The sound of right in movement is recognizable, it does not always proceed from the trembling of excited masses; there are mad rages, there are cracked bells, all tocsins do not give out the sound of bronze. The brawl of passions and ignorances is quite another thing from the shock of progress. Show me in what direction you are going. Rise, if you will, but let it be that you may grow great. There is no insurrection except in a forward direction. Any other sort of rising is bad; every violent step toward the rear is a revolt; to retreat is to commit a deed of violence against the human race. Insurrection is a fit of rage on the part of truth; the pavements which the uprising disturbs give forth the spark of right. These pavements bequeath to the uprising only their mud. Danton against Louis XIV is insurrection; Hébert against Danton is revolt.

Hence it results that if insurrection in given cases may be, as Lafayette says, the most holy of duties, an uprising may be the most fatal of crimes.

There is also a difference in the intensity of heat; insurrection is often a volcano, revolt is often only a fire of straw.

Revolt, as we have said, is sometimes found among those in power. Polignac is a rioter; Camille Desmoulins is one of the governing powers.

Insurrection is sometimes resurrection.

The solution of everything by universal suffrage being an absolutely modern fact, and all history anterior to this fact being, for the space of four thousand years, filled with violated right, and the suffering of peoples, each epoch of history brings with it that protest of which it is capable. Under the Cæsars, there was no insurrection, but there was Juvenal.

The *facit indignatio* replaces the Gracchi.

Under the Cæsars, there is the exile to Syene; there is also the man of the *Annales*. We do not speak of the immense exile of Patmos who, on his part also, overwhelms the real world with a protest in the name of the ideal world, who makes of his vision an enormous satire and casts on Rome-Nineveh, on Rome-Babylon, on Rome-Sodom, the flaming reflection of the Apocalypse. John on his rock is the sphinx on its pedestal; we may understand him, he is a Jew, and it is Hebrew; but the man who writes the *Annales* is of the Latin race, let us rather say he is a Roman.

As the Neros reign in a black way, they should be painted to match. The work of the graving-tool alone would be too pale; there must be poured into the channel a concentrated prose which bites.

Despots count for something in the question of philosophers. A word that is chained is a terrible word. The writer doubles and trebles his style when silence is imposed on a nation by its master. From this silence there arises a certain mysterious plenitude which filters into thought and there congeals into bronze. The compression of history produces conciseness in the historian. The granite solidity of such and such a celebrated prose is nothing but the accumulation effected by the tyrant.

Tyranny constrains the writer to conditions of diameter which are augmentations of force. The Ciceronian period, which hardly sufficed for Verres, would be blunted on Caligula. The less spread of sail in the phrase, the more intensity in the blow. Tacitus thinks with all his might.

The honesty of a great heart, condensed in justice and truth, overwhelms as with lightning.

Be it remarked, in passing, that Tacitus is not historically superposed upon Cæsar. The Tiberii were reserved for him. Cæsar and Tacitus are two successive phenomena, a meeting between whom seems to be mysteriously avoided, by the One who, when He sets the centuries on the stage, regulates the entrances and the exits. Cæsar is great, Tacitus is great; God spares these two greatnesses by not allowing them to clash with one another. The guardian of justice, in striking Cæsar, might strike too hard and be unjust. God does not will it. The great wars of Africa and Spain, the pirates of Sicily destroyed, civilization introduced into Gaul, into Britanny, into Germany—all this glory covers the Rubicon. There is here a sort of delicacy of the divine justice, hesitating to let loose upon the illustrious usurper the formidable historian, sparing Cæsar Tacitus, and according extenuating circumstances to genius.

Certainly, despotism remains despotism, even under the despot of genius. There is corruption under all illustrious tyrants, but the moral pest is still more hideous under infamous tyrants. In such reigns, nothing veils the shame; and those who make examples, Tacitus as well as Juvenal, slap this ignominy which cannot reply, in the face, more usefully in the presence of all humanity.

Rome smells worse under Vitellius than under Sylla. Under Claudius and under Domitian, there is a deformity of baseness corresponding to the repulsiveness of the tyrant. The villainy of slaves is a direct product of the despot; a miasma exhales from these cowering consciences wherein the master is reflected; public powers are unclean; hearts are small; consciences are dull, souls are like vermin; thus it is under Caracalla, thus it is under Commodus, thus it is under Heliogabalus, while, from the Roman Senate, under Cæsar, there comes nothing but the odor of the dung which is peculiar to the eyries of the eagles.

Hence the advent, apparently tardy, of the Tacituses and the Juvenals; it is in the hour for evidence, that the demonstrator makes his appearance.

But Juvenal and Tacitus, like Isaiah in Biblical times, like Dante in the Middle Ages, is man; riot and insurrection are the multitude, which is sometimes right and sometimes wrong.

In the majority of cases, riot proceeds from a material fact; insurrection is always a moral phenomenon. Riot is Masaniello; insurrection, Spartacus. Insurrection borders on mind, riot on the stomach; Gaster grows irritated; but Gaster, assuredly, is not always in the wrong. In questions of famine, riot, Buzançais, for example, holds a true, pathetic, and just point of departure. Nevertheless, it remains a riot. Why? It is because, right at bottom, it was wrong in form. Shy although in the right, violent although strong, it struck at random; it walked like a blind elephant; it left behind it the corpses of old men, of women, and of children; it wished the blood of inoffensive and innocent persons without knowing why. The nourishment of the people is a good object; to massacre them is a bad means.

All armed protests, even the most legitimate, even that of the 10th of August, even that of July 14th, begin with the same troubles. Before the right gets set free, there is foam and tumult. In the beginning, the insurrection is a riot, just as a river is a torrent. Ordinarily it ends in that ocean: revolution. Sometimes, however, coming from those lofty mountains which dominate the moral horizon, justice, wisdom, reason, right, formed of the pure snow of the ideal, after a long fall from rock to rock, after having reflected the sky in its transparency and increased by a hundred affluents in the majestic mien of triumph, insurrection is suddenly lost in some quagmire, as the Rhine is in a swamp.

All this is of the past, the future is another thing. Universal suffrage has this admirable property, that it dissolves riot in its inception, and, by giving the vote to insurrection, it deprives it of its arms. The disappearance of wars, of street wars as well as of wars on the frontiers, such is the inevitable progression. Whatever To-day may be, To-morrow will be peace.

However, insurrection, riot, and points of difference between the former and the latter—the bourgeois, properly speaking, knows nothing of such shades. In his mind, all is sedition, rebellion pure and simple, the revolt of the dog against his master, an attempt to bite whom must be punished by the chain and the kennel, barking, snapping, until such day as the head of the dog, suddenly enlarged, is outlined vaguely in the gloom face to face with the lion.

Then the bourgeois shouts: "Long live the people!"

This explanation given, what does the movement of June, 1832, signify, so far as history is concerned? Is it a revolt? Is it an insurrection?

It may happen to us, in placing this formidable event on the stage, to say revolt now and then, but merely to distinguish superficial facts, and always preserving the distinction between revolt, the form, and insurrection, the foundation.

This movement of 1832 had, in its rapid outbreak and in its melancholy extinction, so much grandeur, that even those who see in it only an uprising, never refer to it otherwise than with respect. For them, it is like a relic of 1830. Excited imaginations, say they, are not to be calmed in a day. A revolution cannot be cut off short. It must needs undergo some undulations before it returns to a state of rest, like a mountain sinking into the plain. There are no Alps without their Jura, nor Pyrenees without the Asturias.

This pathetic crisis of contemporary history which the memory of Parisians calls "the epoch of the riots," is certainly a characteristic hour amid the stormy hours of this century. A last word, before we enter on the recital.

The facts which we are about to relate belong to that dramatic and living reality, which the historian sometimes neglects for lack of time and space. There, nevertheless, we insist upon it, is life, palpitation, human tremor. Petty details, as we think we have already said, are, so to speak, the foliage of great events, and are lost in the distance of history. The epoch, surnamed "of the riots," abounds in details of this nature. Judicial inquiries have not revealed, and perhaps have not sounded, the depths, for another reason than history. We shall therefore bring to light, among the known and published peculiarities, things which have not heretofore been known, about facts over which have passed the forgetfulness of some, and the death of others. The majority of the actors in these gigantic scenes have disappeared; beginning with the very next day they held their peace; but of what we shall relate, we shall be able to say: "We have seen this." We alter a few names, for history relates and does not inform against, but the deed which we shall paint will be genuine. In accordance with the conditions of the book which we are now writing, we shall show only one side and one episode, and certainly, the least known at that, of the two days, the 5th and the 6th of June, 1832, but we shall do it in such wise that the reader may catch a glimpse, beneath the gloomy veil which we are about to lift, of the real form of this frightful public adventure.

Chapter III

A Burial; an Occasion to be Born Again

IN THE SPRING OF 1832, ALTHOUGH THE CHOLERA HAD BEEN CHILLING ALL MINDS FOR THE LAST three months and had cast over their agitation an indescribable and gloomy pacification, Paris had already long been ripe for commotion. As we have said, the great city resembles a piece of artillery; when it is loaded, it suffices for a spark to fall, and the shot is discharged. In June, 1832, the spark was the death of General Lamarque.

Lamarque was a man of renown and of action. He had had in succession, under the Empire and under the Restoration, the sorts of bravery requisite for the two epochs, the bravery of the battlefield and the bravery of the tribune. He was as eloquent as he had been valiant; a sword was discernible in his speech. Like Foy, his predecessor, after upholding the command, he upheld liberty; he sat between the left and the extreme left, beloved of the people because he accepted the chances of the future, beloved of the populace because he had served the Emperor well; he was, in company with Comtes Gérard and Drouet, one of Napoleon's marshals *in petto*. The treaties of 1815 removed him as a personal offense. He hated Wellington with a downright hatred which pleased the multitude; and, for seventeen years, he majestically preserved the sadness of Waterloo, paying hardly any attention to intervening events. In his death-agony, at his last hour, he clasped to his breast a sword which had been presented to him by the officers of the Hundred Days. Napoleon had died uttering the word *army*, Lamarque uttering the word *country*.

His death, which was expected, was dreaded by the people as a loss, and by the government as an occasion. This death was an affliction. Like everything that is bitter, affliction may turn to revolt. This is what took place.

On the preceding evening, and on the morning of the 5th of June, the day appointed for Lamarque's burial, the Faubourg Saint-Antoine, which the procession was to touch at, assumed a formidable aspect. This tumultuous network of streets was filled with rumors. They armed themselves as best they might. Joiners carried off door-weights of their establishment "to break down doors." One of them had made himself a dagger of a stocking-weaver's hook by breaking off the hook and sharpening the stump. Another, who was in a fever "to attack," slept wholly dressed for three days. A carpenter named Lombier met a comrade, who asked him: "Whither are you going?" "Eh! well, I have no weapons." "What then?" "I'm going to my timber-yard to get my compasses." "What for?" "I don't know," said Lombier. A certain Jacqueline, an expeditious man, accosted some passing artisans: "Come here, you!" He treated them to ten sous' worth of wine and said: "Have you work?" "No." "Go to Filspierre, between the Barrière Charonne and the Barrière Montreuil, and you will find work." At Filspierre's they found cartridges and arms. Certain well-known leaders were going the rounds, that is to say, running from one house to another, to collect their men. At Barthélemy's, near the Barrière du Trône, at Capel's, near the Petit-Chapeau, the drinkers accosted each other with a grave air. They were heard to say: "Have you your pistol?" "Under my blouse." "And you?" "Under my shirt." In the Rue Traversière, in front of the Bland workshop, and in the yard of the Maison-Brulée, in front of tool-maker Bernier's, groups whispered together. Among them was observed a certain Mavot, who never remained more than a week in one shop, as the masters always discharged him "because they were obliged to dispute with him every day." Mavot was killed on the following day at the barricade of the Rue Ménilmontant. Pretot, who was destined to perish also in the struggle, seconded Mavot, and to the question: "What is your object?" he replied: *"Insurrection."* Workmen assembled at the corner of the Rue de Bercy, waited for a certain Lemarin, the revolutionary agent for the Faubourg Saint-Marceau. Watchwords were exchanged almost publicly.

On the 5th of June, accordingly, a day of mingled rain and sun, General Lamarque's funeral procession traversed Paris with official military pomp, somewhat augmented through precaution. Two battalions, with draped drums and reversed arms, ten thousand National Guards, with their swords at their sides, escorted the coffin. The hearse was drawn by young men. The officers of the Invalides came immediately behind it, bearing laurel branches. Then came an innumerable, strange, agitated multitude, the sectionaries of the Friends of the People, the Law School, the Medical School, refugees of all nationalities, and Spanish, Italian, German, and Polish flags, tricolored horizontal banners, every possible sort of banner, children waving green boughs, stone-cutters and carpenters who were on strike at the moment, printers who were recognizable by their paper caps, marching two by two, three by three, uttering cries, nearly all of them brandishing sticks, some brandishing sabers, without order and yet with a single soul, now a tumultuous rout, again a column. Squads chose themselves leaders; a man armed with a pair of pistols in full view, seemed to pass the host in review, and the files separated before him. On the side alleys of the boulevards, in the branches of the trees, on balconies, in windows, on the roofs, swarmed the heads of men, women, and children; all eyes were filled with anxiety. An armed throng was passing, and a terrified throng looked on.

The Government, on its side, was taking observations. It observed with its hand on its sword. Four squadrons of carabineers could be seen in the Place Louis XV in their saddles, with their trumpets at their head, cartridge-boxes filled and muskets loaded, all in readiness to march; in the Latin country and at the Jardin des Plantes, the Municipal Guard echelonned from street to street; at the Halle-aux-Vins, a squadron of dragoons; at the Grève half of the 12th Light Infantry, the other half being at the Bastille; the 6th Dragoons at the Célestins; and the courtyard of the Louvre full of artillery. The remainder of the troops were confined to their barracks, without reckoning the regiments of the environs of Paris. Power being uneasy, held suspended over the menacing multitude twenty-four thousand soldiers in the city and thirty thousand in the banlieue.

Divers reports were in circulation in the cortège. Legitimist tricks were hinted at; they spoke of the Duc de Reichstadt, whom God had marked out for death at that very moment when the populace were designating him for the Empire. One personage, whose name has remained unknown, announced that at a given hour two overseers who had been won over, would throw open the doors of a factory of arms to the people. That which predominated on the uncovered brows of the majority of those present was enthusiasm mingled with dejection. Here and there, also, in that multitude given over to such violent but noble emotions, there were visible genuine visages of criminals and ignoble mouths which said: "Let us plunder!" There are certain agitations which stir up the bottoms of marshes and make clouds of mud rise through the water. A phenomenon to which "well drilled" policemen are no strangers.

The procession proceeded, with feverish slowness, from the house of the deceased, by way of the boulevards as far as the Bastille. It rained from time to time; the rain mattered nothing to that throng. Many incidents, the coffin borne round the Vendome column, stones thrown at the Duc de Fitz-James, who was seen on a balcony with his hat on his head, the Gallic cock torn from a popular flag and dragged in the mire, a policeman wounded with a blow from a sword at the Porte Saint-Martin, an officer of the 12th Light Infantry saying aloud: "I am a Republican," the Polytechnic School coming up unexpectedly against orders to remain at home, the shouts of: "Long live the Polytechnique! Long live the Republic!" marked the passage of the funeral train. At the Bastille, long files of curious and formidable people who descended from the Faubourg Saint-Antoine, effected a junction with the procession, and a certain terrible seething began to agitate the throng.

One man was heard to say to another: "Do you see that fellow with a red beard, he's the one who will give the word when we are to fire." It appears that this red beard was present, at another riot, the Quénisset affair, entrusted with this same function.

The hearse passed the Bastille, traversed the small bridge, and reached the esplanade of the bridge of Austerlitz. There it halted. The crowd, surveyed at that moment with a bird's-eye view, would have presented the aspect of a comet whose head was on the esplanade and whose tail spread out over the Quai Bourdon, covered the Bastille, and was prolonged on the boulevard as far as the Porte Saint-Martin. A circle was traced around the hearse. The vast rout held their peace. Lafayette spoke and bade Lamarque farewell. This was a touching and august instant, all heads uncovered, all hearts beat high.

All at once, a man on horseback, clad in black, made his appearance in the middle of the group with a red flag, others say, with a pike surmounted with a red liberty-cap. Lafayette turned aside his head. Exelmans quitted the procession.

This red flag raised a storm, and disappeared in the midst of it. From the Boulevard Bourdon to the bridge of Austerlitz one of those clamors which resemble billows stirred the multitude. Two prodigious shouts went up: "Lamarque to the Panthéon!—Lafayette to the Town-hall!" Some young men, amid the acclamations of the throng, harnessed themselves and began to drag Lamarque in the hearse across the bridge of Austerlitz and Lafayette in a hackney-coach along the Quai Morland.

In the crowd which surrounded and cheered Lafayette, it was noticed that a German showed himself named Ludwig Snyder, who died a centenarian afterwards, who had also been in the war of 1776, and who had fought at Trenton under Washington, and at Brandywine under Lafayette.

In the meantime, the municipal cavalry on the left bank had been set in motion, and came to bar the bridge, on the right bank the dragoons emerged from the Célestins and deployed along the Quai Morland. The men who were dragging Lafayette suddenly caught sight of them at the corner of the quay and shouted: "The dragoons!" The dragoons advanced at a walk, in silence, with their pistols in their holsters, their swords in their scabbards, their guns slung in their leather sockets, with an air of gloomy expectation.

They halted two hundred paces from the little bridge. The carriage in which sat Lafayette advanced to them, their ranks opened and allowed it to pass, and then closed behind it. At that moment the dragoons and the crowd touched. The women fled in terror. What took place during that fatal minute? No one can say. It is the dark moment when two clouds come together. Some declare that a blast of trumpets sounding the charge was heard in the direction of the Arsenal, others that a blow from a dagger was given by a child to a dragoon. The fact is, that three shots were suddenly discharged: the first killed Cholet, chief of the squadron, the second killed an old deaf woman who was in the act of closing her window, the third singed the shoulder of an officer; a woman screamed: "They are beginning too soon!" and all at once, a squadron of dragoons which had remained in the barracks up to this time, was seen to debouch at a gallop with bared swords, through the Rue Bassompierre and the Boulevard Bourdon, sweeping all before them.

Then all is said, the tempest is loosed, stones rain down, a fusillade breaks forth, many precipitate themselves to the bottom of the bank, and pass the small arm of the Seine, now filled in, the timber-yards of the Isle Louviers, that vast citadel ready to hand, bristle with combatants, stakes are torn up, pistol-shots fired, a barricade begun, the young men who are thrust back pass the Austerlitz bridge with the hearse at a run, and the municipal guard, the carabineers rush up, the dragoons ply their swords, the crowd disperses in all directions, a rumor of war flies to all four quarters of Paris, men shout: "To arms!" they run, tumble down, flee, resist. Wrath spreads abroad the riot as wind spreads a fire.

Chapter IV

THE EBULLITIONS OF FORMER DAYS

NOTHING IS MORE EXTRAORDINARY THAN THE FIRST BREAKING OUT OF A RIOT. EVERYTHING bursts forth everywhere at once. Was it foreseen? Yes. Was it prepared? No. Whence comes it? From the pavements. Whence falls it? From the clouds. Here insurrection assumes the character of a plot; there of an improvisation. The first-comer seizes a current of the throng and leads it whither he wills. A beginning full of terror, in which is mingled a sort of formidable gaiety. First come clamors, the shops are closed, the displays of the merchants disappear; then come isolated shots; people flee; blows from gun-stocks beat against portes-cochères, servants can be heard laughing in the courtyards of houses and saying: "There's going to be a row!"

A quarter of an hour had not elapsed when this is what was taking place at twenty different spots in Paris at once.

In the Rue Sainte-Croix-de-la-Bretonnerie, twenty young men, bearded and with long hair, entered a dram-shop and emerged a moment later, carrying a horizontal tricolored flag covered with crape, and having at their head three men armed, one with a sword, one with a gun, and the third with a pike.

In the Rue des Nonaindières, a very well-dressed bourgeois, who had a prominent belly, a sonorous voice, a bald head, a lofty brow, a black beard, and one of these stiff mustaches which will not lie flat, offered cartridges publicly to passers-by.

In the Rue Saint-Pierre-Montmartre, men with bare arms carried about a black flag, on which could be read in white letters this inscription: "Republic or Death!" In the Rue des Jûneurs, Rue du

Cadran, Rue Montorgueil, Rue Mandar, groups appeared waving flags on which could be distinguished in gold letters, the word *section* with a number. One of these flags was red and blue with an almost imperceptible stripe of white between.

They pillaged a factory of small-arms on the Boulevard Saint-Martin, and three armorers' shops, the first in the Rue Beaubourg, the second in the Rue Michel-le-Comte, the other in the Rue du Temple. In a few minutes, the thousand hands of the crowd had seized and carried off two hundred and thirty guns, nearly all double-barreled, sixty-four swords, and eighty-three pistols. In order to provide more arms, one man took the gun, the other the bayonet.

Opposite the Quai de la Grève, young men armed with muskets installed themselves in the houses of some women for the purpose of firing. One of them had a flint-lock. They rang, entered, and set about making cartridges. One of these women relates: "I did not know what cartridges were; it was my husband who told me."

One cluster broke into a curiosity shop in the Rue des Vielles Haudriettes, and seized yataghans and Turkish arms.

The body of a mason who had been killed by a gun-shot lay in the Rue de la Perle.

And then, on the right bank, the left bank, on the quays, on the boulevards, in the Latin country, in the quarter of the Halles, panting men, artisans, students, members of sections read proclamations and shouted: "To arms!" broke street-lanterns, unharnessed carriages, unpaved the streets, broke in the doors of houses, uprooted trees, rummaged cellars, rolled out hogsheads, heaped up paving-stones, rough slabs, furniture and planks, and made barricades.

They forced the bourgeois to assist them in this. They entered the dwellings of women, they forced them to hand over the swords and guns of their absent husbands, and they wrote on the door, with whiting: "The arms have been delivered"; some signed "their names" to receipts for the guns and swords, and said: "Send for them to-morrow at the Mayor's office." They disarmed isolated sentinels and National Guardsmen in the streets on their way to the Town-hall. They tore the epaulets from officers. In the Rue du Cimitière-Saint-Nicholas, an officer of the National Guard, on being pursued by a crowd armed with clubs and foils, took refuge with difficulty in a house, whence he was only able to emerge at nightfall and in disguise.

In the Quartier Saint-Jacques, the students swarmed out of their hôtels and ascended the Rue Saint-Hyacinthe to the Café du Progrèss, or descended to the Café des Sept-Billards, in the Rue des Mathurins. There, in front of the door, young men mounted on the stone corner-posts, distributed arms. They plundered the timber-yard in the Rue Transnonain in order to obtain material for barricades. On a single point the inhabitants resisted, at the corner of the Rue Sainte-Avoye and the Rue Simon-Le-Franc, where they destroyed the barricade with their own hands. At a single point the insurgents yielded; they abandoned a barricade begun in the Rue de Temple after having fired on a detachment of the National Guard, and fled through the Rue de la Corderie. The detachment picked up in the barricade a red flag, a package of cartridges, and three hundred pistol-balls. The National Guardsmen tore up the flag, and carried off its tattered remains on the points of their bayonets.

All that we are here relating slowly and successively took place simultaneously at all points of the city in the midst of a vast tumult, like a mass of tongues of lightning in one clap of thunder. In less than an hour, twenty-seven barricades sprang out of the earth in the quarter of the Halles alone. In the center was that famous house No. 50, which was the fortress of Jeanne and her six hundred companions, and which, flanked on the one hand by a barricade at Saint-Merry, and on the other by a barricade of the Rue Maubuée, commanded three streets, the Rue des Arcis, the Rue Saint-Martin, and the Rue Aubry-le-Boucher, which it faced. The barricades at right angles fell back, the one of the Rue Montorgueil on the Grande-Truanderie, the other of the Rue Geoffroy-Langevin on the Rue Sainte-Avoye. Without reckoning innumerable barricades in twenty other quarters of Paris, in the Marais, at Mont-Sainte-Geneviève; one in the Rue Ménilmontant, where was visible a porte-cochère torn from its hinges; another near the little bridge of the Hôtel-Dieu made with an "écossais," which had been unharnessed and overthrown, three hundred paces from the Prefecture of Police.

At the barricade of the Rue des Ménétriers, a well-dressed man distributed money to the work-men. At the barricade of the Rue Grenetat, a horseman made his appearance and handed to the one who seemed to be the commander of the barricade what had the appearance of a roll of silver. "Here," said he, "this is to pay expenses, wine, et cetera." A light-haired young man, without a cra-vat, went from barricade to barricade, carrying passwords. Another, with a naked sword, a blue po-lice cap on his head, placed sentinels. In the interior, beyond the barricades, the wine-shops and porters' lodges were converted into guard-houses. Otherwise the riot was conducted after the most scientific military tactics. The narrow, uneven, sinuous streets, full of angles and turns, were ad-mirably chosen; the neighborhood of the Halles, in particular, a network of streets more intricate than a forest. The Society of the Friends of the People had, it was said, undertaken to direct the in-surrection in the Quartier Sainte-Avoye. A man killed in the Rue du Ponceau who was searched had on his person a plan of Paris.

That which had really undertaken the direction of the uprising was a sort of strange impetu-osity which was in the air. The insurrection had abruptly built barricades with one hand, and with the other seized nearly all the posts of the garrison. In less than three hours, like a train of powder catching fire, the insurgents had invaded and occupied, on the right bank, the Arsenal, the May-oralty of the Place Royale, the whole of the Marais, the Popincourt arms manufactory, la Galiote, the Château-d'Eau, and all the streets near the Halles; on the left bank, the barracks of the Veter-ans, Sainte-Pélagie, the Place Maubert, the powder magazine of the Deux-Moulins, and all the bar-riers. At five o'clock in the evening, they were masters of the Bastille, of the Lingerie, of the Blancs-Manteaux; their scouts had reached the Place des Victoires, and menaced the Bank, the Petits-Pères barracks, and the Post-Office. A third of Paris was in the hands of the rioters.

The conflict had been begun on a gigantic scale at all points; and, as a result of the disarming domiciliary visits, and armorers' shops hastily invaded, was, that the combat which had begun with the throwing of stones was continued with gun-shots.

About six o'clock in the evening, the Passage du Saumon became the field of battle. The up-rising was at one end, the troops were at the other. They fired from one gate to the other. An ob-server, a dreamer, the author of this book, who had gone to get a near view of this volcano, found himself in the passage between the two fires. All that he had to protect him from the bullets was the swell of the two half-columns which separate the shops; he remained in this delicate situation for nearly half an hour.

Meanwhile the call to arms was beaten, the National Guard armed in haste, the legions emerged from the Mayoralities, the regiments from their barracks. Opposite the passage de l'Ancre a drummer received a blow from a dagger. Another, in the Rue du Cygne, was assailed by thirty young men who broke his instrument, and took away his sword. Another was killed in the Rue Grenier-Saint-Lazare. In the Rue Michel-le-Comte, three officers fell dead one after the other. Many of the Municipal Guards, on being wounded, in the Rue des Lombards, retreated.

In front of the Cour-Batave, a detachment of National Guards found a red flag bearing the following inscription: *Republican revolution, No. 127.* Was this a revolution, in fact?

The insurrection had made of the center of Paris a sort of inextricable, tortuous, colossal citadel.

There was the hearth; there, evidently, was the question. All the rest was nothing but skir-mishes. The proof that all would be decided there lay in the fact that there was no fighting going on there as yet.

In some regiments, the soldiers were uncertain, which added to the fearful uncertainty of the crisis. They recalled the popular ovation which had greeted the neutrality of the 53d of the Line in July, 1830. Two intrepid men, tried in great wars, the Marshal Lobau and General Bugeaud, were in command, Bugeaud under Lobau. Enormous patrols, composed of battalions of the Line, enclosed in entire companies of the National Guard, and preceded by a commissary of police wearing his scarf of office, went to reconnoiter the streets in rebellion. The insurgents, on their side, placed videttes at the corners of all open spaces, and audaciously sent their patrols outside the barricades. Each side was watching the other. The Government, with an army in its hand, hesitated; the night was almost upon them, and the Saint-Merry tocsin began to make itself heard. The Minister of War at that time, Marshal Soult, who had seen Austerlitz, regarded this with a gloomy air.

These old sailors, accustomed to correct maneuvers and having as resource and guide only tactics, that compass of battles, are utterly disconcerted in the presence of that immense foam which is called public wrath.

The National Guards of the suburbs rushed up in haste and disorder. A battalion of the 12th Light came at a run from Saint-Denis, the 14th of the Line arrived from Courbevoie, the batteries of the Military School had taken up their position on the Carrousel; cannons were descending from Vincennes.

Solitude was formed around the Tuileries. Louis Philippe was perfectly serene.

Chapter V

ORIGINALITY OF PARIS

DURING THE LAST TWO YEARS, AS WE HAVE SAID, PARIS HAD WITNESSED MORE THAN ONE INsurrection. Nothing is, generally, more singularly calm than the physiognomy of Paris during an uprising beyond the bounds of the rebellious quarters. Paris very speedily accustoms herself to anything—it is only a riot—and Paris has so many affairs on hand, that she does not put herself out for so small a matter. These colossal cities alone can offer such spectacles. These immense enclosures alone can contain at the same time civil war and an odd and indescribable tranquility. Ordinarily, when an insurrection commences, when the shop-keeper hears the drum, the call to arms, the general alarm, he contents himself with the remark:

"There appears to be a squabble in the Rue Saint-Martin."

Or:

"In the Faubourg Saint-Antoine."

Often he adds carelessly:

"Or somewhere in that direction."

Later on, when the heartrending and mournful hubbub of musketry and firing by platoons becomes audible, the shop-keeper says:

"It's getting hot! Hullo, it's getting hot!"

A moment later, the riot approaches and gains in force, he shuts up his shop precipitately, hastily dons his uniform, that is to say, he places his merchandise in safety and risks his own person.

Men fire in a square, in a passage, in a blind-alley; they take and retake the barricade; blood flows, the grape-shot riddles the fronts of the houses, the balls kill people in their beds, corpses encumber the streets. A few streets away, the shock of billiard-balls can be heard in the cafés.

The theaters open their doors and present vaudevilles; the curious laugh and chat a couple of paces distant from these streets filled with war. Hackney-carriages go their way; passers-by are going to a dinner somewhere in town. Sometimes in the very quarter where the fighting is going on.

In 1831, a fusillade was stopped to allow a wedding-party to pass.

At the time of the insurrection of 1839, in the Rue Saint-Martin, a little, infirm old man, pushing a hand-cart surmounted by a tricolored rag, in which he had carafes filled with some sort of liquid, went and came from barricade to troops and from troops to the barricade, offering his glasses of cocoa impartially—now to the Government, now to anarchy.

Nothing can be stranger; and this is the peculiar character of uprisings in Paris, which cannot be found in any other capital. To this end, two things are requisite, the size of Paris and its gaiety. The city of Voltaire and Napoleon is necessary.

On this occasion, however, in the resort to arms of June 25th, 1832, the great city felt something which was, perhaps, stronger than itself. It was afraid.

Closed doors, windows, and shutters were to be seen everywhere, in the most distant and most "disinterested" quarters. The courageous took to arms, the poltroons hid. The busy and heedless passer-by disappeared. Many streets were empty at four o'clock in the morning.

Alarming details were hawked about, fatal news was disseminated—that *they* were masters of the Bank;—that there were six hundred of them in the Cloister of Saint-Merry alone, entrenched and embattled in the church; that the line was not to be depended on; that Armand Carrel had been to see Marshal Clausel and that the Marshal had said: "Get a regiment first"; that Lafayette was ill, but that he had said to them, nevertheless: "I am with you. I will follow you wherever there is room for a chair"; that one must be on one's guard; that at night there would be people pillaging isolated dwellings in the deserted corners of Paris (there the imagination of the police, that Anne Radcliffe mixed up with the Government was recognizable); that a battery had been established in the Rue Aubry le Boucher; that Lobau and Bugeaud were putting their heads together, and that, at midnight, or at daybreak at latest, four columns would march simultaneously on the center of the uprising, the first coming from the Bastille, the second from the Porte Saint-Martin, the third from the Grève, the fourth from the Halles; that perhaps, also, the troops would evacuate Paris and withdraw to the Champ-de-Mars; that no one knew what would happen, but that this time, it certainly was serious.

People busied themselves over Marshal Soult's hesitations. Why did not he attack at once? It is certain that he was profoundly absorbed. The old lion seemed to scent an unknown monster in that gloom.

Evening came, the theaters did not open; the patrols circulated with an air of irritation; passers-by were searched; suspicious persons were arrested. By nine o'clock, more than eight hundred persons had been arrested, the Prefecture of Police was encumbered with them, so was the Conciergerie, so was La Force.

At the Conciergerie in particular, the long vault which is called the Rue de Paris was littered with trusses of straw upon which lay a heap of prisoners, whom the man of Lyons, Lagrange, harangued valiantly. All that straw rustled by all these men, produced the sound of a heavy shower. Elsewhere prisoners slept in the open air in the meadows, piled on top of each other.

Anxiety reigned everywhere, and a certain tremor which was not habitual with Paris.

People barricaded themselves in their houses; wives and mothers were uneasy; nothing was to be heard but this: "Ah! my God! He has not come home!" There was hardly even the distant rumble of a vehicle to be heard.

People listened on their thresholds, to the rumors, the shouts, the tumult, the dull and indistinct sounds, to the things that were said: "It is cavalry," or: "Those are the caissons galloping," to the trumpets, the drums, the firing, and, above all, to that lamentable alarm peal from Saint-Merry.

They waited for the first cannon-shot. Men sprang up at the corners of the streets and disappeared, shouting: "Go home!" And people made haste to bolt their doors. They said: "How will all this end?" From moment to moment, in proportion as the darkness descended, Paris seemed to take on a more mournful hue from the formidable flaming of the revolt.

BOOK ELEVENTH

THE ATOM FRATERNIZES WITH THE HURRICANE

Chapter I

SOME EXPLANATIONS WITH REGARD TO THE ORIGIN OF GAVROCHE'S POETRY. THE INFLUENCE OF AN ACADEMICIAN ON THIS POETRY

AT THE INSTANT WHEN THE INSURRECTION, ARISING FROM THE SHOCK OF THE POPULACE AND the military in front of the Arsenal, started a movement in advance and toward the rear in the multitude which was following the hearse and which, through the whole length of the boulevards, weighed, so to speak, on the head of the procession, there arose a frightful ebb. The rout was shaken, their ranks were broken, all ran, fled, made their escape, some with shouts of attack, others with the pallor of flight. The great river which covered the boulevards divided in a twinkling, over-flowed to right and left, and spread in torrents over two hundred streets at once with the roar of a sewer that has broken loose.

At that moment, a ragged child who was coming down through the Rue Ménilmontant, holding in his hand a branch of blossoming laburnum which he had just plucked on the heights of Belleville, caught sight of an old holster-pistol in the show-window of a bric-à-brac merchant's shop.

"Mother What's-your-name, I'm going to borrow your machine."

And off he ran with the pistol.

Two minutes later, a flood of frightened bourgeois who were fleeing through the Rue Amelot and the Rue Basse, encountered the lad brandishing his pistol and singing:

> *La nuit on ne voit rien,*
> *Le jour on voit très bien,*
> *D'un écrit apocryphe*
> *Le bourgeois s'ébouriffe,*
> *Pratiquez la vertu,*
> *Tutu, chapeau pointu!*[1]

It was little Gavroche on his way to the wars.

On the boulevard he noticed that the pistol had no trigger.

Who was the author of that couplet which served to punctuate his march, and of all the other songs which he was fond of singing on occasion? We know not. Who does know? Himself, per-haps. However, Gavroche was well up in all the popular tunes in circulation, and he mingled with them his own chirpings. An observing urchin and a rogue, he made a pot-pourri of the voices of nature and the voices of Paris. He combined the repertory of the birds with the repertory of the

---

1. At night one sees nothing, by day one sees very well; the bourgeois gets flurried over an apochryphal scrawl, practice virtue, tutu, pointed hat!

workshops. He was acquainted with thieves, a tribe contiguous to his own. He had, it appears, been for three months apprenticed to a printer. He had one day executed a commission for M. Baour-Lormian, one of the Forty. Gavroche was a gamin of letters.

Moreover, Gavroche had no suspicion of the fact that when he had offered the hospitality of his elephant to two brats on that villainously rainy night, it was to his own brothers that he had played the part of Providence. His brothers in the evening, his father in the morning; that is what his night had been like. On quitting the Rue des Ballets at daybreak, he had returned in haste to the elephant, had artistically extracted from it the two brats, had shared with them some sort of breakfast which he had invented, and had then gone away, confiding them to that good mother, the street, who had brought him up, almost entirely. On leaving them, he had appointed to meet them at the same spot in the evening, and had left them this discourse by way of a farewell: "I break a cane, otherwise expressed, I cut my stick, or, as they say at the court, I file off. If you don't find papa and mamma, young 'uns, come back here this evening. I'll scramble you up some supper, and I'll give you a shakedown." The two children, picked up by some policeman and placed in the refuge, or stolen by some mountebank, or having simply strayed off in that immense Chinese puzzle of a Paris, did not return. The lowest depths of the actual social world are full of these lost traces. Gavroche did not see them again. Ten or twelve weeks had elapsed since that night. More than once he had scratched the back of his head and said: "Where the devil are my two children?"

In the meantime, he had arrived, pistol in hand, in the Rue du Pont-aux-Choux. He noticed that there was but one shop open in that street, and, a matter worthy of reflection, that was a pastry-cook's shop. This presented a providential occasion to eat another apple-turnover before entering the unknown. Gavroche halted, fumbled in his fob, turned his pocket inside out, found nothing, not even a sou, and began to shout: "Help!"

It is hard to miss the last cake.

Nevertheless, Gavroche pursued his way.

Two minutes later, he was in the Rue Saint-Louis. While traversing the Rue du Parc-Royal, he felt called upon to make good the loss of the apple-turnover which had been impossible, and he indulged himself in the immense delight of tearing down the theater posters in broad daylight.

A little further on, on catching sight of a group of comfortable-looking persons, who seemed to be landed proprietors, he shrugged his shoulders and spit out at random before him this mouthful of philosophical bile as they passed:

"How fat those moneyed men are! They're drunk! They just wallow in good dinners. Ask 'em what they do with their money. They don't know. They eat it, that's what they do! As much as their bellies will hold."

Chapter II

GAVROCHE ON THE MARCH

THE BRANDISHING OF A TRIGGERLESS PISTOL, GRASPED IN ONE'S HAND IN THE OPEN STREET, IS so much of a public function that Gavroche felt his fervor increasing with every moment. Amid the scraps of the Marseillaise which he was singing, he shouted: "All goes well. I suffer a great deal in my left paw, I'm all broken up with rheumatism, but I'm satisfied, citizens. All that the bourgeois have to do is to bear themselves well, I'll sneeze them out subversive couplets. What are the police spies? Dogs. And I'd just like to have one of them at the end of my pistol. I'm just from the boulevard, my friends. It's getting hot there, it's getting into a little boil, it's simmering. It's time to skim the pot. Forward march, men! Let an impure blood inundate the furrows! I give my days to my country, I shall never see my concubine more, Nini, finished, yes, Nini? But never mind! Long live joy! Let's fight, crebleu! I've had enough of despotism."

At that moment, the horse of a lancer of the National Guard having fallen, Gavroche laid his pistol on the pavement, and picked up the man, then he assisted in raising the horse. After which he picked up his pistol and resumed his way. In the Rue de Thorigny, all was peace and silence. This apathy, peculiar to the Marais, presented a contrast with the vast surrounding uproar. Four gossips were chatting in a doorway.

Scotland has trios of witches, Paris has quartettes of old gossiping hags; and the "Thou shalt be King" could be quite as mournfully hurled at Bonaparte in the Carrefour Baudoyer as at Macbeth on the heath of Armuyr. The croak would be almost identical.

The gossips of the Rue de Thorigny busied themselves only with their own concerns. Three of them were portresses, and the fourth was a rag-picker with her basket on her back.

All four of them seemed to be standing at the four corners of old age, which are decrepitude, decay, ruin, and sadness.

The rag-picker was humble. In this open-air society, it is the rag-picker who salutes and the portress who patronizes. This is caused by the corner for refuse, which is fat or lean, according to the will of the portresses, and after the fancy of the one who makes the heap. There may be kindness in the broom.

This rag-picker was a grateful creature, and she smiled, with what a smile! on the three portresses. Things of this nature were said:

"Ah, by the way, is your cat still cross?"

"Good gracious, cats are naturally the enemies of dogs, you know. It's the dogs who complain."

"And people also."

"But the fleas from a cat don't go after people."

"That's not the trouble, dogs are dangerous. I remember one year when there were so many dogs that it was necessary to put it in the newspapers. That was at the time when there were at the Tuileries great sheep that drew the little carriage of the King of Rome. Do you remember the King of Rome?"

"I liked the Duc de Bordeau better."

"I knew Louis XVIII. I prefer Louis XVIII."

"Meat is awfully dear, isn't it, Mother Patagon?"

"Ah! don't mention it, the butcher's shop is a horror. A horrible horror—one can't afford anything but the poor cuts nowadays."

Here the rag-picker interposed:

"Ladies, business is dull. The refuse heaps are miserable. No one throws anything away anymore. They eat everything."

"There are poorer people than you, la Vargoulême."

"Ah, that's true," replied the rag-picker, with deference, "I have a profession."

A pause succeeded, and the rag-picker, yielding to that necessity for boasting which lies at the bottom of man, added:

"In the morning, on my return home, I pick over my basket, I sort my things. This makes heaps in my room. I put the rags in a basket, the cores and stalks in a bucket, the linen in my cupboard, the woolen stuff in my commode, the old papers in the corner of the window, the things that are good to eat in my bowl, the bits of glass in my fireplace, the old shoes behind my door, and the bones under my bed."

Gavroche had stopped behind her and was listening.

"Old ladies," said he, "what do you mean by talking politics?"

He was assailed by a broadside, composed of a quadruple howl.

"Here's another rascal."

"What's that he's got in his paddle? A pistol?"

"Well, I'd like to know what sort of a beggar's brat this is?"

"That sort of animal is never easy unless he's overturning the authorities."

Gavroche disdainfully contented himself, by way of reprisal, with elevating the tip of his nose with his thumb and opening his hand wide.

The rag-picker cried:

"You malicious, bare-pawed little wretch!"

The one who answered to the name of Patagon clapped her hands together in horror.

"There's going to be evil doings, that's certain. The errand-boy next door has a little pointed beard, I have seen him pass every day with a young person in a pink bonnet on his arm; to-day I saw him pass, and he had a gun on his arm. Mame Bacheux says, that last week there was a revolution at—at—at—where's the calf!—at Pontoise. And then, there you see him, that horrid scamp, with his pistol! It seems that the Célestins are full of pistols. What do you suppose the Government can do with good-for-nothings who don't know how to do anything but contrive ways of upsetting the world, when we had just begun to get a little quiet after all the misfortunes that have happened, good Lord! to that poor queen whom I saw pass in the tumbril! And all this is going to make tobacco dearer. It's infamous! And I shall certainly go to see him beheaded on the guillotine, the wretch!"

"You've got the sniffles, old lady," said Gavroche. "Blow your promontory."

And he passed on. When he was in the Rue Pavèe, the rag-picker occurred to his mind, and he indulged in this soliloquy:

"You're in the wrong to insult the revolutionists, Mother Dust-Heap-Corner. This pistol is in your interests. It's so that you may have more good things to eat in your basket."

All at once, he heard a shout behind him; it was the portress Patagon who had followed him, and who was shaking her fist at him in the distance and crying:

"You're nothing but a bastard."

"Oh! Come now," said Gavroche, "I don't care a brass farthing for that!"

Shortly afterwards, he passed the Hôtel Lamoignon. There he uttered this appeal:

"Forward march to the battle!"

And he was seized with a fit of melancholy. He gazed at his pistol with an air of reproach which seemed an attempt to appease it:

"I'm going off," said he, "but you won't go off!"

One dog may distract the attention from another dog. A very gaunt poodle came along at the moment. Gavroche felt compassion for him.

"My poor doggy," said he, "you must have gone and swallowed a cask, for all the hoops are visible."

Then he directed his course toward l'Orme-Saint-Gervais.

Chapter III

JUST INDIGNATION OF A HAIR-DRESSER

THE WORTHY HAIR-DRESSER WHO HAD CHASED FROM HIS SHOP THE TWO LITTLE FELLOWS TO whom Gavroche had opened the paternal interior of the elephant was at that moment in his shop engaged in shaving an old soldier of the legion who had served under the Empire. They were talking. The hair-dresser had, naturally, spoken to the veteran of the riot, then of General Lamarque, and from Lamarque they had passed to the Emperor. Thence sprang up a conversation between barber and soldier which Prudhomme, had he been present, would have enriched with arabesques, and which he would have entitled: "Dialogue between the razor and the sword."

"How did the Emperor ride, sir?" said the barber.

"Badly. He did not know how to fall—so he never fell."

"Did he have fine horses? He must have had fine horses!"

"On the day when he gave me my cross, I noticed his beast. It was a racing mare, perfectly white. Her ears were very wide apart, her saddle deep, a fine head marked with a black star, a very long neck, strongly articulated knees, prominent ribs, oblique shoulders, and a powerful crupper. A little more than fifteen hands in height."

"A pretty horse," remarked the hair-dresser.

"It was his Majesty's beast."

The hair-dresser felt, that after this observation, a short silence would be fitting, so he conformed himself to it, and then went on:

"The Emperor was never wounded but once, was he, sir?"

The old soldier replied with the calm and sovereign tone of a man who had been there:

"In the heel. At Ratisbon. I never saw him so well dressed as on that day. He was as neat as a new sou."

"And you, Mr. Veteran, you must have been often wounded?"

"I?" said the soldier, "ah! not to amount to anything. At Marengo, I received two saber-blows on the back of my neck, a bullet in the right arm at Austerlitz, another in the left hip at Jena. At Friedland, a thrust from a bayonet, there—at the Moskowa seven or eight lance-thrusts, no matter where, at Lutzen a splinter of a shell crushed one of my fingers. Ah! and then at Waterloo, a ball from a biscaïen in the thigh, that's all."

"How fine that is!" exclaimed the hair-dresser, in Pindaric accents, "to die on the field of battle! On my word of honor, rather than die in bed, of an illness, slowly, a bit by bit each day, with drugs, cataplasms, syringes, medicines, I should prefer to receive a cannon-ball in my belly!"

"You're not over fastidious," said the soldier.

He had hardly spoken when a fearful crash shook the shop. The show-window had suddenly been fractured.

The wig-maker turned pale.

"Ah, good God!" he exclaimed, "it's one of them!"

"What?"

"A cannon-ball."

"Here it is," said the soldier.

And he picked up something that was rolling about the floor. It was a pebble.

The hair-dresser ran to the broken window and beheld Gavroche fleeing at the full speed, toward the Marché Saint-Jean. As he passed the hair-dresser's shop Gavroche, who had the two brats still in his mind, had not been able to resist the impulse to say good day to him, and had flung a stone through his panes.

"You see!" shrieked the hair-dresser, who from white had turned blue, "that fellow returns and does mischief for the pure pleasure of it. What has anyone done to that gamin?"

Chapter IV

THE CHILD IS AMAZED AT THE OLD MAN

IN THE MEANTIME, IN THE MARCHÉ SAINT-JEAN, WHERE THE POST HAD ALREADY BEEN DISARMED, Gavroche had just "effected a junction" with a band led by Enjolras, Courfeyrac, Combeferre, and Feuilly. They were armed after a fashion. Bahorel and Jean Prouvaire had found them and swelled the group. Enjolras had a double-barreled hunting-gun, Combeferre the gun of a National Guard bearing the number of his legion, and in his belt, two pistols which his unbuttoned coat allowed to be seen, Jean Prouvaire an old cavalry musket, Bahorel a rifle; Courfeyrac was brandishing an unsheathed sword-cane. Feuilly, with a naked sword in his hand, marched at their head shouting: "Long live Poland!"

They reached the Quai Morland. Cravatless, hatless, breathless, soaked by the rain, with lightning in their eyes. Gavroche accosted them calmly:

"Where are we going?"

"Come along," said Courfeyrac.

Behind Feuilly marched, or rather bounded, Bahorel, who was like a fish in water in a riot. He wore a scarlet waistcoat, and indulged in the sort of words which break everything. His waistcoat astounded a passer-by, who cried in bewilderment:

"Here are the reds!"

"The reds, the reds!" retorted Bahorel. "A queer kind of fear, bourgeois. For my part I don't tremble before a poppy, the little red hat inspires me with no alarm. Take my advice, bourgeois, let's leave fear of the red to horned cattle."

He caught sight of a corner of the wall on which was placarded the most peaceable sheet of paper in the world, a permission to eat eggs, a Lenten admonition addressed by the Archbishop of Paris to his "flock."

Bahorel exclaimed:

" 'Flock'; a polite way of saying geese."

And he tore the charge from the nail. This conquered Gavroche. From that instant Gavroche set himself to study Bahorel.

"Bahorel," observed Enjolras, "you are wrong. You should have let that charge alone, he is not the person with whom we have to deal, you are wasting your wrath to no purpose. Take care of your supply. One does not fire out of the ranks with the soul anymore than with a gun."

"Each one in his own fashion, Enjolras," retorted Bahorel. "This bishop's prose shocks me; I want to eat eggs without being permitted. Your style is the hot and cold; I am amusing myself. Besides, I'm not wasting myself, I'm getting a start; and if I tore down that charge, Hercle! 'twas only to whet my appetite."

This word, *Hercle*, struck Gavroche. He sought all occasions for learning, and that tearer-down of posters possessed his esteem. He inquired of him:

"What does *Hercle* mean?"

Bahorel answered:

"It means cursed name of a dog, in Latin."

Here Bahorel recognized at a window a pale young man with a black beard who was watching them as they passed, probably a Friend of the A B C. He shouted to him:

"Quick, cartridges, *para bellum*."

"A fine man! that's true," said Gavroche, who now understood Latin.

A tumultuous retinue accompanied them—students, artists, young men affiliated to the Cougourde of Aix, artisans, longshoremen, armed with clubs and bayonets; some, like Combeferre, with pistols thrust into their trousers.

An old man, who appeared to be extremely aged, was walking in the band.

He had no arms, and he made great haste, so that he might not be left behind, although he had a thoughtful air.

Gavroche caught sight of him:

"Keksekça?" said he to Courfeyrac.

"He's an old duffer."

It was M. Mabeuf.

Chapter V

THE OLD MAN

LET US RECOUNT WHAT HAD TAKEN PLACE. Enjolras and his friends had been on the Boulevard Bourdon, near the public storehouses, at the moment when the dragoons had made their charge. Enjolras, Courfeyrac, and Combeferre were among those who had taken to the Rue Bassompierre, shouting: "To the barricades!" In the Rue Lesdiguières they had met an old man walking along. What had attracted their attention was, that the good man was walking in a zigzag, as though he were intoxicated. Moreover, he had his hat in his hand, although it had been raining all the morning, and was raining pretty briskly at the very time. Courfeyrac had recognized Father Mabeuf. He knew him through having many times accompanied Marius as far as his door. As he was acquainted with the peaceful and more than timid habits of the old beadle-book-collector, and was amazed at the sight of him in the midst of that uproar, a couple of paces from the cavalry charges, almost in the midst of a fusillade, hatless in the rain, and strolling about among the bullets, he had accosted him, and the following dialogue had been exchanged between the rioter of fire and the octogenarian:

"M. Mabeuf, go to your home."

"Why?"

"There's going to be a row."

"That's well."

"Thrusts with the sword and firing, M. Mabeuf."

"That is well."

"Firing from cannon."

"That is good. Where are the rest of you going?"

"We are going to fling the government to the earth."

"That is good."

And he had set out to follow them. From that moment forth he had not uttered a word. His step had suddenly become firm; artisans had offered him their arms; he had refused with a sign of the head. He advanced nearly to the front rank of the column, with the movement of a man who is marching and the countenance of a man who is sleeping.

"What a fierce old fellow!" muttered the students. The rumor spread through the troop that he was a former member of the Convention—an old regicide. The mob had turned in through the Rue de la Verrerie.

Little Gavroche marched in front with that deafening song which made of him a sort of trumpet.

He sang:

> *"Voici la lune qui paraît,*
> *Quand irons-nous dans la forêt?*
> *Demandait Charlot à Charlotte.*
>
> > *Tou tou tou*
> > *Pour Chatou.*
> > *Je n'ai qu'un Dieu, qu'un roi, qu'un liard, et qu'une botte.*
>
> *"Pour avoir bu de grand matin*
> *La rosée à même le thym,*
> *Deux moineaux étaient en ribotte.*
>
> > *Zi zi zi*
> > *Pour Passy.*
> > *Je n'ai qu'un Dieu, qu'un roi, qu'un liard, et qu'une botte.*
>
> *"Et ces deux pauvres petits loups,*
> *Comme deux grives étaient soûls;*
> *Une tigre en riait dans sa grotte.*
>
> > *Don don don*
> > *Pour Meudon.*
> > *Je n'ai qu'un Dieu, qu'un roi, qu'un liard, et qu'une botte.*
>
> *"L'un jurait et l'autre sacrait.*
> *Quand irons-nous dans la forêt?*
> *Demandait Charlot à Charlotte.*
>
> > *Tin tin tin*
> > *Pour Pantin.*
> > *Je n'ai qu'un Dieu, qu'un roi, qu'un liard, et qu'une botte."*[1]

They directed their course toward Saint-Merry.

---

1. Here is the morn appearing. When shall we go to the forest, Charlot asked Charlotte. Tou, tou, tou, for Chatou, I have but one God, one King, one half-farthing, and one boot. And these two poor wolves were as tipsy as sparrows from having drunk dew and thyme very early in the morning. And these two poor little things were as drunk as thrushes in a vineyard; a tiger laughed at them in his cave. The one cursed, the other swore. When shall we go to the forest? Charlot asked Charlotte.

Chapter VI

RECRUITS

THE BAND AUGMENTED EVERY MOMENT. NEAR THE RUE DES BILLETTES, A MAN OF LOFTY STATURE, whose hair was turning gray, and whose bold and daring mien was remarked by Courfeyrac, Enjolras, and Combeferre, but whom none of them knew, joined them. Gavroche, who was occupied in singing, whistling, humming, running on ahead and pounding on the shutters of the shops with the butt of his triggerless pistol, paid no attention to this man.

It chanced that in the Rue de la Verrerie, they passed in front of Courfeyrac's door.

"This happens just right," said Courfeyrac, "I have forgotten my purse, and I have lost my hat."

He quitted the mob and ran up to his quarters at full speed. He seized an old hat and his purse.

He also seized a large square coffer, of the dimensions of a large valise, which was concealed under his soiled linen.

As he descended again at a run, the portress hailed him:

"Monsieur de Courfeyrac!"

"What's your name, portress?"

The portress stood bewildered.

"Why, you know perfectly well, I'm the concierge; my name is Mother Veuvain."

"Well, if you call me Monsieur de Courfeyrac again, I shall call you Mother de Veuvain. Now speak, what's the matter? What do you want?"

"There is someone who wants to speak with you."

"Who is it?"

"I don't know."

"Where is he?"

"In my lodge."

"The devil!" ejaculated Courfeyrac.

"But the person has been waiting your return for over an hour," said the portress.

At the same time, a sort of pale, thin, small, freckled, and youthful artisan, clad in a tattered blouse and patched trousers of ribbed velvet, and who had rather the air of a girl accoutred as a man than of a man, emerged from the lodge and said to Courfeyrac in a voice which was not the least in the world like a woman's voice:

"Monsieur Marius, if you please."

"He is not here."

"Will he return this evening?"

"I know nothing about it."

And Courfeyrac added:

"For my part, I shall not return."

The young man gazed steadily at him and said:

"Why not?"

"Because."

"Where are you going, then?"

"What business is that of yours?"

"Would you like to have me carry your coffer for you?"

"I am going to the barricades."

"Would you like to have me go with you?"

"If you like!" replied Courfeyrac. "The street is free, the pavements belong to everyone."

And he made his escape at a run to join his friends. When he had rejoined them, he gave the coffer to one of them to carry. It was only a quarter of an hour after this that he saw the young man, who had actually followed them.

A mob does not go precisely where it intends. We have explained that a gust of wind carries it away. They overshot Saint-Merry and found themselves, without precisely knowing how, in the Rue Saint-Denis.

BOOK TWELFTH

CORINTHE

Chapter I

HISTORY OF CORINTHE FROM ITS FOUNDATION

THE PARISIANS WHO NOWADAYS ON ENTERING ON THE RUE RAMBUTEAU AT THE END NEAR THE Halles, notice on their right, opposite the Rue Mondétour, a basket-maker's shop having for its sign a basket in the form of Napoleon the Great with this inscription:

NAPOLEON IS MADE
WHOLLY OF WILLOW,

have no suspicion of the terrible scenes which this very spot witnessed hardly thirty years ago.

It was there that lay the Rue de la Chanvrerie, which ancient deeds spell Chanverrerie, and the celebrated public-house called *Corinthe*.

The reader will remember all that has been said about the barricade effected at this point, and eclipsed, by the way, by the barricade Saint-Merry. It was on this famous barricade of the Rue de la Chanvrerie, now fallen into profound obscurity, that we are about to shed a little light.

May we be permitted to recur, for the sake of clearness in the recital, to the simple means which we have already employed in the case of Waterloo. Persons who wish to picture to themselves in a tolerably exact manner the constitution of the houses which stood at that epoch near the Pointe Saint-Eustache, at the northeast angle of the Halles of Paris, where to-day lies the embouchure of the Rue Rambuteau, have only to imagine an N touching the Rue Saint-Denis with its summit and the Halles with its base, and whose two vertical bars should form the Rue de la Grande-Truanderie, and the Rue de la Chanvrerie, and whose transverse bar should be formed by the Rue de la Petite-Truanderie. The old Rue Mondétour cut the three strokes of the N at the most crooked angles. So that the labyrinthine confusion of these four streets sufficed to form, on a space three fathoms square, between the Halles and the Rue Saint-Denis on the one hand, and between the Rue du Cygne and the Rue des Prêcheurs on the other, seven islands of houses, oddly cut up, of varying sizes, placed crosswise and haphazard, and barely separated, like the blocks of stone in a dock, by narrow crannies.

We say narrow crannies, and we can give no more just idea of those dark, contracted, many-angled alleys, lined with eight-story buildings. These buildings were so decrepit that, in the Rue de la Chanvrerie and the Rue de la Petite-Truanderie, the fronts were shored up with beams running from one house to another. The street was narrow and the gutter broad, the pedestrian there walked on a pavement that was always wet, skirting little stalls resembling cellars, big posts encircled with iron hoops, excessive heaps of refuse, and gates armed with enormous, century-old gratings. The Rue Rambuteau has devastated all that.

The name of Mondétour paints marvelously well the sinuosities of that whole set of streets. A little further on, they are found still better expressed by the *Rue Pirouette*, which ran into the Rue Mondétour.

The passer-by who got entangled from the Rue Saint-Denis in the Rue de la Chanvrerie be-held it gradually close in before him as though he had entered an elongated funnel. At the end of this street, which was very short, he found further passage barred in the direction of the Halles by a tall row of houses, and he would have thought himself in a blind-alley, had he not perceived on the right and left two dark cuts through which he could make his escape. This was the Rue Mondé-tour, which on one side ran into the Rue de Prêcheurs, and on the other into the Rue du Cygne and the Petite-Truanderie. At the bottom of this sort of cul-de-sac, at the angle of the cutting on the right, there was to be seen a house which was not so tall as the rest, and which formed a sort of cape in the street. It is in this house, of two stories only, that an illustrious wine-shop had been merrily installed three hundred years before. This tavern created a joyous noise in the very spot which old Theophilus described in the following couplet:

> *Lá branle le squelette horrible*
> *D'un pauvre amant qui se pendit.*[1]

The situation was good, and tavern-keepers succeeded each other there, from father to son.

In the time of Mathurin Regnier, this cabaret was called the *Pot-aux-Roses*, and as the rebus was then in fashion, it had for its sign-board, a post (*poteau*) painted rose-color. In the last century, the worthy Natoire, one of the fantastic masters nowadays despised by the stiff school, having got drunk many times in this wine-shop at the very table where Regnier had drunk his fill, had painted, by way of gratitude, a bunch of Corinth grapes on the pink post. The keeper of the cabaret, in his joy, had changed his device and had caused to be placed in gilt letters beneath the bunch these words: "At the Bunch of Corinth Grapes" (*"Au Raisin de Corinthe"*). Hence the name of Corinthe. Nothing is more natural to drunken men than ellipses. The ellipsis is the zigzag of the phrase. Corinthe gradually dethroned the Pot-aux-Roses. The last proprietor of the dynasty, Father Huche-loup, no longer acquainted even with the tradition, had the post painted blue.

A room on the ground floor, where the bar was situated, one on the first floor containing a billiard-table, a wooden spiral staircase piercing the ceiling, wine on the tables, smoke on the walls, candles in broad daylight—this was the style of this cabaret. A staircase with a trapdoor in the lower room led to the cellar. On the second floor were the lodgings of the Hucheloup family. They were reached by a staircase which was a ladder rather than a staircase, and had for their entrance only a private door in the large room on the first floor. Under the roof, in two mansard attics, were the nests for the servants. The kitchen shared the ground floor with the tap-room.

Father Hucheloup had, possibly, been born a chemist, but the fact is that he was a cook; peo-ple did not confine themselves to drinking alone in his wine-shop, they also ate there. Hucheloup had invented a capital thing which could be eaten nowhere but in his house, stuffed carps, which he called *carpes au gras*. These were eaten by the light of a tallow candle or of a lamp of the time of

---

1. There swings the horrible skelton of a poor lover who hung himself.

Louis XVI, on tables to which were nailed waxed cloths in lieu of table-cloths. People came thither from a distance. Hucheloup, one fine morning, had seen fit to notify passers-by of this "specialty"; he had dipped a brush in a pot of black paint, and as he was an orthographer on his own account, as well as a cook after his own fashion, he had improvised on his wall this remarkable inscription:

CARPES HO GRAS.

One winter, the rainstorms and the showers had taken a fancy to obliterate the S which terminated the first word, and the G which began the third; this is what remained:

CARPE HO RAS.

Time and rain assisting, a humble gastronomical announcement had become a profound piece of advice.

In this way it came about, that though he knew no French, Father Hucheloup understood Latin, that he had evoked philosophy from his kitchen, and that, desirous simply of effacing Lent, he had equaled Horace. And the striking thing about it was, that that also meant: "Enter my wine-shop."

Nothing of all this is in existence now. The Mondétour labyrinth was disemboweled and widely opened in 1847, and probably no longer exists at the present moment. The Rue de la Chanvrerie and Corinthe have disappeared beneath the pavement of the Rue Rambuteau.

As we have already said, Corinthe was the meeting-place if not the rallying-point, of Courfeyrac and his friends. It was Grantaire who had discovered Corinthe. He had entered it on account of the *Carpe horas*, and had returned thither on account of the *Carpes au gras*. There they drank, there they ate, there they shouted; they did not pay much, they paid badly, they did not pay at all, but they were always welcome. Father Hucheloup was a jovial host.

Hucheloup, that amiable man, as was just said, was a wine-shop-keeper with a mustache; an amusing variety. He always had an ill-tempered air, seemed to wish to intimidate his customers, grumbled at the people who entered his establishment, and had rather the mien of seeking a quarrel with them than of serving them with soup. And yet, we insist upon the word, people were always welcome there. This oddity had attracted customers to his shop, and brought him young men, who said to each other: "Come hear Father Hucheloup growl." He had been a fencing-master. All of a sudden, he would burst out laughing. A big voice, a good fellow. He had a comic foundation under a tragic exterior, he asked nothing better than to frighten you, very much like those snuff-boxes which are in the shape of a pistol. The detonation makes one sneeze.

Mother Hucheloup, his wife, was a bearded and a very homely creature.

About 1830, Father Hucheloup died. With him disappeared the secret of stuffed carps. His inconsolable widow continued to keep the wine-shop. But the cooking deteriorated, and became execrable; the wine, which had always been bad, became fearfully bad. Nevertheless, Courfeyrac and his friends continued to go to Corinthe—out of pity, as Bossuet said.

The Widow Hucheloup was breathless and misshapen and given to rustic recollections. She deprived them of their flatness by her pronunciation. She had a way of her own of saying things, which spiced her reminiscences of the village and of her springtime. It had formerly been her delight, so she affirmed, to hear the *loups-de-gorge* (*rouges-gorges*) *chanter dans les ogrepines* (*aubépines*)—to hear the redbreasts sing in the hawthorn-trees.

The hall on the first floor, where "the restaurant" was situated, was a large and long apartment encumbered with stools, chairs, benches, and tables, and with a crippled, lame, old billiard-table. It was reached by a spiral staircase which terminated in the corner of the room at a square hole like the hatchway of a ship.

This room, lighted by a single narrow window, and by a lamp that was always burning, had the air of a garret. All the four-footed furniture comported itself as though it had but three legs— the whitewashed walls had for their only ornament the following quatrain in honor of Mame Hucheloup:

> Elle étonne à dix pas, elle épouvente à deux,
> Une verrue habite en son nez hasardeux;
> On tremble à chaque instant qu'elle ne vous la mouche
> Et qu'un beau jour son nez ne tombe dans sa bouche.[1]

This was scrawled in charcoal on the wall.

Mame Hucheloup, a good likeness, went and came from morning till night before this quatrain with the most perfect tranquility. Two serving-maids, named Matelote and Gibelotte, and who had never been known by any other names, helped Mame Hucheloup to set on the tables the jugs of poor wine, and the various broths which were served to the hungry patrons in earthenware bowls. Matelote, large, plump, red-haired, and noisy, the favorite ex-sultana of the defunct Hucheloup, was homelier than any mythological monster, be it what it may; still, as it becomes the servant to always keep in the rear of the mistress, she was less homely than Mame Hucheloup. Gibelotte, tall, delicate, white with a lymphatic pallor, with circles round her eyes, and drooping lids, always languid and weary, afflicted with what may be called chronic lassitude, the first up in the house and the last in bed, waited on everyone, even the other maid, silently and gently, smiling through her fatigue with a vague and sleepy smile.

Before entering the restaurant room, the visitor read on the door the following line written there in chalk by Courfeyrac:

> Régale si tu peux et mange si tu l'oses.[2]

Chapter II

Preliminary Gaieties

LAIGLE DE MEAUX, AS THE READER KNOWS, LIVED MORE WITH JOLY THAN ELSEWHERE. HE HAD A lodging, as a bird has one on a branch. The two friends lived together, ate together, slept together. They had everything in common, even Musichetta, to some extent. They were, what the subordinate monks who accompany monks are called, *bini*. On the morning of the 5th of June, they went to Corinthe to breakfast. Joly, who was all stuffed up, had a catarrh which Laigle was beginning to share. Laigle's coat was threadbare, but Joly was well dressed.

It was about nine o'clock in the morning, when they opened the door of Corinthe.

They ascended to the first floor.

Matelote and Gibelotte received them.

"Oysters, cheese, and ham," said Laigle.

1. She astounds at ten paces, she frightens at two, a wart inhabits her hazardous nose; you tremble every instant lest she should blow it at you, and lest, some fine day, her nose should tumble into her mouth.
2. Treat if you can, and eat if you dare.

And they seated themselves at a table.

The wine-shop was empty; there was no one there but themselves.

Gibelotte, knowing Joly and Laigle, set a bottle of wine on the table.

While they were busy with their first oysters, a head appeared at the hatchway of the staircase, and a voice said:

"I am passing by. I smell from the street a delicious odor of Brie cheese. I enter." It was Grantaire.

Grantaire took a stool and drew up to the table.

At the sight of Grantaire, Gibelotte placed two bottles of wine on the table.

That made three.

"Are you going to drink those two bottles?" Laigle inquired of Grantaire.

Grantaire replied:

"All are ingenious, thou alone art ingenuous. Two bottles never yet astonished a man."

The others had begun by eating, Grantaire began by drinking. Half a bottle was rapidly gulped down.

"So you have a hole in your stomach?" began Laigle again.

"You have one in your elbow," said Grantaire.

And after having emptied his glass, he added:

"Ah, by the way, Laigle of the funeral oration, your coat is old."

"I should hope so," retorted Laigle. "That's why we get on well together, my coat and I. It has acquired all my folds, it does not bind me anywhere, it is molded on my deformities, it falls in with all my movements, I am only conscious of it because it keeps me warm. Old coats are just like old friends."

"That's true," ejaculated Joly, striking into the dialogue, "an old goat is an old abi" (*ami*, friend).

"Especially in the mouth of a man whose head is stuffed up," said Grantaire.

"Grantaire," demanded Laigle, "have you just come from the boulevard?"

"No."

"We have just seen the head of the procession pass, Joly and I."

"It's a marvelous sight," said Joly.

"How quiet this street is!" exclaimed Laigle. "Who would suspect that Paris was turned upside down? How plainly it is to be seen that in former days there were nothing but convents here! In this neighborhood! Du Breul and Sauval give a list of them, and so does the Abbé Lebeuf. They were all round here, they fairly swarmed, booted and barefooted, shaven, bearded, gray, black, white, Franciscans, Minims, Capuchins, Carmelites, Little Augustines, Great Augustines, old Augustines—there was no end of them."

"Don't let's talk of monks," interrupted Grantaire, "it makes one want to scratch one's self."

Then he exclaimed:

"Bouh! I've just swallowed a bad oyster. Now hypochondria is taking possession of me again. The oysters are spoiled, the servants are ugly. I hate the human race. I just passed through the Rue Richelieu, in front of the big public library. That pile of oyster-shells which is called a library is disgusting even to think of. What paper! What ink! What scrawling! And all that has been written! What rascal was it who said that man was a featherless biped? And then, I met a pretty girl of my acquaintance, who is as beautiful as the spring, worthy to be called Floréal, and who is delighted, enraptured, as happy as the angels, because a wretch yesterday, a frightful banker all spotted with small-pox, deigned to take a fancy to her! Alas! woman keeps on the watch for a protector as much as for a lover; cats chase mice as well as birds. Two months ago that young woman was virtuous in an attic, she adjusted little brass rings in the eyelet-holes of corsets, what do you call it? She sewed, she had a camp bed, she dwelt beside a pot of flowers, she was contented. Now here she is a bankeress. This transformation took place last night. I met the victim this morning in high spirits. The hideous point about it is, that the jade is as pretty to-day as she was yesterday. Her financier did not show in her face. Roses have this advantage or disadvantage over women, that the traces left upon them by caterpillars are visible. Ah! there is no morality on earth. I call to witness the myrtle, the symbol of love, the laurel, the symbol of air, the olive, that ninny, the symbol of peace, the apple-tree which came nearest rangling Adam with its pips, and the fig-tree, the grandfather of petticoats. As for right, do you know what right is? The Gauls covet Clusium, Rome protects Clusium, and demands what wrong Clusium has done to them. Brennus answers: 'The wrong that Alba did to you, the wrong that Fidenæ did to you, the wrong that the Eques, the Volsci, and the Sabines have done to you. They were your neighbors. The Clusians are ours. We understand neighborliness just as you do. You have stolen Alba, we shall take Clusium.' Rome said: 'You shall not take Clusium.' Brennus took Rome. Then he cried: 'Væ victis!' That is what right is. Ah! what beasts of prey there are in this world! What eagles! It makes my flesh creep."

He held out his glass to Joly, who filled it, then he drank and went on, having hardly been interrupted by this glass of wine, of which no one, not even himself, had taken any notice:

"Brennus, who takes Rome, is an eagle; the banker who takes the grisette is an eagle. There is no more modesty in the one case than in the other. So we believe in nothing. There is but one reality: drink. Whatever your opinion may be in favor of the lean cock, like the Canton of Uri, or in favor of the fat cock, like the Canton of Glaris, it matters little, drink. You talk to me of the boulevard, of that procession, *et cetera, et cetera.* Come now, is there going to be another revolution? This poverty of means on the part of the good God astounds me. He has to keep greasing the groove of events every moment. There is a hitch, it won't work. Quick, a revolution! The good God has his hands perpetually black with that cart-grease. If I were in his place, I'd be perfectly simple about it, I would not wind up my mechanism every minute, I'd lead the human race in a straightforward way, I'd weave matters mesh by mesh, without breaking the thread, I would have no provisional arrangements, I would have no extraordinary repertory. What the rest of you call progress advances by means of two motors, men and events. But, sad to say, from time to time, the exceptional becomes necessary. The ordinary troupe suffices neither for event; nor for men: among men geniuses are required, among events revolutions. Great accidents are the law; the order of things cannot do without them; and, judging from the apparition of comets, one would be tempted to think that Heaven itself finds actors needed for its performance. At the moment when one expects it the least, God placards a meteor on the wall of the firmament. Some queer star turns up, underlined by an enormous tail. And that causes the death of Cæsar. Brutus deals him a blow with a knife, and God a blow with a comet. *Crac,* and behold an aurora borealis, behold a revolution, behold a great man; '93 in big letters, Napoleon on guard, the comet of 1811 at the head of the poster. Ah! what a beautiful blue theater all studded with unexpected flashes! Boum! Boum! extraordinary show! Raise your eyes, boobies. Everything is in disorder, the star as well as the drama. Good God, it is too much and not enough. These resources, gathered from exception, seem magnificence and poverty. My friends, Providence has come down to expedients. What does a revolution prove? That God is in a quandary. He effects a *coup d'état* because he, God, has not been able to make both ends meet. In fact, this confirms me in my conjectures as to Jehovah's fortune; and when I see so much distress in heaven and on earth, from the bird who has not a grain of millet to myself without a hundred thousand livres of income, when I see human destiny, which is very badly worn, and even royal destiny, which is threadbare, witness the Prince de Condé hung, when I see winter, which is nothing but a rent in the zenith through which the wind blows, when I see so many rags even in the perfectly new purple of the morning on the crests of hills, when I see the drops of dew, those mock pearls, when I see the frost, that paste, when I see humanity ripped apart and events patched up, and so many spots on the sun and so many holes in the moon, when I see so much misery everywhere, I suspect that God is not rich. The appearance exists, it is true, but I feel that he is hard up. He gives a revolution as a tradesman whose money-box is empty gives a ball. God must not be judged from appearances. Beneath the gilding of heaven I perceive a poverty-stricken universe. Creation is bankrupt. That is why I am discontented. Here it is the 4th of June, it is almost night; ever since this morning I have been waiting for daylight to come; it has not come, and I bet that it won't come all day. This is the inexactness of an ill-paid clerk. Yes, everything is badly arranged, nothing fits anything else, this old world is all warped, I take my stand on the opposition, everything goes awry; the universe is a tease. It's like children, those who want them have none, and those who don't want them have them. Total: I'm vexed. Besides, Laigle de Meaux, that bald-head, offends my sight. It humiliates me to think that I am of the same age as that baldy. However, I criticize, but I do not insult. The universe is what it is. I speak here without evil intent and to ease my conscience. Receive, Eternal Father, the assurance of my distinguished consideration. Ah! by all the saints of Olympus and by all the gods of paradise, I was not intended to be a Parisian, that is to say, to rebound forever, like a shuttlecock between two battledores, from the group of the loungers to the group of the roysterers. I was made to be a Turk, watching oriental houris all day long, executing those exquisite Egyptian dances, as sensuous as the dream of a chaste man, or a Beauceron peasant, or a Venetian gentleman surrounded by gentlewomen, or a petty German prince, furnishing the half of a foot-soldier to the Germanic confederation, and occupying his leisure with drying his breeches on his hedge, that is to say, his frontier. Those are the positions for which I was born! Yes, I have said a Turk, and I will not retract. I do not understand how people can habitually take Turks in bad part; Mohammed had his good points; respect for the inventor of seraglios with houris and paradises with odalisques! Let us not insult Mohammedanism, the only religion which is ornamented with a hen-roost! Now, I insist on a drink. The earth is a great piece of stupidity. And it appears that they are going to fight, all those imbeciles, and to break each other's profiles and to massacre each other in the heart of summer, in the month of June, when they might go off with a creature on their arm, to breathe the immense heaps of new-mown hay in the meadows! Really, people do commit altogether too many follies. An old broken lantern which I have just seen at a bric-à-brac merchant's suggests a reflection to my mind; it is time to enlighten the human race. Yes, behold me sad again. That's what comes of swallowing an oyster and a revolution the wrong way! I am growing melancholy once more. Oh! frightful old world. People strive, turn each other out, prostitute themselves, kill each other, and get used to it!"

And Grantaire, after this fit of eloquence, had a fit of coughing, which was well earned.

"À propos of revolution," said Joly, "it is decidedly abbarent that Barius is in lub."

"Does anyone know with whom?" demanded Laigle.

"Do."

"No?"

"Do! I tell you."

"Marius's love affairs!" exclaimed Grantaire. "I can imagine it. Marius is a fog, and he must have found a vapor. Marius is of the race of poets. He who says poet, says fool, madman, *Tymbræus Apollo.* Marius and his Marie, or his Marion, or his Maria, or his Mariette. They must make a queer pair of lovers. I know just what it is like. Ecstasies in which they forget to kiss. Pure on earth, but joined in heaven. They are souls possessed of senses. They lie among the stars."

Grantaire was attacking his second bottle and, possibly, his second harangue, when a new personage emerged from the square aperture of the stairs. It was a boy less than ten years of age, ragged, very small, yellow, with an odd phiz, a vivacious eye, an enormous amount of hair drenched with rain, and wearing a contented air.

The child unhesitatingly making his choice among the three, addressed himself to Laigle de Meaux.

"Are you Monsieur Bossuet?"

"That is my nickname," replied Laigle. "What do you want with me?"

"This. A tall blonde fellow on the boulevard said to me: 'Do you know Mother Hucheloup?' I said: 'Yes, Rue Chanvrerie, the old man's widow'; he said to me: 'Go there. There you will find M. Bossuet. Tell him from me: "A B C." ' It's a joke that they're playing on you, isn't it. He gave me ten sous."

"Joly, lend me ten sous," said Laigle; and, turning to Grantaire: "Grantaire, lend me ten sous."

This made twenty sous, which Laigle handed to the lad.

"Thank you, sir," said the urchin.

"What is your name?" inquired Laigle.

"Navet, Gavroche's friend."

"Stay with us," said Laigle.

"Breakfast with us," said Grantaire.

The child replied:

"I can't, I belong in the procession, I'm the one to shout 'Down with Polignac!' "

And executing a prolonged scrape of his foot behind him, which is the most respectful of all possible salutes, he took his departure.

The child gone, Grantaire took the word:

"That is the pure-bred gamin. There are a great many varieties of the gamin species. The notary's gamin is called Skip-the-Gutter, the cook's gamin is called a scullion, the baker's gamin is called a *mitron*, the lackey's gamin is called a groom, the marine gamin is called the cabin-boy, the soldier's gamin is called the drummer-boy, the painter's gamin is called paint-grinder, the tradesman's gamin is called an errand-boy, the courtesan gamin is called the minion, the kingly gamin is called the dauphin, the god gamin is called the bambino."

In the meantime, Laigle was engaged in reflection; he said half-aloud:

"A B C, that is to say: the burial of Lamarque."

"The tall blonde," remarked Grantaire, "is Enjolras, who is sending you a warning."

"Shall we go?" ejaculated Bossuet.

"It's raiding," said Joly. "I have sworn to go through fire, but not through water. I don't wand to ged a gold."

"I shall stay here," said Grantaire. "I prefer a breakfast to a hearse."

"Conclusion: we remain," said Laigle. "Well, then, let us drink. Besides, we might miss the funeral without missing the riot."

"Ah! the riot, I am with you!" cried Joly.

Laigle rubbed his hands.

"Now we're going to touch up the revolution of 1830. As a matter of fact, it does hurt the people along the seams."

"I don't think much of your revolution," said Grantaire. "I don't execrate this Government. It is the crown tempered by the cotton nightcap. It is a scepter ending in an umbrella. In fact, I think that to-day, with the present weather, Louis Philippe might utilize his royalty in two directions, he might extend the tip of the scepter end against the people, and open the umbrella end against heaven."

The room was dark, large clouds had just finished the extinction of daylight. There was no one in the wine-shop, or in the street, everyone having gone off "to watch events."

"Is it midday or midnight?" cried Bossuet. "You can't see your hand before your face. Gibelotte, fetch a light."

Grantaire was drinking in a melancholy way.

"Enjolras disdains me," he muttered. "Enjolras said: 'Joly is ill, Grantaire is drunk.' It was to Bossuet that he sent Navet. If he had come for me, I would have followed him. So much the worse for Enjolras! I won't go to his funeral."

This resolution once arrived at, Bossuet, Joly, and Grantaire did not stir from the wine-shop. By two o'clock in the afternoon, the table at which they sat was covered with empty bottles. Two candles were burning on it, one in a flat copper candlestick which was perfectly green, the other in the neck of a cracked carafe. Grantaire had seduced Joly and Bossuet to wine; Bossuet and Joly had conducted Grantaire back toward cheerfulness.

As for Grantaire, he had got beyond wine, that merely moderate inspirer of dreams, ever since midday. Wine enjoys only a conventional popularity with serious drinkers. There is, in fact, in the matter of inebriety, white magic and black magic; wine is only white magic. Grantaire was a daring drinker of dreams. The blackness of a terrible fit of drunkenness yawning before him, far from arresting him, attracted him. He had abandoned the bottle and taken to the beer-glass. The beer-glass is the abyss. Having neither opium nor hashish on hand, and being desirous of filling his brain with twilight, he had had recourse to that fearful mixture of brandy, stout, absinthe, which produces the most terrible of lethargies. It is of these three vapors, beer, brandy, and absinthe, that the lead of the soul is composed. They are three grooms; the celestial butterfly is drowned in them; and there are formed there in a membranous smoke, vaguely condensed into the wing of the bat, three mute furies, Nightmare, Night, and Death, which hover above the slumbering Psyche.

Grantaire had not yet reached that lamentable phase; far from it. He was tremendously gay, and Bossuet and Joly retorted. They clinked glasses. Grantaire added to the eccentric accentuation of words and ideas, a peculiarity of gesture; he rested his left fist on his knee with dignity, his arm forming a right angle, and, with cravat untied, seated astride a stool, his full glass in his right hand, he hurled solemn words at the big maid-servant Matelote:

"Let the doors of the palace be thrown open! Let everyone be a member of the French Academy and have the right to embrace Madame Hucheloup. Let us drink."

And turning to Madame Hucheloup, he added:

"Woman ancient and consecrated by use, draw near that I may contemplate thee!"

And Joly exclaimed:

"Matelote and Gibelotte, dod't gib Grantaire anything more to drink. He has already devoured, since this bording, in wild prodigality, two francs and ninety-five centibes."

And Grantaire began again:

"Who has been unhooking the stars without my permission, and putting them on the table in the guise of candles?"

Bossuet, though very drunk, preserved his equanimity.

He was seated on the sill of the open window, wetting his back in the falling rain, and gazing at his two friends.

All at once, he heard a tumult behind him, hurried footsteps, cries of "To arms!" He turned round and saw in the Rue Saint-Denis, at the end of the Rue de la Chanvrerie, Enjolras passing, gun in hand, and Gavroche with his pistol, Feuilly with his sword, Courfeyrac with his sword, and Jean Prouvaire with his blunderbuss, Combeferre with his gun, Bahorel with his gun, and the whole armed and stormy rabble which was following them.

The Rue de la Chanvrerie was not more than a gun-shot long. Bossuet improvised a speaking-trumpet from his two hands placed around his mouth, and shouted:

"Courfeyrac! Courfeyrac! Hohée!"

Courfeyrac heard the shout, caught sight of Bossuet, and advanced a few paces into the Rue de la Chanvrerie, shouting: "What do you want?" which crossed a "Where are you going?"

"To make a barricade," replied Courfeyrac.

"Well, here! This is a good place! Make it here!"

"That's true, Aigle," said Courfeyrac.

And at a signal from Courfeyrac, the mob flung themselves into the Rue de la Chanvrerie.

Chapter III

NIGHT BEGINS TO DESCEND UPON GRANTAIRE

THE SPOT WAS, IN FACT, ADMIRABLY ADAPTED, THE ENTRANCE TO THE STREET WIDENED OUT, the other extremity narrowed together into a pocket without exit. Corinthe created an obstacle, the Rue Mondétour was easily barricaded on the right and the left, no attack was possible except from the Rue Saint-Denis, that is to say, in front, and in full sight. Bossuet had the comprehensive glance of a fasting Hannibal.

Terror had seized on the whole street at the eruption of the mob. There was not a passer-by who did not get out of sight. In the space of a flash of lightning, in the rear, to right and left, shops, stables, area-doors, windows, blinds, attic skylights, shutters of every description were closed, from the ground floor to the roof. A terrified old woman fixed a mattress in front of her window on two clothes-poles for drying linen, in order to deaden the effect of musketry. The wine-shop alone remained open; and that for a very good reason, that the mob had rushed into it.—"Ah my God! Ah my God!" sighed Mame Hucheloup.

Bossuet had gone down to meet Courfeyrac.

Joly, who had placed himself at the window, exclaimed:

"Courfeyrac, you ought to have brought an umbrella. You will gatch gold."

In the meantime, in the space of a few minutes, twenty iron bars had been wrenched from the grated front of the wine-shop, ten fathoms of street had been unpaved; Gavroche and Bahorel had seized in its passage, and overturned, the dray of a lime-dealer named Anceau; this dray contained three barrels of lime, which they placed beneath the piles of paving-stones: Enjolras raised the cellar trap, and all the widow Hucheloup's empty casks were used to flank the barrels of lime; Feuilly, with his fingers skilled in painting the delicate sticks of fans, had backed up the barrels and the dray with two massive heaps of blocks of rough stone. Blocks which were improvised like the rest and procured no one knows where. The beams which served as props were torn from the neighboring house-fronts and laid on the casks. When Bossuet and Courfeyrac turned round, half the street was already barred with a rampart higher than a man. There is nothing like the hand of the populace for building everything that is built by demolishing.

Matelote and Gibelotte had mingled with the workers. Gibelotte went and came loaded with rubbish. Her lassitude helped on the barricade. She served the barricade as she would have served wine, with a sleepy air.

An omnibus with two white horses passed the end of the street.

Bossuet strode over the paving-stones, ran to it, stopped the driver, made the passengers alight, offered his hand to "the ladies," dismissed the conductor, and returned, leading the vehicle and the horses by the bridle.

"Omnibuses," said he, "do not pass the Corinthe. *Non licet omnibus adire Corinthum.*"

An instant later, the horses were unharnessed and went off at their will, through the Rue Mondétour, and the omnibus lying on its side completed the bar across the street.

Mame Hucheloup, quite upset, had taken refuge in the first story.

Her eyes were vague, and stared without seeing anything, and she cried in a low tone. Her terrified shrieks did not dare to emerge from her throat.

"The end of the world has come," she muttered.

Joly deposited a kiss on Mame Hucheloup's fat, red, wrinkled neck, and said to Grantaire: "My dear fellow, I have always regarded a woman's neck as an infinitely delicate thing."

But Grantaire attained to the highest regions of dithryamb. Matelote had mounted to the first floor once more, Grantaire seized her round her waist, and gave vent to long bursts of laughter at the window.

"Matelote is homely!" he cried: "Matelote is of a dream of ugliness! Matelote is a chimera. This is the secret of her birth: a Gothic Pygmalion, who was making gargoyles for cathedrals, fell in love with one of them, the most horrible, one fine morning. He besought Love to give it life, and this produced Matelote. Look at her, citizens! She has chromate-of-lead-colored hair, like Titian's mistress, and she is a good girl. I guarantee that she will fight well. Every good girl contains a hero. As for Mother Hucheloup, she's an old warrior. Look at her moustaches! She inherited them from her husband. A hussar indeed! She will fight too. These two alone will strike terror to the heart of the banlieue. Comrades, we shall overthrow the government as true as there are fifteen intermediary acids between margaric acid and formic acid; however, that is a matter of perfect indifference to me. Gentlemen, my father always detested me because I could not understand mathematics. I understand only love and liberty. I am Grantaire, the good fellow. Having never had any money, I never acquired the habit of it, and the result is that I have never lacked it; but, if I had been rich, there would have been no more poor people! You would have seen! Oh, if the kind hearts only had fat purses, how much better things would go! I picture myself Jesus Christ with Rothschild's fortune! How much good he would do! Matelote, embrace me! You are voluptuous and timid! You have cheeks which invite the kiss of a sister, and lips which claim the kiss of a lover."

"Hold your tongue, you cask!" said Courfeyrac.

Grantaire retorted:

"I am the capitoul[1] and the master of the floral games!"

Enjolras, who was standing on the crest of the barricade, gun in hand, raised his beautiful, austere face. Enjolras, as the reader knows, had something of the Spartan and of the Puritan in his composition. He would have perished at Thermopylæ with Leonidas, and burned at Drogheda with Cromwell.

"Grantaire," he shouted, "go get rid of the fumes of your wine somewhere else than here. This is the place for enthusiasm, not for drunkenness. Don't disgrace the barricade!"

This angry speech produced a singular effect on Grantaire. One would have said that he had had a glass of cold water flung in his face. He seemed to be rendered suddenly sober.

He sat down, put his elbows on a table near the window, looked at Enjolras with indescribable gentleness, and said to him:

"Let me sleep here."

"Go and sleep somewhere else," cried Enjolras.

But Grantaire, still keeping his tender and troubled eyes fixed on him, replied:

"Let me sleep here—until I die."

Enjolras regarded him with disdainful eyes:

"Grantaire, you are incapable of believing, of thinking, of willing, of living, and of dying."

Grantaire replied in a grave tone:

"You will see."

He stammered a few more unintelligible words, then his head fell heavily on the table, and, as is the usual effect of the second period of inebriety, into which Enjolras had roughly and abruptly thrust him, an instant later he had fallen asleep.

1. Municipal officer of Toulouse.

Chapter IV

AN ATTEMPT TO CONSOLE THE WIDOW HUCHELOUP

BAHOREL, IN ECSTASIES OVER THE BARRICADE, SHOUTED:

"Here's the street in its low-necked dress! How well it looks!"

Courfeyrac, as he demolished the wine-shop to some extent, sought to console the widowed proprietress.

"Mother Hucheloup, weren't you complaining the other day because you had had a notice served on you for infringing the law, because Gibelotte shook a counterpane out of your window?"

"Yes, my good Monsieur Courfeyrac. Ah! good Heavens, are you going to put that table of mine in your horror, too? And it was for the counterpane, and also for a pot of flowers which fell from the attic window into the street, that the government collected a fine of a hundred francs. If that isn't an abomination, what is!"

"Well, Mother Hucheloup, we are avenging you."

Mother Hucheloup did not appear to understand very clearly the benefit which she was to derive from these reprisals made on her account. She was satisfied after the manner of that Arab woman, who, having received a box on the ear from her husband, went to complain to her father, and cried for vengeance, saying: "Father, you owe my husband affront for affront." The father asked: "On which cheek did you receive the blow?" "On the left cheek." The father slapped her right cheek and said: "Now you are satisfied. Go tell your husband that he boxed my daughter's ears, and that I have accordingly boxed his wife's."

The rain had ceased. Recruits had arrived. Workmen had brought under their blouses a barrel of powder, a basket containing bottles of vitriol, two or three carnival torches, and a basket filled with fire-pots, "left over from the King's festival." This festival was very recent, having taken place on the 1st of May. It was said that these munitions came from a grocer in the Faubourg Saint-Antoine named Pépin. They smashed the only street-lantern in the Rue de la Chanvrerie, the lantern corresponding to one in the Rue Saint-Denis, and all the lanterns in the surrounding streets, de Mondétour, du Cygne, des Prêcheurs, and de la Grande and de la Petite-Truanderie.

Enjolras, Combeferre, and Courfeyrac directed everything. Two barricades were now in process of construction at once, both of them resting on the Corinthe house and forming a right angle; the larger shut off the Rue de la Chanvrerie, the other closed the Rue Mondétour, on the side of the Rue de Cygne. This last barricade, which was very narrow, was constructed only of casks and paving-stones. There were about fifty workers on it; thirty were armed with guns; for, on their way, they had effected a wholesale loan from an armorer's shop.

Nothing could be more bizarre and at the same time more motley than this troop. One had a round-jacket, a cavalry saber, and two holster-pistols, another was in his shirt-sleeves, with a round hat, and a powder-horn slung at his side, a third wore a plastron of nine sheets of gray paper and was armed with a saddler's awl. There was one who was shouting: "Let us exterminate them to the last man and die at the point of our bayonet." This man had no bayonet. Another spread out over his coat the cross-belt and cartridge-box of a National Guardsman, the cover of the cartridge-box being ornamented with this inscription in red worsted: *Public Order*. There were a great many guns bearing the numbers of the legions, few hats, no cravats, many bare arms, some pikes. Add to this, all ages, all sorts of faces, small, pale young men, and bronzed longshoremen. All were in haste; and as they helped each other, they discussed the possible chances. That they would receive succor about three o'clock in the morning—that they were sure of one regiment, that Paris would rise.

Terrible sayings with which was mingled a sort of cordial joviality. One would have pronounced them brothers, but they did not know each other's names. Great perils have this fine characteristic, that they bring to light the fraternity of strangers. A fire had been lighted in the kitchen, and there they were engaged in molding into bullets, pewter mugs, spoons, forks, and all the brass tableware of the establishment. In the midst of it all, they drank. Caps and buck-shot were mixed pell-mell on the tables with glasses of wine. In the billiard-hall, Mame Hucheloup, Matelote, and Gibelotte, variously modified by terror, which had stupefied one, rendered another breathless, and roused the third, were tearing up old dish-cloths and making lint; three insurgents were assisting them, three bushy-haired, jolly blades with beards and moustaches, who plucked away at the linen with the fingers of seamstresses and who made them tremble.

The man of lofty stature whom Courfeyrac, Combeferre, and Enjolras had observed at the moment when he joined the mob at the corner of the Rue des Billettes, was at work on the smaller barricade and was making himself useful there. Gavroche was working on the larger one. As for the young man who had been waiting for Courfeyrac at his lodgings, and who had inquired for M. Marius, he had disappeared at about the time when the omnibus had been overturned.

Gavroche, completely carried away and radiant, had undertaken to get everything in readiness. He went, came, mounted, descended, remounted, whistled, and sparkled. He seemed to be there for the encouragement of all. Had he any incentive? Yes, certainly, his poverty; had he wings? yes, certainly, his joy. Gavroche was a whirlwind. He was constantly visible, he was incessantly audible. He filled the air, as he was everywhere at once. He was a sort of almost irritating ubiquity; no halt was possible with him. The enormous barricade felt him on its haunches. He troubled the loungers, he excited the idle, he reanimated the weary, he grew impatient over the thoughtful, he inspired gaiety in some, and breath in others, wrath in others, movement in all, now pricking a student, now biting an artisan; he alighted, paused, flew off again, hovered over the tumult, and the effort, sprang from one party to another, murmuring and humming, and harassed the whole company; a fly on the immense revolutionary coach.

Perpetual motion was in his little arms and perpetual clamor in his little lungs.

"Courage! more paving-stones! more casks! more machines! Where are you now? A hod of plaster for me to stop this hole with! Your barricade is very small. It must be carried up. Put everything on it, fling everything there, stick it all in. Break down the house. A barricade is Mother Gibou's tea. Hullo, here's a glass door."

This elicited an exclamation from the workers.

"A glass door? what do you expect us to do with a glass door, tubercle?"

"Hercules yourselves!" retorted Gavroche. "A glass door is an excellent thing in a barricade. It does not prevent an attack, but it prevents the enemy taking it. So you've never prigged apples over a wall where there were broken bottles? A glass door cuts the corns of the National Guard when they try to mount on the barricade. Pardi! glass is a treacherous thing. Well, you haven't a very wildly lively imagination, comrades."

However, he was furious over his triggerless pistol. He went from one to another, demanding: "A gun, I want a gun! Why don't you give me a gun?"

"Give you a gun!" said Combeferre.

"Come now!" said Gavroche, "why not? I had one in 1830 when we had a dispute with Charles X."

Enjolras shrugged his shoulders.

"When there are enough for the men, we will give some to the children."

Gavroche wheeled round haughtily, and answered:

"If you are killed before me, I shall take yours."

"Gamin!" said Enjolras.

"Greenhorn!" said Gavroche.

A dandy who had lost his way and who lounged past the end of the street created a diversion! Gavroche shouted to him:

"Come with us, young fellow! well now, don't we do anything for this old country of ours?"

The dandy fled.

Chapter V

PREPARATIONS

THE JOURNALS OF THE DAY WHICH SAID THAT THAT *NEARLY IMPREGNABLE STRUCTURE*, OF THE barricade of the Rue de la Chanvrerie, as they call it, reached to the level of the first floor, were mistaken. The fact is, that it did not exceed an average height of six or seven feet. It was built in such a manner that the combatants could, at their will, either disappear behind it or dominate the barrier and even scale its crest by means of a quadruple row of paving-stones placed on top of each other and arranged as steps in the interior. On the outside, the front of the barricade, composed of piles of paving-stones and casks bound together by beams and planks, which were entangled in the wheels of Anceau's dray and of the overturned omnibus, had a bristling and inextricable aspect.

An aperture large enough to allow a man to pass through had been made between the wall of the houses and the extremity of the barricade which was furthest from the wine-shop, so that an exit was possible at this point. The pole of the omnibus was placed upright and held up with ropes, and a red flag, fastened to this pole, floated over the barricade.

The little Mondétour barricade, hidden behind the wine-shop building, was not visible. The two barricades united formed a veritable redoubt. Enjolras and Courfeyrac had not thought fit to barricade the other fragment of the Rue Mondétour which opens through the Rue des Prêcheurs an issue into the Halles, wishing, no doubt, to preserve a possible communication with the outside, and not entertaining much fear of an attack through the dangerous and difficult street of the Rue des Prêcheurs.

With the exception of this issue which was left free, and which constituted what Folard in his strategical style would have termed a branch, and taking into account, also, the narrow cutting arranged on the Rue de la Chanvrerie, the interior of the barricade, where the wine-shop formed a salient angle, presented an irregular square, closed on all sides. There existed an interval of twenty paces between the grand barrier and the lofty houses which formed the background of the street, so that one might say that the barricade rested on these houses, all inhabited, but closed from top to bottom.

All this work was performed without any hindrance, in less than an hour, and without this handful of bold men seeing a single bear-skin cap or a single bayonet make their appearance. The very bourgeois who still ventured at this hour of riot to enter the Rue Saint-Denis, cast a glance at the Rue de la Chanvrerie, caught sight of the barricade, and redoubled their pace.

The two barricades being finished, and the flag run up, a table was dragged out of the wine-shop; and Courfeyrac mounted on the table. Enjolras brought the square coffer, and Courfeyrac opened it. This coffer was filled with cartridges. When the mob saw the cartridges, a tremor ran through the bravest, and a momentary silence ensued.

Courfeyrac distributed them with a smile.

Each one received thirty cartridges. Many had powder, and set about making others with the bullets which they had run. As for the barrel of powder, it stood on a table on one side, near the door, and was held in reserve.

The alarm beat which ran through all Paris, did not cease, but it had finally come to be nothing more than a monotonous noise to which they no longer paid any attention. This noise retreated at times, and again drew near, with melancholy undulations.

They loaded the guns and carbines, all together, without haste, with solemn gravity. Enjolras went and stationed three sentinels outside the barricades, one in the Rue de la Chanvrerie, the second in the Rue des Prêcheurs, the third at the corner of the Rue de la Petite -Truanderie.

Then, the barricades having been built, the posts assigned, the guns loaded, the sentinels stationed, they waited, alone in those redoubtable streets through which no one passed any longer, surrounded by those dumb houses which seemed dead and in which no human movement palpitated, enveloped in the deepening shades of twilight which was drawing on, in the midst of that silence through which something could be felt advancing, and which had about it something tragic and terrifying, isolated, armed, determined, and tranquil.

Chapter VI

WAITING

DURING THOSE HOURS OF WAITING, WHAT DID THEY DO?
    We must needs tell, since this is a matter of history.

While the men made bullets and the women lint, while a large sauce-pan of melted brass and lead, destined to the bullet-mold smoked over a glowing brazier, while the sentinels watched, weapon in hand, on the barricade, while Enjolras, whom it was impossible to divert, kept an eye on the sentinels, Combeferre, Courfeyrac, Jean Prouvaire, Feuilly, Bossuet, Joly, Bahorel, and some others, sought each other out and united as in the most peaceful days of their conversations in their student life, and, in one corner of this wine-shop which had been converted into a casement, a couple of paces distant from the redoubt which they had built, with their carbines loaded and primed resting against the backs of their chairs, these fine young fellows, so close to a supreme hour, began to recite love verses.

What verses? These:

> Vous rappelez-vous notre douce vie,
>   Lorsque nous étions si jeunes tous deux,
> Et que nous n'avions au cœur d'autre envie
>   Que d'être bien mis et d'être amoureux,
>
> Lorsqu'en ajoutant votre age à mon age,
>   Nous ne comptions pas à deux quarante ans,
> Et que, dans notre humble et petit ménage,
>   Tout, même l'hiver, nous était printemps?
>
> Beaux jours! Manuel etait fier et sage,
>   Paris s'asseyait à de saints banquets,
> Foy lançait la foudre, et votre corsage
>   Avait une épingle o je me piquais.

Tout vous contemplait. Avocat sans causes,
  Quand je vous menais au Prado dîner,
Vous étiez jolie au point que les roses
  Me faisaient l'effet de se retourner.

Je les entendais dire: Est elle belle!
  Comme elle sent bon! Quels cheveux à flots!
Sous son mantelet elle cache une aile,
  Son bonnet charmant est à peine éclos.

J'errais avec toi, pressant ton bras souple.
  Les passants croyaient que l'amour charmé
Avait marié, dans notre heureux couple,
  Le doux mois d'avril au beau mois de mai.

Nous vivions cachés, contents, porte close,
  Dévorant l'amour, bon fruit défendu,
Ma bouche n'avait pas dit une chose
  Que déjà ton cœur avait répondu.

La Sorbonne était l'endroit bucolique
  Où je t'adorais du soir au matin.
C'est ainsi qu'une âme amoureuse applique
  La carte du Tendre au pays Latin.

Ô place Maubert! ô place Dauphine!
  Quand, dans le taudis frais et printanier,
Tu tirais ton bas sur ton jambe fine,
  Je voyais un astre au fond du grenier.

J'ai fort lu Platon, mais rien ne m'en reste;
  Mieux que Malebranche et que Lamennais,
Tu me démontrais la bonté céleste
  Avec une fleur que tu me donnais.

Je t'obéissais, tu m'étais soumise;
  O grenier doré! te lacer! te voir
Aller et venir dès l'aube en chemise,
  Mirant ton jeune front à ton vieux miroir.

Et qui donc pourrait perde la mémoire
  De ces temps d'aurore et de firmament,
De rubans, de fleurs, de gaze et de moire,
  Où l'amour bégaye un argot charmant?

Nos jardins étaient un pot de tulipe;
  Tu masquais la vitre avec un jupon;
Je prenais le bol de terre de pipe,
  Et je te donnais le tasse en japon.

Et ces grands malheurs qui nous faisaient rire!
　　　Ton manchon brûlé, ton boa perdu!
Et ce cher portrait du divin Shakespeare
　　　Qu'un soir pour souper nons avons vendu!

J'étais mendiant et toi charitable.
　　　Je baisais au vol tes bras frais et ronds.
Dante in folio nous servait de table
　　　Pour manger gaîment un cent de marrons.

La première fois qu'en mon joyeux bouge
　　　Je pris un baiser a ton lèvre en feu,
Quand tu t'en allais décoiffée et rouge,
　　　Je restai tout pâle et je crus en Dieu!

Te rappelles-tu nos bonheurs sans nombre,
　　　Et tous ces fichus changés en chiffons?
Oh que de soupirs, de nos cœurs pleins d'ombre,
　　　Se sont envolés dans les cieux profonds![1]

The hour, the spot, these souvenirs of youth recalled, a few stars which began to twinkle in the sky, the funeral repose of those deserted streets, the imminence of the inexorable adventure which was in preparation, gave a pathetic charm to these verses murmured in a low tone in the dusk by Jean Prouvaire, who, as we have said, was a gentle poet.

1. Do you remember our sweet life, when we were both so young, and when we had no other desire in our hearts than to be well dressed and in love? When, by adding your age to my age, we could not count forty years between us, and when, in our humble and tiny household, everything was spring to us even in winter. Fair days! Manuel was proud and wise, Paris sat at sacred banquets, Foy launched thunderbolts, and your corsage had a pin on which I pricked myself. Everything gazed upon you. A briefless lawyer when I took you to the Prado to dine, you were so beautiful that the roses seemed to me to turn round, and I heard them say: Is she not beautiful! How good she smells! What billowing hair! Beneath her mantle she hides a wing. Her charming bonnet is hardly unfolded. I wandered with thee, pressing thy supple arm. The passers-by thought that love bewitched had wedded, in our happy couple, the gentle month of April to the fair month of May. We lived concealed, content, with closed doors, devouring love, that sweet forbidden fruit. My mouth had not uttered a thing when thy heart had already responded. The Sorbonne was the bucolic spot where I adored thee from eve till morn. 'Tis thus that an amorous soul applies the chart of the Tender to the Latin country. O Place Maubert! O Place Dauphine! When in the fresh spring-like hut thou didst draw thy stocking on thy delicate leg, I saw a star in the depths of the garret. I have read a great deal of Plato, but nothing of it remains by me; better than Malebranche and than Lamennais thou didst demonstrate to me celestial goodness with a flower which thou gavest to me, I obeyed thee, thou didst submit to me; oh gilded garret! to lace thee! to behold thee going and coming from dawn in thy chemise, gazing at thy young brow in thine ancient mirror! And who, then, would forego the memory of those days of aurora and the firmament, of flowers, of gauze and of moire, when love stammers a charming slang? Our gardens consisted of a pot of tulips; thou didst mask the window with thy petticoat; I took the earthenware bowl and I gave thee the Japanese cup. And those great misfortunes which made us laugh! Thy cuff scorched, thy boa lost! And that dear portrait of the divine Shakespeare which we sold one evening that we might sup! I was a beggar and thou wert charitable. I kissed thy fresh round arms in haste. A folio Danto served us as a table on which to eat merrily a centime's worth of chestnuts. The first time that, in my joyous den, I snatched a kiss from thy fiery lip, when thou wentest forth, disheveled and blushing, I turned deathly pale and I believed in God. Dost thou recall our innumerable joys, and all those fichus changed to rags? Oh! what sighs from the hearts full of gloom fluttered forth to the heavenly depths!

In the meantime, a lamp had been lighted in the small barricade, and in the large one, one of those wax torches such as are to be met with on Shrove-Tuesday in front of vehicles loaded with masks, on their way to la Courtille. These torches, as the reader has seen, came from the Faubourg Saint-Antoine.

The torch had been placed in a sort of cage of paving-stones closed on three sides to shelter it from the wind, and disposed in such a fashion that all the light fell on the flag. The street and the barricade remained sunk in gloom, and nothing was to be seen except the red flag formidably illuminated as by an enormous dark-lantern.

This light enhanced the scarlet of the flag, with an indescribable and terrible purple.

Chapter VII

THE MAN RECRUITED IN THE RUE DES BILLETTES

NIGHT WAS FULLY COME, NOTHING MADE ITS APPEARANCE. ALL THAT THEY HEARD WAS CONfused noises, and at intervals, fusillades; but these were rare, badly sustained and distant. This respite, which was thus prolonged, was a sign that the Government was taking its time, and collecting its forces. These fifty men were waiting for sixty thousand.

Enjolras felt attacked by that impatience which seizes on strong souls on the threshold of redoubtable events. He went in search of Gavroche, who had set to making cartridges in the taproom, by the dubious light of two candles placed on the counter by way of precaution, on account of the powder which was scattered on the tables. These two candles cast no gleam outside. The insurgents had, moreover, taken pains not to have any light in the upper stories.

Gavroche was deeply preoccupied at that moment, but not precisely with his cartridges. The man of the Rue des Billettes had just entered the tap-room and had seated himself at the table which was the least lighted. A musket of large model had fallen to his share, and he held it between his legs. Gavroche, who had been, up to that moment, distracted by a hundred "amusing" things, had not even seen this man.

When he entered, Gavroche followed him mechanically with his eyes, admiring his gun; then, all at once, when the man was seated, the street urchin sprang to his feet. Anyone who had spied upon that man up to that moment, would have seen that he was observing everything in the barricade and in the band of insurgents, with singular attention; but, from the moment when he had entered this room, he had fallen into a sort of brown study, and no longer seemed to see anything that was going on. The gamin approached this pensive personage, and began to step around him on tiptoe, as one walks in the vicinity of a person whom one is afraid of waking. At the same time, over his childish countenance, which was, at once so impudent and so serious, so giddy and so profound, so gay and so heart-breaking, passed all those grimaces of an old man which signify: Ah bah! impossible! My sight is bad! I am dreaming! can this be? no, it is not! but yes! why, no! etc. Gavroche balanced on his heels, clenched both fists in his pockets, moved his neck around like a bird, expended in a gigantic pout all the sagacity of his lower lip. He was astounded, uncertain, incredulous, convinced, dazzled. He had the mien of the chief of the eunuchs in the slave mart, discovering a Venus among the blowsy females, and the air of an amateur recognizing a Raphael in a heap of daubs. His whole being was at work, the instinct which scents out, and the intelligence which combines. It was evident that a great event had happened in Gavroche's life.

It was at the most intense point of this preoccupation that Enjolras accosted him.

"You are small," said Enjolras, "you will not be seen. Go out of the barricade, slip along close to the houses, skirmish about a bit in the streets, and come back and tell me what is going on."

Gavroche raised himself on his haunches.

"So the little chaps are good for something! that's very lucky! I'll go! In the meanwhile, trust to the little fellows, and distrust the big ones." And Gavroche, raising his head and lowering his voice, added, as he indicated the man of the Rue des Billettes:

"Do you see that big fellow there?"

"Well?"

"He's a police spy."

"Are you sure of it?"

"It isn't two weeks since he pulled me off the cornice of the Port Royal, where I was taking the air, by my ear."

Enjolras hastily quitted the urchin and murmured a few words in a very low tone to a long-shoreman from the wine-docks who chanced to be at hand. The man left the room, and returned almost immediately, accompanied by three others. The four men, four porters with broad shoulders, went and placed themselves without doing anything to attract his attention, behind the table on which the man of the Rue des Billettes was leaning with his elbows. They were evidently ready to hurl themselves upon him.

Then Enjolras approached the man and demanded of him:

"Who are you?"

At this abrupt query, the man started. He plunged his gaze deep into Enjolras's clear eyes and appeared to grasp the latter's meaning. He smiled with a smile than which nothing more disdainful, more energetic, and more resolute could be seen in the world, and replied with haughty gravity:

"I see what it is. Well, yes!"

"You are a police spy?"

"I am an agent of the authorities."

"And your name?"

"Javert."

Enjolras made a sign to the four men. In the twinkling of an eye, before Javert had time to turn round, he was collared, thrown down, pinioned and searched.

They found on him a little round card pasted between two pieces of glass, and bearing on one side the arms of France, engraved, and with this motto: *Supervision and vigilance,* and on the other this note: "JAVERT, inspector of police, aged fifty-two," and the signature of the Prefect of Police of that day, M. Gisquet.

Besides this, he had his watch and his purse, which contained several gold pieces. They left him his purse and his watch. Under the watch, at the bottom of his fob, they felt and seized a paper in an envelope, which Enjolras unfolded, and on which he read these five lines, written in the very hand of the Prefect of Police:

"As soon as his political mission is accomplished, Inspector Javert will make sure, by special supervision, whether it is true that the malefactors have instituted intrigues on the right bank of the Seine, near the Jena bridge."

The search ended, they lifted Javert to his feet, bound his arms behind his back, and fastened him to that celebrated post in the middle of the room which had formerly given the wine-shop its name.

Gavroche, who had looked on at the whole of this scene and had approved of everything with a silent toss of his head, stepped up to Javert and said to him:

"It's the mouse who has caught the cat."

All this was so rapidly executed, that it was all over when those about the wine-shop noticed it.

Javert had not uttered a single cry.

At the sight of Javert bound to the post, Courfeyrac, Bossuet, Joly, Combeferre, and the men scattered over the two barricades came running up.

Javert, with his back to the post, and so surrounded with ropes that he could not make a movement, raised his head with the intrepid serenity of the man who has never lied.

"He is a police spy," said Enjolras.

And turning to Javert: "You will be shot ten minutes before the barricade is taken."

Javert replied in his most imperious tone:

"Why not at once?"

"We are saving our powder."

"Then finish the business with a blow from a knife."

"Spy," said the handsome Enjolras, "we are judges and not assassins."

Then he called Gavroche:

"Here you! go about your business! Do what I told you!"

"I'm going!" cried Gavroche.

And halting as he was on the point of setting out:

"By the way, you will give me his gun!" and he added: "I leave you the musician, but I want the clarinet."

The gamin made the military salute and passed gaily through the opening in the large barricade.

Chapter VIII

MANY INTERROGATION POINTS WITH REGARD TO A CERTAIN LE CABUC WHOSE NAME MAY NOT HAVE BEEN LE CABUC

THE TRAGIC PICTURE WHICH WE HAVE UNDERTAKEN WOULD NOT BE COMPLETE, THE READER would not see those grand moments of social birth-pangs in a revolutionary birth, which contain convulsion mingled with effort, in their exact and real relief, were we to omit, in the sketch here outlined, an incident full of epic and savage horror which occurred almost immediately after Gavroche's departure.

Mobs, as the reader knows, are like a snowball, and collect as they roll along, a throng of tumultuous men. These men do not ask each other whence they come. Among the passers-by who had joined the rabble led by Enjolras, Combeferre, and Courfeyrac, there had been a person wearing the jacket of a street porter, which was very threadbare on the shoulders, who gesticulated and vociferated, and who had the look of a drunken savage. This man, whose name or nickname was Le Cabuc, and who was, moreover, an utter stranger to those who pretended to know him, was very drunk, or assumed the appearance of being so, and had seated himself with several others at a table which they had dragged outside of the wine-shop. This Cabuc, while making those who vied with him drunk, seemed to be examining with a thoughtful air the large house at the extremity of the barricade, whose five stories commanded the whole street and faced the Rue Saint-Denis. All at once he exclaimed:

"Do you know, comrades, it is from that house yonder that we must fire. When we are at the windows, the deuce is in it if anyone can advance into the street!"

"Yes, but the house is closed," said one of the drinkers.

"Let us knock!"

"They will not open."

"Let us break in the door!"

Le Cabuc runs to the door, which had a very massive knocker, and knocks. The door opens not. He strikes a second blow. No one answers. A third stroke. The same silence.

"Is there anyone here?" shouts Cabuc.

Nothing stirs.

Then he seizes a gun and begins to batter the door with the butt end.

It was an ancient alley door, low, vaulted, narrow, solid, entirely of oak, lined on the inside with a sheet of iron and iron stays, a genuine prison postern. The blows from the butt end of the gun made the house tremble, but did not shake the door.

Nevertheless, it is probable that the inhabitants were disturbed, for a tiny, square window was finally seen to open on the third story, and at this aperture appeared the reverend and terrified face of a gray-haired old man, who was the porter, and who held a candle.

The man who was knocking paused.

"Gentlemen," said the porter, "what do you want?"

"Open!" said Cabuc.

"That cannot be, gentlemen."

"Open, nevertheless."

"Impossible, gentlemen."

Le Cabuc took his gun and aimed at the porter; but as he was below, and as it was very dark, the porter did not see him.

"Will you open, yes or no?"

"No, gentlemen."

"Do you say no?"

"I say no, my good—"

The porter did not finish. The shot was fired; the ball entered under his chin and came out at the nape of his neck, after traversing the jugular vein.

The old man fell back without a sigh. The candle fell and was extinguished, and nothing more was to be seen except a motionless head lying on the sill of the small window, and a little whitish smoke which floated off toward the roof.

"There!" said Le Cabuc, dropping the butt end of his gun to the pavement.

He had hardly uttered this word, when he felt a hand laid on his shoulder with the weight of an eagle's talon, and he heard a voice saying to him:

"On your knees."

The murderer turned round and saw before him Enjolras's cold, white face.

Enjolras held a pistol in his hand.

He had hastened up at the sound of the discharge.

He had seized Cabuc's collar, blouse, shirt, and suspender with his left hand.

"On your knees!" he repeated.

And, with an imperious motion, the frail young man of twenty years bent the thickset and sturdy porter like a reed, and brought him to his knees in the mire.

Le Cabuc attempted to resist, but he seemed to have been seized by a superhuman hand.

Enjolras, pale, with bare neck and disheveled hair, and his woman's face, had about him at that moment something of the antique Themis. His dilated nostrils, his downcast eyes, gave to his implacable Greek profile that expression of wrath and that expression of Chastity which, as the ancient world viewed the matter, befit Justice.

The whole barricade hastened up, then all ranged themselves in a circle at a distance, feeling that it was impossible to utter a word in the presence of the thing which they were about to behold.

Le Cabuc, vanquished, no longer tried to struggle, and trembled in every limb.

Enjolras released him and drew out his watch.

"Collect yourself," said he. "Think or pray. You have one minute."

"Mercy!" murmured the murderer; then he dropped his head and stammered a few inarticulate oaths.

Enjolras never took his eyes off of him: he allowed a minute to pass, then he replaced his watch in his fob. That done, he grasped Le Cabuc by the hair, as the latter coiled himself into a ball at his knees and shrieked, and placed the muzzle of the pistol to his ear. Many of those intrepid men, who had so tranquilly entered upon the most terrible of adventures, turned aside their heads.

An explosion was heard, the assassin fell to the pavement face downwards.

Enjolras straightened himself up, and cast a convinced and severe glance around him. Then he spurned the corpse with his foot and said:

"Throw that outside."

Three men raised the body of the unhappy wretch, which was still agitated by the last mechanical convulsions of the life that had fled, and flung it over the little barricade into the Rue Mondétour.

Enjolras was thoughtful. It is impossible to say what grandiose shadows slowly spread over his redoubtable serenity. All at once he raised his voice.

A silence fell upon them.

"Citizens," said Enjolras, "what that man did is frightful, what I have done is horrible. He killed, therefore I killed him. I had to do it, because insurrection must have its discipline. Assassination is even more of a crime here than elsewhere; we are under the eyes of the Revolution, we are the priests of the Republic, we are the victims of duty, and must not be possible to slander our combat. I have, therefore, tried that man, and condemned him to death. As for myself, constrained as I am to do what I have done, and yet abhorring it, I have judged myself also, and you shall soon see to what I have condemned myself."

Those who listened to him shuddered.

"We will share thy fate," cried Combeferre.

"So be it," replied Enjolras. "One word more. In executing this man, I have obeyed necessity; but necessity is a monster of the old world, necessity's name is Fatality. Now, the law of progress is, that monsters shall disappear before the angels, and that Fatality shall vanish before Fraternity. It is a bad moment to pronounce the word love. No matter, I do pronounce it. And I glorify it. Love, the future is thine. Death, I make use of thee, but I hate thee. Citizens, in the future there will be neither darkness nor thunderbolts; neither ferocious ignorance, nor bloody retaliation. As there will be no more Satan, there will be no more Michael. In the future no one will kill anyone else, the earth will beam with radiance, the human race will love. The day will come, citizens, when all will be concord, harmony, light, joy and life; it will come, and it is in order that it may come that we are about to die."

Enjolras ceased. His virgin lips closed; and he remained for some time standing on the spot where he had shed blood, in marble immobility. His staring eye caused those about him to speak in low tones.

Jean Prouvaire and Combeferre pressed each other's hands silently, and, leaning against each other in an angle of the barricade, they watched with an admiration in which there was some compassion, that grave young man, executioner and priest, composed of light, like crystal, and also of rock.

Let us say at once that later on, after the action, when the bodies were taken to the morgue and searched, a police agent's card was found on Le Cabuc. The author of this book had in his hands, in 1848, the special report on this subject made to the Prefect of Police in 1832.

We will add, that if we are to believe a tradition of the police, which is strange but probably well founded, Le Cabuc was Claquesous. The fact is, that dating from the death of Le Cabuc, there was no longer any question of Claquesous. Claquesous had nowhere left any trace of his disappearance; he would seem to have amalgamated himself with the invisible. His life had been all shadows, his end was night.

The whole insurgent group was still under the influence of the emotion of that tragic case which had been so quickly tried and so quickly terminated, when Courfeyrac again beheld on the barricade, the small young man who had inquired of him that morning for Marius.

This lad, who had a bold and reckless air, had come by night to join the insurgents.

BOOK THIRTEENTH

MARIUS ENTERS THE SHADOW

Chapter I

FROM THE RUE PLUMET TO THE QUARTIER SAINT-DENIS

THE VOICE WHICH HAD SUMMONED MARIUS THROUGH THE TWILIGHT TO THE BARRICADE OF THE Rue de la Chanvrerie, had produced on him the effect of the voice of destiny. He wished to die; the opportunity presented itself; he knocked at the door of the tomb, a hand in the darkness offered him the key. These melancholy openings which take place in the gloom before despair, are tempting. Marius thrust aside the bar which had so often allowed him to pass, emerged from the garden, and said: "I will go."

Mad with grief, no longer conscious of anything fixed or solid in his brain, incapable of accepting anything thenceforth of fate after those two months passed in the intoxication of youth and love, overwhelmed at once by all the reveries of despair, he had but one desire remaining, to make a speedy end of all.

He set out at rapid pace. He found himself most opportunely armed, as he had Javert's pistols with him.

The young man of whom he thought that he had caught a glimpse, had vanished from his sight in the street.

Marius, who had emerged from the Rue Plumet by the boulevard, traversed the Esplanade and the bridge of the Invalides, the Champs Élysées, the Place Louis XV, and reached the Rue de Rivoli. The shops were open there, the gas was burning under the arcades, women were making their purchases in the stalls, people were eating ices in the Café Laiter, and nibbling small cakes at the English pastry-cook's shop. Only a few posting-chaises were setting out at a gallop from the Hôtel des Princes and the Hôtel Meurice.

Marius entered the Rue Saint-Honoré through the Passage Delorme. There the shops were closed, the merchants were chatting in front of their half-open doors, people were walking about, the street-lanterns were lighted, beginning with the first floor, all the windows were lighted as usual. There was cavalry on the Place du Palais-Royal.

Marius followed the Rue Saint-Honoré. In proportion as he left the Palais-Royal behind him, there were fewer lighted windows, the shops were fast shut, no one was chatting on the thresholds, the street grew somber, and, at the same time, the crowd increased in density. For the passers-by now amounted to a crowd. No one could be seen to speak in this throng, and yet there arose from it a dull, deep murmur.

Near the fountain of the Arbre-Sec, there were "assemblages" motionless and gloomy groups which were to those who went and came as stones in the midst of running water.

At the entrance to the Rue des Prouvaires, the crowd no longer walked. It formed a resisting, massive, solid, compact, almost impenetrable block of people who were huddled together, and conversing in low tones. There were hardly any black coats or round hats now, but smock frocks, blouses, caps, and bristling and cadaverous heads. This multitude undulated confusedly in the nocturnal gloom. Its whisperings had the hoarse accent of a vibration. Although not one of them was walking, a dull trampling was audible in the mire. Beyond this dense portion of the throng, in the Rue du Roule, in the Rue des Prouvaires, and in the extension of the Rue Saint-Honoré, there was no longer a single window in which a candle was burning. Only the solitary and diminishing rows of lanterns could be seen vanishing into the street in the distance. The lanterns of that date resembled large red stars, hanging to ropes, and shed upon the pavement a shadow which had the form of a huge spider. These streets were not deserted. There could be descried piles of guns, moving bayonets, and troops bivouacking. No curious observer passed that limit. There circulation ceased. There the rabble ended and the army began.

Marius willed with the will of a man who hopes no more. He had been summoned, he must go. He found a means to traverse the throng and to pass the bivouac of the troops, he shunned the patrols, he avoided the sentinels. He made a circuit, reached the Rue de Béthisy, and directed his course toward the Halles. At the corner of the Rue des Bourdonnais, there were no longer any lanterns.

After having passed the zone of the crowd, he had passed the limits of the troops; he found himself in something startling. There was no longer a passer-by, no longer a soldier, no longer a light, there was no one; solitude, silence, night, I know not what chill which seized hold upon one. Entering a street was like entering a cellar.

He continued to advance.

He took a few steps. Someone passed close to him at a run. Was it a man? Or a woman? Were there many of them? he could not have told. It had passed and vanished.

Proceeding from circuit to circuit, he reached a lane which he judged to be the Rue de la Poterie; near the middle of this street, he came in contact with an obstacle. He extended his hands. It was an overturned wagon; his foot recognized pools of water, gullies, and paving-stones scattered and piled up. A barricade had been begun there and abandoned. He climbed over the stones and found himself on the other side of the barrier. He walked very near the street-posts, and guided himself along the walls of the houses. A little beyond the barricade, it seemed to him that he could make out something white in front of him. He approached, it took on a form. It was two white horses; the horses of the omnibus harnessed by Bossuet in the morning, who had been straying at random all day from street to street, and had finally halted there, with the weary patience of brutes who no more understand the actions of men, than man understands the actions of Providence.

Marius left the horses behind him. As he was approaching a street which seemed to him to be the Rue du Contrat-Social, a shot coming no one knows whence, and traversing the darkness at random, whistled close by him, and the bullet pierced a brass shaving-dish suspended above his head over a hair-dresser's shop. This pierced shaving-dish was still to be seen in 1848, in the Rue du Contrat-Social, at the corner of the pillars of the market.

This shot still betokened life. From that instant forth he encountered nothing more.

The whole of this itinerary resembled a descent of black steps.

Nevertheless, Marius pressed forward.

Chapter II

AN OWL'S VIEW OF PARIS

A BEING WHO COULD HAVE HOVERED OVER PARIS THAT NIGHT WITH THE WING OF THE BAT OR the owl would have had beneath his eyes a gloomy spectacle.

All that old quarter of the Halles, which is like a city within a city, through which run the Rues Saint-Denis and Saint-Martin, where a thousand lanes cross, and of which the insurgents had made their redoubt and their stronghold, would have appeared to him like a dark and enormous cavity hollowed out in the center of Paris. There the glance fell into an abyss. Thanks to the broken lanterns, thanks to the closed windows, there all radiance, all life, all sound, all movement ceased. The invisible police of the insurrection were on the watch everywhere, and maintained order, that is to say, night. The necessary tactics of insurrection are to drown small numbers in a vast obscurity, to multiply every combatant by the possibilities which that obscurity contains. At dusk, every window where a candle was burning received a shot. The light was extinguished, sometimes the inhabitant was killed. Hence nothing was stirring. There was nothing but fright, mourning, stupor in the houses; and in the streets, a sort of sacred horror. Not even the long rows of windows and stores, the indentations of the chimneys, and the roofs, and the vague reflections which are cast back by the wet and muddy pavements, were visible. An eye cast upward at that mass of shadows might, perhaps, have caught a glimpse here and there, at intervals, of indistinct gleams which brought out broken and eccentric lines, and profiles of singular buildings, something like the lights which go and come in ruins; it was at such points that the barricades were situated. The rest was a lake of obscurity, foggy, heavy, and funereal, above which, in motionless and melancholy outlines, rose the tower of Saint-Jacques, the church of Saint-Merry, and two or three more of those grand edifices of which man makes giants and the night makes phantoms.

All around this deserted and disquieting labyrinth, in the quarters where the Parisian circulation had not been annihilated, and where a few street-lanterns still burned, the aerial observer might have distinguished the metallic gleam of swords and bayonets, the dull rumble of artillery, and the swarming of silent battalions whose ranks were swelling from minute to minute; a formidable girdle which was slowly drawing in and around the insurrection.

The invested quarter was no longer anything more than a monstrous cavern; everything there appeared to be asleep or motionless, and, as we have just seen, any street which one might come to offered nothing but darkness.

A wild darkness, full of traps, full of unseen and formidable shocks, into which it was alarming to penetrate, and in which it was terrible to remain, where those who entered shivered before those whom they awaited, where those who waited shuddered before those who were coming. Invisible combatants were entrenched at every corner of the street; snares of the sepulcher concealed in the density of night. All was over. No more light was to be hoped for, henceforth, except the lightning of guns, no further encounter except the abrupt and rapid apparition of death. Where? How? When? No one knew, but it was certain and inevitable. In this place which had been marked out for the struggle, the Government and the insurrection, the National Guard, and popular societies, the bourgeois and the uprising, groping their way, were about to come into contact. The necessity was the same for both. The only possible issue thenceforth was to emerge thence killed or conquerors. A situation so extreme, an obscurity so powerful, that the most timid felt themselves seized with resolution, and the most daring with terror.

Moreover, on both sides, the fury, the rage, and the determination were equal. For the one party, to advance meant death, and no one dreamed of retreating; for the other, to remain meant death, and no one dreamed of flight.

It was indispensable that all should be ended on the following day, that triumph should rest either here or there, that the insurrection should prove itself a revolution or a skirmish. The Government understood this as well as the parties; the most insignificant bourgeois felt it. Hence a thought of anguish which mingled with the impenetrable gloom of this quarter where all was at the point of being decided; hence a redoubled anxiety around that silence whence a catastrophe was on the point of emerging. Here only one sound was audible, a sound as heartrending as the death-rattle, as menacing as a malediction, the tocsin of Saint-Merry. Nothing could be more blood-curdling than the clamor of that wild and desperate bell, wailing amid the shadows.

As it often happens, nature seemed to have fallen into accord with what men were about to do. Nothing disturbed the harmony of the whole effect. The stars had disappeared, heavy clouds filled the horizon with their melancholy folds. A black sky rested on these dead streets, as though an immense winding-sheet were being outspread over this immense tomb.

While a battle that was still wholly political was in preparation in the same locality which had already witnessed so many revolutionary events, while youth, the secret associations, the schools, in the name of principles, and the middle classes, in the name of interests, were approaching preparatory to dashing themselves together, clasping and throwing each other, while each one hastened and invited the last and decisive hour of the crisis, far away and quite outside of this fatal quarter, in the most profound depths of the unfathomable cavities of that wretched old Paris which disappears under the splendor of happy and opulent Paris, the somber voice of the people could be heard giving utterance to a dull roar.

A fearful and sacred voice which is composed of the roar of the brute and of the word of God, which terrifies the weak and which warns the wise, which comes both from below like the voice of the lion, and from on high like the voice of the thunder.

Chapter III

THE EXTREME EDGE

MARIUS HAD REACHED THE HALLES.

There everything was still calmer, more obscure and more motionless than in the neighboring streets. One would have said that the glacial peace of the sepulcher had sprung forth from the earth and had spread over the heavens.

Nevertheless, a red glow brought out against this black background the lofty roofs of the houses which barred the Rue de la Chanvrerie on the Saint-Eustache side. It was the reflection of the torch which was burning in the Corinthe barricade. Marius directed his steps toward that red light. It had drawn him to the Marché-aux-Poirées, and he caught a glimpse of the dark mouth of the Rue des Prêcheurs. He entered it. The insurgents' sentinel, who was guarding the other end, did not see him. He felt that he was very close to that which he had come in search of, and he walked on tiptoe. In this manner he reached the elbow of that short section of the Rue Mondétour which was, as the reader will remember, the only communication which Enjolras had preserved with the outside world. At the corner of the last house, on his left, he thrust his head forward, and looked into the fragment of the Rue Mondétour.

A little beyond the angle of the lane and the Rue de la Chanvrerie which cast a broad curtain of shadow, in which he was himself engulfed, he perceived some light on the pavement, a bit of the wine-shop, and beyond, a flickering lamp within a sort of shapeless wall, and men crouching down with guns on their knees. All this was ten fathoms distant from him. It was the interior of the barricade.

The houses which bordered the lane on the right concealed the rest of the wine-shop, the large barricade, and the flag from him.

Marius had but a step more to take.

Then the unhappy young man seated himself on a post, folded his arms, and fell to thinking about his father.

He thought of that heroic Colonel Pontmercy, who had been so proud a soldier, who had guarded the frontier of France under the Republic, and had touched the frontier of Asia under Napoleon, who had beheld Genoa, Alexandria, Milan, Turin, Madrid, Vienna, Dresden, Berlin, Moscow, who had left on all the victorious battlefields of Europe drops of that same blood, which he, Marius, had in his veins, who had grown gray before his time in discipline and command, who had lived with his sword-belt buckled, his epaulets falling on his breast, his cockade blackened with powder, his brow furrowed with his helmet, in barracks, in camp, in the bivouac, in ambulances, and who, at the expiration of twenty years, had returned from the great wars with a scarred cheek, a smiling countenance, tranquil, admirable, pure as a child, having done everything for France and nothing against her.

He said to himself that his day had also come now, that his hour had struck, that following his father, he too was about to show himself brave, intrepid, bold, to run to meet the bullets, to offer his breast to bayonets, to shed his blood, to seek the enemy, to seek death, that he was about to wage war in his turn and descend to the field of battle, and that the field of battle upon which he was to descend was the street, and that the war in which he was about to engage was civil war!

He beheld civil war laid open like a gulf before him, and into this he was about to fall. Then he shuddered.

He thought of his father's sword, which his grandfather had sold to a second-hand dealer, and which he had so mournfully regretted. He said to himself that that chaste and valiant sword had done well to escape from him, and to depart in wrath into the gloom; that if it had thus fled, it was because it was intelligent and because it had foreseen the future; that it had had a presentiment of this rebellion, the war of the gutters, the war of the pavements, fusillades through cellar-windows, blows given and received in the rear; it was because, coming from Marengo and Friedland, it did not wish to go to the Rue de la Chanvrerie; it was because, after what it had done with the father, it did not wish to do this for the son! He told himself that if that sword were there, if after taking possession of it at his father's pillow, he had dared to take it and carry it off for this combat of darkness between Frenchmen in the streets, it would assuredly have scorched his hands and burst out aflame before his eyes, like the sword of the angel! He told himself that it was fortunate that it was not there and that it had disappeared, that that was well, that that was just, that his grandfather had been the true guardian of his father's glory, and that it was far better that the colonel's sword should be sold at auction, sold to the old-clothes man, thrown among the old junk, than that it should, to-day, wound the side of his country.

And then he fell to weeping bitterly.

This was horrible. But what was he to do! Live without Cosette he could not. Since she was gone, he must needs die. Had he not given her his word of honor that he would die? She had gone knowing that; this meant that it pleased her that Marius should die. And then, it was clear that she no longer loved him, since she had departed thus without warning, without a word, without a letter, although she knew his address! What was the good of living, and why should he live now? And then, what! should he retreat after going so far! should he flee from danger after having approached it! should he slip away after having come and peeped into the barricade! slip away, all in a tremble, saying: "After all, I have had enough of it as it is. I have seen it, that suffices, this is civil war, and I shall take my leave!" Should he abandon his friends who were expecting him! Who were in need of him possibly! who were a mere handful against an army! Should he be untrue at once to his love, to country, to his word! Should he give to his cowardice the pretext of patriotism! But this was impossible, and if the phantom of his father was there in the gloom, and beheld him retreating, he would beat him on the loins with the flat of his sword, and shout to him: "March on, you poltroon!"

Thus a prey to the conflicting movements of his thoughts, he dropped his head.

All at once he raised it. A sort of splendid rectification had just been effected in his mind. There is a widening of the sphere of thought which is peculiar to the vicinity of the grave; it makes one see clearly to be near death. The vision of the action into which he felt that he was, perhaps, on the point of entering, appeared to him no more as lamentable, but as superb. The war of the street was suddenly transfigured by some unfathomable inward working of his soul, before the eye of his thought. All the tumultuous interrogation points of reverie recurred to him in throngs, but without troubling him. He left none of them unanswered.

Let us see, why should his father be indignant? Are there not cases where insurrection rises to the dignity of duty? What was there that was degrading for the son of Colonel Pontmercy in the combat which was about to begin? It is no longer Montmirail nor Champaubert; it is something quite different. The question is no longer one of sacred territory—but of a holy idea. The country wails, that may be, but humanity applauds. But is it true that the country does wail? France bleeds, but liberty smiles; and in the presence of liberty's smile, France forgets her wound. And then if we look at things from a still more lofty point of view, why do we speak of civil war?

Civil war—what does that mean? Is there a foreign war? Is not all war between men war between brothers? War is qualified only by its object. There is no such thing as foreign or civil war; there is only just and unjust war. Until that day when the grand human agreement is concluded, war, that at least which is the effort of the future, which is hastening on against the past, which is lagging in the rear, may be necessary. What have we to reproach that war with? War does not become a disgrace, the sword does not become a disgrace, except when it is used for assassinating the right, progress, reason, civilization, truth. Then war, whether foreign or civil, is iniquitous; it is called crime. Outside the pale of that holy thing, justice, by what right does one form of man despise another? By what right should the sword of Washington disown the pike of Camille Desmoulins? Leonidas against the stranger, Timoleon against the tyrant, which is the greater? the one is the defender, the other the liberator. Shall we brand every appeal to arms within a city's limits without taking the object into a consideration? Then note the infamy of Brutus, Marcel, Arnould von Blankenheim, Coligny. Hedgerow war? War of the streets? Why not? That was the war of Ambiorix, of Artevelde, of Marnix, of Pelagius. But Ambiorix fought against Rome, Artevelde against France, Marnix against Spain, Pelagius against the Moors; all against the foreigner. Well, the monarchy is a foreigner; oppression is a stranger; the right divine is a stranger. Despotism violates the moral frontier, an invasion violates the geographical frontier. Driving out the tyrant or driving out the English, in both cases, regaining possession of one's own territory. There comes an hour when protestation no longer suffices; after philosophy, action is required; live force finishes what the idea has sketched out; Prometheus chained begins, Aristogeiton ends; the encyclopedia enlightens souls, the 10th of August electrifies them. After Æschylus, Thrasybulus; after Diderot, Danton. Multitudes have a tendency to accept the master. Their mass bears witness to apathy. A crowd is easily led as a whole to obedience. Men must be stirred up, pushed on, treated roughly by the very benefit of their deliverance, their eyes must be wounded by the true, light must be hurled at them in terrible handfuls. They must be a little thunderstruck themselves at their own well-being; this dazzling awakens them. Hence the necessity of tocsins and wars. Great combatants must rise, must enlighten nations with audacity, and shake up that sad humanity which is covered with gloom by the right divine, Cæsarian glory, force, fanaticism, irresponsible power, and absolute majesty; a rabble stupidly occupied in the contemplation, in their twilight splendor, of these somber triumphs of the night. Down with the tyrant! Of whom are you speaking? Do you call Louis Philippe the tyrant? No; no more than Louis XVI. Both of them are what history is in the habit of calling good kings; but principles are not to be parcelled out, the logic of the true is rectilinear, the peculiarity of truth is that it lacks complaisance; no concessions, then; all encroachments on man should be repressed. There is a divine right in Louis XVI, there is *because a Bourbon* in Louis Philippe; both represent in a certain measure the confiscation of right, and, in order to clear away universal insurrection, they must be combated; it must be done, France being always the one to begin. When the master falls in France, he falls everywhere. In short, what cause is more just, and consequently, what war is greater, than that which re-establishes social truth, restores her throne to liberty, restores the people to the people, restores sovereignty to man, replaces the purple on the head of France, restores equity and reason in their plenitude, suppresses every germ of antagonism by restoring each one to himself, annihilates the obstacle which royalty presents to the whole immense universal concord, and places the human race once more on a level with the right? These wars build up peace. An enormous fortress of prejudices, privileges, superstitions, lies, exactions, abuses, violences, iniquities, and darkness still stands erect in this world, with its towers of hatred. It must be cast down. This monstrous mass must be made to crumble. To conquer at Austerlitz is grand; to take the Bastille is immense.

There is no one who has not noticed it in his own case—the soul—and therein lies the marvel of its unity complicated with ubiquity, has a strange aptitude for reasoning almost coldly in the most violent extremities, and it often happens that heartbroken passion and profound despair in the very agony of their blackest monologues, treat subjects and discuss theses. Logic is mingled with convulsion, and the thread of the syllogism floats, without breaking, in the mournful storm of thought. This was the situation of Marius's mind.

As he meditated thus, dejected but resolute, hesitating in every direction, and, in short, shuddering at what he was about to do, his glance strayed to the interior of the barricade. The insurgents were here conversing in a low voice, without moving, and there was perceptible that quasi-silence which marks the last stage of expectation. Overhead, at the small window in the third story, Marius descried a sort of spectator who appeared to him to be singularly attentive. This was the porter who had been killed by Le Cabuc. Below, by the lights of the torch, which was thrust between the paving-stones, this head could be vaguely distinguished. Nothing could be stranger, in that somber and uncertain gleam, than that livid, motionless, astonished face, with its bristling hair, its eyes fixed and staring, and its yawning mouth, bent over the street in an attitude of curiosity. One would have said that the man who was dead was surveying those who were about to die. A long trail of blood which had flowed from that head, descended in reddish threads from the window to the height of the first floor, where it stopped.

BOOK FOURTEENTH

THE GRANDEURS OF DESPAIR

Chapter I

THE FLAG: ACT FIRST

AS YET, NOTHING HAD COME. TEN O'CLOCK HAD SOUNDED FROM SAINT-MERRY. ENJOLRAS AND Combeferre had gone and seated themselves, carbines in hand, near the outlet of the grand barricade. They no longer addressed each other, they listened, seeking to catch even the faintest and most distant sound of marching.

Suddenly, in the midst of the dismal calm, a clear, gay, young voice, which seemed to come from the Rue Saint-Denis, rose and began to sing distinctly, to the old popular air of "By the Light of the Moon," this bit of poetry, terminated by a cry like the crow of a cock:

> *Mon nez est en larmes,*
> *Mon ami Bugeaud,*
> *Prête moi tes gendarmes*
> *Pour leur dire un mot.*
>
> *En capote bleue,*
> *La poule au shako,*
> *Voici la banlieue!*
> *Co-cocorico!*[1]

They pressed each other's hands.

"That is Gavroche," said Enjolras.

"He is warning us," said Combeferre.

A hasty rush troubled the deserted street; they beheld a being more agile than a clown climb over the omnibus, and Gavroche bounded into the barricade, all breathless, saying:

"My gun! Here they are!"

An electric quiver shot through the whole barricade, and the sound of hands seeking their guns became audible.

"Would you like my carbine?" said Enjolras to the lad.

"I want a big gun," replied Gavroche.

And he seized Javert's gun.

Two sentinels had fallen back, and had come in almost at the same moment as Gavroche. They were the sentinels from the end of the street, and the vidette of the Rue de la Petite-Truanderie.

---

1. My nose is in tears, my friend Bugeaud, lend me thy gendarmes that I may say a word to them. With a blue capote and a chicken in his shako, here's the banlieue, co-cocorico.

The vidette of the Lane des Prêcheurs had remained at his post, which indicated that nothing was approaching from the direction of the bridges and Halles.

The Rue de la Chanvrerie, of which a few paving-stones alone were dimly visible in the reflection of the light projected on the flag, offered to the insurgents the aspect of a vast black door vaguely opened into a smoke.

Each man had taken up his position for the conflict.

Forty-three insurgents, among whom were Enjolras, Combeferre, Courfeyrac, Bossuet, Joly, Bahorel, and Gavroche, were kneeling inside the large barricade, with their heads on a level with the crest of the barrier, the barrels of their guns and carbines aimed on the stones as though at loopholes, attentive, mute, ready to fire. Six, commanded by Feuilly, had installed themselves, with their guns leveled at their shoulders, at the windows of the two stories of Corinthe.

Several minutes passed thus, then a sound of footsteps, measured, heavy, and numerous, became distinctly audible in the direction of Saint-Leu. This sound, faint at first, then precise, then heavy and sonorous, approached slowly, without halt, without intermission, with a tranquil and terrible continuity. Nothing was to be heard but this. It was that combined silence and sound, of the statue of the commander, but this stony step had something indescribably enormous and multiple about it which awakened the idea of a throng, and, at the same time, the idea of a specter. One thought one heard the terrible statue Legion marching onward. This tread drew near; it drew still nearer, and stopped. It seemed as though the breathing of many men could be heard at the end of the street. Nothing was to be seen, however, but at the bottom of that dense obscurity there could be distinguished a multitude of metallic threads, as fine as needles and almost imperceptible, which moved about like those indescribable phosphoric networks which one sees beneath one's closed eyelids, in the first mists of slumber at the moment when one is dropping off to sleep. These were bayonets and gun-barrels confusedly illuminated by the distant reflection of the torch.

A pause ensued, as though both sides were waiting. All at once, from the depths of this darkness, a voice, which was all the more sinister, since no one was visible, and which appeared to be the gloom itself speaking, shouted:

"Who goes there?"

At the same time, the click of guns, as they were lowered into position, was heard.

Enjolras replied in a haughty and vibrating tone:

"The French Revolution!"

"Fire!" shouted the voice.

A flash empurpled all the façades in the street as though the door of a furnace had been flung open, and hastily closed again.

A fearful detonation burst forth on the barricade. The red flag fell. The discharge had been so violent and so dense that it had cut the staff, that is to say, the very tip of the omnibus pole.

Bullets which had rebounded from the cornices of the houses penetrated the barricade and wounded several men.

The impression produced by this first discharge was freezing. The attack had been rough, and of a nature to inspire reflection in the boldest. It was evident that they had to deal with an entire regiment at the very least.

"Comrades!" shouted Courfeyrac, "let us not waste our powder. Let us wait until they are in the street before replying."

"And, above all," said Enjolras, "let us raise the flag again."

He picked up the flag, which had fallen precisely at his feet.

Outside, the clatter of the ramrods in the guns could be heard; the troops were reloading their arms.

Enjolras went on:

"Who is there here with a bold heart? Who will plant the flag on the barricade again?"

Not a man responded. To mount on the barricade at the very moment when, without any doubt, it was again the object of their aim, was simply death. The bravest hesitated to pronounce his own condemnation. Enjolras himself felt a thrill. He repeated:

"Does no one volunteer?"

Chapter II

THE FLAG: ACT SECOND

SINCE THEY HAD ARRIVED AT CORINTHE, AND HAD BEGUN THE CONSTRUCTION OF THE BARRI-cade, no attention had been paid to Father Mabeuf. M. Mabeuf had not quitted the mob, however; he had entered the ground floor of the wine-shop and had seated himself behind the counter. There he had, so to speak, retreated into himself. He no longer seemed to look or to think. Courfeyrac and others had accosted him two or three times, warning him of his peril, beseeching him to withdraw, but he did not hear them. When they were not speaking to him, his mouth moved as though he were replying to someone, and as soon as he was addressed, his lips became motionless and his eyes no longer had the appearance of being alive.

Several hours before the barricade was attacked, he had assumed an attitude which he did not afterwards abandon, with both fists planted on his knees and his head thrust forward as though he were gazing over a precipice. Nothing had been able to move him from this attitude; it did not seem as though his mind were in the barricade. When each had gone to take up his position for the combat, there remained in the tap-room where Javert was bound to the post, only a single insurgent with a naked sword, watching over Javert, and himself, Mabeuf. At the moment of the attack, at the detonation, the physical shock had reached him and had, as it were, awakened him; he started up abruptly, crossed the room, and at the instant when Enjolras repeated his appeal: "Does no one volunteer?" the old man was seen to make his appearance on the threshold of the wine-shop. His presence produced a sort of commotion in the different groups. A shout went up:

"It is the voter! It is the member of the Convention! It is the representative of the people!"

It is probable that he did not hear them.

He strode straight up to Enjolras, the insurgents withdrawing before him with a religious fear; he tore the flag from Enjolras, who recoiled in amazement, and then, since no one dared to stop or to assist him, this old man of eighty, with shaking head but firm foot, began slowly to ascend the staircase of paving-stones arranged in the barricade. This was so melancholy and so grand that all around him cried: "Off with your hats!" At every step that he mounted, it was a frightful spectacle; his white locks, his decrepit face, his lofty, bald, and wrinkled brow, his amazed and open mouth, his aged arm upholding the red banner, rose through the gloom and were enlarged in the bloody light of the torch, and the bystanders thought that they beheld the specter of '93 emerging from the earth, with the flag of terror in his hand.

When he had reached the last step, when this trembling and terrible phantom, erect on that pile of rubbish in the presence of twelve hundred invisible guns, drew himself up in the face of death and as though he were more powerful than it, the whole barricade assumed amid the darkness, a supernatural and colossal form.

There ensued one of those silences which occur only in the presence of prodigies. In the midst of this silence, the old man waved the red flag and shouted:

"Long live the Revolution! Long live the Republic! Fraternity! Equality! and Death!"

Those in the barricade heard a low and rapid whisper, like the murmur of a priest who is dispatching a prayer in haste. It was probably the commissary of police who was making the legal summons at the other end of the street.

Then the same piercing voice which had shouted: "Who goes there?" shouted:

"Retire!"

M. Mabeuf, pale, haggard, his eyes lighted up with the mournful flame of aberration, raised the flag above his head and repeated:

"Long live the Republic!"

"Fire!" said the voice.

A second discharge, similar to the first, rained down upon the barricade.

The old man fell on his knees, then rose again, dropped the flag and fell backwards on the pavement, like a log, at full length, with outstretched arms.

Rivulets of blood flowed beneath him. His aged head, pale and sad, seemed to be gazing at the sky.

One of those emotions which are superior to man, which make him forget even to defend himself, seized upon the insurgents, and they approached the body with respectful awe.

"What men these regicides were!" said Enjolras.

Courfeyrac bent down to Enjolras's ear:

"This is for yourself alone, I do not wish to dampen the enthusiasm. But this man was anything rather than a regicide. I knew him. His name was Father Mabeuf. I do not know what was the matter with him to-day. But he was a brave blockhead. Just look at his head."

"The head of a blockhead and the heart of a Brutus," replied Enjolras.

Then he raised his voice:

"Citizens! This is the example which the old give to the young. We hesitated, he came! We were drawing back, he advanced! This is what those who are trembling with age teach to those who tremble with fear! This aged man is august in the eyes of his country. He has had a long life and a magnificent death! Now, let us place the body under cover, that each one of us may defend this old man dead as he would his father living, and may his presence in our midst render the barricade impregnable!"

A murmur of gloomy and energetic assent followed these words.

Enjolras bent down, raised the old man's head, and fierce as he was, he kissed him on the brow, then, throwing wide his arms, and handling this dead man with tender precaution, as though he feared to hurt it, he removed his coat, showed the bloody holes in it to all, and said:

"This is our flag now."

Chapter III

GAVROCHE WOULD HAVE DONE BETTER TO ACCEPT ENJOLRAS'S CARBINE

THEY THREW A LONG BLACK SHAWL OF WIDOW HUCHELOUP'S OVER FATHER MABEUF. SIX MEN made a litter of their guns; on this they laid the body, and bore it, with bared heads, with solemn slowness, to the large table in the tap-room.

These men, wholly absorbed in the grave and sacred task in which they were engaged, thought no more of the perilous situation in which they stood.

When the corpse passed near Javert, who was still impassive, Enjolras said to the spy:

"It will be your turn presently!"

During all this time, Little Gavroche, who alone had not quitted his post, but had remained on guard, thought he spied some men stealthily approaching the barricade. All at once he shouted:

"Look out!"

Courfeyrac, Enjolras, Jean Prouvaire, Combeferre, Joly, Bahorel, Bossuet, and all the rest ran tumultuously from the wine-shop. It was almost too late. They saw a glistening density of bayonets undulating above the barricade. Municipal guards of lofty stature were making their way in, some striding over the omnibus, others through the cut, thrusting before them the urchin, who retreated, but did not flee.

The moment was critical. It was that first, redoubtable moment of inundation, when the stream rises to the level of the levee and when the water begins to filter through the fissures of dike. A second more and the barricade would have been taken.

Bahorel dashed upon the first municipal guard who was entering, and killed him on the spot with a blow from his gun; the second killed Bahorel with a blow from his bayonet. Another had already overthrown Courfeyrac, who was shouting: "Follow me!" The largest of all, a sort of colossus, marched on Gavroche with his bayonet fixed. The urchin took in his arms Javert's immense gun, leveled it resolutely at the giant, and fired. No discharge followed. Javert's gun was not loaded. The municipal guard burst into a laugh and raised his bayonet at the child.

Before the bayonet had touched Gavroche, the gun slipped from the soldier's grasp, a bullet had struck the municipal guardsman in the center of the forehead, and he fell over on his back. A second bullet struck the other guard, who had assaulted Courfeyrac in the breast, and laid him low on the pavement.

This was the work of Marius, who had just entered the barricade.

Chapter IV

THE BARREL OF POWDER

MARIUS, STILL CONCEALED IN THE TURN OF THE RUE MONDÉTOUR, HAD WITNESSED, SHUDDER-ing and irresolute, the first phase of the combat. But he had not long been able to resist that mysterious and sovereign vertigo which may be designated as the call of the abyss. In the presence of the imminence of the peril, in the presence of the death of M. Mabeuf, that melancholy enigma, in the presence of Bahorel killed, and Courfeyrac shouting: "Follow me!" of that child threatened, of his friends to succor or to avenge, all hesitation had vanished, and he had flung himself into the conflict, his two pistols in hand. With his first shot he had saved Gavroche, and with the second delivered Courfeyrac.

Amid the sound of the shots, amid the cries of the assaulted guards, the assailants had climbed the entrenchment, on whose summit Municipal Guards, soldiers of the line and National Guards from the suburbs could now be seen, gun in hand, rearing themselves to more than half the height of their bodies.

They already covered more than two-thirds of the barrier, but they did not leap into the enclosure, as though wavering in the fear of some trap. They gazed into the dark barricade as one would gaze into a lion's den. The light of the torch illuminated only their bayonets, their bear-skin caps, and the upper part of their uneasy and angry faces.

Marius had no longer any weapons; he had flung away his discharged pistols after firing them; but he had caught sight of the barrel of powder in the tap-room, near the door.

As he turned half round, gazing in that direction, a soldier took aim at him. At the moment when the soldier was sighting Marius, a hand was laid on the muzzle of the gun and obstructed it. This was done by someone who had darted forward—the young workman in velvet trousers. The shot sped, traversed the hand and possibly, also, the workman, since he fell, but the ball did not strike Marius. All this, which was rather to be apprehended than seen through the smoke, Marius, who was entering the tap-room, hardly noticed. Still, he had, in a confused way, perceived that gun-barrel aimed at him, and the hand which had blocked it, and he had heard the discharge. But in moments like this, the things which one sees vacillate and are precipitated, and one pauses for nothing. One feels obscurely impelled toward more darkness still, and all is cloud.

The insurgents, surprised but not terrified, had rallied. Enjolras had shouted: "Wait! Don't fire at random!" In the first confusion, they might, in fact, wound each other. The majority of them had ascended to the window on the first story and to the attic windows, whence they commanded the assailants.

The most determined, with Enjolras, Courfeyrac, Jean Prouvaire, and Combeferre, had proudly placed themselves with their backs against the houses at the rear, unsheltered and facing the ranks of soldiers and guards who crowned the barricade.

All this was accomplished without haste, with that strange and threatening gravity which precedes engagements. They took aim, point-blank, on both sides: they were so close that they could talk together without raising their voices.

When they had reached this point where the spark is on the brink of darting forth, an officer in a gorget extended his sword and said:

"Lay down your arms!"

"Fire!" replied Enjolras.

The two discharges took place at the same moment, and all disappeared in smoke.

An acrid and stifling smoke in which dying and wounded lay with weak, dull groans. When the smoke cleared away, the combatants on both sides could be seen to be thinned out, but still in the same positions, reloading in silence. All at once, a thundering voice was heard, shouting:

"Be off with you, or I'll blow up the barricade!"

All turned in the direction whence the voice proceeded.

Marius had entered the tap-room, and had seized the barrel of powder, then he had taken advantage of the smoke, and the sort of obscure mist which filled the entrenched enclosure, to glide along the barricade as far as that cage of paving-stones where the torch was fixed. To tear from it the torch, to replace it by the barrel of powder, to thrust the pile of stones under the barrel, which was instantly staved in, with a sort of horrible obedience—all this had cost Marius but the time necessary to stoop and rise again; and now all, National Guards, Municipal Guards, officers, soldiers, huddled at the other extremity of the barricade, gazed stupidly at him, as he stood with his foot on the stones, his torch in his hand, his haughty face illuminated by a fatal resolution, drooping the flame of the torch toward that redoubtable pile where they could make out the broken barrel of powder, and giving vent to that startling cry:

"Be off with you, or I'll blow up the barricade!"

Marius on that barricade after the octogenarian was the vision of the young revolution after the apparition of the old.

"Blow up the barricade!" said a sergeant, "and yourself with it!"

Marius retorted: "And myself also."

And he dropped the torch toward the barrel of powder.

But there was no longer anyone on the barrier. The assailants, abandoning their dead and wounded, flowed back pell-mell and in disorder toward the extremity of the street, and there were again lost in the night. It was a headlong flight.

The barricade was free.

Chapter V

END OF THE VERSES OF JEAN PROUVAIRE

A LL FLOCKED AROUND MARIUS. COURFEYRAC FLUNG HIMSELF ON HIS NECK.
    "Here you are!"

"What luck!" said Combeferre.

"You came in opportunely!" ejaculated Bossuet.

"If it had not been for you, I should have been dead!" began Courfeyrac again.

"If it had not been for you, I should have been gobbled up!" added Gavroche.

Marius asked:

"Where is the chief?"

"You are he!" said Enjolras.

Marius had had a furnace in his brain all day long; now it was a whirlwind. This whirlwind which was within him, produced on him the effect of being outside of him and of bearing him away. It seemed to him that he was already at an immense distance from life. His two luminous months of joy and love, ending abruptly at that frightful precipice, Cosette lost to him, that barricade, M. Mabeuf getting himself killed for the Republic, himself the leader of the insurgents—all these things appeared to him like a tremendous nightmare. He was obliged to make a mental effort to recall the fact that all that surrounded him was real. Marius had already seen too much of life not to know that nothing is more imminent than the impossible, and that what it is always necessary to foresee is the unforeseen. He had looked on at his own drama as a piece which one does not understand.

In the mists which enveloped his thoughts, he did not recognize Javert, who, bound to his post, had not so much as moved his head during the whole of the attack on the barricade, and who had gazed on the revolt seething around him with the resignation of a martyr and the majesty of a judge. Marius had not even seen him.

In the meanwhile, the assailants did not stir, they could be heard marching and swarming through at the end of the street, but they did not venture into it, either because they were awaiting orders or because they were awaiting reinforcements before hurling themselves afresh on this impregnable redoubt. The insurgents had posted sentinels, and some of them, who were medical students, set about caring for the wounded.

They had thrown the tables out of the wine-shop, with the exception of the two tables reserved for lint and cartridges, and of the one on which lay Father Mabeuf; they had added them to the barricade, and had replaced them in the tap-room with mattresses from the bed of the widow Hucheloup and her servants. On these mattresses they had laid the wounded. As for the three poor creatures who inhabited Corinthe, no one knew what had become of them. They were finally found, however, hidden in the cellar.

A poignant emotion clouded the joy of the disencumbered barricade.

The roll was called. One of the insurgents were missing. And who was it? One of the dearest. One of the most valiant. Jean Prouvaire. He was sought among the wounded, he was not there. He was sought among the dead, he was not there. He was evidently a prisoner. Combeferre said to Enjolras:

"They have our friend; we have their agent. Are you set on the death of that spy?"

"Yes," replied Enjolaras; "but less so than on the life of Jean Prouvaire."

This took place in the tap-room near Javert's post.

"Well," resumed Combeferre, "I am going to fasten my handkerchief to my cane, and go as a flag of truce, to offer to exchange our man for theirs."

"Listen," said Enjolras, laying his hand on Combeferre's arm.

At the end of the street there was a significant clash of arms.

They heard a manly voice shout:

"Vive la France! Long live France! Long live the future!"

They recognized the voice of Prouvaire.

A flash passed, a report rang out.

Silence fell again.

"They have killed him," exclaimed Combeferre.

Enjolras glanced at Javert, and said to him:

"Your friends have just shot you."

Chapter VI

The Agony of Death after the Agony of Life

A PECULIARITY OF THIS SPECIES OF WAR IS, THAT THE ATTACK OF THE BARRICADES IS ALMOST always made from the front, and that the assailants generally abstain from turning the position, either because they fear ambushes, or because they are afraid of getting entangled in the tortuous streets. The insurgents' whole attention had been directed, therefore, to the grand barricade, which was, evidently, the spot always menaced, and there the struggle would infallibly recommence. But Marius thought of the little barricade, and went thither. It was deserted and guarded only by the fire-pot which trembled between the paving-stones. Moreover, the Mondétour alley, and the branches of the Rue de la Petite-Truanderie and the Rue du Cygne were profoundly calm.

As Marius was withdrawing, after concluding his inspection, he heard his name pronounced feebly in the darkness.

"Monsieur Marius!"

He started, for he recognized the voice which had called to him two hours before through the gate in the Rue Plumet.

Only, the voice now seemed to be nothing more than a breath.

He looked about him, but saw no one.

Marius thought he had been mistaken, that it was an illusion added by his mind to the extraordinary realities which were clashing around him. He advanced a step, in order to quit the distant recess where the barricade lay.

"Monsieur Marius!" repeated the voice.

This time he could not doubt that he had heard it distinctly; he looked and saw nothing.

"At your feet," said the voice.

He bent down, and saw in the darkness a form which was dragging itself toward him.

It was crawling along the pavement. It was this that had spoken to him.

The fire-pot allowed him to distinguish a blouse, torn trousers of coarse velvet, bare feet, and something which resembled a pool of blood. Marius indistinctly made out a pale head which was lifted toward him and which was saying to him:

"You do not recognize me?"

"No."

"Éponine."

Marius bent hastily down. It was, in fact, that unhappy child. She was dressed in men's clothes.

"How come you here? What are you doing here?"

"I am dying," said she.

There are words and incidents which arouse dejected beings. Marius cried out with a start:

"You are wounded! Wait, I will carry you into the room! They will attend to you there. Is it serious? How must I take hold of you in order not to hurt you? Where do you suffer? Help! My God! But why did you come hither?"

And he tried to pass his arm under her, in order to raise her.

She uttered a feeble cry.

"Have I hurt you?" asked Marius.

"A little."

"But I only touched your hand."

She raised her hand to Marius, and in the middle of that hand Marius saw a black hole.

"What is the matter with your hand?" said he.

"It is pierced."

"Pierced?"

"Yes."

"What with?"

"A bullet."

"How?"

"Did you see a gun aimed at you?"

"Yes, and a hand stopping it."

"It was mine."

Marius was seized with a shudder.

"What madness! Poor child! But so much the better, if that is all, it is nothing, let me carry you to a bed. They will dress your wound; one does not die of a pierced hand."

She murmured:

"The bullet traversed my hand, but it came out through my back. It is useless to remove me from this spot. I will tell you how you can care for me better than any surgeon. Sit down near me on this stone."

He obeyed; she laid her head on Marius's knees, and, without looking at him, she said:

"Oh! How good this is! How comfortable this is! There; I no longer suffer."

She remained silent for a moment, then she turned her face with an effort, and looked at Marius.

"Do you know what, Monsieur Marius? It puzzled me because you entered that garden; it was stupid, because it was I who showed you that house; and then, I ought to have said to myself that a young man like you—"

She paused, and overstepping the somber transitions that undoubtedly existed in her mind, she resumed with a heart-rending smile:

"You thought me ugly, didn't you?"

She continued:

"You see, you are lost! Now, no one can get out of the barricade. It was I who led you here, by the way! You are going to die, I count upon that. And yet, when I saw them taking aim at you, I put my hand on the muzzle of the gun. How queer it is! But it was because I wanted to die before you. When I received that bullet, I dragged myself here, no one saw me, no one picked me up, I was waiting for you, I said: 'So he is not coming!' Oh, if you only knew. I bit my blouse, I suffered so! Now I am well. Do you remember the day I entered your chamber and when I looked at myself in your mirror, and the day when I came to you on the boulevard near the washerwomen? How the birds sang! That was a long time ago. You gave me a hundred sous, and I said to you: 'I don't want your money.' I hope you picked up your coin? You are not rich. I did not think to tell you to pick it up. The sun was shining bright, and it was not cold. Do you remember, Monsieur Marius? Oh! How happy I am! Everyone is going to die."

She had a mad, grave, and heart-breaking air. Her torn blouse disclosed her bare throat.

As she talked, she pressed her pierced hand to her breast, where there was another hole, and whence there spurted from moment to moment a stream of blood, like a jet of wine from an open bung-hole.

Marius gazed at this unfortunate creature with profound compassion.

"Oh!" she resumed, "it is coming again, I am stifling!"

She caught up her blouse and bit it, and her limbs stiffened on the pavement.

At that moment the young cock's crow executed by little Gavroche resounded through the barricade.

The child had mounted a table to load his gun, and was singing gaily the song then so popular:

"En voyant Lafayette,	*"On beholding Lafayette,*
Le gendarme répète:—	*The gendarme repeats:—*
Sauvons nous! sauvons nous!	*Let us flee! let us flee!*
sauvons nous!"	*let us flee!"*

Éponine raised herself and listened; then she murmured:

"It is he."

And turning to Marius:

"My brother is here. He must not see me. He would scold me."

"Your brother?" inquired Marius, who was meditating in the most bitter and sorrowful depths of his heart on the duties to the Thénardiers which his father had bequeathed to him; "who is your brother?"

"That little fellow."

"The one who is singing?"

"Yes."

Marius made a movement.

"Oh! don't go away," said she, "it will not be long now."

She was sitting almost upright, but her voice was very low and broken by hiccoughs.

At intervals, the death-rattle interrupted her. She put her face as near that of Marius as possible. She added with a strange expression:

"Listen, I do not wish to play you a trick. I have a letter in my pocket for you. I was told to put it in the post. I kept it. I did not want to have it reach you. But perhaps you will be angry with me for it when we meet again presently? Take your letter."

She grasped Marius's hand convulsively with her pierced hand, but she no longer seemed to feel her sufferings. She put Marius's hand in the pocket of her blouse. There, in fact, Marius felt a paper.

"Take it," said she.

Marius took the letter.

She made a sign of satisfaction and contentment.

"Now, for my trouble, promise me—"

And she stopped.

"What?" asked Marius.

"Promise me!"

"I promise."

"Promise to give me a kiss on my brow when I am dead.—I shall feel it."

She dropped her head again on Marius's knees, and her eyelids closed. He thought the poor soul had departed. Éponine remained motionless. All at once, at the very moment when Marius fancied her asleep forever, she slowly opened her eyes in which appeared the somber profundity of death, and said to him in a tone whose sweetness seemed already to proceed from another world:

"And by the way, Monsieur Marius, I believe that I was a little bit in love with you."

She tried to smile once more and expired.

Chapter VII

Gavroche as a Profound Calculator of Distances

MARIUS KEPT HIS PROMISE. HE DROPPED A KISS ON THAT LIVID BROW, WHERE THE ICY PERSPIRATION stood in beads.

This was no infidelity to Cosette; it was a gentle and pensive farewell to an unhappy soul.

It was not without a tremor that he had taken the letter which Éponine had given him. He had immediately felt that it was an event of weight. He was impatient to read it. The heart of man is so constituted that the unhappy child had hardly closed her eyes when Marius began to think of unfolding this paper.

He laid her gently on the ground, and went away. Something told him that he could not peruse that letter in the presence of that body.

He drew near to a candle in the tap-room. It was a small note, folded and sealed with a woman's elegant care. The address was in a woman's hand and ran:

"To Monsieur, Monsieur Marius Pontmercy, at M. Courfeyrac's, Rue de la Verrerie, No. 16."

He broke the seal and read:

"My dearest, alas! my father insists on our setting out immediately. We shall be this evening in the Rue de l'Homme Armé, No. 7. In a week we shall be in England.

COSETTE. June 4th."

Such was the innocence of their love that Marius was not even acquainted with Cosette's handwriting.

What had taken place may be related in a few words. Éponine had been the cause of everything. After the evening of the 3d of June she had cherished a double idea, to defeat the projects of her father and the ruffians on the house of the Rue Plumet, and to separate Marius and Cosette. She had exchanged rags with the first young scamp she came across who had thought it amusing to dress like a woman, while Éponine disguised herself like a man. It was she who had conveyed to Jean Valjean in the Champ de Mars the expressive warning: "Leave your house." Jean Valjean had, in fact, returned home, and had said to Cosette: "We set out this evening and we go to the Rue de l'Homme Armé with Toussaint. Next week, we shall be in London." Cosette, utterly overwhelmed by this unexpected blow, had hastily penned a couple of lines to Marius. But how was she to get the letter to the post? She never went out alone, and Toussaint, surprised at such a commission, would certainly show the letter to M. Fauchelevent. In this dilemma, Cosette had caught sight through the fence, of Éponine in man's clothes, who now prowled incessantly around the garden. Cosette had called to "this young workman" and had handed him five francs and the letter, saying: "Carry this letter immediately to its address." Éponine had put the letter in her pocket. The next day, on the 5th of June, she went to Courfeyrac's quarters to inquire for Marius, not for the purpose of delivering the letter, but—a thing which every jealous and loving soul will comprehend—"to see." There she had waited for Marius, or at least for Courfeyrac, still for the purpose of *seeing*. When Courfeyrac had told her: "We are going to the barricades," an idea flashed through her mind, to fling herself into that death, as she would have done into any other, and to thrust Marius into it also. She had followed Courfeyrac, had made sure of the locality where the barricade was in process of construction; and, quite certain, since Marius had received no warning, and since she had intercepted the letter, that he would go at dusk to his trysting-place for every evening, she had betaken herself to the Rue Plumet, had there awaited Marius, and had sent him, in the name of his friends, the appeal which would, she thought, lead him to the barricade. She reckoned on Marius's despair when he should fail to find Cosette; she was not mistaken. She had returned to the Rue de la Chanvrerie herself. What she did there the reader has just seen. She died with the tragic joy of jealous hearts who drag the beloved being into their own death, and who say: "No one shall have him!"

Marius covered Cosette's letter with kisses. So she loved him! For one moment the idea occurred to him that he ought not to die now. Then he said to himself: "She is going away. Her father is taking her to England, and my grandfather refuses his consent to the marriage. Nothing is changed in our fates." Dreamers like Marius are subject to supreme attacks of dejection, and desperate resolves are the result. The fatigue of living is insupportable; death is sooner over with. Then he reflected that he had still two duties to fulfill: to inform Cosette of his death and send her a final farewell, and to save from the impending catastrophe which was in preparation, that poor child, Éponine's brother and Thénardier's son.

He had a pocket-book about him; the same one which had contained the notebook in which he had inscribed so many thoughts of love for Cosette. He tore out a leaf and wrote on it a few lines in pencil:

"Our marriage was impossible. I asked my grandfather, he refused; I have no fortune, neither hast thou. I hastened to thee, thou wert no longer there. Thou knowest the promise that I gave thee, I shall keep it. I die. I love thee. When thou readest this, my soul will be near thee, and thou wilt smile."

Having nothing wherewith to seal this letter, he contented himself with folding the paper in four, and added the address:

"To Mademoiselle Cosette Fauchelevent, at M. Fauchelevent's, Rue de l'Homme Armé, No. 7."

Having folded the letter, he stood in thought for a moment, drew out his pocket-book again, opened it, and wrote, with the same pencil, these four lines on the first page:

"My name is Marius Pontmercy. Carry my body to my grandfather, M. Gillenormand, Rue des Filles-du-Calvaire, No. 6, in the Marais."

He put his pocket-book back in his pocket, then he called Gavroche.
The gamin, at the sound of Marius's voice, ran up to him with his merry and devoted air.
"Will you do something for me?"
"Anything," said Gavroche. "Good God! if it had not been for you, I should have been done for."
"Do you see this letter?"
"Yes."
"Take it. Leave the barricade instantly" (Gavroche began to scratch his ear uneasily) "and to-morrow morning, you will deliver it at its address to Mademoiselle Cosette, at M. Fauchelevent's, Rue de l'Homme Armé, No. 7."

The heroic child replied:

"Well, but! in the meanwhile the barricade will be taken, and I shall not be there."

"The barricade will not be attacked until daybreak, according to all appearances, and will not be taken before to-morrow noon."

The fresh respite which the assailants were granting to the barricade had, in fact, been prolonged. It was one of those intermissions which frequently occur in nocturnal combats, which are always followed by an increase of rage.

"Well," said Gavroche, "what if I were to go and carry your letter to-morrow?"

"It will be too late. The barricade will probably be blockaded, all the streets will be guarded, and you will not be able to get out. Go at once."

Gavroche could think of no reply to this, and stood there in indecision, scratching his ear sadly.

All at once, he took the letter with one of those bird-like movements which were common with him.

"All right," said he.

And he started off at a run through Mondétour lane.

An idea had occurred to Gavroche which had brought him to a decision, but he had not mentioned it for fear that Marius might offer some objection to it.

This was the idea:

"It is barely midnight, the Rue de l'Homme Armé is not far off; I will go and deliver the letter at once, and I shall get back in time."

BOOK FIFTEENTH

THE RUE DE L'HOMME ARMÉ

Chapter I

A DRINKER IS A BABBLER

WHAT ARE THE CONVULSIONS OF A CITY IN COMPARISON WITH THE INSURRECTIONS OF THE soul? Man is a depth still greater than the people. Jean Valjean at that very moment was the prey of a terrible upheaval. Every sort of gulf had opened again within him. He also was trembling, like Paris, on the brink of an obscure and formidable revolution. A few hours had sufficed to bring this about. His destiny and his conscience had suddenly been covered with gloom. Of him also, as well as of Paris, it might have been said "The two principles are face to face. The white angel and the black angel are about to seize each other on the bridge of the abyss. Which of the two will hurl the other over? Who will carry the day?"

On the evening preceding this same 5th of June, Jean Valjean, accompanied by Cosette and Toussaint had installed himself in the Rue de l'Homme Armé. A change awaited him there.

Cosette had not quitted the Rue Plumet without making an effort at resistance. For the first time since they had lived side by side, Cosette's will and the will of Jean Valjean had proved to be distinct, and had been in opposition, at least, if they had not clashed. There had been objections on one side and inflexibility on the other. The abrupt advice: "Leave your house," hurled at Jean Valjean by a stranger, had alarmed him to the extent of rendering him peremptory. He thought that he had been traced and followed. Cosette had been obliged to give way.

Both had arrived in the Rue de l'Homme Armé without opening their lips, and without uttering a word, each being absorbed in his own personal preoccupation; Jean Valjean so uneasy that he did not notice Cosette's sadness, Cosette so sad that she did not notice Jean Valjean's uneasiness.

Jean Valjean had taken Toussaint with him, a thing which he had never done in his previous absences. He perceived the possibility of not returning to the Rue Plumet, and he could neither leave Toussaint behind nor confide his secret to her. Besides, he felt that she was devoted and trustworthy. Treachery between master and servant begins in curiosity. Now Toussaint, as though she had been destined to be Jean Valjean's servant, was not curious. She stammered in her peasant dialect of Barneville: "I am made so; I do my work; the rest is no affair of mine."

In this departure from the Rue Plumet, which had been almost a flight, Jean Valjean had carried away nothing but the little embalmed valise, baptized by Cosette "the inseparable." Full trunks would have required porters, and porters are witnesses. A fiacre had been summoned to the door on the Rue de Babylone, and they had taken their departure.

It was with difficulty that Toussaint had obtained permission to pack up a little linen and clothes and a few toilet articles. Cosette had taken only her portfolio and her blotting-book.

Jean Valjean, with a view to augmenting the solitude and the mystery of this departure, had arranged to quit the pavilion of the Rue Plumet only at dusk, which had allowed Cosette time to write her note to Marius. They had arrived in the Rue de l'Homme Armé after night had fully fallen.

They had gone to bed in silence.

The lodgings in the Rue de l'Homme Armé were situated on a back court, on the second floor, and were composed of two sleeping-rooms, a dining-room and a kitchen adjoining the dining-room, with a garret where there was a folding-bed, and which fell to Toussaint's share. The dining-room was an antechamber as well, and separated the two bedrooms. The apartment was provided with all necessary utensils.

People reacquire confidence as foolishly as they lose it; human nature is so constituted. Hardly had Jean Valjean reached the Rue de l'Homme Armé when his anxiety was lightened and by degrees dissipated. There are soothing spots which act in some sort mechanically on the mind. An obscure street, peaceable inhabitants. Jean Valjean experienced an indescribable contagion of tranquility in that alley of ancient Paris, which is so narrow that it is barred against carriages by a transverse beam placed on two posts, which is deaf and dumb in the midst of the clamorous city, dimly lighted at midday, and is, so to speak, incapable of emotions between two rows of lofty houses centuries old, which hold their peace like ancients as they are. There was a touch of stagnant oblivion in that street. Jean Valjean drew his breath once more there. How could he be found there?

His first care was to place *the inseparable* beside him.

He slept well. Night brings wisdom; we may add, night soothes. On the following morning he awoke in a mood that was almost gay. He thought the dining-room charming, though it was hideous, furnished with an old round table, a long sideboard surmounted by a slanting mirror, a dilapidated arm-chair, and several plain chairs which were encumbered with Toussaint's packages. In one of these packages Jean Valjean's uniform of a National Guard was visible through a rent.

As for Cosette, she had had Toussaint take some broth to her room, and did not make her appearance until evening.

About five o'clock, Toussaint, who was going and coming and busying herself with the tiny establishment, set on the table a cold chicken, which Cosette, out of deference to her father, consented to glance at.

That done, Cosette, under the pretext of an obstinate sick headache, had bade Jean Valjean good night and had shut herself up in her chamber. Jean Valjean had eaten a wing of the chicken with a good appetite, and with his elbows on the table, having gradually recovered his serenity, had regained possession of his sense of security.

While he was discussing this modest dinner, he had, twice or thrice, noticed in a confused way, Toussaint's stammering words as she said to him: "Monsieur, there is something going on, they are fighting in Paris." But absorbed in a throng of inward calculations, he had paid no heed to it. To tell the truth, he had not heard her. He rose and began to pace from the door to the window and from the window to the door, growing ever more serene.

With this calm, Cosette, his sole anxiety, recurred to his thoughts. Not that he was troubled by this headache, a little nervous crisis, a young girl's fit of sulks, the cloud of a moment, there would be nothing left of it in a day or two; but he meditated on the future, and, as was his habit, he thought of it with pleasure. After all, he saw no obstacle to their happy life resuming its course. At certain hours, everything seems impossible, at others everything appears easy; Jean Valjean was in the midst of one of these good hours. They generally succeed the bad ones, as day follows night, by virtue of that law of succession and of contrast which lies at the very foundation of nature, and which superficial minds call antithesis. In this peaceful street where he had taken refuge, Jean Valjean got rid of all that had been troubling him for some time past. This very fact, that he had seen many shadows, made him begin to perceive a little azure. To have quitted the Rue Plumet without complications or incidents was one good step already accomplished. Perhaps it would be wise to go abroad, if only for a few months, and to set out for London. Well, they would go. What difference did it make to him whether he was in France or in England, provided he had Cosette beside him? Cosette was his nation. Cosette sufficed for his happiness; the idea that he, perhaps, did not suffice for Cosette's happiness, that idea which had formerly been the cause of his fever and sleeplessness, did not even present itself to his mind. He was in a state of collapse from all his past sufferings, and he was fully entered on optimism. Cosette was by his side, she seemed to be his; an optical illusion which everyone has experienced. He arranged in his own mind, with all sorts of felicitous devices, his departure for England with Cosette, and he beheld his felicity reconstituted wherever he pleased, in the perspective of his reverie.

As he paced to and fro with long strides, his glance suddenly encountered something strange. In the inclined mirror facing him which surmounted the sideboard, he saw the four lines which follow:

"My dearest, alas! my father insists on our setting out immediately. We shall be this evening in the Rue de l'Homme Armé, No. 7. In a week we shall be in England.

COSETTE. *June 4th."*

Jean Valjean halted, perfectly haggard.

Cosette on her arrival had placed her blotting-book on the sideboard in front of the mirror, and, utterly absorbed in her agony of grief, had forgotten it and left it there, without even observing that she had left it wide open, and open at precisely the page on which she had laid to dry the four lines which she had penned, and which she had given in charge of the young workman in the Rue Plumet. The writing had been printed off on the blotter.

The mirror reflected the writing.

The result was, what is called in geometry, *the symmetrical image*; so that the writing, reversed on the blotter, was righted in the mirror and presented its natural appearance; and Jean Valjean had beneath his eyes the letter written by Cosette to Marius on the preceding evening.

It was simple and withering.

Jean Valjean stepped up to the mirror. He read the four lines again, but he did not believe them.

They produced on him the effect of appearing in a flash of lightning. It was a hallucination, it was impossible. It was not so.

Little by little, his perceptions became more precise, he looked at Cosette's blotting-book, and the consciousness of the reality returned to him. He caught up the blotter and said: "It comes from there." He feverishly examined the four lines imprinted on the blotter, the reversal of the letters converted into an odd scrawl, and he saw no sense in it. Then he said to himself: "But this signifies nothing; there is nothing written here." And he drew a long breath with inexpressible relief. Who has not experienced those foolish joys in horrible instants? The soul does not surrender to despair until it has exhausted all illusions.

He held the blotter in his hand and contemplated it in stupid delight, almost ready to laugh at the hallucination of which he had been the dupe. All at once his eyes fell upon the mirror again, and again he beheld the vision. There were the four lines outlined with inexorable clearness. This time it was no mirage. The recurrence of a vision is a reality; it was palpable, it was the writing restored in the mirror. He understood.

Jean Valjean tottered, dropped the blotter, and fell into the old arm-chair beside the buffet, with drooping head, and glassy eyes, in utter bewilderment. He told himself that it was plain, that the light of the world had been eclipsed forever, and that Cosette had written that to someone. Then he heard his soul, which had become terrible once more, give vent to a dull roar in the gloom. Try then the effect of taking from the lion the dog which he has in his cage!

Strange and sad to say, at that very moment, Marius had not yet received Cosette's letter; chance had treacherously carried it to Jean Valjean before delivering it to Marius. Up to that day, Jean Valjean had not been vanquished by trial. He had been subjected to fearful proofs; no violence of bad fortune had been spared him; the ferocity of fate, armed with all vindictiveness and all social scorn, had taken him for her prey and had raged against him. He had accepted every extremity when it had been necessary; he had sacrificed his inviolability as a reformed man, had yielded up his liberty, risked his head, lost everything, suffered everything, and he had remained disinterested and stoical to such a point that he might have been thought to be absent from himself like a martyr. His conscience inured to every assault of destiny, might have appeared to be forever impregnable. Well, anyone who had beheld his spiritual self would have been obliged to concede that it weakened at that moment. It was because, of all the tortures which he had undergone in the course of this long inquisition to which destiny had doomed him, this was the most terrible. Never had such pincers seized him hitherto. He felt the mysterious stirring of all his latent sensibilities. He felt the plucking at the strange chord. Alas! the supreme trial, let us say rather, the only trial, is the loss of the beloved being.

Poor old Jean Valjean certainly did not love Cosette otherwise than as a father; but we have already remarked, above, that into this paternity the widowhood of his life had introduced all the shades of love; he loved Cosette as his daughter, and he loved her as his mother, and he loved her as his sister; and, as he had never had either a woman to love or a wife, as nature is a creditor who accepts no protest, that sentiment also, the most impossible to lose, was mingled with the rest, vague, ignorant, pure with the purity of blindness, unconscious, celestial, angelic, divine; less like a sentiment than like an instinct, less like an instinct than like an imperceptible and invisible but real attraction; and love, properly speaking, was, in his immense tenderness for Cosette, like the thread of gold in the mountain, concealed and virgin.

Let the reader recall the situation of heart which we have already indicated. No marriage was possible between them; not even that of souls; and yet, it is certain that their destinies were wedded. With the exception of Cosette, that is to say, with the exception of a childhood, Jean Valjean had never, in the whole of his long life, known anything of that which may be loved. The passions and loves which succeed each other had not produced in him those successive green growths, tender green or dark green, which can be seen in foliage which passes through the winter and in men who pass fifty. In short, and we have insisted on it more than once, all this interior fusion, all this whole, of which the sum total was a lofty virtue, ended in rendering Jean Valjean a father to Cosette. A strange father, forged from the grandfather, the son, the brother, and the husband, that existed in Jean Valjean; a father in whom there was included even a mother; a father who loved Cosette and adored her, and who held that child as his light, his home, his family, his country, his paradise.

Thus when he saw that the end had absolutely come, that she was escaping from him, that she was slipping from his hands, that she was gliding from him, like a cloud, like water, when he had before his eyes this crushing proof: "another is the goal of her heart, another is the wish of her life; there is a dearest one, I am no longer anything but her father, I no longer exist"; when he could no longer doubt, when he said to himself: "She is going away from me!" the grief which he felt surpassed the bounds of possibility. To have done all that he had done for the purpose of ending like this! And the very idea of being nothing! Then, as we have just said, a quiver of revolt ran through him from head to foot. He felt, even in the very roots of his hair, the immense reawakening of egotism, and the *I* in this man's abyss howled.

There is such a thing as the sudden giving way of the inward subsoil. A despairing certainty does not make its way into a man without thrusting aside and breaking certain profound elements which, in some cases, are the very man himself. Grief, when it attains this shape, is a headlong flight of all the forces of the conscience. These are fatal crises. Few among us emerge from them still like ourselves and firm in duty. When the limit of endurance is overstepped, the most imperturbable virtue is disconcerted. Jean Valjean took the blotter again, and convinced himself afresh; he remained bowed and as though petrified and with staring eyes, over those four unobjectionable lines; and there arose within him such a cloud that one might have thought that everything in this soul was crumbling away.

He examined this revelation, athwart the exaggerations of reverie, with an apparent and terrifying calmness, for it is a fearful thing when a man's calmness reaches the coldness of the statue.

He measured the terrible step which his destiny had taken without his having a suspicion of the fact; he recalled his fears of the preceding summer, so foolishly dissipated; he recognized the precipice, it was still the same; only, Jean Valjean was no longer on the brink, he was at the bottom of it.

The unprecedented and heartrending thing about it was that he had fallen without perceiving it. All the light of his life had departed, while he still fancied that he beheld the sun.

His instinct did not hesitate. He put together certain circumstances, certain dates, certain blushes and certain pallors on Cosette's part, and he said to himself: "It is he."

The divination of despair is a sort of mysterious bow which never misses its aim. He struck Marius with his first conjecture. He did not know the name, but he found the man instantly. He distinctly perceived, in the background of the implacable conjuration of his memories, the unknown prowler of the Luxembourg, that wretched seeker of love adventures, that idler of romance, that idiot, that coward, for it is cowardly to come and make eyes at young girls who have beside them a father who loves them.

After he had thoroughly verified the fact that this young man was at the bottom of this situation, and that everything proceeded from that quarter, he, Jean Valjean, the regenerated man, the man who had so labored over his soul, the man who had made so many efforts to resolve all life, all misery, and all unhappiness into love, looked into his own breast and there beheld a specter, Hate.

Great griefs contain something of dejection. They discourage one with existence. The man into whom they enter feels something within him withdraw from him. In his youth, their visits are lugubrious; later on they are sinister. Alas, if despair is a fearful thing when the blood is hot, when the hair is black, when the head is erect on the body like the flame on the torch, when the roll of destiny still retains its full thickness, when the heart, full of desirable love, still possesses beats which can be returned to it, when one has time for redress, when all women and all smiles and all the future and all the horizon are before one, when the force of life is complete, what is it in old age, when the years hasten on, growing ever paler, to that twilight hour when one begins to behold the stars of the tomb?

While he was meditating, Toussaint entered. Jean Valjean rose and asked her:

"In what quarter is it? Do you know?"

Toussaint was struck dumb, and could only answer him:

"What is it, sir?"

Jean Valjean began again: "Did you not tell me that just now that there is fighting going on?"

"Ah! yes, sir," replied Toussaint. "It is in the direction of Saint-Merry."

There is a mechanical movement which comes to us, unconsciously, from the most profound depths of our thought. It was, no doubt, under the impulse of a movement of this sort, and of which he was hardly conscious, that Jean Valjean, five minutes later, found himself in the street.

Bareheaded, he sat upon the stone post at the door of his house. He seemed to be listening. Night had come.

Chapter II

THE STREET URCHIN AN ENEMY OF LIGHT

HOW LONG DID HE REMAIN THUS? WHAT WAS THE EBB AND FLOW OF THIS TRAGIC MEDITATION? Did he straighten up? Did he remain bowed? Had he been bent to breaking? Could he still rise and regain his footing in his conscience upon something solid? He probably would not have been able to tell himself.

The street was deserted. A few uneasy bourgeois, who were rapidly returning home, hardly saw him. Each one for himself in times of peril. The lamp-lighter came as usual to light the lantern which was situated precisely opposite the door of No. 7, and then went away. Jean Valjean would not have appeared like a living man to anyone who had examined him in that shadow. He sat there on the post of his door, motionless as a form of ice. There is congealment in despair. The alarm bells and a vague and stormy uproar were audible. In the midst of all these convulsions of the bell mingled with the revolt, the clock of Saint-Paul struck eleven, gravely and without haste; for the tocsin is man; the hour is God. The passage of the hour produced no effect on Jean Valjean; Jean Valjean did not stir. Still, at about that moment, a brusque report burst forth in the direction of the Halles, a second yet more violent followed; it was probably that attack on the barricade in the Rue de la Chanvrerie which we have just seen repulsed by Marius. At this double discharge, whose fury seemed augmented by the stupor of the night, Jean Valjean started; he rose, turning toward the quarter whence the noise proceeded; then he fell back upon the post again, folded his arms, and his head slowly sank on his bosom again.

He resumed his gloomy dialogue with himself.

All at once, he raised his eyes; someone was walking in the street, he heard steps near him. He looked, and by the light of the lanterns, in the direction of the street which ran into the Rue-aux-Archives, he perceived a young, livid, and beaming face.

Gavroche had just arrived in the Rue l'Homme Armé.

Gavroche was staring into the air, apparently in search of something. He saw Jean Valjean perfectly well, but he took no notice of him.

Gavroche after staring into the air, stared below; he raised himself on tiptoe, and felt of the doors and windows of the ground floor; they were all shut, bolted, and padlocked. After having authenticated the fronts of five or six barricaded houses in this manner, the urchin shrugged his shoulders, and took himself to task in these terms:

"Pardi!"

Then he began to stare into the air again.

Jean Valjean, who, an instant previously, in his then state of mind, would not have spoken to or even answered anyone, felt irresistibly impelled to accost that child.

"What is the matter with you, my little fellow?" he said.

"The matter with me is that I am hungry," replied Gavroche frankly. And he added: "Little fellow yourself."

Jean Valjean fumbled in his fob and pulled out a five-franc piece.

But Gavroche, who was of the wagtail species, and who skipped vivaciously from one gesture to another, had just picked up a stone. He had caught sight of the lantern.

"See here," said he, "you still have your lanterns here. You are disobeying the regulations, my friend. This is disorderly. Smash that for me."

And he flung the stone at the lantern, whose broken glass fell with such a clatter that the bourgeois in hiding behind their curtains in the opposite house cried: "There is 'Ninety-three' come again."

The lantern oscillated violently, and went out. The street had suddenly become black.

"That's right, old street," ejaculated Gavroche, "put on your night-cap."

And turning to Jean Valjean:

"What do you call that gigantic monument that you have there at the end of the street? It's the Archives, isn't it? I must crumble up those big stupids of pillars a bit and make a nice barricade out of them."

Jean Valjean stepped up to Gavroche.

"Poor creature," he said in a low tone, and speaking to himself, "he is hungry."

And he laid the hundred-sou piece in his hand.

Gavroche raised his face, astonished at the size of this sou; he stared at it in the darkness, and the whiteness of the big sou dazzled him. He knew five-franc pieces by hearsay; their reputation was agreeable to him; he was delighted to see one close to. He said:

"Let us contemplate the tiger."

He gazed at it for several minutes in ecstasy; then, turning to Jean Valjean, he held out the coin to him, and said majestically to him:

"Bourgeois, I prefer to smash lanterns. Take back your ferocious beast. You can't bribe me. That has got five claws; but it doesn't scratch me."

"Have you a mother?" asked Jean Valjean.

Gavroche replied:

"More than you have, perhaps."

"Well," returned Jean Valjean, "keep the money for your mother!"

Gavroche was touched. Moreover, he had just noticed that the man who was addressing him had no hat, and this inspired him with confidence.

"Truly," said he, "so it wasn't to keep me from breaking the lanterns?"

"Break whatever you please."

"You're a fine man," said Gavroche.

And he put the five-franc piece into one of his pockets.

His confidence having increased, he added:

"Do you belong in this street?"

"Yes, why?"

"Can you tell me where No. 7 is?"

"What do you want with No. 7?"

Here the child paused, he feared that he had said too much; he thrust his nails energetically into his hair and contented himself with replying:

"Ah! Here it is."

An idea flashed through Jean Valjean's mind. Anguish does have these gleams. He said to the lad:

"Are you the person who is bringing a letter that I am expecting?"

"You?" said Gavroche. "You are not a woman."

"The letter is for Mademoiselle Cosette, is it not?"

"Cosette," muttered Gavroche. "Yes, I believe that is the queer name."

"Well," resumed Jean Valjean, "I am the person to whom you are to deliver the letter. Give it here."

"In that case, you must know that I was sent from the barricade."

"Of course," said Jean Valjean.

Gavroche engulfed his hand in another of his pockets and drew out a paper folded in four. Then he made the military salute.

"Respect for dispatches," said he. "It comes from the Provisional Government."

"Give it to me," said Jean Valjean.

Gavroche held the paper elevated above his head.

"Don't go and fancy it's a love-letter. It is for a woman, but it's for the people. We men fight and we respect the fair sex. We are not as they are in fine society, where there are lions who send chickens[1] to camels."

"Give it to me."

"After all," continued Gavroche, "you have the air of an honest man."

"Give it to me quick."

"Catch hold of it."

And he handed the paper to Jean Valjean.

"And make haste, Monsieur What's-your-name, for Mamselle Cosette is waiting."

Gavroche was satisfied with himself for having produced this remark.

Jean Valjean began again:

"Is it to Saint-Merry that the answer is to be sent?"

"There you are making some of those bits of pastry vulgarly called *brioches* [blunders]. This letter comes from the barricade of the Rue de la Chanvrerie, and I'm going back there. Good evening, citizen."

That said, Gavroche took himself off, or, to describe it more exactly, fluttered away in the direction whence he had come with a flight like that of an escaped bird. He plunged back into the gloom as though he made a hole in it, with the rigid rapidity of a projectile; the alley of l'Homme Armé became silent and solitary once more; in a twinkling, that strange child, who had about him something of the shadow and of the dream, had buried himself in the mists of the rows of black houses, and was lost there, like smoke in the dark; and one might have thought that he had dissipated and vanished, had there not taken place, a few minutes after his disappearance, a startling shiver of glass, and had not the magnificent crash of a lantern rattling down on the pavement once more abruptly awakened the indignant bourgeois. It was Gavroche upon his way through the Rue du Chaume.

1. Love-letters.

Chapter III

WHILE COSETTE AND TOUSSAINT ARE ASLEEP

JEAN VALJEAN WENT INTO THE HOUSE WITH MARIUS'S LETTER.

He groped his way up the stairs, as pleased with the darkness as an owl who grips his prey, opened and shut his door softly, listened to see whether he could hear any noise—made sure that, to all appearances, Cosette and Toussaint were asleep, and plunged three or four matches into the bottle of the Fumade lighter before he could evoke a spark, so greatly did his hand tremble. What he had just done smacked of theft. At last the candle was lighted; he leaned his elbows on the table, unfolded the paper, and read.

In violent emotions, one does not read, one flings to the earth, so to speak, the paper which one holds, one clutches it like a victim, one crushes it, one digs into it the nails of one's wrath, or of one's joy; one hastens to the end, one leaps to the beginning; attention is at fever heat; it takes up in the gross, as it were, the essential points; it seizes on one point, and the rest disappears. In Marius's note to Cosette, Jean Valjean saw only these words.

"I die. When thou readest this, my soul will be near thee."

In the presence of these two lines, he was horribly dazzled; he remained for a moment, crushed, as it were, by the change of emotion which was taking place within him, he stared at Marius's note with a sort of intoxicated amazement, he had before his eyes that splendor, the death of a hated individual.

He uttered a frightful cry of inward joy. So it was all over. The catastrophe had arrived sooner than he had dared to hope. The being who obstructed his destiny was disappearing. That man had taken himself off of his own accord, freely, willingly. This man was going to his death, and he, Jean Valjean, had had no hand in the matter, and it was through no fault of his. Perhaps, even, he is already dead. Here his fever entered into calculations. No, he is not dead yet. The letter had evidently been intended for Cosette to read on the following morning; after the two discharges that were heard between eleven o'clock and midnight, nothing more has taken place; the barricade will not be attacked seriously until daybreak; but that makes no difference, from the moment when "that man" is concerned in this war, he is lost; he is caught in the gearing. Jean Valjean felt himself delivered. So he was about to find himself alone with Cosette once more. The rivalry would cease; the future was beginning again. He had but to keep this note in his pocket. Cosette would never know what had become of that man. All that there requires to be done is to let things take their own course. This man cannot escape. If he is not already dead, it is certain that he is about to die. What good fortune!

Having said all this to himself, he became gloomy.

Then he went downstairs and woke up the porter.

About an hour later, Jean Valjean went out in the complete costume of a National Guard, and with his arms. The porter had easily found in the neighborhood the wherewithal to complete his equipment. He had a loaded gun and a cartridge-box filled with cartridges.

He strode off in the direction of the markets.

Chapter IV

GAVROCHE'S EXCESS OF ZEAL

I N THE MEANTIME, GAVROCHE HAD HAD AN ADVENTURE.

Gavroche, after having conscientiously stoned the lantern in the Rue du Chaume, entered the Rue des Vielles-Haudriettes, and not seeing "even a cat" there, he thought the opportunity a good one to strike up all the song of which he was capable. His march, far from being retarded by his singing, was accelerated by it. He began to sow along the sleeping or terrified houses these incendiary couplets:

> "L'oiseau médit dans les charmilles,
> Et prétend qu'hier Atala
> Avec un Russe s'en alla.
> Où vont les belles filles,
> Lon la.

> "Mon ami Pierrot, tu babilles,
> Parce que l'autre jour Mila
> Cogna sa vitre et m'appela,
> Où vont les belles filles,
> Lon la.

> "Les drôlesses sont fort gentilles,
> Leur poison qui m'ensorcela
> Griserait Monsieur Orfila.
> Où vont les belles filles,
> Lon la.

> "J'aime l'amour et les bisbilles,
> J'aime Agnès, j'aime Paméla,
> Lise en m'allumant se brûla.
> Où vont les belles filles,
> Lon la.

> "Jadis, quand je vis les mantilles
> De Suzette et de Zéila,
> Mon ame à leurs plis se mêla,
> Où vont les belles filles,
> Lon la.

> "Amour, quand dans l'ombre où tu brilles,
> Tu coiffes de roses Lola,
> Je me damnerais pour cela.
> Où vont les belles filles,
> Lon la.

"Jeanne à ton miroir tu t'habilles!
Mon cœur un beau jour s'envola.
Je crois que c'est Jeanne qui l'a.
Où vont les belles filles,
Lon la.

"Le soir, en sortant des quadrilles,
Je montre aux étoiles Stella,
Et je leur dis: 'Régardez-la.'
Où vont les belles filles,
Lon la."[1]

Gavroche, as he sang, was lavish of his pantomime. Gesture is the strong point of the refrain. His face, an inexhaustible repertory of masks, produced grimaces more convulsing and more fantastic than the rents of a cloth torn in a high gale. Unfortunately, as he was alone, and as it was night, this was neither seen nor even visible. Such wastes of riches do occur.

All at once, he stopped short.

"Let us interrupt the romance," said he.

His feline eye had just descried, in the recess of a carriage door what is called in painting, an *ensemble*, that is to say, a person and a thing; the thing was a hand-cart, the person was a man from Auvergene who was sleeping therein.

The shafts of the cart rested on the pavement, and the Auvergnat's head was supported against the front of the cart. His body was coiled up on this inclined plane and his feet touched the ground.

Gavroche, with his experience of the things of this world, recognized a drunken man. He was some corner errand-man who had drunk too much and was sleeping too much.

"There now," thought Gavroche, "that's what the summer nights are good for. We'll take the cart for the Republic, and leave the Auvergnat for the Monarchy."

His mind had just been illuminated by this flash of light:

"How bully that cart would look on our barricade!"

The Auvergnat was snoring.

Gavroche gently tugged at the cart from behind, and at the Auvergnat from the front, that is to say, by the feet, and at the expiration of another minute the imperturbable Auvergnat was reposing flat on the pavement.

The cart was free.

Gavroche, habituated to facing the unexpected in all quarters, had everything about him. He

1. The bird slanders in the elms,
   And pretends that yesterday, Atala
   Went off with a Russian,
     Where fair maids go,
       Lon la.

My friend Pierrot, thou pratest, because Mila knocked at her pane the other day and called me. The jades are very charming, their poison which bewitched me would intoxicate Monsieur Orfila. I'm fond of love and its bickerings, I love Agnes, I love Pamela, Lise burned herself in setting me aflame. In former days when I saw the mantillas of Suzette and of Zeila, my soul mingled with their folds. Love, when thou gleamest in the dark thou crownest Lola with roses, I would lose my soul for that. Jeanne, at thy mirror thou deckest thyself! One fine day, my heart flew forth. I think that it is Jeanne who has it. At night, when I come from the quadrilles, I show Stella to the stars, and I say to them: "Behold her." Where fair maids go, lon la.

fumbled in one of his pockets, and pulled from it a scrap of paper and a bit of red pencil filched from some carpenter.

He wrote:

"French Republic."

"Received thy cart."

And he signed it: "GAVROCHE."

That done, he put the paper in the pocket of the still snoring Auvergnat's velvet vest, seized the cart shafts in both hands, and set off in the direction of the Halles, pushing the cart before him at a hard gallop with a glorious and triumphant uproar.

This was perilous. There was a post at the Royal Printing Establishment. Gavroche did not think of this. This post was occupied by the National Guards of the suburbs. The squad began to wake up, and heads were raised from camp beds. Two street-lanterns broken in succession, that ditty sung at the top of the lungs. This was a great deal for those cowardly streets, which desire to go to sleep at sunset, and which put the extinguisher on their candles at such an early hour. For the last hour, that boy had been creating an uproar in that peaceable arrondissement, the uproar of a fly in a bottle. The sergeant of the banlieue lent an ear. He waited. He was a prudent man.

The mad rattle of the cart, filled to overflowing the possible measure of waiting, and decided the sergeant to make a reconnaisance.

"There's a whole band of them there!" said he, "let us proceed gently."

It was clear that the hydra of anarchy had emerged from its box and that it was stalking abroad through the quarter.

And the sergeant ventured out of the post with cautious tread.

All at once, Gavroche, pushing his cart in front of him, and at the very moment when he was about to turn into the Rue des Vielles-Haudriettes, found himself face to face with a uniform, a shako, a plume, and a gun.

For the second time, he stopped short.

"Hullo," said he, "it's him. Good day, public order."

Gavroche's amazement was always brief and speedily thawed.

"Where are you going, you rascal?" shouted the sergeant.

"Citizen," retorted Gavroche, "I haven't called you 'bourgeois' yet. Why do you insult me?"

"Where are you going, you rogue?"

"Monsieur," retorted Gavroche, "perhaps you were a man of wit yesterday, but you have degenerated this morning."

"I ask you where are you going, you villain?"

Gavroche replied:

"You speak prettily. Really, no one would suppose you as old as you are. You ought to sell all your hair at a hundred francs apiece. That would yield you five hundred francs."

"Where are you going? Where are you going? Where are you going, bandit?"

Gavroche retorted again:

"What villainous words! You must wipe your mouth better the first time that they give you suck."

The sergeant lowered his bayonet.

"Will you tell me where you are going, you wretch?"

"General," said Gavroche "I'm on my way to look for a doctor for my wife who is in labor."

"To arms!" shouted the sergeant.

The master-stroke of strong men consists in saving themselves by the very means that have ruined them; Gavroche took in the whole situation at a glance. It was the cart which had told against him, it was the cart's place to protect him.

At the moment when the sergeant was on the point of making his descent on Gavroche, the cart, converted into a projectile and launched with all the latter's might, rolled down upon him furiously, and the sergeant, struck full in the stomach, tumbled over backwards into the gutter while his gun went off in the air.

The men of the post had rushed out pell-mell at the sergeant's shout; the shot brought on a general random discharge, after which they reloaded their weapons and began again.

This blind-man's-buff musketry lasted for a quarter of an hour and killed several panes of glass.

In the meanwhile, Gavroche, who had retraced his steps at full speed, halted five or six streets distant, and seated himself, panting, on the stone post which forms the corner of the Enfants-Rouges.

He listened.

After panting for a few minutes, he turned in the direction where the fusillade was raging, lifted his left hand to a level with his nose and thrust it forward three times, as he slapped the back of his head with his right hand; an imperious gesture in which Parisian street-urchindom has condensed French irony, and which is evidently efficacious, since it has already lasted half a century.

This gaiety was troubled by one bitter reflection.

"Yes," said he, "I'm splitting with laughter, I'm twisting with delight, I abound in joy, but I'm losing my way, I shall have to take a roundabout way. If I only reach the barricade in season!"

Thereupon he set out again on a run.

And as he ran:

"Ah, by the way, where was I?" said he.

And he resumed his ditty, as he plunged rapidly through the streets, and this is what died away in the gloom:

> *"Mais il reste encore des bastilles,*
> *Et je vais mettre le holà*
> *Dans l'orde public que voilà.*
>   *Où vont les belles filles,*
>   *Lon la.*
>
> *"Quelqu'un veut-il jouer aux quilles?*
> *Tout l'ancien monde s'écroula*
> *Quand la grosse boule roula.*
>   *Où vont les belles filles,*
>   *Lon la.*
>
> *"Vieux bon peuple, à coups de bequilles,*
> *Cassons ce Louvre ou s'étala*
> *La monarchie en falbala.*
>   *Où vont les belles filles,*
>   *Lon la.*
>
> *"Nous en avons forcé les grilles,*
> *Le roi Charles-Dix ce jour là,*
> *Tenait mal et se décolla.*
>   *Où vont les belles filles,*
>   *Lon la."*[1]

1. But some prisons still remain, and I am going to put a stop to this sort of public order. Does anyone wish to play at skittles? The whole ancient world fell in ruin, when the big ball rolled. Good old folks, let us smash with our crutches that Louvre where the monarchy displayed itself in furbelows. We have forced its gates. On that day, King Charles X did not stick well and came unglued.

The post's recourse to arms was not without result. The cart was conquered, the drunken man was taken prisoner. The first was put in the pound, the second was later on somewhat harassed before the councils of war as an accomplice. The public ministry of the day proved its indefatigable zeal in the defense of society, in this instance.

Gavroche's adventure, which has lingered as a tradition in the quarters of the Temple, is one of the most terrible souvenirs of the elderly bourgeois of the Marais, and is entitled in their memories: "The nocturnal attack by the post of the Royal Printing Establishment."

Volume V

Jean Valjean

BOOK FIRST

THE WAR BETWEEN FOUR WALLS

Chapter I

THE CHARYBDIS OF THE FAUBOURG SAINT-ANTOINE AND THE SCYLLA OF THE FAUBOURG DU TEMPLE

THE TWO MOST MEMORABLE BARRICADES WHICH THE OBSERVER OF SOCIAL MALADIES CAN name do not belong to the period in which the action of this work is laid. These two barricades, both of them symbols, under two different aspects, of a redoubtable situation, sprang from the earth at the time of the fatal insurrection of June, 1848, the greatest war of the streets that history has ever beheld.

It sometimes happens that, even contrary to principles, even contrary to liberty, equality, and fraternity, even contrary to the universal vote, even contrary to the government, by all for all, from the depths of its anguish, of its discouragements and its destitutions, of its fevers, of its distresses, of its miasmas, of its ignorances, of its darkness, that great and despairing body, the rabble, protests against, and that the populace wages battle against, the people.

Beggars attack the common right; the ochlocracy rises against demos.

These are melancholy days; for there is always a certain amount of night even in this madness, there is suicide in this duel, and those words which are intended to be insults—beggars, canaille, ochlocracy, populace—exhibit, alas! rather the fault of those who reign than the fault of those who suffer, rather the fault of the privileged than the fault of the disinherited.

For our own part, we never pronounce those words without pain and without respect, for when philosophy fathoms the facts to which they correspond, it often finds many a grandeur beside these miseries. Athens was an ochlocracy; the beggars were the making of Holland; the populace saved Rome more than once; and the rabble followed Jesus Christ.

There is no thinker who has not at times contemplated the magnificences of the lower classes.

It was of this rabble that Saint Jerome was thinking, no doubt, and of all these poor people and all these vagabonds and all these miserable people whence sprang the apostles and the martyrs, when he uttered this mysterious saying: *"Fex urbis, lex orbis"*—the dregs of the city, the law of the earth.

The exasperations of this crowd which suffers and bleeds, its violences contrary to all sense, directed against the principles which are its life, its masterful deeds against the right, are its popular *coups d'état* and should be repressed. The man of probity sacrifices himself, and out of his very love for this crowd, he combats it. But how excusable he feels it even while holding out against it! How he venerates it even while resisting it! This is one of those rare moments, when, while doing that which it is one's duty to do, one feels something which disconcerts one, and which would dissuade one from proceeding further; one persists, it is necessary, but conscience, though satisfied, is sad, and the accomplishment of duty is complicated with a pain at the heart.

June, 1848, let us hasten to say, was an exceptional fact, and almost impossible of classification, in the philosophy of history. All the words which we have just uttered, must be discarded, when it becomes a question of this extraordinary revolt, in which one feels the holy anxiety of toil claiming its rights. It was necessary to combat it, and this was a duty, for it attacked the republic. But what was June, 1848, at bottom? A revolt of the people against itself.

Where the subject is not lost sight of, there is no digression; may we, then, be permitted to arrest the reader's attention for a moment on the two absolutely unique barricades of which we have just spoken and which characterized this insurrection.

One blocked the entrance to the Faubourg Saint-Antoine; the other defended the approach to the Faubourg du Temple; those before whom these two fearful masterpieces of civil war reared themselves beneath the brilliant blue sky of June, will never forget them.

The Saint-Antoine barricade was tremendous; it was three stories high, and seven hundred feet wide. It barred the vast opening of the faubourg, that is to say, three streets, from angle to angle; ravined, jagged, cut up, divided, crenelated, with an immense rent, buttressed with piles that were bastions in themselves, throwing out capes here and there, powerfully backed up by two great promontories of houses of the faubourg, it reared itself like a cyclopean dike at the end of the formidable place which had seen the 14th of July. Nineteen barricades were ranged, one behind the other, in the depths of the streets behind this principal barricade. At the very sight of it, one felt the agonizing suffering in the immense faubourg, which had reached that point of extremity when a distress may become a catastrophe. Of what was that barricade made? Of the ruins of three six-story houses demolished expressly, said some. Of the prodigy of all wraths, said others. It wore the lamentable aspect of all constructions of hatred, ruin. It might be asked: Who built this? It might also be said: Who destroyed this? It was the improvisation of the ebullition. Hold! take this door! this grating! this penthouse! this chimney-piece! this broken brazier! this cracked pot! Give all! cast away all! Push this roll, dig, dismantle, overturn, ruin everything! It was the collaboration of the pavement, the block of stone, the beam, the bar of iron, the rag, the scrap, the broken pane, the unseated chair, the cabbage-stalk, the tatter, the rag, and the malediction. It was grand and it was petty. It was the abyss parodied on the public place by hubbub. The mass beside the atom; the strip of ruined wall and the broken bowl—threatening fraternization of every sort of rubbish. Sisyphus had thrown his rock there and Job his potsherd. Terrible, in short. It was the acropolis of the barefooted. Overturned carts broke the uniformity of the slope; an immense dray was spread out there crossways, its axle pointing heavenward, and seemed a scar on that tumultuous façade; an omnibus hoisted gaily, by main force, to the very summit of the heap, as though the architects of this bit of savagery had wished to add a touch of the street urchin humor to their terror, presented its horseless, unharnessed pole to no one knows what horses of the air. This gigantic heap, the alluvium of the revolt, figured to the mind an Ossa on Pelion of all revolutions; '93 on '89, the 9th of Thermidor on the 10th of August, the 18th of Brumaire on the 11th of January, Vendémiaire on Prairial, 1848 on 1830. The situation deserved the trouble and this barricade was worthy to figure on the very spot whence the Bastille had disappeared. If the ocean made dikes, it is thus that it would build. The fury of the flood was stamped upon this shapeless mass. What flood? The crowd. One thought one beheld hubbub petrified. One thought one heard humming above this barricade as though there had been over their hive, enormous, dark bees of violent progress. Was it a thicket? Was it a bacchanalia? Was it a fortress? Vertigo seemed to have constructed it with blows of its wings. There was something of the cesspool in that redoubt and something Olympian in that confusion. One there beheld in a pell-mell full of despair, the rafters of roofs, bits of garret windows with their figured paper, window sashes with their glass planted there in the ruins awaiting the cannon, wrecks of chimneys, cupboards, tables, benches, a howling topsyturveydom, and those thousand poverty-stricken things, the very refuse of the mendicant, which contain at the same time fury and nothingness. One would have said that it was the tatters of a people, rags of wood, of iron, of bronze, of stone, and that the Faubourg Saint-Antoine had thrust it there at its door, with a colossal flourish of the broom making of its misery its barricade. Blocks resembling headsman's blocks, dislocated chains, pieces of woodwork with brackets having the form of gibbets, horizontal wheels projecting from the rubbish, amalgamated with this edifice of anarchy the somber figure of the old tortures endured by the people. The barricade Saint-Antoine converted everything into a weapon; everything that civil war could throw at the head of society proceeded thence; it was not combat, it was a paroxysm; the carbines which defended this redoubt, among which there were some blunderbusses, sent bits of earthenware, bones, coat-buttons, even the casters from nightstands, dangerous projectiles on account of the brass. This barricade was furious; it hurled to the clouds an inexpressible clamor; at certain moments, when provoking the army, it was covered with throngs and tempest; a tumultuous crowd of flaming heads crowned it; a swarm filled it; it had a thorny crest of guns, of sabers, of cudgels, of axes, of pikes and of bayonets; a vast red flag flapped in the wind; shouts of command, songs of attack, the roll of drums, the sobs of women and bursts of gloomy laughter from the starving were to be heard there. It was huge and living, and, like the back of an electric beast, there proceeded from it little flashes of lightning. The spirit of revolution covered with its cloud this summit where rumbled that voice of the people which resembles the voice of God; a strange majesty was emitted by this titanic basket of rubbish. It was a heap of filth and it was Sinai.

As we have said previously, it attacked in the name of the revolution—what? The revolution. It—that barricade, chance, hazard, disorder, terror, misunderstanding, the unknown—had facing it the Constituent Assembly, the sovereignty of the people, universal suffrage, the nation, the republic; and it was the Carmagnole bidding defiance to the Marseillaise.

Immense but heroic defiance, for the old faubourg is a hero.

The faubourg and its redoubt lent each other assistance. The faubourg shouldered the redoubt, the redoubt took its stand under cover of the faubourg. The vast barricade spread out like a cliff against which the strategy of the African generals dashed itself. Its caverns, its excrescences, its warts, its gibbosities, grimaced, so to speak, and grinned beneath the smoke. The mitraille vanished in shapelessness; the bombs plunged into it; bullets only succeeded in making holes in it; what was the use of cannonading chaos? and the regiments, accustomed to the fiercest visions of war, gazed with uneasy eyes on that species of redoubt, a wild beast in its boar-like bristling and a mountain by its enormous size.

A quarter of a league away, from the corner of the Rue du Temple which debouches on the boulevard near the Château-d'Eau, if one thrust one's head bodily beyond the point formed by the front of the Dallemagne shop, one perceived in the distance, beyond the canal, in the street which mounts the slopes of Belleville at the culminating point of the rise, a strange wall reaching to the second story of the house fronts, a sort of hyphen between the houses on the right and the houses on the left, as though the street had folded back on itself its loftiest wall in order to close itself abruptly. This wall was built of paving-stones. It was straight, correct, cold, perpendicular, leveled with the square, laid out by rule and line. Cement was lacking, of course, but, as in the case of certain Roman walls, without interfering with its rigid architecture. The entablature was mathematically parallel with the base. From distance to distance, one could distinguish on the gray surface, almost invisible loopholes which resembled black threads. These loopholes were separated from each other by equal spaces. The street was deserted as far as the eye could reach. All windows and doors were closed. In the background rose this barrier, which made a blind thoroughfare of the street, a motionless and tranquil wall; no one was visible, nothing was audible; not a cry, not a sound, not a breath. A sepulcher.

The dazzling sun of June inundated this terrible thing with light.

It was the barricade of the Faubourg du Temple.

As soon as one arrived on the spot, and caught sight of it, it was impossible, even for the boldest, not to become thoughtful before this mysterious apparition. It was adjusted, jointed, imbricated, rectilinear, symmetrical and funereal. Science and gloom met there. One felt that the chief of this barricade was a geometrician or a specter. One looked at it and spoke low.

From time to time, if some soldier, an officer or representative of the people, chanced to traverse the deserted highway, a faint, sharp whistle was heard, and the passer-by fell dead or wounded, or, if he escaped the bullet, sometimes a biscaïen was seen to ensconce itself in some closed shutter, in the interstice between two blocks of stone, or in the plaster of a wall. For the men in the barricade had made themselves two small cannons out of two cast-iron lengths of gas-pipe, plugged up at one end with tow and fire-clay. There was no waste of useless powder. Nearly every shot told. There were corpses here and there, and pools of blood on the pavement. I remember a white butterfly which went and came in the street. Summer does not abdicate.

In the neighborhood, the spaces beneath the portes-cochères were encumbered with wounded.

One felt one's self aimed at by some person whom one did not see, and one understood that guns were leveled at the whole length of the street.

Massed behind the sort of sloping ridge which the vaulted canal forms at the entrance to the Faubourg du Temple, the soldiers of the attacking column, gravely and thoughtfully, watched this dismal redoubt, this immobility, this passivity, whence sprang death. Some crawled flat on their faces as far as the crest of the curve of the bridge, taking care that their shakos did not project beyond it.

The valiant Colonel Monteynard admired this barricade with a shudder.—"How that is built!" he said to a Representative. "Not one paving-stone projects beyond its neighbor. It is made of porcelain."—At that moment, a bullet broke the cross on his breast, and he fell.

"The cowards!" people said. "Let them show themselves! Let us see them! They dare not! They are hiding!"

The barricade of the Faubourg du Temple, defended by eighty men, attacked by ten thousand, held out for three days. On the fourth, they did as at Zaatcha, as at Constantine, they pierced the houses, they came over the roofs, the barricade was taken. Not one of the eighty cowards thought of flight, all were killed there with the exception of the leader, Barthélemy, of whom we shall speak presently.

The Saint-Antoine barricade was the tumult of thunders; the barricade of the Temple was silence. The difference between these two redoubts was the difference between the formidable and the sinister. One seemed a maw; the other a mask.

Admitting that the gigantic and gloomy insurrection of June was composed of a wrath and of an enigma, one divined in the first barricade the dragon, and behind the second the sphinx.

These two fortresses had been erected by two men named, the one, Cournet, the other, Barthélemy. Cournet made the Saint-Antoine barricade; Barthélemy the barricade of the Temple. Each was the image of the man who had built it.

Cournet was a man of lofty stature; he had broad shoulders, a red face, a crushing fist, a bold heart, a loyal soul, a sincere and terrible eye. Intrepid, energetic, irascible, stormy; the most cordial of men, the most formidable of combatants. War, strife, conflict, were the very air he breathed and put him in a good humor. He had been an officer in the navy, and, from his gestures and his voice, one divined that he sprang from the ocean, and that he came from the tempest; he carried the hurricane on into battle. With the exception of the genius, there was in Cournet something of Danton, as, with the exception of the divinity, there was in Danton something of Hercules.

Barthélemy, thin, feeble, pale, taciturn, was a sort of tragic street urchin, who, having had his ears boxed by a policeman, lay in wait for him, and killed him, and at seventeen was sent to the galleys. He came out and made this barricade.

Later on, fatal circumstance, in London, proscribed by all, Barthélemy slew Cournet. It was a funeral duel. Sometime afterwards, caught in the gearing of one of those mysterious adventures in which passion plays a part, a catastrophe in which French justice sees extenuating circumstances, and in which English justice sees only death, Barthélemy was hanged. The somber social construction is so made that, thanks to material destitution, thanks to moral obscurity, that unhappy being who possessed an intelligence, certainly firm, possibly great, began in France with the galleys, and ended in England with the gallows. Barthélemy, on occasion, flew but one flag, the black flag.

Chapter II

WHAT IS TO BE DONE IN THE ABYSS IF ONE DOES NOT CONVERSE

SIXTEEN YEARS COUNT IN THE SUBTERRANEAN EDUCATION OF INSURRECTION, AND JUNE, 1848, knew a great deal more about it than June, 1832. So the barricade of the Rue de la Chanvrerie was only an outline, and an embryo compared to the two colossal barricades which we have just sketched; but it was formidable for that epoch.

The insurgents, under the eye of Enjolras, for Marius no longer looked after anything, had made good use of the night. The barricade had been not only repaired, but augmented. They had raised it two feet. Bars of iron planted in the pavement resembled lances in rest. All sorts of rubbish brought and added from all directions complicated the external confusion. The redoubt had been cleverly made over into a wall on the inside and a thicket on the outside.

The staircase of paving-stones which permitted one to mount it like the wall of a citadel had been reconstructed.

The barricade had been put in order, the tap-room disencumbered, the kitchen appropriated for the ambulance, the dressing of the wounded completed, the powder scattered on the ground and on the tables had been gathered up, bullets run, cartridges manufactured, lint scraped, the fallen weapons redistributed, the interior of the redoubt cleaned, the rubbish swept up, corpses removed.

They laid the dead in a heap in the Mondétour lane, of which they were still the masters. The pavement was red for a long time at that spot. Among the dead there were four National Guardsmen of the suburbs. Enjolras had their uniforms laid aside.

Enjolras had advised two hours of sleep. Advice from Enjolras was a command. Still, only three or four took advantage of it.

Feuilly employed these two hours in engraving this inscription on the wall which faced the tavern:

LONG LIVE THE PEOPLES!

These four words, hollowed out in the rough stone with a nail, could still be read on the wall in 1848.

The three women had profited by the respite of the night to vanish definitely; which allowed the insurgents to breathe more freely.

They had found means of taking refuge in some neighboring house.

The greater part of the wounded were able, and wished, to fight still. On a litter of mattresses and trusses of straw in the kitchen, which had been converted into an ambulance, there were five men gravely wounded, two of whom were municipal guardsmen. The municipal guardsmen were attended to first.

In the tap-room there remained only Mabeuf under his black cloth and Javert bound to his post.

"This is the hall of the dead," said Enjolras.

In the interior of this hall, barely lighted by a candle at one end, the mortuary table being behind the post like a horizontal bar, a sort of vast, vague cross resulted from Javert erect and Mabeuf lying prone.

The pole of the omnibus, although snapped off by the fusillade, was still sufficiently upright to admit of their fastening the flag to it.

Enjolras, who possessed that quality of a leader, of always doing what he said, attached to this staff the bullet-ridden and bloody coat of the old man's.

No repast had been possible. There was neither bread nor meat. The fifty men in the barricade had speedily exhausted the scanty provisions of the wine-shop during the sixteen hours which they had passed there. At a given moment, every barricade inevitably becomes the raft of *la Méduse*. They were obliged to resign themselves to hunger. They had then reached the first hours of that Spartan day of the 6th of June when, in the barricade Saint-Merry, Jeanne, surrounded by the insurgents who demanded bread, replied to all combatants crying: "Something to eat!" with: "Why? It is three o'clock; at four we shall be dead."

As they could no longer eat, Enjolras forbade them to drink. He interdicted wine, and portioned out the brandy.

They had found in the cellar fifteen full bottles hermetically sealed. Enjolras and Combeferre examined them. Combeferre when he came up again said: "It's the old stock of Father Hucheloup, who began business as a grocer."—"It must be real wine," observed Bossuet. "It's lucky that Grantaire is asleep. If he were on foot, there would be a good deal of difficulty in saving those bottles."—Enjolras, in spite of all murmurs, placed his veto on the fifteen bottles, and, in order that no one might touch them, he had them placed under the table on which Father Mabeuf was lying.

About two o'clock in the morning, they reckoned up their strength. There were still thirty-seven of them.

The day began to dawn. The torch, which had been replaced in its cavity in the pavement, had just been extinguished. The interior of the barricade, that species of tiny courtyard appropriated from the street, was bathed in shadows, and resembled, athwart the vague, twilight horror, the deck of a disabled ship. The combatants, as they went and came, moved about there like black forms. Above that terrible nesting-place of gloom the stories of the mute houses were lividly outlined; at the very top, the chimneys stood palely out. The sky was of that charming, undecided hue, which may be white and may be blue. Birds flew about in it with cries of joy. The lofty house which formed the back of the barricade, being turned to the East, had upon its roof a rosy reflection. The morning breeze ruffled the gray hair on the head of the dead man at the third-story window.

"I am delighted that the torch has been extinguished," said Courfeyrac to Feuilly. "That torch flickering in the wind annoyed me. It had the appearance of being afraid. The light of torches resembles the wisdom of cowards; it gives a bad light because it trembles."

Dawn awakens minds as it does the birds; all began to talk.

Joly, perceiving a cat prowling on a gutter, extracted philosophy from it.

"What is the cat?" he exclaimed. "It is a corrective. The good God, having made the mouse, said: 'Hullo! I have committed a blunder.' And so he made the cat. The cat is the erratum of the mouse. The mouse, plus the cat, is the proof of creation revised and corrected."

Combeferre, surrounded by students and artisans, was speaking of the dead, of Jean Prouvaire, of Bahorel, of Mabeuf, and even of Cabuc, and of Enjolras's sad severity. He said:

"Harmodius and Aristogiton, Brutus, Chereas, Stephanus, Cromwell, Charlotte Corday, Sand, have all had their moment of agony when it was too late. Our hearts quiver so, and human life is such a mystery that, even in the case of a civic murder, even in a murder for liberation, if there be such a thing, the remorse for having struck a man surpasses the joy of having served the human race."

And, such are the windings of the exchange of speech, that, a moment later, by a transition brought about through Jean Prouvaire's verses, Combeferre was comparing the translators of the Georgics, Raux with Cournand, Cournand with Delille, pointing out the passages translated by Malfilâtre, particularly the prodigies of Cæsar's death; and at that word, Cæsar, the conversation reverted to Brutus.

"Cæsar," said Combeferre, "fell justly. Cicero was severe toward Cæsar, and he was right. That severity is not diatribe. When Zoïlus insults Homer, when Mævius insults Virgil, when Visé insults Molière, when Pope insults Shakespeare, when Frederic insults Voltaire, it is an old law of envy and hatred which is being carried out; geniuses attract insult, great men are always more or less barked at. But Zoïlus and Cicero are two different persons. Cicero is an arbiter in thought, just as Brutus is an arbiter by the sword. For my own part, I blame that last justice, the blade; but antiquity admitted it. Cæsar, the violator of the Rubicon, conferring, as though they came from him, the dignities which emanated from the people, not rising at the entrance of the senate, committed the acts of a king and almost of a tyrant, *regia ac pene tyrannica*. He was a great man; so much the worse, or so much the better; the lesson is but the more exalted. His twenty-three wounds touch me less than the spitting in the face of Jesus Christ. Cæsar is stabbed by the senators; Christ is cuffed by lackeys. One feels the God through the greater outrage."

Bossuet, who towered above the interlocutors from the summit of a heap of paving-stones, exclaimed, rifle in hand:

"Oh Cydathenæum, Oh Myrrhinus, Oh Probalinthus, Oh graces of the Æantides! Oh! Who will grant me to pronounce the verses of Homer like a Greek of Laurium or of Edapteon?"

Chapter III

Light and Shadow

ENJOLRAS HAD BEEN TO MAKE A RECONNAISSANCE. HE HAD MADE HIS WAY OUT THROUGH Mondétour lane, gliding along close to the houses.

The insurgents, we will remark, were full of hope. The manner in which they had repulsed the attack of the preceding night had caused them to almost disdain in advance the attack at dawn. They waited for it with a smile. They had no more doubt as to their success than as to their cause. Moreover, succor was, evidently, on the way to them. They reckoned on it. With that facility of triumphant prophecy which is one of the sources of strength in the French combatant, they divided the day which was at hand into three distinct phases. At six o'clock in the morning a regiment "which had been labored with," would turn; at noon, the insurrection of all Paris; at sunset, revolution.

They heard the alarm bell of Saint-Merry, which had not been silent for an instant since the night before; a proof that the other barricade, the great one, Jeanne's, still held out.

All these hopes were exchanged between the different groups in a sort of gay and formidable whisper which resembled the warlike hum of a hive of bees.

Enjolras reappeared. He returned from his somber eagle flight into outer darkness. He listened for a moment to all this joy with folded arms, and one hand on his mouth. Then, fresh and rosy in the growing whiteness of the dawn, he said:

"The whole army of Paris is to strike. A third of the army is bearing down upon the barricades in which you now are. There is the National Guard in addition. I have picked out the shakos of the fifth of the line, and the standard-bearers of the sixth legion. In one hour you will be attacked. As for the populace, it was seething yesterday, to-day it is not stirring. There is nothing to expect; nothing to hope for. Neither from a faubourg nor from a regiment. You are abandoned."

These words fell upon the buzzing of the groups, and produced on them the effect caused on a swarm of bees by the first drops of a storm. A moment of indescribable silence ensued, in which death might have been heard flitting by.

This moment was brief.

A voice from the obscurest depths of the groups shouted to Enjolras:

"So be it. Let us raise the barricade to a height of twenty feet, and let us all remain in it. Citizens, let us offer the protests of corpses. Let us show that, if the people abandon the republicans, the republicans do not abandon the people."

These words freed the thought of all from the painful cloud of individual anxieties. It was hailed with an enthusiastic acclamation.

No one ever has known the name of the man who spoke thus; he was some unknown blouse-wearer, a stranger, a man forgotten, a passing hero, that great anonymous always mingled in human crises and in social geneses who, at a given moment, utters in a supreme fashion the decisive word, and who vanishes into the shadows after having represented for a minute, in a lightning flash, the people and God.

This inexorable resolution so thoroughly impregnated the air of the 6th of June, 1832, that, almost at the very same hour, on the barricade Saint-Merry, the insurgents were raising that clamor which has become a matter of history and which has been consigned to the documents in the case: "What matters it whether they come to our assistance or not? Let us get ourselves killed here, to the very last man."

As the reader sees, the two barricades, though materially isolated, were in communication with each other.

Chapter IV

MINUS FIVE, PLUS ONE

AFTER THE MAN WHO DECREED THE "PROTEST OF CORPSES" HAD SPOKEN, AND HAD GIVEN THIS formula of their common soul, there issued from all mouths a strangely satisfied and terrible cry, funereal in sense and triumphant in tone:

"Long live death! Let us all remain here!"

"Why all?" said Enjolras.

"All! All!"

Enjolras resumed:

"The position is good; the barricade is fine. Thirty men are enough. Why sacrifice forty?"

They replied:

"Because not one will go away."

"Citizens," cried Enjolras, and there was an almost irritated vibration in his voice, "this republic is not rich enough in men to indulge in useless expenditure of them. Vain-glory is waste. If the duty of some is to depart, that duty should be fulfilled like any other."

Enjolras, the man-principle, had over his co-religionists that sort of omnipotent power which emanates from the absolute. Still, great as was this omnipotence, a murmur arose. A leader to the very finger-tips, Enjolras, seeing that they murmured, insisted. He resumed haughtily:

"Let those who are afraid of not numbering more than thirty say so."

The murmurs redoubled.

"Besides," observed a voice in one group, "it is easy enough to talk about leaving. The barricade is hemmed in."

"Not on the side of the Halles," said Enjolras. "The Rue Mondétour is free, and through the Rue des Prêcheurs one can reach the Marché des Innocents."

"And there," went on another voice, "you would be captured. You would fall in with some grand guard of the line or the suburbs; they will spy a man passing in blouse and cap. 'Whence come you?' 'Don't you belong to the barricade?' And they will look at your hands. You smell of powder. Shot."

Enjolras, without making any reply, touched Combeferre's shoulder, and the two entered the tap-room.

They emerged thence a moment later. Enjolras held in his outstretched hands the four uniforms which he had laid aside. Combeferre followed, carrying the shoulder-belts and the shakos.

"With this uniform," said Enjolras, "you can mingle with the ranks and escape; here is enough for four." And he flung on the ground, deprived of its pavement, the four uniforms.

No wavering took place in his stoical audience. Combeferre took the word.

"Come," said he, "you must have a little pity. Do you know what the question is here? It is a question of women. See here. Are there women or are there not? Are there children or are there not? Are there mothers, yes or no, who rock cradles with their foot and who have a lot of little ones around them? Let that man of you who has never beheld a nurse's breast raise his hand. Ah! you want to get yourselves killed, so do I—I, who am speaking to you; but I do not want to feel the phantoms of women wreathing their arms around me. Die, if you will, but don't make others die. Suicides like that which is on the brink of accomplishment here are sublime; but suicide is narrow, and does not admit of extension; and as soon as it touches your neighbors, suicide is murder. Think of the little blond heads; think of the white locks. Listen, Enjolras has just told me that he saw at the corner of the Rue du Cygne a lighted casement, a candle in a poor window, on the fifth floor, and on the pane the quivering shadow of the head of an old woman, who had the air of having spent the night in watching. Perhaps she is the mother of someone of you. Well, let that man go, and make haste to say to his mother: 'Here I am, mother!' Let him feel at ease, the task here will be performed all the same. When one supports one's relatives by one's toil, one has not the right to sacrifice one's self. That is deserting one's family. And those who have daughters! what are you thinking of? You get yourselves killed, you are dead, that is well. And to-morrow? Young girls without bread—that is a terrible thing. Man begs, woman sells. Ah! those charming and gracious beings, so gracious and so sweet, who have bonnets of flowers, who fill the house with purity, who sing and prattle, who are like a living perfume, who prove the existence of angels in heaven by the purity of virgins on earth, that Jeanne, that Lise, that Mimi, those adorable and honest creatures who are your blessings and your pride, ah! good God, they will suffer hunger! What do you want me to say to you? There is a market for human flesh; and it is not with your shadowy hands, shuddering around them, that you will prevent them from entering it! Think of the street, think of the pavement covered with passers-by, think of the shops past which women go and come with necks all bare, and through the mire. These women, too, were pure once. Think of your sisters, those of you who have them. Misery, prostitution, the police, Saint-Lazare—that is what those beautiful, delicate girls, those fragile marvels of modesty, gentleness and loveliness, fresher than lilacs in the month of May, will come to. Ah! you have got yourselves killed! You are no longer on hand! That is well; you have wished to release the people from Royalty, and you deliver over your daughters to the police. Friends, have a care, have mercy. Women, unhappy women, we are not in the habit of bestowing much thought on them. We trust to the women not having received a man's education, we prevent their reading, we prevent their thinking, we prevent their occupying themselves with politics; will you prevent them from going to the dead-house this evening, and recognizing your bodies? Let us see, those who have families must be tractable, and shake hands with us and take themselves off, and leave us here alone to attend to this affair. I know well that courage is required to leave, that it is hard; but the harder it is, the more meritorious. You say: 'I have a gun, I am at the barricade; so much the worse, I shall remain there.' So much the worse is easily said. My friends, there is a morrow; you will not be here to-morrow, but your families will; and what sufferings! See, here is a pretty, healthy child, with cheeks like an apple, who babbles, prattles, chatters, who laughs, who smells sweet beneath your kiss—and do you know what becomes of him when he is abandoned? I have seen one, a very small creature, no taller than that. His father was dead. Poor people had taken him in out of charity, but they had bread only for themselves. The child was always hungry. It was winter. He did not cry. You could see him approach the stove, in which there was never any fire, and whose pipe, you know, was of mastic and yellow clay. His breathing was hoarse, his face livid, his limbs flaccid, his belly prominent. He said nothing. If you spoke to him, he did not answer. He is dead. He was taken to the Necker Hospital, where I saw him. I was house-surgeon in that hospital. Now, if there are any fathers among you, fathers whose happiness it is to stroll on Sundays holding their child's tiny hand in their robust hand, let each one of those fathers imagine that this child is his own. That poor brat, I remember, and I seem to see him now, when he lay nude on the dissecting table, how his ribs stood out on his skin like the graves beneath the grass in a cemetery. A sort of mud was found in his stomach. There were ashes in his teeth. Come, let us examine ourselves conscientiously and take counsel with our heart. Statistics show that the mortality among abandoned children is fifty-five per cent. I repeat, it is a question of women, it concerns mothers, it concerns young girls, it concerns little children. Who is talking to you of yourselves? We know well what you are; we know well that you are all brave, parbleu! we know well that you all have in your souls the joy and the glory of giving your life for the great cause; we know well that you feel yourselves elected to die usefully and magnificently, and that each one of you clings to his share in the triumph. Very well. But you are not alone in this world. There are other beings of whom you must think. You must not be egoists."

All dropped their heads with a gloomy air.

Strange contradictions of the human heart at its most sublime moments. Combeferre, who spoke thus, was not an orphan. He recalled the mothers of other men, and forgot his own. He was about to get himself killed. He was "an egoist."

Marius, fasting, fevered, having emerged in succession from all hope, and having been stranded in grief, the most somber of shipwrecks, and saturated with violent emotions and conscious that the end was near, had plunged deeper and deeper into that visionary stupor which always precedes the fatal hour voluntarily accepted.

A physiologist might have studied in him the growing symptoms of that febrile absorption known to, and classified by, science, and which is to suffering what voluptuousness is to pleasure. Despair, also, has its ecstasy. Marius had reached this point. He looked on at everything as from without; as we have said, things which passed before him seemed far away; he made out the whole, but did not perceive the details. He beheld men going and coming as through a flame. He heard voices speaking as at the bottom of an abyss.

But this moved him. There was in this scene, a point which pierced and roused even him. He had but one idea now, to die; and he did not wish to be turned aside from it, but he reflected, in his gloomy somnambulism, that while destroying himself, he was not prohibited from saving someone else.

He raised his voice.

"Enjolras and Combeferre are right," said he; "no unnecessary sacrifice. I join them, and you must make haste. Combeferre has said convincing things to you. There are some among you who have families, mothers, sisters, wives, children. Let such leave the ranks."

No one stirred.

"Married men and the supporters of families, step out of the ranks!" repeated Marius.

His authority was great. Enjolras was certainly the head of the barricade, but Marius was its savior.

"I order it," cried Enjolras.

"I entreat you," said Marius.

Then, touched by Combeferre's words, shaken by Enjolras's order, touched by Marius's entreaty, these heroic men began to denounce each other.—"It is true," said one young man to a full grown man, "you are the father of a family. Go."—"It is your duty rather," retorted the man, "you have two sisters whom you maintain."—And an unprecedented controversy broke forth. Each struggled to determine which should not allow himself to be placed at the door of the tomb.

"Make haste," said Courfeyrac, "in another quarter of an hour it will be too late."

"Citizens," pursued Enjolras, "this is the Republic, and universal suffrage reigns. Do you yourselves designate those who are to go."

They obeyed. After the expiration of a few minutes, five were unanimously selected and stepped out of the ranks.

"There are five of them!" exclaimed Marius.

There were only four uniforms.

"Well," began the five, "one must stay behind."

And then a struggle arose as to who should remain, and who should find reasons for the others not remaining. The generous quarrel began afresh.

"You have a wife who loves you."—"You have your aged mother."—"You have neither father nor mother, and what is to become of your three little brothers?"—"You are the father of five children."—"You have a right to live, you are only seventeen, it is too early for you to die."

These great revolutionary barricades were assembling points for heroism. The improbable was simple there. These men did not astonish each other.

"Be quick," repeated Courfeyrac.

Men shouted to Marius from the groups:

"Do you designate who is to remain."

"Yes," said the five, "choose. We will obey you."

Marius did not believe that he was capable of another emotion. Still, at this idea, that of choosing a man for death, his blood rushed back to his heart. He would have turned pale, had it been possible for him to become any paler.

He advanced toward the five, who smiled upon him, and each, with his eyes full of that grand flame which one beholds in the depths of history hovering over Thermopylæ, cried to him:

"Me! me! me!"

And Marius stupidly counted them; there were still five of them! Then his glance dropped to the four uniforms.

At that moment, a fifth uniform fell, as if from heaven, upon the other four.

The fifth man was saved.

Marius raised his eyes and recognized M. Fauchelevent.

Jean Valjean had just entered the barricade.

He had arrived by way of Mondétour lane, whether by dint of inquiries made, or by instinct, or chance. Thanks to his dress of a National Guardsman, he had made his way without difficulty.

The sentinel stationed by the insurgents in the Rue Mondétour, had no occasion to give the alarm for a single National Guardsman, and he had allowed the latter to entangle himself in the street, saying to himself: "Probably it is a reinforcement, in any case it is a prisoner." The moment was too grave to admit of the sentinel abandoning his duty and his post of observation.

At the moment when Jean Valjean entered the redoubt, no one had noticed him, all eyes being fixed on the five chosen men and the four uniforms. Jean Valjean also had seen and heard, and he had silently removed his coat and flung it on the pile with the rest.

The emotion aroused was indescribable.

"Who is this man?" demanded Bossuet.

"He is a man who saves others," replied Combeferre.

Marius added in a grave voice:

"I know him."

This guarantee satisfied everyone.

Enjolras turned to Jean Valjean.

"Welcome, citizen."

And he added:

"You know that we are about to die."

Jean Valjean, without replying, helped the insurgent whom he was saving to don his uniform.

Chapter V

THE HORIZON WHICH ONE BEHOLDS FROM THE SUMMIT OF A BARRICADE

THE SITUATION OF ALL IN THAT FATAL HOUR AND THAT PITILESS PLACE, HAD AS RESULT AND CULminating point Enjolras's supreme melancholy.

Enjolras bore within him the plenitude of the revolution; he was incomplete, however, so far as the absolute can be so; he had too much of Saint-Just about him, and not enough of Anacharsis Cloots; still, his mind, in the society of the Friends of the A B C, had ended by undergoing a certain polarization from Combeferre's ideas; for some time past, he had been gradually emerging from the narrow form of dogma, and had allowed himself to incline to the broadening influence of progress, and he had come to accept, as a definitive and magnificent evolution, the transformation of the great French Republic, into the immense human republic. As far as the immediate means were concerned, a violent situation being given, he wished to be violent; on that point, he never varied; and he remained of that epic and redoubtable school which is summed up in the words: "Eighty-three." Enjolras was standing erect on the staircase of paving-stones, one elbow resting on the stock of his gun. He was engaged in thought; he quivered, as at the passage of prophetic breaths; places where death is have these effects of tripods. A sort of stifled fire darted from his eyes, which were filled with an inward look. All at once he threw back his head, his blond locks fell back like those of an angel on the somber quadriga made of stars, they were like the mane of a startled lion in the flaming of an halo, and Enjolras cried:

"Citizens, do you picture the future to yourselves? The streets of cities inundated with light, green branches on the thresholds, nations sisters, men just, old men blessing children, the past loving the present, thinkers entirely at liberty, believers on terms of full equality, for religion heaven, God the direct priest, human conscience become an altar, no more hatreds, the fraternity of the workshop and the school, for sole penalty and recompense fame, work for all, right for all, peace over all, no more bloodshed, no more wars, happy mothers! To conquer matter is the first step; to realize the ideal is the second. Reflect on what progress has already accomplished. Formerly, the first human races beheld with terror the hydra pass before their eyes, breathing on the waters, the dragon which vomited flame, the griffin who was the monster of the air, and who flew with the wings of an eagle and the talons of a tiger; fearful beasts which were above man. Man, nevertheless, spread his snares, consecrated by intelligence, and finally conquered these monsters. We have vanquished the hydra, and it is called the locomotive; we are on the point of vanquishing the griffin, we already grasp it, and it is called the balloon. On the day when this Promethean task shall be accomplished, and when man shall have definitely harnessed to his will the triple Chimera of antiquity, the hydra, the dragon and the griffin, he will be the master of water, fire, and of air, and he will be for the rest of animated creation that which the ancient gods formerly were to him. Courage, and onward! Citizens, whither are we going? To science made government, to the force of things become the sole public force, to the natural law, having in itself its sanction and its penalty and promulgating itself by evidence, to a dawn of truth corresponding to a dawn of day. We are advancing to the union of peoples; we are advancing to the unity of man. No more fictions; no more parasites. The real governed by the true, that is the goal. Civilization will hold its assizes at the summit of Europe, and, later on, at the center of continents, in a grand parliament of the intelligence. Something similar has already been seen. The amphictyons had two sittings a year, one at Delphos, the seat of the gods, the other at Thermopylæ, the place of heroes. Europe will have her amphictyons; the globe will have its amphictyons. France bears this sublime future in her breast. This is the gestation of the nineteenth century. That which Greece sketched out is worthy of being finished by France. Listen to me, you, Feuilly, valiant artisan, man of the people. I revere you. Yes, you clearly behold the future, yes, you are right. You had neither father nor mother, Feuilly; you adopted humanity for your mother and right for your father. You are about to die, that is to say to triumph, here. Citizens, whatever happens to-day, through our defeat as well as through our victory, it is a revolution that we are about to create. As conflagrations light up a whole city, so revolutions illuminate the whole human race. And what is the revolution that we shall cause? I have just told you, the Revolution of the True. From a political point of view, there is but a single principle; the sovereignty of man over himself. This sovereignty of myself over myself is called Liberty. Where two or three of these sovereignties are combined, the state begins. But in that association there is no abdication. Each sovereignty concedes a certain quantity of itself, for the purpose of forming the common right. This quantity is the same for all of us. This identity of concession which each makes to all, is called Equality. Common right is nothing else than the protection of all beaming on the right of each. This protection of all over each is called Fraternity. The point of intersection of all these assembled sovereignties is called society. This intersection being a junction, this point is a knot. Hence what is called the social bond. Some say social contract; which is the same thing, the word contract being etymologically formed with the idea of a bond. Let us come to an understanding about equality; for, if liberty is the summit, equality is the base. Equality, citizens, is not wholly a surface vegetation, a society of great blades of grass and tiny oaks; a proximity of jealousies which render each other null and void; legally speaking, it is all aptitudes possessed of the same opportunity; politically, it is all votes possessed of the same weight; religiously, it is all consciences possessed of the same right. Equality has an organ: gratuitous and obligatory instruction. The right to the alphabet, that is where the beginning must be made. The primary school imposed on all, the secondary school offered to all, that is the law. From an identical school, an identical society will spring. Yes, instruction! light! light! everything comes from light, and to it everything returns. Citizens, the nineteenth century is great, but the twentieth century will be happy. Then, there will be nothing more like the history of old, we shall no longer, as to-day, have to fear a conquest, an invasion, a usurpation, a rivalry of nations, arms in hand, an interruption of civilization depending on a marriage of kings, on a birth in hereditary tyrannies, a partition of peoples by a congress, a dismemberment because of the failure of a dynasty, a combat of two religions meeting face to face, like two bucks in the dark, on the bridge of the infinite; we shall no longer have to fear famine, farming out, prostitution arising from distress, misery from the failure of work and the scaffold and the sword, and battles and the ruffianism of chance in the forest of events. One might almost say: There will be no more events. We shall be happy. The human race will accomplish its law, as the terrestrial globe accomplishes its law; harmony will be re-established between the soul and the star; the soul will gravitate around the truth, as the planet around the light. Friends, the present hour in which I am addressing you, is a gloomy hour; but these are terrible purchases of the future. A revolution is a toll. Oh! the human race will be delivered, raised up, consoled! We affirm it on this barrier. Whence should proceed that cry of love, if not from the heights of sacrifice? Oh my brothers, this is the point of junction, of those who think and of those who suffer; this barricade is not made of paving-stones, nor of joists, nor of bits of iron; it is made of two heaps, a heap of ideas, and a heap of woes. Here misery meets the ideal. The day embraces the night, and says to it: 'I am about to die, and thou shalt be born again with me.' From the embrace of all desolations faith leaps forth. Sufferings bring hither their agony and ideas their immortality. This agony and this immortality are about to join and constitute our death. Brothers, he who dies here dies in the radiance of the future, and we are entering a tomb all flooded with the dawn."

Enjolras paused rather than became silent; his lips continued to move silently, as though he were talking to himself, which caused them all to gaze attentively at him, in the endeavor to hear more. There was no applause; but they whispered together for a long time. Speech being a breath, the rustling of intelligences resembles the rustling of leaves.

Chapter VI

MARIUS HAGGARD, JAVERT LACONIC

LET US NARRATE WHAT WAS PASSING IN MARIUS'S THOUGHTS.

Let the reader recall the state of his soul. We have just recalled it, everything was a vision to him now. His judgment was disturbed. Marius, let us insist on this point, was under the shadow of the great, dark wings which are spread over those in the death-agony. He felt that he had entered the tomb, it seemed to him that he was already on the other side of the wall, and, he no longer beheld the faces of the living except with the eyes of one dead.

How did M. Fauchelevent come there? Why was he there? What had he come there to do? Marius did not address all these questions to himself. Besides, since our despair has this peculiarity, that it envelops others as well as ourselves, it seemed logical to him that all the world should come thither to die.

Only, he thought of Cosette with a pang at his heart.

However, M. Fauchelevent did not speak to him, did not look at him, and had not even the air of hearing him, when Marius raised his voice to say: "I know him."

As far as Marius was concerned, this attitude of M. Fauchelevent was comforting, and, if such a word can be used for such impressions, we should say that it pleased him. He had always felt the absolute impossibility of addressing that enigmatical man, who was, in his eyes, both equivocal and imposing. Moreover, it had been a long time since he had seen him; and this still further augmented the impossibility for Marius's timid and reserved nature.

The five chosen men left the barricade by way of Mondétour lane; they bore a perfect resemblance to members of the National Guard. One of them wept as he took his leave. Before setting out, they embraced those who remained.

When the five men sent back to life had taken their departure, Enjolras thought of the man who had been condemned to death.

He entered the tap-room. Javert, still bound to the post, was engaged in meditation.

"Do you want anything?" Enjolras asked him.

Javert replied: "When are you going to kill me?"

"Wait. We need all our cartridges just at present."

"Then give me a drink," said Javert.

Enjolras himself offered him a glass of water, and, as Javert was pinioned, he helped him to drink.

"Is that all?" inquired Enjolras.

"I am uncomfortable against this post," replied Javert. "You are not tender to have left me to pass the night here. Bind me as you please, but you surely might lay me out on a table like that other man."

And with a motion of the head, he indicated the body of M. Mabeuf.

There was, as the reader will remember, a long, broad table at the end of the room, on which they had been running bullets and making cartridges. All the cartridges having been made, and all the powder used, this table was free.

At Enjolras's command, four insurgents unbound Javert from the post. While they were loosing him, a fifth held a bayonet against his breast.

Leaving his arms tied behind his back, they placed about his feet a slender but stout whip-cord, as is done to men on the point of mounting the scaffold, which allowed him to take steps about fifteen inches in length, and made him walk to the table at the end of the room, where they laid him down, closely bound about the middle of the body.

By way of further security, and by means of a rope fastened to his neck, they added to the system of ligatures which rendered every attempt at escape impossible, that sort of bond which is called in prisons a martingale, which, starting at the neck, forks on the stomach, and meets the hands, after passing between the legs.

While they were binding Javert, a man standing on the threshold was surveying him with singular attention. The shadow cast by this man made Javert turn his head. He raised his eyes, and recognized Jean Valjean. He did not even start, but dropped his lids proudly and confined himself to the remark: "It is perfectly simple."

Chapter VII

THE SITUATION BECOMES AGGRAVATED

THE DAYLIGHT WAS INCREASING RAPIDLY. NOT A WINDOW WAS OPENED, NOT A DOOR STOOD ajar; it was the dawn but not the awaking. The end of the Rue de la Chanvrerie, opposite the barricade, had been evacuated by the troops, as we have stated, it seemed to be free, and presented itself to passers-by with a sinister tranquility. The Rue Saint-Denis was as dumb as the avenue of Sphinxes at Thebes. Not a living being in the cross-roads, which gleamed white in the light of the sun. Nothing is so mournful as this light in deserted streets. Nothing was to be seen, but there was something to be heard. A mysterious movement was going on at a certain distance. It was evident that the critical moment was approaching. As on the previous evening, the sentinels had come in; but this time all had come.

The barricade was stronger than on the occasion of the first attack. Since the departure of the five, they had increased its height still further.

On the advice of the sentinel who had examined the region of the Halles, Enjolras, for fear of a surprise in the rear, came to a serious decision. He had the small gut of the Mondétour lane, which had been left open up to that time, barricaded. For this purpose, they tore up the pavement for the length of several houses more. In this manner, the barricade, walled on three streets, in front on the Rue de la Chanvrerie, to the left on the Rues du Cygne and de la Petite-Truanderie, to the right on the Rue Mondétour, was really almost impregnable; it is true that they were fatally hemmed in there. It had three fronts, but no exit.—"A fortress but a rat-hole too," said Courfeyrac with a laugh.

Enjolras had about thirty paving-stones "torn up in excess," said Bossuet, piled up near the door of the wine-shop.

The silence was now so profound in the quarter whence the attack must needs come, that Enjolras had each man resume his post of battle.

An allowance of brandy was doled out to each.

Nothing is more curious than a barricade preparing for an assault. Each man selects his place as though at the theater. They jostle, and elbow and crowd each other. There are some who make stalls of paving-stones. Here is a corner of the wall which is in the way, it is removed; here is a redan which may afford protection, they take shelter behind it. Left-handed men are precious; they take the places that are inconvenient to the rest. Many arrange to fight in a sitting posture. They wish to be at ease to kill, and to die comfortably. In the sad war of June, 1848, an insurgent who was a formidable marksman, and who was firing from the top of a terrace upon a roof, had a reclining-chair brought there for his use; a charge of grape-shot found him out there.

As soon as the leader has given the order to clear the decks for action, all disorderly movements cease; there is no more pulling from one another; there are no more coteries; no more asides, there is no more holding aloof; everything in their spirits converges in, and changes into, a waiting for the assailants. A barricade before the arrival of danger is chaos; in danger, it is discipline itself. Peril produces order.

As soon as Enjolras had seized his double-barreled rifle, and had placed himself in a sort of embrasure which he had reserved for himself, all the rest held their peace. A series of faint, sharp noises resounded confusedly along the wall of paving-stones. It was the men cocking their guns.

Moreover, their attitudes were prouder, more confident than ever; the excess of sacrifice strengthens; they no longer cherished any hope, but they had despair, despair—the last weapon, which sometimes gives victory; Virgil has said so. Supreme resources spring from extreme resolutions. To embark in death is sometimes the means of escaping a shipwreck; and the lid of the coffin becomes a plank of safety.

As on the preceding evening, the attention of all was directed, we might almost say leaned upon, the end of the street, now lighted up and visible.

They had not long to wait. A stir began distinctly in the Saint-Leu quarter, but it did not resemble the movement of the first attack. A clashing of chains, the uneasy jolting of a mass, the click of brass skipping along the pavement, a sort of solemn uproar, announced that some sinister construction of iron was approaching. There arose a tremor in the bosoms of these peaceful old streets, pierced and built for the fertile circulation of interests and ideas, and which are not made for the horrible rumble of the wheels of war.

The fixity of eye in all the combatants upon the extremity of the street became ferocious.

A cannon made its appearance.

Artillery-men were pushing the piece; it was in firing trim; the fore-carriage had been detached; two upheld the gun-carriage, four were at the wheels; others followed with the caisson. They could see the smoke of the burning lint-stock.

"Fire!" shouted Enjolras.

The whole barricade fired, the report was terrible; an avalanche of smoke covered and effaced both cannon and men; after a few seconds, the cloud dispersed, and the cannon and men reappeared; the gun-crew had just finished rolling it slowly, correctly, without haste, into position facing the barricade. Not one of them had been struck. Then the captain of the piece, bearing down upon the breech in order to raise the muzzle, began to point the cannon with the gravity of an astronomer leveling a telescope.

"Bravo for the cannoneers!" cried Bossuet.

And the whole barricade clapped their hands.

A moment later, squarely planted in the very middle of the street, astride of the gutter the piece was ready for action. A formidable pair of jaws yawned on the barricade.

"Come, merrily now!" ejaculated Courfeyrac. "That's the brutal part of it. After the fillip on the nose, the blow from the fist. The army is reaching out its big paw to us. The barricade is going to be severely shaken up. The fusillade tries, the cannon takes."

"It is a piece of eight, new model, brass," added Combeferre. "Those pieces are liable to burst as soon as the proportion of ten parts of tin to one hundred of brass is exceeded. The excess of tin renders them too tender. Then it comes to pass that they have caves and chambers when looked at from the vent hole. In order to obviate this danger, and to render it possible to force the charge, it may become necessary to return to the process of the fourteenth century, hooping, and to encircle the piece on the outside with a series of unwelded steel bands, from the breech to the trunnions. In the meantime, they remedy this defect as best they may; they manage to discover where the holes are located in the vent of a cannon, by means of a searcher. But there is a better method, with Gribeauval's movable star."

"In the sixteenth century," remarked Bossuet, "they used to rifle cannon."

"Yes," replied Combeferre, "that augments the projectile force, but diminishes the accuracy of the firing. In firing at short range, the trajectory is not as rigid as could be desired, the parabola is exaggerated, the line of the projectile is no longer sufficiently rectilinear to allow of its striking intervening objects, which is, nevertheless, a necessity of battle, the importance of which increases with the proximity of the enemy and the precipitation of the discharge. This defect of the tension of the curve of the projectile in the rifled cannon of the sixteenth century arose from the smallness of the charge; small charges for that sort of engine are imposed by the ballistic necessities, such, for instance, as the preservation of the gun-carriage. In short, that despot, the cannon, cannot do all that it desires; force is a great weakness. A cannon-ball only travels six hundred leagues an hour; light travels seventy thousand leagues a second. Such is the superiority of Jesus Christ over Napoleon."

"Reload your guns," said Enjolras.

How was the casing of the barricade going to behave under the cannon-balls? Would they effect a breach? That was the question. While the insurgents were reloading their guns, the artillerymen were loading the cannon.

The anxiety in the redoubt was profound.

The shot sped the report burst forth.

"Present!" shouted a joyous voice.

And Gavroche flung himself into the barricade just as the ball dashed against it.

He came from the direction of the Rue du Cygne, and he had nimbly climbed over the auxiliary barricade which fronted on the labyrinth of the Rue de la Petite-Truanderie.

Gavroche produced a greater sensation in the barricade than the cannon-ball.

The ball buried itself in the mass of rubbish. At the most there was an omnibus wheel broken, and the old Anceau cart was demolished. On seeing this, the barricade burst into a laugh.

"Go on!" shouted Bossuet to the artillerists.

Chapter VIII

THE ARTILLERY-MEN COMPEL PEOPLE TO TAKE THEM SERIOUSLY

THEY FLOCKED ROUND GAVROCHE. BUT HE HAD NO TIME TO TELL ANYTHING. MARIUS DREW HIM aside with a shudder.

"What are you doing here?"

"Hullo!" said the child, "what are you doing here yourself?"

And he stared at Marius intently with his epic effrontery. His eyes grew larger with the proud light within them.

It was with an accent of severity that Marius continued:

"Who told you to come back? Did you deliver my letter at the address?"

Gavroche was not without some compunctions in the matter of that letter. In his haste to return to the barricade, he had got rid of it rather than delivered it. He was forced to acknowledge to himself that he had confided it rather lightly to that stranger whose face he had not been able to make out. It is true that the man was bareheaded, but that was not sufficient. In short, he had been administering to himself little inward remonstrances and he feared Marius's reproaches. In order to extricate himself from the predicament, he took the simplest course; he lied abominably.

"Citizen, I delivered the letter to the porter. The lady was asleep. She will have the letter when she wakes up."

Marius had had two objects in sending that letter: to bid farewell to Cosette and to save Gavroche. He was obliged to content himself with the half of his desire.

The dispatch of his letter and the presence of M. Fauchelevent in the barricade, was a coincidence which occurred to him. He pointed out M. Fauchelevent to Gavroche.

"Do you know that man?"

"No," said Gavroche.

Gavroche had, in fact, as we have just mentioned, seen Jean Valjean only at night.

The troubled and unhealthy conjectures which had outlined themselves in Marius's mind, were dissipated. Did he know M. Fauchelevent's opinions? Perhaps M. Fauchelevent was a republican. Hence his very natural presence in this combat.

In the meanwhile, Gavroche was shouting, at the other end of the barricade: "My gun!"

Courfeyrac had it returned to him.

Gavroche warned "his comrades" as he called them, that the barricade was blocked. He had had great difficulty in reaching it. A battalion of the line whose arms were piled in the Rue de la Petite-Truanderie was on the watch on the side of the Rue du Cygne; on the opposite side, the municipal guard occupied the Rue des Prêcheurs. The bulk of the army was facing them in front.

This information given, Gavroche added:

"I authorize you to hit 'em a tremendous whack."

Meanwhile, Enjolras was straining his ears and watching at his embrasure.

The assailants, dissatisfied, no doubt, with their shot, had not repeated it.

A company of infantry of the line had come up and occupied the end of the street behind the piece of ordnance. The soldiers were tearing up the pavement and constructing with the stones a small, low wall, a sort of side-work not more than eighteen inches high, and facing the barricade. In the angle at the left of this epaulement, there was visible the head of the column of a battalion from the suburbs massed in the Rue Saint-Denis.

Enjolras, on the watch, thought he distinguished the peculiar sound which is produced when the shells of grape-shot are drawn from the caissons, and he saw the commander of the piece change the elevation and incline the mouth of the cannon slightly to the left. Then the cannoneers began to load the piece. The chief seized the lint-stock himself and lowered it to the vent.

"Down with your heads, hug the wall!" shouted Enjolras, "and all on your knees along the barricade!"

The insurgents who were straggling in front of the wine-shop, and who had quitted their posts of combat on Gavroche's arrival, rushed pell-mell toward the barricade; but before Enjolras's order could be executed, the discharge took place with the terrifying rattle of a round of grape-shot. This is what it was, in fact.

The charge had been aimed at the cut in the redoubt, and had there rebounded from the wall; and this terrible rebound had produced two dead and three wounded.

If this were continued, the barricade was no longer tenable. The grape-shot made its way in.

A murmur of consternation arose.

"Let us prevent the second discharge," said Enjolras.

And, lowering his rifle, he took aim at the captain of the gun, who, at that moment, was bearing down on the breach of his gun and rectifying and definitely fixing its pointing.

The captain of the piece was a handsome sergeant of artillery, very young, blond, with a very gentle face, and the intelligent air peculiar to that predestined and redoubtable weapon which, by dint of perfecting itself in horror, must end in killing war.

Combeferre, who was standing beside Enjolras, scrutinized this young man.

"What a pity!" said Combeferre. "What hideous things these butcheries are! Come, when there are no more kings, there will be no more war. Enjolras, you are taking aim at that sergeant, you are not looking at him. Fancy, he is a charming young man; he is intrepid; it is evident that he is thoughtful; those young artillery-men are very well educated; he has a father, a mother, a family; he is probably in love; he is not more than five-and-twenty at the most; he might be your brother."

"He is," said Enjolras.

"Yes," replied Combeferre, "he is mine too. Well, let us not kill him."

"Let me alone. It must be done."

And a tear trickled slowly down Enjolras's marble cheek.

At the same moment, he pressed the trigger of his rifle. The flame leaped forth. The artillery-man turned round twice, his arms extended in front of him, his head uplifted, as though for breath, then he fell with his side on the gun, and lay there motionless. They could see his back, from the center of which there flowed directly a stream of blood. The ball had traversed his breast from side to side. He was dead.

He had to be carried away and replaced by another. Several minutes were thus gained, in fact.

Chapter IX

EMPLOYMENT OF THE OLD TALENTS OF A POACHER AND THAT INFALLIBLE MARKMANSHIP WHICH INFLUENCED THE CONDEMNATION OF 1796

OPINIONS WERE EXCHANGED IN THE BARRICADE. THE FIRING FROM THE GUN WAS ABOUT TO begin again. Against that grape-shot, they could not hold out a quarter of an hour longer. It was absolutely necessary to deaden the blows.

Enjolras issued this command:

"We must place a mattress there."

"We have none," said Combeferre, "the wounded are lying on them."

Jean Valjean, who was seated apart on a stone post, at the corner of the tavern, with his gun between his knees, had, up to that moment, taken no part in anything that was going on. He did not appear to hear the combatants saying around him: "Here is a gun that is doing nothing."

At the order issued by Enjolras, he rose.

It will be remembered that, on the arrival of the rabble in the Rue de la Chanvrerie, an old woman, foreseeing the bullets, had placed her mattress in front of her window. This window, an attic window, was on the roof of a six-story house situated a little beyond the barricade. The mattress, placed cross-wise, supported at the bottom on two poles for drying linen, was upheld at the top by two ropes, which, at that distance, looked like two threads, and which were attached to two nails planted in the window frames. These ropes were distinctly visible, like hairs, against the sky.

"Can someone lend me a double-barreled rifle?" said Jean Valjean.

Enjolras, who had just reloaded his, handed it to him.

Jean Valjean took aim at the attic window and fired.

One of the mattress ropes was cut.

The mattress now hung by one thread only.

Jean Valjean fired the second charge. The second rope lashed the panes of the attic window. The mattress slipped between the two poles and fell into the street.

The barricade applauded.

All voices cried:

"Here is a mattress!"

"Yes," said Combeferre, "but who will go and fetch it?"

The mattress had, in fact, fallen outside the barricade, between besiegers and besieged. Now, the death of the sergeant of artillery having exasperated the troop, the soldiers had, for several minutes, been lying flat on their stomachs behind the line of paving-stones which they had erected, and, in order to supply the forced silence of the piece, which was quiet while its service was in course of reorganization, they had opened fire on the barricade. The insurgents did not reply to this musketry, in order to spare their ammunition The fusillade broke against the barricade; but the street, which it filled, was terrible.

Jean Valjean stepped out of the cut, entered the street, traversed the storm of bullets, walked up to the mattress, hoisted it upon his back, and returned to the barricade.

He placed the mattress in the cut with his own hands. He fixed it there against the wall in such a manner that the artillery-men should not see it.

That done, they awaited the next discharge of grape-shot.

It was not long in coming.

The cannon vomited forth its package of buck-shot with a roar. But there was no rebound. The effect which they had foreseen had been attained. The barricade was saved.

"Citizen," said Enjolras to Jean Valjean, "the Republic thanks you."

Bossuet admired and laughed. He exclaimed:

"It is immoral that a mattress should have so much power. Triumph of that which yields over that which strikes with lightning. But never mind, glory to the mattress which annuls a cannon!"

Chapter X

DAWN

AT THAT MOMENT, COSETTE AWOKE.

Her chamber was narrow, neat, unobtrusive, with a long sash-window, facing the East on the back courtyard of the house.

Cosette knew nothing of what was going on in Paris. She had not been there on the preceding evening, and she had already retired to her chamber when Toussaint had said:

"It appears that there is a row."

Cosette had slept only a few hours, but soundly. She had had sweet dreams, which possibly arose from the fact that her little bed was very white. Someone, who was Marius, had appeared to her in the light. She awoke with the sun in her eyes, which, at first, produced on her the effect of being a continuation of her dream. Her first thought on emerging from this dream was a smiling one. Cosette felt herself thoroughly reassured. Like Jean Valjean, she had, a few hours previously, passed through that reaction of the soul which absolutely will not hear of unhappiness. She began to cherish hope, with all her might, without knowing why. Then she felt a pang at her heart. It was three days since she had seen Marius. But she said to herself that he must have received her letter, that he knew where she was, and that he was so clever that he would find means of reaching her. And that certainly to-day, and perhaps that very morning.—It was broad daylight, but the rays of light were very horizontal; she thought that it was very early, but that she must rise, nevertheless, in order to receive Marius.

She felt that she could not live without Marius, and that, consequently, that was sufficient and that Marius would come. No objection was valid. All this was certain. It was monstrous enough already to have suffered for three days. Marius absent three days, this was horrible on the part of the good God. Now, this cruel teasing from on high had been gone through with. Marius was about to arrive, and he would bring good news. Youth is made thus; it quickly dries its eyes; it finds sorrow useless and does not accept it. Youth is the smile of the future in the presence of an unknown quantity, which is itself. It is natural to it to be happy. It seems as though its respiration were made of hope.

Moreover, Cosette could not remember what Marius had said to her on the subject of this absence which was to last only one day, and what explanation of it he had given her. Everyone has noticed with what nimbleness a coin which one has dropped on the ground rolls away and hides, and with what art it renders itself undiscoverable. There are thoughts which play us the same trick; they nestle away in a corner of our brain; that is the end of them; they are lost; it is impossible to lay the memory on them. Cosette was somewhat vexed at the useless little effort made by her memory. She told herself, that it was very naughty and very wicked of her, to have forgotten the words uttered by Marius.

She sprang out of bed and accomplished the two ablutions of soul and body, her prayers and her toilet.

One may, in a case of exigency, introduce the reader into a nuptial chamber, not into a virginal chamber. Verse would hardly venture it, prose must not.

It is the interior of a flower that is not yet unfolded, it is whiteness in the dark, it is the private cell of a closed lily, which must not be gazed upon by man so long as the sun has not gazed upon it. Woman in the bud is sacred. That innocent bud which opens, that adorable half-nudity which is afraid of itself, that white foot which takes refuge in a slipper, that throat which veils itself before a mirror as though a mirror were an eye, that chemise which makes haste to rise up and conceal the shoulder for a creaking bit of furniture or a passing vehicle, those cords tied, those clasps fastened, those laces drawn, those tremors, those shivers of cold and modesty, that exquisite affright in every movement, that almost winged uneasiness where there is no cause for alarm, the successive phases of dressing, as charming as the clouds of dawn—it is not fitting that all this should be narrated, and it is too much to have even called attention to it.

The eye of man must be more religious in the presence of the rising of a young girl, than in the presence of the rising of a star. The possibility of hurting should inspire an augmentation of respect. The down on the peach, the bloom on the plum, the radiated crystal of the snow, the wing of the butterfly powdered with feathers, are coarse compared to that chastity which does not even know that it is chaste. The young girl is only the flash of a dream, and is not yet a statue. Her bedchamber is hidden in the somber part of the ideal. The indiscreet touch of a glance brutalizes this vague penumbra. Here, contemplation is profanation.

We shall, therefore, show nothing of that sweet little flutter of Cosette's rising.

An oriental tale relates how the rose was made white by God, but that Adam looked upon her when she was unfolding, and she was ashamed and turned crimson. We are of the number who fall speechless in the presence of young girls and flowers, since we think them worthy of veneration.

Cosette dressed herself very hastily, combed and dressed her hair, which was a very simple matter in those days, when women did not swell out their curls and bands with cushions and puffs, and did not put crinoline in their locks. Then she opened the window and cast her eyes around her in every direction, hoping to descry some bit of the street, an angle of the house, an edge of pavement, so that she might be able to watch for Marius there. But no view of the outside was to be had. The back court was surrounded by tolerably high walls, and the outlook was only on several gardens. Cosette pronounced these gardens hideous: for the first time in her life, she found flowers ugly. The smallest scrap of the gutter of the street would have met her wishes better. She decided to gaze at the sky, as though she thought that Marius might come from that quarter.

All at once, she burst into tears. Not that this was fickleness of soul; but hopes cut in twain by dejection—that was her case. She had a confused consciousness of something horrible. Thoughts were rife in the air, in fact. She told herself that she was not sure of anything, that to withdraw herself from sight was to be lost; and the idea that Marius could return to her from heaven appeared to her no longer charming but mournful.

Then, as is the nature of these clouds, calm returned to her, and hope and a sort of unconscious smile, which yet indicated trust in God.

Everyone in the house was still asleep. A country-like silence reigned. Not a shutter had been opened. The porter's lodge was closed. Toussaint had not risen, and Cosette, naturally, thought that her father was asleep. She must have suffered much, and she must have still been suffering greatly, for she said to herself, that her father had been unkind; but she counted on Marius. The eclipse of such a light was decidedly impossible. Now and then, she heard sharp shocks in the distance, and she said: "It is odd that people should be opening and shutting their carriage gates so early." They were the reports of the cannon battering the barricade.

A few feet below Cosette's window, in the ancient and perfectly black cornice of the wall, there was a martin's nest; the curve of this nest formed a little projection beyond the cornice, so that from above it was possible to look into this little paradise. The mother was there, spreading her wings like a fan over her brood; the father fluttered about, flew away, then came back, bearing in his beak food and kisses. The dawning day gilded this happy thing, the great law, "Multiply," lay there smiling and august, and that sweet mystery unfolded in the glory of the morning. Cosette, with her hair in the sunlight, her soul absorbed in chimeras, illuminated by love within and by the dawn without, bent over mechanically, and almost without daring to avow to herself that she was thinking at the same time of Marius, began to gaze at these birds, at this family, at that male and female, that mother and her little ones, with the profound trouble which a nest produces on a virgin.

Chapter XI

THE SHOT WHICH MISSES NOTHING AND KILLS NO ONE

THE ASSAILANTS' FIRE CONTINUED. MUSKETRY AND GRAPE-SHOT ALTERNATED, BUT WITHOUT committing great ravages, to tell the truth. The top alone of the Corinthe façade suffered; the window on the first floor, and the attic window in the roof, riddled with buck-shot and biscaïens, were slowly losing their shape. The combatants who had been posted there had been obliged to withdraw. However, this is according to the tactics of barricades; to fire for a long while, in order to exhaust the insurgents' ammunition, if they commit the mistake of replying. When it is perceived, from the slackening of their fire, that they have no more powder and ball, the assault is made. Enjolras had not fallen into this trap; the barricade did not reply.

At every discharge by platoons, Gavroche puffed out his cheek with his tongue, a sign of supreme disdain.

"Good for you," said he, "rip up the cloth. We want some lint."

Courfeyrac called the grape-shot to order for the little effect which it produced, and said to the cannon:

"You are growing diffuse, my good fellow."

One gets puzzled in battle, as at a ball. It is probable that this silence on the part of the redoubt began to render the besiegers uneasy, and to make them fear some unexpected incident, and that they felt the necessity of getting a clear view behind that heap of paving-stones, and of knowing what was going on behind that impassible wall which received blows without retorting. The insurgents suddenly perceived a helmet glittering in the sun on a neighboring roof. A fireman had placed his back against a tall chimney, and seemed to be acting as sentinel. His glance fell directly down into the barricade.

"There's an embarrassing watcher," said Enjolras.

Jean Valjean had returned Enjolras's rifle, but he had his own gun.

Without saying a word, he took aim at the fireman, and, a second later, the helmet, smashed by a bullet, rattled noisily into the street. The terrified soldier made haste to disappear. A second observer took his place. This one was an officer. Jean Valjean, who had reloaded his gun, took aim at the newcomer and sent the officer's casque to join the soldier's. The officer did not persist, and retired speedily. This time the warning was understood. No one made his appearance thereafter on that roof; and the idea of spying on the barricade was abandoned.

"Why did you not kill the man?" Bossuet asked Jean Valjean.

Jean Valjean made no reply.

Chapter XII

DISORDER A PARTISAN OF ORDER

B OSSUET MUTTERED IN COMBEFERRE'S EAR:
  "He did not answer my question."

"He is a man who does good by gun-shots," said Combeferre.

Those who have preserved some memory of this already distant epoch know that the National Guard from the suburbs was valiant against insurrections. It was particularly zealous and intrepid in the days of June, 1832. A certain good dram-shop keeper of Pantin des Vertus or la Cunette, whose "establishment" had been closed by the riots, became leonine at the sight of his deserted dance-hall, and got himself killed to preserve the order represented by a tea-garden. In that bourgeois and heroic time, in the presence of ideas which had their knights, interests had their paladins. The prosiness of the originators detracted nothing from the bravery of the movement. The diminution of a pile of crowns made bankers sing the Marseillaise. They shed their blood lyrically for the counting-house; and they defended the shop, that immense diminutive of the fatherland, with Lacedæmonian enthusiasm.

At bottom, we will observe, there was nothing in all this that was not extremely serious. It was social elements entering into strife, while awaiting the day when they should enter into equilibrium.

Another sign of the times was the anarchy mingled with governmentalism [the barbarous name of the correct party]. People were for order in combination with lack of discipline.

The drum suddenly beat capricious calls, at the command of such or such a Colonel of the National Guard; such and such a captain went into action through inspiration; such and such National Guardsmen fought, "for an idea," and on their own account. At critical moments, on "days" they took counsel less of their leaders than of their instincts. There existed in the army of order, veritable guerilleros, some of the sword, like Fannicot, others of the pen, like Henri Fonfrède.

Civilization, unfortunately represented at this epoch rather by an aggregation of interests than by a group of principles, was or thought itself, in peril; it set up the cry of alarm; each, constituting himself a center, defended it, succored it, and protected it with his own head; and the first-comer took it upon himself to save society.

Zeal sometimes proceeded to extermination. A platoon of the National Guard would constitute itself on its own authority a private council of war, and judge and execute a captured insurgent in five minutes. It was an improvisation of this sort that had slain Jean Prouvaire. Fierce Lynch law, with which no one party had any right to reproach the rest, for it has been applied by the Republic in America, as well as by the monarchy in Europe. This Lynch law was complicated with mistakes. On one day of rioting, a young poet, named Paul Aimé Garnier, was pursued in the Place Royale, with a bayonet at his loins, and only escaped by taking refuge under the porte-cochère of No. 6. They shouted: "There's another of those Saint-Simonians!" and they wanted to kill him. Now, he had under his arm a volume of the memoirs of the Duc de Saint-Simon. A National Guard had read the words *Saint-Simon* on the book, and had shouted: "Death!"

On the 6th of June, 1832, a company of the National Guards from the suburbs, commanded by the Captain Fannicot, above mentioned, had itself decimated in the Rue de la Chanvrerie out of caprice and its own good pleasure. This fact, singular though it may seem, was proved at the judicial investigation opened in consequence of the insurrection of 1832. Captain Fannicot, a bold and impatient bourgeois, a sort of condottiere of the order of those whom we have just characterized, a fanatical and intractable governmentalist, could not resist the temptation to fire prematurely, and the ambition of capturing the barricade alone and unaided, that is to say, with his company. Exasperated by the successive apparition of the red flag and the old coat which he took for the black flag, he loudly blamed the generals and chiefs of the corps, who were holding council and did not think that the moment for the decisive assault had arrived, and who were allowing "the insurrection to fry in its own fat," to use the celebrated expression of one of them. For his part, he thought the barricade ripe, and as that which is ripe ought to fall, he made the attempt.

He commanded men as resolute as himself, "raging fellows," as a witness said. His company, the same which had shot Jean Prouvaire the poet, was the first of the battalion posted at the angle of the street. At the moment when they were least expecting it, the captain launched his men against the barricade. This movement, executed with more good-will than strategy, cost the Fannicot company dear. Before it had traversed two thirds of the street it was received by a general discharge from the barricade. Four, the most audacious, who were running on in front, were mown down point-blank at the very foot of the redoubt, and this courageous throng of National Guards, very brave men but lacking in military tenacity, were forced to fall back, after some hesitation, leaving fifteen corpses on the pavement. This momentary hesitation gave the insurgents time to reload their weapons, and a second and very destructive discharge struck the company before it could regain the corner of the street, its shelter. A moment more and it was caught between two fires, and it received the volley from the battery piece which, not having received the order, had not discontinued its firing.

The intrepid and imprudent Fannicot was one of the dead from this grape-shot. He was killed by the cannon, that is to say, by order.

This attack, which was more furious than serious, irritated Enjolras.—"The fools!" said he. "They are getting their own men killed and they are using up our ammunition for nothing."

Enjolras spoke like the real general of insurrection which he was. Insurrection and repression do not fight with equal weapons. Insurrection, which is speedily exhausted, has only a certain number of shots to fire and a certain number of combatants to expend. An empty cartridge-box, a man killed, cannot be replaced. As repression has the army, it does not count its men, and, as it has Vincennes, it does not count its shots. Repression has as many regiments as the barricade has men, and as many arsenals as the barricade has cartridge-boxes. Thus they are struggles of one against a hundred, which always end in crushing the barricade; unless the revolution, uprising suddenly, flings into the balance its flaming archangel's sword. This does happen sometimes. Then everything rises, the pavements begin to seethe, popular redoubts abound. Paris quivers supremely, the *quid divinum* is given forth, a 10th of August is in the air, a 29th of July is in the air, a wonderful light appears, the yawning maw of force draws back, and the army, that lion, sees before it, erect and tranquil, that prophet, France.

Chapter XIII

PASSING GLEAMS

I N THE CHAOS OF SENTIMENTS AND PASSIONS WHICH DEFEND A BARRICADE, THERE IS A LITTLE OF everything; there is bravery, there is youth, honor, enthusiasm, the ideal, conviction, the rage of the gambler, and, above all, intermittences of hope.

One of these intermittences, one of these vague quivers of hope suddenly traversed the barricade of the Rue de la Chanvrerie at the moment when it was least expected.

"Listen," suddenly cried Enjolras, who was still on the watch, "it seems to me that Paris is waking up."

It is certain that, on the morning of the 6th of June, the insurrection broke out afresh for an hour or two, to a certain extent. The obstinacy of the alarm peal of Saint-Merry reanimated some fancies. Barricades were begun in the Rue du Poirier and the Rue des Gravilliers. In front of the Porte Saint-Martin, a young man, armed with a rifle, attacked alone a squadron of cavalry. In plain sight, on the open boulevard, he placed one knee on the ground, shouldered his weapon, fired, killed the commander of the squadron, and turned away, saying: "There's another who will do us no more harm."

He was put to the sword. In the Rue Saint-Denis, a woman fired on the National Guard from behind a lowered blind. The slats of the blind could be seen to tremble at every shot. A child fourteen years of age was arrested in the Rue de la Cossonerie, with his pockets full of cartridges. Many posts were attacked. At the entrance to the Rue Bertin-Poirée, a very lively and utterly unexpected fusillade welcomed a regiment of cuirassiers, at whose head marched Marshal General Cavaignac de Barague. In the Rue Planche-Mibray, they threw old pieces of pottery and household utensils down on the soldiers from the roofs; a bad sign; and when this matter was reported to Marshal Soult, Napoleon's old lieutenant grew thoughtful, as he recalled Suchet's saying at Saragossa: "We are lost when the old women empty their pots de chambre on our heads."

These general symptoms which presented themselves at the moment when it was thought that the uprising had been rendered local, this fever of wrath, these sparks which flew hither and thither above those deep masses of combustibles which are called the faubourgs of Paris—all this, taken together, disturbed the military chiefs. They made haste to stamp out these beginnings of conflagration.

They delayed the attack on the barricades Maubuée, de la Chanvrerie and Saint-Merry until these sparks had been extinguished, in order that they might have to deal with the barricades only and be able to finish them at one blow. Columns were thrown into the streets where there was fermentation, sweeping the large, sounding the small, right and left, now slowly and cautiously, now at full charge. The troops broke in the doors of houses whence shots had been fired; at the same time, maneuvers by the cavalry dispersed the groups on the boulevards. This repression was not effected without some commotion, and without that tumultuous uproar peculiar to collisions between the army and the people. This was what Enjolras had caught in the intervals of the cannonade and the musketry. Moreover, he had seen wounded men passing the end of the street in litters, and he said to Courfeyrac: "Those wounded do not come from us."

Their hope did not last long; the gleam was quickly eclipsed. In less than half an hour, what was in the air vanished, it was a flash of lightning unaccompanied by thunder, and the insurgents felt that sort of leaden cope, which the indifference of the people casts over obstinate and deserted men, fall over them once more.

The general movement, which seemed to have assumed a vague outline, had miscarried; and the attention of the minister of war and the strategy of the generals could now be concentrated on the three or four barricades which still remained standing.

The sun was mounting above the horizon.

An insurgent hailed Enjolras.

"We are hungry here. Are we really going to die like this, without anything to eat?"

Enjolras, who was still leaning on his elbows at his embrasure, made an affirmative sign with his head, but without taking his eyes from the end of the street.

Chapter XIV

WHEREIN WILL APPEAR THE NAME OF ENJOLRAS'S MISTRESS

COURFEYRAC, SEATED ON A PAVING-STONE BESIDE ENJOLRAS, CONTINUED TO INSULT THE CANnon, and each time that that gloomy cloud of projectiles which is called grape-shot passed overhead with its terrible sound he assailed it with a burst of irony.

"You are wearing out your lungs, poor, brutal, old fellow, you pain me, you are wasting your row. That's not thunder, it's a cough."

And the bystanders laughed.

Courfeyrac and Bossuet, whose brave good humor increased with the peril, like Madame Scarron, replaced nourishment with pleasantry, and, as wine was lacking, they poured out gaiety to all.

"I admire Enjolras," said Bossuet. "His impassive temerity astounds me. He lives alone, which renders him a little sad, perhaps; Enjolras complains of his greatness, which binds him to widowhood. The rest of us have mistresses, more or less, who make us crazy, that is to say, brave. When a man is as much in love as a tiger, the least that he can do is to fight like a lion. That is one way of taking our revenge for the capers that mesdames our grisettes play on us. Roland gets himself killed for Angélique; all our heroism comes from our women. A man without a woman is a pistol without a trigger; it is the woman that sets the man off. Well, Enjolras has no woman. He is not in love, and yet he manages to be intrepid. It is a thing unheard of that a man should be as cold as ice and as bold as fire."

Enjolras did not appear to be listening, but had anyone been near him, that person would have heard him mutter in a low voice: "Patria."

Bossuet was still laughing when Courfeyrac exclaimed:

"News!"

And assuming the tone of an usher making an announcement, he added:

"My name is Eight-Pounder."

In fact, a new personage had entered on the scene. This was a second piece of ordnance.

The artillery-men rapidly performed their maneuvers in force, and placed this second piece in line with the first.

This outlined the catastrophe.

A few minutes later, the two pieces, rapidly served, were firing point-blank at the redoubt; the platoon firing of the line and of the soldiers from the suburbs sustained the artillery.

Another cannonade was audible at some distance. At the same time that the two guns were furiously attacking the redoubt from the Rue de la Chanvrerie, two other cannons, trained one from the Rue Saint-Denis, the other from the Rue Aubry-le-Boucher, were riddling the Saint-Merry barricade. The four cannons echoed each other mournfully.

The barking of these somber dogs of war replied to each other.

One of the two pieces which was now battering the barricade on the Rue de la Chanvrerie was firing grape-shot, the other balls.

The piece which was firing balls was pointed a little high, and the aim was calculated so that the ball struck the extreme edge of the upper crest of the barricade, and crumbled the stone down upon the insurgents, mingled with bursts of grape-shot.

The object of this mode of firing was to drive the insurgents from the summit of the redoubt, and to compel them to gather close in the interior, that is to say, this announced the assault.

The combatants once driven from the crest of the barricade by balls, and from the windows of the cabaret by grape-shot, the attacking columns could venture into the street without being picked off, perhaps, even, without being seen, could briskly and suddenly scale the redoubt, as on the preceding evening, and, who knows? take it by surprise.

"It is absolutely necessary that the inconvenience of those guns should be diminished," said Enjolras, and he shouted: "Fire on the artillery-men!"

All were ready. The barricade, which had long been silent, poured forth a desperate fire; seven or eight discharges followed, with a sort of rage and joy; the street was filled with blinding smoke, and, at the end of a few minutes, athwart this mist all streaked with flame, two thirds of the gunners could be distinguished lying beneath the wheels of the cannons. Those who were left standing continued to serve the pieces with severe tranquility, but the fire had slackened.

"Things are going well now," said Bossuet to Enjolras. "Success."

Enjolras shook his head and replied:

"Another quarter of an hour of this success, and there will not be any cartridges left in the barricade."

It appears that Gavroche overheard this remark.

Chapter XV

GAVROCHE OUTSIDE

COURFEYRAC SUDDENLY CAUGHT SIGHT OF SOMEONE AT THE BASE OF THE BARRICADE, OUTSIDE in the street, amid the bullets.

Gavroche had taken a bottle basket from the wine-shop, had made his way out through the cut, and was quietly engaged in emptying the full cartridge-boxes of the National Guardsmen who had been killed on the slope of the redoubt, into his basket.

"What are you doing there?" asked Courfeyrac.

Gavroche raised his face:

"I'm filling my basket, citizen."

"Don't you see the grape-shot?"

Gavroche replied:

"Well, it is raining. What then?"

Courfeyrac shouted:—"Come in!"

"Instanter," said Gavroche.

And with a single bound he plunged into the street.

It will be remembered that Fannicot's company had left behind it a trail of bodies. Twenty corpses lay scattered here and there on the pavement, through the whole length of the street. Twenty cartouches for Gavroche meant a provision of cartridges for the barricade.

The smoke in the street was like a fog. Whoever has beheld a cloud which has fallen into a mountain gorge between two peaked escarpments can imagine this smoke rendered denser and thicker by two gloomy rows of lofty houses. It rose gradually and was incessantly renewed; hence a twilight which made even the broad daylight turn pale. The combatants could hardly see each other from one end of the street to the other, short as it was.

This obscurity, which had probably been desired and calculated on by the commanders who were to direct the assault on the barricade, was useful to Gavroche.

Beneath the folds of this veil of smoke, and thanks to his small size, he could advance tolerably far into the street without being seen. He rifled the first seven or eight cartridge-boxes without much danger.

He crawled flat on his belly, galloped on all fours, took his basket in his teeth, twisted, glided, undulated, wound from one dead body to another, and emptied the cartridge-box or cartouche as a monkey opens a nut.

They did not dare to shout to him to return from the barricade, which was quite near, for fear of attracting attention to him.

On one body, that of a corporal, he found a powder-flask.

"For thirst," said he, putting it in his pocket.

By dint of advancing, he reached a point where the fog of the fusillade became transparent. So that the sharpshooters of the line ranged on the outlook behind their paving-stone dike and the sharpshooters of the banlieue massed at the corner of the street suddenly pointed out to each other something moving through the smoke.

At the moment when Gavroche was relieving a sergeant, who was lying near a stone doorpost, of his cartridges, a bullet struck the body.

"Fichtre!" ejaculated Gavroche. "They are killing my dead men for me."

A second bullet struck a spark from the pavement beside him.—A third overturned his basket.

Gavroche looked and saw that this came from the men of the banlieue.

He sprang to his feet, stood erect, with his hair flying in the wind, his hands on his hips, his eyes fixed on the National Guardsmen who were firing, and sang:

"On est laid à Nanterre,	*"Men are ugly at Nanterre,*
C'est la faute à Voltaire;	*'Tis the fault of Voltaire;*
Et bête à Palaiseau,	*And dull at Palaiseau,*
C'est la faute à Rousseau."	*'Tis the fault of Rousseau."*

Then he picked up his basket, replaced the cartridges which had fallen from it, without missing a single one, and, advancing toward the fusillade, set about plundering another cartridge-box. There a fourth bullet missed him, again. Gavroche sang:

"Je ne suis pas notaire,	*"I am not a notary,*
C'est la faute à Voltaire;	*'Tis the fault of Voltaire;*
Je suis un petit oiseau,	*I'm a little bird,*
C'est la faute à Rousseau."	*'Tis the fault of Rousseau."*

A fifth bullet only succeeded in drawing from him a third couplet:

"Joie est mon caractère,	*"Joy is my character,*
C'est la faute à Voltaire;	*'Tis the fault of Voltaire;*
Misère est mon trousseau,	*Misery is my trousseau,*
C'est la faute à Rousseau."	*'Tis the fault of Rousseau."*

Thus it went on for some time.

It was a charming and terrible sight. Gavroche, though shot at, was teasing the fusillade. He had the air of being greatly diverted. It was the sparrow pecking at the sportsmen. To each discharge he retorted with a couplet. They aimed at him constantly, and always missed him. The National Guardsmen and the soldiers laughed as they took aim at him. He lay down, sprang to his feet, hid in the corner of a doorway, then made a bound, disappeared, reappeared, scampered away, returned, replied to the grape-shot with his thumb at his nose, and, all the while, went on pillaging the cartouches, emptying the cartridge-boxes, and filling his basket. The insurgents, panting with anxiety, followed him with their eyes. The barricade trembled; he sang. He was not a child, he was not a man; he was a strange gamin-fairy. He might have been called the invulnerable dwarf of the fray. The bullets flew after him, he was more nimble than they. He played a fearful game of hide and seek with death; every time that the flat-nosed face of the specter approached, the urchin administered to it a fillip.

One bullet, however, better aimed or more treacherous than the rest, finally struck the will-o'-the-wisp of a child. Gavroche was seen to stagger, then he sank to the earth. The whole barricade gave vent to a cry; but there was something of Antæus in that pygmy; for the gamin to touch the pavement is the same as for the giant to touch the earth; Gavroche had fallen only to rise again; he remained in a sitting posture, a long thread of blood streaked his face, he raised both arms in the air, glanced in the direction whence the shot had come, and began to sing:

> *"Je suis tombé par terre,*   *"I have fallen to the earth,*
> *C'est la faute à Voltaire;*   *'Tis the fault of Voltaire;*
> *Le nez dans le ruisseau,*   *With my nose in the gutter,*
> *C'est la faute à . . ."*   *'Tis the fault of . . ."*

He did not finish. A second bullet from the same marksman stopped him short. This time he fell face downward on the pavement, and moved no more. This grand little soul had taken its flight.

Chapter XVI

HOW FROM A BROTHER ONE BECOMES A FATHER

AT THAT SAME MOMENT, IN THE GARDEN OF THE LUXEMBOURG—FOR THE GAZE OF THE DRAMA must be everywhere present—two children were holding each other by the hand. One might have been seven years old, the other five. The rain having soaked them, they were walking along the paths on the sunny side; the elder was leading the younger; they were pale and ragged; they had the air of wild birds. The smaller of them said: "I am very hungry."

The elder, who was already somewhat of a protector, was leading his brother with his left hand and in his right he carried a small stick.

They were alone in the garden. The garden was deserted, the gates had been closed by order of the police, on account of the insurrection. The troops who had been bivouacking there had departed for the exigencies of combat.

How did those children come there? Perhaps they had escaped from some guard-house which stood ajar; perhaps there was in the vicinity, at the Barrière d'Enfer, or on the Esplanade de l'Observatoire, or in the neighboring carrefour, dominated by the pediment on which could be read: *In-*

venerunt parvulum pannis involutum, some mountebank's booth from which they had fled; perhaps
they had, on the preceding evening, escaped the eye of the inspectors of the garden at the hour of
closing, and had passed the night in some one of those sentry-boxes where people read the papers?
The fact is, they were stray lambs and they seemed free. To be astray and to seem free is to be lost.
These poor little creatures were, in fact, lost.

These two children were the same over whom Gavroche had been put to some trouble, as the
reader will recollect. Children of the Thénardiers, leased out to Magnon, attributed to M. Gillenormand, and now leaves fallen from all these rootless branches, and swept over the ground by the
wind. Their clothing, which had been clean in Magnon's day, and which had served her as a
prospectus with M. Gillenormand, had been converted into rags.

Henceforth these beings belonged to the statistics as "Abandoned children," whom the police
take note of, collect, mislay and find again on the pavements of Paris.

It required the disturbance of a day like that to account for these miserable little creatures
being in that garden. If the superintendents had caught sight of them, they would have driven such
rags forth. Poor little things do not enter public gardens; still, people should reflect that, as children,
they have a right to flowers.

These children were there, thanks to the locked gates. They were there contrary to the regulations. They had slipped into the garden and there they remained. Closed gates do not dismiss the
inspectors, oversight is supposed to continue, but it grows slack and reposes; and the inspectors,
moved by the public anxiety and more occupied with the outside than the inside, no longer glanced
into the garden, and had not seen the two delinquents.

It had rained the night before, and even a little in the morning. But in June, showers do not
count for much. An hour after a storm, it can hardly be seen that the beautiful blonde day has wept.
The earth, in summer, is as quickly dried as the cheek of a child. At that period of the solstice, the
light of full noonday is, so to speak, poignant. It takes everything. It applies itself to the earth, and
superposes itself with a sort of suction. One would say that the sun was thirsty. A shower is but a
glass of water; a rainstorm is instantly drunk up. In the morning everything was dripping, in the afternoon everything is powdered over.

Nothing is so worthy of admiration as foliage washed by the rain and wiped by the rays of
sunlight; it is warm freshness. The gardens and meadows, having water at their roots, and sun in
their flowers, become perfuming-pans of incense, and smoke with all their odors at once. Everything smiles, sings and offers itself. One feels gently intoxicated. The springtime is a provisional
paradise, the sun helps man to have patience.

There are beings who demand nothing further; mortals, who, having the azure of heaven, say:
"It is enough!" dreamers absorbed in the wonderful, dipping into the idolatry of nature, indifferent
to good and evil, contemplators of cosmos and radiantly forgetful of man, who do not understand
how people can occupy themselves with the hunger of these, and the thirst of those, with the nudity
of the poor in winter, with the lymphatic curvature of the little spinal column, with the pallet, the
attic, the dungeon, and the rags of shivering young girls, when they can dream beneath the trees;
peaceful and terrible spirits they, and pitilessly satisfied. Strange to say, the infinite suffices them.
That great need of man, the finite, which admits of embrace, they ignore. The finite which admits
of progress, and sublime toil, they do not think about. The indefinite, which is born from the human
and divine combination of the infinite and the finite, escapes them. Provided that they are face to
face with immensity, they smile. Joy never, ecstasy forever. Their life lies in surrendering their personality in contemplation. The history of humanity is for them only a detailed plan. All is not there;
the true All remains without; what is the use of busying one's self over that detail, man? Man suffers, that is quite possible; but look at Aldebaran rising! The mother has no more milk, the newborn
babe is dying. I know nothing about that, but just look at this wonderful rosette which a slice of
wood-cells of the pine presents under the microscope! Compare the most beautiful Mechlin lace to

that if you can! These thinkers forget to love. The zodiac thrives with them to such a point that it prevents their seeing the weeping child. God eclipses their souls. This is a family of minds which are, at once, great and petty. Horace was one of them, so was Goethe. La Fontaine perhaps; magnificent egoists of the infinite, tranquil spectators of sorrow, who do not behold Nero if the weather be fair, for whom the sun conceals the funeral pile, who would look on at an execution by the guillotine in the search for an effect of light, who hear neither the cry nor the sob, nor the death-rattle, nor the alarm peal, for whom everything is well, since there is a month of May, who, so long as there are clouds of purple and gold above their heads, declare themselves content, and who are determined to be happy until the radiance of the stars and the songs of the birds are exhausted.

These are dark radiances. They have no suspicion that they are to be pitied. Certainly they are so. He who does not weep does not see. They are to be admired and pitied, as one would both pity and admire a being at once night and day, without eyes beneath his lashes but with a star on his brow.

The indifference of these thinkers, is, according to some, a superior philosophy. That may be; but in this superiority there is some infirmity. One may be immortal and yet limp: witness Vulcan. One may be more than man and less than man. There is incomplete immensity in nature. Who knows whether the sun is not a blind man?

But then, what? In whom can we trust? *Solem quis dicere falsum audeat?* Who shall dare to say that the sun is false? Thus certain geniuses, themselves, certain Very-Lofty mortals, man-stars, may be mistaken? That which is on high at the summit, at the crest, at the zenith, that which sends down so much light on the earth, sees but little, sees badly, sees not at all? Is not this a desperate state of things? No. But what is there, then, above the sun? The god.

On the 6th of June, 1832, about eleven o'clock in the morning, the Luxembourg, solitary and depopulated, was charming. The quincunxes and flower-beds shed forth balm and dazzling beauty into the sunlight. The branches, wild with the brilliant glow of midday, seemed endeavoring to embrace. In the sycamores there was an uproar of linnets, sparrows triumphed, wood-peckers climbed along the chestnut-trees, administering little pecks on the bark. The flower-beds accepted the legitimate royalty of the lilies; the most august of perfumes is that which emanates from whiteness. The peppery odor of the carnations was perceptible. The old crows of Marie de Medici were amorous in the tall trees. The sun gilded, empurpled, set fire to and lighted up the tulips, which are nothing but all the varieties of flame made into flowers. All around the banks of tulips the bees, the sparks of these flame-flowers, hummed. All was grace and gaiety, even the impending rain; this relapse, by which the lilies of the valley and the honeysuckles were destined to profit, had nothing disturbing about it; the swallows indulged in the charming threat of flying low. He who was there aspired to happiness; life smelled good; all nature exhaled candor, help, assistance, paternity, caress, dawn. The thoughts which fell from heaven were as sweet as the tiny hand of a baby when one kisses it.

The statues under the trees, white and nude, had robes of shadow pierced with light; these goddesses were all tattered with sunlight; rays hung from them on all sides. Around the great fountain, the earth was already dried up to the point of being burned. There was sufficient breeze to raise little insurrections of dust here and there. A few yellow leaves, left over from the autumn, chased each other merrily, and seemed to be playing tricks on each other.

This abundance of light had something indescribably reassuring about it. Life, sap, heat, odors overflowed; one was conscious, beneath creation, of the enormous size of the source; in all these breaths permeated with love, in this interchange of reverberations and reflections, in this marvelous expenditure of rays, in this infinite outpouring of liquid gold, one felt the prodigality of the inexhaustible; and, behind this splendor as behind a curtain of flame, one caught a glimpse of God, that millionaire of stars.

Thanks to the sand, there was not a speck of mud; thanks to the rain, there was not a grain of ashes. The clumps of blossoms had just been bathed; every sort of velvet, satin, gold and varnish, which springs from the earth in the form of flowers, was irreproachable. This magnificence was cleanly. The grand silence of happy nature filled the garden. A celestial silence that is compatible with a thousand sorts of music, the cooing of nests, the buzzing of swarms, the flutterings of the breeze. All the harmony of the season was complete in one gracious whole; the entrances and exits of spring took place in proper order; the lilacs ended; the jasmines began; some flowers were tardy, some insects in advance of their time; the vanguard of the red June butterflies fraternized with the rear-guard of the white butterflies of May. The plantain-trees were getting their new skins. The breeze hollowed out undulations in the magnificent enormity of the chestnut-trees. It was splendid. A veteran from the neighboring barracks, who was gazing through the fence, said: "Here is the Spring presenting arms and in full uniform."

All nature was breakfasting; creation was at table; this was its hour; the great blue cloth was spread in the sky, and the great green cloth on earth; the sun lighted it all up brilliantly. God was serving the universal repast. Each creature had his pasture or his mess. The ring-dove found his hemp-seed, the chaffinch found his millet, the goldfinch found chickweed, the red-breast found worms, the green finch found flies, the fly found infusoria, the bee found flowers. They ate each other somewhat, it is true, which is the misery of evil mixed with good; but not a beast of them all had an empty stomach.

The two little abandoned creatures had arrived in the vicinity of the grand fountain, and, rather bewildered by all this light, they tried to hide themselves, the instinct of the poor and the weak in the presence of even impersonal magnificence; and they kept behind the swan-hutch.

Here and there, at intervals, when the wind blew, shouts, clamor, a sort of tumultuous death-rattle, which was the firing, and dull blows, which were discharges of cannon, struck the ear confusedly. Smoke hung over the roofs in the direction of the Halles. A bell, which had the air of an appeal, was ringing in the distance.

These children did not appear to notice these noises. The little one repeated from time to time: "I am hungry."

Almost at the same instant with the children, another couple approached the great basin. They consisted of a good man, about fifty years of age, who was leading by the hand a little fellow of six. No doubt, a father and his son. The little man of six had a big brioche.

At that epoch, certain houses abutting on the river, in the Rues Madame and d'Enfer, had keys to the Luxembourg garden, of which the lodgers enjoyed the use when the gates were shut, a privilege which was suppressed later on. This father and son came from one of these houses, no doubt.

The two poor little creatures watched "that gentleman" approaching, and hid themselves a little more thoroughly.

He was a bourgeois. The same person, perhaps, whom Marius had one day heard, through his love fever, near the same grand basin, counseling his son "to avoid excesses." He had an affable and haughty air, and a mouth which was always smiling, since it did not shut. This mechanical smile, produced by too much jaw and too little skin, shows the teeth rather than the soul. The child, with his brioche, which he had bitten into but had not finished eating, seemed satiated. The child was dressed as a National Guardsman, owing to the insurrection, and the father had remained clad as a bourgeois out of prudence.

Father and son halted near the fountain where two swans were sporting. This bourgeois appeared to cherish a special admiration for the swans. He resembled them in this sense, that he walked like them.

For the moment, the swans were swimming, which is their principal talent, and they were superb.

If the two poor little beings had listened and if they had been of an age to understand, they might have gathered the words of this grave man. The father was saying to his son:

"The sage lives content with little. Look at me, my son. I do not love pomp. I am never seen in clothes decked with gold lace and stones; I leave that false splendor to badly organized souls."

Here the deep shouts which proceeded from the direction of the Halles burst out with fresh force of bell and uproar.

"What is that?" inquired the child.

The father replied:

"It is the Saturnalia."

All at once, he caught sight of the two little ragged boys behind the green swan-hutch.

"There is the beginning," said he.

And, after a pause, he added:

"Anarchy is entering this garden."

In the meanwhile, his son took a bite of his brioche, spit it out, and suddenly burst out crying.

"What are you crying about?" demanded his father.

"I am not hungry anymore," said the child.

The father's smile became more accentuated.

"One does not need to be hungry in order to eat a cake."

"My cake tires me. It is stale."

"Don't you want any more of it?"

"No."

The father pointed to the swans.

"Throw it to those palmipeds."

The child hesitated. A person may not want any more of his cake; but that is no reason for giving it away.

The father went on:

"Be humane. You must have compassion on animals."

And, taking the cake from his son, he flung it into the basin.

The cake fell very near the edge.

The swans were far away, in the center of the basin, and busy with some prey. They had seen neither the bourgeois nor the brioche.

The bourgeois, feeling that the cake was in danger of being wasted, and moved by this useless shipwreck, entered upon a telegraphic agitation, which finally attracted the attention of the swans.

They perceived something floating, steered for the edge like ships, as they are, and slowly directed their course toward the brioche, with the stupid majesty which befits white creatures.

"The swans [cygnes] understand signs [signes]," said the bourgeois, delighted to make a jest.

At that moment, the distant tumult of the city underwent another sudden increase. This time it was sinister. There are some gusts of wind which speak more distinctly than others. The one which was blowing at that moment brought clearly defined drum-beats, clamors, platoon firing, and the dismal replies of the tocsin and the cannon. This coincided with a black cloud which suddenly veiled the sun.

The swans had not yet reached the brioche.

"Let us return home," said the father, "they are attacking the Tuileries."

He grasped his son's hand again. Then he continued:

"From the Tuileries to the Luxembourg, there is but the distance which separates Royalty from the peerage; that is not far. Shots will soon rain down."

He glanced at the cloud.

"Perhaps it is rain itself that is about to shower down; the sky is joining in; the younger branch is condemned. Let us return home quickly."

"I should like to see the swans eat the brioche," said the child.

The father replied:

"That would be imprudent."

And he led his little bourgeois away.

The son, regretting the swans, turned his head back toward the basin until a corner of the quincunxes concealed it from him.

In the meanwhile, the two little waifs had approached the brioche at the same time as the swans. It was floating on the water. The smaller of them stared at the cake, the elder gazed after the retreating bourgeois.

Father and son entered the labyrinth of walks which leads to the grand flight of steps near the clump of trees on the side of the Rue Madame.

As soon as they had disappeared from view, the elder child hastily flung himself flat on his stomach on the rounding curb of the basin, and clinging to it with his left hand, and leaning over the water, on the verge of falling in, he stretched out his right hand with his stick toward the cake. The swans, perceiving the enemy, made haste, and in so doing, they produced an effect of their breasts which was of service to the little fisher; the water flowed back before the swans, and one of these gentle concentric undulations softly floated the brioche toward the child's wand. Just as the swans came up, the stick touched the cake. The child gave it a brisk rap, drew in the brioche, frightened away the swans, seized the cake, and sprang to his feet. The cake was wet; but they were hungry and thirsty. The elder broke the cake into two portions, a large one and a small one, took the small one for himself, gave the large one to his brother, and said to him:

"Ram that into your muzzle."

Chapter XVII

MORTUUS PATER FILIUM MORITURUM EXPECTAT

MARIUS DASHED OUT OF THE BARRICADE, COMBEFERRE FOLLOWED HIM. BUT HE WAS TOO LATE. Gavroche was dead. Combeferre brought back the basket of cartridges; Marius bore the child.

"Alas!" he thought, "that which the father had done for his father, he was requiting to the son; only, Thénardier had brought back his father alive; he was bringing back the child dead."

When Marius re-entered the redoubt with Gavroche in his arms, his face, like the child, was inundated with blood.

At the moment when he had stooped to lift Gavroche, a bullet had grazed his head; he had not noticed it.

Courfeyrac untied his cravat and with it bandaged Marius's brow.

They laid Gavroche on the same table with Mabeuf, and spread over the two corpses the black shawl. There was enough of it for both the old man and the child.

Combeferre distributed the cartridges from the basket which he had brought in.

This gave each man fifteen rounds to fire.

Jean Valjean was still in the same place, motionless on his stone post. When Combeferre offered him his fifteen cartridges, he shook his head.

"Here's a rare eccentric," said Combeferre in a low voice to Enjolras. "He finds a way of not fighting in this barricade."

"Which does not prevent him from defending it," responded Enjolras.

"Heroism has its originals," resumed Combeferre.

And Courfeyrac, who had overheard, added:

"He's another sort from Father Mabeuf."

One thing which must be noted is, that the fire which was battering the barricade hardly dis-

turbed the interior. Those who have never traversed the whirlwind of this sort of war can form no
idea of the singular moments of tranquility mingled with these convulsions. Men go and come, they
talk, they jest, they lounge. Someone whom we know heard a combatant say to him in the midst of
the grape-shot: "We are here as at a bachelor breakfast." The redoubt of the Rue de la Chanvrerie,
we repeat, seemed very calm within. All mutations and all phases had been, or were about to be, exhausted. The position, from critical, had become menacing, and, from menacing, was probably
about to become desperate. In proportion as the situation grew gloomy, the glow of heroism empurpled the barricade more and more. Enjolras, who was grave, dominated it, in the attitude of a
young Spartan sacrificing his naked sword to the somber genius, Epidotas.

Combeferre, wearing an apron, was dressing the wounds: Bossuet and Feuilly were making
cartridges with the powder-flask picked up by Gavroche on the dead corporal, and Bossuet said to
Feuilly: "We are soon to take the diligence for another planet"; Courfeyrac was disposing and arranging on some paving-stones which he had reserved for himself near Enjolras, a complete arsenal, his sword-cane, his gun, two holster pistols, and a cudgel, with the care of a young girl setting
a small dunkerque in order. Jean Valjean stared silently at the wall opposite him. An artisan was fastening Mother Hucheloup's big straw hat on his head with a string, "for fear of sun-stroke," as he
said. The young men from the Cougourde d'Aix were chatting merrily among themselves, as
though eager to speak patois for the last time. Joly, who had taken Widow Hucheloup's mirror from
the wall, was examining his tongue in it. Some combatants, having discovered a few crusts of rather
moldy bread, in a drawer, were eagerly devouring them. Marius was disturbed with regard to what
his father was about to say to him.

Chapter XVIII

THE VULTURE BECOME PREY

WE MUST INSIST UPON ONE PSYCHOLOGICAL FACT PECULIAR TO BARRICADES. NOTHING WHICH
is characteristic of that surprising war of the streets should be omitted.

Whatever may have been the singular inward tranquility which we have just mentioned, the
barricade, for those who are inside it, remains, none the less, a vision.

There is something of the apocalypse in civil war, all the mists of the unknown are commingled with fierce flashes, revolutions are sphinxes, and anyone who has passed through a barricade
thinks he has traversed a dream.

The feelings to which one is subject in these places we have pointed out in the case of Marius,
and we shall see the consequences; they are both more and less than life. On emerging from a barricade, one no longer knows what one has seen there. One has been terrible, but one knows it not.
One has been surrounded with conflicting ideas which had human faces; one's head has been in the
light of the future. There were corpses lying prone there, and phantoms standing erect. The hours
were colossal and seemed hours of eternity. One has lived in death. Shadows have passed by. What
were they?

One has beheld hands on which there was blood; there was a deafening horror; there was also
a frightful silence; there were open mouths which shouted, and other open mouths which held their
peace; one was in the midst of smoke, of night, perhaps. One fancied that one had touched the sinister ooze of unknown depths; one stares at something red on one's finger-nails. One no longer remembers anything.

Let us return to the Rue de la Chanvrerie.

All at once, between two discharges, the distant sound of a clock striking the hour became audible.

"It is midday," said Combeferre.

The twelve strokes had not finished striking when Enjolras sprang to his feet, and from the summit of the barricade hurled this thundering shout:

"Carry stones up into the houses; line the window-sills and the roofs with them. Half the men to their guns, the other half to the paving-stones. There is not a minute to be lost."

A squad of sappers and miners, ax on shoulder, had just made their appearance in battle array at the end of the street.

This could only be the head of a column; and of what column? The attacking column, evidently; the sappers charged with the demolition of the barricade must always precede the soldiers who are to scale it.

They were, evidently, on the brink of that moment which M. Clermont-Tonnerre, in 1822, called "the tug of war."

Enjolras's order was executed with the correct haste which is peculiar to ships and barricades, the only two scenes of combat where escape is impossible. In less than a minute, two thirds of the stones which Enjolras had had piled up at the door of Corinthe had been carried up to the first floor and the attic, and before a second minute had elapsed, these stones, artistically set one upon the other, walled up the sash-window on the first floor and the windows in the roof to half their height. A few loopholes carefully planned by Feuilly, the principal architect, allowed of the passage of the gun-barrels. This armament of the windows could be effected all the more easily since the firing of grape-shot had ceased. The two cannons were now discharging ball against the center of the barrier in order to make a hole there, and, if possible, a breach for the assault.

When the stones destined to the final defense were in place, Enjolras had the bottles which he had set under the table where Mabeuf lay, carried to the first floor.

"Who is to drink that?" Bossuet asked him.

"They," replied Enjolras.

Then they barricaded the window below, and held in readiness the iron cross-bars which served to secure the door of the wine-shop at night.

The fortress was complete. The barricade was the rampart, the wine-shop was the dungeon. With the stones which remained they stopped up the outlet.

As the defenders of a barricade are always obliged to be sparing of their ammunition, and as the assailants know this, the assailants combine their arrangements with a sort of irritating leisure, expose themselves to fire prematurely, though in appearance more than in reality, and take their ease. The preparations for attack are always made with a certain methodical deliberation; after which, the lightning strikes.

This deliberation permitted Enjolras to take a review of everything and to perfect everything. He felt that, since such men were to die, their death ought to be a masterpiece.

He said to Marius: "We are the two leaders. I will give the last orders inside. Do you remain outside and observe."

Marius posted himself on the lookout upon the crest of the barricade.

Enjolras had the door of the kitchen, which was the ambulance, as the reader will remember, nailed up.

"No splashing of the wounded," he said.

He issued his final orders in the tap-room in a curt, but profoundly tranquil tone; Feuilly listened and replied in the name of all.

"On the first floor, hold your axes in readiness to cut the staircase. Have you them?"

"Yes," said Feuilly.

"How many?"

"Two axes and a pole-ax."

"That is good. There are now twenty-six combatants of us on foot. How many guns are there?"

"Thirty-four."

"Eight too many. Keep those eight guns loaded like the rest and at hand. Swords and pistols in your belts. Twenty men to the barricade. Six ambushed in the attic windows, and at the window on the first floor to fire on the assailants through the loopholes in the stones. Let not a single worker remain inactive here. Presently, when the drum beats the assault, let the twenty below stairs rush to the barricade. The first to arrive will have the best places."

These arrangements made, he turned to Javert and said:

"I am not forgetting you."

And, laying a pistol on the table, he added:

"The last man to leave this room will smash the skull of this spy."

"Here?" inquired a voice.

"No, let us not mix their corpses with our own. The little barricade of the Mondétour lane can be scaled. It is only four feet high. The man is well pinioned. He shall be taken thither and put to death."

There was someone who was more impassive at that moment than Enjolras, it was Javert. Here Jean Valjean made his appearance.

He had been lost among the group of insurgents. He stepped forth and said to Enjolras:

"You are the commander?"

"Yes."

"You thanked me a while ago."

"In the name of the Republic. The barricade has two saviors, Marius Pontmercy and yourself."

"Do you think that I deserve a recompense?"

"Certainly."

"Well, I request one."

"What is it?"

"That I may blow that man's brains out."

Javert raised his head, saw Jean Valjean, made an almost imperceptible movement, and said:

"That is just."

As for Enjolras, he had begun to reload his rifle; he cast his eyes about him:

"No objections."

And he turned to Jean Valjean:

"Take the spy."

Jean Valjean did, in fact, take possession of Javert, by seating himself on the end of the table. He seized the pistol, and a faint click announced that he had cocked it.

Almost at the same moment, a blast of trumpets became audible.

"Take care!" shouted Marius from the top of the barricade.

Javert began to laugh with that noiseless laugh which was peculiar to him, and gazing intently at the insurgents, he said to them:

"You are in no better case than I am."

"All out!" shouted Enjolras.

The insurgents poured out tumultuously, and, as they went, received in the back—may we be permitted the expression—this sally of Javert's:

"We shall meet again shortly!"

Chapter XIX

JEAN VALJEAN TAKES HIS REVENGE

WHEN JEAN VALJEAN WAS LEFT ALONE WITH JAVERT, HE UNTIED THE ROPE WHICH FASTENED the prisoner across the middle of the body, and the knot of which was under the table. After this he made him a sign to rise.

Javert obeyed with that indefinable smile in which the supremacy of enchained authority is condensed.

Jean Valjean took Javert by the martingale, as one would take a beast of burden by the breastband, and, dragging the latter after him, emerged from the wine-shop slowly, because Javert, with his impeded limbs, could take only very short steps.

Jean Valjean had the pistol in his hand.

In this manner they crossed the inner trapezium of the barricade. The insurgents, all intent on the attack, which was imminent, had their backs turned to these two.

Marius alone, stationed on one side, at the extreme left of the barricade, saw them pass. This group of victim and executioner was illuminated by the sepulchral light which he bore in his own soul.

Jean Valjean with some difficulty, but without relaxing his hold for a single instant, made Javert, pinioned as he was, scale the little entrenchment in the Mondétour lane.

When they had crossed this barrier, they found themselves alone in the lane. No one saw them. Among the heap they could distinguish a livid face, streaming hair, a pierced hand and the half nude breast of a woman. It was Éponine. The corner of the houses hid them from the insurgents. The corpses carried away from the barricade formed a terrible pile a few paces distant.

Javert gazed askance at this body, and, profoundly calm, said in a low tone:

"It strikes me that I know that girl."

Then he turned to Jean Valjean.

Jean Valjean thrust the pistol under his arm and fixed on Javert a look which it required no words to interpret: "Javert, it is I."

Javert replied:

"Take your revenge."

Jean Valjean drew from his pocket a knife, and opened it.

"A clasp-knife!" exclaimed Javert, "you are right. That suits you better."

Jean Valjean cut the martingale which Javert had about his neck, then he cut the cords on his wrists, then, stooping down, he cut the cord on his feet; and, straightening himself up, he said to him:

"You are free."

Javert was not easily astonished. Still, master of himself though he was, he could not repress a start. He remained open-mouthed and motionless.

Jean Valjean continued:

"I do not think that I shall escape from this place. But if, by chance, I do, I live, under the name of Fauchelevent, in the Rue de l'Homme Armé, No. 7."

Javert snarled like a tiger, which made him half-open one corner of his mouth, and he muttered between his teeth:

"Have a care."

"Go," said Jean Valjean.

Javert began again:

"Thou saidst Fauchelevent, Rue de l'Homme Armé?"

"Number 7."

Javert repeated in a low voice: "Number 7."

He buttoned up his coat once more, resumed the military stiffness between his shoulders, made a half turn, folded his arms and, supporting his chin on one of his hands, he set out in the direction of the Halles. Jean Valjean followed him with his eyes.

A few minutes later, Javert turned round and shouted to Jean Valjean:

"You annoy me. Kill me, rather."

Javert himself did not notice that he no longer addressed Jean Valjean as "thou."

"Be off with you," said Jean Valjean.

Javert retreated slowly. A moment later he turned the corner of the Rue des Prêcheurs.

When Javert had disappeared, Jean Valjean fired his pistol in the air.

Then he returned to the barricade and said:

"It is done."

In the meanwhile, this is what had taken place.

Marius, more intent on the outside than on the interior, had not, up to that time, taken a good look at the pinioned spy in the dark background of the tap-room.

When he beheld him in broad daylight, striding over the barricade in order to proceed to his death, he recognized him. Something suddenly recurred to his mind. He recalled the inspector of the Rue de Pontoise, and the two pistols which the latter had handed to him and which he, Marius, had used in this very barricade, and not only did he recall his face, but his name as well.

This recollection was misty and troubled, however, like all his ideas.

It was not an affirmation that he made, but a question which he put to himself:

"Is not that the inspector of police who told me that his name was Javert?"

Perhaps there was still time to intervene in behalf of that man. But, in the first place, he must know whether this was Javert.

Marius called to Enjolras, who had just stationed himself at the other extremity of the barricade:

"Enjolras!"

"What?"

"What is the name of yonder man?"

"What man?"

"The police agent. Do you know his name?"

"Of course. He told us."

"What is it?"

"Javert."

Marius sprang to his feet.

At that moment, they heard the report of the pistol.

Jean Valjean reappeared and cried: "It is done."

A gloomy chill traversed Marius's heart.

Chapter XX

THE DEAD ARE IN THE RIGHT AND THE LIVING
ARE NOT IN THE WRONG

THE DEATH-AGONY OF THE BARRICADE WAS ABOUT TO BEGIN.

Everything contributed to its tragic majesty at that supreme moment; a thousand mysterious crashes in the air, the breath of armed masses set in movement in the streets which were not visible, the intermittent gallop of cavalry, the heavy shock of artillery on the march, the firing by squads, and the cannonades crossing each other in the labyrinth of Paris, the smokes of battle mounting all gilded above the roofs, indescribable and vaguely terrible cries, lightnings of menace everywhere, the tocsin of Saint-Merry, which now had the accents of a sob, the mildness of the weather, the splendor of the sky filled with sun and clouds, the beauty of the day, and the alarming silence of the houses.

For, since the preceding evening, the two rows of houses in the Rue de la Chanvrerie had become two walls; ferocious walls, doors closed, windows closed, shutters closed.

In those days, so different from those in which we live, when the hour was come, when the people wished to put an end to a situation, which had lasted too long, with a charter granted or with a legal country, when universal wrath was diffused in the atmosphere, when the city consented to the tearing up of the pavements, when insurrection made the bourgeoisie smile by whispering its password in its ear, then the inhabitant, thoroughly penetrated with the revolt, so to speak, was the auxiliary of the combatant, and the house fraternized with the improvised fortress which rested on it. When the situation was not ripe, when the insurrection was not decidedly admitted, when the masses disowned the movement, all was over with the combatants, the city was changed into a desert around the revolt, souls grew chilled, refuges were nailed up, and the street turned into a defile to help the army to take the barricade.

A people cannot be forced, through surprise, to walk more quickly than it chooses. Woe to whomsoever tries to force its hand! A people does not let itself go at random. Then it abandons the insurrection to itself. The insurgents become noxious, infected with the plague. A house is an escarpment, a door is a refusal, a façade is a wall. This wall hears, sees and will not. It might open and save you. No. This wall is a judge. It gazes at you and condemns you. What dismal things are closed houses. They seem dead, they are living. Life which is, as it were, suspended there, persists there. No one has gone out of them for four-and-twenty hours, but no one is missing from them. In the interior of that rock, people go and come, go to bed and rise again; they are a family party there; there they eat and drink; they are afraid, a terrible thing! Fear excuses this fearful lack of hospitality; terror is mixed with it, an extenuating circumstance. Sometimes, even, and this has been actually seen, fear turns to passion; fright may change into fury, as prudence does into rage; hence this wise saying: "The enraged moderates." There are outbursts of supreme terror, whence springs wrath like a mournful smoke.—"What do these people want? What have they come there to do? Let them get out of the scrape. So much the worse for them. It is their fault. They are only getting what they deserve. It does not concern us. Here is our poor street all riddled with balls. They are a pack of rascals. Above all things, don't open the door."—And the house assumes the air of a tomb. The insurgent is in the death-throes in front of that house; he sees the grape-shot and naked swords drawing near; if he cries, he knows that they are listening to him, and that no one will come; there stand walls which might protect him, there are men who might save him; and these walls have ears of flesh, and these men have bowels of stone.

Whom shall he reproach?

No one and everyone.

The incomplete times in which we live.

It is always at its own risk and peril that Utopia is converted into revolution, and from philosophical protest becomes an armed protest, and from Minerva turns to Pallas.

The Utopia which grows impatient and becomes revolt knows what awaits it; it almost always comes too soon. Then it becomes resigned, and stoically accepts catastrophe in lieu of triumph. It serves those who deny it without complaint, even excusing them, and even disculpates them, and its magnanimity consists in consenting to abandonment. It is indomitable in the face of obstacles and gentle toward ingratitude.

Is this ingratitude, however?

Yes, from the point of view of the human race.

No, from the point of view of the individual.

Progress is man's mode of existence. The general life of the human race is called Progress, the collective stride of the human race is called Progress. Progress advances; it makes the great human and terrestrial journey toward the celestial and the divine; it has its halting-places where it rallies the laggard troop, it has its stations where it meditates, in the presence of some splendid Canaan suddenly unveiled on its horizon, it has its nights when it sleeps; and it is one of the poignant anxieties of the thinker that he sees the shadow resting on the human soul, and that he gropes in darkness without being able to awaken that slumbering Progress.

"God is dead, perhaps," said Gerard de Nerval one day to the writer of these lines, confounding progress with God, and taking the interruption of movement for the death of Being.

He who despairs is in the wrong. Progress infallibly awakes, and, in short, we may say that it marches on, even when it is asleep, for it has increased in size. When we behold it erect once more, we find it taller. To be always peaceful does not depend on progress any more than it does on the stream; erect no barriers, cast no boulders; obstacles make water froth and humanity boil. Hence arise troubles; but after these troubles, we recognize the fact that ground has been gained. Until order, which is nothing else than universal peace, has been established, until harmony and unity reign, progress will have revolutions as its halting-places.

What, then, is progress? We have just enunciated it; the permanent life of the peoples.

Now, it sometimes happens, that the momentary life of individuals offers resistance to the eternal life of the human race.

Let us admit without bitterness, that the individual has his distinct interests, and can, without forfeiture, stipulate for his interest, and defend it; the present has its pardonable dose of egotism; momentary life has its rights, and is not bound to sacrifice itself constantly to the future. The generation which is passing in its turn over the earth, is not forced to abridge it for the sake of the generations, its equal, after all, who will have their turn later on.—"I exist," murmurs that someone whose name is All. "I am young and in love, I am old and I wish to repose, I am the father of a family, I toil, I prosper, I am successful in business, I have houses to lease, I have money in the government funds, I am happy, I have a wife and children, I have all this, I desire to live, leave me in peace."—Hence, at certain hours, a profound cold broods over the magnanimous vanguard of the human race.

Utopia, moreover, we must admit, quits its radiant sphere when it makes war. It, the truth of tomorrow, borrows its mode of procedure, battle, from the lie of yesterday. It, the future, behaves like the past. It, pure idea, becomes a deed of violence. It complicates its heroism with a violence for which it is just that it should be held to answer; a violence of occasion and expedient, contrary to principle, and for which it is fatally punished. The Utopia, insurrection, fights with the old military code in its fist; it shoots spies, it executes traitors; it suppresses living beings and flings them into unknown darkness. It makes use of death, a serious matter. It seems as though Utopia had no longer any faith in radiance, its irresistible and incorruptible force. It strikes with the sword. Now, no sword is simple. Every blade has two edges; he who wounds with the one is wounded with the other.

Having made this reservation, and made it with all severity, it is impossible for us not to admire, whether they succeed or not, those the glorious combatants of the future, the confessors of Utopia. Even when they miscarry, they are worthy of veneration; and it is, perhaps, in failure, that they possess the most majesty. Victory, when it is in accord with progress, merits the applause of the people; but a heroic defeat merits their tender compassion. The one is magnificent, the other sublime. For our own part, we prefer martyrdom to success. John Brown is greater than Washington, and Pisacane is greater than Garibaldi.

It certainly is necessary that someone should take the part of the vanquished.

We are unjust toward these great men who attempt the future, when they fail.

Revolutionists are accused of sowing fear abroad. Every barricade seems a crime. Their theories are incriminated, their aim suspected, their ulterior motive is feared, their conscience denounced. They are reproached with raising, erecting, and heaping up, against the reigning social state, a mass of miseries, of griefs, of iniquities, of wrongs, of despairs, and of tearing from the lowest depths blocks of shadow in order therein to embattle themselves and to combat. People shout to them: "You are tearing up the pavements of hell!" They might reply: "That is because our barricade is made of good intentions."

The best thing, assuredly, is the pacific solution. In short, let us agree that when we behold the pavement, we think of the bear, and it is a good-will which renders society uneasy. But it depends on society to save itself; it is to its own good-will that we make our appeal. No violent remedy is necessary. To study evil amiably, to prove its existence, then to cure it. It is to this that we invite it.

However that may be, even when fallen, above all when fallen, these men, who at every point of the universe, with their eyes fixed on France, are striving for the grand work with the inflexible logic of the ideal, are august; they give their life a free offering to progress; they accomplish the will of providence; they perform a religious act. At the appointed hour, with as much disinterestedness as an actor who answers to his cue, in obedience to the divine stage-manager, they enter the tomb. And this hopeless combat, this stoical disappearance they accept in order to bring about the supreme and universal consequences, the magnificent and irresistibly human movement begun on the 14th of July, 1789; these soldiers are priests. The French revolution is an act of God.

Moreover, there are, and it is proper to add this distinction to the distinctions already pointed out in another chapter—there are accepted revolutions, revolutions which are called revolutions; there are refused revolutions, which are called riots.

An insurrection which breaks out, is an idea which is passing its examination before the people. If the people lets fall a black ball, the idea is dried fruit; the insurrection is a mere skirmish.

Waging war at every summons and every time that Utopia desires it, is not the thing for the peoples. Nations have not always and at every hour the temperament of heroes and martyrs.

They are positive. *A priori*, insurrection is repugnant to them, in the first place, because it often results in a catastrophe, in the second place, because it always has an abstraction as its point of departure.

Because, and this is a noble thing, it is always for the ideal, and for the ideal alone, that those who sacrifice themselves do thus sacrifice themselves. An insurrection is an enthusiasm. Enthusiasm may wax wroth; hence the appeal to arms. But every insurrection, which aims at a government or a régime, aims higher. Thus, for instance, and we insist upon it, what the chiefs of the insurrection of 1832, and, in particular, the young enthusiasts of the Rue de la Chanvrerie were combating, was not precisely Louis Philippe. The majority of them, when talking freely, did justice to this king who stood midway between monarchy and revolution; no one hated him. But they attacked the younger branch of the divine right in Louis Philippe as they had attacked its elder branch in Charles X; and that which they wished to overturn in overturning royalty in France, was, as we have explained, the usurpation of man over man, and of privilege over right in the entire universe. Paris without a king has as result the world without despots. This is the manner in which they reasoned. Their aim was distant no doubt, vague perhaps, and it retreated in the face of their efforts; but it was great.

Thus it is. And we sacrifice ourselves for these visions, which are almost always illusions for the sacrificed, but illusions with which, after all, the whole of human certainty is mingled. We throw ourselves into these tragic affairs and become intoxicated with that which we are about to do. Who knows? We may succeed. We are few in number, we have a whole army arrayed against us; but we are defending right, the natural law, the sovereignty of each one over himself from which no abdication is possible, justice and truth, and in case of need, we die like the three hundred Spartans. We do not think of Don Quixote but of Leonidas. And we march straight before us, and once pledged, we do not draw back, and we rush onwards with head held low, cherishing as our hope an unprecedented victory, revolution completed, progress set free again, the aggrandizement of the human race, universal deliverance; and in the event of the worst, Thermopylæ.

These passages of arms for the sake of progress often suffer shipwreck, and we have just explained why. The crowd is restive in the presence of the impulses of paladins. Heavy masses, the multitudes which are fragile because of their very weight, fear adventures; and there is a touch of adventure in the ideal.

Moreover, and we must not forget this, interests which are not very friendly to the ideal and the sentimental are in the way. Sometimes the stomach paralyzes the heart.

The grandeur and beauty of France lies in this, that she takes less from the stomach than other nations: she more easily knots the rope about her loins. She is the first awake, the last asleep. She marches forwards. She is a seeker.

This arises from the fact that she is an artist.

The ideal is nothing but the culminating point of logic, the same as the beautiful is nothing but the summit of the true. Artistic peoples are also consistent peoples. To love beauty is to see the light. That is why the torch of Europe, that is to say of civilization, was first borne by Greece, who passed it on to Italy, who handed it on to France. Divine, illuminating nations of scouts! *Vitaelampada tradunt.*

It is an admirable thing that the poetry of a people is the element of its progress. The amount of civilization is measured by the quantity of imagination. Only, a civilizing people should remain a manly people. Corinth, yes; Sybaris, no. Whoever becomes effeminate makes himself a bastard. He must be neither a dilettante nor a virtuoso: but he must be artistic. In the matter of civilization, he must not refine, but he must sublime. On this condition, one gives to the human race the pattern of the ideal.

The modern ideal has its type in art, and its means is science. It is through science that it will realize that august vision of the poets, the socially beautiful. Eden will be reconstructed by A+B. At the point which civilization has now reached, the exact is a necessary element of the splendid, and the artistic sentiment is not only served, but completed by the scientific organ; dreams must be calculated. Art, which is the conqueror, should have for support science, which is the walker; the solidity of the creature which is ridden is of importance. The modern spirit is the genius of Greece with the genius of India as its vehicle; Alexander on the elephant.

Races which are petrified in dogma or demoralized by lucre are unfit to guide civilization. Genuflection before the idol or before money wastes away the muscles which walk and the will which advances. Hieratic or mercantile absorption lessens a people's power of radiance, lowers its horizon by lowering its level, and deprives it of that intelligence, at once both human and divine of the universal goal, which makes missionaries of nations. Babylon has no ideal; Carthage has no ideal. Athens and Rome have and keep, throughout all the nocturnal darkness of the centuries, halos of civilization.

France is in the same quality of race as Greece and Italy. She is Athenian in the matter of beauty, and Roman in her greatness. Moreover, she is good. She gives herself. Oftener than is the case with other races, is she in the humor for self-devotion and sacrifice. Only, this humor seizes upon her and again abandons her. And therein lies the great peril for those who run when she desires only to walk, or who walk on when she desires to halt. France has her relapses into materialism, and, at certain instants, the ideas which obstruct that sublime brain have no longer anything which recalls French greatness and are of the dimensions of a Missouri or a South Carolina. What is to be done in such a case? The giantess plays at being a dwarf; immense France has her freaks of pettiness. That is all.

To this there is nothing to say. Peoples, like planets, possess the right to an eclipse. And all is well, provided that the light returns and that the eclipse does not degenerate into night. Dawn and resurrection are synonymous. The reappearance of the light is identical with the persistence of the *I*.

Let us state these facts calmly. Death on the barricade or the tomb in exile, is an acceptable occasion for devotion. The real name of devotion is disinterestedness. Let the abandoned allow themselves to be abandoned, let the exiled allow themselves to be exiled, and let us confine ourselves to entreating great nations not to retreat too far, when they do retreat. One must not push too far in descent under pretext of a return to reason.

Matter exists, the minute exists, interest exists, the stomach exists; but the stomach must not be the sole wisdom. The life of the moment has its rights, we admit, but permanent life has its rights also. Alas! the fact that one is mounted does not preclude a fall. This can be seen in history more frequently than is desirable: A nation is great, it tastes the ideal, then it bites the mire, and finds it good; and if it be asked how it happens that it has abandoned Socrates for Falstaff, it replies: "Because I love statesmen."

One word more before returning to our subject, the conflict.

A battle like the one which we are engaged in describing is nothing else than a convulsion toward the ideal. Progress trammeled is sickly, and is subject to these tragic epilepsies. With that malady of progress, civil war, we have been obliged to come in contact in our passage. This is one of the fatal phases, at once act and entr'acte of that drama whose pivot is a social condemnation, and whose veritable title is *Progress*.

Progress!

The cry to which we frequently give utterance is our whole thought; and, at the point of this drama which we have now reached, the idea which it contains having still more than one trial to undergo, it is, perhaps, permitted to us, if not to lift the veil from it, to at least allow its light to shine through.

The book which the reader has under his eye at this moment, is, from one end to the other, as a whole and in detail, whatever may be its intermittences, exceptions and faults, the march from evil to good, from the unjust to the just, from night to day, from appetite to conscience, from rottenness to life, from hell to heaven, from nothingness to God. Point of departure: matter; point of arrival: the soul. The hydra at the beginning, the angel at the end.

Chapter XXI

THE HEROES

ALL AT ONCE, THE DRUM BEAT THE CHARGE.

The attack was a hurricane. On the evening before, in the darkness, the barricade had been approached silently, as by a boa. Now, in broad daylight, in that widening street, surprise was decidedly impossible, rude force had, moreover, been unmasked, the cannon had begun the roar, the army hurled itself on the barricade. Fury now became skill. A powerful detachment of infantry of the line, broken at regular intervals, by the National Guard and the Municipal Guard on foot, and supported by serried masses which could be heard though not seen, debouched into the street at a run, with drums beating, trumpets braying, bayonets leveled, the sappers at their head, and, imperturbable under the projectiles, charged straight for the barricade with the weight of a brazen beam against a wall.

The wall held firm.

The insurgents fired impetuously. The barricade once scaled had a mane of lightning flashes. The assault was so furious, that for one moment, it was inundated with assailants; but it shook off the soldiers as the lion shakes off the dogs, and it was only covered with besiegers as the cliff is covered with foam, to reappear, a moment later, beetling, black and formidable.

The column, forced to retreat, remained massed in the street, unprotected but terrible, and replied to the redoubt with a terrible discharge of musketry. Anyone who has seen fireworks will recall the sheaf formed of interlacing lightnings which is called a bouquet. Let the reader picture to himself this bouquet, no longer vertical but horizontal, bearing a bullet, buck-shot or a biscaïen at the tip of each one of its jets of flame, and picking off dead men one after another from its clusters of lightning. The barricade was underneath it.

On both sides, the resolution was equal. The bravery exhibited there was almost barbarous and was complicated with a sort of heroic ferocity which began by the sacrifice of self.

This was the epoch when a National Guardsman fought like a Zouave. The troop wished to make an end of it, insurrection was desirous of fighting. The acceptance of the death agony in the flower of youth and in the flush of health turns intrepidity into frenzy. In this fray, each one underwent the broadening growth of the death hour. The street was strewn with corpses.

The barricade had Enjolras at one of its extremities and Marius at the other. Enjolras, who carried the whole barricade in his head, reserved and sheltered himself; three soldiers fell, one after the other, under his embrasure without having even seen him; Marius fought unprotected. He made himself a target. He stood with more than half his body above the breastworks. There is no more violent prodigal than the avaricious man who takes the bit in his teeth; there is no man more terrible in action than a dreamer. Marius was formidable and pensive. In battle he was as in a dream. One would have pronounced him a phantom engaged in firing a gun.

The insurgents' cartridges were giving out; but not their sarcasms. In this whirlwind of the sepulcher in which they stood, they laughed.

Courfeyrac was bare-headed.

"What have you done with your hat?" Bossuet asked him.

Courfeyrac replied:

"They have finally taken it away from me with cannon-balls."

Or they uttered haughty comments.

"Can anyone understand," exclaimed Feuilly bitterly, "those men—[and he cited names, well-known names, even celebrated names, some belonging to the old army]—who had promised to join us, and taken an oath to aid us, and who had pledged their honor to it, and who are our generals, and who abandon us!"

And Combeferre restricted himself to replying with a grave smile.

"There are people who observe the rules of honor as one observes the stars, from a great distance."

The interior of the barricade was so strewn with torn cartridges that one would have said that there had been a snowstorm.

The assailants had numbers in their favor; the insurgents had position. They were at the top of a wall, and they thundered point-blank upon the soldiers tripping over the dead and wounded and entangled in the escarpment. This barricade, constructed as it was and admirably buttressed, was really one of those situations where a handful of men hold a legion in check. Nevertheless, the attacking column, constantly recruited and enlarged under the shower of bullets, drew inexorably nearer, and now, little by little, step by step, but surely, the army closed in around the barricade as the vice grasps the wine-press.

One assault followed another. The horror of the situation kept increasing.

Then there burst forth on that heap of paving-stones, in that Rue de la Chanvrerie, a battle worthy of a wall of Troy. These haggard, ragged, exhausted men, who had had nothing to eat for four-and-twenty hours, who had not slept, who had but a few more rounds to fire, who were fumbling in their pockets which had been emptied of cartridges, nearly all of whom were wounded, with head or arm bandaged with black and blood-stained linen, with holes in their clothes from which the blood trickled, and who were hardly armed with poor guns and notched swords, became Titans. The barricade was ten times attacked, approached, assailed, scaled, and never captured.

In order to form an idea of this struggle, it is necessary to imagine fire set to a throng of terrible courages, and then to gaze at the conflagration. It was not a combat, it was the interior of a furnace; there mouths breathed the flame; there countenances were extraordinary. The human form seemed impossible there, the combatants flamed forth there, and it was formidable to behold the going and coming in that red glow of those salamanders of the fray.

The successive and simultaneous scenes of this grand slaughter we renounce all attempts at depicting. The epic alone has the right to fill twelve thousand verses with a battle.

One would have pronounced this that hell of Brahmanism, the most redoubtable of the seventeen abysses, which the Veda calls the Forest of Swords.

They fought hand to hand, foot to foot, with pistol shots, with blows of the sword, with their fists, at a distance, close at hand, from above, from below, from everywhere, from the roofs of the houses, from the windows of the wine-shop, from the cellar windows, whither some had crawled. They were one against sixty.

The façade of Corinthe, half demolished, was hideous. The window, tattooed with grape-shot, had lost glass and frame and was nothing now but a shapeless hole, tumultuously blocked with paving-stones.

Bossuet was killed; Feuilly was killed; Courfeyrac was killed; Combeferre, transfixed by three blows from a bayonet in the breast at the moment when he was lifting up a wounded soldier, had only time to cast a glance to heaven when he expired.

Marius, still fighting, was so riddled with wounds, particularly in the head, that his countenance disappeared beneath the blood, and one would have said that his face was covered with a red kerchief.

Enjolras alone was not struck. When he had no longer any weapon, he reached out his hands to right and left and an insurgent thrust some arm or other into his fist. All he had left was the stumps of four swords; one more than François I at Marignan. Homer says: "Diomedes cuts the throat of Axylus, son of Teuthranis, who dwelt in happy Arisba; Euryalus, son of Mecistæus, exterminates Dresos and Opheltios, Esepius, and that Pedasus whom the naiad Abarbarea bore to the blameless Bucolion; Ulysses overthrows Pidytes of Percosius; Antilochus, Ablerus; Polypætes, Astyalus; Polydamas, Otos, of Cyllene; and Teucer, Aretaon. Meganthios dies under the blows of Euripylus's pike. Agamemnon, king of the heroes, flings to earth Elatos, born in the rocky city which is laved by the sounding river Satnoïs." In our old poems of exploits, Esplandian attacks the giant marquis Swantibore with a cobbler's shoulder-stick of fire, and the latter defends himself by stoning the hero with towers which he plucks up by the roots. Our ancient mural frescoes show us the two Dukes of Bretagne and Bourbon, armed, emblazoned and crested in warlike guise, on horseback and approaching each other, their battle-axes in hand, masked with iron, gloved with iron, booted with iron, the one caparisoned in ermine, the other draped in azure: Bretagne with his lion between the two horns of his crown, Bourbon helmeted with a monster fleur-de-lys on his visor. But, in order to be superb, it is not necessary to wear, like Yvon, the ducal morion, to have in the fist, like Esplandian, a living flame, or, like Phyles, father of Polydamas, to have brought back from Ephyra a good suit of mail, a present from the king of men, Euphetes; it suffices to give one's life for a conviction or a loyalty. This ingenuous little soldier, yesterday a peasant of Bauce or Limousin, who prowls with his clasp-knife by his side, around the children's nurses in the Luxembourg garden, this pale young student bent over a piece of anatomy or a book, a blond youth who shaves his beard with scissors—take both of them, breathe upon them with a breath of duty, place them face to face in the Carrefour Boucherat or in the blind-alley Planche-Mibray, and let the one fight for his flag, and the other for his ideal, and let both of them imagine that they are fighting for their country; the struggle will be colossal; and the shadow which this raw recruit and this sawbones in conflict will produce in that grand epic field where humanity is striving, will equal the shadow cast by Megaryon, King of Lycia, tiger-filled, crushing in his embrace the immense body of Ajax, equal to the gods.

Chapter XXII

FOOT TO FOOT

WHEN THERE WERE NO LONGER ANY OF THE LEADERS LEFT ALIVE, EXCEPT ENJOLRAS AND MARius at the two extremities of the barricade, the center, which had so long sustained Courfeyrac, Joly, Bossuet, Feuilly and Combeferre, gave way. The cannon, though it had not effected a practicable breach, had made a rather large hollow in the middle of the redoubt; there, the summit of the wall had disappeared before the balls, and had crumbled away; and the rubbish which had fallen, now inside, now outside, had, as it accumulated, formed two piles in the nature of slopes on the two sides of the barrier, one on the inside, the other on the outside. The exterior slope presented an inclined plane to the attack.

A final assault was there attempted, and this assault succeeded. The mass bristling with bayonets and hurled forward at a run, came up with irresistible force, and the serried front of battle of the attacking column made its appearance through the smoke on the crest of the battlements. This time, it was decisive. The group of insurgents who were defending the center retreated in confusion.

Then the gloomy love of life awoke once more in some of them. Many, finding themselves under the muzzles of this forest of guns, did not wish to die. This is a moment when the instinct of self-preservation emits howls, when the beast reappears in men. They were hemmed in by the lofty, six-story house which formed the background of their redoubt. This house might prove their salvation. The building was barricaded, and walled, as it were, from top to bottom. Before the troops of the line had reached the interior of the redoubt, there was time for a door to open and shut, the space of a flash of lightning was sufficient for that, and the door of that house, suddenly opened a crack and closed again instantly, was life for these despairing men. Behind this house, there were streets, possible flight, space. They set to knocking at that door with the butts of their guns, and with kicks, shouting, calling, entreating, wringing their hands. No one opened. From the little window on the third floor, the head of the dead man gazed down upon them.

But Enjolras and Marius, and the seven or eight rallied about them, sprang forward and protected them. Enjolras had shouted to the soldiers: "Don't advance!" and as an officer had not obeyed, Enjolras had killed the officer. He was now in the little inner court of the redoubt, with his back planted against the Corinthe building, a sword in one hand, a rifle in the other, holding open the door of the wine-shop which he barred against assailants. He shouted to the desperate men: "There is but one door open; this one."—And shielding them with his body, and facing an entire battalion alone, he made them pass in behind him. All precipitated themselves thither. Enjolras, executing with his rifle, which he now used like a cane, what single-stick players call a "covered rose" round his head, leveled the bayonets around and in front of him, and was the last to enter; and then ensued a horrible moment, when the soldiers tried to make their way in, and the insurgents strove to bar them out. The door was slammed with such violence, that, as it fell back into its frame, it showed the five fingers of a soldier who had been clinging to it, cut off and glued to the post.

Marius remained outside. A shot had just broken his collar-bone, he felt that he was fainting and falling. At that moment, with eyes already shut, he felt the shock of a vigorous hand seizing him, and the swoon in which his senses vanished, hardly allowed him time for the thought, mingled with a last memory of Cosette: "I am taken prisoner. I shall be shot."

Enjolras, not seeing Marius among those who had taken refuge in the wine-shop, had the same idea. But they had reached a moment when each man has not the time to meditate on his own death. Enjolras fixed the bar across the door, and bolted it, and double-locked it with key and chain, while those outside were battering furiously at it, the soldiers with the butts of their muskets, the sappers with their axes. The assailants were grouped about that door. The siege of the wine-shop was now beginning.

The soldiers, we will observe, were full of wrath.

The death of the artillery-sergeant had enraged them, and then, a still more melancholy circumstance, during the few hours which had preceded the attack, it had been reported among them that the insurgents were mutilating their prisoners, and that there was the headless body of a soldier in the wine-shop. This sort of fatal rumor is the usual accompaniment of civil wars, and it was a false report of this kind which, later on, produced the catastrophe of the Rue Transnonain.

When the door was barricaded, Enjolras said to the others:

"Let us sell our lives dearly."

Then he approached the table on which lay Mabeuf and Gavroche. Beneath the black cloth two straight and rigid forms were visible, one large, the other small, and the two faces were vaguely outlined beneath the cold folds of the shroud. A hand projected from beneath the winding sheet and hung near the floor. It was that of the old man.

Enjolras bent down and kissed that venerable hand, just as he had kissed his brow on the preceding evening.

These were the only two kisses which he had bestowed in the course of his life.

Let us abridge the tale. The barricade had fought like a gate of Thebes; the wine-shop fought like a house of Saragossa. These resistances are dogged. No quarter. No flag of truce possible. Men are willing to die, provided their opponent will kill them.

When Suchet says: "Capitulate"—Palafox replies: "After the war with cannon, the war with knives." Nothing was lacking in the capture by assault of the Hucheloup wine-shop; neither paving-stones raining from the windows and the roof on the besiegers and exasperating the soldiers by crushing them horribly, nor shots fired from the attic-windows and the cellar, nor the fury of attack, nor, finally, when the door yielded, the frenzied madness of extermination. The assailants, rushing into the wine-shop, their feet entangled in the panels of the door which had been beaten in and flung on the ground, found not a single combatant there. The spiral staircase, hewn asunder with the ax, lay in the middle of the tap-room, a few wounded men were just breathing their last, everyone who was not killed was on the first floor, and from there, through the hole in the ceiling, which had formed the entrance of the stairs, a terrific fire burst forth. It was the last of their cartridges. When they were exhausted, when these formidable men on the point of death had no longer either powder or ball, each grasped in his hands two of the bottles which Enjolras had reserved, and of which we have spoken, and held the scaling party in check with these frightfully fragile clubs. They were bottles of aqua-fortis.

We relate these gloomy incidents of carnage as they occurred. The besieged man, alas! converts everything into a weapon. Greek fire did not disgrace Archimedes, boiling pitch did not disgrace Bayard. All war is a thing of terror, and there is no choice in it. The musketry of the besiegers, though confined and embarrassed by being directed from below upwards, was deadly. The rim of the hole in the ceiling was speedily surrounded by heads of the slain, whence dripped long, red and smoking streams, the uproar was indescribable; a close and burning smoke almost produced night over this combat. Words are lacking to express horror when it has reached this pitch. There were no longer men in this conflict, which was now infernal. They were no longer giants matched with colossi. It resembled Milton and Dante rather than Homer. Demons attacked, specters resisted.

It was heroism become monstrous.

Chapter XXIII

ORESTES FASTING AND PYLADES DRUNK

AT LENGTH, BY DINT OF MOUNTING ON EACH OTHER'S BACKS, AIDING THEMSELVES WITH THE skeleton of the staircase, climbing up the walls, clinging to the ceiling, slashing away at the very brink of the trapdoor, the last one who offered resistance, a score of assailants, soldiers, National Guardsmen, municipal guardsmen, in utter confusion, the majority disfigured by wounds in the face during that redoubtable ascent, blinded by blood, furious, rendered savage, made an eruption into the apartment on the first floor. There they found only one man still on his feet, Enjolras. Without cartridges, without sword, he had nothing in his hand now but the barrel of his gun whose stock he had broken over the head of those who were entering. He had placed the billiard-table between his assailants and himself; he had retreated into the corner of the room, and there, with haughty eye, and head borne high, with this stump of a weapon in his hand, he was still so alarming as to speedily create an empty space around him. A cry arose:

"He is the leader! It was he who slew the artillery-man. It is well that he has placed himself there. Let him remain there. Let us shoot him down on the spot."

"Shoot me," said Enjolras.

And flinging away his bit of gun-barrel, and folding his arms, he offered his breast.

The audacity of a fine death always affects men. As soon as Enjolras folded his arms and accepted his end, the din of strife ceased in the room, and this chaos suddenly stilled into a sort of sepulchral solemnity. The menacing majesty of Enjolras disarmed and motionless, appeared to oppress this tumult, and this young man, haughty, bloody, and charming, who alone had not a wound, who was as indifferent as an invulnerable being, seemed, by the authority of his tranquil glance, to constrain this sinister rabble to kill him respectfully. His beauty, at that moment augmented by his pride, was resplendent, and he was fresh and rosy after the fearful four-and-twenty hours which had just elapsed, as though he could no more be fatigued than wounded. It was of him, possibly, that a witness spoke afterwards, before the council of war: "There was an insurgent whom I heard called Apollo." A National Guardsman who had taken aim at Enjolras, lowered his gun, saying: "It seems to me that I am about to shoot a flower."

Twelve men formed into a squad in the corner opposite Enjolras, and silently made ready their guns.

Then a sergeant shouted:

"Take aim!"

An officer intervened.

"Wait."

And addressing Enjolras:

"Do you wish to have your eyes bandaged?"

"No."

"Was it you who killed the artillery sergeant?"

"Yes."

Grantaire had waked up a few moments before.

Grantaire, it will be remembered, had been asleep ever since the preceding evening in the upper room of the wine-shop, seated on a chair and leaning on the table.

He realized in its fullest sense the old metaphor of "dead drunk." The hideous potion of absinthe-porter and alcohol, had thrown him into a lethargy. His table being small, and not suitable for the barricade, he had been left in possession of it. He was still in the same posture, with his breast bent over the table, his head lying flat on his arms, surrounded by glasses, beer-jugs and bottles. His was the overwhelming slumber of the torpid bear and the satiated leech. Nothing had had any effect upon it, neither the fusillade, nor the cannon-balls, nor the grape-shot which had made its way through the window into the room where he was. Nor the tremendous uproar of the assault. He merely replied to the cannonade, now and then, by a snore. He seemed to be waiting there for a bullet which should spare him the trouble of waking. Many corpses were strewn around him; and, at the first glance, there was nothing to distinguish him from those profound sleepers of death.

Noise does not rouse a drunken man; silence awakens him. The fall of everything around him only augmented Grantaire's prostration; the crumbling of all things was his lullaby. The sort of halt which the tumult underwent in the presence of Enjolras was a shock to this heavy slumber. It had the effect of a carriage going at full speed, which suddenly comes to a dead stop. The persons dozing within it wake up. Grantaire rose to his feet with a start, stretched out his arms, rubbed his eyes, stared, yawned, and understood.

A fit of drunkenness reaching its end resembles a curtain which is torn away. One beholds, at a single glance and as a whole, all that it has concealed. All suddenly presents itself to the memory; and the drunkard who has known nothing of what has been taking place during the last twenty-four hours, has no sooner opened his eyes than he is perfectly informed. Ideas recur to him with abrupt lucidity; the obliteration of intoxication, a sort of steam which has obscured the brain, is dissipated, and makes way for the clear and sharply outlined importunity of realities.

Relegated, as he was, to one corner, and sheltered behind the billiard-table, the soldiers whose eyes were fixed on Enjolras, had not even noticed Grantaire, and the sergeant was preparing to repeat his order: "Take aim!" when all at once, they heard a strong voice shout beside them:

"Long live the Republic! I'm one of them."

Grantaire had risen. The immense gleam of the whole combat which he had missed, and in which he had had no part, appeared in the brilliant glance of the transfigured drunken man.

He repeated: "Long live the Republic!" crossed the room with a firm stride and placed himself in front of the guns beside Enjolras.

"Finish both of us at one blow," said he.

And turning gently to Enjolras, he said to him:

"Do you permit it?"

Enjolras pressed his hand with a smile.

This smile was not ended when the report resounded.

Enjolras, pierced by eight bullets, remained leaning against the wall, as though the balls had nailed him there. Only, his head was bowed.

Grantaire fell at his feet, as though struck by a thunderbolt.

A few moments later, the soldiers dislodged the last remaining insurgents, who had taken refuge at the top of the house. They fired into the attic through a wooden lattice. They fought under the very roof. They flung bodies, some of them still alive, out through the windows. Two light-infantrymen, who tried to lift the shattered omnibus, were slain by two shots fired from the attic. A man in a blouse was flung down from it, with a bayonet wound in the abdomen, and breathed his last on the ground. A soldier and an insurgent slipped together on the sloping slates of the roof, and, as they would not release each other, they fell, clasped in a ferocious embrace. A similar conflict went on in the cellar. Shouts, shots, a fierce trampling. Then silence. The barricade was captured.

The soldiers began to search the houses round about, and to pursue the fugitives.

Chapter XXIV

PRISONER

MARIUS WAS, IN FACT, A PRISONER.

The hand which had seized him from behind and whose grasp he had felt at the moment of his fall and his loss of consciousness, was that of Jean Valjean.

Jean Valjean had taken no other part in the combat than to expose himself in it. Had it not been for him, no one, in that supreme phase of agony, would have thought of the wounded. Thanks to him, everywhere present in the carnage, like a providence, those who fell were picked up, transported to the tap-room, and cared for. In the intervals, he reappeared on the barricade. But nothing which could resemble a blow, an attack or even personal defense proceeded from his hands. He held his peace and lent succor. Moreover, he had received only a few scratches. The bullets would have none of him. If suicide formed part of what he had meditated on coming to this sepulcher, to that spot, he had not succeeded. But we doubt whether he had thought of suicide, an irreligious act.

Jean Valjean, in the thick cloud of the combat, did not appear to see Marius; the truth is, that he never took his eyes from the latter. When a shot laid Marius low, Jean Valjean leaped forward with the agility of a tiger, fell upon him as on his prey, and bore him off.

The whirlwind of the attack was, at that moment, so violently concentrated upon Enjolras and upon the door of the wine-shop, that no one saw Jean Valjean sustaining the fainting Marius in his arms, traverse the unpaved field of the barricade and disappear behind the angle of the Corinthe building.

The reader will recall this angle which formed a sort of cape on the street; it afforded shelter from the bullets, the grape-shot, and all eyes, and a few square feet of space. There is sometimes a chamber which does not burn in the midst of a conflagration, and in the midst of raging seas, beyond a promontory or at the extremity of a blind-alley of shoals, a tranquil nook. It was in this sort of fold in the interior trapezium of the barricade, that Éponine had breathed her last.

There Jean Valjean halted, let Marius slide to the ground, placed his back against the wall, and cast his eyes about him.

The situation was alarming.

For an instant, for two or three perhaps, this bit of wall was a shelter, but how was he to escape from this massacre? He recalled the anguish which he had suffered in the Rue Polonceau eight years before, and in what manner he had contrived to make his escape; it was difficult then, to-day it was impossible. He had before him that deaf and implacable house, six stories in height, which appeared to be inhabited only by a dead man leaning out of his window; he had on his right the rather low barricade, which shut off the Rue de la Petite-Truanderie; to pass this obstacle seemed easy, but beyond the crest of the barrier a line of bayonets was visible. The troops of the line were posted on the watch behind that barricade. It was evident, that to pass the barricade was to go in quest of the fire of the platoon, and that any head which should run the risk of lifting itself above the top of that wall of stones, would serve as a target for sixty shots. On his left he had the field of battle. Death lurked round the corner of that wall.

What was to be done?

Only a bird could have extricated itself from this predicament.

And it was necessary to decide on the instant, to devise some expedient, to come to some decision. Fighting was going on a few paces away; fortunately, all were raging around a single point, the door of the wine-shop; but if it should occur to one soldier, to one single soldier to turn the corner of the house, or to attack him on the flank, all was over.

Jean Valjean gazed at the house facing him, he gazed at the barricade at one side of him, then he looked at the ground, with the violence of the last extremity, bewildered, and as though he would have liked to pierce a hole there with his eyes.

By dint of staring, something vaguely striking in such an agony began to assume form and outline at his feet, as though it had been a power of glance which made the thing desired unfold. A few paces distant he perceived, at the base of the small barrier so pitilessly guarded and watched on the exterior, beneath a disordered mass of paving-stones which partly concealed it, an iron grating, placed flat and on a level with the soil. This grating, made of stout, transverse bars, was about two feet square. The frame of paving-stones which supported it had been torn up, and it was, as it were, unfastened.

Through the bars a view could be had of a dark aperture, something like the flue of a chimney, or the pipe of a cistern. Jean Valjean darted forward. His old art of escape rose to his brain like an illumination. To thrust aside the stones, to raise the grating, to lift Marius who was as inert as a dead body, upon his shoulders, to descend, with this burden on his loins, and with the aid of his elbows and knees into that sort of well, fortunately not very deep, to let the heavy trap, upon which the loosened stones rolled down afresh, fall into its place behind him, to gain his footing on a flagged surface three meters below the surface—all this was executed like that which one does in dreams, with the strength of a giant and the rapidity of an eagle; this took only a few minutes.

Jean Valjean found himself with Marius, who was still unconscious, in a sort of long, subterranean corridor.

There reigned profound peace, absolute silence, night.

The impression which he had formerly experienced when falling from the wall into the convent, recurred to him. Only, what he was carrying to-day was not Cosette; it was Marius. He could barely hear the formidable tumult in the wine-shop, taken by assault, like a vague murmur overhead.

BOOK SECOND

THE INTESTINE OF THE LEVIATHAN

Chapter I

THE LAND IMPOVERISHED BY THE SEA

P ARIS CASTS TWENTY-FIVE MILLIONS YEARLY INTO THE WATER. AND tHIS WITHOUT METAPHOR. How, and in what manner? Day and night. With what object? With no object. With what intention? With no intention. Why? For no reason. By means of what organ? By means of its intestine. What is its intestine? The sewer.

Twenty-five millions is the most moderate approximative figure which the valuations of special science have set upon it.

Science, after having long groped about, now knows that the most fecundating and the most efficacious of fertilizers is human manure. The Chinese, let us confess it to our shame, knew it before us. Not a Chinese peasant—it is Eckberg who says this—goes to town without bringing back with him, at the two extremities of his bamboo pole, two full buckets of what we designate as filth. Thanks to human dung, the earth in China is still as young as in the days of Abraham. Chinese wheat yields a hundred fold of the seed. There is no guano comparable in fertility with the detritus of a capital. A great city is the most mighty of dung-makers. Certain success would attend the experiment of employing the city to manure the plain. If our gold is manure, our manure, on the other hand, is gold.

What is done with this golden manure? It is swept into the abyss.

Fleets of vessels are dispatched, at great expense, to collect the dung of petrels and penguins at the South Pole, and the incalculable element of opulence which we have on hand, we send to the sea. All the human and animal manure which the world wastes, restored to the land instead of being cast into the water, would suffice to nourish the world.

Those heaps of filth at the gate-posts, those tumbrils of mud which jolt through the street by night, those terrible casks of the street department, those fetid drippings of subterranean mire, which the pavements hide from you—do you know what they are? They are the meadow in flower, the green grass, wild thyme, thyme and sage, they are game, they are cattle, they are the satisfied bellows of great oxen in the evening, they are perfumed hay, they are golden wheat, they are the bread on your table, they are the warm blood in your veins, they are health, they are joy, they are life. This is the will of that mysterious creation which is transformation on earth and transfiguration in heaven.

Restore this to the great crucible; your abundance will flow forth from it. The nutrition of the plains furnishes the nourishment of men.

You have it in your power to lose this wealth, and to consider me ridiculous to boot. This will form the masterpiece of your ignorance.

Statisticians have calculated that France alone makes a deposit of half a milliard every year, in the Atlantic, through the mouths of her rivers. Note this: with five hundred millions we could pay one quarter of the expenses of our budget. The cleverness of man is such that he prefers to get rid of these five hundred millions in the gutter. It is the very substance of the people that is carried off, here drop by drop, there wave after wave, the wretched outpour of our sewers into the rivers, and the gigantic collection of our rivers into the ocean. Every hiccough of our sewers costs us a thousand francs. From this spring two results, the land impoverished, and the water tainted. Hunger arising from the furrow, and disease from the stream.

It is notorious, for example, that at the present hour, the Thames is poisoning London.

So far as Paris is concerned, it has become indispensable of late, to transport the mouths of the sewers downstream, below the last bridge.

A double tubular apparatus, provided with valves and sluices, sucking up and driving back, a system of elementary drainage, simple as the lungs of a man, and which is already in full working order in many communities in England, would suffice to conduct the pure water of the fields into our cities, and to send back to the fields the rich water of the cities, and this easy exchange, the simplest in the world, would retain among us the five hundred millions now thrown away. People are thinking of other things.

The process actually in use, does evil, with the intention of doing good. The intention is good, the result is melancholy. Thinking to purge the city, the population is blanched like plants raised in cellars. A sewer is a mistake. When drainage everywhere, with its double function, restoring what it takes, shall have replaced the sewer, which is a simple impoverishing washing, then, this being combined with the data of a now social economy, the product of the earth will be increased tenfold, and the problem of misery will be singularly lightened. Add the suppression of parasitism, and it will be solved.

In the meanwhile, the public wealth flows away to the river, and leakage takes place. Leakage is the word. Europe is being ruined in this manner by exhaustion.

As for France, we have just cited its figures. Now, Paris, contains one twenty-fifth of the total population of France, and Parisian guano being the richest of all, we understate the truth when we value the loss on the part of Paris at twenty-five millions in the half milliard which France annually rejects. These twenty-five millions, employed in assistance and enjoyment, would double the splendor of Paris. The city spends them in sewers. So that we may say that Paris's great prodigality, its wonderful festival, its Beaujon folly, its orgy, its stream of gold from full hands, its pomp, its luxury, its magnificence, is its sewer system.

It is in this manner that, in the blindness of a poor political economy, we drown and allow to float downstream and to be lost in the gulfs the well-being of all. There should be nets at Saint-Cloud for the public fortune.

Economically considered, the matter can be summed up thus: Paris is a spendthrift. Paris, that model city, that patron of well-arranged capitals, of which every nation strives to possess a copy, that metropolis of the ideal, that august country of the initiative, of impulse and of effort, that center and that dwelling of minds, that nation-city, that hive of the future, that marvelous combination of Babylon and Corinth, would make a peasant of the Fo-Kian shrug his shoulders, from the point of view which we have just indicated.

Imitate Paris and you will ruin yourselves.

Moreover, and particularly in this immemorial and senseless waste, Paris is itself, an imitator.

These surprising exhibitions of stupidity are not novel; this is no young folly. The ancients did like the moderns. "The sewers of Rome," says Liebig, "have absorbed all the well-being of the Roman peasant." When the Campagna of Rome was ruined by the Roman sewer, Rome exhausted Italy, and when she had put Italy in her sewer, she poured in Sicily, then Sardinia, then Africa. The sewer of Rome has engulfed the world. This cesspool offered its engulfment to the city and the universe. *Urbi et orbi.* Eternal city, unfathomable sewer.

Rome sets the example for these things as well as for others.

Paris follows this example with all the stupidity peculiar to intelligent towns.

For the requirements of the operation upon the subject of which we have just explained our views, Paris has beneath it another Paris; a Paris of sewers; which has its streets, its cross-roads, its squares, its blind-alleys, its arteries, and its circulation, which is of mire and minus the human form.

For nothing must be flattered, not even a great people; where there is everything there is also ignominy by the side of sublimity; and, if Paris contains Athens, the city of light, Tyre, the city of might, Sparta, the city of virtue, Nineveh, the city of marvels, it also contains Lutetia, the city of mud.

However, the stamp of its power is there also, and the Titanic sink of Paris realizes, among monuments, that strange ideal realized in humanity by some men like Macchiavelli, Bacon and Mirabeau, grandiose vileness.

The sub-soil of Paris, if the eye could penetrate its surface, would present the aspect of a colossal madrepore. A sponge has no more partitions and ducts than the mound of earth for a circuit of six leagues round about, on which rests the great and ancient city. Not to mention its catacombs, which are a separate cellar, not to mention the inextricable trellis-work of gas pipes, without reckoning the vast tubular system for the distribution of fresh water which ends in the pillar fountains, the sewers alone form a tremendous, shadowy network under the two banks; a labyrinth which has its slope for its guiding thread.

There appears, in the humid mist, the rat which seems the product to which Paris has given birth.

Chapter II

ANCIENT HISTORY OF THE SEWER

LET THE READER IMAGINE PARIS LIFTED OFF LIKE A COVER, THE SUBTERRANEAN NETWORK OF sewers, from a bird's-eye view, will outline on the banks a species of large branch grafted on the river. On the right bank, the belt sewer will form the trunk of this branch, the secondary ducts will form the branches, and those without exit the twigs.

This figure is but a summary one and half exact, the right angle, which is the customary angle of this species of subterranean ramifications, being very rare in vegetation.

A more accurate image of this strange geometrical plan can be formed by supposing that one is viewing some eccentric oriental alphabet, as intricate as a thicket, against a background of shadows, and the misshapen letters should be welded one to another in apparent confusion, and as at haphazard, now by their angles, again by their extremities.

Sinks and sewers played a great part in the Middle Ages, in the Lower Empire and in the Orient of old. The masses regarded these beds of decomposition, these monstrous cradles of death, with a fear that was almost religious. The vermin ditch of Benares is no less conducive to giddiness than the lions' ditch of Babylon. Teglath-Phalasar, according to the rabbinical books, swore by the sink of Nineveh. It was from the sewer of Münster that John of Leyden produced his false moon, and it was from the cesspool of Kekscheb that oriental menalchme, Mokanna, the veiled prophet of Khorassan, caused his false sun to emerge.

The history of men is reflected in the history of sewers. The Gemoniæ[1] narrated Rome. The sewer of Paris has been an ancient and formidable thing. It has been a sepulcher, it has served as an

---

1. Steps on the Aventine Hill, leading to the Tiber, to which the bodies of executed criminals were dragged by hooks to be thrown into the Tiber.

asylum. Crime, intelligence, social protest, liberty of conscience, thought, theft, all that human laws persecute or have persecuted, is hidden in that hole; the *maillotins* in the fourteenth century, the *tire-laine* of the fifteenth, the Huguenots in the sixteenth, Morin's *illuminated* in the seventeenth, the *chauffeurs* [brigands] in the eighteenth. A hundred years ago, the nocturnal blow of the dagger emerged thence, the pickpocket in danger slipped thither; the forest had its cave, Paris had its sewer. Vagrancy, that Gallic *picareria*, accepted the sewer as the adjunct of the Cour des Miracles, and at evening, it returned thither, fierce and sly through the Maubuée outlet, as into a bedchamber.

It was quite natural, that those who had the blind-alley Vide-Gousset [Empty-Pocket] or the Rue Coupe-Gorge [Cut-Throat], for the scene of their daily labor, should have for their domicile by night the culvert of the Chemin-Vert, or the catch basin of Hurepoix. Hence a throng of souvenirs. All sorts of phantoms haunt these long, solitary corridors; everywhere is putrescence and miasma; here and there are breathing-holes, where Villon within converses with Rabelais without.

The sewer in ancient Paris is the rendezvous of all exhaustions and of all attempts. Political economy therein spies a detritus, social philosophy there beholds a residuum.

The sewer is the conscience of the city. Everything there converges and confronts everything else. In that livid spot there are shades, but there are no longer any secrets. Each thing bears its true form, or at least, its definitive form. The mass of filth has this in its favor, that it is not a liar. Ingenuousness has taken refuge there. The mask of Basil is to be found there, but one beholds its cardboard and its strings and the inside as well as the outside, and it is accentuated by honest mud. Scapin's false nose is its next-door neighbor. All the uncleannesses of civilization, once past their use, fall into this trench of truth, where the immense social sliding ends. They are there engulfed, but they display themselves there. This mixture is a confession. There, no more false appearances, no plastering over is possible, filth removes its shirt, absolute denudation puts to the rout all illusions and mirages, there is nothing more except what really exists, presenting the sinister form of that which is coming to an end. There, the bottom of a bottle indicates drunkenness, a basket-handle tells a tale of domesticity; there the core of an apple which has entertained literary opinions becomes an apple-core once more; the effigy on the big sou becomes frankly covered with verdigris, Caiphas's spittle meets Falstaff's puking, the louis-d'or which comes from the gaming-house jostles the nail whence hangs the rope's end of the suicide, a livid fetus rolls along, enveloped in the spangles which danced at the Opera last Shrove-Tuesday, a cap which has pronounced judgment on men wallows beside a mass of rottenness which was formerly Margoton's petticoat; it is more than fraternization, it is equivalent to addressing each other as *thou*. All which was formerly rouged, is washed free. The last veil is torn away. A sewer is a cynic. It tells everything.

The sincerity of foulness pleases us, and rests the soul. When one has passed one's time in enduring upon earth the spectacle of the great airs which reasons of state, the oath, political sagacity, human justice, professional probity, the austerities of situation, incorruptible robes all assume, it solaces one to enter a sewer and to behold the mire which befits it.

This is instructive at the same time. We have just said that history passes through the sewer. The Saint-Barthélemys filter through there, drop by drop, between the paving-stones. Great public assassinations, political and religious butcheries, traverse this underground passage of civilization, and thrust their corpses there. For the eye of the thinker, all historic murderers are to be found there, in that hideous penumbra, on their knees, with a scrap of their winding-sheet for an apron, dismally sponging out their work. Louis XI is there with Tristan, François I with Duprat, Charles IX is there with his mother, Richelieu is there with Louis XIII, Louvois is there, Letellier is there, Hébert, and Maillard are there, scratching the stones, and trying to make the traces of their actions disappear. Beneath these vaults one hears the brooms of specters. One there breathes the enormous fetidness of social catastrophes. One beholds reddish reflections in the corners. There flows a terrible stream, in which bloody hands have been washed.

The social observer should enter these shadows. They form a part of his laboratory. Philosophy is the microscope of the thought. Everything desires to flee from it, but nothing escapes it. Tergiversation is useless. What side of one's self does one display in evasions? the shameful side. Philosophy pursues with its glance, probes the evil, and does not permit it to escape into nothingness. In the obliteration of things which disappear, in the watching of things which vanish, it recognizes all. It reconstructs the purple from the rag, and the woman from the scrap of her dress. From the cesspool, it reconstitutes the city; from mud, it reconstructs manners; from the potsherd it infers the amphora or the jug. By the imprint of a finger-nail on a piece of parchment, it recognizes the difference which separates the Jewry of the Judengasse from the Jewry of the Ghetto. It rediscovers in what remains that which has been, good, evil, the true, the blood-stain of the palace, the ink-blot of the cavern, the drop of sweat from the brothel, trials undergone, temptations welcomed, orgies cast forth, the turn which characters have taken as they became abased, the trace of prostitution in souls of which their grossness rendered them capable, and on the vesture of the porters of Rome the mark of Messalina's elbowing.

Chapter III

BRUNESEAU

T HE SEWER OF PARIS IN THE MIDDLE AGES WAS LEGENDARY. IN THE SIXTEENTH CENTURY, HENRI II attempted a bore, which failed. Not a hundred years ago, the cesspool, Mercier attests the fact, was abandoned to itself, and fared as best it might.

Such was this ancient Paris, delivered over to quarrels, to indecision, and to gropings. It was tolerably stupid for a long time. Later on, '89 showed how understanding comes to cities. But in the good, old times, the capital had not much head. It did not know how to manage its own affairs either morally or materially, and could not sweep out filth any better than it could abuses. Everything presented an obstacle, everything raised a question. The sewer, for example, was refractory to every itinerary. One could no more find one's bearings in the sewer than one could understand one's position in the city; above the unintelligible, below the inextricable; beneath the confusion of tongues there reigned the confusion of caverns; Dædalus backed up Babel.

Sometimes the Paris sewer took a notion to overflow, as though this misunderstood Nile were suddenly seized with a fit of rage. There occurred, infamous to relate, inundations of the sewer. At times, that stomach of civilization digested badly, the cesspool flowed back into the throat of the city, and Paris got an aftertaste of her own filth. These resemblances of the sewer to remorse had their good points; they were warnings; very badly accepted, however; the city waxed indignant at the audacity of its mire, and did not admit that the filth should return. Drive it out better.

The inundation of 1802 is one of the actual memories of Parisians of the age of eighty. The mud spread in cross-form over the Place des Victoires, where stands the statue of Louis XIV; it entered the Rue Saint-Honoré by the two mouths to the sewer in the Champs-Élysées, the Rue Saint-Florentin through the Saint-Florentin sewer, the Rue Pierre-à-Poisson through the sewer de la Sonnerie, the Rue Popincoort, through the sewer of the Chemin-Vert, the Rue de la Roquette, through the sewer of the Rue de Lappe; it covered the drain of the Rue des Champs-Élysées to the height of thirty-five centimeters; and, to the South, through the vent of the Seine, performing its functions in inverse sense, it penetrated the Rue Mazarine, the Rue de l'Échaudé, and the Rue des Marais, where it stopped at a distance of one hundred and nine meters, a few paces distant from the house in which Racine had lived, respecting, in the seventeenth century, the poet more than the

King. It attained its maximum depth in the Rue Saint-Pierre, where it rose to the height of three feet above the flag-stones of the water-spout, and its maximum length in the Rue Saint-Sabin, where it spread out over a stretch two hundred and thirty-eight meters in length.

At the beginning of this century, the sewer of Paris was still a mysterious place. Mud can never enjoy a good fame; but in this case its evil renown reached the verge of the terrible. Paris knew, in a confused way, that she had under her a terrible cavern. People talked of it as of that monstrous bed of Thebes in which swarmed centipedes fifteen long feet in length, and which might have served Behemoth for a bathtub. The great boots of the sewermen never ventured further than certain well-known points. We were then very near the epoch when the scavenger's carts, from the summit of which Sainte-Foix fraternized with the Marquis de Créqui, discharged their loads directly into the sewer. As for cleaning out—that function was entrusted to the pouring rains which encumbered rather than swept away. Rome left some poetry to her sewer, and called it the Gemoniæ; Paris insulted hers, and entitled it the Polypus-Hole. Science and superstition were in accord, in horror. The Polypus hole was no less repugnant to hygiene than to legend. The goblin was developed under the fetid covering of the Mouffetard sewer; the corpses of the Marmousets had been cast into the sewer de la Barillerie; Fagon attributed the redoubtable malignant fever of 1685 to the great hiatus of the sewer of the Marais, which remained yawning until 1833 in the Rue Saint-Louis, almost opposite the sign of the *Gallant Messenger*. The mouth of the sewer of the Rue de la Mortellerie was celebrated for the pestilences which had their source there; with its grating of iron, with points simulating a row of teeth, it was like a dragon's maw in that fatal street, breathing forth hell upon men. The popular imagination seasoned the somber Parisian sink with some indescribably hideous intermixture of the infinite. The sewer had no bottom. The sewer was the lower world. The idea of exploring these leprous regions did not even occur to the police. To try that unknown thing, to cast the plummet into that shadow, to set out on a voyage of discovery in that abyss—who would have dared? It was alarming. Nevertheless, someone did present himself. The cesspool had its Christopher Columbus.

One day, in 1805, during one of the rare apparitions which the Emperor made in Paris, the Minister of the Interior, some Decrès or Crétet or other, came to the master's intimate levee. In the Carrousel there was audible the clanking of swords of all those extraordinary soldiers of the great Republic, and of the great Empire; then Napoleon's door was blocked with heroes; men from the Rhine, from the Escaut, from the Adige, and from the Nile; companions of Joubert, of Desaix, of Marceau, of Hoche, of Kléber; the aérostiers of Fleurus, the grenadiers of Mayence, the pontoon-builders of Genoa, hussars whom the Pyramids had looked down upon, artillerists whom Junot's cannon-ball had spattered with mud, cuirassiers who had taken by assault the fleet lying at anchor in the Zuyderzee; some had followed Bonaparte upon the bridge of Lodi, others had accompanied Murat in the trenches of Mantua, others had preceded Lannes in the hollow road of Montebello. The whole army of that day was present there, in the courtyard of the Tuileries, represented by a squadron or a platoon, and guarding Napoleon in repose; and that was the splendid epoch when the grand army had Marengo behind it and Austerlitz before it.—"Sire," said the Minister of the Interior to Napoleon, "yesterday I saw the most intrepid man in your Empire."— "What man is that?" said the Emperor brusquely, "and what has he done?"—"He wants to do something, Sire."— "What is it?"—"To visit the sewers of Paris."

This man existed and his name was Bruneseau.

Chapter IV

HE VISIT TOOK PLACE. IT WAS A FORMIDABLE CAMPAIGN; A NOCTURNAL BATTLE AGAINST PESTI-
lence and suffocation. It was, at the same time, a voyage of discovery. One of the survivors of
this expedition, an intelligent workingman, who was very young at the time, related curious details
with regard to it, several years ago, which Bruneseau thought himself obliged to omit in his report
to the prefect of police, as unworthy of official style. The processes of disinfection were, at that
epoch, extremely rudimentary. Hardly had Bruneseau crossed the first articulations of that subterranean network, when eight laborers out of the twenty refused to go any further. The operation was
complicated; the visit entailed the necessity of cleaning; hence it was necessary to cleanse and at the
same time, to proceed; to note the entrances of water, to count the gratings and the vents, to lay out
in detail the branches, to indicate the currents at the point where they parted, to define the respective bounds of the divers basins, to sound the small sewers grafted on the principal sewer, to measure the height under the key-stone of each drain, and the width, at the spring of the vaults as well
as at the bottom, in order to determine the arrangements with regard to the level of each water-
entrance, either of the bottom of the arch, or on the soil of the street. They advanced with toil. The
lanterns pined away in the foul atmosphere. From time to time, a fainting sewerman was carried
out. At certain points, there were precipices. The soil had given away, the pavement had crumbled,
the sewer had changed into a bottomless well; they found nothing solid; a man disappeared suddenly; they had great difficulty in getting him out again. On the advice of Fourcroy, they lighted
large cages filled with tow steeped in resin, from time to time, in spots which had been sufficiently
disinfected. In some places, the wall was covered with misshapen fungi—one would have said, tu-
mors; the very stone seemed diseased within this unbreathable atmosphere.

Bruneseau, in his exploration, proceeded downhill. At the point of separation of the two
water-conduits of the Grand-Hurleur, he deciphered upon a projecting stone the date of 1550;
this stone indicated the limits where Philibert Delorme, charged by Henri II with visiting the subterranean drains of Paris, had halted. This stone was the mark of the sixteenth century on the
sewer; Bruneseau found the handiwork of the seventeenth century once more in the Ponceau
drain of the old Rue Vielle-du-Temple, vaulted between 1600 and 1650; and the handiwork of the
eighteenth in the western section of the collecting canal, walled and vaulted in 1740. These two
vaults, especially the less ancient, that of 1740, were more cracked and decrepit than the masonry
of the belt sewer, which dated from 1412, an epoch when the brook of fresh water of Ménilmontant was elevated to the dignity of the Grand Sewer of Paris, an advancement analogous to
that of a peasant who should become first *valet de chambre* to the King; something like Gros-Jean
transformed into Lebel.

Here and there, particularly beneath the Court-House, they thought they recognized the hollows of ancient dungeons, excavated in the very sewer itself. Hideous *in-pace*. An iron neck-collar
was hanging in one of these cells. They walled them all up. Some of their finds were singular;
among others, the skeleton of an orangutan, who had disappeared from the Jardin des Plantes in
1800, a disappearance probably connected with the famous and indisputable apparition of the devil
in the Rue des Bernardins, in the last year of the eighteenth century. The poor devil had ended by
drowning himself in the sewer.

Beneath this long, arched drain which terminated at the Arche-Marion, a perfectly preserved
rag-picker's basket excited the admiration of all connoisseurs. Everywhere, the mire, which the
sewermen came to handle with intrepidity, abounded in precious objects, jewels of gold and silver,
precious stones, coins. If a giant had filtered this cesspool, he would have had the riches of centuries
in his lair. At the point where the two branches of the Rue du Temple and of the Rue Sainte-Avoye

separate, they picked up a singular Huguenot medal in copper, bearing on one side the pig hooded with a cardinal's hat, and on the other, a wolf with a tiara on his head.

The most surprising rencounter was at the entrance to the Grand Sewer. This entrance had formerly been closed by a grating of which nothing but the hinges remained. From one of these hinges hung a dirty and shapeless rag which, arrested there in its passage, no doubt, had floated there in the darkness and finished its process of being torn apart. Bruneseau held his lantern close to this rag and examined it. It was of very fine batiste, and in one of the corners, less frayed than the rest, they made out a heraldic coronet and embroidered above these seven letters: LAVBESP. The crown was the coronet of a Marquis, and the seven letters signified *Laubespine*. They recognized the fact, that what they had before their eyes was a morsel of the shroud of Marat. Marat in his youth had had amorous intrigues. This was when he was a member of the household of the Comte d'Artois, in the capacity of physician to the Stables. From these love affairs, historically proved, with a great lady, he had retained this sheet. As a waif or a souvenir. At his death, as this was the only linen of any fineness which he had in his house, they buried him in it. Some old women had shrouded him for the tomb in that swaddling-band in which the tragic Friend of the people had enjoyed voluptuousness. Bruneseau passed on. They left that rag where it hung; they did not put the finishing touch to it. Did this arise from scorn or from respect? Marat deserved both. And then, destiny was there sufficiently stamped to make them hesitate to touch it. Besides, the things of the sepulcher must be left in the spot which they select. In short, the relic was a strange one. A Marquise had slept in it; Marat had rotted in it; it had traversed the Panthéon to end with the rats of the sewer. This chamber rag, of which Watteau would formerly have joyfully sketched every fold, had ended in becoming worthy of the fixed gaze of Dante.

The whole visit to the subterranean stream of filth of Paris lasted seven years, from 1805 to 1812. As he proceeded, Bruneseau drew, directed, and completed considerable works; in 1808 he lowered the arch of the Ponceau, and, everywhere creating new lines, he pushed the sewer, in 1809, under the Rue Saint-Denis as far as the fountain of the Innocents; in 1810, under the Rue Froidmanteau and under the Salpêtrière; in 1811 under the Rue Neuve-des-Petits-Pères, under the Rue du Mail, under the Rue de l'Écharpe, under the Place Royale; in 1812, under the Rue de la Paix, and under the Chaussée d'Antin. At the same time, he had the whole network disinfected and rendered healthful. In the second year of his work, Bruneseau engaged the assistance of his son-in-law Nargaud.

It was thus that, at the beginning of the century, ancient society cleansed its double bottom, and performed the toilet of its sewer. There was that much clean, at all events.

Tortuous, cracked, unpaved, full of fissures, intersected by gullies, jolted by eccentric elbows, mounting and descending illogically, fetid, wild, fierce, submerged in obscurity, with cicatrices on its pavements and scars on its walls, terrible—such was, retrospectively viewed, the antique sewer of Paris. Ramifications in every direction, crossings, of trenches, branches, goose-feet, stars, as in military mines, cecum, blind-alleys, vaults lined with saltpeter, pestiferous pools, scabby sweats, on the walls, drops dripping from the ceilings, darkness; nothing could equal the horror of this old, waste crypt, the digestive apparatus of Babylon, a cavern, ditch, gulf pierced with streets, a titanic mole-burrow, where the mind seems to behold that enormous blind mole, the past, prowling through the shadows, in the filth which has been splendor.

This, we repeat, was the sewer of the past.

Chapter V

PRESENT PROGRESS

To-DAY THE SEWER IS CLEAN, COLD, STRAIGHT, CORRECT. IT ALMOST REALIZES THE IDEAL OF what is understood in England by the word "respectable." It is proper and grayish; laid out by rule and line; one might almost say as though it came out of a bandbox. It resembles a tradesman who has become a councilor of state. One can almost see distinctly there. The mire there comports itself with decency. At first, one might readily mistake it for one of those subterranean corridors, which were so common in former days, and so useful in flights of monarchs and princes, in those good old times, "when the people loved their kings." The present sewer is a beautiful sewer; the pure style reigns there; the classical rectilinear alexandrine which, driven out of poetry, appears to have taken refuge in architecture, seems mingled with all the stones of that long, dark and whitish vault; each outlet is an arcade; the Rue de Rivoli serves as pattern even in the sewer. However, if the geometrical line is in place anywhere, it is certainly in the drainage trench of a great city. There, everything should be subordinated to the shortest road. The sewer has, nowadays, assumed a certain official aspect. The very police reports, of which it sometimes forms the subject, no longer are wanting in respect toward it. The words which characterize it in administrative language are sonorous and dignified. What used to be called a gut is now called a gallery; what used to be called a hole is now called a surveying orifice. Villon would no longer meet with his ancient temporary provisional lodging. This network of cellars has its immemorial population of prowlers, rodents, swarming in greater numbers than ever; from time to time, an aged and veteran rat risks his head at the window of the sewer and surveys the Parisians; but even these vermin grow tame, so satisfied are they with their subterranean palace. The cesspool no longer retains anything of its primitive ferocity. The rain, which, in former days soiled the sewer, now washes it. Nevertheless, do not trust yourself too much to it. Miasmas still inhabit it. It is more hypocritical than irreproachable. The prefecture of police and the commission of health have done their best. But, in spite of all the processes of disinfection, it exhales, a vague, suspicious odor like Tartuffe after confession.

Let us confess that, taking it all in all, this sweeping is an homage which the sewer pays to civilization, and as, from this point of view, Tartuffe's conscience is a progress over the Augean stables, it is certain that the sewers of Paris have been improved.

It is more than progress; it is transmutation. Between the ancient and the present sewer there is a revolution. What has effected this revolution?

The man whom all the world forgets, and whom we have mentioned, Bruneseau.

Chapter VI

FUTURE PROGRESS

T HE EXCAVATION OF THE SEWER OF PARIS HAS BEEN NO SLIGHT TASK. THE LAST TEN CENTURIES have toiled at it without being able to bring it to a termination, anymore than they have been able to finish Paris. The sewer, in fact, receives all the counter-shocks of the growth of Paris. Within the bosom of the earth, it is a sort of mysterious polyp with a thousand antennae, which expands below as the city expands above. Every time that the city cuts a street, the sewer stretches out an arm. The old monarchy had constructed only twenty-three thousand three hundred meters of sewers; that was where Paris stood in this respect on the 1st of January, 1806. Beginning with this epoch, of which we shall shortly speak, the work was usefully and energetically resumed and prosecuted; Napoleon built—the figures are curious—four thousand eight hundred and four meters; Louis XVIII, five thousand seven hundred and nine; Charles X, ten thousand eight hundred and thirty-six; Louis-Philippe, eighty-nine thousand and twenty; the Republic of 1848, twenty-three thousand three hundred and eighty-one; the present government, seventy thousand five hundred; in all, at the present time, two hundred and twenty-six thousand six hundred and ten meters; sixty leagues of sewers; the enormous entrails of Paris. An obscure ramification ever at work; a construction which is immense and ignored.

As the reader sees, the subterranean labyrinth of Paris is to-day more than ten times what it was at the beginning of the century. It is difficult to form any idea of all the perseverance and the efforts which have been required to bring this cesspool to the point of relative perfection in which it now is. It was with great difficulty that the ancient monarchical provostship and, during the last ten years of the eighteenth century, the revolutionary mayoralty, had succeeded in perforating the five leagues of sewer which existed previous to 1806. All sorts of obstacles hindered this operation, some peculiar to the soil, others inherent in the very prejudices of the laborious population of Paris. Paris is built upon a soil which is singularly rebellious to the pick, the hoe, the bore, and to human manipulation. There is nothing more difficult to pierce and to penetrate than the geological formation upon which is superposed the marvelous historical formation called Paris; as soon as work in any form whatsoever is begun and adventures upon this stretch of alluvium, subterranean resistances abound. There are liquid clays, springs, hard rocks, and those soft and deep quagmires which special science calls *moutardes.*[1] The pick advances laboriously through the calcareous layers alternating with very slender threads of clay, and schistose beds in plates encrusted with oyster-shells, the contemporaries of the pre-Adamite oceans. Sometimes a rivulet suddenly bursts through a vault that has been begun, and inundates the laborers; or a layer of marl is laid bare, and rolls down with the fury of a cataract, breaking the stoutest supporting beams like glass. Quite recently, at Villette, when it became necessary to pass the collecting sewer under the Saint-Martin canal without interrupting navigation or emptying the canal, a fissure appeared in the basin of the canal, water suddenly became abundant in the subterranean tunnel, which was beyond the power of the pumping engines; it was necessary to send a diver to explore the fissure which had been made in the narrow entrance of the grand basin, and it was not without great difficulty that it was stopped up. Elsewhere near the Seine, and even at a considerable distance from the river, as for instance, at Belleville, Grand-Rue and Lumière Passage, quicksands are encountered in which one sticks fast, and in which a man sinks visibly. Add suffocation by miasmas, burial by slides, and sudden crumbling of the earth. Add the typhus, with which the workmen become

---

1. Mustards.

slowly impregnated. In our own day, after having excavated the gallery of Clichy, with a banquette to receive the principal water-conduit of Ourcq, a piece of work which was executed in a trench ten meters deep; after having, in the midst of land-slides, and with the aid of excavations, often putrid, and of shoring up, vaulted the Bièvre from the Boulevard de l'Hôpital, as far as the Seine; after having, in order to deliver Paris from the floods of Montmartre and in order to provide an outlet for that river-like pool nine hectares in extent, which crouched near the Barrière des Martyrs, after having, let us state, constructed the line of sewers from the Barrière Blanche to the road of Aubervilliers, in four months, working day and night, at a depth of eleven meters; after having—a thing heretofore un-seen—made a subterranean sewer in the Rue Barre-du-Bec, without a trench, six meters below the surface, the superintendent, Monnot, died. After having vaulted three thousand meters of sewer in all quarters of the city, from the Rue Traversière-Saint-Antoine to the Rue de l'Ourcine, after having freed the Carrefour Censier-Mouffetard from inundations of rain by means of the branch of the Ar-balète, after having built the Saint-Georges sewer, on rock and concrete in the fluid sands, after hav-ing directed the formidable lowering of the flooring of the vault timber in the Notre-Dame-de-Nazareth branch, Duleau the engineer died. There are no bulletins for such acts of bravery as these, which are more useful, nevertheless, than the brutal slaughter of the field of battle.

The sewers of Paris in 1832, were far from being what they are to-day. Bruneseau had given the impulse, but the cholera was required to bring about the vast reconstruction which took place later on. It is surprising to say, for example, that in 1821, a part of the belt sewer, called the Grand Canal, as in Venice, still stood stagnating uncovered to the sky, in the Rue des Gourdes. It was only in 1821 that the city of Paris found in its pocket the two hundred and sixty-six thousand eighty francs and six centimes required for covering this mass of filth. The three absorbing wells, of the Combat, the Cunette, and Saint-Mandé, with their discharging mouths, their apparatus, their cesspools, and their depuratory branches, only date from 1836. The intestinal sewer of Paris has been made over anew, and, as we have said, it has been extended more than tenfold within the last quarter of a century.

Thirty years ago, at the epoch of the insurrection of the 5th and 6th of June, it was still, in many localities, nearly the same ancient sewer. A very great number of streets, which are now convex were then sunken causeways. At the end of a slope, where the tributaries of a street or cross-roads ended, there were often to be seen large, square gratings with heavy bars, whose iron, polished by the foot-steps of the throng, gleamed dangerous and slippery for vehicles, and caused horses to fall. The of-ficial language of the Roads and Bridges gave to these gratings the expressive name of *Cassis*.[1]

In 1832, in a number of streets, in the Rue de l'Étoile, the Rue Saint-Louis, the Rue du Tem-ple, the Rue Vielle-du-Temple, the Rue Notre-Dame de Nazareth, the Rue Folie-Méricourt, the Quai aux Fleurs, the Rue du Petit-Musc, the Rue du Normandie, the Rue Pont-Aux-Biches, the Rue des Marais, the Faubourg Saint-Martin, the Rue Notre-Dame des-Victoires, the Faubourg Mont-martre, the Rue Grange-Batelière, in the Champs-Élysées, the Rue Jacob, the Rue de Tournon, the ancient Gothic sewer still cynically displayed its maw. It consisted of enormous voids of stone catch-basins sometimes surrounded by stone posts, with monumental effrontery.

Paris in 1806 still had nearly the same sewers numerically as stated in 1663; five thousand three hundred fathoms. After Bruneseau, on the 1st of January, 1832, it had forty thousand three hundred meters. Between 1806 and 1831, there had been built, on an average, seven hundred and fifty me-ters annually, afterwards eight and even ten thousand meters of galleries were constructed every year, in masonry, of small stones, with hydraulic mortar which hardens under water, on a cement foundation. At two hundred francs the meter, the sixty leagues of Paris's sewers of the present day represent forty-eight millions.

In addition to the economic progress which we have indicated at the beginning, grave prob-lems of public hygiene are connected with that immense question: the sewers of Paris.

---

1. From *cassar*, to break: break-necks.

Paris is the center of two sheets, a sheet of water and a sheet of air. The sheet of water, lying at a tolerably great depth underground, but already sounded by two bores, is furnished by the layer of green clay situated between the chalk and the Jurassic lime-stone; this layer may be represented by a disk five-and-twenty leagues in circumference; a multitude of rivers and brooks ooze there; one drinks the Seine, the Marne, the Yonne, the Oise, the Aisne, the Cher, the Vienne and the Loire in a glass of water from the well of Grenelle. The sheet of water is healthy, it comes from heaven in the first place and next from the earth; the sheet of air is unhealthy, it comes from the sewer. All the miasms of the cesspool are mingled with the breath of the city; hence this bad breath. The air taken from above a dung-heap, as has been scientifically proved, is purer than the air taken from above Paris. In a given time, with the aid of progress, mechanisms become perfected, and as light increases, the sheet of water will be employed to purify the sheet of air; that is to say, to wash the sewer. The reader knows, that by "washing the sewer" we mean: the restitution of the filth to the earth; the return to the soil of dung and of manure to the fields. Through this simple act, the entire social community will experience a diminution of misery and an augmentation of health. At the present hour, the radiation of diseases from Paris extends to fifty leagues around the Louvre, taken as the hub of this pestilential wheel.

We might say that, for ten centuries, the cesspool has been the disease of Paris. The sewer is the blemish which Paris has in her blood. The popular instinct has never been deceived in it. The occupation of sewermen was formerly almost as perilous, and almost as repugnant to the people, as the occupation of knacker, which was so long held in horror and handed over to the executioner. High wages were necessary to induce a mason to disappear in that fetid mine; the ladder of the cesspool cleaner hesitated to plunge into it; it was said, in proverbial form: "to descend into the sewer is to enter the grave"; and all sorts of hideous legends, as we have said, covered this colossal sink with terror; a dread sink-hole which bears the traces of the revolutions of the globe as of the revolutions of man, and where are to be found vestiges of all cataclysms from the shells of the Deluge to the rag of Marat.

BOOK THIRD

MUD BUT THE SOUL

Chapter I

THE SEWER AND ITS SURPRISES

IT WAS IN THE SEWERS OF PARIS THAT JEAN VALJEAN FOUND HIMSELF.

Still another resemblance between Paris and the sea. As in the ocean, the diver may disappear there.

The transition was an unheard-of one. In the very heart of the city, Jean Valjean had escaped from the city, and, in the twinkling of an eye, in the time required to lift the cover and to replace it, he had passed from broad daylight to complete obscurity, from midday to midnight, from tumult to silence, from the whirlwind of thunders to the stagnation of the tomb, and, by a vicissitude far more tremendous even than that of the Rue Polonceau, from the most extreme peril to the most absolute obscurity.

An abrupt fall into a cavern; a disappearance into the secret trapdoor of Paris; to quit that street where death was on every side, for that sort of sepulcher where there was life, was a strange instant. He remained for several seconds as though bewildered; listening, stupefied. The waste-trap of safety had suddenly yawned beneath him. Celestial goodness had, in a manner, captured him by treachery. Adorable ambuscades of providence!

Only, the wounded man did not stir, and Jean Valjean did not know whether that which he was carrying in that grave was a living being or a dead corpse.

His first sensation was one of blindness. All of a sudden, he could see nothing. It seemed to him too, that, in one instant, he had become deaf. He no longer heard anything. The frantic storm of murder which had been let loose a few feet above his head, did not reach him, thanks to the thickness of the earth which separated him from it, as we have said, otherwise than faintly and indistinctly, and like a rumbling, in the depths. He felt that the ground was solid under his feet; that was all; but that was enough. He extended one arm and then the other, touched the walls on both sides, and perceived that the passage was narrow; he slipped, and thus perceived that the pavement was wet. He cautiously put forward one foot, fearing a hole, a sink, some gulf; he discovered that the paving continued. A gust of fetidness informed him of the place in which he stood.

After the lapse of a few minutes, he was no longer blind. A little light fell through the man-hole through which he had descended, and his eyes became accustomed to this cavern. He began to distinguish something. The passage in which he had burrowed—no other word can better express the situation—was walled in behind him. It was one of those blind-alleys, which the special jargon terms branches. In front of him there was another wall, a wall like night. The light of the air-hole died out ten or twelve paces from the point where Jean Valjean stood, and barely cast a wan pallor on a few meters of the damp walls of the sewer. Beyond, the opaqueness was massive; to penetrate thither seemed horrible, an entrance into it appeared like an engulfment. A man could, however, plunge into that wall of fog and it was necessary so to do. Haste was even requisite. It occurred to Jean Valjean that the grating which he had caught sight of under the flag-stones, might also catch the eye of the soldiery, and that everything hung upon this chance. They also might descend into that well and search it. There was not a minute to be lost. He had deposited Marius on the ground, he picked him up again—that is the real word for it—placed him on his shoulders once more, and set out. He plunged resolutely into the gloom.

The truth is, that they were less safe than Jean Valjean fancied. Perils of another sort and no less serious were awaiting them, perchance. After the lightning-charged whirlwind of the combat, the cavern of miasmas and traps; after chaos, the sewer. Jean Valjean had fallen from one circle of hell into another.

When he had advanced fifty paces, he was obliged to halt. A problem presented itself. The passage terminated in another gut which he encountered across his path. There two ways presented themselves. Which should he take? Ought he to turn to the left or to the right? How was he to find his bearings in that black labyrinth? This labyrinth, to which we have already called the reader's attention, has a clue, which is its slope. To follow to the slope is to arrive at the river.

This Jean Valjean instantly comprehended.

He said to himself that he was probably, in the sewer des Halles; that if he were to choose the path to the left and follow the slope, he would arrive, in less than a quarter of an hour, at some mouth on the Seine between the Pont au Change and the Pont-Neuf, that is to say, he would make his appearance in broad daylight on the most densely peopled spot in Paris. Perhaps he would come out on some man-hole at the intersection of streets. Amazement of the passers-by at beholding two bleeding men emerge from the earth at their feet. Arrival of the police, a call to arms of the neighboring post of guards. Thus they would be seized before they had even got out. It would be better to plunge into that labyrinth, to confide themselves to that black gloom, and to trust to Providence for the outcome.

He ascended the incline, and turned to the right.

When he had turned the angle of the gallery, the distant glimmer of an air-hole disappeared, the curtain of obscurity fell upon him once more, and he became blind again. Nevertheless, he advanced as rapidly as possible. Marius's two arms were passed round his neck, and the former's feet dragged behind him. He held both these arms with one hand, and groped along the wall with the other. Marius's cheek touched his, and clung there, bleeding. He felt a warm stream which came from Marius trickling down upon him and making its way under his clothes. But a humid warmth near his ear, which the mouth of the wounded man touched, indicated respiration, and consequently, life. The passage along which Jean Valjean was now proceeding was not so narrow as the first. Jean Valjean walked through it with considerable difficulty. The rain of the preceding day had not, as yet, entirely run off, and it created a little torrent in the center of the bottom, and he was forced to hug the wall in order not to have his feet in the water.

Thus he proceeded in the gloom. He resembled the beings of the night groping in the invisible and lost beneath the earth in veins of shadow.

Still, little by little, whether it was that the distant air-holes emitted a little wavering light in this opaque gloom, or whether his eyes had become accustomed to the obscurity, some vague vision returned to him, and he began once more to gain a confused idea, now of the wall which he touched, now of the vault beneath which he was passing. The pupil dilates in the dark, and the soul dilates in misfortune and ends by finding God there.

It was not easy to direct his course.

The line of the sewer re-echoes, so to speak, the line of the streets which lie above it. There were then in Paris two thousand, two hundred streets. Let the reader imagine himself beneath that forest of gloomy branches which is called the sewer. The system of sewers existing at that epoch, placed end to end, would have given a length of eleven leagues. We have said above, that the actual network, thanks to the special activity of the last thirty years, was no less than sixty leagues in extent.

Jean Valjean began by committing a blunder. He thought that he was beneath the Rue Saint-Denis, and it was a pity that it was not so. Under the Rue Saint-Denis there is an old stone sewer which dates from Louis XIII and which runs straight to the collecting sewer, called the Grand Sewer, with but a single elbow, on the right, on the elevation of the ancient Cour des Miracles, and a single branch, the Saint-Martin sewer, whose four arms describe a cross. But the gut of the Petite-Truanderie the entrance to which was in the vicinity of the Corinthe wine-shop has never communicated with the sewer of the Rue Saint-Denis; it ended at the Montmartre sewer, and it was in this that Jean Valjean was entangled. There opportunities of losing one's self abound. The Montmartre sewer is one of the most labyrinthine of the ancient network. Fortunately, Jean Valjean had left behind him the sewer of the markets whose geometrical plan presents the appearance of a multitude of parrots' roosts piled on top of each other; but he had before him more than one embarrassing encounter and more than one street corner—for they are streets—presenting itself in the gloom like an interrogation point; first, on his left, the vast sewer of the Plâtrière, a sort of Chinese puzzle, thrusting out and entangling its chaos of Ts and Zs under the Post-Office and under the rotunda of the Wheat Market, as far as the Seine, where it terminates in a Y; secondly, on his right, the curving corridor of the Rue du Cadran with its three teeth, which are also blind courts; thirdly, on his left, the branch of the Mail, complicated, almost at its inception, with a sort of fork, and proceeding from zigzag to zigzag until it ends in the grand crypt of the outlet of the Louvre, truncated and ramified in every direction; and lastly, the blind-alley of a passage of the Rue des Jeûneurs, without counting little ducts here and there, before reaching the belt sewer, which alone could conduct him to some issue sufficiently distant to be safe.

Had Jean Valjean had any idea of all that we have here pointed out, he would speedily have perceived, merely by feeling the wall, that he was not in the subterranean gallery of the Rue Saint-Denis. Instead of the ancient stone, instead of the antique architecture, haughty and royal even in the sewer, with pavement and string courses of granite and mortar costing eight hundred livres the fathom, he would have felt under his hand contemporary cheapness, economical expedients, porous stone filled with mortar on a concrete foundation, which costs two hundred francs the meter, and the bourgeoise masonry known as *à petits matériaux*—small stuff; but of all this he knew nothing.

He advanced with anxiety, but with calmness, seeing nothing, knowing nothing, buried in chance, that is to say, engulfed in providence.

By degrees, we will admit, a certain horror seized upon him. The gloom which enveloped him penetrated his spirit. He walked in an enigma. This aqueduct of the sewer is formidable; it interlaces in a dizzy fashion. It is a melancholy thing to be caught in this Paris of shadows. Jean Valjean was obliged to find and even to invent his route without seeing it. In this unknown, every step that he risked might be his last. How was he to get out? should he find an issue? should he find it in time? would that colossal subterranean sponge with its stone cavities, allow itself to be penetrated and pierced? should he there encounter some unexpected knot in the darkness? should he arrive at the inextricable and the impassable? would Marius die there of hemorrhage, and he of hunger? should they end by both getting lost, and by furnishing two skeletons in a nook of that night? He did not know. He put all these questions to himself without replying to them. The intestines of Paris form a precipice. Like the prophet, he was in the belly of the monster.

All at once, he had a surprise. At the most unforeseen moment, and without having ceased to walk in a straight line, he perceived that he was no longer ascending; the water of the rivulet was beating against his heels, instead of meeting him at his toes. The sewer was now descending. Why? Was he about to arrive suddenly at the Seine? This danger was a great one, but the peril of retreating was still greater. He continued to advance.

It was not toward the Seine that he was proceeding. The ridge which the soil of Paris forms on its right bank empties one of its water-sheds into the Seine and the other into the Grand Sewer. The crest of this ridge which determines the division of the waters describes a very capricious line. The culminating point, which is the point of separation of the currents, is in the Sainte-Avoye sewer, beyond the Rue Michel-le-Comte, in the sewer of the Louvre, near the boulevards, and in the Montmartre sewer, near the Halles. It was this culminating point that Jean Valjean had reached. He was directing his course toward the belt sewer; he was on the right path. But he did not know it.

Every time that he encountered a branch, he felt of its angles, and if he found that the opening which presented itself was smaller than the passage in which he was, he did not enter but continued his route, rightly judging that every narrower way must needs terminate in a blind-alley, and could only lead him further from his goal, that is to say, the outlet. Thus he avoided the quadruple trap which was set for him in the darkness by the four labyrinths which we have just enumerated.

At a certain moment, he perceived that he was emerging from beneath the Paris which was petrified by the uprising, where the barricades had suppressed circulation, and that he was entering beneath the living and normal Paris. Overhead he suddenly heard a noise as of thunder, distant but continuous. It was the rumbling of vehicles.

He had been walking for about half an hour, at least according to the calculation which he made in his own mind, and he had not yet thought of rest; he had merely changed the hand with which he was holding Marius. The darkness was more profound than ever, but its very depth reassured him.

All at once, he saw his shadow in front of him. It was outlined on a faint, almost indistinct reddish glow, which vaguely empurpled the flooring vault underfoot, and the vault overhead, and gilded to his right and to his left the two viscous walls of the passage. Stupefied, he turned round.

Behind him, in the portion of the passage which he had just passed through, at a distance which appeared to him immense, piercing the dense obscurity, flamed a sort of horrible star which had the air of surveying him.

It was the gloomy star of the police which was rising in the sewer.

In the rear of that star eight or ten forms were moving about in a confused way, black, upright, indistinct, horrible.

Chapter II

EXPLANATION

ON THE DAY OF THE 6TH OF JUNE, A BATTUE OF THE SEWERS HAD BEEN ORDERED. IT WAS FEARED that the vanquished might have taken to them for refuge, and Prefect Gisquet was to search occult Paris while General Bugeaud swept public Paris; a double and connected operation which exacted a double strategy on the part of the public force, represented above by the army and below by the police. Three squads of agents and sewermen explored the subterranean drain of Paris, the first on the right bank, the second on the left bank, the third in the city. The agents of police were armed with carabines, with bludgeons, swords and poignards.

That which was directed at Jean Valjean at that moment, was the lantern of the patrol of the right bank.

This patrol had just visited the curving gallery and the three blind-alleys which lie beneath the Rue du Cadran. While they were passing their lantern through the depths of these blind-alleys, Jean Valjean had encountered on his path the entrance to the gallery, had perceived that it was narrower than the principal passage and had not penetrated thither. He had passed on. The police, on emerging from the gallery du Cadran, had fancied that they heard the sound of footsteps in the direction of the belt sewer. They were, in fact, the steps of Jean Valjean. The sergeant in command of the patrol had raised his lantern, and the squad had begun to gaze into the mist in the direction whence the sound proceeded.

This was an indescribable moment for Jean Valjean.

Happily, if he saw the lantern well, the lantern saw him but ill. It was light and he was shadow. He was very far off, and mingled with the darkness of the place. He hugged the wall and halted. Moreover, he did not understand what it was that was moving behind him. The lack of sleep and food, and his emotions had caused him also to pass into the state of a visionary. He beheld a gleam, and around that gleam, forms. What was it? He did not comprehend.

Jean Valjean having paused, the sound ceased.

The men of the patrol listened, and heard nothing, they looked and saw nothing. They held a consultation.

There existed at that epoch at this point of the Montmartre sewer a sort of cross-roads called *de service*, which was afterwards suppressed, on account of the little interior lake which formed there, swallowing up the torrent of rain in heavy storms. The patrol could form a cluster in this open space. Jean Valjean saw these specters form a sort of circle. These bull-dogs' heads approached each other closely and whispered together.

The result of this council held by the watchdogs was, that they had been mistaken, that there had been no noise, that it was useless to get entangled in the belt sewer, that it would only be a waste of time, but that they ought to hasten toward Saint-Merry; that if there was anything to do, and any "bousingot" to track out, it was in that quarter.

From time to time, parties resole their old insults. In 1832, the word bousingot formed the interim between the word jacobin, which had become obsolete, and the word demagogue which has since rendered such excellent service.

The sergeant gave orders to turn to the left, toward the watershed of the Seine.

If it had occurred to them to separate into two squads, and to go in both directions, Jean Valjean would have been captured. All hung on that thread. It is probable that the instructions of the prefecture, foreseeing a possibility of combat and insurgents in force, had forbidden the patrol to part company. The patrol resumed its march, leaving Jean Valjean behind it. Of all this movement, Jean Valjean perceived nothing, except the eclipse of the lantern which suddenly wheeled round.

Before taking his departure, the sergeant, in order to acquit his policeman's conscience, discharged his gun in the direction of Jean Valjean. The detonation rolled from echo to echo in the crypt, like the rumbling of that titanic entrail. A bit of plaster which fell into the stream and splashed up the water a few paces away from Jean Valjean, warned him that the ball had struck the arch over his head.

Slow and measured steps resounded for some time on the timber work, gradually dying away as they retreated to a greater distance; the group of black forms vanished, a glimmer of light oscillated and floated, communicating to the vault a reddish glow which grew fainter, then disappeared; the silence became profound once more, the obscurity became complete, blindness and deafness resumed possession of the shadows; and Jean Valjean, not daring to stir as yet, remained for a long time leaning with his back against the wall, with straining ears, and dilated pupils, watching the disappearance of that phantom patrol.

Chapter III

THE "SPUN" MAN

THIS JUSTICE MUST BE RENDERED TO THE POLICE OF THAT PERIOD, THAT EVEN IN THE MOST SErious public junctures, it imperturbably fulfilled its duties connected with the sewers and surveillance. A revolt was, in its eyes, no pretext for allowing malefactors to take the bit in their own mouths, and for neglecting society for the reason that the government was in peril. The ordinary service was performed correctly in company with the extraordinary service, and was not troubled by the latter. In the midst of an incalculable political event already begun, under the pressure of a possible revolution, a police agent "spun" a thief without allowing himself to be distracted by insurrection and barricades.

It was something precisely parallel which took place on the afternoon of the 6th of June on the banks of the Seine, on the slope of the right shore, a little beyond the Pont des Invalides.

There is no longer any bank there now. The aspect of the locality has changed.

On that bank, two men, separated by a certain distance, seemed to be watching each other while mutually avoiding each other. The one who was in advance was trying to get away, the one in the rear was trying to overtake the other.

It was like a game of checkers played at a distance and in silence. Neither seemed to be in any hurry, and both walked slowly, as though each of them feared by too much haste to make his partner redouble his pace.

One would have said that it was an appetite following its prey, and purposely without wearing the air of doing so. The prey was crafty and on its guard.

The proper relations between the hunted pole-cat and the hunting dog were observed. The one who was seeking to escape had an insignificant mien and not an impressive appearance; the one who was seeking to seize him was rude of aspect, and must have been rude to encounter.

The first, conscious that he was the more feeble, avoided the second; but he avoided him in a manner which was deeply furious; anyone who could have observed him would have discerned in his eyes the somber hostility of flight, and all the menace that fear contains.

The shore was deserted; there were no passers-by; not even a boatman nor a lighter-man was in the skiffs which were moored here and there.

It was not easy to see these two men, except from the quay opposite, and to any person who had scrutinized them at that distance, the man who was in advance would have appeared like a bristling, tattered, and equivocal being, who was uneasy and trembling beneath a ragged blouse, and the other like a classic and official personage, wearing the frock-coat of authority buttoned to the chin.

Perchance the reader might recognize these two men, if he were to see them closer at hand.

What was the object of the second man?

Probably to succeed in clothing the first more warmly.

When a man clothed by the state pursues a man in rags, it is in order to make of him a man who is also clothed by the state. Only, the whole question lies in the color. To be dressed in blue is glorious; to be dressed in red is disagreeable.

There is a purple from below.

It is probably some unpleasantness and some purple of this sort which the first man is desirous of shirking.

If the other allowed him to walk on, and had not seized him as yet, it was, judging from all appearances, in the hope of seeing him lead up to some significant meeting-place and to some group worth catching. This delicate operation is called "spinning."

What renders this conjecture entirely probable is that the buttoned-up man, on catching sight from the shore of a hackney-coach on the quay as it was passing along empty, made a sign to the driver; the driver understood, evidently recognized the person with whom he had to deal, turned about and began to follow the two men at the top of the quay, at a foot-pace. This was not observed by the slouching and tattered personage who was in advance.

The hackney-coach rolled along the trees of the Champs-Élysées. The bust of the driver whip in hand, could be seen moving along above the parapet.

One of the secret instructions of the police authorities to their agents contains this article: "Always have on hand a hackney-coach, in case of emergency."

While these two men were maneuvering, each on his own side, with irreproachable strategy, they approached an inclined plane on the quay which descended to the shore, and which permitted cab-drivers arriving from Passy to come to the river and water their horses. This inclined plane was suppressed later on, for the sake of symmetry; horses may die of thirst, but the eye is gratified.

It is probable that the man in the blouse had intended to ascend this inclined plane, with a view to making his escape into the Champs-Élysées, a place ornamented with trees, but, in return, much infested with policemen, and where the other could easily exercise violence.

This point on the quay is not very far distant from the house brought to Paris from Moret in 1824, by Colonel Brack, and designated as "the house of François I." A guard-house is situated close at hand.

To the great surprise of his watcher, the man who was being tracked did not mount by the inclined plane for watering. He continued to advance along the quay on the shore.

His position was visibly becoming critical.

What was he intending to do, if not to throw himself into the Seine?

Henceforth, there existed no means of ascending to the quay; there was no other inclined plane, no staircase; and they were near the spot, marked by the bend in the Seine toward the Pont de Jéna, where the bank, growing constantly narrower, ended in a slender tongue, and was lost in the water. There he would inevitably find himself blocked between the perpendicular wall on his right, the river on his left and in front of him, and the authorities on his heels.

It is true that this termination of the shore was hidden from sight by a heap of rubbish six or seven feet in height, produced by some demolition or other. But did this man hope to conceal himself effectually behind that heap of rubbish, which one need but skirt? The expedient would have been puerile. He certainly was not dreaming of such a thing. The innocence of thieves does not extend to that point.

The pile of rubbish formed a sort of projection at the water's edge, which was prolonged in a promontory as far as the wall of the quay.

The man who was being followed arrived at this little mound and went round it, so that he ceased to be seen by the other.

The latter, as he did not see, could not be seen; he took advantage of this fact to abandon all dissimulation and to walk very rapidly. In a few moments, he had reached the rubbish heap and passed round it. There he halted in sheer amazement. The man whom he had been pursuing was no longer there.

Total eclipse of the man in the blouse.

The shore, beginning with the rubbish heap, was only about thirty paces long, then it plunged into the water which beat against the wall of the quay. The fugitive could not have thrown himself into the Seine without being seen by the man who was following him. What had become of him?

The man in the buttoned-up coat walked to the extremity of the shore, and remained there in thought for a moment, his fists clenched, his eyes searching. All at once he smote his brow. He had just perceived, at the point where the land came to an end and the water began, a large iron grating, low, arched, garnished with a heavy lock and with three massive hinges. This grating, a sort of door pierced at the base of the quay, opened on the river as well as on the shore. A blackish stream passed under it. This stream discharged into the Seine.

Beyond the heavy, rusty iron bars, a sort of dark and vaulted corridor could be descried. The man folded his arms and stared at the grating with an air of reproach.

As this gaze did not suffice, he tried to thrust it aside; he shook it, it resisted solidly. It is probable that it had just been opened, although no sound had been heard, a singular circumstance in so rusty a grating; but it is certain that it had been closed again. This indicated that the man before whom that door had just opened, had not a hook but a key.

This evidence suddenly burst upon the mind of the man who was trying to move the grating, and evoked from him this indignant ejaculation:

"That is too much! A government key!"

Then, immediately regaining his composure, he expressed a whole world of interior ideas by this outburst of monosyllables accented almost ironically: "Come! Come! Come! Come!"

That said, and in the hope of something or other, either that he should see the man emerge or other men enter, he posted himself on the watch behind a heap of rubbish, with the patient rage of a pointer.

The hackney-coach, which regulated all its movements on his, had, in its turn, halted on the quay above him, close to the parapet. The coachman, foreseeing a prolonged wait, encased his horses' muzzles in the bag of oats which is damp at the bottom, and which is so familiar to Parisians, to whom, be it said in parenthesis, the Government sometimes applies it. The rare passers-by on the Pont de Jéna, turned their heads, before they pursued their way, to take a momentary glance at these two motionless items in the landscape, the man on the shore, the carriage on the quay.

Chapter IV

HE ALSO BEARS HIS CROSS

J EAN VALJEAN HAD RESUMED HIS MARCH AND HAD NOT AGAIN PAUSED.
This march became more and more laborious. The level of these vaults varies; the average height is about five feet, six inches, and has been calculated for the stature of a man; Jean Valjean was forced to bend over, in order not to strike Marius against the vault; at every step he had to bend, then to rise, and to feel incessantly of the wall. The moisture of the stones, and the viscous nature of the timber framework furnished but poor supports to which to cling, either for hand or foot. He stumbled along in the hideous dung-heap of the city. The intermittent gleams from the air-holes only appeared at very long intervals, and were so wan that the full sunlight seemed like the light of the moon; all the rest was mist, miasma, opaqueness, blackness. Jean Valjean was both hungry and thirsty; especially thirsty; and this, like the sea, was a place full of water where a man cannot drink. His strength, which was prodigious, as the reader knows, and which had been but little decreased by age, thanks to his chaste and sober life, began to give way, nevertheless. Fatigue began to gain on him; and as his strength decreased, it made the weight of his burden increase. Marius, who was, perhaps, dead, weighed him down as inert bodies weigh. Jean Valjean held him in such a manner that his chest was not oppressed, and so that respiration could proceed as well as possible. Between his legs he felt the rapid gliding of the rats. One of them was frightened to such a degree that he bit him. From time to time, a breath of fresh air reached him through the vent-holes of the mouths of the sewer, and reanimated him.

It might have been three hours past midday when he reached the belt sewer.

He was, at first, astonished at this sudden widening. He found himself, all at once, in a gallery where his outstretched hands could not reach the two walls, and beneath a vault which his head did not touch. The Grand Sewer is, in fact, eight feet wide and seven feet high.

At the point where the Montmartre sewer joins the Grand Sewer, two other subterranean galleries, that of the Rue de Provence, and that of the Abattoir, form a square. Between these four ways, a less sagacious man would have remained undecided. Jean Valjean selected the broadest, that is to say, the belt sewer. But here the question again came up—should he descend or ascend? He thought that the situation required haste, and that he must now gain the Seine at any risk. In other terms, he must descend. He turned to the left.

It was well that he did so, for it is an error to suppose that the belt sewer has two outlets, the one in the direction of Bercy, the other toward Passy, and that it is, as its name indicates, the subterranean girdle of the Paris on the right bank. The Grand Sewer, which is, it must be remembered, nothing else than the old brook of Ménilmontant, terminates, if one ascends it, in a blind sack, that is to say, at its ancient point of departure which was its source, at the foot of the knoll of Ménilmontant. There is no direct communication with the branch which collects the waters of Paris beginning with the Quartier Popincourt, and which falls into the Seine through the Amelot sewer above the ancient Isle Louviers. This branch, which completes the collecting sewer, is separated from it, under the Rue Ménilmontant itself, by a pile which marks the dividing point of the waters, between upstream and downstream. If Jean Valjean had ascended the gallery he would have arrived, after a thousand efforts, and broken down with fatigue, and in an expiring condition, in the gloom, at a wall. He would have been lost.

In case of necessity, by retracing his steps a little way, and entering the passage of the Filles-du-Calvaire, on condition that he did not hesitate at the subterranean crossing of the Carrefour

Boucherat, and by taking the corridor Saint-Louis, then the Saint-Gilles gut on the left, then turn-ing to the right and avoiding the Saint-Sebastian gallery, he might have reached the Amelot sewer, and thence, provided that he did not go astray in the sort of F which lies under the Bastille, he might have attained the outlet on the Seine near the Arsenal. But in order to do this, he must have been thoroughly familiar with the enormous madrepore of the sewer in all its ramifications and in all its openings. Now, we must again insist that he knew nothing of that frightful drain which he was tra-versing; and had anyone asked him in what he was, he would have answered: "In the night."

His instinct served him well. To descend was, in fact, possible safety.

He left on his right the two narrow passages which branch out in the form of a claw under the Rue Laffitte and the Rue Saint-Georges and the long, bifurcated corridor of the Chaussée d'Antin.

A little beyond an affluent, which was, probably, the Madeleine branch, he halted. He was ex-tremely weary. A passably large air-hole, probably the man-hole in the Rue d'Anjou, furnished a light that was almost vivid. Jean Valjean, with the gentleness of movement which a brother would exercise toward his wounded brother, deposited Marius on the banquette of the sewer. Marius's blood-stained face appeared under the wan light of the air-hole like the ashes at the bottom of a tomb. His eyes were closed, his hair was plastered down on his temples like a painter's brushes dried in red wash; his hands hung limp and dead. A clot of blood had collected in the knot of his cravat; his limbs were cold, and blood was clotted at the corners of his mouth; his shirt had thrust itself into his wounds, the cloth of his coat was chafing the yawning gashes in the living flesh. Jean Valjean, pushing aside the garments with the tips of his fingers, laid his hand upon Marius's breast; his heart was still beating. Jean Valjean tore up his shirt, bandaged the young man's wounds as well as he was able and stopped the flowing blood; then bending over Marius, who still lay unconscious and almost without breathing, in that half-light, he gazed at him with inexpressible hatred.

On disarranging Marius's garments, he had found two things in his pockets, the roll which had been forgotten there on the preceding evening, and Marius's pocket-book. He ate the roll and opened the pocket-book. On the first page he found the four lines written by Marius. The reader will recall them:

"My name is Marius Pontmercy. Carry my body to my grandfather, M. Gillenormand, Rue des Filles-du-Calvaire, No. 6, in the Marais."

Jean Valjean read these four lines by the light of the air-hole, and remained for a moment as though absorbed in thought, repeating in a low tone: "Rue des Filles-du-Calvaire, number 6, Mon-sieur Gillenormand." He replaced the pocket-book in Marius's pocket. He had eaten, his strength had returned to him; he took Marius up once more upon his back, placed the latter's head carefully on his right shoulder, and resumed his descent of the sewer.

The Grand Sewer, directed according to the course of the valley of Ménilmontant, is about two leagues long. It is paved throughout a notable portion of its extent.

This torch of the names of the streets of Paris, with which we are illuminating for the reader Jean Valjean's subterranean march, Jean Valjean himself did not possess. Nothing told him what zone of the city he was traversing, nor what way he had made. Only the growing pallor of the pools of light which he encountered from time to time indicated to him that the sun was withdrawing from the pavement, and that the day would soon be over; and the rolling of vehicles overhead, hav-ing become intermittent instead of continuous, then having almost ceased, he concluded that he was no longer under central Paris, and that he was approaching some solitary region, in the vicinity of the outer boulevards, or the extreme outer quays. Where there are fewer houses and streets, the sewer has fewer air-holes. The gloom deepened around Jean Valjean. Nevertheless, he continued to advance, groping his way in the dark.

Suddenly this darkness became terrible.

Chapter V

IN THE CASE OF SAND AS IN THAT OF WOMAN, THERE IS A FINENESS WHICH IS TREACHEROUS

HE FELT THAT HE WAS ENTERING THE WATER, AND THAT HE NO LONGER HAD A PAVEMENT UNDER his feet, but only mud.

It sometimes happens, that on certain shores of Bretagne or Scotland a man, either a traveler or a fisherman, while walking at low tide on the beach far from shore, suddenly notices that for several minutes past, he has been walking with some difficulty. The beach underfoot is like pitch; his soles stick fast to it; it is no longer sand, it is bird-lime. The strand is perfectly dry, but at every step that he takes, as soon as the foot is raised, the print is filled with water. The eye, however, has perceived no change; the immense beach is smooth and tranquil, all the sand has the same aspect, nothing distinguishes the soil that is solid from that which is not solid; the joyous little cloud of sand-lice, continues to leap tumultuously under the feet of the passer-by.

The man pursues his way, he walks on, turns toward the land, endeavors to approach the shore. He is not uneasy. Uneasy about what? Only he is conscious that the heaviness of his feet seems to be increasing at every step that he takes. All at once he sinks in. He sinks in two or three inches. Decidedly, he is not on the right road; he halts to get his bearings. Suddenly he glances at his feet; his feet have disappeared. The sand has covered them. He draws his feet out of the sand, he tries to retrace his steps, he turns back, he sinks in more deeply than before. The sand is up to his ankles, he tears himself free from it and flings himself to the left, the sand reaches to mid-leg, he flings himself to the right, the sand comes up to his knees. Then, with indescribable terror, he recognizes the fact that he is caught in a quicksand, and that he has beneath him that frightful medium in which neither man can walk nor fish can swim. He flings away his burden, if he have one, he lightens himself, like a ship in distress; it is too late, the sand is above his knees.

He shouts, he waves his hat, or his handkerchief, the sand continually gains on him; if the beach is deserted, if the land is too far away, if the bank of sand is too ill famed, there is no hero in the neighborhood, all is over, he is condemned to be engulfed. He is condemned to that terrible interment, long, infallible, implacable, which it is impossible to either retard or hasten, which lasts for hours, which will not come to an end, which seizes you erect, free, in the flush of health, which drags you down by the feet, which, at every effort that you attempt, at every shout that you utter, draws you a little lower, which has the air of punishing you for your resistance by a redoubled grasp, which forces a man to return slowly to earth, while leaving him time to survey the horizon, the trees, the verdant country, the smoke of the villages on the plain, the sails of the ships on the sea, the birds which fly and sing, the sun and the sky. This engulfment is the sepulcher which assumes a tide, and which mounts from the depths of the earth toward a living man. Each minute is an inexorable layer-out of the dead. The wretched man tries to sit down, to lie down, to climb; every movement that he makes buries him deeper; he straightens himself up, he sinks; he feels that he is being swallowed up; he shrieks, implores, cries to the clouds, wrings his hands, grows desperate. Behold him in the sand up to his belly, the sand reaches to his breast, he is only a bust now. He uplifts his hands, utters furious groans, clenches his nails on the beach, tries to cling fast to that ashes, supports himself on his elbows in order to raise himself from that soft sheath, and sobs frantically; the sand mounts higher. The sand has reached his shoulders, the sand reaches to his throat; only his face is visible now. His mouth cries aloud, the sand fills it; silence. His eyes still gaze forth, the sand closes them, night. Then his brow decreases, a little hair quivers above the sand; a hand projects, pierces the surface of the beach, waves and disappears. Sinister obliteration of a man.

Sometimes a rider is engulfed with his horse; sometimes the carter is swallowed up with his cart; all founders in that strand. It is shipwreck elsewhere than in the water. It is the earth drowning a man. The earth, permeated with the ocean, becomes a pitfall. It presents itself in the guise of a plain, and it yawns like a wave. The abyss is subject to these treacheries.

This melancholy fate, always possible on certain sea beaches, was also possible, thirty years ago, in the sewers of Paris.

Before the important works, undertaken in 1833, the subterranean drain of Paris was subject to these sudden slides.

The water filtered into certain subjacent strata, which were particularly friable; the foot-way, which was of flag-stones, as in the ancient sewers, or of cement on concrete, as in the new galleries, having no longer an underpinning, gave way. A fold in a flooring of this sort means a crack, means crumbling. The framework crumbled away for a certain length. This crevice, the hiatus of a gulf of mire, was called a *fontis*, in the special tongue. What is a *fontis?* It is the quicksands of the seashore suddenly encountered under the surface of the earth; it is the beach of Mont Saint-Michel in a sewer. The soaked soil is in a state of fusion, as it were; all its molecules are in suspension in soft medium; it is not earth and it is not water. The depth is sometimes very great. Nothing can be more formidable than such an encounter. If the water predominates, death is prompt, the man is swallowed up; if earth predominates, death is slow.

Can anyone picture to himself such a death? If being swallowed by the earth is terrible on the seashore, what is it in a cesspool? Instead of the open air, the broad daylight, the clear horizon, those vast sounds, those free clouds whence rains life, instead of those barks descried in the distance, of that hope under all sorts of forms, of probable passers-by, of succor possible up to the very last moment—instead of all this, deafness, blindness, a black vault, the inside of a tomb already prepared, death in the mire beneath a cover! slow suffocation by filth, a stone box where asphyxia opens its claw in the mire and clutches you by the throat; fetidness mingled with the death-rattle; slime instead of the strand, sulfuretted hydrogen in place of the hurricane, dung in place of the ocean! And to shout, to gnash one's teeth, and to writhe, and to struggle, and to agonize, with that enormous city which knows nothing of it all, over one's head!

Inexpressible is the horror of dying thus! Death sometimes redeems his atrocity by a certain terrible dignity. On the funeral pile, in shipwreck, one can be great; in the flames as in the foam, a superb attitude is possible; one there becomes transfigured as one perishes. But not here. Death is filthy. It is humiliating to expire. The supreme floating visions are abject. Mud is synonymous with shame. It is petty, ugly, infamous. To die in a butt of Malvoisie, like Clarence, is permissible; in the ditch of a scavenger, like Escoubleau, is horrible. To struggle therein is hideous; at the same time that one is going through the death-agony, one is floundering about. There are shadows enough for hell, and mire enough to render it nothing but a slough, and the dying man knows not whether he is on the point of becoming a specter or a frog.

Everywhere else the sepulcher is sinister; here it is deformed.

The depth of the *fontis* varied, as well as their length and their density, according to the more or less bad quality of the sub-soil. Sometimes a *fontis* was three or four feet deep, sometimes eight or ten; sometimes the bottom was unfathomable. Here the mire was almost solid, there almost liquid. In the Lunière fontis, it would have taken a man a day to disappear, while he would have been devoured in five minutes by the Philippeaux slough. The mire bears up more or less, according to its density. A child can escape where a man will perish. The first law of safety is to get rid of every sort of load. Every sewerman who felt the ground giving way beneath him began by flinging away his sack of tools, or his back-basket, or his hod.

The fontis were due to different causes: the friability of the soil; some landslip at a depth beyond the reach of man; the violent summer rains; the incessant flooding of winter; long, drizzling showers. Sometimes the weight of the surrounding houses on a marly or sandy soil forced out the vaults of the subterranean galleries and caused them to bend aside, or it chanced that a flooring vault burst and split under this crushing thrust. In this manner, the heaping up of the Parthénon, obliterated, a century ago, a portion of the vaults of Saint-Geneviève hill. When a sewer was broken in under the pressure of the houses, the mischief was sometimes betrayed in the street above by a sort of space, like the teeth of a saw, between the paving-stones; this crevice was developed in an undulating line throughout the entire length of the cracked vault, and then, the evil being visible, the remedy could be promptly applied. It also frequently happened, that the interior ravages were not revealed by any external scar, and in that case, woe to the sewermen. When they entered without precaution into the sewer, they were liable to be lost. Ancient registers make mention of several scavengers who were buried in fontis in this manner. They give many names; among others, that of the sewerman who was swallowed up in a quagmire under the man-hole of the Rue Carême-Prenant, a certain Blaise Poutrain; this Blaise Poutrain was the brother of Nicholas Poutrain, who was the last gravedigger of the cemetery called the Charnier des Innocents, in 1785, the epoch when that cemetery expired.

There was also that young and charming Vicomte d'Escoubleau, of whom we have just spoken, one of the heroes of the siege of Lerida, where they delivered the assault in silk stockings, with violins at their head. D'Escoubleau, surprised one night at his cousin's, the Duchess de Sourdis's, was drowned in a quagmire of the Beautreillis sewer, in which he had taken refuge in order to escape from the Duke. Madame de Sourdis, when informed of his death, demanded her smelling-bottle, and forgot to weep, through sniffling at her salts. In such cases, there is no love which holds fast; the sewer extinguishes it. Hero refuses to wash the body of Leander. Thisbe stops her nose in the presence of Pyramus and says: "Phew!"

Chapter VI

THE FONTIS

JEAN VALJEAN FOUND HIMSELF IN THE PRESENCE OF A FONTIS.
This sort of quagmire was common at that period in the subsoil of the Champs-Élysées, difficult to handle in the hydraulic works and a bad preservative of the subterranean constructions, on account of its excessive fluidity. This fluidity exceeds even the inconsistency of the sands of the Quartier Saint-Georges, which could only be conquered by a stone construction on a concrete foundation, and the clayey strata, infected with gas, of the Quartier des Martyrs, which are so liquid that the only way in which a passage was effected under the gallery des Martyrs was by means of a cast-iron pipe. When, in 1836, the old stone sewer beneath the Faubourg Saint-Honoré, in which we now see Jean Valjean, was demolished for the purpose of reconstructing it, the quicksand, which forms the subsoil of the Champs-Élysées as far as the Seine, presented such an obstacle, that the operation lasted nearly six months, to the great clamor of the dwellers on the riverside, particularly of those who had hôtels and carriages. The work was more than unhealthy; it was dangerous. It is true that they had four months and a half of rain, and three floods of the Seine.

The fontis which Jean Valjean had encountered was caused by the downpour of the preceding day. The pavement, badly sustained by the subjacent sand, had given way and had produced a stoppage of the water. Infiltration had taken place, a slip had followed. The dislocated bottom had sunk into the ooze. To what extent? Impossible to say. The obscurity was more dense there than else-where. It was a pit of mire in a cavern of night.

Jean Valjean felt the pavement vanishing beneath his feet. He entered this slime. There was water on the surface, slime at the bottom. He must pass it. To retrace his steps was impossible. Mar-ius was dying, and Jean Valjean exhausted. Besides, where was he to go? Jean Valjean advanced. Moreover, the pit seemed, for the first few steps, not to be very deep. But in proportion as he ad-vanced, his feet plunged deeper. Soon he had the slime up to his calves and water above his knees. He walked on, raising Marius in his arms, as far above the water as he could. The mire now reached to his knees, and the water to his waist. He could no longer retreat. This mud, dense enough for one man, could not, obviously, uphold two. Marius and Jean Valjean would have stood a chance of ex-tricating themselves singly. Jean Valjean continued to advance, supporting the dying man, who was, perhaps, a corpse.

The water came up to his arm-pits; he felt that he was sinking; it was only with difficulty that he could move in the depth of ooze which he had now reached. The density, which was his support, was also an obstacle. He still held Marius on high, and with an unheard-of expenditure of force, he advanced still; but he was sinking. He had only his head above the water now, and his two arms holding up Marius. In the old paintings of the deluge there is a mother holding her child thus.

He sank still deeper, he turned his face to the rear, to escape the water, and in order that he might be able to breathe; anyone who had seen him in that gloom would have thought that what he beheld was a mask floating on the shadows; he caught a faint glimpse above him of the drooping head and livid face of Marius; he made a desperate effort and launched his foot forward; his foot struck something solid; a point of support. It was high time.

He straightened himself up, and rooted himself upon that point of support with a sort of fury. This produced upon him the effect of the first step in a staircase leading back to life.

The point of support, thus encountered in the mire at the supreme moment, was the beginning of the other water-shed of the pavement, which had bent but had not given way, and which had curved under the water like a plank and in a single piece. Well built pavements form a vault and pos-sess this sort of firmness. This fragment of the vaulting, partly submerged, but solid, was a verita-ble inclined plane, and, once on this plane, he was safe. Jean Valjean mounted this inclined plane and reached the other side of the quagmire.

As he emerged from the water, he came in contact with a stone and fell upon his knees. He re-flected that this was but just, and he remained there for some time, with his soul absorbed in words addressed to God.

He rose to his feet, shivering, chilled, foul-smelling, bowed beneath the dying man whom he was dragging after him, all dripping with slime, and his soul filled with a strange light.

Chapter VII

ONE SOMETIMES RUNS AGROUND WHEN ONE FANCIES THAT ONE IS DISEMBARKING

HE SET OUT ON HIS WAY ONCE MORE.
However, although he had not left his life in the fontis, he seemed to have left his strength behind him there. That supreme effort had exhausted him. His lassitude was now such that he was obliged to pause for breath every three or four steps, and lean against the wall. Once he was

forced to seat himself on the banquette in order to alter Marius's position, and he thought that he should have to remain there. But if his vigor was dead, his energy was not. He rose again.

He walked on desperately, almost fast, proceeded thus for a hundred paces, almost without drawing breath, and suddenly came in contact with the wall. He had reached an elbow of the sewer, and, arriving at the turn with head bent down, he had struck the wall. He raised his eyes, and at the extremity of the vault, far, very far away in front of him, he perceived a light. This time it was not that terrible light; it was good, white light. It was daylight. Jean Valjean saw the outlet.

A damned soul, who, in the midst of the furnace, should suddenly perceive the outlet of Gehenna, would experience what Jean Valjean felt. It would fly wildly with the stumps of its burned wings, toward that radiant portal. Jean Valjean was no longer conscious of fatigue, he no longer felt Marius's weight, he found his legs once more of steel, he ran rather than walked. As he approached, the outlet became more and more distinctly defined. It was a pointed arch, lower than the vault, which gradually narrowed, and narrower than the gallery, which closed in as the vault grew lower. The tunnel ended like the interior of a funnel; a faulty construction, imitated from the wickets of penitentiaries, logical in a prison, illogical in a sewer, and which has since been corrected.

Jean Valjean reached the outlet.

There he halted.

It certainly was the outlet, but he could not get out.

The arch was closed by a heavy grating, and the grating, which, to all appearance, rarely swung on its rusty hinges, was clamped to its stone jamb by a thick lock, which, red with rust, seemed like an enormous brick. The keyhole could be seen, and the robust latch, deeply sunk in the iron staple. The door was plainly double-locked. It was one of those prison locks which old Paris was so fond of lavishing.

Beyond the grating was the open air, the river, the daylight, the shore, very narrow but sufficient for escape. The distant quays, Paris, that gulf in which one so easily hides one's self, the broad horizon, liberty. On the right, downstream, the bridge of Jéna was discernible, on the left, upstream, the bridge of the Invalides; the place would have been a propitious one in which to await the night and to escape. It was one of the most solitary points in Paris; the shore which faces the Grand-Caillou. Flies were entering and emerging through the bars of the grating.

It might have been half-past eight o'clock in the evening. The day was declining.

Jean Valjean laid Marius down along the wall, on the dry portion of the vaulting, then he went to the grating and clenched both fists round the bars; the shock which he gave it was frenzied, but it did not move. The grating did not stir. Jean Valjean seized the bars one after the other, in the hope that he might be able to tear away the least solid, and to make of it a lever wherewith to raise the door or to break the lock. Not a bar stirred. The teeth of a tiger are not more firmly fixed in their sockets. No lever; no prying possible. The obstacle was invincible. There was no means of opening the gate.

Must he then stop there? What was he to do? What was to become of him? He had not the strength to retrace his steps, to recommence the journey which he had already taken. Besides, how was he to again traverse that quagmire whence he had only extricated himself as by a miracle? And after the quagmire, was there not the police patrol, which assuredly could not be twice avoided? And then, whither was he to go? What direction should he pursue? To follow the incline would not conduct him to his goal. If he were to reach another outlet, he would find it obstructed by a plug or a grating. Every outlet was, undoubtedly, closed in that manner. Chance had unsealed the grating through which he had entered, but it was evident that all the other sewer mouths were barred. He had only succeeded in escaping into a prison.

All was over. Everything that Jean Valjean had done was useless. Exhaustion had ended in failure.

They were both caught in the immense and gloomy web of death, and Jean Valjean felt the terrible spider running along those black strands and quivering in the shadows. He turned his back to the grating, and fell upon the pavement, hurled to earth rather than seated, close to Marius, who still made no movement, and with his head bent between his knees. This was the last drop of anguish.

Of what was he thinking during this profound depression? Neither of himself nor of Marius. He was thinking of Cosette.

Chapter VIII

THE TORN COAT-TAIL

IN THE MIDST OF THIS PROSTRATION, A HAND WAS LAID ON HIS SHOULDER, AND A LOW VOICE SAID to him:

"Half-shares."

Some person in that gloom? Nothing so closely resembles a dream as despair. Jean Valjean thought that he was dreaming. He had heard no footsteps. Was it possible? He raised his eyes.

A man stood before him.

This man was clad in a blouse; his feet were bare; he held his shoes in his left hand; he had evidently removed them in order to reach Jean Valjean, without allowing his steps to be heard.

Jean Valjean did not hesitate for an instant. Unexpected as was this encounter, this man was known to him. The man was Thénardier.

Although awakened, so to speak, with a start, Jean Valjean, accustomed to alarms, and steeled to unforeseen shocks that must be promptly parried, instantly regained possession of his presence of mind. Moreover, the situation could not be made worse, a certain degree of distress is no longer capable of a crescendo, and Thénardier himself could add nothing to this blackness of this night.

A momentary pause ensued.

Thénardier, raising his right hand to a level with his forehead, formed with it a shade, then he brought his eyelashes together, by screwing up his eyes, a motion which, in connection with a slight contraction of the mouth, characterizes the sagacious attention of a man who is endeavoring to recognize another man. He did not succeed. Jean Valjean, as we have just stated, had his back turned to the light, and he was, moreover, so disfigured, so bemired, so bleeding that he would have been unrecognizable in full noonday. On the contrary, illuminated by the light from the grating, a cellar light, it is true, livid, yet precise in its lividness, Thénardier, as the energetic popular metaphor expresses it, immediately "leaped into" Jean Valjean's eyes. This inequality of conditions sufficed to assure some advantage to Jean Valjean in that mysterious duel which was on the point of beginning between the two situations and the two men. The encounter took place between Jean Valjean veiled and Thénardier unmasked.

Jean Valjean immediately perceived that Thénardier did not recognize him.

They surveyed each other for a moment in that half-gloom, as though taking each other's measure. Thénardier was the first to break the silence.

"How are you going to manage to get out?"

Jean Valjean made no reply. Thénardier continued:

"It's impossible to pick the lock of that gate. But still, you must get out of this."

"That is true," said Jean Valjean.

"Well, half-shares then."

"What do you mean by that?"

"You have killed that man; that's all right. I have the key."

Thénardier pointed to Marius. He went on:

"I don't know you, but I want to help you. You must be a friend."

Jean Valjean began to comprehend. Thénardier took him for an assassin.

Thénardier resumed:

"Listen, comrade. You didn't kill that man without looking to see what he had in his pockets. Give me my half. I'll open the door for you."

And half drawing from beneath his tattered blouse a huge key, he added:

"Do you want to see how a key to liberty is made? Look here."

Jean Valjean "remained stupid"—the expression belongs to the elder Corneille—to such a degree that he doubted whether what he beheld was real. It was providence appearing in horrible guise, and his good angel springing from the earth in the form of Thénardier.

Thénardier thrust his fist into a large pocket concealed under his blouse, drew out a rope and offered it to Jean Valjean.

"Hold on," said he, "I'll give you the rope to boot."

"What is the rope for?"

"You will need a stone also, but you can find one outside. There's a heap of rubbish."

"What am I to do with a stone?"

"Idiot, you'll want to sling that stiff into the river, you'll need a stone and a rope, otherwise it would float on the water."

Jean Valjean took the rope. There is no one who does not occasionally accept in this mechanical way.

Thénardier snapped his fingers as though an idea had suddenly occurred to him.

"Ah, see here, comrade, how did you contrive to get out of that slough yonder? I haven't dared to risk myself in it. Phew! you don't smell good."

After a pause he added:

"I'm asking you questions, but you're perfectly right not to answer. It's an apprenticeship against that cursed quarter of an hour before the examining magistrate. And then, when you don't talk at all, you run no risk of talking too loud. That's no matter, as I can't see your face and as I don't know your name, you are wrong in supposing that I don't know who you are and what you want. I twig. You've broken up that gentleman a bit; now you want to tuck him away somewhere. The river, that great hider of folly, is what you want. I'll get you out of your scrape. Helping a good fellow in a pinch is what suits me to a hair."

While expressing his approval of Jean Valjean's silence, he endeavored to force him to talk. He jostled his shoulder in an attempt to catch a sight of his profile, and he exclaimed, without, however, raising his tone:

"Apropos of that quagmire, you're a hearty animal. Why didn't you toss the man in there?"

Jean Valjean preserved silence.

Thénardier resumed, pushing the rag which served him as a cravat to the level of his Adam's apple, a gesture which completes the capable air of a serious man:

"After all, you acted wisely. The workmen, when they come to-morrow to stop up that hole, would certainly have found the stiff abandoned there, and it might have been possible, thread by thread, straw by straw, to pick up the scent and reach you. Someone has passed through the sewer. Who? Where did he get out? Was he seen to come out? The police are full of cleverness. The sewer is treacherous and tells tales of you. Such a find is a rarity, it attracts attention, very few people make use of the sewers for their affairs, while the river belongs to everybody. The river is the true grave. At the end of a month they fish up your man in the nets at Saint-Cloud. Well, what does one care for that? It's carrion! Who killed that man? Paris. And justice makes no inquiries. You have done well."

The more loquacious Thénardier became, the more mute was Jean Valjean.

Again Thénardier shook him by the shoulder.

"Now let's settle this business. Let's go shares. You have seen my key, show me your money."

Thénardier was haggard, fierce, suspicious, rather menacing, yet amicable.

There was one singular circumstance; Thénardier's manners were not simple; he had not the air of being wholly at his ease; while affecting an air of mystery, he spoke low; from time to time he laid his finger on his mouth, and muttered, "hush!" It was difficult to divine why. There was no one there except themselves. Jean Valjean thought that other ruffians might possibly be concealed in some nook, not very far off, and that Thénardier did not care to share with them.

Thénardier resumed:

"Let's settle up. How much did the stiff have in his bags?"

Jean Valjean searched his pockets.

It was his habit, as the reader will remember, to always have some money about him. The mournful life of expedients to which he had been condemned imposed this as a law upon him. On this occasion, however, he had been caught unprepared. When donning his uniform of a National Guardsman on the preceding evening, he had forgotten, dolefully absorbed as he was, to take his pocket-book. He had only some small change in his fob. He turned out his pocket, all soaked with ooze, and spread out on the banquette of the vault one louis d'or, two five-franc pieces, and five or six large sous.

Thénardier thrust out his lower lip with a significant twist of the neck.

"You knocked him over cheap," said he.

He set to feeling the pockets of Jean Valjean and Marius, with the greatest familiarity. Jean Valjean, who was chiefly concerned in keeping his back to the light, let him have his way.

While handling Marius's coat, Thénardier, with the skill of a pickpocket, and without being noticed by Jean Valjean, tore off a strip which he concealed under his blouse, probably thinking that this morsel of stuff might serve, later on, to identify the assassinated man and the assassin. However, he found no more than the thirty francs.

"That's true," said he, "both of you together have no more than that."

And, forgetting his motto: "half-shares," he took all.

He hesitated a little over the large sous. After due reflection, he took them also, muttering:

"Never mind! You cut folks' throats too cheap altogether."

That done, he once more drew the big key from under his blouse.

"Now, my friend, you must leave. It's like the fair here, you pay when you go out. You have paid, now clear out."

And he began to laugh.

Had he, in lending to this stranger the aid of his key, and in making some other man than himself emerge from that portal, the pure and disinterested intention of rescuing an assassin? We may be permitted to doubt this.

Thénardier helped Jean Valjean to replace Marius on his shoulders, then he betook himself to the grating on tiptoe, and barefooted, making Jean Valjean a sign to follow him, looked out, laid his finger on his mouth, and remained for several seconds, as though in suspense; his inspection finished, he placed the key in the lock. The bolt slipped back and the gate swung open. It neither grated nor squeaked. It moved very softly.

It was obvious that this gate and those hinges, carefully oiled, were in the habit of opening more frequently than was supposed. This softness was suspicious; it hinted at furtive goings and comings, silent entrances and exits of nocturnal men, and the wolf-like tread of crime.

The sewer was evidently an accomplice of some mysterious band. This taciturn grating was a receiver of stolen goods.

Thénardier opened the gate a little way, allowing just sufficient space for Jean Valjean to pass out, closed the grating again, gave the key a double turn in the lock and plunged back into the darkness, without making any more noise than a breath. He seemed to walk with the velvet paws of a tiger.

A moment later, that hideous providence had retreated into the invisibility.

Jean Valjean found himself in the open air.

Chapter IX

MARIUS PRODUCES ON SOMEONE WHO IS A JUDGE OF THE MATTER, THE EFFECT OF BEING DEAD

H_{E ALLOWED MARIUS TO SLIDE DOWN UPON THE SHORE.}
    They were in the open air!

The miasmas, darkness, horror lay behind him. The pure, healthful, living, joyous air that was easy to breathe inundated him. Everywhere around him reigned silence, but that charming silence when the sun has set in an unclouded azure sky. Twilight had descended; night was drawing on, the great deliverer, the friend of all those who need a mantle of darkness that they may escape from an anguish. The sky presented itself in all directions like an enormous calm. The river flowed to his feet with the sound of a kiss. The aerial dialogue of the nests bidding each other good night in the elms of the Champs-Élysées was audible. A few stars, daintily piercing the pale blue of the zenith, and visible to reverie alone, formed imperceptible little splendors amid the immensity. Evening was unfolding over the head of Jean Valjean all the sweetness of the infinite.

It was that exquisite and undecided hour which says neither yes nor no. Night was already sufficiently advanced to render it possible to lose one's self at a little distance and yet there was sufficient daylight to permit of recognition at close quarters.

For several seconds, Jean Valjean was irresistibly overcome by that august and caressing serenity; such moments of oblivion do come to men; suffering refrains from harassing the unhappy wretch; everything is eclipsed in the thoughts; peace broods over the dreamer like night; and, beneath the twilight which beams and in imitation of the sky which is illuminated, the soul becomes studded with stars. Jean Valjean could not refrain from contemplating that vast, clear shadow which rested over him; thoughtfully he bathed in the sea of ecstasy and prayer in the majestic silence of the eternal heavens. Then he bent down swiftly to Marius, as though the sentiment of duty had returned to him, and, dipping up water in the hollow of his hand, he gently sprinkled a few drops on the latter's face. Marius's eyelids did not open; but his half-open mouth still breathed.

Jean Valjean was on the point of dipping his hand in the river once more, when, all at once, he experienced an indescribable embarrassment, such as a person feels when there is someone behind him whom he does not see.

We have already alluded to this impression, with which everyone is familiar.

He turned round.

Someone was, in fact, behind him, as there had been a short while before.

A man of lofty stature, enveloped in a long coat, with folded arms, and bearing in his right fist a bludgeon of which the leaden head was visible, stood a few paces in the rear of the spot where Jean Valjean was crouching over Marius.

With the aid of the darkness, it seemed a sort of apparition. An ordinary man would have been alarmed because of the twilight, a thoughtful man on account of the bludgeon. Jean Valjean recognized Javert.

The reader has divined, no doubt, that Thénardier's pursuer was no other than Javert. Javert, after his unlooked-for escape from the barricade, had betaken himself to the prefecture of police, had rendered a verbal account to the Prefect in person in a brief audience, had then immediately gone on duty again, which implied—the note, the reader will recollect, which had been captured on his person—a certain surveillance of the shore on the right bank of the Seine near the Champs-

Élysées, which had, for some time past, aroused the attention of the police. There he had caught sight of Thénardier and had followed him. The reader knows the rest.

Thus it will be easily understood that that grating, so obligingly opened to Jean Valjean was a bit of cleverness on Thénardier's part. Thénardier intuitively felt that Javert was still there; the man spied upon has a scent which never deceives him; it was necessary to fling a bone to that sleuthhound. An assassin, what a godsend! Such an opportunity must never be allowed to slip. Thénardier, by putting Jean Valjean outside in his stead, provided a prey for the police, forced them to relinquish his scent, made them forget him in a bigger adventure, repaid Javert for his waiting, which always flatters a spy, earned thirty francs, and counted with certainty, so far as he himself was concerned, on escaping with the aid of this diversion.

Jean Valjean had fallen from one danger upon another.

These two encounters, this falling one after the other, from Thénardier upon Javert, was a rude shock.

Javert did not recognize Jean Valjean, who, as we have stated, no longer looked like himself. He did not unfold his arms, he made sure of his bludgeon in his fist, by an imperceptible movement, and said in a curt, calm voice:

"Who are you?"

"I."

"Who is 'I'?"

"Jean Valjean."

Javert thrust his bludgeon between his teeth, bent his knees, inclined his body, laid his two powerful hands on the shoulders of Jean Valjean, which were clamped within them as in a couple of vices, scrutinized him, and recognized him. Their faces almost touched. Javert's look was terrible.

Jean Valjean remained inert beneath Javert's grasp, like a lion submitting to the claws of a lynx.

"Inspector Javert," said he, "you have me in your power. Moreover, I have regarded myself as your prisoner ever since this morning. I did not give you my address with any intention of escaping from you. Take me. Only grant me one favor."

Javert did not appear to hear him. He kept his eyes riveted on Jean Valjean. His chin being contracted, thrust his lips upwards toward his nose, a sign of savage reverie. At length he released Jean Valjean, straightened himself stiffly up without bending, grasped his bludgeon again firmly, and, as though in a dream, he murmured rather than uttered this question:

"What are you doing here? And who is this man?"

He still abstained from addressing Jean Valjean as *thou*.

Jean Valjean replied, and the sound of his voice appeared to rouse Javert:

"It is with regard to him that I desire to speak to you. Dispose of me as you see fit; but first help me to carry him home. That is all that I ask of you."

Javert's face contracted as was always the case when anyone seemed to think him capable of making a concession. Nevertheless, he did not say "no."

Again he bent over, drew from his pocket a handkerchief which he moistened in the water and with which he then wiped Marius's blood-stained brow.

"This man was at the barricade," said he in a low voice and as though speaking to himself. "He is the one they called Marius."

A spy of the first quality, who had observed everything, listened to everything, and taken in everything, even when he thought that he was to die; who had played the spy even in his agony, and who, with his elbows leaning on the first step of the sepulcher, had taken notes.

He seized Marius's hand and felt his pulse.

"He is wounded," said Jean Valjean.

"He is a dead man," said Javert.

Jean Valjean replied:

"No. Not yet."

"So you have brought him hither from the barricade?" remarked Javert.

His preoccupation must indeed have been very profound for him not to insist on this alarming rescue through the sewer, and for him not to even notice Jean Valjean's silence after his question.

Jean Valjean, on his side, seemed to have but one thought. He resumed:

"He lives in the Marais, Rue des Filles-du-Calvaire, with his grandfather. I do not recollect his name."

Jean Valjean fumbled in Marius's coat, pulled out his pocket-book, opened it at the page which Marius had penciled, and held it out to Javert.

There was still sufficient light to admit of reading. Besides this, Javert possessed in his eye the feline phosphorescence of night birds. He deciphered the few lines written by Marius, and muttered: "Gillenormand, Rue des Filles-du-Calvaire, No. 6."

Then he exclaimed: "Coachman!"

The reader will remember that the hackney-coach was waiting in case of need.

Javert kept Marius's pocket-book.

A moment later, the carriage, which had descended by the inclined plane of the watering-place, was on the shore. Marius was laid upon the back seat, and Javert seated himself on the front seat beside Jean Valjean.

The door slammed, and the carriage drove rapidly away, ascending the quays in the direction of the Bastille.

They quitted the quays and entered the streets. The coachman, a black form on his box, whipped up his thin horses. A glacial silence reigned in the carriage. Marius, motionless, with his body resting in the corner, and his head drooping on his breast, his arms hanging, his legs stiff, seemed to be awaiting only a coffin; Jean Valjean seemed made of shadow, and Javert of stone, and in that vehicle full of night, whose interior, every time that it passed in front of a street-lantern, appeared to be turned lividly wan, as by an intermittent flash of lightning, chance had united and seemed to be bringing face to face the three forms of tragic immobility, the corpse, the specter, and the statue.

Chapter X

RETURN OF THE SON WHO WAS PRODIGAL OF HIS LIFE

AT EVERY JOLT OVER THE PAVEMENT, A DROP OF BLOOD TRICKLED FROM MARIUS'S HAIR. Night had fully closed in when the carriage arrived at No. 6, Rue des Filles-du-Calvaire.

Javert was the first to alight; he made sure with one glance of the number on the carriage gate, and, raising the heavy knocker of beaten iron, embellished in the old style, with a male goat and a satyr confronting each other, he gave a violent peal. The gate opened a little way and Javert gave it a push. The porter half made his appearance yawning, vaguely awake, and with a candle in his hand.

Everyone in the house was asleep. People go to bed betimes in the Marais, especially on days when there is a revolt. This good, old quarter, terrified at the Revolution, takes refuge in slumber, as children, when they hear the Bugaboo coming, hide their heads hastily under their coverlet.

In the meantime Jean Valjean and the coachman had taken Marius out of the carriage, Jean Valjean supporting him under the armpits, and the coachman under the knees.

As they thus bore Marius, Jean Valjean slipped his hand under the latter's clothes, which were

broadly rent, felt his breast and assured himself that his heart was still beating. It was even beating
a little less feebly, as though the movement of the carriage had brought about a certain fresh access
of life.

Javert addressed the porter in a tone befitting the government, and the presence of the porter
of a factious person.

"Some person whose name is Gillenormand?"

"Here. What do you want with him?"

"His son is brought back."

"His son?" said the porter stupidly.

"He is dead."

Jean Valjean, who, soiled and tattered, stood behind Javert, and whom the porter was surveying with some horror, made a sign to him with his head that this was not so.

The porter did not appear to understand either Javert's words, or Jean Valjean's sign.

Javert continued:

"He went to the barricade, and here he is."

"To the barricade?" ejaculated the porter.

"He has got himself killed. Go waken his father."

The porter did not stir.

"Go along with you!" repeated Javert.

And he added:

"There will be a funeral here to-morrow."

For Javert, the usual incidents of the public highway were categorically classed, which is the
beginning of foresight and surveillance, and each contingency had its own compartment; all possible facts were arranged in drawers, as it were, whence they emerged on occasion, in variable quantities; in the street, uproar, revolt, carnival, and funeral.

The porter contented himself with waking Basque. Basque woke Nicolette; Nicolette roused
great-aunt Gillenormand.

As for the grandfather, they let him sleep on, thinking that he would hear about the matter
early enough in any case.

Marius was carried up to the first floor, without anyone in the other parts of the house being
aware of the fact, and deposited on an old sofa in M. Gillenormand's antechamber; and while
Basque went in search of a physician, and while Nicolette opened the linen-presses, Jean Valjean
felt Javert touch him on the shoulder. He understood and descended the stairs, having behind him
the step of Javert who was following him.

The porter watched them take their departure as he had watched their arrival, in terrified
somnolence.

They entered the carriage once more, and the coachman mounted his box.

"Inspector Javert," said Jean, "grant me yet another favor."

"What is it?" demanded Javert roughly.

"Let me go home for one instant. Then you shall do whatever you like with me."

Javert remained silent for a few moments, with his chin drawn back into the collar of his great-
coat, then he lowered the glass and front:

"Driver," said he, "Rue de l'Homme Armé, No. 7."

Chapter XI

CONCUSSION IN THE ABSOLUTE

THEY DID NOT OPEN THEIR LIPS AGAIN DURING THE WHOLE SPACE OF THEIR RIDE. What did Jean Valjean want? To finish what he had begun; to warn Cosette, to tell her where Marius was, to give her, possibly, some other useful information, to take, if he could, certain final measures. As for himself, so far as he was personally concerned, all was over; he had been seized by Javert and had not resisted; any other man than himself in like situation, would, perhaps, have had some vague thoughts connected with the rope which Thénardier had given him, and of the bars of the first cell that he should enter; but, let us impress it upon the reader, after the Bishop, there had existed in Jean Valjean a profound hesitation in the presence of any violence, even when directed against himself.

Suicide, that mysterious act of violence against the unknown, which may contain, in a measure, the death of the soul, was impossible to Jean Valjean.

At the entrance to the Rue de l'Homme Armé, the carriage halted, the way being too narrow to admit of the entrance of vehicles. Javert and Jean Valjean alighted.

The coachman humbly represented to "monsieur l'Inspecteur," that the Utrecht velvet of his carriage was all spotted with the blood of the assassinated man, and with mire from the assassin. That is the way he understood it. He added that an indemnity was due him. At the same time, drawing his certificate book from his pocket, he begged the inspector to have the goodness to write him "a bit of an attestation."

Javert thrust aside the book which the coachman held out to him, and said:

"How much do you want, including your time of waiting and the drive?"

"It comes to seven hours and a quarter," replied the man, "and my velvet was perfectly new. Eighty francs, Mr. Inspector."

Javert drew four napoleons from his pocket and dismissed the carriage.

Jean Valjean fancied that it was Javert's intention to conduct him on foot to the post of the Blancs-Manteaux or to the post of the Archives both of which are close at hand.

They entered the street. It was deserted as usual. Javert followed Jean Valjean. They reached No. 7. Jean Valjean knocked. The door opened.

"It is well," said Javert. "Go upstairs."

He added with a strange expression, and as though he were exerting an effort in speaking in this manner:

"I will wait for you here."

Jean Valjean looked at Javert. This mode of procedure was but little in accord with Javert's habits. However, he could not be greatly surprised that Javert should now have a sort of haughty confidence in him, the confidence of the cat which grants the mouse liberty to the length of its claws, seeing that Jean Valjean had made up his mind to surrender himself and to make an end of it. He pushed open the door, entered the house, called to the porter who was in bed and who had pulled the cord from his couch: "It is I!" and ascended the stairs.

On arriving at the first floor, he paused. All sorrowful roads have their stations. The window on the landing-place, which was a sash-window, was open. As in many ancient houses, the staircase got its light from without and had a view on the street. The street-lantern, situated directly opposite, cast some light on the stairs, and thus effected some economy in illumination.

Jean Valjean, either for the sake of getting the air, or mechanically, thrust his head out of this window. He leaned out over the street. It is short, and the lantern lighted it from end to end. Jean Valjean was overwhelmed with amazement; there was no longer anyone there.

Javert had taken his departure.

Chapter XII

THE GRANDFATHER

BASQUE AND THE PORTER HAD CARRIED MARIUS INTO THE DRAWING-ROOM, AS HE STILL LAY stretched out, motionless, on the sofa upon which he had been placed on his arrival. The doctor who had been sent for, had hastened thither. Aunt Gillenormand had risen.

Aunt Gillenormand went and came, in affright, wringing her hands and incapable of doing anything but saying: "Heavens! is it possible?" At times she added: "Everything will be covered with blood." When her first horror had passed off, a certain philosophy of the situation penetrated her mind, and took form in the exclamation: "It was bound to end in this way!" She did not go so far as: "I told you so!" which is customary on this sort of occasion. At the physician's orders, a camp bed had been prepared beside the sofa. The doctor examined Marius, and after having found that his pulse was still beating, that the wounded man had no very deep wound on his breast, and that the blood on the corners of his lips proceeded from his nostrils, he had him placed flat on the bed, without a pillow, with his head on the same level as his body, and even a trifle lower, and with his bust bare in order to facilitate respiration. Mademoiselle Gillenormand on perceiving that they were undressing Marius, withdrew. She set herself to telling her beads in her own chamber.

The trunk had not suffered any internal injury; a bullet, deadened by the pocket-book, had turned aside and made the tour of his ribs with a hideous laceration, which was of no great depth, and consequently, not dangerous. The long, underground journey had completed the dislocation of the broken collar-bone, and the disorder there was serious. The arms had been slashed with saber cuts. Not a single scar disfigured his face; but his head was fairly covered with cuts; what would be the result of these wounds on the head? Would they stop short at the hairy cuticle, or would they attack the brain? As yet, this could not be decided. A grave symptom was that they had caused a swoon, and that people do not always recover from such swoons. Moreover, the wounded man had been exhausted by hemorrhage. From the waist down, the barricade had protected the lower part of the body from injury.

Basque and Nicolette tore up linen and prepared bandages; Nicolette sewed them, Basque rolled them. As lint was lacking, the doctor, for the time being, arrested the bleeding with layers of wadding. Beside the bed, three candles burned on a table where the case of surgical instruments lay spread out. The doctor bathed Marius's face and hair with cold water. A full pail was reddened in an instant. The porter, candle in hand, lighted them.

The doctor seemed to be pondering sadly. From time to time, he made a negative sign with his head, as though replying to some question which he had inwardly addressed to himself.

A bad sign for the sick man are these mysterious dialogues of the doctor with himself.

At the moment when the doctor was wiping Marius's face, and lightly touching his still closed eyes with his finger, a door opened at the end of the drawing-room, and a long, pallid figure made its appearance.

This was the grandfather.

The revolt had, for the past two days, deeply agitated, enraged and engrossed the mind of M. Gillenormand. He had not been able to sleep on the previous night, and he had been in a fever all day long. In the evening, he had gone to bed very early, recommending that everything in the house should be well barred, and he had fallen into a doze through sheer fatigue.

Old men sleep lightly; M. Gillenormand's chamber adjoined the drawing-room, and in spite of all the precautions that had been taken, the noise had awakened him. Surprised at the rift of light which he saw under his door, he had risen from his bed, and had groped his way thither.

He stood astonished on the threshold, one hand on the handle of the half-open door, with his head bent a little forward and quivering, his body wrapped in a white dressing-gown, which was straight and as destitute of folds as a winding-sheet; and he had the air of a phantom who is gazing into a tomb.

He saw the bed, and on the mattress that young man, bleeding, white with a waxen whiteness, with closed eyes and gaping mouth, and pallid lips, stripped to the waist, slashed all over with crimson wounds, motionless and brilliantly lighted up.

The grandfather trembled from head to foot as powerfully as ossified limbs can tremble, his eyes, whose corneae were yellow on account of his great age, were veiled in a sort of vitreous glitter, his whole face assumed in an instant the earthy angles of a skull, his arms fell pendent, as though a spring had broken, and his amazement was betrayed by the outspreading of the fingers of his two aged hands, which quivered all over, his knees formed an angle in front, allowing, through the opening in his dressing-gown, a view of his poor bare legs, all bristling with white hairs, and he murmured:

"Marius!"

"Sir," said Basque, "Monsieur has just been brought back. He went to the barricade, and . . ."

"He is dead!" cried the old man in a terrible voice. "Ah! The rascal!"

Then a sort of sepulchral transformation straightened up this centenarian as erect as a young man.

"Sir," said he, "you are the doctor. Begin by telling me one thing. He is dead, is he not?"

The doctor, who was at the highest pitch of anxiety, remained silent.

M. Gillenormand wrung his hands with an outburst of terrible laughter.

"He is dead! He is dead! He is dead! He has got himself killed on the barricades! Out of hatred to me! He did that to spite me! Ah! You blood-drinker! This is the way he returns to me! Misery of my life, he is dead!"

He went to the window, threw it wide open as though he were stifling, and, erect before the darkness, he began to talk into the street, to the night:

"Pierced, sabered, exterminated, slashed, hacked in pieces! Just look at that, the villain! He knew well that I was waiting for him, and that I had had his room arranged, and that I had placed at the head of my bed his portrait taken when he was a little child! He knew well that he had only to come back, and that I had been recalling him for years, and that I remained by my fireside, with my hands on my knees, not knowing what to do, and that I was mad over it! You knew well, that you had but to return and to say: 'It is I,' and you would have been the master of the house, and that I should have obeyed you, and that you could have done whatever you pleased with your old num-skull of a grandfather! you knew that well, and you said:

" 'No, he is a royalist, I will not go!' And you went to the barricades, and you got yourself killed out of malice! To revenge yourself for what I said to you about Monsieur le Duc de Berry. It is infamous! Go to bed then and sleep tranquilly! he is dead, and this is my awakening."

The doctor, who was beginning to be uneasy in both quarters, quitted Marius for a moment, went to M. Gillenormand, and took his arm. The grandfather turned round, gazed at him with eyes which seemed exaggerated in size and bloodshot, and said to him calmly:

"I thank you, sir. I am composed, I am a man, I witnessed the death of Louis XVI, I know how to bear events. One thing is terrible and that is to think that it is your newspapers which do all the mischief. You will have scribblers, chatterers, lawyers, orators, tribunes, discussions, progress, enlightenment, the rights of man, the liberty of the press, and this is the way that your children will be brought home to you. Ah! Marius! It is abominable! Killed! Dead before me! A barricade! Ah, the scamp! Doctor, you live in this quarter, I believe? Oh! I know you well. I see your cabriolet pass my window. I am going to tell you. You are wrong to think that I am angry. One does not fly into a rage against a dead man. That would be stupid. This is a child whom I have reared. I was already old while he was very young. He played in the Tuileries garden with his little shovel and his little chair, and in order that the inspectors might not grumble, I stopped up the holes that he made in the earth with his shovel, with my cane. One day he exclaimed: Down with Louis XVIII! and off he went. It was no fault of mine. He was all rosy and blond. His mother is dead. Have you ever noticed that all little children are blond? Why is it so? He is the son of one of those brigands of the Loire, but children are innocent of their fathers' crimes. I remember when he was no higher than that. He could not manage to pronounce his Ds. He had a way of talking that was so sweet and indistinct that you would have thought it was a bird chirping. I remember that once, in front of the Hercules Farnese, people formed a circle to admire him and marvel at him, he was so handsome, was that child! He had a head such as you see in pictures. I talked in a deep voice, and I frightened him with my cane, but he knew very well that it was only to make him laugh. In the morning, when he entered my room, I grumbled, but he was like the sunlight to me, all the same. One cannot defend one's self against those brats. They take hold of you, they hold you fast, they never let you go again. The truth is, that there never was a cupid like that child. Now, what can you say for your Lafayettes, your Benjamin Constants, and your Tirecuir de Corcelles who have killed him? This cannot be allowed to pass in this fashion."

He approached Marius, who still lay livid and motionless, and to whom the physician had returned, and began once more to wring his hands. The old man's pallid lips moved as though mechanically, and permitted the passage of words that were barely audible, like breaths in the death-agony:

"Ah! heartless lad! Ah! clubbist! Ah! wretch! Ah! Septembrist!"

Reproaches in the low voice of an agonizing man, addressed to a corpse.

Little by little, as it is always indispensable that internal eruptions should come to the light, the sequence of words returned, but the grandfather appeared no longer to have the strength to utter them, his voice was so weak, and extinct, that it seemed to come from the other side of an abyss.

"It is all the same to me, I am going to die too, that I am. And to think that there is not a hussy in Paris who would not have been delighted to make this wretch happy! A scamp who, instead of amusing himself and enjoying life, went off to fight and get himself shot down like a brute! And for whom? Why? For the Republic! Instead of going to dance at the Chaumière, as it is the duty of young folks to do! What's the use of being twenty years old? The Republic, a cursed pretty folly! Poor mothers, beget fine boys, do! Come, he is dead. That will make two funerals under the same carriage gate. So you have got yourself arranged like this for the sake of General Lamarque's handsome eyes! What had that General Lamarque done to you? A slasher! A chatter-box! To get one's self killed for a dead man! If that isn't enough to drive anyone mad! Just think of it! At twenty! And without so much as turning his head to see whether he was not leaving something behind him! That's the way poor, good old fellows are forced to die alone nowadays. Perish in your corner, owl! Well, after all, so much the better, that is what I was hoping for, this will kill me on the spot. I am too old, I am a hundred years old, I am a hundred thousand years old, I ought, by rights, to have been dead long ago. This blow puts an end to it. So all is over, what happiness! What is the good of making him inhale ammonia and all that parcel of drugs? You are wasting your trouble, you fool of a doctor! Come, he's dead, completely dead. I know all about it, I am dead myself too. He hasn't done things by half. Yes, this age is infamous, infamous and that's what I think of you, of your ideas, of your systems, of your masters, of your oracles, of your doctors, of your scape-graces of writers, of your rascally philosophers, and of all the revolutions which, for the last sixty years, have been frightening the flocks of crows in the Tuileries! But you were pitiless in getting yourself killed like this, I shall not even grieve over your death, do you understand, you assassin?"

At that moment, Marius slowly opened his eyes, and his glance, still dimmed by lethargic wonder, rested on M. Gillenormand.

"Marius!" cried the old man. "Marius! My little Marius! my child! my well-beloved son! You open your eyes, you gaze upon me, you are alive, thanks!"

And he fell fainting.

BOOK FOURTH

JAVERT DERAILED

Chapter I

JAVERT PASSED SLOWLY DOWN THE RUE DE L'HOMME ARMÉ.
He walked with drooping head for the first time in his life, and likewise, for the first time in his life, with his hands behind his back.

Up to that day, Javert had borrowed from Napoleon's attitudes, only that which is expressive of resolution, with arms folded across the chest; that which is expressive of uncertainty—with the hands behind the back—had been unknown to him. Now, a change had taken place; his whole person, slow and somber, was stamped with anxiety.

He plunged into the silent streets.

Nevertheless, he followed one given direction.

He took the shortest cut to the Seine, reached the Quai des Ormes, skirted the quay, passed the Grève, and halted at some distance from the post of the Place du Châtelet, at the angle of the Pont Notre-Dame. There, between the Notre-Dame and the Pont au Change on the one hand, and the Quai de la Mégisserie and the Quai aux Fleurs on the other, the Seine forms a sort of square lake, traversed by a rapid.

This point of the Seine is dreaded by mariners. Nothing is more dangerous than this rapid, hemmed in, at that epoch, and irritated by the piles of the mill on the bridge, now demolished. The two bridges, situated thus close together, augment the peril; the water hurries in formidable wise through the arches. It rolls in vast and terrible waves; it accumulates and piles up there; the flood attacks the piles of the bridges as though in an effort to pluck them up with great liquid ropes. Men who fall in there never reappear; the best of swimmers are drowned there.

Javert leaned both elbows on the parapet, his chin resting in both hands, and, while his nails were mechanically twined in the abundance of his whiskers, he meditated.

A novelty, a revolution, a catastrophe had just taken place in the depths of his being; and he had something upon which to examine himself.

Javert was undergoing horrible suffering.

For several hours, Javert had ceased to be simple. He was troubled; that brain, so limpid in its blindness, had lost its transparency; that crystal was clouded. Javert felt duty divided within his conscience, and he could not conceal the fact from himself. When he had so unexpectedly encountered Jean Valjean on the banks of the Seine, there had been in him something of the wolf which regains his grip on his prey, and of the dog who finds his master again.

He beheld before him two paths, both equally straight, but he beheld two; and that terrified him; him, who had never in all his life known more than one straight line. And, the poignant anguish lay in this, that the two paths were contrary to each other. One of these straight lines excluded the other. Which of the two was the true one?

His situation was indescribable.

To owe his life to a malefactor, to accept that debt and to repay it; to be, in spite of himself, on a level with a fugitive from justice, and to repay his service with another service; to allow it to be said to him, "Go," and to say to the latter in his turn: "Be free"; to sacrifice to personal motives duty, that general obligation, and to be conscious, in those personal motives, of something that was also general, and, perchance, superior, to betray society in order to remain true to his conscience; that all these absurdities should be realized and should accumulate upon him—this was what overwhelmed him.

One thing had amazed him—this was that Jean Valjean should have done him a favor, and one thing petrified him—that he, Javert, should have done Jean Valjean a favor.

Where did he stand? He sought to comprehend his position, and could no longer find his bearings.

What was he to do now? To deliver up Jean Valjean was bad; to leave Jean Valjean at liberty was bad. In the first case, the man of authority fell lower than the man of the galleys, in the second, a convict rose above the law, and set his foot upon it. In both cases, dishonor for him, Javert. There was disgrace in any resolution at which he might arrive. Destiny has some extremities which rise perpendicularly from the impossible, and beyond which life is no longer anything but a precipice. Javert had reached one of those extremities.

One of his anxieties consisted in being constrained to think. The very violence of all these conflicting emotions forced him to it. Thought, was something to which he was unused, and which was peculiarly painful.

In thought there always exists a certain amount of internal rebellion; and it irritated him to have that within him.

Thought on any subject whatever, outside of the restricted circle of his functions, would have been for him in any case useless and a fatigue; thought on the day which had just passed, was a torture. Nevertheless, it was indispensable that he should take a look into his conscience, after such shocks, and render to himself an account of himself.

What he had just done made him shudder. He, Javert, had seen fit to decide, contrary to all the regulations of the police, contrary to the whole social and judicial organization, contrary to the entire code, upon a release; this had suited him; he had substituted his own affairs for the affairs of the public; was not this unjustifiable? Every time that he brought himself face to face with this deed without a name which he had committed, he trembled from head to foot. Upon what should he decide? One sole resource remained to him; to return in all haste to the Rue de l'Homme Armé, and commit Jean Valjean to prison. It was clear that that was what he ought to do. He could not.

Something barred his way in that direction.

Something? What? Is there in the world, anything outside of the tribunals, executory sentences, the police and the authorities? Javert was overwhelmed.

A galley-slave sacred! A convict who could not be touched by the law! And that the deed of Javert!

Was it not a fearful thing that Javert and Jean Valjean, the man made to proceed with rigor, the man made to submit—that these two men who were both the things of the law, should have come to such a pass, that both of them had set themselves above the law? What then! such enormities were to happen and no one was to be punished! Jean Valjean, stronger than the whole social order, was to remain at liberty, and he, Javert, was to go on eating the government's bread!

His reverie gradually became terrible.

He might, athwart this reverie, have also reproached himself on the subject of that insurgent who had been taken to the Rue des Filles-du-Calvaire; but he never even thought of that. The lesser fault was lost in the greater. Besides, that insurgent was, obviously, a dead man, and, legally, death puts an end to pursuit.

Jean Valjean was the load which weighed upon his spirit.

Jean Valjean disconcerted him. All the axioms which had served him as points of support all his life long, had crumbled away in the presence of this man. Jean Valjean's generosity toward him, Javert, crushed him. Other facts which he now recalled, and which he had formerly treated as lies and folly, now recurred to him as realities. M. Madeleine reappeared behind Jean Valjean, and the two figures were superposed in such fashion that they now formed but one, which was venerable. Javert felt that something terrible was penetrating his soul—admiration for a convict. Respect for a galley-slave—is that a possible thing? He shuddered at it, yet could not escape from it. In vain did he struggle, he was reduced to confess, in his inmost heart, the sublimity of that wretch. This was odious.

A benevolent malefactor, merciful, gentle, helpful, clement, a convict, returning good for evil, giving back pardon for hatred, preferring pity to vengeance, preferring to ruin himself rather than to ruin his enemy, saving him who had smitten him, kneeling on the heights of virtue, more nearly akin to an angel than to a man. Javert was constrained to admit to himself that this monster existed.

Things could not go on in this manner.

Certainly, and we insist upon this point, he had not yielded without resistance to that monster, to that infamous angel, to that hideous hero, who enraged almost as much as he amazed him. Twenty times, as he sat in that carriage face to face with Jean Valjean, the legal tiger had roared within him. A score of times he had been tempted to fling himself upon Jean Valjean, to seize him and devour him, that is to say, to arrest him. What more simple, in fact? To cry out at the first post that they passed: "Here is a fugitive from justice, who has broken his ban!" to summon the gendarmes and say to them: "This man is yours!" then to go off, leaving that condemned man there, to ignore the rest and not to meddle further in the matter. This man is forever a prisoner of the law; the law may do with him what it will. What could be more just? Javert had said all this to himself; he had wished to pass beyond, to act, to apprehend the man, and then, as at present, he had not been able to do it; and every time that his arm had been raised convulsively toward Jean Valjean's collar, his hand had fallen back again, as beneath an enormous weight, and in the depths of his thought he had heard a voice, a strange voice crying to him: "It is well. Deliver up your savior. Then have the basin of Pontius Pilate brought and wash your claws."

Then his reflections reverted to himself and beside Jean Valjean glorified he beheld himself, Javert, degraded.

A convict was his benefactor!

But then, why had he permitted that man to leave him alive? He had the right to be killed in that barricade. He should have asserted that right. It would have been better to summon the other insurgents to his succor against Jean Valjean, to get himself shot by force.

His supreme anguish was the loss of certainty. He felt that he had been uprooted. The code was no longer anything more than a stump in his hand. He had to deal with scruples of an unknown species. There had taken place within him a sentimental revelation entirely distinct from legal affirmation, his only standard of measurement hitherto. To remain in his former uprightness did not suffice. A whole order of unexpected facts had cropped up and subjugated him. A whole new world was dawning on his soul: kindness accepted and repaid, devotion, mercy, indulgence, violences committed by pity on austerity, respect for persons, no more definitive condemnation, no more conviction, the possibility of a tear in the eye of the law, no one knows what justice according to God, running in inverse sense to justice according to men. He perceived amid the shadows the terrible rising of an unknown moral sun; it horrified and dazzled him. An owl forced to the gaze of an eagle.

He said to himself that it was true that there were exceptional cases, that authority might be put out of countenance, that the rule might be inadequate in the presence of a fact, that everything could not be framed within the text of the code, that the unforeseen compelled obedience, that the virtue of a convict might set a snare for the virtue of the functionary, that destiny did indulge in such ambushes, and he reflected with despair that he himself had not even been fortified against a surprise.

He was forced to acknowledge that goodness did exist. This convict had been good. And he himself, unprecedented circumstance, had just been good also. So he was becoming depraved.

He found that he was a coward. He conceived a horror of himself.

Javert's ideal, was not to be human, to be grand, to be sublime; it was to be irreproachable. Now, he had just failed in this.

How had he come to such a pass? How had all this happened? He could not have told himself. He clasped his head in both hands, but in spite of all that he could do, he could not contrive to explain it to himself.

He had certainly always entertained the intention of restoring Jean Valjean to the law of which Jean Valjean was the captive, and of which he, Javert, was the slave. Not for a single instant while he held him in his grasp had he confessed to himself that he entertained the idea of releasing him. It was, in some sort, without his consciousness, that his hand had relaxed and had let him go free.

All sorts of interrogation points flashed before his eyes. He put questions to himself, and made replies to himself, and his replies frightened him. He asked himself: "What has that convict done, that desperate fellow, whom I have pursued even to persecution, and who has had me under his foot, and who could have avenged himself, and who owed it both to his rancor and to his safety, in leaving me my life, in showing mercy upon me? His duty? No. Something more. And I in showing mercy upon him in my turn—what have I done? My duty? No. Something more. So there is something beyond duty?" Here he took fright; his balance became disjointed; one of the scales fell into the abyss, the other rose heavenward, and Javert was no less terrified by the one which was on high than by the one which was below. Without being in the least in the world what is called Voltairian or a philosopher, or incredulous, being, on the contrary, respectful by instinct, toward the established church, he knew it only as an august fragment of the social whole; order was his dogma, and sufficed for him; ever since he had attained to man's estate and the rank of a functionary, he had centered nearly all his religion in the police. Being—and here we employ words without the least irony and in their most serious acceptation, being, as we have said, a spy as other men are priests. He had a superior, M. Gisquet; up to that day he had never dreamed of that other superior, God.

This new chief, God, he became unexpectedly conscious of, and he felt embarrassed by him. This unforeseen presence threw him off his bearings; he did not know what to do with this superior, he, who was not ignorant of the fact that the subordinate is bound always to bow, that he must not disobey, nor find fault, nor discuss, and that, in the presence of a superior who amazes him too greatly, the inferior has no other resource than that of handing in his resignation.

But how was he to set about handing in his resignation to God?

However things might stand—and it was to this point that he reverted constantly—one fact dominated everything else for him, and that was, that he had just committed a terrible infraction of the law. He had just shut his eyes on an escaped convict who had broken his ban. He had just set a galley-slave at large. He had just robbed the laws of a man who belonged to them. That was what he had done. He no longer understood himself. The very reasons for his action escaped him; only their vertigo was left with him. Up to that moment he had lived with that blind faith which gloomy probity engenders. This faith had quitted him, this probity had deserted him. All that he had believed in melted away. Truths which he did not wish to recognize were besieging him, inexorably. Henceforth, he must be a different man. He was suffering from the strange pains of a conscience abruptly operated on for the cataract. He saw that which it was repugnant to him to behold. He felt himself emptied, useless, put out of joint with his past life, turned out, dissolved. Authority was dead within him. He had no longer any reason for existing.

A terrible situation! to be touched.

To be granite and to doubt! to be the statue of Chastisement cast in one piece in the mold of the law, and suddenly to become aware of the fact that one cherishes beneath one's breast of bronze something absurd and disobedient which almost resembles a heart! To come to the pass of returning good for good, although one has said to one's self up to that day that that good is evil! to be the watch-dog, and to lick the intruder's hand! to be ice and melt! to be the pincers and to turn into a hand! to suddenly feel one's fingers opening! to relax one's grip—what a terrible thing!

The man-projectile no longer acquainted with his route and retreating!

To be obliged to confess this to one's self: infallibility is not infallible, there may exist error in the dogma, all has not been said when a code speaks, society is not perfect, authority is complicated with vacillation, a crack is possible in the immutable, judges are but men, the law may err, tribunals may make a mistake! to behold a rift in the immense blue pane of the firmament!

That which was passing in Javert was the Fampoux of a rectilinear conscience, the derailment of a soul, the crushing of a probity which had been irresistibly launched in a straight line and was breaking against God. It certainly was singular that the stoker of order, that the engineer of authority, mounted on the blind iron horse with its rigid road, could be unseated by a flash of light! that the immovable, the direct, the correct, the geometrical, the passive, the perfect could bend! that there should exist for the locomotive a road to Damascus!

God, always within man, and refractory, He, the true conscience, to the false; a prohibition to the spark to die out; an order to the ray to remember the sun; an injunction to the soul to recognize the veritable absolute when confronted with the fictitious absolute, humanity which cannot be lost; the human heart indestructible; that splendid phenomenon, the finest, perhaps, of all our interior marvels, did Javert understand this? Did Javert penetrate it? Did Javert account for it to himself? Evidently he did not. But beneath the pressure of that incontestable incomprehensibility he felt his brain bursting.

He was less the man transfigured than the victim of this prodigy. In all this he perceived only the tremendous difficulty of existence. It seemed to him that, henceforth, his respiration was repressed forever. He was not accustomed to having something unknown hanging over his head.

Up to this point, everything above him had been, to his gaze, merely a smooth, limpid and simple surface; there was nothing incomprehensible, nothing obscure; nothing that was not defined, regularly disposed, linked, precise, circumscribed, exact, limited, closed, fully provided for; authority was a plane surface; there was no fall in it, no dizziness in its presence. Javert had never beheld the unknown except from below. The irregular, the unforeseen, the disordered opening of chaos, the possible slip over a precipice—this was the work of the lower regions, of rebels, of the wicked, of wretches. Now Javert threw himself back, and he was suddenly terrified by this unprecedented apparition: a gulf on high.

What! one was dismantled from top to bottom! one was disconcerted, absolutely! In what could one trust! That which had been agreed upon was giving way! What! the defect in society's armor could be discovered by a magnanimous wretch! What! an honest servitor of the law could suddenly find himself caught between two crimes—the crime of allowing a man to escape and the crime of arresting him! everything was not settled in the orders given by the State to the functionary! There might be blind-alleys in duty! What—all this was real! was it true that an ex-ruffian, weighed down with convictions, could rise erect and end by being in the right? Was this credible? were there cases in which the law should retire before transfigured crime, and stammer its excuses?—Yes, that was the state of the case! and Javert saw it! and Javert had touched it! and not only could he not deny it, but he had taken part in it. These were realities. It was abominable that actual facts could reach such deformity. If facts did their duty, they would confine themselves to being proofs of the law; facts—it is God who sends them. Was anarchy then, on the point of now descending from on high?

Thus—and in the exaggeration of anguish, and the optical illusion of consternation, all that might have corrected and restrained this impression was effaced, and society, and the human race, and the universe were, henceforth, summed up in his eyes, in one simple and terrible feature—thus the penal laws, the thing judged, the force due to legislation, the decrees of the sovereign courts, the magistracy, the government, prevention, repression, official cruelty, wisdom, legal infallibility, the principle of authority, all the dogmas on which rest political and civil security, sovereignty, justice, public truth, all this was rubbish, a shapeless mass, chaos; he himself, Javert, the spy of order, incorruptibility in the service of the police, the bull-dog providence of society, vanquished and hurled to earth; and, erect, at the summit of all that ruin, a man with a green cap on his head and a halo round his brow; this was the astounding confusion to which he had come; this was the fearful vision which he bore within his soul.

Was this to be endured? No.

A violent state, if ever such existed. There were only two ways of escaping from it. One was to go resolutely to Jean Valjean, and restore to his cell the convict from the galleys. The other . . .

Javert quitted the parapet, and, with head erect this time, betook himself, with a firm tread, toward the station-house indicated by a lantern at one of the corners of the Place du Châtelet.

On arriving there, he saw through the window a sergeant of police, and he entered. Policemen recognize each other by the very way in which they open the door of a station-house. Javert mentioned his name, showed his card to the sergeant, and seated himself at the table of the post on which a candle was burning. On a table lay a pen, a leaden inkstand and paper, provided in the event of possible reports and the orders of the night patrols. This table, still completed by its straw-seated chair, is an institution; it exists in all police stations; it is invariably ornamented with a box-wood saucer filled with sawdust and a wafer-box of cardboard filled with red wafers, and it forms the lowest stage of official style. It is there that the literature of the State has its beginning.

Javert took a pen and a sheet of paper, and began to write. This is what he wrote:

A FEW OBSERVATIONS FOR THE GOOD OF THE SERVICE

In the first place: I beg Monsieur le Préfet to cast his eyes on this.

Secondly: prisoners, on arriving after examination, take off their shoes and stand barefoot on the flag-stones while they are being searched. Many of them cough on their return to prison. This entails hospital expenses.

Thirdly: the mode of keeping track of a man with relays of police agents from distance to distance, is good, but, on important occasions, it is requisite that at least two agents should never lose sight of each other, so that, in case one agent should, for any cause, grow weak in his service, the other may supervise him and take his place.

Fourthly: it is inexplicable why the special regulation of the prison of the Madelonettes interdicts the prisoner from having a chair, even by paying for it.

Fifthly: in the Madelonettes there are only two bars to the canteen, so that the canteen woman can touch the prisoners with her hand.

Sixthly: the prisoners called barkers, who summon the other prisoners to the parlor, force the prisoner to pay them two sous to call his name distinctly. This is a theft.

Seventhly: for a broken thread ten sous are withheld in the weaving shop; this is an abuse of the contractor, since the cloth is none the worse for it.

Eighthly: it is annoying for visitors to La Force to be obliged to traverse the boys' court in order to reach the parlor of Sainte-Marie-l'Égyptienne.

Ninthly: it is a fact that any day gendarmes can be overheard relating in the courtyard of the prefecture the interrogations put by the magistrates to prisoners. For a gendarme, who should be sworn to secrecy, to repeat what he has heard in the examination room is a grave disorder.

Tenthly: Mme. Henry is an honest woman; her canteen is very neat; but it is bad to have a woman keep the wicket to the mouse-trap of the secret cells. This is unworthy of the Conciergerie of a great civilization.

Javert wrote these lines in his calmest and most correct chirography, not omitting a single comma, and making the paper screech under his pen. Below the last line he signed:

JAVERT,
Inspector of the 1st class.

The Post of the Place du Châtelet.
June 7th, 1832, about one o'clock in the morning

Javert dried the fresh ink on the paper, folded it like a letter, sealed it, wrote on the back: *Note for the administration*, left it on the table, and quitted the post. The glazed and grated door fell to behind him.

Again he traversed the Place du Châtelet diagonally, regained the quay, and returned with automatic precision to the very point which he had abandoned a quarter of an hour previously, leaned on his elbows and found himself again in the same attitude on the same paving-stone of the parapet. He did not appear to have stirred.

The darkness was complete. It was the sepulchral moment which follows midnight. A ceiling of clouds concealed the stars. Not a single light burned in the houses of the city; no one was passing; all of the streets and quays which could be seen were deserted; Notre-Dame and the towers of the Court-House seemed features of the night. A street-lantern reddened the margin of the quay. The outlines of the bridges lay shapeless in the mist one behind the other. Recent rains had swollen the river.

The spot where Javert was leaning was, it will be remembered, situated precisely over the rapids of the Seine, perpendicularly above that formidable spiral of whirlpools which loose and knot themselves again like an endless screw.

Javert bent his head and gazed. All was black. Nothing was to be distinguished. A sound of foam was audible; but the river could not be seen. At moments, in that dizzy depth, a gleam of light appeared, and undulated vaguely, water possessing the power of taking light no one knows whence, and converting it into a snake. The light vanished, and all became indistinct once more. Immensity seemed thrown open there. What lay below was not water, it was a gulf. The wall of the quay, abrupt, confused, mingled with the vapors, instantly concealed from sight, produced the effect of an escarpment of the infinite. Nothing was to be seen, but the hostile chill of the water and the stale odor of the wet stones could be felt. A fierce breath rose from this abyss. The flood in the river, divined rather than perceived, the tragic whispering of the waves, the melancholy vastness of the arches of the bridge, the imaginable fall into that gloomy void, into all that shadow was full of horror.

Javert remained motionless for several minutes, gazing at this opening of shadow; he considered the invisible with a fixity that resembled attention. The water roared. All at once he took off his hat and placed it on the edge of the quay. A moment later, a tall black figure, which a belated passer-by in the distance might have taken for a phantom, appeared erect upon the parapet of the quay, bent over toward the Seine, then drew itself up again, and fell straight down into the shadows; a dull splash followed; and the shadow alone was in the secret of the convulsions of that obscure form which had disappeared beneath the water.

BOOK FIFTH

GRANDSON AND GRANDFATHER

Chapter I

IN WHICH THE TREE WITH THE ZINC PLASTER APPEARS AGAIN

SOME TIME AFTER THE EVENTS WHICH WE HAVE JUST RECORDED, SIEUR BOULATRUELLE EXPERI-enced a lively emotion.

Sieur Boulatruelle was that road-mender of Montfermeil whom the reader has already seen in the gloomy parts of this book.

Boulatruelle, as the reader may, perchance, recall, was a man who was occupied with divers and troublesome matters. He broke stones and damaged travelers on the highway.

Road-mender and thief as he was, he cherished one dream; he believed in the treasures buried in the forest of Montfermeil. He hoped someday to find the money in the earth at the foot of a tree; in the meanwhile, he lived to search the pockets of passers-by.

Nevertheless, for an instant, he was prudent. He had just escaped neatly. He had been, as the reader is aware, picked up in Jondrette's garret in company with the other ruffians. Utility of a vice: his drunkenness had been his salvation. The authorities had never been able to make out whether he had been there in the quality of a robber or a man who had been robbed. An order of *nolle prosequi*, founded on his well authenticated state of intoxication on the evening of the ambush, had set him at liberty. He had taken to his heels. He had returned to his road from Gagny to Lagny, to make, under administrative supervision, broken stone for the good of the state, with downcast mien, in a very pensive mood, his ardor for theft somewhat cooled; but he was addicted none the less tenderly to the wine which had recently saved him.

As for the lively emotion which he had experienced a short time after his return to his road-mender's turf-thatched cot, here it is:

One morning, Boulatruelle, while on his way as was his wont, to his work, and possibly also to his ambush, a little before daybreak, caught sight, through the branches of the trees, of a man, whose back alone he saw, but the shape of whose shoulders, as it seemed to him at that distance and in the early dusk, was not entirely unfamiliar to him. Boulatruelle, although intoxicated, had a correct and lucid memory, a defensive arm that is indispensable to anyone who is at all in conflict with legal order.

"Where the deuce have I seen something like that man yonder?" he said to himself. But he could make himself no answer, except that the man resembled someone of whom his memory preserved a confused trace.

However, apart from the identity which he could not manage to catch, Boulatruelle put things together and made calculations. This man did not belong in the countryside. He had just arrived there. On foot, evidently. No public conveyance passes through Montfermeil at that hour. He had walked all night. Whence came he? Not from a very great distance; for he had neither haversack, nor bundle. From Paris, no doubt. Why was he in these woods? why was he there at such an hour? what had he come there for?

Boulatruelle thought of the treasure. By dint of ransacking his memory, he recalled in a vague way that he had already, many years before, had a similar alarm in connection with a man who produced on him the effect that he might well be this very individual.

"By the deuce," said Boulatruelle, "I'll find him again. I'll discover the parish of that parishioner. This prowler of Patron-Minette has a reason, and I'll know it. People can't have secrets in my forest if I don't have a finger in the pie."

He took his pickax which was very sharply pointed.

"There now," he grumbled, "is something that will search the earth and a man."

And, as one knots one thread to another thread, he took up the line of march at his best pace in the direction which the man must follow, and set out across the thickets.

When he had compassed a hundred strides, the day, which was already beginning to break, came to his assistance. Footprints stamped in the sand, weeds trodden down here and there, heather crushed, young branches in the brushwood bent and in the act of straightening themselves up again with the graceful deliberation of the arms of a pretty woman who stretches herself when she wakes, pointed out to him a sort of track. He followed it, then lost it. Time was flying. He plunged deeper into the woods and came to a sort of eminence. An early huntsman who was passing in the distance along a path, whistling the air of Guillery, suggested to him the idea of climbing a tree. Old as he was, he was agile. There stood close at hand a beech-tree of great size, worthy of Tityrus and of Boulatruelle. Boulatruelle ascended the beech as high as he was able.

The idea was a good one. On scrutinizing the solitary waste on the side where the forest is thoroughly entangled and wild, Boulatruelle suddenly caught sight of his man.

Hardly had he got his eye upon him when he lost sight of him.

The man entered, or rather, glided into, an open glade, at a considerable distance, masked by large trees, but with which Boulatruelle was perfectly familiar, on account of having noticed, near a large pile of porous stones, an ailing chestnut-tree bandaged with a sheet of zinc nailed directly upon the bark. This glade was the one which was formerly called the Blaru-bottom. The heap of stones, destined for no one knows what employment, which was visible there thirty years ago, is doubtless still there. Nothing equals a heap of stones in longevity, unless it is a board fence. They are temporary expedients. What a reason for lasting!

Boulatruelle, with the rapidity of joy, dropped rather than descended from the tree. The lair was unearthed, the question now was to seize the beast. That famous treasure of his dreams was probably there.

It was no small matter to reach that glade. By the beaten paths, which indulge in a thousand teasing zigzags, it required a good quarter of an hour. In a bee-line, through the underbrush, which is peculiarly dense, very thorny, and very aggressive in that locality, a full half hour was necessary. Boulatruelle committed the error of not comprehending this. He believed in the straight line; a respectable optical illusion which ruins many a man. The thicket, bristling as it was, struck him as the best road.

"Let's take to the wolves' Rue de Rivoli," said he.

Boulatruelle, accustomed to taking crooked courses, was on this occasion guilty of the fault of going straight.

He flung himself resolutely into the tangle of undergrowth.

He had to deal with holly bushes, nettles, hawthorns, eglantines, thistles, and very irascible brambles. He was much lacerated.

At the bottom of the ravine he found water which he was obliged to traverse.

At last he reached the Blaru-bottom, after the lapse of forty minutes, sweating, soaked, breathless, scratched, and ferocious.

There was no one in the glade. Boulatruelle rushed to the heap of stones. It was in its place. It had not been carried off.

As for the man, he had vanished in the forest. He had made his escape. Where? in what direction? into what thicket? Impossible to guess.

And, heartrending to say, there, behind the pile of stones, in front of the tree with the sheet of zinc, was freshly turned earth, a pickax, abandoned or forgotten, and a hole.

The hole was empty.

"Thief!" shrieked Boulatruelle, shaking his fists at the horizon.

Chapter II

MARIUS, EMERGING FROM CIVIL WAR, MAKES READY FOR DOMESTIC WAR

FOR A LONG TIME, MARIUS WAS NEITHER DEAD NOR ALIVE. FOR MANY WEEKS HE LAY IN A FEVER accompanied by delirium, and by tolerably grave cerebral symptoms, caused more by the shocks of the wounds on the head than by the wounds themselves.

He repeated Cosette's name for whole nights in the melancholy loquacity of fever, and with the somber obstinacy of agony. The extent of some of the lesions presented a serious danger, the suppuration of large wounds being always liable to become reabsorbed, and consequently, to kill the sick man, under certain atmospheric conditions; at every change of weather, at the slightest storm, the physician was uneasy.

"Above all things," he repeated, "let the wounded man be subjected to no emotion." The dressing of the wounds was complicated and difficult, the fixation of apparatus and bandages by cerecloths not having been invented as yet, at that epoch. Nicolette used up a sheet "as big as the ceiling" as she put it, for lint. It was not without difficulty that the chloruretted lotions and the nitrate of silver overcame the gangrene. As long as there was any danger, M. Gillenormand, seated in despair at his grandson's pillow, was, like Marius, neither alive nor dead.

Every day, sometimes twice a day, a very well-dressed gentleman with white hair—such was the description given by the porter—came to inquire about the wounded man, and left a large package of lint for the dressings.

Finally, on the 7th of September, four months to a day, after the sorrowful night when he had been brought back to his grandfather in a dying condition, the doctor declared that he would answer for Marius. Convalescence began. But Marius was forced to remain for two months more stretched out on a long chair, on account of the results called up by the fracture of his collar-bone. There always is a last wound like that which will not close, and which prolongs the dressings indefinitely, to the great annoyance of the sick person.

However, this long illness and this long convalescence saved him from all pursuit. In France, there is no wrath, not even of a public character, which six months will not extinguish. Revolts, in the present state of society, are so much the fault of everyone, that they are followed by a certain necessity of shutting the eyes.

Let us add, that the inexcusable Gisquet order, which enjoined doctors to lodge information against the wounded, having outraged public opinion, and not opinion alone, but the King first of all, the wounded were covered and protected by this indignation; and, with the exception of those who had been made prisoners in the very act of combat, the councils of war did not dare to trouble anyone. So Marius was left in peace.

M. Gillenormand first passed through all manner of anguish, and then through every form of ecstasy. It was found difficult to prevent his passing every night beside the wounded man; he had his big arm-chair carried to Marius's bedside; he required his daughter to take the finest linen in the house for compresses and bandages. Mademoiselle Gillenormand, like a sage and elderly person, contrived to spare the fine linen, while allowing the grandfather to think that he was obeyed. M. Gillenormand would not permit anyone to explain to him, that for the preparation of lint batiste is not nearly so good as coarse linen, nor new linen as old linen. He was present at all the dressings of the wounds from which Mademoiselle Gillenormand modestly absented herself. When the dead flesh was cut away with scissors, he said: "Aïe! aïe!" Nothing was more touching than to see him with his gentle, senile palsy, offer the wounded man a cup of his cooling-draft. He overwhelmed the doctor with questions. He did not observe that he asked the same ones over and over again.

On the day when the doctor announced to him that Marius was out of danger, the good man was in a delirium. He made his porter a present of three louis. That evening, on his return to his own chamber, he danced a gavotte, using his thumb and forefinger as castanets, and he sang the following song:

"*Jeanne est née à Fougère,*   "*Amour, tu vis en elle;*
Vrai nid d'une bergère;   *Car c'est dans sa prunelle*
J'adore son jupon,   *Que tu mets ton carquois.*
Fripon.   *Narquois!*

"*Moi, je la chante, et j'aime,*
Plus que Diane même,
Jeanne et ses durs tetons
Bretons."[1]

Then he knelt upon a chair, and Basque, who was watching him through the half-open door, made sure that he was praying.

Up to that time, he had not believed in God.

At each succeeding phase of improvement, which became more and more pronounced, the grandfather raved. He executed a multitude of mechanical actions full of joy; he ascended and descended the stairs, without knowing why. A pretty female neighbor was amazed one morning at receiving a big bouquet; it was M. Gillenormand who had sent it to her. The husband made a jealous scene. M. Gillenormand tried to draw Nicolette upon his knees. He called Marius, "M. le Baron." He shouted: "Long live the Republic!"

Every moment, he kept asking, the doctor: "Is he no longer in danger?" He gazed upon Marius with the eyes of a grandmother. He brooded over him while he ate. He no longer knew himself, he no longer rendered himself an account of himself. Marius was the master of the house, there was abdication in his joy, he was the grandson of his grandson.

In the state of joy in which he then was, he was the most venerable of children. In his fear lest he might fatigue or annoy the convalescent, he stepped behind him to smile. He was content, joyous, delighted, charming, young. His white locks added a gentle majesty to the gay radiance of his visage. When grace is mingled with wrinkles, it is adorable. There is an indescribable aurora in beaming old age.

1. "Jeanne was born at Fougère, a true shepherd's nest; I adore her petticoat, the rogue.
 "Love, thou dwellest in her; For 'tis in her eyes that thou placest thy quiver, sly scamp!
 "As for me, I sing to her, and I love, more than Diana herself, Jeanne and her firm Breton breasts."

As for Marius, as he allowed them to dress his wounds and care for him, he had but one fixed idea: Cosette.

After the fever and delirium had left him, he did not again pronounce her name, and it might have been supposed that he no longer thought of her. He held his peace, precisely because his soul was there.

He did not know what had become of Cosette; the whole affair of the Rue de la Chanvrerie was like a cloud in his memory; shadows that were almost indistinct, floated through his mind, Éponine, Gavroche, Mabeuf, the Thénardiers, all his friends gloomily intermingled with the smoke of the barricade; the strange passage of M. Fauchelevent through that adventure produced on him the effect of a puzzle in a tempest; he understood nothing connected with his own life, he did not know how nor by whom he had been saved, and no one of those around him knew this; all that they had been able to tell him was, that he had been brought home at night in a hackney-coach, to the Rue des Filles-du-Calvaire; past, present, future were nothing more to him than the mist of a vague idea; but in that fog there was one immovable point, one clear and precise outline, something made of granite, a resolution, a will; to find Cosette once more. For him, the idea of life was not distinct from the idea of Cosette. He had decreed in his heart that he would not accept the one without the other, and he was immovably resolved to exact of any person whatever, who should desire to force him to live—from his grandfather, from fate, from hell—the restitution of his vanished Eden.

He did not conceal from himself the fact that obstacles existed.

Let us here emphasize one detail, he was not won over and was but little softened by all the solicitude and tenderness of his grandfather. In the first place, he was not in the secret; then, in his reveries of an invalid, which were still feverish, possibly, he distrusted this tenderness as a strange and novel thing, which had for its object his conquest. He remained cold. The grandfather absolutely wasted his poor old smile. Marius said to himself that it was all right so long as he, Marius, did not speak, and let things take their course; but that when it became a question of Cosette, he would find another face, and that his grandfather's true attitude would be unmasked. Then there would be an unpleasant scene; a recrudescence of family questions, a confrontation of positions, every sort of sarcasm and all manner of objections at one and the same time, Fauchelevent, Coupelevent, fortune, poverty, a stone about his neck, the future. Violent resistance; conclusion: a refusal. Marius stiffened himself in advance.

And then, in proportion as he regained life, the old ulcers of his memory opened once more, he reflected again on the past, Colonel Pontmercy placed himself once more between M. Gillenormand and him, Marius, he told himself that he had no true kindness to expect from a person who had been so unjust and so hard to his father. And with health, there returned to him a sort of harshness towards his grandfather. The old man was gently pained by this. M. Gillenormand, without however allowing it to appear, observed that Marius, ever since the latter had been brought back to him and had regained consciousness, had not once called him father. It is true that he did not say "monsieur" to him; but he contrived not to say either the one or the other, by means of a certain way of turning his phrases. Obviously, a crisis was approaching.

As almost always happens in such cases, Marius skirmished before giving battle, by way of proving himself. This is called "feeling the ground." One morning it came to pass that M. Gillenormand spoke slightingly of the Convention, àpropos of a newspaper which had fallen into his hands, and gave vent to a royalist harangue on Danton, Saint-Juste and Robespierre.—"The men of '93 were giants," said Marius with severity. The old man held his peace, and uttered not a sound during the remainder of that day.

Marius, who had always present to his mind the inflexible grandfather of his early years, interpreted this silence as a profound concentration of wrath, augured from it a hot conflict, and augmented his preparations for the fray in the inmost recesses of his mind.

He decided that, in case of a refusal, he would tear off his bandages, dislocate his collar-bone, that he would lay bare all the wounds which he had left, and would reject all food. His wounds were his munitions of war. He would have Cosette or die.

He awaited the propitious moment with the crafty patience of the sick.

That moment arrived.

Chapter III

MARIUS ATTACKED

ONE DAY, M. GILLENORMAND, WHILE HIS DAUGHTER WAS PUTTING IN ORDER THE PHIALS AND cups on the marble of the commode, bent over Marius and said to him in his tenderest accents: "Look here, my little Marius, if I were in your place, I would eat meat now in preference to fish. A fried sole is excellent to begin a convalescence with, but a good cutlet is needed to put a sick man on his feet."

Marius, who had almost entirely recovered his strength, collected the whole of it, drew himself up into a sitting posture, laid his two clenched fists on the sheets of his bed, looked his grandfather in the face, assumed a terrible air, and said:

"This leads me to say something to you."

"What is it?"

"That I wish to marry."

"Agreed," said his grandfather.—And he burst out laughing.

"How agreed?"

"Yes, agreed. You shall have your little girl."

Marius, stunned and overwhelmed with the dazzling shock, trembled in every limb.

M. Gillenormand went on:

"Yes, you shall have her, that pretty little girl of yours. She comes everyday in the shape of an old gentleman to inquire after you. Ever since you were wounded, she has passed her time in weeping and making lint. I have made inquiries. She lives in the Rue de l'Homme Armé, No. 7. Ah! There we have it! Ah! so you want her! Well, you shall have her. You're caught. You had arranged your little plot, you had said to yourself: 'I'm going to signify this squarely to my grandfather, to that mummy of the Regency and of the Directory, to that ancient beau, to that Dorante turned Géronte; he has indulged in his frivolities also, that he has, and he has had his love affairs, and his grisettes and his Cosettes; he has made his rustle, he has had his wings, he has eaten of the bread of spring; he certainly must remember it.' Ah! you take the cockchafer by the horns. That's good. I offer you a cutlet and you answer me: 'By the way, I want to marry.' There's a transition for you! Ah! you reckoned on a bickering! You do not know that I am an old coward. What do you say to that? You are vexed? You did not expect to find your grandfather still more foolish than yourself, you are wasting the discourse which you meant to bestow upon me, Mr. Lawyer, and that's vexatious. Well, so much the worse, rage away. I'll do whatever you wish, and that cuts you short, imbecile! Listen. I have made my inquiries, I'm cunning too; she is charming, she is discreet, it is not true about the lancer, she has made heaps of lint, she's a jewel, she adores you, if you had died, there would have been three of us, her coffin would have accompanied mine. I have had an idea, ever since you have been better, of simply planting her at your bedside, but it is only in romances that young girls are brought to the bedsides of handsome young wounded men who interest them.

It is not done. What would your aunt have said to it? You were nude three quarters of the time, my
good fellow. Ask Nicolette, who has not left you for a moment, if there was any possibility of having a woman here. And then, what would the doctor have said? A pretty girl does not cure a man
of fever. In short, it's all right, let us say no more about it, all's said, all's done, it's all settled, take
her. Such is my ferocity. You see, I perceived that you did not love me. I said to myself: 'Here now,
I have my little Cosette right under my hand, I'm going to give her to him, he will be obliged to
love me a little then, or he must tell the reason why.' Ah! so you thought that the old man was going
to storm, to put on a big voice, to shout no, and to lift his cane at all that aurora. Not a bit of it.
Cosette, so be it; love, so be it; I ask nothing better. Pray take the trouble of getting married, sir. Be
happy, my well-beloved child."

That said, the old man burst forth into sobs.

And he seized Marius's head, and pressed it with both arms against his breast, and both fell to
weeping. This is one of the forms of supreme happiness.

"Father!" cried Marius.

"Ah, so you love me!" said the old man.

An ineffable moment ensued. They were choking and could not speak.

At length, the old man stammered:

"Come! his mouth is unstopped at last. He has said: 'Father' to me."

Marius disengaged his head from his grandfather's arms, and said gently:

"But, father, now that I am quite well, it seems to me that I might see her."

"Agreed again, you shall see her to-morrow."

"Father!"

"What?"

"Why not to-day?"

"Well, to-day then. Let it be to-day. You have called me 'father' three times, and it is worth it.
I will attend to it. She shall be brought hither. Agreed, I tell you. It has already been put into verse.
This is the ending of the elegy of the 'Jeune Malade' by André Chénier, by André Chénier whose
throat was cut by the ras . . . by the giants of '93."

M. Gillenormand fancied that he detected a faint frown on the part of Marius, who, in truth,
as we must admit, was no longer listening to him, and who was thinking far more of Cosette than
of 1793.

The grandfather, trembling at having so inopportunely introduced André Chénier, resumed
precipitately:

"Cut his throat is not the word. The fact is that the great revolutionary geniuses, who were not
malicious, that is incontestable, who were heroes, pardi! found that André Chénier embarrassed
them somewhat, and they had him guillot . . . that is to say, those great men on the 7th of Ther-
moidor, besought André Chénier, in the interests of public safety, to be so good as to go . . ."

M. Gillenormand, clutched by the throat by his own phrase, could not proceed. Being able neither to finish it nor to retract it, while his daughter arranged the pillow behind Marius, who was
overwhelmed with so many emotions, the old man rushed headlong, with as much rapidity as his
age permitted, from the bedchamber, shut the door behind him, and, purple, choking and foaming
at the mouth, his eyes starting from his head he found himself nose to nose with honest Basque, who
was blacking boots in the anteroom. He seized Basque by the collar, and shouted full in his face in
fury: "By the hundred thousand Javottes of the devil, those ruffians did assassinate him!"

"Who, sir?"

"André Chénier!"

"Yes, sir," said Basque in alarm.

Chapter IV

MADEMOISELLE GILLENORMAND ENDS BY NO LONGER THINKING IT A BAD THING THAT M. FAUCHELEVENT SHOULD HAVE ENTERED WITH SOMETHING UNDER HIS ARM

COSETTE AND MARIUS BEHELD EACH OTHER ONCE MORE.
What that interview was like we decline to say. There are things which one must not attempt to depict; the sun is one of them.

The entire family, including Basque and Nicolette, were assembled in Marius's chamber at the moment when Cosette entered it.

Precisely at that moment, the grandfather was on the point of blowing his nose; he stopped short, holding his nose in his handkerchief, and gazing over it at Cosette.

She appeared on the threshold; it seemed to him that she was surrounded by a glory.

"Adorable!" he exclaimed.

Then he blew his nose noisily.

Cosette was intoxicated, delighted, frightened, in heaven. She was as thoroughly alarmed as anyone can be by happiness. She stammered all pale, yet flushed, she wanted to fling herself into Marius's arms, and dared not. Ashamed of loving in the presence of all these people. People are pitiless toward happy lovers; they remain when the latter most desire to be left alone. Lovers have no need of any people whatever.

With Cosette, and behind her, there had entered a man with white hair who was grave yet smiling, though with a vague and heartrending smile. It was "Monsieur Fauchelevent"; it was Jean Valjean.

He was very well dressed, as the porter had said, entirely in black, in perfectly new garments, and with a white cravat.

The porter was a thousand leagues from recognizing in this correct bourgeois, in this probable notary, the fear-inspiring bearer of the corpse, who had sprung up at his door on the night of the 7th of June, tattered, muddy, hideous, haggard, his face masked in blood and mire, supporting in his arms the fainting Marius; still, his porter's scent was aroused. When M. Fauchelevent arrived with Cosette, the porter had not been able to refrain from communicating to his wife this aside: "I don't know why it is, but I can't help fancying that I've seen that face before."

M. Fauchelevent in Marius's chamber, remained apart near the door. He had under his arm, a package which bore considerable resemblance to an octavo volume enveloped in paper. The enveloping paper was of a greenish hue, and appeared to be moldy.

"Does the gentleman always have books like that under his arm?" Mademoiselle Gillenormand, who did not like books, demanded in a low tone of Nicolette.

"Well," retorted M. Gillenormand, who had overheard her, in the same tone, "he's a learned man. What then? Is that his fault? Monsieur Boulard, one of my acquaintances, never walked out without a book under his arm either, and he always had some old volume hugged to his heart like that."

And, with a bow, he said aloud:

"Monsieur Tranchelevent . . ."

Father Gillenormand did not do it intentionally, but inattention to proper names was an aristocratic habit of his.

"Monsieur Tranchelevent, I have the honor of asking you, on behalf of my grandson, Baron Marius Pontmercy, for the hand of Mademoiselle."

Monsieur Tranchelevent bowed.

"That's settled," said the grandfather.

And, turning to Marius and Cosette, with both arms extended in blessing, he cried:

"Permission to adore each other!"

They did not require him to repeat it twice. So much the worse! the chirping began. They talked low. Marius, resting on his elbow on his reclining chair, Cosette standing beside him. "Oh, heavens!" murmured Cosette, "I see you once again! it is thou! it is you! The idea of going and fighting like that! But why? It is horrible. I have been dead for four months. Oh! how wicked it was of you to go to that battle! What had I done to you? I pardon you, but you will never do it again. A little while ago, when they came to tell us to come to you, I still thought that I was about to die, but it was from joy. I was so sad! I have not taken the time to dress myself, I must frighten people with my looks! What will your relatives say to see me in a crumpled collar? Do speak! You let me do all the talking. We are still in the Rue de l'Homme Armé. It seems that your shoulder was terrible. They told me that you could put your fist in it. And then, it seems that they cut your flesh with the scissors. That is frightful. I have cried till I have no eyes left. It is queer that a person can suffer like that. Your grandfather has a very kindly air. Don't disturb yourself, don't rise on your elbow, you will injure yourself. Oh! how happy I am! So our unhappiness is over! I am quite foolish. I had things to say to you, and I no longer know in the least what they were. Do you still love me? We live in the Rue de l'Homme Armé. There is no garden. I made lint all the time; stay, sir, look, it is your fault, I have a callous on my fingers."

"Angel!" said Marius.

Angel is the only word in the language which cannot be worn out. No other word could resist the merciless use which lovers make of it.

Then as there were spectators, they paused and said not a word more, contenting themselves with softly touching each other's hands.

M. Gillenormand turned toward those who were in the room and cried:

"Talk loud, the rest of you. Make a noise, you people behind the scenes. Come, a little uproar, the deuce! so that the children can chatter at their ease."

And, approaching Marius and Cosette, he said to them in a very low voice:

"Call each other *thou*. Don't stand on ceremony."

Aunt Gillenormand looked on in amazement at this eruption of light in her elderly household. There was nothing aggressive about this amazement; it was not the least in the world like the scandalized and envious glance of an owl at two turtle-doves, it was the stupid eye of a poor innocent seven-and-fifty years of age; it was a life which had been a failure gazing at that triumph, love.

"Mademoiselle Gillenormand senior," said her father to her, "I told you that this is what would happen to you."

He remained silent for a moment, and then added:

"Look at the happiness of others."

Then he turned to Cosette.

"How pretty she is! how pretty she is! She's a Greuze. So you are going to have that all to yourself, you scamp! Ah! my rogue, you are getting off nicely with me, you are happy; if I were not fifteen years too old, we would fight with swords to see which of us should have her. Come now! I am in love with you, mademoiselle. It's perfectly simple. It is your right. You are in the right. Ah! what a sweet, charming little wedding this will make! Our parish is Saint-Denis du Saint Sacrament, but I will get a dispensation so that you can be married at Saint-Paul. The church is better. It was built by the Jesuits. It is more coquettish. It is opposite the fountain of Cardinal de Birague. The masterpiece of Jesuit architecture is at Namur. It is called Saint-Loup. You must go there after you are married. It is worth the journey. Mademoiselle, I am quite of your mind, I think girls ought to marry, that is what they are made for. There is a certain Sainte-Catherine whom I should always like to see uncoiffed. It's a fine thing to remain a spinster, but it is chilly. The Bible says: Multiply. In order to save the people, Jeanne d'Arc is needed; but in order to make people, what is needed is Mother Goose. So, marry, my beauties. I really do not see the use in remaining a spinster! I know that they have their chapel apart in the church, and that they fall back on the Society of the Virgin; but, sapristi, a handsome husband, a fine fellow, and at the expiration of a year, a big, blond brat who nurses lustily, and who has fine rolls of fat on his thighs, and who musses up your breast in handfuls with his little rosy paws, laughing the while like the dawn—that's better than holding a candle at vespers, and chanting *Turris eburnea!*"

The grandfather executed a pirouette on his eighty-year-old heels, and began to talk again like a spring that has broken loose once more:

> "*Ainsi, bornant les cours de tes rêvasseries,*
> *Alcippe, il est donc vrai, dans peu tu te maries.*"[1]

"By the way!"

"What is it, father?"

"Have not you an intimate friend?"

"Yes, Courfeyrac."

"What has become of him?"

"He is dead."

"That is good."

He seated himself near them, made Cosette sit down, and took their four hands in his aged and wrinkled hands:

"She is exquisite, this darling. She's a masterpiece, this Cosette! She is a very little girl and a very great lady. She will only be a Baroness, which is a come down for her; she was born a Marquise. What eyelashes she has! Get it well fixed in your noddles, my children, that you are in the true road. Love each other. Be foolish about it. Love is the folly of men and the wit of God. Adore each other. Only," he added, suddenly becoming gloomy, "what a misfortune! It has just occurred to me! More than half of what I possess is swallowed up in an annuity; so long as I live, it will not matter, but after my death, a score of years hence, ah! my poor children, you will not have a sou! Your beautiful white hands, Madame la Baronne, will do the devil the honor of pulling him by the tail."

At this point they heard a grave and tranquil voice say:

"Mademoiselle Euphrasie Fauchelevent possesses six hundred thousand francs."

It was the voice of Jean Valjean.

So far he had not uttered a single word, no one seemed to be aware that he was there, and he had remained standing erect and motionless, behind all these happy people.

"What has Mademoiselle Euphrasie to do with the question?" inquired the startled grandfather.

"I am she," replied Cosette.

"Six hundred thousand francs?" resumed M. Gillenormand.

"Minus fourteen or fifteen thousand francs, possibly," said Jean Valjean.

And he laid on the table the package which Mademoiselle Gillenormand had mistaken for a book.

Jean Valjean himself opened the package; it was a bundle of bank-notes. They were turned over and counted. There were five hundred notes for a thousand francs each, and one hundred and sixty-eight of five hundred. In all, five hundred and eighty-four thousand francs.

---

1. "Thus, hemming in the course of thy musings, Alcippus, it is true that thou wilt wed ere long."

"This is a fine book," said M. Gillenormand.

"Five hundred and eighty-four thousand francs!" murmured the aunt.

"This arranges things well, does it not, Mademoiselle Gillenormand senior?" said the grand-father. "That devil of a Marius has ferreted out the nest of a millionaire grisette in his tree of dreams! Just trust to the love affairs of young folks now, will you! Students find studentesses with six hundred thousand francs. Cherubino works better than Rothschild."

"Five hundred and eighty-four thousand francs!" repeated Mademoiselle Gillenormand, in a low tone. "Five hundred and eighty-four! one might as well say six hundred thousand!"

As for Marius and Cosette, they were gazing at each other while this was going on; they hardly heeded this detail.

Chapter V

Deposit Your Money in a Forest Rather Than with a Notary

THE READER HAS, NO DOUBT, UNDERSTOOD, WITHOUT NECESSITATING A LENGTHY EXPLANA-tion, that Jean Valjean, after the Champmathieu affair, had been able, thanks to his first escape of a few days' duration, to come to Paris and to withdraw in season, from the hands of Laffitte the sum earned by him, under the name of Monsieur Madeleine, at Montreuil-sur-Mer; and that fear-ing that he might be recaptured—which eventually happened—he had buried and hidden that sum in the forest of Montfermeil, in the locality known as the Blaru-bottom. The sum, six hundred and thirty thousand francs, all in bank-bills, was not very bulky, and was contained in a box; only, in order to preserve the box from dampness, he had placed it in a coffer filled with chestnut shavings. In the same coffer he had placed his other treasures, the Bishop's candlesticks. It will be remembered that he had carried off the candlesticks when he made his escape from Montreuil-sur-Mer. The man seen one evening for the first time by Boulatruelle, was Jean Valjean. Later on, every time that Jean Valjean needed money, he went to get it in the Blaru-bottom. Hence the absences which we have mentioned. He had a pickax somewhere in the heather, in a hiding-place known to himself alone. When he beheld Marius convalescent, feeling that the hour was at hand, when that money might prove of service, he had gone to get it; it was he again, whom Boulatruelle had seen in the woods, but on this occasion, in the morning instead of in the evening. Boulatruelle inherited his pickax.

The actual sum was five hundred and eighty-four thousand, five hundred francs. Jean Valjean withdrew the five hundred francs for himself.—"We shall see hereafter," he thought.

The difference between that sum and the six hundred and thirty thousand francs withdrawn from Laffitte represented his expenditure in ten years, from 1823 to 1833. The five years of his stay in the convent had cost only five thousand francs.

Jean Valjean set the two candlesticks on the chimney-piece, where they glittered to the great admiration of Toussaint.

Moreover, Jean Valjean knew that he was delivered from Javert. The story had been told in his presence, and he had verified the fact in the *Moniteur*, how a police inspector named Javert had been found drowned under a boat belonging to some laundresses, between the Pont au Change and the Pont-Neuf, and that a writing left by this man, otherwise irreproachable and highly esteemed by his superiors, pointed to a fit of mental aberration and a suicide.—"In fact," thought Jean Valjean, "since he left me at liberty, once having got me in his power, he must have been already mad."

Chapter VI

THE TWO OLD MEN DO EVERYTHING, EACH ONE AFTER HIS OWN FASHION, TO RENDER COSETTE HAPPY

EVERYTHING WAS MADE READY FOR THE WEDDING. THE DOCTOR, ON BEING CONSULTED, DEclared that it might take place in February. It was then December. A few ravishing weeks of perfect happiness passed.

The grandfather was not the least happy of them all. He remained for a quarter of an hour at a time, gazing at Cosette.

"The wonderful, beautiful girl!" he exclaimed. "And she has so sweet and good an air! she is, without exception, the most charming girl that I have ever seen in my life. Later on, she'll have virtues with an odor of violets. How graceful! one cannot live otherwise than nobly with such a creature. Marius, my boy, you are a Baron, you are rich, don't go to pettifogging, I beg of you."

Cosette and Marius had passed abruptly from the sepulcher to paradise. The transition had not been softened, and they would have been stunned, had they not been dazzled by it.

"Do you understand anything about it?" said Marius to Cosette.

"No," replied Cosette, "but it seems to me that the good God is caring for us."

Jean Valjean did everything, smoothed away every difficulty, arranged everything, made everything easy. He hastened toward Cosette's happiness with as much ardor, and, apparently with as much joy, as Cosette herself.

As he had been a mayor, he understood how to solve that delicate problem, with the secret of which he alone was acquainted, Cosette's civil status. If he were to announce her origin bluntly, it might prevent the marriage, who knows? He extricated Cosette from all difficulties. He concocted for her a family of dead people, a sure means of not encountering any objections. Cosette was the only scion of an extinct family; Cosette was not his own daughter, but the daughter of the other Fauchelevent. Two brothers Fauchelevent had been gardeners to the convent of the Petit-Picpus. Inquiry was made at that convent; the very best information and the most respectable references abounded; the good nuns, not very apt and but little inclined to fathom questions of paternity, and not attaching any importance to the matter, had never understood exactly of which of the two Fauchelevents Cosette was the daughter. They said what was wanted and they said it with zeal. An *acte de notoriété* was drawn up. Cosette became in the eyes of the law, Mademoiselle Euphrasie Fauchelevent. She was declared an orphan, both father and mother being dead. Jean Valjean so arranged it that he was appointed, under the name of Fauchelevent, as Cosette's guardian, with M. Gillenormand as supervising guardian over him.

As for the five hundred and eighty thousand francs, they constituted a legacy bequeathed to Cosette by a dead person, who desired to remain unknown. The original legacy had consisted of five hundred and ninety-four thousand francs; but ten thousand francs had been expended on the education of Mademoiselle Euphrasie, five thousand francs of that amount having been paid to the convent. This legacy, deposited in the hands of a third party, was to be turned over to Cosette at her majority, or at the date of her marriage. This, taken as a whole, was very acceptable, as the reader will perceive, especially when the sum due was half a million. There were some peculiarities here and there, it is true, but they were not noticed; one of the interested parties had his eyes blindfolded by love, the others by the six hundred thousand francs.

Cosette learned that she was not the daughter of that old man whom she had so long called father. He was merely a kinsman; another Fauchelevent was her real father. At any other time this would have broken her heart. But at the ineffable moment which she was then passing through, it cast but a slight shadow, a faint cloud, and she was so full of joy that the cloud did not last long. She had Marius. The young man arrived, the old man was effaced; such is life.

And then, Cosette had, for long years, been habituated to seeing enigmas around her; every being who has had a mysterious childhood, is always prepared for certain renunciations.

Nevertheless, she continued to call Jean Valjean: Father.

Cosette, happy as the angels, was enthusiastic over Father Gillenormand. It is true that he overwhelmed her with gallant compliments and presents. While Jean Valjean was building up for Cosette, a normal situation in society and an unassailable status, M. Gillenormand was superintending the basket of wedding gifts. Nothing so amused him as being magnificent. He had given to Cosette a robe of Binche guipure which had descended to him from his own grandmother.

"These fashions come up again," said he, "ancient things are the rage, and the young women of my old age dress like the old women of my childhood."

He rifled his respectable chests of drawers in Coromandel lacquer, with swelling fronts, which had not been opened for years.—"Let us hear the confession of these dowagers," he said, "let us see what they have in their paunches." He noisily violated the pot-bellied drawers of all his wives, of all his mistresses and of all his grandmothers. Pekins, damasks, lampas, painted moires, robes of shot gros de Tours, India kerchiefs embroidered in gold that could be washed, dauphines without a right or wrong side, in the piece, Genoa and Alençon point lace, parures in antique goldsmith's work, ivory bon-bon boxes ornamented with microscopic battles, gewgaws and ribbons—he lavished everything on Cosette. Cosette, amazed, desperately in love with Marius, and wild with gratitude toward M. Gillenormand, dreamed of a happiness without limit clothed in satin and velvet. Her wedding basket seemed to her to be upheld by seraphim. Her soul flew out into the azure depths, with wings of Mechlin lace.

The intoxication of the lovers was only equaled, as we have already said, by the ecstasy of the grandfather. A sort of flourish of trumpets went on in the Rue des Filles-du-Calvaire.

Every morning, a fresh offering of bric-à-brac from the grandfather to Cosette. All possible knickknacks glittered around her.

One day Marius, who was fond of talking gravely in the midst of his bliss, said, à propos of I know not what incident:

"The men of the revolution are so great, that they have the prestige of the ages, like Cato and like Phocion, and each one of them seems to me an antique memory."

"Moire antique!" exclaimed the old gentleman. "Thanks, Marius. That is precisely the idea of which I was in search."

And on the following day, a magnificent dress of tea-rose colored moire antique was added to Cosette's wedding presents.

From these fripperies, the grandfather extracted a bit of wisdom.

"Love is all very well; but there must be something else to go with it. The useless must be mingled with happiness. Happiness is only the necessary. Season that enormously with the superfluous for me. A palace and her heart. Her heart and the Louvre. Her heart and the grand waterworks of Versailles. Give me my shepherdess and try to make her a duchess. Fetch me Phyllis crowned with corn-flowers, and add a hundred thousand francs income. Open for me a bucolic perspective as far as you can see, beneath a marble colonnade. I consent to the bucolic and also to the fairy spectacle of marble and gold. Dry happiness resembles dry bread. One eats, but one does not dine. I want the superfluous, the useless, the extravagant, excess, that which serves no purpose. I remember to have seen, in the Cathedral of Strasburg, a clock, as tall as a three-story house which marked the hours, which had the kindness to indicate the hour, but which had not the air of being made for that; and which, after having struck midday, or midnight—midday, the hour of the sun, or midnight, the hour of love—or any other hour that you like, gave you the moon and the stars, the earth and the

sea, birds and fishes, Phœbus and Phœbe, and a host of things which emerged from a niche, and
the twelve apostles, and the Emperor Charles the Fifth, and Éponine, and Sabinus, and a throng of
little gilded good men, who played on the trumpet to boot. Without reckoning delicious chimes
which it sprinkled through the air, on every occasion, without anyone's knowing why. Is a petty
bald clock-face which merely tells the hour equal to that? For my part, I am of the opinion of the
big clock of Strasburg, and I prefer it to the cuckoo clock from the Black Forest."

M. Gillenormand talked nonsense in connection with the wedding, and all the fripperies of the
eighteenth century passed pell-mell through his dithyrambs.

"You are ignorant of the art of festivals. You do not know how to organize a day of enjoyment in this age," he exclaimed. "Your nineteenth century is weak. It lacks excess. It ignores the
rich, it ignores the noble. In everything it is clean-shaven. Your third estate is insipid, colorless,
odorless, and shapeless. The dreams of your bourgeois who set up, as they express it: a pretty
boudoir freshly decorated, violet, ebony and calico. Make way! Make way! the Sieur Curmudgeon
is marrying Mademoiselle Clutch-penny. Sumptuousness and splendor. A louis d'or has been stuck
to a candle. There's the epoch for you. My demand is that I may flee from it beyond the Sarmatians.
Ah! in 1787, I predict that all was lost, from the day when I beheld the Duc de Rohan, Prince de
Léon, Duc de Chabot, Duc de Montbazon, Marquis de Soubise, Vicomte de Thouars, peer of
France, go to Longchamps in a tapecu! That has borne its fruits. In this century, men attend to business, they gamble on 'Change, they win money, they are stingy. People take care of their surfaces
and varnish them; everyone is dressed as though just out of a band-box, washed, soaped, scraped,
shaved, combed, waked, smoothed, rubbed, brushed, cleaned on the outside, irreproachable, polished as a pebble, discreet, neat, and at the same time, death of my life, in the depths of their consciences they have dung-heaps and cesspools that are enough to make a cow-herd who blows his
nose in his fingers, recoil. I grant to this age the device: 'Dirty Cleanliness.' Don't be vexed, Marius, give me permission to speak; I say no evil of the people as you see, I am always harping on your
people, but do look favorably on my dealing a bit of a slap to the bourgeoisie. I belong to it. He
who loves well lashes well. Thereupon, I say plainly, that nowadays people marry, but that they no
longer know how to marry. Ah! it is true, I regret the grace of the ancient manners. I regret everything about them, their elegance, their chivalry, those courteous and delicate ways, that joyous luxury which everyone possessed, music forming part of the wedding, a symphony above stairs, a
beating of drums below stairs, the dances, the joyous faces round the table, the fine-spun gallant
compliments, the songs, the fireworks, the frank laughter, the devil's own row, the huge knots of
ribbon. I regret the bride's garter. The bride's garter is cousin to the girdle of Venus. On what does
the war of Troy turn? On Helen's garter, parbleu! Why did they fight, why did Diomed the divine
break over the head of Meriones that great brazen helmet of ten points? why did Achilles and Hec-
tor hew each other up with vast blows of their lances? Because Helen allowed Paris to take her
garter. With Cosette's garter, Homer would construct the *Iliad*. He would put in his poem, a loquacious old fellow, like me, and he would call him Nestor. My friends, in bygone days, in those
amiable days of yore, people married wisely; they had a good contract, and then they had a good
carouse. As soon as Cujas had taken his departure, Gamacho entered. But, in sooth! the stomach is
an agreeable beast which demands its due, and which wants to have its wedding also. People supped
well, and had at table a beautiful neighbor without a guimpe so that her throat was only moderately
concealed. Oh! the large laughing mouths, and how gay we were in those days! youth was a bouquet; every young man terminated in a branch of lilacs or a tuft of roses; whether he was a shepherd or a warrior; and if, by chance, one was a captain of dragoons, one found means to call one's
self Florian. People thought much of looking well. They embroidered and tinted themselves. A
bourgeois had the air of a flower, a Marquis had the air of a precious stone. People had no straps to
their boots, they had no boots. They were spruce, shining, waved, lustrous, fluttering, dainty, coquettish, which did not at all prevent their wearing swords by their sides. The humming-bird has

beak and claws. That was the day of the *Gallant Indies*. One of the sides of that century was delicate, the other was magnificent; and by the green cabbages! people amused themselves. To-day,
people are serious. The bourgeois is avaricious, the bourgeoise is a prude; your century is unfortunate. People would drive away the Graces as being too low in the neck. Alas! beauty is concealed
as though it were ugliness. Since the revolution, everything, including the ballet-dancers, has had
its trousers; a mountebank dancer must be grave; your rigadoons are doctrinarian. It is necessary to
be majestic. People would be greatly annoyed if they did not carry their chins in their cravats. The
ideal of an urchin of twenty when he marries, is to resemble M. Royer-Collard. And do you know
what one arrives at with that majesty? at being petty. Learn this: joy is not only joyous; it is great.
But be in love gaily then, what the deuce! marry, when you marry, with fever and giddiness, and tumult, and the uproar of happiness! Be grave in church, well and good. But, as soon as the mass is
finished, sarpejou! you must make a dream whirl around the bride. A marriage should be royal and
chimerical; it should promenade its ceremony from the cathedral of Rheims to the pagoda of
Chanteloup. I have a horror of a paltry wedding. Ventregoulette! be in Olympus for that one day,
at least. Be one of the gods. Ah! people might be sylphs. Games and Laughter, argiraspides; they
are stupids. My friends, every recently made bridegroom ought to be Prince Aldobrandini. Profit
by that unique minute in life to soar away to the empyrean with the swans and the eagles, even if
you do have to fall back on the morrow into the bourgeoisie of the frogs. Don't economize on the
nuptials, do not prune them of their splendors; don't scrimp on the day when you beam. The wedding is not the housekeeping. Oh! if I were to carry out my fancy, it would be gallant, violins would
be heard under the trees. Here is my program: sky-blue and silver. I would mingle with the festival
the rural divinities, I would convoke the Dryads and the Nereids. The nuptials of Amphitrite, a
rosy cloud, nymphs with well-dressed locks and entirely naked, an Academician offering quatrains
to the goddess, a chariot drawn by marine monsters.

> *'Triton trottait devant, et tirait de sa conque*
> *Des sons si ravissants qu'il ravissait quiconque!'*[1]

—there's a festive program, there's a good one, or else I know nothing of such matters, deuce take
it!"

While the grandfather, in full lyrical effusion, was listening to himself, Cosette and Marius
grew intoxicated as they gazed freely at each other.

Aunt Gillenormand surveyed all this with her imperturbable placidity. Within the last five or
six months she had experienced a certain amount of emotions. Marius returned, Marius brought
back bleeding, Marius brought back from a barricade, Marius dead, then living, Marius reconciled,
Marius betrothed, Marius wedding a poor girl, Marius wedding a millionairess. The six hundred
thousand francs had been her last surprise. Then, her indifference of a girl taking her first communion returned to her. She went regularly to service, told her beads, read her euchology, mumbled *Aves* in one corner of the house, while *I love you* was being whispered in the other, and she
beheld Marius and Cosette in a vague way, like two shadows. The shadow was herself.

There is a certain state of inert asceticism in which the soul, neutralized by torpor, a stranger
to that which may be designated as the business of living, receives no impressions, either human,
or pleasant or painful, with the exception of earthquakes and catastrophes. This devotion, as Father
Gillenormand said to his daughter, corresponds to a cold in the head. You smell nothing of life.
Neither any bad, nor any good odor.

Moreover, the six hundred thousand francs had settled the elderly spinster's indecision. Her father had acquired the habit of taking her so little into account, that he had not consulted her in the

---

1. "Triton trotted on before, and drew from his conch-shell sounds so ravishing that he delighted everyone!"

matter of consent to Marius's marriage. He had acted impetuously, according to his wont, having, a despot-turned slave, but a single thought—to satisfy Marius. As for the aunt—it had not even occurred to him that the aunt existed, and that she could have an opinion of her own, and, sheep as she was, this had vexed her. Somewhat resentful in her inmost soul, but impassible externally, she had said to herself: "My father has settled the question of the marriage without reference to me; I shall settle the question of the inheritance without consulting him." She was rich, in fact, and her father was not. She had reserved her decision on this point. It is probable that, had the match been a poor one, she would have left him poor. "So much the worse for my nephew! he is wedding a beggar, let him be a beggar himself!" But Cosette's half-million pleased the aunt, and altered her inward situation so far as this pair of lovers were concerned. One owes some consideration to six hundred thousand francs, and it was evident that she could not do otherwise than leave her fortune to these young people, since they did not need it.

It was arranged that the couple should live with the grandfather—M. Gillenormand insisted on resigning to them his chamber, the finest in the house.—"That will make me young again," he said. "It's an old plan of mine. I have always entertained the idea of having a wedding in my chamber."

He furnished this chamber with a multitude of elegant trifles. He had the ceiling and walls hung with an extraordinary stuff, which he had by him in the piece, and which he believed to have emanated from Utrecht with a buttercup-colored satin ground, covered with velvet auricula blossoms.—"It was with that stuff," said he, "that the bed of the Duchesse d'Anville at la Roche-Guyon was draped."—On the chimney-piece, he set a little figure in Saxe porcelain, carrying a muff against her nude stomach.

M. Gillenormand's library became the lawyer's study which Marius needed; a study, it will be remembered, being required by the council of the order.

Chapter VII

THE EFFECTS OF DREAMS MINGLED WITH HAPPINESS

THE LOVERS SAW EACH OTHER EVERY DAY. COSETTE CAME WITH M. FAUCHELEVENT.—"THIS IS reversing things," said Mademoiselle Gillenormand, "to have the bride come to the house to do the courting like this." But Marius's convalescence had caused the habit to become established, and the arm-chairs of the Rue des Filles-du-Calvaire, better adapted to interviews than the straw chairs of the Rue de l'Homme Armé, had rooted it. Marius and M. Fauchelevent saw each other, but did not address each other. It seemed as though this had been agreed upon. Every girl needs a chaperon. Cosette could not have come without M. Fauchelevent. In Marius's eyes, M. Fauchelevent was the condition attached to Cosette. He accepted it. By dint of discussing political matters, vaguely and without precision, from the point of view of the general amelioration of the fate of all men, they came to say a little more than "yes" and "no." Once, on the subject of education, which Marius wished to have free and obligatory, multiplied under all forms, lavished on everyone, like the air and the sun, in a word, respirable for the entire population, they were in unison, and they almost conversed. M. Fauchelevent talked well, and even with a certain loftiness of language—still, he lacked something indescribable. M. Fauchelevent possessed something less and also something more, than a man of the world.

Marius, inwardly, and in the depths of his thought, surrounded with all sorts of mute questions this M. Fauchelevent, who was, to him, simply benevolent and cold. There were moments when doubts as to his own recollections occurred to him. There was a void in his memory, a black spot, an abyss excavated by four months of agony.—Many things had been lost therein. He had come to the point of asking himself whether it were really a fact that he had seen M. Fauchelevent, so serious and so calm a man, in the barricade.

This was not, however, the only stupor which the apparitions and the disappearances of the past had left in his mind. It must not be supposed that he was delivered from all those obsessions of the memory which force us, even when happy, even when satisfied, to glance sadly behind us. The head which does not turn backwards toward horizons that have vanished contains neither thought nor love. At times, Marius clasped his face between his hands, and the vague and tumultuous past traversed the twilight which reigned in his brain. Again he beheld Mabeuf fall, he heard Gavroche singing amid the grape-shot, he felt beneath his lips the cold brow of Éponine; Enjolras, Courfeyrac, Jean Prouvaire, Combeferre, Bossuet, Grantaire, all his friends rose erect before him, then dispersed into thin air. Were all those dear, sorrowful, valiant, charming or tragic beings merely dreams? had they actually existed? The revolt had enveloped everything in its smoke. These great fevers create great dreams. He questioned himself; he felt himself; all these vanished realities made him dizzy. Where were they all then? was it really true that all were dead? A fall into the shadows had carried off all except himself. It all seemed to him to have disappeared as though behind the curtain of a theater. There are curtains like this which drop in life. God passes on to the following act.

And he himself—was he actually the same man? He, the poor man, was rich; he, the abandoned, had a family; he, the despairing, was to marry Cosette. It seemed to him that he had traversed a tomb, and that he had entered into it black and had emerged from it white, and in that tomb the others had remained. At certain moments, all these beings of the past, returned and present, formed a circle around him, and overshadowed him; then he thought of Cosette, and recovered his serenity; but nothing less than this felicity could have sufficed to efface that catastrophe.

M. Fauchelevent almost occupied a place among these vanished beings. Marius hesitated to believe that the Fauchelevent of the barricade was the same as this Fauchelevent in flesh and blood, sitting so gravely beside Cosette. The first was, probably, one of those nightmares occasioned and brought back by his hours of delirium. However, the natures of both men were rigid, no question from Marius to M. Fauchelevent was possible. Such an idea had not even occurred to him. We have already indicated this characteristic detail.

Two men who have a secret in common, and who, by a sort of tacit agreement, exchange not a word on the subject, are less rare than is commonly supposed.

Once only, did Marius make the attempt. He introduced into the conversation the Rue de la Chanvrerie, and, turning to M. Fauchelevent, he said to him:

"Of course you are acquainted with that street?"

"What street?"

"The Rue de la Chanvrerie."

"I have no idea of the name of that street," replied M. Fauchelevent, in the most natural manner in the world.

The response which bore upon the name of the street and not upon the street itself, appeared to Marius to be more conclusive than it really was.

"Decidedly," thought he, "I have been dreaming. I have been subject to a hallucination. It was someone who resembled him. M. Fauchelevent was not there."

Chapter VIII

TWO MEN IMPOSSIBLE TO FIND

MARIUS'S ENCHANTMENT, GREAT AS IT WAS, COULD NOT EFFACE FROM HIS MIND OTHER PREOC-cupations.

While the wedding was in preparation, and while awaiting the date fixed upon, he caused difficult and scrupulous retrospective researches to be made.

He owed gratitude in various quarters; he owed it on his father's account, he owed it on his own.

There was Thénardier; there was the unknown man who had brought him, Marius, back to M. Gillenormand.

Marius endeavored to find these two men, not intending to marry, to be happy, and to forget them, and fearing that, were these debts of gratitude not discharged, they would leave a shadow on his life, which promised so brightly for the future.

It was impossible for him to leave all these arrears of suffering behind him, and he wished, before entering joyously into the future, to obtain a quittance from the past.

That Thénardier was a villain detracted nothing from the fact that he had saved Colonel Pontmercy. Thénardier was a ruffian in the eyes of all the world except Marius.

And Marius, ignorant of the real scene in the battlefield of Waterloo, was not aware of the peculiar detail, that his father, so far as Thénardier was concerned, was in the strange position of being indebted to the latter for his life, without being indebted to him for any gratitude.

None of the various agents whom Marius employed succeeded in discovering any trace of Thénardier. Obliteration appeared to be complete in that quarter. Madame Thénardier had died in prison pending the trial. Thénardier and his daughter Azelma, the only two remaining of that lamentable group, had plunged back into the gloom. The gulf of the social unknown had silently closed above those beings. On the surface there was not visible so much as that quiver, that trembling, those obscure concentric circles which announce that something has fallen in, and that the plummet may be dropped.

Madame Thénardier being dead, Boulatruelle being eliminated from the case, Claquesous having disappeared, the principal persons accused having escaped from prison, the trial connected with the ambush in the Gorbeau house had come to nothing.

That affair had remained rather obscure. The bench of Assizes had been obliged to content themselves with two subordinates. Panchaud, alias Printanier, alias Bigrenaille, and Demi-Liard, alias Deux-Milliards, who had been inconsistently condemned, after a hearing of both sides of the case, to ten years in the galleys. Hard labor for life had been the sentence pronounced against the escaped and contumacious accomplices.

Thénardier, the head and leader, had been, through contumacy, likewise condemned to death.

This sentence was the only information remaining about Thénardier, casting upon that buried name its sinister light like a candle beside a bier.

Moreover, by thrusting Thénardier back into the very remotest depths, through a fear of being recaptured, this sentence added to the density of the shadows which enveloped this man.

As for the other person, as for the unknown man who had saved Marius, the researches were at first to some extent successful, then came to an abrupt conclusion. They succeeded in finding the carriage which had brought Marius to the Rue des Filles-du-Calvaire on the evening of the 6th of June.

The coachman declared that, on the 6th of June, in obedience to the commands of a police-agent, he had stood from three o'clock in the afternoon until nightfall on the Quai des Champs-Élysées, above the outlet of the Grand Sewer; that, toward nine o'clock in the evening, the grating of the sewer, which abuts on the bank of the river, had opened; that a man had emerged therefrom, bearing on his shoulders another man, who seemed to be dead; that the agent, who was on the watch at that point, had arrested the living man and had seized the dead man; that, at the order of the police-agent, he, the coachman, had taken "all those folks" into his carriage; that they had first driven to the Rue des Filles-du-Calvaire; that they had there deposited the dead man; that the dead man was Monsieur Marius, and that he, the coachman, recognized him perfectly, although he was alive "this time"; that afterwards, they had entered the vehicle again, that he had whipped up his horses; a few paces from the gate of the Archives, they had called to him to halt; that there, in the street, they had paid him and left him, and that the police agent had led the other man away; that he knew nothing more; that the night had been very dark.

Marius, as we have said, recalled nothing. He only remembered that he had been seized from behind by an energetic hand at the moment when he was falling backwards into the barricade; then, everything vanished so far as he was concerned.

He had only regained consciousness at M. Gillenormand's.

He was lost in conjectures.

He could not doubt his own identity. Still, how had it come to pass that, having fallen in the Rue de la Chanvrerie, he had been picked up by the police-agent on the banks of the Seine, near the Pont des Invalides?

Someone had carried him from the Quartier des Halles to the Champs-Élysées. And how? Through the sewer. Unheard-of devotion!

Someone? Who?

This was the man for whom Marius was searching.

Of this man, who was his savior, nothing; not a trace; not the faintest indication.

Marius, although forced to preserve great reserve, in that direction, pushed his inquiries as far as the prefecture of police. There, no more than elsewhere, did the information obtained lead to any enlightenment.

The prefecture knew less about the matter than did the hackney-coachman. They had no knowledge of any arrest having been made on the 6th of June at the mouth of the Grand Sewer.

No report of any agent had been received there upon this matter, which was regarded at the prefecture as a fable. The invention of this fable was attributed to the coachman.

A coachman who wants a gratuity is capable of anything, even of imagination. The fact was assured, nevertheless, and Marius could not doubt it, unless he doubted his own identity, as we have just said.

Everything about this singular enigma was inexplicable.

What had become of that man, that mysterious man, whom the coachman had seen emerge from the grating of the Grand Sewer bearing upon his back the unconscious Marius, and whom the police-agent on the watch had arrested in the very act of rescuing an insurgent? What had become of the agent himself?

Why had this agent preserved silence? Had the man succeeded in making his escape? Had he bribed the agent? Why did this man give no sign of life to Marius, who owed everything to him? His disinterestedness was no less tremendous than his devotion. Why had not that man appeared again? Perhaps he was above compensation, but no one is above gratitude. Was he dead? Who was the man? What sort of a face had he? No one could tell him this.

The coachman answered: "The night was very dark." Basque and Nicolette, all in a flutter, had looked only at their young master all covered with blood.

The porter, whose candle had lighted the tragic arrival of Marius, had been the only one to take note of the man in question, and this is the description that he gave:

"That man was terrible."

Marius had the blood-stained clothing which he had worn when he had been brought back to his grandfather preserved, in the hope that it would prove of service in his researches.

On examining the coat, it was found that one skirt had been torn in a singular way. A piece was missing.

One evening, Marius was speaking in the presence of Cosette and Jean Valjean of the whole of that singular adventure, of the innumerable inquiries which he had made, and of the fruitlessness of his efforts. The cold countenance of "Monsieur Fauchelevent" angered him.

He exclaimed, with a vivacity which had something of wrath in it:

"Yes, that man, whoever he may have been, was sublime. Do you know what he did, sir? He intervened like an archangel. He must have flung himself into the midst of the battle, have stolen me away, have opened the sewer, have dragged me into it, and have carried me through it! He must have traversed more than a league and a half in those frightful subterranean galleries, bent over, weighed down, in the dark, in the cesspool—more than a league and a half, sir, with a corpse upon his back! And with what object? With the sole object of saving the corpse. And that corpse I was. He said to himself: 'There may still be a glimpse of life there, perchance; I will risk my own existence for that miserable spark!' And his existence he risked not once but twenty times! And every step was a danger. The proof of it is, that on emerging from the sewer, he was arrested. Do you know, sir, that that man did all this? And he had no recompense to expect. What was I? An insurgent. What was I? One of the conquered. Oh! if Cosette's six hundred thousand francs were mine . . ."

"They are yours," interrupted Jean Valjean.

"Well," resumed Marius, "I would give them all to find that man once more."

Jean Valjean remained silent.

BOOK SIXTH

THE SLEEPLESS NIGHT

Chapter I

THE 16TH OF FEBRUARY, 1833

THE NIGHT OF THE 16TH TO THE 17TH OF FEBRUARY, 1833, WAS A BLESSED NIGHT. ABOVE ITS SHADows heaven stood open. It was the wedding night of Marius and Cosette.

The day had been adorable.

It had not been the grand festival dreamed by the grandfather, a fairy spectacle, with a confusion of cherubim and Cupids over the heads of the bridal pair, a marriage worthy to form the subject of a painting to be placed over a door; but it had been sweet and smiling.

The manner of marriage in 1833 was not the same as it is to-day. France had not yet borrowed from England that supreme delicacy of carrying off one's wife, of fleeing, on coming out of church, of hiding one's self with shame from one's happiness, and of combining the ways of a bankrupt with the delights of the Song of Songs. People had not yet grasped to the full the chastity, exquisiteness, and decency of jolting their paradise in a posting-chaise, of breaking up their mystery with clic-clacs, of taking for a nuptial bed the bed of an inn, and of leaving behind them, in a commonplace chamber, at so much a night, the most sacred of the souvenirs of life mingled pell-mell with the tête-à-tête of the conductor of the diligence and the maid-servant of the inn.

In this second half of the nineteenth century in which we are now living, the mayor and his scarf, the priest and his chasuble, the law and God no longer suffice; they must be eked out by the Postilion de Lonjumeau; a blue waistcoat turned up with red, and with bell buttons, a plaque like a vantbrace, knee-breeches of green leather, oaths to the Norman horses with their tails knotted up, false galloons, varnished hat, long powdered locks, an enormous whip and tall boots. France does not yet carry elegance to the length of doing like the English nobility, and raining down on the post chaise of the bridal pair a hail storm of slippers trodden down at heel and of worn-out shoes, in memory of Churchill, afterwards Marlborough, or Malbrouck, who was assailed on his wedding-day by the wrath of an aunt which brought him good luck. Old shoes and slippers do not, as yet, form a part of our nuptial celebrations; but patience, as good taste continues to spread, we shall come to that.

In 1833, a hundred years ago, marriage was not conducted at a full trot.

Strange to say, at that epoch, people still imagined that a wedding was a private and social festival, that a patriarchal banquet does not spoil a domestic solemnity, that gaiety, even in excess, provided it be honest, and decent, does happiness no harm, and that, in short, it is a good and a venerable thing that the fusion of these two destinies whence a family is destined to spring, should begin at home, and that the household should thenceforth have its nuptial chamber as its witness.

And people were so immodest as to marry in their own homes.

The marriage took place, therefore, in accordance with this now superannuated fashion, at M. Gillenormand's house.

Natural and commonplace as this matter of marrying is, the banns to publish, the papers to be drawn up, the mayoralty, and the church produce some complication. They could not get ready before the 16th of February.

Now, we note this detail, for the pure satisfaction of being exact, it chanced that the 16th fell on Shrove Tuesday. Hesitations, scruples, particularly on the part of Aunt Gillenormand.

"Shrove Tuesday!" exclaimed the grandfather, "so much the better. There is a proverb:

'Mariage un Mardi gras
N'aura point enfants ingrats.'[1]

Let us proceed. Here goes for the 16th! Do you want to delay, Marius?"

"No, certainly not!" replied the lover.

"Let us marry then," cried the grandfather.

Accordingly, the marriage took place on the 16th, notwithstanding the public merrymaking. It rained that day, but there is always in the sky a tiny scrap of blue at the service of happiness, which lovers see, even when the rest of creation is under an umbrella.

On the preceding evening, Jean Valjean handed to Marius, in the presence of M. Gillenormand, the five hundred and eighty-four thousand francs.

As the marriage was taking place under the régime of community of property, the papers had been simple.

Henceforth, Toussaint was of no use to Jean Valjean; Cosette inherited her and promoted her to the rank of lady's maid.

1. "A Shrove-Tuesday marriage will have no ungrateful children."

As for Jean Valjean, a beautiful chamber in the Gillenormand house had been furnished expressly for him, and Cosette had said to him in such an irresistible manner: "Father, I entreat you," that she had almost persuaded him to promise that he would come and occupy it.

A few days before that fixed on for the marriage, an accident happened to Jean Valjean; he crushed the thumb of his right hand. This was not a serious matter; and he had not allowed anyone to trouble himself about it, nor to dress it, nor even to see his hurt, not even Cosette. Nevertheless, this had forced him to swathe his hand in a linen bandage, and to carry his arm in a sling, and had prevented his signing. M. Gillenormand, in his capacity of Cosette's supervising-guardian, had supplied his place.

We will not conduct the reader either to the mayor's office or to the church. One does not follow a pair of lovers to that extent, and one is accustomed to turn one's back on the drama as soon as it puts a wedding nosegay in its buttonhole. We will confine ourselves to noting an incident which, though unnoticed by the wedding party, marked the transit from the Rue des Filles-du-Calvaire to the church of Saint-Paul.

At that epoch, the northern extremity of the Rue Saint-Louis was in process of repaving. It was barred off, beginning with the Rue du Parc-Royal. It was impossible for the wedding carriages to go directly to Saint-Paul. They were obliged to alter their course, and the simplest way was to turn through the boulevard. One of the invited guests observed that it was Shrove Tuesday, and that there would be a jam of vehicles.—"Why?" asked M. Gillenormand.—"Because of the maskers."— "Capital," said the grandfather, "let us go that way. These young folks are on the way to be married; they are about to enter the serious part of life. This will prepare them for seeing a bit of the masquerade."

They went by way of the boulevard. The first wedding coach held Cosette and Aunt Gillenormand, M. Gillenormand and Jean Valjean. Marius, still separated from his betrothed, according to usage, did not come until the second. The nuptial train, on emerging from the Rue des Filles-du-Calvaire, became entangled in a long procession of vehicles which formed an endless chain from the Madeleine to the Bastille, and from the Bastille to the Madeleine. Maskers abounded on the boulevard. In spite of the fact that it was raining at intervals, merry-andrew, Pantaloon and Clown persisted. In the good humor of that winter of 1833, Paris had disguised itself as Venice. Such Shrove Tuesdays are no longer to be seen nowadays. Everything which exists being a scattered Carnival, there is no longer any Carnival.

The sidewalks were overflowing with pedestrians and the windows with curious spectators. The terraces which crown the peristyles of the theaters were bordered with spectators. Besides the maskers, they stared at that procession—peculiar to Shrove Tuesday as to Longchamps—of vehicles of every description, citadines, tapissières, carioles, cabriolets marching in order, rigorously riveted to each other by the police regulations, and locked into rails, as it were. Anyone in these vehicles is at once a spectator and a spectacle. Police-sergeants maintained, on the sides of the boulevard, these two interminable parallel files, moving in contrary directions, and saw to it that nothing interfered with that double current, those two brooks of carriages, flowing, the one downstream, the other upstream, the one toward the Chaussée d'Antin, the other toward the Faubourg Saint-Antoine. The carriages of the peers of France and of the Ambassadors, emblazoned with coats of arms, held the middle of the way, going and coming freely. Certain joyous and magnificent trains, notably that of the Bœuf Gras, had the same privilege. In this gaiety of Paris, England cracked her whip; Lord Seymour's post-chaise, harassed by a nickname from the populace, passed with great noise.

In the double file, along which the municipal guards galloped like sheep-dogs, honest family coaches, loaded down with great-aunts and grandmothers, displayed at their doors fresh groups of children in disguise, Clowns of seven years of age, Columbines of six, ravishing little creatures, who felt that they formed an official part of the public mirth, who were imbued with the dignity of their harlequinade, and who possessed the gravity of functionaries.

From time to time, a hitch arose somewhere in the procession of vehicles; one or other of the two lateral files halted until the knot was disentangled; one carriage delayed sufficed to paralyze the whole line. Then they set out again on the march.

The wedding carriages were in the file proceeding toward the Bastille, and skirting the right side of the Boulevard. At the top of the Pont-aux-Choux, there was a stoppage. Nearly at the same moment, the other file, which was proceeding toward the Madeleine, halted also. At that point of the file there was a carriage-load of maskers.

These carriages, or to speak more correctly, these wagon-loads of maskers are very familiar to Parisians. If they were missing on a Shrove Tuesday, or at the Mid-Lent, it would be taken in bad part, and people would say: "There's something behind that. Probably the ministry is about to undergo a change." A pile of Cassandras, Harlequins and Columbines, jolted along high above the passers-by, all possible grotesquenesses, from the Turk to the savage, Hercules supporting Marquises, fishwives who would have made Rabelais stop up his ears just as the Mœnads made Aristophanes drop his eyes, tow wigs, pink tights, dandified hats, spectacles of a grimacer, three-cornered hats of Janot tormented with a butterfly, shouts directed at pedestrians, fists on hips, bold attitudes, bare shoulders, immodesty unchained; a chaos of shamelessness driven by a coachman crowned with flowers; this is what that institution was like.

Greece stood in need of the chariot of Thespis, France stands in need of the hackney-coach of Vadé.

Everything can be parodied, even parody. The Saturnalia, that grimace of antique beauty, ends, through exaggeration after exaggeration, in Shrove Tuesday; and the Bacchanal, formerly crowned with sprays of vine leaves and grapes, inundated with sunshine, displaying her marble breast in a divine semi-nudity, having at the present day lost her shape under the soaked rags of the North, has finally come to be called the Jack-pudding.

The tradition of carriage-loads of maskers runs back to the most ancient days of the monarchy. The accounts of Louis XI allot to the bailiff of the palace "twenty sous, Tournois, for three coaches of mascarades in the cross-roads." In our day, these noisy heaps of creatures are accustomed to have themselves driven in some ancient cuckoo carriage, whose imperial they load down, or they overwhelm a hired landau, with its top thrown back, with their tumultuous groups. Twenty of them ride in a carriage intended for six. They cling to the seats, to the rumble, on the cheeks of the hood, on the shafts. They even bestride the carriage lamps. They stand, sit, lie, with their knees drawn up in a knot, and their legs hanging. The women sit on the men's laps. Far away, above the throng of heads, their wild pyramid is visible. These carriage-loads form mountains of mirth in the midst of the rout. Collé, Panard and Piron flow from it, enriched with slang. This carriage which has become colossal through its freight, has an air of conquest. Uproar reigns in front, tumult behind. People vociferate, shout, howl, there they break forth and writhe with enjoyment; gaiety roars; sarcasm flames forth, joviality is flaunted like a red flag; two jades there drag farce blossomed forth into an apotheosis; it is the triumphal car of laughter.

A laughter that is too cynical to be frank. In truth, this laughter is suspicious. This laughter has a mission. It is charged with proving the Carnival to the Parisians.

These fishwife vehicles, in which one feels one knows not what shadows, set the philosopher to thinking. There is government therein. There one lays one's finger on a mysterious affinity between public men and public women.

It certainly is sad that turpitude heaped up should give a sum total of gaiety, that by piling ignominy upon opprobrium the people should be enticed, that the system of spying, and serving as caryatids to prostitution should amuse the rabble when it confronts them, that the crowd loves to behold that monstrous living pile of tinsel rags, half dung, half light, roll by on four wheels howling and laughing, that they should clap their hands at this glory composed of all shames, that there would be no festivals for the populace, did not the police promenade in their midst these sorts twenty-headed ot hydras of joy. But what can be done about it? These be-ribboned and be-flowered tumbrils of mire are insulted and pardoned by the laughter of the public. The laughter of all is the accomplice of universal degradation. Certain unhealthy festivals disaggregate the people and convert them into the populace. And populaces, like tyrants, require buffoons. The King has Roquelaure, the populace has the merry-andrew. Paris is a great, mad city on every occasion that it is a great sublime city. There the Carnival forms part of politics. Paris—let us confess it—willingly allows infamy to furnish it with comedy. She only demands of her masters—when she has masters—one thing: "Paint me the mud." Rome was of the same mind. She loved Nero. Nero was a titanic lighterman.

Chance ordained, as we have just said, that one of these shapeless clusters of masked men and women, dragged about on a vast calash, should halt on the left of the boulevard, while the wedding train halted on the right. The carriage-load of masks caught sight of the wedding carriage containing the bridal party opposite them on the other side of the boulevard.

"Hullo!" said a masker, "here's a wedding."

"A sham wedding," retorted another. "We are the genuine article."

And, being too far off to accost the wedding party, and fearing also, the rebuke of the police, the two maskers turned their eyes elsewhere.

At the end of another minute, the carriage-load of maskers had their hands full, the multitude set to yelling, which is the crowd's caress to masquerades; and the two maskers who had just spoken had to face the throng with their comrades, and did not find the entire repertory of projectiles of the fish-markets too extensive to retort to the enormous verbal attacks of the populace. A frightful exchange of metaphors took place between the maskers and the crowd.

In the meanwhile, two other maskers in the same carriage, a Spaniard with an enormous nose, an elderly air, and huge black moustache, and a gaunt fishwife, who was quite a young girl, masked with a *loup*,[1] had also noticed the wedding, and while their companions and the passers-by were exchanging insults, they had held a dialogue in a low voice.

Their aside was covered by the tumult and was lost in it. The gusts of rain had drenched the front of the vehicle, which was wide open; the breezes of February are not warm; as the fishwife, clad in a low-necked gown, replied to the Spaniard, she shivered, laughed and coughed.

Here is their dialogue:

"Say now."

"What, daddy?"

"Do you see that old cove?"

"What old cove?"

"Yonder, in the first wedding-cart, on our side."

"The one with his arm hung up in a black cravat?"

"Yes."

"Well?"

"I'm sure that I know him."

"Ah!"

"I'm willing that they should cut my throat, and I'm ready to swear that I never said either you, thou, or I, in my life, if I don't know that Parisian." [*pantinois.*]

"Paris in Pantin to-day."

"Can you see the bride if you stoop down?"

"No."

"And the bridegroom?"

"There's no bridegroom in that trap."

"Bah!"

1. A short mask.

"Unless it's the old fellow."

"Try to get a sight of the bride by stooping very low."

"I can't."

"Never mind, that old cove who has something the matter with his paw I know, and that I'm positive."

"And what good does it do to know him?"

"No one can tell. Sometimes it does!"

"I don't care a hang for old fellows, that I don't!"

"I know him."

"Know him, if you want to."

"How the devil does he come to be one of the wedding party?"

"We are in it too."

"Where does that wedding come from?"

"How should I know?"

"Listen."

"Well, what?"

"There's one thing you ought to do."

"What's that?"

"Get off of our trap and spin that wedding."

"What for?"

"To find out where it goes, and what it is. Hurry up and jump down, trot, my girl, your legs are young."

"I can't quit the vehicle."

"Why not?"

"I'm hired."

"Ah, the devil!"

"I owe my fishwife day to the prefecture."

"That's true."

"If I leave the cart, the first inspector who gets his eye on me will arrest me. You know that well enough."

"Yes I do."

"I'm bought by the government for to-day."

"All the same, that old fellow bothers me."

"Do the old fellows bother you? But you're not a young girl."

"He's in the first carriage."

"Well?"

"In the bride's trap."

"What then?"

"So he is the father."

"What concern is that of mine?"

"I tell you that he's the father."

"As if he were the only father."

"Listen."

"What?"

"I can't go out otherwise than masked. Here I'm concealed, no one knows that I'm here. But to-morrow, there will be no more maskers. It's Ash Wednesday. I run the risk of being nabbed. I must sneak back into my hole. But you are free."

"Not particularly."

"More than I am, at any rate."

"Well, what of that?"

"You must try to find out where that wedding party went to."

"Where it went?"

"Yes."

"I know."

"Where is it going then?"

"To the Cadran-Bleu."

"In the first place, it's not in that direction."

"Well! to la Rapée."

"Or elsewhere."

"It's free. Wedding parties are at liberty."

"That's not the point at all. I tell you that you must try to learn for me what that wedding is, who that old cove belongs to, and where that wedding pair lives."

"I like that! that would be queer. It's so easy to find out a wedding party that passed through the street on a Shrove Tuesday, a week afterwards. A pin in a hay-mow! It ain't possible!"

"That don't matter. You must try. You understand me, Azelma."

The two files resumed their movement on both sides of the boulevard, in opposite directions, and the carriage of the maskers lost sight of the "trap" of the bride.

Chapter II

Jean Valjean Still Wears His Arm in a Sling

To realize one's dream. To whom is this accorded? There must be elections for this in heaven; we are all candidates, unknown to ourselves; the angels vote. Cosette and Marius had been elected.

Cosette, both at the mayor's office and at church, was dazzling and touching. Toussaint, assisted by Nicolette, had dressed her.

Cosette wore over a petticoat of white taffeta, her robe of Binche guipure, a veil of English point, a necklace of fine pearls, a wreath of orange flowers; all this was white, and, from the midst of that whiteness she beamed forth. It was an exquisite candor expanding and becoming transfigured in the light. One would have pronounced her a virgin on the point of turning into a goddess.

Marius's handsome hair was lustrous and perfumed; here and there, beneath the thick curls, pale lines—the scars of the barricade—were visible.

The grandfather, haughty, with head held high, amalgamating more than ever in his toilet and his manners all the elegances of the epoch of Barras, escorted Cosette. He took the place of Jean Valjean, who, on account of his arm being still in a sling, could not give his hand to the bride.

Jean Valjean, dressed in black, followed them with a smile.

"Monsieur Fauchelevent," said the grandfather to him, "this is a fine day. I vote for the end of afflictions and sorrows. Henceforth, there must be no sadness anywhere. Pardieu, I decree joy! Evil has no right to exist. That there should be any unhappy men is, in sooth, a disgrace to the azure of the sky. Evil does not come from man, who is good at bottom. All human miseries have for their capital and central government hell, otherwise known as the Devil's Tuileries. Good, here I am uttering demagogical words! As far as I am concerned, I have no longer any political opinions; let all men be rich, that is to say, mirthful, and I confine myself to that."

When, at the conclusion of all the ceremonies, after having pronounced before the mayor and before the priest all possible "yeses," after having signed the registers at the municipality and at the sacristy, after having exchanged their rings, after having knelt side by side under the pall of white moire in the smoke of the censer, they arrived, hand in hand, admired and envied by all, Marius in black, she in white, preceded by the suisse, with the epaulets of a colonel, tapping the pavement with his halberd, between two rows of astonished spectators, at the portals of the church, both leaves of which were thrown wide open, ready to enter their carriage again, and all being finished, Cosette still could not believe that it was real. She looked at Marius, she looked at the crowd, she looked at the sky: it seemed as though she feared that she should wake up from her dream. Her amazed and uneasy air added something indescribably enchanting to her beauty. They entered the same carriage to return home, Marius beside Cosette, M. Gillenormand and Jean Valjean sat opposite them; Aunt Gillenormand had withdrawn one degree, and was in the second vehicle.

"My children," said the grandfather, "here you are, Monsieur le Baron and Madame la Baronne, with an income of thirty thousand livres."

And Cosette, nestling close to Marius, caressed his ear with an angelic whisper: "So it is true. My name is Marius. I am Madame Thou."

These two creatures were resplendent. They had reached that irrevocable and irrecoverable moment, at the dazzling intersection of all youth and all joy. They realized the verses of Jean Prouvaire; they were forty years old taken together. It was marriage sublimated; these two children were two lilies. They did not see each other, they did not contemplate each other. Cosette perceived Marius in the midst of a glory; Marius perceived Cosette on an altar. And on that altar, and in that glory, the two apotheoses mingling, in the background, one knows not how, behind a cloud for Cosette, in a flash for Marius, there was the ideal thing, the real thing, the meeting of the kiss and the dream, the nuptial pillow. All the torments through which they had passed, came back to them in intoxication. It seemed to them that their sorrows, their sleepless nights, their tears, their anguish, their terrors, their despair, converted into caresses and rays of light, rendered still more charming the charming hour which was approaching; and that their griefs were but so many hand-maidens who were preparing the toilet of joy. How good it is to have suffered! Their unhappiness formed a halo round their happiness. The long agony of their love was terminating in an ascension.

It was the same enchantment in two souls, tinged with voluptuousness in Marius, and with modesty in Cosette. They said to each other in low tones: "We will go back to take a look at our little garden in the Rue Plumet." The folds of Cosette's gown lay across Marius.

Such a day is an ineffable mixture of dream and of reality. One possesses and one supposes. One still has time before one to divine. The emotion on that day, of being at midday and of dreaming of midnight is indescribable. The delights of these two hearts overflowed upon the crowd, and inspired the passers-by with cheerfulness.

People halted in the Rue Saint-Antoine, in front of Saint-Paul, to gaze through the windows of the carriage at the orange-flowers quivering on Cosette's head.

Then they returned home to the Rue des Filles-du-Calvaire. Marius, triumphant and radiant, mounted side by side with Cosette the staircase up which he had been borne in a dying condition. The poor, who had trooped to the door, and who shared their purses, blessed them. There were flowers everywhere. The house was no less fragrant than the church; after the incense, roses. They thought they heard voices caroling in the infinite; they had God in their hearts; destiny appeared to them like a ceiling of stars; above their heads they beheld the light of a rising sun. All at once, the clock struck. Marius glanced at Cosette's charming bare arm, and at the rosy things which were vaguely visible through the lace of her bodice, and Cosette, intercepting Marius's glance, blushed to her very hair.

Quite a number of old family friends of the Gillenormand family had been invited; they pressed about Cosette. Each one vied with the rest in saluting her as Madame la Baronne.

The officer, Théodule Gillenormand, now a captain, had come from Chartres, where he was stationed in garrison, to be present at the wedding of his cousin Pontmercy. Cosette did not recognize him.

He, on his side, habituated as he was to have women consider him handsome, retained no more recollection of Cosette than of any other woman.

"How right I was not to believe in that story about the lancer!" said Father Gillenormand to himself.

Cosette had never been more tender with Jean Valjean. She was in unison with Father Gillenormand; while he erected joy into aphorisms and maxims, she exhaled goodness like a perfume. Happiness desires that all the world should be happy.

She regained, for the purpose of addressing Jean Valjean, inflections of voice belonging to the time when she was a little girl. She caressed him with her smile.

A banquet had been spread in the dining-room.

Illumination as brilliant as the daylight, is the necessary seasoning of a great joy. Mist and obscurity are not accepted by the happy. They do not consent to be black. The night, yes; the shadows, no. If there is no sun, one must be made.

The dining-room was full of gay things. In the center, above the white and glittering table, was a Venetian luster with flat plates, with all sorts of colored birds, blue, violet, red, and green, perched amid the candles; around the chandelier, girandoles, on the walls, sconces with triple and quintuple branches; mirrors, silverware, glassware, plate, porcelain, faïence, pottery, gold and silversmith's work, all was sparkling and gay. The empty spaces between the candelabra were filled in with bouquets, so that, where there was not a light, there was a flower.

In the antechamber, three violins and a flute softly played quartettes by Haydn.

Jean Valjean had seated himself on a chair in the drawing-room, behind the door, the leaf of which folded back upon him in such a manner as to nearly conceal him. A few moments before they sat down to table, Cosette came, as though inspired by a sudden whim, and made him a deep curtsy, spreading out her bridal toilet with both hands, and with a tenderly roguish glance, she asked him:

"Father, are you satisfied?"

"Yes," said Jean Valjean, "I am content."

"Well, then, laugh."

Jean Valjean began to laugh.

A few moments later, Basque announced that dinner was served.

The guests, preceded by M. Gillenormand with Cosette on his arm, entered the dining-room, and arranged themselves in the proper order around the table.

Two large arm-chairs figured on the right and left of the bride, the first for M. Gillenormand, the other for Jean Valjean. M. Gillenormand took his seat. The other arm-chair remained empty.

They looked about for M. Fauchelevent.

He was no longer there.

M. Gillenormand questioned Basque.

"Do you know where M. Fauchelevent is?"

"Sir," replied Basque, "I do, precisely. M. Fauchelevent told me to say to you, sir, that he was suffering, his injured hand was paining him somewhat, and that he could not dine with Monsieur le Baron and Madame la Baronne. That he begged to be excused, that he would come to-morrow. He has just taken his departure."

That empty arm-chair chilled the effusion of the wedding feast for a moment. But, if M. Fauchelevent was absent, M. Gillenormand was present, and the grandfather beamed for two. He affirmed that M. Fauchelevent had done well to retire early, if he were suffering, but that it was only a slight ailment. This declaration sufficed. Moreover, what is an obscure corner in such a submersion of joy? Cosette and Marius were passing through one of those egotistical and blessed moments, when no other faculty is left to a person than that of receiving happiness. And then, an idea occurred to M. Gillenormand.—"Pardieu, this arm-chair is empty. Come hither, Marius. Your aunt will permit it, although she has a right to you. This arm-chair is for you. That is legal and delightful. Fortunatus beside Fortunata."—Applause from the whole table. Marius took Jean Valjean's place beside Cosette, and things fell out so that Cosette, who had, at first, been saddened by Jean Valjean's absence, ended by being satisfied with it. From the moment when Marius took his place, and was the substitute, Cosette would not have regretted God himself. She set her sweet little foot, shod in white satin, on Marius's foot.

The arm-chair being occupied, M. Fauchelevent was obliterated; and nothing was lacking.

And, five minutes afterward, the whole table, from one end to the other, was laughing with all the animation of forgetfulness.

At dessert, M. Gillenormand, rising to his feet, with a glass of champagne in his hand—only half full so that the palsy of his eighty years might not cause an overflow—proposed the health of the married pair.

"You shall not escape two sermons," he exclaimed. "This morning, you had one from the curé, this evening you shall have one from your grandfather. Listen to me; I will give you a bit of advice: Adore each other. I do not make a pack of gyrations, I go straight to the mark, be happy. In all creation, only the turtle-doves are wise. Philosophers say: 'Moderate your joys.' I say: 'Give rein to your joys.' Be as much smitten with each other as fiends. Be in a rage about it. The philosophers talk stuff and nonsense. I should like to stuff their philosophy down their gullets again. Can there be too many perfumes, too many open rose-buds, too many nightingales singing, too many green leaves, too much aurora in life? can people love each other too much? can people please each other too much? Take care, Estelle, thou art too pretty! Have a care, Nemorin, thou art too handsome! Fine stupidity, in sooth! Can people enchant each other too much, cajole each other too much, charm each other too much? can one be too much alive, too happy? Moderate your joys. Ah, indeed! Down with the philosophers! Wisdom consists in jubilation. Make merry, let us make merry. Are we happy because we are good, or are we good because we are happy? Is the Sancy diamond called the Sancy because it belonged to Harley de Sancy, or because it weighs six hundred carats? I know nothing about it, life is full of such problems; the important point is to possess the Sancy and happiness. Let us be happy without quibbling and quirking. Let us obey the sun blindly. What is the sun? It is love. He who says love, says woman. Ah! ah! behold omnipotence—women. Ask that demagogue of a Marius if he is not the slave of that little tyrant of a Cosette. And of his own free will, too, the coward! Woman! There is no Robespierre who keeps his place, but woman reigns. I am no longer royalist except toward that royalty. What is Adam? The kingdom of Eve. No '89 for Eve. There has been the royal scepter surmounted by a fleur-de-lys, there has been the imperial scepter surmounted by a globe, there has been the scepter of Charlemagne, which was of iron, there has been the scepter of Louis the Great, which was of gold—the revolution twisted them between its thumb and forefinger, ha'penny straws; it is done with, it is broken, it lies on the earth, there is no longer any scepter, but make me a revolution against that little embroidered handkerchief, which smells of patchouli! I should like to see you do it. Try. Why is it so solid? Because it is a gewgaw. Ah! you are the nineteenth century? Well, what then? And we have been as foolish as you. Do not imagine that you have effected much change in the universe, because your trip-gallant is called the cholera-morbus, and because your pourrée is called the cachuca. In fact, the women must always be loved. I defy you to escape from that. These friends are our angels. Yes, love, woman, the kiss forms a circle from which I defy you to escape; and, for my own part, I should be only too happy to re-enter it. Which of you has seen the planet Venus, the coquette of the abyss, the Célimène of the ocean, rise in the infinite, calming all here below? The ocean is a rough Alcestis. Well, grumble as he will, when Venus appears he is forced to smile. That brute beast submits. We are all made so. Wrath, tempest, claps of thunder, foam to the very ceiling. A woman enters on the scene, a planet rises; flat on your face! Marius was fighting six months ago; to-day he is married. That is well. Yes, Marius, yes, Cosette, you are in the right. Exist boldly for each other, make us burst with rage that we cannot do the same, idealize each other, catch in your beaks all the tiny blades of felicity that exist on earth, and arrange yourselves a nest for life. Pardi, to love, to be loved, what a fine miracle when one is young! Don't imagine that you have invented that. I too, have had my dream, I too, have meditated, I too, have sighed; I too, have had a moonlight soul. Love is a child six thousand years old. Love has the right to a long white beard. Methusalem is a street arab beside Cupid. For sixty centuries, men and women have got out of their scrape by loving. The devil, who is cunning, took to hating man; man, who is still more cunning, took to loving woman. In this way he does more good than the devil does him harm. This craft was discovered in the days of the terrestrial paradise. The invention is old, my friends, but it is perfectly new. Profit by it. Be Daphnis, and Chloe, while waiting to become Philemon and Baucis. Manage so that, when you are with each other, nothing shall be lacking to you, and that Cosette may be the sun for Marius, and that Marius may be the universe to Cosette. Cosette, let your fine weather be the smile of your husband; Marius, let your rain be your wife's tears. And let it never rain in your household. You have filched the winning number in the lottery; you have gained the great prize, guard it well, keep it under lock and key, do not squander it, adore each other and snap your fingers at all the rest. Believe what I say to you. It is good sense. And good sense cannot lie. Be a religion to each other. Each man has his own fashion of adoring God. Saperlotte! the best way to adore God is to love one's wife. *I love thee!* that's my catechism. He who loves is orthodox. The oath of Henri IV places sanctity somewhere between feasting and drunkenness. Ventre-saint-gris! I don't belong to the religion of that oath. Woman is forgotten in it. This astonishes me on the part of Henri IV. My friends, long live women! I am old, they say: it's astonishing how much I feel in the mood to be young. I should like to go and listen to the bagpipes in the woods. Children who contrive to be beautiful and contented—that intoxicates me. I would like greatly to get married, if anyone would have me. It is impossible to imagine that God could have made us for anything but this: to idolize, to coo, to preen ourselves, to be dove-like, to be dainty, to bill and coo our loves from morn to night, to gaze at one's image in one's little wife, to be proud, to be triumphant, to plume one's self; that is the aim of life. There, let not that displease you which we used to think in our day, when we were young folks. Ah! vertu-bamboche! what charming women there were in those days, and what pretty little faces and what lovely lasses! I committed my ravages among them. Then love each other. If people did not love each other, I really do not see what use there would be in having any springtime; and for my own part, I should pray the good God to shut up all the beautiful things that he shows us, and to take away from us and put back in his box, the flowers, the birds, and the pretty maidens. My children, receive an old man's blessing."

The evening was gay, lively and agreeable. The grandfather's sovereign good humor gave the key-note to the whole feast, and each person regulated his conduct on that almost centenarian cordiality. They danced a little, they laughed a great deal; it was an amiable wedding. Goodman Days of Yore might have been invited to it. However, he was present in the person of Father Gillenormand.

There was a tumult, then silence.

The married pair disappeared.

A little after midnight, the Gillenormand house became a temple.

Here we pause. On the threshold of wedding nights stands a smiling angel with his finger on his lips.

The soul enters into contemplation before that sanctuary where the celebration of love takes place.

There should be flashes of light athwart such houses. The joy which they contain ought to make its escape through the stones of the walls in brilliancy, and vaguely illuminate the gloom. It is impossible that this sacred and fatal festival should not give off a celestial radiance to the infinite. Love is the sublime crucible wherein the fusion of the man and the woman takes place; the being one, the being triple, the being final, the human trinity proceeds from it. This birth of two souls into one, ought to be an emotion for the gloom. The lover is the priest; the ravished virgin is terrified. Something of that joy ascends to God. Where true marriage is, that is to say, where there is love, the ideal enters in. A nuptial bed makes a nook of dawn amid the shadows. If it were given to the eye of the flesh to scan the formidable and charming visions of the upper life, it is probable that we should behold the forms of night, the winged unknowns, the blue passers of the invisible, bend down, a throng of somber heads, around the luminous house, satisfied, showering benedictions, pointing out to each other the virgin wife gently alarmed, sweetly terrified, and bearing the reflection of human bliss upon their divine countenances. If at that supreme hour, the wedded pair, dazzled with voluptuousness and believing themselves alone were to listen, they would hear in their chamber a confused rustling of wings. Perfect happiness implies a mutual understanding with the angels. That dark little chamber has all heaven for its ceiling. When two mouths, rendered sacred by love, approach to create, it is impossible, that there should not be, above that ineffable kiss, a quivering throughout the immense mystery of stars.

These felicities are the true ones. There is no joy outside of these joys. Love is the only ecstasy. All the rest weeps.

To love, or to have loved—this suffices. Demand nothing more. There is no other pearl to be found in the shadowy folds of life. To love is a fulfillment.

Chapter III

THE INSEPERABLE

WHAT HAD BECOME OF JEAN VALJEAN?

Immediately after having laughed, at Cosette's graceful command, when no one was paying any heed to him, Jean Valjean had risen, and had gained the antechamber unperceived. This was the very room which, eight months before, he had entered black with mud, with blood and powder, bringing back the grandson to the grandfather. The old wainscoting was garlanded with foliage and flowers; the musicians were seated on the sofa on which they had laid Marius down. Basque, in a black coat, knee-breeches, white stockings and white gloves, was arranging roses round all of the dishes that were to be served. Jean Valjean pointed to his arm in its sling, charged Basque to explain his absence, and went away.

The long windows of the dining-room opened on the street. Jean Valjean stood for several minutes, erect and motionless in the darkness, beneath those radiant windows. He listened. The confused sounds of the banquet reached his ear. He heard the loud, commanding tones of the grandfather, the violins, the clatter of the plates, the bursts of laughter, and through all that merry uproar, he distinguished Cosette's sweet and joyous voice.

He quitted the Rue des Filles-du-Calvaire, and returned to the Rue de l'Homme Armé.

In order to return thither, he took the Rue Saint-Louis, the Rue Culture-Sainte-Catherine, and the Blancs-Manteaux; it was a little longer, but it was the road through which, for the last three months, he had become accustomed to pass every day on his way from the Rue de l'Homme Armé to the Rue des Filles-du-Calvaire, in order to avoid the obstructions and the mud in the Rue Vielle-du-Temple.

This road, through which Cosette had passed, excluded for him, all possibility of any other itinerary.

Jean Valjean entered his lodgings. He lighted his candle and mounted the stairs. The apartment was empty. Even Toussaint was no longer there. Jean Valjean's step made more noise than usual in the chambers. All the cupboards stood open. He penetrated to Cosette's bedroom. There were no sheets on the bed. The pillow, covered with ticking, and without a case or lace, was laid on the blankets folded up on the foot of the mattress, whose covering was visible, and on which no one was ever to sleep again. All the little feminine objects which Cosette was attached to, had been carried away; nothing remained except the heavy furniture and the four walls. Toussaint's bed was despoiled in like manner. One bed only was made up, and seemed to be waiting someone, and this was Jean Valjean's bed.

Jean Valjean looked at the walls, closed some of the cupboard doors, and went and came from one room to another.

Then he sought his own chamber once more, and set his candle on a table.

He had disengaged his arm from the sling, and he used his right hand as though it did not hurt him.

He approached his bed, and his eyes rested, was it by chance? was it intentionally? on the *inseparable* of which Cosette had been jealous, on the little portmanteau which never left him. On his arrival in the Rue de l'Homme Armé, on the 4th of June, he had deposited it on a round table near the head of his bed. He went to this table with a sort of vivacity, took a key from his pocket, and opened the valise.

From it he slowly drew forth the garments in which, ten years before, Cosette had quitted Montfermeil; first the little gown, then the black fichu, then the stout, coarse child's shoes which Cosette might almost have worn still, so tiny were her feet, then the fustian bodice, which was very thick, then the knitted petticoat, next the apron with pockets, then the woolen stockings. These stockings, which still preserved the graceful form of a tiny leg, were no longer than Jean Valjean's hand. All this was black of hue. It was he who had brought those garments to Montfermeil for her. As he removed them from the valise, he laid them on the bed. He fell to thinking. He called up memories. It was in winter, in a very cold month of December, she was shivering, half-naked, in rags, her poor little feet were all red in their wooden shoes. He, Jean Valjean, had made her abandon those rags to clothe herself in these mourning habiliments. The mother must have felt pleased in her grave, to see her daughter wearing mourning for her, and, above all, to see that she was properly clothed, and that she was warm. He thought of that forest of Montfermeil; they had traversed it together, Cosette and he; he thought of what the weather had been, of the leafless trees, of the wood destitute of birds, of the sunless sky; it mattered not, it was charming. He arranged the tiny garments on the bed, the fichu next to the petticoat, the stockings beside the shoes, and he looked at them, one after the other. She was no taller than that, she had her big doll in her arms, she had put her louis d'or in the pocket of that apron, she had laughed, they walked hand in hand, she had no one in the world but him.

Then his venerable, white head fell forward on the bed, that stoical old heart, broke, his face was engulfed, so to speak, in Cosette's garments, and if anyone had passed up the stairs at that moment, he would have heard frightful sobs.

Chapter IV

THE IMMORTAL LIVER

THE OLD AND FORMIDABLE STRUGGLE, OF WHICH WE HAVE ALREADY WITNESSED SO MANY phases, began once more.

Jacob struggled with the angel but one night. Alas! how many times have we beheld Jean Valjean seized bodily by his conscience, in the darkness, and struggling desperately against it!

Unheard-of conflict! At certain moments the foot slips; at other moments the ground crumbles away underfoot. How many times had that conscience, mad for the good, clasped and overthrown him! How many times had the truth, set her knee inexorably upon his breast! How many times, hurled to earth by the light, had he begged for mercy! How many times had that implacable spark, lighted within him, and upon him by the Bishop, dazzled him by force when he had wished to be blind! How many times had he risen to his feet in the combat, held fast to the rock, leaning against sophism, dragged in the dust, now getting the upper hand of his conscience, again overthrown by it! How many times, after an equivoque, after the specious and treacherous reasoning of egotism, had he heard his irritated conscience cry in his ear: "A trip! you wretch!" How many times had his refractory thoughts rattled convulsively in his throat, under the evidence of duty! Resistance to God. Funereal sweats. What secret wounds which he alone felt bleed! What excoriations in his lamentable existence! How many times he had risen bleeding, bruised, broken, enlightened, despair in his heart, serenity in his soul! and, vanquished, he had felt himself the conqueror. And, after having dislocated, broken, and rent his conscience with red-hot pincers, it had said to him, as it stood over him, formidable, luminous, and tranquil: "Now, go in peace!"

But on emerging from so melancholy a conflict, what a lugubrious peace, alas!

Nevertheless, that night Jean Valjean felt that he was passing through his final combat.

A heartrending question presented itself.

Predestinations are not all direct; they do not open out in a straight avenue before the predestined man; they have blind courts, impassable alleys, obscure turns, disturbing cross-roads offering the choice of many ways. Jean Valjean had halted at that moment at the most perilous of these cross-roads.

He had come to the supreme crossing of good and evil. He had that gloomy intersection beneath his eyes. On this occasion once more, as had happened to him already in other sad vicissitudes, two roads opened out before him, the one tempting, the other alarming.

Which was he to take?

He was counseled to the one which alarmed him by that mysterious index finger which we all perceive whenever we fix our eyes on the darkness.

Once more, Jean Valjean had the choice between the terrible port and the smiling ambush.

Is it then true? the soul may recover; but not fate. Frightful thing! an incurable destiny!

This is the problem which presented itself to him:

In what manner was Jean Valjean to behave in relation to the happiness of Cosette and Marius? It was he who had willed that happiness, it was he who had brought it about; he had, himself, buried it in his entrails, and at that moment, when he reflected on it, he was able to enjoy the sort of satisfaction which an armorer would experience on recognizing his factory mark on a knife, on withdrawing it, all smoking, from his own breast.

Cosette had Marius, Marius possessed Cosette. They had everything, even riches. And this was his doing.

But what was he, Jean Valjean, to do with this happiness, now that it existed, now that it was there? Should he force himself on this happiness? Should he treat it as belonging to him? No doubt, Cosette did belong to another; but should he, Jean Valjean, retain of Cosette all that he could retain? Should he remain the sort of father, half seen but respected, which he had hitherto been? Should he, without saying a word, bring his past to that future? Should he present himself there, as though he had a right, and should he seat himself, veiled, at that luminous fireside? Should he take those innocent hands into his tragic hands, with a smile? Should he place upon the peaceful fender of the Gillenormand drawing-room those feet of his, which dragged behind them the disgraceful shadow of the law? Should he enter into participation in the fair fortunes of Cosette and Marius? Should he render the obscurity on his brow and the cloud upon theirs still more dense? Should he place his catastrophe as a third associate in their felicity? Should he continue to hold his peace? In a word, should he be the sinister mute of destiny beside these two happy beings?

We must have become habituated to fatality and to encounters with it, in order to have the daring to raise our eyes when certain questions appear to us in all their horrible nakedness. Good or evil stands behind this severe interrogation point. What are you going to do? demands the sphinx.

This habit of trial Jean Valjean possessed. He gazed intently at the sphinx.

He examined the pitiless problem under all its aspects.

Cosette, that charming existence, was the raft of this shipwreck. What was he to do? To cling fast to it, or to let go his hold?

If he clung to it, he should emerge from disaster, he should ascend again into the sunlight, he should let the bitter water drip from his garments and his hair, he was saved, he should live.

And if he let go his hold?

Then, the abyss.

Thus he took sad council with his thoughts. Or, to speak more correctly, he fought; he kicked furiously internally, now against his will, now against his conviction.

Happily for Jean Valjean that he had been able to weep. That relieved him, possibly. But the beginning was savage. A tempest, more furious than the one which had formerly driven him to Arras, broke loose within him. The past surged up before him facing the present; he compared them and sobbed. The sluice of tears once opened, the despairing man writhed.

He felt that he had been stopped short

Alas! in this fight to the death between our egotism and our duty, when we thus retreat step by step before our immutable ideal, bewildered, furious, exasperated at having to yield, disputing the ground, hoping for a possible flight, seeking an escape, what an abrupt and sinister resistance does the foot of the wall offer in our rear!

To feel the sacred shadow which forms an obstacle!

The invisible inexorable, what an obsession!

Then, one is never done with conscience. Make your choice, Brutus; make your choice, Cato. It is fathomless, since it is God. One flings into that well the labor of one's whole life, one flings in one's fortune, one flings in one's riches, one flings in one's success, one flings in one's liberty or fatherland, one flings in one's well-being, one flings in one's repose, one flings in one's joy! More! more! more! Empty the vase! tip the urn! One must finish by flinging in one's heart.

Somewhere in the fog of the ancient hells, there is a tun like that.

Is not one pardonable, if one at last refuses! Can the inexhaustible have any right? Are not chains which are endless above human strength? Who would blame Sisyphus and Jean Valjean for saying: "It is enough!"

The obedience of matter is limited by friction; is there no limit to the obedience of the soul? If perpetual motion is impossible, can perpetual self-sacrifice be exacted?

The first step is nothing, it is the last which is difficult. What was the Champmathieu affair in comparison with Cosette's marriage and of that which it entailed? What is a re-entrance into the galleys, compared to entrance into the void?

Oh, first step that must be descended, how somber art thou! Oh, second step, how black art thou!

How could he refrain from turning aside his head this time?

Martyrdom is sublimation, corrosive sublimation. It is a torture which consecrates. One can consent to it for the first hour; one seats one's self on the throne of glowing iron, one places on one's head the crown of hot iron, one accepts the globe of red hot iron, one takes the scepter of red hot iron, but the mantle of flame still remains to be donned, and comes there not a moment when the miserable flesh revolts and when one abdicates from suffering?

At length, Jean Valjean entered into the peace of exhaustion.

He weighed, he reflected, he considered the alternatives, the mysterious balance of light and darkness.

Should he impose his galleys on those two dazzling children, or should he consummate his irremediable engulfment by himself? On one side lay the sacrifice of Cosette, on the other that of himself.

At what solution should he arrive? What decision did he come to?

What resolution did he take? What was his own inward definitive response to the unbribable interrogatory of fatality? What door did he decide to open? Which side of his life did he resolve upon closing and condemning? Among all the unfathomable precipices which surrounded him, which was his choice? What extremity did he accept? To which of the gulfs did he nod his head?

His dizzy reverie lasted all night long.

He remained there until daylight, in the same attitude, bent double over that bed, prostrate beneath the enormity of fate, crushed, perchance, alas! with clenched fists, with arms outspread at right angles, like a man crucified who has been un-nailed, and flung face down on the earth. There he remained for twelve hours, the twelve long hours of a long winter's night, ice-cold, without once raising his head, and without uttering a word. He was as motionless as a corpse, while his thoughts wallowed on the earth and soared, now like the hydra, now like the eagle. Anyone to behold him thus motionless, would have pronounced him dead; all at once he shuddered convulsively, and his mouth, glued to Cosette's garments, kissed them; then it could be seen that he was alive.

Who could see? Since Jean Valjean was alone, and there was no one there.

The One who is in the shadows.

BOOK SEVENTH

THE LAST DRAFT FROM THE CUP

Chapter I

THE SEVENTH CIRCLE AND THE EIGHTH HEAVEN

THE DAYS THAT FOLLOW WEDDINGS ARE SOLITARY. PEOPLE RESPECT THE MEDITATIONS OF THE happy pair. And also, their tardy slumbers, to some degree. The tumult of visits and congratulations only begins later on. On the morning of the 17th of February, it was a little past midday when Basque, with napkin and feather-duster under his arm, busy in setting his antechamber to rights, heard a light tap at the door. There had been no ring, which was discreet on such a day. Basque opened the door, and beheld M. Fauchelevent. He introduced him into the drawing-room, still encumbered and topsy-turvy, and which bore the air of a field of battle after the joys of the preceding evening.

"*Dame*, sir," remarked Basque, "we all woke up late."

"Is your master up?" asked Jean Valjean.

"How is Monsieur's arm?" replied Basque.

"Better. Is your master up?"

"Which one? the old one or the new one?"

"Monsieur Pontmercy."

"Monsieur le Baron," said Basque, drawing himself up.

A man is a Baron most of all to his servants. He counts for something with them; they are what a philosopher would call, bespattered with the title, and that flatters them. Marius, be it said in passing, a militant republican as he had proved, was now a Baron in spite of himself. A small revolution had taken place in the family in connection with this title. It was now M. Gillenormand who clung to it, and Marius who detached himself from it. But Colonel Pontmercy had written: "My son will bear my title." Marius obeyed. And then, Cosette, in whom the woman was beginning to dawn, was delighted to be a Baroness.

"Monsieur le Baron?" repeated Basque. "I will go and see. I will tell him that M. Fauchelevent is here."

"No. Do not tell him that it is I. Tell him that someone wishes to speak to him in private, and mention no name."

"Ah!" ejaculated Basque.

"I wish to surprise him."

"Ah!" ejaculated Basque once more, emitting his second "ah!" as an explanation of the first.

And he left the room.

Jean Valjean remained alone.

The drawing-room, as we have just said, was in great disorder. It seemed as though, by lending an air, one might still hear the vague noise of the wedding. On the polished floor lay all sorts of flowers which had fallen from garlands and headdresses. The wax candles, burned to stumps, added stalactites of wax to the crystal drops of the chandeliers. Not a single piece of furniture was in its place. In the corners, three or four arm-chairs, drawn close together in a circle, had the appearance of continuing a conversation. The whole effect was cheerful. A certain grace still lingers round a dead feast. It has been a happy thing. On the chairs in disarray, among those fading flowers, beneath those extinct lights, people have thought of joy. The sun had succeeded to the chandelier, and made its way gaily into the drawing-room.

Several minutes elapsed. Jean Valjean stood motionless on the spot where Basque had left him. He was very pale. His eyes were hollow, and so sunken in his head by sleeplessness that they nearly disappeared in their orbits. His black coat bore the weary folds of a garment that has been up all night. The elbows were whitened with the down which the friction of cloth against linen leaves behind it.

Jean Valjean stared at the window outlined on the polished floor at his feet by the sun.

There came a sound at the door, and he raised his eyes.

Marius entered, his head well up, his mouth smiling, an indescribable light on his countenance, his brow expanded, his eyes triumphant. He had not slept either.

"It is you, father!" he exclaimed, on catching sight of Jean Valjean; "that idiot of a Basque had such a mysterious air! But you have come too early. It is only half-past twelve. Cosette is asleep."

That word: "Father," said to M. Fauchelevent by Marius, signified: supreme felicity. There had always existed, as the reader knows, a lofty wall, a coldness and a constraint between them; ice which must be broken or melted. Marius had reached that point of intoxication when the wall was lowered, when the ice dissolved, and when M. Fauchelevent was to him, as to Cosette, a father.

He continued: his words poured forth, as is the peculiarity of divine paroxysms of joy.

"How glad I am to see you! If you only knew how we missed you yesterday! Good morning, father. How is your hand? Better, is it not?"

And, satisfied with the favorable reply which he had made to himself, he pursued:

"We have both been talking about you. Cosette loves you so dearly! You must not forget that you have a chamber here, We want nothing more to do with the Rue de l'Homme Armé. We will have no more of it at all. How could you go to live in a street like that, which is sickly, which is disagreeable, which is ugly, which has a barrier at one end, where one is cold, and into which one cannot enter? You are to come and install yourself here. And this very day. Or you will have to deal with Cosette. She means to lead us all by the nose, I warn you. You have your own chamber here, it is close to ours, it opens on the garden; the trouble with the clock has been attended to, the bed is made, it is all ready, you have only to take possession of it. Near your bed Cosette has placed a huge, old, easy-chair covered with Utrecht velvet, and she has said to it: 'Stretch out your arms to him.' A nightingale comes to the clump of acacias opposite your windows, every spring. In two months more you will have it. You will have its nest on your left and ours on your right. By night it will sing, and by day Cosette will prattle. Your chamber faces due South. Cosette will arrange your books for you, your Voyages of Captain Cook and the other—Vancouver's—and all your affairs. I believe that there is a little valise to which you are attached, I have fixed upon a corner of honor for that. You have conquered my grandfather, you suit him. We will live together. Do you play whist? you will overwhelm my grandfather with delight if you play whist. It is you who shall take Cosette to walk on the days when I am at the courts, you shall give her your arm, you know, as you used to, in the Luxembourg. We are absolutely resolved to be happy. And you shall be included in it, in our happiness, do you hear, father? Come, will you breakfast with us to-day?"

"Sir," said Jean Valjean, "I have something to say to you. I am an ex-convict."

The limit of shrill sounds perceptible can be overleaped, as well in the case of the mind as in that of the ear. These words: "I am an ex-convict," proceeding from the mouth of M. Fauchelevent and entering the ear of Marius, overshot the possible. It seemed to him that something had just been said to him; but he did not know what. He stood with his mouth wide open.

Then he perceived that the man who was addressing him was frightful. Wholly absorbed in his own dazzled state, he had not, up to that moment, observed the other man's terrible pallor.

Jean Valjean untied the black cravat which supported his right arm, unrolled the linen from around his hand, bared his thumb and showed it to Marius.

"There is nothing the matter with my hand," said he.

Marius looked at the thumb.

"There has not been anything the matter with it," went on Jean Valjean.

There was, in fact, no trace of any injury.

Jean Valjean continued:

"It was fitting that I should be absent from your marriage. I absented myself as much as was in my power. So I invented this injury in order that I might not commit a forgery, that I might not introduce a flaw into the marriage documents, in order that I might escape from signing."

Marius stammered.

"What is the meaning of this?"

"The meaning of it is," replied Jean Valjean, "that I have been in the galleys."

"You are driving me mad!" exclaimed Marius in terror.

"Monsieur Pontmercy," said Jean Valjean, "I was nineteen years in the galleys. For theft. Then, I was condemned for life for theft, for a second offense. At the present moment, I have broken my ban."

In vain did Marius recoil before the reality, refuse the fact, resist the evidence, he was forced to give way. He began to understand, and, as always happens in such cases, he understood too much. An inward shudder of hideous enlightenment flashed through him; an idea which made him quiver traversed his mind. He caught a glimpse of a wretched destiny for himself in the future.

"Say all, say all!" he cried. "You are Cosette's father!"

And he retreated a couple of paces with a movement of indescribable horror.

Jean Valjean elevated his head with so much majesty of attitude that he seemed to grow even to the ceiling.

"It is necessary that you should believe me here, sir; although our oath to others may not be received in law . . ."

Here he paused, then, with a sort of sovereign and sepulchral authority, he added, articulating slowly, and emphasizing the syllables:

". . . You will believe me. I the father of Cosette! before God, no. Monsieur le Baron Pontmercy, I am a peasant of Faverolles. I earned my living by pruning trees. My name is not Fauchelevent, but Jean Valjean. I am not related to Cosette. Reassure yourself."

Marius stammered:

"Who will prove that to me?"

"I. Since I tell you so."

Marius looked at the man. He was melancholy yet tranquil. No lie could proceed from such a calm. That which is icy is sincere. The truth could be felt in that chill of the tomb.

"I believe you," said Marius.

Jean Valjean bent his head, as though taking note of this, and continued:

"What am I to Cosette? A passer-by. Ten years ago, I did not know that she was in existence. I love her, it is true. One loves a child whom one has seen when very young, being old one's self. When one is old, one feels one's self a grandfather toward all little children. You may, it seems to me, suppose that I have something which resembles a heart. She was an orphan. Without either father or mother. She needed me. That is why I began to love her. Children are so weak that the first-comer, even a man like me, can become their protector. I have fulfilled this duty toward Cosette. I do not think that so slight a thing can be called a good action; but if it be a good action, well, say that I have done it. Register this attenuating circumstance. To-day, Cosette passes out of my life;

our two roads part. Henceforth, I can do nothing for her. She is Madame Pontmercy. Her providence has changed. And Cosette gains by the change. All is well. As for the six hundred thousand francs, you do not mention them to me, but I forestall your thought, they are a deposit. How did that deposit come into my hands? What does that matter? I restore the deposit. Nothing more can be demanded of me. I complete the restitution by announcing my true name. That concerns me. I have a reason for desiring that you should know who I am."

And Jean Valjean looked Marius full in the face.

All that Marius experienced was tumultuous and incoherent. Certain gusts of destiny produce these billows in our souls.

We have all undergone moments of trouble in which everything within us is dispersed; we say the first things that occur to us, which are not always precisely those which should be said. There are sudden revelations which one cannot bear, and which intoxicate like baleful wine. Marius was stupefied by the novel situation which presented itself to him, to the point of addressing that man almost like a person who was angry with him for this avowal.

"But why," he exclaimed, "do you tell me all this? Who forces you to do so? You could have kept your secret to yourself. You are neither denounced, nor tracked nor pursued. You have a reason for wantonly making such a revelation. Conclude. There is something more. In what connection do you make this confession? What is your motive?"

"My motive?" replied Jean Valjean in a voice so low and dull that one would have said that he was talking to himself rather than to Marius. "From what motive, in fact, has this convict just said 'I am a convict'? Well, yes! the motive is strange. It is out of honesty. Stay, the unfortunate point is that I have a thread in my heart, which keeps me fast. It is when one is old that that sort of thread is particularly solid. All life falls in ruin around one; one resists. Had I been able to tear out that thread, to break it, to undo the knot or to cut it, to go far away, I should have been safe. I had only to go away; there are diligences in the Rue Bouloy; you are happy; I am going. I have tried to break that thread, I have jerked at it, it would not break, I tore my heart with it. Then I said: 'I cannot live anywhere else than here.' I must stay. Well, yes, you are right, I am a fool, why not simply remain here? You offer me a chamber in this house, Madame Pontmercy is sincerely attached to me, she said to the arm-chair: 'Stretch out your arms to him,' your grandfather demands nothing better than to have me, I suit him, we shall live together, and take our meals in common, I shall give Cosette my arm. . . . Madame Pontmercy, excuse me, it is a habit—we shall have but one roof, one table, one fire, the same chimney-corner in winter, the same promenade in summer, that is joy, that is happiness, that is everything. We shall live as one family. One family!"

At that word, Jean Valjean became wild. He folded his arms, glared at the floor beneath his feet as though he would have excavated an abyss therein, and his voice suddenly rose in thundering tones:

"As one family! No. I belong to no family. I do not belong to yours. I do not belong to any family of men. In houses where people are among themselves, I am superfluous. There are families, but there is nothing of the sort for me. I am an unlucky wretch; I am left outside. Did I have a father and mother? I almost doubt it. On the day when I gave that child in marriage, all came to an end. I have seen her happy, and that she is with a man whom she loves, and that there exists here a kind old man, a household of two angels, and all joys in that house, and that it was well, I said to myself: 'Enter thou not.' I could have lied, it is true, have deceived you all, and remained Monsieur Fauchelevent. So long as it was for her, I could lie; but now it would be for myself, and I must not. It was sufficient for me to hold my peace, it is true, and all would go on. You ask me what has forced me to speak? a very odd thing; my conscience. To hold my peace was very easy, however. I passed the night in trying to persuade myself to it; you questioned me, and what I have just said to you is so extraordinary that you have the right to do it; well, yes, I have passed the night in alleging reasons to myself, and I gave myself very good reasons, I have done what I could. But there are two things in which I have not succeeded; in breaking the thread that holds me fixed, riveted and sealed here by the heart, or in silencing someone who speaks softly to me when I am alone. That is why I have come hither to tell you everything this morning. Everything or nearly everything. It is useless to tell you that which concerns only myself; I keep that to myself. You know the essential points. So I have taken my mystery and have brought it to you. And I have disemboweled my secret before your eyes. It was not a resolution that was easy to take. I struggled all night long. Ah! you think that I did not tell myself that this was no Champmathieu affair, that by concealing my name I was doing no one any injury, that the name of Fauchelevent had been given to me by Fauchelevent himself, out of gratitude for a service rendered to him, and that I might assuredly keep it, and that I should be happy in that chamber which you offer me, that I should not be in anyone's way, that I should be in my own little corner, and that, while you would have Cosette, I should have the idea that I was in the same house with her. Each one of us would have had his share of happiness. If I continued to be Monsieur Fauchelevent, that would arrange everything. Yes, with the exception of my soul. There was joy everywhere upon my surface, but the bottom of my soul remained black. It is not enough to be happy, one must be content. Thus I should have remained Monsieur Fauchelevent, thus I should have concealed my true visage, thus, in the presence of your expansion, I should have had an enigma, thus, in the midst of your full noonday, I should have had shadows, thus, without crying "'ware,' I should have simply introduced the galleys to your fireside, I should have taken my seat at your table with the thought that if you knew who I was, you would drive me from it, I should have allowed myself to be served by domestics who, had they known, would have said: 'How horrible!' I should have touched you with my elbow, which you have a right to dislike, I should have filched your clasps of the hand! There would have existed in your house a division of respect between venerable white locks and tainted white locks; at your most intimate hours, when all hearts thought themselves open to the very bottom to all the rest, when we four were together, your grandfather, you two and myself, a stranger would have been present! I should have been side by side with you in your existence, having for my only care not to disarrange the cover of my dreadful pit. Thus, I, a dead man, should have thrust myself upon you who are living beings. I should have condemned her to myself forever. You and Cosette and I would have had all three of our heads in the green cap! Does it not make you shudder? I am only the most crushed of men; I should have been the most monstrous of men. And I should have committed that crime every day! And I should have had that face of night upon my visage every day! every day! And I should have communicated to you a share in my taint every day! every day! to you, my dearly beloved, my children, to you, my innocent creatures! Is it nothing to hold one's peace? is it a simple matter to keep silence? No, it is not simple. There is a silence which lies. And my lie, and my fraud and my indignity, and my cowardice and my treason and my crime, I should have drained drop by drop, I should have spit it out, then swallowed it again, I should have finished at midnight and have begun again at midday, and my 'good morning' would have lied, and my 'good night' would have lied, and I should have slept on it, I should have eaten it, with my bread, and I should have looked Cosette in the face, and I should have responded to the smile of the angel by the smile of the damned soul, and I should have been an abominable villain! Why should I do it? in order to be happy. In order to be happy. Have I the right to be happy? I stand outside of life, sir."

Jean Valjean paused. Marius listened. Such chains of ideas and of anguishes cannot be interrupted. Jean Valjean lowered his voice once more, but it was no longer a dull voice—it was a sinister voice.

"You ask why I speak? I am neither denounced, nor pursued, nor tracked, you say. Yes! I am denounced! yes! I am tracked! By whom? By myself. It is I who bar the passage to myself, and I drag myself, and I push myself, and I arrest myself, and I execute myself, and when one holds one's self, one is firmly held."

And, seizing a handful of his own coat by the nape of the neck and extending it toward Marius:

"Do you see that fist?" he continued. "Don't you think that it holds that collar in such a wise as not to release it? Well! conscience is another grasp! If one desires to be happy, sir, one must never understand duty; for, as soon as one has comprehended it, it is implacable. One would say that it punished you for comprehending it; but no, it rewards you; for it places you in a hell, where you feel God beside you. One has no sooner lacerated his own entrails than he is at peace with himself."

And, with a poignant accent, he added:

"Monsieur Pontmercy, this is not common sense, I am an honest man. It is by degrading myself in your eyes that I elevate myself in my own. This has happened to me once before, but it was less painful then; it was a mere nothing. Yes, an honest man. I should not be so if, through my fault, you had continued to esteem me; now that you despise me, I am so. I have that fatality hanging over me that, not being able to ever have anything but stolen consideration, that consideration humiliates me, and crushes me inwardly, and, in order that I may respect myself, it is necessary that I should be despised. Then I straighten up again. I am a galley-slave who obeys his conscience. I know well that that is most improbable. But what would you have me do about it? it is the fact. I have entered into engagements with myself; I keep them. There are encounters which bind us, there are chances which involve us in duties. You see, Monsieur Pontmercy, various things have happened to me in the course of my life."

Again Jean Valjean paused, swallowing his saliva with an effort, as though his words had a bitter aftertaste, and then he went on:

"When one has such a horror hanging over one, one has not the right to make others share it without their knowledge, one has not the right to make them slip over one's own precipice without their perceiving it, one has not the right to let one's red blouse drag upon them, one has no right to slyly encumber with one's misery the happiness of others. It is hideous to approach those who are healthy, and to touch them in the dark with one's ulcer. In spite of the fact that Fauchelevent lent me his name, I have no right to use it; he could give it to me, but I could not take it. A name is an *I*. You see, sir, that I have thought somewhat, I have read a little, although I am a peasant; and you see that I express myself properly. I understand things. I have procured myself an education. Well, yes, to abstract a name and to place one's self under it, is dishonest. Letters of the alphabet can be filched, like a purse or a watch. To be a false signature in flesh and blood, to be a living false key, to enter the house of honest people by picking their lock, never more to look straightforward, to forever eye askance, to be infamous within the *I*, no! no! no! no! no! It is better to suffer, to bleed, to weep, to tear one's skin from the flesh with one's nails, to pass nights writhing in anguish, to devour one's self body and soul. That is why I have just told you all this. Wantonly, as you say."

He drew a painful breath, and hurled this final word:

"In days gone by, I stole a loaf of bread in order to live; to-day, in order to live, I will not steal a name."

"To live!" interrupted Marius. "You do not need that name in order to live!"

"Ah! I understand the matter," said Jean Valjean, raising and lowering his head several times in succession.

A silence ensued. Both held their peace, each plunged in a gulf of thoughts. Marius was sitting near a table and resting the corner of his mouth on one of his fingers, which was folded back. Jean Valjean was pacing to and fro. He paused before a mirror, and remained motionless. Then, as though replying to some inward course of reasoning, he said, as he gazed at the mirror, which he did not see:

"While, at present, I am relieved."

He took up his march again, and walked to the other end of the drawing-room. At the moment when he turned round, he perceived that Marius was watching his walk. Then he said, with an inexpressible intonation:

"I drag my leg a little. Now you understand why."

Then he turned fully round toward Marius:

"And now, sir, imagine this: I have said nothing, I have remained Monsieur Fauchelevent, I have taken my place in your house, I am one of you, I am in my chamber, I come to breakfast in the morning in slippers, in the evening all three of us go to the play, I accompany Madame Pontmercy to the Tuileries, and to the Place Royale, we are together, you think me your equal; one fine day you are there, and I am there, we are conversing, we are laughing; all at once, you hear a voice shouting this name: 'Jean Valjean!' and behold, that terrible hand, the police, darts from the darkness, and abruptly tears off my mask!"

Again he paused; Marius had sprung to his feet with a shudder. Jean Valjean resumed:

"What do you say to that?"

Marius's silence answered for him.

Jean Valjean continued:

"You see that I am right in not holding my peace. Be happy, be in heaven, be the angel of an angel, exist in the sun, be content therewith, and do not trouble yourself about the means which a poor damned wretch takes to open his breast and force his duty to come forth; you have before you, sir, a wretched man."

Marius slowly crossed the room, and, when he was quite close to Jean Valjean, he offered the latter his hand.

But Marius was obliged to step up and take that hand which was not offered, Jean Valjean let him have his own way, and it seemed to Marius that he pressed a hand of marble.

"My grandfather has friends," said Marius; "I will procure your pardon."

"It is useless," replied Jean Valjean. "I am believed to be dead, and that suffices. The dead are not subjected to surveillance. They are supposed to rot in peace. Death is the same thing as pardon."

And, disengaging the hand which Marius held, he added, with a sort of inexorable dignity:

"Moreover, the friend to whom I have recourse, is the doing of my duty; and I need but one pardon, that of my conscience."

At that moment, a door at the other end of the drawing-room opened gently halfway, and in the opening Cosette's head appeared. They saw only her sweet face, her hair was in charming disorder, her eyelids were still swollen with sleep. She made the movement of a bird, which thrusts its head out of its nest, glanced first at her husband, then at Jean Valjean, and cried to them with a smile, so that they seemed to behold a smile at the heart of a rose:

"I will wager that you are talking politics. How stupid that is, instead of being with me!"

Jean Valjean shuddered.

"Cosette! . . ." stammered Marius.

And he paused. One would have said that they were two criminals.

Cosette, who was radiant, continued to gaze at both of them. There was something in her eyes like gleams of paradise.

"I have caught you in the very act," said Cosette. "Just now, I heard my father Fauchelevent through the door saying: 'Conscience . . . doing my duty . . .' That is politics, indeed it is. I will not have it. People should not talk politics the very next day. It is not right."

"You are mistaken, Cosette," said Marius, "we are talking business. We are discussing the best investment of your six hundred thousand francs . . ."

"That is not it at all," interrupted Cosette. "I am coming. Does anybody want me here?"

And, passing resolutely through the door, she entered the drawing-room. She was dressed in a voluminous white dressing-gown, with a thousand folds and large sleeves which, starting from the neck, fell to her feet. In the golden heavens of some ancient Gothic pictures, there are these charming sacks fit to clothe the angels.

She contemplated herself from head to foot in a long mirror, then exclaimed, in an outburst of ineffable ecstasy:

"There was once a King and a Queen. Oh! how happy I am!"

That said, she made a curtsey to Marius and to Jean Valjean.

"There," said she, "I am going to install myself near you in an easy-chair, we breakfast in half an hour, you shall say anything you like, I know well that men must talk, and I will be very good."

Marius took her by the arm and said lovingly to her:

"We are talking business."

"By the way," said Cosette, "I have opened my window, a flock of parrots has arrived in the garden—Birds, not maskers. To-day is Ash-Wednesday; but not for the birds."

"I tell you that we are talking business, go, my little Cosette, leave us alone for a moment. We are talking figures. That will bore you."

"You have a charming cravat on this morning, Marius. You are very dandified, monseigneur. No, it will not bore me."

"I assure you that it will bore you."

"No. Since it is you. I shall not understand you, but I shall listen to you. When one hears the voices of those whom one loves, one does not need to understand the words that they utter. That we should be here together—that is all that I desire. I shall remain with you, bah!"

"You are my beloved Cosette! Impossible."

"Impossible!"

"Yes."

"Very good," said Cosette. "I was going to tell you some news. I could have told you that your grandfather is still asleep, that your aunt is at mass, that the chimney in my father Fauchelevent's room smokes, that Nicolette has sent for the chimney-sweep, that Toussaint and Nicolette have already quarreled, that Nicolette makes sport of Toussaint's stammer. Well, you shall know nothing. Ah! it is impossible? you shall see, gentlemen, that I, in my turn, can say: It is impossible. Then who will be caught? I beseech you, my little Marius, let me stay here with you two."

"I swear to you, that it is indispensable that we should be alone."

"Well, am I anybody?"

Jean Valjean had not uttered a single word. Cosette turned to him:

"In the first place, father, I want you to come and embrace me. What do you mean by not saying anything instead of taking my part? who gave me such a father as that? You must perceive that my family life is very unhappy. My husband beats me. Come, embrace me instantly."

Jean Valjean approached.

Cosette turned toward Marius.

"As for you, I shall make a face at you."

Then she presented her brow to Jean Valjean.

Jean Valjean advanced a step toward her.

Cosette recoiled.

"Father, you are pale. Does your arm hurt you?"

"It is well," said Jean Valjean.

"Did you sleep badly?"

"No."

"Are you sad?"

"No."

"Embrace me if you are well, if you sleep well, if you are content, I will not scold you."

And again she offered him her brow.

Jean Valjean dropped a kiss upon that brow whereon rested a celestial gleam.

"Smile."

Jean Valjean obeyed. It was the smile of a specter.

"Now, defend me against my husband."

"Cosette! . . ." ejaculated Marius.

"Get angry, father. Say that I must stay. You can certainly talk before me. So you think me very silly. What you say is astonishing! business, placing money in a bank, a great matter truly. Men make mysteries out of nothing. I am very pretty this morning. Look at me, Marius."

And with an adorable shrug of the shoulders, and an indescribably exquisite pout, she glanced at Marius.

"I love you!" said Marius.

"I adore you!" said Cosette.

And they fell irresistibly into each other's arms.

"Now," said Cosette, adjusting a fold of her dressing-gown, with a triumphant little grimace, "I shall stay."

"No, not that," said Marius, in a supplicating tone. "We have to finish something."

"Still no?"

Marius assumed a grave tone:

"I assure you, Cosette, that it is impossible."

"Ah! you put on your man's voice, sir. That is well, I go. You, father, have not upheld me. Monsieur my father, monsieur my husband, you are tyrants. I shall go and tell grandpapa. If you think that I am going to return and talk platitudes to you, you are mistaken. I am proud. I shall wait for you now. You shall see, that it is you who are going to be bored without me. I am going, it is well."

And she left the room.

Two seconds later, the door opened once more, her fresh and rosy head was again thrust between the two leaves, and she cried to them:

"I am very angry indeed."

The door closed again, and the shadows descended once more.

It was as though a ray of sunlight should have suddenly traversed the night, without itself being conscious of it.

Marius made sure that the door was securely closed.

"Poor Cosette!" he murmured, "when she finds out . . ."

At that word Jean Valjean trembled in every limb. He fixed on Marius a bewildered eye.

"Cosette! oh yes, it is true, you are going to tell Cosette about this. That is right. Stay, I had not thought of that. One has the strength for one thing, but not for another. Sir, I conjure you, I entreat now, sir, give me your most sacred word of honor, that you will not tell her. Is it not enough that you should know it? I have been able to say it myself without being forced to it, I could have told it to the universe, to the whole world—it was all one to me. But she, she does not know what it is, it would terrify her. What, a convict! we should be obliged to explain matters to her, to say to her: 'He is a man who has been in the galleys.' She saw the chain-gang pass by one day. Oh! My God!" . . . He dropped into an arm-chair and hid his face in his hands.

His grief was not audible, but from the quivering of his shoulders it was evident that he was weeping. Silent tears, terrible tears.

There is something of suffocation in the sob. He was seized with a sort of convulsion, he threw himself against the back of the chair as though to gain breath, letting his arms fall, and allowing Marius to see his face inundated with tears, and Marius heard him murmur, so low that his voice seemed to issue from fathomless depths:

"Oh! would that I could die!"

"Be at your ease," said Marius, "I will keep your secret for myself alone."

And, less touched perhaps, than he ought to have been, but forced, for the last hour, to familiarize himself with something as unexpected as it was dreadful, gradually beholding the convict superposed before his very eyes, upon M. Fauchelevent, overcome, little by little, by that lugubrious

- 1178 - VICTOR HUGO

reality, and led, by the natural inclination of the situation, to recognize the space which had just been placed between that man and himself, Marius added:

"It is impossible that I should not speak a word to you, with regard to the deposit which you have so faithfully and honestly remitted. That is an act of probity. It is just that some recompense should be bestowed on you. Fix the sum yourself, it shall be counted out to you. Do not fear to set it very high."

"I thank you, sir," replied Jean Valjean, gently.

He remained in thought for a moment, mechanically passing the tip of his forefinger across his thumb-nail, then he lifted up his voice:

"All is nearly over. But one last thing remains for me . . ."

"What is it?"

Jean Valjean struggled with what seemed a last hesitation, and, without voice, without breath, he stammered rather than said:

"Now that you know, do you think, sir, you, who are the master, that I ought not to see Cosette anymore?"

"I think that would be better," replied Marius coldly.

"I shall never see her more," murmured Jean Valjean.

And he directed his steps toward the door.

He laid his hand on the knob, the latch yielded, the door opened. Jean Valjean pushed it open far enough to pass through, stood motionless for a second, then closed the door again and turned to Marius.

He was no longer pale, he was livid. There were no longer any tears in his eyes, but only a sort of tragic flame. His voice had regained a strange composure.

"Stay, sir," he said. "If you will allow it, I will come to see her. I assure you that I desire it greatly. If I had not cared to see Cosette, I should not have made to you the confession that I have made, I should have gone away; but, as I desired to remain in the place where Cosette is, and to continue to see her, I had to tell you about it honestly. You follow my reasoning, do you not? it is a matter easily understood. You see, I have had her with me for more than nine years. We lived first in that hut on the boulevard, then in the convent, then near the Luxembourg. That was where you saw her for the first time. You remember her blue plush hat. Then we went to the Quartier des Invalides, where there was a railing on a garden, the Rue Plumet. I lived in a little back courtyard, whence I could hear her piano. That was my life. We never left each other. That lasted for nine years and some months. I was like her own father, and she was my child. I do not know whether you understand, Monsieur Pontmercy, but to go away now, never to see her again, never to speak to her again, to no longer have anything, would be hard. If you do not disapprove of it, I will come to see Cosette from time to time. I will not come often. I will not remain long. You shall give orders that I am to be received in the little waiting-room. On the ground floor. I could enter perfectly well by the back door, but that might create surprise perhaps, and it would be better, I think, for me to enter by the usual door. Truly, sir, I should like to see a little more of Cosette. As rarely as you please. Put yourself in my place, I have nothing left but that. And then, we must be cautious. If I no longer come at all, it would produce a bad effect, it would be considered singular. What I can do, by the way, is to come in the afternoon, when night is beginning to fall."

"You shall come every evening," said Marius, "and Cosette will be waiting for you."

"You are kind, sir," said Jean Valjean.

Marius saluted Jean Valjean, happiness escorted despair to the door, and these two men parted.

Chapter II

THE OBSCURITIES WHICH A REVELATION CAN CONTAIN

MARIUS WAS QUITE UPSET.

The sort of estrangement which he had always felt toward the man beside whom he had seen Cosette, was now explained to him. There was something enigmatic about that person, of which his instinct had warned him.

This enigma was the most hideous of disgraces, the galleys. This M. Fauchelevent was the convict Jean Valjean.

To abruptly find such a secret in the midst of one's happiness resembles the discovery of a scorpion in a nest of turtledoves.

Was the happiness of Marius and Cosette thenceforth condemned to such a neighborhood? Was this an accomplished fact? Did the acceptance of that man form a part of the marriage now consummated? Was there nothing to be done?

Had Marius wedded the convict as well?

In vain may one be crowned with light and joy, in vain may one taste the grand purple hour of life, happy love, such shocks would force even the archangel in his ecstasy, even the demigod in his glory, to shudder.

As is always the case in changes of view of this nature, Marius asked himself whether he had nothing with which to reproach himself. Had he been wanting in divination? Had he been wanting in prudence? Had he involuntarily dulled his wits? A little, perhaps. Had he entered upon this love affair, which had ended in his marriage to Cosette, without taking sufficient precautions to throw light upon the surroundings? He admitted—it is thus, by a series of successive admissions of ourselves in regard to ourselves, that life amends us, little by little—he admitted the chimerical and visionary side of his nature, a sort of internal cloud peculiar to many organizations, and which, in paroxysms of passion and sorrow, dilates as the temperature of the soul changes, and invades the entire man, to such a degree as to render him nothing more than a conscience bathed in a mist. We have more than once indicated this characteristic element of Marius's individuality.

He recalled that, in the intoxication of his love, in the Rue Plumet, during those six or seven ecstatic weeks, he had not even spoken to Cosette of that drama in the Gorbeau hovel, where the victim had taken up such a singular line of silence during the struggle and the ensuing flight. How had it happened that he had not mentioned this to Cosette? Yet it was so near and so terrible! How had it come to pass that he had not even named the Thénardiers, and, particularly, on the day when he had encountered Éponine? He now found it almost difficult to explain his silence of that time. Nevertheless, he could account for it. He recalled his benumbed state, his intoxication with Cosette, love absorbing everything, that catching away of each other into the ideal, and perhaps also, like the imperceptible quantity of reason mingled with this violent and charming state of the soul, a vague, dull instinct impelling him to conceal and abolish in his memory that redoubtable adventure, contact with which he dreaded, in which he did not wish to play any part, his agency in which he had kept secret, and in which he could be neither narrator nor witness without being an accuser.

Moreover, these few weeks had been a flash of lightning; there had been no time for anything except love.

In short, having weighed everything, turned everything over in his mind, examined everything, whatever might have been the consequences if he had told Cosette about the Gorbeau ambush, even if he had discovered that Jean Valjean was a convict, would that have changed him, Marius? Would that have changed her, Cosette? Would he have drawn back? Would he have adored her any the less? Would he have refrained from marrying her? No. Then there was nothing to regret, nothing with which he need reproach himself. All was well. There is a deity for those drunken men who are called lovers. Marius blind, had followed the path which he would have chosen had he been in full possession of his sight. Love had bandaged his eyes, in order to lead him whither? To paradise.

But this paradise was henceforth complicated with an infernal accompaniment.

Marius's ancient estrangement toward this man, toward this Fauchelevent who had turned into Jean Valjean, was at present mingled with horror.

In this horror, let us state, there was some pity, and even a certain surprise.

This thief, this thief guilty of a second offense, had restored that deposit. And what a deposit! Six hundred thousand francs.

He alone was in the secret of that deposit. He might have kept it all, he had restored it all.

Moreover, he had himself revealed his situation. Nothing forced him to this. If anyone learned who he was, it was through himself. In this avowal there was something more than acceptance of humiliation, there was acceptance of peril. For a condemned man, a mask is not a mask, it is a shelter. A false name is security, and he had rejected that false name. He, the galley-slave, might have hidden himself forever in an honest family; he had withstood this temptation. And with what motive? Through a conscientious scruple. He himself explained this with the irresistible accents of truth. In short, whatever this Jean Valjean might be, he was, undoubtedly, a conscience which was awakening. There existed some mysterious rehabilitation which had begun; and, to all appearances, scruples had for a long time already controlled this man. Such fits of justice and goodness are not characteristic of vulgar natures. An awakening of conscience is grandeur of soul.

Jean Valjean was sincere. This sincerity, visible, palpable, irrefragable, evident from the very grief that it caused him, rendered inquiries useless, and conferred authority on all that that man had said.

Here, for Marius, there was a strange reversal of situations. What breathed from M. Fauchelevent? distrust. What did Jean Valjean inspire? confidence.

In the mysterious balance of this Jean Valjean which the pensive Marius struck, he admitted the active principle, he admitted the passive principle, and he tried to reach a balance.

But all this went on as in a storm. Marius, while endeavoring to form a clear idea of this man, and while pursuing Jean Valjean, so to speak, in the depths of his thought, lost him and found him again in a fatal mist.

The deposit honestly restored, the probity of the confession—these were good. This produced a lightening of the cloud, then the cloud became black once more.

Troubled as were Marius's memories, a shadow of them returned to him.

After all, what was that adventure in the Jondrette attic? Why had that man taken to flight on the arrival of the police, instead of entering a complaint?

Here Marius found the answer. Because that man was a fugitive from justice, who had broken his ban.

Another question: Why had that man come to the barricade?

For Marius now once more distinctly beheld that recollection which had reappeared in his emotions like sympathetic ink at the application of heat. This man had been in the barricade. He had not fought there. What had he come there for? In the presence of this question a specter sprang up and replied: "Javert."

Marius recalled perfectly now that funereal sight of Jean Valjean dragging the pinioned Javert out of the barricade, and he still heard behind the corner of the little Rue Mondétour that frightful pistol shot. Obviously, there was hatred between that police spy and the galley-slave. The one was in the other's way. Jean Valjean had gone to the barricade for the purpose of revenging himself. He had arrived late. He probably knew that Javert was a prisoner there. The Corsican vendetta has penetrated to certain lower strata and has become the law there; it is so simple that it does not astonish souls which are but half turned toward good; and those hearts are so constituted that a criminal, who is in the path of repentance, may be scrupulous in the matter of theft and unscrupulous in the matter of vengeance. Jean Valjean had killed Javert. At least, that seemed to be evident.

This was the final question, to be sure; but to this there was no reply. This question Marius felt like pincers. How had it come to pass that Jean Valjean's existence had elbowed that of Cosette for so long a period?

What melancholy sport of Providence was that which had placed that child in contact with that man? Are there then chains for two which are forged on high? and does God take pleasure in coupling the angel with the demon? So a crime and an innocence can be roommates in the mysterious galleys of wretchedness? In that defiling of condemned persons which is called human destiny, can two brows pass side by side, the one ingenuous, the other formidable, the one all bathed in the divine whiteness of dawn, the other forever blemished by the flash of an eternal lightning? Who could have arranged that inexplicable pairing off? In what manner, in consequence of what prodigy, had any community of life been established between this celestial little creature and that old criminal?

Who could have bound the lamb to the wolf, and, what was still more incomprehensible, have attached the wolf to the lamb? For the wolf loved the lamb, for the fierce creature adored the feeble one, for, during the space of nine years, the angel had had the monster as her point of support. Cosette's childhood and girlhood, her advent in the daylight, her virginal growth toward life and light, had been sheltered by that hideous devotion. Here questions exfoliated, so to speak, into innumerable enigmas, abysses yawned at the bottoms of abysses, and Marius could no longer bend over Jean Valjean without becoming dizzy. What was this man-precipice?

The old symbols of Genesis are eternal; in human society, such as it now exists, and until a broader day shall effect a change in it, there will always be two men, the one superior, the other subterranean; the one which is according to good is Abel; the one which is according to evil is Cain. What was this tender Cain? What was this ruffian religiously absorbed in the adoration of a virgin, watching over her, rearing her, guarding her, dignifying her, and enveloping her, impure as he was himself, with purity?

What was that cesspool which had venerated that innocence to such a point as not to leave upon it a single spot? What was this Jean Valjean educating Cosette? What was this figure of the shadows which had for its only object the preservation of the rising of a star from every shadow and from every cloud?

That was Jean Valjean's secret; that was also God's secret.

In the presence of this double secret, Marius recoiled. The one, in some sort, reassured him as to the other. God was as visible in this affair as was Jean Valjean. God has his instruments. He makes use of the tool which he wills. He is not responsible to men. Do we know how God sets about the work? Jean Valjean had labored over Cosette. He had, to some extent, made that soul. That was incontestable. Well, what then? The workman was horrible; but the work was admirable. God produces his miracles as seems good to him. He had constructed that charming Cosette, and he had employed Jean Valjean. It had pleased him to choose this strange collaborator for himself. What account have we to demand of him? Is this the first time that the dung-heap has aided the spring to create the rose?

Marius made himself these replies, and declared to himself that they were good. He had not dared to press Jean Valjean on all the points which we have just indicated, but he did not confess to himself that he did not dare to do it. He adored Cosette, he possessed Cosette, Cosette was splendidly pure. That was sufficient for him. What enlightenment did he need? Cosette was a light. Does light require enlightenment? He had everything; what more could he desire? All—is not that enough? Jean Valjean's personal affairs did not concern him.

And bending over the fatal shadow of that man, he clung fast, convulsively, to the solemn declaration of that unhappy wretch: "I am nothing to Cosette. Ten years ago I did not know that she was in existence."

Jean Valjean was a passer-by. He had said so himself. Well, he had passed. Whatever he was, his part was finished.

Henceforth, there remained Marius to fulfill the part of Providence to Cosette. Cosette had sought the azure in a person like herself, in her lover, her husband, her celestial male. Cosette, as she took her flight, winged and transfigured, left behind her on the earth, her hideous and empty chrysalis, Jean Valjean.

In whatever circle of ideas Marius revolved, he always returned to a certain horror for Jean Valjean. A sacred horror, perhaps, for, as we have just pointed out, he felt a *quid divinum* in that man. But do what he would, and seek what extenuation he would, he was certainly forced to fall back upon this: the man was a convict; that is to say, a being who has not even a place in the social ladder, since he is lower than the very lowest rung. After the very last of men comes the convict. The convict is no longer, so to speak, in the semblance of the living. The law has deprived him of the entire quantity of humanity of which it can deprive a man.

Marius, on penal questions, still held to the inexorable system, though he was a democrat and he entertained all the ideas of the law on the subject of those whom the law strikes. He had not yet accomplished all progress, we admit. He had not yet come to distinguish between that which is written by man and that which is written by God, between law and right. He had not examined and weighed the right which man takes to dispose of the irrevocable and the irreparable. He was not shocked by the word *vindicte*. He found it quite simple that certain breaches of the written law should be followed by eternal suffering, and he accepted, as the process of civilization, social damnation. He still stood at this point, though safe to advance infallibly later on, since his nature was good, and, at bottom, wholly formed of latent progress.

In this stage of his ideas, Jean Valjean appeared to him hideous and repulsive. He was a man reproved, he was the convict. That word was for him like the sound of the trump on the Day of Judgment; and, after having reflected upon Jean Valjean for a long time, his final gesture had been to turn away his head. *Vade retro.*

Marius, if we must recognize and even insist upon the fact, while interrogating Jean Valjean to such a point that Jean Valjean had said: "You are confessing me," had not, nevertheless, put to him two or three decisive questions.

It was not that they had not presented themselves to his mind, but that he had been afraid of them. The Jondrette attic? The barricade? Javert? Who knows where these revelations would have stopped? Jean Valjean did not seem like a man who would draw back, and who knows whether Marius, after having urged him on, would not have himself desired to hold him back?

Has it not happened to all of us, in certain supreme conjunctures, to stop our ears in order that we may not hear the reply, after we have asked a question? It is especially when one loves that one gives way to these exhibitions of cowardice. It is not wise to question sinister situations to the last point, particularly when the indissoluble side of our life is fatally intermingled with them. What a terrible light might have proceeded from the despairing explanations of Jean Valjean, and who knows whether that hideous glare would not have darted forth as far as Cosette? Who knows whether a sort of infernal glow would not have lingered behind it on the brow of that angel? The spattering of a lightning-flash is of the thunder also. Fatality has points of juncture where innocence itself is stamped with crime by the gloomy law of the reflections which give color. The purest figures may forever preserve the reflection of a horrible association. Rightly or wrongly, Marius had been afraid. He already knew too much. He sought to dull his senses rather than to gain further light.

In dismay he bore off Cosette in his arms and shut his eyes to Jean Valjean.

That man was the night, the living and horrible night. How should he dare to seek the bottom of it? It is a terrible thing to interrogate the shadow. Who knows what its reply will be? The dawn may be blackened forever by it.

In this state of mind the thought that that man would, henceforth, come into any contact whatever with Cosette was a heartrending perplexity to Marius.

He now almost reproached himself for not having put those formidable questions, before which he had recoiled, and from which an implacable and definitive decision might have sprung. He felt that he was too good, too gentle, too weak, if we must say the word. This weakness had led him to an imprudent concession. He had allowed himself to be touched. He had been in the wrong. He ought to have simply and purely rejected Jean Valjean. Jean Valjean played the part of fire, and that is what he should have done, and have freed his house from that man.

He was vexed with himself, he was angry with that whirlwind of emotions which had deafened, blinded, and carried him away. He was displeased with himself.

What was he to do now? Jean Valjean's visits were profoundly repugnant to him. What was the use in having that man in his house? What did the man want? Here, he became dismayed, he did not wish to dig down, he did not wish to penetrate deeply; he did not wish to sound himself. He had promised, he had allowed himself to be drawn into a promise; Jean Valjean held his promise; one must keep one's word even to a convict, above all to a convict. Still, his first duty was to Cosette. In short, he was carried away by the repugnance which dominated him.

Marius turned over all this confusion of ideas in his mind, passing from one to the other, and moved by all of them. Hence arose a profound trouble.

It was not easy for him to hide this trouble from Cosette, but love is a talent, and Marius succeeded in doing it.

However, without any apparent object, he questioned Cosette, who was as candid as a dove is white and who suspected nothing; he talked of her childhood and her youth, and he became more and more convinced that that convict had been everything good, paternal and respectable that a man can be, toward Cosette. All that Marius had caught a glimpse of and had surmised was real. That sinister nettle had loved and protected that lily.

BOOK EIGHTH

FADING AWAY OF THE TWILIGHT

Chapter I

THE LOWER CHAMBER

ON THE FOLLOWING DAY, AT NIGHTFALL, JEAN VALJEAN KNOCKED AT THE CARRIAGE GATE OF THE Gillenormand house. It was Basque who received him. Basque was in the courtyard at the appointed hour, as though he had received his orders. It sometimes happens that one says to a servant: "You will watch for Mr. So and So, when he arrives."

Basque addressed Jean Valjean without waiting for the latter to approach him:

"Monsieur le Baron has charged me to inquire whether monsieur desires to go upstairs or to remain below?"

"I will remain below," replied Jean Valjean.

Basque, who was perfectly respectful, opened the door of the waiting-room and said:

"I will go and inform Madame."

The room which Jean Valjean entered was a damp, vaulted room on the ground floor, which served as a cellar on occasion, which opened on the street, was paved with red squares and was badly lighted by a grated window.

This chamber was not one of those which are harassed by the feather-duster, the pope's head brush, and the broom. The dust rested tranquilly there. Persecution of the spiders was not organized there. A fine web, which spread far and wide, and was very black and ornamented with dead flies, formed a wheel on one of the window-panes. The room, which was small and low-ceiled, was furnished with a heap of empty bottles piled up in one corner.

The wall, which was daubed with an ochre yellow wash, was scaling off in large flakes. At one end there was a chimney-piece painted in black with a narrow shelf. A fire was burning there; which indicated that Jean Valjean's reply: "I will remain below," had been foreseen.

Two arm-chairs were placed at the two corners of the fireplace. Between the chairs an old bed-side rug, which displayed more foundation thread than wool, had been spread by way of a carpet.

The chamber was lighted by the fire on the hearth and the twilight falling through the window.

Jean Valjean was fatigued. For days he had neither eaten nor slept. He threw himself into one of the arm-chairs.

Basque returned, set a lighted candle on the chimney-piece and retired. Jean Valjean, his head drooping and his chin resting on his breast, perceived neither Basque nor the candle.

All at once, he drew himself up with a start. Cosette was standing beside him.

He had not seen her enter, but he had felt that she was there.

He turned round. He gazed at her. She was adorably lovely. But what he was contemplating with that profound gaze was not her beauty but her soul.

"Well," exclaimed Cosette, "father, I knew that you were peculiar, but I never should have expected this. What an idea! Marius told me that you wish me to receive you here."

"Yes, it is my wish."

"I expected that reply. Good. I warn you that I am going to make a scene for you. Let us begin at the beginning. Embrace me, father."

And she offered him her cheek.

Jean Valjean remained motionless.

"You do not stir. I take note of it. Attitude of guilt. But never mind, I pardon you. Jesus Christ said: Offer the other cheek. Here it is."

And she presented her other cheek.

Jean Valjean did not move. It seemed as though his feet were nailed to the pavement.

"This is becoming serious," said Cosette. "What have I done to you? I declare that I am perplexed. You owe me reparation. You will dine with us."

"I have dined."

"That is not true. I will get M. Gillenormand to scold you. Grandfathers are made to reprimand fathers. Come. Go upstairs with me to the drawing-room. Immediately."

"Impossible."

Here Cosette lost ground a little. She ceased to command and passed to questioning.

"But why? and you choose the ugliest chamber in the house in which to see me. It's horrible here."

"Thou knowest . . ."

Jean Valjean caught himself up.

"You know, madame, that I am peculiar, I have my freaks."

Cosette struck her tiny hands together.

"Madame! . . . You know! . . . more novelties! What is the meaning of this?"

Jean Valjean directed upon her that heartrending smile to which he occasionally had recourse:

"You wished to be Madame. You are so."

"Not for you, father."

"Do not call me father."

"What?"

"Call me 'Monsieur Jean.' 'Jean,' if you like."

"You are no longer my father? I am no longer Cosette? 'Monsieur Jean'? What does this mean? why, these are revolutions, aren't they? what has taken place? come, look me in the face. And you won't live with us! And you won't have my chamber! What have I done to you? Has anything happened?"

"Nothing."

"Well then?"

"Everything is as usual."

"Why do you change your name?"

"You have changed yours, surely."

He smiled again with the same smile as before and added:

"Since you are Madame Pontmercy, I certainly can be Monsieur Jean."

"I don't understand anything about it. All this is idiotic. I shall ask permission of my husband for you to be 'Monsieur Jean.' I hope that he will not consent to it. You cause me a great deal of pain. One does have freaks, but one does not cause one's little Cosette grief. That is wrong. You have no right to be wicked, you who are so good."

He made no reply.

She seized his hands with vivacity, and raising them to her face with an irresistible movement, she pressed them against her neck beneath her chin, which is a gesture of profound tenderness.

"Oh!" she said to him, "be good!"

And she went on:

"This is what I call being good: being nice and coming and living here—there are birds here as there are in the Rue Plumet—living with us, quitting that hole of a Rue de l'Homme Armé, not giving us riddles to guess, being like all the rest of the world, dining with us, breakfasting with us, being my father."

He loosed her hands.

"You no longer need a father, you have a husband."

Cosette became angry.

"I no longer need a father! One really does not know what to say to things like that, which are not common sense!"

"If Toussaint were here," resumed Jean Valjean, like a person who is driven to seek authorities, and who clutches at every branch, "she would be the first to agree that it is true that I have always had ways of my own. There is nothing new in this. I always have loved my black corner."

"But it is cold here. One cannot see distinctly. It is abominable, that it is, to wish to be Monsieur Jean! I will not have you say 'you' to me."

"Just now, as I was coming hither," replied Jean Valjean, "I saw a piece of furniture in the Rue Saint-Louis. It was at a cabinet-maker's. If I were a pretty woman, I would treat myself to that bit of furniture. A very neat toilet table; in the reigning style. What you call rosewood, I think. It is inlaid. The mirror is quite large. There are drawers. It is pretty."

"Hou! the villainous bear!" replied Cosette.

And with supreme grace, setting her teeth and drawing back her lips, she blew at Jean Valjean. She was a Grace copying a cat.

"I am furious," she resumed. "Ever since yesterday, you have made me rage, all of you. I am greatly vexed. I don't understand. You do not defend me against Marius. Marius will not uphold me against you. I am all alone. I arrange a chamber prettily. If I could have put the good God there I would have done it. My chamber is left on my hands. My lodger sends me into bankruptcy. I order a nice little dinner of Nicolette. We will have nothing to do with your dinner, Madame. And my father Fauchelevent wants me to call him 'Monsieur Jean,' and to receive him in a frightful, old, ugly cellar, where the walls have beards, and where the crystal consists of empty bottles, and the curtains are of spiders' webs! You are singular, I admit, that is your style, but people who get married are granted a truce. You ought not to have begun being singular again instantly. So you are going to be perfectly contented in your abominable Rue de l'Homme Armé. I was very desperate indeed there, that I was. What have you against me? You cause me a great deal of grief. Fi!"

And, becoming suddenly serious, she gazed intently at Jean Valjean and added:

"Are you angry with me because I am happy?"

Ingenuousness sometimes unconsciously penetrates deep. This question, which was simple for Cosette, was profound for Jean Valjean. Cosette had meant to scratch, and she lacerated.

Jean Valjean turned pale.

He remained for a moment without replying, then, with an inexpressible intonation, and speaking to himself, he murmured:

"Her happiness was the object of my life. Now God may sign my dismissal. Cosette, thou art happy; my day is over."

"Ah, you have said *thou* to me!" exclaimed Cosette.

And she sprang to his neck.

Jean Valjean, in bewilderment, strained her wildly to his breast. It almost seemed to him as though he were taking her back.

"Thanks, father!" said Cosette.

This enthusiastic impulse was on the point of becoming poignant for Jean Valjean. He gently removed Cosette's arms, and took his hat.

"Well?" said Cosette.

"I leave you, Madame, they are waiting for you."

And, from the threshold, he added:

"I have said *thou* to you. Tell your husband that this shall not happen again. Pardon me."

Jean Valjean quitted the room, leaving Cosette stupefied at this enigmatical farewell.

Chapter II

ANOTHER STEP BACKWARDS

ON THE FOLLOWING DAY, AT THE SAME HOUR, JEAN VALJEAN CAME. Cosette asked him no questions, was no longer astonished, no longer exclaimed that she was cold, no longer spoke of the drawing-room, she avoided saying either "father," or "Monsieur Jean." She allowed herself to be addressed as *you*. She allowed herself to be called Madame. Only, her joy had undergone a certain diminution. She would have been sad, if sadness had been possible to her.

It is probable that she had had with Marius, one of those conversations in which the beloved man says what he pleases, explains nothing, and satisfies the beloved woman. The curiosity of lovers does not extend very far beyond their own love.

The lower room had made a little toilet. Basque had suppressed the bottles, and Nicolette the spiders.

All the days which followed brought Jean Valjean at the same hour. He came every day, because he had not the strength to take Marius's words otherwise than literally. Marius arranged matters so as to be absent at the hours when Jean Valjean came. The house grew accustomed to the novel ways of M. Fauchelevent. Toussaint helped in this direction: "Monsieur has always been like that," she repeated. The grandfather issued this decree: "He's an original." And all was said. Moreover, at the age of ninety-six, no bond is any longer possible, all is merely juxtaposition; a newcomer is in the way. There is no longer any room; all habits are acquired. M. Fauchelevent, M. Tranchelevent, Father Gillenormand asked nothing better than to be relieved from "that gentleman." He added: "Nothing is more common than those originals. They do all sorts of queer things. They have no reason. The Marquis de Canaples was still worse. He bought a palace that he might lodge in the garret. These are fantastic appearances that people affect."

No one caught a glimpse of the sinister foundation. And moreover, who could have guessed such a thing? There are marshes of this description in India. The water seems extraordinary, inexplicable, rippling though there is no wind, and agitated where it should be calm. One gazes at the surface of these causeless ebullitions; one does not perceive the hydra which crawls on the bottom.

Many men have a secret monster in this same manner, a dragon which gnaws them, a despair which inhabits their night. Such a man resembles other men, he goes and comes. No one knows that he bears within him a frightful parasitic pain with a thousand teeth, which lives within the unhappy man, and of which he is dying. No one knows that this man is a gulf. He is stagnant but deep. From time to time, a trouble of which the on-looker understands nothing appears on his surface. A mysterious wrinkle is formed, then vanishes, then reappears; an air-bubble rises and bursts. It is the breathing of the unknown beast.

Certain strange habits: arriving at the hour when other people are taking their leave, keeping in the background when other people are displaying themselves, preserving on all occasions, what may be designated as the wall-colored mantle, seeking the solitary walk, preferring the deserted street, avoiding any share in conversation, avoiding crowds and festivals, seeming at one's ease and living poorly, having one's key in one's pocket, and one's candle at the porter's lodge, however rich one may be, entering by the side door, ascending the private staircase—all these insignificant singularities, fugitive folds on the surface, often proceed from a formidable foundation.

Many weeks passed in this manner. A new life gradually took possession of Cosette: the relations which marriage creates, visits, the care of the house, pleasures, great matters. Cosette's pleasures were not costly, they consisted in one thing: being with Marius. The great occupation of her life was to go out with him, to remain with him. It was for them a joy that was always fresh, to go out arm in arm, in the face of the sun, in the open street, without hiding themselves, before the whole world, both of them completely alone.

Cosette had one vexation. Toussaint could not get on with Nicolette, the soldering of two elderly maids being impossible, and she went away. The grandfather was well; Marius argued a case here and there; Aunt Gillenormand peacefully led that life aside which sufficed for her, beside the new household. Jean Valjean came every day.

The address as *thou* disappeared, the *you*, the "Madame," the "Monsieur Jean," rendered him another person to Cosette. The care which he had himself taken to detach her from him was succeeding. She became more and more gay and less and less tender. Yet she still loved him sincerely, and he felt it.

One day she said to him suddenly: "You used to be my father, you are no longer my father, you were my uncle, you are no longer my uncle, you were Monsieur Fauchelevent, you are Jean.

Who are you then? I don't like all this. If I did not know how good you are, I should be afraid of you."

He still lived in the Rue de l'Homme Armé, because he could not make up his mind to remove to a distance from the quarter where Cosette dwelt.

At first, he only remained a few minutes with Cosette, and then went away.

Little by little he acquired the habit of making his visits less brief. One would have said that he was taking advantage of the authorization of the days which were lengthening: he arrived earlier and departed later.

One day Cosette chanced to say "father" to him. A flash of joy illuminated Jean Valjean's melancholy old countenance. He caught her up: "Say Jean."—"Ah! truly," she replied with a burst of laughter, "Monsieur Jean."—"That is right," said he. And he turned aside so that she might not see him wipe his eyes.

Chapter III

THEY RECALL THE GARDEN OF THE RUE PLUMET

THIS WAS THE LAST TIME. AFTER THAT LAST FLASH OF LIGHT, COMPLETE EXTINCTION ENSUED. No more familiarity, no more good morning with a kiss, never more that word so profoundly sweet: "My father!" He was at his own request and through his own complicity driven out of all his happinesses one after the other; and he had this sorrow, that after having lost Cosette wholly in one day, he was afterwards obliged to lose her again in detail.

The eye eventually becomes accustomed to the light of a cellar. In short, it sufficed for him to have an apparition of Cosette every day. His whole life was concentrated in that one hour.

He seated himself close to her, he gazed at her in silence, or he talked to her of years gone by, of her childhood, of the convent, of her little friends of those bygone days.

One afternoon—it was on one of those early days in April, already warm and fresh, the moment of the sun's great gaiety, the gardens which surrounded the windows of Marius and Cosette felt the emotion of waking, the hawthorn was on the point of budding, a jeweled garniture of gillyflowers spread over the ancient walls, snapdragons yawned through the crevices of the stones, amid the grass there was a charming beginning of daisies, and buttercups, the white butterflies of the year were making their first appearance, the wind, that minstrel of the eternal wedding, was trying in the trees the first notes of that grand, auroral symphony which the old poets called the springtide—Marius said to Cosette: "We said that we would go back to take a look at our garden in the Rue Plumet. Let us go thither. We must not be ungrateful."—And away they flitted, like two swallows toward the spring. This garden of the Rue Plumet produced on them the effect of the dawn. They already had behind them in life something which was like the springtime of their love. The house in the Rue Plumet being held on a lease, still belonged to Cosette. They went to that garden and that house. There they found themselves again, there they forgot themselves. That evening, at the usual hour, Jean Valjean came to the Rue des Filles-du-Calvaire.—"Madame went out with Monsieur and has not yet returned," Basque said to him. He seated himself in silence, and waited an hour. Cosette did not return. He departed with drooping head.

Cosette was so intoxicated with her walk to "their garden," and so joyous at having "lived a whole day in her past," that she talked of nothing else on the morrow. She did not notice that she had not seen Jean Valjean.

"In what way did you go thither?" Jean Valjean asked her.

"On foot."

"And how did you return?"

"In a hackney carriage."

For some time, Jean Valjean had noticed the economical life led by the young people. He was troubled by it. Marius's economy was severe, and that word had its absolute meaning for Jean Valjean. He hazarded a query:

"Why do not you have a carriage of your own? A pretty coupé would only cost you five hundred francs a month. You are rich."

"I don't know," replied Cosette.

"It is like Toussaint," resumed Jean Valjean. "She is gone. You have not replaced her. Why?"

"Nicolette suffices."

"But you ought to have a maid."

"Have I not Marius?"

"You ought to have a house of your own, your own servants, a carriage, a box at the theater. There is nothing too fine for you. Why not profit by your riches? Wealth adds to happiness."

Cosette made no reply.

Jean Valjean's visits were not abridged. Far from it. When it is the heart which is slipping, one does not halt on the downward slope.

When Jean Valjean wished to prolong his visit and to induce forgetfulness of the hour, he sang the praises of Marius; he pronounced him handsome, noble, courageous, witty, eloquent, good. Cosette outdid him. Jean Valjean began again. They were never weary. Marius—that word was inexhaustible; those six letters contained volumes. In this manner, Jean Valjean contrived to remain a long time.

It was so sweet to see Cosette, to forget by her side! It alleviated his wounds. It frequently happened that Basque came twice to announce: "M. Gillenormand sends me to remind Madame la Baronne that dinner is served."

On those days, Jean Valjean was very thoughtful on his return home.

Was there then, any truth in that comparison of the chrysalis which had presented itself to the mind of Marius? Was Jean Valjean really a chrysalis who would persist, and who would come to visit his butterfly?

One day he remained still longer than usual. On the following day he observed that there was no fire on the hearth.—"Hello!" he thought. "No fire."—And he furnished the explanation for himself.—"It is perfectly simple. It is April. The cold weather has ceased."

"Heavens! how cold it is here!" exclaimed Cosette when she entered.

"Why, no," said Jean Valjean.

"Was it you who told Basque not to make a fire then?"

"Yes, since we are now in the month of May."

"But we have a fire until June. One is needed all the year in this cellar."

"I thought that a fire was unnecessary."

"That is exactly like one of your ideas!" retorted Cosette.

On the following day there was a fire. But the two arm-chairs were arranged at the other end of the room near the door. "—What is the meaning of this?" thought Jean Valjean.

He went for the arm-chairs and restored them to their ordinary place near the hearth.

This fire lighted once more encouraged him, however. He prolonged the conversation even beyond its customary limits. As he rose to take his leave, Cosette said to him:

"My husband said a queer thing to me yesterday."

"What was it?"

"He said to me: 'Cosette, we have an income of thirty thousand livres. Twenty-seven that you own, and three that my grandfather gives me.' I replied: 'That makes thirty.' He went on: 'Would you have the courage to live on the three thousand?' I answered: 'Yes, on nothing. Provided that it was with you.' And then I asked: 'Why do you say that to me?' He replied: 'I wanted to know.' "

Jean Valjean found not a word to answer. Cosette probably expected some explanation from him; he listened in gloomy silence. He went back to the Rue de l'Homme Armé; he was so deeply absorbed that he mistook the door and instead of entering his own house, he entered the adjoining dwelling. It was only after having ascended nearly two stories that he perceived his error and went down again.

His mind was swarming with conjectures. It was evident that Marius had his doubts as to the origin of the six hundred thousand francs, that he feared some source that was not pure, who knows? that he had even, perhaps, discovered that the money came from him, Jean Valjean, that he hesitated before this suspicious fortune, and was disinclined to take it as his own—preferring that both he and Cosette should remain poor, rather than that they should be rich with wealth that was not clean.

Moreover, Jean Valjean began vaguely to surmise that he was being shown the door.

On the following day, he underwent something like a shock on entering the ground-floor room. The arm-chairs had disappeared. There was not a single chair of any sort.

"Ah, what's this!" exclaimed Cosette as she entered, "no chairs! Where are the arm-chairs?"

"They are no longer here," replied Jean Valjean.

"This is too much!"

Jean Valjean stammered:

"It was I who told Basque to remove them."

"And your reason?"

"I have only a few minutes to stay to-day."

"A brief stay is no reason for remaining standing."

"I think that Basque needed the chairs for the drawing-room."

"Why?"

"You have company this evening, no doubt."

"We expect no one."

Jean Valjean had not another word to say.

Cosette shrugged her shoulders.

"To have the chairs carried off! The other day you had the fire put out. How odd you are!"

"Adieu!" murmured Jean Valjean.

He did not say: "Adieu, Cosette." But he had not the strength to say: "Adieu, Madame."

He went away utterly overwhelmed.

This time he had understood.

On the following day he did not come. Cosette only observed the fact in the evening.

"Why," said she, "Monsieur Jean has not been here to-day."

And she felt a slight twinge at her heart, but she hardly perceived it, being immediately diverted by a kiss from Marius.

On the following day he did not come.

Cosette paid no heed to this, passed her evening and slept well that night, as usual, and thought of it only when she woke. She was so happy! She speedily dispatched Nicolette to M. Jean's house to inquire whether he were ill, and why he had not come on the previous evening. Nicolette brought back the reply of M. Jean that he was not ill. He was busy. He would come soon. As soon as he was able. Moreover, he was on the point of taking a little journey. Madame must remember that it was his custom to take trips from time to time. They were not to worry about him. They were not to think of him.

Nicolette on entering M. Jean's had repeated to him her mistress's very words. That Madame had sent her to inquire why M. Jean had not come on the preceding evening. "—It is two days since I have been there," said Jean Valjean gently.

But the remark passed unnoticed by Nicolette, who did not report it to Cosette.

Chapter IV

ATTRACTION AND EXTINCTION

DURING THE LAST MONTHS OF SPRING AND THE FIRST MONTHS OF SUMMER IN 1833, THE RARE passers-by in the Marais, the petty shop-keepers, the loungers on thresholds, noticed an old man neatly clad in black, who emerged every day at the same hour, toward nightfall, from the Rue de l'Homme Armé, on the side of the Rue Sainte-Croix-de-la-Bretonnerie, passed in front of the Blancs Manteaux, gained the Rue Culture-Sainte-Catherine, and, on arriving at the Rue de l'Écharpe, turned to the left, and entered the Rue Saint-Louis.

There he walked at a slow pace, with his head strained forward, seeing nothing, hearing nothing, his eye immovably fixed on a point which seemed to be a star to him, which never varied, and which was no other than the corner of the Rue des Filles-du-Calvaire. The nearer he approached the corner of the street the more his eye lighted up; a sort of joy illuminated his pupils like an inward aurora, he had a fascinated and much affected air, his lips indulged in obscure movements, as though he were talking to someone whom he did not see, he smiled vaguely and advanced as slowly as possible. One would have said that, while desirous of reaching his destination, he feared the moment when he should be close at hand. When only a few houses remained between him and that street which appeared to attract him his pace slackened, to such a degree that, at times, one might have thought that he was no longer advancing at all. The vacillation of his head and the fixity of his eyeballs suggested the thought of the magnetic needle seeking the pole. Whatever time he spent on arriving, he was obliged to arrive at last; he reached the Rue des Filles-du-Calvaire; then he halted, he trembled, he thrust his head with a sort of melancholy timidity round the corner of the last house, and gazed into that street, and there was in that tragic look something which resembled the dazzling light of the impossible, and the reflection from a paradise that was closed to him. Then a tear, which had slowly gathered in the corner of his lids, and had become large enough to fall, trickled down his cheek, and sometimes stopped at his mouth. The old man tasted its bitter flavor. Thus he remained for several minutes as though made of stone, then he returned by the same road and with the same step, and, in proportion as he retreated, his glance died out.

Little by little, this old man ceased to go as far as the corner of the Rue des Filles-du-Calvaire; he halted halfway in the Rue Saint-Louis; sometimes a little further off, sometimes a little nearer.

One day he stopped at the corner of the Rue Culture-Sainte-Catherine and looked at the Rue des Filles-du-Calvaire from a distance. Then he shook his head slowly from right to left, as though refusing himself something, and retraced his steps.

Soon he no longer came as far as the Rue Saint-Louis. He got as far as the Rue Pavée, shook his head and turned back; then he went no further than the Rue des Trois-Pavillons; then he did not overstep the Blancs-Manteaux. One would have said that he was a pendulum which was no longer wound up, and whose oscillations were growing shorter before ceasing altogether.

Every day he emerged from his house at the same hour, he undertook the same trip, but he no longer completed it, and, perhaps without himself being aware of the fact, he constantly shortened it. His whole countenance expressed this single idea: What is the use?—His eye was dim; no more radiance. His tears were also exhausted; they no longer collected in the corner of his eyelid; that thoughtful eye was dry. The old man's head was still craned forward; his chin moved at times; the folds in his gaunt neck were painful to behold. Sometimes, when the weather was bad, he had an umbrella under his arm, but he never opened it.

The good women of the quarter said: "He is an innocent." The children followed him and laughed.

BOOK NINTH

SUPREME SHADOW, SUPREME DAWN

Chapter I

PITY FOR THE UNHAPPY, BUT INDULGENCE FOR THE HAPPY

IT IS A TERRIBLE THING TO BE HAPPY! HOW CONTENT ONE IS! HOW ALL-SUFFICIENT ONE FINDS IT! How, being in possession of the false object of life, happiness, one forgets the true object, duty!

Let us say, however, that the reader would do wrong were he to blame Marius.

Marius, as we have explained, before his marriage, had put no questions to M. Fauchelevent, and, since that time, he had feared to put any to Jean Valjean. He had regretted the promise into which he had allowed himself to be drawn. He had often said to himself that he had done wrong in making that concession to despair. He had confined himself to gradually estranging Jean Valjean from his house and to effacing him, as much as possible, from Cosette's mind. He had, in a manner, always placed himself between Cosette and Jean Valjean, sure that, in this way, she would not perceive nor think of the latter. It was more than effacement, it was an eclipse.

Marius did what he considered necessary and just. He thought that he had serious reasons which the reader has already seen, and others which will be seen later on, for getting rid of Jean Valjean without harshness, but without weakness.

Chance having ordained that he should encounter, in a case which he had argued, a former employee of the Laffitte establishment, he had acquired mysterious information, without seeking it, which he had not been able, it is true, to probe, out of respect for the secret which he had promised to guard, and out of consideration for Jean Valjean's perilous position. He believed at that moment, that he had a grave duty to perform: the restitution of the six hundred thousand francs to someone whom he sought with all possible discretion. In the meanwhile, he abstained from touching that money.

As for Cosette, she had not been initiated into any of these secrets; but it would be harsh to condemn her also.

There existed between Marius and her an all-powerful magnetism, which caused her to do, instinctively and almost mechanically, what Marius wished. She was conscious of Marius's will in the direction of "Monsieur Jean," she conformed to it. Her husband had not been obliged to say anything to her; she yielded to the vague but clear pressure of his tacit intentions, and obeyed blindly.

Her obedience in this instance, consisted in not remembering what Marius forgot. She was not obliged to make any effort to accomplish this. Without her knowing why herself, and without his having any cause to accuse her of it, her soul had become so wholly her husband's that that which was shrouded in gloom in Marius's mind became overcast in hers.

Let us not go too far, however; in what concerns Jean Valjean, this forgetfulness and obliteration were merely superficial. She was rather heedless than forgetful. At bottom, she was sincerely attached to the man whom she had so long called her father; but she loved her husband still more dearly. This was what had somewhat disturbed the balance of her heart, which leaned to one side only.

It sometimes happened that Cosette spoke of Jean Valjean and expressed her surprise. Then Marius calmed her; "He is absent, I think. Did not he say that he was setting out on a journey?"— "That is true," thought Cosette. "He had a habit of disappearing in this fashion. But not for so long." Two or three times she dispatched Nicolette to inquire in the Rue de l'Homme Armé whether M. Jean had returned from his journey. Jean Valjean caused the answer "no" to be given.

Cosette asked nothing more, since she had but one need on earth, Marius.

Let us also say that, on their side, Cosette and Marius had also been absent. They had been to Vernon. Marius had taken Cosette to his father's grave.

Marius gradually won Cosette away from Jean Valjean. Cosette allowed it.

Moreover that which is called, far too harshly in certain cases, the ingratitude of children, is not always a thing so deserving of reproach as it is supposed. It is the ingratitude of nature. Nature, as we have elsewhere said, "looks before her." Nature divides living beings into those who are arriving and those who are departing. Those who are departing are turned toward the shadows, those who are arriving toward the light. Hence a gulf which is fatal on the part of the old, and involuntary on the part of the young. This breach, at first insensible, increases slowly, like all separations of branches. The boughs, without becoming detached from the trunk, grow away from it. It is no fault of theirs. Youth goes where there is joy, festivals, vivid lights, love. Old age goes toward the end. They do not lose sight of each other, but there is no longer a close connection. Young people feel the cooling off of life; old people, that of the tomb. Let us not blame these poor children.

Chapter II

LAST FLICKERINGS OF A LAMP WITHOUT OIL

ONE DAY, JEAN VALJEAN DESCENDED HIS STAIRCASE, TOOK THREE STEPS IN THE STREET, SEATED himself on a post, on that same stone post where Gavroche had found him meditating on the night between the 5th and the 6th of June; he remained there a few moments, then went upstairs again. This was the last oscillation of the pendulum. On the following day he did not leave his apartment. On the day after that, he did not leave his bed.

His portress, who prepared his scanty repasts, a few cabbages or potatoes with bacon, glanced at the brown earthenware plate and exclaimed:

"But you ate nothing yesterday, poor, dear man!"

"Certainly I did," replied Jean Valjean.

"The plate is quite full."

"Look at the water jug. It is empty."

"That proves that you have drunk; it does not prove that you have eaten."

"Well," said Jean Valjean, "what if I felt hungry only for water?"

"That is called thirst, and, when one does not eat at the same time, it is called fever."

"I will eat to-morrow."

"Or at Trinity day. Why not to-day? Is it the thing to say: 'I will eat to-morrow'? The idea of leaving my platter without even touching it! My lady-finger potatoes were so good!"

Jean Valjean took the old woman's hand:

"I promise you that I will eat them," he said, in his benevolent voice.

"I am not pleased with you," replied the portress.

Jean Valjean saw no other human creature than this good woman. There are streets in Paris through which no one ever passes, and houses to which no one ever comes. He was in one of those streets and one of those houses.

While he still went out, he had purchased of a copper-smith, for a few sous a little copper crucifix which he had hung up on a nail opposite his bed. That gibbet is always good to look at.

A week passed, and Jean Valjean had not taken a step in his room. He still remained in bed. The portress said to her husband: "The good man upstairs yonder does not get up, he no longer eats, he will not last long. That man has his sorrows, that he has. You won't get it out of my head that his daughter has made a bad marriage."

The porter replied, with the tone of marital sovereignty:

"If he's rich, let him have a doctor. If he is not rich, let him go without. If he has no doctor he will die."

"And if he has one?"

"He will die," said the porter.

The portress set to scraping away the grass from what she called her pavement, with an old knife, and, as she tore out the blades, she grumbled:

"It's a shame. Such a neat old man! He's as white as a chicken."

She caught sight of the doctor of the quarter as he passed the end of the street; she took it upon herself to request him to come upstairs.

"It's on the second floor," said she. "You have only to enter. As the good man no longer stirs from his bed, the door is always unlocked."

The doctor saw Jean Valjean and spoke with him.

When he came down again the portress interrogated him:

"Well, doctor?"

"Your sick man is very ill indeed."

"What is the matter with him?"

"Everything and nothing. He is a man who, to all appearances, has lost some person who is dear to him. People die of that."

"What did he say to you?"

"He told me that he was in good health."

"Shall you come again, doctor?"

"Yes," replied the doctor. "But someone else besides must come."

Chapter III

A PEN IS HEAVY TO THE MAN WHO LIFTED THE FAUCHELEVANT'S CART

ONE EVENING JEAN VALJEAN FOUND DIFFICULTY IN RAISING HIMSELF ON HIS ELBOW; HE FELT OF his wrist and could not find his pulse; his breath was short and halted at times; he recognized the fact that he was weaker than he had ever been before. Then, no doubt under the pressure of some supreme preoccupation, he made an effort, drew himself up into a sitting posture and dressed himself. He put on his old workingman's clothes. As he no longer went out, he had returned to them and preferred them. He was obliged to pause many times while dressing himself; merely putting his arms through his waistcoat made the perspiration trickle from his forehead.

Since he had been alone, he had placed his bed in the antechamber, in order to inhabit that deserted apartment as little as possible.

He opened the valise and drew from it Cosette's outfit.

He spread it out on his bed.

The Bishop's candlesticks were in their place on the chimney-piece. He took from a drawer two wax candles and put them in the candlesticks. Then, although it was still broad daylight—it was summer—he lighted them. In the same way candles are to be seen lighted in broad daylight in chambers where there is a corpse.

Every step that he took in going from one piece of furniture to another exhausted him, and he was obliged to sit down. It was not ordinary fatigue which expends the strength only to renew it; it was the remnant of all movement possible to him; it was life drained which flows away drop by drop in overwhelming efforts and which will never be renewed.

The chair into which he allowed himself to fall was placed in front of that mirror, so fatal for him, so providential for Marius, in which he had read Cosette's reversed writing on the blotting-book. He caught sight of himself in this mirror, and did not recognize himself. He was eighty years old; before Marius's marriage, he would have hardly been taken for fifty; that year had counted for thirty. What he bore on his brow was no longer the wrinkles of age, it was the mysterious mark of death. The hollowing of that pitiless nail could be felt there. His cheeks were pendulous; the skin of his face had the color which would lead one to think that it already had earth upon it; the corners of his mouth drooped as in the mask which the ancients sculptured on tombs. He gazed into space with an air of reproach; one would have said that he was one of those grand tragic beings who have cause to complain of someone.

He was in that condition, the last phase of dejection, in which sorrow no longer flows; it is coagulated, so to speak; there is something on the soul like a clot of despair.

Night had come. He laboriously dragged a table and the old arm-chair to the fireside, and placed upon the table a pen, some ink and some paper.

That done, he had a fainting fit. When he recovered consciousness, he was thirsty. As he could not lift the jug, he tipped it over painfully toward his mouth, and swallowed a draft.

As neither the pen nor the ink had been used for a long time, the point of the pen had curled up, the ink had dried away, he was forced to rise and put a few drops of water in the ink, which he did not accomplish without pausing and sitting down two or three times, and he was compelled to write with the back of the pen. He wiped his brow from time to time.

Then he turned toward the bed, and, still seated, for he could not stand, he gazed at the little black gown and all those beloved objects.

These contemplations lasted for hours which seemed minutes.

All at once he shivered, he felt that a child was taking possession of him; he rested his elbows on the table, which was illuminated by the Bishop's candles and took up the pen. His hand trembled. He wrote slowly the few following lines:

"Cosette, I bless thee. I am going to explain to thee. Thy husband was right in giving me to understand that I ought to go away; but there is a little error in what he believed, though he was in the right. He is excellent. Love him well even after I am dead. Monsieur Pontmercy, love my darling child well. Cosette, this paper will be found; this is what I wish to say to thee, thou wilt see the figures, if I have the strength to recall them, listen well, this money is really thine. Here is the whole matter: White jet comes from Norway, black jet comes from England, black glass jewelery comes from Germany. Jet is the lightest, the most precious, the most costly. Imitations can be made in France as well as in Germany. What is needed is a little anvil two inches square, and a lamp burning spirits of wine to soften the wax. The wax was formerly made with resin and lampblack, and cost four livres the pound. I invented a way of making it with gum shellac and turpentine. It does not cost more than thirty sous, and is much better. Buckles are made with a violet glass which is stuck fast, by means of this wax, to a little framework of black iron. The glass must be violet for iron jewelery, and black for gold jewelery. Spain buys a great deal of it. It is the country of jet . . ."

Here he paused, the pen fell from his fingers, he was seized by one of those sobs which at times, welled up from the very depths of his being; the poor man clasped his head in both hands, and meditated.

"Oh!" he exclaimed within himself [lamentable cries, heard by God alone], "all is over. I shall never see her more. She is a smile which passed over me. I am about to plunge into the night without even seeing her again. Oh! one minute, one instant, to hear her voice, to touch her dress, to gaze upon her, upon her, the angel! and then to die! It is nothing to die, what is frightful is to die without seeing her. She would smile on me, she would say a word to me, would that do any harm to anyone? No, all is over, and forever. Here I am all alone. My God! My God! I shall never see her again!"

At that moment there came a knock at the door.

Chapter IV

A BOTTLE OF INK WHICH ONLY SUCCEEDED IN WHITENING

THAT SAME DAY, OR TO SPEAK MORE ACCURATELY, THAT SAME EVENING, AS MARIUS LEFT THE table, and was on the point of withdrawing to his study, having a case to look over, Basque handed him a letter saying: "The person who wrote the letter is in the antechamber."

Cosette had taken the grandfather's arm and was strolling in the garden.

A letter, like a man, may have an unprepossessing exterior. Coarse paper, coarsely folded— the very sight of certain missives is displeasing.

The letter which Basque had brought was of this sort.

Marius took it. It smelled of tobacco. Nothing evokes a memory like an odor. Marius recognized that tobacco. He looked at the superscription: "To Monsieur, Monsieur le Baron Pommerci. At his hôtel." The recognition of the tobacco caused him to recognize the writing as well. It may be said that amazement has its lightning flashes.

Marius was, as it were, illuminated by one of these flashes.

The sense of smell, that mysterious aid to memory, had just revived a whole world within him.

This was certainly the paper, the fashion of folding, the dull tint of ink; it was certainly the well-known handwriting, especially was it the same tobacco.

The Jondrette garret rose before his mind.

Thus, strange freak of chance! one of the two scents which he had so diligently sought, the one in connection with which he had lately again exerted so many efforts, and which he supposed to be forever lost, had come and presented itself to him of its own accord.

He eagerly broke the seal, and read:

MONSIEUR LE BARON—If the Supreme Being had given me the talents, I might have been baron Thénard, member of the Institute [Aademy of ciences], but I am not. I only bear the same as him, happy if this memory recommends me to the eccellence of your kindnesses. The benefit with which you will honor me will be reciprocle. I am in possession of a secret concerning an individual. This individual concerns you. I hold the secret at your disposal desiring to have the honor to be huseful to you. I will furnish you with the simple means of driving from your honorabel family that individual who has no right there, madame la baronne being of lofty birth. The sanctuary of virtue cannot cohabit longer with crime without abdicating.

I awate in the entichamber the orders of monsieur le baron.

With respect

The letter was signed "Thénard."

This signature was not false. It was merely a trifle abridged.

Moreover, the rigmarole and the orthography completed the revelation. The certificate of origin was complete.

Marius's emotion was profound. After a start of surprise, he underwent a feeling of happiness. If he could now but find that other man of whom he was in search, the man who had saved him, Marius, there would be nothing left for him to desire.

He opened the drawer of his secretary, took out several bank-notes, put them in his pocket, closed the secretary again, and rang the bell. Basque half opened the door.

"Show the man in," said Marius.

Basque announced:

"Monsieur Thénard."

A man entered.

A fresh surprise for Marius. The man who entered was an utter stranger to him.

This man, who was old, moreover, had a thick nose, his chin swathed in a cravat, green spectacles with a double screen of green taffeta over his eyes, and his hair was plastered and flattened down on his brow on a level with his eyebrows like the wigs of English coachmen in "high life." His hair was gray. He was dressed in black from head to foot, in garments that were very threadbare but clean; a bunch of seals depending from his fob suggested the idea of a watch. He held in his hand an old hat! He walked in a bent attitude, and the curve in his spine augmented the profundity of his bow.

The first thing that struck the observer was, that this personage's coat, which was too ample although carefully buttoned, had not been made for him.

Here a short digression becomes necessary.

There was in Paris at that epoch, in a low-lived old lodging in the Rue Beautreillis, near the Arsenal, an ingenious Jew whose profession was to change villains into honest men. Not for too long, which might have proved embarrassing for the villain. The change was on sight, for a day or two, at the rate of thirty sous a day, by means of a costume which resembled the honesty of the world in general as nearly as possible. This costumer was called "the Changer"; the pickpockets of Paris had given him this name and knew him by no other. He had a tolerably complete wardrobe.

The rags with which he tricked out people were almost probable. He had specialties and categories; on each nail of his shop hung a social status, threadbare and worn; here the suit of a magistrate, there the outfit of a Curé, beyond the outfit of a banker, in one corner the costume of a retired military man, elsewhere the habiliments of a man of letters, and further on the dress of a statesman.

This creature was the costumer of the immense drama which knavery plays in Paris. His lair was the green-room whence theft emerged, and into which roguery retreated. A tattered knave arrived at this dressing-room, deposited his thirty sous and selected, according to the part which he wished to play, the costume which suited him, and on descending the stairs once more, the knave was a somebody. On the following day the clothes were faithfully returned, and the Changer, who trusted the thieves with everything, was never robbed. There was one inconvenience about these clothes, they "did not fit"; not having been made for those who wore them, they were too tight for one, too loose for another and did not adjust themselves to anyone. Every pickpocket who exceeded or fell short of the human average was ill at his ease in the Changer's costumes. It was necessary that one should not be either too fat or too lean. The changer had foreseen only ordinary men. He had taken the measure of the species from the first rascal who came to hand, who is neither stout nor thin, neither tall nor short. Hence adaptations which were sometimes difficult and from which the Changer's clients extricated themselves as best they might. So much the worse for the exceptions! The suit of the statesman, for instance, black from head to foot, and consequently proper, would have been too large for Pitt and too small for Castelcicala. The costume of a statesman was designated as follows in the Changer's catalogue; we copy:

"A coat of black cloth, trousers of black wool, a silk waistcoat, boots and linen." On the margin there stood: *ex-ambassador,* and a note which we also copy: "In a separate box, a neatly frizzed peruke, green glasses, seals, and two small quills an inch long, wrapped in cotton." All this belonged to the statesman, the ex-ambassador. This whole costume was, if we may so express ourselves, debilitated; the seams were white, a vague buttonhole yawned at one of the elbows; moreover, one of the coat buttons was missing on the breast; but this was only a detail; as the hand of the statesman should always be thrust into his coat and laid upon his heart, its function was to conceal the absent button.

If Marius had been familiar with the occult institutions of Paris, he would instantly have recognized upon the back of the visitor whom Basque had just shown in, the statesman's suit borrowed from the pick-me-down-that shop of the Changer.

Marius's disappointment on beholding another man than the one whom he expected to see turned to the newcomer's disadvantage.

He surveyed him from head to foot, while that personage made exaggerated bows, and demanded in a curt tone:

"What do you want?"

The man replied with an amiable grin of which the caressing smile of a crocodile will furnish some idea:

"It seems to me impossible that I should not have already had the honor of seeing Monsieur le Baron in society. I think I actually did meet monsieur personally, several years ago, at the house of Madame la Princess Bagration and in the drawing-rooms of his Lordship the Vicomte Dambray, peer of France."

It is always a good bit of tactics in knavery to pretend to recognize someone whom one does not know.

Marius paid attention to the manner of this man's speech. He spied on his accent and gesture, but his disappointment increased; the pronunciation was nasal and absolutely unlike the dry, shrill tone which he had expected.

He was utterly routed.

"I know neither Madame Bagration nor M. Dambray," said he. "I have never set foot in the house of either of them in my life."

The reply was ungracious. The personage, determined to be gracious at any cost, insisted.

"Then it must have been at Chateaubriand's that I have seen Monsieur! I know Chateaubriand very well. He is very affable. He sometimes says to me: 'Thénard, my friend . . . won't you drink a glass of wine with me?' "

Marius's brow grew more and more severe:

"I have never had the honor of being received by M. de Chateaubriand. Let us cut it short. What do you want?"

The man bowed lower at that harsh voice.

"Monsieur le Baron, deign to listen to me. There is in America, in a district near Panama, a village called la Joya. That village is composed of a single house, a large, square house of three stories, built of bricks dried in the sun, each side of the square five hundred feet in length, each story retreating twelve feet back of the story below, in such a manner as to leave in front a terrace which makes the circuit of the edifice, in the center an inner court where the provisions and munitions are kept; no windows, loopholes, no doors, ladders, ladders to mount from the ground to the first terrace, and from the first to the second, and from the second to the third, ladders to descend into the inner court, no doors to the chambers, trapdoors, no staircases to the chambers, ladders; in the evening the traps are closed, the ladders are withdrawn, carbines and blunderbusses trained from the loopholes; no means of entering, a house by day, a citadel by night, eight hundred inhabitants—that is the village. Why so many precautions? because the country is dangerous; it is full of cannibals. Then why do people go there? because the country is marvelous; gold is found there."

"What are you driving at?" interrupted Marius, who had passed from disappointment to impatience.

"At this, Monsieur le Baron. I am an old and weary diplomat. Ancient civilization has thrown me on my own devices. I want to try savages."

"Well?"

"Monsieur le Baron, egotism is the law of the world. The proletarian peasant woman, who toils by the day, turns round when the diligence passes by, the peasant proprietress, who toils in her field, does not turn round. The dog of the poor man barks at the rich man, the dog of the rich man barks at the poor man. Each one for himself. Self-interest—that's the object of men. Gold, that's the loadstone."

"What then? Finish."

"I should like to go and establish myself at la Joya. There are three of us. I have my spouse and my young lady; a very beautiful girl. The journey is long and costly. I need a little money."

"What concern is that of mine?" demanded Marius.

The stranger stretched his neck out of his cravat, a gesture characteristic of the vulture, and replied with an augmented smile:

"Has not Monsieur le Baron perused my letter?"

There was some truth in this. The fact is, that the contents of the epistle had slipped Marius's mind. He had seen the writing rather than read the letter. He could hardly recall it. But a moment ago a fresh start had been given him. He had noted that detail: "my spouse and my young lady."

He fixed a penetrating glance on the stranger. An examining judge could not have done the look better. He almost lay in wait for him.

He confined himself to replying:

"State the case precisely."

The stranger inserted his two hands in both his fobs, drew himself up without straightening his dorsal column, but scrutinizing Marius in his turn, with the green gaze of his spectacles.

"So be it, Monsieur le Baron. I will be precise. I have a secret to sell to you."

"A secret?"

"A secret."

"Which concerns me?"

"Somewhat."

"What is the secret?"

Marius scrutinized the man more and more as he listened to him.

"I commence gratis," said the stranger. "You will see that I am interesting."

"Speak."

"Monsieur le Baron, you have in your house a thief and an assassin."

Marius shuddered.

"In my house? no," said he.

The imperturbable stranger brushed his hat with his elbow, and went on:

"An assassin and a thief. Remark, Monsieur le Baron, that I do not here speak of ancient deeds, deeds of the past which have lapsed, which can be effaced by limitation before the law and by repentance before God. I speak of recent deeds, of actual facts as still unknown to justice at this hour. I continue. This man has insinuated himself into your confidence, and almost into your family under a false name. I am about to tell you his real name. And to tell it to you for nothing."

"I am listening."

"His name is Jean Valjean."

"I know it."

"I am going to tell you, equally for nothing, who he is."

"Say on."

"He is an ex-convict."

"I know it."

"You know it since I have had the honor of telling you."

"No. I knew it before."

Marius's cold tone, that double reply of "I know it," his laconicism, which was not favorable to dialogue, stirred up some smoldering wrath in the stranger. He launched a furious glance on the sly at Marius, which was instantly extinguished. Rapid as it was, this glance was of the kind which a man recognizes when he has once beheld it; it did not escape Marius. Certain flashes can only proceed from certain souls; the eye, that vent-hole of the thought, glows with it; spectacles hide nothing; try putting a pane of glass over hell!

The stranger resumed with a smile:

"I will not permit myself to contradict Monsieur le Baron. In any case, you ought to perceive that I am well informed. Now what I have to tell you is known to myself alone. This concerns the fortune of Madame la Baronne. It is an extraordinary secret. It is for sale—I make you the first offer of it. Cheap. Twenty thousand francs."

"I know that secret as well as the others," said Marius.

The personage felt the necessity of lowering his price a trifle.

"Monsieur le Baron, say ten thousand francs and I will speak."

"I repeat to you that there is nothing which you can tell me. I know what you wish to say to me."

A fresh flash gleamed in the man's eye. He exclaimed:

"But I must dine to-day, nevertheless. It is an extraordinary secret, I tell you. Monsieur le Baron, I will speak. *I* speak. Give me twenty francs."

Marius gazed intently at him:

"I know your extraordinary secret, just as I knew Jean Valjean's name, just as I know your name."

"My name?"

"Yes."

"That is not difficult, Monsieur le Baron. I had the honor to write to you and to tell it to you. Thénard."

"—Dier."

"Hey?"

"Thénardier."

"Who's that?"

In danger the porcupine bristles up, the beetle feigns death, the old guard forms in a square; this man burst into laughter.

Then he flicked a grain of dust from the sleeve of his coat with a fillip.

Marius continued:

"You are also Jondrette the workman, Fabantou the comedian, Genflot the poet, Don Alvaèrès the Spaniard, and Mistress Balizard."

"Mistress what?"

"And you kept a pot-house at Montfermeil."

"A pot-house! Never."

"And I tell you that your name is Thénardier."

"I deny it."

"And that you are a rascal. Here."

And Marius drew a bank-note from his pocket and flung it in his face.

"Thanks! Pardon me! five hundred francs! Monsieur le Baron!"

And the man, overcome, bowed, seized the note and examined it.

"Five hundred francs!" he began again, taken aback. And he stammered in a low voice: "An honest rustler."

Then brusquely:

"Well, so be it!" he exclaimed. "Let us put ourselves at our ease."

And with the agility of a monkey, flinging back his hair, tearing off his spectacles, and withdrawing from his nose by sleight of hand the two quills of which mention was recently made, and which the reader has also met with on another page of this book, he took off his face as the man takes off his hat.

His eye lighted up; his uneven brow, with hollows in some places and bumps in others, hideously wrinkled at the top, was laid bare, his nose had become as sharp as a beak; the fierce and sagacious profile of the man of prey reappeared.

"Monsieur le Baron is infallible," he said in a clear voice whence all nasal twang had disappeared, "I am Thénardier."

And he straightened up his crooked back.

Thénardier, for it was really he, was strangely surprised; he would have been troubled, had he been capable of such a thing. He had come to bring astonishment, and it was he who had received it. This humiliation had been worth five hundred francs to him, and, taking it all in all, he accepted it; but he was none the less bewildered.

He beheld this Baron Pontmercy for the first time, and, in spite of his disguise, this Baron Pontmercy recognized him, and recognized him thoroughly. And not only was this Baron perfectly informed as to Thénardier, but he seemed well posted as to Jean Valjean. Who was this almost beardless young man, who was so glacial and so generous, who knew people's names, who knew all their names, and who opened his purse to them, who bullied rascals like a judge, and who paid them like a dupe?

Thénardier, the reader will remember, although he had been Marius's neighbor, had never seen him, which is not unusual in Paris; he had formerly, in a vague way, heard his daughters talk of a very poor young man named Marius who lived in the house. He had written to him, without knowing him, the letter with which the reader is acquainted.

No connection between that Marius and M. le Baron Pontmercy was possible in his mind.

As for the name Pontmercy, it will be recalled that, on the battlefield of Waterloo, he had heard only the last two syllables, for which he always entertained the legitimate scorn which one owes to what is merely an expression of thanks.

However, through his daughter Azelma, who had started on the scent of the married pair on the 16th of February, and through his own personal researches, he had succeeded in learning many things, and, from the depths of his own gloom, he had contrived to grasp more than one mysterious clue. He had discovered, by dint of industry, or, at least, by dint of induction, he had guessed, who the man was whom he had encountered on a certain day in the Grand Sewer. From the man he had easily reached the name. He knew that Madame la Baronne Pontmercy was Cosette. But he meant to be discreet in that quarter.

Who was Cosette? He did not know exactly himself. He did indeed, catch an inkling of illegitimacy, the history of Fantine had always seemed to him equivocal; but what was the use of talking about that? in order to cause himself to be paid for his silence? He had, or thought he had, better wares than that for sale. And, according to all appearances, if he were to come and make to the Baron Pontmercy this revelation—and without proof: "Your wife is a bastard," the only result would be to attract the boot of the husband toward the loins of the revealer.

From Thénardier's point of view, the conversation with Marius had not yet begun. He ought to have drawn back, to have modified his strategy, to have abandoned his position, to have changed his front; but nothing essential had been compromised as yet, and he had five hundred francs in his pocket. Moreover, he had something decisive to say, and, even against this very well-informed and well-armed Baron Pontmercy, he felt himself strong. For men of Thénardier's nature, every dialogue is a combat. In the one in which he was about to engage, what was his situation? He did not know to whom he was speaking, but he did know of what he was speaking, he made this rapid review of his inner forces, and after having said: "I am Thénardier," he waited.

Marius had become thoughtful. So he had hold of Thénardier at last. That man whom he had so greatly desired to find, was before him. He could honor Colonel Pontmercy's recommendation.

He felt humiliated that that hero should have owned anything to this villain, and that the letter of change drawn from the depths of the tomb by his father upon him, Marius, had been protested up to that day. It also seemed to him, in the complex state of his mind toward Thénardier, that there was occasion to avenge the Colonel for the misfortune of having been saved by such a rascal. In any case, he was content. He was about to deliver the Colonel's shade from this unworthy creditor at last, and it seemed to him that he was on the point of rescuing his father's memory from the debtors' prison. By the side of this duty there was another—to elucidate, if possible, the source of Cosette's fortune. The opportunity appeared to present itself. Perhaps Thénardier knew something. It might prove useful to see the bottom of this man.

He commenced with this.

Thénardier had caused the "honest rustler" to disappear in his fob, and was gazing at Marius with a gentleness that was almost tender.

Marius broke the silence.

"Thénardier, I have told you your name. Now, would you like to have me tell you your secret—the one that you came here to reveal to me? I have information of my own, also. You shall see that I know more about it than you do. Jean Valjean, as you have said, is an assassin and a thief. A thief, because he robbed a wealthy manufacturer, whose ruin he brought about. An assassin, because he assassinated police-agent Javert."

"I don't understand, sir," ejaculated Thénardier.

"I will make myself intelligible. In a certain arrondissement of the Pas de Calais, there was, in 1822, a man who had fallen out with justice, and who, under the name of M. Madeleine, had regained his status and rehabilitated himself. This man had become a just man in the full force of the term. In a trade, the manufacture of black glass goods, he made the fortune of an entire city. As far as his personal fortune was concerned he made that also, but as a secondary matter, and in some sort, by accident. He was the foster-father of the poor. He founded hospitals, opened schools, visited the sick, dowered young girls, supported widows, and adopted orphans; he was like the guardian angel of the country. He refused the cross, he was appointed Mayor. A liberated convict knew the secret of a penalty incurred by this man in former days; he denounced him, and had him arrested, and profited by the arrest to come to Paris and cause the banker Laffitte—I have the fact from the cashier himself—by means of a false signature, to hand over to him the sum of over half a million which belonged to M. Madeleine. This convict who robbed M. Madeleine was Jean Valjean. As for the other fact, you have nothing to tell me about it either. Jean Valjean killed the agent Javert; he shot him with a pistol. I, the person who is speaking to you, was present."

Thénardier cast upon Marius the sovereign glance of a conquered man who lays his hand once more upon the victory, and who has just regained, in one instant, all the ground which he has lost. But the smile returned instantly. The inferior's triumph in the presence of his superior must be wheedling.

Thénardier contented himself with saying to Marius:

"Monsieur le Baron, we are on the wrong track."

And he emphasized this phrase by making his bunch of seals execute an expressive whirl.

"What!" broke forth Marius, "do you dispute that? These are facts."

"They are chimeras. The confidence with which Monsieur le Baron honors me renders it my duty to tell him so. Truth and justice before all things. I do not like to see folks accused unjustly. Monsieur le Baron, Jean Valjean did not rob M. Madeleine and Jean Valjean did not kill Javert."

"This is too much! How is this?"

"For two reasons."

"What are they? Speak."

"This is the first: he did not rob M. Madeleine, because it is Jean Valjean himself who was M. Madeleine."

"What tale are you telling me?"

"And this is the second: he did not assassinate Javert, because the person who killed Javert was Javert."

"What do you mean to say?"

"That Javert committed suicide."

"Prove it! prove it!" cried Marius beside himself.

Thénardier resumed, scanning his phrase after the manner of the ancient Alexandrine measure:

"Police-agent-Ja-vert-was-found-drowned-un-der-a-boat-of-the-Pont-au-Change."

"But prove it!"

Thénardier drew from his pocket a large envelope of gray paper, which seemed to contain sheets folded in different sizes.

"I have my papers," he said calmly.

And he added:

"Monsieur le Baron, in your interests I desired to know Jean Valjean thoroughly. I say that Jean Valjean and M. Madeleine are one and the same man, and I say that Javert had no other assassin than Javert. If I speak, it is because I have proofs. Not manuscript proofs—writing is suspicious, handwriting is complaisant—but printed proofs."

As he spoke, Thénardier extracted from the envelope two copies of newspapers, yellow, faded, and strongly saturated with tobacco. One of these two newspapers, broken at every fold and falling into rags, seemed much older than the other.

"Two facts, two proofs," remarked Thénardier. And he offered the two newspapers, unfolded, to Marius.

The reader is acquainted with these two papers. One, the most ancient, a number of the *Drapeau Blanc* of the 25th of July, 1823, the text of which can be seen in the first volume, established the identity of M. Madeleine and Jean Valjean.

The other, a *Moniteur* of the 15th of June, 1832, announced the suicide of Javert, adding that it appeared from a verbal report of Javert to the prefect that, having been taken prisoner in the barricade of the Rue de la Chanvrerie, he had owed his life to the magnanimity of an insurgent who, holding him under his pistol, had fired into the air, instead of blowing out his brains.

Marius read. He had evidence, a certain date, irrefragable proof, these two newspapers had not been printed expressly for the purpose of backing up Thénardier's statements; the note printed in the *Moniteur* had been an administrative communication from the Prefecture of Police. Marius could not doubt.

The information of the cashier-clerk had been false, and he himself had been deceived.

Jean Valjean, who had suddenly grown grand, emerged from his cloud. Marius could not repress a cry of joy.

"Well, then this unhappy wretch is an admirable man! the whole of that fortune really belonged to him! he is Madeleine, the providence of a whole countryside! he is Jean Valjean, Javert's savior! he is a hero! he is a saint!"

"He's not a saint, and he's not a hero!" said Thénardier. "He's an assassin and a robber."

And he added, in the tone of a man who begins to feel that he possesses some authority: "Let us be calm."

Robber, assassin—those words which Marius thought had disappeared and which returned, fell upon him like an ice-cold shower-bath.

"Again!" said he.

"Always," ejaculated Thénardier. "Jean Valjean did not rob Madeleine, but he is a thief. He did not kill Javert, but he is a murderer."

"Will you speak," retorted Marius, "of that miserable theft, committed forty years ago, and expiated, as your own newspapers prove, by a whole life of repentance, of self-abnegation and of virtue?"

"I say assassination and theft, Monsieur le Baron, and I repeat that I am speaking of actual facts. What I have to reveal to you is absolutely unknown. It belongs to unpublished matter. And perhaps you will find in it the source of the fortune so skillfully presented to Madame la Baronne by Jean Valjean. I say skillfully, because, by a gift of that nature it would not be so very unskillful to slip into an honorable house whose comforts one would then share, and, at the same stroke, to conceal one's crime, and to enjoy one's theft, to bury one's name and to create for one's self a family."

"I might interrupt you at this point," said Marius, "but go on."

"Monsieur le Baron, I will tell you all, leaving the recompense to your generosity. This secret is worth massive gold. You will say to me: 'Why do not you apply to Jean Valjean?' For a very simple reason; I know that he has stripped himself, and stripped himself in your favor, and I consider the combination ingenious; but he has no longer a sou, he would show me his empty hands, and, since I am in need of some money for my trip to la Joya, I prefer you, you who have it all, to him who has nothing. I am a little fatigued, permit me to take a chair."

Marius seated himself and motioned to him to do the same.

Thénardier installed himself on a tufted chair, picked up his two newspapers, thrust them back into their envelope, and murmured as he pecked at the *Drapeau Blanc* with his nail: "It cost me a good deal of trouble to get this one."

That done he crossed his legs and stretched himself out on the back of the chair, an attitude characteristic of people who are sure of what they are saying, then he entered upon his subject gravely, emphasizing his words:

"Monsieur le Baron, on the 6th of June, 1832, about a year ago, on the day of the insurrection, a man was in the Grand Sewer of Paris, at the point where the sewer enters the Seine, between the Pont des Invalides and the Pont de Jéna."

Marius abruptly drew his chair closer to that of Thénardier. Thénardier noticed this movement and continued with the deliberation of an orator who holds his interlocutor and who feels his adversary palpitating under his words:

"This man, forced to conceal himself, and for reasons, moreover, which are foreign to politics, had adopted the sewer as his domicile and had a key to it. It was, I repeat, on the 6th of June; it might have been eight o'clock in the evening. The man hears a noise in the sewer. Greatly surprised, he hides himself and lies in wait. It was the sound of footsteps, someone was walking in the dark, and coming in his direction. Strange to say, there was another man in the sewer besides himself. The grating of the outlet from the sewer was not far off. A little light which fell through it permitted him to recognize the newcomer, and to see that the man was carrying something on his back. He was walking in a bent attitude. The man who was walking in a bent attitude was an ex-convict, and what he was dragging on his shoulders was a corpse. Assassination caught in the very act, if ever there was such a thing. As for the theft, that is understood; one does not kill a man gratis. This convict was on his way to fling the body into the river. One fact is to be noticed, that before reaching the exit grating, this convict, who had come a long distance in the sewer, must, necessarily, have encountered a frightful quagmire where it seems as though he might have left the body, but the sewermen would have found the assassinated man the very next day, while at work on the quagmire, and that did not suit the assassin's plans. He had preferred to traverse that quagmire with his burden, and his exertions must have been terrible, for it is impossible to risk one's life more completely; I don't understand how he could have come out of that alive."

Marius's chair approached still nearer. Thénardier took advantage of this to draw a long breath. He went on:

"Monsieur le Baron, a sewer is not the Champ de Mars. One lacks everything there, even room. When two men are there, they must meet. That is what happened. The man domiciled there and the passer-by were forced to bid each other good day, greatly to the regret of both. The passer-by said to the inhabitant: "You see what I have on my back, I must get out, you have the key, give it to me." That convict was a man of terrible strength. There was no way of refusing. Nevertheless, the man who had the key parleyed, simply to gain time. He examined the dead man, but he could see nothing, except that the latter was young, well dressed, with the air of being rich, and all disfigured with blood. While talking, the man contrived to tear and pull off behind, without the assassin perceiving it, a bit of the assassinated man's coat. A document for conviction, you understand; a means of recovering the trace of things and of bringing home the crime to the criminal. He put this document for conviction in his pocket. After which he opened the grating, made the man go out with his embarrassment on his back, closed the grating again, and ran off, not caring to be mixed up with the remainder of the adventure and above all, not wishing to be present when the assassin threw the assassinated man into the river. Now you comprehend. The man who was carrying the corpse was Jean Valjean; the one who had the key is speaking to you at this moment; and the piece of the coat . . ."

Thénardier completed his phrase by drawing from his pocket, and holding, on a level with his eyes, nipped between his two thumbs and his two forefingers, a strip of torn black cloth, all covered with dark spots.

Marius had sprung to his feet, pale, hardly able to draw his breath, with his eyes riveted on the fragment of black cloth, and, without uttering a word, without taking his eyes from that fragment, he retreated to the wall and fumbled with his right hand along the wall for a key which was in the lock of a cupboard near the chimney.

He found the key, opened the cupboard, plunged his arm into it without looking, and without his frightened gaze quitting the rag which Thénardier still held outspread.

But Thénardier continued:

"Monsieur le Baron, I have the strongest of reasons for believing that the assassinated young man was an opulent stranger lured into a trap by Jean Valjean, and the bearer of an enormous sum of money."

"The young man was myself, and here is the coat!" cried Marius, and he flung upon the floor an old black coat all covered with blood.

Then, snatching the fragment from the hands of Thénardier, he crouched down over the coat, and laid the torn morsel against the tattered skirt. The rent fitted exactly, and the strip completed the coat.

Thénardier was petrified.

This is what he thought: "I'm struck all of a heap."

Marius rose to his feet trembling, despairing, radiant.

He fumbled in his pocket and stalked furiously to Thénardier, presenting to him and almost thrusting in his face his fist filled with bank-notes for five hundred and a thousand francs.

"You are an infamous wretch! you are a liar, a calumniator, a villain. You came to accuse that man, you have only justified him; you wanted to ruin him, you have only succeeded in glorifying him. And it is you who are the thief! And it is you who are the assassin! I saw you, Thénardier Jondrette, in that lair on the Rue de l'Hôpital. I know enough about you to send you to the galleys and even further if I choose. Here are a thousand francs, bully that you are!"

And he flung a thousand-franc note at Thénardier.

"Ah! Jondrette Thénardier, vile rascal! Let this serve you as a lesson, you dealer in second-hand secrets, merchant of mysteries, rummager of the shadows, wretch! Take these five hundred francs and get out of here! Waterloo protects you."

"Waterloo!" growled Thénardier, pocketing the five hundred francs along with the thousand.

"Yes, assassin! You there saved the life of a Colonel . . ."

"Of a General," said Thénardier, elevating his head.

"Of a Colonel!" repeated Marius in a rage. "I wouldn't give a ha'penny for a general. And you come here to commit infamies! I tell you that you have committed all crimes. Go! disappear! Only be happy, that is all that I desire. Ah! monster! here are three thousand francs more. Take them. You will depart to-morrow, for America, with your daughter; for your wife is dead, you abominable liar. I shall watch over your departure, you ruffian, and at that moment I will count out to you twenty thousand francs. Go get yourself hung elsewhere!"

"Monsieur le Baron," replied Thénardier, bowing to the very earth, "eternal gratitude." And Thénardier left the room, understanding nothing, stupefied and delighted with this sweet crushing beneath sacks of gold, and with that thunder which had burst forth over his head in bank-bills.

Struck by lightning he was, but he was also content; and he would have been greatly angered had he had a lightning rod to ward off such lightning as that.

Let us finish with this man at once.

Two days after the events which we are at this moment narrating, he set out, thanks to Marius's care, for America under a false name, with his daughter Azelma, furnished with a draft on New York for twenty thousand francs.

The moral wretchedness of Thénardier, the bourgeois who had missed his vocation, was irremediable. He was in America what he had been in Europe. Contact with an evil man sometimes suffices to corrupt a good action and to cause evil things to spring from it. With Marius's money, Thénardier set up as a slave-dealer.

As soon as Thénardier had left the house, Marius rushed to the garden, where Cosette was still walking.

"Cosette! Cosette!" he cried. "Come! come quick! Let us go. Basque, a carriage! Cosette, come. Ah! My God! It was he who saved my life! Let us not lose a minute! Put on your shawl."

Cosette thought him mad and obeyed.

He could not breathe, he laid his hand on his heart to restrain its throbbing. He paced back and forth with huge strides, he embraced Cosette:

"Ah! Cosette! I am an unhappy wretch!" said he.

Marius was bewildered. He began to catch a glimpse in Jean Valjean of some indescribably lofty and melancholy figure. An unheard-of virtue supreme and sweet, humble in its immensity, appeared to him. The convict was transfigured into Christ.

Marius was dazzled by this prodigy. He did not know precisely what he beheld, but it was grand.

In an instant, a hackney-carriage stood in front of the door.

Marius helped Cosette in and darted in himself.

"Driver," said he, "Rue de l'Homme Armé, Number 7."

The carriage drove off.

"Ah! what happiness!" ejaculated Cosette. "Rue de l'Homme Armé, I did not dare to speak to you of that. We are going to see M. Jean."

"Thy father! Cosette, thy father more than ever. Cosette, I guess it. You told me that you had never received the letter that I sent you by Gavroche. It must have fallen into his hands. Cosette, he went to the barricade to save me. As it is a necessity with him to be an angel, he saved others also; he saved Javert. He rescued me from that gulf to give me to you. He carried me on his back through that frightful sewer. Ah! I am a monster of ingratitude. Cosette, after having been your providence, he became mine. Just imagine, there was a terrible quagmire enough to drown one a hundred times over, to drown one in mire. Cosette! he made me traverse it. I was unconscious; I saw nothing, I heard nothing, I could know nothing of my own adventure. We are going to bring him back, to take him with us, whether he is willing or not, he shall never leave us again. If only he is at home! Provided only that we can find him, I will pass the rest of my life in venerating him. Yes, that is how it should be, do you see, Cosette? Gavroche must have delivered my letter to him. All is explained. You understand."

Cosette did not understand a word.

"You are right," she said to him.

Meanwhile the carriage rolled on.

Chapter V

A NIGHT BEHIND WHICH THERE IS DAY

JEAN VALJEAN TURNED ROUND AT THE KNOCK WHICH HE HEARD ON HIS DOOR.

"Come in," he said feebly.

The door opened.

Cosette and Marius made their appearance.

Cosette rushed into the room.

Marius remained on the threshold, leaning against the jamb of the door.

"Cosette!" said Jean Valjean.

And he sat erect in his chair, his arms outstretched and trembling, haggard, livid, gloomy, an immense joy in his eyes.

Cosette, stifling with emotion, fell upon Jean Valjean's breast.

"Father!" said she.

Jean Valjean, overcome, stammered:

"Cosette! she! you! Madame! it is thou! Ah! my God!"

And, pressed close in Cosette's arms he exclaimed:

"It is thou! thou art here! Thou dost pardon me then!"

Marius, lowering his eyelids, in order to keep his tears from flowing, took a step forward and murmured between lips convulsively contracted to repress his sobs:

"My father!"

"And you also, you pardon me!" Jean Valjean said to him.

Marius could find no words, and Jean Valjean added:

"Thanks."

Cosette tore off her shawl and tossed her hat on the bed.

"It embarrasses me," said she.

And, seating herself on the old man's knees, she put aside his white locks with an adorable movement, and kissed his brow.

Jean Valjean, bewildered, let her have her own way.

Cosette, who only understood in a very confused manner, redoubled her caresses, as though she desired to pay Marius's debt.

Jean Valjean stammered:

"How stupid people are! I thought that I should never see her again. Imagine, Monsieur Pontmercy, at the very moment when you entered, I was saying to myself: 'All is over. Here is her little gown, I am a miserable man, I shall never see Cosette again,' and I was saying that at the very moment when you were mounting the stairs. Was not I an idiot! Just see how idiotic one can be! One reckons without the good God. The good God says:

" 'You fancy that you are about to be abandoned, stupid! No. No, things will not go so. Come, there is a good man yonder who is in need of an angel.' And the angel comes, and one sees one's Cosette again! and one sees one's little Cosette once more! Ah! I was very unhappy."

For a moment he could not speak, then he went on:

"I really needed to see Cosette a little bit now and then. A heart needs a bone to gnaw. But I was perfectly conscious that I was in the way. I gave myself reasons: 'They do not want you, keep in your own course, one has not the right to cling eternally.' Ah! God be praised, I see her once more! Dost thou know, Cosette, thy husband is very handsome? Ah! what a pretty embroidered collar thou hast on, luckily. I am fond of that pattern. It was thy husband who chose it, was it not? And then, thou shouldst have some cashmere shawls. Let me call her thou, Monsieur Pontmercy. It will not be for long."

And Cosette began again:

"How wicked of you to have left us like that! Where did you go? Why have you stayed away so long? Formerly your journeys only lasted three or four days. I sent Nicolette, the answer always was: 'He is absent.' How long have you been back? Why did you not let us know? Do you know that you are very much changed? Ah! what a naughty father! he has been ill, and we have not known it! Stay, Marius, feel how cold his hand is!"

"So you are here! Monsieur Pontmercy, you pardon me!" repeated Jean Valjean.

At that word which Jean Valjean had just uttered once more, all that was swelling Marius's heart found vent.

He burst forth:

"Cosette, do you hear? he has come to that! he asks my forgiveness! And do you know what he has done for me, Cosette? He has saved my life. He has done more—he has given you to me. And after having saved me, and after having given you to me, Cosette, what has he done with himself? He has sacrificed himself. Behold the man. And he says to me the ingrate, to me the forgetful, to me the pitiless, to me the guilty one: Thanks! Cosette, my whole life passed at the feet of this man would be too little. That barricade, that sewer, that furnace, that cesspool—all that he traversed for me, for thee, Cosette! He carried me away through all the deaths which he put aside before me, and accepted for himself. Every courage, every virtue, every heroism, every sanctity he possesses! Cosette, that man is an angel!"

"Hush! hush!" said Jean Valjean in a low voice. "Why tell all that?"

"But you!" cried Marius with a wrath in which there was veneration, "why did you not tell it to me? It is your own fault, too. You save people's lives, and you conceal it from them! You do more, under the pretext of unmasking yourself, you calumniate yourself. It is frightful."

"I told the truth," replied Jean Valjean.

"No," retorted Marius, "the truth is the whole truth; and that you did not tell. You were Monsieur Madeleine, why not have said so? You saved Javert, why not have said so? I owed my life to you, why not have said so?"

"Because I thought as you do. I thought that you were in the right. It was necessary that I should go away. If you had known about that affair of the sewer, you would have made me remain near you. I was therefore forced to hold my peace. If I had spoken, it would have caused embarrassment in every way."

"It would have embarrassed what? embarrassed whom?" retorted Marius. "Do you think that you are going to stay here? We shall carry you off. Ah! good heavens! when I reflect that it was by an accident that I have learned all this. You form a part of ourselves. You are her father, and mine. You shall not pass another day in this dreadful house. Do not imagine that you will be here to-morrow."

"To-morrow," said Jean Valjean, "I shall not be here, but I shall not be with you."

"What do you mean?" replied Marius. "Ah come now, we are not going to permit anymore journeys. You shall never leave us again. You belong to us. We shall not loose our hold of you."

"This time it is for good," added Cosette. "We have a carriage at the door. I shall run away with you. If necessary, I shall employ force."

And she laughingly made a movement to lift the old man in her arms.

"Your chamber still stands ready in our house," she went on. "If you only knew how pretty the garden is now! The azaleas are doing very well there. The walks are sanded with river sand; there are tiny violet shells. You shall eat my strawberries. I water them myself. And no more 'madame,' no more 'Monsieur Jean,' we are living under a Republic, everybody says thou, don't they, Marius? The program is changed. If you only knew, father, I have had a sorrow, there was a robin red-breast which had made her nest in a hole in the wall, and a horrible cat ate her. My poor, pretty, little robin red-breast which used to put her head out of her window and look at me! I cried over it. I should have liked to kill the cat! But now nobody cries anymore. Everybody laughs, everybody is happy. You are going to come with us. How delighted grandfather will be! You shall have your plot in the garden, you shall cultivate it, and we shall see whether your strawberries are as fine as mine. And, then, I shall do everything that you wish, and then, you will obey me prettily."

Jean Valjean listened to her without hearing her. He heard the music of her voice rather than the sense of her words; one of those large tears which are the somber pearls of the soul, welled up slowly in his eyes.

He murmured:

"The proof that God is good is that she is here."

"Father!" said Cosette.

Jean Valjean continued:

"It is quite true that it would be charming for us to live together. Their trees are full of birds. I would walk with Cosette. It is sweet to be among living people who bid each other 'good day,' who call to each other in the garden. People see each other from early morning. We should each cultivate our own little corner. She would make me eat her strawberries. I would make her gather my roses. That would be charming. Only . . ."

He paused and said gently:

"It is a pity."

The tear did not fall, it retreated, and Jean Valjean replaced it with a smile.

Cosette took both the old man's hands in hers.

"My God!" said she, "your hands are still colder than before. Are you ill? Do you suffer?"

"I? No," replied Jean Valjean. "I am very well. Only . . ."

He paused.

"Only what?"

"I am going to die presently."

Cosette and Marius shuddered.

"To die!" exclaimed Marius.

"Yes, but that is nothing," said Jean Valjean.

He took breath, smiled and resumed:

"Cosette, thou wert talking to me, go on, so thy little robin red-breast is dead? Speak, so that I may hear thy voice."

Marius gazed at the old man in amazement.

Cosette uttered a heartrending cry.

"Father! my father! you will live. You are going to live. I insist upon your living, do you hear?"

Jean Valjean raised his head toward her with adoration.

"Oh! yes, forbid me to die. Who knows? Perhaps I shall obey. I was on the verge of dying when you came. That stopped me, it seemed to me that I was born again."

"You are full of strength and life," cried Marius. "Do you imagine that a person can die like this? You have had sorrow, you shall have no more. It is I who ask your forgiveness, and on my knees! You are going to live, and to live with us, and to live a long time. We take possession of you once more. There are two of us here who will henceforth have no other thought than your happiness."

"You see," resumed Cosette all bathed in tears, "that Marius says that you shall not die."

Jean Valjean continued to smile.

"Even if you were to take possession of me, Monsieur Pontmercy, would that make me other than I am? No, God has thought like you and myself, and he does not change his mind; it is useful for me to go. Death is a good arrangement. God knows better than we what we need. May you be happy, may Monsieur Pontmercy have Cosette, may youth wed the morning, may there be around you, my children, lilacs and nightingales; may your life be a beautiful, sunny lawn, may all the enchantments of heaven fill your souls, and now let me, who am good for nothing, die; it is certain that all this is right. Come, be reasonable, nothing is possible now, I am fully conscious that all is over. And then, last night, I drank that whole jug of water. How good thy husband is, Cosette! Thou art much better off with him than with me."

A noise became audible at the door.

It was the doctor entering.

"Good day, and farewell, doctor," said Jean Valjean. "Here are my poor children."

Marius stepped up to the doctor. He addressed to him only this single word: "Monsieur? . . ." But his manner of pronouncing it contained a complete question.

The doctor replied to the question by an expressive glance.

"Because things are not agreeable," said Jean Valjean, "that is no reason for being unjust toward God."

A silence ensued.

All breasts were oppressed.

Jean Valjean turned to Cosette. He began to gaze at her as though he wished to retain her features for eternity.

In the depths of the shadow into which he had already descended, ecstasy was still possible to him when gazing at Cosette. The reflection of that sweet face lighted up his pale visage.

The doctor felt of his pulse.

"Ah! it was you that he wanted!" he murmured, looking at Cosette and Marius.

And bending down to Marius's ear, he added in a very low voice:

"Too late."

Jean Valjean surveyed the doctor and Marius serenely, almost without ceasing to gaze at Cosette.

These barely articulate words were heard to issue from his mouth:

"It is nothing to die; it is dreadful not to live."

All at once he rose to his feet. These accesses of strength are sometimes the sign of the death-agony. He walked with a firm step to the wall, thrusting aside Marius and the doctor who tried to help him, detached from the wall a little copper crucifix which was suspended there, and returned to his seat with all the freedom of movement of perfect health, and said in a loud voice, as he laid the crucifix on the table:

"Behold the great martyr."

Then his chest sank in, his head wavered, as though the intoxication of the tomb were seizing hold upon him.

His hands, which rested on his knees, began to press their nails into the stuff of his trousers.

Cosette supported his shoulders, and sobbed, and tried to speak to him, but could not.

Among the words mingled with that mournful saliva which accompanies tears, they distinguished words like the following:

"Father, do not leave us. Is it possible that we have found you only to lose you again?"

It might be said that agony writhes. It goes, comes, advances toward the sepulcher, and returns toward life. There is groping in the action of dying.

Jean Valjean rallied after this semi-swoon, shook his brow as though to make the shadows fall away from it and became almost perfectly lucid once more.

He took a fold of Cosette's sleeve and kissed it.

"He is coming back! doctor, he is coming back," cried Marius.

"You are good, both of you," said Jean Valjean. "I am going to tell you what has caused me pain. What has pained me, Monsieur Pontmercy, is that you have not been willing to touch that money. That money really belongs to your wife. I will explain to you, my children, and for that reason also, I am glad to see you. Black jet comes from England, white jet comes from Norway. All this is in this paper, which you will read. For bracelets, I invented a way of substituting for slides of soldered sheet iron, slides of iron laid together. It is prettier, better and less costly. You will understand how much money can be made in that way. So Cosette's fortune is really hers. I give you these details, in order that your mind may be set at rest."

The portress had come upstairs and was gazing in at the half-open door. The doctor dismissed her.

But he could not prevent this zealous woman from exclaiming to the dying man before she disappeared: "Would you like a priest?"

"I have had one," replied Jean Valjean.

And, with his finger he seemed to indicate a point above his head where one would have said that he saw someone.

It is probable, in fact, that the Bishop was present at this death-agony.

Cosette gently slipped a pillow under his loins.

Jean Valjean resumed:

"Have no fear, Monsieur Pontmercy, I adjure you. The six hundred thousand francs really belong to Cosette. My life will have been wasted if you do not enjoy them! We managed to do very well with those glass goods. We rivaled what is called Berlin jewelery. However, we could not equal the black glass of England. A gross, which contains twelve hundred very well cut grains, only costs three francs."

When a being who is dear to us is on the point of death, we gaze upon him with a look which clings convulsively to him and which would fain hold him back.

Cosette gave her hand to Marius, and both, mute with anguish, not knowing what to say to the dying man, stood trembling and despairing before him.

Jean Valjean sank moment by moment. He was failing; he was drawing near to the gloomy horizon.

His breath had become intermittent; a little rattling interrupted it. He found some difficulty in moving his forearm, his feet had lost all movement, and in proportion as the wretchedness of limb and feebleness of body increased, all the majesty of his soul was displayed and spread over his brow. The light of the unknown world was already visible in his eyes.

His face paled and smiled. Life was no longer there, it was something else.

His breath sank, his glance grew grander. He was a corpse on which the wings could be felt.

He made a sign to Cosette to draw near, then to Marius; the last minute of the last hour had, evidently, arrived.

He began to speak to them in a voice so feeble that it seemed to come from a distance, and one would have said that a wall now rose between them and him.

"Draw near, draw near both of you. I love you dearly. Oh! how good it is to die like this! And thou lovest me also, my Cosette. I knew well that thou still felt friendly toward thy poor old man. How kind it was of thee to place that pillow under my loins! Thou wilt weep for me a little, wilt thou not? Not too much. I do not wish thee to have any real griefs. You must enjoy yourselves a great deal, my children. I forgot to tell you, that the profit was greater still on the buckles without tongues than on all the rest. A gross of a dozen dozens cost ten francs and sold for sixty. It really was a good business. So there is no occasion for surprise at the six hundred thousand francs, Monsieur Pontmercy. It is honest money. You may be rich with a tranquil mind. Thou must have a carriage, a box at the theaters now and then, and handsome ball-dresses, my Cosette, and then, thou must give good dinners to thy friends, and be very happy. I was writing to Cosette a while ago. She will find my letter. I bequeath to her the two candlesticks which stand on the chimney-piece. They are of silver, but to me they are gold, they are diamonds; they change candles which are placed in them into wax-tapers. I do not know whether the person who gave them to me is pleased with me yonder on high. I have done what I could. My children, you will not forget that I am a poor man, you will have me buried in the first plot of earth that you find, under a stone to mark the spot. This is my wish. No name on the stone. If Cosette cares to come for a little while now and then, it will give me pleasure. And you too, Monsieur Pontmercy. I must admit that I have not always loved you. I ask your pardon for that. Now she and you form but one for me. I feel very grateful to you. I am sure that you make Cosette happy. If you only knew, Monsieur Pontmercy, her pretty rosy cheeks were my delight; when I saw her in the least pale, I was sad. In the chest of drawers, there is a bank-bill for five hundred francs. I have not touched it. It is for the poor. Cosette, dost thou see thy little gown yonder on the bed? dost thou recognize it? That was ten years ago, however. How time flies! We have been very happy. All is over. Do not weep, my children, I am not going very far, I shall see you from there, you will only have to look at night, and you will see me smile. Cosette, dost thou remember Montfermeil? Thou wert in the forest, thou wert greatly terrified; dost thou remember how I took hold of the handle of the water-bucket? That was the first time that I touched thy poor, little hand. It was so cold! Ah! your hands were red then, mademoiselle, they are very white now. And the big doll! dost thou remember? Thou didst call her Catherine. Thou regrettedest not having taken her to the convent! How thou didst make me laugh sometimes, my sweet angel! When it had been raining, thou didst float bits of straw on the gutters, and watch them pass away. One day I gave thee a willow battledore and a shuttlecock with yellow, blue and green feathers. Thou hast forgotten it. Thou wert roguish so young! Thou didst play. Thou didst put cherries in thy ears. Those are things of the past. The forests through which one has passed with one's child, the trees under which one has strolled, the convents where one has concealed one's self, the games, the hearty laughs of childhood, are shadows. I imagined that all that belonged to me. In that lay my stupidity. Those Thénardiers were wicked. Thou must forgive them. Cosette, the moment has come to tell thee the name of thy mother. She was called Fantine. Remember that name—Fantine. Kneel whenever thou utterest it. She suffered much. She loved thee dearly. She had as much unhappiness as thou hast had happiness. That is the way God apportions things. He is there on high, he sees us all, and he knows what he does in the midst of his great stars. I am on the verge of departure, my children. Love each other well and always. There is nothing else but that in the world: love for each other. You will think sometimes of the poor old man who died here. Oh my Cosette, it is not my fault, indeed, that I have not seen thee all this time, it cut me to the heart; I went as far as the corner of the street, I must have produced a queer effect on the people who saw me pass, I was like a madman, I once went out without my hat. I no longer see clearly, my children, I had still other things to say, but never mind. Think a little of me. Come still nearer. I die happy. Give me your dear and well-beloved heads, so that I may lay my hands upon them."

Cosette and Marius fell on their knees, in despair, suffocating with tears, each beneath one of Jean Valjean's hands. Those august hands no longer moved.

He had fallen backwards, the light of the candles illuminated him.

His white face looked up to heaven, he allowed Cosette and Marius to cover his hands with kisses.

He was dead.

The night was starless and extremely dark. No doubt, in the gloom, some immense angel stood erect with wings outspread, awaiting that soul.

Chapter VI

THE GRASS COVERS AND THE RAIN EFFACES

IN THE CEMETERY OF PÈRE-LACHAISE, IN THE VICINITY OF THE COMMON GRAVE, FAR FROM THE ELegant quarter of that city of sepulchers, far from all the tombs of fancy which display in the presence of eternity all the hideous fashions of death, in a deserted corner, beside an old wall, beneath a great yew-tree over which climbs the wild convolvulus, amid dandelions and mosses, there lies a stone. That stone is no more exempt than others from the leprosy of time, of dampness, of the lichens and from the defilement of the birds. The water turns it green, the air blackens it. It is not near any path, and people are not fond of walking in that direction, because the grass is high and their feet are immediately wet. When there is a little sunshine, the lizards come thither. All around there is a quivering of weeds. In the spring, linnets warble in the trees.

This stone is perfectly plain. In cutting it the only thought was the requirements of the tomb, and no other care was taken than to make the stone long enough and narrow enough to cover a man.

No name is to be read there.

Only, many years ago, a hand wrote upon it in pencil these four lines, which have become gradually illegible beneath the rain and the dust, and which are, to-day, probably effaced:

> *Il dort. Quoique le sort fût pour lui bien étrange,*
> *Il vivait. Il mourut quand il n'eut plus son ange.*
> *La chose simplement d'elle-même arriva,*
> *Comme la nuit se fait lorsque le jour s'en va.*[1]

---

1. He sleeps. Although his fate was very strange, he lived. He died when he had no longer his angel. The thing came to pass simply, of itself, as the night comes when day is gone.

THE MAN WHO LAUGHS
A ROMANCE OF ENGLISH HISTORY

CONTENTS

Preliminary Chapter

URSUS

I

URSUS AND HOMO WERE FAST FRIENDS. URSUS WAS A MAN, HOMO A WOLF. THEIR DISPOSI- tions tallied. It was the man who had christened the wolf: probably he had also chosen his own name. Having found *Ursus* fit for himself, he had found *Homo* fit for the beast. Man and wolf turned their partnership to account at fairs, at village fêtes, at the corners of streets where passers-by throng, and out of the need which people seem to feel everywhere to listen to idle gossip, and to buy quack medicine. The wolf, gentle and courteously subordinate, diverted the crowd. It is a pleasant thing to behold the tameness of animals. Our greatest delight is to see all the varieties of domestication parade before us. This it is which collects so many folks on the road of royal processions.

Ursus and Homo went about from cross-road to cross-road, from the High Street of Aberystwith to the High Street of Jedburgh, from countryside to countryside, from shire to shire, from town to town. One market exhausted, they went on to another. Ursus lived in a small van upon wheels, which Homo was civilized enough to draw by day and guard by night. On bad roads, up hills, and where there were too many ruts, or there was too much mud, the man buckled the trace round his neck and pulled fraternally, side by side with the wolf. They had thus grown old together. They encamped at haphazard on a common, in the glade of a wood, on the waste patch of grass where roads intersect, at the outskirts of villages, at the gates of towns, in market-places, in public walks, on the borders of parks, before the entrances of churches. When the cart drew up on a fair green, when the gossips ran up open-mouthed and the curious made a circle round the pair, Ursus harangued and Homo approved. Homo, with a bowl in his mouth, politely made a collection among the audience. They gained their livelihood. The wolf was lettered, likewise the man. The wolf had been trained by the man, or had trained himself unassisted, to divers wolfish arts, which swelled the receipts. "Above all things, do not degenerate into a man," his friend would say to him.

Never did the wolf bite: the man did now and then. At least, to bite was the intent of Ursus. He was a misanthrope, and to italicize his misanthropy he had made himself a juggler. To live, also; for the stomach has to be consulted. Moreover, this juggler-misanthrope, whether to add to the complexity of his being or to perfect it, was a doctor. To be a doctor is little: Ursus was a ventriloquist. You heard him speak without his moving his lips. He counterfeited, so as to deceive you, anyone's accent or pronunciation. He imitated voices so exactly that you believed you heard the people themselves. All alone he simulated the murmur of a crowd, and this gave him a right to the title of Engastrimythos, which he took. He reproduced all sorts of cries of birds, as of the thrush, the wren, the pipit lark, otherwise called the gray cheeper, and the ring ousel, all travelers like himself: so that at times when the fancy struck him, he made you aware either of a public thoroughfare filled with the uproar of men, or of a meadow loud with the voices of beasts—at one time stormy as a multitude, at another fresh and serene as the dawn. Such gifts, although rare, exist. In the last century a man called Touzel, who imitated the mingled utterances of men and animals, and who counterfeited all the cries of beasts, was attached to the person of Buffon—to serve as a menagerie.

Ursus was sagacious, contradictory, odd, and inclined to the singular expositions which we term fables. He had the appearance of believing in them, and this impudence was a part of his humor. He read people's hands, opened books at random and drew conclusions, told fortunes, taught that it is perilous to meet a black mare, still more perilous, as you start for a journey, to hear yourself accosted by one who knows not whither you are going; and he called himself a dealer in superstitions. He used to say: "There is one difference between me and the Archbishop of Canterbury: I avow what I am." Hence it was that the archbishop, justly indignant, had him one day before him; but Ursus cleverly disarmed his grace by reciting a sermon he had composed upon Christmas Day, which the delighted archbishop learnt by heart, and delivered from the pulpit as his own. In consideration thereof the archbishop pardoned Ursus.

As a doctor, Ursus wrought cures by some means or other. He made use of aromatics; he was versed in simples; he made the most of the immense power which lies in a heap of neglected plants, such as the hazel, the catkin, the white alder, the white briony, the mealy-tree, the traveler's joy, the buckthorn. He treated phthisis with the sundew; at opportune moments he would use the leaves of the spurge, which plucked at the bottom are a purgative and plucked at the top, an emetic. He cured sore throat by means of the vegetable excrescence called Jew's ear. He knew the rush which cures the ox and the mint which cures the horse. He was well acquainted with the beauties and virtues of the herb mandragora, which, as everyone knows, is of both sexes. He had many recipes. He cured burns with the salamander wool, of which, according to Pliny, Nero had a napkin. Ursus possessed a retort and a flask; he effected transmutations; he sold panaceas. It was said of him that he had once been for a short time in Bedlam; they had done him the honor to take him for a madman, but had set him free on discovering that he was only a poet. This story was probably not true; we have all to submit to some such legend about us.

The fact is, Ursus was a bit of a savant, a man of taste, and an old Latin poet. He was learned in two forms; he Hippocratized and he Pindarized. He could have vied in bombast with Rapin and Vida. He could have composed Jesuit tragedies in a style not less triumphant than that of Father Bouhours. It followed from his familiarity with the venerable rhythms and meters of the ancients, that he had peculiar figures of speech, and a whole family of classical metaphors. He would say of a mother followed by her two daughters, *There is a dactyl*; of a father preceded by his two sons, *There is an anapaest*; and of a little child walking between its grandmother and grandfather, *There is an amphimacer*. So much knowledge could only end in starvation. The school of Salerno says, "Eat little and often." Ursus ate little and seldom, thus obeying one half the precept and disobeying the other; but this was the fault of the public, who did not always flock to him and, who did not often buy.

Ursus was wont to say: "The expectoration of a sentence is a relief. The wolf is comforted by its howl, the sheep by its wool, the forest by its finch, woman by her love, and the philosopher by his epiphonema." Ursus at a pinch composed comedies, which, in recital, he all but acted; this helped to sell the drugs. Among other works, he had composed an heroic pastoral in honor of Sir Hugh Middleton, who in 1608 brought a river to London. The river was lying peacefully in Hertfordshire, twenty miles from London: the knight came and took possession of it. He brought a brigade of six hundred men, armed with shovels and pickaxes; set to breaking up the ground, scooping it out in one place, raising it in another—now thirty feet high, now twenty feet deep; made wooden aqueducts high in air; and at different points constructed eight hundred bridges of stone, bricks, and timber. One fine morning the river entered London, which was short of water. Ursus transformed all these vulgar details into a fine Eclogue between the Thames and the New River, in which the former invited the latter to come to him, and offered her his bed, saying, "I am too old to please women, but I am rich enough to pay them"—an ingenious and gallant conceit to indicate how Sir Hugh Middleton had completed the work at his own expense.

Ursus was great in soliloquy. Of a disposition at once unsociable and talkative, desiring to see no one, yet wishing to converse with someone, he got out of the difficulty by talking to himself. Anyone who has lived a solitary life knows how deeply seated monologue is in one's nature. Speech imprisoned frets to find a vent. To harangue space is an outlet. To speak out aloud when alone is as it were to have a dialogue with the divinity which is within. It was, as is well known, a custom of Socrates; he declaimed to himself. Luther did the same. Ursus took after those great men. He had the hermaphrodite faculty of being his own audience. He questioned himself, answered himself, praised himself, blamed himself. You heard him in the street soliloquizing in his van. The passersby, who have their own way of appreciating clever people, used to say: He is an idiot. As we have just observed, he abused himself at times; but there were times also when he rendered himself justice. One day, in one of these allocutions addressed to himself, he was heard to cry out, "I have studied vegetation in all its mysteries—in the stalk, in the bud, in the sepal, in the stamen, in the carpel, in the ovule, in the spore, in the theca, and in the apothecium. I have thoroughly sifted chromatics, osmosy, and chymosy; that is to say, the formation of colors, of smell, and of taste." There was something fatuous, doubtless, in this certificate which Ursus gave to Ursus; but let those who have not thoroughly sifted chromatics, osmosy, and chymosy cast the first stone at him.

Fortunately Ursus had never gone into the Low Countries; there they would certainly have weighed him, to ascertain whether he was of the normal weight, above or below which a man is a sorcerer. In Holland this weight was sagely fixed by law. Nothing was simpler or more ingenious. It was a clear test. They put you in a scale, and the evidence was conclusive if you broke the equilibrium. Too heavy, you were hanged; too light, you were burned. To this day the scales in which sorcerers were weighed may be seen at Oudewater, but they are now used for weighing cheeses; how religion has degenerated! Ursus would certainly have had a crow to pluck with those scales. In his travels he kept away from Holland, and he did well. Indeed, we believe that he used never to leave the United Kingdom.

However this may have been, he was very poor and morose, and having made the acquaintance of Homo in a wood, a taste for a wandering life had come over him. He had taken the wolf into partnership, and with him had gone forth on the highways, living in the open air the great life of chance. He had a great deal of industry and of reserve, and great skill in everything connected with healing operations, restoring the sick to health, and in working wonders peculiar to himself. He was considered a clever mountebank and a good doctor. As may be imagined, he passed for a wizard as well—not much indeed; only a little, for it was unwholesome in those days to be considered a friend of the devil. To tell the truth, Ursus, by his passion for pharmacy and his love of plants, laid himself open to suspicion, seeing that he often went to gather herbs in rough thickets where grew Lucifer's salads, and where, as has been proved by the Counselor De l'Ancre, there is a risk of meeting in the evening mist a man who comes out of the earth, "blind of the right eye, barefooted, without a cloak, and a sword by his side." But for the matter of that, Ursus, although eccentric in manner and disposition, was too good a fellow to invoke or disperse hail, to make faces appear, to kill a man with the torment of excessive dancing, to suggest dreams fair or foul and full of terror, and to cause the birth of cocks with four wings. He had no such mischievous tricks. He was incapable of certain abominations, such as, for instance, speaking German, Hebrew, or Greek, without having learned them, which is a sign of unpardonable wickedness, or of a natural infirmity proceeding from a morbid humor. If Ursus spoke Latin, it was because he knew it. He would never have allowed himself to speak Syriac, which he did not know. Besides, it is asserted that Syriac is the language spoken in the midnight meetings at which uncanny people worship the devil. In medicine he justly preferred Galen to Cardan; Cardan, although a learned man, being but an earthworm to Galen.

To sum up, Ursus was not one of those persons who live in fear of the police. His van was long enough and wide enough to allow of his lying down in it on a box containing his not very sumptuous apparel. He owned a lantern, several wigs, and some utensils suspended from nails, among which were musical instruments. He possessed, besides, a bearskin with which he covered himself on his days of grand performance. He called this putting on full dress. He used to say, "I have two skins; this is the real one," pointing to the bearskin.

The little house on wheels belonged to himself and to the wolf. Besides this house, his retort, and his wolf, he had a flute and a violoncello on which he played prettily. He concocted his own elixirs. His wits yielded him enough to sup on sometimes. In the top of his van was a hole, through which passed the pipe of a cast-iron stove; so close to his box as to scorch the wood of it. The stove had two compartments; in one of them Ursus cooked his chemicals, and in the other his potatoes. At night the wolf slept under the van, amicably secured by a chain. Homo's hair was black, that of Ursus, gray; Ursus was fifty, unless, indeed, he was sixty. He accepted his destiny, to such an extent that, as we have just seen, he ate potatoes, the trash on which at that time they fed pigs and convicts. He ate them indignant, but resigned. He was not tall—he was long. He was bent and melancholy. The bowed frame of an old man is the settlement in the architecture of life. Nature had formed him for sadness. He found it difficult to smile, and he had never been able to weep, so that he was deprived of the consolation of tears, as well as of the palliative of joy. An old man is a thinking ruin; and such a ruin was Ursus. He had the loquacity of a charlatan, the leanness of a prophet, the irascibility of a charged mine: such was Ursus. In his youth he had been a philosopher in the house of a lord.

This was 180 years ago, when men were more like wolves than they are now.

Not so very much though.

II

HOMO WAS NO ORDINARY WOLF. FROM HIS APPETITE FOR MEDLARS AND POTATOES HE MIGHT have been taken for a prairie wolf; from his dark hide, for a lycaon; and from his howl prolonged into a bark, for a dog of Chili. But no one has as yet observed the eyeball of a dog of Chili sufficiently to enable us to determine whether he be not a fox, and Homo was a real wolf. He was five feet long, which is a fine length for a wolf, even in Lithuania; he was very strong; he looked at you askance, which was not his fault; he had a soft tongue, with which he occasionally licked Ursus; he had a narrow brush of short bristles on his backbone, and he was lean with the wholesome leanness of a forest life. Before he knew Ursus and had a carriage to draw, he thought nothing of doing his fifty miles a night. Ursus meeting him in a thicket near a stream of running water, had conceived a high opinion of him from seeing the skill and sagacity with which he fished out crayfish, and welcomed him as an honest and genuine Koupara wolf of the kind called crab-eater.

As a beast of burden, Ursus preferred Homo to a donkey. He would have felt repugnance to having his hut drawn by an ass; he thought too highly of the ass for that. Moreover he had observed that the ass, a four-legged thinker little understood by men, has a habit of cocking his ears uneasily when philosophers talk nonsense. In life the ass is a third person between our thoughts and ourselves, and acts as a restraint. As a friend, Ursus preferred Homo to a dog, considering that the love of a wolf is more rare.

Hence it was that Homo sufficed for Ursus. Homo was for Ursus more than a companion, he was an analogue. Ursus used to pat the wolf's empty ribs, saying: "I have found the second volume of myself!" Again he said, "When I am dead, anyone wishing to know me need only study Homo. I shall leave a true copy behind me."

The English law, not very lenient to beasts of the forest, might have picked a quarrel with the wolf, and have put him to trouble for his assurance in going freely about the towns: but Homo took advantage of the immunity granted by a statute of Edward IV to servants: "Every servant in attendance on his master is free to come and go." Besides, a certain relaxation of the law had resulted with regard to wolves, in consequence of its being the fashion of the ladies of the court, under the later Stuarts, to have, instead of dogs, little wolves, called adives, about the size of cats, which were brought from Asia at great cost.

Ursus had communicated to Homo a portion of his talents: such as to stand upright, to restrain his rage into sulkiness, to growl instead of howling, etc.; and on his part, the wolf had taught the man what *he* knew—to do without a roof, without bread and fire, to prefer hunger in the woods to slavery in a palace.

The van, hut, and vehicle in one, which traversed so many different roads, without, however, leaving Great Britain, had four wheels, with shaft for the wolf and a splinter-bar for the man. The splinter-bar came into use when the roads were bad. The van was strong, although it was built of light boards like a dove-cot. In front there was a glass door with a little balcony used for orations, which had something of the character of the platform tempered by an air of the pulpit. At the back there was a door with a practicable panel. By lowering the three steps which turned on a hinge below the door, access was gained to the hut, which at night was securely fastened with bolt and lock. Rain and snow had fallen plentifully on it; it had been painted, but of what color it was difficult to say, change of season being to vans what changes of reign are to courtiers. In front, outside, was a board—a kind of frontispiece, on which the following inscription might once have been deciphered; it was in black letters on a white ground, but by degrees the characters had become confused and blurred:

"By friction gold loses every year a fourteen hundredth part of its bulk. This is what is called the Wear. Hence it follows that on fourteen hundred millions of gold in circulation throughout the world, one million is lost annually. This million dissolves into dust, flies away, floats about, is reduced to atoms, charges, drugs, weighs down consciences, amalgamates with the souls of the rich whom it renders proud, and with those of the poor whom it renders brutish."

The inscription, rubbed and blotted by the rain and by the kindness of nature, was fortunately illegible, for it is possible that its philosophy concerning the inhalation of gold, at the same time both enigmatical and lucid, might not have been to the taste of the sheriffs, the provost-marshals and other big-wigs of the law. English legislation did not trifle in those days. It did not take much to make a man a felon. The magistrates were ferocious by tradition, and cruelty was a matter of routine. The judges of assize increased and multiplied. Jeffreys had become a breed.

III

IN THE INTERIOR OF THE VAN THERE WERE TWO OTHER INSCRIPTIONS ABOVE THE BOY, ON A whitewashed plank, a hand had written in ink as follows—

THE ONLY THINGS NECESSARY TO KNOW

The Baron, peer of England, wears a cap with six pearls. The coronet begins with the rank of Viscount. The Viscount wears a coronet of which the pearls are without number. The Earl a coronet with the pearls upon points, mingled with strawberry leaves placed low between. The Marquis, one with pearls and leaves on the same level. The Duke, one with strawberry leaves alone—no pearls. The Royal Duke, a circlet of crosses and fleurs-de-lys. The Prince of Wales, crown like that of the King, but unclosed.

The Duke is a most high and most puissant prince, the Marquis and Earl most noble and puissant lord, the Viscount noble and puissant lord, the Baron a trusty lord. The Duke is his Grace; the other Peers their Lordships. *Most honorable* is higher than *right honorable*.

Lords who are peers are lords in their own right. Lords who are not peers are lords by courtesy:—there are no real lords, excepting such as are peers.

The House of Lords is a chamber and a court, *Concilium et Curia*, legislature and court of justice. The Commons, who are the people, when ordered to the bar of the Lords, humbly present themselves bareheaded before the peers, who remain covered. The Commons send up their bills by forty members, who present the bill with three low bows. The Lords send their bills to the Commons by a mere clerk. In case of disagreement, the two Houses confer in the Painted Chamber, the Peers seated and covered, the Commons standing and bareheaded.

Peers go to parliament in their coaches in file; the Commons do not. Some peers go to Westminster in open four-wheeled chariots. The use of these and of coaches emblazoned with coats of arms and coronets is allowed only to peers, and forms a portion of their dignity.

Barons have the same rank as bishops. To be a baron peer of England, it is necessary to be in possession of a tenure from the king *per Baroniam integram,* by full barony. The full barony consists of thirteen knights' fees and one third part, each knight's fee being of the value of £20 sterling, which makes in all 400 marks. The head of a barony (*Caput baroniae*) is a castle disposed by inheritance, as England herself, that is to say, descending to daughters if there be no sons, and in that case going to the eldest daughter, *caeteris filiabus aliundè satisfactis.*[1]

Barons have the degree of lord: in Saxon, *laford; dominus* in high Latin; *Lordus* in low Latin. The eldest and younger sons of viscounts and barons are the first esquires in the kingdom. The eldest sons of peers take precedence of knights of the garter. The younger sons do not. The eldest son of a viscount comes after all barons, and precedes all baronets. Every daughter of a peer is a *Lady.* Other English girls are plain *Mistress.*

All judges rank below peers. The sergeant wears a lambskin tippet; the judge one of patchwork, *de minuto vario,* made up of a variety of little white furs, always excepting ermine. Ermine is reserved for peers and the king.

A lord never takes an oath, either to the crown or the law. His word suffices; he says, Upon my honor.

By a law of Edward the Sixth, peers have the privilege of committing manslaughter. A peer who kills a man without premeditation is not prosecuted.

The persons of peers are inviolable.

A peer cannot be held in durance, save in the Tower of London.

A writ of supplicavit cannot be granted against a peer.

A peer sent for by the king has the right to kill one or two deer in the royal park.

A peer holds in his castle a baron's court of justice.

It is unworthy of a peer to walk the street in a cloak, followed by two footmen. He should only show himself attended by a great train of gentlemen of his household.

A peer can be amerced only by his peers, and never to any greater amount than five pounds, excepting in the case of a duke, who can be amerced ten.

A peer may retain six aliens born, any other Englishman but four.

A peer can have wine custom-free; an earl eight tuns.

A peer is alone exempt from presenting himself before the sheriff of the circuit.

A peer cannot be assessed toward the militia.

When it pleases a peer he raises a regiment and gives it to the king; thus have done their graces the Dukes of Athol, Hamilton, and Northumberland.

A peer can hold only of a peer.

In a civil cause he can demand the adjournment of the case, if there be not at least one knight on the jury.

A peer nominates his own chaplains. A baron appoints three chaplains; a viscount four; an earl and a marquis five; a duke six.

A peer cannot be put to the rack, even for high treason. A peer cannot be branded on the hand. A peer is a clerk, though he knows not how to read. In law he knows.

---

1. As much as to say, the other daughters are provided for as best may be. (Note by Ursus on the margin of the wall.)

A duke has a right to a canopy, or cloth of state, in all places where the king is not present; a viscount may have one in his house; a baron has a cover of assay, which may be held under his cup while he drinks. A baroness has the right to have her train borne by a man in the presence of a viscountess.

Eighty-six tables, with five hundred dishes, are served every day in the royal palace at each meal.

If a plebeian strike a lord, his hand is cut off.

A lord is very nearly a king.

The king is very nearly a god.

The earth is a lordship.

The English address God as my lord!

Opposite this writing was written a second one, in the same fashion, which ran thus:

SATISFACTION WHICH MUST SUFFICE THOSE WHO HAVE NOTHING

Henry Auverquerque, Earl of Grantham, who sits in the House of Lords between the Earl of Jersey and the Earl of Greenwich, has a hundred thousand a year. To his lordship belongs the palace of Grantham Terrace, built all of marble and famous for what is called the labyrinth of passages— a curiosity which contains the scarlet corridor in marble of Sarancolin, the brown corridor in lumachel of Astracan, the white corridor in marble of Lani, the black corridor in marble of Alabanda, the gray corridor in marble of Staremma, the yellow corridor in marble of Hesse, the green corridor in marble of the Tyrol, the red corridor, half cherry spotted marble of Bohemia, half lumachel of Cordova, the blue corridor in turquin of Genoa, the violet in granite of Catalonia, the mourning-hued corridor veined black and white in slate of Murviedro, the pink corridor in cipolin of the Alps, the pearl corridor in lumachel of Nonetta, and the corridor of all colors, called the courtiers' corridor, in motley.

Richard Lowther, Viscount Lonsdale, owns Lowther in Westmoreland, which has a magnificent approach, and a flight of entrance steps which seem to invite the ingress of kings.

Richard, Earl of Scarborough, Viscount and Baron Lumley of Lumley Castle, Viscount Lumley of Waterford in Ireland, and Lord Lieutenant and Vice-Admiral of the county of Northumberland and of Durham, both city and county, owns the double castleward of old and new Sandbeck, where you admire a superb railing, in the form of a semicircle, surrounding the basin of a matchless fountain. He has, besides, his castle of Lumley.

Robert Darcy, Earl of Holderness, has his domain of Holderness, with baronial towers, and large gardens laid out in French fashion, where he drives in his coach-and-six, preceded by two outriders, as becomes a peer of England.

Charles Beauclerc, Duke of St. Albans, Earl of Burford, Baron Hedington, Grand Falconer of England, has an abode at Windsor, regal even by the side of the king's.

Charles Bodville Robartes, Baron Robartes of Truro, Viscount Bodmin and Earl of Radnor, owns Wimpole in Cambridgeshire, which is as three palaces in one, having three façades, one bowed and two triangular. The approach is by an avenue of trees four deep.

The most noble and most puissant Lord Philip, Baron Herbert of Cardiff, Earl of Montgomery and of Pembroke, Ross of Kendall, Parr, Fitzhugh, Marmion, St. Quentin, and Herbert of Shurland, Warden of the Stannaries in the counties of Cornwall and Devon, hereditary visitor of Jesus College, possesses the wonderful gardens at Wilton, where there are two sheaf-like fountains, finer than those of his most Christian Majesty King Louis XIV at Versailles.

Charles Seymour, Duke of Somerset, owns Somerset House on the Thames, which is equal to the Villa Pamphili at Rome. On the chimney-piece are seen two porcelain vases of the dynasty of the Yuens, which are worth half a million in French money.

In Yorkshire, Arthur, Lord Ingram, Viscount Irwin, has Temple Newsam, which is entered under a triumphal arch, and which has large wide roofs resembling Moorish terraces.

Robert, Lord Ferrers of Chartly, Bourchier and Luvaine, has Staunton Harold in Leicestershire, of which the park is geometrically planned in the shape of a temple with a façade, and in front of the piece of water is the great church with the square belfry, which belongs to his lordship.

In the county of Northampton, Charles Spencer, Earl of Sunderland, member of his Majesty's Privy Council, possesses Althorp, at the entrance of which is a railing with four columns surmounted by groups in marble.

Laurence Hyde, Earl of Rochester, has, in Surrey, New Park, rendered magnificent by its sculptured pinnacles, its circular lawn belted by trees, and its woodland, at the extremity of which is a little mountain, artistically rounded, and surmounted by a large oak, which can be seen from afar.

Philip Stanhope, Earl of Chesterfield, possesses Bretby Hall in Derbyshire, with a splendid clock tower, falconries, warrens, and very fine sheets of water, long, square, and oval, one of which is shaped like a mirror, and has two jets, which throw the water to a great height.

Charles Cornwallis, Baron Cornwallis of Eye, owns Broome Hall, a palace of the fourteenth century.

The most noble Algernon Capel, Viscount Malden, Earl of Essex, has Cashiobury in Hertfordshire, a seat which has the shape of a capital H, and which rejoices sportsmen with its abundance of game.

Charles, Lord Ossulston, owns Darnley in Middlesex, approached by Italian gardens.

James Cecil, Earl of Salisbury, has, seven leagues from London, Hatfield House, with its four lordly pavilions, its belfry in the center, and its grand courtyard of black and white slabs, like that of St. Germain. This palace, which has a frontage 272 feet in length, was built in the reign of James I by the Lord High Treasurer of England, the great-grandfather of the present earl. To be seen there is the bed of one of the Countesses of Salisbury; it is of inestimable value and made entirely of Brazilian wood, which is a panacea against the bites of serpents, and which is called *milhombres*, that is to say, a thousand men. On this bed is inscribed, *Honi soit qui mal y pense*.

Edward Rich, Earl of Warwick and Holland, is owner of Warwick Castle, where whole oaks are burned in the fireplaces.

In the parish of Sevenoaks, Charles Sackville, Baron Buckhurst, Baron Cranfield, Earl of Dorset and Middlesex, is owner of Knowle, which is as large as a town and is composed of three palaces standing parallel one behind the other, like ranks of infantry. There are six covered flights of steps on the principal frontage, and a gate under a keep with four towers.

Thomas Thynne, Baron Thynne of Warminster, and Viscount Weymouth, possesses Longleat, in which there are as many chimneys, cupolas, pinnacles, pepper-boxes, pavilions, and turrets as at Chambord, in France, which belongs to the king.

Henry Howard, Earl of Suffolk, owns, twelve leagues from London, the palace of Audley End in Essex, which in grandeur and dignity scarcely yields the palm to the Escorial of the King of Spain.

In Bedfordshire, Wrest House and Park, which is a whole district, enclosed by ditches, walls, woodlands, rivers, and hills, belongs to Henry, Marquis of Kent.

Hampton Court, in Herefordshire, with its strong embattled keep, and its gardens bounded by a piece of water which divides them from the forest, belongs to Thomas, Lord Coningsby.

Grimsthorp, in Lincolnshire, with its long façade intersected by turrets in pale, its park, its fish-ponds, its pheasantries, its sheepfolds, its lawns, its grounds planted with rows of trees, its groves, its walks, its shrubberies, its flower-beds and borders, formed in square and lozenge-shape, and resembling great carpets; its racecourses, and the majestic sweep for carriages to turn in at the entrance of the house—belongs to Robert, Earl Lindsey, hereditary lord of the forest of Waltham.

Up Park, in Sussex, a square house, with two symmetrical belfried pavilions on each side of the great courtyard, belongs to the Right Honorable Forde, Baron Grey of Werke, Viscount Glendale and Earl of Tankerville.

Newnham Paddox, in Warwickshire, which has two quadrangular fish-ponds and a gabled archway with a large window of four panes, belongs to the Earl of Denbigh, who is also Count von Rheinfelden, in Germany.

Wytham Abbey, in Berkshire, with its French garden in which there are four curiously trimmed arbors, and its great embattled towers, supported by two bastions, belongs to Montague, Earl of Abingdon, who also owns Rycote, of which he is Baron, and the principal door of which bears the device *Virtus ariete fortior.*

William Cavendish, Duke of Devonshire, has six dwelling-places, of which Chatsworth (two-storied, and of the finest order of Grecian architecture) is one.

The Viscount of Kinalmeaky, who is Earl of Cork, in Ireland, is owner of Burlington House, Piccadilly, with its extensive gardens, reaching to the fields outside London; he is also owner of Chiswick, where there are nine magnificent lodges; he also owns Londesborough, which is a new house by the side of an old palace.

The Duke of Beaufort owns Chelsea, which contains two Gothic buildings, and a Florentine one; he has also Badminton, in Gloucestershire, a residence from which a number of avenues branch out like rays from a star. The most noble and puissant Prince Henry, Duke of Beaufort, is also Marquis and Earl of Worcester, Earl of Glamorgan, Viscount Grosmont, and Baron Herbert of Chepstow, Ragland, and Gower, Baron Beaufort of Caldecott Castle, and Baron de Bottetourt.

John Holles, Duke of Newcastle, and Marquis of Clare, owns Bolsover, with its majestic square keeps; his also is Haughton, in Nottinghamshire, where a round pyramid, made to imitate the Tower of Babel, stands in the center of a basin of water.

William, Earl of Craven, Viscount Uffington, and Baron Craven of Hamstead Marshall, owns Combe Abbey in Warwickshire, where is to be seen the finest water-jet in England; and in Berkshire two baronies, Hamstead Marshall, on the façade of which are five Gothic lanterns sunk in the wall, and Ashdown Park, which is a country seat situate at the point of intersection of cross-roads in a forest.

Linnæus, Lord Clancharlie, Baron Clancharlie and Hunkerville, Marquis of Corleone in Sicily, derives his title from the castle of Clancharlie, built in 912 by Edward the Elder, as a defense against the Danes. Besides Hunkerville House, in London, which is a palace, he has Corleone Lodge at Windsor, which is another, and eight castlewards, one at Burton on Trent, with a royalty on the carriage of plaster of Paris; then Grumdaith Humble, Moricambe, Trewardraith, Hell-Kesters (where there is a miraculous well), Phillinmore, with its turf bogs, Reculver, near the ancient city Vagniac, Vinecaunton, on the Moel-eulle Mountain; besides nineteen boroughs and villages with reeves, and the whole of Penneth chase, all of which bring his lordship £40,000 a year.

The 172 peers enjoying their dignities under James II possess among them altogether a revenue of £1,272,000 sterling a year, which is the eleventh part of the revenue of England.

In the margin, opposite the last name (that of Linnæus, Lord Clancharlie), there was a note in the handwriting of Ursus: *Rebel; in exile; houses, lands, and chattels sequestrated. It is well.*

IV

U RSUS ADMIRED HOMO. ONE ADMIRES ONE'S LIKE. IT IS A LAW.
To be always raging inwardly and grumbling outwardly was the normal condition of Ursus. He was the malcontent of creation. By nature he was a man ever in opposition. He took the world unkindly; he gave his satisfecit to no one and to nothing. The bee did not atone, by its honey-

making, for its sting; a full-blown rose did not absolve the sun for yellow fever and black vomit. It is probable that in secret Ursus criticized Providence a good deal. "Evidently," he would say, "the devil works by a spring, and the wrong that God does is having let go the trigger." He approved of none but princes, and he had his own peculiar way of expressing his approbation. One day, when James II made a gift to the Virgin in a Catholic chapel in Ireland of a massive gold lamp, Ursus, passing that way with Homo, who was more indifferent to such things, broke out in admiration before the crowd, and exclaimed—"It is certain that the blessed Virgin wants a lamp much more than these barefooted children there require shoes."

Such proofs of his loyalty, and such evidences of his respect for established powers, probably contributed in no small degree to make the magistrates tolerate his vagabond life and his low alliance with a wolf. Sometimes of an evening, through the weakness of friendship, he allowed Homo to stretch his limbs and wander at liberty about the caravan. The wolf was incapable of an abuse of confidence, and behaved in society, that is to say among men, with the discretion of a poodle. All the same, if bad-tempered officials had to be dealt with, difficulties might have arisen; so Ursus kept the honest wolf chained up as much as possible.

From a political point of view, his writing about gold, not very intelligible in itself, and now become undecipherable, was but a smear, and gave no handle to the enemy. Even after the time of James II, and under the "respectable" reign of William and Mary, his caravan might have been seen peacefully going its rounds of the little English country towns. He traveled freely from one end of Great Britain to the other, selling his philters and phials, and sustaining, with the assistance of his wolf, his quack mummeries; and he passed with ease through the meshes of the nets which the police at that period had spread all over England in order to sift wandering gangs, and especially to stop the progress of the Comprachicos.

This was right enough. Ursus belonged to no gang. Ursus lived with Ursus, a *tête-à-tête*, into which the wolf gently thrust his nose. If Ursus could have had his way, he would have been a Caribbee; that being impossible, he preferred to be alone. The solitary man is a modified savage, accepted by civilization. He who wanders most is most alone; hence his continual change of place. To remain anywhere long, suffocated him with the sense of being tamed. He passed his life in passing on his way. The sight of towns increased his taste for brambles, thickets, thorns, and holes in the rock. His home was the forest. He did not feel himself much out of his element in the murmur of crowded streets, which is like enough to the bluster of trees. The crowd to some extent satisfies our taste for the desert. What he disliked in his van was its having a door and windows, and thus resembling a house. He would have realized his ideal, had he been able to put a cave on four wheels and travel in a den.

He did not smile, as we have already said, but he used to laugh; sometimes, indeed frequently, a bitter laugh. There is consent in a smile, while a laugh is often a refusal.

His great business was to hate the human race. He was implacable in that hate. Having made it clear that human life is a dreadful thing; having observed the superposition of evils, kings on the people, war on kings, the plague on war, famine on the plague, folly on everything; having proved a certain measure of chastisement in the mere fact of existence; having recognized that death is a deliverance, when they brought him a sick man he cured him; he had cordials and beverages to prolong the lives of the old. He put lame cripples on their legs again, and hurled this sarcasm at them, "There, you are on your paws once more, may you walk long in this valley of tears!" When he saw a poor man dying of hunger, he gave him all the pence he had about him, growling out, "Live on, you wretch! eat! last a long time! It is not I who would shorten your penal servitude." After which, he would rub his hands and say, "I do men all the harm I can."

Through the little window at the back, passers-by could read on the ceiling of the van these words, written within, but visible from without, inscribed with charcoal, in big letters—

URSUS, PHILOSOPHER.

Another Preliminary Chapter

THE COMPRACHICOS

I

WHO NOW KNOWS THE WORD COMPRACHICOS, AND WHO KNOWS ITS MEANING? The Comprachicos or Comprapequeños, were a hideous and nondescript association of wanderers, famous in the 17th century, forgotten in the 18th, unheard of in the 19th. The Comprachicos are like the "succession powder," an ancient social characteristic detail. They are part of old human ugliness. To the great eye of history, which sees everything collectively, the Comprachicos belong to the colossal fact of slavery. Joseph sold by his brethren is a chapter in their story. The Comprachicos have left their traces in the penal laws of Spain and England. You find here and there in the dark confusion of English laws the impress of this horrible truth, like the footprint of a savage in a forest.

Comprachicos, the same as Comprapequeños, is a compound Spanish word signifying Child-buyers.

The Comprachicos traded in children. They bought and sold them. They did not steal them. The kidnapping of children is another branch of industry. And what did they make of these children?

Monsters.

Why monsters?

To laugh at.

The populace must needs laugh, and kings too. The mountebank is wanted in the streets, the jester at the Louvre. The one is called a Clown, the other a Fool.

The efforts of man to procure himself pleasure are at times worthy of the attention of the philosopher.

What are we sketching in these few preliminary pages? A chapter in the most terrible of books; a book which might be entitled—*The Farming of the unhappy by the happy.*

II

A CHILD DESTINED TO BE A PLAYTHING FOR MEN—SUCH A THING HAS EXISTED; SUCH A THING exists even now. In simple and savage times such a thing constituted an especial trade. The 17th century, called the great century, was of those times. It was a century very Byzantine in tone. It combined corrupt simplicity with delicate ferocity; a curious variety of civilization. A tiger with a simper. Madame de Sévigné minces on the subject of the fagot and the wheel. That century traded a good deal in children. Flattering historians have concealed the sore, but have divulged the remedy, Vincent de Paul.

In order that a human toy should succeed, he must be taken early. The dwarf must be fashioned when young. We play with childhood. But a well-formed child is not very amusing; a hunch back is better fun.

Hence grew an art. There were trainers who took a man and made him an abortion; they took a face and made a muzzle; they stunted growth; they kneaded the features. The artificial production of teratological cases had its rules. It was quite a science; what one can imagine as the antithesis of or-thopedy. Where God had put a look, their art put a squint; where God had made harmony, they made discord; where God had made the perfect picture, they re-established the sketch; and, in the eyes of connoisseurs, it was the sketch which was perfect. They debased animals as well; they invented a piebald horse. Turenne rode a piebald horse. In our own days do they not dye dogs blue and green? Nature is our canvas. Man has always wished to add something to God's work. Man retouches cre-ation, sometimes for better, sometimes for worse. The court buffoon was nothing but an attempt to lead back man to the monkey. It was a progress the wrong way. A masterpiece in retrogression. At the same time they tried to make a man of the monkey. Barbara, Duchess of Cleveland and Countess of Southampton, had a marmoset for a page. Frances Sutton, Baroness of Dudley, eighth peeress in the bench of barons, had tea served by a baboon clad in gold brocade, which her ladyship called My Black. Catherine Sedley, Countess of Dorchester, used to go and take her seat in Parliament in a coach with armorial bearings, behind which stood, their muzzles stuck up in the air, three Cape monkeys in grand livery. A Duchess of Medina-Celi, whose toilette Cardinal Pole witnessed, had her stockings put on by an orangutan. These monkeys raised in the scale were a counterpoise to men brutalized and bes-tialized. This promiscuousness of man and beast, desired by the great, was especially prominent in the case of the dwarf and the dog. The dwarf never quitted the dog, which was always bigger than him-self. The dog was the pair of the dwarf; it was as if they were coupled with a collar. This juxtaposi-tion is authenticated by a mass of domestic records; notably by the portrait of Jeffrey Hudson, dwarf of Henrietta of France, daughter of Henri IV, and wife of Charles I.

To degrade man tends to deform him. The suppression of his state was completed by disfig-urement. Certain vivisectors of that period succeeded marvelously well in effacing from the human face the divine effigy. Doctor Conquest, member of the Amen Street College, and judicial visitor of the chemists' shops of London, wrote a book in Latin on this pseudo-surgery, the processes of which he describes. If we are to believe Justus of Carrickfergus, the inventor of this branch of sur-gery was a monk named Avonmore; an Irish word signifying Great River.

The dwarf of the Elector Palatine, Perkeo, whose effigy—or ghost—springs from a magical box in the cave of Heidelberg, was a remarkable specimen of this science, very varied in its appli-cations. It fashioned beings the law of whose existence was hideously simple: it permitted them to suffer, and commanded them to amuse.

III

THE MANUFACTURE OF MONSTERS WAS PRACTICED ON A LARGE SCALE, AND COMPRISED VARIOUS branches.

The Sultan required them, so did the Pope; the one to guard his women, the other to say his prayers. These were of a peculiar kind, incapable of reproduction. Scarcely human beings, they were useful to voluptuousness and to religion. The seraglio and the Sistine Chapel utilized the same species of monsters; fierce in the former case, mild in the latter.

They knew how to produce things in those days which are not produced now; they had talents which we lack, and it is not without reason that some good folk cry out that the decline has come. We no longer know how to sculpture living human flesh; this is consequent on the loss of the art of torture. Men were once virtuosi in that respect, but are so no longer; the art has become so simpli-fied that it will soon disappear altogether. In cutting the limbs of living men, in opening their bel-lies and in dragging out their entrails, phenomena were grasped on the moment and discoveries made. We are obliged to renounce these experiments now, and are thus deprived of the progress which surgery made by aid of the executioner.

The vivisection of former days was not limited to the manufacture of phenomena for the market-place, of buffoons for the palace (a species of augmentative of the courtier), and eunuchs for sultans and popes. It abounded in varieties. One of its triumphs was the manufacture of cocks for the king of England.

It was the custom, in the palace of the kings of England, to have a sort of watchman, who crowed like a cock. This watcher, awake while all others slept, ranged the palace, and raised from hour to hour the cry of the farmyard, repeating it as often as was necessary, and thus supplying a clock. This man, promoted to be cock, had in childhood undergone the operation of the pharynx which was part of the art described by Dr. Conquest. Under Charles II the salivation inseparable to the operation having disgusted the Duchess of Portsmouth, the appointment was indeed preserved, so that the splendor of the crown should not be tarnished, but they got an unmutilated man to represent the cock. A retired officer was generally selected for this honorable employment. Under James II the functionary was named William Sampson, Cock, and received for his crow £9. 2d. 6s. annually.

The memoirs of Catherine II inform us that at St. Petersburg, scarcely a hundred years since, whenever the czar or czarina was displeased with a Russian prince, he was forced to squat down in the great antechamber of the palace, and to remain in that posture a certain number of days, mewing like a cat, or clucking like a sitting hen, and pecking his food from the floor.

These fashions have passed away; but not so much, perhaps, as one might imagine. Nowadays, courtiers slightly modify their intonation in clucking to please their masters. More than one picks up from the ground—we will not say from the mud—what he eats.

It is very fortunate that kings cannot err. Hence their contradictions never perplex us. In approving always, one is sure to be always right—which is pleasant. Louis XIV would not have liked to see at Versailles either an officer acting the cock, or a prince acting the turkey. That which raised the royal and imperial dignity in England and Russia would have seemed to Louis the Great incompatible with the crown of St. Louis. We know what his displeasure was when Madame Henriette forgot herself so far as to see a hen in a dream—which was, indeed, a grave breach of good manners in a lady of the court. When one is of the court, one should not dream of the courtyard. Bossuet, it may be remembered, was nearly as scandalized as Louis XIV.

IV

THE COMMERCE IN CHILDREN IN THE 17TH CENTURY, AS WE HAVE EXPLAINED, WAS CONNECTED with a trade. The Comprachicos engaged in the commerce, and carried on the trade. They bought children, worked a little on the raw material, and resold them afterwards.

The venders were of all kinds: from the wretched father, getting rid of his family, to the master, utilizing his stud of slaves. The sale of men was a simple matter. In our own time we have had fighting to maintain this right. Remember that it is less than a century ago since the Elector of Hesse sold his subjects to the King of England, who required men to be killed in America. Kings went to the Elector of Hesse as we go to the butcher to buy meat. The Elector had food for powder in stock, and hung up his subjects in his shop. Come buy, it is for sale. In England, under Jeffreys, after the tragical episode of Monmouth, there were many lords and gentlemen beheaded and quartered. Those who were executed left wives and daughters, widows and orphans, whom James II gave to the queen, his wife. The queen sold these ladies to William Penn. Very likely the king had so much per cent on the transaction. The extraordinary thing is not that James II should have sold the women, but that William Penn should have bought them. Penn's purchase is excused, or explained, by the fact that having a desert to sow with men, he needed women as farming implements.

Her Gracious Majesty made a good business out of these ladies. The young sold dear. We may imagine, with the uneasy feeling which a complicated scandal arouses, that probably some old duchesses were thrown in cheap.

The Comprachicos were also called the Cheylas, a Hindu word, which conveys the image of harrying a nest.

For a long time the Comprachicos only partially concealed themselves. There is sometimes in the social order a favoring shadow thrown over iniquitous trades, in which they thrive. In our own day we have seen an association of the kind in Spain, under the direction of the ruffian Ramon Selles, last from 1834 to 1866, and hold three provinces under terror for thirty years—Valencia, Alicante, and Murcia.

Under the Stuarts, the Comprachicos were by no means in bad odor at court. On occasions they were used for reasons of state. For James II they were almost an *instrumentum regni*. It was a time when families, which were refractory or in the way, were dismembered; when a descent was cut short; when heirs were suddenly suppressed. At times one branch was defrauded to the profit of another. The Comprachicos had a genius for disfiguration which recommended them to state policy. To disfigure is better than to kill. There was, indeed, the Iron Mask, but that was a mighty measure. Europe could not be peopled with iron masks, while deformed tumblers ran about the streets without creating any surprise. Besides, the iron mask is removable; not so the mask of flesh. You are masked forever by your own flesh—what can be more ingenious? The Comprachicos worked on man as the Chinese work on trees. They had their secrets, as we have said; they had tricks which are now lost arts. A sort of fantastic stunted thing left their hands; it was ridiculous and wonderful. They would touch up a little being with such skill that its father could not have known it. *Et que méconnáitrait l'oeil même de son père,* as Racine says in bad French. Sometimes they left the spine straight and remade the face. They unmarked a child as one might unmark a pocket-handkerchief. Products, destined for tumblers, had their joints dislocated in a masterly manner—you would have said they had been boned. Thus gymnasts were made.

Not only did the Comprachicos take away his face from the child, they also took away his memory. At least they took away all they could of it; the child had no consciousness of the mutilation to which he had been subjected. This frightful surgery left its traces on his countenance, but not on his mind. The most he could recall was that one day he had been seized by men, that next he had fallen asleep, and then that he had been cured. Cured of what? he did not know. Of burnings by sulfur and incisions by the iron he remembered nothing. The Comprachicos deadened the little patient by means of a stupefying powder which was thought to be magical, and suppressed all pain. This powder has been known from time immemorial in China, and is still employed there in the present day. The Chinese have been beforehand with us in all our inventions—printing, artillery, aerostation, chloroform. Only the discovery which in Europe at once takes life and birth, and becomes a prodigy and a wonder, remains a chrysalis in China, and is preserved in a deathlike state. China is a museum of embryos.

Since we are in China, let us remain there a moment to note a peculiarity. In China, from time immemorial, they have possessed a certain refinement of industry and art. It is the art of molding a living man. They take a child, two or three years old, put him in a porcelain vase, more or less grotesque, which is made without top or bottom, to allow egress for the head and feet. During the day the vase is set upright, and at night is laid down to allow the child to sleep. Thus the child thickens without growing taller, filling up with his compressed flesh and distorted bones the reliefs in the vase. This development in a bottle continues many years. After a certain time it becomes irreparable. When they consider that this is accomplished, and the monster made, they break the vase. The child comes out—and, behold, there is a man in the shape of a mug!

This is convenient; by ordering your dwarf betimes you are able to have it of any shape you wish.

V

JAMES II TOLERATED THE COMPRACHICOS FOR THE GOOD REASON THAT HE MADE USE OF THEM; AT least it happened that he did so more than once. We do not always disdain to use what we despise. This low trade, an excellent expedient sometimes for the higher one which is called state policy, was willingly left in a miserable state, but was not persecuted. There was no surveillance, but a certain amount of attention. Thus much might be useful—the law closed one eye, the king opened the other.

Sometimes the king went so far as to avow his complicity. These are audacities of monarchical terrorism. The disfigured one was marked with the fleur-de-lys; they took from him the mark of God; they put on him the mark of the king. Jacob Astley, knight and baronet, lord of Melton Constable, in the county of Norfolk, had in his family a child who had been sold, and upon whose forehead the dealer had imprinted a fleur-de-lys with a hot iron. In certain cases in which it was held desirable to register for some reason the royal origin of the new position made for the child, they used such means. England has always done us the honor to utilize, for her personal service, the fleur-de-lys.

The Comprachicos, allowing for the shade which divides a trade from a fanaticism, were analogous to the Stranglers of India. They lived among themselves in gangs, and to facilitate their progress, affected somewhat of the merry-andrew. They encamped here and there, but they were grave and religious, bearing no affinity to other nomads, and incapable of theft. The people for a long time wrongly confounded them with the Moors of Spain and the Moors of China. The Moors of Spain were coiners, the Moors of China were thieves. There was nothing of the sort about the Comprachicos; they were honest folk. Whatever you may think of them, they were sometimes sincerely scrupulous. They pushed open a door, entered, bargained for a child, paid, and departed. All was done with propriety.

They were of all countries. Under the name of Comprachicos fraternized English, French, Castilians, Germans, Italians. A unity of idea, a unity of superstition, the pursuit of the same calling, make such fusions. In this fraternity of vagabonds, those of the Mediterranean seaboard represented the East, those of the Atlantic seaboard the West. Many Basques conversed with many Irishmen. The Basque and the Irishman understand each other, they speak the old Punic jargon; add to this the intimate relations of Catholic Ireland with Catholic Spain—relations such that they terminated by bringing to the gallows in London one almost King of Ireland, the Celtic Lord de Brany; from which resulted the conquest of the county of Leitrim.

The Comprachicos were rather a fellowship than a tribe; rather a residuum than a fellowship. It was all the riffraff of the universe, having for their trade a crime. It was a sort of harlequin people, all composed of rags. To recruit a man was to sew on a tatter.

To wander was the Comprachicos' law of existence—to appear and disappear. What is barely tolerated cannot take root. Even in the kingdoms where their business supplied the courts, and, on occasions, served as an auxiliary to the royal power, they were now and then suddenly ill-treated. Kings made use of their art, and sent the artists to the galleys. These inconsistencies belong to the ebb and flow of royal caprice. "For such is our pleasure."

A rolling stone and a roving trade gather no moss. The Comprachicos were poor. They might have said what the lean and ragged witch observed, when she saw them setting fire to the stake, "Le jeu n'en vaut pas la chandelle." It is possible, nay probable (their chiefs remaining unknown), that the wholesale contractors in the trade were rich. After the lapse of two centuries, it would be difficult to throw any light on this point.

It was, as we have said, a fellowship. It had its laws, its oaths, its formulae—it had almost its cabala. Anyone nowadays wishing to know all about the Comprachicos need only go into Biscaya or Galicia; there were many Basques among them, and it is in those mountains that one hears their history. To this day the Comprachicos are spoken of at Oyarzun, at Urbistondo, at Leso, at Astigarraga. *Aguardate niño, que voy a llamar al Comprachicos*—Take care, child, or I'll call the Comprachicos—is the cry with which mothers frighten their children in that country.

The Comprachicos, like the Zigeuner and the Gypsies, had appointed places for periodical meetings. From time to time their leaders conferred together. In the seventeenth century they had four principal points of rendezvous. One in Spain, the pass of Pancorbo; one in Germany, the glade called the Wicked Woman, near Diekirsch, where there are two enigmatic bas-reliefs, representing a woman with a head and a man without one; one in France, the hill where was the colossal statue of Massue-la-Promesse in the old sacred wood of Borvo Tomona, near Bourbonne les Bains; one in England, behind the garden wall of William Challoner, Squire of Gisborough in Cleveland, Yorkshire, behind the square tower and the great wing which is entered by an arched door.

VI

THE LAWS AGAINST VAGABONDS HAVE ALWAYS BEEN VERY RIGOROUS IN ENGLAND. ENGLAND, IN her Gothic legislation, seemed to be inspired with this principle, *Homo errans fera errante pejor*. One of the special statutes classifies the man without a home as "more dangerous than the asp, dragon, lynx, or basilisk" (*atrocior aspide, dracone, lynce, et basilico*). For a long time England troubled herself as much concerning the gypsies, of whom she wished to be rid, as about the wolves of which she had been cleared. In that the Englishman differed from the Irishman, who prayed to the saints for the health of the wolf, and called him my godfather.

English law, nevertheless, in the same way as (we have just seen) it tolerated the wolf, tamed, domesticated, and become in some sort a dog, tolerated the regular vagabond, become in some sort a subject. It did not trouble itself about either the mountebank or the traveling barber, or the quack doctor, or the peddler, or the open-air scholar, as long as they had a trade to live by. Further than this, and with these exceptions, the description of freedom which exists in the wanderer terrified the law. A tramp was a possible public enemy. That modern thing, the lounger, was then unknown; that ancient thing, the vagrant, was alone understood. A suspicious appearance, that indescribable something which all understand and none can define, was sufficient reason that society should take a man by the collar. "Where do you live? How do you get your living?" And if he could not answer, harsh penalties awaited him. Iron and fire were in the code: the law practiced the cauterization of vagrancy.

Hence, throughout English territory, a veritable "loi des suspects" was applicable to vagrants (who, it must be owned, readily became malefactors), and particularly to gypsies, whose expulsion has erroneously been compared to the expulsion of the Jews and the Moors from Spain, and the Protestants from France. As for us, we do not confound a battue with a persecution.

The Comprachicos, we insist, had nothing in common with the gypsies. The gypsies were a nation; the Comprachicos were a compound of all nations—the lees of a horrible vessel full of filthy waters. The Comprachicos had not, like the gypsies, an idiom of their own; their jargon was a promiscuous collection of idioms: all languages were mixed together in their language; they spoke a medley. Like the gypsies, they had come to be a people winding through the peoples; but their common tie was association, not race. At all epochs in history one finds in the vast liquid mass which constitutes humanity some of these streams of venomous men exuding poison around them. The gypsies were a tribe; the Comprachicos a freemasonry—a masonry having not a noble aim, but a hideous handicraft. Finally, their religions differ—the gypsies were Pagans, the Comprachicos were Christians, and more than that, good Christians, as became an association which, although a mixture of all nations, owed its birth to Spain, a devout land.

They were more than Christians, they were Catholics; they were more than Catholics, they were Romans, and so touchy in their faith, and so pure, that they refused to associate with the Hungarian nomads of the comitate of Pesth, commanded and led by an old man, having for scepter a wand with a silver ball, surmounted by the double-headed Austrian eagle. It is true that these Hungarians were schismatics, to the extent of celebrating the Assumption on the 29th August, which is an abomination.

In England, so long as the Stuarts reigned, the confederation of the Comprachicos was (for motives of which we have already given you a glimpse) to a certain extent protected. James II, a devout man, who persecuted the Jews and trampled out the gypsies, was a good prince to the Comprachicos. We have seen why. The Comprachicos were buyers of the human wares in which he was dealer. They excelled in disappearances. Disappearances are occasionally necessary for the good of the State. An inconvenient heir of tender age whom they took and handled lost his shape. This facilitated confiscation; the transfer of titles to favorites was simplified. The Comprachicos were, moreover, very discreet and very taciturn. They bound themselves to silence, and kept their word, which is necessary in affairs of state. There was scarcely an example of their having betrayed the secrets of the king. This was, it is true, for their interest; and if the king had lost confidence in them, they would have been in great danger. They were thus of use in a political point of view. Moreover these artists furnished singers for the Holy Father. The Comprachicos were useful for the *Miserere* of Allegri. They were particularly devoted to Mary. All this pleased the papistry of the Stuarts. James II could not be hostile to holy men who pushed their devotion to the Virgin to the extent of manufacturing eunuchs. In 1688 there was a change of dynasty in England. Orange supplanted Stuart. William III replaced James II.

James II went away to die in exile, miracles were performed on his tomb, and his relics cured the Bishop of Autun of fistula—a worthy recompense of the Christian virtues of the prince.

William, having neither the same ideas nor the same practices as James, was severe to the Comprachicos. He did his best to crush out the vermin.

A statute of the early part of William and Mary's reign hit the association of child-buyers hard. It was as the blow of a club to the Comprachicos, who were from that time pulverized. By the terms of this statute those of the fellowship taken and duly convicted, were to be branded with a red-hot iron, imprinting R, on the shoulder, signifying rogue; on the left hand T, signifying thief; and on the right hand M, signifying man-slayer. The chiefs, "supposed to be rich, although beggars in appearance," were to be punished in the *collistrigium*—that is, the pillory—and branded on the forehead with a P, besides having their goods confiscated, and the trees in their woods rooted up. Those who did not inform against the Comprachicos were to be punished by confiscation and imprisonment for life, as for the crime of misprision. As for the women found among these men, they were to suffer the cucking-stool—this is a tumbrel, the name of which is composed of the French word *coquine*, and the German *stuhl*. English law being endowed with a strange longevity, this punishment still exists in English legislation for quarrelsome women. The cucking-stool is suspended over a river or a pond, the woman seated on it. The chair is allowed to drop into the water, and then pulled out. This dipping of the woman is repeated three times, "to cool her anger," says the commentator, Chamberlayne.

PART I

BOOK THE FIRST

NIGHT NOT SO BLACK AS MAN

Chapter 1

PORTLAND BILL

AN OBSTINATE NORTH WIND BLEW WITHOUT CEASING OVER THE MAINLAND OF EUROPE, AND yet more roughly over England, during all the month of December, 1689, and all the month of January, 1690. Hence the disastrous cold weather, which caused that winter to be noted as "memorable to the poor," on the margin of the old Bible in the Presbyterian chapel of the Non-jurors in London. Thanks to the lasting qualities of the old monarchical parchment employed in official registers, long lists of poor persons, found dead of famine and cold, are still legible in many local repositories, particularly in the archives of the Liberty of the Clink, in the borough of Southwark, of Pie Powder Court (which signifies Dusty Feet Court), and in those of Whitechapel Court, held in the village of Stepney by the bailiff of the Lord of the Manor. The Thames was frozen over—a thing which does not happen once in a century, as the ice forms on it with difficulty owing to the action of the sea. Coaches rolled over the frozen river, and a fair was held with booths, bear-baiting and bull-baiting. An ox was roasted whole on the ice. This thick ice lasted two months. The hard year 1690 surpassed in severity even the famous winters at the beginning of the seventeenth century, so minutely observed by Dr. Gideon Delane, the same who was, in his quality of apothecary to King James, honored by the city of London with a bust and a pedestal.

One evening, toward the close of one of the most bitter days of the month of January, 1690, something unusual was going on in one of the numerous inhospitable bights of the bay of Portland, which caused the sea-gulls and wild geese to scream and circle round its mouth, not daring to re-enter.

In this creek, the most dangerous of all which line the bay, during the continuance of certain winds, and consequently the most lonely—convenient by reason of its very danger, for ships in hiding—a little vessel, almost touching the cliff, so deep was the water, was moored to a point of rock. We are wrong in saying, the night falls; we should say the night rises, for it is from the earth that obscurity comes. It was already night at the bottom of the cliff; it was still day at top. Anyone approaching the vessel's moorings would have recognized a Biscayan hooker.

The sun, concealed all day by the mist, had just set. There was beginning to be felt that deep and sombrous melancholy which might be called anxiety for the absent sun. With no wind from the sea, the water of the creek was calm.

This was, especially in winter, a lucky exception. Almost all the Portland creeks have sand-bars; and in heavy weather the sea becomes very rough, and, to pass in safety, much skill and practice are necessary. These little ports (ports more in appearance than fact) are of small advantage. They are hazardous to enter, fearful to leave. On this evening, for a wonder, there was no danger.

The Biscay hooker is of an ancient model, now fallen into disuse. This kind of hooker, which has done service even in the navy, was stoutly built in its hull; a boat in size, a ship in strength. It figured in the Armada. Sometimes the war-hooker attained to a high tonnage; thus the *Great Grif-*

fin, bearing a captain's flag, and commanded by Lopez de Medina, measured six hundred and fifty good tons, and carried forty guns. But the merchant and contraband hookers were very feeble specimens. Sea-folk held them at their true value, and esteemed the model a very sorry one, The rigging of the hooker was made of hemp, sometimes with wire inside, which was probably intended as a means, however unscientific, of obtaining indications, in the case of magnetic tension. The lightness of this rigging did not exclude the use of heavy tackle, the cabrias of the Spanish galleon, and the cameli of the Roman triremes. The helm was very long, which gives the advantage of a long arm of leverage, but the disadvantage of a small arc of effort. Two wheels in two pulleys at the end of the rudder corrected this defect, and compensated, to some extent, for the loss of strength. The compass was well housed in a case perfectly square, and well-balanced by its two copper frames placed horizontally, one in the other, on little bolts, as in Cardan's lamps. There was science and cunning in the construction of the hooker, but it was ignorant science and barbarous cunning. The hooker was primitive, just like the praam and the canoe; was kindred to the praam in stability and to the canoe in swiftness, and, like all vessels born of the instinct of the pirate and fisherman, it had remarkable sea qualities; it was equally well suited to landlocked and to open waters. Its system of sails, complicated in stays, and very peculiar, allowed of its navigating trimly in the close bays of Asturias (which are little more than enclosed basins, as Pasages for instance), and also freely out at sea. It could sail round a lake, and sail round the world—a strange craft with two objects, good for a pond and good for a storm. The hooker is among vessels what the wagtail is among birds, one of the smallest and one of the boldest. The wagtail perching on a reed scarcely bends it, and, flying away, crosses the ocean.

These Biscay hookers, even to the poorest, were gilt and painted. Tattooing is part of the genius of those charming people, savages to some degree. The sublime coloring of their mountains, variegated by snows and meadows, reveals to them the rugged spell which ornament possesses in itself. They are poverty-stricken and magnificent; they put coats-of-arms on their cottages; they have huge asses, which they bedizen with bells, and huge oxen, on which they put headdresses of feathers. Their coaches, which you can hear grinding the wheels two leagues off, are illuminated, carved, and hung with ribbons. A cobbler has a bas-relief on his door; it is only St. Crispin, and an old shoe; but it is in stone. They trim their leathern jackets with lace. They do not mend their rags, but they embroider them. Vivacity profound and superb! The Basques are like the Greeks, children of the sun; while the Valencian drapes himself, bare and sad, in his russet woolen rug, with a hole to pass his head through, the natives of Galicia and Biscay have the delight of fine linen shirts, bleached in the dew. Their thresholds and their windows teem with faces fair and fresh, laughing under garlands of maize; a joyous and proud serenity shines out in their ingenious arts, in their trades, in their customs, in the dress of their maidens, in their songs. The mountain, that colossal ruin, is all aglow in Biscay: the sun's rays go in and out of every break. The wild Jaïzquivel is full of Idylls. Biscay is Pyrenean grace as Savoy is Alpine grace. The dangerous bays—the neighbors of St. Sebastian, Leso, and Fontarabia—with storms, with clouds, with spray flying over the capes, with the rages of the waves and the winds, with terror, with uproar, mingle boat-women crowned with roses. He who has seen the Basque country wishes to see it again. It is the blessed land. Two harvests a year; villages resonant and gay; a stately poverty; all Sunday the sound of guitars, dancing, castanets, love-making; houses clean and bright; storks in the belfries.

Let us return to Portland—that rugged mountain in the sea.

The peninsula of Portland, looked at geometrically, presents the appearance of a bird's head, of which the bill is turned toward the ocean, the back of the head toward Weymouth; the isthmus is its neck.

Portland, greatly to the sacrifice of its wildness, exists now but for trade. The coasts of Portland were discovered by quarrymen and plasterers toward the middle of the seventeenth century. Since that period what is called Roman cement has been made of the Portland stone—a useful industry, enriching the district, and disfiguring the bay. Two hundred years ago these coasts were eaten away as a cliff; to-day, as a quarry. The pick bites meanly, the wave grandly; hence a diminution of beauty. To the magnificent ravages of the ocean have succeeded the measured strokes of men. These measured strokes have worked away the creek where the Biscay hooker was moored. To find any vestige of the little anchorage, now destroyed, the eastern side of the peninsula should be searched, toward the point beyond Folly Pier and Dirdle Pier, beyond Wakeham even, between the place called Church Hope and the place called Southwell.

The creek, walled in on all sides by precipices higher than its width, was minute by minute becoming more overshadowed by evening. The misty gloom, usual at twilight, became thicker; it was like a growth of darkness at the bottom of a well. The opening of the creek seaward, a narrow passage, traced on the almost night-black interior a pallid rift where the waves were moving. You must have been quite close to perceive the hooker moored to the rocks, and, as it were, hidden by the great cloaks of shadow. A plank thrown from on board on to a low and level projection of the cliff, the only point on which a landing could be made, placed the vessel in communication with the land. Dark figures were crossing and recrossing each other on this tottering gangway, and in the shadow some people were embarking.

It was less cold in the creek than out at sea, thanks to the screen of rock rising over the north of the basin, which did not, however, prevent the people from shivering. They were hurrying. The effect of the twilight defined the forms as though they had been punched out with a tool. Certain indentations in their clothes were visible, and showed that they belonged to the class called in England, The ragged.

The twisting of the pathway could be distinguished vaguely in the relief of the cliff. A girl who lets her stay-lace hang down trailing over the back of an arm-chair, describes, without being conscious of it, most of the paths of cliffs and mountains. The pathway of this creek, full of knots and angles, almost perpendicular, and better adapted for goats than men, terminated on the platform where the plank was placed. The pathways of cliffs ordinarily imply a not very inviting declivity; they offer themselves less as a road than as a fall; they sink rather than incline. This one—probably some ramification of a road on the plain above—was disagreeable to look at, so vertical was it. From underneath you saw it gain by zigzag the higher layer of the cliff where it passed out through deep passages on to the high plateau by a cutting in the rock; and the passengers for whom the vessel was waiting in the creek must have come by this path.

Excepting the movement of embarkation which was being made in the creek, a movement visibly scared and uneasy, all around was solitude; no step, no noise, no breath was heard. At the other side of the roads, at the entrance of Ringstead Bay, you could just perceive a flotilla of shark-fishing boats, which were evidently out of their reckoning. These polar boats had been driven from Danish into English waters by the whims of the sea. Northerly winds play these tricks on fishermen. They had just taken refuge in the anchorage of Portland—a sign of bad weather expected and danger out at sea. They were engaged in casting anchor. The chief boat, placed in front after the old manner of Norwegian flotillas, all her rigging standing out in black, above the white level of the sea; and in front might be perceived the hook-iron, loaded with all kinds of hooks and harpoons, destined for the Greenland shark, the dogfish, and the spinous shark, as well as the nets to pick up the sunfish.

Except a few other craft, all swept into the same corner, the eye met nothing living on the vast horizon of Portland. Not a house, not a ship. The coast in those days was not inhabited, and the roads, at that season, were not safe.

Whatever may have been the appearance of the weather, the beings who were going to sail away in the Biscayan urca, pressed on the hour of departure all the same. They formed a busy and confused group, in rapid movement on the shore. To distinguish one from another was difficult; impossible to tell whether they were old or young. The indistinctness of evening intermixed and blurred them; the mask of shadow was over their faces. They were sketches in the night. There were eight of them, and there were seemingly among them one or two women, hard to recognize under the rags and tatters in which the group was attired—clothes which were no longer man's or woman's. Rags have no sex.

A smaller shadow, flitting to and fro among the larger ones, indicated either a dwarf or a child. It was a child.

Chapter II

LEFT ALONE

THIS IS WHAT AN OBSERVER CLOSE AT HAND MIGHT HAVE NOTED.
All wore long cloaks, torn and patched, but covering them, and at need concealing them up to the eyes; useful alike against the north wind and curiosity. They moved with ease under these cloaks. The greater number wore a handkerchief rolled round the head, a sort of rudiment which marks the commencement of the turban in Spain. This headdress was nothing unusual in England. At that time the South was in fashion in the North; perhaps this was connected with the fact that the North was beating the South. It conquered and admired. After the defeat of the Armada, Castilian was considered in the halls of Elizabeth to be elegant court talk. To speak English in the palace of the Queen of England was held almost an impropriety. Partially to adopt the manners of those upon whom we impose our laws is the habit of the conquering barbarian toward conquered civilization. The Tartar contemplates and imitates the Chinese. It was thus Castilian fashions penetrated into England; in return, English interests crept into Spain.

One of the men in the group embarking appeared to be a chief. He had sandals on his feet, and was bedizened with gold lace tatters and a tinsel waistcoat, shining under his cloak like the belly of a fish. Another pulled down over his face a huge piece of felt, cut like a somberro; this felt had no hole for a pipe, thus indicating the wearer to be a man of letters.

On the principle that a man's vest is a child's cloak, the child was wrapped over his rags in a sailor's jacket, which descended to his knees.

By his height you would have guessed him to be a boy of ten or eleven; his feet were bare.

The crew of the hooker was composed of a captain and two sailors.

The hooker had apparently come from Spain, and was about to return thither. She was beyond a doubt engaged in a stealthy service from one coast to the other.

The persons embarking in her whispered among themselves.

The whispering interchanged by these creatures was of composite sound—now a word of Spanish, then of German, then of French, then of Gaelic, at times of Basque. It was either a patois or a slang. They appeared to be of all nations, and yet of the same band.

The motley group appeared to be a company of comrades, perhaps a gang of accomplices.

The crew was probably of their brotherhood. Community of object was visible in the embarkation.

Had there been a little more light, and if you could have looked at them attentively, you might have perceived on these people rosaries and scapulars half-hidden under their rags; one of the semi-women mingling in the group had a rosary almost equal for the size of its beads to that of a dervish, and easy to recognize for an Irish one made at Llanymthefry, which is also called Llanandriffy.

You might also have observed, had it not been so dark, a figure of Our Lady and Child carved and gilt on the bow of the hooker. It was probably that of the Basque Notre-Dame, a sort of Pana-gia of the old Cantabri. Under this image, which occupied the position of a figure-head, was a lantern, which at this moment was not lighted—an excess of caution which implied an extreme de-sire of concealment. This lantern was evidently for two purposes. When alight, it burned before the Virgin, and at the same time illumined the sea, a beacon doing duty as a taper.

Under the bowsprit the cutwater, long, curved, and sharp, came out in front like the horn of a crescent. At the top of the cutwater, and at the feet of the Virgin, a kneeling angel, with folded wings, leaned her back against the stem, and looked through a spyglass at the horizon. The angel was gilded like Our Lady. In the cutwater were holes and openings to let the waves pass through, which afforded an opportunity for gilding and arabesques.

Under the figure of the Virgin was written, in gilt capitals, the word *Matutina*—the name of the vessel, not to be read just now on account of the darkness.

Amid the confusion of departure there were thrown down in disorder, at the foot of the cliff, the goods which the voyagers were to take with them, and which, by means of a plank serving as a bridge across, were being passed rapidly from the shore to the boat. Bags of biscuit, a cask of stock-fish, a case of portable soup, three barrels—one of fresh water, one of malt, one of tar—four or five bottles of ale, an old portmanteau buckled up by straps, trunks, boxes, a ball of tow for torches and signals. Such was the lading. These ragged people had valises, which seemed to indicate a rov-ing life. Wandering rascals are obliged to own something; at times they would prefer to fly away like birds, but they cannot do so without abandoning the means of earning a livelihood. They of necessity possess boxes of tools and instruments of labor, whatever their errant trade may be. Those of whom we speak were dragging their baggage with them, often an encumbrance.

It could not have been easy to bring these movables to the bottom of the cliff. This, however, revealed the intention of a definite departure.

No time was lost; there was one continued passing to and fro from the shore to the vessel, and from the vessel to the shore; each one took his share of the work; one carried a bag, another a chest. Those amidst the promiscuous company who were possibly or probably women worked like the rest. They overloaded the child.

It was doubtful if the child's father or mother were in the group; no sign of life was vouch-safed him. They made him work, nothing more. He appeared not a child in a family, but a slave in a tribe. He waited on everyone, and no one spoke to him.

However, he made haste, and, like the others of this mysterious troop, he seemed to have but one thought—to embark as quickly as possible. Did he know why? probably not, he hurried me-chanically because he saw the others hurry.

The hooker was decked. The stowing of the lading in the hold was quickly finished, and the moment to put off arrived. The last case had been carried over the gangway, and nothing was left to embark but the men. The two objects among the group who seemed women were already on board; six, the child among them, were still on the low platform of the cliff. A movement of de-parture was made in the vessel, the captain seized the helm, a sailor took up an ax to cut the hawser; to cut is an evidence of haste; when there is time it is unknotted.

"Andamos," said, in a low voice, he who appeared chief of the six, and who had the spangles on his tatters. The child rushed toward the plank in order to be the first to pass. As he placed his foot on it, two of the men hurried by, at the risk of throwing him into the water, got in before him and passed on; the fourth drove him back with his fist and followed the third; the fifth, who was the chief, bounded into rather than entered the vessel, and, as he jumped in, kicked back the plank, which fell into the sea, a stroke of the hatchet cut the moorings, the helm was put up, the vessel left the shore, and the child remained on land.

Chapter III

Alone

THE CHILD REMAINED MOTIONLESS ON THE ROCK, WITH HIS EYES FIXED; NO CALLING OUT, NO appeal. Though this was unexpected by him, he spoke not a word. The same silence reigned in the vessel. No cry from the child to the men—no farewell from the men to the child. There was on both sides a mute acceptance of the widening distance between them. It was like a separation of ghosts on the banks of the Styx. The child, as if nailed to the rock, which the high tide was beginning to bathe, watched the departing bark. It seemed as if he realized his position. What did he realize? —Darkness.

A moment later, the hooker gained the neck of the creek and entered it. Against the clear sky the masthead was visible, rising above the split blocks between which the strait wound as between two walls. The truck wandered to the summit of the rocks and appeared to run into them. Then it was seen no more—all was over—the bark had gained the sea.

The child watched its disappearance—he was astounded but dreamy. His stupefaction was complicated by a sense of the dark reality of existence. It seemed as if there were experience in this dawning being. Did he, perchance, already exercise judgment? Experience coming too early constructs, sometimes, in the obscure depths of a child's mind, some dangerous balance—we know not what—in which the poor little soul weighs God.

Feeling himself innocent, he yielded. There was no complaint—the irreproachable does not reproach.

His rough expulsion drew from him no sign—he suffered a sort of internal stiffening. The child did not bow under this sudden blow of fate, which seemed to put an end to his existence ere it had well begun; he received the thunderstroke standing.

It would have been evident to anyone who could have seen his astonishment unmixed with dejection, that, in the group which abandoned him, there was nothing which loved him, nothing which he loved.

Brooding, he forgot the cold. Suddenly the wave wetted his feet—the tide was flowing; a gust passed through his hair—the north wind was rising. He shivered. There came over him, from head to foot, the shudder of awakening.

He cast his eyes about him.

He was alone.

Up to this day there had never existed for him any other men than those who were now in the hooker. Those men had just stolen away.

Let us add what seems a strange thing to state. Those men, the only ones he knew, were unknown to him.

He could not have said who they were. His childhood had been passed among them, without his having the consciousness of being of them. He was in juxtaposition to them, nothing more.

He had just been—forgotten—by them.

He had no money about him, no shoes to his feet, scarcely a garment to his body, not even a piece of bread in his pocket.

It was winter—it was night. It would be necessary to walk several leagues before a human habitation could be reached.

He did not know where he was.

He knew nothing, unless it was that those who had come with him to the brink of the sea had gone away without him.

He felt himself put outside the pale of life.

He felt that man failed him.

He was ten years old.

The child was in a desert, between depths where he saw the night rising, and depths where he heard the waves murmur.

He stretched his little thin arms and yawned.

Then, suddenly, as one who makes up his mind, bold, and throwing off his numbness—with the agility of a squirrel—or perhaps of an acrobat—he turned his back on the creek, and set himself to climb up the cliff. He escaladed the path, left it, returned to it, quick and venturous. He was hurrying landward, just as though he had a destination marked out; nevertheless he was going nowhere.

He hastened without an object—a fugitive before Fate.

To climb is the function of a man; to clamber is that of an animal—he did both. As the slopes of Portland face southward, there was scarcely any snow on the path; the intensity of cold had, however, frozen that snow into dust very troublesome to the walker. The child freed himself of it. His man's jacket, which was too big for him, complicated matters, and got in his way. Now and then on an overhanging crag or in a declivity he came upon a little ice, which caused him to slip down. Then, after hanging some moments over the precipice, he would catch hold of a dry branch or projecting stone. Once he came on a vein of slate, which suddenly gave way under him, letting him down with it. Crumbling slate is treacherous. For some seconds the child slid like a tile on a roof; he rolled to the extreme edge of the decline; a tuft of grass which he clutched at the right moment saved him. He was as mute in sight of the abyss as he had been in sight of the men; he gathered himself up and reascended silently. The slope was steep; so he had to tack in ascending. The precipice grew in the darkness; the vertical rock had no ending. It receded before the child in the distance of its height. As the child ascended, so seemed the summit to ascend. While he clambered he looked up at the dark entablature placed like a barrier between heaven and him. At last he reached the top.

He jumped on the level ground, or rather landed, for he rose from the precipice.

Scarcely was he on the cliff when he began to shiver. He felt in his face that bite of the night, the north wind. The bitter north-wester was blowing; he tightened his rough sailor's jacket about his chest.

It was a good coat, called in ship language a sou' wester, because that sort of stuff allows little of the south-westerly rain to penetrate.

The child, having gained the table-land, stopped, placed his feet firmly on the frozen ground and looked about him.

Behind him was the sea; in front the land; above, the sky—but a sky without stars; an opaque mist masked the zenith.

On reaching the summit of the rocky wall he found himself turned toward the land, and looked at it attentively. It lay before him as far as the sky-line, flat, frozen, and covered with snow. Some tufts of heather shivered in the wind. No roads were visible. Nothing, not even a shepherd's cot. Here and there, pale, spiral vortices might be seen, which were whirls of fine snow, snatched from the ground by the wind and blown away. Successive undulations of ground, become suddenly misty, rolled themselves into the horizon. The great dull plains were lost under the white fog. Deep silence. It spread like infinity, and was hush as the tomb.

The child turned again toward the sea.

The sea, like the land, was white, the one with snow, the other with foam. There is nothing so melancholy as the light produced by this double whiteness.

Certain lights of night are very clearly cut in their hardness; the sea was like steel, the cliff like ebony. From the height where the child was, the bay of Portland appeared almost like a geographical map, pale, in a semi-circle of hills. There was something dreamlike in that nocturnal landscape—a wan disk belted by a dark crescent. The moon sometimes has a similar appearance. From cape to cape, along the whole coast, not a single spark indicating a hearth with a fire, not a lighted window, not an inhabited house, was to be seen. As in heaven so on earth, no light. Not a lamp below, not a star above. Here and there came sudden risings in the great expanse of waters in the gulf, as the wind disarranged and wrinkled the vast sheet. The hooker was still visible in the bay as she fled.

It was a black triangle gliding over the livid waters.

Far away the waste of waters stirred confusedly in the ominous clear-obscure of immensity. The *Matutina* was making quick way. She seemed to grow smaller every minute. Nothing appears so rapid as the flight of a vessel melting into the distance of ocean.

Suddenly she lit the lantern at her prow. Probably the darkness falling round her made those on board uneasy, and the pilot thought it necessary to throw light on the waves. This luminous point, a spark seen from afar, clung like a corpse light to the high and long black form. You would have said it was a shroud raised up and moving in the middle of the sea, under which someone wandered with a star in his hand.

A storm threatened in the air: the child took no account of it, but a sailor would have trembled. It was that moment of preliminary anxiety, when it seems as though the elements are changing into persons, and one is about to witness the mysterious transfiguration of the wind into the wind-god. The sea becomes Ocean: its power reveals itself as Will: that which one takes for a thing, is a soul. It will become visible: Hence the terror. The soul of man fears to be thus confronted with the soul of nature.

Chaos was about to appear. The wind rolling back the fog, and making a stage of the clouds behind, set the scene for that fearful drama of wave and winter, which is called a Snowstorm. Vessels putting back hove in sight. For some minutes past the roads had no longer been deserted. Every instant troubled barks hastening toward an anchorage appeared from behind the capes; some were doubling Portland Bill, the others St. Albans head. From afar ships were running in. It was a race for refuge. Southwards the darkness thickened, and clouds, full of night, bordered on the sea. The weight of the tempest hanging overhead made a dreary lull on the waves. It certainly was no time to sail. Yet the hooker had sailed.

She had made the south of the cape. She was already out of the gulf, and in the open sea. Suddenly there came a gust of wind. The *Matutina*, which was still clearly in sight, made all sail, as if resolved to profit by the hurricane. It was the nor'-wester, a wind sullen and angry. Its weight was felt instantly. The hooker, caught broadside on, staggered, but recovering held her course to sea. This indicated a flight rather than a voyage, less fear of sea than of land, and greater heed of pursuit from man than from wind.

The hooker, passing through every degree of diminution, sank into the horizon. The little star which she carried into shadow paled. More and more the hooker became amalgamated with the night, then disappeared.

This time for good and all.

At least the child seemed to understand it so; he ceased to look at the sea. His eyes turned back upon the plains, the wastes, the hills, toward the space where it might not be impossible to meet something living.

Into this unknown he set out.

Chapter IV

QUESTIONS

WHAT KIND OF BAND WAS IT WHICH HAD LEFT THE CHILD BEHIND IN ITS FLIGHT? Were those fugitives Comprachicos?

We have already seen the account of the measures taken by William III, and passed by Parliament against the malefactors, male and female, called Comprachicos, otherwise Comprapequeños, otherwise Cheylas.

There are laws which disperse. The law acting against the Comprachicos determined, not only the Comprachicos, but vagabonds of all sorts, on a general flight.

It was the devil take the hindmost. The greater number of the Comprachicos returned to Spain; many of them, as we have said, being Basques.

The law for the protection of children had at first this strange result: it caused many children to be abandoned.

The immediate effect of the penal statute was to produce a crowd of children, found or rather lost. Nothing is easier to understand. Every wandering gang containing a child was liable to suspicion. The mere fact of the child's presence was in itself a denunciation.

"They are very likely Comprachicos." Such was the first idea of the sheriff, of the bailiff, of the constable. Hence arrest and inquiry. People simply unfortunate, reduced to wander and to beg, were seized with a terror of being taken for Comprachicos although they were nothing of the kind. But the weak have grave misgivings of possible errors in justice. Besides, these vagabond families are very easily scared. The accusation against the Comprachicos was that they traded in other people's children. But the promiscuousness caused by poverty and indigence is such that at times it might have been difficult for a father and mother to prove a child their own.

How came you by this child? how were they to prove that they held it from God? The child became a peril—they got rid of it. To fly unencumbered was easier; the parents resolved to lose it—now in a wood, now on a strand, now down a well.

Children were found drowned in cisterns.

Let us add that, in imitation of England, all Europe henceforth hunted down the Comprachicos. The impulse of pursuit was given. There is nothing like belling the cat. From this time forward the desire to seize them made rivalry and emulation among the police of all countries, and the alguazil was not less keenly watchful than the constable.

One could still read, twenty-three years ago, on a stone of the gate of Otero, an untranslatable inscription—the words of the code outraging propriety. In it, however, the shade of difference which existed between the buyers and the stealers of children is very strongly marked. Here is part of the inscription in somewhat rough Castillan, *Aqui quedan las orejas de los Comprachicos, y las bolsas de los robaniños, mientras que se van ellos al trabajo de mar.* You see the confiscation of ears, etc., did not prevent the owners going to the galleys. Whence followed a general rout among all vagabonds. They started frightened; they arrived trembling. On every shore in Europe their furtive advent was watched. Impossible for such a band to embark with a child, since to disembark with one was dangerous.

To lose the child was much simpler of accomplishment.

And this child, of whom we have caught a glimpse in the shadow of the solitudes of Portland, by whom had he been cast away?

To all appearance by Comprachicos.

Chapter V

THE TREE OF HUMAN INVENTION

IT MIGHT BE ABOUT SEVEN O'CLOCK IN THE EVENING. THE WIND WAS NOW DIMINISHING, A SIGN, however, of a violent recurrence impending. The child was on the table-land at the extreme south point of Portland.

Portland is a peninsula; but the child did not know what a peninsula is, and was ignorant even of the name of Portland. He knew but one thing, which is, that one can walk until one drops down. An idea is a guide; he had no idea. They had brought him there, and left him there. *They* and *there*. These two enigmas represented his doom. *They*, were humankind. *There*, was the universe. For him in all creation there was absolutely no other basis to rest on but the little piece of ground where he placed his heel, ground hard and cold to his naked feet. In the great twilight world, open on all sides, what was there for the child? Nothing.

He walked toward this Nothing. Around him was the vastness of human desertion.

He crossed the first plateau diagonally, then a second, then a third. At the extremity of each plateau the child came upon a break in the ground. The slope was sometimes steep, but always short; the high, bare plains of Portland resemble great flagstones overlapping each other. The south side seems to enter under the protruding slab, the north side rises over the next one; these made ascents, which the child stepped over nimbly. From time to time he stopped, and seemed to hold counsel with himself. The night was becoming very dark. His radius of sight was contracting. He now only saw a few steps before him.

All of a sudden he stopped, listened for an instant, and with an almost imperceptible nod of satisfaction, turned quickly and directed his steps toward an eminence of moderate height, which he dimly perceived on his right, at the point of the plain nearest the cliff. There was on the eminence a shape which in the mist looked like a tree. The child had just heard a noise in this direction, which was the noise neither of the wind nor of the sea, nor was it the cry of animals. He thought that someone was there, and in a few strides he was at the foot of the hillock.

In truth, someone was there.

That which had been indistinct on the top of the eminence was now visible. It was something like a great arm thrust straight out of the ground; at the upper extremity of the arm a sort of forefinger, supported from beneath by the thumb, pointed out horizontally; the arm, the thumb, and the forefinger drew a square against the sky. At the point of juncture of this peculiar finger and this peculiar thumb there was a line, from which hung something black and shapeless. The line moving in the wind sounded like a chain. This was the noise the child had heard. Seen closely, the line was that which the noise indicated, a chain—a single chain cable.

By that mysterious law of amalgamation which throughout nature causes appearances to exaggerate realities, the place, the hour, the mist, the mournful sea, the cloudy turmoils on the distant horizon, added to the effect of this figure, and made it seem enormous.

The mass linked to the chain presented the appearance of a scabbard. It was swaddled like a child, and long like a man. There was a round thing at its summit, about which the end of the chain was rolled. The scabbard was riven asunder at the lower end, and shreds of flesh hung out between the rents.

A feeble breeze stirred the chain, and that which hung to it swayed gently. The passive mass obeyed the vague motions of space. It was an object to inspire indescribable dread. Horror, which disproportions everything, blurred its dimensions while retaining its shape. It was a condensation of darkness, which had a defined form. Night was above and within the specter; it was a prey of ghastly exaggeration. Twilight and moon-rise, stars setting behind the cliff, floating things in space, the clouds, winds from all quarters, had ended by penetrating into the composition of this visible nothing. The species of log hanging in the wind partook of the impersonality diffused far over sea and sky, and the darkness completed this phase of the *thing* which had once been a man.

It was that which is no longer.

To be naught but a remainder! Such a thing is beyond the power of language to express. To exist no more, yet to persist; to be in the abyss, yet out of it; to reappear above death as if indissoluble. There is a certain amount of impossibility mixed with such reality. Thence comes the inexpressible. This being—was it a being? This black witness was a remainder, and an awful remainder—a remainder of what? Of nature first, and then of society. Naught, and yet total.

The lawless inclemency of the weather held it at its will; the deep oblivion of solitude environed it; it was given up to unknown chances; it was without defense against the darkness, which did with it what it willed. It was forever the patient; it submitted; the hurricane (that ghastly conflict of winds) was upon it.

The specter was given over to pillage. It underwent the horrible outrage of rotting in the open air; it was an outlaw of the tomb. There was no peace for it even in annihilation: in the summer it fell away into dust, in the winter into mud. Death should be veiled, the grave should have its reserve. Here was neither veil nor reserve: but cynically avowed putrefaction. It is effrontery in death to display its work, it offends all the calmness of shadow when it does its task outside its laboratory, the grave.

This dead being had been stripped. To strip one already stripped—relentless act! His marrow was no longer in his bones; his entrails were no longer in his body; his voice was no longer in his throat. A corpse is a pocket which death turns inside out and empties. If he ever had a Me, where was the Me? There still, perchance, and this was fearful to think of. Something wandering about something in chains—can one imagine a more mournful lineament in the darkness?

Realities exist here below which serve as issues to the unknown, which seem to facilitate the egress of speculation, and at which hypothesis snatches. Conjecture has its *compelle intrare*. In passing by certain places and before certain objects one cannot help stopping—a prey to dreams into the realms of which the mind enters. In the invisible there are dark portals ajar. No one could have met this dead man without meditating.

In the vastness of dispersion he was wearing silently away. He had had blood which had been drunk, skin which had been eaten, flesh which had been stolen. Nothing had passed him by without taking somewhat from him. December had borrowed cold of him; midnight, horror; the iron, rust; the plague, miasma; the flowers, perfume. His slow disintegration was a toll paid to all—a toll of the corpse to the storm, to the rain, to the dew, to the reptiles, to the birds. All the dark hands of night had rifled the dead.

He was, indeed, an inexpressibly strange tenant, a tenant of the darkness. He was on a plain and on a hill, and *he was not*. He was palpable, yet vanished. He was a shadow accruing to the night. After the disappearance of day into the vast of silent obscurity, he became in lugubrious accord with all around him. By his mere presence he increased the gloom of the tempest, and the calm of stars. The unutterable which is in the desert was condensed in him. Waif of an unknown fate, he commingled with all the wild secrets of the night. There was in his mystery a vague reverberation of all enigmas.

About him life seemed sinking to its lowest depths. Certainty and confidence appeared to diminish in his environs. The shiver of the brushwood and the grass, a desolate melancholy, an anxiety in which a conscience seemed to lurk, appropriated with tragic force the whole landscape to that black figure suspended by the chain. The presence of a specter in the horizon is an aggravation of solitude.

He was a Sign. Having unappeasable winds around him, he was implacable. Perpetual shuddering made him terrible. Fearful to say, he seemed to be a center in space, with something immense leaning on him. Who can tell? Perhaps that equity, half seen and set at defiance, which transcends human justice. There was in his unburied continuance the vengeance of men and his own vengeance. He was a testimony in the twilight and the waste. He was in himself a disquieting substance, since we tremble before the substance which is the ruined habitation of the soul. For dead matter to trouble us, it must once have been tenanted by spirit. He denounced the law of earth to the law of Heaven. Placed there by man, he there awaited God. Above him floated, blended with all the vague distortions of the cloud and the wave, boundless dreams of shadow.

Who could tell what sinister mysteries lurked behind this phantom? The illimitable circumscribed by nought, nor tree, nor roof, nor passer-by, was around the dead man. When the unchangeable broods over us, when Heaven, the abyss, the life, grave, and eternity appear patent, then it is we feel that all is inaccessible, all is forbidden, all is sealed. When infinity opens to us, terrible indeed is the closing of the gate behind.

Chapter VI

STRUGGLE BETWEEN DEATH AND NIGHT

THE CHILD WAS BEFORE THIS THING, DUMB, WONDERING, AND WITH EYES FIXED.

To a man it would have been a gibbet; to the child it was an apparition.

Where a man would have seen a corpse the child saw a specter.

Besides, he did not understand.

The attractions of the obscure are manifold. There was one on the summit of that hill. The child took a step, then another; he ascended, wishing all the while to descend; and approached, wishing all the while to retreat.

Bold, yet trembling, he went close up to survey the specter.

When he got close under the gibbet, he looked up and examined it.

The specter was tarred; here and there it shone. The child distinguished the face. It was coated over with pitch; and this mask, which appeared viscous and sticky, varied its aspect with the night shadows. The child saw the mouth, which was a hole; the nose, which was a hole; the eyes, which were holes. The body was wrapped, and apparently corded up, in coarse canvas, soaked in naphtha. The canvas was moldy and torn. A knee protruded through it. A rent disclosed the ribs; partly corpse, partly skeleton. The face was the color of earth; slugs, wandering over it, had traced across it vague ribbons of silver. The canvas, glued to the bones, showed in reliefs like the robe of a statue. The skull, cracked and fractured, gaped like a rotten fruit. The teeth were still human, for they retained a laugh. The remains of a cry seemed to murmur in the open mouth. There were a few hairs of beard on the cheek. The inclined head had an air of attention.

Some repairs had recently been done; the face had been tarred afresh, as well as the ribs and the knee which protruded from the canvas. The feet hung out below.

Just underneath, in the grass, were two shoes, which snow and rain had rendered shapeless. These shoes had fallen from the dead man.

The barefooted child looked at the shoes.

The wind, which had become more and more restless, was now and then interrupted by those pauses which foretell the approach of a storm. For the last few minutes it had altogether ceased to blow. The corpse no longer stirred; the chain was as motionless as a plumb line.

Like all newcomers into life, and taking into account the peculiar influences of his fate, the child no doubt felt within him that awakening of ideas characteristic of early years, which endeavors to open the brain and which resembles the pecking of the young bird in the egg. But all that there was in his little consciousness just then was resolved into stupor. Excess of sensation has the effect of too much oil, and ends by putting out thought. A man would have put himself questions; the child put himself none; he only looked.

The tar gave the face a wet appearance; drops of pitch, congealed in what had once been the eyes, produced the effect of tears. However, thanks to the pitch, the ravage of death, if not annulled, was visibly slackened and reduced to the least possible decay. That which was before the child was a thing of which care was taken: the man was evidently precious. They had not cared to keep him alive, but they cared to keep him dead.

The gibbet was old, wormeaten, although strong, and had been in use many years.

It was an immemorial custom in England to tar smugglers. They were hanged on the seaboard, coated over with pitch and left swinging. Examples must be made in public, and tarred examples last longest. The tar was mercy; by renewing it they were spared making too many fresh examples. They placed gibbets from point to point along the coast, as nowadays they do beacons. The hanged man did duty as a lantern. After his fashion, he guided his comrades, the smugglers. The smugglers from far out at sea perceived the gibbets. There is one, first warning; another, second warning. It did not stop smuggling; but public order is made up of such things. The fashion lasted in England up to the beginning of this century. In 1822 three men were still to be seen hanging in front of Dover Castle. But, for that matter, the preserving process was employed not only with smugglers. England turned robbers, incendiaries and murderers to the same account. Jack Painter, who set fire to the government storehouses at Portsmouth, was hanged and tarred in 1776. L'Abbe Coyer, who describes him as Jean le Peintre, saw him again in 1777; Jack Painter was hanging above the ruin he had made, and was retarred from time to time. His corpse lasted—I had almost said lived—nearly fourteen years. It was still doing good service in 1788; in 1790, however, they were obliged to replace it by another. The Egyptians used to value the mummy of the king; a plebeian mummy can also, it appears, be of service.

The wind, having great power on the hill, had swept it of all its snow. Herbage reappeared on it, interspersed here and there with a few thistles; the hill was covered by that close short grass which grows by the sea, and causes the tops of cliffs to resemble green cloth. Under the gibbet, on the very spot over which hung the feet of the executed criminal, was a long and thick tuft, uncommon on such poor soil. Corpses, crumbling there for centuries past, accounted for the beauty of the grass. Earth feeds on man.

A dreary fascination held the child; he remained there open-mouthed. He only dropped his head a moment when a nettle, which felt like an insect, stung his leg; then he looked up again—he looked above him at the face which looked down on him. It appeared to regard him the more steadfastly because it had no eyes. It was a comprehensive glance, having an indescribable fixedness in which there were both light and darkness, and which emanated from the skull and teeth, as well as the empty arches of the brow. The whole head of a dead man seems to have vision, and this is awful. No eyeball, yet we feel that we are looked at. A horror of worms.

Little by little the child himself was becoming an object of terror. He no longer moved. Torpor was coming over him. He did not perceive that he was losing consciousness—he was becoming benumbed and lifeless. Winter was silently delivering him over to night. There is something of the traitor in winter. The child was all but a statue. The coldness of stone was penetrating his bones; darkness, that reptile, was crawling over him. The drowsiness resulting from snow creeps over man like a dim tide. The child was being slowly invaded by a stagnation resembling that of the corpse. He was falling asleep.

On the hand of sleep is the finger of death. The child felt himself seized by that hand. He was on the point of falling under the gibbet. He no longer knew whether he was standing upright.

The end always impending, no transition between to be and not to be, the return into the crucible, the slip possible every minute. Such is the precipice which is Creation.

Another instant, the child and the dead, life in sketch and life in ruin, would be confounded in the same obliteration.

The specter appeared to understand, and not to wish it. Of a sudden it stirred. One would have said it was warning the child. It was the wind beginning to blow again. Nothing stranger than this dead man in movement.

The corpse at the end of the chain, pushed by the invisible gust, took an oblique attitude; rose to the left, then fell back, reascended to the right, and fell and rose with slow and mournful precision. A weird game of see-saw. It seemed as though one saw in the darkness the pendulum of the clock of Eternity.

This continued for some time. The child felt himself waking up at the sight of the dead; through his increasing numbness he experienced a distinct sense of fear.

The chain at every oscillation made a grinding sound, with hideous regularity. It appeared to take breath, and then to resume. This grinding was like the cry of a grasshopper.

An approaching squall is heralded by sudden gusts of wind. All at once the breeze increased into a gale. The corpse emphasized its dismal oscillations. It no longer swung, it tossed; the chain, which had been grinding, now shrieked. It appeared that its shriek was heard. If it was an appeal, it was obeyed. From the depths of the horizon came the sound of a rushing noise.

It was the noise of wings.

An incident occurred, a stormy incident, peculiar to graveyards and solitudes. It was the arrival of a flight of ravens. Black flying specks pricked the clouds, pierced through the mist, increased in size, came near, amalgamated, thickened, hastening toward the hill, uttering cries. It was like the approach of a Legion. The winged vermin of the darkness alighted on the gibbet; the child, scared, drew back.

Swarms obey words of command; the birds crowded on the gibbet, not one was on the corpse. They were talking among themselves. The croaking was frightful. The howl, the whistle and the roar, are signs of life; the croak is a satisfied acceptance of putrefaction. In it you can fancy you hear the tomb breaking silence. The croak is night-like in itself.

The child was frozen even more by terror than by cold.

Then the ravens held silence. One of them perched on the skeleton. This was a signal: they all precipitated themselves upon it. There was a cloud of wings, then all their feathers closed up, and the hanged man disappeared under a swarm of black blisters struggling in the obscurity. Just then the corpse moved. Was it the corpse? Was it the wind? It made a frightful bound. The hurricane, which was increasing, came to its aid. The phantom fell into convulsions. The squall, already blowing with full lungs, laid hold of it, and moved it about in all directions.

It became horrible; it began to struggle. An awful puppet, with a gibbet chain for a string. Some humorist of night must have seized the string and been playing with the mummy. It turned and leapt as if it would fain dislocate itself; the birds, frightened, flew off. It was like an explosion of all those unclean creatures. Then they returned; and a struggle began.

The dead man seemed possessed with hideous vitality. The winds raised him as though they meant to carry him away. He seemed struggling and making efforts to escape, but his iron collar held him back. The birds adapted themselves to all his movements, retreating, then striking again, scared but desperate. On one side a strange flight was attempted, on the other the pursuit of a chained man. The corpse, impelled by every spasm of the wind, had shocks, starts, fits of rage: it went, it came, it rose, it fell, driving back the scattered swarm. The dead man was a club, the swarms were dust. The fierce, assailing flock would not leave their hold, and grew stubborn; the man, as if maddened by the cluster of beaks, redoubled his blind chastisement of space. It was like the blows of a stone held in a sling. At times the corpse was covered by talons and wings; then it was free. There were disappearances of the horde; then sudden furious returns. A frightful torment continuing after life was past. The birds seemed frenzied. The air-holes of hell must surely give passage to such swarms. Thrusting of claws, thrusting of beaks, croakings, rendings of shreds no longer flesh, creakings of the gibbet, shudderings of the skeleton, jingling of the chain, the voices of the storm and tumult. What conflict more fearful? A hobgoblin warring with devils! A combat with a specter!

At times the storm redoubling its violence, the hanged man revolved on his own pivot, turning every way at once toward the swarm, as if he wished to run after the birds; his teeth seemed to try and bite them. The wind was for him, the chain against him. It was as if black deities were mixing themselves up in the fray. The hurricane was in the battle. As the dead man turned himself about, the flock of birds wound round him spirally. It was a whirl in a whirlwind. A great roar was heard from below. It was the sea.

The child saw this nightmare. Suddenly he trembled in all his limbs; a shiver thrilled his frame; he staggered, tottered, nearly fell, recovered himself, pressed both hands to his forehead, as if he felt his forehead a support; then, haggard, his hair streaming in the wind, descending the hill with long strides, his eyes closed, himself almost a phantom, he took flight, leaving behind that torment in the night.

Chapter VII

The North Point of Portland

HE RAN UNTIL HE WAS BREATHLESS, AT RANDOM, DESPERATE, OVER THE PLAIN INTO THE SNOW, into space. His flight warmed him. He needed it. Without the run and the fright he had died.

When his breath failed him, he stopped, but he dared not look back. He fancied that the birds would pursue him, that the dead man had undone his chain and was perhaps hurrying behind him, and no doubt the gibbet itself was descending the hill, running after the dead man; he feared to see these things if he turned his head.

When he had somewhat recovered his breath, he resumed his flight.

To account for facts does not belong to childhood. He received impressions which were magnified by terror, but he did not link them together in his mind, nor form any conclusion on them. He was going on, no matter how or where; he ran in agony and difficulty as one in a dream. During the three hours or so since he had been deserted, his onward progress, still vague, had changed its purpose. At first it was a search, now it was a flight. He no longer felt hunger nor cold—he felt fear. One instinct had given place to another. To escape was now his whole thought—to escape from what? From everything. On all sides life seemed to enclose him like a horrible wall. If he could have fled from all things, he would have done so. But children know nothing of that breaking from prison which is called suicide. He was running. He ran on for an indefinite time; but fear dies with lack of breath.

All at once, as if seized by a sudden accession of energy and intelligence, he stopped. One would have said he was ashamed of running away. He drew himself up, stamped his foot, and, with head erect, looked round. There was no longer hill, nor gibbet, nor flights of crows. The fog had resumed possession of the horizon. The child pursued his way: he now no longer ran but walked. To say that meeting with a corpse had made a man of him would be to limit the manifold and confused impression which possessed him. There was in his impression much more and much less.

The gibbet, a mighty trouble in the rudiment of comprehension, nascent in his mind, still seemed to him an apparition; but a trouble overcome is strength gained, and he felt himself stronger. Had he been of an age to probe self, he would have detected within him a thousand other germs of meditation; but the reflection of children is shapeless, and the utmost they feel is the bitter after-taste of that which, obscure to them, the man later on calls indignation. Let us add that a child has the faculty of quickly accepting the conclusion of a sensation; the distant fading boundaries which amplify painful subjects escape him. A child is protected by the limit of feebleness against emotions which are too complex. He sees the fact, and little else beside. The difficulty of being satisfied by half-ideas does not exist for him. It is not until later that experience comes, with its brief, to conduct the lawsuit of life. *Then* he confronts groups of facts which have crossed his path—the understanding, cultivated and enlarged, draws comparisons—the memories of youth reappear under the passions, like the traces of a palimpsest under the erasure; these memories form the bases of logic, and that which was a vision in the child's brain becomes a syllogism in the man's. Experience is, however, various, and turns to good or evil according to natural disposition. With the good it ripens, with the bad it rots.

The child had run quite a quarter of a league, and walked another quarter, when suddenly he felt the craving of hunger. A thought which altogether eclipsed the hideous apparition on the hill occurred to him forcibly, that he must eat. Happily there is in man a brute which serves to lead him back to reality.

But what to eat, where to eat, how to eat?

He felt his pockets mechanically, well knowing that they were empty. Then he quickened his steps, without knowing whither he was going. He hastened toward a possible shelter. This faith in an inn is one of the convictions enrooted by God in man. To believe in a shelter is to believe in God.

However, in that plain of snow there was nothing like a roof. The child went on, and the waste continued bare as far as eye could see. There had never been a human habitation on the table-land. It was at the foot of the cliff, in holes in the rocks, that, lacking wood to build themselves huts, had dwelt long ago the aboriginal inhabitants, who had slings for arms, dried cow-dung for firing, for a god the idol Heil standing in a glade at Dorchester, and for trade the fishing of that false gray coral which the Gauls called *plin*, and the Greeks *isidis plocamos*.

The child found his way as best he could. Destiny is made up of cross-roads. An option of path is dangerous. This little being had an early choice of doubtful chances.

He continued to advance, but although the muscles of his thighs seemed to be of steel, he began to tire. There were no tracks in the plain, or if there were any, the snow had obliterated them. Instinctively he inclined eastwards. Sharp stones had wounded his heels. Had it been daylight pink stains made by his blood might have been seen in the footprints he left in the snow.

He recognized nothing. He was crossing the plain of Portland from south to north, and it is probable that the band with which he had come, to avoid meeting anyone, had crossed it from east to west; they had most likely sailed in some fisherman's or smuggler's boat, from a point on the coast of Uggescombe, such as St. Catherine's Cape, or Swancry, to Portland to find the hooker which awaited them, and they must have landed in one of the creeks of Weston, and re-embarked in one of those of Easton. That direction was intersected by the one the child was now following. It was impossible for him to recognize the road.

On the plain of Portland there are, here and there, raised strips of land, abruptly ended by the shore and cut perpendicular to the sea. The wandering child reached one of these culminating points and stopped on it, hoping that a larger space might reveal further indications. He tried to see around him. Before him in place of a horizon, was a vast livid opacity. He looked at this attentively, and under the fixedness of his glance it became less indistinct. At the base of a distant fold of land toward the east, in the depths of that opaque lividity (a moving and wan sort of precipice, which resembled a cliff of the night), crept and floated some vague black rents, some dim shreds of vapor.

The pale opacity was fog, the black shreds were smoke. Where there is smoke there are men. The child turned his steps in that direction.

He saw some distance off a descent, and at the foot of the descent, among shapeless conformations of rock, blurred by the mist, what seemed to be either a sandbank or a tongue of land, joining probably to the plains of the horizon the table-land he had just crossed. It was evident he must pass that way.

He had, in fact, arrived at the Isthmus of Portland, a diluvian alluvium which is called Chess Hill.

He began to descend the side of the plateau.

The descent was difficult and rough. It was (with less of ruggedness, however) the reverse of the ascent he had made on leaving the creek. Every ascent is balanced by a decline. After having clambered up he crawled down.

He leapt from one rock to another at the risk of a sprain, at the risk of falling into the vague depths below. To save himself when he slipped on the rock or on the ice, he caught hold of handfuls of weeds and furze, thick with thorns, and their points ran into his fingers. At times he came on an easier declivity, taking breath as he descended; then came on the precipice again, and each step necessitated an expedient. In descending precipices, every movement solves a problem. One must be skillful under pain of death. These problems the child solved with an instinct which would have made him the admiration of apes and mountebanks. The descent was steep and long. Nevertheless he was coming to the end of it.

Little by little it was drawing nearer the moment when he should land on the Isthmus, of which from time to time he caught a glimpse. At intervals, while he bounded or dropped from rock to rock, he pricked up his ears, his head erect, like a listening deer. He was hearkening to a diffused and faint uproar, far away to the left, like the deep note of a clarion. It was a commotion of winds, preceding that fearful north blast which is heard rushing from the pole, like an inroad of trumpets. At the same time the child felt now and then on his brow, on his eyes, on his cheeks, something which was like the palms of cold hands being placed on his face. These were large frozen flakes, sown at first softly in space, then eddying, and heralding a snowstorm. The child was covered with them. The snowstorm, which for the last hour had been on the sea, was beginning to gain the land. It was slowly invading the plains. It was entering obliquely, by the north-west, the table-land of Portland.

BOOK THE SECOND

THE HOOKER AT SEA

Chapter I

SUPERHUMAN LAWS

THE SNOWSTORM IS ONE OF THE MYSTERIES OF THE OCEAN. IT IS THE MOST OBSCURE OF THINGS meteorological; obscure in every sense of the word. It is a mixture of fog and storm; and even in our days we cannot well account for the phenomenon. Hence many disasters.

We try to explain all things by the action of wind and wave; yet in the air there is a force which is not the wind, and in the waters a force which is not the wave. That force, both in the air and in the water, is effluvium. Air and water are two nearly identical liquid masses, entering into the composition of each other by condensation and dilatation, so that to breathe is to drink. Effluvium alone is fluid. The wind and the wave are only impulses; effluvium is a current. The wind is visible in clouds, the wave is visible in foam; effluvium is invisible. From time to time, however, it says, "I am here." Its "I am here" is a clap of thunder.

The snowstorm offers a problem analogous to the dry fog. If the solution of the callina of the Spaniards and the quobar of the Ethiopians be possible, assuredly that solution will be achieved by attentive observation of magnetic effluvium.

Without effluvium a crowd of circumstances would remain enigmatic. Strictly speaking, the changes in the velocity of the wind, varying from 3 feet per second to 220 feet, would supply a reason for the variations of the waves rising from 3 inches in a calm sea to 36 feet in a raging one. Strictly speaking, the horizontal direction of the winds, even in a squall, enables us to understand how it is that a wave 30 feet high can be 1,500 feet long. But why are the waves of the Pacific four times higher near America than near Asia; that is to say, higher in the East than in the West? Why is the contrary true of the Atlantic? Why, under the Equator, are they highest in the middle of the sea? Wherefore these deviations in the swell of the ocean? This is what magnetic effluvium, combined with terrestrial rotation and sidereal attraction, can alone explain.

Is not this mysterious complication needed to explain an oscillation of the wind veering, for instance, by the west from south-east to north-east, then suddenly returning in the same great curve from north-east to south-east, so as to make in thirty-six hours a prodigious circuit of 560 degrees? Such was the preface to the snowstorm of March 17, 1867.

The storm-waves of Australia reach a height of 80 feet; this fact is connected with the vicinity of the Pole. Storms in those latitudes result less from disorder of the winds than from submarine electrical discharges. In the year 1866 the transatlantic cable was disturbed at regular intervals in its working for two hours in the twenty-four, from noon to two o'clock, by a sort of intermittent fever. Certain compositions and decompositions of forces produce phenomena, and impose themselves on the calculations of the seaman under pain of shipwreck. The day that navigation, now a routine, shall become a mathematic; the day we shall, for instance, seek to know why it is that in our regions hot winds come sometimes from the north, and cold winds from the south; the day we shall

understand that diminutions of temperature are proportionate to oceanic depths; the day we realize that the globe is a vast loadstone polarized in immensity, with two axes—an axis of rotation, and
an axis of effluvium, intersecting each other at the center of the earth, and that the magnetic poles
turn round the geographical poles; when those who risk life will choose to risk it scientifically;
when men shall navigate assured from studied uncertainty; when the captain shall be a meteorolo-
gist; when the pilot shall be a chemist; then will many catastrophes be avoided. The sea is magnetic
as much as aquatic: an ocean of unknown forces floats in the ocean of the waves, or, one might say,
on the surface. Only to behold in the sea a mass of water is not to see it at all: the sea is an ebb and
flow of fluid, as much as a flux and reflux of liquid. It is, perhaps, complicated by attractions even
more than by hurricanes; molecular adhesion manifested among other phenomena by capillary attraction, although microscopic, takes in ocean, its place in the grandeur of immensity; and the wave
of effluvium sometimes aids, sometimes counteracts, the wave of the air and the wave of the waters. He who is ignorant of electric law is ignorant of hydraulic law; for the one intermixes with the
other. It is true there is no study more difficult nor more obscure; it verges on empiricism, just as
astronomy verges on astrology; and yet without this study there is no navigation. Having said this
much we will pass on.

One of the most dangerous components of the sea is the snowstorm. The snowstorm is above
all things magnetic. The pole produces it as it produces the aurora borealis. It is in the fog of the one
as in the light of the other; and in the flake of snow as in the streak of flame, effluvium is visible.

Storms are the nervous attacks and delirious frenzies of the sea. The sea has its ailments. Tempests may be compared to maladies. Some are mortal, others not; some may be escaped, others not.
The snowstorm is supposed to be generally mortal. Jarabija, one of the pilots of Magellan, termed
it "a cloud issuing from the devil's sore side."

The old Spanish navigators called this kind of squall *la nevada*, when it came with snow; *la
helada*, when it came with hail. According to them, bats fell from the sky, with the snow.

Snowstorms are characteristic of polar latitudes; nevertheless, at times they glide—one might
almost say tumble—into our climates; so much ruin is mingled with the chances of the air.

The *Matutina*, as we have seen, plunged resolutely into the great hazard of the night, a hazard
increased by the impending storm. She had encountered its menace with a sort of tragic audacity;
nevertheless, it must be remembered that she had received due warning.

Chapter II

OUR FIRST ROUGH SKETCHES FILLED IN

WHILE THE HOOKER WAS IN THE GULF OF PORTLAND, THERE WAS BUT LITTLE SEA ON; THE
ocean, if gloomy, was almost still, and the sky was yet clear. The wind took little effect on
the vessel; the hooker hugged the cliff as closely as possible; it served as a screen to her.

There were ten on board the little Biscayan felucca, three men in crew, and seven passengers,
of whom two were women. In the light of the open sea (which broadens twilight into day) all the
figures on board were clearly visible. Besides they were not hiding now, they were all at ease, each
one reassumed his freedom of manner, spoke in his own note, showed his face: departure was to
them a deliverance.

The motley nature of the group shone out. The women were of no age. A wandering life produces premature old age, and indigence is made up of wrinkles. One of them was a Basque of the

Dry-ports. The other, with the large rosary, was an Irishwoman. They wore that air of indifference common to the wretched. They had squatted down close to each other when they got on board, on chests at the foot of the mast. They talked to each other. Irish and Basque are, as we have said, kindred languages. The Basque woman's hair was scented with onions and basil. The skipper of the hooker was a Basque of Guipuzcoa. One sailor was a Basque of the northern slope of the Pyrenees, the other was of the southern slope—that is to say, they were of the same nation, although the first was French and the latter Spanish. The Basques recognize no official country. *Mi madre se llama Montaña,* my mother is called the mountain, as Zalareus, the muleteer, used to say. Of the five men who were with the two women, one was a Frenchman of Languedoc, one a Frenchman of Provence, one a Genoese; one an old man, he who wore the somberro without a hole for a pipe, appeared to be a German. The fifth, the chief, was a Basque of the Landes from Biscarrosse. It was he who, just as the child was going on board the hooker, had, with a kick of his heel, cast the plank into the sea. This man, robust, agile, sudden in movement, covered, as may be remembered, with trimmings, slashings, and glistening tinsel, could not keep in his place; he stooped down, rose up, and continually passed to and fro from one end of the vessel to the other, as if debating uneasily on what had been done and what was going to happen.

This chief of the band, the captain and the two men of the crew, all four Basques, spoke sometimes Basque, sometimes Spanish, sometimes French—these three languages being common on both slopes of the Pyrenees. But generally speaking, excepting the women, all talked something like French, which was the foundation of their slang. The French language about this period began to be chosen by the peoples as something intermediate between the excess of consonants in the north and the excess of vowels in the south. In Europe, French was the language of commerce, and also of felony. It will be remembered that Gibby, a London thief, understood Cartouche.

The hooker, a fine sailer, was making quick way; still, ten persons, besides their baggage, were a heavy cargo for one of such light draft.

The fact of the vessel's aiding the escape of a band did not necessarily imply that the crew were accomplices. It was sufficient that the captain of the vessel was a Vascongado, and that the chief of the band was another. Among that race mutual assistance is a duty which admits of no exception. A Basque, as we have said, is neither Spanish nor French; he is Basque, and always and everywhere he must succor a Basque. Such is Pyrenean fraternity.

All the time the hooker was in the gulf, the sky, although threatening, did not frown enough to cause the fugitives any uneasiness. They were flying, they were escaping, they were brutally gay. One laughed, another sang; the laugh was dry but free, the song was low but careless.

The Languedocian cried, *"Caoucagno!" "Cocagne"* expresses the highest pitch of satisfaction in Narbonne. He was a longshore sailor, a native of the waterside village of Gruissan, on the southern side of the Clappe, a bargeman rather than a mariner, but accustomed to work the reaches of the inlet of Bages, and to draw the dragnet full of fish over the salt sands of St. Lucie. He was of the race who wear a red cap, make complicated signs of the cross after the Spanish fashion, drink wine out of goat-skins, eat scraped ham, kneel down to blaspheme, and implore their patron saint with threats—"Great saint, grant me what I ask, or I'll throw a stone at thy head, *ou té feg un pic.*" He might be, at need, a useful addition to the crew.

The Provençal in the caboose was blowing up a turf fire under an iron pot, and making broth. The broth was a kind of puchero, in which fish took the place of meat, and into which the Provençal threw chick peas, little bits of bacon cut in squares, and pods of red pimento; concessions made by the eaters of *bouillabaisse* to the eaters of *olla podrida.* One of the bags of provisions was beside him unpacked. He had lighted over his head an iron lantern, glazed with talc, which swung on a hook from the ceiling. By its side, on another hook, swung the weather-cock halcyon. There was a popular belief in those days that a dead halcyon, hung by the beak, always turned its breast to the quarter whence the wind was blowing. While he made the broth, the Provençal put the neck of a gourd into his mouth, and now and then swallowed a draft of aguardiente. It was one of those gourds covered with wicker, broad and flat, with handles, which used to be hung to the side by a strap, and which were then called hip-gourds. Between each gulp he mumbled one of those country songs of which the subject is nothing at all: a hollow road, a hedge; you see in the meadow, through a gap in the bushes, the shadow of a horse and cart, elongated in the sunset, and from time to time, above the hedge, the end of a fork loaded with hay appears and disappears—you want no more to make a song.

A departure, according to the bent of one's mind, is a relief or a depression. All seemed lighter in spirits excepting the old man of the band, the man with the hat that had no pipe.

This old man, who looked more German than anything else, although he had one of those unfathomable faces in which nationality is lost, was bald, and so grave that his baldness might have been a tonsure. Every time he passed before the Virgin on the prow, he raised his felt hat, so that you could see the swollen and senile veins of his skull. A sort of full gown, torn and threadbare, of brown Dorchester serge, but half-hid his closely fitting coat, tight, compact, and hooked up to the neck like a cassock. His hands inclined to cross each other, and had the mechanical junction of habitual prayer. He had what might be called a wan countenance; for the countenance is above all things a reflection, and it is an error to believe that idea is colorless. That countenance was evidently the surface of a strange inner state, the result of a composition of contradictions, some tending to drift away in good, others in evil, and to an observer it was the revelation of one who was less and more than human—capable of falling below the scale of the tiger, or of rising above that of man. Such chaotic souls exist. There was something inscrutable in that face. Its secret reached the abstract. You felt that the man had known the foretaste of evil which is the calculation, and the aftertaste which is the zero. In his impassibility, which was perhaps only on the surface, were imprinted two petrifactions: the petrifaction of the heart proper to the hangman, and the petrifaction of the mind proper to the mandarin. One might have said (for the monstrous has its mode of being complete) that all things were possible to him, even emotion. In every savant there is something of the corpse, and this man was a savant. Only to see him you caught science imprinted in the gestures of his body and in the folds of his dress. His was a fossil face, the serious cast of which was counteracted by that wrinkled mobility of the polyglot which verges on grimace. But a severe man withal; nothing of the hypocrite, nothing of the cynic. A tragic dreamer. He was one of those whom crime leaves pensive, he had the brow of an incendiary tempered by the eyes of an archbishop. His sparse gray locks turned to white over his temples. The Christian was evident in him, complicated with the fatalism of the Turk. Chalkstones deformed his fingers, dissected by leanness. The stiffness of his tall frame was grotesque. He had his sea-legs, he walked slowly about the deck, not looking at anyone, with an air decided and sinister. His eyeballs were vaguely filled with the fixed light of a soul studious of the darkness and afflicted by reapparitions of conscience.

From time to time the chief of the band, abrupt and alert, and making sudden turns about the vessel, came to him and whispered in his ear. The old man answered by a nod. It might have been the lightning consulting the night.

Chapter III

TROUBLED MEN ON THE TROUBLED SEA

TWO MEN ON BOARD THE CRAFT WERE ABSORBED IN THOUGHT—THE OLD MAN, AND THE SKIP-
per of the hooker, who must not be mistaken for the chief of the band. The captain was occupied by the sea, the old man by the sky. The former did not lift his eyes from the waters; the latter
kept watch on the firmament. The skipper's anxiety was the state of the sea; the old man seemed to
suspect the heavens. He scanned the stars through every break in the clouds.

It was the time when day still lingers, but some few stars begin faintly to pierce the twilight.
The horizon was singular. The mist upon it varied. Haze predominated on land, clouds at sea.

The skipper, noting the rising billows, hauled all taut before he got outside Portland Bay. He
would not delay so doing, until he should pass the headland. He examined the rigging closely, and
satisfied himself that the lower shrouds were well set up, and supported firmly the futtock-shrouds;
precautions of a man who means to carry on with a press of sail, at all risks.

The hooker was not trimmed, being two feet by the head. This was her weak point.

The captain passed every minute from the binnacle to the standard compass, taking the bearings of objects on shore. The *Matutina* had at first a soldier's wind which was not unfavorable,
though she could not lie within five points of her course. The captain took the helm as often as possible, trusting no one but himself to prevent her from dropping to leeward, the effect of the rudder
being influenced by the steerage-way.

The difference between the true and apparent course being relative to the way on the vessel,
the hooker seemed to lie closer to the wind than she did in reality. The breeze was not a-beam, nor
was the hooker close-hauled; but one cannot ascertain the true course made, except when the wind
is abaft. When you perceive long streaks of clouds meeting in a point on the horizon, you may be
sure that the wind is in that quarter; but this evening the wind was variable; the needle fluctuated;
the captain distrusted the erratic movements of the vessel. He steered carefully but resolutely, luffed
her up, watched her coming to, prevented her from yawing, and from running into the wind's eye:
noted the leeway, the little jerks of the helm: was observant of every roll and pitch of the vessel, of
the difference in her speed, and of the variable gusts of wind. For fear of accidents, he was constantly on the lookout for squalls from off the land he was hugging, and above all he was cautious
to keep her full; the direction of the breeze indicated by the compass being uncertain from the small
size of the instrument. The captain's eyes, frequently lowered, remarked every change in the waves.

Once nevertheless he raised them toward the sky, and tried to make out the three stars of
Orion's belt. These stars are called the three magi, and an old proverb of the ancient Spanish pilots
declares that, "He who sees the three magi is not far from the Savior."

This glance of the captain's tallied with an aside growled out, at the other end of the vessel,
by the old man, "We don't even see the pointers, nor the star Antares, red as he is. Not one is
distinct."

No care troubled the other fugitives.

Still, when the first hilarity they felt in their escape had passed away, they could not help remembering that they were at sea in the month of January, and that the wind was frozen. It was impossible to establish themselves in the cabin. It was much too narrow and too much encumbered by
bales and baggage. The baggage belonged to the passengers, the bales to the crew, for the hooker
was no pleasure boat, and was engaged in smuggling. The passengers were obliged to settle themselves on deck, a condition to which these wanderers easily resigned themselves. Open-air habits

make it simple for vagabonds to arrange themselves for the night. The open air (*la belle étoile*) is their friend, and the cold helps them to sleep—sometimes to die.

This night, as we have seen, there was no *belle étoile*.

The Languedocian and the Genoese, while waiting for supper, rolled themselves up near the women, at the foot of the mast, in some tarpaulin which the sailors had thrown them.

The old man remained at the bow motionless, and apparently insensible to the cold.

The captain of the hooker, from the helm where he was standing, uttered a sort of guttural call somewhat like the cry of the American bird called the exclaimer; at his call the chief of the band drew near, and the captain addressed him thus—

"Etcheco Jaüna." These two words, which mean "tiller of the mountain," form with the old Cantabri a solemn preface to any subject which should command attention.

Then the captain pointed the old man out to the chief, and the dialogue continued in Spanish; it was not, indeed, a very correct dialect, being that of the mountains. Here are the questions and answers.

"Etcheco jaüna, que es este hombre?"

"Un hombre."

"Que lenguas habla?"

"Todas."

"Que cosas sabe?"

"Todas."

"Qual païs?"

"Ningun, y todos."

"Qual dios?"

"Dios."

"Como le llamas?"

"El tonto."

"Como dices que le llamas?"

"El sabio."

"En vuestre tropa que esta?"

"Esta lo que esta."

"El gefe?"

"No."

"Pues que esta?"

"La alma."[1]

The chief and the captain parted, each reverting to his own meditation, and a little while afterwards the *Matutina* left the gulf.

Now came the great rolling of the open sea. The ocean in the spaces between the foam was slimy in appearance. The waves, seen through the twilight in indistinct outline, somewhat resembled plashes of gall. Here and there a wave floating flat showed cracks and stars, like a pane of glass

---

1. Tiller of the mountain, who is that man?—A man.
  What tongue does he speak?—All.
  What things does he know?—All.
  What is his country?—None and all.
  Who is his God?—God.
  What do you call him?—The madman.
  What do you say you call him?—The wise man.
  In your band, what is he?—He is what he is.
  The chief?—No.
  Then what is he?—The soul.

broken by stones; in the center of these stars, in a revolving orifice, trembled a phosphorescence, like that feline reflection of vanished light which shines in the eyeballs of owls.

Proudly, like a bold swimmer, the *Matutina* crossed the dangerous Shambles shoal. This bank, a hidden obstruction at the entrance of Portland roads, is not a barrier, it is an amphitheater—a circus of sand under the sea, its benches cut out by the circling of the waves—an arena, round and symmetrical, as high as a Jungfrau—only drowned—a coliseum of the ocean, seen by the diver in the vision-like transparency which engulfs him, such is the Shambles shoal. There hydras fight, leviathans meet. There, says the legend, at the bottom of the gigantic shaft, are the wrecks of ships, seized and sunk by the huge spider Kraken, also called the fish-mountain. Such things lie in the fearful shadow of the sea.

These spectral realities, unknown to man, are manifested at the surface by a slight shiver.

In this nineteenth century, the Shambles bank is in ruins; the breakwater recently constructed has overthrown and mutilated, by the force of its surf, that high submarine architecture, just as the jetty, built at the Croisic in 1760, changed, by a quarter of an hour, the course of the tides. And yet the tide is eternal. But eternity obeys man more than man imagines.

Chapter IV

A CLOUD DIFFERENT FROM THE OTHERS ENTERS ON THE SCENE

THE OLD MAN WHOM THE CHIEF OF THE BAND HAD NAMED FIRST THE MADMAN, THEN THE SAGE, now never left the forecastle. Since they crossed the Shambles shoal, his attention had been divided between the heavens and the waters. He looked down, he looked upwards, and above all watched the north-east.

The skipper gave the helm to a sailor, stepped over the after hatchway, crossed the gangway, and went on to the forecastle. He approached the old man, but not in front. He stood a little behind, with elbows resting on his hips, with outstretched hands, the head on one side, with open eyes and arched eyebrows, and a smile in the corners of his mouth, an attitude of curiosity hesitating between mockery and respect.

The old man, either that it was his habit to talk to himself, or that hearing someone behind incited him to speech, began to soliloquize while he looked into space.

"The Meridian, from which the right ascension is calculated, is marked in this century by four stars, the Polar, Cassiopeia's Chair, Andromeda's Head, and the star Algenib, which is in Pegasus. But there is not one visible."

These words followed each other mechanically, confused, and scarcely articulated, as if he did not care to pronounce them. They floated out of his mouth and dispersed. Soliloquy is the smoke exhaled by the inmost fires of the soul.

The skipper broke in, "My lord!"

The old man, perhaps rather deaf as well as very thoughtful, went on—

"Too few stars, and too much wind. The breeze continually changes its direction and blows inshore; thence it rises perpendicularly. This results from the land being warmer than the water. Its atmosphere is lighter. The cold and dense wind of the sea rushes in to replace it. From this cause, in the upper regions the wind blows toward the land from every quarter. It would be advisable to make long tacks between the true and apparent parallel. When the latitude by observation differs from the latitude by dead reckoning, by not more than three minutes in thirty miles, or by four minutes in sixty miles, you are in the true course."

The skipper bowed, but the old man saw him not. The latter, who wore what resembled an Oxford or Gottingen university gown, did not relax his haughty and rigid attitude. He observed the waters as a critic of waves and of men. He studied the billows, but almost as if he was about to demand his turn to speak amidst their turmoil, and teach them something. There was in him both pedagogue and soothsayer. He seemed an oracle of the deep.

He continued his soliloquy, which was perhaps intended to be heard.

"We might strive if we had a wheel instead of a helm. With a speed of twelve miles an hour, a force of twenty pounds exerted on the wheel produces three hundred thousand pounds' effect on the course. And more too. For in some cases, with a double block and runner, they can get two more revolutions."

The skipper bowed a second time, and said, "My lord!"

The old man's eye rested on him, he had turned his head without moving his body.

"Call me Doctor."

"Master Doctor, I am the skipper."

"Just so," said the doctor.

The doctor, as henceforward we shall call him, appeared willing to converse.

"Skipper, have you an English sextant?"

"No."

"Without an English sextant you cannot take an altitude at all."

"The Basques," replied the captain, "took altitudes before there were any English."

"Be careful you are not taken aback."

"I keep her away when necessary."

"Have you tried how many knots she is running?"

"Yes."

"When?"

"Just now."

"How?"

"By the log."

"Did you take the trouble to look at the triangle?"

"Yes."

"Did the sand run through the glass in exactly thirty seconds?"

"Yes."

"Are you sure that the sand has not worn the hole between the globes?"

"Yes."

"Have you proved the sand-glass by the oscillations of a bullet?"

"Suspended by a rope yarn drawn out from the top of a coil of soaked hemp? Undoubtedly."

"Have you waxed the yarn lest it should stretch?"

"Yes."

"Have you tested the log?"

"I tested the sand-glass by the bullet, and checked the log by a round shot."

"Of what size was the shot?"

"One foot in diameter."

"Heavy enough?"

"It is an old round shot of our war hooker, *La Casse de Par-Grand*."

"Which was in the Armada?"

"Yes."

"And which carried six hundred soldiers, fifty sailors, and twenty-five guns?"

"Shipwreck knows it."

"How did you compute the resistance of the water to the shot?"

"By means of a German scale."

"Have you taken into account the resistance of the rope supporting the shot to the waves?"

"Yes."

"What was the result?"

"The resistance of the water was 170 pounds."

"That's to say she is running four French leagues an hour."

"And three Dutch leagues."

"But that is the difference merely of the vessel's way and the rate at which the sea is running?"

"Undoubtedly."

"Whither are you steering?"

"For a creek I know, between Loyola and St. Sebastian."

"Make the latitude of the harbor's mouth as soon as possible."

"Yes, as near as I can."

"Beware of gusts and currents. The first cause the second."

"Traidores."[1]

"No abuse. The sea understands. Insult nothing. Rest satisfied with watching."

"I have watched, and I do watch. Just now the tide is running against the wind; by and by, when it turns, we shall be all right."

"Have you a chart?"

"No; not for this channel."

"Then you sail by rule of thumb?"

"Not at all. I have a compass."

"The compass is one eye, the chart the other."

"A man with one eye can see."

"How do you compute the difference between the true and apparent course?"

"I've got my standard compass, and I make a guess."

"To guess is all very well. To know for certain is better."

"Christopher guessed."

"When there is a fog and the needle revolves treacherously, you can never tell on which side you should look out for squalls, and the end of it is that you know neither the true nor apparent day's work. An ass with his chart is better off than a wizard with his oracle."

"There is no fog in the breeze yet, and I see no cause for alarm."

"Ships are like flies in the spider's web of the sea."

"Just now both winds and waves are tolerably favorable."

"Black specks quivering on the billows, such are men on the ocean."

"I dare say there will be nothing wrong to-night."

"You may get into such a mess that you will find it hard to get out of it."

"All goes well at present."

The doctor's eyes were fixed on the north-east. The skipper continued—

"Let us once reach the Gulf of Gascony, and I answer for our safety. Ah! I should say I am at home there. I know it well, my Gulf of Gascony. It is a little basin, often very boisterous; but there, I know every sounding in it and the nature of the bottom; mud opposite San Cipriano, shells opposite Cizarque, sand off Cape Peñas, little pebbles off Boncaut de Mimizan, and I know the color of every pebble."

The skipper broke off, the doctor was no longer listening.

The doctor gazed at the north-east. Over that icy face passed an extraordinary expression. All the agony of terror possible to a mask of stone was depicted there. From his mouth escaped this word, "Good!"

---

1. Traitors.

His eyeballs, which had all at once become quite round like an owl's, were dilated with stupor on discovering a speck on the horizon. He added—

"It is well. As for me, I am resigned."

The skipper looked at him. The doctor went on talking to himself, or to someone in the deep—

"I say, Yes."

Then he was silent, opened his eyes wider and wider with renewed attention on that which he was watching, and said—

"It is coming from afar, but not the less surely will it come."

The arc of the horizon which occupied the visual rays and thoughts of the doctor, being opposite to the west, was illuminated by the transcendent reflection of twilight, as if it were day. This arc, limited in extent, and surrounded by streaks of grayish vapor, was uniformly blue, but of a leaden rather than cerulean blue. The doctor, having completely returned to the contemplation of the sea, pointed to this atmospheric arc, and said—

"Skipper, do you see?"

"What?"

"That."

"What?"

"Out there."

"A blue spot? Yes."

"What is it?"

"A niche in heaven."

"For those who go to heaven; for those who go elsewhere—it is another affair." And he emphasized these enigmatical words with an appalling expression which was unseen in the darkness.

A silence ensued. The skipper, remembering the two names given by the chief to this man, asked himself the question—

"Is he a madman, or is he a sage?"

The stiff and bony finger of the doctor remained immovably pointing, like a sign-post, to the misty blue spot in the sky.

The skipper looked at this spot.

"In truth," he growled out, "it is not sky but clouds."

"A blue cloud is worse than a black cloud," said the doctor; "and," he added, "it's a snow-cloud."

"La nube de la nieve," said the skipper, as if trying to understand the word better by translating it.

"Do you know what a snow-cloud is?" asked the doctor.

"No."

"You'll know by and by."

The skipper again turned his attention to the horizon.

Continuing to observe the cloud, he muttered between his teeth—

"One month of squalls, another of wet; January with its gales, February with its rains, that's all the winter we Asturians get. Our rain even is warm. We've no snow but on the mountains. Ay, ay, look out for the avalanche. The avalanche is no respecter of persons. The avalanche is a brute."

"And the waterspout is a monster," said the doctor, adding, after a pause, "Here it comes." He continued, "Several winds are getting up together. A strong wind from the west, and a gentle wind from the east."

"That last is a deceitful one," said the skipper.

The blue cloud was growing larger.

"If the snow," said the doctor, "is appalling when it slips down the mountain, think what it is when it falls from the Pole!"

His eye was glassy. The cloud seemed to spread over his face and simultaneously over the horizon. He continued, in musing tones—

"Every minute the fatal hour draws nearer. The will of heaven is about to be manifested."

The skipper asked himself again this question—"Is he a madman?"

"Skipper," began the doctor, without taking his eyes off the cloud, "have you often crossed the Channel?"

"This is the first time."

The doctor, who was absorbed by the blue cloud, and who, as a sponge can take up but a definite quantity of water, had but a definite measure of anxiety, displayed no more emotion at this answer of the skipper than was expressed by a slight shrug of his shoulders.

"How is that?"

"Master Doctor, my usual cruise is to Ireland. I sail from Fontarabia to Black Harbor, or to the Achill Islands. I go sometimes to Braich-y-Pwll, a point on the Welsh coast. But I always steer outside the Scilly Islands. I do not know this sea at all."

"That's serious. Woe to him who is inexperienced on the ocean! One ought to be familiar with the Channel: the Channel is the Sphinx. Look out for shoals."

"We are in twenty-five fathoms here."

"We ought to get into fifty-five fathoms to the west, and avoid even twenty fathoms to the east."

"We'll sound as we get on."

"The Channel is not an ordinary sea. The water rises fifty feet with the spring tides, and twenty-five with neap tides. Here we are in slack water. I thought you looked scared."

"We'll sound to-night."

"To sound you must heave to, and that you cannot do."

"Why not?"

"On account of the wind."

"We'll try."

"The squall is close on us."

"We'll sound, Master Doctor."

"You could not even bring to."

"Trust in God."

"Take care what you say. Pronounce not lightly the awful name."

"I will sound, I tell you."

"Be sensible; you will have a gale of wind presently."

"I say that I will try for soundings."

"The resistance of the water will prevent the lead from sinking, and the line will break. Ah! so this is your first time in these waters?"

"The first time."

"Very well; in that case listen, skipper."

The tone of the word Listen was so commanding that the skipper made an obeisance.

"Master Doctor, I am all attention."

"Port your helm, and haul up on the starboard tack."

"What do you mean?"

"Steer your course to the west."

"Caramba!"

"Steer your course to the west."

"Impossible."

"As you will. What I tell you is for the others' sake. As for myself, I am indifferent."

"But, Master Doctor, steer west?"

"Yes, skipper."

"The wind will be dead ahead."

"Yes, skipper."

"She'll pitch like the devil."

"Moderate your language. Yes, skipper."

"The vessel would be in irons."

"Yes, skipper."

"That means very likely the mast will go."

"Possibly."

"Do you wish me to steer west?"

"Yes."

"I cannot."

"In that case settle your reckoning with the sea."

"The wind ought to change."

"It will not change all night."

"Why not?"

"Because it is a wind 1200 leagues in length."

"Make headway against such a wind. Impossible."

"To the west, I tell you."

"I'll try, but in spite of everything she will fall off."

"That's the danger."

"The wind sets us to the east."

"Don't go to the east."

"Why not?"

"Skipper, do you know what is for us the word of death?"

"No."

"Death is the east."

"I'll steer west."

This time the doctor, having turned right round, looked the skipper full in the face, and with his eyes resting on him, as though to implant the idea in his head, pronounced slowly, syllable by syllable, these words—

"If to-night out at sea, we hear the sound of a bell, the ship is lost."

The skipper pondered in amaze.

"What do you mean?"

The doctor did not answer. His countenance, expressive for a moment, was now reserved. His eyes became vacuous. He did not appear to hear the skipper's wondering question. He was now attending to his own monologue. His lips let fall, as if mechanically, in a low murmuring tone, these words—

"The time has come for sullied souls to purify themselves."

The skipper made that expressive grimace, which raises the chin toward the nose.

"He is more madman than sage," he growled, and moved off.

Nevertheless he steered west.

But the wind and the sea were rising.

Chapter V

HARDQUANONNE

THE MIST WAS DEFORMED BY ALL SORTS OF INEQUALITIES, BULGING OUT AT ONCE ON EVERY point of the horizon, as if invisible mouths were busy puffing out the bags of wind. The formation of the clouds was becoming ominous. In the west, as in the east, the sky's depths were now invaded by the blue cloud: it advanced in the teeth of the wind. These contradictions are part of the wind's vagaries.

The sea, which a moment before wore scales, now wore a skin—such is the nature of that dragon. It was no longer a crocodile, it was a boa. The skin, lead-colored and dirty, looked thick, and was crossed by heavy wrinkles. Here and there, on its surface, bubbles of surge, like pustules, gathered and then burst. The foam was like a leprosy. It was at this moment that the hooker, still seen from afar by the child, lighted her signal.

A quarter of an hour elapsed.

The skipper looked for the doctor: he was no longer on deck. Directly the skipper had left him, the doctor had stooped his somewhat ungainly form under the hood, and had entered the cabin: there he had sat down near the stove, on a block. He had taken a shagreen ink-bottle and a cordwain pocket-book from his pocket; he had extracted from his pocket-book a parchment folded four times, old, stained, and yellow; he had opened the sheet, taken a pen out of his ink-case, placed the pocket-book flat on his knee, and the parchment on the pocket-book; and by the rays of the lantern, which was lighting the cook, he set to writing on the back of the parchment. The roll of the waves inconvenienced him. He wrote thus for some time.

As he wrote, the doctor remarked the gourd of aguardiente, which the Provençal tasted every time he added a grain of pimento to the puchero, as if he were consulting it in reference to the seasoning. The doctor noticed the gourd, not because it was a bottle of brandy, but because of a name which was plaited in the wickerwork with red rushes on a background of white. There was light enough in the cabin to permit of his reading the name.

The doctor paused, and spelled it in a low voice—

"Hardquanonne."

Then he addressed the cook.

"I had not observed that gourd before; did it belong to Hardquanonne?"

"Yes," the cook answered; "to our poor comrade, Hardquanonne."

The doctor went on.

"To Hardquanonne, the Fleming of Flanders?"

"Yes."

"Who is in prison?"

"Yes."

"In the dungeon at Chatham?"

"It is his gourd," replied the cook; "and he was my friend. I keep it in remembrance of him. When shall we see him again? It is the bottle he used to wear slung over his hip."

The doctor took up his pen again, and continued laboriously tracing somewhat straggling lines on the parchment. He was evidently anxious that his handwriting should be very legible; and, at length, notwithstanding the tremulousness of the vessel and the tremulousness of age, he finished what he wanted to write.

It was time, for, suddenly, a sea struck the craft, a mighty rush of waters besieged the hooker, and they felt her break into that fearful dance in which ships lead off with the tempest.

The doctor arose and approached the stove, meeting the ship's motion with his knees dexterously bent, dried as best he could, at the stove where the pot was boiling, the lines he had written, refolded the parchment in the pocket-book, and replaced the pocket-book and the inkhorn in his pocket.

The stove was not the least ingenious piece of interior economy in the hooker. It was judiciously isolated. Meanwhile, the pot heaved—the Provençal was watching it.

"Fish broth," said he.

"For the fishes," replied the doctor. Then he went on deck again.

Chapter VI

THEY THINK THAT HELP IS AT HAND

THROUGH HIS GROWING PREOCCUPATION, THE DOCTOR IN SOME SORT REVIEWED THE SITUATION; and anyone near to him might have heard these words drop from his lips—

"Too much rolling, and not enough pitching."

Then recalled to himself by the dark workings of his mind, he sank again into thought, as a miner into his shaft. His meditation in nowise interfered with his watch on the sea. The contemplation of the sea is in itself a reverie.

The dark punishment of the waters, eternally tortured, was commencing. A lamentation arose from the whole main. Preparations, confused and melancholy, were forming in space. The doctor observed all before him, and lost no detail. There was, however, no sign of scrutiny in his face. One does not scrutinize hell.

A vast commotion, yet half latent, but visible through the turmoils in space, increased and irritated, more and more, the winds, the vapors, the waves. Nothing is so logical and nothing appears so absurd as the ocean. Self dispersion is the essence of its sovereignty, and is one of the elements of its redundance. The sea is ever for and against. It knots, that it may unravel itself; one of its slopes attacks, the other relieves. No apparition is so wonderful as the waves. Who can paint the alternating hollows and promontories, the valleys, the melting bosoms, the sketches? How render the thickets of foam, blendings of mountains and dreams? The indescribable is everywhere there, in the rending, in the frowning, in the anxiety, in the perpetual contradiction, in the chiaroscuro, in the pendants of the cloud, in the keys of the ever-open vault, in the disaggregation without rupture, in the funereal tumult caused by all that madness!

The wind had just set due north. Its violence was so favorable and so useful in driving them away from England that the captain of the *Matutina* had made up his mind to set all sail. The hooker slipped through the foam as at a gallop, the wind right aft, bounding from wave to wave in a gay frenzy. The fugitives were delighted, and laughed; they clapped their hands, applauded the surf, the sea, the wind, the sails, the swift progress, the flight, all unmindful of the future. The doctor appeared not to see them, and dreamt on.

Every vestige of day had faded away. This was the moment when the child, watching from the distant cliff, lost sight of the hooker. Up to then, his glance had remained fixed, and, as it were, leaning on the vessel. What part had that look in fate? When the hooker was lost to sight in the distance, and when the child could no longer see aught, the child went north and the ship went south.

All were plunged in darkness.

Chapter VII

SUPERHUMAN HORRORS

O N THEIR PART IT WAS WITH WILD JUBILEE AND DELIGHT THAT THOSE ON BOARD THE HOOKER saw the hostile land recede and lessen behind them. By degrees the dark ring of ocean rose higher, dwarfing in twilight Portland, Purbeck, Tineham, Kimmeridge, the Matravers, the long streaks of dim cliffs, and the coast dotted with lighthouses.

England disappeared. The fugitives had now nothing round them but the sea.

All at once night grew awful.

There was no longer extent nor space; the sky became blackness, and closed in round the vessel. The snow began to fall slowly; a few flakes appeared. They might have been ghosts. Nothing else was visible in the course of the wind. They felt as if yielded up. A snare lurked in every possibility.

It is in this cavernous darkness that in our climate the polar waterspout makes its appearance.

A great muddy cloud, like to the belly of a hydra, hung over ocean, and in places its lividity adhered to the waves. Some of these adherences resembled pouches with holes, pumping the sea, disgorging vapor, and refilling themselves with water. Here and there these suctions drew up cones of foam on the sea.

The boreal storm hurled itself on the hooker. The hooker rushed to meet it. The squall and the vessel met as though to insult each other.

In the first mad shock not a sail was clewed up, not a jib lowered, not a reef taken in, so much is flight a delirium. The mast creaked and bent back as if in fear.

Cyclones, in our northern hemisphere, circle from left to right, in the same direction as the hands of a watch, with a velocity which is sometimes as much as 60 miles an hour. Although she was entirely at the mercy of that whirling power, the hooker behaved as if she were out in moderate weather, without any further precaution than keeping her head on to the rollers, with the wind broad on the bow so as to avoid being pooped or caught broadside on. This semi-prudence would have availed her nothing in case of the wind's shifting and taking her aback.

A deep rumbling was brewing up in the distance. The roar of the abyss, nothing can be compared to it. It is the great brutish howl of the universe. What we call matter, that unsearchable organism, that amalgamation of incommensurable energies, in which can occasionally be detected an almost imperceptible degree of intention which makes us shudder, that blind, benighted cosmos, that enigmatical Pan, has a cry, a strange cry, prolonged, obstinate, and continuous, which is less than speech and more than thunder. That cry is the hurricane. Other voices, songs, melodies, clamors, tones, proceed from nests, from broods, from pairings, from nuptials, from homes. This one, a trumpet, comes out of the Naught, which is All. Other voices express the soul of the universe, this one expresses the monster. It is the howl of the formless. It is the inarticulate, finding utterance in the indefinite. A thing it is full of pathos and terror. Those clamors converse above and beyond man. They rise, fall, undulate, determine waves of sound, form all sorts of wild surprises for the mind, now burst close to the ear with the importunity of a peal of trumpets, now assail us with the rumbling hoarseness of distance. Giddy uproar which resembles a language, and which, in fact, is a language. It is the effort which the world makes to speak. It is the lisping of the wonderful. In this wail is manifested vaguely all that the vast dark palpitation endures, suffers, accepts, rejects. For the most part it talks nonsense; it is like an access of chronic sickness, and rather an epilepsy diffused than a force employed; we fancy that we are witnessing the descent of supreme evil into the infinite. At moments we seem to discern a reclamation of the elements, some vain effort of chaos to reassert itself over creation. At times it is a complaint. The void bewails and justifies itself. It is as the pleading of the world's cause. We can fancy that the universe is engaged in a lawsuit; we listen, we try to grasp the reasons given, the redoubtable for and against. Such a moaning of the shadows has the tenacity of a syllogism. Here is a vast trouble for thought. Here is the *raison d'être* of mythologies and polytheisms. To the terror of those great murmurs are added superhuman outlines melting away as they appear—Eumenides which are almost distinct, throats of furies shaped in the clouds, Plutonian chimeras almost defined. No horrors equal those sobs, those laughs, those tricks of tumult, those inscrutable questions and answers, those appeals to unknown aid. Man knows not what to become in the presence of that awful incantation. He bows under the enigma of those Draconian intonations. What latent meaning have they? What do they signify? What do they threaten? What do they implore? It would seem as though all bonds were loosened. Vociferations from precipice to precipice, from air to water, from the wind to the wave, from the rain to the rock, from the zenith to the nadir, from the stars to the foam—the abyss unmuzzled—such is that tumult, complicated by some mysterious strife with evil consciences.

The loquacity of night is not less lugubrious than its silence. One feels in it the anger of the unknown.

Night is a presence. Presence of what?

For that matter we must distinguish between night and the shadows. In the night there is the absolute; in the darkness the multiple. Grammar, logic as it is, admits of no singular for the shadows. The night is one, the shadows are many.

This mist of nocturnal mystery is the scattered, the fugitive, the crumbling, the fatal; one feels earth no longer, one feels the other reality.

In the shadow, infinite and indefinite, lives something or someone; but that which lives there forms part of our death. After our earthly passage, when that shadow shall be light for us, the life which is beyond our life shall seize us. Meanwhile it appears to touch and try us. Obscurity is a pressure. Night is, as it were, a hand placed on our soul. At certain hideous and solemn hours we feel that which is beyond the wall of the tomb encroaching on us.

Never does this proximity of the unknown seem more imminent than in storms at sea. The horrible combines with the fantastic. The possible interrupter of human actions, the old Cloud compeller, has it in his power to mold, in whatsoever shape he chooses, the inconsistent element, the limitless incoherence, the force diffused and undecided of aim. That mystery the tempest every instant accepts and executes some unknown changes of will, apparent or real.

Poets have, in all ages, called this the caprice of the waves. But there is no such thing as caprice. The disconcerting enigmas which in nature we call caprice, and in human life chance, are splinters of a law revealed to us in glimpses.

Chapter VIII

NIL ET NOX

THE CHARACTERISTIC OF THE SNOWSTORM IS ITS BLACKNESS. NATURE'S HABITUAL ASPECT DURing a storm, the earth or sea black and the sky pale, is reversed; the sky is black, the ocean white, foam below, darkness above; a horizon walled in with smoke; a zenith roofed with crape. The tempest resembles a cathedral hung with mourning, but no light in that cathedral: no phantom lights on the crests of the waves, no spark, no phosphorescence, naught but a huge shadow. The polar cyclone differs from the tropical cyclone, inasmuch as the one sets fire to every light, and the other extinguishes them all. The world is suddenly converted into the arched vault of a cave. Out of the night falls a dust of pale spots, which hesitate between sky and sea. These spots, which are flakes of snow, slip, wander, and float. It is like the tears of a winding-sheet putting themselves into lifelike motion. A mad wind mingles with this dissemination. Blackness crumbling into whiteness, the furious into the obscure, all the tumult of which the sepulcher is capable, a whirlwind under a catafalque—such is the snowstorm. Underneath trembles the ocean, forming and reforming over portentous unknown depths.

In the polar wind, which is electrical, the flakes turn suddenly into hailstones, and the air becomes filled with projectiles; the water crackles, shot with grape.

No thunderstrokes: the lightning of boreal storms is silent. What is sometimes said of the cat, "it swears," may be applied to this lightning. It is a menace proceeding from a mouth half-open, and strangely inexorable. The snowstorm is a storm blind and dumb; when it has passed, the ships also are often blind and the sailors dumb.

To escape from such an abyss is difficult.

It would be wrong, however, to believe shipwreck to be absolutely inevitable. The Danish fishermen of Disco and the Balesin; the seekers of black whales; Hearn, steering toward Behring Strait, to discover the mouth of Coppermine River; Hudson, Mackenzie, Vancouver, Ross, Dumont D'Urville, all underwent at the Pole itself the wildest hurricanes, and escaped out of them.

It was into this description of tempest that the hooker had entered, triumphant and in full sail. Frenzy against frenzy. When Montgomery, escaping from Rouen, threw his galley, with all the force of its oars, against the chain barring the Seine at La Bouille, he showed similar effrontery.

The *Matutina* sailed on fast; she bent so much under her sails that at moments she made a fearful angle with the sea of fifteen degrees; but her good bellied keel adhered to the water as if glued to it. The keel resisted the grasp of the hurricane. The lantern at the prow cast its light ahead.

The cloud, full of winds, dragging its tumor over the deep, cramped and eat more and more into the sea round the hooker. Not a gull, not a sea-mew, nothing but snow. The expanse of the field of waves was becoming contracted and terrible; only three or four gigantic ones were visible.

Now and then a tremendous flash of lightning of a red copper color broke out behind the obscure superposition of the horizon and the zenith; that sudden release of vermilion flame revealed the horror of the clouds; that abrupt conflagration of the depths, to which for an instant the first tiers of clouds and the distant boundaries of the celestial chaos seemed to adhere, placed the abyss in perspective. On this ground of fire the snow-flakes showed black; they might have been compared to dark butterflies flying about in a furnace—then all was extinguished.

The first explosion over, the squall, still pursuing the hooker, began to roar in thorough bass. This phase of grumbling is a perilous diminution of uproar. Nothing is so terrifying as this monologue of the storm. This gloomy recitative appears to serve as a moment of rest to the mysterious combating forces, and indicates a species of patrol kept in the unknown.

The hooker held wildly on her course. Her two mainsails especially were doing fearful work. The sky and sea were as of ink with jets of foam running higher than the mast. Every instant masses of water swept the deck like a deluge, and at each roll of the vessel, the hawse-holes, now to starboard now to larboard, became as so many open mouths vomiting back the foam into the sea. The women had taken refuge in the cabin, but the men remained on deck; the blinding snow eddied round, the spitting surge mingled with it. All was fury.

At that moment the chief of the band, standing abaft on the stern-frames, holding on with one hand to the shrouds, and with the other taking off the kerchief he wore round his head and waving it in the light of the lantern, gay and arrogant, with pride in his face, and his hair in wild disorder, intoxicated by all the darkness, cried out—

"We are free!"

"Free, free, free," echoed the fugitives, and the band, seizing hold of the rigging, rose up on deck.

"Hurrah!" shouted the chief.

And the band shouted in the storm—

"Hurrah!"

Just as this clamor was dying away in the tempest, a loud solemn voice rose from the other end of the vessel, saying—

"Silence!"

All turned their heads. The darkness was thick, and the doctor was leaning against the mast so that he seemed part of it, and they could not see him.

The voice spoke again—

"Listen!"

All were silent.

Then did they distinctly hear through the darkness the toll of a bell.

Chapter IX

THE CHARGE CONFIDED TO A RAGING SEA

THE SKIPPER, AT THE HELM, BURST OUT LAUGHING—

"A bell, that's good. We are on the larboard tack. What does the bell prove? Why, that we have land to starboard."

The firm and measured voice of the doctor replied—

"You have not land to starboard."

"But we have," shouted the skipper.

"No!"

"But that bell tolls from the land."

"That bell," said the doctor, "tolls from the sea."

A shudder passed over these daring men, the haggard faces of the two women appeared above the companion like two hobgoblins conjured up: the doctor took a step forward, separating his tall form from the mast. From the depth of the night's darkness came the toll of the bell.

The doctor resumed—

"There is in the midst of the sea, halfway between Portland and the Channel Islands, a buoy, placed there as a caution; that buoy is moored by chains to the shoal, and floats on the top of the water. On the buoy is fixed an iron trestle, and across the trestle a bell is hung. In bad weather heavy seas toss the buoy, and the bell rings. That is the bell you hear."

The doctor paused to allow an extra-violent gust of wind to pass over, waited until the sound of the bell reasserted itself, and then went on—

"To hear that bell in a storm, when the nor'-wester is blowing, is to be lost. Wherefore? For this reason: if you hear the bell, it is because the wind brings it to you. But the wind is nor'-westerly, and the breakers of Aurigny lie east. You hear the bell only because you are between the buoy and the breakers. It is on those breakers the wind is driving you. You are on the wrong side of the buoy. If you were on the right side, you would be out at sea on a safe course, and you would not hear the bell. The wind would not convey the sound to you. You would pass close to the buoy without knowing it. We are out of our course. That bell is shipwreck sounding the tocsin. Now, look out!"

As the doctor spoke the bell, soothed by a lull of the storm, rang slowly stroke by stroke, and its intermitting toll seemed to testify to the truth of the old man's words. It was as the knell of the abyss.

All listened breathless. Now to the voice. Now to the bell.

Chapter X

THE COLOSSAL SAVAGE, THE STORM

IN THE MEANTIME THE SKIPPER HAD CAUGHT UP HIS SPEAKING-TRUMPET.

"Strike every sail, my lads; let go the sheets, man the down-hauls, lower ties and brails. Let us steer to the west, let us regain the high sea; head for the buoy, steer for the bell, there's an offing down there. We've yet a chance."

"Try," said the doctor.

Let us remark here, by the way, that this ringing buoy, a kind of bell tower on the deep, was removed in 1802. There are yet alive very old mariners who remember hearing it. It forewarned, but rather too late.

The orders of the skipper were obeyed. The Languedocian made a third sailor. All bore a hand. Not satisfied with brailing up, they furled the sails, lashed the earrings, secured the clew-lines, bunt-lines, and leech-lines, and clapped preventor-shrouds on the block straps, which thus might serve as back-stays. They fished the mast. They battened down the ports and bulls' eyes, which is a method of walling up a ship. These evolutions, though executed in a lubberly fashion, were, nevertheless, thoroughly effective. The hooker was stripped to bare poles. But, in proportion as the vessel, stowing every stitch of canvas, became more helpless, the havoc of both winds and waves increased. The seas ran mountains high. The hurricane, like an executioner hastening to his victim, began to dismember the craft. There came, in the twinkling of an eye, a dreadful crash: the top-sails were blown from the bolt-ropes, the chess-trees were hewn asunder, the deck was swept clear, the shrouds were carried away, the mast went by the board, all the lumber of the wreck was flying in shivers. The main shrouds gave out although they were turned in, and stoppered to four fathoms.

The magnetic currents common to snowstorms hastened the destruction of the rigging. It broke as much from the effect of effluvium as the violence of the wind. Most of the chain gear, fouled in the blocks, ceased to work. Forward the bows, aft the quarters, quivered under the terrific shocks. One wave washed overboard the compass and its binnacle. A second carried away the boat, which, like a box slung under a carriage, had been, in accordance with the quaint Asturian custom, lashed to the bow-sprit. A third breaker wrenched off the spritsail yard. A fourth swept away the figurehead and signal light. The rudder only was left.

To replace the ship's bow lantern they set fire to, and suspended at the stem, a large block of wood covered with oakum and tar.

The mast, broken in two, all bristling with quivering splinters, ropes, blocks, and yards, cumbered the deck. In falling it had stove in a plank of the starboard gunwale. The skipper, still firm at the helm, shouted—

"While we can steer we have yet a chance. The lower planks hold good. Axes, axes! Overboard with the mast! Clear the decks!"

Both crew and passengers worked with the excitement of despair.

A few strokes of the hatchets, and it was done. They pushed the mast over the side. The deck was cleared.

"Now," continued the skipper, "take a rope's end and lash me to the helm." To the tiller they bound him.

While they were fastening him he laughed, and shouted—

"Blow, old hurdy-gurdy, bellow. I've seen your equal off Cape Machichaco."

And when secured, he clutched the helm with that strange hilarity which danger awakens.

"All goes well, my lads. Long live our Lady of Buglose; let us steer west."

An enormous wave came down abeam, and fell on the vessel's quarter. There is always in storms a tiger-like wave, a billow fierce and decisive, which, attaining a certain height, creeps horizontally over the surface of the waters for a time, then rises, roars, rages, and falling on the distressed vessel, tears it limb from limb.

A cloud of foam covered the entire poop of the *Matutina*.

There was heard above the confusion of darkness and waters a crash.

When the spray cleared off, when the stern again rose in view, the skipper and the helm had disappeared. Both had been swept away.

The helm and the man they had but just secured to it had passed with the wave into the hissing turmoil of the hurricane.

The chief of the band, gazing intently into the darkness, shouted—

"Te burlas de nosotros?"

To this defiant exclamation there followed another cry—

"Let go the anchor. Save the skipper."

They rushed to the capstan and let go the anchor.

Hookers carry but one. In this case the anchor reached the bottom, but only to be lost. The bottom was of the hardest rock. The billows were raging with resistless force. The cable snapped like a thread.

The anchor lay at the bottom of the sea. At the cutwater there remained but the cable end protruding from the hawse-hole.

From this moment the hooker became a wreck. The *Matutina* was irrevocably disabled. The vessel, just before in full sail, and almost formidable in her speed, was now helpless. All her evolutions were uncertain and executed at random. She yielded passively and like a log to the capricious fury of the waves. That in a few minutes there should be in place of an eagle a useless cripple, such a transformation is to be witnessed only at sea.

The howling of the wind became more and more frightful. A hurricane has terrible lungs; it makes unceasingly mournful additions to darkness, which cannot be intensified. The bell on the sea rang despairingly, as if tolled by a weird hand.

The *Matutina* drifted like a cork at the mercy of the waves. She sailed no longer—she merely floated. Every moment she seemed about to turn over on her back, like a dead fish. The good condition and perfectly water-tight state of the hull alone saved her from this disaster. Below the wateline not a plank had started. There was not a cranny, chink, nor crack; and she had not made a single drop of water in the hold. This was lucky, as the pump, being out of order, was useless.

The hooker pitched and roared frightfully in the seething billows. The vessel had throes as of sickness, and seemed to be trying to belch forth the unhappy crew.

Helpless they clung to the standing rigging, to the transoms, to the shank painters, to the gaskets, to the broken planks, the protruding nails of which tore their hands, to the warped riders, and to all the rugged projections of the stumps of the masts. From time to time they listened. The toll of the bell came over the waters fainter and fainter; one would have thought that it also was in distress. Its ringing was no more than an intermittent rattle. Then this rattle died away. Where were they? At what distance from the buoy? The sound of the bell had frightened them—its silence terrified them. The north-wester drove them forward in, perhaps, a fatal course. They felt themselves wafted on by maddened and ever-recurring gusts of wind. The wreck sped forward in the darkness. There is nothing more fearful than being hurried forward blindfolded. They felt the abyss before them, over them, under them. It was no longer a run, it was a rush.

Suddenly, through the appalling density of the snowstorm, there loomed a red light.

"A lighthouse!" cried the crew.

Chapter XI

THE CASKETS

IT WAS INDEED THE CASKETS LIGHT.

A lighthouse of the nineteenth century is a high cylinder of masonry, surmounted by scientifically constructed machinery for throwing light. The Caskets lighthouse in particular is a triple white tower, bearing three light-rooms. These three chambers revolve on clockwork wheels, with such precision that the man on watch who sees them from sea, can invariably take ten steps during their irradiation, and twenty-five during their eclipse. Everything is based on the focal plan, and on the rotation of the octagon drum, formed of eight wide simple lenses, in range, having above and below it two series of dioptric rings; an algebraic gear, secured from the effects of the beating of winds and waves by glass a millimeter thick, yet sometimes broken by the sea-eagles, which dash themselves like great moths against these gigantic lanterns. The building which encloses and sustains this mechanism, and in which it is set, is also mathematically constructed. Everything about it is plain, exact, bare, precise, correct. A lighthouse is a mathematical figure.

In the seventeenth century a lighthouse was a sort of plume of the land on the seashore. The architecture of a lighthouse tower was magnificent and extravagant. It was covered with balconies, balusters, lodges, alcoves, weathercocks. Nothing but masks, statues, foliage, volutes, reliefs, figures large and small, medallions with inscriptions. *Pax in bello,* said the Eddystone lighthouse. We may as well observe, by the way, that this declaration of peace did not always disarm the ocean. Winstanley repeated it on a lighthouse which he constructed at his own expense, on a wild spot near Plymouth. The tower being finished, he shut himself up in it to have it tried by the tempest. The storm came and carried off the lighthouse, and Winstanley in it. Such excessive adornment gave too great a hold to the hurricane, as generals too brilliantly equipped in battle draw the enemy's fire. Besides whimsical designs in stone, they were loaded with whimsical designs in iron, copper, and wood. The ironwork was in relief, the woodwork stood out. On the sides of the lighthouse there jutted out, clinging to the walls among the arabesques, engines of every description, useful and useless, windlasses, tackles, pulleys, counterpoises, ladders, cranes, grapnels. On the pinnacle around the light, delicately-wrought ironwork held great iron chandeliers, in which were placed pieces of rope steeped in resin; wicks which burned doggedly, and which no wind extinguished; and from top to bottom the tower was covered by a complication of sea standards, banderoles, banners, flags, pennons, colors which rose from stage to stage, from story to story, a medley of all hues, all shapes, all heraldic devices, all signals, all confusion, up to the light chamber, making, in the storm, a gay riot of tatters about the blaze. That insolent light on the brink of the abyss showed like a defiance, and inspired shipwrecked men with a spirit of daring. But the Caskets light was not after this fashion.

It was, at that period, merely an old barbarous lighthouse, such as Henry I had built it after the loss of the *White Ship*—a flaming pile of wood under an iron trellis, a brazier behind a railing, a head of hair flaming in the wind.

The only improvement made in this lighthouse since the twelfth century was a pair of forge-bellows worked by an indented pendulum and a stone weight, which had been added to the light chamber in 1610.

The fate of the sea-birds who chanced to fly against these old lighthouses was more tragic than those of our days. The birds dashed against them, attracted by the light, and fell into the brazier, where they could be seen struggling like black spirits in a hell, and at times they would fall back again between the railings upon the rock, red hot, smoking, lame, blind, like half-burned flies out of a lamp.

To a full-rigged ship in good trim, answering readily to the pilot's handling, the Caskets light is useful; it cries—Look out; it warns her of the shoal. To a disabled ship it is simply terrible. The hull, paralyzed and inert, without resistance, without defense against the impulse of the storm, or the mad heaving of the waves, a fish without fins, a bird without wings, can but go where the wind wills. The lighthouse shows the end—points out the spot where it is doomed to disappear—throws light upon the burial. It is the torch of the sepulcher.

To light up the inexorable chasm—to warn against the inevitable—what more tragic mockery!

Chapter XII

FACE TO FACE WITH THE ROCK

THE WRETCHED PEOPLE IN DISTRESS ON BOARD THE *MATUTINA* UNDERSTOOD AT ONCE THE MYS-terious derision which mocked their shipwreck. The appearance of the lighthouse raised their spirits at first, then overwhelmed them. Nothing could be done, nothing attempted. What has been said of kings, we may say of the waves—we are their people, we are their prey. All that they rave must be borne. The nor'-wester was driving the hooker on the Caskets. They were nearing them; no evasion was possible. They drifted rapidly toward the reef; they felt that they were getting into shallow waters; the lead, if they could have thrown it to any purpose, would not have shown more than three or four fathoms. The shipwrecked people heard the dull sound of the waves being sucked within the submarine caves of the steep rock. They made out, under the lighthouse, like a dark cut-ting between two plates of granite, the narrow passage of the ugly wild-looking little harbor, sup-posed to be full of the skeletons of men and carcasses of ships. It looked like the mouth of a cavern, rather than the entrance of a port. They could hear the crackling of the pile on high within the iron grating. A ghastly purple illuminated the storm, the collision of the rain and hail disturbed the mist. The black cloud and the red flame fought, serpent against serpent; live ashes, reft by the wind, flew from the fire, and the sudden assaults of the sparks seemed to drive the snowflakes be-fore them. The breakers, blurred at first in outline, now stood out in bold relief, a medley of rocks with peaks, crests, and vertebrae. The angles were formed by strongly-marked red lines, and the inclined planes in blood-like streams of light. As they neared it, the outline of the reefs increased and rose—sinister.

One of the women, the Irishwoman, told her beads wildly.

In place of the skipper, who was the pilot, remained the chief, who was the captain. The Basques all know the mountain and the sea. They are bold on the precipice, and inventive in catastrophes.

They neared the cliff. They were about to strike. Suddenly they were so close to the great north rock of the Caskets that it shut out the lighthouse from them. They saw nothing but the rock and the red light behind it. The huge rock looming in the mist was like a gigantic black woman with a hood of fire.

That ill-famed rock is called the Biblet. It faces the north side of the reef, which on the south is faced by another ridge, L'Etacqaux-giulmets. The chief looked at the Biblet, and shouted—

"A man with a will to take a rope to the rock! Who can swim?"

No answer.

No one on board knew how to swim, not even the sailors. An ignorance not uncommon among sea-faring people.

A beam nearly free of its lashings was swinging loose. The chief clasped it with both hands, crying, "Help me."

They unlashed the beam. They had now at their disposal the very thing they wanted. From the defensive, they assumed the offensive.

It was a longish beam of heart of oak, sound and strong, useful either as a support or as an engine of attack, a lever for a burden, a ram against a tower.

"Ready!" shouted the chief.

All six, getting foothold on the stump of the mast, threw their weight on the spar projecting over the side, straight as a lance toward a projection of the cliff.

It was a dangerous maneuver. To strike at a mountain is audacity indeed. The six men might well have been thrown into the water by the shock.

There is variety in struggles with storms. After the hurricane, the shoal, after the wind, the rock. First the intangible, then the immovable, to be encountered.

Some minutes passed, such minutes as whiten men's hair.

The rock and the vessel were about to come in collision. The rock, like a culprit, awaited the blow.

A resistless wave rushed in; it ended the respite. It caught the vessel underneath, raised it, and swayed it for an instant as the sling swings its projectile.

"Steady!" cried the chief, "it is only a rock, and we are men."

The beam was couched, the six men were one with it, its sharp bolts tore their arm-pits, but they did not feel them.

The wave dashed the hooker against the rock.

Then came the shock.

It came under the shapeless cloud of foam which always hides such catastrophes.

When this cloud fell back into the sea, when the waves rolled back from the rock, the six men were tossing about the deck, but the *Matutina* was floating alongside the rock—clear of it. The beam had stood and turned the vessel; the sea was running so fast that in a few seconds she had left the Caskets behind.

Such things sometimes occur. It was a straight stroke of the bowsprit that saved Wood of Largo at the mouth of the Tay. In the wild neighborhood of Cape Winterton, and under the command of Captain Hamilton, it was the appliance of such a lever against the dangerous rock, Branodu-um, that saved the *Royal Mary* from shipwreck, although she was but a Scotch-built frigate. The force of the waves can be so abruptly discomposed that changes of direction can be easily managed, or at least are possible even in the most violent collisions. There is a brute in the tempest. The hurricane is a bull, and can be turned.

The whole secret of avoiding shipwreck is to try and pass from the secant to the tangent.

Such was the service rendered by the beam to the vessel. It had done the work of an oar, had taken the place of a rudder. But the maneuver once performed could not be repeated. The beam was overboard; the shock of the collision had wrenched it out of the men's hands, and it was lost in the waves. To loosen another beam would have been to dislocate the hull.

The hurricane carried off the *Matutina*. Presently the Caskets showed as a harmless encumbrance on the horizon. Nothing looks more out of countenance than a reef of rocks under such circumstances. There are in nature, in its obscure aspects, in which the visible blends with the invisible, certain motionless, surly profiles, which seem to express that a prey has escaped.

Thus glowered the Caskest while the *Matutina* fled.

The lighthouse paled in distance, faded, and disappeared.

There was something mournful in its extinction. Layers of mist sank down upon the now uncertain light. Its rays died in the waste of waters, the flame floated, struggled, sank, and lost its form. It might have been a drowning creature. The brazier dwindled to the snuff of a candle; then nothing more but a weak, uncertain flutter. Around it spread a circle of extravasated glimmer; it was like the quenching of light in the pit of night.

The bell which had threatened was dumb. The lighthouse which had threatened had melted away. And yet it was more awful now that they had ceased to threaten. One was a voice, the other a torch. There was something human about them.

They were gone, and naught remained but the abyss.

Chapter XIII

FACE TO FACE WITH NIGHT

AGAIN WAS THE HOOKER RUNNING WITH THE SHADOW INTO IMMEASURABLE DARKNESS. The *Matutina*, escaped from the Caskets, sank and rose from billow to billow. A respite, but in chaos.

Spun round by the wind, tossed by all the thousand motions of the wave, she reflected every mad oscillation of the sea. She scarcely pitched at all, a terrible symptom of a ship's distress. Wrecks merely roll. Pitching is a convulsion of the strife. The helm alone can turn a vessel to the wind.

In storms, and more especially in the meteors of snow, sea and night end by melting into amalgamation, resolving into nothing but a smoke. Mists, whirlwinds, gales, motion in all directions, no basis, no shelter, no stop. Constant recommencement, one gulf succeeding another. No horizon visible; intense blackness for background. Through all these the hooker drifted.

To have got free of the Caskets, to have eluded the rock, was a victory for the shipwrecked men; but it was a victory which left them in stupor. They had raised no cheer; at sea such an imprudence is not repeated twice. To throw down a challenge where they could not cast the lead, would have been too serious a jest.

The repulse of the rock was an impossibility achieved. They were petrified by it. By degrees, however, they began to hope again. Such are the insubmergable mirages of the soul! There is no distress so complete but that even in the most critical moments the inexplicable sunrise of hope is seen in its depths. These poor wretches were ready to acknowledge to themselves that they were saved. It was on their lips.

But suddenly something terrible appeared to them in the darkness.

On the port bow arose, standing stark, cut out on the background of mist, a tall, opaque mass, vertical, right-angled, a tower of the abyss. They watched it open-mouthed.

The storm was driving them toward it.

They knew not what it was. It was the Ortach rock.

Chapter XIV

ORTACH

HE REEF REAPPEARED. AFTER THE CASKETS COMES ORTACH. THE STORM IS NO ARTIST; BRUTAL
and all-powerful, it never varies its appliances. The darkness is inexhaustible. Its snares and
perfidies never come to an end. As for man, he soon comes to the bottom of his resources. Man expends his strength, the abyss never.

The shipwrecked men turned toward the chief, their hope. He could only shrug his shoulders.
Dismal contempt of helplessness.

A pavement in the midst of the ocean, such is the Ortach rock. The Ortach, all of a piece, rises
up in a straight line to eighty feet above the angry beating of the waves. Waves and ships break
against it. An immovable cube, it plunges its rectilinear planes a peak into the numberless serpentine curves of the sea.

At night it stands an enormous block resting on the folds of a huge black sheet. In time of
storm it awaits the stroke of the ax, which is the thunderclap.

But there is never a thunderclap during the snowstorm. True, the ship has the bandage round
her eyes; darkness is knotted about her; she is like one prepared to be led to the scaffold. As for the
thunderbolt, which makes quick ending, it is not to be hoped for.

The *Matutina,* nothing better than a log upon the waters, drifted toward this rock, as she had
drifted toward the other. The poor wretches on board, who had for a moment believed themselves
saved, relapsed into their agony. The destruction they had left behind faced them again. The reef
reappeared from the bottom of the sea. Nothing had been gained.

The Caskets are a figuring iron with a thousand compartments. The Ortach is a wall. To be
wrecked on the Caskets is to be cut into ribbons; to strike on the Ortach is to be crushed into
powder.

Nevertheless, there was one chance.

On a straight frontage such as that of the Ortach, neither the wave nor the cannon-ball can ric-
ochet. The operation is simple; first the flux, then the reflux; a wave advances, a billow returns.

In such cases the question of life and death is balanced thus; if the wave carries the vessel on
the rock, she breaks on it and is lost; if the billow retires before the ship has touched, she is carried
back, she is saved.

It was a moment of great anxiety; those on board saw through the gloom the great decisive
wave bearing down on them. How far was it going to drag them? If the wave broke upon the ship,
they were carried on the rock and dashed to pieces. If it passed under the ship. . . .

The wave *did* pass under.

They breathed again.

But what of the recoil? What would the surf do with them? The surf carried them back. A few
minutes later the *Matutina* was free of the breakers. The Ortach faded from their view, as the Caskets had done. It was their second victory. For the second time the hooker had verged on destruction, and had drawn back in time.

Chapter XV

PORTENTOSUM MARE

MEANWHILE A THICKENING MIST HAD DESCENDED ON THE DRIFTING WRETCHES. THEY WERE ignorant of their whereabouts, they could scarcely see a cable's length around. Despite a furious storm of hail which forced them to bend down their heads, the women had obstinately refused to go below again. No one, however hopeless, but wishes, if shipwreck be inevitable, to meet it in the open air. When so near death, a ceiling above one's head seems like the first outline of a coffin.

They were now in a short and chopping sea. A turgid sea indicates its constraint. Even in a fog the entrance into a strait may be known by the boiling-like appearance of the waves. And thus it was, for they were unconsciously coasting Aurigny. Between the west of Ortach and the Caskets and the east of Aurigny the sea is hemmed in and cramped, and the uneasy position determines locally the condition of storms. The sea suffers like others, and when it suffers it is irritable. That channel is a thing to fear.

The *Matutina* was in it.

Imagine under the sea a tortoise shell as big as Hyde Park or the Champs-Élysées, of which every striature is a shallow, and every embossment a reef. Such is the western approach of Aurigny. The sea covers and conceals this shipwrecking apparatus. On this conglomeration of submarine breakers the cloven waves leap and foam—in calm weather, a chopping sea; in storms, a chaos.

The shipwrecked men observed this new complication without endeavoring to explain it to themselves. Suddenly they understood it. A pale vista broadened in the zenith; a wan tinge overspread the sea; the livid light revealed on the port side a long shoal stretching eastward, toward which the power of the rushing wind was driving the vessel. The shoal was Aurigny.

What was that shoal? They shuddered. They would have shuddered even more had a voice answered them—Aurigny.

No isle is so well defended against man's approach as Aurigny. Below and above water it is protected by a savage guard, of which Ortach is the outpost. To the west, Burhou, Sauteriaux, Anfroque, Niangle, Fond du Croc, Les Jumelles, La Grosse, La Clanque, Les Eguillons, Le Vrac, La Fosse-Malière; to the east, Sauquet, Hommeau Floreau, La Brinebetais, La Queslingue, Croquelihou, La Fourche, Le Saut, Noire Pute, Coupie, Orbue. These are hydra-monsters of the species reef.

One of these reefs is called Le But, the goal, as if to imply that every voyage ends there.

This obstruction of rocks, simplified by night and sea, appeared to the shipwrecked men in the shape of a single dark band, a sort of black blot on the horizon.

Shipwreck is the ideal of helplessness; to be near land, and unable to reach it; to float, yet not to be able to do so in any desired direction; to rest the foot on what seems firm and is fragile; to be full of life, when o'ershadowed by death; to be the prisoner of space; to be walled in between sky and ocean; to have the infinite overhead like a dungeon; to be encompassed by the eluding elements of wind and waves; and to be seized, bound, paralyzed—such a load of misfortune stupefies and crushes us. We imagine that in it we catch a glimpse of the sneer of the opponent who is beyond our reach. That which holds you fast is that which releases the birds and sets the fishes free. It appears nothing, and is everything. We are dependent on the air which is ruffled by our mouths; we are dependent on the water which we catch in the hollow of our hands. Draw a glassful from the storm, and it is but a cup of bitterness—a mouthful is nausea, a waveful is extermination. The grain of sand in the desert, the foam-flake on the sea, are fearful symptoms. Omnipotence takes no care to hide its atom, it changes weakness into strength, fills naught with all; and it is with the infinitely little that the infinitely great crushes you. It is with its drops the ocean dissolves you. You feel you are a plaything.

A plaything: ghastly epithet!

The *Matutina* was a little above Aurigny, which was not an unfavorable position; but she was drifting toward its northern point, which was fatal. As a bent bow discharges its arrow, the nor'-wester was shooting the vessel toward the northern cape. Off that point, a little beyond the harbor of Corbelets, is that which the seamen of the Norman archipelago call a "*singe*."

The "*singe*," or race, is a furious kind of current. A wreath of funnels in the shallows produces in the waves a wreath of whirlpools. You escape one to fall into another. A ship caught hold of by the race, winds round and round until some sharp rock cleaves her hull; then the shattered vessel stops, her stern rises from the waves, the stem completes the revolution in the abyss, the stern sinks in, and all is sucked down. A circle of foam broadens and floats, and nothing more is seen on the surface of the waves but a few bubbles here and there rising from the smothered breathings below.

The three most dangerous races in the whole Channel are, one close to the well-known Girdler Sands, one at Jersey between the Pignonnet and the Point of Noirmont, and the race of Aurigny.

Had a local pilot been on board the *Matutina*, he could have warned them of their fresh peril. In place of a pilot, they had their instinct. In situations of extreme danger men are endowed with second sight. High contortions of foam were flying along the coast in the frenzied raid of the wind. It was the spitting of the race. Many a bark has been swamped in that snare. Without knowing what awaited them, they approached the spot with horror.

How to double that cape? There were no means of doing it.

Just as they had seen, first the Caskets, then Ortach, rise before them, they now saw the point of Aurigny, all of steep rock. It was like a number of giants, rising up one after another—a series of frightful duels.

Charybdis and Scylla are but two; the Caskets, Ortach, and Aurigny are three.

The phenomenon of the horizon being invaded by the rocks was thus repeated with the grand monotony of the abyss. The battles of the ocean have the same sublime tautology as the combats of Homer.

Each wave, as they neared it, added twenty cubits to the cape, awfully magnified by the mist; the fast decreasing distance seemed more inevitable—they were touching the skirts of the race! The first fold which seized them would drag them in—another wave surmounted, and all would be over.

Suddenly the hooker was driven back, as by the blow of a Titan's fist. The wave reared up under the vessel and fell back, throwing the waif back in its mane of foam. The *Matutina*, thus impelled, drifted away from Aurigny.

She was again on the open sea.

Whence had come the succor? From the wind. The breath of the storm had changed its direction.

The wave had played with them, now it was the wind's turn. They had saved themselves from the Caskets. Off Ortach it was the wave which had been their friend. Now it was the wind. The wind had suddenly veered from north to south. The sou'-wester had succeeded the nor'-wester.

The current is the wind in the waters; the wind is the current in the air. These two forces had just counteracted each other, and it had been the wind's will to snatch its prey from the current.

The sudden fantasies of ocean are uncertain. They are, perhaps, an embodiment of the perpetual; when at their mercy man must neither hope nor despair. They do, and they undo. The ocean amuses itself. Every shade of wild, untamed ferocity is phased in the vastness of that cunning sea, which Jean Bart used to call the "great brute." To its claws and their gashings succeed soft intervals of velvet paws. Sometimes the storm hurries on a wreck, at others it works out the problem with care; it might almost be said that it caresses it. The sea can afford to take its time, as men in their agonies find out.

We must own that occasionally these lulls of the torture announce deliverance. Such cases are rare. However this may be, men in extreme peril are quick to believe in rescue; the slightest pause in the storm's threats is sufficient; they tell themselves that they are out of danger. After believing themselves buried, they declare their resurrection; they feverishly embrace what they do not yet possess; it is clear that the bad luck has turned; they declare themselves satisfied; they are saved; they cry quits with God. They should not be in so great a hurry to give receipts to the Unknown.

The sou'-wester set in with a whirlwind. Shipwrecked men have never any but rough helpers. The *Matutina* was dragged rapidly out to sea by the remnant of her rigging—like a dead woman trailed by the hair. It was like the enfranchisement granted by Tiberius, at the price of violation. The wind treated with brutality those whom it saved; it rendered service with fury; it was help without pity.

The wreck was breaking up under the severity of its deliveries.

Hailstones, big and hard enough to charge a blunderbuss, smote the vessel; at every rotation of the waves these hailstones rolled about the deck like marbles. The hooker, whose deck was almost flush with the water, was being beaten out of shape by the rolling masses of water and its sheets of spray. On board it was each man for himself.

They clung on as best they could. As each sea swept over them, it was with a sense of surprise they saw that all were still there. Several had their faces torn by splinters.

Happily despair has stout hands. In terror a child's hand has the grasp of a giant. Agony makes a vice of a woman's fingers. A girl in her fright can almost bury her rose-colored fingers in a piece of iron. With hooked fingers they hung on somehow, as the waves dashed on and passed off them; but every wave brought them the fear of being swept away.

Suddenly they were relieved.

Chapter XVI

THE PROBLEM SUDDENLY WORKS IN SILENCE

THE HURRICANE HAD JUST STOPPED SHORT. THERE WAS NO LONGER IN THE AIR SOU'-WESTER OR nor'-wester. The fierce clarions of space were mute. The whole of the waterspout had poured from the sky without any warning of diminution, as if it had slided perpendicularly into a gulf beneath. None knew what had become of it; flakes replaced the hailstones, the snow began to fall slowly. No more swell: the sea flattened down.

Such sudden cessations are peculiar to snowstorms. The electric effluvium exhausted, all becomes still, even the wave, which in ordinary storms often remains agitated for a long time. In snowstorms it is not so. No prolonged anger in the deep. Like a tired-out worker it becomes drowsy directly, thus almost giving the lie to the laws of statics, but not astonishing old seamen, who know that the sea is full of unforeseen surprises.

The same phenomenon takes place, although very rarely, in ordinary storms. Thus, in our time, on the occasion of the memorable hurricane of July 27th, 1867, at Jersey the wind, after fourteen hours' fury, suddenly relapsed into a dead calm.

In a few minutes the hooker was floating in sleeping waters.

At the same time (for the last phase of these storms resembles the first) they could distinguish nothing; all that had been made visible in the convulsions of the meteoric cloud was again dark. Pale outlines were fused in vague mist, and the gloom of infinite space closed about the vessel. The wall of night—that circular occlusion, that interior of a cylinder the diameter of which was lessening minute by minute—enveloped the *Matutina*, and, with the sinister deliberation of an encroaching iceberg, was drawing in dangerously. In the zenith nothing—a lid of fog closing down. It was as if the hooker were at the bottom of the well of the abyss.

In that well the sea was a puddle of liquid lead. No stir in the waters—ominous immobility! The ocean is never less tamed than when it is still as a pool.

All was silence, stillness, blindness.

Perchance the silence of inanimate objects is taciturnity.

The last ripples glided along the hull. The deck was horizontal, with an insensible slope to the sides. Some broken planks were shifting about irresolutely. The block on which they had lighted the tow steeped in tar, in place of the signal light which had been swept away, swung no longer at the prow, and no longer let fall burning drops into the sea. What little breeze remained in the clouds was noiseless. The snow fell thickly, softly, with scarce a slant. No foam of breakers could be heard. The peace of shadows was over all.

This repose succeeding all the past exasperations and paroxysms was, for the poor creatures so long tossed about, an unspeakable comfort. It was as though the punishment of the rack had ceased. They caught a glimpse about them and above them of something which seemed like a consent that they should be saved. They regained confidence. All that had been fury was now tranquility. It appeared to them a pledge of peace. Their wretched hearts dilated. They were able to let go the end of rope or beam to which they had clung, to rise, hold themselves up, stand, walk, move about. They felt inexpressibly calmed. There are in the depths of darkness such phases of paradise, preparations for other things. It was clear that they were delivered out of the storm, out of the foam, out of the wind, out of the uproar. Henceforth all the chances were in their favor. In three or four hours it would be sunrise. They would be seen by some passing ship; they would be rescued. The worst was over; they were re-entering life. The important feat was to have been able to keep afloat until the cessation of the tempest. They said to themselves, "It is all over this time."

Suddenly they found that all was indeed over.

One of the sailors, the northern Basque, Galdeazun by name, went down into the hold to look for a rope, then came above again and said—

"The hold is full."

"Of what?" asked the chief.

"Of water," answered the sailor.

The chief cried out—

"What does that mean?"

"It means," replied Galdeazun, "that in half an hour we shall founder."

Chapter XVII

THE LAST RESOURCE

THERE WAS A HOLE IN THE KEEL. A LEAK HAD BEEN SPRUNG. WHEN IT HAPPENED NO ONE COULD have said. Was it when they touched the Caskets? Was it off Ortach? Was it when they were whirled about the shallows west of Aurigny? It was most probable that they had touched some rock there. They had struck against some hidden buttress which they had not felt in the midst of the convulsive fury of the wind which was tossing them. In tetanus who would feel a prick?

The other sailor, the southern Basque, whose name was Ave Maria, went down into the hold, too, came on deck again, and said—

"There are two varas of water in the hold."

About six feet.

Ave Maria added, "In less than forty minutes we shall sink."

Where was the leak? They couldn't find it. It was hidden by the water which was filling up the hold. The vessel had a hole in her hull somewhere under the waterline, quite forward in the keel. Impossible to find it—impossible to check it. They had a wound which they could not staunch. The water, however, was not rising very fast.

The chief called out—

"We must work the pump."

Galdeazun replied, "We have no pump left."

"Then," said the chief, "we must make for land."

"Where is the land?"

"I don't know."

"Nor I."

"But it must be somewhere."

"True enough."

"Let someone steer for it."

"We have no pilot."

"Stand to the tiller yourself."

"We have lost the tiller."

"Let's rig one out of the first beam we can lay hands on. Nails—a hammer—quick—some tools."

"The carpenter's box is overboard; we have no tools."

"We'll steer all the same; no matter where."

"The rudder is lost."

"Where is the boat? We'll get in and row."

"The boat is lost."

"We'll row the wreck."

"We have lost the oars."

"We'll sail."

"We have lost the sails, and the mast."

"We'll rig one up with a pole and a tarpaulin for sail. Let's get clear of this and trust in the wind."

"There is no wind."

The wind, indeed, had left them, the storm had fled, and its departure, which they had believed to mean safety, meant, in fact, destruction. Had the sou'-wester continued it might have driven them wildly on some shore, might have beaten the leak in speed—might, perhaps, have carried them to some propitious sandbank, and cast them on it before the hooker foundered. The swiftness of the storm, bearing them away, might have enabled them to reach land; but no more wind, no more hope. They were going to die because the hurricane was over.

The end was near!

Wind, hail, the hurricane, the whirlwind—these are wild combatants that may be overcome; the storm can be taken in the weak point of its armor; there are resources against the violence which continually lays itself open, is off its guard, and often hits wide. But nothing is to be done against a calm; it offers nothing to the grasp of which you can lay hold.

The winds are a charge of Cossacks; stand your ground and they disperse. Calms are the pincers of the executioner.

The water, deliberate and sure, irrepressible and heavy, rose in the hold, and as it rose, the vessel sank—it was happening slowly.

Those on board the wreck of the *Matutina* felt that most hopeless of catastrophes—an inert catastrophe undermining them. The still and sinister certainty of their fate petrified them. No stir in the air, no movement on the sea. The motionless is the inexorable. Absorption was sucking them down silently. Through the depths of the dumb waters—without anger, without passion, not willing, not knowing, not caring—the fatal center of the globe was attracting them downwards. Horror in repose amalgamating them with itself. It was no longer the wide open mouth of the sea, the double jaw of the wind and the wave, vicious in its threat, the grin of the waterspout, the foaming appetite of the breakers—it was as if the wretched beings had under them the black yawn of the infinite.

They felt themselves sinking into Death's peaceful depths. The height between the vessel and the water was lessening—that was all. They could calculate her disappearance to the moment. It was the exact reverse of submersion by the rising tide. The water was not rising toward them, they were sinking toward it. They were digging their own grave. Their own weight was their sexton.

They were being executed, not by the law of man, but by the law of things.

The snow was falling, and as the wreck was now motionless, this white lint made a cloth over the deck and covered the vessel as with a winding-sheet.

The hold was becoming fuller and deeper—no means of getting at the leak. They struck a light and fixed three or four torches in holes as best they could. Galdeazun brought some old leathern buckets, and they tried to bale the hold out, standing in a row to pass them from hand to hand, but the buckets were past use, the leather of some was unstitched, there were holes in the bottoms of the others, and the buckets emptied themselves on the way. The difference in quantity between the water which was making its way in and that which they returned to the sea was ludicrous—for a ton that entered a glassful was baled out; they did not improve their condition. It was like the expenditure of a miser, trying to exhaust a million, halfpenny by halfpenny.

The chief said, "Let us lighten the wreck."

During the storm, they had lashed together the few chests which were on deck. These remained tied to the stump of the mast. They undid the lashings and rolled the chests overboard through a breach in the gunwale. One of these trunks belonged to the Basque woman, who could not repress a sigh.

"Oh, my new cloak lined with scarlet! Oh, my poor stockings of birchen-bark lace! Oh, my silver earrings to wear at mass on May Day!"

The deck cleared, there remained the cabin to be seen to. It was greatly encumbered; in it were, as may be remembered, the luggage belonging to the passengers, and the bales belonging to the sailors. They took the luggage, and threw it over the gunwale. They carried up the bales and cast them into the sea.

Thus they emptied the cabin. The lantern, the cap, the barrels, the sacks, the bales, and the water-butts, the pot of soup, all went over into the waves.

They unscrewed the nuts of the iron stove, long since extinguished: they pulled it out, hoisted it on deck, dragged it to the side, and threw it out of the vessel.

They cast overboard everything they could pull out of the deck—chains, shrouds, and torn rigging.

From time to time the chief took a torch, and throwing its light on the figures painted on the prow to show the draft of water, looked to see how deep the wreck had settled down.

Chapter XVIII

THE HIGHEST RESOURCE

T HE WRECK BEING LIGHTENED, WAS SINKING MORE SLOWLY, BUT NONE THE LESS SURELY. The hopelessness of their situation was without resource—without mitigation; they had exhausted their last expedient.

"Is there anything else we can throw overboard?"

The doctor, whom everyone had forgotten, rose from the companion, and said—

"Yes."

"What?" asked the chief.

The doctor answered, "Our Crime."

They shuddered, and all cried out—

"Amen."

The doctor standing up, pale, raised his hand to heaven, saying

"Kneel down."

They wavered—to waver is the preface to kneeling down.

The doctor went on—

"Let us throw our crimes into the sea, they weigh us down; it is they that are sinking the ship. Let us think no more of safety—let us think of salvation. Our last crime, above all, the crime which we committed, or rather completed, just now; oh, wretched beings who are listening to me, it is that which is overwhelming us. For those who leave intended murder behind them, it is an impious insolence to tempt the abyss. He who sins against a child, sins against God. True, we were obliged to put to sea, but it was certain perdition. The storm, warned by the shadow of our crime, came on. It is well. Regret nothing, however. There, not far off in the darkness, are the sands of Vauville and Cape La Hogue. It is France. There was but one possible shelter for us, which was Spain. France is no less dangerous to us than England. Our deliverance from the sea would have led but to the gibbet. Hanged or drowned—we had no alternative. God has chosen for us; let us give Him thanks. He has vouchsated us the grave which cleanses. Brethren, the inevitable hand is in it. Remember that it was we who just now did our best to send on high that child, and that at this very moment, now as I speak, there is perhaps, above our heads, a soul accusing us before a Judge whose eye is on us. Let us make the best use of this last respite; let us make an effort, if we still may, to repair, as far as we are able, the evil that we have wrought. If the child survives us, let us come to his aid; if he is dead, let us seek his forgiveness. Let us cast our crime from us. Let us ease our consciences of its weight. Let us strive that our souls be not swallowed up before God, for that is the awful shipwreck. Bodies go to the fishes, souls to the devils. Have pity on yourselves. Kneel down, I tell you. Repentance is the bark which never sinks. You have lost your compass! You are wrong! You still have prayer."

The wolves became lambs—such transformations occur in last agonies; tigers lick the crucifix; when the dark portal opens ajar, belief is difficult, unbelief impossible. However imperfect may be the different sketches of religion essayed by man, even when his belief is shapeless, even when the outline of the dogma is not in harmony with the lineaments of the eternity he foresees, there comes in his last hour a trembling of the soul. There is something which will begin when life is over; this thought impresses the last pang.

A man's dying agony is the expiration of a term. In that fatal second he feels weighing on him a diffused responsibility. That which has been complicates that which is to be. The past returns and enters into the future. What is known becomes as much an abyss as the unknown. And the two chasms, the one which is full by his faults, the other of his anticipations, mingle their reverberations. It is this confusion of the two gulfs which terrifies the dying man.

They had spent their last grain of hope on the direction of life; hence they turned in the other. Their only remaining chance was in its dark shadow. They understood it. It came on them as a lugubrious flash, followed by the relapse of horror. That which is intelligible to the dying man is as what is perceived in the lightning. Everything, then nothing; you see, then all is blindness. After death the eye will reopen, and that which was a flash will become a sun.

They cried out to the doctor—

"Thou, thou, there is no one but thee. We will obey thee, what must we do? Speak."

The doctor answered—

"The question is how to pass over the unknown precipice, and reach the other bank of life, which is beyond the tomb. Being the one who knows the most, my danger is greater than yours. You do well to leave the choice of the bridge to him whose burden is the heaviest."

He added—

"Knowledge is a weight added to conscience."

He continued—

"How much time have we still?"

Galdeazun looked at the water-mark, and answered—

"A little more than a quarter of an hour."

"Good," said the doctor.

The low hood of the companion on which he leant his elbows made a sort of table; the doctor took from his pocket his inkhorn and pen, and his pocket-book out of which he drew a parchment, the same one on the back of which he had written, a few hours before, some twenty cramped and crooked lines.

"A light," he said.

The snow, falling like the spray of a cataract, had extinguished the torches one after another; there was but one left. Ave Maria took it out of the place where it had been stuck, and holding it in his hand, came and stood by the doctor's side.

The doctor replaced his pocket-book in his pocket, put down the pen and inkhorn on the hood of the companion, unfolded the parchment, and said—

"Listen."

Then in the midst of the sea, on the failing bridge (a sort of shuddering flooring of the tomb), the doctor began a solemn reading, to which all the shadows seemed to listen. The doomed men bowed their heads around him. The flaming of the torch intensified their pallor. What the doctor read was written in English. Now and then, when one of those woe-begone looks seemed to ask an explanation, the doctor would stop, to repeat—whether in French, or Spanish, Basque, or Italian—the passage he had just read. Stifled sobs and hollow beatings of the breast were heard. The wreck was sinking more and more.

The reading over, the doctor placed the parchment flat on the companion, seized his pen, and on a clear margin which he had carefully left at the bottom of what he had written, he signed himself, GERNADUS GEESTEMUNDE: Doctor.

Then, turning toward the others, he said—

"Come, and sign."

The Basque woman approached, took the pen, and signed herself, ASUNCION.

She handed the pen to the Irish woman, who, not knowing how to write, made a cross.

The doctor, by the side of this cross, wrote, BARBARA FERMOY, *of Tyrrif Island, in the Hebrides.*

Then he handed the pen to the chief of the band.

The chief signed, GAIZDORRA: *Captal.*

The Genoese signed himself under the chief's name, GIANGIRATE.

The Languedocian signed, JACQUES QUARTOURZE: *alias, the Narbonnais.*

The Provençal signed, LUC-PIERRE CAPGAROUPE, *of the Galleys of Mahon.*

Under these signatures the doctor added a note—

Of the crew of three men, the skipper having been washed overboard by a sea, but two remain, and they have signed.

The two sailors affixed their names underneath the note. The northern Basque signed himself, GALDEAZUN.

The southern Basque signed, AVE MARIA: *Robber.*

Then the doctor said—

"Capgaroupe."

"Here," said the Provençal.

"Have you Hardquanonne's flask?"

"Yes."

"Give it me."

Capgaroupe drank off the last mouthful of brandy, and handed the flask to the doctor.

The water was rising in the hold; the wreck was sinking deeper and deeper into the sea. The sloping edges of the ship were covered by a thin gnawing wave, which was rising. All were crowded on the center of the deck.

The doctor dried the ink on the signatures by the heat of the torch, and folding the parchment into a narrower compass than the diameter of the neck, put it into the flask. He called for the cork.

"I don't know where it is," said Capgaroupe.

"Here is a piece of rope," said Jacques Quartourze.

The doctor corked the flask with a bit of rope, and asked for some tar. Galdeazun went forward, extinguished the signal light with a piece of tow, took the vessel in which it was contained from the stern, and brought it, half-full of burning tar, to the doctor.

The flask holding the parchment which they had all signed was corked and tarred over.

"It is done," said the doctor.

And from out all their mouths, vaguely stammered in every language, came the dismal utterances of the catacombs.

"Ainsi soit-il!"

"Meâ culpâ!"

"Asi sea!"

"Aro raï!"

"Amen!"

It was as though the somber voices of Babel were scattered through the shadows as Heaven uttered its awful refusal to hear them.

The doctor turned away from his companions in crime and distress, and took a few steps toward the gunwale. Reaching the side, he looked into space, and said, in a deep voice—

"Bist du bei mir?"[1]

Perchance he was addressing some phantom.

The wreck was sinking.

Behind the doctor all the others were in a dream. Prayer mastered them by main force. They did not bow, they were bent. There was something involuntary in their condition; they wavered as a sail flaps when the breeze fails. And the haggard group took by degrees, with clasping of hands

1. Art thou near me?

and prostration of foreheads, attitudes various, yet of humiliation. Some strange reflection of the deep seemed to soften their villainous features.

The doctor returned toward them. Whatever had been his past, the old man was great in the presence of the catastrophe.

The deep reserve of nature which enveloped him preoccupied without disconcerting him. He was not one to be taken unawares. Over him was the calm of a silent horror: on his countenance the majesty of God's will comprehended.

This old and thoughtful outlaw unconsciously assumed the air of a pontiff.

He said—

"Attend to me."

He contemplated for a moment the waste of water, and added—

"Now we are going to die."

Then he took the torch from the hands of Ave Maria, and waved it.

A spark broke from it and flew into the night.

Then the doctor cast the torch into the sea.

The torch was extinguished: all light disappeared. Nothing left but the huge, unfathomable shadow. It was like the filling up of the grave.

In the darkness the doctor was heard saying—

"Let us pray."

All knelt down.

It was no longer on the snow, but in the water, that they knelt.

They had but a few minutes more.

The doctor alone remained standing.

The flakes of snow falling on him had sprinkled him with white tears, and made him visible on the background of darkness. He might have been the speaking statue of the shadow.

The doctor made the sign of the cross and raised his voice, while beneath his feet he felt that almost imperceptible oscillation which prefaces the moment in which a wreck is about to founder. He said—

"Pater noster qui es in coelis."

The Provençal repeated in French—

"Notre Père êqui tes aux cieux."

The Irishwoman repeated in Gaelic, understood by the Basque woman—

"Ar nathair ata ar neamh."

The doctor continued—

"Sanctificetur nomen tuum."

"Que votre nom soit sanctifié," said the Provençal.

"Naomhthar hainm," said the Irishwoman.

"Adveniat regnum tuum," continued the doctor.

"Que votre règne arrive," said the Provençal.

"Tigeadh do rioghachd," said the Irishwoman.

As they knelt, the waters had risen to their shoulders. The doctor went on—

"Fiat voluntas tua."

"Que votre volonté soit faite," stammered the Provençal.

And the Irishwoman and Basque woman cried—

"Deuntar do thoil ar an Hhalàmb."

"Sicut in coelo, sicut in terra," said the doctor.

No voice answered him.

He looked down. All their heads were under water. They had let themselves be drowned on their knees.

The doctor took in his right hand the flask which he had placed on the companion, and raised it above his head.

The wreck was going down. As he sank, the doctor murmured the rest of the prayer.

For an instant his shoulders were above water, then his head, then nothing remained but his arm holding up the flask, as if he were showing it to the Infinite.

His arm disappeared; there was no greater fold on the deep sea than there would have been on a tun of oil. The snow continued falling.

One thing floated, and was carried by the waves into the darkness. It was the tarred flask, kept afloat by its osier cover.

BOOK THE THIRD

THE CHILD IN THE SHADOW

Chapter I

CHESIL

THE STORM WAS NO LESS SEVERE ON LAND THAN ON SEA. THE SAME WILD ENFRANCHISEMENT OF the elements had taken place around the abandoned child. The weak and innocent become their sport in the expenditure of the unreasoning rage of their blind forces. Shadows discern not, and things inanimate have not the clemency they are supposed to possess.

On the land there was but little wind. There was an inexplicable dumbness in the cold. There was no hail. The thickness of the falling snow was fearful.

Hailstones strike, harass, bruise, stun, crush. Snowflakes do worse: soft and inexorable, the snowflake does its work in silence, touch it, and it melts. It is pure, even as the hypocrite is candid. It is by white particles slowly heaped upon each other that the flake becomes an avalanche and the knave a criminal.

The child continued to advance into the mist. The fog presents but a soft obstacle; hence its danger. It yields, and yet persists. Mist, like snow, is full of treachery. The child, strange wrestler at war with all these risks, had succeeded in reaching the bottom of the descent, and had gained Chesil. Without knowing it he was on an isthmus, with the ocean on each side; so that he could not lose his way in the fog, in the snow, or in the darkness, without falling into the deep waters of the gulf on the right hand, or into the raging billows of the high sea on the left. He was traveling on, in ignorance, between these two abysses.

The Isthmus of Portland was at this period singularly sharp and rugged. Nothing remains at this date of its past configuration. Since the idea of manufacturing Portland stone into Roman cement was first seized, the whole rock has been subjected to an alteration which has completely changed its original appearance. Calcareous lias, slate, and trap, are still to be found there, rising from layers of conglomerate, like teeth from a gum; but the pickax has broken up and leveled those bristling, rugged peaks which were once the fearful perches of the ossifrage. The summits exist no longer where the labbes and the skua gulls used to flock together, soaring, like the envious, to sully high places. In vain might you seek the tall monolith called Godolphin, an old British word, signifying "white eagle." In summer you may still gather on those surfaces, pierced and perforated like a sponge, rosemary, penny-royal, wild hyssop, and sea-fennel which when infused makes a good cordial, and that herb full of knots, which grows in the sand and from which they make matting; but you no longer find gray amber, or black tin, or that triple species of slate—one sort green, one blue, and the third the color of sage-leaves. The foxes, the badgers, the otters, and the martens have taken themselves off; on the cliffs of Portland, as well as at the extremity of Cornwall, where there were at one time chamois, none remain. They still fish in some inlets for plaice and pilchards; but the scared salmon no longer ascend the Wey, between Michaelmas and Christmas, to spawn. No more are seen there, as during the reign of Elizabeth, those old unknown birds as large as hawks, who could cut an apple in two, but ate only the pips. You never meet those crows with yellow beaks, called Cornish choughs in English, *pyrrocorax* in Latin, who, in their mischief, would drop burning twigs on thatched roofs. Nor that magic bird, the fulmar, a wanderer from the Scottish archipelago, dropping from his bill an oil which the islanders used to burn in their lamps. Nor do you ever find in the evening, in the plash of the ebbing tide, that ancient, legendary neitse, with the feet of a hog and the bleat of a calf. The tide no longer throws up the whiskered seal, with its curled ears and sharp jaws, dragging itself along on its nailless paws. On that Portland—nowadays so changed as scarcely to be recognized—the absence of forests precluded nightingales; but now the falcon, the swan, and the wild goose have fled. The sheep of Portland, nowadays, are fat and have fine wool; the few scattered ewes, which nibbled the salt grass there two centuries ago, were small and tough and coarse in the fleece, as became Celtic flocks brought there by garlic-eating shepherds, who lived to a hundred, and who, at the distance of half a mile, could pierce a cuirass with their yard-long arrows. Uncultivated land makes coarse wool. The Chesil of to-day resembles in no particular the Chesil of the past, so much has it been disturbed by man and by those furious winds which gnaw the very stones.

At present this tongue of land bears a railway, terminating in a pretty square of houses, called Chesilton, and there is a Portland station. Railway carriages roll where seals used to crawl.

The Isthmus of Portland two hundred years ago was a back of sand, with a vertebral spine of rock.

The child's danger changed its form. What he had had to fear in the descent was falling to the bottom of the precipice; in the isthmus, it was falling into the holes. After dealing with the precipice, he must deal with the pitfalls. Everything on the seashore is a trap—the rock is slippery, the strand is quicksand. Resting-places are but snares. It is walking on ice which may suddenly crack and yawn with a fissure, through which you disappear. The ocean has false stages below, like a well-arranged theater.

The long backbone of granite, from which fall away both slopes of the isthmus, is awkward of access. It is difficult to find there what, in scene-shifters' language, are termed *practicables*. Man has no hospitality to hope for from the ocean; from the rock no more than from the wave. The sea is provident for the bird and the fish alone. Isthmuses are especially naked and rugged; the wave, which wears and mines them on either side, reduces them to the simplest form. Everywhere there were sharp relief ridges, cuttings, frightful fragments of torn stone, yawning with many points, like the jaws of a shark; breaknecks of wet moss, rapid slopes of rock ending in the sea. Whosoever undertakes to pass over an isthmus meets at every step misshapen blocks, as large as houses, in the forms of shin-bones, shoulder-blades, and thigh-bones, the hideous anatomy of dismembered rocks. It is not without reason that these *striae* of the seashore are called *côtes*.[1]

The wayfarer must get out as he best can from the confusion of these ruins. It is like journeying over the bones of an enormous skeleton.

1. Ribs.

Put a child to this labor of Hercules.

Broad daylight might have aided him. It was night. A guide was necessary. He was alone. All the vigor of manhood would not have been too much. He had but the feeble strength of a child. In default of a guide, a footpath might have aided him; there was none.

By instinct he avoided the sharp ridge of the rocks, and kept to the strand as much as possible. It was there that he met with the pitfalls. They were multiplied before him under three forms: the pitfall of water, the pitfall of snow, and the pitfall of sand. This last is the most dangerous of all, because the most illusory. To know the peril we face is alarming; to be ignorant of it is terrible. The child was fighting against unknown dangers. He was groping his way through something which might, perhaps, be the grave.

He did not hesitate. He went round the rocks, avoided the crevices, guessed at the pitfalls, obeyed the twistings and turnings caused by such obstacles; yet he went on. Though unable to advance in a straight line, he walked with a firm step. When necessary, he drew back with energy. He knew how to tear himself in time from the horrid bird-lime of the quicksands. He shook the snow from about him. He entered the water more than once up to the knees. Directly that he left it, his wet knees were frozen by the intense cold of the night. He walked rapidly in his stiffened garments; yet he took care to keep his sailor's coat dry and warm on his chest. He was still tormented by hunger.

The chances of the abyss are illimitable. Everything is possible in it, even salvation. The issue may be found, though it be invisible. How the child, wrapped in a smothering winding-sheet of snow, lost on a narrow elevation between two jaws of an abyss, managed to cross the isthmus is what he could not himself have explained. He had slipped, climbed, rolled, searched, walked, persevered, that is all. Such is the secret of all triumphs. At the end of somewhat less than half an hour he felt that the ground was rising. He had reached the other shore. Leaving Chesil, he had gained terra firma.

The bridge which now unites Sandford Castle with Smallmouth Sands did not then exist. It is probable that in his intelligent groping he had reascended as far as Wyke Regis, where there was then a tongue of sand, a natural road crossing East Fleet.

He was saved from the isthmus; but he found himself again face to face with the tempest, with the cold, with the night.

Before him once more lay the plain, shapeless in the density of impenetrable shadow. He examined the ground, seeking a footpath. Suddenly he bent down. He had discovered, in the snow, something which seemed to him a track.

It was indeed a track—the print of a foot. The print was cut out clearly in the whiteness of the snow, which rendered it distinctly visible. He examined it. It was a naked foot; too small for that of a man, too large for that of a child.

It was probably the foot of a woman. Beyond that mark was another, then another, then another. The footprints followed each other at the distance of a step, and struck across the plain to the right. They were still fresh, and slightly covered with little snow. A woman had just passed that way.

This woman was walking in the direction in which the child had seen the smoke. With his eyes fixed on the footprints, he set himself to follow them.

Chapter II

THE EFFECT OF SNOW

HE JOURNEYED SOME TIME ALONG THIS COURSE. UNFORTUNATELY THE FOOTPRINTS WERE BE- coming less and less distinct. Dense and fearful was the falling of the snow. It was the time when the hooker was so distressed by the snowstorm at sea.

The child, in distress like the vessel, but after another fashion, had, in the inextricable inter- section of shadows which rose up before him, no resource but the footsteps in the snow, and he held to it as the thread of the labyrinth.

Suddenly, whether the snow had filled them up or for some other reason, the footsteps ceased. All became even, level, smooth, without a stain, without a detail. There was now nothing but a white cloth drawn over the earth and a black one over the sky. It seemed as if the foot-passenger had flown away. The child, in despair, bent down and searched; but in vain.

As he arose he had a sensation of hearing some indistinct sound, but he could not be sure of it. It resembled a voice, a breath, a shadow. It was more human than animal; more sepulchral than living. It was a sound, but the sound of a dream.

He looked, but saw nothing.

Solitude, wide, naked and livid, was before him. He listened. That which he had thought he heard had faded away. Perhaps it had been but fancy. He still listened. All was silent.

There was illusion in the mist.

He went on his way again. He walked forward at random, with nothing thenceforth to guide him.

As he moved away the noise began again. This time he could doubt it no longer. It was a groan, almost a sob.

He turned. He searched the darkness of space with his eyes. He saw nothing. The sound arose once more. If limbo could cry out, it would cry in such a tone.

Nothing so penetrating, so piercing, so feeble as the voice—for it was a voice. It arose from a soul. There was palpitation in the murmur. Nevertheless, it seemed uttered almost unconsciously. It was an appeal of suffering, not knowing that it suffered or that it appealed.

The cry—perhaps a first breath, perhaps a last sigh—was equally distant from the rattle which closes life and the wail with which it commences. It breathed, it was stifled, it wept, a gloomy sup- plication from the depths of night. The child fixed his attention everywhere, far, near, on high, below. There was no one. There was nothing. He listened. The voice arose again. He perceived it distinctly. The sound somewhat resembled the bleating of a lamb.

Then he was frightened, and thought of flight.

The groan again. This was the fourth time. It was strangely miserable and plaintive. One felt that after that last effort, more mechanical than voluntary, the cry would probably be extinguished. It was an expiring exclamation, instinctively appealing to the amount of aid held in suspense in space. It was some muttering of agony, addressed to a possible Providence.

The child approached in the direction from whence the sound came.

Still he saw nothing.

He advanced again, watchfully.

The complaint continued. Inarticulate and confused as it was, it had become clear—almost vi- brating. The child was near the voice; but where was it?

He was close to a complaint. The trembling of a cry passed by his side into space. A human moan floated away into the darkness. This was what he had met. Such at least was his impression, dim as the dense mist in which he was lost.

Whilst he hesitated between an instinct which urged him to fly, and an instinct which commanded him to remain, he perceived in the snow at his feet, a few steps before him, a sort of undulation of the dimensions of a human body—a little eminence, low, long, and narrow, like the mold over a grave—a sepulcher in a white churchyard.

At the same time the voice cried out. It was from beneath the undulation that it proceeded. The child bent down, crouching before the undulation, and with both his hands began to clear it away.

Beneath the snow which he removed a form grew under his hands; and suddenly in the hollow he had made, there appeared a pale face.

The cry had not proceeded from that face. Its eyes were shut, and the mouth open but full of snow.

It remained motionless; it stirred not under the hands of the child. The child, whose fingers were numbed with frost, shuddered when he touched its coldness. It was that of a woman. Her disheveled hair was mingled with the snow. The woman was dead.

Again the child set himself to sweep away the snow. The neck of the dead woman appeared; then her shoulders, clothed in rags. Suddenly he felt something move feebly under his touch. It was something small that was buried, and which stirred. The child swiftly cleared away the snow, discovering a wretched little body—thin, wan with cold, still alive, lying naked on the dead woman's naked breast.

It was a little girl.

It had been swaddled up, but in rags so scanty that in its struggles it had freed itself from its tatters. Under it, its attenuated limbs, and above it, its breath, had somewhat melted the snow. A nurse would have said that it was five or six months old, but perhaps it might be a year, for growth, in poverty, suffers heart-breaking reductions which sometimes even produce rachitis. When its face was exposed to the air, it gave a cry, the continuation of its sobs of distress. For the mother not to have heard that sob, proved her irrevocably dead.

The child took the infant in his arms. The stiffened body of the mother was a fearful sight; a spectral light proceeded from her face. The mouth, apart and without breath, seemed to form in the indistinct language of shadows her answer to the questions put to the dead by the Invisible. The ghastly reflection of the icy plains was on that countenance. There was the youthful forehead under the brown hair, the almost indignant knitting of the eyebrows, the pinched nostrils, the closed eyelids, the lashes glued together by the rime, and from the corners of the eyes to the corners of the mouth, a deep channel of tears. The snow lighted up the corpse. Winter and the tomb are not adverse. The corpse is the icicle of man. The nakedness of her breasts was pathetic. They had fulfilled their purpose. On them was a sublime blight of the life infused into one being by another from whom life has fled, and maternal majesty was there instead of virginal purity. At the point of one of the nipples was a white pearl. It was a drop of milk frozen.

Let us explain at once. On the plains over which the deserted boy was passing in his turn, a beggar woman, nursing her infant and searching for a refuge, had lost her way a few hours before. Benumbed with cold she had sunk under the tempest, and could not rise again. The falling snow had covered her. So long as she was able she had clasped her little girl to her bosom, and thus died.

The infant had tried to suck the marble breast. Blind trust, inspired by nature, for it seems that it is possible for a woman to suckle her child even after her last sigh.

But the lips of the infant had been unable to find the breast, where the drop of milk, stolen by death, had frozen, whilst under the snow the child, more accustomed to the cradle than the tomb, had wailed.

The deserted child had heard the cry of the dying child.

He disinterred it.

He took it in his arms.

When she felt herself in his arms she ceased crying. The faces of the two children touched each other, and the purple lips of the infant sought the cheek of the boy, as it had been a breast. The little girl had nearly reached the moment when the congealed blood stops the action of the heart. Her mother had touched her with the chill of her own death—a corpse communicates death; its numbness is infectious. Her feet, hands, arms, knees, seemed paralyzed by cold. The boy felt the terrible chill. He had on him a garment dry and warm—his pilot jacket. He placed the infant on the breast of the corpse, took off his jacket, wrapped the infant in it, took it up again in his arms, and now, almost naked, under the blast of the north wind which covered him with eddies of snowflakes, carrying the infant, he pursued his journey.

The little one having succeeded in finding the boy's cheek, again applied her lips to it, and, soothed by the warmth, she slept. First kiss of those two souls in the darkness.

The mother lay there, her back to the snow, her face to the night; but perhaps at the moment when the little boy stripped himself to clothe the little girl, the mother saw him from the depths of infinity.

Chapter III

A BURDEN MAKES A ROUGH ROAD ROUGHER

IT WAS LITTLE MORE THAN FOUR HOURS SINCE THE HOOKER HAD SAILED FROM THE CREEK OF PORT-land, leaving the boy on the shore. During the long hours since he had been deserted, and had been journeying onwards, he had met but three persons of that human society into which he was, perchance, about to enter. A man—the man on the hill—a woman—the woman in the snow—and the little girl whom he was carrying in his arms.

He was exhausted by fatigue and hunger, yet advanced more resolutely than ever, with less strength and an added burden. He was now almost naked. The few rags which remained to him, hardened by the frost, were sharp as glass, and cut his skin. He became colder, but the infant was warmer. That which he lost was not thrown away, but was gained by her. He found out that the poor infant enjoyed the comfort which was to her the renewal of life. He continued to advance.

From time to time, still holding her securely, he bent down, and taking a handful of snow he rubbed his feet with it, to prevent their being frostbitten. At other times, his throat feeling as if it were on fire, he put a little snow in his mouth and sucked it; this for a moment assuaged his thirst, but changed it into fever—a relief which was an aggravation.

The storm had become shapeless from its violence. Deluges of snow are possible. This was one. The paroxysm scourged the shore at the same time that it uptore the depths of ocean. This was, perhaps, the moment when the distracted hooker was going to pieces in the battle of the breakers.

He traveled under this north wind, still toward the east, over wide surfaces of snow. He knew not how the hours had passed. For a long time he had ceased to see the smoke. Such indications are soon effaced in the night; besides, it was past the hour when fires are put out. Or he had, perhaps, made a mistake, and it was possible that neither town nor village existed in the direction in which he was traveling. Doubting, he yet persevered.

Two or three times the little infant cried. Then he adopted in his gait a rocking movement, and the child was soothed and silenced. She ended by falling into a sound sleep. Shivering himself, he felt her warm. He frequently tightened the folds of the jacket round the babe's neck, so that the frost should not get in through any opening, and that no melted snow should drop between the garment and the child.

The plain was unequal. In the declivities into which it sloped, the snow, driven by the wind into the dips of the ground, was so deep, in comparison with a child so small, that it almost engulfed him, and he had to struggle through it, half buried. He walked on, working away the snow with his knees.

Having cleared the ravine, he reached the high lands swept by the winds, where the snow lay thin. Then he found the surface a sheet of ice. The little girl's lukewarm breath, playing on his face, warmed it for a moment, then lingered, and froze in his hair, stiffening it into icicles.

He felt the approach of another danger. He could not afford to fall. He knew that if he did so, he should never rise again. He was overcome by fatigue, and the weight of the darkness would, as with the dead woman, have held him to the ground, and the ice glued him alive to the earth.

He had tripped upon the slopes of precipices, and had recovered himself: he had stumbled into holes, and had got out again. Thenceforth the slightest fall would be death; a false step opened for him a tomb. He must not slip. He had not strength to rise even to his knees. Now everything was slippery; everywhere there was rime and frozen snow. The little creature whom he carried made his progress fearfully difficult. She was not only a burden, which his weariness and exhaustion made excessive, but was also an embarrassment. She occupied both his arms: and, to him who walks over ice, both arms are a natural and necessary balancing power.

He was obliged to do without this balance.

He did without it and advanced, bending under his burden, not knowing what would become of him.

This little infant was the drop causing the cup of distress to overflow.

He advanced, reeling at every step, as if on a spring board, and accomplishing, without spectators, miracles of equilibrium. Let us repeat that he was, perhaps, followed on this path of pain by eyes unsleeping in the distances of the shadows—the eyes of the mother and the eyes of God. He staggered, slipped, recovered himself, took care of the infant, and, gathering the jacket about her, he covered up her head; staggered again, advanced—slipped—then drew himself up. The cowardly wind drove against him. Apparently, he made much more way than was necessary. He was, to all appearance, on the plains where Bincleaves Farm was afterwards established, between what are now called Spring Gardens and the Parsonage House. Homesteads and cottages occupy the place of waste lands. Sometimes less than a century separates a steppe from a city.

Suddenly, a lull having occurred in the icy blast which was blinding him, he perceived, at a short distance in front of him, a cluster of gables and of chimneys shown in relief by the snow. The reverse of a silhouette—a city painted in white on a black horizon, something like what we call nowadays a negative proof. Roofs—dwellings—shelter! He had arrived somewhere at last. He felt the ineffable encouragement of hope. The watch of a ship which has wandered from her course feels some such emotion when he cries, "Land ho!"

He hurried his steps.

At length, then, he was near mankind. He would soon be amidst living creatures. There was no longer anything to fear. There glowed within him that sudden warmth—security; that out of which he was emerging was over; thenceforth there would no longer be night, nor winter, nor tempest. It seemed to him that he had left all evil chances behind him. The infant was no longer a burden. He almost ran.

His eyes were fixed on the roofs. There was life there. He never took his eyes off them. A dead man might gaze thus on what might appear through the half-open lid of his sepulcher. There were the chimneys of which he had seen the smoke.

No smoke arose from them now. He was not long before he reached the houses. He came to the outskirts of a town—an open street. At that period bars to streets were falling into disuse.

The street began by two houses. In those two houses neither candle nor lamp was to be seen; nor in the whole street; nor in the whole town, so far as eye could reach. The house to the right was a roof rather than a house—nothing could be more mean. The walls were of mud, the roof was of straw, and there was more thatch than wall. A large nettle, springing from the bottom of the wall, reached the roof. The hovel had but one door, which was like that of a dog-kennel; and a window, which was but a hole. All was shut up. At the side an inhabited pigsty told that the house was also inhabited.

The house on the left was large, high, built entirely of stone, with a slated roof. It was also closed. It was the rich man's home, opposite to that of the pauper.

The boy did not hesitate. He approached the great mansion. The double folding-door of massive oak, studded with large nails, was of the kind that leads one to expect that behind it there is a stout armory of bolts and locks. An iron knocker was attached to it. He raised the knocker with some difficulty, for his benumbed hands were stumps rather than hands. He knocked once.

No answer.

He struck again; and two knocks.

No movement was heard in the house.

He knocked a third time.

There was no sound. He saw that they were all asleep, and did not care to get up.

Then he turned to the hovel. He picked up a pebble from the snow, and knocked against the low door.

There was no answer.

He raised himself on tiptoe, and knocked with his pebble against the pane too softly to break the glass, but loud enough to be heard.

No voice was heard; no step moved; no candle was lighted.

He saw that there, as well, they did not care to awake.

The house of stone and the thatched hovel were equally deaf to the wretched.

The boy decided on pushing on further, and penetrating the strait of houses which stretched away in front of him, so dark that it seemed more like a gulf between two cliffs than the entrance to a town.

Chapter IV

ANOTHER FORM OF DESERT

IT WAS WEYMOUTH WHICH HE HAD JUST ENTERED. WEYMOUTH THEN WAS NOT THE RESPECTABLE and fine Weymouth of to-day.

Ancient Weymouth did not present, like the present one, an irreproachable rectangular quay, with an inn and a statue in honor of George III. This resulted from the fact that George III had not yet been born. For the same reason, they had not yet designed on the slope of the green hill toward the east, fashioned flat on the soil by cutting away the turf and leaving the bare chalk to the view, the white horse, an acre long, bearing the king upon his back, and always turning, in honor of George III, his tail to the city. These honors, however, were deserved. George III, having lost in his old age the intellect he had never possessed in his youth, was not responsible for the calamities of his reign. He was an innocent. Why not erect statues to him?

Weymouth, a hundred and eighty years ago, was about as symmetrical as a game of spillikins in confusion. In legends it is said that Astaroth traveled over the world, carrying on her back a wallet which contained everything, even good women in their houses; a pell-mell of sheds thrown from her devil's bag would give an idea of that irregular Weymouth—the good women in the sheds included. The Music Hall remains as a specimen of those buildings; a confusion of wooden dens, carved, and eaten by worms (which carve in another fashion)—shapeless, overhanging buildings, some with pillars, leaning one against the other for support against the sea wind and leaving between them awkward spaces of narrow and winding channels, lanes, and passages, often flooded by the equinoctial tides. A heap of old grandmother houses, crowded round a grandfather church, such was Weymouth; a sort of old Norman village thrown up on the coast of England.

The traveler, who entered the tavern, now replaced by the hôtel, instead of paying royally his twenty-five francs for a fried sole and a bottle of wine, had to suffer the humiliation of eating a pennyworth of soup made of fish—which soup, by the by, was very good. Wretched fare!

The deserted child, carrying the foundling, passed through the first street, then the second, then the third. He raised his eyes, seeking in the higher stories and in the roofs a lighted window-pane, but all were closed and dark. At intervals he knocked at the doors. No one answered. Nothing makes the heart so like a stone as being warm between sheets. The noise and the shaking had at length awakened the infant. He knew this because he felt her suck his cheek. She did not cry, believing him her mother.

He was about to turn and wander long, perhaps, in the intersections of the Scrambridge lanes, where there were then more cultivated plots than dwellings, more thorn hedges than houses; but fortunately he struck into a passage which exists to this day near Trinity schools. This passage led him to a water-brink, where there was a roughly built quay with a parapet, and to the right he made out a bridge. It was the bridge over the Wey, connecting Weymouth with Melcombe Regis, and under the arches of which the Backwater joins the harbor.

Weymouth, a hamlet, was then the suburb of Melcombe Regis, a city and port. Now Melcombe Regis is a parish of Weymouth. The village has absorbed the city. It was the bridge which did the work. Bridges are strange vehicles of suction, which inhale the population, and sometimes swell one riverbank at the expense of its opposite neighbor.

The boy went to the bridge, which at that period was a covered timber structure. He crossed it. Thanks to its roofing, there was no snow on the planks. His bare feet had a moment's comfort as they crossed them. Having passed over the bridge, he was in Melcombe Regis. There were fewer wooden houses than stone ones there. He was no longer in the village, he was in the city.

The bridge opened on a rather fine street called St. Thomas's Street. He entered it. Here and there were high carved gables and shop-fronts. He set to knocking at the doors again: he had no strength left to call or shout.

At Melcombe Regis, as at Weymouth, no one was stirring. The doors were all carefully double-locked. The windows were covered by their shutters, as the eyes by their lids. Every precaution had been taken to avoid being roused by disagreeable surprises. The little wanderer was suffering the indefinable depression made by a sleeping town. Its silence, as of a paralyzed ants' nest, makes the head swim. All its lethargies mingle their nightmares, its slumbers are a crowd, and from its human bodies lying prone, there arises a vapor of dreams. Sleep has gloomy associates beyond this life: the decomposed thoughts of the sleepers float above them in a mist which is both of death and of life, and combine with the Possible, which has also, perhaps, the power of thought, as it floats in space. Hence arise entanglements. Dreams, those clouds, interpose their folds and their transparencies over that star, the mind. Above those closed eyelids, where vision has taken the place of sight, a sepulchral disintegration of outlines and appearances dilates itself into impalpability. Mysterious, diffused existences amalgamate themselves with life on that border of death, which sleep is. Those larvae and souls mingle in the air. Even he who sleeps not feels a medium press upon him full of sinister life. The surrounding chimera, in which he suspects a reality, impedes him. The waking man, wending his way amidst the sleep phantoms of others, unconsciously pushes back passing shadows, has, or imagines that he has, a vague fear of adverse contact with the invisible, and feels at every moment the obscure pressure of a hostile encounter which immediately dissolves. There is something of the effect of a forest in the nocturnal diffusion of dreams.

This is what is called being afraid without reason.

What a man feels, a child feels still more.

The uneasiness of nocturnal fear, increased by the spectral houses, increased the weight of the sad burden under which he was struggling.

He entered Conycar Lane, and perceived at the end of that passage the Backwater, which he took for the ocean. He no longer knew in what direction the sea lay. He retraced his steps, struck to the left by Maiden Street, and returned as far as St. Albans Row.

There, by chance and without selection, he knocked violently at any house that he happened to pass. His blows, on which he was expending his last energies, were jerky and without aim; now ceasing altogether for a time, now renewed as if in irritation. It was the violence of his fever striking against the doors.

One voice answered.

That of Time.

Three o'clock tolled slowly behind him from the old belfry of St. Nicholas.

Then all sank into silence again.

That no inhabitant should have opened the lattice may appear surprising. Nevertheless that silence is in a great measure to be explained. We must remember that in January, 1790, they were just over a somewhat severe outbreak of the plague in London, and that the fear of receiving sick vagabonds caused a diminution of hospitality everywhere. People would not even open their windows for fear of inhaling the poison.

The child felt the coldness of men more terribly than the coldness of night. The coldness of men is intentional. He felt a tightening on his sinking heart which he had not known on the open plains. Now he had entered into the midst of life, and remained alone. This was the summit of misery. The pitiless desert he had understood; the unrelenting town was too much to bear.

The hour, the strokes of which he had just counted, had been another blow. Nothing is so freezing in certain situations as the voice of the hour. It is a declaration of indifference. It is Eternity saying, "What does it matter to me?"

He stopped, and it is not certain that, in that miserable minute, he did not ask himself whether it would not be easier to lie down there and die. However, the little infant leaned her head against his shoulder, and fell asleep again.

This blind confidence set him onwards again. He whom all supports were failing felt that he was himself a basis of support. Irresistible summons of duty!

Neither such ideas nor such a situation belonged to his age. It is probable that he did not understand them. It was a matter of instinct. He did what he chanced to do.

He set out again in the direction of Johnstone Row. But now he no longer walked; he dragged himself along. He left St. Mary's Street to the left, made zigzags through lanes, and at the end of a winding passage found himself in a rather wide, open space. It was a piece of waste land not built upon; probably the spot where Chesterfield Place now stands. The houses ended there. He perceived the sea to the right, and scarcely anything more of the town to his left.

What was to become of him? Here was the country again. To the east great inclined planes of snow marked out the wide slopes of Radipole. Should he continue this journey? Should he advance and re-enter the solitudes? Should he return and re-enter the streets? What was he to do between those two silences—the mute plain and the deaf city? Which of the two refusals should he choose?

There is the anchor of mercy. There is also the look of piteousness. It was that look which the poor little despairing wanderer threw around him.

All at once he heard a menace.

Chapter V

MISANTHROPY PLAYS ITS PRANKS

A STRANGE AND ALARMING GRINDING OF TEETH REACHED HIM THROUGH THE DARKNESS. It was enough to drive one back: he advanced. To those to whom silence has become dreadful, a howl is comforting.

That fierce growl reassured him—that threat was a promise. There was there a being alive and awake, though it might be a wild beast. He advanced in the direction whence came the snarl.

He turned the corner of a wall, and, behind in the vast sepulchral light made by the reflection of snow and sea, he saw a thing placed as if for shelter. It was a cart, unless it was a hovel. It had wheels—it was a carriage. It had a roof—it was a dwelling. From the roof arose a funnel, and out of the funnel smoke. This smoke was red, and seemed to imply a good fire in the interior. Behind, projecting hinges indicated a door, and in the center of this door a square opening showed a light inside the caravan. He approached.

Whatever had growled perceived his approach, and became furious. It was no longer a growl which he had to meet, it was a roar. He heard a sharp sound, as of a chain violently pulled to its full length, and suddenly, under the door, between the hind wheels, two rows of sharp white teeth appeared. At the same time as the mouth between the wheels, a head was put through the window.

"Peace there!" said the head.

The mouth was silent.

The head began again—

"Is anyone there?"

The child answered—

"Yes."

"Who?"

"I."

"You? Who are you? whence do you come?"

"I am weary," said the child.

"What o'clock is it?"

"I am cold."

"What are you doing there?"

"I am hungry."

The head replied—

"Everyone cannot be as happy as a lord. Go away."

The head was withdrawn and the window closed.

The child bowed his forehead, drew the sleeping infant closer in his arms, and collected his strength to resume his journey; he had taken a few steps, and was hurrying away.

However, at the same time that the window closed the door had opened; a step had been let down, the voice which had spoken to the child cried out angrily from the inside of the van.

"Well! why do you not enter?"

The child turned back.

"Come in," resumed the voice. "Who has sent me a fellow like this, who is hungry and cold, and who does not come in?"

The child, at once repulsed and invited, remained motionless.

The voice continued—

"You are told to come in, you young rascal."

He made up his mind, and placed one foot on the lowest step.

There was a great growl under the van. He drew back. The gaping jaws appeared.

"Peace!" cried the voice of the man.

The jaws retreated, the growling ceased.

"Come up!" continued the man.

The child with difficulty climbed up the three steps. He was impeded by the infant so be-numbed, rolled up and enveloped in the jacket that nothing could be distinguished of her, and that she was but a little shapeless mass.

He passed over the three steps; and having reached the threshold, stopped.

No candle was burning in the caravan, probably from the economy of want. The hut was lighted only by a red tinge, arising from the opening at the top of the stove, in which sparkled a peat fire. On the stove were smoking a porringer and a saucepan, containing to all appearance something to eat. The savory odor was perceptible. The hut was furnished with a chest, a stool, and an unlighted lantern which hung from the ceiling. Besides, to the partition were attached some boards on brackets and some hooks, from which hung a variety of things. On the boards and nails were rows of glasses, coppers, an alembic, a vessel rather like those used for graining wax, which are called granulators, and a confusion of strange objects of which the child under-stood nothing, and which were utensils for cooking and chemistry. The caravan was oblong in shape, the stove being in front. It was not even a little room; it was scarcely a big box. There was more light outside from the snow than inside from the stove. Everything in the caravan was in-distinct and misty. Nevertheless, a reflection of the fire on the ceiling enabled the spectator to read in large letters—

URSUS, PHILOSOPHER.

The child, in fact, was entering the house of Homo and Ursus. The one he had just heard growling, the other speaking.

The child having reached the threshold, perceived near the stove a man, tall, smooth, thin and old, dressed in gray, whose head, as he stood, reached the roof. The man could not have raised him-self on tiptoe. The caravan was just his size.

"Come in!" said the man, who was Ursus.

The child entered.

"Put down your bundle."

The child placed his burden carefully on the top of the chest, for fear of awakening and terri-fying it.

The man continued—

"How gently you put it down! You could not be more careful were it a case of relics. Is it that you are afraid of tearing a hole in your rags? Worthless vagabond! in the streets at this hour! Who are you? Answer! But no. I forbid you to answer. There! You are cold. Warm yourself as quick as you can," and he shoved him by the shoulders in front of the fire.

"How wet you are! You're frozen through! A nice state to come into a house! Come, take off those rags, you villain!" and as with one hand, and with feverish haste, he dragged off the boy's rags which tore into shreds, with the other he took down from a nail a man's shirt, and one of those knit-ted jackets which are up to this day called kiss-me-quicks.

"Here are clothes."

He chose out of a heap a woolen rag, and chafed before the fire the limbs of the exhausted and bewildered child, who at that moment, warm and naked, felt as if he were seeing and touching heaven. The limbs having been rubbed, he next wiped the boy's feet.

"Come, you limb! you have nothing frostbitten! I was a fool to fancy you had something frozen, hindlegs or forepaws. You will not lose the use of them this time. Dress yourself!"

The child put on the shirt, and the man slipped the knitted jacket over it.

"Now. . . ."

The man kicked the stool forward and made the little boy sit down, again shoving him by the shoulders; then he pointed with his finger to the porringer which was smoking upon the stove. What the child saw in the porringer was again heaven to him—namely, a potato and a bit of bacon.

"You are hungry—eat!"

The man took from the shelf a crust of hard bread and an iron fork, and handed them to the child.

The boy hesitated.

"Perhaps you expect me to lay the cloth," said the man, and he placed the porringer on the child's lap.

"Gobble that up."

Hunger overcame astonishment. The child began to eat. The poor boy devoured rather than ate. The glad sound of the crunching of bread filled the hut. The man grumbled—

"Not so quick, you horrid glutton! Isn't he a greedy scoundrel? When such scum are hungry, they eat in a revolting fashion. You should see a lord sup. In my time, I have seen dukes eat. They don't eat; that's noble. They drink, however. Come, you pig! stuff yourself!"

The absence of ears, which is the concomitant of a hungry stomach, caused the child to take little heed of these violent epithets, tempered as they were by charity of action involving a contradiction resulting in his benefit. For the moment he was absorbed by two exigencies and by two ecstasies—food and warmth.

Ursus continued his imprecations, muttering to himself—

"I have seen King James, supping in *propriâ personâ*, in the Banqueting House, where are to be admired the paintings of the famous Rubens. His Majesty touched nothing. This beggar here browses—browses, a word derived from brute. What put it into my head to come to this Weymouth seven times devoted to the infernal deities? I have sold nothing since morning. I have harangued the snow. I have played the flute to the hurricane. I have not pocketed a farthing; and now, to-night, beggars drop in. Horrid place! There is battle, struggle, competition between the fools in the street and myself. They try to give me nothing but farthings. I try to give them nothing but drugs. Well! to-day I've made nothing. Not an idiot on the highway. Not a penny in the till. Eat away! Hell-born boy! Tear and crunch! We have fallen on times when nothing can equal the cynicism of spongers. Fatten at my expense, parasite! This wretched boy is more than hungry; he is mad. It is not appetite, it is ferocity. He is carried away by a rabid virus. Perhaps he has the plague. Have you the plague, you thief? Suppose he were to give it to Homo! No, never! Let the populace die, but not my wolf. But by the by I am hungry myself. I declare that this is all very disagreeable. I have worked far into the night. There are seasons in a man's life when he is hard pressed. I was to-night, by hunger. I was alone. I made a fire. I had but one potato, one crust of bread, a mouthful of bacon, and a drop of milk, and I put it to warm. I said to myself, 'Good.' I think I am going to eat, and bang! this crocodile falls upon me at the very moment. He installs himself clean between my food and myself. Behold! how my larder is devastated! Eat! pike, eat! You shark! how many teeth have you in your jaws? Guzzle, wolf-cub; no, I withdraw that word. I respect wolves. Swallow up my food, boa. I have worked all day, and far into the night, on an empty stomach; my throat is sore; my pancreas in distress; my entrails torn; and my reward is to see another eat. 'Tis all one, though! We will divide. He shall have the bread, the potato and the bacon, but I will have the milk."

Just then a wail, touching and prolonged, arose in the hut. The man listened.

"You cry! sycophant! Why do you cry?"

The boy turned toward him. It was evident that it was not he who cried. He had his mouth full.

The cry continued.

The man went to the chest.

"So it is your bundle that wails! Vale of Jehoshaphat! Behold a vociferating parcel! What the devil has your bundle got to croak about?"

He unrolled the jacket, an infant's head appeared, the mouth open and crying.

"Well! Who goes there?" said the man. "Here is another of them. When is this to end? Who is there? To arms! corporal, call out the guard; another bang! What have you brought me, thief? Don't you see it is thirsty?

"Come! the little one must have a drink. So now I shall not have even the milk!"

He took down from the things lying in disorder on the shelf a bandage of linen, a sponge, and a phial, muttering savagely, "What an infernal place!"

Then he looked at the little infant. " 'Tis a girl! one can tell that by her scream, and she is drenched as well." He dragged away, as he had done from the boy, the tatters in which she was knotted up rather than dressed, and swathed her in a rag, which, though of coarse linen, was clean and dry. This rough and sudden dressing made the infant angry.

"She mews relentlessly," said he.

He bit off a long piece of sponge, tore from the roll a square piece of linen, drew from it a bit of thread, took the saucepan containing the milk from the stove, filled the phial with milk, drove down the sponge halfway into its neck, covered the sponge with linen, tied this cork in with the thread, applied his cheeks to the phial to be sure that it was not too hot, and seized under his left arm the bewildered bundle which was still crying. "Come! take your supper, creature! Let me suckle you," and he put the neck of the bottle to its mouth.

The little infant drank greedily.

He held the phial at the necessary incline, grumbling, "They are all the same, the cowards! When they have all they want they are silent."

The child had drunk so ravenously, and had seized so eagerly this breast offered by a cross-grained Providence, that she was taken with a fit of coughing.

"You are going to choke!" growled Ursus. "A fine gobbler this one, too!"

He drew away the sponge which she was sucking, allowed the cough to subside, and then replaced the phial to her lips, saying, "Suck! you little wretch!"

In the meantime the boy had laid down his fork. Seeing the infant drink had made him forget to eat. The moment before, while he ate, the expression in his face was satisfaction—now it was gratitude. He watched the infant's renewal of life; the completion of the resurrection begun by himself filled his eyes with an ineffable brilliancy. Ursus went on muttering angry words between his teeth. The little boy now and then lifted toward Ursus his eyes moist with the unspeakable emotion which the poor little being felt but was unable to express. Ursus addressed him furiously.

"Well, will you eat?"

"And you?" said the child, trembling all over, and with tears in his eyes. "You will have nothing!"

"Will you be kind enough to eat it all up, you cub! There is not too much for you, since there was not enough for me."

The child took up his fork, but did not eat.

"Eat," shouted Ursus. "What has it got to do with me? Who speaks of me? Wretched little barefooted clerk of Penniless Parish, I tell you, eat it all up. You are here to eat, drink, and sleep—eat, or I will kick you out, both of you."

The boy, under this menace, began to eat again. He had not much trouble in finishing what was left in the porringer. Ursus muttered, "This building is badly joined. The cold comes in by the window-pane." A pane had indeed been broken in front, either by a jolt of the caravan or by a stone thrown by some mischievous boy. Ursus had placed a star of paper over the fracture, which had become unpasted. The blast entered there.

He was half-seated on the chest. The infant in his arms, and at the same time on his lap, was sucking rapturously at the bottle, in the happy somnolency of cherubim before their Creator, and infants at their mothers' breast.

"She is drunk," said Ursus; and he continued, "After this, preach sermons on temperance!"

The wind tore from the pane the plaster of paper, which flew across the hut; but this was nothing to the children who were entering life anew; whilst the little girl drank, and the little boy ate, Ursus grumbled—

"Drunkenness begins in the infant in swaddling clothes. What useful trouble Bishop Tillotson gives himself, thundering against excessive drinking. What an odious draft of wind! And then my stove is old. It allows puffs of smoke to escape enough to give you trichiasis. One has the inconvenience of cold, and the inconvenience of fire. One cannot see clearly. That being over there abuses my hospitality. Well! I have not been able to distinguish the animal's face yet. Comfort is wanting here. By Jove! I am a great admirer of exquisite banquets in well closed rooms. I have missed my vocation. I was born to be a sensualist. The greatest of stoics was Philoxenus, who wished to possess the neck of a crane, so as to be longer in tasting the pleasures of the table. Receipts to-day, naught. Nothing sold all day. Inhabitants, servants, and tradesmen, here is the doctor, here are the drugs. You are losing your time, old friend. Pack up your physic. Everyone is well down here. It's a cursed town, where everyone is well! The skies alone have diarrhoea—what snow! Anaxagoras taught that the snow was black; and he was right, cold being blackness. Ice is night. What a hurricane! I can fancy the delight of those at sea. The hurricane is the passage of demons. It is the row of the tempest fiends galloping and rolling head over heels above our bone-boxes. In the cloud this one has a tail, that one has horns, another a flame for a tongue, another claws to its wings, another a lord chancellor's paunch, another an academician's pate. You may observe a form in every sound. To every fresh wind a fresh demon. The ear hears, the eye sees, the crash is a face. Zounds! There are folks at sea—that is certain. My friends! get through the storm as best you can. I have enough to do to get through life. Come now, do I keep an inn, or do I not? Why should I trade with these travelers? The universal distress sends its spatterings even as far as my poverty. Into my cabin fall hideous drops of the far-spreading mud of mankind. I am given up to the voracity of travelers. I am a prey—the prey of those dying of hunger. Winter, night, a pasteboard hut, an unfortunate friend below and without, the storm, a potato, a fire as big as my fist, parasites, the wind penetrating through every cranny, not a halfpenny, and bundles which set to howling. I open them, and find beggars inside. Is this fair? Besides, the laws are violated. Ah! vagabond with your vagabond child! Mischievous pickpocket, evil-minded abortion, so you walk the streets after curfew? If our good king only knew it, would he not have you thrown into the bottom of a ditch, just to teach you better? My gentleman walks out at night with my lady, and with the glass at fifteen degrees of frost, bareheaded and barefooted. Understand that such things are forbidden. There are rules and regulations, you lawless wretches. Vagabonds are punished, honest folks who have houses are guarded and protected. Kings are the fathers of their people. I have my own house. You would have been whipped in the public street had you chanced to have been met, and quite right, too. There must be order in an established city. For my own part, I did wrong not to denounce you to the constable. But I am such a fool! I understand what is right and do what is wrong. Oh, the ruffian! to come here in such a state! I did not see the snow upon them when they came in; it had melted, and here's my whole house swamped. I have an inundation in my home. I shall have to burn an incredible amount of coals to dry up this lake—coals at twelve farthings, the miners' standard! How am I going to manage to fit three into this caravan? Now it is over; I enter the nursery; I am going to have in my house the weaning of the future beggardom of England. I shall have for employment, office, and function, to fashion the miscarried fortunes of that colossal Prostitute, Misery, to bring to perfection future gallows' birds, and to give young thieves the forms of philosophy. The tongue of the wolf is the warning of God. And to think that if I had not been eaten up by creatures of this kind for the last thirty years, I should be rich; Homo would be fat; I should have a medicine-chest full of rarities; as many surgical instruments as Doctor Linacre, surgeon to King Henry VIII; divers animals of all kinds; Egyptian mummies, and similar curiosities; I should be a member of the College of Physicians, and have the right of using the library, built in 1652 by the celebrated Hervey, and of studying in the lantern of that dome whence you can see the whole of London. I could continue my observations of solar obfuscation, and prove that a caligenous vapor arises from the planet. Such was the opinion of John Kepler, who was born the year before the Massacre of St. Bartholomew, and who was mathematician to the emperor. The sun is a chimney which sometimes smokes; so does my stove. My stove is no better than the sun. Yes, I should have made my fortune: my part would have been a different one—I should not be the insignificant fellow I am. I should not degrade science in the highways, for the crowd is not worthy of the doctrine, the crowd being nothing better than a confused mixture of all sorts of ages, sexes, humors, and conditions, that wise men of all periods have not hesitated to despise, and whose extravagance and passion the most moderate men in their justice detest! Oh, I am weary of existence! After all, one does not live long! The human life is soon done with. But, no—it is long. At intervals, that we should not become too discouraged, that we may have the stupidity to consent to bear our being, and not profit by the magnificent opportunities to hang ourselves which cords and nails afford, nature puts on an air of taking a little care of man—not to-night, though. The rogue causes the wheat to spring up, ripens the grape, gives her song to the nightingale. From time to time a ray of morning or a glass of gin, and that is what we call happiness! It is a narrow border of good round a huge winding-sheet of evil. We have a destiny of which the devil has woven the stuff, and God has sewn the hem. In the meantime, you have eaten my supper, you thief!"

In the meantime the infant whom he was holding all the time in his arms very tenderly whilst he was vituperating shut its eyes languidly; a sign of repletion. Ursus examined the phial, and grumbled—

"She has drunk it all up, the impudent creature!"

He arose, and sustaining the infant with his left arm, with his right he raised the lid of the chest and drew from beneath it a bear-skin, the one he called, as will be remembered, his real skin. Whilst he was doing this he heard the other child eating, and looked at him sideways.

"It will be something to do if, henceforth, I have to feed that growing glutton. It will be a worm gnawing at the vitals of my industry."

He spread out, still with one arm, the bear-skin on the chest, working his elbow and managing his movements so as not to disturb the sleep into which the infant was just sinking.

Then he laid her down on the fur, on the side next the fire. Having done so, he placed the phial on the stove, and exclaimed—

"I'm thirsty, if you like!"

He looked into the pot. There were a few good mouthfuls of milk left in it; he raised it to his lips. Just as he was about to drink, his eye fell on the little girl. He replaced the pot on the stove, took the phial, uncorked it, poured into it all the milk that remained, which was just sufficient to fill it, replaced the sponge and the linen rag over it, and tied it round the neck of the bottle.

"All the same, I'm hungry and thirsty," he observed.

And he added—

"When one cannot eat bread, one must drink water."

Behind the stove there was a jug with the spout off. He took it and handed it to the boy.

"Will you drink?"

The child drank, and then went on eating.

Ursus seized the pitcher again, and conveyed it to his mouth. The temperature of the water which it contained had been unequally modified by the proximity of the stove.

He swallowed some mouthfuls and made a grimace.

"Water! pretending to be pure, thou resemblest false friends. Thou art warm at the top and cold at bottom."

In the meantime the boy had finished his supper. The porringer was more than empty, it was cleaned out. He picked up and ate pensively a few crumbs caught in the folds of the knitted jacket on his lap.

Ursus turned toward him.

"That is not all. Now, a word with you. The mouth is not made only for eating, it is made for speaking. Now that you are warmed and stuffed, you beast, take care of yourself. You are going to answer my questions. Whence do you come?"

The child replied—

"I do not know."

"How do you mean, you don't know?"

"I was abandoned this evening on the seashore."

"You little scamp! what's your name? He is so good for nothing that his relations desert him."

"I have no relations."

"Give in a little to my tastes, and observe that I do not like those who sing to a tune of fibs. Thou must have relatives since you have a sister."

"It is not my sister."

"It is not your sister?"

"No."

"Who is it then?"

"It is a baby that I found."

"Found?"

"Yes."

"What! did you pick her up?"

"Yes."

"Where? If you lie I will exterminate you."

"On the breast of a woman who was dead in the snow."

"When?"

"An hour ago."

"Where?"

"A league from here."

The arched brow of Ursus knitted and took that pointed shape which characterizes emotion on the brow of a philosopher.

"Dead! Lucky for her! We must leave her in the snow. She is well off there. In which direction?"

"In the direction of the sea."

"Did you cross the bridge?"

"Yes."

Ursus opened the window at the back and examined the view.

The weather had not improved. The snow was falling thickly and mournfully.

He shut the window.

He went to the broken glass; he filled the hole with a rag; he heaped the stove with peat; he spread out as far as he could the bear-skin on the chest; took a large book which he had in a corner, placed it under the skin for a pillow, and laid the head of the sleeping infant on it.

Then he turned to the boy.

"Lie down there."

The boy obeyed, and stretched himself at full length by the side of the infant.

Ursus rolled the bear-skin over the two children, and tucked it under their feet.

He took down from a shelf, and tied round his waist, a linen belt with a large pocket containing, no doubt, a case of instruments and bottles of restoratives.

Then he took the lantern from where it hung to the ceiling and lighted it. It was a dark lantern. When lighted it still left the children in shadow.

Ursus half-opened the door, and said—

"I am going out; do not be afraid. I shall return. Go to sleep."

Then letting down the steps, he called Homo. He was answered by a loving growl.

Ursus, holding the lantern in his hand, descended. The steps were replaced, the door was re-closed. The children remained alone.

From without, a voice, the voice of Ursus, said—

"You, boy, who have just eaten up my supper, are you already asleep?"

"No," replied the child.

"Well, if she cries, give her the rest of the milk."

The clinking of a chain being undone was heard, and the sound of a man's footsteps, mingled with that of the pads of an animal, died off in the distance. A few minutes after, both children slept profoundly.

The little boy and girl, lying naked side by side, were joined through the silent hours, in the seraphic promiscuousness of the shadows; such dreams as were possible to their age floated from one to the other; beneath their closed eyelids there shone, perhaps, a starlight; if the word marriage were not inappropriate to the situation, they were husband and wife after the fashion of the angels. Such innocence in such darkness, such purity in such an embrace, such foretastes of heaven are possible only to childhood, and no immensity approaches the greatness of little children. Of all gulfs this is the deepest. The fearful perpetuity of the dead chained beyond life, the mighty animosity of the ocean to a wreck, the whiteness of the snow over buried bodies, do not equal in pathos two children's mouths meeting divinely in sleep, and the meeting of which is not even a kiss. A betrothal perchance, perchance a catastrophe. The unknown weighs down upon their juxtaposition. It charms, it terrifies; who knows which? It stays the pulse. Innocence is higher than virtue. Innocence is holy ignorance. They slept. They were in peace. They were warm. The nakedness of their bodies, embraced each in each, amalgamated with the virginity of their souls. They were there as in the nest of the abyss.

Chapter VI

THE AWAKING

THE BEGINNING OF DAY IS SINISTER. A SAD PALE LIGHT PENETRATED THE HUT. IT WAS THE FROZEN dawn. That wan light which throws into relief the mournful reality of objects which are blurred into spectral forms by the night, did not awake the children, so soundly were they sleeping. The caravan was warm. Their breathings alternated like two peaceful waves. There was no longer a hurricane without. The light of dawn was slowly taking possession of the horizon. The constellations were being extinguished, like candles blown out one after the other. Only a few large stars resisted. The deep-toned song of the Infinite was coming from the sea.

The fire in the stove was not quite out. The twilight broke, little by little, into daylight. The boy slept less heavily than the girl. At length, a ray brighter than the others broke through the pane, and he opened his eyes. The sleep of childhood ends in forgetfulness. He lay in a state of semistupor, without knowing where he was or what was near him, without making an effort to remember, gazing at the ceiling, and setting himself an aimless task as he gazed dreamily at the letters of the inscription—Ursus, Philosopher—which, being unable to read, he examined without the power of deciphering.

The sound of the key turning in the lock caused him to turn his head.

The door turned on its hinges, the steps were let down. Ursus was returning. He ascended the steps, his extinguished lantern in his hand. At the same time the pattering of four paws fell upon the steps. It was Homo, following Ursus, who had also returned to his home.

The boy awoke with somewhat of a start. The wolf, having probably an appetite, gave him a morning yawn, showing two rows of very white teeth. He stopped when he had got halfway up the steps, and placed both forepaws within the caravan, leaning on the threshold, like a preacher with his elbows on the edge of the pulpit. He sniffed the chest from afar, not being in the habit of finding it occupied as it then was. His wolfine form, framed by the doorway, was designed in black against the light of morning. He made up his mind, and entered. The boy, seeing the wolf in the caravan, got out of the bear-skin, and, standing up, placed himself in front of the little infant, who was sleeping more soundly than ever.

Ursus had just hung the lantern up on a nail in the ceiling. Silently, and with mechanical deliberation, he unbuckled the belt in which was his case, and replaced it on the shelf. He looked at nothing, and seemed to see nothing. His eyes were glassy. Something was moving him deeply in his mind. His thoughts at length found breath, as usual, in a rapid outflow of words. He exclaimed—

"Happy, doubtless! Dead! stone dead!"

He bent down, and put a shovelful of turf mold into the stove; and as he poked the peat, he growled out—

"I had a deal of trouble to find her. The mischief of the unknown had buried her under two feet of snow. Had it not been for Homo, who sees as clearly with his nose as Christopher Columbus did with his mind, I should be still there, scratching at the avalanche, and playing hide and seek with Death. Diogenes took his lantern and sought for a man; I took my lantern and sought for a woman. He found a sarcasm, and I found mourning. How cold she was. I touched her hand—a stone! What silence in her eyes. How can anyone be such a fool as to die and leave a child behind! It will not be convenient to pack three into this box. A pretty family I have now! A boy and a girl!"

Whilst Ursus was speaking, Homo sidled up close to the stove. The hand of the sleeping infant was hanging down between the stove and the chest. The wolf set to licking it. He licked it so softly that he did not awake the little infant.

Ursus turned round.

"Well done, Homo. I shall be father, and you shall be uncle."

Then he betook himself again to arranging the fire with philosophical care, without interrupting his aside.

"Adoption! It is settled; Homo is willing."

He drew himself up.

"I should like to know who is responsible for that woman's death? Is it man? or. . . ."

He raised his eyes, but looked beyond the ceiling, and his lips murmured—

"Is it Thou?"

Then his brow dropped, as if under a burden, and he continued—

"The night took the trouble to kill the woman."

Raising his eyes, they met those of the boy, just awakened, who was listening. Ursus addressed him abruptly—

"What are you laughing about?"

The boy answered—

"I am not laughing."

Ursus felt a kind of shock, looked at him fixedly for a few minutes and said—

"Then you are frightful."

The interior of the caravan, on the previous night, had been so dark that Ursus had not yet seen the boy's face. The broad daylight revealed it. He placed the palms of his hands on the two shoulders of the boy, and, examining his countenance more and more piercingly, exclaimed—

"Do not laugh any more!"

"I am not laughing," said the child.

Ursus was seized with a shudder from head to foot.

"You do laugh, I tell you."

Then seizing the child with a grasp which would have been one of fury had it not been one of pity, he asked him, roughly—

"Who did that to you?"

The child replied—

"I don't know what you mean."

"How long have you had that laugh?"

"I have always been thus," said the child.

Ursus turned toward the chest, saying in a low voice—

"I thought that work was out of date."

He took from the top of it, very softly, so as not to awaken the infant, the book which he had placed there for a pillow.

"Let us see Conquest," he murmured.

It was a bundle of paper in folio, bound in soft parchment. He turned the pages with his thumb, stopped at a certain one, opened the book wide on the stove, and read—

" *'De Denasatis,'* it is here."

And he continued—

"Bucca fissa usque ad aures, genezivis denudatis, nasoque murdridato, masca eris, et ridebis semper."

"There it is for certain."

Then he replaced the book on one of the shelves, growling.

"It might not be wholesome to inquire too deeply into a case of the kind. We will remain on the surface; laugh away, my boy!"

Just then the little girl awoke. Her good day was a cry.

"Come, nurse, give her the breast," said Ursus.

The infant sat up. Ursus taking the phial from the stove, gave it to her to suck.

Then the sun arose. He was level with the horizon. His red rays gleamed through the glass, and struck against the face of the infant, which was turned toward him. Her eyeballs, fixed on the sun, reflected his purple orbit like two mirrors. The eyeballs were immovable, the eyelids also.

"See!" said Ursus. "She is blind."

PART II

BOOK THE FIRST

THE EVERLASTING PRESENCE OF THE PAST: MAN REFLECTS MAN

Chapter 1

LORD CLANCHARLIE

I

THERE WAS, IN THOSE DAYS, AN OLD TRADITION.

That tradition was Lord Linnæus Clancharlie.

Linnæus Baron Clancharlie, a contemporary of Cromwell, was one of the peers of England, few in number, be it said, who accepted the republic. The reason of his acceptance of it might, indeed, for want of a better, be found in the fact that for the time being, the republic was triumphant. It was a matter of course that Lord Clancharlie should adhere to the republic, as long as the republic had the upper hand; but after the close of the revolution and the fall of the parliamentary government, Lord Clancharlie had persisted in his fidelity to it. It would have been easy for the noble patrician to re-enter the reconstituted upper house, repentance being ever well received on restorations, and Charles II being a kind prince enough to those who returned to their allegiance to him; but Lord Clancharlie had failed to understand what was due to events. While the nation overwhelmed with acclamation the king come to retake possession of England; while unanimity was recording its verdict, while the people were bowing their salutation to the monarchy, while the dynasty was rising anew amidst a glorious and triumphant recantation, at the moment when the past was becoming the future, and the future becoming the past, that nobleman remained refractory. He turned his head away from all that joy, and voluntarily exiled himself. While he could have been a peer, he preferred being an outlaw. Years had thus passed away. He had grown old in his fidelity to the dead republic, and was therefore crowned with the ridicule which is the natural reward of such folly.

He had retired into Switzerland, and dwelt in a sort of lofty ruin on the banks of the Lake of Geneva. He had chosen his dwelling in the most rugged nook of the lake, between Chillon, where is the dungeon of Bonnivard, and Vevay, where is Ludlow's tomb. The rugged Alps, filled with twilight, winds, and clouds, were around him; and he lived there, hidden in the great shadows that fall from the mountains. He was rarely met by any passer-by. The man was out of his country, almost out of his century. At that time, to those who understood and were posted in the affairs of the period, no resistance to established things was justifiable. England was happy; a restoration is as the reconciliation of husband and wife, prince and nation return to each other, no state can be more graceful or more pleasant. Great Britain beamed with joy; to have a king at all was a good deal— but furthermore, the king was a charming one. Charles II was amiable, a man of pleasure, yet able to govern, and great, if not after the fashion of Louis XIV. He was essentially a gentleman. Charles II was admired by his subjects. He had made war in Hanover for reasons best known to himself; at least, no one else knew them. He had sold Dunkirk to France, a maneuver of state policy. The Whig peers, concerning whom Chamberlain says, "The cursed republic infected with its stinking breath several of the high nobility," had had the good sense to bow to the inevitable, to conform to the times, and to resume their seats in the House of Lords. To do so it sufficed that they should take the oath of allegiance to the king. When these facts were considered, the glorious reign, the excellent king, august princes given back by divine mercy to the people's love; when it was remembered that persons of such consideration as Monk, and, later on, Jeffreys, had rallied round the throne; that they had been properly rewarded for their loyalty and zeal by the most splendid appointments and the most lucrative offices; that Lord Clancharlie could not be ignorant of this, and that it only depended on himself to be seated by their side, glorious in his honors; that England had, thanks to her king, risen again to the summit of prosperity; that London was all banquets and carousals; that everybody was rich and enthusiastic, that the court was gallant, gay, and magnificent—if by chance, far from these splendors, in some melancholy, indescribable half-light, like nightfall, that old man, clad in the same garb as the common people, was observed pale, absent-minded, bent toward the grave, standing on the shore of the lake, scarce heeding the storm and the winter, walking as though at random, his eye fixed, his white hair tossed by the wind of the shadow, silent, pensive, solitary, who could forbear to smile?

It was the sketch of a madman.

Thinking of Lord Clancharlie, of what he might have been and what he was, a smile was indulgent; some laughed out aloud, others could not restrain their anger. It is easy to understand that men of sense were much shocked by the insolence implied by his isolation.

One extenuating circumstance: Lord Clancharlie had never had any brains. Everyone agreed on that point.

II

IT IS DISAGREEABLE TO SEE ONE'S FELLOWS PRACTICE OBSTINACY. IMITATIONS OF REGULUS ARE NOT popular, and public opinion holds them in some derision. Stubborn people are like reproaches, and we have a right to laugh at them.

Besides, to sum up, are these perversities, these rugged notches, virtues? Is there not in these excessive advertisements of self-abnegation and of honor a good deal of ostentation? It is all parade more than anything else. Why such exaggeration of solitude and exile? to carry nothing to extremes is the wise man's maxim. Be in opposition if you choose, blame if you will, but decently, and crying out all the while "Long live the King." The true virtue is common sense—what falls ought to fall, what succeeds ought to succeed. Providence acts advisedly, it crowns him who deserves the crown; do you pretend to know better than Providence? When matters are settled—when one rule has replaced another—when success is the scale in which truth and falsehood are weighed, in one side the catastrophe, in the other the triumph; then doubt is no longer possible, the honest man rallies to the winning side, and although it may happen to serve his fortune and his family, he does not allow himself to be influenced by that consideration, but thinking only of the public weal, holds out his hand heartily to the conqueror.

What would become of the state if no one consented to serve it? Would not everything come to a standstill? To keep his place is the duty of a good citizen. Learn to sacrifice your secret preferences. Appointments must be filled, and someone must necessarily sacrifice himself. To be faithful to public functions is true fidelity. The retirement of public officials would paralyze the state. What! banish yourself!—how weak! As an example?—what vanity! As a defiance?—what audacity! What do you set yourself up to be, I wonder? Learn that we are just as good as you. If we chose we too could be intractable and untameable, and do worse things than you; but we prefer to be sensible people. Because I am a Trimalcion, you think that I could not be a Cato! What nonsense.

III

NEVER WAS A SITUATION MORE CLEARLY DEFINED OR MORE DECISIVE THAN THAT OF 1660. NEVER had a course of conduct been more plainly indicated to a well-ordered mind. England was out of Cromwell's grasp. Under the republic many irregularities had been committed. British preponderance had been created. With the aid of the Thirty Years' War, Germany had been overcome; with the aid of the Fronde, France had been humiliated; with the aid of the Duke of Braganza, the power of Spain had been lessened. Cromwell had tamed Mazarin; in signing treaties the Protector of England wrote his name above that of the King of France. The United Provinces had been put under a fine of eight millions; Algiers and Tunis had been attacked; Jamaica conquered; Lisbon humbled; French rivalry encouraged in Barcelona, and Masaniello in Naples; Portugal had been made fast to England; the seas had been swept of Barbary pirates from Gibraltar to Crete; maritime domination had been founded under two forms, Victory and Commerce. On the 10th of August, 1653, the man of thirty-three victories, the old Admiral who called himself the sailors' grandfather, Martin Happertz van Tromp, who had beaten the Spanish, had been destroyed by the English fleet. The Atlantic had been cleared of the Spanish navy, the Pacific of the Dutch, the Mediterranean of the Venetian, and by the patent of navigation, England had taken possession of the seacoast of the world. By the ocean she commanded the world; at sea the Dutch flag humbly saluted the British flag. France, in the person of the Ambassador Mancini, bent the knee to Oliver Cromwell; and Cromwell played with Calais and Dunkirk as with two shuttlecocks on a battledore. The continent had been taught to tremble, peace had been dictated, war declared, the British Ensign raised on every pinnacle. By itself the Protector's regiment of Ironsides weighed in the fears of Europe against an army. Cromwell used to say, *"I wish the Republic of England to be respected, as was respected the Republic of Rome."* No longer were delusions held sacred: speech was free, the press was free. In the public street men said what they listed; they printed what they pleased without control or censorship. The equilibrium of thrones had been destroyed. The whole order of European monarchy, in which the Stuarts formed a link, had been overturned. But at last England had emerged from this odious order of things, and had won its pardon.

The indulgent Charles II had granted the declaration of Breda. He had conceded to England oblivion of the period in which the son of the Huntingdon brewer placed his foot on the neck of Louis XIV. England said its meâ culpâ, and breathed again. The cup of joy was, as we have just said, full; gibbets for the regicides adding to the universal delight. A restoration is a smile; but a few gibbets are not out of place, and satisfaction is due to the conscience of the public. To be good subjects was thenceforth the people's sole ambition. The spirit of lawlessness had been expelled. Royalty was reconstituted. Men had recovered from the follies of politics. They mocked at revolution, they jeered at the republic, and as to those times when such strange words as *Right, Liberty, Progress,* had been in the mouth—why, they laughed at such bombast! Admirable was the return to common sense. England had been in a dream. What joy to be quit of such errors! Was ever anything so mad? Where should we be if everyone had his rights? Fancy everyone's having a hand in the government? Can you imagine a city ruled by its citizens? Why, the citizens are the team, and the team cannot be driver. To put to the vote is to throw to the winds. Would you have states driven like clouds? Disorder cannot build up order. With chaos for an architect, the edifice would be a Babel. And, besides, what tyranny is this pretended liberty! As for me, I wish to enjoy myself; not to govern. It is a bore to have to vote; I want to dance. A prince is a providence, and takes care of us all. Truly the king is generous to take so much trouble for our sakes. Besides, he is to the manner born. He knows what it is. It's his business. Peace, War, Legislation, Finance—what have the people to do with such things? Of course the people have to pay; of course the people have to serve; but that should suffice them. They have a place in policy; from them come two essential things, the army and the budget. To be liable to contribute, and to be liable to serve; is not that enough? What more should they want? They are the military and the financial arm. A magnificent *rôle*. The king reigns for them, and they must reward him accordingly. Taxation and the civil list are the salaries paid by the peoples and earned by the prince. The people give their blood and their money, in return for which they are led. To wish to lead themselves! what an absurd idea! They require a guide; being ignorant, they are blind. Has not the blind man his dog? Only the people have a lion, the king, who consents to act the dog. How kind of him! But why are the people ignorant? because it is good for them. Ignorance is the guardian of Virtue. Where there is no perspective there is no ambition. The ignorant man is in useful darkness, which, suppressing sight, suppresses covetousness: whence innocence. He who reads, thinks; who thinks, reasons. But not to reason is duty; and happiness as well. These truths are incontestable; society is based on them.

Thus had sound social doctrines been re-established in England; thus had the nation been reinstated. At the same time a correct taste in literature was reviving. Shakespeare was despised, Dryden admired. *"Dryden is the greatest poet of England, and of the century,"* said Atterbury, the translator of *Achitophel*. It was about the time when M. Huet, Bishop of Avranches, wrote to Saumaise, who had done the author of *Paradise Lost* the honor to refute and abuse him—*"How can you trouble yourself about so mean a thing as that Milton?"* Everything was falling into its proper place: Dryden above, Shakespeare below; Charles II on the throne, Cromwell on the gibbet. England was raising herself out of the shame and the excesses of the past. It is a great happiness for nations to be led back by monarchy to good order in the state and good taste in letters.

That such benefits should be misunderstood is difficult to believe. To turn the cold shoulder to Charles II, to reward with ingratitude the magnanimity which he displayed in ascending the throne—was not such conduct abominable? Lord Linnæus Clancharlie had inflicted this vexation upon honest men. To sulk at his country's happiness, alack, what aberration!

We know that in 1650 Parliament had drawn up this form of declaration: *"I promise to remain faithful to the republic, without king, sovereign, or lord."* Under pretext of having taken this monstrous oath, Lord Clancharlie was living out of the kingdom, and, in the face of the general joy, thought that he had the right to be sad. He had a morose esteem for that which was no more, and was absurdly attached to things which had been.

To excuse him was impossible. The kindest-hearted abandoned him; his friends had long done him the honor to believe that he had entered the republican ranks only to observe the more closely the flaws in the republican armor, and to smite it the more surely when the day should come, for the sacred cause of the king. These lurkings in ambush for the convenient hour to strike the enemy a death-blow in the back are attributes of loyalty. Such a line of conduct had been expected of Lord Clancharlie, so strong was the wish to judge him favorably; but, in the face of his strange persistence in republicanism, people were obliged to lower their estimate. Evidently Lord Clancharlie was confirmed in his convictions—that is to say, an idiot!

The explanation given by the indulgent, wavered between puerile stubbornness and senile obstinacy.

The severe and the just went further; they blighted the name of the renegade. Folly has its rights, but it has also its limits. A man may be a brute, but he has no right to be a rebel. And, after all, what was this Lord Clancharlie? A deserter. He had fled his camp, the aristocracy, for that of the enemy, the people. This faithful man was a traitor. It is true that he was a traitor to the stronger, and faithful to the weaker; it is true that the camp repudiated by him was the conquering camp, and the camp adopted by him, the conquered; it is true that by his treason he lost everything—his political privileges and his domestic hearth, his title and his country. He gained nothing but ridicule, he attained no benefit but exile. But what does all this prove?—that he was a fool. Granted.

Plainly a dupe and traitor in one. Let a man be as great a fool as he likes, so that he does not set a bad example. Fools need only be civil, and in consideration thereof they may aim at being the basis of monarchies. The narrowness of Clancharlie's mind was incomprehensible. His eyes were still dazzled by the phantasmagoria of the revolution. He had allowed himself to be taken in by the republic—yes; and cast out. He was an affront to his country. The attitude he assumed was down-right felony. Absence was an insult. He held aloof from the public joy as from the plague. In his voluntary banishment he found some indescribable refuge from the national rejoicing. He treated loyalty as a contagion: over the widespread gladness at the revival of the monarchy, denounced by him as a lazaretto, he was the black flag. What! could he look thus askance at order reconstituted, a nation exalted, and a religion restored? Over such serenity why cast his shadow? Take umbrage at England's contentment! Must he be the one blot in the clear blue sky! Be as a threat! Protest against a nation's will! refuse his Yes to the universal consent! It would be disgusting, if it were not the part of a fool. Clancharlie could not have taken into account the fact that it did not matter if one had taken the wrong turn with Cromwell, as long as one found one's way back into the right path with Monk.

Take Monk's case. He commands the republican army. Charles II, having been informed of his honesty, writes to him. Monk, who combines virtue with tact, dissimulates at first, then suddenly at the head of his troops dissolves the rebel parliament, and re-establishes the king on the throne. Monk is created Duke of Albemarle, has the honor of having saved society, becomes very rich, sheds a glory over his own time, is created Knight of the Garter, and has the prospect of being buried in Westminster Abbey. Such glory is the reward of British fidelity!

Lord Clancharlie could never rise to a sense of duty thus carried out. He had the infatuation and obstinacy of an exile. He contented himself with hollow phrases. He was tongue-tied by pride. The words conscience and dignity are but words, after all. One must penetrate to the depths. These depths Lord Clancharlie had not reached. His "eye was single," and before committing an act he wished to observe it so closely as to be able to judge it by more senses than one. Hence arose absurd disgust to the facts examined. No man can be a statesman who gives way to such over-strained delicacy. Excess of conscientiousness degenerates into infirmity. Scruple is one-handed when a scepter is to be seized, and a eunuch when fortune is to be wedded. Distrust scruples; they drag you too far. Unreasonable fidelity is like a ladder leading into a cavern—one step down, an-other, then another, and there you are in the dark. The clever reascend; fools remain in it. Con-science must not be allowed to practice such austerity. If it be, it will fall until, from transition to transition, it at length reaches the deep gloom of political prudery. Then one is lost. Thus it was with Lord Clancharlie.

Principles terminate in a precipice.

He was walking, his hands behind him, along the shores of the Lake of Geneva. A fine way of getting on!

In London they sometimes spoke of the exile. He was accused before the tribunal of public opinion. They pleaded for and against him. The cause having been heard, he was acquitted on the ground of stupidity.

Many zealous friends of the former republic had given their adherence to the Stuarts. For this they deserve praise. They naturally calumniated him a little. The obstinate are repulsive to the com-pliant. Men of sense, in favor and good places at court, weary of his disagreeable attitude, took pleasure in saying, *"If he has not rallied to the throne, it is because he has not been sufficiently paid,"* etc. *"He wanted the chancellorship which the king has given to Hyde."* One of his old friends went so far as to whisper, *"He told me so himself."* Remote as was the solitude of Linnæus Clancharlie, something of this talk would reach him through the outlaws he met, such as old regicides like Andrew Broughton, who lived at Lausanne. Clancharlie confined himself to an imperceptible shrug of the shoulders, a sign of profound deterioration. On one occasion he added to the shrug these few words, murmured in a low voice, "I pity those who believe such things."

IV

CHARLES II, GOOD MAN! DESPISED HIM. THE HAPPINESS OF ENGLAND UNDER CHARLES II WAS more than happiness, it was enchantment. A restoration is like an old oil painting, blackened by time, and revarnished. All the past reappeared, good old manners returned, beautiful women reigned and governed. Evelyn notices it. We read in his journal, "Luxury, profaneness, contempt of God. I saw the king on Sunday evening with his courtesans, Portsmouth, Cleveland, Mazarin, and two or three others, all nearly naked, in the gaming-room." We feel that there is ill-nature in this description, for Evelyn was a grumbling Puritan, tainted with republican reveries. He did not appreciate the profitable example given by kings in those grand Babylonian gaieties, which, after all, maintain luxury. He did not understand the utility of vice. Here is a maxim: Do not extirpate vice, if you want to have charming women; if you do you are like idiots who destroy the chrysalis whilst they delight in the butterfly.

Charles II, as we have said, scarcely remembered that a rebel called Clancharlie existed; but James II was more heedful. Charles II governed gently, it was his way; we may add, that he did not govern the worse on that account. A sailor sometimes makes on a rope intended to baffle the wind, a slack knot which he leaves to the wind to tighten. Such is the stupidity of the storm and of the people.

The slack knot very soon becomes a tight one. So did the government of Charles II.

Under James II the throttling began; a necessary throttling of what remained of the revolution. James II had a laudable ambition to be an efficient king. The reign of Charles II was, in his opinion, but a sketch of restoration. James wished for a still more complete return to order. He had, in 1660, deplored that they had confined themselves to the hanging of ten regicides. He was a more genuine reconstructor of authority. He infused vigor into serious principles. He installed true justice, which is superior to sentimental declamations, and attends, above all things, to the interests of society. In his protecting severities we recognize the father of the state. He entrusted the hand of justice to Jeffreys, and its sword to Kirke. That useful Colonel, one day, hung and rehung the same man, a republican, asking him each time, "Will you renounce the republic?" The villain, having each time said "No," was dispatched—"*I hanged him four times,*" said Kirke, with satisfaction. The renewal of executions is a great sign of power in the executive authority. Lady Lisle, who, though she had sent her son to fight against Monmouth, had concealed two rebels in her house, was executed; another rebel, having been honorable enough to declare that an Anabaptist female had given him shelter, was pardoned, and the woman was burned alive. Kirke, on another occasion, gave a town to understand that he knew its principles to be republican, by hanging nineteen burgesses. These reprisals were certainly legitimate, for it must be remembered that, under Cromwell, they cut off the noses and ears of the stone saints in the churches. James II, who had had the sense to choose Jeffreys and Kirke, was a prince imbued with true religion; he practiced mortification in the ugliness of his mistresses; he listened to le Père la Colombière, a preacher almost as unctuous as le Père Cheminais, but with more fire, who had the glory of being, during the first part of his life, the counselor of James II, and, during the latter, the inspirer of Mary Alcock. It was, thanks to this strong religious nourishment, that later on, James II was enabled to bear exile with dignity, and to exhibit, in his retirement at Saint Germain, the spectacle of a king rising superior to adversity, calmly touching for king's evil, and conversing with Jesuits.

It will be readily understood that such a king would trouble himself to a certain extent about such a rebel as Lord Linnæus Clancharlie. Hereditary peerages have a certain hold on the future, and it was evident that if any precautions were necessary with regard to that lord, James II was not the man to hesitate.

Chapter II

LORD DAVID DIRRY-MOIR

LORD LINNÆUS CLANCHARLIE HAD NOT ALWAYS BEEN OLD AND PROSCRIBED; HE HAD HAD HIS phase of youth and passion. We know from Harrison and Pride that Cromwell, when young, loved women and pleasure, a taste which, at times (another reading of the text *Woman*), betrays a seditious man. Distrust the loosely-clasped girdle. *Male proecinctam juvenem cavete*. Lord Clancharlie, like Cromwell, had had his wild hours and his irregularities. He was known to have had a natural child, a son. This son was born in England in the last days of the republic, just as his father was going into exile. Hence he had never seen his father. This bastard of Lord Clancharlie had grown up as page at the court of Charles II. He was styled Lord David Dirry-Moir: he was a lord by courtesy, his mother being a woman of quality. The mother, while Lord Clancharlie was becoming an owl in Switzerland, made up her mind, being a beauty, to give over sulking, and was forgiven that Goth, her first lover, by one undeniably polished and at the same time a royalist, for it was the king himself.

She had been but a short time the mistress of Charles II, sufficiently long however to have made his Majesty—who was delighted to have won so pretty a woman from the republic—bestow on the little Lord David, the son of his conquest, the office of keeper of the stick, which made that bastard officer, boarded at the king's expense, by a natural revulsion of feeling, an ardent adherent of the Stuarts. Lord David was for some time one of the hundred and seventy wearing the great sword, while afterwards, entering the corps of pensioners, he became one of the forty who bear the gilded halberd. He had, besides being one of the noble company instituted by Henry VIII as a bodyguard, the privilege of laying the dishes on the king's table. Thus it was that whilst his father was growing gray in exile, Lord David prospered under Charles II.

After which he prospered under James II.

The king is dead. Long live the king! It is the *non deficit alter, aureus*.

It was on the accession of the Duke of York that he obtained permission to call himself Lord David Dirry-Moir, from an estate which his mother, who had just died, had left him, in that great forest of Scotland, where is found the krag, a bird which scoops out a nest with its beak in the trunk of the oak.

II

JAMES II WAS A KING, AND AFFECTED TO BE A GENERAL. HE LOVED TO SURROUND HIMSELF WITH young officers. He showed himself frequently in public on horseback, in a helmet and cuirass, with a huge projecting wig hanging below the helmet and over the cuirass—a sort of equestrian statue of imbecile war. He took a fancy to the graceful mien of the young Lord David. He liked the royalist for being the son of a republican. The repudiation of a father does not damage the foundation of a court fortune. The king made Lord David gentleman of the bedchamber, at a salary of a thousand a year.

It was a fine promotion. A gentleman of the bedchamber sleeps near the king every night, on a bed which is made up for him. There are twelve gentlemen who relieve each other.

Lord David, whilst he held that post, was also head of the king's granary, giving out corn for the horses and receiving a salary of £260. Under him were the five coachmen of the king, the five postilions of the king, the five grooms of the king, the twelve footmen of the king, and the four chair-bearers of the king. He had the management of the racehorses which the king kept at Newmarket, and which cost his Majesty £600 a year. He worked his will on the king's wardrobe, from which the Knights of the Garter are furnished with their robes of ceremony. He was saluted to the ground by the usher of the Black Rod, who belongs to the king. That usher, under James II, was the knight of Duppa. Mr. Baker, who was clerk of the crown, and Mr. Brown, who was clerk of the Parliament, kowtowed to Lord David. The court of England, which is magnificent, is a model of hospitality. Lord David presided, as one of the twelve, at banquets and receptions. He had the glory of standing behind the king on offertory days, when the king give to the church the golden *byzantium*; on collar-days, when the king wears the collar of his order; on communion days, when no one takes the sacrament excepting the king and the princes. It was he who, on Holy Thursday, introduced into his Majesty's presence the twelve poor men to whom the king gives as many silver pence as the years of his age, and as many shillings as the years of his reign. The duty devolved on him when the king was ill, to call to the assistance of his Majesty the two grooms of the almonry, who are priests, and to prevent the approach of doctors without permission from the council of state. Besides, he was lieutenant-colonel of the Scotch regiment of Guards, the one which plays the Scottish march. As such, he made several campaigns, and with glory, for he was a gallant soldier. He was a brave lord, well-made, handsome, generous, and majestic in look and in manner. His person was like his quality. He was tall in stature, as well as high in birth.

At one time he stood a chance of being made groom of the stole, which would have given him the privilege of putting the king's shirt on his Majesty: but to hold that office it was necessary to be either prince or peer. Now, to create a peer is a serious thing; it is to create a peerage, and that makes many people jealous. It is a favor; a favor which gives the king one friend and a hundred enemies, without taking into account that the one friend becomes ungrateful. James II, from policy, was indisposed to create peerages, but he transferred them freely. The transfer of a peerage produces no sensation. It is simply the continuation of a name. The order is little affected by it.

The good-will of royalty had no objection to raise Lord David Dirry-Moir to the Upper House so long as it could do so by means of a substituted peerage. Nothing would have pleased his Majesty better than to transform Lord David Dirry-Moir, lord by courtesy, into a lord by right.

III

THE OPPORTUNITY OCCURRED.

One day it was announced that several things had happened to the old exile, Lord Clancharlie, the most important of which was that he was dead. Death does just this much good to folks: it causes a little talk about them. People related what they knew, or what they thought they knew, of the last years of Lord Linnæus. What they said was probably legend and conjecture. If these random tales were to be credited, Lord Clancharlie must have had his republicanism intensified toward the end of his life, to the extent of marrying (strange obstinacy of the exile!) Ann Bradshaw, the daughter of a regicide; they were precise about the name. She had also died, it was said, but in giving birth to a boy. If these details should prove to be correct, his child would of course be the legitimate and rightful heir of Lord Clancharlie. These reports, however, were extremely vague in form and were rumors rather than facts. Circumstances which happened in Switzerland, in those days, were as remote from the England of that period as those which take place in China from the England of to-day. Lord Clancharlie must have been fifty-nine at the time of his marriage, they said, and sixty at the birth of his son, and must have died shortly after, leaving his infant orphaned both of father and mother. This was possible, perhaps, but improbable. They added that the child was beautiful as the day—just as we read in all the fairy tales. King James put an end to these rumors, evidently without foundation, by declaring, one fine morning, Lord David Dirry-Moir sole and positive heir *in default of legitimate issue,* and by his royal pleasure, of Lord Linnæus Clancharlie, his natural father, *the absence of all other issue and descent being established,* patents of which grant were registered in the House of Lords. By these patents the king instituted Lord David Dirry-Moir, in the titles, rights, and prerogatives of the late Lord Linnæus Clancharlie, on the sole condition that Lord David should wed, when she attained a marriageable age, a girl who was, at that time, a mere infant a few months old, and whom the king had, in her cradle, created a duchess, no one knew exactly why; or, rather, everyone knew why. This little infant was called the Duchess Josiana.

The English fashion then ran on Spanish names. One of Charles II's bastards was called Carlos, Earl of Plymouth. It is likely that Josiana was a contraction for Josefa-y-Ana. Josiana, however, may have been a name—the feminine of Josias. One of Henry VIII's gentlemen was called Josias du Passage.

It was to this little duchess that the king granted the peerage of Clancharlie. She was a peeress till there should be a peer; the peer should be her husband. The peerage was founded on a double castleward, the barony of Clancharlie and the barony of Hunkerville; besides, the barons of Clancharlie were, in recompense of an ancient feat of arms, and by royal license, Marquises of Corleone, in Sicily.

Peers of England cannot bear foreign titles; there are, nevertheless, exceptions; thus—Henry Arundel, Baron Arundel of Wardou, was, as well as Lord Clifford, a Count of the Holy Roman Empire, of which Lord Cowper is a prince. The Duke of Hamilton is Duke of Chatelherault, in France; Basil Fielding, Earl of Denbigh, is Count of Hapsburg, of Lauffenberg, and of Rheinfelden, in Germany. The Duke of Marlborough was Prince of Mindelheim, in Suabia, just as the Duke of Wellington was Prince of Waterloo, in Belgium. The same Lord Wellington was a Spanish Duke of Ciudad Rodrigo, and Portuguese Count of Vimiera.

There were in England, and there are still, lands both noble and common. The lands of the Lords of Clancharlie were all noble. These lands, burghs, bailiwicks, fiefs, rents, freeholds, and domains, adherent to the peerage of Clancharlie-Hunkerville, belonged provisionally to Lady Josiana, and the king declared that, once married to Josiana, Lord David Dirry-Moir should be Baron Clancharlie.

Besides the Clancharlie inheritance, Lady Josiana had her own fortune. She possessed great wealth, much of which was derived from the gifts of *Madame sans queue* to the Duke of York. *Madame sans queue* is short for Madame. Henrietta of England, Duchess of Orleans, the lady of highest rank in France after the queen, was thus called.

IV

HAVING PROSPERED UNDER CHARLES AND JAMES, LORD DAVID PROSPERED UNDER WILLIAM. HIS Jacobite feeling did not reach to the extent of following James into exile. While he continued to love his legitimate king, he had the good sense to serve the usurper; he was, moreover, although sometimes disposed to rebel against discipline, an excellent officer. He passed from the land to the sea forces, and distinguished himself in the White Squadron. He rose in it to be what was then called captain of a light frigate. Altogether he made a very fine fellow, carrying to a great extent the elegancies of vice: a bit of a poet, like everyone else; a good servant of the state, a good servant to the prince; assiduous at feasts, at galas, at ladies' receptions, at ceremonies, and in battle; servile in a gentlemanlike way; very haughty; with eyesight dull or keen, according to the object examined; inclined to integrity; obsequious or arrogant, as occasion required; frank and sincere on first acquaintance, with the power of assuming the mask afterwards; very observant of the smiles and frowns of the royal humor; careless before a sword's point; always ready to risk his life on a sign from his Majesty with heroism and complacency, capable of any insult but of no impoliteness; a man of courtesy and etiquette, proud of kneeling at great regal ceremonies; of a gay valor; a courtier on the surface, a paladin below; quite young at forty-five. Lord David sang French songs, an elegant gaiety which had delighted Charles II. He loved eloquence and fine language. He greatly admired those celebrated discourses which are called the funeral orations of Bossuet.

From his mother he had inherited almost enough to live on, about £10,000 a year. He managed to get on with it—by running into debt. In magnificence, extravagance, and novelty he was without a rival. Directly he was copied he changed his fashion. On horseback he wore loose boots of cow-hide, which turned over, with spurs. He had hats like nobody else's; unheard-of lace, and bands of which he alone had the pattern.

Chapter III

THE DUCHESS JOSIANA

TOWARD 1705, ALTHOUGH LADY JOSIANA WAS TWENTY-THREE AND LORD DAVID FORTY-FOUR, THE wedding had not yet taken place, and that for the best reasons in the world. Did they hate each other? Far from it; but what cannot escape from you inspires you with no haste to obtain it. Josiana wanted to remain free, David to remain young. To have no tie until as late as possible appeared to him to be a prolongation of youth. Middle-aged young men abounded in those rakish times. They grew gray as young fops. The wig was an accomplice: later on, powder became the auxiliary. At fifty-five Lord Charles Gerrard, Baron Gerrard, one of the Gerrards of Bromley, filled London with his successes. The young and pretty Duchess of Buckingham, Countess of Coventry, made a fool of herself for love of the handsome Thomas Bellasys, Viscount Faulconberg, who was sixty-seven. People quoted the famous verses of Corneille, the septuagenarian, to a girl of twenty—"Marquise, si mon visage." Women, too, had their successes in the autumn of life. Witness Ninon and Marion. Such were the models of the day.

Josiana and David carried on a flirtation of a particular shade. They did not love, they pleased, each other. To be at each other's side sufficed them. Why hasten the conclusion? The novels of those days carried lovers and engaged couples to that kind of stage which was the most becoming. Besides, Josiana, while she knew herself to be a bastard, felt herself a princess, and carried her authority over him with a high tone in all their arrangements. She had a fancy for Lord David. Lord David was handsome, but that was over and above the bargain. She considered him to be fashionable.

To be fashionable is everything. Caliban, fashionable and magnificent, would distance Ariel, poor. Lord David was handsome; so much the better. The danger in being handsome is being insipid; and that he was not. He betted, boxed, ran into debt. Josiana thought great things of his horses, his dogs, his losses at play, his mistresses. Lord David, on his side, bowed down before the fascinations of the Duchess Josiana—a maiden without spot or scruple, haughty, inaccessible, and audacious. He addressed sonnets to her, which Josiana sometimes read. In these sonnets he declared that to possess Josiana would be to rise to the stars, which did not prevent his always putting the ascent off to the following year. He waited in the antechamber outside Josiana's heart; and this suited the convenience of both. At court all admired the good taste of this delay. Lady Josiana said, "It is a bore that I should be obliged to marry Lord David; I, who would desire nothing better than to be in love with him!"

Josiana was "the flesh." Nothing could be more resplendent. She was very tall—too tall. Her hair was of that tinge which might be called red gold. She was plump, fresh, strong, and rosy, with immense boldness and wit. She had eyes which were too intelligible. She had neither lovers nor chastity. She walled herself round with pride. Men! oh, fie! a god only would be worthy of her, or a monster. If virtue consists in the protection of an inaccessible position, Josiana possessed all possible virtue, but without any innocence. She disdained intrigues; but she would not have been displeased had she been supposed to have engaged in some, provided that the objects were uncommon, and proportioned to the merits of one so highly placed. She thought little of her reputation, but much of her glory. To appear yielding, and to be unapproachable, is perfection. Josiana felt herself majestic and material. Hers was a cumbrous beauty. She usurped rather than charmed. She trod upon hearts. She was earthly. She would have been as much astonished at being proved to have a soul in her bosom as wings on her back. She discoursed on Locke; she was polite; she was suspected of knowing Arabic.

To be "the flesh" and to be woman are two different things. Where a woman is vulnerable, on the side of pity, for instance, which so readily turns to love, Josiana was not. Not that she was unfeeling. The ancient comparison of flesh to marble is absolutely false. The beauty of flesh consists in not being marble: its beauty is to palpitate, to tremble, to blush, to bleed, to have firmness without hardness, to be white without being cold, to have its sensations and its infirmities; its beauty is to be life, and marble is death.

Flesh, when it attains a certain degree of beauty, has almost a claim to the right of nudity; it conceals itself in its own dazzling charms as in a veil. He who might have looked upon Josiana nude would have perceived her outlines only through a surrounding glory. She would have shown herself without hesitation to a satyr or a eunuch. She had the self-possession of a goddess. To have made her nudity a torment, ever eluding a pursuing Tantalus, would have been an amusement to her.

The king had made her a duchess, and Jupiter a Nereid—a double irradiation of which the strange brightness of this creature was composed. In admiring her you felt yourself becoming a pagan and a lackey. Her origin had been bastardy and the ocean. She appeared to have emerged from the foam. From the stream had risen the first jet of her destiny; but the spring was royal. In her there was something of the wave, of chance, of the patrician, and of the tempest. She was well read and accomplished. Never had a passion approached her, yet she had sounded them all. She had a disgust for realizations, and at the same time a taste for them. If she had stabbed herself, it would, like Lucretia, not have been until afterwards. She was a virgin stained with every defilement in its visionary stage. She was a possible Astarte in a real Diana. She was, in the insolence of high birth, tempting and inaccessible. Nevertheless, she might find it amusing to plan a fall for herself. She dwelt in a halo of glory, half-wishing to descend from it, and perhaps feeling curious to know what a fall was like. She was a little too heavy for her cloud. To err is a diversion. Princely unconstraint has the privilege of experiment; and what is frailty in a plebeian is only frolic in a duchess. Josiana was in everything—in birth, in beauty, in irony, in brilliancy—almost a queen. She had felt a moment's enthusiasm for Louis de Bouffles, who used to break horse-shoes between his fingers. She regretted that Hercules was dead. She lived in some undefined expectation of a voluptuous and supreme ideal.

Morally, Josiana brought to one's mind the line—

Un beau torse de femme en hydre se termine.

Hers was a noble neck, a splendid bosom, heaving harmoniously over a royal heart, a glance full of life and light, a countenance pure and haughty, and who knows? below the surface was there not, in a semi-transparent and misty depth, an undulating, supernatural prolongation, perchance deformed and dragon-like—a proud virtue ending in vice in the depth of dreams.

II

WITH ALL THAT SHE WAS A PRUDE.
          It was the fashion.
Remember Elizabeth.

Elizabeth was of a type that prevailed in England for three centuries: the sixteenth, seventeenth, and eighteenth. Elizabeth was more than English, she was Anglican. Hence the deep respect of the Episcopalian Church for that queen—a respect resented by the Church of Rome, which counterbalanced it with a dash of excommunication. In the mouth of Sixtus V, when anathematizing Elizabeth, malediction turned to madrigal: *"Un gran cervello di principessa,"* he says. Mary Stuart, less concerned with the church and more with the woman part of the question, had little respect for her sister Elizabeth; and wrote to her as queen to queen and coquette to prude: "Your disinclination to marriage arises from your not wishing to lose the liberty of being made love to." Mary Stuart played with the fan, Elizabeth with the ax. An uneven match. They were rivals, besides, in literature. Mary Stuart composed French verses; Elizabeth translated Horace. The ugly Elizabeth decreed herself beautiful; liked quatrains and acrostics; had the keys of towns presented to her by cupids; bit her lips, after the Italian fashion, rolled her eyes after the Spanish; had in her wardrobe three thousand dresses, and costumes, of which several were for the character of Minerva and Amphitrite; esteemed the Irish for the width of their shoulders; covered her farthingale with braids and spangles; loved roses; cursed, swore, and stamped; struck her maids of honor with her clenched fists; used to send Dudley to the devil; beat Burleigh, the Chancellor, who would cry—poor old fool! spat on Matthew; collared Hatton; boxed the ears of Essex; showed her legs to Bassompierre; and was a virgin.

What she did for Bassompierre, the Queen of Sheba had done for Solomon, consequently she was right, Holy Writ having created the precedent. That which is biblical may well be Anglican. Biblical precedent goes so far as to speak of a child who was called Ebnehaquem or Melilechet—that is to say, the Wise Man's son.

Why object to such manners? Cynicism is at least as good as hypocrisy.

Nowadays England, whose Loyola is named Wesley, casts down her eyes a little at the remembrance of that past age. She is vexed at the memory, yet proud of it.

Amidst such manners as these, a taste for deformity existed, especially amongst women, and singularly amongst beautiful women. Where is the use of being beautiful if one does not possess a baboon? Where is the charm of being a queen if one cannot bandy words with a dwarf? Mary Stuart had "been kind" to the bandy-legged Rizzio. Maria Theresa, of Spain, had been "somewhat familiar" with a negro. Whence the *black abbess*. In the alcoves of the great century, a hump was the fashion; witness the Marshal of Luxembourg, and before Luxembourg, Condé, "such a pretty little man!"

Beauties themselves might be ill-made without detriment; it was admitted. Anne Boleyn had one breast bigger than the other, six fingers to one hand, and a projecting tooth; Lavallière was bandy-legged; which did not hinder Henry VIII from going mad for the one, and Louis XIV for the other.

Morals were equally awry. There was not a woman of high rank who was not teratological. Agnes possessed the principles of Messalina. They were women by day, ghouls by night. They sought the scaffold to kiss the heads of the newly beheaded on their iron stakes. Marguerite de Valois, a predecessor of the prudes, wore, fastened to her belt, the hearts of her lovers in tin boxes, padlocked. Henry IV had hidden himself under her farthingale.

In the eighteenth century the Duchess de Berry, daughter of the Regent, was in herself an abstract, of obscene and royal type, all of these creatures.

These fine ladies, moreover, knew Latin. From the 16th century this had been accounted a feminine accomplishment. Lady Jane Grey had carried fashion to the point of knowing Hebrew. The Duchess Josiana Latinized. Then (another fine thing) she was secretly a Catholic; after the manner of her uncle, Charles II, rather than her father, James II. James II had lost his crown for his Catholicism, and Josiana did not care to risk her peerage. Thus it was that while a Catholic amongst her intimate friends and the refined of both sexes, she was outwardly a Protestant for the benefit of the riffraff.

This is the pleasant view to take of religion. You enjoy all the good things belonging to the official Episcopalian church, and later on you die, like Grotius, in the odor of Catholicity, having the glory of a mass being said for you by le Père Petau.

Although plump and healthy, Josiana was, we repeat, a perfect prude.

At times her sleepy and voluptuous way of dragging out the end of her phrases was like the creeping of a tiger's paws in the jungle.

The advantage of prudes is that they disorganize the human race. They deprive it of the honor of their adherence. Beyond all, keep the human species at a distance. This is a point of the greatest importance.

When one has not got Olympus, one must take the Hôtel de Rambouillet. Juno resolves herself into Araminta. A pretension to divinity not admitted creates affectation. In default of thunderclaps there is impertinence. The temple shrivels into the boudoir. Not having the power to be a goddess, she is an idol.

There is besides, in prudery, a certain pedantry which is pleasing to women. The coquette and the pedant are neighbors. Their kinship is visible in the fop. The subtle is derived from the sensual. Gluttony affects delicacy, a grimace of disgust conceals cupidity. And then woman feels her weak point guarded by all that casuistry of gallantry which takes the place of scruples in prudes. It is a line of circumvallation with a ditch. Every prude puts on an air of repugnance. It is a protection. She will consent, but she disdains—for the present.

Josiana had an uneasy conscience. She felt such a leaning toward immodesty that she was a prude. The recoils of pride in the direction opposed to our vices lead us to those of a contrary nature. It was the excessive effort to be chaste which made her a prude. To be too much on the defensive points to a secret desire for attack; the shy woman is not strait-laced. She shut herself up in the arrogance of the exceptional circumstances of her rank, meditating, perhaps, all the while, some sudden lapse from it.

It was the dawn of the eighteenth century. England was a sketch of what France was during the regency. Walpole and Dubois are not unlike. Marlborough was fighting against his former king, James II, to whom it was said he had sold his sister, Miss Churchill. Bolingbroke was in his meridian, and Richelieu in his dawn. Gallantry found its convenience in a certain medley of ranks. Men were equalized by the same vices as they were later on, perhaps, by the same ideas. Degradation of rank, an aristocratic prelude, began what the revolution was to complete. It was not very far off the time when Jelyotte was seen publicly sitting, in broad daylight, on the bed of the Marquise d'Epinay. It is true (for manners re-echo each other) that in the sixteenth century Smeton's nightcap had been found under Anne Boleyn's pillow.

If the word woman signifies fault, as I forget what Council decided, never was woman so womanlike as then. Never, covering her frailty by her charms, and her weakness by her omnipotence, has she claimed absolution more imperiously. In making the forbidden the permitted fruit, Eve fell; in making the permitted the forbidden fruit, she triumphs. That is the climax. In the eighteenth century the wife bolts out her husband. She shuts herself up in Eden with Satan. Adam is left outside.

III

ALL JOSIANA'S INSTINCTS IMPELLED HER TO YIELD HERSELF GALLANTLY, RATHER THAN TO GIVE herself legally. To surrender on the score of gallantry implies learning, recalls Menalcas and Amaryllis, and is almost a literary act. Mademoiselle de Scudéry, putting aside the attraction of ugliness for ugliness' sake, had no other motive for yielding to Pélisson.

The maiden a sovereign, the wife a subject, such was the old English notion. Josiana was deferring the hour of this subjection as long as she could. She must eventually marry Lord David, since such was the royal pleasure. It was a necessity, doubtless; but what a pity! Josiana appreciated Lord David, and showed him off. There was between them a tacit agreement, neither to conclude nor to break off the engagement. They eluded each other. This method of making love, one step in advance, and two back, is expressed in the dances of the period, the minuet and the gavotte.

It is unbecoming to be married—fades one's ribbons, and makes one look old. An espousal is a dreary absorption of brilliancy. A woman handed over to you by a notary, how commonplace! The brutality of marriage creates definite situations; suppresses the will; kills choice; has a syntax, like grammar; replaces inspiration by orthography; makes a dictation of love; disperses all Life's mysteries; diminishes the rights both of sovereign and subject; by a turn of the scale destroys the charming equilibrium of the sexes, the one robust in bodily strength, the other all-powerful in feminine weakness: strength on one side, beauty on the other; makes one a master and the other a servant, while without marriage one is a slave, the other a queen.

To make Love prosaically decent, how gross! to deprive it of all impropriety, how dull!

Lord David was ripening. Forty; 'tis a marked period. He did not perceive this, and in truth he looked no more than thirty. He considered it more amusing to desire Josiana than to possess her. He possessed others. He had mistresses. On the other hand, Josiana had dreams.

The Duchess Josiana had a peculiarity, less rare than it is supposed. One of her eyes was blue and the other black. Her pupils were made for love and hate, for happiness and misery. Night and day were mingled in her look.

Her ambition was this: to show herself capable of impossibilities. One day she said to Swift, "You people fancy that you know what scorn is." "You people" meant the human race.

She was a skin-deep Papist. Her Catholicism did not exceed the amount necessary for fashion. She would have been a Puseyite in the present day. She wore great dresses of velvet, satin, or moire, some composed of fifteen or sixteen yards of material, with embroideries of gold and silver; and round her waist many knots of pearls, alternating with other precious stones. She was extravagant in gold lace. Sometimes she wore an embroidered cloth jacket like a bachelor. She rode on a man's saddle, notwithstanding the invention of side-saddles, introduced into England in the fourteenth century by Anne, wife of Richard II. She washed her face, arms, shoulders, and neck, in sugar-candy, diluted in white of egg, after the fashion of Castile. There came over her face, after anyone had spoken wittily in her presence, a reflective smile of singular grace. She was free from malice, and rather good-natured than otherwise.

Chapter IV

THE LEADER OF FASHION

J OSIANA WAS BORED. THE FACT IS SO NATURAL AS TO BE SCARCELY WORTH MENTIONING.
Lord David held the position of judge in the gay life of London. He was looked up to by
the nobility and gentry. Let us register a glory of Lord David's. He was daring enough to wear his
own hair. The reaction against the wig was beginning. Just as in 1824 Eugene Deveria was the first
to allow his beard to grow, so in 1702 Prince Devereux was the first to risk wearing his own hair in
public disguised by artful curling. For to risk one's hair was almost to risk one's head. The indignation was universal. Nevertheless Prince Devereux was Viscount Hereford, and a peer of England. He was insulted, and the deed was well worth the insult. In the hottest part of the row Lord
David suddenly appeared without his wig and in his own hair. Such conduct shakes the foundations
of society. Lord David was insulted even more than Viscount Hereford. He held his ground. Prince
Devereux was the first, Lord David Dirry-Moir the second. It is sometimes more difficult to be second than first. It requires less genius, but more courage. The first, intoxicated by the novelty, may
ignore the danger; the second sees the abyss, and rushes into it. Lord David flung himself into the
abyss of no longer wearing a wig. Later on these lords found imitators. Following these two revolutionists, men found sufficient audacity to wear their own hair, and powder was introduced as an
extenuating circumstance.

In order to establish, before we pass on, an important period of history, we should remark that
the first blow in the war of wigs was really struck by a Queen, Christina of Sweden, who wore
man's clothes, and had appeared in 1680, in her hair of golden brown, powdered, and brushed up
from her head. She had, besides, says Misson, a slight beard. The Pope, on his part, by a bull of
March, 1694, had somewhat let down the wig, by taking it from the heads of bishops and priests,
and in ordering churchmen to let their hair grow.

Lord David, then, did not wear a wig, and did wear cow-hide boots. Such great things made
him a mark for public admiration. There was not a club of which he was not the leader, not a boxing match in which he was not desired as referee. The referee is the arbitrator.

He had drawn up the rules of several clubs in high life. He founded several resorts of fashionable society, of which one, the Lady Guinea, was still in existence in Pall Mall in 1772. The Lady
Guinea was a club in which all the youth of the peerage congregated. They gamed there. The lowest stake allowed was a rouleau of fifty guineas, and there was never less than 20,000 guineas on the
table. By the side of each player was a little stand on which to place his cup of tea, and a gilt bowl
in which to put the rouleaux of guineas. The players, like servants when cleaning knives, wore
leather sleeves to save their lace, breast-plates of leather to protect their ruffles, shades on their
brows to shelter their eyes from the great glare of the lamps, and, to keep their curls in order, broad-
brimmed hats covered with flowers. They were masked to conceal their excitement, especially when
playing the game of *quinze*. All, moreover, had their coats turned the wrong way, for luck. Lord
David was a member of the Beefsteak Club, the Surly Club, and of the Splitfarthing Club, of the
Cross Club, the Scratchpenny Club, of the Sealed Knot, a Royalist Club, and of the Martinus Scrib-
blerus, founded by Swift, to take the place of the Rota, founded by Milton.

Though handsome, he belonged to the Ugly Club. This club was dedicated to deformity. The
members agreed to fight, not about a beautiful woman, but about an ugly man. The hall of the club
was adorned by hideous portraits—Thersites, Triboulet, Duns, Hudibras, Scarron; over the chimney was Aesop, between two men, each blind of an eye, Cocles and Camoëns (Cocles being blind

of the left, Camoëns of the right eye), so arranged that the two profiles without eyes were turned to each other. The day that the beautiful Mrs. Visart caught the smallpox, the Ugly Club toasted her. This club was still in existence in the beginning of the nineteenth century, and Mirabeau was elected an honorary member.

Since the restoration of Charles II, revolutionary clubs had been abolished. The tavern in the little street by Moorfields where the Calf's Head Club was held, had been pulled down; it was so called because on the 30th of January, the day on which the blood of Charles I flowed on the scaffold, the members had drunk red wine out of the skull of a calf to the health of Cromwell. To the republican clubs had succeeded monarchical clubs. In them people amused themselves with decency.

* * * * * * *

There was the Hell-fire Club, where they played at being impious. It was a joust of sacrilege. Hell was at auction there to the highest bidder in blasphemy.

There was the Butting Club, so called from its members butting folks with their heads. They found some street porter with a wide chest and a stupid countenance. They offered him, and compelled him, if necessary, to accept a pot of porter, in return for which he was to allow them to butt him with their heads four times in the chest, and on this they betted. One day a man, a great brute of a Welshman named Gogangerdd, expired at the third butt. This looked serious. An inquest was held, and the jury returned the following verdict: "Died of an inflation of the heart, caused by excessive drinking." Gogangerdd had certainly drunk the contents of the pot of porter.

There was the Fun Club. *Fun* is like *cant*, like *humor*, a word which is untranslatable. Fun is to farce what pepper is to salt. To get into a house and break a valuable mirror, slash the family portraits, poison the dog, put the cat in the aviary, is called "cutting a bit of fun." To give bad news which is untrue, whereby people put on mourning by mistake, is fun. It was fun to cut a square hole in the Holbein at Hampton Court. Fun would have been proud to have broken the arm of the Venus of Milo. Under James II a young millionaire lord who had during the night set fire to a thatched cottage, a feat which made all London burst with laughter, was proclaimed the King of Fun. The poor devils in the cottage were saved in their night clothes. The members of the Fun Club, all of the highest aristocracy, used to run about London during the hours when the citizens were asleep, pulling the hinges from the shutters, cutting off the pipes of pumps, filling up cisterns, digging up cultivated plots of ground, putting out lamps, sawing through the beams which supported houses, breaking the window-panes, especially in the poor quarters of the town. It was the rich who acted thus toward the poor. For this reason no complaint was possible. That was the best of the joke. Those manners have not altogether disappeared. In many places in England and in English possessions—at Guernsey, for instance—your house is now and then somewhat damaged during the night, or a fence is broken, or the knocker twisted off your door. If it were poor people who did these things, they would be sent to jail; but they are done by pleasant young gentlemen.

The most fashionable of the clubs was presided over by an emperor, who wore a crescent on his forehead, and was called the Grand Mohawk. The Mohawk surpassed the Fun. Do evil for evil's sake was the program. The Mohawk Club had one great object—to injure. To fulfill this duty, all means were held good. In becoming a Mohawk, the members took an oath to be hurtful. To injure at any price, no matter when, no matter whom, no matter where, was a matter of duty. Every member of the Mohawk Club was bound to possess an accomplishment. One was "a dancing master"; that is to say he made the rustics frisk about by pricking the calves of their legs with the point of his sword. Others knew how to make a man sweat; that is to say, a circle of gentlemen with drawn rapiers would surround a poor wretch, so that it was impossible for him not to turn his back upon someone. The gentleman behind him chastised him for this by a prick of his sword, which made him spring round; another prick in the back warned the fellow that one of noble blood was behind him, and so on, each one wounding him in his turn. When the man, closed round by the circle of swords and covered with blood, had turned and danced about enough, they ordered their servants to beat him with sticks, to change the course of his ideas. Others "hit the lion"; that is, they gaily stopped a passenger, broke his nose with a blow of the fist, and then shoved both thumbs into his eyes. If his eyes were gouged out, he was paid for them.

Such were, toward the beginning of the eighteenth century, the pastimes of the rich idlers of London. The idlers of Paris had theirs. M. de Charolais was firing his gun at a citizen standing on his own threshold. In all times youth has had its amusements.

Lord David Dirry-Moir brought into all these institutions his magnificent and liberal spirit. Just like anyone else he would gaily set fire to a cot of woodwork and thatch, and just scorch those within; but he would rebuild their houses in stone. He insulted two ladies. One was unmarried: he gave her a portion; the other was married: he had her husband appointed chaplain.

Cockfighting owed him some praiseworthy improvements. It was marvelous to see Lord David dress a cock for the pit. Cocks lay hold of each other by the feathers, as men by the hair. Lord David, therefore, made his cock as bald as possible. With a pair of scissors he cut off all the feathers from the tail and from the head to the shoulders, and all those on the neck. So much less for the enemy's beak, he used to say. Then he extended the cock's wings, and cut each feather, one after another, to a point, and thus the wings were furnished with darts. So much for the enemy's eyes, he would say. Then he scraped its claws with a penknife, sharpened its nails, fitted it with spurs of sharp steel, spat on its head, spat on its neck, anointed it with spittle, as they used to rub oil over athletes; then set it down in the pit, a redoubtable champion, exclaiming, "That's how to make a cock an eagle, and a bird of the poultry yard a bird of the mountain."

Lord David attended prize-fights, and was their living law. On occasions of great performances it was he who had the stakes driven in and ropes stretched, and who fixed the number of feet for the ring. When he was a second, he followed his man step by step, a bottle in one hand, a sponge in the other, crying out to him to *hit hard*, suggesting stratagems, advising him as he fought, wiping away the blood, raising him when overthrown, placing him on his knee, putting the mouth of the bottle between his teeth, and from his own mouth, filled with water, blowing a fine rain into his eyes and ears, a thing which reanimates even a dying man. If he was referee, he saw that there was no foul play, prevented anyone, whosoever he might be, from assisting the combatants, excepting the seconds, declared the man beaten who did not fairly face his opponent, watched that the time between the rounds did not exceed half a minute, prevented butting, and declared whoever resorted to it beaten, and forbade a man's being hit when down. All this science, however, did not render him a pedant, nor destroy his ease of manner in society.

When he was referee, rough, pimple-faced, unshorn friends of either combatant never dared to come to the aid of their failing man, nor, in order to upset the chances of the betting, jumped over the barrier, entered the ring, broke the ropes, pulled down the stakes, and violently interposed in the battle. Lord David was one of the few referees whom they dared not thrash.

No one could train like him. The pugilist whose trainer he consented to become was sure to win. Lord David would choose a Hercules—massive as a rock, tall as a tower—and make him his child. The problem was to turn that human rock from a defensive to an offensive state. In this he excelled. Having once adopted the Cyclops, he never left him. He became his nurse; he measured out his wine, weighed his meat, and counted his hours of sleep. It was he who invented the athlete's admirable rules, afterwards reproduced by Morley. In the mornings, a raw egg and a glass of sherry; at twelve, some slices of a leg of mutton, almost raw, with tea; at four, toast and tea; in the evening, pale ale and toast; after which he undressed his man, rubbed him, and put him to bed. In the street, he never allowed him to leave his sight, keeping him out of every danger, runaway horses, the wheels of carriages, drunken soldiers, pretty girls. He watched over his virtue. This maternal solicitude continually brought some new perfection into the pupil's education. He taught him the blow with the fist which breaks the teeth, and the twist of the thumb which gouges out the eye. What could be more touching?

Thus he was preparing himself for public life to which he was to be called later on. It is no easy matter to become an accomplished gentleman.

Lord David Dirry-Moir was passionately fond of open-air exhibitions, of shows, of circuses with wild beasts, of the caravans of mountebanks, of clowns, tumblers, merrymen, open-air farces, and the wonders of a fair. The true noble is he who smacks of the people. Therefore it was that Lord David frequented the taverns and low haunts of London and the Cinque Ports. In order to be able at need, and without compromising his rank in the white squadron, to be cheek-by-jowl with a topman or a calker, he used to wear a sailor's jacket when he went into the slums. For such disguise, his not wearing a wig was convenient; for even under Louis XIV the people kept to their hair like the lion to his mane. This gave him great freedom of action. The low people whom Lord David used to meet in the stews, and with whom he mixed, held him in high esteem, without ever dreaming that he was a lord. They called him Tom-Jim-Jack. Under this name he was famous and very popular amongst the dregs of the people. He played the blackguard in a masterly style: when necessary, he used his fists. This phase of his fashionable life was highly appreciated by Lady Josiana.

Chapter V

QUEEN ANNE

ABOVE THIS COUPLE THERE WAS ANNE, QUEEN OF ENGLAND. AN ORDINARY WOMAN WAS QUEEN Anne. She was gay, kindly, august—to a certain extent. No quality of hers attained to virtue, none to vice. Her stoutness was bloated; her fun, heavy; her good-nature, stupid. She was stubborn and weak. As a wife she was faithless and faithful, having favorites to whom she gave up her heart, and a husband for whom she kept her bed. As a Christian, she was a heretic and a bigot. She had one beauty—the well-developed neck of a Niobe. The rest of her person was indifferently formed. She was a clumsy coquette, and a chaste one. Her skin was white and fine; she displayed a great deal of it. It was she who introduced the fashion of necklaces of large pearls clasped round the throat. She had a narrow forehead, sensual lips, fleshy cheeks, large eyes, short sight. Her short sight extended to her mind. Beyond a burst of merriment now and then, almost as ponderous as her anger, she lived in a sort of taciturn grumble and a grumbling silence. Words escaped from her which had to be guessed at. She was a mixture of a good woman and a mischievous devil. She liked surprises, which is extremely woman-like. Anne was a pattern—just sketched roughly—of the universal Eve. To that sketch had fallen that chance, the throne. She drank. Her husband was a Dane, thoroughbred. A Tory, she governed by the Whigs; like a woman, like a mad woman. She had fits of rage. She was violent, a brawler. Nobody more awkward than Anne in directing affairs of state. She allowed events to fall about as they might chance. Her whole policy was cracked. She excelled in bringing about great catastrophes from little causes. When a whim of authority took hold of her, she called it giving a stir with the poker. She would say with an air of profound thought, "No peer may keep his hat on before the king except De Courcy, Baron Kingsale, an Irish peer." Or, "It would be an injustice were my husband not to be Lord High Admiral, since my father was." And she made George of Denmark High Admiral of England and of all her Majesty's plantations. She was perpetually perspiring bad humor; she did not explain her thought, she exuded it. There was something of the Sphinx in this goose.

She rather liked fun, teasing, and practical jokes. Could she have made Apollo a hunchback, it would have delighted her. But she would have left him a god. Good-natured, her ideal was to allow none to despair, and to worry all. She had often a rough word in her mouth; a little more, and she would have sworn like Elizabeth. From time to time she would take from a man's pocket, which she wore in her skirt, a little round box, of chased silver, on which was her portrait, in profile, between the two letters Q. A.; she would open this box, and take from it, on her finger, a little pomade, with which she reddened her lips; and, having colored her mouth, would laugh. She was greedily fond of the flat Zealand ginger-bread cakes. She was proud of being fat.

More of a Puritan than anything else, she would, nevertheless, have liked to devote herself to stage plays. She had an absurd academy of music, copied after that of France. In 1700 a Frenchman, named Forteroche, wanted to build a royal circus at Paris, at a cost of 400,000 francs, which scheme was opposed by D'Argenson. This Forteroche passed into England, and proposed to Queen Anne, who was immediately charmed by the idea, to build in London a theater with machinery, with a fourth under-stage finer than that of the King of France. Like Louis XIV, she liked to be driven at a gallop. Her teams and relays would sometimes do the distance between London and Windsor in less than an hour and a quarter.

II

IN ANNE'S TIME, NO MEETING WAS ALLOWED WITHOUT THE PERMISSION OF TWO JUSTICES OF THE peace. The assembly of twelve persons, were it only to eat oysters and drink porter, was a felony. Under her reign, otherwise relatively mild, pressing for the fleet was carried on with extreme violence: a gloomy evidence that the Englishman is a subject rather than a citizen. For centuries England suffered under that process of tyranny which gave the lie to all the old charters of freedom, and out of which France especially gathered a cause of triumph and indignation. What in some degree diminishes the triumph is, that while sailors were pressed in England, soldiers were pressed in France. In every great town of France, any able-bodied man, going through the streets on his business, was liable to be shoved by the crimps into a house called the oven. There he was shut up with others in the same plight, those fit for service were picked out, and the recruiters sold them to the officers. In 1695, there were thirty of these ovens in Paris.

The laws against Ireland, emanating from Queen Anne, were atrocious. Anne was born in 1664, two years before the great fire of London, on which the astrologers (there were some left, and Louis XIV was born with the assistance of an astrologer, and swaddled in a horoscope) predicted that, being the elder sister of fire, she would be queen. And so she was, thanks to astrology and the revolution of 1688. She had the humiliation of having only Gilbert, Archbishop of Canterbury, for godfather. To be godchild of the Pope was no longer possible in England. A mere primate is but a poor sort of godfather. Anne had to put up with one, however. It was her own fault. Why was she a Protestant?

Denmark had paid for her virginity (*virginitas empta,* as the old charters expressed it) by a dowry of £6,250 a year, secured on the bailiwick of Wardinburg and the island of Fehmarn. Anne followed, without conviction, and by routine, the traditions of William. The English, under that royalty born of a revolution, possessed as much liberty as they could lay hands on between the Tower of London, into which they put orators, and the pillory, into which they put writers. Anne spoke a little Danish in her private chats with her husband, and a little French in her private chats with Bolingbroke. Wretched gibberish; but the height of English fashion, especially at court, was to talk French. There was never a *bon mot* but in French. Anne paid a deal of attention to her coins, especially to copper coins, which are the low and popular ones; she wanted to cut a great figure on them. Six farthings were struck during her reign. On the back of the first three she had merely a throne struck, on the back of the fourth she ordered a triumphal chariot, and on the back of the sixth a goddess holding a sword in one hand and an olive branch in the other, with the scroll, *Bello et pace.* Her father, James II, was candid and cruel; she was brutal.

At the same time she was mild at bottom. A contradiction which only appears such. A fit of anger metamorphosed her. Heat sugar and it will boil.

Anne was popular. England liked feminine rulers. Why? France excludes them. There is a reason at once. Perhaps there is no other. With English historians Elizabeth embodies grandeur, Anne good-nature. As they will. Be it so. But there is nothing delicate in the reigns of these women. The lines are heavy. It is gross grandeur and gross good-nature. As to their immaculate virtue, England is tenacious of it, and we are not going to oppose the idea. Elizabeth was a virgin tempered by Essex; Anne, a wife complicated by Bolingbroke.

III

ONE IDIOTIC HABIT OF THE PEOPLE IS TO ATTRIBUTE TO THE KING WHAT THEY DO THEMSELVES. They fight. Whose the glory? The king's. They pay. Whose the generosity? The king's. Then the people love him for being so rich. The king receives a crown from the poor, and returns them a farthing. How generous he is! The colossus which is the pedestal contemplates the pigmy which is the statue. How great is this myrmidon! he is on my back. A dwarf has an excellent way of being taller than a giant: it is to perch himself on his shoulders. But that the giant should allow it, there is the wonder—and that he should admire the height of the dwarf, there is the folly. Simplicity of mankind! The equestrian statue, reserved for kings alone, is an excellent figure of royalty: the horse is the people. Only that the horse becomes transfigured by degrees. It begins in an ass; it ends in a lion. Then it throws its rider, and you have 1642 in England and 1789 in France; and sometimes it devours him, and you have in England 1649, and in France 1793. That the lion should relapse into the donkey is astonishing; but it is so. This was occurring in England. It had resumed the pack-saddle, idolatry of the crown. Queen Anne, as we have just observed, was popular. What was she doing to be so? Nothing. Nothing!—that is all that is asked of the sovereign of England. He receives for that nothing £1,250,000 a year. In 1705, England, which had had but thirteen men of war under Elizabeth, and thirty-six under James I, counted a hundred and fifty in her fleet. The English had three armies, 5,000 men in Catalonia; 10,000 in Portugal; 50,000 in Flanders; and besides, was paying £1,666,666 a year to monarchical and diplomatic Europe, a sort of prostitute the English people has always had in keeping. Parliament having voted a patriotic loan of thirty-four million francs of annuities, there had been a crush at the exchequer to subscribe it. England was sending a squadron to the East Indies, and a squadron to the West of Spain under Admiral Leake, without mentioning the reserve of four hundred sail, under Admiral Sir Cloudesley Shovel. England had lately annexed Scotland. It was the interval between Hochstadt and Ramillies, and the first of these victories was foretelling the second. England, in its cast of the net at Hochstadt, had made prisoners of twenty-seven battalions and four regiments of dragoons, and deprived France of one hundred leagues of country—France drawing back dismayed from the Danube to the Rhine. England was stretching her hand out toward Sardinia and the Balearic Islands. She was bringing into her ports in triumph ten Spanish line-of-battle ships, and many a galleon laden with gold. Hudson Bay and Straits were already half-given over by Louis XIV. It was felt that he was about to give up his hold over Acadia, St. Christopher's and Newfoundland, and that he would be but too happy if England would only tolerate the King of France fishing for cod at Cape Breton. England was about to impose upon him the shame of demolishing himself the fortifications of Dunkirk. Meanwhile, she had taken Gibraltar, and was taking Barcelona. What great things accomplished! How was it possible to refuse Anne admiration for taking the trouble of living at the period?

From a certain point of view, the reign of Anne appears a reflection of the reign of Louis XIV. Anne, for a moment even with that king in the race which is called history, bears to him the vague resemblance of a reflection. Like him, she plays at a great reign; she has her monuments, her arts, her victories, her captains, her men of letters, her privy purse to pension celebrities, her gallery of chefs-d'oeuvre, side by side with those of his Majesty. Her court, too, was a cortége, with the features of a triumph, an order and a march. It was a miniature copy of all the great men of Versailles, not giants themselves. In it there is enough to deceive the eye; add God save the Queen, which might have been taken from Lulli, and the ensemble becomes an illusion. Not a personage is missing. Christopher Wren is a very passable Mansard; Somers is as good as Lamoignon; Anne has a Racine in Dryden, a Boileau in Pope, a Colbert in Godolphin, a Louvois in Pembroke, and a Turenne in Marlborough. Heighten the wigs and lower the foreheads. The whole is solemn and pompous, and the Windsor of the time has a faded resemblance to Marly. Still the whole was effeminate, and Anne's Père Tellier was called Sarah Jennings. However, there is an outline of incipient irony, which fifty years later was to turn to philosophy, in the literature of the age, and the Protestant Tartuffe is unmasked by Swift just in the same way as the Catholic Tartuffe is denounced by Molière. Although the England of the period quarrels and fights France, she imitates her and draws enlightenment from her; and the light on the façade of England is French light. It is a pity that Anne's reign lasted but twelve years, or the English would not hesitate to call it the century of Anne, as we say the century of Louis XIV. Anne appeared in 1702, as Louis XIV declined. It is one of the curiosities of history, that the rise of that pale planet coincides with the setting of the planet of purple, and that at the moment in which France had the king Sun, England should have had the queen Moon.

A detail to be noted. Louis XIV, although they made war with him, was greatly admired in England. "He is the kind of king they want in France," said the English. The love of the English for their own liberty is mingled with a certain acceptance of servitude for others. That favorable regard of the chains which bind their neighbors sometimes attains to enthusiasm for the despot next door.

To sum up, Anne rendered her people *hureux*, as the French translator of Beeverell's book repeats three times, with graceful reiteration at the sixth and ninth page of his dedication, and the third of his preface.

IV

QUEEN ANNE BORE A LITTLE GRUDGE TO THE DUCHESS JOSIANA, FOR TWO REASONS. FIRSTLY, because she thought the Duchess Josiana handsome. Secondly, because she thought the Duchess Josiana's betrothed handsome. Two reasons for jealousy are sufficient for a woman. One is sufficient for a queen. Let us add that she bore her a grudge for being her sister. Anne did not like women to be pretty. She considered it against good morals. As for herself, she was ugly. Not from choice, however. A part of her religion she derived from that ugliness. Josiana, beautiful and philosophical, was a cause of vexation to the queen. To an ugly queen, a pretty duchess is not an agreeable sister.

There was another grievance, Josiana's "improper" birth. Anne was the daughter of Anne Hyde, a simple gentlewoman, legitimately, but vexatiously, married by James II when Duke of York. Anne, having this inferior blood in her veins, felt herself but half royal, and Josiana, having come into the world quite irregularly, drew closer attention to the incorrectness, less great, but really existing, in the birth of the queen. The daughter of *mésalliance* looked without love upon the daughter of bastardy, so near her. It was an unpleasant resemblance. Josiana had a right to say to Anne, "My mother was at least as good as yours." At court no one said so, but they evidently thought it. This was a bore for her royal Majesty. Why this Josiana? What had put it into her head to be born? What good was a Josiana? Certain relationships are detrimental. Nevertheless, Anne smiled on Josiana. Perhaps she might even have liked her, had she not been her sister.

Chapter VI

BARKILPHEDRO

IT IS USEFUL TO KNOW WHAT PEOPLE DO, AND A CERTAIN SURVEILLANCE IS WISE. JOSIANA HAD Lord David watched by a little creature of hers, in whom she reposed confidence, and whose name was Barkilphedro.

Lord David had Josiana discreetly observed by a creature of his, of whom he was sure, and whose name was Barkilphedro.

Queen Anne, on her part, kept herself secretly informed of the actions and conduct of the Duchess Josiana, her bastard sister, and of Lord David, her future brother-in-law by the left hand, by a creature of hers, on whom she counted fully, and whose name was Barkilphedro.

This Barkilphedro had his fingers on that keyboard—Josiana, Lord David, a queen. A man between two women. What modulations possible! What amalgamation of souls!

Barkilphedro had not always held the magnificent position of whispering into three ears.

He was an old servant of the Duke of York. He had tried to be a churchman but had failed. The Duke of York, an English and a Roman prince, compounded of royal Popery and legal Anglicanism, had his Catholic house and his Protestant house, and might have pushed Barkilphedro in one or the other hierarchy; but he did not judge him to be Catholic enough to make him almoner, or Protestant enough to make him chaplain. So that between two religions, Barkilphedro found himself with his soul on the ground.

Not a bad posture, either, for certain reptile souls.

Certain ways are impracticable, except by crawling flat on the belly.

An obscure but fattening servitude had long made up Barkilphedro's whole existence. Service is something; but he wanted power besides. He was, perhaps, about to reach it when James II fell. He had to begin all over again. Nothing to do under William III, a sullen prince, and exercising in his mode of reigning a prudery which he believed to be probity. Barkilphedro, when his protector, James II, was dethroned, did not lapse all at once into rags. There is a something which survives deposed princes, and which feeds and sustains their parasites. The remains of the exhaustible sap causes leaves to live on for two or three days on the branches of the uprooted tree; then, all at once, the leaf yellows and dries up: and thus it is with the courtier.

Thanks to that embalming which is called legitimacy, the prince himself, although fallen and cast away, lasts and keeps preserved; it is not so with the courtier, much more dead than the king. The king, beyond there, is a mummy; the courtier, here, is a phantom. To be the shadow of a shadow is leanness indeed. Hence Barkilphedro became famished. Then he took up the character of a man of letters.

But he was thrust back even from the kitchens. Sometimes he knew not where to sleep. "Who will give me shelter?" he would ask. He struggled on. All that is interesting in patience in distress he possessed. He had, besides, the talent of the termite—knowing how to bore a hole from the bottom to the top. By dint of making use of the name of James II, of old memories, of fables of fidelity, of touching stories, he pierced as far as the Duchess Josiana's heart.

Josiana took a liking to this man of poverty and wit, an interesting combination. She presented him to Lord Dirry-Moir, gave him a shelter in the servants' hall among her domestics, retained him in her household, was kind to him, and sometimes even spoke to him. Barkilphedro felt neither hunger nor cold again. Josiana addressed him in the second person; it was the fashion for great ladies to do so to men of letters, who allowed it. The Marquise de Mailly received Roy, whom she had never seen before, in bed, and said to him, "C'est toi qui as fait l'Année galante! Bonjour." Later on, the men of letters returned the custom. The day came when Fabre d'Eglantine said to the Duchesse de Rohan, "N'est-tu pas la Chabot?"

For Barkilphedro to be "thee'd" and "thou'd" was a success; he was overjoyed by it. He had aspired to this contemptuous familiarity. "Lady Josiana thees-and-thous me," he would say to himself. And he would rub his hands. He profited by this theeing-and-thouing to make further way. He became a sort of constant attendant in Josiana's private rooms; in no way troublesome; unperceived; the duchess would almost have changed her shift before him. All this, however, was precarious. Barkilphedro was aiming at a position. A duchess was halfway; an underground passage which did not lead to the queen was having bored for nothing.

One day Barkilphedro said to Josiana—

"Would your Grace like to make my fortune?"

"What dost thou want?"

"An appointment."

"An appointment? for thee!"

"Yes, madam."

"What an idea! *thou* to ask for an appointment! thou, who art good for nothing."

"That's just the reason."

Josiana burst out laughing.

"Among the offices to which thou art unsuited, which dost thou desire?"

"That of cork drawer of the bottles of the ocean."

Josiana's laugh redoubled.

"What meanest thou? Thou art fooling."

"No, madam."

"To amuse myself, I shall answer you seriously," said the duchess. "What dost thou wish to be? Repeat it."

"Uncorker of the bottles of the ocean."

"Everything is possible at court. Is there an appointment of that kind?"

"Yes, madam."

"This is news to me. Go on."

"There is such an appointment."

"Swear it on the soul which thou dost not possess."

"I swear it."

"I do not believe thee."

"Thank you, madam."

"Then thou wishest?—Begin again."

"To uncork the bottles of the ocean."

"That is a situation which can give little trouble. It is like grooming a bronze horse."

"Very nearly."

"Nothing to do. Well 'tis a situation to suit thee. Thou art good for that much."

"You see I am good for something."

"Come! thou art talking nonsense. Is there such an appointment?"

Barkilphedro assumed an attitude of deferential gravity.

"Madam, you had an august father, James II, the king, and you have an illustrious brother-in-law, George of Denmark, Duke of Cumberland; your father was, and your brother is, Lord High Admiral of England—"

"Is what thou tellest me fresh news? I know all that as well as thou."

"But here is what your Grace does not know. In the sea there are three kinds of things: those at the bottom, *lagan*; those which float, *flotsam*; those which the sea throws up on the shore, *jetsam*."

"And then?"

"These three things—*lagan, flotsam,* and *jetsam*—belong to the Lord High Admiral."

"And then?"

"Your Grace understands."

"No."

"All that is in the sea, all that sinks, all that floats, all that is cast ashore—all belongs to the Admiral of England."

"Everything! Really? And then?"

"Except the sturgeon, which belongs to the king."

"I should have thought," said Josiana, "all that would have belonged to Neptune."

"Neptune is a fool. He has given up everything. He has allowed the English to take everything."

"Finish what thou wert saying."

" 'Prizes of the sea' is the name given to such *treasure trove.*"

"Be it so."

"It is boundless: there is always something floating, something being cast up. It is the contribution of the sea—the tax which the ocean pays to England."

"With all my heart. But pray conclude."

"Your Grace understands that in this way the ocean creates a department."

"Where?"

"At the Admiralty."

"What department?"

"The Sea Prize Department."

"Well?"

"The department is subdivided into three offices—Lagan, Flotsam, and Jetsam—and in each there is an officer."

"And then?"

"A ship at sea writes to give notice on any subject to those on land—that it is sailing in such a latitude—that it has met a sea monster—that it is in sight of shore—that it is in distress—that it is about to founder—that it is lost, etc. The captain takes a bottle, puts into it a bit of paper on which he has written the information, corks up the flask, and casts it into the sea. If the bottle goes to the bottom, it is in the department of the lagan officer; if it floats, it is in the department of the flotsam officer; if it be thrown upon shore, it concerns the jetsam officer."

"And wouldst thou like to be the jetsam officer?"

"Precisely so."

"And that is what thou callest uncorking the bottles of the ocean?"

"Since there is such an appointment."

"Why dost thou wish for the last-named place in preference to both the others?"

"Because it is vacant just now."

"In what does the appointment consist?"

"Madam, in 1598 a tarred bottle, picked up by a man, conger-fishing on the strand of Epidium Promontorium, was brought to Queen Elizabeth; and a parchment drawn out of it gave information to England that Holland had taken, without saying anything about it, an unknown country, Nova Zembla; that the capture had taken place in June, 1596; that in that country people were eaten by bears; and that the manner of passing the winter was described on a paper enclosed in a musket-case hanging in the chimney of the wooden house built in the island, and left by the Dutchmen, who were all dead: and that the chimney was built of a barrel with the end knocked out, sunk into the roof."

"I don't understand much of thy rigmarole."

"Be it so. Elizabeth understood. A country the more for Holland was a country the less for England. The bottle which had given the information was held to be of importance; and thenceforth an order was issued that anybody who should find a sealed bottle on the seashore should take it to the Lord High Admiral of England, under pain of the gallows. The admiral entrusts the opening of such bottles to an officer, who presents the contents to the Queen, if there be reason for so doing."

"Are many such bottles brought to the Admiralty?"

"But few. But it's all the same. The appointment exists. There is for the office a room and lodgings at the Admiralty."

"And for that way of doing nothing, how is one paid?"

"One hundred guineas a year."

"And thou wouldst trouble me for that much?"

"It is enough to live upon."

"Like a beggar."

"As it becomes one of my sort."

"One hundred guineas! It's a bagatelle."

"What keeps you for a minute, keeps us for a year. That's the advantage of the poor."

"Thou shalt have the place."

A week afterwards, thanks to Josiana's exertions, thanks to the influence of Lord David Dirry-Moir, Barkilphedro—safe thenceforth, drawn out of his precarious existence, lodged, and boarded, with a salary of a hundred guineas—was installed at the Admiralty.

Chapter VII

BARKILPHEDRO GNAWS HIS WAY

THERE IS ONE THING THE MOST PRESSING OF ALL: TO BE UNGRATEFUL. Barkilphedro was not wanting therein.

Having received so many benefits from Josiana, he had naturally but one thought—to revenge himself on her. When we add that Josiana was beautiful, great, young, rich, powerful, illustrious, while Barkilphedro was ugly, little, old, poor, dependent, obscure, he must necessarily revenge himself for all this as well.

When a man is made out of night, how is he to forgive so many beams of light?

Barkilphedro was an Irishman who had denied Ireland—a bad species.

Barkilphedro had but one thing in his favor—that he had a very big belly. A big belly passes for a sign of kind-heartedness. But his belly was but an addition to Barkilphedro's hypocrisy; for the man was full of malice.

What was Barkilphedro's age? None. The age necessary for his project of the moment. He was old in his wrinkles and gray hairs, young in the activity of his mind. He was active and ponderous; a sort of hippopotamus-monkey. A royalist, certainly; a republican—who knows? a Catholic, perhaps; a Protestant, without doubt. For Stuart, probably; for Brunswick, evidently. To be For, is a power only on the condition of being at the same time Against. Barkilphedro practiced this wisdom.

The appointment of drawer of the bottles of the ocean was not as absurd as Barkilphedro had appeared to make out. The complaints, which would in these times be termed declamations, of Garcia Fernandez in his *Chart-Book of the Sea*, against the robbery of jetsam, called right of wreck, and against the pillage of wreck by the inhabitants of the coast, had created a sensation in England, and had obtained for the shipwrecked this reform—that their goods, chattels, and property, instead of being stolen by the country-people, were confiscated by the Lord High Admiral. All the *débris* of the sea cast upon the English shore—merchandise, broken hulls of ships, bales, chests, etc.—belonged to the Lord High Admiral; but—and here was revealed the importance of the place asked for by Barkilphedro—the floating receptacles containing messages and declarations awakened particularly the attention of the Admiralty. Shipwrecks are one of England's gravest cares. Navigation being her life, shipwreck is her anxiety. England is kept in perpetual care by the sea. The little glass bottle thrown to the waves by the doomed ship contains final intelligence, precious from every point of view. Intelligence concerning the ship, intelligence concerning the crew, intelligence concerning the place, the time, the manner of loss, intelligence concerning the winds which have broken up the vessel, intelligence concerning the currents which bore the floating flask ashore. The situation filled by Barkilphedro has been abolished more than a century, but it had its real utility. The last holder was William Hussey, of Doddington, in Lincolnshire. The man who held it was a sort of guardian of the things of the sea. All the closed and sealed-up vessels, bottles, flasks, jars, thrown upon the English coast by the tide were brought to him. He alone had the right to open them; he was first in the secrets of their contents; he put them in order, and ticketed them with his signature. The expression *"loger un papier au greffe,"* still used in the Channel Islands, is thence derived. However, one precaution was certainly taken. Not one of these bottles could be unsealed except in the presence of two jurors of the Admiralty sworn to secrecy, who signed, conjointly with the holder of the jetsam office, the official report of the opening. But these jurors being held to secrecy, there resulted for Barkilphedro a certain discretionary latitude; it depended upon him, to a certain extent, to suppress a fact or bring it to light.

These fragile floating messages were far from being what Barkilphedro had told Josiana, rare and insignificant. Sometimes they reached land with little delay; at others, after many years. That depended on the winds and the currents. The fashion of casting bottles on the surface of the sea has somewhat passed away, like that of vowing offerings, but in those religious times, those who were about to die were glad thus to send their last thought to God and to men, and at times these messages from the sea were plentiful at the Admiralty. A parchment preserved in the hall at Audlyene (ancient spelling), with notes by the Earl of Suffolk, Grand Treasurer of England under James I, bears witness that in the one year, 1615, fifty-two flasks, bladders, and tarred vessels, containing mention of sinking ships, were brought and registered in the records of the Lord High Admiral.

Court appointments are the drop of oil in the widow's cruse, they ever increase. Thus it is that the porter has become chancellor, and the groom, constable. The special officer charged with the appointment desired and obtained by Barkilphedro was invariably a confidential man. Elizabeth had wished that it should be so. At court, to speak of confidence is to speak of intrigue, and to speak of intrigue is to speak of advancement. This functionary had come to be a personage of some consideration. He was a clerk, and ranked directly after the two grooms of the almonry. He had the right of entrance into the palace, but we must add, what was called the humble entrance—*humilis introïtus*—and even into the bedchamber. For it was the custom that he should inform the monarch, on occasions of sufficient importance, of the objects found, which were often very curious: the wills of men in despair—farewells cast to fatherland—revelations of falsified logs, bills of lading, and crimes committed at sea, legacies to the crown, etc., that he should maintain his records in communication with the court, and should account, from time to time, to the king or queen, concerning the opening of these ill-omened bottles. It was the black cabinet of the ocean.

Elizabeth, who was always glad of an opportunity of speaking Latin, used to ask Tonfield, of Coley in Berkshire, jetsam officer of her day, when he brought her one of these papers cast up by the sea, *"Quid mihi scribit Neptunus?"* (What does Neptune write me?)

The way had been eaten, the insect had succeeded. Barkilphedro approached the queen.

This was all he wanted.

To make his fortune?

No.

To unmake that of others?

A greater happiness.

To hurt is to enjoy.

To have within one the desire of injuring, vague but implacable, and never to lose sight of it, is not given to all.

Barkilphedro possessed that fixity of intention.

As the bulldog holds on with his jaws, so did his thought.

To feel himself inexorable gave him a depth of gloomy satisfaction. As long as he had a prey under his teeth, or in his soul, a certainty of evil-doing, he wanted nothing.

He was happy, shivering in the cold which his neighbor was suffering. To be malignant is an opulence. Such a man is believed to be poor, and, in truth, is so; but he has all his riches in malice, and prefers having them so. Everything is in what contents one. To do a bad turn, which is the same as a good turn, is better than money. Bad for him who endures, good for him who does it. Catesby, the colleague of Guy Fawkes, in the Popish powder plot, said: "To see Parliament blown upside down, I wouldn't miss it for a million sterling."

What was Barkilphedro? That meanest and most terrible of things—an envious man.

Envy is a thing ever easily placed at court.

Courts abound in impertinent people, in idlers, in rich loungers hungering for gossip, in those who seek for needles in trusses of hay, in triflers, in banterers bantered, in witty ninnies, who cannot do without converse with an envious man.

What a refreshing thing is the evil spoken to you of others.

Envy is good stuff to make a spy. There is a profound analogy between that natural passion, envy, and that social function, espionage. The spy hunts on others' account, like the dog. The envious man hunts on his own, like the cat.

A fierce Myself, such is the envious man.

He had other qualities. Barkilphedro was discreet, secret, concrete. He kept in everything and racked himself with his hate. Enormous baseness implies enormous vanity. He was liked by those whom he amused, and hated by all others; but he felt that he was disdained by those who hated him, and despised by those who liked him. He restrained himself. All his gall simmered noiselessly in his hostile resignation. He was indignant, as if rogues had the right to be so. He was the furies' silent prey. To swallow everything was his talent. There were deaf wraths within him, frenzies of interior rage, black and brooding flames unseen; he was a *smoke-consuming* man of passion. The surface was smiling. He was kind, prompt, easy, amiable, obliging. Never mind to whom, never mind where, he bowed. For a breath of wind he inclined to the earth. What a source of fortune to have a reed for a spine! Such concealed and venomous beings are not so rare as is believed. We live surrounded by ill-omened crawling things. Wherefore the malevolent? A keen question! The dreamer constantly proposes it to himself, and the thinker never resolves it. Hence the sad eye of the philosophers ever fixed upon that mountain of darkness which is destiny, and from the top of which the colossal specter of evil casts handfuls of serpents over the earth.

Barkilphedro's body was obese, and his face lean. A fat bust and a bony countenance. His nails were channeled and short, his fingers knotted, his thumbs flat, his hair coarse, his temples wide apart, and his forehead a murderer's, broad and low. The littleness of his eye was hidden under his bushy eyebrows. His nose, long, sharp, and flabby, nearly met his mouth. Barkilphedro, properly attired as an emperor, would have somewhat resembled Domitian. His face of muddy yellow might have been modeled in slimy paste—his immovable cheeks were like putty; he had all kinds of ugly refractory wrinkles; the angle of his jaw was massive, his chin heavy, his ear underbred. In repose, and seen in profile, his upper lip was raised at an acute angle, showing two teeth. Those teeth seemed to look at you. The teeth can look, just as the eye can bite.

Patience, temperance, continence, reserve, self-control, amenity, deference, gentleness, politeness, sobriety, chastity, completed and finished Barkilphedro. He culumniated those virtues by their possession.

In a short time Barkilphedro took a foothold at court.

Chapter VIII

INFERI

THERE ARE TWO WAYS OF MAKING A FOOTING AT COURT. IN THE CLOUDS, AND YOU ARE AUGUST; in the mud, and you are powerful.

In the first case, you belong to Olympus.

In the second case, you belong to the private closet.

He who belongs to Olympus has but the thunderbolt, he who is of the private closet has the police.

The private closet contains all the instruments of government, and sometimes, for it is a traitor, its chastisement. Heliogabalus goes there to die. Then it is called the latrines.

Generally it is less tragic. It is there that Alberoni admires Vendôme. Royal personages willingly make it their place of audience. It takes the place of the throne. Louis XIV receives the Duchess of Burgundy there. Philip V is shoulder to shoulder there with the queen. The priest penetrates into it. The private closet is sometimes a branch of the confessional. Therefore it is that at court there are underground fortunes—not always the least. If, under Louis XI, you would be great, be Pierre de Rohan, Marshal of France; if you would be influential, be Olivier le Daim, the barber; if you would, under Mary de Medicis, be glorious, be Sillery, the Chancellor; if you would be a person of consideration, be La Hannon, the maid; if you would, under Louis XV, be illustrious, be Choiseul, the minister; if you would be formidable, be Lebel, the valet. Given, Louis XIV, Bontemps, who makes his bed, is more powerful than Louvois, who raises his armies, and Turenne, who gains his victories. From Richelieu, take Père Joseph, and you have Richelieu nearly empty. There is the mystery the less. His Eminence in scarlet is magnificent; his Eminence in gray is terrible. What power in being a worm! All the Narvaez amalgamated with all the O'Donnells do less work than one Sor Patrocinio.

Of course the condition of this power is littleness. If you would remain powerful, remain petty. Be Nothingness. The serpent in repose, twisted into a circle, is a figure at the same time of the infinite and of naught.

One of these viper-like fortunes had fallen to Barkilphedro.

He had crawled where he wanted.

Flat beasts can get in everywhere. Louis XIV had bugs in his bed and Jesuits in his policy.

The incompatibility is nil.

In this world everything is a clock. To gravitate is to oscillate. One pole is attracted to the other. Francis I is attracted by Triboulet; Louis XIV is attracted by Lebel. There exists a deep affinity between extreme elevation and extreme debasement.

It is abasement which directs. Nothing is easier of comprehension. It is he who is below who pulls the strings. No position more convenient. He is the eye, and has the ear. He is the eye of the government; he has the ear of the king. To have the eye of the king is to draw and shut, at one's whim, the bolt of the royal conscience, and to throw into that conscience whatever one wishes. The mind of the king is his cupboard; if he be a rag-picker, it is his basket. The ears of kings belong not to kings, and therefore it is that, on the whole, the poor devils are not altogether responsible for their actions. He who does not possess his own thought does not possess his own deed. A king obeys— what? Any evil spirit buzzing from outside in his ear; a noisome fly of the abyss.

This buzzing commands. A reign is a dictation.

The loud voice is the sovereign; the low voice, sovereignty. Those who know how to distinguish, in a reign, this low voice, and to hear what it whispers to the loud, are the real historians.

Chapter IX

HATE IS AS STRONG AS LOVE

QUEEN ANNE HAD SEVERAL OF THESE LOW VOICES ABOUT HER. BARKILPHEDRO WAS ONE. Besides the queen, he secretly worked, influenced, and plotted upon Lady Josiana and Lord David. As we have said, he whispered in three ears, one more than Dangeau. Dangeau whispered in but two, in the days when, thrusting himself between Louis XIV, in love with Henrietta, his sister-in-law, and Henrietta, in love with Louis XIV, her brother-in-law, he being Louis's secretary, without the knowledge of Henrietta, and Henrietta's without the knowledge of Louis, he wrote the questions and answers of both the love-making marionettes.

Barkilphedro was so cheerful, so accepting, so incapable of taking up the defense of anybody, possessing so little devotion at bottom, so ugly, so mischievous, that it was quite natural that a regal personage should come to be unable to do without him. Once Anne had tasted Barkilphedro she would have no other flatterer. He flattered her as they flattered Louis the Great, by stinging her neighbors. "The king being ignorant," says Madame de Montchevreuil, "one is obliged to mock at the savants."

To poison the sting, from time to time, is the acme of art. Nero loves to see Locusta at work.

Royal palaces are very easily entered; these madrepores have a way in soon guessed at, contrived, examined, and scooped out at need by the gnawing thing which is called the courtier. A pretext to enter is sufficient. Barkilphedro, having found this pretext, his position with the queen soon became the same as that with the Duchess Josiana—that of an indispensable domestic animal. A witticism risked one day by him immediately led to his perfect understanding of the queen and how to estimate exactly her kindness of heart. The queen was greatly attached to her Lord Steward, William Cavendish, Duke of Devonshire, who was a great fool. This lord, who had obtained every Oxford degree and did not know how to spell, one fine morning committed the folly of dying. To die is a very imprudent thing at court, for there is then no further restraint in speaking of you. The queen, in the presence of Barkilphedro, lamented the event, finally exclaiming, with a sigh—

"It is a pity that so many virtues should have been borne, and served by so poor an intellect."

"Dieu veuille avoir son âne!" whispered Barkilphedro, in a low voice, and in French.

The queen smiled. Barkilphedro noted the smile. His conclusion was that biting pleased. Free license had been given to his spite. From that day he thrust his curiosity everywhere, and his malignity with it. He was given his way, so much was he feared. He who can make the king laugh makes the others tremble. He was a powerful buffoon. Every day he worked his way forward underground. Barkilphedro became a necessity. Many great people honored him with their confidence, to the extent of charging him, when they required him, with their disgraceful commissions.

There are wheels within wheels at court. Barkilphedro became the motive power. Have you remarked, in certain mechanisms, the smallness of the motive wheel?

Josiana, in particular, who, as we have explained, made use of Barkilphedro's talents as a spy, reposed such confidence in him that she had not hesitated to entrust him with one of the master-keys of her apartments, by means of which he was able to enter them at any hour. This excessive license of insight into private life was in fashion in the seventeenth century. It was called "giving the key." Josiana had given two of these confidential keys—Lord David had one, Barkilphedro the other. However, to enter straight into a bedchamber was, in the old code of manners, a thing not in the least out of the way. Thence resulted incidents. La Ferté, suddenly drawing back the bed curtains of Mademoiselle Lafont, found, inside, Sainson, the black musketeer, etc., etc.

Barkilphedro excelled in making the cunning discoveries which place the great in the power of the little. His walk in the dark was winding, soft, clever. Like every perfect spy, he was composed of the inclemency of the executioner and the patience of a micograph. He was a born courtier. Every courtier is a noctambulist. The courtier prowls in the night, which is called power. He carries a dark lantern in his hand. He lights up the spot he wishes, and remains in darkness himself. What he seeks with his lantern is not a man, it is a fool. What he finds is the king.

Kings do not like to see those about them pretend to greatness. Irony aimed at anyone except themselves has a charm for them. The talent of Barkilphedro consisted in a perpetual dwarfing of the peers and princes to the advantage of her Majesty's stature, thus increased in proportion. The master-key held by Barkilphedro was made with two sets of wards, one at each end, so as to open the inner apartments in both Josiana's favorite residences—Hunkerville House in London, Corleone Lodge at Windsor. These two houses were part of the Clancharlie inheritance. Hunkerville House was close to Oldgate. Oldgate was a gate of London, which was entered by the Harwich road, and on which was displayed a statue of Charles II, with a painted angel on his head, and beneath his feet a carved lion and unicorn. From Hunkerville House, in an easterly wind, you heard the peals of St. Marylebone. Corleone Lodge was a Florentine palace of brick and stone, with a marble colonnade, built on pilework, at Windsor, at the head of the wooden bridge, and having one of the finest courts in England.

In the latter palace, near Windsor Castle, Josiana was within the queen's reach. Nevertheless, Josiana liked it.

Scarcely anything in appearance, everything in the root; such was the influence of Barkilphedro over the queen. There is nothing more difficult than to drag up these bad grasses of the court— they take a deep root, and offer no hold above the surface. To root out a Roquelaure, a Triboulet, or a Brummel, is almost impossible.

From day to day, and more and more, did the queen take Barkilphedro into her good graces. Sarah Jennings is famous; Barkilphedro is unknown. His existence remains ignored. The name of Barkilphedro has not reached as far as history. All the moles are not caught by the mole-trapper.

Barkilphedro, once a candidate for orders, had studied a little of everything. Skimming all things leaves naught for result. One may be victim of the *omnis res scibilis*. Having the vessel of the Danaïdes in one's head is the misfortune of a whole race of learned men, who may be termed the sterile. What Barkilphedro had put into his brain had left it empty.

The mind, like nature, abhors vacuum. Into emptiness nature puts love; the mind often puts hate. Hate occupies.

Hate for hate's sake exists. Art for art's sake exists in nature more than is believed. A man hates—he must do something. Gratuitous hate—formidable word! It means hate which is itself its own payment. The bear lives by licking his claws. Not indefinitely, of course. The claws must be revictualed. Something must be put under them.

Hate indistinct is sweet and suffices for a time; but one must end by having an object. An animosity diffused over creation is exhausting, like every solitary pleasure. Hate without an object is like a shooting-match without a target. What lends interest to the game is a heart to be pierced. One cannot hate solely for honor; some seasoning is necessary—a man, a woman, somebody, to destroy. This service of making the game interesting; of offering an end; of throwing passion into hate by fixing it on an object; of amusing the hunter by the sight of his living prey; giving the watcher the hope of the smoking and boiling blood about to flow; of amusing the birdcatcher by the credulity of the uselessly-winged lark; of being a victim, unknowingly reared for murder by a master mind; all this exquisite and horrible service, of which the person rendering it is unconscious, Josiana rendered Barkilphedro.

Thought is a projectile. Barkilphedro had, from the first day, begun to aim at Josiana the evil intentions which were in his mind. An intention and a carbine are alike. Barkilphedro aimed at Josiana, directing against the duchess all his secret malice. That astonishes you! What has the bird done at which you fire? You want to eat it, you say. And so it was with Barkilphedro.

Josiana could not be struck in the heart—the spot where the enigma lies is hard to wound: but she could be struck in the head—that is, in her pride. It was there that she thought herself strong, and that she was weak.

Barkilphedro had found it out. If Josiana had been able to see clearly through the night of Barkilphedro, if she had been able to distinguish what lay in ambush behind his smile, that proud woman, so highly situated, would have trembled. Fortunately for the tranquility of her sleep, she was in complete ignorance of what was in the man.

The unexpected spreads, one knows not whence. The profound depths of life are dangerous. There is no small hate. Hate is always enormous. It preserves its stature in the smallest being, and remains a monster. An elephant hated by a worm is in danger.

Even before he struck, Barkilphedro felt, with joy, the foretaste of the evil action which he was about to commit. He did not as yet know what he was going to do to Josiana; but he had made up his mind to do something. To have come to this decision was a great step taken.

To crush Josiana utterly would have been too great a triumph. He did not hope for so much; but to humiliate her, lessen her, bring her grief, redden her proud eyes with tears of rage—what a success! He counted on it. Tenacious, diligent, faithful to the torment of his neighbor, not to be torn from his purpose, nature had not formed him for nothing. He well understood how to find the flaw in Josiana's golden armor, and how to make the blood of that Olympian flow.

What benefit, we ask again, would accrue to him in so doing? An immense benefit; doing evil to one who had done good to him. What is an envious man? An ungrateful one. He hates the light which lights and warms him. Zoilus hated that benefit to man, Homer. To inflict on Josiana what would nowadays be called vivisection—to place her, all convulsed, on his anatomical table; to dissect her alive, at his leisure, in some surgery; to cut her up, as an amateur, while she should scream; this dream delighted Barkilphedro!

To arrive at this result it was necessary to suffer somewhat himself; he did so willingly. We may pinch ourselves with our own pincers. The knife as it shuts cuts our fingers. What does it matter? That he should partake of Josiana's torture was a matter of little moment. The executioner handling the red-hot iron, when about to brand a prisoner, takes no heed of a little burn. Because another suffers much, he suffers nothing. To see the victim's writhings takes all pain from the inflicter.

Do harm, whatever happens.

To plan evil for others is mingled with an acceptance of some hazy responsibility. We risk our-

selves in the danger which we impel toward another, because the chain of events sometimes, of
course, brings unexpected accidents. This does not stop the man who is truly malicious. He feels as
much joy as the patient suffers agony. He is tickled by the laceration of the victim. The malicious
man blooms in hideous joy. Pain reflects itself on him in a sense of welfare. The Duke of Alva used
to warm his hands at the stake. The pile was torture, the reflection of it pleasure. That such trans-
positions should be possible makes one shudder. Our dark side is unfathomable. *Supplice exquis* (exquisite torture)—the expression is in Bodin—has perhaps this terrible triple sense: search for the
torture; suffering of the tortured; delight of the torturer.

Ambition, appetite; all such words signify someone sacrificed to someone satiated. It is sad that
hope should be wicked. Is it that the outpourings of our wishes flow naturally to the direction to
which we most incline, that of evil? One of the hardest labors of the just man is to expunge from
his soul a malevolence which it is difficult to efface. Almost all our desires, when examined, contain
what we dare not avow.

In the completely wicked man this exists in hideous perfection. So much the worse for others,
signifies so much the better for himself. The shadows of the caverns of man's mind.

Josiana, in a plenitude of security the fruit of ignorant pride, had a contempt for all danger.
The feminine faculty of disdain is extraordinary. Josiana's disdain, unreasoning, involuntary, and
confident. Barkilphedro was to her so contemptible that she would have been astonished had anyone remarked to her that such a creature existed. She went, and came, and laughed before this man
who was looking at her with evil eyes. Thoughtful, he bided his time.

In proportion as he waited, his determination to cast a despair into this woman's life augmented. Inexorable high tide of malice.

In the meantime he gave himself excellent reasons for his determination. It must not be
thought that scoundrels are deficient in self-esteem. They enter into details with themselves in their
lofty monologues, and they take matters with a high hand. How? This Josiana had bestowed charity on him! She had thrown some crumbs of her enormous wealth to him, as to a beggar. She had
nailed and riveted him to an office which was unworthy him. Yes; that he, Barkilphedro, almost a
clergyman, of varied and profound talent, a learned man, with the material in him for a bishop,
should have for employ the registration of nasty patience-trying shards, that he should have to pass
his life in the garret of a register-office, gravely uncorking stupid bottles, encrusted with all the nas-
tiness of the sea, deciphering musty parchments, like filthy conjuring-books, dirty wills, and other
illegible stuff of the kind, was the fault of this Josiana. Worst of all! this creature "thee'd" and
"thou'd" him! And he should not revenge himself!—he should not punish such conduct! Well, in
that case there would no longer be justice on earth!

Chapter X

THE FLAME WHICH WOULD BE SEEN IF MAN WERE TRANSPARENT

WHAT! THIS WOMAN, THIS EXTRAVAGANT THING, THIS LIBIDINOUS DREAMER, A VIRGIN UNTIL
the opportunity occurred, this bit of flesh as yet unfreed, this bold creature under a
princess's coronet; this Diana by pride, as yet untaken by the first comer, just because chance had
so willed it; this bastard of a low-lived king who had not the intellect to keep his place; this duchess
by a lucky hit, who, being a fine lady, played the goddess, and who, had she been poor, would have
been a prostitute; this lady, more or less, this robber of a proscribed man's goods, this overbearing

strumpet, because one day he, Barkilphedro, had not money enough to buy his dinner, and to get a lodging, she had had the impudence to seat him in her house at the corner of a table, and to put him up in some hole in her intolerable palace; where? never mind where; perhaps in the barn, perhaps in the cellar, what does it matter? a little better than her valets, a little worse than her horses. She had abused his distress; his, Barkilphedro's; in hastening to do him treacherous good, a thing which the rich do in order to humiliate the poor, and to tie them, like curs led by a string. Besides, what did the service she rendered him cost her? A service is worth what it costs. She had spare rooms in her house. She came to Barkilphedro's aid! A great thing, indeed; had she eaten a spoonful the less of turtle soup for it? had she deprived herself of anything in the hateful overflowing of her super-fluous luxuries? No. She had added to it a vanity, a luxury, a good action like a ring on her finger, the relief of a man of wit, the patronization of a clergyman. She could give herself airs; say, "I lav-ish kindness; I fill the mouths of men of letters; I am his benefactress. How lucky the wretch was to find me out! What a patroness of the arts I am!" All for having set up a truckle bed in a wretched garret in the roof. As for the place in the Admiralty, Barkilphedro owed it to Josiana; by Jove, a pretty appointment! Josiana had made Barkilphedro what he was. She had created him. Be it so. Yes, created nothing. Less than nothing. For in his absurd situation he felt borne down, tongue-tied, dis-figured. What did he owe Josiana? The thanks due from a hunchback to the mother who bore him deformed. Behold your privileged ones, your folks overwhelmed with fortune, your parvenus, your favorites of that horrid stepmother, Fortune! And that man of talent, Barkilphedro, was obliged to stand on staircases, to bow to footmen, to climb to the top of the house at night, to be courteous, assiduous, pleasant, respectful, and to have ever on his muzzle a respectful grimace! Was not it enough to make him gnash his teeth with rage! And all the while she was putting pearls round her neck, and making amorous poses to her fool, Lord David Dirry-Moir; the hussy!

Never let anyone do you a service. They will abuse the advantage it gives them. Never allow yourself to be taken in the act of inanition. They would relieve you. Because he was starving, this woman had found it a sufficient pretext to give him bread. From that moment he was her servant; a craving of the stomach, and there is a chain for life! To be obliged is to be sold. The happy, the powerful, make use of the moment you stretch out your hand to place a penny in it, and at the cri-sis of your weakness make you a slave, and a slave of the worst kind, the slave of an act of charity. a slave forced to love the enslaver. What infamy! what want of delicacy; what an assault on your self respect! Then all is over. You are sentenced for life to consider this man good, that woman beautiful; to remain in the back rows; to approve, to applaud, to admire, to worship, to prostrate yourself, to blister your knees by long genuflections, to sugar your words when you are gnawing your lips with anger, when you are biting down your cries of fury, and when you have within you more savage turbulence and more bitter foam than the ocean!

It is thus that the rich make prisoners of the poor.

This slime of a good action performed toward you bedaubs and bespatters you with mud forever.

An alms is irremediable. Gratitude is paralysis. A benefit is a sticky and repugnant adherence which deprives you of free movement. Those odious, opulent, and spoiled creatures whose pity has thus injured you are well aware of this. It is done—you are their creature. They have bought you—and how? By a bone taken from their dog and cast to you. They have flung that bone at your head. You have been stoned as much as benefited. It is all one. Have you gnawed the bone—yes or no? You have had your place in the dog-kennel as well. Then be thankful. Be ever thankful. Adore your masters. Kneel on indefinitely. A benefit implies an understood inferiority accepted by you. It means that you feel them to be gods and yourself a poor devil. Your diminution augments them. Your bent form makes theirs more upright. In the tones of their voices there is an impertinent in-flexion. Their family matters, their marriages, their baptisms, their child-bearings, their progeny, all concern you. A wolf cub is born to them. Well! you have to compose a sonnet. You are a poet because you are low. Isn't it enough to make the stars fall! A little more, and they would make you wear their old shoes.

"Who have you got there, my dear? How ugly he is! Who is that man?"

"I do not know. A sort of scholar, whom I feed."

Thus converse these idiots, without even lowering their voice. You hear, and remain mechanically amiable. If you are ill, your masters will send for the doctor—not their own. Occasionally they may even inquire after you. Being of a different species from you, and at an inaccessible height above you, they are affable. Their height makes them easy. They know that equality is impossible. By force of disdain they are polite. At table they give you a little nod. Sometimes they absolutely know how your name is spelled! They only show that they are your protectors by walking unconsciously over all the delicacy and susceptibility you possess. They treat you with good-nature. Is all this to be borne?

No doubt he was eager to punish Josiana. He must teach her with whom she had to deal!

Oh! my rich gentry, because you cannot eat up everything, because opulence produces indigestion seeing that your stomachs are no bigger than ours, because it is, after all, better to distribute the remainder than to throw it away, you exalt a morsel flung to the poor into an act of magnificence. Oh! you give us bread, you give us shelter, you give us clothes, you give us employment, and you push audacity, folly, cruelty, stupidity, and absurdity to the pitch of believing that we are grateful. The bread is the bread of servitude, the shelter is a footman's bedroom, the clothes are a livery, the employment is ridiculous, paid for, it is true, but brutalizing.

Oh! you believe in the right to humiliate us with lodging and nourishment, and you imagine that we are your debtors, and you count on our gratitude? Very well! we will eat up your substance, we will devour you alive and gnaw your heartstrings with our teeth.

This Josiana! was it not absurd? what merit had she? She had accomplished the wonderful work of coming into the world as a testimony of the folly of her father, and the shame of her mother. She had done us the favor to exist, and for her kindness in becoming a public scandal, they paid her millions; she had estates and castles, warrens, parks, lakes, forests, and I know not what besides, and with all that she was making a fool of herself, and verses were addressed to her! And Barkilphedro, who had studied and labored and taken pains, and stuffed his eyes and his brain with great books, who had grown moldy in old works and in science, who was full of wit, who could command armies, who could, if he would, write tragedies like Otway and Dryden, who was made to be an emperor, Barkilphedro had been reduced to permit this nobody to prevent him from dying of hunger. Could the usurpation of the rich, the hateful elect of chance, go farther? They put on the semblance of being generous to us, of protecting us, and of smiling on us, and we would drink their blood and lick our lips after it! That this low woman of the court should have the odious power of being a benefactress, and that a man so superior should be condemned to pick up such bribes falling from such a hand, what a frightful iniquity! and what social system is this which has for its base disproportion and injustice? Would it not be best to take it by the four corners, and to throw pell-mell to the ceiling the damask table-cloth, and the festival, and the orgies, and the tippling and drunkenness, and the guests, and those with their elbows on the table, and those with their paws under it, and the insolent who give and the idiots who accept, and to spit it all back again in the face of Providence, and fling all the earth to the heavens? In the meantime let us stick our claws into Josiana.

Thus dreamed Barkilphedro. Such were the ragings of his soul. It is the habit of the envious man to absolve himself, amalgamating with his personal grievance the public wrongs.

All the wild forms of hateful passions went and came in the intellect of this ferocious being. At the corners of old maps of the world of the fifteenth century, are great vague spaces without shape or name, on which are written these three words, *Hic sunt leones*. Such a dark corner is there also in man. Passions grow and growl somewhere within us, and we may say of an obscure portion of our souls, there are lions here.

Is this scaffolding of wild reasoning absolutely absurd? does it lack a certain justice? We must confess it does not.

It is fearful to think that judgment within us is not justice. Judgment is the relative, justice is the absolute. Think of the difference between a judge and a just man.

Wicked men lead conscience astray with authority. There are gymnastics of untruth. A sophist is a forger, and this forger sometimes brutalizes good sense.

A certain logic, very supple, very implacable, and very agile, is at the service of evil, and excels in stabbing truth in the dark. These are blows struck by the devil at Providence.

The worst of it was that Barkilphedro had a presentiment. He was undertaking a heavy task, and he was afraid that after all the evil achieved might not be proportionate to the work.

To be corrosive as he was, to have within himself a will of steel, a hate of diamond, a burning curiosity for the catastrophe, and to burn nothing, to decapitate nothing, to exterminate nothing; to be what he was, a force of devastation, a voracious animosity, a devourer of the happiness of others, to have been created (for there is a creator, whether God or devil), to have been created Barkilphedro all over, and to inflict perhaps after all but a fillip of the finger—could this be possible? could it be that Barkilphedro should miss his aim? To be a lever powerful enough to heave great masses of rock, and when sprung to the utmost power, to succeed only in giving an affected woman a bump in the forehead! to be a catapult dealing ruin on a pole-kitten! To accomplish the task of Sisyphus, to crush an ant; to sweat all over with hate, and for nothing at all. Would not this be humiliating, when he felt himself a mechanism of hostility capable of reducing the world to powder! To put into movement all the wheels within wheels, to work in the darkness all the mechanism of a Marly machine, and to succeed perhaps in pinching the end of a little rosy finger! He was to turn over and over blocks of marble, perchance with the result of ruffling a little the smooth surface of the court! Providence has a way of thus expending forces grandly. The movement of a mountain often only displaces a molehill.

Besides this, when the court is the dangerous arena, nothing is more dangerous than to aim at your enemy and miss him. In the first place, it unmasks you and irritates him; but besides and above all, it displeases the master. Kings do not like the unskillful. Let us have no contusions, no ugly gashes. Kill anybody, but give no one a bloody nose. He who kills is clever, he who wounds awkward. Kings do not like to see their servants lamed. They are displeased if you chip a porcelain jar on their chimney-piece, or a courtier in their cortége. The court must be kept neat. Break and replace; that does not matter. Besides, all this agrees perfectly with the taste of princes for scandal. Speak evil, do none; or if you do, let it be in grand style.

Stab, do not scratch, unless the pin be poisoned. This would be an extenuating circumstance, and was, we may remember, the case with Barkilphedro.

Every malicious pigmy is a phial in which is enclosed the dragon of Solomon. The phial is microscopic, the dragon immense. A formidable condensation, awaiting the gigantic hour of dilation! Ennui consoled by the premeditation of explosion! The prisoner is larger than the prison. A latent giant! how wonderful! A minnow in which is contained a hydra. To be this fearful magical box, to contain within him a leviathan, is to the dwarf both a torture and a delight.

Nor would anything have caused Barkilphedro to let go his hold. He awaited his time. Was it to come? What mattered that? He watched for it. Self-love is mixed up in the malice of the very wicked man. To make holes and gaps in a court fortune higher than your own, to undermine it at all risks and perils, while encased and concealed yourself, is, we repeat, exceedingly interesting. The player at such a game becomes eager, even to passion. He throws himself into the work as if he were composing an epic. To be very mean, and to attack that which is great, is in itself a brilliant action. It is a fine thing to be a flea on a lion.

The noble beast feels the bite, and expends his mighty anger against the atom. An encounter with a tiger would weary him less; see how the actors exchange their parts. The lion, humiliated, feels the sting of the insect, and the flea can say, "I have in my veins the blood of a lion."

However, these reflections but half appeased the cravings of Barkilphedro's pride. Consolations, palliations at most. To vex is one thing; to torment would be infinitely better. Barkilphedro had a thought which returned to him without ceasing; his success might not go beyond just irritating the epidermis of Josiana. What could he hope for more; he so obscure, against her so radiant! A scratch is worth but little to him who longs to see the crimson blood of his flayed victim, and to hear her cries as she lies before him more than naked, without even that garment the skin! With such a craving, how sad to be powerless!

Alas, there is nothing perfect!

However, he resigned himself. Not being able to do better, he only dreamed half his dream. To play a treacherous trick is an object after all.

What a man is he who revenges himself for a benefit received! Barkilphedro was a giant among such men. Usually, ingratitude is forgetfulness. With this man, patented in wickedness, it was fury. The vulgar ingrate is full of ashes: what was within Barkilphedro? A furnace. A furnace walled round by hate, silence, and rancor, awaiting Josiana for fuel. Never had a man abhorred a woman to such a point without reason. How terrible! She was his dream, his preoccupation, his ennui, his rage.

Perhaps he was a little in love with her.

Chapter XI

BARKILPHEDRO IN AMBUSCADE

To find the vulnerable spot in Josiana, and to strike her there, was, for all the causes we have just mentioned, the imperturbable determination of Barkilphedro. The wish is sufficient; the power is required. How was he to set about it? There was the question.

Vulgar vagabonds set the scene of any wickedness they intend to commit with care. They do not feel themselves strong enough to seize the opportunity as it passes, to take possession of it by fair means or foul, and to constrain it to serve them. Deep scoundrels disdain preliminary combinations. They start from their villainies alone, merely arming themselves all round, prepared to avail themselves of various chances which may occur, and then, like Barkilphedro, await the opportunity. They know that a ready-made scheme runs the risk of fitting ill into the event which may present itself. It is not thus that a man makes himself master of possibilities, and guides them as one pleases. You can come to no previous arrangement with destiny. To-morrow will not obey you. There is a certain want of discipline in chance.

Therefore they watch for it, and summon it suddenly, authoritatively, on the spot. No plan, no sketch, no rough model; no ready-made shoe ill-fitting the unexpected. They plunge headlong into the dark. To turn to immediate and rapid profit any circumstance that can aid him is the quality which distinguishes the able scoundrel, and elevates the villain into the demon. To strike suddenly at fortune, *that* is true genius.

The true scoundrel strikes you from a sling with the first stone he can pick up. Clever malefactors count on the unexpected, that senseless accomplice of so many crimes. They grasp the incident and leap on it; there is no better *Ars poetica* for this species of talent. Meanwhile be sure with whom you have to deal. Survey the ground.

With Barkilphedro the ground was Queen Anne. Barkilphedro approached the queen, and so close, that sometimes he fancied he heard the monologues of her Majesty. Sometimes he was present unheeded at conversations between the sisters. Neither did they forbid his sliding in a word. He profited by this to lessen himself—a way of inspiring confidence. Thus, one day in the garden at Hampton Court being behind the duchess, who was behind the queen, he heard Anne, following the fashion, awkwardly enunciating sentiments.

"Animals are happy," said the queen. "They run no risk of going to hell."

"They are there already," replied Josiana.

This answer, which bluntly substituted philosophy for religion, displeased the queen. If, perchance, there was depth in the observation, Anne felt shocked.

"My dear," said she to Josiana, "we talk of hell like a couple of fools. Ask Barkilphedro all about it. He ought to know such things."

"As a devil?" said Josiana.

"As a beast," replied Barkilphedro, with a bow.

"Madam," said the queen to Josiana, "he is cleverer than we."

For a man like Barkilphedro to approach the queen was to obtain a hold on her. He could say, "I hold her." Now, he wanted a means of taking advantage of his power for his own benefit. He had his foothold in the court. To be settled there was a fine thing. No chance could now escape him. More than once he had made the queen smile maliciously. This was having a license to shoot. But was there any preserved game? Did this license to shoot permit him to break the wing or the leg of one like the sister of her Majesty? The first point to make clear was, did the queen love her sister? One false step would lose all. Barkilphedro watched.

Before he plays, the player looks at the cards. What trumps has he? Barkilphedro began by examining the age of the two women. Josiana, twenty-three; Anne, forty-one. So far so good. He held trumps. The moment that woman ceases to count by springs, and begins to count by winters, she becomes cross. A dull rancor possesses her against the time of which she carries the proofs. Fresh-blown beauties, perfumes for others, are to such a one but thorns. Of the roses she feels but the prick. It seems as if all the freshness is stolen from her, and that beauty decreases in her because it increases in others.

To profit by this secret ill-humor, to dive into the wrinkle on the face of this woman of forty, who was a queen, seemed a good game for Barkilphedro.

Envy excels in exciting jealousy, as a rat draws the crocodile from its hole.

Barkilphedro fixed his wise gaze on Anne. He saw into the queen, as one sees into a stagnant pool. The marsh has its transparency. In dirty water we see vices, in muddy water we see stupidity; Anne was muddy water.

Embryos of sentiments and larvae of ideas moved in her thick brain. They were not distinct; they had scarcely any outline. But they were realities, however shapeless. The queen thought this; the queen desired that. To decide what, was the difficulty. The confused transformations which work in stagnant water are difficult to study. The queen, habitually obscure, sometimes made sudden and stupid revelations. It was on these that it was necessary to seize. He must take advantage of them on the moment. How did the queen feel toward the Duchess Josiana? Did she wish her good or evil?

Here was the problem. Barkilphedro set himself to solve it. This problem solved, he might go further.

Divers chances served Barkilphedro; his tenacity at the watch above all.

Anne was, on her husband's side, slightly related to the new Queen of Prussia, wife of the king with the hundred chamberlains. She had her portrait painted on enamel, after the process of Turquet of Mayerne. This Queen of Prussia had also a younger illegitimate sister, the Baroness Drika.

One day, in the presence of Barkilphedro, Anne asked the Russian ambassador some question about this Drika.

"They say she is rich?"

"Very rich."

"She has palaces?"

"More magnificent than those of her sister, the queen."

"Whom will she marry?"

"A great lord, the Count Gormo."

"Pretty?"

"Charming."

"Is she young?"

"Very young."

"As beautiful as the queen?"

The ambassador lowered his voice, and replied—

"More beautiful."

"That is insolent," murmured Barkilphedro.

The queen was silent, then she exclaimed—

"Those bastards!"

Barkilphedro noticed the plural.

Another time, when the queen was leaving the chapel, Barkilphedro kept pretty close to her Majesty, behind the two grooms of the almonry. Lord David Dirry-Moir, crossing the ranks of women, made a sensation by his handsome appearance. As he passed there was an explosion of feminine exclamations.

"How elegant! How gallant! What a noble air! How handsome!"

"How disagreeable!" grumbled the queen.

Barkilphedro overheard this; it decided him.

He could hurt the duchess without displeasing the queen. The first problem was solved; but now the second presented itself.

What could he do to harm the duchess? What means did his wretched appointment offer to attain so difficult an object?

Evidently none.

Chapter XII

SCOTLAND, IRELAND, AND ENGLAND

LET US NOTE A CIRCUMSTANCE. JOSIANA HAD *LE TOUR*.
This is easy to understand when we reflect that she was, although illegitimate, the queen's sister—that is to say, a princely personage.

To have *le tour*, what does it mean?

Viscount St. John, otherwise Bolingbroke, wrote as follows to Thomas Lennard, Earl of Sussex—

"Two things mark the great—in England, they have *le tour*; in France, *le pour*."

When the King of France traveled, the courier of the court stopped at the halting-place in the evening, and assigned lodgings to his Majesty's suite.

Amongst the gentlemen some had an immense privilege. "They have *le pour*," says the *Journal Historique* for the year 1694, page 6; "which means that the courier who marks the billets puts '*Pour*' before their names—as '*Pour* M. le Prince de Soubise'; instead of which, when he marks the lodging of one who is not royal, he does not put *pour*, but simply the name—as 'Le Duc de Gesvres, le Duc de Mazarin.' " This *pour* on a door indicated a prince or a favorite. A favorite is worse than a prince. The king granted *le pour*, like a blue ribbon or a peerage.

Avoir le tour in England was less glorious, but more real. It was a sign of intimate communication with the sovereign. Whoever might be, by birth or favor, in a position to receive direct communications from majesty, had in the wall of their bedchamber a shaft, in which was adjusted a bell. The bell sounded, the shaft opened, a royal missive appeared on a gold plate or on a cushion of velvet, and the shaft closed. This was intimate and solemn, the mysterious in the familiar. The shaft was used for no other purpose. The sound of the bell announced a royal message. No one saw who brought it. It was of course merely the page of the king or the queen. Leicester *avait le tour* under Elizabeth; Buckingham under James I. Josiana had it under Anne, though not much in favor. Never was a privilege more envied.

This privilege entailed additional servility. The recipient was more of a servant. At court that which elevates, degrades. *Avoir le tour* was said in French; this circumstance of English etiquette having, probably, been borrowed from some old French folly.

Lady Josiana, a virgin peeress as Elizabeth had been a virgin queen, led—sometimes in the city, and sometimes in the country, according to the season—an almost princely life, and kept nearly a court, at which Lord David was courtier, with many others.

Not being married, Lord David and Lady Josiana could show themselves together in public without exciting ridicule, and they did so frequently. They often went to plays and racecourses in the same carriage, and sat together in the same box. They were chilled by the impending marriage, which was not only permitted to them, but imposed upon them; but they felt an attraction for each other's society. The privacy permitted to the engaged has a frontier easily passed. From this they abstained; that which is easy is in bad taste.

The best pugilistic encounters then took place at Lambeth, a parish in which the Lord Archbishop of Canterbury has a palace though the air there is unhealthy, and a rich library open at certain hours to decent people.

One evening in winter there was in a meadow there, the gates of which were locked, a fight, at which Josiana, escorted by Lord David, was present. She had asked—

"Are women admitted?"

And David had responded

"*Sunt faeminae magnates!*"

Liberal translation, "Not shopkeepers." Literal translation, "Great ladies exist. A duchess goes everywhere!"

This is why Lady Josiana saw a boxing match.

Lady Josiana made only this concession to propriety—she dressed as a man, a very common custom at that period. Women seldom traveled otherwise. Out of every six persons who traveled by the coach from Windsor, it was rare that there were not one or two amongst them who were women in male attire; a certain sign of high birth.

Lord David, being in company with a woman, could not take any part in the match himself, and merely assisted as one of the audience.

Lady Josiana betrayed her quality in one way; she had an opera-glass, then used by gentlemen only.

This encounter in the noble science was presided over by Lord Germaine, great-grandfather, or granduncle, of that Lord Germaine who, toward the end of the eighteenth century, was colonel, ran away in a battle, was afterwards made Minister of War, and only escaped from the bolts of the enemy, to fall by a worse fate, shot through and through by the sarcasm of Sheridan.

Many gentlemen were betting. Harry Bellew, of Carleton, who had claims to the extinct peerage of Bella-aqua, with Henry, Lord Hyde, member of Parliament for the borough of Dunhivid, which is also called Launceston; the Honorable Peregrine Betrie, member for the borough of Truro, with Sir Thomas Colpepper, member for Maidstone; the Laird of Lamyrbau, which is on the borders of Lothian, with Samuel Trefusis, of the borough of Penryn; Sir Bartholomew Gracedieu, of the borough of Saint Ives, with the Honorable Charles Bodville, who was called Lord Robartes, and who was Custos Rotulorum of the county of Cornwall; besides many others.

Of the two combatants, one was an Irishman, named after his native mountain in Tipperary, Phelem-ghe-Madone, and the other a Scot, named Helmsgail.

They represented the national pride of each country. Ireland and Scotland were about to set to; Erin was going to fisticuff Gajothel. So that the bets amounted to over forty thousand guineas, besides the stakes.

The two champions were naked, excepting short breeches buckled over the hips, and spiked boots laced as high as the ankles.

Helmsgail, the Scot, was a youth scarcely nineteen, but he had already had his forehead sewn up, for which reason they laid 2⅓ to 1 on him. The month before he had broken the ribs and gouged out the eyes of a pugilist named Sixmileswater. This explained the enthusiasm he created. He had won his backers twelve thousand pounds. Besides having his forehead sewn up Helmsgail's jaw had been broken. He was neatly made and active. He was about the height of a small woman, upright, thick set, and of a stature low and threatening. And nothing had been lost of the advantages given him by nature; not a muscle which was not trained to its object, pugilism. His firm chest was compact, and brown and shining like brass. He smiled, and three teeth which he had lost added to this smile.

His adversary was tall and overgrown—that is to say, weak.

He was a man of forty years of age, six feet high, with the chest of a hippopotamus, and a mild expression of face. The blow of his fist would break in the deck of a vessel, but he did not know how to use it.

The Irishman, Phelem-ghe-Madone, was all surface, and seemed to have entered the ring to receive, rather than to give, blows. Only it was felt that he would take a deal of punishment. Like underdone beef, tough to chew, and impossible to swallow. He was what was termed, in local slang, raw meat. He squinted. He seemed resigned.

The two men had passed the preceding night in the same bed, and had slept together. They had each drunk port wine from the same glass, to the three-inch mark.

Each had his group of seconds—men of savage expression, threatening the umpires when it suited their side. Amongst Helmsgail's supporters was to be seen John Gromane, celebrated for having carried an ox on his back; and one called John Bray, who had once carried on his back ten bushels of flour, at fifteen pecks to the bushel, besides the miller himself, and had walked over two hundred paces under the weight. On the side of Phelem-ghe-Madone, Lord Hyde had brought from Launceston a certain Kilter, who lived at Green Castle, and could throw a stone weighing twenty pounds to a greater height than the highest tower of the castle.

These three men, Kilter, Bray, and Gromane, were Cornishmen by birth, and did honor to their county.

The other seconds were brutal fellows, with broad backs, bowed legs, knotted fists, dull faces; ragged, fearing nothing, nearly all jail-birds.

Many of them understood admirably how to make the police drunk. Each profession should have its peculiar talents.

The field chosen was further off than the bear garden, where they formerly baited bears, bulls, and dogs; it was beyond the line of the furthest houses, by the side of the ruins of the Priory of Saint Mary Overy, dismantled by Henry VIII. The wind was northerly, and biting; a small rain fell, which was instantly frozen into ice. Some gentlemen present were evidently fathers of families, recognized as such by their putting up their umbrellas.

On the side of Phelem-ghe-Madone was Colonel Moncreif, as umpire; and Kilter, as second, to support him on his knee.

On the side of Helmsgail, the Honorable Pughe Beaumaris was umpire, with Lord Desertum, from Kilcarry, as bottle-holder, to support him on his knee.

The two combatants stood for a few seconds motionless in the ring, whilst the watches were being compared. They then approached each other and shook hands.

Phelem-ghe-Madone said to Helmsgail—

"I should prefer going home."

Helmsgail answered, handsomely—

"The gentlemen must not be disappointed on any account."

Naked as they were, they felt the cold. Phelem-ghe-Madone shook. His teeth chattered.

Dr. Eleanor Sharpe, nephew of the Archbishop of York, cried out to them—

"Set to, boys; it will warm you."

Those friendly words thawed them.

They set to.

But neither one nor the other was angry. There were three ineffectual rounds. The Rev. Dr. Gumdraith, one of the forty Fellows of All Souls' College, cried—

"Spirit them up with gin."

But the two umpires and the two seconds adhered to the rule. Yet it was exceedingly cold.

First blood was claimed.

They were again set face to face.

They looked at each other, approached, stretched their arms, touched each other's fists, and then drew back.

All at once, Helmsgail, the little man, sprang forward. The real fight had begun.

Phelem-ghe-Madone was struck in the face, between the eyes. His whole face streamed with blood. The crowd cried—

"Helmsgail has tapped his claret!"

There was applause. Phelem-ghe-Madone, turning his arms like the sails of a windmill, struck out at random.

The Honorable Peregrine Bertie said, "Blinded"; but he was not blind yet.

Then Helmsgail heard on all sides these encouraging words—

"Bung up his peepers!"

On the whole, the two champions were really well matched; and, notwithstanding the unfavorable weather, it was seen that the fight would be a success.

The great giant, Phelem-ghe-Madone, had to bear the inconveniences of his advantages; he moved heavily. His arms were massive as clubs; but his chest was a mass. His little opponent ran, struck, sprung, gnashed his teeth; redoubling vigor by quickness, from knowledge of the science.

On the one side was the primitive blow of the fist—savage, uncultivated, in a state of ignorance; on the other side, the civilized blow of the fist. Helmsgail fought as much with his nerves as with his muscles, and with as much intention as force. Phelem-ghe-Madone was a kind of sluggish mauler—somewhat mauled himself, to begin with. It was art against nature. It was cultivated ferocity against barbarism.

It was clear that the barbarian would be beaten, but not very quickly. Hence the interest.

A little man against a big one, and the chances are in favor of the little one. The cat has the best of it with a dog. Goliaths are always vanquished by Davids.

A hail of exclamations followed the combatants.

"Bravo, Helmsgail! Good! Well done, Highlander! Now, Phelem!"

And the friends of Helmsgail repeated their benevolent exhortation—

"Bung up his peepers!"

Helmsgail did better. Rapidly bending down and back again, with the undulation of a serpent, he struck Phelem-ghe-Madone in the sternum. The Colossus staggered.

"Foul blow!" cried Viscount Barnard.

Phelem-ghe-Madone sank down on the knee of his second, saying—

"I am beginning to get warm."

Lord Desertum consulted the umpires, and said—

"Five minutes before time is called."

Phelem-ghe-Madone was becoming weaker. Kilter wiped the blood from his face and the sweat from his body with a flannel, and placed the neck of a bottle to his mouth. They had come to the eleventh round. Phelem, besides the scar on his forehead, had his breast disfigured by blows, his belly swollen, and the fore part of the head scarified. Helmsgail was untouched.

A kind of tumult arose among the gentlemen.

Lord Barnard repeated, "Foul blow."

"Bets void!" said the Laird of Lamyrbau.

"I claim my stake!" replied Sir Thomas Colpepper.

And the honorable member for the borough of Saint Ives, Sir Bartholomew Gracedieu, added, "Give me back my five hundred guineas, and I will go. Stop the fight."

Phelem arose, staggering like a drunken man, and said—

"Let us go on fighting, on one condition—that I also shall have the right to give one foul blow."

They cried "Agreed!" from all parts of the ring. Helmsgail shrugged his shoulders. Five minutes elapsed, and they set to again.

The fighting, which was agony to Phelem, was play to Helmsgail. Such are the triumphs of science.

The little man found means of putting the big one into chancery—that is to say, Helmsgail suddenly took under his left arm, which was bent like a steel crescent, the huge head of Phelem-ghe-Madone, and held it there under his arm-pits, the neck bent and twisted, whilst Helmsgail's right fist fell again and again like a hammer on a nail, only from below and striking upwards, thus smashing his opponent's face at his ease. When Phelem, released at length, lifted his head, he had no longer a face.

That which had been a nose, eyes, and a mouth, now looked only like a black sponge soaked in blood. He spat, and on the ground lay four of his teeth.

Then he fell. Kilter received him on his knee.

Helmsgail was hardly touched: he had some insignificant bruises, and a scratch on his collar-bone.

No one was cold now. They laid sixteen and a quarter to one on Helmsgail.

Harry Carleton cried out—

"It is all over with Phelem-ghe-Madone. I will lay my peerage of Bella-aqua, and my title of Lord Bellew, against the Archbishop of Canterbury's old wig, on Helmsgail."

"Give me your muzzle," said Kilter to Phelem-ghe-Madone. And stuffing the bloody flannel into the bottle, he washed him all over with gin. The mouth reappeared, and he opened one eyelid. His temples seemed fractured.

"One round more, my friend," said Kilter; and he added, "for the honor of the low town."

The Welsh and the Irish understand each other, still Phelem made no sign of having any power of understanding left.

Phelem arose, supported by Kilter. It was the twenty-fifth round. From the way in which this Cyclops, for he had but one eye, placed himself in position, it was evident that this was the last round, for no one doubted his defeat. He placed his guard below his chin, with the awkwardness of a failing man.

Helmsgail, with a skin hardly sweating, cried out—

"I'll back myself, a thousand to one."

Helmsgail, raising his arm, struck out; and, what was strange, both fell. A ghastly chuckle was heard. It was Phelem-ghe-Madone's expression of delight. While receiving the terrible blow given him by Helmsgail on the skull, he had given him a foul blow on the navel.

Helmsgail, lying on his back, rattled in his throat.

The spectators looked at him as he lay on the ground, and said, "Paid back!" All clapped their hands, even those who had lost. Phelem-ghe-Madone had given foul blow for foul blow, and had only asserted his right.

They carried Helmsgail off on a hand-barrow. The opinion was that he would not recover.

Lord Robartes exclaimed, "I win twelve hundred guineas."

Phelem-ghe-Madone was evidently maimed for life.

As she left, Josiana took the arm of Lord David, an act which was tolerated amongst people engaged. She said to him—

"It is very fine, but—"

"But what?"

"I thought it would have driven away my spleen. It has not."

Lord David stopped, looked at Josiana, shut his mouth, and inflated his cheeks, whilst he nodded his head, which signified attention, and said to the duchess—

"For spleen there is but one remedy."

"What is it?"

"Gwynplaine."

The duchess asked—

"And who is Gwynplaine?"

BOOK THE SECOND

GWYNPLAINE AND DEA

Chapter I

WHEREIN WE SEE THE FACE OF HIM OF WHOM WE HAVE HITHERTO SEEN ONLY THE ACTS

NATURE HAD BEEN PRODIGAL OF HER KINDNESS TO GWYNPLAINE. SHE HAD BESTOWED ON HIM A mouth opening to his ears, ears folding over to his eyes, a shapeless nose to support the spectacles of the grimace maker, and a face that no one could look upon without laughing.

We have just said that nature had loaded Gwynplaine with her gifts. But was it nature? Had she not been assisted?

Two slits for eyes, a hiatus for a mouth, a snub protuberance with two holes for nostrils, a flattened face, all having for the result an appearance of laughter; it is certain that nature never produces such perfection single-handed.

But is laughter a synonym of joy?

If, in the presence of this mountebank—for he was one—the first impression of gaiety wore off, and the man was observed with attention, traces of art were to be recognized. Such a face could never have been created by chance, it must have resulted from intention. Such perfect completeness is not in nature. Man can do nothing to create beauty, but everything to produce ugliness. A Hottentot profile cannot be changed into a Roman outline, but out of a Grecian nose you may make a Calmuck's. It only requires to obliterate the root of the nose, and to flatten the nostrils. The dog Latin of the Middle Ages had a reason for its creation of the verb *denasare*. Had Gwynplaine when a child been so worthy of attention that his face had been subjected to transmutation? Why not? Needed there a greater motive than the speculation of his future exhibition? According to all appearance, industrious manipulators of children had worked upon his face. It seemed evident that a mysterious and probably occult science, which was to surgery what alchemy was to chemistry, had chiseled his flesh, evidently at a very tender age, and manufactured his countenance with premeditation. That science, clever with the knife, skilled in obtusions and ligatures, had enlarged the mouth, cut away the lips, laid bare the gums, distended the ears, cut the cartilages, displaced the eyelids and the cheeks, enlarged the zygomatic muscle, pressed the scars and cicatrices to a level, turned back the skin over the lesions whilst the face was thus stretched, from all which resulted that powerful and profound piece of sculpture, the mask, Gwynplaine.

Man is not born thus.

However it may have been, the manipulation of Gwynplaine had succeeded admirably. Gwynplaine was a gift of Providence to dispel the sadness of man.

Of what providence? Is there a providence of demons as well as of God? We put the question without answering it.

Gwynplaine was a mountebank. He showed himself on the platform. No such effect had ever before been produced. Hypochondriacs were cured by the sight of him alone. He was avoided by folks in mourning, because they were compelled to laugh when they saw him, without regard to their decent gravity. One day the executioner came, and Gwynplaine made him laugh. Everyone who saw Gwynplaine held his sides; he spoke, and they rolled on the ground. He was removed from sadness as is pole from pole. Spleen at the one; Gwynplaine at the other.

Thus he rose rapidly in the fairground and at the cross-roads to the very satisfactory renown of a horrible man.

It was Gwynplaine's laugh which created the laughter of others, yet he did not laugh himself. His face laughed; his thoughts did not. The extraordinary face which chance or a special and weird industry had fashioned for him, laughed alone. Gwynplaine had nothing to do with it. The outside did not depend on the interior. The laugh which he had not placed, himself, on his brow, on his eyelids, on his mouth, he could not remove. It had been stamped forever on his face. It was automatic, and the more irresistible because it seemed petrified. No one could escape from this rictus. Two convulsions of the face are infectious; laughing and yawning. By virtue of the mysterious operation to which Gwynplaine had probably been subjected in his infancy, every part of his face contributed to that rictus; his whole physiognomy led to that result, as a wheel centers in the nave. All his emotions, whatever they might have been, augmented his strange face of joy, or to speak more correctly, aggravated it. Any astonishment which might seize him, any suffering which he might feel, any anger which might take possession of him, any pity which might move him, would only increase this hilarity of his muscles. If he wept, he laughed; and whatever Gwynplaine was, whatever he wished to be, whatever he thought, the moment that he raised his head, the crowd, if crowd there was, had before them one impersonation: an overwhelming burst of laughter.

It was like a head of Medusa, but Medusa hilarious. All feeling or thought in the mind of the spectator was suddenly put to flight by the unexpected apparition, and laughter was inevitable. Antique art formerly placed on the outsides of the Greek theater a joyous brazen face, called Comedy.

It laughed and occasioned laughter, but remained pensive. All parody which borders on folly, all irony which borders on wisdom, were condensed and amalgamated in that face. The burden of care, of disillusion, anxiety, and grief were expressed in its impassive countenance, and resulted in a lugubrious sum of mirth. One corner of the mouth was raised, in mockery of the human race; the other side, in blasphemy of the gods. Men confronted that model of the ideal sarcasm and exemplification of the irony which each one possesses within him; and the crowd, continually renewed round its fixed laugh, died away with delight before its sepulchral immobility of mirth.

One might almost have said that Gwynplaine was that dark, dead mask of ancient comedy, adjusted to the body of a living man. That infernal head of implacable hilarity he supported on his neck. What a weight for the shoulders of a man—an everlasting laugh!

An everlasting laugh!

Let us understand each other; we will explain. The Manichaeans believed the absolute occasionally gives way, and that God himself sometimes abdicates for a time. So also of the will. We do not admit that it can ever be utterly powerless. The whole of existence resembles a letter modified in the postscript. For Gwynplaine the postscript was this: by the force of his will, and by concentrating all his attention, and on condition that no emotion should come to distract and turn away the fixedness of his effort, he could manage to suspend the everlasting rictus of his face, and to throw over it a kind of tragic veil, and then the spectator laughed no longer; he shuddered.

This exertion Gwynplaine scarcely ever made. It was a terrible effort, and an insupportable tension. Moreover, it happened that on the slightest distraction, or the slightest emotion, the laugh, driven back for a moment, returned like a tide with an impulse which was irresistible in proportion to the force of the adverse emotion.

With this exception, Gwynplaine's laugh was everlasting.

On seeing Gwynplaine, all laughed. When they had laughed they turned away their heads. Women especially shrank from him with horror. The man was frightful. The joyous convulsion of laughter was as a tribute paid; they submitted to it gladly, but almost mechanically. Besides, when once the novelty of the laugh had passed over, Gwynplaine was intolerable for a woman to see, and impossible to contemplate.

But he was tall, well made, and agile, and no way deformed, excepting in his face.

This led to the presumption that Gwynplaine was rather a creation of art than a work of nature. Gwynplaine, beautiful in figure, had probably been beautiful in face. At his birth he had no doubt resembled other infants. They had left the body intact, and retouched only the face.

Gwynplaine had been made to order—at least, that was probable. They had left him his teeth; teeth are necessary to a laugh. The death's-head retains them. The operation performed on him must have been frightful. That he had no remembrance of it was no proof that it had not taken place. Surgical sculpture of the kind could never have succeeded except on a very young child, and consequently on one having little consciousness of what happened to him, and who might easily take a wound for a sickness. Besides, we must remember that they had in those times means of putting patients to sleep, and of suppressing all suffering; only then it was called magic, while now it is called anaesthesia.

Besides this face, those who had brought him up had given him the resources of a gymnast and an athlete. His articulations usefully displaced and fashioned to bending the wrong way, had received the education of a clown, and could, like the hinges of a door, move backwards and forwards. In appropriating him to the profession of mountebank nothing had been neglected. His hair had been dyed with ochre once for all; a secret which has been rediscovered at the present day. Pretty women use it, and that which was formerly considered ugly is now considered an embellishment. Gwynplaine had yellow hair. His hair having probably been dyed with some corrosive preparation, had left it woolly and rough to the touch. Its yellow bristles, rather a mane than a head of hair, covered and concealed a lofty brow, evidently made to contain thought. The operation, whatever it had been, which had deprived his features of harmony, and put all their flesh into disorder, had had no effect on the bony structure of his head. The facial angle was powerful and surprisingly grand. Behind his laugh there was a soul, dreaming, as all our souls dream.

However, his laugh was to Gwynplaine quite a talent. He could do nothing with it, so he turned it to account. By means of it he gained his living.

Gwynplaine, as you have doubtless already guessed, was the child abandoned one winter evening on the coast of Portland, and received into a poor caravan at Weymouth.

Chapter II

DEA

THAT BOY WAS AT THIS TIME A MAN. FIFTEEN YEARS HAD ELAPSED. IT WAS IN 1705. GWYNPLAINE was in his twenty-fifth year.

Ursus had kept the two children with him. They were a group of wanderers. Ursus and Homo had aged. Ursus had become quite bald. The wolf was growing gray. The age of wolves is not ascertained like that of dogs. According to Molière, there are wolves which live to eighty, amongst others the little koupara, and the rank wolf, the *Canis nubilus* of Say.

The little girl found on the dead woman was now a tall creature of sixteen, with brown hair, slight, fragile, almost trembling from delicacy, and almost inspiring fear lest she should break; admirably beautiful, her eyes full of light, yet blind. That fatal winter night which threw down the beggar woman and her infant in the snow had struck a double blow. It had killed the mother and blinded the child. Gutta serena had forever paralyzed the eyes of the girl, now become woman in her turn. On her face, through which the light of day never passed, the depressed corners of the mouth indicated the bitterness of the privation. Her eyes, large and clear, had a strange quality: extinguished forever to her, to others they were brilliant. They were mysterious torches lighting only the outside. They gave light but possessed it not. These sightless eyes were resplendent. A captive of shadow, she lighted up the dull place she inhabited. From the depth of her incurable darkness, from behind the black wall called blindness, she flung her rays. She saw not the sun without, but her soul was perceptible from within.

In her dead look there was a celestial earnestness. She was the night, and from the irremediable darkness with which she was amalgamated, she came out a star.

Ursus, with his mania for Latin names, had christened her Dea. He had taken his wolf into consultation. He had said to him, "You represent man, I represent the beasts. We are of the lower world, this little one shall represent the world on high. Such feebleness is all-powerful. In this manner the universe shall be complete in our hut in its three orders—human, animal and Divine." The wolf made no objection. Therefore the foundling was called Dea.

As to Gwynplaine, Ursus had not the trouble of inventing a name for him. The morning of the day on which he had realized the disfigurement of the little boy and the blindness of the infant, he had asked him, "Boy, what is your name?" and the boy had answered, "They call me Gwynplaine." "Be Gwynplaine, then," said Ursus.

Dea assisted Gwynplaine in his performances. If human misery could be summed up, it might have been summed up in Gwynplaine and Dea. Each seemed born in a compartment of the sepulcher; Gwynplaine in the horrible, Dea in the darkness. Their existences were shadowed by two different kinds of darkness, taken from the two formidable sides of night. Dea had that shadow in her,

Gwynplaine had it on him. There was a phantom in Dea, a specter in Gwynplaine. Dea was sunk
in the mournful, Gwynplaine in something worse. There was for Gwynplaine, who could see, a
heartrending possibility that existed not for Dea, who was blind; he could compare himself with
other men. Now, in a situation such as that of Gwynplaine, admitting that he should seek to examine it, to compare himself with others was to understand himself no more. To have, like Dea, empty
sight from which the world is absent, is a supreme distress, yet less than to be an enigma to one's
self; to feel that something is wanting here as well, and that something, one's self; to see the universe and not to see one's self. Dea had a veil over her, the night; Gwynplaine a mask, his face. Inexpressible fact, it was by his own flesh that Gwynplaine was masked! What his visage had been, he
knew not. His face had vanished. They had affixed to him a false self. He had for a face, a disappearance. His head lived, his face was dead. He never remembered to have seen it. Mankind was for
Gwynplaine, as for Dea, an exterior fact. It was far-off. She was alone, he was alone. The isolation
of Dea was funereal, she saw nothing; that of Gwynplaine sinister, he saw all things. For Dea creation never passed the bounds of touch and hearing; reality was bounded, limited, short, immediately lost. Nothing was infinite to her but darkness. For Gwynplaine to live was to have the crowd
forever before him and outside him. Dea was the proscribed from light, Gwynplaine the banned of
life. They were beyond the pale of hope, and had reached the depth of possible calamity; they had
sunk into it, both of them. An observer who had watched them would have felt his reverie melt into
immeasurable pity. What must they not have suffered! The decree of misfortune weighed visibly
on these human creatures, and never had fate encompassed two beings who had done nothing to deserve it, and more clearly turned destiny into torture, and life into hell.

They were in a Paradise.

They were in love.

Gwynplaine adored Dea. Dea idolized Gwynplaine.

"How beautiful you are!" she would say to him.

Chapter III

"Oculos non Habet, et Videt"

ONLY ONE WOMAN ON EARTH SAW GWYNPLAINE. IT WAS THE BLIND GIRL. SHE HAD LEARNED
what Gwynplaine had done for her, from Ursus, to whom he had related his rough journey
from Portland to Weymouth, and the many sufferings which he had endured when deserted by the
gang. She knew that when an infant dying upon her dead mother, suckling a corpse, a being scarcely
bigger than herself had taken her up; that this being, exiled, and, as it were, buried under the refusal
of the universe to aid him, had heard her cry; that all the world being deaf to him, he had not been
deaf to her; that the child, alone, weak, cast off, without resting-place here below, dragging himself
over the waste, exhausted by fatigue, crushed, had accepted from the hands of night a burden, another child; that he, who had nothing to expect in that obscure distribution which we call fate, had
charged himself with a destiny; that naked, in anguish and distress, he had made himself a Providence; that when Heaven had closed he had opened his heart; that, himself lost, he had saved; that
having neither roof-tree nor shelter, he had been an asylum; that he had made himself mother and
nurse; that he who was alone in the world had responded to desertion by adoption; that lost in the
darkness he had given an example; that, as if not already sufficiently burdened, he had added to his
load another's misery; that in this world, which seemed to contain nothing for him, he had found a

duty; that where everyone else would have hesitated, he had advanced; that where everyone else would have drawn back, he consented; that he had put his hand into the jaws of the grave and drawn out her—Dea. That, himself half naked, he had given her his rags, because she was cold; that famished, he had thought of giving her food and drink; that for one little creature, another little creature had combated death; that he had fought it under every form; under the form of winter and snow, under the form of solitude, under the form of terror, under the form of cold, hunger, and thirst, under the form of whirlwind, and that for her, Dea, this Titan of ten had given battle to the immensity of night. She knew that as a child he had done this, and that now as a man, he was strength to her weakness, riches to her poverty, healing to her sickness, and sight to her blindness. Through the mist of the unknown by which she felt herself encompassed, she distinguished clearly his devotion, his abnegation, his courage. Heroism in immaterial regions has an outline; she distinguished this sublime outline. In the inexpressible abstraction in which thought lives unlighted by the sun, Dea perceived this mysterious lineament of virtue. In the surrounding of dark things put in motion, which was the only impression made on her by reality; in the uneasy stagnation of a creature, always passive, yet always on the watch for possible evil; in the sensation of being ever defenseless, which is the life of the blind; she felt Gwynplaine above her; Gwynplaine never cold, never absent, never obscured; Gwynplaine sympathetic, helpful, and sweet-tempered. Dea quivered with certainty and gratitude, her anxiety changed into ecstasy, and with her shadowy eyes she contemplated on the zenith from the depth of her abyss the rich light of his goodness. In the ideal, kindness is the sun; and Gwynplaine dazzled Dea.

To the crowd, which has too many heads to have a thought, and too many eyes to have a sight—to the crowd who, superficial themselves, judge only of the surface, Gwynplaine was a clown, a merry-andrew, a mountebank, a creature grotesque, a little more and a little less than a beast. The crowd knew only the face.

For Dea, Gwynplaine was the savior who had gathered her into his arms in the tomb, and borne her out of it; the consoler who made life tolerable; the liberator, whose hand, holding her own, guided her through that labyrinth called blindness. Gwynplaine was her brother, friend, guide, support; the personification of heavenly power, the husband, winged and resplendent. Where the multitude saw the monster, Dea recognized the archangel. It was that Dea, blind, perceived his soul.

Chapter IV

WELL-MATCHED LOVERS

URSUS BEING A PHILOSOPHER UNDERSTOOD. HE APPROVED OF THE FASCINATION OF DEA. HE SAID: the blind see the invisible. He said: conscience is vision. Then, looking at Gwynplaine, he murmured: semi-monster, but demi-god.

Gwynplaine, on the other hand, was madly in love with Dea.

There is the invisible eye, the spirit, and the visible eye, the pupil. He saw her with the visible eye. Dea was dazzled by the ideal; Gwynplaine, by the real. Gwynplaine was not ugly; he was frightful. He saw his contrast before him: in proportion as he was terrible, Dea was sweet. He was horror; she was grace. Dea was his dream. She seemed a vision scarcely embodied. There was in her whole person, in her Grecian form, in her fine and supple figure, swaying like a reed; in her shoulders, on which might have been invisible wings; in the modest curves which indicated her sex, to the soul rather than to the senses; in her fairness, which amounted almost to transparency; in the august and reserved serenity of her look, divinely shut out from earth; in the sacred innocence of her smile, she was almost an angel, and yet just a woman.

Gwynplaine, we have said, compared himself and compared Dea.

His existence, such as it was, was the result of a double and unheard-of choice. It was the point of intersection of two rays; one from below and one from above—a black and a white ray. To the same crumb, perhaps pecked at, at once, by the beaks of evil and good, one gave the bite, the other the kiss. Gwynplaine was this crumb—an atom, wounded and caressed. Gwynplaine was the product of fatality combined with Providence. Misfortune had placed its finger on him; happiness as well. Two extreme destinies composed his strange lot. He had on him an anathema and a benediction. He was the elect, cursed. Who was he? He knew not. When he looked at himself, he saw one he knew not; but this unknown was a monster. Gwynplaine lived as it were beheaded, with a face which did not belong to him. This face was frightful, so frightful that it was absurd. It caused as much fear as laughter. It was a hell-concocted absurdity. It was the shipwreck of a human face into the mask of an animal. Never had been seen so total an eclipse of humanity in a human face; never parody more complete; never had apparition more frightful grinned in nightmare; never had everything repulsive to woman been more hideously amalgamated in a man. The unfortunate heart, masked and calumniated by the face, seemed forever condemned to solitude under it, as under a tombstone.

Yet no! Where unknown malice had done its worst, invisible goodness had lent its aid. In the poor fallen one, suddenly raised up, by the side of the repulsive, it had placed the attractive; on the barren shoal it had set the loadstone; it had caused a soul to fly with swift wings toward the deserted one; it had sent the dove to console the creature whom the thunderbolt had overwhelmed, and had made beauty adore deformity. For this to be possible it was necessary that beauty should not see the disfigurement. For this good fortune, misfortune was required. Providence had made Dea blind.

Gwynplaine vaguely felt himself the object of a redemption. Why had he been persecuted? He knew not. Why redeemed? He knew not. All he knew was that a halo had encircled his brand. When Gwynplaine had been old enough to understand, Ursus had read and explained to him the text of Dr. Conquest, *de Denasatis,* and in another folio, Hugo Plagon, the passage, *Nares habens mutilas*; but Ursus had prudently abstained from "hypotheses," and had been reserved in his opinion of what it might mean. Suppositions were possible. The probability of violence inflicted on Gwynplaine when an infant was hinted at, but for Gwynplaine the result was the only evidence. His destiny was to live under a stigma. Why this stigma? There was no answer.

Silence and solitude were around Gwynplaine. All was uncertain in the conjectures which could be fitted to the tragical reality; excepting the terrible fact, nothing was certain. In his discouragement Dea intervened a sort of celestial interposition between him and despair. He perceived, melted and inspirited by the sweetness of the beautiful girl who turned to him, that, horrible as he was, a beautified wonder affected his monstrous visage. Having been fashioned to create dread, he was the object of a miraculous exception, that it was admired and adored in the ideal by the light; and, monster that he was, he felt himself the contemplation of a star.

Gwynplaine and Dea were united, and these two suffering hearts adored each other. One nest and two birds, that was their story. They had begun to feel a universal law—to please, to seek, and to find each other.

Thus hatred had made a mistake. The persecutors of Gwynplaine, whoever they might have been—the deadly enigma, from wherever it came—had missed their aim. They had intended to drive him to desperation; they had succeeded in driving him into enchantment. They had affianced him beforehand to a healing wound. They had predestined him for consolation by an infliction. The pincers of the executioner had softly changed into the delicately-molded hand of a girl. Gwynplaine was horrible; artificially horrible—made horrible by the hand of man. They had hoped to exile him forever: first, from his family, if his family existed, and then from humanity. When an infant, they had made him a ruin; of this ruin Nature had repossessed herself, as she does of all ruins. This solitude Nature had consoled, as she consoles all solitudes. Nature comes to the succor of the deserted; where all is lacking, she gives back her whole self. She flourishes and grows green amid ruins: she has ivy for the stones and love for man.

Profound generosity of the shadows!

Chapter V

THE BLUE SKY THROUGH THE BLACK CLOUD

T HUS LIVED THESE UNFORTUNATE CREATURES TOGETHER, DEA, RELYING; GWYNPLAINE, AC-cepted. These orphans were all in all to each other, the feeble and the deformed. The widowed were betrothed. An inexpressible thanksgiving arose out of their distress. They were grateful. To whom? To the obscure immensity. Be grateful in your own hearts. That suffices. Thanksgiving has wings, and flies to its right destination. Your prayer knows its way better than you can.

How many men have believed that they prayed to Jupiter, when they prayed to Jehovah! How many believers in amulets are listened to by the Almighty! How many atheists there are who know not that, in the simple fact of being good and sad, they pray to God!

Gwynplaine and Dea were grateful. Deformity is expulsion. Blindness is a precipice. The expelled one had been adopted; the precipice was habitable.

Gwynplaine had seen a brilliant light descending on him, in an arrangement of destiny which seemed to put, in the perspective of a dream, a white cloud of beauty having the form of a woman, a radiant vision in which there was a heart; and the phantom, almost a cloud and yet a woman, clasped him; and the apparition embraced him; and the heart desired him. Gwynplaine was no longer deformed. He was beloved. The rose demanded the caterpillar in marriage, feeling that within the caterpillar there was a divine butterfly. Gwynplaine the rejected was chosen. To have one's desire is everything. Gwynplaine had his, Dea hers.

The abjection of the disfigured man was exalted and dilated into intoxication, into delight, into belief; and a hand was stretched out toward the melancholy hesitation of the blind girl, to guide her in her darkness.

It was the penetration of two misfortunes into the ideal, which absorbed them. The rejected found a refuge in each other. Two blanks, combining, filled each other up. They held together by what they lacked: in that in which one was poor, the other was rich. The misfortune of the one made the treasure of the other. Had Dea not been blind, would she have chosen Gwynplaine? Had Gwynplaine not been disfigured, would he have preferred Dea? She would probably have rejected the deformed, as he would have passed by the infirm. What happiness for Dea that Gwynplaine was hideous! What good fortune for Gwynplaine that Dea was blind! Apart from their providential matching, they were impossible to each other. A mighty want of each other was at the bottom of their loves. Gwynplaine saved Dea. Dea saved Gwynplaine. Apposition of misery produced adherence. It was the embrace of those swallowed in the abyss; none closer, none more hopeless, none more exquisite.

Gwynplaine had a thought. "What should I be without her?" Dea had a thought. "What should I be without him?"

The exile of each made a country for both. The two incurable fatalities, the stigmata of Gwynplaine and the blindness of Dea, joined them together in contentment. They sufficed to each other. They imagined nothing beyond each other. To speak to one another was a delight, to approach was beatitude; by force of reciprocal intuition they became united in the same reverie, and thought the same thoughts. In Gwynplaine's tread, Dea believed that she heard the step of one deified. They tightened their mutual grasp in a sort of sidereal *chiaroscuro*, full of perfumes, of gleams, of music, of the luminous architecture of dreams. They belonged to each other; they knew themselves to be forever united in the same joy and the same ecstasy; and nothing could be stranger than this construction of an Eden by two of the damned.

They were inexpressibly happy. In their hell they had created heaven. Such was thy power, O Love! Dea heard Gwynplaine's laugh; Gwynplaine saw Dea's smile. Thus ideal felicity was found, the perfect joy of life was realized, the mysterious problem of happiness was solved; and by whom? By two outcasts.

For Gwynplaine, Dea was splendor. For Dea, Gwynplaine was presence. Presence is that profound mystery which renders the invisible world divine, and from which results that other mystery—confidence. In religions this is the only thing which is irreducible; but this irreducible thing suffices. The great motive power is not seen; it is felt.

Gwynplaine was the religion of Dea. Sometimes, lost in her sense of love toward him, she knelt, like a beautiful priestess before a gnome in a pagoda, made happy by her adoration.

Imagine to yourself an abyss, and in its center an oasis of light, and in this oasis two creatures shut out of life, dazzling each other. No purity could be compared to their loves. Dea was ignorant what a kiss might be, though perhaps she desired it; because blindness, especially in a woman, has its dreams, and though trembling at the approaches of the unknown, does not fear them all. As to Gwynplaine, his sensitive youth made him pensive. The more delirious he felt, the more timid he became. He might have dared anything with this companion of his early youth, with this creature as innocent of fault as of the light, with this blind girl who saw but one thing—that she adored him! But he would have thought it a theft to take what she might have given; so he resigned himself with a melancholy satisfaction to love angelically, and the conviction of his deformity resolved itself into a proud purity.

These happy creatures dwelt in the ideal. They were spouses in it at distances as opposite as the spheres. They exchanged in its firmament the deep effluvium which is in infinity attraction, and on earth the sexes. Their kisses were the kisses of souls.

They had always lived a common life. They knew themselves only in each other's society. The infancy of Dea had coincided with the youth of Gwynplaine. They had grown up side by side. For a long time they had slept in the same bed, for the hut was not a large bedchamber. They lay on the chest, Ursus on the floor; that was the arrangement. One fine day, whilst Dea was still very little, Gwynplaine felt himself grown up, and it was in the youth that shame arose. He said to Ursus, "I will also sleep on the floor." And at night he stretched himself, with the old man, on the bear-skin. Then Dea wept. She cried for her bedfellow; but Gwynplaine, become restless because he had begun to love, decided to remain where he was. From that time he always slept by the side of Ursus on the planks. In the summer, when the nights were fine, he slept outside with Homo.

When thirteen, Dea had not yet become resigned to the arrangement. Often in the evening she said, "Gwynplaine, come close to me; that will put me to sleep." A man lying by her side was a necessity to her innocent slumbers.

Nudity is to see that one is naked. She ignored nudity. It was the ingenuousness of Arcadia or Otaheite. Dea untaught, made Gwynplaine wild. Sometimes it happened that Dea, when almost reaching youth, combed her long hair as she sat on her bed—her chemise unfastened and falling off revealed indications of a feminine outline, and a vague commencement of Eve—and would call Gwynplaine. Gwynplaine blushed, lowered his eyes, and knew not what to do in presence of this innocent creature. Stammering, he turned his head, feared, and fled. The Daphnis of darkness took flight before the Chloe of shadow.

Such was the idyll blooming in a tragedy.

Ursus said to them—

"Old brutes! adore each other!"

Chapter VI

URSUS AS TUTOR, AND URSUS AS GUARDIAN

URSUS ADDED—

"Some of these days I will play them a nasty trick. I will marry them."

Ursus taught Gwynplaine the theory of love. He said to him—

"Do you know how the Almighty lights the fire called love? He places the woman underneath, the devil between, and the man at the top. A match—that is to say, a look—and behold, it is all on fire."

"A look is unnecessary," answered Gwynplaine, thinking of Dea.

And Ursus replied—

"Booby! do souls require mortal eyes to see each other?"

Ursus was a good fellow at times. Gwynplaine, sometimes madly in love with Dea, became melancholy, and made use of the presence of Ursus as a guard on himself. One day Ursus said to him—

"Bah! do not put yourself out. When in love, the cock shows himself."

"But the eagle conceals himself," replied Gwynplaine.

At other times Ursus would say to himself, apart—

"It is wise to put spokes in the wheels of the Cytherean car. They love each other too much. This may have its disadvantages. Let us avoid a fire. Let us moderate these hearts."

Then Ursus had recourse to warnings of this nature, speaking to Gwynplaine when Dea slept, and to Dea when Gwynplaine's back was turned—

"Dea, you must not be so fond of Gwynplaine. To live in the life of another is perilous. Egoism is a good root of happiness. Men escape from women. And then Gwynplaine might end by becoming infatuated with you. His success is so great! You have no idea how great his success is!"

"Gwynplaine, disproportions are no good. So much ugliness on one side and so much beauty on another ought to compel reflection. Temper your ardor, my boy. Do not become too enthusiastic about Dea. Do you seriously consider that you are made for her? Just think of your deformity and her perfection! See the distance between her and yourself! She has everything, this Dea. What a white skin! What hair! Lips like strawberries! And her foot! her hand! Those shoulders, with their exquisite curve! Her expression is sublime. She walks diffusing light; and in speaking, the grave tone of her voice is charming. But for all this, to think that she is a woman! She would not be such a fool as to be an angel. She is absolute beauty. Repeat all this to yourself, to calm your ardor."

These speeches redoubled the love of Gwynplaine and Dea, and Ursus was astonished at his want of success, just as one who should say, "It is singular that with all the oil I throw on fire, I cannot extinguish it."

Did he, then, desire to extinguish their love, or to cool it even?

Certainly not. He would have been well punished had he succeeded. At the bottom of his heart this love, which was flame for them and warmth for him, was his delight.

But it is natural to grate a little against that which charms us; men call it wisdom.

Ursus had been, in his relations with Gwynplaine and Dea, almost a father and a mother. Grumbling all the while, he had brought them up; grumbling all the while, he had nourished them. His adoption of them had made the hut roll more heavily, and he had been oftener compelled to harness himself by Homo's side, to help to draw it.

We may observe, however, that after the first few years, when Gwynplaine was nearly grown up, and Ursus had grown quite old, Gwynplaine had taken his turn, and drawn Ursus.

Ursus, seeing that Gwynplaine was becoming a man, had cast the horoscope of his deformity. *"It has made your fortune!"* he had told him.

This family of an old man and two children, with a wolf, had become, as they wandered, a group more and more intimately united. Their errant life had not hindered education. "To wander is to grow," Ursus said. Gwynplaine was evidently made to exhibit at fairs. Ursus had cultivated in him feats of dexterity, and had encrusted him as much as possible with all he himself possessed of science and wisdom.

Ursus, contemplating the perplexing mask of Gwynplaine's face, often growled—

"He has begun well." It was for this reason that he had perfected him with every ornament of philosophy and wisdom.

He repeated constantly to Gwynplaine—

"Be a philosopher. To be wise is to be invulnerable. You see what I am. I have never shed a tear. This is the result of my wisdom. Do you think that occasion for tears has been wanting had I felt disposed to weep?"

Ursus, in one of his monologues in the hearing of the wolf, said—

"I have taught Gwynplaine everything, Latin included. I have taught Dea nothing, music included."

He had taught them both to sing. He had himself a pretty talent for playing on the oaten reed, a little flute of that period. He played on it agreeably, as also on the *chiffonie*, a sort of beggar's hurdy-gurdy, mentioned in the Chronicle of Bertrand Duguesclin as the "truant instrument," which started the symphony. These instruments attracted the crowd. Ursus would show them the chiffonie, and say, "It is called *organistrum* in Latin."

He had taught Dea and Gwynplaine to sing according to the method of Orpheus and of Egide Binchois. Frequently he interrupted the lessons with cries of enthusiasm, such as "Orpheus, musician of Greece! Binchois, musician of Picardy!"

These branches of careful culture did not occupy the children so as to prevent their adoring each other. They had mingled their hearts together as they grew up, as two saplings planted near mingle their branches as they become trees.

"No matter," said Ursus. "I will marry them."

Then he grumbled to himself—

"They are quite tiresome with their love."

The past, their little past, at least, had no existence for Dea and Gwynplaine. They knew only what Ursus had told them of it. They called Ursus father. The only remembrance which Gwynplaine had of his infancy was as of a passage of demons over his cradle. He had an impression of having been trodden in the darkness under deformed feet. Was this intentional or not? He was ignorant on this point. That which he remembered clearly and to the slightest detail were his tragical adventures when deserted at Portland. The finding of Dea made that dismal night a radiant date for him.

The memory of Dea, even more than that of Gwynplaine, was lost in clouds. In so young a child all remembrance melts away. She recollected her mother as something cold. Had she ever seen the sun? Perhaps so. She made efforts to pierce into the blank which was her past life.

"The sun!—what was it?"

She had some vague memory of a thing luminous and warm, of which Gwynplaine had taken the place.

They spoke to each other in low tones. It is certain that cooing is the most important thing in the world. Dea often said to Gwynplaine—

"Light means that you are speaking."

Once, no longer containing himself, as he saw through a muslin sleeve the arm of Dea, Gwynplaine brushed its transparency with his lips; ideal kiss of a deformed mouth! Dea felt a deep delight; she blushed like a rose. This kiss from a monster made Aurora gleam on that beautiful brow full of night. However, Gwynplaine sighed with a kind of terror, and as the neckerchief of Dea gaped, he could not refrain from looking at the whiteness visible through that glimpse of Paradise.

Dea pulled up her sleeve, and stretching toward Gwynplaine her naked arm, said—

"Again!"

Gwynplaine fled.

The next day the game was renewed, with variations.

It was a heavenly subsidence into that sweet abyss, called love.

At such things, heaven smiles philosophically.

Chapter VII

BLINDNESS GIVES LESSONS IN CLAIRVOYANCE

AT TIMES GWYNPLAINE REPROACHED HIMSELF. HE MADE HIS HAPPINESS A CASE OF CONSCIENCE. He fancied that to allow a woman who could not see him to love him, was to deceive her.

What would she have said could she have suddenly obtained her sight? How she would have felt repulsed by what had previously attracted her! How she would have recoiled from her frightful loadstone! What a cry! What covering of her face! What a flight! A bitter scruple harassed him. He told himself that such a monster as he had no right to love. He was a hydra idolized by a star. It was his duty to enlighten the blind star.

One day he said to Dea—

"You know that I am very ugly."

"I know that you are sublime," she answered.

He resumed—

"When you hear all the world laugh, they laugh at me because I am horrible."

"I love you," said Dea.

After a silence, she added—

"I was in death, you brought me to life. When you are here, heaven is by my side. Give me your hand, that I may touch heaven."

Their hands met and grasped each other. They spoke no more, but were silent in the plenitude of love.

Ursus, who was crabbed, had overheard this. The next day when the three were together, he said—

"For that matter, Dea is ugly also."

The word produced no effect. Dea and Gwynplaine were not listening. Absorbed in each other, they rarely heeded such exclamations of Ursus. Their depth was a dead loss.

This time, however, the precaution of Ursus, "Dea is also ugly," indicated in this learned man a certain knowledge of women. It is certain that Gwynplaine, in his loyalty, had been guilty of an imprudence. To have said, *I am ugly*, to any other blind girl than Dea, might have been dangerous. To be blind, and in love, is to be twofold blind. In such a situation, dreams are dreamt. Illusion is the food of dreams. Take illusion from love, and you take from it its aliment. It is compounded of every enthusiasm, of both physical and moral admiration.

Moreover, you should never tell a woman a word difficult to understand. She will dream about it, and she often dreams falsely. An enigma in a reverie spoils it. The shock caused by the fall of a careless word displaces that against which it strikes. At times it happens, without our knowing why, that because we have received the obscure blow of a chance word, the heart empties itself insensibly of love. He who loves, perceives a decline in his happiness. Nothing is to be feared more than this slow exudation from the fissure in the vase.

Happily, Dea was not formed of such clay. The stuff of which other women are made had not been used in her construction. She had a rare nature. The frame, but not the heart, was fragile. A divine perseverance in love, was in the heart of her being.

The whole disturbance which the word used by Gwynplaine had produced in her ended in her saying one day—

"To be ugly—what is it? It is to do wrong. Gwynplaine only does good. He is handsome."

Then, under the form of interrogation so familiar to children and to the blind, she resumed—

"To see?—what is it that you call seeing? For my own part, I cannot see; I know. It seems that *to see*, means to hide."

"What do you mean?" said Gwynplaine.

Dea answered—

"To see is a thing which conceals the true."

"No," said Gwynplaine.

"But yes," replied Dea, "since you say you are ugly."

She reflected a moment, and then said, "Storyteller!"

Gwynplaine felt the joy of having confessed, and of not being believed. Both his conscience and his love were consoled.

Thus they had reached, Dea sixteen, Gwynplaine nearly twenty-five. They were not, as it would now be expressed, "more advanced" than the first day. Less even; for it may be remembered that on their wedding night she was nine months and he ten years old. A sort of holy childhood had continued in their love. Thus it sometimes happens that the belated nightingale prolongs her nocturnal song till dawn.

Their caresses went no further than pressing hands, or lips brushing a naked arm. Soft, half-articulate whispers sufficed them.

Twenty-four and sixteen! So it happened that Ursus, who did not lose sight of the ill-turn he intended to do them, said—

"One of these days you must choose a religion."

"Wherefore?" inquired Gwynplaine.

"That you may marry."

"That is already done," said Dea.

Dea did not understand that they could be more man and wife than they were already.

At bottom, this chimerical and virginal content, this innocent union of souls, this celibacy taken for marriage, was not displeasing to Ursus. He had said what he had said because he thought it necessary. But the medical knowledge he possessed convinced him that Dea, if not too young, was too fragile and delicate for what he called "Hymen in flesh and bone."

That would come soon enough. Besides, were they not already married? If the indissoluble existed anywhere, was it not in their union? Gwynplaine and Dea! They were creatures worthy of the love they mutually felt, flung by misfortune into each other's arms. And as if they were not enough in this first link, love had survened on misfortune, and had attached them, united and bound them together. What power could ever break that iron chain, bound with knots of flowers? They were indeed bound together.

Dea had beauty, Gwynplaine had sight. Each brought a dowry. They were more than coupled; they were paired; separated solely by the sacred interposition of innocence.

Though dream as Gwynplaine would, however, and absorb all meaner passions as he could, in the contemplation of Dea and before the tribunal of conscience, he was a man. Fatal laws are not to be eluded. He underwent, like everything else in nature, the obscure fermentations willed by the Creator. At times, therefore, he looked at the women who were in the crowd, but he immediately felt that the look was a sin, and hastened to retire, repentant, into his own soul.

Let us add that he met with no encouragement. On the face of every woman who looked upon him he saw aversion, antipathy, repugnance, and rejection. It was clear that no other than Dea was possible for him. This aided his repentance.

Chapter VIII

Not Only Happiness, but Prosperity

WHAT TRUE THINGS ARE TOLD IN STORIES! THE BURNED SCAR OF THE INVISIBLE FIEND WHO HAS touched you is remorse for a wicked thought. In Gwynplaine evil thoughts never ripened, and he had therefore no remorse. Sometimes he felt regret.

Vague mists of conscience.

What was this?

Nothing.

Their happiness was complete; so complete, that they were no longer even poor.

From 1689 to 1704 a great change had taken place.

It happened sometimes, in the year 1704, that as night fell on some little village on the coast, a great, heavy van, drawn by a pair of stout horses, made its entry. It was like the shell of a vessel reversed, the keel for a roof, the deck for a floor, placed on four wheels. The wheels were all of the same size, and high as wagon wheels. Wheels, pole, and van were all painted green, with a rhythmical gradation of shades, which ranged from bottle green for the wheels, to apple green for the roofing. This green color had succeeded in drawing attention to the carriage, which was known in all the fairgrounds as The Green Box. The Green Box had but two windows, one at each extremity, and at the back a door with steps to let down. On the roof, from a tube painted green like the rest, smoke arose. This moving house was always varnished and washed afresh. In front, on a ledge fastened to the van, with the window for a door, behind the horses and by the side of an old man who held the reins and directed the team, two gypsy women, dressed as goddesses, sounded their trumpets. The astonishment with which the villagers regarded this machine was overwhelming.

This was the old establishment of Ursus, its proportions augmented by success, and improved from a wretched booth into a theater. A kind of animal, between dog and wolf, was chained under the van. This was Homo. The old coachman who drove the horses was the philosopher himself.

Whence came this improvement from the miserable hut to the Olympic caravan?

From this;—Gwynplaine had become famous.

It was with a correct scent of what would succeed amongst men that Ursus had said to Gwynplaine—

"They made your fortune."

Ursus, it may be remembered, had made Gwynplaine his pupil. Unknown people had worked upon his face; he, on the other hand, had worked on his mind; and behind this well-executed mask, he had placed all that he could of thought. So soon as the growth of the child had rendered him fitted for it, he had brought him out on the stage; that is, he had produced him in front of the van.

The effect of his appearance had been surprising. The passers-by were immediately struck with wonder. Never had anything been seen to be compared to this extraordinary mimic of laughter. They were ignorant how the miracle of infectious hilarity had been obtained. Some believed it to be natural, others declared it to be artificial, and as conjecture was added to reality, everywhere, at every cross-road on the journey, in all the grounds of fairs and fêtes, the crowd ran after Gwynplaine. Thanks to this great attraction, there had come into the poor purse of the wandering group, first a rain of farthings, then of heavy pennies, and finally of shillings. The curiosity of one place exhausted, they passed on to another. Rolling does not enrich a stone, but it enriches a caravan; and year by year, from city to city, with the increased growth of Gwynplaine's person and of his ugliness, the fortune predicted by Ursus had come.

"What a good turn they did you there, my boy," said Ursus.

This "fortune" had allowed Ursus, who was the administrator of Gwynplaine's success, to have the chariot of his dreams constructed—that is to say, a caravan large enough to carry a theater, and to sow science and art in the highways. Moreover, Ursus had been able to add to the group composed of himself, Homo, Gwynplaine, and Dea, two horses and two women, who were the goddesses of the troupe, as we have just said, and its servants. A mythological frontispiece was, in those days, a service to a caravan of mountebanks.

"We are a wandering temple," said Ursus.

These two gypsies, picked up by the philosopher from amongst the vagabondage of cities and suburbs, were ugly and young, and were called, by order of Ursus, the one Phœbe, and the other Venus.

For these read Fibi and Vinos, that we may conform to English pronunciation.

Phœbe cooked; Venus scrubbed the temple.

Moreover, on days of performance they dressed Dea.

Mountebanks have their public life as well as princes, and on these occasions Dea was arrayed, like Fibi and Vinos, in a Florentine petticoat of flowered stuff, and a woman's jacket without sleeves, leaving the arms bare. Ursus and Gwynplaine wore men's jackets, and, like sailors on board a man-of-war, great loose trousers. Gwynplaine had, besides, for his work and for his feats of strength, round his neck and over his shoulders, an esclavine of leather. He took charge of the horses. Ursus and Homo took charge of each other.

Dea, being used to the Green Box, came and went in the interior of the wheeled house, with almost as much ease and certainty as those who saw.

The eye which could penetrate within this structure and its internal arrangements might have perceived in a corner, fastened to the planks, and immovable on its four wheels, the old hut of Ursus, placed on half-pay, allowed to rust, and from thenceforth dispensed the labor of rolling, as Ursus was relieved from the labor of drawing it.

This hut, in a corner at the back, to the right of the door, served as bedchamber and dressing-room to Ursus and Gwynplaine. It now contained two beds. In the opposite corner was the kitchen.

The arrangement of a vessel was not more precise and concise than that of the interior of the Green Box. Everything within it was in its place, arranged, foreseen, and intended.

The caravan was divided into three compartments, partitioned from each other. These communicated by open spaces without doors. A piece of stuff fell over them, and answered the purpose of concealment. The compartment behind belonged to the men, the compartment in front to the women, the compartment in the middle, separating the two sexes, was the stage. The instruments of the orchestra and the properties were kept in the kitchen. A loft under the arch of the roof contained the scenes, and on opening a trapdoor lamps appeared, producing wonders of light.

Ursus was the poet of these magical representations; he wrote the pieces. He had a diversity of talents; he was clever at sleight of hand. Besides the voices he imitated, he produced all sorts of unexpected things; shocks of light and darkness; spontaneous formations of figures or words, as he willed, on the partition; vanishing figures in chiaroscuro; strange things, amidst which he seemed to meditate, unmindful of the crowd who marveled at him.

One day Gwynplaine said to him—

"Father, you look like a sorcerer!"

And Ursus replied—

"Then I look, perhaps, like what I am."

The Green Box, built on a clear model of Ursus's, contained this refinement of ingenuity—that between the fore and hind wheels, the central panel of the left side turned on hinges by the aid of chains and pulleys, and could be let down at will like a drawbridge. As it dropped it set at liberty three legs on hinges, which supported the panel when let down, and which placed themselves straight on the ground like the legs of a table, and supported it above the earth like a platform. This exposed the stage, which was thus enlarged by the platform in front.

This opening looked for all the world like a "mouth of hell," in the words of the itinerant Puritan preachers, who turned away from it with horror. It was, perhaps, for some such impious invention that Solon kicked out Thespis.

For all that Thespis has lasted much longer than is generally believed. The traveling theater is still in existence. It was on those stages on wheels that, in the sixteenth and seventeenth centuries, they performed in England the ballets and dances of Amner and Pilkington; in France, the pastorals of Gilbert Colin; in Flanders, at the annual fairs, the double choruses of Clement, called Non Papa; in Germany, the "Adam and Eve" of Theiles; and, in Italy, the Venetian exhibitions of Animuccia and of Cafossis, the "Silvæ" of Gesualdo, the "Prince of Venosa," the "Satyr" of Laura Guidiccioni, the "Despair of Philene," the "Death of Ugolina," by Vincent Galileo, father of the astronomer, which Vincent Galileo sang his own music, and accompanied himself on his viol de gamba; as well as all the first attempts of the Italian opera which, from 1580, substituted free inspiration for the madrigal style.

The chariot, of the color of hope, which carried Ursus, Gwynplaine, and their fortunes, and in front of which Fibi and Vinos trumpeted like figures of Fame, played its part of this grand Bohemian and literary brotherhood. Thespis would no more have disowned Ursus than Congrio would have disowned Gwynplaine.

Arrived at open spaces in towns or villages, Ursus, in the intervals between the too-tooing of Fibi and Vinos, gave instructive revelations as to the trumpetings.

"This symphony is Gregorian," he would exclaim, "citizens and townsmen; the Gregorian form of worship, this great progress, is opposed in Italy to the Ambrosial ritual, and in Spain to the Mozarabic ceremonial, and has achieved its triumph over them with difficulty."

After which the Green Box drew up in some place chosen by Ursus, and evening having fallen, and the panel stage having been let down, the theater opened and the performance began.

The scene of the Green Box represented a landscape painted by Ursus; and, as he did not know how to paint, it represented a cavern just as well as a landscape. The curtain, which we call drop nowadays, was a checked silk, with squares of contrasted colors.

The public stood without, in the street, in the fair, forming a semi-circle round the stage, exposed to the sun and the showers; an arrangement which made rain less desirable for theaters in those days than now. When they could, they acted in an inn-yard, on which occasions the windows of the different stories made rows of boxes for the spectators. The theater was thus more enclosed, and the audience a more paying one. Ursus was in everything—in the piece, in the company, in the kitchen, in the orchestra. Vinos beat the drum, and handled the sticks with great dexterity. Fibi played on the *morache*, a kind of guitar. The wolf had been promoted to be a utility gentleman, and played, as occasion required, his little parts. Often when they appeared side by side on the stage, Ursus in his tightly-laced bear's skin, Homo with his wolf's skin fitting still better, no one could tell which was the beast. This flattered Ursus.

Chapter IX

ABSURDITIES WHICH FOLKS WITHOUT TASTE CALL POETRY

THE PIECES WRITTEN BY URSUS WERE INTERLUDES—A KIND OF COMPOSITION OUT OF FASHION nowadays. One of these pieces, which has not come down to us, was entitled *Ursus Rursus*. It is probable that he played the principal part himself. A pretended exit, followed by a reappearance, was apparently its praiseworthy and sober subject. The titles of the interludes of Ursus were sometimes Latin, as we have seen, and the poetry frequently Spanish. The Spanish verses written by Ursus were rhymed, as was nearly all the Castilian poetry of that period. This did not puzzle the people. Spanish was then a familiar language; and the English sailors spoke Castilian even as the Roman sailors spoke Carthaginian (see Plautus). Moreover, at a theatrical representation, as at mass, Latin, or any other language unknown to the audience, is by no means a subject of care with them. They get out of the dilemma by adapting to the sounds familiar words. Our old Gallic France was particularly prone to this manner of being devout. At church, under cover of an *Immolatus*, the faithful chanted, "I will make merry"; and under a *sanctus*, "Kiss me, sweet."

The Council of Trent was required to put an end to these familiarities.

Ursus had composed expressly for Gwynplaine an interlude, with which he was well pleased. It was his best work. He had thrown his whole soul into it. To give the sum of all one's talents in the production is the greatest triumph that anyone can achieve. The toad which produces a toad achieves a grand success. You doubt it? Try, then, to do as much.

Ursus had carefully polished this interlude. This bear's cub was entitled *Chaos Vanquished*. Here it was: a night scene. When the curtain drew up, the crowd, massed around the Green Box, saw nothing but blackness. In this blackness three confused forms moved in the reptile state: a wolf, a bear, and a man. The wolf acted the wolf; Ursus, the bear; Gwynplaine, the man. The wolf and the bear represented the ferocious forces of Nature—unreasoning hunger and savage ignorance. Both rushed on Gwynplaine. It was chaos combating man. No face could be distinguished. Gwynplaine fought enfolded in a winding-sheet, and his face was covered by his thickly-falling locks. All else was shadow. The bear growled, the wolf gnashed his teeth, the man cried out. The man was down; the beasts overwhelmed him. He cried for aid and succor; he hurled to the unknown an agonized appeal. He gave a death-rattle. To witness this agony of the prostrate man, now scarcely distinguishable from the brutes, was appalling. The crowd looked on breathless; in one minute more the wild beasts would triumph, and chaos reabsorb man. A struggle—cries—howlings; then, all at once, silence.

A song in the shadows. A breath had passed, and they heard a voice. Mysterious music floated, accompanying this chant of the invisible; and suddenly, none knowing whence or how, a white apparition arose. This apparition was a light; this light was a woman; this woman was a spirit. Dea—calm, fair, beautiful, formidable in her serenity and sweetness—appeared in the center of a luminous mist. A profile of brightness in a dawn! She was a voice: a voice light, deep, indescribable. She sang in the newborn light; she, invisible, made visible. They thought that they heard the hymn of an angel, or the song of a bird. At this apparition the man, starting up in his ecstasy, struck the beasts with his fists, and overthrew them.

Then the vision, gliding along in a manner difficult to understand, and therefore the more admired, sang these words in Spanish sufficiently pure for the English sailors who were present—

> *"Ora! llora!*
> *De palabra*
> *Nace razon.*
> *De luz el son."*[1]

Then looking down, as if she saw a gulf beneath, she went on—

> *"Noche, quita te de alli!*
> *El alba canta hallali."*[2]

As she sang, the man raised himself by degrees; instead of lying he was now kneeling, his hands elevated toward the vision, his knees resting on the beasts, which lay motionless, and as if thunder-stricken.

She continued, turning toward him—

> *"Es menester a cielos ir,*
> *Y tu que llorabas reir."*[3]

And approaching him with the majesty of a star, she added—

> *"Gebra barzon;*
> *Deja, monstruo,*
> *A tu negro*
> *Caparazon."*[4]

And she put her hand on his brow. Then another voice arose deeper, and consequently, still sweeter—a voice broken and enwrapped with a gravity both tender and wild. It was the human chant responding to the chant of the stars. Gwynplaine, still in obscurity, his head under Dea's hand, and kneeling on the vanquished bear and wolf, sang—

> *"O ven! ama!*
> *Eres alma,*
> *Soy corazon."*[5]

And suddenly from the shadow a ray of light fell full upon Gwynplaine. Then, through the darkness, was the monster full exposed.

1. Pray! weep! Reason is born of the word. Song creates light.

2. Night, away! the dawn sings hallali.

3. Thou must go to heaven, and smile, thou that weepest.

4. Break the yolk; throw off, monster, thy dark clothing.

5. O, come, and love! thou art soul, I am heart.

To describe the commotion of the crowd is impossible.

A sun of laughter rising, such was the effect. Laughter springs from unexpected causes, and nothing could be more unexpected than this termination. Never was sensation comparable to that produced by the ray of light striking on that mask, at once ludicrous and terrible. They laughed all around his laugh. Everywhere: above, below, behind, before, at the uttermost distance; men, women, old gray-heads, rosy-faced children; the good, the wicked, the gay, the sad, everybody. And even in the streets, the passers-by who could see nothing, hearing the laughter, laughed also. The laughter ended in clapping of hands and stamping of feet. The curtain dropped: Gwynplaine was recalled with frenzy. Hence an immense success. Have you seen *Chaos Vanquished*? Gwynplaine was run after. The listless came to laugh, the melancholy came to laugh, evil consciences came to laugh—a laugh so irresistible that it seemed almost an epidemic. But there is a pestilence from which men do not fly, and that is the contagion of joy. The success, it must be admitted, did not rise higher than the populace. A great crowd means a crowd of nobodies. *Chaos Vanquished* could be seen for a penny. Fashionable people never go where the price of admission is a penny.

Ursus thought a good deal of his work, which he had brooded over for a long time. "It is in the style of one Shakespeare," he said, modestly.

The juxtaposition of Dea added to the indescribable effect produced by Gwynplaine. Her white face by the side of the gnome represented what might have been called divine astonishment. The audience regarded Dea with a sort of mysterious anxiety. She had in her aspect the dignity of a virgin and of a priestess, not knowing man and knowing God. They saw that she was blind, and felt that she could see. She seemed to stand on the threshold of the supernatural. The light that beamed on her seemed half earthly and half heavenly. She had come to work on earth, and to work as heaven works, in the radiance of morning. Finding a hydra, she formed a soul. She seemed like a creative power, satisfied, but astonished at the result of her creation; and the audience fancied that they could see in the divine surprise of that face desire of the cause, and wonder at the result. They felt that she loved this monster. Did she know that he was one? Yes; since she touched him. No; since she accepted him. This depth of night and this glory of day united, formed in the mind of the spectator a chiaroscuro in which appeared endless perspectives. How much divinity exists in the germ, in what manner the penetration of the soul into matter is accomplished, how the solar ray is an umbilical cord, how the disfigured is transfigured, how the deformed becomes heavenly, all these glimpses of mysteries added an almost cosmical emotion to the convulsive hilarity produced by Gwynplaine. Without going too deep, for spectators do not like the fatigue of seeking below the surface, something more was understood than was perceived. And this strange spectacle had the transparency of an avatar.

As to Dea, what she felt cannot be expressed by human words; she knew that she was in the midst of a crowd, and knew not what a crowd was. She heard a murmur, that was all. For her the crowd was but a breath. Generations are passing breaths. Man respires, aspires, and expires. In that crowd Dea felt herself alone, and shuddering as one hanging over a precipice. Suddenly, in this trouble of innocence in distress, prompt to accuse the unknown, in her dread of a possible fall, Dea, serene notwithstanding, and superior to the vague agonies of peril, but inwardly shuddering at her isolation, found confidence and support. She had seized her thread of safety in the universe of shadows; she put her hand on the powerful head of Gwynplaine.

Joy unspeakable! she placed her rosy fingers on his forest of crisp hair. Wool when touched gives an impression of softness. Dea touched a lamb which she knew to be a lion. Her whole heart poured out an ineffable love. She felt out of danger, she had found her savior. The public believed that they saw the contrary. To the spectators the being loved was Gwynplaine, and the savior was Dea. What matters! thought Ursus, to whom the heart of Dea was visible. And Dea, reassured, consoled and delighted, adored the angel whilst the people contemplated the monster, and endured, fascinated herself as well, though in the opposite sense, that dread Promethean laugh.

True love is never weary. Being all soul it cannot cool. A brazier comes to be full of cinders; not so a star. Her exquisite impressions were renewed every evening for Dea, and she was ready to weep with tenderness whilst the audience was in convulsions of laughter. Those around her were but joyful; she was happy.

The sensation of gaiety due to the sudden shock caused by the rictus of Gwynplaine was evidently not intended by Ursus. He would have preferred more smiles and less laughter, and more of a literary triumph. But success consoles. He reconciled himself every evening to his excessive triumph, as he counted how many shillings the piles of farthings made, and how many pounds the piles of shillings; and besides, he said, after all, when the laugh had passed, *Chaos Vanquished* would be found in the depths of their minds, and something of it would remain there.

Perhaps he was not altogether wrong; the foundations of a work settle down in the mind of the public. The truth is, that the populace, attentive to the wolf, the bear, to the man, then to the music, to the howlings governed by harmony, to the night dissipated by dawn, to the chant releasing the light, accepted with a confused, dull sympathy, and with a certain emotional respect, the dramatic poem of *Chaos Vanquished*, the victory of spirit over matter, ending with the joy of man.

Such were the vulgar pleasures of the people.

They sufficed them. The people had not the means of going to the noble matches of the gentry, and could not, like lords and gentlemen, bet a thousand guineas on Helmsgail against Phelemghe-Madone.

Chapter X

AN OUTSIDER'S VIEW OF MEN AND THINGS

MAN HAS A NOTION OF REVENGING HIMSELF ON THAT WHICH PLEASES HIM. HENCE THE CONtempt felt for the comedian.

This being charms me, diverts, distracts, teaches, enchants, consoles me, flings me into an ideal world, is agreeable and useful to me. What evil can I do him in return? Humiliate him. Disdain is a blow from afar. Let us strike the blow. He pleases me, therefore he is vile. He serves me, therefore I hate him. Where can I find a stone to throw at him? Priest, give me yours. Philosopher, give me yours. Bossuet, excommunicate him. Rousseau, insult him. Orator, spit the pebbles from your mouth at him. Bear, fling your stone. Let us cast stones at the tree, hit the fruit and eat it. Bravo! and down with him! To repeat poetry is to be infected with the plague. Wretched playactor, we will put him in the pillory for his success. Let him follow up his triumph with our hisses. Let him collect a crowd, and create a solitude. Thus it is that the wealthy, termed the higher classes, have invented for the actor that form of isolation, applause.

The crowd is less brutal. They neither hated nor despised Gwynplaine. Only the meanest calker of the meanest crew of the meanest merchantman, anchored in the meanest English seaport, considered himself immeasurably superior to this amuser of the "scum," and believed that a calker is as superior to an actor as a lord is to a calker.

Gwynplaine was, therefore, like all comedians, applauded and kept at a distance. Truly, all success in this world is a crime, and must be expiated. He who obtains the medal has to take its reverse side as well.

For Gwynplaine there was no reverse. In this sense, both sides of his medal pleased him. He was satisfied with the applause, and content with the isolation. In Applause, he was rich. In Isolation, happy.

To be rich in his low estate means to be no longer wretchedly poor, to have neither holes in his clothes, nor cold at his hearth, nor emptiness in his stomach. It is to eat when hungry, and drink when thirsty. It is to have everything necessary, including a penny for a beggar. This indigent wealth, enough for liberty, was possessed by Gwynplaine. So far as his soul was concerned, he was opulent. He had love. What more could he want? Nothing.

You may think that had the offer been made to him to remove his deformity he would have grasped at it. Yet he would have refused it emphatically. What! to throw off his mask and have his former face restored, to be the creature he had perchance been created, handsome and charming? No, he would never have consented to it. For what would he have to support Dea? what would have become of that poor child, the sweet blind girl who loved him? Without his rictus, which made him a clown without parallel, he would have been a mountebank, like any other; a common athlete, a picker up of pence from the chinks in the pavement, and Dea would perhaps not have had bread every day. It was with deep and tender pride that he felt himself the protector of the helpless and heavenly creature. Night, solitude, nakedness, weakness, ignorance, hunger, and thirst—seven yawning jaws of misery—were raised around her, and he was the St. George fighting the dragon. He triumphed over poverty. How? By his deformity. By his deformity he was useful, helpful, victorious, great. He had but to show himself, and money poured in. He was a master of crowds, the sovereign of the mob. He could do everything for Dea. Her wants he foresaw, her desires, her tastes, her fancies, in the limited sphere in which wishes are possible to the blind, he fulfilled. Gwynplaine and Dea were, as we have already shown, Providence to each other. He felt himself raised on her wings, she felt herself carried in his arms. To protect the being who loves you, to give what she requires to her who shines on you as your star, can anything be sweeter? Gwynplaine possessed this supreme happiness, and he owed it to his deformity. His deformity had raised him above all. By it he had gained the means of life for himself and others; by it he had gained independence, liberty, celebrity, internal satisfaction and pride. In his deformity he was inaccessible. The Fates could do nothing beyond this blow in which they had spent their whole force, and which he had turned into a triumph. This lowest depth of misfortune had become the summit of Elysium. Gwynplaine was imprisoned in his deformity, but with Dea. And this was, as we have already said, to live in a dungeon of paradise. A wall stood between them and the living world. So much the better. This wall protected as well as enclosed them. What could affect Dea, what could affect Gwynplaine, with such a fortress around them? To take from him his success was impossible. They would have had to deprive him of his face. Take from him his love. Impossible. Dea could not see him. The blindness of Dea was divinely incurable. What harm did his deformity do Gwynplaine? None. What advantage did it give him? Every advantage. He was beloved, notwithstanding its horror, and perhaps for that very cause. Infirmity and deformity had by instinct been drawn toward and coupled with each other. To be beloved, is not that everything? Gwynplaine thought of his disfigurement only with gratitude. He was blessed in the stigma. With joy he felt that it was irremediable and eternal. What a blessing that it was so! While there were highways and fairgrounds, and journeys to take, the people below, and the sky above, they would be sure to live, Dea would want nothing, and they should have love. Gwynplaine would not have changed faces with Apollo. To be a monster was his form of happiness.

Thus, as we said before, destiny had given him all, even to overflowing. He who had been rejected had been preferred.

He was so happy that he felt compassion for the men around him. He pitied the rest of the world. It was, besides, his instinct to look about him, because no one is always consistent, and a man's nature is not always theoretic; he was delighted to live within an enclosure, but from time to time he lifted his head above the wall. Then he retreated again with more joy into his loneliness with Dea, having drawn his comparisons. What did he see around him?

What were those living creatures of which his wandering life showed him so many specimens, changed every day? Always new crowds, always the same multitude, ever new faces, ever the same miseries. A jumble of ruins. Every evening every phase of social misfortune came and encircled his happiness.

The Green Box was popular.

Low prices attract the low classes. Those who came were the weak, the poor, the little. They rushed to Gwynplaine as they rushed to gin. They came to buy a penny-worth of forgetfulness. From the height of his platform Gwynplaine passed those wretched people in review. His spirit was enwrapped in the contemplation of every succeeding apparition of widespread misery. The physiognomy of man is modeled by conscience, and by the tenor of life, and is the result of a crowd of mysterious excavations. There was never a suffering, not an anger, not a shame, not a despair, of which Gwynplaine did not see the wrinkle. The mouths of those children had not eaten. That man was a father, that woman a mother, and behind them, their families might be guessed to be on the road to ruin. There was a face already marked by vice, on the threshold of crime, and the reasons were plain—ignorance and indigence. Another showed the stamp of original goodness, obliterated by social pressure, and turned to hate. On the face of an old woman he saw starvation. On that of a girl, prostitution. The same fact, and although the girl had the resource of her youth, all the sadder for that! In the crowd were arms without tools; the workers asked only for work, but the work was wanting. Sometimes a soldier came and seated himself by the workmen, sometimes a wounded pensioner; and Gwynplaine saw the specter of war. Here Gwynplaine read want of work; there man-farming, slavery. On certain brows he saw an indescribable ebbing back toward animalism, and that slow return of man to beast, produced on those below by the dull pressure of the happiness of those above. There was a break in the gloom for Gwynplaine. He and Dea had a loophole of happiness; the rest was damnation. Gwynplaine felt above him the thoughtless trampling of the powerful, the rich, the magnificent, the great, the elect of chance. Below he saw the pale faces of the disinherited. He saw himself and Dea, with their little happiness, so great to themselves, between two worlds. That which was above went and came, free, joyous, dancing, trampling under foot; above him the world which treads, below the world which is trodden upon. It is a fatal fact, and one indicating a profound social evil, that light should crush the shadow! Gwynplaine thoroughly grasped this dark evil. What! a destiny so reptile! Shall a man drag himself thus along with such adherence to dust and corruption, with such vicious tastes, such an abdication of right, or such abjectness that one feels inclined to crush him under foot? Of what butterfly is, then, this earthly life the grub?

What! in the crowd which hungers and which denies everywhere, and before all, the questions of crime and shame (the inflexibility of the law producing laxity of conscience), is there no child that grows but to be stunted, no virgin but matures for sin, no rose that blooms but for the slime of the snail?

His eyes at times sought everywhere, with the curiosity of emotion, to probe the depths of that darkness, in which there died away so many useless efforts, and in which there struggled so much weariness: families devoured by society, morals tortured by the laws, wounds gangrened by penalties, poverty gnawed by taxes, wrecked intelligence swallowed up by ignorance, rafts in distress alive with the famished, feuds, dearth, death-rattles, cries, disappearances. He felt the vague oppression of a keen, universal suffering. He saw the vision of the foaming wave of misery dashing over the crowd of humanity. He was safe in port himself, as he watched the wreck around him. Sometimes he laid his disfigured head in his hands and dreamed.

What folly to be happy! How one dreams! Ideas were born within him. Absurd notions crossed his brain.

Because formerly he had succored an infant, he felt a ridiculous desire to succor the whole world. The mists of reverie sometimes obscured his individuality, and he lost his ideas of proportion so far as to ask himself the question, "What can be done for the poor?" Sometimes he was so absorbed in his subject as to express it aloud. Then Ursus shrugged his shoulders and looked at him fixedly. Gwynplaine continued his reverie.

"Oh! were I powerful, would I not aid the wretched? But what am I?—An atom. What can I do?—Nothing."

He was mistaken. He was able to do a great deal for the wretched. He could make them laugh; and, as we have said, to make people laugh is to make them forget. What a benefactor on earth is he who can bestow forgetfulness!

Chapter XI

GWYNPLAINE THINKS JUSTICE, AND URSUS TALKS TRUTH

A PHILOSOPHER IS A SPY. URSUS, A WATCHER OF DREAMS, STUDIED HIS PUPIL.
Our monologues leave on our brows a faint reflection, distinguishable to the eye of a physiognomist. Hence what occurred to Gwynplaine did not escape Ursus. One day as Gwynplaine was meditating, Ursus pulled him by his jacket, and exclaimed—

"You strike me as being an observer! You fool! Take care. It is no business of yours. You have one thing to do—to love Dea. You have two causes of happiness—the first is, that the crowd sees your muzzle; the second is, that Dea does not. You have no right to the happiness you possess, for no woman who saw your mouth would consent to your kiss; and that mouth which has made your fortune, and that face which has given you riches, are not your own. You were not born with that countenance. It was borrowed from the grimace which is at the bottom of the infinite. You have stolen your mask from the devil. You are hideous; be satisfied with having drawn that prize in the lottery. There are in this world (and a very good thing too) the happy by right, and the happy by luck. You are happy by luck. You are in a cave wherein a star is enclosed. The poor star belongs to you. Do not seek to leave the cave, and guard your star, O spider! You have in your web the carbuncle, Venus. Do me the favor to be satisfied. I see your dreams are troubled. It is idiotic of you. Listen, I am going to speak to you in the language of true poetry. Let Dea eat beefsteaks and muttonchops, and in six months she will be as strong as a Turk; marry her immediately, give her a child, two children, three children, a long string of children. That is what I call philosophy. Moreover, it is happiness, which is no folly. To have children is a glimpse of heaven. Have brats—wipe them, blow their noses, dirt them, wash them and put them to bed. Let them swarm about you. If they laugh, it is well; if they howl, it is better—to cry is to live. Watch them suck at six months, crawl at a year, walk at two, grow tall at fifteen, fall in love at twenty. He who has these joys has everything. For myself, I lacked the advantage; and that is the reason why I am a brute. God, a composer of beautiful poems and the first of men of letters, said to his fellow-workman, Moses: 'Increase and multiply.' Such is the text. Multiply, you beast! As to the world, it is as it is; you cannot make nor mar it. Do not trouble yourself about it. Pay no attention to what goes on outside. Leave the horizon alone. A comedian is made to be looked at, not to look. Do you know what there is outside? The happy, by right. You, I repeat, are the happy by chance. You are the pickpocket of the happiness of which they are the proprietors. They are the legitimate possessors; you are the intruder. You live in concubinage with luck. What do you want that you have not already? Shibboleth help me! This fellow is a rascal. To multiply himself by Dea would be pleasant, all the same. Such happiness is like a swindle. Those above who possess happiness by privilege do not like folks below them to have so much enjoyment. If they ask you what right you have to be happy, you will not know what to answer. You have no patent, and they have. Jupiter, Allah, Vishnu, Sabaoth, it does not matter who, has given them the passport to happiness. Fear them. Do not meddle with them, lest they should meddle with you. Wretch! do you know what the man is who is happy by right? He is a terrible being. He is a lord. A lord! He must have intrigued pretty well in the devil's unknown country before he was born, to enter life by the door he did. How difficult it must have been to him to be born! It is the only trouble he has given himself; but, just heaven, what a one!—to obtain from destiny, the blind blockhead, to mark him in his cradle a master of men. To bribe the box-keeper to give him the best place at the show. Read the memoranda in the old hut, which I have placed on half-pay. Read that breviary of my wisdom, and you will see what it is to be a lord. A lord is one who has all, and is all. A lord is one who exists above his own nature. A lord is one who has when young the rights of an old man; when old, the success in intrigue of a young one; if vicious, the homage of respectable people; if a coward, the command of brave men; if a do-nothing, the fruits of labor; if ignorant, the diploma of Cambridge or Oxford; if a fool, the admiration of poets; if ugly, the smiles of women; if a Thersites, the helm of Achilles; if a hare, the skin of a lion. Do not misunderstand my words. I do not say that a lord must necessarily be ignorant, a coward, ugly, stupid, or old. I only mean that he may be all those things without any detriment to himself. On the contrary. Lords are princes. The King of England is only a lord, the first peer of the peerage; that is all, but it is much. Kings were formerly called lords—the Lord of Denmark, the Lord of Ireland, the Lord of the Isles. The Lord of Norway was first called king three hundred years ago. Lucius, the most ancient king in England, was spoken to by Saint Telesphorus as my Lord Lucius. The Lords are peers—that is to say, equals—of whom?—Of the king. I do not commit the mistake of confounding the lords with parliament. The assembly of the people which the Saxons before the Conquest called *wittenagemote*, the Normans, after the Conquest, entitled *parliamentum*. By degrees the people were turned out. The king's letters clause convoking the Commons, addressed formerly *ad concilium impendendum*, are now addressed *ad consentiendum*. To say yes is their liberty. The peers can say No; and the proof is that they have said it. The peers can cut off the king's head. The people cannot. The stroke of the hatchet which decapitated Charles I is an encroachment, not on the king, but on the peers, and it was well to place on the gibbet the carcass of Cromwell. The lords have power. Why? Because they have riches. Who has turned over the leaves of the Doomsday Book? It is the proof that the lords possess England. It is the registry of the estates of subjects, compiled under William the Conqueror; and it is in the charge of the Chancellor of the Exchequer. To copy anything in it, you have to pay twopence a line. It is a proud book. Do you know that I was domestic doctor to a lord, who was called Marmaduke, and who had thirty-six thousand a year? Think of that, you hideous idiot! Do you know that, with rabbits only from the warrens of Earl Lindsay, they could feed all the riffraff of the Cinque Ports? And the good order kept! Every poacher is hung. For two long, furry ears sticking out of a game bag, I saw the father of six children hanging on the gibbet. Such is the peerage. The rabbit of a great lord is of more importance than God's image in a man.

"Lords exist, you trespasser, do you see? and we must think it good that they do; and even if we do not, what harm will it do them? The people object, indeed! Why? Plautus himself would never have attained the comicality of such an idea. A philosopher would be jesting if he advised the poor devil of the masses to cry out against the size and weight of the lords. Just as well might the gnat dispute with the foot of an elephant. One day I saw a hippopotamus tread upon a molehill; he crushed it utterly. He was innocent. The great soft-headed fool of a mastodon did not even know of the existence of moles. My son, the moles that are trodden on are the human race. To crush is a law. And do you think that the mole himself crushes nothing? Why, it is the mastodon of the flesh-worm, who is the mastodon of the globeworm. But let us cease arguing. My boy, there are coaches in the world; my lord is inside, the people under the wheels; the philosopher gets out of the way. Stand aside, and let them pass. As to myself, I love lords, and shun them. I lived with one; the beauty of my recollections suffices me. I remember his country-house, like a glory in a cloud. My dreams are all retrospective. Nothing could be more admirable than Marmaduke Lodge in grandeur, beautiful symmetry, rich avenues, and the ornaments and surroundings of the edifice. The houses, country seats, and palaces of the lords present a selection of all that is greatest and most magnificent in this flourishing kingdom. I love our lords. I thank them for being opulent, powerful, and prosperous. I myself am clothed in shadow, and I look with interest upon the shred of heavenly blue which is called a lord. You enter Marmaduke Lodge by an exceedingly spacious courtyard, which forms an oblong square, divided into eight spaces, each surrounded by a balustrade; on each side is a wide approach, and a superb hexagonal fountain plays in the midst; this fountain is formed of two basins, which are surmounted by a dome of exquisite openwork, elevated on six columns. It was there that I knew a learned Frenchman, Monsieur l'Abbé du Cros, who belonged to the Jacobin monastery in the Rue Saint Jacques. Half the library of Erpenius is at Marmaduke Lodge, the other half being at the theological gallery at Cambridge. I used to read the books, seated under the ornamented portal. These things are only shown to a select number of curious travelers. Do you know, you ridiculous boy, that William North, who is Lord Grey of Rolleston, and sits fourteenth on the bench of Barons, has more forest trees on his mountains than you have hairs on your horrible noddle? Do you know that Lord Norreys of Rycote, who is Earl of Abingdon, has a square keep a hundred feet high, having this device—*Virtus ariete fortior*; which you would think meant that virtue is stronger than a ram, but which really means, you idiot, that courage is stronger than a battering-machine. Yes, I honor, accept, respect, and revere our lords. It is the lords who, with her royal Majesty, work to procure and preserve the advantages of the nation. Their consummate wisdom shines in intricate junctures. Their precedence over others I wish they had not; but they have it. What is called principality in Germany, grandeeship in Spain, is called peerage in England and France. There being a fair show of reason for considering the world a wretched place enough, heaven felt where the burden was most galling, and to prove that it knew how to make happy people, created lords for the satisfaction of philosophers. This acts as a set-off, and gets heaven out of the scrape, affording it a decent escape from a false position. The great are great. A peer, speaking of himself, says *we*. A peer is a plural. The king qualifies the peer *consanguinei nostri*. The peers have made a multitude of wise laws; amongst others, one which condemns to death anyone who cuts down a three-year-old poplar-tree. Their supremacy is such that they have a language of their own. In heraldic style, black, which is called sable for gentry, is called saturne for princes, and diamond for peers. Diamond dust, a night thick with stars, such is the night of the happy! Even amongst themselves these high and mighty lords have their own distinctions. A baron cannot wash with a viscount, without his permission. These are indeed excellent things, and safeguards to the nation. What a fine thing it is for the people to have twenty-five dukes, five marquises, seventy-six earls, nine viscounts, and sixty-one barons; making altogether a hundred and seventy-six peers, of which some are your grace, and some my lord. What matter a few rags here and there, withal: everybody cannot be dressed in gold. Let the rags be. Cannot you see the purple? One balances the other. A thing must be built of something. Yes, of course, there are the poor—what of them! They line the happiness of the wealthy. Devil take it! our lords are our glory! The pack of hounds belonging to Charles, Baron Mohun, costs him as much as the hospital for lepers in Moorgate, and for Christ's Hospital, founded for children, in 1553, by Edward VI. Thomas Osborne, Duke of Leeds, spends yearly on his liveries five thousand golden guineas. The Spanish grandees have a guardian appointed by law to prevent their ruining themselves. That is cowardly. Our lords are extravagant and magnificent. I esteem them for it. Let us not abuse them like envious folks. I feel happy when a beautiful vision passes. I have not the light, but I have the reflection. A reflection thrown on my ulcer, you will say. Go to the devil! I am a Job, delighted in the contemplation of Trimalcion. Oh, that beautiful and radiant planet up there! But the moonlight is something. To suppress the lords was an idea which Orestes, mad as he was, would not have dared to entertain. To say that the lords are mischievous or useless is as much as to say that the state should be revolutionized, and that men are not made to live like cattle, browsing the grass and bitten by the dog. The field is shorn by the sheep, the sheep by the shepherd. It is all one to me. I am a philosopher, and I care about life as much as a fly. Life is but a lodging. When I think that Henry Bowes Howard, Earl of Berkshire, has in his stable twenty-four state carriages, of which one is mounted in silver and another in gold—good heavens! I know that everyone has not got twenty-four state carriages; but there is no need to complain for all that. Because you were cold one night, what was that to him? It concerns you only. Others besides you suffer cold and hunger. Don't you know that without that cold, Dea would not have been blind, and if Dea were not blind she would not love you? Think of that, you fool! And, besides, if all the people who are lost were to complain, there would be a pretty tumult! Silence is the rule. I have no doubt that heaven imposes silence on the damned, otherwise heaven itself would be punished by their ever-lasting cry. The happiness of Olympus is bought by the silence of Cocytus. Then, people! be silent! I do better myself; I approve and admire. Just now I was enumerating the lords, and I ought to add to the list two archbishops and twenty-four bishops. Truly, I am quite affected when I think of it! I remember to have seen at the tithe-gathering of the Rev. Dean of Raphoe, who combined the peer-age with the church, a great tithe of beautiful wheat taken from the peasants in the neighborhood, and which the dean had not been at the trouble of growing. This left him time to say his prayers. Do you know that Lord Marmaduke, my master, was Lord Grand Treasurer of Ireland, and High Seneschal of the sovereignty of Knaresborough in the county of York? Do you know that the Lord High Chamberlain, which is an office hereditary in the family of the Dukes of Ancaster, dresses the king for his coronation, and receives for his trouble forty yards of crimson velvet, besides the bed on which the king has slept; and that the Usher of the Black Rod is his deputy? I should like to see you deny this, that the senior viscount of England is Robert Brent, created a viscount by Henry V. The lords' titles imply sovereignty over land, except that of Earl Rivers, who takes his title from his family name. How admirable is the right which they have to tax others, and to levy, for instance, four shillings in the pound sterling income-tax, which has just been continued for another year. And all the time taxes on distilled spirits, on the excise of wine and beer, on tonnage and poundage, on cider, on perry, on mum, malt, and prepared barley, on coals, and on a hundred things besides. Let us venerate things as they are. The clergy themselves depend on the lords. The Bishop of Man is subject to the Earl of Derby. The lords have wild beasts of their own, which they place in their ar-morial bearings. God not having made enough, they have invented others. They have created the heraldic wild boar, who is as much above the wild boar as the wild boar is above the domestic pig, and the lord is above the priest. They have created the griffin, which is an eagle to lions, and a lion to eagles, terrifying lions by his wings, and eagles by his mane. They have the guivre, the unicorn, the serpent, the salamander, the tarask, the dree, the dragon, and the hippogriff. All these things, terrible to us, are to them but an ornament and an embellishment. They have a menagerie which they call the blazon, in which unknown beasts roar. The prodigies of the forest are nothing com-pared to the inventions of their pride. Their vanity is full of phantoms which move as in a sublime night, armed with helm and cuirass, spurs on their heels and the scepters in their hands, saying in a grave voice, 'We are the ancestors!' The cankerworms eat the roots, and panoplies eat the people. Why not? Are we to change the laws? The peerage is part of the order of society. Do you know that there is a duke in Scotland who can ride ninety miles without leaving his own estate? Do you know that the Archbishop of Canterbury has a revenue of £40,000 a year? Do you know that her Majesty has £700,000 sterling from the civil list, besides castles, forests, domains, fiefs, tenancies, freeholds, prebendaries, tithes, rent, confiscations, and fines, which bring in over a million sterling? Those who are not satisfied are hard to please."

"Yes," murmured Gwynplaine sadly; "the paradise of the rich is made out of the hell of the poor."

Chapter XII

URSUS THE POET DRAGS ON URSUS THE PHILOSOPHER

THEN DEA ENTERED. HE LOOKED AT HER, AND SAW NOTHING BUT HER. THIS IS LOVE; ONE MAY BE carried away for a moment by the importunity of some other idea, but the beloved one enters, and all that does not appertain to her presence immediately fades away, without her dreaming that perhaps she is effacing in us a world.

Let us mention a circumstance. In *Chaos Vanquished*, the word *monstruo*, addressed to Gwynplaine, displeased Dea. Sometimes, with the smattering of Spanish, which everyone knew at the period, she took it into her head to replace it by *quiero*, which signifies, I wish it. Ursus tolerated, although not without an expression of impatience, this alteration in his text. He might have said to Dea, as in our day Moessard said to Vissot, *Tu manques de respect au repertoire.*

"The Laughing Man."

Such was the form of Gwynplaine's fame. His name, Gwynplaine, little known at any time, had disappeared under his nickname, as his face had disappeared under its grin.

His popularity was like his visage—a mask.

His name, however, was to be read on a large placard in front of the Green Box, which offered the crowd the following narrative composed by Ursus:—

"Here is to be seen Gwynplaine, who was deserted at the age of ten, on the night of the 29th of January, 1690, by the villainous Comprachicos, on the coast of Portland. The little boy has grown up, and is called now—

THE LAUGHING MAN."

The existence of these mountebanks was as an existence of lepers in a leper-house, and of the blessed in one of the Pleiades. There was every day a sudden transition from the noisy exhibition outside, into the most complete seclusion. Every evening they made their exit from this world. They were like the dead, vanishing on condition of being reborn next day. A comedian is a revolving light, appearing one moment, disappearing the next, and existing for the public but as a phantom or a light, as his life circles round. To exhibition succeeded isolation. When the performance was finished, whilst the audience were dispersing, and their murmur of satisfaction was dying away in the streets, the Green Box shut up its platform, as a fortress does its drawbridge, and all communication with mankind was cut off. On one side, the universe; on the other, the caravan; and this caravan contained liberty, clear consciences, courage, devotion, innocence, happiness, love—all the constellations.

Blindness having sight and deformity beloved sat side by side—hand pressing hand, brow touching brow, and whispered to each other, intoxicated with love.

The compartment in the middle served two purposes—for the public it was a stage, for the actors a dining-room.

Ursus, ever delighting in comparisons, profited by the diversity of its uses to liken the central compartment in the Green Box to the arradach in an Abyssinian hut.

Ursus counted the receipts, then they supped. In love all is ideal. In love, eating and drinking together afford opportunities for many sweet promiscuous touches, by which a mouthful becomes a kiss. They drank ale or wine from the same glass, as they might drink dew out of the same lily. Two souls in love are as full of grace as two birds. Gwynplaine waited on Dea, cut her bread, poured out her drink, approached her too close.

"Hum!" cried Ursus, and he turned away, his scolding melting into a smile.

The wolf supped under the table, heedless of everything which did actually not concern his bone.

Fibi and Vinos shared the repast, but gave little trouble. These vagabonds, half wild and as uncouth as ever, spoke in the gypsy language to each other.

At length Dea re-entered the women's apartment with Fibi and Vinos. Ursus chained up Homo under the Green Box; Gwynplaine looked after the horses, the lover becoming a groom, like a hero of Homer's or a paladin of Charlemagne's. At midnight, all were asleep, except the wolf, who, alive to his responsibility, now and then opened an eye. The next morning they met again. They breakfasted together, generally on ham and tea. Tea was introduced into England in 1698. Then Dea, after the Spanish fashion, took a siesta, acting on the advice of Ursus, who considered her delicate, and slept some hours, while Gwynplaine and Ursus did all the little jobs of work, without and within, which their wandering life made necessary. Gwynplaine rarely wandered away from the Green Box, except on unfrequented roads and in solitary places. In cities he went out only at night, disguised in a large slouched hat, so as not to exhibit his face in the street.

His face was to be seen uncovered only on the stage.

The Green Box had frequented cities but little. Gwynplaine at twenty-four had never seen towns larger than the Cinque Ports. His renown, however, was increasing. It began to rise above the populace, and to percolate through higher ground. Amongst those who were fond of, and ran after, strange foreign curiosities and prodigies, it was known that there was somewhere in existence, leading a wandering life, now here, now there, an extraordinary monster. They talked about him, they sought him, they asked where he was. The laughing man was becoming decidedly famous. A certain luster was reflected on *Chaos Vanquished*.

So much so, that, one day, Ursus, being ambitious, said—

"We must go to London."

BOOK THE THIRD

THE BEGINNING OF THE FISSURE

Chapter I

THE TADCASTER INN

AT THAT PERIOD LONDON HAD BUT ONE BRIDGE—LONDON BRIDGE, WITH HOUSES BUILT UPON it. This bridge united London to Southwark, a suburb which was paved with flint pebbles taken from the Thames, divided into small streets and alleys, like the city, with a great number of buildings, houses, dwellings, and wooden huts jammed together, a pell-mell mixture of combustible matter, amidst which fire might take its pleasure, as 1666 had proved. Southwark was then pronounced Soudric, it is now pronounced Sousouorc, or near it; indeed, an excellent way of pronouncing English names is not to pronounce them. Thus, for Southampton, say Stpntn.

It was the time when "Chatham" was pronounced *je t'aime*.

The Southwark of those days resembles the Southwark of to-day about as much as Vaugirard resembles Marseilles. It was a village—it is a city. Nevertheless, a considerable trade was carried on there. The long old Cyclopean wall by the Thames was studded with rings, to which were anchored the river barges.

This wall was called the Effroc Wall, or Effroc Stone. York, in Saxon times, was called Effroc. The legend related that a Duke of Effroc had been drowned at the foot of the wall. Certainly the water there was deep enough to drown a duke. At low water it was six good fathoms. The excellence of this little anchorage attracted sea vessels, and the old Dutch tub, called the *Vograat*, came to anchor at the Effroc Stone. The *Vograat* made the crossing from London to Rotterdam, and from Rotterdam to London, punctually once a week. Other barges started twice a day, either for Deptford, Greenwich, or Gravesend, going down with one tide and returning with the next. The voyage to Gravesend, though twenty miles, was performed in six hours.

The *Vograat* was of a model now no longer to be seen, except in naval museums. It was almost a junk. At that time, while France copied Greece, Holland copied China. The *Vograat*, a heavy hull with two masts, was partitioned perpendicularly, so as to be water-tight, having a narrow hold in the middle, and two decks, one fore and the other aft. The decks were flush as in the iron turret-vessels of the present day, the advantage of which is that in foul weather, the force of the wave is diminished, and the inconvenience of which is that the crew is exposed to the action of the sea, owing to there being no bulwarks. There was nothing to save anyone on board from falling over. Hence the frequent falls overboard and the losses of men, which have caused the model to fall into disuse. The *Vograat* went to Holland direct, and did not even call at Gravesend.

An old ridge of stones, rock as much as masonry, ran along the bottom of the Effroc Stone, and being passable at all tides, was used as a passage on board the ships moored to the wall. This wall was, at intervals, furnished with steps. It marked the southern point of Southwark. An embankment at the top allowed the passers-by to rest their elbows on the Effroc Stone, as on the parapet of a quay. Thence they could look down on the Thames; on the other side of the water London dwindled away into fields.

Up the river from the Effroc Stone, at the bend of the Thames which is nearly opposite St. James's Palace, behind Lambeth House, not far from the walk then called Foxhall (Vauxhall, probably), there was, between a pottery in which they made porcelain, and a glass-blower's, where they made ornamental bottles, one of those large unenclosed spaces covered with grass, called formerly in France *cultures* and *mails*, and in England bowling-greens. Of bowling-green, a green on which to roll a ball, the French have made *boulingrin*. Folks have this green inside their houses nowadays, only it is put on the table, is a cloth instead of turf, and is called billiards.

It is difficult to see why, having boulevard (boule-vert), which is the same word as bowling-green, the French should have adopted *boulingrin*. It is surprising that a person so grave as the Dictionary should indulge in useless luxuries.

The bowling-green of Southwark was called Tarrinzeau Field, because it had belonged to the Barons Hastings, who are also Barons Tarrinzeau and Mauchline. From the Lords Hastings the Tarrinzeau Field passed to the Lords Tadcaster, who had made a speculation of it, just as at a later date, a Duke of Orleans made a speculation of the Palais Royal. Tarrinzeau Field afterwards became waste ground and parochial property.

Tarrinzeau Field was a kind of permanent fairground, covered with jugglers, athletes, mountebanks, and music on platforms; and always full of "fools going to look at the devil," as Archbishop Sharp said. To look at the devil means to go to the play.

Several inns, which harbored the public and sent them to these outlandish exhibitions, were established in this place, which kept holiday all the year round, and thereby prospered. These inns were simply stalls, inhabited only during the day. In the evening the tavern-keeper put into his pocket the key of the tavern and went away.

One only of these inns was a house, the only dwelling in the whole bowling-green, the caravans of the fairground having the power of disappearing at any moment, considering the absence of any ties in the vagabond life of all mountebanks.

Mountebanks have no roots to their lives.

This inn, called the Tadcaster, after the former owners of the ground, was an inn rather than a tavern, a hôtel rather than an inn, and had a carriage entrance and a large yard.

The carriage entrance, opening from the court on the field, was the legitimate door of the Tadcaster Inn, which had, beside it, a small bastard door, by which people entered. To call it bastard is to mean preferred. This lower door was the only one used. It opened into the tavern, properly so called, which was a large tap-room, full of tobacco smoke, furnished with tables, and low in the ceiling. Over it was a window on the first floor, to the iron bars of which was fastened and hung the sign of the inn. The principal door was barred and bolted, and always remained closed.

It was thus necessary to cross the tavern to enter the courtyard.

At the Tadcaster Inn there was a landlord and a boy. The landlord was called Master Nicless, the boy Govicum. Master Nicless—Nicholas, doubtless, which the English habit of contraction had made Nicless, was a miserly widower, and one who respected and feared the laws. As to his appearance, he had bushy eyebrows and hairy hands. The boy, aged fourteen, who poured out drink, and answered to the name of Govicum, wore a merry face, and an apron. His hair was cropped close, a sign of servitude.

He slept on the ground floor, in a nook in which they formerly kept a dog. This nook had for window a bull's-eye looking on the bowling-green.

Chapter II

Open-Air Eloquence

ONE VERY COLD AND WINDY EVENING, ON WHICH THERE WAS EVERY REASON WHY FOLKS SHOULD hasten on their way along the street, a man, who was walking in Tarrinzeau Field close under the walls of the tavern, stopped suddenly. It was during the last months of winter between 1704 and 1705. This man, whose dress indicated a sailor, was of good mien and fine figure, things imperative to courtiers, and not forbidden to common folk.

Why did he stop? To listen. What to? To a voice apparently speaking in the court on the other side of the wall, a voice a little weakened by age, but so powerful, notwithstanding, that it reached the passer-by in the street. At the same time might be heard in the enclosure, from which the voice came, the hubbub of a crowd.

This voice said—

"Men and women of London, here I am! I cordially wish you joy of being English. You are a great people. I say more: you are a great populace. Your fisticuffs are even better than your sword thrusts. You have an appetite. You are the nation which eats other nations—a magnificent function! This suction of the world makes England pre-eminent. As politicians and philosophers, in the management of colonies, populations, and industry, and in the desire to do others any harm which may turn to your own good, you stand alone. The hour will come when two boards will be put up on earth—inscribed on one side, Men; on the other, Englishmen. I mention this to your glory, I, who am neither English nor human, having the honor to be a bear. Still more—I am a doctor. That follows. Gentlemen, I teach. What? Two kinds of things—things which I know, and things which I do not. I sell my drugs and I sell my ideas. Approach and listen. Science invites you. Open your ear; if it is small, it will hold but little truth; if large, a great deal of folly will find its way in. Now, then, attention! I teach the Pseudoxia Epidemica. I have a comrade who will make you laugh, but I can make you think. We live in the same box, laughter being of quite as old a family as thought. When people asked Democritus, 'How do you know?' he answered, 'I laugh.' And if I am asked, 'Why do you laugh?' I shall answer, 'I know.' However, I am not laughing. I am the rectifier of popular errors. I take upon myself the task of cleaning your intellects. They require it. Heaven permits people to deceive themselves, and to be deceived. It is useless to be absurdly modest. I frankly avow that I believe in Providence, even where it is wrong. Only when I see filth—errors are filth—I sweep them away. How am I sure of what I know? That concerns only myself. Everyone catches wisdom as he can. Lactantius asked questions of, and received answers from, a bronze head of Virgil. Sylvester II conversed with birds. Did the birds speak? Did the Pope twitter? That is a question. The dead child of the Rabbi Eleazer talked to Saint Augustine. Between ourselves, I doubt all these facts except the last. The dead child might perhaps talk, because under its tongue it had a gold plate, on which were engraved divers constellations. Thus he deceived people. The fact explains itself. You see my moderation. I separate the true from the false. See! here are other errors in which, no doubt, you partake, poor ignorant folks that you are, and from which I wish to free you. Dioscorides believed that there was a god in the henbane; Chrysippus in the cynopaste; Josephus in the root bauras; Homer in the plant moly. They were all wrong. The spirits in herbs are not gods but devils. I have tested this fact. It is not true that the serpent which tempted Eve had a human face, as Cadmus relates. Garcias de Horto, Cadamosto, and John Hugo, Archbishop of Trèves, deny that it is sufficient to saw down a tree to catch an elephant. I incline to their opinion. Citizens, the efforts of Lucifer are the cause of all false impressions. Under the reign of such a prince, it is natural that meteors of error and of perdition should arise. My friends, Claudius Pulcher did not die because the fowls refused to come out of the fowl-house. The fact is, that Lucifer, having foreseen the death of Claudius Pulcher, took care to prevent the birds feeding. That Beelzebub gave the Emperor Vespasian the virtue of curing the lame and giving sight to the blind, by his touch, was an act praiseworthy in itself, but of which the motive was culpable. Gentlemen, distrust those false doctors, who sell the root of the briony and the white snake, and who make washes with honey and the blood of a cock. See clearly through that which is false. It is not quite true that Orion was the result of a natural function of Jupiter. The truth is that it was Mercury who produced this star in that way. It is not true that Adam had a navel. When St. George killed the dragon he had not the daughter of a saint standing by his side. St. Jerome had not a clock on the chimney-piece of his study; first, because living in a cave, he had no study; secondly, because he had no chimney-piece; thirdly, because clocks were not yet invented. Let us put these things right. Put them right. O gentlefolks, who listen to me, if anyone tells you that a lizard will be born in your head if you smell the herb valerian—that the rotting carcase of the ox changes into bees, and that of the horse into hornets—that a man weighs more when dead than when alive—that the blood of the he-goat dissolves emeralds—that a caterpillar, a fly, and a spider, seen on the same tree, announces famine, war, and pestilence—that the falling sickness is to be cured by a worm found in the head of a buck—do not believe him. These things are errors. But now listen to truths. The skin of a sea-calf is a safeguard against thunder. The toad feeds upon earth, which causes a stone to come into his head. The rose of Jericho blooms on Christmas Eve. Serpents cannot endure the shadow of the ash tree. The elephant has no joints, and sleeps resting upright against a tree. Make a toad sit upon a cock's egg, and he will hatch a scorpion which will become a salamander. A blind person will recover sight by putting one hand on the left side of the altar and the other on his eyes. Virginity does not hinder maternity. Honest people, lay these truths to heart. Above all, you can believe in Providence in either of two ways, either as thirst believes in the orange, or as the ass believes in the whip. Now I am going to introduce you to my family."

Here a violent gust of wind shook the window-frames and shutters of the inn, which stood detached. It was like a prolonged murmur of the sky. The orator paused a moment, and then resumed.

"An interruption; very good. Speak, north wind. Gentlemen, I am not angry. The wind is loquacious, like all solitary creatures. There is no one to keep him company up there, so he jabbers. I resume the thread of my discourse. Here you see associated artists. We are four—*a lupo principium*. I begin by my friend, who is a wolf. He does not conceal it. See him! He is educated, grave, and sagacious. Providence, perhaps, entertained for a moment the idea of making him a doctor of the university; but for that one must be rather stupid, and that he is not. I may add that he has no prejudices, and is not aristocratic. He chats sometimes with bitches; he who, by right, should consort only with she-wolves. His heirs, if he have any, will no doubt gracefully combine the yap of their mother with the howl of their father. Because he does howl. He howls in sympathy with men. He barks as well, in condescension to civilization—a magnanimous concession. Homo is a dog made perfect. Let us venerate the dog. The dog—curious animal! sweats with its tongue and smiles with its tail.—Gentlemen, Homo equals in wisdom, and surpasses in cordiality, the hairless wolf of Mexico, the wonderful xoloïtzeniski. I may add that he is humble. He has the modesty of a wolf who is useful to men. He is helpful and charitable, and says nothing about it. His left paw knows not the good which his right paw does. These are his merits. Of the other, my second friend, I have but one word to say. He is a monster. You will admire him. He was formerly abandoned by pirates on the shores of the wild ocean. This third one is blind. Is she an exception? No, we are all blind. The miser is blind; he sees gold, and he does not see riches. The prodigal is blind; he sees the beginning, and does not see the end. The coquette is blind; she does not see her wrinkles. The learned man is blind; he does not see his own ignorance. The honest man is blind; he does not see the thief. The thief is blind; he does not see God. God is blind; the day that he created the world, He did not see the devil manage to creep into it. I myself am blind; I speak, and do not see that you are deaf. This blind girl who accompanies us is a mysterious priestess. Vesta has confided to her her torch. She has in her character depths as soft as a division in the wool of a sheep. I believe her to be a king's daughter, though I do not assert it as a fact. A laudable distrust is the attribute of wisdom. For my own part, I reason and I doctor, I think and I heal. *Chirurgus sum.* I cure fevers, miasmas, and plagues. Almost all our melancholy and sufferings are issues, which if carefully treated relieve us quietly from other evils which might be worse. All the same I do not recommend you to have an anthrax, otherwise called carbuncle. It is a stupid malady, and serves no good end. One dies of it—that is all. I am neither uncultivated nor rustic. I honor eloquence and poetry, and I live in an innocent union with these goddesses. I conclude by a piece of advice. Ladies and gentlemen—on the sunny side of your dispositions, cultivate virtue, modesty, honesty, probity, justice and love. Each one here below may thus have his little pot of flowers on his window-sill. My lords and gentlemen, I have spoken. The play is about to begin."

The man who was apparently a sailor, and who had been listening outside, entered the lower room of the inn, crossed it, paid the necessary entrance money, reached the courtyard which was full of people, saw at the bottom of it a caravan on wheels, wide open, and on the platform an old man dressed in a bear-skin, a young man looking like a mask, a blind girl, and a wolf.

"Gracious heaven!" he cried, "what delightful people!"

Chapter III

WHERE THE PASSER-BY REAPPEARS

THE GREEN BOX, AS WE HAVE JUST SEEN, HAD ARRIVED IN LONDON. IT WAS ESTABLISHED AT Southwark. Ursus had been tempted by the bowling-green, which had one great recommendation, that it was always fair-day there, even in winter.

The dome of St. Paul's was a delight to Ursus.

London, take it all in all, has some good in it. It was a brave thing to dedicate a cathedral to St. Paul. The real cathedral saint is St. Peter. St. Paul is suspected of imagination, and in matters ecclesiastical imagination means heresy. St. Paul is a saint only with extenuating circumstances. He entered heaven only by the artists' door.

A cathedral is a sign. St. Peter is the sign of Rome, the city of the dogma; St. Paul that of London, the city of schism.

Ursus, whose philosophy had arms so long that it embraced everything, was a man who appreciated these shades of difference, and his attraction toward London arose, perhaps, from a certain taste of his for St. Paul.

The yard of the Tadcaster Inn had taken the fancy of Ursus. It might have been ordered for the Green Box. It was a theater ready-made. It was square, with three sides built round, and a wall forming the fourth. Against this wall was placed the Green Box, which they were able to draw into the yard, owing to the height of the gate. A large wooden balcony, roofed over, and supported on posts, on which the rooms of the first story opened, ran round the three fronts of the interior façades of the house, making two right angles. The windows of the ground floor made boxes, the pavement of the court the pit, and the balcony the gallery. The Green Box, reared against the wall, was thus in front of a theater. It was very like the Globe, where they played *Othello*, *King Lear*, and *The Tempest*.

In a corner behind the Green Box was a stable.

Ursus had made his arrangements with the tavern-keeper, Master Nicless, who, owing to his respect for the law, would not admit the wolf without charging him extra.

The placard, "Gwynplaine, the Laughing Man," taken from its nail in the Green Box, was hung up close to the sign of the inn. The sitting-room of the tavern had, as we have seen, an inside door which opened into the court. By the side of the door was constructed off-hand, by means of an empty barrel, a box for the money-taker, who was sometimes Fibi, and sometimes Vinos. This was managed much as at present. Pay and pass in. Under the placard announcing the Laughing Man was a piece of wood, painted white, hung on two nails, on which was written in charcoal in large letters the title of Ursus's grand piece, *Chaos Vanquished*.

In the center of the balcony, precisely opposite the Green Box, and in a compartment having for entrance a window reaching to the ground, there had been partitioned off a space "for the nobility." It was large enough to hold, in two rows, ten spectators.

"We are in London," said Ursus. "We must be prepared for the gentry."

He had furnished this box with the best chairs in the inn, and had placed in the center a grand arm-chair of yellow Utrecht velvet, with a cherry-colored pattern, in case some alderman's wife should come.

They began their performances. The crowd immediately flocked to them, but the compartment for the nobility remained empty. With that exception their success became so great that no mountebank memory could recall its parallel. All Southwark ran in crowds to admire the Laughing Man.

The merry-andrews and mountebanks of Tarrinzeau Field were aghast at Gwynplaine. The effect he caused was as that of a sparrow-hawk flapping his wings in a cage of goldfinches, and feeding in their seed-trough. Gwynplaine ate up their public.

Besides the small fry, the swallowers of swords and the grimace makers, real performances took place on the green. There was a circus of women, ringing from morning till night with a magnificent peal of all sorts of instruments—psalteries, drums, rebecks, micamons, timbrels, reeds, dulcimers, gongs, chevrettes, bagpipes, German horns, English eschaqueils, pipes, flutes, and flageolets.

In a large round tent were some tumblers, who could not have equaled our present climbers of the Pyrenees—Dulma, Bordenave, and Meylonga—who from the peak of Pierrefitte descend to the plateau of Limaçon, an almost perpendicular height. There was a traveling menagerie, where was to be seen a performing tiger, who, lashed by the keeper, snapped at the whip and tried to swallow the lash. Even this comedian of jaws and claws was eclipsed in success.

Curiosity, applause, receipts, crowds, the Laughing Man monopolized everything. It happened in the twinkling of an eye. Nothing was thought of but the Green Box.

"*Chaos Vanquished* is *Chaos Victor*," said Ursus, appropriating half Gwynplaine's success, and taking the wind out of his sails, as they say at sea. That success was prodigious. Still it remained local. Fame does not cross the sea easily. It took a hundred and thirty years for the name of Shakespeare to penetrate from England into France. The sea is a wall; and if Voltaire—a thing which he very much regretted when it was too late—had not thrown a bridge over to Shakespeare, Shakespeare might still be in England, on the other side of the wall, a captive in insular glory.

The glory of Gwynplaine had not passed London Bridge. It was not great enough yet to reecho throughout the city. At least not at first. But Southwark ought to have sufficed to satisfy the ambition of a clown. Ursus said—

"The money bag grows palpably bigger."

They played *Ursus Rursus* and *Chaos Vanquished*.

Between the acts Ursus exhibited his power as an engastrimist, and executed marvels of ventriloquism. He imitated every cry which occurred in the audience—a song, a cry, enough to startle, so exact the imitation, the singer or the crier himself; and now and then he copied the hubbub of the public, and whistled as if there were a crowd of people within him. These were remarkable talents. Besides this he harangued like Cicero, as we have just seen, sold his drugs, attended sickness, and even healed the sick.

Southwark was enthralled.

Ursus was satisfied with the applause of Southwark, but by no means astonished.

"They are the ancient Trinobantes," he said.

Then he added—"I must not mistake them, for delicacy of taste, for the Atrobates, who people Berkshire, or the Belgians, who inhabited Somersetshire, nor for the Parisians, who founded York."

At every performance the yard of the inn, transformed into a pit, was filled with a ragged and enthusiastic audience. It was composed of watermen, chairmen, coachmen, and bargemen, and sailors, just ashore, spending their wages in feasting and women. In it there were felons, ruffians, and blackguards, who were soldiers condemned for some crime against discipline to wear their red coats, which were lined with black, inside out, and from thence the name of blackguard, which the French turn into *blagueurs*. All these flowed from the street into the theater, and poured back from the theater into the tap. The emptying of tankards did not decrease their success.

Amidst what it is usual to call the scum, there was one taller than the rest, bigger, stronger, less poverty-stricken, broader in the shoulders; dressed like the common people, but not ragged.

Admiring and applauding everything to the skies, clearing his way with his fists, wearing a disordered periwig, swearing, shouting, joking, never dirty, and, at need, ready to blacken an eye or pay for a bottle.

This frequenter was the passer-by whose cheer of enthusiasm has been recorded.

This connoisseur was suddenly fascinated, and had adopted the Laughing Man. He did not come every evening, but when he came he led the public—applause grew into acclamation—success rose not to the roof, for there was none, but to the clouds, for there were plenty of them. Which clouds (seeing that there was no roof) sometimes wept over the masterpiece of Ursus.

His enthusiasm caused Ursus to remark this man, and Gwynplaine to observe him.

They had a great friend in this unknown visitor.

Ursus and Gwynplaine wanted to know him; at least, to know who he was.

One evening, Ursus was in the side scene, which was the kitchen-door of the Green Box, seeing Master Nicless standing by him, showed him this man in the crowd, and asked him—

"Do you know that man?"

"Of course I do."

"Who is he?"

"A sailor."

"What is his name?" said Gwynplaine, interrupting.

"Tom-Jim-Jack," replied the inn-keeper.

Then as he redescended the steps at the back of the Green Box, to enter the inn, Master Nicless let fall this profound reflection, so deep as to be unintelligible—

"What a pity that he should not be a lord. He would make a famous scoundrel."

Otherwise, although established in the tavern, the group in the Green Box had in no way altered their manner of living, and held to their isolated habits. Except a few words exchanged now and then with the tavern-keeper, they held no communication with any of those who were living, either permanently or temporarily, in the inn; and continued to keep to themselves.

Since they had been at Southwark, Gwynplaine had made it his habit, after the performance and the supper of both family and horses—when Ursus and Dea had gone to bed in their respective compartments—to breathe a little the fresh air of the bowling-green, between eleven o'clock and midnight.

A certain vagrancy in our spirits impels us to take walks at night, and to saunter under the stars. There is a mysterious expectation in youth. Therefore it is that we are prone to wander out in the night, without an object.

At that hour there was no one in the fairground, except, perhaps, some reeling drunkard, making staggering shadows in dark corners. The empty taverns were shut up, and the lower room in the Tadcaster Inn was dark, except where, in some corner, a solitary candle lighted a last reveler. An indistinct glow gleamed through the window-shutters of the half-closed tavern, as Gwynplaine, pensive, content, and dreaming, happy in a haze of divine joy, passed backwards and forwards in front of the half-open door.

Of what was he thinking? Of Dea—of nothing—of everything—of the depths.

He never wandered far from the Green Box, being held, as by a thread, to Dea. A few steps away from it was far enough for him.

Then he returned, found the whole Green Box asleep, and went to bed himself.

Chapter IV

CONTRARIES FRATERNIZE IN HATE

S UCCESS IS HATEFUL, ESPECIALLY TO THOSE WHOM IT OVERTHROWS. IT IS RARE THAT THE EATEN
adore the eaters.

The Laughing Man had decidedly made a hit. The mountebanks around were indignant. A theatrical success is a syphon—it pumps in the crowd and creates emptiness all round. The shop opposite is done for. The increased receipts of the Green Box caused a corresponding decrease in the receipts of the surrounding shows. Those entertainments, popular up to that time, suddenly collapsed. It was like a low-water mark, showing inversely, but in perfect concordance, the rise here, the fall there. Theaters experience the effect of tides: they rise in one only on condition of falling in another. The swarming foreigners who exhibited their talents and their trumpetings on the neighboring platforms, seeing themselves ruined by the Laughing Man, were despairing, yet dazzled. All the grimacers, all the clowns, all the merry-andrews envied Gwynplaine. How happy he must be with the snout of a wild beast! The buffoon mothers and dancers on the tightrope, with pretty children, looked at them in anger, and pointing out Gwynplaine, would say—"What a pity you have not a face like that!" Some beat their babes savagely for being pretty. More than one, had she known the secret, would have fashioned her son's face in the Gwynplaine style. The head of an angel, which brings no money in, is not as good as that of a lucrative devil. One day the mother of a little child who was a marvel of beauty, and who acted a cupid, exclaimed—

"Our children are failures! They only succeeded with Gwynplaine." And shaking her fist at her son, she added—"If I only knew your father, wouldn't he catch it!"

Gwynplaine was the goose with the golden eggs! What a marvelous phenomenon! There was an uproar through all the caravans. The mountebanks, enthusiastic and exasperated, looked at Gwynplaine and gnashed their teeth. Admiring anger is called envy. Then it howls! They tried to disturb *Chaos Vanquished*; made a cabal, hissed, scolded, shouted! This was an excuse for Ursus to make out-of-door harangues to the populace, and for his friend Tom-Jim-Jack to use his fists to reestablish order. His pugilistic marks of friendship brought him still more under the notice and regard of Ursus and Gwynplaine. At a distance, however, for the group in the Green Box sufficed to themselves, and held aloof from the rest of the world, and because Tom-Jim-Jack, this leader of the mob, seemed a sort of supreme bully, without a tie, without a friend; a smasher of windows, a manager of men, now here, now gone, hail-fellow-well-met with everyone, companion of none.

This raging envy against Gwynplaine did not give in for a few friendly hits from Tom-Jim-Jack. The outcries having miscarried, the mountebanks of Tarrinzeau Field fell back on a petition. They addressed to the authorities. This is the usual course. Against an unpleasant success we first try to stir up the crowd and then we petition the magistrate.

With the merry-andrews the reverends allied themselves. The Laughing Man had inflicted a blow on the preachers. There were empty places not only in the caravans, but in the churches. The congregations in the churches of the five parishes in Southwark had dwindled away. People left before the sermon to go to Gwynplaine. *Chaos Vanquished*, the Green Box, the Laughing Man, all the abominations of Baal, eclipsed the eloquence of the pulpit. The voice crying in the desert, *vox clamantis in deserto*, is discontented, and is prone to call for the aid of the authorities. The clergy of the five parishes complained to the Bishop of London, who complained to her Majesty.

The complaint of the merry-andrews was based on religion. They declared it to be insulted. They described Gwynplaine as a sorcerer, and Ursus as an atheist. The reverend gentlemen invoked social order. Setting orthodoxy aside they took action on the fact that acts of parliament were violated. It was clever. Because it was the period of Mr. Locke, who had died but six months previously—28th October, 1704—and when skepticism, which Bolingbroke had imbibed from Voltaire, was taking root. Later on Wesley came and restored the Bible, as Loyola restored the papacy.

Thus the Green Box was battered on both sides; by the merry-andrews, in the name of the Pentateuch, and by chaplains in the name of the police. In the name of heaven and of the inspectors of nuisances. The Green Box was denounced by the priests as an obstruction, and by the jugglers as sacrilegious.

Had they any pretext? Was there any excuse? Yes. What was the crime? This: there was the wolf. A dog was allowable; a wolf forbidden. In England the wolf is an outlaw. England admits the dog which barks, but not the dog which howls—a shade of difference between the yard and the woods.

The rectors and vicars of the five parishes of Southwark called attention in their petitions to numerous parliamentary and royal statutes putting the wolf beyond the protection of the law. They moved for something like the imprisonment of Gwynplaine and the execution of the wolf, or at any rate for their banishment. The question was one of public importance, the danger to persons passing, etc. And, on this point, they appealed to the Faculty. They cited the opinion of the Eighty physicians of London, a learned body which dates from Henry VIII, which has a seal like that of the State, which can raise sick people to the dignity of being amenable to their jurisdiction, which has the right to imprison those who infringe its law and contravene its ordinances, and which, amongst other useful regulations for the health of the citizens, put beyond doubt this fact acquired by science: that if a wolf sees a man first, the man becomes hoarse for life. Besides, he may be bitten.

Homo, then, was a pretext.

Ursus heard of these designs through the inn-keeper. He was uneasy. He was afraid of two claws—the police and the justices. To be afraid of the magistracy, it is sufficient to be afraid, there is no need to be guilty. Ursus had no desire for contact with sheriffs, provosts, bailiffs, and coroners. His eagerness to make their acquaintance amounted to nil. His curiosity to see the magistrates was about as great as the hare's to see the greyhound.

He began to regret that he had come to London. " 'Better' is the enemy of 'good,' " murmured he apart. "I thought the proverb was ill-considered. I was wrong. Stupid truths are true truths."

Against the coalition of powers—merry-andrews taking in hand the cause of religion, and chaplains, indignant in the name of medicine—the poor Green Box, suspected of sorcery in Gwynplaine and of hydrophobia in Homo, had only one thing in its favor (but a thing of great power in England), municipal inactivity. It is to the local authorities letting things take their own course that Englishmen owe their liberty. Liberty in England behaves very much as the sea around England. It is a tide. Little by little manners surmount the law. A cruel system of legislation drowned under the wave of custom; a savage code of laws still visible through the transparency of universal liberty: such is England.

The Laughing Man, *Chaos Vanquished*, and Homo might have mountebanks, preachers, bishops, the House of Commons, the House of Lords, her Majesty, London, and the whole of England against them, and remain undisturbed so long as Southwark permitted.

The Green Box was the favorite amusement of the suburb, and the local authorities seemed disinclined to interfere. In England, indifference is protection. So long as the sheriff of the county of Surrey, to the jurisdiction of which Southwark belongs, did not move in the matter, Ursus breathed freely, and Homo could sleep on his wolf's ears.

So long as the hatred which it excited did not occasion acts of violence, it increased success. The Green Box was none the worse for it, for the time. On the contrary, hints were scattered that it contained something mysterious. Hence the Laughing Man became more and more popular. The public follow with gusto the scent of anything contraband. To be suspected is a recommendation. The people adopt by instinct that at which the finger is pointed. The thing which is denounced is like the savor of forbidden fruit; we rush to eat it. Besides, applause which irritates someone, especially if that someone is in authority, is sweet. To perform, whilst passing a pleasant evening, both an act of kindness to the oppressed, and of opposition to the oppressor, is agreeable. You are protecting at the same time that you are being amused. So the theatrical caravans on the bowling-green continued to howl and to cabal against the Laughing Man. Nothing could be better calculated to enhance his success. The shouts of one's enemies are useful, and give point and vitality to one's triumph. A friend wearies sooner in praise than an enemy in abuse. To abuse does not hurt. Enemies are ignorant of this fact. They cannot help insulting us, and this constitutes their use. They cannot hold their tongues, and thus keep the public awake.

The crowds which flocked to *Chaos Vanquished* increased daily.

Ursus kept what Master Nicless had said of intriguers and complaints in high places to himself, and did not tell Gwynplaine, lest it should trouble the ease of his acting by creating anxiety. If evil was to come, he would be sure to know it soon enough.

Chapter V

THE WAPENTAKE

ONCE, HOWEVER, HE THOUGHT IT HIS DUTY TO DEROGATE FROM THIS PRUDENCE, FOR PRUdence's sake, thinking that it might be well to make Gwynplaine uneasy. It is true that this idea arose from a circumstance much graver, in the opinion of Ursus, than the cabals of the fair or of the church.

Gwynplaine, as he picked up a farthing which had fallen when counting the receipts, had, in the presence of the inn-keeper, drawn a contrast between the farthing, representing the misery of the people, and the die, representing, under the figure of Anne, the parasitical magnificence of the throne—an ill-sounding speech. This observation was repeated by Master Nicless, and had such a run that it reached to Ursus through Fibi and Vinos. It put Ursus into a fever. Seditious words, lèse Majesté. He took Gwynplaine severely to task. "Watch over your abominable jaws. There is a rule for the great—to do nothing; and a rule for the small—to say nothing. The poor man has but one friend, silence. He should only pronounce one syllable: 'yes.' To confess and to consent is all the right he has. 'Yes,' to the judge; 'yes,' to the king. Great people, if it pleases them to do so, beat us. I have received blows from them. It is their prerogative; and they lose nothing of their greatness by breaking our bones. The ossifrage is a species of eagle. Let us venerate the scepter, which is the first of staves. Respect is prudence, and mediocrity is safety. To insult the king is to put one's self in the same danger as a girl rashly paring the nails of a lion. They tell me that you have been prattling about the farthing, which is the same thing as the liard, and that you have found fault with the august medallion, for which they sell us at market the eighth part of a salt herring. Take care; let us be serious. Consider the existence of pains and penalties. Suck in these legislative truths. You are in a country in which the man who cuts down a tree three years old is quietly taken off to the gallows. As to swearers, their feet are put into the stocks. The drunkard is shut up in a barrel with the bottom out, so that he can walk, with a hole in the top, through which his head is passed, and with two in the bung for his hands, so that he cannot lie down. He who strikes another one in Westminster Hall is imprisoned for life and has his goods confiscated. Whoever strikes anyone in the king's palace has his hand struck off. A fillip on the nose chances to bleed, and, behold! you are maimed for life. He who is convicted of heresy in the bishop's court is burned alive. It was for no great matter that Cuthbert Simpson was quartered on a turnstile. Three years since, in 1702, which is not long ago, you see, they placed in the pillory a scoundrel, called Daniel Defoe, who had had the audacity to print the names of the Members of Parliament who had spoken on the previous evening. He who commits high treason is disemboweled alive, and they tear out his heart and buffet his cheeks with it. Impress on yourself notions of right and justice. Never allow yourself to speak a word, and at the first cause of anxiety, run for it. Such is the bravery which I counsel and which I practice. In the way of temerity, imitate the birds; in the way of talking, imitate the fishes. England has one admirable point in her favor, that her legislation is very mild."

His admonition over, Ursus remained uneasy for some time. Gwynplaine not at all. The intrepidity of youth arises from want of experience. However, it seemed that Gwynplaine had good reason for his easy mind, for the weeks flowed on peacefully, and no bad consequences seemed to have resulted from his observations about the queen.

Ursus, we know, lacked apathy, and, like a roebuck on the watch, kept a lookout in every direction. One day, a short time after his sermon to Gwynplaine, as he was looking out from the window in the wall which commanded the field, he became suddenly pale.

"Gwynplaine?"

"What?"

"Look."

"Where?"

"In the field."

"Well?"

"Do you see that passer-by?"

"The man in black?"

"Yes."

"Who has a kind of mace in his hand?"

"Yes."

"Well?"

"Well, Gwynplaine, that man is a wapentake."

"What is a wapentake?"

"He is the bailiff of the hundred."

"What is the bailiff of the hundred?"

"He is the *proepositus hundredi.*"

"And what is the *proepositus hundredi?*"

"He is a terrible officer."

"What has he got in his hand?"

"The iron weapon."

"What is the iron weapon?"

"A thing made of iron."

"What does he do with that?"

"First of all, he swears upon it. It is for that reason that he is called the wapentake."

"And then?"

"Then he touches you with it."

"With what?"

"With the iron weapon."

"The wapentake touches you with the iron weapon?"

"Yes."

"What does that mean?"

"That means, follow me."

"And must you follow?"

"Yes."

"Whither?"

"How should I know?"

"But he tells you where he is going to take you?"

"No."

"How is that?"

"He says nothing and you say nothing."

"But—"

"He touches you with the iron weapon. All is over then. You must go."

"But where?"

"After him."

"But where?"

"Wherever he likes, Gwynplaine."

"And if you resist?"

"You are hanged."

Ursus looked out of the window again, and drawing a long breath, said—

"Thank God! He has passed. He was not coming here."

Ursus was perhaps unreasonably alarmed about the indiscreet remark, and the consequences likely to result from the unconsidered words of Gwynplaine.

Master Nicless, who had heard them, had no interest in compromising the poor inhabitants of the Green Box. He was amassing, at the same time as the Laughing Man, a nice little fortune. *Chaos Vanquished* had succeeded in two ways. While it made art triumph on the stage, it made drunkenness prosper in the tavern.

Chapter VI

THE MOUSE EXAMINED BY THE CATS

URSUS WAS SOON AFTERWARDS STARTLED BY ANOTHER ALARMING CIRCUMSTANCE. THIS TIME IT was he himself who was concerned. He was summoned to Bishopsgate before a commission composed of three disagreeable countenances. They belonged to three doctors, called overseers. One was a Doctor of Theology, delegated by the Dean of Westminster; another, a Doctor of Medicine, delegated by the College of Surgeons; the third, a Doctor in History and Civil Law, delegated by Gresham College. These three experts *in omne re scibile* had the censorship of everything said in public throughout the bounds of the hundred and thirty parishes of London, the seventy-three of Middlesex, and, by extension, the five of Southwark.

Such theological jurisdictions still subsist in England, and do good service. In December, 1868, by sentence of the Court of Arches, confirmed by the decision of the Privy Council, the Reverend Mackonochie was censured, besides being condemned in costs, for having placed lighted candles on a table. The liturgy allows no jokes.

Ursus, then, one fine day received from the delegated doctors an order to appear before them, which was, luckily, given into his own hands, and which he was therefore enabled to keep secret. Without saying a word, he obeyed the citation, shuddering at the thought that he might be considered culpable to the extent of having the appearance of being suspected of a certain amount of rashness. He who had so recommended silence to others had here a rough lesson. *Garrule, sana teipsum.*

The three doctors, delegated and appointed overseers, sat at Bishopsgate, at the end of a room on the ground floor, in three arm-chairs covered with black leather, with three busts of Minos, Æacus, and Rhadamanthus, in the wall above their heads, a table before them, and at their feet a form for the accused.

Ursus, introduced by a tipstaff, of placid but severe expression, entered, perceived the doctors, and immediately in his own mind, gave to each of them the name of the judge of the infernal regions represented by the bust placed above his head. Minos, the president, the representative of theology, made him a sign to sit down on the form.

Ursus made a proper bow—that is to say, bowed to the ground; and knowing that bears are charmed by honey, and doctors by Latin, he said, keeping his body still bent respectfully —

"*Tres faciunt capitulum!*"

Then, with head inclined (for modesty disarms) he sat down on the form.

Each of the three doctors had before him a bundle of papers, of which he was turning the leaves.

Minos began.

"You speak in public?"

"Yes," replied Ursus.

"By what right?"

"I am a philosopher."

"That gives no right."

"I am also a mountebank," said Ursus.

"That is a different thing."

Ursus breathed again, but with humility.

Minos resumed—

"As a mountebank, you may speak; as a philosopher, you must keep silence."

"I will try," said Ursus.

Then he thought to himself—

"I may speak, but I must be silent. How complicated."

He was much alarmed.

The same overseer continued—

"You say things which do not sound right. You insult religion. You deny the most evident truths. You propagate revolting errors. For instance, you have said that the fact of virginity excludes the possibility of maternity."

Ursus lifted his eyes meekly, "I did not say that. I said that the fact of maternity excludes the possibility of virginity."

Minos was thoughtful, and mumbled, "True, that is the contrary."

It was really the same thing. But Ursus had parried the first blow.

Minos, meditating on the answer just given by Ursus, sank into the depths of his own imbecility, and kept silent.

The overseer of history, or, as Ursus called him, Rhadamanthus, covered the retreat of Minos by this interpolation, "Accused! your audacity and your errors are of two sorts. You have denied that the battle of Pharsalia would have been lost because Brutus and Cassius had met a negro."

"I said," murmured Ursus, "that there was something in the fact that Cæsar was the better captain."

The man of history passed, without transition, to mythology.

"You have excused the infamous acts of Actæon."

"I think," said Ursus, insinuatingly, "that a man is not dishonored by having seen a naked woman."

"Then you are wrong," said the judge, severely. Rhadamanthus returned to history.

"Apropos of the accidents which happened to the cavalry of Mithridates, you have contested the virtues of herbs and plants. You have denied that a herb like the securiduca, could make the shoes of horses fall off."

"Pardon me," replied Ursus. "I said that the power existed only in the herb sferra cavallo. I never denied the virtue of any herb," and he added, in a low voice, "nor of any woman."

By this extraneous addition to his answer Ursus proved to himself that, anxious as he was, he was not disheartened. Ursus was a compound of terror and presence of mind.

"To continue," resumed Rhadamanthus; "you have declared that it was folly in Scipio, when he wished to open the gates of Carthage, to use as a key the herb aethiopis, because the herb aethiopis has not the property of breaking locks."

"I merely said that he would have done better to have used the herb lunaria."

"That is a matter of opinion," murmured Rhadamanthus, touched in his turn. And the man of history was silent.

The theologian, Minos, having returned to consciousness, questioned Ursus anew. He had had time to consult his notes.

"You have classed orpiment amongst the products of arsenic, and you have said that it is a poison. The Bible denies this."

"The Bible denies, but arsenic affirms it," sighed Ursus.

The man whom Ursus called Æacus, and who was the envy of medicine, had not yet spoken, but now looking down on Ursus, with proudly half-closed eyes, he said—

"The answer is not without some show of reason."

Ursus thanked him with his most cringing smile. Minos frowned frightfully. "I resume," said Minos. "You have said that it is false that the basilisk is the king of serpents, under the name of cockatrice."

"Very reverend sir," said Ursus, "so little did I desire to insult the basilisk that I have given out as certain that it has a man's head."

"Be it so," replied Minos, severely; "but you added that Poerius had seen one with the head of a falcon. Can you prove it?"

"Not easily," said Ursus.

Here he had lost a little ground.

Minos, seizing the advantage, pushed it.

"You have said that a converted Jew has not a nice smell."

"Yes. But I added that a Christian who becomes a Jew has a nasty one."

Minos lost his eyes over the accusing documents.

"You have affirmed and propagated things which are impossible. You have said that Elien had seen an elephant write sentences."

"Nay, very reverend gentleman! I simply said that Oppian had heard a hippopotamus discuss a philosophical problem."

"You have declared that it is not true that a dish made of beech-wood will become covered of itself with all the viands that one can desire."

"I said, that if it has this virtue, it must be that you received it from the devil."

"That I received it!"

"No, most reverend sir. I, nobody, everybody!"

Aside, Ursus thought, "I don't know what I am saying."

But his outward confusion, though extreme, was not distinctly visible. Ursus struggled with it.

"All this," Minos began again, "implies a certain belief in the devil."

Ursus held his own.

"Very reverend sir, I am not an unbeliever with regard to the devil. Belief in the devil is the reverse side of faith in God. The one proves the other. He who does not believe a little in the devil, does not believe much in God. He who believes in the sun must believe in the shadow. The devil is the night of God. What is night? The proof of day."

Ursus here extemporized a fathomless combination of philosophy and religion. Minos remained pensive, and relapsed into silence.

Ursus breathed afresh.

A sharp onslaught now took place. Æacus, the medical delegate, who had disdainfully protected Ursus against the theologian, now turned suddenly from auxiliary into assailant. He placed his closed fist on his bundle of papers, which was large and heavy. Ursus received this apostrophe full in the breast—

"It is proved that crystal is sublimated ice, and that the diamond is sublimated crystal. It is averred that ice becomes crystal in a thousand years, and crystal diamond in a thousand ages. You have denied this."

"Nay," replied Ursus, with sadness. "I only said that in a thousand years ice had time to melt, and that a thousand ages were difficult to count."

The examination went on; questions and answers clashed like swords.

"You have denied that plants can talk."

"Not at all. But to do so they must grow under a gibbet."

"Do you own that the mandragora cries?"

"No; but it sings."

"You have denied that the fourth finger of the left hand has a cordial virtue."

"I only said that to sneeze to the left was a bad sign."

"You have spoken rashly and disrespectfully of the phoenix."

"Learned judge, I merely said that when he wrote that the brain of the phoenix was a delicate morsel, but that it produced headache, Plutarch was a little out of his reckoning, inasmuch as the phoenix never existed."

"A detestable speech! The cinnamalker which makes its nest with sticks of cinnamon, the rhintacus that Parysatis used in the manufacture of his poisons, the manucodiatas which is the bird of paradise, and the semenda, which has a threefold beak, have been mistaken for the phoenix; but the phoenix has existed."

"I do not deny it."

"You are a stupid ass."

"I desire to be thought no better."

"You have confessed that the elder-tree cures the quinsy, but you added that it was not because it has in its root a fairy excrescence."

"I said it was because Judas hung himself on an elder-tree."

"A plausible opinion," growled the theologian, glad to strike his little blow at Æacus.

Arrogance repulsed soon turns to anger. Æacus was enraged.

"Wandering mountebank! you wander as much in mind as with your feet. Your tendencies are out of the way and suspicious. You approach the bounds of sorcery. You have dealings with unknown animals. You speak to the populace of things that exist but for you alone, and the nature of which is unknown, such as the hoemorrhoues."

"The hoemorrhoues is a viper which was seen by Tremellius."

This repartee produced a certain disorder in the irritated science of Doctor Æacus.

Ursus added, "The existence of the hoemorrhoues is quite as true as that of the odoriferous hyena, and of the civet described by Castellus."

Æacus got out of the difficulty by charging home.

"Here are your own words, and very diabolical words they are. Listen."

With his eyes on his notes, Æacus read—

"Two plants, the thalagssigle and the aglaphotis, are luminous in the evening, flowers by day, stars by night"; and looking steadily at Ursus, "What have you to say to that?"

Ursus answered—

"Every plant is a lamp. Its perfume is its light."

Æacus turned over other pages.

"You have denied that the vesicles of the otter are equivalent to castoreum."

"I merely said that perhaps it may be necessary to receive the teaching of Ætius on this point with some reserve."

Æacus became furious.

"You practice medicine?"

"I practice medicine," sighed Ursus, timidly.

"On living things?"

"Rather than on dead ones," said Ursus.

Ursus defended himself stoutly, but dully; an admirable mixture, in which meekness predominated. He spoke with such gentleness that Doctor Æacus felt that he must insult him.

"What are you murmuring there?" said he, rudely.

Ursus was amazed, and restricted himself to saying—

"Murmurings are for the young, and moans for the aged. Alas, I moan!"

Æacus replied—

"Be assured of this—if you attend a sick person, and he dies, you will be punished by death."

Ursus hazarded a question.

"And if he gets well?"

"In that case," said the doctor, softening his voice, "you will be punished by death."

"There is little difference," said Ursus.

The doctor replied—

"If death ensues, we punish gross ignorance; if recovery, we punish presumption. The gibbet in either case."

"I was ignorant of the circumstance," murmured Ursus. "I thank you for teaching me. One does not know all the beauties of the law."

"Take care of yourself."

"Religiously," said Ursus.

"We know what you are about."

"As for me," thought Ursus, "that is more than I always know myself."

"We could send you to prison."

"I see that perfectly, gentlemen."

"You cannot deny your infractions nor your encroachments."

"My philosophy asks pardon."

"Great audacity has been attributed to you."

"That is quite a mistake."

"It is said that you have cured the sick."

"I am the victim of calumny."

The three pairs of eyebrows which were so horribly fixed on Ursus contracted. The three wise faces drew near to each other and whispered. Ursus had the vision of a vague fool's cap sketched out above those three empowered heads. The low and requisite whispering of the trio was of some minutes' duration, during which time Ursus felt all the ice and all the scorch of agony. At length Minos, who was president, turned to him and said angrily—

"Go away!"

Ursus felt something like Jonas when he was leaving the belly of the whale.

Minos continued—

"You are discharged."

Ursus said to himself—

"They won't catch me at this again. Good bye, medicine!"

And he added, in his innermost heart—

"From henceforth I will carefully allow them to die."

Bent double, he bowed everywhere; to the doctors, to the busts, the tables, the walls, and re-tiring backwards through the door, disappeared almost as a shadow melting into air.

He left the hall slowly, like an innocent man, and rushed from the street rapidly, like a guilty one. The officers of justice are so singular and obscure in their ways, that even when acquitted, one flies from them.

As he fled he mumbled—

"I am well out of it. I am the savant untamed; they the savant civilized. Doctors cavil at the learned. False science is the excrement of the true, and is employed to the destruction of philoso-phers. Philosophers, as they produce sophists, produce their own scourge. Of the dung of the thrush is born the mistletoe, with which is made birdlime, with which the thrush is captured. *Turdus sibi malum cacat.*"

We do not represent Ursus as a refined man. He was imprudent enough to use words which expressed his thoughts. He had no more taste than Voltaire.

When Ursus returned to the Green Box, he told Master Nicless that he had been delayed by following a pretty woman, and let not a word escape him concerning his adventure.

Except in the evening when he said in a low voice to Homo—

"See here, I have vanquished the three heads of Cerberus."

Chapter VII

WHY SHOULD A GOLD PIECE LOWER ITSELF BY MIXING WITH A HEAP OF PENNIES?

AN EVENT HAPPENED.

The Tadcaster Inn became more and more a furnace of joy and laughter. Never was there more resonant gaiety. The landlord and his boy were become insufficient to draw the ale, stout, and porter. In the evening in the lower room, with its windows all aglow, there was not a va-cant table. They sang, they shouted; the great old hearth, vaulted like an oven, with its iron bars piled with coals, shone out brightly. It was like a house of fire and noise.

In the yard—that is to say, in the theater—the crowd was greater still.

Crowds as great as the suburb of Southwark could supply so thronged the performances of *Chaos Vanquished* that directly the curtain was raised—that is to say, the platform of the Green Box was lowered—every place was filled. The windows were alive with spectators, the balcony was crammed. Not a single paving-stone in the paved yard was to be seen. It seemed paved with faces.

Only the compartment for the nobility remained empty.

There was thus a space in the center of the balcony, a black hole, called in metaphorical slang, an oven. No one there. Crowds everywhere except in that one spot.

One evening it was occupied.

It was on a Saturday, a day on which the English make all haste to amuse themselves before the *ennui* of Sunday. The hall was full.

We say *hall*. Shakespeare for a long time had to use the yard of an inn for a theater, and he called it *hall*.

Just as the curtain rose on the prologue of *Chaos Vanquished*, with Ursus, Homo, and Gwynplaine on the stage, Ursus, from habit, cast a look at the audience, and felt a sensation.

The compartment for the nobility was occupied. A lady was sitting alone in the middle of the box, on the Utrecht velvet arm-chair. She was alone, and she filled the box. Certain beings seem to give out light. This lady, like Dea, had a light in herself, but a light of a different character.

Dea was pale, this lady was pink. Dea was the twilight, this lady, Aurora. Dea was beautiful, this lady was superb. Dea was innocence, candor, fairness, alabaster—this woman was of the purple, and one felt that she did not fear the blush. Her irradiation overflowed the box, she sat in the midst of it, immovable, in the spreading majesty of an idol.

Amidst the sordid crowd she shone out grandly, as with the radiance of a carbuncle. She inundated it with so much light that she drowned it in shadow, and all the mean faces in it underwent eclipse. Her splendor blotted out all else.

Every eye was turned toward her.

Tom-Jim-Jack was in the crowd. He was lost like the rest in the nimbus of this dazzling creature.

The lady at first absorbed the whole attention of the public, who had crowded to the performance, thus somewhat diminishing the opening effects of *Chaos Vanquished*.

Whatever might be the air of dreamland about her, for those who were near she was a woman; perchance, too much a woman.

She was tall and amply formed, and showed as much as possible of her magnificent person. She wore heavy earrings of pearls, with which were mixed those whimsical jewels called "keys of England." Her upper dress was of Indian muslin, embroidered all over with gold—a great luxury, because those muslin dresses then cost six hundred crowns. A large diamond brooch closed her chemise, the which she wore so as to display her shoulders and bosom, in the immodest fashion of the time; the chemisette was made of that lawn of which Anne of Austria had sheets so fine that they could be passed through a ring. She wore what seemed like a cuirass of rubies—some uncut, but polished, and precious stones were sewn all over the body of her dress. Then, her eyebrows were blackened with Indian ink; and her arms, elbows, shoulders, chin, and nostrils, with the top of her eyelids, the lobes of her ears, the palms of her hands, the tips of her fingers, were tinted with a glowing and provoking touch of color. Above all, she wore an expression of implacable determination to be beautiful. This reached the point of ferocity. She was like a panther, with the power of turning cat at will, and caressing. One of her eyes was blue, the other black.

Gwynplaine, as well as Ursus, contemplated her.

The Green Box somewhat resembled a phantasmagoria in its representations. *Chaos Vanquished* was rather a dream than a piece; it generally produced on the audience the effect of a vision. Now, this effect was reflected on the actors. The house took the performers by surprise, and they were thunderstruck in their turn. It was a rebound of fascination.

The woman watched them, and they watched her.

At the distance at which they were placed, and in that luminous mist which is the half-light of a theater, details were lost, and it was like a hallucination. Of course it was a woman, but was it not a chimera as well? The penetration of her light into their obscurity stupefied them. It was like the appearance of an unknown planet. It came from a world of the happy. Her irradiation amplified her figure. The lady was covered with nocturnal glitterings, like a milky way. Her precious stones were stars. The diamond brooch was perhaps a pleiad. The splendid beauty of her bosom seemed supernatural. They felt, as they looked upon the star-like creature, the momentary but thrilling approach of the regions of felicity. It was out of the heights of a Paradise that she leant toward their mean-looking Green Box, and revealed to the gaze of its wretched audience her expression of inexorable serenity. As she satisfied her unbounded curiosity, she fed at the same time the curiosity of the public.

It was the Zenith permitting the Abyss to look at it.

Ursus, Gwynplaine, Vinos, Fibi, the crowd, everyone had succumbed to her dazzling beauty, except Dea, ignorant in her darkness.

An apparition was indeed before them; but none of the ideas usually evoked by the word were realized in the lady's appearance.

There was nothing about her diaphanous, nothing undecided, nothing floating, no mist. She was an apparition; rose-colored and fresh, and full of health. Yet, under the optical condition in which Ursus and Gwynplaine were placed, she looked like a vision. There are fleshy phantoms, called vampires. Such a queen as she, though a spirit to the crowd, consumes twelve hundred thousand a year, to keep her health.

Behind the lady, in the shadow, her page was to be perceived, *el mozo*, a little child-like man, fair and pretty, with a serious face. A very young and very grave servant was the fashion at that period. This page was dressed from top to toe in scarlet velvet, and had on his skull-cap, which was embroidered with gold, a bunch of curled feathers. This was the sign of a high class of service, and indicated attendance on a very great lady.

The lackey is part of the lord, and it was impossible not to remark, in the shadow of his mistress, the train-bearing page. Memory often takes notes unconsciously; and, without Gwynplaine's suspecting it, the round cheeks, the serious mien, the embroidered and plumed cap of the lady's page left some trace on his mind. The page, however, did nothing to call attention to himself. To do so is to be wanting in respect. He held himself aloof and passive at the back of the box, retiring as far as the closed door permitted.

Notwithstanding the presence of her train-bearer, the lady was not the less alone in the compartment, since a valet counts for nothing.

However powerful a diversion had been produced by this person, who produced the effect of a personage, the dénouement of *Chaos Vanquished* was more powerful still. The impression which it made was, as usual, irresistible. Perhaps, even, there occurred in the hall, on account of the radiant spectator (for sometimes the spectator is part of the spectacle), an increase of electricity. The contagion of Gwynplaine's laugh was more triumphant than ever. The whole audience fell into an indescribable epilepsy of hilarity, through which could be distinguished the sonorous and magisterial ha! ha! of Tom-Jim-Jack.

Only the unknown lady looked at the performance with the immobility of a statue, and with her eyes, like those of a phantom, she laughed not. A specter, but sun-born.

The performance over, the platform drawn up, and the family reassembled in the Green Box, Ursus opened and emptied on the supper-table the bag of receipts. From a heap of pennies, there slid suddenly forth a Spanish gold onza.

"Hers!" cried Ursus.

The onza amidst the pence covered with verdigris was a type of the lady amidst the crowd.

"She has paid an onza for her seat," cried Ursus, with enthusiasm.

Just then the hotel-keeper entered the Green Box, and, passing his arm out of the window at the back of it, opened the loophole in the wall of which we have already spoken, which gave a view over the field, and which was level with the window; then he made a silent sign to Ursus to look out. A carriage, swarming with plumed footmen carrying torches and magnificently appointed, was driving off at a fast trot.

Ursus took the piece of gold between his forefinger and thumb respectfully, and, showing it to Master Nicless, said—

"She is a goddess."

Then his eyes falling on the carriage which was about to turn the corner of the field, and on the imperial of which the footmen's torches lighted up a golden coronet, with eight strawberry leaves, he exclaimed—

"She is more. She is a duchess."

The carriage disappeared. The rumbling of its wheels died away in the distance.

Ursus remained some moments in an ecstasy, holding the gold piece between his finger and thumb, as in a monstrance, elevating it as the priest elevates the host.

Then he placed it on the table, and, as he contemplated it, began to talk of "Madam."

The inn-keeper replied—

"She was a duchess." Yes. They knew her title. But her name? Of that they were ignorant. Master Nicless had been close to the carriage, and seen the coat-of-arms and the footmen covered with lace. The coachman had a wig on which might have belonged to a Lord Chancellor. The carriage was of that rare design called, in Spain, *cochetumbon*, a splendid build, with a top like a tomb, which makes a magnificent support for a coronet. The page was a man in miniature, so small that he could sit on the step of the carriage outside the door. The duty of those pretty creatures was to bear the trains of their mistresses. They also bore their messages. And did you remark the plumed cap of the page? How grand it was! You pay a fine if you wear those plumes without the right of doing so. Master Nicless had seen the lady, too, quite close. A kind of queen. Such wealth gives beauty. The skin is whiter, the eye more proud, the gait more noble, and grace more insolent. Nothing can equal the elegant impertinence of hands which never work. Master Nicless told the story of all the magnificence of the white skin with the blue veins, the neck, the shoulders, the arms, the touch of paint everywhere, the pearl earrings, the headdress powdered with gold, the profusion of stones, the rubies, the diamonds.

"Less brilliant than her eyes," murmured Ursus.

Gwynplaine said nothing.

Dea listened.

"And do you know," said the tavern-keeper, "the most wonderful thing of all?"

"What?" said Ursus.

"I saw her get into her carriage."

"What then?"

"She did not get in alone."

"Nonsense!"

"Someone got in with her."

"Who?"

"Guess."

"The king," said Ursus.

"In the first place," said Master Nicless, "there is no king at present. We are not living under a king. Guess who got into the carriage with the duchess."

"Jupiter," said Ursus.

The hotel-keeper replied—

"Tom-Jim-Jack!"

Gwynplaine, who had not said a word, broke silence.

"Tom-Jim-Jack!" he cried.

There was a pause of astonishment, during which the low voice of Dea was heard to say—

"Cannot this woman be prevented coming?"

Chapter VIII

SYMPTOMS OF POISONING

THE "APPARITION" DID NOT RETURN. IT DID NOT REAPPEAR IN THE THEATER, BUT IT REAPPEARED to the memory of Gwynplaine. Gwynplaine was, to a certain degree, troubled. It seemed to him that for the first time in his life he had seen a woman.

He made that first stumble, a strange dream. We should beware of the nature of the reveries that fasten on us. Reverie has in it the mystery and subtlety of an odor. It is to thought what perfume is to the tuberose. It is at times the exudation of a venomous idea, and it penetrates like a vapor. You may poison yourself with reveries, as with flowers. An intoxicating suicide, exquisite and malignant. The suicide of the soul is evil thought. In it is the poison. Reverie attracts, cajoles, lures, entwines, and then makes you its accomplice. It makes you bear your half in the trickeries which it plays on conscience. It charms; then it corrupts you. We may say of reverie as of play, one begins by being a dupe, and ends by being a cheat.

Gwynplaine dreamed.

He had never before seen Woman. He had seen the shadow in the women of the populace, and he had seen the soul in Dea.

He had just seen the reality.

A warm and living skin, under which one felt the circulation of passionate blood; an outline with the precision of marble and the undulation of the wave; a high and impassive mien, mingling refusal with attraction, and summing itself up in its own glory; hair of the color of the reflection from a furnace; a gallantry of adornment producing in herself and in others a tremor of voluptuousness, the half-revealed nudity betraying a disdainful desire to be coveted at a distance by the crowd; an irradicable coquetry; the charm of impenetrability, temptation seasoned by the glimpse of perdition, a promise to the senses and a menace to the mind; a double anxiety, the one desire, the other fear. He had just seen these things. He had just seen Woman.

He had seen more and less than a woman; he had seen a female.

And at the same time an Olympian. The female of a god.

The mystery of sex had just been revealed to him.

And where? On inaccessible heights—at an infinite distance.

O mocking destiny! The soul, that celestial essence, he possessed; he held it in his hand. It was Dea. Sex, that terrestrial embodiment, he perceived in the heights of heaven. It was that woman.

A duchess!

"More than a goddess," Ursus had said.

What a precipice! Even dreams dissolved before such a perpendicular height to escalade.

Was he going to commit the folly of dreaming about the unknown beauty?

He debated with himself.

He recalled all that Ursus had said of high stations which are almost royal. The philosopher's disquisitions, which had hitherto seemed so useless, now became landmarks for his thoughts. A very thin layer of forgetfulness often lies over our memory, through which at times we catch a glimpse of all beneath it. His fancy ran on that august world, the peerage, to which the lady belonged, and which was so inexorably placed above the inferior world, the common people, of which he was one.

And was he even one of the people? Was not he, the mountebank, below the lowest of the low? For the first time since he had arrived at the age of reflection, he felt his heart vaguely contracted by a sense of his baseness, and of that which we nowadays call abasement. The paintings and the catalogues of Ursus, his lyrical inventories, his dithyrambics of castles, parks, fountains, and colonnades, his catalogues of riches and of power, revived in the memory of Gwynplaine in the relief of reality mingled with mist. He was possessed with the image of this zenith. That a man should be a lord!—it seemed chimerical. It was so, however. Incredible thing! There were lords! But were they of flesh and blood, like ourselves? It seemed doubtful. He felt that he lay at the bottom of all darkness, encompassed by a wall, while he could just perceive in the far distance above his head, through the mouth of the pit, a dazzling confusion of azure, of figures, and of rays, which was Olympus. In the midst of this glory the duchess shone out resplendent.

He felt for this woman a strange, inexpressible longing, combined with a conviction of the impossibility of attainment. This poignant contradiction returned to his mind again and again, notwithstanding every effort. He saw near to him, even within his reach, in close and tangible reality, the soul; and in the unattainable—in the depths of the ideal—the flesh. None of these thoughts attained to certain shape. They were as a vapor within him, changing every instant its form, and floating away. But the darkness which the vapor caused was intense.

He did not form even in his dreams any hope of reaching the heights where the duchess dwelt. Luckily for him.

The vibration of such ladders of fancy, if ever we put our foot upon them, may render our brains dizzy forever. Intending to scale Olympus, we reach Bedlam; any distinct feeling of actual desire would have terrified him. He entertained none of that nature.

Besides, was he likely ever to see the lady again? Most probably not. To fall in love with a passing light on the horizon, madness cannot reach to that pitch. To make loving eyes at a star even, is not incomprehensible. It is seen again, it reappears, it is fixed in the sky. But can anyone be enamored of a flash of lightning?

Dreams flowed and ebbed within him. The majestic and gallant idol at the back of the box had cast a light over his diffused ideas, then faded away. He thought, yet thought not of it; turned to other things—returned to it. It rocked about in his brain—nothing more. It broke his sleep for several nights. Sleeplessness is as full of dreams as sleep.

It is almost impossible to express in their exact limits the abstract evolutions of the brain. The inconvenience of words is that they are more marked in form than ideas. All ideas have indistinct boundary lines, words have not. A certain diffused phase of the soul ever escapes words. Expression has its frontiers, thought has none.

The depths of our secret souls are so vast that Gwynplaine's dreams scarcely touched Dea. Dea reigned sacred in the center of his soul; nothing could approach her.

Still (for such contradictions make up the soul of man), there was a conflict within him. Was he conscious of it? Scarcely.

In his heart of hearts he felt a collision of desires. We all have our weak points. Its nature would have been clear to Ursus; but to Gwynplaine it was not.

Two instincts—one the ideal, the other sexual—were struggling within him. Such contests occur between the angels of light and darkness on the edge of the abyss.

At length the angel of darkness was overthrown. One day Gwynplaine suddenly thought no more of the unknown woman.

The struggle between two principles—the duel between his earthly and his heavenly nature—had taken place within his soul, and at such a depth that he had understood it but dimly. One thing was certain, that he had never for one moment ceased to adore Dea.

He had been attacked by a violent disorder, his blood had been fevered; but it was over. Dea alone remained.

Gwynplaine would have been much astonished had anyone told him that Dea had ever been, even for a moment, in danger; and in a week or two the phantom which had threatened the hearts of both their souls faded away.

Within Gwynplaine nothing remained but the heart, which was the hearth, and the love, which was its fire.

Besides, we have just said that "the duchess" did not return.

Ursus thought it all very natural. "The lady with the gold piece" is a phenomenon. She enters, pays, and vanishes. It would be too much joy were she to return.

As to Dea, she made no allusion to the woman who had come and passed away. She listened, perhaps, and was sufficiently enlightened by the sighs of Ursus, and now and then by some significant exclamation, such as—

"One does not get ounces of gold every day!"

She spoke no more of "the woman." This showed deep instinct. The soul takes obscure precautions, in the secrets of which it is not always admitted itself. To keep silence about anyone seems to keep them afar off. One fears that questions may call them back. We put silence between us, as if we were shutting a door.

So the incident fell into oblivion.

Was it ever anything? Had it ever occurred? Could it be said that a shadow had floated between Gwynplaine and Dea? Dea did not know of it, nor Gwynplaine either. No; nothing had occurred. The duchess herself was blurred in the distant perspective like an illusion. It had been but a momentary dream passing over Gwynplaine, out of which he had awakened.

When it fades away, a reverie, like a mist, leaves no trace behind; and when the cloud has passed on, love shines out as brightly in the heart as the sun in the sky.

Chapter IX

ABYSSUS ABYSSUM VOCAT

ANOTHER FACE DISAPPEARED; TOM-JIM-JACK'S. SUDDENLY HE CEASED TO FREQUENT THE TAD-caster Inn.

Persons so situated as to be able to observe other phases of fashionable life in London, might have seen that about this time the *Weekly Gazette*, between two extracts from parish registers, announced the departure of Lord David Dirry-Moir, by order of her Majesty, to take command of his frigate in the white squadron then cruising off the coast of Holland.

Ursus, perceiving that Tom-Jim-Jack did not return, was troubled by his absence. He had not seen Tom-Jim-Jack since the day on which he had driven off in the same carriage with the lady of the gold piece. It was, indeed, an enigma who this Tom-Jim-Jack could be, who carried off duchesses under his arm. What an interesting investigation! What questions to propound! What things to be said. Therefore Ursus said not a word.

Ursus, who had had experience, knew the smart caused by rash curiosity. Curiosity ought always to be proportioned to the curious. By listening, we risk our ear; by watching, we risk our eye. Prudent people neither hear nor see. Tom-Jim-Jack had got into a princely carriage. The tavern-keeper had seen him. It appeared so extraordinary that the sailor should sit by the lady that it made Ursus circumspect. The caprices of those in high life ought to be sacred to the lower orders. The reptiles called the poor had best squat in their holes when they see anything out of the way. Quiescence is a power. Shut your eyes, if you have not the luck to be blind; stop up your ears, if you have not the good fortune to be deaf; paralyze your tongue, if you have not the perfection of being mute. The great do what they like, the little what they can. Let the unknown pass unnoticed. Do not importune mythology. Do not interrogate appearances. Have a profound respect for idols. Do not let us direct our gossiping toward the lessenings or increasings which take place in superior regions, of the motives of which we are ignorant. Such things are mostly optical delusions to us inferior creatures. Metamorphoses are the business of the gods: the transformations and the contingent disorders of great persons who float above us are clouds impossible to comprehend, and perilous to study. Too much attention irritates the Olympians engaged in their gyrations of amusement or fancy; and a thunderbolt may teach you that the bull you are too curiously examining is Jupiter. Do not lift the folds of the stone-colored mantles of those terrible powers. Indifference is intelligence. Do not stir and you will be safe. Feign death, and they will not kill you. Therein lies the wisdom of the insect. Ursus practiced it.

The tavern-keeper, who was puzzled as well, questioned Ursus one day.

"Do you observe that Tom-Jim-Jack never comes here now?"

"Indeed!" said Ursus. "I have not remarked it."

Master Nicless made an observation in an undertone, no doubt touching the intimacy between the ducal carriage and Tom-Jim-Jack; a remark which, as it might have been irreverent and dangerous, Ursus took care not to hear.

Still Ursus was too much of an artist not to regret Tom-Jim-Jack. He felt some disappointment. He told his feeling to Homo, of whose discretion alone he felt certain. He whispered into the ear of the wolf, "Since Tom-Jim-Jack ceased to come, I feel a blank as a man, and a chill as a poet." This pouring out of his heart to a friend relieved Ursus.

His lips were sealed before Gwynplaine, who, however, made no allusion to Tom-Jim-Jack. The fact was that Tom-Jim-Jack's presence or absence mattered not to Gwynplaine, absorbed as he was in Dea.

Forgetfulness fell more and more on Gwynplaine. As for Dea, she had not even suspected the existence of a vague trouble. At the same time, no more cabals or complaints against the Laughing Man were spoken of. Hate seemed to have let go its hold. All was tranquil in and around the Green Box. No more opposition from strollers, merry-andrews, nor priests; no more grumbling outside. Their success was unclouded. Destiny allows of such sudden serenity. The brilliant happiness of Gwynplaine and Dea was for the present absolutely cloudless. Little by little it had risen to a degree which admitted of no increase. There is one word which expresses the situation: apogee. Happiness, like the sea, has its high tide. The worst thing for the perfectly happy, is that it recedes.

There are two ways of being inaccessible; being too high and being too low. At least as much, perhaps, as the first is the second to be desired. More surely than the eagle escapes the arrow, the animalcule escapes being crushed. This security of insignificance, if it had ever existed on earth, was enjoyed by Gwynplaine and Dea, and never before had it been so complete. They lived on, daily more and more ecstatically wrapped in each other. The heart saturates itself with love as with a divine salt that preserves it, and from this arises the incorruptible constancy of those who have loved each other from the dawn of their lives, and the affection which keeps its freshness in old age. There is such a thing as the embalmment of the heart. It is of Daphnis and Chloë that Philemon and Baucis are made. The old age, of which we speak, evening resembling morning, was evidently reserved for Gwynplaine and Dea. In the meantime they were young.

Ursus looked on this love as a doctor examines his case. He had what was in those days termed a hippocratical expression of face. He fixed his sagacious eyes on Dea, fragile and pale, and growled out, "It is lucky that she is happy." At other times he said, "She is lucky for her health's sake." He shook his head, and at times read attentively a portion treating of heart-disease in Aviccunas, translated by Vossiscus Fortunatus, Louvain, 1650, an old wormeaten book of his.

Dea, when fatigued, suffered from perspirations and drowsiness, and took a daily *siesta*, as we have already seen. One day, while she was lying asleep on the bear-skin, Gwynplaine was out, and Ursus bent down softly and applied his ear to Dea's heart. He seemed to listen for a few minutes, and then stood up, murmuring, "She must not have any shock. It would find out the weak place."

The crowd continued to flock to the performance of *Chaos Vanquished*. The success of the Laughing Man seemed inexhaustible. Everyone rushed to see him; no longer from Southwark only, but even from other parts of London. The general public began to mingle with the usual audience, which no longer consisted of sailors and drivers only; in the opinion of Master Nicless, who was well acquainted with crowds, there were in the crowd gentlemen and baronets disguised as common people. Disguise is one of the pleasures of pride, and was much in fashion at that period. This mixing of the aristocratic element with the mob was a good sign, and showed that their popularity was extending to London. The fame of Gwynplaine has decidedly penetrated into the great world. Such was the fact. Nothing was talked of but the Laughing Man. He was talked about even at the Mohawk Club, frequented by noblemen.

In the Green Box they had no idea of all this. They were content to be happy. It was intoxication to Dea to feel, as she did every evening, the crisp and tawny head of Gwynplaine. In love there is nothing like habit. The whole of life is concentrated in it. The reappearance of the stars is the custom of the universe. Creation is nothing but a mistress, and the sun is a lover. Light is a dazzling caryatid supporting the world. Each day, for a sublime minute, the earth covered by night rests on the rising sun. Dea, blind, felt a like return of warmth and hope within her when she placed her hand on the head of Gwynplaine.

To adore each other in the shadows, to love in the plenitude of silence; who could not become reconciled to such an eternity?

One evening Gwynplaine, feeling within him that overflow of felicity which, like the intoxication of perfumes, causes a sort of delicious faintness, was strolling, as he usually did after the performance, in the meadow some hundred paces from the Green Box. Sometimes in those high tides of feeling in our souls we feel that we would fain pour out the sensations of the overflowing heart. The night was dark but clear. The stars were shining. The whole fairground was deserted. Sleep and forgetfulness reigned in the caravans which were scattered over Tarrinzeau Field.

One light alone was unextinguished. It was the lamp of the Tadcaster Inn, the door of which was left ajar to admit Gwynplaine on his return.

Midnight had just struck in the five parishes of Southwark, with the breaks and differences of tone of their various bells. Gwynplaine was dreaming of Dea. Of whom else should he dream? But that evening, feeling singularly troubled, and full of a charm which was at the same time a pang, he thought of Dea as a man thinks of a woman. He reproached himself for this. It seemed to be failing in respect to her. The husband's attack was forming dimly within him. Sweet and imperious impatience! He was crossing the invisible frontier, on this side of which is the virgin, on the other, the wife. He questioned himself anxiously. A blush, as it were, overspread his mind. The Gwynplaine of long ago had been transformed, by degrees, unconsciously in a mysterious growth. His old modesty was becoming misty and uneasy. We have an ear of light, into which speaks the spirit; and an ear of darkness, into which speaks the instinct. Into the latter strange voices were making their proposals. However pure-minded may be the youth who dreams of love, a certain grossness of the flesh eventually comes between his dream and him. Intentions lose their transparency. The unavowed desire implanted by nature enters into his conscience. Gwynplaine felt an indescribable yearning of the flesh, which abounds in all temptation, and Dea was scarcely flesh. In this fever, which he knew to be unhealthy, he transfigured Dea into a more material aspect, and tried to exaggerate her seraphic form into feminine loveliness. It is thou, O woman, that we require.

Love comes not to permit too much of paradise. It requires the fevered skin, the troubled life, the unbound hair, the kiss electrical and irreparable, the clasp of desire. The sidereal is embarrassing, the ethereal is heavy. Too much of the heavenly in love is like too much fuel on a fire: the flame suffers from it. Gwynplaine fell into an exquisite nightmare; Dea to be clasped in his arms—Dea clasped in them! He heard nature in his heart crying out for a Woman. Like a Pygmalion in a dream modeling a Galatea out of the azure, in the depths of his soul he worked at the chaste contour of Dea—a contour with too much of heaven, too little of Eden. For Eden is Eve, and Eve was a female, a carnal mother, a terrestrial nurse; the sacred womb of generations; the breast of unfailing milk; the rocker of the cradle of the newborn world, and wings are incompatible with the bosom of woman. Virginity is but the hope of maternity. Still, in Gwynplaine's dreams, Dea, until now, had been enthroned above flesh. Now, however, he made wild efforts in thought to draw her downwards by that thread, sex, which ties every girl to earth. Not one of those birds is free. Dea, like all the rest, was within this law; and Gwynplaine, though he scarcely acknowledged it, felt a vague desire that she should submit to it. This desire possessed him in spite of himself, and with an ever-recurring relapse. He pictured Dea as woman. He came to the point of regarding her under a hitherto unheard-of form; as a creature no longer of ecstasy only, but of voluptuousness; as Dea, with her head resting on the pillow. He was ashamed of this visionary desecration. It was like an attempt at profanation. He resisted its assault. He turned from it, but it returned again. He felt as if he were committing a criminal assault. To him, Dea was encompassed by a cloud. Cleaving that cloud, he shuddered, as though he were raising her chemise. It was in April. The spine has its dreams. He rambled at random with the uncertain step caused by solitude. To have no one by is a provocative to wander. Whither flew his thoughts? He would not have dared to own it to himself. To heaven? No. To a bed. You were looking down upon him, O ye stars.

Why talk of a man in love? Rather say a man possessed. To be possessed by the devil, is the exception; to be possessed by a woman, the rule. Every man has to bear this alienation of himself. What a sorceress is a pretty woman! The true name of love is captivity.

Man is made prisoner by the soul of a woman; by her flesh as well, and sometimes even more by the flesh than by the soul. The soul is the true-love, the flesh, the mistress.

We slander the devil. It was not he who tempted Eve. It was Eve who tempted him. The woman began. Lucifer was passing by quietly. He perceived the woman, and became Satan.

The flesh is the cover of the unknown. It is provocative (which is strange) by its modesty. Nothing could be more distracting. It is full of shame, the hussey!

It was the terrible love of the surface which was then agitating Gwynplaine, and holding him in its power. Fearful the moment in which man covets the nakedness of woman. What dark things lurk beneath the fairness of Venus!

Something within him was calling Dea aloud, Dea the maiden, Dea the other half of a man, Dea flesh and blood, Dea with uncovered bosom. That cry was almost driving away the angel. Mysterious crisis through which all love must pass and in which the Ideal is in danger! Therein is the predestination of Creation. Moment of heavenly corruption! Gwynplaine's love of Dea was becoming nuptial. Virgin love is but a transition. The moment was come. Gwynplaine coveted the woman.

He coveted a woman!

Precipice of which one sees but the first gentle slope!

The indistinct summons of nature is inexorable. The whole of woman, what an abyss!

Luckily, there was no woman for Gwynplaine but Dea. The only one he desired, the only one who could desire him.

Gwynplaine felt that vague and mighty shudder which is the vital claim of infinity. Besides there was the aggravation of the spring. He was breathing the nameless odors of the starry darkness. He walked forward in a wild feeling of delight. The wandering perfumes of the rising sap, the heady irradiations which float in shadow, the distant opening of nocturnal flowers, the complicity of little hidden nests, the murmurs of waters and of leaves, soft sighs rising from all things, the freshness, the warmth, and the mysterious awakening of April and May, is the vast diffusion of sex murmuring, in whispers, their proposals of voluptuousness, till the soul stammers in answer to the giddy provocation. The ideal no longer knows what it is saying.

Anyone observing Gwynplaine walk would have said, "See!—a drunken man!"

He almost staggered under the weight of his own heart, of spring and of the night.

The solitude in the bowling-green was so peaceful that at times he spoke aloud. The consciousness that there is no listener induces speech.

He walked with slow steps, his head bent down, his hands behind him, the left hand in the right, the fingers open.

Suddenly he felt something slipped between his fingers.

He turned round quickly.

In his hand was a paper, and in front of him a man.

It was the man who, coming behind him with the stealth of a cat, had placed the paper in his fingers.

The paper was a letter.

The man, as he appeared pretty clearly in the starlight, was small, chubby-cheeked, young, sedate, and dressed in a scarlet livery, exposed from top to toe through the opening of a long gray cloak, then called a capenoche, a Spanish word contracted; in French it was *cape-de-nuit*. His head was covered by a crimson cap, like the skull-cap of a cardinal, on which servitude was indicated by a strip of lace. On this cap was a plume of tissern feathers. He stood motionless before Gwynplaine, like a dark outline in a dream.

Gwynplaine recognized the duchess's page.

Before Gwynplaine could utter an exclamation of surprise, he heard the thin voice of the page, at once childlike and feminine in its tone, saying to him—

"At this hour to-morrow, be at the corner of London Bridge. I will be there to conduct you—"

"Whither?" demanded Gwynplaine.

"Where you are expected."

Gwynplaine dropped his eyes on the letter, which he was holding mechanically in his hand.

When he looked up, the page was no longer with him.

He perceived a vague form lessening rapidly in the distance. It was the little valet. He turned the corner of the street, and solitude reigned again.

Gwynplaine saw the page vanish, then looked at the letter. There are moments in our lives when what happens seems not to happen. Stupor keeps us for a moment at a distance from the fact.

Gwynplaine raised the letter to his eyes, as if to read it, but soon perceived that he could not do so for two reasons—first, because he had not broken the seal; and, secondly, because it was too dark.

It was some minutes before he remembered that there was a lamp at the inn. He took a few steps sideways, as if he knew not whither he was going.

A somnambulist, to whom a phantom had given a letter, might walk as he did.

At last he made up his mind. He ran, rather than walked, toward the inn, stood in the light which broke through the half-open door, and by it again examined the closed letter. There was no design on the seal, and on the envelope was written, "*To Gwynplaine.*" He broke the seal, tore the envelope, unfolded the letter, put it directly under the light, and read as follows—

You are hideous; I am beautiful. You are a player; I am a duchess. I am the highest; you are the lowest. I desire you! I love you! Come!

BOOK THE FOURTH

THE CELL OF TORTURE

Chapter I

THE TEMPTATION OF ST. GWYNPLAINE

ONE JET OF FLAME HARDLY MAKES A PRICK IN THE DARKNESS: ANOTHER SETS FIRE TO A VOLCANO. Some sparks are gigantic.

Gwynplaine read the letter, then he read it over again. Yes, the words were there, "I love you!" Terrors chased each other through his mind.

The first was, that he believed himself to be mad.

He was mad; that was certain. He had just seen what had no existence. The twilight specters were making game of him, poor wretch! The little man in scarlet was the will-o'-the-wisp of a dream. Sometimes, at night, nothings condensed into flame come and laugh at us. Having had his laugh out, the visionary being had disappeared, and left Gwynplaine behind him, mad.

Such are the freaks of darkness.

The second terror was, to find out that he was in his right senses.

A vision? Certainly not. How could that be? Had he not a letter in his hand? Did he not see an envelope, a seal, paper, and writing? Did he not know from whom that came? It was all clear enough. Someone took a pen and ink, and wrote. Someone lighted a taper, and sealed it with wax. Was not his name written on the letter— *"To Gwynplaine?"* The paper was scented. All was clear.

Gwynplaine knew the little man. The dwarf was a page. The gleam was a livery. The page had given him a rendezvous for the same hour on the morrow, at the corner of London Bridge.

Was London Bridge an illusion?

No, no. All was clear. There was no delirium. All was reality. Gwynplaine was perfectly clear in his intellect. It was not a phantasmagoria, suddenly dissolving above his head, and fading into nothingness. It was something which had really happened to him. No, Gwynplaine was not mad, nor was he dreaming. Again he read the letter.

Well, yes! But then?

That then was terror-striking.

There was a woman who desired him! If so, let no one ever again pronounce the word incredible! A woman desire him! A woman who had seen his face! A woman who was not blind! And who was this woman? An ugly one? No; a beauty. A gypsy? No; a duchess!

What was it all about; and what could it all mean? What peril in such a triumph! And how was he to help plunging into it headlong?

What! that woman! The siren, the apparition, the lady in the visionary box, the light in the darkness! It was she! Yes; it was she!

The crackling of the fire burst out in every part of his frame. It was the strange, unknown lady, she who had previously so troubled his thoughts; and his first tumultuous feelings about this woman returned, heated by the evil fire. Forgetfulness is nothing but a palimpsest: an incident happens unexpectedly, and all that was effaced revives in the blanks of wondering memory.

Gwynplaine thought that he had dismissed that image from his remembrance, and he found that it was still there; and she had put her mark in his brain, unconsciously guilty of a dream. Without his suspecting it the lines of the engraving had been bitten deep by reverie. And now a certain amount of evil had been done, and this train of thought, thenceforth, perhaps, irreparable, he took up again eagerly. What! she desired him! What! the princess descend from her throne, the idol from its shrine, the statue from its pedestal, the phantom from its cloud! What! from the depths of the impossible had this chimera come! This deity of the sky! This irradiation! This nereid all glistening with jewels! This proud and unattainable beauty, from the height of her radiant throne, was bending down to Gwynplaine! What! had she drawn up her chariot of the dawn, with its yoke of turtle-doves and dragons, before Gwynplaine, and said to him, "Come!" What! this terrible glory of being the object of such abasement from the empyrean, for Gwynplaine! This woman, if he could give that name to a form so starlike and majestic, this woman proposed herself, gave herself, delivered herself up to him! Wonder of wonders! A goddess prostituting herself for him! The arms of a courtesan opening in a cloud to clasp him to the bosom of a goddess, and that without degradation! Such majestic creatures cannot be sullied. The gods bathe themselves pure in light; and this goddess who came to him knew what she was doing. She was not ignorant of the incarnate hideousness of Gwynplaine. She had seen the mask which was his face; and that mask had not caused her to draw back. Gwynplaine was loved notwithstanding it!

Here was a thing surpassing all the extravagance of dreams. He was loved in consequence of his mask. Far from repulsing the goddess, the mask attracted her. Gwynplaine was not only loved, he was desired. He was more than accepted, he was chosen. He, chosen!

What! there, where this woman dwelt, in the regal region of irresponsible splendor, and in the power of full, free will; where there were princes, and she could take a prince; nobles, and she could take a noble; where there were men handsome, charming, magnificent, and she could take an Adonis: whom did she take? Gnafron! She could choose from the midst of meteors and thunders, the mighty six-winged seraphim, and she chose the larva crawling in the slime. On one side were highnesses and peers, all grandeur, all opulence, all glory. On the other, a mountebank. The mountebank carried it! What kind of scales could there be in the heart of this woman? By what measure did she weigh her love? She took off her ducal coronet, and flung it on the platform of a clown! She took from her brow the Olympian aureola, and placed it on the bristly head of a gnome! The world had turned topsy turvy. The insects swarmed on high, the stars were scattered below, whilst the wonder-stricken Gwynplaine, overwhelmed by a falling ruin of light and lying in the dust, was enshrined in a glory. One all-powerful, revolting against beauty and splendor, gave herself to the damned of night; preferred Gwynplaine to Antinoüs; excited by curiosity, she entered the shadows, and descending within them, and from this abdication of goddess-ship was rising, crowned and prodigious, the royalty of the wretched. "You are hideous. I love you." These words touched Gwynplaine in the ugly spot of pride. Pride is the heel in which all heroes are vulnerable. Gwynplaine was flattered in his vanity as a monster. He was loved for his deformity. He, too, was the Exception, as much and perhaps more than the Jupiters and the Apollos. He felt superhuman, and so much a monster as to be a god. Fearful bewilderment!

Now, who was this woman? What did he know about her? Everything and nothing. She was a duchess, that he knew; he knew, also, that she was beautiful and rich; that she had liveries, lackeys, pages, and footmen running with torches by the side of her coroneted carriage. He knew that she was in love with him; at least she said so. Of everything else he was ignorant. He knew her title, but not her name. He knew her thought; he knew not her life. Was she married, widow, maiden? Was she free? Of what family was she? Were there snares, traps, dangers about her? Of the gallantry existing on the idle heights of society; the caves on those summits, in which savage charmers dream amid the scattered skeletons of the loves which they have already preyed on; of the extent of tragic cynicism to which the experiments of a woman may attain who believes herself to be beyond the reach of man; of things such as these Gwynplaine had no idea. Nor had he even in his mind materials out of which to build up a conjecture, information concerning such things being very scanty in the social depths in which he lived. Still he detected a shadow; he felt that a mist hung over all this brightness. Did he understand it? No. Could he guess at it? Still less. What was there behind that letter? One pair of folding doors opening before him, another closing on him, and causing him a vague anxiety. On the one side an avowal; on the other an enigma. Avowal and enigma, which, like two mouths, one tempting, the other threatening, pronounce the same word: Dare!

Never had perfidious chance taken its measures better, nor timed more fitly the moment of temptation. Gwynplaine, stirred by spring, and by the sap rising in all things, was prompt to dream the dream of the flesh. The old man who is not to be stamped out, and over whom none of us can triumph, was awaking in that backward youth, still a boy at twenty-four.

It was just then, at the most stormy moment of the crisis, that the offer was made him, and the naked bosom of the Sphinx appeared before his dazzled eyes. Youth is an inclined plane. Gwynplaine was stooping, and something pushed him forward. What? the season and the night. Who? the woman.

Were there no month of April, man would be a great deal more virtuous. The budding plants are a set of accomplices! Love is the thief, Spring the receiver.

Gwynplaine was shaken.

There is a kind of smoke of evil, preceding sin, in which the conscience cannot breathe. The obscure nausea of hell comes over virtue in temptation. The yawning abyss discharges an exhalation which warns the strong, and turns the weak giddy. Gwynplaine was suffering its mysterious attack.

Dilemmas, transient and at the same time stubborn, were floating before him. Sin, presenting itself obstinately again and again to his mind, was taking form. The morrow, midnight? London Bridge, the page? Should he go? "Yes," cried the flesh; "no," cried the soul.

Nevertheless, we must remark that, strange as it may appear at first sight, he never once put himself the question: "Should he go?" quite distinctly. Reprehensible actions are like over-strong brandies; you cannot swallow them at a draft. You put down your glass; you will see to it presently; there is a strange taste even about that first drop. One thing is certain: he felt something behind him pushing him forward toward the unknown. And he trembled. He could catch a glimpse of a crumbling precipice, and he drew back, stricken by the terror encircling him. He closed his eyes. He tried hard to deny to himself that the adventure had ever occurred, and to persuade himself into doubting his reason. This was evidently his best plan; the wisest thing he could do was to believe himself mad.

Fatal fever! Every man, surprised by the unexpected, has at times felt the throb of such tragic pulsations. The observer ever listens with anxiety to the echoes resounding from the dull strokes of the battering-ram of destiny striking against a conscience.

Alas! Gwynplaine put himself questions. Where duty is clear, to put one's self questions is to suffer defeat.

One detail, however, is noteworthy; the effrontery of the adventure, which might, perhaps, have shocked a depraved man, never struck him. He was utterly unconscious of what cynicism is composed. He had no idea of prostitution as referred to above. He had not the power to conceive it. He was too pure to admit complicated hypoteheses. He saw but the grandeur of the woman. Alas! he felt flattered. His vanity assured him of victory only. To dream that he was the object of unchaste desire, rather than of love, would have required much greater wit than innocence possesses. Close to *I love you*, he could not perceive the frightful corrective, *I desire you*. He could not grasp the animal side of the goddess's nature.

There are invasions which the mind may have to suffer. There are the Vandals of the soul, evil thoughts coming to devastate our virtue. A thousand contrary ideas rushed into Gwynplaine's brain, now following each other singly, now crowding together. Then silence reigned again, and he would lean his head on his hands, in a kind of mournful attention, as of one who contemplates a landscape by night.

Suddenly he felt that he was no longer thinking. His reverie had reached that point of utter darkness in which all things disappear.

He remembered, too, that he had not entered the inn. It might be about two o'clock in the morning.

He placed the letter which the page had brought him in his side-pocket, but perceiving that it was next his heart, he drew it out again, crumpled it up, and placed it in a pocket of his hose. He then directed his steps toward the inn, which he entered stealthily, and without awaking little Govicum, who, while waiting up for him, had fallen asleep on the table, with his arms for a pillow. He closed the door, lighted a candle at the lamp, fastened the bolt, turned the key in the lock, taking, mechanically, all the precautions usual to a man returning home late, ascended the staircase of the Green Box, slipped into the old hovel which he used as a bedroom, looked at Ursus, who was asleep, blew out his candle, and did not go to bed.

Thus an hour passed away. Weary, at length, and fancying that bed and sleep were one, he laid his head upon the pillow without undressing, making darkness the concession of closing his eyes. But the storm of emotions which assailed him had not waned for an instant. Sleeplessness is a cruelty which night inflicts on man. Gwynplaine suffered greatly. For the first time in his life, he was not pleased with himself. Ache of heart mingled with gratified vanity. What was he to do? Day broke at last; he heard Ursus get up, but did not raise his eyelids. No truce for him, however. The letter was ever in his mind. Every word of it came back to him in a kind of chaos. In certain violent storms within the soul, thought becomes a liquid. It is convulsed, it heaves, and something rises from it, like the dull roaring of the waves. Flood and flow, sudden shocks and whirls, the hesitation of the wave before the rock; hail and rain; clouds with the light shining through their breaks; the petty flights of useless foam; wild swell broken in an instant; great efforts lost; wreck appearing all around; darkness and universal dispersion: as these things are of the sea, so are they of man. Gwynplaine was a prey to such a storm.

At the acme of his agony, his eyes still closed, he heard an exquisite voice saying, "Are you asleep, Gwynplaine?" He opened his eyes with a start, and sat up. Dea was standing in the half-open doorway. Her ineffable smile was in her eyes and on her lips. She was standing there, charming in the unconscious serenity of her radiance. Then came, as it were, a sacred moment. Gwynplaine watched her, startled, dazzled, awakened. Awakened from what? from sleep? no, from sleeplessness. It was she, it was Dea; and suddenly he felt in the depths of his being the indescribable wane of the storm and the sublime descent of good over evil; the miracle of the look from on high was accomplished; the blind girl, the sweet light-bearer, with no effort beyond her mere presence, dissipated all the darkness within him; the curtain of cloud was dispersed from his soul as if drawn by an invisible hand, and a sky of azure, as though by celestial enchantment, again spread over Gwynplaine's conscience. In a moment he became by the virtue of that angel, the great and good Gwynplaine, the innocent man. Such mysterious confrontations occur to the soul as they do to creation. Both were silent; she, who was the light; he, who was the abyss; she, who was divine; he, who was appeased; and over Gwynplaine's stormy heart Dea shone with the indescribable effect of a star shining on the Sea.

Chapter II

FROM GAY TO GRAVE

HOW SIMPLE IS A MIRACLE! IT WAS BREAKFAST HOUR IN THE GREEN BOX, AND DEA HAD MERELY come to see why Gwynplaine had not joined their little breakfast table.

"It is you!" exclaimed Gwynplaine; and he had said everything. There was no other horizon, no vision for him now but the heavens where Dea was. His mind was appeased; appeased in such a manner as he alone can understand, who has seen the smile spread swiftly over the sea when the hurricane has passed away. Over nothing does the calm come so quickly as over the whirlpool. This results from its power of absorption. And so it is with the human heart. Not always, however.

Dea had but to show herself, and all the light that was in Gwynplaine left him and went to her, and behind the dazzled Gwynplaine there was but a flight of phantoms. What a peacemaker is adoration! A few minutes afterwards they were sitting opposite each other, Ursus between them, Homo at their feet. The teapot, hung over a little lamp, was on the table. Fibi and Vinos were outside, waiting.

They breakfasted as they supped, in the center compartment. From the position in which the narrow table was placed, Dea's back was turned toward the aperture in the partition which was opposite the entrance door of the Green Box. Their knees were touching. Gwynplaine was pouring out tea for Dea. Dea blew gracefully on her cup. Suddenly she sneezed. Just at that moment a thin smoke rose above the flame of the lamp, and something like a piece of paper fell into ashes. It was the smoke which had caused Dea to sneeze.

"What was that?" she asked.

"Nothing," replied Gwynplaine.

And he smiled. He had just burned the duchess's letter.

The conscience of the man who loves, is the guardian angel of the woman whom he loves.

Unburdened of the letter, his relief was wondrous, and Gwynplaine felt his integrity as the eagle feels its wings.

It seemed to him as if his temptation had evaporated with the smoke, and as if the duchess had crumbled into ashes with the paper.

Taking up their cups at random, and drinking one after the other from the same one, they talked. A babble of lovers, a chattering of sparrows! Child's talk, worthy of Mother Goose or of Homer! With two loving hearts, go no further for poetry; with two kisses for dialogue, go no further for music.

"Do you know something?"

"No."

"Gwynplaine, I dreamt that we were animals, and had wings."

"Wings; that means birds," murmured Gwynplaine.

"Fools! it means angels," growled Ursus.

And their talk went on.

"If you did not exist, Gwynplaine?"

"What then?"

"It could only be because there was no God."

"The tea is too hot; you will burn yourself, Dea."

"Blow on my cup."

"How beautiful you are this morning!"

"Do you know that I have a great many things to say to you?"

"Say them."

"I love you."

"I adore you."

And Ursus said aside, "By heaven, they are polite!"

Exquisite to lovers are their moments of silence! In them they gather, as it were, masses of love, which afterwards explode into sweet fragments.

"Do you know! In the evening, when we are playing our parts, at the moment when my hand touches your forehead—oh, what a noble head is yours, Gwynplaine!—at the moment when I feel your hair under my fingers, I shiver; a heavenly joy comes over me; and I say to myself, In all this world of darkness which encompasses me, in this universe of solitude, in this great obscurity of ruin in which I am, in this quaking fear of myself and of everything, I have one prop; and he is there. It is he. It is you."

"Oh! you love me," said Gwynplaine. "I, too, have but you on earth. You are all in all to me. Dea, what would you have me do? What do you desire? What do you want?"

Dea answered—

"I do not know. I am happy."

"Oh," replied Gwynplaine, "we are happy."

Ursus raised his voice severely—

"Oh, you are happy, are you? That's a crime. I have warned you already. You are happy! Then take care you aren't seen. Take up as little room as you can. Happiness ought to stuff itself into a hole. Make yourselves still less than you are, if that can be. God measures the greatness of happiness by the littleness of the happy. The happy should conceal themselves like malefactors. Oh, only shine out like the wretched glowworms that you are, and you'll be trodden on; and quite right, too! What do you mean by all that love-making nonsense? I'm no duenna, whose business it is to watch lovers billing and cooing. I'm tired of it all, I tell you; and you may both go to the devil."

And feeling that his harsh tones were melting into tenderness, he drowned his emotion in a loud grumble.

"Father," said Dea, "how roughly you scold!"

"It's because I don't like to see people too happy."

Here Homo re-echoed Ursus. His growl was heard from beneath the lovers' feet.

Ursus stooped down, and placed his hand on Homo's head.

"That's right; you're in bad humor, too. You growl. The bristles are all on end on your wolf's pate. You don't like all this love-making. That's because you are wise. Hold your tongue all the same. You have had your say, and given your opinion; be it so. Now be silent."

The wolf growled again. Ursus looked under the table at him.

"Be still, Homo! Come, don't dwell on it, you philosopher!"

But the wolf sat up, and looked toward the door, showing his teeth.

"What's wrong with you now?" said Ursus. And he caught hold of Homo by the skin of the neck.

Heedless of the wolf's growls, and wholly wrapped up in her own thoughts and in the sound of Gwynplaine's voice, which left its aftertaste within her, Dea was silent, and absorbed by that kind of ecstasy peculiar to the blind, which seems at times to give them a song to listen to in their souls, and to make up to them for the light which they lack, by some strain of ideal music. Blindness is a cavern, to which reaches the deep harmony of the Eternal.

While Ursus, addressing Homo, was looking down, Gwynplaine had raised his eyes. He was about to drink a cup of tea, but did not drink it. He placed it on the table with the slow movement of a spring drawn back; his fingers remained open, his eyes fixed. He scarcely breathed.

A man was standing in the doorway, behind Dea. He was clad in black, with a hood. He wore a wig down to his eyebrows, and held in his hand an iron staff with a crown at each end. His staff was short and massive. He was like Medusa thrusting her head between two branches in Paradise.

Ursus, who had heard someone enter and raised his head without loosing his hold of Homo, recognized the terrible personage. He shook from head to foot, and whispered to Gwynplaine—

"It's the wapentake."

Gwynplaine recollected. An exclamation of surprise was about to escape him, but he restrained it. The iron staff, with the crown at each end, was called the iron weapon. It was from this iron weapon, upon which the city officers of justice took the oath when they entered on their duties, that the old wapentakes of the English police derived their qualification.

Behind the man in the wig, the frightened landlord could just be perceived in the shadow.

Without saying a word, a personification of the muta Themis of the old charters, the man stretched his right arm over the radiant Dea, and touched Gwynplaine on the shoulder with the iron staff, at the same time pointing with his left thumb to the door of the Green Box behind him. These gestures, all the more imperious for their silence, meant, follow me.

Pro signo exeundi, sursum trahe, says the old Norman record.

He who was touched by the iron weapon had no right but the right of obedience. To that mute order there was no reply. The harsh penalties of the English law threatened the refractory. Gwynplaine felt a shock under the rigid touch of the law; then he sat as though petrified.

If, instead of having been merely grazed on the shoulder, he had been struck a violent blow on the head with the iron staff, he could not have been more stunned. He knew that the police officer summoned him to follow; but why? *That* he could not understand.

On his part Ursus, too, was thrown into the most painful agitation, but he saw through matters pretty distinctly. His thoughts ran on the jugglers and preachers, his competitors, on informations laid against the Green Box, on that delinquent the wolf, on his own affair with the three Bishopsgate commissioners, and who knows?—perhaps—but that would be too fearful—Gwynplaine's unbecoming and factious speeches touching the royal authority.

He trembled violently.

Dea was smiling.

Neither Gwynplaine nor Ursus pronounced a word. They had both the same thought: not to frighten Dea. It may have struck the wolf as well, for he ceased growling. True, Ursus did not loose him.

Homo, however, was a prudent wolf when occasion required. Who is there who has not remarked a kind of intelligent anxiety in animals? It may be that to the extent to which a wolf can understand mankind he felt that he was an outlaw.

Gwynplaine rose.

Resistance was impracticable, as Gwynplaine knew. He remembered Ursus's words, and there was no question possible. He remained standing in front of the wapentake. The latter raised the iron staff from Gwynplaine's shoulder, and drawing it back, held it out straight in an attitude of command: a constable's attitude which was well understood in those days by the whole people, and which expressed the following order: "Let this man, and no other, follow me. The rest remain where they are. Silence!"

No curious followers were allowed. In all times the police have had a taste for arrests of the kind. This description of seizure was termed sequestration of the person.

The wapentake turned round in one motion, like a piece of mechanism revolving on its own pivot, and with grave and magisterial step proceeded toward the door of the Green Box.

Gwynplaine looked at Ursus. The latter went through a pantomime composed as follows: he shrugged his shoulders, placed both elbows close to his hips, with his hands out, and knitted his brows into chevrons, all which signifies—we must submit to the unknown.

Gwynplaine looked at Dea. She was in her dream. She was still smiling. He put the ends of his fingers to his lips, and sent her an unutterable kiss.

Ursus, relieved of some portion of his terror now that the wapentake's back was turned, seized the moment to whisper in Gwynplaine's ear—

"On your life, do not speak until you are questioned."

Gwynplaine, with the same care to make no noise as he would have taken in a sick-room, took his hat and cloak from the hook on the partition, wrapped himself up to the eyes in the cloak, and pushed his hat over his forehead. Not having been to bed, he had his working clothes still on, and his leather esclavin round his neck. Once more he looked at Dea. Having reached the door, the wapentake raised his staff and began to descend the steps; then Gwynplaine set out as if the man was dragging him by an invisible chain. Ursus watched Gwynplaine leave the Green Box. At that moment the wolf gave a low growl, but Ursus silenced him and whispered, "He is coming back."

In the yard, Master Nicless was stemming, with servile and imperious gestures, the cries of terror raised by Vinos and Fibi, as in great distress they watched Gwynplaine led away, and the mourning-colored garb and the iron staff of the wapentake.

The two girls were like petrifactions: they were in the attitude of stalactites. Govicum, stunned, was looking open-mouthed out of a window.

The wapentake preceded Gwynplaine by a few steps, never turning round or looking at him, in that icy ease which is given by the knowledge that one is the law.

In death-like silence they both crossed the yard, went through the dark tap-room, and reached the street. A few passers-by had collected about the inn door, and the justice of the quorum was there at the head of a squad of police. The idlers, stupefied, and without breathing a word, opened out and stood aside, with English discipline, at the sight of the constable's staff. The wapentake moved off in the direction of the narrow street then called the Little Strand, running by the Thames; and Gwynplaine, with the justice of the quorum's men in ranks on each side, like a double hedge, pale, without a motion except that of his steps, wrapped in his cloak as in a shroud, was leaving the inn further and further behind him as he followed the silent man, like a statue following a specter.

Chapter III

LEX, REX, FEX

UNEXPLAINED ARREST, WHICH WOULD GREATLY ASTONISH AN ENGLISHMAN NOWADAYS, WAS then a very usual proceeding of the police. Recourse was had to it, notwithstanding the Habeas Corpus Act, up to George II's time, especially in such delicate cases as were provided for by *lettres de cachet* in France; and one of the accusations against which Walpole had to defend himself was that he had caused or allowed Neuhoff to be arrested in that manner. The accusation was probably without foundation, for Neuhoff, King of Corsica, was put in prison by his creditors.

These silent captures of the person, very usual with the Holy Væhme in Germany, were admitted by German custom, which rules one half of the old English laws, and recommended in certain cases by Norman custom, which rules the other half. Justinian's chief of the palace police was called *"Silentiarius Imperialis."* The English magistrates who practiced the captures in question relied upon numerous Norman texts—*Canes latrant, sergentes silent. Sergenter agere, id est tacere.* They quoted Lundulphus Sagax, paragraph 16: *Facit Imperator silentium.* They quoted the charter of King Philip in 1307: *Multos tenebimus bastonerios qui, obmutescentes, sergentare valeant*. They quoted the statutes of Henry I of England, cap. 53: *Surge signo jussus. Taciturnior esto. Hoc est esse in captione regis*. They took advantage especially of the following description, held to form part of the ancient feudal franchises of England—"Sous les viscomtes sont les serjans de l'espée, lesquels doivent justicier vertueusement à l'espée tous ceux qui suient malveses compagnies, gens diffamez d'aucuns crimes, et gens fuites et forbannis. . . . et les doivent si vigoureusement et discrètement ap-préhender, que la bonne gent qui sont paisibles soient gardez paisiblement et que les malfeteurs soient espoantés." To be thus arrested was to be seized "à le glaive de l'espée." (*Vetus Consuetudo Normanniae*, MS. part 1, sect. 1, ch. 11.) The jurisconsults referred besides "*in Charta Ludovici Hutuni pro Normannis*, chapter *Servientes spathae*." *Servientes spathae*, in the gradual approach of base Latin to our idioms, became *sergentes spadae*.

These silent arrests were the contrary of the *Clameur de Haro*, and gave warning that it was advisable to hold one's tongue until such time as light should be thrown upon certain matters still in the dark. They signified questions reserved, and showed in the operation of the police a certain amount of *raison d'état*.

The legal term "private" was applied to arrests of this description. It was thus that Edward III according to some chroniclers, caused Mortimer to be seized in the bed of his mother, Isabella of France. This, again, we may take leave to doubt; for Mortimer sustained a siege in his town before being captured.

Warwick, the king-maker, delighted in practicing this mode of "attaching people." Cromwell made use of it, especially in Connaught; and it was with this precaution of silence that Trailie Ar-cklo, a relation of the Earl of Ormond, was arrested at Kilmacaugh.

These captures of the body by the mere motion of justice represented rather the *mandat de comparution* than the warrant of arrest. Sometimes they were but processes of inquiry, and even argued, by the silence imposed upon all, a certain consideration for the person seized. For the mass of the people, little versed as they were in the estimate of such shades of difference, they had pe-culiar terrors.

It must not be forgotten that, in 1705 and even much later, England was far from being what she is to-day. The general features of its constitution were confused and, at times, very oppressive. Daniel Defoe, who had himself had a taste of the pillory, characterizes the social order of England, somewhere in his writings, as the "iron hands of the law." There was not only the law; there was its arbitrary administration. We have but to recall Steele, ejected from Parliament; Locke, driven from his chair; Hobbes and Gibbon, compelled to flight; Charles Churchill, Hume, and Priestley, persecuted; John Wilkes sent to the Tower. The task would be a long one, were we to count over the victims of the statute against seditious libel. The Inquisition had, to some extent, spread its arrangements throughout Europe, and its police practice was taken as a guide. A monstrous attempt against all rights was possible in England. We have only to recall the *Gazetier Cuirassé*. In the midst of the eighteenth century, Louis XV had writers, whose works displeased him, arrested in Pic-cadilly. It is true that George II laid his hands on the Pretender in France, right in the middle of the hall at the opera. Those were two long arms! that of the King of France reaching London! that of the King of England, Paris! Such was the liberty of the period.

We may add, that they were fond of putting people to death privately in prisons, sleight of hand mingled with capital punishment; a hideous expedient, to which England is reverting at the present moment, thus giving to the world the strange spectacle of a great people, which, in its de-sire to take the better part, chooses the worse; and which, having before it the past on one side and progress on the other, mistakes its way, and takes night for day.

Chapter IV

URSUS SPIES THE POLICE

As WE HAVE ALREADY SAID, ACCORDING TO THE VERY SEVERE LAWS OF THE POLICE OF THOSE days, the summons to follow the wapentake, addressed to an individual, implied to all other persons present the command not to stir.

Some curious idlers, however, were stubborn, and followed from afar off the *cortége* which had taken Gwynplaine into custody.

Ursus was of them. He had been as nearly petrified as anyone has a right to be. But Ursus, so often assailed by the surprises incident to a wandering life, and by the malice of chance, was, like a ship-of-war, prepared for action, and could call to the post of danger the whole crew—that is to say, the aid of all his intelligence.

He flung off his stupor, and began to think. He strove not to give way to emotion, but to stand face to face with circumstances.

To look fortune in the face is the duty of everyone not an idiot; to seek not to understand, but to act.

Presently he asked himself—What could he do?

Gwynplaine being taken, Ursus was placed between two terrors—a fear for Gwynplaine, which instigated him to follow; and a fear for himself, which urged him to remain where he was.

Ursus had the intrepidity of a fly, and the impassibility of a sensitive plant. His agitation was not to be described. However, he took his resolution heroically, and decided to brave the law, and to follow the wapentake, so anxious was he concerning the fate of Gwynplaine.

His terror must have been great to prompt so much courage.

To what valiant acts will not fear drive a hare!

The chamois in despair jumps a precipice. To be terrified into imprudence is one of the forms of fear.

Gwynplaine had been carried off rather than arrested. The operation of the police had been executed so rapidly that the Fair field, generally little frequented at that hour of the morning, had scarcely taken cognizance of the circumstance.

Scarcely anyone in the caravans had any idea that the wapentake had come to take Gwynplaine. Hence the smallness of the crowd.

Gwynplaine, thanks to his cloak and his hat, which nearly concealed his face, could not be recognized by the passers-by.

Before he went out to follow Gwynplaine, Ursus took a precaution. He spoke to Master Nicless, to the boy Govicum, and to Fibi and Vinos, and insisted on their keeping absolute silence before Dea, who was ignorant of everything. That they should not utter a syllable that could make her suspect what had occurred; that they should make her understand that the cares of the management of the Green Box necessitated the absence of Gwynplaine and Ursus; that, besides, it would soon be the time of her daily siesta, and that before she awoke he and Gwynplaine would have returned; that all that had taken place had arisen from a mistake; that it would be very easy for Gwynplaine and himself to clear themselves before the magistrate and police; that a touch of the finger would put the matter straight, after which they should both return; above all, that no one should say a word on the subject to Dea. Having given these directions he departed.

Ursus was able to follow Gwynplaine without being remarked. Though he kept at the greatest possible distance, he so managed as not to lose sight of him. Boldness in ambuscade is the bravery of the timid.

After all, notwithstanding the solemnity of the attendant circumstances, Gwynplaine might have been summoned before the magistrate for some unimportant infraction of the law.

Ursus assured himself that the question would be decided at once.

The solution of the mystery would be made under his very eyes by the direction taken by the *cortége* which took Gwynplaine from Tarrinzeau Field when it reached the entrance of the lanes of the Little Strand.

If it turned to the left, it would conduct Gwynplaine to the justice hall in Southwark. In that case there would be little to fear, some trifling municipal offense, an admonition from the magistrate, two or three shillings to pay, and Gwynplaine would be set at liberty, and the representation of *Chaos Vanquished* would take place in the evening as usual. In that case no one would know that anything unusual had happened.

If the *cortége* turned to the right, matters would be serious.

There were frightful places in that direction.

When the wapentake, leading the file of soldiers between whom Gwynplaine walked, arrived at the small streets, Ursus watched them breathlessly. There are moments in which a man's whole being passes into his eyes.

Which way were they going to turn?

They turned to the right.

Ursus, staggering with terror, leant against a wall that he might not fall.

There is no hypocrisy so great as the words which we say to ourselves, *"I wish to know the worst!"* At heart we do not wish it at all. We have a dreadful fear of knowing it. Agony is mingled with a dim effort not to see the end. We do not own it to ourselves, but we would draw back if we dared; and when we have advanced, we reproach ourselves for having done so.

Thus did Ursus. He shuddered as he thought—

"Here are things going wrong. I should have found it out soon enough. What business had I to follow Gwynplaine?"

Having made this reflection, man being but self-contradiction, he increased his pace, and, mastering his anxiety, hastened to get nearer the *cortége*, so as not to break, in the maze of small streets, the thread between Gwynplaine and himself.

The *cortége* of police could not move quickly on account of its solemnity.

The wapentake led it.

The justice of the quorum closed it.

This order compelled a certain deliberation of movement.

All the majesty possible in an official shone in the justice of the quorum. His costume held a middle place between the splendid robe of a doctor of music of Oxford and the sober black habiliments of a doctor of divinity of Cambridge. He wore the dress of a gentleman under a long godebert, which is a mantle trimmed with the fur of the Norwegian hare. He was half Gothic and half modern, wearing a wig like Lamoignon, and sleeves like Tristan l'Hermite. His great, round eye watched Gwynplaine with the fixedness of an owl's.

He walked with a cadence. Never did honest man look fiercer.

Ursus, for a moment thrown out of his way in the tangled skein of streets, overtook, close to Saint Mary Overy, the *cortége*, which had fortunately been retarded in the churchyard by a fight between children and dogs, a common incident in the streets in those days. *"Dogs and boys,"* say the old registers of police, placing the dogs before the boys.

A man being taken before a magistrate by the police was, after all, an everyday affair, and each one having his own business to attend to, the few who had followed soon dispersed. There remained but Ursus on the track of Gwynplaine.

They passed before two chapels opposite to each other, belonging the one to the Recreative Religionists, the other to the Hallelujah League, sects which flourished then, and which exist to the present day.

Then the *cortége* wound from street to street, making a zigzag, choosing by preference lanes not yet built on, roads where the grass grew, and deserted alleys.

At length it stopped.

It was in a little lane with no houses except two or three hovels. This narrow alley was composed of two walls, one on the left, low; the other on the right, high. The high wall was black, and built in the Saxon style with narrow holes, scorpions, and large square gratings over narrow loopholes. There was no window on it, but here and there slits, old embrasures of picrriers and archegayes. At the foot of this high wall was seen, like the hole at the bottom of a rat-trap, a little wicket gate, very elliptical in its arch.

This small door, encased in a full, heavy girding of stone, had a grated peephole, a heavy knocker, a large lock, hinges thick and knotted, a bristling of nails, an armor of plates, and hinges, so that altogether it was more of iron than of wood.

There was no one in the lane. No shops, no passengers; but in it there was heard a continual noise, as if the lane ran parallel to a torrent. There was a tumult of voices and of carriages. It seemed as if on the other side of the black edifice there must be a great street, doubtless the principal street of Southwark, one end of which ran into the Canterbury road, and the other on to London Bridge.

All the length of the lane, except the *cortége* which surrounded Gwynplaine, a watcher would have seen no other human face than the pale profile of Ursus hazarding a half advance from the shadow of the corner of the wall, looking, yet fearing to see. He had posted himself behind the wall at a turn of the lane.

The constables grouped themselves before the wicket. Gwynplaine was in the center, the wapentake and his baton of iron being now behind him.

The justice of the quorum raised the knocker, and struck the door three times. The loophole opened.

The justice of the quorum said—

"By order of her Majesty."

The heavy door of oak and iron turned on its hinges, making a chilly opening, like the mouth of a cavern. A hideous depth yawned in the shadow.

Ursus saw Gwynplaine disappear within it.

Chapter V

A FEARFUL PLACE

THE WAPENTAKE ENTERED BEHIND GWYNPLAINE.

Then the justice of the quorum.

Then the constables.

The wicket was closed.

The heavy door swung to, closing hermetically on the stone sills, without anyone seeing who had opened or shut it. It seemed as if the bolts re-entered their sockets of their own act. Some of these mechanisms, the inventions of ancient intimidation, still exist in old prisons; doors of which you saw no door-keeper. With them the entrance to a prison becomes like the entrance to a tomb.

This wicket was the lower door of Southwark Jail.

There was nothing in the harsh and wormeaten aspect of this prison to soften its appropriate air of rigor.

Originally a pagan temple, built by the Catieuchlans for the Mogons, ancient English gods, it became a palace for Ethelwolfe and a fortress for Edward the Confessor; then it was elevated to the dignity of a prison, in 1199, by John Lackland. Such was Southwark Jail. This jail, at first intersected by a street, like Chenonceaux by a river, had been for a century or two a gate, that is to say, the gate of the suburb; the passage had then been walled up. There remain in England some prisons of this nature. In London, Newgate; at Canterbury, Westgate; at Edinburgh, Canongate. In France the Bastile was originally a gate.

Almost all the jails of England present the same appearance—a high wall without and a hive of cells within. Nothing could be more funereal than the appearance of those prisons, where spiders and justice spread their webs, and where John Howard, that ray of light, had not yet penetrated. Like the old Gehenna of Brussels, they might well have been designated Treurenberg—*the house of tears.*

Men felt before such buildings, at once so savage and inhospitable, the same distress that the ancient navigators suffered before the hell of slaves mentioned by Plautus, islands of creaking chains, *ferricrepiditae insulae,* when they passed near enough to hear the clank of the fetters.

Southwark Jail, an old place of exorcisms and torture, was originally used solely for the imprisonment of sorcerers, as was proved by two verses engraved on a defaced stone at the foot of the wicket—

> *Sunt arreptitii, vexati daemone multo*
> *Est energumenus, quem daemon possidet unus.*

Lines which draw a subtle delicate distinction between the demoniac and man possessed by a devil.

At the bottom of this inscription, nailed flat against the wall, was a stone ladder, which had been originally of wood, but which had been changed into stone by being buried in earth of petrifying quality at a place called Apsley Gowis, near Woburn Abbey.

The prison of Southwark, now demolished, opened on two streets, between which, as a gate, it formerly served as means of communication. It had two doors. In the large street a door, apparently used by the authorities; and in the lane the door of punishment, used by the rest of the living and by the dead also, because when a prisoner in the jail died, it was by that issue that his corpse was carried out. A liberation not to be despised. Death is release into infinity.

It was by the gate of punishment that Gwynplaine had been taken into prison. The lane, as we have said, was nothing but a little passage, paved with flints, confined between two opposite walls. There is one of the same kind at Brussels called *Rue d'une Personne.* The walls were unequal in height. The high one was the prison; the low one, the cemetery—the enclosure for the mortuary remains of the jail—was not higher than the ordinary stature of a man. In it was a gate almost opposite the prison wicket. The dead had only to cross the street; the cemetery was but twenty paces from the jail. On the high wall was affixed a gallows; on the low one was sculptured a death's-head. Neither of these walls made its opposite neighbor more cheerful.

Chapter VI

THE KIND OF MAGISTRACY UNDER THE WIGS OF FORMER DAYS

ANYONE OBSERVING AT THAT MOMENT THE OTHER SIDE OF THE PRISON—ITS FAÇADES—WOULD have perceived the high street of Southwark, and might have remarked, stationed before the monumental and official entrance to the jail, a traveling carriage, recognized as such by its imperial. A few idlers surrounded the carriage. On it was a coat-of-arms, and a personage had been seen to descend from it and enter the prison. "Probably a magistrate," conjectured the crowd. Many of the English magistrates were noble, and almost all had the right of bearing arms. In France blazon and robe were almost contradictory terms. The Duke Saint-Simon says, in speaking of magistrates, "People of that class." In England a gentleman was not despised for being a judge.

There are traveling magistrates in England; they are called judges of circuit, and nothing was easier than to recognize the carriage as the vehicle of a judge on circuit. That which was less comprehensible was, that the supposed magistrate got down, not from the carriage itself, but from the box, a place which is not habitually occupied by the owner. Another unusual thing. People traveled at that period in England in two ways. By coach, at the rate of a shilling for five miles, and by post, paying three halfpence per mile, and twopence to the postilion after each stage. A private carriage, whose owner desired to travel by relays, paid as many shillings per horse per mile as the horseman paid pence. The carriage drawn up before the jail in Southwark had four horses and two postilions, which displayed princely state. Finally, that which excited and disconcerted conjectures to the utmost was the circumstance that the carriage was sedulously shut up. The blinds of the windows were closed up. The glasses in front were darkened by blinds; every opening by which the eye might have penetrated was masked. From without, nothing within could be seen, and most likely from within, nothing could be seen outside. However, it did not seem probable that there was anyone in the carriage.

Southwark being in Surrey, the prison was within the jurisdiction of the sheriff of the county.

Such distinct jurisdictions were very frequent in England. Thus, for example, the Tower of London was not supposed to be situated in any county; that is to say, that, legally, it was considered to be in air. The Tower recognized no authority of jurisdiction except in its own constable, who was qualified as *custos curris*. The Tower had its jurisdiction, its church, its court of justice, and its government apart. The authority of its *custos*, or constable, extended, beyond London, over twenty-one hamlets. As in Great Britain legal singularities engraft one upon another the office of the master gunner of England was derived from the Tower of London. Other legal customs seem still more whimsical. Thus, the English Court of Admiralty consults and applies the laws of Rhodes and of Oleron, a French island which was once English.

The sheriff of a county was a person of high consideration. He was always an esquire, and sometimes a knight. He was called *spectabilis* in the old deeds, "a man to be looked at," a kind of intermediate title between *illustris* and *clarissimus*—less than the first, more than the second. Long ago the sheriffs of the counties were chosen by the people; but Edward II, and after him Henry VI, having claimed their nomination for the crown, the office of sheriff became a royal emanation.

They all received their commissions from majesty, except the sheriff of Westmoreland, whose office was hereditary, and the sheriffs of London and Middlesex, who were elected by the livery in the common hall. Sheriffs of Wales and Chester possessed certain fiscal prerogatives. These appointments are all still in existence in England, but, subjected little by little to the friction of manners and ideas, they have lost their old aspects. It was the duty of the sheriff of the county to escort and protect the judges on circuit. As we have two arms, he had two officers; his right arm the under-sheriff, his left arm the justice of the quorum. The justice of the quorum, assisted by the bailiff of the hundred, termed the wapentake, apprehended, examined, and, under the responsibility of the sheriff, imprisoned, for trial by the judges of circuit, thieves, murderers, rebels, vagabonds, and all sorts of felons.

The shade of difference between the under-sheriff and the justice of the quorum, in their hierarchical service toward the sheriff, was that the under-sheriff accompanied and the justice of the quorum assisted.

The sheriff held two courts, one fixed and central, the county court; and a movable court, the sheriff's turn. He thus represented both unity and ubiquity. He might as judge be aided and informed on legal questions by the sergeant of the coif, called *sergens coifae,* who is a sergeant-at-law, and who wears under his black skull-cap a fillet of white Cambray lawn.

The sheriff delivered the jails. When he arrived at a town in his province, he had the right of summary trial of the prisoners, of which he might cause either their release or the execution. This was called a jail delivery. The sheriff presented bills of indictment to the twenty-four members of the grand jury. If they approved, they wrote above, *billa vera*; if the contrary, they wrote *ignoramus.* In the latter case the accusation was annulled, and the sheriff had the privilege of tearing up the bill. If during the deliberation a juror died, this legally acquitted the prisoner and made him innocent, and the sheriff, who had the privilege of arresting the accused, had also that of setting him at liberty.

That which made the sheriff singularly feared and respected was that he had the charge of executing all the orders of her Majesty, a fearful latitude. An arbitrary power lodges in such commissions.

The officers termed vergers, the coroners making part of the sheriff's *cortége,* and the clerks of the market as escort, with gentlemen on horseback and their servants in livery, made a handsome suite. The sheriff, says Chamberlayne, is the "life of justice, of law, and of the country."

In England an insensible demolition constantly pulverizes and dissevers laws and customs. You must understand in our day that neither the sheriff, the wapentake, nor the justice of the quorum could exercise their functions as they did then. There was in the England of the Past a certain confusion of powers, whose ill-defined attributes resulted in their overstepping their real bounds at times, a thing which would be impossible in the present day. The usurpation of power by police and justices has ceased. We believe that even the word wapentake has changed its meaning. It implied a magisterial function; now it signifies a territorial division: it specified the centurion; it now specifies the hundred (*centum*).

Moreover, in those days the sheriff of the county combined with something more and something less, and condensed in his own authority, which was at once royal and municipal, the two magistrates formerly called in France the civil lieutenant of Paris and the lieutenant of police. The civil lieutenant of Paris, Monsieur, is pretty well described in an old police note: "The civil lieutenant had no dislike to domestic quarrels, because he always has the pickings."—(22d July, 1704). As to the lieutenant of police, he was a redoubtable person, multiple and vague. The best personification of him was René d'Argenson, who, as was said by Saint-Simon, displayed in his face the three judges of hell united.

The three judges of hell sat, as has already been seen, at Bishopsgate, London.

Chapter VII

SHUDDERING

W HEN GWYNPLAINE HEARD THE WICKET SHUT, CREAKING IN ALL ITS BOLTS, HE TREMBLED. IT seemed to him that the door which had just closed was the communication between light and darkness; opening on one side on the living, human crowd, and on the other on a dead world; and now that everything illumined by the sun was behind him, that he had stepped over the boundary of life and was standing without it, his heart contracted. What were they going to do with him? What did it all mean? Where was he?

He saw nothing around him; he found himself in perfect darkness. The shutting of the door had momentarily blinded him. The window in the door had been closed as well. No loophole, no lamp. Such were the precautions of old times. It was forbidden to light the entrance to the jails, so that the newcomers should take no observations.

Gwynplaine extended his arms, and touched the wall on the right side and on the left. He was in a passage. Little by little a cavernous daylight exuding, no one knows whence, and which floats about dark places, and to which the dilatation of the pupil adjusts itself slowly, enabled him to distinguish a feature here and there, and the corridor was vaguely sketched out before him.

Gwynplaine, who had never had a glimpse of penal severities, save in the exaggerations of Ursus, felt as though seized by a sort of vague gigantic hand. To be caught in the mysterious toils of the law is frightful. He who is brave in all other dangers is disconcerted in the presence of justice. Why? Is it that the justice of man works in twilight, and the judge gropes his way? Gwynplaine remembered what Ursus had told him of the necessity for silence. He wished to see Dea again; he felt some discretionary instinct, which urged him not to irritate. Sometimes to wish to be enlightened is to make matters worse; on the other hand, however, the weight of the adventure was so overwhelming that he gave way at length and could not restrain a question.

"Gentlemen," said he, "whither are you taking me?"

They made no answer.

It was the law of silent capture, and the Norman text is formal: *A silentiarus ostio praepositis introducti sunt.*

This silence froze Gwynplaine. Up to that moment he had believed himself to be firm: he was self-sufficing. To be self-sufficing is to be powerful. He had lived isolated from the world, and imagined that being alone he was unassailable; and now all at once he felt himself under the pressure of a hideous collective force. How was he to combat that horrible anonyma, the law? He felt faint under the perplexity; a fear of an unknown character had found a fissure in his armor; besides, he had not slept, he had not eaten, he had scarcely moistened his lips with a cup of tea. The whole night had been passed in a kind of delirium, and the fever was still on him. He was thirsty; perhaps hungry. The craving of the stomach disorders everything. Since the previous evening all kinds of incidents had assailed him. The emotions which had tormented had sustained him. Without the storm a sail would be a rag. But his was the excessive feebleness of the rag, which the wind inflates till it tears it. He felt himself sinking. Was he about to fall without consciousness on the pavement? To faint is the resource of a woman, and the humiliation of a man. He hardened himself, but he trembled. He felt as one losing his footing.

Chapter VIII

LAMENTATION

THEY BEGAN TO MOVE FORWARD.
    They advanced through the passage.

There was no preliminary registry, no place of record. The prisons in those times were not overburdened with documents. They were content to close round you without knowing why. To be a prison, and to hold prisoners, sufficed.

The procession was obliged to lengthen itself out, taking the form of the corridor. They walked almost in single file; first the wapentake, then Gwynplaine, then the justice of the quorum, then the constables, advancing in a group, and blocking up the passage behind Gwynplaine as with a bung. The passage narrowed. Now Gwynplaine touched the walls with both his elbows. In the roof, which was made of flints, dashed with cement, was a succession of granite arches jutting out, and still more contracting the passage. He had to stoop to pass under them. No speed was possible in that corridor. Anyone trying to escape through it would have been compelled to move slowly. The passage twisted. All entrails are tortuous; those of a prison as well as those of a man. Here and there, sometimes to the right and sometimes to the left, spaces in the wall, square and closed by large iron gratings, gave glimpses of flights of stairs, some descending and some ascending.

They reached a closed door; it opened. They passed through, and it closed again. Then they came to a second door, which admitted them, then to a third, which also turned on its hinges. These doors seemed to open and shut of themselves. No one was to be seen. While the corridor contracted, the roof grew lower, until at length it was impossible to stand upright. Moisture exuded from the wall. Drops of water fell from the vault. The slabs that paved the corridor were clammy as an intestine. The diffused pallor that served as light became more and more a pall. Air was deficient, and what was singularly ominous, the passage was a descent.

Close observation was necessary to perceive that there was such a descent. In darkness a gentle declivity is portentous. Nothing is more fearful than the vague evils to which we are led by imperceptible degrees.

It is awful to descend into unknown depths.

How long had they proceeded thus? Gwynplaine could not tell.

Moments passed under such crushing agony seem immeasurably prolonged.

Suddenly they halted.

The darkness was intense.

The corridor widened somewhat. Gwynplaine heard close to him a noise of which only a Chinese gong could give an idea; something like a blow struck against the diaphragm of the abyss. It was the wapentake striking his wand against a sheet of iron.

That sheet of iron was a door.

Not a door on hinges, but a door which was raised and let down.

Something like a portcullis.

There was a sound of creaking in a groove, and Gwynplaine was suddenly face to face with a bit of square light. The sheet of metal had just been raised into a slit in the vault, like the door of a mouse-trap.

An opening had appeared.

The light was not daylight, but glimmer; but on the dilated eyeballs of Gwynplaine the pale and sudden ray struck like a flash of lightning.

It was some time before he could see anything. To see with dazzled eyes is as difficult as to see in darkness.

At length, by degrees, the pupil of his eye became proportioned to the light, just as it had been proportioned to the darkness, and he was able to distinguish objects. The light, which at first had seemed too bright, settled into its proper hue and became livid. He cast a glance into the yawning space before him, and what he saw was terrible.

At his feet were about twenty steps, steep, narrow, worn, almost perpendicular, without balustrade on either side, a sort of stone ridge cut out from the side of a wall into stairs, entering and leading into a very deep cell. They reached to the bottom.

The cell was round, roofed by an ogee vault with a low arch, from the fault of level in the top stone of the frieze, a displacement common to cells under heavy edifices.

The kind of hole acting as a door, which the sheet of iron had just revealed, and on which the stairs abutted, was formed in the vault, so that the eye looked down from it as into a well.

The cell was large, and if it was the bottom of a well, it must have been a cyclopean one. The idea that the old word *"cul-de-basse-fosse"* awakens in the mind can only be applied to it if it were a lair of wild beasts.

The cell was neither flagged nor paved. The bottom was of that cold, moist earth peculiar to deep places.

In the midst of the cell, four low and disproportioned columns sustained a porch heavily ogival, of which the four moldings united in the interior of the porch, something like the inside of a miter. This porch, similar to the pinnacles under which sarcophagi were formerly placed, rose nearly to the top of the vault, and made a sort of central chamber in the cavern, if that could be called a chamber which had only pillars in place of walls.

From the key of the arch hung a brass lamp, round and barred like the window of a prison. This lamp threw around it—on the pillars, on the vault, on the circular wall which was seen dimly behind the pillars—a wan light, cut by bars of shadow.

This was the light which had at first dazzled Gwynplaine; now it threw out only a confused redness.

There was no other light in the cell—neither window, nor door, nor loophole.

Between the four pillars, exactly below the lamp, in the spot where there was most light, a pale and terrible form lay on the ground.

It was lying on its back; a head was visible, of which the eyes were shut; a body, of which the chest was a shapeless mass; four limbs belonging to the body, in the position of the cross of Saint Andrew, were drawn toward the four pillars by four chains fastened to each foot and each hand.

These chains were fastened to an iron ring at the base of each column. The form was held immovable, in the horrible position of being quartered, and had the icy look of a livid corpse.

It was naked. It was a man.

Gwynplaine, as if petrified, stood at the top of the stairs, looking down. Suddenly he heard a rattle in the throat.

The corpse was alive.

Close to the specter, in one of the ogives of the door, on each side of a great seat, which stood on a large flat stone, stood two men swathed in long black cloaks; and on the seat an old man was sitting, dressed in a red robe—wan, motionless, and ominous, holding a bunch of roses in his hand.

The bunch of roses would have enlightened anyone less ignorant that Gwynplaine. The right of judging with a nosegay in his hand implied the holder to be a magistrate, at once royal and municipal. The Lord Mayor of London still keeps up the custom. To assist the deliberations of the judges was the function of the earliest roses of the season.

The old man seated on the bench was the sheriff of the county of Surrey.

His was the majestic rigidity of a Roman dignitary.

The bench was the only seat in the cell.

By the side of it was a table covered with papers and books, on which lay the long, white wand of the sheriff. The men standing by the side of the sheriff were two doctors, one of medicine, the other of law; the latter recognizable by the sergeant's coif over his wig. Both wore black robes—one of the shape worn by judges, the other by doctors.

Men of these kinds wear mourning for the deaths of which they are the cause.

Behind the sheriff, at the edge of the flat stone under the seat, was crouched—with a writing-table near to him, a bundle of papers on his knees, and a sheet of parchment on the bundle—a secretary, in a round wig, with a pen in his hand, in the attitude of a man ready to write.

This secretary was of the class called keeper of the bag, as was shown by a bag at his feet.

These bags, in former times employed in law processes, were termed bags of justice.

With folded arms, leaning against a pillar, was a man entirely dressed in leather, the hangman's assistant.

These men seemed as if they had been fixed by enchantment in their funereal postures round the chained man. None of them spoke or moved.

There brooded over all a fearful calm.

What Gwynplaine saw was a torture chamber. There were many such in England.

The crypt of Beauchamp Tower long served this purpose, as did also the cell in the Lollards' prison. A place of this nature is still to be seen in London, called "The Vaults of Lady Place." In this last-mentioned chamber there is a grate for the purpose of heating the irons.

All the prisons of King John's time (and Southwark Jail was one) had their chambers of torture.

The scene which is about to follow was in those days a frequent one in England, and might even, by criminal process, be carried out to-day, since the same laws are still unrepealed. England offers the curious sight of a barbarous code living on the best terms with liberty. We confess that they make an excellent family party.

Some distrust, however, might not be undesirable. In the case of a crisis, a return to the penal code would not be impossible. English legislation is a tamed tiger with a velvet paw, but the claws are still there. Cut the claws of the law, and you will do well. Law almost ignores right. On one side is penalty, on the other humanity. Philosophers protest; but it will take some time yet before the justice of man is assimilated to the justice of God.

Respect for the law: that is the English phrase. In England they venerate so many laws, that they never repeal any. They save themselves from the consequences of their veneration by never putting them into execution. An old law falls into disuse like an old woman, and they never think of killing either one or the other. They cease to make use of them; that is all. Both are at liberty to consider themselves still young and beautiful. They may fancy that they are as they were. This politeness is called respect.

Norman custom is very wrinkled. That does not prevent many an English judge casting sheep's eyes at her. They stick amorously to an antiquated atrocity, so long as it is Norman. What can be more savage than the gibbet? In 1867 a man was sentenced to be cut into four quarters and offered to a woman—the Queen.

Still, torture was never practiced in England. History asserts this as a fact. The assurance of history is wonderful.

Matthew of Westminster mentions that the "Saxon law, very clement and kind," did not punish criminals by death; and adds that "it limited itself to cutting off the nose and scooping out the eyes." That was all!

Gwynplaine, scared and haggard, stood at the top of the steps, trembling in every limb. He shuddered from head to foot. He tried to remember what crime he had committed. To the silence of the wapentake had succeeded the vision of torture to be endured. It was a step, indeed, forward;

but a tragic one. He saw the dark enigma of the law under the power of which he felt himself increasing in obscurity.

The human form lying on the earth rattled in its throat again.

Gwynplaine felt someone touching him gently on his shoulder.

It was the wapentake.

Gwynplaine knew that meant that he was to descend.

He obeyed.

He descended the stairs step by step. They were very narrow, each eight or nine inches in height. There was no hand-rail. The descent required caution. Two steps behind Gwynplaine followed the wapentake, holding up his iron weapon; and at the same interval behind the wapentake, the justice of the quorum.

As he descended the steps, Gwynplaine felt an indescribable extinction of hope. There was death in each step. In each one that he descended there died a ray of the light within him. Growing paler and paler, he reached the bottom of the stairs.

The larva lying chained to the four pillars still rattled in its throat.

A voice in the shadow said—

"Approach!"

It was the sheriff addressing Gwynplaine.

Gwynplaine took a step forward.

"Closer," said the sheriff.

The justice of the quorum murmured in the ear of Gwynplaine so gravely that there was solemnity in the whisper, "You are before the sheriff of the county of Surrey."

Gwynplaine advanced toward the victim extended in the center of the cell. The wapentake and the justice of the quorum remained where they were, allowing Gwynplaine to advance alone.

When Gwynplaine reached the spot under the porch, close to that miserable thing which he had hitherto perceived only from a distance, but which was a living man, his fear rose to terror. The man who was chained there was quite naked, except for that rag so hideously modest, which might be called the vineleaf of punishment, the *succingulum* of the Romans, and the *christipannus* of the Goths, of which the old Gallic jargon made *cripagne*. Christ wore but that shred on the cross.

The terror-stricken sufferer whom Gwynplaine now saw seemed a man of about fifty or sixty years of age. He was bald. Grizzly hairs of beard bristled on his chin. His eyes were closed, his mouth open. Every tooth was to be seen. His thin and bony face was like a death's-head. His arms and legs were fastened by chains to the four stone pillars in the shape of the letter X. He had on his breast and belly a plate of iron, and on this iron five or six large stones were laid. His rattle was at times a sigh, at times a roar.

The sheriff, still holding his bunch of roses, took from the table with the hand which was free his white wand, and standing up said, "Obedience to her Majesty."

Then he replaced the wand upon the table.

Then in words long-drawn as a knell, without a gesture, and immovable as the sufferer, the sheriff, raising his voice, said—

"Man, who liest here bound in chains, listen for the last time to the voice of justice; you have been taken from your dungeon and brought to this jail. Legally summoned in the usual forms, *formaliis verbis pressus*; not regarding to lectures and communications which have been made, and which will now be repeated, to you; inspired by a bad and perverse spirit of tenacity, you have preserved silence, and refused to answer the judge. This is a detestable license, which constitutes, among deeds punishable by cashlit, the crime and misdemeanor of overseness."

The sergeant of the coif on the right of the sheriff interrupted him, and said, with an indifference indescribably lugubrious in its effect, " *Overhernessa*. Laws of Alfred and of Godrun, chapter the sixth."

The sheriff resumed.

"The law is respected by all except by scoundrels who infest the woods where the hinds bear young."

Like one clock striking after another, the sergeant said—

"Qui faciunt vastum in foresta ubi damae solent founinare."

"He who refuses to answer the magistrate," said the sheriff, "is suspected of every vice. He is reputed capable of every evil."

The sergeant interposed.

"Prodigus, devorator, profusus, salax, ruffianus, ebriosus, luxuriosus, simulator, consumptor patrimonii, elluo, ambro, et gluto."

"Every vice," said the sheriff, "means every crime. He who confesses nothing, confesses everything. He who holds his peace before the questions of the judge is in fact a liar and a parricide."

"Mendax et parricida," said the sergeant.

The sheriff said—

"Man, it is not permitted to absent one's self by silence. To pretend contumaciousness is a wound given to the law. It is like Diomede wounding a goddess. Taciturnity before a judge is a form of rebellion. Treason to justice is high treason. Nothing is more hateful or rash. He who resists interrogation, steals truth. The law has provided for this. For such cases, the English have always enjoyed the right of the foss, the fork, and chains."

"Anglica Charta, year 1088," said the sergeant. Then with the same mechanical gravity, he added, *"Ferrum, et fossam, et furcas cum aliis libertatibus."*

The sheriff continued—

"Man! Forasmuch as you have not chosen to break silence, though of sound mind and having full knowledge in respect of the subject concerning which justice demands an answer, and forasmuch as you are diabolically refractory, you have necessarily been put to torture, and you have been, by the terms of the criminal statutes, tried by the *'Peine forte et dure.'* This is what has been done to you, for the law requires that I should fully inform you. You have been brought to this dungeon. You have been stripped of your clothes. You have been laid on your back naked on the ground, your limbs have been stretched and tied to the four pillars of the law; a sheet of iron has been placed on your chest, and as many stones as you can bear have been heaped on your belly, 'and more,' says the law."

"Plusque," affirmed the sergeant.

The sheriff continued—

"In this situation, and before prolonging the torture, a second summons to answer and to speak has been made you by me, sheriff of the county of Surrey, and you have satanically kept silent, though under torture, chains, shackles, fetters, and irons."

"Attachiamenta legalia," said the sergeant.

"On your refusal and contumacy," said the sheriff, "it being right that the obstinacy of the law should equal the obstinacy of the criminal, the proof has been continued according to the edicts and texts. The first day you were given nothing to eat or drink."

"Hoc est superjejunare," said the sergeant.

There was silence, the awful hiss of the man's breathing was heard from under the heap of stones.

The sergeant-at-law completed his quotation.

"Adde augmentum abstinentiae ciborum diminutione. Consuetudo brittanica, art. 504."

The two men, the sheriff and the sergeant, alternated. Nothing could be more dreary than their imperturbable monotony. The mournful voice responded to the ominous voice; it might be said that the priest and the deacon of punishment were celebrating the savage mass of the law.

The sheriff resumed.

"On the first day you were given nothing to eat or drink. On the second day you were given food, but nothing to drink. Between your teeth were thrust three mouthfuls of barley bread. On the third day they gave you to drink, but nothing to eat. They poured into your mouth at three different times, and in three different glasses, a pint of water taken from the common sewer of the prison. The fourth day is come. It is to-day. Now, if you do not answer, you will be left here till you die. Justice wills it."

The sergeant, ready with his reply, appeared.

"*Mors rei homagium est bonae legi.*"

"And while you feel yourself dying miserably," resumed the sheriff, "no one will attend to you, even when the blood rushes from your throat, your chin, and your armpits, and every pore, from the mouth to the loins."

"*A throtabolla,*" said the sergeant, "*et pabu et subhircis et a grugno usque ad crupponum.*"

The sheriff continued—

"Man, attend to me, because the consequences concern you. If you renounce your execrable silence, and if you confess, you will only be hanged, and you will have a right to the meldefeoh, which is a sum of money."

"*Damnum confitens,*" said the sergeant, "*habeat le meldefeoh. Leges Inae,* chapter the twentieth."

"Which sum," insisted the sheriff, "shall be paid in doitkins, suskins, and galihalpens, the only case in which this money is to pass, according to the terms of the statute of abolition, in the third of Henry V, and you will have the right and enjoyment of *scortum ante mortem,* and then be hanged on the gibbet. Such are the advantages of confession. Does it please you to answer to justice?"

The sheriff ceased, and waited.

The prisoner lay motionless.

The sheriff resumed.

"Man, silence is a refuge in which there is more risk than safety. The obstinate man is damnable and vicious. He who is silent before justice is a felon to the crown. Do not persist in this unfilial disobedience. Think of her Majesty. Do not oppose our gracious queen. When I speak to you, answer her; be a loyal subject."

The patient rattled in the throat.

The sheriff continued.

"So, after the seventy-two hours of the proof, here we are at the fourth day. Man, this is the decisive day. The fourth day has been fixed by the law for the confrontation."

"*Quarta die, frontem ad frontem adduce,*" growled the sergeant.

"The wisdom of the law," continued the sheriff, "has chosen this last hour to hold what our ancestors called 'judgment by mortal cold,' seeing that it is the moment when men are believed on their yes or their no."

The sergeant on the right confirmed his words.

"*Judicium pro frodmortell, quod homines credendi sint per suum ya et per suum no.* Charter of King Adelstan, volume the first, page one hundred and sixty-three."

There was a moment's pause; then the sheriff bent his stern face toward the prisoner.

"Man, who art lying there on the ground—"

He paused.

"Man," he cried, "do you hear me?"

The man did not move.

"In the name of the law," said the sheriff, "open your eyes."

The man's lids remained closed.

The sheriff turned to the doctor, who was standing on his left.

"Doctor, give your diagnostic."

"*Probe, da diagnosticum,*" said the sergeant.

The doctor came down with magisterial stiffness, approached the man, leant over him, put his ear close to the mouth of the sufferer, felt the pulse at the wrist, the armpit, and the thigh, then rose again.

"Well?" said the sheriff.

"He can still hear," said the doctor.

"Can he see?" inquired the sheriff.

The doctor answered, "He can see."

On a sign from the sheriff, the justice of the quorum and the wapentake advanced. The wapentake placed himself near the head of the patient. The justice of the quorum stood behind Gwynplaine.

The doctor retired a step behind the pillars.

Then the sheriff, raising the bunch of roses as a priest about to sprinkle holy water, called to the prisoner in a loud voice, and became awful.

"O, wretched man, speak! The law supplicates before she exterminates you. You, who feign to be mute, remember how mute is the tomb. You, who appear deaf, remember that damnation is more deaf. Think of the death which is worse than your present state. Repent: you are about to be left alone in this cell. Listen! you who are my likeness; for I am a man! Listen, my brother, because I am a Christian! Listen, my son, because I am an old man! Look at me; for I am the master of your sufferings, and I am about to become terrible. The terrors of the law make up the majesty of the judge. Believe that I myself tremble before myself. My own power alarms me. Do not drive me to extremities. I am filled by the holy malice of chastisement. Feel, then, wretched man, the salutary and honest fear of justice, and obey me. The hour of confrontation is come, and you must answer. Do not harden yourself in resistance. Do not that which will be irrevocable. Think that your end belongs to me. Half man, half corpse, listen! At least, let it not be your determination to expire here, exhausted for hours, days, and weeks, by frightful agonies of hunger and foulness, under the weight of those stones, alone in this cell, deserted, forgotten, annihilated, left as food for the rats and the weasels, gnawed by creatures of darkness while the world comes and goes, buys and sells, whilst carriages roll in the streets above your head. Unless you would continue to draw painful breath without remission in the depths of this despair—grinding your teeth, weeping, blaspheming—without a doctor to appease the anguish of your wounds, without a priest to offer a divine draft of water to your soul. Oh! if only that you may not feel the frightful froth of the sepulcher ooze slowly from your lips, I adjure and conjure you to hear me. I call you to your own aid. Have pity on yourself. Do what is asked of you. Give way to justice. Open your eyes, and see if you recognize this man!"

The prisoner neither turned his head nor lifted his eyelids.

The sheriff cast a glance first at the justice of the quorum and then at the wapentake.

The justice of the quorum, taking Gwynplaine's hat and mantle, put his hands on his shoulders and placed him in the light by the side of the chained man. The face of Gwynplaine stood out clearly from the surrounding shadow, in its strange relief.

At the same time, the wapentake bent down, took the man's temples between his hands, turned the inert head toward Gwynplaine, and with his thumbs and his first fingers lifted the closed eyelids.

The prisoner saw Gwynplaine. Then, raising his head voluntarily, and opening his eyes wide, he looked at him.

He quivered as much as a man can quiver with a mountain on his breast, and then cried out—

" 'Tis he! Yes; 'tis he!"

And he burst into a horrible laugh.

" 'Tis he!" he repeated.

Then his head fell back on the ground, and he closed his eyes again.

"Registrar, take that down," said the justice.

Gwynplaine, though terrified, had, up to that moment, preserved a calm exterior. The cry of the prisoner—" 'Tis he!" overwhelmed him completely. The words "Registrar, take that down!" froze him. It seemed to him that a scoundrel had dragged him to his fate without his being able to guess why, and that the man's unintelligible confession was closing round him like the clasp of an iron collar. He fancied himself side by side with him in the posts of the same pillory. Gwynplaine lost his footing in his terror, and protested. He began to stammer incoherent words in the deep distress of an innocent man, and quivering, terrified, lost, uttered the first random outcries that rose to his mind, and words of agony like aimless projectiles.

"It is not true. It was not me. I do not know the man. He cannot know me, since I do not know him. I have my part to play this evening. What do you want of me? I demand my liberty. Nor is that all. Why have I been brought into this dungeon? Are there laws no longer? You may as well say at once that there are no laws. My Lord Judge, I repeat that it is not I. I am innocent of all that can be said. I know I am. I wish to go away. This is not justice. There is nothing between this man and me. You can find out. My life is not hidden up. They came and took me away like a thief. Why did they come like that? How could I know the man? I am a traveling mountebank, who plays farces at fairs and markets. I am the Laughing Man. Plenty of people have been to see me. We are staying in Tarrinzeau Field. I have been earning an honest livelihood these fifteen years. I am five-and-twenty. I lodge at the Tadcaster Inn. I am called Gwynplaine. My lord, let me out. You should not take advantage of the low estate of the unfortunate. Have compassion on a man who has done no harm, who is without protection, and without defense. You have before you a poor mountebank."

"I have before me," said the sheriff, "Lord Fermain Clancharlie, Baron Clancharlie and Hunkerville, Marquis of Corleone in Sicily, and a peer of England."

Rising, and offering his chair to Gwynplaine, the sheriff added—

"My lord, will your lordship deign to seat yourself?"

BOOK THE FIFTH

THE SEA AND FATE ARE MOVED BY THE SAME BREATH

Chapter 1

THE DURABILITY OF FRAGILE THINGS

DESTINY SOMETIMES PROFFERS US A GLASS OF MADNESS TO DRINK. A HAND IS THRUST OUT OF the mist, and suddenly hands us the mysterious cup in which is contained the latent intoxication.

Gwynplaine did not understand.

He looked behind him to see who it was who had been addressed.

A sound may be too sharp to be perceptible to the ear; an emotion too acute conveys no meaning to the mind. There is a limit to comprehension as well as to hearing.

The wapentake and the justice of the quorum approached Gwynplaine, and took him by the arms. He felt himself placed in the chair which the sheriff had just vacated. He let it be done, without seeking an explanation.

When Gwynplaine was seated, the justice of the quorum and the wapentake retired a few steps, and stood upright and motionless, behind the seat.

Then the sheriff placed his bunch of roses on the stone table, put on spectacles which the secretary gave him, drew from the bundles of papers which covered the table a sheet of parchment, yellow, green, torn, and jagged in places, which seemed to have been folded in very small folds, and of which one side was covered with writing; standing under the light of the lamp, he held the sheet close to his eyes, and in his most solemn tone read as follows—

"In the name of the Father, the Son, and the Holy Ghost.

"This present day, the twenty-ninth of January, one thousand six hundred and ninetieth year of Our Lord.

"Has been wickedly deserted on the desert coast of Portland, with the intention of allowing him to perish of hunger, of cold, and of solitude, a child ten years old.

"That child was sold at the age of two years, by order of his most gracious Majesty, King James the Second.

"That child is Lord Fermain Clancharlie, the only legitimate son of Lord Linnæus Clancharlie, Baron Clancharlie and Hunkerville, Marquis of Corleone in Sicily, a Peer of England, and of Ann Bradshaw, his wife, both deceased. That child is the inheritor of the estates and titles of his father. For this reason he was sold, mutilated, disfigured, and put out of the way by desire of his most gracious Majesty.

"That child was brought up, and trained to be a mountebank at markets and fairs.

"He was sold at the age of two, after the death of the peer, his father, and ten pounds sterling were given to the king as his purchase-money, as well as for divers concessions, tolerations, and immunities.

"Lord Fermain Clancharlie, at the age of two years, was bought by me, the undersigned, who write these lines, and mutilated and disfigured by a Fleming of Flanders, called Hardquanonne, who alone is acquainted with the secrets and modes of treatment of Doctor Conquest.

"The child was destined by us to be a laughing mask (*masca ridens*).

"With this intention Hardquanonne performed on him the operation, *Bucca fissa usque ad aures*, which stamps an everlasting laugh upon the face.

"The child, by means known only to Hardquanonne, was put to sleep and made insensible during its performance, knowing nothing of the operation which he underwent.

"He does not know that he is Lord Clancharlie.

"He answers to the name of Gwynplaine.

"This fact is the result of his youth, and the slight powers of memory he could have had when he was bought and sold, being then barely two years old.

"Hardquanonne is the only person who knows how to perform the operation *Bucca fissa*, and the said child is the only living subject upon which it has been essayed.

"The operation is so unique and singular that though after long years this child should have come to be an old man instead of a child, and his black locks should have turned white, he would be immediately recognized by Hardquanonne.

"At the time that I am writing this, Hardquanonne, who has perfect knowledge of all the facts, and participated as principal therein, is detained in the prisons of his highness the Prince of Orange, commonly called King William III. Hardquanonne was apprehended and seized as being one of the band of Comprachicos or Cheylas. He is imprisoned in the dungeon of Chatham.

"It was in Switzerland, near the Lake of Geneva, between Lausanne and Vévey, in the very house in which his father and mother died, that the child was, in obedience with the orders of the king, sold and given up by the last servant of the deceased Lord Linnæus, which servant died soon after his master, so that this secret and delicate matter is now unknown to anyone on earth, excepting Hardquanonne, who is in the dungeon of Chatham, and ourselves, now about to perish.

"We, the undersigned, brought up and kept, for eight years, for professional purposes, the little lord bought by us of the king.

"To-day, flying from England to avoid Hardquanonne's ill fortune, our fear of the penal indictments, prohibitions, and fulminations of Parliament has induced us to desert, at night-fall, on the coast of Portland, the said child Gwynplaine, who is Lord Fermain Clancharlie.

"Now, we have sworn secrecy to the king, but not to God.

"To-night, at sea, overtaken by a violent tempest by the will of Providence, full of despair and distress, kneeling before Him who could save our lives, and may, perhaps, be willing to save our souls, having nothing more to hope from men, but everything to fear from God, having for only anchor and resource repentance of our bad actions, resigned to death, and content if Divine justice be satisfied, humble, penitent, and beating our breasts, we make this declaration, and confide and deliver it to the furious ocean to use as it best may according to the will of God. And may the Holy Virgin aid us, Amen. And we attach our signatures."

The sheriff interrupted, saying—

"Here are the signatures. All in different handwritings."

And he resumed.

"Doctor Gernardus Geestemunde.—Asuncion.—A cross, and at the side of it, Barbara Fermoy, from Tyrryf Isle, in the Hebrides; Gaizdorra, Captain; Giangirate; Jacques Quartourze, *alias* le Narbonnais; Luc-Pierre Capgaroupe, from the galleys of Mahon."

The sheriff, after a pause, resumed, a "note written in the same hand as the text and the first signature," and he read—

"Of the three men comprising the crew, the skipper having been swept off by a wave, there remain but two, and we have signed, Galdeazun; Ave Maria, Thief."

The sheriff, interspersing his reading with his own observations, continued, "At the bottom of the sheet is written—

" 'At sea, on board of the *Matutina*, Biscay hooker, from the Gulf de Pasages.' This sheet," added the sheriff, "is a legal document, bearing the mark of King James the Second. On the margin of the declaration, and in the same handwriting, there is this note, 'The present declaration is written by us on the back of the royal order, which was given us as our receipt when we bought the child. Turn the leaf and the order will be seen.' "

The sheriff turned the parchment, and raised it in his right hand, to expose it to the light.

A blank page was seen, if the word blank can be applied to a thing so moldy, and in the middle of the page three words were written, two Latin words, *Jussu regis*, and a signature, *Jeffreys*.

"*Jussu regis, Jeffreys,*" said the sheriff, passing from a grave voice to a clear one.

Gwynplaine was as a man on whose head a tile falls from the palace of dreams.

He began to speak, like one who speaks unconsciously.

"Gernardus, yes, the doctor. An old, sad-looking man. I was afraid of him. Gaïzdorrá, Captain, that means chief. There were women, Asuncion, and the other. And then the Provençal. His name was Capgaroupe. He used to drink out of a flat bottle on which there was a name written in red."

"Behold it," said the sheriff.

He placed on the table something which the secretary had just taken out of the bag. It was a gourd, with handles like ears, covered with wicker. This bottle had evidently seen service, and had sojourned in the water. Shells and seaweed adhered to it. It was encrusted and damascened over with the rust of ocean. There was a ring of tar round its neck, showing that it had been hermetically sealed. Now it was unsealed and open. They had, however, replaced in the flask a sort of bung made of tarred oakum, which had been used to cork it.

"It was in this bottle," said the sheriff, "that the men about to perish placed the declaration which I have just read. This message addressed to justice has been faithfully delivered by the sea."

The sheriff increased the majesty of his tones, and continued—

"In the same way that Harrow Hill produces excellent wheat, which is turned into fine flour for the royal table, so the sea renders every service in its power to England, and when a nobleman is lost, finds and restores him."

Then he resumed—

"On this flask, as you say, there is a name written in red."

He raised his voice, turning to the motionless prisoner—

"Your name, malefactor, is here. Such are the hidden channels by which truth, swallowed up in the gulf of human actions, floats to the surface."

The sheriff took the gourd, and turned to the light one of its sides, which had, no doubt, been cleaned for the ends of justice. Between the interstices of wicker was a narrow line of red reed, blackened here and there by the action of the water and of time.

The reed, notwithstanding some breakages, traced distinctly in the wickerwork these twelve letters—Hardquanonne.

Then the sheriff, resuming that monotonous tone of voice which resembles nothing else, and which may be termed a judicial accent, turned toward the sufferer.

"Hardquanonne! when by us, the sheriff, this bottle on which is your name, was for the first time shown, exhibited, and presented to you, you at once, and willingly, recognized it as having belonged to you. Then, the parchment being read to you which was contained, folded and enclosed within it, you would say no more; and in the hope, doubtless, that the lost child would never be recovered, and that you would escape punishment, you refused to answer. As the result of your refusal, you have had applied to you the *peine forte et dure;* and the second reading of the said parchment, on which is written the declaration and confession of your accomplices, was made to you—but in vain.

"This is the fourth day, and that which is legally set apart for the confrontation, and he who was deserted on the twenty-ninth of January, one thousand six hundred and ninety, having been brought into your presence, your devilish hope has vanished, you have broken silence, and recognized your victim."

The prisoner opened his eyes, lifted his head, and, with a voice strangely resonant of agony, but which had still an indescribable calm mingled with its hoarseness, pronounced in excruciating accents, from under the mass of stones, words to pronounce each of which he had to lift that which was like the slab of a tomb placed upon him. He spoke—

"I swore to keep the secret. I have kept it as long as I could. Men of dark lives are faithful, and hell has its honor. Now silence is useless. So be it! For this reason I speak. Well—yes; 'tis he! We did it between us—the king and I! The king, by his will; I, by my art!"

And looking at Gwynplaine—

"Now laugh forever!"

And he himself began to laugh.

This second laugh, wilder yet than the first, might have been taken for a sob.

The laughed ceased, and the man lay back. His eyelids closed.

The sheriff, who had allowed the prisoner to speak, resumed—

"All which is placed on record."

He gave the secretary time to write, and then said—

"Hardquanonne, by the terms of the law, after confrontation followed by identification, after the third reading of the declarations of your accomplices, since confirmed by your recognition and confession, and after your renewed avowal, you are about to be relieved from these irons, and placed at the good pleasure of her Majesty to be hung as *plagiary.*"

"*Plagiary,*" said the sergeant of the coif. "That is to say, a buyer and seller of children. Law of the Visigoths, seventh book, third section, paragraph *Usurpaverit,* and Salic law, section the forty-first, paragraph the second, and law of the Frisons, section the twenty-first, *Deplagio;* and Alexander Nequam says—

" '*Qui pueros vendis, plagiarius est tibi nomen.*' "

The sheriff placed the parchment on the table, laid down his spectacles, took up the nosegay, and said—

"End of *la peine forte et dure.* Hardquanonne, thank her Majesty."

By a sign, the justice of the quorum set in motion the man dressed in leather.

This man, who was the executioner's assistant, "groom of the gibbet," the old charters call him, went to the prisoner, took off the stones, one by one, from his chest, and lifted the plate of iron up, exposing the wretch's crushed sides. Then he freed his wrists and ankle-bones from the four chains that fastened him to the pillars.

The prisoner, released alike from stones and chains, lay flat on the ground, his eyes closed, his arms and legs apart, like a crucified man taken down from a cross.

"Hardquanonne," said the sheriff, "arise!"

The prisoner did not move.

The groom of the gibbet took up a hand and let it go; the hand fell back. The other hand, being raised, fell back likewise.

The groom of the gibbet seized one foot and then the other, and the heels fell back on the ground.

The fingers remained inert, and the toes motionless. The naked feet of an extended corpse seem, as it were, to bristle.

The doctor approached, and drawing from the pocket of his robe a little mirror of steel, put it to the open mouth of Hardquanonne. Then with his fingers he opened the eyelids. They did not close again. The glassy eyeballs remained fixed.

The doctor rose up and said—

"He is dead."

And he added—

"He laughed; that killed him."

" 'Tis of little consequence," said the sheriff. "After confession, life or death is a mere formality."

Then, pointing to Hardquanonne by a gesture with the nosegay of roses, the sheriff gave the order to the wapentake—

"A corpse to be carried away to-night."

The wapentake acquiesced by a nod.

And the sheriff added—

"The cemetery of the jail is opposite."

The wapentake nodded again.

The sheriff, holding in his left hand the nosegay and in his right the white wand, placed himself opposite Gwynplaine, who was still seated, and made him a low bow; then assuming another solemn attitude, he turned his head over his shoulder and looking Gwynplaine in the face, said—

"To you here present, we Philip Denzill Parsons, knight, sheriff of the county of Surrey, assisted by Aubrey Dominick, Esq., our clerk and registrar, and by our usual officers, duly provided by the direct and special commands of her Majesty, in virtue of our commission, and the rights and duties of our charge, and with authority from the Lord Chancellor of England, the affidavits having been drawn up and recorded, regard being had to the documents communicated by the Admiralty, after verification of attestations and signatures, after declarations read and heard, after confrontation made, all the statements and legal information having been completed, exhausted, and brought to a good and just issue, we signify and declare to you, in order that right may be done, that you are Fermain Clancharlie, Baron Clancharlie and Hunkerville, Marquis de Corleone in Sicily, and a peer of England; and God keep your lordship!"

And he bowed to him.

The sergeant on the right, the doctor, the justice of the quorum, the wapentake, the secretary, all the attendants except the executioner, repeated his salutation still more respectfully, and bowed to the ground before Gwynplaine.

"Ah," said Gwynplaine; "awake me!"

And he stood up, pale as death.

"I come to awake you indeed," said a voice which had not yet been heard.

A man came out from behind the pillars. As no one had entered the cell since the sheet of iron had given passage to the *cortége* of police, it was clear that this man had been there in the shadow before Gwynplaine had entered, that he had a regular right of attendance, and had been present by appointment and mission. The man was fat and pursy, and wore a court wig and a traveling cloak.

He was rather old than young, and very precise.

He saluted Gwynplaine with ease and respect—with the ease of a gentleman-in-waiting, and without the awkwardness of a judge.

"Yes," he said; "I have come to awaken you. For twenty-five years you have slept. You have been dreaming. It is time to awake. You believe yourself to be Gwynplaine; you are Clancharlie. You believe yourself to be one of the people; you belong to the peerage. You believe yourself to be of the lowest rank; you are of the highest. You believe yourself a player; you are a senator. You believe yourself poor; you are wealthy. You believe yourself to be of no account; you are important. Awake, my lord!"

Gwynplaine, in a low voice, in which a tremor of fear was to be distinguished, murmured—

"What does it all mean?"

"It means, my lord," said the fat man, "that I am called Barkilphedro; that I am an officer of the Admiralty; that this waif, the flask of Hardquanonne, was found on the beach, and was brought to be unsealed by me, according to the duty and prerogative of my office; that I opened it in the presence of two sworn jurors of the Jetsam Office, both members of parliament, William Brathwait, for the city of Bath, and Thomas Jervois, for Southampton; that the two jurors deciphered and attested the contents of the flask, and signed the necessary affidavit conjointly with me; that I made my report to her Majesty, and by order of the queen all necessary and legal formalities were carried out with the discretion necessary in a matter so delicate; that the last form, the confrontation, has just been carried out; that you have £40,000 a year; that you are a peer of the United Kingdom of Great Britain, a legislator and a judge, a supreme judge, a sovereign legislator, dressed in purple and ermine, equal to princes, like unto emperors; that you have on your brow the coronet of a peer, and that you are about to wed a duchess, the daughter of a king."

Under this transfiguration, overwhelming him like a series of thunderbolts, Gwynplaine fainted.

Chapter II

THE WAIF KNOWS ITS OWN COURSE

ALL THIS HAD OCCURRED OWING TO THE CIRCUMSTANCE OF A SOLDIER HAVING FOUND A BOTtle on the beach.

We will relate the facts.

In all facts there are wheels within wheels.

One day one of the four gunners composing the garrison of Castle Calshor picked up on the sand at low water a flask covered with wicker, which had been cast up by the tide. This flask, covered with mold, was corked by a tarred bung. The soldier carried the waif to the colonel of the castle, and the colonel sent it to the High Admiral of England. The Admiral meant the Admiralty; with waifs, the Admiralty meant Barkilphedro.

Barkilphedro, having uncorked and emptied the bottle, carried it to the queen. The queen immediately took the matter into consideration.

Two weighty counselors were instructed and consulted; viz., the Lord Chancellor, who is by law the guardian of the king's conscience, and the Lord Marshal, who is referee in Heraldry and in the pedigrees of the nobility. Thomas Howard, Duke of Norfolk, a Catholic peer, who is hereditary Earl Marshal of England, had sent word by his deputy Earl Marshal, Henry Howard, Earl Bindon, that he would agree with the Lord Chancellor. The Lord Chancellor was William Cowper. We must not confound this chancellor with his namesake and contemporary William Cowper, the anatomist and commentator on Bidloo, who published a treatise on muscles, in England, at the very time that Etienne Abeille published a history of bones, in France. A surgeon is a very different thing from a lord. Lord William Cowper is celebrated for having, with reference to the affair of Talbot Yelverton, Viscount Longueville, propounded this opinion: That in the English constitution, the restoration of a peer is more important than the restoration of a king. The flask found at Calshor had awakened his interest in the highest degree. The author of a maxim delights in opportunities to which it may be applied. Here was a case of the restoration of a peer. Search was made. Gwynplaine, by the inscription over his door, was soon found. Neither was Hardquanonne dead. A prison rots a man, but preserves him; if to keep is to preserve. People placed in Bastiles were rarely removed. There is little more change in the dungeon than in the tomb. Hardquanonne was still in the prison at Chatham. They had only to put their hands on him. He was transferred from Chatham to London. In the meantime, information was sought in Switzerland. The facts were found to be correct. They obtained from the local archives at Vévey, at Lausanne, the certificate of Lord Linnæus's marriage in exile, the certificate of his child's birth, the certificate of the decease of the father and mother; and they had duplicates, duly authenticated, made to answer all necessary requirements.

All this was done with the most rigid secrecy, with what is called royal promptitude, and with that mole-like silence recommended and practiced by Bacon, and later on made law by Blackstone, for affairs connected with the Chancellorship and the State, and in matters termed parliamentary. The *jussu regis* and the signature *Jeffreys* were authenticated. To those who have studied pathologically the cases of caprice called "our good-will and pleasure," this *jussu regis* is very simple. Why should James II, whose credit required the concealment of such acts, have allowed that to be written which endangered their success? The answer is, cynicism—haughty indifference. Oh! you believe that effrontery is confined to abandoned women? The *raison d'état* is equally abandoned. *Et se cupit ante videri.* To commit a crime and emblazon it—there is the sum total of history. The king tattooes himself like the convict. Often when it would be to a man's greatest advantage to escape from the hands of the police, or the records of history, he would seem to regret the escape, so great is the love of notoriety. Look at my arm! Observe the design! *I* am Lacenaire! See, a temple of love and a burning heart pierced through with an arrow! *Jussu regis.* It is I, James the Second. A man commits a bad action, and places his mark upon it. To fill up the measure of crime by effrontery, to denounce himself, to cling to his misdeeds, is the insolent bravado of the criminal. Christina seized Monaldeschi, had him confessed and assassinated, and said—

"I am the Queen of Sweden, in the palace of the King of France."

There is the tyrant who conceals himself, like Tiberius; and the tyrant who displays himself, like Philip II. One has the attributes of the scorpion, the other those rather of the leopard. James II was of this latter variety. He had, we know, a gay and open countenance, differing so far from Philip. Philip was sullen, James jovial. Both were equally ferocious. James II was an easy-minded tiger; like Philip II, his crimes lay light upon his conscience. He was a monster by the grace of God. Therefore he had nothing to dissimulate nor to extenuate, and his assassinations were by divine right. He, too, would not have minded leaving behind him those archives of Simancas, with all his misdeeds dated, classified, labeled, and put in order, each in its compartment, like poisons in the cabinet of a chemist. To set the sign-manual to crimes is right royal.

Every deed done is a draft drawn on the great invisible paymaster. A bill had just come due with the ominous endorsement, *Jussu regis.*

Queen Anne, in one particular unfeminine, seeing that she could keep a secret, demanded a confidential report of so grave a matter from the Lord Chancellor; one of the kind specified as "report to the royal ear." Reports of this kind have been common in all monarchies. At Vienna there was "a counselor of the ear"—an aulic dignitary. It was an ancient Carlovingian office—the *auricularius* of the old palatine deeds. He who whispers to the emperor.

William, Baron Cowper, Chancellor of England, whom the Queen believed in because he was short-sighted like herself, or even more so, had committed to writing a memorandum commencing thus: "Two birds were subject to Solomon, a lapwing, the Hudbud, who could speak all languages, and an eagle, the Simourganka, who covered with the shadow of his wings a caravan of twenty thousand men. Thus, under another form, Providence," etc. The Lord Chancellor proved the fact that the heir to a peerage had been carried off, mutilated, and then restored. He did not blame James II, who was, after all, the Queen's father. He even went so far as to justify him. First, there are ancient monarchical maxims. *E senioratu eripimus. In roturagio cadat.* Secondly, there is a royal right of mutilation. Chamberlayne asserts the fact. *Corpora et bona nostrorum subjectorum nostra sunt,* said James I, of glorious and learned memory. The eyes of dukes of the blood royal have been plucked out for the good of the kingdom. Certain princes, too near to the throne, have been conveniently stifled between mattresses, the cause of death being given out as apoplexy. Now, to stifle is worse than to mutilate. The King of Tunis tore out the eyes of his father, Muley Assem, and his ambassadors have not been the less favorably received by the Emperor. Hence the king may order the suppression of a limb like the suppression of a state, etc. It is legal. But one law does not destroy another. "If a drowned man is cast up by the water, and is not dead, it is an act of God readjusting one of the king. If the heir be found, let the coronet be given back to him. Thus was it done for Lord Alla, King of Northumberland, who was also a mountebank. Thus should be done to Gwynplaine, who is also a king, seeing that he is a peer. The lowness of the occupation which he has been obliged to follow, under constraint of superior power, does not tarnish the blazon: as in the case of Abdolmumen, who was a king, although he had been a gardener; that of Joseph, who was a saint, although he had been a carpenter; that of Apollo, who was a god, although he had been a shepherd."

In short, the learned chancellor concluded by advising the reinstatement, in all his estates and dignities, of Lord Fermain Clancharlie, miscalled Gwynplaine, on the sole condition that he should be confronted with the criminal Hardquanonne, and identified by the same. And on this point the chancellor, as constitutional keeper of the royal conscience, based the royal decision. The

Lord Chancellor added in a postscript that if Hardquanonne refused to answer, he should be subjected to the *peine forte et dure*, until the period called the *frodmortell*, according to the statute of King Athelstane, which orders the confrontation to take place on the fourth day. In this there is a certain inconvenience, for if the prisoner dies on the second or third day the confrontation becomes difficult; still the law must be obeyed. The inconvenience of the law makes part and parcel of it. In the mind of the Lord Chancellor, however, the recognition of Gwynplaine by Hardquanonne was indubitable.

Anne, having been made aware of the deformity of Gwynplaine, and not wishing to wrong her sister, on whom had been bestowed the estates of Clancharlie, graciously decided that the Duchess Josiana should be espoused by the new lord—that is to say, by Gwynplaine.

The reinstatement of Lord Fermain Clancharlie was, moreover, a very simple affair, the heir being legitimate, and in the direct line.

In cases of doubtful descent and of peerages in abeyance claimed by collaterals, the House of Lords must be consulted. This (to go no further back) was done in 1782, in the case of the barony of Sydney, claimed by Elizabeth Perry; in 1798, in that of the barony of Beaumont, claimed by Thomas Stapleton; in 1803, in that of the barony of Chandos, claimed by the Reverend Tymewell Brydges; in 1813, in that of the earldom of Banbury, claimed by General Knollys, etc., etc. But the present was no similar case. Here there was no pretence for litigation; the legitimacy was undoubted; the right clear and certain. There was no point to submit to the House, and the Queen, assisted by the Lord Chancellor, had power to recognize and admit the new peer.

Barkilphedro managed everything.

The affair, thanks to him, was kept so close, the secret was so hermetically sealed, that neither Josiana nor Lord David caught sight of the fearful abyss which was being dug under them. It was easy to deceive Josiana, entrenched as she was behind a rampart of pride. She was self-isolated. As to Lord David, they sent him to sea, off the coast of Flanders. He was going to lose his peerage, and had no suspicion of it. One circumstance is noteworthy.

It happened that at six leagues from the anchorage of the naval station commanded by Lord David, a captain called Halyburton broke through the French fleet. The Earl of Pembroke, President of the Council, proposed that this Captain Halyburton should be made vice-admiral. Anne struck out Halyburton's name, and put Lord David Dirry-Moir's in its place, that he might, when no longer a peer, have the satisfaction of being a vice-admiral.

Anne was well pleased. A hideous husband for her sister, and a fine step for Lord David. Mischief and kindness combined.

Her Majesty was going to enjoy a comedy. Besides, she argued to herself that she was repairing an abuse of power committed by her august father. She was reinstating a member of the peerage. She was acting like a great queen; she was protecting innocence according to the will of God; that Providence in its holy and impenetrable ways, etc., etc. It is very sweet to do a just action which is disagreeable to those whom we do not like.

To know that the future husband of her sister was deformed, sufficed the queen. In what manner Gwynplaine was deformed, and by what kind of ugliness, Barkilphedro had not communicated to the queen, and Anne had not deigned to inquire. She was proudly and royally disdainful. Besides, what could it matter? The House of Lords could not but be grateful. The Lord Chancellor, its oracle, had approved. To restore a peer is to restore the peerage. Royalty on this occasion had shown itself a good and scrupulous guardian of the privileges of the peerage. Whatever might be the face of the new lord, a face cannot be urged in objection to a right. Anne said all this to herself, or something like it, and went straight to her object, an object at once grand, womanlike, and regal; namely, to give herself a pleasure.

The queen was then at Windsor, a circumstance which placed a certain distance between the intrigues of the court and the public. Only such persons as were absolutely necessary to the plan were in the secret of what was taking place. As to Barkilphedro, he was joyful, a circumstance which gave a lugubrious expression to his face. If there be one thing in the world which can be more hideous than another, 'tis joy.

He had had the delight of being the first to taste the contents of Hardquanonne's flask. He seemed but little surprised, for astonishment is the attribute of a little mind. Besides, was it not all due to him, who had waited so long on duty at the gate of chance? Knowing how to wait, he had fairly won his reward.

This *nil admirari* was an expression of face. At heart we may admit that he was very much astonished. Anyone who could have lifted the mask with which he covered his inmost heart even before God would have discovered this: that at the very time Barkilphedro had begun to feel finally convinced that it would be impossible—even to him, the intimate and most infinitesimal enemy of Josiana—to find a vulnerable point in her lofty life. Hence an access of savage animosity lurked in his mind. He had reached the paroxysm which is called discouragement. He was all the more furious, because despairing. To gnaw one's chain!—how tragic and appropriate the expression! A villain gnawing at his own powerlessness!

Barkilphedro was perhaps just on the point of renouncing, not his desire to do evil to Josiana, but his hope of doing it; not the rage, but the effort. But how degrading to be thus baffled! To keep hate thenceforth in a case, like a dagger in a museum! How bitter the humiliation!

All at once to a certain goal—Chance, immense and universal, loves to bring such coincidences about—the flask of Hardquanonne came, driven from wave to wave, into Barkilphedro's hands. There is in the unknown an indescribable fealty which seems to be at the beck and call of evil. Barkilphedro, assisted by two chance witnesses, disinterested jurors of the Admiralty, uncorked the flask, found the parchment, unfolded, read it. What words could express his devilish delight!

It is strange to think that the sea, the wind, space, the ebb and flow of the tide, storms, calms, breezes, should have given themselves so much trouble to bestow happiness on a scoundrel. That cooperation had continued for fifteen years. Mysterious efforts! During fifteen years the ocean had never for an instant ceased from its labors. The waves transmitted from one to another the floating bottle. The shelving rocks had shunned the brittle glass; no crack had yawned in the flask; no friction had displaced the cork; the seaweeds had not rotted the osier; the shells had not eaten out the word "Hardquanonne"; the water had not penetrated into the waif; the mold had not rotted the parchment; the wet had hot effaced the writing. What trouble the abyss must have taken! Thus that which Gernardus had flung into darkness, darkness had handed back to Barkilphedro. The message sent to God had reached the devil. Space had committed an abuse of confidence, and a lurking sarcasm which mingles with events had so arranged that it had complicated the loyal triumph of the lost child's becoming Lord Clancharlie with a venomous victory—in doing a good action, it had mischievously placed justice at the service of iniquity. To save the victim of James II was to give a prey to Barkilphedro. To reinstate Gwynplaine was to crush Josiana. Barkilphedro had succeeded; and it was for this that for so many years the waves, the surge, the squalls had buffeted, shaken, thrown, pushed, tormented, and respected this bubble of glass, which bore within it so many commingled fates. It was for this that there had been a cordial cooperation between the winds, the tides, and the tempests: a vast agitation of all prodigies for the pleasure of a scoundrel; the infinite cooperating with an earthworm! Destiny is subject to such grim caprices.

Barkilphedro was struck by a flash of Titanic pride. He said to himself that it had all been done to fulfill his intentions. He felt that he was the object and the instrument.

But he was wrong. Let us clear the character of chance.

Such was not the real meaning of the remarkable circumstance of which the hatred of Barkilphedro was to profit. Ocean had made itself father and mother to an orphan, had sent the hurricane against his executioners, had wrecked the vessel which had repulsed the child, had swallowed up the clasped hands of the storm-beaten sailors, refusing their supplications and accepting only their repentance; the tempest received a deposit from the hands of death. The strong vessel containing the crime was replaced by the fragile phial containing the reparation. The sea changed its character, and, like a panther turning nurse, began to rock the cradle, not of the child, but of his destiny, whilst he grew up ignorant of all that the depths of ocean were doing for him.

The waves to which this flask had been flung watching over that past which contained a future; the whirlwind breathing kindly on it; the currents directing the frail waif across the fathomless wastes of water; the caution exercised by seaweed, the swells, the rocks; the vast froth of the abyss, taking under its protection an innocent child; the wave imperturbable as a conscience; chaos reestablishing order; the worldwide shadows ending in radiance; darkness employed to bring to light the star of truth; the exile consoled in his tomb; the heir given back to his inheritance; the crime of the king repaired; divine premeditation obeyed; the little, the weak, the deserted child with infinity for a guardian! All this Barkilphedro might have seen in the event on which he triumphed. This is what he did not see. He did not believe that it had all been done for Gwynplaine. He fancied that it had been effected for Barkilphedro, and that he was well worth the trouble. Thus it is ever with Satan.

Moreover, ere we feel astonished that a waif so fragile should have floated for fifteen years undamaged, we should seek to understand the tender care of the ocean. Fifteen years is nothing. On the 4th of October, 1867, on the coast of Morbihan, between the Isle de Croix, the extremity of the peninsula de Gavres, and the Rocher des Errants, the fishermen of Port Louis found a Roman amphora of the fourth century, covered with arabesques by the encrustations of the sea. That amphora had been floating fifteen hundred years.

Whatever appearance of indifference Barkilphedro tried to exhibit, his wonder had equaled his joy. Everything he could desire was there to his hand. All seemed ready made. The fragments of the event which was to satisfy his hate were spread out within his reach. He had nothing to do but to pick them up and fit them together—a repair which it was an amusement to execute. He was the artificer.

Gwynplaine! He knew the name. *Masca Ridens*. Like everyone else, he had been to see the Laughing Man. He had read the sign nailed up against the Tadcaster Inn, as one reads a playbill that attracts a crowd. He had noted it. He remembered it directly in its most minute details; and, in any case, it was easy to compare them with the original. That notice, in the electrical summons which arose in his memory, appeared in the depths of his mind, and placed itself by the side of the parchment signed by the shipwrecked crew, like an answer following a question, like the solution following an enigma; and the lines—"Here is to be seen Gwynplaine, deserted at the age of ten, on the 29th of January, 1690, on the coast at Portland"—suddenly appeared to his eyes in the splendor of an apocalypse. His vision was the light of *Mene, Tekel, Upharsin*, outside a booth. Here was the destruction of the edifice which made the existence of Josiana. A sudden earthquake. The lost child was found. There was a Lord Clancharlie; David Dirry-Moir was nobody. Peerage, riches, power, rank—all these things left Lord David and entered Gwynplaine. All the castles, parks, forests, town-houses, palaces, domains, Josiana included, belonged to Gwynplaine. And what a climax for Josiana! What had she now before her? Illustrious and haughty, a player; beautiful, a monster. Who could have hoped for this? The truth was that the joy of Barkilphedro had become enthusiastic. The most hateful combinations are surpassed by the infernal munificence of the unforeseen. When reality likes, it works masterpieces. Barkilphedro found that all his dreams had been nonsense; reality were better.

The change he was about to work would not have seemed less desirable had it been detrimental to him. Insects exist which are so savagely disinterested that they sting, knowing that to sting is to die. Barkilphedro was like such vermin.

But this time he had not the merit of being disinterested. Lord David Dirry-Moir owed him nothing, and Lord Fermain Clancharlie was about to owe him everything. From being a *protége*, Barkilphedro was about to become a protector. Protector of whom? Of a peer of England. He was going to have a lord of his own, and a lord who would be his creature. Barkilphedro counted on giving him his first impressions. His peer would be the morganatic brother-in-law of the queen. His ugliness would please the queen in the same proportion as it displeased Josiana. Advancing by such favor, and assuming grave and modest airs, Barkilphedro might become a somebody. He had always been destined for the church. He had a vague longing to be a bishop.

Meanwhile he was happy.

Oh, what a great success! and what a deal of useful work had chance accomplished for him! His vengeance—for he called it his vengeance—had been softly brought to him by the waves. He had not lain in ambush in vain.

He was the rock, Josiana was the waif. Josiana was about to be dashed against Barkilphedro, to his intense villainous ecstasy.

He was clever in the art of suggestion, which consists in making in the minds of others a little incision into which you put an idea of your own—holding himself aloof, and without appearing to mix himself up in the matter, it was he who arranged that Josiana should go to the Green Box and see Gwynplaine. It could do no harm. The appearance of the mountebank, in his low estate, would be a good ingredient in the combination; later on it would season it.

He had quietly prepared everything beforehand. What he most desired was something unspeakably abrupt. The work on which he was engaged could only be expressed in these strange words: the construction of a thunderbolt.

All preliminaries being complete, he had watched till all the necessary legal formalities had been accomplished. The secret had not oozed out, silence being an element of law.

The confrontation of Hardquanonne with Gwynplaine had taken place. Barkilphedro had been present. We have seen the result.

The same day a post-chaise belonging to the royal household was suddenly sent by her Majesty to fetch Lady Josiana from London to Windsor, where the queen was at the time residing.

Josiana, for reasons of her own, would have been very glad to disobey, or at least to delay obedience, and put off her departure till next day: but court life does not permit of these objections. She was obliged to set out at once, and to leave her residence in London, Hunkerville House, for her residence at Windsor, Corleone Lodge.

The Duchess Josiana left London at the very moment that the wapentake appeared at the Tadcaster Inn to arrest Gwynplaine and take him to the torture cell of Southwark.

When she arrived at Windsor, the Usher of the Black Rod, who guards the door of the presence chamber, informed her that her Majesty was in audience with the Lord Chancellor, and could not receive her until the next day; that, consequently, she was to remain at Corleone Lodge, at the orders of her Majesty; and that she should receive the queen's commands direct, when her Majesty awoke the next morning. Josiana entered her house feeling very spiteful, supped in a bad humor, had the spleen, dismissed everyone except her page, then dismissed him, and went to bed while it was yet daylight.

When she arrived she had learned that Lord David Dirry-Moir was expected at Windsor the next day, owing to his having, whilst at sea, received orders to return immediately and receive her Majesty's commands.

Chapter III

AN AWAKENING

No man could pass suddenly from Siberia into Senegal without losing consciousness.

—HUMBOLDT

THE SWOON OF A MAN, EVEN OF ONE THE MOST FIRM AND ENERGETIC, UNDER THE SUDDEN SHOCK of an unexpected stroke of good fortune, is nothing wonderful. A man is knocked down by the unforeseen blow, like an ox by the poleax. Francis d'Albescola, he who tore from the Turkish ports their iron chains, remained a whole day without consciousness when they made him pope. Now the stride from a cardinal to a pope is less than that from a mountebank to a peer of England.

No shock is so violent as a loss of equilibrium.

When Gwynplaine came to himself and opened his eyes it was night. He was in an arm-chair, in the midst of a large chamber lined throughout with purple velvet, over walls, ceiling, and floor. The carpet was velvet. Standing near him, with uncovered head, was the fat man in the traveling cloak, who had emerged from behind the pillar in the cell at Southwark. Gwynplaine was alone in the chamber with him. From the chair, by extending his arms, he could reach two tables, each bearing a branch of six lighted wax candles. On one of these tables there were papers and a casket, on the other refreshments; a cold fowl, wine, and brandy, served on a silver-gilt salver.

Through the panes of a high window, reaching from the ceiling to the floor, a semi-circle of pillars was to be seen, in the clear April night, encircling a courtyard with three gates, one very wide, and the other two low. The carriage gate, of great size, was in the middle; on the right, that for equestrians, smaller; on the left, that for foot passengers, still less. These gates were formed of iron railings, with glittering points. A tall piece of sculpture surmounted the central one. The columns were probably in white marble, as well as the pavement of the court, thus producing an effect like snow, and framed in its sheet of flat flags was a mosaic, the pattern of which was vaguely marked in the shadow. This mosaic, when seen by daylight, would no doubt have disclosed to the sight, with much emblazonry and many colors, a gigantic coat-of-arms, in the Florentine fashion. Zigzags of balustrades rose and fell, indicating stairs of terraces. Over the court frowned an immense pile of architecture, now shadowy and vague in the starlight. Intervals of sky, full of stars, marked out clearly the outline of the palace. An enormous roof could be seen, with the gable ends vaulted; garret windows, roofed over like visors; chimneys like towers; and entablatures covered with motionless gods and goddesses.

Beyond the colonnade there played in the shadow one of those fairy fountains in which, as the water falls from basin to basin, it combines the beauty of rain with that of the cascade, and as if scattering the contents of a jewel box, flings to the wind its diamonds and its pearls as though to divert the statues around. Long rows of windows ranged away, separated by panoplies in relievo, and by busts on small pedestals. On the pinnacles, trophies and morions with plumes cut in stone alternated with statues of heathen deities.

In the chamber where Gwynplaine was, on the side opposite the window, was a fireplace as high as the ceiling, and on another, under a dais, one of those old spacious feudal beds which were reached by a ladder, and where you might sleep lying across; the joint-stool of the bed was at its side; a row of arm-chairs by the walls, and a row of ordinary chairs, in front of them, completed the furniture. The ceiling was domed. A great wood fire in the French fashion blazed in the fireplace; by the richness of the flames, variegated of rose color and green, a judge of such things would have seen that the wood was ash—a great luxury. The room was so large that the branches of candles failed to light it up. Here and there curtains over doors, falling and swaying, indicated communications with other rooms. The style of the room was altogether that of the reign of James I—a style square and massive, antiquated and magnificent. Like the carpet and the lining of the chamber, the dais, the baldaquin, the bed, the stool, the curtains, the mantelpiece, the coverings of the table, the sofas, the chairs, were all of purple velvet.

There was no gilding, except on the ceiling. Laid on it, at equal distance from the four angles, was a huge round shield of embossed metal, on which sparkled, in dazzling relief, various coats of arms; amongst the devices, on two blazons, side by side, were to be distinguished the cap of a baron and the coronet of a marquis; were they of brass or of silver-gilt? You could not tell. They seemed to be of gold. And in the center of this lordly ceiling, like a gloomy and magnificent sky, the gleaming escutcheon was as the dark splendor of a sun shining in the night.

The savage, in whom is embodied the free man, is nearly as restless in a palace as in a prison. This magnificent chamber was depressing. So much splendor produces fear. Who could be the inhabitant of this stately palace? To what colossus did all this grandeur appertain? Of what lion is this the lair? Gwynplaine, as yet but half-awake, was heavy at heart.

"Where am I?" he said.

The man who was standing before him answered—

"You are in your own house, my lord."

Chapter IV

FASCINATION

IT TAKES TIME TO RISE TO THE SURFACE. AND GWYNPLAINE HAD BEEN THROWN INTO AN ABYSS OF stupefaction.

We do not gain our footing at once in unknown depths.

There are routs of ideas, as there are routs of armies. The rally is not immediate.

We feel as it were scattered; as though some strange evaporation of self were taking place.

God is the arm. Chance is the sling. Man is the pebble. How are you to resist, once flung?

Gwynplaine, if we may coin the expression, ricocheted from one surprise to another. After the love-letter of the duchess came the revelation in the Southwark dungeon.

In destiny, when wonders begin, prepare yourself for blow upon blow. The gloomy portals once open, prodigies pour in. A breach once made in the wall, and events rush upon us pell-mell. The marvelous never comes singly.

The marvelous is an obscurity. The shadow of this obscurity was over Gwynplaine. What was happening to him seemed unintelligible. He saw everything through the mist which a deep commotion leaves in the mind, like the dust caused by a falling ruin. The shock had been from top to bottom. Nothing was clear to him. However, light always returns by degrees. The dust settles. Moment by moment the density of astonishment decreases. Gwynplaine was like a man with his eyes open and fixed in a dream, as if trying to see what may be within it. He dispersed the mist. Then he reshaped it. He had intermittances of wandering. He underwent that oscillation of the mind in the unforeseen, which alternately pushes us in the direction in which we understand, and then throws us back in that which is incomprehensible. Who has not at some time felt this pendulum in his brain?

By degrees his thoughts dilated in the darkness of the event, as the pupil of his eye had done in the underground shadows at Southwark. The difficulty was to succeed in putting a certain space between accumulated sensations. Before that combustion of hazy ideas called comprehension can take place, air must be admitted between the emotions. There, air was wanting. The event, so to speak, could not be breathed.

In entering that terrible cell at Southwark, Gwynplaine had expected the iron collar of a felon; they had placed on his head the coronet of a peer. How could this be? There had not been space of time enough between what Gwynplaine had feared and what had really occurred; it had succeeded too quickly—his terror changing into other feelings too abruptly for comprehension. The contrasts were too tightly packed one against the other. Gwynplaine made an effort to withdraw his mind from the vice.

He was silent. This is the instinct of great stupefaction, which is more on the defensive than it is thought to be. Who says nothing is prepared for everything. A word of yours allowed to drop may be seized in some unknown system of wheels, and your utter destruction be compassed in its complex machinery.

The poor and weak live in terror of being crushed. The crowd ever expect to be trodden down. Gwynplaine had long been one of the crowd.

A singular state of human uneasiness can be expressed by the words: Let us see what will happen. Gwynplaine was in this state. You feel that you have not gained your equilibrium when an unexpected situation surges up under your feet. You watch for something which must produce a result. You are vaguely attentive. We will see what happens. What? You do not know. Whom? You watch.

The man with the paunch repeated, "You are in your own house, my lord."

Gwynplaine felt himself. In surprises, we first look to make sure that things exist; then, we feel ourselves, to make sure that we exist ourselves. It was certainly to him that the words were spoken; but he himself was somebody else. He no longer had his jacket on, or his esclavine of leather. He had a waistcoat of cloth of silver; and a satin coat, which he touched and found to be embroidered. He felt a heavy purse in his waistcoat pocket. A pair of velvet trunk hose covered his clown's tights. He wore shoes with high red heels. As they had brought him to this palace, so had they changed his dress.

The man resumed—

"Will your lordship deign to remember this: I am called Barkilphedro; I am clerk to the Admiralty. It was I who opened Hardquanonne's flask, and drew your destiny out of it. Thus, in the *Arabian Nights* a fisherman releases a giant from a bottle."

Gwynplaine fixed his eyes on the smiling face of the speaker.

Barkilphedro continued—

"Besides this palace, my lord, Hunkerville House, which is larger, is yours. You own Clancharlie Castle, from which you take your title, and which was a fortress in the time of Edward the Elder. You have nineteen bailiwicks belonging to you, with their villages and their inhabitants. This puts under your banner, as a landlord and a nobleman, about eighty thousand vassals and tenants. At Clancharlie you are a judge—judge of all, both of goods and of persons—and you hold your baron's court. The king has no right which you have not, except the privilege of coining money. The king, designated by the Norman law as chief signor, has justice, court, and coin. Coin is money. So that you, excepting in this last, are as much a king in your lordship as he is in his kingdom. You have the right, as a baron, to a gibbet with four pillars in England; and, as a marquis, to a scaffold with seven posts in Sicily: that of the mere lord having two pillars; that of a lord of the manor, three; and that of a duke, eight. You are styled prince in the ancient charters of Northumberland. You are related to the Viscounts Valentia in Ireland, whose name is Power, and to the Earls of Umfraville in Scotland, whose name is Angus. You are chief of a clan, like Campbell, Ardmannach, and Macallummore. You have eight barons' courts: Reculver, Baston, Hell-Kerters, Homble, Moricambe, Grundraith, Trenwardraith and others. You have a right over the turf-cutting of Pillinmore, and over the alabaster quarries near Trent. Moreover, you own all the country of Penneth Chase; and you have a mountain with an ancient town on it. The town is called Vinecaunton; the mountain is called Moil-enlli. All which gives you an income of forty thousand pounds a year. That is to say, forty times the five-and-twenty thousand francs with which a Frenchman is satisfied."

Whilst Barkilphedro spoke, Gwynplaine, in a crescendo of stupor, remembered the past. Memory is a gulf that a word can move to its lowest depths. Gwynplaine knew all the words pronounced by Barkilphedro. They were written in the last lines of the two scrolls which lined the van in which his childhood had been passed, and, from so often letting his eyes wander over them mechanically, he knew them by heart. On reaching, a forsaken orphan, the traveling caravan at Weymouth, he had found the inventory of the inheritance which awaited him; and in the morning, when the poor little boy awoke, the first thing spelled by his careless and unconscious eyes was his own title and its possessions. It was a strange detail added to all his other surprises, that, during fifteen years, rolling from highway to highway, the clown of a traveling theater, earning his bread day by day, picking up farthings, and living on crumbs, he should have traveled with the inventory of his fortune placarded over his misery.

Barkilphedro touched the casket on the table with his forefinger.

"My lord, this casket contains two thousand guineas which her gracious Majesty the Queen has sent you for your present wants."

Gwynplaine made a movement.

"That shall be for my Father Ursus," he said.

"So be it, my lord," said Barkilphedro. "Ursus, at the Tadcaster Inn. The Sergeant of the Coif, who accompanied us hither, and is about to return immediately, will carry them to him. Perhaps I may go to London myself. In that case I will take charge of it."

"I shall take them to him myself," said Gwynplaine.

Barkilphedro's smile disappeared, and he said—

"Impossible!"

There is an impressive inflection of voice which, as it were, underlines the words. Barkilphedro's tone was thus emphasized; he paused, so as to put a full stop after the word he had just uttered. Then he continued, with the peculiar and respectful tone of a servant who feels that he is master—

"My lord, you are twenty-three miles from London, at Corleone Lodge, your court residence, contiguous to the Royal Castle of Windsor. You are here unknown to anyone. You were brought here in a close carriage, which was awaiting you at the gate of the jail at Southwark. The servants who introduced you into this palace are ignorant who you are; but they know me, and that is sufficient. You may possibly have been brought to these apartments by means of a private key which is in my possession. There are people in the house asleep, and it is not an hour to awaken them. Hence we have time for an explanation, which, nevertheless, will be short. I have been commissioned by her Majesty—"

As he spoke, Barkilphedro began to turn over the leaves of some bundles of papers which were lying near the casket.

"My lord, here is your patent of peerage. Here is that of your Sicilian marquisate. These are the parchments and title-deeds of your eight baronies, with the seals of eleven kings, from Baldret, King of Kent, to James the Sixth of Scotland, and first of England and Scotland united. Here are your letters of precedence. Here are your rent-rolls, and titles and descriptions of your fiefs, freeholds, dependencies, lands, and domains. That which you see above your head in the emblazonment on the ceiling are your two coronets: the circlet with pearls for the baron, and the circlet with strawberry leaves for the marquis.

"Here, in the wardrobe, is your peer's robe of red velvet, bordered with ermine. To-day, only a few hours since, the Lord Chancellor and the Deputy Earl Marshal of England, informed of the result of your confrontation with the Comprachico Hardquanonne, have taken her Majesty's commands. Her Majesty has signed them, according to her royal will, which is the same as the law. All formalities have been complied with. To-morrow, and no later than to-morrow, you will take your seat in the House of Lords, where they have for some days been deliberating on a bill, presented by the Crown, having for its object the augmentation, by a hundred thousand pounds sterling yearly, of the annual allowance to the Duke of Cumberland, husband of the queen. You will be able to take part in the debate."

Barkilphedro paused, breathed slowly, and resumed.

"However, nothing is yet settled. A man cannot be made a peer of England without his own consent. All can be annulled and disappear, unless you acquiesce. An event nipped in the bud ere it ripens often occurs in state policy. My lord, up to this time silence has been preserved on what has occurred. The House of Lords will not be informed of the facts until to-morrow. Secrecy has been kept about the whole matter for reasons of state, which are of such importance that the influential persons who alone are at this moment cognizant of your existence, and of your rights, will forget them immediately should reasons of state command their being forgotten. That which is in darkness may remain in darkness. It is easy to wipe you out; the more so as you have a brother, the natural son of your father and of a woman who afterwards, during the exile of your father, became mistress to King Charles II, which accounts for your brother's high position at court; for it is to this brother, bastard though he be, that your peerage would revert. Do you wish this? I cannot think so. Well, all depends on you. The queen must be obeyed. You will not quit the house till to-morrow in a royal carriage, and to go to the House of Lords. My lord, will you be a peer of England; yes or no? The queen has designs for you. She destines you for an alliance almost royal. Lord Fermain Clancharlie, this is the decisive moment. Destiny never opens one door without shutting another. After a certain step in advance, to step back is impossible. Whoso enters into transfiguration, leaves behind him evanescence. My lord, Gwynplaine is dead. Do you understand?"

Gwynplaine trembled from head to foot.

Then he recovered himself.

"Yes," he said.

Barkilphedro, smiling, bowed, placed the casket under his cloak, and left the room.

Chapter V

We Think We Remember; We Forget

WHENCE ARISE THOSE STRANGE, VISIBLE CHANGES WHICH OCCUR IN THE SOUL OF MAN? Gwynplaine had been at the same moment raised to a summit and cast into an abyss.

His head swam with double giddiness. The giddiness of ascent and descent. A fatal combination.

He felt himself ascend, and felt not his fall.

It is appalling to see a new horizon.

A perspective affords suggestions—not always good ones.

He had before him the fairy glade, a snare perhaps, seen through opening clouds, and showing the blue depths of sky; so deep, that they are obscure.

He was on the mountain, whence he could see all the kingdoms of the earth. A mountain all the more terrible that it is a visionary one. Those who are on its apex are in a dream.

Palaces, castles, power, opulence, all human happiness extending as far as eye could reach; a map of enjoyments spread out to the horizon; a sort of radiant geography of which he was the center. A perilous mirage!

Imagine what must have been the haze of such a vision, not led up to, not attained to as by the gradual steps of a ladder, but reached without transition and without previous warning.

A man going to sleep in a mole's burrow, and awaking on the top of the Strasbourg steeple; such was the state of Gwynplaine.

Giddiness is a dangerous kind of glare, particularly that which bears you at once toward the day and toward the night, forming two whirlwinds, one opposed to the other.

He saw too much and not enough.

He saw all, and nothing.

His state was what the author of this book has somewhere expressed as the blind man dazzled.

Gwynplaine, left by himself, began to walk with long strides. A bubbling precedes an explosion.

Notwithstanding his agitation, in this impossibility of keeping still, he meditated. His mind liquefied as it boiled. He began to recall things to his memory. It is surprising how we find that we have heard so clearly that to which we scarcely listened. The declaration of the shipwrecked men, read by the sheriff in the Southwark cell, came back to him clearly and intelligibly. He recalled every word, he saw under it his whole infancy.

Suddenly he stopped, his hands clasped behind his back, looking up to the ceilings—the sky—no matter what—whatever was above him.

"Quits!" he cried.

He felt like one whose head rises out of the water. It seemed to him that he saw everything—the past, the future, the present—in the accession of a sudden flash of light.

"Oh!" he cried, for there are cries in the depths of thought. "Oh! it was so, was it? I was a lord. All is discovered. They stole, betrayed, destroyed, abandoned, disinherited, murdered me! The corpse of my destiny floated fifteen years on the sea; all at once it touched the earth, and it started up, erect and living. I am reborn. I am born. I felt under my rags that the breast there palpitating was not that of a wretch; and when I looked on crowds of men, I felt that they were the flocks, and that I was not the dog, but the shepherd! Shepherds of the people, leaders of men, guides and masters, such were my fathers; and what they were I am! I am a gentleman, and I have a sword; I am a baron, and I have a casque; I am a marquis, and I have a plume; I am a peer, and I have a coronet. Lo! they deprived me of all this. I dwelt in light, they flung me into darkness. Those who proscribed the father, sold the son. When my father was dead, they took from beneath his head the stone of exile which he had placed for his pillow, and, tying it to my neck, they flung me into a sewer. Oh! those scoundrels who tortured my infancy! Yes, they rise and move in the depths of my memory. Yes; I see them again. I was that morsel of flesh pecked to pieces on a tomb by a flight of crows. I bled and cried under all those horrible shadows. Lo! it was there that they precipitated me, under the crush of those who come and go, under the trampling feet of men, under the undermost of the human race, lower than the serf, baser than the serving man, lower than the felon, lower than the slave, at the spot where Chaos becomes a sewer, in which I was engulfed. It is from thence that I come; it is from this that I rise; it is from this that I am risen. And here I am now. Quits!"

He sat down, he rose, clasped his head with his hands, began to pace the room again, and his tempestuous monologue continued within him.

"Where am I?—on the summit? Where is it that I have just alighted?—on the highest peak? This pinnacle, this grandeur, this dome of the world, this great power, is my home. This temple is in air. I am one of the gods. I live in inaccessible heights. This supremacy, which I looked up to from below, and from whence emanated such rays of glory that I shut my eyes; this ineffaceable peerage; this impregnable fortress of the fortunate, I enter. I am in it. I am of it. Ah, what a decisive turn of the wheel! I was below, I am on high—on high forever! Behold me a lord! I shall have a scarlet robe. I shall have an earl's coronet on my head. I shall assist at the coronation of kings. They will take the oath from my hands. I shall judge princes and ministers. I shall exist. From the depths into which I was thrown, I have rebounded to the zenith. I have palaces in town and country: houses, gardens, chases, forests, carriages, millions. I will give fêtes. I will make laws. I shall have the choice of joys and pleasures. And the vagabond Gwynplaine, who had not the right to gather a flower in the grass, may pluck the stars from heaven!"

Melancholy overshadowing of a soul's brightness! Thus it was that in Gwynplaine, who had been a hero, and perhaps had not ceased to be one, moral greatness gave way to material splendor. A lamentable transition! Virtue broken down by a troop of passing demons. A surprise made on the weak side of man's fortress. All the inferior circumstances called by men superior, ambition, the purblind desires of instinct, passions, covetousness, driven far from Gwynplaine by the wholesome restraints of misfortune, took tumultuous possession of his generous heart. And from what had this arisen? From the discovery of a parchment in a waif drifted by the sea. Conscience may be violated by a chance attack.

Gwynplaine drank in great drafts of pride, and it dulled his soul. Such is the poison of that fatal wine.

Giddiness invaded him. He more than consented to its approach. He welcomed it. This was the effect of previous and long-continued thirst. Are we an accomplice of the cup which deprives us of reason? He had always vaguely desired this. His eyes had always turned toward the great. To watch is to wish. The eaglet is not born in the eyrie for nothing.

Now, however, at moments, it seemed to him the simplest thing in the world that he should be a lord. A few hours only had passed, and yet the past of yesterday seemed so far off! Gwynplaine had fallen into the ambuscade of Better, who is the enemy of Good.

Unhappy is he of whom we say, how lucky he is! Adversity is more easily resisted than prosperity. We rise more perfect from ill fortune than from good. There is a Charybdis in poverty, and a Scylla in riches. Those who remain erect under the thunderbolt are prostrated by the flash. Thou who standest without shrinking on the verge of a precipice, fear lest thou be carried up on the innumerable wings of mists and dreams. The ascent which elevates will dwarf thee. An apotheosis has a sinister power of degradation.

It is not easy to understand what is good luck. Chance is nothing but a disguise. Nothing deceives so much as the face of fortune. Is she Providence? Is she Fatality?

A brightness may not be a brightness, because light is truth, and a gleam may be a deceit. You believe that it lights you; but no, it sets you on fire.

At night—a candle made of mean tallow becomes a star if placed in an opening in the darkness. The moth flies to it.

In what measure is the moth responsible?

The sight of the candle fascinates the moth as the eye of the serpent fascinates the bird.

Is it possible that the bird and the moth should resist the attraction? Is it possible that the leaf should resist the wind? Is it possible that the stone should refuse obedience to the laws of gravitation?

These are material questions, which are moral questions as well.

After he had received the letter of the duchess, Gwynplaine had recovered himself. The deep love in his nature had resisted it. But the storm having wearied itself on one side of the horizon, burst out on the other, for in destiny, as in nature, there are successive convulsions. The first shock loosens, the second uproots.

Alas! how do the oaks fall?

Thus he who, when a child of ten, stood alone on the shore of Portland, ready to give battle, who had looked steadfastly at all the combatants whom he had to encounter, the blast which bore away the vessel in which he had expected to embark, the gulf which had swallowed up the plank, the yawning abyss, of which the menace was its retrocession, the earth which refused him a shelter, the sky which refused him a star, solitude without pity, obscurity without notice, ocean, sky, all the violence of one infinite space, and all the mysterious enigmas of another; he who had neither trembled nor fainted before the mighty hostility of the unknown; he who, still so young, had held his own with night, as Hercules of old had held his own with death; he who in the unequal struggle had thrown down this defiance, that he, a child, adopted a child, that he encumbered himself with a load, when tired and exhausted, thus rendering himself an easier prey to the attacks on his weakness, and, as it were, himself unmuzzling the shadowy monsters in ambush around him—he who, a precocious warrior, had immediately, and from his first steps out of the cradle, struggled breast to breast with destiny; he, whose disproportion with strife had not discouraged from striving; he who, perceiving in everything around him a frightful occultation of the human race, had accepted that eclipse, and proudly continued his journey; he who had known how to endure cold, thirst, hunger, valiantly; he who, a pigmy in stature, had been a colossus in soul: this Gwynplaine, who had conquered the great terror of the abyss under its double form, Tempest and Misery, staggered under a breath—Vanity.

Thus, when she has exhausted distress, nakedness, storms, catastrophes, agonies on an unflinching man, Fatality begins to smile, and her victim, suddenly intoxicated, staggers.

The smile of Fatality! Can anything more terrible be imagined? It is the last resource of the pitiless trier of souls in his proof of man. The tiger, lurking in destiny, caresses man with a velvet paw. Sinister preparation, hideous gentleness in the monster!

Every self-observer has detected within himself mental weakness coincident with aggrandizement. A sudden growth disturbs the system, and produces fever.

In Gwynplaine's brain was the giddy whirlwind of a crowd of new circumstances; all the light and shade of a metamorphosis; inexpressibly strange confrontations; the shock of the past against the future. Two Gwynplaines, himself doubled; behind, an infant in rags crawling through night— wandering, shivering, hungry, provoking laughter; in front, a brilliant nobleman—luxurious, proud, dazzling all London. He was casting off one form, and amalgamating himself with the other. He was casting the mountebank, and becoming the peer. Change of skin is sometimes change of soul. Now and then the past seemed like a dream. It was complex; bad and good. He thought of his father. It was a poignant anguish never to have known his father. He tried to picture him to himself. He thought of his brother, of whom he had just heard. Then he had a family! He, Gwynplaine! He lost himself in fantastic dreams. He saw visions of magnificence; unknown forms of solemn grandeur moved in mist before him. He heard flourishes of trumpets.

"And then," he said, "I shall be eloquent."

He pictured to himself a splendid entrance into the House of Lords. He should arrive full to the brim with new facts and ideas. What could he not tell them? What subjects he had accumulated! What an advantage to be in the midst of them, a man who had seen, touched, undergone, and suffered; who could cry aloud to them, "I have been near to everything, from which you are so far removed." He would hurl reality in the face of those patricians, crammed with illusions. They should tremble, for it would be the truth. They would applaud, for it would be grand. He would arise amongst those powerful men, more powerful than they. "I shall appear as a torch-bearer, to show them truth; and as a sword-bearer, to show them justice!" What a triumph!

And, building up these fantasies in his mind, clear and confused at the same time, he had attacks of delirium—sinking on the first seat he came to; sometimes drowsy, sometimes starting up. He came and went, looked at the ceiling, examined the coronets, studied vaguely the hieroglyphics of the emblazonment, felt the velvet of the walls, moved the chairs, turned over the parchments, read the names, spelled out the titles, Buxton, Homble, Grundraith, Hunkerville, Clancharlie; compared the wax, the impression, felt the twist of silk appended to the royal privy seal, approached the window, listened to the splash of the fountain, contemplated the statues, counted, with the patience of a somnambulist, the columns of marble, and said—

"It is real."

Then he touched his satin clothes, and asked himself—

"Is it I? Yes."

He was torn by an inward tempest.

In this whirlwind, did he feel faintness and fatigue? Did he drink, eat, sleep? If he did so, he was unconscious of the fact. In certain violent situations instinct satisfies itself, according to its requirements, unconsciously. Besides, his thoughts were less thoughts than mists. At the moment that the black flame of an eruption disgorges itself from depths full of boiling lava, has the crater any consciousness of the flocks which crop the grass at the foot of the mountain?

The hours passed.

The dawn appeared, and brought the day. A bright ray penetrated the chamber, and at the same instant broke on the soul of Gwynplaine.

And Dea! said the light.

BOOK THE SIXTH

URSUS UNDER DIFFERENT ASPECTS

Chapter I

WHAT THE MISANTHROPE SAID

AFTER URSUS HAD SEEN GWYNPLAINE THRUST WITHIN THE GATES OF SOUTHWARK JAIL, HE REmained, haggard, in the corner from which he was watching. For a long time his ears were haunted by the grinding of the bolts and bars, which was like a howl of joy that one wretch more should be enclosed within them.

He waited. What for? He watched. What for? Such inexorable doors, once shut, do not reopen so soon. They are tongue-tied by their stagnation in darkness, and move with difficulty, especially when they have to give up a prisoner. Entrance is permitted. Exit is quite a different matter. Ursus knew this. But waiting is a thing which we have not the power to give up at our own will. We wait in our own despite. What we do disengages an acquired force, which maintains its action when its object has ceased, which keeps possession of us and holds us, and obliges us for some time longer to continue that which has already lost its motive. Hence the useless watch, the inert position that we have all held at times, the loss of time which every thoughtful man gives mechanically to that which has disappeared. None escapes this law. We become stubborn in a sort of vague fury. We know not why we are in the place, but we remain there. That which we have begun actively, we continue passively, with an exhausting tenacity from which we emerge overwhelmed. Ursus, though differing from other men, was, as any other might have been, nailed to his post by that species of conscious reverie into which we are plunged by events all important to us, and in which we are impotent. He scrutinized by turns those two black walls, now the high one, then the low; sometimes the door near which the ladder to the gibbet stood, then that surmounted by a death's-head. It was as if he were caught in a vice, composed of a prison and a cemetery. This shunned and unpopular street was so deserted that he was unobserved.

At length he left the arch under which he had taken shelter, a kind of chance sentry-box, in which he had acted the watchman, and departed with slow steps. The day was declining, for his guard had been long. From time to time he turned his head and looked at the fearful wicket through which Gwynplaine had disappeared. His eyes were glassy and dull. He reached the end of the alley, entered another, then another, retracing almost unconsciously the road which he had taken some hours before. At intervals he turned, as if he could still see the door of the prison, though he was no longer in the street in which the jail was situated. Step by step he was approaching Tarrinzeau Field. The lanes in the neighborhood of the fairground were deserted pathways between enclosed gardens. He walked along, his head bent down, by the hedges and ditches. All at once he halted, and drawing himself up, exclaimed, "So much the better!"

At the same time he struck his fist twice on his head and twice on his thigh, thus proving himself to be a sensible fellow, who saw things in their right light; and then he began to growl inwardly, yet now and then raising his voice.

"It is all right! Oh, the scoundrel! the thief! the vagabond! the worthless fellow! the seditious scamp! It is his speeches about the government that have sent him there. He is a rebel. I was harboring a rebel. I am free of him, and lucky for me; he was compromising us. Thrust into prison! Oh, so much the better! What excellent laws! Ungrateful boy! I who brought him up! To give oneself so much trouble for this! Why should he want to speak and to reason? He mixed himself up in politics. The ass! As he handled pennies he babbled about the taxes, about the poor, about the people, about what was no business of his. He permitted himself to make reflections on pennies. He commented wickedly and maliciously on the copper money of the kingdom. He insulted the farthings of her Majesty. A farthing! Why, 'tis the same as the queen. A sacred effigy! Devil take it! a sacred effigy! Have we a queen, yes or no? Then respect her verdigris! Everything depends on the government: one ought to know that. I have experience, I have. I know something. They may say to me, But you give up politics, then? Politics, my friends, I care as much for them as for the rough hide of an ass. I received, one day, a blow from a baronet's cane. I said to myself, that is enough. I understand politics. The people have but a farthing, they give it; the queen takes it, the people thank her. Nothing can be more natural. It is for the peers to arrange the rest; their lordships, the lords spiritual and temporal. Oh! so Gwynplaine is locked up! So he is in prison. That is just as it should be. It is equitable, excellent, well-merited, and legitimate. It is his own fault. To criticize is forbidden. Are you a lord, you idiot? The constable has seized him, the justice of the quorum has carried him off, the sheriff has him in custody. At this moment he is probably being examined by a sergeant of the coif. They pluck out your crimes, those clever fellows! Imprisoned, my wag! So much the worse for him, so much the better for me! Faith, I am satisfied. I own frankly that fortune favors me. Of what folly was I guilty when I picked up that little boy and girl! We were so quiet before, Homo and I! What had they to do in my caravan, the little blackguards? Didn't I brood over them when they were young! Didn't I draw them along with my harness! Pretty foundlings, indeed; he as ugly as sin, and she blind of both eyes! Where was the use of depriving myself of everything for their sakes? The beggars grow up, forsooth, and make love to each other. The flirtations of the deformed! It was to that we had come. The toad and the mole; quite an idyl! That was what went on in my household. All which was sure to end by going before the justice. The toad talked politics! But now I am free of him. When the wapentake came I was at first a fool; one always doubts one's own good luck. I believed that I did not see what I did see; that it was impossible, that it was a nightmare, that a daydream was playing me a trick. But no! Nothing could be truer. It is all clear. Gwynplaine is really in prison. It is a stroke of Providence. Praise be to it! He was the monster who, with the row he made, drew attention to my establishment, and denounced my poor wolf. Be off, Gwynplaine; and, see, I am rid of both! Two birds killed with one stone. Because Dea will die, now that she can no longer see Gwynplaine. For she sees him, the idiot! She will have no object in life. She will say, 'What am I to do in the world?' Good-bye! To the devil with both of them. I always hated the creatures! Die, Dea! Oh, I am quite comfortable!"

Chapter II

WHAT HE DID

H E RETURNED TO THE TADCASTER INN.
It struck half-past six. It was a little before twilight.

Master Nicless stood on his doorstep.

He had not succeeded, since the morning, in extinguishing the terror which still showed on his scared face.

He perceived Ursus from afar.

"Well!" he cried.

"Well! what?"

"Is Gwynplaine coming back? It is full time. The public will soon be coming. Shall we have the performance of 'The Laughing Man' this evening?"

"I am the laughing man," said Ursus.

And he looked at the tavern-keeper with a loud chuckle.

Then he went up to the first floor, opened the window next to the sign of the inn, leant over toward the placard about Gwynplaine, the laughing man, and the bill of *Chaos Vanquished*; unnailed the one, tore down the other, put both under his arm, and descended.

Master Nicless followed him with his eyes.

"Why do you unhook that?"

Ursus burst into a second fit of laughter.

"Why do you laugh?" said the tavern-keeper.

"I am re-entering private life."

Master Nicless understood, and gave an order to his lieutenant, the boy Govicum, to announce to everyone who should come that there would be no performance that evening. He took from the door the box made out of a cask, where they received the entrance money, and rolled it into a corner of the lower sitting-room.

A moment after, Ursus entered the Green Box.

He put the two signs away in a corner, and entered what he called the woman's wing.

Dea was asleep.

She was on her bed, dressed as usual, excepting that the body of her gown was loosened, as when she was taking her siesta.

Near her Vinos and Fibi were sitting—one on a stool, the other on the ground—musing. Notwithstanding the lateness of the hour, they had not dressed themselves in their goddesses' gauze, which was a sign of deep discouragement. They had remained in their drugget petticoats and their dress of coarse cloth.

Ursus looked at Dea.

"She is rehearsing for a longer sleep," murmured he.

Then, addressing Fibi and Vinos—

"You both know all. The music is over. You may put your trumpets into the drawer. You did well not to equip yourselves as deities. You look ugly enough as you are, but you were quite right. Keep on your petticoats—no performance to-night, nor to-morrow, nor the day after to-morrow. No Gwynplaine. Gwynplaine is clean gone."

Then he looked at Dea again.

"What a blow to her this will be! It will be like blowing out a candle."

He inflated his cheeks.

"Puff! nothing more."

Then, with a little dry laugh—

"Losing Gwynplaine, she loses all. It would be just as if I were to lose Homo. It will be worse. She will feel more lonely than anyone else could. The blind wade through more sorrow than we do."

He looked out of the window at the end of the room.

"How the days lengthen! It is not dark at seven o'clock. Nevertheless, we will light up."

He struck the steel and lighted the lamp which hung from the ceiling of the Green Box.

Then he leaned over Dea.

"She will catch cold; you have unlaced her bodice too low. There is a proverb—

> *" 'Though April skies be bright,*
> *Keep all your wrappers tight.' "*

Seeing a pin shining on the floor, he picked it up, and pinned up her sleeve. Then he paced the Green Box, gesticulating.

"I am in full possession of my faculties. I am lucid, quite lucid. I consider this occurrence quite proper, and I approve of what has happened. When she awakes I will explain everything to her clearly. The catastrophe will not be long in coming. No more Gwynplaine. Good night, Dea. How well all has been arranged! Gwynplaine in prison, Dea in the cemetery, they will be *vis-á-vis!* A dance of death! Two destinies going off the stage at once. Pack up the dresses. Fasten the valise. For valise, read coffin. It was just what was best for them both. Dea without eyes, Gwynplaine without a face. On high the Almighty will restore sight to Dea and beauty to Gwynplaine. Death puts things to rights. All will be well. Fibi, Vinos, hang up your tambourines on the nail. Your talents for noise will go to rust; my beauties, no more playing, no more trumpeting *Chaos Vanquished* is vanquished. 'The Laughing Man' is done for. 'Taratantara' is dead. Dea sleeps on. She does well. If I were she I would never awake. Oh! she will soon fall asleep again. A skylark like her takes very little killing. This comes of meddling with politics. What a lesson! Governments are right. Gwynplaine to the sheriff. Dea to the gravedigger. Parallel cases! Instructive symmetry! I hope the tavern-keeper has barred the door. We are going to die to-night quietly at home, between ourselves—not I, nor Homo, but Dea. As for me, I shall continue to roll on in the caravan. I belong to the meanderings of vagabond life. I shall dismiss these two women. I shall not keep even one of them. I have a tendency to become an old scoundrel. A maidservant in the house of a libertine is like a loaf of bread on the shelf. I decline the temptation. It is not becoming at my age. *Turpe senilis amor.* I will follow my way alone with Homo. How astonished Homo will be! Where is Gwynplaine? Where is Dea? Old comrade, here we are once more alone together. Plague take it! I'm delighted. Their bucolics were an encumbrance. Oh! that scamp Gwynplaine, who is never coming back. He has left us stuck here. I say All right. And now 'tis Dea's turn. That won't be long. I like things to be done with. I would not snap my fingers to stop her dying—her dying! I tell you! See, she awakes!"

Dea opened her eyelids; many blind persons shut them when they sleep. Her sweet unwitting face wore all its usual radiance.

"She smiles," whispered Ursus, "and I laugh. That is as it should be."

Dea called—

"Fibi! Vinos! It must be the time for the performance. I think I have been asleep a long time. Come and dress me."

Neither Fibi nor Vinos moved.

Meanwhile, the ineffable blind look of Dea's eyes met those of Ursus. He started.

"Well!" he cried; "what are you about? Vinos! Fibi! Do you not hear your mistress? Are you deaf? Quick! the play is going to begin."

The two women looked at Ursus in stupefaction.

Ursus shouted—

"Do you not hear the audience coming in? Fibi, dress Dea. Vinos, take your tambourine."

Fibi was obedient; Vinos, passive. Together, they personified submission. Their master, Ursus, had always been to them an enigma. Never to be understood is a reason for being always obeyed. They simply thought he had gone mad, and did as they were told. Fibi took down the costume, and Vinos the tambourine.

Fibi began to dress Dea. Ursus let down the door-curtain of the women's room, and from behind the curtain continued—

"Look there, Gwynplaine! the court is already more than half full of people. They are in heaps in the passages. What a crowd! And you say that Fibi and Vinos look as if they did not see them. How stupid the gypsies are! What fools they are in Egypt! Don't lift the curtain from the door. Be decent. Dea is dressing."

He paused, and suddenly they heard an exclamation—

"How beautiful Dea is!"

It was the voice of Gwynplaine.

Fibi and Vinos started, and turned round. It was the voice of Gwynplaine, but in the mouth of Ursus.

Ursus, by a sign which he made through the door ajar, forbade the expression of any astonishment.

Then, again taking the voice of Gwynplaine—

"Angel!"

Then he replied in his own voice—

"Dea an angel! You are a fool, Gwynplaine. No mammifer can fly except the bats."

And he added—

"Look here, Gwynplaine! Let Homo loose; that will be more to the purpose."

And he descended the ladder of the Green Box very quickly, with the agile spring of Gwynplaine, imitating his step so that Dea could hear it.

In the court he addressed the boy, whom the occurrences of the day had made idle and inquisitive.

"Spread out both your hands," said he, in a loud voice.

And he poured a handful of pence into them.

Govicum was grateful for his munificence.

Ursus whispered in his ear—

"Boy, go into the yard; jump, dance, knock, bawl, whistle, coo, neigh, applaud, stamp your feet, burst out laughing, break something."

Master Nicless, saddened and humiliated at seeing the folks who had come to see "The Laughing Man" turned back and crowding toward other caravans, had shut the door of the inn. He had even given up the idea of selling any beer or spirits that evening, that he might have to answer no awkward questions; and, quite overcome by the sudden close of the performance, was looking, with his candle in his hand, into the court from the balcony above.

Ursus, taking the precaution of putting his voice between parentheses fashioned by adjusting the palms of his hands to his mouth, cried out to him—

"Sir! do as your boy is doing; yelp, bark, howl."

He reascended the steps of the Green Box, and said to the wolf—

"*Talk* as much as you can."

Then, raising his voice—

"What a crowd there is! We shall have a crammed performance."

In the meantime Vinos played the tambourine. Ursus went on—

"Dea is dressed. Now we can begin. I am sorry they have admitted so many spectators. How thickly packed they are! Look, Gwynplaine, what a mad mob it is. I will bet that to-day we shall take more money than we have ever done yet. Come, gypsies, play up, both of you. Come here. Fibi, take your clarion. Good. Vinos, drum on your tambourine. Fling it up and catch it again. Fibi, put yourself into the attitude of Fame. Young ladies, you have too much on. Take off those jackets. Replace stuff by gauze. The public like to see the female form exposed. Let the moralists thunder. A little indecency. Devil take it! What of that? Look voluptuous, and rush into wild melodies. Snort, blow, whistle, flourish, play the tambourine. What a number of people, my poor Gwynplaine!"

He interrupted himself.

"Gwynplaine, help me. Let down the platform." He spread out his pocket-handkerchief. "But first let me roar in my rag," and he blew his nose violently, as a ventriloquist ought. Having returned his handkerchief to his pocket, he drew the pegs out of the pulleys, which creaked as usual as the platform was let down.

"Gwynplaine, do not draw the curtain until the performance begins. We are not alone. You two come on in front. Music, ladies! tum, tum, tum. A pretty audience we have! the dregs of the people. Good heavens!"

The two gypsies, stupidly obedient, placed themselves in their usual corners of the platform. Then Ursus became wonderful. It was no longer a man, but a crowd. Obliged to make abundance out of emptiness, he called to aid his prodigious powers of ventriloquism. The whole orchestra of human and animal voices which was within him he called into tumult at once.

He was legion. Anyone with his eyes closed would have imagined that he was in a public place on some day of rejoicing, or in some sudden popular riot. A whirlwind of clamor proceeded from Ursus; he sang, he shouted, he talked, he coughed, he spat, he sneezed, took snuff, talked and responded, put questions and gave answers, all at once. The half-uttered syllables ran one into another. In the court, untenanted by a single spectator, were heard men, women, and children. It was a clear confusion of tumult. Strange laughter wound, vapor-like, through the noise, the chirping of birds, the swearing of cats, the wailings of children at the breast. The indistinct tones of drunken men were to be heard, and the growls of dogs under the feet of people who stamped on them. The cries came from far and near, from top to bottom, from the upper boxes to the pit. The whole was an uproar, the detail was a cry. Ursus clapped his hands, stamped his feet, threw his voice to the end of the court, and then made it come from underground. It was both stormy and familiar. It passed from a murmur to a noise, from a noise to a tumult, from a tumult to a tempest. He was himself, any, everyone else. Alone, and polyglot. As there are optical illusions, there are also auricular illusions. That which Proteus did to sight Ursus did to hearing. Nothing could be more marvelous than his facsimile of multitude. From time to time he opened the door of the women's apartment and looked at Dea. Dea was listening. On his part the boy exerted himself to the utmost. Vinos and Fibi trumpeted conscientiously, and took turns with the tambourine. Master Nicless, the only spectator, quietly made himself the same explanation as they did, that Ursus was gone mad, which was, for that matter, but another sad item added to his misery. The good tavern-keeper growled out, "What insanity!" And he was serious as a man might well be who has the fear of the law before him.

Govicum, delighted at being able to help in making a noise, exerted himself almost as much as Ursus. It amused him, and, moreover, it earned him pence.

Homo was pensive.

In the midst of the tumult Ursus now and then uttered such words as these—"Just as usual, Gwynplaine. There is a cabal against us. Our rivals are undermining our success. Tumult is the seasoning of triumph. Besides there are too many people. They are uncomfortable. The angles of their neighbors' elbows do not dispose them to good-nature. I hope the benches will not give way. We shall be the victims of an incensed population. Oh! if our friend Tom-Jim-Jack were only here! but he never comes now. Look at those heads rising one above the other. Those who are forced to stand don't look very well pleased, though the great Galen pronounced it to be strengthening. We will shorten the entertainment; as only *Chaos Vanquished* was announced in the playbill, we will not play *Ursus Rursus*. There will be something gained in that. What an uproar! O blind turbulence of the masses. They will do us some damage. However, they can't go on like this. We should not be able to play. No one can catch a word of the piece. I am going to address them. Gwynplaine, draw the curtain a little aside.—Gentlemen." Here Ursus addressed himself with a shrill and feeble voice—

"Down with that old fool!"

Then he answered in his own voice—

"It seems that the mob insult me. Cicero is right: *plebs fex urbis*. Never mind, we will admonish the mob, though I shall have a great deal of trouble to make myself heard. I will speak, notwithstanding. Man, do your duty. Gwynplaine, look at that scold grinding her teeth down there."

Ursus made a pause, in which he placed a gnashing of his teeth. Homo, provoked, added a second, and Govicum a third.

Ursus went on—

"The women are worse than the men. The moment is unpropitious, but it doesn't matter! Let us try the power of a speech; an eloquent speech is never out of place. Listen, Gwynplaine, to my attractive exordium. Ladies and gentlemen, I am a bear. I take off my head to address you. I humbly appeal to you for silence." Ursus, lending a cry to the crowd, said, "Grumphl?!"

Then he continued—

"I respect my audience. Grumphll is an epiphonema as good as any other welcome. You growlers. That you are all of the dregs of the people, I do not doubt. That in no way diminishes my esteem for you. A well-considered esteem. I have a profound respect for the bullies who honor me with their custom. There are deformed folks amongst you. They give me no offense. The lame and the humpbacked are works of nature. The camel is gibbous. The bison's back is humped. The badger's left legs are shorter than the right, That fact is decided by Aristotle, in his treatise on the walking of animals. There are those amongst you who have but two shirts. one on his back, and the other at the pawnbroker's. I know that to be true. Albuquerque pawned his moustache, and St. Denis his glory. The Jews advanced money on the glory. Great examples. To have debts is to have something. I revere your beggardom."

Ursus cut short his speech, interrupting it in a deep bass voice by the shout—

"Triple ass!"

And he answered in his politest accent—

"I admit it. I am a learned man. I do my best to apologize for it. I scientifically despise science. Ignorance is a reality on which we feed; science is a reality on which we starve. In general one is obliged to choose between two things. To be learned and grow thin, or to browse and be an ass. O gentlemen! browse! Science is not worth a mouthful of anything nice. I had rather eat a sirloin of beef than know what they call the psoas muscle. I have but one merit. A dry eye. Such as you see me, I have never wept. It must be owned that I have never been satisfied—never satisfied—not even with myself. I despise myself; but I submit this to the members of the opposition here present—if Ursus is only a learned man, Gwynplaine is an artist."

He groaned again—

"Grumphll!"

And resumed—

"Grumphll again! it is an objection. All the same, I pass it over. Near Gwynplaine, gentlemen and ladies, is another artist, a valued and distinguished personage who accompanies us. His lordship Homo, formerly a wild dog, now a civilized wolf, and a faithful subject of her Majesty's. Homo is a mine of deep and superior talent. Be attentive and watch. You are going to set Homo play as well as Gwynplaine, and you must do honor to art. That is an attribute of great nations. Are you men of the woods? I admit the fact. In that case, *sylvae sunt consule dignae*. Two artists are well worth one consul. All right! Someone has flung a cabbage stalk at me, but did not hit me. That will not stop my speaking; on the contrary, a danger evaded makes folks garrulous, *Garrula pericula*, says Juvenal. My hearers! there are amongst you drunken men and drunken women. Very well. The men are unwholesome. The women are hideous. You have all sorts of excellent reasons for stowing yourselves away here on the benches of the pothouse. Want of work, idleness, the spare time between two robberies, porter, ale, stout, malt, brandy, gin, and the attraction of one sex for the other. What could be better? A wit prone to irony would find this a fair field. But I abstain. 'Tis luxury; so be it, but even an orgy should be kept within bounds. You are gay, but noisy. You imitate successfully the cries of beasts; but what would you say if, when you were making love to a lady, I passed my time in barking at you? It would disturb you, and so it disturbs us. I order you to hold your tongues. Art is as respectable as debauch. I speak to you civilly."

He apostrophized himself—

"May the fever strangle you, with your eyebrows like the beard of rye."

And he replied—

"Honorable gentlemen, let the rye alone. It is impious to insult the vegetables, by likening them either to human creatures or animals. Besides, the fever does not strangle. 'Tis a false metaphor. For pity's sake, keep silence. Allow me to tell you that you are slightly wanting in the repose which characterizes the true English gentleman. I see that some amongst you who have shoes out of which their toes are peeping, take advantage of the circumstance to rest their feet on the shoulders of those who are in front of them, causing the ladies to remark that the soles of shoes divide always at the part at which is the head of the metatarsal bones. Show more of your hands, and less of your feet. I perceive scamps who plunge their ingenious fists into the pockets of their foolish neighbors. Dear pickpockets, have a little modesty. Fight those next to you if you like; do not plunder them. You will vex them less by blackening an eye, than by lightening their purses of a penny. Break their noses if you like. The shopkeeper thinks more of his money than of his beauty. Barring this, accept my sympathies, for I am not pedantic enough to blame thieves. Evil exists. Everyone endures it, everyone inflicts it. No one is exempt from the vermin of his sins. That's what I keep saying. Have we not all our itch? I, myself, have made mistakes. *Plaudite, cives*."

Ursus uttered a long groan, which he overpowered by these concluding words—

"My lords and gentlemen, I see that my address has unluckily displeased you. I take leave of your hisses for a moment. I shall put on my head, and the performance is going to begin."

He dropped his oratorical tone, and resumed his usual voice.

"Close the curtains. Let me breathe. I have spoken like honey. I have spoken well. My words were like velvet; but they were useless. I called them my lords and gentlemen. What do you think of all this scum, Gwynplaine? How well may we estimate the ills which England has suffered for the last forty years through the ill-temper of these irritable and malicious spirits. The ancient Britons were warlike, these are melancholy and learned. They glory in despising the laws and contemning royal authority. I have done all that human eloquence can do. I have been prodigal of metonymics, as gracious as the blooming cheek of youth. Were they softened by them? I doubt it. What can affect a people who eat so extraordinarily, who stupefy themselves by tobacco so completely that their literary men often write their works with a pipe in their mouths? Never mind. Let us begin the play."

The rings of the curtain were heard being drawn over the rod. The tambourines of the gypsies were still. Ursus took down his instrument, executed his prelude, and said, in a low tone: "Alas! Gwynplaine, how mysterious it is"; then he flung himself down with the wolf.

When he had taken down his instrument, he had also taken from the nail a rough wig which he had, and which he had thrown on the stage in a corner within his reach. The performance of *Chaos Vanquished* took place as usual, minus only the effect of the blue light and the brilliancy of the fairies. The wolf played his best. At the proper moment Dea made her appearance, and, in her voice so tremulous and heavenly, invoked Gwynplaine. She extended her arms, feeling for that head.

Ursus rushed at the wig, ruffled it, put it on, advanced softly, and holding his breath, his head bristled thus under the hand of Dea.

Then calling all his art to his aid, and copying Gwynplaine's voice, he sang with ineffable love the response of the monster to the call of the spirit. The imitation was so perfect that again the gypsies looked for Gwynplaine, frightened at hearing without seeing him.

Govicum, filled with astonishment, stamped, applauded, clapped his hands, producing an Olympian tumult, and himself laughed as if he had been a chorus of gods. This boy, it must be confessed, developed a rare talent for acting an audience.

Fibi and Vinos, being automatons of which Ursus pulled the strings, rattled their instruments, composed of copper and ass's skin, the usual sign of the performance being over and of the departure of the people.

Ursus arose, covered with perspiration. He said, in a low voice, to Homo, "You see it was necessary to gain time. I think we have succeeded. I have not acquitted myself badly. I, who have as much reason as anyone to go distracted. Gwynplaine may perhaps return to-morrow. It is useless to kill Dea directly. I can explain matters to you."

He took off his wig and wiped his forehead.

"I am a ventriloquist of genius," murmured he. "What talent I displayed! I have equaled Brabant, the engastrimist of Francis I of France. Dea is convinced that Gwynplaine is here."

"Ursus," said Dea, "where is Gwynplaine?"

Ursus started, and turned round. Dea was still standing at the back of the stage, alone under the lamp which hung from the ceiling. She was pale, with the pallor of a ghost.

She added, with an ineffable expression of despair—

"I know. He has left us. He is gone. I always knew that he had wings."

And raising her sightless eyes on high, she added—

"When shall I follow?"

Chapter III

COMPLICATIONS

URSUS WAS STUNNED.
He had not sustained the illusion.

Was it the fault of ventriloquism? Certainly not. He had succeeded in deceiving Fibi and Vinos, who had eyes, although he had not deceived Dea, who was blind. It was because Fibi and Vinos saw with their eyes, while Dea saw with her heart. He could not utter a word. He thought to himself, *Bos in linguá*. The troubled man has an ox on his tongue.

In his complex emotions, humiliation was the first which dawned on him. Ursus, driven out of his last resource, pondered.

"I lavish my onomatopies in vain." Then, like every dreamer, he reviled himself. "What a frightful failure! I wore myself out in a pure loss of imitative harmony. But what is to be done next?"

He looked at Dea. She was silent, and grew paler every moment, as she stood perfectly motionless. Her sightless eyes remained fixed in depths of thought.

Fortunately, something happened. Ursus saw Master Nicless in the yard, with a candle in his hand, beckoning to him.

Master Nicless had not assisted at the end of the phantom comedy played by Ursus. Someone had happened to knock at the door of the inn. Master Nicless had gone to open it. There had been two knocks, and twice Master Nicless had disappeared. Ursus, absorbed by his hundred-voiced monologue, had not observed his absence.

On the mute call of Master Nicless, Ursus descended.

He approached the tavern-keeper. Ursus put his finger on his lips. Master Nicless put his finger on his lips.

The two looked at each other thus.

Each seemed to say to the other, "We will talk, but we will hold our tongues."

The tavern-keeper silently opened the door of the lower room of the tavern. Master Nicless entered. Ursus entered. There was no one there except these two. On the side looking on the street, both doors and window-shutters were closed.

The tavern-keeper pushed the door behind him, and shut it in the face of the inquisitive Govicum.

Master Nicless placed the candle on the table.

A low, whispering dialogue began.

"Master Ursus?"

"Master Nicless?"

"I understand at last."

"Nonsense!"

"You wished the poor blind girl to think that all going on as usual."

"There is no law against my being a ventriloquist."

"You are a clever fellow."

"No."

"It is wonderful how you manage all that you wish to do."

"I tell you, it is not."

"Now, I have something to tell you."

"Is it about politics?"

"I don't know."

"Because, in that case I could not listen to you."

"Look here: whilst you were playing actors and audience by yourself, someone knocked at the door of the tavern."

"Someone knocked at the door?"

"Yes."

"I don't like that."

"Nor I, either."

"And then?"

"And then I opened it."

"Who was it that knocked?"

"Someone who spoke to me."

"What did he say?"

"I listened to him."

"What did you answer?"

"Nothing. I came back to see you play."

"And——?"

"Someone knocked a second time."

"Who——he same person?"

"No, another."

"Someone else to speak to you?"

"Someone who said nothing."

"I like that better."

"I do not."

"Explain yourself, Master Nicless."

"Guess who called the first time."

"I have no leisure to be an Œdipus."

"It was the proprietor of the circus."

"Over the way?"

"Over the way."

"Whence comes all that fearful noise. Well?"

"Well, Master Ursus, he makes you a proposal."

"A proposal?"

"A proposal."

"Why?"

"Because——"

"You have an advantage over me, Master Nicless; just now you solved my enigma, and now I cannot understand yours."

"The proprietor of the circus commissioned me to tell you that he had seen the *cortége* of police pass this morning, and that he, the proprietor of the circus, wishing to prove that he is your friend, offers to buy of you, for fifty pounds, ready money, your caravan, the Green Box, your two horses, your trumpets, with the women that blow them, your play, with the blind girl who sings in it, your wolf, and yourself."

Ursus smiled a haughty smile.

"Inn-keeper, tell the proprietor of the circus that Gwynplaine is coming back."

The inn-keeper took something from a chair in the darkness, and turning toward Ursus with both arms raised, dangled from one hand a cloak, and from the other a leather esclavine, a felt hat, and a jacket.

And Master Nicless said, "The man who knocked the second time was connected with the police; he came in and left without saying a word, and brought these things."

Ursus recognized the esclavine, the jacket, the hat, and the cloak of Gwynplaine.

Chapter IV

MOENIBUS SURDIS CAMPANA MUTA

URSUS SMOOTHED THE FELT OF THE HAT, TOUCHED THE CLOTH OF THE CLOAK, THE SERGE OF the coat, the leather of the esclavine, and no longer able to doubt whose garments they were, with a gesture at once brief and imperative, and without saying a word, pointed to the door of the inn.

Master Nicless opened it.

Ursus rushed out of the tavern.

Master Nicless looked after him, and saw Ursus run as fast as his old legs would allow, in the direction taken that morning by the wapentake who carried off Gwynplaine.

A quarter of an hour afterwards, Ursus, out of breath, reached the little street in which stood the back wicket of the Southwark Jail, which he had already watched so many hours. This alley was lonely enough at all hours, but if dreary during the day, it was portentous in the night. No one ventured through it after a certain hour. It seemed as though people feared that the walls should close in, and that if the prison or the cemetery took a fancy to embrace, they should be crushed in their clasp. Such are the effects of darkness. The pollard willows of the Ruelle Vauvert in Paris were thus ill-famed. It was said that during the night the stumps of those trees changed into great hands, and caught hold of the passers-by.

By instinct the Southwark folks shunned, as we have already mentioned, this alley between a prison and a churchyard. Formerly it had been barricaded during the night by an iron chain. Very uselessly; because the strongest chain which guarded the street was the terror it inspired.

Ursus entered it resolutely.

What intention possessed him? None.

He came into the alley to seek intelligence.

Was he going to knock at the gate of the jail? Certainly not. Such an expedient, at once fearful and vain, had no place in his brain. To attempt to introduce himself to demand an explanation. What folly! Prisons do not open to those who wish to enter, anymore than to those who desire to get out. Their hinges never turn except by law. Ursus knew this. Why, then, had he come there? To see. To see what? Nothing. Who can tell? Even to be opposite the gate through which Gwynplaine had disappeared was something.

Sometimes the blackest and most rugged of walls whispers, and some light escapes through a cranny. A vague glimmering is now and then to be perceived through solid and somber piles of building. Even to examine the envelope of a fact may be to some purpose. The instinct of us all is to leave between the fact which interests us and ourselves but the thinnest possible cover. Therefore it was that Ursus returned to the alley in which the lower entrance to the prison was situated.

Just as he entered it he heard one stroke of the clock, then a second.

"Hold," thought he; "can it be midnight already?"

Mechanically he set himself to count.

"Three, four, five."

He mused.

"At what long intervals this clock strikes!—how slowly! Six; seven!"

Then he remarked—

"What a melancholy sound! Eight, nine! Ah! nothing can be more natural; it's dull work for a clock to live in a prison. Ten! Besides, there is the cemetery. This clock sounds the hour to the living, and eternity to the dead. Eleven! Alas! to strike the hour to him who is not free, is also to chronicle an eternity! Twelve!"

He paused.

"Yes, it is midnight."

The clock struck a thirteenth stroke.

Ursus shuddered.

"Thirteen!"

Then followed a fourteenth; then a fifteenth.

"What can this mean?"

The strokes continued at long intervals. Ursus listened.

"It is not the striking of a clock: it is the bell Muta. No wonder I said, 'How long it takes to strike midnight.' This clock does not strike: it tolls. What fearful thing is about to take place?"

Formerly all prisons, and all monasteries, had a bell called Muta, reserved for melancholy occasions. La Muta (the mute) was a bell which struck very low, as if doing its best not to be heard.

Ursus had reached the corner which he had found so convenient for his watch and whence he had been able, during a great part of the day, to keep his eye on the prison.

The strokes followed each other at lugubrious intervals.

A knell makes an ugly punctuation in space. It breaks the preoccupation of the mind into funereal paragraphs. A knell, like a man's death-rattle, notifies an agony. If in the houses about the neighborhood where a knell is tolled there are reveries straying in doubt, its sound cuts them into rigid fragments. A vague reverie is a sort of refuge. Some indefinable diffuseness in anguish allows now and then a ray of hope to pierce through it. A knell is precise and desolating. It concentrates this diffusion of thought, and precipitates the vapors in which anxiety seeks to remain in suspense. A knell speaks to each one in the sense of his own grief or of his own fear. Tragic bell! it concerns you. It is a warning to you.

There is nothing so dreary as a monologue on which its cadence falls. The even returns of sound seem to show a purpose.

What is it that this hammer, the bell, forges on the anvil of thought?

Ursus counted, vaguely and without motive, the tolling of the knell. Feeling that his thoughts were sliding from him, he made an effort not to let them slip into conjecture. Conjecture is an inclined plane, on which we slip too far to be to our own advantage. Still, what was the meaning of the bell?

He looked through the darkness in the direction in which he knew the gate of the prison to be.

Suddenly, in that very spot which looked like a dark hole, a redness showed. The redness grew larger, and became a light.

There was no uncertainty about it. It soon took a form and angles. The gate of the jail had just turned on its hinges. The glow painted the arch and the jambs of the door. It was a yawning rather than an opening. A prison does not open; it yawns—perhaps from ennui. Through the gate passed a man with a torch in his hand.

The bell rang on. Ursus felt his attention fascinated by two objects. He watched—his ear the knell, his eye the torch. Behind the first man the gate, which had been ajar, enlarged the opening suddenly, and allowed egress to two other men; then to a fourth. This fourth was the wapentake, clearly visible in the light of the torch. In his grasp was his iron staff.

Following the wapentake, there filed and opened out below the gateway in order, two by two, with the rigidity of a series of walking posts, ranks of silent men.

This nocturnal procession stepped through the wicket in file, like a procession of penitents, without any solution of continuity, with a funereal care to make no noise, gravely—almost gently; a serpent issues from its hole with similar precautions.

The torch threw out their profiles and attitudes into relief. Fierce looks, sullen attitudes.

Ursus recognized the faces of the police who had that morning carried off Gwynplaine.

There was no doubt about it. They were the same. They were reappearing.

Of course, Gwynplaine would also reappear. They had led him to that place. They would bring him back.

It was all quite clear.

Ursus strained his eyes to the utmost. Would they set Gwynplaine at liberty?

The files of police flowed from the low arch very slowly, and, as it were, drop by drop. The toll of the bell was uninterrupted, and seemed to mark their steps. On leaving the prison, the procession turned their backs on Ursus, went to the right, into the bend of the street opposite to that in which he was posted.

A second torch shone under the gateway, announcing the end of the procession.

Ursus was now about to see what they were bringing with them. The prisoner. The man.

Ursus was soon, he thought, to see Gwynplaine.

That which they carried appeared.

It was a bier.

Four men carried a bier, covered with black cloth.

Behind them came a man, with a shovel on his shoulder.

A third lighted torch, held by a man reading a book, probably the chaplain, closed the procession.

The bier followed the ranks of the police, who had turned to the right.

Just at that moment the head of the procession stopped.

Ursus heard the grating of a key.

Opposite the prison, in the low wall which ran along the other side of the street, another opening was illuminated by a torch passing beneath it.

This gate, over which a death's-head was placed, was that of the cemetery.

The wapentake passed through it, then the men, then the second torch. The procession decreased therein, like a reptile entering his retreat.

The files of police penetrated into that other darkness which was beyond the gate; then the bier; then the man with the spade; then the chaplain with his torch and his book, and the gate closed.

There was nothing left but a haze of light above the wall.

A muttering was heard. Then some dull sounds. Doubtless the chaplain and the gravedigger. The one throwing on the coffin some verses of Scripture, the other some clods of earth.

The muttering ceased; the heavy sounds ceased. A movement was made. The torches shone. The wapentake reappeared, holding high his weapon, under the reopened gate of the cemetery; then the chaplain with his book, and the gravedigger with his spade. The *cortége* reappeared without the coffin.

The files of men crossed over in the same order, with the same taciturnity, and in the opposite direction. The gate of the cemetery closed. That of the prison opened. Its sepulchral architecture stood out against the light. The obscurity of the passage became vaguely visible. The solid and deep night of the jail was revealed to sight; then the whole vision disappeared in the depths of shadow.

The knell ceased. All was locked in silence. A sinister incarceration of shadows.

A vanished vision; nothing more.

A passage of specters, which had disappeared.

The logical arrangement of surmises builds up something which at least resembles evidence. To the arrest of Gwynplaine, to the secret mode of his capture, to the return of his garments by the police officer, to the death-bell of the prison to which he had been conducted, was now added, or rather adjusted—portentous circumstance—a coffin carried to the grave.

"He is dead!" cried Ursus.

He sank down upon a stone.

"Dead! They have killed him! Gwynplaine! My child! My son!"

And he burst into passionate sobs.

Chapter V

STATE POLICY DEALS WITH LITTLE MATTERS AS WELL AS WITH GREAT

U RSUS, ALAS! HAD BOASTED THAT HE HAD NEVER WEPT. HIS RESERVOIR OF TEARS WAS FULL. SUCH plenitude as is accumulated drop on drop, sorrow on sorrow, through a long existence is not to be poured out in a moment. Ursus wept long.

The first tear is a letting out of waters. He wept for Gwynplaine, for Dea, for himself, Ursus, for Homo. He wept like a child. He wept like an old man. He wept for everything at which he had ever laughed. He paid off arrears. Man is never nonsuited when he pleads his right to tears.

The corpse they had just buried was Hardquanonne's; but Ursus could not know that.

The hours crept on.

Day began to break. The pale clothing of the morning was spread out, dimly creased with shadow, over the bowling-green. The dawn lighted up the front of the Tadcaster Inn. Master Nicless had not gone to bed, because sometimes the same occurrence produces sleeplessness in many.

Troubles radiate in every direction. Throw a stone in water, and count the splashes.

Master Nicless felt himself impeached. It is very disagreeable that such things should happen in one's house. Master Nicless, uneasy, and foreseeing misfortunes, meditated. He regretted having received such people into his house. Had he but known that they would end by getting him into mischief! But the question was how to get rid of them? He had given Ursus a lease. What a blessing if he could free himself from it. How should he set to work to drive them out?

Suddenly the door of the inn resounded with one of those tumultuous knocks which in England announces "Somebody." The gamut of knocking corresponds with the ladder of hierarchy.

It was not quite the knock of a lord; but it was the knock of a justice.

The trembling inn-keeper half opened his window. There was, indeed, the magistrate. Master Nicless perceived at the door a body of police, from the head of which two men detached themselves, one of whom was the justice of the quorum.

Master Nicless had seen the justice of the quorum that morning, and recognized him.

He did not know the other, who was a fat gentleman, with a waxen-colored face, a fashionable wig, and a traveling cloak. Nicless was much afraid of the first of these persons, the justice of the quorum. Had he been of the court, he would have feared the other most, because it was Barkilphedro.

One of the subordinates knocked at the door again violently.

The inn-keeper, with great drops of perspiration on his brow, from anxiety, opened it.

The justice of the quorum, in the tone of a man who is employed in matters of police, and who is well acquainted with various shades of vagrancy, raised his voice, and asked, severely, for—

"Master Ursus!"

The host, cap in hand, replied—

"Your honor; he lives here."

"I know it," said the justice.

"No doubt, your honor."

"Tell him to come down."

"Your honor, he is not here."

"Where is he?"

"I do not know."

"How is that?"

"He has not come in."

"Then he must have gone out very early?"

"No; but he went out very late."

"What vagabonds!" replied the justice.

"Your honor," said Master Nicless, softly, "here he comes."

Ursus, indeed, had just come in sight, round a turn of the wall. He was returning to the inn. He had passed nearly the whole night between the jail, where at midday he had seen Gwynplaine, and the cemetery, where at midnight he had heard the grave filled up. He was pallid with two pallors—that of sorrow and of twilight.

Dawn, which is light in a chrysalis state, leaves even those forms which are in movement in the uncertainty of night. Ursus, wan and indistinct, walked slowly, like a man in a dream. In the wild distraction produced by agony of mind, he had left the inn with his head bare. He had not even found out that he had no hat on. His spare, gray locks fluttered in the wind. His open eyes appeared sightless. Often when awake we are asleep, and as often when asleep we are awake.

Ursus looked like a lunatic.

"Master Ursus," cried the inn-keeper, "come; their honors desire to speak to you."

Master Nicless, in his endeavor to soften matters down, let slip, although he would gladly have omitted, this plural, "their honors"—respectful to the group, but mortifying, perhaps, to the chief, confounded therein, to some degree, with his subordinates.

Ursus started like a man falling off a bed, on which he was sound asleep.

"What is the matter?" said he.

He saw the police, and at the head of the police the justice. A fresh and rude shock.

But a short time ago, the wapentake, now the justice of the quorum. He seemed to have been cast from one to the other, as ships by some reefs of which we have read in old stories.

The justice of the quorum made him a sign to enter the tavern. Ursus obeyed.

Govicum, who had just got up, and who was sweeping the room, stopped his work, got into a corner behind the tables, put down his broom, and held his breath. He plunged his fingers into his hair, and scratched his head, a symptom which indicated attention to what was about to occur.

The justice of the quorum sat down on a form, before a table. Barkilphedro took a chair. Ursus and Master Nicless remained standing. The police officers, left outside, grouped themselves in front of the closed door.

The justice of the quorum fixed his eye, full of the law, upon Ursus. He said—

"You have a wolf."

Ursus answered—

"Not exactly."

"You have a wolf," continued the justice, emphasizing "wolf" with a decided accent.

Ursus answered—

"You see—"

And he was silent.

"A misdemeanor!" replied the justice.

Ursus hazarded an excuse—

"He is my servant."

The justice placed his hand flat on the table, with his fingers spread out, which is a very fine gesture of authority.

"Merry-andrew! to-morrow, by this hour, you and your wolf must have left England. If not, the wolf will be seized, carried to the register office, and killed."

Ursus thought, "More murder!" but he breathed not a syllable, and was satisfied with trembling in every limb.

"You hear?" said the justice.

Ursus nodded.

The justice persisted—

"Killed."

There was silence.

"Strangled, or drowned."

The justice of the quorum watched Ursus.

"And yourself in prison."

Ursus murmured—

"Your worship!"

"Be off before to-morrow morning; if not, such is the order."

"Your worship!"

"What?"

"Must we leave England, he and I?"

"Yes."

"To-day?"

"To-day."

"What is to be done?"

Master Nicless was happy. The magistrate, whom he had feared, had come to his aid. The police had acted as auxiliary to him, Nicless. They had delivered him from "such people." The means he had sought were brought to him. Ursus, whom he wanted to get rid of, was being driven away by the police, a superior authority. Nothing to object to. He was delighted. He interrupted—

"Your honor, that man—"

He pointed to Ursus with his finger.

"That man wants to know how he is to leave England to-day. Nothing can be easier. There are night and day at anchor on the Thames, both on this and on the other side of London Bridge, vessels that sail to the Continent. They go from England to Denmark, to Holland, to Spain; not to France, on account of the war, but everywhere else. To-night several ships will sail, about one o'clock in the morning, which is the hour of high tide, and, amongst others, the V U of Rotterdam."

The justice of the quorum made a movement of his shoulder toward Ursus.

"Be it so. Leave by the first ship—by the U."

"Your worship," said Ursus.

"Well?"

"Your worship, if I had, as formerly, only my little box on wheels, it might be done. A boat would contain that; but—"

"But what?"

"But now I have got the Green Box, which is a great caravan drawn by two horses, and however wide the ship might be, we could not get it into her."

"What is that to me?" said the justice. "The wolf will be killed."

Ursus shuddered, as if he were grasped by a hand of ice.

"Monsters!" he thought. "Murdering people is their way of settling matters."

The inn-keeper smiled, and addressed Ursus.

"Master Ursus, you can sell the Green Box."

Ursus looked at Nicless.

"Master Ursus, you have the offer."

"From whom?"

"An offer for the caravan, an offer for the two horses, an offer for the two gypsy women, an offer—"

"From whom?" repeated Ursus.

"From the proprietor of the neighboring circus."

Ursus remembered it.

"It is true."

Master Nicless turned to the justice of the quorum.

"Your honor, the bargain can be completed to-day. The proprietor of the circus close by wishes to buy the caravan and the horses."

"The proprietor of the circus is right," said the justice, "because he will soon require them. A caravan and horses will be useful to him. He, too, will depart to-day. The reverend gentlemen of the parish of Southwark have complained of the indecent riot in Tarrinzeau field. The sheriff has taken his measures. To-night there will not be a single juggler's booth in the place. There must be an end of all these scandals. The honorable gentleman who deigns to be here present—"

The justice of the quorum interrupted his speech to salute Barkilphedro, who returned the bow.

"The honorable gentleman who deigns to be present has just arrived from Windsor. He brings orders. Her Majesty has said, 'It must be swept away.' "

Ursus, during his long meditation all night, had not failed to put himself some questions. After all, he had only seen a bier. Could he be sure that it contained Gwynplaine? Other people might have died besides Gwynplaine. A coffin does not announce the name of the corpse, as it passes by. A funeral had followed the arrest of Gwynplaine. That proved nothing. *Post hoc, non propter hoc, etc.* Ursus had begun to doubt.

Hope burns and glimmers over misery like naphtha over water. Its hovering flame ever floats over human sorrow. Ursus had come to this conclusion, "It is probable that it was Gwynplaine whom they buried, but it is not certain. Who knows?—perhaps Gwynplaine is still alive."

Ursus bowed to the justice.

"Honorable judge, I will go away, we will go away, all will go away, by the *Vograat* of Rotterdam, to-day. I will sell the Green Box, the horses, the trumpets, the gypsies. But I have a comrade, whom I cannot leave behind—Gwynplaine."

"Gwynplaine is dead," said a voice.

Ursus felt a cold sensation, such as is produced by a reptile crawling over the skin. It was Barkilphedro who had just spoken.

The last gleam was extinguished. No more doubt now. Gwynplaine was dead. A person in authority must know. This one looked ill-favored enough to do so.

Ursus bowed to him.

Master Nicless was a good-hearted man enough, but a dreadful coward. Once terrified he became a brute. The greatest cruelty is that inspired by fear.

He growled out—

"This simplifies matters."

And he indulged, standing behind Ursus, in rubbing his hands, a peculiarity of the selfish, signifying "I am well out of it," and suggestive of Pontius Pilate washing his hands.

Ursus, overwhelmed, bent down his head.

The sentence on Gwynplaine had been executed: Death. His sentence was pronounced: Exile. Nothing remained but to obey. He felt as in a dream.

Someone touched his arm. It was the other person, who was with the justice of the quorum. Ursus shuddered.

The voice which had said, "Gwynplaine is dead," whispered in his ear—

"Here are ten guineas, sent you by one who wishes you well."

And Barkilphedro placed a little purse on a table before Ursus. We must not forget the casket that Barkilphedro had taken with him.

Ten guineas out of two thousand! It was all that Barkilphedro could make up his mind to part with. In all conscience it was enough. If he had given more, he would have lost. He had taken the trouble of finding out a lord; and having sunk the shaft it was but fair that the first proceeds of the mine should belong to him. Those who see meanness in the act are right, but they would be wrong to feel astonished. Barkilphedro loved money, especially money which was stolen. An envious man is an avaricious one. Barkilphedro was not without his faults. The commission of crimes does not preclude the possession of vices. Tigers have their lice.

Besides, he belonged to the school of Bacon.

Barkilphedro turned toward the justice of the quorum, and said to him—

"Sir, be so good as to conclude this matter. I am in haste. A carriage and horses belonging to her Majesty await me. I must go full gallop to Windsor, for I must be there within two hours' time. I have intelligence to give, and orders to take."

The justice of the quorum arose.

He went to the door, which was only latched, opened it, and, looking silently toward the police, beckoned to them authoritatively. They entered with that silence which heralds severity of action.

Master Nicless—satisfied with the rapid *dénouement* which cut short his difficulties—charmed to be out of the entangled skein, was afraid, when he saw the muster of officers, that they were going to apprehend Ursus in his house. Two arrests—one after the other—made in his house, first that of Gwynplaine, then that of Ursus, might be injurious to the inn. Customers dislike police raids.

Here then was a time for a respectful appeal, suppliant and generous. Master Nicless turned toward the justice of the quorum a smiling face, in which confidence was tempered by respect.

"Your honor, I venture to observe to your honor that these honorable gentlemen, the police officers, might be dispensed with now that the wolf is about to be carried away from England, and that this man, Ursus, makes no resistance; and since your honor's orders are being punctually carried out, your honor will consider that the respectable business of the police, so necessary to the good of the kingdom, does great harm to an establishment, and that my house is innocent. The merry-andrews of the Green Box having been swept away, as her Majesty says, there is no longer any criminal here, as I do not suppose that the blind girl and the two women are criminals; therefore, I implore your honor to deign to shorten your august visit, and to dismiss these worthy gentlemen who have just entered, because there is nothing for them to do in my house; and, if your honor will permit me to prove the justice of my speech under the form of a humble question, I will prove the inutility of these revered gentlemen's presence by asking your honor, if the man, Ursus, obeys orders, and departs, who there can be to arrest here?"

"Yourself," said the justice.

A man does not argue with a sword which runs him through and through. Master Nicless subsided—he cared not on what, on a table, on a form, on anything that happened to be there—prostrate.

The justice raised his voice, so that if there were people outside, they might hear.

"Master Nicless Plumptree, keeper of this tavern, this is the last point to be settled. This mountebank and the wolf are vagabonds. They are driven away. But the person most in fault is yourself. It is in your house, and with your consent, that the law has been violated; and you, a man licensed, invested with a public responsibility, have established the scandal here. Master Nicless, your license is taken away; you must pay the penalty, and go to prison."

The policemen surrounded the inn-keeper.

The justice continued, pointing out Govicum—

"Arrest that boy as an accomplice." The hand of an officer fell upon the collar of Govicum, who looked at him inquisitively. The boy was not much alarmed, scarcely understanding the occurrence; having already observed many things out of the way, he wondered if this were the end of the comedy.

The justice of the quorum forced his hat down on his head, crossed his hands on his stomach, which is the height of majesty, and added—

"It is decided, Master Nicless; you are to be taken to prison, and put into jail, you and the boy; and this house, the Tadcaster Inn, is to remain shut up, condemned and closed. For the sake of example. Upon which, you will follow us."

BOOK THE SEVENTH

THE TITANESS

Chapter I

THE AWAKENING

A ND DEA!
It seemed to Gwynplaine, as he watched the break of day at Corleone Lodge, while the things we have related were occurring at the Tadcaster Inn, that the call came from without; but it came from within.

Who has not heard the deep clamors of the soul?

Moreover, the morning was dawning.

Aurora is a voice.

Of what use is the sun if not to reawaken that dark sleeper—the conscience?

Light and virtue are akin.

Whether the god be called Christ or Love, there is at times an hour when he is forgotten, even by the best. All of us, even the saints, require a voice to remind us, and the dawn speaks to us, like a sublime monitor. Conscience calls out before duty, as the cock crows before the dawn of day.

That chaos, the human heart, hears the *fiat lux!*

Gwynplaine—we will continue thus to call him (Clancharlie is a lord, Gwynplaine is a man)—Gwynplaine felt as if brought back to life. It was time that the artery was bound up.

For a while his virtue had spread its wings and flown away.

"And Dea!" he said.

Then he felt through his veins a generous transfusion. Something healthy and tumultuous rushed upon him. The violent eruption of good thoughts is like the return home of a man who has not his key, and who forces his own look honestly. It is an escalade, but an escalade of good. It is a burglary! but a burglary of evil.

"Dea! Dea! Dea!" repeated he.

He strove to assure himself of his heart's strength. And he put the question with a loud voice—"Where are you?"

He almost wondered that no one answered him.

Then again, gazing on the walls and the ceiling, with wandering thoughts, through which reason returned.

"Where are you? Where am I?"

And in the chamber which was his cage he began to walk again, to and fro, like a wild beast in captivity.

"Where am I? At Windsoayou? In Southwark. Alas! this is the first time that there has been distance between us. Who has dug this gulf? I here, thou there. Oh, it cannot be; it shall not be! What is this that they have done to me?"

He stopped.

"Who talked to me of the queen? What do I know of such things? *I* changed! Why? Because I am a lord. Do you know what has happened, Dea? You are a lady. What has come to pass is astounding. My business now is to get back into my right road. Who is it who led me astray? There is a man who spoke to me mysteriously. I remember the words which he addressed to me. 'My lord, when one door opens another is shut. That which you have left behind is no longer yours.' In other words, you are a coward. That man, the miserable wretch! said that to me before I was well awake. He took advantage of my first moment of astonishment. I was as it were a prey to him. Where is he, that I may insult him? He spoke to me with the evil smile of a demon. But see, I am myself again. That is well. They deceive themselves if they think that they can do what they like with Lord Clancharlie, a peer of England. Yes, with a peeress, who is Dea! Conditions! Shall I accept them? The queen. What is the queen to me? I never saw her. I am not a lord to be made a slave. I enter my position unfettered. Did they think they had unchained me for nothing? They have unmuzzled me. That is all. Dea! Ursus! we are together. That which you were, I was. That which I am, you are. Come. No. I will go to you directly—directly. I have already waited too long. What can they think, not seeing me return! That money. When I think I sent them that money! It was myself that they wanted. I remember the man said that I could not leave this place. We shall see that. Come! a carriage, a carriage! put to the horses. I am going to look for them. Where are the servants? I ought to have servants here since I am a lord. I am master here. This is my house. I will twist off the bolts, I will break the locks, I will kick down the doors, I will run my sword through the body of anyone who bars my passage. I should like to see who shall stop me. I have a wife, and she is Dea. I have a father, who is Ursus. My house is a palace, and I give it to Ursus. My name is a diadem, and I give it to Dea. Quick, directly, Dea, I am coming—yes, you may be sure that I shall soon stride across the intervening space!"

And raising the first piece of tapestry he came to, he rushed from the chamber impetuously.

He found himself in a corridor.

He went straight forward.

A second corridor opened out before him.

All the doors were open.

He walked on at random, from chamber to chamber, from passage to passage, seeking an exit.

Chapter II

THE RESEMBLANCE OF A PALACE TO A WOOD

IN PALACES AFTER THE ITALIAN FASHION, AND CORLEONE LODGE WAS ONE, THERE WERE VERY FEW doors, but abundance of tapestry screens and curtained doorways. In every palace of that date there was a wonderful labyrinth of chambers and corridors, where luxury ran riot; gilding, marble, carved wainscoting, Eastern silks; nooks and corners, some secret and dark as night, others light and pleasant as the day. There were attics, richly and brightly furnished; burnished recesses, shining with Dutch tiles and Portuguese azulejos. The tops of the high windows were converted into small rooms and glass attics, forming pretty habitable lanterns. The thickness of the walls was such that there were rooms within them. Here and there were closets, nominally wardrobes. They were called "The Little Rooms." It was within them that evil deeds were hatched.

When a Duke of Guise had to be killed, the pretty Présidente of Sylvecane abducted, or the cries of little girls brought thither by Lebel, smothered, such places were convenient for the purpose. They were labyrinthine chambers, impracticable to a stranger; scenes of abductions; unknown depths, receptacles of mysterious disappearances. In those elegant caverns princes and lords stored their plunder. In such a place the Count de Charolais hid Madame Courchamp, the wife of the Clerk of the Privy Council; Monsieur de Monthulé, the daughter of Haudry, the farmer of la Croix Saint Lenfroy; the Prince de Conti, the two beautiful baker women of l'Ile Adam; the Duke of Buckingham, poor Pennywell, etc. The deeds done there were such as were designated by the Roman law as committed *vi, clam, et precario*—by force, in secret, and for a short time. Once in, an occupant remained there till the master of the house decreed his or her release. They were gilded oubliettes, savoring both of the cloister and the harem. Their staircases twisted, turned, ascended, and descended. A zigzag of rooms, one running into another, led back to the starting-point. A gallery terminated in an oratory. A confessional was grafted on to an alcove. Perhaps the architects of "the little rooms," building for royalty and aristocracy, took as models the ramifications of coral beds, and the openings in a sponge. The branches became a labyrinth. Pictures turning on false panels were exits and entrances. They were full of stage contrivances, and no wonder—considering the dramas that were played there! The floors of these hives reached from the cellars to the attics. Quaint madrepore inlaying every palace, from Versailles downwards, like cells of pygmies in dwelling-places of Titans. Passages, niches, alcoves, and secret recesses. All sorts of holes and corners, in which was stored away the meanness of the great.

These winding and narrow passages recalled games, blindfolded eyes, hands feeling in the dark, suppressed laughter, blind man's bluff, hide and seek, while, at the same time, they suggested memories of the Atrides, of the Plantagenets, of the Medicis, the brutal knights of Eltz, of Rizzio, of Monaldeschi, of naked swords, pursuing the fugitive flying from room to room.

The ancients, too, had mysterious retreats of the same kind, in which luxury was adapted to enormities. The pattern has been preserved underground in some sepulchers in Egypt, notably in the tomb of King Psammetichus, discovered by Passalacqua. The ancient poets have recorded the horrors of these suspicious buildings. *Error circumflexus. Locus implicitus gyris.*

Gwynplaine was in the "little rooms" of Corleone Lodge. He was burning to be off, to get outside, to see Dea again. The maze of passages and alcoves, with secret and bewildering doors, checked and retarded his progress. He strove to run, he was obliged to wander. He thought that he had but one door to thrust open, while he had a skein of doors to unravel. To one room succeeded another. Then a crossway, with rooms on every side.

Not a living creature was to be seen. He listened. Not a sound.

At times he thought that he must be returning toward his starting-point. Then, that he saw someone approaching. It was no one. It was only the reflection of himself in a mirror, dressed as a nobleman. *That* he?—Impossible! Then he recognized himself, but not at once.

He explored every passage that he came to.

He examined the quaint arrangements of the rambling building, and their yet quainter fittings. Here, a cabinet, painted and carved in a sentimental, but vicious style; there, an equivocal-looking chapel, studded with enamels and mother-of-pearl, with miniatures on ivory wrought out in relief, like those on old-fashioned snuff-boxes; there, one of those pretty Florentine retreats, adapted to the hypochondriasis of women, and even then called *boudoirs*. Everywhere—on the ceilings, on the walls, and on the very floors—were representations, in velvet or in metal, of birds, of trees; of luxuriant vegetation, picked out in reliefs of lacework; tables covered with jet carvings, representing warriors, queens, and tritons armed with the scaly terminations of a hydra. Cut crystals combining prismatic effects with those of reflection. Mirrors repeated the light of precious stones, and sparkles glittered in the darkest corners. It was impossible to guess whether those many-sided, shining surfaces, where emerald green mingled with the golden hues of the rising sun, where floated a glimmer of ever-varying colors, like those on a pigeon's neck, were miniature mirrors, or enormous beryls. Everywhere was magnificence, at once refined and stupendous; if it was not the most diminutive of palaces, it was the most gigantic of jewel-cases. A house for Mab, or a jewel for Geo.

Gwynplaine sought an exit. He could not find one. Impossible to make out his way. There is nothing so confusing as wealth seen for the first time. Moreover, this was a labyrinth. At each step he was stopped by some magnificent object which appeared to retard his exit, and to be unwilling to let him pass. He was encompassed by a net of wonders. He felt himself bound and held back.

What a horrible palace! he thought. Restless, he wandered through the maze, asking himself what it all meant—whether he was in prison? chafing, thirsting for the fresh air. He repeated Dea! Dea! as if that word was the thread of the labyrinth, and must be held unbroken, to guide him out of it. Now and then he shouted, "Ho! Anyone there?" No one answered. The rooms never came to an end. All was deserted, silent, splendid, sinister. It realized the fables of enchanted castles. Hidden pipes of hot air maintained a summer temperature in the building. It was as if some magician had caught up the month of June, and imprisoned it in a labyrinth. There were pleasant odors now and then, and he crossed currents of perfume, as though passing by invisible flowers. It was warm. Carpets everywhere. One might have walked about there, unclothed.

Gwynplaine looked out of the windows. The view from each one was different. From one he beheld gardens, sparkling with the freshness of a spring morning; from another, a plot decked with statues; from a third, a patio in the Spanish style, a little square, flagged, moldy, and cold. At times he saw a river—it was the Thames; sometimes a great tower—it was Windsor.

It was still so early that there were no signs of life without.

He stood still and listened.

"Oh! I will get out of this place," said he. "I will return to Dea! They shall not keep me here by force. Woe to him who bars my exits. What is that great tower yonder? If there was a giant, a hell-hound, a minotaur, to keep the gates of this enchanted palace, I would annihilate him. If an army, I would exterminate it. Dea! Dea!"

Suddenly he heard a gentle noise, very faint. It was like dropping water. He was in a dark, narrow passage, closed, some few paces farther on, by a curtain. He advanced to the curtain, pushed it aside, entered. He leaped before he looked.

Chapter III

EVE

An OCTAGON ROOM, WITH A VAULTED CEILING, WITHOUT WINDOWS, BUT LIGHTED BY A SKYLIGHT; walls, ceiling, and floors faced with peach-colored marble; a black marble canopy, like a pall, with twisted columns in the solid but pleasing Elizabethan style, overshadowing a vase-like bath of the same black marble—this was what he saw before him. In the center of the bath arose a slender jet of tepid and perfumed water, which, softly and slowly, was filling the tank. The bath was black to augment fairness into brilliancy.

It was the water which he had heard. A waste-pipe, placed at a certain height in the bath, prevented it from overflowing. Vapor was rising from the water, but not sufficient to cause it to hang in drops on the marble. The slender jet of water was like a supple wand of steel, bending at the slightest current of air. There was no furniture, except a chair-bed with pillows, long enough for a woman to lie on at full length, and yet have room for a dog at her feet. The French, indeed, borrow their word *canapé* from *can-al-pie.* This sofa was of Spanish manufacture. In it silver took the place of woodwork. The cushions and coverings were of rich white silk.

On the other side of the bath, by the wall, was a lofty dressing-table of solid silver, furnished with every requisite for the table, having in its center, and in imitation of a window, eight small Venetian mirrors, set in a silver frame. In a panel on the wall was a square opening, like a little window, which was closed by a door of solid silver. This door was fitted with hinges, like a shutter. On the shutter there glistened a chased and gilt royal crown. Over it, and affixed to the wall, was a bell, silver gilt, if not of pure gold.

Opposite the entrance of the chamber, in which Gwynplaine stood as if transfixed, there was an opening in the marble wall, extending to the ceiling, and closed by a high and broad curtain of silver tissue. This curtain, of fairy-like tenuity, was transparent, and did not interrupt the view. Through the center of this web, where one might expect a spider, Gwynplaine saw a more formidable object—a naked woman. Yet not quite naked; for she was covered—covered from head to foot. Her dress was a long chemise; so long, that it floated over her feet, like the dresses of angels in holy pictures; but so fine that it seemed liquid. More treacherous and more perilous was this covering than naked beauty could have been. History has registered the procession of princesses and of great ladies between files of monks; under pretext of naked feet and of humility, the Duchess de Montpensier showed herself to all Paris in a lace shift, a wax taper in her hand as a corrective.

The silver tissue, transparent as glass and fastened only at the ceiling, could be lifted aside. It separated the marble chamber, which was a bathroom, from the adjoining apartment, which was a bedchamber. This tiny dormitory was as a grotto of mirrors. Venetian glasses, close together, mounted with gold moldings, reflected on every side the bed in the center of the room. On the bed, which, like the toilet-table, was of silver, lay the woman; she was asleep.

She was sleeping with her head thrown back, one foot peeping from its covering, like the Succuba, above whose heads dreams flap their wings.

Her lace pillow had fallen on the floor. Between her nakedness and the eye of the spectator were two obstacles—her chemise and the curtain of silver gauze; two transparencies. The room, rather an alcove than a chamber, was lighted with some reserve by the reflection from the bathroom. Perhaps the light was more modest than the woman.

The bed had neither columns, nor dais, nor top; so that the woman, when she opened her eyes, could see herself reflected a thousand times in the mirrors above her head.

The crumpled clothes bore evidence of troubled sleep. The beauty of the folds was proof of the quality of the material.

It was a period when a queen, thinking that she should be damned, pictured hell to herself as a bed with coarse sheets.

A dressing-gown, of curious silk, was thrown over the foot of the couch. It was apparently Chinese; for a great golden lizard was partly visible in between the folds.

Beyond the couch, and probably masking a door, was a large mirror, on which were painted peacocks and swans.

Shadow seemed to lose its nature in this apartment, and glistened. The spaces between the mirrors and the gold work were lined with that sparkling material called at Venice thread of glass— *i.e.,* spun glass.

At the head of the couch stood a reading-desk, on a movable pivot, with candles, and a book lying open, bearing this title, in large red letters, *Alcoranus Mahumedis.*

Gwynplaine saw none of these details. He had eyes only for the woman. He was at once stupefied and filled with tumultuous emotions, states apparently incompatible, yet sometimes coexistent. He recognized her. Her eyes were closed, but her face was turned toward him. It was the duchess. She, the mysterious being in whom all the splendors of the unknown were united; she who had occasioned him so many unavowable dreams; she who had written him so strange a letter! The only woman in the world of whom he could say, "She has seen me, and she desires me!"

He had dismissed the dreams from his mind; he had burned the letter. He had, as far as lay in his power, banished the remembrance of her from his thoughts and dreams. He no longer thought of her. He had forgotten her. . . .

Again he saw her, and saw her terrible in power. A woman naked, is a woman armed. His breath came in short catches. He felt as if he were in a storm-driven cloud. He looked. This woman before him! Was it possible? At the theater, a duchess; here a nereid, a nymph, a fairy. Always an apparition. He tried to fly, but felt the futility of the attempt. His eyes were riveted on the vision, as though he were bound. Was she a woman? Was she a maiden? Both. Messalina was perhaps present, though invisible, and smiled, while Diana kept watch.

Over all her beauty was the radiance of inaccessibility. No purity could compare with her chaste and haughty form. Certain snows, which have never been touched, give an idea of it—such as the sacred whiteness of the Jungfrau. That which was represented by that unconscious brow; by that rich, disheveled hair; by the drooping lids; by those blue veins, dimly visible; by the sculptured roundness of her bosom, her hips, and her knees, indicated by delicate pink undulations seen through the folds of her drapery, was the divinity of a queenly sleep. Immodesty was merged in splendor. She was as calm in her nakedness, as if she had the right to a godlike effrontery. She felt the security of an Olympian, who knew that she was daughter of the depths, and might say to the ocean, "Father!" And she exposed herself, unattainable and proud, to everything that should pass— to looks, to desires, to ravings, to dreams; as proud in her languor, on her boudoir couch, as Venus in the immensity of the sea-foam.

She had slept all night, and was prolonging her sleep into the daylight; her boldness, begun in shadow, continued in light.

Gwynplaine shuddered. He admired her with an unhealthy and absorbing admiration, which ended in fear. Misfortunes never come singly. Gwynplaine thought he had drained to the dregs the cup of his ill-luck. Now it was refilled. Who was it who was hurling all those unremitting thunderbolts on his devoted head, and who had now thrown against him, as he stood trembling there, a sleeping goddess? What! was the dangerous and desirable object of his dream lurking all the while behind these successive glimpses of heaven? Did these favors of the mysterious tempter tend to inspire him with vague aspirations and confused ideas, and overwhelm him with an intoxicating series of realities proceeding from apparent impossibilities? Wherefore did all the shadows conspire against him, a wretched man; and what would become of him, with all those evil smiles of fortune beaming on him? Was his temptation prearranged? This woman, how and why was she there? No explanation! Why him? Why her? Was he made a peer of England expressly for this duchess? Who had brought them together? Who was the dupe? Who the victim? Whose simplicity was being abused? Was it God who was being deceived? All these undefined thoughts passed confusedly, like a flight of dark shadows, through his brain. That magical and malevolent abode, that strange and prison-like palace, was it also in the plot? Gwynplaine suffered a partial unconsciousness. Suppressed emotions threatened to strangle him. He was weighed down by an overwhelming force. His will became powerless. How could he resist? He was incoherent and entranced. This time he felt he was becoming irremediably insane. His dark, headlong fall over the precipice of stupefaction continued.

But the woman slept on.

What aggravated the storm within him was, that he saw not the princess, not the duchess, not the lady; but the woman.

Deviations from right exist in man, in a latent state. There is an invisible tracing of vice, ready prepared, in our organizations. Even when we are innocent, and apparently pure, it exists within us. To be stainless, is not to be faultless. Love is a law. Desire is a snare. There is a great difference between getting drunk once and habitual drunkenness. To desire a woman, is the former; to desire women, the latter.

Gwynplaine, losing all self-command, trembled. What could he do against such a temptation? Here were no skillful effects of dress, no silken folds, no complex and coquettish adornments, no affected exaggeration of concealment or of exhibition, no cloud. It was nakedness in fearful simplicity—a sort of mysterious summons—the shameless audacity of Eden. The whole of the dark side of human nature was there. Eve worse than Satan; the human and the superhuman commingled. A perplexing ecstasy, winding up in a brutal triumph of instinct over duty. The sovereign contour of beauty is imperious. When it leaves the ideal and condescends to be real, its proximity is fatal to man.

Now and then the duchess moved softly on the bed, with the vague movement of a cloud in the heavens, changing as a vapor changes its form. She undulated, composing and discomposing the charming curves of her body. Woman is as supple as water; and, like water, this one had an indescribable appearance of its being impossible to grasp her. Absurd as it may appear, though he saw her present in the flesh before him, yet she seemed a chimera; and, palpable as she was, she seemed to him afar off. Scared and livid, he gazed on. He listened for her breathing, and fancied he heard only a phantom's respiration. He was attracted, though against his will. How arm himself against her—or against himself? He had been prepared for everything except this danger. A savage doorkeeper, a raging monster of a jailer—such were his expected antagonists. He looked for Cerberus, he saw Hebe. A sleeping woman! What an opponent! He closed his eyes. Too bright a dawn blinds the eyes. But through his closed eyelids there penetrated at once the woman's form—not so distinct, but beautiful as ever.

Fly! Easier said than done. He had already tried and failed. He was rooted to the ground, as if in a dream. When we try to draw back, temptation clogs our feet, and glues them to the earth. We can still advance, but to retire is impossible. The invisible arms of sin rise from below and drag us down.

There is a commonplace idea, accepted by everyone, that feelings become blunted by experience. Nothing can be more untrue. You might as well say that by dropping nitric acid slowly on a sore it would heal and become sound, and that torture dulled the sufferings of Damiens. The truth is, that each fresh application intensifies the pain.

From one surprise after another, Gwynplaine had become desperate. That cup, his reason, under this new stupor, was overflowing. He felt within him a terrible awakening. Compass he no longer possessed. One idea only was before him—the woman. An indescribable happiness appeared, which threatened to overwhelm him. He could no longer decide for himself. There was an irresistible current and a reef. The reef was not a rock, but a siren. A magnet at the bottom of the abyss. He wished to tear himself away from this magnet—but how was he to carry out his wish? He had ceased to feel any basis of support. Who can foresee the fluctuations of the human mind! A man may be wrecked, as is a ship. Conscience is an anchor. It is a terrible thing, but, like the anchor, conscience may be carried away.

He had not even the chance of being repulsed on account of his terrible disfigurement. The woman had written to say that she loved him.

In every crisis there is a moment when the scale hesitates before kicking the beam. When we lean to the worst side of our nature, instead of strengthening our better qualities, the moral force which has been preserving the balance gives way, and down we go. Had this critical moment in Gwynplaine's life arrived?

How could he escape?

So it is she! the duchess! the woman! There she was in that lonely room—asleep, far from succor, helpless, alone, at his mercy—yet he was in her power! The duchess! We have, perchance, observed a star in the distant firmament. We have admired it. It is so far off. What can there be to make us shudder in a fixed star? Well, one day—one night, rather—it moves. We perceive a trembling gleam around it. The star which we imagined to be immovable is in motion. It is no longer a star, but a comet—the incendiary giant of the skies. The luminary moves on, grows bigger, shakes off a shower of sparks and fire, and becomes enormous. It advances toward us. Oh, horror! it is coming our way! The comet recognizes us, marks us for its own, and will not be turned aside. Irresistible attack of the heavens! What is it which is bearing down on us? An excess of light, which blinds us; an excess of life, which kills us. That proposal which the heavens make we refuse; that unfathomable love we reject. We close our eyes; we hide; we tear ourselves away; we imagine the danger is past. We open our eyes—the formidable star is still before us; but, no longer a star, it has become a world. A world unknown, a world of lava and ashes; the devastating prodigy of space. It fills the sky, allowing no compeers. The carbuncle of the firmament's depths, a diamond in the distance, when drawn close to us becomes a furnace. You are caught in its flames. And the first sensation of burning is that of a heavenly warmth.

Chapter IV

SATAN

SUDDENLY THE SLEEPER AWOKE. SHE SAT UP WITH A SUDDEN AND GRACIOUS DIGNITY OF MOVEment, her fair silken tresses falling in soft disorder on her hips; her loosened nightdress disclosed her shoulder; she toucher her pink toes with her little hand, and gazed for some moments on the naked foot, worthy to be worshipped by Pericles, and copied by Phidias. Then stretching herself, she yawned like a tigress in the rising sun.

Perhaps Gwynplaine breathed heavily, as we do when we endeavor to restrain our respiration.

"Is anyone there?" said she.

She yawned as she spoke, and her very yawn was graceful. Gwynplaine listened to the unfamiliar voice; the voice of a charmer, its accents exquisitely haughty, its caressing intonation softening its native arrogance. Then rising on her knees—there is an antique statue kneeling thus in the midst of a thousand transparent folds—she drew the dressing-gown toward her, and springing from the couch stood upright by it—nude; then, suddenly, with the swiftness of an arrow's flight, she was clothed. In the twinkling of an eye the silken robe was around her. The trailing sleeve concealed her hands; only the tips of her toes, with little pink nails like those of an infant, were left visible. Having drawn from underneath the dressing-gown a mass of hair which had been imprisoned by it, she crossed behind the couch to the end of the room, and placed her ear to the painted mirror, which was, apparently, a door. Tapping the glass with her finger, she called, "Is anyone there? Lord David? Are you come already? What time is it then? Is that you, Barkilphedro?" She turned from the glass. "No! it was not there. Is there anyone in the bathroom? Will you answer? Of course not. No one could come that way."

Going to the silver lace curtain, she raised it with her foot, thrust it aside with her shoulder, and entered the marble room. An agonized numbness fell upon Gwynplaine. No possibility of concealment. It was too late to fly. Moreover, he was no longer equal to the exertion. He wished that the earth might open and swallow him up. Anything to hide him.

She saw him. She stared, immensely astonished, but without the slightest nervousness. Then, in a tone of mingled pleasure and contempt, she said, "Why, it is Gwynplaine!" Suddenly with a rapid spring, for this cat was a panther, she flung herself on his neck. She clasped his head between her naked arms, from which the sleeves, in her eagerness, had fallen back.

Suddenly, pushing him back, and holding him by both shoulders with her small claw-like hands, she stood up face to face with him, and began to gaze at him with a strange expression.

It was a fatal glance she gave him with her Aldebaran-like eyes—a glance at once equivocal and starlike. Gwynplaine watched the blue eye and the black eye, distracted by the double ray of heaven and of hell that shone in the orbs thus fixed on him. The man and the woman threw a malign dazzling reflection one on the other. Both were fascinated, he by her beauty, she by his deformity. Both were in a measure awe-stricken. Pressed down, as by an overwhelming weight, he was speechless.

"Oh!" she cried. "How clever you are. You are come. You found out that I was obliged to leave London. You followed me. That was right. Your being here proves you to be a wonder."

The simultaneous return of self-possession acts like a flash of lightning. Gwynplaine, indistinctly warned by a vague, rude, but honest misgiving, drew back, but the pink nails clung to his shoulders and restrained him. Some inexorable power proclaimed its sway over him. He himself, a wild beast, was caged in a wild beast's den. She continued, "Anne, the fool, you know whom I mean—the queen—ordered me to Windsor without giving any reason. When I arrived she was closeted with her idiot of a Chancellor. But how did you contrive to obtain access to me? That's what I call being a man—obstacles, indeed—there are no such things! You come at a call. You found things out. My name, the Duchess Josiana, you knew, I fancy. Who was it brought you in? No doubt it was the page. Oh, he is clever! I will give him a hundred guineas. Which way did you get in? Tell me! No, don't tell me. I don't want to know. Explanations diminish interest. I prefer the marvelous, and you are hideous enough to be wonderful. You have fallen from the highest heavens, or you have risen from the depths of hell through the devil's trapdoor. Nothing can be more natural. The ceiling opened or the floor yawned. A descent in a cloud, or an ascent in a mass of fire and brimstone, that is how you have traveled. You have a right to enter like the gods. Agreed; you are my lover."

Gwynplaine was scared, and listened; his mind growing more irresolute every moment. Now all was certain. Impossible to have any further doubt. That letter! the woman confirmed its meaning. Gwynplaine the lover and the beloved of a duchess! Mighty pride, with its thousand baleful heads, stirred his wretched heart. Vanity, that powerful agent within us, works us measureless evil.

The duchess went on, "Since you are here, it is so decreed. I ask nothing more. There is someone on high, or in hell, who brings us together. The betrothal of Styx and Aurora! Unbridled ceremonies beyond all laws! The very day I first saw you, I said, it is he! I recognize him. He is the monster of my dreams. He shall be mine. We should give destiny a helping hand. Therefore I wrote to you. One question, Gwynplaine: do you believe in predestination? For my part, I have believed in it since I read, in Cicero, Scipio's dream. Ah! I did not observe it. Dressed like a gentleman! You in fine clothes! Why not! You are a mountebank. All the more reason. A juggler is as good as a lord. Moreover, what are lords? Clowns. You have a noble figure; you are magnificently made. It is wonderful that you should be here. When did you arrive? How long have you been here? Did you see me naked? I am beautiful, am I not? I was going to take my bath. Oh! how I love you! You read my letter! Did you read it yourself? Did anyone read it to you? Can you read? Probably you are ignorant. I ask questions, but don't answer them. I don't like the sound of your voice. It is soft. An extraordinary thing like you should snarl, and not speak. You sing harmoniously. I hate it. It is the only thing about you that I do not like. All the rest is terrible—is grand. In India you would be a god. Were you born with that frightful laugh on your face? No! No doubt it is a penal brand. I do hope you have committed some crime. Come to my arms."

She sank on the couch and made him sit beside her. They found themselves close together unconsciously. What she said passed over Gwynplaine like a mighty storm. He hardly understood the meaning of her whirlwind of words. Her eyes were full of admiration. She spoke tumultuously, frantically, with a voice broken and tender. Her words were music, but their music was to Gwynplaine as a hurricane. Again she fixed her gaze upon him and continued—

"I feel degraded in your presence, and oh ! what happiness that is. How insipid it is to be a grandee! I am noble; what can be more tiresome? Disgrace is a comfort. I am so satiated with respect that I long for contempt. We are all a little erratic, from Venus, Cleopatra, Mesdames de Chevreuse and de Longueville, down to myself. I will make a display of you, I declare. Here's a love affair which will be a blow to my family, the Stuarts. Ah! I breathe again. I have discovered a secret. I am clear of royalty. To be free from its trammels is indeed deliverance. To break down, defy, make and destroy at will, that is true enjoyment. Listen, I love you."

She paused; then with a frightful smile, went on, "I love you, not only because you are deformed, but because you are low. I love monsters, and I love mountebanks. A lover despised, mocked, grotesque, hideous, exposed to laughter on that pillory called a theater, has for me an extraordinary attraction. It is tasting the fruit of hell. An infamous lover, how exquisite! To taste the apple, not of Paradise, but of hell; such is my temptation. It is for that I hunger and thirst. I am that Eve, the Eve of the depths. Probably you are, unknown to yourself, a devil. I am in love with a nightmare. You are a moving puppet, of which the strings are pulled by a specter. You are the incarnation of infernal mirth. You are the master I require. I wanted a lover such as those of Medea and Canidia. I felt sure that some night would bring me such a one. You are all that I want. I am talking of a heap of things of which you probably know nothing. Gwynplaine, hitherto I have remained untouched; I give myself to you, pure as a burning ember. You evidently do not believe me; but if you only knew how little I care!"

Her words flowed like a volcanic eruption. Pierce Mount Etna, and you may obtain some idea of that jet of fiery eloquence.

Gwynplaine stammered, "Madame—"

She placed her hand on his mouth. "Silence," she said. "I am studying you. I am unbridled desire, immaculate. I am a vestal bacchante. No man has known me, and I might be the virgin pythoness at Delphos, and have under my naked foot the bronze tripod, where the priests lean their elbows on the skin of the python, whispering questions to the invisible god. My heart is of stone, but it is like those mysterious pebbles which the sea washes to the foot of the rock called Huntly Nabb, at the mouth of the Tees, and which if broken are found to contain a serpent. That serpent is my love. A love which is all-powerful, for it has brought you to me. An impossible distance was between us. I was in Sirius, and you were in Allioth. You have crossed the immeasurable space, and here you are. 'Tis well. Be silent. Take me."

She ceased; he trembled. Then she went on, smiling, "You see, Gwynplaine, to dream is to create; to desire is to summon. To build up the chimera is to provoke the reality. The all-powerful and terrible mystery will not be defied. It produces result. You are here. Do I dare to lose caste? Yes. Do I dare to be your mistress? Your concubine? Your slave? Your chattel? Joyfully. Gwynplaine, I am woman. Woman is clay longing to become mire. I want to despise myself. That lends a zest to pride. The alloy of greatness is baseness. They combine in perfection. Despise me, you who are despised. Nothing can be better. Degradation on degradation. What joy! I pluck the double blossom of ignominy. Trample me under foot. You will only love me the more. I am sure of it. Do you understand why I idolize you? Because I despise you. You are so immeasurably below me that I place you on an altar. Bring the highest and lowest depths together, and you have Chaos, and I delight in Chaos, Chaos, the beginning and end of everything. What is Chaos? A huge blot. Out of that blot God made light, and out of that sink the world. You don't know how perverse I can be. Knead a star in mud, and you will have my likeness."

Thus spoke the siren; the loosened robe revealing her virgin bosom.

She went on

"A wolf to all beside; a faithful dog to you. How astonished they will all be! The astonishment of fools is amusing. I understand myself. Am I a goddess? Amphitrite gave herself to the Cyclops. *Fluctivoma Amphitrite.* Am I a fairy? Urgele gave herself to Bugryx, a winged man, with eight webbed hands. Am I a princess? Marie Stuart had Rizzio. Three beauties, three monsters. I am greater than they, for you are lower than they. Gwynplaine, we were made for one another. The monster that you are outwardly, I am within. Thence my love for you. A caprice? Just so. What is a hurricane but a caprice? Our stars have a certain affinity. Together we are things of night—you in your face, I in my mind. As your countenance is defaced, so is my mind. You, in your turn, create me. You come, and my real soul shows itself. I did not know it. It is astonishing. Your coming has evoked the hydra in me, who am a goddess. You reveal my real nature. See how I resemble you. Look at me as if I were a mirror. Your face is my mind. I did not know I was so terrible. I am also, then, a monster. Oh! Gwynplaine, you do amuse me!"

She laughed, a strange and childlike laugh; and putting her mouth close to his ear, whispered—

"Do you want to see a mad woman? look at me."

She poured her searching look into Gwynplaine. A look is a philter. Her loosened robe provoked a thousand dangerous feelings. Blind, animal ecstasy was invading his mind, ecstasy combined with agony.

Whilst she spoke, though he felt her words like burning coals, his blood froze within his veins. He had not strength to utter a word.

She stopped and looked at him.

"O, monster!" she cried. She grew wild.

Suddenly she seized his hands.

"Gwynplaine, I am the throne; you are the footstool. Let us join on the same level. Oh, how happy I am in my fall! I wish all the world could know how abject I am become. It would bow down all the lower. The more man abhors, the more does he cringe. It is human nature. Hostile, but reptile; dragon, but worm. Oh, I am as depraved as are the gods! They can never say that I am not a king's bastard. I act like a queen. Who was Rodope, but a queen loving Pteh, a man with a crocodile's head? She raised the third pyramid in his honor. Penthesilea loved the centaur, who, being now a star, is named Sagittarius. And what do you say about Anne of Austria? Mazarin was ugly enough! Now, you are not only ugly, you are deformed. Ugliness is mean, deformity is grand. Ugliness is the devil's grin behind beauty; deformity is the reverse of sublimity. It is the back view. Olympus has two aspects. One, by day, shows Apollo; the other, by night, shows Polyphemus. You! you are a Titan. You would be Behemoth in the forests, Leviathan in the deep, and Typhon in the sewer. You surpass everything. There is the trace of lightning in your deformity; your face has been battered by the thunderbolt. The jagged contortion of forked lightning has imprinted its mark on your face. It struck you and passed on. A mighty and mysterious wrath has, in a fit of passion, cemented your spirit in a terrible and superhuman form. Hell is a penal furnace, where the iron called Fatality is raised to a white heat. You have been branded with it. To love you is to understand grandeur. I enjoy that triumph. To be in love with Apollo, a fine effort, forsooth! Glory is to be measured by the astonishment it creates. I love you. I have dreamt of you night after night. This is my palace. You shall see my gardens. There are fresh springs under the shrubs; arbors for lovers; and beautiful groups of marble statuary by Bernini. Flowers! there are too many—during the spring the place is on fire with roses. Did I tell you that the queen is my sister? Do what you like with me. I am made for Jupiter to kiss my feet, and for Satan to spit in my face. Are you of any religion? I am a Papist. My father, James II, died in France, surrounded by Jesuits. I have never felt before as I feel now that I am near you. Oh, how I should like to pass the evening with you, in the midst of music, both reclining on the same cushion, under a purple awning, in a gilded gondola on the soft expanse of ocean. Insult me, beat me, kick me, cuff me, treat me like a brute! I adore you."

Caresses can roar. If you doubt it, observe the lion's. The woman was horrible, and yet full of grace. The effect was tragic. First he felt the claw, then the velvet of the paw. A feline attack, made up of advances and retreats. There was death as well as sport in this game of come and go. She idolized him, but arrogantly. The result was contagious frenzy. Fatal language, at once inexpressible, violent, and sweet. The insulter did not insult; the adorer outraged the object of adoration. She, who buffeted, deified him. Her tones imparted to her violent yet amorous words an indescribable Promethean grandeur. According to Æschylus, in the orgies in honor of the great goddess, the women were smitten by this evil frenzy when they pursued the satyrs under the stars. Such paroxysms raged in the mysterious dances in the grove of Dodona. This woman was as if transfigured— if, indeed, we can term that transfiguration which is the antithesis of heaven.

Her hair quivered like a mane; her robe opened and closed. Nothing could be more attractive than that bosom, full of wild cries. The sunshine of the blue eye mingled with the fire of the black one. She was unearthly.

Gwynplaine, giving way, felt himself vanquished by the deep subtlety of this attack.

"I love you!" she cried.

And she bit him with a kiss.

Homeric clouds were, perhaps, about to be required to encompass Gwynplaine and Josiana, as they did Jupiter and Juno. For Gwynplaine to be loved by a woman who could see, and who saw him; to feel on his deformed mouth the pressure of divine lips, was exquisite and maddening. Before this woman, full of enigmas, all else faded away in his mind. The remembrance of Dea struggled in the shadows with weak cries. There is an antique bas-relief representing the Sphinx devouring a Cupid. The wings of the sweet celestial are bleeding between the fierce, grinning fangs.

Did Gwynplaine love this woman? Has man, like the globe, two poles? Are we, on our inflexible axis, a moving sphere, a star when seen from afar, mud when seen more closely, in which night alternates with day? Has the heart two aspects—one on which its love is poured forth in light; the other in darkness? Here a woman of light, there a woman of the sewer. Angels are necessary. Is it possible that demons are also essential? Has the soul the wings of the bat? Does twilight fall fatally for all? Is sin an integral and inevitable part of our destiny? Must we accept evil as part and portion of our whole? Do we inherit sin as a debt? What awful subjects for thought!

Yet a voice tells us that weakness is a crime. Gwynplaine's feelings are not to be described. The flesh, life, terror, lust, an overwhelming intoxication of spirit, and all the shame possible to pride. Was he about to succumb?

She repeated, "I love you!" and flung her frenzied arms around him. Gwynplaine panted.

Suddenly close at hand there rang, clear and distinct, a little bell. It was the little bell inside the wall. The duchess, turning her head, said—

"What does she want of me?"

Quickly with the noise of a spring door, the silver panel, with the golden crown chased on it, opened. A compartment of a shaft, lined with royal blue velvet, appeared, and, on a golden salver, a letter. The letter, broad and weighty, was placed so as to exhibit the seal, which was a large impression in red wax. The bell continued to tinkle. The open panel almost touched the couch where the duchess and Gwynplaine were sitting.

Leaning over, but still keeping her arm round his neck, she took the letter from the plate, and touched the panel. The compartment closed in, and the bell ceased ringing.

The duchess broke the seal, and, opening the envelope, drew out two documents contained therein, and flung it on the floor at Gwynplaine's feet. The impression of the broken seal was still decipherable, and Gwynplaine could distinguish a royal crown over the initial A. The torn envelope lay open before him, so that he could read, "To Her Grace the Duchess Josiana." The envelope had contained both vellum and parchment. The former was a small, the latter a large, document. On the parchment was a large Chancery seal in green wax, called Lords' sealing-wax.

The face of the duchess, whose bosom was palpitating, and whose eyes were swimming with passion, became overspread with a slight expression of dissatisfaction.

"Ah!" she said. "What does she send me? A lot of papers! What a spoil-sport that woman is!"

Pushing aside the parchment, she opened the vellum.

"It is her handwriting. It is my sister's hand. It is quite provoking. Gwynplaine, I asked you if you could read. Can you?"

Gwynplaine nodded assent.

She stretched herself at full length on the couch, carefully drew her feet and arms under her robe, with a whimsical affectation of modesty, and, giving Gwynplaine the vellum, watched him with an impassioned look.

"Well! you are mine. Begin your duties, my beloved. Read me what the queen writes."

Gwynplaine took the vellum, unfolded it, and, in a voice tremulous with many emotions, began to read—

"MADAM—We are graciously pleased to send to you herewith, sealed and signed by our trusty and well-beloved William Cowper, Lord High Chancellor of England, a copy of a report showing forth the very important fact that the legitimate son of Linnæus Lord Clancharlie has just been discovered and recognized, bearing the name of Gwynplaine, in the lowest rank of a wandering and vagabond life, among strollers and mountebanks. His false position dates from his earliest days. In accordance with the laws of the country, and in virtue of his hereditary rights, Lord Fermain Clancharlie, son of Lord Linnæus, will be this day admitted, and installed in his position in the House of Lords. Therefore, having regard to your welfare, and wishing to preserve for your use the property and estates of Lord Clancharlie of Hunkerville, we substitute him in the place of Lord David Dirry-Moir, and recommend him to your good graces. We have caused Lord Fermain to be conducted to Corleone Lodge. We will and command, as sister and as Queen, that the said Fermain Lord Clancharlie, hitherto called Gwynplaine, shall be your husband, and that you shall marry him. Such is our royal pleasure."

While Gwynplaine, in tremulous tones which varied at almost every word, was reading the document, the duchess, half risen from the couch, listened with fixed attention. When Gwynplaine finished, she snatched the letter from his hands.

"Anne R," she murmured in a tone of abstraction. Then picking up from the floor the parchment she had thrown down, she ran her eye over it. It was the confession of the shipwrecked crew of the *Matutina*, embodied in a report signed by the sheriff of Southwark and by the lord chancellor.

Having perused the report, she read the queen's letter over again. Then she said, "Be it so." And calmly pointing with her finger to the door of the gallery through which he had entered, she added, "Begone."

Gwynplaine was petrified, and remained immovable. She repeated, in icy tones, "Since you are my husband, begone." Gwynplaine, speechless, and with eyes downcast like a criminal, remained motionless. She added, "You have no right to be here; it is my lover's place." Gwynplaine was like a man transfixed. "Very well," said she, "I must go myself. So you are my husband. Nothing can be better. I hate you." She rose, and with an indescribably haughty gesture of adieu, left the room. The curtain in the doorway of the gallery fell behind her.

Chapter V

THEY RECOGNIZE, BUT DO NOT KNOW, EACH OTHER

GWYNPLAINE WAS ALONE. ALONE, AND IN THE PRESENCE OF THE TEPID BATH AND THE DESERTED couch. The confusion in his mind had reached its culminating point. His thoughts no longer resembled thoughts. They overflowed and ran riot; it was the anguish of a creature wrestling with perplexity. He felt as if he were awaking from a horrid nightmare. The entrance into unknown spheres is no simple matter.

From the time he had received the duchess's letter, brought by the page, a series of surprising adventures had befallen Gwynplaine, each one less intelligible than the other. Up to this time, though in a dream, he had seen things clearly. Now he could only grope his way. He no longer thought, nor even dreamed. He collapsed. He sank down upon the couch which the duchess had vacated.

Suddenly, he heard a sound of footsteps, and those of a man. The noise came from the opposite side of the gallery to that by which the duchess had departed. The man approached, and his footsteps, though deadened by the carpet, were clear and distinct. Gwynplaine, in spite of his abstraction, listened.

Suddenly, beyond the silver web of curtain which the duchess had left partly open, a door, evidently concealed by the painted glass, opened wide, and there came floating into the room the refrain of an old French song, caroled at the top of a manly and joyous voice—

"Trois petits gorets sur leur fumier
Juraient comme de porteurs de chaise,"

and a man entered. He wore a sword by his side, a magnificent naval uniform, covered with gold lace, and held in his hand a plumed hat with loops and cockade. Gwynplaine sprang up erect as if moved by springs. He recognized the man, and was, in turn, recognized by him. From their astonished lips came, simultaneously, this double exclamation—

"Gwynplaine!"

"Tom-Jim-Jack!"

The man with the plumed hat advanced toward Gwynplaine, who stood with folded arms.

"What are you doing here, Gwynplaine?"

"And you, Tom-Jim-Jack, what are you doing here?"

"Oh! I understand. Josiana! a caprice. A mountebank and a monster! The double attraction is too powerful to be resisted. You disguised yourself in order to get here, Gwynplaine?"

"And you, too, Tom-Jim-Jack?"

"Gwynplaine, what does this gentleman's dress mean?"

"Tom-Jim-Jack, what does that officer's uniform mean?"

"Gwynplaine, I answer no questions."

"Neither do I, Tom-Jim-Jack."

"Gwynplaine, my name is not Tom-Jim-Jack."

"Tom-Jim-Jack, my name is not Gwynplaine."

"Gwynplaine, I am here in my own house."

"I am here in my own house, Tom-Jim-Jack."

"I will not have you echo my words. You are ironical; but I've got a cane. An end to your jokes, you wretched fool."

Gwynplaine became ashy pale. "You are a fool yourself, and you shall give me satisfaction for this insult."

"In your booth as much as you like, with fisticuffs."

"Here, and with swords?"

"My friend, Gwynplaine, the sword is a weapon for gentlemen. With it I can only fight my equals. At fisticuffs we are equal, but not so with swords. At the Tadcaster Inn, Tom-Jim-Jack could box with Gwynplaine. At Windsor, the case is altered. Understand this: I am a rear-admiral."

"And I am a peer of England."

The man whom Gwynplaine recognized as Tom-Jim-Jack burst out laughing. "Why not a king? Indeed, you are right. An actor plays every part. You'll tell me next that you are Theseus, Duke of Athens."

"I am a peer of England, and we are going to fight."

"Gwynplaine, this becomes tiresome. Don't play with one who can order you to be flogged. I am Lord David Dirry-Moir."

"And I am Lord Clancharlie."

Again Lord David burst out laughing.

"Well said! Gwynplaine is Lord Clancharlie. That is indeed the name the man must bear who is to win Josiana. Listen, I forgive you, and do you know the reason? It's because we are both lovers of the same woman."

The curtain in the door was lifted, and a voice exclaimed, "You are the two husbands, my lords."

They turned.

"Barkilphedro!" cried Lord David.

It was indeed he; he bowed low to the two lords, with a smile on his face. Some few paces behind him was a gentleman with a stern and dignified countenance, who carried in his hand a black wand. This gentleman advanced, and, bowing three times to Gwynplaine, said, "I am the Usher of the Black Rod. I come to fetch your lordship, in obedience to her Majesty's commands."

BOOK THE EIGHTH

THE CAPITOL AND THINGS AROUND IT

Chapter I

ANALYSIS OF MAJESTIC MATTERS

IRRESISTIBLE FATE EVER CARRYING HIM FORWARD, WHICH HAD NOW FOR SO MANY HOURS SHOW-ered its surprises on Gwynplaine, and which had transported him to Windsor, transferred him again to London. Visionary realities succeeded each other without a moment's intermission. He could not escape from their influence. Freed from one he met another. He had scarcely time to breathe. Anyone who has seen a juggler throwing and catching balls can judge the nature of fate.

Those rising and falling projectiles are like men tossed in the hands of Destiny—projectiles and playthings.

On the evening of the same day, Gwynplaine was an actor in an extraordinary scene. He was seated on a bench covered with fleurs-de-lys; over his silken clothes he wore a robe of scarlet velvet, lined with white silk, with a cape of ermine, and on his shoulders two bands of ermine embroidered with gold. Around him were men of all ages, young and old, seated like him on benches covered with fleurs-de-lys, and dressed like him in ermine and purple. In front of him other men were kneeling, clothed in black silk gowns. Some of them were writing; opposite, and a short distance from him, he observed steps, a raised platform, a dais, a large escutcheon glittering between a lion and a unicorn, and at the top of the steps, on the platform under the dais, resting against the escutcheon, was a gilded chair with a crown over it. This was a throne. The throne of Great Britain.

Gwynplaine, himself a peer of England, was in the House of Lords. How Gwynplaine's introduction to the House of Lords came about, we will now explain. Throughout the day, from morning to night, from Windsor to London, from Corleone Lodge to Westminster Hall, he had step by step mounted higher in the social grade. At each step he grew giddier. He had been conveyed from Windsor in a royal carriage with a peer's escort. There is not much difference between a guard of honor and a prisoner's. On that day, travelers on the London and Windsor road saw a galloping cavalcade of gentlemen pensioners of her Majesty's household, escorting two carriages drawn at a rapid pace. In the first carriage sat the Usher of the Black Rod, his wand in his hand. In the second was to be seen a large hat with white plumes, throwing into shadow and hiding the face underneath it. Who was it who was thus being hurried on—a prince? a prisoner? It was Gwynplaine.

It looked as if they were conducting someone to the Tower, unless, indeed, they were escorting him to the House of Lords. The queen had done things well. As it was for her future brother-in-law, she had provided an escort from her own household. The officer of the Usher of the Black Rod rode on horseback at the head of the cavalcade. The Usher of the Black Rod carried, on a cushion placed on a seat of the carriage, a black portfolio stamped with the royal crown. At Brentford, the last relay before London, the carriages and escort halted. A four-horse carriage of tortoise-shell, with two postilions, a coachman in a wig, and four footmen, was in waiting. The wheels, steps, springs, pole, and all the fittings of this carriage were gilt. The horses' harness was of silver. This state coach was of an ancient and extraordinary shape, and would have been distinguished by its grandeur among the fifty-one celebrated carriages of which Roubo has left us drawings.

The Usher of the Black Rod and his officer alighted. The latter, having lifted the cushion, on which rested the royal portfolio, from the seat in the postchaise, carried it on outstretched hands, and stood behind the Usher. He first opened the door of the empty carriage, then the door of that occupied by Gwynplaine, and, with downcast eyes, respectfully invited him to descend. Gwynplaine left the chaise, and took his seat in the carriage. The Usher carrying the rod, and the officer supporting the cushion, followed, and took their places on the low front seat provided for pages in old state coaches. The inside of the carriage was lined with white satin trimmed with Binche silk, with tufts and tassels of silver. The roof was painted with armorial bearings. The postilions of the chaises they were leaving were dressed in the royal livery. The attendants of the carriage they now entered wore a different but very magnificent livery.

Gwynplaine, in spite of his bewildered state in which he felt quite overcome, remarked the gorgeously-attired footmen, and asked the Usher of the Black Rod—

"Whose livery is that?"

He answered—

"Yours, my lord."

The House of Lords was to sit that evening. *Curia erat serena,* run the old records. In England parliamentary work is by preference undertaken at night. It once happened that Sheridan began a speech at midnight and finished it at sunrise.

The two postchaises returned to Windsor. Gwynplaine's carriage set out for London. This ornamented four-horse carriage proceeded at a walk from Brentford to London, as befitted the dignity of the coachman. Gwynplaine's servitude to ceremony was beginning in the shape of his solemn-looking coachman. The delay was, moreover, apparently prearranged; and we shall see presently its probable motive.

Night was falling, though it was not quite dark, when the carriage stopped at the King's Gate, a large sunken door between two turrets, connecting Whitehall with Westminster. The escort of gentlemen pensioners formed a circle around the carriage. A footman jumped down from behind it and opened the door. The Usher of the Black Rod, followed by the officer carrying the cushion, got out of the carriage, and addressed Gwynplaine.

"My lord, be pleased to alight. I beg your lordship to keep your hat on."

Gwynplaine wore under his traveling cloak the suit of black silk, which he had not changed since the previous evening. He had no sword. He left his cloak in the carriage. Under the arched way of the King's Gate there was a small side door, raised some few steps above the road. In ceremonial processions the greatest personage never walks first.

The Usher of the Black Rod, followed by his officer, walked first; Gwynplaine followed. They ascended the steps, and entered by the side door. Presently they were in a wide, circular room, with a pillar in the center, the lower part of a turret. The room, being on the ground floor, was lighted by narrow windows in the pointed arches, which served but to make darkness visible. Twilight often lends solemnity to a scene. Obscurity is in itself majestic.

In this room, thirteen men, disposed in ranks, were standing; three in the front row, six in the second row, and four behind. In the front row one wore a crimson velvet gown; the other two, gowns of the same color, but of satin. All three had the arms of England embroidered on their shoulders. The second rank wore tunics of white silk, each one having a different coat-of-arms emblazoned in front. The last row were clad in black silk, and were thus distinguished. The first wore a blue cape. The second had a scarlet St. George embroidered in front. The third, two embroidered crimson crosses, in front and behind. The fourth had a collar of black sable fur. All were uncovered, wore wigs, and carried swords. Their faces were scarcely visible in the dim light, neither could they see Gwynplaine's face.

The Usher of the Black Rod, raising his wand, said—

"My Lord Fermain Clancharlie, Baron Clancharlie and Hunkerville, I, the Usher of the Black Rod, first officer of the presence chamber, hand your lordship over to Garter King-at-Arms."

The person clothed in velvet, quitting his place in the ranks, bowed to the ground before Gwynplaine, and said—

"My Lord Fermain Clancharlie, I am Garter, Principal King-at-Arms of England. I am the officer appointed and installed by his grace the Duke of Norfolk, hereditary Earl Marshal. I have sworn obedience to the king, peers, and knights of the garter. The day of my installation, when the Earl Marshal of England anointed me by pouring a goblet of wine on my head, I solemnly promised to be attentive to the nobility; to avoid bad company; to excuse, rather than accuse, gentlefolks; and to assist widows and virgins. It is I who have the charge of arranging the funeral ceremonies of peers, and the supervision of their armorial bearings. I place myself at the orders of your lordship."

The first of those wearing satin tunics, having bowed deeply, said—

"My lord, I am Clarenceaux, Second King-at-Arms of England. I am the officer who arranges the obsequies of nobles below the rank of peers. I am at your lordship's disposal."

The other wearer of the satin tunic bowed and spoke thus—

"My lord, I am Norroy, Third King-at-Arms of England. Command me."

The second row, erect and without bowing, advanced a pace. The right-hand man said—

"My lord, we are the six Dukes-at-Arms of England. I am York."

Then each of the heralds, or Dukes-at-Arms, speaking in turn, proclaimed his title.

"I am Lancaster."

"I am Richmond."

"I am Chester."

"I am Somerset."

"I am Windsor."

The coats-of-arms embroidered on their breasts were those of the counties and towns from which they took their names.

The third rank, dressed in black, remained silent. Garter King-at-Arms, pointing them out to Gwynplaine, said—

"My lord, these are the four Pursuivants-at-Arms. Blue Mantle."

The man with the blue cape bowed.

"Rouge Dragon."

He with the St. George inclined his head.

"Rouge Croix."

He with the scarlet crosses saluted.

"Portcullis."

He with the sable fur collar made his obeisance.

On a sign from the King-at-Arms, the first of the pursuivants, Blue Mantle, stepped forward and received from the officer of the Usher the cushion of silver cloth and crown-emblazoned portfolio. And the King-at-Arms said to the Usher of the Black Rod—

"Proceed; I leave in your hands the introduction of his lordship!"

The observance of these customs, and also of others which will now be described, were the old ceremonies in use prior to the time of Henry VIII, and which Anne for some time attempted to revive. There is nothing like it in existence now. Nevertheless, the House of Lords thinks that it is unchangeable; and, if Conservatism exists anywhere, it is there.

It changes, nevertheless. *E pur si muove.* For instance, what has become of the maypole—which the citizens of London erected on the 1st of May, when the peers went down to the House? The last one was erected in 1713. Since then the maypole has disappeared. Disuse.

Outwardly, unchangeable; inwardly, mutable. Take, for example, the title of Albemarle. It sounds eternal. Yet it has been through six different families—Odo, Mandeville, Bethune, Plantagenet, Beauchamp, Monck. Under the title of Leicester five different names have been merged—Beaumont, Breose, Dudley, Sydney, Coke. Under Lincoln, six; under Pembroke, seven. The families change, under unchanging titles. A superficial historian believes in immutability. In reality it does not exist. Man can never be more than a wave; humanity is the ocean.

Aristocracy is proud of what women consider a reproach—age! Yet both cherish the same illusion, that they do not change. It is probable the House of Lords will not recognize itself in the foregoing description, nor yet in that which follows, thus resembling the once pretty woman, who objects to having any wrinkles. The mirror is ever a scapegoat, yet its truths cannot be contested. To portray exactly, constitutes the duty of a historian. The King-at-Arms, turning to Gwynplaine, said—

"Be pleased to follow me, my lord." And added, "You will be saluted. Your lordship, in returning the salute, will be pleased merely to raise the brim of your hat."

They moved off, in procession, toward a door at the far side of the room. The Usher of the Black Rod walked in front; then Blue Mantle, carrying the cushion; then the King-at-Arms; and after him came Gwynplaine, wearing his hat. The rest, kings-at-arms, heralds, and pursuivants, remained in the circular room. Gwynplaine, preceded by the Usher of the Black Rod, and escorted by the King-at-Arms, passed from room to room, in a direction which it would now be impossible to trace, the old Houses of Parliament having been pulled down. Amongst others, he crossed that Gothic state-chamber in which took place the last meeting of James II and Monmouth, and whose walls witnessed the useless debasement of the cowardly nephew at the feet of his vindictive uncle.

On the walls of this chamber hung, in chronological order, nine fell-length portraits of former peers, with their dates—Lord Nansladron, 1305; Lord Baliol, 1306; Lord Benestede, 1314; Lord Cantilupe, 1356; Lord Montbegon, 1357; Lord Tibotot, 1373; Lord Zouch of Codnor, 1615; Lord Bella-Aqua, with no date; Lord Harren and Surrey, Count of Blois, also without date.

It being now dark, lamps were burning at intervals in the galleries. Brass chandeliers, with wax candles, illuminated the rooms, lighting them like the side aisles of a church. None but officials were present. In one room, which the procession crossed, stood, with heads respectfully lowered, the four clerks of the signet, and the Clerk of the Council. In another room stood the distinguished Knight Banneret, Philip Sydenham of Brympton, in Somersetshire. The Knight Banneret is a title conferred in time of war, under the unfurled royal standard. In another room was the senior baronet of England, Sir Edmund Bacon of Suffolk, heir of Sir Nicholas Bacon, styled, *Primus baronetorum Anglicae*. Behind Sir Edmund was an armor-bearer with an arquebus, and an esquire carrying the arms of Ulster, the baronets being the hereditary defenders of the province of Ulster in Ireland. In another room was the Chancellor of the Exchequer, with his four accountants, and the two deputies of the Lord Chamberlain, *appointed to cleave the tallies*.

At the entrance of a corridor covered with matting, which was the communication between the Lower and the Upper House, Gwynplaine was saluted by Sir Thomas Mansell of Margam, Comptroller of the Queen's Household and Member for Glamorgan; and at the exit from the corridor by a deputation of one for every two of the Barons of the Cinque Ports, four on the right and four on the left, the Cinque Ports being eight in number. William Hastings did obeisance for Hastings; Matthew Aylmor, for Dover; Josias Burchett, for Sandwich; Sir Philip Boteler, for Hythe; John Brewer, for New Rumney; Edward Southwell, for the town of Rye; James Hayes, for Winchelsea; George Nailor, for Seaford. As Gwynplaine was about to return the salute, the King-at-Arms reminded him in a low voice of the etiquette, "Only the brim of your hat, my lord." Gwynplaine did as directed. He now entered the so-called Painted Chamber, in which there was no painting, except a few of saints, and amongst them St. Edward, in the high arches of the long and deep-pointed windows, which were divided by what formed the ceiling of Westminster Hall and the floor of the Painted Chamber. On the far side of the wooden barrier which divided the room from end to end, stood the three Secretaries of State, men of mark. The functions of the first of these officials comprised the supervision of all affairs relating to the south of England, Ireland, the Colonies, France, Switzerland, Italy, Spain, Portugal, and Turkey. The second had charge of the north of England, and watched affairs in the Low Countries, Germany, Denmark, Sweden, Poland, and Russia. The third, a Scot, had charge of Scotland. The two first-mentioned were English: one of them being the Honorable Robert Harley, Member for the borough of New Radnor. A Scotch member, Mungo Graham, Esquire, a relation of the Duke of Montrose, was present. All bowed, without speaking, to Gwynplaine, who returned the salute by touching his hat. The barrier-keeper lifted the wooden arm which, pivoting on a hinge, formed the entrance to the far side of the Painted Chamber, where stood the long table, covered with green cloth, reserved for peers. A branch of lighted candles stood on the table. Gwynplaine, preceded by the Usher of the Black Rod, Garter King-at-Arms, and Blue Mantle, penetrated into this privileged compartment. The barrier-keeper closed the opening immediately Gwynplaine had passed. The King-at-Arms, having entered the precincts of the privileged compartment, halted. The Painted Chamber was a spacious apartment. At the further end, upright, beneath the royal escutcheon which was placed between the two windows, stood two old men, in red velvet robes, with two rows of ermine trimmed with gold lace on their shoulders, and wearing wigs, and hats with white plumes. Through the openings of their robes might be detected silk garments and sword hilts. Motionless behind them stood a man dressed in black silk, holding on high a great mace of gold surmounted by a crowned lion. It was the Mace-bearer of the Peers of England. The lion is their crest. *Et les Lions ce sont les Barons et li Per*, runs the manuscript chronicle of Bertrand Duguesclin.

The King-at-Arms pointed out the two persons in velvet, and whispered to Gwynplaine—

"My lord, these are your equals. Be pleased to return their salute exactly as they make it. These two peers are barons, and have been named by the Lord Chancellor as your sponsors. They are very old, and almost blind. They will, themselves, introduce you to the House of Lords. The first is Charles Mildmay, Lord Fitzwalter, sixth on the roll of barons; the second is Augustus Arundel, Lord Arundel of Trerice, thirty-eighth on the roll of barons." The King-at-Arms having advanced a step toward the two old men, proclaimed "Fermain Clancharlie, Baron Clancharlie, Baron Hunkerville, Marquis of Corleone in Sicily, greets your lordships!" The two peers raised their hats to the full extent of the arm, and then replaced them. Gwynplaine did the same. The Usher of the Black Rod stepped forward, followed by Blue Mantle and Garter King at-Arms. The Mace-bearer took up his post in front of Gwynplaine, the two peers at his side, Lord Fitzwalter on the right, and Lord Arundel of Trerice on the left. Lord Arundel, the elder of the two, was very feeble. He died the following year, bequeathing to his grandson John, a minor, the title which became extinct in 1768. The procession, leaving the Painted Chamber, entered a gallery in which were rows of pilasters, and between the spaces were sentinels, alternately pikemen of England and halberdiers of Scotland. The Scotch halberdiers were magnificent kilted soldiers, worthy to encounter later on at Fontenoy the French cavalry, and the royal cuirassiers, whom their colonel thus addressed: *"Messieurs les maitres, assurez vos chapeaux. Nous allons avoir l'honneur de charger."* The captain of these soldiers saluted Gwynplaine, and the peers, his sponsors, with their swords. The men saluted with their pikes and halberds.

At the end of the gallery shone a large door, so magnificent that its two folds seemed to be masses of gold. On each side of the door, there stood, upright and motionless, men who were called door-keepers. Just before you came to this door, the gallery widened out into a circular space. In this space was an arm-chair with an immense back, and on it, judging by his wig and from the amplitude of his robes, was a distinguished person. It was William Cowper, Lord Chancellor of England. To be able to cap a royal infirmity with a similar one has its advantages. William Cowper was short-sighted. Anne had also defective sight, but in a lesser degree. The near-sightedness of William Cowper found favor in the eyes of the short-sighted queen, and induced her to appoint him Lord Chancellor, and Keeper of the Royal Conscience. William Cowper's upper lip was thin, and his lower one thick—a sign of semi-good-nature.

This circular space was lighted by a lamp hung from the ceiling. The Lord Chancellor was sitting gravely in his large arm-chair; at his right was the Clerk of the Crown, and at his left the Clerk of the Parliaments.

Each of the clerks had before him an open register and an inkhorn.

Behind the Lord Chancellor was his mace-bearer, holding the mace with the crown on the top, besides the train-bearer and purse-bearer, in large wigs.

All these officers are still in existence. On a little stand, near the woolsack, was a sword, with a gold hilt and sheath, and belt of crimson velvet.

Behind the Clerk of the Crown was an officer holding in his hands the coronation robe.

Behind the Clerk of the Parliaments another officer held a second robe, which was that of a peer.

The robes, both of scarlet velvet, lined with white silk, and having bands of ermine trimmed with gold lace over the shoulders, were similar, except that the ermine band was wider on the coronation robe.

The third officer, who was the librarian, carried on a square of Flanders leather the red book, a little volume bound in red morocco, containing a list of the peers and commons, besides a few blank leaves and a pencil, which it was the custom to present to each new member on his entering the House.

Gwynplaine, between the two peers, his sponsors, brought up the procession, which stopped before the woolsack.

The two peers, who introduced him, uncovered their heads, and Gwynplaine did likewise.

The King-at-Arms received from the hands of Blue Mantle the cushion of silver cloth, knelt down, and presented the black portfolio on the cushion to the Lord Chancellor.

The Lord Chancellor took the black portfolio, and handed it to the Clerk of the Parliament.

The Clerk received it ceremoniously, and then sat down.

The Clerk of the Parliament opened the portfolio, and arose.

The portfolio contained the two usual messages—the royal patent addressed to the House of Lords, and the writ of summons.

The Clerk read aloud these two messages, with respectful deliberation, standing.

The writ of summons, addressed to Fermain Lord Clancharlie, concluded with the accustomed formalities—

"We strictly enjoin you, on the faith and allegiance that you owe, to come and take your place in person among the prelates and peers sitting in our Parliament at Westminster, for the purpose of giving your advice, in all honor and conscience, on the business of the kingdom and of the Church."

The reading of the messages being concluded, the Lord Chancellor raised his voice—

"The message of the Crown has been read. Lord Clancharlie, does your lordship renounce transubstantiation, adoration of saints, and the mass?"

Gwynplaine bowed.

"The test has been administered," said the Lord Chancellor.

And the Clerk of the Parliament resumed—

"His lordship has taken the test."

The Lord Chancellor added—

"My Lord Clancharlie, you can take your seat."

"So be it," said the two sponsors.

The King-at-Arms rose, took the sword from the stand, and buckled it round Gwynplaine's waist.

"Ce faict," says the old Norman charter, "le pair prend son espée, et monte aux hauts siéges, et assiste a l'audience."

Gwynplaine heard a voice behind him, which said—

"I array your lordship in a peer's robe."

At the same time, the officer who spoke to him, who was holding the robe, placed it on him, and tied the black strings of the ermine cape round his neck.

Gwynplaine, the scarlet robe on his shoulders, and the golden sword by his side, was attired like the peers on his right and left.

The librarian presented to him the red book, and put it in the pocket of his waistcoat.

The King-at-Arms murmured in his ear—

"My lord, on entering, will bow to the royal chair."

The royal chair is the throne.

Meanwhile the two clerks were writing, each at his table—one on the register of the Crown, the other on the register of the House.

Then both—the Clerk of the Crown preceding the other—brought their books to the Lord Chancellor, who signed them. Having signed the two registers, the Lord Chancellor rose.

"Fermain Lord Clancharlie, Baron Clancharlie, Baron Hunkerville, Marquis of Corleone in Sicily, be you welcome among your peers, the lords spiritual and temporal of Great Britain."

Gwynplaine's sponsors touched his shoulder.

He turned round.

The folds of the great gilded door at the end of the gallery opened.

It was the door of the House of Lords.

Thirty-six hours only had elapsed since Gwynplaine, surrounded by a different procession, had entered the iron door of Southwark Jail.

What shadowy chimeras had passed, with terrible rapidity through his brain! Chimeras which were hard facts; rapidity, which was a capture by assault!

Chapter II

IMPARTIALITY

THE CREATION OF AN EQUALITY WITH THE KING, CALLED PEERAGE, WAS, IN BARBAROUS EPOCHS, a useful fiction. This rudimentary political expedient produced in France and England different results. In France, the peer was a mock king; in England, a real prince—less grand than in France, but more genuine: we might say less, but worse.

Peerage was born in France; the date is uncertain—under Charlemagne, says the legend; under Robert le Sage, says history; and history is not more to be relied on than legend. Favin writes: "The King of France wished to attach to himself the great of his kingdom, by the magnificent title of peers, as if they were his equals."

Peerage soon thrust forth branches, and from France passed over to England.

The English peerage has been a great fact, and almost a mighty institution. It had for precedent the Saxon wittenagemote. The Danish thane and the Norman vavassour commingled in the baron. Baron is the same as vir, which is translated into Spanish by *varon*, and which signifies, *par excellence*, "Man." As early as 1075, the barons made themselves felt by the king—and by what a king! By William the Conqueror. In 1086 they laid the foundation of feudality, and its basis was the "Doomsday Book." Under John Lackland came conflict. The French peerage took the high hand with Great Britain, and demanded that the king of England should appear at their Bar. Great was the indignation of the English barons. At the coronation of Philip Augustus, the King of England, as Duke of Normandy, carried the first square banner, and the Duke of Guyenne the second. Against this king, a vassal of the foreigner, the War of the Barons burst forth. The barons imposed on the weak-minded King John, Magna Charta, from which sprang the House of Lords. The pope took part with the king, and excommunicated the lords. The date was 1215, and the pope was Innocent III, who wrote the "Veni Sancte Spiritus," and who sent to John Lackland the four cardinal virtues in the shape of four gold rings. The Lords persisted. The duel continued through many generations. Pembroke struggled. 1248 was the year of "the provisions of Oxford." Twenty-four barons limited the king's powers, discussed him, and called a knight from each county to take part in the widened breach. Here was the dawn of the Commons. Later on, the Lords added two citizens from each city, and two burgesses from each borough. It arose from this, that up to the time of Elizabeth the peers were judges of the validity of elections to the House of Commons. From their jurisdiction sprang the proverb that the members returned ought to be without the three P's—*sine Prece, sine Pretio, sine Poculo*. This did not obviate rotten boroughs. In 1293, the Court of Peers in France had still the King of England under their jurisdiction; and Philippe le Bel cited Edward I to appear before him. Edward I was the king who ordered his son to boil him down after death, and to carry his bones to the wars. Under the follies of their kings the Lords felt the necessity of fortifying parliament. They divided it into two chambers, the upper and the lower. The Lords arrogantly kept the Supremacy. "If it happens that any member of the Commons should be so bold as to speak to the prejudice of the House of Lords, he is called to the bar of the House to be reprimanded, and, occasionally, to be sent to the Tower." There is the same distinction in voting. In the House of Lords they vote one by one, beginning with the junior, called the puisne baron. Each peer answers *"Content,"* or *"non-Content."* In the Commons they vote together, by "Aye," or "No," in a crowd. The Commons accuse, the peers judge. The peers, in their disdain of figures, delegated to the Commons, who were to profit by it, the superintendence of the Exchequer, thus named, according to some, after the table-cover, which was like a chess-board, and according to others, from the drawers of the old safe, where was kept, behind an iron grating, the treasure of the kings of England. The "Year-book" dates from the end of the thirteenth century. In the War of the Roses the weight of the Lords was thrown, now on the side of John of Gaunt, Duke of Lancaster, now on the side of Edmund, Duke of York. Wat Tyler, the Lollards, Warwick the King-maker, all that anarchy from which freedom is to spring, had for foundation, avowed or secret, the English feudal system. The Lords were usefully jealous of the Crown; for to be jealous is to be watchful. They circumscribed the royal initiative, diminished the category of cases of high treason, raised up pretended Richards against Henry IV, appointed themselves arbitrators, judged the question of the three crowns between the Duke of York and Margaret of Anjou, and at need levied armies, and fought their battles of Shrewsbury, Tewkesbury, and St. Albans, sometimes winning, sometimes losing. Before this, in the thirteenth century, they had gained the battle of Lewes, and had driven from the kingdom the four brothers of the king, bastards of Queen Isabella by the Count de la Marche; all four usurers, who extorted money from Christians by means of the Jews; half princes, half sharpers—a thing common enough in more recent times, but not held in good odor in those days. Up to the fifteenth century the Norman Duke peeped out in the King of England, and the acts of Parliament were written in French. From the reign of Henry VII, by the will of the Lords, these were written in English. England, British under Uther Pendragon; Roman under Cæsar; Saxon under the Heptarchy; Danish under Harold; Norman after William; then became, thanks to the Lords, English. After that she became Anglican. To have one's religion at home is a great power. A foreign pope drags down the national life. A Mecca is an octopus, and devours it. In 1534, London bowed out Rome. The peerage adopted the reformed religion, and the Lords accepted Luther. Here we have the answer to the excommunication of 1215. It was agreeable to Henry VIII; but, in other respects, the Lords were a trouble to him. As a bulldog to a bear, so was the House of Lords to Henry VIII. When Wolsey robbed the nation of Whitehall, and when Henry robbed Wolsey of it, who complained? Four lords—Darcie of Chichester; Saint John of Bletsho; and (two Norman names) Mountjoie and Mounteagle. The king usurped. The peerage encroached. There is something in hereditary power which is incorruptible. Hence the insubordination of the Lords. Even in Elizabeth's reign the barons were restless. From this resulted the tortures at Durham. Elizabeth was as a farthingale over an executioner's block. Elizabeth assembled Parliament as seldom as possible, and reduced the House of Lords to sixty-five members, amongst whom there was but one marquis (Winchester), and not a single duke. In France the kings felt the same jealousy and carried out the same elimination. Under Henry III there were no more than eight dukedoms in the peerage, and it was to the great vexation of the king that the Baron de Mantes, the Baron de Courcy, the Baron de Coulommiers, the Baron de Chateauneuf-en-Thimerais, the Baron de la Ferè-en-Lardenois, the Baron de Mortagne, and some others besides, maintained themselves as barons—peers of France. In England the crown saw the peerage diminish with pleasure. Under Anne, to quote but one example, the peerages become extinct since the twelfth century amounted to five hundred and sixty-five. The War of the Roses had begun the extermination of dukes, which the ax of Mary Tudor completed. This was, indeed, the decapitation of the nobility. To prune away the dukes was to cut off its head. Good policy, perhaps; but it is better to corrupt than to decapitate. James I was of this opinion. He restored dukedoms. He made a duke of his favorite Villiers, who had made him a pig; a transformation from the duke feudal to the duke courtier. This sowing was to bring forth a rank harvest: Charles II was to make two of his mistresses duchesses—Barbara of Southampton, and

Louise de la Querouel of Portsmouth. Under Anne there were to be twenty-five dukes, of whom three were to be foreigners, Cumberland, Cambridge, and Schomberg. Did this court policy, invented by James I, succeed? No. The House of Peers was irritated by the effort to shackle it by intrigue. It was irritated against James I, it was irritated against Charles I, who, we may observe, may have had something to do with the death of his father, just as Marie de Medicis may have had something to do with the death of her husband. There was a rupture between Charles I. and the peerage. The Lords who, under James I, had tried at their bar extortion, in the person of Bacon, under Charles I, tried treason, in the person of Strafford. They had condemned Bacon, they condemned Strafford. One had lost his honor, the other lost his life. Charles I was first beheaded in the person of Strafford. The Lords lent their aid to the Commons. The king convokes Parliament to Oxford, the revolution convokes it to London. Forty-four peers side with the King, twenty-two with the Republic. From this combination of the people with the Lords arose the Bill of Rights—a sketch of the French *Droits de l'homme*, a vague shadow flung back from the depths of futurity by the revolution of France on the revolution of England.

Such were the services of the peerage. Involuntary ones, we admit, and dearly purchased, because the said peerage is a huge parasite. But considerable services, nevertheless.

The despotic work of Louis XI, of Richelieu, and of Louis XIV, the creation of a sultan, leveling taken for true equality, the bastinado given by the scepter, the common abasement of the people, all these Turkish tricks in France the peers prevented in England. The aristocracy was a wall, banking up the king on one side, sheltering the people on the other. They redeemed their arrogance toward the people by their insolence toward the king. Simon, Earl of Leicester, said to Henry III— *"King, thou hast lied!"* The Lords curbed the crown, and grated against their kings in the tenderest point, that of venery. Every lord, passing through a royal park, had the right to kill a deer: in the house of the king the peer was at home; in the Tower of London the scale of allowance for the king was no more than that for a peer, viz., twelve pounds sterling per week. This was the House of Lords' doing.

Yet more. We owe to it the deposition of kings. The Lords ousted John Lackland, degraded Edward II, deposed Richard II, broke the power of Henry VI, and made Cromwell a possibility. What a Louis XIV there was in Charles I! Thanks to Cromwell, it remained latent. By the by, we may here observe that Cromwell himself, though no historian seems to have noticed the fact, aspired to the peerage. This was why he married Elizabeth Bouchier, descendant and heiress of a Cromwell, Lord Bouchier, whose peerage became extinct in 1471, and of a Bouchier, Lord Robesart, another peerage extinct in 1429. Carried on with the formidable increase of important events, he found the suppression of a king a shorter way to power than the recovery of a peerage. A ceremonial of the Lords, at times ominous, could reach even to the king. Two men-at-arms from the Tower, with their axes on their shoulders, between whom an accused peer stood at the bar of the house, might have been there in like attendance on the king as on any other nobleman. For five centuries the House of Lords acted on a system, and carried it out with determination. They had their days of idleness and weakness, as, for instance, that strange time when they allowed themselves to be seduced by the vessels loaded with cheeses, hams, and Greek wines sent them by Julius II. The English aristocracy was restless, haughty, ungovernable, watchful, and patriotically mistrustful. It was that aristocracy which, at the end of the seventeenth century, by act the tenth of the year 1694, deprived the borough of Stockbridge, in Hampshire, of the right of sending members to Parliament, and forced the Commons to declare null the election for that borough, stained by papistical fraud. It imposed the test on James, Duke of York, and, on his refusal to take it, excluded him from the throne. He reigned, notwithstanding; but the Lords wound up by calling him to account and banishing him. That aristocracy has had, in its long duration, some instinct of progress. It has always given out a certain quantity of appreciable light, except now toward its end, which is at hand. Under James II it maintained in the Lower House the proportion of three hundred and forty-six burgesses against ninety-two knights. The sixteen barons, by courtesy, of the Cinque Ports were more than counterbalanced by the fifty citizens of the twenty-five cities. Though corrupt and egotistic, that aristocracy was, in some instances, singularly impartial. It is harshly judged. History keeps all its compliments for the Commons. The justice of this is doubtful. We consider the part played by the Lords a very great one. Oligarchy is the independence of a barbarous state, but it is an independence. Take Poland, for instance, nominally a kingdom, really a republic. The peers of England held the throne in suspicion and guardianship. Time after time they have made their power more felt than that of the Commons. They gave check to the king. Thus, in that remarkable year, 1694, the Triennial Parliament Bill, rejected by the Commons, in consequence of the objections of William III, was passed by the Lords. William III, in his irritation, deprived the Earl of Bath of the governorship of Pendennis Castle, and Viscount Mordaunt of all his offices. The House of Lords was the republic of Venice in the heart of the royalty of England. To reduce the king to a doge was its object; and, in proportion as it decreased the power of the crown, it increased that of the people. Royalty knew this, and hated the peerage. Each endeavored to lessen the other. What was thus lost by each was proportionate profit to the people. Those two blind powers, monarchy and oligarchy, could not see that they were working for the benefit of a third, which was democracy. What a delight it was to the crown, in the last century, to be able to hang a peer, Lord Ferrers!

However, they hung him with a silken rope. How polite!

"They would not have hung a peer of France," the Duke of Richelieu haughtily remarked. Granted. They would have beheaded him. Still more polite!

Montmorency Tancarville signed himself *peer of France and England*; thus throwing the English peerage into the second rank. The peers of France were higher and less powerful, holding to rank more than to authority, and to precedence more than to domination. There was between them and the Lords that shade of difference which separates vanity from pride. With the peers of France, to take precedence of foreign princes, of Spanish grandees, of Venetian patricians; to see seated on the lower benches the Marshals of France, the Constable and the Admiral of France, were he even Comte de Toulouse and son of Louis XIV; to draw a distinction between duchies in the male and female line; to maintain the proper distance between a simple *comté*, like Armagnac or Albret, and a *comté pairié*, like Evreux; to wear by right, at five-and-twenty, the blue ribbon of the golden fleece; to counterbalance the Duke de la Tremoille, the most ancient peer of the court, with the Duke Uzès, the most ancient peer of the Parliament; to claim as many pages and horses to their carriages as an elector; to be called *monseigneur* by the first President; to discuss whether the Duke de Maine dates his peerage as the Comte d'Eu, from 1458; to cross the grand chamber diagonally, or by the side—such things were grave matters. Grave matters with the Lords were the Navigation Act, the Test Act, the enrollment of Europe in the service of England, the command of the seas, the expulsion of the Stuarts, war with France. On one side, etiquette above all; on the other, empire above all. The peers of England had the substance, the peers of France the shadow.

To conclude, the House of Lords was a starting point; toward civilization this is an immense thing. It had the honor to found a nation. It was the first incarnation of the unity of the people: English resistance, that obscure but all-powerful force, was born in the House of Lords. The barons, by a series of acts of violence against royalty, have paved the way for its eventual downfall. The House of Lords at the present day is somewhat sad and astonished at what it has unwillingly and unintentionally done, all the more that it is irrevocable.

What are concessions? Restitutions—and nations know it.

"I grant," says the king.

"I get back my own," says the people.

The House of Lords believed that it was creating the privileges of the peerage, and it has produced the rights of the citizen. That vulture, aristocracy, has hatched the eagle's egg of liberty.

And now the egg is broken, the eagle is soaring, the vulture dying.

Aristocracy is at its last gasp; England is growing up.

Still, let us be just toward the aristocracy. It entered the scale against royalty, and was its counterpoise. It was an obstacle to despotism. It was a barrier. Let us thank and bury it.

Chapter III

THE OLD HALL

NEAR WESTMINSTER ABBEY WAS AN OLD NORMAN PALACE WHICH WAS BURNED IN THE TIME OF Henry VIII. Its wings were spared. In one of them Edward VI placed the House of Lords, in the other the House of Commons. Neither the two wings nor the two chambers are now in existence. The whole has been rebuilt.

We have already said, and we must repeat, that there is no resemblance between the House of Lords of the present day and that of the past. In demolishing the ancient palace they somewhat demolished its ancient usages. The strokes of the pickax on the monument produce their counterstrokes on customs and charters. An old stone cannot fall without dragging down with it an old law. Place in a round room a parliament, which has been hitherto held in a square room, and it will no longer be the same thing. A change in the shape of the shell changes the shape of the fish inside.

If you wish to preserve an old thing, human or divine, a code or a dogma, a nobility or a priesthood, never repair anything about it thoroughly, even its outside cover. Patch it up, nothing more. For instance, Jesuitism is a piece added to Catholicism. Treat edifices as you would treat institutions. Shadows should dwell in ruins. Worn-out powers are uneasy in chambers freshly decorated. Ruined palaces accord best with institutions in rags. To attempt to describe the House of Lords of other days would be to attempt to describe the unknown. History is night. In history there is no second tier. That which is no longer on the stage immediately fades into obscurity. The scene is shifted, and all is at once forgotten. The past has a synonym, the unknown.

The peers of England sat as a court of justice in Westminster Hall, and as the higher legislative chamber in a chamber specially reserved for the purpose, called *The House of Lords*.

Besides, the house of peers of England, which did not assemble as a court, unless convoked by the crown, two great English tribunals, inferior to the house of peers, but superior to all other jurisdiction, sat in Westminster Hall. At the end of that hall they occupied adjoining compartments. The first was the Court of King's Bench, in which the king was supposed to preside; the second, the Court of Chancery, in which the Chancellor presided. The one was a court of justice, the other a court of mercy. It was the Chancellor who counseled the King to pardon; only rarely, though.

These two courts, which are still in existence, interpreted legislation, and reconstructed it somewhat, for the art of the judge is to carve the code into jurisprudence; a task from which equity results as it best may. Legislation was worked up and applied in the severity of the great hall of Westminster, the rafters of which were of chestnut wood, over which spiders could not spread their webs. There are enough of them in all conscience in the laws.

To sit as a court and to sit as a chamber are two distinct things. This double function constitutes supreme power. The Long Parliament, which began in November, 1640, felt the revolutionary necessity for this two-edged sword. So it declared that, as House of Lords, it possessed judicial as well as legislative power.

This double power has been, from time immemorial, vested in the House of Peers. We have just mentioned that as judges they occupied Westminster Hall; as legislators, they had another chamber. This other chamber, properly called the House of Lords, was oblong and narrow. All the light in it came from four windows in deep embrasures, which received their light through the roof, and a bull's-eye, composed of six panes with curtains, over the throne. At night there was no other light than twelve half candelabra, fastened to the wall. The chamber of Venice was darker still. A certain obscurity is pleasing to those owls of supreme power.

A high ceiling adorned with many-faced relievos and gilded cornices, circled over the chamber where the Lords assembled. The Commons had but a flat ceiling. There is a meaning in all monarchical buildings. At one end of the long chamber of the Lords was the door; at the other, opposite to it, the throne. A few paces from the door, the bar, a transverse barrier, and a sort of frontier, marked the spot where the people ended and the peerage began. To the right of the throne was a fireplace with emblazoned pinnacles, and two bas-reliefs of marble, representing, one, the victory of Cuthwolf over the Britons, in 572; the other, the geometrical plan of the borough of Dunstable, which had four streets, parallel to the four quarters of the world. The throne was approached by three steps. It was called the royal chair. On the two walls, opposite each other, were displayed in successive pictures, on a huge piece of tapestry given to the Lords by Elizabeth, the adventures of the Armada, from the time of its leaving Spain, until it was wrecked on the coasts of Great Britain. The great hulls of the ships were embroidered with threads of gold and silver, which had become blackened by time. Against this tapestry, cut at intervals by the candelabra fastened in the wall, were placed, to the right of the throne, three rows of benches for the bishops, and to the left three rows of benches for the dukes, marquises, and earls, in tiers, and separated by gangways. On the three benches of the first section sat the dukes; on those of the second, the marquises; on those of the third, the earls. The viscounts' bench was placed across, opposite the throne, and behind, between the viscounts and the bar, were two benches for the barons.

On the highest bench to the right of the throne sat the two archbishops of Canterbury and York; on the middle bench three bishops, London, Durham, and Winchester, and the other bishops on the lowest bench. There is between the Archbishop of Canterbury and the other bishops this considerable difference, that he is bishop "by divine providence," whilst the others are only so "by divine permission." On the right of the throne was a chair for the Prince of Wales, and on the left, folding chairs for the royal dukes, and behind the latter, a raised seat for minor peers, who had not the privilege of voting. Plenty of fleurs-de-lys everywhere, and the great escutcheon of England over the four walls, above the peers, as well as above the king.

The sons of peers and the heirs to peerages assisted at the debates, standing behind the throne, between the dais and the wall. A large square space was left vacant between the tiers of benches placed along three sides of the chamber and the throne. In this space, which was covered with the state carpet, interwoven with the arms of Great Britain, were four woolsacks—one in front of the throne, on which sat the Lord Chancellor, between the mace and the seal; one in front of the bishops, on which sat the judges, counselors of state, who had the right to vote, but not to speak; one in front of the dukes, marquises, and earls, on which sat the Secretaries of State; and one in front of the viscounts and barons, on which sat the Clerk of the Crown and the Clerk of the Parliament, and on which the two under-clerks wrote, kneeling.

In the middle of the space was a large covered table, heaped with bundles of papers, registers, and summonses, with magnificent inkstands of chased silver, and with high candlesticks at the four corners.

The peers took their seats in chronological order, each according to the date of the creation of his peerage. They ranked according to their titles, and within their grade of nobility according to seniority. At the bar stood the Usher of the Black Rod, his wand in his hand. Inside the door was the Deputy-Usher; and outside, the Crier of the Black Rod, whose duty it was to open the sittings of the Courts of Justice, with the cry, "Oyez!" in French, uttered thrice, with a solemn accent upon the first syllable. Near the Crier stood the Sergeant Mace-Bearer of the Chancellor.

In royal ceremonies the temporal peers wore coronets on their heads, and the spiritual peers, miters. The archbishops wore miters, with a ducal coronet; and the bishops, who rank after viscounts, miters, with a baron's cap.

It is to be remarked, as a coincidence at once strange and instructive, that this square formed by the throne, the bishops, and the barons, with kneeling magistrates within it, was in form similar to the ancient parliament in France under the two first dynasties. The aspect of authority was the same in France as in England. Hincmar, in his treatise, "De Ordinatione Sacri Palatii," described in 853 the sittings of the House of Lords at Westminster in the eighteenth century. Strange, indeed! a description given nine hundred years before the existence of the thing described.

But what is history? An echo of the past in the future; a reflex from the future on the past.

The assembly of Parliament was obligatory only once in every seven years.

The Lords deliberated in secret, with closed doors. The debates of the Commons were public. Publicity entails diminution of dignity.

The number of the Lords was unlimited. To create Lords was the menace of royalty; a means of government.

At the beginning of the eighteenth century the House of Lords already contained a very large number of members. It has increased still further since that period. To dilute the aristocracy is politic. Elizabeth most probably erred in condensing the peerage into sixty-five lords. The less numerous, the more intense is a peerage. In assemblies, the more numerous the members, the fewer the heads. James II understood this when he increased the Upper House to a hundred and eighty-eight lords; a hundred and eighty-six if we subtract from the peerages the two duchies of royal favorites, Portsmouth and Cleveland. Under Anne the total number of the lords, including bishops, was two hundred and seven. Not counting the Duke of Cumberland, husband of the Queen, there were twenty-five dukes, of whom the premier, Norfolk, did not take his seat, being a Catholic; and of whom the junior, Cambridge, the Elector of Hanover, did, although a foreigner. Winchester, termed first and sole marquis of England, as Astorga was termed sole Marquis of Spain, was absent, being a Jacobite; so that there were only five marquises, of whom the premier was Lindsay, and the junior Lothian; seventy-nine earls, of whom Derby was premier and Islay junior; nine viscounts, of whom Hereford was premier, and Lonsdale junior, and sixty-two barons, of whom Abergavenny was premier, and Hervey junior. Lord Hervey, the junior baron, was what was called the "Puisné of the House." Derby, of whom Oxford, Shrewsbury, and Kent took precedence, and who was therefore but the fourth under James II, became (under Anne) premier earl. Two chancellors' names had disappeared from the list of barons—Verulam, under which designation history finds us Bacon; and Wem, under which it finds us Jeffreys. Bacon and Jeffreys! both names overshadowed, though by different crimes. In 1705, the twenty-six bishops were reduced to twenty-five, the See of Chester being vacant. Amongst the bishops some were peers of high rank, such as William Talbot, Bishop of Oxford, who was head of the Protestant branch of that family. Others were eminent Doctors, like John Sharp, Archbishop of York, formerly Dean of Norwich; the poet, Thomas Spratt, Bishop of Rochester, an apoplectic old man; and that Bishop of Lincoln, who was to die Archbishop of Canterbury, Wake, the adversary of Bossuet. On important occasions, and when a message from the Crown to the House was expected, the whole of this august assembly—in robes, in wigs, in miters, or plumes—formed out, and displayed their rows of heads, in tiers, along the walls of the House, where the storm was vaguely to be seen exterminating the Armada—almost as much as to say, "The storm is at the orders of England."

Chapter IV

THE OLD CHAMBER

T HE WHOLE CEREMONY OF THE INVESTITURE OF GWYNPLAINE, FROM HIS ENTRY UNDER THE King's Gate to his taking the test under the nave window, was enacted in a sort of twilight.

Lord William Cowper had not permitted that he, as Lord Chancellor of England, should receive too many details of circumstances connected with the disfigurement of the young Lord Fermain Clancharlie, considering it below his dignity to know that a peer was not handsome; and feeling that his dignity would suffer if an inferior should venture to intrude on him information of such a nature. We know that a common fellow will take pleasure in saying: "that prince is hump-backed"; therefore, it is abusive to say that a lord is deformed. To the few words dropped on the subject by the queen the Lord Chancellor had contented himself with replying—

"The face of a peer is in his peerage!"

Ultimately, however, the affidavits he had read and certified enlightened him. Hence the precautions which he took. The face of the new lord, on his entrance into the House, might cause some sensation. This it was necessary to prevent; and the Lord Chancellor took his measures for the purpose. It is a fixed idea, and a rule of conduct in grave personages, to allow as little disturbance as possible. Dislike of incident is a part of their gravity. He felt the necessity of so ordering matters that the admission of Gwynplaine should take place without any hitch, and like that of any other successor to the peerage.

It was for this reason that the Lord Chancellor directed that the reception of Lord Fermain Clancharlie should take place at the evening sitting. The Chancellor being the door-keeper— "Quodammodo ostiarus," says the Norman charter; "Januarum cancellorumque," says Tertullian— he can officiate outside the room on the threshold; and Lord William Cowper had used his right by carrying out under the nave the formalities of the investiture of Lord Fermain Clancharlie. Moreover, he had brought forward the hour for the ceremonies; so that the new peer actually made his entrance into the House before the House had assembled.

For the investiture of a peer on the threshold, and not in the chamber itself, there were precedents. The first hereditary baron, John de Beauchamp, of Holt Castle, created by patent by Richard II, in 1387, Baron Kidderminster, was thus installed. In renewing this precedent the Lord Chancellor was creating for himself a future cause for embarrassment, of which he felt the inconvenience less than two years afterwards on the entrance of Viscount Newhaven into the House of Lords.

Short-sighted as we have already stated him to be, Lord William Cowper scarcely perceived the deformity of Gwynplaine; while the two sponsors, being old and nearly blind, did not perceive it at all.

The Lord Chancellor had chosen them for that very reason.

More than this, the Lord Chancellor, having only seen the presence and stature of Gwynplaine, thought him a fine-looking man. When the door-keeper opened the folding doors to Gwynplaine there were but few peers in the House; and these few were nearly all old men. In assemblies the old members are the most punctual, just as toward women they are the most assiduous.

On the dukes' benches there were but two, one white-headed, the other gray: Thomas Osborne, Duke of Leeds, and Schomberg, son of that Schomberg, German by birth, French by his marshal's bâton, and English by his peerage, who was banished by the edict of Nantes, and who, having fought against England as a Frenchman, fought against France as an Englishman. On the benches of the lords spiritual there sat only the Archbishop of Canterbury, Primate of England, above; and below,

Dr. Simon Patrick, Bishop of Ely, in conversation with Evelyn Pierrepoint, Marquis of Dorchester, who was explaining to him the difference between a gabion considered singly and when used in the parapet of a field work, and between palisades and fraises; the former being a row of posts driven info the ground in front of the tents, for the purpose of protecting the camp; the latter sharp-pointed stakes set up under the wall of a fortress, to prevent the escalade of the besiegers and the desertion of the besieged; and the marquis was explaining further the method of placing fraises in the ditches of redoubts, half of each stake being buried and half exposed. Thomas Thynne, Viscount Weymouth, having approached the light of a chandelier, was examining a plan of his architect's for laying out his gardens at Longleat, in Wiltshire, in the Italian style—as a lawn, broken up into plots, with squares of turf alternating with squares of red and yellow sand, of river shells, and of fine coal dust. On the viscounts' benches was a group of old peers, Essex, Ossulstone, Peregrine, Osborne, William Zulestein, Earl of Rochford, and amongst them, a few more youthful ones, of the faction which did not wear wigs, gathered round Prince Devereux, Viscount Hereford, and discussing the question whether an infusion of apalaca holly was tea. "Very nearly," said Osborne.—"Quite," said Essex. This discussion was attentively listened to by Paulet St. John, a cousin of Bolingbroke, of whom Voltaire was, later on, in some degree the pupil; for Voltaire's education, commenced by Père Porée, was finished by Bolingbroke. On the marquises' benches, Thomas de Grey, Marquis of Kent, Lord Chamberlain to the Queen, was informing Robert Bertie, Marquis of Lindsay, Lord Chamberlain of England, that the first prize in the great English lottery of 1694 had been won by two French refugees, Monsieur Le Coq, formerly councilor in the parliament of Paris, and Monsieur Ravenel, a gentleman of Brittany. The Earl of Wemyss was reading a book, entitled *Pratique Curieuse des Oracles des Sybilles.* John Campbell, Earl of Greenwich, famous for his long chin, his gaiety, and his eighty-seven years, was writing to his mistress. Lord Chandos was trimming his nails.

The sitting which was about to take place, being a royal one, where the crown was to be represented by commissioners, two assistant door-keepers were placing in front of the throne a bench covered with purple velvet. On the second woolsack sat the Master of the Rolls, *sacrorum scriniorum magister,* who had then for his residence the house formerly belonging to the converted Jews. Two under-clerks were kneeling, and turning over the leaves of the registers which lay on the fourth woolsack. In the meantime the Lord Chancellor took his place on the first woolsack. The members of the chamber took theirs, some sitting, others standing; when the Archbishop of Canterbury rose and read the prayer, and the sitting of the House began.

Gwynplaine had already been there for some time without attracting any notice. The second bench of barons, on which was his place, was close to the bar, so that he had had to take but a few steps to reach it. The two peers, his sponsors, sat, one on his right, the other on his left, thus almost concealing the presence of the newcomer.

No one having been furnished with any previous information, the Clerk of the Parliament had read in a low voice, and, as it were, mumbled through the different documents concerning the new peer, and the Lord Chancellor had proclaimed his admission in the midst of what is called, in the reports, "general inattention." Everyone was talking. There buzzed through the House that cheerful hum of voices during which assemblies pass things which will not bear the light, and at which they wonder when they find out what they have done, too late.

Gwynplaine was seated in silence, with his head uncovered, between the two old peers, Lord Fitzwalter and Lord Arundel. On entering, according to the instructions of the King-at-Arms—afterwards renewed by his sponsors—he had bowed to the throne.

Thus all was over. He was a peer. That pinnacle, under the glory of which he had, all his life, seen his master, Ursus, bow himself down in fear—that prodigious pinnacle was under his feet. He was in that place, so dark and yet so dazzling in England. Old peak of the feudal mountain, looked up to for six centuries by Europe and by history! Terrible nimbus of a world of shadow! He had entered into the brightness of its glory, and his entrance was irrevocable.

He was there in his own sphere, seated on his throne, like the king on his. He was there and nothing in the future could obliterate the fact. The royal crown, which he saw under the dais, was brother to his coronet. He was a peer of that throne. In the face of majesty he was peerage; less, but like. Yesterday, what was he? A player. To-day, what was he? A prince.

Yesterday, nothing; to-day, everything.

It was a sudden confrontation of misery and power, meeting face to face, and resolving themselves at once into the two halves of a conscience. Two specters, Adversity and Prosperity, were taking possession of the same soul, and each drawing that soul toward itself.

Oh, pathetic division of an intellect, of a will, of a brain, between two brothers who are enemies! the Phantom of Poverty and the Phantom of Wealth! Abel and Cain in the same man!

Chapter V

ARISTROCRATIC GOSSIP

B Y DEGREES THE SEATS OF THE HOUSE FILLED AS THE LORDS ARRIVED. THE QUESTION WAS THE vote for augmenting, by a hundred thousand pounds sterling, the annual income of George of Denmark, Duke of Cumberland, the queen's husband. Besides this, it was announced that several bills assented to by her Majesty were to be brought back to the House by the Commissioners of the Crown empowered and charged to sanction them. This raised the sitting to a royal one. The peers all wore their robes over their usual court or ordinary dress. These robes, similar to that which had been thrown over Gwynplaine, were alike for all, excepting that the dukes had five bands of ermine, trimmed with gold; marquises, four; earls and viscounts, three; and barons, two. Most of the lords entered in groups. They had met in the corridors, and were continuing the conversations there begun. A few came in alone. The costumes of all were solemn; but neither their attitudes nor their words corresponded with them. On entering, each one bowed to the throne.

The peers flowed in. The series of great names marched past with scant ceremonial, the public not being present. Leicester entered, and shook Lichfield's hand; then came Charles Mordaunt, Earl of Peterborough and Monmouth, the friend of Locke, under whose advice he had proposed the recoinage of money; then Charles Campbell, Earl of Loudoun, listening to Fulke Greville, Lord Brooke; then Dorme, Earl of Carnarvon; then Robert Sutton, Baron Lexington, son of that Lexington who recommended Charles II to banish Gregorio Leti, the historiographer, who was so ill-advised as to try to become a historian; then Thomas Bellasys, Viscount Falconberg, a handsome old man; and the three cousins, Howard, Earl of Bindon, Bowes Howard, Earl of Berkshire, and Stafford Howard, Earl of Stafford—all together; then John Lovelace, Baron Lovelace, which peerage became extinct in 1736, so that Richardson was enabled to introduce Lovelace in his book, and to create a type under the name. All these personages—celebrated each in his own way, either in politics or in war, and of whom many were an honor to England—were laughing and talking.

It was history, as it were, seen in undress.

In less than half an hour the House was nearly full. This was to be expected, as the sitting was a royal one. What was more unusual was the eagerness of the conversations. The House, so sleepy not long before, now hummed like a hive of bees.

The arrival of the peers who had come in late had woke them up. These lords had brought news. It was strange that the peers who had been there at the opening of the sitting knew nothing of what had occurred, while those who had not been there knew all about it. Several lords had come from Windsor.

For some hours past the adventures of Gwynplaine had been the subject of conversation. A secret is a net; let one mesh drop, and the whole goes to pieces. In the morning, in consequence of the incidents related above, the whole story of a peer found on the stage, and of a mountebank become a lord, had burst forth at Windsor in Royal places. The princes had talked about it, and then the lackeys. From the court the news soon reached the town. Events have a weight, and the mathematical rule of velocity, increasing in proportion to the squares of the distance, applies to them. They fall upon the public, and work themselves through it with the most astounding rapidity. At seven o'clock no one in London had caught wind of the story. By eight, Gwynplaine was the talk of the town. Only the lords who had been so punctual that they were present before the assembling of the House were ignorant of the circumstances, not having been in the town when the matter was talked of by everyone , and having been in the House, where nothing had been perceived. Seated quietly on their benches, they were addressed by the eager newcomers.

"Well!" said Francis Brown, Viscount Montacute, to the Marquis of Dorchester.

"What?"

"Is it possible?"

"What?"

"The Laughing Man!"

"Who is the Laughing Man?"

"Don't you know the Laughing Man?"

"No."

"He is a clown, a fellow performing at fairs. He has an extraordinary face, which people gave a penny to look at. A mountebank."

"Well, what then?"

"You have just installed him as a peer of England."

"You are the laughing man, my Lord Montacute!"

"I am not laughing, my Lord Dorchester."

Lord Montacute made a sign to the Clerk of the Parliament, who rose from his woolsack, and confirmed to their lordships the fact of the admission of the new peer. Besides, he detailed the circumstances.

"How wonderful!" said Lord Dorchester. "I was talking to the Bishop of Ely all the while."

The young Earl of Annesley addressed old Lord Eure, who had but two years more to live, as he died in 1707.

"My Lord Eure."

"My Lord Annesley."

"Did you know Lord Linnæus Clancharlie?"

"A man of bygone days. Yes, I did."

"He died in Switzerland."

"Yes; we were relations."

"He was a republican under Cromwell, and remained a republican under Charles II?"

"A republican? Not at all! He was sulking. He had a personal quarrel with the king. I know from good authority that Lord Clancharlie would have returned to his allegiance, if they had given him the office of Chancellor, which Lord Hyde held."

"You astonish me, Lord Eure. I had heard that Lord Clancharlie was an honest politician."

"An honest politician! does such a thing exist? Young man, there is no such thing."

"And Cato?"

"Oh, you believe in Cato, do you?"

"And Aristides?"

"They did well to exile him."

"And Thomas More?"

"They did well to cut off his head."

"And in your opinion Lord Clancharlie was a man as you describe. As for a man remaining in exile, why, it is simply ridiculous."

"He died there."

"An ambitious man disappointed?"

"You ask if I knew him? I should think so indeed. I was his dearest friend."

"Do you know, Lord Eure, that he married when in Switzerland?"

"I am pretty sure of it."

"And that he had a lawful heir by that marriage?"

"Yes; who is dead."

"Who is living."

"Living?"

"Living."

"Impossible!"

"It is a fact—proved, authenticated, confirmed, registered."

"Then that son will inherit the Clancharlie peerage?"

"He is not going to inherit it."

"Why?"

"Because he has inherited it. It is done."

"Done?"

"Turn your head, Lord Eure; he is sitting behind you, on the barons' benches."

Lord Eure turned, but Gwynplaine's face was concealed under his forest of hair.

"So," said the old man, who could see nothing but his hair, "he has already adopted the new fashion. He does not wear a wig."

Grantham accosted Colepepper.

"Someone is finely sold."

"Who is that?"

"David Dirry-Moir."

"How is that?"

"He is no longer a peer."

"How can that be?"

And Henry Auverquerque, Earl of Grantham, told John Baron Colepepper the whole anecdote—how the waif-flask had been carried to the Admiralty, about the parchment of the Comprachicos, the *Jussu regis,* countersigned *Jeffreys,* and the confrontation in the torture-cell at Southwark, the proof of all the facts acknowledged by the Lord Chancellor and by the Queen; the taking the test under the nave, and finally the admission of Lord Fermain Clancharlie at the commencement of the sitting. Both the lords endeavored to distinguish his face as he sat between Lord Fitzwalter and Lord Arundel, but with no better success than Lord Eure and Lord Annesley.

Gwynplaine, either by chance or by the arrangement of his sponsors, forewarned by the Lord Chancellor, was so placed in shadow as to escape their curiosity.

"Who is it? Where is he?"

Such was the exclamation of all the newcomers, but no one succeeded in making him out distinctly. Some, who had seen Gwynplaine in the Green Box, were exceedingly curious, but lost their labor; as it sometimes happens that a young lady is entrenched within a troop of dowagers, Gwynplaine was, as it were, enveloped in several layers of lords, old, infirm, and indifferent. Good livers, with the gout, are marvelously indifferent to stories about their neighbors.

There passed, from hand to hand, copies of a letter three lines in length, written, it was said, by the Duchess Josiana to the Queen, her sister, in answer to the injunction made by her Majesty, that she should espouse the new peer, the lawful heir of the Clancharlies, Lord Fermain. This letter was couched in the following terms—

MADAME—The arrangement will suit me just as well. I can have Lord David for my lover.—(Signed, JOSIANA.

This note, whether a true copy or a forgery, was received by all with the greatest enthusiasm. A young lord, Charles Okehampton, Baron Mohun, who belonged to the wigless faction, read and reread it with delight. Lewis de Duras, Earl of Faversham, an Englishman with a Frenchman's wit, looked at Mohun and smiled.

"That is a woman I should like to marry!" exclaimed Lord Mohun.

The lords around them overheard the following dialogue between Duras and Mohun.

"Marry the Duchess Josiana, Lord Mohun!"

"Why not?"

"Plague take it."

"She would make one very happy!"

"She would make many very happy."

"But is it not always a question of many?"

"Lord Mohun, you are right. With regard to women, we have always the leavings of others. Has anyone ever had a beginning?"

"Adam, perhaps."

"Not he."

"Then Satan."

"My dear lord," concluded Lewis de Duras, "Adam only lent his name. Poor dupe! He endorsed the human race. Man was begotten on the woman by the devil."

Hugh Cholmondeley, Earl of Cholmondeley, strong in points of law, was asked from the bishops' benches by Nathaniel Crew, who was doubly a peer, being a temporal peer, as Baron Crew, and a spiritual peer, as Bishop of Durham.

"Is it possible?" said Crew.

"Is it regular?" said Cholmondeley.

"The investiture of this peer was made outside the House," replied the Bishop; "but it is stated that there are precedents for it."

"Yes. Lord Beauchamp, under Richard II; Lord Chenay, under Elizabeth: and Lord Broghill, under Cromwell."

"Cromwell goes for nothing."

"What do you think of it all?"

"Many different things."

"My Lord Cholmondeley, what will be the rank of this young Lord Clancharlie in the House?"

"My Lord Bishop, the interruption of the Republic having displaced ancient rights of precedence, Clancharlie now ranks in the peerage between Barnard and Somers, so that should each be called upon to speak in turn, Lord Clancharlie would be the eighth in rotation."

"Really! he, a mountebank from a public show!"

"The act, per se, does not astonish me, my Lord Bishop. We meet with such things. Still more wonderful circumstances occur! Was not the War of the Roses predicted by the sudden drying up of the river Ouse, in Bedfordshire, on January 1st, 1399. Now, if a river dries up, a peer may, quite as naturally, fall into a servile condition. Ulysses, King of Ithaca, played all kinds of different parts. Fermain Clancharlie remained a lord under his player's garb. Sordid garments touch not the soul's nobility. But taking the test and the investiture outside the sitting, though strictly legal, might give rise to objections. I am of opinion that it will be necessary to look into the matter, to see if there be any ground to question the Lord Chancellor in Privy Council, later on. We shall see in a week or two what is best to be done."

And the Bishop added—

"All the same. It is an adventure such as has not occurred since Earl Gesbodus's time."

Gwynplaine, the Laughing Man; the Tadcaster Inn; the Green Box; *Chaos Vanquished*; Switzerland; Chillon; the Comprachicos; exile; mutilation; the Republic; Jeffreys; James II; the *jussu regis*; the bottle opened at the Admiralty; the father, Lord Linnæus; the legitimate son, Lord Fermain; the bastard son, Lord David; the probable lawsuits; the Duchess Josiana; the Lord Chancellor; the Queen—all these subjects of conversation ran from bench to bench.

Whispering is like a train of gunpowder.

They seized on every incident. All the details of the occurrence caused an immense murmur through the House. Gwynplaine, wandering in the depths of his reverie, heard the buzzing, without knowing that he was the cause of it. He was strangely attentive to the depths, not to the surface. Excess of attention becomes isolation.

The buzz of conversation in the House impedes its usual business no more than the dust raised by a troop impedes its march. The judges—who in the Upper House were mere assistants, without the privilege of speaking, except when questioned—had taken their places on the second woolsack; and the three Secretaries of State theirs on the third.

The heirs to peerages flowed into their compartment, at once without and within the House, at the back of the throne.

The peers in their minority were on their own benches. In 1705 the number of these little lords amounted to no less than a dozen—Huntingdon, Lincoln, Dorset, Warwick, Bath, Barlington, Derwentwater—destined to a tragical death—Longueville, Lonsdale, Dudley, Ward, and Carteret: a troop of brats made up of eight earls, two viscounts, and two barons.

In the center, on the three stages of benches, each lord had taken his seat. Almost all the bishops were there. The dukes mustered strong, beginning with Charles Seymour, Duke of Somerset; and ending with George Augustus, Elector of Hanover, and Duke of Cambridge, junior in date of creation, and consequently junior in rank. All were in order, according to right of precedence: Cavendish, Duke of Devonshire, whose grandfather had sheltered Hobbes, at Hardwicke, when he was ninety-two; Lennox, Duke of Richmond; the three Fitzroys, the Duke of Southampton, the Duke of Grafton, and the Duke of Northumberland; Butler, Duke of Ormond; Somerset, Duke of Beaufort; Beauclerk, Duke of St. Albans; Paulet, Duke of Bolton; Osborne, Duke of Leeds; Wrottesley Russell, Duke of Bedford, whose motto and device was *che sara sara*, which expresses a determination to take things as they come; Sheffield, Duke of Buckingham; Manners, Duke of Rutland; and others. Neither Howard, Duke of Norfolk, nor Talbot, Duke of Shrewsbury, were present, being Catholics; nor Churchill, Duke of Marlborough, the French Malbrouck, who was at that time fighting the French and beating them. There were no Scotch dukes then—Queensberry, Montrose, and Roxburgh not being admitted till 1707.

Chapter VI

THE HIGH AND THE LOW

ALL AT ONCE A BRIGHT LIGHT BROKE UPON THE HOUSE. FOUR DOOR-KEEPERS BROUGHT AND placed on each side of the throne four high candelabra filled with wax-lights. The throne, thus illuminated, shone in a kind of purple light. It was empty, but august. The presence of the queen herself could not have added much majesty to it.

The Usher of the Black Rod entered with his wand, and announced—

"The Lords Commissioners of her Majesty."

The hum of conversation immediately subsided.

A clerk, in a wig and gown, appeared at the great door, holding a cushion worked with fleurs-de-ys, on which lay parchment documents. These documents were bills. From each hung the *bille*, or *bulle*, by a silken string, from which laws are called bills in England and bulls at Rome. Behind the clerk walked three men in peers' robes, and wearing plumed hats.

These were the Royal Commissioners. The first was the Lord High Treasurer of England, Godolphin; the second, the Lord President of the Council, Pembroke; the third, the Lord of the Privy Seal, Newcastle.

They walked one by one, according to precedence, not of their rank, but of their commission— Godolphin first, Newcastle last, although a duke.

They reached the bench in front of the throne, to which they bowed, took off and replaced their hats, and sat down on the bench.

The Lord Chancellor turned toward the Usher of the Black Rod, and said—

"Order the Commons to the bar of the House."

The Usher of the Black Rod retired.

The clerk, who was one of the clerks of the House of Lords, placed on the table, between the four woolsacks, the cushion on which lay the bills.

Then there came an interruption, which continued for some minutes.

Two door-keepers placed before the bar a stool with three steps.

This stool was covered with crimson velvet, on which *fleurs-de-lys* were designed in gilt nails.

The great door, which had been closed, was reopened; and a voice announced—

"The faithful Commons of England."

It was the Usher of the Black Rod announcing the other half of Parliament.

The lords put on their hats.

The members of the House of Commons entered, preceded by their Speaker, all with uncovered heads.

They stopped at the bar. They were in their ordinary garb; for the most part dressed in black, and wearing swords.

The Speaker, the Right Honorable John Smith, an esquire, member for the borough of Andover, got up on the stool which was at the center of the bar. The Speaker of the Commons wore a robe of black satin, with large hanging sleeves, embroidered before and behind with brandenburgs of gold, and a wig smaller than that of the Lord Chancellor. He was majestic, but inferior.

The Commons, both Speaker and members, stood waiting, with uncovered heads, before the peers, who were seated, with their hats on.

Amongst the members of Commons might have been remarked the Chief Justice of Chester, Joseph Jekyll; the Queen's three Sergeants-at-Law—Hooper, Powys, and Parker; James Montagu,

Solicitor-General; and the Attorney-General, Simon Harcourt. With the exception of a few baronets and knights, and nine lords by courtesy—Hartington, Windsor, Woodstock, Mordaunt, Granby, Scudamore, Fitzhardinge, Hyde, and Berkeley—sons of peers and heirs to peerages—all were of the people—a sort of gloomy and silent crowd.

When the noise made by the trampling of feet had ceased, the Crier of the Black Rod, standing by the door, exclaimed—

"Oyez!"

The Clerk of the Crown arose. He took, unfolded, and read the first of the documents on the cushion. It was a message from the Queen, naming three commissioners to represent her in Parliament with power to sanction the bills.

"To wit—"

Here the Clerk raised his voice.

"Sidney Earl Godolphin."

The Clerk bowed to Lord Godolphin. Lord Godolphin raised his hat.

The Clerk continued—

"Thomas Herbert, Earl of Pembroke and Montgomery."

The Clerk bowed to Lord Pembroke. Lord Pembroke touched his hat.

The Clerk resumed—

"John Holles, Duke of Newcastle."

The Duke of Newcastle nodded.

The Clerk of the Crown resumed his seat.

The Clerk of the Parliaments arose. His under-clerk, who had been on his knees behind him, got up also. Both turned their faces to the throne, and their backs to the Commons.

There were five bills on the cushion. These five bills, voted by the Commons and agreed to by the Lords, awaited the royal sanction.

The Clerk of the Parliaments read the first bill.

It was a bill passed by the Commons, charging the country with the costs of the improvements made by the Queen to her residence at Hampton Court, amounting to a million sterling.

The reading over, the Clerk bowed low to the throne. The under-clerk bowed lower still; then, half-turning his head toward the Commons, he said—

"The Queen accepts your bounty—*et ainsi le veut*."

The Clerk read the second bill.

It was a law condemning to imprisonment and fine whosoever withdrew himself from the service of the trainbands. The trainbands were a militia, recruited from the middle and lower classes, serving gratis, which in Elizabeth's reign furnished, on the approach of the Armada, one hundred and eighty-five thousand foot-soldiers and forty thousand horse.

The two clerks made a fresh bow to the throne, after which, the under-clerk, again half-turning his face to the Commons, said—

"*La Reine le veut*."

The third bill was for increasing the tithes and prebends of the Bishopric of Lichfield and Coventry, which was one of the richest in England; for making an increased yearly allowance to the cathedral, for augmenting the number of its canons, and for increasing its deaneries and benefices, "to the benefit of our holy religion," as the preamble set forth. The fourth bill added to the budget fresh taxes: one on marbled paper; one on hackney-coaches, fixed at the number of eight hundred in London, and taxed at a sum equal to fifty-two francs yearly each; one on barristers, attorneys and solicitors, at forty-eight francs a year a head; one on tanned skins, notwithstanding, said the preamble, the complaints of the workers in leather. One on soap, notwithstanding the petitions of the City of Exeter and of the whole of Devonshire, where great quantities of cloth and serge were manufactured; one on wine at four shillings; one on flour; one on barley and hops; and one renewing for four years "the necessities of the State," said the pre-amble, "requiring to be attended to before the remonstrances of commerce"—tonnage-dues, varying from six francs per ton, for ships coming from the westward, to eighteen francs on those coming from the eastward. Finally, the bill, declaring the sums already levied for the current year insufficient, concluded by decreeing a poll-tax on each subject throughout the kingdom of four shillings per head, adding that a double tax would be levied on everyone who did not take the fresh oath to Government. The fifth bill forbade the admission into the hospital of any sick person who on entering did not deposit a pound sterling to pay for his funeral, in case of death. These last three bills, like the first two, were one after the other sanctioned and made law by a bow to the throne, and the four words pronounced by the under-clerk, *"la Reine le veut,"* spoken over his shoulder to the Commons. Then the under-clerk knelt down again before the fourth woolsack, and the Lord Chancellor said—

"Soit fait comme il est désiré."

This terminated the royal sitting. The Speaker, bent double before the Chancellor, descended from the stool, backwards, lifting up his robe behind him; the members of the House of Commons bowed to the ground, and as the Upper House resumed the business of the day, heedless of all these marks of respect, the Commons departed.

Chapter VII

STORMS OF MEN ARE WORSE THAN STORMS OF OCEANS

THE DOORS WERE CLOSED AGAIN, THE USHER OF THE BLACK ROD RE-ENTERED; THE LORDS COM-missioners left the bench of State, took their places at the top of the dukes' benches, by right of their commission, and the Lord Chancellor addressed the House.

"My Lords, the House having deliberated for several days on the Bill which proposes to aug-ment by £100,000 sterling the annual provision for his Royal Highness the Prince, her Majesty's Consort, and the debate having been exhausted and closed, the House will proceed to vote; the votes will be taken according to custom, beginning with the puisne Baron. Each Lord, on his name being called, will rise and answer *content*, or *non-content*, and will be at liberty to explain the mo-tives of his vote, if he thinks fit to do so. Clerk, take the vote."

The Clerk of the House, standing up, opened a large folio, and spread it open on a gilded desk. This book was the list of the peerage.

The puisne of the House of Lords at that time was John Hervey, created Baron and Peer in 1703, from whom is descended the Marquis of Bristol.

The clerk called,

"My Lord John, Baron Hervey."

An old man in a fair wig rose, and said, "Content."

Then he sat down.

The Clerk registered his vote.

The Clerk continued—

"My Lord Francis Seymour, Baron Conway, of Killultagh."

"Content," murmured, half-rising, an elegant young man, with a face like a page, who little thought that he was to be ancestor to the Marquises of Hertford.

"My Lord John Leveson, Baron Gower," continued the Clerk.

This Baron, from whom were to spring the Dukes of Sutherland, rose, and, as he reseated himself, said "Content."

The Clerk went on—

"My Lord Heneage Finch, Baron Guernsey."

The ancestor of the Earls of Aylesford, neither older nor less elegant than the ancestor of the Marquises of Hertford, justified his device, *aperto vivere voto*, by the proud tone in which he exclaimed, "Content."

Whilst he was resuming his seat, the Clerk called the fifth Baron—

"My Lord John, Baron Granville."

Rising and resuming his seat quickly, "Content," exclaimed Lord Granville, of Potheridge, whose peerage was to become extinct in 1709.

The Clerk passed to the sixth.

"My Lord Charles Montague, Baron Halifax."

"Content," said Lord Halifax, the bearer of a title which had become extinct in the Saville family, and was destined to become extinct again in that of Montague. Montague is distinct from Montagu and Montacute. And Lord Halifax added, "Prince George has an allowance as her Majesty's Consort; he has another as Prince of Denmark; another as Duke of Cumberland; another as Lord High Admiral of England and Ireland; but he has not one as Commander-in-Chief. This is an injustice and a wrong which must be set right, in the interest of the English people."

Then Lord Halifax passed a eulogium on the Christian religion, abused popery, and voted the subsidy.

Lord Halifax sat down, and the Clerk resumed—

"My Lord Christopher, Baron Barnard."

Lord Barnard, from whom were to descend the Dukes of Cleveland, rose to answer to his name.

"Content."

He took some time in reseating himself, for he wore a lace band which was worth showing. For all that, Lord Barnard was a worthy gentleman and a brave officer.

While Lord Barnard was resuming his seat, the Clerk, who read by routine, hesitated for an instant; he readjusted his spectacles, and leaned over the register with renewed attention; then, lifting up his head, he said—

"My Lord Fermain Clancharlie, Baron Clancharlie and Hunkerville."

Gwynplaine arose.

"Non-content," said he.

Every face was turned toward him. Gwynplaine remained standing. The branches of candles, placed on each side of the throne, lighted up his features, and marked them against the darkness of the august chamber in the relief with which a mask might show against a background of smoke.

Gwynplaine had made that effort over himself which, it may be remembered, was possible to him in extremity. By a concentration of will equal to that which would be needed to cow a tiger, he had succeeded in obliterating for a moment the fatal grin upon his face. For an instant he no longer laughed. This effort could not last long. Rebellion against that which is our law or our fatality must be short-lived; at times, the waters of the sea resist the power of gravitation, swell into a waterspout and become a mountain, but only on the condition of falling back again.

Such a struggle was Gwynplaine's. For an instant, which he felt to be a solemn one, by a prodigious intensity of will, but for not much longer than a flash of lightning lasts, he had thrown over his brow the dark veil of his soul—he held in suspense his incurable laugh. From that face upon which it had been carved, he had withdrawn the joy. Now it was nothing but terrible.

"Who is this man?" exclaimed all.

That forest of hair, those dark hollows under the brows, the deep gaze of eyes which they could not see, that head, on the wild outlines of which light and darkness mingled weirdly, were a wonder indeed. It was beyond all understanding; much as they had heard of him, the sight of Gwynplaine was a terror. Even those who expected much found their expectations surpassed. It was as though on the mountain reserved for the gods, during the banquet on a serene evening, the whole of the all-powerful body being gathered together, the face of Prometheus, mangled by the vulture's beak, should have suddenly appeared before them, like a blood-colored moon on the horizon. Olympus looking on Caucasus! What a vision! Old and young, open-mouthed with surprise, fixed their eyes upon Gwynplaine.

An old man, respected by the whole House, who had seen many men and many things, and who was intended for a dukedom—Thomas, Earl of Wharton—rose in terror.

"What does all this mean?" he cried. "Who has brought this man into the House? Let him be put out."

And addressing Gwynplaine haughtily—

"Who are you? Whence do you come?"

Gwynplaine answered—

"Out of the depths."

And, folding his arms, he looked at the lords.

"Who am I? I am wretchedness. My lords, I have a word to say to you."

A shudder ran through the House. Then all was silence. Gwynplaine continued—

"My lords, you are highly placed. It is well. We must believe that God has His reasons that it should be so. You have power, opulence, pleasure, the sun ever shining in your zenith; authority unbounded, enjoyment without a sting, and a total forgetfulness of others. So be it. But there is something below you—above you, it may be. My lords, I bring you news; news of the existence of mankind."

Assemblies are like children. A strange occurrence is as a jack-in-the-box to them. It frightens them; but they like it. It is as if a spring were touched, and a devil jumps up. Mirabeau, who was also deformed, was a case in point in France.

Gwynplaine felt within himself, at that moment, a strange elevation. In addressing a body of men, one's foot seems to rest on them; to rest, as it were, on a pinnacle of souls—on human hearts, that quiver under one's heel. Gwynplaine was no longer the man who had been, only the night before, almost mean. The fumes of the sudden elevation which had disturbed him had cleared off and become transparent, and in the state in which Gwynplaine had been seduced by a vanity, he now saw but a duty. That which had at first lessened, now elevated him. He was illuminated by one of those great flashes which emanate from duty.

All round Gwynplaine arose cries of "Hear, hear!"

Meanwhile, rigid and superhuman, he succeeded in maintaining on his features that severe and sad contraction under which the laugh was fretting like a wild horse struggling to escape.

He resumed—

"I am he who cometh out of the depths. My lords, you are great and rich. There lies your danger. You profit by the night; but beware! The Dawn is all-powerful. You cannot prevail over it. It is coming. Nay! it is come. Within it is the dayspring of irresistible light. And who shall hinder that sling from hurling the sun into the sky? The sun I speak of is Right. You are Privilege. Tremble! The real master of the house is about to knock at the door. What is the father of Privilege? Chance. What is his son? Abuse. Neither Chance nor Abuse are abiding. For both a dark morrow is at hand. I am come to warn you. I am come to impeach your happiness. It is fashioned out of the misery of your neighbor. You have everything, and that everything is composed of the nothing of others. My lords, I am an advocate without hope, pleading a cause that is lost; but that cause God will gain on appeal. As for me, I am but a voice. Mankind is a mouth, of which I am the cry. You shall hear me! I am about to open before you, peers of England, the great assize of the people; of that sovereign who is the subject; of that criminal who is the judge. I am weighed down under the load of all that I have to say. Where am I to begin? I know not. I have gathered together, in the vast diffusion of suffering, my innumerable and scattered pleas. What am I to do with them now? They overwhelm me, and I must cast them to you in a confused mass. Did I foresee this? No. You are astonished. So am I. Yesterday, I was a mountebank. To-day, I am a peer. Deep play! Of whom? Of the Unknown. Let us all tremble. My lords, all the blue sky is for you. Of this immense universe you see but the sunshine. Believe me, it has its shadows. Amongst you I am called Lord Fermain Clancharlie; but my true name is one of poverty—Gwynplaine. I am a wretched thing carved out of the stuff of which the great are made, for such was the pleasure of a king. That is my history. Many amongst you knew my father. I knew him not. His connection with you was his feudal descent; his outlawry is the bond between him and me. What God willed was well. I was cast into the abyss. For what end? To search its depths. I am a diver, and I have brought back the pearl, truth. I speak, because I know. You shall hear me, my lords. I have seen, I have felt! Suffering is not a mere word, ye happy ones! Poverty I grew up in; winter has frozen me; hunger I have tasted; contempt I have suffered; pestilence I have undergone; shame I have drunk of. And I will vomit all these up before you, and this ejection of all misery shall sully your feet and flame about them. I hesitated before I allowed myself to be brought to the place where I now stand, because I have duties to others elsewhere, and my heart is not here. What passed within me has nothing to do with you. When the man, whom you call Usher of the Black Rod, came to seek me by order of the woman whom you call the Queen, the idea struck me for a moment that I would refuse to come. But it seemed to me that the hidden hand of God pressed me to the spot, and I obeyed. I felt that I must come amongst you. Why? Because of my rags of yesterday. It is to raise my voice among those who have eaten their fill that God mixed me up with the famished. Oh, have pity! Of this fatal world to which you believe yourselves to belong, you know nothing. Placed so high, you are out of it. But I will tell you what it is; I have had experience enough. I come from beneath the pressure of your feet. I can tell you your weight. Oh, you who are masters, do you know what you are? do you see what you are doing? No. Oh, it is dreadful! One night, one night of storm, a little deserted child, an orphan alone in the immeasurable creation, I made my entrance into that darkness which you call society. The first thing that I saw was the law, under the form of a gibbet; the second was riches, your riches, under the form of a woman dead of cold and hunger; the third, the future, under the form of a child left to die; the fourth, goodness, truth, and justice, under the figure of a vagabond, whose sole friend and companion was a wolf."

Just then, Gwynplaine, stricken by a sudden emotion, felt the sobs rising in his throat, causing him most unfortunately to burst into an uncontrollable fit of laughter.

The contagion was immediate. A cloud had hung over the assembly. It might have broken into terror; it broke into delight. Mad merriment seized the whole House. Nothing pleases the great chambers of sovereign man so much as buffoonery. It is their revenge upon their graver moments.

The laughter of kings is like the laughter of the gods. There is always a cruel point in it. The lords set to play. Sneers gave sting to their laughter. They clapped their hands around the speaker, and insulted him. A volley of merry exclamations assailed him like bright, but wounding hailstones.

"Bravo, Gwynplaine!"—"Bravo, Laughing Man!"—"Bravo, Snout of the Green Box!"— "Mask of Tarrinzeau Field!"—"You are going to give us a performance."—"That's right; talk away!"—"There's a funny fellow!"—"How the beast does laugh, to be sure!"— "Good day, pantaloon!"—"How d'ye do, my lord clown!"—"Go on with your speech!"— "That fellow a peer of England!"—"Go on!"—"No, no!"—"Yes, yes!"

The Lord Chancellor was much disturbed.

A deaf peer, James Butler, Duke of Ormond, placing his hand to his ear like an ear trumpet, asked Charles Beauclerk, Duke of St. Albans—

"How has he voted?"

"Non-content."

"By heavens!" said Ormond, "I can understand it, with such a face as his."

Do you think that you can ever recapture a crowd once it has escaped your grasp? And all assemblies are crowds alike. No, eloquence is a bit; and if the bit breaks, the audience runs away, and rushes on till it has thrown the orator. Hearers naturally dislike the speaker, which is a fact not as clearly understood as it ought to be. Instinctively he pulls the reins, but that is a useless expedient. However, all orators try it, as Gwynplaine did.

He looked for a moment at those men who were laughing at him. Then he cried—

"So, you insult misery! Silence, Peers of England! Judges, listen to my pleading! Oh! I conjure you, have pity. Pity for whom? Pity for yourselves. Who is in danger? Yourselves! Do you not see that you are in a balance, and that there is in one scale your power, and in the other your responsibility? It is God who is weighing you. Oh, do not laugh. Think. The trembling of your consciences is the oscillation of the balance in which God is weighing your actions. You are not wicked; you are like other men, neither better nor worse. You believe yourselves to be gods, but be ill to-morrow, and see your divinity shivering in fever! We are worth one as much as the other. I address myself to honest men; there are such here. I address myself to lofty intellects; there are such here. I address myself to generous souls; there are such here. You are fathers, sons, and brothers; therefore you are often touched. He amongst you who has this morning watched the awaking of his little child is a good man. Hearts are all alike. Humanity is nothing but a heart. Between those who oppress and those who are oppressed, there is but a difference of place. Your feet tread on the heads of men. The fault is not yours; it is that of the social Babel. The building is faulty, and out of the perpendicular. One floor bears down the other. Listen, and I will tell you what to do. Oh! as you are powerful, be brotherly. As you are great, be tender. If you only knew what I have seen! Alas! what gloom is there beneath! The people are in a dungeon. How many are condemned who are innocent! No daylight, no air, no virtue! They are without hope, and yet—there is the danger! they expect something. Realize all this misery. There are beings who live in death. There are little girls who at twelve begin by prostitution, and who end in old age at twenty. As to the severities of the criminal code, they are fearful. I speak somewhat at random, and do not pick my words. I say everything that comes into my head. No later than yesterday I, who stand here, saw a man lying in chains, naked, with stones piled on his chest, expire in torture. Do you know of these things? No. If you knew what goes on, you would not dare to be happy. Who of you have been to Newcastle-upon-Tyne? There, in the mines, are men who chew coals to fill their stomachs and deceive hunger. Look here! in Lancashire, Ribblechester has sunk, by poverty, from a town to a village. I do not see that Prince George of Denmark requires a hundred thousand pounds extra. I should prefer receiving a poor sick man into the hospital, without compelling him to pay his funeral expenses in advance. In Carnarvon, and at Strathmore, as well as at Strathbickan, the exhaustion of the poor is horrible. At Stratford, they cannot drain the marsh, for want of money. The manufactories are shut up all over Lancashire. There is forced idleness everywhere. Do you know that the herring fishers at Harlech eat grass when the fishery fails? Do you know that at Burton-Lazars there are still lepers confined, on whom they fire if they leave their tan houses! At Ailesbury, a town of which one of you is lord, destitution is chronic. At Penkridge, in Coventry, where you have just endowed a cathedral and enriched a bishop, there are no beds in the cabins, and they dig holes in the earth, in which to put the little children to lie, so that instead of beginning life in the cradle, they begin it in the grave. I have seen these things! My lords, do you know who pays the taxes you vote? The dying! Alas! you deceive yourselves. You are going the wrong road. You augment the poverty of the poor to increase the riches of the rich. You should do the reverse. What! take from the worker to give to the idle, take from the tattered to give to the well-clad; take from the beggar to give to the prince! Oh, yes! I have old republican blood in my veins. I have a horror of these things. How I execrate kings! And how shameless are the women! I have been told a sad story. How I hate Charles II! A woman whom my father loved gave herself to that king whilst my father was dying in exile. The prostitute! Charles II, James II! After a scamp, a scoundrel. What is there in a king? A man, feeble and contemptible, subject to wants and infirmities. Of what good is a king? You cultivate that parasite, royalty; you make a serpent of that worm, a dragon of that insect. Oh, pity the poor! You increase the weight of the taxes for the profit of the throne. Look to the laws which you decree. Take heed of the suffering swarms which you crush. Cast your eyes down. Look at what is at your feet. O ye great, there are the little. Have pity! yes, have pity on yourselves; for the people is in its agony, and when the lower part of the trunk dies, the higher parts die too. Death spares no limb. When night comes no one can keep his corner of daylight. Are you selfish? then save others. The destruction of the vessel cannot be a matter of indifference to any passenger. There can be no wreck for some that is not wreck for all. Oh! believe it, the abyss yawns for all!"

The laughter increased and became irresistible. For that matter, such extravagance as there was in his words was sufficient to amuse any assembly. To be comic without and tragic within, what suffering can be more humiliating? what pain deeper? Gwynplaine felt it. His words were an appeal in one direction, his face in the other. What a terrible position was his!

Suddenly, his voice rang out in strident bursts.

"How gay these men are! Be it so. Here is irony face to face with agony; a sneer mocking the death-rattle. They are all-powerful. Perhaps so; be it so. We shall see. Behold! I am one of them; but I am, also, one of you, O ye poor! A king sold me. A poor man sheltered me. Who mutilated me? A prince. Who healed and nourished me? A pauper. I am Lord Clancharlie; but I am still Gwynplaine. I take my place amongst the great; but I belong to the mean. I am amongst those who rejoice; but I am with those who suffer. Oh, this system of society is false! Some day will come that which is true. Then there will be no more lords; and there shall be free and living men. There will be no more masters; there will be fathers. Such is the future. No more prostration; no more baseness; no more ignorance; no more human beasts of burden; no more courtiers; no more toadies! no more kings; but Light! In the meantime, see me here. I have a right, and I will use it. Is it a right? No, if I use it for myself. Yes, if I use it for all. I will speak to you, my lords, being one of you. O my brothers below, I will tell them of your nakedness. I will rise up with a bundle of the people's rags in my hand. I will shake off over the masters the misery of the slaves; and these favored and arrogant ones shall no longer be able to escape the remembrance of the wretched, nor the princes the itch of the poor; and so much the worse, if it be the bite of vermin; and so much the better, if it awake the lions from their slumber."

Here Gwynplaine turned toward the kneeling under-clerks, who were writing on the fourth woolsack.

"Who are those fellows kneeling down? What are you doing? Get up; you are men."

These words, suddenly addressed to inferiors whom a lord ought not even to perceive, increased the merriment to the utmost.

They had cried, "Bravo!" Now, they shouted, "Hurrah!" From clapping their hands, they proceeded to stamping their feet. One might have been back in the Green Box, only that there the laughter applauded Gwynplaine; here it exterminated him. The effort of ridicule is to kill. Men's laughter sometimes exerts all its power to murder.

The laughter proceeded to action. Sneering words rained down upon him. Humor is the folly of assemblies. Their ingenious and foolish ridicule shuns facts instead of studying them, and condemns questions instead of solving them. Any extraordinary occurrence is a point of interrogation; to laugh at it is like laughing at an enigma. But the Sphynx, which never laughs, is behind it.

Contradictory shouts arose—

"Enough! enough!" "Encore! encore!"

William Farmer, Baron Leimpster, flung at Gwynplaine the insult cast by Ryc Quiney at Shakespeare—

"Histrio, mima!"

Lord Vaughan, a sententious man, twenty-ninth on the barons' bench, exclaimed—

"We must be back in the days when animals had the gift of speech. In the midst of human tongues the jaw of a beast has spoken."

"Listen to Balaam's ass," added Lord Yarmouth.

Lord Yarmouth presented that appearance of sagacity produced by a round nose and a crooked mouth.

"The rebel Linnæus is chastised in his tomb. The son is the punishment of the father," said John Hough, Bishop of Lichfield and Coventry, whose prebendary Gwynplaine's attack had glanced.

"He lies!" said Lord Cholmondeley, the legislator so well read up in the law. "That which he calls torture is only the *peine forte et dure*, and a very good thing, too. Torture is not practiced in England."

Thomas Wentworth, Baron Raby, addressed the Chancellor.

"My Lord Chancellor, adjourn the House."

"No, no. Let him go on. He is amusing. Hurrah! hip! hip! hip!"

Thus shouted the young lords, their fun amounting to fury. Four of them especially were in the full exasperation of hilarity and hate. These were Laurence Hyde, Earl of Rochester; Thomas Tufton, Earl of Thanet; Viscount Hatton; and the Duke of Montagu.

"To your tricks, Gwynplaine!" cried Rochester.

"Put him out, put him out!" shouted Thanet.

Viscount Hatton drew from his pocket a penny, which he flung to Gwynplaine.

And John Campbell, Earl of Greenwich; Savage, Earl Rivers; Thompson, Baron Haversham; Warrington, Escrick Rolleston, Rockingham, Carteret, Langdale, Barcester, Maynard, Hunsdon, Carnarvon, Cavendish, Burlington, Robert Darcy, Earl of Holderness, Other Windsor, Earl of Plymouth, applauded.

There was a tumult as of pandemonium or of pantheon, in which the words of Gwynplaine were lost.

Amidst it all, there was heard but one word of Gwynplaine's: "Beware!"

Ralph, Duke of Montagu, recently down from Oxford, and still a beardless youth, descended from the bench of dukes, where he sat the nineteenth in order, and placed himself in front of Gwynplaine, with his arms folded. In a sword there is a spot which cuts sharpest, and in a voice an accent which insults most keenly. Montagu spoke with that accent, and sneering with his face close to that of Gwynplaine, shouted—

"What are you talking about?"

"I am prophesying," said Gwynplaine.

The laughter exploded anew; and below this laughter, anger growled its continued bass. One of the minors, Lionel Cranfield Sackville, Earl of Dorset and Middlesex, stood upon his seat, not smiling, but grave as became a future legislator, and, without saying a word, looked at Gwynplaine with his fresh twelve-year old face, and shrugged his shoulders. Whereat the Bishop of St. Asaph's whispered in the ear of the Bishop of St. David's, who was sitting beside him, as he pointed to Gwynplaine, "There is the fool"; then pointing to the child, "there is the sage."

A chaos of complaint rose from amidst the confusion of exclamations—

"Gorgon's face!"—"What does it all mean?"—"An insult to the House!"—"The fellow ought to be put out!"—"What a madman!"— "Shame! shame!"—"Adjourn the House!"—"No; let him finish his speech!"—"Talk away, you buffoon!"

Lord Lewis of Duras, with his arms akimbo, shouted—

"Ah! it does one good to laugh. My spleen is cured. I propose a vote of thanks in these terms: 'The House of Lords returns thanks to the Green Box.'"

Gwynplaine, it may be remembered, had dreamt of a different welcome.

A man who, climbing up a steep and crumbling acclivity of sand above a giddy precipice, has felt it giving way under his hands, his nails, his elbows, his knees, his feet; who—losing instead of gaining on his treacherous way, a prey to every terror of the danger, slipping back instead of ascending, increasing the certainty of his fall by his very efforts to gain the summit, and losing ground in every struggle for safety—has felt the abyss approaching nearer and nearer, until the certainty of his coming fall into the yawning jaws open to receive him, has frozen the marrow of his bones—that man has experienced the sensations of Gwynplaine.

He felt the ground he had ascended crumbling under him, and his audience was the precipice.

There is always someone to say the word which sums all up.

Lord Scarsdale translated the impression of the assembly in one exclamation—

"What is the monster doing here?"

Gwynplaine stood up, dismayed and indignant, in a sort of final convulsion. He looked at them all fixedly.

"What am I doing here? I have come to be a terror to you! I am a monster, do you say? No! I am the people! I am an exception? No! I am the rule; you are the exception! You are the chimera; I am the reality! I am the frightful man who laughs! Who laughs at what? At you, at himself, at everything! What is his laugh? Your crime and his torment! That crime he flings at your head! That punishment he spits in your face! I laugh, and that means I weep!"

He paused. There was less noise. The laughter continued, but it was more subdued. He may have fancied that he had regained a certain amount of attention. He breathed again, and resumed—

"This laugh which is on my face a king placed there. This laugh expresses the desolation of mankind. This laugh means hate, enforced silence, rage, despair. This laugh is the production of torture. This laugh is a forced laugh. If Satan were marked with this laugh, it would convict God. But the Eternal is not like them that perish. Being absolute, He is just; and God hates the acts of kings. Oh! you take me for an exception; but I am a symbol. Oh, all-powerful men, fools that you are! open your eyes. I am the incarnation of All. I represent humanity, such as its masters have made it. Mankind is mutilated. That which has been done to me has been done to it. In it have been deformed right, justice, truth, reason, intelligence, as eyes, nostrils, and ears have been deformed in me; its heart has been made a sink of passion and pain, like mine, and, like mine, its features have been hidden in a mask of joy. Where God had placed his finger, the king set his sign-manual. Monstrous superposition! Bishops, peers, and princes, the people is a sea of suffering, smiling on the surface. My lords, I tell you that the people are as I am. To-day you oppress them; to-day you hoot at me. But the future is the ominous thaw, in which that which was as stone shall become wave. The appearance of solidity melts into liquid. A crack in the ice, and all is over. There will come an hour when convulsion shall break down your oppression; when an angry roar will reply to your jeers. Nay, that hour did come! Thou wert of it, O my Father! That hour of God did come, and was called the Republic! It was destroyed, but it will return. Meanwhile, remember that the line of kings armed with the sword was broken by Cromwell, armed with the ax. Tremble! Incorruptible solutions are at hand: the talons which were cut are growing again; the tongues which were torn out are floating away, they are turning to tongues of fire, and, scattered by the breath of darkness, are shouting through infinity; those who hunger are showing their idle teeth; false heavens, built over real hells, are tottering. The people are suffering—they are suffering; and that which is on high totters, and that which is below yawns. Darkness demands its change to light; the damned discuss the elect. Behold! it is the coming of the people, the ascent of mankind, the beginning of the end, the red dawn of the catastrophe! Yes, all these things are in this laugh of mine, at which you laugh to-day! London is one perpetual fête. Be it so. From one end to the other, England rings with acclamation. Well! but listen. All that you see is I. You have your fêtes—they are my laugh; you have your public rejoicings—they are my laugh; you have your weddings, consecrations, and coronations—they are my laugh. The births of your princes are my laugh. But above you is the thunderbolt—it is my laugh."

How could they stand such nonsense? The laughter burst out afresh; and now it was overwhelming. Of all the lava which that crater, the human mouth, ejects, the most corrosive is joy. To inflict evil gaily is a contagion which no crowd can resist. All executions do not take place on the scaffold; and men, from the moment they are in a body, whether in mobs or in senates, have always a ready executioner amongst them, called sarcasm. There is no torture to be compared to that of the wretch condemned to execution by ridicule. This was Gwynplaine's fate. He was stoned with their jokes, and riddled by the scoffs shot at him. He stood there a mark for all. They sprang up; they cried, "Encore"; they shook with laughter; they stamped their feet; they pulled each other's bands. The majesty of the place, the purple of the robes, the chaste ermine, the dignity of the wigs, had no effect. The lords laughed, the bishops laughed, the judges laughed, the old men's benches derided, the children's benches were in convulsions. The Archbishop of Canterbury nudged the Archbishop of York; Henry Compton, Bishop of London, brother of Lord Northampton, held his sides; the Lord Chancellor bent down his head, probably to conceal his inclination to laugh; and, at the bar, that statue of respect, the Usher of the Black Rod, was laughing also.

Gwynplaine, become pallid, had folded his arms; and, surrounded by all those faces, young and old, in which had burst forth this grand Homeric jubilee; in that whirlwind of clapping hands, of stamping feet, and of hurrahs; in that mad buffoonery, of which he was the center; in that splendid overflow of hilarity; in the midst of that unmeasured gaiety, he felt that the sepulcher was within him. All was over. He could no longer master the face which betrayed, nor the audience which insulted him.

That eternal and fatal law, by which the grotesque is linked with the sublime—by which the laugh re-echoes the groan, parody rides behind despair, and seeming is opposed to being—had never found more terrible expression. Never had a light more sinister illumined the depths of human darkness.

Gwynplaine was assisting at the final destruction of his destiny by a burst of laughter. The irremediable was in this. Having fallen, we can raise ourselves up; but, being pulverized, never. And the insult of their sovereign mockery had reduced him to dust. From thenceforth nothing was possible. Everything is in accordance with the scene. That which was triumph in the Green Box was disgrace and catastrophe in the House of Lords. What was applause there, was insult here. He felt something like the reverse side of his mask. On one side of that mask he had the sympathy of the people, who welcomed Gwynplaine; on the other, the contempt of the great, rejecting Lord Fermain Clancharlie. On one side, attraction; on the other, repulsion; both leading him toward the shadows. He felt himself, as it were, struck from behind. Fate strikes treacherous blows. Everything will be explained hereafter, but, in the meantime, destiny is a snare, and man sinks into its pitfalls. He had expected to rise, and was welcomed by laughter. Such apotheoses have lugubrious terminations. There is a dreary expression—to be sobered; tragical wisdom born of drunkenness! In the midst of that tempest of gaiety commingled with ferocity, Gwynplaine fell into a reverie.

An assembly in mad merriment drifts as chance directs, and loses its compass when it gives itself to laughter. None knew whither they were tending, or what they were doing. The House was obliged to rise, adjourned by the Lord Chancellor, "owing to extraordinary circumstances," to the next day. The peers broke up. They bowed to the royal throne and departed. Echoes of prolonged laughter were heard losing themselves in the corridors.

Assemblies, besides their official doors, have—under tapestry, under projections, and under arches—all sorts of hidden doors, by which the members escape like water through the cracks in a vase. In a short time the chamber was deserted. This takes place quickly and almost imperceptibly, and those places, so lately full of voices, are suddenly given back to silence.

Reverie carries one far; and one comes by long dreaming to reach, as it were, another planet.

Gwynplaine suddenly awoke from such a dream. He was alone. The chamber was empty. He had not even observed that the House had been adjourned. All the peers had departed, even his sponsors. There only remained here and there some of the lower officers of the House, waiting for his lordship to depart before they put the covers on and extinguished the lights.

Mechanically he placed his hat on his head, and, leaving his place, directed his steps to the great door opening into the gallery. As he was passing through the opening in the bar, a door-keeper relieved him of his peer's robes. This he scarcely felt. In another instant, he was in the gallery.

The officials who remained observed with astonishment that the peer had gone out without bowing to the throne!

Chapter VIII

HE WOULD BE A GOOD BROTHER, WERE HE NOT A GOOD SON

THERE WAS NO ONE IN THE GALLERY.

Gwynplaine crossed the circular space, from whence they had removed the arm-chair and the tables, and where there now remained no trace of his investiture. Candelabra and lusters, placed at certain intervals, marked the way out. Thanks to this string of light, he retraced without difficulty, through the suite of saloons and galleries, the way which he had followed on his arrival with the King-at-Arms and the Usher of the Black Rod. He saw no one, except here and there some old lord with tardy steps, plodding along heavily in front of him.

Suddenly, in the silence of those great deserted rooms, bursts of indistinct exclamations reached him, a sort of nocturnal clatter unusual in such a place. He directed his steps to the place whence this noise proceeded, and found himself in a spacious hall, dimly lighted, which was one of the exits from the House of Lords. He saw a great glass door open, a flight of steps, footmen and links, a square outside, and a few coaches waiting at the bottom of the steps.

This was the spot from which the noise which he had heard had proceeded.

Within the door, and under the hall lamp, was a noisy group in a storm of gestures and of voices.

Gwynplaine approached in the gloom.

They were quarrelling. On one side there were ten or twelve young lords, who wanted to go out; on the other, a man, with his hat on, like themselves, upright and with a haughty brow, who barred their passage.

Who was this man? Tom-Jim-Jack.

Some of these lords were still in their robes, others had thrown them off, and were in their usual attire. Tom-Jim-Jack wore a hat with plumes—not white, like the peers; but green tipped with orange. He was embroidered and laced from head to foot, had flowing bows of ribbon and lace round his wrists and neck, and was feverishly fingering with his left hand the hilt of the sword which hung from his waistbelt, and on the billets and scabbard of which were embroidered an admiral's anchors.

It was he who was speaking and addressing the young lords; and Gwynplaine overheard the following—

"I have told you you are cowards. You wish me to withdraw my words. Be it so. You are not cowards; you are idiots. You all combined against one man. That was not cowardice. All right. Then it was stupidity. He spoke to you, and you did not understand him. Here, the old are hard of hearing, the young devoid of intelligence. I am one of your own order to quite sufficient extent to tell you the truth. This newcomer is strange, and he has uttered a heap of nonsense, I admit; but amidst all that nonsense there were some things which were true. His speech was confused, undigested, ill-delivered. Be it so. He repeated, 'You know, you know,' too often; but a man who was but yesterday a clown at a fair cannot be expected to speak like Aristotle or like Doctor Gilbert Burnet, Bishop of Salisbury. The vermin, the lions, the address to the under-clerks—all that was in bad taste. Zounds! who says it wasn't? It was a senseless and fragmentary and topsy-turvy harangue; but here and there came out facts which were true. It is no small thing to speak even as he did, seeing it is not his trade. I should like to see you do it. Yes; you! What he said about the lepers at Burton-Lazars is an undeniable fact. Besides, he is not the first man who has talked nonsense. In fine, my lords, I do not like to see the many set upon one. Such is my humor; and I ask your lordships' permission to take offense. You have displeased me; I am angry. I am grateful to God for having drawn up from the depth of his low existence this peer of England, and for having given back his inheritance to the heir; and, without heeding whether it will or will not affect my own affairs, I consider it a beautiful sight to see an insect transformed into an eagle, and Gwynplaine into Lord Clancharlie. My lords, I forbid you holding any opinion but mine. I regret that Lord Lewis Duras should not be here. I should like to insult him. My lords, it is Fermain Clancharlie who has been the peer, and you who have been the mountebanks. As to his laugh, it is not his fault. You have laughed at that laugh; men should not laugh at misfortune. If you think that people cannot laugh at you as well, you are very much mistaken. You are ugly. You are badly dressed. My Lord Haversham, I saw your mistress the other day; she is hideous—a duchess, but a monkey. Gentlemen who laugh, I repeat that I should like to hear you try to say four words running! many men jabber; very few speak. You imagine you know something, because you have kept idle terms at Oxford or Cambridge, and because, before being peers of England on the benches of Westminster, you have been asses on the benches at Gonville and Caius. Here I am; and I choose to stare you in the face. You have just been impudent to this new peer. A monster, certainly; but a monster given up to beasts. I had rather be that man than you. I was present at the sitting, in my place as a possible heir to a peerage. I heard all. I have not the right to speak; but I have the right to be a gentleman. Your jeering airs annoyed me. When I am angry I would go up to Mount Pendlehill, and pick the cloudberry which brings the thunderbolt down on the gatherer. That is the reason why I have waited for you at the door. We must have a few words, for we have arrangements to make. Did it strike you that you failed a little in respect toward myself? My lords, I entertain a firm determination to kill a few of you. All you who are here—Thomas Tufton, Earl of Thanet; Savage, Earl Rivers; Charles Spencer, Earl of Sunderland; Laurence Hyde, Earl of Rochester; you Barons, Gray of Rolleston, Cary Hunsdon, Escrick, Rockingham, little Carteret; Robert Darcy, Earl of Holderness; William, Viscount Hutton; and Ralph, Duke of Montagu; and any who choose, I, David Dirry-Moir, an officer of the fleet, summon, call, and command you to provide yourselves, in all haste, with seconds and umpires, and I will meet you face to face and hand to hand, to-night, at once, to-morrow, by day or night, by sunlight or by candlelight, where, when, or how you please, so long as there is two sword-lengths' space; and you will do well to look to the flints of your pistols and the edges of your rapiers, for it is my firm intention to cause vacancies in your peerages. Ogle Cavendish, take your measures, and think of your motto, *Cavendo tutus*; Marmaduke Langdale, you will do well, like your ancestor, Grindold, to order a coffin to be brought with you. George Booth, Earl of Warrington, you will never again see the County Palatine of Chester, or your labyrinth like that of Crete, or the high towers of Dunham Massy! As to Lord Vaughan, he is young enough to talk impertinently, and too old to answer for it. I shall demand satisfaction for his words of his nephew Richard Vaughan, Member of Parliament for the Borough of Merioneth. As for you, John Campbell, Earl of Greenwich, I will kill you as Achon killed Matas; but with a fair cut, and not from behind, it being my custom to present my heart and not my back to the point of the sword. I have spoken my mind, my lords. And so use witchcraft, if you like. Consult the fortune-tellers. Grease your skins with oint-ments and drugs to make them invulnerable; hang round your necks charms of the devil or the Vir-gin; I will fight you blest or curst, and I will not have you searched to see if you are wearing any wizard's tokens. On foot or on horseback, on the highroad if you wish it, in Piccadilly, or at Char-ing Cross; and they shall take up the pavement for our meeting, as they unpaved the court of the Louvre for the duel between Guise and Bassompierre. All of you! Do you hear? I mean to fight you all. Dorme, Earl of Carnarvon, I will make you swallow my sword up to the hilt, as Marolles did to Lisle Mariveaux, and then we shall see, my lord, whether you will laugh or not. You, Burlington, who look like a girl of seventeen, you shall choose between the lawn of your house in Middlesex, and your beautiful garden at Londesborough in Yorkshire, to be buried in. I beg to inform your lordships that it does not suit me to allow your insolence in my presence. I will chastise you, my lords. I take it ill that you should have ridiculed Lord Fermain Clancharlie. He is worth more than you. As Clancharlie, he has nobility, which you have. As Gwynplaine, he has intellect, which you have not. I make his cause my cause, insult to him insult to me, and your ridicule my wrath. We shall see who will come out of this affair alive, because I challenge you to the death. Do you understand? With any arm, in any fashion, and you shall choose the death that pleases you best; and since you are clowns as well as gentlemen, I proportion my defiance to your qualities, and I give you your choice of any way in which a man can be killed, from the sword of the prince to the fist of the black-guard."

To this furious onslaught of words, the whole group of young noblemen answered by a smile. "Agreed," they said.

"I choose pistols," said Burlington.

"I," said Escrick, "the ancient combat of the lists, with the mace and the dagger."

"I," said Holderness, "the duel with two knives, long and short, stripped to the waist, and breast to breast."

"Lord David," said the Earl of Thanet, "you are a Scot. I choose the claymore."

"I, the sword," said Rockingham.

"I," said Duke Ralph, "prefer the fists; 'tis noblest."

Gwynplaine came out from the shadow. He directed his steps toward him whom he had hith-erto called Tom-Jim-Jack, but in whom now, however, he began to perceive something more. "I thank you," said he, "but this is my business."

Every head turned toward him.

Gwynplaine advanced. He felt himself impelled toward the man whom he heard called Lord David; his defender, and perhaps something nearer. Lord David drew back.

"Oh!" said he. "It is you, is it? This is well-timed. I have a word for you as well. Just now you spoke of a woman, who, after having loved Lord Linnæus Clancharlie, loved Charles II."

"It is true."

"Sir, you insulted my mother."

"Your mother!" cried Gwynplaine. "In that case, as I guessed, we are—"

"Brothers," answered Lord David, and he struck Gwynplaine. "We are brothers," said he; "so we can fight. One can only fight one's equal; who is one's equal if not one's brother? I will send you my seconds; to-morrow we will cut each other's throats."

BOOK THE NINTH

IN RUINS

Chapter I

IT IS THROUGH EXCESS OF GREATNESS THAT MAN REACHES EXCESS OF MISERY

As MIDNIGHT TOLLED FROM ST. PAUL'S, A MAN WHO HAD JUST CROSSED LONDON BRIDGE STRUCK into the lanes of Southwark. There were no lamps lighted, it being at that time the custom in London, as in Paris, to extinguish the public lamps at eleven o'clock; that is, to put them out just as they became necessary. The streets were dark and deserted. When the lamps are out, men stay in. He whom we speak of advanced with hurried strides. He was strangely dressed for walking at such an hour. He wore a coat of embroidered silk, a sword by his side, a hat with white plumes, and no cloak. The watchmen, as they saw him pass, said, "It is a lord walking for a wager," and they moved out of his way with the respect due to a lord and to a better.

The man was Gwynplaine. He was making his escape. Where was he? He did not know. We have said that the soul has its cyclones; fearful whirlwinds, in which heaven, the sea, day, night, life, death, are all mingled in unintelligible horror. It can no longer breathe Truth; it is crushed by things in which it does not believe. Nothingness becomes hurricane. The firmament pales. Infinity is empty. The mind of the sufferer wanders away. He feels himself dying. He craves for a star. What did Gwynplaine feel? a thirst; a thirst to see Dea.

He felt but that. To reach the Green Box again, and the Tadcaster Inn, with its sounds and light; full of the cordial laughter of the people; to find Ursus and Homo, to see Dea again, to re-enter life. Disillusion, like a bow, shoots its arrow, man, toward the True. Gwynplaine hastened on. He approached Tarrinzeau Field. He walked no longer now; he ran. His eyes pierced the darkness before him. His glance preceded him, eagerly seeking the harbor on the horizon. What a moment for him when he should see the lighted windows of Tadcaster Inn!

He reached the bowling-green. He turned the corner of the wall, and saw before him, at the other end of the field, some distance off, the inn—the only house, it may be remembered, in the field where the fair was held.

He looked. There was no light; nothing but a black mass.

He shuddered. Then he said to himself that it was late, that the tavern was shut up, that it was very natural, that everyone was asleep, that he had only to awaken Nicless or Govicum, that he must go up to the inn and knock at the door. He did so, running no longer now, but rushing.

He reached the inn, breathless. It is when, storm-beaten and struggling in the invisible convulsions of the soul until he knows not whether he is in life or in death, that all the delicacy of a man's affection for his loved ones, being yet unimpaired, proves a heart true. When all else is swallowed up, tenderness still floats unshattered. Not to awaken Dea too suddenly was Gwynplaine's first thought. He approached the inn with as little noise as possible. He recognized the nook, the old dog kennel, where Govicum used to sleep. In it, contiguous to the lower room, was a window opening on to the field. Gwynplaine tapped softly at the pane. It would be enough to awaken Govicum, he thought.

There was no sound in Govicum's room.

"At his age," said Gwynplaine, "a boy sleeps soundly."

With the back of his hand he knocked against the window gently. Nothing stirred.

He knocked louder twice. Still nothing stirred. Then, feeling somewhat uneasy, he went to the door of the inn and knocked. No one answered. He reflected, and began to feel a cold shudder come over him.

"Master Nicless is old, children sleep soundly, and old men heavily. Courage! louder!"

He had tapped, he had knocked, he had kicked the door; now he flung himself against it.

This recalled to him a distant memory of Weymouth, when, a little child, he had carried Dea, an infant, in his arms.

He battered the door again violently, like a lord, which, alas! he was.

The house remained silent. He felt that he was losing his head. He no longer thought of caution. He shouted—

"Nicless! Govicum!"

At the same time he looked up at the windows, to see if any candle was lighted. But the inn was blank. Not a voice, not a sound, not a glimmer of light. He went to the gate and knocked at it, kicked against it, and shook it, crying out wildly—

"Ursus! Homo!"

The wolf did not bark.

A cold sweat stood in drops upon his brow. He cast his eyes around. The night was dark; but there were stars enough to render the fair-green visible. He saw—a melancholy sight to him—that everything on it had vanished.

There was not a single caravan. The circus was gone. Not a tent, not a booth, not a cart remained. The strollers, with their thousand noisy cries, who had swarmed there, had given place to a black and sullen void.

All were gone.

The madness of anxiety took possession of him. What did this mean? What had happened? Was no one left? Could it be that life had crumbled away behind him? What had happened to them all? Good heavens! Then he rushed like a tempest against the house. He struck the small door, the gate, the windows, the window-shutters, the walls with fists and feet, furious with terror and agony of mind.

He called Nicless, Govicum, Fibi, Vinos, Ursus, Homo. He tried every shout and every sound against this wall. At times he waited and listened; but the house remained mute and dead. Then, exasperated, he began again with blows, shouts, and repeated knockings, re-echoed all around. It might have been thunder trying to awake the grave.

There is a certain stage of fright in which a man becomes terrible. He who fears everything fears nothing. He would strike the Sphynx. He defies the Unknown.

Gwynplaine renewed the noise in every possible form, stopping, resuming, unwearying in the shouts and appeals by which he assailed the tragic silence. He called a thousand times on the names of those who should have been there. He shrieked out every name except that of Dea, a precaution of which he could not have explained the reason himself, but which instinct inspired even in his distraction.

Having exhausted calls and cries, nothing was left but to break in.

"I must enter the house," he said to himself; "but how?"

He broke a pane of glass in Govicum's room by thrusting his hand through it, tearing the flesh; he drew the bolt of the sash and opened the window. Perceiving that his sword was in the way, he tore it off angrily, scabbard, blade, and belt, and flung it on the pavement. Then he raised himself by the inequalities in the wall, and, though the window was narrow, he was able to pass through it.

He entered the inn. Govicum's bed, dimly visible in its nook, was there; but Govicum was not in it. If Govicum was not in his bed, it was evident that Nicless could not be in his.

The whole house was dark. He felt in that shadowy interior the mysterious immobility of emptiness, and that vague fear which signifies—"There is no one here."

Gwynplaine, convulsed with anxiety, crossed the lower room, knocking against the tables, upsetting the earthenware, throwing down the benches, sweeping against the jugs, and, striding over the furniture, reached the door leading into the court, and broke it open with one blow from his knee, which sprung the lock. The door turned on its hinges. He looked into the court. The Green Box was no longer there.

Chapter II

THE DREGS

GWYNPLAINE LEFT THE HOUSE, AND BEGAN TO EXPLORE TARRINZEAU FIELD IN EVERY DIRECTION. He went to every place where, the day before, the tents and caravans had stood. He knocked at the stalls, though he knew well that they were uninhabited. He struck everything that looked like a door or a window. Not a voice arose from the darkness. Something like death had been there.

The anthill had been razed. Some measures of police had apparently been carried out. There had been what, in our days, would be called a razzia. Tarrinzeau Field was worse than a desert; it had been scoured, and every corner of it scratched up, as it were, by pitiless claws. The pocket of the unfortunate fair-green had been turned inside out, and completely emptied.

Gwynplaine, after having searched every yard of ground, left the green, struck into the crooked streets abutting on the site called East Point, and directed his steps toward the Thames. He had threaded his way through a network of lanes, bounded only by walls and hedges, when he felt the fresh breeze from the water, heard the dull lapping of the river, and suddenly saw a parapet in front of him. It was the parapet of the Effroc stone.

This parapet bounded a block of the quay, which was very short and very narrow. Under it the high wall, the Effroc stone, buried itself perpendicularly in the dark water below.

Gwynplaine stopped at the parapet, and, leaning his elbows on it, laid his head in his hands and set to thinking, with the water beneath him.

Did he look at the water? No. At what then? At the shadow; not the shadow without, but within him. In the melancholy night-bound landscape, which he scarcely marked, in the outer depths, which his eyes did not pierce, were the blurred sketches of masts and spars. Below the Effroc stone there was nothing on the river; but the quay sloped insensibly downwards till, some distance off, it met a pier, at which several vessels were lying, some of which had just arrived, others which were on the point of departure. These vessels communicated with the shore by little jetties, constructed for the purpose, some of stone, some of wood, or by movable gangways. All of them, whether moored to the jetties or at anchor, were wrapped in silence. There was neither voice nor movement on board, it being a good habit of sailors to sleep when they can, and awake only when wanted. If any of them were to sail during the night at high tide, the crews were not yet awake. The hulls, like large black bubbles, and the rigging, like threads mingled with ladders, were barely visible. All was livid and confused. Here and there a red cresset pierced the haze.

Gwynplaine saw nothing of all this. What he was musing on was destiny.

He was in a dream—a vision—giddy in presence of an inexorable reality.

He fancied that he heard behind him something like an earthquake. It was the laughter of the Lords.

From that laughter he had just emerged. He had come out of it, having received a blow, and from whom?

From his own brother!

Flying from the laughter, carrying with him the blow, seeking refuge, a wounded bird, in his nest, rushing from hate and seeking love, what had he found?

Darkness.

No one.

Everything gone.

He compared that darkness to the dream he had indulged in.

What a crumbling away!

Gwynplaine had just reached that sinister bound—the void. The Green Box gone, was his universe vanished.

His soul had been closed up.

He reflected.

What could have happened? Where were they? They had evidently been carried away. Destiny had given him, Gwynplaine, a blow, which was greatness; its reaction had struck them another, which was annihilation. It was clear that he would never see them again. Precautions had been taken against that. They had scoured the fair-green, beginning by Nicless and Govicum, so that he should gain no clue through them. Inexorable dispersion! That fearful social system, at the same time that it had pulverized him in the House of Lords, had crushed them in their little cabin. They were lost; Dea was lost—lost to him forever. Powers of heaven! where was she? And he had not been there to defend her!

To have to make guesses as to the absent whom we love is to put oneself to the torture. He inflicted this torture on himself. At every thought that he fathomed, at every supposition which he made, he felt within him a moan of agony.

Through a succession of bitter reflections he remembered a man who was evidently fatal to him, and who had called himself Barkilphedro. That man had inscribed on his brain a dark sentence which reappeared now, he had written it in such terrible ink that every letter had turned to fire; and Gwynplaine saw flaming at the bottom of his thought the enigmatical words, the meaning of which was at length solved: "Destiny never opens one door, without closing another."

All was over. The final shadows had gathered about him. In every man's fate there may be an end of the world for himself alone. It is called despair. The soul is full of falling stars.

This, then, was what he had come to.

A vapor had passed. He had been mingled with it. It had lain heavily on his eyes, it had disordered his brain. He had been outwardly blinded, intoxicated within. This had lasted the time of a passing vapor. Then everything melted away, the vapor and his life. Awaking from the dream, he found himself alone.

All vanished, all gone, all lost. Night. Nothingness. Such was his horizon.

He was alone.

Alone has a synonym, which is Dead. Despair is an accountant. It sets itself to find its total, it adds up everything, even to the farthings. It reproaches Heaven with its thunderbolts and its pinpricks. It seeks to find what it has to expect from fate. It argues, weighs, and calculates, outwardly cool, while the burning lava is still flowing on within.

Gwynplaine examined himself, and examined his fate.

The backward glance of thought; terrible recapitulation!

When at the top of a mountain, we look down the precipice; when at the bottom, we look up at heaven. And we say, I was there.

Gwynplaine was at the very bottom of misfortune. How sudden, too, had been his fall!

Such is the hideous swiftness of misfortune, although it is so heavy that we might fancy it slow. But no! It would likewise appear that snow, from its coldness, ought to be the paralysis of winter, and, from its whiteness, the immobility of the winding-sheet. Yet this is contradicted by the avalanche.

The avalanche is snow become a furnace. It remains frozen, but it devours. The avalanche had enveloped Gwynplaine. He had been torn like a rag, uprooted like a tree, precipitated like a stone. He recalled all the circumstances of his fall. He put himself questions, and returned answers. Grief is an examination. There is no judge so searching as conscience conducting its own trial.

What amount of remorse was there in his despair? This he wished to find out, and dissected his conscience. Excruciating vivisection!

His absence had caused a catastrophe. Had this absence depended on him? In all that had happened, had he been a free agent? No! He had felt himself captive. What was that which had arrested and detained him—a prison? No. A chain? No. What then? Sticky slime! He had sunk into the slough of greatness.

To whom has it not happened to be free in appearance, yet to feel that his wings are hampered?

There had been something like a snare spread for him. What is at first temptation, ends by captivity.

Nevertheless (and his conscience pressed him on this point) had he merely submitted to what had been offered him? No; he had accepted it.

Violence and surprise had been used with him in a certain measure, it was true; but he, in a certain measure, had given in. To have allowed himself to be carried off, was not his fault; but to have allowed himself to be inebriated, was his weakness. There had been a moment—a decisive moment—when the question was proposed. This Barkilphedro had placed a dilemma before Gwynplaine, and had given him clear power to decide his fate by a word. Gwynplaine might have said, "No." He had said, "Yes."

From that "Yes," uttered in a moment of dizziness, everything had sprung. Gwynplaine realized this now in the bitter aftertaste of that consent.

Nevertheless—for he debated with himself—was it then so great a wrong to take possession of his right, of his patrimony, of his heritage, of his house; and, as a patrician, of the rank of his ancestors; as an orphan, of the name of his father? What had he accepted? A restitution. Made by whom? By Providence.

Then his mind revolted. Senseless acceptance! What a bargain had he struck! what a foolish exchange! He had trafficked with Providence at a loss. How now! For an income of £80,000 a year; for seven or eight titles; for ten or twelve palaces; for houses in town, and castles in the country; for a hundred lackeys; for packs of hounds, and carriages, and armorial bearings; to be a judge and legislator; for a coronet and purple robes, like a king; to be a baron and a marquis; to be a peer of England, he had given the hut of Ursus and the smile of Dea. For shipwreck and destruction in the surging immensity of greatness, he had bartered happiness. For the ocean he had given the pearl. O madman! O fool! O dupe!

Yet nevertheless—and here the objection reappeared on firmer ground—in this fever of high fortune which had seized him, all had not been unwholesome. Perhaps there would have been selfishness in renunciation; perhaps he had done his duty in the acceptance. Suddenly transformed into a lord, what ought he to have done? The complication of events produces perplexity of mind. This had happened to him. Duty gave contrary orders. Duty on all sides at once, duty multiple and contradictory; this was the bewilderment which he had suffered. It was this that had paralyzed him, especially when he had not refused to take the journey from Corleone Lodge to the House of Lords. What we call rising in life is leaving the safe for the dangerous path. Which is, thenceforth, the straight line? Toward whom is our first duty? Is it toward those nearest to ourselves, or is it toward mankind generally? Do we not cease to belong to our own circumscribed circle, and become part of the great family of all? As we ascend, we feel an increased pressure on our virtue. The higher we rise, the greater is the strain. The increase of right is an increase of duty. We come to many cross-ways, phantom roads perchance, and we imagine that we see the finger of conscience pointing each one of them out to us. Which shall we take? Change our direction, remain where we are, advance, go back? What are we to do? That there should be cross-roads in conscience is strange enough; but responsibility may be a labyrinth. And when a man contains an idea, when he is the incarnation of a fact—when he is a symbolical man, at the same time that he is a man of flesh and blood—is not the responsibility still more oppressive? Thence the care-laden docility and the dumb anxiety of Gwynplaine; thence his obedience when summoned to take his seat. A pensive man is often a passive man. He had heard what he fancied was the command of duty itself. Was not that entrance into a place where oppression could be discussed and resisted the realization of one of his deepest aspirations? When he had been called upon to speak, he, the fearful human scantling, he, the living specimen of the despotic whims under which, for six thousand years, mankind has groaned in agony—had he the right to refuse? Had he the right to withdraw his head from under the tongue of fire descending from on high to rest upon him?

In the obscure and giddy debate of conscience, what had he said to himself? This: "The people are a silence. I will be the mighty advocate of that silence; I will speak for the dumb; I will speak of the little to the great—of the weak to the powerful. This is the purpose of my fate. God wills what He wills, and does it. It was a wonder that Hardquanonne's flask, in which was the metamorphosis of Gwynplaine into Lord Clancharlie, should have floated for fifteen years on the ocean, on the billows, in the surf, through the storms, and that all the raging of the sea did it no harm. But I can see the reason. There are destinies with secret springs. I have the key of mine, and know its enigma. I am predestined; I have a mission; I will be the poor man's lord; I will speak for the speechless with despair; I will translate inarticulate remonstrance; I will translate the mutterings, the groans, the murmurs, the voices of the crowd, their ill-spoken complaints, their unintelligible words, and those animal-like cries which ignorance and suffering put into men's mouths. The clamor of men is as inarticulate as the howling of the wind. They cry out, but they are understood; so that cries become equivalent to silence, and silence with them means throwing down their arms. This forced disarmament calls for help. I will be their help; I will be the Denunciation; I will be the Word of the people. Thanks to me, they shall be understood. I will be the bleeding mouth from which the gag has been torn. I will tell everything. This will be great, indeed."

Yes; it is fine to speak for the dumb; but to speak to the deaf is sad. And that was his second part in the drama.

Alas! he had failed irremediably. The elevation in which he had believed, the high fortune, had melted away like a mirage. And what a fall! To be drowned in a surge of laughter!

He had believed himself strong, he who, during so many years, had floated with observant mind on the wide sea of suffering; he who had brought back out of the great shadow so touching a cry. He had been flung against that huge rock, the frivolity of the fortunate. He believed himself an avenger; he was but a clown. He thought that he wielded the thunderbolt; he did but tickle. In place of emotion, he met with mockery. He sobbed; they burst into gaiety, and under that gaiety, he had sunk fatally submerged.

And what had they laughed at? At his laugh. So, that trace of a hateful act, of which he must keep the mark forever—mutilation carved in everlasting gaiety; the stigmata of laughter, image of the sham contentment of nations under their oppressors; that mask of joy produced by torture; that abyss of grimace which he carried on his features; the scar which signified *Jussu regis,* the attestation of a crime committed by the king toward him, and the symbol of crime committed by royalty toward the people—that it was which had triumphed over him—that it was which had overwhelmed him; so that the accusation against the executioner turned into sentence upon the victim.

What a prodigious denial of justice! Royalty, having had satisfaction of his father, had had satis-faction of him! The evil that had been done had served as pretext and as motive for the evil which remained to be done. Against whom were the lords angered? Against the torturer? No. Against the tortured. Here is the throne; there, the people. Here, James II; there, Gwynplaine. That confronta-tion, indeed, brought to light an outrage and a crime. What was the outrage? Complaint. What was the crime? Suffering. Let misery hide itself in silence, otherwise it becomes treason. And those men who had dragged Gwynplaine on the hurdle of sarcasm, were they wicked? No; but they, too, had their fatality: they were happy. They were executioners, ignorant of the fact. They were good-humored; they saw no use in Gwynplaine. He opened himself to them. He tore out his heart to show them, and they cried, "Go on with your play!" But, sharpest sting! he had laughed himself. The frightful chain which tied down his soul hindered his thoughts from rising to his face. His dis-figurement reached even his senses; and, while his conscience was indignant, his face gave it the lie, and jested. Then all was over. He was the laughing man, the caryatid of the weeping world. He was an agony petrified in hilarity, carrying the weight of a universe of calamity, and walled up forever with the gaiety, the ridicule, and the amusement of others; of all the Oppressed, of whom he was the Incarnation, he partook the hateful fate, to be a desolation not believed in; they jeered at his dis-tress; to them he was but an extraordinary buffoon lifted out of some frightful condensation of mis-ery, escaped from his prison, changed to a deity, risen from the dregs of the people to the foot of the throne, mingling with the stars, and who, having once amused the damned, now amused the elect. All that was in him of generosity, of enthusiasm, of eloquence, of heart, of soul, of fury, of anger, of love, of inexpressible grief, ended in—a burst of laughter! And he proved, as he had told the lords, that this was not the exception; but that it was the normal, ordinary, universal, unlimited, sovereign fact, so amalgamated with the routine of life, that they took no account of it. The hun-gry pauper laughs, the beggar laughs, the felon laughs, the prostitute laughs, the orphan laughs to gain his bread; the slave laughs, the soldier laughs, the people laugh. Society is so constituted that every perdition, every indigence, every catastrophe, every fever, every ulcer, every agony, is re-solved on the surface of the abyss into one frightful grin of joy. Now, he was that universal grin, and that grin was himself. The law of heaven, the unknown power which governs, had willed that a specter visible and palpable, a specter of flesh and bone, should be the synopsis of the monstrous parody which we call the world; and he was that specter. Immutable fate!

He had cried: "Pity for those who suffer." In vain! He had striven to awake pity—he had awakened horror. Such is the law of apparitions.

But while he was a specter, he was also a man; here was the heartrending complication. A specter without, a man within. A man more than any other, perhaps, since his double fate was the synopsis of all humanity. And he felt that humanity was at once present in him, and absent from him. There was in his existence something insurmountable. What was he? A disinherited heir? No; for he was a lord. Was he a lord? No; for he was a rebel. He was the light-bearer; a terrible spoil-sport. He was not Satan, certainly; but he was Lucifer. His entrance, with his torch in his hand, was sinister.

Sinister for whom? for the sinister. Terrible to whom? to the terrible. Therefore, they rejected him. Enter their order? be accepted by them? Never. The obstacle which he carried in his face was frightful; but the obstacle which he carried in his ideas was still more insurmountable. His speech was to them more deformed than his face. He had no possible thought in common with the world of the great and powerful, in which he had by a freak of fate been born, and from which another freak of fate had driven him out. There was between men and his face a mask, and between society and his mind a wall. In mixing, from infancy, a wandering mountebank, with that vast and tough substance which is called the crowd, in saturating himself with the attraction of the multitude, and impregnating himself with the great soul of mankind, he had lost, in the common sense of the whole of mankind, the particular sense of the reigning classes. On their heights, he was impossible.

He had reached them wet with water from the well of Truth; the odor of the abyss was on him. He was repugnant to those princes perfumed with lies. To those who live on fiction, truth is disgusting; and he who thirsts for flattery vomits the real, when he has happened to drink it by mistake. That which Gwynplaine brought was not fit for their table. For what was it? Reason, wisdom, justice; and they rejected them with disgust.

There were bishops there. He brought God into their presence. Who was this intruder?

The two poles repel each other. They can never amalgamate, for transition is wanting. Hence the result—a cry of anger—when they were brought together in terrible juxtaposition: all misery concentrated in a man, face to face with all pride concentrated in a caste.

To accuse is useless. To state is sufficient. Gwynplaine, meditating on the limits of his destiny, proved the total uselessness of his effort. He proved the deafness of high places. The privileged have no hearing on the side next the disinherited. Is it their fault? Alas! no. It is their law. Forgive them! To be moved would be to abdicate. Of lords and princes expect nothing. He who is satisfied is inexorable. For those that have their fill, the hungry do not exist. The happy ignore and isolate themselves. On the threshold of their paradise, as on the threshold of hell, must be written, "Leave all hope behind."

Gwynplaine had met with the reception of a specter entering the dwelling of the gods.

Here all that was within him rose in rebellion. No, he was no specter; he was a man. He told them, he shouted to them, that he was Man.

He was not a phantom. He was palpitating flesh. He had a brain, and he thought; he had a heart, and he loved; he had a soul, and he hoped. Indeed, to have hoped overmuch was his whole crime.

Alas! he had exaggerated hope into believing in that thing at once so brilliant and so dark, which is called Society. He who was without had re-entered it. It had at once, and at first sight, made him its three offers, and given him its three gifts—marriage, family, and caste. Marriage? He had seen prostitution on the threshold. Family? His brother had struck him, and was awaiting him the next day, sword in hand. Caste? It had burst into laughter in his face, at him, the patrician, at him, the wretch. It had rejected, almost before it had admitted, him. So that his first three steps into the dense shadow of society had opened three gulfs beneath him.

And it was by a treacherous transfiguration that his disaster had begun; and catastrophe had approached him with the aspect of apotheosis!

Ascend! had signified Descend!

His fate was the reverse of Job's. It was through prosperity that adversity had reached him.

O tragical enigma of life! Behold what pitfalls! A child, he had wrestled against the night, and had been stronger than it; a man, he had wrestled against destiny, and had overcome it. Out of disfigurement he had created success; and out of misery, happiness. Of his exile he had made an asylum. A vagabond, he had wrestled against space; and, like the birds of the air, he had found his crumb of bread. Wild and solitary, he had wrestled against the crowd, and had made it his friend. An athlete, he had wrestled against that lion, the people; and he had tamed it. Indigent, he had wrestled against distress, he had faced the dull necessity of living, and from amalgamating with misery every joy of his heart, he had at length made riches out of poverty. He had believed himself the conqueror of life. Of a sudden he was attacked by fresh forces, reaching him from unknown depths; this time, with menaces no longer, but with smiles and caresses. Love, serpent-like and sensual, had appeared to him, who was filled with angelic love. The flesh had tempted him, who had lived on the ideal. He had heard words of voluptuousness like cries of rage; he had felt the clasp of a woman's arms, like the convolutions of a snake; to the illumination of truth had succeeded the fascination of falsehood; for it is not the flesh that is real, but the soul. The flesh is ashes, the soul is flame. For the little circle allied to him by the relationship of poverty and toil, which was his true and natural family, had been substituted the social family—his family in blood, but of tainted blood; and even be-

fore he had entered it, he found himself face to face with an intended fractricide. Alas! he had allowed himself to be thrown back into that society of which Brantôme, whom he had not read,
wrote: *"The son has a right to challenge his father!"* A fatal fortune had cried to him, "Thou art not
of the crowd, thou art of the chosen!" and had opened the ceiling above his head like a trap in the
sky, and had shot him up through this opening, causing him to appear, wild, and unexpected, in the
midst of princes and masters. Then suddenly he saw around him, instead of the people who applauded him, the lords who cursed him. Mournful metamorphosis! Ignominious ennobling! Rude
spoliation of all that had been his happiness! Pillage of his life by derision; Gwynplaine, Clancharlie, the lord, the mountebank, torn out of his old lot, out of his new lot, by the beaks of those eagles.

What availed it that he had commenced life by immediate victory over obstacle? Of what good
had been his early triumphs? Alas! the fall must come ere destiny be complete.

So, half against his will, half of it—because after he had done with the wapentake he had to
do with Barkilphedro, and he had given a certain amount of consent to his abduction—he had left
the real for the chimerical; the true for the false; Dea for Josiana; love for pride; liberty for power;
labor proud and poor, for opulence full of unknown responsibilities; the shade in which is God, for
the lurid flames in which the devils dwell; Paradise for Olympus!

He had tasted the golden fruit. He was now spitting out the ashes to which it turned.

Lamentable result! Defeat, failure, fall into ruin, insolent expulsion of all his hopes, frustrated
by ridicule. Immeasurable disillusion! and what was there for him in the future? If he looked forward to the morrow, what did he see? A drawn sword the point of which was against his breast, and
the hilt in the hand of his brother. He could see nothing but the hideous flash of that sword. Josiana
and the House of Lords made up the background in a monstrous chiaroscuro full of tragic shadows.

And that brother seemed so brave and chivalrous! Alas! he had hardly seen the Tom-Jim-Jack,
who had defended Gwynplaine, the Lord David, who had defended Lord Clancharlie; but he had
had time to receive a blow from him and to love him.

He was crushed.

He felt it impossible to proceed further. Everything had crumbled about him. Besides, what
was the good of it? All weariness dwells in the depths of despair.

The trial had been made. It could not be renewed.

Gwynplaine was like a gamester who has played all his trumps away, one after the other. He
had allowed himself to be drawn to a fearful gambling-table, without thinking what he was about;
for, so subtle is the poison of illusion! he had staked Dea against Josiana, and had gained a monster;
he had staked Ursus against a family, and had gained an insult; he had played his mountebank platform against his seat in the Lords; for the applause which was his, he had gained insult. His last card
had fallen on that fatal green cloth, the deserted bowling-green. Gwynplaine had lost. Nothing remained but to pay. Pay up, wretched man!

The thunderstricken lie still. Gwynplaine remained motionless. Anybody perceiving him from
afar, in the shadow, stiff and without movement, might have fancied that he saw an upright stone.

Hell, the serpent, and reverie are tortuous. Gwynplaine was descending the sepulchral spirals
of the deepest thought.

He reflected on that world of which he had just caught a glimpse, with the icy contemplation
of a last look. Marriage, but no love; family, but no brotherly affection; riches, but no conscience;
beauty, but no modesty; justice, but no equity; order, but no equilibrium; authority, but no right;
power, but no intelligence; splendor, but no light. Inexorable balance-sheet! He went throughout
the supreme vision in which his mind had been plunged. He examined successively destiny, situation, society, and himself. What was destiny? A snare. Situation? Despair. Society? Hatred. And
himself? A defeated man. In the depths of his soul he cried. Society is the stepmother, Nature is the
mother. Society is the world of the body, Nature is the world of the soul. The one tends to the coffin, to the deal box in the grave, to the earthworms, and ends there. The other tends to expanded

wings, to transformation into the morning light, to ascent into the firmament, and there revives into new life.

By degrees a paroxysm came over him, like a sweeping surge. At the close of events there is always a last flash, in which all stands revealed once more.

He who judges meets the accused face to face. Gwynplaine reviewed all that society and all that nature had done for him. How kind had nature been to him! How she, who is the soul, had succored him! All had been taken from him, even his features. The soul had given him all back—all, even his features; because there was on earth a heavenly blind girl made expressly for him, who saw not his ugliness, and who saw his beauty.

And it was from this that he had allowed himself to be separated; from that adorable girl, from his own adopted one, from her tenderness, from her divine blind gaze, the only gaze on earth that saw him, that he had strayed! Dea was his sister, because he felt between them the grand fraternity of above—the mystery which contains the whole of heaven. Dea, when he was a little child, was his virgin; because every child has his virgin, and at the commencement of life a marriage of souls is always consummated in the plenitude of innocence. Dea was his wife, for theirs was the same nest on the highest branch of the deep-rooted tree of Hymen. Dea was still more—she was his light, for without her all was void, and nothingness; and for him her head was crowned with rays. What would become of him without Dea? What could he do with all that was himself? Nothing in him could live without her. How, then, could he have lost sight of her for a moment? Oh, unfortunate man! He allowed distance to intervene between himself and his star; and, by the unknown and terrible laws of gravitation in such things, distance is immediate loss.

Where was she, the star? Dea! Dea! Dea! Dea! Alas! he had lost her light. Take away the star, and what is the sky? A black mass. But why, then, had all this befallen him? Oh, what happiness had been his! For him God had remade Eden. Too close was the resemblance, alas! even to allowing the serpent to enter; but this time it was the man who had been tempted. He had been drawn without, and then, by a frightful snare, had fallen into a chaos of murky laughter, which was hell. Oh, grief! Oh, grief! How frightful seemed all that had fascinated him! That Josiana, fearful creature!—half beast, half goddess! Gwynplaine was now on the reverse side of his elevation, and he saw the other aspect of that which had dazzled him. It was baleful! His peerage was deformed; his coronet was hideous; his purple robe, a funeral garment; those palaces, infected; those trophies, those statues, those armorial bearings, sinister; the unwholesome and treacherous air poisoned those who breathed it, and turned them mad. How brilliant the rags of the mountebank, Gwynplaine, appeared to him now! Alas! where was the Green Box, poverty, joy, the sweet wandering life—wandering together, like the swallows? They never left each other then; he saw her every minute, morning, evening. At table their knees, their elbows, touched; they drank from the same cup; the sun shone through the pane, but it was only the sun, and Dea was Love. At night they slept not far from each other; and the dream of Dea came and hovered over Gwynplaine, and the dream of Gwynplaine spread itself mysteriously above the head of Dea. When they awoke they could be never quite sure that they had not exchanged kisses in the azure mists of dreams. Dea was all innocence; Ursus, all wisdom. They wandered from town to town; and they had for provision and for stimulant the frank, loving gaiety of the people. They were angel vagabonds, with enough of humanity to walk the earth and not enough of wings to fly away; and now all had disappeared! Where was it gone? Was it possible that it was all effaced? What wind from the tomb had swept over them? All was eclipsed! All was lost! Alas! power, irresistible and deaf to appeal, which weighs down the poor, flings its shadow over all, and is capable of anything. What had been done to them? And he had not been there to protect them, to fling himself in front of them, to defend them, as a lord, with his title, his peerage, and his sword; as a mountebank, with his fists and his nails!

And here arose a bitter reflection, perhaps the most bitter of all. Well! no; he could not have defended them. It was he himself who had destroyed them; it was to save him, Lord Clancharlie, from them; it was to isolate his dignity from contact with them, that the infamous omnipotence of society had crushed them. The best way in which he could protect them would be to disappear, and then the cause of their persecution would cease. He out of the way, they would be allowed to remain in peace. Into what icy channel was his thought beginning to run! Oh! why had he allowed himself to be separated from Dea? Was not his first duty toward her? To serve and to defend the people? But Dea was the people. Dea was an orphan. She was blind; she represented humanity. Oh! what had they done to them? Cruel smart of regret! His absence had left the field free for the catastrophe. He would have shared their fate; either they would have been taken and carried away with him, or he would have been swallowed up with them. And, now, what would become of him without them? Gwynplaine without Dea. Was it possible? Without Dea was to be without everything. It was all over now. The beloved group was forever buried in irreparable disappearance. All was spent. Besides, condemned and damned as Gwynplaine was, what was the good of further struggle? He had nothing more to expect either of men or of heaven. Dea! Dea! Where is Dea? Lost! What? lost? He who has lost his soul can regain it but through one outlet—death.

Gwynplaine, tragically distraught, placed his hand firmly on the parapet, as on a solution, and looked at the river.

It was his third night without sleep. Fever had come over him. His thoughts, which he believed to be clear, were blurred. He felt an imperative need of sleep. He remained for a few instants leaning over the water. Its darkness offered him a bed of boundless tranquility in the infinity of shadow. Sinister temptation!

He took off his coat, which he folded and placed on the parapet; then he unbuttoned his waistcoat. As he was about to take it off, his hand struck against something in the pocket. It was the red book which had been given him by the librarian of the House of Lords: he drew it from the pocket, examined it in the vague light of the night, and found a pencil in it, with which he wrote on the first blank that he found these two lines—

"I depart. Let my brother David take my place, and may he be happy!"

Then he signed, "Fermain Clancharlie, peer of England."

He took off his waistcoat and placed it upon the coat; then his hat, which he placed upon the waistcoat. In the hat he laid the red book open at the page on which he had written. Seeing a stone lying on the ground, he picked it up and placed it in the hat. Having done all this, he looked up into the deep shadow above him. Then his head sank slowly, as if drawn by an invisible thread toward the abyss.

There was a hole in the masonry near the base of the parapet; he placed his foot in it, so that his knee stood higher than the top, and scarcely an effort was necessary to spring over it. He clasped his hands behind his back and leaned over. "So be it," said he.

And he fixed his eyes on the deep waters. Just then he felt a tongue licking his hands.

He shuddered, and turned round.

Homo was behind him.

CONCLUSION

THE NIGHT AND THE SEA

Chapter I

A WATCH-DOG MAY BE A GUARDIAN ANGEL

G WYNPLAINE UTTERED A CRY.
    "Is that you, wolf?"

Homo wagged his tail. His eyes sparkled in the darkness. He was looking earnestly at Gwynplaine.

Then he began to lick his hands again. For a moment Gwynplaine was like a drunken man, so great is the shock of Hope's mighty return.

Homo! What an apparition! During the last forty-eight hours he had exhausted what might be termed every variety of the thunderbolt. But one was left to strike him—the thunderbolt of joy. And it had just fallen upon him. Certainty, or at least the light which leads to it, regained; the sudden intervention of some mysterious clemency possessed, perhaps, by destiny; life saying, "Behold me!" in the darkest recess of the grave; the very moment in which all expectation has ceased bringing back health and deliverance; a place of safety discovered at the most critical instant in the midst of crumbling ruins; Homo was all this to Gwynplaine. The wolf appeared to him in a halo of light.

Meanwhile, Homo had turned round. He advanced a few steps, and then looked back to see if Gwynplaine was following him.

Gwynplaine was doing so. Homo wagged his tail, and went on.

The road taken by the wolf was the slope of the quay of the Effroc stone. This slope shelved down to the Thames; and Gwynplaine, guided by Homo, descended it.

Homo turned his head now and then, to make sure that Gwynplaine was behind him.

In some situations of supreme importance nothing approaches so near an omniscient intelligence as the simple instinct of a faithful animal. An animal is a lucid somnambulist.

There are cases in which the dog feels that he should follow his master; others, in which he should precede him. Then the animal takes the direction of sense. His imperturbable scent is a confused power of vision in what is twilight to us. He feels a vague obligation to become a guide. Does he know that there is a dangerous pass, and that he can help his master to surmount it? Probably not. Perhaps he does. In any case, someone knows it for him. As we have already said, it often happens in life that some mighty help which we have held to have come from below has, in reality, come from above. Who knows all the mysterious forms assumed by God?

What was this animal? Providence.

Having reached the river, the wolf led down the narrow tongue of land which bordered the Thames.

Without noise or bark he pushed forward on his silent way. Homo always followed his instinct and did his duty; but with the pensive reserve of an outlaw.

Some fifty paces more, and he stopped. A wooden platform appeared on the right. At the bottom of this platform, which was a kind of wharf on piles, a black mass could be made out, which was a tolerably large vessel. On the deck of the vessel, near the prow, was a glimmer, like the last flicker of a night-light.

The wolf, having finally assured himself that Gwynplaine was there, bounded on to the wharf. It was a long platform, floored and tarred, supported by a network of joists, and under which flowed the river. Homo and Gwynplaine shortly reached the brink.

The ship moored to the wharf was a Dutch vessel, of the Japanese build, with two decks, fore and aft, and between them an open hold, reached by an upright ladder, in which the cargo was laden. There was thus a forecastle and an afterdeck, as in our old river boats, and a space between them ballasted by the freight. The paper boats made by children are of a somewhat similar shape. Under the decks were the cabins, the doors of which opened into the hold and were lighted by glazed port-holes. In stowing the cargo a passage was left between the packages of which it consisted. These vessels had a mast on each deck. The foremast was called Paul, the mainmast Peter; the ship being sailed by these two masts, as the Church was guided by her two apostles. A gangway was thrown, like a Chinese bridge, from one deck to the other, over the center of the hold. In bad weather, both flaps of the gangway were lowered, on the right and left, on hinges, thus making a roof over the hold; so that the ship, in heavy seas, was hermetically closed. These sloops, being of very massive construction, had a beam for a tiller, the strength of the rudder being necessarily proportioned to the height of the vessel. Three men, the skipper and two sailors, with a cabin-boy, sufficed to navigate these ponderous sea-going machines. The decks, fore and aft, were, as we have already said, without bulwarks. The great lumbering hull of this particular vessel was painted black, and on it, visible even in the night, stood out, in white letters, the words, *Vograat, Rotterdam.*

About that time many events had occurred at sea, and amongst others, the defeat of the Baron de Pointi's eight ships off Cape Carnero, which had driven the whole French fleet into refuge at Gibraltar; so that the Channel was swept of every man-of-war, and merchant vessels were able to sail backwards and forwards between London and Rotterdam, without a convoy.

The vessel on which was to be read the word *Vograat*, and which Gwynplaine was now close to, lay with her main-deck almost level with the wharf. But one step to descend, and Homo in a bound, and Gwynplaine in a stride, were on board.

The deck was clear, and no stir was perceptible. The passengers, if, as was likely, there were any, were already on board, the vessel being ready to sail, and the cargo stowed, as was apparent from the state of the hold, which was full of bales and cases. But they were, doubtless, lying asleep in the cabins below, as the passage was to take place during the night. In such cases the passengers do not appear on deck till they awake the following morning. As for the crew, they were probably having their supper in the men's cabin, whilst awaiting the hour fixed for sailing, which was now rapidly approaching. Hence the silence on the two decks connected by the gangway.

The wolf had almost run across the wharf; once on board, he slackened his pace into a discreet walk. He still wagged his tail—no longer joyfully, however, but with the sad and feeble wag of a dog troubled in his mind. Still preceding Gwynplaine, he passed along the afterdeck, and across the gangway.

Gwynplaine, having reached the gangway, perceived a light in front of him. It was the same that he had seen from the shore. There was a lantern on the deck, close to the foremast, by the gleam of which was sketched in black, on the dim background of the night, what Gwynplaine recognized to be Ursus's old four-wheeled van.

This poor wooden tenement, cart and hut combined, in which his childhood had rolled along, was fastened to the bottom of the mast by thick ropes, of which the knots were visible at the wheels. Having been so long out of service, it had become dreadfully rickety; it leant over feebly on one side; it had become quite paralytic from disuse; and, moreover, it was suffering from that incurable malady—old age. Moldy and out of shape, it tottered in decay. The materials of which it was built were all rotten. The iron was rusty, the leather torn, the woodwork wormeaten. There were lines of cracks across the window in front, through which shone a ray from the lantern. The wheels were warped. The lining, the floor, and the axletrees seemed worn out with fatigue. Altogether, it presented an indescribable appearance of beggary and prostration. The shafts, stuck up, looked like two arms raised to heaven. The whole thing was in a state of dislocation. Beneath it was hanging Homo's chain.

Does it not seem that the law and the will of nature would have dictated Gwynplaine's headlong rush to throw himself upon life, happiness, love regained? So they would, except in some case of deep terror such as his. But he who comes forth, shattered in nerve and uncertain of his way, from a series of catastrophes, each one like a fresh betrayal, is prudent even in his joy; hesitates, lest he should bear the fatality of which he has been the victim to those whom he loves; feels that some evil contagion may still hang about him, and advances toward happiness with wary steps. The gates of Paradise reopen; but before he enters he examines his ground.

Gwynplaine, staggering under the weight of his emotion, looked around him, while the wolf went and lay down silently by his chain.

Chapter II

BARKILPHEDRO, HAVING AIMED AT THE EAGLE, BRINGS DOWN THE DOVE

THE STEP OF THE LITTLE VAN WAS DOWN—THE DOOR AJAR—THERE WAS NO ONE INSIDE. THE faint light which broke through the pane in front sketched the interior of the caravan vaguely in melancholy chiaroscuro. The inscriptions of Ursus, gloryifying the grandeur of Lords, showed distinctly on the worn-out boards, which were both the wall without and the wainscot within. On a nail, near the door, Gwynplaine saw his esclavine and his cape hung up, as they hang up the clothes of a corpse in a dead-house. Just then he had neither waistcoat nor coat on.

Behind the van something was laid out on the deck at the foot of the mast, which was lighted by the lantern. It was a mattress, of which he could make out one corner. On this mattress someone was probably lying, for he could see a shadow move.

Someone was speaking. Concealed by the van, Gwynplaine listened. It was Ursus's voice. That voice, so harsh in its upper, so tender in its lower, pitch; that voice, which had so often upbraided Gwynplaine, and which had taught him so well, had lost the life and clearness of its tone. It was vague and low, and melted into a sigh at the end of every sentence. It bore but a confused resemblance to his natural and firm voice of old. It was the voice of one in whom happiness is dead. A voice may become a ghost.

He seemed to be engaged in monologue rather than in conversation. We are already aware, however, that soliloquy was a habit with him. It was for that reason that he passed for a madman.

Gwynplaine held his breath, so as not to lose a word of what Ursus said, and this was what he heard.

"This is a very dangerous kind of craft, because there are no bulwarks to it. If we were to slip, there is nothing to prevent our going overboard. If we have bad weather, we shall have to take her below, and that will be dreadful. An awkward step, a fright, and we shall have a rupture of the aneurism. I have seen instances of it. O my God! what is to become of us? Is she asleep? Yes. She is asleep. Is she in a swoon? No. Her pulse is pretty strong. She is only asleep. Sleep is a reprieve. It is the happy blindness. What can I do to prevent people walking about here? Gentlemen, if there be anybody on deck, I beg of you to make no noise. Do not come near us, if you do not mind. You know a person in delicate health requires a little attention. She is feverish, you see. She is very young. 'Tis a little creature who is rather feverish. I put this mattress down here so that she may have a little air. I explain all this so that you should be careful. She fell down exhausted on the mattress as if she had fainted. But she is asleep. I do hope that no one will awake her. I address myself to the ladies, if there are any present. A young girl, it is pitiful! We are only poor mountebanks, but I beg a little kindness, and if there is anything to pay for not making a noise, I will pay it. I thank you, ladies and gentlemen. Is there anyone there? No. I don't think there is. My talk is mere loss of breath. So much the better. Gentlemen, I thank you, if you are there; and I thank you still more if you are not. Her forehead is all in perspiration. Come, let us take our places in the galleys again. Put on the chain. Misery is come back. We are sinking again. A hand, the fearful hand which we cannot see, but the weight of which we feel ever upon us, has suddenly struck us back toward the dark point of our destiny. Be it so. We will bear up. Only I will not have her ill. I must seem a fool to talk aloud like this, when I am alone; but she must feel she has someone near her when she awakes. What shall I do if somebody awakes her suddenly! No noise, in the name of heaven! A sudden shock which would awake her suddenly would be of no use. It will be a pity if anybody comes by. I believe that everyone on board is asleep. Thanks be to Providence for that mercy. Well, and Homo? Where is he, I wonder? In all this confusion I forgot to tie him up. I do not know what I am doing. It is more than an hour since I have seen him. I suppose he has been to look for his supper somewhere ashore. I hope nothing has happened to him. Homo! Homo!"

Homo struck his tail softly on the planks of the deck.

"You are there. Oh! you are there! Thank God for that. If Homo had been lost, it would have been too much to bear. She has moved her arm. Perhaps she is going to awake. Quiet, Homo! The tide is turning. We shall sail directly. I think it will be a fine night. There is no wind: the flag droops. We shall have a good passage. I do not know what moon it is, but there is scarcely a stir in the clouds. There will be no swell. It will be a fine night. Her cheek is pale; it is only weakness! No, it is flushed; it is only the fever? Stay! It is rosy. She is well! I can no longer see clearly. My poor Homo, I no longer see distinctly. So we must begin life afresh. We must set to work again. There are only we two left, you see. We will work for her, both of us! She is our child. Ah! the vessel moves! We are off! Good-bye, London! Good evening! good night! To the devil with horrible London!"

He was right. He heard the dull sound of the unmooring as the vessel fell away from the wharf. Abaft on the poop a man, the skipper, no doubt, just come from below, was standing. He had slipped the hawser and was working the tiller. Looking only to the rudder, as befitted the combined phlegm of a Dutchman and a sailor, listening to nothing but the wind and the water, bending against the resistance of the tiller, as he worked it to port or starboard, he looked in the gloom of the afterdeck, like a phantom bearing a beam upon its shoulder. He was alone there. So long as they were in the river the other sailors were not required. In a few minutes the vessel was in the center of the current, with which she drifted without rolling or pitching. The Thames, little disturbed by the ebb, was calm. Carried onwards by the tide, the vessel made rapid way. Behind her the black scenery of London was fading in the mist.

Ursus went on talking.

"Never mind, I will give her digitalis. I am afraid that delirium will supervene. She perspires in the palms of her hands. What sin can we have committed in the sight of God? How quickly has all this misery come upon us! Hideous rapidity of evil! A stone falls. It has claws. It is the hawk swooping on the lark. It is destiny. There you lie, my sweet child! One comes to London. One says: What a fine city! What fine buildings! Southwark is a magnificent suburb. One settles there. But now they are horrid places. What would you have me do there? I am going to leave. This is the 30th of April. I always distrusted the month of April. There are but two lucky days in April, the 5th and the 27th; and four unlucky ones—the 10th, the 20th, the 29th, and the 30th. This has been placed beyond doubt by the calculations of Cardan. I wish this day were over. Departure is a comfort. At dawn we shall be at Gravesend, and to-morrow evening at Rotterdam. Zounds! I will begin life again in the van. We will draw it, won't we, Homo?"

A light tapping announced the wolf's consent.

Ursus continued—

"If one could only get out of a grief, as one gets out of a city! Homo, we must yet be happy. Alas! there must always be the one who is no more. A shadow remains on those who survive. You know whom I mean, Homo. We were four, and now we are but three. Life is but a long loss of those whom we love. They leave behind them a train of sorrows. Destiny amazes us by a prolixity of unbearable suffering; who then can wonder that the old are garrulous? It is despair that makes the dotard, old fellow! Homo, the wind continues favorable. We can no longer see the dome of St. Paul's. We shall pass Greenwich presently. That will be six good miles over. Oh! I turn my back forever on those odious capitals, full of priests, of magistrates, and of people. I prefer looking at the leaves rustling in the woods. Her forehead is still in perspiration. I don't like those great violet veins in her arm. There is fever in them. Oh! all this is killing me. Sleep, my child. Yes; she sleeps."

Here a voice spoke: an ineffable voice, which seemed from afar, and appeared to come at once from the heights and the depths—a voice divinely fearful, the voice of Dea.

All that Gwynplaine had hitherto felt seemed nothing. His angel spoke. It seemed as though he heard words spoken from another world in a heaven-like trance.

The voice said—

"He did well to go. This world was not worthy of him. Only I must go with him. Father! I am not ill; I heard you speak just now. I am very well, quite well. I was asleep. Father, I am going to be happy."

"My child," said Ursus in a voice of anguish, "what do you mean by that?"

The answer was—

"Father, do not be unhappy."

There was a pause, as if to take breath, and then these few words, pronounced slowly, reached Gwynplaine.

"Gwynplaine is no longer here. It is now that I am blind. I knew not what night was. Night is absence."

The voice stopped once more, and then continued—

"I always feared that he would fly away. I felt that he belonged to Heaven. He has taken flight suddenly. It was natural that it should end thus. The soul flies away like a bird. But the nest of the soul is in the height, where dwells the Great Loadstone, who draws all toward Him. I know where to find Gwynplaine. I have no doubt about the way. Father, it is yonder. Later on you will rejoin us, and Homo, too."

Homo, hearing his name pronounced, wagged his tail softly against the deck.

"Father!" resumed the voice, "you understand that once Gwynplaine is no longer here, all is over. Even if I would remain, I could not, because one must breathe. We must not ask for that which is impossible. I was with Gwynplaine. It was quite natural, I lived. Now Gwynplaine is no more, I die. The two things are alike: either he must come, or I must go. Since he cannot come back, I am going to him. It is good to die. It is not at all difficult. Father, that which is extinguished here, shall be rekindled elsewhere. It is a heartache to live in this world. It cannot be that we shall always be unhappy. When we go to what you call the stars, we shall marry, we shall never part again, and we shall love, love, love; and that is what is God."

"There, there, do not agitate yourself," said Ursus.

The voice continued—

"Well, for instance; last year. In the spring of last year we were together, and we were happy. How different it is now! I forget what little village we were in, but there were trees, and I heard the linnets singing. We came to London; all was changed. This is no reproach, mind. When one comes to a fresh place, how is one to know anything about it? Father, do you remember that one day there was a woman in the great box; you said: 'It is a duchess.' I felt sad. I think it might have been better had we kept to the little towns. Gwynplaine has done right, withal. Now my turn has come. Besides, you have told me yourself, that when I was very little, my mother died, and that I was lying on the ground with the snow falling upon me, and that he, who was also very little then, and alone, like myself, picked me up, and that it was thus that I came to be alive; so you cannot wonder that now I should feel it absolutely necessary to go and search the grave to see if Gwynplaine be in it. Because the only thing which exists in life is the heart; and after life, the soul. You take notice of what I say, father, do you not? What is moving? It seems as if we are in something that is moving, yet I do not hear the sound of the wheels."

After a pause the voice added—

"I cannot exactly make out the difference between yesterday and to-day. I do not complain. I do not know what has occurred, but something must have happened."

These words, uttered with deep and inconsolable sweetness, and with a sigh which Gwynplaine heard, wound up thus—

"I must go, unless he should return."

Ursus muttered gloomily, "I do not believe in ghosts."

He went on—

"This is a ship. You ask why the house moves, it is because we are on board a vessel. Be calm; you must not talk so much. Daughter, if you have any love for me, do not agitate yourself, it will make you feverish. I am so old, I could not bear it if you were to have an illness. Spare me! do not be ill!"

Again the voice spoke—

"What is the use of searching the earth, when we can only find in Heaven?"

Ursus replied, with a half attempt at authority—

"Be calm. There are times when you have no sense at all. I order you to rest. After all, you cannot be expected to know what it is to rupture a blood-vessel. I should be easy if you were easy. My child, do something for me as well. If he picked you up, I took you in. You will make me ill. That is wrong. You must calm yourself, and go to sleep. All will come right. I give you my word of honor, all will come right. Besides, it is very fine weather. The night might have been made on purpose. To-morrow we shall be at Rotterdam, which is a city in Holland, at the mouth of the Meuse."

"Father," said the voice, "look here; when two beings have always been together from infancy, their state should not be disturbed, or death must come, and it cannot be otherwise. I love you all the same, but I feel that I am no longer altogether with you, although I am as yet not altogether with him."

"Come! try to sleep," repeated Ursus.

The voice answered—

"I shall have sleep enough soon."

Ursus replied, in trembling tones—

"I tell you that we are going to Holland, to Rotterdam, which is a city."

"Father," continued the voice, "I am not ill; if you are anxious about that, you may rest easy. I have no fever. I am rather hot; it is nothing more."

Ursus stammered out—

"At the mouth of the Meuse—"

"I am quite well, father; but look here! I feel that I am going to die!"

"Do nothing so foolish," said Ursus. And he added, "Above all, God forbid she should have a shock!"

There was a silence. Suddenly Ursus cried out—

"What are you doing? Why are you getting up? Lie down again, I implore of you."

Gwynplaine shivered, and stretched out his head.

Chapter III

PARADISE REGAINED BELOW

HE SAW DEA. SHE HAD JUST RAISED HERSELF UP ON THE MATTRESS. SHE HAD ON A LONG WHITE dress, carefully closed, and showing only the delicate form of her neck. The sleeves covered her arms, the folds, her feet. The branch-like tracery of blue veins, hot and swollen with fever, were visible on her hands. She was shivering and rocking, rather than reeling, to and fro, like a reed. The lantern threw up its glancing light on her beautiful face. Her loosened hair floated over her shoulders. No tears fell on her cheeks. In her eyes there was fire, and darkness. She was pale, with that paleness which is like the transparency of a divine life in an earthly face. Her fragile and exquisite form was, as it were, blended and interfused with the folds of her robe. She wavered like the flicker of a flame, while, at the same time, she was dwindling into shadow. Her eyes, opened wide, were resplendent. She was as one just freed from the sepulcher; a soul standing in the dawn.

Ursus, whose back only was visible to Gwynplaine, raised his arms in terror. "Oh! my child! Oh! heavens! she is delirious. Delirium is what I feared worst of all. She must have no shock, for that might kill her; yet nothing but a shock can prevent her going mad. Dead or mad! what a situation. O God! what can I do? My child, lie down again."

Meanwhile, Dea spoke. Her voice was almost indistinct, as if a cloud already interposed between her and earth.

"Father, you are wrong. I am not in the least delirious. I hear all you say to me, distinctly. You tell me that there is a great crowd of people, that they are waiting, and that I must play to-night. I am quite willing. You see that I have my reason; but I do not know what to do, since I am dead, and Gwynplaine is dead. I am coming all the same. I am ready to play. Here I am; but Gwynplaine is no longer here."

"Come, my child," said Ursus, "do as I bid you. Lie down again."

"He is no longer here, no longer here. Oh! how dark it is!"

"Dark," muttered Ursus. "This is the first time she has ever uttered that word!"

Gwynplaine, with as little noise as he could help making as he crept, mounted the step of the caravan, entered it, took from the nail the cape and the esclavine, put the esclavine round his neck, and redescended from the van, still concealed by the projection of the cabin, the rigging, and the mast.

Dea continued murmuring. She moved her lips, and by degrees the murmur became a melody. In broken pauses, and with the interrupted cadences of delirium, her voice broke into the mysterious appeal she had so often addressed to Gwynplaine in *Chaos Vanquished*. She sang, and her voice was low and uncertain as the murmur of the bee—

> *"Noche, quita te de alli,*
> *El alba canta. . . ."*[1]

She stopped. "No, it is not true. I am not dead. What was I saying? Alas! I am alive. I am alive. He is dead. I am below. He is above. He is gone. I remain. I shall hear his voice no more, nor his footstep. God, who had given us a little Paradise on earth, has taken it away. Gwynplaine, it is over. I shall never feel you near me again. Never! And his voice! I shall never hear his voice again. And she sang—

1. "Depart, O night! sings the dawn."

> "*Es menester a cielos ir—*
> *Deja, quiero,*
> *A tu negro*
> *Caparazon.*"

> "*We must go to heaven.*
> *Take off, I entreat thee,*
> *Thy black cloak.*"

She stretched out her hand, as if she sought something in space on which she might rest.

Gwynplaine, rising by the side of Ursus, who had suddenly become as though petrified, knelt down before her.

"Never," said Dea, "never shall I hear him again."

She began, wandering, to sing again—

> "*Deja, quiero,*
> *A tu negro*
> *Caparazon.*"

Then she heard a voice—even the beloved voice—answering—

> "*O ven! ama!*
> *Eres alma,*
> *Soy corazon.*"

> "*O come and love*
> *Thou art the soul,*
> *I am the heart.*"

And at the same instant Dea felt under her hand the head of Gwynplaine. She uttered an indescribable cry.

"Gwynplaine!"

A light, as of a star, shone over her pale face, and she tottered. Gwynplaine received her in his arms.

"Alive!" cried Ursus.

Dea repeated "Gwynplaine"; and with her head bowed against Gwynplaine's cheek, she whispered faintly—

"You have come down to me again; I thank you, Gwynplaine."

And seated on his knee, she lifted up her head. Wrapped in his embrace, she turned her sweet face toward him, and fixed on him those eyes so full of light and shadow, as though she could see him.

"It is you," she said.

Gwynplaine covered her sobs with kisses. There are words which are at once words, cries, and sobs, in which all ecstasy and all grief are mingled and burst forth together. They have no meaning, and yet tell all.

"Yes! it is! It is I, Gwynplaine, of whom you are the soul. Do you hear me? I, of whom you are the child, the wife, the star, the breath of life. I, to whom you are eternity. It is I. I am here. I hold you in my arms. I am alive. I am yours. Oh! when I think that in a moment all would have been over—one minute more, but for Homo! I will tell you everything. How near is despair to joy! Dea, we live! Dea, forgive me. Yes. Yours forever. You are right. Touch my forehead. Make sure that it is I. If you only knew—but nothing can separate us now. I rise out of hell, and ascend into heaven. Am I not with you? You said that I descended. Not so; I reascend. Once more with you! Forever! I tell you forever! Together! We are together! Who would have believed it? We have found each other again. All our troubles are past. Before us now there is nothing but enchantment. We will renew our happy life, and we will shut the door so fast that misfortune shall never enter again. I will tell you all. You will be astonished. The vessel has sailed. No one can prevent that now. We are on our voyage, and at liberty. We are going to Holland. We will marry. I have no fear about gaining a livelihood. What can hinder it? There is nothing to fear. I adore you!"

"Not so quick!" stammered Ursus.

Dea, trembling, and with the rapture of an angelic touch, passed her hand over Gwynplaine's profile. He overheard her say to herself, "It is thus that gods are made."

Then she touched his clothes.

"The esclavine," she said, "the cape. Nothing changed. All as it was before."

Ursus, stupefied, delighted, smiling, drowned in tears, looked at them, and addressed an aside to himself.

"I don't understand it in the least. I am a stupid idiot—I, who saw him carried to the grave! I cry, and I laugh. That is all I know. I am as great a fool as if I were in love myself. But that is just what I am. I am in love with them both. Old fool! Too much emotion. Too much emotion. It is what I was afraid of. No, it is that I wished for. Gwynplaine, be careful of her. Yes, let them kiss! it is no affair of mine. I am but a spectator. What I feel is droll. I am the parasite of their happiness, and I am nourished by it."

Whilst Ursus was talking to himself, Gwynplaine exclaimed—

"Dea, you are too beautiful! I don't know where my wits were gone these last few days. Truly, there is but you on earth. I see you again, but as yet I can hardly believe it. In this ship! But tell me, how did it all happen? To what a state have they reduced you. But where is the Green Box? They have robbed you. They have driven you away. It is infamous. Oh! I will avenge you. I will avenge you, Dea. They shall answer for it. I am a peer of England."

Ursus, as if stricken by a planet full in his breast, drew back, and looked at Gwynplaine attentively.

"It is clear that he is not dead; but can he have gone mad?" and he listened to him doubtfully.

Gwynplaine resumed.

"Be easy, Dea; I will carry my complaint to the House of Lords."

Ursus looked at him again, and struck his forehead with the tip of his forefinger. Then making up his mind—

"It is all one to me," he said. "It will be all right, all the same. Be as mad as you like, my Gwynplaine. It is one of the rights of man. As for me, I am happy; but how came all this about?"

The vessel continued to sail smoothly and fast. The night grew darker and darker. The mists, which came inland from the ocean, were invading the zenith, from which no wind blew them away. Only a few large stars were visible, and they disappeared one after another, so that soon there were none at all, and the whole sky was dark, infinite, and soft. The river broadened until the banks on each side were nothing but two thin brown lines mingling with the gloom. Out of all this shadow rose a profound peace. Gwynplaine, half seated, held Dea in his embrace. They spoke, they cried, they babbled, they murmured in a mad dialogue of joy! How are we to paint thee, O joy!

"My life!"

"My heaven!"

"My love!"

"My whole happiness!"

"Gwynplaine!"

"Dea, I am drunk. Let me kiss your feet."

"Is it you, then, for certain!"

"I have so much to say to you now that I do not know where to begin."

"One kiss!"

"O, my wife!"

"Gwynplaine, do not tell me that I am beautiful. It is you who are handsome."

"I have found you again. I hold you to my heart. This is true. You are mine. I do not dream. Is it possible? Yes, it is. I recover possession of life. If you only knew! I have met with all sorts of adventures, Dea!"

"Gwynplaine, I love you!"

And Ursus murmured—

"Mine is the joy of a grandfather."

Homo, having come from under the van, was going from one to the other discreetly, exacting no attention, licking them left and right—now Ursus's thick shoes, now Gwynplaine's cape, now Dea's dress, now the mattress. This was his way of giving his blessing.

They had passed Chatham and the mouth of the Medway. They were approaching the sea. The shadowy serenity of the atmosphere was such that the passage down the Thames was being made without trouble: no maneuver was needful, nor was any sailor called on deck. At the other end of the vessel the skipper, still alone, was steering. There was only this man aft. At the bow the lantern lighted up the happy group of beings who, from the depths of misery, had suddenly been raised to happiness by a meeting so unhoped for.

Chapter IV

NAY; ON HIGH!

SUDDENLY DEA, DISENGAGING HERSELF FROM GWYNPLAINE'S EMBRACE, AROSE. SHE PRESSED BOTH her hands against her heart, as if to still its throbbings.

"What is wrong with me?" said she. "There is something the matter. Joy is suffocating. No, it is nothing! That is lucky. Your reappearance, O my Gwynplaine, has given me a blow—a blow of happiness. All this heaven of joy which you have put into my heart has intoxicated me. You being absent, I felt myself dying. The true life which was leaving me you have brought back. I felt as if something was being torn away within me. It is the shadows that have been torn away, and I feel life dawn in my brain—a glowing life, a life of fever and delight. This life which you have just given me is wonderful. It is so heavenly that it makes me suffer somewhat. It seems as though my soul is enlarged, and can scarcely be contained in my body. This life of seraphim, this plenitude, flows into my brain and penetrates it. I feel like a beating of wings within my breast. I feel strangely, but happy. Gwynplaine, you have been my resurrection."

She flushed, became pale, then flushed again, and fell.

"Alas!" said Ursus, "you have killed her."

Gwynplaine stretched his arms toward Dea. Extremity of anguish coming upon extremity of ecstasy, what a shock! He would himself have fallen, had he not had to support her.

"Dea!" he cried, shuddering, "what is the matter?"

"Nothing," said she, "I love you!"

She lay in his arms, lifeless, like a piece of linen; her hands were hanging down helplessly.

Gwynplaine and Ursus placed Dea on the mattress. She said, feebly—

"I cannot breathe lying down."

They lifted her up.

Ursus said—

"Fetch a pillow."

She replied—

"What for? I have Gwynplaine!"

She laid her head on Gwynplaine's shoulder, who was sitting behind, and supporting her, his eyes wild with grief.

"Oh," said she, "how happy I am!"

Ursus took her wrist, and counted the pulsation of the artery. He did not shake his head. He said nothing, nor expressed his thoughts except by the rapid movement of his eyelids, which were opening and closing convulsively, as if to prevent a flood of tears from bursting out.

"What is the matter?" asked Gwynplaine.

Ursus placed his ear against Dea's left side.

Gwynplaine repeated his question eagerly, fearful of the answer.

Ursus looked at Gwynplaine, then at Dea. He was livid. He said—

"We ought to be parallel with Canterbury. The distance from here to Gravesend cannot be very great. We shall have fine weather all night. We need fear no attack at sea, because the fleets are all on the coast of Spain. We shall have a good passage."

Dea, bent, and growing paler and paler, clutched her robe convulsively. She heaved a sigh of inexpressible sadness, and murmured—

"I know what this is; I am dying!"

Gwynplaine rose in terror. Ursus held Dea.

"Die! You die! No; it shall not be! You cannot die! Die now! Die at once! It is impossible! God is not ferociously cruel—to give you and to take you back in the same moment. No; such a thing cannot be. It would make one doubt in Him. Then, indeed, would everything be a snare—the earth, the sky, the cradles of infants, the human heart, love, the stars. God would be a traitor, and man a dupe. There would be nothing in which to believe. It would be an insult to the creation. Everything would be an abyss. You know not what you say, Dea. You shall live! I command you to live! You must obey me! I am your husband and your master, I forbid you to leave me! Oh, heavens! Oh, wretched Man! No, it cannot be; I to remain in the world after you! Why, it is as monstrous as that there should be no sun! Dea! Dea! recover! It is but a moment of passing pain. One feels a shudder at times, and thinks no more about it. It is absolutely necessary that you should get well and cease to suffer. *You* die! What have I done to you? The very thought of it drives me mad. We belong to each other, and we love each other. You have no reason for going! It would be unjust! Have I committed crimes? Besides, you have forgiven me. Oh, you would not make me desperate—have me become a villain, a madman, drive me to perdition? Dea, I entreat you! I conjure you! I supplicate you! Do not die!"

And clenching his hands in his hair, agonized with fear, stifled with tears, he threw himself at her feet.

"My Gwynplaine," said Dea, "it is no fault of mine."

There then rose to her lips a red froth, which Ursus wiped away with the fold of her robe, before Gwynplaine, who was prostrate at her feet, could see it.

Gwynplaine took her feet in his hands, and implored her in all kinds of confused words.

"I tell you, I will not have it! *You* die? I have no strength left to bear it. Die? Yes; but both of us together—not otherwise. *You* die, my Dea? I will never consent to it! My divinity! my love! Do you understand that I am with you? I swear that you shall live! Oh, but you cannot have thought what would become of me after you were gone. If you had an idea of the necessity which you are to me, you would see that it is absolutely impossible! Dea! you see I have but you! The most ex-traordinary things have happened to me. You will hardly believe that I have just explored the whole of life in a few hours! I have found out one thing—that there is nothing in it! You exist! if you did not, the universe would have no meaning. Stay with me! Have pity on me! Since you love me, live on! If I have just found you again, it is to keep you. Wait a little longer; you cannot leave me like this, now that we have been together but a few minutes! Do not be impatient! Oh, Heaven, how I suffer! You are not angry with me, are you? You know that I could not help going when the wapen-take came for me. You will breathe more easily presently, you will see. Dea, all has been put right. We are going to be happy. Do not drive me to despair, Dea! I have done nothing to you!"

These words were not spoken, but sobbed out. They rose from his breast—now in a lament which might have attracted the dove, now in a roar which might have made lions recoil.

Dea answered him in a voice growing weaker and weaker, and pausing at nearly every word.

"Alas! it is of no use, my beloved! I see that you are doing all you can. An hour ago I wanted to die; now I do not. Gwynplaine—my adored Gwynplaine! how happy we have been! God placed you in my life, and He takes me out of yours. You see, I am going. You will remember the Green Box, won't you; and poor blind little Dea? You will remember my song? Do not forget the sound of my voice, and the way in which I said, 'I love you!' I will come back and tell it to you again, in the night while you are asleep. Yes, we found each other again; but it was too much joy. It was to end at once. It is decreed that I am to go first. I love my father, Ursus, and my brother, Homo, very dearly. You are all so good. There is no air here. Open the window. My Gwynplaine, I did not tell you, but I was jealous of a woman who came one day. You do not even know of whom I speak. Is it not so? Cover my arms, I am rather cold. And Fibi and Vinos, where are they? One comes to love everybody. One feels a friendship for all those who have been mixed up in one's happiness. We have a kindly feeling toward them for having been present in our joys. Why has it all passed away? I have not clearly understood what has happened during the last two days. Now I am dying. Leave me in my dress. When I put it on I foresaw that it would be my shroud. I wish to keep it on. Gwynplaine's kisses are upon it. Oh, what would I not have given to have lived on! What a happy life we led in our poor caravan! How we sang! How I listened to the applause! What joy it was never to be sepa-rated from each other! It seemed to me that I was living in a cloud with you: I knew one day from another, although I was blind. I knew that it was morning, because I heard Gwynplaine; I felt that it was night, because I dreamed of Gwynplaine. I felt that I was wrapped up in something, which was his soul. We adored each other so sweetly. It is all fading away; and there will be no more songs. Alas! that I cannot live on! You will think of me, my beloved!"

Her voice was growing fainter. The ominous waning, which was death, was stealing away her breath. She folded her thumbs within her fingers, a sign that her last moments were approaching. It seemed as though the first uncertain words of an angel just created were blended with the last fail-ing accents of the dying girl.

She murmured—

"You will think of me, won't you? It would be very sad to be dead, and to be remembered by no one. I have been wayward at times; I beg pardon of you all. I am sure that, if God had so willed it, we might yet have been happy, my Gwynplaine; for we take up but very little room, and we might have earned our bread together in another land. But God has willed it otherwise. I cannot make out in the least why I am dying. I never complained of being blind, so that I cannot have of-fended anyone. I should never have asked for anything, but always to be blind as I was, by your side. Oh, how sad it is to have to part!"

Her words were more and more inarticulate, evaporating into each other, as if they were being blown away. She had become almost inaudible.

"Gwynplaine," she resumed, "you will think of me, won't you? I shall crave it when I am dead."

And she added—

"Oh, keep me with you!"

Then after a pause, she said—

"Come to me as soon as you can. I shall be very unhappy without you, even in heaven. Do not leave me long alone, my sweet Gwynplaine! My Paradise was here. Above there is only heaven! Oh! I cannot breathe! My beloved! My beloved! My beloved!"

"Mercy!" cried Gwynplaine.

"Farewell!" murmured Dea.

And he pressed his mouth to her beautiful icy hands. For a moment it seemed as if she had ceased to breathe. Then she raised herself on her elbows, and an intense splendor flashed across her eyes, and through an ineffable smile her voice rang out clearly.

"Light!" she cried. "I see!"

And she expired. She fell back rigid and motionless on the mattress.

"Dead!" said Ursus.

And the poor old man, as if crushed by his despair, bowed his bald head and buried his swollen face in the folds of the gown which covered Dea's feet. He lay there in a swoon.

Then Gwynplaine became awful. He arose, lifted his eyes, and gazed into the vast gloom above him. Seen by none on earth, but looked down upon, perhaps, as he stood in the darkness, by some invisible presence, he stretched his hands on high, and said—

"I come!"

And he strode across the deck, toward the side of the vessel as if beckoned by a vision.

A few paces off was the abyss. He walked slowly, never casting down his eyes. A smile came upon his face, such as Dea's had just worn. He advanced straight before him, as if watching something. In his eyes was a light like the reflection of a soul perceived from afar off. He cried out, "Yes!" At every step he was approaching nearer to the side of the vessel. His gait was rigid, his arms were lifted up, his head was thrown back, his eyeballs were fixed. His movement was ghost-like. He advanced without haste and without hesitation, with fatal precision, as though there were before him no yawning gulf and open grave. He murmured, "Be easy. I follow you. I understand the sign that you are making me." His eyes were fixed upon a certain spot in the sky, where the shadow was deepest. The smile was still upon his face. The sky was perfectly black; there was no star visible in it, and yet he evidently saw one. He crossed the deck. A few stiff ominous steps, and he had reached the very edge.

"I come," said he; "Dea, behold, I come!"

One step more, there was no bulwark; the void was before him; he strode into it. He fell. The night was thick and dull, the water deep. It swallowed him up. He disappeared calmly and silently. None saw nor heard him. The ship sailed on, and the river flowed.

Shortly afterwards the ship reached the sea.

When Ursus returned to consciousness, he found that Gwynplaine was no longer with him, and he saw Homo by the edge of the deck baying in the shadow and looking down upon the water.

ABOUT THE AUTHOR

Victor Hugo (1802-1855) was born in Paris and grew up in garrison towns in France and Spain where his father, an officer in Napoleon's army, was posted. He decided upon a writing career while a teenager and published his first novel, the historical romance *Hans of Iceland*, in 1825. Its popularity spurred his literary ambitions and he became a prolific writer of poetry, essays, dramas, and novels, many of them informed by his criticism of the penal system and disdain for the death penalty. With the production of his play *Hernani* in 1830 and the publication of *The Hunchback of Notre-Dame* the following year, Hugo was recognized as a major literary writer whose fiction served as vehicles for social and political criticism. He was inducted into the Académie Française in 1841 and made a peer of France in 1845. Hugo was elected a deputy of the legislative assembly of the Second Republic in 1849 but was forced to flee to Belgium two years later owing to his outspoken opposition to president Louis-Napoleon Bonaparte. Although he continued to live in exile from France for nineteen years he wrote ceaselessly. In 1862, he published his masterpiece *Les Misérables*, the novel that crystallized his concerns as a writer and citizen regarding the judicial and political system of his native country. *The Man Who Laughs*, his sympathetic portrait of the underclass, was published in 1869. With the fall of the Second Republic the following year, Hugo returned to France and a hero's welcome. He remained politically active for the rest of his life, serving in the French government, and was regarded as France's most popular writer and leading man of letters.

THE LIBRARY OF ESSENTIAL WRITERS

JANE AUSTEN *Seven Novels*

CHARLOTTE BRONTË *Four Novels*

LEWIS CARROLL *Complete Works*

JOSEPH CONRAD *Complete Short Stories*

JAMES FENIMORE COOPER *Five Novels*

DANIEL DEFOE *Five Novels*

CHARLES DICKENS *Five Novels*

ALEXANDRE DUMAS *Three Novels*

GEORGE ELIOT *Four Novels*

GUSTAVE FLAUBERT *Five Novels*

E. M. FORSTER *Four Novels*

THOMAS HARDY *Five Novels*

NATHANIEL HAWTHORNE *Five Novels*

ERNEST HEMINGWAY *Four Novels*

O. HENRY *The Fiction*

VICTOR HUGO *Three Novels*

HENRY JAMES *Five Novels*

JACK LONDON *Six Novels*

H.P. LOVECRAFT *The Fiction*

W. SOMERSET MAUGHAM *Five Novels*

HERMAN MELVILLE *Seven Novels*

EDGAR ALLAN POE *Fiction and Poetry*

SAKI *The Fiction*

ROBERT LOUIS STEVENSON *Seven Novels*

BRAM STOKER *Five Novels*

LEO TOLSTOY *Three Novels*

MARK TWAIN *Five Novels*

JULES VERNE *Seven Novels*

H. G. WELLS *Seven Novels*

EDITH WHARTON *Five Novels*

OSCAR WILDE *Collected Works*